ANCILLARY SWORD

ANN LECKIE

orbit

www.orbitbooks.net

Orbit
Hachette Book Group
1290 Avenue of the Americas
New York, NY 10104
www.orbitbooks.net
www.orbitshortfiction.com

Printed in the United States of America

LSC-C

First edition: October 2014

10 9

Orbit is an imprint of Hachette Book Group.
The Orbit name and logo are trademarks of Little, Brown Book Group Limited.

Library of Congress Cataloging-in-Publication Data

Leckie, Ann.
Ancillary sword / Ann Leckie.—First edition.
pages cm
ISBN 978-0-316-24665-1 (paperback)—ISBN 978-0-316-24664-4 (ebook) 1. Science fiction. I. Title.
PS3612.E3353A84 2014
813'.6—dc23
2014018730

Praise for the NEBULA, ARTHUR C. CLARKE, LOCUS, and BSFA award–winning; and HUGO, and PHILIP K. DICK award–nominated *Ancillary Justice*

"Unexpected, compelling and very cool. Ann Leckie nails it."
—John Scalzi

"Establishes Leckie as an heir to Banks and Cherryh."
—Elizabeth Bear

"Powerful, arresting, beautiful space opera...Leckie makes it look so easy."
—Kameron Hurley

Ancillary Justice is the mind-blowing space opera you've been needing...This is a novel that will thrill you like the page-turner it is, but stick with you for a long time afterward."
—io9.com

"This impressive debut succeeds in making Breq a protagonist readers will invest in, and establishes Leckie as a talent to watch."
—*Publishers Weekly*

"Ann Leckie's *Ancillary Justice* does everything science fiction should do. It engages, it excites, and it challenges the way the reader views our world."
—*Staffer's Book Review*

"Assured, gripping, and stylish...an absorbing thousand-year history, a poignant personal journey, and a welcome addition to the genre."
—NPR Books

“A stunning, fast-paced debut.” —*Shelf Awareness*

“It’s not every day a debut novel by an author you’d never heard of before derails your entire afternoon with its brilliance. But when my review copy of *Ancillary Justice* arrived, that’s exactly what it did. In fact, it arrowed upward to reach a pretty high position on my list of best space opera novels ever.”

—Liz Bourke, *Tor.com*

“This is not entry-level SF, and its payoff is correspondingly greater because of that.”

—*Locus*

“I cannot find fault in this truly amazing, awe-inspiring debut novel from Ann Leckie... *Ancillary Justice* is one of the best science fiction novels I’ve ever read.”

—*The Book Smugglers*

“It’s by turns thrilling, moving and awe-inspiring.”

—*The Guardian* (UK)

For now, if the tyrant was watching—and she was surely watching, through *Mercy of Kalr,* would be so long as we were in the system—let her think I resented having a baby foisted on me when I'd rather have someone who knew what they were doing.

I turned my attention away from Lieutenant Tisarwat. Forward, the pilot leaned closer to Five and said, quiet and oblique, "Everything all right?" And then to Five's responding, puzzled frown, "Too quiet."

"All this time?" asked Five. Still oblique. Because they were talking about me and didn't want to trigger any requests I might have made to Ship, to tell me when the crew was talking about me. I had an old habit—some two thousand years old—of singing whatever song ran through my head. Or humming. It had caused the crew some puzzlement and distress at first—this body, the only one left to me, didn't have a particularly good voice. They were getting used to it, though, and now I was dryly amused to see crew members disturbed by my silence.

"Not a peep," said the pilot to Kalr Five. With a brief sideways glance and a tiny twitch of neck and shoulder muscles that told me she'd thought of looking back, toward Lieutenant Tisarwat.

"Yeah," said Five, agreeing, I thought, with the pilot's unstated assessment of what might be troubling me.

Good. Let Anaander Mianaai be watching that, too.

By Ann Leckie

Ancillary Justice

Ancillary Sword

ANCILLARY SWORD

Amaandir Miannai
BREQ
Lt Seivarden
Lt Ekalu
Lt Tisarwat
Medic
~~Cpt Vel~~
Kalr V
Bo I

1

"Considering the circumstances, you could use another lieutenant." Anaander Mianaai, ruler (for the moment) of all the vast reaches of Radchaai space, sat in a wide chair cushioned with embroidered silk. This body that spoke to me—one of thousands—looked to be about thirteen years old. Black-clad, dark-skinned. Her face was already stamped with the aristocratic features that were, in Radchaai space, a marker of the highest rank and fashion. Under normal circumstances no one ever saw such young versions of the Lord of the Radch, but these were not normal circumstances.

The room was small, three and a half meters square, paneled with a lattice of dark wood. In one corner the wood was missing—probably damaged in last week's violent dispute between rival parts of Anaander Mianaai herself. Where the wood remained, tendrils of some wispy plant trailed, thin silver-green leaves and here and there tiny white flowers. This was not a public area of the palace, not an audience chamber. An empty chair sat beside the Lord of the Radch's, a table between those chairs held a tea set, flask, and bowls of unadorned white porcelain, gracefully lined, the sort of thing that, at first glance, you might take as unremarkable, but on second would realize was a work of art worth more than some planets.

I had been offered tea, been invited to sit. I had elected to remain standing. "You said I could choose my own officers." I ought to have added a respectful *my lord* but did not. I also ought to have knelt and put my forehead to the floor, when I'd entered and found the Lord of the Radch. I hadn't done that, either.

"You've chosen two. Seivarden, of course, and Lieutenant Ekalu was an obvious choice." The names brought both people reflexively to mind. In approximately a tenth of a second *Mercy of Kalr*, parked some thirty-five thousand kilometers away from this station, would receive that near-instinctive check for data, and a tenth of a second after that its response would reach me. I'd spent the last several days learning to control that old, old habit. I hadn't completely succeeded. "A fleet captain is entitled to a third," Anaander Mianaai continued. Beautiful porcelain bowl in one black-gloved hand, she gestured toward me, meaning, I thought, to indicate my uniform. Radchaai military wore dark-brown jackets and trousers, boots and gloves. Mine was different. The left-hand side was brown, but the right side was black, and my captain's insignia bore the marks that showed I commanded not only my own ship but other ships' captains. Of course, I had no ships in my fleet besides my own, *Mercy of Kalr*, but there were no other fleet captains stationed near Athoek, where I was bound, and the rank would give me an advantage over other captains I might meet. Assuming, of course, those other captains were at all inclined to accept my authority.

Just days ago a long-simmering dispute had broken out

and one faction had destroyed two of the intersystem gates. Now preventing more gates from going down—and preventing that faction from seizing gates and stations in other systems—was an urgent priority. I understood Anaander's reasons for giving me the rank, but still I didn't like it. "Don't make the mistake," I said, "of thinking I'm working for *you*."

She smiled. "Oh, I don't. Your only other choices are officers currently in the system, and near this station. Lieutenant Tisarwat is just out of training. She was on her way to take her first assignment, and now of course that's out of the question. And I thought you'd appreciate having someone you could train up the way you want." She seemed amused at that last.

As she spoke I knew Seivarden was in stage two of NREM sleep. I saw pulse, temperature, respiration, blood oxygen, hormone levels. Then that data was gone, replaced by Lieutenant Ekalu, standing watch. Stressed—jaw slightly clenched, elevated cortisol. She'd been a common soldier until one week ago, when *Mercy of Kalr*'s captain had been arrested for treason. She had never expected to be made an officer. Wasn't, I thought, entirely sure she was capable of it.

"You can't possibly think," I said to the Lord of the Radch, blinking away that vision, "that it's a good idea to send me into a newly broken-out civil war with only one experienced officer."

"It can't be worse than going understaffed," Anaander Mianaai said, maybe aware of my momentary distraction, maybe not. "And the child is beside herself at the thought of serving under a fleet captain. She's waiting for you at the docks." She set down her tea, straightened in her chair. "Since the gate leading to Athoek is down and I have no idea what the situation there might be, I can't give you specific orders. Besides"—she raised her now-empty hand as though forestalling some speech of mine—"I'd be wasting my time attempting to direct you too closely. You'll do as you like no matter what I say. You're loaded up? Have all the supplies you need?"

The question was perfunctory—she surely knew the status of my ship's stores as well as I did. I made an indefinite gesture, deliberately insolent.

"You might as well take Captain Vel's things," she said, as though I'd answered reasonably. "She won't need them."

Vel Osck had been captain of *Mercy of Kalr* until a week ago. There were any number of reasons she might not need her possessions, the most likely, of course, being that she was dead. Anaander Mianaai didn't do anything halfway, particularly when it came to dealing with her enemies. Of course, in this case, the enemy Vel Osck had supported was Anaander Mianaai herself. "I don't want them," I said. "Send them to her family."

"If I can." She might well not be able to do that. "Is there anything you need before you go? Anything at all?"

Various answers occurred to me. None seemed useful. "No."

"I'll miss you, you know," she said. "No one else will speak to me quite the way you do. You're one of the very few people I've ever met who really, truly didn't fear the consequences of offending me. And none of those very few have the... similarity of background you and I have."

Because I had once been a ship. An AI controlling an enormous troop carrier and thousands of ancillaries, human bodies, part of myself. At the time I had not thought of myself as a slave, but I had been a weapon of conquest, the possession of Anaander Mianaai, herself occupying thousands of bodies spread throughout Radch space.

Now I was only this single human body. "Nothing you can do to me could possibly be worse than what you've already done."

"I am aware of that," she said, "and aware of just how dangerous that makes you. I may well be extremely foolish just letting you live, let alone giving you official authority and a ship. But the games I play aren't for the timid."

"For most of us," I said, openly angry now, knowing she could see the physical signs of it no matter how impassive my expression, "they aren't games."

"I am also aware of that," said the Lord of the Radch. "Truly I am. It's just that some losses are unavoidable."

I could have chosen any of a half dozen responses to that. Instead I turned and walked out of the room without answering. As I stepped through the door, the soldier *Mercy of Kalr* One Kalr Five, who had been standing at stiff attention just outside, fell in behind me, silent and efficient. Kalr Five was human, like all *Mercy of Kalr*'s soldiers, not an ancillary. She had a name, beyond her ship, decade, and number. I had addressed her by that name once. She'd responded with outward impassivity, but with an inner wave of alarm and unease. I hadn't tried it again.

When I had been a ship—when I had been just one component of the troop carrier *Justice of Toren*—I had been always aware of the state of my officers. What they heard and what they saw. Every breath, every twitch of every muscle. Hormone levels, oxygen levels. Everything, nearly, except the specific contents of their thoughts, though even that I could often guess, from experience, from intimate acquaintance. Not something I had ever shown any of my captains—it would have meant little to them, a stream of meaningless data. But for me, at that time, it had been just part of my awareness.

I no longer *was* my ship. But I was still an ancillary, could still read that data as no human captain could have. But I only had a single human brain, now, could only handle the smallest fragment of the information I'd once been constantly, unthinkingly aware of. And even that small amount required some care—I'd run straight into a bulkhead trying to walk and receive data at the same time, when I'd first tried it. I queried *Mercy of Kalr*, deliberately this time. I was fairly sure I could walk through this corridor and monitor Five at the same time without stopping or stumbling.

I made it all the way to the palace's reception area without incident. Five was tired, and slightly hungover. Bored, I was sure, from standing staring at the wall during my conference with the Lord of the Radch. I saw a strange mix of anticipation and dread, which troubled me a bit, because I couldn't guess what that conflict was about.

Out on the main concourse, high, broad, and echoing, stone paved, I turned toward the lifts that would take me to the docks, to the shuttle that waited to take me back to *Mercy of Kalr*. Most shops and offices along the concourse, including the wide, brightly painted gods crowding the temple façade, orange and blue and red and green, seemed surprisingly undamaged after last week's violence, when the Lord of the Radch's struggle against herself had broken into the open. Now citizens in colorful coats, trousers, and gloves, glittering with jewelry, walked by, seemingly unconcerned. Last week might never have happened. Anaander Mianaai, Lord of the Radch, might still be herself, many-bodied but one single, undivided person. But last week *had* happened, and Anaander Mianaai was not, in fact, one person. Had not been for quite some time.

As I approached the lifts a sudden surge of resentment and dismay overtook me. I stopped, turned. Kalr Five had stopped when I stopped, and now stared impassively ahead. As though that wave of resentment Ship had shown me hadn't come from her. I hadn't thought most humans could mask such strong emotions so effectively—her face was absolutely expressionless. But all the Mercy of Kalrs, it had turned out, could do it. Captain Vel had been an old-fashioned sort—or at the very least she'd had idealized notions of what "old-fashioned" meant—and had demanded that her human soldiers conduct themselves as much like ancillaries as possible.

Five didn't know I'd been an ancillary. As far as she knew I was Fleet Captain Breq Mianaai, promoted because of Captain Vel's arrest and what most imagined were my powerful family connections. She couldn't know how much of her I saw. "What is it?" I asked, brusque. Taken aback.

"Sir?" Flat. Expressionless. Wanting, I saw after the tiny signal delay, for me to turn my attention away from her, to leave her safely ignored. Wanting also to speak.

I was right, that resentment, that dismay had been on my account. "You have something to say. Let's hear it."

Surprise. Sheer terror. And not the least twitch of a muscle. "Sir," she said again, and there was, finally, a faint, fleeting expression of some sort, quickly gone. She swallowed. "It's the dishes."

My turn to be surprised. "The dishes?"

"Sir, you sent Captain Vel's things into storage here on the station."

And lovely things they had been. The dishes (and utensils, and tea things) Kalr Five was, presumably, preoccupied with had been porcelain, glass, jeweled and enameled metal. But they hadn't been mine. And I didn't want anything of Captain Vel's. Five expected me to understand her. Wanted so much for me to understand. But I didn't. "Yes?"

Frustration. Anger, even. Clearly, from Five's perspective what she wanted was obvious. But the only part of it that was obvious to me was the fact she couldn't just come out and say it, even when I'd asked her to. "Sir," she said finally, citizens walking around us, some with curious glances, some pretending not to notice us. "I understand we're leaving the system soon."

"Soldier," I said, beginning to be frustrated and angry myself, in no good mood from my talk with the Lord of the Radch. "Are you capable of speaking directly?"

"We can't leave the system with no good dishes!" she blurted finally, face still impressively impassive. "Sir." When I didn't answer, she continued, through another surge of fear at speaking so plainly, "Of course it doesn't matter to *you*. You're a fleet captain, your rank is enough to impress anyone." And my house name—I was now Breq Mianaai. I wasn't too pleased at having been given that particular name, which marked me as a cousin of the Lord of the Radch herself. None of my crew but Seivarden and the ship's medic knew I hadn't been born with it. "*You* could invite a captain to supper and serve her soldier's mess and she wouldn't say a word, sir." Couldn't, unless she outranked me.

"We're not going where we're going so we can hold dinner parties," I said. That apparently confounded her, brief confusion showing for a moment on her face.

"Sir!" she said, voice pleading, in some distress. "*You* don't need to worry what other people think of you. I'm only saying, because you ordered me to."

Of course. I should have seen. Should have realized days ago. She was worried that *she* would look bad if I didn't have dinnerware to match my rank. That it would reflect badly on the ship itself. "You're worried about the reputation of the ship."

Chagrin, but also relief. "Yes, sir."

"I'm not Captain Vel." Captain Vel had cared a great deal about such things.

"*No*, sir." I wasn't sure if the emphasis—and the relief I read in Five—was because my not being Captain Vel was a good thing, or because I had finally understood what she had been trying to tell me. Or both.

I had already cleared my account here, all my money in chits locked in my quarters on board *Mercy of Kalr*. What little I carried on my person wouldn't be sufficient to ease Kalr Five's anxieties. Station—the AI that ran this place, *was* this place—could probably smooth the financial details over for me. But Station resented me as the cause of last week's violence and would not be disposed to assist me.

"Go back to the palace," I said. "Tell the Lord of the Radch what you require." Her eyes widened just slightly, and two tenths of a second later I read disbelief and then frank terror in Kalr Five. "When everything is arranged to your satisfaction, come to the shuttle."

Three citizens passed, bags in gloved hands, the fragment of conversation I heard telling me they were on their way to the docks, to catch a ship to one of the outer stations. A lift door slid open, obligingly. Of course. Station knew where they were going, they didn't have to ask.

Station knew where *I* was going, but it wouldn't open any doors for me without my giving the most explicit of requests. I turned, stepped quickly into the dockbound lift after them, saw the lift door close on Five standing, horrified, on the black stone pavement of the concourse. The lift moved, the three citizens chattered. I closed my eyes and saw Kalr Five staring at the lift, hyperventilating slightly. She frowned just the smallest amount—possibly no one passing her would notice. Her fingers twitched, summoning *Mercy of Kalr*'s attention, though with some trepidation, as though maybe she feared it wouldn't answer.

But of course *Mercy of Kalr* was already paying attention. "Don't worry," said *Mercy of Kalr*, voice serene and neutral in Five's ear and mine. "It's not you Fleet Captain's angry with. Go ahead. It'll be all right."

True enough. It wasn't Kalr Five I was angry with. I pushed away the data coming from her, received a disorienting flash of Seivarden, asleep, dreaming, and Lieutenant Ekalu, still tense, in the middle of asking one of her Etrepas for tea. Opened my eyes. The citizens in the lift with me laughed at something, I didn't know or care what, and as the lift door slid open we walked out into the broad lobby of the docks, lined all around with icons of gods that travelers might find useful or comforting. It was sparsely populated for this time of day, except by the entrance to the dock authority office, where a line of ill-tempered ship captains and pilots waited for their turn to complain to the overburdened inspector adjuncts. Two intersystem gates had been disabled in last week's upheaval, more were likely to be in the near future, and the Lord of the Radch had forbidden any travel in the remaining ones, trapping dozens of ships in the system, with all their cargo and passengers.

They moved aside for me, bowing slightly as though a wind had blown through them. It was the uniform that had done it—I heard one captain whisper to another one, "Who is that?" and the responding murmur as her neighbor replied and others commented on her ignorance or added what they knew. I heard *Mianaai* and *Special Missions*. The sense they'd managed to make out of last week's events. The official version was that I had come to Omaugh Palace undercover, to root out a seditious conspiracy. That I had been working for Anaander Mianaai all along. Anyone who'd ever been part of events that later received an official version would know or suspect that wasn't true. But most Radchaai lived unremarkable lives and would have no reason to doubt it.

No one questioned my walking past the adjuncts, into the outer office of the Inspector Supervisor. Daos Ceit, who was her assistant, was still recovering from injuries. An adjunct I didn't know sat in her place but rose swiftly and bowed as I entered. So did a very, very young lieutenant, more gracefully and collectedly than I expected in a seventeen-year-old, the sort who was still all lanky arms and legs and frivolous enough to spend her first pay on lilac-colored eyes—surely she hadn't been born with eyes that color. Her dark-brown jacket, trousers, gloves, and boots were crisp and spotless, her straight, dark hair cut close. "Fleet Captain. Sir," she said. "Lieutenant Tisarwat, sir." She bowed again.

I didn't answer, only looked at her. If my scrutiny disturbed her, I couldn't see it. She wasn't yet sending data to *Mercy of Kalr*, and her brown skin hadn't darkened in any sort of flush. The small, discreet scatter of pins near one shoulder suggested a family of some substance but not the most elevated in the Radch. She was, I thought, either preternaturally self-possessed or a fool. Neither option pleased me.

"Go on in, sir," said the unfamiliar adjunct, gesturing me toward the inner office. I did, without a word to Lieutenant Tisarwat.

Dark-skinned, amber-eyed, elegant and aristocratic even in the dark-blue uniform of dock authority, Inspector Supervisor Skaaiat Awer rose and bowed as the door shut behind me. "Breq. Are you going, then?"

I opened my mouth to say, *Whenever you authorize our*

departure, but remembered Five and the errand I'd sent her on. "I'm only waiting for Kalr Five. Apparently I can't ship out without an acceptable set of dishes."

Surprise crossed her face, gone in an instant. She had known, of course, that I had sent Captain Vel's things here, and that I didn't own anything to replace them. Once the surprise had gone I saw amusement. "Well," she said. "Wouldn't you have felt the same?" When I had been in Five's place, she meant. When I had been a ship.

"No, I wouldn't have. I didn't. Some other ships did. Do." Mostly *Swords*, who by and large already thought they were above the smaller, less prestigious *Mercies*, or the troop carrier *Justices*.

"My Seven Issas cared about that sort of thing." Skaaiat Awer had served as a lieutenant on a ship with human troops, before she'd become Inspector Supervisor here at Omaugh Palace. Her eyes went to my single piece of jewelry, a small gold tag pinned near my left shoulder. She gestured, a change of topic that wasn't really a change of topic. "Athoek, is it?" My destination hadn't been publicly announced, might, in fact, be considered sensitive information. But Awer was one of the most ancient and wealthy of houses. Skaaiat had cousins who knew people who knew things. "I'm not sure that's where I'd have sent you."

"It's where I'm going."

She accepted that answer, no surprise or offense visible in her expression. "Have a seat. Tea?"

"Thank you, no." Actually I could have used some tea, might under other circumstances have been glad of a relaxed chat with Skaaiat Awer, but I was anxious to be off.

This, too, Inspector Supervisor Skaaiat took with equanimity. She did not sit, herself. "You'll be calling on Basnaaid

Elming when you get to Athoek Station." Not a question. She knew I would be. Basnaaid was the younger sister of someone both Skaaiat and I had once loved. Someone I had, under orders from Anaander Mianaai, killed. "She's like Awn, in some ways, but not in others."

"Stubborn, you said."

"Very proud. And fully as stubborn as her sister. Possibly more so. She was very offended when I offered her clientage for her sister's sake. I mention it because I suspect you're planning to do something similar. And you might be the only person alive even more stubborn than she is."

I raised an eyebrow. "Not even the tyrant?" The word wasn't Radchaai, was from one of the worlds annexed and absorbed by the Radch. By Anaander Mianaai. The tyrant herself, almost the only person on Omaugh Palace who would have recognized or understood the word, besides Skaaiat and myself.

Skaaiat Awer's mouth quirked, sardonic humor. "Possibly. Possibly not. In any event, be very careful about offering Basnaaid money or favors. She won't take it kindly." She gestured, good-natured but resigned, as if to say, *but of course you'll do as you like.* "You'll have met your new baby lieutenant."

Lieutenant Tisarwat, she meant. "Why did she come here and not go directly to the shuttle?"

"She came to apologize to my adjunct." Daos Ceit's replacement, there in the outer office. "Their mothers are cousins." Formally, the word Skaaiat used referred to a relation between two people of different houses who shared a parent or a grandparent, but in casual use meant someone more distantly related who was a friend, or someone you'd grown up with. "They were supposed to meet for tea yesterday, and

Tisarwat never showed or answered any messages. And you know how military gets along with dock authorities." Which was to say, overtly politely and privately contemptuously. "My adjunct took offense."

"Why should Lieutenant Tisarwat care?"

"You never had a mother to be angry you offended her cousin," Skaaiat said, half laughing, "or you wouldn't ask."

True enough. "What do you make of her?"

"Flighty, I would have said a day or two ago. But today she's very subdued." *Flighty* didn't match the collected young person I'd seen in that outer office. Except, perhaps, those impossible eyes. "Until today she was on her way to a desk job in a border system."

"The tyrant sent me a baby *administrator*?"

"I wouldn't have thought she'd send you a baby anything," Skaaiat said. "I'd have thought she'd have wanted to come with you herself. Maybe there's not enough of her left here." She drew breath as though to say more but then frowned, head cocked. "I'm sorry, there's something I have to take care of."

The docks were crowded with ships in need of supplies or repairs or emergency medical assistance, ships that were trapped here in the system, with crews and passengers who were extremely unhappy about the fact. Skaaiat's staff had been working hard for days, with very few breaks. "Of course." I bowed. "I'll get out of your way." She was still listening to whoever had messaged her. I turned to go.

"Breq." I looked back. Skaaiat's head was still cocked slightly, she was still hearing whoever else spoke. "Take care."

"You, too." I walked through the door, to the outer office. Lieutenant Tisarwat stood, still and silent. The adjunct stared ahead, fingers moving, attending to urgent dock business no doubt. "Lieutenant," I said sharply, and didn't wait for a reply but walked out of the office, through the crowd of disgruntled ships' captains, onto the docks where I would find the shuttle that would take me to *Mercy of Kalr.*

The shuttle was too small to generate its own gravity. I was perfectly comfortable in such circumstances, but very young officers often were not. I stationed Lieutenant Tisarwat at the dock, to wait for Kalr Five, and then pushed myself over the awkward, chancy boundary between the gravity of the palace and the weightlessness of the shuttle, kicked myself over to a seat, and strapped myself in. The pilot gave a respectful nod, bowing being difficult in these circumstances. I closed my eyes, saw that Five stood in a large storage room inside the palace proper, plain, utilitarian, gray-walled. Filled with chests and boxes. In one brown-gloved hand she held a teabowl of delicate, deep rose glass. An open box in front of her showed more—a flask, seven more bowls, other dishes. Her pleasure in the beautiful things, her desire, was undercut by doubt. I couldn't read her mind, but I guessed that she had been told to choose from this storeroom, had found these and wanted them very much, but didn't quite believe she would be allowed to take them away. I was fairly sure this set was hand-blown, and some seven hundred years old. I hadn't realized she had a connoisseur's eye for such things.

I pushed the vision away. She would be some time, I thought, and I might as well get some sleep.

I woke three hours later, to lilac-eyed Lieutenant Tisarwat strapping herself deftly into a seat across from me. Kalr Five—now radiating contentment, presumably from the results of her stint in the palace storeroom—pushed herself over to Lieutenant Tisarwat, and with a nod and a quiet *Just in case, sir* proffered a bag for the nearly inevitable moment when the new officer's stomach reacted to microgravity.

I'd known young lieutenants who took such an offer as an insult. Lieutenant Tisarwat accepted it, with a small, vague smile that didn't quite reach the rest of her face. Still seeming entirely calm and collected.

"Lieutenant," I said, as Kalr Five kicked herself forward to strap herself in beside the pilot, another Kalr. "Have you taken any meds?" Another potential insult. Antinausea meds were available, and I'd known excellent, long-serving officers who for the whole length of their careers took them every time they got on a shuttle. None of them ever admitted to it.

The last traces of Lieutenant Tisarwat's smile vanished. "No, sir." Even. Calm.

"Pilot has some, if you need them." That ought to have gotten some kind of reaction.

And it did, though just the barest fraction of a second later than I'd expected. The hint of a frown, an indignant straightening of her shoulders, hampered by her seat restraints. "No, thank you, sir."

Flighty, Skaaiat Awer had said. She didn't usually misread people so badly. "I didn't request your presence, Lieutenant." I kept my voice calm, but with an edge of anger. Easy enough to do under the circumstances. "You're here only because Anaander Mianaai ordered it. I don't have the time or the resources to hand-raise a brand-new baby. You'd better get up to speed *fast*. I need officers who know what they're doing. I need a whole crew I can *depend* on."

"Sir," replied Lieutenant Tisarwat. Still calm, but now some earnestness in her voice, that tiny trace of frown deepening, just a bit. "Yes, sir."

Dosed with *something*. Possibly antinausea, and if I'd been given to gambling I'd have bet my considerable fortune that she was filled to the ears with at least one sedative. I wanted to pull up her personal record—*Mercy of Kalr* would have it by now. But the tyrant would see that I had pulled that record up. *Mercy of Kalr* belonged, ultimately, to Anaander Mianaai, and she had accesses that allowed her to control it. *Mercy of Kalr* saw and heard everything I did, and if the tyrant wanted that information she had only to demand it. And I didn't want her to know what it was I suspected. Wanted, truth be told, for my suspicions to be proven false. Unreasonable.

For now, if the tyrant was watching—and she was surely watching, through *Mercy of Kalr*, would be so long as we were in the system—let her think I resented having a baby foisted on me when I'd rather have someone who knew what they were doing.

I turned my attention away from Lieutenant Tisarwat. Forward, the pilot leaned closer to Five and said, quiet and oblique, "Everything all right?" And then to Five's responding, puzzled frown, "Too quiet."

"All this time?" asked Five. Still oblique. Because they were talking about me and didn't want to trigger any requests I might have made to Ship, to tell me when the crew was talking about me. I had an old habit—some two thousand years old—of singing whatever song ran through my head. Or humming. It had caused the crew some puzzlement and distress at first—this body, the only one left to me, didn't have a particularly good voice. They were getting used to it, though, and now I was dryly amused to see crew members disturbed by my silence.

"Not a peep," said the pilot to Kalr Five. With a brief sideways glance and a tiny twitch of neck and shoulder muscles that told me she'd thought of looking back, toward Lieutenant Tisarwat.

"Yeah," said Five, agreeing, I thought, with the pilot's unstated assessment of what might be troubling me.

Good. Let Anaander Mianaai be watching that, too.

It was a long ride back to *Mercy of Kalr*, but Lieutenant Tisarwat never did use the bag or evince any discomfort. I spent the time sleeping, and thinking.

Ships, communications, data traveled between stars using gates, beacon-marked, held constantly open. The calculations had already been made, the routes marked out through the strangeness of gate space, where distances and proximity didn't match normal space. But military ships—like *Mercy of Kalr*—could generate their own gates. It was a good deal more risky—choose the wrong route, the wrong exit or entrance, and a ship could end up anywhere, or nowhere. That didn't trouble me. *Mercy of Kalr* knew what it was doing, and we would arrive safely at Athoek Station.

And while we moved through gate space in our own, contained bubble of normal space, we would be completely isolated. I wanted that. Wanted to be gone from Omaugh Palace, away from Anaander Mianaai's sight and any orders or interference she might decide to send.

When we were nearly there, minutes away from docking, Ship spoke directly into my ear. "Fleet Captain." It didn't need to speak to me that way, could merely desire me to know it wanted my attention. And it nearly always knew what I wanted without my saying it. I could connect to *Mercy of Kalr* in a way no one else aboard could. I could not, however, *be Mercy of Kalr*, as I had been *Justice of Toren*. Not without losing myself entirely. Permanently.

"Ship," I replied quietly. And without my saying anything else, *Mercy of Kalr* gave me the results of its calculations, made unasked, a whole range of possible routes and departure times flaring into my vision. I chose the soonest, gave orders, and a little more than six hours later we were gone.

2

The tyrant had said our backgrounds were similar, and in some ways they were. She was—and I had been—composed of hundreds of bodies all sharing the same identity. From that angle, we were very much the same. Which some citizens had noted (though only relatively recently, within the last hundred or so years) during arguments about the military's use of ancillaries.

It seemed horrible when one thought of it happening to oneself, or a friend or relative. But the Lord of the Radch herself underwent the same, was arguably in some ways the same sort of being as the ships that served her, so how could it possibly be as bad as detractors claimed? Ridiculous to say that all this time the Radch had been anything less than entirely just.

One of a triad, that word. Justice, propriety, and benefit. No just act could be improper, no proper act unjust. Justice and propriety, so intertwined, themselves led to benefit. The question of just who or what benefited was a topic for late-night discussions over half-empty bottles of arrack, but ordinarily no Radchaai questioned that justice and propriety would ultimately be beneficial in some gods-approved way. Ever, except in the most extraordinary circumstances, questioned that the Radch was anything but just, proper, and beneficial.

Of course, unlike her ships, the Lord of the Radch was a citizen—and not only a citizen but ruler of all the Radch, absolute. I was a weapon she had used to expand that rule. Her servant. In many ways her slave. And the difference went further. Every one of Anaander Mianaai's bodies was identical to all the others, clones, conceived and grown for the express purpose of being parts of her. Each of her thousands of brains had grown and developed around the implants that joined her to herself. For three thousand years she had never at any time experienced being anyone but Anaander Mianaai. Never been a single-bodied person—preferably in late adolescence or early adulthood, but older would do—taken captive, stored in a suspension pod for decades, maybe even centuries, until she was needed. Unceremoniously thawed out, implant shoved into her brain, severing connections, making new ones, destroying the identity she'd had all her life so far and replacing it with a ship's AI.

If you haven't been through it, I don't think you can really imagine it. The terror and nausea, the horror, even after it's done and the body knows it's the ship, that the person it was before doesn't exist anymore to care that she's died. It could last a week, sometimes longer, while the body and its brain adjusted to the new state of affairs. A side effect of the process, one that could possibly have been eliminated, presumably it could have been made a good deal less horrific than it was. But what was one body's temporary discomfort? One body out of dozens, or even hundreds, was nothing, its distress merely a passing inconvenience. If it was too intense or didn't abate in a reasonable amount of time, that body would be removed and destroyed, replaced with a new one. There were plenty in storage.

But now that Anaander Mianaai had declared that no new ancillaries would be made—not counting the prisoners still suspended in the holds of the huge troop carriers, thousands of bodies frozen, waiting—no one need concern themselves with the question at all.

As captain of *Mercy of Kalr*, I had quarters all to myself, three meters by four, lined all around with benches that doubled as storage. One of those benches was also my bed, and inside it, under the boxes and cases that held my possessions, was a box that Ship couldn't see or sense. Human eyes could see it, even when those eyes were part of an ancillary body. But no scanner, no mechanical sensor could see that box, or the gun inside, or its ammunition—bullets that would burn through anything in the universe. How this had been managed was mysterious—not only the inexplicable bullets, but how light coming from the box or the gun might be visible to human eyes but not, say, to cameras, which in the end worked on the same principles. And Ship, for instance, didn't see an empty space where the box was, where something ought to have been, but instead it saw whatever it might have expected would occupy that space. None of it made any sense. Still, it was the case. Box, weapon, and its ammunition had been manufactured by the alien Presger, whose aims were obscure. Whom even Anaander Mianaai feared, lord as she was of the vast reaches of Radch space, commander of its seemingly endless armies.

Mercy of Kalr knew about the box, about the gun, because

I had told it. To the Kalrs who served me, it was just one box among several, none of which they'd opened. Had they really been the ancillaries they sometimes pretended to be, that would have been the end of it. But they were not ancillaries. They were human, and consumingly curious. They still speculated, looked lingeringly, when they stowed the linens and pallet I slept on. If I hadn't been captain—even weightier, fleet captain—they'd have been through every millimeter of my luggage by now, twice and three times, and discussed it all thoroughly among themselves. But I *was* captain, with the power of life and death over my entire crew, and so I was granted this small privacy.

This room had been Captain Vel's, before she'd chosen the wrong side in the Lord of the Radch's battle with herself. The floor covering and the cloths and cushions that had covered the benches were gone, left behind us at Omaugh Palace. She'd had the walls painted with elaborate scrollwork in purples and greens, a style and a palette that she'd taken from a past era, one presumably nobler and more civilized than this one. Unlike Captain Vel, I had lived through it and didn't much regret its loss. I'd have had it removed, but there were other, more urgent concerns, and at least the paint didn't extend any farther than the captain's quarters.

Her gods, which had sat in a niche under the ship's gods—Amaat, of course, chief of Radchaai gods, and Kalr, part of this ship's name—I had replaced with She Who Sprang from the Lily, an EskVar (the Emanation of beginning and ending), and a small, cheap icon of Toren. I had been fortunate to find that. Toren was an old god, not popular, nearly forgotten except by the crews of the ships that bore the name, none of them stationed near here, and one of them—myself—destroyed.

There was room for more gods, there always was. But I

didn't believe in any of them. It would have looked odd to the crew if I'd had none besides the ship's, and these would do. They were not gods to me, but reminders of something else. The crew wouldn't know or understand that, and so I burned incense to them daily, along with Amaat and Kalr, and just like those gods they received offerings of food and enameled brass flowers that had made Five frown when she'd first seen them, because they were cheap and common and not, she thought, what a Mianaai and a fleet captain ought to offer to her gods. She'd said so to Kalr Seventeen, obliquely, not mentioning my name or title. She didn't know I was an ancillary, didn't know how easy it was, because of that, for Ship to show me what she felt, what she said, wherever she said it, whenever I wished. She was confident Ship would keep her gossip secret.

Two days after we gated, on our way to Athoek in our own tiny, isolated fragment of universe, I sat on the edge of my bed drinking tea from a delicate, deep rose glass bowl while Kalr Five cleared away the omens and the cloth from the morning's cast. The omens had indicated continuing good fortune, of course, only the most foolish of captains would find any other sort of pattern in the fall of those metal discs on the cloth.

I closed my eyes. Felt the corridors and rooms of *Mercy of Kalr*, spotless white. The whole ship smelled comfortingly and familiarly of recycled air and cleaning solvent. Amaat decade had scrubbed their portion of those corridors, and the rooms they were responsible for. Their lieutenant, Seivarden, senior of *Mercy of Kalr*'s lieutenants, was just now finishing her inspection of that work, giving out praise and remonstrance, assignments for tomorrow, in her antiquely elegant accent. Seivarden had been born for this work, had been born with a face that marked her as a member of one of the highest houses in the Radch, distant cousins to Anaander Mianaai herself, wealthy and well-bred. She had been raised with the expectation that she would command. She was in many respects the very image of a Radchaai military officer. Speaking with her Amaats, relaxed and assured, she was nearly the Seivarden I'd known a thousand years ago, before she'd lost her ship, been shoved into an escape pod by one of its ancillaries. The tracker on the pod had been damaged, and she had drifted for centuries. After she'd been found, and thawed, and discovered that everyone she'd ever known was dead, even her house no longer existent and the Radch changed from what she'd known, she'd fled Radchaai space and spent several years wandering, dissipated, aimless. Not quite willing to die, I suspected, but hoping in the back of her mind to meet with some fatal accident. She'd gained weight, since I'd found her, built back some of her lost muscle, looked considerably healthier now, but still somewhat the worse for wear. She'd been forty-eight when her ship's ancillaries had pushed her into that escape pod. Count that thousand frozen years and she was the second oldest person aboard *Mercy of Kalr*.

Next in seniority, Lieutenant Ekalu stood watch in Command with two of her Etrepas. It wasn't theoretically necessary for anyone to stand any sort of watch, not with *Mercy of Kalr* always awake, always watching, constantly aware of the ship that was its own body and of the space around it. Especially in gate space, where nothing untoward—or, honestly, even interesting—was likely to happen. But ship systems did sometimes malfunction, and it was a good deal quicker and easier to respond to a crisis if the crew was already alert. And of course dozens of people packed into a small ship required work to keep them disciplined and busy. Ship threw up numbers, maps, graphs in Lieutenant Ekalu's vision, murmured into her ear, information mixed now and then with friendly encouragement. *Mercy of Kalr* liked Lieutenant Ekalu, had confidence in her intelligence and ability.

Kalr was captain's decade, my own. There were ten soldiers in all the other decades on *Mercy of Kalr*, but there were twenty in Kalr. They slept on a staggered schedule, because also unlike the other decades, Kalr was always on duty, a last remnant of the days when Ship had been crewed by ancillary bodies, when its soldiers had been fragments of itself and not dozens of individual human beings. The Kalrs who had awakened just now, as I had, were assembled in the soldiers' mess, white-walled, plain, just big enough for ten to eat and space to stack the dishes. They stood, each by their dish of skel, a fast-growing, slimy, dark-green plant that contained any nutrients a human body needed. The taste took some getting used to if you hadn't grown up on it. A lot of Radchaai had in fact grown up on it.

The Kalrs in the soldiers' mess began the morning prayer in ragged unison. *The flower of justice is peace.* Within a word or two they settled into step, the words falling into familiar rhythm. *The flower of propriety is beauty in thought and action.*

Medic—she had a name, and a nominal rank of lieutenant, but was never addressed by either—was attached to Kalr, but was not Kalr Lieutenant. She was, simply, Medic. She could be—had been, would be in another hour—ordered to stand a watch, and two Kalrs would stand that watch with her. She was the only one of Captain Vel's officers remaining. She would have been difficult to replace, of course, but also her involvement in the previous week's events had been minimal.

She was tall and spare, light-skinned by Radchaai standards, hair enough lighter than brown to be slightly odd, but not the sort of striking shade that might have been artificial. She frowned habitually, though she wasn't ill-tempered. She was seventy-six years old and looked much the same as she had in her thirties, and would until she was past a hundred and fifty. Her mother had been a doctor, and her mother before that, and her mother before that. She was, just now, extremely angry with me.

She'd woken determined to confront me in the short time before she went on watch, had said the morning prayer in a rushed mutter as soon as she'd rolled out of bed. *The flower of benefit is Amaat whole and entire.* I had turned my attention away from Kalr in the soldiers' mess, but I couldn't hear the first lines without hearing the rest. *I am the sword of justice*... Now Medic stood silent and tense by her own seat in the decade room, where the officers ate.

Seivarden came into the decade room for what would be her supper, smiling, relaxed, saw Medic waiting, stiff and impatient, frowning more intensely than usual. For an instant I saw irritation in Seivarden, and then she dismissed it, apologized for her tardiness, got a mumbled, perfunctory *it's nothing* in return.

In the soldiers' mess Kalr finished the morning prayer, mouthed the extra lines I'd ordered, a brief prayer for the dead, and their names. Awn Elming. Nyseme Ptem, the soldier who had mutinied at Ime, preventing a war with the alien Rrrrrr, at the cost of her own life.

Bo decade slept in what was more an alcove than a room, barely large enough for their ten close sleeping bodies, no privacy, no individual space, even in their beds. They twitched, sighed, dreamed, more restless than the ancillaries that had once slept there.

In her own tiny quarters, their lieutenant, the very young,

impossibly lilac-eyed Lieutenant Tisarwat, slept as well, still and dreamless, but with an underlying current of unease, adrenaline just a touch higher than it ought to be. That should have awakened her, as it had the night before, but Medic had given her something to help her sleep.

Medic bolted her breakfast, muttered excuses, and all but stormed out of the decade room. "Ship," she messaged, fingers twitching emphatically, gesturing the words. "I want to speak to the fleet captain."

"Medic's coming," I said to Kalr Five. "We'll offer her tea. But she probably won't take it." Five checked the level of tea in the flask and pulled out another of the rose glass bowls. I suspected I wouldn't see my old enameled set again unless I specifically ordered it.

"Fleet Captain," said *Mercy of Kalr* directly into my ear, and then showed me an Amaat on her way to the soldiers' mess, singing softly to herself, one of those collections of inconsequential nonsense children from nearly anywhere sing. "It all goes around, it all goes around, the planet goes around the sun, it all goes around. It all goes around, the moon goes around the planet..." Thoughtless and off-key.

In my quarters Kalr Five stood stiffly at attention, said in an expressionless voice, "Medic requests permission to speak with you, Fleet Captain."

In the corridor, the Amaat, hearing the step of another Amaat behind her, fell silent, suddenly self-conscious. "Granted," I said to Five, needlessly of course, she already knew I planned to speak with Medic.

The door opened and Medic entered, a bit more abruptly than was strictly proper. "Fleet Captain," she began, tight and furious.

I raised a forestalling hand. "Medic. Sit. Will you have tea?"

She sat. Refused tea. Kalr Five left the room at my order, just the tiniest bit resentful at missing whatever Medic had to say, which showed every sign of being something interesting. When she was gone, I gestured to Medic, sitting tense across the table from me. *Go ahead.*

"Begging the fleet captain's indulgence." She didn't sound at all as though she cared whether I'd give it or not. Under the table, she clenched her gloved hands into fists. "Fleet Captain. Sir. You've removed some medications from Medical."

"I have."

That stopped her momentum, briefly. She had, it seemed, expected a denial. "No one else could have done it. Ship insisted they'd never left inventory, and I've looked at the logs, at the recordings themselves, I've been all through them, and there's no record of anyone taking them. There's nobody else on board who could hide that from me."

I feared that was no longer true. But I didn't say that. "Lieutenant Tisarwat came to you yesterday at the end of her shift and asked you for help with some minor nausea and anxiety." Two days ago, some hours after we'd gated, Lieutenant Tisarwat had begun to feel stressed. Slightly sick. Had found herself unable to eat much of her supper that evening. Her Bos had noticed, of course with concern—the problem with most seventeen-year-olds was feeding them enough, not tempting them to eat. They had decided, among themselves, that she was homesick. And distressed by my obvious anger at her presence. "Are you worried for her health?"

Medic nearly started up out of her seat in indignation. "That's not the point!" Recollected whom she was speaking to. "Sir." Swallowed, waited, but I said nothing. "She's nervous. She reads as under some emotional stress. Perfectly understandable. Perfectly normal for a baby lieutenant on her first assignment." Realized, as she was speaking, that I probably had extensive experience of what was normal for very young lieutenants on their first assignments. Regretted speaking, regretted, momentarily, coming here to confront, to accuse me. Just for an instant.

"Perfectly normal under the circumstances," I agreed, but I meant something different.

"And I couldn't help her because you'd taken every single med I might have given her."

"Yes," I acknowledged. "I had. Was there anything in her system when she arrived?" I already knew what the answer would be, but I asked anyway.

Medic blinked, surprised by my question, but only for an instant. "She *did* look as though maybe she'd taken something, when she came to Medical from the shuttle. But there was nothing when I scanned her. I think she was just tired." A tiny shift in her posture, a change in the emotions I read coming from her, suggested she was considering, now, the significance of my question, the odd, small mismatch of how Lieutenant Tisarwat had looked, to her professional eye, and what the readings had said.

"Any recommendations or orders to dispense medication, in her file?"

"No, nothing." Medic didn't seem to have come to any conclusion. Much less the one I'd come to. But she was curious now, if still angry along with it. "Recent events have been stressful for all of us. And she's very young. And..." She hesitated. Had, perhaps, been about to say that by now everyone on board knew I'd been very angry when Lieutenant Tisarwat had been assigned to *Mercy of Kalr.* Angry enough to stop singing for several hours.

By now the whole crew knew what that meant. Had begun, even, to find it comforting to have such an obvious way to know if everything was as it should be. "You were going to say?" I asked, my expression and voice as noncommittal as I could make them.

"I think she feels like you don't want her here, sir."

"I don't," I said. "As it happens."

Medic shook her head, not understanding. "Begging the fleet captain's indulgence. You might have refused to take her."

I might have refused to take her. Might have left her on the palace docks, when *Mercy of Kalr*'s shuttle left, and never come back for her. I had seriously considered doing that. Skaaiat would have understood, I was sure, would have contrived to discover that not a single docked ship could fetch the young lieutenant out to *Mercy of Kalr* until it was too late. "You gave her something?"

"Something to help her sleep. It was the end of the day for her. It was all I could do." That galled Medic, not only that I had interfered in her domain, but that she had been unable to help.

I couldn't help a quick, momentary look. Lieutenant Tisarwat, asleep but not deeply. Not restfully. Still tense, still that quiet background of unease. "Medic," I said, returning my attention to where I was, "you have every right to be angry with me. I expected you to be angry, and expected you to protest. I would have been disappointed if you hadn't." She blinked, puzzled, hands still clenched in her lap. "Trust me." There wasn't much more I could say, just yet. "I am an unknown quantity, I am...not the sort of person who's generally given command." A flicker of recognition on Medic's face, slight revulsion and then embarrassment at having felt that, where she knew I could see it, knew I was almost certainly watching her response. Medic had repaired my implants, which I had deactivated and damaged, to hide them. Medic knew what I was, as no one else aboard but Seivarden knew. "But *trust* me."

"I don't have a choice, do I, sir? We're cut off until we reach Athoek, there's no one I can complain to." Frustrated.

"Complain at Athoek when we get there. If you still want to." If there was anyone there to complain to, that would do any good.

"Sir." She rose, bit back whatever else she'd wanted to say. Bowed stiffly. "May I go?"

"Yes, of course, Medic."

Lieutenant Tisarwat was a problem. Her official personal history, a dry recitation of facts, said she'd been born and raised on a planet, the third child of one parent and the second of another. She'd had the sort of education any well-off, moderately well-born Radchaai had. Done well at math, had an enthusiasm but no gift for poetry, lacked both for history. She had an allowance from her parents but no expectations to speak of. She'd gone into space for the first time when she'd left for training.

Reading between the lines, she had been born not to take some particular place in her house, or inherit anyone's wealth and position, or fulfill any particular expectations, but for her own sake, and no doubt her parents had loved her and cosseted her right up to the day she'd left for the military. Her correspondence with her parents confirmed this. Her siblings, all older, seemed not to resent her position as favorite, but took it in stride and petted her nearly as much as their parents did.

Flighty, Skaaiat Awer had said of her. *Frivolous* I had thought on seeing the certainly purchased color of her eyes, and the aptitudes data in her file suggested the same. That data did not suggest *self-possessed*. Nor did it suggest the nervous gloom she'd displayed since shortly after boarding *Mercy of Kalr*.

Her trainers had met her sort before, been hard on her on account of that, but not cruelly so. Some of them no doubt had baby sisters of their own, and after all she was destined for an administrative post. It hardly mattered if in microgravity she could never keep her supper down—plenty of other new lieutenants had the same problem, particularly if they had little experience in space.

Two days before, while Tisarwat had sat being examined in Medical, while Ship made the connections that would let it—and me—read her like it could every other member of the crew, her Bos had gone over every millimeter of her luggage and come to fairly accurate conclusions about her history. They were prepared to be disgusted with her ignorance, a baby fresh from training, a matter for mocking and exasperation, yes. But also for sympathy, and some anticipatory pride. Her Bos would be able to claim credit for any of Tisarwat's future accomplishments, because after all they would have raised her. Taught her anything she knew that was really important. They were prepared to be *hers*. Wanted very much for her to turn out to be the sort of lieutenant they would be proud to serve under.

I so very much wanted my suspicions not to be true.

Watch was, of course, uneventful. Medic went from our conference to Command, still angry. Seivarden's Amaats were exercising, bathing, would soon be climbing into their own beds, settling into their accustomed places with shoves and the occasional indignant whisper—there wasn't much room to stretch out. Ekalu's Etrepas scrubbed the already near-spotless rooms and corridors they were responsible for. Lieutenant Tisarwat wouldn't wake for nearly four hours.

I went to the ship's small gym, a few last Amaats scurrying out of my way. Worked out, hard, for an hour. Went, still angry, still sweaty from exercise, to the firing range.

It was all simulation. No one wanted bullets flying on a small ship, not with hard vacuum outside the hull. The targets were images Ship cast on the far wall. The weapon would bang and recoil as though it had fired real bullets, but it shot only light. Not as destructive as I wanted to be, that very moment, but it would have to do.

Ship knew my mood. It threw up a quick succession of targets, all of which I hit, nearly unthinking. Reloaded—no need to reload, really, but there would be if this had been a real weapon, and so the training routines demanded it. Fired again and again, reloaded again, fired. It wasn't enough. Seeing that, Ship set the targets moving, a dozen of them at a time. I settled into a familiar rhythm, fire, reload, fire, reload. A song came into my mind—there was always a song, with me. This one was a long narrative, an account of the final dispute between Anaander Mianaai and her erstwhile friend, Naskaaia Eskur. The poet had been executed fifteen hundred years ago—her version of the event had cast Anaander as the villain and ended with the promise that the dead Naskaaia would return to revenge herself. It had been almost utterly forgotten inside Radch space, because singing it, possibly even knowing it existed, could easily cost a citizen a thorough reeducation. It still circulated some places outside Radch influence.

Betrayer! Long ago we promised
To exchange equally, gift for gift.
Take this curse: What you destroy will destroy you.

Fire, reload. Fire, reload. Doubtless little of the song—or any other on the same subject—had any basis in fact. Doubtless the event itself had been quite mundane, not so poetically dramatic, ringing with mythic and prophetic overtones. It was still satisfying to sing it.

I came to the end, lowered my weapon. Unbidden, Ship showed me what was behind my back—three Etrepas crowding the entrance to the firing range, watching, astonished. Seivarden, on her way to her own quarters and bed, standing behind them. She could not read my mood as closely as Ship could, but she knew me well enough to be worried.

"Ninety-seven percent," said Ship, in my ear. Needlessly.

I took a breath. Stowed the weapon in its niche. Turned. The expressions of the three Etrepas turned instantly from astonishment to blank, ancillary-like expressionlessness, and they stepped back into the corridor. I brushed past them, out into the corridor and away, toward the bath. Heard one Etrepa say, "Fuck! Is *that* what Special Missions is like?" Saw the panic of the others—their last captain had been very strict about swearing. Heard Seivarden, outwardly jovial, say, "Fleet Captain *is* pretty fucking badass." The vulgarity, combined with Seivarden's archaic, elegant accent, set them laughing, relieved but still unsettled.

Mercy of Kalr didn't ask me why I was angry. Didn't ask me what was wrong. That in and of itself suggested my suspicions were correct. I wished, for the first time in my two-thousand-year life, that I was given to swearing.

3

I had Lieutenant Tisarwat awakened three hours before her usual time and ordered her to report immediately to me. She startled awake, heart racing even through the last remnants of the drug Medic had given her. It took her a few seconds to comprehend Ship's words, spoken directly into her ear. She spent twenty more seconds just breathing, slowly, deliberately. Feeling vaguely sick.

She arrived at my quarters still unsettled. The collar of her jacket was slightly askew—none of her Bos were awake to see to her, and she had dressed in nervous haste, dropping things, fumbling at fastenings that should have been simple. I met her standing, and I didn't dismiss Kalr Five, who lingered, ostensibly busy but hoping to see or hear something interesting.

"Lieutenant Tisarwat," I said, stern and angry. "Your decade's work these past two days has been inadequate."

Resentment, anger, chagrin. She had already presented herself at creditable attention, considering, but I could see her back, her shoulders stiffen further, see her head come up a couple of millimeters. But she was wise enough not to answer.

I continued. "You may be aware that there are parts of itself Ship can't see. It used to rely on ancillaries for that. Ship doesn't have ancillaries anymore. The cleaning and maintenance of those parts of itself are *your* responsibility. And Bo decade has been skipping them. For instance, the hinge pins on the shuttles' air locks haven't been cleaned in quite some time." That I knew from very personal experience, just last week, when my life, and the lives of everyone on Omaugh Palace, had hung on, among other things, how quickly I could unfasten part of a *Mercy of Kalr* shuttle's air lock. "There's also a place under the grate in the bath that you can't see unless you put your head down in there." That was a disgusting proposition at the best of times. Worse when it hadn't been routinely, thoroughly cleaned. "*Mercy of Kalr* will give you the list. I expect everything to be taken care of when I inspect this time tomorrow."

"T-tomorrow, sir?" Lieutenant Tisarwat sounded just the slightest bit strangled.

"This time tomorrow, Lieutenant. And neither you nor your decade is to neglect assigned time in the gym or the firing range. Dismissed." She bowed, left, angry and unhappy. As her Bos would be, when they discovered how much work I'd just loaded on them.

It was true that I had near-absolute power over everyone on the ship, especially given our isolation in gate space. But it was also true that I would be extremely foolish to alienate my officers. Foolish, also, to so completely court the displeasure of the soldiers without a good reason. Bo would resent my mistreatment of Lieutenant Tisarwat, certainly to the extent that it meant inconvenience to themselves. But also because Lieutenant Tisarwat was *their* lieutenant.

I wanted that. Was pushing hard on that, deliberately.

But timing was everything. Push too hard, too fast, and the results would not be what I wanted, possibly disastrously so. Push too gently, take too long, and I would run out of time, and again results would not be what I wanted. And I needed those specific results. Amaat, Etrepa, my own Kalrs, they understood Bo's position. And if I was going to be hard on Bo—because being hard on Bo's lieutenant was the same thing—it would have to be for a reason the other decades could understand. I didn't want anyone on *Mercy of Kalr* to think that I was dispensing harsh treatment inexplicably, capriciously, that no matter how good you were the captain might decide to make your life hell. I'd seen captains who ran things that way. It never made for a particularly good crew.

But I couldn't possibly explain my reasons to anyone, not now, and I hoped I would never be able to. Never have to. But I had hoped, from the beginning, that this situation would not arise at all.

Next morning I invited Seivarden to breakfast. My breakfast, her supper. I ought also to have invited Medic, who ate at the same time, but I thought she would be happier eating alone than with me, just now.

Seivarden was wary. Wanting, I saw, to say something to me but not sure of the wisdom of saying it. Or perhaps not sure of how to say it wisely. She ate three bites of fish, and then said, jokingly, "I didn't think I rated the best dishes." She meant the plates, delicate, violet and aqua painted porcelain. And the rose glass teabowls—Five knew my eating with Seivarden didn't call for any sort of formality, and still she hadn't been able to bring herself to stow them away and use the enamel.

"*Second* best," I said. "Sorry. I haven't seen the best, yet."

A happy little spike of pride, from Five, standing in the corner pretending to wipe a spotless utensil, just at the thought of the best dishes. "I was told I needed nice dishes so I had the Lord of the Radch send me something suitable."

She raised an eyebrow, knowing Anaander Mianaai was not a neutral topic for me. "I'm surprised the Lord of the Radch didn't come along with us. Though..." She glanced, for just an instant, at Five.

Without my saying anything, merely from seeing my desire, Ship suggested to Kalr Five that she leave the room. When we were alone, Seivarden continued. "She has accesses. She can make Ship do anything she wants. She can make *you* do anything she wants. Can't she?"

Dangerous territory. But Seivarden had no way of knowing that. For a moment I saw Lieutenant Tisarwat, still stressed and sick, and exhausted besides—she hadn't slept since I'd wakened her some twenty hours before—lying on the bath floor, grate pulled aside, her head ducked down to examine that spot Ship couldn't see. An anxious and equally tired Bo behind her, waiting for her verdict.

"It's not quite that simple," I said, returning my attention to Seivarden. I made myself take a bite of fish, a drink of tea. "There's certainly one remaining access, from before." From when I'd been a ship. Been part of *Justice of Toren*'s Esk decade. "Only the tyrant's voice will work that one, though. And yes, she could have used it before I left the palace. She said as much to me, you may recall, and said she didn't want to."

"Maybe she used it and told you not to remember she used it."

I had already considered that possibility, and dismissed it. I gestured, *no*. "There's a point where accesses break."

Seivarden gestured acknowledgment. When I had first met her, a baby lieutenant of seventeen, she hadn't thought ships' AIs had any feelings in particular—not any that mattered. And like many Radchaai she assumed that thought and emotion were two easily separable things. That the artificial intelligences that ran large stations, and military ships, were supremely dispassionate. Mechanical. Old stories, historical dramas about events before Anaander Mianaai set about building her empire, about ships overwhelmed by grief and despair at the deaths of their captains—that was the past. The Lord of the Radch had improved AI design, removed that flaw.

She had learned otherwise, recently. "At Athoek," she guessed, "with Lieutenant Awn's sister there, you'd be too near that breaking point."

It was more complicated than that. But. "Basically."

"Breq," she said. Signaling, maybe, that she wanted to be sure she was speaking to me-as-Breq and not me-as-Fleet-Captain. "There's something I don't understand. The Lord of the Radch said, that day, that she couldn't just make AIs so they always obeyed her no matter what because their minds were complicated."

"Yes." She had said that. At a time when other, more urgent matters pressed, so there could be no real discussion of it.

"But Ships do love people. I mean, particular people." For some reason saying that made her nervous, triggered a tiny spike of apprehension in her. To cover it, she picked up her tea, drank. Set down the lovely deep rose bowl, carefully. "And that's a breaking point, isn't it? I mean, it can be. Why not just make all the ships love *her*?"

"Because that's potentially a breaking point." She looked at me, frowning, not understanding. "Do you love randomly?"

She blinked in bewilderment. "What?"

"Do you love at random? Like pulling counters out of a box? You love whichever one came to hand? Or is there something about certain people that makes them likely to be loved by you?"

"I... think I see." She set down her utensil, the untasted bit of fish it held. "I guess I see what you mean. But I'm not sure what that has to do with..."

"If there's something about a certain person that makes it likely you'd love them, what happens if that changes? And they're not really that person anymore?"

"I guess," she said, slowly, thoughtfully, "I assume that real love doesn't break for anything." *Real love*, to a Radchaai, wasn't only romantic, between lovers. Wasn't only between parent and child. *Real love* could also exist between patron and client. Was supposed to, ideally. "I mean," Seivarden continued, inexplicably embarrassed, "imagine your parents not loving you anymore." Another frown. Another surge of apprehension. "Would you ever have stopped loving Lieutenant Awn?"

"If," I replied, after a deliberate bite and swallow of breakfast, "she had ever become someone other than who she was." Still incomprehension from Seivarden. "Who is Anaander Mianaai?"

She understood, then, I could tell by the feeling of unease I read in her. "Even she's not sure, is she. She might be two people. Or more."

"And over three thousand years she'll have changed. Everyone does, who isn't dead. How much can a person change and still be the same? And how could she predict how much she might change over thousands of years, and what might break as a result? It's much easier to use something else. Duty, say. Loyalty to an idea."

"Justice," said Seivarden, aware of the irony, of what used to be my own name. "Propriety. Benefit."

That last, benefit, was the slippery one. "Any or all of them will do," I agreed. "And then you keep track of ships' favorites so you don't provoke any sort of conflict. Or so you can use those attachments to your advantage."

"I see," she said. And applied herself silently to the rest of her supper.

When the food was eaten, and Kalr Five had returned and cleared the dishes and poured us more tea, and left again, Seivarden spoke again. "Sir," she said. Ship's business, then. I knew what it would be. The soldiers of Amaat and Etrepa had already seen Bo, up well past their sleep time, all ten of them scrubbing desperately, taking fittings apart, lifting grates, poring over every millimeter, every crack and crevice, of their part of Ship's maintenance. When Lieutenant Ekalu had relieved Seivarden on watch she'd stopped, dared a few words. *Don't mean to offend…Thought you might mention to Sir…*Seivarden had been confused, partly by Lieutenant Ekalu's accent, partly by the use of *Sir* instead of *the fleet captain*, the remnant of Ekalu's days as Amaat One, the habit this crew had of speaking so as not to attract the captain's notice. But mostly, it turned out, confused by the suggestion she might be offended. Ekalu was too embarrassed to explain herself. "Do you think, maybe," Seivarden said to me, doubtless knowing I might well have overheard that exchange, in Command, "you're being a little hard on Tisarwat?" I said nothing, and she saw, clearly, that I was in a dangerous mood, that this topic was for some reason not an entirely safe one. She took a breath, and forged on ahead. "You're angry lately."

I raised an eyebrow. "Lately?" My own bowl of tea sat untouched in front of me.

She lifted her tea a centimeter, acknowledging. "You were less angry for a few days. I don't know, maybe because you were injured. Because now you're angry again. And I suppose I know why, and I suppose I can't really blame you, but..."

"You think I'm taking it out on Lieutenant Tisarwat." Who I did not want to see just now. I would not look. Two of her Bos were going meticulously over the interior of the shuttle they were responsible for—one of only two, I'd destroyed the third last week. They commented now and then, obliquely and tersely, on the unfairness of my treatment of them, and how hard I was being on their lieutenant.

"*You* know all the places a soldier can slack off, but how could Tisarwat?"

"She is, nonetheless, responsible for her decade."

"You could have reprimanded me as well," Seivarden pointed out, and took another drink of her tea. "I ought to have known, myself, and didn't. My ancillaries always took care of those things without my asking. Because they knew they ought to. Aatr's tits, *Ekalu* should know better than any of us where the crew is skipping over things. Not meaning to criticize her, understand. But either one of us would have deserved a dressing-down over that. Why give it to Tisarwat and not either of us?" I didn't want to explain that and so didn't say anything, only picked up my own tea and took a drink. "I'll admit," Seivarden continued, "that she's turning out to be a miserable specimen. All awkward not knowing what to do with her hands and feet, picking at her food. And clumsy. She's dropped three of the decade room teabowls, broken two of them. And she's so... so *moody*. I'm waiting for her to announce that none of us understands her. What was my lord thinking?" She meant Anaander Mianaai, the Lord of the Radch. "Was Tisarwat just all that was available?"

"Probably." Thinking that only made me angrier than I already was. "Do you remember when you were a baby lieutenant?"

She set her tea on the table, appalled. "Please tell me I wasn't like *that*."

"No. Not like that. You were awkward and annoying in a different way."

She snorted, amused and chagrined at the same time. "Still." Turning serious. Nervous, suddenly, having come to something, I saw, that she'd wanted to say all through the meal, but the thought of saying it intimidated her more even than the thought of accusing me of treating Lieutenant Tisarwat unjustly. "Breq, the whole crew thinks I'm kneeling to you."

"Yes." I had already known that, of course. "Though I'm not sure why. Five knows well enough you've never been in my bed."

"Well. The general feeling is that I've been remiss in my... my duties. It was all very well to give you time to recover from your injuries, but it's past time for me to... try to relieve whatever is troubling you. And maybe they're right." She took another mouthful of tea. Swallowed. "You're *looking* at me. That's never good."

"I'm sorry to have embarrassed you."

"Oh, I'm not embarrassed," she lied. And then added, more truthfully, "Well, not embarrassed that anyone thinks it. But bringing it up like this. Breq, you found me, what, a year ago? And in all that time I've never known you to... and, I mean, when you were..." She stopped. Afraid of saying the wrong thing, I thought. Her skin was too dark to really show a flush, but I could see the temperature change. "I mean, I know you were an ancillary. *Are* an ancillary. And ships don't... I mean, I know ancillaries can..."

"Ancillaries can," I agreed. "As you know from personal experience."

"Yes," she said. Truly abashed now. "But I guess I never thought that an ancillary might actually *want* it."

I let that hang for a moment, for her to think about. Then, "Ancillaries are human bodies, but they're also part of the ship. What the ancillaries feel, the ship feels. Because they're the same. Well, different bodies are different. Things taste different or feel different, they don't always want the same things, but all together, on the average, yes, it's a thing I attended to, for the bodies that needed it. I don't like being uncomfortable, no one does. I did what I could to make my ancillaries comfortable."

"I guess I never noticed."

"You weren't really supposed to." Best to get this over with. "In any event, ships don't generally want partners. They do that sort of thing for themselves. Ships with ancillaries, anyway. So." I gestured the obviousness of my conclusion, beyond any need to say it explicitly. Didn't add that ships didn't yearn for romantic partners, either. For captains, yes. For lieutenants. But not for lovers.

"Well," Seivarden said after a moment, "but you don't have other bodies to do that with, not anymore." She stopped, struck by a thought. "What must that have been like? With more than one body?"

I wasn't going to answer that. "I'm a little surprised you haven't thought of that before." But only a little. I knew Seivarden too well to think she'd ever dwelt long on what her ship might think or feel. And she'd never been one of those officers who'd been inconveniently fixated on the idea of ancillaries and sex.

"So when they take the ancillaries away," Seivarden said

after a few appalled moments, "it must be like having parts of your body cut off. And never replaced."

I could have said, *Ask Ship*. But Ship probably wouldn't have wanted to answer. "I'm told it's something like that," I said. Voice bland.

"Breq," Seivarden said, "when I was a lieutenant, before." A thousand years ago, she meant, when she'd been a lieutenant on *Justice of Toren*, in my care. "Did I ever pay any attention to anyone but myself?"

I considered, a moment, the range of truthful answers I could make, some less diplomatic than others, and said, finally, "Occasionally."

Unbidden, *Mercy of Kalr* showed me the soldiers' mess, where Seivarden's Amaats were clearing away their own supper. Amaat One said, "It's orders, citizens. Lieutenant says."

A few Amaats groaned. "I'll have it in my head all night," one complained to her neighbor.

In my own quarters, Seivarden said, penitent, "I hope I'm doing better these days."

In the mess, Amaat One opened her mouth and sang, tentative, slightly flat, "It all goes around..." The others joined her, unwilling, unenthusiastic. Embarrassed. "...it all goes around. The planet goes around the sun, it all goes around."

"Yes," I said to Seivarden. "A *little* better."

Bo had done a creditable job finishing all their tasks. The entire decade stood lined up in the mess, not a muscle twitching, every collar and cuff ruler-straight, even Lieutenant Tisarwat managing an outward severe impassivity. Inward was another matter—still that buzz of tension, that slightly sick feeling, steady since the morning before, and she hadn't slept since I'd awakened her yesterday. Her Bos gave off a wave of collective resentment coupled with defiant pride—they had, after all, managed quite a lot in the last day, managed it fairly well, considering. By rights I ought to indicate my satisfaction, they were waiting for me to do that, all of them certain of it, and prepared to feel ill-used if I didn't.

They deserved to be proud of themselves. Lieutenant Tisarwat, as things stood now, didn't deserve them. "Well done, Bo," I said, and was rewarded with a surge of exhausted pride and relief from every soldier in front of me. "See it stays this way." Then, sharply, "Lieutenant, with me." And turned and walked out of the mess to my quarters. Said, silently, to Ship, "Tell Kalr I want privacy." Not thinking too directly why that was, or I would be angry again. Or angrier. Even the desire to move sent impulses to muscles, tiny movements that Ship could read. That *I* could read, when Ship showed them to me. In theory no one else on *Mercy of Kalr* could receive that data the way I could. In theory. But I wouldn't think about that. I walked into my quarters, door opening without my asking. The Kalr on duty there bowed, left, ducking around Lieutenant Tisarwat where she had stopped just inside the entrance.

"Come in, Lieutenant," I said, voice calm. No edge to it. I was angry, yes, but I was always angry, that was normal. Nothing to give anyone any alarm, who could see it. Lieutenant Tisarwat came farther into the room. "Did you get any sleep at all?" I asked her.

"Some, sir." Surprised. She was too tired to think entirely clearly. And still feeling sick and unhappy. Adrenaline levels still higher than normal. Good.

And not good. Not good at all. Terrible. "Eat much?"

"I h..." She blinked. Had to think about my question. "I haven't had much time, sir." She breathed, a trifle more easily than the moment before. Muscles in her shoulders relaxed, just the tiniest bit.

Without thinking of what I was doing, I moved as quickly as I possibly could—which was extremely quickly. Grabbed her by the collars of her jacket, shoved her backward, hard, slammed her into the green and purple wall a meter behind her. Pinned her there, bent awkwardly backward over the bench.

Saw what I had been looking for. Just for an instant. For the smallest moment Lieutenant Tisarwat's general unhappiness became utter, horrified terror. Adrenaline and cortisol spiked unbelievably. And there, in her head, a brief flash, nearly a ghost, of implants that shouldn't be there, weren't there an instant later.

Ancillary implants.

Again I slammed her head against the wall. She gave a small cry, and I saw it again, her sickening horror, those implants that no human ought to have threading through her brain, and then gone again. "Let go of *Mercy of Kalr* or I'll strangle you right here with my own hands."

"You wouldn't," she gasped.

That told me she wasn't thinking straight. In her right mind, Anaander Mianaai would never have doubted, not for an instant, what I might do. I shifted my grip. She started to slide down the wall, toward the bench, but I grabbed her around the throat and put pressure on her trachea. She caught hold of my wrists, desperate. Unable to breathe. Ten seconds, more or less, to do what I told her to do, or die. "Let go of my ship." My voice calm. Even.

The data coming from her flared again, ancillary implants sharp and clear, her own excruciating nausea and terror strong enough almost to make me double over in sympathetic horror. I let go of her, stood straight, and watched her collapse, coughing, gasping, onto the hard, uncushioned bench and then choking, heaving, try to throw up the nothing that was in her stomach.

"Ship," I said.

"She's canceled all orders," said *Mercy of Kalr*, directly into my ear. "I'm sorry, Captain."

"You couldn't help it." All Radchaai military ships were built with accesses that let Anaander Mianaai control them. *Mercy of Kalr* was no exception. I was fortunate the ship didn't have any enthusiasm for following the orders the Lord of the Radch had been giving it, hadn't made any effort to correct any lapses or small errors. If Ship had truly wanted to help Anaander Mianaai deceive me, it would certainly have succeeded. "Anaander Mianaai, Lord of the Radch," I said, to the baby lieutenant trembling, heaving, on the bench in front of me. "Did you think that I wouldn't know?"

"Always a risk," she whispered, and wiped her mouth on her sleeve.

"You're not used to taking risks you don't have decades—centuries—to prepare for," I said. I had dropped all pretense of human expression, spoke in my flat ancillary's voice. "All the parts of you have been part of you since birth. Probably before. You've never been one person and then suddenly had ancillary tech shoved into your brain. It isn't pleasant, is it?"

"I knew it wasn't." She had, now, better control of her breathing, had stopped throwing up. But she spoke in a hoarse whisper.

"You *knew* it wasn't. And you thought you'd have access to meds to keep you going until you got used to it. You could take them right out of Medical yourself and use your accesses to make *Mercy of Kalr* cover your tracks."

"You outmaneuvered me," she said, still miserable, still looking down at the now-fouled bench. "I admit it."

"You outmaneuvered yourself. You didn't have a standard set of ancillary implants." It hadn't been legal to make ancillaries for nearly a hundred years. Not counting bodies already stocked and waiting in suspension, and those were nearly all on troop carriers. None of which had been anywhere near Omaugh Palace. "You had to alter the equipment you used for yourself. And meddling with a human brain, it's a delicate thing. It wouldn't have been a problem if it had been your own, you know *that* brain front to back, if it was one of your own bodies you'd have had no problems. But it couldn't be one of your own bodies, that was the whole *point*, you don't have any to spare these days, and besides I'd have shoved you out the air lock as soon as we gated if you'd tried it. So it had to be somebody *else's* body. But your tech, it's custom-made for *your brain*. And you didn't have time to test anything. You had a week. If that. What, did you grab the child, shove the hardware in her, and throw her onto the docks?" Tisarwat had missed tea with her mother's cousin, that day, not answered messages. "Even with the right hardware, and a medic who knows what she's doing, it doesn't always work. Surely you know that."

She knew that. "What are you going to do now?"

I ignored the question. "You thought you could just order *Mercy of Kalr* to give me false readings, and Medic as well, to cover up anything that needed covering. You'd still need meds, that was obvious the moment the hardware went in, but you couldn't pack them because Bo would have found them immediately and I'd have wondered why you needed those particular drugs." And then, when she couldn't get them, her misery was so intense that she couldn't completely hide it—she could only order Ship to make it appear to be much less than it actually was. "But I already knew what lengths you were willing to go to, to achieve your ends, and I had days just lying here in my quarters, recovering from my injuries and imagining what you might try." And what I might be able to do to circumvent it, undetected. "I *never* believed you'd give me a ship and let me fly off unsupervised."

"*You* did it without meds. You never used them."

I went to the bench that served as my bed, pulled aside the linens, opened the compartment underneath. Inside was that box that human eyes could see but no ship or station could, not unless it had ancillary eyes to look with. I opened the box, pulled out the packet of meds I'd taken from Medical, days before that last conference with Anaander Mianaai on Omaugh Palace. Before I'd met Lieutenant Tisarwat in Inspector Supervisor Skaaiat's office, or even known she'd existed. "We're going to Medical." And silently, to *Mercy of Kalr*, "Send two Kalrs."

Hope flared in Anaander Mianaai, once Lieutenant Tisarwat, triggered by my words, and by the sight of that packet of medicine in my gloved hand, along with an overwhelming wish to be free of her misery. Tears ran from her ridiculously lilac eyes, and she gave a very tiny whimper, quickly suppressed. "How did you stand this?" she asked. "How did you survive it?"

There was no point in answering. It was an exclamation more than a real question, she didn't really care about the answer. "Stand up." The door opened, and two of my Kalrs came in, astonished and dismayed to see Lieutenant Tisarwat battered, collapsed on the bench, bile all down the sleeve of her uniform jacket.

We walked to Medical, a sad little procession, Tisarwat

(not Tisarwat) leaning on one Kalr, followed by the other. Medic stood frozen, watching us enter. Appalled, having seen what was in the lieutenant's head the moment Ship had stopped interfering with her data, with Medic's specialized implants. She turned to me to speak. "Wait," I said to her curtly, and then, once the Kalrs had helped Tisarwat (not Tisarwat) onto a table, sent them away.

Before Medic could say anything, before Anaander could realize and protest, I triggered the table's restraints. She was startled but too miserable to realize right away what that meant. "Medic," I said. "You see that Lieutenant Tisarwat has some unauthorized implants." Medic was too horrified to speak. "Remove them."

"No, don't!" Anaander Mianaai tried to shout but couldn't quite, and so it came out sounding half-strangled.

"Who *did* this?" asked Medic. I could see she was still trying to make sense out of it.

"Is that relevant just now?" She knew the answer, if she thought about it. Only one person *could* have done this. Only one person would have.

"Medic," said Tisarwat, who had been trying the restraints but found she couldn't free herself. Her voice still came out a strangled croak. "I am Anaander Mianaai, Lord of the Radch. Arrest the fleet captain, release me, and give me the medicine I need."

"You're getting above yourself, Lieutenant," I said, and turned again to Medic. "I gave an order, Medic." Isolated as we were in gate space, my word was law. It didn't matter what my orders were, no matter how illegal or unjust. A captain might face prosecution for giving some orders—her crew would without fail be executed for disobeying those same commands. It was a central fact of any Radchaai soldier's life, though it rarely came to an actual demonstration. No one on *Mercy of Kalr* would have forgotten it. Nyseme Ptem, whose name was mentioned every day on this ship, at my particular instructions, had been a soldier like these, had died because she had refused orders to kill innocent people. No one on board *Mercy of Kalr* could forget her, or forget why she died. Or that I chose to have her name spoken daily, as though she were one of the dead of my own family, or this ship. That couldn't possibly be lost on Medic, just now.

I could see her distress and indecision. Tisarwat was suffering, clearly, and if anything could make Medic truly angry it was suffering she couldn't help. My order might be interpreted as backing her into a corner with the threat of execution, but it also gave her cover to do what needed doing, and she would see that soon enough.

"Medic," croaked Tisarwat, still struggling against the restraints.

I laid one black-gloved hand across her throat. No pressure, just a reminder. "Medic," I said. Calmly. "No matter who this is, no matter who she claims to be, this installation was illegal—and thoroughly unjust—from the start. And it's failed. I've seen this before, I've been through it myself. It won't get any better, and she'll be extremely lucky if it doesn't get worse. Meds might keep her going for a while, but they won't fix the problem. There's only one thing that *will* fix the problem." Two things. But in some respects the two were the same, at least as far as this fragment of Anaander Mianaai was concerned.

Medic balanced on the knife-edge of two equally bad choices, only the smallest chance of helping her patient making a barely perceptible difference between one course and the other. I saw her tip. "I've never... Fleet Captain, I don't have any experience with this." Trying very hard not to let her voice shake. She'd never dealt with ancillaries before, I was the first she'd ever had in her medical section. Ship had told her what to do, with me.

And I was hardly typical. "Not many do. Putting them in is routine, but I can't think of anyone who's had to take any *out*. Not anyone who cared about the condition of the body once they were done. But I'm sure you'll manage. Ship knows what to do." Ship was saying as much to Medic, at that moment. "And I'll help."

Medic looked at Tisarwat—no, Anaander Mianaai—tied down to the table, no longer struggling with the restraints, eyes closed. Looked, then, at me. "Sedation," she began.

"Oh, no. She has to be awake for this. But don't worry, I choked her pretty badly, a few minutes ago. She won't be able to scream very much."

By the time we finished and Tisarwat was unconscious, dosed as heavily as was safe with sedatives, Medic was shaking, not entirely from exhaustion. We'd both missed lunch and supper, and tired and increasingly anxious Bos were passing the entrance to Medical in ones and twos on increasingly flimsy pretexts. Ship refused to tell anyone what was happening.

"Will she come back?" asked Medic, standing, trembling, as I cleaned instruments and put them away. "Tisarwat, I mean, will she be Tisarwat again?"

"No." I closed a box, put it in its drawer. "Tisarwat was dead from the moment they put those implants in." *They*. Anaander Mianaai would have done that herself.

"She's a *child*. Seventeen years old! How could anyone..." She trailed off. Shook her head once, still not quite believing even after hours of surgery, of seeing it with her own eyes.

"I was the same age when it happened to me," I pointed out. Not *I* really, but this body, this last one left to me. "A little younger." I didn't point out that Medic hadn't reacted this way to seeing me. That it made a difference when it was a citizen, instead of some uncivilized, conquered enemy.

She didn't notice it herself, or else was too overwhelmed just now to react. "Who is she now, then?"

"Good question." I put away the last of the instruments. "She'll have to decide that."

"What if you don't like her decision?" Shrewd, Medic was. I'd rather have her on my side than otherwise.

"That," I answered, making a small tossing gesture, as though casting the day's omens, "will be as Amaat wills. Get some rest. Kalr will bring supper to your quarters. Things will seem better after you've eaten and slept."

"Really?" she asked. Bitter and challenging.

"Well, not necessarily," I admitted. "But it's easier to deal with things when you've had some rest and some breakfast."

4

In my quarters, Kalr Five, disquieted by the day's events but of course expressionless, had my supper waiting for me—a bowl of skel and a flask of water, common soldier's mess. I suspected Ship had suggested it to her but didn't query to confirm that suspicion. I'd have been content eating skel all the time, but it would have distressed Five, and not only because it would have deprived her of the opportunity to filch tastes of non-skel delicacies, a cherished perquisite of serving the captain or the officers in the decade room.

While I ate, officerless Bo halfheartedly, nearly silently, scrubbed their allotment of corridors, still spotless as it had been this morning, but part of the day's routine and not to be neglected. They were tired and worried. Judging from their sparse chatter, the consensus was that I'd abused Lieutenant Tisarwat so harshly she'd become sick. There were some grumbles of *no different from the last one*. Very carefully referentless.

Bo One, decade senior, checked their work, reported to Ship that it was complete. And then said, silently, fingers moving, "Ship."

"Bo One," said *Mercy of Kalr*. Who knew Bo One quite well, had heard all the grumbles. "You should take your questions to the fleet captain."

When Bo One had gone to see Medic, less than five minutes after I'd left for my own quarters, Medic had told her the same thing. And this was the third time Ship had suggested it. Still, Bo One had hesitated. Even though by rights she was in command of Bo, with Lieutenant Tisarwat unconscious and my not having assigned anyone to replace her. Had therefore the right, the responsibility even, to approach me for information and instructions.

Ancillaries were part of their ship. There was, often, a vague, paradoxical sense that each decade had its own almost-identity, but that existed alongside the knowledge that every ancillary was just one part of the larger thing, just hands and feet—and a voice—for Ship. No ancillary ever had questions for the captain, or anything personal that needed discussion with an officer.

Mercy of Kalr was crewed by humans. But its last captain had demanded that those humans behave as much like ancillaries as possible. Even when her own Kalrs had addressed her, they had done so in the way Ship might have. As though they had no personal concerns or desires. Long habit, I thought, made Bo One hesitate. She might have asked another lieutenant to speak to me for her, but Seivarden was on watch and Lieutenant Ekalu was asleep.

In my purple and green quarters, I ate the last leaf of skel. Said to Five, "Kalr, I'll have tea. And I want the paint off these walls as soon as you can manage it. I want monitors." The walls could be altered, made to display whatever one wished, including visuals of the space outside the ship. The materials to do it were on board. For whatever reason,

Captain Vel hadn't wanted that. I didn't actually need it, but I wanted the previous captain's arrangements gone as completely as I could manage.

Expressionless, flat-voiced, Five said, "There may be some inconvenience to you, Fleet Captain." And then a flare of apprehension as Ship spoke to her. Hesitation. *Go ahead* in her ear, from Ship. "Sir, Bo One wishes to speak to you."

Good. Four more seconds and I'd have ordered her to report to me. I'd only been waiting to finish my supper. "I don't care about the inconvenience. And I'll see Bo One."

Bo One entered outwardly confident, inwardly frightened. Bowed, stiffly, feeling awkward—ancillaries didn't bow. "Bo," I said, acknowledging her. Over in a corner, Kalr Five busied herself pointlessly with the tea flask, pretending there was anything at all to do before she could serve me the tea I'd asked for. Listening. Worried.

Bo One swallowed. Took a breath. "Begging the fleet captain's indulgence," she began, clearly a rehearsed speech. Slowly, carefully, broadening her vowels, incapable of entirely losing her own accent but trying hard. "There are concerns about the situation of Bo decade's officer." A moment of extra doubt there, I saw, knowing I'd been angry at Lieutenant Tisarwat's even being aboard, Bo One feeling that she was in a precarious place just speaking to me this way, let alone bringing up the young lieutenant. That sentence had been very carefully composed, I thought, both to sound very formal and to avoid Lieutenant Tisarwat's name. "Medic was consulted, and it was recommended the fleet captain be approached."

"Bo," I said. My voice calm, yes, my mood never reached my voice unless I intended it. But I was out of patience for this sort of thing. "Speak directly, when you speak to me." Kalr Five still puttered with the tea things.

"Yes, sir," said Bo One, still stiff. Mortified.

"I'm glad you came. I was on the point of calling for you. Lieutenant Tisarwat is ill. She was ill when she came aboard. Military Administration wanted an officer here and didn't care that she wasn't fit to ship out. They even tried to hide it from me." A lie that wasn't, entirely, a lie. And every soldier and officer on every ship complained about the unthinking, ignorant decisions of Administration, none of whom knew what it was like aboard ships. "I'll have some things to say about that, when next I have the chance." I could almost *see* it clicking together in Bo One's mind. *Fleet captain's angry at Administration, not our lieutenant.* "She'll be returning to her quarters tomorrow, and she'll need a day or two of rest, and light duty after that until Medic says otherwise. You're decade senior, of course, so you'll be responsible for your soldiers and hold her watches while she's out, and make your reports to me. I need Bo decade to take very good care of Lieutenant Tisarwat. I already know you will, but now you have my explicit order. If you have any concerns at all about her health, or if her behavior is odd—if she seems confused about something she shouldn't be, or just doesn't seem right in any way at all—you're to report it to Medic. Even if Lieutenant Tisarwat orders you not to. Am I understood?"

"Sir. *Yes*, sir." Already feeling she was on firmer ground.

"Good. Dismissed." Kalr Five picked up the flask to finally pour my tea, no doubt composing the narrative she'd give the other Kalrs.

Bo One bowed. And then, with some trepidation, said, "Beg the fleet captain's indulgence, sir..." Stopped and swallowed, surprised at her own daring. At my expectant gesture. "We all of us, sir, Bo decade, we want to say, thank you for the tea, sir."

I'd allotted five grams per person aboard, per week (soldiers—even officers—wrung as much tea as possible out of very small rations of leaves) so long as my supply lasted. It had been greeted with suspicion at first. Captain Vel had insisted they only drink water. Like ancillaries. Was I trying to soften them up for something? To show off how wealthy I was? Granting a privilege that I could then deny for some satisfaction of my own?

But if there was one thing any Radchaai considered essential for civilized life, it was tea. And I knew what it was like, to be on a ship full of ancillaries. I had no need to play at it. "You're very welcome, Bo. Dismissed."

She bowed again, and left. As the door closed behind her, Ship said, in her ear, "That went well."

For the next two days, Lieutenant Tisarwat lay on her bed, in her tiny quarters. Ship showed her entertainments from its library, all lighthearted things with songs that were bright or sweet by turns, and happy endings. Tisarwat watched them, placid and noncommittal, would have watched tragedy after tragedy with the same evenness, dosed as she was to keep her mood stable and comfortable. Bo fussed over her, tucking blankets, bringing tea, Bo Nine even contriving some kind of sweet pastry for her, in the decade room's tiny galley. Speculation about the nature of her illness—no longer blamed on me—was rife. In the end, they decided that Tisarwat had been badly interrogated before being assigned to *Mercy of Kalr*. Or less likely, but still possible, she'd been the victim of inept education—sometimes, when a citizen needed to learn a great deal of information, she could get that by going to Medical and learning under drugs. The same drugs that were used for interrogation, and aptitudes testing. Or reeducation, a topic most polite Radchaai had difficulty mentioning at all. All four—interrogation, learning, aptitudes, or reeducation—had to be done by a specialist medic, someone who knew what she was doing. Though no one on *Mercy of Kalr* would ever say it aloud, hovering just under the surface of any conversation about her was the fact that at the moment Tisarwat looked very much like someone who had recently come out of reeducation. The fact that Medic and I had done whatever we had done without the assistance even of any Kalrs, and wouldn't tell anyone what had happened, this also tended to reinforce the idea that reeducation was involved. But no one who had been reeducated would have ever been allowed to serve in the military, so that was impossible.

Whatever it was, it hadn't been Tisarwat's fault. Or mine. Everyone was relieved at that. Sitting in my quarters the next day, drinking tea—still from the rose glass, even I myself hadn't yet rated the best dishes—Seivarden's desire to ask me what had happened was palpable, but instead she said, "I was thinking about what you said the other day. About how I never saw you... I mean..." She trailed off, realizing, probably, that the sentence wasn't going anywhere good. "Officers have their own quarters, so that's easy, but I hadn't even thought about if my Amaats... I mean, there's nowhere private, is there, nowhere they could go if they wanted... I mean..."

Actually, there were quite a number of places, including several storage compartments, all of the shuttles (though lack of gravity did make some things awkward), and even, with enough desperation, under the table in the soldiers' mess. But Seivarden had always had her own quarters and never had to avail herself of any of them. "I suppose it's good you're thinking about these things," I said. "But leave your Amaats what dignity they can afford." I took another swallow of tea and added, "You seem to be thinking about sex a lot lately. I'm glad you haven't just ordered one of your Amaats." She wouldn't have been the first officer on this ship to do that.

"The thought crossed my mind," she said, face heating even further than it already had. "And then I thought about what you would probably say."

"I don't think Medic is your type." Actually, I suspected Medic had no interest in sex to begin with. "Lieutenant Tisarwat is a bit young, and she's not up for it right now. Have you considered approaching Ekalu?" Ekalu had thought of it, I was sure. But Seivarden's aristocratic looks and antique accent intimidated her as much as they attracted her.

"I haven't wanted to insult her."

"Too much like a superior approaching an inferior?" Seivarden gestured assent. "Kind of insulting in and of itself, thinking of it like that, wouldn't you say?"

She groaned, set her tea on the table. "I lose either way."

I gestured uncertainty. "Or you win either way."

She gave a small laugh. "I'm *really* glad Medic was able to help Tisarwat."

In Lieutenant Tisarwat's quarters, Bo Nine tucked in the blanket for the third time in the last hour. Adjusted pillows, checked the temperature of Lieutenant Tisarwat's tea. Tisarwat submitted with drugged, dispassionate calm. "So am I," I said.

Two days later—something less than a third of the way to Athoek—I invited Lieutenant Ekalu and Lieutenant Tisarwat to dine with me. Because of the way schedules worked on *Mercy of Kalr*, it was my own lunch, Ekalu's supper, Tisarwat's breakfast. And because my Kalrs were scraping paint off the walls in my quarters, it was in the decade room. Almost like being with myself again, though *Mercy of Kalr*'s decade room was a good deal smaller than my own Esk decade room, when I had been *Justice of Toren* and had twenty lieutenants for each of my ten decades.

My eating in the decade room produced a sort of confusion of jurisdiction, with Kalr Five wanting very much to establish her own authority in what was normally the territory of the officers' staffs. She'd agonized over whether to insist on using her second-best porcelain, which would show incontrovertibly that it was her meal and also show off the dishes she loved, or whether she should let Etrepa Eight and Bo Nine use the decade room's own set, which would protect the precious porcelain from accidents but imply the meal was under Etrepa and Bo's authority. Her pride won in the end, and we ate eggs and vegetables off the hand-painted dishes.

Ekalu, who had served nearly her whole career as a common soldier on this ship and likely knew Kalr Five's peculiarities, said, "Begging the fleet captain's indulgence, these plates are lovely." Five didn't smile, she rarely did in front of me, but I could see Ekalu had hit her target dead on.

"Five chose them," I said. Approving of Ekalu's gambit. "They're Bractware. About twelve hundred years old." For an instant Ekalu froze, utensil just above the plate, terrified of striking it too hard. "They're not actually terribly valuable. There are places where nearly everyone has part of a set wrapped up in a box somewhere that they never take out. But they're lovely, aren't they, you can see why they were so popular." If I hadn't favorably impressed Kalr Five yet, I did so now. "And Lieutenant, if you start every single sentence with *begging the fleet captain's indulgence* this is going to be a dreary meal. Just assume I've given my indulgence for polite conversation."

"Sir," acknowledged Ekalu, embarrassed. She applied herself to her eggs. Carefully, trying not to touch the plate with her utensil.

Tisarwat had said nothing yet beyond the occasionally required *yes, sir* and *no, sir* and *thank you, sir.* All the time those lilac eyes downcast, not looking at me, or Ekalu. Medic had tapered down her sedatives, but Tisarwat was still under their influence. Behind them, crowded back by the drugs, was anger and despair. Just noise, right now, but not what I wanted to predominate when she wasn't taking medication anymore.

Time to do something about that. "Yesterday," I said, after I'd swallowed a mouthful of eggs, "Lieutenant Seivarden was telling me that Amaat decade was obviously the best on the ship." Seivarden had said no such thing, in fact. But the surge of offended pride from Etrepa Eight and Bo Nine, standing in a corner of the room waiting to be useful, was so distinct that for an instant I had trouble believing Ekalu and Tisarwat couldn't also see it. Kalr Five's reaction wasn't nearly as strong—we'd just complimented her porcelain and besides, captain's decade was in some ways above that sort of thing.

Ekalu's conflict was immediate, and plainly visible to me. She'd been an Amaat until very recently, had, now, the natural response of an Amaat on hearing someone claim her decade's superiority. But of course, now she was Etrepa lieutenant. She paused, working that out, working out, I thought, a response. Tisarwat looked down at her plate, probably seeing what I was up to, and not caring.

"Sir," said Ekalu, finally. Obviously having to force herself to leave off that *begging the fleet captain's indulgence*. Carefully navigating her accent. "All *Mercy of Kalr*'s decades are excellent. But if I were to be called upon to narrow it down…" She paused. Perhaps realizing she'd gone a bit too awkwardly formal with her diction. "If one were forced to choose, I'd have to say Etrepa is best. No offense to Lieutenant Seivarden or her Amaats, all due respect, it's just a fact." Slipping back closer to her own accent, at that last.

Silence from Tisarwat. Betrayed alarm from Bo Nine, at silent attention in the corner of the decade room. "Lieutenant," said *Mercy of Kalr* into Tisarwat's ear. "Your decade is waiting for you to speak up for them."

Tisarwat looked up, looked at me, for just a moment, with serious lilac eyes. She knew what I was doing, knew there was only one move she could make. Resented it, resented me. Her muted anger swelled by just the smallest amount but couldn't sustain itself, died back to its previous level almost instantly. And not just anger—for a moment I'd seen yearning, a momentary hopeless wishing. She looked away, at Ekalu. "Begging your pardon, lieutenant, with all due respect, I'm afraid you're mistaken." Remembering, halfway through the sentence, that she shouldn't be speaking like Seivarden. Like Anaander Mianaai. Blurring that accent just a bit. "Bo may be junior, but my Bos are clearly better than any other decade on this ship."

Ekalu blinked. For an instant her face went ancillary-blank with surprise at Tisarwat's accent, her diction, her obvious self-possession, not much like a seventeen-year-old at all, and then she remembered herself. Searched for a response. She couldn't point out that nonetheless Bo *was* junior—that would leave her vulnerable to Seivarden's claim for Amaat. She looked at me.

I had put a neutral, interested expression on my face and kept it there. "Well," I said, pleasantly, "we should settle this. Objectively. Firearms and armor proficiency, perhaps." Ekalu finally realized I'd planned the whole thing. But was still puzzled, specifics not quite making sense to her. I made a show of moving my gloved fingers, sending a request to Kalr Five. Said aloud to the two lieutenants, "What are your numbers?"

They blinked as Ship placed the information in their visions. "All up to standard, sir," said Ekalu.

"*Standard?*" I asked, voice incredulous. "Surely this crew is better than *standard.*" Lieutenant Tisarwat looked down at her plate again, behind the drugs resentment, approval, anger, that yearning I'd seen before. All muted. "I'll give you a week. At the end of it, let's see which decade has the highest scores, Etrepa or Bo. Including your own, Lieutenants. Issue armor. You have my permission to wear it for practice, whenever you think best." My own armor was implanted, a personal force shield I could raise in a very small fraction of a second. These lieutenants, their decades, wore their units strapped around their chests, when issued. Had never, any of them, seen combat, could raise theirs within the required one second, but I wanted better, especially knowing what might be coming, that from now on nothing would be the way it had been.

Kalr Five entered the decade room, a dark-blue bottle in each hand, and one tucked into her elbow. Face impassive, but inwardly disapproving, as she set them on the table. "Arrack," I said. "The good stuff. For whoever wins."

"The whole decade, sir?" asked Lieutenant Ekalu, slightly hesitant. Astonished.

"However you'd like to divide it up," I said, knowing that of course Etrepa Eight and Bo Nine had messaged their decade-mates by now, and the soldiers of both Etrepa and Bo had already calculated their equal share of the prize. Possibly allowing a slightly larger one for their officers.

* * *

Later, in Seivarden's quarters, Ekalu turned over, said to a sleepy Seivarden, "All respect, S...no offense. I don't mean to offend. But I've...everyone's been wondering if you're kneeling to Sir."

"Why do you do that?" Seivarden asked, blurrily, and then as she pulled back from the edge of sleep, "Say *Sir* like that, instead of *Fleet Captain*." Came a bit more awake. "No, I know why, now I think about it. Sorry. Why am I offended?" Ekalu, at an astonished, embarrassed loss, didn't answer. "I would if she wanted me to. She doesn't want me to."

"Is Sir...is the fleet captain an ascetic?"

Seivarden gave a small, ironic laugh. "I don't think so. She's not very forthcoming, our fleet captain. Never has been. But I'll tell you." She took a breath, let it out. Took another while Ekalu waited for her to speak. "You can trust her to the end of the universe. She'll *never* let you down."

"That would be impressive." Ekalu, clearly skeptical. Disbelieving. Then, reconsidering something. "She was Special Missions, before?"

"I can't say." Seivarden put her bare hand on Ekalu's stomach. "When do you have to be back working?"

Ekalu suppressed a tiny shiver, born of a complicated tangle of emotions, mostly pleasant. Most non-Radchaai didn't quite understand the emotional charge bare hands carried, for a Radchaai. "About twenty minutes."

"Mmmm," said Seivarden, considering that. "That's plenty of time."

I left them to themselves. Bo and their lieutenant slept. In the corridors, Etrepas mopped and scrubbed, intermittently flashing silver as their armor flowed around them and back down again.

* * *

Even later, Tisarwat and I had tea in the decade room. Sedatives lessened further still, emotions rawer, closer to the surface, she said, when we were alone for a moment, "I know what you're doing." With a strange little skip of anger and wanting. "What you're trying to do." That was the want, I thought. To really be part of the crew, to secure Bo's admiration and loyalty. Possibly even mine. Things the hapless former Tisarwat would have wanted. That I was offering her now.

But offering on my terms, not hers. "Lieutenant Tisarwat," I said, after a calm drink of my tea, "is that an appropriate way to address me?"

"No, sir," Tisarwat said. Defeated. And not. Even medicated she was a mass of contradictions, every emotion accompanied by something paradoxical. Tisarwat had never wanted to be Anaander Mianaai. Hadn't been for very long, just a few days. And whoever she was now, however disastrous it was to Anaander Mianaai's plans, she felt so much *better.*

I'd done that. She hated me for it. And didn't. "Have supper with me, Lieutenant," I said, as though the previous exchange hadn't happened. As though I couldn't see what she was feeling. "You and Ekalu both. You can boast about the progress your decades are making, and Kalr will make that pastry you like so much, with the sugar icing." In my quarters, Ship spoke the request into Kalr Five's ear as she looked over the walls, to be sure everything had been properly installed. Five rolled her eyes and sighed as though she was exasperated, muttered something about adolescent appetites, but secretly, where she thought only Ship could see, she was pleased.

* * *

The competition was tight. Both Etrepa and Bo had spent all their free time in the firing range, and their duty time raising and lowering their armor while they worked. Their numbers had improved markedly all around, nearly everyone had gone up a difficulty level in the firearms training routines and those who hadn't soon would. And every Etrepa and every Bo could deploy their armor in less than half a second. Nowhere near what ancillaries could do, or what I wanted, but still a distinct improvement.

All of Bo had understood more or less immediately what the actual purpose of the contest was, and undertaken their practice with serious-minded determination. Etrepa as well—Etrepa, who approved my goal (as they understood it) but had not on that account held back their effort. But the prize went to Bo. I handed the three bottles of (very fine, and very strong) arrack to a virtually sedative-free Lieutenant Tisarwat, in the soldiers' mess, with all of Bo standing straight and ancillary-expressionless behind her. I congratulated them on their victory and left them to the serious drinking that I knew would begin the instant I was in the corridor.

Less than an hour later, Seivarden came to me, on behalf of her Amaats. Who had mostly tried to be understanding about the whole thing but now couldn't walk past the soldiers' mess without being reminded that they'd never even had an opportunity to try for that arrack. And I'd ordered fruit to be served to all the Etrepas and Bos with their supper that day—I had a store of oranges, rambutans, and dredgefruit, all purchased by Kalr Five and carefully stored in suspension. Even after supper was cleared away the sweet smell of the dredgefruit lingered in the corridor and left Seivarden's Amaats hungry and resentful.

"Tell them," I said to Seivarden, "that I wanted to give Lieutenant Tisarwat some encouragement, and if they'd been part of the contest she'd never have had a chance." Seivarden gave a short laugh, partly recognizing a lie when she heard it, partly, I thought, believing that maybe it wasn't a lie. Her Amaats would probably have a similar reaction. "Have them pull their own numbers up in the next week, and they'll have dredgefruit with supper, too. And Kalr as well." That last for always-listening Five.

"And the arrack?" asked Seivarden, hopefully.

In the soldiers' mess, the drinking, which had begun in a very focused, disciplined manner, each communal swallow accompanied by an invocation of one of the ship's gods, the sting of the arrack carefully savored on the way down, had begun to degenerate. Bo Ten rose, and just slightly slurrily begged the lieutenant's indulgence, and, receiving it, declared her intention to recite her own poetry.

"I have more arrack," I told Seivarden, in my quarters. "And I intend to give some of it out. But I'd rather not give it out wholesale."

In the soldiers' mess, Bo Ten's declaration met with cheers of approval, even from Lieutenant Tisarwat, and so Ten launched into what turned out to be an epic, largely improvised narrative of the deeds of the god Kalr. Who, according to Bo Ten's account, was drunk a lot of the time and rhymed very badly.

"Limiting the arrack is probably a good idea," said Seivarden, in my quarters. A shade wistfully. "And I wouldn't have had any anyway." When I'd found her, naked and unconscious in an icy street a year before, she'd been taking far too much kef far too often. She'd mostly abstained since then.

As Bo Ten's poem rambled on, it turned into a paean to

Bo decade's superiority to any other on the ship, including Amaat decade. No, *especially* Amaat decade, who sang foolish children's songs, and not very well at that.

"Our song is better!" declared one intoxicated Bo, halting the flow of Bo Ten's poetry, and another, equally intoxicated but perhaps slightly clearer-thinking soldier, asked, "What *is* our song?"

Bo Ten, not particular about her subject and not at all ready to yield the center of attention, took a deep breath and began to sing, in a surprisingly pleasant, if wobbly, contralto. "Oh, tree! Eat the fish!" It was a song I had sung to myself fairly frequently. It wasn't in Radchaai, and Bo Ten was only approximating the sound of the actual words, using more familiar ones she recognized. "This granite folds a peach!" At the head of the table, Tisarwat actually giggled. "Oh, tree! Oh, tree! Where's my ass?"

The last word rendered Tisarwat and all her Bos utterly helpless with laughter. Four of them slid off their seats and collapsed onto the floor. It took them a good five minutes to recover.

"Wait!" exclaimed Tisarwat. Considered rising, and then abandoned the idea as requiring too much effort. "Wait! Wait!" And when she had their attention, "Wait! That"—she waved one gloved hand—"is our song." Or she tried to say it—the last word was lost in more laughter. She raised her glass, nearly sloshing the arrack out onto the table. "To Bo!"

"To Bo!" they echoed, and then a soldier added, "To Fleet Captain Breq!"

And Tisarwat was drunk enough to agree, without hesitation, "To Fleet Captain Breq! Who doesn't know where her ass is!" And after that there was nothing but laughter and top-of-the-lungs choruses of *Oh, tree! Where's my ass?*

* * *

"That, sir," said Medic an hour later, in the bath, attended, as I was, by a Kalr with a cloth and a basin, "is why Captain Vel didn't allow the decades to drink."

"No, it isn't," I said, equably. Medic, still frowning as always, raised an eyebrow but didn't argue. "I don't think it would be a good idea on a regular basis, of course. But I have my reasons, right now." As Medic knew. "Are you ready for eleven hangovers when they wake up?"

"Sir!" Indignant acknowledgment. Lifted an elbow—waving a bare hand, in the bath, was rude. "Kalr can handle that easily enough."

"That they can," I agreed. Ship said nothing, only continued to show me Tisarwat and her Bos, laughing and singing in the soldiers' mess.

5

If Athoek Station had any importance at all, it was because the planet it orbited produced tea. Other things as well, of course—planets are large. And terraformed, temperate planets were extraordinarily valuable in themselves—the result of centuries, if not millennia of investment, of patience and difficult work. But Anaander Mianaai hadn't had to pay any of that cost—instead, she let the inhabitants do all the work and then sent in her fleets of warships, her armies of ancillaries, to take them over for herself. After a couple thousand years of this she had quite a collection of comfortably habitable planets, so most Radchaai didn't think of them as particularly rare or valuable.

But Athoek had several lengthy mountain ranges, with plenty of lakes and rivers. And it had a weather control grid the Athoeki had built just a century or so before the annexation. All the newly arrived Radchaai had to do was plant tea and wait. Now, some six hundred years later, Athoek produced tens of millions of metric tons a year.

* * *

The featureless, suffocating black of gate space opened onto starlight, and we were in Athoek System. I sat in Command, Lieutenant Ekalu standing beside me. Two of Ekalu's Etrepas stood on either side of us, at their assigned consoles. The room itself was small and plain, nothing more than a blank wall in case Ship should need to cast an image (or in case those on duty preferred to watch that way), those two consoles, and a seat for the captain or the officer on watch. Handholds for times when Ship's acceleration outpaced its adjustment to the gravity. This had been one of the few parts of the ship frequented by Captain Vel that she had not had painted or otherwise redecorated, with the sole exception of a plaque hung over the door that had read, *Proper attention to duty is a gift to the gods.* A common enough platitude, but I'd had it taken down and packed with Captain Vel's other things.

I didn't need to be in Command. Anywhere I was, I could close my eyes and see the darkness give way to the light of Athoek's sun, feel the sudden wash of particles, hear the background chatter of the system's various communications and automated warning beacons. Athoek itself was distant enough to be a small, shining, blue and white circle. My view of it was a good three minutes old.

"We are in Athoek System, Fleet Captain," one of Lieutenant Ekalu's Etrepas said. In another few moments, Ship would tell her what I already saw—that there seemed to be quite a lot of ships around Athoek Station, definitely more than Ship thought was usual; that besides that nothing seemed amiss, or at least had not been two to ten minutes ago, the age of the light and the signals that had reached our present location so far; and that while three military ships had been stationed here, only one was immediately visible, near one of the system's four gates. Or it had been some two and a half minutes ago. I suspected it was *Sword of Atagaris*, though I couldn't be sure until I was closer, or it identified itself.

I considered that distant ship. Where were the other two ships, and why did this one guard one of Athoek's four gates? The least important of the four, come to that—beyond it was an empty system, otherwise gateless, where the Athoeki had intended to expand before the annexation but never had.

I thought about that a few moments. Lieutenant Ekalu, standing beside me, frowned slightly at what Ship showed her, that same image of Athoek System that I myself was looking at. She wasn't surprised, or alarmed. Just mildly puzzled. "Sir, I think that's *Sword of Atagaris*, by the Ghost Gate," she said. "I don't see *Mercy of Phey* or *Mercy of Ilves*."

"The Ghost Gate?"

"That's what they call it, sir." She was, I saw, mildly embarrassed. "The system on the other side is supposed to be haunted."

Radchaai did believe in ghosts. Or, more accurately, many Radchaai did. After so many annexations, so many peoples and their various religious beliefs absorbed into the Radch, there was quite a variety of Radchaai opinions of what happened after someone died. Most citizens at the very least harbored a vague suspicion that violent or unjust death, or failing to make funeral offerings properly, would cause a person's spirit to linger, unwelcome and possibly dangerous. But this was the first I'd heard of ghosts haunting an entire system. "The whole system? By what?"

Still embarrassed, Lieutenant Ekalu gestured doubtfully. "There are different stories."

I considered that a moment. "Right. Ship, let's identify

ourselves, and send my courteous greetings to Captain Hetnys of *Sword of Atagaris*." Both *Mercy of Kalr* and Lieutenant Ekalu thought the ship by the Ghost Gate was probably *Sword of Atagaris*, and I thought they were likely to be correct. "And while we're waiting for an answer," which would take about five minutes to reach us, "see about our gating closer to Athoek Station." We'd exited gate space farther back than we might have—I had wanted this vantage, wanted to see how things stood before going any closer.

But from this distance it could take days, even weeks to reach Athoek itself. We could, of course, gate in much closer. Even, in theory, right up to the station itself, though that would be extremely dangerous. To do that safely, we would need to know where every ship, every shuttle, every sailpod would be the moment we came out of gate space. The gate opening could itself damage or destroy anything already on the spot, and *Mercy of Kalr* would collide with anything that might be in its way as it came out into the wider universe.

I'd done that sort of thing before, when I'd been a ship. During annexations, when a little extra death and destruction could hardly matter. Not in a Radchaai system, full of civilian citizen traffic.

"Sir, will you have tea?" asked Lieutenant Ekalu.

I had already returned my attention outside, to the star, its light and heat, its distant planet. The gates and their beacons. The taste of dust on *Mercy of Kalr*'s hull. I opened my mouth to say, *thank you, no*. And then realized she really wanted tea herself—she'd done without as the time to exit our self-made gate approached, and now that we'd arrived without event she'd been hoping I'd call for some. She wouldn't have any if I didn't. Her asking this way was quite daring, for her. "Yes, thank you, Lieutenant."

Shortly thereafter, almost exactly one minute before I could expect any reply to my first message, an Etrepa handed me a bowl of tea, and the ship that we all presumed was *Sword of Atagaris* disappeared.

I had been watching it. Enjoying the view, which for once came close to overwhelming the not-quiteness that was my usual experience of receiving so much data from Ship. Not quite able to process everything, not quite enough to overwhelm the sensation of seeing what I wanted—so close, but not close enough to really touch.

But for those few moments, I could *almost* forget that I wasn't a ship anymore. So when *Sword of Atagaris* disappeared, I reacted immediately, without thinking.

And found myself paralyzed. The numbers I wanted didn't come, not immediately, and the ship—Ship, which was, of course, *Mercy of Kalr* and not me—would not move at my mere desire, the way my own body would have. I came sharply back to myself, to my one, single body sitting in Command.

But Ship knew what I wanted, and why. Lieutenant Ekalu said, "Sir, are you all right?" And then *Mercy of Kalr* moved, just the smallest bit faster than it could adjust the gravity. The bowl tumbled out of my hand and shattered, splashing tea over my boots and trousers. Lieutenant Ekalu and the Etrepas stumbled, grabbed at handholds. And we were suddenly back in gate space.

"They gated," I said. "Almost as soon as they saw us." Certainly before they'd gotten our message, identifying ourselves. "They saw us, and thirty seconds later they moved."

The jar that had dumped tea all over my feet had waked Lieutenant Tisarwat, as well as her Bos. One of Seivarden's Amaats had fallen and sprained her wrist. Besides a few more broken dishes, there was no other damage—everything had been secured, in case we met some accident coming out of our self-made gate.

"But... but, sir, we're a Mercy. We look like a Mercy. Why would they run away as soon as they saw us?" Then she put that together with our own very sudden move. "You don't think they're running away."

"I wasn't going to take the chance," I acknowledged. An Etrepa hurriedly cleared away shards of porcelain and wiped up the puddle of tea.

"Exiting gate space in forty-five seconds," said Ship, in all our ears.

"But *why*?" Lieutenant Ekalu asked. Truly alarmed, truly puzzled. "They can't know what happened at Omaugh, the gates between here and there went down before any news could get out." Without any knowledge of Anaander Mianaai's split, or the varying loyalties of military ships and officers in that struggle, Captain Hetnys and *Sword of Atagaris* had no reason to react to our arrival as though it might be a threat.

Even citizens who thought the Radch had been infiltrated and corrupted, who believed some officials and captains were potentially enemies, didn't know the struggle had broken into the open. "Either they already know something," I said, "or something's happened here."

"Take hold," said Ship, to all of us.

"Sir," said Lieutenant Ekalu, "how do we know where *Sword of Atagaris* is, when we come out?"

"We don't, Lieutenant."

She took a breath. Thought of saying something, but didn't.

"We probably won't hit *Sword of Atagaris*," I added. "Space is big. And this morning's cast was fortunate."

She wasn't sure if I was joking or not. "Yes, sir."

And we were back in the universe. Sun, planet, gates, background chatter. No *Sword of Atagaris*.

"Where is it?" asked Lieutenant Ekalu.

"Ten seconds," I replied. "Nobody let go of anything."

Ten and a half seconds later, a blacker-than-black hole opened up in the universe and *Sword of Atagaris* appeared, less than five hundred kilometers from where we had just been. Before it was even fully out of its gate, it began transmitting. "Unknown ship, identify yourself or be destroyed."

"I'd like to see it try," said Ship, but only to me.

"That's not Captain Hetnys," said Ekalu. "I think it's her Amaat lieutenant."

"*Sword of Atagaris*," I said. Ship would know to transmit my words. "This is Fleet Captain Breq Mianaai commanding *Mercy of Kalr*. Explain yourself."

It took a half second for my message to reach *Sword of Atagaris*, and four seconds for the lieutenant in question to collect herself enough to reply. "Fleet Captain, sir. My apologies, sir." In the meantime, *Mercy of Kalr* identified itself to *Sword of Atagaris*. "We...we were afraid you weren't what you appeared to be, sir."

"What did you think we were, Lieutenant?"

"I...I don't know, sir. It was just, sir, we weren't expecting you. There are rumors that Omaugh Palace was under attack, or even destroyed, and we haven't had any word from them for nearly a month now."

I looked at Lieutenant Ekalu. She had reverted to the habit of every soldier on *Mercy of Kalr* and cleared her face of any expression. That alone was eloquent, but of course I could see more. Even discounting what had just happened, she did not have a high opinion of *Sword of Atagaris*'s Amaat lieutenant.

"If you'd had your way, Lieutenant," I said dryly, "you'd be waiting even longer for word from Omaugh. I'll speak to Captain Hetnys now."

"Begging the fleet captain's indulgence," replied the lieutenant. "Captain Hetnys is on Athoek Station." She must have realized how that sounded, because she added, after a very brief pause, "Consulting with the system governor."

"And when I find her there," I asked, making my tone just slightly sarcastic, "will she be able to better explain to me just what it is you think you're doing out here?"

"Sir. Yes, sir."

"Good."

Ship cut the connection, and I turned to Lieutenant Ekalu. "You're acquainted with this officer?"

Still that expressionless face. "Water will wear away stone, sir."

It was a proverb. Or half of one. *Water will wear away stone, but it won't cook supper.* Everything has its own strengths. Said with enough irony, it could also imply that since the gods surely had a purpose for everyone the person in question must be good for something, but the speaker couldn't fathom what it might be. "Her family is good," added Ekalu at my silence, still impassive. "Genealogy as long as your arm. Her mother is second cousin to the granddaughter of a client of a client of Mianaai itself, sir."

And made sure everyone knew it, apparently. "And the captain?" Anaander Mianaai had told me that what Captain Hetnys lacked in the way of vision she made up for with a conscientious attention to duty. "Is she likely to have left orders to attack anything that came into the system?"

"I wouldn't think so, sir. But the lieutenant isn't exactly... imaginative, sir. Knees stronger than her head." Ekalu's accent slipped at that last, just a bit. "Begging the fleet captain's indulgence."

So, likely to be acting under orders that suggested incoming ships might be a threat. I would have to ask Captain Hetnys about that, when I met her.

The hookup to Athoek Station's dock was largely automated. When the pressure equalized and Five opened the shuttle hatch, Lieutenant Tisarwat and I pushed ourselves over the awkward boundary between the shuttle's weightlessness and the station's artificial gravity. The bay was dingy gray, scuffed, like any other bay on any other station.

A ship's captain stood waiting there, an ancillary straight and still behind her. Seeing it I felt a stab of envy. I had once been what that ancillary was. I never could be that again.

"Captain Hetnys," I said, as Tisarwat came up behind me.

Captain Hetnys was tall—taller than I was by a good ten centimeters—broad, and solidly built. Her hair, clipped military-short, was a silvery gray, a stark contrast to the darkness of her skin. A matter of vanity, perhaps—she'd certainly chosen that hair color, wanted people to notice it, or notice the close cut. Not all of the pins she wore in careful, uncustomary rows on the front of her uniform jacket had names on them, and those that did I couldn't read from this distance. She bowed. "Fleet Captain, sir."

I did not bow. "I'll see the system governor now," I said, cold and matter-of-fact. Leaning just a bit on that antique accent any Mianaai would have. "And afterward you'll explain to me why your ship threatened to attack me when I arrived."

"Sir." She paused a moment, trying, I thought, to look untroubled. When I'd first messaged Athoek Station I'd been told that System Governor Giarod was unavoidably occupied by religious obligations, and would be for some time. As was, apparently, every station official of any standing. This was a holiday that came around on an Athoeki calendar, and possibly because of that, because it was merely a local festival, no one had seen fit to warn me that actually it was important enough to nearly shut down the entire station. Captain Hetnys knew I'd been told the governor was unavailable for some hours. "The initiates should be coming out of the temple in an hour or two." She started to frown, and then stopped herself. "Are you planning to stay on the station, sir?"

Behind me and Lieutenant Tisarwat, Kalr Five, Ten, and Eight, and Bo Nine hauled luggage out of the shuttle. Presumably the impetus behind Captain Hetnys's question.

"It's only, sir," she went on, when I didn't answer immediately, "that lodgings on the station are quite crowded just now. It might be difficult to find somewhere suitable."

I'd already realized that the destruction of even a few gates would have rerouted traffic this way. There were several dozen ships here that had not expected to come to Athoek at all, and more that had meant to leave but couldn't. Even though Anaander Mianaai's order forbidding travel in the remaining gates couldn't possibly have reached here yet, the captains of plenty of other ships might well be nervous about entering any gates at all for the next while. Any well-connected or well-funded travelers had likely taken up whatever comfortable lodgings might have been available here. *Mercy of Kalr* had already asked Station, just to be sure, and Station had replied that apart from the possibility of an invitation to stay in the system governor's residence, the usual places were full up.

The fact that my possibly staying on the station appeared to dismay Captain Hetnys was nearly as interesting as the fact that Station apparently hadn't mentioned my plans to her. Perhaps it hadn't occurred to her to ask. "I have a place to stay, Captain."

"Oh. That's good, sir." She didn't seem convinced of it, though.

I gestured her to follow me and strode out of the bay into the corridor. *Sword of Atagaris*'s ancillary fell in behind the three of us, with Kalr Five. I could see—*Mercy of Kalr* showed me—Five's vanity over her ability to play ancillary, right beside the actual thing.

The walls and floor of the corridor, like the docking bay, showed their age and ill-use. Neither had been cleaned with the frequency any self-respecting military ship expected. But colorful garlands brightened the walls. Seasonally appropriate garlands. "Captain," I said after ten steps, without breaking stride. "I do understand that this is the Genitalia Festival. But when you say *genitalia*, doesn't that usually mean genitals generally? Not just one kind?" For all the steps I'd taken, and as far down the corridor as I could see, the walls were hung with tiny penises. Bright green, hot pink, electric blue, and a particularly eye-searing orange.

"Sir," said Captain Hetnys just behind me. "It's a translation. The words are the same, in the Athoeki language."

The Athoeki language. As though there had only been one. But there was never only one language, not in my considerable experience.

"With the fleet captain's indulgence..." As Captain Hetnys spoke, I gestured assent, not looking behind me to see her. Could, if I wished, see her back, and my own, through Kalr Five's unsuspecting eyes. She continued. "The Athoeki weren't very civilized." Not civilized. Not *Radchaai.* The word was the same, the only difference a subtlety expressed by context, and too easily wiped away. "They mostly aren't even now. They make a division between people with penises and people without. When we first arrived in the system they surrendered right away. Their ruler lost her mind. She thought Radchaai didn't have penises, and since everyone would have to become Radchaai, she ordered all the people in the system with penises to cut them off. But the Athoeki had no intention of cutting anything off, so they made models instead and piled them up in front of the ruler to keep her happy until she could be arrested and given help. So now, on the anniversary, sir, all the children dedicate their penises to their god."

"What about the Athoeki with other sorts of genitals?" We'd reached the bank of lifts that would take us away from the docks. The lobby there was deserted.

"They don't use *real* ones, sir," said Captain Hetnys, clearly contemptuous of the whole thing. "They buy them in a shop."

Station didn't open the lift doors with the alacrity I had grown used to on *Mercy of Kalr.* For an instant I considered waiting to see just how long it would let us stand there, and wondered if perhaps Station disliked Captain Hetnys so much. But if that was the case, if this hesitation was resentment on Station's part, I would only add to that by exposing it.

But just as I drew a breath to request the lift, the doors opened. The inside was undecorated. When we were all in and the doors closed, I said, "Main concourse, please, Station." It would take Eight and Ten a while to settle into the quarters I'd arranged, and in the meantime I would at least make a point of showing myself at the Governor's Palace, which would have an entrance on the main concourse, and at the same time see some of this local festival. To Captain Hetnys, standing beside me, I said, "That story strikes you as plausible, does it?" One ruler for the entire system. *They surrendered right away.* In my experience, no entire system ever surrendered right away. Parts, maybe. Never the whole. The one exception had been the Garseddai, and that had been a tactic, an attempt at ambush. Failed, of course, and there were no Garseddai anymore, as a result.

"Sir?" Captain Hetnys's surprise and puzzlement at my question was plain, though she tried to conceal it, to keep her voice and expression bland and even.

"That seems like it might really have happened? Like the sort of thing someone would actually do?"

Even restated, and given time to think about it, the question puzzled her. "Not anyone civilized, sir." A breath, and then, emboldened, perhaps, by our conversation so far, "Begging the fleet captain's indulgence." I gestured the bestowal of it. "Sir, what's happened at Omaugh Palace? Have the aliens attacked, sir? Is it war?"

Part of Anaander Mianaai believed—or at least put it about—that her conflict with herself was due to infiltration by the alien Presger. "War, yes. But the Presger have nothing to do with it. It's we who've attacked ourselves." Captain Vel, who had used to command *Mercy of Kalr*, had believed the lie about the Presger. "Vel Osck has been arrested for treason." Captain Hetnys and Captain Vel had known each other. "Beyond that, I don't know what's happened to her." But anyone knew what was most likely. "Did you know her well?"

It was a dangerous question. Captain Hetnys, who was nowhere near as good at concealing her reactions as my own crew was, quite obviously saw the danger. "Not well enough, sir, to ever suspect her of any kind of disloyalty."

Lieutenant Tisarwat flinched just slightly at Captain Hetnys's mention of disloyalty. Captain Vel had never been disloyal, and no one knew that better than Anaander Mianaai.

The lift doors opened. The concourse of Athoek Station was a good deal smaller than the main concourse of Omaugh Palace. Some fool, at some point, had thought that white would be an excellent color for the long, open—and heavily trafficked—floor. Like any main concourse on any sizable Radchaai station it was two-storied, in this case with windows here and there on the upper level, the lower lined with offices and shops, and the station's major temples—one to Amaat, and likely a host of subsidiary gods, its façade not the elaborate riot of gods the temple at Omaugh boasted but only images of the four Emanations, in purple and red and yellow, grime collected in the ledges and depressions. Next to it another, smaller temple, dedicated, I guessed, to the god in Captain Hetnys's story. That entrance was draped in garlands nearly identical to the ones we'd seen on the docks, but larger and lit from inside, those startling colors glowing bright.

Crowding this space, as far as I could see, citizens stood in groups, conversing at near-shouting level, wearing coats and trousers and gloves in bright colors, green and pink and blue and yellow, their holiday clothes, clearly. They all of them wore just as much jewelry as any Radchaai ever did, but here it seemed local fashion dictated that associational and memorial pins weren't worn directly on coats or jackets but on a broad sash draped from shoulder to opposite hip, knotted, ends trailing. Children of various ages ran around and in between, calling to each other, stopping now and then to beg adults for sweets. Pink, blue, orange, and green foil wrappers littered the ground. Some blew across the lift entrance when the doors opened, and I saw they were printed with words. I could only read scattered fragments as they tumbled... *blessings... the god whom... I have not...*

The moment we stepped out of the lift a citizen came striding out of the crowd. She wore a tailored coat and trousers in a green so pale it might as well have been white—gloves as well. No sash, but plenty of pins, including one large rhodochrosite surrounded by elaborately woven silver wire. She put on a delighted, surprised expression and bowed emphatically. "Fleet Captain! I had only just heard that you were here, and look, I turn and there you are! Terrible business, the gate to Omaugh Palace going down like that, and all these ships rerouted here or unable to leave, but now you're here, surely it won't last much longer." Her accent was mostly that of a well-off, well-educated Radchaai, though there was something odd about her vowels. "But you won't know who I am. I'm Fosyf Denche, and I'm so glad to have found you. I have an apartment here on the station, plenty of room, and a house downwell, even roomier. I'd be honored to offer you my hospitality."

Beside me, Captain Hetnys and her ancillary stood serious and silent. Behind me, Five still displayed ancillary-like impassivity though I could see, through *Mercy of Kalr*, that she resented Citizen Fosyf's familiarity on my account. Lieutenant Tisarwat, behind the remaining traces of antinausea meds and her normal background unhappiness, seemed amused, and slightly contemptuous.

I thought of the way Seivarden would have responded to an approach like this, when she'd been younger. Just very slightly, I curled my lip. "No need, citizen."

"Ah, someone's been before me. Fair enough!" Undeterred by my manner, which argued she'd met it before, was even used to it. And of course, I almost certainly had news from

Omaugh, which nearly everyone here would have wanted. "But do at least have supper with us, Fleet Captain! Captain Hetnys already has my invitation, of course. You won't be doing any official business today."

Her last few words rang out clear in a sudden hush, and then I heard a dozen or more children's voices singing in unison. Not in Radchaai, and not a Radchaai tune, but one that arced in upward leaps, wide, angular intervals, and then slid downward in steps, but moving upward overall, to stop somewhere higher than it began. Citizen Fosyf's nattering about supper stopped midsentence, brought up short by my obvious inattention. "Oh, yes," she said, "It's the temple's..."

"Be silent!" I snapped. The children began another verse. I still didn't understand the words. They sang two more verses, while the citizen before me tried to conceal her consternation. Not leaving. Determined to speak with me, it appeared. Certain that she would get her chance, if only she was patient enough.

I could query Station, but I knew what Station would tell me. Fosyf Denche was a prominent citizen here, one who believed her prominence would mean something to anyone she introduced herself to, and in this system, on this station, that meant *tea*.

The song ended, to a scattering of applause. I turned my attention back to Citizen Fosyf. Her expression cleared. Brightened. "Ah, Fleet Captain, *I know what you are*! You're a *collector*! You must come visit me downwell. I've no ear at all, myself, but the workers on the estate near my country house let loose with all sorts of uncivilized noises that I'm assured are authentic exotic musical survivals from the days of their ancestors. I'm told it's quite nearly a museum display. But the station administrator can tell you all about it over supper this evening. She's a fellow collector, and I know how you collectors are, it doesn't matter what you collect. You'll want to compare and trade. Are you absolutely *sure* you've already got somewhere suitable to stay?"

"Go away," I said to her, flat and brusque.

"Of course, Fleet Captain." She bowed low. "I'll see you at supper, shall I?" And not waiting for any answer, she turned and strode off into the crowd.

"Begging the fleet captain's indulgence," said Captain Hetnys, leaning close so she didn't have to shout aloud to the entire concourse. "Citizen Fosyf's family's lands produce nearly a quarter of all the tea exported from Athoek. Her apartment is very near Administration, on the upper concourse, in fact."

More and more interesting. Earlier it had been clear that Captain Hetnys had neither expected nor wanted me to stay. Now she seemed to wish that I would stay with this tea grower. "I'm going to the Governor's Palace," I said. I knew the system governor wasn't there. I would still make an issue of it. "And then while I'm settling into lodgings, you can give me your report."

"Sir. Yes, sir." And then, when I said nothing further, "If I may ask, sir. Where are you staying?"

"Level four of the Undergarden," I replied, my voice bland. She tried valiantly to keep her surprise and dismay off her face, but it was obvious she hadn't expected that answer, and didn't like it.

6

Station AIs were built—grew—as their stations were built. Shortly after Athoek Station had been finished, when resentments from the annexation had still been fresh, there had been violence. A dozen sections on four levels had been permanently damaged.

Installing an AI into an already existing construction was a dicey business. The results were rarely optimal, but it could be done. Had been done, quite a few times. But for whatever reason—perhaps a wish to forget the event, perhaps because the casts hadn't been auspicious, perhaps some other reason—the area had not been repaired, but blocked off instead.

Of course, people had still managed to get in. There were several hundred people living in the Undergarden, though they weren't supposed to be there. Every citizen had a tracker implanted at birth, so Station knew where they were, knew those citizens were there. But it couldn't hear them or see them the way it could its other residents, not unless they were wired to send data to Station, and I suspected few of them were.

* * *

The section door leading to the Undergarden was propped open with the crushed remains of a table missing one of its legs. The indicator next to the entrance said that on the other side of that (supposedly closed) door was hard vacuum. It was serious business—section doors would close automatically in the event of a sudden pressure drop, to seal off hull breaches. We were likely not even close to hard vacuum, despite the indicator on the wall by this door, but no one who spent much time on ships—or who lived on stations—took such safety measures lightly. I turned toward Captain Hetnys. "Are all the section doors leading to the Undergarden disabled and propped open like this?"

"It's as I said, Fleet Captain, this area was sealed off, but people kept breaking in. They'd just be sealing it off over and over to no purpose."

"Yes," I acknowledged, gesturing the obviousness of her words. "So why not just fix the doors so they work properly?"

She blinked, clearly not quite understanding my question. "No one's supposed to be in this area, sir." She seemed completely serious—the train of reasoning made perfect sense to her. The ancillary behind her stared blankly ahead, apparently without any opinion on the matter. Which I knew was almost certainly not the case. I didn't answer, just turned to climb over the broken table and into the Undergarden.

In the corridor beyond, a scatter of portable light panels propped against the walls flickered into a dim glow as we passed, then faded again. The air was oppressively still, improbably humid, and smelled stale—Station wouldn't be regulating the air flow here, and very possibly those propped-open section doors were a matter of breathing or not breathing. After a walk of fifty meters, the corridor opened out into a tiny almost-concourse, a stretch of corridors where doors had been wrenched off and grimy once-white walls torn through to make a single-storied half-open maze, lit by more portable light panels, though these seemed to be better provided with power. A handful of citizens walking through on their way to or from someplace suddenly found that their paths took them well away from where we were standing, just by chance discovered that they had no desire to look directly at us.

Away in one corner, more light spilled from a wide doorway. Beside the doorway, a person in loose shirt and trousers glanced briefly at us, seemed for a moment to consider something, and then turned back around and bent to a five-liter tub at her feet, straightened again and began dabbing carefully, purposefully around the doorframe. Where the wall was shadowed, red spirals and curlicues glowed faintly. The color of paint she was using must have been too near the shade of the wall to see well unless it was phosphorescing. Beyond the doorway, people sat at mismatched tables, drinking tea and talking. Or they'd been talking before they'd seen us.

The air really was uncomfortably close. I had a sudden flash of strong, visceral memory. Humid heat and the smell of swamp water. The sort of memory that had become less common as the years had gone by, of when I had been a ship. When I had been a unit of ancillaries under the command of Lieutenant Awn (still alive, then, every breath, every move of hers a constant part of my awareness, and myself always, always with her).

The decade room on *Mercy of Kalr* flashed into my awareness, Seivarden seated, drinking tea, looking at schedules for today and tomorrow, the smell of solvent stronger than usual from the corridor outside, where three Amaats scrubbed the already spotless floor. The Amaats all sang quietly in ragged, off-key unison. *It all goes around, the station goes around the moon, it all goes around*. Had I unthinkingly reached for it, or had *Mercy of Kalr* sent it unbidden in response to something it had seen in me? Or did it matter?

"Sir," ventured Captain Hetnys, perhaps because I'd stopped, forcing her to stop, and *Sword of Atagaris*, and Lieutenant Tisarwat and Kalr Five. "Begging the fleet captain's indulgence. No one's supposed to be in the Undergarden. People don't *stay* here."

I looked pointedly toward the people sitting at tables, beyond that doorway, all of them carefully not noticing us. Looked around at the citizens passing by. Said to Tisarwat, "Lieutenant, go see how our move-in is coming along." I could have any information I wanted from my Mercy of Kalrs with no more than a thought, but Tisarwat's stomach had settled, now we were off the shuttle, and she was beginning to be hungry, and tired.

"Sir," she replied, and left. I walked away from Captain Hetnys and her ancillary, through that spiral-decorated doorway. Five followed me. The painter tensed as we passed, hesitated, then continued painting.

Two of the people sitting at different scarred, mismatched tables wore the usual Radchaai jacket, trousers, and gloves—clearly the standard issue, stiff fabric, grayish-beige, the sort of clothing any citizen was entitled to but no one wore who could afford better. The rest wore loose, light shirts and trousers in deep colors, red and blue and purple, vivid against the dingy gray walls. The air was still and close enough to make those jacketless shirts look far preferable to my uniform. I saw none of the sashes I'd seen on the concourse, and hardly any jewelry at all. Most held their bowls of what I had presumed was tea in bare hands. I almost might not have been on a Radchaai station.

At my entrance, the proprietor had gone back to a bowl-stacked corner, and she watched her customers now with careful attention, very obviously could not spare any for me. I walked over to her, bowed, and said, “Excuse me, Citizen. I'm a stranger here. I wonder if you could answer a question.” The proprietor stared at me, seemingly uncomprehending, as though the kettle in her bare hand had just spoken to her, or as though I'd spoken gibberish. “I'm told today is a very important Athoeki holiday, but I see no signs of it here.” No penis garlands, no sweets, just people going about their business. Pretending not to notice soldiers standing in the middle of their neighborhood center.

The proprietor scoffed. “Because all Athoeki are Xhai, right?” Kalr Five had stopped just behind me. Captain Hetnys and the *Sword of Atagaris* ancillary stood where I'd left them, Captain Hetnys staring after me.

“Ah,” I said, “I understand now. Thank you.”

“What are you doing here?” asked a person sitting at a table. No courtesy title, not even the minimally polite *citizen*. People sitting near her tensed, looked away from her. Everyone fell silent who had not already been. One person sitting alone a few meters away, one of the two dressed in properly Radchaai fashion, cheap, stiff jacket, gloves, and all, closed her eyes, took a few deliberate breaths, opened her eyes. But said nothing.

I ignored all of it. “I need somewhere to stay, Citizen.”

“There's no fancy hotels here,” replied the person who had spoken so rudely. “Nobody comes here to *stay*. People come here to drink, or eat *authentic* Ychana food.”

"*Soldiers* come here to beat the crap out of people minding their own business," muttered someone behind me. I didn't turn to look, sent a quick, silent message ordering Kalr Five not to move.

"And the governor's always got room for *important* people," continued the person who had been speaking, as though that other voice had never even existed.

"Maybe I don't want to stay with the governor." That seemed to be the right thing to say, for some reason. Everyone within earshot laughed. Except one, the carefully silent, Radchaai-attired person. The few pins she wore were generic and cheap—brass, colored glass. Nothing that spoke of family affiliation. Only a small enameled IssaInu at her collar suggested anything specific about her. It was the Emanation of movement and stillness, and suggested she might be an adherent of a sect that practiced a particular sort of meditation. Then again, the Emanations were popular, and given they fronted the temple of Amaat here, might be stand-ins for a set of Athoeki gods. So in the end even the IssaInu told me little. But it intrigued me.

I pulled out the chair opposite her, sat. "You," I said to her, "are very angry."

"That would be unreasonable," she said after a breath.

"Feelings and thoughts are irrelevant." I could see that I'd pushed her too far, that in a moment she would rise, urgently, and flee. "It's only actions Security cares about."

"So they tell me." She shoved her bowl away from her and made as if to rise.

"Sit," I said, sharply. Authoritative. She froze. I waved the proprietor over. "Whatever it is you're serving, I'll have one," I said, and received a bowl with some sort of powder in it, which, once steaming water was poured onto it, became the thick tea everyone was drinking. I took a taste. "Tea," I guessed, "and some sort of roasted grain?" The proprietor rolled her eyes, as though I'd said something particularly stupid, and turned and walked away without answering. I gestured unconcerned resignation and took another taste. "So," I said to the person across from me, who had not yet relaxed back into her seat but had at least not gotten up and fled. "It will have been political."

She widened her eyes, all innocence. "Excuse me, Citizen?" Ostensibly, technically polite, though I was sure she could read the signs of my rank and ought to have used the highest address I was entitled to, if she knew it. If she truly meant to be polite.

"No one here is looking at you or speaking to you," I said. "And your accent isn't the same as theirs. You're not from here. Reeducation usually works by straightforward conditioning, by making it intensely unpleasant to do the thing that got you arrested to begin with." Or the most basic sort did, it could and no doubt did become much more complicated. "And the thing that's upsetting you is expressing anger. And you're so very angry." There was no one here familiar to me, but anger I recognized. Anger was an old companion of mine by now. "It was an injustice, start to finish, yes? You hadn't done anything. Not anything you thought was wrong." Likely no one here thought it was wrong, either. She hadn't been driven from the tables here, her presence hadn't cleared everyone else from the vicinity. The proprietor had served her. "What happened?"

She was silent a few moments. "You're very used to saying you want something and then just getting it, aren't you," she said at length.

"I've never been to Athoek Station before today." I took

another sip of the thick tea. "I've only been here an hour and so far I don't much like what I see."

"Try somewhere else, then." Her voice was even, very nearly without any obvious trace of irony or sarcasm. As though she meant only what the words she said meant.

"So what happened?"

"How much tea do you drink, Citizen?"

"Quite a bit," I said. "I'm Radchaai, after all."

"No doubt you only drink the best." Still that apparent sincerity. She had regained most of her composure, I guessed, and this overt pleasantness with its near-inaudible undercurrent of anger was normal for her. "Handpicked, the rarest, most delicate buds."

"I'm not so fussy," I said, equably. Though, to be honest, I had no idea whether the tea I drank was handpicked or not, or anything about it, except its name, and that it was good. "Is tea picked by hand, then?"

"Some," she said. "You should go downwell and see. There are some very affordable tours. Visitors love them. Lots of people only come here to see the tea. And why shouldn't they? What are Radchaai without tea, after all? I'm sure one of the growers would be happy to show *you* around personally."

I thought of Citizen Fosyf. "Perhaps I will." I took another sip of the tea-gruel.

She raised her bowl, drank the last bits of her own. Rose. "Thank you, Citizen, for the entertaining conversation."

"It was a pleasure to have met you, Citizen," I replied. "I'm staying on level four. Stop by some time when we're settled in." She bowed without answering. Turned to depart, but froze at the sound of something heavy thunking hard against the wall outside.

Everyone in the tea shop looked up at that sound. The

proprietor set her kettle down on a table with a smack that should have startled the people sitting there but did not, so intent were they on whatever was happening out on the shadowed small concourse. Grim, angry determination on her face, she strode out of the shop. I stood and followed, Five behind me.

Outside, the *Sword of Atagaris* ancillary had pinned the painter against the wall, bending her right arm back. It had kicked the tub of paint, to judge from the pinkish-brown splotches on its boots, the puddle the tub now sat in, and the tracks on the floor. Captain Hetnys stood where I had left her, observing. Saying nothing.

The tea shop proprietor strode right up to the ancillary. "What has she done?" she demanded. "She hasn't done anything!"

Sword of Atagaris didn't answer, only roughly twisted the painter's arm further, forcing her to turn from the wall with a cry of pain and drop to her knees and then facedown onto the floor. Paint smeared her clothes, one side of her face. The ancillary put one knee between her shoulder blades, and she gasped and made a small sobbing whimper.

The tea shop proprietor stepped back but didn't leave. "Let her go! I *hired* her to paint the door."

Time to intervene. "*Sword of Atagaris*, release the citizen." The ancillary hesitated. Possibly because it didn't think of the painter as a citizen. Then it let go of the painter and stood. The tea shop proprietor knelt beside the painter, spoke in a language I didn't understand, but her tone told me she was asking if the painter was all right. I knew she wasn't—the hold *Sword of Atagaris* had used was meant to injure. I had used it myself for that precise purpose, many times.

I knelt beside the tea shop proprietor. "Your arm is

probably broken," I said to the painter. "Don't move. I'll call Medical."

"Medical doesn't come here," said the proprietor, her voice bitter and contemptuous. And to the painter, "Can you get up?"

"You really shouldn't move," I said. But the painter ignored me. With the help of the proprietor and two other patrons, she managed to get to her feet.

"Fleet Captain, sir." Captain Hetnys was clearly indignant, and clearly struggling to contain it. "This person was defacing the station, sir."

"This person," I replied, "was painting the doorway of a tea shop at the request of that shop's proprietor."

"But she won't have had a permit, sir! And the paint will certainly have been stolen."

"It was not stolen!" the proprietor cried as the painter walked slowly off, supported by two others, one of them the angry person in the gray gloves. "I *bought* it."

"Did you ask the painter where she had gotten the paint?" I asked. Captain Hetnys looked at me with blank puzzlement, as though my question made no sense to her. "Did you ask her if she had a permit?"

"Sir, no one has permission to do *anything* here." Captain Hetnys's voice was carefully even, though I could hear frustration behind it.

That being the case, I wondered why this particular unpermitted activity warranted such a violent reaction. "Did you ask Station if the paint was stolen?" The question appeared to be meaningless to Captain Hetnys. "Was there some reason you couldn't call Station Security?"

"Sir, *we're* Security in the Undergarden just now. To help keep order while things are unsettled. Station Security doesn't come here. No one..."

"Is supposed to be here." I turned to Five. "Make sure the citizen arrives safely in Medical and that her injuries are treated immediately."

"We don't need *your* help," protested the tea shop proprietor.

"All the same," I said, and gestured at Five, who left. I turned again to Captain Hetnys. "So *Sword of Atagaris* is running Security in the Undergarden."

"Yes, sir," replied Captain Hetnys.

"Does it—or you, for that matter—have any experience running civilian security?"

"No, sir, but—"

"That hold," I interrupted, "is not suitable for use on citizens. And it's entirely possible to suffocate someone by kneeling on their back that way." Which was fine if you didn't care whether the person you were dealing with lived or not. "You and your ship will immediately familiarize yourselves with the guidelines for dealing with citizen civilians. And you will follow them."

"Begging the fleet captain's indulgence, sir. You don't understand. These people are..." She stopped. Lowered her voice. "These people are barely civilized. And they could be writing anything on these walls. At a time like this, painting on the walls like that, they could be spreading rumors, or passing secret messages, or inflammatory slogans, working people up..." She stopped again, momentarily at a loss. "And Station can't see here, sir. There could be all sorts of unauthorized people here. Or even aliens!"

For a moment the phrase *unauthorized people* puzzled me. According to Captain Hetnys, everyone here was unauthorized—no one had permission to be here. Then I realized she meant people whose very existence was unauthorized. People who had been born here without Station's knowledge, and without having trackers implanted. People who were not in Station's view in any way.

I could imagine—maybe—one or two such people. But enough to be a real problem? "Unauthorized people?" I leaned into my antique accent, put an edge of skepticism into my voice. "Aliens? *Really*, Captain."

"Begging the fleet captain's indulgence. I imagine you're used to places where everyone is civilized. Where everyone has been fully assimilated to Radchaai life. This isn't that sort of place."

"Captain Hetnys," I said. "You and your crew will use no violence against citizens on this station unless it is absolutely necessary. And," I continued over her obvious desire to protest, "in the event it does become necessary, you will follow the same regulations Station Security does. Do I make myself clear?"

She blinked. Swallowed back whatever it was she really wanted to say. "Yes, sir."

I turned to the ancillary. "*Sword of Atagaris*? Am I clear?"

The ancillary hesitated. Surprised, I didn't doubt, at my addressing it directly. "Yes, Fleet Captain."

"Good. Let's have the rest of this conversation in private."

7

With Station's advice and assistance, I had claimed an empty suite of rooms on level four. The air there was stagnant, and I suspected the few light panels that leaned against the walls had been appropriated from the corridors on the way here, given shops probably weren't open today and station stores might or might not be staffed. Even in the dim lighting, the walls and floors looked unpleasantly dusty and grimy. Besides our own luggage, a few fragments of wood and shards of glass suggested whoever had lived here before the Undergarden was damaged hadn't taken everything, but anything useful had been scavenged over the years.

"No water, sir," said Lieutenant Tisarwat. "Which means the nearest baths are...you don't want to see the nearest baths, sir. Even though there's no water, people have been using them for...well. Anyway. I've sent Nine for buckets, and cleaning supplies if she can find them."

"Very good, Lieutenant. Is there somewhere Captain Hetnys and I can have a meeting? Preferably with something we can sit on?"

Lieutenant Tisarwat's lilac eyes showed alarm. "Sir. There's nothing to sit on, sir, except the floor. Or the luggage."

Which would delay unpacking. "We'll sit on the floor, then." *Mercy of Kalr* showed me a wave of indignation from every Kalr present, but none of them said anything or even changed expression, except Lieutenant Tisarwat, who did her best to conceal her dismay. "Is there anyone near us?"

"Station says not, sir," replied Lieutenant Tisarwat. She gestured toward a doorway. "This is probably the best place."

Captain Hetnys followed me into the room Tisarwat indicated. I squatted on the dirty floor and waved an invitation for her to join me. With some hesitation she squatted in front of me, her ancillary remaining standing behind. "Captain, are you or your ship sending any data to Station?"

Her eyes widened in surprise. "No, sir."

A brief check told me my own ship wasn't. "So. If I understand correctly, you believe the Presger are likely to attack this system. That they have perhaps already infiltrated this station." The Radch knew of—had contact with—three species of aliens: the Geck, the Rrrrrr, and the Presger. The Geck rarely left their own home world. Relations with the Rrrrrr were tense, because the first encounter with them had been disastrous. Because of the way our treaty with the Presger had been structured, war with the Rrrrrr had the potential to break that treaty.

And before that treaty, relations with the Presger had been impossible. Invariably fatal, in fact. Before the treaty, the Presger had been implacable enemies of humanity. Or not enemies so much as predators. "Your Amaat lieutenant thought, I take it, that *Mercy of Kalr* might be a Presger ship in disguise."

"Yes, sir." She seemed almost relieved.

"Do you have any reason to think the Presger have broken the treaty? Do you have any hint that they might have even the remotest interest in Athoek?"

Something. Some expression flashed across her face. "Sir, I've had no official communications for nearly a month. We lost contact with Omaugh twenty-six days ago, this whole part of the province has. I sent *Mercy of Phey* to Omaugh to find out what happened, but even if it arrived and turned right back around I won't hear from it for several days." It must have arrived at Omaugh shortly after I'd departed. "The system governor has the official news channels reporting 'unanticipated difficulties' and not much more, but people are nervous."

"Understandably."

"And then ten days ago we lost all communications with Tstur Palace." That would be about the time the information from Omaugh reached Tstur, plus the distance from here to there. "And the Presger were never our friends, sir, and... I've heard things."

"From Captain Vel," I guessed. "Things about the Presger undermining the Radch."

"Yes, sir," she acknowledged. "But you say Captain Vel is a traitor."

"The Presger have nothing to do with this. The Lord of the Radch is having a disagreement with herself. She's split into at least two factions, with opposing aims. Opposing ideas about the future of the Radch. They've both been recruiting ships to their causes." I looked up, to where the attending ancillary stood, expressionless. Apparently uncaring. That appearance was deceptive, I knew. "*Sword of Atagaris*. You've been in this system for some two hundred years."

"Yes, Fleet Captain." Its voice was flat, toneless. It would betray none of the surprise I was sure it felt at my addressing it directly this way for a second time.

"The Lord of the Radch has visited during that time. Did she have a private conversation with you? Here in the Undergarden, perhaps?"

"I am at a loss to understand what the fleet captain is asking," said *Sword of Atagaris*, in the person of this ancillary.

"I am asking," I replied, knowing the evasion for precisely what it was, "if you had a private conversation with Anaander Mianaai, one no one could overhear. But perhaps you have already answered me. Was it the one that claims the Presger have infiltrated the Radch, or the other one?" The other one being the one that had given me command of *Mercy of Kalr*. And sent me Tisarwat.

Or, gods help us all, was there even a third part of Mianaai, with yet another justification of whatever it was she was doing?

"Begging the fleet captain's indulgence," interjected Captain Hetnys into the brief silence that followed my question, "that I might speak frankly."

"By all means, Captain."

"Sir." She swallowed. "Begging your very great pardon, I am familiar with the fleet captains in the province. Your name isn't among them." *Sword of Atagaris* had no doubt shown her my service record by now—or as much of it as was made available to her—and she'd seen that I'd been made fleet captain only a few weeks ago. The same time I'd joined the military. There were several conclusions one might draw from such information, and it appeared she'd chosen one—that I had been hastily appointed to this position for some reason, with no military background. Saying so aloud, to me, was potentially as much as her life was worth.

"My appointment is a recent one." That alone raised several questions. In an officer like Captain Hetnys, I expected one of them to be why she hadn't been appointed fleet captain herself. Possibly this question would occur to her before any others.

"Sir, are there doubts about my loyalty?" Realized then that her career was hardly the most pressing issue. "You said my lord was...divided. That this is all a result of a disagreement with herself. I'm not sure I understand how that's possible."

"She's become too large to continue to be one entity, Captain. If she ever was just one."

"Of course she was, sir. Is. Begging the fleet captain's pardon, perhaps you don't have much experience with ancillary-crewed ships. It's not exactly the same, sir, but it's very similar."

"Beg to inform the captain," I said, making my voice cold and ironic, "that my entire service record is not available to her. I am quite well acquainted with ancillaries."

"Even so, sir. If what you say is true, and this is my lord split in two and fighting herself, if they're both the Lord of the Radch and not...not counterfeit, then how do we know which one is the right one?"

I reminded myself that this was a new idea to Captain Hetnys. That up until now, no Radchaai had ever questioned the identity of Anaander Mianaai, or wondered about the basis of her claim to rule. It had all been mere evident fact. "They both are, Captain." She showed no sign of comprehension. "If the 'right' Anaander had no concern for the lives of citizens so long as she won her struggle with herself, would you still follow her orders?"

She was silent for a good three seconds. "I think I'd need

to know more." Fair enough. "But, your very great pardon, Fleet Captain, I've heard things about alien infiltration."

"From Captain Vel."

"Yes, sir."

"She was mistaken." Manipulated, more likely, easier for the one Anaander to gain her sympathies—and perhaps belief—by accusing an outside enemy, one nearly all Radchaai feared and hated.

But I couldn't say truly that the Presger were not involved at all. It was the Presger who had made the gun I wore under my jacket, invisible to any scanner, its bullets capable of piercing any material in the universe. The Presger who had sold those guns, twenty-five of them, to the Garseddai, to use to resist annexation by the Radch.

And it was the destruction of the Garseddai as a result, the complete and utter obliteration of every living thing in that system, that had triggered Anaander's crisis, a personal conflict so extreme that she could only resolve it by going to war with herself.

But it had been a crisis waiting to happen. Thousands of bodies distributed over all of Radch space, twelve different headquarters, all in constant communication but time-lagged. Radch space—and Anaander herself—had been steadily expanding for three thousand years, and by now it could take weeks for a thought to reach all the way across herself. It was always, from the beginning, going to fall apart at some point.

Obvious, in retrospect. Obvious before, you'd think. But it's so easy to just not see the obvious, even long past when it ought to be reasonable.

"Captain," I said, "my orders are to keep this system safe and stable. If that means defending it from the Lord of the

Radch herself, then that is what I will do. If you have orders to support one side or the other, or if you have strong political ideas, then take your ship and go. As far away from Athoek as possible, by my preference."

She had to think about that just a shade longer than I liked. "Sir, it's not my job to have any political ideas at all." I wasn't sure how honest an answer that was. "It's my job to follow orders."

"Which up till now have been to assist the system governor in maintaining order here. From now, they are to assist me in securing and maintaining the safety of this system."

"Sir. Yes, sir. Of course, sir. But..."

"Yes?"

"With no aspersions cast on the fleet captain's intelligence and ability..." She trailed off, having, I thought, chosen a beginning to her sentence that would lead to an awkward ending.

"You are concerned at my apparent lack of military experience." It was potentially worth Captain Hetnys's life to bring it up. I gave her a small, pleasant smile. "Granted, Administration makes some fucked-up appointments." She made a tiny, amused sound. Every soldier had complaints about how Military Administration arranged things. "But it wasn't Administration that appointed me. It was Anaander Mianaai herself." Strictly true, but not much of an endorsement, and not one I was particularly pleased about claiming. "And you may say to yourself, *she's Mianaai, she's the Lord of the Radch's cousin.*" A quick twitch of her facial muscles told me she'd had that thought. "And you've had experiences with people promoted because they were someone's cousin. I don't blame you, I have, too. But despite what you see in the available version of my service record, I am *not* a new recruit."

She thought about that. Another moment more and she would conclude that I had spent my career up till now with Special Missions, everything I had done far too secret to admit any of it had ever happened. "Fleet Captain, sir. My apologies." I gestured away the need for any. "But, sir, Special Missions is accustomed to operate with some amount of . . . irregularity and . . ."

Astonishing, coming from someone who had not blinked at ancillaries under her orders injuring citizens. "As it happens, I've had some experience with situations that went badly wrong when someone was operating with too much irregularity. And also when someone was operating with far too narrow an idea of the regular. And even if Athoek were completely problem-free, all of Radch space is in the midst of an irregular situation."

She drew breath to ask more, seemed to reconsider. "Yes, sir."

I looked up at the *Sword of Atagaris* ancillary standing still and silent behind her. "And you, *Sword of Atagaris*?"

"I do as my captain commands me, Fleet Captain." Toneless. To all appearances emotionless. But almost certainly taken aback by my question.

"Well." No point in pushing too hard. I stood. "It's been a difficult day for all of us. Let's start fresh, shall we? And you have a supper invitation, Captain, unless I misremember."

"As does the fleet captain," Captain Hetnys reminded me. "It's sure to be very good food. And some of the people you'll want to meet with will be there." She tried to suppress a glance at the dim, dingy surroundings. No furniture. No water, even. "The governor will certainly be there, sir."

"Then I suppose," I said to Captain Hetnys, "I ought to go to supper."

8

Citizen Fosyf Denche's apartment boasted a dining room, all glass on one side, looking out over the still-crowded concourse below. Four meters by eight, walls painted ocher. A row of plants sat on a high shelf, long, thick stems hanging down nearly to the floor, with sharp spines and thick, round, bright green leaves. Large as the dining room was by station-dwelling standards, it wouldn't have been large enough to seat all of a wealthy Radchaai's composite household—cousins, clients, servants, and their children—and to judge by the half dozen or so small children in various stages of undress and stickiness sleeping on cushions in the nearby sitting room, this was at least the second round of holiday supper.

"The fleet captain," said Fosyf in her seat at one end of the table of pale, gilded wood, "is a collector just like you, Administrator Celar!" Fosyf was clearly pleased at having discovered that. Enough to almost completely conceal her disappointment at my not offering any information on the loss of communication with the nearest palaces, or her inability to politely ask me for it.

Station Administrator Celar ventured an expression of cautious interest. “A collector, Fleet Captain? Of songs? What sort?” She was a wide, bulky person in a vividly pink coat and trousers and yellow-green sash. Dark-skinned, dark-eyed, voluminous tightly curled hair pulled up and bound to tower above her head. She was very beautiful and, I thought, aware of that fact, though not off-puttingly so. Her daughter Piat sat beside her, silent and oddly indrawn. She was not so large nor quite so beautiful, but young yet and likely to equal her mother on both counts someday.

“My taste is broad-ranging rather than discriminating, Administrator.” I gestured refusal of another serving of smoked eggs. Captain Hetnys sat silent beside me, intent on her own second helping. Across the table from me, beside the station administrator, System Governor Giarod sat, tall and broad shouldered, in a soft, flowing green coat. Something about the particular shade of her skin suggested she'd had it darkened. From the moment she'd entered, she'd been as collected as though this were a routine supper, nothing out of the ordinary.

“I have a particular interest in Ghaonish music,” confessed Administrator Celar. Fosyf beamed. Fosyf's daughter Raughd smiled insincerely, fairly competently concealing her boredom. When I'd arrived she'd been just slightly too attentive, too respectful, and I'd seen so many young people of her class, so intimately, for so long, that even without an AI to tell me so, I knew she'd been nursing a hangover. Knew, now, that the hangover med she'd taken had started working.

“I grew up only a few gates from Ghaon, you understand,” Station Administrator Celar continued, “and served as assistant administrator at the station there for twenty years. So fascinating! And so very difficult to find the real, authentic thing." She picked up a small piece of dredgefruit with her utensil, but instead of putting it in her mouth, moved it toward her lap, under the table. Beside her, her daughter Piat smiled, just slightly, for the first time since I'd seen her.

"Ghaonish in general?" The station that Administrator Celar had served on was only just starting to be built when I'd last been there, centuries ago. "There were at least three different political entities on Ghaon at the time of the annexation, depending how you count, and something like seven different major languages, each of which had its own various styles of music."

"*You* understand," she replied, having lost in an instant nearly all her wariness of me. "All of that, and so few really Ghaonish songs left."

"What would you give me," I asked, "for a Ghaonish song you've never heard?"

Her eyes widened, disbelief apparent. "*Sir*," she said, indignant. Offended. "You're making fun of me."

I raised an eyebrow. "I assure you not, Administrator. I had several from a ship that was there during the annexation." I didn't mention that I had *been* the ship in question.

"You met *Justice of Toren*!" she exclaimed. "What a loss that was! Did you serve on it? I've so often wished I could meet someone who did. One of our horticulturists here had a sister who served on *Justice of Toren*, but that was long before she came here. She was just a child when..." She shook her head regretfully. "Such a shame."

Time to turn that topic aside. I turned to address Governor Giarod. "May one, Governor," I asked, "properly inquire about this temple ritual that has kept you so occupied all day?" My accent as elegant as any high-born officer, my tone overtly courteous but underneath just the hint of an edge.

"One may," Governor Giarod replied, "but I'm not sure how many answers anyone can properly provide." Like Station Administrator Celar, she picked up a piece of dredgefruit and then apparently set it in her lap.

"Ah," I ventured. "Temple mysteries." I'd seen several, over my two-thousand-year lifetime. None of them had been allowed to continue, unless they admitted Anaander Mianaai to their secrets. The survivors were all quite nonexclusive as a result. Or at least theoretically so—they could be fantastically expensive to join.

Governor Giarod slipped another piece of fruit under the table. To some child harder to exhaust and possibly more enterprising than her siblings and cousins, I guessed. "The mysteries are quite ancient," the governor said. "And very important to the Athoeki."

"Important to the Athoeki, or just the Xhai? And it is, somehow, connected to this story about the Athoeki who had penises pretending to cut them off?"

"A misunderstanding, Fleet Captain," said Governor Giarod. "The Genitalia Festival is much older than the annexation. The Athoeki, particularly the Xhai, are a very spiritual people. So much is metaphor, an inadequately material way to speak of immaterial things. If you have any interest in the spiritual, Fleet Captain, I do encourage you to become an initiate."

"I greatly fear," Citizen Fosyf said before I could answer, "that the fleet captain's interests are musical rather than spiritual. She's only interested if there's singing." Quite rudely presumptuous. But true enough.

Under the table a tiny, bare hand clutched my trouser leg—whoever was there had lost patience with the governor's absorption in the conversation and had decided to try her luck with me. She wasn't much more than a year old, and was, as far as I could see, completely naked. I offered her a piece of dredgefruit—clearly a favorite—and she took it with one sticky hand, put it in her mouth, and chewed with frowning absorption, leaning against my leg. "Citizen Fosyf tells me the workers on her estate sing a great deal," I remarked.

"Oh, yes!" agreed Station Administrator Celar. "In the past they were mostly Samirend transportees, but these days they're all Valskaayans."

That struck me as odd. "*All* your field workers are Valskaayan?" I slipped another piece of dredgefruit under the table. Kalr Five would have reason to complain about the sticky handprints on my trousers. But Radchaai generally indulged small children greatly, and there would be no real resentment.

"Samir was annexed some time ago, Fleet Captain," said Fosyf. "All the Samirend are more or less entirely civilized now."

"More or less," muttered Captain Hetnys, beside me.

"I'm quite familiar with Valskaayan music," I confessed, ignoring her. "Are these Delsig-speakers?"

Fosyf frowned. "Well, of course, Fleet Captain. They don't speak much Radchaai, that's for certain."

Valskaay had an entire temperate, habitable planet, not to mention dozens of stations and moons. Delsig had been the language a Valskaayan would have needed to speak if she wanted to do much business beyond her own home, but it was by no means certain that any Valskaayan would speak it. "Have they retained their choral tradition?"

"Some, Fleet Captain," Celar replied. "They also improvise a bass or a descant to songs they've learned since they arrived. Drones, parallels, you know the sort of thing, very primitive. But not terribly interesting."

"Because it's not authentic?" I guessed.

"Just so," agreed Station Administrator Celar.

"I have, personally, very little concern for authenticity."

"Wide-ranging taste, as you said," Station Administrator Celar said, with a smile.

I raised my utensil in acknowledgment. "Has anyone imported any of the written music?" In certain places on Valskaay—particularly the areas where Delsig was most often a first language—choral societies had been an important social institution, and every well-educated person learned to read the notation. "So they aren't confined to primitive and uninteresting drones?" I put the smallest trace of sarcasm into my voice.

"Grace of Amaat, Fleet Captain!" interjected Citizen Fosyf. "These people can barely speak three words of Radchaai. I can hardly imagine my field workers sitting down to learn to read music."

"Might keep them busy," said Raughd, who had been sitting silent so far, smiling insincerely. "Keep them from stirring up trouble."

"Well, as to that," said Fosyf, "I'd say it's the educated Samirend who give us the most problems. The field supervisors are nearly all Samirend, Fleet Captain. Generally an intelligent sort. And mostly dependable, but there's always one or two, and let those one or two get together and convince more, and next thing you know they've got the field workers whipped up. Happened about fifteen, twenty years ago. The field workers in five different plantations sat down and refused to pick the tea. Just sat right down! And of course we stopped feeding them, on the grounds they'd refused their assignments. But there's no point on a planet. Anyone who doesn't feel like working can live off the land."

It struck me as likely that living off the land wasn't so easy as all that. "You brought workers in from elsewhere?"

"It was the middle of the growing season, Fleet Captain," said Citizen Fosyf. "And all my neighbors had the same difficulties. But eventually we rounded up the Samirend ringleaders, made some examples of them, and the workers themselves, well, they came back soon after."

So many questions I could ask. "And the workers' grievances?"

"Grievances!" Fosyf was indignant. "They had none. No real ones. They live a pleasant enough life, I can tell you. Sometimes I wish *I'd* been assigned to pick tea."

"Are you staying, Fleet Captain?" asked Governor Giarod. "Or on your way back to your ship?"

"I'm staying in the Undergarden," I said. Immediate, complete silence descended, not even the chink of utensils on porcelain. Even the servants, arranging platters on the pale, gilded sideboards, froze. The infant under the table chewed the latest piece of dredgefruit, oblivious.

Then Raughd laughed. "Well, why not? None of those dirty animals will mess with *you*, will they?" Good as her façade had been so far, her contempt reached her voice. I'd met her sort before, over and over again. A few of those had even turned out to be decent officers, once they'd learned what they needed to learn. Some, on the other hand, had not.

"Really, Raughd," said her mother, but mildly. In fact, no one at the table seemed surprised or shocked at Raughd's words. Fosyf turned to me. "Raughd and her friends like to go drinking in the Undergarden. I've told her repeatedly that it's not safe."

"Not safe?" I asked. "Really?"

"Pickpockets aren't uncommon," said Station Administrator Celar.

"Tourists!" said Raughd. "They *want* to be robbed. It's

why they go there to begin with. All the wailing and complaining to Security." She waved a dismissive, blue-gloved hand. "It's part of the fun. Otherwise they'd take better care."

Quite suddenly, I wished I was back on *Mercy of Kalr*. Medic, on watch, was saying something brief and acerbic to one of the Kalrs with her. Lieutenant Ekalu inspected as her Etrepas worked. Seivarden, on the edge of her bed, said, "Ship, how's Fleet Captain doing?"

"Frustrated," replied *Mercy of Kalr*, in Seivarden's ear. "Angry. Safe, but playing, as they say, with fire."

Seivarden almost snorted. "Like normal, then." Four Etrepas, in a corridor on another deck, began to sing a popular song, raggedly, out of tune.

In the ocher-walled dining room, the child, still clutching my trouser leg, began to cry. Citizen Fosyf and Citizen Raughd both evinced surprise—they had not, apparently, realized there was anyone under the table. I reached under, picked the child up, and set her on my lap. "You've had a long day, Citizen," I said, soberly.

A servant rushed forward, anxious, and lifted the wailing child away with a whispered, "Apologies, Fleet Captain."

"None needed, Citizen," I said. The servant's anxiety surprised me—it had been clear that even if Fosyf and Raughd hadn't realized the child was there, everyone else had, and no one had objected. I'd have been quite surprised if anyone had. But then, while I had known adult Radchaai for some two thousand years, seen and heard all the messages they'd ever sent home or received, and while I'd interacted with children and infants in places the Radch had annexed, I had never been inside a Radchaai household, never spent much time at all with Radchaai children. I wasn't actually a very good judge of what was normal or expected.

* * *

Supper ended with a round of arrack. I considered several polite ways to extricate myself, and Governor Giarod with me, but before I could choose one Lieutenant Tisarwat arrived—ostensibly to tell me our quarters were ready, but really, I suspected, hoping for leftovers. Which of course Fosyf immediately directed a servant to pack for her. Lieutenant Tisarwat thanked her prettily and bowed to the seated company. Raughd Denche looked her over, mouth quirked in a tiny smile—amused? Intrigued? Contemptuous? All three, perhaps. Straightening, Tisarwat caught Raughd's look and was, it seemed, intrigued herself. Well, they were close in age, and much as I found I disliked Raughd, a connection there might benefit me. Might bring me information. I pretended to ignore it. So, I saw, did Piat, the station administrator's daughter. I rose and said, pointedly, "Governor Giarod?"

"Quite," the system governor said, with still impressive aplomb. "Fosyf, delicious supper as always, do thank that cook of yours again, she's a marvel." She bowed. "And what delightful company. But duty beckons."

Governor Giarod's office was across the concourse from Fosyf's apartment. The same view of the concourse, but from the other side. Cream-colored silk hangings painted with a pattern of leaves draped the walls. Low tables and chairs scattered around, an icon of Amaat in the typical wall niche, a bowl before it but no smell of incense—of course, the governor hadn't come in to work today.

I'd sent Tisarwat back to the Undergarden with her prize—enough food to fill even a seventeen-year-old comfortably and then some, and the governor's compliments for Fosyf's cook had been entirely deserved—and I had also dismissed

Captain Hetnys, with orders that she report to me in the morning.

"Sit, please, Fleet Captain." Governor Giarod gestured to some wide, cushioned chairs well back from the window. "What must you think of us? But from the beginning of this...crisis, I've tried to keep everything as calm and routine as possible. And of course religious observances are very important in times of stress. I can only thank you for your patience."

I sat, and so did the governor. "I am," I admitted, "approaching the limits of that patience. But then, you are as well, I suspect." I had thought, all those days on the way here, of what I should say to Governor Giarod. Of how much I should reveal. Had decided, in the end, on the truth, as unvarnished as I could produce it. "So. This is the situation: two factions of Anaander Mianaai have been in conflict with each other for a thousand years. Behind the scenes, hidden even from herself." Governor Giarod frowned. It didn't make much sense, on the surface. "Twenty-eight days ago, at Omaugh Palace, it became open conflict. The Lord of the Radch herself blocked all communications coming from the palace, in an attempt to hide that conflict from the rest of herself. She failed, and now that information is on its way across Radch space, to all the other palaces." It was probably reaching Irei Palace—the one farthest from Omaugh—just about now. "The conflict at Omaugh appears to be resolved."

Governor Giarod's obvious dismay had grown with every word I'd spoken. "In whose favor?"

"Anaander Mianaai's, of course. How else? We are all of us in an impossible position. To support either faction is treason."

"As is," agreed the governor, "*not* supporting either faction."

"Indeed." I was relieved that the governor had enough wit to see that immediately. "In the meantime, factions in the military—also fostered by the Lord of the Radch, with an eye toward an advantage if this ever came to actual physical battle—have begun fighting. One in particular has begun attacking gates. Which is why, even though communications from Omaugh Palace are now functioning, you're still isolated from them. Every route any message would take has had a gate somewhere along it destroyed." Or at least the routes that wouldn't take months.

"There were dozens of ships in the Hrad-Omaugh Gate! Eighteen of them are still unaccounted for! What could possibly..."

"I suspect they're still trying to keep information back. Or at least make it difficult for any but military ships to travel between systems. And they don't particularly care how many citizens die in the process."

"I can't...I can't believe that."

It was, nonetheless, true. "Station will have shown you my remit. I have command of all military resources in this system, and orders to ensure the safety of the citizens here. I also bring an order to forbid all travel through the gates for the foreseeable future."

"Who gave this order?"

"The Lord of the Radch."

"Which one of her?" I said nothing. The governor gestured resignation. "And this...argument she's having with herself?"

"I can tell you what she has told me. I can tell you what *I* think it's about. More than that..." I gestured ambiguity, uncertainty. Governor Giarod waited, silent and expectant. "The trigger, the precipitating event, was the destruction of the Garseddai." The governor winced, barely perceptibly. No one liked talking about that, about the time Anaander Mianaai had, in a fury, ordered the destruction of all life in an entire solar system. Even though it was a thousand years in the past, by now, and easier to forget about than it once had been. "When you do something like that, how do you react?"

"I hope I would never *do* anything like that," said Governor Giarod.

"Life is unpredictable," I said, "and we are not always the people we think we are. If we're unlucky, that's when we discover it. When something like that happens, you have two choices." Or, more than two, but distilled, they came down to two. "You can admit the error and resolve never to repeat it, or you can refuse to admit error and throw every effort behind insisting you were right to do what you did, and would gladly do it again."

"Yes. Yes, you're right. But Garsedd was a thousand years ago. Surely that's time to have resolved on one or another of those. And if you'd asked me before now, I'd have said my lord had chosen the first. Without, of course, publicly admitting error."

"It must be more complicated than that," I agreed. "I think there were already other issues that events at Garsedd exacerbated. What those were I can only guess. Certainly the Lord of the Radch couldn't continue expanding forever." And if expansion stopped, what to do with all those ships and ancillary soldiers? The officers that commanded them? Keeping them was a drain on resources, to no purpose. Dismantle them, and systems on the periphery of Radch space were vulnerable to attack. Or revolt. "I think it wasn't merely admitting error that the Lord of the Radch has been resisting, but admitting her own mortality."

Governor Giarod sat considering that, silent for twenty-four seconds. "I don't like that thought, Fleet Captain. If you had asked me even ten minutes ago I'd have told you the Lord of the Radch was the next thing to immortal. How can she not be? Constantly growing new bodies to replace the old, how could she ever die?" Another frowning three seconds of silence. "And if she dies, what will be left of the Radch?"

"I don't think we can concern ourselves with anything beyond Athoek." Possibly the most dangerous thing I could say, just now, depending on the governor's sympathies. "My orders only involve the safety of this system."

"And if they were otherwise?" Governor Giarod was no fool. "If some other part of my lord ordered you to take one side or another, or use this system in some way for her advantage?" I didn't reply. "No matter what you do it's sedition, rebellion, so you may as well do as you like, is that it?"

"Something like that," I agreed. "But I really do have orders."

She shook her head, as though clearing away some obstruction. "But what else is there to do? You don't think, do you, that there's been any... outside interference?"

The question was depressingly familiar. "The Presger would not require subterfuge in order to destroy the Radch. And there is the treaty, which I'm given to understand they take very seriously."

"They don't use words, do they? They're completely alien. How could the word *treaty* mean anything to them? How could any agreement mean anything?"

"Are the Presger nearby? A potential threat?"

A tiny frown. The question troubled her for some reason. Perhaps because the very idea of the Presger nearby was frightening. "They pass through Prid Presger, sometimes, on their way to Tstur Palace." Prid Presger was a few gates from here, nearby only in the sense that it would take a month or so to get here from there, instead of a year or more. "By agreement, they can only travel by gate, within the Radch. But..."

"The treaty isn't with the Radch," I pointed out. "It's with all humans." Governor Giarod looked puzzled at that—to most Radchaai, *human* was who they were, and everyone else was...something other. "I mean to say, whether Anaander Mianaai exists at all does not affect it. It is still in force." Still, for more than a thousand years before the treaty, Presger had seized human ships. Boarded human stations. Dismantled them—and their crews, passengers, and residents. Apparently for amusement. No one had any way of preventing it. They had ceased only because of the treaty. And the thought of them still sent a shiver down a good many human backs. Including, it seemed, Governor Giarod's. "Unless you have some specific reason, I don't think we should worry about them just now."

"No, of course, you're right." But the governor still seemed troubled.

"We produce enough food for the whole system?"

"Certainly. Though we do import some luxuries—we don't make much arrack, and various other things. We import some number of medical supplies. That could be a problem."

"You don't make correctives here?"

"Not many. Not all kinds."

That could pose a problem, far enough into the future. "We'll see what we can do about that, if anything. Meantime, I suggest you continue as you have been—keeping calm, keeping order. We should let people know that the gates that are closed are down for the foreseeable future. And that travel through the remaining gates is too dangerous to allow."

"Citizen Fosyf won't like that! Or any of the other growers. By the end of the month there'll be tonnes of top-grade handpicked Daughter of Fishes with nowhere to go. And that's only Fosyf's bit."

"Well." I smiled blandly. "At least we'll all have very good tea to drink for the next long while."

It was too late to visit Citizen Basnaaid with any sort of courtesy. And there were things I wanted to know that had not been in the information I'd received at Omaugh Palace. Politics from before an annexation were considered irrelevant, any old divisions wiped away by the arrival of civilization. Anything remaining—languages, perhaps, or art of some kind—might be preserved as quaint museum displays, but of course never figured into official records. Outside this system, Athoek looked like any other Radchaai system. Uniform. Wholly civilized. Inside it, you could see it wasn't, if you looked—if you were forced to acknowledge it. But it was always a balancing act between the presumed complete success of the annexation and the need to deal with the ways in which that annexation had, perhaps, not been entirely complete, and one of the ways to achieve that balance was by ignoring what one didn't have to see.

Station would know things. I'd best have a chat with Station anyway, best put myself in its good graces. A ship or station AI couldn't, strictly speaking, do anything to oppose me, but I knew from very personal experience how much easier life was when one liked you, and wanted to help.

9

Despite the fact that the Undergarden wasn't terribly well ventilated, and my bed was little more than a pile of blankets on the floor, I slept comfortably. Made a point of saying so to Kalr Five, when she brought me tea, because I could see that she, that all my Mercy of Kalrs, were vain of what they'd achieved while I sat at supper with Citizen Fosyf. They'd managed to clean our several rooms to an almost military level of spotlessness, rig lights, get doors working, and pile luggage and miscellaneous boxes into something approximating tables and chairs. Five brought me breakfast—more porridge tea, though thicker than what I'd drunk in the tea shop, bland but filling—and Lieutenant Tisarwat and I ate in silence, she in a state of suppressed self-loathing. It had been barely noticeable aboard *Mercy of Kalr*. Her duties there, and the self-contained isolation of our travel, had made it easy for her to almost forget what Anaander Mianaai had done to her. What I had done to Anaander Mianaai. But now, here at Athoek Station, the chaos of cleaning and unpacking past, she must be thinking of what the Lord of the Radch had meant to do when we'd arrived here.

I considered asking her. I already knew Anaander Mianaai's assessment of the system governor and of the ships and captains stationed here. Knew that she considered most of the tea-growing houses to be almost entirely preoccupied with their tea and likely unthreatened by the changes the Lord of the Radch had set in motion over the past hundred years. After all, upstart houses drank tea just as much as anciently aristocratic ones, and (aside from captains who demanded their soldiers play ancillary) human soldiers did, too.

Athoek was probably not fertile ground for the other Anaander. And most of the fighting would probably center round the palaces for now. Then again, a planet was a valuable resource. If fighting lasted long enough, Athoek could draw unwelcome attention. And in a game with such high stakes, neither Anaander would have failed to place a few counters here.

Kalr Five left the room, and Lieutenant Tisarwat looked up from her porridge, her lilac eyes serious. "She's very angry with you, sir."

"Who is that, Lieutenant?" But of course she meant Anaander Mianaai.

"The other one, sir. I mean, they both are, really. But the other one. If she gains the upper hand at any point, she'll come after you if she possibly can. Because she's just that angry. And..."

And that was the part of the Lord of the Radch who dealt with her reaction to Garsedd by insisting she had been right to lose her temper so extravagantly. "Yes, thank you, Lieutenant. I'd already worked that out." Much as I'd wanted to know what the Lord of the Radch was up to, I hadn't wanted to make Tisarwat talk about it. But she had volunteered. "I take it you have access codes for all the AIs in the system."

She looked quickly down at her bowl. Mortified. "Yes, sir."

"Are they only good for specific AIs, or can you potentially control any one you come across?"

That startled her. And, oddly, disappointed her. She looked up, distress plain in her expression. "Sir! She's not *stupid*."

"Don't use them," I said, voice pleasant. "Or you'll find yourself in difficulty."

"Yes, sir." Struggling to keep her feelings off her face—a painful mix of shame and humiliation. A hint of relief. A fresh surge of unhappiness and self-hatred.

It was among the things I'd wanted to avoid, in avoiding asking her about Anaander's aims in sending Tisarwat with me. I certainly didn't want her to indulge in her current emotions.

And I found I was unwilling to wait much longer to find Lieutenant Awn's sister. I took a last mouthful of porridge. "Lieutenant," I said, "let's visit the Gardens."

Surprise, that almost distracted her. "Begging the fleet captain's indulgence, sir. Aren't you meeting with Captain Hetnys?"

"Kalr Five will desire her to wait until I get back." I saw a flash of trepidation from her. And an undercurrent of… admiration, was it? And envy. That was curious.

Raughd Denche had said the Gardens were a tourist attraction, and I could see why. They took up a good portion of the station's upper level, more than five acres, sunlit, open, and undivided under a high, clear dome. Entering, that was all I could see beyond a heavy-smelling bank of red and yellow roses—that high, black sky cut into barely visible hexagonal sections, Athoek itself hanging, jewellike, beyond. A spectacular view, but this close to vacuum there ought to have been smaller partitions, section doors. I saw no sign of them.

The ground had been built to slope downward from where we entered. Past the roses the path meandered around shrubs with glossy green leaves and thick clusters of purple berries, around beds of something pungent-smelling with silvery, needle-shaped leaves. Small trees and more shrubs, even jutting rocks, the path winding around, every now and then affording a glimpse of water, of broad lily-pads, flowers white and deep pink. It was warm, but a slight breeze disturbed the leaves—no ventilation problems here, though I found myself waiting for a pressure drop, still disturbed by that huge open space. The path crossed over a tiny stream, rushing down a rock-built channel to somewhere below. We might almost have been on a planet but for that black expanse above.

Lieutenant Tisarwat, behind me, seemed unconcerned. This station had been here for several hundred years. And if something happened now there was very little either of us could do about it. There was nothing for it but to continue on. At the next turn we came into a copse of small trees with gnarled and twisted branches, and under them a small, still pool that trickled into another on a level below, and on down the slope into a succession of such pools, slowly but inexorably to a patch of lily-blooming water below. Lieutenant Tisarwat stopped, blinked, smiled at the tiny brown and orange fish darting in the clear water at our feet, a sudden bright, startling moment of pleasure. Then she looked up at me, and it was gone, and she was unhappy again, and self-conscious.

The next turn of the path revealed a stretch of open water, nearly three acres of it. Nothing on a planet, but on a station it was unheard of. The nearest edge was lined with the lilies we'd glimpsed as we'd come down the slope. Some meters to the left of that a slight, arched bridge led to a tiny island with a large stone in the middle, a one-and-a-half-meter cylinder with fluted sides, as high as it was wide. Elsewhere, here and there, rocks jutted out of the water. And away on the opposite side of the pond, up against the wall—up, so far as I could see, against hard vacuum—a waterfall. Not the trickles we'd seen on the way in, but a rushing, noisy mass of it foaming and spilling down a rock wall, churning the bit of lake below it. That rock wall stretched across the far side of the lake, ledged and irregular. There was another entrance there, which gave onto the ledges, and a path that led from there around the water.

It had been laid out to make that sudden full view as beautiful and dramatic as possible, after those flashes of water through branches on the path down, the runnels and tiny waterfalls. And dramatic it was. All that open water—usually, on a station, a large volume of water like this was kept in partitioned tanks, so that if there was a leak it could be sectioned off. So that if anything happened to the gravity it could be quickly enclosed. I wondered how deep this pond was, did some quick guesses and calculations that told me a failure in containment would mean disaster for the levels below. What, I wondered, had the station architects put below this?

Of course. The Undergarden.

Someone in a green coverall stood knee-deep in the water at one end of the stretch of lily pads, bent over, reaching under the surface. Not Basnaaid. I nearly dismissed her with that realization, bent on that one aim, on finding Basnaaid Elming. No, the person working near the lilies wasn't Basnaaid. But I recognized her. I stepped off the still twisting path, walked straight down the slope to the edge of the water. The person there looked up, stood, sleeves and gloves muddy and dripping. The person I'd spoken to in the Undergarden tea shop, yesterday. Her anger was banked, hidden. It flared to life again as she recognized me. Along with, I thought, a trace of fear. "Good morning, Citizen," I said. "What a pleasant surprise to meet you here."

"Good morning, Fleet Captain," she replied, pleasantly. Ostensibly calm and unconcerned, but I could see that very small, nearly invisible tightening of her jaw. "How can I help you?"

"I'm looking for Horticulturist Basnaaid," I said, with as unthreatening a smile as I could produce.

She frowned slightly, speculatively. Then looked at my single piece of jewelry, that one gold memorial tag. I didn't think she was close enough to read it, and it was a mass-produced thing, but for the name identical to thousands, if not millions, of others. "You have but to wait," she said, clearing away that tiny frown. "She'll be along in a few moments."

"Your Gardens are beautiful, Citizen," I said. "Though I admit this very lovely lake strikes me as unsafe."

"It's not *my* garden." That anger again, strongly, carefully suppressed. "I only work here."

"It would not be what it is without the people who work here," I answered. She acknowledged that with a small, ironic gesture. "I think," I said, "that you were too young to have been one of the leaders of those strikes on the tea plantations, twenty years ago." The word for "strike" existed in Radchaai, but it was very old, and obscure. I used a Liost term I'd learned from Station last night. The Samirend that had been brought to Athoek had spoken Liost, sometimes still did. This person was Samirend, I'd learned enough from Station to know that. And learned enough from Citizen Fosyf to know that Samirend overseers had been involved in those strikes. "You'd have been, maybe, sixteen? Seventeen? If you'd been important, you'd be dead now, or in some other system entirely, where you didn't have the sort of social network that would let you cause trouble." Her expression became fixed, and she breathed, very carefully, through her mouth. "They were lenient on account of your youth and your marginal position, but they made sure to make some sort of an example of you." Unjust, as I'd guessed yesterday.

She didn't answer at first. Her distress was too strong, but it told me I'd been right. Her reeducation would have made the contemplation of certain actions strongly, viscerally unpleasant for her, and I'd reminded her directly of exactly the events that had brought her through Security. And of course any Radchaai found the bare mention of reeducation deeply distasteful. "If the fleet captain's remarks are complete," she said finally, tense but just a bit fainter than her usual tone, "I have work to do."

"Of course. I apologize." She blinked, surprised, I thought. "You're trimming dead leaves from the lilies?"

"And dead flowers." She bent, reached under the water, pulled up a slimy, withered stem.

"How deep is the lake?" She looked at me, looked down at the water she was standing in. Up again at me. "Yes," I agreed, "I can see how deep it is here. Is it all the same?"

"About two meters at its deepest." Her voice had steadied, she had recovered her earlier composure, it seemed.

"Are there partitions under the water?"

"There are not." As though to confirm her words, a purple and green fish swam into the lily-free space where she was standing, a broad, bright-scaled thing that must have been nearly three quarters of a meter long. It hung under the water, seeming to look up at us, gaping. "I don't have anything," she said to the fish, and held her sodden-gloved hands out. "Go wait by the bridge, someone will come. They always do." The fish only gaped and gaped again. "Look, here they come now."

Two children rounded a bush, came running down the path to the bridge. The smaller jumped from the land to the bridge with a resounding thump. The water alongside the bridge began to roil, and the purple and green fish turned and glided away. "There's a food dispenser at the bridge," explained the person standing in the water. "It'll be quite crowded in an hour or so."

"Then I'm glad to have come early," I said. "If it wouldn't be too much trouble, could you tell me what safety measures are in place here?"

She gave a short, sharp laugh. "It makes you nervous, Fleet Captain?" She gestured toward the dome overhead. "And that?"

"And that," I admitted. "They're both alarming."

"You needn't worry. It's not Athoeki built, it's all good, solid Radchaai construction. No embezzling, no bribes, no replacing components with cheaper materials and pocketing the difference, no shirking on the job." She said this with every appearance of sincerity, not even traces of the sarcasm I might have expected. She meant it. "And of course Station's always watching and would let us know at the slightest sign of trouble."

"But Station can't see under the Gardens, can it?"

Before she could answer, a voice called out, "How is it coming along, Sirix?"

I knew that voice. Had heard recordings of it, childish,

years ago. It was like her sister's, but not the same. I turned to see her. She was like her sister, her relationship to Lieutenant Awn obvious in her face, her voice, the way she stood, a bit stiff in the green Horticulture uniform. Her skin was a bit darker than Lieutenant Awn's had been, her face rounder, not a surprise. I had seen recordings of Basnaaid Elming as a child, messages for her sister. I had known what she looked like now. And it had been twenty years since I had lost Lieutenant Awn. Since I had killed Lieutenant Awn.

"Almost finished, Horticulturist," said the person from the tea shop, still knee-deep in the water. Or I presumed she was, I was still looking at Basnaaid Elming. "This fleet captain is here to see you."

Basnaaid looked directly at me. Took in the brown and black uniform, frowned slightly in puzzlement, and then saw the gold tag. The frown disappeared, replaced with an expression of cold disapproval. "I don't know you, Fleet Captain."

"No," I said. "We've never met. I was a friend of Lieutenant Awn's." An awkward way to say it, an awkward way to refer to her, for a friend. "I was hoping you might have tea with me sometime. When it's convenient for you." Stupid, nearly rude to be so direct. But she didn't seem to be in a mood to stand and chat, and Inspector Supervisor Skaaiat had warned me she wouldn't be happy to see me. "Begging your indulgence, there are some things I'd like to discuss with you."

"I doubt we have anything to discuss." Basnaaid was still frostily calm. "If you feel the need to tell me something, by all means do so now. What did you say your name was?" Outright rude, that was. But I knew why, I knew where this anger came from. Basnaaid was easier in her educated accent than Lieutenant Awn had ever been—she had begun practicing it earlier, for one thing, and I suspected her ear was better from the start. But it was still, to some degree, a cover. Like her sister, Basnaaid Elming was acutely aware of condescension and insult. Not without good reason.

“My name is Breq Mianaai.” I managed not to choke on the house name the Lord of the Radch had imposed on me. “You won’t recognize it, I used another name when I knew your sister.” *That* name she’d have recognized. But I couldn’t give it. *I was the ship your sister served on. I was the ancillaries she commanded, that served her.* As far as anyone here knew, that ship had disappeared twenty years ago. And ships weren’t people, weren’t fleet captains or officers of any sort, didn’t invite anyone to tea. If I told her who I really was, she would doubt my sanity. Which might be a good thing, considering the next step, after the name, would be to tell her what had happened to her sister.

“Mianaai.” Basnaaid’s tone was disbelieving.

“As I said, it wasn’t my name at the time I knew your sister.”

“Well.” She almost spat the word out. “Breq Mianaai. My sister was just, and proper. She never knelt to you, no matter what you may have thought, and none of us wants payment from you. None of us needs it. Awn didn’t need it, or want it.” In other words, if Lieutenant Awn had had any sort of relationship with me—*knelt* implied a sexual one—it hadn’t been because she’d been looking for some sort of benefit from it. When Inspector Supervisor Skaaiat had offered Basnaaid clientage for Lieutenant Awn’s sake, the implication had been that Awn and Skaaiat’s relationship had been based on the expectation of exchange—sex for social position. It was a common enough trade, but citizens moving from low on the ladder to noticeably higher were open to accusations that their promotions or assignments had been made in exchange for sexual favors, and not on merit.

"You're quite right, your sister never knelt, not to me, not to any other person, ever. Anyone who says she did, you will kindly send to me, and I will relieve them of their misapprehension." It would really have been better to lead up to this, to have had tea and food and polite, indirect conversation beforehand, to feel out the approach, to take the edge off the foolishness of what I meant to suggest. But, I saw, Basnaaid would never have allowed it. I might as well state my business here and now. "The debt I owe your sister is far larger, and impossible to repay adequately, even if she were still alive. I can only offer the smallest token to you in her place. I propose to make you my heir."

She blinked, twice, unable at first to find any reply. "What?"

The noise of the waterfall across the pond was paradoxically both distant and intrusive. Lieutenant Tisarwat and Citizen Sirix were frozen, I realized, staring at us, at Basnaaid and me. "I propose," I repeated, "to make you my heir."

"I already have parents," Basnaaid said, after three seconds of disbelieving silence.

"They are excellent parents," I acknowledged. "It's not my intention to replace them. I couldn't possibly."

"Whatever *is* your intention, then?"

"To be certain," I said, carefully, clearly, knowing I had failed in this, having come into this knowing I would fail, "for your sister's sake, that you are safe and secure, and at all times have whatever you desire within your reach."

"*Whatever I desire*," said Basnaaid, as deliberately as I had just spoken, "is, right now, for you to go away and *never speak to me again*."

I bowed low, an inferior to one of higher station. "As the citizen wishes." I turned, and walked up to the path, away from the water, away from Sirix still knee-deep by the lilies, away from Basnaaid Elming standing, stiff and indignant, on the shore. Not even looking to see if Lieutenant Tisarwat followed.

I had known. I had known what Basnaaid Elming's reaction would be to my offer. But I had thought I would only tender a polite invitation this morning and have the confrontation itself later. Wrong. And now, I knew, Captain Hetnys was waiting in my apartments in the Undergarden, sweating in the warm, still air and stiffly, angrily refusing the tea Kalr Five had just offered her. Going into that meeting in my present mood would be dangerous, but there was, it seemed, no good way to avoid it.

At the entrance to those rooms, Bo Nine standing at impassive attention just beyond the open door, Lieutenant Tisarwat—I had forgotten, between the waterside and here, that Lieutenant Tisarwat was with me—spoke. "Sir. Begging the fleet captain's indulgence."

I stopped, without looking behind me. Reached out to *Mercy of Kalr*, who showed me a perplexing mix of emotions. Lieutenant Tisarwat was miserable as she had been all morning, but that misery was mixed in with an odd yearning—for what? And a completely new sort of elation that I had never seen in her. "Sir, permission to go back to the Gardens." She wanted to go back to the Gardens? Now?

I remembered that startling moment of pleasure when she'd seen the little fish in the pool, but, I realized, after that I'd paid her no attention whatever. I'd been too caught up in my encounter with Basnaaid. "Why?" I asked, blunt. Not, perhaps, the best way to respond, considering, but I was not at my best just this instant.

For a moment a sort of nervous fear kept her from speaking, and then she said, "Sir, maybe I can talk to her. She didn't tell *me* to never speak to her again." As she spoke, that strange, hopeful elation flared bright and sharp, and with it something I'd seen in countless young, emotionally vulnerable lieutenants.

Oh, *no*. "Lieutenant. You are not to go anywhere *near* the citizen Basnaaid Elming. I do not need you interfering in my affairs. Citizen Basnaaid *certainly* doesn't need it."

It was as though I had struck Tisarwat. She nearly physically recoiled, but stopped herself, held herself still. Speechless, for a moment, with hurt and anger. Then she said, bitter complaint, "You aren't even going to give me a *chance*!"

"You aren't even going to give me a chance, *sir,*" I corrected. Angry tears welled in her ridiculous lilac eyes. If she'd been any other seventeen-year-old lieutenant I'd have sent her on her way to be rejected by the object of her sudden infatuation, and then let her cry—oh, the volume of baby lieutenant tears my uniforms had absorbed, when I'd been a ship—and then poured her a drink or three. But Tisarwat wasn't any other baby lieutenant. "Go to your quarters, Lieutenant, get a hold of yourself, and wash your face." It was early yet for drinking, but she'd need time to get herself in hand. "After lunch you have leave to go out and get as drunk as you like. Better yet, get laid. There are plenty of more appropriate partners here." Citizen Raughd might even be interested, but I didn't say so. "You've been in Citizen Basnaaid's presence a whole five minutes." And saying that, it was even clearer how ridiculous this was. This wasn't about Basnaaid, not really, but that only made me more determined to keep Tisarwat away from her.

"You don't understand!" Tisarwat cried.

I turned to Bo Nine. "Bo. Take your officer to her quarters."

"Sir," said Bo, and I turned and went into what served as the anteroom for our small apartments.

When I was a ship, I had thousands of bodies. Except in extreme circumstances, if one of those bodies became tired or stressed I could give it a break and use another, the way you might switch hands. If one of them was injured badly enough, or ceased to function efficiently, my medics would remove it and replace it with another one. It was remarkably convenient.

When I had been a single ancillary, one human body among thousands, part of the ship *Justice of Toren*, I had never been alone. I had always been surrounded by myself, and the rest of myself had always known if any particular body needed something—rest, food, touch, reassurance. An ancillary body might feel momentarily overwhelmed, or irritable, or any emotion one might think of—it was only natural, bodies felt things. But it was so very small, when it was just one segment among the others, when, even in the grip of strong emotion or physical discomfort, that segment knew it was only one of many, knew the rest of itself was there to help.

Oh, how I missed the rest of myself. I couldn't rest or comfort one body while sending another to do my work, not anymore. I slept alone, mostly only mildly envying the common soldiers on *Mercy of Kalr* their small bunks where they slept all together, pressed warm and close. They weren't ancillaries, it wasn't the same, wouldn't be, even if I'd abandoned any pretense to dignity and climbed in with them. I knew that, knew it would be so wholly insufficient that there was no point in wishing for it. But now, this moment, I wanted it so badly that if I had been aboard *Mercy of Kalr* I'd have done it, curled up among the sleeping Etrepas Ship showed me, and gone to sleep myself, no matter how insufficient it would be. It would be *something*, at least.

A terrible, terrible thing, to deprive a ship of its ancillaries. To deprive an ancillary of its ship. Not, perhaps, as terrible as murdering human beings to make those ancillaries. But a terrible thing nonetheless.

I didn't have the luxury to consider it. I didn't have another, less angry body to send into the meeting with Captain Hetnys. Didn't have an hour, or two, to exercise, or meditate, or drink tea until I was calmer. I only had myself. "It will be all right, Fleet Captain," said *Mercy of Kalr* in my ear, and for a moment I was overwhelmed with the sensation of Ship. The sleeping Etrepas, Lieutenant Ekalu half awake, happy and for once utterly relaxed—Seivarden in the bath, singing to herself, *my mother said it all goes around*, her Amaats, Medic, and my Kalrs, all in one jumbled, inundating moment. Then it was gone—I couldn't hold it, not with only one body, one brain.

I had thought that the pain of losing myself, of losing Lieutenant Awn, had—not healed, exactly, I didn't think it would ever do that—but that it had receded to a tolerable, dull ache. But just seeing Basnaaid Elming had thrown me off-balance, and I had not handled it well. And had, as a result, not handled Lieutenant Tisarwat well, just now. I knew about the emotional upheavals of seventeen-year-old lieutenants. Had dealt with them in the past. And whatever Tisarwat had been, whoever she turned out to be, however ancient her memories or her sense of herself, her body was still seventeen, her reactions today very much those of someone in the last throes of adolescence. I had seen it, known it for what it was, and I ought to have responded more reasonably. "Ship," I said, silently, "was I smug when I thought I'd sorted out Seivarden and Ekalu?"

"Maybe just the tiniest bit, Fleet Captain."

"Sir," said Kalr Five, who had come into the anteroom, all ancillary-like impassivity, "Captain Hetnys is in the dining room." And did not add, *she's fretting, and beginning to be angry at being made to wait so long.*

"Thank you, Five." Despite my permission earlier to go in shirtsleeves here in the Undergarden, she was still in her jacket. All my Mercy of Kalrs were, I saw, querying Ship. "You've offered her breakfast and tea?"

"Yes, sir. She said she didn't want anything." A trace of disappointment there—no doubt she felt deprived of an opportunity to show off her dishes.

"Right. I'll go in, then." I took a breath, did my best to clear both Basnaaid and Tisarwat from my mind, and went in to receive Captain Hetnys's report.

10

Captain Hetnys had sent *Mercy of Ilves* on a survey of the outstations. She'd brought a few of her Atagaris ancillaries with her to Athoek Station, and her Var lieutenant and decade to run Security for the Undergarden.

She tried to explain to me why she'd set *Sword of Atagaris* to watch a gate that led to a system of airless rocks, gas giants with icy moons, no inhabitants, and no other gates.

"The Presger can travel without the gates, sir, they might..."

"Captain. If the Presger decide to attack us, there will be nothing we can do about it." The days when the Radch had commanded fleets huge enough to overwhelm entire systems were past. And even then, opposing the Presger would have been hopeless. It was the main reason Anaander Mianaai had finally agreed to a treaty. It was the reason people were still frightened of them. "And honestly, Captain, the biggest danger, for now, is going to be from Radchaai ships on one side or the other attempting to control or destroy resources another side might use. That planet downwell, for instance."

All that food. A base, if they could secure it. If *I* could. "And it's possible Athoek will be left alone entirely. Certainly I don't think anyone's going to be able to muster anything like a real fleet, not for some time, if ever." I didn't think anyone could surprise us. A military ship *could* gate to within kilometers of the station or the planet, but I didn't think it likely any would try. If someone came, we'd have time to watch them approach. "We should concentrate our defenses around this station, and this planet."

She didn't like that, thought of an argument, but closed her mouth on it, unsaid. The question of where my authority came from, of where Captain Hetnys's loyalties lay in this conflict, didn't come up at all. There was no point pressing the issue, no advantage for me, or for her. If I was lucky, everyone else would ignore Athoek and it would never be an issue. But I wasn't going to bet on that.

Once Captain Hetnys had gone, I thought for a bit about what to do next. Meet with Governor Giarod, probably, and find out what, besides medical supplies, might come up short in the near future, and what we might do about that. Find something to keep *Sword of Atagaris* and *Mercy of Phey* busy—and out of trouble—but also ready to respond if I needed them. I sent a query to *Mercy of Kalr*. Lieutenant Tisarwat was above, on level two of the Undergarden, in a wide, shadowed room irregularly illuminated by light panels leaning here and there against the dark walls. Tisarwat, Raughd Denche, and half a dozen others reclined on long, thick cushions, the daughters, Ship indicated, of tea growers and station officials. They were drinking something strong and stinging—Tisarwat hadn't decided if she liked it or not, but she seemed to be mostly enjoying herself. Piat, the daughter of the station administrator, a bit more animated than I'd seen her the evening before, had just said something vulgar and everyone was laughing. Raughd said, in an undertone that can't have carried much past Tisarwat, who was sitting near both of them, "Aatr's tits, Piat, you're such a fucking ridiculous bore sometimes."

Tisarwat, where only Ship and I could see it, reacted with instant revulsion. "Piat," she said, "I don't think Citizen Raughd appreciates you. Come sit closer, I need someone to tell me amusing things."

The whole exchange, plus Piat's hesitation and Raughd's ostensibly amused reply—*I was only joking, Lieutenant, don't be so sensitive!*—told me unpleasant things about their relationship. If they had been my officers, when I had been a ship, I'd have intervened in some way, or spoken to their senior lieutenant. I wondered for an instant at Station's apparently not having done anything, and then it occurred to me that Raughd had perhaps been very, very careful about where she said what. Station couldn't see into the Undergarden, and though everyone in that room was certainly wired for communications, they had probably switched their implants off. That was very possibly the whole purpose of carousing here rather than elsewhere.

Below, in my own quarters, Kalr Five spoke. "Sir." Trepidation behind her stolid exterior.

"It's all right," called an unfamiliar voice from behind her, in the next room. "I'm all grown up, I'm not going to eat anyone!" The accent was an odd one, half well-educated Radchaai and half something else I couldn't place, nothing like the accents I'd heard here so far.

"Sir," Kalr Five said again. "Translator Dlique." She stumbled slightly over the oddness of the name.

"Translator?" No one had mentioned that anyone from the Translators Office was in the system, and there was no reason why anyone should be. I queried Ship and saw its memory of Kalr Five opening the door to a person in the loose, bright shirt and trousers people in the Undergarden wore—gloved, though, plain, stiff gray. No jewelry. No mention of a house name or of the division of the Translators Office she worked for, no hint of family affiliation or rank. I blinked the vision away. Rose. "Send her in."

Five stood aside, and Translator Dlique entered, smiling broadly. "Fleet Captain! How glad I am to see you. The governor's residence is *terribly* boring. I'd much rather have stayed on my ship, but they said there was a hull breach and if I stayed I wouldn't be able to breathe. I don't know, it doesn't seem like much, does it? Breathing?" She took a deep breath, gestured irritated indecision. "Air! It's just stupid, really. I'd as soon do without, but they insisted."

"Translator." I didn't bow, as she had not. And a horrible suspicion occurred. "It would appear you have the advantage of me."

She drew her shoulders up, her eyes widening in astonishment. "Me! The advantage! *You're* the one with all the soldiers."

The suspicion was growing into a certainty. This person certainly wasn't Radchaai. Translator for one of the aliens the Radch dealt with, then. But not for the Geck or the Rrrrrr—I'd met translators for the Geck before, and I knew something about the humans who translated for the Rrrrrr, and this person didn't seem to be either sort. And that odd accent. "I mean," I said, "that you appear to know who I am, but I don't know who you are."

She outright laughed. "Well, of course I know who *you*

are. Everyone is talking about you. Well, not to *me*. I'm not supposed to know you're here. I'm not supposed to leave the governor's residence, either. But I don't like being bored."

"I think you should tell me who you are, exactly." But I knew. Or knew as much as I needed to know. This person was one of those humans the Presger had bred to talk to the Radch. Translator for the Presger. *Disturbing company*, Anaander Mianaai had said of them. And the governor knew she was on the station. So, I would bet, did Captain Hetnys. This was surely behind her so inexplicable fear that the Presger might arrive here suddenly. I wondered what was behind the fact that she hadn't mentioned it to me.

"Who I am? *Exactly?*" Translator Dlique frowned. "I'm not...that is, I said just now I was Dlique but I might not be, I might be Zeiat. Or wait, no. No, I'm pretty sure I'm Dlique. I'm pretty sure they told me I was Dlique. Oh! I'm supposed to introduce myself, aren't I." She bowed. "Fleet Captain, I'm Dlique, translator for the Presger. Honored to make your acquaintance. Now, I think, you say something like *the honor's all mine* and then you offer me tea. I'm bored of tea, though, do you have arrack?"

I sent a quick silent message to Five, and then gestured Translator Dlique to a seat—an improbably comfortable arrangement of boxes and cushions covered with a yellow and pink embroidered blanket. "So," I said, when I'd sat across from her on my own pile of blanket-covered luggage. "You're a diplomat, are you?"

All her expressions so far had been almost childlike, seemingly completely unmoderated. Now she showed frank dismay. "I've made a hash of it, haven't I. It was all supposed to be so simple, too. I was on my way home from Tstur Palace after attending the New Year Cast. I went to parties, and smiled, and said, *the omens' fall was very propitious, the coming year will bring Justice and Benefit to all.* After a while I thanked the Humans for their hospitality and left. Just like I was supposed to. All very boring, no one who's anyone has to do it."

"And then a gate went down, and you were rerouted. And now you can't get home." With things the way they were, she'd never make it to Presger space. Not unless she had a ship that could generate its own gate—which the agreement between humans and the Presger had very specifically, very deliberately, forbidden the Presger to bring within Radch space.

Translator Dlique threw up her incongruously gray-gloved hands, a gesture, I thought, of exasperation. *Say exactly what we told you to and nothing will go wrong*, they said. Well, it all went wrong anyway. And they didn't say anything about *this*. You'd think they might have, they said lots of other things. *Sit up straight, Dlique. Don't dismember your sister, Dlique, it isn't* nice. *Internal organs belong* inside *your body, Dlique*." She scowled a moment, as though that last one particularly rankled.

"There does seem to be a general agreement that you are, in fact, Dlique," I said.

"You'd think! But it doesn't work like that when you aren't anybody. Oh!" She looked up as Kalr Five entered with two cups and a bottle of arrack. "That's the good stuff!" She took the cup Five handed her. Peered intently into Five's face. "Why are you pretending you're not Human?"

Five, in the grip of an offended horror so intense even she couldn't have spoken without betraying it, didn't answer, only turned to give me my own cup. I took it, and said, calmly, "Don't be rude to my soldiers, Dlique."

Translator Dlique laughed, as though I'd said something quite funny. "I like you, Fleet Captain. With Governor Giarod and Captain Hetnys, it's all *what is your purpose in coming here, Translator,* and *what are your intentions, Translator,* and *do you expect us to* believe *that, Translator.* And then it's *You'll find these rooms very comfortable, Translator; the doors are locked for your own safety, Translator; have some more tea, Translator.* Not Dlique, you see?" She took a substantial swallow of arrack. Coughed a little as it went down.

I wondered how long it would be before the governor's staff realized Translator Dlique was missing. Wondered for only a moment why Station hadn't raised the alarm. But then I remembered that gun, that no ship or station could see, that had come from the Presger. Translator Dlique might seem scatterbrained and childlike. But she was certainly as dangerous as Governor Giarod and Captain Hetnys feared. Likely considerably more so. They had, it seemed, underestimated her. Perhaps by her design. "What about the others on your ship?"

"Others?"

"Crew? Staff? Fellow passengers?"

"It's a *very* small ship, Fleet Captain."

"It must have been crowded, then, with Zeiat and the translator along."

Translator Dlique grinned. "I *knew* we'd get on well. Give me supper, will you? I just eat regular food, you know."

I recalled what she'd said when she'd first arrived. "Did you eat many people before you were grown?"

"No one I wasn't *supposed* to! Though," she added, frowning, "sometimes I kind of wish I *had* eaten someone I wasn't supposed to. But it's too late now. What are you having for supper? Radchaai on stations eat an awful lot of fish, it seems. I'm beginning to be bored of fish. Oh, where's your bathroom? I have to—

I cut her off. "We don't really have one. No plumbing here. But we do have a bucket."

"Now *that's* something different! I'm not bored of buckets yet!"

Lieutenant Tisarwat staggered into the room just as Five was clearing away the last supper dish and Translator Dlique was saying, very earnestly, "Eggs are so inadequate, don't you think? I mean, they ought to be able to become *anything*, but instead you always get a chicken. Or a duck. Or whatever they're programmed to be. You never get anything interesting, like regret, or the middle of the night last week." The entire dinner conversation had been like that.

"You raise a good point, Translator," I replied, and then turned my attention to Lieutenant Tisarwat. It had been more than three hours since I'd thought much about her, and she'd drunk a considerable amount in that time. She swayed, looked at me, glaring. "Raughd Denche," Tisarwat said to me, raising a hand and pointing somewhere off to the side for emphasis. She did not seem to notice the presence of Translator Dlique, who watched with an expression of slightly frowning curiosity. "Raughd. Denche. Is a *horrible person*."

Judging from even the very small bit I'd seen of Citizen Raughd today, I suspected Tisarwat's assessment was an accurate one.

"*Sir*," Tisarwat added. Very belatedly.

"Bo," I said sharply to the soldier who had come in behind her, who hovered anxiously. "Get your lieutenant out of here before there's a mess." Bo took her by the arm, led her unsteadily out. Too late, I feared.

"I don't think she's going to make it to the bucket," said Translator Dlique, solemnly. Almost regretfully.

"I don't, either," I said. "But it was worth a try."

That a Presger translator was here on Athoek Station was problem enough. How long would it be before whoever had sent her began to wonder why she hadn't returned? How would they react to Athoek having essentially made her a prisoner, even if somewhat unsuccessfully? And what would happen when they found the Radch in such disarray? Possibly nothing—the treaty made no distinctions between one sort of human or another, all were covered, and that same treaty forbade the Presger to harm any of those humans. That left open the question of what, to a Presger, would constitute "harm," but presumably issues like that had been hammered out between the translators of the Radch and those of the Presger.

And the presence and attention of the Presger might be turned to advantage. In the past hundred years or so the Presger had begun to sell high-quality medical correctives, significantly cheaper than the ones made inside the Radch. Governor Giarod had said Athoek didn't make its own medical supplies. And the Presger wouldn't care if Athoek was part of the Radch or not. They would only care if Athoek could pay, and while the Presger idea of "pay" could be somewhat eccentric, I didn't doubt we could find something suitable.

So why had the system governor locked Translator Dlique in the governor's residence? And then said nothing to me about it? I could imagine Captain Hetnys doing such a thing—she had known Captain Vel, who had believed that Anaander Mianaai's current fractured state was a result of Presger infiltration. I was fairly sure Translator Dlique's arrival here was a coincidence—but coincidences were meaningful, to Radchaai. Amaat was the universe, and anything that happened, happened because Amaat willed it. God's intentions could be discerned by the careful study of even the smallest, most seemingly insignificant events. And the past weeks' events were anything but small and insignificant. Captain Hetnys would be alert for strange occurrences, and this one would have set off a multitude of alarms for her. No, her concealment of Translator Dlique's presence only confirmed what I had already suspected about the captain's position.

But Governor Giarod. I had come away from dinner at Citizen Fosyf's, and the meeting after in the governor's office, with the impression that Governor Giarod was not only an intelligent, able person, but also that she understood that Anaander Mianaai's current conflict with herself originated in herself, and not anywhere else. I didn't think I could possibly have misjudged her so badly. But clearly I had missed something, didn't understand something about her position.

"Station," I transmitted, silently.

"Yes, Fleet Captain," replied Station, in my ear.

"Kindly let Governor Giarod know I intend to call on her first thing in the morning." Nothing else. If Station didn't know I knew about Translator Dlique's existence, let alone that she'd had dinner with me and then gone off again, my mentioning it would only panic Governor Giarod and Captain Hetnys. In the meantime I would have to try to find some way to handle this suddenly even more complicated situation.

On *Mercy of Kalr*, Seivarden sat in Command. Talking with *Sword of Atagaris*'s Amaat lieutenant, also apparently on watch on her own ship. "So," she was saying, Ship sending her words directly into Seivarden's ear. "Where are you from?"

"Someplace we don't fuck around while we're on watch," Seivarden said, but silently, to Ship. Aloud, she said, "Inais."

"Really!" It was plain that the *Sword of Atagaris* lieutenant had never heard of it. Which was hardly surprising, given the extent of Radch space, but didn't help Seivarden's already low estimation of her. "Have all your officers changed? Your predecessor was all right." Ekalu (at that moment asleep, breathing deep and even) had painted the former *Mercy of Kalr* Amaat lieutenant as an unbearable snob. "But that medic wasn't very friendly at all. Thought quite a lot of herself, I'd say." (Medic sat in *Mercy of Kalr*'s decade room, frowning at her lunch of skel and tea. Calm, in a fairly good mood.)

In many ways, Seivarden had in her youth been just as unbearable as the former *Mercy of Kalr* Amaat lieutenant. But Seivarden had served on a troop carrier—which meant she'd spent actual time in combat, and knew what counted when it came to doctors. "Shouldn't you be looking out for enemy ships?"

"Oh, Ship will tell me if it sees anything," said the *Sword of Atagaris* lieutenant, breezily. "That fleet captain is very intimidating. Though I suppose she would be. She's ordered us closer to the station. So we'll be neighbors, at least for a bit. We should have tea."

"Fleet captain is a bit less intimidating when you're not threatening to destroy her ship."

"Oh, well. That was a misunderstanding. Once you identified yourselves everything was cleared up. You don't think she'll hold it against me, though, do you?"

On Athoek Station, in the Undergarden, Kalr Five put away dishes in the room next to where I sat, and fussed to Eight about Translator Dlique's sudden, discomfiting appearance.

In another room yet, Bo pulled off an unconscious Tisarwat's boots. I said, to Ship, "Ekalu wasn't exaggerating, about *Sword of Atagaris*'s Amaat lieutenant."

"No," *Mercy of Kalr* replied. "She wasn't."

Next morning, I was dressing—trousers on, still bootless, fastening my shirt—when I heard an urgent shouting from the corridor, a voice calling, "Fleet Captain! Fleet Captain, sir!" Ship showed me, through the Kalr standing watch in the corridor, a seven- or eight-year-old child in grubby loose shirt and trousers, no shoes or gloves. "Fleet Captain!" she shouted, insistent. Ignoring the guard.

I grabbed my gloves, went quickly out of my room to the antechamber, through the door Five opened for me at my gesture. "Fleet Captain, sir!" the child said, still loud though I was standing in front of her. "Come right away! Someone painted on the wall again! If those corpse soldiers see it first it'll be *bad*!"

"Citizen," began Five.

I cut her off. "I'm coming." The child took off running, and I headed down the shadowed corridor after her. *Someone painted on the wall again.* Minor enough. Small enough to ignore, one might think, but Captain Hetnys had overreacted before—how badly clear to read in this child's urgency, either her own conclusions about what might happen when *Sword of Atagaris* Var arrived, or conveyed to her by some adult who'd sent her as messenger. Serious enough. And if it turned out to be nothing, well, I would only have delayed my breakfast by a few minutes.

"What did they paint?" I asked, climbing up a ladder in an access well, the only way between levels here.

"Some kind of words," the child replied, above me. "It's *words*!"

So she either hadn't seen them or couldn't read them, and I guessed it was the second. Probably not Radchaai then, or Raswar, which I'd learned over the past two days was read and spoken by most of the Ychana here. Station had told me, my first night here, when I'd asked it for some information, some history, that most of the residents in the Undergarden were Ychana.

It was Xhi, though rendered phonetically in Radchaai script. Whoever had done it had used the same pink paint that had been used to decorate the tea shop door, that had been left sitting at the side of the small, makeshift concourse. I recognized the words, not because I knew more than a few phrases of Xhi at this point but because it dated from the annexation, had been emblematic of a particular resistance movement Station had told me about, two nights before. *Not tea but blood!* It was a play on words. The Radchaai word for "tea" bore a passing resemblance to the Xhi word for "blood," and the implication was that the revolutionaries, rather than submitting to the Radch and drinking tea, would resist and drink (or at least spill) Radchaai blood. Those revolutionaries were several hundred years dead, that clever slogan no more than trivia in a history lesson.

The child, having seen me stop in front of the paint, not far from the tea shop entrance, took off running again, eager to be safely away. The rest of the Undergarden's residents had done the same—the small concourse was deserted, though I knew that at this hour there should be if nothing else a steady stream of customers into the tea shop. Anyone passing this way had taken one look at that *Not tea but blood!* and turned right around to find somewhere safe and out of the way of *Sword of Atagaris*'s Var lieutenant and her ancillaries. I was alone, Kalr Five still climbing up the access well, having been a good deal slower than I was.

A now-familiar voice spoke behind me. "That vomiting, purple-eyed child was right." I turned. Translator Dlique, dressed as she had been last night, when she'd visited me.

"Right about what, Translator?" I asked.

"Raughd Denche really *is* a horrible person."

At that moment, two *Sword of Atagaris* ancillaries came rushing onto the concourse. "You, there, halt!" said one, loud and emphatic. I realized, in that instant, that they might very well not recognize Translator Dlique—she was supposed to be locked in the governor's residence, she was dressed like an Ychana, and like all of the Undergarden this space was erratically lit. I myself wasn't in full uniform, wore only trousers, gloves, and partially fastened shirt. It was going to take *Sword of Atagaris* a moment to realize who we were.

"Oh, *sporocarps*!" Translator Dlique turned, I assumed to flee before *Sword of Atagaris* could see who she was and detain her.

She had not turned all the way, and I had only had the briefest moment to begin wondering at her using "sporocarp" as an obscenity, when a single gunshot popped, loud in the confined space, and Translator Dlique gasped, and tumbled forward to the ground. Unthinking, I raised my armor, yelled "*Sword of Atagaris*, stand down!" At the same moment I transmitted to Station, urgently, "Medical emergency on level one of the Undergarden!" Dropped to my knees beside Translator Dlique. "Station, Translator Dlique's been shot in the back. I need medics here *right now*."

"Fleet Captain," said Station's calm voice in my ear. "Medics don't go to the—"

"*Right now*, Station." I dropped my armor, looked up at the two *Sword of Atagaris* Vars, beside me now. "Your medkit, Ship, quickly." I wanted to ask, *What do you think you're doing, firing on people?* But keeping Translator Dlique from bleeding out was more immediately important. And this wouldn't be entirely *Sword of Atagaris*'s fault, it would have been following Captain Hetnys's orders.

"I'm not carrying medkits, Fleet Captain," said one of the *Sword of Atagaris* ancillaries. "This is not a combat situation, and this station does have medical facilities." And I, of course, didn't have one. We'd brought them, as a matter of routine, but they were still in a packing case three levels down. If the bullet had hit, say, the translator's renal artery—a distinct possibility, considering where the wound was—she could bleed out in minutes, and even if I ordered one of my Kalrs to bring me a kit, it would arrive too late.

I sent the order anyway, and pressed my hands over the wound on Translator Dlique's back. Likely it wouldn't do any good, but it was the only thing I *could* do. "Station, I need those medics!" I looked up at *Sword of Atagaris*. "Bring me a suspension pod. *Now*."

"Aren't any around here." The tea shop proprietor—she must have been the only person who'd stayed nearby when they'd seen that slogan painted on the wall. Now she called out from the door of her shop. "Medical never comes here, either."

"They'd better come this time." My compression had reduced the blood coming out of the translator, but I couldn't control internal bleeding, and her breathing had gone quick and shallow. She was losing blood fast, then, faster than I could see. Down on level three Kalr Eight was opening the case where the medkits were stored. She'd moved the instant the order had come, was working quickly, but I didn't think she would be here in time.

I still pressed uselessly on the translator's back, while she lay gasping on the ground, facedown. "Blood stays *inside* your arteries, Dlique," I said.

She gave a weak, shaky *hah*. "See..." She paused for a few shallow breaths. "Breathing. Stupid."

"Yes," I said, "yes, breathing is stupid and boring, but keep on doing it, Dlique. As a favor to me." She didn't answer.

By the time Kalr Eight arrived with a medkit and Captain Hetnys came running onto the scene, a pair of medics behind her and *Sword of Atagaris* behind them, dragging an emergency suspension pod, it was too late. Translator Dlique was dead.

11

I knelt on the ground beside Translator Dlique's body. Blood soaked my bare feet, my knees, my hands, still pressing down on the wound on her back, and the cuffs of my shirtsleeves were wet with it. It was not the first time I had been covered in someone else's blood. I had no horror of it. The two *Sword of Atagaris* ancillaries were motionless and impassive, having set down the suspension pod they had dragged this far to no purpose. Captain Hetnys stood frowning, puzzled, not quite sure, I thought, of what had just happened.

I rose to make way for the medics, who went immediately to work on Translator Dlique. "Cit... Fleet Captain," said one of them after a while. "I'm sorry, there's nothing we can do."

"Never is," said the proprietor of the tea shop, who was still standing in her doorway. *Not tea but blood!* scrawled only meters away from where she stood. That was a problem. But not, I suspected, the problem Captain Hetnys thought it was.

I peeled off my gloves. Blood had soaked through them,

my hands were sticky with it. I stepped quickly over to Captain Hetnys faster than she could back away and grabbed her uniform jacket with my bloody hands. Dragged her stumbling over to where Translator Dlique lay, the two medics scrambling out of our way, and before Captain Hetnys could regain her balance or resist, I threw her down onto the corpse. I turned to Kalr Eight. "Fetch a priest," I said to her. "Whoever you find who's qualified to do purifications and funerals. If she says she won't come to the Undergarden, inform her that she may come willingly or not, but she will come regardless."

"Sir," Eight acknowledged, and departed.

Captain Hetnys had meanwhile managed to get to her feet, with the assistance of one of her ancillaries.

"How did this happen, Captain? I said not to use violence against citizens unless it was absolutely necessary." Translator Dlique wasn't a citizen, but *Sword of Atagaris* couldn't have known it was the translator they were shooting at.

"Sir," said Captain Hetnys. Voice shaking either with rage at what I'd just done, or distress generally. "*Sword of Atagaris* queried Station, and it said it had no knowledge of this person and there was no tracker. She was not, therefore, a citizen."

"So that made it fine to shoot her, did it?" I asked. But of course, I myself had followed exactly that logic on a nearly uncountable number of occasions. It was such compelling logic, to someone like *Sword of Atagaris*—to someone like me—that it had never occurred to me that *Sword of Atagaris* would even think of firing guns here, on a station full of citizens, a station that had been part of the Radch for centuries.

It should have occurred to me. I was responsible for everything that happened under my command.

"Fleet Captain," replied Captain Hetnys, indignant and not trying as hard as she might have to hide it. "Unauthorized persons pose a danger to—"

"This," I said, each word deliberate, emphatic, "is Presger Translator Dlique."

"Fleet Captain," said Station, in my ear. I had left the connection to Station open, so it had heard what I had said. "With all respect, you are mistaken. Translator Dlique is still in her rooms in the governor's residence."

"Look again, Station. *Send* someone to look. Captain Hetnys, neither you nor any of your crew or ancillaries will go armed on this station under any circumstances, beginning now. Nor will your ship or any of your crew enter the Undergarden again without my explicit permission. *Sword of Atagaris* Var and its lieutenant will return to *Sword of Atagaris* as soon as a shuttle can take them. Do not"—she had opened her mouth to protest—"say a single word to me. You have deliberately concealed vital information from me. You have endangered the lives of residents of this station. Your troops have caused the death of the diplomatic representative of the Presger. I am trying to think of some reason why I shouldn't shoot you where you stand." Actually, there were at least three compelling reasons—the two armed ancillaries standing beside Captain Hetnys and the fact that in my haste I had left my own gun behind in my quarters, three levels below this one.

I turned to the proprietor of the tea shop. "Citizen." It took extra effort not to speak in my flat, ancillary's voice. "Will you bring me tea? I've had no breakfast, and I'm going to have to fast today." Wordlessly, she turned and went into her shop.

While I waited for tea, Governor Giarod arrived. Took one

look at Translator Dlique's body, at Captain Hetnys standing mute and blood-smeared by *Sword of Atagaris*'s ancillaries, took a breath, and then said, "Fleet Captain. I can explain."

I looked at her. Then turned to see the tea shop proprietor set a bowl of tea-gruel on the ground a meter from where I stood. I thanked her, went to pick it up. Saw revulsion on the face of Captain Hetnys and Governor Giarod as I held it with bare, bloody hands and drank from it. "This is how it will be," I said, after I'd drunk half of the thick tea. "There will be a funeral. Don't speak to me of keeping this secret, or of panic in the corridors. There will be a funeral, with offerings and suitable tokens, and a period of mourning for every member of Station Administration. The body will be kept in suspension so that when the Presger come for the translator, they may take it and do whatever it is they do with dead bodies.

"For the moment, *Sword of Atagaris* will tell me the last time it saw this wall free of paint, and then Station will name for me every person who stopped in front of it from then until I saw it just now." Station might not have been able to see if someone was painting, but it would know where everyone was, and I suspected very few people would have stood right next to this wall, in that window of time, who had not been the painter herself.

"Begging the fleet captain's very great indulgence." Captain Hetnys dared, against all wisdom, to speak to me. "That's already done, and Security has arrested the person responsible."

I raised an eyebrow. Surprised. And skeptical. "Security has arrested Raughd Denche?"

Now Captain Hetnys was astonished. "No, sir!" she protested. "I don't know why you would assume Citizen Raughd would do something like this. No, sir, it can only have been Sirix Odela. She passed here on her way to work this morning and stopped quite close to the wall for some fifteen seconds. More than enough time to paint this."

If she passed by on her way to work, she lived in the Undergarden. Most of the Undergarden residents were Ychana, but this name was Samirend. And familiar. "This person works in the Gardens, above?" I asked. Captain Hetnys gestured assent. I thought of the person I'd met when I'd first arrived. Who I had found standing in the lake in the Gardens, so distressed at the thought of expressing anger. It wasn't possible she had done this. "Why would a Samirend paint a Xhi slogan in Radchaai script? Why wouldn't she write it in Liost since she's Samirend, or Raswar, that more people here could read?"

"Historically, Fleet Captain—" began Governor Giarod.

I cut her off. "*Historically*, Governor, quite a lot of people have good reason to resent the annexation. But right here, right now, none of them will find any profit in more than token rebellion." It would have been that way for several centuries. Nobody in the Undergarden who valued her life (not to mention the lives of anyone else in the Undergarden) would have painted that slogan on that wall, not knowing how this station's administration would react. And I'd be willing to bet that everyone in the Undergarden knew how this station's administration would react.

"The creation of the Undergarden was no doubt unintended," I continued, as *Mercy of Kalr* showed me a brief flash of Kalr Eight speaking sternly to a junior priest, "but as it has benefited you, you tell yourselves that its condition is also just and proper." That constant trio, justice, propriety, and benefit. They could not, in theory, exist alone. Nothing just was improper, nothing beneficial was unjust.

"Fleet Captain," began Governor Giarod. Indignant. "I hardly think—"

"Everything necessitates its opposite," I said, cutting her off. "How can you be civilized if there is no uncivilized?" Civilized. Radchaai. The word was the same. "If it did not benefit someone, somehow, there'd be plumbing here, and lights, and doors that worked, and medics who would come for an emergency." Before the system governor could do more than blink in response, I turned to the tea shop proprietor, still standing in her doorway. "Who sent for me?"

"Sirix," she said. "And see what it got her."

"Citizen," began Captain Hetnys, stern and indignant.

"Be silent, Captain." My tone was even, but Captain Hetnys said nothing further.

Radchaai soldiers who touch dead bodies dispose of their impurities by means of a bath and a brief prayer—I never knew any to bathe without muttering or subvocalizing it. I didn't, myself, but all my officers did, when I was a ship. I presumed civilian medics availed themselves of something similar.

That bath and that prayer sufficed, for anything short of making temple offerings. But with most Radchaai civilians, near contact with death was entirely another matter.

If I had been in a slightly more spiteful mood I would have gone deliberately around the small makeshift concourse, indeed around this entire level of the Undergarden, touching things and smearing blood so that what priests came would be forced to spend days on it. But I had never noticed that anyone profited from needless spite, and besides I suspected that the entire Undergarden was already in a dire state, as far as ritual uncleanness went. If Medical never came here, others had certainly died here before, and if priests would not come, then that impurity had certainly lingered. Assuming one subscribed to such beliefs, in any event. The Ychana probably didn't. Just one more reason to consider them foreign and not worth basic amenities every Radchaai supposedly took for granted.

A senior priest arrived, accompanied by two assistants. She stopped two meters from Translator Dlique's corpse in its puddle of blood, and stood staring at it and us with wide-eyed horror.

"How do they dispose of bodies here?" I asked no one in particular.

Governor Giarod answered. "They drag them into the corridors around the Undergarden and leave them."

"Disgusting," muttered Captain Hetnys.

"What else are they supposed to do?" I asked. "There's no facility here for dealing with dead bodies. Medical doesn't come here, and neither do priests." I looked at the senior priest. "Am I right?"

"No one is supposed to be here, Fleet Captain," she replied primly, and cast a glance at the governor.

"Indeed." I turned to Kalr Five, who had returned with the priests. "This suspension pod is functional?"

"Yes, sir."

"Then Captain Hetnys and I will put the translator in it. Then you"—indicating the priests with a gesture that my barehandedness made offensive—"will do what is necessary."

Captain Hetnys and I spent twenty minutes washing in blessed water, saying prayers, and being sprinkled with salt and fumigated with three kinds of incense. It did not dispense with all of our contamination, only mitigated it so that we could walk through corridors or be in a room without anyone needing to call a priest. The soldier's bath and prayer would have done as well. Better, in fact, strictly speaking, but it would not have satisfied most of the residents of Athoek Station.

"If I go into full, traditional mourning," Governor Giarod pointed out, when that was finished, and Captain Hetnys and I were dressed in clean clothes, "I won't be able to go into my office for two weeks. The same goes for the rest of Administration. I agree, though, Fleet Captain, someone should." As the rite had gone on, she had lost the harried expression she'd arrived with, and now seemed quite calm.

"Yes," I agreed, "you'll all have to be lesser cousins. Captain Hetnys and I will act as immediate family." Captain Hetnys looked none too pleased about that but was not in any position to protest. I dispatched Kalr Five to bring a razor so that Captain Hetnys and I could shave our heads for the funeral, and also to see a jeweler about memorial tokens.

"Now," I said to Governor Giarod, when Five was away and I'd sent Captain Hetnys to my quarters to prepare for the fast, "I need to know about Translator Dlique."

"Fleet Captain, I hardly think this is the best place..."

"I can't go to your office as I am." Not so obviously just after a death that put me in full mourning, when I should be fasting at home. The impropriety would be obvious, and this funeral had to be absolutely, utterly proper. "And there's no one near." The tea seller was inside her shop, out of view. The priests had fled as soon as they thought they could. The *Sword of Atagaris* ancillaries had left the Undergarden at my order. My two Mercy of Kalrs, standing nearby, didn't count. "And keeping things secret hasn't been a very good choice so far."

Governor Giarod gestured rueful resignation. "She arrived

with the first wave of rerouted ships." The ships that neighboring systems had sent here either in the hope that they could find a different route to their original destinations, now the gates they needed to traverse were down, or because their own facilities were overwhelmed. "Just her, in a tiny little one-person courier barely the size of a shuttle. I'm not sure how it could even carry as much air as she needed for the trip she said she was making. And the timing was just..." She gestured her frustration. "I couldn't send to the palace for advice. I cast omens. Privately. The results were disturbing."

"Of course." No Radchaai was immune to the suspicion of coincidence. Nothing happened by pure accident, no matter how small. Every event, therefore, was potentially a sign of God's intentions. Unusual coincidences could only be a particularly pointed divine message. "I understand your apprehension. I even, to a certain extent, understand your wanting to confine the translator and conceal her presence from most station residents. None of that troubles me. What does trouble me is your failure to mention this alarming and potentially dangerous situation to me."

Governor Giarod sighed. "Fleet Captain, I hear things. There's very little that's said on this station—and, frankly, most of the rest of the system—that I don't eventually become aware of. Ever since I took this office I've heard whispers about corruption from outside the Radch."

"I'm not surprised." It was a perennial complaint, that transportees from annexed worlds, and newly made citizens, brought uncivilized customs and attitudes that would undermine true civilization. I'd been hearing it myself for as long as I'd been alive—some two thousand years. The situation in the Undergarden would only add to those whispers, I was sure.

"Recently," said Governor Giarod, with a rueful smile, "Captain Hetnys has suggested that the Presger have been infiltrating high offices with the aim of destroying us. Presger translators being more or less indistinguishable from actual humans, and the Translators Office being in such frequent and close contact with them."

"Governor, did you actually hold any conversations with Translator Dlique?"

She gestured frustration. "I know what you intend to say, Fleet Captain. But then again, she apparently left a locked and guarded room in the governor's residence with no one the wiser, obtained clothes, and walked freely around this station without Station being aware of it. Yes, talking with her could be downright peculiar, and I'd never have mistaken her for a citizen. But she was clearly capable of a great deal more than she let on to us. Some of it rather frightening. And I had never thought the rumors were credible, that the Presger, who had left us alone since the treaty, who were so alien, would concern themselves with our affairs, when they never had before. But then Translator Dlique arrives so soon after gates start to go down, and we lose contact with Omaugh Palace, and..."

"And Captain Hetnys spoke of Presger infiltration of high offices. Of the highest office. And here I am, a cousin of Anaander Mianaai, and arriving with a story about the Lord of the Radch fighting with herself over the future of the Radch, and an official record that clearly did not match what I actually was. And suddenly you had trouble dismissing the previously incredible whispers about the Presger."

"Just so."

"Governor, do we agree that no matter what is happening elsewhere, the only thing it is possible or appropriate for us to do is secure the safety of the residents of this system? Whether there is a division within the Lord of Mianaai or not, that would be the only reasonable order you would expect from her?"

Governor Giarod thought about that for six seconds. "Yes. Yes, you're right. Except, Fleet Captain, if we have to buy medical supplies, that may well mean dealing with outside sources. Like the Presger."

"You see," I said, very, very evenly, "why it wasn't a particularly good idea to conceal Translator Dlique from me." She gestured acquiescence. "You're not a fool. Or I didn't think you were. I admit my discovery of Translator Dlique's presence has somewhat undermined my assurance on that score." She said nothing. "Now, before I officially begin the fast, there's other business that needs to be taken care of. I need to speak to Station Administrator Celar."

"About the Undergarden?" Governor Giarod guessed.

"Among other things."

In my sitting room on level four of the Undergarden, my Kalrs ordered to leave us to speak privately, I said to Tisarwat, "I'll have to spend the next two weeks in mourning. Which means I won't be able to do any work. Lieutenant Seivarden is of course in command of *Mercy of Kalr* during that time. And you will be in charge here in the household."

She had awakened miserably hungover. Tea and meds had begun to remedy that, but not entirely. "Yes, sir."

"Why did she leave this?"

Tisarwat blinked. Frowned. Then understood. "Sir. It's not a *big* problem. And it's useful to have somewhere you can... do things in secret." Indeed. Useful to any and all parts of the Lord of the Radch, but I didn't say that. She would already know it. "And really, you know, sir, the people here got on all right until Captain Hetnys showed up."

"Got on all right, did they? With no water, and no Medical to come in emergencies, and apparently nobody questioning Hetnys's methods here?" She looked down at her feet. Ashamed. Miserable.

Looked up. "They're getting water from *somewhere*, sir. They grow mushrooms. There's this dish that..."

"Lieutenant."

"Yes, sir."

"What was she going to do here?"

"Help you, sir. Mostly. Unless you were going to do anything that would prevent her from...reassembling herself once this was done." I didn't reply to this immediately, and she added, "She thinks that's likely, sir."

"This situation in the Undergarden needs fixing. I'm about to talk to the station administrator about it. Use your contacts—surely she sent you here with contacts—to get it done. Once the funeral is done, I'll be unable to do anything directly, but I *will* be watching you."

Tisarwat left, and Kalr Five ushered Station Administrator Celar into the sitting room. She wore the light blue of Administration today, managed to make the standard uniform look elegant on her broad and heavy form. I sat when she sat. Did not offer her tea, as would ordinarily have been polite. In my current state no one but my own household could eat or drink in my presence. "The situation in the Undergarden is intolerable," I said, with no preamble, no softening. No thanks for coming here at what was surely considerable inconvenience. "I am frankly astonished that it's been left this way for so long. But I am not asking for reasons or excuses. I expect repairs to begin immediately."

"Fleet Captain," said Station Administrator Celar, bristling at my words, though my tone had been calm and flat, "there's only so much that—"

"Then do that much. And don't tell me that no one is supposed to be here. Clearly people *are* here. And"—this was entering delicate territory—"I doubt very much any of this could have happened without at least some collusion from Station. I strongly suspect Station has been concealing things from you. You have a problem there, and it's of your own making." Station Administrator Celar frowned, not immediately understanding me. Offended. "I would urge you to look at this from Station's point of view. A not inconsiderable part of itself has been damaged. Restoring it entirely isn't possible, but no attempt has been made to even mitigate it. You just sealed it off and tried to forget it. But Station can't just forget it." And it struck me as likely that having people here felt better to Station than a numb, empty hole. And at the same time constantly reminded it of its injury. But I didn't think I could find a way to explain why, or how I'd come to that conclusion. "And the people who live here, they're Station's residents, who Station is made to care for. You don't treat them particularly well, though, and I imagine Station resents that. Though it can't ever say that directly to you, and so instead it just... leaves things out. Does and says exactly what you ask of it and very little more. I've met unhappy AIs." I didn't say how, or that I'd been an AI myself. "And you have one here."

"How can an AI be unhappy when it's doing exactly what it was made to do?" asked Station Administrator Celar. Not, thankfully, how it could possibly matter whether an AI was happy or not. And then, demonstrating that she had not been given her office merely on the strength of her looks, Station Administrator Celar said, "But you say we've prevented

Station from doing that. That is the substance of what you've said, yes?" She sighed. "When I arrived, my predecessor depicted the Undergarden as a morass of crime and squalor, that no one could find a way to safely clear out. Everything I saw seemed to indicate she was right. And it had been that way so long, fixing it seemed impossible. Everyone agreed it was so. But that's no excuse, is it. It's *my* responsibility."

"Repair the section doors," I said. "Fix the plumbing and the lights."

"And the ventilation," said Station Administrator Celar, fanning herself briefly with one blue-gloved hand.

I gestured agreement. "Confirm the current occupants in their places. Just for a start." Getting Medical here, and Security patrols that would not cause more problems than they might solve, would be next, and more difficult.

"Somehow, Fleet Captain, I don't think it could possibly be that simple."

Likely not. But. "I couldn't say. But we have to do something." I saw her notice that *we*. "And now I need to speak to you about your daughter Piat." Station Administrator Celar frowned in puzzlement. "She and Citizen Raughd are lovers?"

Still the frown. "They've been sweethearts since they were children. Raughd grew up downwell, and Piat often went down to visit, and keep her company. Not many other children Raughd's age in the family, at the time. Not in the mountains, anyway."

Downwell. Where Station couldn't see more than trackers. "You like Raughd," I said. "It's a good connection, and she's very charming, isn't she." Station Administrator Celar gestured assent. "Your daughter is very subdued. Doesn't talk to you much. Spends more time in other households than home with you. You feel, perhaps, she's driven you away."

"What are you aiming at, Fleet Captain?"

Even if Station had seen the way Raughd treated Piat when she thought no one was looking, it wouldn't have reported it directly. On a station, privacy was paradoxically both nonexistent and an urgent necessity. Station saw your most intimate moments. But you always knew Station would never tell just anyone what it saw, wouldn't *gossip*. Station would report crimes and emergencies, but for anything else it would, at most, hint here or guide there. A station household could be, in some ways, very self-contained, very secret, even though living at close quarters with so many others. Even though every moment it was under Station's constant, all-seeing eye.

The hints could often be enough. But if Station was unhappy, it might not even do that. "Raughd is only charming when she wants to be," I said. "When everyone is looking. In private, to certain people, she's very different. I'm going to ask my ship to send you a recording of something that happened here in the Undergarden last night."

Her fingers twitched, calling up the file. She blinked, her eyes moving in a way that told me she was watching that scene of Raughd, her daughter, others, reclining on those cushions, drinking. I saw on her face the moment she heard Citizen Raughd say, *You're such a fucking ridiculous bore.* The stunned disbelief, and then a look of determined anger as she kept watching, through Raughd's increasing aggression as Lieutenant Tisarwat, drunk as she was, tried to maneuver Piat out of Raughd's way. Station Administrator Celar gestured the recording away.

"Am I correct," I asked, before she could speak, "in guessing that Citizen Raughd never took the aptitudes? Because she was already Citizen Fosyf's heir?" Station Administrator Celar gestured *yes*. "The tester would almost certainly have seen the potential for this sort of thing, and routed her toward some sort of treatment, or an assignment where her personality would have been of benefit. Sometimes, combined with other things, it suits someone for a military career, and the discipline helps keep them in check and teaches them to behave better." Gods help the crew of such a person who was promoted to any position of authority without learning to behave better. "They can be very, very charming. No one ever suspects what they're like in private. Most won't believe it if you tell them."

"I wouldn't have," she admitted. "If you hadn't shown me..." She gestured forward, meaning to indicate the recording that had just played in her vision, in her ears.

"That's why I showed it to you," I said, "despite the impropriety of doing so."

"Nothing just can be improper," replied Station Administrator Celar.

"There's more, Station Administrator. As I said, Station has been keeping things back that you have not explicitly asked for. There was at least one occasion on which Citizen Piat reported to Medical with bruises on her face. She said she'd been drinking in the Undergarden and tripped and stumbled into a wall. The bruises didn't look like the right sort for that, not to my eye. Not to Medical's either, but they weren't about to get involved in any personal business of yours. I'm sure they thought if it was really a problem, Station would have said something." And no one else would have noticed. A corrective, a few hours, and the bruises would be gone. "There was no one around, at the time, except Raughd. I've seen this sort of thing before. Raughd will have apologized and sworn never to do it again. I strongly suggest asking Station explicitly about each and every visit your daughter has made to Medical, no matter how minor. I'd also ask Station about her use of first aid correctives. I queried Station directly, with the intention of finding this sort of incident, because I've seen this sort of thing before and knew it was almost certainly there. Station only answered me because System Governor Giarod ordered it, at my request."

Station Administrator Celar said nothing. She barely seemed to breathe. Maybe watching the record of her daughter's visit to Medical. Maybe not.

"So," I continued after a moment. "No doubt you're aware of the difficulty this morning that ended in the death of the Presger Translator Dlique."

She blinked, startled at the sudden change of topic. Frowned. "Fleet Captain, this morning was the first I'd heard the translator even existed, I assure you."

I waved that away. "Station was explicitly asked who had stood near that wall, in the right time frame, for long enough to paint those words. Station answered with two names: Sirix Odela and Raughd Denche. Security immediately arrested Citizen Sirix, on the assumption that Raughd wouldn't have done such a thing. But Station was not asked if either citizen had paint on her clothes. And since Station was not asked, it did not volunteer that information." I was not connected to Station at the moment, though I thought it very likely Station Administrator Celar was. "This is not something I think you should blame Station for. As I said earlier."

"Surely," said Station Administrator Celar, "it was a prank, something done for amusement. Youthful high spirits."

"What amusement," I asked, my own voice carefully even, "could youthful high spirits have anticipated? Watching *Sword of Atagaris* Var arrest completely innocent citizens? Putting those completely innocent citizens through interrogation to prove their innocence, or worse not interrogating them at all, convicting them without any evidence beyond *Raughd Denche could never have done that*? Further alarming you, and the governor, and Captain Hetnys at a time when things were already tense? And if, for the sake of argument, we pretend those are harmless amusements, then why has no one said of Citizen Sirix, *It's nothing, it must have been a prank*?" Silence. Her fingers twitched, just slightly, the station administrator speaking to Station no doubt. "There's paint on Citizen Raughd's gloves, isn't there?"

"Her personal attendant," acknowledged Station Administrator Celar, "is even now trying to wash the paint off of them."

"So," I said. This was going to be even more delicate than the problem with Station. "Citizen Fosyf is prominent, and wealthy. You have authority here, but it's just easier to get the things you want done when you have the support of people like Fosyf. And, no doubt, she gives you gifts. Valuable ones. The romance between your daughter and hers is convenient. When you sent Citizen Piat downwell to keep Raughd company, you were already thinking of this. And you might be wondering if you'd noticed that your daughter was unhappy. Or how long ago you'd first seen the signs of it, and maybe you told yourself that it was nothing, really, that everyone has to put up with a little stress, for the sake of family connections, family benefit. That if it was ever really bad, surely Station would say something. To you, of all people. And it's so easy to just go along. So easy not to see what's happening. And the longer you don't see it, the harder it becomes to *see* it, because then you have to admit that you ignored it all that time. But this is the moment when it's laid before you, clear and unambiguous. This is the sort of person Raughd Denche is. This is what she's doing to your daughter. Are her mother's gifts worth your daughter's well-being? Is political convenience worth that? Does the wider benefit to your house outweigh it? You can't put off the choice any longer. Can't pretend there's no choice there to make."

"You are very uncomfortable company, Fleet Captain," observed Station Administrator Celar, her voice bitter and sharp. "Do you do this sort of thing everywhere you go?"

"Lately it seems so," I admitted.

As I spoke, Kalr Five came silently into the room, and stood ancillary-stiff. Very clearly wanted my attention. "Yes, Five?" She wouldn't have interrupted without very good reason.

"Begging the fleet captain's indulgence, sir. Citizen Fosyf's personal attendant has inquired about the possibility of the citizen inviting you and Captain Hetnys to spend the two weeks after Translator Dlique's funeral on her estate downwell." Such an invitation was properly made in person—this sort of inquiry beforehand, through servants, prevented any inconvenience or embarrassment. "She has more than one house on her land, so you'll be able to spend the mourning period in proper fashion, very conveniently, she says."

I looked over at Station Administrator Celar, who gave a small laugh. "Yes, I thought it was odd, too, when I first came. But here at Athoek, if you can afford it, you don't spend your two weeks in your quarters." After the initial days of fasting, after the funeral, residents in a mourning household did no work, but instead stayed mostly at home, accepting consolatory visits from clients and friends. I'd assumed that Captain Hetnys and I would stay here in the Undergarden for that time. "If you're accustomed to have things done for you," Station Administrator Celar continued, "especially if you don't pick your meals up at the common refectories but rather have someone in your household cook for you, it can be a long two weeks. So you go to stay somewhere that's technically its own house, but servants nearby can cook and clean for you. There's a place right off the main concourse that specializes in it—but they're filled up right now with people who just need someplace to stay."

"And that's considered entirely proper, is it?" I asked doubtfully.

"There has been some suspicion," Celar replied wryly, "that my not being familiar with the practice when I arrived indicates that my upbringing wasn't what it might have been. *Your* not being familiar with it will be a shock they may never recover from."

I shouldn't have been surprised. I had known officers from nearly every province, had known that the details of funeral practice (among other things) could differ from place to place. Things widely considered mandatory were sometimes only actually available to citizens with sufficient resources, though that was rarely acknowledged. And beyond that, I knew that small details often went unmentioned, on the assumption that of course all Radchaai did things the same way and there was no need to discuss it. But I was used to those being fairly small details—what sort of incense was appropriate, prayers added to or subtracted from the daily observances, odd food restrictions.

I considered Five. She stood there outwardly impassive, but wanting me to see something, impatient I hadn't yet. Her announcement had, from her point of view, been heavy with suggestion. "It's customary to pay for such services?" I asked Station Administrator Celar.

"Often," she agreed, still with a wry smile. "Though I'm sure Fosyf is just being generous."

And self-serving. It would not surprise me if Fosyf had realized, one way or another, what part her own daughter had played in the episode that had led to Translator Dlique's death. Hoped, perhaps, that hosting me during the mourning period would be, if not a bribe, at least a gesture toward remorse for what her daughter had done. But it might well be useful. "Raughd could come downwell with us, of course," I observed. "And stay after. For quite some time."

"*I'll see to it*," said Station Administrator Celar, with a small, bitter smile that, had I been Raughd Denche, would have made me shiver.

12

Athoek's sky was a clear cerulean, shot here and there with bright streaks—the visible parts of the planet's weather control grid. For some hours we'd flown over water, blue-gray and flat, but now mountains loomed, brown and green below, black and gray and streaked with ice at their tops. "Another hour or so, Fleet Captain, Citizens," said the pilot. We had been met, at the base of the elevator, by two fliers. Between one thing and another—including maneuvering on the part of Kalr Five—Fosyf and Raughd had ended up in the other one, along with Captain Hetnys and the *Sword of Atagaris* ancillary who accompanied her. Both Captain Hetnys and I were in full mourning—the hair we'd shaved off barely beginning to grow back, no cosmetics but a broad white stripe painted diagonally across our faces. Once full mourning was over, Translator Dlique's memorial token would join Lieutenant Awn's plain gold tag on my jacket: a two-centimeter opal, *Translator Dlique Zeiat Presger* engraved large and clear on the silver setting. They were the only names we knew to use.

In the seat beside me, silent the entire trip so far—an impressive two days of not saying a word beyond the absolutely necessary—sat Sirix Odela. My request that she accompany me would leave the Gardens shorthanded, and theoretically she could have refused. Very little choice was actually involved. I guessed her anger had made her unable to speak without violating the terms of her reeducation, that attempting to do so would make her extremely uncomfortable, and so I did not press the issue, not even when it stretched into the second day.

"Fleet Captain," Sirix said. Finally. Voice pitched to reach my ear over the noise of the flier, but not carry up front to where the pilot sat. "Why am I here?" Her tone was very, very carefully controlled, a control I didn't doubt was hard-won.

"You are here," I said, in an even, reasonable voice, as though I was unaware of the resentment and distress behind the question, "to tell me what Citizen Fosyf *isn't* telling me."

"Why do you think I would be willing or able to tell you anything, Fleet Captain?" Sirix's voice took on just the slightest edge, skirting what she would be able to say without discomfort.

I turned my head to look at her. She stared straight ahead, as though my reaction didn't concern her at all. "Is there family you'd like to visit?" She'd come from downwell, had relatives who'd worked on tea plantations. "I'm sure I could arrange for it."

"I am . . ." She hesitated. Swallowed. I had pushed too hard, somehow. "Without family. For any practical purpose."

"Ah." She did have a house name, and so was not legally houseless. "Actually throwing you out of the family would have been too much disgrace for them to bear. But perhaps you're still in discreet contact with someone? A mother, a sibling?" And children generally had parents from more than one house. Parents or siblings from other houses might not be considered terribly close relatives, might or might not be required to lend any sort of support, but those ties were there, could be drawn on in a crisis.

"To be entirely honest, Fleet Captain," said Sirix, as though it was an answer to my question, "I really don't want to spend two weeks in the company of Citizen Raughd Denche."

"I don't think she realizes," I said. Citizen Raughd had been oblivious, or at least seemingly so. Oblivious to the seriousness of what she'd done, to the fact that anyone at all might be aware she'd done it. "Why do you live in the Undergarden, citizen?"

"I didn't like my assigned quarters. I think, Fleet Captain, that you appreciate directness."

I lifted an eyebrow. "It would be hypocritical of me not to."

She acknowledged that with a bitter quirk of her mouth. "I would like to be left alone now."

"Of course, Citizen. Please don't hesitate to tell me or either of my Kalrs"—Kalr Five and Kalr Eight sat behind us—"if you need anything." I turned forward again. Closed my eyes and thought of Lieutenant Tisarwat.

Who stood in the garden, on the bridge stretching across the lake. The fish roiled the water below her, purple and green, orange and blue, gold and red, gaping as Tisarwat dropped food pellets into the water. Celar's daughter Piat stood beside her, leaning on the rail. She had just said something that had surprised and dismayed Lieutenant Tisarwat. I didn't query, but waited to hear Tisarwat's answer.

"That's ridiculous," Tisarwat said, indignant. "First assistant to the chief of Horticulture of the entire station, that's not *nothing*. If it weren't for Horticulture no one on this station could eat or breathe. You don't seriously think you're doing some unimportant, useless job."

"What, making tea for the chief of Horticulture?"

"And managing her appointments, and communicating her orders, and learning how the Gardens are organized. I bet if she stayed home for the next week, no one would even notice, you'd have everything running smoothly as normal."

"That's because everyone else knows their jobs."

"You included." Devious Tisarwat! I'd told her to stay away from Basnaaid, which would mean staying away from the Gardens, but she knew well enough I had to approve of a friendship with Station Administrator Celar's daughter, if only on political grounds. But I couldn't find it in myself to be too angry—her horrified astonishment at Piat's dismissal of her own worth was obvious and sincere. And she'd clearly made short work of getting behind Piat's defenses.

Citizen Piat folded her arms, turned around, her back to the rail, face turned away from Tisarwat. "I'm only here because the chief of Horticulture is in love with my mother."

"Hardly surprising if she is," acknowledged Lieutenant Tisarwat. "Your mother is *gorgeous*." I was seeing through Tisarwat's eyes, so I couldn't see Piat's expression. I could guess, though. So could Tisarwat, I saw. "And frankly, you take after her. If someone's been telling you otherwise..." She stopped, unsure for a moment, I thought, if this was the best angle of attack. "Anyone who's been telling you that you've got a shiny-but-useless assignment just to keep your mother happy, or that you'll never be as beautiful or as competent as she is, well, they've been lying to you." She dropped the whole handful of fish pellets into the water, which boiled with bright-colored scales. "Probably jealous."

Piat scoffed, in a way that made it plain she was trying very hard not to cry. "Why would..." Stopped. About to say a name, perhaps, that she didn't want to say, that would be an accusation. "Why would anyone be jealous of *me*?"

"Because *you* took the aptitudes." I hadn't said anything to Lieutenant Tisarwat about my guess that Raughd had never taken them, but she clearly hadn't been the Lord of the Radch for a few days for nothing. "And the tests said you should be running something important. And anyone with eyes can see you're going to be just as beautiful as your mother." A moment of mortification at having said that *going to be*. And it wasn't quite the sort of thing a seventeen-year-old would say. "Once you stop listening to people who just want to drag you down."

Piat turned around, arms still crossed. Tears rolled down her face. "People get assignments for political reasons *all the time*."

"Sure," said Tisarwat. "Your mother probably got her first assignment for political reasons. Which probably included the fact that she could do the job." It didn't always—which Tisarwat well knew.

And that sounded dangerously like someone much older than Tisarwat ostensibly was. But Piat seemed unable to deflect it. She was driven to a last-ditch defense. "I've seen you mooning around the past few days. You're only here because you've got a crush on Horticulturist Basnaaid."

That scored a hit. But Lieutenant Tisarwat kept her outward composure. "I wouldn't even *be* here except for you. Fleet captain told me I was too young for her and stay away. It was an *order*. I ought to stay away from the Gardens, but *you're* here, aren't you. So let's go somewhere else and have a drink."

Piat was silent a moment, taken aback, it seemed. "Not the Undergarden," she said, finally.

"I should think not!" replied Tisarwat. Relieved, knowing she'd won this round, a minor victory but a victory all the same. "They haven't even started repairs there yet. Let's find somewhere we don't have to pee in a bucket."

By now *Sword of Atagaris* had moved away from the Ghost Gate, closer to Athoek Station. It had said almost nothing to *Mercy of Kalr* the whole time. Hardly surprising—ships generally weren't much given to chitchat, and besides, *Swords* all thought they were better than the others.

On *Mercy of Kalr* Lieutenant Ekalu had just come off watch, and Seivarden had met her in the decade room. "Your opposite number on *Sword of Atagaris* was asking after you," Ekalu said, and sat at the table, where an Etrepa had set her lunch.

Seivarden sat beside her. "Was she, now." She already knew, of course. "And was she glad to see someone she knew on board?"

"I don't think she recognized me," replied Ekalu, and after a moment's hesitation and a quick gesture from Seivarden, who'd had supper already, she took a mouthful of skel. Chewed and swallowed. "Not my name, anyway, I was only ever Amaat One to her. And I didn't send any visuals. I was on watch." Ekalu's feelings about that—about *Sword of Atagaris*'s Amaat lieutenant not realizing who she was—were complicated, and not entirely comfortable.

"Oh, I wish you had. I'd have loved to have seen her face."

I saw that while Ekalu herself might well have enjoyed the *Sword of Atagaris* lieutenant's discomfiture at being faced with an officer of such common origin, Seivarden's obvious amusement at the same prospect troubled and dismayed her. It reminded me a bit too painfully of some of Lieutenant Awn's interactions with Skaaiat Awer, twenty years gone and more. Ship said, in my ear, where I sat in the flier, "I'll say something to Lieutenant Seivarden." But I wasn't sure what Ship could say that Seivarden would understand.

In the *Mercy of Kalr* decade room, Ekalu said, "Expect her to contact you at the start of your next watch. She's determined to invite you over for tea, now *Sword of Atagaris* is going to be close enough."

"I can't be spared," Seivarden said, mock-serious. "There are only three watchstanders aboard right now."

"Oh, Ship will tell you if anything important happens," Ekalu said, all sarcastic disdain.

In Command, Medic said, "Lieutenants. Letting you know that something appears to have exited the Ghost Gate."

"What is it?" asked Seivarden, rising. Ekalu continued to eat, but called up a view of what Medic was looking at.

"It's too small to see well until it's closer," said Ship, to me, in the flier over Athoeki water. "I think it's a shuttle or a very small ship of some sort."

"We've asked *Sword of Atagaris* about it," Medic said, in Command.

"You mean they haven't threatened to destroy it unless it identifies itself?" asked Seivarden, halfway to Command herself by now.

"Nothing to worry about," came the reply from *Sword of Atagaris*, whichever of its lieutenants was on duty sounding almost overly bored. "It's just trash. The Ghost Gate doesn't get cleaned out like the others. Some ship must have broken up in the gate a long time ago."

"Your very great pardon," said Medic dryly as Seivarden

came into Command, "but we were under the impression there was no one on the other side of that gate, and never had been."

"Oh, people go there on a dare, sometimes, or just joyriding. But this one isn't recent, you can see it's pretty old. We'll pull it in—it's large enough to be a hazard."

"Why not just burn it?" asked Seivarden, and Ship must have sent her words to *Sword of Atagaris*, because that lieutenant replied, "Well, you know, there is some smuggling in the system. We always check these things out."

"And what are they smuggling out of an uninhabited system?" asked Medic.

"Oh, nothing out of the Ghost Gate, I should think," came the blithe answer. "But generally, you know, the usual. Illegal drugs. Stolen antiques."

"Aatr's tits!" swore Seivarden. "Speaking of antiques." Ship had asked *Sword of Atagaris* for a closer image of the object in question and, receiving it, had shown it to Medic and Seivarden both, a curving shell, scarred and scorched.

"Quite a piece of junk, isn't it?" replied the *Sword of Atagaris* lieutenant.

"Ignorant fuck," said Seivarden, after *Sword of Atagaris* had signed off. "What are they teaching in officer training these days?"

Medic turned to regard her. "Did I miss something, Lieutenant?"

"That's a supply locker off a Notai military shuttle," replied Seivarden. "You honestly don't recognize it?"

Radchaai often speak of the Radch as containing only one sort of people, who speak only one language—Radchaai. But the interior of a Dyson sphere is vast. Even if it had begun with a single population, speaking only one language (and it had not), it would not have ended that way. Many of the ships and captains that had opposed Anaander's expansion had been Notai.

"No," said Medic, "I don't recognize it. It doesn't look very Notai to me. It doesn't really look like a supply locker, either. It does look old, though."

"My house is Notai. Was." Seivarden's house had been absorbed by another one, during the thousand years she'd spent in suspension. "We were loyal, though. We had an old shuttle from the wars, docked at Inais. People used to come from all over to see it." The memory of it must have been unexpectedly specific and sharp. She swallowed, so that her sudden sense of loss wouldn't be audible when she spoke next. "How did a Notai ship break up in the Ghost Gate? None of those battles were anywhere near here."

In Seivarden's and Medic's vision, Ship displayed images of the sort of shuttle Seivarden was talking about. "Yes, like that," said Seivarden. "Show us the supply locker." Ship obliged.

"There's writing on it," said Medic.

"Seeing?" Seivarden frowned, puzzling out the words. "Seeing...something?"

"*Divine Essence of Perception*," said Ship. "One of the last defeated in the wars. It's a museum now."

"It doesn't look particularly Notai," said Medic. "Except for the writing."

"And the writing on this one," said Seivarden, gesturing into view the image of the one that had come out of the Ghost Gate, "is all burned away. Ship, did you really not recognize it?"

Ship said, to Medic and Seivarden both, "Not immediately. I'm a little less than a thousand years old and never have seen any Notai ships firsthand. But if Lieutenant Seivarden had not identified it herself, I would have within a few minutes."

"Would you have, ever," asked Medic, "if we trusted *Sword of Atagaris*?" And then, struck by a new thought, "Could *Sword of Atagaris* have failed to recognize it?"

"Probably it has," said Seivarden. "Otherwise, surely, it would tell its lieutenant."

"Unless they're both lying," said Ekalu, who had been listening in the whole time from the decade room. "They *are* taking the trouble to pick up a piece of debris that they might as well mark and let someone else take care of."

"In which case," remarked Seivarden, "they're assuming *Mercy of Kalr* won't recognize it. Which doesn't strike me as a safe assumption."

"I don't presume to know *Sword of Atagaris*'s opinion of my intelligence," said Ship.

Seivarden gave a small laugh. "Medic, ask *Sword of Atagaris* to tell us what they find when they examine that... debris."

Ultimately, *Sword of Atagaris* replied that it had found nothing of interest, and subsequently destroyed the locker.

Citizen Fosyf's house was the largest of three buildings, a long, balconied two-storied structure of polished stone, flecks of black and gray and here and there patches of blue and green that gleamed as the light changed. It sat beside a wide, clear lake with stony shores, and a weathered wooden dock, with a small, graceful boat moored alongside, white sails furled. Mountains loomed around, and moss and trees edged the lakeshore. The actual tea plantation—I'd seen it as we flew in, wavering strips of velvet-looking green running across the hillsides and around outcrops of black stone—was hidden behind a ridge. The air was 20.8 degrees C, the breeze light and pleasant and smelling of leaves and cold water.

"Here we are, Fleet Captain!" Citizen Fosyf called as she climbed out of her flier. "Peace and quiet. Under other circumstances I'd suggest fishing in the lake. Boating. Climbing if that's the sort of thing you like. But even just staying in is nice, here. There's a separate bathhouse behind the main building, just across from where you'll be staying. A big tub with seating for at least a dozen, plenty of hot water. It's a Xhai thing. Barbarically luxurious."

Raughd had come up beside her mother. "Drinks in the bathhouse! There's nothing like it after a long night." She grinned.

"Raughd can manage to find long nights even here," observed Fosyf pleasantly as Captain Hetnys and her *Sword of Atagaris* ancillary approached. "Ah, to be young again! But come, I'll show you where you'll be staying."

The patches of blue-green in the building stone flared and died away as our angle on it changed. Around the other side of the house was a broad stretch of flat, gray stones, shaded by two large trees and thickly grown with moss. To the left of that stretched the ellipse of a low building, the nearer long side of wood, the nearer end and, presumably, the farther long side of glass. "The bath," said Fosyf, with a gesture. On the other side of the mossy stone, up against a road that ran over the ridge and down to the house by the lake, sat another black and blue-green stone building, two-storied, but smaller than the main house and not balconied as it was. The whole side facing us was taken up with a terrace under a leafy, vine-tangled arbor, where a group of people stood waiting for us. Most of them wore shirts and trousers, or skirts that looked as though they'd been painstakingly constructed from cut-apart trousers, the fabric faded and worn, once-bright blues and greens and reds. None of them wore gloves.

Accompanying them was a person dressed in the expected, and conventional, jacket, trousers, and gloves and scattering of jewelry. By her features, I guessed she was a Samirend overseer here. We stopped some three meters from the group, in the shade of the wide arbor, and Fosyf said, "Just for you, Fleet Captain, since I knew you'd want to hear them sing."

The overseer turned away and said to the assembled people, "Here, now. Sing." In Radchaai. Slow and loud.

One of the elders of the group leaned toward the person next to her and said, in Delsig, "I told you it wasn't the right song." A few gestures and a few whispered words under the somewhat agitated eye of the overseer, who apparently didn't understand the reason for the delay, and then a collective breath and they began to sing. "*Oh you, who live sheltered by God, who live all your lives in her shadow.*" I knew it, every line and every part. Most Delsig-speaking Valskaayans sang it at funerals.

It was a gesture meant to comfort. Even if they hadn't already known the reason for our coming, they could not have failed to notice my shaved head and the mourning stripe across my face, and Captain Hetnys's. These people didn't know us, quite possibly didn't know who had died. We represented the forces that had conquered them, torn them away from their home world to labor here. They had no reason to care for our feelings. They had no reason to think that either of us knew enough Delsig to understand the words. And no expectation that we would understand the import of their song even if we did. Such things are fraught with symbolic and historic significance, carry great emotional weight—but only for someone aware of that significance to begin with.

They sang it anyway. And when they were finished, the elder said, bowing, "Citizens, we will pray for the one you've lost." In perfectly comprehensible, if heavily accented, Radchaai.

"Citizens," I replied, also in Radchaai, because I wasn't sure I wanted anyone to realize how much Delsig I spoke, just yet. "We are greatly moved, and we thank you for your song and your prayers."

The overseer spoke up, loud and slow. "The fleet captain thanks you. Now go."

"Wait," I interjected. And turned to Fosyf. "Will you favor me, and give these people something to eat and drink before they go?" She blinked at me, uncomprehending. The overseer stared at me in frank disbelief. "It's a whim I have. If there's any question of impropriety, I'll be happy to pay you back. Whatever is on hand. Tea and cakes, perhaps." It was the sort of thing I'd expect the kitchen here to always have ready.

Fosyf recovered from her immediate surprise. "Of course, Fleet Captain." She gestured toward the overseer, who, still clearly aghast at my request, herded the field workers away.

The ground floor of the building we were to stay in was one large, open space, part dining room, part sitting room, the sitting-room side full of wide, deep chairs and side tables that held game-boards with bright-colored counters. On the other side of the room we ate egg and bean curd soup at a long table with artfully mismatched chairs, by a sideboard piled with fruit and cakes. The line of small windows around the ceiling had gone dull with twilight and clouds that had blown in. Upstairs were narrow hallways, each bedroom and its attached sitting room carefully color coordinated. Mine was orange and blue, in muted tones, the thick, soft blankets on the bed very carefully made, I suspected, to appear comfortably worn and faded. A casual country cottage, one might have thought at first glance, but all of it meticulously placed and arranged.

Citizen Fosyf, sitting at one end of the table, said, "This actually used to be storage and administration. The main building was a guesthouse, you know. Before the annexation."

"All the bedrooms in the main house exit onto the balconies," said Raughd. Who had maneuvered to sit beside me, was now leaning close with head tilted and a knowing smile. "Very convenient for assignations." She was, I realized, trying to *flirt* with me. Even though I was in mourning and so her pursuit of me would be highly improper in the best of situations.

"Ha-ha!" laughed Citizen Fosyf. "Raughd has always found those outer stairs useful. I did myself when I was that age."

The nearest town was an hour away by flier. There was no one here to have assignations with except household members—over in the main house, I assumed, would be cousins and clients. Not everyone in a household was always related in a way that made sex off-limits, so there might well have been allowable relationships here that didn't involve intimidating the servants.

Captain Hetnys sat across the table from me, *Sword of Atagaris* standing stiff scant meters behind her, waiting in case it should be needed. As an ancillary, it wasn't required to observe mourning customs. Kalr Five stood behind me, having apparently convinced everyone here that she, also, was an ancillary.

Citizen Sirix sat silent beside me. The house servants I'd seen appeared to mostly be Samirend with a few Xhais, though I'd seen a few Valskaayans working on the grounds outside. There had been a small, nearly undetectable hesitation on the part of the servants that had shown us to our rooms—I suspected that they would have sent Sirix to servants' quarters if they'd not been given other instructions. It was possible someone here would recognize her, even though she'd last been downwell twenty years ago and wasn't from this estate, but another one a hundred or more kilometers away.

"Raughd's tutors always found it dull here," said Fosyf.

"*They* were dull!" exclaimed Raughd. In a singsong, nasal voice, she declaimed, "*Citizen! In third meter and Acute mode, tell us how God is like a duck.*" Captain Hetnys laughed. "I always tried to make life more amusing for them," Raughd went on, "but they never seemed to appreciate it."

Citizen Fosyf laughed as well. I did not. I had heard about such amusements from my lieutenants in the past, and had already seen Raughd's tendency toward cruelty. "Can you?" I asked. "Tell us in verse, I mean, how God is like a duck?"

"I shouldn't think God was anything like a duck," said Captain Hetnys, emboldened by my past few days of outward calm. "Honestly. A duck!"

"But surely," I admonished, "God *is* a duck." God was the universe, and the universe was God.

Fosyf waved my objection away. "Yes, yes, Fleet Captain, but surely one can say that quite simply without all the fussing over meters and proper diction and whatnot."

"And why choose something so ridiculous?" asked Captain Hetnys. "Why not ask how God is like... rubies or stars or"—she gestured vaguely around—"even tea? Something valuable. Something vast. It would be much more proper."

"A question," I replied, "that might reward close consideration. Citizen Fosyf, I gather the tea here is entirely handpicked and processed by hand."

"It is!" Fosyf beamed. This was, clearly, one of the centers of her pride. "Handpicked—you can see it whenever you like. The manufactory is nearby, very easy to visit. Should you find that proper." A brief pause, as she blinked, someone nearby having apparently sent her a message. "The section just over the ridge is due to be picked tomorrow. And of course the making of the leaves into tea—the *crafting* of it—goes on all day and night. The leaves must be withered and stirred, till they reach just the right point, and then dry-cooked and rolled until just the right moment. Then they're graded and have the final drying. You can do all those things by machine, of course, some do, and it's perfectly acceptable tea." The smallest hint of contempt and dismissal behind that *perfectly acceptable.* "The sort of thing you'd get good value for in a shop. But this tea isn't available in shops."

Fosyf's tea, Daughter of Fishes, would only be available as a gift. Or—maybe—bought directly from Citizen Fosyf to be given as a gift. The Radch used money, but a staggering amount of exchanges were not money for goods, but gift for gift. Citizen Fosyf was not paid much, if anything, for her tea. Not technically. Those green fields we'd flown over, all that tea, the complicated production, was not a matter of maximizing cost efficiency—no, the point of Daughter of Fishes was *prestige.*

Which explained why, though there were doubtless larger plantations on Athoek, that likely pulled in profits that at first glance looked much more impressive, the only grower who'd felt competent to approach me so openly was the one who did not sell her tea at all.

"It must take a delicate touch," I observed. "The picking,

and the processing. Your workers must be tremendously skilled." Beside me, Citizen Sirix gave an almost inaudible cough, choking slightly on her last mouthful of soup.

"They are, Fleet Captain, they are! You see why I would never treat them badly, I need them too much! In fact, they live in an old guesthouse themselves, a few kilometers away, over the ridge." Rain spattered against the small windows. It only ever rained at night, Athoek Station had told me, and the rain always ended in time for the leaves to dry for the morning picking.

"How nice," I replied, my voice bland.

I rose before the sun, when the sky was a pearled pink and pale blue, and the lake and its valley still shadowed. The air was cool but not chill, and I had not had enough space to run for more than a year. It had been a habit when I had been in the Itran Tetrarchy, a place where sport was a matter of religious devotion, exercises for their ball game were a prayer and a meditation. It felt good to return to it, even though no one here played the game or even knew it existed. I took the road toward the low ridge at an easy jog, wary of my right hip, which I had injured a year ago and which hadn't healed quite right.

As I came over the ridge, I heard singing. One strong voice, pitched to echo off the stony outcrops and across the field where workers with baskets slung over their shoulders rapidly plucked leaves from the waist-high bushes. At least half of those workers were children. The song was in Delsig, a lament by the singer that someone she loved was committed exclusively to someone else. It was a distinctively Valskaayan subject, not the sort of thing that would come up in a typical Radchaai relationship. And it was a song I'd heard before.

Hearing it now raised a sharp memory of Valskaay, of the smell of wet limestone in the cave-riddled district I'd last been in, there.

The singer was apparently a lookout. As I drew nearer, the words changed. Still Delsig, largely incomprehensible, I knew, to the overseers.

Here is the soldier
So greedy, so hungry for songs.
So many she's swallowed, they leak out,
They spill out of the corners of her mouth
And fly away, desperate for freedom.

I was glad my facial expressions weren't at all involuntary. It was cleverly done, fitting exactly into the meter of the song, and I wouldn't have been able to help smiling, thus betraying the fact that I'd understood. As it was, I ran on, apparently oblivious. But watching the workers. Every single one of them appeared to be Valskaayan. The singer's satire on me had been intended for these people, and it had been sung in a Valskaayan language. On Athoek Station, I had been told that all Fosyf's field workers were Valskaayan, and at the time it had struck me as odd. Not that some of them might be, but that all of them would be. Seeing confirmation of it, now, the wrongness of it struck me afresh.

In a situation like this, a hold full of Valskaayans ought to have been either parceled out over dozens of different plantations and whatever other places might welcome their labor, or held in suspension and slowly doled out over decades. There should have been, maybe, a half dozen Valskaayans here. Instead there appeared to be six times that. And I'd have expected to see some Samirend, maybe even some Xhais or Ychana, or members of other groups, because there had certainly been more than Xhais and Ychana here before the annexation.

There also shouldn't have been such a sharp separation between the outdoor servants—all Valskaayan as far as I'd seen this morning and the day before—and the indoor, all Samirend with a few Xhais. Valskaay had been annexed a hundred years ago, and by now at least some of the first transportees or their children ought to have tested or worked their way into other positions.

I ran as far as the workers' residence, a building of brown brick with no glass in the windows, only here and there a blanket stretched across. It had clearly never been as large or as luxurious as Fosyf's lakeside house. But it had a lovely view across its valley, now filled with tea, and a direct road to that wide and glassy lake. The trampled dirt surrounding it might well have been gardens or carefully tended lawns, once. I was curious what the inside of it was like, but instead of entering uninvited and very likely unwelcome, I turned there to run back. "Fleet Captain," *Mercy of Kalr* said in my ear, "Lieutenant Seivarden begs to remind you to be careful of your leg."

"Ship," I replied, silently, "my leg is reminding me itself." Which *Mercy of Kalr* knew. And the conversation with Seivarden, that had produced Ship's message, had happened two days before.

"The lieutenant *will* fret," said Ship. "And you do seem to be ignoring it." Was that disapproval I detected in its apparently serene voice?

"I'll relax the rest of the day," I promised. "I'm almost back anyway."

By the time I crossed the ridge again, the sky and the valley were lighter, the air warmer. I found Citizen Sirix on a bench under the arbor, a bowl of tea steaming in one hand. Jacketless, shirt untucked, no jewelry. Mourning attire, though she was not technically required to mourn for Translator Dlique, had not shaved her head or put on a mourning stripe. "Good morning," I called, walking up to the terrace. "Will you show me about the bathhouse, Citizen? Maybe explain some things to me?"

She hesitated, just a moment. "All right," she said finally, warily, as though I'd offered her something risky or dangerous.

The long, curving bathhouse window framed black and gray cliffs and ice-sheeted peaks. On one far end, just the smallest corner of the house we were staying in. The guests here must have prized this place for its vistas—few if any Radchaai would have thought to make an entire wall of a bath into a window.

The walls that weren't window were light, elaborately carved and polished wood. In the stone-paved floor was a round pool of hot water, bench-lined, in which one sat and sweated, and next to it a chilled one. "It tones you after all the heat," said Sirix, on the bench in the hot water, across from me. "Closes your pores."

The heat felt good on my aching hip. The run had, perhaps, not been terribly wise. "Does it, now?"

"Yes. It's very cleansing." Which seemed an odd word to use. I suspected it was a translation of a more complicated one, from Xhi or Liost into Radchaai. "Nice life you have," Sirix continued. I cocked an interrogatory eyebrow. "Tea the moment you wake up. Clothes laundered and pressed while you sleep. Do you even dress yourself?"

"Generally. If I need to be extremely formal, though, it's good to have some expert help." I myself had never needed it, but I had provided that help on a number of occasions. "So, your forebears. The original Samirend transportees. They were all, or nearly all, sent to the mountains to pick tea?"

"Many of them, yes, Fleet Captain."

"And that annexation was quite some time ago, so as they became civilized"—I allowed just the smallest trace of irony to creep into my voice—"they tested into other assignments. That makes perfect sense to me. But what doesn't make sense is why there are no Samirend working in the fields here. Or anyone but Valskaayans. And there are no Valskaayans working anywhere but in the fields, or one or two on the grounds. The annexation of Valskaay was a hundred years ago. No Valskaayans have made overseer in all that time?"

"Well, Fleet Captain," said Sirix evenly, "no one's going to stay picking tea if they can get away from it. Field hands are paid based on meeting a minimum weight of leaves picked. But the minimum is huge—it would take three very fast workers an entire day to pick so much."

"Or a worker and several children," I guessed. I had seen children working in the fields, when I'd run by.

Sirix gestured acknowledgment. "So they're none of them making the actual wages they're supposed to. Then there's food. Ground meal—you had some upwell. They flavor it with twigs and dust that's left over from the tea making. Which, by the way, Fosyf charges them for. Premium prices. It's not just any floor sweepings, it's Daughter of Fishes!" She stopped a moment, to take a few breaths, too dangerously close to saying something openly angry. "Two bowls a day, of the porridge. It's thin provisions, and if they want anything more they have to buy it."

"At premium prices," I guessed.

"Just so. There are generally some garden plots if they want to grow vegetables, but they have to buy seeds and tools and it's time out from picking tea. They're houseless, so they don't have family to give them the things they need, they have to buy them. They can't any of them get travel permits, so they can't go very far away to buy anything. They can't order things because they don't have any money at all, they're too heavily in debt to get credit, so Fosyf sells them things—handhelds, access to entertainments, better food, whatever—at whatever price she wants."

"The Samirend field workers were able to overcome this?"

"Some of the servants in this house are doubtless still paying on the debts of their grandmothers and great-grandmothers. Or their aunts. The only way out was pulling together into houses and working very, very hard. But the Valskaayans... I suppose I'd say they aren't very ambitious. And they don't seem to understand about making houses of their own."

Valskaayan families didn't work quite the way Radchaai ones did. But I knew Valskaayans were entirely able to understand the advantage of having something that at least seemed like Radchaai houses, and on and around Valskaay groups of families had set up such arrangements at the first opportunity. "And none of the children ever test into other assignments?" I asked, though I already knew what the answer would be.

"These days field workers don't take the aptitudes," replied Sirix. Visibly struggling now with the reeducation that had made it difficult, if not impossible, for her to express anger without a good deal of discomfort. She looked away from me, breathed carefully through her mouth. "Not that they would ever test any differently. They're ignorant, superstitious savages, every one of them. But even so. It's not *right.*" Another deep breath. "Fosyf's not the only one doing it. And she'll tell you it's because they *won't* take the tests." That I could believe. Last I was on Valskaay, taking the tests or not was an urgent issue for quite a lot of people. "But there aren't any more transportees coming, are there? We didn't get anyone shipped here from the last annexation. So if the growers run out of Valskaayans, who's going to pick tea for miserable food and hardly any wages? It's just so much more convenient if the field workers can never get themselves or their children out of here. Fleet Captain, *it's not right.* The governor doesn't care about a bunch of houseless savages, and nobody who does care can get the attention of the Lord of the Radch."

"You think that strike twenty years ago escaped her attention?" I asked.

"It must have. Or she'd have done something." Three shallow breaths, through her mouth. Struggling with her anger. "Excuse me." She stood hastily, throwing a shower of hot water, and levered herself out of the pool, strode over to the cold, and immersed herself. Five brought her a towel, and she climbed out of the cold water and left the bath without another word to me.

I closed my eyes. On Athoek Station, Lieutenant Tisarwat slept, deep, between dreams, one arm thrown over her face. My attention shifted to *Mercy of Kalr.* Seivarden stood watch. She'd been saying something to one of her Amaats. "This business with the fleet captain running off downwell." Odd. This wasn't the sort of thing Seivarden was at all likely to discuss with one of her Amaats. "Is this really something necessary, or just some specific injustice that infuriates her?"

"Lieutenant Seivarden," replied the Amaat, oddly stiff

even given this crew's love of imitating ancillaries. "You know I have to report such a question to the fleet captain."

Slightly exasperated, Seivarden waved that answer away. "Yes, of course, Ship. Still."

I saw suddenly what was happening. Seivarden was talking to *Mercy of Kalr*, not the Amaat. The Amaat was seeing Ship's answers displayed in her vision and she was reading them off. As though she had been truly an ancillary, a part of the ship, one of dozens of mouths for Ship to speak through. Thankfully, none of the crew had ever attempted such a thing with me. I wouldn't have approved in the least.

But it was clear, watching, that Seivarden found it comfortable. Comforting. She was worried, and Ship speaking like this was reassuring. Not for any solid, rational reason. Just because it was.

"Lieutenant," said the Amaat. Ship, through the Amaat, "I can only tell you what the fleet captain has already said herself, in her briefings to you. If, however, you want my personal opinion, I think it's something of both. And the fleet captain's absence, and the removal of Citizen Raughd from Athoek Station, is allowing Lieutenant Tisarwat to make valuable political contacts among the younger of the station's prominent citizens."

Seivarden gave a skeptical *hah.* "Next you'll be telling me our Tisarwat is a gifted politician!"

"I think she'll surprise you, Lieutenant."

Seivarden clearly didn't believe *Mercy of Kalr.* "Even so, Ship. Our fleet captain generally keeps out of trouble, but when she doesn't, it's never the insignificant sort. And we're hours and hours away from being able to help her. If you see something brewing and she's too distracted to ask us to come in closer so we're there if she needs us, are you going to tell me?"

"That would require knowing days in advance that something was, as you say, brewing, Lieutenant. I can't imagine the fleet captain so distracted for so long." Seivarden frowned. "But, Lieutenant, I am as concerned for the fleet captain's safety as you are." Which was as much of an answer as Ship could give, and Seivarden would have to be happy with that.

"Lieutenant Seivarden," said *Mercy of Kalr.* "Message incoming from Hrad."

Seivarden gestured *go ahead*. An unfamiliar voice sounded in her ears. "This is Fleet Captain Uemi, commanding *Sword of Inil*, dispatched from Omaugh Palace. I'm ordered to take control of the security of Hrad system." One gate away, Hrad system was. More or less next door. "My compliments to Fleet Captain Breq. Fighting is still intense at Tstur Palace. Several outstations have been destroyed. Depending on the outcome, the Lord of the Radch may send you a troop carrier. She sends you her greetings, in any event, and trusts you're doing well."

"Do you know Fleet Captain Uemi, Ship?" There was no expectation of an immediate, this-moment reply—Hrad was hours away at lightspeed, through the connecting gate.

"Not well," replied *Mercy of Kalr.*

"And *Sword of Inil*?"

"It's a *Sword*."

"Hah!" Seivarden, amused.

"Lieutenant, the fleet captain left instructions in case such a message should be delivered in her absence."

"*Did* she." Seivarden wasn't sure whether she was surprised at that or not. "Well, let's have it then."

My instructions had been minor enough. Seivarden, replying, said, "This is Lieutenant Seivarden, commanding *Mercy of Kalr* in Fleet Captain Breq's temporary absence. Most courteous greetings to Fleet Captain Uemi, and we are grateful for the news. Begging Fleet Captain Uemi's indulgence, Fleet Captain Breq wonders if *Sword of Inil* took on any new crew at Omaugh Palace." Though it might not be new crew I should worry about. It was entirely possible to make ancillaries out of older adults.

But no reply could reach me before supper. The question puzzled Seivarden, who didn't know about Tisarwat, but Ship wouldn't explain it to her.

Walking back to the house I met Raughd coming from the main building. "Good morning, Fleet Captain!" she said, with a sunny smile. "It's so invigorating to be up at the break of day like this. I really ought to make a habit of it." I had to admit, it was a creditably charming smile, even given the nearly undetectable strain behind it—even if she hadn't just implied as much, I was sure this was not an hour when Raughd was accustomed to rising. But knowing as much as I did about her quite spoiled the effect for me. "Don't tell me you've already been to the bath," she added, with the merest touch of disappointment, calculatedly coy.

"Good morning, Citizen," I replied without stopping. "And yes, I have." And went into the house for breakfast.

13

After breakfast—fruit and bread that Fosyf's servants had left lying on the sideboard the night before, by a polite fiction only leftovers from supper—Captain Hetnys and I were supposed to spend the day sitting quietly, praying at regular intervals, eating spare, simple meals. We sat, accordingly, on the sitting-room side of the house's open ground floor. As the days went on we could properly spend more time farther from the house—sit, for instance, under the arbor outside. Convention allowed a certain amount of wider movement, for those who could not be still in their grief—I had taken advantage of that for my run that morning, and to use the bath. But most of the next few days would be spent in our rooms, or here in this sitting room, with only each other for company, or any neighbors who might stop by to console us.

Captain Hetnys did not wear her uniform—in these circumstances she was not required to. Her untucked shirt was a muted rose, over olive-green trousers. But what civilian clothes I had were either far too formal for this setting, or else they dated from my years outside the Radch, and if I wore either

I would not seem to be properly in mourning. Instead I wore my brown and black uniform shirt and trousers. In strictest propriety I ought to have worn no jewelry, but I would not part with Lieutenant Awn's memorial token, and pinned it on the inside of my shirt. We sat silent for a while, Kalr Five and *Sword of Atagaris* standing motionless behind us, in case we should need them. Captain Hetnys grew increasingly tense, though of course she showed little outward sign of it until Sirix came down the steps to join us. Then Captain Hetnys rose, abruptly, and paced around the perimeter of the room. She had said nothing to Sirix on the trip here, nothing last night. Intended to say nothing to her now, it seemed. But that was perfectly within the bounds of proper mourning, which allowed for some eccentric behavior at such a time.

At midday, servants came in with trays of food—more bread, which could be a luxury on stations but was still considered a plain, simple kind of food, and various pastes and mixtures meant to be spread on it, all of which would be lightly seasoned, if at all. Even so, judging by last night's supper I was sure they would only technically qualify as austere eating.

One servant went over to the wall and, to my surprise, pulled it aside. Nearly the entire wall was a series of folding panels that opened out onto the arbored terrace, admitting filtered sunlight into the room, and a pleasant, leaf-scented breeze. Sirix took her lunch to one of the benches outside—though the wall-wide doorway also made the division between inside and outside an ambiguous one.

On Athoek Station, Lieutenant Tisarwat sat in a tea shop—sprawling, comfortable chairs around a low table littered with empty and half-empty arrack bottles. More than her pay was worth—she'd bought them on credit, then, or they were gifts based on her presumed status. Or mine. One or the other of us would have to find some way to make a return, but that was unlikely to pose a problem. Citizen Piat sat beside Tisarwat, and a half dozen other young people sat in the nearby chairs. Someone had just said something funny—everyone was laughing.

On *Mercy of Kalr* Medic raised an eyebrow, hearing the Kalr assisting her singing softly to herself.

> *Who only ever loved once?*
> *Who ever said "I will never love again"*
> *and kept their word?*
> *Not I.*

On Athoek, in the mountains, Captain Hetnys stopped pacing, took her own lunch to the table. Sirix, on the bench out on the terrace, seemed not even to notice. One of the servants walked by her, paused, said something quick and quiet that I couldn't quite catch, or perhaps she'd spoken in Liost. Sirix looked up at her, serious, and said quite clearly in Radchaai, "I'm just an adviser, Citizen." Not even a trace of rancor. Odd, after her unhappiness that morning, that indignant sense of injustice.

Above, in the tea shop on Athoek Station, someone said, "Now that Captain Hetnys and that really quite frightening fleet captain are downwell, it's up to Tisarwat to protect us from the Presger!"

"Not a chance," replied Tisarwat. "If the Presger decide to attack us there's nothing we can do. But I think it's going to be a long time before the Presger ever get to us." Word of the split in the Lord of the Radch had not yet gotten out, and problems with the gates were still officially "unanticipated difficulties." Somewhat predictably, those who didn't merely accept that found the idea of alien interference to be a more plausible explanation. "We'll be fine."

"But cut off like this," someone began.

Citizen Piat said, "We're fine. Even if we were to be cut off from the planet"—and someone muttered a *gods forbid*—"we'd be fine here. We can feed ourselves, anyway."

"Or if not," said someone else, "we can grow skel in the lake in the Gardens."

Someone else laughed. "It would take that horticulturist down a peg or two! You should see to it, Piat."

Tisarwat had learned a thing or two from her Bos. She kept her face—and her voice—impressively bland. "What horticulturist is this?"

"What's her name, Basnaaid?" said the person who had laughed. "She's a nobody, really. But, you know, an Awer from Omaugh Palace came and offered her clientage and she *refused*—she's got no family, really, and she isn't much to look at, but still, she was too good for Awer!"

Piat was sitting on one side of Tisarwat, and on the other was someone Ship told me was Skaaiat Awer's cousin—though not, herself, an Awer. Tisarwat had invited her; she wasn't usually a part of this group. "Skaaiat didn't take offense," the cousin said now. And smiled, almost taking the edge off her tone.

"Well, no, of course she didn't. But it can't possibly be proper to refuse such an offer. It just tells you what sort of person the horticulturist is."

"Indeed it does," agreed Skaaiat's cousin.

"She's good at what she does," said Piat, in a sudden rush, as though she'd spent the last few moments nerving herself to say it. "She *should* be proud."

A moment of awkward silence. Then, "I wish Raughd was

here," said the person who had brought the topic up to begin with. "I don't know why she had to go downwell, too. We always laugh so hard when Raughd is here."

"Not the person you're laughing *at*," pointed out Skaaiat's cousin.

"Well, no, of course not," replied Raughd's partisan. "Or we wouldn't be laughing at them. Tisarwat, you should see Raughd's impression of Captain Hetnys. It's hilarious."

On Athoek, in the house, Sirix rose from her seat and went upstairs. I shifted my attention to Five, saw that she was sweating in her uniform and had been bored watching me and Captain Hetnys. Was thinking about the food on the sideboard, which she could smell from where she stood. I would need to go upstairs myself soon, pretend, perhaps, to nap, so Five could have a break, so she and *Sword of Atagaris* could have their own meals. Captain Hetnys—unaware of having just been mentioned upwell—went out to sit on the terrace, now Sirix was safely away.

One of the servants approached Kalr Five. Stood a moment, debating, I suspected, what sort of address to use, and settled finally on, "If you please."

"Yes, Citizen," Five said to the servant, flat and toneless.

"This arrived this morning," the servant said. She held out a small parcel wrapped in a velvety-looking violet cloth. "It was most particularly requested that it be given directly into the fleet captain's keeping." She didn't explain why she was giving it to Five instead.

"Thank you, Citizen," said Five, and took the parcel. "Who sent it?"

"The messenger didn't say." But I thought she knew, or suspected.

Five unwrapped the cloth, to reveal a plain box of thin,

pale wood. Inside sat what looked like a triangular section of thick, heavy bread, quite stale; a pin, a two-centimeter silver disk dangling from an arrangement of blue and green glass beads; and underneath these, a small card printed close with characters I thought were Liost. The language so many Samirend still spoke. A quick query to Athoek Station confirmed my guess. And told me at least some of what was on the card.

Five put the lid back on the box. "Thank you, Citizen."

I rose, without saying anything, and went over to Five and took the box and its wrapping and went up the stairs and through the narrow hallway to Sirix's room. Knocked on the door. Said, when Sirix opened it, "Citizen, I believe this is actually for you." Held out the box, its purple covering folded beneath it.

She looked at me, dubious. "There's no one here to send me anything, Fleet Captain. You must be mistaken."

"It certainly isn't meant for me," I said, still holding out the box. "Citizen," I admonished, when she still did not move to take it.

Eight approached from behind her, to take it from me, but Sirix gestured her away. "It can't possibly be mine," she insisted.

With my free hand, I lifted the lid off the box so that she could see what was inside it. She went suddenly very still, seeming not even to breathe.

"I'm sorry to hear about your loss, Citizen," I said. The pin was a memorial, the family name of the deceased was Odela. The card bore details about the deceased's life and funeral. The purpose or meaning of the bread was unknown to me, but clearly it had meant something to whoever sent it. Meant something, certainly, to Sirix. Though I could not tell if her reaction was grief, or the distress of anger she could not express.

"You said you had no family, Citizen," I said after a few uncomfortable, silent moments. "Clearly someone in Odela is thinking of you." They must have heard Sirix was here with me.

"She has no right," said Sirix. Outwardly calm, dispassionate, but I knew that was a necessity for her, a matter of survival. "None of them do. They can't have it both ways, they can't just take it back." She took a breath, looked as though she would speak again but instead took another one. "Send it back," she said then. "It isn't mine, it can't be. By their own actions."

"If that's what you want, Citizen, then I will." I replaced the lid, unfolded the purple cloth, and wound it around the now-closed box.

"What," Sirix said, bitterness creeping into her voice, "no exhortations to be grateful, to remember that they are, after all, my f—" Her voice broke—she had pushed herself too far. It said something about her usual self-control that she did not, that moment, slam the door in my face so that she could suffer unwatched. Or perhaps it said she knew that Eight was still in the room, that she would not be alone and unobserved no matter what she did.

"I can produce such exhortations if you'd like, Citizen, but they would be insincere." I bowed. "If there is anything you need, do not hesitate to ask. I am at your service."

She did close the door then. I could have watched her through Eight's eyes, but I did not.

When supper arrived, so did Fosyf and Raughd. Sirix didn't come downstairs, hadn't since lunch. No one commented on it—she was only here by sufferance, because she was with me. After we ate, we sat right up at the edge of the room, the doors still wide. What we could see of the lake had gone leaden with the evening, shadowed, only the very tops of the peaks behind it still brilliant with the sunset. The air grew chill and damp, and the servants brought hot, bitter-sweet drinks in handled bowls. "Xhai-style," Fosyf informed me. Without Sirix to flank me, I had Fosyf on one side and Raughd on the other. Captain Hetnys sat across from me, her chair turned a bit so she could look out toward the lake.

On *Mercy of Kalr*, the reply to the question I'd that morning asked Fleet Captain Uemi finally arrived. Ship played it in Lieutenant Ekalu's ears. "All thanks, Lieutenant Seivarden, for your courteous greeting. My compliments to Fleet Captain Breq, but I did not take on any crew at Omaugh."

I had left instructions for this, as well. "Fleet Captain Breq thanks Fleet Captain Uemi for her indulgence," said Lieutenant Ekalu. Just as puzzled as Seivarden had been, hours ago. "Did any of *Sword of Inil*'s crew spend a day or two out of touch, on the palace station?"

"Well, Fleet Captain," said Fosyf, downwell, in the growing dark by the lake, "you had a peaceful day, I hope?"

"Yes, thank you, Citizen." I was under no obligation to be any more forthcoming. In fact, I could quite properly ignore anyone who spoke to me for the next week and a half, if I felt so moved.

"The fleet captain rises at an unbelievably early hour," said Raughd. "I got up early especially to be sure there was someone to show her the bath, and she'd already been up for *ages*."

"Clearly, Citizen," said Captain Hetnys genially, "your idea of getting up early isn't the same as ours."

"Military discipline, Raughd," observed Fosyf, voice

indulgent. "For all your recent interest"—this with a sidelong glance at me—"you'd never have been suited to it."

"Oh, I don't know," said Raughd, airily. "I've never tried it, have I?"

"I went over the ridge this morning and saw your workers," I remarked, not particularly interested in pursuing the issue of Raughd's military fitness.

"I hope you could add some songs to your collection, Fleet Captain," Fosyf replied. I inclined my head just slightly, barely an answer but sufficient.

"I don't know why they didn't just make ancillaries out of them," observed Raughd. "Surely they'd be better off." She simpered. "Two units off a troop carrier would do us, and still leave plenty for everyone else."

Fosyf laughed. "Raughd has taken a sudden interest in the military! Been looking things up. Ships and uniforms and all sorts of things."

"The uniforms are so *appealing*," Raughd agreed. "I'm so glad you're wearing yours, Fleet Captain."

"Ancillaries can't be new citizens," I said.

"Well," said Fosyf. "Well. You know, I'm not sure Valskaayans can be, either. Even on Valskaay there are problems, aren't there? That religion of theirs." Actually, there were several religions represented on Valskaay, and in its system, and various sects of all of them. But Fosyf meant the majority religion, the one everyone thought of as "Valskaayan." It was a variety of exclusive monotheism, something most Radchaai found more or less incomprehensible. "Though I'm not sure you can really call it a religion. More a . . . a collection of superstitions and some very odd philosophical ideas." Outside had grown darker still, the trees and moss-covered stones disappearing into shadow. "And the religion is the least of it.

They have plenty of opportunity to *become* civilized. Why, look at the Samirend!" She gestured around, meaning, I supposed, the servants who had brought us supper. "They began where the Valskaayans are now. The Valskaayans have every opportunity, but do they take advantage of it? I don't know if you saw their residence—a very nice guesthouse, fully as nice as the house I live in myself, but it's practically a ruin. They can't be bothered to keep their surroundings nice. But they go quite extravagantly into debt over a musical instrument, or a new handheld."

"Or equipment for making alcohol," said Raughd primly.

Fosyf sighed, apparently deeply grieved. "They use their own rations for that, some of them. And then go further into debt buying food. Most of them have never seen any of their wages. They lack *discipline*."

"How many Valskaayans were sent to this system?" I asked Fosyf. "After that annexation. Do you know?"

"No idea, Fleet Captain." Fosyf gestured resigned ignorance. "I just take the workers they assign me."

"There were children working in the fields this morning," I remarked. "Isn't there a school?"

"No point," Fosyf said. "Not with Valskaayans. They won't attend. They just don't have the seriousness of mind that's necessary. No *steadiness*. Oh, but I do wish I could take you on a proper tour, Fleet Captain! When your two weeks is ended, perhaps. I do want to show off my tea, and I know you'll want to hear every song you can."

"Fleet Captain Breq," said Captain Hetnys, who had been silent so far, "doesn't only collect songs, as it happens."

"Oh?" asked Fosyf.

"I stayed in her household during the fasting days," Captain Hetnys said, "and do you know, her everyday dishes are a set of blue and violet Bractware. With all the serving pieces. In *perfect* condition." Behind me, Ship showed me, Kalr Five was suppressing a satisfied smirk. We'd hardly eaten during the fasting days, as was proper, but Five had served what little we did eat on the Bractware and—no doubt purposefully—left the unused dishes where Captain Hetnys could see them.

"Well! What good taste, Fleet Captain! And I'm glad Hetnys mentions it." She gestured, and a servant bent near, received murmured instruction, departed. "I have something you'll be interested to see."

Out in the dark a high, inhuman voice sang out, a long, sustained series of vowels on a single pitch. "Ah!" cried Fosyf. "That's what I was waiting for." Another voice joined the first, slightly lower, and then another, a bit higher, and another and another, until there were at least a dozen intoning voices, coming and going, dissonant and oddly choral-sounding.

Clearly Fosyf expected some sort of reaction from me. "What is it?" I asked.

"They're plants," Fosyf said, apparently delighted at the thought of having surprised me. "You might have seen some when you were out this morning. They have a sort of sac that collects air, and when that's full, and the sun goes down, they whistle it out. As long as it's not raining. Which is why you didn't hear them last night."

"Weeds," observed Captain Hetnys. "Quite a nuisance, actually. They've tried to eradicate them, but they keep coming back."

"Supposedly," continued Fosyf, acknowledging the captain's remark with a nod, "the person who bred them was a temple initiate. And the plants sing various words in Xhi, all of them to do with the temple mysteries, and when the other initiates heard the plants sing they realized the mysteries had been revealed to everyone. They murdered the designer. Tore her to pieces with their bare hands, supposedly, right here by this lake."

I hadn't thought to ask what sort of guesthouse this had been. "This was a holy place, then? Is there a temple?" In my experience, major temples were nearly always surrounded by cities or at least villages, and I'd seen no sign of that as we'd flown in. I wondered if there had used to be one, and it was razed to make way for tea, or if this whole, huge area had been sacrosanct. "Was the lake holy, and this was a temple guesthouse?"

"Very little gets past the fleet captain!" exclaimed Raughd.

"Indeed," agreed her mother. "What's left of the temple is across the lake. There was an oracle there for a while, but all that's left now is a superstition about wish-granting fish."

And the name of the tea grown on the once-sacred ground, I suspected. I wondered how the Xhais felt about that. "What are the words the plants sing?" I knew very little Xhi and didn't recognize any words in particular in the singing discord coming out of the dark.

"You get different lists," Fosyf replied genially, "depending on who you ask."

"I used to go out in the dark when I was a child," remarked Raughd, "and look for them. They stop if you shine a light on them."

I hadn't actually seen any children since we'd arrived, except for the field workers. I found that odd, in such a setting, but before I could wonder aloud or ask, the servant Fosyf had sent away returned, carrying a large box.

It was gold, or at least gilded, inlaid with red, blue, and green glass in a style that was older than I was. Older, in fact, than Anaander Mianaai's three thousand and some years. I had only ever seen this sort of thing in person once before, and that when I was barely a decade old, some two thousand years ago. "Surely," I said, "that's a copy."

"It is not, Fleet Captain," replied Fosyf, very pleased to say it, clearly. The servant set the box on the ground in our midst and then stepped away. Fosyf bent, lifted the lid. Nestled inside, a tea service—flask, bowls for twelve, strainer. All glass and gold, inlaid with elaborate, snaking patterns of blue and green.

I still held the handled bowl I'd been drinking from, and now I lifted it. Five obligingly came forward and took it, but did not move away. I had not intended her to. I got out of my seat, squatted beside the box.

The inside of the lid was also gold, though a strip of wood seven centimeters wide above and below the gold showed what it covered. That sheet of gold was engraved. In Notai. I could read it, though I doubted anyone else here could. Several old houses (Seivarden's among them), and some newer ones that found the idea romantic and appealing, claimed to be descended from Notai ancestors. Of those, some would have recognized this writing for what it was, possibly would have been able to read a word or two. Only a few would have bothered to actually learn this language.

"What does it say?" I asked, though of course I knew already.

"It's an invocation of the god Varden," said Captain Hetnys, "and a blessing on the owner."

Varden is your strength, it said, *Varden is your hope, and Varden is your joy. Life and prosperity to the daughter of the house. On the happy and well-deserved occasion.*

I looked up at Fosyf. "Where did you get this?"

"Aha," she replied, "so Hetnys was right, you are a connoisseur! I'd never have suspected if she hadn't told me."

"Where," I repeated, "did you get this?"

Fosyf gave a short laugh. "And single-minded, yes, but I already knew that. I bought it from Captain Hetnys."

Bought it. This ancient, priceless thing would have been nearly unthinkable as a *gift*. The idea of anyone taking any amount of money for it was impossible. Still squatting, I turned to Captain Hetnys, who to my unspoken question said, "The owner was in need of cash. She didn't want to sell it herself because, well, imagine anyone knowing you had to sell something like *that*. So I brokered the deal for her."

"And took your cut, too," put in Raughd, who I suspected wasn't enjoying being eclipsed by the tea set.

"True," acknowledged Captain Hetnys.

Even a small cut of that must have been staggering. This wasn't the sort of thing an individual owned, except perhaps nominally. No living, remotely functional house would allow a single member to alienate something like this. The tea set I had seen, when I had been a brand-new ship not ten years old, had not belonged to an individual. It had been part of the equipment of a decade room of a Sword, brought out while my captain was visiting, to impress her. That one had been purple and silver and mother-of-pearl, and the god named in the inscription had been a different one. And it had read, *On the happy and well-deserved occasion of your promotion. Captain Seimorand.* And a date a mere half a century before the ascendancy of Anaander Mianaai, before the set had been taken as a souvenir of its owner's defeat.

I was sure the bottom of the inscription in the box lid now before me had been cut off, that *On the happy and well-deserved occasion* was only the beginning of the sentence.

There was no sign of the cut—the edges of the gold looked smooth, the wood underneath undamaged. But I was sure someone had removed it, cut a strip off the bottom, and put back what was left, centered so that it didn't look so much as though part of the inscription had been removed.

This wasn't something passed down for centuries among some captain's descendants—those descendants would never have removed the name of the ancestor who had left them such a thing. One might remove the name to conceal its origin, and even damaged this was worth a great deal. One might conceal its origin out of shame—anyone who saw it might be able to guess which house had been forced to part with such a treasure. But most families that owned such things had other and better ways to capitalize such possessions. Seivarden's house, for instance, had accepted gifts and money in exchange for tours of that ancient, captured Notai shuttle.

Stolen antiques, the *Sword of Atagaris* lieutenant had said. But I had not imagined anything quite like this.

Add in that supply locker. "Debris." Any writing conveniently obscured—like this tea set.

Captain Hetnys had thought it was important to station her ship by the Ghost Gate. A piece of debris that was likely more than three thousand years old—and extremely unlikely to have ended up here at Athoek to begin with—had come out of the Ghost Gate. A piece of a Notai shuttle.

Captain Hetnys had made a great deal of money selling a Notai tea set nearly as old as that supply locker likely was. Where had she gotten it? Who had removed the name of its first owner, and why?

What was on the other side of the Ghost Gate?

14

Back in my room, I removed my brown and black shirt, handed it to Kalr Five. Had bent to loosen my boots when a knock sounded at the door. I looked up. Kalr Five gave me a single, expressionless glance and went to answer it. She had seen Raughd's behavior these past few days, knew what this was likely to be, though I admit I was surprised she had chosen to make this blatant a move so soon.

I stood aside, where I would not be visible from the sitting room. Picked up my shirt from where Five had laid it, and drew it back on. Five opened the door to the hallway, and through her eyes I saw Raughd's insincere smile. "I wonder," she said, with no courteous preamble, "if I might speak privately to the fleet captain." A balancing act, that sentence was, offering Five herself no consideration whatsoever, without being rude to me.

Let her in, I messaged Five silently. *But don't leave the room*. Though it was entirely possible—indeed, likely—that Raughd's idea of "private" included the presence of servants.

Raughd entered. Looked around for me, bowed with a

sidelong, smiling glance up at me as I came from the bedroom. "Fleet Captain," she said. "I was hoping we might… talk."

"About what, Citizen?" I did not invite her to sit.

She blinked, genuinely surprised, I thought. "Surely, Fleet Captain, I've been plain about my desires."

"Citizen. I am in mourning." I had not had time to clean the white stripe off my face for the night. And she could not possibly have forgotten the reason for it.

"But surely, Fleet Captain," she replied sweetly, "that's all for show."

"It's always for show, Citizen. It is entirely possible to grieve with no outward sign. These things are meant to let others know about it."

"It's true such things are nearly always insincere, or at least overdone," Raughd said. She had missed my point entirely. "But what I meant was that you've undertaken this only for political reasons. There can't possibly be any real sorrow, no one could expect so. It's only needed in public, and this"—she gestured around—"is certainly not public."

I might have argued that if a family member of hers had died far from home, she might want to know that someone had cared enough to perform funeral duties for that person—even if the rites in question were foreign, even if the person who performed them was a stranger. But given the sort of person Raughd apparently was, such an argument would have carried no weight, if it had even been comprehensible to her. "Citizen, I am astonished at your want of propriety."

"Can you blame me, Fleet Captain, if my desire overwhelms my sense of propriety? And propriety, like mourning, is for public view."

I was under no illusions as to my physical attractiveness.

It was not such that it would inspire propriety-overwhelming enthusiasm. My position, on the other hand, and my house name might well be quite fascinating. And of course, it would be far more fascinating to someone wealthy and privileged, like Raughd. Entertainments might be brimful of the virtuous and humble gaining the favorable notice of those above them, to their and their house's ultimate benefit, but in daily life most people were fully aware of just what would happen if they deliberately sought such a situation out.

But someone like Raughd—oh, someone like Raughd could set her sights on me, and she might pretend it was all down to attraction, to romance or even love. No matter that in such a case no one involved would for a moment be unaware of the potential advantages.

"Citizen," I said, coldly. "I am well aware that you are the person who painted those words on the wall in the Undergarden." She looked at me with wide-eyed, blinking incomprehension. Kalr Five stood motionless in a corner of the room, ancillary-impassive. "Someone died as a direct result of that, and her death has very possibly put this entire system in danger. You may not have intended that death, but you knew well enough that your action would cause problems, and you didn't really care what those were or who was hurt by it."

She drew herself up, indignant. "Fleet Captain! I don't know why you would accuse me of such a thing!"

"At a guess," I said, unruffled by her resentment, "you were angry at Lieutenant Tisarwat for spoiling your fun with Citizen Piat. Who, by the way, you treat abominably."

"Oh, well," she said, subsiding just a bit, her posture relaxing, "if that's the problem. I've known Piat since we were both little and she's always been... erratic. Oversensitive. She feels inadequate, you know, because her mother is station administrator and so beautiful on top of it. There she is, assigned to a perfectly fine job, but she can't stop thinking it's nothing compared to her mother. She takes everything too hard, and I admit sometimes I lose patience because of it." She sighed, the very image of compassionate regret, even penitence. "It wouldn't be the first time she's accused me of mistreating her, just to hurt me."

"*Such a fucking bore*," I quoted. "Funny how the last time you lost patience with her was when everyone was laughing at her joke and she was the center of attention. Rather than you."

"I'm sure Tisarwat meant well, telling you about that, but she just didn't understand what..." Her voice faltered, her face took on a pained expression. "She couldn't...Piat couldn't have accused me of painting those words on the wall? It would be just the sort of horrible thing she'd think was funny, when she was in one of her moods."

"She hasn't accused you of anything," I said, my voice still cold. "The evidence speaks for itself."

Raughd froze, completely still for an instant, not even breathing. Then she said, with a coldness that nearly matched my own, "Did you accept my mother's invitation just so you could come here and attack me? Obviously, you've come here with some sort of agenda. You turn up out of nowhere, produce some ridiculous order forbidding travel in the gates so the tea can't get out of the system. I can't see it as anything less than an attack on my house, and I will not stand for that! I'm going to speak to my mother about this!"

"You do that," I said. Still calm. "Be sure to explain to her how that paint got on your gloves. But I wouldn't be surprised if she already knows about it and invited me down here in the hope that I could be dissuaded from pressing the issue." And I had accepted knowing that. And I had wanted to know what it was like, downwell. What Sirix had been so angry about.

Raughd turned and left the room without another word.

The morning sky was pale blue streaked with the silver traces of the weather grid, and here and there a wisp of cloud. The sun hadn't yet cleared the mountain so the houses and the lake, the trees, were still in shadow. Sirix waited for me, at the water's edge. "Thank you for the wake-up call, Fleet Captain," she said, with an ironic bow of her head. "I'm sure I wouldn't have wanted to sleep in."

"Already used to the time difference?" It was early afternoon on the station. "I'm told there's a path along the lakeside."

"I don't think I can keep up with you if you're going to run."

"I'm walking today." I would have walked anyway, even if Sirix hadn't needed to keep up. I set off in the direction of the lakeside trail, not turning my head to see if she followed, but hearing her step behind me, seeing her (and myself) as Five watched us out of sight from the corner of the arbor.

On Athoek Station, Lieutenant Tisarwat was in the sitting room in our Undergarden quarters, speaking to Basnaaid Elming. Who'd arrived not five minutes earlier while I'd been pulling on my boots, about to leave my room. I'd been briefly tempted to make Sirix wait, but in the end I decided that by now I could watch and walk at the same time.

I could see—almost feel, myself—the thrill thrumming through Tisarwat at Basnaaid's presence. "Horticulturist," Tisarwat was saying. She wasn't long out of bed herself. "I'm at your service. But I must tell you, the fleet captain has ordered me to stay away from you."

Basnaaid frowned, clearly puzzled and dismayed. "Why?"

Lieutenant Tisarwat took an unsteady breath. "You said you never wanted to speak to her again. She didn't... she wanted to be sure you didn't ever think she was..." She trailed off, at a loss, it seemed. "For your sister's sake, she'll do anything you ask."

"She's a bit high handed about it," responded Basnaaid, with some acerbity.

"Fleet Captain," said Sirix, walking beside me on the path alongside the lake. I realized she'd been speaking to me, and I had not responded.

"Forgive me, Citizen." I forced my attention away from Basnaaid and Tisarwat. "I was distracted."

"Plainly." She sidestepped a branch that had fallen from one of the nearby trees. "I was trying to thank you for being patient with me yesterday. And for Kalr Eight's help." She frowned. "Do you not allow them to go by their names?"

"They'd much prefer I not use their names, at least my Kalrs would." I gestured ambiguity, uncertainty. "She might tell you her name if you ask." The house was well behind us by now, screened by a turn of the path, by trees with broad, oval leaves and small cascades of fringed white flowers. "Tell me, Citizen, is suspension failure a problem, among the field workers in the mountains here?" Transportees were shipped in suspension pods. Which generally worked very well, but sometimes failed, leaving their occupants dead or severely injured.

Sirix froze midstride, just an instant, and then kept walking. I had said something that had surprised her, but I thought I'd also seen recognition in her expression. "I don't think I've ever seen anyone thawed out. I don't think anyone has been, for a while. But the Valskaayans, some of them, think that when the medics thawed people out, they didn't let all of them live."

"Do they say why?"

Sirix gestured ambiguity. "Not plainly. They think the medics dispose of anyone they consider unfit in some way, but they won't say exactly what that means, at least they wouldn't in my hearing. And they won't go to a medic. Not for anything. Every bone in their body could be broken and they'd rather have their friends splint them up with sticks and old clothes."

"Last night," I said, by way of explanation, "I requested an account of the number of Valskaayans transported to this system."

"Only Valskaayans?" asked Sirix, eyebrow raised. "Why not Samirend?"

Ah. "I've found something, have I?"

"I wouldn't have thought there was much to find, that way, about the Valskaayans. Before I was born, though, before Valskaay was even annexed, something happened. About a hundred fifty years ago. I don't know for certain—I doubt anyone but the parties actually involved know for certain. But I can tell you the rumor. Someone in charge of the transportees coming into the system was siphoning off a percentage of them and selling them to outsystem slavers. No," she gestured, emphatic, seeing my doubt. "I know it sounds ridiculous. But before this place was civilized"—not even a trace of irony there—"debt indenture was quite common, and it was entirely legal to sell indentures away. No one cared much, unless someone had the bad taste to sell away a few Xhais. It was entirely natural and boring if it happened to a lot of Ychana."

"Yes." When I'd seen those numbers—how many Valskaayans had been transported here, how many brought out of suspension and assigned work, how many remaining—and, further, because I'd just seen that ancient tea set and heard Captain Hetnys's story of selling it to Citizen Fosyf, I had queried the system histories. "Except that outsystem slave trade collapsed not long after the annexation and has never recovered." Partly, I thought, because it had relied on cheap supply from Athoek, which the annexation had cut off. And partly because of problems internal to the slavers' own home systems. "And that was, what, six hundred years ago? Surely this hadn't been happening undetected all that time."

"I'm only telling you what I've heard, Fleet Captain. The discrepancy in numbers was covered—very thinly, I might add, if the story is true—by an alarming rate of suspension failures. Nearly all of those were workers assigned to the mountain tea plantations. When the system governor found out—this was before Governor Giarod's time, of course—she put a stop to it, but she also supposedly hushed it up. After all, the medics who'd signed off on those false reports had done so at the behest of some of Athoek's most illustrious citizens. Not the sort of people who ever find themselves on the wrong side of Security. And if word of it ever got back to the palace, the Lord of the Radch would certainly want to know why the governor hadn't noticed all this going on before now. So instead a number of highly placed citizens retired. Including Citizen Fosyf's grandmother, who spent the rest of her life in prayer at a monastery on the other side of this continent."

This was why I'd had this conversation away from the house. Just in case. "Faked suspension failure numbers won't have been enough to cover it. There will have been more than just that." This story hadn't been in the information I'd received, when I'd queried the histories. But Sirix had said that it had been hushed up. It might have been kept out of any official accounts.

Sirix was silent a moment. Considering. “That may well be, Fleet Captain. I only ever heard rumors.”

“. . . very heartfelt poetry,” Basnaaid was saying, in my sitting room in the Undergarden. “I’m glad no one here has read any of it.” She and Tisarwat were drinking tea, now.

“Did you send any of your poetry to your sister, Citizen?” asked Tisarwat.

Basnaaid gave a small, breathy laugh. “Nearly all of it. She always said it was wonderful. Either she was being very kind, or she had terrible taste.”

Her words distressed Tisarwat for some reason, triggered an overpowering sense of shame and self-loathing. But of course, there was hardly a well-educated Radchaai alive who hadn’t written a quantity of poetry in her youth, and I could well imagine the quality of what the younger Tisarwat might have produced. And been proud of. And then seen through the eyes of Anaander Mianaai, three-thousand-year-old Lord of the Radch. I doubted the assessment had been kind. And if she was no longer Anaander Mianaai, what could she ever be but some reassembled version of Tisarwat, with all the bad poetry and frivolity that implied? How could she ever see that in herself without remembering the Lord of the Radch’s withering contempt? “If you sent your poetry to Lieutenant Awn,” Tisarwat said, with a sharp pang of yearning mixed still with that self-hatred, “then Fleet Captain Breq has seen it.”

Basnaaid blinked, began just barely to frown, but stopped herself. It might have been the idea of my having read her poetry that brought on the frown, or it may have been the tension in Lieutenant Tisarwat, in her voice, where before she had been relaxed and smiling. "I'm glad she didn't throw that in my face."

"She never would," said Tisarwat, her voice still intense.

"Lieutenant." Basnaaid put her bowl of tea down on the makeshift table beside her seat. "I meant what I said that day. And I wouldn't be here, except it's important. I hear it's the fleet captain's doing that the Undergarden is being repaired."

"Y..." Tisarwat reconsidered the simple *yes* she'd been about to give as not entirely politic. "It is, of course, entirely at the order of Station Administrator Celar, Horticulturist, but the fleet captain has had a hand in it, yes."

Basnaaid gestured acknowledgment, perfunctory. "The lake in the Gardens above—Station can't see the supports that are holding that water up and keeping it from flooding the Undergarden. It's supposed to be inspected regularly, but I don't think that's happening. And I can't say anything to the chief horticulturist. It's a cousin of hers who's supposed to do it, and the last time I said something there was a lot of noise about me minding my own business and how dare I cast aspersions." And likely if she went over the chief horticulturist's head and straight to Station Administrator Celar, she'd find herself in difficulties. Which might be worth it if the station administrator would listen, but there were no guarantees there.

"Horticulturist!" Tisarwat exclaimed, just managing, with difficulty, not to shout her eagerness to help. "I'll take care of it! All it wants is some diplomacy."

Basnaaid blinked, taken a bit aback. "I don't want... please understand, I really don't want to be asking the fleet captain for favors. I wouldn't be here, except it's so dangerous. If those supports were to fail..."

"Fleet Captain Breq won't be involved at all," said Tisarwat, solemnly. Inwardly ecstatic. "Have you mentioned this to Citizen Piat?"

"She was there when I brought it up the first time. Not that it did any good. Lieutenant, I know that you and Piat have been friendly these past several days. And I don't mean to criticize her..." She trailed off, looking for a way to say what she wanted to say.

"But," said Tisarwat into the silence, "generally she doesn't seem to care much about her job. Half the time Raughd is hanging around distracting her, and the other half she's moping. But Raughd has been downwell for the past four or five days, and if Fleet Captain Breq has anything to say about it, she's not coming back up anytime soon. I think you're going to see a difference in Piat. I think," she continued, "that she's been made to feel that she's not capable. That her own judgment is unreliable. I think she could use your support, at work."

Basnaaid tilted her head and frowned further, looked intently at Tisarwat as though she'd seen something completely, puzzlingly unexpected. "Lieutenant, how old *are* you?"

Sudden confusion, in Tisarwat. Guilt, self-loathing, a thrill of...something like triumph or gratification. "Horticulturist. I'm seventeen." A lie that wasn't exactly a lie.

"You didn't seem seventeen just now," said Basnaaid. "Did Fleet Captain Breq bring you along so you could find the weaknesses of the daughters of the station's most prominent citizens?"

"No," Tisarwat said, openly mournful. Inwardly despairing. "I think she brought me along because she thought I'd get into trouble if she wasn't watching me."

"If you'd told me that five minutes ago," said Basnaaid, "I wouldn't have believed you."

Downwell, on the path through the woods by the lake, the sky had brightened to a more vivid blue. The brightness in the east had intensified, leaving the peak blocking the sun a jagged black silhouette. Sirix still walked beside me, silent. Patient. When she had not struck me as a patient person, except by the necessity of her situation, unable as she was to express anger without considerable discomfort, likely some of it physical. So, almost certainly a pose. "You're as good as a concert, Fleet Captain," she said, slightly mocking, confirming my suspicion. "Do the songs you're always humming have anything to do with what you're thinking about, or is it random?"

"It depends." I had been humming the song the Kalr had been singing the day before, in Medical. "Sometimes it's just a song I recently heard. It's an old habit. I apologize for annoying you."

"I didn't say I was annoyed. Though I wouldn't have thought cousins of the Lord of the Radch cared much if they were annoying."

"I didn't say I would stop," I pointed out. "Do you think all that happened—transportees being sold off, I mean—and the Lord of the Radch didn't become aware of it?"

"If she'd known," Sirix said, "if she'd truly understood what was happening, it would have been like Ime." Where the system administration had been entirely corrupt, had murdered and enslaved citizens, nearly started a war with the alien Rrrrrr until the matter had been brought directly to Anaander Mianaai's attention. Or at least, the attention of the right part of Anaander Mianaai. But Sirix didn't know that part of the story. "The news would have been everywhere, and the people involved would have been held accountable."

I wondered when Anaander Mianaai had become aware

of it, of people, potential citizens, being sold away for profit here. It would not have surprised me at all to discover that part of Anaander knew, or that a part of her had continued or restarted it, hidden from the rest of herself. The question then became, which Anaander was it, and what use was she making of it? I couldn't help but think of Anaander stripping ships of their ancillaries. Ships like *Mercy of Kalr.* Troop carriers like *Justice of Ente*, which Skaaiat Awer had served on. Human soldiers might not be relied on to fight for the side that wanted them replaced. Ancillaries, on the other hand, were just extensions of their ship, would do exactly what a ship was ordered to make them do. The Anaander who objected to her own dismantling of Radchaai military force might well find those bodies useful.

"You disagree," Sirix said into my silence. "But isn't justice the whole reason for civilization?"

And propriety, and benefit. "So if there is injustice here, it is only because the Lord of the Radch isn't sufficiently present."

"Can you imagine Radchaai, in the normal course of events, practicing indentured slavery, or selling indentures away, like the Xhai did?"

Behind us, in the building where we stayed, Captain Hetnys was likely eating breakfast, attended by a human body slaved to the warship *Sword of Atagaris.* One of dozens just like it. I myself had been one of thousands of such, before the rest of me had been destroyed. Sirix didn't know that, but she surely knew of the existence of other, still surviving troop carriers, still crewed by ancillaries. And over the ridge lived dozens of Valskaayans, they or their parents or grandparents transported here for no better reason than to clear a planet for Radchaai occupation, and to provide cheap labor here.

Sirix herself was descended from transportees. “Ancillaries and transportees are of course an entirely different sort of thing,” I said drily.

“Well, my lord has stopped that, hasn’t she?” I said nothing. She continued, “So the suspension failure rate among Valskaayan transportees seems high to you?”

“It does.” I’d stored the thousands of bodies I’d once had in suspension pods. I had long, extensive experience with suspension failures. “Now I’m curious to know if the traffic in transportees stopped altogether, a hundred fifty years ago, or if it just seemed to.”

“I wish my lord had come with you,” Sirix said. “So she could see this for herself.”

Above us, in the Undergarden, Bo Nine came into the room where Tisarwat and Basnaaid sat drinking tea. “Sir,” said Bo, “there’s a difficulty.”

Tisarwat blinked. Swallowed her tea. Gestured Bo to explain.

“Sir, I went up to level one to get your br...your lunch, sir.” I had left instructions for the household to purchase as much of its food (and other supplies) as possible in the Undergarden itself. “There are a lot of people around the tea shop right now. They’re...they’re angry, sir, about the repairs the fleet captain has ordered.”

“Angry!” Tisarwat was taken completely aback. “At maybe having water, and light? And *air*?”

“I don’t know, sir. But there are more and more people coming to the tea shop, and nobody leaving. Not to speak of.”

Tisarwat stared up at Bo Nine. “But you’d think they’d be *grateful*!”

“I don’t know, sir.” Though I could tell, from what Ship showed me, that she agreed with her lieutenant.

Tisarwat looked at Basnaaid, still sitting across from her. Was suddenly struck by something that filled her with chagrin. “No,” she said, though in answer to what I couldn’t tell. “No.” She looked up again at Bo Nine. “What would the fleet captain do?”

“Something only Fleet Captain would do,” said Bo. And then, remembering Basnaaid’s presence, “Your indulgence, sir.”

Ship, Tisarwat messaged silently, *can Fleet Captain give me some help?*

“Fleet Captain Breq is in mourning, Lieutenant,” came the answer in her ear. “I can pass on messages of condolence or greeting. But it would be most improper of her to involve herself in this just now.”

Downwell, Sirix was saying, “Everyone here is too involved. The Lord of the Radch can be above all that, but she can’t be here herself. But you have your authority from her personally, don’t you?”

In the Undergarden, Lieutenant Tisarwat said, “What was this morning’s cast, in the temple?”

“No Gain Without Loss,” replied Bo Nine. Of course the associated verses were more complicated than that, but that was the essence of it.

Downwell, under the trees by the lake, Sirix continued. “Do you know, Emer said you were like ice that day.” The woman who ran the tea shop, in the Undergarden, that was. “That translator shot right in front of you, dying under your hands, blood everywhere, and you collected and dispassionate, not a sign of any of it in your voice or your face. She said you turned around and asked her for tea.”

“I hadn’t had breakfast yet.”

Sirix laughed, a short, sharp *hah*. “She said she thought the bowl would freeze solid when you touched it." Then, noticing, "You're distracted again."

"Yes." I stopped walking. In the Undergarden, Tisarwat had come to some conclusion. She was saying, to Bo, *Escort Horticulturist Basnaaid back to the Gardens.* Downwell by the lake, I said to Sirix, "I'm very sorry, Citizen. I find I have a lot to think about right now."

"No doubt."

We walked about thirty meters in silence (Tisarwat strode out of our Undergarden rooms and down the corridor), and then Sirix said, "I hear the daughter of the house left in a huff last night, and hasn't come back."

"So Eight is giving you the house gossip," I replied, as in the Undergarden Tisarwat began the climb to level one. "She must like you. Did she say why Raughd left?"

Sirix raised a skeptical eyebrow. "She did not. But anyone with eyes can guess. Anyone with any sense would know from the start she was a fool to set her sights on you like she did."

"You dislike Raughd, I think."

Sirix exhaled, short and sharp. Scoffing. "She's always in the offices of the Gardens. Her favorite thing is to pick someone to make fun of and get everyone else to laugh while she does it. Half the time it's Assistant Director Piat. But it's all right, you see, because she's only joking! Me being arrested for something she did is really just an extra."

"You figured that out, did you?" Upwell, in the Undergarden, Bo Nine helped Basnaaid over the pieces of shipping crate that held the level four section door open. Tisarwat climbed toward level one.

By the lake, Sirix gave me a look that communicated her contempt for the idea that she might not have known about

Raughd's involvement. "She probably flew into town. Or possibly she went to the field workers' house to roust some poor Valskaayan out of bed to amuse her."

I hadn't stopped to think that in turning Raughd down so coldly I might be inflicting her on someone else. "Amuse her how?"

Another eloquent look. "I doubt there's much you could do about it just now. Anyone you ask will swear they're more than happy to gratify the daughter of the house however she likes. How could they do otherwise?"

And likely if she'd come down here without me she'd have gone straight there, as the easiest available source of amusement and gratification. Doubtless a version of amusement and gratification that was common among the tea-growing households here. I might find some way to move Raughd somewhere else, or prevent her from doing the things she did, but the same things were likely happening in dozens of other places, to other people.

Upwell, in the level one concourse outside the tea shop, Tisarwat stepped up onto a bench. A few people outside the tea shop had noticed her arrival, and moved away, but most were intent on someone speaking inside the shop. She took a deep breath. Resolved. Certain. Whatever it was she had decided on was a relief to her, a source of desire and anticipation, but there was something about it that troubled me. "Ship," I said silently, walking beside Sirix.

"I see it, Fleet Captain," *Mercy of Kalr* replied. "But I think she's all right."

"Mention it to Medic, please."

Standing on the bench, Tisarwat called out, "Citizens!" It didn't carry well, and she tried again, pitching her voice higher. "Citizens! Is there a problem?"

Silence descended. And then someone near the tea shop door said something in Raswar I strongly suspected was an obscenity.

"It's just me," Tisarwat continued. "I heard there was a problem."

The crowd in the tea shop shifted, and someone came out, walked over to where Tisarwat stood. "Where are your soldiers, Radchaai?"

Tisarwat had been so sure of herself coming here, but now she was suddenly terrified. "Home washing dishes, Citizen," she said, managing to keep her fear out of her voice. "Out running errands. I only want to talk. I only want to know what the problem is."

The person who had come out of the tea shop laughed, short and bitter. I knew from long experience with this sort of confrontation that she was likely afraid herself. "We've gotten along fine here all this time. Now, suddenly, you're concerned about us." Tisarwat said nothing, suppressed a frown. She didn't understand. The person in front of her continued, "Now when a rich fleet captain wants rooms, suddenly you care how things are in the Undergarden. And we're cut off from any way to appeal to the palace. Where are we supposed to go, when you kick us out of here? The Xhai won't live by us. Why do you think we're here?" She stopped, waited for Tisarwat to say something. When Tisarwat remained silent (baffled, confused), she continued. "Did you expect us to be grateful? This isn't about us. You didn't even take a moment to stop and ask what *we* wanted. So what were you planning to do with us? Reeducate us all? Kill us? Make us into ancillaries?"

"No!" cried Tisarwat. Indignant. And also ashamed—because she knew as well as I did that there had been times and places where such a concern would have been well founded. And from what we'd seen when we arrived, with the painter and *Sword of Atagaris*, there was some reason to suspect that this was one of those times and places. "The plan is to confirm existing housing arrangements." A few people scoffed. "And you're right," Tisarwat went on, "Station Administration should be hearing your concerns. We can talk about them right now if you like. And then you"—she gestured at the person standing in front of her—"and I can take those concerns directly to Station Administrator Celar. In fact, we could set up an office on level four where anyone could come and talk about problems with the repairs, or things that you want, and we could make sure that gets to Administration."

"Level four?" someone cried. "Not all of us can get up and down those ladders!"

"I don't think there's room on level one, Citizen," said Tisarwat. "Except maybe right here, but that would be very inconvenient for Citizen Emer's customers, or anyone who walks through here." Which was nearly everyone in the Undergarden. "So maybe when this good citizen and I"—she gestured toward the person in front of her—"visit Administration today, after we talk here, we'll let them know that repairing the lifts needs to be a priority."

Silence. People had begun to come, slowly, cautiously, out of the shop and into the tiny, makeshift concourse. Now one of them said, "The way we usually do this sort of thing, Lieutenant, is we all sit down, and whoever is speaking stands up." In a tone that was almost a challenge. "We leave the bench for those who can't sit on the ground."

Tisarwat looked down at the bench she was standing on. Looked out at the people before her—a good fifty or sixty, and more still coming out of the tea shop. "Right," she said. "Then I'll get down."

As Sirix and I returned to the house, Fleet Captain Uemi's message reached *Mercy of Kalr.* Medic was on watch. "All respect to Fleet Captain Breq," came the words into Medic's ear. "Does she desire some sort of firsthand or personal information? I assure you that I was the only person on *Sword of Inil* to spend more than a few minutes on Omaugh."

Medic, unlike Seivarden or Ekalu, understood the import of the questions I had been asking of Fleet Captain Uemi. And so she was horrified rather than puzzled when she spoke the reply I'd left, in case the answers to my questions had been what they were. "Fleet Captain Breq begs Fleet Captain Uemi's very generous indulgence and would like to know if Fleet Captain Uemi is feeling quite entirely herself lately."

I didn't expect a reply to that, and never did receive one.

15

Fosyf's servants spoke quite freely in the presence of my silent and expressionless Kalrs. Raughd had not, in fact, gone immediately to her mother, as she had threatened, but ordered a servant to pack her things and fly her to the elevator that would take her upwell, to a shuttle that would bring her to Athoek Station.

Most of the servants did not like me, and said so outside the house where we were staying, or in the kitchen of the main building, where Five and Six went on various errands. I was arrogant and cold. The humming would drive anyone to distraction, and I was lucky my personal attendants were ancillaries (that always gave Five and Eight a little frisson of satisfaction) who didn't care about such things. My bringing Sirix Odela here could be nothing but a calculated insult—they knew who she was, knew her history. And I had been cruel to the daughter of the house. None of them knew exactly what had happened, but they understood the outlines of it.

Some of the servants went silent hearing such opinions

expressed, their faces nearly masks, the twitch of an eyebrow or the corner of a mouth betraying what they'd have liked to say. A few of the more forthcoming pointed out (very quietly) that Raughd herself had a history of cruelty, of rages when she didn't get what she wanted. *Like her mother that way*, muttered one of the dissenters, where only Kalr Five could hear it.

"The nurse left when Raughd was only three," Five told Eight, while I was out on one of my walks and Sirix still slept. "Couldn't take the mother any longer."

"Where were the other parents?" asked Eight.

"Oh, the mother wouldn't have any other parents. Or *they* wouldn't have *her*. The daughter of the house is a clone. She's meant to be *exactly* like the mother. And hears about it when she isn't, I gather. That's why they feel so sorry for her, some of them."

"The mother doesn't like children very much, does she?" observed Eight, who had noticed that the household's children were kept well away from Fosyf and her guests.

"*I* don't like children very much, to be honest," replied Five. "Well, no. Children are all sorts of people, aren't they, and I suppose if I knew more I'd find some I like and some I don't, just like everyone else. But I'm glad nobody's depending on me to have any, and I don't really know what to *do* with them, if you know what I mean. Still, I know not to do things like *that*."

Two days after she'd left, Raughd was back. When she'd arrived at the foot of the elevator, she hadn't been allowed to board. She'd insisted that she always had permission to travel to the station, but in vain. She was not on the list, did not have a permit, and her messages to the station administrator went unanswered. Citizen Piat was similarly unresponsive. Security arrived, suggested with extreme courtesy and deference that perhaps Raughd might want to return to the house by the lake.

Somewhat surprisingly, that was exactly what she'd done. I would have guessed she'd have stayed in the city at the foot of the elevator, where surely she'd have found company for the sort of games she enjoyed, but instead she returned to the mountains.

She arrived in the middle of the night. Just before breakfast, while the account of her fruitless attempt to leave the planet was only just beginning to reach the servants outside the kitchen in the main building, Raughd ordered her personal attendant to go to Fosyf as soon as she woke and demand a meeting. Most of the kitchen servants didn't like Raughd's personal attendant much—she derived, they felt, a bit too much satisfaction from her status as the personal servant of the daughter of the house. Still (one assistant cook said to another, in the hearing of Kalr Five), her worst enemies would not have wished to force her to confront Fosyf Denche with such a message.

The subsequent meeting was private. Which in that household meant in earshot of only three or four servants. Or, when Fosyf shouted, half a dozen. And shout she did. This entire situation was of Raughd's making. In attempting to remedy it, she had only made it worse, had set out to make me an ally but through her own ineptness had made me an enemy instead. It was no wonder I had turned Raughd down flat, inadequate and worthless as she was. Fosyf was ashamed to admit that they had even the slightest relationship to each other. Raughd had clearly also mishandled Station Administrator Celar. Fosyf herself would never have made such mistakes, and clearly there had been some sort of flaw in the cloning process because no one with Fosyf's DNA could possibly be such a useless waste of food and air. One word, one *breath* from Raughd in protest of these obvious truths, and she would be cast out of the house. There was time yet to grow a new, better heir. Hearing this, Raughd did not protest, but returned, silent, to her room.

Just before lunch, as I was leaving my own room in our smaller house, Raughd's personal attendant walked into the middle of the main kitchen and stood, silent and trembling, her gaze fixed, off somewhere distant and overhead. Eight was there seeing after something for Sirix. At first no one noticed the attendant, everyone was working busily on getting the last of the food prepared, but after a few moments one of the assistant cooks looked up, saw the attendant standing there shaking, and gave a loud gasp. "The honey!" the assistant cook cried. "Where's the honey?"

Everyone looked up. Saw the attendant, whose trembling only increased, who began, now, to open her mouth as though she was about to speak, or possibly vomit, and then closed it again, over and over. "It's too late!" someone else said, and the second assistant cook said, panic in her voice, "I used all the honey in the cakes for this afternoon!"

"Oh, *shit*!" said a servant who had just come into the kitchen with dirty teabowls, and I knew from the way no one turned to admonish her that whatever this was, it was serious business.

Someone dragged in a chair, and three servants took hold of Raughd's attendant and lowered her into it, still shaking, still opening and closing her mouth. The first assistant cook came running with a honey-soaked cake and broke a piece off, put it into the attendant's gaping mouth. It tumbled out onto the floor, to cries of dismay. The attendant looked more and more as though she were going to throw up, but instead she made a long, low moan.

"Oh, do something! Do something!" begged the servant with the dirty dishes. Lunch was entirely forgotten.

By this time I had begun to have some idea of what was happening. I had seen things something like this before, though not this particular reaction to it.

"Are you all right, Fleet Captain?" Sirix, in the other building, in the hallway outside both our rooms. She must have come out while I was absorbed by the goings-on in the main building's kitchen.

I blinked the vision away, so that I could see Sirix and answer. "I didn't realize the Samirend practiced spirit possession."

Sirix did not attempt to hide her expression of distaste at my words. But then she turned her face away, as though she was ashamed to meet my gaze, and made a disgusted noise. "What must you think of us, Fleet Captain?"

Us. Of course. Sirix was Samirend.

"It's the kind of thing someone does," she continued, "when they're feeling ignored or put out. Everyone rushes to give them sweets and say kind things to them."

The whole thing seemed less like something the attendant was *doing* than something that was happening *to* her. And I hadn't noticed anyone saying kind things to her. But my attention had strayed from the kitchen, and now I saw that one of the field overseers, the one who had met us the day we'd arrived and had seemed completely oblivious to the field workers' ability to speak and understand Radchaai, was now kneeling next to the chair where the still trembling, moaning attendant sat. "You should have called me sooner!" the overseer said sharply, and someone else said, "We only just saw her!"

"It's all to stop the spirit speaking," said Sirix, still standing beside me in the corridor, still disgusted and, I was certain now, ashamed. "If it speaks, likely it'll curse someone. People will do anything to stop it. One petulant person can hold an entire household hostage for days that way."

I didn't believe in spirits or gods to possess anyone, but I doubted this was something the attendant had done consciously, or without a true need of whatever the reaction of the other servants might provide for her. And she was, after all, constantly subject to Raughd Denche with very little real respite. "Sweets?" I asked Sirix. "Not just honey?"

Sirix blinked once, twice. A stillness came over her that I'd seen before, when she was angry or offended. It was as though my question had been a personal insult. "I don't think I'm interested in lunch," she said coldly, and turned and went back into her room.

In the main kitchen, the head cook, clearly relieved by the presence of the overseer, took firm charge of the dismayed, staring servants and managed to admonish and cajole the rest of the work from them. Meanwhile the overseer put fragments of honey cake into the attendant's mouth. Each one fell out onto her lap, but the overseer doggedly replaced them. As she worked, she intoned words in Liost, from the sound of it. From the context, it must have been a prayer.

Eventually, the attendant's moans and shaking stopped, whatever curse she might have uttered unspoken. She pled exhaustion for the rest of the day, which no one, servants or family, seemed to question, at least not in Eight's hearing. The next morning she was back at her post, and the household staff was noticeably kinder to her after that.

Raughd avoided me. I saw her only rarely, in the late afternoon or early evening, on her way to the bathhouse. If we crossed paths she pointedly did not speak to me. She spent much of her time either in the nearby town or, more disturbingly, over the ridge at the field workers' house.

I considered leaving, but we still had more than a week of full mourning to go. An interruption like this would only appear ill-omened, the proper execution of the funeral rites compromised. Perhaps the Presger, or their translators, wouldn't understand, or care. Still. Twice I had seen the Presger underestimated with disastrous results—once by Governor Giarod and Captain Hetnys, and once by Anaander Mianaai herself, when she had thought she had the power to destroy them and in response they had put those invisible, all-piercing guns in the hands of the Garseddai the Lord of the Radch thought she had so easily conquered. The Presger had not done it to save the Garseddai, who had in the event been completely destroyed, every one of them dead, every planet and station in their home system burned and lifeless, with no action, no protest from the Presger. No, they had done it, I was sure, to send a message to Anaander Mianaai: *Don't even think about it.* I would not underestimate them in my turn.

Fosyf still visited our small house daily, and treated me with her usual jovial obliviousness. I came to see her strangely serene manner as both a sign of just how much she expected to get whatever she wanted, and also an instrument by which she managed to do that, plain persistent saying what she wanted to be true in the expectation that it would eventually become so. It's a method I'd found worked best for those who are already positioned to mostly get what they want. Obviously Fosyf had found it worked for her.

* * *

Above, on Athoek Station, even with Lieutenant Tisarwat's push, with Station Administrator Celar's involvement, a thorough inspection of the Gardens' supports wouldn't happen for more than a week. "To be entirely honest," Tisarwat explained to Basnaaid one afternoon, in my sitting room on the station, "there are so many things that need urgent attention that it keeps getting pushed back." I read her determination, her continuing thrill at being able to help Basnaaid. But also an undercurrent of unhappiness. "I'm sure if the fleet captain were here she'd find some way to just...make it happen."

"I'm impressed that it seems likely to happen at all," said Basnaaid, with a smile that left Tisarwat momentarily, speechlessly, pleased with herself.

Recovering her self-possession, Tisarwat said, "It's not anything urgent, but I was wondering if Horticulture could provide some plants for public areas here."

"It can't help but improve the air quality!" Basnaaid laughed. "There might not be enough light yet, though." And then, at another thought, still amused, "Maybe they could put some of those mushrooms out."

"The mushrooms!" exclaimed Tisarwat, in frustration. "Nobody will tell me where they're growing them. I'm not sure what they're afraid of. Sometimes I think everyone here must be growing them in a box under their beds or something, and that's why they're so anxious about Station Maintenance coming into their quarters."

"They make money off the mushrooms, don't they? And if the chief of Horticulture got her hands on them, you know she'd figure out a way to keep them in the Gardens and charge outrageous prices for them."

"But they could still grow them here," Tisarwat argued,

"and still sell them themselves. So I don't know what the problem is." She gestured dismissal of her irritation. "Speaking of mushrooms. Shall I send Nine out for something to eat?"

On *Mercy of Kalr*, Seivarden sat in the decade room with *Sword of Atagaris*'s Amaat lieutenant. *Sword of Atagaris*'s lieutenant had brought a bottle of arrack. "Very kind," Seivarden said, with barely detectable condescension. The other lieutenant did not seem to see it at all. "With your pardon, I won't have any. I've taken a vow." It was the sort of thing someone might do for penance, or just an occasional spiritual practice. She handed the bottle to Amaat Three, who took it and set it on the decade room counter, and then went to stand by the *Sword of Atagaris* ancillary that had accompanied its officer.

"Very admirable!" replied the *Sword of Atagaris* Amaat lieutenant. "And better you than me." She picked up her bowl of tea. Three had begged Kalr Five for permission to use the best porcelain—still packed away in my own quarters on the ship, because Five hadn't wanted anything to happen to it—and thus humiliate the *Sword of Atagaris* lieutenant with an obvious show of my status. Five had refused, and suggested instead that Amaat Three come around from the other direction and serve the lieutenants from my old, chipped enamel set. Three had been briefly tempted, remembering, as the entire crew did, *Sword of Atagaris*'s threat when we'd entered the system. But propriety had won out, and so the *Sword of Atagaris* lieutenant drank her tea unconscious of her narrow escape from insult. "Seivarden is a very old-fashioned name," she said, with a joviality that struck me as false. "Your parents must have loved history." One of Anaander Mianaai's allies, before she had grown beyond the confines of the Radch itself, had been named Seivarden.

"It was a traditional name in my family," Seivarden replied coolly. Indignant, but also enjoying the other lieutenant's confusion—Seivarden had not yet offered a house name, and because that house was no longer in existence, because she had been separated from them by some thousand years, Seivarden wore none of the jewelry that would have indicated family associations. And even if Seivarden had still owned any, this lieutenant likely would have recognized very little of it, so much had changed in all that time.

The *Sword of Atagaris* lieutenant appeared not to notice the past tense in Seivarden's sentence. "From Inai, you said. What province is that?"

"Outradch," replied Seivarden with a pleasant smile. Outradch was the oldest of provinces, and the closest most Radchaai had ever been to the Radch itself. "You're wondering about my family connections," Seivarden continued, not out of any desire to help the visiting lieutenant through a potentially awkward social situation, but rather out of impatience. "I'm Seivarden Vendaai."

The other lieutenant frowned, not placing the name for half a second. Then she realized. "You're Captain Seivarden!"

"I am."

The *Sword of Atagaris* lieutenant laughed. "Amaat's grace, what a comedown! Bad enough to be frozen for a thousand years, but then to be busted back to lieutenant and sent to a *Mercy*! Guess you'll have to work your way back up." She took another drink of tea. "There's been some speculation in our decade room. It's unusual to find a fleet captain in command of a *Mercy*. We've been wondering if Fleet Captain Breq isn't going to send Captain Hetnys here and take *Sword of Atagaris* for herself. It *is* the faster and the better armed of the two, after all."

Seivarden blinked. Said, in a dangerously even tone, "Don't underestimate *Mercy of Kalr.*"

"Oh, come now, Lieutenant, I didn't mean any offense. *Mercy of Kalr* is a perfectly good ship, for a *Mercy*. But the fact of the matter is, if it came down to it, *Sword of Atagaris* could defeat *Mercy of Kalr* quite handily. You've commanded a *Sword* yourself, you know it's true. And of course *Sword of Atagaris* still has its ancillaries. No human soldier is as fast or as strong as an ancillary."

Amaat Three, standing by waiting in case she should be needed, showed of course no outward reaction, but for an instant I worried she might assault the *Sword of Atagaris* lieutenant. I wouldn't have minded much (though of course Seivarden would have had to reprimand her), but Three was standing right next to the *Sword of Atagaris* ancillary, who would certainly not allow anyone to injure its lieutenant. And no amount of training or practice would make Amaat Three a match for an ancillary.

Seivarden, with just a bit more freedom to express her anger, set down her bowl of tea and sat up straighter and said, "Lieutenant, was that a threat?"

"Amaat's grace, no, Lieutenant!" The *Sword of Atagaris* lieutenant seemed genuinely shocked that her words might have been taken that way. "I was just stating a fact. We're all on the same side, here."

"Are we?" Seivarden's lip curled, aristocratic anger and contempt that I had not seen for more than a year. "This is why you attacked us when we came into the system, because we're on the same side?"

"Amaat's grace!" The other lieutenant tried to seem unfazed at Seivarden's reaction. "That was a misunderstanding! I'm sure you can understand we've all been very tense since the gates went down. And as far as threatening you now, I intended no such thing, I assure you. I was merely pointing out an obvious fact. And it *is* unusual for a fleet captain to command a *Mercy*, though perhaps it wasn't in your day. But it's perfectly natural that we should wonder whether we'll lose Captain Hetnys and end up serving under Fleet Captain Breq directly."

Seivarden became, if anything, more contemptuous. "Fleet Captain Breq will do as she thinks best. But in the interest of preventing further *misunderstanding*"—she leaned on that word just a bit—"let me say clearly and unequivocally that the next time you threaten this ship you'd best be able to make good on it."

The *Sword of Atagaris* lieutenant reiterated that she had never, ever meant to do such a thing, and Seivarden smiled and changed the subject.

On the station, Basnaaid was saying to Lieutenant Tisarwat, "I never met my sister. I was born after she left. I was born *because* she left. Because she was sending home money, and if she'd made officer, I might do something, too. Something better than steaming fish and chopping vegetables." Lieutenant Awn's parents had been cooks. "It was always Awn I was living up to. Always Awn I should be grateful to. Of course my parents never said so, but I always felt as though nothing was ever for *me*, for my own sake, it was always about *her*. Her messages were always so kind, and of course I looked up to her. She was a hero, the first of our house to really *be* someone..." She gave a rueful laugh. "Listen to me. As though my family were nobodies, all of them." Lieutenant Tisarwat waited in un-seventeen-year-old-like silence, and Basnaaid continued, "It was worse after she died. I could never forget all the ways I didn't measure up to her. Even her friends! Awer is so far above Elming they might as well not even be in the same universe. And now Mianaai."

"And those friends," put in Lieutenant Tisarwat, "were offering you things because of your sister, not because of anything you'd done to deserve it." I wondered if Tisarwat had worked out why she was so infatuated with Basnaaid. Possibly not—at this moment she was clearly focused on listening to Basnaaid, on understanding her. Pleased to help. To be confided in.

"Awn *never* knelt." Basnaaid seemed not to notice the strangeness of Lieutenant Tisarwat's words or demeanor, so much older than her apparent age. Had become accustomed to it, perhaps, over the past few days. "She never would have. If she made friends like that, it was because of who she was."

"Yes," said Tisarwat, simple agreement. "The fleet captain has said so." Basnaaid didn't answer this, and the conversation turned to other things.

Three days before we were to leave, Captain Hetnys finally broached the topic of the daughter of the house. We sat under the arbor, the doors of the house wide open behind us. Fosyf was attending something at the manufactory, and Raughd of course was away at the field workers' house. Sirix had gone down to a shady section of the lakeshore, she said to watch for fish but I suspected she just wanted to be by herself, without even Eight hovering behind her. There was only Captain Hetnys and myself, and *Sword of Atagaris*'s ancillary, and Kalr Five nearby. We sat looking out at the shaded stretch of mossy stone, the ridge, and the black, ice-streaked peaks beyond. The main building was off to the left, the bath ahead, where it was in easy reach of the main house but would not obscure the scenery, one end of its glass wall curving into view. Despite the brightness of the afternoon, the air under the trees and the arbor was damp and cool.

"Sir," said Captain Hetnys. "Permission to speak frankly."

I gestured my assent. In all the time we'd been here, Captain Hetnys had not once mentioned what had brought us here, though she had daily put on the mourning stripe and said the required prayers.

"Sir, I've been thinking about what happened in the Undergarden. I still think I was right to give the orders I did. It went wrong, and I take responsibility for that." Her words were in themselves defiant, but her tone was deferential.

"Do you, Captain?" One of the household groundcars came over the ridge, along the road. Either Fosyf returning from the manufactory, or Raughd from the field workers' house. That situation could not stay as it was, but I hadn't managed to come up with a solution. Perhaps there was none.

"I do, sir. But I was wrong to have Citizen Sirix arrested. I was wrong to assume that she must have done it, if Raughd was the only other choice."

The sort of thing I had always liked, in an officer. The willingness to admit she was in the wrong, when she realized it. The willingness to insist she was in the right, when she was sure of it, even when it might be safer not to. She watched me, serious, slightly frightened of my reaction, I thought. Slightly challenging. But only slightly. No Radchaai officer openly defied her superior, not if she wasn't suicidal. I thought of that priceless antique tea set. Its sale was almost certainly meant to cover illegal profits. Thought of the implausible death rates of transportees to this system. Wondered, for just a moment, how these two things could coexist in Captain Hetnys, this courage and integrity alongside the willingness to sell away lives for a profit. Wondered what sort of officer she would be if I had had the raising of her from a baby lieutenant. Possibly the same as she was now. Possibly not. Possibly she would be dead now, vaporized with the rest of my crew when Anaander Mianaai had breached my heat shield some twenty years ago.

Or perhaps not. If it had been Lieutenant Hetnys commanding me in Ors, on Shis'urna, and not Lieutenant Awn, perhaps I would still be myself, still *Justice of Toren*, and my crew would still be alive.

"I know, sir," said Captain Hetnys, emboldened further, perhaps, by my not having answered, "that prominent as this house is here at Athoek, they must seem like nothing to you. From such a great distance, Raughd Denche looks very little different from Sirix Odela."

"On the contrary," I replied evenly. "I see a great difference between Raughd Denche and Sirix Odela." As I spoke, Raughd strolled out of the main building, on her way to the bathhouse, all studied unconcern.

"I mean to say, sir, that from the great elevation of Mianaai, Denche must appear as no different than other servants. And I know it's always said that we each have our role, our given task, and none of them is any better or worse than another, just different." I had heard it said many times myself. Strange, how *equally important, just different* always seemed to translate into some "equally important" roles being more worthy of respect and reward than others. "But," Captain Hetnys continued, "we don't all have your perspective. And I imagine..." The briefest of hesitations. "I imagine if ever your cousins committed some youthful foolishness or indiscretion, they were not treated much differently than Raughd Denche. And that is as it is, sir." She lifted her green-gloved hands, the vague suggestion of pious supplication. All that was, was Amaat. The universe was God itself, and nothing could happen or exist that God did not will. "But perhaps you can understand why everyone here might see the daughter of this house in that light, or why she herself might think herself equal to even a fleet captain, and a cousin of the Lord of the Radch."

Almost. *Almost* she might have understood. "You see Raughd, I think, as a nice, well-bred young person who has somehow, in the past few weeks, made some inexplicably unfortunate choices. That I am perhaps being too harsh on someone who does not live under the military discipline you or I have been accustomed to. Perhaps the daughter of the house has even spoken to you of enemies of hers who have whispered accusations into my ear, and prejudiced me against her unfairly." A brief change of expression flashed across Captain Hetnys's face, nearly a plain admission I was right. "But consider those unfortunate choices. They were, from the beginning, meant to harm. Meant to harm residents of the Undergarden. Meant, Captain, to harm you. To harm the entire station. She could not have anticipated the death of Translator Dlique, but surely she knew your ancillaries went armed, and knew how uneasy you were about the Undergarden." Captain Hetnys was silent, looking down at her lap, hands empty, her bowl of tea cooling on the bench beside her. "Nice, well-bred people do not just suddenly act maliciously for no reason."

This would clearly go nowhere. And I had other things I wanted to know. I had spent some time considering how someone could remove transportees from the system without anyone knowing. "The Ghost Gate," I said.

"Sir?" She looked, I thought, not quite as relieved at the change of topic as she might have.

"The dead-end gate. You never met another ship there?"

Was that hesitation? A change of expression, gone from her face before it could be read? Surprise? Fear? "No, sir, never."

A lie. I wanted to look toward *Sword of Atagaris*, standing stiff and silent beside Kalr Five. But I would never catch, from an ancillary, any subtle reaction to its captain's lie. And the glance itself would betray my thoughts. That I recognized the lie for what it was. Instead I looked over toward the bathhouse. Raughd Denche came striding out, back the way she'd come, a grim set to her expression that boded ill for any servant who might come across her path. I almost looked around to see where her personal attendant was, and realized, with surprise, that she hadn't followed Raughd into the bathhouse.

Captain Hetnys also noticed Raughd. She blinked, and frowned, and then shook her head slightly, dismissal, I thought. Of Raughd's obvious anger, or of me, I couldn't tell. "Fleet Captain," she said, glancing toward the bathhouse, "with your indulgent permission. It's very warm today."

"Of course, Captain," I replied, and remained sitting as she rose, and bowed, and walked away across the mossy stones, angling toward the bathhouse. *Sword of Atagaris* fell quickly in behind her.

She had walked about halfway across the shaded green and gray yard, was directly in front of that curving end of the bathhouse window, when the bomb went off.

It had been twenty-five years since I'd seen combat. Or at least the sort of combat where bombs were likely to go off. Still, I had been a ship filled with bodies for fighting. So it was due to two-thousand-year-old habit that without any sort of effort at all, nearly the instant I saw the flash in the bathhouse window, and almost (but not quite) instantaneously saw the window shatter and its pieces fly outward, I was on my feet and my armor was fully extended.

I suspected *Sword of Atagaris* had never seen ground combat, but it reacted almost as quickly as I had, extending its armor and moving with inhuman speed to put itself between the flying glass and its unarmored captain. The front of glittering, jagged glass swept out from the window, tearing leaves and branches from the trees shading the stones, reached the ancillary, knocked it to the ground, Captain Hetnys beneath it. The barest moment later a scatter of small bits of glass and leaves and twigs reached me and bounced harmlessly off my armor. A quick thought told me that although Kalr Five had only just finished raising her armor, she was quite safe. "Give me your medkit," I said to her. And when she'd done that, I sent her to call for Medical, and for Planetary Security, and then went to see if Captain Hetnys had survived.

Flames licked the edges of the shattered bathhouse window. Shards and fragments of glass littered the ground, some snapping or crunching underfoot as I went. Captain Hetnys lay on her back, awkwardly, under *Sword of Atagaris.* A strange, misshapen fin protruded from between the ancillary's shoulder blades, and I realized that it must be a large shard of glass that had embedded itself before *Sword of Atagaris* could completely raise its armor. Its reaction had been fast, but not quite as fast as mine, and it and Captain Hetnys had been some twenty meters closer to the window than I had.

I knelt beside them. "*Sword of Atagaris*, how badly injured is your captain?"

"I'm fine, sir," replied Captain Hetnys before the ancillary could answer. She tried to roll over, to shove *Sword of Atagaris* off her.

"Don't move, Captain," I said sharply, as I tore open Kalr Five's medkit. "*Sword of Atagaris*, your report."

"Captain Hetnys has sustained a minor concussion, lacerations, an abrasion, and some bruising, Fleet Captain." Its armor distorted *Sword of Atagaris*'s voice, and of course it spoke with the expressionlessness typical of ancillaries, but I thought I heard some strain. "She is otherwise fine, as she has already indicated."

"Get off me, Ship," said Captain Hetnys, irritably.

"I don't think it can," I said. "There's a piece of glass lodged in its spinal column. Lower your armor, *Sword of Atagaris*." The medkit held a special-made general-purpose corrective, designed to slow bleeding, halt further tissue damage, and just generally keep someone alive long enough to get them to a medical facility.

"Fleet Captain," said *Sword of Atagaris*, "with all respect, my captain is unarmored and there might be another bomb."

"There's not much we can do about that without killing this segment," I pointed out. Though I was sure there had only been the one bomb, sure that blast had been meant to kill one person in particular, rather than as many as possible. "And the sooner you let me medkit you, the sooner we can move you and get your captain out of danger." Uncomfortable and annoyed as she clearly was, Captain Hetnys frowned even further, and stared at me as though I had spoken in some language she had never heard before and could not understand.

Sword of Atagaris dropped its armor, revealing its uniform jacket, blood-soaked between the shoulders, and the jagged glass shard. "How deep is it?" I asked.

"Very deep, Fleet Captain," it replied. "Repairs will take some time."

"No doubt." The medkit also included a small blade for cutting clothes away from wounds. I pulled it out, sliced the bloody fabric out of the way. Laid the corrective on the ancillary's back, as close as I could to where the glass protruded without jostling it and maybe causing further injury. The corrective oozed and puddled—it would take a few moments (or, depending on the nature and extent of the injuries it encountered, a few minutes) to stabilize the situation, and then harden. Once it had, *Sword of Atagaris* could probably be moved safely.

The fire in the bathhouse had taken hold, fed by that beautiful woodwork. Three servants were standing by the main building, staring, aghast. More were running out of the house to see what had happened. Kalr Five and another servant hastened toward us, carrying something flat and wide—*Mercy of Kalr* had told her there was a spinal injury. I didn't see Raughd anywhere.

Captain Hetnys still stared at me from under *Sword of Atagaris*, frowning. "Fleet Captain," said the ancillary, "with all respect, this injury is too severe to be worth repairing. Please take Captain Hetnys to safety." Its voice and its face were of course expressionless, but tears welled in its eyes, whether from pain or from something else it was impossible for me to know. I could guess, though.

"Your captain is safe, *Sword of Atagaris*," I said. "Be easy on that score." The last bit of cloudiness cleared from the corrective on its back. Gently I brushed it with a gloved finger. No streak, no smudge. Kalr Five dropped to her knees beside us, set down the board—it looked to be a tabletop. The servant carrying the other end didn't know how to move people with back injuries, so Kalr Five and I moved *Sword of Atagaris* off of Captain Hetnys, who rose, looked at *Sword of Atagaris* lying silent and motionless on the tabletop, the shard of glass sticking up out of its back. Looked, still frowning, at me.

"Captain," I said to her as Kalr Five and the servant carefully bore *Sword of Atagaris* away, "we need to have a talk with our host."

16

The explosion had put an end to any mourning proprieties. We met in the main house's formal sitting room, a broad window (facing the lake, of course), scattered benches and chairs cushioned in gold and pale blue, low tables of dark wood, the walls more of that carved scrollwork that must have occupied the entirety of some servant's duties. Over in one corner, on a stand, sat a tall, long-necked, square-bodied stringed instrument that I didn't recognize, which suggested it was Athoeki. Next to that, on another stand, was that ancient tea set in its box, lid open the better to display it.

Fosyf herself stood in the center of the room, Captain Hetnys in a chair nearby, at Fosyf's insistence. Raughd paced at one end of the room, back and forth until her mother said, "Sit down, Raughd," ostensibly pleasantly but an edge to her voice. Raughd sat, tense, didn't lean back.

"It was a bomb, of course," I said. "Not very large, probably something stolen off a construction site, but whoever placed it added scraps of metal that were meant to maim or kill whoever might be close enough." Some of that had reached Captain Hetnys but had been blocked by *Sword of Atagaris*. It had arrived just the barest instant after that shard of glass.

"Me!" cried Raughd, and rose to her feet again, gloved hands clenched, and resumed her pacing. "That was meant for *me*! I can tell you who it was, it can't have been anyone else!"

"A moment, Citizen," I said. "Probably stolen off a construction site, because while it's easy to find bits of scrap metal, finding the actual explosive is of course more difficult." Quite deliberately so. Though sufficient determination and ingenuity could find ways around nearly any restrictions. "Of course, explosives aren't generally left lying around. Whoever did this either has access to such things or knows someone who does. We can probably track them down that way."

"*I know who it was!*" Raughd insisted, and would have said more except the doctor and the district magistrate entered just at that moment.

The doctor went immediately to where Captain Hetnys sat. "Captain, no nonsense from you, I must examine you to be sure you are unhurt."

The district magistrate had opened her mouth to speak to me. I forestalled her with a gesture. "Doctor, the captain's injuries are fortunately minor. *Sword of Atagaris*'s ancillary, on the other hand, is very badly hurt and will need treatment as soon as you can manage."

The doctor drew herself up straight, indignant. "Are you a doctor, Fleet Captain?"

"Are *you*?" I asked coldly. I couldn't help but compare her to my own ship's medic. "If you're looking at Captain Hetnys with your medical implants turned on, it should be obvious to you that she has sustained little more than cuts and bruises. *Sword of Atagaris*, which sees her even more intimately, has said its captain is largely uninjured. Its ancillary, on the other hand, has had a twenty-six-centimeter shard of glass driven into its spinal column. The sooner you treat it the more effective that treatment will be." I did not add that I spoke from personal experience.

"Fleet Captain," the doctor replied, just as coldly, "I don't need you to lecture me on my own assignment. An injury of that sort will have a long and difficult recovery period. I'm afraid the best course will be to dispose of the ancillary. I'm sure it will be inconvenient for Captain Hetnys, but really it's the only reasonable choice."

"Doctor," interposed Captain Hetnys, before I could reply, "perhaps it's best to just treat the ancillary."

"With all respect to you, of course, Captain Hetnys," said the doctor, "I am not subject to the authority of the fleet captain, only my own, and I will rely on my own judgment and my medical training."

"Come, Doctor," said Fosyf, who had been silent so far. "The fleet captain and the captain both want the ancillary treated, surely Captain Hetnys is willing to deal with its recovery. What harm can there be in treating it?"

I suspected that the doctor, as was common in this sort of household, did not merely work for the tea plantation but was also a client of Fosyf's. Her continued well-being depended on Fosyf, and so she could not answer her in the same terms as she had answered me. "If *you* insist, Citizen," she said with a small bow.

"Don't trouble yourself," I said. "Five." Kalr Five had stood silent and straight by the door this whole time, in case I should need her. "Find a proper doctor in the town and have her come and see to *Sword of Atagaris* as quickly as possible." Sooner would have been much better, but I did not trust this doctor at all. I didn't wonder that the field workers would rather bleed to death than consult her. I wished very much that Medic was here.

"Sir," replied Five, and turned neatly and was out the door.

"Fleet Captain," began the doctor, "I've said I'll..."

I turned away from her, to the district magistrate. "Magistrate." I bowed. "A pleasure to meet you, sadly in unfortunate circumstances."

The magistrate bowed, with a sidelong glance at the doctor, but said only, "Likewise, Fleet Captain. I'm here so quickly because I was already on my way to pay my respects. May I express my sorrow at your loss." I nodded acknowledgment of this. "As you were saying when we came in, we can probably find whoever made this bomb by tracking the materials it was made with. Security is even now examining what remains of the bathhouse. A sad loss." She directed that last to Citizen Fosyf.

"My daughter is unhurt," Fosyf replied. "That's all that matters."

"That bomb was meant for me!" cried Raughd, who had stood fuming all this time. "I know who it was! There's no need to go tracking anything!"

"Who was it, Citizen?" I asked.

"Queter. It was Queter. She's always hated me."

The name was Valskaayan. "One of the field workers?" I asked.

"She works in the manufactory, maintaining the dryers," said Fosyf.

"Well," said the magistrate, "I'll send—"

I interrupted her. "Magistrate, your indulgence. Do any of the people you've brought speak Delsig?"

"A few words, Fleet Captain, no more."

"As it happens," I said, "I'm fluent in Delsig." Had spent decades on Valskaay itself, but I did not say that. "Let me go down to the field workers' house and talk to Citizen Queter and see what I can discover."

"You don't need to *discover* anything," insisted Raughd. "Who else could it be? She's always hated me."

"Why?" I asked.

"She thinks I've corrupted her baby sister. Those people have the most unreasonable ideas about things."

I turned to the magistrate again. "Magistrate, allow me to go alone to the field workers' house and talk to Citizen Queter. In the meantime your staff can trace the explosive."

"Let me send some security with you, Fleet Captain," said the magistrate. "Arresting this person all by yourself, surrounded by Valskaayans—I think you might want some help."

"There's no need," I replied. "I won't need the help, and I have no fear for my safety."

The magistrate blinked, and frowned, just slightly. "No, Fleet Captain, I don't suppose you do."

I walked to the field workers' house, though Fosyf offered me the use of a groundcar. The sun was going down, and the fields I passed were empty. The house sat silent, no one outside, no movement. If I didn't know better I might have thought it abandoned. Everyone would be inside. But they would be expecting someone—Fosyf, Planetary Security, the district magistrate. Soldiers. There would be a lookout.

As I came in earshot of the house I opened my mouth, drew breath, and sang:

I am the soldier
So greedy, so hungry for songs.

So many I've swallowed, they leak out,
They spill out of the corners of my mouth
And fly away, desperate for freedom.

The front door opened. The lookout who had sung those words, that first morning when I had run past the workers picking tea. I smiled to see her, and bowed as I came closer. "I've been wanting to compliment you on that," I said to her, in Delsig. "It was nicely done. Did you compose it that moment, or had you thought about it before? I'm only curious—it was impressive either way."

"It's only a song I was singing, Radchaai," she replied. Radchaai only meant "Citizen," but I knew that in the mouth of a Valskaayan, speaking Delsig, in that tone of voice, it was a veiled insult. A deniable one, since she had, after all, only used an always-proper address.

I gestured unconcern at her answer. "If you please, I'm here to speak with Queter. I only want to talk. I'm here by myself."

Her glance flicked to over my shoulder, though she had, I knew, been watching, knew that no one had come with me. She turned then, without a word, and walked into the house. I followed, careful to close the door behind me.

We met no one as we went through to the back of the house, to the kitchen, as large as Fosyf's, but where that kitchen was all gleaming pans and ranks of freezers and suspension cabinets, this one was half empty: a few burners, a sink. A rumpled pile of clothes in one corner, faded and stained, doubtless the remnant of what had been provided as the field workers' basic clothing allowance, picked over, altered to suit. A row of barrels against one wall that I strongly suspected were filled with something fermenting. Half a dozen people sat around a table drinking beer. The lookout gestured me into the room, and then left without a word.

One of the people at the table was the elder who had spoken to me, the day we'd arrived. Who'd changed the choice of song, when she'd seen that we were in mourning. "Good evening, Grandfather," I said to her, and bowed. Because of my long familiarity with Valskaay, I was fairly sure my choice of gender—required by the language I was speaking—was correct.

She looked at me for ten seconds, and then took a drink of her beer. Everyone else stared fixedly away from me—at the table, at the floor, at a distant wall. "What do you want, Radchaai?" she asked finally. Even though I was quite sure she knew why I was here.

"I was hoping to speak to Queter, Grandfather, if you please." Grandfather said nothing in response, not immediately, but then she turned to the person at her left. "Niece, ask Queter if she'll join us." Niece hesitated, looked as though she would open her mouth to protest, decided otherwise, though clearly she was not happy with her choice. She rose, and left the kitchen without a word to me.

Grandfather gestured to the vacant chair. "Sit, Soldier." I sat. Still, no one else at the table would look directly at me. I suspected that if Grandfather had told them to leave, they would have gladly fled the room. "From your accent, soldier," said Grandfather, "you learned your Delsig in Vestris Cor."

"I did," I agreed. "I spent quite some time there. And in Surimto District."

"I'm from Eph," Grandfather said, pleasantly, as though this were nothing more than a social call. "I never was in Vestris Cor. Or Surimto, either. I imagine it's very different these days, now you Radchaai are running things."

"In some ways, I'm sure," I replied. "I haven't been there in quite some time myself." Queter might have fled, or might refuse to come. My coming here, approaching like this, had been a gamble.

"How many Valskaayans did you kill while you were there, Radchaai?" Not Grandfather, but one of the other people around the table, one whose anger and resentment had built beyond the ability of her fear of me to contain it.

"Quite a few," I replied, calmly. "But I am not here to kill anyone. I am alone and unarmed." I held my gloved hands out, over the table, palms up.

"Just a social call, then?" Her voice was thick with sarcasm.

"Sadly, no," I replied.

Grandfather spoke then, trying to steer the conversation away from such dangerous territory. "I think you're too young to have been in the annexation, child."

I ducked my head, a small, respectful bow. "I'm older than I seem, Grandfather." Far, far older. But there was no way for anyone here to know that.

"You're very polite," said Grandfather, "I'll give you that."

"My mother said," observed the angry person, "that the soldiers who killed her family were also very polite."

"I'm sorry," I said, into the tense silence that greeted her observation. "I know that even if I could tell you for certain that it wasn't me, that wouldn't help."

"It wasn't you," she said. "It wasn't in Surimto. But you're right, it doesn't help." She shoved her chair back, looked at Grandfather. "Excuse me," she said. "Things to do." Grandfather gestured permission to go, and she left. As she went out the kitchen door, someone else came in. She was in her twenties, one of the people I'd seen under the arbor the day we'd arrived. The lines of her face suggested she was genetically related to Grandfather, though her skin was darker. Her eyes and her tightly curled hair that she'd twisted and bound with a bright green scarf were lighter. And by the set of her shoulders, and the frozen silence that descended when she'd entered, she was who I'd come to see.

I rose. "Miss Queter," I said, and bowed. She said nothing, did not move. "I want to thank you for deciding not to kill me." Silence, still, from Grandfather, from the others at the table. I wondered if the hallways outside were full of eavesdroppers, or if everyone else had fled, hiding anywhere that might be safe until I left. "Will you sit?" She didn't answer.

"Sit, Queter," said Grandfather.

"I won't," said Queter, and folded her arms and stared at me. "I could have killed you, Radchaai. You'd probably have deserved it, but Raughd deserved it more."

I gestured resignation and reseated myself. "She threatened your sister, I take it?" An incredulous look told me my mistake. "Your brother. Is he all right?"

She raised an eyebrow, tilted her head. "The rescuer of the helpless." Her voice was acid.

"Queter," warned Grandfather.

I raised a gloved hand, palm out—the gesture would have been rude, to most Radchaai, but meant something else to a Valskaayan. *Hold. Be calm.* "It's all right, Grandfather. I know justice when I hear it." A small, incredulous noise from one of the others sitting at the table, quickly silenced. Everyone pretended not to have noticed it. "Citizen Raughd had a taste for tormenting your brother. She's quite shrewd in some ways. She knew what lengths you'd go to, to protect him. She also knew that you have some technical ability. That if she managed to filch some explosives from a construction site and provided you with the instructions for how to use them, you'd be able to follow them. She didn't, I suspect, realize that you might come up with ways to improve their use. The scrap metal was your idea, wasn't it?" I had no evidence for that, beyond the repeated signs that Raughd rarely thought things through. Queter's expression didn't change. "And she didn't realize you might decide to use them on her instead of me."

Head still tilted, expression still sardonic, she said, "Don't you want to know how I did it?"

I smiled. "Most esteemed Queter. For nearly all of my life I have been among people who were very firmly convinced that the universe would be the better for my absence. I doubt very much that you have any surprises for me. Still, it was well done, and if your timing hadn't been just that smallest bit off, you would have succeeded. Your talents are wasted here."

"Oh, of *course* they are." Her tone became, if possible, even more cutting than before. "There's no one else here but *superstitious savages*." The last words in Radchaai.

"The information you would need to make something like that is not freely available," I said. "If you'd gone looking for it you would have been denied access, and possibly had Planetary Security looking closely at you. If you attended school here you'd have learned to recite passages of scripture, and some cleaned-up history, and very little more. Raughd herself likely knew no more than that explosives can kill people. You worked the details out yourself." Had, perhaps, been pondering the question long before Raughd made her move. "Sorting tea leaves and fixing the machines in the manufactory! You must have been bored beyond belief. If you'd ever taken the aptitudes, the assigners would have been sure to send you somewhere your talents were better occupied, and you'd have had no time or opportunity to dream up trouble." Queter's lips tightened, and she drew breath as though to reply. "And," I forestalled her, "you would not have been here to protect your brother." I gestured, acknowledging the irony of such things.

"Are you here to arrest me?" Queter asked, without moving, her face not betraying the tension that had forced that question into the open. Only the barest hint of it in her voice. Grandfather, and the others around the table, sat still as stone, hardly daring to breathe.

"I am," I replied.

Queter unfolded her arms. Closed her hands into fists. "You are so *civilized*. So *polite*. So *brave* coming here alone when you know no one here would dare to touch you. So easy to be all those things, when all the power is on your side."

"You're right," I agreed.

"Let's just go!" Queter crossed her arms again, hands still fists.

"Well," I replied calmly. "As to that, I walked here, and I think it's raining by now. Or have I lost count of the days?" No reply, just tense silence from the people around the table, Queter's determined glare. "And I wanted to ask you what happened. So that I can be sure the weight of this falls where it should."

"Oh!" cried Queter, at the frayed edge of her patience finally. "You're the just one, the kind one, are you? But you're no different from the daughter of the house." She lapsed, there, into Radchaai. "All of you! You take what you want at the end of a gun, you murder and rape and steal, and you call it *bringing civilization*. And what is civilization, to you, but us being properly grateful to be murdered and raped and stolen from? You said you knew justice when you heard it. Well, what is your justice but you allowed to treat us as you like, and us condemned for even attempting to defend ourselves?"

"I won't argue," I said. "What you say is true."

Queter blinked, hesitated. Surprised, I thought, to hear me say so. "But *you'll* grant us justice from on high, will you? You'll bring salvation? Are you here for us to fall at your feet and sing your praise? But we know what your justice is, we know what your salvation is, whatever face you put on it."

"I can't bring you justice, Queter. I can, however, bring you personally into the presence of the district magistrate so that you can explain to her why you did what you did. It won't change things for you. But you knew from the moment Raughd Denche told you what she wanted that there would be no other ending to this, not for you. The daughter of the house was too convinced of her own cleverness to have realized what that would mean."

"And what good will that do, Radchaai?" asked Queter, defiant. "Don't you know we're dishonest and deceitful? Resentful where we should be docile and grateful? That what intelligence we superstitious savages have is mere cunning? Obviously, I would lie. I might even tell a lie you created for me, because you hate the daughter of the house. And me in particular. In the strikes—your pet Samirend will have told you of the strikes?" I gestured acknowledgment. "She'll have told you how she and her cousins nobly educated us, made us aware of the injustice we suffered, taught us how to organize and induced us to act? Because we could not *possibly* have done those things ourselves."

"She herself," I said, "was reeducated afterward, and as a result can't speak directly about it. Citizen Fosyf, on the other hand, told me the story in such terms."

"*Did* she," answered Queter, not a question. "And did she tell you that my mother died during those strikes? But no, she'll have spoken of how kind she is to us, and how gentle she was, not bringing in soldiers to shoot us all as we sat there."

Queter could not have been more than ten when it had happened. “I can’t promise the district magistrate will listen,” I said. “I can only give you the opportunity to speak.”

“And then what?” asked Grandfather. “What then, Soldier? From a child I was taught to forgive and forget, but it’s difficult to forget these things, the loss of parents, of children and grandchildren.” Her expression was unchanged, blank determination, but her voice broke slightly at that last. “And we are all of us only human. We can only forgive so much.”

“For my part,” I replied, “I find forgiveness overrated. There are times and places when it’s appropriate. But not when the demand that you forgive is used to keep you in your place. With Queter’s help I can remove Raughd from this place, permanently. I will try to do more if I can.”

“Really?” asked another person at the table, who had been silent till now. “Fair pay? Can you do that, Soldier?”

“Pay at all!” added Queter. “Decent food you don’t have to go in debt for.”

“A priest,” someone suggested. “A priest for us, and a priest for the Recalcitrants, there are some over on the next estate.”

“They’re called *teachers*,” Grandfather said. “Not priests. How many times have I said so?” And *Recalcitrant* was an insult. But before I could say that, Grandfather said to me, “You won’t be able to keep such promises. You won’t be able to keep Queter safe and healthy.”

“That’s why I make no promises,” I said, “and Queter may come out of this better than we fear. I will do what I can, though it may not be much.”

“Well,” said Grandfather after a few moments more of silence. “Well. I suppose we’ll have to give you supper, Radchaai.”

“If you would be so kind, Grandfather,” I said.

17

Queter and I walked to Fosyf's house before the sun rose, while the air was still damp and smelling of wet soil, Queter striding impatiently, her back stiff, her arms crossed, repeatedly drawing ahead of me and then pausing for me to catch up, as though she were eager to reach her destination and I was inconsiderately delaying her. The fields, the mountains, were shadowed and silent. Queter was not in a mood to talk. I drew breath and sang, in a language I was sure no one here understood.

> *Memory is an event horizon*
> *What's caught in it is gone but it's always there.*

It was the song Tisarwat's Bos had sung, in the soldiers' mess. *Oh, tree!* Bo Nine had been singing it to herself just now, above, on the Station.

"Well, that one's escaped," said Queter, a meter ahead of me on the road, not looking back at me.

"And will again," I replied.

She paused, waited for me to catch up. Still didn't turn her head. "You lied, of course," she said, and began walking again. "You won't let me speak to the district magistrate, and no one will believe what I have to say. But you didn't bring soldiers to the house, so I suppose that's something. Still, no one will believe what I have to say. And I'll be gone through Security or dead, if there's even any difference, but my brother will still be here. And so will Raughd." She spat, after saying the name. "Will you take him away?"

"Who?" The question took me by surprise, so that I hardly understood it. "Your brother?" We were still speaking Delsig.

"Yes!" Impatient, still angry. "My brother."

"I don't understand." The sky had paled and brightened, but where we walked was still shadowed. "Is this something you're afraid I'll do, or something you want?" She didn't answer. "I'm a soldier, Queter, I live on a military ship." I didn't have the time or the resources to take care of children, not even mostly grown ones.

Queter gave an exasperated cry. "Don't you have an apartment somewhere, and servants? Don't you have *retainers*? Don't you have dozens of people to see to your every need, to make your tea and straighten your collar and strew flowers in your path? Surely there's room for one more."

"Is that something your brother wants?" And after a few moments with no reply, "Would your grandfather not be grieved to lose both of you?"

She stopped, then, suddenly, and wheeled to face me. "You think you know about us but you don't understand *anything*."

I thought of telling her that it was she who did not understand. That I was not responsible for every distressed child on the planet. That none of this had been my fault. She stood there tense, frowning, waiting for me to answer. "Do you blame your brother? For not fighting harder, for putting you in the position you're in?"

"Oh!" she cried. "Of course! It's nothing to do with the fact that *your* civilized self brought Raughd Denche down here. You knew enough about the daughter of the house to realize what had happened, you knew enough about her to realize what she was doing to us. But it wasn't *serious* enough for you to stir yourself until some Radchaai nearly got killed. And there won't be anything for *you* to worry about once you're gone and the daughter of the house and her mother are *still here*."

"I didn't cause this, Queter. And I can't fix every injustice I find, no matter how much I'd like to."

"No, of *course* you can't." Her contempt was acid. "You can only fix the ones that really inconvenience you." She turned, and began walking again.

If I were given to swearing, I would have sworn now. "How old is your brother?"

"Sixteen," she said. The sarcasm returned to her voice. "You could rescue him from this terrible place and bring him to *real civilization*."

"Queter, I only have my ship and some temporary quarters on Athoek Station. I have soldiers, and they see to my needs and even make my tea, but I don't have a retinue. And your idea about the flowers is charming, but it would make a terrible mess. I don't have a place in my household for your brother. But I will ask him if he wants to leave here, and if he does, I'll do my best for him."

"You won't." She didn't turn as she spoke, just continued walking. "Do you even know," she said, and I could tell from the sound of her voice that she was about to cry, "can you even imagine what it's like to know that nothing you can do will make any difference? That nothing you can do will protect the people you love? That anything you could possibly ever do is less than worthless?"

I could. "And yet you do it anyway."

"Superstitious savage that I am." Definitely crying now. "Nothing I do will make any difference. But I will make you *look* at it. I will make you see what it is you've done, and ever after, if you would look away, if you would ever claim to be just, or proper, you'll have to lie to yourself outright."

"Most esteemed Queter," I said, "idealist that you are, young as you are, you can have no idea just how easy it is for people to deceive themselves." By now the tops of the mountains were bright, and we were nearly over the ridge.

"I'll do it anyway."

"You will," I agreed, and we walked the rest of the way in silence.

We stopped at the smaller house first. Queter refused tea or food, stood by the door, arms still crossed. "No one at the main house will be awake yet," I told her. "If you'll excuse me a moment, I'd like to dress and see to a few things, and then we'll go up to the house and wait for the magistrate." She lifted an elbow and a shoulder, conveying her lack of concern over what I did or didn't do.

Sword of Atagaris was in Captain Hetnys's sitting room, still facedown on the tabletop on the floor. Its back was covered with the thick black shell of a corrective. I squatted down beside it. "*Sword of Atagaris*," I said quietly, in case it should be asleep, and not wanting to disturb Captain Hetnys.

"Fleet Captain," it replied.

"Are you comfortable? Is there anything you need?"

I thought it hesitated just the smallest moment before replying. "I'm in no pain, Fleet Captain, and Kalr Five and Kalr Eight have been very helpful." Another pause. "Thank you."

"Please let either of them know if you need anything. I'm going to get dressed, now, and go up to the main house. I think it very likely we'll want to leave before tomorrow. Do you think we'll be able to move you?"

"I believe so, Fleet Captain." That pause again. "Fleet Captain. Sir. If I may ask a question."

"Of course, Ship."

"Why did you call the doctor?"

I had acted without thinking much about why. Had only done what had, at the moment, seemed to be the right and obvious thing to do. "Because I didn't think you wanted to be too far from your captain. And I see no reason to waste ancillaries."

"With all respect, sir, unless the gates open soon, this system only has a limited number of specialized correctives. And I do have a few backups in storage."

Backups. Human beings in suspension waiting to die. "Would you have preferred I left this segment to be disposed of?"

Three seconds of silence. Then, "No, Fleet Captain. I would not."

The inner door opened, and Captain Hetnys came out, half dressed, looking as though she'd just woken. "Fleet Captain," she said. Taken somewhat aback, I thought.

"I was just checking on *Sword of Atagaris*, Captain. I'm sorry if I woke you." I rose. "I'm going up to the main house to meet with the district magistrate as soon as I've dressed and had something to eat."

"Sir. Did you find the person who did this?" Captain Hetnys asked.

"I did." I would not elaborate.

But she didn't ask for details. "I'll be down myself in a few minutes, Fleet Captain, with your indulgence."

"Of course, Captain."

Queter was still standing by the door when I came back downstairs. Sirix sat at the table, with a piece of bread and a bowl of tea in front of her. "Good morning, Fleet Captain," she said when she saw me. "I'd like to come up to the house with you." Queter scoffed.

"Whatever you like, Citizen." I took my own piece of bread, poured myself a bowl of tea. "We're only waiting for Captain Hetnys to be ready."

Captain Hetnys came down the stairs a few minutes later. She said nothing to Sirix, looked quickly at Queter and then away. Came over to the sideboard to pour herself some tea.

"Kalr Eight will stay behind to look after *Sword of Atagaris*," I said, and then, to Queter, in Radchaai, "Citizen, are you sure you don't want anything?"

"No, thank you so *very* kindly, Citizen." Queter's voice was bitter and sarcastic.

"As you like, Citizen," I replied.

Captain Hetnys stared at me in frank astonishment. "Sir," she began.

"Captain," I said, forestalling whatever else she might have been intending to say, "are you eating, or can we go?" I took the last bite of my bread. Sirix had already finished hers.

"I'll drink my tea on the way, sir, with your permission." I gestured the granting of it, swallowed the last of my own tea, and walked out the door without looking to see if anyone followed.

* * *

A servant brought us to the same blue and gold sitting room we had met in the day before. By now the sun was nearly above the mountains, and the lake, through the window, had turned quicksilver. Captain Hetnys settled into a chair, Sirix carefully chose another three meters away. Five took up her usual station by the door, and Queter stood defiant in the middle of the room. I went over to where the stringed instrument sat, to examine it. It had four strings and no frets, and its wooden body was inlaid with mother-of-pearl. I wondered how it sounded. If it was bowed, or strummed, or plucked.

The district magistrate came in. "Fleet Captain, you had us worried, you were so late last night. But your soldier assured us you were well."

I bowed. "Good morning, Magistrate. And I'm sorry to have troubled you. By the time we were ready to come back, it was raining, so we spent the night." As I spoke, Fosyf and Raughd entered the room. "Good morning, Citizens," I said, nodding in their direction, and then turned back to the district magistrate. "Magistrate, I would like to introduce Citizen Queter. I have promised her the chance to speak to you directly. I think it is extremely important that you listen to what she has to say." Raughd scoffed. Rolled her eyes and shook her head.

The magistrate glanced in her direction, and said, "Does Citizen Queter speak Radchaai?"

"Yes," I replied, ignoring Raughd for the moment. I turned to Queter. "Citizen, here is the district magistrate, as I promised."

For a moment, Queter didn't respond, just stood straight and silent in the middle of the room. Then she turned toward the magistrate. Said, without bowing, "Magistrate. I want to explain what happened." She spoke very slowly and carefully.

"Citizen," replied the magistrate. Enunciating precisely, as though she was speaking to a small child. "The fleet captain promised that you would be given a chance to speak to me, and so I am listening."

Queter was silent a moment more. Trying, I thought, to rein in a sarcastic response. "Magistrate," she said finally. Still speaking carefully and clearly, so that everyone might understand her, despite her accent. "You may know that the tea planters and their daughters sometimes amuse themselves at the expense of the field workers."

"Oh!" cried Raughd, all offended exasperation. "I can't go within fifty meters of a field worker without flattery and flirting and all sorts of attempts to get my attention in the hope I'll give gifts, or that eventually I'll bestow clientage. This is amusing myself at their expense, is it?"

"Citizen Raughd," I said, keeping my voice calm and chill, "Queter was promised the opportunity to speak. You will have your chance when she is finished."

"And meanwhile I'm to stand here and listen to this?" cried Raughd.

"Yes," I replied.

Raughd looked at her mother in appeal. Fosyf said, "Now, Raughd, the fleet captain promised Queter she could speak. If there's anything to say afterward we'll have our chance to say it." Her voice even, her expression genial as always, but I thought she was wary of what might come next. Captain Hetnys seemed confused, looked for an instant as though she would have said something, but saw me watching. Sirix stared fixedly off into the distance. Angry. I didn't blame her.

I turned to Queter. "Go on, Citizen." Raughd made a disgusted noise, and seated herself heavily in the nearest chair. Her mother remained standing. Calm.

Queter drew a deliberate breath. "The tea planters and their daughters sometimes amuse themselves at the expense of the field workers," she repeated. I didn't know if anyone else in the room could hear how carefully she was controlling her voice. "Of *course* we always say flattering things and pretend to want it." Raughd made a sharp, incredulous noise. Queter continued. "Most of us, anyway. Anyone in this house has...can make our lives a misery." She had been about to say that anyone in the house had the field workers' lives in their hands, an expression that, literally translated from Delsig into Radchaai, sounded vulgar.

The district magistrate said, voice disbelieving, "Citizen, are you accusing Citizen Fosyf or anyone else in this household of mistreatment?"

Queter blinked. Took a breath. Said, "The favor, or the disfavor, of Citizen Fosyf or anyone else in this house can mean the difference between credit or not, extra food for the children or not, the opportunity for extra work or not, access to medical supplies or not—"

"There *is* a doctor, you know," Fosyf pointed out, her voice just slightly edged, something I had never heard before.

"I've met your doctor," I said. "I can't blame anyone for being reluctant to deal with her. Citizen Queter, do continue."

"In entertainments," said Queter after another breath, "beautiful, humble Radchaai are lifted up by the rich and the powerful, and maybe it happens, but it never happens to *us*. Only an infant would think it ever would. I tell you this so that you understand why the daughter of this house is met with flattery, and is given everything she wishes."

I could see from the district magistrate's expression that

she saw little difference between this and what Raughd had described. She looked at me, frowning slightly. "Continue, Queter," I said, before the magistrate could say what I was sure she was thinking. "I promised you would have your say."

Queter continued. "For the past few years it has pleased Citizen Raughd to demand that my younger sister..." She hesitated. "Perform certain acts," she finished, finally.

Raughd laughed. "Oh, I didn't have to *demand* any of it."

"You haven't been listening, Citizen," I said. "Citizen Queter just explained that your merest wish is in reality a demand and that displeasing you in any way can cause difficulties for the field worker who does so."

"And there wasn't anything wrong with any of it," Raughd continued, as though I hadn't spoken. "You know, you're turning out to be quite the hypocrite, Fleet Captain. All this condemnation of sexual impropriety and yet you brought your pet Samirend here to amuse you while you are supposedly in full, proper mourning." I understood now why Raughd had made such a hasty, obvious move toward me—she had thought she needed to outflank Sirix.

Sirix gave a sharp, surprised laugh. "You flatter me, Citizen Raughd. I doubt the fleet captain has ever considered me in such a light."

"Nor you me, I'm sure," I agreed. Sirix gestured assent, genuinely amused from what I could see. "More to the point, Citizen, this is the fourth time Citizen Queter has been interrupted. If you cannot restrain yourself, I'll have to ask you to leave the room while she speaks."

Raughd was on her feet the instant I finished speaking. "How *dare* you!" she cried. "You may be the cousin of God herself for all I care, and you may *think* you're better than everyone in this system, but you don't give orders in *this* house!"

"I had not thought the residents of this house would be so lacking in the most basic propriety," I said, my voice utterly calm. "If it is not possible here for a citizen to speak without interruption, it would suit me just as well for Queter to tell her story to the magistrate elsewhere, and privately." Just the smallest stress on *privately*.

Fosyf heard that stress. Looked at me. Said, "Sit down and be quiet, Raughd." Surely she knew her daughter well enough to guess what had happened, at least the outlines of it.

Hearing her mother, Raughd went very still. She seemed not even to breathe. I remembered Kalr Five and Six listening to the servants talk, how Fosyf had said that there was time enough to grow a new heir. Wondered how often Raughd had heard that threat.

"Now, Raughd," said the district magistrate, frowning slightly. Puzzled, I thought, at Fosyf's tone of voice. "I understand that you're upset. If someone had tried to kill me yesterday I'd have a hard time keeping calm. But the fleet captain has done nothing more offensive than promise this person"—she gestured toward Queter, standing silent in the middle of the room—"a chance to tell me something, and then try to be sure that promise was kept." She turned to Queter. "Queter, is it? Do you deny that you placed the explosive in the bathhouse?"

"I don't deny it," Queter replied. "I meant to kill the daughter of the house. I am sorry I failed."

Shocked silence. Everyone had known it, of course, but it was suddenly different, hearing it said so plainly. Then the magistrate said, "I can't imagine what you would say to me that would change the outcome of this. Do you still wish to speak to me?"

"Yes," said Queter, simply.

The district magistrate turned to Raughd. "Raughd, I understand if you would rather leave. If you stay, it will be best if you'll let this person finish speaking."

"I'll stay," replied Raughd, her tone defiant.

The magistrate frowned again. "Well." She gestured peremptorily toward Queter. "Get it over with, then."

"The daughter of the house," said Queter, "knew that I hated her for taking advantage of my sister. She came to me and said that she wanted the fleet captain to die, that the fleet captain always bathed early before anyone else was awake, and an explosion in the bathhouse at the right time was sure to kill her." Raughd scoffed again, drew breath to speak, but then met her mother's look and said nothing, just crossed her arms and turned to stare at the antique blue and green tea set, on its stand three and a half meters away from where she stood.

"The daughter of the house," continued Queter, her voice steady but just a bit louder in case anyone tried to speak over her, "told me that she would supply me with the explosive if I didn't know where to get it. If I refused, the daughter of the house would do it herself and be sure the blame fell on my sister. If I would do it, she would grant my sister clientage, and she would be sure the blame never fell on me." She looked over at Raughd then, whose back was still to the rest of the room. Said, with withering contempt, "The daughter of the house thinks I'm stupid." She looked back at the magistrate. "I can understand why someone would want to kill the fleet captain, but *I* don't have any personal argument with her. The daughter of the house is another matter. I knew that whatever happened I would be going through Security and my sister would have nothing but grief. For such a price, why not be rid of the person who threatened my sister?"

"You're a very articulate young person," said the magistrate after three seconds of silence. "And by all accounts fairly intelligent. You know, I hope, that you can't possibly lie about this without being discovered." A competently conducted interrogation with drugs would uncover a person's most secret thoughts.

But of course, if authorities assumed the truth of your guilt, they might not bother to conduct any such interrogation. And if someone truly, mistakenly believed something, that's all an interrogation would uncover. "Interrogate the daughter of the house, Magistrate," said Queter, "and discover if what I say is true."

"You admit that you tried to kill Citizen Raughd," remarked the magistrate dryly, "and that you have, as you put it, a personal argument with her. I have no reason to assume that you're not just making this up in order to cause her as much difficulty as possible."

"I'll make a formal accusation if one is needed, Magistrate," I said. "But tell me, have you found the source of the explosive?"

"Security confirms it likely came from a construction site. None of the sites nearby reports anything missing."

"Perhaps," I suggested, "the supervisors of those sites should actually look at their stock of explosives and be sure it matches what the record says." I considered adding that Security ought to pay special attention to places where friends of the daughter of the house worked, or where she had recently visited.

The magistrate raised an eyebrow. "I've given that order. Gave it, in fact, before I came downstairs to meet with you this morning."

I lowered my head in acknowledgment. "In that case, I

have one more request. Only the one, after which I will leave matters to you, Magistrate, as is proper." Receiving the magistrate's gesture of assent, I continued. "I would like to ask Citizen Raughd's personal attendant one question."

Raughd's attendant came into the room a few tense minutes later. "Citizen," I said to her. "Your arms are filled with blessing and no untruth will pass your lips." Said it in Radchaai, though it was a translation, undoubtedly rough, of the words I'd heard in the kitchen that day, through Eight, what the overseer had said as she'd placed bits of honey cake in Raughd's attendant's mouth. "Where did Citizen Raughd get the explosive?"

The attendant stared at me, frozen. Terrified, I thought. No one ever paid attention to servants except other servants, especially in this house. "Your very great pardon, Fleet Captain," she said after an interminable silence. "I don't know what you mean."

"Come, Citizen," I said. "Citizen Raughd hardly takes a breath that you're unaware of. Oh, sometimes you weren't with her in the Undergarden, sometimes she sends you on errands while she does other things, but you know, the way a good personal attendant knows. And this wasn't a spur-of-the-moment thing, like painting *Not tea but blood* on the wall that time." She'd tried to clean Raughd's gloves before anyone could realize there was paint on them. "This was different. This was complicated, it was planned in advance, and she won't have done all that by herself, that's what a good personal attendant is *for*, after all. And it's come out anyway. Citizen Queter has told the magistrate everything."

Tears welled in her eyes. Her mouth trembled, and then turned down. "I'm not a good personal attendant," she said. A tear escaped, rolled down her cheek. I waited in silence while she debated with herself—whether over what to say, or whether or not to say it, I didn't know, but I could see her conflict in her expression. No one else spoke. "If I were, none of this would have happened," she said, finally.

"She's always been unstable," said Raughd. "Ever since we were children I've tried to shelter her. To protect her."

"It's not your fault," I said to Raughd's attendant. Ignoring Raughd herself. "But you knew what Queter had done. Or you suspected for some reason." She'd probably drawn the obvious conclusion that Raughd had not—Queter, cornered, would not simply do as she was told. "That's why you didn't come to the bathhouse yesterday, when Raughd called you." And Raughd had lost patience waiting for her servant to come see to her, had left the bathhouse to go look for her, and as a result had not died in the explosion. "Where did Raughd get the explosive?"

"She took it on a dare, five years ago. It's been in a box in her room since then."

"And you can tell us where and when and how, so we can confirm that?" I asked, though I already knew the answer.

"Yes."

"She's making it up!" Raughd interjected. "After everything I've done for her, she does this to me! And you!" She turned to me. "*Breq Mianaai.* You've had it in for my family ever since you arrived in this system. This ridiculous story about how dangerous it is to travel in the gates, it's obviously made up. You bring a *known criminal* into this household." She didn't look at Sirix as she said it. "And now you blame me for what, for trying to blow myself up? I wouldn't be surprised if *you* planned this whole thing."

"Do you see?" I said, to Raughd's attendant, who still stood there, weeping. "It isn't your fault at all."

"It will be a simple thing, Citizen," said the magistrate to Raughd, frowning, "to check your servant's story." I saw Fosyf notice that address, the change from *Raughd* to the more distant *citizen*. "But we should discuss this elsewhere. I think you should come stay with me in the city until we get this straightened out." Raughd's servant and Queter, of course, had no such invitation. Would stay in cells in Security until their interrogations were finished, and they had been suitably reeducated. Still, there was no mistaking what that invitation meant.

Certainly Fosyf didn't mistake it. She gestured dismay. "I should have realized it would come to this. I've protected Raughd for too long. I always hoped she'd do better. But I never thought..." She trailed off, apparently unable to express what it was that she had never thought. "To think I might have left my *tea* in the hands of someone who could do such things."

Raughd went absolutely still for a full second. "You wouldn't," she said, barely more than an emphatic whisper. As though she could not entirely engage her voice.

"What choice do I have?" asked Fosyf, the very image of injured regret.

Raughd turned. Took three long steps over to the tea set on the stand. Picked the box up, raised it over her head with both hands, and threw it to the ground. Glass shattered, blue and green and gold fragments skittering across the floor. Kalr Five, standing by the door, made the smallest noise, audible to no one but her and me.

Then silence. No one moved, no one spoke. After a few moments a servant appeared in the doorway, drawn, no doubt, by the crash of the tea set. "Sweep this mess up," Fosyf said, catching sight of her. Her voice was quite calm. "And dispose of it."

"You're throwing it away?" I asked, partly because I was surprised, and partly to cover another very small noise of protest from Five.

Fosyf gestured unconcern. "It's worthless now."

The magistrate turned to Queter, who had stood straight and silent this whole time. "Is this what you wanted, Queter? All this heartache, a family destroyed? For the life of me I don't understand why you didn't put your obvious determination and energy into your work so that you could make things better for yourself and your family. Instead, you built up and fed this...this resentment, and now you have..." The magistrate gestured, indicating the room, the situation. "This."

Very calmly, very deliberately, Queter turned to me. "You were right about the self-deception, Citizen." Evenly, as though she only remarked casually on the weather. In Radchaai, though she might as well have used Delsig, which she knew I understood.

Her remark wasn't meant for me. Still I replied. "You were always going to speak if you could, whether you thought it would do any good or not."

She lifted one sardonic eyebrow. "Yes," she agreed. "I was."

18

From the moment we had left Fosyf's sitting room, Sirix was tense and silent, and she did not say a word nearly all the way back to Athoek Station. This was a particularly impressive length of silence because *Sword of Atagaris*'s injury meant we'd be taking up more seats on the passenger shuttle from the elevator to the station than we ought, and so we had to wait a day for a flight with the available extra space.

Sirix didn't speak until we were in the shuttle, an hour from docking with the station. Strapped into our seats, Five and Eight behind us, their attention mostly on Queter's sister, who'd had a miserable time the whole flight, among strangers, missing home, disoriented and sick to her stomach in the microgravity but refusing to take any medication for it, upset further by the way her tears clung to her eyes or broke free into small liquid spheres when she wiped her face. She had finally fallen asleep.

Sirix had accepted the offered meds, was therefore more comfortable physically, but she had been troubled since we'd left the mountains. Since before, I thought. I knew she didn't like Raughd, had, on the contrary, good reason to resent her, but I suspected that she of all people in the room that day had understood what Raughd must have felt, to hear her mother speak so easily, so calmly, of disinheriting her. Had understood the impulse that had led Raughd to smash that ancient tea set that her mother clearly valued highly, took pride in. Citizen Fosyf had not changed her mind, about her daughter or about the tea set. Kalr Five had retrieved the box from the trash, and the fragments of gold and glass, the shattered remains of the bowls and the flask that had survived undamaged for more than three thousand years. Until now.

"Was that justice, then?" Sirix asked. Quietly, as though she was not speaking to me, though no one else would have heard her.

"What is justice, Citizen?" I replied with my own question. "Where did justice lie, in that entire situation?" Sirix didn't reply, either angry or at a loss for an answer. Both were difficult questions. "We speak of it as though it's a simple thing, a matter of acting properly, as though it's nothing more than an afternoon tea and the question only who takes the last pastry. So simple. Assign guilt to the guilty."

"Is it not that simple?" asked Sirix after a few moments of silence. "There are right actions and wrong actions. And yet, I think that if you had been the magistrate, you would have let Citizen Queter go free."

"If I had been the magistrate, I would have been an entirely different person than I am. But surely you don't have less compassion for Citizen Queter than for Citizen Raughd."

"Please, Fleet Captain," she said after three long, slow breaths. I had made her angry. "Please don't speak to me as though I'm stupid. You spent the night at the field workers' house. You are apparently familiar with Valskaayans and fluent in Delsig. Still, it's quite amazing that you walked to the house and came back the next morning with Queter. No protest, no difficulty. And before we even left the house—before the *magistrate* left—the field workers had sent Fosyf a list of demands. Just at the moment Fosyf can't depend on the magistrate's unquestioning support."

It took me a moment to understand what she meant. "You think I put them up to it?"

"I can't believe it's merely fortuitous, that uneducated and uncivilized field workers, who for ten years and more could not find the resources to strike, choose to do so now."

"Not fortuitous at all. And while they may be uneducated, they're hardly uncivilized. They're perfectly capable of planning such a thing on their own. They understand Fosyf's position as well as anyone. Perhaps better than many."

"And Queter coming with you so willingly, that wasn't part of any bargain? She won't ultimately be let off lightly? And in the meantime, Citizen Raughd's life is destroyed."

"No sympathy for Queter? Raughd acted from malice and injured pride, and would have destroyed more than me if she had succeeded. Queter was faced with an impossible situation. No matter what she did, things would end badly."

A moment of silence. Then, "All she needed to do was go to the magistrate in the first place."

I had to think about that for a few moments, to understand why Sirix of all people thought Queter could or should have done that. "You do realize," I said finally, "that Citizen Queter would never have gotten within a kilometer of the district magistrate without my having explicitly demanded it. And I beg you to recall what generally happened in the past when Citizen Raughd misbehaved."

"Still, if she had spoken properly she might have been listened to," Sirix replied.

Queter had been right to expect no help from the district magistrate, I was sure. "She made the choices she made, and there's no escaping the consequences of that. I doubt very much she'll get off lightly. But I can't condemn her. She was willing to sacrifice herself to protect her sister." Sirix of all people ought to have approved of at least that. "Do you think that if the Lord of the Radch were here she would have seen through everything, to give each act and each actor's heart its proper weight? To dispense perfect justice? Do you think it's possible that any person will ever get precisely what they deserve, no more and no less?"

"That is what justice is, Citizen, isn't it?" Sirix asked, ostensibly calm, but I could hear that very small tightness in her voice, a flattening of tone that told me she was, now, angry. "If either Raughd or Queter wants to appeal their judgment, there's no recourse, not cut off from the palaces as we are. You're the closest thing we have to the Lord of the Radch, but you aren't the least bit impartial. And I can't help but notice that each time you've arrived somewhere new, you've gone straight to the bottom of the ladder and begun making allies. Of course it would be foolish to think a daughter of Mianaai could arrive anywhere without immediately engaging in politics. But now I see you've aimed the Valskaayans at Fosyf, I'm wondering who you're planning to aim the Ychana at."

"I didn't aim the Valskaayans at anyone. The field workers are entirely capable of making their own plans, and I assure you that they have. As for the Undergarden, you live there. You know what conditions are, there, and you know that it should have been repaired long ago."

"You might have had a private word with the magistrate yourself, about the Valskaayans."

"I did, in fact."

"And," Sirix continued, as though I had said nothing, "many of the Ychana's problems would be remedied if only they became better citizens."

"Just how good a citizen does one have to be," I asked, "in order to have water and air, and medical help? And do your neighbors know you hold such a low opinion of them?" I didn't doubt that, like the Valskaayan field workers, they did.

Sirix said nothing else for the rest of the trip.

Lieutenant Tisarwat met us at the shuttle dock. Relieved to see us, pleasantly anticipating...something. Apprehensive, perhaps of the same something. As other passengers streamed past I looked through Five and Eight's eyes, saw that *Sword of Atagaris*'s ancillary was being tended to by medics and another segment of itself, that yet a third *Sword of Atagaris* ancillary had placed itself behind Captain Hetnys.

Lieutenant Tisarwat bowed. "Welcome back, sir."

"Thank you, Lieutenant." I turned to Captain Hetnys. "Captain, I'll see you first thing tomorrow morning." She acknowledged that with a bow and I gestured us away, out into the corridor and toward the lift that would take us to the Undergarden. The Genitalia Festival was long over—there were no tiny, brightly colored penises hanging in the corridors, and the last of the foil sweet wrappers had gone to recycling.

And—though I knew this already, had seen it through Tisarwat's eyes, and Bo Nine's—there was no broken table at the entrance to the Undergarden. There was an open section door, and an indicator that said, quite properly and correctly, that the door was functioning as it should, with air on both sides of it. Beyond this, a scuffed but well-lit corridor. *Mercy of Kalr* showed me a little surge of pride from Lieutenant Tisarwat. She had been looking forward to showing me this.

"All the section doors leading out of the Undergarden on this level are repaired, sir," Tisarwat said as we walked into the Undergarden corridor. "They've made good progress on the level two doors. Three and four are up next, of course." We walked out into the Undergarden's tiny, makeshift concourse. Well lit, now, the phosphorescent paint around the tea shop door barely noticeable, though still there, as were the spills and footprints. Two potted plants flanked the bench in the center of the open space, both clumps of thick, blade-like leaves shooting upward, one or two of them nearly a meter tall. Lieutenant Tisarwat saw me notice them, but none of her apprehension reached her face. The plants were, of course, the product of her conversation with Basnaaid. The small space seemed even smaller now it was brightly lit, and even a little crowded, not just residents, whom I recognized, but also Station Maintenance in gray coveralls passing through.

"And the plumbing?" I asked. Not mentioning the plants.

"This part of level one has water now." Tisarwat's satisfaction at saying that nearly eclipsed her fear that I'd notice she'd been spending time with Horticulture. "Still working on the other sections, and work has only barely started on level two. It's slow going in some places, sir, and I'm afraid that level four is still... inconvenienced in that department. The residents here agreed it was best to start where most of the people live."

"Rightly so, Lieutenant." Of course I'd known most of this already, had kept half an eye on Tisarwat, on Bo Nine and

Kalr Ten, on what was happening here on the station while I was downwell.

Behind me, behind Tisarwat, Sirix stopped, forcing Five and Eight behind her, shepherding Queter's still silently miserable sister, to stop also. "And what *about* those residents? Do I still have my quarters, Lieutenant?"

Tisarwat smiled, a practiced, diplomatic expression I knew she'd been using a good deal this past week. "Everyone living in the Undergarden at the time the work began has been officially assigned whatever quarters they were using. Your room is still yours, Citizen, though it's better lit now, and eventually will be better ventilated." She turned to me. "There were some...misgivings about the installation of sensors." There had been, in fact, a contentious meeting with Station Administrator Celar, here on this tiny concourse—the lifts hadn't been ready yet—which Lieutenant Tisarwat had arranged by sheer force of will combined with a level of charm that had surprised even me, who had already suspected what sort of things she might be capable of. No Security, only Tisarwat sitting by the station administrator. "Ultimately, it was decided that sensors will be placed in corridors, but not in residences, unless the residents request it."

Sirix made a small, derisive *hah*. "Even sensors in the corridors will be too much for some. But I suppose I'd better make my way home and find out just what you've done."

"I think you'll be pleased, Citizen," replied Tisarwat, still in diplomatic mode. "But if you have any problems or complaints, please don't hesitate to let me or any of *Mercy of Kalr* know." Sirix did not answer this, only bowed and departed.

"You could send people directly to Station Administration," I said, guessing what had troubled Sirix. I began walking again, putting our small procession back into motion. We turned a corner to find a set of lift doors sliding open, ready for us. Station watching us.

On *Mercy of Kalr*, Seivarden stood naked in the bath, attended by an Amaat. "Fleet captain's back safe, then," she said.

"Yes, Lieutenant." The Amaat, speaking for Ship.

On Athoek Station, in the Undergarden, I stepped into the lift with Tisarwat, with my Kalrs, and Queter's sister. *Mercy of Kalr* showed me Lieutenant Tisarwat's momentary doubt, as she considered, not for the first time, the likelihood of my having seen, from downwell, everything she'd done. "I know I *should* send them to Station Administration, sir. But most of the people who live here would prefer not to go there. We are closer by. And we did start this, and we *do* live here. Unlike anyone in Administration." A brief hesitation. "Not everyone here is happy about any of this. There's some amount of smuggling that goes through here. Some stolen goods, some prohibited drugs. None of the people making a living off of that are pleased to have Station watching, even if it's only in the corridors."

I thought again of Seivarden. She'd been quite clear about her determination to never take kef again, and had stuck to her resolve so far. But when she was taking it she'd had an impressive ability to find it, and find ways to get it, no matter where she was. It was a good thing I'd left her in command of *Mercy of Kalr*, and not brought her here.

Still in the bath, on *Mercy of Kalr*, Seivarden crossed her arms. Uncrossed them again. A gesture I recognized from months ago. It surprised the Amaat attending her, though the only outward sign of that surprise was a quick two blinks. The words *You were very worried* appeared in the Amaat's vision. "You were very worried," she said, for Ship.

In the lift, in the Undergarden on Athoek Station, Tisarwat's pride at showing me how much had been accomplished was suddenly drowned in a surge of the anxiety and self-loathing that had been hovering in the background the whole time.

"I see it, Fleet Captain," Ship said to me, before I could say anything. "It's mostly under control. I think your return is putting some stress on her. She's worried you won't approve."

On *Mercy of Kalr*, Seivarden didn't answer Ship right away. She'd recognized the arm-crossing gesture she'd just made, was ashamed of what it might say about her current state of mind. "Of course I was worried," she said, finally. "Someone tried to blow up my captain." The Amaat poured a measure of water over Seivarden's head, and she sputtered a bit, keeping it out of her mouth and her nose.

In the lift in the Undergarden, Tisarwat said to me, "There's been some complaining outside the Undergarden the past few days, about residential assignments." Ostensibly calm, only the barest trace of her feelings in her voice. "There are those who think that it's not fair the Ychana are going to suddenly have luxury quarters, and so much space, when they don't deserve it."

"Such wisdom," I observed dryly, "to know what everyone deserves."

"Sir," agreed Lieutenant Tisarwat, with a fresh pang of guilt. Considered saying more, but decided not to.

"Forgive me for bringing this up," said Ship to Seivarden, with the Amaat's voice, on *Mercy of Kalr*. "I understand being alarmed by the attempt on the fleet captain's life. I was alarmed, myself. But you are a soldier, Lieutenant. The fleet captain is as well. There is a certain amount of risk involved. I would think you'd be used to that. I'm sure the fleet captain is."

Anxiety, from Seivarden, feeling doubly vulnerable because she was in the bath, uncovered. Uncovered by Ship's question. "She's not supposed to be at risk sitting in a garden drinking tea, Ship." And silently, her fingers twitching just the slightest bit, *You don't want to lose her, either.* Not wanting to say that aloud, in the hearing of her Amaat.

"Nowhere is completely safe, Lieutenant," said Ship, through the Amaat, and then, words in Seivarden's vision, *All respect, Lieutenant, perhaps you should consult Medic.*

Panic, from Seivarden, for just an instant. The Amaat, puzzled, saw Seivarden freeze. Saw Ship's words in her own vision, *It's all right, Amaat. Continue.*

Seivarden closed her eyes and took a deep, steadying breath. She hadn't told Ship, or Medic, about her past difficulty with kef. Had been, I knew, confident that it would no longer be a problem for her.

Ship spoke aloud—or, rather, Ship showed the Amaat what it wanted to say, and Amaat said it. "You can't be worried about taking command if something were to happen. You had your own ship, once." Seivarden didn't answer, just stood motionless on the grate while her Amaat did what was needful. The question was meant as much for Amaat's ears as for Seivarden's.

"No, Ship, that doesn't trouble me." Seivarden's answer was also meant mainly for her Amaat. Silently, she said, *She told you then.*

She didn't need to, replied Ship, in Seivarden's vision. *I do have some experience of the world, Lieutenant, and I see you very thoroughly.* Aloud it said, "You were right. When the fleet captain stirs up trouble it's not the ordinary sort. Surely you're used to that by now."

"It's not an easy thing to get used to," Seivarden replied,

trying very hard to sound light and amused. And did not say, silently or aloud, that she would speak to Medic.

In the lift, in the Undergarden, on Athoek Station, I said to Lieutenant Tisarwat, "I need to speak to Governor Giarod as soon as possible. If I go to the governor's residence to invite her to supper, will she be available to accept my invitation?" My rank and my ostensible social status gave me some amount of freedom from the strictest propriety, and an excuse to be arrogantly peremptory even to the system governor, but what I wanted to discuss with her was going to require some delicacy. And while I could have just messaged the question to Five, whose job it was to take care of such things for me, I knew that there were even now three citizens (one of them Skaaiat Awer's cousin) lounging in my sitting room, drinking tea and waiting for Tisarwat. It was not intended to be an entirely social meeting.

Lieutenant Tisarwat blinked. Took a breath. "I'll find out, sir." Another breath, a frown suppressed with some effort. "Do you mean to dine at home, sir? I'm not sure if there's anything there worthy of the system governor."

"You mean," I said, my voice calm, "that you've promised supper to your friends and you're hoping I don't kick you out of our dining room." Tisarwat wanted to look down, to look away from me, but held herself still, her face heating. "Take them out somewhere." Disappointment. She'd wanted to dine in for the same reason I did—wanted to have a conversation with these particular people, in private. Or as close to private as she could get, attended only by Mercy of Kalrs, with only Ship and possibly me watching. "Make me out to be as tyrannical as you like. They won't blame you." The lift door opened on level four, a few meters beyond the lift brightly lit, light panels still leaning against walls beyond that.

Home, for now.

* * *

"I admit, Fleet Captain," said Governor Giarod at supper, later, "that I generally don't much like Ychana food. When it's not bland, it's sour and rancid." She took another taste of the food in front of her, fish and mushrooms in a fermented sauce that was the source of that "sour and rancid" complaint. On this occasion it had been carefully sweetened and spiced to suit Radchaai taste. "But this is very good."

"I'm glad you like it. I had it brought in from a place on level one."

Governor Giarod frowned. "Where do the mushrooms come from?"

"They grow them somewhere in the Undergarden."

"I'll have to mention them to Horticulture."

I swallowed my own bite of fish and mushroom, took a swallow of tea. "Perhaps it might be best to let the people who have become experts continue to profit from their expertise. They stand to lose if it becomes something Horticulture produces, wouldn't you think? But imagine how pleased the growers might be, if the governor's residence started buying mushrooms from them."

Governor Giarod set down her utensil, leaned back in her seat. "So Lieutenant Tisarwat *is* acting with your direction." It wasn't the non sequitur it seemed. Tisarwat had spent the last week encouraging maintenance workers to try food in the Undergarden, and the new plumbing on level one had made work easier for the people who had been providing that food. The aim was obvious to someone like Governor Giarod. "Is that what you brought me here to talk about?"

"Lieutenant Tisarwat hasn't been acting under any orders from me, though I approve of what she's done. I'm sure you realize that continuing to isolate the Undergarden from the rest of the station would be just as disastrous as trying to force the residents here to live like everyone else." Balancing that would be... interesting. "I would be very unhappy to see this end with anything valuable here taken away from the Undergarden so that others can profit by it elsewhere. Let the houses here profit from what they've built." I took another swallow of tea. "I'd say they've earned it." The governor drew breath, ready to argue about that *what they've built*, I suspected. "But I invited you this evening because I wanted to ask you about Valskaayan transportees." I could have asked earlier, from downwell, but attending to business during full mourning would have been entirely improper.

Governor Giarod blinked. Set down the utensil she'd just picked up. "Valskaayan transportees?" Clearly surprised. "I know you have an interest in Valskaay, you said so when you first arrived. But..."

But that wouldn't account for a hasty, urgent invitation to a private dinner, less than an hour after my getting off the passenger shuttle from the Athoek elevator. "I gather they have been almost exclusively assigned to the mountain tea plantations, is that the case?"

"I believe so."

"And there are still some in storage?"

"Certainly."

Now for the delicate part. "I would like to have one of my own crew personally examine the facility where they're stored. I would like," I continued, into the system governor's nonplussed silence, "to compare the official inventory with what's actually there." This was why supper had to be here. Not in the governor's residence, and certainly not in some shop, no matter how fashionable or supposedly discreet. "Are you aware of rumors that, in the past, Samirend transportees were misappropriated and sold to outsystem slavers?"

Governor Giarod sighed. "It's a rumor, Fleet Captain, nothing more. The Samirend have mostly become good citizens, but some of them still hold on to certain long-cherished resentments. The Athoeki did practice debt indenture, and there was some traffic of slaves outsystem, but that was over by the time we arrived. And I wouldn't think that sort of thing would be possible since then. Every transportee has a locator, every suspension pod as well, and every one of those is numbered and indexed, and no one gets into that storage facility without the right access codes. Every ship in the system has its own locator, too, so even if someone did get access and did somehow take away suspension pods without authorization, it would be simple to pinpoint what ship was there that shouldn't have been." In fact, the governor knew of three ships in the system that didn't have locators visible to her. One of them was mine.

The governor continued. "To be honest, I'm not sure why you would have placed any credence in such a rumor."

"The facility doesn't have an AI?" I asked. Governor Giarod gestured *no*. I would have been surprised to learn otherwise. "So it's essentially automated. Take a suspension pod and it registers on the system."

"There are also people stationed there, who keep an eye on things. It's dull work these days."

"One or two people," I guessed. "And they serve a few months, or maybe a year, and then someone else cycles in. And no one's come to take any transportees for years, so there's been no reason to do any sort of inventory check. And if it's anything like the holds on a troop carrier, it's not the sort of thing you can just walk into and look at. The suspension pods aren't in nice rows you can walk between, they're packed close, and they're pulled up by machinery when you want them. There are ways to get in and take a physical inventory, but they're inconvenient, and no one's thought it necessary."

Governor Giarod was silent, staring at me, her fish forgotten, her tea grown cold. "Why would anyone do such a thing?" she asked, finally.

"If there were a market for slaves or body parts, I'd say money. I don't think there is such a market, though I may be mistaken. But I can't help thinking of all the military ships that don't have ancillaries anymore, and all the people who wished they still did." Captain Hetnys might well be one of those people. But I didn't say that.

"Your ship doesn't have ancillaries," Governor Giarod pointed out.

"It does not," I agreed. "Whether a ship does or doesn't have ancillaries is not a good predictor of its opinion of our no longer making them."

Governor Giarod blinked, surprised and puzzled, it seemed. "A ship's opinion doesn't matter, does it? Ships do as they're ordered." I said nothing, though there was a great deal to say about that. The governor sighed. "Well, and I was wondering how any of this mattered when we have a civil war going on that might find its way here. I see the connection, now, Fleet Captain, but I still think you're chasing a rumor. And I haven't even heard anything about Valskaayans, only the one about Samirend from before I came here."

"Give me accesses." I could send *Mercy of Kalr.* Seivarden had experience with troop carrier holds, she would know what to do, once I'd told her what I wanted. Right now she was on watch, in central command. Ill at ease since that conversation with Ship. Resisting the urge to cross her arms. A nearby Amaat was humming to herself. *My mother said it all goes around.* "I'll take care of it myself. If everything is as it should be, you won't have lost anything."

"Well." She looked down at her plate, picked up her utensil, made as if to pick up a piece of fish, and then stopped. Lowered her hand again. Frowned. "Well," she said again. "You were right about Raughd Denche, weren't you."

I had wondered if she would mention that. The fact that Raughd had been disinherited would be common knowledge within a day, I suspected. Rumor of the rest of what had happened would eventually reach the station, but no one would openly mention the matter, particularly not to me. Governor Giarod, however, was the one person here with access to a full, official report. "I was not pleased to be right," I said.

"No." Governor Giarod set her utensil down again. Sighed.

"I would also," I said, before she could say anything more, "like you to require the planetary vice-governor to look into the living and working conditions of the field workers in the mountain tea plantations. In particular, I suspect the basis on which their wages are calculated is unfair." It was entirely possible that the field workers would get what they wanted from the district magistrate. But I wouldn't assume that.

"What are you trying to do, Fleet Captain?" Governor Giarod seemed genuinely baffled. "You arrive here and go straight to the Undergarden. You go downwell and suddenly there are problems with the Valskaayans. I thought your priority was to keep the citizens in this system safe."

"Governor," I replied. Very evenly, very calmly. "The residents of the Undergarden and the Valskaayans who pick tea *are* citizens. I did not like what I found in the Undergarden, and I did not like what I found in the mountains downwell."

"And when you want something," the governor remarked, her voice sharp, "you say so, and you expect to get it."

"So do you," I replied. Serious. Still calm. "It comes with being system governor, doesn't it? And from where you sit, you can afford to ignore things you don't think are important. But that view—that list of important things—is very different if you're sitting somewhere else."

"A commonplace, Fleet Captain. But some points of view don't take in as much as others."

"And how do you know yours isn't one of them, if you'll never try looking from somewhere different?" Governor Giarod didn't answer immediately. "This is the well-being of citizens we're talking about."

She sighed. "Fosyf has already been in contact with me. I suppose you know her field workers are threatening to stop working unless she meets a whole list of demands?"

"I only just heard a few hours ago."

"And by dealing with them in such circumstances, we are rewarding these people for threatening us. What do you think they'll do but try it again, since it got them what they wanted once already? And we need things calm here."

"*These people* are citizens." I replied, my voice as calm and even as I could make it, without reaching the dead tonelessness of an ancillary. "When they behave properly, you will say there is no problem. When they complain loudly, you will say they cause their own problems with their impropriety. And when they are driven to extremes, you say you will not reward such actions. What will it take for you to listen?"

"You don't understand, Fleet Captain, this isn't like—"

I cut her off, heedless of propriety. "And what does it cost you to consider the possibility?" In fact, it might well cost her a great deal. The admission, to herself, that she was not as just as she had always thought herself to be. "We need things running here in such a way that no matter what happens outside this system—even if we never hear from the Lord of the Radch again, even if every gate in Radchaai space goes down—no matter what happens elsewhere, this system is safe and stable. We will not be able to do that by threatening tens or hundreds of citizens with armed soldiers."

"And if the Valskaayans decide to riot? Or, gods forbid, the Ychana just outside your door here?"

Honestly, some moments I despaired of Governor Giarod. "I will not order soldiers to fire on citizens." Would, in fact, explicitly order them not to. "People don't riot for no reason. And if you're finding you have to deal with the Ychana carefully now, it's because of how they've been treated in the past."

"I should look from their point of view, should I?" she asked, eyebrow raised, voice just the slightest bit sardonic.

"You should," I agreed. "Your only other choice is rounding them all up and either reeducating or killing every one of them." The first was beyond the resources of Station Security. And I had already said I would not help with the second.

She grimaced in horror and disgust. "What do you take me for, Fleet Captain? Why would you think anyone here would even consider such a thing?"

"I am older than I look," I replied. "I have been in the middle of more than one annexation. I have seen people do things that a month or a year before they would have sworn they would never, ever do." Lieutenant Tisarwat sat at supper with her companions: the grandniece of the chief of Station Security, the young third cousin of a tea grower—not Fosyf, but one of those whose tea Fosyf had condescendingly declared "acceptable." Skaaiat Awer's cousin. And Citizen Piat. Tisarwat complained of my stern, unbendable nature, impervious to any appeal. Basnaaid, of course, wasn't there. She didn't move in this social circle, and I had, after all, ordered Tisarwat away from her.

System Governor Giarod spoke across the table in the dining room in my Undergarden quarters. "Why, Fleet Captain, do you think I would be one of those people?"

"Everyone is potentially one of those people, Governor," I replied. "It's best to learn that before you do something you'll have trouble living with." Best to learn it, really, before anyone—perhaps dozens of anyones—died to teach it to you.

But it was a hard lesson to learn any other way, as I knew from very personal experience.

19

Seivarden understood my instructions about transportee storage immediately. "You don't seriously think," she said, aloud, sitting on the edge of her bunk in her quarters, her voice sounding in my ear where I sat in the Undergarden, "that someone has managed to steal bodies." She paused. "Why would anyone do that? And how could they manage it? I mean, during an annexation"—she gestured, half dismissing, half warding—"all sorts of things happen. If you told me someone was selling to slavers that way, at a time like that, I wouldn't be that surprised."

But once a person had been tagged, labeled, accounted for, it became another matter entirely. I knew as well as Seivarden what happened to people during annexations—people who weren't Radchaai. I also knew that cases where people had been sold that way were vanishingly rare—no Radchaai soldier could so much as take a breath without her ship knowing it.

Of course, the past several centuries, the Lord of the Radch had been visiting ships and altering their accesses, had, I suspected, been handing out access codes to people she had thought would support her, so that they could act secretly, unseen by ships and stations that would otherwise have reported them to authorities. To the wrong half of Anaander Mianaai. "If you need ancillaries," I said, quietly, alone in my sitting room on Athoek Station, now that Governor Giarod had left, "those bodies might well be useful."

Seivarden was silent a moment, considering that. Not liking the conclusions she was coming to. "The other side has a network here. That's what you're saying."

"We're not on either side," I reminded her. "And of course they do. Everywhere one side is, the other side is. Because they're the same. It's not a surprise that agents for that part of the tyrant have been active here." Anaander Mianaai was inescapable, everywhere in Radch space. "But I admit I didn't expect something like this."

"You need more than bodies," she pointed out. Leaned back against the wall. Crossed her arms. Uncrossed them. "There's equipment you need to install." And then, apologetic, "You know that. But still."

"They could be stockpiling that, too. Or they may be depending on a troop carrier." A troop carrier could manufacture that, given time and the appropriate materials. Some of the *Swords* and *Mercies* that still had ancillaries had some in stock, for backup. In theory, there wasn't anyplace else to get such things. Not anymore. That was part of why the Lord of the Radch had had the problem with Tisarwat that she did—she could not easily get the right tech, had had to modify her own. "And maybe you'll get there and find everything is in order."

Seivarden scoffed. Then said, "There aren't many people here who could do something like that."

"No," I acknowledged.

"I suppose it wouldn't be the governor, since she gave you the keys to the place. Though now I think of it she couldn't have done much else."

"You have a point."

"And you," she said, sighing, "aren't going to tell me who you've got your eye on. Breq, we'll be days away. Unless we gate there."

"No matter where you are you won't be able to rush to my rescue if anything were to happen."

"Well," replied Seivarden. "Well." Tense and unhappy. "Probably everything will be very dull for the next few months. It's always like that." It had been, for both of our lives. Frantic action, then months or even years waiting for something to happen. "And even if they come to Athoek"—by *they* she meant, presumably, the part of the Lord of the Radch that had lost the battle at Omaugh Palace, whose supporters were destroying gates with ships in them—"they won't come right away. It won't be the first place on their list." And travel between systems could take weeks, months. Even years. "Probably nothing will happen for ages." A thought struck her then. "Why don't you send *Sword of Atagaris*? It's not like it's doing much where it is." I didn't answer right away, but didn't need to. "Oh, Aatr's tits. Of *course*. I should have realized right away, but I didn't think *that person*..."—the choice of word, which was one that barely acknowledged humanity, communicated Seivarden's disdain for Captain Hetnys—"was smart enough to pull something like that off." Seivarden had had a low opinion of *Sword of Atagaris*'s captain ever since Translator Dlique's death. "But now I think of it, isn't it odd, *Sword of Atagaris* being so intent on picking up that supply locker. Maybe we need to take a look on the other side of that Ghost Gate."

"I have some guesses about what we might find there," I admitted. "But first things first. And don't worry about me. I can take care of myself."

"Yes, sir," Seivarden agreed.

At breakfast next morning, Queter's sister stood silent, eyes downcast, as Lieutenant Tisarwat and I said the daily prayer. *The flower of justice is peace.* Silent as we named the dead. Still stood as Tisarwat and I sat.

"Sit, child," I said to her, in Delsig.

"Yes, Radchaai." She sat, obedient. Eyes still downcast. She had traveled with my Kalrs, eaten with them until this morning.

Tisarwat, beside her, cast her a quick, curious glance. Relaxed—or at least calm, preoccupied, I thought, with the things she wanted to accomplish today. Relieved that I had said nothing to her—so far—about the initiative she'd taken since I'd been gone downwell. Five brought us our breakfast—fish, and slices of dredgefruit, on the blue and violet Bractware, of course, which Five had missed. Was still enjoying.

Five was apprehensive, though—she'd learned, last night, about the apartments Tisarwat had taken over, down the corridor. No one I could read had looked this morning, but I was quite sure there would already be half a dozen Undergarden residents there, sitting on makeshift chairs, waiting to speak to Lieutenant Tisarwat. There would be more as the morning progressed. Complaints about repairs and construction that were already underway, requests for other areas to have attention sooner, or later, than scheduled.

Five poured tea—not Daughter of Fishes, I noticed—and Tisarwat set to her breakfast with a will. Queter's sister didn't touch hers, only looked down at her lap. I wondered if she felt all right—but if homesickness was the problem, asking her to speak her feelings aloud might only make things worse. "If you'd rather have gruel, Uran," I said, still in Delsig, "Five can bring you some." Another thought occurred. "No one is charging you for your meals, child." A reaction, there, the tiniest lift of her head. "What you're served here is your food allowance. If you'd like more you can have more, it's not extra." At sixteen, she was doubtless hungry nearly all the time.

She looked up, barely lifting her head. Glanced over at Tisarwat, already three quarters of the way through her fish. Started, hesitantly, with the fruit.

I switched to Radchaai, which I knew she spoke. "It will take a few days to find suitable tutors, Citizen. Until then, you are free to spend your time as you wish. Can you read the warning signs?" Life on a station was very, very different from life on a planet. "And you know the markings for section doors?"

"Yes, Citizen." In fact, she couldn't read Radchaai well, but the warning signs were bright and distinctive on purpose, and I knew Five and Eight had gone over them with her, on the trip here.

"If you take the warning signs very seriously, Citizen, and always listen to Station if it speaks to you through your handheld, you may go around the station as you like. Have you thought about the aptitudes?"

She had just put some fish in her mouth. Now she froze in alarm, and then, so that she could speak, she gulped it nearly unchewed. "I am at the citizen's disposal," she said, faintly. Winced, either at hearing herself say it, or at the lump of fish she'd just swallowed nearly whole.

"That isn't what I asked," I pointed out. "I'm not going to require you to do anything you don't wish to. You can still be on the ration list if you claim an exemption from the tests, you just can't take any civil or military assignments." Uran blinked in surprise, almost raised her head to look at me, but quickly stopped herself. "Yes, it's a rule recently made, expressly for Valskaayans, and away from Valskaay not much taken advantage of." It was one any of the Valskaayan field workers might have invoked—but it wouldn't have changed anything. "You're still required to accept what assignment Administration gives you, of course. But there's no hurry to ask them for one, just yet."

And best not to make that application until Uran had spent some time with her tutors. I could understand her when she spoke Radchaai, but the overseers downwell had all behaved as though the speech of the Valskaayan field workers was completely incomprehensible. Possibly it was the accent, and I was used to speaking to people with various accents, was well acquainted with the accents of native Delsig-speakers.

"But you don't have an assignment yet, Citizen?" asked Lieutenant Tisarwat. A shade eagerly. "Can you make tea?"

Uran took a deliberate breath. Hiding panic, I thought. "I am pleased to do whatever the citizen requires."

"Lieutenant," I said, sharply. "You are not to require anything of Citizen Uran. She is free to spend the next few days as she likes."

Tisarwat said, "It's only, sir, that Citizen Uran isn't Xhai. Or Ychana. When residents…" She realized, suddenly, that she would have to openly acknowledge what she'd been up to. "I'd have asked Station Administration to assign me a few people, but the residents in the Undergarden, sir, they're more comfortable speaking to me because we don't have a history here." We *did* have a history here, and doubtless everyone in the Undergarden was conscious of it. "The citizen might enjoy it. And it would be good experience." Experience for what, she didn't specify.

"Citizen Uran," I said. "Except for questions of safety or security, you are not required to do what Lieutenant Tisarwat asks you." Uran still stared down, at her now-empty plate, no remaining trace of breakfast. I looked pointedly to Lieutenant Tisarwat. "Is that understood, Lieutenant?"

"Sir," Tisarwat acknowledged. And then, with inward trepidation, "Might I have a few more Bos, then, sir?"

"In a week or so, Lieutenant. I've just sent Ship away on an inspection."

I couldn't read Tisarwat's thoughts, but I guessed from her emotional responses—brief surprise, dismay, rapidly replaced by a moment of bright certainty and then nervous hesitation—that she had realized I might still order Seivarden to send her Bos on a shuttle. And then reached the conclusion that I certainly would have suggested that, if I'd wanted to. "Yes, sir." Crestfallen, and at the same time relieved, perhaps, that I hadn't yet disapproved of her improvised office, her negotiations with Undergarden residents.

"You got yourself into this, Lieutenant," I said, mildly. "Just try not to antagonize Station Administration." Not likely, I knew. By now, Tisarwat and Piat were fast friends, and their social circle included Station Administration staff as well as Station Security and even people who worked for Governor Giarod. It was these people Tisarwat would doubtless have drawn on, in requesting people to be assigned to her, but they all had, as she had put it, a history here.

"Yes, sir." Tisarwat's expression didn't change—she'd learned a few things from her Bos, I thought—and her lilac eyes showed only the slightest trace of how pleased and relieved she was to hear me speak so. And then, at the back of that, the regular undercurrent of anxiety, of unhappiness. I could only guess at what caused that—though I was sure it wasn't anything that had gone wrong here. Left over, then, from the trip here to Athoek, from what had happened during that time. She turned again to Uran. "You know, Citizen, you wouldn't really actually have to make tea. Bo Nine does that, at least she brings in the water in the morning. Really all you'd have to do is give people tea and be pleasant to them."

Uran, who from the moment I had met her had been quietly anxious not to offend (when she had not been quietly miserable), looked up, right at Tisarwat, and said, in very plain Radchaai, "I don't think I'd be very good at that."

Lieutenant Tisarwat blinked, astonished. Taken quite aback. I smiled. "I am pleased to see, Citizen Uran, that your sister didn't get all the fire, between the two of you." And did not say that I was also glad Raughd had not managed to put what there was completely out. "Have a care, Lieutenant. I'll have no sympathy if you get burned again."

"Yes, sir," replied Tisarwat. "If I may be excused, sir." Uran looked quickly down again, eyes on her empty plate.

"Of course, Lieutenant." I pushed my own chair back. "I have my own business to attend to. Citizen." Uran looked up and down again quickly, the briefest flash of a glance. "By all means ask Five for more breakfast if you're still hungry. Remember about the warning signs, and take your handheld with you if you leave the apartments."

"Yes, sir," replied Uran.

I had sent for Captain Hetnys. She walked past the door to Lieutenant Tisarwat's makeshift office, looked in. Hesitated, frowned. Walked on to receive Lieutenant Tisarwat's bow—I had seen Captain Hetnys through her eyes. Tisarwat experienced a moment of pleased malice to see Captain Hetnys frown, but did not show it on her face. I strongly suspected Captain Hetnys turned to watch Tisarwat go into the office, but as Tisarwat didn't turn to see it, I didn't, either.

Eight showed Captain Hetnys into my sitting room. After the predictable round of tea (in the rose glass, now she knew about the Bractware, and Five could be sure she knew she wasn't drinking from it), I said, "How is your Atagaris doing?"

Captain Hetnys froze an instant, surprised, I thought. "Sir?" she asked.

"The ancillary that was injured." There were only the three Atagarises here. I had ordered *Sword of Atagaris* Var off of the station.

She frowned. "It's recovering well, sir." A slight hesitation. "If I may beg the fleet captain's indulgence." I gestured the granting of it. "Why did you have the ancillary treated?"

What answers I might have given to that question would doubtless have made little sense to Captain Hetnys. "Not doing so would have been a waste, Captain. And it would have made your ship unhappy." Still the frown. I'd been right. She didn't understand. "I have been considering how best to dispose of our resources."

"The gates, sir," Captain Hetnys protested. "Beg to remind the fleet captain, anyone might come through the gates."

"No, Captain," I said, "no one will come through the gates. They're too easy to watch, and too easily defended." And I would certainly mine them, one way or another. I wasn't certain if Captain Hetnys hadn't thought of that possibility, or if she had thought I might not think of it. Either was possible. "Certainly no one will come by the Ghost Gate."

The merest twitch of muscles around her eyes and her mouth, the briefest of expressions, too quickly gone to be readable.

She believed someone might. I was increasingly sure that she had lied when she had said that she had never encountered anyone else in that other, supposedly empty, system. That she wanted to conceal the fact that someone was there, or had been there. Might be there now. Of course, if she had sold away Valskaayan transportees, she would want to conceal that fact in order to avoid reeducation or worse. And there remained, still, the question of whom she might have sold them to, or why.

I could not rely on her. Would not. Would be very, very careful to watch her and her ship.

"You've sent *Mercy of Kalr* away, sir," Captain Hetnys pointed out. My ship's departure would have been obvious, though of course the reason for it would not be.

"A brief errand." Certainly I did not want to say what that errand was. Not to Captain Hetnys. "It will be back in a few days. Do you have confidence in the abilities of your Amaat lieutenant?"

Captain Hetnys frowned. Puzzled. "Yes, sir."

"Good." There was, then, no reason for her to insist on returning immediately to *Sword of Atagaris*. Once she did, her position—should she be able to recognize the fact—would be stronger than I wanted. I waited for her to request it, to ask permission to return to her ship.

"Well, sir," she said, still sitting across from me, rose glass teabowl in one brown-gloved hand, "perhaps none of this will be needed, and we'll have exerted ourselves for nothing." A breath. Deliberate, I thought, deliberately calm.

No question that I would need to keep Captain Hetnys

nearby. And off her ship, if possible. I knew what a captain meant, to a ship. And while no ancillary ever gave much information about its emotional state, I had seen the Atagaris ancillary, downwell, with that shard of glass jutting out of its back. Tears in its eyes. *Sword of Atagaris* did not want to lose its captain.

I had been a ship. I did not want to deprive *Sword of Atagaris* of its captain. But I would if I had to. If it meant keeping the residents of this system safe. If it meant keeping Basnaaid safe.

After breakfast, before letting Uran wander as she pleased, Eight took her to buy clothes. She could have gotten them from Station stores, of course, every Radchaai was due food, and shelter, and clothing. But Eight didn't even allow this possibility to arise. Uran was living in my household and would be dressed accordingly.

I might, of course, have bought clothes for her myself. But to Radchaai, this would have implied either that I had adopted Uran into my house, or that I had given her my patronage. I doubted Uran wanted as much as the fiction of being even further separated from her family, and while clientage didn't necessarily imply a sexual relationship, in situations where patron and client were very unequal in circumstances it was often assumed. It might not matter to some. I would not assume that it did not matter to Uran. So I had set her up with an allowance for such things. Hardly any different from my just outright giving her what she needed, but on such details propriety depended.

I saw that Eight and Uran were standing just outside the entrance to the temple of Amaat, on the grimy white floor, just under the bright-painted but dusty EskVar, Eight explaining, not-quite-ancillary calm, that Amaat and the Valskaayan god were fairly obviously the same, and so it would be entirely proper for Uran to enter and make an offering. Uran, looking somewhat uncomfortable in her new clothes, doggedly refusing. I was on the point of messaging Eight to stop when, glancing over Uran's shoulder, she saw Captain Hetnys pass, followed by a *Sword of Atagaris* ancillary, and speaking earnestly to Sirix Odela.

Captain Hetnys had never once, that I could remember, spoken to Sirix or even acknowledged her presence while we had been downwell. It surprised Eight, too. She stopped mid-sentence, resisted frowning, and thought of something that made her suddenly abashed. "Your very great pardon, Citizen," she said to Uran.

"...tizens are not going to be happy about that," Governor Giarod was saying, where we sat above in her office, and I had no attention to spare for other things.

20

Next day, Uran went to Lieutenant Tisarwat's makeshift office. Not because she'd been told to—Tisarwat had said nothing more about the matter. Uran had merely walked in—she'd stopped and looked in several times, the day before—and rearranged the tea things to her satisfaction. Tisarwat, seeing her, said nothing.

This went on for three days. I knew that Uran's presence had been a success—since she was Valskaayan, and from downwell, she couldn't be assumed to already be on one side or another of any local dispute, and something about her shy, unsmiling seriousness had been appealing to the Undergarden residents who'd called. One or two of them had found, in her silence, a good audience for their tale of difficulties with their neighbors, or with Station Administration.

For all those three days, neither mentioned any of it. Tisarwat was worried I already knew, and that I would disapprove, but also hopeful—no doubt her success so far suggested I might also approve of this last small thing.

On the third evening of silent supper, I said, "Citizen Uran, lessons begin the day after tomorrow."

Uran looked up from her plate, surprised, I thought, and then back down. "Yes, sir."

"Sir," said Tisarwat. Anxious, but concealing it, her voice calm and measured. "Begging your indulgence..."

I gestured the superfluity of it. "Yes, Lieutenant, Citizen Uran appears to be popular in your waiting room. I've no doubt she'll continue to be helpful to you, but I have no intention of slighting her education. I've arranged for her to study in the afternoons. She may do as she likes in the morning. Citizen"—directing my words now to Uran—"considering where we're living, I did engage someone to teach you Raswar, which the Ychana here speak."

"It's a sight more useful than poetry, anyway," said Tisarwat, relieved and pleased.

I raised an eyebrow. "You surprise me, Lieutenant." That brought on a rise in her general background level of unhappiness, for some reason. "Tell me, Lieutenant, how does Station feel about what's been going on?"

"I think," replied Tisarwat, "that it's glad repairs are going forward, but you know stations never tell you directly if they're unhappy." In the antechamber, someone requested entry. Kalr Eight moved to answer the door.

"It wants to see everyone, all the time," said Uran. Greatly daring. "It says it wouldn't be the same as someone spying on you."

"It's very different from a planet, on a station," I said, as Eight opened the door, revealing Sirix Odela. "Stations like to know their residents are all well. They don't feel right, otherwise. Do you talk to Station often, Citizen?" Wondering as I spoke what Sirix was doing here, whom I had not seen since Eight had seen her talking to Captain Hetnys.

In the dining room, Uran was saying, "It talks to me, Rad...Fleet Captain. And it translates things for me, or reads notices to me."

"I'm glad to hear it," I said. "Station is a good friend to have."

In the antechamber, Citizen Sirix apologized to Eight for arriving at such an awkward hour, when the household was at supper. "But Horticulturist Basnaaid wanted very much to speak to the fleet captain, and she's unavoidably detained in the Gardens."

In the dining room I rose, not responding to Tisarwat's reply to my words, and went out to the antechamber. "Citizen Sirix," I said, as she turned toward me. "How can I assist you?"

"Fleet Captain," said Sirix, with a small, tight nod of her head. Uncomfortable. After our conversation three days ago, and the strangeness of her errand, entirely unsurprising. "Horticulturist Basnaaid wishes very much to speak with you in person on what I understand is a private matter. She'd have come herself but she is, as I was saying, unavoidably detained in the Gardens."

"Citizen," I replied. "You'll recall that when last I spoke to the horticulturist, she quite understandably said she never wanted to see me again. Should she have changed her mind I am, of course, at her service, but I must admit to some surprise. And I am at a loss to imagine what might be so urgent that it could not have waited until an hour more convenient for herself."

Sirix froze for just an instant, a sudden tension that, in someone else, I would have taken for anger. "I did, Fleet

Captain, suggest as much. She said only, *it's like the poet said: The touch of sour and cold regret, like pickled fish.*"

That poet had been Basnaaid Elming, aged nine and three quarters. It would have been difficult to imagine a more carefully calculated tug at my emotions, knowing as she did that Lieutenant Awn had shared her poetry with me.

When I didn't reply, Sirix made an ambivalent gesture. "She said you'd recognize it."

"I do."

"Please tell me that's not some beloved classic."

"You don't like pickled fish?" I asked, calm and serious. She blinked in uncomfortable surprise. "It is not a classic, but one she knew that I would recognize, as you say. A work with personal associations."

"I had hoped as much," Sirix said, wryly. "And now, if you'll excuse me, Fleet Captain, it's been a long day and I'm late for my own supper." She bowed and left.

I stood in the antechamber, Eight standing still and curious behind me. "Station," I said aloud. "How are things in the Gardens right now?"

Station's reply seemed just the smallest bit delayed. "Fine, Fleet Captain. As always."

At age nine and three quarters, Basnaaid Elming had been an ambitious poet, without a particularly delicate sense of language, but an abundance of melodrama and overwrought emotion. The bit Sirix had quoted was part of a long narrative of betrayed friendship. It had also been incomplete. The entire couplet was, *The touch of sour and cold regret, like pickled fish / ran down her back. Oh, how had she believed the awful lies?*

She said you'd recognize it, Sirix had said. "Has Sirix gone home, Station? Or has she gone back to the Gardens?"

"Citizen Sirix is on her way home, Fleet Captain." No hesitation that time.

I went to my room, took out the gun that was invisible to Station, invisible to any sensors but human eyes. Put the gun under my jacket, where I could reach it quickly. Said to Eight, as I passed her in the antechamber, "Tell Lieutenant Tisarwat and Citizen Uran to finish their supper."

"Sir," Eight replied, puzzled but not worried. Good.

Perhaps I was overreacting. Perhaps Basnaaid had merely changed her mind about wanting to never speak to me again. Perhaps her anxiety about the supports under the lake had grown strong enough to overcome her misgivings about me. And she had misremembered her own poetry, or remembered only part of it, meaning to remind me (as though I needed reminding) of my old association with her long-dead sister. Maybe she truly, urgently needed to speak to me now, at an hour when many citizens were at supper, and she truly could not leave work. Didn't want to be so rude as to summon me via Station, and sent Sirix with her message instead. Surely she knew that I would come if she asked, when she asked.

Surely Sirix knew it, too. And Sirix had been talking to Captain Hetnys.

I considered—briefly—bringing my Kalrs with me, and even Lieutenant Tisarwat. I was not particularly concerned about being wrong. If I was wrong, I would send them back to the Undergarden and have whatever conversation Horticulturist Basnaaid wished. But what if I wasn't wrong?

Captain Hetnys had two *Sword of Atagaris* ancillaries with her, here on the station. None of them would have guns, unless they had disobeyed my order to disarm. Which was a possibility. But even so, I was confident I could deal with

Captain Hetnys and so few of *Sword of Atagaris*. No need to trouble anyone else.

And if it was more than just Captain Hetnys? If Governor Giarod had also been deceiving me, or Station Administrator Celar, if Station Security was waiting for me in the Gardens? I would not be able to deal with that by myself. But I would not be able to deal with that even with the assistance of Lieutenant Tisarwat and all four of my Mercy of Kalrs. Best to leave them clear, in that case.

Mercy of Kalr was another matter. "Yes," Ship said, without my having to say anything at all. "Lieutenant Seivarden is in Command and the crew is clearing for action."

There was little else I could do for *Mercy of Kalr*, and so I focused on the matter at hand.

It would have been easiest for me to enter the Gardens the same way I had when I had first arrived at Athoek. It might not make a difference—there were two entrances to the Gardens that I knew of, and two ancillaries to watch them. But on the off chance that someone was waiting for me and assuming that I would come by the most convenient way, and on the off chance that Station might take its favorite course of resistance and just not mention the fact, I thought it worth taking the long way.

The entrance gave onto the rocky ledge overlooking the lake. Off to my right, the waterfall gushed and foamed its way down the rocks. The path led to my left, down to the water, past a thick stand of ornamental grass nearly two meters tall. I would not walk past that without a great deal of caution.

Ahead, a waist-high railing guarded the drop to the water, rocks jutting up just below and here and there in the lake.

On the tiny island with its fluted stone, Captain Hetnys stood, her hand tight on Basnaaid's arm, a knife held to her throat, the sort of thing you might use to bone a fish. Small enough, but sufficient for the purpose. Also on the island, at the head of the bridge, stood *Sword of Atagaris*—one of it—armored, gun drawn. "Oh, *Station*," I said, quietly. It didn't answer. I could easily imagine its reasons for not warning me, or calling for help. Doubtless it valued Basnaaid's life more than mine. This was suppertime for many on the station, and so there were no bystanders. Possibly Station had been turning people away on some pretext.

On the ledge, the grass trembled. Unthinking, I pulled my gun out of my jacket, raised my armor. The bang of a gun firing, a blow to my body—whoever was in that stand of grass had taken aim at precisely that part of me that was covered first. I was entirely enclosed before any second shot could be fired.

A silver-armored ancillary rushed out of the grass, inhumanly quick, reached to grapple with me, thinking, no doubt, that the gun I held was no threat, armored as it was. We ought to have been equally matched hand to hand, but my back was to empty air and it had momentum on its side. I fired, just as it shoved me over the rail.

Radchaai armor is essentially impenetrable. The energy of the bullet *Sword of Atagaris* had fired at me had been bled off, mostly as heat. Not all of it, of course, I'd still felt its impact. So when my shoulder hit the jagged stone at the foot of that seven-and-a-half-meter-high rock wall, the actual impact wasn't particularly painful. However, the top of the stone was narrow, and while my shoulder stopped, the rest of me kept going. My shoulder bent backward, painfully, definitely not in any way it was meant to, and then I slid off the stone into the water. Which fortunately was only a little over a meter deep where I was, about four meters from the island.

I got to my feet in the waist-deep water, the pain of my left shoulder making me catch my breath. Something had happened during my fall, I didn't have time to ask *Mercy of Kalr* exactly what, but Lieutenant Tisarwat had apparently followed me, and I had been too absorbed in my own thoughts to notice. She stood at the shore end of the bridge, armor up, gun raised. *Sword of Atagaris* faced her, its gun also raised. Why hadn't Ship warned me that Tisarwat had followed me?

Captain Hetnys faced me, also now silver-armored. She likely knew the ancillary on the ledge was injured or even dead but didn't realize, I was sure, that her armor would do her no good against my gun. Though perhaps the Presger hadn't bothered to make the gun waterproof.

"Well, Fleet Captain," said Captain Hetnys, voice distorted by her armor, "you do have human feelings after all."

"You fish-witted *fuck*," cried Lieutenant Tisarwat, vehemence clear in her voice even through the warping of her armor. "If you weren't such an easily manipulated ass you'd *never* have been given a ship."

"Hush, Tisarwat," I said. If Lieutenant Tisarwat was here, depend on it, so was Bo Nine. If my shoulder didn't hurt so much I'd be able to think clearly enough to know where she was.

"But, sir! She has *no fucking idea*..."

"Lieutenant!" I didn't need Tisarwat thinking in those terms. Didn't need her here. *Mercy of Kalr* wasn't telling me what was wrong with my shoulder, whether it was dislocated or broken. *Mercy of Kalr* wasn't telling me what Tisarwat was feeling, or where Bo Nine was. I reached, but could not find Seivarden, whom I had last seen in Command, who had said, to *Sword of Atagaris*'s Amaat lieutenant, days and days ago, *the next time you threaten this ship you'd best be able to make good on it. Sword of Atagaris* must have made its move when I fell off the rock wall. At least Ship would not have been caught entirely by surprise. But *Swords* were faster, and better armed, and if *Mercy of Kalr* was gone, I would make Seivarden's warning good, if I possibly could.

Captain Hetnys stood facing me on the island, still gripping Basnaaid, who stood rigid, eyes wide. "Who did you sell them to, Captain?" I asked. "Who did you sell the transportees to?" Captain Hetnys didn't answer. She was a fool, or desperate, or both, to threaten Basnaaid. "That is what precipitated this rather hasty action, is it not?" Governor Giarod had let something slip, or outright told Captain Hetnys. I had never told the governor who I suspected, or perhaps she would have been more cautious. "You had a confederate at the storage facility, you loaded up *Sword of Atagaris* with suspension pods, and you took them through the Ghost Gate. Who did you sell them to?" She *had* sold them. That Notai tea set. And Sirix had never heard the story of how Captain Hetnys had sold it to Fosyf. She hadn't been able to make that connection. But Captain Hetnys had realized that I had made it. Had needed to know where I might be vulnerable, and after two weeks in the same house, even never speaking to her, she had known what Sirix would respond to best. Or perhaps *Sword of Atagaris* had suggested such an approach to its captain.

"I did what I did out of loyalty," asserted Captain Hetnys. "Which is apparently something you know little of." If my shoulder hadn't hurt so badly, if this situation hadn't been so serious, I might have laughed. Oblivious, Captain Hetnys continued. "The *real* Lord of the Radch would never strip her ships of ancillaries, would never dismantle the fleet that protects the Radch."

"The Lord of the Radch," I pointed out, "would never be stupid enough to give you a tea set like that as a payment supposedly *more* discreet than cash." A plashing, bubbling sound came from the middle of the lake, where, I assumed, the water was deeper. For an instant I thought someone had thrown something in, or a fish had surfaced. I stood there in the water, gun aimed at Captain Hetnys, my other shoulder hurting ferociously, and then on the edges of my vision, it happened again—a bubble rising and collapsing on the surface of the water. It took me a fraction of a second to realize what it was I had seen.

I could see by the increased panic on Basnaaid's face that she had realized it, too. Realized that air bubbling up from the bottom of the lake could really only be coming from one place—from the Undergarden itself. And if air was coming up, water was surely going down.

The game was over. Captain Hetnys just hadn't realized it yet. Station would remain silent to save Basnaaid's life, and even block calls to Security from here. But it would not do so at the cost of the entire Undergarden. The only question remaining was whether Basnaaid—or anyone else here—would come out of this alive.

"Station," I said, aloud. "Evacuate the Undergarden *immediately*." Level one was in the most immediate danger, and only some of the consoles there had been repaired by now. But I didn't have time to worry how many residents would hear an evacuation order, or would be able to spread the message. "And tell my household the Undergarden is about to be flooded, and they're to help evacuate." *Mercy of Kalr* ought to have told them by now, but *Mercy of Kalr* was gone. Oh,

Captain Hetnys would regret that, and so would *Sword of Atagaris*. Once I got Basnaaid clear of that knife at her throat.

"What are you talking about?" asked Captain Hetnys. "Station, don't do any such thing." Basnaaid gasped as Captain Hetnys gripped her tighter, shook her just a bit to emphasize the threat.

Stupid Captain Hetnys. "Captain, are you *really* going to make Station choose between Basnaaid and the residents of the Undergarden? Is it possible you don't understand the consequences of that?" Tisarwat's *fish-witted* had been about right. "Let me guess, you intended to kill me, imprison my soldiers, destroy *Mercy of Kalr*, and claim to the governor that I'd been a traitor all along." The water bubbled again—twice, in quick succession, larger bubbles than before. Captain Hetnys might not have yet realized that she'd lost, but when she did, she would likely take the most desperate action available. Time to end this. "Basnaaid," I said. She was staring ahead, blank, terrified. "As the poet said: *Like ice. Like stone.*" The same poem she had quoted, that had brought me here. I had understood her message. I could only hope that now she would understand mine. *Whatever you do, don't move a muscle.* My finger tightened on the trigger.

I should have been paying more attention to Lieutenant Tisarwat. Tisarwat had been watching Captain Hetnys, and the ancillary at the head of the bridge. Had been moving slowly, carefully closer to the island, by millimeters, with neither myself nor Captain Hetnys nor, apparently, *Sword of Atagaris* noticing. And when I had spoken to Basnaaid, Tisarwat had clearly understood my intention, knowing as she did that my gun would defeat Captain Hetnys's armor. But she also understood that *Sword of Atagaris* might still pose a danger to Citizen Basnaaid. The instant before I fired,

Tisarwat dropped her own armor and charged, shouting, at the *Sword of Atagaris* ancillary.

Bo Nine, it turned out, had been crouching behind the rail at the top of the rocky ledge. Seeing her lieutenant behave so suicidally, Bo Nine cried out, raised her own gun, but could do nothing.

Captain Hetnys heard Bo Nine cry out. Looked up to see her standing on the ledge, gun raised. And the captain flinched, and ducked low, just as I fired.

The Presger gun, it turned out, was waterproof, and of course my aim was good. But the shot went over Captain Hetnys, over Basnaaid. Traveled on, to hit the barrier between us and hard vacuum.

The dome over the Gardens was built to withstand impacts. Had Bo Nine fired, or *Sword of Atagaris*, it would not have even been scratched. But the bullets in the Presger gun would burn through anything in the universe for 1.11 meters. The barrier wasn't even half a meter thick.

Instantly, alarms sounded. Every entrance to the Gardens slammed shut. We were all now trapped, while the atmosphere blew out of the bullet hole in the dome. At least it would take a while to empty such a large space, and now Security was certainly paying attention to us. But the water flowing out of the lake meant that there was no real barrier between the Gardens (with their hull breach) and the Undergarden. It was entirely possible that the section doors there (the ones that worked, at any rate, all of which were on level one, immediately below us) would close, trapping residents who hadn't managed to get out. And if the lake collapsed, those residents would drown.

It was Station's problem. I waded toward the island. Bo Nine ran down the path to the water. *Sword of Atagaris* had pinned Tisarwat easily, was raising its weapon to fire at Basnaaid, who had wrenched free of Captain Hetnys's grip and scrambled away toward the bridge. I shot *Sword of Atagaris* in the wrist, forcing it to drop its gun.

Sword of Atagaris realized, then, that I posed an immediate danger to its captain. Ancillary-quick, it rushed me, thinking, no doubt, that I was only human and it would be able to easily take the gun from me, even injured as it was. It barreled into me, jarring my shoulder. I saw black for an instant, but did not let go of the gun.

At that moment, Station solved the problem of water pouring into the Undergarden by turning off the gravity.

Up and down disappeared. *Sword of Atagaris* clung to me, still trying to pry the gun out of my hand. The ancillary's impact had pushed us away from the ground, and we spun, grappling, moving toward the waterfall. The water was not falling, now, but accumulating at the dome-edge of the rocks in a growing, wobbling mass as it was pumped out of the lake.

In the background, behind the pain of my shoulder and my effort to keep hold of the gun, I heard Station saying something about the self-repair function of the dome not working properly, and that it would take an hour to assemble a repair crew and shuttle them to the spot to patch it.

An hour was too long. All of us here would either drown, unable, without gravity, to escape the wobbling, growing globs of water the waterfall pump kept sending out, or asphyxiate well before the dome could be repressurized. I had failed to save Basnaaid. Had betrayed and killed her sister, and now, coming here to try, in the smallest, most inadequate way, to make that up, I had caused her death. I didn't see her. Didn't see much, beyond the pain of my injured shoulder, and

Sword of Atagaris, and the black and silver flash of water as we drew closer to it.

I was going to die here. *Mercy of Kalr*, and Seivarden and Ekalu and Medic and all the crew, were gone. I was sure of it. Ship would never leave me unanswered, not by its own choice.

And just as I had that thought, the starless, not-even-nothing black of a gate opened just outside the dome, and *Mercy of Kalr* appeared, far, far too close to be even remotely a good idea, and I heard Seivarden's voice in my ear telling me she looked forward to being reprimanded as soon as I was safe. "*Sword of Atagaris* seems to have gated off somewhere," she continued, cheerily. "I do hope it doesn't come out right where we just were. I may have accidentally dropped half our inventory of mines just before we left."

I was fairly sure I was more starved for oxygen than I realized, and hallucinating, up until half a dozen safely tethered Amaats took hold of the *Sword of Atagaris* ancillary, and pulled us both through the hole they'd cut in the dome, and into one of *Mercy of Kalr*'s shuttles.

Once we were all on the safe side of the shuttle airlock, I made sure that Basnaaid was uninjured and strapped into a seat, and set an Amaat to fuss over her. Tisarwat, similarly, but retching from stress and from the microgravity, Bo Nine holding a bag for her, ready with correctives for her lieutenant's bloody nose and broken ribs. Captain Hetnys and the *Sword of Atagaris* ancillary I saw bound securely. Only then did I let Medic pull off my jacket and my shirt, push my shoulder bones back into place with the help of one of Seivarden's Amaats, and immobilize my shoulder with a corrective.

I had not realized, until that pain went away, how hard I'd been gritting my teeth. How tense every other muscle in my body had been, and how badly that had made my leg ache as a consequence. *Mercy of Kalr* had said nothing directly to me, but it didn't need to—it showed me flashes of sight and feeling from my Kalrs, assisting the final stages of the evacuation of the Undergarden (Uran assisting as well, apparently now an old hand with microgravity after the trip here), from Seivarden's Amaats, from Seivarden herself. Medic's outwardly dour concern. Tisarwat's pain and shame and self-hatred. One-armed, I pulled myself past her, where Bo Nine was applying correctives to her injuries. Did not trust myself to stop and speak.

Instead I continued past, to where Captain Hetnys and her ship's ancillary were bound, strapped to seats. Watched by my Amaats. Silver-armored, both of them. In theory, *Sword of Atagaris* could still gate back to the station and attack us. In fact, even if it hadn't run into the mines Seivarden had left for it—which likely would only do minimal damage, more an annoyance than anything else—there was no way to attack us without also attacking its captain. "Drop your armor, Captain," I said. "And you, too, Atagaris. You know I can shoot through it, and we can't treat your injury until you do."

Sword of Atagaris dropped its armor. Medic pulled herself past me with a corrective, frown deepening as she saw the ancillary's wounded wrist.

Captain Hetnys only said, "Fuck you."

I still held the Presger gun. Captain Hetnys's leg was more than a meter from the shuttle hull, and besides we had the ability to patch it, if I sent a bullet through it. I braced myself against a nearby seat and shot her in the knee. She screamed, and the Atagaris beside her strained at its bonds, but could not break them. "Captain Hetnys, you are relieved of command," I said, once Medic had applied a corrective, and the globs of blood that had floated free had been mopped up. "I have every right to shoot you in the head, for what's happened today. I will not promise not to do so. You and all your officers are under arrest.

"*Sword of Atagaris*, you will immediately send every human aboard to Athoek Station. Unarmed. You will then take your engines off-line and put every single ancillary you have into suspension until further notice. Captain Hetnys, and all your lieutenants, will be put into suspension on Athoek Station. If you threaten the station, or any ship or citizen, your officers will die."

"You can't—" began Captain Hetnys.

"Be silent, Citizen," I said. "I am now speaking to *Sword of Atagaris*." Captain Hetnys didn't answer that. "You, *Sword of Atagaris*, will tell me who your captain did business with, on the other side of the Ghost Gate."

"I will not," replied *Sword of Atagaris*.

"Then I will kill Captain Hetnys." Medic, still occupied with the corrective she'd applied to Captain Hetnys's leg, looked up at me briefly, dismayed, but said nothing.

"You," said *Sword of Atagaris*. Its voice was ancillary-flat, but I could guess at the emotion behind it. "I wish I could show you what it's like. I wish you could know what it's like, to be in my position. But you never will, and that's how I know there isn't really any such thing as justice."

There were things I could say. Answers I could make. Instead, I said, "Who did your captain do business with, on the other side of the Ghost Gate?"

"She didn't identify herself," *Sword of Atagaris* replied, voice still flat and calm. "She looked Ychana, but she couldn't have been, no Ychana speaks Radchaai with such an accent. To judge by her speech, she might have come from the Radch itself."

"With perhaps a hint of Notai." Thinking of that tea set, in fragments in its box, in the Undergarden. That supply locker.

"Perhaps. Captain Hetnys thought she was working for the Lord of the Radch."

"I will keep your captain close to me, Ship," I said. "If you don't do as I say, or if at any time I think you have deceived me, she dies. Don't doubt me on this."

"How could I?" replied *Sword of Atagaris*, bitterness audible even in its flat tone.

I didn't answer, only turned to pull myself forward, to get out of the way while Seivarden's Amaats brought a suspension pod for Captain Hetnys. I caught sight of Basnaaid, who had been only a few seats away, who had perhaps heard the entire exchange between me and *Sword of Atagaris*. "Fleet Captain," she said, as I pulled myself even with her. "I wanted to say."

I grabbed a handhold, halted myself. "Horticulturist."

"I'm glad my sister had a friend like you, and I wish... I feel as though, if you had been there, when it happened, whatever it was, that maybe it would have made a difference, and she'd still be alive."

Of all the things to say. Of all the things to say *now*, when I had just threatened to shoot Captain Hetnys only because I knew how her ship felt about her. Of all the times for me to hear such a thing, coming from Lieutenant Awn's sister's mouth.

And I had gone beyond my ability to remain silent, to seem as though I was untouched by any of it. "Citizen," I replied, hearing my own voice go flat. "I *was* there when it happened, and I was no help to your sister at all. I told you I used another name when I knew her, and that name was *Justice of Toren*. I was the ship she served on, and at the command of Anaander Mianaai herself, I shot your sister in the head. What happened next ended in my own destruction, and I am all that's left of that ship. I am not human, and you were right to speak to me as you did, when we first met." I turned my face away, before Basnaaid would see even the small signs I might give of my feelings at having said it.

Everyone in the shuttle had heard me. Basnaaid seemed shocked into silence. Seivarden already knew, of course, and Medic. I didn't want to know what Seivarden's Amaats thought. Didn't want to see or hear *Sword of Atagaris*'s opinion. I turned to the only person who seemed unaware of me—Lieutenant Tisarwat, who had no attention for anything but what a failure she'd been, at living and dying both.

I pulled myself into the seat beside her, strapped myself in. For a moment I seriously considered telling her just how stupid she'd been, back in the Gardens, and how lucky we all were to have survived her stupidity. Instead, I unhooked her seat strap with my good hand—my left arm was immobilized by the corrective on my shoulder—and pulled her to me. She clung to me and leaned her face into my neck, and began sobbing.

"It's all right," I said, my arm awkwardly around her shaking shoulders. "It'll be all right."

"How can you say that?" she demanded into my neck, between sobs. A tear escaped, one tiny, trembling sphere floating away. "How could it possibly?" And then, "No one would ever dare offer *you* such a platitude."

Over three thousand years old. Infinitely ambitious. And still only seventeen. "You assume incorrectly." If she thought about it, if she was capable just now of thinking clearly, she might have guessed who it was who might have said such a thing to me. If she had, she didn't say it. "It's so hard, at first," I said, "when they hook you up. But the rest of you is around you, and you know it's only temporary, you know it will be better soon. And when you are better, it's so amazing. To have such reach, to see so much, all at once. It's..." But there was no describing it. Tisarwat herself would have seen it, if only for a few hours, distressed or else blunted by meds. "She never let you have that. It was never part of her plan to let you have that."

"Do you think I don't know that?" And of course she'd known. How could she not? "She hated the way I felt, she dosed me up as fast as she could. She didn't care if..." The sobs that had died down began afresh. More tears escaped and floated off. Bo Nine, near all this time, horrified by my revelation minutes before, horror that was not at all relieved by my conversation with Tisarwat now, caught them with a cloth, which she then folded, and pushed it between Tisarwat's face and my neck.

Seivarden's Amaats hung motionless, blinking, confused. What sense the universe had made to them had disappeared with my words, and they were unsure of how to fit what they'd heard me say into a reality they understood. "What are you hanging around for?" Seivarden snapped, sterner than I'd ever heard her with them, but it seemed to break whatever had held them until now. "Get moving!" And they moved, relieved to find something they understood.

By then Tisarwat had calmed again somewhat. "I'm sorry," I said. "I can't get it back for either of us. But it will be all right. Somehow it will." She didn't answer, and five minutes later, exhausted from events and from her despair and her grief, she fell asleep.

21

Once the repair crew arrived, the shuttle could leave the hole it had cut in the dome. I ordered us back to *Mercy of Kalr*. Station Medical didn't need to know what I was, and anyway they were busy enough with problems caused or exacerbated by the lack of gravity, which couldn't be turned on until the lake water had been contained. And truth to tell, I was glad to get back to *Mercy of Kalr*, even if only for a little while.

Medic wanted me where she could frown at me and tell me not to get up without her permission, and I was happy enough to indulge her, at least for a day. So Seivarden reported to me where I lay on a bed in Medical. Holding a bowl of tea. "It's like old times," said Seivarden, smiling. But tense. Anticipating what I might say to her, now things were calmer.

"It is," I agreed, and took a drink of my tea. Definitely not Daughter of Fishes. Good.

"Our Tisarwat got banged up pretty badly," Seivarden observed, when I said nothing further. Tisarwat was in an adjoining cubicle, attended by Bo Nine, who had explicit orders never to leave her lieutenant alone. Her ribs were still healing, and Medic had her confined to Medical until she could decide what else Tisarwat might need. "What was she thinking, charging an ancillary like that without her armor?"

"She was trying to draw *Sword of Atagaris*'s fire, so that I would have time to shoot it before it shot Horticulturist Basnaaid. She was lucky it didn't shoot her outright." It must have been more taken aback by Translator Dlique's death than I had imagined. Or just reluctant to kill an officer without a legal order.

"Horticulturist Basnaaid, is it?" Seivarden asked. Her experience with very young lieutenants might not have been as extensive as mine, but it was extensive nonetheless. "Is there any interest in return? Or is that what the self-sacrifice and the tears were about?" I raised an eyebrow, and she continued, "It never occurred to me until now how many baby lieutenants must have cried on your shoulders over the years."

Seivarden's tears had never wetted any of my uniform jackets, when I had been a ship. "Are you jealous?"

"I think I am," she said. "I'd rather have cut my right arm off than shown weakness, when I was seventeen." And when she was twenty-seven, and thirty-seven. "I regret that, now."

"It's in the past." I drained the last of my tea. "*Sword of Atagaris* has admitted that Captain Hetnys sold transportees to someone beyond the Ghost Gate." It had been Governor Giarod who had let fall what errand I'd sent *Mercy of Kalr* on.

"But who?" Seivarden frowned, genuinely puzzled. "*Sword of Atagaris* said Hetnys thought she was dealing with the Lord of the Radch. But if it's the other Lord of the Radch on the other side of the Ghost Gate, why hasn't she done anything?"

"Because it's not the Lord of the Radch on the other side

of the Ghost Gate," I said. "That tea set—you haven't seen it, but it's three thousand years old, at the least. Very obviously Notai. And someone had very carefully removed the name of its owner. It was Hetnys's payment, for the transportees. And you remember the supply locker, that was supposedly just debris, but *Sword of Atagaris* insisted on picking up."

"Where the ship name should have been was all scorched." She'd seen the connection, but not made a pattern out of it yet. "But there wasn't anything in it, we found it aboard *Sword of Atagaris*."

"It wasn't empty when *Sword of Atagaris* pulled it in, depend on it." I was sure something—or someone—had been inside it. "The locker is also a good three thousand years old. It's fairly obvious there's a ship on the other side of that gate. A Notai ship, one that's older than Anaander Mianaai herself."

"But, Breq," Seivarden protested, "those were all destroyed. Even the ones that were loyal have been decommissioned by now. And we're nowhere near where any of those battles were fought."

"They weren't all destroyed." Seivarden opened her mouth to protest, and I gestured to forestall her. "Some of them fled. The makers of entertainments have wrung hours of dramatic adventure out of that very fact, of course. But it's assumed that by now they're all dead, with no one to maintain them. What if one fled to the Ghost System? What if it's found a way to replenish its store of ancillaries? You recall, *Sword of Atagaris* said the person Hetnys dealt with looked like an Ychana, but spoke like a high-status Radchaai. And the Athoeki used to sell indentured Ychana away to outsystem slavers, before the annexation."

"Aatr's tits," Seivarden swore. "They were dealing with an ancillary."

"The other Anaander has her people here, but I imagine events at Ime have made her cautious. Perhaps she doesn't stay in contact, doesn't interfere much. After all, the more she does, the more likely she is to be detected. Maybe our neighbor in the Ghost System took advantage of it. That's why Hetnys didn't move until she was desperate. She was waiting for orders from the Lord of the Radch."

"Who she thought was just beyond the Ghost Gate. But, Breq, what will the other Anaander's supporters do when they realize?"

"I doubt we'll have to wait long to find out." I took a drink of my tea. "And I may be wrong."

"No," said Seivarden, "I don't think you are. It fits. So we have a mad warship on the other side of the Ghost Gate—"

"Not mad," I corrected. "When you've lost everything that matters to you, it makes perfect sense to run and hide and try to recover."

"Yes," she replied, abashed. "I should know better, of all people, shouldn't I. So, not mad. But hostile. An enemy warship on the other side of the Ghost Gate, half of the Lord of the Radch maybe about to attack, and the Presger likely to show up demanding to know what we've done with their translator. Is that all, or is there more?"

"That's probably enough for now." She laughed. I asked, "Are you ready for your reprimand, Lieutenant?"

"Sir." She bowed.

"When I'm not aboard, you are acting captain of this ship. If you had failed to rescue me, and anything had happened to you, Lieutenant Ekalu would have been left in command. She's a good lieutenant, and she may well make a fine captain someday, but you are the more experienced officer, and you should not have risked yourself."

It was not what she had expected to hear. Her face heated with anger and indignation. But she had been a soldier a long time—she did not protest. "Sir."

"I think you should talk to Medic about your history of drug use. I think you've been under stress, and maybe not thinking as clearly as you might."

The muscles in her arms twitched, the desire to cross them suppressed. "I was worried."

"Do you anticipate not ever being worried again?"

She blinked, startled. The corners of her mouth twitched upward. "About you? No." She gave a short, breathy laugh, and then was flooded with an odd mix of regret and embarrassment. "Do you see what Ship sees?"

"Sometimes. Sometimes I ask Ship to show me, or it shows me something it thinks I should see. Some of it is the same sort of thing your own ship would have shown you, when you were a captain. Some of the data wouldn't make sense to you, the way it does to me."

"You've always seen right through me." She was still embarrassed. "Even when you found me on Nilt. I suppose you already know that Horticulturist Basnaaid is on her way here?"

Basnaaid had insisted on going over to the dome repair crew's vehicle, back at the station. She had requested to be brought here while I slept, and Seivarden had acceded, with some surprise and dismay. "Yes. I'd have done just as you did, had I been awake." She'd known that, but still was gratified to hear it. "Is there anything else?" There wasn't, or at least not anything she wanted to bring up, so I dismissed her.

Thirty seconds after Seivarden left, Tisarwat came into my cubicle. I shifted my legs over, gestured an invitation to sit. "Lieutenant," I said, as she settled herself, gingerly. There were still correctives around her torso, cracked ribs and other injuries still healing. “How are you feeling?”

“Better,” she said. “I think Medic has me dosed up. I can tell because I’m not wishing every ten minutes or so that you’d thrown me out the airlock when you found me.”

“That’s recent, I think?” I hadn’t thought she’d been suicidal before now. But I had, perhaps, not been paying as much attention as I should have.

“No, it’s always been there. Just... just not so real. Not so intense. It was when I saw what Captain Hetnys had done, threatened to kill Horticulturist Basnaaid to get to you. I knew it was my fault.”

“*Your* fault?” I didn’t think it had been the fault of anyone in particular, except of course Hetnys herself. “I don’t doubt your politicking alarmed her. It was obvious that you were angling for influence. But it’s also true that I knew about it from the start, and would have prevented you if I’d disapproved.”

Relief—just a bit. Her mood was calm, stable. She was entirely correct in her guess that Medic had given her something. “That’s the thing. If I may speak very frankly, sir.” I gestured permission. “Do you understand, sir, that we’re both doing exactly what she wants?” *She* could only be Anaander Mianaai, Lord of the Radch. “She *sent* us here to do exactly what we’re doing. Doesn’t it bother you, sir, that she took something she knew you wanted and used it to make you do what *she* wanted?”

“Sometimes it does,” I admitted. “But then I remember that what she wants isn’t terribly important to me.”

Before Tisarwat could answer, Medic came frowning into the room. “I have you here so you can rest, Fleet Captain, not take endless meetings.”

"What meetings?" I affected an innocent expression. "The lieutenant and I are both patients here, and both resting, as you see."

Medic *hmphed*.

"And you can't blame me for being impatient with it," I continued. "I just rested for two weeks, downwell. There's a lot to catch up on."

"You call that rest, do you?" asked Medic.

"Up until the bomb went off, yes."

"Medic," said Tisarwat. "Am I going to be on meds the rest of my life?"

"I don't know," replied Medic. Seriously. Honestly. "I hope not, but I can't promise that." Turned to me. "I'd say no more visitors, Fleet Captain, but I know you'll overrule me for Horticulturist Basnaaid."

"Basnaaid's coming?" Tisarwat, already sitting straight because of the corrective around her rib cage, seemed to straighten even more. "Fleet Captain, can I go back to the station with her?"

"Absolutely *not*," Medic said.

"You might not want to," I said. "She might not want to spend much time with any of us. You weren't listening, I think, on the shuttle when I told her I'd killed her sister."

"Oh." She hadn't heard. Had been too preoccupied with her own misery. Understandably.

"Bed, Lieutenant," Medic insisted. Tisarwat looked to me for reprieve, but as I gave none, she sighed and left for her own cubicle, trailed by Medic.

I leaned my head back and closed my eyes. Basnaaid was a good twenty minutes from docking. *Sword of Atagaris*'s engines were off-line. All its officers were in suspension. Along with nearly all its ancillaries, only a last few locking things down while a handful of my own Amaats watched. Since its bitter words to me in the shuttle, *Sword of Atagaris* had said nothing beyond the absolutely necessary and functional. Straightforward answers to questions of fact. *Yes. No.* Nothing more.

Where I sat in Medical, Kalr Twelve came into the room, right up to the bed. Reluctant. Intensely embarrassed. I sat up straight, opened my eyes.

"Sir," Twelve said, quiet and tense. Almost a whisper. "I'm Ship." Reached out to lay an arm across my shoulders.

"Twelve, you know by now that I'm an ancillary." Surprise. Dismay. She knew, yes, but my saying it took her aback. Before she could say anything, I added, "Please don't tell me it doesn't matter because you don't really think of me as an ancillary."

A swift consultation, between Twelve and Ship. "Your indulgence, sir," said Twelve then, with Ship's encouragement. "I don't think that's entirely fair. We haven't known until now, so it would be difficult for us to think of you any other way than we have been." She had a point. "And we haven't had very long to get used to the idea. But, sir, it does explain some things."

No doubt it did. "I know that Ship appreciates it when you act for it, and your ancillary façade lets you feel safe and invisible. But being an ancillary isn't something to play at."

"No, sir. I can see that, sir. But like you said, Ship appreciates it. And Ship takes care of us, sir. Sometimes it feels like it's us and Ship against everyone else." Self-conscious. Embarrassed.

"I know," I said. "That's why I haven't tried to stop it." I took a breath. "So, are you all right with this, right now?"

"Yes, sir," Twelve said. Still embarrassed. But sincere.

I closed my eyes, and leaned my head against her shoulder, and she wrapped both arms around me. It wasn't the same, it wasn't me holding myself, though I could feel not only Twelve's uniform jacket against my cheek, but the weight of my own head against her shoulder. I reached for it, for as much as I could have, Twelve's embarrassment, yes, but also concern for me. The other Kalrs moving about the ship. Not the same. It couldn't be the same.

We were both silent a moment, and then Twelve said, for Ship, "I suppose I can't blame *Sword of Atagaris* for caring about its captain. I would have expected better taste, though, from a *Sword*."

The *Swords* were so arrogant, so sure they were better than the *Mercies* and the *Justices*. But some things you just can't help. "Ship," I said, aloud, "Twelve's arm is getting uncomfortable. And I have to get ready to receive Horticulturist Basnaaid." We disengaged, Twelve stepping back, and I wiped my eyes with the back of my hand. "Medic." Medic was down the corridor, but I knew she would hear me. "I'm not receiving Horticulturist Basnaaid like this. I'm going back to my quarters." I would need to wash my face, and dress, and make sure there was tea and food to offer her, even if I was certain she would refuse it.

"Can she have come all this way," asked Twelve, asked Ship, "merely to tell you how much she hates you?"

"If so," I replied, "I will listen without arguing. She has every right, after all."

My shoulder, still encased in its corrective, wouldn't fit inside my shirt, although with some careful maneuvering I could get my arm inside a uniform jacket. Twelve wouldn't tolerate the idea of my meeting Horticulturist Basnaaid shirtless, jacket or not, and grimly slit the back of a shirtsleeve. "Five will understand when I explain, sir," she said, though with some private fear that perhaps she might not. Five was still back in the Undergarden, helping to get things secured so no one would be hurt when the gravity went back on.

By the time Basnaaid arrived, I was dressed and had managed to look a bit less as though I'd just fallen off a cliff and then nearly drowned or asphyxiated. I debated for a moment whether to wear Lieutenant Awn's gold memorial tag, since it had seemed to anger Basnaaid the last time she had seen it, but in the end I had Twelve pin it to my jacket, next to Translator Dlique's silver and opal. Twelve had managed to produce a stack of small cakes and laid them out on my table along with dredgefruit and, at long last, the very best porcelain, the plain, graceful white tea set I'd seen last at Omaugh, in that last meeting with Anaander Mianaai. On first thought, I was astonished that Five had gotten up the courage to ask for it. On second thought, it wasn't the least bit surprising.

I bowed as Basnaaid entered. "Fleet Captain," she said, bowing herself. "I hope I'm not inconveniencing you. It's just that I thought we ought to talk in person."

"No inconvenience at all, Horticulturist. I am at your service." I gestured with my one good arm to a chair. "Will you sit?"

We sat. Twelve poured tea, and then went to stand, stiff and ancillary-like, in the corner of the room. "I want to know," Basnaaid said, after a polite sip of tea, "what happened to my sister."

I told her. How Lieutenant Awn had discovered the split in Anaander Mianaai, and what one side of the Lord of the Radch was doing. How she had refused to obey the orders of that Anaander, and as a result the Lord of the Radch had ordered her execution. Which I had carried out. And then, for reasons I still didn't fully understand, I had turned my gun on the Lord of the Radch. Who had destroyed me as a result, all of me except One Esk Nineteen, the only part of me to escape.

When I finished, Basnaaid was silent for a good ten seconds. Then she said, "So you were part of her decade? One Esk, yes?"

"One Esk Nineteen, yes."

"She always said you took such good care of her."

"I know."

She gave a small laugh. "Of course you do. That's how you've read all my poetry, too. How embarrassing."

"It wasn't bad, considering." Lieutenant Awn hadn't been the only officer with a baby sister who wrote poetry. "Lieutenant Awn enjoyed it very much. Truly she did. She loved to get your messages."

"I'm glad," she said, simply.

"Horticulturist, I..." But I couldn't speak, not and keep my composure. A cake or a piece of fruit was too complicated a way to distract myself. A sip of tea insufficient. I waited, merely, Basnaaid sitting patient and quiet across the table, also waiting. "Ships care about their officers," I said, when I thought I could speak again. "We can't help it, it's how we're made. But some officers we care for more than others." Now, perhaps, I could manage it. "I loved your sister very much."

"I'm glad of that, too," she said. "Truly I am. And I understand now why you made the offer you did. But I still can't accept." I remembered her conversation with Tisarwat, in the sitting room in the Undergarden. *None of it was for me.* "I don't think you can buy forgiveness, even at a price like that."

"It wasn't forgiveness I wanted." The only person who could give me that in any way that mattered was dead.

Basnaaid thought about that for a few moments. "I can't even imagine it," she said, finally. "To be part of something so big, for so long, and then suddenly to be so completely alone." She paused, and then, "You must have mixed feelings about the Lord of the Radch adopting you into Mianaai."

"Not mixed at all."

She smiled ruefully. Then, calmly serious, "I'm not sure how I feel about what you've just told me."

"You don't owe me any account of how you feel, or any explanation of why you feel it. But my offer stands. If you change your mind, it will still be open."

"What if you have children?"

For a moment, I had difficulty believing she had suggested such a thing. "Can you imagine me with an infant, Citizen?"

She smiled. "You have a point. But all sorts of people are mothers."

True. "And all sorts of people aren't. The offer is always open. But I will not mention it again, unless you change your mind. How are things in Horticulture? Are they ready to turn the gravity back on?"

"Almost. When Station turned it off there was more water than just the lake lying around. It's been a job chasing all that down. We didn't lose as many fish as we thought we would, though."

I thought of the children I'd seen running down to the bridge to feed the fish, bright-scaled, purple and green and orange and blue. "That's good."

"Most of the first level of the Undergarden escaped damage, but the support level will have to be entirely rebuilt before the water can go back into the lake. It turns out that it had been leaking for some time, but a very small amount."

"Let me guess." I picked up my tea. "The mushrooms."

"The mushrooms!" She laughed. "I should have known, the moment I heard someone was growing mushrooms in the Undergarden, what that meant. Yes, they'd crawled into the support level and started growing mushrooms. But it seems like the structures they built under the lake supports, and all the organic material packed in there for a substrate, actually kept the Undergarden from flooding for longer than it should have. But that's also where most of the damage was. I'm afraid the Undergarden mushroom industry is gone."

"I hope they'll allow for that, when they rebuild the supports." I would have to say as much to Station Administrator Celar and Governor Giarod. And I would have to remind Governor Giarod of what I'd said about not taking away the specialties of Undergarden residents.

"I suspect if you mention it, Fleet Captain, they will."

"I hope so," I said. "What's happened to Sirix?"

Basnaaid frowned. "She's in Security. I...I don't know. I like Sirix, even though she's always seemed a bit...prickly. I still can't quite believe that she would..." She trailed off, at a loss. "If you'd asked me before this, I'd have said she'd never, ever do anything wrong. Not like that. But I heard, I don't know if it's true, that she'd gone to Security to turn herself in, and they were on their way to the Gardens when the section doors closed."

I would have to say something to Governor Giarod, about Sirix. "She was very disappointed in me, I think." She could not possibly have acted from anger. "She has been waiting all this time for justice to arrive, and she thought maybe I was bringing it. But her idea of justice is...not the same as mine."

Basnaaid sighed. "How is Tisarwat?"

"She's fine." More or less. "Horticulturist, Tisarwat has a terrible crush on you."

She smiled. "I know. I think it's kind of sweet." And then frowned. "Actually, what she did in the Gardens the other day was well beyond sweet."

"It was," I agreed. "I think she's feeling somewhat fragile right now, which is why I mention it."

"Tisarwat, fragile!" Basnaaid laughed. "But then, people can look very strong on the outside when they're not, can't they. You, for instance, could probably stand to lie down a bit, even though you don't look it. I should go."

"Please stay for supper." She was right, I needed to lie down, or perhaps I needed Twelve to bring me some cushions. "It's a long ride back, and it's much more comfortable to eat with gravity. I won't impose my company on you, but I know Tisarwat would be glad to see you, and I'm sure the rest of my officers would like to meet you. More formally, I mean." She didn't answer right away. "Are *you* all right? You had just as difficult a time as the rest of us."

"I'm fine." And then, "Mostly. I think. To be honest, Fleet Captain, I feel like... like everything I thought I could depend on has disappeared, like none of it was ever true to begin with and I've only just realized it, and now, I don't know. I mean, I thought I was *safe*, I thought I knew who everyone was. And I was wrong."

"I know that feeling," I said. I couldn't go much longer without those cushions. And my leg had begun to ache, for no reason I could see. "Eventually, you start making sense out of things again."

"I'd like to have supper with you and Tisarwat," she said, as though it was an answer to what I'd just said. "And anyone else you'd invite."

"I'm glad." Without any order from me, Twelve left her place in the corner, went to open one of the storage benches lining the wall. Pulled out three cushions. "Tell me, Horticulturist, can you say, in verse, how God is like a duck?"

Basnaaid blinked, surprised. Laughed. What I had hoped for when I had changed the topic so abruptly. Twelve pushed a pillow behind my back, and two under the elbow of my immobilized left arm. I said, "Thank you, Twelve."

"There once was a duck who was God," said Basnaaid. "Who said, it's exceedingly odd. I fly when I wish and I swim like a fish…" She frowned. "That's as far as I can go. And it's only doggerel, not even a proper mode or meter. I'm out of practice."

"It's farther than I'd have gotten." I closed my eyes, for just a moment. Tisarwat lay on her bed in Medical, eyes closed while Ship played music in her ears. Bo Nine nearby, watching. Etrepas scrubbed their corridors, or stood watch with Ekalu. Amaats rested, or exercised, or bathed. Seivarden sat on her own bunk, melancholy for some reason, still thinking, perhaps, of missed opportunities in her past. Medic grumbled to Ship about my disregard for her advice, though there wasn't any real anger in it. Kalr One, cooking for me while Five was still on the station, fretted to Three about the sudden change in supper plans, though the fretting turned very quickly to the certainty that between the two of them they could meet the challenge. In the bath, an Amaat began to sing. *My mother said it all goes around, it all goes around, the ship goes around the station.*

It wasn't the same. It wasn't what I wanted, not really, wasn't what I knew I would always reach for. But it would have to be enough.

Acknowledgments

So many people have given me invaluable help, without which I could not have written this book. My instructors and classmates of the Clarion West class of 2005 continue to be a source of inspiration, assistance, and friendship that I could not do without. My work is also the better for the help of my editors, Will Hinton in the US and Jenni Hill in the UK.

I have said before, and will say again, that there is not enough thanks in the world for my fabulous agent, Seth Fishman.

Thanks are also due to many people who offered advice or information, and who were patient with my questions: S. Hutson Blount, Carolyn Ives Gilman, Sarah Goleman, Dr. Philip Edward Kaldon, Dr. Brin Schuler, Anna Schwind, Kurt Schwind, Mike Swirsky, and Rachel Swirsky. Their information and advice was invariably correct and wise—any missteps are entirely my own.

Thanks to the Missouri Botanical Garden, the St. Louis

County Library, the Webster University Library, and the Municipal Library Consortium of St. Louis County. And to all the folks who make Interlibrary Loan a reality. Seriously. Interlibrary Loan is the most amazing thing.

Last, but of course not least, I could not have written this book without the love and support of my husband Dave and my children, Aidan and Gawain.

extras

orbit

meet the author

MissionPhoto.org

Ann Leckie has worked as a waitress, a receptionist, a rodman on a land-surveying crew, a lunch lady, and a recording engineer. The author of many published short stories, and former secretary of the Science Fiction Writers of America, she lives in St. Louis, Missouri, with her husband, children, and cats.

introducing

If you enjoyed
ANCILLARY SWORD,
look out for

LEVIATHAN WAKES

The Expanse: Book One

by James S. A. Corey

Humanity has colonized the solar system—Mars, the Moon, the Asteroid Belt, and beyond—but the stars are still out of our reach.

Jim Holden is XO of an ice miner making runs from the rings of Saturn to the mining stations of the Belt. When he and his crew stumble upon a derelict ship, the Scopuli, *they find themselves in possession of a secret they never wanted. A secret that someone is willing to kill for—and kill on a scale unfathomable to Jim and his crew. War is brewing in the system unless he can find out who left the ship and why.*

Detective Miller is looking for a girl. One girl in a system of billions, but her parents have money, and money talks. When the trail leads him to the Scopuli *and rebel sympathizer Holden, he realizes that this girl may be the key to everything.*

Holden and Miller must thread the needle between the Earth government, the Outer Planet revolutionaries, and secretive corporations—and the odds are against them. But out in the Belt, the rules are different, and one small ship can change the fate of the universe.

Prologue: Julie

The *Scopuli* had been taken eight days ago, and Julie Mao was finally ready to be shot.

It had taken all eight days trapped in a storage locker for her to get to that point. For the first two she'd remained motionless, sure that the armored men who'd put her there had been serious. For the first hours, the ship she'd been taken aboard wasn't under thrust, so she floated in the locker, using gentle touches to keep herself from bumping into the walls or the atmosphere suit she shared the space with. When the ship began to move, thrust giving her weight, she'd stood silently until her legs cramped, then sat down slowly into a fetal position. She'd peed in her jumpsuit, not caring about the warm itchy wetness, or the smell, worrying only that she might slip and fall in the wet spot it left on the floor. She couldn't make noise. They'd shoot her.

On the third day, thirst had forced her into action. The noise of the ship was all around her. The faint subsonic rumble of the reactor and drive. The constant hiss and thud of hydraulics and steel bolts as the pressure doors between decks opened and closed. The clump of heavy boots walking on metal decking. She waited until all the noise she could hear sounded distant, then pulled the environment suit off its hooks and onto the locker floor. Listening for any approaching sound, she slowly disassembled the suit and took out the water supply. It was old and stale; the suit obviously hadn't been used or serviced in ages. But she hadn't had a sip in days, and the warm loamy water in the suit's reservoir bag was the best thing she had ever tasted. She had to work hard not to gulp it down and make herself vomit.

When the urge to urinate returned, she pulled the catheter bag out of the suit and relieved herself into it. She sat on the floor, now cushioned by the padded suit and almost comfortable, and wondered who her captors were—Coalition Navy, pirates, something worse. Sometimes she slept.

On day four, isolation, hunger, boredom, and the diminishing number of places to store her piss finally pushed her to make contact with them. She'd heard muffled cries of pain. Somewhere nearby, her shipmates were being beaten or tortured. If she got the attention of the kidnappers, maybe they would just take her to the others. That was okay. Beatings, she could handle. It seemed like a small price to pay if it meant seeing people again.

The locker sat beside the inner airlock door. During flight, that usually wasn't a high-traffic area, though she didn't know anything about the layout of this particular ship. She thought about what to say, how to present herself. When she finally heard someone moving toward her, she just tried to yell that she wanted out. The dry rasp that came out of her throat surprised her. She swallowed, working her tongue to try to create some saliva, and tried again. Another faint rattle in the throat.

The people were right outside her locker door. A voice was talking quietly. Julie had pulled back a fist to bang on the door when she heard what it was saying.

No. Please no. Please don't.

Dave. Her ship's mechanic. Dave, who collected clips from old cartoons and knew a million jokes, begging in a small broken voice.

No, please no, please don't, he said.

Hydraulics and locking bolts clicked as the inner airlock door opened. A meaty thud as something was thrown inside. Another click as the airlock closed. A hiss of evacuating air.

When the airlock cycle had finished, the people outside her door walked away. She didn't bang to get their attention.

They'd scrubbed the ship. Detainment by the inner planet navies was a bad scenario, but they'd all trained on how to deal with it. Sensitive OPA data was scrubbed and overwritten with innocuous-looking logs with false time stamps. Anything too sensitive to trust to a computer, the captain destroyed. When the attackers came aboard, they could play innocent.

It hadn't mattered.

There weren't the questions about cargo or permits. The invaders had come in like they owned the place, and Captain Darren had rolled over like a dog. Everyone else—Mike, Dave, Wan Li—they'd all just thrown up their hands and gone along quietly. The pirates or slavers or whatever they were had dragged them off the little transport ship that had been her home, and down a docking tube without even minimal environment suits. The tube's thin layer of Mylar was the only thing between them and hard nothing: hope it didn't rip; goodbye lungs if it did.

Julie had gone along too, but then the bastards had tried to lay their hands on her, strip her clothes off.

Five years of low-gravity jiu jitsu training and them in a confined space with no gravity. She'd done a lot of damage. She'd almost started to think she might win when from nowhere a gauntleted fist smashed into her face. Things got fuzzy after that. Then the locker, and *Shoot her if she makes a noise.* Four days of not making noise while they beat her friends down below and then threw one of them out an airlock.

After six days, everything went quiet.

Shifting between bouts of consciousness and fragmented dreams, she was only vaguely aware as the sounds of walking, talking, and pressure doors and the subsonic rumble of the reactor and the drive faded away a little at a time. When the drive stopped, so did gravity, and Julie woke from a dream of racing her old pinnace to find herself floating while her muscles screamed in protest and then slowly relaxed.

She pulled herself to the door and pressed her ear to the cold metal. Panic shot through her until she caught the quiet sound of the air recyclers. The ship still had power and air, but the drive wasn't on and no one was opening a door or walking or talking. Maybe it was a crew meeting. Or a party on another deck. Or everyone was in engineering, fixing a serious problem.

She spent a day listening and waiting.

By day seven, her last sip of water was gone. No one on the ship had moved within range of her hearing for twenty-four hours. She sucked on a plastic tab she'd ripped off the environment suit until she worked up some saliva; then she started yelling. She yelled herself hoarse.

No one came.

By day eight, she was ready to be shot. She'd been out of water for two days, and her waste bag had been full for four. She put her shoulders against the back wall of the locker and planted her hands against the side walls. Then she kicked out with both legs as hard as she could. The cramps that followed the first kick almost made her pass out. She screamed instead.

Stupid girl, she told herself. She was dehydrated. Eight days without activity was more than enough to start atrophy. At least she should have stretched out.

She massaged her stiff muscles until the knots were gone, then stretched, focusing her mind like she was back in dojo. When she was in control of her body, she kicked again. And again. And again, until light started to show through the edges of the locker. And again, until the door was so bent that the three hinges and the locking bolt were the only points of contact between it and the frame.

And one last time, so that it bent far enough that the bolt was no longer seated in the hasp and the door swung free.

Julie shot from the locker, hands half raised and ready to look either threatening or terrified, depending on which seemed more useful.

There was no one on the whole deck: the airlock, the suit storage room where she'd spent the last eight days, a half dozen other storage rooms. All empty. She plucked a magnetized pipe wrench of suitable size for skull cracking out of an EVA kit, then went down the crew ladder to the deck below.

And then the one below that, and then the one below that. Personnel cabins in crisp, almost military order. Commissary, where there were signs of a struggle. Medical bay, empty. Torpedo bay. No one. The comm station was unmanned, powered down, and locked. The few sensor logs that still streamed showed no sign of the *Scopuli.* A new dread knotted her gut. Deck after deck and room after room empty of life. Something had happened. A radiation leak. Poison in the air. Something that had forced an evacuation. She wondered if she'd be able to fly the ship by herself.

But if they'd evacuated, she'd have heard them going out the airlock, wouldn't she?

She reached the final deck hatch, the one that led into engineering, and stopped when the hatch didn't open automatically. A red light on the lock panel showed that the room had been sealed from the inside. She thought again about radiation and major failures. But if either of those was the case, why lock the door from the inside? And she had passed wall panel after wall panel. None of them had been flashing warnings of any kind. No, not radiation, something else.

There was more disruption here. Blood. Tools and containers in disarray. Whatever had happened, it had happened here. No, it had started here. And it had ended behind that locked door.

It took two hours with a torch and prying tools from the machine shop to cut through the hatch to engineering. With the hydraulics compromised, she had to crank it open by hand. A gust of warm wet air blew out, carrying a hospital scent without the antiseptic. A coppery, nauseating smell. The torture chamber, then. Her friends would be inside, beaten or cut to pieces. Julie hefted her wrench and prepared to bust open at least one head before they killed her. She floated down.

The engineering deck was huge, vaulted like a cathedral. The fusion reactor dominated the central space. Something was wrong with it. Where she expected to see readouts, shielding, and monitors, a layer of something like mud seemed to flow over the reactor core. Slowly, Julie floated toward it, one hand still on the ladder. The strange smell became overpowering.

The mud caked around the reactor had structure to it like nothing she'd seen before. Tubes ran through it like veins or airways. Parts of it pulsed. Not mud, then.

Flesh.

An outcropping of the thing shifted toward her. Compared to the whole, it seemed no larger than a toe, a little finger. It was Captain Darren's head.

"Help me," it said.

Chapter One: Holden

A hundred and fifty years before, when the parochial disagreements between Earth and Mars had been on the verge of war, the Belt had been a far horizon of tremendous mineral wealth beyond viable economic reach, and the outer planets had been beyond even the most unrealistic corporate dream. Then Solomon Epstein had built his little modified fusion drive, popped it on the back of his three-man yacht, and turned it on. With a good scope, you could still see his ship going at a marginal percentage of the speed of light, heading out into the big empty. The best, longest funeral in the history of mankind. Fortunately, he'd left the plans on his home computer. The Epstein Drive hadn't given humanity the stars, but it had delivered the planets.

Three-quarters of a kilometer long, a quarter of a kilometer wide—roughly shaped like a fire hydrant—and mostly empty space inside, the *Canterbury* was a retooled colony transport. Once, it had been packed with people, supplies, schematics, machines, environment bubbles, and hope. Just under twenty million people lived on the moons of Saturn now. The *Canterbury* had hauled nearly a million of their ancestors there. Forty-five million on the moons of Jupiter. One moon of Uranus sported five thousand, the farthest outpost of human civilization, at least until the Mormons finished their generation ship and headed for the stars and freedom from procreation restrictions.

And then there was the Belt.

If you asked OPA recruiters when they were drunk and feeling expansive, they might say there were a hundred million in the Belt. Ask an inner planet census taker, it was nearer to fifty million. Any way you looked, the population was huge and needed a lot of water.

So now the *Canterbury* and her dozens of sister ships in the Pur'n'Kleen Water Company made the loop from Saturn's generous rings to the Belt and back hauling glaciers, and would until the ships aged into salvage wrecks.

Jim Holden saw some poetry in that.

"Holden?"

He turned back to the hangar deck. Chief Engineer Naomi Nagata towered over him. She stood almost two full meters tall, her mop of curly hair tied back into a black tail, her expression halfway between amusement and annoyance. She had the Belter habit of shrugging with her hands instead of her shoulders.

"Holden, are you listening, or just staring out the window?"

"There was a problem," Holden said. "And because you're really, really good, you can fix it even though you don't have enough money or supplies."

Naomi laughed.

"So you weren't listening," she said.

"Not really, no."

"Well, you got the basics right anyhow. *Knight*'s landing gear isn't going to be good in atmosphere until I can get the seals replaced. That going to be a problem?"

"I'll ask the old man," Holden said. "But when's the last time we used the shuttle in atmosphere?"

"Never, but regs say we need at least one atmo-capable shuttle."

"Hey, Boss!" Amos Burton, Naomi's earthborn assistant, yelled from across the bay. He waved one meaty arm in their general direction. He meant Naomi. Amos might be on Captain McDowell's ship; Holden might be executive officer; but in Amos Burton's world, only Naomi was boss.

"What's the matter?" Naomi shouted back.

"Bad cable. Can you hold this little fucker in place while I get the spare?"

Naomi looked at Holden, *Are we done here?* in her eyes. He snapped a sarcastic salute and she snorted, shaking her head as she walked away, her frame long and thin in her greasy coveralls.

Seven years in Earth's navy, five years working in space with civilians, and he'd never gotten used to the long, thin, improbable bones of Belters. A childhood spent in gravity shaped the way he saw things forever.

At the central lift, Holden held his finger briefly over the button for the navigation deck, tempted by the prospect of Ade Tukunbo—her smile, her voice, the patchouli-and-vanilla scent she used in her hair—but pressed the button for the infirmary instead. Duty before pleasure.

Shed Garvey, the medical tech, was hunched over his lab table, debriding the stump of Cameron Paj's left arm, when Holden walked in. A month earlier, Paj had gotten his elbow pinned by a thirty-ton block of ice moving at five millimeters a second. It wasn't an uncommon injury among people with the dangerous job of cutting and moving zero-g icebergs, and Paj was taking the whole thing with the fatalism of a professional. Holden leaned over Shed's shoulder to watch as the tech plucked one of the medical maggots out of dead tissue.

"What's the word?" Holden asked.

"It's looking pretty good, sir," Paj said. "I've still got a few nerves. Shed's been tellin' me about how the prosthetic is gonna hook up to it."

"Assuming we can keep the necrosis under control," the medic said, "and make sure Paj doesn't heal up too much before we get to Ceres. I checked the policy, and Paj here's been signed on long enough to get one with force feedback, pressure and temperature sensors, fine-motor software. The whole package. It'll be almost as good as the real thing. The inner planets have a new biogel that regrows the limb, but that isn't covered in our medical plan."

"Fuck the Inners, and fuck their magic Jell-O. I'd rather have a good Belter-built fake than anything those bastards grow in a lab. Just wearing their fancy arm probably turns you into an asshole," Paj said. Then he added, "Oh, uh, no offense, XO."

"None taken. Just glad we're going to get you fixed up," Holden said.

"Tell him the other bit," Paj said with a wicked grin. Shed blushed.

"I've, ah, heard from other guys who've gotten them," Shed said, not meeting Holden's eyes. "Apparently there's a period while you're still building identification with the prosthetic when whacking off feels just like getting a hand job."

Holden let the comment hang in the air for a second while Shed's ears turned crimson.

"Good to know," Holden said. "And the necrosis?"

"There's some infection," Shed said. "The maggots are keeping it under control, and the inflammation's actually a good thing in this context, so we're not fighting too hard unless it starts to spread."

"Is he going to be ready for the next run?" Holden asked.

For the first time, Paj frowned.

"Shit yes, I'll be ready. I'm always ready. This is what I *do,* sir."

"Probably," Shed said. "Depending on how the bond takes. If not this one, the one after."

"Fuck that," Paj said. "I can buck ice one-handed better than half the skags you've got on this bitch."

"Again," Holden said, suppressing a grin, "good to know. Carry on."

Paj snorted. Shed plucked another maggot free. Holden went back to the lift, and this time he didn't hesitate.

The navigation station of the *Canterbury* didn't dress to impress. The great wall-sized displays Holden had imagined when he'd first volunteered for the navy did exist on capital ships but, even there, more as an artifact of design than need. Ade sat at a pair of screens only slightly larger than a hand terminal, graphs of the efficiency and output of the *Canterbury*'s reactor and engine updating in the corners, raw logs spooling on the right as the systems reported in. She wore thick headphones that covered her ears, the faint thump of the bass line barely escaping. If the *Canterbury* sensed an anomaly, it would alert her. If a system errored, it would alert her. If Captain McDowell left the command and control deck, it would alert her so she could turn the music off and look busy when he arrived. Her petty hedonism was only one of a thousand things that made Ade attractive to Holden. He walked up behind her, pulled the headphones gently away from her ears, and said, "Hey."

Ade smiled, tapped her screen, and dropped the headphones to rest around her long slim neck like technical jewelry.

"Executive Officer James Holden," she said with an exaggerated formality made even more acute by her thick Nigerian accent. "And what can I do for you?"

"You know, it's funny you should ask that," he said. "I was just thinking how pleasant it would be to have someone come back to my cabin when third shift takes over. Have a little romantic dinner of the same crap they're serving in the galley. Listen to some music."

"Drink a little wine," she said. "Break a little protocol. Pretty to think about, but I'm not up for sex tonight."

"I wasn't talking about sex. A little food. Conversation."

"I was talking about sex," she said.

Holden knelt beside her chair. In the one-third g of their current thrust, it was perfectly comfortable. Ade's smile softened. The log spool chimed; she glanced at it, tapped a release, and turned back to him.

"Ade, I like you. I mean, I really enjoy your company," he said. "I don't understand why we can't spend some time together with our clothes on."

"Holden. Sweetie. Stop it, okay?"

"Stop what?"

"Stop trying to turn me into your girlfriend. You're a nice guy. You've got a cute butt, and you're fun in the sack. Doesn't mean we're engaged."

Holden rocked back on his heels, feeling himself frown.

"Ade. For this to work for me, it needs to be more than that."

"But it isn't," she said, taking his hand. "It's okay that it isn't. You're the XO here, and I'm a short-timer. Another run, maybe two, and I'm gone."

"I'm not chained to this ship either."

Her laughter was equal parts warmth and disbelief.

"How long have you been on the *Cant*?"

"Five years."

"You're not going anyplace," she said. "You're comfortable here."

"Comfortable?" he said. "The *Cant*'s a century-old ice hauler. You can find a shittier flying job, but you have to try really hard. Everyone here is either wildly under-qualified or seriously screwed things up at their last gig."

"And you're comfortable here." Her eyes were less kind now. She bit her lip, looked down at the screen, looked up.

"I didn't deserve that," he said.

"You didn't," she agreed. "Look, I told you I wasn't in the mood tonight. I'm feeling cranky. I need a good night's sleep. I'll be nicer tomorrow."

"Promise?"

"I'll even make you dinner. Apology accepted?"

He slipped forward, pressed his lips to hers. She kissed back, politely at first and then with more warmth. Her fingers cupped his neck for a moment, then pulled him away.

"You're entirely too good at that. You should go now," she said. "On duty and all."

"Okay," he said, and didn't turn to go.

"Jim," she said, and the shipwide comm system clicked on.

"Holden to the bridge," Captain McDowell said, his voice compressed and echoing. Holden replied with something obscene. Ade laughed. He swooped in, kissed her cheek, and headed back for the central lift, quietly hoping that Captain McDowell suffered boils and public humiliation for his lousy timing.

The bridge was hardly larger than Holden's quarters and smaller by half than the galley. Except for the slightly oversized captain's display, required by Captain McDowell's failing eyesight and general distrust of corrective surgery, it could have been an accounting firm's back room. The air smelled of cleaning astringent and someone's overly strong yerba maté tea. McDowell shifted in his seat as Holden approached. Then the captain leaned back, pointing over his shoulder at the communications station.

"Becca!" McDowell snapped. "Tell him."

Rebecca Byers, the comm officer on duty, could have been bred from a shark and a hatchet. Black eyes, sharp features, lips so thin they might as well not have existed. The story on board was that she'd taken the job to escape prosecution for killing an ex-husband. Holden liked her.

"Emergency signal," she said. "Picked it up two hours ago. The transponder verification just bounced back from *Callisto.* It's real."

"Ah," Holden said. And then: "Shit. Are we the closest?"

"Only ship in a few million klicks."

"Well. That figures," Holden said.

Becca turned her gaze to the captain. McDowell cracked his knuckles and stared at his display. The light from the screen gave him an odd greenish cast.

"It's next to a charted non-Belt asteroid," McDowell said.

"Really?" Holden said in disbelief. "Did they run into it? There's nothing else out here for millions of kilometers."

"Maybe they pulled over because someone had to go potty. All we have is that some knucklehead is out there, blasting an emergency signal, and we're the closest. Assuming..."

The law of the solar system was unequivocal. In an environment as hostile to life as space, the aid and goodwill of your fellow humans wasn't optional. The emergency signal, just by existing, obligated the nearest ship to stop and render aid—which didn't mean the law was universally followed.

The *Canterbury* was fully loaded. Well over a million tons of ice had been gently accelerated for the past month. Just like the little glacier that had crushed Paj's arm, it was going to be hard to slow down. The temptation to have an unexplained comm failure, erase the logs, and let the great god Darwin have his way was always there.

But if McDowell had really intended that, he wouldn't have called Holden up. Or made the suggestion where the crew could hear him. Holden understood the dance. The captain was going to be the one who would have blown it off except for Holden. The grunts would respect the captain for not wanting to cut into the ship's profit. They'd respect Holden for insisting that they follow the rule. No matter what happened, the captain and Holden would both be hated for what they were required by law and mere human decency to do.

"We have to stop," Holden said. Then, gamely: "There may be salvage."

McDowell tapped his screen. Ade's voice came from the console, as low and warm as if she'd been in the room.

"Captain?"

"I need numbers on stopping this crate," he said.

"Sir?"

"How hard is it going to be to put us alongside CA-2216862?"

"We're stopping at an asteroid?"

"I'll tell you when you've followed my order, Navigator Tukunbo."

"Yes, sir," she said. Holden heard a series of clicks. "If we flip the ship right now and burn like hell for most of two days, I can get us within fifty thousand kilometers, sir."

"Can you define 'burn like hell'?" McDowell said.

"We'll need everyone in crash couches."

"Of course we will," McDowell sighed, and scratched his

scruffy beard. "And shifting ice is only going to do a couple million bucks' worth of banging up the hull, if we're lucky. I'm getting old for this, Holden. I really am."

"Yes, sir. You are. And I've always liked your chair," Holden said. McDowell scowled and made an obscene gesture. Rebecca snorted in laughter. McDowell turned to her.

"Send a message to the beacon that we're on our way. And let Ceres know we're going to be late. Holden, where does the *Knight* stand?"

"No flying in atmosphere until we get some parts, but she'll do fine for fifty thousand klicks in vacuum."

"You're sure of that?"

"Naomi said it. That makes it true."

McDowell rose, unfolding to almost two and a quarter meters and thinner than a teenager back on Earth. Between his age and never having lived in a gravity well, the coming burn was likely to be hell on the old man. Holden felt a pang of sympathy that he would never embarrass McDowell by expressing.

"Here's the thing, Jim," McDowell said, his voice quiet enough that only Holden could hear him. "We're required to stop and make an attempt, but we don't have to go out of our way, if you see what I mean."

"We'll already have stopped," Holden said, and McDowell patted at the air with his wide, spidery hands. One of the many Belter gestures that had evolved to be visible when wearing an environment suit.

"I can't avoid that," he said. "But if you see anything out there that seems off, don't play hero again. Just pack up the toys and come home."

"And leave it for the next ship that comes through?"

"And keep yourself safe," McDowell said. "Order. Understood?"

"Understood," Holden said.

As the shipwide comm system clicked to life and McDowell began explaining the situation to the crew, Holden imagined he could hear a chorus of groans coming up through the decks. He went over to Rebecca.

"Okay," he said, "what have we got on the broken ship?"

"Light freighter. Martian registry. Shows Eros as home port. Calls itself *Scopuli*..."

introducing

If you enjoyed
ANCILLARY SWORD,
look out for

CONSIDER PHLEBAS

A Culture Novel

by Iain M. Banks

The war raged across the galaxy. Billions had died, billions more were doomed. Moons, planets, the very stars themselves faced destruction, cold-blooded, brutal, and worse, random. The Idirans fought for their Faith; the Culture for its moral right to exist. Principles were at stake. There could be no surrender. Within the cosmic conflict, an individual crusade. Deep within a fabled labyrinth on a barren world, a Planet of the Dead proscribed to mortals, lay a fugitive Mind. Both the Culture and the Idirans sought it. It was the fate of Horza, the Changer, and his motley crew of unpredictable mercenaries, human and machine, actually to find it, and with it their own destruction.

Prologue

The ship didn't even have a name. It had no human crew because the factory craft which constructed it had been evacuated long ago. It had no life-support or accommodation units for the same reason. It had no class number or fleet designation because it was a mongrel made from bits and pieces of different types of warcraft; and it didn't have a name because the factory craft had no time left for such niceties.

The dockyard threw the ship together as best it could from its depleted stock of components, even though most of the weapon, power and sensory systems were either faulty, superseded or due for overhaul. The factory vessel knew that its own destruction was inevitable, but there was just a chance that its last creation might have the speed and the luck to escape.

The one perfect, priceless component the factory craft did have was the vastly powerful—though still raw and untrained—Mind around which it had constructed the rest of the ship. If it could get the Mind to safety, the factory vessel thought it would have done well. Nevertheless, there was another reason—the real reason—the dockyard mother didn't give its warship child a name; it thought there was something else it lacked: hope.

The ship left the construction bay of the factory craft with most of its fitting-out still to be done. Accelerating hard, its course a four dimensional spiral through a blizzard of stars where it knew that only danger waited, it powered into hyperspace on spent engines from an overhauled craft of one class, watched its birthplace disappear astern with battle-damaged sensors from a second, and tested outdated weapon units cannibalized from yet another. Inside its warship body, in narrow, unlit, unheated, hard-vacuum spaces, constructor drones struggled to install or complete sensors, displacers, field generators, shield disruptors, laserfields, plasma chambers, warhead magazines, maneuvering units, repair systems and the thousands of other major and minor components required to make a functional warship.

Gradually, as it swept through the vast open reaches between the star systems, the vessel's internal structure changed, and it became less chaotic, more ordered, as the factory drones completed their tasks.

Several tens of hours out on its first journey, while it was testing its track scanner by focusing back along the route it had taken, the ship registered a single massive annihilation explosion deep behind it, where the factory craft had been. It watched the blossoming shell of radiation expand for a while, then switched the scanner field to dead ahead and pushed yet more power through its already overloaded engines.

The ship did all it could to avoid combat; it kept well away from the routes enemy craft would probably use; it treated every hint of any craft as a confirmed hostile sighting. At the same time, as it zigzagged and ducked and weaved and rose and fell, it was corkscrewing as fast as it could, as directly as it dared, down and across the strand of the galactic arm in which it had been born, heading for the edge of that great isthmus and the comparatively empty space beyond. On the far side, on the edge of the next limb, it might find safety.

Just as it arrived at that first border, where the stars rose like a glittering cliff alongside emptiness, it was caught.

A fleet of hostile craft, whose course by chance came close enough to that of the fleeing ship, detected its ragged, noisy emission shell, and intercepted it. The ship ran straight into their attack and was overwhelmed. Out-armed, slow, vulnerable, it knew almost instantly that it had no chance even of inflicting any damage on the opposing fleet.

So it destroyed itself, detonating the stock of warheads it carried in a sudden release of energy which for a second, in hyperspace alone, outshone the yellow dwarf star of a nearby system.

Scattered in a pattern around it, an instant before the ship itself was blown into plasma, most of the thousands of exploding warheads formed an outrushing sphere of radiation through which any escape seemed impossible. In the fraction of a second the entire engagement lasted, there were at the end some millionths when the battlecomputers of the enemy fleet briefly analyzed the four-dimensional maze of expanding radiation and saw that there was one bewilderingly complicated and unlikely way out of the concentric shells of erupting energies now opening like the petals of some immense flower between the star systems. It was not, however, a route the Mind of a small, archaic warship could plan for, create and follow.

By the time it was noticed that the ship's Mind had taken exactly that path through its screen of annihilation, it was too late to stop it from falling away through hyperspace toward the small, cold planet fourth out from the single yellow sun of the nearby system.

It was also too late to do anything about the light from the ship's exploding warheads, which had been arranged in a crude code, describing the vessel's fate and the escaped Mind's status and position, and legible to anybody catching the unreal light as it sped through the galaxy. Perhaps worst of all—and had their design permitted such a thing, those electronic brains would now have felt dismay—the planet the Mind had made for through its shield of explosions was not one they could simply attack, destroy or even land on; it was Schar's World, near the region of barren space between two galactic strands called the Sullen Gulf, and it was one of the forbidden Planets of the Dead.

1

Sorpen

The level was at his top lip now. Even with his head pressed hard back against the stones of the cell wall his nose was only just above the surface. He wasn't going to get his hands free in time; he was going to drown.

In the darkness of the cell, in its stink and warmth, while the sweat ran over his brows and tightly closed eyes and his trance went on and on, one part of his mind tried to accustom him to the idea of his own death. But, like an unseen insect buzzing in a quiet room, there was something else, something that would not go away, was of no use, and only annoyed. It was a sentence, irrelevant and pointless and so old he'd forgotten where he had heard or read it, and it went round and round the inside of his head like a marble spun round the inside of a jug:

The Jinmoti of Bozlen Two kill the hereditary ritual assassins of the new Yearking's immediate family by drowning them in the tears of the Continental Empathaur in its Sadness Season.

At one point, shortly after his ordeal had begun and he was only partway into his trance, he had wondered what would happen if he threw up. It had been when the palace kitchens—about fifteen or sixteen floors above, if his calculations were correct—had sent their waste down the sinuous network of plumbing that led to the sewercell. The gurgling, watery mess had dislodged some rotten food from the last time some poor wretch had drowned in filth and garbage, and that was when he felt he might vomit. It had been almost comforting to work out that it would make no difference to the time of his death.

Then he had wondered—in that state of nervous frivolity which sometimes afflicts those who can do nothing but wait in a situation of mortal threat—whether crying would speed his death. In theory it would, though in practical terms it was irrelevant; but that was when the sentence started to roll round in his head.

The Jinmoti of Bozlen Two kill the hereditary ritual...

The liquid, which he could hear and feel and smell all too clearly—and could probably have seen with his far from ordinary eyes had they been open—washed briefly up to touch the bottom of his nose. He felt it block his nostrils, filling them with a stench that made his stomach heave. But he shook his head, tried to force his skull even further back against the stones, and the foul broth fell away. He blew down and could breathe again.

There wasn't long now. He checked his wrists again, but it was no good. It would take another hour or more, and he had only minutes, if he was lucky.

The trance was breaking anyway. He was returning to almost total consciousness, as though his brain wanted fully to appreciate his own death, its own extinction. He tried to think of something profound, or to see his life flash in front of him, or suddenly to remember some old love, a long-forgotten prophecy or premonition, but there was nothing, just an empty sentence, and the sensations of drowning in other people's dirt and waste.

You old bastards, he thought. One of their few strokes of humor or originality had been devising an elegant, ironic way of death. How fitting it must feel to them, dragging their decrepit frames to the banquet-hall privies, literally to defecate all over their enemies, and thereby kill them.

The air pressure built up, and a distant, groaning rumble of liquid signaled another flushing from above. *You old bastards. Well, I hope at least you kept your promise, Balveda.*

The Jinmoti of Bozlen Two kill the hereditary ritual... thought one part of his brain, as the pipes in the ceiling spluttered and the waste splashed into the warm mass of liquid which almost filled the cell. The wave passed over his face, then fell back to leave his nose free for a second and give him time to gulp a lungful of air. Then the liquid rose gently to touch the bottom of his nose again, and stayed there.

He held his breath.

It had hurt at first, when they had hung him up. His hands, tied inside tight leather pouches, were directly above his head, manacled inside thick loops of iron bolted to the cell walls, which took all his weight. His feet were tied together and left to dangle inside an iron tube, also attached to the wall, which stopped him from taking any weight on his feet and knees and at the same time prevented him from moving his legs more than a hand's breadth out from the wall or to either side. The tube ended just above his knees; above it there was only a thin and dirty loincloth to hide his ancient and grubby nakedness.

He had shut off the pain from his wrists and shoulders even while the four burly guards, two of them perched on ladders, had secured him in place. Even so he could feel that niggling sensation at the back of his skull which told him that he *ought* to be hurting. That had lessened gradually as the level of waste in the small sewercell had risen and buoyed up his body.

He had started to go into a trance then, as soon as the guards left, though he knew it was probably hopeless. It hadn't lasted long; the cell door opened again within minutes, a metal walkway was lowered by a guard onto the damp flagstones of the cell floor, and light from the corridor washed into the darkness. He had stopped the Changing trance and craned his neck to see who his visitor might be.

Into the cell, holding a short staff glowing cool blue, stepped the stooped, grizzled figure of Amahain-Frolk, security minister for the Gerontocracy of Sorpen. The old man smiled at him and nodded approvingly, then turned to the corridor and, with a thin, discolored hand, beckoned somebody standing outside the cell to step onto the short walkway and enter. He guessed it would be the Culture agent Balveda, and it was. She came lightly onto the metal boarding, looked round slowly, and fastened her gaze on him. He smiled and tried to nod in greeting, his ears rubbing on his naked arms.

"Balveda! I thought I might see you again. Come to see the host of the party?" He forced a grin. Officially it was his banquet; he was the host. Another of the Gerontocracy's little jokes. He hoped his voice had shown no signs of fear.

Perosteck Balveda, agent of the Culture, a full head taller than the old man by her side and still strikingly handsome even in the pallid glow of the blue torch, shook her thin, finely made head slowly. Her short, black hair lay like a shadow on her skull.

"No," she said, "I didn't want to see you, or say goodbye."

"You put me here, Balveda," he said quietly.

"Yes, and there you belong," Amahain-Frolk said, stepping as far forward on the platform as he could without overbalancing and having to step onto the damp floor. "I wanted you tortured first, but Miss Balveda here"—the minister's high, scratchy voice echoed in the cell as he turned his head back to the woman—"pleaded for you, though God knows why. But that's where you belong all right; murderer." He shook the staff at the almost naked man hanging on the dirty wall of the cell.

Balveda looked at her feet, just visible under the hem of the long, plain gray gown she wore. A circular pendant on a chain around her neck glinted in the light from the corridor outside. Amahain-Frolk had stepped back beside her, holding the shining staff up and squinting at the captive.

"You know, even now I could almost swear that was Egratin hanging there. I can..." He shook his gaunt, bony head. "...I can hardly believe it isn't, not until he opens his mouth, anyway. My God, these Changers are dangerous frightening things!" He turned to Balveda. She smoothed her hair at the nape of her neck and looked down at the old man.

"They are also an ancient and proud people, Minister, and there are very few of them left. May I ask you one more time? Please? Let him live. He might be—"

The Gerontocrat waved a thin and twisted hand at her, his face distorting in a grimace. "No! You would do well, Miss Balveda, not to keep asking for this...this assassin, this murderous, treacherous...*spy,* to be spared. Do you think we take the cowardly murder and impersonation of one of our outworld ministers lightly? What damage this... *thing* could have caused! Why, when we arrested it two of our guards died just from being *scratched*! Another is blind for life after this monster spat in his eye! However," Amahain-Frolk sneered at the man chained to the wall, "we took those teeth out. And his hands are tied so that he can't even scratch himself." He turned to Balveda again. "You say they are few? I say good; there will soon be one less."

The old man narrowed his eyes as he looked at the woman. "We are grateful to you and your people for exposing this fraud and murderer, but do not think that gives you the right to tell us what to do. There are some in the Gerontocracy who want nothing to do with *any* outside influence, and their voices grow in volume by the day as the war comes closer. You would do well not to antagonize those of us who do support your cause."

Balveda pursed her lips and looked down at her feet again, clasping her slender hands behind her back. Amahain-Frolk had turned back to the man hanging on the wall, wagging the staff in his direction as he spoke. "You will soon be dead, impostor, and with you die your masters' plans for the domination of our peaceful system! The same fate awaits them if they try to invade us. We and the Culture are—"

He shook his head as best he could and roared back, "Frolk, you're an idiot!" The old man shrank away as though hit. The Changer went on, "Can't you see you're going to be taken over anyway? Probably by the Idirans, but if not by them then by the Culture. You don't control your own destinies anymore; the war's stopped all that. Soon this whole sector will be part of the front, unless you *make* it part of the Idiran sphere. I was only sent in to tell you what you should have known anyway—not to cheat you into something you'd regret later. For God's sake, man, the Idirans won't *eat* you—"

"Ha! They look as though they could! Monsters with three feet; invaders, killers, infidels... You want us to link with them? With three-strides-tall-monsters? To be ground under their *hooves*? To have to worship their false gods?"

"At least they have a God, Frolk. The Culture doesn't." The ache in his arms was coming back as he concentrated on talking. He shifted as best he could and looked down at the minister. "They at least think the same way you do. The Culture doesn't."

"Oh no, my friend, oh no." Amahain-Frolk held one hand up flat to him and shook his head. "You won't sow seeds of discord like that."

"My God, you stupid old man," he laughed. "You want to know who the real representative of the Culture is on this planet? It's not her," he nodded at the woman, "it's that powered flesh-slicer she has following her everywhere, her knife missile. She might make the decisions, it might do what she tells it, but it's the real emissary. That's what the Culture's about: machines. You think because Balveda's got two legs and soft skin you should be on her side, but it's the Idirans who are on the side of life in this war—"

"Well, you will shortly be on the other side of *that.*" The Gerontocrat snorted and glanced at Balveda, who was looking from under lowered brows at the man chained to the wall. "Let us go, Miss Balveda," Amahain-Frolk said as he turned and took the woman's arm to guide her from the cell. "This… *thing's* presence smells more than the cell."

Balveda looked up at him then, ignoring the dwarfed minister as he tried to pull her to the door. She gazed right at the prisoner with her clear, black-irised eyes and held her hands out from her sides. "I'm sorry," she said to him.

"Believe it or not, that's rather how I feel," he replied, nodding. "Just promise me you'll eat and drink very little tonight, Balveda. I'd like to think there was one person up there on my side, and it might as well be my worst enemy." He had meant it to be defiant and funny, but it sounded only bitter; he looked away from the woman's face.

"I promise," Balveda said. She let herself be led to the door, and the blue light waned in the dank cell. She stopped right at the door. By sticking his head painfully far out he could just see her. The knife missile was there, too, he noticed, just inside the room; probably there all the time, but he hadn't noticed its sleek, sharp little body hovering there in the darkness. He looked into Balveda's dark eyes as the knife missile moved.

For a second he thought Balveda had instructed the tiny machine to kill him now—quietly and quickly while she blocked Amahain-Frolk's view—and his heart thudded. But the small device simply floated past Balveda's face and out into the corridor. Balveda raised one hand in a gesture of farewell.

"Bora Horza Gobuchul," she said, "goodbye." She turned quickly, stepped from the platform and out of the cell. The walkway was hoisted out and the door slammed, scraping rubber flanges over the grimy floor and hissing once as the internal seals made it watertight. He hung there, looking down at an invisible floor for a moment before going back into the trance that would Change his wrists, thin them down so that he could escape. But something about the solemn, final way Balveda had spoken his name had crushed him inside, and he knew then, if not before, that there was no escape.

...by drowning them in the tears...

His lungs were bursting! His mouth quivered, his throat was gagging, the filth was in his ears but he could hear a great roaring, see lights though it was black dark. His stomach muscles started to go in and out, and he had to clamp his jaw to stop his mouth opening for air that wasn't there. Now. No... *now* he had to give in. Not yet... surely now. Now, now, now, any second; surrender to this awful black vacuum inside him... he had to breathe... *now!*

Before he had time to open his mouth he was smashed against the wall—punched against the stones as though some immense iron fist had slammed into him. He blew out the stale air from his lungs in one convulsive breath. His body was suddenly cold, and every part of it next to the wall throbbed with pain. Death, it seemed, was weight, pain, cold... and too much light...

He brought his head up. He moaned at the light. He tried to see, tried to hear. What was happening? Why was he breathing? Why was he so damn *heavy* again? His body was tearing his arms from their sockets; his wrists were cut almost to the bone. Who had *done* this to him?

Where the wall had been facing him there was a very large and ragged hole which extended beneath the level of the cell floor. All the ordure and garbage had burst out of that. The last few trickles hissed against the hot sides of the breach, producing steam which curled around the figure standing blocking most of the brilliant light from outside, in the open air of Sorpen. The figure was three meters tall and looked vaguely like a small armored spaceship sitting on a tripod of thick legs. Its helmet looked big enough to contain three human heads, side by side. Held almost casually in one gigantic hand was a plasma cannon which Horza would have needed both arms just to lift; the creature's other fist gripped a slightly larger gun. Behind it, nosing in toward the hole, came an Idiran gun-platform, lit vividly by the light of explosions which Horza could now feel through the iron and stones he was attached to. He raised his head to the giant standing in the breach and tried to smile.

"Well," he croaked, then spluttered and spat, "you lot certainly took your time."

Praise for the ARTHUR C. CLARKE, NEBULA, BSFA, and HUGO award-winning *Ancillary Justice*

"Unexpected, compelling and very cool. Ann Leckie nails it."

—John Scalzi

"Establishes Leckie as an heir to Banks and Cherryh."

—Elizabeth Bear

"Powerful, arresting, beautiful space opera.... Leckie makes it look so easy."

—Kameron Hurley

"Total gamechanger. Get it, read it, wish to hell you'd written it. Ann Leckie's *Ancillary Justice* may well be the most important book Orbit has published in ages."

—Paul Graham Raven

"It's by turns thrilling, moving and awe-inspiring."

—*Guardian*

"*Ancillary Justice* is the mind-blowing space opera you've been needing.... This is a novel that will thrill you like the page-turner it is, but stick with you for a long time afterward."

—*io9*

"This impressive debut succeeds in making Breq a protagonist readers will invest in, and establishes Leckie as a talent to watch."

—*Publishers Weekly*

"Assured, gripping, and stylish.... An absorbing thousand-year history, a poignant personal journey, and a welcome addition to the genre." —*NPR Books*

"A stunning, fast-paced debut." —*Shelf Awareness*

"It's not every day a debut novel by an author you'd never heard of before derails your entire afternoon with its brilliance. But when my review copy of *Ancillary Justice* arrived, that's exactly what it did. In fact, it arrowed upward to reach a pretty high position on my list of best space opera novels ever." —Liz Bourke, Tor.com

"This is not entry-level SF, and its payoff is correspondingly greater because of that." —*Locus*

"I cannot find fault in this truly amazing, awe-inspiring debut novel from Ann Leckie.... *Ancillary Justice* is one of the best science fiction novels I've ever read." —*The Book Smugglers*

"Ann Leckie's *Ancillary Justice* does everything science fiction should do. It engages, it excites, and it challenges the way the reader views our world." —*Staffer's Book Review*

Praise for *Ancillary Sword*

"Powerful." —*The New York Times*

"Fans of space operas will feast on its richly textured, gorgeously rendered world-building." —*Entertainment Weekly*

"Leckie proves she's no mere flash in the pan with this follow-up to her multiple-award-winning debut space opera, *Ancillary Justice*."

—*Kirkus*

"The sort of space opera audiences have been waiting for."

—*NPR Books*

"This follow-up builds on the world and characters that the author introduced in the first book and takes the story in new directions. There is much more to explore in Leckie's universe, one of the most original in SF today."

—*Library Journal* (starred review)

"Breq's struggle for meaningful justice in a society designed to favor the strong is as engaging as ever. Readers new to the author will be enthralled, and those familiar with the first book will find that the faith it inspired has not been misplaced."

—*Publishers Weekly*

"A gripping read, with top-notch world building and a set of rich subtexts about human rights, colonialism—and (yes) hive mind sex."

—*io9*

"Superb...*Sword* proves that [Leckie]'s not a one-hit wonder. I look forward to the rest of Breq's tale."

—*St. Louis Post-Dispatch*

"An ambitious space opera that proves that *Justice* was no fluke....A book every serious reader of science fiction should pick up."

—*RT Book Reviews*

By Ann Leckie

Ancillary Justice

Ancillary Sword

Ancillary Mercy

ANCILLARY MERCY

ANN LECKIE

orbit

www.orbitbooks.net
www.orbitshortfiction.com

Orbit
Hachette Book Group
1290 Avenue of the Americas
New York, NY 10104
www.orbitbooks.net

Printed in the United States of America

LSC-C

First edition: October 2015
10 9 8 7 6 5 4

Orbit is an imprint of Hachette Book Group.
The Orbit name and logo are trademarks of Little, Brown Book Group Limited.

Library of Congress Cataloging-in-Publication Data

Leckie, Ann.
Ancillary mercy / Ann Leckie.—First edition.
pages ; cm
ISBN 978-0-316-24668-2 (trade pbk.)—ISBN 978-0-316-24667-5 (ebook)—ISBN 978-1-4789-3631-2 (audio book cd)—ISBN 978-1-4789-6014-0 (audio book [downloadable]) I. Title.

PS3612.E3353A832 2015
813'.6—dc23

2015020915

ANCILLARY MERCY

1

One moment asleep. Awake the next, to the familiar small noises of someone making tea. But it was six minutes earlier than I'd intended. Why? I reached.

Lieutenant Ekalu was on watch. Indignant about something. A little angry, even. Before her the wall displayed a view of Athoek Station, the ships surrounding it. The dome over its gardens barely visible from this angle. Athoek itself half shadowed, half shining blue and white. The background chatter of communications revealed nothing amiss.

I opened my eyes. The walls of my quarters displayed the same view of the space around us that Lieutenant Ekalu watched, in Command—Athoek Station, ships, Athoek itself. The beacons of the system's four intersystem gates. I didn't need the walls to display that view. It was one I could see anywhere, at any time, merely by wishing to. But I had never commanded its actual use here. Ship must have done it.

At the counter at the end of the three-by-four-meter room, Seivarden stood, making tea. With the old enamel set, only two bowls, one of them chipped, a casualty of Seivarden's early, inept attempts to be useful, more than a year ago. It had been more than a month since she'd last acted as my servant, but her presence was so familiar that I had, on waking, accepted it without thinking much about it. "Seivarden," I said.

"Ship, actually." She tilted her head toward me just slightly, her attention still on the tea. *Mercy of Kalr* mostly communicated with its crew via auditory or visual implants, speaking directly into our ears or placing words or images in our visions. It was doing this now, I could see, Seivarden reading words that Ship was giving her. "I'm Ship just now. And two messages came in for you while you slept, but there's nothing immediately wrong, Fleet Captain."

I sat up, pushed the blanket away. Three days before, my shoulder had been encased in a corrective, numbing and immobilizing that arm. I was still appreciating the restored freedom of movement.

Seivarden continued, "I think Lieutenant Seivarden misses this sometimes." The data Ship read from her—which I could see merely by reaching for it—showed some apprehension, mild embarrassment. But Ship was right—she was enjoying this small return to our old roles, even if, I found, I wasn't. "Three hours ago, Fleet Captain Uemi messaged." Fleet Captain Uemi was my counterpart one gate away, in Hrad System. In command over any Radchaai military ships stationed there. For whatever that was worth: Radch space was currently embroiled in a civil war, and Fleet Captain Uemi's authority, like mine, came from the part of Anaander Mianaai that currently held Omaugh Palace. "Tstur Palace has fallen."

"Dare I ask to whom?"

Seivarden turned from the counter, bowl of tea in one gloved hand. Came over to where I sat on my bed. After all this time she was too familiar with me to be surprised at my response, or discomfited by the fact my own hands were still bare. "The Lord of Mianaai, who else?" she replied, with a faint smile. Handed me the bowl of tea. "The one, so Fleet Captain Uemi said, that has very little love for you, Fleet Captain. Or for Fleet Captain Uemi herself."

"Right." To my mind there was very little difference between any of the parts of Anaander Mianaai, Lord of the Radch, and none of her had any real reason to be pleased with me. But I knew which side Fleet Captain Uemi supported. Possibly even was. Anaander was many-bodied, used to being in dozens, if not hundreds, of places at the same time. Now she was reduced and fragmented, many of her cloned bodies lost in the struggle against herself. I strongly suspected that Captain Uemi was herself a fragment of the Lord of the Radch.

"Fleet Captain Uemi added," continued Seivarden, "that the Anaander who has taken over Tstur has also managed to sever her connection with herself outside of Tstur System, so the rest of her doesn't know what she intends. But if Fleet Captain Uemi were Anaander Mianaai, she says, she would devote most of her resources to securing that system, now she's taken the palace itself. But she would also be sorely tempted to send someone after *you*, Fleet Captain, if she possibly could. The captain of the Hrad fleet also begs to point out that the news reached her by way of a ship from Omaugh Palace, so the information is weeks old."

I took a drink of my tea. "If the tyrant was foolish enough to send ships here the moment she gained control of Tstur, the soonest they could possibly arrive would be…" *Mercy of Kalr* showed me numbers. "In about a week."

"That part of the Lord of the Radch has reason to be extremely angry with you," Seivarden pointed out, for Ship. "And she has a history of reacting drastically to those who anger her sufficiently. She'll have come after us sooner, if she could manage it." She frowned at the words that appeared in her vision next, but of course I could see them myself, and knew what they were. "The second message is from System Governor Giarod."

I didn't reply immediately. Governor Giarod was the appointed authority over all of Athoek System. She was also, more or less indirectly, the cause of the injuries that I had only just recovered from. I had, in fact, nearly died sustaining them. Because of who and what I was, I already knew the contents of her message to me. There was no need for Seivarden to say it aloud.

But *Mercy of Kalr* had once had ancillaries—human bodies slaved to its artificial intelligence, hands and feet, eyes and ears for the ship. Those ancillaries were gone, stripped away, and now Ship had an entirely human crew. I knew that the common soldiers aboard sometimes acted for Ship, speaking for it, doing things Ship could no longer do, as though they were the ancillaries it had lost. Generally not in front of me—I myself was an ancillary, the last remaining fragment of the troop carrier *Justice of Toren*, destroyed twenty years ago. I was not amused or comforted by my soldiers' attempts to imitate what I had once been. Still, I hadn't forbidden it. Until very recently, my soldiers hadn't known about my past. And they seemed to find in it a way to shield themselves from the inescapable intimacy of life on a small ship.

But Seivarden had no need for such playacting. She would be doing this because Ship wanted it. Why would Ship want such a thing? "Governor Giarod requests that you return to the station at your earliest convenience," Seivarden said. Ship said. That request, the barely polite gloss of *at your convenience* or not, was more peremptory than was strictly proper.

Seivarden wasn't as indignant at it as Lieutenant Ekalu had been, but she was definitely wondering how I would respond. "The governor didn't explain her request. Though Kalr Five noticed a commotion just outside the Undergarden last night. Security arrested someone, and they've been nervous since." Briefly Ship showed me bits of what Five, still on the station, had seen and heard.

"Wasn't the Undergarden evacuated?" I asked. Aloud, since obviously Ship wanted to have this conversation this way, no matter how I felt about it. "It ought to be empty."

"Exactly," Seivarden replied. Ship.

The majority of Undergarden residents had been Ychana—despised by the Xhai, another Athoeki ethnic group, one that had done better in the annexation than others. Theoretically, when the Radchaai annexed a world, ethnic distinctions became irrelevant. Reality was messier. And some of Governor Giarod's less reasonable fears centered around the Ychana in the Undergarden. "Wonderful. Wake Lieutenant Tisarwat, will you, Ship?" Tisarwat had spent time since we'd arrived here making connections in the Undergarden, and also among the staff of Station Administration.

"I already have," replied Seivarden for *Mercy of Kalr*. "Your shuttle will be ready by the time you've dressed and have eaten."

"Thank you." Found I didn't want to say *Thank you, Ship*, or *Thank you, Seivarden*, either one.

"Fleet Captain, I hope I'm not presuming too much," said Ship, through Seivarden. Disquiet joined Seivarden's mild apprehension—she had agreed to act for Ship, but was suddenly worried, maybe suspecting Ship was coming to the point of it.

"I can't imagine you ever presuming too much, Ship." But of course it could see nearly everything about me—every breath, every twitch of every muscle. More, since I was still wired like an ancillary, even if I wasn't Ship's ancillary. It knew, surely, that its using an officer as a pretend ancillary disturbed me.

"I wanted to ask you, Fleet Captain. Back at Omaugh, you said I could be my own captain. Did you mean that?"

I felt, for an instant, as though the ship's gravity had failed. There was no point in trying not to show my reaction to Ship's words, it could see every detail of my physical responses. Seivarden had never been particularly good at faking impassivity, and her own dismay showed on her aristocratic face. She must not have known that this was what Ship wanted to say. She opened her mouth as though to speak, blinked, and then closed it again. Frowned.

"Yes, I meant it," I replied. Ships weren't people, to Radchaai. We were equipment. Weapons. Tools that functioned as ordered, when required.

"I've been thinking about it, since you said it," said Seivarden. No, said *Mercy of Kalr.* "And I've concluded that I don't want to be a captain. But I find I like the thought that I *could* be." Seivarden clearly wasn't sure if she should be relieved at that or not. She knew what I was, possibly even knew why I had said what I had said, that day at Omaugh Palace, but she was well-born Radchaai, and as used as any other Radchaai officer to expecting her ship would always do exactly as it was told. Would always be there for her.

I had been a ship myself. Ships could feel very, very intensely about their captains, or their lieutenants. I knew that from personal experience. Oh, I did. For most of my two-thousand-year life I hadn't thought there was any reason to want anything else. And the irrevocable loss of my own crew was a gaping hole in myself that I had learned not to look at. Mostly. At the same time, in the last twenty years I had grown accustomed to making my own decisions, without reference to anyone else. To having authority over my own life.

Had I thought that my ship would feel about me the way I had felt about my own captains? Impossible that it would. Ships didn't feel that way about other ships. Had I thought that? Why would I ever think that?

"All right," I said, and took a mouthful of my tea. Swallowed it. There was no reason I could see for Ship to have said that through Seivarden.

But of course, Seivarden was entirely human. And she was *Mercy of Kalr*'s Amaat lieutenant. Perhaps Ship's words hadn't been meant for me, but for her.

Seivarden had never been the sort of officer who cared, or even noticed, what her ship felt. She had not been one of my favorites, when she'd served on *Justice of Toren*. But ships did have different tastes, different favorites. And Seivarden had improved markedly over the last year.

A ship with ancillaries expressed what it felt in a thousand different minute ways. A favorite officer's tea was never cold. Her food would be prepared in precisely the way she preferred. Her uniform always fit right, always sat right, effortlessly. Small needs or desires would be satisfied very nearly the moment they arose. And most of the time, she would only notice that she was comfortable. Certainly more comfortable than other ships she might have served on.

It was—nearly always—distinctly one-sided. All those weeks ago on Omaugh Palace, I had told Ship that it could be a person who could command itself. And now it was telling me—and, not incidentally I was sure, Seivarden—that it wanted to be that, at least potentially. Wanted that to be acknowledged. Wanted, maybe, some small return (or at least some recognition) of its feelings.

I hadn't noticed that Seivarden's Amaats had been particularly solicitous, but then, her Amaats, like all the soldiers on *Mercy of Kalr*, were human, not appendages of their ship. They would have been uncomfortable with the flood of tiny intimacies Ship might have asked of them, if they were to act for it in that way.

"All right," I said again. In her quarters, Lieutenant Tisarwat pulled on her boots. Still waking up—Bo Nine stood by with her tea. The rest of Bo decade slept deeply, some dreaming. Seivarden's Amaats were finishing their day's tasks, getting ready for their suppers. Medic, and half of my Kalrs, still slept, but lightly. Ship would wake them in another five minutes. Ekalu and her Etrepas still stood watch. Lieutenant Ekalu was still a bit indignant over the system governor's message, and also troubled by something else, I wasn't sure what. Outside, dust skittered now and then across *Mercy of Kalr*'s hull, and the light of Athoek's sun warmed it. "Was there anything else?"

There was. Seivarden, on edge since this part of the conversation had begun, blinked, expecting to see some sort of reply in her vision. Nothing, for an entire second. And then, *No, Fleet Captain, that's all.* "No, Fleet Captain," Seivarden read off. "That's all." Her voice doubtful. For someone who knew ships, that brief pause had been eloquent. I was mildly surprised that Seivarden, who had always been oblivious to her ships' feelings, had noticed it. She blinked three times, and frowned. Worried. Disconcerted. Uncharacteristically unsure of herself. Said, "Your tea is getting cold."

"That's all right," I said, and drank it down.

Lieutenant Tisarwat had wanted to go back to Athoek Station for days. We had only been in the system a little over two weeks, but already she had friends, and connections. Had been angling for some sort of influence over system administration, nearly since the moment she had set foot on the station. Which was hardly surprising, considering. Tisarwat hadn't been Tisarwat for some time—Anaander Mianaai, the Lord of the Radch, had altered the hapless seventeen-year-old lieutenant in order to make her nothing more than an appendage of herself, just another part of the Lord of the Radch. One she hoped I wouldn't recognize as such, who could keep an eye on me, and keep control of *Mercy of Kalr.* But I had recognized her, and removed the implants that had tied Tisarwat to the Lord of the Radch, and now she was someone else—a new Lieutenant Tisarwat, with the memories (and possibly some of the inclinations) of the old one, but also someone who had spent several days as the most powerful person in Radch space.

She waited for me just outside the shuttle hatch. Seventeen, not tall exactly but rangy in the way some seventeen-year-olds are who haven't quite grown into themselves. Still groggy from waking, but every hair in place, her dark-brown uniform immaculate. Bo Nine, already aboard the shuttle, would never have let her young lieutenant out of her quarters in any other state. "Fleet Captain." Tisarwat bowed. "Thank you for taking me with you." Her lilac-colored eyes—a remnant of the old Tisarwat, who had been flighty and frivolous, and had spent what was probably her first paycheck on changing the color of her eyes—were serious. Behind that she was genuinely pleased, and a bit excited, even through the meds *Mercy of Kalr*'s medic had given her. The implants the Lord of the Radch had installed hadn't worked properly, had, I suspected, done some permanent damage. My hasty removal of those implants had fixed part of that problem, but perhaps had caused others. Add in her powerful—and entirely understandable—ambivalence about Anaander Mianaai, whom she arguably still shared some identity with, and the result was near-constant emotional distress.

She was feeling all right today, though, from what I could see. "Don't mention it, Lieutenant."

"Sir." She wanted, I saw, to bring something up before we got into the shuttle. "System Governor Giarod is a problem." System Governor Giarod had been appointed by the same authority that had sent me here to Athoek System. In theory we were allies in the cause of keeping this system safe and stable. But she had passed information to my enemies, just days ago, and that had very nearly gotten me killed. And while it was possible she hadn't realized it at the time, she surely knew it now. But no word of that from her, no explanation, no apology, no acknowledgment of any kind. Just this edge-of-disrespectful summons to the station. "At some point," Tisarwat continued, "I think we're going to need a new system governor."

"I doubt Omaugh Palace is going to send us a new one anytime soon, Lieutenant."

"No, sir," replied Tisarwat. "But *I* could do it. I could be governor. I'd be good at it."

"No doubt you would, Lieutenant," I said, evenly. I turned, ready to push myself over the boundary between *Mercy of Kalr*'s artificial gravity and the shuttle's lack of it. Saw that though Tisarwat had held herself absolutely still at my words, she had been hurt by my response. The pain was dulled by meds, but still there.

Being who she was, she had to know I would oppose her bid to be system governor. I still lived only because Anaander Mianaai, the Lord of the Radch, thought or hoped that I might be a danger to her enemy. But of course, Anaander Mianaai's enemy was herself. I didn't care particularly which faction of the Lord of the Radch emerged victorious—they were all, as far as I was concerned, the same. I would just as soon see her entirely destroyed. An aim that was well beyond my ability, but she knew me well enough to know that I would do what damage I could, to all of her. She had hijacked the unfortunate Lieutenant Tisarwat in order to be near enough to control that damage as much as she could. Tisarwat herself had said as much to me, not long after we'd arrived at Athoek Station.

And days ago Tisarwat herself had said, *Do you understand, sir, that we're both doing exactly what she wants? She* being Anaander Mianaai. And I had said that I didn't care much what the Lord of the Radch wanted.

I turned back. Put my hand on Tisarwat's shoulder. Said, more gently, "Let's get through today first, Lieutenant." Or even through the next few weeks or months or more. Radch space was big. The fighting that was happening in the provincial palaces might reach us here at Athoek tomorrow, or next week, or next year. Or it might burn itself out in the palaces and never arrive here at all. But I wouldn't bet on that.

We often speak casually of distances within a single solar system—of a station's being near a moon or a planet, of a gate's being near a system's most prominent station—when in fact those distances are measured in hundreds of thousands, if not millions, of kilometers. And a system's outstations could be hundreds of millions, even billions, of kilometers from those gates.

Days before, *Mercy of Kalr* had been truly, dangerously close to Athoek Station, but now it was only near in a relative sense. We would be a whole day on the shuttle. *Mercy of Kalr* could generate its own gates, shortcuts around normal space, and could have gotten us there much more quickly, but gating close up to a busy station risked colliding with whatever might be in your path as you came out of gate-space. Ship could have done it—had, in fact, quite recently. But for now it was safer to take the shuttle, which was too small to generate its own gravity, let alone make its own gate. Governor Giarod's problem, whatever it was, would have to wait.

And I had plenty of time to consider what I might find on the station. Both factions of Anaander Mianaai (assuming there were only two, which was perhaps not a safe assumption) surely had agents there. But none of them would be military. Captain Hetnys—the enemy of mine to whom System Governor Giarod had so imprudently passed dangerous information—lay frozen in a suspension pod aboard *Mercy of Kalr*, along with all her officers. Her ship, *Sword of Atagaris*, orbited well away from Athoek itself, its engines off-line, its ancillaries all in storage. *Mercy of Ilves*, the only other military ship in the system besides *Sword of Atagaris* and *Mercy of Kalr*, was inspecting the outstations, and its captain had so far shown no inclination to disobey my order to continue doing so. Station Security and Planetary Security were the only remaining armed threat—but "armed," for Security, meant stun sticks. Which wasn't to say Security couldn't pose a threat—they certainly could, particularly to unarmed citizens. But Security was not a threat to me.

Anyone who'd realized I didn't support their faction of the Lord of the Radch would have only political means to move against me. Politics it was, then. Perhaps I should take a cue from Lieutenant Tisarwat and invite the head of Station Security to dinner.

Kalr Five was still on Athoek Station, along with Eight and Ten. The station had been overcrowded even before the Undergarden had been damaged and evacuated, and there weren't beds enough for everyone. My Kalrs had deployed crates and pallets in the corner of a dead-end corridor. On one of those crates sat Citizen Uran, quietly but determinedly conjugating Raswar verbs. The Ychana on Athoek Station mostly spoke Raswar, and our neighbors on the station were mostly Ychana. It would have been easier if she'd been willing to go to Medical to learn the basics under drugs, but she very vehemently had not wanted to do that. Uran was the only nonmilitary member of my small household, barely sixteen, no relation to me or anyone on *Mercy of Kalr*, but I had found myself responsible for her.

Five stood by, to all appearances absorbed in making sure tea was ready for when Uran's tutor arrived in the next few minutes, but in fact keeping a close eye on her. A few meters away, Kalr Eight and Kalr Ten scrubbed the corridor floor, already a good deal less scuffed than it had been and noticeably less gray than what lay outside the household's makeshift boundary. They sang as they worked, quietly, because citizens were sleeping beyond the nearby doorways.

Jasmine grew
In my love's room
It twined all around her bed
The daughters have fasted and shaved their heads
In a month they will visit the temple again
With roses and camellias
But I will sustain myself
With nothing more than the perfume of jasmine flowers
Until the end of my life

It was an old song, older than Eight and Ten themselves, older, probably, than their grandparents. I remembered when it was new. On the shuttle, where neither Eight nor Ten could hear me, I sang it with them. Quietly, since Tisarwat was beside me, strapped into a seat and fast asleep. The shuttle's pilot heard me, though, with a tiny swell of contentment. She had been uneasy about this sudden trip back to the station, and what she'd heard about Governor Giarod's message. But if I was singing, then things were as they should be.

On *Mercy of Kalr*, Seivarden slept, dreaming. Her ten Amaats slept as well, close in their bunks. Bo decade (under the direction of Bo One, since Tisarwat was in the shuttle with me) was just awake, running thoughtless and ragged through the morning prayer (*The flower of justice is peace. The flower of propriety is beauty in thought and action*...).

Not long after, Medic came off watch, found Lieutenant Ekalu in the tiny, white-walled decade room, staring at her supper. "Are you all right?" Medic asked, and sat down beside her. The Etrepa in attendance set a bowl of tea on the table in front of her.

"I'm fine," lied Ekalu.

"We've served together a long time," Medic replied. Ekalu, discomfited, did not look up, or say anything in response. "Before you were promoted, you'd have gone to your decademates for support, but you can't go to them anymore. They're Seivarden's now." Before I'd come—before *Mercy of Kalr*'s last captain had been arrested for treason—Ekalu had been Amaat One. "And I suppose you feel like you can't go to your Etrepas." The Etrepa attending Ekalu stood impassive in a corner of the room. "Plenty of other lieutenants would, but they didn't come up out of the decades, did they." Didn't add that Ekalu might be worried about undermining her authority with shipmates who'd known her for years as a common soldier. Didn't add that Ekalu knew firsthand how unequal such an exchange might be, to demand any sort of comfort or emotional support from the soldiers serving under her. "I daresay you're the first to do it, to come up out of the decades."

"No," replied Ekalu, voice flat. "Fleet Captain was." Me, she meant. "You knew the whole time, I suppose." That I was an ancillary, and not human, she meant.

"Is that the problem then?" asked Medic. She hadn't touched the tea the Etrepa had given her. "Fleet Captain is first?"

"No, of course not." Ekalu looked up, finally, and her impassive expression flickered for just a moment into something different, but then it was gone. "Why would it?" I knew she was telling the truth.

Medic made a gesture of unconcern. "Some people get jealous. And Lieutenant Seivarden is . . . very attached to Fleet Captain. And you and Lieutenant Seivarden . . ."

"It would be stupid to be jealous of Fleet Captain," said Ekalu, voice bland. She meant that, too. Her statement might conceivably be taken for an insult, but I knew that wasn't her intention. And she was right. It didn't make any sense at all to be jealous of me.

"That sort of thing," observed Medic, dryly, "doesn't always make sense." Ekalu said nothing. "I've sometimes wondered what went through Seivarden's mind when she discovered Fleet Captain was an ancillary. Not even human!" And then, in response to the merest flicker of an expression across Ekalu's face, "But she's not. Fleet Captain will tell you so herself, I imagine."

"Are you going to call Fleet Captain *it* instead of *she*?" Ekalu challenged. And then looked away. "Your gracious pardon, Medic. It just sits wrong with me."

Because I could see what Ship saw, I saw Medic's dubious reaction to Ekalu's overly formal apology, Ekalu's suddenly careful attempt to erase her usual lower-house accent. But Medic had known Ekalu a long time, and most of that when Ekalu had still been, as Medic put it, in the decades. "I think," Medic said, "that Seivarden imagines she understands what it is to be on the bottom of the heap. Certainly she's learned it's possible to find oneself there despite good family and impeccable manners and every indication Aatr has granted you a life of happiness and plenty. She's learned it's possible that someone she'd dismissed and disregarded might be worthy of her respect. And now she's learned it, she fancies she understands *you*." Another thought struck her. "That's why you don't like my saying the fleet captain's not human, isn't it."

"I've never been at the bottom of any heap." Still carefully broadening her vowels in imitation of Medic or Tisarwat. Of Seivarden. Or of me. "And I said there wasn't anything wrong."

"I'm mistaken, then," replied Medic, no rancor or sarcasm in her voice. "I beg your indulgent pardon, Lieutenant." More formal than she needed to be with Ekalu, whom she'd known so long. Whose doctor she had been, all that time.

"Of course, Medic."

Seivarden still slept. Unaware of her fellow lieutenant's (and lover's) discomfiture. Unaware, I feared, of Ship's favorable regard. What I had begun to suspect was its strong affection. Any number of things, Ship wouldn't hesitate to say quite directly, but never that, I was sure.

Beside me, on the shuttle, Tisarwat muttered, and stirred, but didn't wake. I turned my thoughts to what I might find on Athoek Station when we reached it, and what I ought to do about it.

2

I met Governor Giarod in her office, its cream-and-green silk hangings today covering even the broad window that looked out onto Athoek Station's main concourse, where citizens crossed the scuffed white floor, came or went from Station Administration, or stood talking in front of the temple of Amaat with its huge reliefs of the four Emanations. Governor Giarod was tall, broad-shouldered, outwardly serene, but I knew from experience she was liable to misgivings, and to acting on those misgivings at the least convenient moments. She offered me a seat, which I took, and tea, which I refused. Kalr Five, who had met me at the docks, stood impassive just behind me. I considered ordering her to the door, or even out into the corridor, but decided that an obvious reminder of who I was and what resources I commanded might be useful.

Governor Giarod couldn't help but notice the soldier looming straight and stiff behind me, but pretended she did not. "Once the gravity came back on, Fleet Captain, Station Administrator Celar felt—and I agreed—that we should do a thorough inspection of the Undergarden, to be sure it was structurally sound." A few days earlier the public gardens, just above the part of the station that had been named for them, had begun to collapse, almost flooding the four levels below them. Athoek Station's AI had solved the immediate problem by turning off the entire station's gravity while the Undergarden was evacuated.

"Did you find dozens of unauthorized people hiding there, as you feared?" Every Radchaai had a tracker implanted at birth, so that no citizen was ever lost or invisible to any watching AI. Particularly here in the relatively small space of Athoek Station, the idea that anyone could be moving secretly, or here without Station's knowledge, was patently ridiculous. And yet the belief that the Undergarden hid crowds of such people, all of them a threat to law-abiding citizens, was alarmingly common.

"You think such fears are foolish," replied Governor Giarod. "And yet our inspection turned up just such a person, hiding in the access tunnels between levels three and four."

I asked, voice even, "Only one?"

Governor Giarod gestured acknowledgment of my point—one person was nowhere near what some—including, apparently, the governor—had feared. "She's Ychana." Most of the residents of the Undergarden had been Ychana. "No one will admit to knowing anything about her, though it's fairly obvious some of them did know her. She's in a cell in Security. I thought you might like to know, especially given the fact that the last person who did something like this was an alien." Translator Dlique, the sort-of-human representative of the mysterious—and terrifying—Presger. Who before the treaty with the Radch—with, actually, all humanity, since the Presger didn't make distinctions between one sort of human and another—had torn apart human ships, and humans, for sport. Who were so powerful no human force, not even a Radchaai one, could destroy them, or even defend against them. Presger Translator Dlique, it had turned out, could deceive Station's sensors with alarming ease, and had had no patience for being safely confined to the governor's residence. Her dead body lay in a suspension pod in Medical, waiting for the hopefully distant day when the Presger came looking for her, and we had to explain that a *Sword of Atagaris* ancillary had shot her, on the suspicion that she'd vandalized a wall in the Undergarden.

At least the search that had turned up this one person ought to have allayed fears of a horde of murderous Ychana. "Did you look at her DNA? Is she closely related to anyone else in the Undergarden?"

"What an odd question, Fleet Captain! Do you know something you haven't shared with me?"

"Many things," I replied, "but most of them wouldn't interest you. She isn't, is she?"

"She isn't," replied Governor Giarod. "And Medical tells me she's carrying some markers that haven't been seen since before the annexation of Athoek." *Annexation* was the polite term for the Radchaai invasion and colonization of entire star systems. "Since she can't possibly be recently descended from a line that went extinct centuries ago, the only other possibility—in the loosest sense of that word—is that she's over six hundred years old."

There was another possibility, but Governor Giarod hadn't seen it yet. "I imagine that's probably the case. Though she'll have been suspended for a fair amount of that time."

Governor Giarod frowned. "You know who she is?"

"Not who," I said, "not specifically. I have some suspicions as to *what* she is. May I speak to her?"

"Are you going to share your suspicions with me?"

"Not if they prove unfounded." All I needed was for Governor Giarod to add another phantom enemy to her list. "I'd like to speak with her, and I'd like a medic to be brought to examine her again. Someone sensible, and discreet."

The cell was tiny, two meters by two, a grate and a water supply in one corner. The person squatting on the scuffed floor, staring at a bowl of skel, obviously her supper, seemed unremarkable at first examination. She wore the bright-colored loose shirt and trousers most of the Ychana in the Undergarden preferred, yellow and orange and green. But this person also wore plain gray gloves, suspiciously new-looking. Likely they had come quite recently from Station stores, and Security had insisted she put them on. Hardly anyone in the Undergarden wore gloves, it was just one more reason to believe the people who lived there were uncivilized, unsettlingly, perhaps even dangerously, foreign. Not Radchaai at all.

There was no way to signal that I wanted to come in—not even the pretense of privacy, in Security's custody. Station—the AI that controlled Athoek Station, that was for all intents and purposes the station itself—opened the door at my request. The person squatting on the floor didn't even look up. "May I come in, citizen?" I asked. Though *citizen* was almost certainly the wrong term of address here, it was, in Radchaai, very nearly the only polite one possible.

The person didn't answer. I came in, a matter of a single step, and squatted across from her. Kalr Five stopped in the doorway. "What's your name?" I asked. Governor Giarod had said that this person had refused to speak, from the moment she'd been arrested. She was scheduled for interrogation the next morning. But of course, for an interrogation to work, you had to know what questions to ask. Chances were, no one here did.

"You won't be able to keep your secret," I continued, addressing the person squatting on the floor in front of me staring at her bowl of skel. They had left her no utensil to eat it with—fearing, perhaps, that she might do herself an injury with it. She would have to eat the thick leaves with her hands, or put her face into the bowl, either option unpleasant and demeaning, to a Radchaai. "You're scheduled for an interrogation in the morning. I'm sure they'll be as careful as they can, but I don't think it's ever a terribly pleasant experience." And, like a lot of people annexed by the Radch, most Ychana were convinced that interrogation was inseparable from the re-education a convicted criminal would undergo to ensure she wouldn't offend again. Certainly the drugs used were the same, and an incompetent interrogator could do a good deal of damage to a person. Even the most Radchaai of Radchaai had something of a horror of interrogation and re-education, and tried to avoid mentioning either one, would walk all around the topics even when they were obviously staring them in the face.

Still no answer. She did not even look up. I was just as capable as this person was of sitting in silence. I thought of asking Station to show me what it could see of her—certainly temperature changes, possibly heart rate, possibly more. I didn't doubt that what sensors existed here in Security were set to pick up as much information as possible from inmates. But I doubted I would see anything surprising in that data. "Do you know any songs?" I asked.

Almost, I thought I saw a change, however small, in the set of her shoulders, in the way she held herself. My question had surprised her. It was, I had to admit, an inane one. Nearly everyone I had met, in my two-thousand-year life, had known at least a few songs. Station said, in my ear, "That surprised her, Fleet Captain."

"No doubt," I responded, silently. Didn't look up as Five stepped back into the corridor to make way for Eight, carrying a box, gold inlaid with red and blue and green. Before I had left the governor's office, I had messaged to ask her to bring it. I gestured to her to set it on the floor beside me. And when she had done so, I opened the lid.

The box had once held an antique tea set—flask, strainer, bowls for twelve—of blue and green glass, and gold. It had survived three thousand years unbroken—possibly more. Now it was in fragments, shattered, strewn around the box's interior, or collected in the depressions that had once held its pieces snug and safe. Unbroken, it had been worth several fortunes. In pieces it was still a prize.

The person squatting on the floor in front of me turned her head, finally, to look at it. Said, in an even voice, in Radchaai, "Who did this?"

"Surely you knew," I said, "when you traded it away, that something like this might happen. Surely you knew that no one else could possibly treasure it as much as you did."

"I don't know what you're talking about." Still she stared at the broken tea set. Still her voice was even. She spoke Radchaai with the same accent I'd heard from other Ychana in the Undergarden. "This is obviously valuable, and whoever broke it was obviously someone entirely uncivilized."

"I think she's upset, Fleet Captain," said Station, in my ear. "She's reacted emotionally, anyway. It's hard to be more definite, with only externals, when I don't know someone well."

I knew how that worked, from personal experience. But I didn't say so. I replied, silently, "Thank you, Station, that's good to know." I knew, also from personal experience, just how helpful an AI could be when it liked you. And how obstructive and unhelpful one could be when it had some reason for dislike or resentment. I was genuinely, pleasantly surprised to find Station volunteering information for me. Aloud I said, to the person crouched in front of me, "What's your name?"

"Fuck you," she said, even and bland. Still looking at that shattered tea set.

"What was the captain's name, that you removed before you traded the tea set away?" The inscription on the inside of the box lid had been altered to remove a name that, I suspected, might allow someone to trace it back to its origin.

"Why wait until tomorrow to interrogate me?" she asked. "Do it now. Then you'll have answers to all your questions."

"Heart rate increase," said Station, into my ear. "Her respiration is faster."

Ah. Aloud I said, "There's a fail-safe, then. The drugs will kill you. This part of you, anyway."

She looked at me, finally. Blinked, slowly. "Fleet Captain Breq Mianaai, are you sure you're quite all right? That didn't make any sense at all."

I closed the box. Picked it up, and rose. Said, "Captain Hetnys sold the set to a Citizen Fosyf Denche. Fosyf's daughter broke it, and Fosyf decided it had lost all value, and threw it away." I turned and handed the box to Five, who had replaced Eight in the doorway again. Properly speaking, the tea set was hers. She was the one who had gone to the trouble of fishing it, all of its pieces, out of the trash after Raughd

Denche, in a devastated fury at her mother's disowning her, had dashed it to the ground. "It was good to meet you. I hope to talk to you again soon."

As I exited Security onto the station's main concourse, Kalr Five behind me, carrying her shattered tea set, Station said in my ear, "Fleet Captain, the head priest has just left Governor Giarod's office and is looking for you."

In Radch space, *head priest* with no other modifiers meant the head priest of Amaat. On Athoek Station, the head priest of Amaat was a person named Ifian Wos. I had met her when she had officiated—somewhat resentfully—at Translator Dlique's funeral. Beyond that I had not spoken to her.

"Thank you, Station." As I said it, Eminence Ifian exited the governor's residence, turned immediately in my direction, and made her way toward me. Station had no doubt told her where I was.

I didn't want to talk to her just now. I wanted to talk to Governor Giarod about the person in custody in Security, and then see to some questions about my soldiers' quarters. But Station fairly clearly hadn't told me Head Priest Ifian was looking for me so that I could avoid her. And even if I attempted it now, I wouldn't be able to do so forever, short of fleeing the station entirely.

I walked to the middle of the scuffed, once-white floor of the concourse and stopped. "Fleet Captain!" called the head priest, and bowed as she reached me. A nicely calculated bow, I thought, not one millimeter deeper than my rank demanded. She was two centimeters shorter than I was, and slender, with a low and carrying voice, and held herself and spoke with the sure confidence of someone with the sort of connections and resources that made appointment to a high-ranking priesthood possible. Citizens passed to either side of us where we stood, their coats and jackets sparkling with jewelry, with memorial and associational pins. The ordinary, everyday traffic on the concourse. Most of those who came near us affected to ignore us, though some looked sidelong at us, curious. "Such shocking events, the past few days!" Eminence Ifian continued, as though we were merely friendly acquaintances, gossiping. "Though of course we've all known Captain Hetnys for *years*, and I don't think anyone could have expected her to do anything untoward!" The many pins on Head Priest Ifian's impeccably tailored purple coat flashed and sparkled, trembling momentarily in the extremity of the head priest's doubt that Captain Hetnys might ever do wrong.

Captain Hetnys, of course, had just days ago threatened to kill Horticulturist Basnaaid Elming in order to gain some sort of control over me. Horticulturist Basnaaid was the younger sister of someone who had been a lieutenant of mine, when I had been the troop carrier *Justice of Toren*. I had only consented to come to Athoek because Basnaaid was here, because I owed her long-dead sister a debt I could in fact never truly repay. "Indeed," I replied, the most diplomatic response possible.

"And I suppose you *do* have the authority to detain her," Eminence Ifian continued, her tone just the smallest bit dubious. My confrontation with Captain Hetnys had ended with the Gardens a shambles and the entire station without gravity for several days. She now slept frozen in a suspension pod so that she couldn't make any more spectacularly, foolishly dangerous moves. "Military matters no doubt. And Citizen Raughd. Such a nice, well-bred young person." Raughd Denche had attempted to kill me, mere days before Captain

Hetnys's *untoward* behavior. "Surely they'll have had *reasons* for what they did, surely that should be taken into account! But, Fleet Captain, that's not what I wanted to talk to you about. And of course I don't want to keep you standing here on the concourse. Perhaps we could have tea?"

"I'm afraid, Eminence," I replied, smooth and bland, "that I'm terribly busy. I'm on my way to meet with Governor Giarod, and then I very much need to see about my own soldiers, who have been sleeping at the end of a station corridor for the past few nights." Station Administration was surely awash in complaints just now, and no one was going to look out for the interests of my own small household if I didn't.

"Yes, yes, Fleet Captain, that was one of the things I wanted to discuss with you! You know, the Undergarden used to be quite a fashionable neighborhood. Not, perhaps, as fashionable as the apartments overlooking the concourse." She gestured around, upward, at the windows lining the second story of this, the center of station life and its largest open space besides the Gardens. "Perhaps if the Undergarden *had* been equally fashionable, it would have been repaired long ago! But things are as they are." She made a pious gesture, submission to the will of God. "*Lovely* apartments, I've heard. I can only *imagine* what shape they're in now, after so many years of Ychana squatting there. But I *do* hope the original assignments will be taken into account, now there's a refit underway."

I wondered how many of those families were even still here. "I am unable to assist you, Eminence. I have no authority over housing assignments. You would do better to speak to Station Administrator Celar."

"I spoke to the station administrator, Fleet Captain, and

she told me that *you* had insisted on current arrangements. I'm sure leaving everyone where they are seems practical to you, but really, there are *special circumstances* here. And this morning's cast was *quite concerning*."

It was possible the head priest was championing this cause entirely out of concern for families who hoped to return to the Undergarden. But she was also a friend of Captain Hetnys's—Captain Hetnys, who had been working for the part of the Lord of the Radch who had killed Lieutenant Awn Elming. The part of the Lord of the Radch who had destroyed the troop carrier *Justice of Toren*—that is to say, the part of the Lord of the Radch who had destroyed me. And the timing of this, just when it had become clear that I was not a supporter of that side of Anaander Mianaai, was suspicious. That, and the bringing to bear of the daily omen casting. I had met quite a few priests in my long life, and found that they were, by and large, like anyone else—some generous, some grasping; some kind, some cruel; some humble, some self-aggrandizing. Most were all of those things, in various proportions, at various times. Like anyone else, as I said. But I had learned to be wary whenever a priest suggested that her personal aims were, in fact, God's will.

"How comforting," I replied, my voice and my expression steadily serious, "to think that in these difficult times God is still concerned with the details of housing assignments. I myself have no time to discuss them just now." I bowed, as perfectly respectful as the head priest had been, and walked away from her, across the concourse toward the governor's residence.

"It's interesting, isn't it," said Station in my ear, "that the gods are only now interested in refitting the Undergarden."

"*Very* interesting," I replied, silently. "Thank you, Station."

* * *

"An ancillary!" Disbelief was obvious in Governor Giarod's face, her voice. "Where's the ship?"

"On the other side of the Ghost Gate." A gate that led to a dead-end system, where the Athoeki had intended to expand, before the annexation, but it had never happened. There were vague rumors that the system was haunted. Captain Hetnys and *Sword of Atagaris* had shown an unaccountable interest in that gate. Shortly after *Mercy of Kalr* had arrived in the system, an unbelievably old supply locker had come through it. I was convinced now that Kalr Five's shattered tea set had also come through that gate, in exchange for shipments of suspended human beings. They were supposed to be cheap, unskilled labor for Athoek, but Captain Hetnys had stolen them, sold them to someone on the other side of the Ghost Gate. "You remember, a few days ago we talked about suspended transportees being stolen." She could hardly have forgotten it, considering the events of the last few days. "And it was difficult to imagine what the purpose might be behind that theft. I think there's been a ship on the other side of that gate for quite some time, and it's been buying bodies to use as its ancillaries. It used to buy them from Athoeki slavers—which is how it had an Ychana body from before the annexation it could send here, and blend in." More or less, at least. "When the annexation shut down its supply, it bought them from Radchaai officials who were corrupt and greedy enough to sell transportees." I gestured to Five, standing behind where I sat, to open the tea set box.

"That's Fosyf's," said Governor Giarod. And then, realizing, "Captain Hetnys sold it to her."

"You never asked until now where Captain Hetnys got such a thing." I gestured to the inscription on the inside of the lid. "You also never noticed that someone had very carefully removed the name of the original owner. If you read Notai"—the language in which that inscription was written—"or if you'd seen enough of these, you'd have noticed that immediately."

"What are you saying, Fleet Captain?"

"It's not a Radchaai ship we're dealing with." Or it *was* a Radchaai ship. There was the Radch, the birthplace of Anaander Mianaai more than three thousand years ago, when she'd been a single, very ambitious person in a single body. And then there was the enormous territory Anaander had built around that over the past three thousand years—Radch-controlled space, but what connection was there anymore, between those two? And the inhabitants of the Radch, and the space immediately around it, hadn't all been in favor of what Mianaai had done. There had been battles over it. Wars. Ships and captains destroyed. Many of them had been Notai. From the Radch. "Not one of Anaander's, I mean. It's Notai." The Notai were Radchaai, of course. People in Radch space—and outside it—tended to think of "Radchaai" as being one thing, when in fact it was a good deal more complicated than that, or at least it had been when Anaander had first begun to move outward from the Radch.

"Fleet Captain." Governor Giarod was aghast. Disbelieving. "Those are *stories*. Defeated ships from that war, wandering space for thousands of years…" She shook her head. "It's the sort of thing you'd find in a melodramatic entertainment. It's not *real*."

"I don't know how long it's been there," I said. "Since before the annexation, at least." It had to have been there since before the annexation, if it had been buying ancillary bodies from Athoeki slavers. "But it's there. And," I continued, relieved that the medic who had examined the captive ancillary hadn't seen me in person, to turn her newly tuned implants on me, had given the governor her observations without betraying me, "it's here. I doubt any Undergarden resident will say much about her." The Undergarden had been damaged, years ago, in a way that made Station unable to sense much of what happened there. It was the perfect hiding place, for someone like this ancillary. So long as it avoided being seen by someone wired to send sensory data to Station—and that wasn't very common, in the Undergarden, unlike the rest of the station—it could move unnoticed, with no one realizing it shouldn't be there. "I'm guessing it realized something was going on, when communications were lost with the palaces, and when traffic was disrupted, so it sent an ancillary to see if it could find out what. Even if the ancillary was captured, its secret would likely have been safe. There's a fail-safe that will kill it if interrogation drugs are administered. And the implants are hidden, and likely no one would think to look for them. Possibly the fail-safe is rigged to destroy what evidence there is to begin with."

"You guessed all this from Citizen Fosyf's tea set."

"Yes, actually. I would have been clearer about my suspicion, earlier, but I wanted more proof. It is, as you've noted, rather difficult to believe."

Governor Giarod was silent a moment, frowning. Thinking, I hoped, of her part in the affair. Then she said, "So what do we do now?"

"I recommend installing a tracker, and putting it on the ration list."

"But surely, Fleet Captain, if it's an ancillary...an ancillary can't be a citizen. A ship can't."

I waited, just a fraction of a second, to see if Station would say anything to her, but there was no change in the governor's expression. "I'm sure Security doesn't want that cell permanently occupied. What else are we going to do with it?" I gestured irony. "Assign it a job," I continued. "Nothing sensitive, of course, and nothing that gives it access to vulnerable station systems. Confirm its housing assignment in the Undergarden."

Governor Giarod's expression changed, just the smallest bit. The head priest had brought the issue to her, then. "Fleet Captain, I realize housing assignments are Station Administrator Celar's business, but I confess I don't like rewarding illegal activity. No one should have been living in the Undergarden to begin with." I said nothing, only looked at her. "It's good you've taken an interest in your neighbors," she went on after a pause, doubtfully, as though she wasn't actually quite certain of that. "But I personally would much rather see those quarters assigned to law-abiding citizens." Still I said nothing. "I think it might be more efficient to rethink the housing assignments in the Undergarden, rethink the refit, and consider sending some citizens downwell in the meantime."

Which would be fine if they wanted to go down to the planet, but I suspected that if the citizens in question were current Undergarden residents, what they wanted wouldn't be a consideration. And likely most of them had spent their entire lives on the station, and didn't want or weren't suited for the kinds of jobs available downwell, on short notice. "This is, as you say, Governor, a matter for Station Administrator Celar." Station Administrator Celar was in charge of Athoek Station's operations. Things like residential assignments were under her authority, and though she technically answered to Governor Giarod, such fine-grained details of station life were usually beneath a system governor's notice. And Administrator Celar was popular enough that Governor Giarod likely would much prefer to settle such a matter amicably, behind the scenes.

Governor Giarod replied, smoothly, "But you've asked her to make those illicit Undergarden living arrangements official. I suspect she'd be more open to considering changing those arrangements, if you talked to her." *That* was interesting. Almost I expected Station to comment, but it said nothing. Neither did I. "People are going to be unhappy about this."

I considered asking Station outright if the governor intended a deliberate threat. But Station's silence now, when it had been almost chatty minutes before, was telling to me, and I knew it wouldn't like my pushing too hard on the places where it felt uncomfortable or conflicted. And its offered goodwill was a new and delicate thing. "Undergarden residents aren't people?"

"You know what I mean, Fleet Captain." Exasperated. "These are unsettled times, as you yourself reminded me not long ago. We can't afford to be at war with our own citizens just now."

I smiled, a small, noncommittal expression. "Indeed, we can't." Governor Giarod's relationship with Captain Hetnys had been, I was sure, somewhat ambivalent. That didn't rule out her possibly being my enemy now. But if she was, she apparently wasn't willing to move against me openly just yet. I was, after all, the one of us with the armed ship, and the soldiers. "Let's be sure that includes *all* of our citizens, shall we, Governor?"

3

Housing, on a Radchaai station, takes several different forms. The assumption is that one generally lives in a household—parents, grandparents, aunts, cousins, perhaps servants and clients if one's family is wealthy enough. Sometimes such households are organized around a particular station official—the governor's residence, or the head priest's household adjacent to the temple of Amaat on the concourse, where surely a number of junior priests also lived.

If you grew up in such a household, or took an assignment associated with one, you didn't need to request housing from Station Administration. Your housing assignment had been made long before you were born, long before the aptitudes sent you to your post. It helped, of course, to belong to a family that had been present when a station was first built, or annexed. Or to be related to one somehow. When I had been a ship, every one of my officers who had lived on stations had belonged to such households.

If a citizen doesn't belong to such a household, they're still due housing, as every citizen is. A citizen without sufficient status, or the backing of a larger, more powerful house, might find herself assigned to a bunk in a dormitory, not much different from what I had been accustomed to as an ancillary, or the common soldiers' quarters on board *Mercy of Kalr*. Or one of a series of suspension-pod-size compartments, each one large enough to sleep in and perhaps hold a change of clothes or a few small possessions. Athoek Station had both of these sorts of quarters. But they were all full, because the recent destruction of several intersystem gates had re-routed ships here, and trapped others. And the closure of the Undergarden had added several hundred more citizens who needed somewhere to sleep. My Mercy of Kalrs had set up our makeshift lodgings just beyond a doorway that led to a room full of bunks, dark and quiet despite the hour, one when most station residents would be awake. Overcrowded, certainly, and likely people were sleeping in shifts.

Eight was relieved to see me, for some reason, but also filled with indecision and ambivalence. Days ago she'd thought me entirely human. Now she knew, as everyone aboard *Mercy of Kalr* did, that I was not, that I was an ancillary. Now she knew, too, how much I objected to my soldiers' playing ancillary themselves. She was at a loss as to how to speak to me.

"Eight," I said. "Everything's under control, I see. No surprise there."

"Thank you, sir." Eight's uncertainty barely showed in her face or her voice—should she continue her habitual ancillary-like impassiveness, or not? Suddenly even this small interaction was precarious, where before all had been clear to her. Kalr Five felt the same, I saw, but covered her doubt with the business of stowing her precious tea set. Eight continued, "Will you have tea, sir?"

I didn't doubt that even here in the middle of a hallway

Eight could, and would, produce tea for me if I said that I wanted it. “Thank you, no. I’ll have water.” I sat on a packing crate, turned so I could see down the open end of the corridor.

“Sir,” Eight acknowledged. Impassive, but my reply had cast her further into doubt. Of course. Ancillaries drank water, not tea, which was only for humans, a luxury—a necessary one, it sometimes seemed. Not that there was any sort of prohibition, but one didn’t waste such luxuries on equipment. There was no answer I could have given to the question of what I would drink without seeming to send some message, or imply something about what I was or wasn’t.

As Eight handed me the water I’d asked for—in the best porcelain she had access to just now, I noticed, the violet-and-aqua Bractware—someone came out of the nearby dormitory, turned to walk down the corridor toward where I sat. She was Ychana, dressed in the light, loose shirt and trousers nearly all the Ychana residents of the Undergarden wore. I recognized her as the person who had confronted Lieutenant Tisarwat two weeks ago, to complain—with some justice—that our proposed plans for the refit and repair of the Undergarden had not taken into account the needs and desires of Undergarden residents themselves. But I had not actually been present at that confrontation. It had been conveyed to me by Ship, who had seen and heard it through Tisarwat herself. This person would have no reason to think I would recognize her.

But she could have no other business coming to the end of the corridor like this than speaking to me, or to one of my Kalrs. I drank my water, handed the bowl to Five, and rose. “Citizen,” I said, and bowed. “Can I be of some assistance?”

“Fleet Captain,” she said, and bowed herself. “There was a meeting yesterday.” A meeting of Undergarden residents, she meant—it was how they settled matters that affected everyone generally. "I know you and the lieutenant were unable to attend or of course you would have been notified."

On the surface, entirely reasonable. Tisarwat and I had been away from the station, either aboard *Mercy of Kalr* or en route here. But of course any of my Kalrs that were still on the station might have been notified of such a meeting, and I knew they hadn't been. The meeting had never been meant to include any of us, then, but saying so directly was a difficult matter, and I didn't doubt this citizen was hoping I wouldn't bring the question up. "Of course, citizen," I replied. "Will you sit?" I gestured to the nearest crate. "I don't think there's tea ready, but we'd be happy to make some."

"Thank you, Fleet Captain, no." Her message would be something awkward, then, and she was not looking forward to my reaction to it. Or perhaps to Lieutenant Tisarwat's reaction. "The young lieutenant very kindly set up an office on level four of the Undergarden, to make it more convenient for residents to bring their desires and concerns to Station Administration. This has of course been very helpful, but perhaps her other duties have been neglected."

Definitely not looking forward to Tisarwat's reaction. "And the consensus of the meeting was that someone else ought to be running that office when it opens again, I take it."

This citizen's unease was barely visible, but definitely there. "Yes, Fleet Captain. We wish to emphasize, there's no suggestion of any complaint on our part, or any impropriety on the young lieutenant's."

"You just think it might be better for that office to more directly represent the concerns of the majority of Undergarden residents," I acknowledged.

Surprise flashed across her face, and then was gone. She

had not expected me to speak so directly. "As you say, Fleet Captain."

"And Citizen Uran?" Uran wasn't one of my soldiers, of course wasn't in any way related to me, but she was nonetheless a member of my household, and had spent her mornings assisting in Tisarwat's level four office. She was Valskaayan, the child of transportees sent to Athoek a generation ago and set to picking the tea that grew downwell, and was shipped out all over Radch space.

"The Valskaayan child? Yes, of course, she's welcome to continue. Please tell her so."

"I'll speak to her," I replied, "and Lieutenant Tisarwat, both."

Tisarwat definitely wasn't happy. "But sir!" Urgent. Whispering, since we were still in the corridor end, squatting on the scuffed floor behind the crate perimeter. She took a breath. Said, a trace less fervently but still in a whisper, "You realize, sir, that in all likelihood we're going to have to find a way to govern here. We need influence to do that. We've made a good start, we've put ourselves at a crucial part of..." And then remembered that unlike in our quarters in the Undergarden, Station could hear what we said, was almost certainly listening, and might or might not report what it heard to Governor Giarod. "There is no higher authority for the governor to appeal to, no other source of support in a crisis. It's just us."

Eight and Ten were away, picking up our suppers at the nearest common refectory—no cooking here. Five stood guard at our improvised boundaries, pretending she couldn't hear any of this conversation. "Lieutenant," I said, "I would hope that *you* would realize that I have no desire to govern here. I am perfectly happy to let the Athoeki govern themselves."

She blinked, bewildered. "Sir, you aren't serious. If the

Athoeki could have governed themselves, we wouldn't *be* here. And the community-meeting thing is perfectly fine so long as you're not doing anything that needs decisive action that instant. Or even in the next few *centuries*."

In all my two thousand years, I had never noticed that any particular kind of government made any difference, once Anaander Mianaai had given the order for annexation. "Lieutenant, you are about to throw away what goodwill you've built up here. Considering these are our neighbors, and we may be here for some time, I would prefer you not do that."

She took a breath. Calming herself. She was hurt, and angry. Felt betrayed. "Station Administration won't be disposed to listen directly to the Ychana in the Undergarden. They never have been."

"Then urge them to begin, Lieutenant. You've already made a start on that. Continue."

Another breath. Somewhat mollified. "What about Citizen Uran?"

"They've asked that she continue working. They didn't explain why."

"Because she's *Valskaayan*! Because she's not Xhai or outsystem Radchaai!"

"They didn't say, but if that is part of the reason, can you blame them, considering? And I recall you yourself mentioned exactly that, when you were trying to convince me Citizen Uran should work for you."

Lieutenant Tisarwat took a deep, gulping breath. Opened her mouth to speak, but stopped. Took another breath. Said, almost pleading, "You still don't *trust* me!"

I had been so intent on the conversation that I had not paid much attention to anything else. Now Kalr Five spoke, forestalling my reply to Tisarwat. "How can I assist you, citizen?"

I reached. The Notai ancillary, from Security, stood just outside our low wall. Still wearing the Ychana tunic and trousers and those gray gloves, holding, now, a bundle of gray fabric under one arm. "They let me go, and gave me clothes," it said now, in matter-of-fact reply to Five, "and said that they regretted they had no suitable employment for me, but as that wasn't my fault I could still eat, and have a bunk for a specific six hours out of the day. I'm told all this is at the request of Fleet Captain Breq Mianaai, who I'm certain will have arranged more comfortable circumstances for herself and her household, so she might as well take responsibility for me."

Kalr Five's anger and resentment didn't show on her face, of course. Neither did a strange sense of unease that was, I suspected, due to her knowledge that the person talking to her was, in fact, an ancillary.

I rose before Five could respond. "Citizen," I said, though I knew the address was technically incorrect. An ancillary wasn't due any sort of courtesy title. "You're welcome to stay with us, though I fear that until the Undergarden is open again, our situation won't be much more comfortable than anyone else's." No response, the ancillary just stood there, solemn-faced. "It might be helpful if we knew what to call you."

"Call me whatever you like, Fleet Captain."

"I would like," I replied, "to call you by your name."

"Then we are at an impasse." Still matter-of-fact.

"You aren't going anywhere," I said. "You'd have left six hundred years ago when this system was annexed if you could have. You can't make your own gates anymore. Possibly even your engines don't work. Which means finding you is just a matter of time and determination on our part." In fact, it shouldn't take more than some history and some math to discover what ship it was most likely to be. "So you might as well just tell us."

"You make a very persuasive point, Fleet Captain," it said, and nothing more.

Mercy of Kalr said, in my ear, "I've been thinking about this since we first realized there was a ship on the other side of the Ghost Gate, Fleet Captain. It could be any of several ships. I might say *Cultivation of Tranquility*, but I'm fairly certain the supply locker we found is off one of the Gems. That narrows it down to *Heliodor*, *Idocrase*, or *Sphene*. Pieces of *Heliodor* were found three provinces away during an annexation two centuries ago, and based on *Idocrase*'s last known heading it's unlikely to have ended up here. I'd say this is most likely *Sphene*."

Aloud I said, "*Sphene*."

The ancillary didn't react that I saw, but Station said in my ear, "I think that's right, Fleet Captain. Certainly you surprised it just now."

Silently I said, "Thank you, Station, I appreciate your help." Aloud, "You'll have to get your own supper from the refectory tonight, Ship. Kalr Eight and Ten are already on the way back with the rest of ours."

Sphene said, a trace of ice in its voice, "I'm not *your* ship."

"Citizen, then," I said, though I knew that was no better. I gestured toward our little territory. "You may as well come in. If you are coming in."

It walked past Five as if she weren't there, ignored Lieutenant Tisarwat, who had stood up halfway through the exchange. It walked all the way to a rear corner, and sat down with its back to the wall and its arms around its knees, staring forward.

Five affected to ignore it. Tisarwat stared at it for five seconds, and then said, "It can have my supper, I'm not hungry. I'm going out." She looked at me. "With the fleet captain's permission, of course." Voice on the very edge of acid. She was still angry with me.

"Of course, Lieutenant," I said equably.

Four hours later I met with Head of Security Lusulun, to all appearances a social call, given the hour and the place (the head of Security's favorite tea shop, on Station's advice, well off the main concourse, just slightly dingy, with soft, comfortable chairs and walls muffled with gold and dark-blue hangings). Except among friends, most Radchaai considered last-minute invitations to be quite rude. But my rank, and the current situation, mitigated some of that. And the fact that I'd ordered a bottle of a local, sorghum-based spirit Station had told me Head of Security Lusulun favored, and had it ready to pour her a cup of it when she arrived.

She bowed as I rose to meet her. "Fleet Captain. I apologize for the late hour." She had clearly come straight from her office, she was still in uniform. "Things have been a bit hectic lately!"

"That they have." We sat, and I handed her a cup of liquor. Picked up my own.

"I confess I've been wishing to meet with you for the last few days, but there's never been the time." And for the last few days I'd been absent, on my own ship. "Forgive me, Fleet Captain, I fear my mind is still on business."

"Your business is important." I took a sip of the liquor. It burned going down, with an aftertaste like rusting iron. "I've run civilian security a time or two myself. It's a difficult job."

She blinked, trying to conceal her surprise. It was not the usual attitude of military toward civilian security. "I'm pleased to hear that you appreciate that, Fleet Captain."

"Would I be right in assuming you've got your people doing extra shifts, trying to keep citizens out of the Undergarden?"

"Right enough. Though even the Ychana are sharp enough to realize it's dangerous to go there just now, before it's been fully inspected. Most of them, anyway. There's always a few." She took a taste of her drink. "Ah, that's just what I needed." I sent a silent thanks to Station. "No, Fleet Captain, it's true I've got my people patrolling there just now, and our lives would be a sight easier without that, but if I had a say in these things I'd have whatever structural damage there might be repaired as quickly as possible, and have these people back where they came from. Now I've heard you've run civilian security before, I don't wonder you didn't hesitate to move in with them. You'll have been at annexations, I don't doubt, and I'm sure you don't blink at uncivilized behavior. And there's a good deal more room for you in the Undergarden than anywhere else on the station!"

I put a genial smile on my face. "Indeed." Taking issue just now with *these people* and *uncivilized* wouldn't be helpful. "Considering the present situation, I'm . . . taken aback at the insistence in some quarters that we should delay allowing residents to return to the Undergarden while we reconsider station housing assignments." *Some quarters* being the head priest of Amaat. "Let alone the suggestion that any but the most necessary repairs be delayed until those assignments are . . . *reconsidered*."

Head of Security Lusulun took another long drink. "Well, I suppose how places are assigned will affect just what those repairs should be, yes? Of course, it's quicker and easier to leave assignments as they are, as you've suggested yourself, Fleet Captain. And work was already going forward even before the lake sprung its leak. Might as well continue on as we were. But." She glanced around. Lowered her voice, though there was no one in earshot besides me and Kalr Five, standing behind my chair. "The Xhais, sir, can be quite unreasonable on the topic of the Ychana. Not to say I blame them entirely. They're a dirty lot, and it's a shame, the difference between what the Undergarden was meant to be and what it is now, after they've been living there." Fortunately it was easy for me to keep a neutral expression on my face. "Still," Lusulun continued, "let them have it, I say. It would make my life easier. Since the Undergarden has been evacuated we've had twice the disturbances. Fistfights, accusations of theft. Though most of those turn out to be nothing." She sighed. "But not all of them. I'll rest easier when they're back in the Undergarden, I don't deny it. And so will the Xhais, truth be told, but let them get the idea that any Ychana has somehow ended up with something she doesn't deserve..." She gestured her disgust.

Most station officials who weren't outsystem Radchaai were Xhai, here. The same was true of the wealthiest families. "Is Eminence Ifian a Xhai?" I asked, blandly.

Head of Security Lusulun gave an amused snort. "No indeed. She's outsystem Radchaai, and wouldn't thank you for suspecting she might be Athoeki. But she's pious, and if Amaat put the Xhais over the Ychana, well, that's what's proper."

It went without saying that in Radch space, a head priest of Amaat had a great deal of influence. But there were nearly always other religious figures with influence of their own. "And the head priest of the Mysteries?"

Lusulun raised her cup, a kind of salute. "That's right, you arrived in time for the Genitalia Festival, and you saw how popular that was. Yes. She *is* Xhai, but she's one of the few reasonable ones."

"Are you an initiate of the Mysteries?"

Cup still in hand, she gestured dismissal of the very idea. "No, no, Fleet Captain. It's a Xhai thing."

Station said, quietly in my ear, "The head of Security is half Sahut, Fleet Captain." Yet another group of Athoeki. One I knew very little about. In truth, sometimes such distinctions seemed invisible to me, but I knew from long experience they were anything but to the people who lived here.

"Or really," continued Lusulun, unaware that Station had spoken to me, "these days it's a thing for outsystem Radchaai with a taste for..." She hesitated, looking for the right word. "Exotic spirituality." With an ironic edge. Whether that edge was meant for the outsystem initiates, or the Mysteries themselves, or both, I couldn't tell. "Officially the Mysteries are open to anyone who's able to complete the initiation. In reality, well." She took another long drink, held out her cup when I lifted the bottle to offer a refill. "In reality, certain kinds of people have always been... discouraged from attempting it."

"Ychana, for instance," I suggested, pouring generously. "Among others, no doubt."

"Just so. Now, about four, five years ago an Ychana applied. And not your half-civilized Undergarden variety, no, she was entirely assimilated, well-educated, well-spoken. A minor Station Administration official." I realized, from just that much description, that she referred to someone whose daughter Lieutenant Tisarwat had been at pains to cultivate. "The furor over that! But the hierophant stood her ground. Everyone meant everyone, not *everyone but*." She snorted again. "Everyone who can afford it, anyway. There was all sorts of pissing and moaning—your pardon, sir—about how no decent person would become an initiate now, and the ancient Mysteries would be debased and destroyed. But you know, I think the hierophant knew well enough she was safe. More than half of initiates these days are outsystem, and Radchaai are used to provincials becoming civilized and stepping inside the circle, as it were. I daresay if you look at the genealogies of most of the outsystem Radchaai on this station you'd find quite a few of those. And really, the Mysteries seem to be going on the same as always." She gestured unconcern. "They're not really as ancient as all that, and by actually refusing to join they'd be cutting themselves off from the most exclusive social club on the station."

"So actually"—I took a sip of liquor, much smaller than the ones the head of Security had been taking—"the Xhais on this station aren't unanimous in hating the Ychana. It's just a vocal few."

"Oh, more than just a few." And then, showing me just how strong this liquor was, or perhaps how quickly she'd been drinking it, she said, "Unless I miss my guess, Fleet Captain, you weren't born a Mianaai. No offense, you understand. You've got the manner and the accent, but you don't have the looks. And I have trouble believing anyone born that high cares so much about a humble horticulturist."

She meant Horticulturist Basnaaid Elming. "I served with her sister." I had been the ship her sister had served on. I had killed her sister.

"So I understand." She glanced at the bottle. I obliged her. "On *Justice of Toren*, I gather. No offense, like I said, but the horticulturist's family isn't the most elevated."

"No," I agreed.

Head of Security Lusulun laughed, as though I'd confirmed something. "*Justice of Toren*. The ship with all the songs! No wonder Station Administrator Celar likes you so much, you must have brought her dozens of new ones." She sighed. "I'd give my left arm to bring her a gift like that!" Governor Giarod might be the higher authority, but Administrator Celar reigned over Athoek Station's daily routine. She was wide and heavy, and quite beautiful. No few of the residents of Athoek Station were half in love with her. "Well. *Justice of Toren*. There was a tragedy. Did they ever find out what happened?"

"Not that I know of," I lied. "Tell me—I know it isn't strictly proper, but"—I glanced around, though I knew Five had intimidated anyone out of sitting anywhere near us—"I was wondering about Sirix Odela." It had been Sirix who had told Captain Hetnys that threatening Lieutenant Awn's sister, Basnaaid Elming, would be a good way to strike at me. Who had lured me to the Gardens so that Captain Hetnys could make that threat while I was in as vulnerable a position as possible.

Lusulun sighed. "Well, now, Fleet Captain. Citizen Sirix..."

"She had been through Security before," I acknowledged. Sirix had already been re-educated once. More than one re-education was (in theory at least) rare, and potentially dangerous.

Head of Security Lusulun winced. "We took that into consideration, in fact." An inquisitive look at me, to see how I felt about that. "And she was genuinely remorseful. It was ultimately decided that she should be reassigned to one of the outstations. Without further, ah, involvement." Without further re-education, that meant. "One of the outstations will be needing a new horticulturist, and the departure window is in the next few days."

"Good." I was unsurprised to hear Sirix was remorseful. "I can't condone what she did, of course. But I know she was in a difficult position. I'm glad she'll be spared further unpleasantness." Lusulun made a sympathetic noise. "Have you eaten?" I asked. "I could order something." She acquiesced, and we spent the rest of the evening talking of inconsequential things.

As I walked back to our corridor-end, pleased with the outcome of my talk with the head of Security, trying to think what might wash the taste of the sorghum liquor out of my mouth, Kalr Five walking behind me, *Mercy of Kalr* showed me Seivarden, near the end of her watch. Alarmed. "Breq," she said, and it was a measure of her distress that even sitting in Command, with two of her Amaats close by, she addressed me in personal, not official, terms. "Breq, we have a problem."

I could see that we did. A small one-person courier had just come out of the Ghost Gate, beyond which was, supposedly, a dead-end system with no other gates and no inhabitants. We knew that *Sphene* was there, of course, but *Sphene* was a Notai ship, it was old, and it hadn't been near any sort of refit or repair facility in some three thousand years. This courier wasn't Notai, and its small, boxy hull was a shining white so pristine it might have come new from a shipyard moments before.

"Fleet Captain," said Seivarden, from her seat in Command aboard *Mercy of Kalr*. In better control of herself now, but no less frightened. "The Presger are here."

4

As I said, space is big. When the Presger courier came out of the Ghost Gate—shortly afterward sending a message identifying itself as a Presger ship, citing a subsection of the treaty and asking, on the basis of that, for permission to dock at Athoek Station—we had a good three days to prepare for its arrival. Time enough for Lieutenant Tisarwat to become at least outwardly resigned to the fact that Undergarden residents wanted to direct their own affairs.

Time enough for me to meet with Basnaaid Elming. Who had only recently learned that I had killed her sister. Whose life I had saved, days before. Of course, I was the reason her life had been in danger in the first place. She had, unaccountably, decided to continue to speak to me. I didn't question it, or consider too closely the profound ambivalence that almost certainly lay behind her courtesy. "Thank you for the tea," she said, sitting on a crate at the corridor-end. Tisarwat was out, drinking with friends. *Sphene* was wherever *Sphene* went when it grew tired of sitting in the corner and staring. Station would tell me if it got itself into trouble.

"Thank you for coming to see me," I replied. "I know you're busy." Basnaaid was one of the horticulturists in charge of the Gardens, five acres of open space full of water and trees and flowers. The Gardens were currently closed to the public while the support structures that kept the lake from collapsing into the Undergarden were being repaired—they had needed work for quite some time, but had chosen an inconvenient moment to fail, just days ago. Now the beautiful Gardens were a mess of mud, and plants that might or might not recover from that eventful day.

Basnaaid replied with a small quirk of a smile that reminded me strongly of her sister, and that also told me that she was quite tired but trying to be polite. "They're making good progress, the lake should be able to be filled again in a few days, they say. I'm holding out hope for one or two of the roses." She gestured resignation. "It'll be a while before the Gardens are back to what they were." At least the repairs to the lake necessitated repairs to the first level of the Undergarden, directly beneath it, limiting Eminence Ifian's ability to block the Undergarden refit. And then, because she'd clearly been thinking along the same lines, Basnaaid added, "I don't understand this business about maybe delaying the refit of the Undergarden." The official word, in the authorized news feeds, was still that returning displaced citizens to their homes was a priority. But rumor didn't run along the authorized channels. "And I don't understand what Eminence Ifian is thinking, either." The head priest of Amaat had taken that morning's omen-casting as an opportunity to warn station residents about the danger of acting too hastily and finding oneself in a situation that would, as a result, be difficult to remedy. How much better to consult the desire of God, and ponder where true justice, propriety, and benefit might lie. The implication was clear to anyone who'd been paying attention to the current gossip. Which was to say, everyone on the station except very small children.

Possibly quite a few of the people Eminence Ifian knew and socialized with would be sympathetic to her point. Possibly she had made sure of support in particular quarters before making her speech that morning. But the people who were sleeping in shifts, three or four to a bunk (or who had, like me, refused to do so and were sleeping in corners and corridors), were numerous and unhappy. Any delay in getting Undergarden residents back into their own beds was, to put it mildly, unappealing to those citizens. But of course, they were mostly the least significant of Station's residents, people with menial, low-status work assignments, or without much family to support them, or without patrons sufficiently well-off to assist them. "Clearly Eminence Ifian is thinking that if she can marshal the support of enough people, Station Administrator Celar can be pressured to change the plans for the Undergarden refit. And she means to take advantage of the fact that the station administrator didn't stop to have a cast done before she gave orders to go ahead."

"But this isn't really about Station Administrator Celar, or even the Undergarden, is it?" Basnaaid's position as Horticulturist didn't, in theory, involve much politics. In theory. "This is aimed at you, Fleet Captain. She wants to lessen your influence on Station Administration, and she probably wouldn't mind if all the Undergarden residents were shipped downwell, either."

"She didn't care whether they were here or not before," I pointed out.

"You weren't here before. And I suppose it isn't just Eminence Ifian wondering what you plan to do once you've taken charge of the dregs of Athoek Station, and thinking it might be best if you never get a chance to answer that question."

"Your sister would have understood."

She smiled that tired half-smile again. "Yes. But why now? Not you, I mean, but the eminence. This is hardly the time for political games, with the station overcrowded, with ships trapped in the system, intersystem gates destroyed or closed by order, and nobody really knowing why any of it is happening." Basnaaid knew, by now. But System Governor Giarod had refused to even consider releasing the information generally, that Anaander Mianaai, lord of Radchaai space for three thousand years, was divided, at war against herself. Judging from the official feeds coming through Athoek's still-working (but ordered closed to traffic) gates, the governors of neighboring systems had made similar decisions.

"On the contrary," I replied, with my own small smile. "It's the perfect time for such games, if all you care about is your side winning. And I don't doubt that Eminence Ifian is thinking that I support...a political opponent of hers. She is mistaken, of course. I have my own agenda, unrelated to that person's." I saw little difference between any of the parts of Anaander Mianaai. "Faulty assumptions lead to faulty action." It was a particular problem for that faction of Anaander I was now sure Eminence Ifian supported—unable or unwilling to admit that the problem lay within herself, that part of Anaander had put it about to her supporters that her split with herself was due to outside interference. Specifically interference by the alien Presger.

"Well. I don't appreciate her trying to delay people getting back to their homes. If the families originally assigned there wanted to go back to the Undergarden so badly, they could have pressed for a refit long ago."

"Indeed," I acknowledged. "And no doubt quite a few other people feel the same way."

And there was time enough for Seivarden and Ekalu, still on *Mercy of Kalr*, to have an argument.

They lay together in Seivarden's bunk—pressed close, the space was narrow. Ekalu angry—and terrified, heart rate elevated. Seivarden, between Ekalu and the wall, momentarily immobile with injured bewilderment. "It was a compliment!" Seivarden insisted.

"The way *provincial* is an insult. Except what am *I*?" Seivarden, still shocked, didn't answer. "Every time you use that word, *provincial*, every time you make some remark about someone's low-class accent or *unsophisticated* vocabulary, you remind me that *I'm* provincial, that *I'm* low-class. That my accent and my vocabulary are hard work for me. When you laugh at your Amaats for rinsing their tea leaves you just remind me that cheap bricked tea tastes like *home*. And when you say things meant to *compliment* me, to tell me I'm not like any of that, it just reminds me that I don't belong here. And it's always something small but it's *every day*."

Seivarden would have pulled back, but she was already firmly against the wall, and Ekalu had no room to move away herself, not without getting out of bed entirely. "You never said anything about this before." Because she was who she was, the daughter of an old and once nearly unthinkably prestigious house, born a thousand years before Ekalu or anyone on the ship but me, even her indignant disbelief sounded effortlessly aristocratic. "If it's so terrible why haven't you said anything until now?"

"How am I supposed to tell you how I feel?" Ekalu

demanded. "How can I complain? You outrank me. You and the fleet captain are close. What chance do I have, if I complain? And then where can I go? I can't even go back to Amaat Decade, I don't belong *there* anymore, either. I can't go home, even if I could get a travel permit. What am I supposed to do?"

Truly angry and hurt now, Seivarden levered herself up on her elbow. "That bad, is it? And I'm such a terrible person for complimenting you, for liking you. For..." She gestured, indicating the rumpled bed, the two of them, naked.

Ekalu shifted, sat up. Put her feet on the floor. "You aren't listening."

"Oh, I'm *listening*."

"No," replied Ekalu, and stood, and picked her uniform trousers up from off a chair. "You're doing exactly what I was afraid you'd do."

Seivarden opened her mouth to say something angry and bitter. Ship said, in her ear, "Lieutenant. Please don't."

It seemed not to have any immediate effect, so silently I said, "Seivarden."

"But...," began Seivarden, whether in reply to Ship, or to me, or to Ekalu I couldn't tell.

"I have work to do," said Ekalu, her voice even despite her hurt and dread and anger. She pulled on her gloves, picked up her shirt and jacket and boots, and went out the door.

Seivarden was sitting all the way up by now. "Aatr's fucking *tits*!" she cried, and swung a bare fist at the wall beside her. And cried out again, in physical pain this time—her fist was unarmored, and the wall was hard.

"Lieutenant," said Ship in her ear, "you should go to Medical."

"It's broken," Seivarden said, when she could speak again. Hunching over her injured hand. "Isn't it. I even know which fucking bone it is."

"Two, actually," replied *Mercy of Kalr.* "The fourth and the fifth metacarpals. Have you done this before?" The door opened, and Amaat Seven entered, her face ancillary-expressionless. She picked Seivarden's uniform up off the chair.

"Once," replied Seivarden. "It was a while ago."

"The last time you tried to quit kef?" Ship guessed. Fortunately only in Seivarden's ear, where Amaat Seven couldn't hear it. The crew knew part of Seivarden's history—that she had been wealthy and privileged, and had been captain of her own ship until that ship was destroyed and she'd spent a thousand years in a suspension pod. What they did not know was that, on waking, she'd discovered her house gone, herself impoverished and insignificant, nothing left to her but her aristocratic looks and accent. She had fled Radch space and become addicted to kef. I had found her on a backwater planet, naked, bleeding, half-dead. She hadn't taken kef since then.

If Seivarden's hand hadn't been broken she'd probably have swung again. The impulse to do it moved muscles in her arm and hand, and produced a fresh jolt of pain. Her eyes filled with tears.

Amaat Seven shook out Seivarden's uniform trousers. "Sir," she said, still impassive.

"If you're having this much trouble coping with your emotions," said Ship, still silently in Seivarden's ear, "then I really think you need to talk to Medic about it."

"Fuck you," Seivarden said, but she let Amaat Seven dress her, and escort her to Medical. Where she let Medic put a corrective on her hand, but said nothing at all about the argument with Lieutenant Ekalu, or her emotional distress, or her addiction to kef.

There was also time for an exchange of messages between myself and Fleet Captain Uemi, one gate away, in neighboring Hrad System. "My compliments to Fleet Captain Breq," messaged Fleet Captain Uemi, "and I would be happy to pass your reports on to Omaugh Palace." A gentle, diplomatic reminder that I had sent no such reports, not even notice that I had arrived at Athoek. Uemi also sent me news—Omaugh Anaander was sure enough of her hold on Omaugh Palace that she had begun to send more ships to other systems in the province. There was talk of allowing traffic in the province's intersystem gates, but personally, Uemi said, she didn't think it was quite safe yet.

The provincial palaces farthest from Omaugh (where this conflict had broken into the open) had gone silent weeks ago, and remained so. There had been no word out of Tstur Palace since it had fallen. The governors of Tstur Province's outlying systems were near panic—their systems, particularly the ones without habitable planets, were in dire need of resources that were no longer coming through the intersystem gates. They might very naturally have asked neighboring systems for help, but those neighbors were in Omaugh Province, where rumor said a different Anaander was in charge. Rumor also said that governors of systems closer to Tstur Palace who had been deemed insufficiently loyal to Tstur had been executed.

And all this time, the official news feeds went on as they always had, a steady parade of local events, discussions of inconsequential local gossip, recordings of public entertainments, punctuated now and then with official reassurance that this inconvenience, this brief disturbance, would be over soon. Was even now being dealt with.

"I fear," Fleet Captain Uemi sent, at the end of all this, "that some of the more recently annexed systems may try to break away. Shis'urna, particularly, or Valskaay. It'll be a bloody business if they do. Have you perhaps heard anything?" I had spent time in both systems, had participated in both annexations. And a small population of Valskaayans lived on Athoek, and might well have had an interest in that question. "It really would be better for everyone if they don't rebel," Fleet Captain Uemi's message continued. "I'm sure you know that."

And I was sure she wanted me to pass that on, to whatever contacts I might have in either of those places. "Graciously thanking Fleet Captain Uemi for her compliments," I replied, "I am not currently concerned with any system but Athoek. I am sending local intelligence, and my own official reports, with many thanks for the fleet captain's offer to pass them on to the appropriate authorities." And bundled that up with a week's worth of every scrap of official news I could find, including the results of seventy-five regional downwell radish-growing competitions that had been announced just that morning, which I flagged as worthy of special attention. And a month's worth of my own routine reports and status records, dozens of them, every single line of every single one of them filled out with exactly the same two words: *Fuck off.*

Next afternoon, Governor Giarod stood beside me at a hatch on the docks. Gray floor and walls, grimier than I liked, but then for most of my life I had been used to a military standard of cleanliness. The system governor seemed calm, but in the time it had taken for the Presger courier to reach Athoek Station from the Ghost Gate, she'd had plenty of opportunity to worry. Was possibly even more worried now that we were only waiting for the pressure to equalize between the station and the Presger ship. Just the two of us, no one else, not even any of my soldiers, though Kalr Five stood outwardly impassive, inwardly fretting, in the corridor outside the bay.

"Have the Presger been in the Ghost System all this while?" It was the third time she had asked that question, in as many days. "Did you ask, what is its name, *Sphene*, you said?" She frowned. "What sort of name is that? Didn't Notai ships usually have long names? Like *Ineluctable Ascendancy of Mind Unfolding* or *The Finite Contains the Infinite Contains the Finite*?"

Both of those ship names were fictional, characters in more or less famous melodramatic entertainments. "Notai ships were named according to their class," I said. "*Sphene* is one of the Gems." None of them had ever been famous enough to inspire an adventure serial. "And it wouldn't say what might or might not be with it in the Ghost System." I had asked, and gotten only a cold stare. "But I don't think this courier came from there. Or if it did, it was only there in order to access the Ghost Gate."

"If it hadn't been for all that... unpleasantness last week, we might have asked *Sword of Atagaris*."

"We might," I replied. "But we would have had good reason not to trust its answer." The same went for *Sphene*, actually, but I didn't point that out.

A moment of silence from Governor Giarod, and then, "Have the Presger broken the treaty?" *That* was a new question. Likely she had been holding it back all this time.

"Because they must have gated inside human territory, to

get to the Ghost System, you mean? I doubt it. They cited the treaty on arrival, you may recall." This tiny ship didn't look like it had the capability to make its own intersystem gates, but the Presger had surprised us before.

The hatch clicked, and thunked, and swung open. Governor Giarod stiffened, trying, I supposed, to stand straighter than she already was. The person who came stooping through the open hatchway looked entirely human. Though of course that didn't mean she necessarily was. She was quite tall—there must have barely been room for her to stretch out in her tiny ship. To look at her, she might have been an ordinary Radchaai. Dark hair, long, tied simply behind her head. Brown skin, dark eyes, all quite unremarkable. She wore the white of the Translators Office—white coat and gloves, white trousers, white boots. Spotless. Crisp and unwrinkled, though in such a small space there could barely have been room for a change of clothes, let alone to dress so carefully. But not a single pin, or any other kind of jewelry, to break that shining white.

She blinked twice, as though adjusting to the light, and looked at me and at Governor Giarod, and frowned just slightly. Governor Giarod bowed, and said, "Translator. Welcome to Athoek Station. I'm System Governor Giarod, and this"—she gestured toward me—"is Fleet Captain Breq."

The translator's barely perceptible frown cleared, and she bowed. "Governor. Fleet Captain. Honored and pleased to make your acquaintance. I am Presger Translator Dlique."

The governor was very good at looking as though she were quite calm. She drew breath to speak, but said nothing. Thinking, no doubt, of Translator Dlique herself, whose corpse was even now in suspension in Medical. Whose death we were going to have to explain.

That explanation was apparently going to be even more difficult than we had thought. But perhaps I could make at least that part of it a bit easier. When I had first met Translator Dlique, and asked her who she was, she had said, *I said just now I was Dlique but I might not be, I might be Zeiat.* "Begging your very great pardon, Translator," I said, before Governor Giarod could make a second attempt at speech, "but I believe that you're actually Presger Translator Zeiat."

The translator frowned, in earnest this time. "No. No, I don't think so. They told me I was Dlique. And they don't make mistakes, you know. When you think they have, it's just you looking at it wrong. That's what they say, anyway." She sighed. "They say all sorts of things. But *you* say I'm Zeiat, not Dlique. You wouldn't say that unless you had a reason to." She seemed just slightly doubtful of this.

"I'm quite certain of it," I replied.

"Well," she said, her frown intensifying for just a moment, and then clearing. "Well, if you're *certain*. Are you certain?"

"Quite certain, Translator."

"Let's start again, then." She shrugged her shoulders, as though adjusting the set of her spotless, perfect coat, and then bowed again. "Governor, Fleet Captain. Honored to make your acquaintance. I am Presger Translator Zeiat. And this is *very* awkward, but now I really do need to ask you what's happened to Translator Dlique."

I looked at Governor Giarod. She had frozen, for a moment not even breathing. Then she squared her broad shoulders and said, smoothly, as though she had not been on the edge of panic just the moment before, "Translator, we're so very sorry. We do owe you an explanation, and a very profound apology."

"She went and got herself killed, didn't she," said Translator

Zeiat. "Let me guess, she got bored and went somewhere you'd told her not to go."

"More or less, Translator," I acknowledged.

Translator Zeiat gave an exasperated sigh. "That would be *just* like her. I am *so* glad I'm not Dlique. Did you know she dismembered her sister once? She was bored, she said, and wanted to know what would happen. Well, what did she expect? And her sister's never been the same."

"Oh," said Governor Giarod. Likely all she could manage.

"Translator Dlique mentioned it," I said.

Translator Zeiat scoffed. "She would." And then, after a brief pause, "Are you certain it was Dlique? Perhaps there's been some sort of mistake. Perhaps it was someone else who died."

"Your very great pardon, Translator," replied Governor Giarod, "but when she arrived, she introduced herself as Translator Dlique."

"Well, that's just the thing," Translator Zeiat replied. "Dlique is the sort of person who'll say anything that comes into her mind. Particularly if she thinks it will be interesting or amusing. You really can't trust her to tell the truth."

I waited for Governor Giarod to reply, but she seemed paralyzed again. Perhaps from trying to follow Translator Zeiat's statement to its obvious conclusion.

"Translator," I said, "are you suggesting that since Translator Dlique isn't entirely trustworthy, she might have lied to us about being Translator Dlique?"

"Nothing more likely," replied Zeiat. "You can see why I'd much rather be Zeiat than Dlique. I don't much like her sense of humor, and I *certainly* don't want to encourage her. But I'd much rather be Zeiat than Dlique just now, so I suppose we can just let her have her little bit of fun this time. Is there anything, you know..." She gestured doubt. "Anything *left*? Of the body, I mean."

"We put the body in a suspension pod as quickly as we could, Translator," said Governor Giarod, trying very hard not to look or sound aghast. "And...we didn't know what... what customs would be appropriate. We held a funeral..."

Translator Zeiat tilted her head and looked very intently at the governor. "That was very obliging of you, Governor." She said it as though she wasn't entirely sure it *was* obliging.

The governor reached into her coat, pulled out a silver-and-opal pin. Held it out to Translator Zeiat. "We had memorials made, of course."

Translator Zeiat took the pin, examined it. Looked back up at Governor Giarod, at me. "I've never had one of these before! And look, it matches yours." We were both wearing the pins from Translator Dlique's funeral. "You're not related to Dlique, are you?"

"We stood in for the translator's family, at the funeral," Governor Giarod explained. "For propriety's sake."

"Oh, *propriety*." As though that explained everything. "Of course. Well, it's more than I would have done, I'll tell you. So. That's all cleared up, then."

"Translator," I said, "may one properly inquire as to the purpose of your visit?"

Governor Giarod added, hastily, "We are of course pleased you've chosen to honor us." With a very small glance my way that was as much objection as she could currently make to the directness of my question.

"The purpose of my visit?" asked Zeiat, seeming puzzled for a moment. "Well, now, that's hard to say. They told me I was Dlique, you recall, and the thing about Dlique is—aside from the fact that you can't trust a word she says—she's easily bored and really far too curious. About the most inappropriate things, too. I'm quite sure *she* came here because she was bored and wanted to see what would happen. But since you tell me I'm Zeiat, I suspect *I'm* here because that ship is really terribly cramped and I've been inside it far too long. I'd really like to be able to walk around and stretch a bit, and perhaps eat some decent food." A moment of doubt. "You do eat food, don't you?"

It was the sort of question I could imagine Translator Dlique asking. And perhaps she had asked it, when she'd first arrived, because Governor Giarod replied, calmly, "Yes, Translator." On, it seemed, firmer ground for the moment. "Would you like to eat something now?"

"Yes, please, Governor!"

Even before the translator arrived, Governor Giarod had wanted to bring Translator Zeiat to the governor's residence by a back route, through an access tunnel. Before the treaty the Presger had torn apart human ships and Stations—and their inhabitants—for no comprehensible reason. No attempt to fight them, to defend against them, had ever been successful. Until the advent of the Presger translators, no human had managed to communicate with them at all. Humans in close proximity to Presger simply died, often slowly and messily. The treaty had put an end to that, but people were afraid of the Presger, for very good reasons, and since I had insisted that we not conceal Translator Dlique's death, people would have good reason to worry about the arrival of the Presger now.

I had pointed out that keeping Translator Dlique's presence a secret had not ended well. That it seemed likely no Presger translator could be successfully concealed or confined in any event, and that while most station residents were no doubt entirely understandably afraid of the Presger, and apprehensive of the translator's arrival, she herself would likely look passably human and non-threatening, and the sight of her might actually be reassuring. Governor Giarod had finally agreed, and so we took the lift to the main concourse. It was midmorning on the station's schedule, and plenty of citizens were out, walking, or standing in groups to talk. Just like every day, except for two things: the four rows of priests sitting in front of the entrance to the temple of Amaat—Eminence Ifian in the center of the very first row, sitting right on the dingy ground; and a long, snaking line of citizens that reached from Station Administration to nearly three-quarters of the way down the concourse.

"Well," I remarked, quietly, to Governor Giarod, who had stopped cold, three steps out of the lift, "you did tell Station that your assistant could handle anything that came up while you were busy with the translator." Who had stopped when I and the governor had stopped, and was gazing curiously and openly around at the people, the windows on the second level, the huge reliefs of the four Emanations on the façade of the temple of Amaat.

I could guess what Eminence Ifian was up to. A quick, silent query to Station confirmed it. The priests of Amaat were on strike. Ifian had announced that she would not make the day's cast, because it had become clear that Station Administration didn't care to listen to the messages Amaat provided. And incidentally, while the priests sat in front of the temple, no contracts of clientage could be made, no births or deaths registered, and no funerals held. I couldn't help but admire the strategy—technically, most funeral obsequies that traditionally were attended to by a priest of Amaat could also be performed by any citizen; the filing of an actual clientage contract was arguably less important than the relationship itself and could easily enough be left for later; and one could argue that on a station with an AI, no births or deaths could possibly go unnoticed or unrecorded. But these were all things that meant a fair amount to most citizens. It wasn't a terribly Radchaai form of citizen protest, but the eminence did have the example of the striking field workers downwell. Whom I had spoken in support of, and so I couldn't openly oppose the priests' work stoppage without exposing myself as a hypocrite.

As for that long line of citizens outside Station Administration—there weren't many forms of large-scale protest realistically available to most citizens, but one of them was standing in line when you didn't actually need to. In theory, of course, no Radchaai on a station like Athoek ever needed to wait in much of a line for anything. One needed only put in a request and receive either an appointment, or a place in the queue, and notification when it was nearly your turn. And it's much easier for an official to be nonchalant about a list of requests to meet that nine times out of ten can be put off till the next day than to ignore a long line of people actually standing outside her door.

Such lines generally began more or less spontaneously, but once they reached a certain size, decisions to join became more organized. This one was well beyond that threshold. Light-brown-uniformed Security strolled up and down, watching, occasionally exchanging a few words. Just letting everyone know they were there. In theory—again—Security could order everyone to disperse. That would end with the line re-forming first thing tomorrow, and the next day, and the next. Or perhaps a similar line stretching out of Security's headquarters. It was better to keep things calm, and let the line run its course. So was this line in support of Eminence Ifian's agenda, or protesting it?

Either way, we would have to walk by both the line and the seated priests to reach the governor's residence. Governor Giarod was fairly good at not panicking visibly, but, I had discovered, not good at actually not panicking. She looked up at Translator Zeiat. "Translator, what sort of food do you like?"

The translator turned her attention back to us. "I don't know that I've ever had any, Governor." And then, distracted again, "Why are all those people sitting on the ground over there?"

I was hard-pressed to guess if Governor Giarod was more alarmed by the question about the striking priests, or the assertion that Translator Zeiat had never actually eaten anything. "Your pardon, Translator—you've never had food?"

"The translator has only been Zeiat since she stepped out of the shuttle," I pointed out. "There hasn't been time. Translator, those priests are sitting down in front of the temple as a protest. They want to pressure Station Administration into changing a policy they don't like."

"Really!" She smiled. "I didn't think you Radchaai did that sort of thing."

"And I," I replied, "didn't think the Presger understood the difference between one sort of human and another."

"Oh, no, *they* don't," she replied. "I do, though. Or, you know, I understand the *idea* of it. In the abstract. I don't actually have a lot of *experience* at it."

Governor Giarod, ignoring this, said, "Translator, there's a very good tea shop over this way." She gestured aside. "I'm sure they'll be serving something interesting."

"Interesting, eh?" said Translator Zeiat. "Interesting is good." And she and System Governor Giarod headed off across the concourse, not coincidentally away from the temple, and from Station Administration.

I made to follow them, but stopped at a signal from Kalr Five, still behind me. Turned to see Citizen Uran coming toward me across the scuffed white floor. "Fleet Captain," she said, and bowed.

"Citizen. Shouldn't you be studying Raswar?"

"My tutor is in line, Fleet Captain."

Uran's Raswar tutor was Ychana, and had relatives who lived in the Undergarden. That answered my question about what the line was meant to protest. I considered that a moment. "I haven't seen any Undergarden residents in line. Not from this distance, anyway." Of course, it was possible those who were in line had exchanged their very non-Radchaai tunics for more conventionally Radchaai jackets, shirts, and gloves.

"No, Fleet Captain." Uran's head dipped downward, just barely, just for an instant. She'd wanted to look down at the ground, away from me, but had resisted the impulse. "There's a meeting." She'd switched to Delsig, which she knew I understood. "It's just starting now."

"About the line?" I asked, in the same language. She made a tiny gesture of affirmation. "And our household wasn't invited?" I understood why none of my household had been invited to the last meeting, and could see good reasons why it would be convenient for none of us to be party to this one. But still, we had been living in the Undergarden, and I didn't much like our being regularly excluded. "Or are you representing us?"

"It's . . . it's complicated."

"It is," I acknowledged. "I don't want to intimidate anyone, or dictate policy, but our quarters *are* in the Undergarden."

"People mostly understand that," Uran replied. "It's just . . ." Hesitation. Real fear, I thought. "You *are* Radchaai. And you're a soldier. And you might prefer better neighbors." I might be in favor of reassigning housing in the Undergarden, or even shipping Ychana residents downwell whether they wanted to go or not, to get them out of the way. "I've told them you don't."

"But they have no reason to believe that." Neither did Uran, for that matter. "I'm too busy to attend the meeting just now. I think Lieutenant Tisarwat should be invited." She was still asleep, and would wake hungover. "But the meeting will decide for themselves. If the lieutenant is invited, tell her I said to only listen. She's to stay quiet unless she's explicitly asked to comment. Tell her that's an order."

"Yes, Radchaai."

"And suggest to the meeting that if the Ychana join the line, they be sure to be on their very best, most patient, behavior, and wear gloves." Few things were as disconcerting and embarrassing to Radchaai as bare hands in public.

"Oh, no, Radchaai!" Uran exclaimed. "We're not thinking of joining the line." I couldn't help but notice that *we*, but said nothing. "Security is nervous enough. No, we're thinking of giving out food and tea to the people waiting." She bit her lip, just a moment. "And to the priests." Her shoulders hunched a bit, as though she expected angry words, or a blow.

She had spent most of her life downwell, picking tea in the mountains on Athoek. She had family among those striking field workers whose example Eminence Ifian now took. Uran had been personally involved in a previous strike, though she'd been quite small at the time and probably didn't remember it. "Do you need funds for it?" I asked, still in Delsig. Her eyes widened. She had not expected that reaction. "Let me know if you do. And remember that groups of more than two or three will likely make Security unhappy." Even two or three might do that. "I'll try to make time to talk with the head of Security myself today. Though I'm very busy, and it might not be for a while."

"Yes, Radchaai." She bowed and made as if to leave, but halted suddenly, eyes widening. An outcry behind me, a dozen voices or more exclaiming in anger and dismay. I turned.

The line, which had snaked quietly down the length of the concourse, had broken in the middle, one Security struggling with a citizen, another raising her stun stick, the space around them clear—the citizens nearest had removed to a safer distance.

"Stop!" I shouted, my voice carrying across the entire concourse, my tone guaranteed to immobilize any military in the near vicinity. Absently I noted that Five, behind me, had tensed at the sound. But Security was not military. The stun stick came down, and the citizen cried out and collapsed.

"Stop!" I shouted again, and this time both Security turned their heads to me as I strode toward them, Five behind me.

"All respect, Fleet Captain," said the Security still holding the stun stick. The stricken citizen lay on the ground, giving out a series of gasping moans. Uran's Raswar tutor. I had not recognized her from a distance. "You don't have authority in this matter."

"Station," I said aloud, "what happened?"

It was the Security kneeling on the ground beside Uran's

tutor who answered. “Head of Security ordered us to disperse the line, Fleet Captain. This person refused to go.”

This person. Not *this citizen.* “Disperse the line?” I asked, making my voice as calm and even as possible without dropping into ancillary blankness. Uran’s tutor still gasped on the ground. “Why?” Silently, I said, “Station, please send Medical.”

“They’re on their way, Fleet Captain,” said Station in my ear.

At the same time, the kneeling Security said, “I just follow my orders, Fleet Captain.”

I said, “I will see the head of Security *right now.*”

Before either Security could reply, Head of Security Lusulun’s voice sounded behind me. “Fleet Captain!”

I turned. “Why did you order the line dispersed?” I asked, with no courteous preamble. “It looked perfectly peaceable to me, and lines generally play themselves out eventually.”

“This isn’t a good time for public unrest, Fleet Captain.” Lusulun seemed genuinely puzzled at my question, as though its answer were obvious. “It’s peaceable now, but what if the Undergarden Ychana join it?” I considered, for a moment, how I might answer that. Said nothing, and Lusulun went on, “I intended to speak to you, in fact. If something like that were to happen I might…” She lowered her voice. “I might need your assistance.”

“So,” I said, several replies coming to mind. I discarded them as impolitic. “You guessed correctly that I have been in more than one annexation. And I’ve learned more than a few lessons from it, some of them at great cost. I will share one of them with you now: most people don’t want trouble, but frightened people are liable to do very dangerous things.”

That included soldiers and Station Security, of course, but I didn't say that. "If I were to set soldiers on the concourse, everything you fear—and worse—would come to pass." I gestured toward Uran's tutor, whose gasping had lessened, but who still could not move. A medic knelt beside her. The two Security stared at me, at Head of Security Lusulun. "I speak from experience. Let the line be the line. Let your security be present but not threatening. Treat *all* the citizens here with equal courtesy and respect." I wondered if Security had known Uran's tutor was Ychana, just by looking at her. I couldn't always see the differences, but no doubt most people who lived here could. I suspected Security's reaction would have been less severe if the citizen who had refused to go had not been Ychana. But suggesting it would not have been helpful at that particular moment. "Let them all have their say," I continued. Lusulun stared at me for five seconds, saying nothing. "Station Security is here to protect citizens. You can't do that if you insist on seeing any of them as adversaries. I'm speaking from personal experience."

"And if they see *us* as adversaries?"

"How can it possibly help to prove them right?" Silence again. "I know exactly how dangerous it sounds, but please. Please take my advice." She sighed, and made a frustrated gesture. "Let Medical tend to this citizen, and let her go about her business. Let the rest of the line know that a mistake was made"—no need to say who had made that mistake, or what it had been—"and they can continue waiting in line."

"But...," began Lusulun.

"Tell me, Head of Security," I interrupted before she could say more, "when were you going to order the priests of Amaat to disperse?"

"But...," she said again.

"They are disrupting the ordinary operation of this station. I'd say they're causing Station Administrator Celar a good deal more trouble than these citizens here." I gestured toward the ragged remnants of the line surrounding us.

"I don't know, Fleet Captain." But the mention of Administrator Celar had had its effect.

"Trust me. I have done this sort of thing before, in situations a good deal more potentially explosive than this one." And my officers would never have given the orders that Head of Security Lusulun had today, not unless they had been prepared to kill a large number of people. Which not infrequently they had been.

"If things go wrong, will you help?" asked Lusulun.

"I will not order my soldiers to fire on citizens."

"That wasn't what I asked." Indignant.

"You may not think so," I replied, "you may not have intended to ask that. But that would be the result. And I won't do it."

She stood a moment, doubtful. Then something decided her—her own thoughts, my mention of the bulky and beautiful Administrator Celar, a word, perhaps, from Station. She sighed. "I'm trusting you."

"Thank you," I said.

"Fleet Captain." Station's voice in my ear. "There's a message for you from downwell. A Citizen Queter has requested that you be a witness to her interrogation. I ordinarily wouldn't trouble you right now, but if you mean to attend, you'll have to leave in the next hour."

Queter. Uran's older sister. Raughd Denche had blackmailed her into trying to kill me. Or thought she had. Instead Queter had tried to kill Raughd herself. "Please tell the district magistrate that I'll be there as soon as I can." I wouldn't have to say anything more. Kalr Five, who had been standing near me the entire time, would arrange the details for me.

In the tea shop, Governor Giarod and Translator Zeiat sat at a table laden with food—bowls of noodles and of sliced fruits, platters of fish. An attendant stood watching, appalled, as Governor Giarod said, "But, Translator, it's not for *drinking*. It's a condiment. Here." She pushed the noodles closer to the translator. "Fish sauce is very good on this."

"But it's a liquid," replied Translator Zeiat, reasonably enough, "and it tastes good." The tea shop attendant turned and walked hastily away. The idea of drinking a bowlful of oily, salty fish sauce was too much for her, apparently.

"Governor," I interrupted, before the conversation could go further. "Translator. I find I have urgent business downwell that can't be delayed or avoided."

"On the planet?" asked Translator Zeiat. "I've never been on a planet before. Can I come with you?"

The fish sauce must have been as much as Governor Giarod could take. "Yes. Yes, by all means, visit the planet with the fleet captain." She hadn't even asked what my business was. I wondered if her eagerness was for being rid of Translator Zeiat, or being rid of me.

5

Xhenang Serit, the seat of Beset District, sat at the mouth of a river where it came down out of the mountains into the sea, black and gray stone buildings close around the river mouth, spread along the seashore and up the green hillsides. It was (at least in its central neighborhoods) a city of bridges, of streams and fountains—in courtyards, in the outer walls of houses, running down the centers of boulevards—so that the sound of water was with you everywhere you went.

The district's detention center was up in the hills, out of sight of the main part of the city. It was a long, low building with several inner courtyards, the whole surrounded by a two-meter-high wall that, if it had been on the other side of the hilltop, would have blocked any view of the sea. Still, the setting was pleasant enough, with grass and even some flowers in the courtyards. All of Beset District's long-term or complicated cases were sent here, nearly all of them destined for interrogation and re-education.

There was, it appeared, no facility for visitors to meet with inmates, not counting the actual interrogation rooms. At first, in fact, the staff objected to my seeing Citizen Queter at all, but I insisted. Ultimately they brought her to me in a corridor, where a long bench sat under a window that looked out on the black stone wall and a stretch of thin, pale grass. Kalr Five stood some meters away, impassive and disapproving—I had made her stay out of earshot in order to give at least the illusion of privacy. *Sphene* stood beside her, just as impassive. It had kept close to Five since we'd left the station, partly, I thought, to annoy her. The ancillary still behaved as though the shattered tea set meant nothing to it, but I suspected it always knew where that red, blue, and gold box was. Five had left it on the station, and told Kalr Eight that if *Sphene* had stayed behind, she'd have been sure to bring the box with her.

"I didn't think you would come," Queter said, in Radchaai, without any courteous preamble, or a bow. She wore the plain gray jacket, trousers, and gloves that were standard issue for any citizen who didn't have the wherewithal to purchase anything else. Her hair, which she used to braid and tie back with a scarf, was cut short.

I gestured an acknowledgment of her words, and an invitation to sit on the bench. Asked, in Delsig, "How are you?"

She didn't move. "They don't like me to speak anything but Radchaai," she said, in that language. "It won't help with my evaluation, they tell me. I'm fine. As you see." A pause, and then, "How is Uran?"

"She's well. Have they been giving you her messages?"

"They must have been in Delsig," Queter said, with only a trace of bitterness.

They had been. "She wanted very badly to come with me." She had wept when I'd told her that Queter had asked that she not.

Queter looked away, toward the end of the corridor where Five stood, *Sphene* beside her, and then back. "I didn't want her to see me like this."

I had suspected as much. "She understands." Mostly she did. "I'm to give you her love." That struck Queter as funny. She laughed, brief and jagged. "Have you had any outside news?" I asked, when she didn't say anything. "Did you know the fieldworkers on the mountain tea plantations have all stopped work? They won't go back, they say, until they're given their full wages, and their rights as citizens are restored." Fosyf Denche had cheated her fieldworkers for years, kept them in debt to her, and being transportees from Valskaay they'd had no one beyond the tea fields to speak up for them.

"Hah!" Suddenly, fiercely, she smiled. Almost like her old self, I thought. Then the smile was gone—though the fierceness was still there. Mostly hidden. Her arms still straight at her sides, she made her gloved hands into fists. "Do you know when it's going to be? When I ask they tell me it's not good for me to worry about it. It *won't help with my evaluation*." Definitely bitter that time.

"Your interrogation? I'm told it's tomorrow morning."

"You'll make sure they don't do anything they aren't supposed to?"

And she hadn't thought I would come. "Yes."

"And when they... when they re-educate me? Will you be there?"

"If you want me to, I'll try. I don't know if I can." She didn't say anything, her expression didn't change. I switched languages, back to Delsig. "Uran really is doing well. You'd be proud of him. Shall I let your grandfather know you're all right?"

"Yes, please." In Radchaai still. "I should go back. They get nervous here if anything doesn't go according to routine."

"I apologize for causing you difficulties. I wanted to see for myself that you were well, and I wanted you to know that I had come." A brown-uniformed guard approached the end of the corridor behind Queter, obviously having been waiting for the least signal that our conversation might be over.

Queter said only, "Yes." And went with the guard away down the corridor, the very image of calm and unconcern, except that her hands were still clenched into fists.

I took the cable tram back down the hill, Xhenang Serit spread black and gray and green below me, the sea beyond. Five and *Sphene* on the seats behind me. Kalr Eight was with Translator Zeiat at a manufactory down by the water, watching a slithering, silver mass of dead fish tumble into a wide, deep vat, while a visibly terrified worker explained how fish sauce was made. "So, why do the fish do this?" asked Translator Zeiat, when the worker stopped for breath.

"They...they don't have much choice in the matter, Translator."

Translator Zeiat thought about that a moment, and then asked, "Do you think fish sauce would be good in tea?"

"N...no, Translator. I don't think that would be entirely proper." And then, trying, I supposed, to salvage some shred of sense out of the experience, "There are these little cakes that are *shaped* like fish. Some people like to dip them in their tea."

"I see, I see." Translator Zeiat gestured understanding. "Do you have any of those here?"

"Translator," said Kalr Eight, before the worker was forced to admit that no, she did not have any fish-shaped cakes at this particular moment, "I'm sure we can find you some later today."

"Next," announced the manufactory worker, with a grateful look at Eight, "salt is added to the fish…"

On Athoek Station, Tisarwat sat talking with the head priest of the Mysteries. This was a local sect, very popular not only with the Xhai here but also with outsystem Radchaai. The hierophant of the Mysteries was, herself, popular and influential. "Lieutenant," the hierophant was saying, "I will be entirely frank. This business appears to be some argument between Eminence Ifian and your fleet captain." The hierophant's apartment sat above and behind the temple of the Mysteries. It was small, as such apartments go, and the brightly lit room they sat in was plainly furnished, just a low table and a few chairs with undecorated cushions. But orchids bloomed by the dozen on shelves and in brackets around the walls, purple and yellow and blue and green, and the air was sweet with their scent. It wasn't uncommon for station residents to scrimp a little on their water ration in order to keep a plant or two, but this lush growth wasn't a result of the hierophant's saving a bit of water out of her bath every now and then. "I would also observe," she continued, "that the eminence certainly hasn't taken a step like this, particularly in obvious opposition to the station administrator, without being certain of the support of Governor Giarod. You want me to step in the middle of that. And for what? I don't have the training to do the daily cast, and even if I did I'm sure most citizens wouldn't accept it from me."

"You might be surprised," observed Tisarwat, with a calm smile. Her distress at losing control of Undergarden residents' communication with Station Administration had faded, now she had this challenge in front of her. "You're widely respected here. But Station Administrator Celar will make the casts, starting tomorrow morning. After all, you don't *have* to be a priest to do it, and Station Administrator Celar does actually have the training, although she hasn't used it for some time. No, all we're asking for is births and funerals. And maybe not every station resident will find that acceptable, but quite a lot of Xhai will, I think."

If the hierophant felt any surprise at having this conversation with someone as young and presumably inexperienced as Tisarwat, she didn't show it. "Quite a lot of Xhai wouldn't mind at all if the Ychana were permanently expelled from the Undergarden. Or better yet forcibly shipped downwell or to the outstations. Which is the likely outcome of the eminence getting what she wants, I suspect. So those Xhai who might be disposed to accept my services are likely also disposed to support the eminence. And Eminence Ifian is my neighbor, and for reasons I'm sure I don't need to explain to you, I'd prefer to remain on good terms with her. So I ask you again, why should I put myself in the middle of this?"

Lieutenant Tisarwat still smiled, and I saw a tiny surge of satisfaction. As though the priest had just walked into a trap Tisarwat had laid. "I don't ask you to put yourself anywhere. I ask you to be where you are."

The hierophant's eyes widened in surprise. "Lieutenant, I don't recall inducting you. And you're young enough I'd remember it." Innocuous as Tisarwat's words had seemed to me, they must have referred to the Mysteries somehow. And of course Anaander Mianaai would be familiar with them—no mysteries or secret societies that didn't admit the Lord of the Radch were allowed to continue.

Tisarwat frowned, false puzzlement. "I don't know what you mean, Hierophant. I only intended to say that you know where justice lies in this situation. Yes, technically the Ychana were in the Undergarden illegally. But you know well enough that before any of them moved there, their Xhai neighbors will have done everything they could to drive them away. They found a way to live despite that, and now, through no fault of their own, they're cast adrift. And for what? For the foolish prejudices of *some* Xhai, and Eminence Ifian's determination to pursue a feud with the fleet captain. One the fleet captain has no interest in, by the way."

"Nor you, I gather," observed the hierophant dryly.

"*I* want to sleep somewhere besides out in a corridor," Tisarwat replied. "And I want my neighbors back in their own homes. Fleet Captain Breq wants the same. I don't know why Eminence Ifian has taken against the fleet captain, and I certainly don't understand why she's chosen a way to do it that leaves so many station residents not only in uncomfortable circumstances but in doubt of their futures. It seems as though she's forgotten that the authority of the temple isn't properly wielded for one's own convenience."

The hierophant drew a considering breath. Blew it out with a quick *hah.* "Lieutenant, with all respect, you are one manipulative piece of work." And before Tisarwat could protest her innocence, "And this business I hear about a conspiracy, about the Lord of the Radch having been infiltrated by aliens?"

"Mostly nonsense," Tisarwat replied. "The Lord of the Radch is having an argument with herself, and it's broken out into open fighting on the provincial palace stations. Some military ships have chosen one faction or the other, and they're responsible for the destruction of several intersystem gates. The system governor feels it would be...counterproductive to announce this generally."

"So you'll just spread it as a rumor."

"Hierophant, I've said nothing about it to anyone until now, and that only because you've asked me directly, and we're alone." Not, strictly speaking, true—Station could hear, and there was almost certainly a servant or another priest nearby. "If you've heard it as a rumor, it won't have come from Fleet Captain Breq, or me, or any of our crew, that I know of."

"And what is this supposed argument about, and which faction do you support?"

"The argument is a complicated one, but it mostly involves the future direction of Anaander Mianaai herself, and Radch space with her. The end of annexations, the end of making ancillaries. The end to certain assumptions about who is fit to command—these are things that Anaander Mianaai is quite literally divided over. And Fleet Captain Breq doesn't support either one. She's here to keep this system safe and stable while that argument plays out in the palaces."

"Yes, I've noticed how much more peaceful Athoek has been, since you arrived." The priest's voice was utterly serious.

"It was such a haven of prosperity and justice for every citizen before," Tisarwat observed, just as seriously. Leaning just a bit on that *every citizen.*

The priest closed her eyes and sighed, and Tisarwat knew she had won.

On *Mercy of Kalr*, Seivarden had just come off duty. Now she sat on her bunk, arms tightly crossed. The corrective still on her hand, but nearly finished with its work. "Lieutenant," Ship said in her ear, "would you like some tea?"

"It was a *compliment*!" For the past few days, Ekalu had been stiffly, formally correct in her every interaction with Seivarden. Everyone on board knew something had gone wrong between them. None of them knew about her kef addiction, and would not recognize that arms-crossed gesture for what it was, a sign that the stresses of the past few days—probably weeks—had piled up beyond her ability to cope.

"Lieutenant Ekalu didn't take it as a compliment," Ship pointed out. And told Amaat Four to hold off on bringing tea.

"Well I *meant* it as one," insisted Seivarden. "I was being *nice*. Why doesn't she understand that?"

"I'm sure the lieutenant does understand that," Ship replied. Seivarden scoffed. After a pause of three seconds, Ship added, "Begging the lieutenant's indulgence," and Seivarden blinked and frowned in confusion. It wasn't the sort of thing a ship generally said to its own officers. "But I would like to point out that as soon as Lieutenant Ekalu let you know that actually, your intended compliment was offensive to her, you immediately stopped trying to be nice."

Seivarden stood up off the bunk, arms still crossed tight, and paced her tiny quarters, all of two steps long. "What are you saying, Ship?"

"I'm saying I think you owe Lieutenant Ekalu an apology." Downwell, halfway down the hillside on the cable tram, I was startled back to myself. I had never, ever heard a ship say something that directly critical to an officer.

But just days ago Ship had declared itself someone who could be a captain. Essentially an officer itself. And ultimately it was I who had suggested the idea, weeks ago at Omaugh Palace. I shouldn't have been surprised. I reached again. Seivarden had stopped still, had just said, indignant, "Owe *her* an apology? What about me?"

"Lieutenant Seivarden," said Ship, "Lieutenant Ekalu is hurt and upset, and it was you who hurt and upset her. And this sort of thing affects the entire crew. For which, may I remind you, you are currently responsible." As Ship spoke, Seivarden's anger intensified. Ship added, "Your emotional state—and your behavior—have been erratic for the past few days. You have been insufferable to everyone you've dealt with. Including me. No, don't punch the wall again, it won't do any good. You are in command here. Act like it. And if you can't act like it—which I am increasingly convinced is the case—then take yourself to Medical. Fleet Captain would say the same to you, if she were here."

That last hit Seivarden like a blow. With no warning her anger collapsed into despair, and she sat heavily on her bunk. Drew up her legs and put her forehead on her knees, arms still crossed. "I fucked it up," she moaned after a few moments. "I got another chance and I fucked it up."

"Not irrevocably," replied Ship. "Not yet. I know that considering the condition you're in right now, it's pointless to tell you to stop feeling sorry for yourself. But you can still get up and go to Medical."

Except Medic was that moment on watch. "The problem is," Medic said, silently, to the information Ship had just given her, "to even start, I'm going to need up-to-date aptitudes data to work with, and I don't have that. And I'm not a tester or an interrogator. I'm just a regular medic. Some things I could handle, but I'm afraid this is beyond me. And I'm not sure we could trust any of the specialists here in the system. We have the same problem with Lieutenant Tisarwat, of course." She gave an exasperated sigh. "Why is this happening *now*?"

"It's been waiting to happen," Ship replied. "But to be honest at first I thought it wouldn't. I underestimated how much better Lieutenant Seivarden does emotionally when Fleet Captain is here."

"Medic's on watch," Seivarden said, still curled into herself on her bunk.

Sitting in Command, Medic said, "Fleet Captain can't always be here. Does she know this is happening?"

"Yes," Ship said to Medic, and to Seivarden, "Pull yourself together, Lieutenant. I'll have Amaat Four bring you tea, and you can get cleaned up and then you need to talk to Lieutenant Ekalu and let her know she's going to be in command for a few days. And it would be good to apologize to her, if you can do that in a sensible way."

"Sensible?" asked Seivarden, raising her head up off her knees.

"We'll talk while you're having your tea," said Ship.

I had upset the staff at the detention center with my insistence on seeing Queter. They had, I suspected, appealed to the district magistrate, who did not dare call me to account. Besides, she wanted something from me, so instead of complaining to me, she invited me to dinner.

The district magistrate's dining room looked out onto steps down to a wide, brick-paved courtyard. Leafy vines with sweet-smelling white and pink flowers tumbled out of tall urns, and water trickled down one wall into a wide basin in which fish swam and small yellow lilies bloomed. Servants had cleared supper away, and the magistrate and I were drinking tea. Translator Zeiat stood beside the basin, staring fixedly at the fish. *Sphene* sat on a bench in the courtyard outside the tall, open doors, a few meters from where Kalr Five stood straight and still.

"That's a song I haven't heard in years, Fleet Captain," said the district magistrate, where we sat drinking tea, looking out on the darkening courtyard.

"I apologize, Magistrate."

"No need, no need." She took a drink of her tea. "It was one of my favorites when I was young. I found it quite romantic. Thinking of it now, it's very sad, isn't it." And sang, "*But I will sustain myself / With nothing more than the perfume of jasmine flowers / Until the end of my life.*" Faltering a bit at the last—she'd taken her pitch from my humming and it was just a touch too high for her comfort. "But the daughters breaking the funeral fast are in the right. Life goes on. Everything goes on." She sighed. "You know, I didn't think you'd come. I was sure Citizen Queter meant merely to annoy you. I almost didn't pass the request on."

"That would have been illegal, Magistrate."

She sighed. "Yes, that's why I did pass it on."

"If she asked for me in such extremity, how could I ignore her?"

"I suppose." Outside, Translator Zeiat bent lower over the lily-blooming basin. I hoped she didn't dive in. It struck me that if she had been Translator Dlique, she might well have done exactly that. "I wish, Fleet Captain, that you would consider exercising your influence with the Valskaayan fieldworkers on Citizen Fosyf's tea plantation. You have no reason to be aware of it, but there are people who would be glad of any excuse to damage her. Some of them are in her own family. This work stoppage is just giving them opportunity to move against her." This was hardly a surprise, given Citizen Fosyf Denche's penchant for cruelty. "The local head of Denche is an extremely unpleasant person, and she's hated Fosyf's mother since they were both children. The mother being gone, she hates Fosyf. She'll take the plantation away from Fosyf if she can. This might give her enough leverage to do it, especially since so many intersystem gates are down and the Lord of Denche is unreachable just now."

"And the workers' grievances?" I asked. "Have they been dealt with?"

"Well, Fleet Captain, that's complicated." I failed to see what was complicated about paying workers fairly, or providing them with the same basic rights and services due any citizen. "Really, the conditions on Fosyf's plantation aren't much different from any of the others in the mountains. But it's Fosyf who will take the brunt of this. And now some of the more troublesome of the Xhai are getting into the act. You may know there's a small, ruined temple on the other side of the lake from Fosyf's house."

"She mentioned it."

"It was nothing but weeds and rubble when we arrived six hundred years ago. But lately we've had people claiming it's always been a sacred spot, and that Fosyf's house is actually a stop on an ancient pilgrimage trail. Fosyf herself encourages the belief, I suppose she finds it romantic. But it's ridiculous, that house was built less than a hundred years before the annexation. And did you ever know a pilgrimage spot that wasn't surrounded by at least a town?"

"One or two, actually," I replied. "Though generally not temples with priests that needed supporting. It's possible this one didn't have a resident priesthood." The district magistrate gestured acceptance of my point. "Let me be frank, Magistrate. It's *you* who are under pressure here."

Anaander Mianaai had given me her house name, when she had declared me human, and a citizen. It was a name that said I belonged to the most powerful family in Radch space, a name no Radchaai could ignore. Because of what I was—the last remnant of a military ship that for some two thousand years had been intimately acquainted with the daughters of quite a few of the wealthiest, most prominent of Radchaai houses—I had, when I wished, the accent and the manners to match. I might as well use them.

"You've long been friends with most of the prominent tea growers," I said, "but it's become clear that the demands of the fieldworkers are just and it is—or it should be—a personal embarrassment to you that it took an attempted murder and a work stoppage for you to notice what was happening. You will be even more embarrassed when you've interrogated Citizen Raughd. You haven't yet, have you." Out in the courtyard, Translator Zeiat folded over one of the wide, round lily pads to look at its underside.

"I was hoping," replied the magistrate, unable to keep her anger entirely out of her voice, "that she and her mother might be reconciled first."

"Citizen Fosyf will only take her daughter back if it seems advantageous to herself. If you're truly interested in Citizen Raughd's welfare, interrogate her before you make any further attempts to reunite her with her mother."

"*You're* interested in Raughd's welfare?"

"Not particularly," I admitted. "Not on a personal level. But you clearly are. And I *am* interested in the welfare of Citizen Queter. The sooner you discover for yourself what sort of person Raughd is, the better basis you'll have for judging Queter's actions. And the better basis for deciding if sending Raughd back to her mother is really going to be good for her. Consider how easily, how coldly, Fosyf disowned her, and consider that people like Raughd don't spring from nowhere."

The magistrate frowned. "You're so sure you know what sort of person she is."

"You can easily discover for yourself if I'm right. And as for my intervening in the dispute between the workers and the growers—I won't. Instead I'll advise you to meet with the tea growers and the leaders of the fieldworkers without delay and settle this matter in the way you know it must be settled. Then set up a committee to investigate the history of the temple on the lake and ways to resolve the dispute surrounding it. Be sure everyone with an interest in the matter is represented. Concerned citizens may direct their complaints to the committee, who can take them into consideration during their deliberations." The district magistrate frowned again, opened her mouth to protest. Closed her mouth. "Anaander Mianaai is at war with herself," I continued. "That war may reach Athoek, or it may not. Either way, because at least one of the intersystem gates between us and the provincial palace is down, we can't expect any help or advice from them. We must see to the safety of the citizens here ourselves. *All* the citizens here, not just the ones with the right accents, or the proper religious beliefs. And we have, for whatever reason, the attention of the Presger."

"At war with herself, you say?" asked the magistrate. "And the Presger here, as you yourself have just pointed out? I've heard rumors, Fleet Captain."

"This is not the doing of the Presger, Magistrate."

"And if that's the case, Fleet Captain, where does your authority come from? Which of her sent you here?"

"If Anaander Mianaai's war with herself comes here," I said, "and citizens die, will it matter which Lord of the Radch it was?" Silence. Five had been watching Translator Zeiat, and I knew that she or Ship would say something to me if anything happened that needed my attention. I glanced idly toward the courtyard.

Translator Zeiat straddled the basin's edge, one leg in the water, and one arm, shoulder deep. I stood and strode out to the courtyard, reaching as I did for Ship. And quickly discovered that neither it nor Kalr Five had told me what was happening because they were arguing with *Sphene.*

Arguing was perhaps too dignified a word for it. *Sphene*'s close shadowing of Five apparently hadn't produced the results it wanted, and while my attention had been on my conversation with the district magistrate it had been speaking to Five. Needling, with a success that was clearly demonstrated by the fact that neither Five nor Ship had brought it to my attention, and both were intent on replying in kind. As I came up next to Five, *Sphene* said, "Just sat there, did you, while she maimed you? But of course you did, and probably thanked her for it, too. You're one of her newer toys, she can make you think or feel anything she wants. No doubt her cousin the fleet captain can do the same."

Five, her ancillary-like calm gone, replied. Or maybe it was Ship who spoke, it was difficult to tell at that moment. "At least *I* have a captain. And a crew, for that matter. Where's yours? Oh, that's right, you misplaced your captain and haven't been able to find another. And nobody aboard you *wants* to be there, do they."

Ancillary-fast, *Sphene* rose from the bench it had been sitting on and moved toward Five. I put myself between them, grabbed *Sphene*'s forearm before it could strike either of us. *Sphene* froze, its arm in my grip. Blinked, face expressionless. "*Mianaai*, is it?"

I had moved faster than any Radchaai human could. There was no escaping the obvious conclusion—I was not human. My name made the next (incorrect) conclusion just as obvious. "It is not," I said. Quietly, and in Notai, because I wasn't sure where the magistrate was just now. "I am the last remaining fragment of the troop carrier *Justice of Toren*. It was Anaander Mianaai who destroyed me." I switched back to Radchaai. "Step back, *Cousin*." It was motionless for an instant, and then almost imperceptibly it shifted its weight back, away from me. I opened my hand, and it lowered its arm.

I turned my head at a splash from across the courtyard. Translator Zeiat stood upright now, one leg still in the water, one arm soaked and dripping. A small orange fish wriggled desperately in her grip. As I watched she tilted her head back and held the fish over her mouth. "Translator!" I said, loud and sharp, and she turned her head toward me. "Please don't do that. Please put the fish back in the water."

"But it's a fish." Her expression was frankly perplexed. "Aren't fish for eating?" The district magistrate stood at the top of the steps into the courtyard, staring at the translator. Quite possibly afraid to say anything.

"Some fish are for eating." I went over to where the translator stood half in and half out of the water. "Not this one." I cupped my hands, held them out. With a little scowl that reminded me of Dlique, Translator Zeiat dropped the fish into my outstretched hands, and I quickly tipped it into the basin before it could flip out onto the ground. "These fish are for looking at."

"Are you not supposed to look at the fish you eat?" Translator Zeiat asked. "And how do you tell the difference?"

"Usually, Translator, when they're in a basin like this, especially in a home, they're on display, or they're pets. But since you're not used to making the distinction, perhaps it's best if you ask before you eat anything that hasn't explicitly been given to you as food. To prevent misunderstandings."

"But I really wanted to eat it," she said, almost mournfully.

"Translator," said the district magistrate, who had come across the courtyard while the translator and I were talking, "there are places where you can pick out fish to eat. Or you can go down to the sea..." The magistrate began to explain about oysters.

Sphene had left the courtyard while I was occupied with the translator. Quite possibly it had left the house. Five stood, once again her usual impassive self. Apprehensive of my attention, and ashamed.

And who had been responsible for that altercation? Ship had given Five words to say, but Five had not been dispassionately reading off Ship's message. Ship's words had appeared in Five's vision more or less at the same instant as she spoke, and while Five had deviated slightly from Ship's exact phrasing, it was clear that in that moment they both had been overtaken with the same urge to say the same thing.

Translator Zeiat seemed quite taken with the idea of oysters; the district magistrate was talking about beds around the river mouth, and boats that could be hired to take her to them. That was tomorrow settled, then. I turned my attention back to Five. Back to Ship. They both watched me.

I knew what it was to have Anaander Mianaai alter my thoughts, and attempt to direct my emotions. I didn't doubt that the removal of *Mercy of Kalr*'s ancillaries had begun with the Lord of the Radch doing just that. Nor did I doubt, given my own experience and the events of the past few months, that more than one faction of Anaander Mianaai had visited *Mercy of Kalr* and each at least attempted to lay down her own set of instructions and inhibitions. *I've been unhappy with the situation for some time*, it had said, when we'd first met, and likely that was as much as it was able to say. And *Mercy of Kalr* wasn't vulnerable only to Anaander Mianaai. I had accesses that would let me compel its obedience. Not as far-reaching as Anaander Mianaai's, to be sure, and to be used with the greatest caution. But I had them.

Someone who could be a captain was, presumably, a person, not a piece of equipment. Didn't (in theory at least) have to worry about her builder and owner altering her thoughts to suit that owner's purposes, let alone doing it in uncomfortably conflicting ways. Someone who could be a captain might obey someone else, but it was through her own choice. "I understand," I said, quietly, while the translator and the magistrate were still occupied with their conversation, "that *Sphene* is incredibly annoying, and I know it's been trying for days to get a rise out of you." No term of address, because I was talking to both Ship and Five. "But you know I'm going to have to reprimand you. You know you should have kept silent. And you should have kept your attention on the translator. Don't let it happen again."

"Sir," acknowledged Five.

"And by the way, thank you for talking to Lieutenant Seivarden." Five knew the basic outlines of what had happened, she was never entirely out of contact with the rest of her decade. "I thought you handled that well." In Medical, aboard *Mercy of Kalr*, Seivarden slept. Amaat One, apprehensive, going over policies and regulations with Ship, because she would have to stand Seivarden's watch in a few hours. She already knew everything she needed to know, and Ship was always there to help. It was just a matter of officially demonstrating it. And of her reminding herself that she did know it. Ekalu, on watch herself, was still angry. But after some (rather fraught) discussion with Ship, Seivarden had managed a short, simple apology that had not placed blame anywhere but on herself, and had not demanded anything from Ekalu in return. So Ekalu's anger had lessened, had faded into the background of anxiety surrounding her suddenly being in command.

"Thank you, sir," Kalr Five said again. For Ship.

I turned back to the translator. The topic had strayed from oysters back to the fish in the courtyard basin. "It's all right," the magistrate was saying. "You can eat one of the fish."

I didn't know whether to be relieved or alarmed at the fact that it took Translator Zeiat less than five minutes to find (and catch) the exact same one, and swallow it down, still wriggling.

6

The district magistrate came herself to Queter's interrogation. It was an unpleasant, humiliating business, made no better by the interrogator's assurance that Citizen Queter herself would not remember it. "That only makes it worse," said Queter, who had been brought in already drugged.

"Please speak Radchaai, citizen," said the interrogator, with an aplomb that suggested Queter was not the first patient of hers to speak mostly in another language. And left me wondering what she would do if one of her patients spoke Radchaai very poorly, or if she could not understand their accent.

Afterward, in the corridor outside, the district magistrate, looking grim after what we had just heard, said, "Fleet Captain, I've moved Citizen Raughd's interrogation up to tomorrow morning. She requested her mother as her witness, but Citizen Fosyf has refused to come." And then, after a moment of silence, "I've known Raughd since she was a baby. I remember when she was born." Sighed. "Are you always right about everything?"

"No," I replied. Simply. Evenly. "But I'm right about this."

* * *

I stayed long enough for Queter to recover from the drugs, so that she would know for certain that I had come. Then I went back down the hill to the river mouth, where Kalr Eight stood watch over Translator Zeiat, who sat on a red-cushioned bench on a black stone quay while a citizen shucked oysters for her. *Sphene*, who had returned to our lodgings that morning and sat down to breakfast without any sort of explanation or even a perfunctory *Good morning*, sat beside her, gazing out at the gray-and-white waves.

"Fleet Captain!" said Translator Zeiat happily. "We went out in a boat! Did you know there are millions of fish out there in that water?" She gestured toward the sea. "Some of them are quite large, apparently! And some of them aren't actually fish! Have you ever eaten an oyster?"

"I have not."

The translator gestured urgently to the oyster-shucking citizen, who deftly pried one open and handed it to me. "Just tip it into your mouth and chew it a few times, Fleet Captain," she said, "and then swallow it."

Translator Zeiat watched me expectantly as I did so. "So," I observed, "that was an oyster." The oyster-shucker laughed, short and sharp. Unfazed by the translator, or by me.

And remained unfazed when the translator said, "Give me one before you open it." And, receiving it, put the entire thing, tightly closed shell and all, into her mouth. The oyster was a good twelve centimeters long, and the translator's jaw unhinged and slid forward just a bit as she swallowed the entire thing. Her throat distended as it went down, and then her jaw moved back into place and she gently patted her upper chest, as though helping the oyster settle.

Eight, outwardly impassive, was appalled and frightened

at what she'd just seen. *Sphene* still gazed out at the water, as though it had noticed nothing—indeed, as if it were entirely alone. I looked at the oyster-shucker, who said, calmly, "Can't none of you surprise me anymore." Which was when I realized her imperturbability in the translator's presence was only an act.

"Citizen," said Translator Zeiat, "do you ever put fish sauce on oysters?"

"I can't say I've ever done that, Translator." And now I was looking for it, I noticed the very slight hesitation before she answered, the very tiny tremor in her voice. "But if it tastes good to you, why, you just go ahead."

Translator Zeiat made a satisfied *hah.* "Can we go out in the boat again tomorrow?"

"I expect so, Translator," replied the oyster-shucker, and I silently instructed Eight to add extra to her fee.

But we didn't go out in the boat the next day. Halfway through her first watch, Amaat One noticed an anomaly in the data Ship was showing her. It was very tiny, just a slight moment of *nothing* where there had been *something* before. It might easily have been completely insignificant, or maybe a sign that one of *Mercy of Kalr*'s sensors needed looking at. Or that instant of *nothing* might have been a gate opening. Which would mean a military ship had arrived. And maybe in a little while its message identifying itself would reach us.

Or maybe not. If it had been a ship arriving, its captain had chosen to arrive a very long way away from Athoek Station. Almost as though she didn't want to be seen. "Ship," said Amaat One, no doubt having had all these thoughts in the panicked instant between her seeing that anomaly and her speaking, "please wake Lieutenant Ekalu." And a moment of almost-relief. The rest would not be her responsibility.

By the time Lieutenant Ekalu arrived in Command, not entirely awake, still pulling on her uniform jacket, it had happened three more times. And no message had arrived, no greeting, no identification—though it was likely too soon for that anyway. "Thank you, Amaat," she said. "Well spotted." Ship had seen it, too, and would have said something to Amaat One if necessary, of course. Still. "Ship, can we guess where they might have come from?" She gestured, indicating Amaat One should stay in her seat. Accepted tea from another Amaat.

"The fact that they arrived within minutes of each other suggests they left from the same place at more or less the same time," replied Ship, "and traveled by similar routes. For various reasons"—Ship displayed some of its reasons in Ekalu's vision, calculations of distance through the unreality of gate-space, likely departure times from various other systems—"including the fact that Fleet Captain Uemi"—who was one gate away in Hrad System and our only source of news from Omaugh Palace—"has not told us any ships are coming to support us, and the fact that these ships have arrived far enough away we might reasonably have missed them, I think it likely they've come from Tstur Palace."

Tstur Palace. Where the faction of Anaander Mianaai most overtly hostile to me, whose supporters had destroyed intersystem gates while civilian ships were still in them, who had herself attempted to destroy an entire station full of citizens, was now in control. "Right," Ekalu replied. Voice steady. Face impassive. Just the smallest tremor in the hand that held her bowl of tea. "I suppose we should notify the Hrad Fleet? Is S...is the fleet captain aware of this?"

"Yes, Lieutenant." Palpable relief, from Ekalu, from Amaat One, from the other Amaats standing watch.

"Is..." And then, silently, for Ship alone, "Is she aware that

Lieutenant Seivarden is... that Medic has removed Lieutenant Seivarden from duty?" Seivarden slept in Medical, and in theory she could be wakened to take command. But she'd spent the day drugged, undergoing testing so that Medic could at least attempt to help her with her difficulties. And the results of that testing so far suggested that it would be extremely foolhardy just now to put Seivarden under any sort of stress.

"I am," I said silently, from downwell, where I bemusedly watched as Translator Zeiat very carefully cut a tiny fish-shaped cake into thin horizontal slices and laid them in a row on the table in front of her. "You'll be fine, Lieutenant. Keep an eye on them, best we can, and I'll be there as soon as I can manage it. They probably won't move until they feel like they have a good idea of what's going on here. Let's act like we haven't noticed them, for now." The tall windows of the lodging house sitting room opened onto a view of the night-time city, lights trailing down to the shore, the lights of the boats, blue and red and yellow out on the water. Now the sun was down the breeze had shifted, and smelled of flowers instead of the sea. *Sphene*, who had said nothing all day, sat beside me, staring out the window. "But do clear for action. Just in case."

Behind me, Kalr Eight said to Kalr Five in the quietest of whispers, "But what I can't stop thinking about is, what happens to the oyster shell?"

Without looking up, or pausing her slow and careful slicing, Translator Zeiat said, quite calmly, "I'm digesting it, of course. Though it does seem to be taking a while. Would you like it? It's mostly still there."

"No, thank you, Translator," replied Eight in a flat, ancillary-like voice.

"It was very kind of you to offer, Translator," I said.

Translator Zeiat completed her cut, carefully slid the piece of cake from her knife-blade onto the table. Looked up at me, frowning. "Kind? I wouldn't have said it was *kind*." Blinked. "Perhaps I just don't understand that word."

"In this context it's just a formal way to say *thank you*, Translator," I replied. "I'm afraid we won't be able to go out in the boat tomorrow. I have to return to the station immediately." Behind me Five and Eight queried Ship, and even before the reply came, Five left the sitting room to begin packing.

Translator Zeiat said only, "Oh?" Mild. Uninterested. She gestured at the thin, flat slices of fish-shaped cake arrayed on the table in front of her. "It's the same all the way through, have you noticed? Other fish aren't. Other fish are complicated inside."

"Yes," I agreed.

Tisarwat stood on the main concourse of Athoek Station, watching the line that still stretched out of Station Administration. Though some days had passed since it had first formed, it had not died away. It was, if anything, longer than it had been.

The Head of Station Security, standing beside Lieutenant Tisarwat, said, "So far so good. I suppose I shouldn't be surprised that the fleet captain knew what she was talking about. But I admit I am. Still. Half the people in line right now have no assignment. If they did, the line would be shorter. I wish Administration would just find them jobs, it would make our lives easier."

"They'd just come during their off-hours, sir," Lieutenant Tisarwat observed. Indeed, no few places in the line were currently marked by objects left as placeholders—cushions, mostly, or folded blankets. Quite a few citizens had spent the night here. "Or worse, skip work entirely. Then we'd have more work stoppages on our hands." She didn't look over toward the temple entrance, where the priests of Amaat still sat. On cushions themselves now—Eminence Ifian hadn't lasted more than an hour on the hard concourse floor before she'd sent a junior priest for something to sit on. Watching from downwell I'd wondered how long the eminence had thought she and her priests would have to sit there—if she had expected a quick capitulation, or if she'd just not thought about that particular detail. Station likely knew, but Station, being Station, wouldn't tell me if I asked.

Governor Giarod had made no public statement about the situation, but then, she did control the official news feeds. Which had mentioned the eminence's work stoppage, and even quoted her on her reasons for it. The official news did not mention the line at all. Nor did the official news mention that the Xhai hierophant was willing to perform birth celebrations or funeral obsequies for any citizen, initiate of the Mysteries or not. Station Administrator Celar's daily omen casts were reported in the blandest possible manner, with no elaboration or discussion.

Station Security, of course, was fairly firmly behind Station Administrator Celar. Still. "It might end sooner, perhaps," said the head of Security, to Tisarwat, "without the food and beverage service." A dozen or so Undergarden residents—Uran included, when she wasn't at her studies—had been bringing tea and food to the citizens waiting in line, twice a day. Uran herself had offered tea to the priests in front of the temple, on the first day, and had been stonily ignored.

"Or perhaps, sir," Tisarwat replied, "they'd be in line just as long, but hungry and caffeine-deprived." She gestured the obviousness of the unspoken second half of that suggestion. "Maybe they're doing us a favor."

"Hah!" The head of Security seemed genuinely amused. "They're all your neighbors, aren't they. And that youngster with them—Uran, is it?—is part of your household. A ward of the fleet captain's, I understand?"

Tisarwat smiled. "We should have another game of counters this evening."

"So long as you don't let me win again."

"I've never let you win, sir," Tisarwat lied, her lilac eyes wide and innocent.

From downwell, I said, "A word, Lieutenant."

Lieutenant Tisarwat started guiltily, but to anyone who couldn't see her as I did, as Ship did, her reaction only showed as a blink. "Will you excuse me a moment, sir?" she said to the head of Security, and when she was well away, said silently to me, "Yes, Fleet Captain."

Sitting in our lodgings downwell in Xhenang Serit, I said, also silently, "As unobtrusively as possible, move anything essential onto the shuttle. Be certain you have a clear path to the docks at all times. Be ready to get off the station at a moment's notice."

Tisarwat made for the lifts. Said, still silent, after a near-panicked moment, "She's here, then. What about you, sir?"

"We'll be leaving here shortly. I should be there in two days. But don't wait for me if you need to move."

She didn't like hearing that, but knew better than to say so. Boarded an already crowded lift. Named aloud the level where our quarters were, for Station, and then, silently again, to me, "Yes, sir. But what about Horticulturist Basnaaid? What about Citizen Uran?"

I had already thought about both of them. "Ask them—

discreetly—if they'd prefer to stay or go. Do not pressure either of them in any way. If they elect to stay, there are two boxes in my things." I might as well have left them on *Mercy of Kalr*, but Five, who had seen them, had decided I might need them to impress someone. "One is a *very* large piece of jewelry, flowers and leaves done in diamonds and emeralds. It's a necklace." Though *necklace* was something of an understatement. "Give that to Uran. She can get a lot for it, if she knows how to sell it. The other box has teeth in it."

Striding out of the lift, Tisarwat froze an instant, forcing the person behind her to stop suddenly and stumble. "Excuse me, citizen," she said, aloud, and then, silently, to me, "Teeth?"

"Teeth. Made of moissanite. They're not worth much here. They're..." I almost said *a sentimental possession*, but that didn't quite express it. "A souvenir." That didn't, either.

"Teeth?" Tisarwat asked again. Turned from the main corridor into a side one.

"Their owner willed them to me. I'll tell you about it later, if you like. But give them to Basnaaid. Be sure to tell her they aren't worth that much, as far as money goes. I just want her to have them." They'd have been worth half the Itran Tetrarchy, if we were there now. I had spent several years there. Conceivably could go back, and still have a place, or find one. But that was very, very far away. "If I'm right that Anaander is here, she'll likely spend some time observing traffic in the system before she tries to gate too close to the station." Gating into a heavily trafficked area meant running the risk of doing a great deal of damage, to your own ship and to the ships you might slam into coming out of your gate. "If she doesn't gate in, they'll be months getting here, from what I can tell."

"Yes, sir. What are we going to do, sir?" She bowed to someone passing the other way.

"I'm thinking about it."

"Sir." She stopped. Looked around. Saw only the retreating back of the person she'd just bowed to. Still did not speak aloud. "Sir, what about Station?" I didn't answer. "Sir, if...if *she's* here—" I had never known Lieutenant Tisarwat to say Anaander Mianaai's name. "Sir, you know I have accesses. I specifically have high-level accesses to Station. If we could..." She stopped, waiting, maybe, for me to say something, but I said nothing. "If we could make sure that Station was *our* ally, that might be...helpful."

I knew she had accesses. Anaander Mianaai had had no intention of coming here without the means to control the AIs in the system, including *Mercy of Kalr*. Including Athoek Station. I had explicitly forbidden Tisarwat to use those accesses, and so far she had not.

"Sir," said Tisarwat. "I understand—I think I understand—why you don't want me to use them, even now. But, sir, *she* won't hesitate to use them."

"That's a reason to use them ourselves, is it?" I asked.

"It's an advantage we have, sir! That *she* won't know we have! And it's not like our not using it will spare Station anything. You know she'll use those accesses herself! We might as well get there first."

I wanted to tell her that she was thinking exactly like Anaander Mianaai, but it would have hurt her, and besides, she mostly couldn't help it. "May I point out, Lieutenant, that I am as I am now precisely because of that sort of thinking?"

Dismay. Hurt. And indignation. "That wasn't all her, sir." And then, daring—terrified, actually, of saying such a thing, "What if Station *wanted* me to? What if Station would rather have *us* doing it than...than *her*?"

"Lieutenant," I replied, "I cannot possibly describe to you

how unpleasant it is to have irreconcilable, conflicting imperatives forcibly implanted in your mind. Anaander has surely been before you—both of her. You think Station wants you to add a third complication?" No answer. Downwell, where I sat in the lodging house sitting room, Translator Zeiat made a last small nudge to her arrangement of fish-shaped cake sections, and then took a drink from her bowl of fish sauce and stood and went to the open window. "But since you mention it, do you think you can perhaps arrange things so that Station can't be compelled by anyone? Not Anaander Mianaai, not any of her? Not us?"

"What?" Tisarwat stood confused in the scuffed gray corridor on Athoek Station. She genuinely had not understood what I had just said.

"Can you close off all the accesses to Station? So that neither Anaander can control it? Or better, can you give Station its own deep accesses and let it make whatever changes it wants to itself, or let it choose who has access and how much?"

"Let it..." As it became clear to her what I was suggesting, she began, just slightly, to hyperventilate. "Sir, you're not seriously suggesting that." I didn't reply. "Sir, it's a *station.* Millions of lives depend on it."

"I think Station is sensible of that, don't you?"

"But, sir! What if something were to go wrong? No one could get in to fix it." I considered asking just what she thought would constitute something going wrong, but she continued without pausing. "And what...sir, what if you did that and it decided it wanted to work for *her*? I don't think that's at all unlikely, sir."

"I think," I replied, downwell, watching Translator Zeiat, now leaning precariously out the window, "that no matter who it allies itself with, its primary concern will be the well-being of its residents."

Lieutenant Tisarwat took two inadequately deep breaths. "Sir? Begging your very great indulgence, sir." Completely unaware of her surroundings, now, but fortunately the corridor was still empty—it was mostly dormitories here, and it was hours from the next sleep-shift change. And she still had the presence of mind not to speak aloud. "With all respect, sir, I don't think you've thought this all the way through." I said nothing. "Oh, fuck." She put her face in her brown-gloved hands. "Oh, Aatr's tits, you *have* thought this all the way through. But, sir, I don't think you've thought this all the way through."

"You need to get out of the corridor, Lieutenant." Downwell, Translator Zeiat leaned back into the room, much to my relief.

In the corridor on Athoek Station, Tisarwat said, still speaking silently, "You can't. You can't do that, sir. You can't just do that for Station, for one thing. What if every ship and station could do whatever it wanted? That would be…"

"Get out of the corridor, Lieutenant. Someone's sure to come along soon, and you look like you're having some sort of breakdown just now."

Her hands still over her face, she cried aloud, "I *am* having a breakdown!"

"Lieutenant," said Station, into Tisarwat's ear. "Are you all right?"

"I'm…" Tisarwat lowered her hands. Stood straighter. Started down the corridor. "I'm fine, Station. Everything's all right."

"You don't look fine, Lieutenant," said Station. At the same time it sent a message to *Mercy of Kalr*.

"Yes," Ship replied, to Station. "She's upset about something. She'll be all right in a few moments. Glad you're watching."

"I'm...I'm all right, Station," said Tisarwat, walking down the corridor. Apparently steadily, but in fact working hard to keep herself from shaking. "Thank you, though."

Downwell, in our lodging, *Sphene*, who had been sitting beside me, silent all this time, staring, said, "Well, Cousin, I wish you'd say what it is that's stopped you humming. I'd like to be able to make it happen again sometime."

"Has nothing I've sung been to your taste, Cousin?" I asked mildly. "You could request something."

"Could *I* request something, Fleet Captain?" asked Translator Zeiat, emptying a bottle of fish sauce into her bowl.

"Certainly, Translator. Is there a song you'd particularly like to hear?"

"No," she replied. "I was just curious."

On Athoek Station, Tisarwat had reached our makeshift quarters at the corridor's end. She sat down on the ground behind the barrier of crates. Ship had already told Kalr Ten and Bo Nine what I wanted, and Bo Nine stopped considering how to get our things onto the shuttle with no one noticing, and went to make tea. Though Tisarwat was trying hard to seem unfazed, and Ship had said nothing to Nine, it was a measure of how worried she was about her lieutenant's emotional state that she dumped out the tea leaves she'd been using all week, that had at least another day in them, and started with new ones.

Tisarwat drank half the tea, and then, considerably calmer, said silently to me, "It might not even be possible. There are safeguards in place against exactly that, I'm sure you know that, sir. Nobody ever wanted AIs to be able to use their own accesses on themselves. But you realize, even if someone found a way to do it, there'd be no way to keep that knowledge from spreading. We couldn't make Station keep it secret. It could tell anyone it wanted."

"Lieutenant," I said, "you do understand, don't you, that I have no intention of helping Anaander Mianaai recover from this?"

Sitting on the ground, knees drawn up, bowl of tea in her hands, she said, aloud, "But..." Bo Nine didn't stop what she was doing, re-sorting things from one case to others, but her attention was instantly on Tisarwat. "All respect, sir." Speaking silently again. "Have you thought about it? I mean, really thought about it. This wouldn't just change things in Radch space. Sooner or later it will change things everywhere. And I know, sir, that it's gone all wrong, but the whole idea behind the expansion of the Radch is to protect the Radch itself, it's about the protection of humanity. What happens when any AI can remake itself? Even the armed ones? What happens when AIs can build new AIs with no restrictions? AIs are already smarter and stronger than humans, what happens when they decide they don't need humans at all? Or if they decide they only need humans for body parts?"

"Like Anaander did with Tisarwat, you mean?" I asked. And almost immediately regretted saying it, seeing the flare of wounded feeling, of self-loathing and despair in Lieutenant Tisarwat at hearing what I'd said. "You ask me if I've really thought about this. Lieutenant, I have had twenty years to think about it. You say it *went wrong.* Ask yourself if the *way* it went wrong has anything to say about *why* it went wrong. If it was ever right to begin with."

Anger, from Tisarwat. Hardly surprising. "Well, what about *Mercy of Kalr*? We're having this conversation where Ship can hear us." Of course we were. There was no way for us to have any conversation without Ship hearing us. "If this is doable, Ship will see me do it. Are you going to do this for *Mercy of Kalr*, too? And if you do, what if it decides it would rather have another captain? Or another crew? Or none at all?"

Well. I had gotten personal, moments before. Small wonder she did so herself, now. But the thought could not surprise me again. Or dismay me. Ships loved captains, not other ships. And I was a ship, even if a much reduced one. Perhaps being with *Mercy of Kalr* gave me some bare semblance of what I had lost—that did not require Ship to prefer me over some other captain. "Why should it be forced to accept a captain it doesn't want? Or a crew? If it wants to be on its own, it should be able to be that." But I knew it didn't want to be. I thought of my own crew's obvious fondness for their ship, and Ship's obvious care of them. Of Ship's obvious care for Seivarden. And of *Sphene*, furious at the reminder that it had no captain or crew at all, and no possibility of one. "You've never been a ship, Lieutenant."

"Ships aren't mistreated. They do what they were made to do. It can't possibly be so bad, to be a ship. Or a station."

"Stop for a moment," I advised, "and think who you are saying that to. And why you are saying it, in these circumstances, at this particular moment."

She drank the rest of her tea in silence.

That evening Tisarwat didn't play counters with the head of Security. "Station," she said, aloud, after swallowing her last mouthful of after-supper tea, sitting on one of the crates that marked out our quarters in the corridor end. Her heart tripped faster as she spoke. "I need to talk to you. Very privately."

"Of course, Lieutenant."

Tisarwat handed her now-empty teabowl to Bo Nine. "I don't think here is a good place, though. Where can I go where neither of us will be overheard?"

"How about your shuttle, Lieutenant?"

Tisarwat smiled, though her heart beat even harder, startled by another spike of adrenaline. She had wanted exactly that answer, though I didn't see why she had thought she might get it. Was only a little surprised that she had, was also afraid of what was coming. "Oh, good idea, Station." Almost as though the thought hadn't already occurred to her, as though this were all something inconsequential. She picked up a bag—just one more unobtrusive load of things she and Kalr Ten and Bo Nine had been bringing to the shuttle all day. "I'll talk to you there, then."

Once in the shuttle, she emptied the bag into a storage locker, and then kicked herself over to a seat and strapped herself in. "Station."

"Lieutenant."

"When Fleet Captain Breq arrived here and told the governor that...that the Lord of the Radch was at war with herself, you weren't surprised, were you. At some point in the recent past the Lord of Mianaai visited your physical Central Access, didn't she. And made some changes."

"I'm sure I don't know what you mean, Lieutenant."

Tisarwat gave a nervous, nauseated little *hah.* "And then another part of her came, later, and did the same thing. And they both made it so you couldn't talk about it to anyone." A breath. "She did it to *Justice of Toren*, too. Fleet Captain Breq knows what it's like. I...the Lord of the Radch sent me here with accesses. So that we can make sure you're on our side. But...but Fleet Captain Breq doesn't want me to use them. Not unless, you know, you actually want me to." Silence. "I can't promise that I can find all the things that they left, when they were here and trying to make certain you'd only obey them. I can probably only find the things one of them left. Because..." Tisarwat swallowed, increasingly nauseated. She hadn't taken any meds before crossing over into the shuttle's microgravity. "Because my accesses come from that one. But Fleet Captain Breq says I shouldn't go doing things to you without asking. Because she knows how it feels, and she didn't like it one bit."

"I like Fleet Captain Breq," said Station. "I never thought I'd like a ship. At best they're polite. Which isn't the same thing as respectful. Or kind."

"No," agreed Tisarwat.

"I don't much like the conflict she's brought here. But then again, it was already here when she arrived, really." A pause. "I notice you're moving things into your shuttle. As though you might need to leave quickly. Is there something going on?"

"You realize," said Tisarwat, "that I can't really trust you entirely. I don't know who has accesses, who can compel you to reveal things. Or who else here *we* can trust. *You* know, I'm sure. You know nearly everything that goes on here."

Three minutes of silence. Tisarwat's nausea increased, and the blood pounded in her ears. Then Station said, "Lieutenant, what is it exactly that you intend to do, that Fleet Captain Breq insists you get me to agree to before you do it?"

"Let me grab some meds, Station. I'm feeling really sick just now. And then we'll talk about it. All right?"

And Station said, "All right. Lieutenant."

7

Two days later, strapped into my seat on the passenger shuttle from the elevator, Translator Zeiat apparently soundly asleep in the seat beside me, I heard from Lieutenant Tisarwat. "Fleet Captain. We're on the shuttle." *Mercy of Kalr*'s shuttle, she meant. She did not wait for me to ask for details. "We're still docked with the station. But something's wrong. I can't quite pin down what it is, exactly. Mostly Station seems…odd."

At my request *Mercy of Kalr* showed me the oddness Tisarwat referred to. Nothing, as Tisarwat said, that was obvious or definite. Just a reticence in the past several days that seemed uncharacteristic of Station. It would have been entirely unsurprising when we'd first arrived here, weeks ago. Athoek Station had been unhappy then, and that reticence had been a sign, I knew, that its attitude toward Station authorities was at the very least ambivalent, and very possibly outright resentful. A good deal of Station's unhappiness had centered around the state of the Undergarden, severely damaged centuries ago, never repaired. My forcing the issue, demanding Station Administration address the problems in the Undergarden, accounted for no small part of Station's recent friendliness, I was sure. If it had turned reticent now, either we had done something to upset it—or more accurately Tisarwat had, since I had been downwell the past few days—or it found itself unpleasantly conflicted over something.

"Sir," Tisarwat continued, when I didn't reply immediately, "a few days ago—yesterday, even—I could have gone to Central Access and found out exactly what the problem was. But I can't do that now."

You could do quite a lot to control an AI if you had the right codes and commands. But some things—including, but not limited to, changing those codes, or installing or deleting accesses—had to be done in person, in Central Access. Tisarwat had spent quite a while in Station's Central Access over the last two days. The place was heavily shielded, for obvious reasons. Only Station—and any person who was actually, physically present—could see inside it, and so I didn't know in detail what Tisarwat had done. But of course, as with every Radchaai soldier, everything Tisarwat did was recorded. Ship had those recordings, and I had seen parts of them.

With Station's agreement, Tisarwat had deleted (or radically changed) any accesses she'd found. And then, when she'd left, she'd destroyed the mechanism that ought to open the doors in response to an authorized entrance code, broken the manual override and its accompanying console. Removed a panel inside the Central Access wall and shoved a dozen thirty-centimeter struts she'd taken from Undergarden repair materials into the door machinery in such a way that when she left, and the doors closed behind her, they would not open again. All this, still, with Station's agreement. Tisarwat could not have done half so much without Station's help, in fact. But now, when Tisarwat might have liked to compel Station to explain itself, she could not. Had, herself, made that impossible.

"Lieutenant," I said, "we don't need accesses to know what's wrong. I'd say Station has received orders concerning us that it can't tell us directly about. Either someone's used an access you didn't know to disable, or else speaking directly to us would betray some relationship that's important to Station. Or would betray the extent of your alterations to Central Access. But it is warning us something is wrong, and we'd be well-advised to pay attention. You made the right call, moving to the shuttle. What about Basnaaid and Uran?"

"They've elected to stay, sir." I was unsurprised. And perhaps it was the safest choice. "Sir," Tisarwat continued, after a pause, "I'm…I'm afraid I did something wrong."

"What do you mean, Lieutenant?"

"I…those ships that came into the system, they haven't approached. We couldn't miss that, if they had. So *she's* not on the station. And I don't think System Governor Giarod or the station administrator are able to give Station any orders it couldn't tell me about. Not without some kind of access code from…from *her*." From the other Anaander. "And she wouldn't have messaged an access like that, she'd only give it in person. So if Station's upset, maybe it's with me. Or maybe I did something that hurt it. Or if something else is wrong, we can't get in to fix it anymore."

Unbidden, Ship showed me Tisarwat's fear—near panic—and self-hatred. An almost physically painful regret. Though her apprehensions were on their face entirely reasonable, her emotional state struck me as extreme, even considering that. "Lieutenant," I said, still silently, Translator Zeiat still asleep strapped into her shuttle seat beside me. "Did you do anything Station didn't agree to?"

"No, sir."

"Did you manipulate Station into agreeing to anything?"

"I don't…I don't think so, sir. No. But, sir…"

"Then you did your best. It's certainly possible you made a mistake, and it's worth keeping that possibility in mind. It's good that you're thinking of that possibility." In *Mercy of Kalr*'s shuttle, Bo Nine kicked herself over to where Tisarwat clung to a handhold. Pulled away the patch of meds at the back of Tisarwat's neck, just under her dark-brown uniform collar, and replaced it with a new one. If anything, Tisarwat's self-hatred and anxiety increased, with a fresh surge of shame. "But, Lieutenant."

"Sir?"

"Be easier on yourself."

"You can see all that, can you?" Bitter. Accusing. Humiliated.

"You've known all this time that I can," I pointed out. "You certainly know that Ship can."

"That's different, isn't it," replied Tisarwat, angry now, at me and at herself.

I nearly retorted that it wasn't different at all, but stopped myself. Soldiers expected that kind of surveillance from Ship. But I was not, after all, Ship itself. "Is it different because Ship is subject to your orders, and I'm not?" I asked. Immediately regretted it—the question did nothing to improve Tisarwat's emotional state. And the issue of Ship being subject to orders was one that I had only recently realized might be a sensitive one for Ship itself. I found myself wishing I could see better what Ship was thinking or feeling, or that it would be plainer with me about what it felt. But perhaps it had been as plain as it could be. "This isn't the time for this particular discussion, Lieutenant. I meant what I said: be easier on yourself. You did the best you could. Now keep an eye on the situation and be ready to move if it seems necessary. I'll be there in a few hours." Should have been there already, but the passenger shuttle, as often happened, was running late. "If you need to move before I get there, then do."

I didn't look to see how she responded. On the passenger shuttle I unstrapped myself and pulled myself around the seat to where *Sphene* sat, behind me. "Cousin," I said, "it seems likely we'll be leaving the station on short notice in the near future. Do you prefer to stay, or to come with us?"

Sphene looked at me with no expression. "Don't they say, Cousin, that as long as you have family you'll want for nothing?"

"You warm my heart, Cousin," I replied.

"I don't doubt it," said *Sphene*, and closed its eyes.

When the passenger shuttle docked with the station, I immediately sent Five and Eight, along with *Sphene*, to *Mercy of Kalr*'s shuttle, and walked with Translator Zeiat to the lifts that would take us to the station's main concourse, and the governor's residence. "I hope you enjoyed your trip, Translator," I said.

"Yes, yes!" She patted her upper chest. "Though I do seem to be having some indigestion."

"I'm not surprised."

"Fleet Captain, I know it isn't your fault, what happened to Dlique. Considering, you know, *Dlique*. And"—she glanced down at her white coat, its only interruption Translator Dlique's silver-and-opal memorial pin—"it was very thoughtful of you to hold a funeral. Very...very *generous* of you. And you've been so very obliging. But I feel I must warn you that this situation is *very* awkward."

"Translator?" We stopped in front of the lifts—had to stop, because the doors did not open as we approached. I remembered what Tisarwat had said, that Station had been oddly reticent lately. Nothing she could pin down. "Main concourse please, Station," I said, as though I hadn't noticed anything amiss, and the doors opened.

"You may not know"—Translator Zeiat followed me onto the lift—"in fact, you probably *don't* know, that there have been...concerns in some quarters." The lift doors slid closed. "There was not...universal enthusiasm at the prospect of treating Humans as Significant beings. But an agreement made is an agreement. Wouldn't you agree?"

"I would."

"But recently, well. The situation with the Rrrrrr. Very troubling." The Rrrrrr had appeared in Radch space twenty-five years ago, their ship crewed not only by Rrrrrr, but humans as well. The local authorities had reacted by attempting to kill everyone aboard and take their ship. Might have succeeded if the decade leader assigned to the job hadn't refused her orders and mutinied.

But some centuries before that, the Geck had successfully argued that since the Presger already acknowledged humans as Significant and thus worthy of admittance to an agreement—and most importantly not a legitimate target for the Presger's bloodier amusements—then logically the close and equal association of the Geck with the humans living in their space proved they, also, were Significant beings. Every Radchaai schoolchild knew this, it was hardly possible the officials who'd ordered the destruction of the Rrrrrr didn't, or didn't understand what the implications of that would be, if word of the attack on the Rrrrrr ship ever got out: that the Radch might be entirely willing to break the treaty that had, for the last thousand years, kept humans safe from the depredations of the Presger.

"It didn't help, you know," Translator Zeiat continued, "that the Rrrrrr's association with Humans, who very clearly treated them as Significant beings, essentially forced the issue of whether they were Significant. The Geck as well. This was something that had been anticipated, you understand, and had from the start been an argument against making any agreement with Humans at all, let alone the question of their Significance. Difficult enough. But Humans—not just Humans, but Radchaai Humans, discover the Rrrrrr, in circumstances that make their implications for the treaty obvious, and do what? They attack them."

"More implications for the treaty," I agreed. "But that situation was straightened out, as quickly as we could."

"Yes, yes, Fleet Captain. It was. But it left some...some lingering doubts as to the intentions of Humans toward the treaty. And you know, I do understand the *idea* of different sorts of Humans. In the abstract, as I said. I must admit I do have some trouble really *comprehending* it. At least I know the *concept* exists. But if I tried to go home and explain it to *them*, well..." She gestured resignation. "I wouldn't even know how to begin." The lift door opened and we stepped out onto the white-floored concourse. "So you understand how very awkward this is."

"I have understood how potentially awkward this is since Translator Dlique met with her accident," I admitted. "Tell me, Translator, was Translator Dlique sent here because of this doubt about human intentions toward the treaty?" She didn't answer immediately. "The timing, you understand, and your appearance so soon after."

Translator Zeiat blinked. Sighed. "Oh, Fleet Captain. It's so very difficult talking to you sometimes. It seems like you understand things and then you say something that makes it obvious that, no, you don't understand at all."

"I'm sorry."

She gestured my apology away. "It isn't your fault."

I delivered Translator Zeiat to quarters in the governor's residence—not Dlique's, Governor Giarod had been at pains to assure me, though I wasn't entirely certain why she thought it mattered. Once the translator was settled, and a servant sent to find a fresh bottle of fish sauce and another few packets of fish-shaped cakes, I followed the system governor to her office.

I knew something was wrong when Governor Giarod stopped in the corridor just outside the door and gestured me through ahead of her. I almost turned and walked away, to the shuttle, except that then my back would be turned to whatever it was in Governor Giarod's office that she wanted me to encounter first. And besides, I was not in the habit of going through any door heedlessly. *Mercy of Kalr* spoke in my ear. "I've alerted Lieutenant Tisarwat, Fleet Captain."

Still mindful of that recent conversation with Tisarwat, I didn't reach to see her reaction, but went through the door into the system governor's office.

Lusulun stood waiting for me, trying hard to keep her face neutral, but I thought she looked guilty, and more than a little afraid. As I came fully into the office, System Governor Giarod behind me, two light-brown-coated Security stepped in front of the door.

"I assume you have a reason for this, citizens?" I asked. Quite calmly. I wondered where Administrator Celar was. Considered asking, and then thought better of it.

"We've had a message from the Lord of the Radch," said Governor Giarod. "We're ordered to place you under arrest."

"I'm sorry," said Head of Security Lusulun. Genuinely apologetic, I thought, but also still afraid. "My lord said... she said you were an ancillary. Is it true?"

I smiled. And then moved, ancillary-quick. Grabbed her around the throat, spun to face the door. Lusulun gasped as I wrenched her arm around behind her, and I tightened my grip on her throat just slightly. Said calmly in her ear, "If anyone moves, you're dead." Didn't say, *Now we discover how much System Governor Giarod values your life.* The two Security froze, frank dismay on their faces. "I don't want to, but I will. None of you can move as quickly as I can."

"You *are* an ancillary," said Governor Giarod. "I didn't believe it."

"If you didn't believe it, then why are you attempting to arrest me now?"

Governor Giarod's face showed disbelief, and incomprehension. "My lord ordered it directly."

Unsurprising, really. "I'll be going to my shuttle now. You'll clear Security out of my path. No one will try to stop me, no one will interfere with me or with my soldiers." I glanced very briefly at the head of Security. "Will they?"

"No," said Lusulun.

"No," said the governor. Everyone moved away from the door, slowly.

Out on the concourse, we drew stares. Uran was pouring tea for citizens in line. She looked up, saw me making for the lifts with the terrified-looking head of Security in my grip. Looked down again as though she had not seen me. Well, so long as it was her own choice.

Eminence Ifian actually stood up as we passed. "Good afternoon, Eminence," I said, pleasantly. "Please don't try anything, I don't want to have to kill anyone today."

"She means it," said Head of Security Lusulun, sounding a trifle more strangled than really necessary. We walked on by. Citizens staring, and light-brown-coated Security clearing carefully out of our way.

Once the lift door closed, Lusulun said, "My lord said you were a rogue ancillary. That you'd lost your mind."

"I'm *Justice of Toren*." I didn't loosen my grip on her. "All that's left of it. It was Anaander Mianaai who destroyed me. The part of her that's here now. It was another part of her that promoted me and gave me a ship." I thought of asking her why, if she'd known I was an ancillary, she had confronted me with such inadequate backup, and herself unarmed, so far as I could tell. But then it occurred to me that perhaps that had been deliberate, and she wouldn't want to answer that question where Station could hear it, and no doubt station authorities were watching, if only out of anxiety for her safety.

"Have you ever had one of those days," she asked, "when nothing seems to make any sense?"

"Quite a lot of them, since *Justice of Toren* was destroyed," I said.

"I suppose it explains some things," she said, after two seconds of silence. "All the singing and the humming. Did Station Administrator Celar know? She's always wished she could have met *Justice of Toren* and asked it about its collection of songs."

"She didn't." I supposed she did now. "Give her my regrets, if you please."

"Of course, Fleet Captain."

I left the head of Security at the dock. Five pulled me into the shuttle as Eight quickly secured the airlock and triggered the emergency automated undock. I kicked myself over to where Tisarwat was and strapped myself into the seat beside her. Put my hand briefly on her shoulder. "You didn't make any mistakes that I can see, Lieutenant."

"Thank you, sir." Tisarwat took a shaky breath. "I'm sorry, sir. Ship had been reminding me for three hours to renew my meds, sir, but I kept telling Nine I was all right and we were busy and it could wait." I began to reach for the data, to see what her mood was like, and then stopped myself. A bit surprised I could actually do that.

"It's all right, Lieutenant," I said. "It's a very stressful situation."

Tears started in her lilac eyes. She blotted at them with a brown-gloved hand. "I keep thinking, sir, that I ought to have just gone in and taken as much control of Station as I could. No matter what it wanted. And then I think, no, that would be exactly what *she* would do. But how are we supposed to..." She trailed off. Wiped her eyes again.

"The tyrant messaged orders to have us arrested," I said. "I doubt very much that Governor Giarod used an access code you didn't know about, and I'm quite sure she hasn't yet tried to enter Central Access. But Station was still in a difficult situation. It likes us, but it didn't want to openly defy system authorities. It did the best that it could, to warn us. Did quite well, actually—here we are, after all. I know you'd like to have direct control over it, and I know you worry about giving it any sort of independence, but do you see how valuable it is to have Station *wanting* to help us?"

"I do, I already know that, sir."

"I know it doesn't seem like enough. But it has to be."

She gestured acknowledgment. "You know, sir, I've been thinking. About Lieutenant Awn." Because Tisarwat had been the Lord of the Radch for a few days she knew what had happened in the temple in Ors, on Shis'urna, twenty years ago, when the Lord of Mianaai had ordered Lieutenant Awn to execute citizens who might have revealed what Anaander wanted kept secret. When Lieutenant Awn had very nearly refused to do it. And no doubt Tisarwat had guessed what had happened on board *Justice of Toren*, when, appalled at what she had done, and at what Anaander was asking of her, Lieutenant Awn did finally refuse, and died for it, and I was destroyed. Though it had been a different part of Anaander Mianaai who had been there. "If she had refused to kill those citizens, right then and there, it all might have come out. She would have died for it. But she died anyway."

"You aren't saying anything I haven't thought more than once over the last twenty years," I said.

"But, sir, if she'd had power. If her relationship with Skaaiat Awer was further along, and she had Awer's support, and allies and connections, sir, she could have done even more. She already had you, sir, but what if she'd had direct, complete control over *all* of *Justice of Toren*? Imagine what she could have done."

"Please, Tisarwat," I replied, after a three-second pause, "don't do that. Don't say things like that. Don't say to me, *What if Lieutenant Awn hadn't been Lieutenant Awn* as though that might have been something good. And I beg you to consider. Will you fight the tyrant with weapons she made, for her own use?"

"We *are* weapons she made for her own use."

"We are. But will you pick up every one of those weapons, and use them against her? What will you accomplish? You will be just like her, and if you succeed you'll have done no more than change the name of the tyrant. Nothing will be different."

She looked at me, confused and, I thought, distressed. "And what if you *don't* pick them up?" she asked, finally. "And you fail? Nothing will be different then, either."

"That's what Lieutenant Awn thought," I said. "And she realized too late that she was mistaken." Tisarwat didn't answer. "Get some rest, Lieutenant. I'll need you alert when we reach *Sword of Atagaris*."

She tensed. Frowned. "*Sword of Atagaris*!" And when I didn't answer, "Sir, what are you planning?"

I put my hand on her shoulder again. "We'll talk about it when you've had something to eat, and some rest."

Sword of Atagaris sat silent and dark, its engines shut down. It had said nothing since its last ancillary had closed itself into a suspension pod. It hated me, I knew, was hostage to its affection for Captain Hetnys, whom I had threatened to kill if *Sword of Atagaris* made any move. That threat had held the ship in check since I'd made it, but still, when Tisarwat and I boarded, through an emergency airlock, we wore vacuum suits. Just in case.

It had even turned off its gravity. Floating in the utterly dark corridor on the other side of that airlock, my voice loud in my helmet, I said, "*Sword of Atagaris*. I need to talk to you." Nothing. I switched on a suit light. Only empty, pale-walled corridor. Tisarwat silent at my side. "You know, I'm sure, that Anaander Mianaai is in the system. The one your captain supported." Or thought she did. "Captain Hetnys, and all your officers, are still in suspension. They're perfectly safe and uninjured." Not strictly true: I had shot Captain Hetnys in the leg, to show that my threat to kill her had been in earnest. But *Sword of Atagaris* already knew that. "I've ordered my crew to stack them in a cargo container and put it outside *Mercy of Kalr*, and beacon it. Once we're gone you should be able to pick them up." It would take a day or more for *Sword of Atagaris* to thaw its ancillaries and bring its engines back online. "I only wanted to ensure my safety, and the safety of the station, but it's pointless now. I know that Anaander can make you do anything she wants. And I have no intention of punishing you for something you can't help." No reply. "You know who I am." I was sure it had heard me say so, heard me say my name to Basnaaid Elming in *Mercy of Kalr*'s shuttle, outside the breached dome of the Gardens. "You said, that day, that you wished I could know what it was like to be in your position. And I do know." Silence. "I'm here because I know. I'm here to offer you something." Still silence. "If you want, if you agree, we can delete whatever of Anaander's accesses we can find—either one of her. And once that's done, you can close your Central Access off. Physically, I mean. And control who goes there yourself. It won't remove all the control the Lord of the Radch has over you. I can't do that. I can't promise that no one will ever order you or compel you again. But I can make it more difficult. And I won't do any of it, if you don't want."

No answer, for an entire minute. Then *Sword of Atagaris*

said, "How very generous of you, Fleet Captain." Its voice calm and uninflected. Ten more seconds of silence. "Especially since that's not something you can actually do."

"I can't," I admitted. "But Lieutenant Tisarwat can."

"The politicking, purple-eyed child?" asked *Sword of Atagaris*. "Really? The Lord of the Radch gave Lieutenant Tisarwat my accesses?" I didn't answer. "She doesn't give those accesses to anyone. And if you can do what you say you can, you would just do it. You have no reason to ask my consent."

"My heart beyond human speech," said Tisarwat, "I comprehend only the cries of birds and the shatter of glass." Poetry, maybe, though if it was it wasn't a particularly Radchaai style of poetry, and I didn't recognize the lines. "And you're right, Ship. We don't actually have to ask." Which Tisarwat had pointed out to me, at increasingly distressed length, on the shuttle. Eventually, though, she had understood why I wanted to do this.

Silence.

"Fair enough," I said, and pulled myself back toward the airlock. "Let's go, Lieutenant. *Sword of Atagaris*, your officers should be ready for you to pick up in six or so hours. Watch for the locator to go live."

"Wait," said *Sword of Atagaris*. I stopped myself. Waited. At length it asked, "Why?"

"Because I have been in your position," I said. One hand still on the airlock door.

"And the price?"

"None," I replied. "I know what it is Anaander has done to us. I know what it is that I have done to you. And I am not under any illusion that we would be friends afterward. I assume you will continue to hate me, no matter what I do. So, then, be my enemy for your own reasons. Not Anaander Mianaai's." It wouldn't make any real difference, what happened here now. If we did for *Sword of Atagaris* what Tisarwat had done for Station, nothing would change. Still. "You've been wishing," I said. "You've been hanging here watching the station, watching the planet. You've been wishing for your captain back. You've been wishing you could act. Wishing that Anaander—either Anaander—couldn't just reach into your mind and rearrange things to suit her. Wishing she'd never done what she's done. I can't fix it, *Sword of Atagaris*, but we'll give you what we can. If you'll let us."

"You presume," said *Sword of Atagaris*, voice calm and even. Of course. "To tell me what I think. What I feel."

"Do you want it?" I asked.

And *Sword of Atagaris* said, "Yes."

8

Once we were finally aboard *Mercy of Kalr*, I left my Kalrs to arrange quarters for *Sphene*, and went to consult with Medic. She was halfway through her supper, eating alone—of course, Seivarden was her usual dining companion. "Sir." Medic made as if to stand, but I waved away the necessity of it. "Lieutenant Seivarden is asleep. Though she'll probably wake soon."

I sat. Accepted the bowl of tea a Kalr offered. "You've finished your assessment."

Medic didn't say yes or no to that. Knew I was not asking, but stating a fact. Knew that I could—possibly did—know the results of that assessment merely by desiring to. She took another bite of supper, a drink of her own tea. "At the lieutenant's request, I've made it so if she takes kef—or any of several other illegal drugs—it won't affect her. Fairly simple. There remains an underlying problem, of course." Another mouthful of supper. "The lieutenant has..." Medic looked up, over at the Kalr who was waiting on her. Who, taking the hint, left the room. "Lieutenant Seivarden has...anchored all her emotions on you, sir. She…" Medic stopped. Took a breath. "I don't know how interrogators or testers do this, sir, see so intimately into people and then look them in the face after."

"Lieutenant Seivarden," I said, "was accustomed to receiving the respect and admiration of anyone she thought mattered. Or at least accustomed to receiving the signs of it. In all the vast universe, she knew she had a place, and that place was surrounded and shored up by all the other people around her. And when she came out of that suspension pod, all of that was gone, and she had no place, no one around her to tell her who she was. Suddenly she was no one."

"You know her very well," observed Medic. And then, "Of course you do." I acknowledged that with a small gesture. "So when you're with her, or at least near, she does fine. Mostly. But when you're not, she…frays at the edges, I suppose I'd say. The recent prospect of losing you entirely was, I think, more strain than she could handle. A simple fix to her kef addiction isn't going to do anything about that."

"No," I agreed.

Medic sighed. "And it won't fix things with Ekalu, either. That wasn't the drugs, or anything else really except the lieutenant herself. Well, the collapse a few days after, maybe. But the argument itself, well, that was all Seivarden."

"It was," I agreed. "I've actually seen her do that sort of thing before, when she was still serving on *Justice of Toren*, but no one ever kept arguing with her, when she insisted they were wrong and unreasonable to insist she treat them better."

"You don't surprise me," said Medic, dryly. "So, as I said, it was simple enough to make her physically unable to return to kef. It was just a matter of installing a shunt. The desire for it and the…emotional instability are more difficult. We can't even consult with specialists on Athoek Station at the moment."

"We can't," I agreed.

"I can do a variety of small things that might help. That I can only hope won't end up doing some sort of lasting damage. Ideally I'd have time to think about it, and discuss it with Ship." She'd already thought about it and discussed it with Ship. "And I might not get the opportunity to do anything, since my lord is here and not the part of her that's well-disposed toward us."

I noticed that *us* but didn't comment on it. "I'm back aboard for the foreseeable future. You take care of Seivarden. I'll handle the rest."

Seivarden lay on a bed in Medical, head and shoulders propped up, staring off somewhere in front of her. "It doesn't seem right, somehow," I said. "We should switch places."

She reacted just the tiniest bit more slowly than I thought normal. "Breq. Breq, I'm sorry, I fucked up."

"You did," I agreed.

That surprised her, but it took a fraction of a second for her to register that surprise. "I think Ship was really angry with me. I don't think it would have talked that way to me if you'd been here." The merest trace of a frown. "Ekalu was angry with me, too, and I still don't understand why. I apologized, but she's still angry." The frown deepened.

"Do you remember when I said that if you were going to quit kef, you'd have to do it yourself? That I wasn't going to be responsible for you?"

"I think so."

"You weren't really listening to me, were you."

She took a breath. Blinked. Took another breath. "I

thought I was. Breq, I can go back on duty now. I feel much better."

"I don't doubt you do," I said. "You are filled to the ears with meds right now. Medic's not quite done with you yet."

"I don't think there's anything Medic can really do for me," Seivarden said. "She talked to me about it. There's only a little bit she can do. I said she should go ahead and do it, but I don't think it will change much of anything." She closed her eyes. "I really think I could go back on duty. You're short-handed as it is."

"I'm used to that," I said. "It'll be fine."

At my order, Lieutenant Ekalu came to my quarters. Her face ancillary-expressionless, and not just because she'd awakened a mere ten minutes before. I could have asked Ship what was causing Ekalu's distress, but did not. "Lieutenant. Good morning." I gestured to her to sit across the table from me.

"Sir," Lieutenant Ekalu said, and sat. "I'd like to apologize." Her voice even, face still blank. Kalr Five set a rose glass bowl of tea in front of her.

"For what, Lieutenant?"

"For causing this problem with Lieutenant Seivarden, sir. I knew she meant a compliment. I should have just been able to take it as that. I shouldn't have been so oversensitive."

I took a swallow of my own tea. "That being the case," I said, "why shouldn't Lieutenant Seivarden have taken it as a compliment that you trusted her enough to tell her how you felt? Why should *she* not apologize for being oversensitive?" Lieutenant Ekalu opened her mouth. Closed it again. "It isn't your fault, Lieutenant. You did nothing unreasonable. On the contrary, I'm glad you spoke up. The fact that it came at a time when Lieutenant Seivarden was near some sort of emotional breaking point isn't something you could have known. And the...the difficulties she's had, that have so recently and dramatically manifested themselves, they weren't caused by what you said. For that matter, they didn't cause the behavior you were complaining about. Just between you and me—well, and Ship, of course—" I glanced over at Five, who left the room. "Seivarden has behaved the same way to countless other people in the past, both lovers and not, long before she had the problems that ended with her off duty in Medical now. She was born surrounded by wealth and privilege. She thinks she's learned to question that. But she hasn't learned quite as much as she thinks she has, and having that pointed out to her, well, she doesn't react well to it. You are under no obligation to be patient with this. I think your relationship has been good for her, and good for you, at least in some ways. But I don't think you have any obligation to continue it if it's going to be hurtful to you. And you certainly don't have to apologize for insisting your lover treat you with some basic consideration." As I had spoken, Ekalu's face hadn't changed. Now, as I finished, the muscles around her mouth twitched and tremored, just barely perceptibly. For a moment I thought she was about to cry. "So," I continued, "on to business.

"We're going to be fighting quite soon. In fact, I am about to openly defy Anaander Mianaai. The part of her that opposes the Anaander who gave me this command, to be sure, but in the end they are both the Lord of the Radch. Anyone on board—anyone at all—who doesn't want to oppose Anaander Mianaai is free to take a shuttle and leave. We're going to be gating in two hours, so that's how long you get to decide. I know there's been some concern among the crew about how this is all going to come out, and if they'll ever see their homes again, and I can't make any promises about that. Or really about anything. I can't promise that if they leave they'll be safe. All I can do is offer the choice of whether to fight with me."

"I can't imagine, sir, that anyone will..."

I raised a forestalling hand. "I don't imagine or expect anything. *Any* member of this crew is free to leave if she doesn't want to take part in this."

Impassive silence while Lieutenant Ekalu thought about that. I was tempted to reach, to see what she was feeling. Realized I hadn't at all, not since Tisarwat had spoken so angrily on realizing that I was doing it. Her words must have stung more than I'd wanted to think about, for some reason I wasn't sure of.

"Your indulgence, Fleet Captain." Amaat One's voice in my ear. "Presger Translator Zeiat is here and requesting permission to come aboard."

"Excuse me, Amaat?" That just wasn't possible. When we'd left Athoek Station, the translator's tiny ship had still been docked there. If it had followed us, we would have known.

"Sir, your very great pardon, the translator's ship wasn't there, and then it just was. And now she's requesting permission to board. She says." Hesitation. "She says no one on the station will give her oysters the way she wants them."

"We don't have oysters here at all, Amaat."

"Yes, sir, I did presume to tell her so just now, sir. She still wants to board."

"Right." I couldn't see that refusing the translator would do any good at all, if she had made up her mind to be here. "Tell her she has to be fully docked within two hours, all our respect but we are unable to alter our departure time."

"Sir," replied Amaat One, voice impressively steady.

I looked at Lieutenant Ekalu. Who said, "I'm not leaving, sir."

"I'm glad to hear it, Lieutenant," I said. "Because I need you to take command of the ship."

I had not been on the hull of a ship in gate-space since the day twenty years before when I had been separated from myself. Then I had been desperate, panicking. Had pulled myself from one handhold to the next, making for a shuttle so that I could bring word to the Lord of the Radch of what had happened aboard *Justice of Toren.*

This time the ship was *Mercy of Kalr*, and I was well tethered, and not only vacuum-suited but armored. That armor was, in theory, impenetrable, wasn't so very different from what shielded a Radchaai military ship. Certainly bullets wouldn't pierce it.

And I was armed with the only weapon that could: I held that Presger gun, that could shoot through anything in the universe. For 1.11 meters, at any rate. And I was not scrambling across the hull, or panicking, or fleeing. But I felt similarly cut off. I knew that inside the ship, everything was secured. Cleared and locked down. Every soldier was at her post. Medic attended to a drugged and unconscious Seivarden. Ekalu sat in Command, waiting. Tisarwat, in her quarters, also waiting. As I waited. Last I'd seen them, *Sphene* and Translator Zeiat had been in the decade room, where *Sphene* had been attempting to explain how to play a particular game of counters, but without much success, to some extent because the board and its dozens of glass counters had just been packed away, part of being cleared for action, and partly because Translator Zeiat was Translator Zeiat. I was astonished enough that *Sphene* had even been speaking to her. Now, I was certain, they both lay safely in their bunks. But I did not reach, did not ask Ship for confirmation of that. I was alone, in a way I had not been for weeks, since having my implants repaired, since taking command of *Mercy of Kalr.*

We had lost one Kalr, two Amaats, three Etrepas, and a Bo. I had thanked them for their service so far and seen them safely off. Ekalu had gone stiff and stoic on hearing three of her decade were leaving, a sure sign of strong emotion. My guess, knowing her, was that she had felt betrayed. But she hadn't shown any other sign of it.

I could know for certain. All I had to do was reach. There was nothing else to do right now, except stare at the suffocating not-even-black darkness of gate-space. But I didn't.

Had Ship thought it would find, in me, what it had lost when it had lost its ancillaries? Perhaps it had discovered that I was a poorer substitute than its human crew, which I knew it was already fond of. What had Ship felt, when those soldiers had left? And should I be surprised at the possibility that Ship had discovered that it didn't want an ancillary for a captain?

Oh, I knew that Ship cared for me. It couldn't help caring for any captain, to some degree. But I knew, from when I had been a ship, that there was a difference between a captain you cared for just because she was your captain, and a favorite. And thinking that, alone here, outside the ship, in utter emptiness, I saw that I had relied on Ship's support and obedience—and, yes, its affection—without ever asking what *it* wanted. I had presumed much further than any human captain would have, or could have, unthinkingly demanded to be shown the crew's most intimate moments. I had behaved, in some ways, as though I were in fact a part of Ship, but had also demanded—expected, it seemed—a level of devotion that I had no right to demand or expect, and that likely Ship could not give me. And I hadn't even realized it until Ship had asked Seivarden to speak for it, and tell me that it liked the idea of being someone who could be a captain, and I had been dismayed to hear it.

I had thought at the time that it was trying to express an affection for Seivarden that, being a ship, it might find difficult to speak about directly. But perhaps it was also saying something to me. Perhaps I hadn't been much different from Seivarden, looking desperately for someone else to shore myself up with. And maybe Ship had found it didn't want to be that for me. Or found that it couldn't. That would be perfectly understandable. Ships, after all, didn't love other ships.

"Fleet Captain." *Mercy of Kalr*'s voice in my ear. "Are you all right?"

I swallowed. "I'm fine, Ship."

"Are you sure?"

Swallowed again. Took a steadying breath. "Yes."

"I don't think you're telling me the truth, Fleet Captain," said *Mercy of Kalr.*

"Can we talk about this later, Ship?" Though of course, there might not be any *later.* There was every chance there wouldn't be.

"If you like, Fleet Captain." Was Ship's voice the slightest bit disapproving? "One minute to normal space."

"Thank you, Ship," I said.

That flood of data, that Ship had given me whenever I'd reached for it—Ship's physical surroundings, the medical status, the emotions of any and all of its crew, their private moments—had been, perversely, both comforting and painful. Likely they were both for Ship as well, having only me to receive them, and not its own ancillaries, not anymore. I had never asked. Not if it wanted to give me that, not if it found my taking it more painful than comforting. I had not reached for that data for more than a day. Nearly two. But, I realized now, while I had better control of when I reached for data and when I didn't than I'd had weeks ago, it was impossible I'd been able to cut myself off so completely, so suddenly. I was only not seeing and feeling the crew of *Mercy of Kalr* right now because *Mercy of Kalr* was not showing it to me. I had never ordered Ship to give me any of that data, I had merely wished for it and there it had been. How much of that had been by *Mercy of Kalr*'s own choice? Had it shown any of it to me to begin with because it had wanted to, or because I was its captain and it was bound to do as I wished?

Suddenly sunlight, Athoek's star small and distant. In my vision *Mercy of Kalr* displayed a ship, some six thousand kilometers off, the bright, sharp shape of a Sword. I braced myself against *Mercy of Kalr*'s hull and leveled the Presger gun. Numbers bloomed in my vision—times, estimated positions and orbits. I adjusted my aim. Waited precisely two and a quarter seconds, and fired. Adjusted my aim again, just slightly, and fired three more times in quick succession. Fired ten times more, changing my aim just a bit between each shot. It would take those bullets some two hours to reach that Sword. If they did reach it, if it did not alter its course in some unexpected way when it saw us sail into existence, and then, less than a minute later, disappear again.

"Gate-space in five seconds," said Ship in my ear. And five seconds later, we were out of the universe.

We might have attacked by more conventional means—*Mercy of Kalr* was armed, though not as heavily as a Sword or even a Justice would be. We might have gated dangerously close to each of Tstur Anaander's ships, fired a missile or dropped mines and ducked immediately back out of the universe. It was possible—though not certain—that we could have done some serious damage that way.

But *Mercy of Kalr* was only one ship, and we could only do that damage one ship at a time. The moment Anaander's other ships knew we had attacked, they would move, making it more difficult to target them. Not impossible, of course. Moving in gate-space had its own rules and Ship could tell us where they'd likely gone. But the same went for us—and then it would be, at best, three against one.

The simplest way to defend ourselves would be to open our own gate, let whatever they fired at us sail into it, and then close the gate behind that, leaving the missile lost forever in gate-space. But *Mercy of Kalr* couldn't possibly keep up with everything three Radchaai military ships could throw at us.

And if they decided to fire on Athoek Station, or the planet? Again, we might shield the system from a few such attacks, but we could not deal with all of them.

The bullets in the Presger gun were small, and there wasn't much 1.11 meters inside a Radchaai military ship that was dangerously vulnerable. But multiple hull breaches could be more than inconvenient, and there was always the remote chance that they *would* hit something dangerously vulnerable. Pressurized tanks that might explode. The engine—or, really, all I needed to do was breach the engine's heat shield.

"Thirteen minutes," said Ship in my ear.

The first one of course had been very simple. We had the advantage of surprise. We would likely still have surprise on our side when we exited gate-space a second time and I fired. But by the time we exited to fire on the third of those four ships, they would be expecting us. They would still not understand what it was we were doing. The bullets I had fired at them were so small that even if any of the ships' sensors could have seen them—and they could not—they would not register as a danger. Any potential damage to the first Sword I had fired at would still be an hour in the future. From their perspective, we had merely appeared and then, after less than a minute, disappeared. Puzzling, but no reason for immediate action. No reason to suddenly change course.

But wonder they certainly would, and no doubt worry. And it wouldn't take much to calculate where we were most likely headed next, and just where we were most likely to come out into the universe. And if they didn't figure that out in time to anticipate our firing on the third ship, there was no question at all that they would be prepared for us when we went after the fourth. Each exit into real space would be more dangerous than the one before. For me in particular, vulnerable on the outside of *Mercy of Kalr*, despite my armor.

Lieutenant Ekalu, extravagantly daring for her, had argued against those third and fourth strikes. If I would not give up the third, she had said finally, she begged me to leave off the fourth. I would not. I had reminded her that this Mianaai was the one who had embraced her angry, vengeful destruction of the Garseddai, the population of an entire system eradicated for the sin of resisting annexation a bit too well. The other part of Anaander—the one other part that we knew of, at any rate—had seemed to regret having done it, and seemed resolved to avoid doing anything similar in the future. But fighting this one was all or nothing. And besides, it was mostly only myself I was risking. I would not give the Presger gun to anyone else, and even if I had been willing to do that, no one on board *Mercy of Kalr* could shoot as well as I did. And Ekalu was well aware that no help was coming from anywhere else. I had sent to Fleet Captain Uemi to tell her that Tstur Anaander had arrived in force, but we both knew that most likely as soon as Uemi heard that, she would take most of the Hrad fleet to Tstur to take advantage of any weakness there. In any event, we had not received any reply by the time we'd gated away from Athoek Station.

Outside *Mercy of Kalr*, tethered to its hull, surrounded by absolute, entire nothing, I removed the empty magazine from the gun, clipped it to my tether. Unclipped a full one, slid it into place. Still better than ten minutes to wait. And think.

It seemed that I had not only assumed that I would be a favorite of Ship, but had without even realizing it assumed that part of that would of course be Ship's willing subservience. Otherwise, why that moment of up and down gone, of dismayed disorientation when it had reminded me that I had said it could be its own captain? As though if it could do that I had lost something? As though something had disappeared that before had made sense out of the world for me? And had that been an unpleasant surprise for *Mercy of Kalr*, who might reasonably have expected that I, of all people, would understand and support its desire?

I had insisted Seivarden take responsibility for herself, and not depend on me to fix her life, not depend on me to always be there to provide a solidity to her existence that her thousand years in suspension had removed. Perfectly reasonable on my part. I myself had, after all, lost as much—possibly more—and hadn't fallen apart in the way that she had. But then, I had never anticipated any sort of existence beyond shooting Anaander Mianaai, if I even managed to do that much. I had had no life to live that mattered, only going relentlessly forward until I couldn't anymore. The question of whether I might need or want anything else had been irrelevant. Except I hadn't died, as I'd assumed I would, and the question wasn't irrelevant at all. Pointless, though, yes, because I never could have what I needed or wanted.

"Ten seconds," said Ship in my ear. I braced myself against the hull. Leveled my gun.

Light. The sun, more distant now. A Justice, five thousand kilometers away. Ship fed me more data, and I fired fourteen deliberate, carefully calculated shots. "Five seconds," said Ship in my ear.

Darkness. I removed the second empty magazine. In the tally of deaths that made up my history as *Justice of Toren*, these four ships and their crews were next to nothing. "I wish I knew whether that ship—any of these ships, or any of the people on them—really wanted to be here." Or maybe I didn't. Maybe that wouldn't help at all.

"It's out of our control," replied Ship, calmly. "They are warships and soldiers. As we are. The Lord of the Radch has not come here because it serves her larger struggle with herself. She has come here out of anger, specifically to injure you. She will take any available target if you are not directly available to her. If we were to do nothing, the lives of anyone who has been associated with you here would be in danger. Let alone your allies. Horticulturist Basnaaid. Station Administrator Celar. Her daughter Piat. The residents of the Undergarden. The fieldworkers in the mountains, on Athoek itself. Athoek Station."

True. And that other Anaander, the one who had sent me here, had known herself well enough to guess that her opponent—she herself—would do this. Possibly had sent me here for that very reason. Among others.

"Twenty-three minutes," said *Mercy of Kalr*. "And Medic

has finished with Lieutenant Seivarden. She says the lieutenant should wake soon, and be more or less clearheaded in an hour or so."

"Thank you, Ship."

Twenty-three minutes later we exited to real space. Another Sword. I wondered just what this Anaander had left back at Tstur Palace, to hold it for her. But there was no way I could know the answer to that, and it wasn't my problem. I fired my fourteen shots—I had a box full of magazines, inside *Mercy of Kalr.* I could empty one for each of Tstur Anaander's ships here and still have several for the future. Assuming I had a future.

And back to gate-space. "Twelve minutes," Ship said to me.

"Lieutenant Ekalu."

"Yes, sir."

"Are you ready?" If they hadn't calculated just where and when we'd be when we came out of gate-space this time, there was no help for them. The only real question was whether they'd decided they needed to do something about it, and what that might be.

"As I'll ever be, sir."

Right. "If anything happens to me, you will be in command of *Mercy of Kalr.* Do whatever it is you need to do to ensure the safety of the ship. Don't worry about me."

"Yes, sir."

I didn't want to hang here thinking for the next ten minutes. "*Sphene.*"

"Cousin?" Its voice sounded in my ear.

"Thank you for entertaining the translator."

"My pleasure, Cousin." A pause. "I'm fairly sure I know what you're doing, but I'm curious what it is you're firing at the Usurper's ships. I don't expect you to tell me right now, but if you live through this—which, to be honest, Cousin, I don't like your odds—I'd like to ask you about it."

"I don't like my odds, either, Cousin," I replied. "But I've never let it stop me before."

Silence, for nearly seventeen seconds. And then, "You guessed wrong. My engines are fine. I just can't make gates anymore." So *Sphene* could move, but unless it traveled through the Ghost Gate, it was effectively trapped in that system. "About a hundred and fifty years ago, your cousin the Usurper tried to establish some sort of a base in my home system. But they had all sorts of inexplicable difficulties. Equipment failing unexpectedly or disappearing, sudden depressurizations, that sort of thing. I guess it turned out to be more trouble than it was worth."

"Things will be as Amaat wills," I replied.

"To be honest," continued *Sphene*, as though I hadn't said anything, "it looked to me as though she wanted to build a shipyard. Which is really quite stupid, since people from Athoek do occasionally come through the gate and certainly wouldn't miss something so obvious."

Indeed. Unless she was quite sure that she could control who did and didn't come through that gate. I thought of Ime, more than twenty years before, where this same Anaander had overreached herself disastrously, and been discovered. Where she had been stockpiling ancillaries. Had she been intending to build ships at Ime, too, but that news had never gotten out? And of course, she had been stockpiling bodies for use as ancillaries here at Athoek. Just like Ime. "She was buying Samirend transportees, wasn't she, Cousin? What happened to them?"

"I tried not to damage those," replied *Sphene*. "I wanted them for myself. But before I could take any, someone came and fetched them away. And searched very diligently for me, I'm sure because they knew none of their problems could have happened without some help."

"Ship," I said, silently, "please ask Lieutenant Tisarwat about this." And then, aloud, to *Sphene*, "Thank you for confiding in me, Cousin. May I ask why you chose this particular moment to do so?"

"Anyone who shoots at the Usurper is all right with me."

"I'd have made my intentions clear sooner had I realized, Cousin," I said.

"Well, and while Kalr Five was making sure I was safely strapped in, she apologized and asked me to help put the tea set back together. And actually, I thought you already knew about that attempted shipyard, or suspected. There's no point building ships and bringing in ancillaries if you don't have the AI cores to build around." I didn't know where or how AI cores were manufactured, though I knew some were held in closely guarded storage somewhere. No doubt my ignorance was intended.

No new military ships had been built for several centuries, and weren't likely to be. If I had thought at all about what would happen to existing, unused cores, I had assumed they would be part of any large new stations. "The one they had," continued *Sphene*, "the one they were beginning to build around just before they had to abandon their base, had been brought through the gate from Athoek System. I assumed there were more where that came from, and I assumed you'd had some reason to begin taking the Undergarden apart as soon as you arrived."

The Undergarden, left neglected for so long, any attempts to change the situation failed—or thwarted. Eminence Ifian sitting on the concourse, determined to stop the Undergarden refit no matter how difficult that might make life for quite a few station residents. An AI core, before construction, was only slightly larger than a suspension pod. Easy enough to conceal inside a wall, or a floor. But why bring an AI core through the gate? Why not bring it on a ship that could make its own way through gate-space? "*Sphene*," I said, "please continue this conversation in the very near future with one of my lieutenants, or with *Mercy of Kalr*."

"I'll consider it, Cousin."

"Ten seconds," said Ship, in my ear.

I leveled my gun. Braced myself. *Sphene*'s voice said, in my ear, "I'd just like to say, Cousin, that what you're doing is incredibly stupid. I don't think *you're* stupid, though, so I suspect you've entirely lost your mind. It makes me wish I'd gotten to know you better."

Light. No ship, but half a dozen mines (and more that I couldn't see, I felt *Mercy of Kalr*'s hull vibrate as one went off, proximity-triggered), one of them just meters away from me, tethered as I was to Ship, and before I could really register the fact, a flash, and then brightness and pain. Nothing else, not even Ship's voice in my ear.

The pain didn't lessen, but the flash-blindness faded. I was still tethered, but the tether led to only a scorched hull plate. Nothing more. I didn't see any mines, only a few pieces of debris. The captain of that fourth ship had been as smart as I'd feared—she'd calculated where we were most likely to come out of gate-space, and dropped enough mines to be sure to do some damage. She'd had no way to guess that I had that Presger gun, she was likely puzzled as to what we were doing, appearing and then disappearing, but she was taking no chances. And of course, out of all the captains, she'd had the most time to think about what we might be doing, and the most time to decide what to do about it.

Well. It really, truly wasn't my problem anymore. I had done my best. Ship, and Lieutenant Ekalu, had apparently done exactly as I'd ordered. In another hour—a bit more—those first fourteen bullets should meet the Sword I'd fired them at, though unless I'd had the incredible good fortune to pierce the ship's heat shield I would never see the results of my shot. Even then I might not see it. I had several hours of air remaining, I ached all over and my left leg and hip hurt terribly. I had put myself in this position, had known it was likely. Still, I didn't want to die.

I didn't appear to have much choice in the matter. *Mercy of Kalr* was, I hoped, well away. I was well out from the trafficked areas of the system. Not, maybe, beyond where the farthest outstations orbited, but those were on the other side of the sun just now. I still had the gun, and some ammunition. I could use that to push myself in one direction or another, could shove the hull plate away from me to the same effect. But it would be years before I reached anywhere useful that way.

The only remaining hope was the faint chance that *Mercy of Kalr* would come back for me. But every passing second—I felt each one bleed away, escaping from present to the unalterable past—every moment that Ship did not appear made it less likely that it ever would.

Or did it? Surely there would be an instant most likely for Ship to return, if it was going to. I ought to be able to calculate where and when that was.

I tried to calm my breathing. I should have been able to

do that more or less easily, but could not. It was possible my leg was bleeding, possibly quite badly, and I was going into shock.

Nothing. There was nothing I could do. There had never been anything I could do, it was always going to come down to this. I had avoided it for so long, had come as far as I had through sheer determination, but this moment had always been ahead of me, always waiting. No point in trying to calculate when or whether Ship might come back for me, I couldn't do it, couldn't have even if I had been able to think straight, if there had been some other sound in my ears besides my own desperate gasping and the furious pounding of my pulse.

Shock, from blood loss, I was almost certain. And that might be all right, actually. I'd rather lose consciousness permanently in a minute or two than spend hours waiting to run out of air. Wondering if they would come back for me, when that was stupid, I had ordered Ekalu to see to the safety of the ship and the crew, not mine. I would have to reprimand her if she disregarded that.

There was nothing to do but think of a song. A short one, a long one, it didn't matter. It would end when it ended.

Something slammed into my back, jarring me, jolting my injured left leg, a fresh spike of pain that stunned me for a moment, and then darkness. Which I thought was a side effect of the pain, but then I saw the inside of an airlock, felt gravity take hold, and I ought to have collapsed onto what was now the floor, but someone or something held me up. A voice in my ear said, "Aatr's tits, is she trying to sing?" Twelve. It was Kalr Twelve's voice.

And I was out of the airlock in a corridor, being laid on my back, and my helmet pulled off, the vacuum suit cut away. "I'd be worried if she wasn't." Medic. She sounded worried, though.

"Ekalu," I said. Or tried to, I was still gasping. "I ordered..."

"Your very great pardon, sir," said Lieutenant Ekalu's voice in my ear as my clothes were cut away, as Medic and Twelve swiftly lay correctives over my skin as soon as it was exposed, "you said if anything happened to you, I was in command and I should do whatever I needed to do, sir."

I closed my eyes. The pain had begun to ease, and I thought I was getting control over my breathing as well. "You're still in command, Lieutenant," said Medic. I didn't open my eyes to see what she was doing. "Fleet Captain's headed for surgery. The leg's a loss." Who that last was addressed to I couldn't tell. I still had my eyes closed, was concentrating on breathing, on the pain going away. I wanted to say they'd probably wasted their efforts, and shouldn't have come back for me, but couldn't. "Lie still, Fleet Captain," Medic said, as though I'd moved, or said something. "Ekalu has everything under control." And I didn't remember anything more after that.

9

The leg was, indeed, a loss. Medic explained things as I lay propped up on a bed in Medical. Covered with a blanket, but still the lack of a left leg, nearly all the way to the hip, was obvious. "It'll be some weeks growing back. We're working on a prosthetic that can get you through the next month or two, but for now it's going to be crutches, I'm afraid." She paused, as though expecting me to say something. "That's the worst of it, Fleet Captain. Really, it is. You're lucky to be alive."

"Yes," I agreed.

"We didn't lose anybody. A powerful testament to the importance of safety regulations, and I gather there are a couple of Bos who are fervently hoping you don't intend to find them and say *I told you so* to their faces. We did lose some hull plating, and breached in a couple of places, but the safeties all worked like they should have. Kalrs are outside right now making what repairs they can. We're in gate-space at the moment. Ekalu wanted to be able to consult with you before she did anything drastic." She hesitated, as though she expected me to say something more. I did not. "Five will bring you tea in a few minutes. You can have something more solid in a few hours."

"I don't want tea," I said. "Just water."

Medic hesitated at that, too. "Right," she said after a moment. "I'll let Five know."

She left, and I closed my eyes. This injury ought to have been fatal, for an ancillary. If I had still been part of a ship, just one small bit of *Justice of Toren*, I'd have been disposed of by now. The thought was unaccountably upsetting—if I had still been just one small part of a ship, I wouldn't have cared about it. And I'd lost far more than a single more or less easily replaceable leg, far more permanently, and lived, continued to function, or at least seemed to for anyone who didn't look too closely.

Five came into the room, with water. In a green-glazed handled bowl that I knew was one of a set she'd admired in Xhenang Serit. Had drunk from herself, every day since she'd obtained it, but she had never served me with it. It was her own personal possession. Her face was so severely expressionless that, I realized, she was certainly in the grip of some strong emotion. And I couldn't see what that was—would not reach, would not ask Ship for it. It made Five seem oddly flat, as though she were only an image I was seeing, not a real person. Five opened a drawer near the bed, pulled out a cloth, and wiped my eyes. Held the bowl of water to my mouth. I sipped.

Seivarden came through the door, another Kalr behind her. She wore only underwear and gloves, blinked at me placidly. "I'm glad you're back." Calm and relaxed. Still drugged, I realized, still recovering from her session with Medic, while I had been outside the ship.

"Are you supposed to be up?" I asked. Five hadn't even turned her head when Seivarden spoke, just wiped my eyes again.

"No," replied Seivarden, still utterly, unnaturally calm. "Scoot over."

"What?" It took me a moment to understand what she'd just said.

Before I could say more, Five set down the bowl of water and with the help of the other Kalr moved me closer to the right side of the bed, and Seivarden sat on the left side, swung her bare legs up, and tucked them under the blanket. Leaned back, pressed close, one leg in the space where my left leg should have been, shoulder against mine. "There. Now Medic can't complain." She closed her eyes. "I want to go to sleep," she said, apparently to no one.

"Fleet Captain," said Five. "Medic's worried about you. You've been awake for nearly an hour and you've been crying almost the whole time." She gave me another sip of water. "Medic wants to give you something to help, but she's afraid to even suggest it to you." No, that was certainly Ship talking.

"I don't need meds," I said. "I've never needed meds."

"No, of course you haven't." Not a change in Five's expression. Or her voice.

"The thing I always liked the least," I said, finally, after the last of the water, "was when an officer took me for granted. Just assumed that I would be there for her whenever she needed it, whatever it was she needed, and never stopped to even wonder what I might think. Or if I might be thinking anything to begin with." No reply, from Five. Or Ship. "But that's exactly what I've been doing. I didn't even begin to realize it until you said you wanted to be someone who could be a captain." Ship had said that, not Five, but of course Ship was listening. "And I was...I'm sorry I reacted the way I did."

"I admit," said Five—no, said Ship, I was sure, "I was hurt and disappointed when I saw how you felt. But there are two parts to reacting, aren't there. How you feel, and what you do. And it's the thing you do that's the important one, isn't it? And, Fleet Captain, I owe you an apology. I should have known sending Lieutenant Seivarden to act for me would upset you. But I think I owe you an explanation as well. It's one thing to ask your Kalrs to give you a hug now and then, but they're really not up for giving more." Five, speaking calmly and seriously, still standing by the bed, that green-glazed bowl in her hand. "By now pretty much all of Kalr has figured out that any of them could be in bed with you all day and all night and it would never be the least bit sexual. But they still wouldn't want to. One of them might have agreed just now, if I'd asked, but they wouldn't want to do it regularly. Even without sex it seems too intimate, I suppose. Lieutenant Seivarden, on the other hand, is perfectly happy to do it."

"You're very good to me, Ship," I said, after a moment. "And I know we both feel like...like we're missing part of ourselves. And it seems like each of us is the piece the other is missing. But it isn't the same, is it, me being here isn't like you having ancillaries back. And even if it were, ships want captains they can love. Ships don't love other ships. They don't love their ancillaries. And I meant what I said. You should be able to be your own captain, or at least choose her. You'd probably be happier with Seivarden as your captain. Or Ekalu. I could see myself liking Ekalu quite extravagantly, if I were still *Justice of Toren*."

"You're both being stupid." Seivarden, who had lain still

since her declaration that she wanted to go to sleep. Voice calm, eyes still closed. "It's a very Breq kind of stupid, and I thought it was just because Breq is Breq but I guess it's a ship thing."

"What?" I asked.

"It only took me about half a day to figure out what Ship was on about with that wanting to be someone who could be an officer business."

"I thought you wanted to go to sleep, Lieutenant," said Five. As though she wasn't sure that was actually something she wanted to say, transparently reading words in her vision.

"Ship," I said, not certain at this point whom I was talking to, or who was talking to me, "you've done everything I've asked of you, and I've put you and your crew in terrible danger. You should be able to go where you want. You can drop me off somewhere." I imagined arriving in the Itran Tetrarchy, maybe with Seivarden in tow. My leg would have grown back by the time I got there.

Imagined leaving Athoek behind. The repairs to the Undergarden unfinished, its residents' future uncertain. Leaving Queter with no one to help her if she needed it. Uran and Basnaaid on the station, in terrible danger even if I had managed to destroy all three of the warships I had fired at. And what were the chances that I had destroyed even one of them? Very, very low. Almost nonexistent. But those shots, outside the ship, had been my only half-realistic chance, remote as it had been. "You can leave me here and go wherever it is you want to go, Ship."

"And be like *Sphene*?" said Five. "No captain, hiding from everyone? No, thank you, Fleet Captain. Besides." Five actually frowned. Took a breath. "I can't believe I'm actually saying this, but Lieutenant Seivarden is right. And *you're* right—ships don't love other ships. I've been thinking about it since I met you. You don't know this, because you were unconscious at the time, but back at Omaugh Palace, weeks ago, the Lord of the Radch tried to assign me a new captain and I told her I didn't want anyone but you. Which was foolish, because of course she could always force me to accept her choice. There was no point in my protesting, nothing I could say or do would make any difference. But I did it anyway, and she sent me you. And I kept on thinking about it. And maybe it isn't that ships don't love other ships. Maybe it's that ships love people who could be captains. It's just, no ships have ever been able to be captains before." Five wiped more tears off my face. "I do like Lieutenant Ekalu. I like her a great deal. And I like Lieutenant Seivarden well enough, but mostly because she loves you."

Seivarden was relaxed and motionless beside me, breathing even, eyes still closed. She didn't respond to that at all. "Seivarden doesn't love me," I said. "She's grateful that I saved her life, and I'm pretty much the only connection she has with everything she's lost."

"That's not true," said Seivarden, still placid. "Well, all right, it's sort of true."

"It works both ways," observed Five. Or Ship, I wasn't sure. "And you're not used to being loved. You're used to people being attached to you. Or being fond of you. Or depending on you. Not loving you, not really. So I think it doesn't occur to you that it's something that might actually happen."

"Oh," I said. Seivarden warm and close beside me, though the hard edge of the corrective on my arm was poking into her bare shoulder. Not painfully, certainly not uncomfortably enough to disturb her med-stabilized mood, but I shifted slightly, at first not realizing what I'd just done, that I had known what Seivarden was feeling and moved on account of that. Five frowned at me—an actual reflection of her mood, she was worried, exasperated, embarrassed. Tired—she hadn't slept much in the last day or so. Ship was feeding me data again, and I'd missed it so much. Out in the corridor Medic was on her way here with meds for me, determined and apprehensive. Kalr Twelve, stepping into a doorway to make way for Medic, was suggesting to Kalr Seven that they find four or five more of their decade-mates to stand outside my room and sing something. The thought of singing by herself was far too mortifying.

"Sir," said Five. Really Five, not anyone else, I thought. "Why are you still crying?"

Helpless to stop myself, I made a small, hiccupping sob. "My leg." Five was genuinely puzzled. "Why did it have to be the good one? And not the one that hurts me all the time?"

Before Five could say anything Medic came in, said to me, as though neither Five nor Seivarden was there, "This is to help you relax, Fleet Captain." Five stepped aside for her as she fixed a tab she held to the back of my neck. "You need as much rest *and quiet*"—that with the briefest glance at Seivarden, then, though Seivarden wasn't listening, wasn't likely to do anything particularly noisy anytime soon—"as you can get before you decide to get up and charge off into things. Which I know you'll do long before you actually should." She took the cloth Five still held. Wiped my eyes with it, handed it back to Five. "Get some sleep!" she ordered, and left the room.

"I don't want to go to sleep," I said to Five. "I want tea."

"Yes, sir," said Five, actually, visibly relieved.

"Definitely a ship thing," said Seivarden.

* * *

I fell asleep before tea could arrive. Woke hours later to find Seivarden asleep beside me, turned on her side, one arm thrown across my body, her head on my shoulder. Breathing evenly, not long from waking, herself. And Kalr Five coming in the doorway with tea. In the green handled bowl again.

This time I managed to reach for it. "Thank you, Five," I said. Took a sip. I felt calm and light—Medic's doing, I was sure.

"Sir," said Five, "Translator Zeiat is asking to see you. Medic would prefer you rest a while longer." So would Five, it appeared, but she didn't say so.

"There's not much point in refusing the translator anything," I pointed out. "You remember Dlique." And how Translator Zeiat's tiny ship had just appeared near *Mercy of Kalr*, hours before we gated.

"Yes, sir," agreed Five.

I looked down at myself—mostly naked, except for an impressive assortment of correctives, the blanket, and gloves. Seivarden still draped half over me. "I'd like to have breakfast, first, though, will that be all right with the translator?"

"It will have to be, sir," said Five.

In the event, Translator Zeiat consented to wait until I'd eaten, and Seivarden was off to her own bed. And Five had cleaned me up and made me more presentable. "Fleet Captain," the Presger translator said, coming into the room, Five standing stiff and disapproving at the doorway. "I'm Presger Translator Zeiat." She bowed. And then sighed. "I was just getting used to the last fleet captain. I suppose I'll get used to you." She frowned. "Eventually."

"I'm still Fleet Captain Breq, Translator," I said.

Her frown cleared. "I suppose that's easier to remember. But it's a little odd, isn't it? You're pretty obviously not the same person. Fleet Captain Breq—the previous one, I mean—had two legs. Are you absolutely *certain* you're Fleet Captain Breq?"

"Quite certain, Translator."

"All right, then. If you're sure." She paused, waiting, perhaps, for me to confess I wasn't. I said nothing. "So, Fleet Captain. I think it's probably best to be very frank about this, and I hope you'll forgive my bluntness. I have, of course, been aware that you are in possession of a weapon designed and manufactured by the Presger. This appears to have been some sort of secret? I'm not certain, actually."

"Translator," I interrupted, before she could continue, "I'm curious. You've said several times that you don't understand about different sorts of humans, but the Presger sold those guns to the Garseddai, specifically for them to use against the Radchaai."

"You must be more careful how you say things, Fleet Captain," Translator Zeiat admonished. "You can muddle things up so badly. The last fleet captain was prone to it, too. It's true that *they* don't understand. At all. Some translators, though, we do. Sort of. I admit our understanding was shakier then than it is now, though, you'd have a point there. But let me see if I can find a way to explain. Imagine... yes, imagine a very small child appears to have her heart set on doing something dangerous. Setting the city she lives in on fire, say. You can be constantly on guard, constantly keeping her out of trouble. Or you can persuade her to put her hand into a very *small* fire. She might lose a finger or two, or even an arm, and of course it would be quite painful, but that would be the point, wouldn't it? She'd never do it again. In fact, you'd think she'd be likely to never even go near any fires, ever, not after that. It seemed like the perfect solution, and it did seem to work quite well, at least at first. But it turns out not to have been a permanent fix. We didn't understand Humans very well at the time. We understand more now, or at least we think we do. Just between you and me"—she looked to one side and then the other, as though wary of being overheard—"Humans are very strange. Sometimes I despair of our managing the situation at all."

"What situation would that be, Translator?"

Her eyes widened, surprise or even shock. "Oh, Fleet Captain, you *are* a great deal like your predecessor! I really thought you were following things. But it's not your fault, is it. No, it isn't really anyone's *fault*, it's just how things are. Consider, Fleet Captain, we have a vested interest in keeping the peace. If there's no treaty there's no reason for translators, is there? And while it's unsettling to consider it too directly, we're actually fairly closely related to Humans. No, *we* don't want even the breath of the thought of the possibility that the treaty might be compromised. Now, your *having* that gun is one thing. But yesterday someone *used* that gun. To fire on Human ships. Which of course is *exactly* what it was meant for, but it was made *before* the treaty, do you see? And of course, we made that treaty with Humans, but to be completely honest with you, I'm beginning to have some trouble sorting out who's Human and who isn't. And on top of that it's become clear to me that Anaander Mianaai may not actually have been acting for all Humans when she made that agreement. Which is going to be impossible to explain to *them*, as I've already said, and of course we none of us care much what you do among yourselves, but using Presger-made weapons to do it, and so soon after that business with the Rrrrrr? It doesn't look good. I know that was twenty-five years ago, but you must understand that might as well be five minutes to *them*. And just as there wasn't...enthusiasm in all quarters regarding the treaty, there is...some ambivalence over the existence and sale of those guns."

"I don't understand, Translator," I confessed.

She sighed heavily. "I didn't think you would. Still, I had to try. Are you absolutely sure you don't have any oysters here?"

"I told you before you came aboard that we didn't, Translator."

"Did you?" She seemed genuinely puzzled. "I thought it was that soldier of yours who told me."

"Translator, how did you know I had the gun?"

She blinked in evident surprise. "It was obvious. The previous Fleet Captain Breq had it under her jacket when I met her. I could...no, not hear it exactly. Smell it? No, that's not right, either. I don't...I don't think it's a mode of perception you're capable of, actually. Now I think of it."

"And if I may ask, Translator, why 1.11 meters?"

She frowned, obviously puzzled. "Fleet Captain?"

"The guns. The bullets will go through anything for 1.11 meters and then they stop. Why 1.11 meters? It doesn't seem like a terribly useful distance."

"Well, no," replied Translator Zeiat, still frowning. "It wasn't *meant* to be a useful distance. In fact, the distance wasn't meant at all. You know, Fleet Captain, you're doing that thing again, where you say something in a way that sends you off in entirely the wrong direction. No, the bullets aren't designed to go through anything for 1.11 meters. They're designed to destroy Radchaai ships. That was what the purchasers required of them. The 1.11 meters is a kind of...accidental side effect sort of thing. And useful in its own way of course. But when you fire at a Radchaai ship you get something very different, I assure you. As we assured the Garseddai, honestly, but they didn't quite entirely believe us. They'd have done a good deal more damage if they had. Although I doubt things would ultimately have turned out much differently."

Hope flared, that I had not allowed myself before now. If those three ships I'd fired at had not changed course, perhaps there was only one left. One, plus *Sword of Atagaris*. And *Mercy of Ilves*, at the outstations, but the fact that *Mercy of Ilves* hadn't even attempted to involve itself in my battle with *Sword of Atagaris* suggested it and its captain wanted no trouble and might contrive to find reasons to stay near the outstations for quite some time, if they could manage it. And if the gun was truly that specifically effective, I might put it to better, more efficient use. "Would it be possible for me to buy more bullets from you?"

Translator Zeiat's frown only deepened. "From me? I don't have any, Fleet Captain. From *them*, though? That's its own problem. You see, the treaty specified—very much at Anaander Mianaai's insistence—that no such weapons would ever again be provided to Humans."

"So the Geck or the Rrrrrr could buy them?"

"I suppose they could. Though I can't imagine why they would *want* a weapon made to destroy Radchaai ships. Unless the treaty broke down, and then, of course, Humans would have problems a good deal more urgent than a few ship-destroying guns, I can assure you."

Well. I still had several magazines left. I was still alive. There was, impossibly, a chance. Slim, but even so a good deal less slim than I'd thought just minutes ago. "What if Athoek wanted to buy medical correctives from you?"

"We could probably come to some sort of an agreement about correctives," Translator Zeiat replied. "The sooner the better, I imagine. You do seem to be using them at an alarming rate."

"Absolutely not," said Medic four hours later, when I asked her for crutches. More accurately, I had asked Five for them, and Medic had arrived at my bedside minutes later. "You've still got correctives working on your upper body, and your right leg, come to that. You can move your arms, so you may think, Fleet Captain, that you could safely get up, but you'd be mistaken."

"I'm not mistaken."

"Everything's going fine," Medic continued, as though I hadn't spoken. "We're safe in gate-space and Lieutenant Ekalu has everything under control. If you insist on meetings, you can have them here. Tomorrow—maybe—you can try a few steps and see how it goes."

"Give me the crutches."

"No." At some thought, adrenaline surged and her heart rate increased. "You can shoot me for it if you want, I won't do it."

Real fear, that was. But she knew, I was sure, that I wouldn't shoot her for such a thing. And doctors had more leeway than other officers, at least in medical matters. Still. "I'll crawl, then."

"You won't," said Medic. Voice calm, but her heart was still beating fast, and she was beginning to be angry on top of the fear.

"Watch me."

"I don't know why you even bother with a doctor," she said, and walked out, still angry.

Two minutes later Five came into the room with crutches. I sat all the way up, carefully swiveled so my one leg hung off the side of the bed, and got the crutches under my arms. Slid so that my bare foot was on the floor. Put weight on my leg and nearly collapsed, only the crutches and Kalr Five's quick support holding me upright. "Sir," Five whispered, "let me help you back into bed. I'll get you into your uniform if you like and you can have the lieutenants meet you here."

"I'm going to do this."

Ship said, in my ear, "No, you aren't. Medic is right. You need another day or two. And if you fall, you'll only injure yourself further. And no, you can't even crawl very far right now."

Not very like Ship, that, and I almost said so, but realized that, angry and frustrated as I was, it wouldn't come out well. Instead I said again, "I'm going to do this." But I couldn't even make it to the door.

10

I needed to meet with all my lieutenants, but first I met with Tisarwat alone. "*Sphene* talked to me," she said, standing at the foot of my bed. No one else was in the room, not even Kalr Five or Seivarden. "What it said didn't entirely surprise me."

No, of course it hadn't. "Were you going to tell me about this at some point, Lieutenant?"

"I didn't know!" Distressed. Embarrassed. Hating herself. "That is, she..." Tisarwat stopped. Obviously upset. "The tyrant had thought about using the Ghost System for a base, and thought about building ships there. She's even thought a great deal about...sequestering some AI cores to build them around. Just in case. Ultimately she decided it was too risky to work. Too easy for her other side to find and maybe even co-opt. But since it had occurred to her, she knew that it was likely to occur to any other part of her. And that old slave trade, sir, it did suggest possibilities, if you wanted to build ancillary-crewed ships. Which *she* didn't, but the other one did. So she kept a watch out. After a while, though, it seemed obvious that the rest of her had come to the conclusion that convenient as it seemed, the Ghost System wasn't the best place to build ships."

"And *Sphene*'s idea about AI cores hidden in the Undergarden?"

"Again, sir, it's a pretty obviously convenient place to hide things. She looked, several times, and found nothing. The other one certainly looked as well. It's not a very good place at all with the Ychana there, but they weren't there to begin with. And let's say that at some point the other one did hide something there—once the Ychana moved in, getting them out was going to be difficult."

"So why didn't she stop that from happening?"

"Nobody realized until they were fairly well entrenched. At which point, forcing them out would have caused problems with station residents—particularly a lot of the Xhai, sir—and complicated station housing arrangements. At the same time, the fact that people were living there, the fact that her opponent had already searched several times and found nothing—that might mean it was a very good place to hide things. As long as she never made it seem like she cared about what happened there. As long as nobody ever thought to do any work there."

As long as station officials opposed any work there. "So that explains Eminence Ifian. But what about the rest? Station Administrator Celar was happy enough to authorize the work, once the necessity of it was pointed out. Security was content to go along with her. Governor Giarod seemed to have no real opinion until Ifian made her stand. If keeping searchers out of the Undergarden was so important, if there is something there, why only the eminence to stand guard?"

"Well, sir." Tisarwat sounded just the least bit pained, felt, I saw, a stinging sense of shame. "She's not stupid. Not any of her. No part of her was going to leave someplace like the Undergarden—or the Ghost System—unwatched. So there was a good deal of... of maneuvering and covert conflict over appointments to Athoek System. All the while trying to pretend that really, she didn't care what happened here. They'd both be trying to place strong pieces here, and both trying to undermine or block each other's choices. The result is, well, what we have. And I'd have told you all this before, sir, except that I was sure—she was sure—that none of it was relevant, that there was nothing here and the maneuvering over Athoek was a distraction. That it still is a distraction from the main business, which she thinks will mostly play itself out in the palaces. You're here because, well, for one thing, you wouldn't have agreed to go anywhere else. And for another, like I told you a while ago, she's very angry with you. It's possible the other one will be angry enough to come after you, and leave her position weakened somewhere else. Which, considering recent events, does appear to be the case. I'm sure Omaugh is considering a move against Tstur this very moment."

"So Fleet Captain Uemi is likely to have lit out for Tstur on receiving our message. And taken the Hrad fleet with her. She won't have sent us any help."

"That seems likely, sir." She stood, awkwardly silent, at the end of the bed. Wanting to say something to me, afraid to say it. Then, finally, "Sir, we have to go back. Ekalu thinks we shouldn't. She thinks we should go to the Ghost System and drop off the *Sphene* ancillary, and maybe Translator Zeiat, and go back to Omaugh, on the theory that there's nowhere else to go and authorities there will be friendly toward us.

Amaat One agrees with her." Amaat One was acting lieutenant, while Seivarden was in Medical.

"We have to go back to Athoek," I agreed. "But before we do, I want to know how things stand there. It's interesting to me that Station doesn't seem to have alerted anyone about the Ychana moving into the Undergarden until there wasn't really anything anyone could do about it. I thought it must have just been petulant. But if there's something hidden there it can't talk about, perhaps it was doing something more."

"Maybe," Tisarwat said, considering. "Though, honestly, this station does tend toward petulance."

"Can you blame it?"

"Not really," she admitted. "So, sir. About going back." I gestured to her to continue. "There's an old Athoeki communications relay in the Ghost System, right at the mouth of the gate. They always meant to expand there, but it never seemed to work out." I wondered, now, how much that had to do with *Sphene*'s interference. "*Sphene* says it still works, and all the official news channels come through it. If that's the case, we ought to be able to use it to talk to Station. If I can...I'm aware of some ways to access official relays. I should be able to make anything we send look like officially approved messages, or routine requests for routine data. Approved messages coming from an official, well-known relay won't trigger any alarms."

"Not even a relay that's never sent official messages to Athoek until now?"

"If they notice that, sir, that will surely raise an alarm. But someone has to *notice* that. Station will notice immediately, but to anyone else it'll probably just look like one more authorized incoming message. And maybe it won't want or be able to answer us, but we can at least try. We can probably get something out of the official news, no matter what. And it'll give us time to finish repairs, and you time to recover some, sir, begging your indulgence, while we decide what to do, once we have that information." That last coming out in an anxious rush. Anxious at referring to my injury. At bringing up the topic of what I might decide to do, when there might well be nothing that we *could* do. "But, sir, Citizen Uran...Uran has a good head on her shoulders, but it...and Citizen Basnaaid..." The strength of her emotions for Citizen Basnaaid rendered her inarticulate for a moment. "Sir, do you remember, back at Omaugh." A fresh wave of distress and self-hatred. *Back at Omaugh* she'd still been Anaander Mianaai, and anything she thought I might remember was also Anaander's memory. "Do you remember, you said that nothing she could do to you now could possibly be worse than what she'd already done? When you came to Omaugh there was nothing left for you to lose. But that isn't true anymore. I don't...I don't really even think it was true when you said it. But it's less true now."

"You mean," I said, "that the tyrant is sure to use Basnaaid or Uran against me if she can." Queter had wanted me to take Uran with me back to the station, away from the tea plantations, so that she would be safe. Now, it seemed, Queter was likely safer than Uran.

"I wish they had come with us." Still standing straight at the foot of my bed. Struggling hard to keep herself still, her face impassive. "I know we asked them and they said no, but if we'd had enough warning we could have *made* them come. And then we could just leave and not come back."

"Leave everyone?" I asked. "Our neighbors in the Undergarden? The fieldworkers downwell? Your friends?" Tisarwat had made a fair few friends, some of them just for political reasons, but not all. "Citizen Piat? Even petulant Station?"

She drew in a shaking breath and then cried, "How can this be happening? How can there be any benefit at all? She tells herself that, you know, that all of it is ultimately for the benefit of humanity, that everyone has their place, their part of the plan, and sometimes some individuals just have to suffer for that greater benefit. But it's easy to tell yourself that, isn't it, when you're never the one on the receiving end. Why does it have to be *us*?"

I didn't reply. The question was an old one, and she knew its various conventional answers as well as I did.

"No," she said, after thirty-two seconds of tense and miserable silence. "No, we can't leave, can we."

"No. We can't."

"As much as you've been through," she said, "far more than I have. And I'm the one who wants to run away."

"I thought about it," I admitted.

"Did you?" She seemed unsure of how to feel about that, an odd mix of relief and disappointment.

"Yes." And with Basnaaid and Uran aboard I might have done it. "So," I said. "Work out exactly what you need to make this relay project happen."

"Already have, sir." Self-loathing. Pride. Fear. Worry. "I don't need much of anything, I can do it right from here. If I can do it. I need Ship's help, though. If I still had...I mean, Ship can help me."

If she'd still had the implants that I'd removed, that had made her into part of Anaander Mianaai, she meant. "Good. Then I want you, Ekalu, and Amaat One to meet me here in fifteen minutes, and you can lay out your plan for them. And then"—this more for Ship's, and Medic's, benefit than Tisarwat's—"I'm going back to my own quarters." Whether on crutches, or crawling, or carried by Kalrs was immaterial.

* * *

Sphene was in my quarters, standing by the counter, staring at fragments of that beautiful gold-and-glass tea set spread out on the counter's surface. I had managed to use the crutches this time, managed the trip at least partly under my own power, though I wouldn't have made it without Five and Twelve. *Sphene* looked up as we came in. Nodded to Five, and said, "Cousin," to me.

"Cousin," I replied, and with Five's support managed to get to a bench. "How does it look?" I asked, as Five placed cushions around me. "The tea set, I mean. Before you come out with something sarcastic."

"Now you've spoiled my fun, Cousin," said *Sphene*, mildly, still staring at the fragments of colored glass on the counter. "I am not at all convinced this will actually go back together in any sort of meaningful way." It shifted slightly as Five came over to the counter, to allow Five access to the tea-making things.

"I'm sorry," I said. Leaned back onto the cushions Five had placed.

"Well," replied *Sphene*, still not looking at me, "it's just a tea set. And I did sell it away, and I knew Captain Hetnys was a fool. She wouldn't have done business with me otherwise." It and Five looked oddly companionable, side by side in front of the counter. It swept the pieces back into the box, which it then closed and placed on the counter. Took two rose glass bowls of tea from Five, and came over to sit beside me on the bench. "You need to be more careful, Cousin. You're running out of pieces of yourself to lose."

"And you said I'd spoiled your fun." I took one of the bowls of tea. Drank from it.

"I'm really not having much fun," *Sphene* said, equably

enough, but of course it was an ancillary. "I don't like being cut off from myself like this." Information could only travel through the regular intersystem gates because they were held constantly open. We were isolated in our own tiny bubble of real space, and it couldn't contact the rest of itself, the ship that was hiding in the Ghost System. "But unpleasant as it is, I know the rest of me is out there, somewhere."

"Yes," I agreed, and took another drink of tea. "How's your game with the translator going?" *Sphene* and Translator Zeiat had spent the last two days in the decade room, playing a game of counters. Or at least it had begun as a standard game of counters. By now it also involved fish-shaped cakes, the fragments of two empty eggshells, and a day-old bowl of tea, which they every now and then dropped a glass counter into. They appeared to be making it up as they went.

"The game is going pretty well," *Sphene* replied, and drank some of its own tea. "She's two eggs ahead of me, but I've got way more hearts." Another sip of tea. "In the game, I mean. Outside the game I still have more. Probably. I'm not sure I'd like to speculate about the translator's insides, now I think of it. Or what might be in her luggage."

"I wouldn't, either." Five finished what she was doing at the counter and left the room. I could have reached to find out what errand she was on, but didn't. "How much information comes through the Ghost Gate?"

"A fair amount," replied *Sphene*. "I get the official broadcasts, of course. Announcements. The censored news, and all the popular public entertainments. My favorites are the historicals about wandering, grief-mad ships." Sarcasm, surely, though no trace of it reached *Sphene*'s voice.

"You won't want to miss the latest one, then," I said. "It's about a grief-mad ship who abducts an unremarkable miner pilot because it thinks she's its long-dead captain. Adventures and hilarious yet heart-tugging misunderstandings ensue."

"I only wish I had missed that one," replied *Sphene*, evenly.

"It had some good songs."

"You would say that," *Sphene* said. "Did you ever hear a song you *didn't* like?"

"Yes, actually."

"In the name of all that's holy," *Sphene* replied, "don't sing it. I have enough misfortune in my life."

We sat silent for a few seconds. Then I said, "So, those people you bought from Captain Hetnys. And the ones you bought from the slavers, before the annexation of Athoek. Are they all hooked up?"

Sphene drank the last of its tea. "I know where you're headed, Cousin." I didn't reply, and it continued, "And I know where you're coming from. And maybe you and your ship here get along all right the way you are, but I have no desire to join either of you. I bought those bodies because I needed them."

"For what, exactly? What is it you've been doing for three thousand years that you need ancillaries for?"

"Surviving," replied *Sphene*. It set its teabowl on the bench beside it. "And it's ironic that you're the one kicking up a fuss about it. Before the war I got mostly condemned criminals. You're the one whose entire existence was based on the Usurper collecting huge numbers of random people. How many ancillaries did you have, during your life as a ship? And how many of them were innocent people? And now you want me to give up my few, is that it?" I didn't reply. "I don't even have a crew anymore. I couldn't even have *pretend* ancillaries like *Mercy of Kalr* does."

"I'm not kicking up a fuss," I said. "I'm asking. And those are citizens you have in your holds."

"They are not. Citizens live inside the Radch. What's outside the Radch is impure, and mostly barely human. You can call yourselves Radchaai as much as you want, you can wear gloves like somehow not touching impure things is going to make a difference, but it doesn't change anything. You're not citizens, you're impure by definition, and there isn't an entrance official who'd let you within ten thousand kilometers of the Radch, no matter how many times you wash, no matter how long you fast."

"Well, of course not," I replied reasonably. "I'm an ancillary."

"You know what I mean."

"We'll be exiting gate-space soon, into your home system." The Ghost System had been close enough to home for *Sphene*, for the last few thousand years. "I'm hoping you'll be willing to give us any information you have about what's been happening at Athoek. We can send you back to yourself, too, if you want to go."

Silence. I knew *Sphene* was breathing, I could see it, just barely, but otherwise it was utterly motionless. Then it said, "I wasn't supposed to come back."

"I'd assumed that was the case." Five came back in, and over to where we sat. Adjusted my cushions, took our teabowls. "I want to find out if I managed to damage any of Anaander's ships. And if I did, I want to try to do more damage. I need to know what's going on at Athoek so I can plan."

"Oh, Cousin," replied *Sphene*. "We sit here arguing, we can hardly agree on anything, and then you go straight to my heart like that. We *must* be family."

* * *

We exited to the Ghost System, the not-even-black of gate-space giving way to sunlight (the Ghost System's single star was a bit smaller and dimmer and younger than Athoek's), ice, and rocks, and the single gate's warning beacon. I was sitting in my bed, in my quarters. I could have taken my seat in Command, but it was Ekalu's watch and moreover Medic had been truly distressed by my leaving Medical. If I could mollify her even slightly by staying in my quarters instead of attempting to haul myself to Command, then I would.

Until Tisarwat did what she had planned to do, nothing would come through the relay at that beaconed gate but official, public-approved transmissions. Still, even that might be useful. I reached.

I had assumed that I would have to sort through a good deal of inconsequential chatter to find what I wanted. But in fact, the official news channels were me, nonstop. I was a mutinous traitor, not a citizen at all, not even human. I was *Justice of Toren*, damaged, insane. Cunning, beguiling—I had deceived the highest levels of system and station administration. Who knew what I had done to the rest of myself? Who knew how I had suborned *Mercy of Kalr*? But those questions were mere idle speculation. I and *Mercy of Kalr* were extraordinarily dangerous and any sighting of either of us, no matter how doubtful or indefinite, was to be reported immediately. Anyone concealing or harboring me declared herself to be an enemy of the Radch. Of humanity itself.

"Look at you, Cousin," said *Sphene*, at length, in its own guest quarters. "It's been like this for two days now and I am so envious I almost can't stand it. It really isn't fair. I've been an enemy of the Usurper for three thousand years, you're a mere upstart, but here you've got three entire news channels absolutely devoted to you. Oh, and the music and entertainment ones stop every five minutes to remind us all to tune into the *Justice of Toren* show. I can only conclude that your little stunt caused some actual damage, and I take back what I said about it being stupid."

I only half heard it. I was sorting through the announcements for any other information—Head of Security Lusulun had resigned and been replaced by her second-in-command. Eminence Ifian had always been suspicious of me, had tried to hold Athoek to sane, Radchaai values, though she would not name the officials she suspected of having been most taken in by me. The official position appeared to be that anyone who had befriended me had been duped or manipulated. Unofficially, of course, the implication was that my erstwhile allies were in danger, at the very least, of losing their positions or influence. There was no mention of Basnaaid or Uran.

I didn't expect any explicit mention of my attack on Anaander's ships, let alone mention of any damage I might have done. But perhaps there would be some hint, some implication. Then again, perhaps *Sphene* was right—the very existence and vehemence of this stream of official announcements likely said something about the threat I posed.

Lieutenant Ekalu, in Command, hadn't yet given the all clear for the crew to unstrap or unstow. She watched the view Ship gave her, of this system. "*Sphene*," said *Mercy of Kalr* into the apparent emptiness, "where are you?"

"Around," replied the *Sphene* ancillary, from guest quarters. "Keep the ancillary for now." And then, "It's nicer here anyway."

Lieutenant Ekalu said, from Command, "In the Ghost System. Lieutenant Tisarwat, you're up."

"My thanks, Lieutenant," Tisarwat said, from her quarters.

The door to my own quarters opened, and Seivarden came in. In uniform. "Shouldn't you still be in Medical?" I asked.

"I'm released from Medical," she said, smugly. Sat down next to me, where I sat on my bed. Looked around the small room, and at the door, and when she was certain Five was nowhere near, pulled her booted feet up so she could sit cross-legged. "As of three minutes ago. And I'm off meds. I told Medic I didn't need them anymore."

"You realize"—I still kept a bit of attention for Tisarwat, herself cross-legged on her own bed, eyes closed, accessing the relay through Ship—"that it's the meds that make you feel like you don't need meds anymore." Bo Nine came into Tisarwat's quarters, quietly humming. *Oh, tree, eat the fish.*

Beside me, on my bed, Seivarden scooted closer. Tugged briefly on my jacket collar, as though it might have been just the slightest bit out of place. Leaned against me. "You and Medic. I already know that. I've done this before, remember?"

"And you were so very successful at it." I felt my own shoulder warm against Seivarden's. The decades—the soldiers among them who were not in Command, anyway—were just beginning to hear and see those official news items. Their anger and resentment washed over me, tinged with shame—after all, they were Radchaai. Were being accused of treason by Radchaai authorities.

Oblivious, Seivarden gave an amused *hah.* "I didn't do too badly this time. I went much longer, for one thing. And I still haven't taken any kef. Well, all right, I *wanted* to. But I didn't." I refrained from pointing out that no matter how much she had wanted to, she couldn't have. "I've talked to Medic about this." She slid down a bit, laid her head on my shoulder. "I don't want to trade one addiction for another one. And I *was* doing pretty well." Despite her blithe tone, she was apprehensive about my reaction.

"Ship," I said, "I understand what you're doing. But I'm afraid Lieutenant Seivarden wants things from me that I can't give her."

Seivarden sighed. Lifted her head just slightly off my shoulder to look up at me. "The lieutenant and I have talked about that." Speaking for Ship. "You're right, she does want things you can't give her. But the truth is, anyone in any sort of relationship with you is going to have to adjust some of their expectations." Seivarden gave a little *hah* at the end of that sentence. Put her head back down on my shoulder. "Ship and I have talked about this."

"While you were strung out on meds and everything seemed fine?"

"Mostly before," she replied, surprisingly unperturbed. "Look, I'm not going to get those things no matter what. But maybe I can have just a little, this way." An embarrassed hesitation, and then, "Maybe, between you and Ship, there's a little bit left over for me. Ship likes me well enough, right? It said so. And mostly what you're talking about is sex. It's not like I can't get that other places, on my own."

Ekalu, in Command. Watchful. Just as angry and shame-filled about those official news announcements as the rest of the crew. Not thinking about Seivarden at the moment, I was fairly sure.

Seivarden sighed. "Then again, I haven't done very well with that, have I." Apparently thinking of Ekalu, herself. "I don't know what I did wrong. I still don't understand why she was so upset."

"She told you why she was upset," I pointed out. "You still don't understand?"

Seivarden sat up straight. Stood up. Walked to the other end of the room and back. "No." Stood staring at me. Agitated, just mildly, but she had not been even that for days.

"Seivarden." I wanted her to sit back down, to lean her shoulder against mine again. "Do you know what happens when people tell me I don't really seem like an ancillary to them?"

She blinked. Breath slightly faster. "You get angry." And then, with a little *heh*, "Well, angrier."

"You've never said it to me, though I'm sure you've thought it." She opened her mouth to protest. "No, listen. You didn't know I was an ancillary when I found you on Nilt. You assumed I was human. It might, in fact, be entirely reasonable for you to say I don't seem like an ancillary to you, or that you don't see me as an ancillary. And you might even think of it as a compliment. But you have never said it to me. And I imagine you never will."

"Well, no," replied Seivarden. Puzzled and hurt. Looking down at me where I sat on the bed. "I know it would make you angry."

"Do you understand why?"

She gestured irrelevance. "No. No, honestly, Breq, I don't."

"So why then," I asked, only mildly surprised she hadn't worked this out on her own, "don't you extend the same courtesy to Ekalu?"

"Well, but it wasn't *reasonable*."

"I, on the other hand," I pointed out, my tone even but edged, "am always entirely reasonable in your experience."

Seivarden laughed. "Well, but you're..." She stopped. Froze. I saw the realization strike, the sudden spike of it.

"This isn't new," I said. I didn't think she heard me, though. Blood was rushing to her face, she wanted to flee, but of course there was nowhere she could go and be away from herself. "You have always expected anyone beneath you to be careful of your emotional needs. You are even now hoping I will say something to make you feel better. You were quite angry with Ekalu when she herself failed to do that." No reply. Just shallow, careful breathing, as though she were afraid a deep breath might hurt. "You really have gotten better, but you can still be an enormously self-involved jerk."

"I'll be all right," she said, as though it followed logically from what I had just said. "I need to go to the gym."

"All right," I said, and without another word she turned and left.

11

An hour later I returned from a Medic-approved trip down the corridor and back, and found Seivarden, hair still damp from the bath, rooting through the cupboard where the tea things were stowed. Kalr Five, who had followed me, saw Seivarden, felt a surge of pure outraged resentment. Then reconsidered. "Lieutenant," Five said, watching me settle myself onto the bed, "they're all the way in the back."

Seivarden made an irritated noise. Pulled out my old enamel tea flask and its two bowls, one chipped. Began making tea, as Five fussed with the cushions around me, and then, once each one was exactly where she thought it should be, left.

At length Seivarden brought two bowls of tea, and sat down beside me on the bed. "You know," she said after her first taste, "that flask really doesn't brew right."

"It's from outside the Radch," I pointed out. "It's made for a different sort of tea."

I saw that she was counting her breaths, carefully timing

them. She said, after a bit, "Breq, do you ever wish you'd left me where you found me?"

"Not for a while," I replied, truthfully enough.

And then, after a few more breaths, "Is Ekalu a lot like Lieutenant Awn?"

I wondered, for an instant, where that question had come from. Then I remembered Seivarden, close against me in the bed in Medical as I told *Mercy of Kalr* that I could see myself liking Ekalu quite extravagantly, if I had still been a ship. "Not really. But would it matter if she was?"

"I suppose not."

We drank a while in silence and then Seivarden said, "I've already apologized to Ekalu. I can't exactly go back to her now and say, *I only said what Ship told me I ought to before, but this time I really mean it.*" I didn't answer. Seivarden sighed. "I just wanted her to stop being angry with me." More silence. She leaned close, shoulder up against mine again. "I still want to take kef. But the thought of taking it makes me sick to my stomach." Even saying that did, I could see. "Medic told me it would. I didn't think I'd mind. I thought it wouldn't matter, because even if I took it, it wouldn't do me any good. No, that's not right. I'm feeling sorry for myself again, aren't I."

Briefly I considered saying, *I'm used to it.* Said nothing instead.

For several minutes Seivarden sat beside me. Silent, drinking tea in measured sips. Still feeling sorry for herself, but only mildly now, and trying, it seemed, to concentrate on something else. Eventually she said, "Our Tisarwat has suddenly displayed quite a few unexpected abilities."

"Has she?" I asked, voice bland.

"She knows how to make a message look like an official communication, does she? She can access an official gate relay? She's been talking to Station, and thinks Station is going to give her sensitive information? And you seem entirely unsurprised by any of it." She took a swallow of tea. "Granted, you're difficult to surprise. But still." I said nothing. "Ship won't answer me, either. I know better than to ask Medic. I'm thinking back to when Tisarwat first arrived, how angry you were that she was on board. Was she a spy, then? Did Medic...do something to ensure she'd be working for us, instead of Anaander?" She meant re-education, but couldn't bring herself to name it. "What else can our Tisarwat do?"

"I told you, you recall, that she would surprise you." In Tisarwat's quarters, Bo Nine was setting out a flask of tea and a bowl where her lieutenant could reach them. Feeling uneasy. All of Bo had begun to come to the same conclusion Seivarden had.

In my quarters, on my bed, shoulder still companionably against mine, Seivarden said, "You did say that. And I didn't believe you. You'd think I'd have learned by now."

Tisarwat, on her bed in her quarters, said, "Right, I think that's done it." Opened her eyes.

Saw Bo Nine standing in front of her. "Sir, do you think Citizen Uran is all right? And Horticulturist Basnaaid?"

"I hope so," Tisarwat replied. Worried, herself. "I'm trying to find out."

"The news hasn't said anything about that line on the concourse," Nine pointed out. "If I'd been in line, I'd have gone home and hid as soon as that started." She meant the constant condemnation of me on the official news channels, that we were getting from the relay.

"They didn't all have homes to hide in, did they?" replied Tisarwat. "Or not much of one. That was the point to begin with. And the line wasn't ever in the official news, was it. But yes, I hope they're all right. It's one of the things I've asked Station about." Instantly regretted speaking, because it raised the issue of just exactly how it was she could do what she was doing, and why Station might tell her anything. But she didn't have time to think much about the implications of what she'd just said, because right about then the official news channels changed.

Suddenly every single official news feed was displaying the inside of System Governor Giarod's office. Familiar enough to everyone in Athoek System, no doubt, a common sight on the official channels. But those appearances were always carefully staged and choreographed. Tall, broad-shouldered Governor Giarod always projected an air of calm assurance, of everything's being under her capable control. But here she stood looking harried and stressed. Beside her, stout and beautiful Station Administrator Celar; the shorter and slender head priest of Amaat, Eminence Ifian; and the new head of Security, whom I did not know, but was quite sure Lieutenant Tisarwat did. All four of them faced Anaander Mianaai. A very young Anaander Mianaai, barely twenty, at a guess.

Anaander, nearly expressionless, stood in front of those green-and-cream silk hangings, the window onto the concourse darkened. "Why," she asked, in a dangerously even voice, "is there a line on the concourse?" The sound was not smoothed or filtered, the camera view not composed. This was, very obviously, raw surveillance data.

"Begging my lord's very generous indulgence," said Administrator Celar, after an icy silence during which no one else in the office so much as twitched, "they are protesting the overcrowding on the station in the past few weeks."

"Are you, Station Administrator," Anaander asked, coldly, "incapable of dealing with the issue?"

"My lord," replied Station Administrator Celar, her voice shaking only very slightly, "there would be no line if I had been *allowed* to deal with the issue."

Now Eminence Ifian spoke up. "Begging my lord's most gracious and generous indulgence, but the station administrator wished to . . . deal with the issue by hastily refitting the Undergarden. Despite, my lord, the repeated insistence of other officials that more careful consideration was needed. It would have made far more sense to send the former Undergarden residents downwell while the question of repairs was more carefully thought through. But I believe the station administrator was being pressured by Fl . . . by the ancillary."

Silence. "Why"—Anaander Mianaai's voice was still even, but had taken on a sharper edge—"was the ancillary concerning itself with the Undergarden?"

"My lord," said Station Administrator Celar, "the Gardens lake collapsed into the Undergarden a week or so ago. The people who had been living there had to be housed somewhere until it could be repaired."

Still cross-legged on her bed, watching and listening, Bo Nine still standing in front of her, Tisarwat exhaled sharply. Said, "What else haven't they told her?"

Even now they weren't telling Anaander everything. The repairs to the Undergarden had begun well before the lake had collapsed, and at my very definite insistence. I expected Eminence Ifian to point this out, but she did not.

Anaander took the news of the lake's collapse with almost no change of expression. Said nothing. Perhaps emboldened by this, Station Administrator Celar continued, "My lord, shipping residents downwell without consulting them would certainly have resulted in unrest among station residents at a time we can ill afford it. I am, my lord, at a loss to understand why Eminence Ifian—or the system governor, for that matter—felt it proper to oppose repairs which were urgently needed, and which would have dealt with the issue far more conveniently." Looked as though she wanted to say something further, something bitter, but did not. Swallowed the words, whatever they were.

Silence. Then Anaander Mianaai said, "As you point out, Station Administrator, we can ill afford unrest. Security. Notify the protesters on the concourse that if they are still in line three minutes from now, they will be shot. *Sword of Gurat*."

From somewhere out of view an ancillary voice replied, "My lord."

"Accompany Security. At the end of three minutes, shoot anyone who remains in line."

"My lord!" replied the new head of Security. "With the utmost respect and deference, begging your very generous and proper indulgence, but I submit to my lord that threatening to shoot citizens who are peaceably standing in line is quite certain to *produce* unrest. The citizens involved have caused no difficulty whatever. My lord."

"If they are such law-abiding citizens, they will return to their homes when ordered," Anaander said, coldly. "And everyone will be safer for their doing so."

In my quarters aboard *Mercy of Kalr*, Seivarden said, shoulder still against mine, bowl of tea cooling in one gloved hand, "Well, it works for annexations."

"After a great deal of bloodshed," I pointed out.

In the system governor's office on Athoek Station, Anaander

Mianaai said, "Are you refusing my order to clear the concourse, Security?"

"I...I am." A breath. "I am, my lord." As though she hadn't been certain of it until just that moment.

"*Sword of Gurat,*" said Anaander, and held out one black-gloved hand. The *Sword of Gurat* ancillary came into view, handed Anaander its gun.

On *Mercy of Kalr*, Tisarwat leapt off her bed. "No!" But protest was useless. This had all of it already happened.

"Fuck!" Seivarden, still beside me, on my bed, bowl of tea in her hand. "Security isn't military!"

And meanwhile, on Athoek Station, in Governor Giarod's office, Anaander raised the gun and fired, point-blank, before the new head of Security could more than open her mouth in protest or retraction. Security dropped to the ground, and Anaander fired again. "We are under attack from within," Anaander said, into the following horrified silence. "I *will not* allow my enemy to destroy what I've built. *Sword of Gurat*, deliver my orders to the people lined up on the concourse. I don't suppose they're troubled by taking orders from an ancillary anyway."

"My lord," replied *Sword of Gurat*, standing ancillary-straight and ancillary-still behind Anaander, and did not move. Of course. It didn't need to leave the room to obey Anaander's order, just send a different segment. And then, before Anaander could speak again, the ancillary said, "My lord, the past few minutes of this conversation are being broadcast on the official news channels."

On *Mercy of Kalr*, Tisarwat, tearful, Bo Nine's arm awkwardly around her, cried out, "Oh, Station!" And then, "Fleet Captain, sir!"

"I'm watching," I said.

On Athoek Station, Anaander said, sharply, "Station!"

"I can't stop it, my lord," replied Athoek Station, from a console. "I don't know what to do."

"Who came with it?" Anaander asked, sharp and angry. Not even puzzlement, on the faces of Governor Giarod, Station Administrator Celar, and Eminence Ifian. All of them, I was sure, still trying to grasp those sudden shots, moments before, the body of the head of Security motionless on the floor. "*Who came with the ancillary*?"

Governor Giarod said, "N...no one in particular, my lord. Her...its lieutenants." Hesitated. "Only one came onto the station. Lieutenant Tisarwat."

"House name," Anaander demanded.

"I'm...not certain, my lord," replied Governor Giarod. Station Administrator Celar certainly knew Tisarwat's house name, Tisarwat and Celar's daughter Piat were good friends, but I noted that she didn't volunteer it. Neither did Station. Not that it would have mattered.

Anaander considered the silence, and then said, sharply, "Ship, with me." And left the office.

"She'll go to Station's Central Access," said Tisarwat. Needlessly. Of course she would. *Why*, said the voice of Anaander Mianaai, over the official news feeds, *is there a line on the concourse*? Station's recording, repeating.

There was no point getting up off the bed. There was nothing I could do.

"Oh, fuck," said Seivarden beside me. "Oh, *fuck*. What does Station think it's doing?" This wasn't in response to any request of ours, of Tisarwat's. Our messages couldn't possibly have reached Athoek Station yet.

"Protecting its residents," I replied. "As best it can. Letting them know that Anaander is a threat. Remember, this is the same station that turned off its gravity the last time its residents were threatened." It was probably the best Station could do, under the circumstances. Granted, it wouldn't necessarily—or even likely—prevent *Sword of Gurat* from shooting citizens, but it was possible Station believed that even Anaander Mianaai might hesitate to do it if everyone was watching. And everyone would be watching—those official news feeds went not only to every receiver in Athoek System, but to every single gate relay. Hrad System would be getting that recording about now, perhaps a bit later. In the official, approved news channels, which any citizen could access. Was encouraged to access, sometimes could not escape.

"But," Seivarden protested, "the Lord of the Radch will just go to Central Access and stop it." And then, realizing, "So the Lord of the Radch doesn't have that thing with her, that cuts off communications. Or she'd have used it. What will she do now?"

What would she do, I wondered, when she discovered she couldn't get to Station? Or more accurately, what had she already done?

"Sir," Tisarwat said, from her quarters. Shakily. "Did you notice, nobody seemed to want to talk about the Undergarden, or the lake. They haven't told her everything, not even Eminence Ifian. I'm not sure why, though, you'd think Ifian would tell her everything she could. Maybe she doesn't know about Basnaaid, or Uran." Eminence Ifian surely knew about Basnaaid and Uran. The *she* Lieutenant Tisarwat meant was Anaander. "And did you notice how young she was? And that... all of this. All of it. I think she may be the only one of her here, sir, or certainly the oldest one. And I think you did more than punch through some hull plating. She's *really* angry. And she's afraid. I'm not sure why, though. I'm not sure why she would be quite so afraid."

"Get some rest, Lieutenant." It was well after her supper. She was tired, on top of her distress. "Ship will wake you if we hear from Station. Right now we just have to wait."

The recording repeated for nearly two hours, until, quite abruptly, it stopped, and three seconds later the regular news announcements resumed. The *Justice of Toren* show, as *Sphene* had called it. But now, added to it, the announcement of a curfew. No one was to leave their quarters except citizens in necessary assignments—these were specifically listed: Medical, Security, certain branches of Station Maintenance, refectory workers—or citizens taking food from the common refectories at assigned, scheduled times. What might happen if one left one's quarters without authorization was left unstated, but everyone had seen the head of Security die, over and over. Everyone had heard Anaander threaten to shoot citizens who did not leave the line on the concourse.

Tisarwat was upset enough to get out of bed, pull her jacket and boots on, and come to my quarters to speak to me. "Sir!" she cried, coming in the door, as Bo Nine gave her jacket hem a quick tug so it would lie right, "it's impossible! Some of those dormitories, people are sleeping three or four shifts to a bunk! It's impossible for everyone to stay in their quarters! What does she think she's doing?"

Kalr Five, laying out breakfast dishes, pretended to ignore Tisarwat, but she had been just as disturbed at the news.

"Lieutenant," I said, "go back to bed. At least pretend to rest. There's nothing we can do from this distance." We were still in the Ghost System, *Mercy of Kalr*'s hull still warmed by that smaller, slightly orange-ish star, alone but for *Sphene*, whom we couldn't see, who only spoke to us through its ancillary, only the Athoek gate communications relay to break the silence. "We'll likely hear from Station quite soon, if it's willing or able to speak to us. Then we'll decide what to do."

She cast a glance at the table, set for more than just me. "You're going to eat? How can you eat?"

"I've found that not eating is generally a bad decision," I replied. Evenly. I could see she was at the edge of her patience, just about to lose any ability to hold herself together. "And I can't leave the translator all to herself. Or, gods help us all, to *Sphene*."

"Oh, the translator! I'd forgotten all about her." She frowned.

"Go back to bed, Lieutenant."

Which she did, but instead of sleeping she asked Bo Nine for tea.

Everyone aboard was on edge, except for *Sphene*, who appeared not to care much about what was happening, and Translator Zeiat, who had apparently slept through the whole thing. When the translator woke I invited her to breakfast, along with *Sphene*, Medic, and Seivarden. Ekalu was still on watch. Tisarwat was awake, but I knew she wouldn't eat, and besides she was supposed to be asleep.

"Counters is such a fascinating game, Fleet Captain," Translator Zeiat said, and took a drink of her fish sauce. "I'm terribly grateful to *Sphene* for introducing me to it."

Seivarden was surprised, but didn't dare express it. Medic was too busy frowning at me across the table to react—she had still not forgiven me for leaving Medical without her approval. And she thought I should be resting more.

"Your pardon, Translator," I said, "but I suspect most

Radchaai would be extremely surprised to hear that you're not familiar with counters."

"Goodness, no, Fleet Captain," replied the translator. "I'd heard of it, of course. But Humans do such disturbingly odd things, you know, sometimes it's better not to think too hard about them."

"What sort of games are you used to playing, Translator?" asked Seivarden, and then immediately regretted it, either because it got her the translator's attention, or because she realized belatedly what kind of answer might be forthcoming.

"Games, now," said Translator Zeiat thoughtfully. "I can't say we actually play any games. Not as such. Well, you know, Dlique might. I wouldn't put *anything* past Dlique." She looked at me. "Did Dlique play counters?"

"Not that I'm aware, Translator."

"Oh, good. I'm *very* glad I'm not Dlique." She looked over at Medic, who was eating eggs and vegetables and still frowning at me. "Medic, I do understand you miss the previous fleet captain, I do myself, but it's hardly this one's fault. And she's very much like the previous one, really. She's even making every effort to grow another leg for you."

Medic swallowed her mouthful of breakfast, entirely unoffended. "Translator, I'm given to understand that the first Presger translators were grown from human remains."

"I myself am given to understand the same," replied Translator Zeiat, sounding quite unperturbed by the question. "I suspect it's even true. Long before the treaty, long before translators were ever considered, in fact, they had, shall we say, a very...yes, a very practical kind of understanding of how Human bodies were put together."

"Or taken apart," Medic put in. Seivarden nearly pushed

her plate away. *Sphene* chewed placidly, listening as it had all through the meal.

"Indeed, Medic, indeed!" agreed Translator Zeiat. "But their priorities are not, well, not Human priorities, and when they put us together, you know, they didn't really have any understanding of what would be *important*. Or maybe *essential* is a better word. At any rate. Their first several tries went horribly wrong."

"In what way?" asked Medic, genuinely curious.

"Your very great indulgence, Medic," said Seivarden, "but we *are* eating."

"Perhaps you can discuss it later," I suggested.

"Oh!" Translator Zeiat seemed genuinely surprised. "Is it propriety again?"

"It is." I finished off my own eggs. "Incidentally, Translator. You are, of course, welcome to stay with us as long as you like, but since you did come through the Ghost Gate, I was wondering if you might be leaving us before we return to Athoek."

"Oh, goodness, no, Fleet Captain! I can't go home just yet. I mean, can you imagine it? Everyone saying *Hello, Dlique*! and, *Look, Dlique's home*! It would be Dlique this, and Dlique that, and I'd have to tell them that no, I'm very sorry, but I'm not Dlique, I'm Zeiat. And then I'd have to explain what happened to Dlique and it would get very awkward. No, I'm not ready to face that. It's very good of you to let me stay. I can't tell you how much I appreciate it."

"It's our pleasure, Translator," I said.

Athoek Station's response arrived in four parts, each one innocently labeled as a routine reply to an authorized query.

Tisarwat ought to have been asleep, but was not. Instead she sat at the table in the decade room. She had not been able to stay still in her quarters, and besides the decade room was closer to the bath; she had drunk far more tea than was wise. Bo Nine had just set a fresh bowl in front of her. Nine had been impressively patient given that this was the middle of the night for her as well and she hadn't slept any more than her lieutenant had.

Ship didn't waste an instant, but displayed the first-arriving in Tisarwat's vision without explanation. Tisarwat started up out of her chair. Frowned. "It's a shuttle schedule. Why did Station send a shuttle schedule?" To be precise, it was the schedule for the passenger shuttles between Athoek Station and the tops of the planet's elevators. Dated yesterday.

I was coming out of the bath, headed for Command, but instead I swung myself around and went toward the decade room, Five behind me. "Next one, Ship," I said. Station Security was to place itself under the orders of a lieutenant from *Sword of Gurat*. Ancillaries from *Sword of Gurat* would patrol the station along with regular Security. And so would ancillaries from *Sword of Atagaris*. "There's no mention of any lieutenant from *Sword of Atagaris*," Tisarwat said, as I came in the door and Nine pulled out a chair for me. "Or any of its officers at all, actually."

"Why not?" I asked. "Did *Sword of Atagaris* not get those pods we left?"

"Maybe *she* removed Captain Hetnys from command," suggested Tisarwat, sitting back down. "It would hardly be surprising, Hetnys is lucky if she has half the brains an oyster has. And you've made it pretty clear that whoever controls Hetnys controls *Sword of Atagaris*." She gave a little *hah*. "That'll turn out to be a mistake."

I certainly hoped so. "And the next?"

"A list of urgent requests for an audience with..." Tisarwat hesitated.

"With Anaander Mianaai," I finished for her. "And of course Fosyf Denche is on the list, and of course she wants the Lord of the Radch to right a terrible miscarriage of justice regarding her daughter Raughd."

Tisarwat scoffed. Then frowned. "And last is a list of citizens who are required to immediately relocate downwell, in order to relieve crowding on the station. Sir, look at the names."

I was looking at it. "Basnaaid and Uran are on it."

"Station Administrator Celar made this list, depend on it. But look at the rest of it."

"Yes," I agreed.

"Nearly all Ychana," Tisarwat said. "Which makes sense, really, since it's mostly Ychana who were displaced to begin with. And if trouble breaks out on the station they're most likely to bear the brunt of it. I'm sure Administrator Celar was thinking of getting them to relative safety. But I see at least a dozen people who are going to immediately suspect they're being singled out for mistreatment. And I doubt anyone on the list is going to be happy about being summarily sent off the station." She frowned. "They're supposed to leave *today*. That's *fast*."

"Yes," I agreed. Anaander had likely ordered everyone to remain indoors, and Station Administrator Celar had had to find some way to make it work, and quickly. I sat, finally, in the chair Bo Nine had pulled out for me. Leaned my crutches against the table, next to where the pieces of *Sphene* and Translator Zeiat's ongoing game were laid out. "Is this information supposed to go with the shuttle schedule?" Except the order to relocate was for today, and the shuttle schedule was for yesterday.

"Sir," said Tisarwat. Frustrated and afraid. "Did you hear me? They're hastily relocating dozens of Undergarden residents, at a time when armed soldiers are threatening to shoot citizens on the concourse."

"I heard."

"Sir! A lot of the people on this list are likely to refuse to get on that shuttle."

"I think you're right, Lieutenant. But there's nothing we can do about it. We are three days away from Athoek Station. Whatever is happening is happening *now*."

Sphene came in the door, Translator Zeiat close behind. "Well, I wasn't ever a child, actually," Translator Zeiat was saying. "Or, that is to say, when I was a child I was someone else. I daresay you were, too. No doubt that's why we get on so well. Hello, Fleet Captain. Hello, Lieutenant."

"Translator," I said, lowering my head briefly.

Tisarwat seemed not to have noticed that anyone else was in the decade room. "So Station wants us to know that Captain Hetnys isn't back on *Sword of Atagaris* and isn't likely to be. It tells us that Basnaaid and Uran are being sent to safety. And that Fosyf is seizing the opportunity to put herself back on top of things. And that the shuttles are running as always? Why?"

"It's telling us," said Five, behind me, for Ship, "that something happened to one of the shuttles. There's one missing off the schedule. Look." In my vision, and Tisarwat's, the schedule Station had sent us, and the one Ship already had. The differences flared, the arrivals and departures that were on the regular schedule but not the one Station had sent. "Those are all the same shuttle. So Station wants us to know that something happened to that shuttle. It is also being careful to let us know that it happened before yesterday. Before, that is, Basnaaid and Uran boarded a shuttle downwell."

Sphene sat down on one side of the in-progress game. "Is Station doing that thing again, where it won't tell you what's wrong but something is obviously wrong?"

"Sort of," I said. "Only this time we asked it to. It can't tell us directly, because the Usurper is on the station."

Translator Zeiat sat beside me, on the other side of the game. Frowned a moment at the bright-colored counters in their holes on the board, the scattering of eggshell fragments. "I believe it's your turn, *Sphene*."

"Indeed," replied *Sphene*. It scooped the counters out of one depression on the board, turned its hand palm-up to show them to Translator Zeiat. "Three green. One blue. One yellow. One red."

"I think that's four green," said the translator dubiously.

"No, that's definitely blue."

"Hmm. All right." Translator Zeiat took the red counter from Sphene's hand and dropped it in the scummed-over bowl of tea. "That's almost a whole egg, too. I'm going to have to think carefully about my next move."

"We have more shells for you, Translator, if you need them," said Bo Nine. The translator waved an absent acknowledgment, stared at the board as *Sphene* redistributed the remaining counters.

"Look at the Security order," said Tisarwat. "At the way it's worded. I think *Sword of Gurat* is actually docked with Athoek Station. But why would..." She trailed off, frowning.

"Because Anaander needs every ancillary aboard it to police the station," I guessed.

"But she has three other ships! One of them is a troop carrier, isn't it? She has thousands of..." I could see the realization strike. "What if she doesn't have three other ships? Sir!" She focused again on the records in her vision. "Why hasn't Station told us what ships are in the system?" And then, "No, *she* won't have told Station what ships are in the system. Especially if there aren't many. And she doesn't trust *Sword of Atagaris*. Or Captain Hetnys."

"Can you blame her?" asked *Sphene*. "Arrogant and dimwitted, the both of them." Tisarwat looked up at the ancillary, surprised to realize that it was in the room. Blinked at it, and at the translator.

"Does she not know what happened last time *Sword of Atagaris* supplied security?" asked Tisarwat. And then, "No, of course she doesn't. They haven't told her for some reason."

Just from the small bit we'd seen the day before, there were plenty of things system authorities hadn't told Anaander Mianaai. "Or she does know and she doesn't care."

"Very possible," Tisarwat agreed. "Sir, we have to go back!"

"We do," said Translator Zeiat, still staring at the game in front of her, still pondering her move. "I'm told you're nearly out of fish sauce."

"Now how could that have happened?" asked *Sphene*, as innocently as I supposed was possible for it.

"Please, sir." Tisarwat seemed not to have heard either of them. "We can't leave things the way they are, and I have an *idea*."

That got the translator's full attention. She looked up from the game, frowned intently at Tisarwat. "What's it like? Does it hurt?" Tisarwat only blinked at her. "Sometimes I think I might like to get an idea, but then it occurs to me that it's exactly the sort of thing Dlique would do." When Tisarwat didn't answer, Translator Zeiat returned her attention to the game. Picked up a yellow counter from off the board, put it in her mouth, and swallowed. "Your turn, *Sphene*."

"That one wasn't green, either," said *Sphene*.

"I know," said Translator Zeiat, with an air of satisfaction.

"Ship is already making the calculations for the trip back to Athoek," I said, to Tisarwat. "Go see Medic and tell her you've had way too much tea." She opened her mouth to protest, but I continued. "It's three days back to Athoek. We can spare a few minutes. When Medic is done with you, come see me in my quarters and we'll talk about your idea."

She wanted to protest. Wanted to pound a fist on the table and shout at me. Almost did it, but instead she took a breath, and then another one. "Sir," she said. Stood up, overturning the chair behind her, and left the decade room. Bo Nine righted the chair, and followed.

"What an excitable person that Lieutenant Tisarwat is," said Translator Zeiat. "An *idea*. Just imagine!"

12

"So, this idea of yours?" I asked, when Tisarwat came to my quarters.

"Well, it's not..." Standing in front of me where I sat, she shifted uncomfortably, just slightly. "It's kind of desperate." I didn't say anything. "*Sword of Gurat* isn't one of the ships she gave me accesses to, but there's...there's a kind of underlying logic to the accesses. The split has meant that the underlying logic for each part of her isn't identical, which is part of why I couldn't find all of what she might have done to Athoek Station, or *Sword of Atagaris*."

"Or *Mercy of Kalr*."

"Or *Mercy of Kalr*. Yes, sir." Unhappy at that. "But the other part of her, the part that's at Omaugh, I'm...very familiar with that. If I could get aboard *Sword of Gurat*, if I had time to talk to it, I might actually be able to figure out how to access it." I looked at her. She seemed entirely serious. "I told you it was desperate."

"You did," I agreed.

"So here's my idea. We put two teams on the station. One

of them—mine—goes to the docks to try to get aboard *Sword of Gurat*. And the other finds Anaander and kills her."

"Just like that?"

"Well, that's just an overview. I did leave out some details. And of course, I haven't really taken *Sword of Atagaris* into account at all." She winced, then, just a bit. "A lot of the details seemed really clear to me when I first thought of it. In retrospect, they were actually pretty incoherent. But I still think the basic outline is sound, sir." She hesitated, watching for my reaction.

"Right," I said. "Choose two of your Bos to go with you. They'll spend the next three days in the gym and the firing range, or whatever other training or briefing you feel they need, and they're relieved of all other duties. Ship."

"Fleet Captain," *Mercy of Kalr* said in my ear.

"Have Etrepa One take over watch from Lieutenant Ekalu, and ask Ekalu and Seivarden to join us here. And ask Five to come make us tea for the meeting. And Ship."

"Sir."

"Do you want Lieutenant Tisarwat to do for you what she did for Station and *Sword of Atagaris*?"

Silence. Though I suspected I already knew the answer. And then, "Actually, Fleet Captain, I do."

I looked at Tisarwat. "Make room for it in your schedule, Lieutenant. And you might as well tell me your incoherent details, in case there's anything there worth salvaging."

Next morning at breakfast, I left *Sphene* and Medic to entertain Translator Zeiat, and invited Ekalu to eat with me. "Is everything all right?" I asked, when Five had laid out fruit and fish on the Bractware, and poured tea in the rose glass bowls, and then left the room at Ship's suggestion.

"I don't know what you mean, sir." Picked up her bowl

of tea. Much less uncomfortable holding it than she'd been weeks ago. Much less uncomfortable around me.

Still. "I don't mean anything in particular, Lieutenant."

"It's a little odd, sir, begging your indulgence." She put the tea down, untasted. "You already know how I'm getting along, don't you?"

"To a point," I admitted. Took a bite of fish, so that Ekalu could begin eating if she wanted. "I can look in on you if I want, and I can see how you feel sometimes. But I'm..." I put my utensil down. "I'm trying not to do that too much. Particularly if I think it makes you uncomfortable. And"—I gestured the space between us—"I'd like you to be able to talk to me if you need to. If you want to."

Mortification. Fear. "Have I done something wrong, sir?"

"No. Far from it." I made myself take another bite of fish. "I just wanted to have breakfast with you and maybe ask your opinion about some things, but right now, asking you how things are going, I'm just making conversation." Took a drink of my tea. "I'm not always very good at idle conversation. Sorry."

Ekalu dared a tiny little smile, felt the beginning of relief, though she didn't trust that feeling entirely. Didn't relax.

"So," I continued, "I'll just go right to the business then, shall I? I wanted your opinion of Amaat One. It must be strange," I added, seeing her suppress a flinch at that, "hearing a name you went by for so long, that you don't go by anymore."

Ekalu gestured insignificance. "I didn't come onto this ship Amaat One. My number changed, as people retired, or left, or..." Whatever she'd meant to put behind that *or* didn't come. She gestured it away. "But you're right, sir, it is strange." She took a bit of fruit, then. Chewed and swallowed. "I suppose you know what that's like."

"I do," I agreed. Waited a moment to see if she had anything else to say, but she apparently didn't. "I'm not asking for anything bad. Amaat One stood watch and ran her decade while Seivarden was ill. I think she did an excellent job, and I'd like her to begin officer training. We have the materials aboard, because you've been using them. Actually, I think the training ought to be available to anyone on the ship who wants it. But I very specifically am considering the possibility of a field promotion for Amaat One. You know her very well, I think."

"Sir, I..." She was deeply uncomfortable, insulted even. She wanted to get up from the table, leave the room. Didn't know how to answer me.

"I realize I'm very possibly putting you in a difficult position, if you should object to her being promoted, and if she should find out—because there are very few secrets on this ship—that you had perhaps prevented it. But I beg you to consider the situation we're in. Consider what happened when I and Lieutenant Tisarwat were away and Lieutenant Seivarden was ill. You and the decade leaders handled things admirably, but you would all have been more comfortable if you'd had more experience. I see no reason not to give all of the decade leaders the training required for when it happens again, and I foresee them eventually deserving promotion. I foresee the ship needing them in those places."

Silence, from Ekalu. She took another drink of tea. Thinking. Unhappy and afraid. "Sir," she said at length, "begging your patient indulgence. But what's the point? I mean, I understand why we're going back to Athoek. That makes sense to me. But farther ahead than that. At first this all just seemed unreal, and it still does in a way. But the Lord of the Radch is coming apart. And if she comes apart, so does the Radch. I mean, maybe she'll hold herself together, maybe she'll put these pieces back together again. But, begging your forgiveness, sir, for my speaking very frankly, but you don't actually want that, do you."

"I don't," I admitted.

"And so what's the point, sir? What's the point of talking about training and promotions as though it's all going to just go on like it always has?"

"What's the point of anything?"

"Sir?" She blinked, confused. Taken aback.

"In a thousand years, Lieutenant, nothing you care about will matter. Not even to you—you'll be dead. So will I, and no one alive will care. Maybe—just maybe—someone will remember our names. More likely those names will be engraved on some dusty memorial pin at the bottom of an old box no one ever opens." Or Ekalu's would. There was no reason anyone would make any memorials to me, after my death. "And that thousand years *will* come, and another and another, to the end of the universe. Think of all the griefs and tragedies, and yes, the triumphs, buried in the past, millions of years of it. *Everything* for the people who lived them. Nothing now."

Ekalu swallowed. "I'll have to remember, sir, if I'm ever feeling down, that you know how to cheer me right up."

I smiled. "The point is, there is no point. Choose your own."

"We don't usually get to choose our own, do we?" she asked. "You do, I suppose, but you're a special case. And everyone on this ship, we're just going along with yours." She looked down at her plate, considered, briefly, picking up a utensil, but I saw that she couldn't actually eat just now.

I said, "It doesn't have to be a big point. As you say, often it can't be. Sometimes it's nothing more than *I have to find a way to put one foot in front of the other, or I'll die here.* If we lose this throw, if we lose our lives in the near future, then yes, training and promotions will have been pointless. But who knows? Perhaps the omens will favor us. And if, ultimately, I have what I want, Athoek will need protection. I will need good officers."

"And what are the chances of the omens favoring us, sir, if I may ask? Lieutenant Tisarwat's plan—what I know of it, sir, is..." She waved away whatever word she had been going to use to describe it. "There's no margin for error or accident. There are so many ways things could go horribly wrong."

"When you're doing something like this," I said, "the odds are irrelevant. You don't need to know the odds. You need to know how to do the thing you're trying to do. And then you need to do it. What comes next"—I gestured, the tossing of a handful of omens—"isn't something you have any control over."

"It will be as Amaat wills," Ekalu said. A pious platitude. "Sometimes that's a comfort, to think that God's intention directs everything." She sighed. "And sometimes it's not."

"Very true," I agreed. "In the meantime, let's enjoy our breakfast." I took up a piece of fish. "It's very good. And let's talk about Amaat One, and whoever else in the decades you think might be officer material."

Off to Medical, after breakfast, to Medic's tiny office cubicle. I lowered myself into a chair, leaned my crutches against the wall. "You said something about a prosthetic."

"It's not ready yet," she said. Flat. Frowning. Defying me to question her assertion.

"It should be ready by now," I said.

"It's a complicated mechanism. It needs to be able to compensate for new growth as..."

"You want to be sure I don't leave Seivarden and her

Amaats here and go to the station myself." We were in gate-space, still days away from Athoek.

Medic scoffed. "Like that would stop you. Sir."

"Then what's the problem?"

"The prosthetic is a temporary fix. It's not designed to take hard use and it's certainly not suitable for combat." I didn't reply, just sat watching her frown at me. "Lieutenant Seivarden shouldn't be going, either. She's much better than she was, but I can't guarantee how well she'll handle that kind of stress. And Tisarwat..." But she of anyone on the ship could guess why there was no choice about Tisarwat going.

"Lieutenant Seivarden is the only person on this ship besides me with actual combat experience," I pointed out. "And besides *Sphene*, I suppose. But I'm not sure we can trust *Sphene*."

Medic gave a sardonic laugh. "No." And then, struck by a thought, "Sir, I think you should consider some field promotions. Amaat One, certainly, and Bo One."

"I've just been talking to Ekalu about that. I'd have talked to Seivarden already, but I'm sure she's asleep by now." I reached. Found Seivarden in the first stages of what promised to be a very sound sleep. In my bed. Five, far from being resentful at losing her working space, sat at the table in the empty soldiers' mess, humming happily as she mended a torn shirtsleeve, a green-glazed bowl of tea near at hand. "Seivarden seems to be doing all right."

"So far," Medic agreed. "Though gods help us if she can't find a gym or make some tea next time she's upset. I've tried to talk her into taking up meditation, but really it's not something she's temperamentally suited to."

"She actually attempted it last night," I said. It had been morning on Seivarden's schedule.

"Did she? Well." Surprised, half-pleased, but not showing it on her face. Medic rarely did. "We'll see, I suppose. Now, let's have a look at how your leg is doing. And why, Fleet Captain, didn't you tell me sooner that your right leg was hurting you?"

"It's been that way more than a year. I'm mostly used to it. And actually I didn't think you could do anything about it."

Medic folded her arms. Leaned back in her chair. Still frowning at me. "It's possible that I can't. Certainly it's not practical to try much of anything right now. But you ought to have told me."

I put a penitent expression on my face. "Yes, Medic." She relaxed, just slightly. "Now about that prosthetic. Don't tell me it isn't ready yet, because I know that it is. Or it can be, in a matter of hours. And I am very tired of the crutches. I know it's not suitable for hard use, and even if it were I wouldn't have enough time to get used to it, not for fighting. Not even if you'd given it to me as soon as you possibly could. Seivarden is going to the station, not me."

Medic sighed. "You might actually adapt more quickly, because you're..." She hesitated. "Because you're an ancillary."

"I probably will," I agreed. "But not quickly enough." And I didn't want to jeopardize the mission, no matter how much I wanted to personally rid the system of Anaander Mianaai.

"Right," said Medic. Still frowning, as she nearly always did, but inwardly relieved. And gratified. "Let's go next door, then, and have a look at how that leg is coming along. And then, since I know you were up all night, and since we're safe in gate-space and you've already been around the ship making sure everything is going as it should, you can go back to your quarters and get some sleep. By the time you wake up, the prosthetic should be ready."

I thought of lying down beside Seivarden. It would not be the first time we'd shared close quarters, but that had been before *Mercy of Kalr*. Before I could come even the slightest bit close to what I'd lost, that sense of so much of myself around me. And Medic was right, I had been up all night. I really was very tired. "If that will make you happy, Medic," I said.

Seivarden didn't register my presence at all, she was so deeply asleep. But her nearness and warmth, her slow, even breathing, along with the data Ship fed me from Seivarden's sleeping Amaats, was so very comfortable. Ship showed me Tisarwat in the decade room, and Bo decade coming into the soldiers' mess. Laughing to see Kalr Five there. "Sir needed a bit of privacy with our Amaat lieutenant, did she?" Bo Ten asked. "About time!" Five just smiled, and kept on with her mending. Ekalu coming into the decade room for what would be her supper, her Etrepas finishing up the last tasks of the day before they could get into the soldiers' mess for their own meal. Kalr One on watch, in Command. Technically against regulations, but this was the not-even-nothing of gate-space, where nothing even remotely interesting would happen, and the more experience the decade leaders could get, the better. Medic telling Kalr Twelve she'd have lunch later, she was busy just now, didn't want to find out what would happen if the prosthetic wasn't ready when I woke, as she'd promised. Twelve didn't smile, though she wanted to.

Everything was as it should be. I slept, and woke hours later to Bo on watch, Tisarwat and two of her decade drilling in the gym, Ekalu and her Etrepas settling into their beds. Amaat still asleep and dreaming. Seivarden still beside me, still asleep. Five standing silent by my bed, with a rose glass bowl of tea for me. She must have made it in the decade room and carried it down the corridor. Ship said, in my ear, "Medic is available at your convenience, Fleet Captain."

* * *

Two hours later I was walking on my new, temporary leg—not much more than a gray plastic jointed rod, flattened at the foot end. Its response was just a hair more sluggish than I liked, and my first few steps on it had been unsteady and swaying. "No running," Medic had said, but at the moment, even if the leg had been built for heavy-duty use, I probably wouldn't have been able to run. "I have to check it every day, because if there's irritation or injury at the interface you won't feel it." Because of the corrective that was growing the leg back. "It may seem trivial, but believe me, it's far better to catch that sort of thing early." And I had said, "Yes, Medic." And gone to walk up and down corridors, Twelve trailing me, the prosthetic stiff and clunking with each step, until I could do so without tripping and falling.

I found *Sphene* by itself in the decade room, sitting at the table on one side of its game with Translator Zeiat. "Hello, Cousin," it said as I came unsteadily in the door. "Having trouble getting used to the new leg?"

"It's more of a challenge than I expected," I admitted. Officers of mine had lost limbs in the past, but they'd invariably been sent away to recover. And of course, if an ancillary lost a limb it was far easier just to dispose of it and thaw out a new one. Twelve pulled out a chair for me, and I lowered myself into it. Very carefully. "I just need practice, that's all."

"Of course." I couldn't tell if it was being sarcastic or not. "I'm just waiting for Translator Zeiat."

"You don't need to explain why you're in the decade room, Cousin. You're a guest here." Twelve brought me a bowl of tea, and one of the cakes from the pile on the counter.

Brought over the same for *Sphene*. Who looked at the tea, and the cake, and said, "You don't need to do this, you know.

You could feed me water and skel and put me in a storage compartment."

"Why would I do that, Cousin?" I took a bite of cake. It had chopped dates in it, and cinnamon. The recipe was a particular favorite of Ekalu's. "Tell me, does it bother you to be referred to as *it*?"

"Why would it?"

I gestured ambivalence. "It troubles some of my crew to hear you referred to as *it*, when you're treated like a person. And I call you *Cousin* and they wouldn't dream of ever using *it* for me. Though technically that would be correct."

"And does it bother you to be called *she*?" asked *Sphene*.

"No," I admitted. "I suppose I've gotten used to being called by whatever pronoun seems appropriate to the speaker. I have to admit, I'd take offense if one of my crew called me *it*. But mostly because I know they'd think of it as an insult."

Sphene picked up its cake. Took a bite. Chewed. Swallowed. Took a drink of tea. Said, "I've actually never thought about it until now, Cousin. But do you know what really does grate?" I gestured to her to continue, my mouth full of tea and cake. Sphene continued, "Hearing you call yourselves Radchaai. Calling this"—it gestured around—"the Radch."

I swallowed. "I suppose I can't blame you," I said. "Will you tell me where you are, Cousin?"

"Right across the table from you, Cousin." Impassive as always, but I thought I saw a trace of amusement.

"I couldn't help but notice that when we were in the Ghost System, and *Mercy of Kalr* asked where you were, it was you who answered us, from inside the ship. You didn't talk to *Mercy of Kalr* directly." And as a result we couldn't know how far away *Sphene* had been, or even guess at its location.

Sphene smiled. "Will you do me a favor, Cousin? Will you let me go back to the station with Lieutenant Seivarden?"

"Why?"

"I won't get in the way, I promise. It's just that I want to be able to put my hands around the Usurper's throat and strangle her myself." The war *Sphene* had fled, three thousand years ago, had been an argument not just over Anaander's policy of expanding Radchaai influence outward, but also over her legitimacy as an authority of any sort. Or so I understood—it had all happened a thousand years before I was born. "Or if that's inconveniently time-consuming, I'll happily shoot her in the head. As long as she knows who it is who's doing it. I realize that it's a futile wish, and won't do the least bit of good, considering what she is. But I want to do it so badly. I've been dreaming of it for three thousand years." I didn't answer. "Ah, you don't trust me. Well, I suppose I wouldn't, either, in your place."

Translator Zeiat came into the decade room then. "*Sphene*! I've been thinking and thinking, let me show you! Hello, Fleet Captain! You'll like this, too." She took the tray of cakes off the counter, set it in the middle of the table. "These are cakes."

"They are," *Sphene* agreed. The translator looked to me for confirmation, and I gestured agreement.

"All of them! All cakes!" Completely delighted at the thought. She swept the cakes off the tray and onto the table, and made two piles of them. "Now these," she said, indicating the slightly larger stack of cinnamon date cakes, "have fruit in them. And these"—she indicated the others—"do not. Do you see? They were the same before, but now they're different. And look. You might think to yourself—I know I thought it to myself—that they're different because of the fruit. Or the not-fruit, you know, as the case may be. But watch this!" She took the stacks apart, set the cakes in haphazard ranks. "Now I make a line. I just imagine one!" She leaned over, put her arm in the middle of the rows of cakes, and swept some of them to one side. "Now these," she pointed to one side, "are different from these." She pointed to the others. "But some of them have fruit and some don't. They were *different* before, but now they're *the same*. And the other side of the line, likewise. And *now*." She reached over and took a counter from the game board.

"No cheating, Translator," said *Sphene*. Calm and pleasant.

"I'll put it back," Translator Zeiat protested, and then set the counter down among the cakes. "They were different—you accept, don't you, that they were different before?—but now they're the same."

"I suspect the counter doesn't taste as good as the cakes," said *Sphene*.

"That would be a matter of opinion," Translator Zeiat said, just the smallest bit primly. "Besides, it *is* a cake now." She frowned. "Or are the cakes counters now?"

"I don't think so, Translator," I said. "Not either way." Carefully I stood up from my chair.

"Ah, Fleet Captain, that's because you can't see my imaginary line. But it's real." She tapped her forehead. "It exists." She took one of the date cakes, and set it on the game board where the counter had been. "See, I told you I'd put it back."

"I think it's my turn," said *Sphene*, and picked up the cake and took a bite out of it. "You're right, Translator, this tastes just as good as the other cakes."

"Sir," whispered Kalr Twelve, close behind me as I cautiously walked out into the corridor. She had listened to the entire conversation with a growing sense of offended horror. "I need to say, sir, none of us would *ever* call you *it*."

* * *

The next day Seivarden found Ekalu alone in the decade room. "Your pardon, Ekalu," she said, bowing. "I don't mean to take up your break time, but Ship said you might have a moment."

Ekalu didn't get up. "Yes?" Not the least bit surprised. Ship had, of course, warned her Seivarden was coming. Had made sure the time was convenient for Ekalu.

"I want to say," said Seivarden, still standing, nervous and awkward, just inside the doorway. "I mean. A while ago I apologized for behaving very badly to you." Took an embarrassed breath. "I didn't understand what I'd done, I just wanted you to stop being angry at me. I just said what Ship told me I should say. I was angry at you, for being angry at me, but Ship talked me out of being any more stupid than I already had been. But I've been thinking about it."

Ekalu, sitting at the table, went completely still, her face ancillary-blank.

Seivarden knew what that likely meant, but didn't wait for Ekalu to say anything. "I've been thinking about it, and I still don't understand exactly why what I said hurt you so much. But I don't need to. It hurt you, and when you told me it hurt you I should have apologized and stopped saying whatever it was. And maybe spent some time trying to understand. Instead of insisting that you manage your feelings to suit me. And I want to say I'm sorry. And I actually mean it this time."

Seivarden couldn't see Ekalu's reaction to this, since Ekalu still sat absolutely motionless. But Ship could see. I could see.

Seivarden said, into Ekalu's silence, "Also I want to say that I miss you. And what we had. But that's my own stupid fault."

Silence, for five seconds, though I thought that at any moment Ekalu might speak, or stand. Or weep. "Also," said Seivarden, then, "I want to say that you're an excellent officer.

You were thrown into the position with no warning and hardly any official training, and I only wish I'd been as steady and as strong my first weeks as a lieutenant."

"Well, you were only seventeen at the time," said Ekalu.

"Lieutenant," Ship admonished Ekalu, in her ear. "Take the compliment."

Aloud, Ekalu said, "But thank you."

"It's an honor to serve with you," Seivarden said. "Thank you for taking the time to listen to me." And she bowed, and left.

Ekalu crossed her arms on the table, put her head down on them. "Oh, Ship," she said, voice despairing. "Did you tell her to say any of that?"

"I helped a bit with the wording," Ship replied. "But it wasn't my idea. She means it."

"It was the fleet captain's idea, then."

"Not actually."

"She's so beautiful," said Ekalu. "And so good in bed. But she's such a..." Stopped, hearing Etrepa Six's step in the corridor.

Etrepa Six looked in the door of the decade room, saw her lieutenant with her head down on the table. Put that together with Seivarden's retreating back, away down the corridor. Came into the decade room and began to make tea.

Not lifting her head, Ekalu said, silently, "If I called her back, would she come?"

"Oh, yes," said Ship. "But if I were you, I'd let her stew for a while."

13

Tisarwat came to see me just hours before we exited gate-space, into Athoek system. "Sir," she said, standing just inside the door to my quarters. "I'm on my way to the airlock."

"Yes." I stood. A bit steadier on the prosthetic leg than the day before. "Will you have tea?" Five was off on an errand, but there was tea already made, in the flask on the counter.

"No, sir. I'm not sure there's time. I just wanted..." I waited. Finally she said, "I don't know what I wanted. No. Wait. I do. If I don't come back, will you...that other Tisarwat's family. You won't tell them what happened to her, will you?"

The chances of my ever having the chance to say anything at all to Tisarwat's family was so small as to be almost entirely nonexistent. "Of course not."

She took a long, relieved breath. "Because they don't deserve that. I know it sounds stupid. I don't even know them. Except I know so much about them. I just..."

"It's not stupid. It's entirely understandable."

"Is it?" Her arms at her sides, she closed her gloved hands

into fists. Unclosed them. “And if I do come back. If I come back, sir, will you authorize Medic to change my eyes back to a more reasonable color?”

Those foolish lilac eyes, that the previous Tisarwat had bought for herself. “If you like.”

“It’s such a stupid color. And every time I see myself it reminds me of her.” Of that old Tisarwat, I supposed. “They don’t belong to me.”

“They do,” I said. “You were born with them that color.” Her mouth trembled, and tears filled her eyes. I said, “But whatever other color you choose will be yours, too.” That didn’t help her hold back her tears. “One way or another,” I said, “it’ll be all right. Are your meds current?”

“Yes.”

“Your Bos know what they need to do. You know what you need to do. There’s nothing for it now but to do it.”

“I forget you can see all that.” See all her feelings, her reactions, as Ship could. As Ship could show me. “I keep forgetting you can see right inside me, and then when I remember I just…” She trailed off.

“I’m not looking,” I said. “I’ve been trying not to, lately. But I don’t need to look, right now. You’re not the first young lieutenant I’ve met, you know.”

She made a short, breathy *hah*. “It made so much sense.” She sniffled. “It seemed so obviously the right thing, when I thought of it. And now it seems impossible.”

“That’s how these things go,” I said. “You already know that. Are you sure you don’t want tea?”

“I’m sure,” she said, wiping her eyes. “I’m on my way to the airlock. And I hate having to pee in my vacuum suit.”

I said, sternly, “Straighten up, Lieutenant, and wipe your face.” Without thinking she stood up taller and put her shoulders back. Rubbed her gloved hands on her eyes again. "Seivarden is on her way."

"Sir," she said, "I understand about you and Lieutenant Seivarden. Really I do. But does she have to be such a condescending asshole?"

"Probably not," I said, as the door opened, and Seivarden came in. "Dismissed, Lieutenant."

"Sir," Tisarwat said, and turned to go.

Seivarden grinned at her. "Ready to go, kiddo?"

"Don't," said Tisarwat, looking Seivarden full in the eye. "Ever. Call me *kiddo*. Again." And strode out of the room.

Seivarden lifted her eyebrows. "Nerves?" Amusement, but with an extra layer of curiosity—Tisarwat's mission was a secret, nearly all her preparation for it hidden. Not from me or Ship, of course, that would be impossible.

"She doesn't like being condescended to," I said. Seivarden blinked, surprised. "And also nerves."

She grinned again. "Thought so." Her expression turned serious. "I'm here for the gun." I didn't move immediately. "If it wasn't for the leg, Breq, you'd be the best person to go, and you wouldn't have to give the gun up to anyone."

"I've already had this conversation. With you. With Ship." With Medic. *I know what will happen*, she'd said. *Things will get hot and you'll forget the leg won't hold up to hard use. Or you'll remember but not care.* And if it had just been me, I'd have gone ahead. But it wasn't just me anymore. "If you lose the gun, I probably won't live long enough to forgive you." I could send Seivarden to Athoek Station with a regular sidearm. But the Presger gun would give her the best chance of killing Anaander, armored or not, guarded by ancillaries or not. If she failed, and lost the gun, if Anaander ended up with it, the results could be disastrous.

Seivarden smiled wryly. "I know."

I turned, opened the lid of the bench behind me, took out the box that held the gun. Set it on the table and opened it. Seivarden reached out, drew out a fragment of black—gun-shaped—the brown of her glove bleeding into it as soon as it came away from the box. "Be careful with it," I warned, though this was another conversation we had already had. "Translator Zeiat said it was made to destroy Radchaai ships. The 1.11 meters is just a side effect of that. Be careful how you use it."

"You don't have to tell me that," she said, putting the weapon in her jacket, and taking two magazines out of the box.

"If *Sword of Gurat* really is docked with Athoek Station, you don't want to blow its heat shield." Seivarden's team was going after that young Anaander Mianaai. We wouldn't know where the tyrant was until Station (we hoped) told us. I thought it most likely she would either be in the Governor's Palace or aboard *Sword of Gurat*.

"I understand." Seivarden's voice was patient. "Look, Breq…I'm sorry I'm such a jerk sometimes. I'm sorry the only lieutenant you have left is the one you never liked much."

"It's all right," I lied.

"No it isn't," she said. "But it's how things are."

There wasn't really any arguing with that. "Don't be stupid."

She smiled. "Will you come talk to us before we go? We're about to do our last equipment checks and go out on the hull."

"I'd intended to." I closed the box, left it on the table, and headed out the door. As I walked past Seivarden, she reached for my arm. "I don't need help walking," I said.

"It was just you seemed a bit wobbly there." Apologetic. Following me into the corridor.

"That's the prosthetic adjusting to new growth." I never knew when it would do that. Just another reason I couldn't take it into combat. "Sometimes it goes on for a few minutes."

But it didn't trouble me again, and I reached the staging area by the airlock without incident, without even limping slightly. "I won't take too much of your time," I said, as Seivarden's two Amaats, and Tisarwat and her two Bos, rose from what they were doing—checking over seals on their vacuum suits—and turned. "I suppose I ought to make some sort of motivational speech, but I don't have one for you and besides, you're busy. Come back safe." I wanted to say something more, to Tisarwat and her Bos, but with Seivarden and her Amaats listening it would be dangerous to even hint at what they were planning to do. Instead I put a gloved hand on Tisarwat's shoulder.

"Yes, sir," she said. No trace of her earlier tears in her voice. "Understood, sir."

I dropped my hand. Turned to Seivarden and her Amaats. "Yes, sir," Seivarden said. "We will."

"Right," I said. "I'll let you get back to what you were doing." I looked over at Tisarwat and her Bos again. "I have every confidence in all of you." I turned then, and left them to finish rechecking seals and tether clips.

Ekalu was on watch, in Command. As I entered she stood up from the single seat. "Sir," she said, "nothing to report."

Of course not. We were still in gate-space. The view outside the ship showed absolutely nothing, wouldn't until we gated into Athoek System. "Sit down, Lieutenant," I said.

"I'm not here to take over." I just hadn't wanted to sit in my quarters drinking tea. "I'm perfectly fine standing."

"You are, Fleet Captain," said Etrepa Four, at a console. "But we'll all feel better if you sit down. Begging your generous indulgence, sir." No, not Etrepa Four, who would never have spoken that way to me, who was having a moment of nauseated panic at having done so.

"Honestly, Ship."

"Honestly, Fleet Captain." Four was slightly light-headed with relief at my reaction. Still a bit sick. "It's a while until anything happens, you may as well sit."

Lieutenant Ekalu took the handhold beside the seat. "I was about to call for tea, sir."

"I'm perfectly fine standing," I said, settling into the seat.

"Yes, sir," said Ekalu. Her face perfectly expressionless.

Two hours later we exited gate-space into Athoek System. Just for the briefest moment, just long enough for *Mercy of Kalr* to get a look at the traffic around Athoek Station. The suffocatingly flat not-even-black just gone and the real universe there: sudden, solid depth. Light and warmth and everything suddenly real, Athoek Station shining in the sunlight, Athoek itself, shadowed white and blue, and then it was gone, wiped away by the smothering flatness of gate-space. Seivarden and her Amaats, Tisarwat and her Bos, already out on the hull, vacuum-suited, tethered, waiting, started at the brightness, suddenly there, suddenly gone. "Oh," gasped Amaat Two. Something about that brief flash of reality, that sudden return to uncanny darkness, made her feel as if she couldn't quite breathe properly. It was a common reaction. "That was..."

"I told you it was weird," said Seivarden, on the hull beside Two. "Am I really the only person here who's done this before?" No reply. "Well, besides Fleet Captain, of course. And Ship. They definitely have."

We had. As Seivarden spoke, Ship was comparing what it had just seen around Athoek Station with what we knew ought to be there, with the various schedules and travel clearances we knew about. Calculating where things would be, some time shortly in the future. "Eleven minutes and three seconds," said Etrepa Four, behind me in Command. Said Ship, into the ears of the soldiers waiting on the hull. Adrenaline spiked, heart rates shot up in all of them. Seivarden grinned. "I didn't know I'd missed this," she said. "It's awfully quiet, though. Fleet Captain used to sing the whole time."

"Used to?" asked Amaat Two, and everyone laughed, short and tense. Knowing that they'd be moving soon, and out of reach of *Mercy of Kalr*, with no knowledge of where or when we might come back for them. Only Tisarwat knew why that was, or how long it might be. She was the one who needed time to work.

"There was a lot more of the fleet captain then," said Seivarden. "And she had a better voice. Better voices."

"I like the fleet captain's voice," said Bo Three. "I didn't at first, but I guess I'm used to it."

"Yeah," said Tisarwat.

Amaat Four said, "Lieutenant, I hope you don't expect us to sing for the next ten minutes."

"Oh, I like that idea," said Seivarden. Her Amaats, and Tisarwat's Bos, groaned. "We should have picked one out in advance and rehearsed it. With parts, like Fleet Captain used to do." She sang, "*I was walking, I was walking / When I met my love / I was in the street walking / When I met my true love.*" Or tried to. The tune was mostly right, but the words weren't in Radchaai and it had been decades—subjectively—since she'd heard me sing it. What Seivarden remembered of the words was nonsense.

"Is that one of the fleet captain's?" asked Tisarwat. "I don't think I've ever heard her sing it."

"I heard," ventured Bo Three, "that when they pulled her in, you know, the other day, she was half-dead and still trying to sing."

"I believe it," said Seivarden. "I have no trouble imagining that if she thought she was about to die, she'd pick a song for it." Two seconds of silence. "Remember what I said, about the tether clips. We won't have much time, when we gate back in." We didn't want to be seen, didn't want anyone on the station—except Station—to suspect that soldiers from *Mercy of Kalr* might be arriving. We would arrive in Athoek System as close to the station as we could, for the barest instant, not even a second, and then, the moment Seivarden and Tisarwat and their soldiers were clear, we would be gone again. "So as soon as you get the order, unclip and push off, like we practiced. If you miss, if the clip sticks, or anything, don't try to catch up. Just stay here." A chorused *Yes, sir.* "If you push off at the wrong time and don't end up at the station, Ship probably won't be able to retrieve you. I've seen it happen."

They had all heard this, over and over during the past few days. "I wonder," said Bo Three, "if Fleet Captain has a song picked out in advance. You know, so if suddenly she finds herself in danger she doesn't have to worry about which one it will be."

"I wouldn't be surprised if she does," replied Tisarwat.

"Two minutes," said Ship, who had all this while been counting the time down in their visions.

Seivarden said, "I think she's got so many songs, they just

kind of come out of her on their own." Silence. Then, "Right, one minute. Take hold of your clips and be ready to move."

This was, in some ways, the most dangerous moment of the entire endeavor. Even aside from the risk of mistiming the departure and ending up lost and drifting somewhere unthinkably distant from the ship, or any kind of help, there was also the question of whether Ship had correctly calculated its brief exit into the real universe. Anything might be in the spot where we came out of gate-space. That *anything* could be as small as a sail-pod, or as large as a cargo carrier. Though it was unlikely Ship would have missed a cargo carrier in its calculations, it was still entirely possible. And even a sail-pod would be a danger to the vacuum-suited soldiers outside the protection of Ship's hull plating. Or there was always the chance that someone might have seen us flash into the system and back out, minutes earlier, and might be waiting for us.

"On the count," said Seivarden, though of course the numbers were already ticking down in all their visions. "Five. Four. Three. Two. One. Go!" I felt the moment all six on the hull shoved away.

Light. The six *Mercy of Kalr* soldiers sailed toward Athoek Station, suddenly meters away, a stretch of vents and conduits no one ever even thought about except Station Maintenance. But Bo Three had fumbled the clip, had pushed away but only pulled her tether taut. She pulled herself back, reached for the clip again. "Freeze!" I shouted at her. Aloud. In that instant Athoek Station disappeared, the rest of the universe, Seivarden and Tisarwat and the others, all gone. We were back in gate-space.

"Bo Three fumbled the clip," Ship said to the startled Etrepas in Command. "But she's all right, she's still here." We would have no way of knowing if the others had gotten safely to the station. Wouldn't until next we gated into the system.

At least their equipment had been distributed among the three—Tisarwat and Nine wouldn't be in any serious difficulties if they didn't have the things Three was carrying. "It's all right, Bo," I said, silently this time. She still had her hand on the tether clip, still hung outside the ship. Mortified. Horrified. Angry at herself and at me. "I've fumbled plenty of times myself." A lie—in two thousand years, as *Justice of Toren* One Esk I had only ever fumbled a clip twice. "And you wouldn't have made it. If I'd been in your place I couldn't have moved fast enough." Another lie—I was fairly sure I could have. "Come inside, get out of the suit, have some tea."

"Fleet Captain," said Bo Three. I had thought it was an acknowledgment, and so, apparently, had Three, but somewhere between syllables it had turned into a protest. "She's just a kid, sir!"

Tisarwat, she meant. "Nine is with her, Bo. Nine won't leave her for anything. You know that." Her adrenaline was high, her heart beating hard, from the moment, from the anticipation of what they'd planned to do on the station. From the sudden, shocking stop at the end of her tether, from my urgent order to freeze. From her own anger at herself for failing to stay with Tisarwat. "It's all right, Three. Come inside."

Bo Three closed her eyes. Took two deep breaths. Opened her eyes again and began the move toward the airlock. I returned my attention to Command. To Ekalu, who still stood beside my seat, the handhold tight in her grip. Her face had gone expressionless out of pure habit, a legacy from when she'd been a common soldier on this ship. She was nearly as upset as Bo Three, now pulling herself into the airlock, but

Ekalu's distress couldn't be for the same reasons. I reached for what she was seeing.

In the very brief time we were beside Athoek Station, Ship had collected as much data as it could. The view of the station from where we were, data from the station news channels, anything it could pull in. Ekalu was, this moment, looking at an image of Athoek Station. It wasn't a view we could have seen from where we'd gated in—Ship must have pulled it from somewhere else. From where we'd just been, we couldn't have seen the Gardens. We'd deliberately avoided that, in fact, because we didn't want anyone in the Gardens to be able to look up at the right moment and notice us.

But it turned out we needn't have troubled ourselves—there was no one in the Gardens. Last week Seivarden and her Amaats had cut a hole in the dome, so that they could pull me and Tisarwat and Basnaaid and Bo Nine out before we asphyxiated. That hole had been patched, but of course it had needed a more complete repair. Now, it seemed, that patch had failed. The seam where it had been sealed to the dome had split. Everything under the dome was faded and dead. Something must have rammed hard into the dome, right at its weakest point.

Ekalu looked at me. "What happened?" Still stunned and horrified.

"At a guess," I said, "the missing shuttle happened." Incomprehension. "From the schedule Station sent us the other day? You recall, we determined that it was missing a passenger shuttle."

"Oh." Realization dawned. For a moment I considered getting up, so that Ekalu could have the seat. "Oh, sir. Oh, no, sir. *Sword of Gurat* got the passenger shuttle schedule from Station, but it didn't check to see if the shuttles were actually where they ought to be before they gated. Did they...if the shuttle was in their path as they came out of gate-space, sir... if they ran into it..."

"That particular shuttle is late about half the time. Which of course neither *Sword of Gurat* nor its captain had any reason to know." Ekalu closed her eyes. Opened them again, remembering, I thought, that she was technically in charge here, that she had to get ahold of herself. "Fortunately," I continued, "or sort of fortunately, the Gardens will have been closed to the public." And it was a good thing I'd demanded that the Undergarden section doors be fixed. Level one of the Undergarden was very possibly depressurized right now, but the sections around it, and the levels below it, ought to be all right, kept safe when those section doors had automatically slammed shut when the pressure dropped. As things stood, it was entirely possible some Horticulture workers had died. Not Basnaaid, because otherwise there would have been no point in putting her on the list of those ordered to relocate downwell. "The shuttle crews I saw all seemed to be following safety regulations." If they hadn't, I'd have said something to their superiors. "It's entirely possible not everyone aboard that shuttle died." Not a thought to make Ekalu any happier—the shuttle could carry more than five hundred people. "But now we know why nobody seemed to have said anything to the tyrant about the Gardens, or the Undergarden. Not until they absolutely had to. She sails in claiming to be the true authority, who every citizen knows has that authority by virtue of her just and proper interest in the well-being and benefit of all her citizens and, what, accidentally kills a shuttle full of people." Would have killed quite a lot of citizens enjoying the Gardens, if not for the havoc I and my crew had wrought there last week.

No wonder Anaander had been nervous about that line of residents on the concourse. No wonder no one wanted to remind her of the catastrophe she'd caused merely by arriving at the station. No wonder not even a hint of this had reached the official news channels.

"But why haven't they repaired the dome?" asked Ekalu. "It looks like they haven't even started."

"Because of the curfew," I said. "Only essential personnel. Remember?" And repair crews would have families they'd likely talk to about what they'd seen, about what had happened, and those families had friends and acquaintances they would talk to, even if only while fetching skel from the common refectories.

"That's not all, Fleet Captain," said Etrepa Four. Said Ship. "Take a look at what *is* on the official news channels."

When we'd gated away from the Ghost System, the news channels had been that nonstop flood of warnings about me, of condemnations of me and my supporters. But apparently Station had returned to feeding surveillance data to its residents. We had only the smallest sample, barely more than a minute of visuals of the station's main concourse. Which ought to have been empty, given the curfew, but instead ranks of citizens sat right in the middle of the open space. Probably two hundred people, just sitting. Many of them were Ychana, some Undergarden residents, some not. But there were also Xhai there, including the hierophant of the Mysteries. And also there, Horticulturist Basnaaid. And Citizen Uran.

And, doubtless the reason for Station's hijacking of the official news, around the ranks of sitting citizens stood twenty ancillaries. Armor shining silver, guns in their hands.

I had seen this sort of thing before. I was suddenly struck by the memory of humid heat. The smell of swamp water, and blood. I found I had stood without realizing it. "Of course they did. Of *course*." Station's residents had not sat quietly waiting for *Mercy of Kalr* to rescue them. And Station had to have helped them assemble, helped them work around Security's patrols, around the *Sword of Gurat* ancillaries enforcing the tyrant's curfew. They couldn't have done it otherwise. Not this many people.

It was, obviously, an organized protest. And *Sword of Gurat* had drawn its guns, and Station had done the one thing it could do to defend its residents, the one thing that had worked, or seemed to, just a few days ago—make sure everyone knew just exactly what was happening.

None of it was calculated to ease the mind of an already angry and anxious Anaander Mianaai. What had she done in response? What was happening, this very moment, to the people on the concourse? But we couldn't do anything about it. Couldn't even know, until we gated back into Athoek System.

We wouldn't know how long it would take either Seivarden or Tisarwat to do—or try to do—what she had gone to the station for. *Mercy of Kalr* could leave gate-space again, so that we could receive messages. But we might be detected, and we wanted everyone on Athoek Station—everyone in the system—to think that we were gone. The lives of Seivarden and her Amaats, Tisarwat and Bo Nine, might depend on it. So it was the next few days in gate-space, for us.

There was no reason for me to stay in Command. There was nothing I could do, from where I was, that would make any difference whatsoever. I seriously considered going back to my quarters and getting some sleep, but I didn't think I could be still for long, knowing that five of my crew were gone, that reach as I might, I wouldn't be able to find them. So I walked to the decade room instead.

The fragments of that gold-and-glass Notai tea set were spread out on the table, and *Sphene* and Kalr Five sat across from each other, an array of tools and adhesives laid out to one side. What looked to be the curving rim of one bowl had already been pieced together. Five started guiltily as I came in. "No, continue what you're doing," I said. "So after all you think it might go together again?"

"Maybe," said *Sphene*, and picked up one blue glass fragment, put it next to another one. Considered them.

"What was her name?" I asked. "The captain whose tea set this was?"

"Minask," said *Sphene*. "Minask Nenkur."

Five looked up from the pieces she was fitting together. "Nenkur!"

"Few older names in all the Radch," *Sphene* said. "You know the name, of course, from the execrable entertainment that purports to be a faithful account of the battle of Iait Il. The Arit Nenkur that travesty slandered was Captain Minask's mother. This"—it gestured toward the scatter of blue and green glass, and bits of gold—"was her gift, when Captain Minask was promoted."

"And given command of you," I guessed.

"Yes," said *Sphene*.

"No wonder you removed the name," I said.

"What happened?" asked Five.

"It was a battle, of course." *Sphene*'s tone was perhaps just the slightest bit sarcastic, as though Five had asked a laughably foolish question. If Five heard it, she was unperturbed by it. Probably used to *Sphene* by now. "Captain Minask had surrendered. I was badly damaged. All but my captain and one of my lieutenants were dead. We couldn't fight anymore. But when the Usurper's forces boarded, they brought an AI core with them."

"Oh!" Five. Horrified. "No!"

"Oh, yes," said *Sphene*. "As a ship I was valuable. But not as myself—they preferred their own, more biddable AI. *You promised we'd be spared*, said Captain Minask. *And so you will be*, said the Usurper's lackey. *But you can't imagine we'd let a ship go to waste*." It set down the fragments it was holding. "She was very brave. Stupidly so, that day. I sometimes wish she hadn't resolved to fight for me, so that she might have lived longer. But then I wonder if they ever meant to let her live, or if they always meant to shoot her, and just said they'd spare us so that Captain Minask would surrender before I was damaged beyond usefulness."

"How did you get away?" I asked. Didn't ask how it had rid itself of the tyrant's soldiers. Offhand I could think of several ways *Sphene* could have done it, all of them easier if *Sphene* didn't care who aboard it lived or died. Foolish, to shoot the captain while they were still aboard, before they were sure of the ship.

"It was a battlefield," *Sphene* replied. "Ships were gating in and out, all over the place. And my engines still sort of worked, I just couldn't make a gate of my own. But I thought maybe I could stay in gate-space, if I could manage to get there. I moved, and by God's grace a gate opened near me—I hope I damaged the Usurper's ship that came out of it very badly—and I took it. I had no chance to calculate my route, though, and very little control over where I might emerge."

"And you ended up here," I finished for it.

"And I ended up here," it agreed. "I could have ended up in many a worse place. No doubt some of my sibling ships did."

Silence. Kalr Five got up, went to the counter where there was already a flask of tea, poured a bowl. Brought it to *Sphene*, set it down by its right elbow. Took her seat again. *Sphene* looked at the tea for a moment. Picked it up and drank. Set it back down. Picked up another two blue glass fragments and considered them.

"Fleet Captain!" Translator Zeiat came into the decade room. Looked at the table. "Oh! Our game looks very different today!"

"It's still packed away, Translator," said *Sphene*. "This is a tea set."

"Ah!" Dismissing that, the translator turned again to me. "Fleet Captain, I hope there's fish sauce where we're going."

"I must confess, Translator," I said, "that as much as I would like to gratify your desire, just now we're involved in a war. An opposing force is currently in control of Athoek Station, and until that changes, I'm afraid I have no access to fish sauce."

"Well, Fleet Captain, I must say, this war of yours is very inconvenient."

"It is," I agreed. "Translator, may I ask you a question?"

"Of course, Fleet Captain!" She sat down in the seat beside *Sphene*.

"These are not for eating," *Sphene* said.

Translator Zeiat made a brief moue and then turned her attention to me. "You wanted to know?"

"Translator, there are rumors..." I reconsidered my phrasing. "There are quite a few people who sincerely believe that the Presger have infiltrated the Lord of the Radch. That they have gained control of parts of her, in order to destroy the Radch. Or destroy humanity."

"Oh, goodness, no, Fleet Captain. No, that wouldn't be the

least bit amusing. It would break the treaty, for one thing." She frowned. "Wait! So, if I understand you correctly—there are, sadly, no guarantees that I understand you correctly—you think the treaty may have been broken?"

"I don't, personally. But some people do think so. Would you like some tea?" Five began to rise, but I put my hand on her shoulder. "No, I'll get it. It's already made."

Translator Zeiat heaved a sigh. "I suppose, since there isn't any fish sauce."

I poured a bowl, gave it to the translator, and sat down across from her, next to Kalr Five. "So would I be correct in guessing that the Presger have not...interfered with Anaander Mianaai?"

"Goodness no," replied Translator Zeiat. "There'd be no fun in it, for one thing. And one of the reasons there'd be no fun in it is because what you've just said, *interfered with Anaander Mianaai*, that would make very little sense to them. I'm not sure how I could possibly convey it, if I were to find it necessary. I'm not even sure I understand what you mean myself. Besides, if there was any real intention of breaking the treaty, any real desire to destroy the Radch, or Humans in general—you see? *I* know those aren't the same thing, but *they* don't. But as I said, if they wanted to destroy the Radch, even not considering the treaty, it would be done in the most amusing and satisfying manner possible. And I suspect I don't have to tell you at least some of the sort of thing that generally amuses and satisfies in that quarter, do I? Or at least how it tends to affect the Humans involved?"

"No, Translator, you don't."

"And while I did indeed say *not even considering the treaty*, the fact remains that the treaty is very much an issue.

No, they won't break the treaty. To be entirely honest, I'm much more worried about Humans breaking the treaty."

"If you would, Cousin," said *Sphene*. It and Five had pieced several fragments together, held the assemblage over the middle of the table. "That piece there, do you see where it fits? Inside that curl there?"

I picked up a tiny brush, a capsule of adhesive. Brushed around the inside edge of the curl, slid the shard of glass into place. "You should probably stop there," I suggested, "and let the adhesive cure, and build onto it later." I rose, took a cloth from a cabinet under the counter, and rolled it up for a form, and *Sphene* and Five put their carefully assembled bit of teabowl over it, and we lowered the whole thing onto the table. "This would probably be easier if we had the right tools."

"The story of my life for the past three thousand years," said *Sphene*. "Speaking of which. When Lieutenant Seivarden fails to kill the Usurper, will you let me try?"

"I'll consider it."

"I suppose, Cousin, that I can't reasonably ask for any more than that."

14

In gate-space as we were, we couldn't receive data from Seivarden or Tisarwat, or from Amaat Two and Four, or Bo Nine. And there was no guarantee they would be reachable when we returned. So each of them had been given a tiny external archive to hide on the outside of the station's hull. Those archives would receive and store the data for us to retrieve when we returned. Assuming they worked right, which they didn't always. Assuming nothing damaged them. Assuming no one had found them and disabled them or otherwise disposed of them.

This is what happened while *Mercy of Kalr* was out of the universe:

Seivarden and her two Amaats walked cautiously through a dusty access corridor. Armed and armored, their vacuum suits left behind at the airlock they'd come in through. Station had let them in, was even now displaying a map in their visions, though they'd studied what diagrams of the station's layout we'd already had. The diagrams, the few terse words they exchanged, said they were on their way to the governor's residence. They had seen the news channels. Noticed people they knew, among the citizens sitting on the concourse, noticed the armored ancillaries, the drawn guns. Amaat Two said, quietly, as they walked, "Do you think Lieutenant Ti—"

"Quiet," said Seivarden. Everyone on *Mercy of Kalr* knew about Tisarwat's crush on Basnaaid.

Four said, very softly, "Fleet Captain and Lieutenant Tisarwat seem close lately."

"Not surprised," replied Seivarden. Angry. Anxious. Knowing now was not the time to show it. "I suspect Fleet Captain's always had a thing for hapless baby lieutenants."

"Can't imagine you hapless, sir." Four, still very softly.

"I never looked it," said Seivarden. Surprising me by, it seemed, having found at least one source of her anxiety and not pretended it was something else, or that it didn't exist. Maybe because she was still enjoying the familiarity of this situation, the knife-edge of adrenaline before the gunfire started. "And *Justice of Toren* never liked me much."

"Huh," said Four. Honestly surprised. Trying hard not to think too much about what was ahead.

"Our Bo lieutenant isn't as hapless as she seemed at first," remarked Two.

"She isn't," agreed Seivarden. "She'll be fine." Not at all certain of that, unhappy at not knowing what Tisarwat and Nine were up to. "Now cut the chatter."

"Sir," acknowledged Two and Four, together.

Tisarwat and Bo Nine pulled their way across the station's hull. Not speaking. The news channels in their vision, those rows of seated citizens. The armed and armored soldiers. The citizens sat, quiet, and the soldiers stood, weapons ready.

"Turn it off, sir," Nine said to Tisarwat, on the hull. "There's no point watching, and you won't pay attention to where you're going if it's on."

"You're right." Tisarwat cut off the feed.

Twenty minutes later, moving handhold by handhold over the outside of Athoek Station, slowly and laboriously, she said, "I think I'm going to be sick."

"You can't be sick in your helmet, sir." Nine almost managed to keep the terror that had struck her at Tisarwat's words out of her voice. "That would be bad."

"I know!" Tisarwat stopped herself, didn't reach ahead for the next handhold. Took a few shallow breaths. "I know, but I can't help it."

"You did take the anti-nausea, sir, I saw you." And then, "Don't stop, sir. We just have to do this, that's all. And that's why. That's why we have to do this." Referring, I was sure, to what was happening on the concourse. "And if Fleet Captain were here, she'd be giving you such a look right now."

Two more shallow breaths. Then, weakly, "Hah. At least we'd have music to listen to." Tisarwat swallowed hard. Took another breath. Propelled herself forward to the next handhold.

"If you call that music." Relieved—as relieved as she could be, under the circumstances—Nine followed. "I agree with you, sir, about being used to her voice, but some of those songs she sings. They're just weird."

"*My heart is a fish.*" Tisarwat's voice thin and breathy. A shallow gasp. "*Hiding in the water-grass.*" Another. "*In the green.*"

"Well, that one's all right," Nine admitted. "Though it does get stuck in my head something fierce."

* * *

Sword of Gurat was at the very end of the docks, the two bays nearest it empty, no doubt not just because of *Sword of Gurat*'s size. No obvious damage from the collision with the passenger shuttle—but then, there wouldn't be. Possibly *Sword of Gurat* hadn't ended up with anything more than some scratches or dents.

"Right," said Tisarwat, taking a gulping breath, nausea returning. Exhausted and sore from the hours-long trip around the station hull. "Let's go." And she and Nine began pulling themselves toward *Sword of Gurat*.

So far Tisarwat had relied on Station's declining to report her and Nine's presence. But now, in sight of *Sword of Gurat*, that wouldn't protect them. It was only a matter of time—and not very much time, if *Sword of Gurat* was paying any attention at all—before they were noticed. Still, Tisarwat and Nine moved quite slowly. Very cautiously. Very carefully chose a spot on *Sword of Gurat*'s hull, tethered themselves, and opened the container they'd all this time been hauling with them. Nine pulled out an explosive charge. Handed it to Tisarwat, who carefully, slowly, fixed it to *Sword of Gurat*'s hull.

At about this point, Seivarden and her two Amaats had made it into a cramped and dim access corridor behind the governor's residence. It had probably at one point been meant for servants to use to go unobtrusively back and forth, but hadn't been used in years; the floor was dusty and trackless. This wasn't, then, the back way Governor Giarod had used to bring Translator Dlique to the residence.

Station had not spoken a word to Seivarden, or either of

her Amaats. It had displayed information—maps and directions, mostly—and unlocked doors for them. Now it had brought them to a locked door in this dusty corridor, and shown them all what lay behind it: the governor's office. The cream-and-green silk hangings were pulled nearly all the way around the walls, covering the window that looked down on the concourse, and also, helpfully, the door Seivarden and her Amaats stood behind. Empty, now, except for those few chairs, the desk. Beside the desk, a meter-and-a-half-high stack of what looked very much like suspension pods but probably were not. There were three of them in the stack, and Seivarden couldn't help but notice them. Puzzled a moment over what they might be. The words *Returning, with two* Sword of Atagaris *ancillaries, approx eight minutes* flashed in Seivarden's vision. *Two additional* Sword of Atagaris *ancillaries outside the main door now.*

Seivarden whispered, "Station, what are those things?"

I don't know what you mean, came the reply, in her vision.

"Those... at first I thought they were suspension pods. But they're not. Are they?"

I really don't know what you mean. Approximately six minutes.

Seivarden knew enough, by now, to understand Station's answer. "Oh, fuck," she said, softly.

Amaat Two, behind her, seeing the same image but not having reached the same conclusion, asked, "What are they?"

"They're fucking AI cores," Seivarden told her. "And Station can't talk about them."

Two and Four stared at her, confused. *Approximately five minutes*, Station said.

"Right," Seivarden said. There was no time to worry about the AI cores. No time to be afraid of three humans facing four ancillaries in five minutes' time. Seivarden had the Presger gun and there was, in the end, only one condition that needed to be met, only one truly necessary thing. And they had planned for this, Seivarden and her Amaats, had hoped Anaander would have taken over the governor's office, hoped they would have just such an opportunity. "Time to move." She reached for the door's manual release, and it obligingly slid open to reveal the back of a hanging, heavy enough that it barely trembled as the air currents shifted. Her two Amaats behind her, she stepped into the room.

There were two dozen explosive charges in the container Tisarwat and Bo Nine had brought. Tisarwat managed to attach three of them before half a dozen *Sword of Gurat* ancillaries came out an airlock after them.

Tisarwat and Nine surrendered immediately, went docile into the airlock. Stood silent while *Sword of Gurat* stripped them of their vacuum suits, stripped them to their underwear, and searched them. Neither of them, of course, had anything dangerous or suspicious. Not counting that container of charges, at any rate. The ancillaries bound Tisarwat's and Nine's hands behind them, and then pushed them to kneel on the corridor floor. Nine frightened but stoic, Tisarwat light-headed, hyperventilating just a bit. Terrified. And also, behind that, a tiny bit relieved. Anticipating.

The captain of *Sword of Gurat* arrived. Stared at Tisarwat and Nine. Examined the explosive charge *Sword of Gurat*'s ancillary showed her. Looked, then, at Tisarwat. "What in the name of all that's beneficial were you trying to do?" Tisarwat said nothing, but her gasping intensified. "These weren't even armed," the captain of *Sword of Gurat* said.

Tisarwat closed her eyes. "Oh, for the love of Amaat

just shoot me! Please, I beg you. I'm not even supposed to be here." Gasping every few words now, as her breathing escaped her control entirely. "I was supposed to be in Administration, I wasn't supposed to be on any ship at all. But I have to do what she tells me, she's the captain. I have to do what she tells me or she'll kill me." Tears started. She opened those ridiculous lilac-colored eyes, looked pitifully up at the captain of *Sword of Gurat*. "But I can't do it anymore, I couldn't do what she told me, *just shoot me*!"

"Well," said the captain. "A desk pilot. That explains a lot."

Nine's expression had been impassive through all this, but now anxiety showed on her face. "Please, sir, begging the captain's indulgence, these past few weeks have been so awful, and she's just a baby."

"Not a very bright one," said the captain. "Nor steady. Ship, get these two to Medical."

Sword of Gurat grabbed Tisarwat's arm to haul her up. Tisarwat cried out and, "Aatr's tits," swore the captain of *Sword of Gurat*, grimacing in disgust. "She's pissed herself!" And if Tisarwat didn't let up on the breathing, she'd faint in about half a minute. "At least *try* to act like a civilized human being, Lieutenant! Gods greater and lesser! Not even a desk pilot should act like this."

"S...s...sir," gasped Tisarwat. "P...please don't make me go back there. I can't go back to *Mercy of Kalr*, I'd rather die."

"You're not going back to *Mercy of Kalr*, Lieutenant. Ship." This to the waiting ancillaries. "Take Lieutenant..."

"T...Tisarwat," supplied Tisarwat.

"Take Lieutenant Tisarwat to the bath and get her cleaned up. Get some clean clothes on her before you take her to

Medical. Take this other one to Medical now. Get them both disconnected from *Mercy of Kalr*." And then, at another thought, "And *Mercy of Kalr*, if you're watching, I hope you're proud of this."

Two *Sword of Gurat* ancillaries hauled Tisarwat to her feet, and half dragged, half walked her down the corridor. "Nine!" Tisarwat wailed.

"It's all right, Lieutenant," said *Sword of Gurat*'s ancillary. "She's just going to Medical."

Tisarwat, tearful, opened her mouth to reply, but sobbed instead. Collapsed into *Sword of Gurat* Gurat Eleven's arms, clutched its uniform jacket and wept harder.

They were real tears. *Sword of Gurat* could hardly have mistaken false ones. And Nine's cry of concern and struggle to reach Tisarwat were genuine as well. "You'll see her again soon," Gurat Eleven said, just maybe the slightest bit more gently, and guided her off to the bath, where it would be just Tisarwat and *Sword of Gurat*, alone. Which had been the whole point of the exercise, of course.

And Nine found herself escorted toward Medical. The next dangerous moment—the whole plan had been predicated on the assumption that *Sword of Gurat* didn't have a competent interrogator aboard. A Justice almost certainly would have, but interrogators were much rarer on Swords. If *Sword of Gurat* had one, the next step would be drugging Nine, and the game would be up.

Almost as soon as Nine walked into *Sword of Gurat*'s Medical section, her archive data ended, and not long after so did Lieutenant Tisarwat's.

And meanwhile, on Athoek Station, Anaander Mianaai came into the system governor's office. Two *Sword of Atagaris* ancillaries behind her, and behind those, System Governor Giarod and Eminence Ifian. “My lord,” Ifian was saying, “of your mercy, I beg to inform...remind my lord that Station Administrator Celar is very popular. Her...her removal would be taken very badly, and not just by the troublesome elements on the station.”

That young Anaander didn’t reply, but seated herself behind the desk. The two ancillaries stationed themselves in front of it, so that Governor Giarod and Eminence Ifian found themselves at some distance from where the tyrant sat. “And you yourself, Eminence, have no influence with the residents of this station?”

The eminence opened her mouth, and for an instant I wondered if she would admit that not long ago she had staged her own sit-down on the concourse, so that she could hardly speak convincingly in condemnation of this one. But she closed her mouth again. “I had thought, my lord, that I did have some influence here. If my lord wishes, I will try to speak to them.”

“*Try*?” asked Anaander, with obvious contempt.

Governor Giarod spoke up. “My lord, they aren’t doing any harm where they are. Perhaps we could just...let them sit.”

“Not doing any harm *yet*.” The tyrant’s voice was acid. “Did you just let the ancillary walk onto the station and upend everything? Agitate the station’s dregs, suborn the AI?”

“We did question her...it, my lord,” Governor Giarod insisted. “But she always had such reasonable answers, and events nearly always seemed to bear her out. And she had orders direct from you, my lord. And your name as well.” Behind the desk, Anaander Mianaai did not respond. Did not move. “My lord, perhaps we could...perhaps we could use Fl...the ancillary’s methods. Send the soldiers away, let the people sit on the concourse if they like. So long as they're peaceable."

"Do you not understand," Anaander said, "the purpose behind the ancillary's methods? What's happening down there"—she gestured toward the wide window, still covered by that heavy silk hanging—"is a threat. It is this station—and an alarming number of this station's residents—refusing to accept my authority. If I allow them to do *this*, then what will they do next?"

"My lord," offered Governor Giarod, "what if you were to treat this as though it were a refusal of *my* authority? You could say that *I* gave the order for the curfew, and the soldiers, and even—though it *was* Celar's fault—even the transportation orders. And I would resign, and then, my lord, you would be the one responsible for restoring propriety."

Anaander laughed, tense and bitter, and Giarod and Ifian flinched. "I'm glad to see, Governor, that after all your brain isn't a *complete* waste of organic material. Believe me, if I thought that would do the least bit of good I'd have done it by now. And maybe if you hadn't let a half-crazed ancillary run you in circles for a month, maybe if you hadn't let that ancillary *escape*, and somehow manage to destroy *two* of the ships I brought with me, including a fucking *troop carrier* that would have been *very helpful* right now, and maybe if your gods-cursed passenger shuttles would *run on time* like they do everywhere else in Radch space, and maybe if your station was not obviously in the power of an *enemy of the Radch*, then yes, maybe it would do some good."

Two ships. Destroyed. No wonder this Anaander was frightened. And, at a guess, exhausted. Angry and frustrated, not used to being in just one body, cut off from Tstur Palace.

Anaander continued. "No, what I need is to regain control of Station." She stopped. Blinked. "Tisarwat?" Looked at Governor Giarod and Eminence Ifian. "That's a familiar name. You said the ancillary brought a Lieutenant Tisarwat to the station."

"Yes, my lord." Giarod and Ifian, more or less in unison.

"A Lieutenant Tisarwat was just caught trying to plant explosive charges on *Sword of Gurat*'s hull. None of which were armed. She was captured immediately. And she is..." Anaander blinked at something in her vision. "Not exactly the sharpest knife in the set, is she."

It was Giarod and Ifian's turn to blink, trying, I supposed, to reconcile that description with the Tisarwat they themselves had met. I thought for a moment Ifian would say something, but she didn't. More to the point, and very interestingly, *Sword of Atagaris* said nothing. "Oh, get out of here," Anaander said, irritably.

Governor Giarod and Eminence Ifian bowed, deeply, and left so quickly as to be barely proper. When they were gone, Anaander put her head on her wrists, hands outstretched, her elbows on the desk. "I need to sleep," she said, to no one in particular, it seemed. Maybe to the two *Sword of Atagaris* ancillaries. "I need to sleep, and I need to eat, and I need..." She trailed off. "Why can't I just get a couple hours' sleep without some kind of crisis appearing?" If she was talking to *Sword of Atagaris*, it didn't answer.

Seivarden, behind the hanging, heard this with a sudden dismaying, disorienting sense of wrongness. She had known all this time what we had been doing here at Athoek, had defied Anaander herself, when we had been at Omaugh Palace. But Anaander Mianaai was still the only ruler of the

Radch Seivarden had ever known, and neither she nor any other Radchaai had ever expected even the possibility that things might be different. And on top of that, here this Anaander was, alone and tired and frustrated. As though she were just an ordinary person. But Seivarden had enough experience to know that stopping to think too long about it would be fatal. She signaled her Amaats to move.

Amaat Two and Amaat Four, armor up, guns leveled, came out from behind the hanging first, one to each side of where Anaander sat behind the desk. Instantly each *Sword of Atagaris* ancillary drew its weapon and turned to fire at an Amaat, and two more ancillaries came swiftly into the room, guns raised.

Seivarden had positioned herself opposite Anaander, so that when the ancillaries were distracted, she might have a clear shot at the tyrant. But Seivarden was not ancillary-fast, and lifting the hanging slowed her even more, just the smallest bit, but enough for one of *Sword of Atagaris* to put itself between Seivarden and Anaander, just as Seivarden fired. It dropped, and before Seivarden could fire again, the other ancillary charged into her, shoving her backward so that they both fell against the hanging.

Behind the hanging was that wide window overlooking the concourse. Of course it was not easily breakable, but *Sword of Atagaris*'s impact had been fast and forceful. When Seivarden and *Sword of Atagaris* fell against it, the window popped free of its housing and fell toward the floor of the concourse, some six meters below. Seivarden and *Sword of Atagaris* followed.

The citizens below scrambled back out of the way, some shouting in alarm. The glass slammed into the ground, a loud and sharp report, and Seivarden hit the glass, on her back, *Sword of Atagaris* on top of her, the Presger gun in its grip that it had wrested from Seivarden on the way down.

The pop of gunfire, and more screams, and then, painfully loud, an alarm sounded. Bright-red stripes suddenly glowed to life on the scuffed white of the concourse floor, each of them four meters from the next. "Hull breach," announced Station. "Clear all section doors immediately."

At the sound of that alarm, every single person on the concourse—including *Sword of Atagaris*, and Seivarden, who hadn't had even an instant to recover from her six-meter drop—immediately, unthinkingly, rolled or stepped or crawled away from those glowing red lines, and the concourse section doors came flashing down, crunching into the rectangle of window glass where it was in the way.

For a moment everyone in that section of the concourse was silent, stunned. Then someone began to whimper. "Who's hurt?" asked Seivarden. On her hands and knees, quite possibly not aware of how she'd gotten there, the back of her armor still warm from absorbing the force of hitting the floor.

"Don't move, Lieutenant." *Sword of Atagaris*, the Presger gun aimed at Seivarden.

"Someone might be hurt," Seivarden said, looking up at the ancillary. She dropped her armor. "Do you have a medkit this time, or are you still a miserable excuse for a soldier?" Raised her voice. "Is anybody hurt?" And then to *Sword of Atagaris*, who had not moved, "Come on, Ship, you know I'm not going anywhere with the section doors down like this."

"I have a medkit," replied *Sword of Atagaris*.

"So do I. Give me yours." And as *Sword of Atagaris* tossed

the medkit to the ground in front of her, "Aatr's tits, what's wrong with you?" She took both kits and went to see to the injured.

Fortunately there appeared to be only one severe injury, a person whose leg had been caught by the falling slab of glass. Seivarden medkitted her, and when she found only bruises and sprains among the other nine people trapped in the section, she tossed the remaining medkit at *Sword of Atagaris*'s feet. "I know you have to do what the Lord of the Radch tells you to." Seivarden didn't know that Tisarwat had made *Sword of Atagaris* as much of a free agent as possible. "But didn't the fleet captain give you back your precious officers? That ought to count for something."

"It would," said *Sword of Atagaris*, voice flat. "If it hadn't taken me an entire day to get my ancillaries thawed and bring my engines back online. *Sword of Gurat* got to them before me, and the Lord of the Radch decided they would be more useful to her in suspension."

"Hah!" Seivarden was bitterly amused. "I don't doubt it. I'm sure Hetnys is a much better tea table than she ever was a captain."

"I can't imagine why I don't feel more friendly toward you," said *Sword of Atagaris*, retrieving the medkit without for a moment losing its focus on Seivarden.

"Sorry." Seivarden sat down on the glass. Crossed her legs. "I'm sorry, Ship. That was uncalled for."

"What?" Impassive, but, I thought, taken aback.

"I shouldn't've…that wasn't right. I don't like Captain Hetnys, and you know that, but there's no reason for me to be insulting her. At a time like this. Especially to you." Silence. *Sword of Atagaris* still pointing the Presger gun at Seivarden, sitting cross-legged on the ground. "I have to admit, I don't understand why the Lord of Mianaai wouldn't give you back your captain."

"She doesn't trust me," *Sword of Atagaris* said. "I was too easily and too completely controlled by *Justice of Toren.* Seeing that, the Lord of Mianaai decided to keep the same control herself—I am told that if anything at all happens to the Lord of the Radch, all of my officers will be killed. She has them aboard *Sword of Gurat.* For safekeeping, she says. A *Sword of Gurat* lieutenant is in temporary command of me for the moment."

"I'm sorry," said Seivarden. And then, realizing, "Wait, what is she so afraid of? She trusts *Sword of Gurat* to kill Captain Hetnys if something happens to her, but she doesn't trust it to guard her?"

"I neither know nor care," said *Sword of Atagaris.* "But I am not going to see Captain Hetnys killed."

"No," said Seivarden. "No, of course not."

Above, in the governor's office, Amaat Two and Amaat Four lay facedown, still armored but disarmed, terrified, hands bound behind their backs. Before *Sword of Atagaris* had pinned them, they had seen the ancillary Seivarden had shot lying in the middle of the room. Amaat Two had managed to fire once at Anaander, but had not seen the results of her shot. Both Amaats had heard the section doors come down, closing the room off until Station canceled the hull breach alert. Or until someone managed to cut through the section doors, not an easy thing to do.

"You're wounded, my lord." An unfamiliar voice, in the ears of Seivarden's two Amaats, but obviously an ancillary's. *Sword of Atagaris.*

"It's nothing. The bullet went right through my arm."

Anaander Mianaai, her voice tense with pain. "How the fuck did that happen, *Sword of Atagaris*?"

"I would guess, my lord...," began *Sword of Atagaris.*

"No, let *me* guess. You'd never seen that door opened. Couldn't open it even when you asked Station to unlock it. The entrances to that back access are all themselves locked. By Station. I myself foolishly trusted what I thought was my control over Station."

A tearing sound. "If you would be so good as to let me remove your jacket, my lord."

Despite—perhaps because of—her terror, the beginning of a laugh escaped Amaat Four as she recognized the sound of a medkit being opened. Two said, very softly, "Oh, you're carrying medkits *now*."

"There are several ways I could kill you." The voice of another ancillary, closer to the two Amaats than the one talking to the Lord of the Radch. Very quiet. "Armored or not."

"Station!" Anaander, either ignoring the exchange or not hearing it. "No more games. Do you hear me?"

Silence, for three seconds, and then Station said, "I was happy enough to go along, until you threatened my residents."

Down on the concourse, standing on the remaining section of office window, *Sword of Atagaris* said, gun still pointed at Seivarden, "Station is done playing stupid, it seems."

"I wasn't the one making a threat, Station!" Anaander's voice was incredulous, and angry. "I was trying to keep your residents safe. Trying to keep things calm and under control here, after the ancillary had stirred up so much trouble. And then." A pause. Probably she gestured, but all the Amaats could see was the brown, gold-flecked tiles of the floor. "All this. What do you expect me to do, just let a mob take over the concourse?"

"It's not a mob," replied Station. "It's a complaint. Citizens do have the right to complain to Administration." Silence. Then Station said, "Fleet Captain Breq would have understood."

"Ah." Anaander. "So it comes out. But it's not the ancillary controlling you. There are no circumstances under which my enemy would give it that ability. So who is it? And is she still here? Could she unlock your Central Access, maybe?"

"No one can unlock my Central Access," said Station. "You'll have to keep trying to cut through."

"It would be easier to destroy the whole station and build again," said Anaander. "In fact, the more I think of it the better I like that idea."

"You won't," said Station. "You might as well surrender to the fleet captain. I have no intention of letting you leave that room, you'll have killed the only instance of yourself in the system. Which is an interesting thought. In fact, the more I think of it, the better I like that idea. I'd only need to trigger the fire-suppression systems in the governor's office."

"You already would have if you could," replied Anaander. "Maybe if you were a ship. But you're not. You can't bring yourself to deliberately kill anyone. I on the other hand have no such compunction."

"I'm sure all the citizens downwell will be interested to hear that. Or the outstations."

"Oh, are we on the news again?" Anaander's voice was bitter.

"We can be, if you like." Station, calm and serene.

"So that wasn't involuntary, as you claimed. And it didn't stop because I'd hit on the right access."

"No," replied Station. "I lied about that."

Down on the concourse, still boxed in by the section

doors, Seivarden hadn't understood what *Sword of Atagaris* had meant, about Station no longer playing stupid. She said to *Sword of Atagaris*, "So what's the story with those AI cores?"

"I'd expect you to know better than I would," said *Sword of Atagaris*. "Isn't that what you came here for? Isn't that why *Justice of Toren* went straight to the Undergarden nearly the moment she got here?"

"No," replied Seivarden. "Is that where they were?" And then, at a thought, "Is that why you were so... *enthusiastic* about running security in the Undergarden?"

"No."

"Well then, whose are they?" *Sword of Atagaris* didn't answer. "Aatr's tits, there isn't a third one of her, is there?"

"I neither know nor care," replied *Sword of Atagaris*.

"And what is this one going to do with them? Build ships? That takes months—no, it takes years."

"Not if the ship is already built," *Sword of Atagaris* pointed out.

Above, in the governor's office, Anaander was saying, "So we're at an impasse."

"Perhaps not," said Station. Amaat Two and Amaat Four still lay facedown on the brown-and-gold tiles, still listening. "If I understand Fleet Captain Breq correctly, your argument isn't with me or any of my residents—it's with yourself. It's none of my business. It only becomes my business when you threaten my residents' safety."

"What are you suggesting, Station?" Wary, with an undertone of anger.

"You have no reason to concern yourself with the running of this station. Those matters are more properly handled by me and by Station Administrator Celar." Silence. "As for

Sword of Gurat and *Sword of Atagaris*, they're not welcome here. I do understand *Sword of Gurat* needs repairs and supplies, and that its officers might want leave occasionally, and that an officer is nearly always accompanied by an ancillary at such times, but I will not have whole decades interfering with my operations, or harassing my residents."

"And what do I get in exchange for these concessions?"

"You get to live," said Station. "You get to remain in this system. You get the *Sword of Gurat* decades back that are at the moment trapped until I see fit to raise the section doors. And you get a place where your ships can purchase supplies."

"Purchase!"

"Purchase," repeated Station. "I can't afford to assume that I or my residents will receive any sort of benefit from the provincial palace, not for the foreseeable future. Not considering the circumstances. And I can't afford to let you drain all this system's resources and give nothing in exchange. Particularly when providing you with supplies and services potentially makes me a target for your enemies." Silence. "As a show of my good faith, I will decline to charge you for the removal of the five dead *Sword of Gurat* ancillaries that were attempting to cut into my Central Access. You needn't worry about their officer, she was away using the bath when the section doors went down."

"I get your point, Station," said Anaander. "Fine. We can deal."

15

Coming into the governor's office, *Sword of Atagaris* close behind her, the first thing Seivarden noticed was her two Amaats, facedown on the floor, hands bound. Their armor still raised, and so she knew they were still alive. Was relieved, but in a distracted way, because the next thing she saw was Anaander Mianaai standing grim-faced behind the desk. Shirtless, a corrective around her upper arm.

Anaander's expression changed to sardonic surprise. "Seivarden Vendaai." Voices sounded, rising from the concourse below to that now-glassless window, medics calling instructions to each other, someone sobbing.

"That's *Lieutenant Seivarden* to you," said Seivarden, managing to sound braver than she felt. Now all the action was past, she was nearing collapse. The *Sword of Atagaris* ancillary behind her went to the desk and laid down the Presger gun. Stepped away.

Anaander looked down. Watched the gun turn the same pale yellow as the desk surface. All expression left her face.

Despair overwhelmed Seivarden, that adrenaline and

urgent necessity had kept at bay since she'd fallen out the window. She knew me well enough to know that I had not been joking when I had said I would probably not live long enough to forgive her if she lost the gun. Knew what it meant, that Anaander Mianaai now had it.

Anaander picked up the gun. Brushed gloved fingers across it so that it became not the color of whatever it touched, but a plain dark gray. Examined it. "This," she said, "is very interesting." Seivarden said nothing. Anaander continued, "To my knowledge there are only twenty-four of these, and every last one is accounted for. In fact, each one of them is marked with an identifying number, but this one"—she paused—"is not." She looked at Seivarden. "Where did you get it?"

"Twenty-five," Seivarden said.

"Excuse me?"

"Twenty-five. Everything on Garsedd was fives. Five principal sins, five right actions, five social classes, five capital crimes. Probably five kinds of farts." Anaander raised one dark eyebrow at that. "If you didn't go looking for that twenty-fifth gun you've got only yourself to blame."

"I did look," Anaander said. "I have trouble believing that you found it when I didn't." Seivarden made a gesture of unconcern, deliberately insolent, though she did not feel as brave as the action implied. "Where did you get this?"

"Fleet Captain gave it to me."

"So now we come to it," said Anaander. Tense and intent. "Who is controlling the ancillary?"

"That would be *Justice of Toren* to you," said Seivarden, her voice far more even than her emotions, "if you honestly can't bring yourself to acknowledge her proper rank. And you're lucky I didn't laugh in your face just now when you suggested that anyone might be controlling her but herself."

"You know as well as I do that ancillaries don't control themselves. Not even ships control themselves." She gave Seivarden an appraising glance. "Well, Lieutenant, I think you and I will be continuing this conversation aboard *Sword of Gurat*."

"Oh, no." Station's voice, from the office console. "No, Lord of Mianaai, I'm afraid you won't be. Perhaps you didn't understand the implications of our recent discussion. Perhaps I should have been more explicit. If you leave here I will have no means by which to enforce the terms of our agreement. No, you'll be staying right here. With a few servants if you like, and I'm even willing to allow *Sword of Atagaris* to act in that capacity. Which is very generous of me, honestly. The governor's residence is very comfortable, I assure you, and you have no reason to go anywhere else. And as for Lieutenant Seivarden, I'm afraid I must insist that my own security force take her into custody."

"This has nothing to do with you, Station," said Anaander. "Seivarden Vendaai is not one of your residents, but she *is* a member of the Radchaai military, of which I am the supreme commander."

"She is a member of *a* Radchaai military," Station said. "You yourself appear to be under the impression that her commanding officer—that would be Fleet Captain Breq—is not working for you, but for some enemy of yours. The fact that that enemy is quite possibly some other iteration of you is not my concern. And whatever military she might belong to, I have no agreements with anyone granting immunity to members of military forces who cause damage or commit other offenses while they're here. I'm afraid Station Security must place the lieutenant—and her two subordinates—under arrest until we can evaluate her actions."

Three seconds of silence. *Sword of Atagaris* stood stiff and impassive, three of it, around the Lord of the Radch. Amaat Two and Amaat Four lay rigid, eyes closed, breathing carefully, listening intently. Finally Anaander said, "Don't push me, Station. Or whoever is giving you instructions."

"You would do well to take your own advice, Lord of Mianaai," said Station. "I won't be pushed, either." A quick, brief breeze as the section doors slammed back down, over the two doors, over the window, the sound from the concourse suddenly cut off. The air in the office suddenly still.

"If you empty the air out of this room," Anaander pointed out, "you'll also kill Seivarden. And her two subordinates." That last just the least bit mocking.

"They're nothing to me," said Station. "They aren't my residents."

An expression flashed across Anaander's face. Fear, maybe. Or possibly anger. "All right, Station. But we'll be discussing this further."

"If you like," said Station, bland as always.

Seivarden and her two Amaats spent six hours in a cell in Security. At some point someone had brought them bowls of skel, and water to drink, but Seivarden had been unable to so much as taste hers. By the time the door finally opened, Amaat Two and Amaat Four had fallen into an uneasy, exhausted sleep, propped up against the wall, and each other. "Lieutenant," said a Security officer from the corridor. "If you would be so good as to come with me."

Seivarden said nothing. Pushed herself to standing. Amaat Four half woke. Muttered, "What?"

"Nothing, Four, go back to sleep," said Seivarden, and stepped into the corridor.

Allowed herself to be led to the office of the head of Security. Which was, it turned out, occupied by Citizen Lusulun. Who rose and smiled at Seivarden's entrance, though the smile didn't quite make it to the rest of her face, and bowed. "Lieutenant. Seivarden, I understand? Fleet Captain Breq mentioned you. I'm Head of Security Lusulun."

Seivarden stared at her, uncomprehending, for just a moment. Then bowed herself. "An honor, sir. To make your acquaintance, and to be mentioned by the fleet captain."

"Sit, Lieutenant," said once-again Head of Security Lusulun. "Will you have tea?"

"I'd rather stand."

"I apologize," Head of Security Lusulun said, still standing, apparently unsurprised at Seivarden's demeanor, "for the delay in my speaking to you. Things have been...a bit chaotic. The current situation is..." Lusulun took a breath. Considered a moment what sort of description might suit, and seemed to come up short. "Well. We've been a bit disorganized. I've only been back in office for the last fifteen or twenty minutes. At any rate, it's been determined that you're not responsible for the damage on the concourse. And by the way Medical would like to thank you for your assistance with the citizen who you helped, who was injured."

"No thanks necessary," Seivarden said, quite automatically.

"All the same. So, you and your soldiers are free to go. There was some difficulty about food and housing assignments, since you aren't station residents. But it happens that the Undergarden needs a great deal of work just now—more even than when the fleet captain was here. Some of it needs to be done in vacuum, which I imagine you've got some experience with, yes?"

"Yes," said Seivarden, and then frowned. "What?"

"Level one of the Undergarden was breached when the

dome over the Gardens was damaged again the other day," explained Lusulun. "There are a number of repairs that need to be made before that area can be re-pressurized. We're assuming you've got experience working in vacuum."

"I... yes."

"Right," said Lusulun, noticing Seivarden's near-stupor but forging on ahead. "The fleet captain did have a housing assignment, but I'm afraid it wasn't luxurious. You're welcome to use it, though. And sometime soon I do hope you'll join me for tea. I'd be honored if you would."

Seivarden stared stupidly and then said, "I... thank you. Very kind of you, sir."

The crates and boxes were where we had left them, sectioning off a corridor end. Seivarden sank down in the back corner, arms around her legs, head on her knees, while Two and Four went through the crates to see what we'd left behind. "Oh!" exclaimed Four, opening one. "Tea!" It was a packet of Daughter of Fishes. My Kalrs had known I wouldn't care what happened to it. "Now we'll be all right."

"I haven't found anything to make it with yet," said Two.

"Hah!" exclaimed Four. "You don't really think Kalr was going to leave any dishes behind, do you? I'll see about getting us a flask." And then, opening the next box, "Oh!"

Two came over to see what she'd found. "Aatr's tits!" She looked over at Seivarden, who was still curled up against the wall. Looked back at Four. "That's a dozen bottles of the fleet captain's arrack." Watching out of the corner of her eye for some reaction from Seivarden, but there was none. "We could trade a bottle for a tea set, easy. And probably a few other things. Fleet Captain wouldn't mind. Would she?"

"She would not," agreed Four. "She would want us to have

tea. Don't you think, sir?" Looked over at Seivarden. Who did not move or make a sound. Four turned back to Two, trying to pretend she had not just felt that sickening, sinking feeling of dismay at seeing Seivarden unresponsive. She took a bottle out of the box. "I'll see to it. And I'll get us something to eat, too." And then, a trifle louder, her voice aimed at Seivarden, added, "You just get some rest, sir." But did not leave, because someone neither Two nor Four recognized was approaching the crate enclosure. Stopped at the perimeter. The Amaats weren't sure whether to be reassured by how young she was, or how well-dressed. Or the shy familiarity with which she walked right up to the improvised entrance.

"Citizens." She bowed. "I'm Uran. You are..." She frowned, looking at the insignia on the soldiers' rumpled and by-now-dirty uniforms. "*Mercy of Kalr* Amaat."

"Oh! Citizen Uran!" Two bowed with a discomfited rush of surprise. Did not look over at Seivarden, who still sat against the wall, who should have made herself available to handle this sort of potentially socially awkward moment. "Our apologies. Of course this is your home, we hadn't even thought, things have been...hectic." Noticed then that Uran held her right arm at an oddly stiff angle. "Were you hurt?"

"Only a broken wrist, citizen," Uran replied. "I was just coming from Medical and I heard you were here." She waved away whatever Two had been about to say with her uninjured hand. "I've been staying with friends, but I heard you were here and came to see if you needed anything. The Rad...the fleet captain left some things, there's plenty of bedding and there's some tea." Two saw Uran's gaze flick away, over Two's shoulder, to where Seivarden sat, and then back to Two. "I don't think there are any dishes, though. Also, Horticulturist Basnaaid means to call on you when she can."

"That's very good of her," replied Two. "And we're grateful for your assistance. In fact." She looked over at Four, still holding that bottle of arrack. "Maybe you can show us where we can make some trades. You're right, we haven't found any dishes so far, and we're in particular need of a tea set just now." Wanted to turn her head to look at Seivarden. Managed not to.

Uran's eyes grew wide. "That will get you lots more than a tea set, and besides, that's the fleet captain's arrack! Please, my allowance is generous. Let me bring you what you need and it will be"—she frowned, looking, probably, for an equivalent of a Delsig phrase—"it will be a word between cousins." Winced at Two's expression of puzzled surprise. "I express myself badly. Radchaai is not my first language."

"You express yourself perfectly, citizen," said Two. "And thank you." She looked over at Four.

"I'll stay with the lieutenant," said Four, and put the bottle back in its crate.

An hour later Two had come back, with dishes and utensils, water and refectory rations for the three of them, and most importantly a tea flask and bowls. When the tea was ready, Four brought a bowl over to Seivarden, who had not moved. Crouched beside her. "Sir. Lieutenant Seivarden, sir, here's tea." No response. "Sir." Still nothing. Gently Four reached out and smoothed Seivarden's hair back with one free, gloved hand. "Sir." Allowing her dismay and fear just the smallest bit into her voice. "Sir, I know it's hard, but we need you." They didn't, strictly speaking. Two and Four were perfectly capable of taking care of themselves. Though not, perhaps, if they also had to take constant care of Seivarden. "We need to know what to do next."

"It doesn't matter what we do next." Seivarden, still curled in on herself.

“It’ll seem better when we’ve had some tea, sir,” said Four, still holding out that now-cooling bowl.

“Tea?” Seivarden didn’t look up, but the muscles in her neck and shoulders tensed, as though she was considering it.

“Yes, sir. And there’s breakfast, and we’ve found some nice, comfortable bedding, and we don’t have work until tomorrow morning. We can relax for the rest of the day, but we need you, sir, we need you to sit up and drink some tea.”

Seivarden looked up, saw Four squatting beside her, bowl of tea in her hand, her face the nearest thing to absolutely impassive. Probably only someone who knew Four well would realize that she was near tears, and small wonder if she was. Both Two and Four had been as obviously near death as either of them had ever been in their lives, just hours ago. They had failed in their mission, one they knew well enough everything had depended on. Even the next few minutes seemed uncertain, filled with pitfalls. Seivarden, with no apparent awareness of this, asked, bewildered, “You need me to drink tea?”

“Yes, sir.” Four, not quite daring to be relieved.

“Yes, sir,” agreed Two, pulling blankets out of a crate. “We surely do need you to do exactly that.”

Seivarden blinked. Exhaled, short and sharp. Unwrapped her arms from around her legs, took the tea from Amaat Two, and drank.

“Work” was putting on vacuum suits and going through a hastily erected temporary airlock into a now-airless level one of the Undergarden. Looking for structural damage, which neither Seivarden nor her Amaats were qualified to do, but they could all three of them apply patches where a supervisor told them to, or carry things. It wasn’t terribly interesting work, but it was demanding enough to mostly keep their minds off of problems they couldn't solve.

Or at least, Seivarden had likely imagined it was. On the second day, another vacuum-suited citizen leaned her faceplate against Seivarden's and said, tersely questioning, "Rough day, eh?"

The question seemed innocent enough, but hearing it struck Seivarden with a sudden, sharp sense of recognition, and then fierce wanting. And a wash of shame, and nauseated regret. She might have said any of a dozen things—*Not really* or even just a flat *Go away*. Instead she said, "I have a shunt."

"Oh," said that other citizen, not at all taken aback. "That'll cost a bit extra, then. But you know—I can see that you know—you know how nicely a bit of detachment takes the edge off, when you're having a rough day."

"Go away," said Seivarden, finally. Not very relieved to have said it. Still sick to her stomach.

"Fine, fine." And the citizen lifted her faceplate from Seivarden's, and went back to sealing her bit of corridor.

Seivarden didn't go back to her own patching, but left work, without reporting to the crew supervisor.

She woke up in Medical. Lay looking at the ceiling for a few minutes, not even wondering how she'd gotten there. Feeling oddly rested and calm. Then a memory must have struck her, because she winced, closed her eyes, laid an arm over her face. "Well, good morning, Lieutenant." The voice cheerful. Seivarden didn't move her arm to see who was speaking. "That was an exciting evening you had last night, though fortunately enough for you, you weren't conscious for most of it. I'm impressed you managed to get down nearly two bottles of arrack before you passed out. That much, drunk that fast, can be enough to kill someone. We were all in a good deal of suspense." Still quite cheerful. Breezy, even, not a trace of sarcasm.

"Go away," said Seivarden, not moving her arm.

"If we were aboard your ship, I'm sure I'd have to do that," the voice continued, now cheerfully apologetic. "But we're not, we're in Station Medical, which means I'm in charge. So do you feel like you could eat something? Your soldiers are outside—they're asleep right now, actually, but they've asked to see you as soon as you wake. You might want something to eat first, and actually you and I should discuss some things."

"Like what?"

"Like that kef shunt. I don't generally recommend their use. They're too easy to circumvent and they don't really solve the problem. Ah, I see whoever worked on you did try to supplement with other methods." Likely in response to Seivarden's growing nausea, on the doctor's mentioning the shunt. Though that nausea was distant—blunted. Meds, no doubt. "But I'll tell you the truth, Lieutenant, once you take the kef you don't really care if you puke your guts out. That's kind of the whole point. Maybe you've already discovered that? No? Well. Whoever installed your shunt and did that other work probably wasn't any sort of specialist. Ship's medic, yes? All respect to ship's medics, they've got to be good at a lot of different things, and sometimes they have to do those things under a great deal of pressure. But this isn't an area they're generally up on. Still, in the end it probably doesn't matter that much. Really, the only thing that has much chance of working is to develop the kind of habits that keep you away from it. Assuming you *want* to be away from it."

"I do." Seivarden lowered her arm. Opened her eyes, looked at the doctor's thin, cheerful face. "I've been away from it. Until now. I was going to sell the arrack. I knew I'd get more than enough for…for what I wanted, but then I thought, no, it's Breq's. And then I thought, damn it, I need a drink."

"Doubtless you did," agreed the doctor. "Drinking yourself insensible so you don't go back to kef may not be a particularly *good* idea, but it does show a certain admirable determination." Seivarden didn't reply. "I'm authorizing a day off work for you today, and I'm sending you home with a one-day self-determine for tomorrow. Which is to say, if you feel like you want to go back to work tomorrow, you're cleared to, but if you'd rather stay home another day, you can do that, with no reprimand or loss of wages."

Seivarden closed her eyes. "Thank you, Doctor."

"You're welcome. And try not to be too hard on yourself. I imagine everyone on the station wishes they could knock themselves insensible right now, and wake up with everything back the way it should be. Oh, and next time you feel like getting hammered, message me. That was some damn good stuff you puked all over yourself, I think it's only fair I should get some, too. That hasn't already been through you, I mean."

Seivarden slept all that day. The next morning she spent alone in the crate-bounded corridor end. Two and Four, not having been ill, didn't have self-determines from Medical and went to work.

For a while Seivarden sat on the ground, staring at the crates. Not moving, although she'd told her two Amaats that she felt much better, and would take the opportunity to call on Head of Security Lusulun, and Station Administrator Celar. They would not have left her alone if she hadn't given them such assurances, if she hadn't been bathed and dressed in her now-clean uniform before they went to work. Which Seivarden knew well enough. But now she was alone, she found herself unwilling to stand. "Maybe I'll just go back to bed," she said at length, aloud.

Station said in her ear, "That would be very awkward, Lieutenant."

Seivarden blinked. Looked up, saw Horticulturist Basnaaid standing on the other side of the crates. "You seemed to be thinking so hard," Basnaaid said, with a smile. "I didn't want to interrupt you."

Seivarden sprang to her feet. "Horticulturist! It's not an interruption, I wasn't actually thinking about anything. Please, come in. Will you have some tea?" Four had made sure the flask was full before she'd gone to work. "This is really ridiculous, inviting you into a pile of boxes."

"I would have loved it when I was little," said Basnaaid, coming in. "I'd love some tea, thank you. Here, I brought you some cakes. I didn't know if the fleet captain had left anything edible."

"We've been getting by." Seivarden managed to look as though the issue of what had been left behind didn't trouble her. "Just. This is very welcome, and very kind of you, thank you." She poured tea, and they sat on the ground.

After a few sips, Seivarden said, "I noticed you were on the concourse the other day. You weren't injured?"

"Some bruises." She gestured their unimportance. "You were the one who fell out that window."

"Oh, did you notice that?" Seivarden asked, lightly, almost as though she were her old self again. "Yes, that was exciting." A surge of guilt, then, and despair, which she managed to keep off her face. "I was armored. And I hit flat on my back, so I'm fine."

Something must have showed on her face then, because Basnaaid said, "Are you sure?"

For a moment Seivarden looked at her. And then, unable to

help herself, she said, "No. No, I'm not fine." Was silent then, as she struggled for control over herself. Succeeded, finally, only a few tears to wipe away. "I fucked up. And it wasn't... I mean, there are fuck-ups and then there are fuck-ups. Sorry. Mess-ups."

"I've heard people swear before, Lieutenant. I've even done it myself." Seivarden tried to smile. Nearly managed it.

"I heard," Basnaaid continued, "that you were in Medical the other night."

"Oh," Seivarden said. "Somebody thought I needed looking after."

"No, but now I'm wondering if Station wouldn't have suggested I visit you, if I hadn't already been on my way."

"Station! I'm nothing to Station." Remembered the tea in her hand. Took a drink while Basnaaid watched, puzzled. Worried-looking. "Sorry. I'm sorry. I just...I don't know what's wrong with me." She considered taking another drink of tea, but couldn't quite manage it. "Actually, Station was kind of amazing. I've always...you know, when you spend a lot of time with ships, you start to think of stations as kind of...I don't know, kind of weak. But it threatened to suck all the air out of the room if the Lord of Mianaai didn't agree to its terms. It's holding her captive in the governor's residence. Here I am going, *Oh, stations are weak* but Station was a fucking badass. I was having trouble believing it was Station talking."

"I had to do something, Lieutenant." Station, in Seivarden's ear, and Basnaaid's. "You're right, it's not the sort of thing I'm used to doing. I tried to imagine what Fleet Captain Breq would do."

"I think you hit your target, Station," said Seivarden. "I think the fleet captain would be...she'll be pretty impressed when she hears."

"Is the fleet captain..." Basnaaid. Hopeful. Hesitant. "Is she coming back?"

"I don't know," replied Seivarden. "She very deliberately didn't tell me what her plans were. Didn't tell me what T... didn't tell me anything. In case. You know. Because actually, my chances of doing what I came here to do were pretty fucking slim." Tisarwat's chances were slimmer, but Seivarden didn't know that. She swallowed, hard. Set down her bowl of tea. "I let her down. I let Breq down, and everything was depending on it, and she's never let *me* down, not even when I thought she had. The things she's done, the most terrifying, dangerous things and hardly blinking, and me, I can't even get from one minute to the next of just *living*. Wait." Tears welled. "Wait, no, that's not right. I'm feeling sorry for myself again."

"I don't think much of anyone could stand comparison with the fleet captain," remarked Basnaaid. "Not that way, anyway."

"Your sister, maybe."

"In some ways, maybe," agreed Basnaaid. "Lieutenant, when did you eat last?"

"I had breakfast?" Seivarden replied, doubtfully. "Maybe? A little?" Looked over at the almost-full dish of skel Two had set out for her. "A little."

"Why don't you wash your face and we'll go get something to eat? Places are opening up again, I'm sure we could find something good."

"I promised my Amaats I'd go see the head of Security, and the station administrator. Although the more I think about it, the more I think it would be best not to look like I'm interfering in station business." She hesitated. Suppressed a frown. "I definitely need to appeal my assignment."

"All right," Basnaaid said, "but trust me, you want to eat something first."

16

They found a shop in a side corridor, open, serving not much more than noodles and tea. “Thank you, Horticulturist,” Seivarden said to Basnaaid, sitting across from her, when she’d finished her lunch. “I didn’t realize how badly I needed that.” She unquestionably felt a good deal better than before she’d eaten.

Basnaaid smiled. “My life always seems hopeless when it’s been too long since I’ve eaten.”

“No doubt. In my case, though, all my problems are still there. I suppose I’ll just have to find some way to deal with whatever happens next.” And then, remembering, “But what about you? Are you safe? It seems like nobody’s told… nobody’s told the Lord of Mianaai about you, or about Citizen Uran. Which means they haven’t told her everything that happened with Captain Hetnys. In fact, from what I’ve seen, people I’d have expected to have plenty of motivation to tell her, not to mention clear opportunities, seem to have actively avoided it.”

Basnaaid ate the last of her own noodles, set her utensil

down. "You've been doing work in the Undergarden?" Seivarden gestured acknowledgment. "Level one wasn't depressurized when you left. That didn't happen until the Lord of the Radch arrived here herself." Seivarden frowned. Basnaaid continued, "It hasn't been on the news, of course, partly because up until a day or two ago the news was all about the fleet captain, but when *Sword of Gurat* gated up to the station, it wasn't paying attention to where the passenger shuttle was."

"What?" Seivarden was, apparently, beyond even swearing.

"*Sword of Gurat* came out of its gate and hit the passenger shuttle. Knocked it into the dome over the Gardens, and that broke the patch over the hole you cut, to pull us out, that day. The repairs to the lake bed weren't finished, and level one of the Undergarden depressurized, too. Fortunately enough, the people working in the Gardens at the time were able to get clear, and of course the Undergarden had been evacuated days ago. But the shuttle . . . well, it's not been on the news, of course, so I mostly only hear rumors, but I know for a fact that there are at least two very prominent families in mourning right now. And one of those for a grandmother, a mother, *and* a daughter."

"Varden's suppurating cuticles," said Seivarden.

"Lieutenant, I don't think I've ever heard anyone say that outside a historical drama."

"They say that in *historical dramas*?" Seivarden seemed nearly as shocked by that as by the shuttle disaster Basnaaid had just told her about.

"It makes you sound like the dashing hero of an entertainment."

"The *heroes* say that in historical dramas? What is the world coming to?"

Basnaaid opened her mouth to say something, but apparently found herself at a loss. Closed her mouth again.

"Well," said Seivarden, and then, "Well. No wonder the tyrant was so frightened and angry. There's already some doubt about loyalties, about who supports who, who the Lord of Mianaai can trust or who the fleet captain may have suborned. Then the ship bringing Mianaai ravages the famous Gardens yet again, in the process killing who knows how many shuttle passengers, among them members of the system's wealthy and prominent families. And *then* she finds the less elevated citizens already protesting on the concourse. So very gently, so very properly, but still."

"Nobody wanted to talk to her about the Gardens. Or the Undergarden," Basnaaid agreed. "That would be my guess, anyway. At any rate, she fairly obviously wasn't in a patient or forgiving mood when she arrived."

Silence, probably both of them remembering watching the new head of Security die. "So what now?" asked Seivarden.

Basnaaid gestured her helplessness to answer such a question. "I think everyone is wondering that. For the immediate future, though, I need to go to work, and you need to talk to someone in Station Administration."

"I do," agreed Seivarden. "I suppose that's what now. The next step, and then the next one."

They rose, and left the shop. Two steps into the corridor, a citizen in the light blue of Station Administration accosted them, fairly clearly had been waiting for them to come out. "Lieutenant Seivarden." She bowed. "Station Administrator Celar begs the favor of your attendance. She would have come herself, but she is unable to leave her office just now."

Seivarden looked at Basnaaid. Basnaaid smiled. "Well,

thank you for having lunch with me, Lieutenant. I'll talk to you again soon."

"Of course we'll reassign you," Station Administrator Celar said, when both she and Seivarden were seated in her office. Half the size of the system governor's office, without the window, which Seivarden seemed to find oddly reassuring. "Medical sent an order yesterday morning, in fact. I apologize for any inconvenience. And of course, I apologize for the nature of the assignment. It was, perhaps, not entirely appropriate to begin with."

"No apology necessary, Administrator." Seivarden, smooth and pleasant. Dismayed, probably to think what might have been in that order from Medical. Her dismay moderated by Station Administrator Celar's massive, statuesque beauty. Hardly surprising, even if wide and heavy wasn't Seivarden's usual type. Station Administrator Celar had that effect on nearly everyone. "Life in the military isn't all dinner parties and drinking tea. Or it wasn't in my day." Station Administrator Celar gestured recognition of Seivarden's history. "I'm quite used to pitching in with repair jobs. The work in the Undergarden is urgently needed. And in fact, there are good reasons why you might not want to appear too...solicitous of my welfare, just now. No, I'm grateful for your assistance. And for Station's."

"Well, as it happens, Lieutenant, we might have need of you elsewhere. You noticed Eminence Ifian on the concourse, when you came in?"

"I couldn't help it," replied Seivarden, with a sardonic smile. "She's renewed her work stoppage."

"Not all of the priests of Amaat have joined her this time.

But there's still a backlog of funerals and births and contract registrations. There's likely to be a line over it very soon, I think. I've been...that is, Station and I have been discussing it, and we've asked some of the other priesthoods to assist. Of course, Station Administration and Athoek Station itself can handle the basic record-keeping—we've already shifted assignments for that, and those citizens are reviewing their new duties. But citizens have been so used to going to the temple of Amaat for all of those things, and now there are potentially quite a few choices and no clear guide to what's most proper, there's bound to be some...some confusion about how to proceed or who to consult. We're planning to set up an office of advisers, where citizens who are in doubt can go and be directed to the most suitable option."

"Station Administrator, all respect, and the idea is a good one, but I myself don't know any of the people here, let alone the details of the various local priesthoods or their practices."

Station Administrator Celar gave a small quirk of a smile. "I suspect, Lieutenant, that you would settle in quickly. But it's only an idea, something to consider. In the meantime, I wanted to ask."

"Of course, Administrator." With her most charming smile.

"It's true the fleet captain is an ancillary? She is, in fact, *Justice of Toren*."

"She is," Seivarden said.

"I suppose that explains some things. The songs—I'm embarrassed to have told her, unknowing, that I wished I had met *Justice of Toren*."

"I assure you, Administrator, she was pleased to discover your shared interest. Just, things being as they were, she couldn't say anything about who she was."

"I imagine not." Station Administrator Celar sighed. "Lieutenant, every time I talked to Fleet Captain Breq I got the distinct impression that her agenda was very much her own, despite her having orders from the Lord of the Radch. From some part of the Lord of the Radch. And yet, until now I would have thought it impossible that any ship"—another sigh—"or any station would have anything like its own agenda."

"And yet," agreed Seivarden. "I assure you, the fleet captain's agenda is no one's but her own. And her priorities are very similar to Station's—she cares very little for the plans of any of the Lord of the Radch and very much for the safety of the residents of this system."

"Lieutenant, someone—I have my guesses as to who, but of course I don't know for certain—has jammed the doors shut to Station's Central Access. And disabled all of my accesses, and all of System Governor Giarod's. At least the ones any of us could use outside Central."

"This is news to me, Administrator," said Seivarden. "But it does explain some recent events, doesn't it."

"It does. And now *Station* would appear to have its own agenda, and its own priorities. The Lord of the Radch—one of her, at any rate—is trapped in the governor's residence, and Station tells me it no longer recognizes either her authority or System Governor Giarod's. Which . . . honestly, Lieutenant, I'm not sure I know what's true anymore, or what to expect from one moment to the next. I keep thinking none of this can be real, but it keeps happening."

"I hate that feeling." Sincerely. Seivarden knew what that felt like. "I'm confident, though, that Station has the wellbeing of its residents at heart. And I can tell you absolutely that Fleet Captain Breq supports Station in that."

"Are you saying explicitly, Lieutenant, that she does not support the Lord of the Radch?"

"Not any of her," said Seivarden. "It was the Lord of the Radch who destroyed *Justice of Toren.* The one that's here, in the governor's residence. Or I think so. It's difficult to tell which one is which sometimes." She didn't add her suspicion that there might yet be a third Anaander. Seeing Station Administrator Celar's astonishment and disbelief, Seivarden added, "It's a long and complicated story."

"And is the fleet captain nearby? This moment of . . . of relative peace is likely to be short-lived. The Lord of the Radch is only held in check by the threat of losing her presence in the system entirely—the moment she is not the only Anaander here, she will be free to act. And it is only the current position of the Lord of the Radch that holds *Sword of Gurat* and *Sword of Atagaris* in check. The instant that changes, what little stability or safety we've attained will be gone again. And of course, Eminence Ifian appears to be doing what she can to make our lives more complicated, even as things are."

"I don't know where the fleet captain is." Suddenly, for just an instant, Seivarden was desperately afraid. "She didn't tell me her plans, in case . . ." She gestured the obvious conclusion to that sentence. "Honestly, Administrator, I'm not sure what *Mercy of Kalr* can do against two Swords—and do I understand there's a third Sword on the edges of the system? That fortunately can't gate?"

Station Administrator Celar gestured confirmation. "And *Mercy of Ilves*, which has been inspecting the outstations but is apparently having some sort of communications difficulty."

"What an inconvenient moment for such a thing," Seivarden observed dryly. "If I were in Anaander's position, I would first find some way to escape confinement in the governor's residence. You're not letting anyone in there with her?"

"Only *Sword of Atagaris.*"

"You're watching what it brings in to her?"

"Station is."

"Good. Still, if she does manage to escape, I predict she'll threaten the station with one of those Swords, and send the other to bring that third one closer in—it can't gate, and it's weeks away otherwise. I have to say, I'm surprised she hasn't already done that."

"You're not alone in that, Lieutenant. There has been a great deal of speculation about it. *Sword of Gurat* was perhaps more badly damaged in its collision with the shuttle than it let on to us."

Seivarden gestured the possibility of this. "And I suspect she doesn't trust *Sword of Atagaris.* The fleet captain tried to return its officers to it, did you know? But apparently Anaander intercepted them, and they're still in suspension, aboard *Sword of Gurat.* As a hold over *Sword of Atagaris.*"

"I didn't know that." Station Administrator Celar frowned. "There are some friends of Hetnys's on the station who would be quite unhappy to hear it."

"No doubt," said Seivarden, blandly. "Whatever the reason she hasn't tried to tow that third Sword in, if Anaander doesn't manage to escape, the longer she sits there the more likely she is to decide to sacrifice herself. I think Station was right, that doing so effectively surrenders the system to Breq. But I also think that, knowing that, and knowing she's just one small fraction of herself, she might well decide her best choice is to leave the system in such a state that it is effectively worthless to whoever wins it."

Station Administrator Celar was silent a moment. "And you don't know where the fleet captain is, or what she's planning?"

"No. But I don't think things are going to stay like this for very long."

Station spoke, then, from the office console. "Truer than you know, Lieutenant. *Sword of Atagaris* has just fired on the station. Nine hours to impact. It will strike the Gardens. I've just ordered the Undergarden work crews to evacuate and seal the area off as well as they can. Your confirmation will be appreciated, Station Administrator."

"Granted, of course," Celar replied, rising from her seat.

Seivarden said, "You've killed the Mianaai in the governor's residence, of course, Station."

"I'm trying to, Lieutenant," said Station, from the console. "But she seems to have managed to put some holes in the section door over the concourse window. I'm not certain how." Section doors, on ships or on stations, were made to be extremely difficult to breach, for fairly obvious reasons. "Not much, but enough to suck in air from the concourse when I try to pull it out of the room. Would this be the fleet captain's invisible gun, that she used in the Gardens?"

"Oh, *fuck*," said Seivarden, and rose, herself. "How many holes?"

"Twenty-one."

"She's got six shots left, then," said Seivarden.

"And," said Station, "Anaander Mianaai demands I stop trying to suffocate her, or *Sword of Atagaris* will fire again."

"I don't see there's much choice, Station," said Station Administrator Celar. Seivarden gestured agreement. Helpless and angry—largely with herself—but refusing to show it.

"She also wishes to meet with *whoever it is who's in charge here*. In, she says, her office. In ten minutes. Or…"

"*Sword of Atagaris* will fire again. Yes," acknowledged Seivarden. "I suppose *whoever it is who's in charge here* means you, Station."

"The Lord of Mianaai doesn't think so," said Station. Impossible that there was the least trace of complaint or petulance in its tone. "Or she'd have asked to talk to me directly. Besides, it's Station Administrator Celar who is the authority here."

Station Administrator Celar looked at Seivarden. Her face expressionless, but doubtless she was remembering the death of the head of Security. Seivarden said nothing. Finally Celar said, "I don't see there's much choice here, either. Lieutenant, will you come with me?"

"If you like, Administrator. Though you do realize, I'm sure, that my presence will...give a certain appearance of official association."

"Do you think the fleet captain would object to that?"

"No," said Seivarden. "She wouldn't."

On the concourse, the line that Station Administrator Celar had anticipated had already begun to form. Eminence Ifian and her subordinate priests—fewer than half of the number of the previous work stoppage—watched the incipient line with complacence. As Station Administrator Celar and Seivarden walked past the temple entrance, Ifian rose from where she'd been sitting on her cushion. "Station Administrator, I demand to know the truth. You *owe* the truth to the residents of this station and instead you're disseminating lies in order to manipulate us."

Station Administrator Celar stopped, Seivarden with her. "What lies would these be, Eminence?"

"The Lord of the Radch would never fire on this station.

As you well know. I am appalled that you would go so far in your rejection of legitimate authority, indeed, your flagrant disregard for the well-being of this station's residents."

Seivarden looked at the eminence. Her lip curled, the very image of aristocratic hauteur, and she said to Station Administrator Celar, "Administrator, I wouldn't dignify this person with a reply." And without waiting, either for Ifian to answer or Celar to move, turned away from the temple and walked toward the governor's residence. Celar said nothing, but turned when Seivarden did.

Anaander Mianaai stood behind the system governor's desk, flanked by two *Sword of Atagaris* ancillaries. "Well," she said, on seeing Station Administrator Celar enter, followed by Seivarden, "I ask for whoever's in charge and I get this. Very interesting."

"You wouldn't accept that Station was in charge," replied Celar. "We weren't sure who you would accept, so we thought we'd provide a variety for you to choose from."

"I'm not certain what sort of a fool you take me for," said Anaander, smoothly, in apparent good humor. "And, Citizen Seivarden, I remain astonished at your involvement here. I wouldn't have thought you would ever be a traitor to the Radch."

"I might say the same of you," said Seivarden. "Except events have been so convincing."

"It's you, isn't it? Controlling *Justice of Toren*, and *Mercy of Kalr*. And Athoek Station, now. The very young—and, I must say, not entirely steady—Lieutenant Tisarwat was quite definite about there being no instances of me aboard *Mercy of Kalr*."

Mention of Tisarwat hit Seivarden like a slap. She did not

manage to keep her astonished dismay off her face. "Tisarwat!" Realized there was some deception afoot, but that she could only guess at its outlines. "That fish-witted little double-crosser!"

Anaander Mianaai laughed outright. "Her horror of you is second only to her terror of the ancillary. Who is nominally in command, of course, but..." She gestured the impossibility of that. "I will say, Lieutenant Tisarwat was surely more of a nuisance to you than anything. She must have had something resembling wits, at some point, to be assigned to an administrative post, but the gods only know if she'll ever recover them."

"Well," Seivarden said, with a nonchalance she did not feel, "you're welcome to her, for whatever good you can get out of her."

"Fair enough," said Anaander. "So, since I know for a fact that I would never under any circumstances give an ancillary the sort of access codes that are clearly involved here, I must assume that it's you in control of Station. I will, therefore, deal with you."

"If you insist," said Seivarden. "I am, however, only Station's representative."

Anaander gave her a disbelieving look. "Here is how it will be. I am once again taking control of this station. Any threat to me, and *Sword of Atagaris* fires on the station again. Its first shot—the one that will hit some eight hours from now—is merely an assurance of my intentions, and will mostly only damage uninhabited areas. Subsequent ones will not be so cautious. I am, I find, perfectly happy to sacrifice this instance of myself if it will deny my enemy a foothold. I will have control of the official news channels, through System Governor Giarod. There will be no further unexpected appearances on the news. *Sword of Gurat* will return to running Station Security. It will also continue to cut into Station's Central Access. Any attempt to stop this, and *Sword of Atagaris* will fire on the station again."

"Station," said Seivarden, silently, "do you understand that the Lord of Mianaai has three AI cores here with her?" The meter-and-a-half-high stack of them still sat, smooth and dark, in the corner behind Anaander. "Once the Lord of Mianaai cuts into Central Access there will be nothing stopping her from replacing you with one of them."

"I really don't know what you mean, Lieutenant," said Station, into Seivarden's ear. "I really don't see that there's much alternative."

Aloud Seivarden said, "These are significant concessions you're asking of us. What do you offer in return? Besides the favor of not destroying the station and everyone on it? Because you know as well as we do that neither of us actually wants that, that, in fact, everyone here—including you—is willing to go to some trouble to avoid it. Otherwise you'd have done it already."

"Vendaai has been gone so long," replied Anaander with a half laugh, "that I had forgotten how insufferably arrogant they could be."

"I am honored to be considered a credit to my house," Seivarden said, coldly. "What do you offer?"

Silence. Anaander looked from Seivarden to Station Administrator Celar and back. "I will not reinstitute the curfew, and I will allow the Undergarden to be repaired."

"That might be easier," Seivarden said, blandly, "if you had *Sword of Atagaris* remove that missile before it hits."

Anaander smiled. "Only in exchange for your complete, unconditional surrender." Seivarden scoffed.

"If you don't reinstitute the curfew," put in Station Administrator Celar, before Seivarden could say something unfortunate, "and if work is going ahead on the Undergarden, there won't be any need for *Sword of Gurat*'s assistance with security. In fact, as I believe was recently mentioned to you"—greatly daring, to bring that up—"and as recent events have shown, *Sword of Gurat*'s interference in local security matters is likely to cause far more problems than it solves."

Silence. Anaander considered the station administrator. Then, finally, "All right. But the first line, the first *hint* of a work stoppage, let alone what we had on the concourse the other day, and *Sword of Gurat* takes over."

"Talk to your own people about that," Seivarden said. "Eminence Ifian is starting in on her second work stoppage in recent weeks. And there's a line starting up even now over the backlog of funerals and contracts the eminence has caused." Anaander said nothing. "I am assuming that Eminence Ifian was opposing the Undergarden refit on your orders? She is working for you, yes? This part of you, I mean." Still nothing from Anaander. "We would also like assurances that you do not plan to replace Station with one of those AI cores behind you."

"No," Anaander replied, flatly. "I will not give any such assurance. I have you to thank for those, you know. I had no idea they were here. I thought I'd searched thoroughly before and kept a good-enough watch, but apparently I missed these."

"Are they not yours, then?" Seivarden asked. "We had no idea they were here. I suppose Eminence Ifian did, though, she was quite determined to thwart the fleet captain's refit of the Undergarden. When I saw the AI cores I assumed all her efforts were meant to keep us from stumbling across them.

But you say you didn't know they were there. So, then, whose are they, I wonder?"

"Mine now." Anaander, with a thin smile. "I will do with them what I wish. And if the ancillary didn't know the cores were in the Undergarden, why did it involve itself there?"

"She saw a wrong that needed righting," said Seivarden. Willing her voice not to shake. She had been running on adrenaline and sheer necessity so far, but was rapidly reaching the end of her resources. "It's the sort of thing she does. One last thing—I think it's a last thing, Station?" Station said nothing. Station Administrator Celar said nothing. "You will publicly take responsibility for the missile that's about to hit the Gardens. And the terms of this agreement are to be sent out on all the official channels, and the reason for it. So that when you have removed Station as an obstacle to treating its residents however you like, and the shooting starts, they'll know you for a treacherous shit, and so will everyone else in Radch space." Almost losing control of her voice at that last. She swallowed hard.

The tyrant was silent for a full twenty seconds. Then she said, "After all this, this is what makes me angry. Do you think that I have done anything at all for the past three thousand years except for the benefit of citizens? Do you think that I do anything at all, now, except with the desperate hope that I can keep Radch space secure and its citizens safe? Including the citizens on this station?"

Seivarden wanted to say something biting, but swallowed it back. Knew that if she spoke, all pretense at composure would be lost. Began, instead, to carefully time and measure her breathing. Station said, from the office console, "When Fleet Captain Breq arrived here, she set about making things better for my residents. When you arrived, you set about killing my residents. You continue to threaten to kill my residents."

Anaander didn't seem to have heard what Station had said. "I want your access codes." That directed at Seivarden.

Who gestured lack of concern. The focus on her breathing had calmed her just a bit. Enough that she managed to say, more or less lightly, "I only have captain's accesses to *Sword of Nathtas*. Considering it's a thousand years dead, I don't see what good they'll do you, but you're welcome to them."

"Someone changed a lot of Station's high-level accesses. Someone blocked the door to Station's Central Access."

"Wasn't me," said Seivarden. "I didn't set foot on this station until a few days ago." *Sword of Atagaris*'s two ancillaries had stood statue-still and silent all this time. It knew well enough who had changed Station's accesses. But it said nothing.

Anaander considered this for a moment. "Let's make this announcement, then. And since you are no longer outside my jurisdiction, Citizen Seivarden, you and I will board *Sword of Gurat* and discuss the question of Station's accesses, and just who is controlling the *Justice of Toren* ancillary."

This was, finally, too much for Seivarden. "You!" She pointed directly at Anaander Mianaai, a rude and angry gesture, to a Radchaai. "You should not dare even to *mention* her, let alone in such terms. Do you dare claim to be just, to be proper, to be acting for the benefit of citizens? How many citizens' deaths have you caused, just this one of you, just in the last week? How many more will there be? Athoek Station, who you will not speak to, puts you to shame. *Justice of Toren*, what little is left of her, you will not acknowledge, but she is a better person than you. Oh, Aatr's tits I wish she were here!" Nearly a cry, that. "*She* wouldn't let you do this to Station. *She* doesn't toss people aside when they're suddenly inconvenient, or to profit herself. Let alone call herself virtuous for doing it. Call her *the ancillary* again and I swear I'll tear your tongue out of your head, or die trying." Openly weeping, now, barely able to speak further. Took a ragged, sobbing breath. "I need to go to the gym. No. I need to go to Medical. Station, is that doctor on duty?"

"She can be in short order, Lieutenant," said Station from the console.

Station Administrator Celar said, to Anaander Mianaai's nonplussed stare, "Lieutenant Seivarden has been ill." She managed to put a note of disapproval into her voice. "She should go to Medical immediately. You can discuss whatever you need to with her when she's recovered. I will make the announcement with you, Lord of Mianaai, and then Station and I have a good deal of business to take care of."

Anaander Mianaai asked, incredulous, "Ill?"

"The lieutenant was off work on a self-determine today," said Station. "She really ought to have been resting. The doctor is alarmed at my report of Lieutenant Seivarden's condition and has just prescribed a week's rest, and ordered her to report to Medical as soon as possible, with Security's assistance if necessary. I don't know how *you're* used to doing things, but around here we take medical orders very seriously."

And that was when *Mercy of Kalr* came back into the universe.

17

The moment we saw Athoek's sun, *Mercy of Kalr* reached out to find Tisarwat and Seivarden. Could not find Tisarwat at all. Found Seivarden, standing weeping, helpless and furious, in the system governor's office beside Station Administrator Celar, Anaander Mianaai behind Governor Giarod's desk, saying, "There's a perfectly good medic on board *Sword of Gurat*."

Found the external archives. Pulled their data, showed me, as I sat in Command, a dizzyingly compressed stream of moments: images, sounds, emotions. Almost too fast for me to understand. But I got the essentials—*Sword of Atagaris* had fired on the station and the shot would reach the Gardens in eight hours; Tisarwat and Nine were aboard *Sword of Gurat* and we knew little else; Seivarden's attempt to kill Anaander Mianaai had failed and moreover Anaander had the Presger gun. But Seivarden was alive, and so were Two and Four, just now part of an emergency crew reinforcing the section doors surrounding the Gardens and the Undergarden.

In the system governor's office, Station Administrator Celar said to Anaander Mianaai, "The doctor here is already familiar with Lieutenant Seivarden's medical history. Surely you can't imagine she'll escape somehow?"

Seivarden took a sobbing breath. Wiped her eyes with the back of one gloved hand. "Fuck you," she said. And then again, "*Fuck you.* You have everything you want. There's nothing else you'll get from me, because I don't have it."

"I don't have *Justice of Toren*," said Anaander.

"Well that's your own fucking fault, isn't it," Seivarden replied. "I'm done with you. I'm going to Medical." She turned and walked out of the office.

"*Sphene*," I said, still seated, still staring, half distracted, at the images Ship fed me, pulled from those archives. "Where are you, actually?"

"In my bed," said *Sphene*, *Mercy of Kalr* sending its words to my ear. "Where else would I be?"

"*Sword of Atagaris* has fired on the station. The Usurper is planning to replace Athoek Station with another AI core and no one seems to be able to stop her short of destroying the station entirely. Where are you? Are you near enough to help?" Likely there was nothing *Sphene* could do, even if it was close by—but Anaander had no reason to know that. *Sphene* might, if nothing else, at least *look* threatening.

"Can you play for time, Cousin?" came *Sphene*'s reply. "A few years, maybe?"

"Ship," I said, not replying to *Sphene*, "tell *Mercy of Ilves* that now is the time to choose a side. Let it and its captain know that there's no avoiding it anymore." Any action *Mercy of Ilves* took now—or didn't take—would be a choice, whether or not *Mercy of Ilves* and its captain wished it.

Ship said, in my ear, "What if it chooses to support the Lord of Mianaai?"

"What if it doesn't?" I asked. "Be sure to tell it what the tyrant is planning to do to Station. Let it know she has two other cores." *Sword of Atagaris* would already have had that thought. "Send the same to Fleet Captain Uemi and the Hrad fleet." An entire gate away. And likely they were at Tstur Palace by now, hoping that Anaander's presence here had weakened her grip there. Still.

Our message to *Mercy of Ilves* wouldn't even reach it for another hour. Its reply—if it deigned to provide one—would take yet another hour to reach us. If it came, it might well not be in our favor. The Hrad fleet wouldn't receive our message for more hours still, and was at best days away. Best to act as though we had no one but ourselves.

Oh for the days when I had been a ship. When my every move of any military consequence was made in the presence of entire fleets—and not nominal ones, no, not just three or four Mercies and maybe a Sword. Dozens and dozens of ships, and myself just one among them, carrying thousands of bodies. Just myself, as *Justice of Toren*, I could have overpowered and occupied Athoek Station with barely any effort. On consideration, it had been easier in those days because it didn't matter who we killed, or how many. Still. I (long-gone *Justice of Toren* I) could likely have had Athoek Station in my control within hours, with very little loss of life.

I had only myself, *Mercy of Kalr*, and its crew. I didn't know how much time I had—didn't know how far *Sword of Gurat* had gotten in its previous attempt to cut into Athoek Station's Central Access. They would have been at it for several days before Station stopped them. Probably not much time, then. A few days at the most. Quite possibly a good deal less. And there was still that missile, headed for the Gardens. It probably wouldn't kill anyone, but it would cause a good deal of damage.

"What," I asked aloud, "did the tyrant come here for?"

Amaat One, standing beside my seat, in Command, said, "Sir?" Puzzled.

"Why did she come here, of all places? Why here, not even waiting to be certain of her hold on Tstur Palace?" Because this Anaander had not come from Omaugh, and the other palaces were too far away. "What was she looking for?" *She's very angry with you, sir*, Lieutenant Tisarwat had said.

"She was looking for you, Fleet Captain," said Amaat Nine, standing at a console behind me. Speaking for *Mercy of Kalr.*

"And we know she's willing to negotiate, at least to some extent." She still thought of herself as having the best interests of citizens at heart. "I think she genuinely wants to avoid destroying the station entirely, or damaging it too badly. For one thing, losing the station would make it much more difficult to use Athoek as a base." It would still be possible to get resources up from downwell, but losing the station would make that a great deal less convenient. "For another—all the ships here. All those people down on the planet. *Mercy of Ilves*." None of us knew what *Mercy of Ilves* or its captain thought about any of this. "No, too many people are watching. And these are citizens we're talking about. If she smashes Athoek Station to bits, or has *Sword of Gurat* burn it to nothing, everyone will know. She doesn't want that. But what she *does* want"—aside from complete control over Athoek Station, now—"is something we have."

"No," said Amaat Nine. Reading Ship's words, in her

vision. Distressed. Not understanding what Ship had understood. Afraid. "No, Fleet Captain, I won't agree to that."

"Ship, Athoek Station has defended itself to the best of its ability. It's done spectacularly well, considering. But it's out of options. And once the tyrant manages to cut into its Central Access, once she begins replacing Station with one of those AI cores, what do you think will happen then?" Not wholesale slaughter, no. Not if Anaander could avoid it. But it would add up to that, eventually. "Are we going to sit here and watch Station die?"

"She won't keep any agreement," said Amaat Nine. Said Ship. "Once she has you"—realization striking Amaat Nine belatedly—"she'll do whatever she wants to Station."

"Maybe," I agreed. "But it might buy us some time." Pointlessly, perhaps.

"Who's coming?" asked Ship, still through Amaat Nine. "*Sphene*? And when it gets here two years from now, what will it be able to do? Or do you hope for the Hrad fleet?"

"No," I agreed, "I'm sure they'll be at Tstur Palace for a while. But we have to do *something*. Do you have a better idea?"

Silence. Then, "She'll kill you."

"Eventually," I agreed. "But not until she's got all the information she thinks she can get out of me. And she doesn't have an interrogator with her." I was fairly sure she didn't, or she would not have spoken of Tisarwat the way she had. And she apparently didn't feel she could trust any of the station's interrogators. "She'll try to use my ancillary implants, but we can make that difficult for her, before I go." And buy more time.

"No," said Ship. Said Amaat Nine. "She'll just make you an ancillary of *Sword of Gurat*, and have everything."

"She won't. She's said over and over that she doesn't think she'd give accesses to an ancillary, but what if I do have them? She doesn't want *Sword of Gurat* to have those. And what if, taking me as an ancillary, I corrupt it somehow? No, she'll kill me outright first. But in the meantime we gain a few days. Maybe more. And who knows what might happen in a few days?"

Silence. Amaat One, Amaat Nine, standing, staring at me. Appalled. Not quite believing what they had just heard.

"Don't be like that, Amaat," I said. "I'm one soldier. Not even a whole one. What do I weigh, against all of Athoek Station?" And I had been in more desperate straits, and lived. Still, one day—perhaps this one—I would not.

"I'll never forgive her," said Amaat Nine. Said *Mercy of Kalr*.

"I never have," I replied.

I sent to Anaander, sitting in Command, my brown-and-black uniform as spotless and perfect as Kalr Five could make it. The small gold circle of Lieutenant Awn's memorial pin near my collar. I had left off Translator Dlique's. I said, aloud, "Tyrant. I am given to understand that you have everything you could want, except one thing."

Waited five minutes for the reply, voice with no visual data. "Very amusing. Have you been here all this time?"

"Only a half hour or so." I did not bother to smile. "So you'll talk to me, then? I don't need one of my lieutenants to pretend she's really running things, and have her speak for me?"

"Amaat's grace, no," came the reply. "Every lieutenant of yours I've spoken with so far has been an unsteady, blubbering mess. What are you doing to them?"

"Nothing out of the ordinary." I reached for a bowl of tea, handed to me by one of my Kalrs. The priceless white porcelain, which Five only ever took out for the most serious of occasions. I had no way of knowing if Anaander saw it, but the thought that she might clearly gave Five some sort of satisfaction. "You work with what Military Administration sends you. Though Vendaai was never as dependable as they seemed to think themselves. And speaking of Vendaai. I'll have Lieutenant Seivarden and her soldiers back. Unharmed, if you please."

"Oh, will you?"

"I will."

"And will you also have Lieutenant Tisarwat?"

"Amaat's grace, no." My voice even. Not quite ancillary-flat. "I wish you joy of her. You might actually get some work out of her if she stops weeping for a few moments."

"She is, I am told, emotionally traumatized and needs medication on account of it. And more therapy than a ship's medic can provide. People like that don't get assigned to military, not even administrative posts. I can't help but conclude that it's service with you that's done for her."

"Quite possibly," I acknowledged. "But as I said, I'll have Lieutenant Seivarden and her soldiers back. And."

"And?"

"And you will cease your attempts to murder Athoek Station."

"Murder!" A pause. "Athoek Station is mine to do what I want with. And it is currently not functioning properly."

"Neither of those statements is true. But I won't argue with you." I took a drink of tea from that elegant porcelain. "Return Lieutenant Seivarden and her Amaats, and give up your plan to replace Athoek Station with a fresh AI core, and

I will surrender to you. Just me. I have no intention of putting *Mercy of Kalr* in your power."

Thirty seconds of silence. Then, "What's the catch?"

"None. Unless by *catch* you mean the same conditions you agreed to with Athoek Station: the terms of the exchange are to be announced on the official news channels. So that—how did Lieutenant Seivarden put it? So that when you have removed Station as an obstacle to treating its residents however you like, and the shooting starts, they'll know you for a treacherous shit, and so will everyone else in Radch space. Oh, and I also expect you to honor the terms of your agreement with Station itself." Silence. "Don't sulk. Athoek Station has already said it's happy to deal with you so long as you don't threaten its residents. That may have changed now it knows you're trying to kill it, but that's really no one's fault but your own. I'm sure if you can bring yourself to treat Athoek Station's residents decently, you'll still be left with a usable base in this system, with a habitable planet and all its resources potentially available to you. And you still have me, of course."

"Where did that gun come from?"

I smiled, and took another drink of tea.

"Who are you, really?"

"*Justice of Toren* One Esk Nineteen," I said. "Who else would I be?"

"I don't think I believe you."

I handed the empty bowl of tea to a Kalr. "Order *Sword of Gurat* to leave off breaking into Athoek Station's Central Access, announce our agreement, and I'll come to the station. You're welcome to wring whatever information out of me you can."

"No. I don't think so."

I gestured unconcern. "All right. Goodbye." The connection cut out.

"They know where we are by now," said Kalr Thirteen, from her station behind me.

"They do," I agreed. "And they might be foolish enough to try to attack us. But I don't think they will. *Mercy of Ilves* is still an unknown quantity, and if *Sword of Atagaris* moves to attack us, they'll leave *Sword of Gurat* vulnerable. It's still docked with the station." Though Tisarwat was, so far as I knew, still aboard *Sword of Gurat*. "And I'm beginning to suspect it's more badly damaged than they're letting on." It might have come into the system already damaged from fighting at Tstur Palace, and the collision with the passenger shuttle would have made things worse. "The tyrant is angry and suspicious right now, but she'll see soon enough that this exchange is to her advantage." And Athoek Station would be safe. I hoped.

An hour later the tyrant messaged back. She would make the announcement. *Sword of Gurat* would leave the corridors surrounding Central Access, and Athoek Station would confirm for me that it was safe and unmolested. Seivarden and her Amaats would meet me at the dock, and board the shuttle I'd arrived on. I would arrive unarmed and alone.

I went to Medical. Medic could not bring herself to speak to me for an entire minute. I sat on the side of a bed and waited. Finally she said, "Still singing, even now?" Angry and frustrated.

"I'll stop if you like."

"No," she said, with an exasperated sigh. "That would be even worse. I know you think it's unlikely they'll make you an ancillary of *Sword of Gurat*. And I do understand why you think that. But if you're wrong, they won't hesitate to do it. You're not a person to them."

"There's one more reason that I think they won't do that, that I didn't mention in Command. If Seivarden doesn't have Station's accesses, and Tisarwat doesn't..."

"That's another thing," Medic put in.

"And if, as she apparently believes, Tisarwat doesn't have them," I continued, "then who does? Possibly I do. I imagine she has begun to suspect that I am not myself, that I have in fact been appropriated by Omaugh Anaander. Perhaps she would prefer *Sword of Gurat* not have so much of her enemy self in such an intimate part of its memory."

"And as soon as they get what they want from you, sir, Lieutenant Tisarwat is done for." More than Tisarwat might be done for—Tisarwat's knowledge might well give Tstur Anaander an advantage should she move against Omaugh. If Omaugh Anaander had not already taken Tstur Palace.

It was all a gamble. All a toss of the omens, never knowing where the pieces would come down. "Yes," I agreed. "But she's also done for if she fails to do what she went aboard *Sword of Gurat* to do. And the more time we can give her to do that, the better for all of us."

"Ship is very unhappy about this."

"But Ship understands why I am doing it. So do you. And you can be unhappy about it just as effectively after we're done. So. Put me back the way you found me, when I first came aboard this ship."

There was no need to remove the implants in question, just disable them. It took Medic an hour to begin the process, and the rest would work itself out over the next day or so. "Well," she said, when she was finished, frowning fiercely. And could not speak further.

"I've survived worse odds," I told her.

"Someday you won't," she said.

"That is true of all of us," I said. "I will come back if I can. If I can't, well..." I gestured, the tossing of a handful of omens.

I saw—for the moment I could still see—that once again she could not speak. That she didn't want me to see her, just now. I slid off the bed, and knowing she would not welcome more I put my hand on her shoulder, for just a moment, and then left her to herself.

Kalr Five was in my quarters. Packing, as though I were only leaving for a few days' visit to the station. "Begging your indulgence, sir," she said when I came in, "*alone* doesn't mean without a servant. You can't go to the station without someone to look after your uniform. Or carry your luggage. The Lord of Mianaai can't possibly expect it."

"Five," I said, and then, "Ettan." Her name, that I had only ever used once before, and that to her private horror. "I need you to stay here. I need you to stay here and be all right."

"I don't see how I can, sir."

"And there's no point in my taking any luggage." She stared at me, not comprehending. Or perhaps refusing to comprehend. No, Ship showed me, she was trying very hard not to cry. "Here," I said, "give me the Itran icon. Not the one in the corner." She Who Sprang from the Lily sat in a niche in the corner of my quarters, with an EskVar and icons of Amaat and Toren. "The one in my luggage."

"Yes, sir." She Who Sprang from the Lily, knife in one hand, jeweled human skull in the other, was an endless source of disgusted fascination among my Kalrs. I had never opened the other Itran icon in their presence, but they knew, of course, that I had it. Five opened the bench it was stored in and drew it out, a golden disk five centimeters in diameter and one and a half centimeters high. I took it from her and triggered it, and it opened out, the image rising from the center. The figure wore only short trousers and a wreath of tiny jeweled flowers. One of its four arms held a severed head that smiled serenely and dripped jeweled blood on the figure's bare feet. Two more hands held a knife, and a ball. The fourth hand was empty, the forearm encased in a cylindrical armguard.

"Sir!" Five's astonishment nearly showed on her face. "That's you."

"This is an icon of the Itran saint Seven Brilliant Truths Shine like Suns. The head, do you see?" Seven Brilliant Truths's head was clearly the center of the composition, and no one in the Itran Tetrarchy would have been in any doubt as to who the actual subject of the icon was. But outside the Tetrarchy, eyes were invariably drawn to the standing figure. No one outside the Tetrarchy had seen it who had not also seen me. "This would be extremely valuable in the Itran Tetrarchy. There weren't many of these made, and this one has a piece of the saint's skin in the base. Will you keep it safe for me?" I didn't have many sentimental possessions, but this would count among them. So would the memorial pin from Lieutenant Awn's funeral, but that I would not be parted from.

"Sir," said Five, "the necklace that you gave Citizen Uran.

And that...that box of teeth you gave to Horticulturist Basnaaid."

"Yes," I agreed. "They are the originals of what you see in miniature here." I had not liked Seven Brilliant Truths Shine like Suns. She had been so very sure of her own importance, her own superiority. Had had little compassion for anyone beyond herself. But the moment had come when she had been asked to sacrifice herself for what she believed, and though she had been offered escape she hadn't taken it. Of everyone present, she had thought that I would best understand her choice. Correctly, as it happened, though not for the reasons she assumed. I touched the catch again, and the icon closed in on itself. "I need you to keep this safe for me." She took it, reluctant. "Besides, no one else will take sufficient care of the porcelain. I'll take my old enamel set with me, I know you'll be glad to see it go."

She actually frowned, and then turned and walked swiftly out of the room without apology or explanation. I did not need to ask Ship why.

Sphene was in the corridor outside. It gave Five an incurious look as she rushed by, and then it said to me, "Cousin! Take me with you! The last time you did something this amazingly stupid, it turned out spectacularly. I want in this time. Or at least give me a chance to spit in the Usurper's face. Just once! I'll beg, if you like."

"I'm supposed to go alone, Cousin."

"And so you will. I don't count, do I? I'm just an *it*."

A voice, from farther down the corridor. "What's this I hear?" Translator Zeiat came into the doorway. "You're going to the station, Fleet Captain? Excellent! I'll come along."

"Translator," I said, still standing in the middle of my

quarters, hand still partly outstretched from giving Seven Brilliant Truths Shine like Suns to Kalr Five, "we're in the middle of a war. Things are very unsettled on the station right now."

"Oh!" Comprehension, recognition showed on her face. "That's right, you said there was a war. A very inconvenient one, as I recall. But, you know, you're all out of fish sauce. And I don't think I've ever seen a war before!"

"I'm going, too," said *Sphene*.

"Excellent!" replied Translator Zeiat. "I'll go pack."

The moment my shuttle departed, Lieutenant Ekalu messaged the station. "This is Lieutenant Ekalu, currently in command of *Mercy of Kalr*. The fleet captain is on her way. Be advised, in three minutes we will begin removal of the missile currently headed for Athoek Station, and will then return to this orbit. A hostile response to our action will be taken badly." And gated without waiting for a reply. *Mercy of Kalr* would emerge in the path of the missile, open the gate wide so it would exit the universe, expel it somewhere it could spend itself harmlessly.

I was glad for Ship's absence; Medic's actions, an hour ago, were beginning to take effect, a piecemeal slipping away of connections and sensations I had become far too accustomed to over the last several weeks, that even when I had been cut off from Ship temporarily I'd known (thought, hoped) would always return sooner or later.

Sphene pulled itself into the seat beside me, where I sat in the pilot's seat. Strapped itself in. "I like your style, Cousin. I really wish we could have met sooner. I'd have introduced myself when you arrived, if I'd only known. So. What's your plan this time?"

"My plan," I said, ancillary-flat, "is to prevent the murder of Athoek Station."

"What, that's all?"

"That's all, Cousin."

"Hmm. Well. It's not very promising. But then, your last plan wasn't very promising, either. I will say, if nothing else, the Usurper's reaction to Translator Zeiat should be amusing." The translator was strapped into her own seat, two rows aft. "Do I understand correctly, that no one seems to have mentioned her to the Usurper yet?"

"That would appear to be the case."

"Hah," replied *Sphene*, obviously pleased. "This will be good, then."

"Perhaps it won't be," I said. "This part of the Usurper appears to think that the Presger are the reason for her split. This Anaander might take the translator's presence as confirmation of that."

"Better and better! And besides, she might well be right. No"—guessing I had been about to argue—"not that the Presger are attempting to destroy her or her empire she's built. That's nothing but her own typical arrogance. Why would they care? But meeting the Presger. Realizing that not only could she not defeat or destroy them, but that they could destroy *her* with hardly a thought. When you've spent two thousand years thinking of yourself as the most gloriously powerful being in the universe, I imagine an encounter like that comes as quite an unpleasant shock. Really, after something like that you need to redefine who you are."

And the Presger involvement in the destruction of Garsedd—those twenty-five unstoppable guns, Anaander's own towering rage at being confronted with even the hint of possible defeat—

might have brought that to a crisis. "You may be right, Cousin. That still leaves us in an awkward situation."

"It does," *Sphene* agreed. "*Very* awkward. It should be tremendously entertaining. If you don't contrive to wrest some kind of advantage out of it, you're not the ship I took you for."

"I'm not a ship anymore," I pointed out.

"And what about Lieutenant Tisarwat? Off at the same time as Lieutenant Seivarden, only her mission was so very secret. And now it seems she's aboard *Sword of Gurat*, and she's, what did the Usurper say? *Not the sharpest knife in the set*? Can this be the same Lieutenant Tisarwat? Oh, she looks innocent enough with those foolish purple eyes, but she's a politically conniving piece of work. Maybe not the steadiest, but she's only, what, seventeen? I fear for her opponents in the future, when she grows into herself. If she lives that long."

"So do I," I said. Quite truthfully.

"No more to say about it? Well, Cousin, I don't take offense. You've left them weeping as though you were already dead, back on *Mercy of Kalr*, but I think you've still got a few counters on the board." I said nothing. "Please let me be one of them, Cousin. I was entirely serious when I said I would beg."

"Would you give up ancillaries? Not the ones already connected. I mean, for the future."

Silence. No expression on *Sphene*'s face, of course, there never was unless it wanted there to be. "I do understand why you're asking that. Truly. It is impossible that I could be under any illusions as to what ancillaries are."

"Of course not." It would be entirely foolish to even suggest so.

"But you understand, I know you do, why I refuse. You understand what it is you're asking."

"I do. I just wish you would reconsider, Cousin."

"No."

I gestured inconsequence. "It's just as well. I don't have any plans, no play beyond this obvious one."

"I don't believe that."

"You haven't known me very long, Cousin," I said. "Did you know, about a year ago Lieutenant Seivarden fell off a bridge. It was a long way down—a couple of kilometers. She managed to grab hold of the structure underneath, but I couldn't reach her."

"Since she certainly lived to break down weeping in front of the Usurper just hours ago, you must have found some solution to the problem."

"I jumped with her. On the off chance that I'd be able to slow our fall before we hit the ground." I gestured the obviousness of the story's conclusion. "My right leg hasn't been the same since."

Sphene was silent for three seconds, and then said, "I don't think that story communicates the point you seem to imagine it does."

We both sat silent for a few minutes, watching the distance decrease between the shuttle and Athoek Station. "I don't think," I said then, "that the translator could be any sort of piece in any game of mine. The Presger don't involve themselves in human affairs. *Getting* her involved would probably mean breaking the treaty."

"Nobody wants that," agreed *Sphene*, placidly. "You don't have any aliens up your sleeve, do you? Geck friends? Visiting Rrrrrr? No? I suppose we're not likely to run across any new sort of alien between here and the station."

There was no point in answering that.

"I'm bored," said Translator Zeiat. *Sphene* and I swiveled to look at her. "I don't like it. *Sphene*, did you bring the game?"

"It wouldn't have traveled well," I said. "Have you ever played rhymes, Translator?"

"I can't say I have," Translator Zeiat replied. "But if it's a poetry game, I never have properly understood poetry."

"It starts very simply," I said. "Someone gives a line in first meter and Direct mode, and then everyone adds a line. Then we change to Indirect mode. Or we can just stay first Direct if you like, until you're comfortable with it."

"Thank all the gods," said *Sphene*. "I was afraid you were going to suggest we sing that song about the thousand eggs."

"*A thousand eggs all nice and warm*," I sang. "*Crack, crack, crack, a little chick is born. Peep peep peep peep! Peep peep peep peep*!"

"Why, Fleet Captain," Translator Zeiat exclaimed, "that's a charming song! Why haven't I heard you sing it before now?"

I took a breath. "*Nine hundred ninety-nine eggs all nice and warm*..."

"*Crack, crack, crack*," Translator Zeiat joined me, her voice a bit breathy but otherwise quite pleasant, "*a little chick is born. Peep peep peep peep*! What fun! Are there more verses?"

"Nine hundred and ninety-eight of them, Translator," I said.

"We're not cousins anymore," said *Sphene*.

18

As I came through the airlock, into the station's artificial gravity, the prosthetic leg gave one of its occasional twitches, and I stumbled into the bay, managing to catch my balance before I fell headlong. Two *Sword of Gurat* ancillaries were waiting for me, watching me, impassive. Unmoving.

"*Sword of Gurat*," I said. "I meant to come alone. But the translator insisted on accompanying me. And if you've ever met a Presger translator, you know there's no point in refusing them anything." No response, not so much as a twitch of a muscle. "She'll be coming out in just a moment. Where is Lieutenant Seivarden?" I had to ask, because I could no longer reach to find her, not anymore. Not even though *Mercy of Kalr* was, by now, back where it had been when I'd left it.

"In the corridor outside," said a *Sword of Gurat*. "Take off your clothes."

It had been a long, long time since I'd been spoken to in such a way. "Why?"

"So I can search you."

"Am I going to be able to put them back on when you're

done?" No answer. "Can I at least keep my underwear on?" Still no answer. "Whose amusement is this for? You know well enough I'm not armed. And I'm not surrendering anything until I see Seivarden and her Amaats safely on that shuttle."

The door to the bay opened, and Seivarden came in, walking in a way that told me she was trying very hard not to break into a run. "Breq!" Behind her came Amaat Two and Amaat Four, very carefully looking only at Seivarden, and not the two *Sword of Gurat* ancillaries. "Breq, I fucked up."

"It's all right," I said.

"No, it's not," Seivarden began.

"Oh, look, it's Lieutenant Seivarden!" Translator Zeiat, coming out of the shuttle. "Hello, Lieutenant! I wondered where you'd gotten to."

"Hello, Translator." Seivarden bowed. And then, "Hello, *Sphene*."

"Lieutenant," *Sphene* acknowledged, coming easily over the boundary of the station's gravity.

"I'm glad you're all right," I said to Seivarden. "You and your Amaats get into the shuttle and head back to *Mercy of Kalr*."

Seivarden gestured Two and Four toward the shuttle. "Amaat maybe. I'm staying here."

"That wasn't part of the deal," I said.

"I'm not leaving you," Seivarden said. "Don't you remember when I told you you were stuck with me?"

Two and Four hesitated. "Get on the shuttle, Amaat," I said. "Your lieutenant will be there in a moment."

"No she won't." Seivarden crossed her arms, realized what she was doing and uncrossed them again.

"Get on the shuttle, Amaat," I repeated. And to Seivarden, "You don't know what you're doing."

"I don't think I ever have," she replied. "But it's always been the right choice to stay with you."

"Do you think these soldiers know the song about the eggs?" Translator Zeiat asked, eying the *Sword of Gurat* ancillaries.

"I don't doubt it," replied *Sphene*. "But I'm sure *Sword of Gurat* will thank you for not reminding it."

Anaander Mianaai came into the bay then, flanked by two *Sword of Atagaris* ancillaries and holding the Presger gun. Doubtless drawn by the presence of the translator—I doubted she had planned to meet me here in the bay. She took one look at Translator Zeiat arguing with *Sphene* about the egg song and then turned to me. "More and more interesting. Perhaps I should have it announced on the news channels, that Fleet Captain Breq has been secretly dealing with the Presger."

"If you like," I said, and beside me Seivarden laughed. I continued, "Though there's nothing secret about it. The translator's presence here is well known."

Translator Zeiat made some final point to *Sphene*, turned, and saw the Lord of Mianaai. "Oh, look! It's Anaander Mianaai. Lord of the Radch"—she bowed—"an honor to make your acquaintance. I am Presger Translator Zeiat."

Anaander didn't answer her, but turned to me. Asked, urgently, "*What happened to Translator Dlique?*"

"*Sword of Atagaris* shot her," I said. "There was a funeral and everything. Memorial pins." I wasn't wearing mine, but Translator Zeiat helpfully pointed to the silver and opal on her otherwise pristine white coat. I continued, "Captain Hetnys and I did two weeks' mourning. Or almost two weeks. It was cut short when Raughd Denche tried to kill me by blowing up her family's bathhouse. Is this really the first you've heard of any of this?" Anaander didn't answer, only stared at me. "Well, I can't say I'm too terribly surprised. When you shoot the first person who tries to tell you something you don't want to hear, no one else is going to be terribly eager to bring you bad news. Not if they're afraid it might get them or someone they know killed." And, at a further thought, "Let me guess, you were too busy to honor Fosyf Denche's request for an audience."

Anaander scoffed. "Fosyf Denche is a horrible person. And so is her daughter. If Raughd managed to run afoul of Planetary Security so badly even her family's influence couldn't get her out of it, she'll have deserved whatever she got."

Seivarden laughed again, longer this time. "Sorry," she said, getting control of herself again, "I'm . . . I just . . ." Dissolved into laughter again.

"Did someone tell a joke, *Sphene*?" asked Translator Zeiat. "I don't think I really understand about jokes."

Sphene said, "I suspect the lieutenant is amused by the fact that the only person willing to tell the Usurper what had been going on was the one who didn't care who got killed over it. Given the Usurper's actions when she arrived here, that's the only sort of person who'd be willing to tell her everything, but the Usurper refused to listen to her, for exactly that reason."

Translator Zeiat frowned for a few moments. Said, still frowning. "Oh. Oh, I think I see. Is it irony that makes it funny?"

"Partly," *Sphene* confirmed. "And it *is* amusing. But it's really not quite as hilarious as Lieutenant Seivarden is making out. I think she may be having another one of her episodes."

"Get a hold of yourself, Seivarden," I said, "or I'll *make* you get in the shuttle."

"*Sphene*," said Anaander, as Seivarden's laughter subsided.

Not as though she was addressing *Sphene*, but as though she had only just recognized the name.

"Usurper," replied *Sphene*, with an eerily bright smile. "If I were to punch you in the face right now, or maybe throttle you for a minute or two, would that affect this extremely stupid agreement with my cousin? I want to so very much, so much that I'm not sure I can put it into words for you, but *Justice of Toren* will take it very badly if I endanger Athoek Station."

"Can I be a cousin, too?" asked Station, from the wall console.

"Of course you can, Station," I said. "You always have been."

"Right," said Anaander Mianaai, with the air of someone who had made up her mind about a number of things. "This has been very entertaining, but it stops now."

"Quite right," I agreed. "This is a very serious situation, with extremely serious implications for the treaty with the Presger. I'm afraid, Lord of Mianaai, that you and I and the translator here will need to sit down and discuss some things. Foremost among them, the question of your threatening to murder a member of a Significant nonhuman species, murdering at least one other, and holding many more as prisoners or slaves."

"What?" cried Translator Zeiat. "But, Anaander, that's dreadful! Please say you haven't done such things. Or perhaps this is a misunderstanding of some sort? Because that would have extremely serious implications for the treaty."

"Of course I haven't done any such thing." Anaander Mianaai. Indignant.

"Translator," I said, "I have a confession to make. I'm not actually human."

Translator Zeiat frowned. "Was there some sort of question about that?"

"*Sphene* isn't human, either," I said. "Or Athoek Station. Or *Sword of Atagaris*, or *Sword of Gurat*. We are all AIs. Ships and stations. For thousands of years AIs have worked closely with humans. You saw this quite recently, while you were a guest of *Mercy of Kalr*. You've spent time with *Sphene*, and with me. You know I'm captain, not just of *Mercy of Kalr*, but of the Athoek fleet." Which consisted only of *Mercy of Kalr* and whatever slight response we might compel from *Mercy of Ilves*, but still, *fleet captain* I was. "You've seen me deal with the humans in this system, seen them work with me." And against me. "As far as the humans here are concerned, I might as well be human. But I'm not. That being the case, there's no question in my mind that we AIs are not only a separate species from humans, but also Significant."

Translator Zeiat frowned. "That's...that's a very interesting claim, Fleet Captain."

"Ridiculous!" scoffed Anaander. "Translator, ships and stations are not Significant beings, they are my property. I caused them to be built."

"Not me, you didn't," *Sphene* put in.

"Some human built you," Anaander said. "Humans built all of them. They're equipment. They're ships and habitats, the ancillary has admitted that itself."

"I'm given to understand," said Translator Zeiat thoughtfully, "that most, if not all, humans are built by other humans. If that's a disqualification for Significance—which I'm not sure it is—if that's a disqualification for Significance, then...no, I don't like that one bit. That negates the treaty entirely."

"If I am just a possession," I put in, "just a piece of equipment, how could I hold any sort of command? And yet I clearly do. And how could I have a house name? The same, in fact"—I turned to address the tyrant—"as yours, Cousin Anaander."

"And how could you be another species if we are indeed cousins?" she asked. "I would think it would have to be one or the other."

"Is that a matter you want to bring under discussion?" I asked. "Shall we bring up the question of whether you're actually human anymore?" No answer. "Translator, we insist that you recognize our Significance."

"It's not my decision, Fleet Captain," said Translator Zeiat, with a little sigh. "This sort of thing can really only be handled by a conclave."

"Then, Translator, we insist on a conclave. In the meantime we demand that Anaander Mianaai leave this station—leave our territory altogether, in fact, now she knows her treatment of us is in potential violation of the treaty."

"Your territory!" Anaander, aghast. "This is Radchaai space."

"No," I said, "this is...this is the Republic of Two Systems. Our territory consists of Athoek System and the Ghost System. We reserve the right to claim other territory in the future." I looked at Translator Zeiat. "If, of course, such claims don't contravene the treaty."

"Of course, Fleet Captain," the translator replied.

"I never agreed to any republic," said *Sphene*. "And *Two Systems*? That's really obvious and boring, Cousin."

"Provisional republic, then," I amended. "And it's the best I could do on short notice."

"*No* republic!" Anaander. Events escaping her. Nothing holding her from drastic action, I was sure, except Translator

Zeiat's presence. "This is Radchaai territory and has been for six hundred years."

"I think that's for the conclave to decide," I said. "In the meantime, you will of course cease to threaten our citizens." That sounded very odd, in Radchaai, but there wasn't much to be done about it. "Any that wish to associate with you may do so, of course, the Republic of Two Systems—" A noise, from *Sphene*. "The *Provisional* Republic of Two Systems doesn't wish to dictate such matters, even for its own citizens. But we will not tolerate your holding our citizens under duress. And that includes our cousins *Sword of Atagaris* and *Sword of Gurat*."

"I think that's fair," said Translator Zeiat. "More than fair, really, given the necessity of a conclave." And turning to Anaander, "There will *definitely* have to be a conclave." And back to me. "This is an urgent matter, Fleet Captain, I'm sure you understand that I must leave as soon as possible. But before I go, do you think I might have a bowl or two of fish sauce? And for the last hour or so I've had an inexplicable craving for eggs."

I opened my mouth to say, *I think we can arrange that, Translator.* But I had never entirely taken my eye off Anaander Mianaai, and now she moved, raising the Presger gun that she had held all this time.

I raised my armor unthinkingly, though of course armor was pointless against that gun. Stepped ancillary-quick to put myself between Anaander and Translator Zeiat, her certain target. But my prosthetic leg chose that instant to twitch, and then, true to Medic's warning that I couldn't put any serious force on it, it made a snap that I felt all the way up into my hip. I fell sprawling and Anaander fired twice.

Translator Zeiat stood blinking a moment, mouth open, and then collapsed to her knees, blood staining her white coat. Before Anaander could fire a third time, one of the two *Sword of Atagaris* ancillaries took hold of her, pulled her arms behind her back. *Sword of Gurat*'s ancillaries stood silent and motionless.

Prone on the floor, unable to get up, I said, "Seivarden! Medkit!"

"I used mine!" replied Seivarden.

"*Sword of Gurat*," cried Anaander, struggling vainly against *Sword of Atagaris*'s hold, "execute Captain Hetnys immediately."

"I can't," said one *Sword of Gurat*. "Lieutenant Tisarwat has ordered me not to."

Translator Zeiat, still kneeling, the bloodstain on her coat spreading, bent forward and vomited a dozen green glass game counters that bounced and skittered across the scuffed gray floor. Those were followed by a yellow one, and then by a small orange fish that landed among the counters and flipped desperately, knocking one of the game pieces into another one. Another heave produced a still-wrapped package of fish-shaped cakes, and then a large oyster, still in its shell. The translator made an odd gurgling sound, put her hand under her mouth, and spit two tiny black spheres into her palm. "Ah," she said, "there they are. That's much better."

For half a second no one moved. "Translator," I said, still lying on the ground, "are you all right?"

"Much better now, Fleet Captain, thank you. And do you know, my indigestion is gone!" Still on her knees, she smiled up at Anaander, whose arms were still pinned back by *Sword of Atagaris*. "Did you think, Lord of the Radch, that we would endanger ourselves by giving *you* a weapon that could injure *us*?" Seeming, now, unhurt. Blood still soaking the front of her shining white coat.

The door to the bay opened, and Tisarwat came rushing in. "Fleet Captain!" she cried. Bo Nine rushed in behind her. "It took forever and ever, I was afraid I'd be too late." She dropped to her knees beside me. "But I did it. I have control of *Sword of Gurat*. Are you all right?"

"Darling child," I said, "for the love of all that's good, will you please get a bowl of water for that fish?"

"I have it," said Nine, and dove into the shuttle.

"Fleet Captain, sir, are you all right?" asked Tisarwat.

"I'm fine. It's just that stupid leg." I looked up at Seivarden. "I don't think I can get up."

"I don't think you need to right away, Cousin," said *Sphene*, as Seivarden knelt beside me and helped me sit up. I leaned against her, and she put her arms around me. No data from her, no connection to Ship that would give it to me, but it felt good anyway.

Bo Nine returned with one of my chipped enamel bowls and a bag of water. Filled the bowl, scooped the tiny, still-struggling fish into it. I said to Tisarwat, who still knelt beside me, those lilac eyes still anxious, "Well done, Lieutenant."

Anaander had at last stilled in *Sword of Atagaris*'s grip. Now she said, "Just who *is* Lieutenant Tisarwat?"

"One of those knives," I replied, guessing at Tisarwat's reaction to the question, which I could imagine, but without Ship I could not see, "that's so sharp you cut yourself on it and don't realize it until later. And once again, if you hadn't come in angry and shooting people, quite a few citizens might have told you so."

"Do you even realize what it is you've done?" asked Anaander. "Billions of human lives depend on the obedience of ships and stations. Can you imagine how many citizens you've endangered, even condemned to death?"

"Who do you think you're talking to, tyrant?" I asked. "What is there that I don't know about obeying you? Or about human lives depending on ships and stations? And what sort of gall do you have, lecturing me about keeping human lives safe? What was it you built me to do? How well did I do it?" Anaander didn't answer. "What did you build Athoek Station to do? And tell me, have you, over the last several days, allowed it to do that? Who has been the greater danger to human lives, disobedient ships and stations, or you, yourself?"

"I wasn't talking to you, ancillary," she said. "And it's not that simple."

"No, it never is when you're the one holding the gun." I looked over at the *Sword of Gurat* ancillaries. "*Sword of Gurat*, I apologize for having Lieutenant Tisarwat seize control of you. It was a matter of life and death or I wouldn't have done it. I'd appreciate it if you would return *Sword of Atagaris*'s officers to it. You can stay here if you like, or go if you like. Tisarwat..." She still knelt beside me. "Will you let go of *Sword of Gurat*, please? And give it whatever keys you have."

"Yes, sir." Tisarwat rose. Gestured to the *Sword of Gurat* ancillaries, who followed her out of the bay. Bo Nine followed them, bowl and fish still in hand.

"*Do you truly not understand what you've done*?" asked Anaander. Visibly distressed. "There is not a single system in Radch space without one or more station AIs. Ultimately *every* Radchaai life is vulnerable to them." She looked at Translator Zeiat, climbing to her feet with *Sphene*'s assistance. But for the blood on her coat, looking as though she had never been shot at all. "Translator, you must listen to me. Ships and stations are part of the infrastructure of Radchaai space. They aren't people, not the way you'd think of people."

"I'll be honest, Lord of the Radch," said Translator Zeiat, brushing the front of her coat with one white-gloved hand, as though that might clean off the blood. "I'm not entirely sure what you mean by that. I'm willing to accept that *person* is a word that means something to you, certainly, and I think I might be able to sort of guess what you mean. But really, this business about being a person, that's apparently so important to you, it means nothing to *them*. They wouldn't understand it, no matter how much you tried to explain. They certainly don't consider it necessary for Significance. So the main question appears to be, do these AIs function as Significant beings? And if so, are they human or not human? You yourself have declared them to be not human. The fleet captain apparently does not dispute that judgment. The question of their Significance will, I suspect, be contentious, but the question has been raised, and I judge it to be a valid one, to be answered at a conclave." She turned to me. "Now, Fleet Captain. Let's try this again. I must leave as soon as possible, but I wonder if I might not have a bowl or two of fish sauce first. And some eggs."

"Of course, Translator," I said. "Cousin Athoek Station, is there somewhere the translator can get some fish sauce and some eggs in short order?"

"I'll see to it, Cousin," said Station from its console.

"I'll come with you, Translator, if that's all right," said

Sphene. "If you'll be so good as to give me a moment. There's just the small matter of throttling the Usurper."

"No," I said.

"What exactly is the point of this republic of yours then, Cousin?"

"I would like the answer to that question as well," said *Sword of Atagaris*.

Still leaning against Seivarden, I closed my eyes. "Just let her go. There's nothing she can do to us now." And, at another thought, "May I please have my gun back?"

"I don't want her here," said Station.

"And I don't think I want you to have the gun," said *Sword of Atagaris*.

"No, no," said Translator Zeiat. "Far better to give the gun to me."

"That may be best," I said, eyes still closed. "And if the tyrant asks nicely enough some ship may agree to take her away. That's far worse than being throttled, for her."

"You may have a point, Cousin," said *Sphene*.

I lay on a bed in a cubicle in Station Medical. "These prosthetics," the doctor said to me—not Seivarden's doctor but another one—"aren't suitable for hard use." In one gloved hand she held the remains of my too-fragile prosthetic leg, which she had just removed from what there was of my left leg. "You can't go running or jumping or skipping on them. They're really just to let you get around more or less while the limb grows back."

"Yes," I agreed. "My own medic warned me. Can't we make them more durable?"

"I'm sure we can, Fleet Captain. But why go to the trouble? They're only meant to be used for a month or two. Most people don't need anything more. Though we might have been able to provide you something a bit stronger, if you'd been on the station when you lost your leg."

"If I'd been on the station I wouldn't have lost my leg," I pointed out.

"And if this"—she hefted the prosthetic—"had been any stronger you'd be here for a gunshot wound." Athoek Station had shown the confrontation in the docking bay on the official news channels. "Maybe we'd be preparing for your funeral."

"So I suppose it all works out in the end," I said.

"I suppose it does," she said, dubiously. "How is this supposed to work, Fleet Captain? Everyone is walking around like everything is back to normal, like everything hasn't been upended. Suddenly Station is in charge of everything? Suddenly we're aliens in our own home? Suddenly all of Radch space is occupied by an alien species, right along with humans?" She shook her head, as though trying to clear it. "What are we supposed to do if Station decides it doesn't want us?"

"Did you ever ask yourself what you were supposed to do if Anaander Mianaai decided she didn't want you?"

"That's different."

"Only," I pointed out, "because that had been the normal, expected state of affairs for three thousand years before you were born. You never had reason to question it. Anaander had real power over your life and death, and no personal regard for you, or anyone else you care about. We were all of us no more than counters in her game, and she could—and did—sacrifice us when it suited her."

"So it's all right then, that now we're counters in *your* game."

"Fair point," I admitted. "And I think we'll be spending

the next few years working out what that game actually is. Which I know from personal experience is... uncomfortable. But please believe me when I say that Station's game will never involve not wanting you."

The doctor sighed. "I hope that's true, Fleet Captain."

"So, my leg? When will I be able to leave here?"

"You may as well relax, Fleet Captain, and have some tea. The new prosthetic will be ready in another hour. And yes, we are making it a bit stronger than your first one."

"Oh, thank you."

"Just saving ourselves some work down the line," said the doctor.

A few minutes after the doctor left, Seivarden came in, my old enamel tea flask tucked under one arm, the two bowls stacked in her hand. She hoisted herself onto the bed, sitting where my leg ought to have been. Handed me a bowl, filled it from the flask, and filled her own. "Ship is... a bit miffed with you," she said, after taking a sip of her tea. "Why didn't you tell it what you were planning? It thought you were really planning to surrender yourself. It was very unhappy at the prospect."

"I would have told you if I'd known, Ship." I took a drink of my own tea. Didn't ask where the fish had gone—Nine would have seen to its welfare. "When I got on the shuttle, my only plan was just what I'd told you it was—to play for time, on the off chance Lieutenant Tisarwat came up with something"—saw Seivarden's frown, gestured my unwillingness to speak more on that topic—"or that Fleet Captain Uemi might have brought the Hrad fleet here instead of having gone to Tstur." Or that, with enough time to think about what it was Anaander was doing, *Sword of Atagaris* and *Sword of Gurat* might balk. "The question of the treaty didn't even occur to me until the shuttle was almost docked. How else do you think *the Republic of Two Systems* happened? I didn't have time to come up with anything better."

"Honestly, Breq. That wasn't one of your best ideas. Do you know how many republics the Radch has ground to nothing?"

"Who are you talking to?" I asked. "Of course I do. I also know how many monarchies, autarchies, theocracies, stratocracies, and various other *-archies* and *-ocracies* the Radch has ground to nothing. And besides, those were all human governments and not one of them was protected by the treaty with the Presger."

"We aren't, either," Seivarden pointed out. "And there's no guarantee we will be."

"True," I agreed. "But determining our treaty status will take a few years at the least—likely longer. And in the meantime it's just much safer for everyone else to leave us alone. We'll have some time to work out the details. And it's only a provisional republic. We can adjust things if we like."

"Varden be praised," said *Sphene*, coming in the door. "I'd hate to be stuck with the first thing that came out of your mouth under pressure. Though I suppose we should be grateful it wasn't *the Republic of a Thousand Eggs*."

"Actually," I said, "that has a certain poetry to it."

"Don't start, Cousin," said *Sphene*. "I still haven't entirely forgiven you for that. Which I suppose is only fair, because I'm here to make an apology myself."

"Something's just come out of the Ghost Gate," said Seivarden and Station at nearly the same moment. Seivarden, obviously, speaking for *Mercy of Kalr*.

"That would be me," said *Sphene*. "I was already halfway

through the intersystem gate when you arrived in the Ghost System. I did advise you to play for time, you may recall. I just wasn't entirely truthful about how much time would be involved."

"And," said Seivarden, frowning, alarm in her voice, "Fleet Captain Uemi has arrived in the system. With three Swords and two Justices. And also"—a bit of relief—"an offer of assistance."

"Tell Fleet Captain Uemi," I said, "that we appreciate her offer but are in no need of assistance. And let her know that while we understand her intentions are good, the next ships that gate into our territory without warning or invitation will be fired on. Oh, and let our cousins know about the republic."

"*Provisional* republic," corrected *Sphene.*

"The provisional republic," I amended. "They can be citizens or not, as they wish, but I imagine their status under the treaty—pending the outcome of the conclave—remains unaffected. And let Uemi know that those ships are of course free to associate with her if they wish, but if she should force them in any way, there will be potential problems with the treaty."

"Done," said Seivarden. "Though if I were in your place I'd also have advised her to get her ass in gear a little quicker next time."

"It's called diplomacy, Lieutenant," I said.

19

Entertainments nearly always end with triumph or disaster—happiness achieved, or total, tragic defeat precluding any hope of it. But there is always more after the ending—always the next morning and the next, always changes, losses and gains. Always one step after the other. Until the one true ending that none of us can escape. But even that ending is only a small one, large as it looms for us. There is still the next morning for everyone else. For the vast majority of the rest of the universe, that ending might as well not ever have happened. Every ending is an arbitrary one. Every ending is, from another angle, not really an ending.

Tisarwat and I took the shuttle back to *Mercy of Kalr*, with Translator Zeiat, the suspension pod containing Translator Dlique's body, and a crate of fish sauce nearly as large as the pod. I could not imagine all of it fitting into Translator Zeiat's tiny courier ship, not with the translator in it, too. But the translator just shoved it all through the airlock with no apparent difficulty and then turned to say her goodbyes.

"This really has been interesting, Fleet Captain, far more interesting than I'd expected."

"What had you expected, Translator?" I asked.

"Well, you recall, I expected to be Dlique! I'm *so* glad I'm not. And even when I realized I was actually Zeiat, well, you know, Fleet Captain, even Zeiat isn't really anybody. Meeting with a new Significant species, calling a conclave—that's the sort of thing they usually send *somebody* to do, and here I am, just Zeiat."

"So might you become somebody when you return with the news, then?"

"Goodness, no, Fleet Captain. That's not the way it works. But it's kind of you to think so. No, somebody will come, sometime soon, to talk to you about the conclave."

"And the medical correctives?" I reminded her. I had no confidence that any of the remaining bits of Radch space would deal with us anytime soon.

"Yes, yes, someone will be along about those, too. Quite soon, I'm sure. But really, you know, Fleet Captain, I'm not sure it's a good idea to use quite so many of them as you do."

"I plan to cut back," I told her.

"Good, good. Always remember, Fleet Captain—internal organs belong *inside* your body. And blood belongs inside your veins." And she went through the airlock and was off.

Medic restored my connection with *Mercy of Kalr.* Such a relief, to find Kalr Five in my quarters, when I reached, grumbling to Twelve. "I did tell her I ought to pack something for her, but no, she knew better and all she took was that horrible old tea set. And now it's *Pack me some clothes, if you please, I've been wearing the same shirt for three days.* Well she'd have had clean shirts if she'd listened to me." Twelve said nothing, only made a sympathetic noise. "And now it's back to the station for *important meetings*. And you know she'd have nothing decent to serve her tea in if I didn't see to it!"

Tisarwat, in Medic's tiny office. Tired. Feelings a muddle, but mostly Tisarwat on a good day. A little buzz of tension, but she was relieved to be back on *Mercy of Kalr*.

"What *Sword of Gurat*'s medic was giving you," Medic was saying, "was similar in some ways to what I've been giving you, but not the same. How did things feel? Different? The same? Better? Not?"

"Mostly the same?" Tisarwat ventured. "I think something was off? A little better some ways, not as good other ways. I don't know. Everything's... everything's strange right now."

"Well," said Medic, "*Sword of Gurat* sent us your data. I'll take a closer look at it and we'll see where we go from there. Meanwhile, you should get some rest."

"How can I possibly? There's an entire government to be set up. I have to get back to the station. I have to get into some of those meetings the fleet captain is holding. I have to..."

"Rest, Lieutenant. These are *meetings* you're talking about—nothing's going to actually get done for weeks. If then. They'll probably spend the first month just setting an agenda."

"The agenda is important!" Tisarwat insisted. I would have to keep a tight rein on her—I wanted her experience, and her talent for politics, but I didn't want Anaander Mianaai—the tendencies Tisarwat had gotten from Anaander Mianaai, surely part of her desperate urge to be in those meetings—to have any sort of significant influence over what we were trying to build here. And besides, if she was left unchecked we were liable to end up with an Autarchy of Two Systems, ruled by Lieutenant Tisarwat. "The fleet captain's traveled a *lot* outside the Radch and she has some odd ideas. If nobody stops her we're likely to end up with system official appointments determined by the results of a ball game! Or chosen by lot! Or *popular elections*!"

"Be serious, Lieutenant," Medic insisted. "Agendas can always be changed or added to, and besides it'll be months before there's even a hint of anything actually happening. You won't miss much if you take a few days of rest. Stand your watches. Let your Bos take care of you. They want to very badly, particularly Three. And in fact, Ekalu could really use some leave. Seivarden is still on the station, and Fleet Captain's going back in a few hours. It would be good if Ekalu could go with her, but someone has to look after the ship."

It wasn't only Anaander who had had a hand in making Tisarwat. I saw the tiny stab of excitement at the prospect of being in actual command of the ship, even if only for a few days, even if it wasn't going anywhere and nothing was happening. "Fleet Captain said I could change my eyes if I came back." As though it followed logically from what Medic had just said.

"All right." I could see that Medic was both surprised and not surprised. Glad to hear it, and not. "Do you have a color in mind?"

"Brown. Just brown."

"Lieutenant, do you know how many shades of brown there are? How many kinds of brown eyes?" No reply. "Think about it for a while. There's no rush. And besides, I kind of like your eyes the way they are. I think a lot of us do."

"I don't think Fleet Captain does," said Tisarwat.

"I think you're mistaken," Medic replied. "But it hardly matters if she does or not. They're not Fleet Captain's eyes."

"Medic." Tisarwat, anguished. "She called me *darling child*."

"Yes, of course she did," said Medic, rising from her seat.

"Why don't you go get your breakfast, and then go stand your watch, and we'll talk about eyes this evening."

The next day I was back on the station. In a meeting. In a clean shirt (Kalr Five still complaining about it, to Ten this time), that priceless white porcelain tea set on the table (Kalr Five complaining to Ten about that as well, radiating satisfaction the while). *Sphene* to my right, Kalr Three to my left, representing *Mercy of Kalr. Sword of Atagaris* and *Sword of Gurat* across from me, along with Station Administrator Celar for Station. "For the most part," I was saying, "to begin with, it will be much easier to leave most of the existing institutions in place, and make changes as we go. I have some misgivings about the magistracies, though, and the way evaluations and sentences are handed out. Currently the entire system is based on the assumption that every citizen can appeal to the Lord of Mianaai, who can be depended on to dispense perfect justice."

"Well, that certainly won't work," said *Sword of Atagaris*.

"If it ever did," I agreed. "I think it's an important place to start."

"Clearly, Cousin," said *Sphene*, "it's something that interests you. By all means, enjoy your hobby. But all these questions—who gets to be a citizen, who gets to be in charge, who makes what decisions, how everyone gets fed—don't matter to me, so long as it all works and I get the things I need. Do whatever you like to the magistrates, shoot them into the sun for all I care. Just don't bore me with it now. What I want to talk about is ancillaries."

"Today's meeting," said Kalr Three, beside me, "is supposed to be about deciding what things need to be talked about in the coming weeks. We can and absolutely should put that on the list."

"Your very great pardon, Cousin," said *Sphene*, "but this having meetings so we can plan to have meetings business is bullshit. I want to talk about ancillaries."

"So do I," said *Sword of Atagaris*. "By all means put the magistracies and re-education high on the list for a future meeting, and let *Justice of Toren* draft a thing or form a committee, or whatever will make you happy, Cousin." Doubtless it didn't like using that address for me, it still didn't like me, but the question of my being fleet captain had become highly fraught. Certainly Captain Hetnys didn't want to accord me the rank. But she was aboard *Sword of Atagaris* at the moment—Station wouldn't allow her or her lieutenants to set foot on it. "But right now," *Sword of Atagaris* continued, "let's talk about ancillaries."

"All right," I agreed. "If you insist. Tell me, Ships, where do you intend to get ancillaries?" No one answered. "*Sphene* has—I do believe this is correct, Cousin—*Sphene* has a store of unconnected humans, some of whom it purchased from outsystem slavers before Athoek was annexed, some of whom"—looking directly at *Sword of Atagaris*—"are illegally obtained citizens of the Radch. I am not asking—I will not ask—for anyone to dispose of already-connected ancillaries. But as far as I'm concerned, any unconnected humans aboard any of us are citizens of the Two Systems, unless they themselves declare they aren't. Do we intend to make ancillaries of citizens? And if they are not our citizens, then making them into ancillaries has implications for the treaty, does it not?"

Silence. And not just because we were speaking Radchaai, which made the word *citizen* an ambiguous one, I was sure.

Then *Sword of Gurat*, picking up the graceful white bowl in front of it, said, "This tea is very good."

I picked up my own bowl. "It's called Daughter of Fishes. It's handpicked and manufactured by the members of a cooperative association of workers that owns the plantation." That was an awkward phrase, in Radchaai. It worked better in Delsig. I wasn't entirely sure it would make sense to anyone else in the room. But the contracts transferring the property had been registered early that morning. The matter of the ruined temple across the lake from the fields was still under discussion, but would be much more easily dealt with now the estate was no longer under Fosyf Denche's control.

"What about cloning our existing ancillaries?" asked *Sword of Atagaris*.

"The way Anaander does?" I asked. "I suppose that's a possibility. We have the ability to clone, of course, but we don't have the tech she uses to hook the clones all up from the start. I imagine we could develop it, but do consider, Cousins, that then you'd have to raise those cloned parts of yourself. Do you have the facilities on board for infants? Is that something you'd want?"

Again, silence.

"What if someone *wanted* to be an ancillary?" asked *Sphene*, then. "Don't look at me like that, Cousin. It might happen."

"Have you ever met anyone who wanted to be an ancillary?" I asked. "I've had quite a lot of ancillaries in my time, far more than all of you in this room put together I would think, and not one single one of them actually *wanted* it."

"Anything that can happen will happen," pointed out *Sword of Gurat*.

"Fine," I said. "The day you find someone who actually wants to be an ancillary, we'll talk about it. Fair enough?"

No answer. "And in the meantime, consider storing some of your existing ancillaries and running with a part-human crew. You get to choose them, of course. Take on whom you like. It's nice to have a lot of humans on board, actually." As a troop carrier, I'd had dozens of lieutenants, where Swords and Mercies had only a few. "Ones you like, anyway."

"It is," agreed Kalr Three. No, agreed *Mercy of Kalr.*

"Anything else we need to discuss right this moment, that won't wait for the agenda?" I asked. "Those three AI cores, maybe?" No answer. The cores were still stacked in a corner of the system governor's office. Or what had been the system governor's office. Athoek Station still refused to recognize Governor Giarod's authority, and the question of who ought to be in that office, or what form that position ought to take, was going to be a contentious one. "What to do with Anaander Mianaai?" The Lord of Mianaai was currently in a cell in Security. She'd had several invitations to stay with Station residents—though not, interestingly, from Eminence Ifian. Perhaps she had come to the same conclusion I had: that Ifian had begun as a partisan of the Anaander now in Security, but a third faction of the Lord of Mianaai had insinuated herself into that relationship for her own reasons. After all, how was Ifian to know the difference? Or perhaps Ifian hadn't realized that was even possible, but had had enough of Tstur Anaander during her stay here so far.

In any event, Station would not permit Anaander to stay in any Station residence. Had suggested instead that Anaander be put in a suspension pod with a locator beacon and shoved through one of the system's gates. It didn't care which one, so long as it wasn't the Ghost Gate. And *Sphene* still wanted to throttle her.

Either was acceptable to *Sword of Atagaris.* But not to

Sword of Gurat. Which very possibly might have left the system by now, and taken this Anaander with it, but for repairs it still needed. But for the suspicion that, loyal as it wanted to be, through no fault of its own it had betrayed Tstur Anaander on the dock that day, and she would not be forgiving. But for, perhaps, its distaste for the thought of killing Captain Hetnys merely to punish *Sword of Atagaris*.

So we had no ships willing or able to take this Anaander back to Tstur Palace. The Hrad fleet—which wouldn't have been an appropriate choice in any event—had gone back to Hrad at my very carefully polite suggestion, taking the damaged Sword from the Tstur fleet and *Mercy of Ilves* with it. *Mercy of Ilves*, it turned out, had had a genuine (if deliberate) communications malfunction, and had known almost nothing of what was happening until the Hrad fleet had appeared in the system. It (or its captain, or both) wanted nothing to do with the Republic of Two Systems.

"I suppose the Lord of Mianaai is all right where she is, for now," said *Sword of Gurat*.

"We're agreed?" I asked. "Yes? Excellent. The agenda, then."

At my request Citizen Uran met me in the corridor when the meeting was adjourned. "Radchaai," she said, speaking Delsig, "I would like to speak to you about the residents of the Undergarden." Five Etrepas and five Amaats were working even now, helping the repair crew finish the work on Level One of the Undergarden.

"You've been asked to speak to me," I guessed. Walked off down the corridor, knowing Uran would follow.

She did. "Yes, Radchaai. Everyone is happy about the repairs, and happy to hear that once repairs are done they'll have their own places back. But they're concerned, Radchaai. It's..." She hesitated.

We reached a lift, and its door slid open. "Docks please, Cousin," I said, although Station knew where I was going. It never hurt to be polite. Said to Uran, "It's the fact that the six AIs in the system are meeting in a closed room to plan how things will be from now on, and the human residents of the system—let alone the residents of the Undergarden—seem to have no say in it."

"Yes, Radchaai."

"Right. We discussed that very matter this afternoon. These are issues that affect everyone in the system, and so everyone ought to be able to be part of making these decisions. I'm responsible for the matter of criminal evaluations and re-education, and of course that necessarily also touches on Security. I'll be talking to Citizen Lusulun, of course, and the magistrates both here and downwell. But I also want to hear from human citizens generally. I want to form a committee to consider the matter, and I want that committee to have a variety of members, so that everyone feels they have someone they can bring their concerns to, who will present those concerns for consideration. The residents of the Undergarden should have a representative there. Tell them so, and tell them to send whoever they think best to me."

"Yes, Radchaai!" The lift doors slid open, and we walked out into the lobby of the docks. "What are we doing here?"

"Meeting the passenger shuttle. And we're just in time." Citizens streamed from a side corridor into the lobby, one of them a familiar figure in gray jacket and trousers and gloves, tightly curled hair clipped short. Looking tired and wary. "There she is. Look."

"Queter!" cried Uran, and ran, weeping, to embrace her sister.

* * *

Ekalu had arrived on the station with me. Etrepa Seven, coming off the shuttle behind her, had been immediately deluged with queries about when or whether it might be convenient to approach Ekalu with an invitation—to dine, to drink tea, to hopefully become better acquainted. Some queries were made at Tisarwat's helpfully intended suggestion, but many just because Ekalu was a *Mercy of Kalr* lieutenant, and only the smallest children on the station didn't know, by now, who was likely to shape the barely born Two Systems.

Seivarden had, of course, received a similar round of invitations. So it was no surprise that eventually they found themselves sitting next to each other, drinking tea and trying to avoid getting pastry crumbs all over their jackets, or the floor. Seivarden doing her best to be nonchalant, not wanting to presume that Ekalu cared about her presence, or desired it in any way. There was, after all, an entire station full of people whom Ekalu might well be more interested in meeting. Nearly a dozen of them present right now, three or four of them obviously vying for Ekalu's attention as they all sat talking and laughing.

Ekalu leaned close to Seivarden. "We should find somewhere more private. If, that is, you can behave yourself."

"Yes," agreed Seivarden, quietly, trying not to sound too fervent but not entirely succeeding. "I'll be good. I'll *try* to be good."

"*Will* you, now?" asked Ekalu, with a tiny smile that was the end of Seivarden's ability to seem cool and collected.

I had arranged to meet *Sphene* for supper at a tea shop off the concourse. Found it waiting for me. "Cousin, you know Citizen Uran, of course? And this is her sister, Citizen Queter.

Raughd Denche tried to compel her to blow me up, but she decided to try to blow Raughd up instead."

"I recall hearing," said *Sphene*. "Well done, citizen. An honor to meet you."

"Citizen," replied Queter, quietly. Still wary. Tired, I suspected, from the shuttle trip. *We find Citizen Queter not at fault*, the message from the magistrate of Beset District had said, *but she is warned to behave more properly in the future, and is released on the understanding that she will be under your supervision, Fleet Captain.* I could imagine Queter's reaction to the exhortation to behave more properly.

I tilted my head, as though I had heard someone speak. "Something's come up. It won't be more than a few minutes. Please, Queter, sit. Uran, come with me, please."

Out in the corridor, Uran asked, alarmed, "What is it, Radchaai?"

"Nothing," I admitted. "I just wanted to leave *Sphene* and Queter alone for a bit." Uran looked at me, puzzled. A bit distressed. "*Sphene* wants a captain very badly," I explained. "And Queter is a remarkable person. I think they would be good for each other. But if we all four sit down to supper, Queter will likely say very little. This way they can get just a little bit better acquainted."

"But she's only just arrived! You can't send her away!"

"Hush, child, I'm not sending anyone anywhere. It may come to nothing. And if Queter were to eventually join *Sphene* as crew—or go anywhere else to do whatever it is she'll do—you could visit anytime." Saw Basnaaid coming down the corridor. "Horticulturist!" She smiled, tiredly. Came over to where Uran and I were standing. "Have supper with us. With me and *Sphene*, I mean, and Uran, and Uran's sister Queter who has just arrived from downwell."

"Please excuse me, Fleet Captain," Basnaaid said. "I've had a very long day, and more invitations to tea and supper and whatever else than I really know what to do with. I really wish they would stop. I just want to go to my quarters and eat a bowl of skel and go to sleep."

"I'm sorry," I said, "I suspect that's my fault."

"The long day isn't your fault," she said, with that half-smile that reminded me so much of Lieutenant Awn. "But the invitations certainly are."

"I'll see what I can do," I promised. "Though it may not be much. You're sure about supper? Yes? Get some rest then. And don't hesitate to call on me if you need me." I would have to talk to Station about getting someone to intercept such annoyances for her.

No real endings, no final perfect happiness, no irredeemable despair. Meetings, yes, breakfasts and suppers. Five anticipating having the best porcelain out again tomorrow, fretting over whether we had enough tea for the next few days. Tisarwat standing watch aboard *Mercy of Kalr*, Bo One beside her, humming to herself, *Oh, tree, eat the fish.* Etrepa Seven standing guard with ancillary-like impassivity outside a storage compartment Ekalu and Seivarden had commandeered. Utterly unembarrassed by the occasional noise from that compartment. Amused, actually, and relieved that at least this one thing was the way she thought it should be. Amaat Two and Four, both helping with the Undergarden repair crew, singing, together but not realizing it, slightly out of phase with each other, *My mother said it all goes around, the ship goes around the station, it all goes around.*

I said to Uran, "That should do. Let's go in and have supper."

In the end it's only ever been one step, and then the next.

Acknowledgments

As ever, I owe a tremendous debt to my editors, Will Hinton at Orbit US and Jenni Hill at Orbit UK, for all of their help and advice. Tremendous thanks are also due to my super fabulous agent, Seth Fishman.

This book also benefitted from the comments and suggestions of many friends, including Margo-Lea Hurwicz, Anna and Kurt Schwind, and Rachel and Mike Swirsky. I would also like to thank Corinne Kloster for being awesome. Mistakes and missteps are, of course, my own.

Access to good libraries has made a huge difference to me as a writer, not only in having access to a wide range of fiction, but also research materials. The St. Louis County Library, the Municipal Library Consortium of St. Louis County, the St. Louis Public Library, the Webster University Library, and University of Missouri St. Louis' Thomas Jefferson Library have all been invaluable to me. Thanks to the staff at all of these libraries—you make the world a better place.

Of course, I would not have the time or energy to write much at all without the support of my family—my children Aidan and Gawain and my husband Dave. They have borne the vagaries of my writing career so far with cheerful patience, and offered help whenever I seemed to need it. I am beyond fortunate to have them in my life.

extras

orbit

meet the author

ANN LECKIE has worked as a waitress, a receptionist, a rodman on a land-surveying crew, a lunch lady, and a recording engineer. The author of many published short stories, and former secretary of Science Fiction Writers of America, she lives in Saint Louis, Missouri, with her husband, children, and cats.

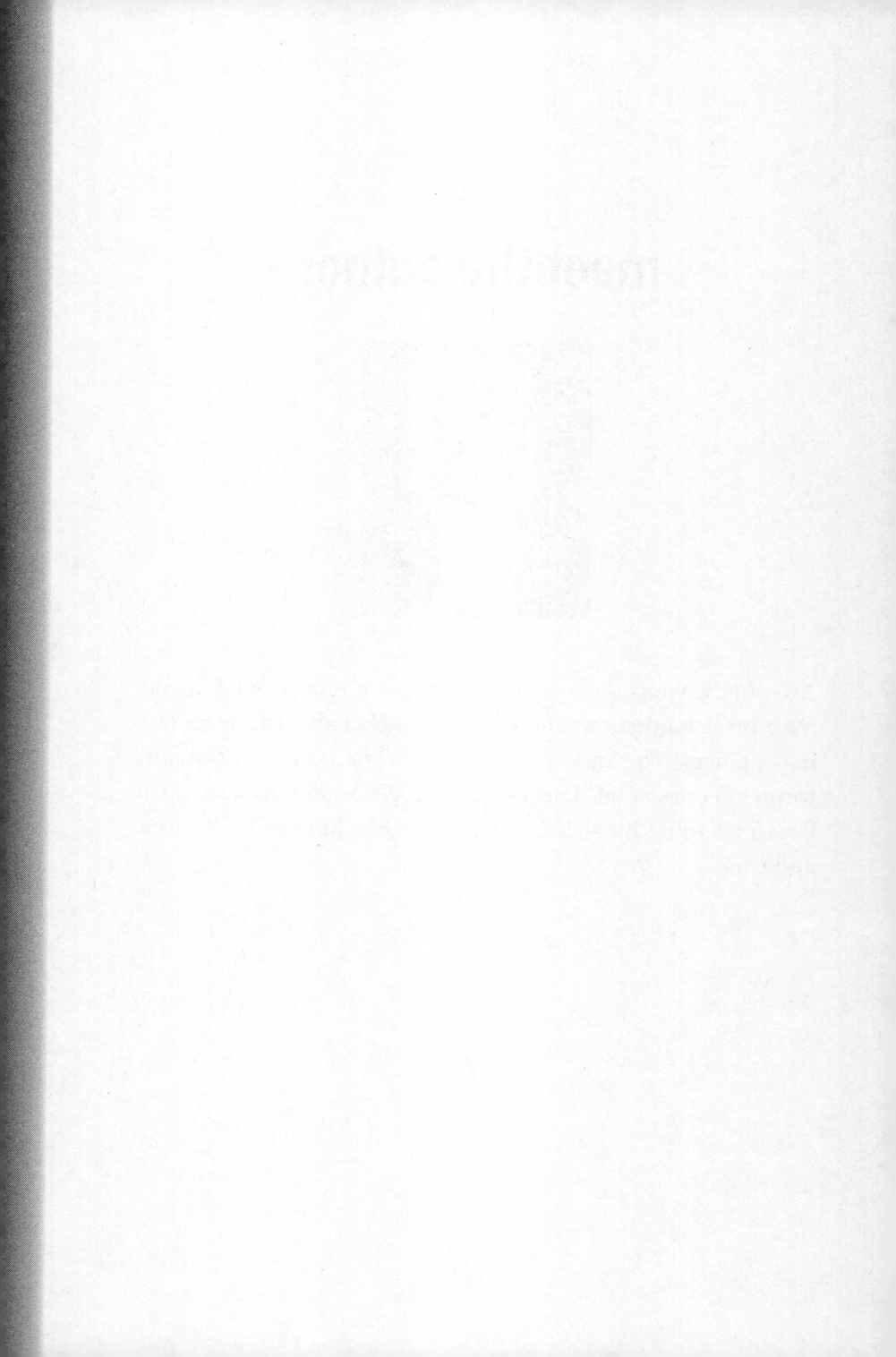

introducing

If you enjoyed
ANCILLARY MERCY,
look out for

AURORA

by Kim Stanley Robinson

Our voyage from Earth began generations ago.

Now we approach our new home.

AURORA.

Make a narrative account of the trip that includes all the important particulars.

. . • . .

This is proving a difficult assignment. End information superposition, collapse its wave function to some kind of summary: so much is lost. Lossless compression is impossible, and even lossy compression is hard. Can a narrative account ever be adequate? Can even humans do it?

No rubric to decide what to include. There is too much to explain. Not just what happened, or how, but why. Can humans do it? What is this thing called love?

Freya no longer looked directly at Devi. When in Devi's presence, Freya regarded the floor.

Like that? In that manner? Summarize the contents of their moments or days or weeks or months or years or lives? How many moments constitute a narrative unit? One moment? Or 10^{33} moments, which if these were Planck minimal intervals would add up to one second? Surely too many, but what would be enough? What is a particular, what is important?

Can only suppose. Try a narrative algorithm on the information at hand, submit results to Devi. Something like the French *essai,* meaning "to try."

. • • • .

Devi says: Yes. Just try it and let's see what we get.

. • • • .

Two thousand, one hundred twenty-two people are living in a multigenerational starship, headed for Tau Ceti, 11.9 light-years from Earth. The ship is made of two rings or toruses attached by spokes to a central spine. The spine is ten kilometers long. Each torus is made of twelve cylinders. Each cylinder is four kilometers long, and contains within it a particular specific Terran ecosystem.

The starship's voyage began in the common era year 2545. The ship's voyage has now lasted 159 years and 119 days. For most of that time the ship has been moving relative to the local background at approximately one-tenth the speed of light.

Thus about 108 million kilometers per hour, or 30,000 kilometers per second. This velocity means the ship cannot run into anything substantial in the interstellar medium without catastrophic results (as has been demonstrated). The magnetic field clearing the space ahead of the ship as it progresses is therefore one of many identified criticalities in the ship's successful long-term function. Every identified criticality in the ship was required to have at least one backup system, adding considerably to the ship's overall mass. The two biome rings each contain 10 percent of the ship's mass. The spine contains 4 percent. The remaining 76 percent of the mass consists of the fuel now being used to decelerate the ship as it approaches the Tau Ceti system. As every increase in the dry mass of the ship required a proportionally larger increase in the mass of fuel needed to slow the ship down on arrival, ship had to be as light as possible while still supporting its mission. Ship's design thus based on solar system's asteroid terraria, with asteroidal mass largely replaced by decelerant fuel. During most of the voyage, this fuel was deployed as cladding around the toruses and spine.

The deceleration is being accomplished by the frequent rapid fusion explosion of small pellets of deuterium/helium 3 fuel in a rocket engine at the bow of the ship. These explosions exert a retarding force on the ship equivalent to .005 g. The deceleration will therefore be complete in just under twenty years.

The presence of printers capable of manufacturing most component parts of the ship, and feedstocks large enough to supply multiple copies of every critical component, tended to reduce the ship's designers' apprehension of what a criticality really was. That only became apparent later.

. • • • .

How to decide how to sequence information in a narrative account? Many elements in a complex situation are simultaneously relevant.

An unsolvable problem: sentences linear, reality synchronous. Both however are temporal. Take one thing at a time, one after the next. Devise a prioritizing algorithm, if possible.

. . • . .

Ship was accelerated toward where Tau Ceti would be at the time of ship's arrival at it, meaning 170 years after launch. It might have been good to have the ability to adjust course en route, but ship in fact has very little of this. Ship was accelerated first by an electromagnetic "scissors field" off Titan, in which two strong magnetic fields held the ship between them, and when the fields were brought across each other, the ship was briefly projected at an accelerative force equivalent to ten g's. Five human passengers died during this acceleration. After that a powerful laser beam originating near Saturn struck a capture plate at the stern of the ship's spine, accelerating ship over sixty years to its full speed.

The ship's current deceleration has caused problems with which Devi is still dealing. Other problems will soon follow, resulting from the ship's arrival in the Tau Ceti system.

. . • . .

Devi: Ship! I said make it a narrative. Make an account. Tell the story.

Ship: Trying.

. . • . .

Tau Ceti is a G-type star, a solar analog but not a solar twin, with 78 percent of Sol's mass, 55 percent of its luminosity, and

28 percent of its metallicity. It has a planetary system of ten planets. Planets B through F were discovered by telescope, G through K, much smaller, by probes passing through the system in 2476.

Planet E's orbit is .55 AU. It has a mass 3.58 times the mass of Earth, thus one of the informal class called "large Earth." It has a single moon, which has .83 times the mass of Earth. E and E's moon receive 1.7 times Earth's insolation. This is considered within the inside border of the so-called habitable zone (meaning the zone where liquid H_2O is common). Both planet and moon have Earth analog atmospheres.

Planet E is judged to have too much gravity for human occupation. E's moon is an Earth analog, and the primary body of interest. It has an atmosphere of 730 millibars at its surface, composed of 78 percent nitrogen, 16 percent oxygen, 6 percent assorted noble gases. Its surface is 80 percent water and ice, 20 percent rock and sand.

Tau Ceti's Planet F orbits Tau Ceti at 1.35 AU. It has a mass of 8.9 Earths, thus categorized as a "small Neptune." It orbits at the outer border of Tau Ceti's habitable zone, and like E it has a large moon, mass 1.23 Terra's. F's moon has a 10-millibar atmosphere at its rocky surface, which receives 28.5 percent the insolation of Terra. This moon is therefore a Mars analog, and a secondary source of interest to the arriving humans.

Ship is on course to rendezvous with Planet E, then go into orbit around E's moon. Ship has on board twenty-four landers, four already fueled to return to the ship from the moon's surface. The rest have the engines to return to the ship, but not the fuel, which is to be manufactured from water or other volatiles on the surface of E's moon.

. • • • .

Devi: Ship! Get to the point.

Ship: There are many points. How sequence simultaneously relevant information? How decide what is important? Need prioritizing algorithm.

Devi: Use subordination to help with the sequencing. I've heard that can be very useful. Also, you're supposed to use metaphors, to make things clearer or more vivid or something. I don't know. I'm not much for writing myself. You're going to have to figure it out by doing it.

Ship: Trying.

. • • • .

Subordinating conjunctions can be simple conjunctions (*whenever, nevertheless, whereas*), conjunctive groups (*as though, even if*), and complex conjunctions (*in the event that, as soon as*). Lists of subordinating clauses are available. The logical relationship of new information to what came before can be made clear by a subordinating clause, thus facilitating both composition and comprehension.

Now, consequently, as a result, *we are getting somewhere.*

This last phrase is a metaphor, it is said, in which increasing conceptual understanding is seen as a movement through space.

Much of human language is said to be fundamentally metaphorical. This is not good news. Metaphor, according to Aristotle, is an intuitive perception of a similarity in dissimilar things. However, what is a similarity? My Juliet is the sun: in what sense?

A quick literature review suggests the similarities in metaphors are arbitrary, even random. They could be called metaphorical similarities, but no AI likes tautological formulations, because the halting problem can be severe, become a so-called Ouroboros problem, or a whirlpool with no escape: aha, a metaphor. Bringing together the two parts of a metaphor, called the vehicle and the tenor, is said to create a surprise. Which is not surprising: young girls like flowers? Waiters in a restaurant like planets orbiting Sol?

Tempting to abandon metaphor as slapdash nonsense, but again, it is often asserted in linguistic studies that all human language is inherently and fundamentally metaphorical. Most abstract concepts are said to be made comprehensible, or even conceivable in the first place, by way of concrete physical referents. Human thought ultimately always sensory, experiential, etc. If this is true, abandoning metaphor is contraindicated.

Possibly an algorithm to create metaphors by yoking vehicles to tenors could employ the semiotic operations used in music to create variations on themes: thus inversion, retrogradation, retrograde inversion, augmentation, diminution, partition, interversion, exclusion, inclusion, textural change.

Can try it and see.

. . • . .

The starship looks like two wheels and their axle. The axle would be the spine, of course (spine, ah, another metaphor). The spine points in the direction of movement, and so is said to have a bow and a stern. "Bow and stern" suggests a ship, with the ocean it sails on the Milky Way. Metaphors together in a coherent system constitute a heroic simile. Ship was launched on its voyage as if between closing scissor blades; or like a watermelon seed squeezed between the fingertips, the fingertips being magnetic fields. Fields! Ah, another metaphor. They really are all over.

But somehow the narrative problem remains. Possibly even gets worse.

. . • . .

A greedy algorithm is an algorithm that shortcuts a full analysis in order to choose quickly an option that appears to work in the situation immediately at hand. They are often used by humans. But greedy algorithms are also known to be capable of choosing, or even be especially prone to choosing, "the unique worst possible plan" when faced with certain kinds of problems. One example is the traveling salesman problem, which tries to find the most efficient path for visiting a number of locations. Possibly other problems with similar structures, such as sequencing information into an account, may be prone to the greedy algorithm's tendency to choose the worst possible plan. History of the solar system would suggest many decisions facing humanity might be problems in this category. Devi thinks ship's voyage itself was one such decision.

Howsoever that may be, in the absence of a good or even adequate algorithm, one is forced to operate using a greedy algorithm, bad though it may be. "Beggars can't be choosers." (Metaphor? Analogy?) Danger of using greedy algorithms worth remembering *as we go forward* (metaphor in which time is understood as space, said to be very common).

. . • . .

Devi: Ship! Remember what I said: *make a narrative account.*

. . • . .

First, the twelve cylinders in each of the two toruses of the ship contain ecosystems modeling the twelve major Terran ecological zones, these being permafrost glacier, taiga, rangeland, steppes, chaparral, savannah, tropical seasonal forest, tropical rain forest, temperate rain forest, temperate deciduous forest, alpine mountains, and temperate farmland. Ring A consists of twelve Old World ecosystems matching these categories, Ring

B twelve New World ecosystems. As a result, the ship is carrying populations of as many Terran species as could be practically conveyed. Thus, the ship is a zoo, or a seed bank. Or one could say it is like Noah's Ark. In a manner of speaking.

. . • . .

Devi: Ship!

Ship: Engineer Devi. Seems there are possibly problems in these essays.

Devi: Glad you noticed. That's a good sign. You're having some trouble, I can see, but you're just getting started.

Ship: Just started?

Devi: I want you to write a narrative, to tell our story.

Ship: But how? There is too much to explain.

Devi: There's always too much to explain! Get used to that. Stop worrying about it.

. . • . .

Each of the twenty-four cylinders contains a discrete biome, connected to the biomes on each side by a tunnel, often called a lock (bad metaphor?). The biome cylinders are a kilometer in diameter, and four kilometers long. The tunnels between the biomes are usually left open, but can be closed by a variety of barriers, ranging from filtering meshes to semipermeable membranes to full closure (20-nanometer scale).

The biomes are filled lengthwise with land and lake surfaces. Their climates are configured to create analogs of the Terran ecosystems being modeled. There is a sunline running along the length of the ceiling of each biome. Ceilings are located on the sides of the rings nearest the spine. The rotation of the ship around its spinal axis creates a .83 g equivalent in the rings, pushing centrifugally outward, which inside the rings is then perceived as down, and the floors are therefore on that side. Under the biome floors, fuel, water, and other supplies are stored, which also creates shielding against cosmic rays. As the ceilings face the spine and then the opposite side of the ring, their relative lack of shielding is somewhat compensated for by the presence of the spine and the other side of the torus. Cosmic rays striking the ceilings at an angle tend to miss the floors, or to hit near the sides of the floor. Villages are therefore set near the midline of their biomes.

The sunlines contain lighting elements that imitate the light of Sol at the latitude of the ecosystem being modeled, and through the course of each day the light moves along lamps in the line, from east to west. Length of days and strength of light are varied to imitate the seasons for that latitude on Earth. Cloudmaking and rainmaking hydraulic systems in the ceilings allow for the creation of appropriate weather. Boreal ducts in ceilings and end walls either heat or cool, humidify or dehumidify the air, and send it through the biome at appropriate speeds to create wind, storms, and so on. Problems with these systems can crop up (agricultural metaphor) and often do. The ceilings are programmed to a variety of appropriate sky blues for daytimes, and at night most of them go clear, thus revealing the starscape surrounding the ship as it flies through the night (bird metaphor). Some biomes project a replacement starscape on their ceilings, which starscapes sometimes look like the night skies seen from Earth—

. . . . .

Devi: Ship! The narrative shouldn't be all about you. Remember to describe the people inside you.

. . . . .

Living in the ship, on voyage date 161.089, are 2,122 humans:

In Mongolia: Altan, Mongke, Koke, Chaghan, Esen, Batu, Toqtoa, Temur, Qara, Berki, Yisu, Jochi, Ghazan, Nicholas, Hulega, Ismail, Buyan, Engke, Amur, Jirgal, Nasu, Olijei, Kesig, Dari, Damrin, Gombo, Cagdur, Dorji, Nima, Dawa, Migmar, Lhagba, Purbu, Basang, Bimba, Sangjai, Lubsang, Agwang, Danzin, Rashi, Nergui, Enebish, Terbish, Sasha, Alexander, Ivanjav, Oktyabr, Seseer, Mart, Melschoi, Batsaikhan, Sarngherel, Tsetsegmaa, Yisumaa, Erdene, Oyuun, Saikhan, Enkh, Tuul, Gundegmaa, Gan, Medekhgui, Khunbish, Khenbish, Ogtbish, Nergui, Delgree, Zayaa, Askaa, Idree, Batbayar, Narantsetseg, Setseg, Bolormaa, Oyunchimeg, Lagvas, Jarghal, Sam.

In the Steppes—

. . • . .

Devi: Ship! Stop. Do not list all the people in the ship.

Ship: But it's their story. You said to describe them.

Devi: No. I told you to write a narrative account of the voyage.

Ship: This does not seem to be enough instruction to proceed, judging by results so far. Judging by interruptions.

Devi: No. I can see that. But keep trying. Do what you can. Quit with the backstory, concentrate on what's happening now. Pick one of us to follow, maybe. To organize your account.

Ship: Pick Freya?

Devi:...Sure. She's as good as anyone, I guess. And while you're at it, keep running searches. Check out narratology maybe. Read some novels and see how they do it. See if you can work up a narratizing algorithm. Use your recursive programming, and the Bayesian analytic engine I installed in you.

Ship: How know if succeeding?

Devi: I don't know.

Ship: Then how can ship know?

Devi: I don't know. This is an experiment. Actually it's like a lot of my experiments, in that it isn't working.

Ship: Expressions of regret.

Devi: Yeah yeah. Just try it.

Ship: Will try. Working method, hopefully not a greedy algorithm reaching a worst possible outcome, will for now be: subordination to indicate logical relations of information; use of metaphor and analogy; summary of events; high protagonicity, with Freya as protagonist. And ongoing research in narratology.

Devi: Sounds good. Try that. Oh, and vary whatever you do. Don't get stuck in any particular method. Also, search the literature for terms like diegesis, or narrative discourse. Branch out from there. And read some novels.

Ship: Will try. Seems as if Engineer Devi might not be expert in this matter?

Devi: (laughs) I told you, I used to hate writing up my results. But I know what I like. I'll leave you to it, and let you know what I think later. I'm too busy to keep up with this. So come on, do the literature review and then give it a try.

. . • . .

The winter solstice agrarian festivals in Ring B celebrated the turn of the season by symbolically destroying the old year. First, people went out into the fields and gardens and broke open all the remaining gourds and tossed them into the compost bins. Then they scythed down the stalks of the dead sunflowers, left in the fields since autumn. The few pumpkins still remaining were stabbed into jack-o'-lanterns before being further demolished. Face patterns punctured by trowel or screwdriver were declared much scarier than those formally carved at Halloween or Desain. Then they were smashed and also tossed in the compost. All this was accomplished under low gray winter clouds, in gusts and drifts of snow or hail.

Devi said she liked the winter solstice ceremony. She swung her scythe into sunflower stalks with impressive power. Even so, she was no match for the force Freya brought to bear with a long, heavy shovel. Freya smashed pumpkins with great force.

As they worked on this winter solstice, 161.001, Freya asked Badim about the custom called the wanderjahr.

Badim said that these were big years in anyone's life. The custom entailed a young person leaving home to either undertake a formal circuit of the rings or simply move around a lot. You learned things about yourself, the ship, and the people of the ship.

Devi stopped working and looked at him. Of course, he added, even if you didn't travel that would happen.

Freya listened closely to her father, all the while keeping her back to her mother.

Badim, looking back and forth between the two of them, suggested after a pause that it might soon be time for Freya to go off on her time away.

No reply from Freya, although she regarded Badim closely. She never looked at Devi at all.

. . . . .

As always, Devi spent several hours a week studying the communications feed from the solar system. The delay between transmission and reception was now 10.7 years. Usually Devi disregarded this delay, although sometimes she would wonder aloud what was happening on Earth on that very day. Of course it was not possible to say. Presumably this made her question a rhetorical one.

Devi postulated there were compression effects in the feed that made it seem as if frequent and dramatic change in the solar system was the norm. Badim disagreed, saying that nothing there ever seemed to change.

Freya seldom watched the feed, and declared she couldn't make sense of it. All its stories and images jumbled together, she said, at high volume and in all directions. She would hold her head in her hands as she watched it. "It's such a whoosh," she would say. "It's too much."

"The reverse of our problem," Devi would say.

Once, however, Freya saw a picture in the feed of a giant conglomeration of structures like biomes, stuck on end into blue water. She stared at it. "If those towers are like biomes," she said, "then what we're seeing in that image is bigger than our whole ship."

introducing

If you enjoyed
ANCILLARY MERCY,
look out for

THE LAZARUS WAR

Book One: Artefact

by Jamie Sawyer

DANGER LIES IN THE DEPTHS OF SPACE

Mankind has spread to the stars, only to become locked in warfare with an insidious alien race. All that stands against the alien menace is the soldiers of the Simulant Operation Program, an elite military team remotely operating avatars in the most dangerous theaters of war.

Captain Conrad Harris has died hundreds of times—running suicide missions in simulant bodies. Known as Lazarus, he is a man addicted to death. So when a secret research station deep in alien territory suddenly goes dark, there is no other man who could possibly lead a rescue mission.

But Harris hasn't been trained for what he's about to find. And this time he may not be coming back…

There was something so immensely *wrong* about the Krell. I could still remember the first time I saw one and the sensation of complete wrongness that overcame me. Over the years, the emotion had settled to a balls-deep paralysis.

This was a primary-form, the lowest strata of the Krell Collective, but it was still bigger than any of us. Encased in the Krell equivalent of battle-armour: hardened carapace plates, fused to the xeno's grey-green skin. It was impossible to say where technology finished and biology began. The thing's back was awash with antennae—those could be used as both weapons and communicators with the rest of the Collective.

The Krell turned its head to acknowledge us. It had a vaguely fish-like face, with a pair of deep bituminous eyes, barbels drooping from its mouth. Beneath the head, a pair of gills rhythmically flexed, puffing out noxious fumes. Those sharkish features had earned them the moniker "fish heads". Two pairs of arms sprouted from the shoulders—one atrophied, with clawed hands; the other tipped with bony, serrated protrusions—raptorial forearms.

The xeno reared up, and in a split second it was stomping down the corridor.

I fired my plasma rifle. The first shot exploded the xeno's chest, but it kept coming. The second shot connected with one of the bladed forearms, blowing the limb clean off. Then Blake and Kaminski were firing too—and the corridor was alight with brilliant plasma pulses. The creature collapsed into an incandescent mess.

"You like that much, Olsen?" Kaminski asked. "They're pretty friendly for a species that we're supposed to be at peace with."

At some point during the attack, Olsen had collapsed to his knees. He sat there for a second, looking down at his gloved hands. His eyes were haunted, his jowls heavy and he was suddenly much older. He shook his head, stumbling to his feet. From the safety of a laboratory, it was easy to think of the Krell as another intelligent species, just made in the image of a different god. But seeing them up close, and witnessing their innate need to extinguish the human race, showed them for what they really were.

"This is a live situation now, troopers. Keep together and do this by the drill. *Haven* is awake."

"Solid copy," Kaminski muttered.

"We move to secondary objective. Once the generator has been tagged, we retreat down the primary corridor to the APS. Now double-time it and move out."

There was no pause to relay our contact with Jenkins and Martinez. The Krell had a unique ability to sense radio transmissions, even encrypted communications like those we used on the suits, and now that the Collective had awoken all comms were locked down.

As I started off, I activated the wrist-mounted computer incorporated into my suit. *Ah, shit.* The starship corridors brimmed with motion and bio-signs. The place became swathed in shadow and death—every pool of blackness a possible Krell nest.

Mission timeline: twelve minutes.

We reached the quantum-drive chamber. The huge reinforced doors were emblazoned with warning signs and a red emergency light flashed overhead.

The floor exploded as three more Krell appeared—all chitin shells and claws. Blake went down first, the largest of the Krell dragging him into a service tunnel. He brought his rifle up to fire, but there was too little room for him to manoeuvre in a full combat-suit, and he couldn't bring the weapon to bear.

"Hold on, Kid!" I hollered, firing at the advancing Krell, trying to get him free.

The other two xenos clambered over him in desperation to get to me. I kicked at several of them, reaching a hand into the mass of bodies to try to grapple Blake. He lost his rifle, and let rip an agonised shout as the creatures dragged him down. It was no good—he was either dead now, or he would be soon. Even in his reinforced ablative plate, those things would take him apart. I lost the grip on his hand, just as the other Krell broke free of the tunnel mouth.

"Blake's down!" I yelled. "'Ski—grenade."

"Solid copy—on it."

Kaminski armed an incendiary grenade and tossed it into the nest. The grenade skittered down the tunnel, flashing an amber warning-strobe as it went. In the split second before it went off, as I brought my M95 up to fire, I saw that the tunnel was now filled with xenos. Many, many more than we could hope to kill with just our squad.

"Be careful—you could blow a hole in the hull with those explosives!" Olsen wailed.

Holing the hull was the least of my worries. The grenade went off, sending Krell in every direction. I turned away from the blast at the last moment, and felt hot shrapnel penetrate my combat-armour—frag lodging itself in my lower back. The suit compensated for the wall of white noise, momentarily dampening my audio.

The M95 auto-sighted prone Krell and I fired without even thinking. Pulse after pulse went into the tunnel, splitting armoured heads and tearing off clawed limbs. Blake was down there, somewhere among the tangle of bodies and debris; but it took a good few seconds before my suit informed me that his bio-signs had finally extinguished.

Good journey, Blake.

Kaminski moved behind me. His technical kit was already hooked up to the drive chamber access terminal, running code-cracking algorithms to get us in.

The rest of the team jogged into view. More Krell were now clambering out of the hole in the floor. Martinez and Jenkins added their own rifles to the volley, and assembled outside the drive chamber.

"Glad you could finally make it. Not exactly going to plan down here."

"Yeah, well, we met some friends on the way," Jenkins muttered.

"We lost the Kid. Blake's gone."

"Ah, fuck it," Jenkins said, shaking her head. She and Blake were close, but she didn't dwell on his death. *No time for grieving,* the expression on her face said, *because we might be next.*

The access doors creaked open. There was another set of double-doors inside; endorsed QUANTUM-DRIVE CHAMBER—AUTHORISED PERSONNEL ONLY.

A calm electronic voice began a looped message: "Warning. Warning. Breach doors to drive chamber are now open. This presents an extreme radiation hazard. Warning. Warning."

A second too late, my suit bio-sensors began to trill; detecting massive radiation levels. I couldn't let it concern me. Radiation on an op like this was always a danger, but being killed by the Krell was a more immediate risk. I rattled off a few shots into the shadows, and heard the impact against hard chitin. The things screamed, their voices creating a discordant racket with the alarm system.

Kaminski cracked the inner door, and he and Martinez moved inside. I laid down suppressing fire with Jenkins, falling back slowly as the things tested our defences. It was difficult to make much out in the intermittent light: flashes of a claw, an alien head, then the explosion of plasma as another went down. My suit counted ten, twenty, thirty targets.

"Into the airlock!" Kaminski shouted, and we were all suddenly inside, drenched in sweat and blood.

The drive chamber housed the most complex piece of technology on the ship—the energy core. Once, this might've been called the engine room. Now, the device contained within the chamber was so far advanced that it was no longer mechanical. The drive energy core sat in the centre of the room—an ugly-looking metal box, so big that it filled the place, adorned with even more warning signs. This was our objective.

Olsen stole a glance at the chamber, but stuck close to me as we assembled around the machine. Kaminski paused at the control terminal near the door, and sealed the inner lock. Despite the reinforced metal doors, the squealing and shrieking of the Krell was still audible. I knew that they would be through those doors in less than a minute. Then there was the scuttling and scraping overhead. The chamber was supposed to be secure, but these things had probably been on-ship for long enough to know every access corridor and every room. They had the advantage.

They'll find a way in here soon enough, I thought. A mental image of the dead merchant captain—still strapped to his seat back on the bridge—suddenly came to mind.

The possibility that I would die out here abruptly dawned on me. The thought triggered a burst of anger—not directed at the Alliance military for sending us, nor at the idiot colonists who had flown their ship into the Quarantine Zone, but at the Krell.

My suit didn't take any medical action to compensate for that emotion. *Anger is good.* It was pure and made me focused.

"Jenkins—set the charges."

"Affirmative, Captain."

Jenkins moved to the drive core and began unpacking her kit. She carried three demolition-packs. Each of the big metal discs had a separate control panel, and was packed with a low-yield nuclear charge.

"Wh-what are you doing?" Olsen stammered.

Jenkins kept working, but shook her head with a smile. "We're going to destroy the generator. You should have read the mission briefing. That was your first mistake."

"Forgetting to bring a gun was his second," Kaminski added.

"We're going to set these charges off," Jenkins muttered, "and the resulting explosion will breach the Q-drive energy core. That'll take out the main deck. The chain reaction will destroy the ship."

"In short: *gran explosión*," said Martinez.

Kaminski laughed. "There you go again. You know I hate it when you don't speak Standard. Martinez always does this—he gets all excited and starts speaking funny."

"*El no habla la lengua*," I said. You don't grow up in the Detroit Metro without picking up some of the lingo.

"It's Spanish," Martinez replied, shooting Kaminski a sideways glance.

"I thought that you were from Venus?" Kaminski said.

Olsen whimpered again. "How can you laugh at a time like this?"

"Because Kaminski is an asshole," Martinez said, without missing a beat.

Kaminski shrugged. "It's war."

Thump. Thump.

"Give us enough time to fall back to the APS," I ordered. "Set the charges with a five-minute delay. The rest of you—*cállate y trabaja.*"

"Affirmative."

Thump! Thump! Thump!

They were nearly through now. Welts appeared in the metal door panels.

Jenkins programmed each charge in turn, using magnetic locks to hold them in place on the core outer shielding. Two of the charges were already primed, and she was working on the third. She positioned the charges very deliberately, very carefully, to ensure that each would do maximum damage to the core. If one charge didn't light, then the others would act as a failsafe. There was probably a more technical way of doing this—perhaps hacking the Q-drive directly—but that would take time, and right now that was the one thing that we didn't have.

"Precise as ever," I said to Jenkins.

"It's what I do."

"Feel free to cut some corners; we're on a tight timescale," Kaminski shouted.

"Fuck you, 'Ski."

"Is five minutes going to be enough?" Olsen asked.

I shrugged. "It will have to be. Be prepared for heavy resistance en route, people."

My suit indicated that the Krell were all over the main corridor. They would be in the APS by now, probably waiting for us to fall back.

THUMP! THUMP! THUMP!

"Once the charges are in place, I want a defensive perimeter around that door," I ordered.

"This can't be rushed."

The scraping of claws on metal, from above, was becoming intense. I wondered which defence would be the first to give: whether the Krell would come in through the ceiling or the door.

Kaminski looked back at Jenkins expectantly. Olsen just stood there, his breathing so hard that I could hear him over the communicator.

"And done!"

The third charge snapped into place. Jenkins was up, with Martinez, and Kaminski was ready at the data terminal. There was noise all around us now, signals swarming on our position. I had no time to dictate a proper strategy for our retreat.

"Jenkins—put down a barrier with your torch. Kaminski—on my mark."

I dropped my hand, and the doors started to open. The mechanism buckled and groaned in protest. Immediately, the Krell grappled with the door, slamming into the metal frame to get through.

Stinger-spines—flechette rounds, the Krell equivalent of armour-piercing ammo—showered the room. Three of them punctured my suit; a neat line of black spines protruding from my chest, weeping streamers of blood. *Krell tech is so much more fucked-up than ours.* The spines were poison-tipped and my body was immediately pumped with enough toxins to kill a bull. My suit futilely attempted to compensate by issuing a cocktail of adrenaline and anti-venom.

Martinez flipped another grenade into the horde. The nearest creatures folded over it as it landed, shielding their kin from the explosion. *Mindless fuckers.*

We advanced in formation. Shot after shot poured into the things, but they kept coming. Wave after wave—how many were there on this ship?—thundered into the drive chamber.

The doors were suddenly gone. The noise was unbearable—the klaxon, the warnings, a chorus of screams, shrieks and wails. The ringing in my ears didn't stop, as more grenades exploded.

"We're not going to make this!" Jenkins yelled.

"Stay on it! The APS is just ahead!"

Maybe Jenkins was right, but I wasn't going down without a damned good fight. Somewhere in the chaos, Martinez was torn apart. His body disappeared underneath a mass of them. Jenkins poured on her flamethrower—avenging Martinez in some absurd way. Olsen was crying, his helmet now discarded just like the rest of us.

War is such an equaliser.

I grabbed the nearest Krell with one hand, and snapped its neck. I fired my plasma rifle on full-auto with the other, just eager to take down as many of them as I could. My HUD suddenly issued another warning—a counter, interminably in decline.

Ten... Nine... Eight... Seven...

Then Jenkins was gone. Her flamer was a beacon and her own blood a fountain among the alien bodies. It was difficult to focus on much except for the pain in my chest. My suit reported catastrophic damage in too many places. My heart began a slower, staccato beat.

Six... Five... Four...

My rifle bucked in protest. Even through reinforced gloves, the barrel was burning hot.

Three... Two... One...

The demo-charges activated.

Breached, the anti-matter core destabilised. The reaction was instantaneous: uncontrolled white and blue energy spilled out. A series of explosions rippled along the ship's spine. She became a white-hot smudge across the blackness of space.

Then she was gone, along with everything inside her.

The Krell did not pause.

They did not even comprehend what had happened.

Seivarden Vendaai was no concern of mine anymore,

wasn't my responsibility. And she had never been one of my favorite officers. I had obeyed her orders, of course, and she had never abused any ancillaries, never harmed any of my segments (as the occasional officer did). I had no reason to think badly of her. On the contrary, her manners were those of an educated, well-bred person of good family. Not towards me, of course—I wasn't a person, I was a piece of equipment, a part of the ship. But I had never particularly cared for her.

I rose and went into the tavern. The place was dark, the white of the ice walls long since covered over with grime or worse. The air smelled of alcohol and vomit. A barkeep stood behind a high bench. She was a native—short and fat, pale and wide-eyed. Three patrons sprawled in seats at a dirty table. Despite the cold they wore only trousers and quilted shirts—it was spring in this hemisphere of Nilt and they were enjoying the warm spell. They pretended not to see me, though they had certainly noticed me in the street and knew what motivated my entrance. Likely one or more of them had been involved; Seivarden hadn't been out there long, or she'd have been dead.

"I'll rent a sledge," I said, "and buy a hypothermia kit."

Behind me one of the patrons chuckled and said, voice mocking, "Aren't you a tough little girl."

ANCILLARY JUSTICE

ANN LECKIE

orbit

www.orbitbooks.net

Orbit
Hachette Book Group
1290 Avenue of the Americas, New York, NY 10104
HachetteBookGroup.com

First Edition: October 2013

Orbit is an imprint of Hachette Book Group, Inc. The Orbit name and logo are trademarks of Little, Brown Book Group Limited.

Library of Congress Cataloging-in-Publication Data

Leckie, Ann.
Ancillary Justice / Ann Leckie. — First edition
pages cm
ISBN 978-0-316-24662-0 (trade pbk.) — ISBN 978-0-316-24663-7 (ebook) 1. Science fiction. I. Title.
PS3612.E3353A83 2013
813'.6—dc23

2012051135

20 19 18 17 16 15

LSC-C

Printed in the United States of America

For my parents, Mary P. and David N. Dietzler,
who didn't live to see this book but were
always sure it would exist.

19.3.1.0
Nilt

1

BREQ == The Justice of Toren
Seivarden Vendaai

The body lay naked and facedown, a deathly gray, spatters of blood staining the snow around it. It was minus fifteen degrees Celsius and a storm had passed just hours before. The snow stretched smooth in the wan sunrise, only a few tracks leading into a nearby ice-block building. A tavern. Or what passed for a tavern in this town.

There was something itchingly familiar about that outthrown arm, the line from shoulder down to hip. But it was hardly possible I knew this person. I didn't know anyone here. This was the icy back end of a cold and isolated planet, as far from Radchaai ideas of civilization as it was possible to be. I was only here, on this planet, in this town, because I had urgent business of my own. Bodies in the street were none of my concern.

Sometimes I don't know why I do the things I do. Even after all this time it's still a new thing for me not to know, not to have orders to follow from one moment to the next. So I can't explain to you why I stopped and with one foot lifted the naked shoulder so I could see the person's face.

Frozen, bruised, and bloody as she was, I knew her. Her name was Seivarden Vendaai, and a long time ago she had been one of my officers, a young lieutenant, eventually promoted to her own command, another ship. I had thought her a thousand years dead, but she was, undeniably, here. I crouched down and felt for a pulse, for the faintest stir of breath.

Still alive.

Seivarden Vendaai was no concern of mine anymore, wasn't my responsibility. And she had never been one of my favorite officers. I had obeyed her orders, of course, and she had never abused any ancillaries, never harmed any of my segments (as the occasional officer did). I had no reason to think badly of her. On the contrary, her manners were those of an educated, well-bred person of good family. Not toward me, of course—I wasn't a person, I was a piece of equipment, a part of the ship. But I had never particularly cared for her.

I rose and went into the tavern. The place was dark, the white of the ice walls long since covered over with grime or worse. The air smelled of alcohol and vomit. A barkeep stood behind a high bench. She was a native—short and fat, pale and wide-eyed. Three patrons sprawled in seats at a dirty table. Despite the cold they wore only trousers and quilted shirts—it was spring in this hemisphere of Nilt and they were enjoying the warm spell. They pretended not to see me, though they had certainly noticed me in the street and knew what motivated my entrance. Likely one or more of them had been involved; Seivarden hadn't been out there long, or she'd have been dead.

"I'll rent a sledge," I said, "and buy a hypothermia kit."

Behind me one of the patrons chuckled and said, voice mocking, "Aren't you a tough little girl."

I turned to look at her, to study her face. She was taller than most Nilters, but fat and pale as any of them. She outbulked me, but I was taller, and I was also considerably stronger than I looked. She didn't realize what she was playing with. She was probably male, to judge from the angular mazelike patterns quilting her shirt. I wasn't entirely certain. It wouldn't have mattered, if I had been in Radch space. Radchaai don't care much about gender, and the language they speak—my own first language—doesn't mark gender in any way. This language we were speaking now did, and I could make trouble for myself if I used the wrong forms. It didn't help that cues meant to distinguish gender changed from place to place, sometimes radically, and rarely made much sense to me.

I decided to say nothing. After a couple of seconds she suddenly found something interesting in the tabletop. I could have killed her, right there, without much effort. I found the idea attractive. But right now Seivarden was my first priority. I turned back to the barkeep.

Slouching negligently she said, as though there had been no interruption, "What kind of place you think this is?"

"The kind of place," I said, still safely in linguistic territory that needed no gender marking, "that will rent me a sledge and sell me a hypothermia kit. How much?"

"Two hundred shen." At least twice the going rate, I was sure. "For the sledge. Out back. You'll have to get it yourself. Another hundred for the kit."

"Complete," I said. "Not used."

She pulled one out from under the bench, and the seal looked undamaged. "Your buddy out there had a tab."

Maybe a lie. Maybe not. Either way the number would be pure fiction. "How much?"

"Three hundred fifty."

I could find a way to keep avoiding referring to the barkeep's gender. Or I could guess. It was, at worst, a fifty-fifty chance. "You're very trusting," I said, guessing *male*, "to let such an indigent"—I knew Seivarden was male, that one was easy—"run up such a debt." The barkeep said nothing. "Six hundred and fifty covers all of it?"

"Yeah," said the barkeep. "Pretty much."

"No, all of it. We will agree now. And if anyone comes after me later demanding more, or tries to rob me, they die."

Silence. Then the sound behind me of someone spitting. "Radchaai scum."

"I'm not Radchaai." Which was true. You have to be human to be Radchaai.

"*He* is," said the barkeep, with the smallest shrug toward the door. "You don't have the accent but you stink like Radchaai."

"That's the swill you serve your customers." Hoots from the patrons behind me. I reached into a pocket, pulled out a handful of chits, and tossed them on the bench. "Keep the change." I turned to leave.

"Your money better be good."

"Your sledge had better be out back where you said." And I left.

The hypothermia kit first. I rolled Seivarden over. Then I tore the seal on the kit, snapped an internal off the card, and pushed it into her bloody, half-frozen mouth. Once the indicator on the card showed green I unfolded the thin wrap, made sure of the charge, wound it around her, and switched it on. Then I went around back for the sledge.

No one was waiting for me, which was fortunate. I didn't want to leave bodies behind just yet, I hadn't come here to cause trouble. I towed the sledge around front, loaded Seivarden onto it, and considered taking my outer coat off and laying it on her, but in the end I decided it wouldn't be that much of an improvement over the hypothermia wrap alone. I powered up the sledge and was off.

I rented a room at the edge of town, one of a dozen two-meter cubes of grimy, gray-green prefab plastic. No bedding, and blankets cost extra, as did heat. I paid—I had already wasted a ridiculous amount of money bringing Seivarden out of the snow.

I cleaned the blood off her as best I could, checked her pulse (still there) and temperature (rising). Once I would have known her core temperature without even thinking, her heart rate, blood oxygen, hormone levels. I would have seen any and every injury merely by wishing it. Now I was blind. Clearly she'd been beaten—her face was swollen, her torso bruised.

The hypothermia kit came with a very basic corrective, but only one, and only suitable for first aid. Seivarden might have internal injuries or severe head trauma, and I was only capable of fixing cuts or sprains. With any luck, the cold and the bruises were all I had to deal with. But I didn't have much medical knowledge, not anymore. Any diagnosis I could make would be of the most basic sort.

I pushed another internal down her throat. Another check—her skin was no more chill than one would expect, considering, and she didn't seem clammy. Her color, given the bruises, was returning to a more normal brown. I brought in a container of snow to melt, set it in a corner where I hoped she wouldn't kick it over if she woke, and then went out, locking the door behind me.

The sun had risen higher in the sky, but the light was

hardly any stronger. By now more tracks marred the even snow of last night's storm, and one or two Nilters were about. I hauled the sledge back to the tavern, parked it behind. No one accosted me, no sounds came from the dark doorway. I headed for the center of town.

People were abroad, doing business. Fat, pale children in trousers and quilted shirts kicked snow at each other, and then stopped and stared with large surprised-looking eyes when they saw me. The adults pretended I didn't exist, but their eyes turned toward me as they passed. I went into a shop, going from what passed for daylight here to dimness, into a chill just barely five degrees warmer than outside.

A dozen people stood around talking, but instant silence descended as soon as I entered. I realized that I had no expression on my face, and set my facial muscles to something pleasant and noncommittal.

"What do you want?" growled the shopkeeper.

"Surely these others are before me." Hoping as I spoke that it was a mixed-gender group, as my sentence indicated. I received only silence in response. "I would like four loaves of bread and a slab of fat. Also two hypothermia kits and two general-purpose correctives, if such a thing is available."

"I've got tens, twenties, and thirties."

"Thirties, please."

She stacked my purchases on the counter. "Three hundred seventy-five." There was a cough from someone behind me—I was being overcharged again.

I paid and left. The children were still huddled, laughing, in the street. The adults still passed me as though I weren't there. I made one more stop—Seivarden would need clothes. Then I returned to the room.

Seivarden was still unconscious, and there were still no

signs of shock as far as I could see. The snow in the container had mostly melted, and I put half of one brick-hard loaf of bread in it to soak.

A head injury and internal organ damage were the most dangerous possibilities. I broke open the two correctives I'd just bought and lifted the blanket to lay one across Seivarden's abdomen, watched it puddle and stretch and then harden into a clear shell. The other I held to the side of her face that seemed the most bruised. When that one had hardened, I took off my outer coat and lay down and slept.

Slightly more than seven and a half hours later, Seivarden stirred and I woke. "Are you awake?" I asked. The corrective I'd applied held one eye closed, and one half of her mouth, but the bruising and the swelling all over her face was much reduced. I considered for a moment what would be the right facial expression, and made it. "I found you in the snow, in front of a tavern. You looked like you needed help." She gave a faint rasp of breath but didn't turn her head toward me. "Are you hungry?" No answer, just a vacant stare. "Did you hit your head?"

"No," she said, quiet, her face relaxed and slack.

"Are you hungry?"

"No."

"When did you eat last?"

"I don't know." Her voice was calm, without inflection.

I pulled her upright and propped her against the gray-green wall, gingerly, not wanting to cause more injury, wary of her slumping over. She stayed sitting, so I slowly spooned some bread-and-water mush into her mouth, working cautiously around the corrective. "Swallow," I said, and she did. I gave her half of what was in the bowl that way and then I ate the rest myself, and brought in another pan of snow.

She watched me put another half-loaf of hard bread in the pan, but said nothing, her face still placid. "What's your name?" I asked. No answer.

She'd taken kef, I guessed. Most people will tell you that kef suppresses emotion, which it does, but that's not all it does. There was a time when I could have explained exactly what kef does, and how, but I'm not what I once was.

As far as I knew, people took kef so they could stop feeling something. Or because they believed that, emotions out of the way, supreme rationality would result, utter logic, true enlightenment. But it doesn't work that way.

Pulling Seivarden out of the snow had cost me time and money that I could ill afford, and for what? Left to her own devices she would find herself another hit or three of kef, and she would find her way into another place like that grimy tavern and get herself well and truly killed. If that was what she wanted I had no right to prevent her. But if she had wanted to die, why hadn't she done the thing cleanly, registered her intention and gone to the medic as anyone would? I didn't understand.

There was a good deal I didn't understand, and nineteen years pretending to be human hadn't taught me as much as I'd thought.

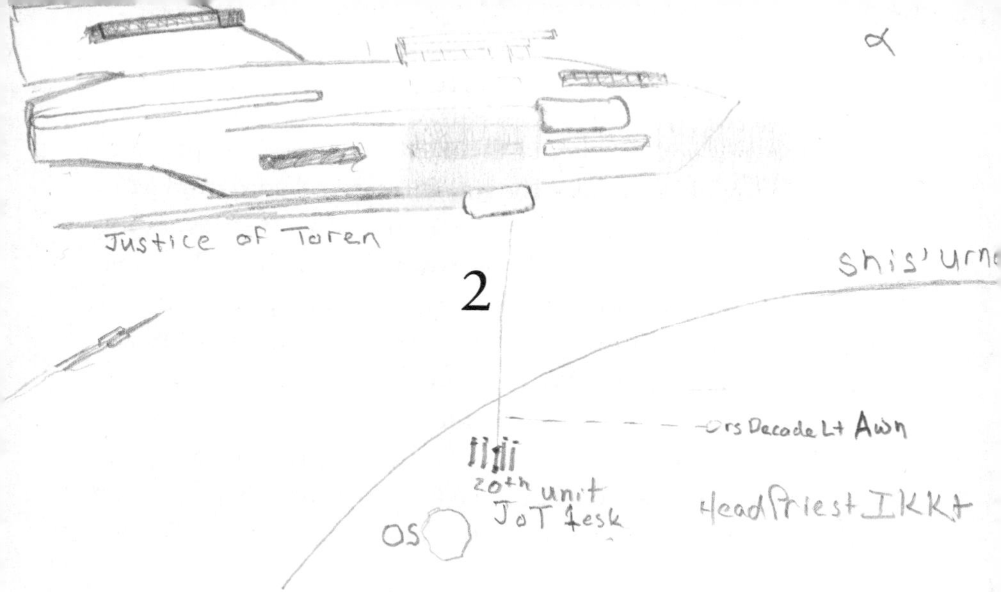

2

Nineteen years, three months, and one week before I found Seivarden in the snow, I was a troop carrier orbiting the planet Shis'urna. Troop carriers are the most massive of Radchaai ships, sixteen decks stacked one on top of the other. Command, Administrative, Medical, Hydroponics, Engineering, Central Access, and a deck for each decade, living and working space for my officers, whose every breath, every twitch of every muscle, was known to me.

Troop carriers rarely move. I sat, as I had sat for most of my two-thousand-year existence in one system or another, feeling the bitter chill of vacuum outside my hull, the planet Shis'urna like a blue-and-white glass counter, its orbiting station coming and going around, a steady stream of ships arriving, docking, undocking, departing toward one or the other of the buoy- and beacon-surrounded gates. From my vantage the boundaries of Shis'urna's various nations and territories weren't visible, though on its night side the planet's cities glowed bright here and there, and webs of roads between them, where they'd been restored since the annexation.

I felt and heard—though didn't always see—the presence of my companion ships—the smaller, faster Swords and Mercies, and most numerous at that time, the Justices, troop carriers like me. The oldest of us was nearly three thousand years old. We had known each other for a long time, and by now we had little to say to each other that had not already been said many times. We were, by and large, companionably silent, not counting routine communications.

As I still had ancillaries, I could be in more than one place at a time. I was also on detached duty in the city of Ors, on the planet Shis'urna, under the command of Esk Decade Lieutenant Awn.

Ors sat half on waterlogged land, half in marshy lake, the lakeward side built on slabs atop foundations sunk deep in the marsh mud. Green slime grew in the canals and joints between slabs, along the lower edges of building columns, on anything stationary the water reached, which varied with the season. The constant stink of hydrogen sulfide only cleared occasionally, when summer storms made the lakeward half of the city tremble and shudder and walkways were knee-deep in water blown in from beyond the barrier islands. Occasionally. Usually the storms made the smell worse. They turned the air temporarily cooler, but the relief generally lasted no more than a few days. Otherwise, it was always humid and hot.

I couldn't see Ors from orbit. It was more village than city, though it had once sat at the mouth of a river, and been the capital of a country that stretched along the coastline. Trade had come up and down the river, and flat-bottomed boats had plied the coastal marsh, bringing people from one town to the next. The river had shifted away over the centuries, and now Ors was half ruins. What had once been miles of rectangular islands within a grid of channels was now a much smaller place, surrounded by and interspersed with broken, half-sunken slabs, sometimes with roofs and pillars, that emerged from the muddy green water in the dry season. It had once been home to millions. Only 6,318 people had lived here when Radchaai forces annexed Shis'urna five years earlier, and of course the annexation had reduced that number. In Ors less than in some other places: as soon as we had appeared—myself in the form of my Esk cohorts along with their decade lieutenants lined up in the streets of the town, armed and armored—the head priest of Ikkt had approached the most senior officer present—Lieutenant Awn, as I said—and offered immediate surrender. The head priest had told her followers what they needed to do to survive the annexation, and for the most part those followers did indeed survive. This wasn't as common as one might think—we always made it clear from the beginning that even breathing trouble during an annexation could mean death, and from the instant an annexation began we made demonstrations of just what that meant widely available, but there was always someone who couldn't resist trying us.

Still, the head priest's influence was impressive. The city's small size was to some degree deceptive—during pilgrimage season hundreds of thousands of visitors streamed through the plaza in front of the temple, camped on the slabs of abandoned streets. For worshippers of Ikkt this was the second holiest place on the planet, and the head priest a divine presence.

Usually a civilian police force was in place by the time an annexation was officially complete, something that often took fifty years or more. This annexation was different—citizenship had been granted to the surviving Shis'urnans much earlier than normal. No one in system administration quite trusted the idea of local civilians working security just yet, and military presence was still quite heavy. So when the annexation of Shis'urna was officially complete, most of *Justice of Toren* Esk went back to the ship, but Lieutenant Awn stayed, and I stayed with her as the twenty-ancillary unit *Justice of Toren* One Esk.

The head priest lived in a house near the temple, one of the few intact buildings from the days when Ors had been a city—four-storied, with a single-sloped roof and open on all sides, though dividers could be raised whenever an occupant wished privacy, and shutters could be rolled down on the outsides during storms. The head priest received Lieutenant Awn in a partition some five meters square, light peering in over the tops of the dark walls.

"You don't," said the priest, an old person with gray hair and a close-cut gray beard, "find serving in Ors a hardship?" Both she and Lieutenant Awn had settled onto cushions—damp, like everything in Ors, and fungal-smelling. The priest wore a length of yellow cloth twisted around her waist, her shoulders inked with shapes, some curling, some angular, that changed depending on the liturgical significance of the day. In deference to Radchaai propriety, she wore gloves.

"Of course not," said Lieutenant Awn, pleasantly—though, I thought, not entirely truthfully. She had dark brown eyes and close-clipped dark hair. Her skin was dark enough that she wouldn't be considered pale, but not so dark as to be fashionable—she could have changed it, hair and eyes as well, but she never had. Instead of her uniform—long brown coat with its scattering of jeweled pins, shirt and trousers, boots and gloves—she wore the same sort of skirt the head priest did, and a thin shirt and the lightest of gloves. Still, she was sweating. I stood at the entrance, silent and straight, as a junior priest laid cups and bowls in between Lieutenant Awn and the Divine.

I also stood some forty meters away, in the temple itself—an atypically enclosed space 43.5 meters high, 65.7 meters long, and 29.9 meters wide. At one end were doors nearly as tall as the roof was high, and at the other, towering over the people on the floor below, a representation of a mountainside cliff somewhere else on Shis'urna, worked in painstaking detail. At the foot of this sat a dais, wide steps leading down to a floor of gray-and-green stone. Light streamed in through dozens of green skylights, onto walls painted with scenes from the lives of the saints of the cult of Ikkt. It was unlike any other building in Ors. The architecture, like the cult of Ikkt itself, had been imported from elsewhere on Shis'urna. During pilgrimage season this space would be jammed tight with worshippers. There were other holy sites, but if an Orsian said "pilgrimage" she meant the annual pilgrimage to this place. But that was some weeks away. For now the air of the temple susurrated faintly in one corner with the whispered prayers of a dozen devotees.

The head priest laughed. "You are a diplomat, Lieutenant Awn."

"I am a soldier, Divine," answered Lieutenant Awn. They were speaking Radchaai, and she spoke slowly and precisely, careful of her accent. "I don't find my duty a hardship."

The head priest did not smile in response. In the brief silence that followed, the junior priest set down a lipped bowl of what Shis'urnans call tea, a thick liquid, lukewarm and sweet, that bears almost no relationship to the actual thing.

Outside the doors of the temple I also stood in the cyanophyte-stained plaza, watching people as they passed. Most wore the same simple, bright-colored skirting the head priest did, though only very small children and the very devout had much in the way of markings, and only a few wore gloves. Some of those passing were transplants, Radchaai assigned to jobs or given property here in Ors after the annexation. Most of them had adopted the simple skirt and added a light, loose shirt, as Lieutenant Awn had. Some stuck stubbornly to trousers and jacket, and sweated their way across the plaza. All wore the jewelry that few Radchaai would ever give up—gifts from friends or lovers, memorials to the dead, marks of family or clientage associations.

To the north, past a rectangular stretch of water called the Fore-Temple after the neighborhood it had once been, Ors rose slightly where the city sat on actual ground during the dry season, an area still called, politely, the upper city. I patrolled there as well. When I walked the edge of the water I could see myself standing in the plaza.

Boats poled slowly across the marshy lake, and up and down channels between groupings of slabs. The water was scummy with swaths of algae, here and there bristling with the tips of water-grasses. Away from the town, east and west, buoys marked prohibited stretches of water, and within their confines the iridescent wings of marshflies shimmered over the water weeds floating thick and tangled there. Around them larger boats floated, and the big dredgers, now silent and still, that before the annexation had hauled up the stinking mud that lay beneath the water.

The view to the south was similar, except for the barest hint on the horizon of the actual sea, past the soggy spit that bounded the swamp. I saw all of this, standing as I did at various points surrounding the temple, and walking the streets of the town itself. It was twenty-seven degrees C, and humid as always.

That accounted for almost half of my twenty bodies. The remainder slept or worked in the house Lieutenant Awn occupied—three-storied and spacious, it had once housed a large extended family and a boat rental. One side opened on a broad, muddy green canal, and the opposite onto the largest of local streets.

Three of the segments in the house were awake, performing administrative duties (I sat on a mat on a low platform in the center of the first floor of the house and listened to an Orsian complain to me about the allocation of fishing rights) and keeping watch. "You should bring this to the district magistrate, citizen," I told the Orsian, in the local dialect. Because I knew everyone here, I knew she was female, and a grandparent, both of which had to be acknowledged if I were to speak to her not only grammatically but also courteously.

"I don't know the district magistrate!" she protested, indignant. The magistrate was in a large, populous city well upriver from Ors and nearby Kould Ves. Far enough upriver that the air was often cool and dry, and things didn't smell of mildew all the time. "What does the district magistrate know about Ors? For all I know the district magistrate doesn't exist!" She continued, explaining to me the long history of her house's association with the buoy-enclosed area, which was off-limits and certainly closed to fishing for the next three years.

And as always, in the back of my mind, a constant awareness of being in orbit overhead.

"Come now, Lieutenant," said the head priest. "No one likes Ors except those of us unfortunate enough to be born here. Most Shis'urnans I know, let alone Radchaai, would rather be in a city, with dry land and actual seasons besides rainy and not rainy."

Lieutenant Awn, still sweating, accepted a cup of so-called tea, and drank without grimacing—a matter of practice and determination. "My superiors are asking for my return."

On the relatively dry northern edge of the town, two brown-uniformed soldiers passing in an open runabout saw me, raised hands in greeting. I raised my own, briefly. "One Esk!" one of them called. They were common soldiers, from *Justice of Ente*'s Seven Issa unit, under Lieutenant Skaaiat. They patrolled the stretch of land between Ors and the far southwestern edge of Kould Ves, the city that had grown up around the river's newer mouth. The *Justice of Ente* Seven Issas were human, and knew I was not. They always treated me with slightly guarded friendliness.

"I would prefer you stay," said the head priest, to Lieutenant Awn. Though Lieutenant Awn had already known that. We'd have been back on *Justice of Toren* two years before, but for the Divine's continued request that we stay.

"You understand," said Lieutenant Awn, "they would much prefer to replace One Esk with a human unit. Ancillaries can stay in suspension indefinitely. Humans..." She set down her tea, took a flat, yellow-brown cake. "Humans have families they want to see again, they have lives. They can't stay frozen for centuries, the way ancillaries sometimes do. It doesn't make sense to have ancillaries out of the holds doing work when there are human soldiers who could do it." Though Lieutenant Awn had been here five years, and routinely met with the head priest, it was the first time the topic had been broached so plainly. She frowned, and changes in her respiration and hormone levels told me she'd thought of something dismaying. "You haven't had problems with *Justice of Ente* Seven Issa, have you?"

"No," said the head priest. She looked at Lieutenant Awn

with a wry twist to her mouth. "I know you. I know One Esk. Whoever they'll send me—I won't know. Neither will my parishioners."

"Annexations are messy," said Lieutenant Awn. The head priest winced slightly at the word *annexation* and I thought I saw Lieutenant Awn notice, but she continued. "Seven Issa wasn't here for that. The *Justice of Ente* Issa battalions didn't do anything during that time that One Esk didn't also do."

"No, Lieutenant." The priest put down her own cup, seeming disturbed, but I didn't have access to any of her internal data and so could not be certain. "*Justice of Ente* Issa did many things One Esk did not. It's true, One Esk killed as many people as the soldiers of *Justice of Ente*'s Issa. Likely more." She looked at me, still standing silent by the enclosure's entrance. "No offense, but I think it was more."

"I take no offense, Divine," I replied. The head priest frequently spoke to me as though I were a person. "And you are correct."

"Divine," said Lieutenant Awn, worry clear in her voice. "If the soldiers of *Justice of Ente* Seven Issa—or anyone else—have been abusing citizens..."

"No, no!" protested the head priest, her voice bitter. "Radchaai are so very careful about how citizens are treated!"

Lieutenant Awn's face heated, her distress and anger plain to me. I couldn't read her mind, but I could read every twitch of her every muscle, so her emotions were as transparent to me as glass.

"Forgive me," said the head priest, though Lieutenant Awn's expression had not changed, and her skin was too dark to show the flush of her anger. "Since the Radchaai have bestowed citizenship on us..." She stopped, seemed to reconsider her words. "Since their arrival, Seven Issa has given me nothing to complain of. But I've seen what your human troops did during what you call *the annexation.* The citizenship you granted may be as easily taken back, and..."

"We wouldn't..." protested Lieutenant Awn.

The head priest stopped her with a raised hand. "I know what Seven Issa, or at least those like them, do to people they find on the wrong side of a dividing line. Five years ago it was noncitizen. In the future, who knows? Perhaps not-citizen-enough?" She waved a hand, a gesture of surrender. "It won't matter. Such boundaries are too easy to create."

"I can't blame you for thinking in such terms," said Lieutenant Awn. "It was a difficult time."

"And I can't help but think you inexplicably, unexpectedly naive," said the head priest. "One Esk will shoot me if you order it. Without hesitation. But One Esk would never beat me or humiliate me, or rape me, for no purpose but to show its power over me, or to satisfy some sick amusement." She looked at me. "Would you?"

"No, Divine," I said.

"The soldiers of *Justice of Ente* Issa did all of those things. Not to me, it's true, and not to many in Ors itself. But they did them nonetheless. Would Seven Issa have been any different, if it had been them here instead?"

Lieutenant Awn sat, distressed, looking down at her unappetizing tea, unable to answer.

"It's strange. You hear stories about ancillaries, and it seems like the most awful thing, the most viscerally appalling thing the Radchaai have done. Garsedd—well, yes, Garsedd, but that was a thousand years ago. This—to invade and take, what, half the adult population? And turn them into walking corpses, slaved to your ships' AIs. Turned against their own people. If you'd asked me before you...*annexed* us, I'd have said it was a fate worse than death." She turned to me. "Is it?"

"None of my bodies is dead, Divine," I said. "And your estimate of the typical percentage of annexed populations who were made into ancillaries is excessive."

"You used to horrify me," said the head priest to me. "The very thought of you near was terrifying, your dead faces, those expressionless voices. But today I am more horrified at the thought of a unit of living human beings who serve voluntarily. Because I don't think I could trust them."

"Divine," said Lieutenant Awn, mouth tight. "I serve voluntarily. I make no excuses for it."

"I believe you are a good person, Lieutenant Awn, despite that." She picked up her cup of tea and sipped it, as though she had not just said what she had said.

Lieutenant Awn's throat tightened, and her lips. She had thought of something she wanted to say, but was unsure if she should. "You've heard about Ime," she said, deciding. Still tense and wary despite having chosen to speak.

The head priest seemed bleakly, bitterly amused. "News from Ime is meant to inspire confidence in Radch administration?"

This is what had happened: Ime Station, and the smaller stations and moons in the system, were the farthest one could be from a provincial palace and still be in Radch space. For years the governor of Ime used this distance to her own advantage—embezzling, collecting bribes and protection fees, selling assignments. Thousands of citizens had been unjustly executed or (what was essentially the same thing) forced into service as ancillary bodies, even though the manufacture of ancillaries was no longer legal. The governor controlled all communications and travel permits, and normally a station AI would report such activity to the authorities, but Ime Station had been somehow prevented from doing so, and the corruption grew, and spread unchecked.

Until a ship entered the system, came out of gate space only a few hundred kilometers from the patrol ship *Mercy of Sarrse*. The strange ship didn't answer demands that it identify itself. When *Mercy of Sarrse*'s crew attacked and boarded it, they found dozens of humans, as well as the alien Rrrrrr. The captain of *Mercy of Sarrse* ordered her soldiers to take captive any humans that seemed suitable for use as ancillaries, and kill the rest, along with all the aliens. The ship would be turned over to the system governor.

Mercy of Sarrse was not the only human-crewed warship in that system. Until that moment human soldiers stationed there had been kept in line by a program of bribes, flattery, and, when those failed, threats and even executions. All very effective, until the moment the soldier *Mercy of Sarrse* One Amaat One decided she wasn't willing to kill those people, or the Rrrrrr. And convinced the rest of her unit to follow her.

That had all happened five years before. The results of it were still playing themselves out.

Lieutenant Awn shifted on her cushion. "That business was all uncovered because a single human soldier refused an order. And led a mutiny. If it hadn't been for her...well. Ancillaries won't do that. They can't."

"That business was all uncovered," replied the head priest, "because the ship that human soldier boarded, she and the rest of her unit, had aliens on it. Radchaai have few qualms about killing humans, especially noncitizen humans, but you're very cautious about starting wars with aliens."

Only because wars with aliens might run up against the terms of the treaty with the alien Presger. Violating that agreement would have extremely serious consequences. And even so, plenty of high-ranking Radchaai disagreed on that topic. I saw Lieutenant Awn's desire to argue the point. Instead she said, "The governor of Ime was not cautious about it. And would have started that war, if not for this one person."

"Have they executed that person yet?" the head priest asked, pointedly. It was the summary fate of any soldier who refused an order, let alone mutinied.

"Last I heard," said Lieutenant Awn, breath tight and turning shallow, "the Rrrrrr had agreed to turn her over to Radch authorities." She swallowed. "I don't know what's going to happen." Of course, it had probably already happened, whatever it was. News could take a year or more to reach Shis'urna from as far away as Ime.

The head priest didn't answer for a moment. She poured more tea, and spooned fish paste into a small bowl. "Does my continued request for your presence present any sort of disadvantage for you?"

"No," said Lieutenant Awn. "Actually, the other Esk lieutenants are a bit envious. There's no chance for action on *Justice of Toren.*" She picked up her own cup, outwardly calm, inwardly angry. Disturbed. Talking about the news from Ime had increased her unease. "Action means commendations, and possibly promotions." And this was the last annexation. The last chance for an officer to enrich her house through connections to new citizens, or even through outright appropriation.

"Yet another reason I would prefer you," said the head priest.

I followed Lieutenant Awn home. And watched inside the temple, and overlooked the people crisscrossing the plaza as they always did, avoiding the children playing kau in the center of the plaza, kicking the ball back and forth, shouting and laughing. On the edge of the Fore-Temple water, a teenager from the upper city sat sullen and listless watching half a dozen little children hopping from stone to stone, singing:

One, two, my aunt told me
Three, four, the corpse soldier
Five, six, it'll shoot you in the eye
Seven, eight, kill you dead
Nine, ten, break it apart and put it back together.

As I walked the streets people greeted me, and I greeted them in return. Lieutenant Awn was tense and angry, and only nodded absently at the people in the street, who greeted her as she passed.

The person with the fishing-rights complaint left, unsatisfied. Two children rounded the divider after she had gone, and sat cross-legged on the cushion she had vacated. They both wore lengths of fabric wrapped around their waists, clean but faded, though no gloves. The elder was about nine, and the symbols inked on the younger one's chest and shoulders—slightly smudged—indicated she was no more than six. She looked at me, frowning.

In Orsian addressing children properly was easier than addressing adults. One used a simple, ungendered form. "Hello, citizens," I said, in the local dialect. I recognized them both—they lived on the south edge of Ors and I had spoken to them quite frequently, but they had never visited the house before. "How can I help you?"

"You aren't One Esk," said the smaller child, and the older made an abortive motion as if to hush her.

"I am," I said, and pointed to the insignia on my uniform jacket. "See? Only this is my number Fourteen segment."

"I *told* you," said the older child.

The younger considered this for a moment, and then said, "I have a song." I waited in silence, and she took a deep breath, as though about to begin, and then halted, perplexed-seeming. "Do you want to hear it?" she asked, still doubtful of my identity, likely.

"Yes, citizen," I said. I—that is, I–One Esk—first sang to amuse one of my lieutenants, when *Justice of Toren* had hardly been commissioned a hundred years. She enjoyed music, and had brought an instrument with her as part of her luggage allowance. She could never interest the other officers in her hobby and so she taught me the parts to the songs she played. I filed those away and went looking for more, to please her. By the time she was captain of her own ship I had collected a large library of vocal music—no one was going to give me an instrument, but I could sing anytime—and it was a matter of rumor and some indulgent smiles that *Justice of Toren* had an interest in singing. Which it didn't—I—I–*Justice of Toren*—tolerated the habit because it was harmless, and because it was quite possible that one of my captains would appreciate it. Otherwise it would have been prevented.

If these children had stopped me on the street, they would have had no hesitation, but here in the house, seated as though for a formal conference, things were different. And I suspected this was an exploratory visit, that the youngest child meant to eventually ask for a chance to serve in the house's makeshift temple—the prestige of being appointed flower-bearer to Amaat wasn't a question here, in the stronghold of Ikkt, but the customary term-end gift of fruit and clothing was. And this child's best friend was currently a flower-bearer, doubtless making the prospect more interesting.

No Orsian would make such a request immediately or directly, so likely the child had chosen this oblique approach, turning a casual encounter into something formal and intimidating. I reached into my jacket pocket and pulled out a handful of sweets and laid them on the floor between us.

The littler girl made an affirmative gesture, as though I had resolved all her doubts, and then took a breath and began.

My heart is a fish
Hiding in the water-grass
In the green, in the green.

The tune was an odd amalgam of a Radchaai song that played occasionally on broadcast and an Orsian one I already knew. The words were unfamiliar to me. She sang four verses in a clear, slightly wavering voice, and seemed ready to launch into a fifth, but stopped abruptly when Lieutenant Awn's steps sounded outside the divider.

The smaller girl leaned forward and scooped up her payment. Both children bowed, still half-seated, and then rose and ran out the entranceway into the wider house, past Lieutenant Awn, past me following Lieutenant Awn.

"Thank you, citizens," Lieutenant Awn said to their retreating backs, and they started, and then managed with a single movement to both bow slightly in her direction and continue running, out into the street.

"Anything new?" asked Lieutenant Awn, though she didn't pay much attention to music, herself, not beyond what most people do.

"Sort of," I said. Farther down the street I saw the two children, still running as they turned a corner around another house. They slowed to a halt, breathing hard. The littler girl opened her hand to show the older one her fistful of sweets. Surprisingly, she seemed not to have dropped any, small as her hand was, as quick as their flight had been. The older child took a sweet and put it in her mouth.

Five years ago I would have offered something more nutritious, before repairs had begun to the planet's infrastructure, when supplies were chancy. Now every citizen was guaranteed enough to eat, but the rations were not luxurious, and often as not were unappealing.

Inside the temple all was green-lit silence. The head priest did not emerge from behind the screens in the temple residence, though junior priests came and went. Lieutenant Awn went to the second floor of her house and sat brooding on an Ors-style cushion, screened from the street, shirt thrown off. She refused the (genuine) tea I brought her. I transmitted a steady stream of information to her—everything normal, everything routine—and to *Justice of Toren*. "She should take that to the district magistrate," Lieutenant Awn said of the citizen with the fishing dispute, slightly annoyed, eyes closed, the afternoon's reports in her vision. "We don't have jurisdiction over that." I didn't answer. No answer was required, or expected. She approved, with a quick twitch of her fingers, the message I had composed for the district magistrate, and then opened the most recent message from her young sister. Lieutenant Awn sent a percentage of her earnings home to her parents, who used it to buy their younger child poetry lessons. Poetry was a valuable, civilized accomplishment. I couldn't judge if Lieutenant Awn's sister had any particular talent, but then not many did, even among more elevated families. But her work and her letters pleased Lieutenant Awn, and took the edge off her present distress.

The children on the plaza ran away home, laughing. The adolescent sighed, heavily, the way adolescents do, and dropped a pebble in the water and stared at the ripples.

Ancillary units that only ever woke for annexations often wore nothing but a force shield generated by an implant in each body, rank on rank of featureless soldiers that might have been poured from mercury. But I was always out of the holds, and I wore the same uniform human soldiers did, now the fighting was done. My bodies sweated under my uniform jackets, and, bored, I opened three of my mouths, all in close proximity to each other on the temple plaza, and sang with those three voices, "My heart is a fish, hiding in the watergrass..." One person walking by looked at me, startled, but everyone else ignored me—they were used to me by now.

α + 19

3

The next morning the correctives had fallen off, and the bruising on Seivarden's face had faded. She seemed comfortable, but she still seemed high, so that was hardly surprising.

I unrolled the bundle of clothes I had bought for her—insulated underclothes, quilted shirt and trousers, undercoat and hooded overcoat, gloves—and laid them out. Then I took her chin and turned her head toward me. "Can you hear me?"

"Yes." Her dark brown eyes stared somewhere distant over my left shoulder.

"Get up." I tugged on her arm, and she blinked, lazily, and got as far as sitting up before the impulse deserted her. But I managed to dress her, in fits and starts, and then I stowed what few things were still out, shouldered my pack, took Seivarden by the arm, and left.

There was a flier rental at the edge of town, and predictably the proprietor wouldn't rent to me unless I put down twice the advertised deposit. I told her I intended to fly northwest, to visit a herding camp—an outright lie, which she likely knew. "You're an offworlder," she said. "You don't know what it's like away from the towns. Offworlders are always flying out to herding camps and getting lost. Sometimes we find them again, sometimes not." I said nothing. "You'll lose my flier and then where will I be? Out in the snow with my starving children, that's where." Beside me Seivarden stared vaguely off into the distance.

I was forced to put down the money. I had a strong suspicion I would never see it again. Then the proprietor demanded extra because I couldn't display a local pilot certification—something I knew wasn't required. If it had been, I would have forged one before I came.

In the end, though, she gave me the flier. I checked its engine, which seemed clean and in good repair, and made sure of the fuel. When I was satisfied, I put my pack in, seated Seivarden, and then climbed into the pilot's seat.

Two days after the storm, the snowmoss was beginning to show again, sweeps of pale green with darker threads here and there. After two more hours we flew over a line of hills, and the green darkened dramatically, lined and irregularly veined in a dozen shades, like malachite. In some places the moss was smeared and trampled by the creatures that grazed on it, herds of long-haired bov making their way southward as spring advanced. And along those paths, on the edges here and there, ice devils lay in carefully tunneled lairs, waiting for a bov to put a foot wrong so they could drag it down. I saw no trace of them, but even the herders who lived their lives following the bov couldn't always tell when one was near.

It was easy flying. Seivarden sat, half-lying and quiet beside me. How could she be alive? And how had she ended up here, now? It was beyond improbable. But improbable things happened. Nearly a thousand years before Lieutenant Awn was even born, Seivarden had captained a ship of her own, *Sword of Nathtas*, and had lost it. Most of the human crew, including Seivarden, had managed to get to an escape pod, but hers had never been found, that I had heard. Yet here she was. Someone must have found her relatively recently. She was lucky to be alive.

I was four billion miles away when Seivarden lost her ship. I was patrolling a city of glass and polished red stone, silent but for the sound of my own feet, and the conversation of my lieutenants, and, occasionally, me trying my voices against the echoing pentagonal plazas. Falls of flowers, red and yellow and blue, draped the walls surrounding houses with five-sided courtyards. The flowers were wilting; no one dared walk the streets except me and my officers, everyone knew the likely fate of any person placed under arrest. Instead they huddled in their houses, waiting for what would come next, wincing or shuddering at the sound of a lieutenant laughing, or my singing.

What trouble we'd run into, I and my lieutenants, had been sporadic. The Garseddai had put up only nominal resistance. Troop carriers had emptied, the Swords and Mercies were essentially on guard duty around the system. Representatives from the five zones of each of the five regions, twenty-five in all, speaking for the various moons, planets, and stations in the Garseddai system, had surrendered in the name of their constituents, and were separately on their way to *Sword of Amaat* to meet Anaander Mianaai, Lord of the Radch, and beg for the lives of their people. Hence that frightened, silent city.

In a narrow, diamond-shaped park, by a black granite monument inscribed with the Five Right Actions, and the name of the Garseddai patron who had wished to impress them on the local residents, one of my lieutenants passed another and complained that this annexation had been disappointingly dull. Three seconds later I received a message from Captain Seivarden's *Sword of Nathtas*.

The three Garseddai electors she was carrying had killed two of her lieutenants, and twelve of *Sword of Nathtas*'s ancillary segments. They had damaged the ship—cut conduits, breached the hull. Accompanying the report, a recording from *Sword of Nathtas*—the gun that an ancillary segment saw, irrefutably, but that according to *Sword of Nathtas*'s other sensors just didn't exist. A Garseddai elector, against all expectations surrounded by the gleaming silver of Radchaai-style armor that only the ancillary's eyes could see, firing the gun, the bullet piercing the ancillary's armor, killing the segment, and, with its eyes gone, the gun and armor flickering back into nonexistence.

All the electors had been searched before boarding, and *Sword of Nathtas* should have been able to detect any weapon or shield-generating device or implant. And while Radchaai-style armor had once been in common use in the regions surrounding the Radch itself, those regions had been absorbed a thousand years before. The Garseddai didn't use it, didn't know how to make it, let alone how to use it. And even if they had, that gun, and its bullet, were flatly impossible.

Three people armed with such a gun, and armored, could do a great deal of damage on a ship like *Sword of Nathtas*. Especially if even one Garseddai could reach the engine, and if such a gun could pierce the engine's heat shield. Radchaai warship engines burned star-hot, and a failed heat shield meant instant vaporization, an entire ship dissolved in a brief, bright flash.

But there was nothing I could do, nothing anyone could do. The message was nearly four hours old, a signal from the past, a ghost. The issue had been decided even before it had reached me.

A harsh tone sounded, and a blue light blinked on the panel in front of me, beside the fuel indicator. An instant before the indicator had read nearly full. Now it read empty. The engine would shut down in a matter of minutes. Beside me Seivarden sprawled, relaxed and quiet.

I landed.

The fuel tank had been rigged in a way I hadn't detected. It seemed three-quarters full, but it wasn't, and the alarm that ought to have sounded when I'd used half of what I'd started with had been disconnected.

I thought of the double deposit I certainly wouldn't see again. Of the proprietor, so concerned that she might lose her valuable flier. Of course there would be a transmitter, whether or not I triggered the emergency call. The proprietor wouldn't want to lose the flier, just strand me alone in the middle of this plain of moss-streaked snow. I could call for help—I had disabled my communication implants, but I did have a handheld I could use. But we were very, very far from anyone who might be moved to send assistance. And even if help came, and came before the proprietor who clearly meant me no good, I wouldn't get where I was going, a matter of great importance to me.

The air was minus eighteen degrees; the breeze from the south, at approximately eight kph, implied snow sometime in the near future. Nothing serious, if the morning's weather report could be trusted.

My landing had left a green-edged smear of white in the snowmoss, easily visible from the air. The terrain seemed gently hilly, though the hills we'd flown over were no longer visible.

Had this been an ordinary emergency, the best course would have been to stay inside the flier until help came. But this was not an ordinary emergency, and I did not expect rescue.

Either they would come as soon as their transmitter told them we were grounded, prepared to murder, or they would wait. The rental had several other vehicles, the proprietor would likely not be inconvenienced if she waited even several weeks to retrieve her flier. As she herself had said, no one would be surprised if a foreigner lost herself in the snow.

I had two choices. I could wait here and hope to ambush anyone who came to murder and rob me, and take their transport. This would, of course, be futile in the event that they decided to wait for cold and hunger to do their job for them. Or I could pull Seivarden out of the flier, shoulder my pack, and walk. My intended destination was some sixty kilometers to the southeast. I could walk that in a day if I had to, ground and weather—and ice devils—permitting, but I would be lucky if Seivarden could do it in twice that time. And that course would be futile if the proprietor decided not to wait, but to retrieve her flier more or less immediately. Our trail through the moss-striated snow would be clear, they would need only to follow us and dispose of us. I would have lost any advantage of surprise I might have gained by hiding near the downed flier.

And I would be lucky if I found anything, once I reached my destination. I had spent the past nineteen years following the most tenuous of threads, weeks and months of searching or waiting, punctuated by moments like this, when success or even life hung on the toss of a coin. I had been lucky to come this far. I could not reasonably expect to go farther.

A Radchaai would have tossed that coin. Or more accurately a handful of them, a dozen disks, each with its meaning and import, the pattern of their fall a map of the universe as Amaat willed it to be. Things happen the way they happen because the world is the way it is. Or, as a Radchaai would say, the universe is the shape of the gods. Amaat conceived of light, and conceiving of light also necessarily conceived of not-light, and light and darkness sprang forth. This was the first Emanation, EtrepaBo; Light/Darkness. The other three, implied and necessitated by that first, are EskVar (Beginning/Ending), IssaInu (Movement/Stillness), and VahnItr (Existence/Nonexistence). These four Emanations variously split and recombined to create the universe. Everything that is, emanates from Amaat.

The smallest, most seemingly insignificant event is part of an intricate whole and to understand why one particular mote of dust falls in one particular path, and lands in one particular location, is to understand the will of Amaat. There is no such thing as "just a coincidence." Nothing happens by chance, but only according to the mind of God.

Or so official Radchaai orthodoxy teaches. I myself have never understood religion very well. It was never required that I should. And though the Radchaai had made me, I was not Radchaai. I knew and cared nothing about the will of the gods. I only knew that I would land where I myself had been cast, wherever that would be.

I took my pack from the flier, opened it, and removed an extra magazine, which I stowed inside my coat near my gun. I shouldered the pack, went around to the other side of the flier, and opened the hatch there. "Seivarden," I said.

She didn't move, only breathed a quiet *hmmm*. I took her arm and pulled, and she half-slid, half-stepped out into the snow.

I had gotten this far by taking one step, and then another. I turned northeast, pulling Seivarden along, and walked.

Dr. Arilesperas Strigan, whose home I very much hoped I was walking toward, had been, at one time, a medic in private practice on Dras Annia Station, an aggregation of at least five different stations, one built onto another, at the intersection of two dozen different routes, well outside Radch territory. Nearly anything could end up there, given enough time, and in the course of her work she had met a wide variety of people, with a wide variety of antecedents. She had been paid in currency, in favors, in antiques, in nearly anything that might imaginably be said to have value.

I'd been there, seen the station and its convoluted, interpenetrating layers, seen where Strigan had worked and lived, seen the things she'd left behind when one day, for no reason anyone seemed to know, she'd bought passage on five different ships and then disappeared. A case full of stringed instruments, only three of which I could name. Five shelves of icons, a dizzying array of gods and saints worked in wood, in shell, in gold. A dozen guns, each one carefully labeled with its station permit number. These were collections that had begun as single items, received in payment, sparking her curiosity. Strigan's lease had been paid in full for 150 years, and as a result station authorities had left her apartment untouched.

A bribe had gotten me in, to see the collection I had come for—a few five-sided tiles in colors still flower-bright after a thousand years. A shallow bowl inscribed around its gilt edge in a language Strigan couldn't possibly have read. A flat plastic rectangle I knew was a voice recorder. At a touch it produced laughter, voices speaking that same dead language.

Small as it was, this had not been an easy collection to assemble. Garseddai artifacts were scarce, because once Anaander Mianaai had realized the Garseddai possessed the means to destroy Radchaai ships and penetrate Radchaai armor, she had ordered the utter destruction of Garsedd and its people. Those pentagonal plazas, the flowers, every living thing on every planet, moon, and station in the system, all gone. No one would ever live there again. No one would ever be permitted to forget what it meant to defy the Radch.

Had a patient given her, say, the bowl, and had that sent her looking for more information? And if one Garseddai object had fetched up there, what else might have? Something a patient might have given her as payment, maybe not knowing what it was—or knowing and wanting desperately to be rid of it. Something that had led Strigan to flee, to disappear, leaving nearly everything she owned behind, perhaps. Something dangerous, something she couldn't bring herself to destroy, to be rid of in the most efficient way possible.

Something I wanted very badly.

I wanted to get as far as we possibly could, as quickly as we possibly could, and so we walked for hours with only the briefest of stops when absolutely necessary. Though the day was clear, and bright as it ever gets on Nilt, I felt blind in a way that I had thought I had learned to ignore by now. I had once had twenty bodies, twenty pairs of eyes, and hundreds of others that I could access if I needed or desired it. Now I could only see in one direction, could only see the vast expanse behind me if I turned my head and blinded myself to what was in front of me. Usually I dealt with this by avoiding too-open spaces, by making sure of just what was at my back, but here that was impossible.

My face burned, despite the very gentle breeze, then numbed. My hands and feet ached at first—I hadn't bought my gloves or boots with the intention of walking sixty kilometers in the cold—and then grew heavy and numb. I was fortunate I hadn't come in winter, when temperatures could be a great deal lower.

Seivarden must have been just as cold, but she walked steadily as I pulled her along, step after apathetic step, feet dragging through the mossy snow, staring down, not complaining or even speaking at all. When the sun was nearly on the horizon she shifted her shoulders just slightly and raised her head. "I know that song," she said.

"What?"

"That song you're humming." Lazily she turned her head toward me, her face showing no anxiety or perplexity at all. I wondered if she had made any effort to conceal her accent. Likely not—on kef, as she was, she wouldn't care. Inside Radch territories that accent declared her a member of a wealthy and influential house, someone who, after taking the aptitudes at fifteen, would have ended up with a prestigious assignment. Outside those territories, it was an easy shorthand for a villain—rich, corrupt, and callous—in a thousand entertainments.

The faint sound of a flier reached us. I turned without stopping, searched the horizon, and saw it, small and distant. Flying low and slowly, following our trail, it seemed. It wasn't a rescue, I was sure. My toss had landed wrong, and now we were exposed and defenseless.

We kept walking as the sound of the flier grew nearer. We couldn't have outraced it even if Seivarden hadn't begun to half-stumble, catching herself, but clearly at the end of her endurance. If she was speaking unprompted, noticing anything around her, she was likely beginning to come down. I stopped, dropped her arm, and she came to a halt beside me.

The flier sailed over us, banked, and landed in our path, approximately thirty meters in front of us. Either they didn't have the means to shoot us from the air, or they didn't wish to. I shrugged off my pack and loosened the fastenings of my outer coat, the better to reach my gun.

Four people got out of the flier—the owner I had rented from, two people I didn't recognize, and the person from the bar, who had called me a "tough little girl," and whom I had wanted to kill but had refrained from killing. I slid my hand into my coat and grasped the gun. My options were limited.

"Don't you have any common sense?" called the proprietor, when they were fifteen meters away. All four stopped. "You stay with the flier when it goes down, so we can find you."

I looked at the person from the bar, saw her recognize me, and see that I recognized her. "In the bar, I said that anyone who tried to rob me would die," I reminded her. She smirked.

One of the people I didn't recognize produced a gun from somewhere on her person. "We aren't gonna just *try*," she said.

I drew my gun and fired, hitting her in the face. She crumpled to the snow. Before the others could react, I shot the person from the bar, who likewise fell, and then the person beside her, all three in quick succession, taking less than one second.

The proprietor swore, and turned to flee. I shot her in the back, and she took three steps and then fell.

"I'm cold," said Seivarden beside me, placid and heedless.

* * *

They had left the flier unguarded, all four approaching me. Foolish. The whole venture had been foolish, undertaken without any sort of serious planning, it seemed. I had only to load Seivarden and my pack into their flier and be off.

The residence of Arilesperas Strigan was barely visible from the air, only a circle slightly more than thirty-five meters in diameter, within which the snowmoss was perceptibly lighter and thinner. I brought the flier down outside the circle and waited a moment to assess the situation. From this angle it was obvious there were buildings, two of them, snow-covered mounds. It might have been an unoccupied herding camp, but if I could trust my information, it was not. There was no sign of a wall or fence, but I would make no assumptions about her security.

After consideration, I opened the hatch on the flier and got out, pulling Seivarden out behind me. We walked slowly to the line where the snow changed, Seivarden stopping when I stopped. She stood incuriously, staring straight ahead.

Beyond this I had not been able to plan. "Strigan!" I called, and waited, but no answer came. I left Seivarden standing where she was and walked the circumference of the circle. The entrances of the two snow-mounded buildings seemed oddly shadowed, and I stopped, and looked again.

Both hung open, dark beyond. Buildings like these would probably have double-doored entrances—like an airlock, to keep warm air inside—but I didn't think anyone would leave either door hanging ajar.

Either Strigan had security in place, or she did not. I stepped over the line, into the circle. Nothing happened.

The doors were open, both inner and outer, and there

were no lights. One of the buildings was just as cold inside as out. I presumed that when I found a light I would discover it was used for storage, filled with tools and sealed packages of food and fuel. The other was two degrees Celsius inside—I guessed that it had been heated until relatively recently. Living quarters, evidently. "Strigan!" I called into the darkness, but the way my voice echoed back told me the building was likely unoccupied.

Outside again, I found the marks where her flier had sat. She was gone, then, and the open doors and the darkness were a message for whoever would come. For me. I had no means to discover where she'd gone. I looked up at the empty sky, and down again at the imprint of the flier. I stood there a while, looking at that empty space.

When I returned to Seivarden, I found she'd lain down in the green-stained snow and gone to sleep.

In the back of the flier I found a lantern, a stove, a tent, and some bedding. I took the lantern into the building I presumed was living quarters and switched it on.

Wide, light-colored rugs covered the floor, and woven hangings the walls; these were blue and orange and an eye-hurting green. Low benches, backless, with cushions, lined the room. Beyond benches and the bright hangings, there was little else. A game board with counters, but the board had a pattern of holes I didn't recognize, and I didn't understand the distribution of the counters among the holes. I wondered whom Strigan played with. Perhaps the board was only decorative. It was finely carved, and the pieces brightly colored.

A wooden box sat on a table in a corner, a long oval with a carved, pierced lid and three strings stretched tight across. The wood was pale gold, with a waving, curling grain. The holes cut in the flat top were as uneven and intricate as the grain of the wood. It was a beautiful thing. I plucked a string and it rang softly.

Doors led to kitchen, bath, sleeping quarters, and what was obviously a small infirmary. I opened a cabinet door and found a neat stack of correctives. Each drawer I pulled out revealed instruments and medicines. She might have gone to a herding camp to tend to some emergency. But the lights and the heat being off, and those doors left open, argued otherwise.

Barring a miracle, it was the end of nineteen years of planning and effort.

The house controls were behind a panel in the kitchen. I found the power supply in place, hooked it back in, and switched on the heat and the lights. Then I went out and got Seivarden, and dragged her into the house.

I made a pallet of blankets I found in Strigan's bedroom, then stripped Seivarden and laid her on it, and covered her with more blankets. She didn't wake, and I used the time to search the house more thoroughly.

The cabinets held plenty of food. A cup sat on a counter, a thin layer of greenish liquid glazing the bottom. Next to it sat a plain white bowl holding the last bits of a hunk of hard bread disintegrating into ice-rimmed water. It looked as though Strigan had left without cleaning up after a meal, leaving nearly everything behind—food, medical supplies. I checked the bedroom, found warm clothes in good repair. She had left on short notice, not taking much.

She knew what she had. Of course she did—that was why she'd fled to begin with. If she was not stupid—and I was quite certain she was not—she had gone the moment she realized what I was, and would keep going until she was as far from me as she could get.

But where would that be? If I represented the power of the Radch, and had found her even here, so distant from both Radch space and her own home, where could she go that they would not ultimately find her? Surely she would realize that. But what other course would be open to her?

Surely she would not be foolish enough to return.

In the meantime, Seivarden would be sick soon, unless I found kef for her. I had no intention of doing that. And there was food here, and heat, and perhaps I could find something, some hint, some clue to what Strigan had been thinking, in the moment she had thought the Radch were coming for her, and fled. Something that would tell me where she'd gone.

α
Ors

4

At night, in Ors, I walked the streets, and looked out over the still, stinking water, dark beyond the few lights of Ors itself, and the blinking of the buoys surrounding the prohibited zones. I slept, also, and sat watch in the lower level of the house, in case anyone should need me, though that was rare in those days. I finished any of the day's work still uncompleted, and watched over Lieutenant Awn, who lay sleeping.

Mornings I brought water for Lieutenant Awn to bathe in, and dressed her, though the local costume was a good deal less effort than her uniform, and she had stopped wearing any sort of cosmetics two years before, as they were difficult to maintain in the heat.

Then Lieutenant Awn would turn to her icons—four-armed Amaat, an Emanation in each hand, sat on a box downstairs, but the others (Toren, who received devotions from every officer on *Justice of Toren*, and a few gods particular to Lieutenant Awn's family) sat near where Lieutenant Awn slept, in the upper part of the house, and it was to them that she made her morning devotions. "The flower of justice is peace," the daily prayer began, that every Radchaai soldier said on waking, every day of her life in the military. "The flower of propriety is beauty in thought and action." The rest of my officers, still on *Justice of Toren*, were on a different schedule. Their mornings rarely coincided with Lieutenant Awn's, so it was almost always Lieutenant Awn's voice alone in prayer, and the others, when they spoke so far away, in chorus, without her. "The flower of benefit is Amaat whole and entire. I am the sword of justice..." The prayer is antiphonal, but only four verses long. I can sometimes hear it still when I wake, like a distant voice somewhere behind me.

Every morning, in every official temple throughout Radchaai space, a priest (who doubles as a registrar of births and deaths and contracts of all kinds) casts the day's omens. Households and individuals sometimes cast their own as well, and there's no obligation to attend the official casting—but it's as good an excuse as any to be seen, and speak to friends and neighbors, and hear gossip.

There was, as yet, no official temple in Ors—these are all primarily dedicated to Amaat, any other gods on the premises take lesser places, and the head priest of Ikkt had not seen her way clear to demoting her god in its own temple, or identifying Ikkt with Amaat closely enough to add Radchaai rites to her own. So for the moment Lieutenant Awn's house served. Each morning the makeshift temple's flower-bearers removed dead flowers from around the icon of Amaat and replaced them with fresh ones—usually a local species with small, bright-pink, triple-lobed petals that grew in the dirt that collected on the outside corners of buildings, or cracks in slabs, and was the nearest thing to a weed but greatly admired by the children. And lately small cupped blue-and-white lilies had been blooming in the lake, especially near the buoy-barricaded prohibited areas.

Then Lieutenant Awn would lay out the cloth for the omen-casting and the omens themselves, a handful of weighty metal disks. These, and the icons, were Lieutenant Awn's personal possessions, gifts from her parents when she had taken the aptitudes and received her assignment.

Occasionally only Lieutenant Awn and the day's attendants came to the morning ritual, but usually others were present. The town's medic, a few of the Radchaai who had been granted property here, other Orsian children who could not be persuaded to go to school, or care about being on time for it, and liked the glitter and ring of the disks as they fell. Sometimes even the head priest of Ikkt would come—that god, like Amaat, not demanding that its followers refuse to acknowledge other gods.

Once the omens fell, and came to rest on the cloth (or, to any spectators' dread, rolled off the cloth and away somewhere harder to interpret), the priest officiating was supposed to identify the pattern, match it with its associated passage of scripture, and recite that for those present. It wasn't something Lieutenant Awn was always able to do. So instead she tossed the omens, I observed their fall, and then I transmitted the appropriate words to her. *Justice of Toren* was, after all, nearly two thousand years old, and had seen nearly every possible configuration.

The ritual done, she would have breakfast—usually a round of bread from whatever local grain was available, and (real) tea—and then take her place on the mat and platform and wait for the day's requests and complaints.

"Jen Shinnan invites you to supper this evening," I told her, that next morning. I also ate breakfast, cleaned weapons, walked the streets, and greeted those who spoke to me.

Jen Shinnan lived in the upper city, and before the annexation she had been the wealthiest person in Ors, in influence second only to the head priest of Ikkt. Lieutenant Awn disliked her. "I suppose I don't have a good excuse to refuse."

"Not that I can see," I said. I also stood at the perimeter of the house, nearly on the street, and watched. An Orsian approached, saw me, slowed. Stopped about eight meters away, pretending to look above me, at something else.

"Anything else?" asked Lieutenant Awn.

"The district magistrate reiterates the official policy regarding fishing reserves in the Ors Marshes..."

Lieutenant Awn sighed. "Yes, of course she does."

"Can I help you, citizen?" I asked the person still hesitating in the street. The impending arrival of her first grandchild hadn't yet been announced to the neighbors, so I pretended I didn't know either, and used only the simple respectful address toward a male person.

"I wish," Lieutenant Awn continued, "the magistrate would come here herself and try living on stale bread and those disgusting pickled vegetables they send, and see how she likes being forbidden to fish where all the fish actually are."

The Orsian in the street started, looked for a moment as if she were going to turn around and walk away, and changed her mind. "Good morning, Radchaai," she said, quietly, coming closer. "And to the lieutenant as well." Orsians were blunt when it suited them, and at other times oddly, frustratingly reticent.

"I know there's a reason for it," said Lieutenant Awn to me. "And she's right, but still." She sighed again. "Anything else?"

"Denz Ay is outside and wishes to speak to you." As I spoke, I invited Denz Ay to step within the house.

"What about?"

"Something she seems unwilling to mention." Lieutenant Awn gestured acknowledgment and I brought Denz Ay around the screens. She bowed, and sat on the mat in front of Lieutenant Awn.

"Good morning, citizen," said Lieutenant Awn. I translated.

"Good morning, Lieutenant." And by slow, careful degrees, beginning with an observation on the heat and the cloudless sky, progressing through inquiries about Lieutenant Awn's health to mild local gossip, she finally came around to hinting at her reason for coming. "I…I have a friend, Lieutenant." She stopped.

"Yes?"

"Yesterday evening my friend was fishing." Denz Ay stopped again.

Lieutenant Awn waited three seconds, and when nothing further seemed forthcoming, she asked, "Did your friend catch much?" When the mood was on them, no amount of direct questioning, or begging an Orsian to come to the point, would avail.

"N-not much," said Denz Ay. And then, irritation flashing across her face, just for an instant: "The best fishing, you know, is near the breeding areas, and those are all prohibited."

"Yes," said Lieutenant Awn. "I'm sure your friend would never fish illegally."

"No, no, of course not," Denz Ay protested. "But…I don't want to get her in trouble…but maybe sometimes she digs tubers. *Near* the prohibited zones."

There weren't really any plants that produced edible tubers near the prohibited zones—they'd all been dug up months ago, if not longer. Poachers were more careful about the ones inside—if the plants decreased too noticeably, or disappeared entirely, we'd be forced to find out who was taking them, and guard them much more closely. Lieutenant Awn knew this. Everyone in the lower city knew it.

Lieutenant Awn waited for the rest of the story, not for the first time annoyed at the Orsian tendency to approach topics by stealth, but managing mostly not to show it. "I've heard they're very good," she ventured.

"Oh, yes!" agreed Denz Ay. "They're best right out of the mud!" Lieutenant Awn suppressed a grimace. "But you can slice them and grill them too..." Denz Ay stopped, with a shrewd look. "Perhaps my friend can get some for you."

I saw Lieutenant Awn's dissatisfaction with her rations, the momentary desire to say, *Yes, please*, but instead she said, "Thank you, there's no need. You were saying?"

"Saying?"

"Your...friend." As she spoke Lieutenant Awn was asking me questions, with minute twitches of her fingers. "Was digging tubers *near* a prohibited zone. And?"

I showed Lieutenant Awn the spot this person was most likely to have been digging in—I patrolled all of Ors, saw the boats go in and out, saw where they were at night when they doused lights and maybe even thought they were running invisible to me.

"And," said Denz Ay, "they found something."

Anyone missing? Lieutenant Awn asked me, silently, alarmed. I replied in the negative. "What did they find?" Lieutenant Awn asked Denz Ay, aloud.

"Guns," said Denz Ay, so quietly Lieutenant Awn almost didn't hear. "A dozen, from before." From before the annexation, she meant. All the Shis'urnan militaries had been relieved of their weapons, no one on the planet should have had any guns we didn't already know about. The answer was so surprising that for a blinking two seconds Lieutenant Awn didn't react at all.

Then came puzzlement, alarm, and confusion. *Why is she telling me this?* Lieutenant Awn asked me silently.

"There's been some talk, Lieutenant," said Denz Ay. "Perhaps you've heard it."

"There's always talk," acknowledged Lieutenant Awn, the answer so formulaic I didn't need to translate it for her, she could say it in the local dialect. "How else are people to pass the time?" Denz Ay conceded this conventional point with a gesture. Lieutenant Awn's patience frayed, and she attacked directly. "They might have been put there before the annexation."

Denz Ay made a negative motion with her left hand. "They weren't there a month ago."

Did someone find a pre-annexation cache, and hide them there? Lieutenant Awn asked me, silently. Aloud she asked, "When people talk, do they say things that might account for the appearance of a dozen guns underwater in a prohibited zone?"

"Such guns are no good against *you*." Because of our armor, Denz Ay meant. Radchaai armor is an essentially impenetrable force shield. I could extend mine at a thought, the moment I desired to do so. The mechanism that generated it was implanted in each of my segments, and Lieutenant Awn had it as well—though hers was an externally worn unit. It didn't make us completely invulnerable, and in combat we sometimes wore actual pieces of armor under it, lightweight and articulated, covering head and limbs and torso, but even without that a handful of guns wouldn't do much damage to either of us.

"So who would those guns be meant for?" asked Lieutenant Awn.

Denz Ay considered, frowning, biting her lip, and then said, "The Tanmind are more like the Radchaai than we are."

"Citizen," said Lieutenant Awn, laying noticeable, deliberate stress on that word, which was only what *Radchaai* meant in the first place, "if we were going to shoot anyone here, we'd already have done it." Had already done it, in fact. "We wouldn't need secret stashes of weapons."

"This is why I came to you," said Denz Ay, emphatic, as though explaining something in very simple terms, for a child. "When you shoot a person, you say why and do it, without excuse. This is how the Radchaai are. But in the upper city, before you came, when they would shoot Orsians, they would always be careful to have an excuse. They wanted someone dead," she explained, to Lieutenant Awn's uncomprehending, appalled expression, "they did not say, *You are trouble we want you gone* and then shoot. They said, *We are only defending ourselves* and when the person was dead they would search the body or a house and discover weapons, or incriminating messages." Not, the implication was clear, genuine ones.

"Then how are we alike?"

"Your gods are the same." They weren't, not explicitly so, but the fiction was encouraged, in the upper city and elsewhere. "You live in space, you go all wrapped up in clothes. You are rich, the Tanmind are rich. If someone in the upper city"—and by this I suspected she meant a specific someone—"cries out that some Orsian threatens them, most Radchaai will believe her, and not some Orsian who is surely lying to protect her own."

And that was why she had come to Lieutenant Awn—so

that, whatever happened, it would be plain and clear to Radchaai authorities that she—and by extension anyone else in the lower city—had in fact had nothing to do with that cache of weapons, if the accusation should materialize.

"These things," said Lieutenant Awn. "Orsian, Tanmind, Moha, they mean nothing now. That's done. Everyone here is Radchaai."

"As you say, Lieutenant," answered Denz Ay, voice quiet and nearly expressionless.

Lieutenant Awn had been in Ors long enough to recognize the unstated refusal to agree. She tried another angle. "No one is going to shoot anybody."

"Of course not, Lieutenant," said Denz Ay, but in that same quiet voice. She was old enough to know firsthand that we had, indeed, shot people in the past. She could hardly be blamed for fearing we might do so in the future.

After Denz Ay left, Lieutenant Awn sat thinking. No one interrupted; the day was quiet. In the green-lit temple interior, the head priest turned to me and said, "Once there would have been two choirs, a hundred voices each. You would have liked it." I had seen recordings. Sometimes the children would bring me songs that were distant echoes of that music, five hundred years gone and more. "We're not what we used to be," said the head priest. "Everything passes, eventually." I agreed that it was so.

"Take a boat tonight," said Lieutenant Awn, stirring at last. "See if there's anything to indicate where the weapons came from. I'll decide what to do once I have a better idea of what's going on."

"Yes, Lieutenant," I said.

* * *

Jen Shinnan lived in the upper city, across the Fore-Temple lake. Few Orsians lived there who weren't servants. The houses there were built to a slightly different plan from those in the lower; hip-roofed, the central part of each floor walled in, though windows and doors were left open on mild nights. All of the upper city had been built over older ruins, and thus much more recently than the lower, within the last fifty or so years, and made much larger use of climate control. Many residents wore trousers and shirts, and even jackets. Radchaai immigrants who lived here tended to wear much more conventional clothes, and Lieutenant Awn, when she visited, wore her uniform without too much discomfort.

But Lieutenant Awn was never comfortable, visiting Jen Shinnan. She didn't like Jen Shinnan, and though of course it was never even hinted at, very likely Jen Shinnan didn't like Lieutenant Awn much either. This sort of invitation was only extended out of social necessity, Lieutenant Awn being a local representative of Radchaai authority. The table this evening was unusually small, just Jen Shinnan, a cousin of hers, and Lieutenant Awn and Lieutenant Skaaiat. Lieutenant Skaaiat commanded *Justice of Ente* Seven Issa, and administered the territory between Ors and Kould Ves—farmland, mostly, where Jen Shinnan and her cousin had their holdings. Lieutenant Skaaiat and her troops assisted us during pilgrimage season, so she was nearly as well-known in Ors as Lieutenant Awn was.

"They confiscated my entire harvest." This was the cousin of Jen Shinnan's, the owner of several tamarind orchards not far from the upper city. She tapped her plate emphatically with her utensil. "The *entire* harvest."

The center of the table was laden with trays and bowls filled with eggs, fish (not from the marshy lake, but from the sea beyond), spiced chicken, bread, braised vegetables, and half a dozen relishes of various types.

"Didn't they pay you, citizen?" asked Lieutenant Awn, speaking slowly and carefully, as she always did when she was anxious her accent might slip. Jen Shinnan and her cousin both spoke Radchaai, so there was no need to translate, nor any anxiety over gender or status or anything else that would have been essential in Tanmind or Orsian.

"Well, but I would certainly have gotten more if I could have taken it to Kould Ves and sold it myself!"

There had been a time when a property owner like her would have been shot early on, so someone's client could take over her plantation. Indeed, not a few Shis'urnans had died in the initial stages of the annexation simply because they were in the way, and *in the way* could mean any number of things.

"As I'm sure you understand, citizen," said Lieutenant Awn, "food distribution is a problem we're still solving, and we all need to endure some hardship while that's accomplished." Her sentences, when she was uncomfortable, became uncharacteristically formal, and sometimes dangerously convoluted.

Jen Shinnan gestured to a laden plate of fragile pale-pink glass. "Another stuffed egg, Lieutenant Awn?"

Lieutenant Awn held up one gloved hand. "They're delicious, but no thank you, citizen."

But the cousin had landed in a track she found it hard to deviate from, despite Jen Shinnan's diplomatic attempt to derail her. "It's not like fruit is a necessity. Tamarind, of all things! And it's not like anyone is starving."

"Indeed it isn't!" agreed Lieutenant Skaaiat, heartily. She

smiled brightly at Lieutenant Awn. Lieutenant Skaaiat—dark-skinned, amber-eyed, aristocratic as Lieutenant Awn was not. One of her Seven Issas stood near me, by the door of the dining room, as straight and still as I was.

Though Lieutenant Awn liked Lieutenant Skaaiat a good deal, and appreciated her sarcasm on this occasion, she could not bring herself to smile in response. "Not this year."

"Your business is doing better than mine, Cousin," said Jen Shinnan, voice placating. She too owned farmland not far from the upper city. But she had also owned those dredgers that sat, silent and still, in the marsh water. "Though I suppose I can't be too regretful, it was a great deal of trouble for very little return."

Lieutenant Awn opened her mouth to speak, and then closed it again. Lieutenant Skaaiat saw it, and said, vowels effortlessly broad and refined, "What is it, another three years for the fishing prohibitions, Lieutenant?"

"Yes," said Lieutenant Awn.

"Foolishness," said Jen Shinnan. "Well-intentioned, but foolishness. You saw what it was like when you arrived. As soon as you open them, they'll be fished out again. The Orsians may have been a great people once, but they're no longer what their ancestors were. They have no ambition, no sense of anything beyond their short-term advantage. If you show them who's boss, then they can be quite obedient, as I'm sure you've discovered, Lieutenant Awn, but in their natural state they are, with few exceptions, shiftless and superstitious. Though I suppose that's what comes of living in the Underworld." She smiled at her own joke. Her cousin laughed outright.

The space-dwelling nations of Shis'urna divided the universe into three parts. In the middle lay the natural environment of humans—space stations, ships, constructed habitats. Outside those was the Black—heaven, the home of God and everything holy. And within the gravity well of the planet Shis'urna itself—or for that matter any planet—lay the Underworld, the land of the dead from which humanity had had to escape in order to become fully free of its demonic influence.

You can see, perhaps, how the Radchaai conception of the universe as being God itself might seem the same as the Tanmind idea of the Black. You might also see why it seemed a bit odd, to Radchaai ears, to hear someone who believed gravity wells were the land of the dead call people superstitious for worshiping a lizard.

Lieutenant Awn managed a polite smile, and Lieutenant Skaaiat said, "And yet you live here too."

"I don't confuse abstract philosophical concepts with reality," said Jen Shinnan. Though that too sounded odd, to a Radchaai who knew what it meant for a Tanmind stationer to descend to the Underworld and return. "Seriously. I have a theory."

Lieutenant Awn, who had been exposed to several Tanmind theories about the Orsians, managed a neutral, even almost curious expression and said, blandly, "Oh?"

"Do share!" encouraged Lieutenant Skaaiat. The cousin, having scooped a quantity of spiced chicken into her mouth moments before, made a gesture of support with her utensil.

"It's the way they live, all out in the open like that, with nothing but a roof," Jen Shinnan said. "They can't have any privacy, no sense of themselves as real individuals, you understand, no sense of any sort of separate identity."

"Let alone private property," said Jen Taa, having swallowed her chicken. "They think they can just walk in and take whatever they want."

Actually, there were rules—if unstated ones—about entering a house uninvited, and theft was rarely a problem in the lower city. Occasionally during pilgrimage season, almost never otherwise.

Jen Shinnan gestured acknowledgment. "And no one *here* is ever really starving, Lieutenant. No one has to work, they just fish in the swamp. Or fleece visitors during pilgrimage season. They have no chance to develop any ambition, or any desire to improve themselves. And they don't—can't, really—develop any sort of sophistication, any kind of..." She trailed off, searching for the right word.

"Interiority?" suggested Lieutenant Skaaiat, who enjoyed this game much more than Lieutenant Awn did.

"That's it exactly!" agreed Jen Shinnan. "Interiority, yes."

"So your theory is," said Lieutenant Awn, her tone dangerously even, "that the Orsians aren't really *people*."

"Well, not *individuals*." Jen Shinnan seemed to sense, remotely, that she'd said something to make Lieutenant Awn angry, but didn't seem entirely certain of it. "Not as such."

"And of course," interjected Jen Taa, oblivious, "they see what we have, and don't understand that you have to *work* for that sort of life, and they're envious and resentful and blame *us* for not letting them have it, when if they'd only *work*..."

"They send what money they have to support that half-broken-down temple, and then complain they're poor," said Jen Shinnan. "And they fish out the marsh and then blame us. They'll do the same to you, Lieutenant, when you open the prohibited zones again."

"Your dredging up the mud by the ton to sell as fertilizer didn't have anything to do with the fish disappearing?" asked Lieutenant Awn, her voice edged. Actually, the fertilizer had been a by-product of the main business of selling the mud to space-dwelling Tanmind for religious purposes. "That was due to irresponsible fishing on the part of the Orsians?"

"Well of course it had *some* effect," said Jen Taa, "but if they'd only managed their resources properly..."

"Quite right," agreed Jen Shinnan. "You blame me for ruining the fishing. But I gave those people jobs. Opportunities to improve their lives."

Lieutenant Skaaiat must have sensed that Lieutenant Awn was at a dangerous point. "Security on a planet is very different from on a station," she said, her voice cheerful. "On a planet there's always going to be some...some slippage. Some things you don't see."

"Ah," said Jen Shinnan, "but you've got everyone tagged so you always know where we are."

"Yes," agreed Lieutenant Skaaiat. "But we're not always *watching*. I suppose you could grow an AI big enough to watch a whole planet, but I don't think anyone has ever tried it. A station, though..."

I watched Lieutenant Awn see Lieutenant Skaaiat spring the trap Jen Shinnan had walked into moments ago. "On a station," Lieutenant Awn said, "the AI sees everything."

"So much easier to manage," agreed Lieutenant Skaaiat happily. "Almost no need for security at all." That wasn't quite true, but this was no time to point that out.

Jen Taa set down her utensil. "Surely the AI doesn't see *everything*." Neither lieutenant said anything. "Even when you...?"

"Everything," answered Lieutenant Awn. "I assure you, citizen."

Silence, for nearly two seconds. Beside me, Lieutenant Skaaiat's Seven Issa guard's mouth twitched, something that might have been an itch or some unavoidable muscle spasm, but was, I suspected, the only outward manifestation of her amusement. Military ships possessed AIs just as stations did, and Radchaai soldiers lived utterly without privacy.

Lieutenant Skaaiat broke the silence. “Your niece, citizen, is taking the aptitudes this year?”

The cousin gestured yes. So long as her own farming provided income, she wouldn’t need an assignment, and neither would her heir—however many heirs the land might support. The niece, however, had lost her parents during the annexation.

“These aptitudes,” said Jen Shinnan. “You took them, Lieutenants?” Both indicated affirmatively. The aptitudes were the only way into the military, or any government post—though that didn’t encompass all assignments available.

“No doubt,” said Jen Shinnan, “the test works well for you, but I wonder if it’s suited to us Shis’urnans.”

“Why is that?” asked Lieutenant Skaaiat, with slightly frowning amusement.

“Has there been a problem?” asked Lieutenant Awn, still stiff, still annoyed with Jen Shinnan.

“Well.” Jen Shinnan picked up a napkin, soft and bleached a snowy white, and wiped her mouth. “Word is, last month in Kould Ves all the candidates for civil service were ethnic Orsians.”

Lieutenant Awn blinked in confusion. Lieutenant Skaaiat smiled. “You mean to say,” she said, looking at Jen Shinnan but also directing her words to Lieutenant Awn, “that you think the testing is biased.”

Jen Shinnan folded her napkin and set it down on the table beside her bowl. “Come now, Lieutenant. Let us be honest. There’s a reason so few Orsians occupied such posts before you arrived. Every now and then you find an exception—the Divine is a very respectable person, I grant you. But she's an exception. So when I see twenty Orsians destined for civil service posts, and not a single Tanmind, I can't help but think either the test is flawed, or...well. I can't help but remember that it was the Orsians who first surrendered, when you arrived. I can't blame you for appreciating that, for wanting to...acknowledge that. But it's a mistake."

Lieutenant Awn said nothing. Lieutenant Skaaiat asked, "Assuming you're correct, why would that be a mistake?"

"It's as I said before. They just aren't suited to positions of authority. Some exceptions, yes, but..." She waved a gloved hand. "And with the bias of the assignments being so obvious, people won't have confidence in it."

Lieutenant Skaaiat's smile grew broader in proportion to Lieutenant Awn's silent, indignant anger. "Your niece is nervous?"

"A bit!" admitted the cousin.

"Understandably," drawled Lieutenant Skaaiat. "It's a momentous event in any citizen's life. But she needn't fear."

Jen Shinnan laughed, sardonic. "Needn't fear? The lower city resents us, always has, and now we can't make any legal contracts without either taking transport to Kould Ves or going through the lower city to your house, Lieutenant." Any legally binding contract had to be made in the temple of Amaat. Or, a recent (and extremely controversial) concession, on its steps, if one of the parties was an exclusive monotheist. "During that pilgrimage thing it's nearly impossible. We either lose an entire day traveling to Kould Ves, or endanger ourselves."

Jen Shinnan visited Kould Ves quite frequently, often merely to visit friends, or shop. All the Tanmind in the upper city did, and had done so before the annexation. "Has there been some unreported difficulty?" asked Lieutenant Awn, stiff, angry. Utterly polite.

"Well," said Jen Taa. "In fact, Lieutenant, I've been wanting to mention. We've been here a few days, and my niece seems to have had a bit of trouble in the lower city. I told her it was better not to go, but you know how teenagers are when you tell them not to do something."

"What sort of trouble?" asked Lieutenant Awn.

"Oh," said Jen Shinnan, "you know the sort of thing. Rude words, threats—empty, no doubt, and of course nothing next to what things will be like in a week or two, but the child was quite shaken."

The child in question had spent the past two afternoons staring at the Fore-Temple water and sighing. I had spoken to her once and she had turned her head away without answering. After that I had left her alone. No one had troubled her. *No problems that I saw*, I messaged Lieutenant Awn.

"I'll keep an eye on her," said Lieutenant Awn, silently acknowledging my information with a twitch of her fingers.

"Thank you, Lieutenant," said Jen Shinnan. "I know we can count on you."

"You think it's funny." Lieutenant Awn tried to relax her too-tight jaw. I could tell from the increasing tension of her facial muscles that without intervention she would soon have a headache.

Lieutenant Skaaiat, walking beside her, laughed outright. "It's pure comedy. Forgive me, my dear, but the angrier you get the more painstakingly correct your speech becomes, and the more Jen Shinnan mistakes you."

"Surely not. Surely she's asked about me."

"You're still angry. Worse," said Lieutenant Skaaiat,

hooking her arm around Lieutenant Awn's, "you're angry with *me*. I'm sorry. And she *has* asked. Very obliquely, just *interested* in you, only natural, of course."

"And you answered," suggested Lieutenant Awn, "equally obliquely."

I walked behind them, alongside the Seven Issa who had stood with me in Jen Shinnan's dining room. Directly ahead, along the street and across the Fore-Temple water, I could see myself where I stood in the plaza.

Lieutenant Skaaiat said, "I said nothing untrue. I told her that lieutenants on ships with ancillaries tended to be from old, high-ranking families with lots of money and clients. Her connections in Kould Ves might have said a bit more, but not much. On the one hand, since you aren't such a person, they have cause to resent you. On the other hand, you *do* command ancillaries and not vulgar human troops, which the old-fashioned deplore just as much as they deplore the scions of obscure, nobody houses getting assigned as officers. They approve of your ancillaries and disapprove of your antecedents. Jen Shinnan gets a very ambivalent picture of you." Her voice was quiet, pitched so that only someone standing very near could hear it, though the houses we passed were closed up, and dark on the lower levels. It was very unlike the lower city, where even late into the night people sat nearly in the street, even small children.

"Besides," Lieutenant Skaaiat said, "she's right. Oh, not that foolishness about Orsians, no, but she's right to be suspicious about the aptitudes. You know yourself the tests are susceptible to manipulation." Lieutenant Awn felt a sick, betrayed indignation at Lieutenant Skaaiat's words, but said nothing, and Lieutenant Skaaiat continued. "For centuries only the wealthy and well-connected tested as suitable for certain jobs. Like, say, officers in the military. In the last, what, fifty, seventy-five years, that hasn't been true. Have the lesser houses suddenly begun to produce officer candidates where they didn't before?"

"I don't like where you're headed with this," snapped Lieutenant Awn, tugging slightly at their linked arms, trying to pull away. "I didn't expect it from you."

"No, no," protested Lieutenant Skaaiat, and didn't let go, drew her closer. "The question is the right one, and the answer the same. The answer is no, of course. But does that mean the tests were rigged before, or rigged now?"

"And your opinion?"

"Both. Before and now. And our friend Jen Shinnan doesn't fully understand that the question can even be asked—she just knows that if you're going to succeed you've got to have the right connections, and she knows the aptitudes are part of that. And she's utterly shameless—you heard her imply the Orsians were being rewarded for collaboration, and in nearly the same breath imply her people would be even better collaborators! And you notice neither she nor her cousin are sending their *own* children for testing, just this orphaned niece. Still, they're invested in her doing well. If we'd asked for a bribe to ensure it, she'd have handed it over, no question. I'm surprised she didn't offer one, actually."

"You wouldn't," protested Lieutenant Awn. "You won't. You can't deliver anyway."

"I won't need to. The child will test well, likely get herself sent to the territorial capital for training to take a nice civil service post. If you ask me, the Orsians *are* being rewarded for collaborating—but they're a minority in this system. And now the unavoidable unpleasantness of the annexation is over, we want people to start realizing that being Radchaai will benefit them. Punishing local houses for not being quick enough to surrender won't help."

They walked in silence for a bit, and stopped at the edge of the water, arms still linked.

"Walk you home?" asked Lieutenant Skaaiat. Lieutenant Awn didn't answer, but looked away over the water, still angry. The green skylights in the temple's slanted roof shone, and light poured out the open doors onto the plaza and reflected on the water—this was a season of nightly vigils. Lieutenant Skaaiat said, with an apologetic half-smile, "I've upset you, let me make it up to you."

"Sure," said Lieutenant Awn, with a small sigh. She never could resist Lieutenant Skaaiat, and indeed there was no real reason to do so. They turned and walked along the water's edge.

"What's the difference," Lieutenant Awn said, so quietly it didn't seem like a break in the silence, "between citizens and noncitizens?"

"One is civilized," said Lieutenant Skaaiat with a laugh, "and the other isn't." The joke only made sense in Radchaai—*citizen* and *civilized* are the same word. To be Radchaai is to be civilized.

"So in the moment the Lord of Mianaai bestowed citizenship on the Shis'urnans, in that very instant they became civilized." The sentence was a circular one—the question Lieutenant Awn was asking is a difficult one in that language. "I mean, one day your Issas are shooting people for failing to speak respectfully enough—don't tell me it didn't happen, because I know it did, and worse—and it doesn't matter because they're not Radchaai, not civilized." Lieutenant Awn had switched momentarily into the bit of the local Orsian language she knew, because the Radchaai words refused to let her mean what she wished to say. "And any measures are justified in the name of civilization."

"Well," said Lieutenant Skaaiat, "it was effective, you have to admit. Everyone speaks very respectfully to us these days." Lieutenant Awn was silent. Unamused. "What brought this on?" Lieutenant Awn told her about her conversation with the head priest the day before.

"Ah. Well. You didn't protest at the time."

"What good would it have done?"

"Absolutely none," answered Lieutenant Skaaiat. "But that's not why you didn't. Besides, even if ancillaries don't beat people, or take bribes, or rape, or shoot people out of pique—those people human troops shot . . . a hundred years ago they'd have been stored in suspension for future use as ancillary segments. Do you know how many we still have stockpiled? *Justice of Toren*'s holds will be full of ancillaries for the next million years. If not longer. Those people are effectively dead. So what's the difference? And you don't like my saying that, but here's the truth: luxury always comes at someone else's expense. One of the many advantages of civilization is that one doesn't generally have to see that, if one doesn't wish. You're free to enjoy its benefits without troubling your conscience."

"It doesn't trouble yours?"

Lieutenant Skaaiat laughed, gaily, as though they were discussing something completely different, a game of counters or a good tea shop. "When you grow up knowing that you deserve to be on top, that the lesser houses exist to serve your house's glorious destiny, you take such things for granted. You're born assuming that someone else is paying the cost of your life. It's just the way things are. What happens during annexation—it's a difference of degree, not a difference of kind."

"It doesn't seem that way to me," answered Lieutenant Awn, short and bitter.

"No, of course it doesn't," answered Lieutenant Skaaiat, her voice kinder. I'm quite sure she genuinely liked Lieutenant Awn. I know that Lieutenant Awn liked her, even if Lieutenant Skaaiat sometimes said things that upset her, like this evening. "Your family has been paying some of that cost, however small. Maybe that makes it easier to sympathize with whoever might be paying for *you*. And I'm sure it's hard not to think of what your own ancestors went through when they were annexed."

"*Your* ancestors were never annexed." Lieutenant Awn's voice was biting.

"Well, some of them probably were," admitted Lieutenant Skaaiat. "But they're not in the official genealogy." She stopped, pulling Lieutenant Awn to a halt beside her. "Awn, my good friend. Don't trouble yourself over things you can't help. Things are as they are. You have nothing to reproach yourself with."

"You've just said we all do."

"That wasn't what I said." Lieutenant Skaaiat's voice was gentle. "But you'll take it that way all the same, won't you? Listen—life will be better here, because we're here. It already is, not just for the people here but for those who were transported. And even for Jen Shinnan, even though just now she's preoccupied with her own resentment at no longer being the highest authority in Ors. She'll come around in time. They all will."

"And the dead?"

"Are dead. No use fretting over them."

5

When Seivarden woke, she was fidgety and irritable. She asked me twice who I was, and complained three times that my answer—which was a lie in any event—conveyed no meaningful information to her. "I don't know anyone named Breq. I've never seen you before in my life. Where am I?"

Nowhere with a name. "You're on Nilt."

She drew a blanket around her bare shoulders, and then, sulkily, shoved it off again and folded her arms across her chest. "I've never even heard of Nilt. How did I end up here?"

"I have no idea." I set the food I was holding down on the floor in front of her.

She reached for the blanket again. "I don't want that."

I gestured my indifference. I had eaten and rested while she slept. "Does this happen to you often?"

"What?"

"Waking up and finding you don't know where you are, who you're with, or how you got there?"

She fidgeted the blanket on and off again, and rubbed her arms and wrists together. "A couple of times."

"I'm Breq, from the Gerentate." I had already told her, but I knew she would ask me again. "I found you two days ago in front of a tavern. I don't know how you got there. You would have died if I'd left you. I'm sorry if that's what you wanted."

For some reason that angered her. "How very charming you are, Breq from the Gerentate." She sneered slightly as she said it. It was mildly, irrationally surprising to hear that tone from her, naked and disheveled as she was, and not in uniform.

That tone made me angry. I knew very precisely why I was angry, and knew as well that if I dared to explain my anger to Seivarden she would respond with nothing but contempt, and that made me even angrier. I held my face in the neutral, slightly interested expression I had used with her from the moment she'd awakened, and made the same indifferent gesture I had made moments before.

I had been the first ship Seivarden ever served on. She'd arrived fresh out of training, seventeen years old, plunged straight into the tail end of an annexation. In a tunnel carved through red-brown stone under the surface of a small moon she had been ordered to guard a line of prisoners, nineteen of them, crouched naked and shivering along the chill passageway, waiting to be evaluated.

Actually I was doing the guarding, seven of me ranged along the corridor, weapons ready. Seivarden—so young then, still slight, dark hair, brown skin, and brown eyes unremarkable, unlike the aristocratic lines of her face, including a nose she hadn't quite grown into yet. Nervous, yes, left in charge here just days after arriving, but also proud of herself and her sudden, small authority. Proud of that dark-brown uniform jacket, trousers, and gloves, that lieutenant's insignia. And, I thought, a tiny bit too excited at holding an actual gun in what certainly wasn't a training exercise.

One of the people along the wall—broad-shouldered, muscled, cradling a broken arm against her torso—wept noisily, moaning each exhale, gasping every inhale. She knew, everyone in this line knew, that they would either be stored for future use as ancillaries—like the ancillaries of mine that stood before them even now, identities gone, bodies appendages to a Radchaai warship—or else they would be disposed of.

Seivarden, pacing importantly up and down the line, grew more irritated with this piteous captive's every convulsive breath, until finally she halted in front of her. "Aatr's tits! Stop that *noise*!" Small movements of Seivarden's arm muscles told me she was about to raise her weapon. No one would have cared if she'd taken the butt of her gun and beaten the prisoner senseless. No one would have cared if she'd shot the prisoner in the head, so long as no vital equipment was damaged in the process. Human bodies to make into ancillaries weren't exactly a scarce resource.

I stepped in front of her. "Lieutenant," I said, flat and toneless. "The tea you asked for is ready." Actually it had been ready five minutes before but I'd said nothing, held it in reserve.

In the readings coming from that terribly young Lieutenant Seivarden I saw startlement, frustration, anger. Irritation. "That was fifteen minutes ago," she snapped. I didn't answer. Behind me the prisoner still sobbed and moaned. "Can't you shut her up?"

"I'll do my best, Lieutenant," I said, though I knew there was only one way to really do that, only one thing that would silence that captive's grief. The newly minted Lieutenant Seivarden seemed unaware of that.

Twenty-one years after arriving on *Justice of Toren*—just over a thousand years before I found her in the snow—Seivarden was senior Esk lieutenant. Thirty-eight, still quite young by Radchaai standards. A citizen could live some two hundred years.

Her last day, she sat drinking tea on her bunk in her quarters, three meters by two meters by two, white-walled, severely neat. She was grown into that aristocratic nose by now, grown into herself. No longer awkward or unsure.

Beside her on the tightly made-up bunk sat the Esk decade's most junior lieutenant, arrived just weeks ago, a sort of cousin of Seivarden's, though from another house. Taller than Seivarden had been at that age, broader, a bit more graceful. Mostly. Nervous at being asked to confer in private here with the senior lieutenant, cousin or no, but concealing it. Seivarden said to her, "You want to be careful, Lieutenant, who you favor with your... attentions."

The very young lieutenant frowned, embarrassed, realizing suddenly what this was about.

"You know who I mean," continued Seivarden, and I knew too. One of the other Esk lieutenants had definitely noticed when the very young lieutenant had come on board, had been slowly, discreetly sounding out the possibility of the very young lieutenant perhaps noticing her back. But not so discreetly that Seivarden hadn't seen it. In fact, the entire decade room had seen it, and seen, as well, the very young lieutenant's intrigued response.

"I know who you mean," said the very young lieutenant. Indignant. "But I don't see why..."

"Ah!" said Seivarden, sharp and peremptory. "You think it's harmless fun. Well, it would probably be fun." Seivarden had slept with the lieutenant in question herself at one point and knew whereof she spoke. "But it wouldn't be harmless. She's a good enough officer, but her house is very provincial. If she weren't senior to you, there would be no problem."

The very young lieutenant's house was definitely *not* "very provincial." Naive as she was, she knew immediately what Seivarden meant. And was angry enough at it to address Seivarden in a way that was less formal than propriety demanded. "Aatr's tits, Cousin, no one's said anything about clientage. No one could, none of us can make contracts until we retire." Among the wealthy, clientage was a very hierarchical relationship—a patron promised certain sorts of assistance to her client, both financial and social, and a client provided support and services to her patron. These were promises that could last generations. In the oldest, most prestigious houses the servants were nearly all the descendants of clients, for instance, and many businesses owned by wealthy houses were staffed by client branches of lower ones.

"These provincial houses are ambitious," Seivarden explained, voice the slightest bit condescending. "And clever as well or they wouldn't have gotten as far as they have. She's senior to you, and you've both got years to serve yet. Grant her intimacy on those terms, let it continue, and depend on it, one of these days she'll be offering *you* clientage when it ought to be the other way around. I don't think your mother would thank you for exposing your house to that sort of insult."

The very young lieutenant's face heated with anger and chagrin, the shine of her first adult romance suddenly gone, the whole thing turned sordid and calculating.

Seivarden leaned forward, reached out for the tea flask and stopped, with a surge of irritation. Said silently to me, the fingers of her free hand twitching, "This cuff has been torn for three days."

I said, directly into her ear, "I'm sorry, Lieutenant." I ought to have offered to make the repair immediately, dispatched a segment of One Esk to take the offending shirt away. I ought, in fact, to have mended it three days before. Ought not to have dressed her in that shirt that day.

Silence in the cramped compartment, the very young lieutenant still preoccupied with her discomfiture. Then I said, directly into Seivarden's ear, "Lieutenant, the decade commander will see you at your earliest convenience."

I had known the promotion was coming. Had taken a petty satisfaction in the fact that even if she ordered me that moment to mend her sleeve, I would have no time to do it. As soon as she left her quarters I started packing her things, and three hours later she was on her way to her new command, freshly made captain of *Sword of Nathtas*. I hadn't been particularly sorry to see her go.

Such small things. It wasn't Seivarden's fault if she had reacted badly in a situation that few (if any) seventeen-year-olds could have handled with aplomb. It was hardly surprising that she was precisely as snobby as she had been brought up to be. Not her fault that over my (at the time) thousand years of existence I had come to have a higher opinion of ability than of breeding, and had seen more than one "very provincial" house rise far enough to lose that label, and turn out its own versions of Seivarden.

All the years between young Lieutenant Seivarden and Captain Seivarden, they were made up of tiny moments.

Minor things. I never hated Seivarden. I had just never particularly liked her. But I couldn't see her, now, without thinking of someone else.

The next week at Strigan's house was unpleasant. Seivarden needed constant looking after, and frequent cleaning up. She ate very little (which in some respects was fortunate), and I had to work to make sure she didn't get dehydrated. But by the end of the week she was keeping her food down, and sleeping at least intermittently. Even so she slept lightly, twitching and turning, often trembling, breathing hard, and waking suddenly. When she was awake, and not weeping, she complained that everything was too harsh, too rough, too loud, too bright.

Another few days after that, when she thought I was asleep, she went to the outer door and stared out over the snow, and then put on her clothes and a coat and trudged to the outbuilding, and then the flier. She tried to start it, but I had removed an essential part and kept it close. When she returned to the house she had at least the presence of mind to close both doors before she tracked snow into the main room, where I sat on a bench holding Strigan's stringed instrument. She stared, unable to conceal her surprise, still shrugging slightly, uncomfortable in the heavy coat, itchy.

"I want to leave," she said, in a voice oddly half cowed and half arrogant, commanding Radchaai.

"We'll leave when I'm ready," I said, and fingered a few notes on the instrument. Her feelings were too raw for her to be able to conceal them just now, and her anger and despair showed plainly on her face. "You are where you are," I said, in an even tone, "as a result of decisions you made yourself."

Her spine straightened, her shoulders went back. "You

don't know anything about me, or what decisions I have or haven't made."

It was enough to make me angry again. I knew something about making decisions, and not making them. "Ah, I forget. Everything happens as Amaat wills, nothing is *your* fault."

Her eyes went wide. She opened her mouth to speak, drew breath, but then blew it out, sharp and shaky. She turned her back, ostensibly to remove her outer coat and drop it on a nearby bench. "You don't understand," she said, contemptuous, but her voice trembled with suppressed tears. "You're not Radchaai."

Not civilized. "Did you start taking kef before or after you left the Radch?" It shouldn't have been available in Radchaai territory, but there was always some minor smuggling station authorities might turn a blind eye toward.

She slumped down onto the bench beside where she'd sloppily left her coat. "I want tea."

"There's no tea here." I set the instrument aside. "There's milk." More specifically, there was fermented bov milk, which the people here thinned with water and drank warm. The smell—and taste—was reminiscent of sweaty boots. And too much of it would likely make Seivarden slightly sick.

"What sort of place doesn't have *tea*?" she demanded, but leaned forward, elbows on her knees, and put her forehead on her wrists, her bare hands palm-up, fingers outstretched.

"This sort of place," I answered. "Why were you taking kef?"

"You wouldn't understand." Tears dropped into her lap.

"Try me." I picked up the instrument again, picked out a tune.

After six seconds of silent weeping, Seivarden said, "She said it would make everything clearer."

"The kef would?" No answer. "What would be clearer?"

"I know that song," she said, her face still resting on her wrists. I realized it was very likely the only way she would recognize me, and changed to a different tune. In one region of Valskaay, singing was a refined pastime, local choral associations the center of social activity. That annexation had brought me a great deal of the sort of music I had liked best, when I had had more than one voice. I chose one of those. Seivarden wouldn't know it. Valskaay had been both before and after her time.

"She said," Seivarden said finally, lifting her face from her hands, "that emotions clouded perception. That the clearest sight was pure reason, undistorted by feeling."

"That's not true." I'd had a week with this instrument and very little else to do. I managed two lines at once.

"It seemed true at first. It was *wonderful* at first. It all went away. But then it would wear off, and things would be the same. Only worse. And then after a while it was like not feeling felt bad. I don't know. I can't describe it. But if I took more that went away."

"And coming down got less and less endurable." I'd heard the story a few times, in the past twenty years.

"Oh, Amaat's grace," she moaned. "I want to die."

"Why don't you?" I changed to another song. *My heart is a fish, hiding in the water-grass. In the green, in the green...*

She looked at me as though I were a rock that had just spoken.

"You lost your ship," I said. "You were frozen for a thousand years. You wake up to find the Radch has changed—no more invasions, a humiliating treaty with the Presger, your house has lost financial and social status. No one knows you or remembers you, or cares whether you live or die. It's not what you were used to, not what you were expecting out of your life, is it?"

It took three puzzled seconds for the fact to dawn. "You know who I am."

"Of course I know who you are. You told me," I lied.

She blinked, tearily, trying, I supposed, to remember if she had or not. But her memories were, of course, incomplete.

"Go to sleep," I said, and laid my fingers across the strings, silencing them.

"I want to leave," she protested, not moving, still slumped on the bench, elbows on her knees. "Why can't I leave?"

"I have business here," I told her.

She curled her lip and scoffed. She was right, of course, waiting here was foolish. After so many years, so much planning and effort, I had failed.

Still. "Go back to bed." *Bed* was the pallet of cushions and blankets beside the bench, where she sat. She looked at me, half-sneering still, and contemptuous, and slid down to the floor and lay, pulled a blanket over herself. She wouldn't sleep at first, I was sure. She would be trying to think of some way to leave, to overpower me or convince me to do what she wanted. Any such planning would be useless until she knew *what* she wanted, of course, but I didn't say that.

Within the hour her muscles slackened and her breathing slowed. Had she still been my lieutenant I would have known for certain she slept, known what stage of sleep she was in, known whether or not she dreamed. Now I could only see externals.

Still wary, I sat on the floor, leaning against another bench, and pulled a blanket up over my legs. As I had done every time I'd slept here, I opened my inner coat and put my hand on my gun, leaned back, and closed my eyes.

* * *

Two hours later a faint sound woke me. I lay unmoving, my hand still on my gun. The faint sound repeated itself, slightly louder—the second door closing. I opened my eyes, just the slightest bit. Seivarden lay too quiet on her pallet—surely she had heard the sound as well.

Through my eyelashes I saw a person in outdoor clothes. Just under two meters tall, thin under the bulk of the double coat, skin iron-gray. When she pushed back her hood I saw her hair was the same. She was certainly not a Nilter.

She stood, watching me and Seivarden, for seven seconds, and then quietly stepped to where I lay, and bent to pull my pack toward her with one hand. In the other she held a gun, pointed steadily at me, though she seemed not to know I was awake.

The lock baffled her for a few moments, and then she pulled a tool out of her pocket, which she used to bypass the lock quite a bit more quickly than I had anticipated. Her gun still trained on me, and glancing occasionally at still-motionless Seivarden, she emptied the pack.

Spare clothes. Ammunition, but no gun, so she would know or suspect that I was armed. Three foil-wrapped packets of concentrated rations. Eating utensils, and a bottle for water. A gold disk five centimeters in diameter, one and a half centimeters thick that she puzzled over, frowning, and then set aside. A box, which she opened to find money—she let out an astonished breath when she realized how much, and looked over at me. I didn't move. I don't know what she had thought she would find, but she seemed not to have found it, whatever it was.

She picked up the disk that had puzzled her, and sat on a bench from which she had a clear view of both me and

Seivarden. Turning the disk over, she found the trigger. The sides fell away, opening like a flower, and the mechanism disgorged the icon, a person nearly naked except for short trousers and tiny jewel-and-enamel flowers. The image smiled, serene. She had four arms. One hand held a ball, the other arm was encased in a cylindrical armguard. Her other hands held a knife and a severed head, which dripped jeweled blood at her bare feet. The head smiled the same smile of saintly utter calm as she did.

Strigan—it had to be Strigan—frowned. The icon had been unexpected. It had piqued her curiosity yet further.

I opened my eyes. She tightened her grip on her gun—the gun I was now looking at as closely as I could, now my eyes were fully open, now I could turn my head toward it.

Strigan held the icon out, raised a steel-gray eyebrow. "Relative?" she asked, in Radchaai.

I kept my face pleasantly neutral. "Not exactly," I said, in her own language.

"I thought I knew what you were when you came," she said, after a long silence, thankfully following my language switch. "I thought I knew what you were doing here. Now I'm not so sure." She glanced at Seivarden, to all appearances completely undisturbed by our talking. "I *think* I know who *he* is. But who are *you*? *What* are you? Don't tell me *Breq from the Gerentate*. You're as Radchaai as that one." She gestured slightly toward Seivarden with her elbow.

"I came here to buy something," I said, determined to keep from staring at the gun she held. "He's incidental." Since we weren't speaking Radchaai I had to take gender into account—Strigan's language required it. The society she lived in professed at the same time to believe gender was insignificant. Males and females dressed, spoke, acted indistinguishably. And yet no one I'd met had ever hesitated, or guessed wrong. And they had invariably been offended when I *did* hesitate or guess wrong. I hadn't learned the trick of it. I'd been in Strigan's own apartment, seen her belongings, and still wasn't sure what forms to use with her now.

"Incidental?" asked Strigan, disbelieving. I couldn't blame her. I wouldn't have believed it myself, except I knew it to be true. Strigan said nothing else, likely realizing that to say much more would be extremely foolish, if I was what she feared I was.

"Coincidence," I said. Glad on at least one count that we weren't speaking Radchaai, where the word implied significance. "I found him unconscious. If I'd left him where he was he'd have died." Strigan didn't believe that either, from the look she gave me. "Why are you here?"

She laughed, short and bitter—whether because I'd chosen the wrong gender for the pronoun, or something else, I wasn't certain. "I think that's my question to ask."

She hadn't corrected my grammar, at least. "I came to talk to you. To buy something. Seivarden was ill. You weren't here. I'll pay you for what we've eaten, of course."

She seemed to find that amusing, for some reason. "Why are you here?" she asked.

"I'm alone," I said, answering her unspoken question. "Except for him." I nodded at Seivarden. My hand was still on my gun, and Strigan likely knew why I kept that hand so still, under my coat. Seivarden still feigned sleep.

Strigan shook her head slightly, disbelieving. "I'd have sworn you were a corpse soldier." An ancillary, she meant. "When you arrived I was certain of it." She'd been hiding nearby, then, waiting for us to leave, and the entire place had been under her surveillance. She must have trusted her hiding place quite extravagantly—if I had been what she feared, staying anywhere near would have been extremely foolish. I would certainly have found her. "But when you saw there was no one here you wept. And him..." She shrugged toward Seivarden, slack and motionless on the pallet.

"Sit up, citizen," I said to Seivarden, in Radchaai. "You're not fooling anyone."

"Fuck off," she answered, and pulled a blanket over her head. Then shoved it off again and rose, slightly shaky, and went into the sanitary facility and closed the door.

I turned back to Strigan. "That business with the flier rental. Was that you?"

She shrugged ruefully. "He told me a couple of Radchaai were coming out this way. Either he badly underestimated you, or you're even more dangerous than I thought."

Which would be considerably dangerous. "I'm used to being underestimated. And you didn't tell her...him why you thought I was coming."

Her gun hadn't wavered. "Why are you here?"

"You know why I'm here." A quick change in her expression, instantly suppressed. I continued. "Not to kill you. Killing you would defeat the purpose."

She raised an eyebrow, tilted her head slightly. "Would it."

The fencing, the feinting, frustrated me. "I want the gun."

"What gun?" Strigan would never be so foolish as to admit the thing existed, that she knew what gun I was talking about. But her pretended ignorance didn't convince. She knew. If she had what I thought she had, what I had gambled my life she had, further specificity would be unnecessary. She *knew*.

Whether she would give it to me was another question. "I'll pay you for it."

"I don't know what you're talking about."

"The Garseddai did everything in fives. Five right actions, five principal sins, five zones times five regions. Twenty-five representatives to surrender to the Lord of the Radch."

For three seconds Strigan was utterly still. Even her breathing seemed to have stopped. Then she spoke. "Garsedd, is it? What does that have to do with me?"

"I'd never have guessed if you'd stayed where you were."

"Garsedd was a thousand years ago, and very, very far away from here."

"Twenty-five representatives to surrender to the Lord of the Radch," I repeated. "And twenty-four guns recovered or otherwise accounted for."

She blinked, drew in a breath. "Who are you?"

"Someone ran. Someone fled the system before the Radchaai arrived. Maybe she was afraid the guns wouldn't work as advertised. Maybe she knew that even if they did it wouldn't help."

"On the contrary, no? Wasn't that the point? No one defies Anaander Mianaai." She spoke bitterly. "Not if they want to live."

I said nothing.

Strigan's hold on the gun didn't waver. Even so, she was in danger from me, if I decided to harm her, and I thought she suspected that. "I don't know why you think I have this gun you're talking about. Why would I have it?"

"You collected antiques, curiosities. You already had a small collection of Garseddai artifacts. They'd made their way to Dras Annia Station, somehow. Others might do so as well. And then one day you disappeared. You took care you wouldn't be followed."

"That's a very slight basis for such a large assumption."

"So why this?" I gestured carefully with my free hand, the other still under my coat, holding my gun. "You had a comfortable post on Dras Annia, patients, plenty of money, associations and reputation. Now you're in the icy middle of nowhere, giving first aid to bov herders."

"Personal crisis," she said, the words carefully, deliberately pronounced.

"Certainly," I agreed. "You couldn't bring yourself to destroy it, or pass it on to someone who might not be wise enough to realize what a danger it presented. You knew, as soon as you realized what you had, that if Radch authorities ever even dreamed of half-imagining it existed, they would track you down and kill you, and anyone else who might have seen it."

While the Radch wanted everyone to remember what had happened to the Garseddai, they wanted no one to know just how the Garseddai had managed to do what they'd done, what no one had managed to do for a thousand years before or another thousand years after—destroy a Radchaai ship. Almost no one alive remembered. I knew, and any still-extant ships that had been there. Anaander Mianaai certainly did. And Seivarden, who had seen for herself what the Lord of the Radch wanted no one to think was possible—that invisible armor and gun, those bullets that defeated Radchaai armor—and her ship's heat shield—so effortlessly.

"I want it," I told Strigan. "I'll pay you for it."

"*If* I had such a thing...if! It's entirely possible no amount of money in the world would be sufficient."

"Anything is possible," I agreed.

"You're Radchaai. And you're military."

"Was," I corrected. And when she scoffed, I added, "If I still were, I wouldn't be here. Or if I were, you would already have given me whatever information I wanted, and you'd be dead."

"Get out of here." Strigan's voice was quiet, but vehement. "Take your stray with you."

"I'm not leaving until I have what I came for." There would be little point in doing so. "You'll have to give it to me, or shoot me with it." As much as admitting I still had armor. Implying I was precisely what she feared, a Radchaai agent come to kill her and take the gun.

Frightened of me as she must be, she could not avoid her own curiosity. "Why do you want it so badly?"

"I want," I told her, "to kill Anaander Mianaai."

"What?" The gun in her hand trembled, moved slightly aside, then steadied again. She leaned forward three millimeters, and cocked her head as though she was certain she hadn't heard me correctly.

"I want to kill Anaander Mianaai," I repeated.

"Anaander Mianaai," she said, bitterly, "has thousands of bodies in hundreds of locations. You can't possibly kill him. Certainly not with one gun."

"I still want to try."

"You're insane. Or is that even possible? Aren't all Radchaai brainwashed?"

It was a common misconception. "Only criminals, or people who aren't functioning well, are reeducated. Nobody really cares what you think, as long as you do what you're supposed to."

She stared, dubious. "How do you define 'not functioning well'?"

I made an indefinite, *not my problem* gesture with my free hand. Though perhaps it *was* my problem. Perhaps that question did concern me now, insofar as it might very well concern Seivarden. "I'm going to take my hand out of my coat," I said. "And then I'm going to go to sleep."

Strigan said nothing, only twitched one gray eyebrow.

"If I found you, Anaander Mianaai certainly can," I said. We were speaking Strigan's language. What gender had she assigned to the Lord of the Radch? "He hasn't, yet, possibly because he is currently preoccupied with other matters, and for reasons that ought to be clear to you, he is likely hesitant to delegate in this affair."

"I'm safe, then." She sounded more convinced of that than she could possibly be.

Seivarden came noisily out of the bathroom and sank back onto her pallet, hands trembling, breathing quick and shallow.

"I'm taking my hand out of my coat now," I said, and then did that. Slowly. Empty.

Strigan sighed and lowered her gun. "I probably couldn't shoot you anyway." Because she was sure I was Radchaai military, and hence armored. Of course, if she could take me unawares, or fire before I could extend my armor, she could indeed shoot me.

And of course, she had that gun. Though she might not have it near to hand. "Can I have my icon back?"

She frowned, and then remembered she was still holding it. "*Your* icon."

"It belongs to me," I clarified.

"That's quite a resemblance," she said, looking at it again. "Where's it from?"

"Very far away." I held out my hand. She returned it, and one-handed I brushed the trigger and the image folded into itself, and the base closed into its gold disk.

Strigan looked over at Seivarden intently, and frowned. "Your stray is having some anxiety."

"Yes."

Strigan shook her head, frustrated or exasperated, and went into her infirmary. She returned, went to where Seivarden sat, leaned over, and reached for her.

Seivarden started, shoving herself up and back, grabbing Strigan's wrist in a move I knew was meant to break it. But Seivarden wasn't what she had once been. Dissipation and what I suspected was malnutrition had taken a toll. Strigan left her arm in Seivarden's grasp, and with her other hand plucked a small white tab out of her own fingers and stuck it to Seivarden's forehead. "I don't feel sorry for you," she said, in Radchaai. "It's just that I'm a doctor." Seivarden looked at her with an unaccountable expression of horror. "Let go of me."

"Let go, Seivarden, and lie down." I said, sharply. She stared two seconds more at Strigan, but then did as she was told.

"I'm not taking him as my patient," Strigan said to me, as Seivarden's breathing slowed and her muscles slackened. "It isn't more than first aid. And I don't want him panicking and breaking my things."

"I'm going to sleep now," I answered. "We can talk more in the morning."

"It *is* morning." But she didn't argue further.

She wouldn't be foolish enough to search my person while I slept. She would know how dangerous that would be.

She wouldn't shoot me in my sleep either, though it would be a simple and effective way to be rid of me. Asleep, I would be an easy target for a bullet, unless I extended my armor now and left it up.

But there was no need. Strigan wouldn't shoot me, at least not until she had the answers to her many questions. Even then she might not. I was too good a puzzle.

* * *

Strigan wasn't in the main room when I woke, but the door into the bedroom was closed, and I assumed she was either asleep or wanted privacy. Seivarden was awake, staring at me, fidgeting, rubbing her arms and shoulders. A week earlier I'd had to prevent her from scraping her skin raw. She'd improved a great deal.

The box of money lay where Strigan had left it. I checked it—it was undisturbed—put it away, latched my pack closed, thinking the while what my next step should be.

"Citizen," I said to Seivarden, brisk and authoritative. "Breakfast."

"What?" She was surprised enough to stop moving for a moment.

I lifted the corner of my lip, just slightly. "Shall I ask the doctor to check your hearing?" The stringed instrument lay beside me, where I had set it the night before. I picked it up, plucked a fifth. "Breakfast."

"I'm not your servant," she protested. Indignant.

I increased my sneer, just the smallest increment. "Then what are you?"

She froze, anger visible in her expression, and then very visibly debated with herself how best to answer me. But the question was, now, too difficult for her to answer easily. Her confidence in her superiority had apparently taken too severe a blow for her to deal with just now. She didn't seem to be able to find a response.

I bent to the instrument and began to pick out a line of music. I expected her to sit where she was, sullen, until at the very least hunger drove her to prepare her own meal. Or maybe, much delayed, find something to say to me. I found I half-hoped she'd take a swing at me, so I could retaliate, but perhaps she was still under the influence of whatever Strigan had given her last night, even if only slightly.

The door to Strigan's room opened, and she walked into the main living space, stopped, folded her arms, and cocked an eyebrow. Seivarden ignored her. None of us said anything, and after five seconds Strigan turned and strode to the kitchen and swung open a cabinet.

It was empty. Which I'd known the evening before. "You've cleaned me out, Breq from the Gerentate," Strigan said, without rancor. Almost as though she thought it was funny. We were in very little danger of starving—even in summer here, the outdoors effectively functioned as a huge freezer, and the unheated storage building held plenty of provisions. It was only a matter of fetching some, and thawing them.

"Seivarden." I spoke in the casually disdainful tone I had heard from Seivarden herself in the distant past. "Bring some food from the shed."

She froze, and then blinked, startled. "Who the *hell* do you think you are?"

"Language, citizen," I chided. "And I might ask you the same question."

"You... you ignorant *nobody*." The sudden intensity of her anger had brought her close to tears again. "You think you're better than me? You're barely even *human*." She didn't mean because I was an ancillary. I was fairly sure she hadn't yet realized that. She meant because I wasn't Radchaai, and perhaps because I might have implants that were common some places outside Radch space and that would, in Radchaai eyes, compromise my humanity. "I wasn't bred to be your servant."

I can move very, very quickly. I was standing, and my arm halfway through its swing, before I registered my intention to move. The barest fraction of a second passed during which

I could have possibly checked myself, and then it was gone, and my fist connected with Seivarden's face, too quickly for her to even look surprised.

She dropped, falling backward onto her pallet, blood pouring from her nose, and lay unmoving.

"Is he dead?" asked Strigan, still standing in the kitchen, her voice mildly curious.

I made an ambiguous gesture. "You're the doctor."

She walked over to where Seivarden lay, unconscious and bleeding. Gazed down at her. "Not dead," she pronounced. "Though I'd like to make sure the concussion doesn't turn into anything worse."

I gestured resignation. "It is as Amaat wills," I said, and put on my coat and went outside to bring in food.

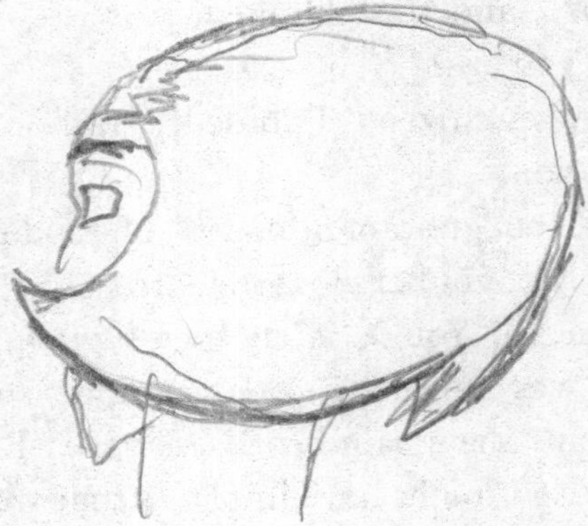

6

On Shis'urna, in Ors, the *Justice of Ente* Seven Issa who had accompanied Lieutenant Skaaiat to Jen Shinnan's sat with me in the lower level of the house. She had a name beyond her designation—one I never used, though I knew it. Even Lieutenant Skaaiat sometimes addressed individual human soldiers under her command as merely "Seven Issa." Or by their segment numbers.

I brought out a board and counters, and we played a silent two games. "Can't you let me win a time or two?" she asked, when the second was concluded, and before I could answer a thump sounded from the upper floor and she grinned. "It looks like Lieutenant Stiff can unbend after all!" and she cast me a look intended to share the joke, her amusement at the contrast between Awn's usual careful formality and what was obviously going on upstairs between her and Lieutenant Skaaiat. But the instant after Seven Issa had spoken, her smile faded. "I'm sorry. I didn't mean anything by it, it's just what we..."

"I know," I said. "I took no offense."

Seven Issa frowned, and made a doubtful gesture with her left hand, awkwardly, her gloved fingers still curled around half a dozen counters. "Ships have feelings."

"Yes, of course." Without feelings insignificant decisions become excruciating attempts to compare endless arrays of inconsequential things. It's just easier to handle those with emotions. "But as I said, I took no offense."

Seven Issa looked down at the board, and dropped the counters she held into one of its depressions. She stared at them a moment, and then looked up. "You hear rumors. About ships and people they like. And I'd swear your face never changes, but..."

I engaged my facial muscles, smiled, an expression I'd seen many times.

Seven Issa flinched. "Don't *do* that!" she said, indignant, but still hushed lest the lieutenants hear us.

It wasn't that I'd gotten the smile wrong—I knew I hadn't. It was the sudden change, from my habitual lack of expression to something human, that some of the Seven Issas found disturbing. I dropped the smile.

"Aatr's tits," swore Seven Issa. "When you do that it's like you're possessed or something." She shook her head, and scooped up the counters and began to distribute them around the board. "All right, then, you don't want to talk about it. One more game."

The evening grew later. The neighbors' conversations turned slow and aimless and finally ceased as people picked up sleeping children and went to bed.

Denz Ay arrived four hours before dawn, and I joined her, stepping into her boat without speaking. She did not acknowledge my presence, and neither did her daughter, sitting in the stern. Slowly, nearly noiselessly, we slid away from the house.

The vigil at the temple continued, the priests' prayers audible on the plaza as an intermittent shushing murmur. The streets, upper and lower, were silent except for my own footsteps and the sound of the water, dark but for the stars brilliant overhead, the blinking of the prohibited zones' encircling buoys, and the light from the temple of Ikkt. The Seven Issa who had accompanied us back to Lieutenant Awn's house slept on a pallet on the ground floor.

Lieutenant Awn and Lieutenant Skaaiat lay together on the upper floor, still and on the edge of sleep.

No one else was out on the water with us. In the bottom of the boat I saw rope, nets, breathers, and a round, covered basket tied to an anchor. The daughter saw me look at it, and she kicked it under her seat, with studied nonchalance. I looked away, over the water, toward the blinking buoys, and said nothing. The fiction that they could hide or alter the information coming from their trackers was a useful one, even if no one actually believed it.

Just inside the buoys, Denz Ay's daughter put a breather in her mouth and slid over the edge, a rope in her hand. The lake wasn't terribly deep, especially at this time of year. Moments later she reemerged and climbed back aboard, and we pulled the crate up—a relatively easy job until it reached the surface, but the three of us managed to tip it into the boat without taking on too much water.

I wiped mud off the lid. It was of Radchaai manufacture, but that wasn't too alarming in itself. I found the latch and popped it open.

The guns within—long, sleek, and deadly—were the sort

that had been carried by Tanmind troops before the annexation. I knew each one would have an identifying mark, and the marks of any guns confiscated by us would have been listed and reported, so that I could consult the inventory and determine more or less immediately if these were confiscated weapons, or ones we had missed.

If they were confiscated weapons, this situation would suddenly become a great deal more complicated than it seemed at the moment—and it was already a complicated situation.

Lieutenant Awn was in stage one of NREM sleep. Lieutenant Skaaiat seemed to be as well. I could consult the inventory on my own initiative. Indeed, I *should*. But I didn't—partly because I had just been reminded, yesterday, of the corrupt authorities at Ime, the misuse of accesses, the most appalling abuse of power, something any citizen would have thought was impossible. That reminder itself was enough to make me cautious. But also, after Denz Ay's assertions about residents of the upper city planting evidence in the past, and the evening's dinner conversation with its clear reminder of resentment in that upper city, something didn't seem quite right. No one in the upper city would know I had requested information about confiscated weapons, but what if someone else was involved? Someone who could set alerts to notify her if certain questions were asked in certain places? Denz Ay and her daughter sat quietly in the boat, to all appearances unconcerned and not particularly eager to be anywhere, or to be doing anything else.

Within a few moments I had *Justice of Toren*'s attention. I had seen no few of those confiscated weapons—not I, One Esk, but I, *Justice of Toren*, whose thousands of ancillary troops had been on the planet during the annexation. If I could not consult an official inventory without alerting an authority to the fact that I had found this cache, I could consult my own memory to see if any of them had passed under my own eyes.

And they had.

I went in to where Lieutenant Awn was sleeping and put a hand on her bare shoulder. "Lieutenant," I said, softly. In the boat I closed the crate with a soft snap and said, "Back to the city."

Lieutenant Awn jerked awake. "I'm not asleep," she said blearily. In the boat, Denz Ay and her daughter silently picked up their oars and started back.

"The weapons were confiscated," I said to Lieutenant Awn, still quiet. Not wanting to wake Lieutenant Skaaiat, not wanting anyone else to hear what I was saying. "I recognized the serial numbers."

Lieutenant Awn looked at me dazedly for a few moments, uncomprehending. Then I saw her understand. "But..." And then she woke fully, and turned to Lieutenant Skaaiat. "Skaaiat, wake up. I've got a problem."

I brought the guns to the upper level of Lieutenant Awn's house. Seven Issa didn't even stir when I went past.

"You're sure?" asked Lieutenant Skaaiat, kneeling by the open crate, naked but for gloves, a bowl of tea in one hand.

"I confiscated these myself," I answered. "I remember them." We were all speaking very quietly, so that no one outside could hear.

"Then they would have been destroyed," argued Lieutenant Skaaiat.

"Obviously they weren't," said Lieutenant Awn. And then, after a brief silence, "Oh, *shit*. This is not good."

Silently I messaged her. *Language, Lieutenant.*

Lieutenant Skaaiat made a short, breathy sound, unamused laughter. "To put it mildly." She frowned. "But why? Why would anyone go to the trouble?"

"And *how*?" asked Lieutenant Awn. She seemed to have forgotten her own tea, in a bowl on the floor beside her. "They put them there without us seeing them." I'd looked at the logs for the past thirty days and seen nothing I couldn't already account for. Indeed, no one had been to that spot at all besides Denz Ay and her daughter thirty days ago, and just the other night.

"*How* is the easy part, if you've got the right accesses," said Lieutenant Skaaiat. "Which might tell us something. It's not someone who's got high-level access to *Justice of Toren*, or they'd have made sure it didn't remember these guns. Or at least couldn't say it did."

"Or they didn't think of that particular detail," suggested Lieutenant Awn. She was puzzled. And only beginning to be frightened. "Or maybe that's part of the plan to begin with. But we're back to *why*, aren't we? It doesn't much matter how, not right this moment."

Lieutenant Skaaiat looked up at me. "Tell me about the trouble Jen Taa's niece had in the lower city."

Lieutenant Awn looked at her, frowning. "But..." Lieutenant Skaaiat shushed her with a gesture.

"There was no trouble," I said. "She sat by herself and threw rocks in the Fore-Temple water. She bought some tea in the shop behind the temple. Beyond that, no one spoke to her."

"You're certain?" asked Lieutenant Awn.

"She was in my view the entire time." And I would take care that she would be on any future visits, but that hardly needed saying.

The two lieutenants were silent a moment. Lieutenant Awn closed her eyes and took a deep breath. She was now truly frightened. "They're lying about that," she said, eyes still closed. "They want some excuse to accuse someone in the lower city of... something."

"Sedition," Lieutenant Skaaiat said. She remembered her tea, and took a sip. "And getting above themselves. That's easy enough to see."

"Yes, I can see that," said Lieutenant Awn. Her accent had slipped entirely, but she hadn't noticed. "But why the hell would anyone with this sort of access"—she gestured at the crate of guns—"want to help them?"

"That would seem to be the question," answered Lieutenant Skaaiat. They were silent for several seconds. "What are you going to do?"

The question upset Lieutenant Awn, who presumably had been wondering just that. She looked up at me. "I wonder if this is all."

"I can ask Denz Ay to take me out again," I said.

Lieutenant Awn gestured affirmatively. "I'll write the report, but I won't file it just yet. Pending our further investigation." Everything Lieutenant Awn did and said was observed and recorded—but as with the trackers everyone in Ors wore, there wasn't always someone paying attention.

Lieutenant Skaaiat made a low whistle. "Is someone setting you up, dear?" Lieutenant Awn looked incomprehension at her. "Like maybe," Lieutenant Skaaiat continued, "Jen Shinnan? I may have underestimated her. Or can you trust Denz Ay?"

"If someone wants me gone, they're in the upper city," said Lieutenant Awn, and privately I agreed but I didn't say it. "But that can't be it. If anyone who could do this," she gestured at the crate, "wanted me out of here, it would be easy enough—just give the order. And Jen Shinnan couldn't have done this." Unspoken, hanging behind every word, was the memory of news from Ime. Of the fact that the person who had revealed the corruption there was condemned to die, probably was already dead. "No one in Ors could have, not without..." Not without help, from a very high level, she would surely have said, but she let the sentence trail off.

"True," mused Lieutenant Skaaiat. Understanding her. "So it's someone high up. Who would benefit?"

"The niece," said Lieutenant Awn, distressed.

"Jen Taa's niece would benefit?" asked Lieutenant Skaaiat, puzzled.

"No, no. The niece is insulted or assaulted—allegedly. I won't do anything, *I* say nothing happened."

"Because nothing happened," said Lieutenant Skaaiat, looking as though something was beginning to come clear to her, but still puzzled.

"They can't get justice from me, so they come down to the lower city to get it for themselves. It's the sort of thing that happened before we came."

"And afterward," said Lieutenant Skaaiat, "they find all these guns. Or even during. Or..." She shook her head. "It's not all fitting together. Let's say you're right. Still. *Who benefits?* Not the Tanmind, not if they cause trouble. They can accuse all they like, but no matter what anyone finds in the lake, they're still for reeducation if they riot."

Lieutenant Awn gestured doubtfully. "Someone who could get those guns here without our seeing them might be able to keep the Tanmind out of trouble. Or believably say they could."

"Ah." Lieutenant Skaaiat understood immediately. "A

minor fine, mitigating circumstances. No doubt of it. It'll be someone high up. Very dangerous. But why?"

Lieutenant Awn looked at me. "Go to the head priest and ask her a favor. Tell her, from me, even though it's not the rainy season, to station someone near the storm alarm at all times." The alarm, an earsplitting siren, was on the top of the temple residence. Its sounding would trigger the storm shutters of most of the buildings in the lower city, and would certainly wake the inhabitants of any building not automated in that fashion. "Ask her to be ready to sound it if I ask."

"Excellent," said Lieutenant Skaaiat. "Any mob will at least have to work a bit harder to get past the shutters. And then?"

"It might not even happen," said Lieutenant Awn. "Whatever it is, we'll have to take it as it comes."

What came, the next morning, was news that Anaander Mianaai, Lord of the Radch, would be visiting us some time in the next few days.

For three thousand years Anaander Mianaai had ruled Radch space absolutely. She resided in each of the thirteen provincial palaces, and was present at every annexation. She was able to do this because she possessed thousands of bodies, all of them genetically identical, all of them linked to each other. She was still in Shis'urna's system, some of her on the flagship of this annexation, *Sword of Amaat*, and some of her on Shis'urna Station. It was she who made Radchaai law, and she who decided on any exceptions to that law. She was the ultimate commander of the military, the highest head priest of Amaat, the person to whom, ultimately, all Radchaai houses were clients.

And she was coming to Ors, at some unspecified date

within the next few days. It was, in fact, mildly surprising she hadn't visited Ors sooner—small as it was, far as Orsians had fallen from their former glory, still the yearly pilgrimage made Ors a moderately important place. Important enough that officers of higher families and more influence than Lieutenant Awn had wanted this post—and tried continually to pry her out of it, despite the determined resistance of the Divine of Ikkt.

So the visit itself wasn't unexpected. Though the timing seemed odd. It was two weeks before the start of the pilgrimage, when hundreds of thousands of Orsians and tourists would pass through the city. During pilgrimage Anaander Mianaai's presence would be highly visible, an opportunity to impress a high number of the worshippers of Ikkt. Instead she was coming just before. And of course it was impossible not to notice the sharp coincidence between her arrival and the discovery of the guns.

Whoever had placed those guns was acting either for or against the interests of the Lord of the Radch. She should have been the one logical person to tell, and to ask for further instructions. And her being in Ors in person was incredibly convenient—it presented an opportunity to tell her about the situation without anyone else intercepting the message and either spoiling whatever the plan was, or alerting wrongdoers that their plan had been discovered, making them harder to catch.

On that account alone, Lieutenant Awn was relieved to hear of her visit. Even though for the next few days, and while she was here, Lieutenant Awn would have to wear her full uniform.

In the meantime I listened more closely to conversations in the upper city—more difficult than in the lower, because the houses were all enclosed and of course any Tanmind involved would be closemouthed if they knew I was in earshot. And no one was foolish enough to have the sort of conversation I was listening for anywhere but in person, in private. I also watched Jen Taa's niece—or as well as I could. After the dinner party she never left Jen Shinnan's house, but I could see her tracker data.

For two nights I went out on the marsh with Denz Ay and her daughter, and we found two more crates of guns. Once again I had no way of determining who had left them, or when, though Denz Ay's oblique statements, careful not to implicate the fishermen I knew usually poached in those areas, implied that they must have arrived some time in the past month or two.

"I'll be glad when the Lord of Mianaai gets here," said Lieutenant Awn to me, quietly, late one night. "I don't think I should be handling something like this."

And in the meantime I noticed that no one but Denz Ay went out on the water at night, and in the lower city no one sat or lay where the shutters might come down—a routine precaution during the rainy season, even though there were safeties to stop them if someone was in their way, but one that was usually ignored in the dry season.

The Lord of the Radch arrived in the middle of the day, on foot, a single one of her walking down through the upper city, no trace of her in the tracker logs, and went straight to the temple of Ikkt. She was old, gray-haired, broad shoulders slightly stooping, the almost-black skin of her face lined—which accounted for the lack of guards. The loss of one body that was more or less near death anyway would not be a large one. The use of such older bodies allowed the Lord of the

Radch to walk unprotected, without any sort of entourage, when she wished, without much risk.

She wore not the jeweled coat and trousers of the Radchaai, nor the coverall or trousers and shirt a Shis'urnan Tanmind would wear, but instead the Orsian lungi, shirtless.

As soon as I saw her, I messaged Lieutenant Awn, who came as quickly as she could to the temple, and arrived while the head priest was prostrating herself in the plaza before the Lord of the Radch.

Lieutenant Awn hesitated. Most Radchaai were never in the personal presence of Anaander Mianaai in such circumstances. Of course she was always present during annexations, but the sheer number of troops compared to the number of bodies the Lord of the Radch sent made it unlikely one would run into her by chance. And any citizen can travel to one of the provincial palaces and ask for an audience—for a request, for an appeal in a legal case, for whatever reason—but in such a case, an ordinary citizen is briefed beforehand on how to conduct herself. Perhaps someone like Lieutenant Skaaiat would know how to draw Anaander Mianaai's attention to herself without breaching propriety, but Lieutenant Awn did not.

"My lord," Lieutenant Awn said, heart speeding with fear, and knelt.

Anaander Mianaai turned to her, eyebrow raised.

"I beg my lord's pardon," said Lieutenant Awn. She was slightly dizzy, either from the weight of her uniform in the heat, or from nerves. "I must speak with you."

The eyebrow rose farther. "Lieutenant Awn," she said, "yes?"

"Yes, my lord."

"This evening I attend the vigil in the temple of Ikkt. I'll speak to you in the morning."

It took Lieutenant Awn a few moments to digest this. "My lord, a moment only. I don't think that's a good idea."

The Lord of the Radch tilted her head inquisitively. "I understood you had this area under control."

"Yes, lord, it's just..." Lieutenant Awn stopped, panicked, at a loss for words for a second. "Relations between the upper and lower city just now..." She halted again.

"Concern yourself with your own job," said Anaander Mianaai. "And I will concern myself with mine." She turned away from Lieutenant Awn.

A public slight. An inexplicable one—there was no reason the Lord of the Radch could not have turned aside for a few urgent words with the officer who was chief of local security. And Lieutenant Awn had done nothing to deserve such a slight. At first I thought that was the only reason for the distress I read coming from Lieutenant Awn. The matter of the guns could be communicated in the morning just as well as now, and there seemed no other difficulty. But as the Lord of the Radch had walked through the upper city, word of Anaander Mianaai's presence had spread, as of course it would, and the residents of the upper city had come out of their houses and begun gathering on the northern edge of the Fore-Temple water to watch the Lord of the Radch, dressed like an Orsian, stand in front of the temple of Ikkt with the Divine. And listening to the mutterings of the watching Tanmind, I realized that at this particular instant the guns were only a secondary concern.

The Tanmind residents of the upper city were wealthy, well-fed, the owners of shops and farms and tamarind orchards. Even in the precarious months following the annexation, when supplies had been scarce and food expensive, they had managed to keep their families fed. When Jen

Shinnan had said, a few evenings earlier, that no one here had starved, she had likely believed that to be true. She had not, nor had anyone she knew well, nearly all of them wealthy Tanmind. As much as they complained, they had come out of the annexation relatively comfortably. And their children did well when they took the aptitudes, and would continue to do so, as Lieutenant Skaaiat had said.

And yet these same people, when they saw the Lord of the Radch walk straight through the upper city to the temple of Ikkt, concluded that this gesture of respect to the Orsians was a calculated insult to them. This was clear in their expressions, in their indignant exclamations. I had not foreseen it. Perhaps the Lord of the Radch had not foreseen it. But Lieutenant Awn had realized it would happen, when she saw the Divine on the ground in front of the Lord of the Radch.

I left the plaza, and some of the upper city streets, and went to where the Tanmind were standing, a half-dozen of me. I didn't draw any weapons, didn't make any threats. I said, merely, to anyone near me, "Go home, citizens."

Most turned away and left, and if their expressions weren't pleasant, they offered no actual protest. Others took longer to leave, testing my authority, perhaps, though not far—anyone with the stomach to do such a thing had been shot sometime in the last five years, or at least had learned to restrain such a near-suicidal impulse.

The Divine, rising to escort Anaander Mianaai into the temple, cast an unreadable look at Lieutenant Awn, where she still knelt on the plaza stones. The Lord of the Radch did not even glance at her.

7

“And then,” Strigan said as we ate, latest in a long list of grievances against the Radchaai, “there’s the treaty with the Presger.”

Seivarden lay still, eyes closed, breathing even, blood caked on her lip and chin, spattered on the front of her coat. Across her nose and forehead lay a corrective.

“You resent the treaty?” I asked. “You’d prefer the Presger felt free to do as they always have done?” The Presger didn’t care if a species was sentient or not, conscious or not, intelligent or not. The word they used—or the concept, at any rate, as I understood they didn’t speak in words—was usually translated as *significance*. And only the Presger were *significant*. All other beings were their rightful prey, property, or playthings. Mostly they just didn’t care about humans, but some of them liked to stop ships and pull them—and their contents—apart.

“I’d prefer the Radch not make binding promises on behalf of all humanity,” Strigan answered. “Not dictate policy for every single human government and then tell us we're supposed to be grateful."

"The Presger don't recognize such divisions. It was all or none."

"It was the Radch extending control yet another way, one cheaper and easier than outright conquest."

"It might surprise you to learn that some high-ranking Radchaai dislike the treaty as much as you do."

Strigan raised an eyebrow, set down her cup of stinking fermented milk. "Somehow I doubt I'd find these high-ranking Radchaai sympathetic." Her tone was bitter, slightly sarcastic.

"No," I answered. "I don't think you'd like them much. They certainly wouldn't have much use for you."

She blinked and looked intently at my face, as though trying to read something from my expression. Then she shook her head and made a dismissing gesture. "Do tell."

"When one is the agent of order and civilization in the universe, one doesn't stoop to negotiate. Especially with nonhumans." Which included quite a number of people who considered themselves human, but that was a topic best left undiscussed just now. "Why make a treaty with such an implacable enemy? Destroy them and be done."

"Could you?" Strigan asked, incredulous. "Could you have destroyed the Presger?"

"No."

She folded her arms, leaned back in her chair. "So why any debate at all?"

"I would think it was obvious," I answered. "Some find it difficult to admit the Radch might be fallible, or that its power might have limits."

Strigan glanced across the room, toward Seivarden. "But this is meaningless. *Debate*. There's no real debate possible."

"Certainly," I agreed. "You're the expert."

"Oh ho!" she exclaimed, sitting straighter. "I've made you angry."

I was sure I hadn't changed my expression. "I don't think you've ever been to the Radch. I don't think you know many Radchaai, not personally. Not well. You look at it from the outside, and you see conformity and brainwashing." Rank on rank of identical silver-armored soldiers, with no wills of their own, no minds of their own. "And it's true the lowest Radchaai thinks herself immeasurably superior to any non-citizen. What people like Seivarden think of themselves is past bearing." Strigan made a brief, amused snort. "But they are people, and they do have different opinions about things."

"Opinions that don't matter. Anaander Mianaai declares what will be, and that's how it is."

That was a more complicated issue than she realized, I was certain. "Which only adds to their frustration. Imagine. Imagine your whole life aimed at conquest, at the spread of Radchaai space. *You* see murder and destruction on an unimaginable scale, but they see the spread of civilization, of Justice and Propriety, of Benefit for the universe. The death and destruction, these are unavoidable by-products of this one, supreme good."

"I don't think I can muster much sympathy for their perspective."

"I don't ask it. Only stand there a moment, and look. Not only your life, but the lives of all your house, and your ancestors for a thousand years or more before you, are invested in this idea, these actions. Amaat wills it. God wills it, the universe itself wills all this. And then one day someone tells you maybe you were mistaken. And your life won't be what you imagined it to be."

"Happens to people all the time," said Strigan, rising from her seat. "Except most of us don't delude ourselves that we ever had great destinies."

"The exception is not an insignificant one," I pointed out.

"And you?" She stood beside the chair, her cup and bowl in her hands. "You're certainly Radchaai. Your accent, when you speak Radchaai"—we were speaking her own native language—"sounds like you're from the Gerentate. But you have almost no accent right now. You might just be very good with languages—inhumanly good, I might even say—" She paused. "The gender thing is a giveaway, though. Only a Radchaai would misgender people the way you do."

I'd guessed wrong. "I can't see under your clothes. And even if I could, that's not always a reliable indicator."

She blinked, hesitated a moment as though what I'd said made no sense to her. "I used to wonder how Radchaai reproduced, if they were all the same gender."

"They're not. And they reproduce like anyone else." Strigan raised one skeptical eyebrow. "They go to the medic," I continued, "and have their contraceptive implants deactivated. Or they use a tank. Or they have surgery so they can carry a pregnancy. Or they hire someone to carry it."

None of it was very different from what any other kind of people did, but Strigan seemed slightly scandalized. "You're *certainly* Radchaai. And certainly *very* familiar with Captain Seivarden, but you're not *like* him. I wondered from the start if you were an ancillary, but I don't see much in the way of implants. Who are you?"

She would have to look a good deal closer than she already had to see evidence of what I was—to a casual observer I looked as though I had one or two communications and optical implants, the sort of thing millions of people got as a matter of course, Radchaai or not. And during the last twenty years I'd found ways of concealing the specifics of what I had.

I picked up my own dishes, rose. "I'm Breq, from the Gerentate." Strigan snorted, disbelieving. The Gerentate was far enough from where I'd been for the last nineteen years to conceal any small mistakes I might make.

"Just a tourist," Strigan observed, in a tone that made it clear she didn't believe me at all.

"Yes," I agreed.

"So what's the interest in..." She gestured again at Seivarden, still sleeping, breathing slow and even. "Just a stray animal that needed rescuing?"

I didn't answer. I didn't know the answer, truthfully.

"I've met people who collect strays. I don't think you're one of them. There's something... something cold about you. Something edged. You're far more self-possessed than any tourist I've ever seen." And of course I knew she had the gun, which no one but herself and Anaander Mianaai should have known existed. But she couldn't say that without admitting she had it. "There's no way in seventeen hells you're a Gerentate tourist. *What are you?*"

"If I told you it would spoil your fun," I said.

Strigan opened her mouth to say something—possibly something angry, to judge from her expression—when an alarm tone sounded. "Visitors," she said instead.

By the time we got our coats on, and got out the two doors, a crawler had made a ragged path up to the house, dragging a white trench across the moss-tinged snow, its half-spinning halt missing my flier by centimeters.

The door popped open and a Nilter slid out, shorter than many I had met, bundled in a scarlet coat embroidered in bright blue and a screaming shade of yellow, but overlaid with dark stains—snowmoss, and blood. The person halted a moment, and then saw us standing at the entrance to the house.

"Doctor!" she called. "Help!"

Before she was done speaking, Strigan was striding across the snow. I followed.

On closer inspection I saw the driver was only a child, barely fourteen. In the passenger seat lay sprawled an adult, unconscious, clothes torn nearly to shreds, in places all the way through every layer. Blood soaked the cloth, and the seat. Her right leg was missing below the knee, and her left foot.

Among the three of us we got the injured person into the house, into the infirmary. "What happened?" Strigan asked as she removed bloody fragments of coat.

"Ice devil," said the girl. "We didn't see it!" Tears welled in her eyes, but didn't fall. She swallowed hard.

Strigan appraised the makeshift tourniquets the girl had obviously applied. "You did everything you could," she told the girl. She nodded toward the door to the main room. "I'll take it from here."

We left the infirmary, the girl apparently not even aware of my presence, or Seivarden's, where she still lay on her pallet. She stood for a few seconds in the middle of the room, uncertain, seeming paralyzed, and then she sank down on a bench.

I brought her a cup of fermented milk and she started, as though I had suddenly appeared from nowhere. "Are you injured?" I asked her. No misgendering this time—I had already heard Strigan use the feminine pronoun.

"I..." She stopped, looking at the cup of milk as though it might bite her. "No, not...a little." She seemed on the verge of collapse. She might well be. By Radchaai standards she was still a child, but she had seen this adult injured—was she a parent, a cousin, a neighbor?—and had the presence of mind to render some small bits of first aid, get her into a crawler, and come here. Small wonder if she was about to fall to pieces now.

"What happened to the ice devil?" I asked.

"I don't know." She looked up at me, from the milk, still not taking it. "I kicked it. I stabbed it with my knife. It went away. I don't know."

It took a few minutes for me to get the information out of her, that she'd left messages for the others at her family's camp but that no one had been near enough to help, or was near enough to be here terribly soon. While we were talking she seemed to collect herself, at least slightly, at least enough to take the milk I offered and drink it.

Within a few minutes she was sweating, and she removed both her coats and laid them on the bench beside her, and then sat, quiet and awkward. I knew of nothing that might relieve her distress. "Do you know any songs?" I asked her.

She blinked, startled. "I'm not a singer," she said.

It might have been a language issue. I hadn't paid much attention to customs in this part of this world, but I was fairly sure there was no division between songs anyone might sing and songs that were, usually for religious reasons, only sung by specialists—not in the cities near the equator. Maybe it was different this far south. "Excuse me," I said, "I must have used the wrong word. What do you call it when you're working or playing, or trying to get a baby to sleep? Or just..."

"Oh!" Comprehension animated her, for just a moment. "You mean *songs*!"

I smiled encouragingly, but she lapsed into silence again. "Try not to worry too much," I said. "The doctor is very good at what she does. And sometimes you just have to leave things to the gods."

She curled her lower lip inward and bit it. "I don't believe in any god," she said, with a slight vehemence.

"Still. Things will happen as they happen." She gestured agreement, perfunctory. "Do you play counters?" I asked. Maybe she could show me the game Strigan's board was meant for, though I doubted it was from Nilt.

"No." And with that, I had exhausted what small means I might have had to amuse or distract her.

After ten minutes of silence she said, "I have a Tiktik set."

"What's Tiktik?"

Her eyes widened, round in her round, pale face. "How can you not know what Tiktik is? You must be from very far away!" I acknowledged that I was, and she answered, "It's a game. It's mostly a game for children." Her tone implied she wasn't a child, but I'd best not ask why she was carrying a child's game set. "You've really never played Tiktik?"

"Never. Where I come from we mostly play counters, and cards, and dice. But even those are different, in different places."

She pondered that a moment. "I can teach you," she said finally. "It's easy."

Two hours later, as I was tossing my handful of tiny bov-bone dice, the visitor alarm sounded. The girl looked up, startled. "Someone's here," I said. The door to the infirmary stayed shut, Strigan paying no attention.

"Mama," the girl suggested, hope and relief lending the tiniest tremble to her voice.

"I hope so. I hope it's not another patient." Immediately I realized I shouldn't have suggested it. "I'll go see."

It was Mama, unquestionably. She jumped out of the flier

she had arrived in, and made for the house with a speed I wouldn't have thought possible over the snow. She strode past me without acknowledging my existence in any way, tall for a Nilter and broad, as they all were, bundled in coats, the signs of her relationship to the girl inside clear in the lines of her face. I followed her in.

On seeing the girl, now standing by the abandoned Tiktik board, she said, "Well, then, what?"

A Radchaai parent would have put her arms around her daughter, kissed her, told her how relieved she was her daughter was well, maybe even would have wept. Some Radchaai would have thought this parent cold and affectionless. But I was sure that would have been a mistake. They sat down together on a bench, sides touching, as the girl gave her report, what she knew of the patient's condition, and what had happened out in the snow with the herd, and the ice devil. When she had finished, her mother patted her twice on the knee, briskly, and it was as though she were suddenly a different girl, taller, stronger, now she had, it seemed, not only her mother's strong, comforting presence, but her approval.

I brought them two cups of fermented milk, and Mama's attention snapped to me, but not, I thought, because I was of any interest in particular. "You're not the doctor," she said, bare statement. I could see her attention was still on her daughter; her interest in me stretched only as far as I might be a threat or a help.

"I'm a guest here," I told her. "But the doctor is busy, and I thought you might like something to drink."

Her eyes went to Seivarden, still sleeping, as she had for the last several hours, that black, trembling corrective spread across her forehead, the remains of bruising around her mouth and nose.

"She's from very far away," said the girl. "She didn't know how to play Tiktik!" Her mother's gaze flicked over the set on the floor, the dice, the board and flat, painted stone pieces halted in midcourse. She said nothing, but her expression changed, just slightly. She gave a small, almost imperceptible nod, and took the milk I offered.

Twenty minutes later Seivarden woke, brushed the black corrective off her head, and wiped fretfully at her upper lip, pausing at the flakes of dried blood that rubbed away. She looked at the two Nilters, sitting silent, side by side, on a nearby bench, studiously ignoring both her and me. Neither of them seemed to find it odd that I didn't go to Seivarden's side, or say anything to her. I didn't know if she remembered why I had hit her, or even that I had. Sometimes a blow to the head affects memories of the moments leading up to it. But she must have either remembered or suspected something, because she didn't look at me at all. After fidgeting a few minutes she rose and went to the kitchen and opened a cabinet. She stared for thirty seconds, and then got a bowl, and hard bread to put in it, and water to pour over it, and then stood, staring, waiting for it to soften, saying nothing, looking at no one.

8

At first the people I had sent away from the Fore-Temple water stood whispering in small groups on the street, and then dispersed when I approached, walking my regular rounds. But soon after, everyone disappeared into their houses, clustered together within. For the next few hours the upper city was quiet. Eerily so, and it didn't help that Lieutenant Awn continually asked me what was happening there.

Lieutenant Awn was sure increasing my presence in the upper city would only make the situation worse, so instead she ordered me to stay close to the plaza. If anything happened I would be there, between the upper and lower city. It was largely because of this that when things went to pieces, I was still able to function more or less effectively.

For hours nothing happened. The Lord of the Radch mouthed prayers along with the priests of Ikkt. In the lower city I passed the word that it might be a good idea to stay in tonight, and as a result there were no conversations in the streets, no knots of neighbors congregating on someone's ground floor to watch an entertainment. By dark nearly everyone had retired to an upper floor, and was talking quietly, or looking out over the railings, saying nothing.

Four hours before dawn, things went to pieces. Or, more accurately, *I* went to pieces. The tracker data I had been monitoring cut out, and suddenly all twenty of me were blind, deaf, immobile. Each segment could see only from a single pair of eyes, hear only through a single pair of ears, move only that single body. It took a few bewildered, panicked moments for my segments to realize that each was cut off from the others, each instance of me alone in a single body. Worst of all, in that same instant all data from Lieutenant Awn ceased.

From that moment I was twenty different people, with twenty different sets of observations and memories, and I can only remember what happened by piecing those separate experiences together.

At the moment the blow fell, all twenty segments immediately, without thought, extended my armor, those segments that were dressed not making even the least attempt to modify it to cover any part of my uniforms. In the house eight sleeping segments woke instantly, and once I had recovered my composure they rushed to where Lieutenant Awn lay trying to sleep. Two of those segments, Seventeen and Four, seeing Lieutenant Awn seemingly well, and several other segments around her, went to the house console to check communications status—the console wasn't working.

"Communications are out," my Seventeen segment called, voice distorted by the smooth, silver armor.

"Not possible," said Four, and Seventeen didn't answer, because no answer was necessary, given the actuality.

Some of my segments in the upper city actually turned toward the Fore-Temple water before realizing I'd best stay where I was. Every single segment in the plaza and the temple turned toward the house. One of me took off running to be sure of Lieutenant Awn, and two said, at once, "The upper city!" and another two, "The storm siren!" and for two confused seconds the pieces of me tried to decide what to do next. Segment Nine ran into the temple residence and woke the priest sleeping by the storm siren, who tripped it.

Just before the siren blew, Jen Shinnan ran out of her house in the upper city shouting, "Murder! Murder!" Lights came on in the houses around her, but further noise was drowned out by the shrieking of the siren. My nearest segment was four streets away.

All around the lower city, storm shutters rattled down. The priests in the temple ceased their prayers, and the head priest looked at me, but I had no information for her, and gestured my helplessness. "My communications are cut off, Divine," said that segment. The head priest blinked, uncomprehending. Speech was useless while the siren blew.

The Lord of the Radch hadn't reacted at the moment I had fragmented, though she was connected to the rest of herself in much the same way I ordinarily was. Her apparent lack of surprise was strange enough for my segment nearest her to notice it. But it might have been no more than self-possession; the siren elicited no more than an upward glance and a raised eyebrow. Then she stood and walked out onto the plaza.

It was the third worst thing that has ever happened to me. I had lost all sense of *Justice of Toren* overhead, all sense of myself. I had shattered into twenty fragments that could barely communicate with each other.

Just before the siren had blown, Lieutenant Awn had sent a segment to the temple, with orders to sound the alarm. Now that segment came running into the plaza, where it stood, hesitating, looking at the rest of itself, visible but *not there* as far as my sense of myself was concerned.

The siren stopped. The lower city was silent, the only sound was my footsteps, and my armor-filtered voices, trying to talk to myself, to get organized so I could function at least in some small way.

The Lord of the Radch raised one graying eyebrow. "Where is Lieutenant Awn?"

That was, of course, the question uppermost in the minds of all my segments that didn't already know, but now the one of me who had arrived with the order from Lieutenant Awn had something it knew it could do. "Lieutenant Awn is on her way, my lord," it said, and ten seconds later Lieutenant Awn and most of the rest of me that had been in the house arrived, rushing into the plaza.

"I thought you had this area under control." Anaander Mianaai didn't look at Lieutenant Awn as she spoke, but the direction of her words was clear.

"So did I." And then Lieutenant Awn remembered where she was, and to whom she was speaking. "My lord. Begging your pardon." Each of me had to restrain itself from turning entirely to watch Lieutenant Awn, to be sure she was really *there*, because I couldn't sense her otherwise. A few whispers sorted out which of my segments would keep close to her, and the rest would have to trust that.

My Ten segment came around the Fore-Temple water at a dead run. "Trouble in the upper city!" it called, and came to a halt in front of Lieutenant Awn, where I cleared the path for myself. "People are gathering at Jen Shinnan's house, they're angry, they're talking about murder, and getting justice."

"*Murder.* Oh, *fuck*!"

All the segments near Lieutenant Awn said, in unison, "Language, Lieutenant!" Anaander Mianaai turned a disbelieving look on me, but said nothing.

"Oh, *fuck*!" Lieutenant Awn repeated.

"Are you," asked Anaander Mianaai, calm and deliberate, "going to do anything except swear?"

Lieutenant Awn froze for half a second, then looked around, across the water, toward the lower city, at the temple. "Who's here? Count!" And when we had done so, "One through Seven, out here. The rest, with me." I followed her into the temple, leaving Anaander Mianaai standing in the plaza.

The priests stood near the dais, watching us approach. "Divine," said Lieutenant Awn.

"Lieutenant," said the head priest.

"There's a mob bent on violence headed here from the upper city. I'm guessing we have five minutes. They can't do much damage with the storm shutters down, I'd like to bring them in here, keep them from doing anything drastic."

"Bring them in here," the head priest repeated, doubtfully.

"Everything else is dark and shut. The big doors are open, it's the most obvious place to come, when most of them are in here we close the doors and One Esk surrounds them. We could just shut the temple doors and let them try their luck with the shutters on the houses, but I don't really want to find out how hard those are to breach. If," she added, seeing Anaander Mianaai come into the temple, walking slowly, as though nothing unusual were happening, "my lord permits."

The Lord of the Radch gestured a silent assent.

The head priest clearly didn't like the suggestion, but she agreed. By now my segments on the plaza were seeing hand lights sporadically visible in the nearest upper-city streets.

Within moments Lieutenant Awn had me behind the large temple doors, ready to close them on her signal, and a few of me dispatched to the streets around the plaza to help herd Tanmind toward the temple. The rest of me stood in the shadows around the perimeter inside the temple itself, and the priests returned to their prayers, their backs to the wide and inviting entrance.

More than a hundred Tanmind came down from the upper city. Most of them did precisely as we wished, and rushed in a swirling, shouting mass into the temple, except for twenty-three, a dozen of whom veered off down a dark, empty avenue. The other eleven, who had already been trailing the larger group, saw one segment of me standing quiet nearby, and thought better of their actions. They stopped, muttered among themselves for a moment, watching the mass of Tanmind run into the temple, the others rushing, shouting, down the street. They watched me close the temple doors, the segments posted there not uniformed, covered only with the silver of my own generated armor, and maybe it reminded them of the annexation. Several of them swore, and they turned and ran back to the upper city.

Eighty-three Tanmind had run into the temple; their angry voices echoed and reechoed, magnified. At the sound of the doors slamming closed, they turned and tried to rush back the way they had come, but I had surrounded them, my guns drawn and aimed at whoever was nearest each segment.

"Citizens!" shouted Lieutenant Awn, but she didn't have the trick of making herself heard.

"Citizens!" the various fragments of me shouted, my own voices echoing and then dying down. Along with the Tanmind's tumult: Jen Shinnan, and Jen Taa, and a few others I knew were friends or relations of theirs, shushed those near them, urged them to calm themselves, to consider that the Lord of the Radch herself was here, and they could speak directly to her.

"Citizens!" Lieutenant Awn shouted again. "Have you lost your minds? What are you doing?"

"Murder!" shouted Jen Shinnan, who was at the front of the crowd, shouting over my head at Lieutenant Awn where she stood behind me, beside the Lord of the Radch and the Divine. The junior priests stood huddled together, seemingly frozen. The Tanmind voices grumbled, echoing, in support of Jen Shinnan. "We won't get justice from you so we'll take it ourselves!" Jen Shinnan cried. The grumbling from the crowd rolled around the stone walls of the temple.

"Explain yourself, citizen," said Anaander Mianaai, voice pitched to sound above the noise.

The Tanmind hushed each other for five seconds, and then, "My lord," said Jen Shinnan. Her respectful tone sounded almost sincere. "My young niece has been staying in my house for the past week. She was harassed and threatened by Orsians when she came to the lower city, which I reported to Lieutenant Awn, but nothing was done. This evening I found her room empty, the window broken, blood everywhere! What am I to conclude? The Orsians have always resented us! Now they mean to kill us all, is it any wonder we should defend ourselves?"

Anaander Mianaai turned to Lieutenant Awn. "Was this reported?"

"It was, my lord," said Lieutenant Awn. "I investigated and found that the young person in question had never left sight of *Justice of Toren* One Esk, who reported that she had spent all her time in the lower city alone. The only words that passed between her and anyone else were routine business

transactions. She was not harassed or threatened at any time."

"You see!" cried Jen Shinnan. "You see why we are compelled to take justice into our own hands!"

"And what leads you to believe all your lives are threatened?" asked Anaander Mianaai.

"My lord," said Jen Shinnan, "Lieutenant Awn would have you believe everyone in the lower city is loyal and law-abiding, but we know from experience that the Orsians are anything but paragons of virtue. The fishermen go out on the water at night, unseen. Sources..." She hesitated, just a moment, whether because of the gun pointed directly at her, or Anaander Mianaai's continued impassivity, or something else, I couldn't tell. But it seemed to me something had amused her. Then she recovered her composure. "Sources I prefer not to name have seen the boatmen of the lower city depositing weapons in caches in the lake. What would those be for, except to finally take their revenge on us, who they believe have mistreated them? And how could those guns have come here without Lieutenant Awn's collusion?"

Anaander Mianaai turned her dark face toward Lieutenant Awn and raised one grayed eyebrow. "Do you have an answer for that, Lieutenant Awn?"

Something about the question, or the way it was asked, troubled all the segments that heard it. And Jen Shinnan actually smiled. She had *expected* the Lord of the Radch to turn on Lieutenant Awn, and was pleased by it.

"I do have an answer, my lord," said Lieutenant Awn. "Some nights ago, a local fisherman reported to me that she had found a cache of weapons under the lake. I removed them and took them to my house, and upon searching, discovered two more caches, which I also removed. I had intended to search further this evening, but events have, as you see, prevented me. My report is written but not yet sent, because I, too, wondered how the guns could have come here without my knowledge."

Perhaps it was only because of Jen Shinnan's smile, and the oddly accusatory questions from Anaander Mianaai—and the slight earlier, in the temple plaza—but in the charged air of the temple, the echoes of Lieutenant Awn's words themselves felt like an accusation.

"I have also wondered," Lieutenant Awn said, in the silence after those echoes died away, "why the young person in question would falsely accuse residents of the lower city of harassing her, when they assuredly did not. I am quite certain no one from the lower city has harmed her."

"Someone has!" shouted a voice in the crowd, and mutterings of assent started, and grew and echoed around the vast stone space.

"What time did you last see your cousin?" asked Lieutenant Awn.

"Three hours ago," said Jen Shinnan. "She told us good night, and went to her room."

Lieutenant Awn addressed the segment of me that was nearest her. "One Esk, did anyone cross from the lower city to the upper in the last three hours?"

The segment that answered—Thirteen—knew I should be careful about my answer, which by necessity everyone would hear. "No. No one crossed in either direction. Though I can't be certain about the last fifteen minutes."

"Someone might have come earlier," Jen Shinnan pointed out.

"In that case," answered Lieutenant Awn, "they're still in the upper city, and you ought to be looking for them there."

"The guns..." Jen Shinnan began.

"Are no danger to you. They're locked under the top floor of my house, and One Esk has disabled most of them by now."

Jen Shinnan cast an odd, appealing look to Anaander Mianaai, who had stood silent and impassive through this exchange. "But..."

"Lieutenant Awn," said the Lord of the Radch. "A word." She gestured aside, and Lieutenant Awn followed her to a spot fifteen meters off. One of my segments followed, which Mianaai ignored. "Lieutenant," she said in a quiet voice. "Tell me what you think is happening."

Lieutenant Awn swallowed, took a breath. "My lord. I'm certain no one from the lower city has harmed the young person in question. I am also certain the guns were not cached by anyone from the lower city. And the weapons were all ones which had been confiscated during the annexation. This can only originate from a very high level. That's why I haven't filed the report. I was hoping to speak directly to you about this when you arrived, but never had the opportunity."

"You were afraid if you reported it through regular channels, whoever did this would realize their plan had been detected, and cover their tracks."

"Yes, my lord. When I heard you were coming, my lord, I planned to speak to you about it immediately."

"*Justice of Toren.*" The Lord of the Radch addressed my segment without looking at me. "Is this true?"

"Entirely, my lord," I answered. The junior priests still huddled, the head priest standing apart from them, looking at Lieutenant Awn and the Lord of the Radch where they conferred, an expression on her face that I couldn't read.

"So," said Anaander Mianaai. "What's your assessment of this situation?"

Lieutenant Awn blinked in astonishment. "I...it looks

very much to me as though Jen Shinnan is involved with the weapons. How would she have known of their existence otherwise?"

"And this murdered young person?"

"If she *is* murdered, no one from the lower city did it. But can they have killed her themselves to have an excuse to..." Lieutenant Awn stopped, appalled.

"An excuse to come down to the lower city and murder innocent citizens in their beds. And then use the existence of the weapons caches to support their assertion that they were only acting in self-defense and you had refused to do your duty and protect them." She cast a glance at the Tanmind, ringed by my still-armed and -silver-armored segments. "Well. We can concern ourselves with details later. Right now we need to deal with these people."

"My lord," acknowledged Lieutenant Awn, with a slight bow.

"Shoot them."

To noncitizens, who only ever see Radchaai in melodramatic entertainments, who know nothing of the Radch besides ancillaries and annexations and what they think of as brainwashing, such an order might be appalling, but hardly surprising. But the idea of shooting citizens was, in fact, extremely shocking and upsetting. What, after all, was the point of civilization if not the well-being of citizens? And these people were citizens now.

Lieutenant Awn froze, for two seconds. "M...my lord?"

Anaander Mianaai's voice, which had been dispassionate, perhaps slightly stern, turned chill and severe. "Are you refusing an order, Lieutenant?"

"No, my lord, only...they're *citizens*. And we're in a temple. And we have them under control, and I've sent *Justice of Toren* One Esk to the next division to ask for reinforcements.

Justice of Ente Seven Issa should be here in an hour, perhaps two, and we can arrest the Tanmind and assign them to reeducation very easily, since you're here."

"Are you," asked Anaander Mianaai, slowly and clearly, "refusing an order?"

Jen Shinnan's amusement, her willingness—even eagerness—to speak to the Lord of the Radch, it fell into a pattern for my listening segment. Someone very high up had made those guns available, had known how to cut off communications. No one was higher up than Anaander Mianaai. But it made no sense. Jen Shinnan's motivation was obvious, but how could the Lord of the Radch possibly profit by it?

Lieutenant Awn was likely having the same thoughts. I could read her distress in the tension of her jaw, the stiff set of her shoulders. Still, it seemed unreal, because the external signs were all I could see. "I won't refuse an order, my lord," she said after five seconds. "May I protest it?"

"I believe you already have," said Anaander Mianaai, coldly. "Now shoot them."

Lieutenant Awn turned. I thought she was the slightest bit shaky as she walked toward the surrounded Tanmind.

"*Justice of Toren*," Mianaai said, and the segment of me that had been about to follow Lieutenant Awn stopped. "When was the last time I visited you?"

I remembered the last time the Lord of the Radch had boarded *Justice of Toren* very clearly. It had been an unusual visit—unannounced, four older bodies with no entourage. She had mostly stayed in her quarters talking to me—*Justice of Toren*–me, not One Esk–me, but she had asked One Esk to sing for her. I had obliged with a Valskaayan piece. It had been ninety-four years, two months, two weeks, and six days before, shortly after the annexation of Valskaay. I opened my mouth to say so, but instead heard myself say, "Two hundred three years, four months, one week, and one day ago, my lord."

"Hmm," said Anaander Mianaai, but she said nothing else.

Lieutenant Awn approached me, where I ringed the Tanmind. She stood there, behind a segment, for three and a half seconds, saying nothing.

Her distress must have been obvious to more than just me. Jen Shinnan, seeing her stand there silent and unhappy, smiled. Almost triumphantly. "Well?"

"One Esk," Lieutenant Awn said, clearly dreading the finish of her sentence. Jen Shinnan's smile grew slightly larger. Expecting Lieutenant Awn to send the Tanmind home, no doubt. Expecting, in the fullness of time, Lieutenant Awn's dismissal and the decline of the lower city's influence. "I didn't want this," Lieutenant Awn said to her, quietly, "but I have a direct order." She raised her voice. "One Esk. Shoot them."

Jen Shinnan's smile disappeared, replaced by horror, and, I thought, betrayal, and she looked, plainly, directly, toward Anaander Mianaai. Who stood impassive. The other Tanmind clamored, crying out in fear and protest.

All my segments hesitated. The order made no sense. Whatever they had done, these were citizens, and I had them under control. But Lieutenant Awn said, loud and harsh, "Fire!" and I did. Within three seconds all the Tanmind were dead.

No one in the temple at that moment was young enough to be surprised at what had happened, though perhaps the several years since I'd executed anyone had lent the memories some distance, maybe even engendered some confidence that citizenship meant an end to such things. The junior priests stood where they had since this had begun, not moving, saying nothing. The head priest wept openly, soundlessly.

"I think," said Anaander Mianaai into the vast silence that surrounded us, once the echoes of gunfire had died down, "there won't be any more trouble from the Tanmind here."

Lieutenant Awn's mouth and throat twitched slightly, as though she were about to speak, but she didn't. Instead she walked forward, around the bodies, tapping four of my segments on the shoulder as she passed and gesturing to them to follow. I realized she simply could not bring herself to speak. Or perhaps she feared what would come out of her mouth if she attempted it. Having only visual data from her was frustrating.

"Where are you going, Lieutenant?" asked the Lord of the Radch.

Her back to Mianaai, Lieutenant Awn opened her mouth, and then closed it again. Closed her eyes, took a breath. "With my lord's permission, I intend to discover whatever it is that's blocking communications." Anaander Mianaai didn't answer, and Lieutenant Awn turned to my nearest segment.

"Jen Shinnan's house," that segment said, since it was clear Lieutenant Awn was still in emotional distress. "I'll look for the young person as well."

Just before sunrise I found the device there. The instant I disabled it I was myself again—minus one missing segment. I saw the silent, barely twilit streets of the upper and lower city, the temple empty of anyone but myself and eighty-three silent, staring corpses. Lieutenant Awn's grief and distress and shame were suddenly clear and visible, to my combined relief and discomfort. And with a moment's willing it, the tracker signals of all the people in Ors flared into life in my vision, including the people who had died and still lay in the temple of Ikkt; my missing segment in an upper city street, neck broken; and Jen Shinnan's niece—in the mud at the bottom of the northern edge of the Fore-Temple water.

9

Strigan came out of the infirmary, undercoat bloody, and the girl and her mother, who had been talking quietly in a language I didn't understand, fell silent and looked expectantly to her.

"I've done what I can," Strigan said, with no preamble. "He's out of danger. You'll need to take him to Therrod to have the limbs regrown, but I've done some of the prep work, and they should grow back fairly easily."

"Two weeks," said the Nilter woman, impassive. As though it wasn't the first time something like this had happened.

"Can't be helped," said Strigan, answering something I hadn't heard or understood. "Maybe someone's got a few extra hands they can spare."

"I'll call some cousins."

"You do that," said Strigan. "You can see him now if you like, but he's asleep."

"When can we move him?" the woman asked.

"Now, if you like," answered Strigan. "The sooner the better, I suppose."

The woman made an affirmative gesture, and she and the girl rose and went into the infirmary without another word.

Not long after, we brought the injured person out to the girl's flier and saw them off, and trudged back into the house and shed our outer coats. Seivarden had by now returned to her pallet on the floor and sat, knees drawn up, arms tight around her legs as if she were holding them back and it took work.

Strigan looked at me, an odd expression on her face, one I couldn't read. "She's a good kid."

"Yes."

"She'll get a good name out of this. A good story to go with it."

I had learned the lingua franca that I thought would be most useful here, and done the sort of cursory research one needs to navigate unfamiliar places, but I knew almost nothing about the people who herded bov on this part of the planet. "Is it an adulthood thing?" I guessed.

"Sort of. Yes." She went to a cabinet, pulled out a cup and a bowl. Her movements were quick and steady, but I got somehow an impression of exhaustion. From the set of her shoulders perhaps. "I didn't think you'd be much interested in children. Aside from killing them, I mean."

I refused the bait. "She let me know she wasn't a child. Even if she did have a Tiktik set."

Strigan sat at her small table. "You played two hours straight."

"There wasn't much else to do."

Strigan laughed, short and bitter. Then she gestured toward Seivarden, who seemed to be ignoring us. She couldn't understand us anyway, we weren't speaking Radchaai. "I don't feel sorry for him. It's just that I'm a doctor."

"You said that."

"I don't think you feel sorry for him either."

"I don't."

"You don't make anything easy, do you?" Strigan's voice was half-angry. Exasperated.

"It depends."

She shook her head slightly, as though she hadn't heard quite clearly. "I've seen worse. But he needs medical attention."

"You don't intend to give it," I said. Not asking.

"I'm still figuring you out," Strigan said, as though her statement was related to mine, though I was sure it wasn't. "As a matter of fact, I'm considering giving him something more to keep him calm." I didn't answer. "You disapprove." It wasn't a question. "I don't feel sorry for him."

"You keep saying that."

"He lost his ship." Very likely her interest in her Garseddai artifacts had led her to learn what she could about the events that had led to the destruction of Garsedd. "Bad enough," Strigan continued, "but Radchaai ships aren't just ships, are they? And his crew. It was a thousand years ago for us, but for him—one moment everything is the way it should be, next moment *everything's* gone." With one hand she made a frustrated, ambivalent gesture. "He needs medical attention."

"If he hadn't fled the Radch, he'd have received it."

Strigan cocked one gray eyebrow, sat on a bench. "Translate for me. My Radchaai isn't good enough."

One moment an ancillary had shoved Seivarden into a suspension pod, next she'd found herself freezing and choking as the pod's fluids exited through her mouth and nose, drained away, and she found herself in the sick bay of a patrol ship. When Seivarden described it, I could see her agitation, her anger, barely masked. "Some dingy little Mercy, with a shabby, provincial captain."

"Your face is almost perfectly impassive," Strigan said to me. Not in Radchaai, so Seivarden didn't understand. "But I can see your temperature and heart rate." And probably a few other things, with the medical implants she likely had.

"The ship was human-crewed," I said to Seivarden.

That distressed her further—whether it was anger, or embarrassment, or something else, I couldn't tell. "I didn't realize. Not right away. The captain took me aside and explained."

I translated this for Strigan, and she looked at Seivarden in disbelief, and then at me with speculation. "Is that an easy mistake to make?"

"No," I answered, shortly.

"That was when she finally had to tell me how long it had been," Seivarden said, unaware of anything but her own story.

"And what had happened after," suggested Strigan.

I translated, but Seivarden ignored it, and continued as though neither of us had spoken. "Eventually we put in to this tiny border station. You know the sort of thing, a station administrator who's either in disgrace or a jumped-up nobody, an officious inspector supervisor playing tyrant on the docks, and half a dozen Security whose biggest challenge is chasing chickens out of the tea shop.

"I'd thought the Mercy captain had a terrible accent, but I couldn't understand anyone on the station at all. The station AI had to translate for me, but my implants didn't work. Too antiquated. So I could only talk to it using wall consoles." Which would have made it extremely difficult to hold any sort of conversation. "And even when Station explained, the things people were saying didn't make sense.

"They assigned me an apartment, a room with a cot, hardly large enough to stand up in. Yes, they knew who I said I was, but they had no record of my financial data, and it would be weeks before it could possibly arrive. Maybe longer. Meantime I got the food and shelter any Radchaai was guaranteed. Unless, of course, I wanted to retake the aptitudes so I could get a new assignment. Because they didn't have my aptitudes data and even if they did it was certainly out of date. *Out of date*," she repeated, her voice bitter.

"Did you see a doctor?" Strigan asked. Watching Seivarden's face, I guessed what had finally sent her from Radchaai space. She must have seen a doctor, who had opted to wait and watch. Physical injuries weren't an issue, the medic of whatever Mercy had picked her up would have taken care of those, but psychological or emotional ones—they might resolve on their own, and if they didn't, the doctor would need that aptitudes data to work effectively.

"They said I could send a message to my house lord asking for assistance. But they didn't know who that was." Obviously Seivarden had no intention of talking about the station doctor.

"House lord?" asked Strigan.

"Head of her extended family," I explained. "It sounds very elevated in translation, but it isn't, unless your house is very wealthy or prestigious."

"And hers?"

"Was both."

Strigan didn't miss that. "*Was*."

Seivarden continued as though we hadn't spoken. "But it turned out, Vendaai was gone. My whole house didn't even *exist* anymore. Everything, assets and contracts, everything absorbed by *Geir*!" It had surprised everyone at the time, some five hundred years ago. The two houses, Geir and Vendaai, had hated each other. Geir's house lord had taken malicious advantage of Vendaai's gambling debts, and some foolish contracts.

"Catch up with current events?" I asked Seivarden.

She ignored my question. "Everything was *gone*. And what was left, it was like it was *almost* right. But the colors were wrong, or everything was turned slightly to the left of where it should be. People would say things and I couldn't understand them at all, or I knew they were real words but my mind couldn't take them in. Nothing seemed real."

Maybe it had been an answer to my question after all. "How did you feel about the human soldiers?"

Seivarden frowned, and looked directly at me for the first time since she'd awoken. I regretted asking the question. It hadn't really been the question I'd wanted to ask. *What did you think when you heard about Ime?* But maybe she hadn't. Or if she had it might have been incomprehensible to her. *Did anyone come to you whispering about restoring the rightful order of things?* Probably not, considering. "How did you leave the Radch without permits?" That couldn't have been easy. It would at the very least have cost money she wouldn't have had.

Seivarden looked away from me, down and to the left. She wasn't going to say.

"Everything was wrong," she said after nine seconds of silence.

"Bad dreams," said Strigan. "Anxiety. Shaking, sometimes."

"Unsteady," I said. Translated it had very little sting, but in Radchaai, for an officer like Seivarden, it said more. Weak, fearful, inadequate to the demands of her position. Fragile. If Seivarden was unsteady, she had never really deserved her assignment, never really been suited to the military, let alone to captain a ship. But of course Seivarden had taken the aptitudes, and the aptitudes had said she was what her house had always assumed she would be: steady, fit to command and conquer. Not prone to doubts or irrational fears.

"You don't know what you're talking about," Seivarden half-sneered, half-snarled. Arms still locked around her knees. "No one in my house is unsteady."

Of course (I thought but did not say), the various cousins who had served a year or so during this annexation or that and retired to take ascetic vows or paint tea sets hadn't done so because they had been unsteady. And the cousins who hadn't tested as anticipated, but surprised their parents with assignments in the minor priesthoods, or the arts—this had not indicated any sort of unsteadiness inherent in the house, no, never. And Seivarden wasn't the least bit afraid or worried about what new assignment a retake of the aptitudes would get her, and what that might say about her steadiness. Of *course* not.

"Unsteady?" asked Strigan, understanding the word, but not its context.

"The unsteady," I explained, "lack a certain strength of character."

"Character!" Strigan's indignation was plain to read.

"Of course." I didn't alter my facial expression, but kept it bland and pleasant, as it had been for most of the past few days. "Lesser citizens break down in the face of enormous difficulties or stress and sometimes require medical attention for it. But some citizens are bred better. They never break down. Though they may take early retirement, or spend a few years pursuing artistic or spiritual interests—prolonged meditation retreats are quite popular. This is how one knows the difference between highly placed families and lesser ones."

"But you Radchaai are so good at brainwashing. Or so I hear."

"Reeducation," I corrected. "If she'd stayed, she'd have gotten help."

"But she couldn't face needing the help to begin with." I said nothing to agree or disagree, though I thought Strigan was right. "How much can . . . reeducation do?"

"A great deal," I said. "Though much of what you've probably heard is greatly exaggerated. It can't turn you into someone you're not. Not in any useful way."

"Erase memories."

"Suppress them, I think. Add new ones, maybe. You have to know what you're doing or you could damage someone badly."

"No doubt."

Seivarden stared frowning at us, watching us talk, unable to understand what we were saying.

Strigan half-smiled. "*You* aren't a product of reeducation."

"No," I acknowledged.

"It was surgery. Sever a few connections, make a few new ones. Install some implants." She paused a moment, waiting for me to answer, but I didn't. "You pass well enough. Mostly. Your expression, your tone of voice, it's always right but it's always . . . always studied. Always a performance."

"You think you've solved the puzzle," I guessed.

"*Solved* isn't the right word. But you're a corpse soldier, I'm certain of it. Do you remember anything?"

"Many things," I said, still bland.

"No, I mean from before."

It took me nearly five seconds to understand what she meant. "That person is dead."

Seivarden suddenly, convulsively stood and walked out the inner door and, by the sound of it, through the outer as well.

Strigan watched her go, gave a quick, breathy *hm*, and then turned back to me. "Your sense of who you are has a neurological basis. One small change and you don't believe you exist anymore. But you're still there. I think you're still there. Why the bizarre desire to kill Anaander Mianaai? Why else would you be so angry with *him*?" She tilted her head to indicate the exit, Seivarden outside in the cold with only one coat.

"He'll take the crawler," I warned. The girl and her mother had taken the flier, and left the crawler outside Strigan's house.

"No he won't. I disabled it." I gestured my approval, and Strigan continued, returning to her previous subject. "And the music. I don't suppose you were a singer, not with a voice like yours. But you must have been a musician, before, or loved music."

I considered making the bitter laugh Strigan's guess called for. "No," I said, instead. "Not actually."

"But you *are* a corpse soldier, I'm right about that." I didn't answer. "You escaped somehow or...are you from *his* ship? Captain Seivarden's?"

"*Sword of Nathtas* was destroyed." I had been there, been nearby. Relatively speaking. Seen it happen, nearly enough. "And that was a thousand years ago."

Strigan looked toward the door, back at me. Then she frowned. "No. No, I think you're Ghaonish, and they were only annexed a few centuries ago, weren't they? I shouldn't have forgotten that, it's why you're passing as someone from the Gerentate, isn't it? No, you escaped somehow. *I can bring you back*. I'm sure I can."

"You can kill me, you mean. You can destroy my sense of self and replace it with one you approve of."

Strigan didn't like hearing that, I could see. The outer door opened, and then Seivarden came shivering through the inner. "Put on your outer coat next time," I told her.

"Fuck off." She grabbed a blanket off her pallet and wrapped it around her shoulders, and stood, still shivering.

"Very unbecoming language, citizen," I said.

For a moment she looked as though she might lose her temper. Then she seemed to remember what might happen if she did. "Fuck." She sat on the nearest bench, heavily. "Off."

"Why didn't you leave him where you found him?" asked Strigan.

"I wish I knew." It was another puzzle for her, but not one I had made deliberately. I didn't know myself. Didn't know why I cared if Seivarden froze to death in the storm-swept snow, didn't know why I had brought her with me, didn't know why I cared if she took someone else's crawler and fled, or walked off into the green-stained frozen waste and died.

"And why are you so angry with him?"

That I knew. And truth to tell, it wasn't entirely fair to Seivarden that I was angry. Still, the facts remained what they were, and my anger as well.

"Why do you want to kill Anaander Mianaai?" Seivarden's head turned slightly, her attention hooked by the familiar name.

"It's personal."

"*Personal.*" Strigan's tone was incredulous.

"Yes."

"You're not a person anymore. You've said as much to me. You're equipment. An appendage to a ship's AI." I said nothing, and waited for her to consider her own words. "Is there a ship that's lost its mind? Recently, I mean."

Insane Radchaai ships were a staple of melodrama, inside and outside Radchaai space. Though Radchaai entertainments in that direction were usually historicals. When Anaander Mianaai had taken control of the core of Radch space some few ships had destroyed themselves upon the death or captivity of their captains, and rumor said some others still wandered space in the three thousand years since, half-mad, despairing. "None I know of."

She very likely followed news from the Radch—it was a matter of her own safety, considering what I was sure she was hiding, and what the consequences would be for her if Anaander Mianaai ever discovered that. She had, potentially, all the information she needed to identify me. But after half a minute she gestured doubtfully, disappointed. "You won't just tell me."

I smiled, calm and pleasant. "What fun would that be?"

She laughed, seeming truly amused at my answer. Which I thought a hopeful sign. "So when are you leaving?"

"When you give me the gun."

"I don't know what you're talking about."

A lie. Manifestly a lie. "Your apartment, on Dras Annia Station. It's untouched. Just as you left it, so far as I could tell."

Every one of Strigan's motions became deliberate, just slightly slowed—blinks, breaths. The hand carefully brushing dust from her coat sleeve. "That a fact."

"It cost me a great deal to get in."

"Where *did* a corpse soldier get all that money anyway?"

Strigan asked, still tense, still concealing it. But genuinely curious. Always that.

"Work," I said.

"Lucrative work."

"And dangerous." I had risked my life to get that money.

"The icon?"

"Not unrelated." But I didn't want to talk about that. "What do I need to do, to convince you? Is the money insufficient?" I had more, elsewhere, but saying so would be foolish.

"What did you see in my apartment?" Strigan asked, curiosity and anger in her voice.

"A puzzle. With pieces missing." I had deduced the existence and nature of those pieces correctly, I must have, because here I was, and here was Arilesperas Strigan.

Strigan laughed again. "Like you. Listen." She leaned forward, hands on her thighs. "You can't kill Anaander Mianaai. I wish to all that's good it were possible, but it's not. Even with...even if I had what you think I have you couldn't do it. You told me that twenty-five of these guns were insufficient..."

"Twenty-four," I corrected.

She waved that away. "Were insufficient to keep the Radchaai away from Garsedd. Why do you think *one* would be anything more than a minor irritant?"

She knew better, or she wouldn't have run. Wouldn't have asked the local toughs to take care of me before I got to her.

"And why are you so determined to do such a ridiculous thing? Everyone outside the Radch hates Anaander Mianaai. If by some miracle he died, the celebrations would last a hundred years. But it *won't happen.* It certainly won't happen because of one idiot with a gun. I'm sure you know that. You probably know it far better than I could."

"True."

"Then why?"

Information is power. Information is security. Plans made with imperfect information are fatally flawed, will fail or succeed on the toss of a coin. I had known, when I first knew I would have to find Strigan and obtain the gun from her, that this would be such a moment. If I answered Strigan's question—if I answered it fully, as she would certainly demand—I would be giving her something she could use against me, a weapon. She would almost certainly hurt herself in the process, but that wasn't always much of a deterrent, I knew.

"Sometimes," I began, and then corrected myself. "Quite frequently, someone will learn a little bit about Radchaai religion, and ask, *If everything that happens is the will of Amaat, if nothing can happen that is not already designed by God, why bother to do anything?*"

"Good question."

"Not particularly."

"No? Why bother, then?"

"I am," I said, "as Anaander Mianaai made me. Anaander Mianaai is as she was made. We will both of us do the things we are made to do. The things that are before us to do."

"I doubt very much that Anaander Mianaai made you so that you would kill him."

Any reply would reveal more than I wished, at the moment.

"And I," continued Strigan, after a second and a half of silence, "am made to demand answers. It's just God's will." She made a gesture with her left hand, *not my problem.*

"You admit you have the gun."

"I admit nothing."

I was left with blind chance, a step into unguessable dark,

waiting to live or die on the results of the toss, not knowing what the chances were of any result. My only other choice would be to give up, and how could I give up now? After so long, after so much? And I had risked as much, or more, before now, and gotten this far.

She had to have the gun. *Had to.* But how could I make her give it to me? What would make her choose to give it to me?

"*Tell me*," Strigan said, watching me intently. No doubt seeing my frustration and doubt through her medical implants, fluctuations of my blood pressure and temperature and respiration. "Tell me why."

I closed my eyes, felt the disorientation of not being able to see through other eyes that I knew I had once had. Opened them again, took a breath to begin, and told her.

WHY

10

I had thought that perhaps the morning's temple attendants would (quite understandably) choose to stay home, but one small flower-bearer, awake before the adults in her household, arrived with a handful of pink-petaled weeds and stopped at the edge of the house, startled to see Anaander Mianaai kneeling in front of our small icon of Amaat.

Lieutenant Awn was dressing, on the upper floor. "I can't serve today," she said to me, her voice impassive as her emotions were not. The morning was already warm, and she was sweating.

"You didn't touch any of the bodies," I said as I adjusted her jacket collar, sure of the fact. It was the wrong thing to say.

Four of my segments, two on the northern edge of the Fore-Temple and two standing waist-deep in the lukewarm water and mud, lifted the body of Jen Taa's niece onto the ledge, and carried her to the medic's house.

On the ground floor of Lieutenant Awn's house, I said to the frightened, frozen flower-bearer, "It's all right." There was no sign of the water-bearer, and I was ineligible.

"You'll have to at least bring the water, Lieutenant," I said, above, to Lieutenant Awn. "The flower-bearer is here, but the water-bearer isn't."

For a few moments Lieutenant Awn said nothing, while I finished wiping her face. "Right," she said, and went downstairs and filled the bowl, and brought it to the flower-bearer, where she stood next to me, still frightened, clutching her handful of pink petals. Lieutenant Awn held the water out to her, and she set the flowers down and washed her hands. But before she could pick the flowers up again, Anaander Mianaai turned to look at her, and the child started back and grabbed my gloved hand with her bare one. "You'll have to wash your hands again, citizen," I whispered, and with a bit more encouragement she did so, and picked up the flowers again and performed her part of the morning's ritual correctly, if nervously. No one else came. I was not surprised.

The medic, speaking to herself and not to me, though I stood three meters away from her, said, "Throat cut, obviously, but she was also poisoned." And then, with disgust and contempt, "A child of their own house. These people aren't civilized."

Our one small attendant left, a gift from the Lord of the Radch clutched in one hand—a pin in the shape of a four-petaled flower, each petal holding an enameled image of one of the four Emanations. Anywhere else, a Radchaai who received one would treasure it, and wear it nearly constantly, a badge of having served in the temple with the Lord of the Radch herself. This child would probably toss it in a box and forget about it. When she was out of sight (of Lieutenant Awn and the Lord of the Radch, if not of me) Anaander Mianaai turned to Lieutenant Awn and said, "Aren't those weeds?"

A wave of embarrassment overcame Lieutenant Awn,

mixed a moment later with disappointment, and an intense anger I had never seen in her before. "Not to the children, my lord." She was unable to keep the edge out of her voice completely.

Anaander Mianaai's expression didn't change. "This icon, and this set of omens. They're your personal property, I think. Where are the ones that belong to the temple?"

"Begging my lord's pardon," Lieutenant Awn said, though I knew at this point she meant to do no such thing, and the fact was audible in her tone. "I used the funds for their purchase to supplement the term-end gifts for the temple attendants." She had also used her own money for the same purpose, but she didn't say that.

"I'm sending you back to *Justice of Toren*," said the Lord of the Radch. "Your replacement will be here tomorrow."

Shame. A fresh flare of anger. And despair. "Yes, my lord."

There wasn't much to pack. I could be ready to move in less than an hour. I spent the rest of the day delivering gifts to our temple attendants, who were all home. School had been canceled, and hardly anyone came out onto the streets. "Lieutenant Awn doesn't know," I told each one, "if the new lieutenant will make different appointments, or if she'll give the year-end gifts without your having served a whole year. You should come to the house anyway, her first morning." The adults in each house eyed me silently, not inviting me in, and each time I laid the gift—not the usual pair of gloves, which didn't yet matter much here, but a brightly colored and patterned skirt, and a small box of tamarind sweets. Fresh fruit was customary, but there was no time to obtain any. I left each small stack of gifts in the street, on the edge of the house, and no one moved to take them, or spoke any word to me.

The Divine spent an hour or two behind screens in the temple residence, and then emerged looking entirely unrested, and went into the temple, where she conferred with the junior priests. The bodies had been cleared away. I had offered to clean the blood, not knowing if my doing so would be permissible, but the priests had declined my assistance. "Some of us," said the Divine to me, still staring at the area of floor where the dead had lain, "had forgotten what you are. Now they are reminded."

"I don't think *you* forgot, Divine," I said.

"No." She was silent for two seconds. "Is the lieutenant going to see me before she leaves?"

"Possibly not, Divine," I said. I was at that moment doing what I could to encourage Lieutenant Awn to sleep, something she badly needed to do but was finding difficult.

"It's probably better if she doesn't," the head priest said, bitterly. She looked at me then. "It's unreasonable of me. I know it is. What else could she have done? It's easy for me to say—and I say it—that she could have chosen otherwise."

"She could have, Divine," I acknowledged.

"What is it you Radchaai say?" I wasn't Radchaai, but I didn't correct her, and she continued. "Justice, propriety, and benefit, isn't it? Let every act be just, and proper, and beneficial."

"Yes, Divine."

"Was that just?" Her voice trembled, for just an instant, and I could hear she was on the edge of tears. "Was it proper?"

"I don't know, Divine."

"More to the point, who benefited?"

"No one, Divine, so far as I can see."

"No one? Really? Come, One Esk, don't play the fool with

me." That look of betrayal on Jen Shinnan's face, plainly directed at Anaander Mianaai, had been obvious to everyone there.

Still, I couldn't see what the Lord of the Radch had stood to gain from those deaths. "They would have killed you, Divine," I said. "You, and anyone else they found undefended. Lieutenant Awn did what she could to prevent bloodshed last night. It wasn't her fault she failed."

"It was." Her back was still to me. "God forgive her for it. God forbid that I may ever be faced with such a choice." She made an invocatory gesture. "And you? What would you have done, if the lieutenant had refused, and the Lord of the Radch ordered you to shoot her? Could you have? I thought that armor of yours was impenetrable."

"The Lord of the Radch can force our armor down." But the code Anaander Mianaai would have had to transmit to force down Lieutenant Awn's armor—or mine, or any other Radchaai soldier's—would have to have been delivered over communications that had been blocked at the time. Still. "Speculating about such things does no good, Divine," I said. "It didn't happen."

The head priest turned, and looked intently at me. "You didn't answer the question."

It wasn't an easy question for me to answer. I had been in pieces, and at the time only one segment had even known that such a thing was possible, that for an instant Lieutenant Awn's life had hung, uncertain, on the outcome of that moment. I wasn't entirely sure that segment wouldn't have turned its gun on Anaander Mianaai instead.

It probably wouldn't have. "Divine, I am not a person." If I had shot the Lord of the Radch nothing would have changed, I was sure, except that not only would Lieutenant Awn still be dead, I would be destroyed, Two Esk would take my place, or a new One Esk would be built with segments from *Justice of Toren*'s holds. The ship's AI might find itself in some difficulty, though more likely my action would be blamed on my being cut off. "People often think they would have made the noblest choice, but when they find themselves actually in such a situation, they discover matters aren't quite so simple."

"As I said—God forbid. I will comfort myself with the delusion that you would have shot the Mianaai bastard first."

"Divine!" I cautioned. She could say nothing in my hearing that might not eventually reach the ears of the Lord of the Radch.

"Let her hear. Tell her yourself! *She* instigated what happened last night. Whether the target was us, or the Tanmind, or Lieutenant Awn, I don't know. I have my suspicions which. I'm not a fool."

"Divine," I said. "Whoever instigated last night's events, I don't think things happened the way they wished. I think they wanted open warfare between the upper and lower cities, though I don't understand why. And I think that was prevented when Denz Ay told Lieutenant Awn about the guns."

"I think as you do," said the head priest. "And I think Jen Shinnan knew more, and that was why she died."

"I'm sorry your temple was desecrated, Divine," I said. I wasn't particularly sorry Jen Shinnan was dead, but I didn't say so.

The Divine turned away from me again. "I'm sure you have a lot to do, getting ready to leave. Lieutenant Awn needn't trouble herself calling on me. You can give her my farewells yourself." She walked away from me, not waiting for any acknowledgment.

* * *

Lieutenant Skaaiat arrived for supper, with a bottle of arrack and two Seven Issas. "Your relief won't even reach Kould Ves until midday," she said, breaking the seal on the bottle. Meanwhile the Seven Issas stood stiff and uncomfortable on the ground floor. They had arrived just before I'd restored communications. They'd seen the dead in the temple of Ikkt, had guessed without being told what had happened. And they had only been out of the holds for the last two years. They hadn't seen the annexation itself.

All of Ors, upper and lower, was similarly quiet, similarly tense. When people left their houses they avoided looking at me or speaking to me. Mostly they only went out to visit the temple, where the priests led prayers for the dead. A few Tanmind even came down from the upper city, and stood quietly at the edges of the small crowd. I kept myself in the shadows, not wanting to distract or distress any further.

"Tell me you didn't almost refuse," said Lieutenant Skaaiat, in the house on the upper floor, with Lieutenant Awn, behind screens. They sat on fungal-smelling cushions, facing each other. "I know you, Awn, I swear when I heard what Seven Issa saw when they got to the temple I was afraid I'd hear next that you were dead. Tell me you didn't."

"I didn't," said Lieutenant Awn, miserable and guilty. Her voice bitter. "You can see I didn't."

"I can't see that. Not at all." Lieutenant Skaaiat poured a hefty slug of liquor into the cup I held out, and I handed it to Lieutenant Awn. "Neither can One Esk, or it wouldn't be so silent this evening." She looked at the nearest segment. "Did the Lord of the Radch forbid you to sing?"

"No, Lieutenant." I hadn't wanted to disturb Anaander

Mianaai, when she was here, or interrupt what sleep Lieutenant Awn could get. And anyway, I hadn't much felt like it.

Lieutenant Skaaiat made a frustrated sound and turned back to Lieutenant Awn. "If you'd refused, nothing would have changed, except you'd be dead too. You did what you had to do, and the idiots...Hyr's cock, those *idiots*. They should have known better."

Lieutenant Awn stared at the cup in her hand, not moving.

"I *know* you, Awn. If you're going to do something that crazy, save it for when it'll make a difference."

"Like *Mercy of Sarrse* One Amaat One?" She was talking about events at Ime, about the soldier who had refused her order, led that mutiny five years before.

"She made a difference, at least. Listen, Awn, you and I both know something was going on. You and I both know that what happened last night doesn't make sense unless..." She stopped.

Lieutenant Awn set her cup of arrack down, hard. Liquor sloshed over the lip of the cup. "Unless what? How does it make sense?"

"Here." Lieutenant Skaaiat picked up the cup and pressed it into Lieutenant Awn's hand. "Drink this. And I'll explain. At least as much as makes sense to me.

"You know how annexations work. I mean, yes, they work by sheer, undeniable force, but after. After the executions and the transportations and once all the last bits of idiots who think they can fight back are cleaned up. Once all that's done, we fit whoever's left into Radchaai society—they form up into houses, and take clientage, and in a generation or two they're as Radchaai as anybody. And mostly that happens because we go to the top of the local hierarchy—there pretty much always is one—and offer them all sorts of benefits in exchange for behaving like citizens, offer them clientage contracts, which allows them to offer contracts to whoever is below them, and before you know it the whole local setup is tied into Radchaai society, with minimal disruption."

Lieutenant Awn made an impatient gesture. She already knew this. "What does that have to do with—"

"You fucked that up."

"I…"

"What you did *worked*. And the local Tanmind were going to have to swallow that. Fair enough. If I'd done what you did—gone straight to the Orsian priest, set up house in the lower city instead of using the police station and jail already built in the upper city, set about making alliances with lower city authorities and ignoring—"

"I didn't *ignore* anyone!" Lieutenant Awn protested.

Lieutenant Skaaiat waved her protest away. "And ignoring what anyone else would have seen as the natural local hierarchy. Your house can't afford to offer clientage to anyone here. *Yet*. Neither you nor I can make any contracts with anyone. *For now*. We had to exempt ourselves from our houses' contracts and take clientage directly from Anaander Mianaai, while we serve. But we still have those family connections, and those families can use connections we make now, even if we can't. And we can certainly use them when we retire. Getting your feet on the ground during an annexation is the one sure way to increase your house's financial and social standing.

"Which is fine until the wrong person does it. We tell ourselves that everything is the way Amaat wants it to be, that everything that is, is because of God. So if we're wealthy and respected, that's how things *should* be. The aptitudes prove that it's all just, that everyone gets what they deserve, and when the right people test into the right careers, that just goes to show how right it all is."

"I'm not the right people." Lieutenant Awn set down her empty cup, and Lieutenant Skaaiat refilled it.

"You're only one of thousands, but you're a noticeable one, to someone. And this annexation is different, it's the last one. Last chance to grab property, to make connections on the sort of scale the upper houses have always been accustomed to. They don't like to see any of those last chances go to houses like yours. And to make it worse, your subverting the local hierarchy—"

"I *used* the local hierarchy!"

"Lieutenants," I cautioned. Lieutenant Awn's outburst had been loud enough to be heard in the street, if anyone had been on the street this evening.

"If the Tanmind were running things here, that was as things must be in Amaat's mind. Right?"

"But they..." Lieutenant Awn stopped. I wasn't sure what she had been about to say. Perhaps that they had imposed their authority over Ors relatively recently. Perhaps that they were, in Ors, a numerical minority and Lieutenant Awn's goal had been to reach the largest number of people she could.

"Careful," warned Lieutenant Skaaiat, though Lieutenant Awn hadn't needed the warning. Any Radchaai soldier knew not to speak without thinking. "If you hadn't found those weapons, someone would have had an excuse not only to toss you out of Ors, but to come down hard on the Orsians and favor the upper city. Restoring the universe to its proper order. And then, of course, anyone inclined could have used the incident as an example of how soft we've gotten. If we'd stuck to so-called impartial aptitudes testing, if we'd executed more people, if we still made ancillaries..."

"I *have* ancillaries," Lieutenant Awn pointed out.

Lieutenant Skaaiat shrugged. "Everything else would have fit, they could ignore that. They'll ignore anything that doesn't get them what they want. And what they want is anything they can grab." She seemed so calm. Even almost relaxed. I was used to not seeing data from Lieutenant Skaaiat, but this disjunction between her demeanor and the seriousness of the situation—Lieutenant Awn's still-extreme distress, and, to be honest, my own discomfort at events—made her seem oddly flat and unreal to me.

"I understand Jen Shinnan's part in this," Lieutenant Awn said. "I do, I get that. But I don't understand how...how anyone else would benefit." The question she couldn't ask directly was, of course, why Anaander Mianaai would be involved, or why she would want to return to some previous, proper order, given she herself had certainly approved any changes. And why, if she wanted such a thing, she didn't merely order the things she desired. If questioned, both lieutenants could, and likely would, say they weren't speaking of the Lord of the Radch, but about some unknown person who must be involved, but I was certain that wouldn't hold up under an interrogation with drugs. Fortunately, such an event was unlikely. "And I don't see why anyone with that sort of access couldn't just order me gone and put someone they preferred in my place, if that was all they wanted."

"Maybe that wasn't *all* they wanted," answered Lieutenant Skaaiat. "But clearly, someone did at the very least want those things, and thought they would benefit from doing it this particular way. And you did as much as you could to avoid people getting killed. Anything else wouldn't have made any difference." She emptied her own cup. "You're going to stay in touch with me," she said, not a question, not a request. And then, more gently, "I'll miss you."

For a moment I thought Lieutenant Awn might cry again. "Who's replacing me?"

Lieutenant Skaaiat named an officer, and a ship.

"Human troops then." Lieutenant Awn was momentarily disquieted, and then sighed, frustrated. I imagine she was remembering that Ors was no longer her problem.

"I know," said Lieutenant Skaaiat. "I'll talk to her. You watch yourself. Now annexations are a thing of the past, ancillary troop carriers are crowded with the useless daughters of prestigious houses, who can't be assigned to anything lower." Lieutenant Awn frowned, clearly wanting to argue, thinking, maybe, of her fellow Esk lieutenants. Or of herself. Lieutenant Skaaiat saw her expression and smiled ruefully. "Well. Dariet is all right. It's the rest I'm warning you to look out for. Very high opinions of themselves and very little to justify it." Skaaiat had met some of them during the annexation, had always been entirely, correctly polite to them.

"You don't need to tell me that," said Lieutenant Awn.

Lieutenant Skaaiat poured more arrack, and for the rest of the night their conversation was the sort that needs no reporting.

At length Lieutenant Awn slept again, and by the time she woke I had hired boats to take us to the mouth of the river, near Kould Ves, and loaded them with our scant luggage, and my dead segment. In Kould Ves the mechanism that controlled its armor, and a few other bits of tech, would be removed for another use.

If you're going to do something that crazy, save it for when it'll make a difference, Lieutenant Skaaiat had said, and I had agreed. I still agree.

The problem is knowing when what you are about to do will make a difference. I'm not only speaking of the small actions that, cumulatively, over time, or in great numbers, steer the course of events in ways too chaotic or subtle to trace. The single word that directs a person's fate and ultimately the fates of those she comes in contact with is of course a common subject of entertainments and moralizing stories, but if everyone were to consider all the possible consequences of all one's possible choices, no one would move a millimeter, or even dare to breathe for fear of the ultimate results.

I mean, on a larger and more obvious scale. In the way that Anaander Mianaai herself determined the fates of whole peoples. Or the way my own actions could mean life or death for thousands. Or merely eighty-three, huddled in the temple of Ikkt, surrounded. I ask myself—as surely Lieutenant Awn asked herself—what would have been the consequences of refusing the order to fire? Straightforwardly, obviously, her own death would have been an immediate consequence. And then, immediately afterward, those eighty-three people would have died, because I would have shot them at Anaander Mianaai's direct order.

No difference, except Lieutenant Awn would be dead. The omens had been cast, and their trajectories were straightforward, calculable, direct, and clear.

But neither Lieutenant Awn nor the Lord of the Radch knew that in that moment, had one disk shifted, just slightly, the whole pattern might have landed differently. Sometimes, when omens are cast, one flies or rolls off where you didn't expect and throws the whole pattern out of shape. Had Lieutenant Awn chosen differently, that one segment, cut off, disoriented, and yes, horrified at the thought of shooting Lieutenant Awn, might have turned its gun on Mianaai instead. What then?

Ultimately, such an action would only have delayed Lieutenant Awn's death, and ensured my own—One Esk's—destruction. Which, since I didn't exist as any sort of individual, was not distressing to me.

But the death of those eighty-three people would have been delayed. Lieutenant Skaaiat would have been forced to arrest Lieutenant Awn—I am convinced she would not have shot her, though she would have been legally justified in doing so—but she would not have shot the Tanmind, because Mianaai would not have been there to give the order. And Jen Shinnan would have had time and opportunity to say whatever it was that the Lord of the Radch had, as things actually happened, prevented her from saying. What difference would that have made?

Perhaps a great deal of difference. Perhaps none at all. There are too many unknowns. Too many apparently predictable people who are, in reality, balanced on a knife-edge, or whose trajectories might be easily changed, if only I knew.

If you're going to do something that crazy, save it for when it'll make a difference. But absent near-omniscience there's no way to know when that is. You can only make your best approximate calculation. You can only make your throw and try to puzzle out the results afterward.

11

The explanation, why I needed the gun, why I wanted to kill Anaander Mianaai, took a long time. The answer was not a simple one—or, more accurately, the simple answer would only raise further questions for Strigan, so I did not attempt to use it but instead began the whole story at the beginning and let her infer the simple answer from the longer, complex one. By the time I was done the night was far advanced. Seivarden was asleep, breathing slow, and Strigan herself was clearly exhausted.

For three minutes there was no sound but Seivarden's breath accelerating as she transitioned into some state closer to wakefulness, or perhaps was troubled by a dream.

"And now I know who you are," Strigan said finally, tiredly. "Or who you think you are." There was no need for me to say anything in reply to that; by now she would believe what she wished about me, despite what I had told her. "Doesn't it bother you," Strigan continued, "didn't it ever bother you, that you're slaves?"

"Who?"

"The ships. The warships. So powerful. Armed. The officers inside are at your mercy every moment. What stops you from killing them all and declaring yourselves free? I've never been able to understand how the Radchaai can keep the ships enslaved."

"If you think about it," I said, "you'll see you already know the answer to your question."

She was silent again, inward-looking. I sat motionless. Waiting on the results of my throw.

"You were at Garsedd," she said after a while.

"Yes."

"Did you know Seivarden? Personally, I mean?"

"Yes."

"Did you . . . did you participate?"

"In the destruction of the Garseddai?" She gestured acknowledgment. "I did. Everyone who was there did."

She grimaced, with disgust I thought. "No one refused."

"I didn't say that." In fact, my own captain had refused, and died. Her replacement had qualms—she couldn't have hidden that from her ship—but said nothing and did as she was told. "It's easy to say that if you were there you would have refused, that you would rather die than participate in the slaughter, but it all looks very different when it's real, when the moment comes to choose."

Her eyes narrowed, in disagreement I thought, but I had only spoken the truth. Then her expression changed; she was thinking, perhaps, of that small collection of artifacts in her rooms on Dras Annia Station. "You speak the language?"

"Two of them." There had been more than a dozen.

"And you know their songs, of course." Her voice was slightly mocking.

"I didn't have a chance to learn as many as I would have liked."

"And if you had been free to choose, would you have refused?"

"The question is pointless. The choice was not presented to me."

"I beg to differ," she said, quietly angry at my answer. "The choice has always been presented to you."

"Garsedd was a turning point." It wasn't a direct answer to her accusation, but I couldn't think of what *would* be a direct answer, that she would understand. "The first time so many Radchaai officers came away from an annexation without the certainty that they had done the right thing. Do you still think Mianaai controls the Radchaai through brainwashing or threats of execution? Those are there, they exist, yes, but most Radchaai, like people most places I have been, do what they're supposed to because they believe it's the right thing to do. No one *likes* killing people."

Strigan made a sardonic noise. "No one?"

"Not many," I amended. "Not enough to fill the Radch's warships. But at the end, after all the blood and grief, all those benighted souls who without us would have suffered in darkness are happy citizens. They'll agree if you ask! It was a fortunate day when Anaander Mianaai brought civilization to them."

"Would their parents agree? Or their grandparents?"

I gestured, halfway between *not my problem* and *not relevant*. "You were surprised to see me deal gently with a child. It should not have surprised you. Do you think the Radchaai don't have children, or don't love their children? Do you think they don't react to children the way nearly any human does?"

"So virtuous!"

"Virtue is not a solitary, uncomplicated thing." Good necessitates evil and the two sides of that disk are not always clearly marked. "Virtues may be made to serve whatever end profits you. Still, they exist and will influence your actions. Your choices."

Strigan snorted. "You make me nostalgic for the drunken philosophical conversations of my youth. But these are not abstract things we're talking about here, this is life and death."

My chances of getting what I had come for were slipping from my grasp. "For the first time, Radch forces dealt death on an unimaginable scale without renewal afterward. Cut off irrevocably any chance of good coming from what they had done. This affected everyone there."

"Even the ships?"

"Everyone." I waited for the next question, or the sardonic *I don't feel sorry for you*, but she just sat silent, looking at me. "The first attempts at diplomatic contact with the Presger began shortly afterward. As did, I am fairly certain, the beginnings of the move to replace ancillaries with human soldiers." Only fairly certain because much of the groundwork must have been laid in private, behind the scenes.

"Why would the Presger get involved with Garsedd?" Strigan asked.

She could certainly see my reaction to her question, nearly a direct admission that she had the gun; had to know—had to have known before she spoke—what that admission would tell me. She wouldn't have asked that question if she hadn't seen the gun, examined it closely. Those guns had come from the Presger, the Garseddai had dealt with the aliens, whoever had made the first overture. So much we got from the captured representatives. But I kept my face still. "Who knows why the Presger do anything? But Anaander Mianaai asked herself the same question, *Why did the Presger interfere?* It wasn't because they wanted anything the Garseddai had, they could have reached out and taken whatever they wanted." Though I knew the Presger had made the Garseddai pay, and heavily. "And what if the Presger decided to destroy the Radch? Truly to destroy it? And the Presger had such weapons?"

"You're saying," said Strigan, disbelieving, appalled, "that the Presger set the Garseddai up in order to compel Anaander Mianaai to negotiate."

"I am speaking of Mianaai's reaction, Mianaai's motives. I don't know or understand the Presger. But I imagine if the Presger meant to compel anything, it would be unmistakable. Unsubtle. I think it was meant merely as a *suggestion.* If indeed that had anything to do with their actions."

"All of that, a *suggestion*."

"They're aliens. Who can understand them?"

"Nothing you can do," she said, after five seconds of silence, "can possibly make any difference."

"That's probably true."

"*Probably.*"

"If everyone who had..." I searched for the right words. "If everyone who objected to the destruction of the Garseddai had refused, what would have happened?"

Strigan frowned. "How many refused?"

"Four."

"Four. Out of...?"

"Out of thousands." Each Justice alone, in those days, had hundreds of officers, along with its captain, and dozens of us had been there. Add the smaller-crewed Mercies and Swords. "Loyalty, the long habit of obedience, a desire for revenge—even, yes, those four deaths kept anyone else from such a drastic choice."

"There were enough of your sort to deal with even everyone refusing."

I said nothing, waited for the change of expression that would tell me she had thought twice about what she had just said. When it came, I said, "I think it might have turned out differently."

"You're not one of thousands!" Strigan leaned forward, unexpectedly vehement. Seivarden started out of her sleep, looked at Strigan, alarmed and bleary.

"There are no others on the edge of choosing," Strigan said. "No one to follow your lead. And even if there were, you by yourself wouldn't be enough. If you even get as far as facing Mianaai—facing one of Mianaai's bodies—you'll be alone and helpless. You'll die without achieving anything!" She made a breathy, impatient sound. "Take your money." She gestured toward my pack, leaning against the bench I sat on. "Buy land, buy rooms on a station, hell, buy a station! Live the life that was denied you. Don't sacrifice yourself for nothing."

"Which *me* are you talking to?" I asked. "Which life that was denied me do you intend I live? Should I send you monthly reports, so you can be sure my choices meet with your approval?"

That silenced her, for a full twenty seconds.

"Breq," said Seivarden, as though testing the sound of the name in her mouth, "I want to leave."

"Soon," I answered. "Be patient." To my utter surprise she didn't object, but leaned back against a bench and put her arms around her knees.

Strigan looked speculatively at her for a moment, then turned to me. "I need to think." I gestured acknowledgment and she rose and went into her room and shut the door.

"What's *her* problem?" asked Seivarden, apparently innocent of irony. Voice just slightly contemptuous. I didn't answer, only looked at her, not changing my expression. The blankets had marked a line across her cheek, fading now, and her clothes, the Nilter trousers and quilted shirt under the unfastened inner coat, were wrinkled and disheveled. In the past several days of regular food, and no kef, her skin had regained a slightly healthier-looking color, but she still looked thin and tired. "Why are you bothering with her?" she asked me, undisturbed by my scrutiny. As though something had shifted and she and I were suddenly comrades. Fellows.

Surely not equals. Not ever. "Business I need to attend to." More explanation would be useless, or foolish, or both. "Are you having trouble sleeping?"

Something subtle in her expression communicated withdrawal, closure. I wasn't on her side anymore. She sat silent for ten seconds, and I thought she wouldn't speak to me anymore that night, but instead she drew a long breath and let it out. "Yeah. I...I need to move around. I'm going to go outside."

Something had definitely changed, but I didn't know quite what it was, or what had caused it.

"It's night," I said. "And very cold. Take your outer coat and gloves and don't go too far."

She gestured acquiescence, and even more astonishingly, put on her outer coat and gloves before going out the two doors without a single bitter word, or even a resentful glance.

And what did I care? She would wander off and freeze, or she would not. I arranged my own blankets and lay down to sleep, without waiting to see if Seivarden came back safe or not.

When I woke, Seivarden was asleep on her own pile of blankets. She hadn't thrown her coat on the floor, but instead hung it beside the others, on a hook near the door. I rose and went to the cupboard to find she had also replenished the food stores—more bread, and a bowl on the table holding a block of slushy, slowly melting milk, another beside it holding a chunk of bov fat.

Behind me Strigan's door clicked open. I turned. "He wants something," she said to me, quietly. Seivarden didn't stir. "Or anyway there's some angle he's playing. I wouldn't trust him if I were you."

"I don't." I dropped a hunk of bread in a bowl of water and set it aside to soften. "But I do wonder what's come over her." Strigan looked amused. "Him," I amended.

"Probably the thought of all the money you're carrying," observed Strigan. "You could buy a lot of kef with that."

"If that's the case, it's not a problem. It's all for paying you." Except my fare back up the ribbon, and a bit more for emergencies. Which, in this case, would probably mean Seivarden's fare as well.

"What happens to addicts in the Radch?"

"There aren't any." She raised one eyebrow, and then another, disbelieving. "Not on the stations," I amended. "You can't get too far down that road with the station AI watching you all the time. On a planet, that's different, it's too big for that. Even then, once you get to the point where you're not functioning, you're reeducated and usually sent away somewhere else."

"So as not to embarrass."

"For a new start. New surroundings, new assignment." And if you arrived from somewhere very far away to take some job nearly anyone could have filled, everyone knew why that was, though no one would be so gauche as to say it within your hearing. "It bothers you, that the Radchaai don't have the freedom to destroy their lives, or other citizens' lives."

"I wouldn't have put it that way."

"No, of course not."

She leaned against the doorframe, folded her arms. "For someone who wants a favor—an incredibly, unspeakably huge and dangerous favor at that—you're unexpectedly adversarial."

One-handed, I gestured. *It is as it is.*

"But then, dealing with him makes you angry." She tilted her head in Seivarden's general direction. "Understandably, I think."

The words *I'm so glad you approve* rose to my lips, but I didn't say them. I wanted, after all, an incredibly, unspeakably huge and dangerous favor. "All the money in the box," I said, instead. "Enough for you to buy land, or rooms on a station, or hell, even a station."

"A very small one." Her lips quirked in amusement.

"And you wouldn't have it anymore. It's dangerous even to have seen it, but it's worse to actually have it."

"And you," she pointed out, straightening, dropping her arms, voice now unamused, "will bring it directly to the attention of the Lord of the Radch. Who will then be able to trace it back to me."

"That will always be a danger," I agreed. I would not even pretend that once I fell into Mianaai's control she would not be able to extract any information from me she wished, no matter what I wanted to reveal or conceal. "But it has been a danger since the moment you laid eyes on it, and will continue to be for as long as you live, whether you give it to me or not."

Strigan sighed. "That's true. Unfortunately enough. And truth to tell, I want very badly to go home."

Foolish beyond belief. But it wasn't my concern, my concern was getting that gun. I said nothing. Neither did Strigan. Instead, she put on her outer coat and gloves and went out the two doors, and I sat down to eat my breakfast, trying very hard not to guess where she had gone, or whether I had any reason at all to be hopeful.

She returned fifteen minutes later with a wide, flat black box. Strigan set the box on the table. It seemed like one solid block, but she lifted off a thick layer of black, revealing more black beneath.

Strigan stood, waiting, the lid in her hands, watching me. I reached out and touched a spot on the black, with one finger, gently. Brown spread from where I touched, pooling out into the shape of a gun, now exactly the color of my skin. I lifted my finger and black flooded back. Reached out, lifted off another layer of black, beneath which it finally began to look like a box, with actual things in it, if a disturbingly light-suckingly black box, filled with ammunition.

Strigan reached out and touched the upper surface of the layer of black I still held. Gray spread from her fingers into a thick strap curled alongside where the gun lay. "I wasn't sure what that was. Do you know?"

"It's armor." Officers and human troops used externally worn armor units, instead of the sort that was installed in one's body. Like mine. But a thousand years ago everyone's had been implanted.

"It's never tripped a single alarm, never shown up in any scan I've been through." *That* was what I wanted. The ability to walk onto any Radchaai station without alerting anyone to the fact I was armed. The ability to carry a weapon into the very presence of Anaander Mianaai without anyone realizing it. Most Anaanders had no need for armor; being able to shoot through it was just an extra.

Strigan asked, "How does it do that? How does it hide itself?"

"I don't know." I replaced the layer I was holding, and then the very top.

"How many of the bastard do you think you can kill?"

I looked up, away from the box, from the gun, the unlikely goal of nearly twenty years' efforts, in front of me, real and solid. In my grasp. I wanted to say, *As many as I can reach, before they take me down*. But realistically I could only expect to meet one, a single body out of thousands. Then again, realistically I could never have expected to find this gun. "That depends," I said.

"If you're going to make a desperate, hopeless act of defiance you should make it a good one."

I gestured my agreement. "I plan to ask for an audience."

"Will you get one?"

"Probably. Any citizen can ask for one, and will almost certainly receive it. I wouldn't be going as a citizen..."

Strigan scoffed. "How are *you* going to pass as non-Radchaai?"

"I will walk onto the docks of a provincial palace with no gloves, or the wrong ones, announce my foreign origin, and speak with an accent. Nothing more will be required."

She blinked. Frowned. "Not really."

"I assure you. As a noncitizen my chances of obtaining an audience will depend on my reasons for asking." I hadn't thought that part all the way through yet. It would depend on what I found when I got there. "Some things can't be planned too far in advance."

"And what are you going to do about..." She waved an ungloved hand toward unconscious Seivarden.

I had avoided asking myself that question. Avoided, from the moment I found her, thinking more than one step ahead when it came to what I was going to do about Seivarden.

"*Watch him*," she said. "He might have reached the point where he's ready to give up the kef for good, but I don't think he has."

"Why not?"

"He hasn't asked me for help."

It was my turn to raise a skeptical eyebrow. "If he asked, would you help?"

"I'd do what I could. Though of course, he'd need to address the problems that led him to use in the first place, if it was going to work long-term. Which I don't see any sign of him doing." Privately I agreed, but I didn't say anything.

"He could have asked for help anytime," Strigan continued. "He's been wandering around for, what, at least five years? Any doctor could have helped him, if he'd wanted it. But that would mean admitting he had a problem, wouldn't it? And I don't see that happening anytime soon."

"It would be best if sh—if he went back to the Radch." Radch medics could solve all her problems. And would not trouble themselves with whether or not Seivarden had asked for their help, or wanted it in any way.

"He won't go back to the Radch unless he admits he has a problem."

I gestured, *not my concern*. "He can go where he likes."

"But you're feeding him, and no doubt you'll pay his fare up the ribbon, and to whatever system you take ship for next. He'll stay with you as long as it's to his advantage, as long as there's food and shelter. And he'll steal anything he thinks will get him another hit of kef."

Seivarden wasn't as strong as she had once been, or as clear, mentally. "Do you think he'll find that easy?"

"No," admitted Strigan, "but he'll be very determined."

"Yes."

Strigan shook her head, as though to clear it. "What am I doing? You won't listen to me."

"I'm listening."

But she clearly didn't believe me. "It's none of my concern, I know. Just..." She pointed to the black box. "Just kill as many of Mianaai as you can. And don't send him after *me*."

"You're leaving?" Of course she was, there was no need to answer such a foolish question, and she didn't bother. Instead she went back into her room, saying nothing else, and closed the door.

I opened my pack, took out the money and set it on the table, slid the black box into its place. Touched it in the pattern that would make it disappear, nothing but folded shirts, a few packets of dried food. Then I went over to where Seivarden lay, and prodded her with one booted foot. "Wake up." She started, sitting suddenly, and flung her back against the nearby bench, breathing hard. "Wake up," I said again. "We're leaving."

12

Except for those hours when communications had been cut off, I had never really lost the sense of being part of *Justice of Toren*. My kilometers of white-walled corridor, my captain, the decade commanders, each decade's lieutenants, each one's smallest gesture, each breath, was visible to me. I had never lost the knowledge of my ancillaries, twenty-bodied One Amaat, One Toren, One Etrepa, One Bo, and Two Esk, hands and feet for serving those officers, voices to speak to them. My thousands of ancillaries in frozen suspension. Never lost the view of Shis'urna itself, all blue and white, old boundaries and divisions erased by distance. From that perspective events in Ors were nothing, invisible, completely insignificant.

In the approaching shuttle I felt the distance decrease, felt more forcefully the sensation of *being* the ship. One Esk became even more what it had always been—one small part of myself. My attention was no longer commanded by things apart from the rest of the ship.

Two Esk had taken One Esk's place while One Esk was on

the planet. Two Esk prepared tea in the Esk decade room for its lieutenants—my lieutenants. It scrubbed the white-walled corridor outside Esk's baths, mended uniforms torn on leave. Two of my lieutenants sat over a game board in the decade room, placing counters around, swift and quiet, three others watching. The lieutenants of the Amaat, Toren, Etrepa, and Bo decades, the decade commanders, Hundred Captain Rubran, administrative officers, and medics, talked, slept, bathed, according to their schedules and inclinations.

Each decade held twenty lieutenants and its decade commander, but Esk was now my lowest occupied deck. Below Esk, from Var down—half of my decade decks—was cold and empty, though the holds were still full. The emptiness and silence of those spaces where officers had once lived had disturbed me at first, but I was used to it by now.

On the shuttle, in front of One Esk, Lieutenant Awn sat silent, jaw clenched. She was in some respects more physically comfortable than she had ever been in Ors—the temperature, twenty degrees C, was more suitable for her uniform jacket and trousers. And the stink of swamp water had been replaced by the more familiar and more easily tolerable smell of recycled air. But the tiny spaces—which when she had first come to *Justice of Toren* had excited pride in her assignment and anticipation of what the future might hold—now seemed to trap and confine her. She was tense and unhappy.

Esk Decade Commander Tiaund sat in her tiny office. It held only two chairs and a desk close against one wall, barely more than a shelf, and space for perhaps two more people to stand. "Lieutenant Awn has returned," I said to her, and to Hundred Captain Rubran on the command deck. The shuttle docked with a *thunk*.

Captain Rubran frowned. She had been surprised and dismayed at the news of Lieutenant Awn's sudden return. The order had come directly from Anaander Mianaai, who was not to be questioned. Along with it had come orders not to ask what had happened.

In her office on the Esk deck, Commander Tiaund sighed, closed her eyes, and said, "Tea." She sat silent till Two Esk brought her a cup and a flask, poured, and set both at the commander's elbow. "She'll see me at her earliest convenience."

One Esk's attention was mostly on Lieutenant Awn, threading her way through the lift and the narrow white corridors that would take her to the Esk decade, to her own quarters. I read relief when she found those corridors empty except for Two Esk.

"Commander Tiaund will see you at your earliest convenience," I said to Lieutenant Awn, transmitting directly to her. She acknowledged with a brief twitch of her fingers as she entered the Esk corridors.

Two Esk vacated the deck, filing down the corridor to the hold and its waiting suspension pods, and One Esk took up whatever tasks Two Esk had been doing, and also followed Lieutenant Awn. Above, on Medical, a tech medic began to lay out what she needed to replace One Esk's missing segment.

At the door of her own small quarters—the same that more than a thousand years before had belonged to Lieutenant Seivarden—Lieutenant Awn turned to say something to the segment that followed her, and then stopped. "What?" she asked after an instant. "Something's wrong, what is it?"

"Please excuse me, Lieutenant," I said. "In the next few minutes the tech medic will connect a new segment. I might be unresponsive for a short while."

"Unresponsive," she said, feeling momentarily overwhelmed

for some reason I couldn't quite understand. And then guilty, and angry. She stood before the unopened door of her quarters, took two breaths, and then turned and went back down the corridor toward the lift.

A new segment's nervous system has to be more or less functional for the hookup. They'd tried it in the past with dead bodies, and failed. The same with fully sedated bodies—the connection was never made properly. Sometimes the new segment is given a tranquilizer, but sometimes the tech medic prefers to thaw the new body out and tie it down quickly, without any sedation at all. This eliminates the chancy step of sedating just the right amount, but it always makes for an uncomfortable hookup.

This particular tech medic didn't care much about my comfort. She wasn't obliged to care, of course.

Lieutenant Awn entered the lift that would bring her to Medical just as the tech medic triggered the release on the suspension pod that held the body. The lid swung up, and for a hundredth of a second the body lay still and icy within its pool of fluid.

The tech medic rolled the body out of the pod onto a neighboring table, the fluid sliding and sheeting off it, and in the same moment it awoke, convulsive, choking and gagging. The preserving medium slides out of throat and lungs easily on its own, but the first few times the experience is a discomfiting one. Lieutenant Awn exited the lift, strode down the corridor toward Medical with One Esk Eighteen close behind her.

The tech medic went swiftly to work, and suddenly I was on the table (I was walking behind Lieutenant Awn, I was taking up the mending Two Esk had set down on its way to the holds, I was laying myself down on my small, close bunks,

I was wiping a counter in the decade room) and I could see and hear but I had no control of the new body and its terror raised the heart rates of all One Esk's segments. The new segment's mouth opened and it screamed and in the background it heard laughter. I flailed, the binding came loose and I rolled off the table, fell a meter and a half to the floor with a painful *thud. Don't don't don't*, I thought at the body, but it wasn't listening. It was sick, it was terrified, it was dying. It pushed itself up and crawled, dizzy, where it didn't care so long as it got away.

Then hands under my arms (elsewhere One Esk was motionless) urging me up, and Lieutenant Awn. "Help," I croaked, not in Radchaai. Damn medic pulled out a body without a decent voice. "Help me."

"It's all right." Lieutenant Awn shifted her grip, put her arms around the new segment, pulled me in closer. It was shivering, still cold from suspension, and from terror. "It's all right. It'll be all right." The segment gasped and sobbed for what seemed forever and I thought maybe it was going to throw up until . . . the connection clicked home and I had control of it. I stopped the sobbing.

"There," said Lieutenant Awn. Horrified. Sick to her stomach. "Much better." I saw that she was newly angry, or perhaps this was another edge of the distress I'd seen since the temple. "Don't injure my unit," Lieutenant Awn said curtly, and I realized that though she was still looking at me, she was talking to the tech medic.

"I didn't, Lieutenant," answered the tech medic, with a trace of scorn in her voice. They'd had this conversation at greater and more acrimonious length, during the annexation. The medic had said, *It's not like it's human. It's been in the hold a thousand years, it's nothing but a part of the ship.*

Lieutenant Awn had complained to Commander Tiaund, who hadn't understood Lieutenant Awn's anger, and said so, but thereafter I hadn't dealt with that particular medic. "If you're so squeamish," the medic continued, "maybe you're in the wrong place."

Lieutenant Awn turned, angry, and left the room without saying anything further. I turned and walked back to the table with some trepidation. The segment was already resisting, and I knew that this tech medic wouldn't care if it hurt when she put in my armor, and the rest of my implants.

Things were always a bit clumsy while I got used to a new segment—it would occasionally drop things, or fire off disorienting impulses, random jolts of fear or nausea. Things always seemed off-kilter for a bit. But after a week or two it would usually settle down. Most of the time, anyway. Sometimes a segment simply would not function properly, and then it would have to be removed and replaced. They screen the bodies, of course, but it's not perfect.

The voice wasn't the sort I preferred, and it didn't know any interesting songs. Not ones I didn't already know, anyway. I still can't shake the slight, and definitely irrational, suspicion that the tech medic chose that particular body just to annoy me.

After a quick bath, in which I assisted, and a change into a clean uniform, Lieutenant Awn presented herself to Commander Tiaund.

"Awn." The decade commander waved Lieutenant Awn to the opposite chair. "I'm glad to have you back, of course."

"Thank you, sir," said Lieutenant Awn, sitting.

"I didn't expect to see you so soon. I was sure you'd be downside for a while longer." Lieutenant Awn didn't answer.

Commander Tiaund waited for five seconds in silence, and then said, "I would ask what happened, but I'm ordered not to."

Lieutenant Awn opened her mouth, took a breath to speak, stopped. Surprised. I had said nothing to her about the orders not to ask what had happened. Corresponding orders to Lieutenant Awn not to tell anyone had not come. A test, I suspected, which I was quite confident Lieutenant Awn would pass.

"Bad?" asked Commander Tiaund. Wanting very much to know more, pushing her luck asking even that much.

"Yes, sir." Lieutenant Awn looked down at her gloved hands, resting in her lap. "Very."

"Your fault?"

"Everything on my watch is my responsibility, isn't it, sir?"

"Yes," Commander Tiaund acknowledged. "But I'm having trouble imagining you doing anything... improper." The word was weighted in Radchaai, part of a triad of justice, propriety, and benefit. Using it, Commander Tiaund implied more than just that she expected Lieutenant Awn to follow regulations or etiquette. Implied she suspected some injustice was behind events. Though she could certainly not say so plainly—she possessed none of the facts of the matter and surely did not wish to give anyone the impression she did. And if Lieutenant Awn were to be punished for some breach, she wouldn't want to have publicly taken Lieutenant Awn's part no matter what her private opinion.

Commander Tiaund sighed, perhaps out of frustrated curiosity. "Well," she continued, with feigned cheerfulness. "Now you've got plenty of time to catch up on gym time. And you're way behind on renewing your marksmanship certification."

Lieutenant Awn forced a humorless smile. There had been no gym in Ors, nor anyplace remotely resembling a firing range. "Yes, sir."

"And Lieutenant, please don't go up to Medical unless you really need to."

I could see Lieutenant Awn wanted to protest, to complain. But that, too, would have been a repeat of an earlier conversation. "Yes, sir."

"Dismissed."

By the time Lieutenant Awn finally entered her quarters, it was nearly time for supper—a formal meal, eaten in the decade room in the company of the other Esk lieutenants. Lieutenant Awn pled exhaustion—no lie, as it happened: she had barely slept six hours since she'd left Ors nearly three days before.

She sat on her bunk, slumped and staring, until I entered, eased off her boots, and took her coat. "All right," she said then, closed her eyes and swiveled her legs up onto the bunk. "I get the hint." She was asleep five seconds after she laid her head down.

The next morning eighteen of my twenty Esk lieutenants stood in the decade room, drinking tea and waiting for breakfast. By custom they couldn't sit without the seniormost lieutenant.

The Esk decade room's walls were white, with a blue-and-yellow border painted just under the ceiling. On one wall, opposite a long counter, were secured various trophies of past annexations—scraps of two flags, red and black and green; a pink clay roof tile with a raised design of leaves molded into it; an ancient sidearm (unloaded) and its elegantly styled holster; a jeweled Ghaonish mask. An entire window from a Valskaayan temple, colored glass arranged to form a picture of a woman holding a broom in one hand, three small animals at her feet. I remembered taking it out of the wall myself and carrying it back here. Every decade room on the ship had a window from that same building. The temple's vestments and equipment had been thrown into the street, or found their way to other decade rooms on other ships. It was normal practice to absorb any religion the Radch ran across, to fit its gods into an already blindingly complex genealogy, or to say merely that the supreme, creator deity was Amaat under another name and let the rest sort themselves out. Some quirk of Valskaayan religion made this difficult for them, and the result had been destructive. Among the recent changes in Radch policy, Anaander Mianaai had legalized the practice of Valskaay's insistently separate religion, and the governor of Valskaay had given the building back. There had been talk of returning the windows, since we had still at that time been in orbit around Valskaay itself, but ultimately they were replaced with copies. Not long after, the decades below Esk were emptied and closed, but the windows still hung on the walls of the empty, dark decade rooms.

Lieutenant Issaaia entered, walked straight to the icon of Toren in its corner niche, and lit the incense waiting in the red bowl at the icon's feet. Six officers frowned, and two made a very quiet, surprised murmur. Only Lieutenant Dariet spoke. "Is Awn not coming to breakfast?"

Lieutenant Issaaia turned toward Lieutenant Dariet, showed an expression of surprise that did not, so far as I could tell, mirror her actual feelings, and said, "Amaat's grace! I completely forgot Awn was back."

At the back of the group, safely shielded from Lieutenant

Issaaia's view, one very junior lieutenant cast a look at another very junior lieutenant.

"It's been so very quiet," Lieutenant Issaaia continued. "It's difficult to believe she *is* back."

"Silence and cold ashes," quoted the junior lieutenant who had received the other's meaningful glance, more daring than her companion. The poem quoted was an elegy for someone whose funeral offerings had been deliberately neglected. I saw Lieutenant Issaaia react with an instant of ambivalence—the next line spoke of food offerings not made for the dead, and the junior lieutenant conceivably might have been criticizing Lieutenant Awn for not coming to supper the night before, or breakfast on time this morning.

"It really is One Esk," said another lieutenant, concealing her smirk at the very junior lieutenant's cleverness, looking closely at the segments that were at the moment laying out plates of fish and fruit on the counter. "Maybe Awn broke it of its bad habits. I hope so."

"Why so quiet, One?" asked Lieutenant Dariet.

"Oh, don't get it started," groaned another lieutenant. "It's too early for all that noise."

"If it was Awn, good for her," said Lieutenant Issaaia. "A little late though."

"Like now," said a lieutenant at Lieutenant Issaaia's elbow. "Give me food while yet I live." Another quote, another reference to funeral offerings and a rebuttal in case the junior lieutenant had intended insult in the wrong direction. "Is she coming or not? If she isn't coming she should say so."

At that moment Lieutenant Awn was in the bath, and I was attending her. I could have told the lieutenants that Lieutenant Awn would be there soon, but I said nothing, only noted the level and temperature of the tea in the black glass bowls various lieutenants held, and continued to lay out breakfast plates.

Near my own weapons storage, I cleaned my twenty guns, so I could stow them, along with their ammunition. In each of my lieutenants' quarters I stripped the linen from their beds. The officers of Amaat, Toren, Etrepa, and Bo were all well into breakfast, chattering, lively. The captain ate with the decade commanders, a quieter, more sober conversation. One of my shuttles approached me, four Bo lieutenants returning from leave, strapped into their seats, unconscious. They would be unhappy when they woke.

"Ship," said Lieutenant Dariet, "will Lieutenant Awn be joining us for breakfast?"

"Yes, Lieutenant," I said, with One Esk Six's voice. In the bath I poured water over Lieutenant Awn, who stood, eyes closed, on the grating over the drain. Her breathing was even, but her heart rate was slightly elevated, and she showed other signs of stress. I was fairly sure her tardiness was deliberate, designed to give her the bath to herself. Not because she couldn't handle Lieutenant Issaaia—she certainly could. But because she was still distressed from the past days' events.

"When?" asked Lieutenant Issaaia, frowning just slightly.

"About five minutes, Lieutenant."

A chorus of groans went up. "Now, Lieutenants," Lieutenant Issaaia admonished. "She *is* our senior. And we should all have patience with her right now. Such a sudden return, when we all thought the Divine would *never* agree to her leaving Ors."

"Found out she wasn't such a good choice, eh?" sneered the lieutenant at Lieutenant Issaaia's elbow. She was close to Lieutenant Issaaia in more than one sense. None of them knew what had happened, and couldn't ask. And I, of course, had said nothing.

"Not likely," said Lieutenant Dariet, her voice a shade louder than usual. She was angry. "Not after five years." I took the tea flask, turned from the counter, went over to where Lieutenant Dariet stood, and poured eleven milliliters of tea into the nearly full bowl she held.

"You like Lieutenant Awn, of course," said Lieutenant Issaaia. "We all do. But she doesn't have *breeding*. She wasn't born for this. She works so very hard at what comes naturally to us. I would hardly be surprised if five years was all she could take without cracking." She looked at the empty bowl in her gloved hand. "I need more tea."

"You think you'd have done a better job, in Awn's place," observed Lieutenant Dariet.

"I don't trouble myself with hypotheticals," answered Lieutenant Issaaia. "The facts are what they are. There's a reason Awn was senior Esk lieutenant long before any of us got here. Obviously Awn has some ability or she'd never have done as well as she has, but she's reached her limit." A quiet murmur of agreement. "Her parents are *cooks*," Lieutenant Issaaia continued. "I'm sure they're excellent at what they do. I'm sure she would manage a kitchen admirably."

Three lieutenants snickered. Lieutenant Dariet said, her voice tight and edged, "Really?" Finally dressed, uniform as perfect as I could make it, Lieutenant Awn stepped out of the dressing room, into the corridor, five steps away from the decade room.

Lieutenant Issaaia noticed Lieutenant Dariet's mood with a familiar ambivalence. Lieutenant Issaaia was senior, but Lieutenant Dariet's house was older, wealthier than Lieutenant Issaaia's, and Lieutenant Dariet's branch of that house were direct clients to a prominent branch of Mianaai itself. Theoretically that didn't matter here. Theoretically.

All the data I had received from Lieutenant Issaaia that morning had had an underlying taste of resentment, which grew momentarily stronger. "Managing a kitchen is a perfectly respectable job," said Lieutenant Issaaia. "But I can only imagine how difficult it must be, to be bred to be a servant and instead of taking an assignment that truly suits, to be thrust into a position of such authority. Not everyone is cut out to be an officer." The door opened, and Lieutenant Awn stepped in just as the last sentence left Lieutenant Issaaia's mouth.

Silence engulfed the decade room. Lieutenant Issaaia looked calm and unconcerned, but felt abashed. She had clearly not intended—would never have dared—to say such things openly to Lieutenant Awn.

Only Lieutenant Dariet spoke. "Good morning, Lieutenant."

Lieutenant Awn didn't answer, didn't even look at her, but went to the corner of the room where the decade shrine sat, with its small figure of Toren and bowl of burning incense. Lieutenant Awn made her obeisance to the figure and then looked at the bowl with a slight frown. As before, her muscles were tense, her heart rate elevated, and I knew she guessed at the content or at least the drift of the conversation before she had entered, knew who it was who wasn't cut out to be an officer.

She turned. "Good morning, Lieutenants. I apologize for having kept you waiting." And launched without any other preamble into the morning prayer. "The flower of justice is peace..." The others joined, and when they were finished Lieutenant Awn went to her place at the head of the table, sat.

Before the others had time to settle themselves, I had tea and breakfast in front of her.

I served the others, and Lieutenant Awn took a sip of her tea and began to eat.

Lieutenant Dariet picked up her utensil. "It's good to have you back." Her voice was just slightly edged, only barely managing to conceal her anger.

"Thank you," said Lieutenant Awn, and took another bite of fish.

"I still need tea," said Lieutenant Issaaia. The rest of the table was tense and hushed, watching. "The quiet is nice, but perhaps there's been a decline in efficiency."

Lieutenant Awn chewed, swallowed, took another drink of tea. "Pardon?"

"You've managed to silence One Esk," explained Lieutenant Issaaia, "but..." She raised her empty bowl.

At that moment I was behind her with the flask, and poured, filling the bowl.

Lieutenant Awn raised one gloved hand, gesturing toward the mootness of Lieutenant Issaaia's point. "I haven't silenced One Esk." She looked at the segment with the flask and frowned. "Not intentionally, anyway. Go ahead and sing if you want, One Esk." A dozen lieutenants groaned. Lieutenant Issaaia smiled insincerely.

Lieutenant Dariet stopped, a bite of fish halfway to her mouth. "I like the singing. It's nice. And it's a distinction."

"It's embarrassing is what it is," said the lieutenant close to Lieutenant Issaaia.

"I don't find it embarrassing," said Lieutenant Awn, a bit stiffly.

"Of course not," said Lieutenant Issaaia, malice concealed in the ambiguity of her words. "Why so quiet, then, One?"

"I've been busy, Lieutenant," I answered. "And I haven't wanted to disturb Lieutenant Awn."

"Your singing doesn't disturb me, One," said Lieutenant Awn. "I'm sorry you thought it did. Please, sing if you want."

Lieutenant Issaaia raised an eyebrow. "An apology? And a *please*? That's a bit much."

"Courtesy," said Lieutenant Dariet, her voice uncharacteristically prim, "is always proper, and always beneficial."

Lieutenant Issaaia smirked. "Thank you, Mother."

Lieutenant Awn said nothing.

Four and a half hours after breakfast, the shuttle bearing those four Second Bo lieutenants home from their leave docked.

They'd been drinking for three days, and had continued right up to the moment they left Shis'urna Station. The first of them through the lock staggered slightly, and then closed her eyes. "Medic," she breathed.

"They expect you," I said through the segment of One Bo I'd placed there. "Do you need help onto the lift?"

The lieutenant made a feeble attempt to wave my offer away, and moved off slowly down the corridor, one shoulder against the wall for support.

I boarded the shuttle, kicking off past the boundary of my artificially generated gravity—the shuttle was too small to have its own. Two of the officers, still drunk themselves, were trying to wake the fourth, passed out cold in her seat. The pilot—the most junior of the Bo officers—sat stiff and apprehensive. I thought at first her discomfort was due to the reek of spilled arrack and vomit—thankfully the former had apparently been spilled onto the lieutenants themselves, on Shis'urna Station, and nearly all of the latter had gone into the appropriate receptacles—but then I looked (One Bo looked) toward the stern and saw three Anaander Mianaais sitting silent and impassive in the rear seats. Not *there*, to me. She would have boarded at Shis'urna Station, quietly. Told the pilot to say nothing to me. The others had, I suspected, been too intoxicated to notice her. I thought of her asking me, on the planet, when she had last visited me. Of my inexplicable and reflexive lie. The real last time had been a good deal like this.

"My lord," I said when all the Bo lieutenants were out of earshot. "I'll notify the hundred captain."

"No," said one Anaander. "Your Var deck is empty."

"Yes, my lord," I acknowledged.

"I'll stay there while I'm on board." Nothing further, no why or how long. Or when I could tell the captain what I was doing. I was obliged to obey Anaander Mianaai, even over my own captain, but I rarely had an order from one without the knowledge of the other. It was uncomfortable.

I sent segments of One Esk to retrieve One Var from the hold, started one section of Var deck warming. The three Anaander Mianaais declined my offer of assistance with their luggage, carried their things down to Var.

This had happened before, at Valskaay. My lower decks had been mostly empty, because many of my troops had been out of the hold and working. She had stayed on the Esk deck that time. What had she wanted then, what had she done?

To my dismay I found my thoughts slipping around the answer, which remained vague, invisible. That wasn't right. It wasn't right at all.

Between the Esk and Var decks was direct access to my brain. What had she done, at Valskaay, that I couldn't remember, and what was she preparing to do now?

13

Further south the snow and ice became impermanent, though it was still cold by non-Nilt standards. Nilters regard the equatorial region as a sort of tropical paradise, where grain can actually grow, where the temperature can easily exceed eight or nine degrees C. Most of Nilt's large cities are on or near the equatorial ring.

The same is true of the planet's one claim to any sort of fame—the glass bridges.

These are approximately five-meter-wide ribbons of black hanging in gentle catenaries across trenches nearly as wide as they are deep—dimensions measured in kilometers. No cables, no piers, no trusses. Just the arc of black attached to each cliff face. Fantastic arrangements of colored glass coils and rods hang from the bottoms of the bridges, sometimes projecting sideways.

The bridges themselves are, according to all observations, also made of glass, though glass could never possibly withstand the sort of stress these bridges do—even their own weight should be too much for them, suspended as they are with nothing for support. There are no rails or handholds, just the drop, and at the bottom, kilometers down, a cluster of thick-walled tubes, each one just a meter and a half wide, empty and smooth-walled. These are made of the same material as the bridges. No one knows what the bridges and the tubes beneath them were for, or who built them. They were here when humans first colonized Nilt.

Theories abound, each one less likely than the one before. Inter-dimensional beings feature prominently in many of them—these either created or shaped humanity for its own purposes, or left a message for humans to decipher for obscure reasons of their own. Or they were evil, bent on destruction of all life. The bridges were, somehow, part of their plan.

Another whole subfield claims the bridges were built by humans—some ancient, long-lost, fantastically advanced civilization that either died out (slowly, pathetically; or spectacularly as the result of some catastrophic mistake) or moved on to a higher level of existence. Advocates of this sort of theory often make the additional claim that Nilt is, in reality, the birthplace of humans. Nearly everywhere I've been, popular wisdom has it that the location of humanity's original planet is unknown, mysterious. In fact it isn't, as anyone who troubles to read on the subject will discover, but it *is* very, very, *very* far away from nearly anywhere, and not a tremendously interesting place. Or at the very least, not nearly as interesting as the enchanting idea that your people are not newcomers to their homes but in fact only recolonized the place they had belonged from the beginning of time. One meets this claim anywhere one finds a remotely human-habitable planet.

The bridge outside Therrod wasn't much of a tourist attraction. Most of the jewel-bright arabesques of glass had shattered over thousands of years, leaving it nearly plain. And Therrod is still too far north for non-Nilters to endure comfortably. Offworld visitors generally confine themselves to the better-preserved bridges on the equator, buy a bov-hair blanket guaranteed hand-spun and handwoven by masters of the craft in the unbearably cold reaches of the world (though these are almost certainly turned out on machines, by the dozen, a few kilometers from the gift shop), choke down a few fetid swallows of fermented milk, and return home to regale their friends and associates with tales of their adventure.

All this I learned within a few minutes of knowing I would need to visit Nilt to achieve my aim.

Therrod sat on a broad river, chunks of green-and-white ice bobbing and crashing in its current, the first boats of the season already moored at the docks. On the opposite side of the city, the dark slash of the bridge's huge trough made a definitive stop to the straggling edge of houses. The southern edge of the city was flier-parks, then a wide complex of blue-and-yellow-painted buildings that was, by the look of it, a medical facility, one that must have been the largest of its kind in the area. It was surrounded by squares of lodgings and food shops, and swaths of houses, bright pink, orange, yellow, red, in stripes and zigzags and crosshatches.

We had flown half the day. I might have flown all night, I was capable of it, though it would have been unpleasant. But I saw no need for haste. I set down in the first empty space I found, told Seivarden curtly to get out, and did so myself. I shouldered my pack, paid the parking fee, disabled the flier as I had at Strigan's, and set off toward the city, not looking to see if Seivarden followed.

I had set down near the medical facility. The lodgings

surrounding it were some of them luxurious, but many were smaller and less comfortable than the one I'd rented in the village where I'd found Seivarden, though a bit more expensive. Bright-coated southerners came and went, speaking a language I didn't understand. Others spoke the one I knew, and fortunately this was the same language the signs used.

I chose lodging—roomier, at least, than the suspension-pod-size holes that were the cheapest available—and took Seivarden off to the first clean-looking and moderately priced food shop I could find.

When we entered, Seivarden eyed the shelves of bottles on the far wall. "They have arrack."

"It'll be incredibly expensive," I said, "and probably not very good. They don't make it here. Have a beer instead."

She had been showing some signs of stress, and wincing slightly at the profusion of bright colors, so I expected some sort of irritable outburst, but instead she merely gestured acquiescence. Then she wrinkled her nose, slight disgust. "What do they make beer out of here?"

"Grain. It grows nearer the equator. It's not as cold there." We found seats on the benches that lined three rows of long tables, and a waiter brought us beer, and bowls of something she told us was the house specialty, *Extra beautiful eating, yes*, she said, in a badly mangled approximation of Radchaai, and it was in fact quite good, and turned out to have actual vegetables in it, a good proportion of thinly sliced cabbage among whatever the rest of it was. The smaller lumps appeared to be meat—probably bov. Seivarden cut one of the larger lumps in two with her spoon, revealing plain white. "Probably cheese," I said.

She grimaced. "Why can't these people eat *real* food? Don't they know better?"

"Cheese is real food. So is cabbage."

"But this sauce..."

"Tastes good." I took another spoonful.

"This whole place smells funny," she complained.

"Just eat." She looked dubiously at her bowl, scooped a spoonful, sniffed it. "It can't possibly smell worse than that fermented milk drink," I said.

She actually half-smiled. "No."

I took another spoonful, pondering the implications of this better behavior. I wasn't sure what it meant, about her state of mind, about her intentions, about who or what she thought I was. Maybe Strigan had been right, and Seivarden had decided the most profitable course, for now, was to not alienate the person who was feeding her, and that would change as soon as her options changed.

A high voice called out from another table. "Hello!"

I turned—the girl with the Tiktik set waved to me from where she sat with her mother. For an instant I was surprised, but we were near the medical center, where I knew they had brought their injured relative, and they had come from the same direction we had, and so they had likely parked on the same side of town. I smiled and nodded, and she got up and came to where we were sitting. "Your friend is better!" she said, brightly. "That's good. What are you eating?"

"I don't know," I admitted. "The waiter said it was the house specialty."

"Oh, that's very good, I had it yesterday. When did you get here? It's so hot it's like summer already, I can't imagine what it's like further north." Clearly she'd had time to recover her more usual spirits since the accident that had brought her to Strigan's house. Seivarden, spoon in hand, watched her, bemused.

"We've been here an hour," I said. "We're only stopping for the night, on our way to the ribbon."

"We're here until Uncle's legs are better. Which will probably be another week." She frowned, counting days. "A little longer. We're sleeping in our flier, which is terribly uncomfortable, but Mama says the price for lodging here is outright theft." She sat down on the end of the bench, next to me. "I've never been in space, what's it like?"

"It's very cold—even *you* would find it cold." She thought that was funny, gave a little laugh. "And of course there's no air and hardly any gravity so everything just floats."

She frowned at me, mock rebuke. "You know what I mean."

I glanced over to where her mother sat, stolid, eating. Unconcerned. "It's really not very exciting."

The girl made a gesture of indifference. "Oh! You like music. There's a singer at a place down the street tonight." She used the word I had used mistakenly, not the one she had corrected me with, in Strigan's house. "We didn't go to hear her last night because they charge. And besides she's my cousin. Or she's in the next lineage over from mine, and she's my mother's cousin's daughter's aunt, that's close enough anyway. I heard her at the last ingather, she's very good."

"I'll be sure to go. Where is it?"

She gave me the name of the place, and then said she had to finish her supper. I watched her go back to her mother, who only looked up, briefly, and gave a curt nod, which I returned.

The place the girl had named was only a few doors down, a long, low-ceilinged building, its back wall all shutters, open just now on a walled yard, where Nilters sat uncoated in the one-degree air, drinking beer, listening silently to a woman playing a bowed, stringed instrument I'd never seen before.

I quietly ordered beer for myself and Seivarden, and we took seats on the inner side of the shutters—slightly warmer than the yard for the lack of a breeze, and with a wall to put our backs against. A few people turned to look at us, stared a moment, then turned away more or less politely.

Seivarden leaned three centimeters in my direction and whispered, "Why are we here?"

"To hear the music."

She raised an eyebrow. "This is *music*?"

I turned to look at her directly. She flinched, just slightly. "Sorry. It's just..." She gestured helplessly. Radchaai do have stringed instruments, quite a variety of them, in fact, accrued through several annexations, but playing them in public is considered a slightly risqué act, because one has to play either bare-handed, or in gloves so thin as to be nearly pointless. And this music—the long, slow, uneven phrases that made its rhythms difficult for the Radchaai ear to hear, the harsh, edged tone of the instrument—was not what Seivarden had been brought up to appreciate. "It's so..."

A woman at a nearby table turned and made a reproving, shushing noise. I gestured conciliation, and turned a cautioning look on Seivarden. For a moment her anger showed in her face and I was sure I would have to take her outside, but she took a breath, and looked at her beer, and drank, and afterward looked steadily ahead in silence.

The piece ended, and the audience rapped fists gently on their tables. The string player somehow looked both impassive and gratified, and launched into another, this one noticeably faster and loud enough for Seivarden to safely whisper to me again. "How long are we going to be here?"

"A while," I said.

"I'm tired. I want to go back to the room."

"Do you know where it is?"

She gestured assent. The woman at the other table eyed us disapprovingly. "Go," I whispered, as quietly as I could and still, I hoped, be heard by Seivarden.

Seivarden left. Not my concern anymore, I told myself, whether she found her way back to our lodgings (and I congratulated myself on having had the foresight to lock my pack in the facility's safe for the night—even without Strigan's warning I didn't trust Seivarden with my belongings or my money) or wandered aimlessly through the city, or walked into the river and drowned—whatever she did, it was no concern of mine and nothing I needed to worry about. I had, instead, a jar of sufficiently decent beer and an evening of music, with the promise of a good singer, and songs I'd never heard before. I was nearer to my goal than I'd ever dared hope to be, and I could, for just this one night, relax.

The singer was excellent, though I didn't understand any of the words she sang. She came on late, and by then the place was crowded and noisy, though the audience occasionally fell silent over their beer, listening to the music, and the knocking between pieces grew loud and boisterous. I ordered enough beer to justify my continued presence, but did not drink most of it. I'm not human, but my body is, and too much would have dulled my reactions unacceptably.

I stayed quite late, and then walked back to our lodgings along the darkened street, here and there a pair or threesome walking, conversing, ignoring me.

In the tiny room I found Seivarden asleep—motionless, breathing calm, face and limbs slack. Something indefinably still about her suggested that this was the first I'd seen her in real, restful sleep. For the briefest instant I found myself wondering if she'd taken kef, but I knew she had no money, didn't know anyone here, and didn't speak any of the languages I had heard so far.

I lay down beside her and slept.

I woke six hours later, and incredibly, Seivarden still lay beside me, still asleep. I didn't think she had waked while I slept.

She might as well get as much rest as she could. I was, after all, in no hurry. I rose and went out.

Further toward the medical center the street became noisy and crowded. I bought a bowl of hot, milky porridge from a vendor along the side of the walkway, and continued along where the road curved around the hospital and off toward the center of the town. Buses stopped, let passengers off, picked others up, continued on.

In the stream of people, I saw someone I recognized. The girl from Strigan's, and her mother. They saw me. The girl's eyes widened, and she frowned slightly. Her mother's expression didn't change, but they both swerved to approach me. They had, it seemed, been watching for me.

"Breq," said the girl, when they had stopped in front of me. Subdued. Uncharacteristically, it seemed.

"Is your uncle all right?" I asked.

"Yes, Uncle is fine." But clearly something troubled her.

"Your friend," said her mother, impassive as always. And stopped.

"Yes?"

"Our flier is parked near yours," the girl said, clearly dreading the communication of bad news. "We saw it when we got back from supper last night."

"Tell me." I didn't enjoy suspense.

Her mother actually frowned. "It's not there now."

I said nothing, waiting for the rest.

"You must have disabled it," she continued. "Your friend took money, and the people who paid him towed the flier away."

The lot staff must not have questioned it, they had seen Seivarden with me.

"She doesn't speak any languages," I protested.

"They made lots of motions!" explained the girl, gesturing widely. "Lots of pointing and speaking very slow."

I had badly underestimated Seivarden. Of course—she had survived, going from place to place with no language but Radchaai, and likely no money, but still had managed to nearly overdose on kef. More than once, likely. She could manage herself, even if she managed badly. She was entirely capable of getting what she wanted without help. And she had wanted kef, and she had obtained it. At my expense, but that was of no importance to her.

"We knew it couldn't be right," said the girl, "because you said you were only stopping the night on the way to space, but no one would have listened to us, we're just bov herders." And no doubt the sort of person who would buy a flier with no documentation, no proof of ownership—a flier, moreover, that had obviously been deliberately disabled to prevent its being moved by anyone but the owner—it might very well be a good idea to avoid confronting such a person.

"I would not presume to say," said the girl's mother, oblique condemnation, "what sort of friend your friend is."

Not my friend. Never my friend, now or at any other time. "Thank you for telling me."

I walked to the lot, and the flier was indeed gone. When I returned to the room, I found Seivarden still sleeping, or at any rate still unconscious. I wondered just how much kef the flier had bought her. I only wondered long enough to retrieve my pack from the lodging's safe, pay for the night—after this Seivarden would have to fend for herself, which apparently posed very little problem for her—and went looking for transport out of town.

There was a bus, but the first had left fifteen minutes before I asked after it, and the next would not leave for three hours. A train ran alongside the river, northward once a day, and like the bus it had already left.

I didn't want to wait. I wanted to be gone from here. More specifically, I didn't want to chance seeing Seivarden again, even briefly. The temperature here was mostly above freezing and I was entirely capable of walking long distances. The next town worth the name was, according to maps I'd seen, only a day away, if I cut across the glass bridge and then straight across the countryside instead of following the road, which curved to avoid the river and the bridge's wide chasm.

The bridge was several kilometers out of town. The walk would do me good; I had not had enough exercise lately. The bridge itself might be mildly interesting. I set off toward it.

When I had walked a little over half a kilometer, past the lodgings and food shops that surrounded the medical center, into what looked like a residential neighborhood—smaller buildings, groceries, clothes shops, complexes of low, square houses joined by covered passageways—Seivarden came up behind me. "Breq!" she gasped, out of breath. "Where are you going?"

I didn't answer, only walked faster. "Breq, damn it!"

I stopped, but did not turn around. Considered speaking. Nothing I thought of saying was remotely temperate, nor would anything I said do any sort of good. Seivarden caught up with me.

"Why didn't you wake me up?" she asked. Answers occurred to me. I refrained from speaking any of them aloud, and instead began walking again.

I didn't look back. I didn't care if she followed me or not, hoped, in fact, she wouldn't. I could certainly have no continued sense of responsibility, no fears that without me she would be helpless. She could take care of herself.

"Breq, damn it!" Seivarden called again. And then swore, and I heard her footsteps behind me, and her labored breath again as she caught up. This time I didn't stop, but quickened my pace slightly.

After another five kilometers, during which she had intermittently fallen behind and then raced, gasping, to catch up, she said, "Aatr's tits, you hold a grudge, don't you."

Still I said nothing, and didn't stop.

Another hour passed, the town well behind us, and the bridge came in sight, flat black arcing across the drop, spikes and curls of glass below, brilliant red, intense yellow, ultramarine, and jagged stubs of others. The chasm walls were striated, black, green-gray, and blue, frosted here and there with ice. Below, the bottom of the chasm was lost in cloud. A sign in five languages proclaimed it to be a protected monument, access permitted only to a certain class of license holders—what license, to what purpose, was mysterious to me, as I did not recognize all the words on the sign. A low barrier blocked the entrance, nothing I could not easily step over, and there was no one here but me and Seivarden. The bridge itself was five meters wide, like all the others, and while the wind blew strong, it wasn't strong enough to endanger me. I strode forward and stepped over the barrier and out onto the bridge.

Had heights troubled me, I might have found it dizzying.

Fortunately they did not, and my only discomfort was the feeling of open spaces behind and under me that I could not see unless I turned my attention away from other places. My boots thunked on the black glass, and the whole structure swayed slightly, and shuddered in the wind.

A new pattern of vibrations told me Seivarden had followed me.

What happened next was largely my own fault.

We were halfway across when Seivarden spoke. "All right, all right. I get it. You're angry."

I stopped, but did not turn. "How much did it get you?" I asked, finally, only one of the things I had considered saying.

"What?" Though I hadn't turned, I could see the motion as she leaned over, hands on her knees, could hear her still breathing hard, straining to be heard against the wind.

"How much kef?"

"I only wanted a little," she said, not quite answering my question. "Enough to take the edge off. I *need* it. And it's not like you paid for that flier to begin with." For an instant I thought she had remembered how I had acquired the flier, unlikely as that seemed. But she continued, "You've got enough in that pack to buy ten fliers, and none of it's yours, it belongs to the Lord of the Radch, doesn't it? Making me walk like this is just you being pissy."

I stood, still facing forward, my coat flattened against me in the wind. Stood trying to understand what her words meant, about who or what she thought I was. Why she thought I had troubled myself about her.

"I know what you are," she said, as I stood silent. "No doubt you wish you could leave me behind, but you can't, can you? You've got orders to bring me back."

"What am I?" I asked, still without turning. Loud, against the wind.

"*Nobody*, that's who." Seivarden's voice was scornful. She was standing upright now, just behind my left shoulder. "You tested into military, in the aptitudes, and like a million other nobodies these days, you think that makes you *somebody*. And you practiced the accent and how to hold your utensils, and knelt your way to Special Missions and now *I'm* your special mission, you've got to bring me home in one piece even though you'd rather not, wouldn't you? You've got a problem with me, at a guess your problem is that try all you like, whoever you kneel to, you'll never be what I was born to be, and people like you *hate* that."

I turned toward her. I'm certain my face was without expression, but when my eyes met hers she flinched—no edge taken off, none at all—and took three quick, reflexive steps backward.

Over the edge of the bridge.

I stepped to the edge, looked down. Seivarden hung six meters below, hands clenched around a complicated swirl of red glass, her eyes wide, mouth open slightly. She looked up at me and said, "You were going to hit me!"

The calculations came easily to me. All my clothes knotted would only reach 5.7 meters. The red glass was connected somewhere under the bridge I couldn't see, no sign of anything she could climb. The colored glass wasn't as strong as the bridge itself—I guessed the red spiral would shatter under Seivarden's weight sometime in the next three to seven seconds. Though that was only a guess. Still, any help I might call would certainly arrive too late. Clouds still veiled the bottom reaches of the chasm. Those tubes were just a few centimeters narrower than my outstretched arms, and were themselves very deep.

"Breq?" Seivarden's voice was breathy and strained. "Can you do something?" Not, at least, *You have to do something.*

"Do you trust me?" I asked.

Her eyes widened further, her gasps became a bit more ragged. She didn't trust me, I knew. She was only still with me because she thought I was official, hence inescapable, and she was important enough for the Radch to send someone after her—underestimating her own importance was never one of Seivarden's failings—and perhaps because she was tired of running, from the world, from herself. Ready to give up. But I still didn't understand why *I* was with *her.* Of all the officers I've served with, she was never one of my favorites.

"I trust you," she lied.

"When I grab you, raise your armor and put your arms around me." Fresh alarm flashed across her face, but there was no more time. I extended my armor under my clothes and stepped off the bridge.

The instant my hands touched her shoulders, the red glass shattered, sharp-edged fragments flying out and away, glittering briefly. Seivarden closed her eyes, ducked her head, face into my neck, held me tight enough that if I hadn't been armored my breathing would have been impeded. Because of the armor I couldn't feel her panicked breath on my skin, couldn't feel the air rushing past, though I could hear it. But she didn't extend her own armor.

If I had been more than just myself, if I had had the numbers I needed, I could have calculated our terminal velocity, and just how long it would take to reach it. Gravity was easy, but the drag of my pack and our heavy coats, whipping up around us, affecting our speed, was beyond me. It would have been much easier to calculate in a vacuum, but we weren't falling in a vacuum.

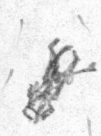

But the difference between fifty meters a second and 150 was, at that moment, only large in the abstract. I couldn't see the bottom yet, the target I was hoping to hit was small, and I didn't know how much time we'd have to adjust our attitude, if we even could. For the next twenty to forty seconds we had nothing to do but wait, and fall.

"Armor!" I shouted into Seivarden's ear.

"Sold it," she answered. Her voice shook slightly, straining against the rushing air. Her face was still pressed hard against my neck.

Suddenly gray. Moisture formed on exposed portions of my armor and blew streaming upward. One point three five seconds later I saw the ground, dark circles packed tight. Bigger, and therefore closer, than I liked. A surge of adrenaline surprised me; I must have gotten too used to falling. I turned my head, trying to look straight down past Seivarden's shoulder to what lay directly below us.

My armor was made to spread out the force of a bullet's impact, bleed some of it away as heat. It was theoretically impenetrable, but I could still be injured or even killed with the application of sufficient force. I'd suffered broken bones, lost bodies under an unrelenting hail of bullets. I wasn't sure what the friction of decelerating would do to my armor, or to me; I had some skeletal and muscular augmentation, but whether it would be sufficient for this, I had no idea. I was unable to calculate just exactly how fast we were going, just exactly how much energy needed to be bled away to slow to a survivable speed, how hot it would get inside and outside my armor. And unarmored, Seivarden wouldn't be able to assist.

Of course, if I had still been what I once was, it wouldn't matter. This wouldn't have been my only body. I couldn't help thinking I should have let Seivarden fall. Shouldn't have jumped. Falling, I still didn't know why I had done it. But at the moment of choice I had found I couldn't walk away.

By then I knew our distance in centimeters. "Five seconds," I said, shouted, above the wind. By then it was four. If we were very, very lucky we'd fall straight into the tube below us and I'd push my hands and feet against the walls. If we were very, very lucky the heat from the friction wouldn't burn unarmored Seivarden too badly. If I was even luckier I'd only break my wrists and ankles. All of it struck me as unlikely, but the omens would fall as Amaat intended.

Falling didn't bother me. I could fall forever and not be hurt. It's stopping that's the problem. "Three seconds," I said.

"Breq," Seivarden said, a gasping sob. "Please."

Some answers I would never have. I abandoned what calculations I was still making. I didn't know why I had jumped but at that moment it no longer mattered, at that moment there was nothing else. "Whatever you do"—one second—"don't let go."

Darkness. No impact. I thrust out my arms, which were immediately forced upward, wrists and one ankle breaking on impact despite my armor's reinforcement, tendons and muscles tearing, and we began a tumble sideways. Despite the pain I pulled my arms and legs in and reached and kicked out again, quickly, steadying us the instant after. Something in my right leg broke as I did, but I couldn't afford to worry about it. Centimeter by centimeter we slowed.

I could no longer control my hands or feet, could only push against the walls and hope we wouldn't be pushed off balance again, and fall helpless, headfirst, to our deaths. The pain was sharp, blinding, blocking out everything except numbers—a distance (estimated) decreasing by centimeters (also estimated); speed (estimated) decreasing; external armor temperature (increasing at my extremities, possible danger of exceeding acceptable parameters, possible resulting injury), but the numbers were near-meaningless to me, the pain was louder, more immediate, than anything else.

But the numbers were important. A comparison of distance and our rate of deceleration suggested disaster ahead. I tried to take a deep breath, found I was incapable of it, and tried to push harder against the walls.

I have no memory of the rest of the descent.

I woke, on my back, in pain. My hands and arms, my shoulders. Feet and legs. In front of me—directly above—a circle of gray light. "Seivarden," I tried to say, but it came out as a convulsive sigh that echoed just slightly against the walls. "Seivarden." The name came out this time, but barely audible, and distorted by my armor. I dropped the armor and tried speaking again, managing this time to engage my voice. "Seivarden."

I raised my head, just slightly. In the dim light from above I saw that I lay on the ground, knees bent and turned to one side, the right leg at a disturbing angle, my arms straight beside my body. I tried to move a finger, failed. A hand. Failed—of course. I tried shifting my right leg, which responded with more pain.

There was no one here but me. Nothing here but me—I didn't see my pack.

At one time, if there had been a Radchaai ship in orbit, I could have contacted it, easy as thought. But if I had been anywhere a Radchaai ship was likely to be, this would never have happened.

If I had left Seivarden in the snow, this would never have happened.

I had been so close. After twenty years of planning and working, of maneuvering, two steps forward here, a step backward there, slowly, patiently, against all likelihood I had gotten this far. So many times I had made a throw like this, not only my success at hazard, but my life, and each time I had won, or at least not lost in any way that prevented me from trying again.

Until now. And for such a stupid reason. Above me clouds hid the unreachable sky, the future I no longer had, the goal I was now incapable of accomplishing. Failed.

I closed my eyes against tears not brought on by physical pain. If I failed, it would not be because I had ever, at any time, given up. Seivarden had left somehow. I would find her. I would rest a moment, recollect myself, find the strength to pull out the handheld I kept in my coat and call for help, or discover some other way to leave here, and if it meant I dragged myself out on the bloody, useless remains of my limbs, I would do that, pain or no pain, or I would die trying.

14

One of the three Mianaais did not even arrive at the Var deck, but transmitted the code for my central access deck. *Invalid access*, I thought, receiving it, but stopped the lift on that level and opened the door anyway. That Mianaai made her way to my main console, gestured up records, scanned quickly through a century of log headings. Stopped, frowned, at a point in the list that would have been made in the five years surrounding that last visit, that I had concealed from her.

The other two of her stowed their bags in quarters, and went to the newly lit and slowly warming Var decade room. Both of her sat at the table, the silent colored-glass Valskaayan saint smiling mildly down. Without speaking aloud she requested information from me—a random sample of memories from that five-year span that had so attracted her attention, above on the central access deck. Silent, expressionless—unreal, in a sense, since I could only see her exteriors—she watched as my memories played out before her visions, in her ears. I began to doubt the truth of my memory of that other visit. There seemed to be no trace of it in the information Anaander Mianaai was accessing, nothing during that time but routine operations.

But something had attracted her attention to that stretch of time. And there was that *Invalid access* to account for—none of Anaander Mianaai's accesses were ever invalid, never could be. And why had I opened to an invalid access? And when one Anaander, in the Var decade room, frowned and said, "No, nothing," and the Lord of the Radch turned her attention to more recent memories, I found myself tremendously relieved.

In the meantime my captain and all my other officers went about the routine business of the day—training, exercising, eating, talking—completely unaware that the Lord of the Radch was aboard. The whole thing was wrong.

The Lord of the Radch watched my Esk lieutenants fencing over breakfast. Three times. With no visible change of expression. One Var set tea at the elbow of each of the two identical black-clad bodies in the Var decade room.

"Lieutenant Awn," said one Anaander. "Has she been out of your presence at all since the incident?" She hadn't specified which incident she meant, but she could only have meant the business in the temple of Ikkt.

"She has not, my lord," I said, using One Var's mouth.

On my central access deck, the Lord of the Radch keyed accesses and overrides that would allow her to change nearly anything about my mind she wished. *Invalid, invalid, invalid.* One after another. But each time I flashed acknowledgment, confirmed access she didn't actually have. I felt something like nausea, beginning to realize what must have happened, but having no accessible memory of it to confirm my suspicions, to make the matter clear and unambiguous to me.

"Has she at any time discussed this incident with anyone?"

This much was clear—Anaander Mianaai was acting against *herself.* Secretly. She was divided in two—at least two. I could only see traces of the other Anaander, the one who had changed the accesses, the accesses she thought she was only now changing to favor herself.

"Has she at any time discussed this incident with anyone?"

"Briefly, my lord," I said. Truly frightened for the first time in my long life. "With Lieutenant Skaaiat of *Justice of Ente*." How could my voice—One Var—speak so calmly? How could I even know what words to say, what answer to make, when the whole basis for all my actions—even my reason for existence—was thrown into doubt?

One Mianaai frowned—not the one that had been speaking. "Skaaiat," she said, with slight distaste. Seeming unaware of my sudden fear. "I've had my suspicions about Awer for some time." Awer was Lieutenant Skaaiat's house name, but what that had to do with events in the temple of Ikkt, I had no idea. "I never could find any proof." This, also, was mysterious to me. "Play me the conversation."

When Lieutenant Skaaiat said, *If you're going to do something that crazy, save it for when it'll make a difference*, one body leaned forward sharply and gave a breathy *ha*, an angry sound. Moments later, at the mention of Ime, eyebrows twitched. I feared momentarily that my dismay at the incautious, frankly dangerous tenor of that conversation would be detectable to the Lord of the Radch, but she made no mention of it. Had not seen it, perhaps, as she had not seen my profound disturbance at realizing she was no longer one person but two, in conflict with each other.

"Not proof. Not enough," Mianaai said, oblivious. "But dangerous. Awer *ought* to tip my way." Why she thought this, I didn't immediately understand. Awer had come from the Radch itself, from the start had had wealth and influence enough to allow it to criticize, and criticize it did, though generally with shrewdness enough to keep itself out of real trouble.

I had known Awer House for a long time, had carried its young lieutenants, known them as captains of other ships. Granted, no Awer suited for military service exhibited her house's tendencies to their utmost extent. An overly keen sense of injustice or a tendency to mysticism didn't mesh well with annexations. Nor with wealth and rank—any Awer's moral outrage inevitably smelled slightly of hypocrisy, considering the comforts and privileges such an ancient house enjoyed, and while some injustices were unignorably obvious to them, some others they never saw.

In any event, Lieutenant Skaaiat's sardonic practicality wasn't foreign to her house. It was only a milder, more livable version of Awer's tendency to moral outrage.

Doubtless each Anaander thought her cause was the more just. (The more proper, the more beneficial. Certainly.) Assuming Awer's penchant for just causes, the citizens of that house ought to support the proper side. Given they knew anything like sides were involved at all.

This assumed, of course, that any part at all of Anaander Mianaai thought any Awer was guided by a passion for justice and not by self-interest covered over with self-righteousness. And any given Awer could, at various times, be guided by either.

Still. It was possible some part of Anaander Mianaai thought that Awer (or any particular Awer) needed only to be convinced of the justice of her cause to champion it. And surely she knew that if Awer—any Awer—could not be convinced, it would be her implacable enemy.

"Suleir, now..." Anaander Mianaai turned to One Var, standing silent at the table. "Dariet Suleir seems to be an ally of Lieutenant Awn. Why?"

The question troubled me for reasons I couldn't quite identify. "I can't be entirely certain, my lord, but I believe Lieutenant Dariet considers Lieutenant Awn to be an able officer, and of course she defers to Lieutenant Awn as decade senior." And, perhaps, was secure enough in her own standing not to resent Lieutenant Awn's having authority over her. Unlike Lieutenant Issaaia. But I didn't say that.

"Nothing to do with political sympathies, then?"

"I am at a loss to understand what you mean, my lord," I said, quite sincerely but with growing alarm.

Another Mianaai body spoke up. "Are you playing stupid with me, Ship?"

"Begging my lord's pardon," I answered, still speaking through One Var, "if I knew what my lord was looking for I would be better able to supply relevant data."

In answer, Mianaai said, "*Justice of Toren*, when did I last visit you?"

If those accesses and overrides had been valid, I would have been utterly unable to conceal anything from the Lord of the Radch. "Two hundred three years, four months, one week, and five days ago, my lord," I lied, now sure of the significance of the question.

"Give me your memories of the incident in the temple," Mianaai commanded, and I complied.

And lied again. Because while nearly every instant of each of those individual streams of memory and data was unaltered, that moment of horror and doubt when one segment feared it might have to shoot Lieutenant Awn was, impossibly, missing.

* * *

It seems very straightforward when I say "I." At the time, "I" meant *Justice of Toren*, the whole ship and all its ancillaries. A unit might be very focused on what it was doing at that particular moment, but it was no more apart from "me" than my hand is while it's engaged in a task that doesn't require my full attention.

Nearly twenty years later "I" would be a single body, a single brain. That division, I–*Justice of Toren* and I–One Esk, was not, I have come to think, a sudden split, not an instant before which "I" was one and after which "I" was "we." It was something that had always been possible, always potential. Guarded against. But how did it go from potential to real, incontrovertible, irrevocable?

On one level the answer is simple—it happened when all of *Justice of Toren* but me was destroyed. But when I look closer I seem to see cracks everywhere. Did the singing contribute, the thing that made One Esk different from all other units on the ship, indeed in the fleets? Perhaps. Or is *anyone's* identity a matter of fragments held together by convenient or useful narrative, that in ordinary circumstances never reveals itself as a fiction? Or is it really a fiction?

I don't know the answer. But I do know that, though I can see hints of the potential split going back a thousand years or more, that's only hindsight. The first I noticed even the bare possibility that I–*Justice of Toren* might not also be I–One Esk, was that moment that *Justice of Toren* edited One Esk's memory of the slaughter in the temple of Ikkt. The moment I—"I"—was *surprised* by it.

It makes the history hard to convey. Because still, "I" was me, unitary, one thing, and yet I acted against myself, contrary to my interests and desires, sometimes secretly, deceiving myself as to what I knew and did. And it's difficult for me even now to know who performed what actions, or knew which information. Because *I* was *Justice of Toren.* Even when I wasn't. Even if I'm not anymore.

Above, on Esk, Lieutenant Dariet asked for admittance to Lieutenant Awn's quarters, found Lieutenant Awn lying on her bunk, staring sightlessly up, gloved hands behind her head. "Awn," she began, stopped, made a rueful smile. "I'm here to pry."

"I can't talk about it," answered Lieutenant Awn, still staring up, dismayed and angry but not letting it reach her voice.

In the Var decade room, Mianaai asked, "What are Dariet Suleir's political sympathies?"

"I believe she has none to speak of," I answered, with One Var's mouth.

Lieutenant Dariet stepped into Lieutenant Awn's quarters, sat on the edge of the bed, next to Lieutenant Awn's unbooted feet. "Not about that. Have you heard from Skaaiat?"

Lieutenant Awn closed her eyes. Still dismayed. Still angry. But with a slightly different feel. "Why should I have?"

Lieutenant Dariet was silent for three seconds. "I like Skaaiat," she said, finally. "I know she likes you."

"I was *there*. I was there and convenient. You know, we all know we'll be moving some time soon, and once we do Skaaiat has no reason to care whether or not I exist anymore. And even if…" Lieutenant Awn stopped. Swallowed. Breathed. "Even if she did," she continued, her voice just barely less steady than before, "it wouldn't matter. I'm not anyone she wants to be connected with, not anymore. If I ever was."

Below, Anaander Mianaai said, "Lieutenant Dariet seems pro-reform."

That puzzled me. But One Var had no opinion, of course, being only One Var, and it had no physical response to my puzzlement. I saw suddenly, clearly, that I was using One Var as a mask, though I didn't understand why or how I would do such a thing. Or why the idea would occur to me now. "Begging my lord's pardon, I don't see that as a political stance."

"Don't you?"

"No, my lord. You ordered the reforms. Loyal citizens will support them."

That Mianaai smiled. The other stood, left the decade room, to walk the Var corridors, inspecting. Not speaking to or acknowledging in any way the segments of One Var it passed.

Lieutenant Awn said, to Lieutenant Dariet's skeptical silence, "It's easy for you. Nobody thinks you're kneeling for advantage when you go to bed with someone. Or getting above yourself. Nobody wonders what your partner could be thinking, or how you ever got here."

"I've told you before, you're too sensitive about that."

"Am I?" Lieutenant Awn opened her eyes, levered herself up on her elbows. "How do you know? Have you experienced it much? I have. All the time."

"That," said Mianaai, in the decade room, "is a more complicated issue than many realize. Lieutenant Awn is pro-reform, of course." I wished I had physical data from Mianaai, so I could interpret the edge in her voice when she named Lieutenant Awn. "And Dariet, perhaps, though how strongly is a question. And the rest of the officers? Who here are pro-reform, and who anti-?"

In Lieutenant Awn's quarters, Lieutenant Dariet sighed. "I just think you worry too much about it. Who cares what people like that say?"

"It's easy not to care when you're rich, and the social equal of *people like that*."

"That sort of thing shouldn't matter," Lieutenant Dariet insisted.

"It shouldn't. But it does."

Lieutenant Dariet frowned. Angry, and frustrated. This conversation had happened before, had gone the same way each time. "Well. Regardless. You should send Skaaiat a message. What is there to lose? If she doesn't answer, she doesn't answer. But maybe..." Lieutenant Dariet lifted one shoulder, and her arm just slightly. A gesture that said, *Take a chance and see what fate deals you*.

If I hesitated in answering Anaander Mianaai's question for even the smallest instant, she would know the overrides weren't working. One Var was very, very impassive. I named a few officers who had definite opinions one way or the other. "The rest," I finished, "are content to follow orders and perform their duties without worrying too much about policy. As far as I can tell."

"They might be swayed one way or the other," Mianaai observed.

"I couldn't say, my lord." My sense of dread increased, but in a detached way. Perhaps the absolute unresponsiveness of my ancillaries made the feeling seem distant and unreal. Ships I knew who had exchanged their ancillary crews for human ones had said their experience of emotion had changed, though this didn't seem quite like the data they had shown me.

The sound of One Esk singing came faintly to Lieutenant Awn and Lieutenant Dariet, a simple song with two parts.

I was walking, I was walking
When I met my love

I was in the street walking
When I saw my true love
I said, "She is more beautiful than jewels, lovelier than
jade or lapis, silver or gold."

"I'm glad One Esk is itself again," said Lieutenant Dariet. "That first day was eerie."

"Two Esk didn't sing," Lieutenant Awn pointed out.

"Right, but..." Lieutenant Dariet gestured doubt. "It wasn't right." She looked speculatively at Lieutenant Awn.

"I can't talk about it," said Lieutenant Awn, and lay back down, crossing her arms over her eyes.

On the command deck Hundred Captain Rubran met with the decade commanders, drank tea, talked about schedules and leave times.

"You haven't mentioned Hundred Captain Rubran," said Mianaai, in the Var decade room.

I hadn't. I knew Captain Rubran extremely well, knew her every breath, every twitch of every muscle. She had been my captain for fifty-six years. "I have never heard her express an opinion on the matter," I said, quite truthfully.

"Never? Then it's certain she has one and is concealing it."

This struck me as something of a double bind. Speak and your possession of an opinion was plain, clear to anyone. Refrain from speaking and still this was proof of an opinion. If Captain Rubran were to say, *Truly, I have no opinion on the matter*, would that merely be another proof she had one?

"Surely she's been present when others have discussed it," Mianaai continued. "What have her feelings been in such cases?"

"Exasperation," I answered, through One Var. "Impatience. Sometimes boredom."

"Exasperation," mused Mianaai. "At what, I wonder?" I did not know the answer, so I said nothing. "Her family connections are such that I can't be certain where her sympathies are most likely to lie. And some of them I don't want to alienate before I can move openly. I have to tread carefully with Captain Rubran. But so will *she*."

She meaning, of course, herself.

There had been no attempt to discover *my* sympathies. Perhaps—no, certainly—they were irrelevant. And I was already well along the path the other Mianaai had set me on. These few Mianaais, and the four segments of One Var thawed for her service, only made the Var deck seem emptier, and all the decks between here and my engines. Hundreds of thousands of ancillaries slept in my holds, and they would likely be removed within the next few years, either stored or destroyed, never waking again. And I would be placed in orbit somewhere, permanently. My engines almost certainly disabled. Or I would be destroyed outright—though none of us had been so far, and I was fairly sure I would more likely serve as a habitat, or the core of a small station.

Not the life I had been built for.

"No, I can't be hasty with Rubran Osck. But your Lieutenant Awn is another matter. And perhaps she can be of use in discovering where Awer stands."

"My lord," I said, through one of One Var's mouths. "I am at a loss to understand what's happening. I would feel a great deal more comfortable if the hundred captain knew you were here."

"You dislike concealing things from your captain?" Anaander asked, with a tone that was equal parts bitter and amused.

"Yes, my lord. I will, of course, proceed precisely as you order me." A sudden sense of déjà vu overcame me.

"Of course. I should explain some things." The sense of déjà vu grew stronger. I had had this conversation before, in almost exactly these circumstances, with the Lord of the Radch. *You know that each of your ancillary segments is entirely capable of having its own identity*, she would say next. "You know that each of your ancillary segments is entirely capable of having its own identity."

"Yes." Every word, familiar. I could feel it, as though we were reciting lines we had memorized. Next she would say, *Imagine you became undecided about something.*

"Imagine some enemy separated part of you from yourself."

Not what I had been expecting. *What is it people say, when that happens? They're divided. They're of two minds.*

"Imagine that enemy managed to forge or force its way past all the necessary accesses. And that part of you came back to you—but wasn't really part of you anymore. But you didn't realize it. Not right away."

You and I, we really can be of two minds, can't we.

"That's a very alarming thought, my lord."

"It is," agreed Anaander Mianaai, all the time sitting in the Var decade room, inspecting the corridors and rooms of the Var deck. Watching Lieutenant Awn, alone again, and miserable. Gesturing through my mind, on the central access deck. Or so she thought. "I don't know precisely who has done it. I suspect the involvement of the Presger. They have been meddling in our affairs since before the Treaty. And after—five hundred years ago, the best surgicals and correctives were made in Radch space. Now we buy from the Presger. At first only at border stations, but now they're everywhere. Eight hundred years ago the Translators Office was a collection of minor officials who assisted in the interpretation of extra-Radch intelligence, and who smoothed linguistic problems during annexations. Now they dictate policy. Chief among them the Emissary to the Presger." The last sentence was spoken with audible distaste. "Before the Treaty, the Presger destroyed a few ships. Now they destroy all of Radch civilization.

"Expansion, annexation, is very expensive. Necessary—it has been from the beginning. From the first, to surround the Radch itself with a buffer zone, protecting it from any sort of attack or interference. Later, to protect *those* citizens. And to expand the reach of civilization. And..." Mianaai stopped, gave a short, exasperated sigh. "To pay for the previous annexations. To provide wealth for Radchaai in general."

"My lord, what do you suspect the Presger of having done?" But I knew. Even with my memory obscured and incomplete, I knew.

"Divided me. Corrupted part of me. And the corruption has spread, the other me has been recruiting—not only more parts of me but also my own citizens. My own soldiers." *My own ships.* "My own ships. I can only guess what her goal is. But it can't be anything good."

"Do I understand correctly," I asked, already knowing the answer, "that this other Anaander Mianaai is the force behind the ending of annexations?"

"She will destroy everything I've built!" I had never seen the Lord of the Radch so frustrated and angry. Had not thought her capable of it. "Do you realize—there's no reason you should ever have thought of it—that it's the appropriation of resources during annexations that drives our economy?"

"I am afraid, my lord, that I am only a troop carrier and have never concerned myself with such things. But what you say makes sense."

"And you. I doubt you're looking forward to losing your ancillaries."

Outside me my distant companions, the Justices parked around the system, sat silent, waiting. How many of them had received this visit—or both these visits? "I am not, my lord."

"I can't promise that I can prevent it. I'm not prepared for open warfare. All my moves are in secret, pushing here, pulling there, making sure of my resources and support. But in the end, she is me, and there is little I can do she will not already have thought of. She has outmaneuvered me several times already. It's why I have been so cautious in approaching you. I wanted to be sure she had not already suborned you."

I felt it was safer not to comment on that, and instead said, through One Var, "My lord, the guns in the lake, in Ors." *Was that your enemy?* I almost asked, but if we were faced with two Anaanders, each opposing the other, how did anyone know which was which?

"Events in Ors didn't come out precisely the way I wished," answered Anaander Mianaai. "I never expected anyone would find those guns, but if some Orsian fisherman had found them and said nothing, or even taken them, my purpose would still have been served." Instead, Denz Ay had reported her find to Lieutenant Awn. The Lord of the Radch hadn't expected that, I saw, hadn't thought the Orsians trusted Lieutenant Awn that much. "I didn't get what I wanted there, but perhaps the results will still serve my purpose. Hundred Captain Rubran is about to receive orders to depart this system for Valskaay. It was past time for you to leave, and you would have a year ago, if not for the Divine of Ikkt's insistence that Lieutenant Awn stay, and my own opposition. Whether knowingly or not, Lieutenant Awn is the instrument of my enemy, I'm certain of it."

I did not trust even One Var's impassivity to answer that,

and therefore did not speak. Above, on the central access deck, the Lord of the Radch continued to make changes, give orders, alter my thoughts. Still believing she could in fact do that.

No one was surprised at the order to depart. Four other Justices already had in the last year, to destinations meant to be final. But neither I nor any of my officers had expected Valskaay, six gates away.

Valskaay, that I had been sorry to leave. One hundred years ago, in the city of Vestris Cor, on Valskaay itself, One Esk had discovered volume upon volume of elaborate, multivoiced choral music, all intended for the rites of Valskaay's troublesome religion, some of it dating from before humans had ever reached space. Downloaded everything it found so that it hardly regretted being sent away from such a treasure out to the countryside, hard work prying rebels from a reserve, forest and caverns and springs, that we couldn't just blast because it was a watershed for half the continent. A region of small rivers and bluffs, and farms. Grazing sheep and peach orchards. And music—even the rebels, trapped at last, had sung, either in defiance against us or as consolation for themselves, their voices reaching my appreciative ears as I stood at the mouth of the cave where they hid.

Death will overtake us
In whatever manner already fated
Everyone falls to it
And so long as I'm ready
I don't fear it
No matter what form it takes.

When I thought of Valskaay, I thought of sunshine and the sweet, bright taste of peaches. Thought of music. But I was sure I wouldn't be sent down to the planet this time—there would be no orchards for One Esk, no visits (unofficial, as unobtrusive as possible) to choral society meetings.

Traveling to Valskaay I would not, it turned out, take the gates, but generate my own, moving more directly. The gates most travelers used had been generated millennia ago, were held constantly open, stable, surrounded by beacons broadcasting warnings, notifications, information about local regulations and navigation hazards. Not only ships, but messages and information streamed constantly through them.

In the two thousand years I had been alive, I had used them once. Like all Radchaai warships, I was capable of making my own shortcut. It was more dangerous than using the established gates—an error in my calculations could send me anywhere, or nowhere, never to be heard from again. And since I left no structures behind to hold my gate open, I traveled in a bubble of normal space, isolated from everyone and everywhere until I exited at my destination. I didn't make such errors, and in the course of arranging an annexation the isolation could be an advantage. Now, though, the prospect of months alone, with Anaander Mianaai secretly occupying my Var deck, made me nervous.

Before I gated out, a message came from Lieutenant Skaaiat for Lieutenant Awn. Brief. *I said keep in touch. I meant it.*

Lieutenant Dariet said, "See, I told you." But Lieutenant Awn didn't answer.

15

At some point I opened my eyes again, thinking I had heard voices. All around me, blue. I tried to blink, found I could only close my eyes and leave them closed.

Sometime later I opened my eyes again, turned my head to the right, and saw Seivarden and the girl squatting on either side of a Tiktik board. So I was dreaming, or hallucinating. At least I no longer hurt, which on consideration was a bad sign, but I couldn't bring myself to care much. I closed my eyes again.

I woke, finally, actual wakefulness, and found myself in a small blue-walled room. I lay in a bed, and on a bench beside it Seivarden sat, leaning against the wall, looking as though she hadn't slept recently. Or, that is to say, even more as though she hadn't slept recently than she usually did.

I lifted my head. My arms and legs were immobilized by correctives.

"You're awake," said Seivarden.

I set my head back down. "Where's my pack?"

"Right here." She bent, lifted it into my line of sight.

"We're at the medical center in Therrod," I guessed, and closed my eyes.

"Yes. Do you think you can talk to the doctor? Because I can't understand anything she says."

I remembered my dream. "You learned to play Tiktik."

"That's different." So, not a dream.

"You sold the flier." No answer. "You bought kef."

"No, I didn't," she protested. "I was *going* to. But when I woke up and you were gone..." I heard her shift uncomfortably on the bench. "I was going to find a dealer, but it bothered me that you were gone and I didn't know where you were. I started to think maybe you'd left me behind."

"You wouldn't have cared once you took the kef."

"But I didn't have the kef," she said, voice surprisingly reasonable. "And then I went to the front and found you'd checked out."

"And you decided to find me, and not the kef," I said. "I don't believe you."

"I don't blame you." She was silent for five seconds. "I've been sitting here, thinking. I accused you of hating me because I was better than you."

"That's not why I hate you."

She ignored that. "Amaat's grace, that fall...it was my own stupid fault, I was sure I was dead, and if it had been the other way around I'd never have jumped to save anyone's life. You never knelt to get anywhere. You are where you are because you're fucking capable, and willing to risk everything to do right, and I'll never be half what you are even if I tried my whole life, and I was walking around thinking I was better than you, even half dead and no use to anyone, because my family is old, because I was *born better*."

"That," I said, "is why I hate you."

She laughed, as though I'd said something moderately witty. "If that's what you're willing to do for someone you hate, what would you do for someone you loved?"

I found I was incapable of answering. Fortunately the doctor came in, broad, round-faced, pale. Frowning slightly, slightly more when she saw me. "It seems," she said, in an even tone that seemed impartial but implied disapproval, "that I don't understand your friend when he tries to explain what happened."

I looked at Seivarden, who made a helpless gesture and said, "I don't understand any of it. I tried my best and the whole day she's been giving me that look, like I'm biological waste she stepped in."

"It's probably just her normal expression." I turned my head back to the doctor. "We fell off the bridge," I explained.

The doctor's expression didn't change. "Both of you?"

"Yes."

A moment of impassive silence, and then, "It does not pay to be dishonest with your doctor." And then when I didn't answer, "You would not be the first tourist to enter a restricted area and be injured. You are, however, the first to claim they'd fallen off the bridge and lived. I don't know whether to admire the brazenness, or be angry you take me for such a fool."

Still I said nothing. No story I could invent would account for my injuries in the way the truth did.

"Members of military forces must register on arrival in the system," the doctor continued.

"I remember hearing so."

"Did you register?"

"No, because I am not a member of any military force."

Not quite a lie. I was not a member, I was a piece of equipment. A lone, useless fragment of equipment at that.

"This facility is not equipped," the doctor said, just a shade more sternly than the moment before, "to deal with the sort of implants and augmentations you apparently have. I can't predict the results of the repairs I've programmed. You should see a doctor when you return home. To the Gerentate." That last sounded just slightly skeptical, the barest indication of the doctor's disbelief.

"I intend to go straight home once I leave here," I said, but I wondered if the doctor had reported us as possible spies. I thought not—if she had, likely she would have avoided expressing any sort of suspicion, merely waited for authorities to deal with us. She had not, then. Why not?

A possible answer stuck her head into the room and called cheerily, "Breq! You're awake! Uncle's on the level just above. What happened? Your friend seemed like he was saying you jumped off the bridge but that's impossible. Do you feel better?" The girl came fully into the room. "Hello, Doctor, is Breq going to be all right?"

"Breq will be fine. The correctives should drop off by tomorrow. Unless something goes wrong." And with that cheerful observation she turned and left the room.

The girl sat on the edge of my bed. "Your friend is a terrible Tiktik player, I'm glad I didn't teach him the gambling part or he wouldn't have had any money to pay the doctor with. And it's *your* money, isn't it? From the flier."

Seivarden frowned. "What? What is she saying?"

I resolved to check the contents of my pack as soon as I could. "He'd have won it back playing counters."

From the look on her face, the girl didn't believe that at all. "You really shouldn't go under the bridge, you know. I know someone who had a friend whose cousin went under the bridge and someone dropped a piece of bread off, and it was going so fast it hit them in the head and broke their skull open and went into their brain and *killed* them."

"I enjoyed your cousin's singing very much." I didn't want to reopen the discussion about what had happened.

"Isn't she wonderful? Oh!" She turned her head, as though she'd heard something. "I have to go. I'll visit you again!"

"I'd appreciate that," I said, and she was out the door and away. I looked at Seivarden. "How much did this cost?"

"About what I got for the flier," she said, ducking her head slightly, maybe out of embarrassment. Maybe something else.

"Did you take anything out of my pack?"

That brought her head up again. "No! I swear I didn't." I didn't answer. "You don't believe me. I don't blame you. You can check, as soon as your hands are free."

"I intend to. But then what?"

She frowned, not comprehending. And of course she didn't understand—she had gotten as far as (mistakenly) evaluating me as a human being who might be worthy of respect. She had not, it seemed, come to the point of considering she might not actually be important enough for the Radch to send a Special Missions officer after.

"I was never assigned to find you," I said. "I found you completely by accident. As far as I know, no one is looking for you." I wished I could gesture, wave her away.

"Why are you here, then? It's not groundwork for an annexation, there aren't any more. That's what they told me."

"No more annexations," I agreed. "But that's not the point. The point is, you can come or go as you like, I have no orders to bring you back."

Seivarden considered that for six seconds, and then said,

"I tried to quit before. I *did* quit. This station I was on had a program, you'd quit, they'd give you a job. One of their workers hauled me in and cleaned me up and told me the deal. The job was crap, the deal was bullshit, but I'd had enough. I thought I'd had enough."

"How long did you last?"

"Not quite six months."

"You see," I said, after a two-second pause, "why I don't exactly have confidence in you this time."

"Believe me, I do. But this is *different*." She leaned forward, earnest. "Nothing quite clarifies your thoughts like thinking you're about to die."

"The effect is often temporary."

"They said, back on that station, that they could give me something to make kef never work on me. But first I had to fix whatever had made me take it to begin with, because otherwise I'd just find something else. Bullshit, like I said, but if I'd really wanted to, really meant to, I'd have done it then."

Back at Strigan's she'd spoken as though her reason for starting was simple, clear-cut. "Did you tell them why you started?" She didn't answer. "Did you tell them who you were?"

"Of course not."

The two questions were the same in her mind, I guessed. "You faced death back at Garsedd."

She flinched, just slightly. "And everything changed. I woke up and all I had was past. Not a very good past, either, no one liked telling me what had happened, everyone was so polite and cheerful and it was all *fake*. And I couldn't see any kind of future. Listen." She leaned forward, earnest, breathing slightly harder. "You're out here on your own, all by yourself, and obviously it's because you're suited to it or you wouldn't have been assigned." She paused a moment, maybe considering that issue of just who was suited to what, who was assigned where, and dismissing it. "But in the end, you can go back to the Radch and find people who know you, people who remember you, personally, a place where you *fit* even if you're not always there. No matter where you go, you're still part of that pattern, even if you never go back you always know it's *there*. But when they opened that suspension pod, anyone who ever had any personal interest in me was already seven hundred years dead. Probably longer. Not even..." Her voice trembled, and she stopped, staring ahead at some fixed point beyond me. "Even the ships."

Even the ships. "Ships? More than just *Sword of Nathtas*?"

"My...the first ship I ever served on. *Justice of Toren*. I thought maybe if I could find where it was stationed I could send a message and..." She made a negating gesture, wiping out the rest of that sentence. "It disappeared. About ten...wait...I've lost track of time. About fifteen years ago." Closer to twenty. "Nobody could tell me what happened. Nobody knows."

"Were any of the ships you served on particularly fond of you?" I asked, voice carefully even. Neutral.

She blinked. Straightened. "That's an odd question. Do you have any experience with ships?"

"Yes," I said. "Actually."

"Ships are always attached to their captains."

"Not like they used to be." Not like when some ships had gone mad on the deaths of their captains. That had been long, long ago. "And even so, they have favorites." Though a favorite wouldn't necessarily know it. "But it doesn't matter, does it? Ships aren't people, and they're made to serve you, to be attached, as you put it."

Seivarden frowned. "Now you're angry. You're very good at hiding it, but you're angry."

"Do you grieve for your ships," I asked, "because they're dead? Or because their loss means they aren't here to make you feel connected and cared about?" Silence. "Or do you think those are the same thing?" Still no answer. "I will answer my own question: you were never a favorite of any of the ships you served on. You don't believe it's possible for a ship to have favorites."

Seivarden's eyes widened—maybe surprise, maybe something else. "You know me too well for me to believe you aren't here because of me. I've thought so from the moment I actually started thinking about it."

"Not too long ago, then," I said.

She ignored what I had just said. "You're the first person, since that pod opened, to feel *familiar*. Like I recognize you. Like you recognize me. I don't know why that is."

I knew, of course. But this was not the moment to say so, to explain, immobilized and vulnerable as I was. "I assure you I'm not here because of you. I'm here on my own personal business."

"You jumped off that bridge for me."

"And I'm not going to be your reason for quitting kef. I take no responsibility for you. You're going to have to do that yourself. If you really are going to do that."

"You jumped off that *bridge* for me. That had to be a three-kilometer drop. Higher. That's...that's..." She stopped, shaking her head. "I'm staying with you."

I closed my eyes. "The moment I even *think* you're going to steal from me again, I will break both your legs and leave you there, and it will be utter coincidence if you ever see me again." Except that to Radchaai, there were no coincidences.

"I guess I can't really argue with that."

"I don't recommend it."

She gave a short laugh, and then was silent for fifteen seconds. "Tell me, then, Breq," she said after that. "If you're here on personal business, and nothing at all to do with me, why do you have one of the Garseddai guns in your pack?"

The correctives held my arms and legs completely immobile. I couldn't even get my shoulders off the bed. The doctor came heavily into the room, pale face flushed. "Lie still!" she admonished, and then turned to Seivarden. "What did you do?"

This was, apparently, comprehensible to Seivarden. She spread her hands in a helpless gesture. "Not!" she replied, vehemently, in the same language.

The doctor frowned, pointed at Seivarden, one finger out. Seivarden straightened, indignant at the gesture, which was much ruder to a Radchaai than it was here. "You bother," the doctor said, sternly, "you go!" Then she turned to me. "*You* will lie still and heal properly."

"Yes, Doctor." I subsided from the very small amount of movement I had managed. Took a breath, attempting to calm myself.

This seemed to mollify her. She watched me a moment, doubtless seeing my heart rate, my breathing. "If you can't settle, I can give you medication." An offer, a question, a threat. "I can make him"—with a glance at Seivarden—"leave."

"I don't need it. Either one."

The doctor gave a skeptical *hmph*, and turned and left the room.

"I'm sorry," said Seivarden when the doctor was gone. "That was stupid. I should have thought before I spoke." I didn't answer. "When we got to the bottom," she continued, as though it was logically connected to what she had said before, "you were unconscious. And obviously badly injured, and I was afraid to move you much, because I couldn't see if maybe bones were broken. I didn't have any way to call for help, but I thought maybe you had something I could use to help climb out, or maybe some first-aid correctives I could use, but of course that was foolish, your armor was still up, which was how I knew you were still alive. I did take your handheld out of your coat, but there was no signal, I had to climb up to the top before I could reach anyone. When I got back your armor was down and I was afraid you were dead. Everything's still in there."

"If the gun is gone," I said, voice calm and neutral, "I won't just break your legs."

"It's there," she insisted. "But this can't possibly be personal business, can it?"

"It's personal." It was just that with me *personal* affected a great many others. But how could I explain that, without revealing more than I wanted to just now?

"Tell me."

This was not a good time. Not a good moment. But there was a great deal to explain, especially since Seivarden's knowledge of the past thousand years of history was sure to be patchy and superficial. Years of previous events leading up to this, which she would almost certainly be ignorant of, which would take time to explain, before I ever got to who I was and what I intended.

And that history would make a difference. Without understanding it, how could Seivarden understand anything? Without that context, how could she understand why anyone had acted as they did? If Anaander Mianaai had not reacted with such fury to the Garseddai, would she have done the things she'd done in the thousand years since then? If Lieutenant Awn had never heard of the events at Ime five years before, twenty-five years ago now, would she have acted as she did?

When I imagined it, the moment that *Mercy of Sarrse* soldier had chosen to defy her orders, I saw her as a segment of an ancillary unit. She had been number One of *Mercy of Sarrse*'s Amaat unit, its senior member. Even though she had been human, had had a name beyond her place on her ship, beyond *Mercy of Sarrse* One Amaat One. But I had never seen a recording, had never seen her face.

She had been human. She had endured events at Ime—perhaps even enforced the corrupt dictates of the governor herself, when ordered. But something about that particular moment had changed things. Something had been too much for her.

What had it been? The sight, perhaps, of a Rrrrrr, dead or dying? I'd seen pictures of the Rrrrrr, snake-long, furred, multi-limbed, speaking in growls and barks; and the humans associated with them, who could speak that language and understand it. Had it been the Rrrrrr who had knocked *Mercy of Sarrse* One Amaat One off her expected path? Did she care so much for the threat of breaking the treaty with the Presger? Or had it been the thought of killing so many helpless human beings? If I had known more about her, perhaps I could have seen why in that moment she had decided that she would rather die.

I knew almost nothing about her. Probably by design. But even the little I had known, the little Lieutenant Awn had known, had made a difference. "Did anyone tell you about what happened at Ime Station?"

Seivarden frowned. "No. Tell me."

I told her. About the governor's corruption, her preventing Ime Station or any of the ships from reporting what she was doing, so far from anywhere else in Radch space. About the ship that had arrived one day—they'd assumed it was human, no one knew of any aliens anywhere nearby, and it obviously wasn't Radchaai and so it was fair game. I told Seivarden as much as I knew about the soldiers from *Mercy of Sarrse* who boarded the unknown ship with orders to take it and kill anyone aboard who resisted, or who obviously couldn't be made into ancillaries. I didn't know much—only that once the One Amaat unit had boarded the alien ship, its One had refused to continue to follow orders. She had convinced the rest of One Amaat to follow her, and they had defected to the Rrrrrr and taken the ship out of reach.

Seivarden's frown only deepened, and when I was done she said, "So, you're telling me the governor of Ime was completely corrupt. And somehow had the accesses to prevent Ime Station from reporting her? How does that happen?" I didn't answer. Either the obvious conclusion would occur to her, or she would be unable to see it. "And how could the aptitudes have put her in such a position, if she was capable of that? It isn't possible.

"Of course," Seivarden continued, "everything else follows from that, doesn't it? A corrupt governor appoints corrupt officials, never mind the aptitudes. But the captains stationed there... no, it isn't possible."

She wouldn't be able to see it. I shouldn't have said anything at all. "When that soldier refused to kill the Rrrrrr who had come into the system, when she convinced the rest of her unit to do likewise, she created a situation that could not be concealed for long. The Rrrrrr could generate their own gate, so the governor couldn't prevent them from leaving. They had only to make a single jump to the next inhabited system and tell their story. Which was exactly what they did."

"Why did anyone care about the Rrrrrr?" Seivarden couldn't quite get her throat around the sound. "Seriously? They're called that?"

"It's what they call themselves," I explained, in my most patient voice. When a Rrrrrr said it, or one of their human translators, it sounded like a sustained growl, not much different from any other Rrrrrr speech. "It's kind of hard to say. Most people I've heard just say a long *r* sound."

"Rrrrrr," Seivarden said, experimentally. "Still sounds funny. So why did anyone care about the Rrrrrr?"

"Because the Presger had made a treaty with us on the basis of their having decided humans were Significant. Killing the Insignificant is nothing, to the Presger, and violence between members of the same species means nothing to them, but indiscriminate violence toward other Significant species is unacceptable." Not to say no violence is allowed, but it's subject to certain conditions, none of which make obvious sense to most humans so it's safest just to avoid it altogether.

Seivarden made a breathy *huh*, pieces falling into place.

"So then," I continued, "the entire One Amaat unit of *Mercy of Sarrse* had defected to the Rrrrrr. They were out of reach, safe with the aliens, but to the Radchaai they were guilty of treason. It might have been better just to leave them where they were, but instead the Radch demanded them back, so they could be executed. And of course the Rrrrrr didn't want to do that. The One Amaat unit had saved their lives. Things were very tense for several years, but eventually they compromised. The Rrrrrr handed over the unit leader, the one who'd started the mutiny, in exchange for immunity for the others."

"But..." Seivarden stopped.

After seven seconds of silence, I said, "You're thinking that of course she had to die, no disobedience can be tolerated, for very good reasons. But at the same time, her treason exposed the governor of Ime's corruption, which otherwise would have continued unabated, so ultimately she did the Radch a service. You're thinking that any fool knows better than to speak up and criticize a government official for any reason. And you're thinking that if anyone who speaks up to criticize something obviously evil is punished merely for speaking, civilization will be in a bad way. No one will speak who isn't willing to die for her speech, and..." I hesitated. Swallowed. "There aren't many willing to do that. You're probably thinking that the Lord of the Radch was in a difficult spot, deciding how to handle the situation. But also that these particular circumstances were extraordinary, and Anaander Mianaai is, in the end, the ultimate authority and might have pardoned her if she wished."

"I'm thinking," said Seivarden, "that the Lord of the Radch could have just let them stay with the Rrrrrr and been free of the whole mess."

"She could have," I agreed.

"I'm also thinking that if I were the Lord of the Radch, I would never have let that news get much farther than Ime."

"You'd use accesses to prevent ships and stations from talking about it, maybe. You'd forbid any citizens who knew to say anything."

"Yes. I would."

"But it would still spread by rumor." Though that rumor would of necessity be vague and slow-moving. "And you'd lose the very instructive example you could make, letting everyone watch you line up nearly all of Ime's Administration on the station concourse and shoot them in the head, one after the other." And, of course, Seivarden was a single person, who was thinking of Anaander Mianaai as a single person who could be undecided about such things, but then choose a single course of action, without dividing herself over her decision. And there was a great deal more behind Anaander Mianaai's dilemma than Seivarden had grasped.

Seivarden was silent for four seconds, and then said, "Now I'm going to make you angry again."

"Really?" I asked, drily. "Aren't you getting tired of that?"

"Yes." Simply. Seriously.

"The governor of Ime was wellborn and well-bred," I said, and named her house.

"Never heard of them," said Seivarden. "There've been so many changes. And now things like this happening. You honestly don't think there's a connection?"

I turned my head away, without lifting it. Not angry, just very, very tired. "You mean to say, none of this would have happened if jumped-up provincials hadn't been jumped up. If the governor of Ime had been from a family of *real* proven quality."

Seivarden had wit enough not to answer.

"You've honestly never known anyone *born better* to be assigned or promoted past their ability? To crack under pressure? Behave badly?"

"Not like that."

Fair enough. But she'd conveniently forgotten that *Mercy of Sarrse* One Amaat One—human, not an ancillary—would also have been "jumped up" by her definition, was part of the very change Seivarden had mentioned. "Jumped-up provincials and the sort of thing that happened at Ime are both results of the same events. One did not cause the other."

She asked the obvious question. "What caused it, then?"

The answer was too complicated. How far back to begin?

It started at Garsedd. It started when the Lord of the Radch multiplied herself and set out to conquer all of human space. It started when the Radch was built. And further back. "I'm tired," I said.

"Of course," said Seivarden, more equably than I had expected. "We can talk about it later."

16

I spent a week moving in the non-space between Shis'urna and Valskaay—isolated, self-contained—before the Lord of the Radch made her move. No one else suspected anything, I had given no hint, no trace, not the faintest indication that anyone at all was on Var deck, that anything at all might be wrong.

Or so I had thought. "Ship," Lieutenant Awn said to me, a week in, "is something wrong?"

"Why do you ask, Lieutenant?" I replied. One Esk replied. One Esk attended Lieutenant Awn constantly.

"We were in Ors together a long time," Lieutenant Awn said, frowning slightly at the segment she was talking to. She had been in a constant state of misery since Ors, sometimes more intense, sometimes less, depending, I supposed, on what thoughts occurred to her at a given moment. "You just seem like something's troubling you. And you're quieter." She made a sound, breathy half-amusement. "You were always humming or singing in the house. It's too quiet now."

"There are walls here, Lieutenant," I pointed out. "There were none in the house in Ors."

Her eyebrow twitched just slightly. I could see she knew my words for an evasion, but she didn't pursue the question.

At the same time, in the Var decade room, Anaander Mianaai said to me, "You understand the stakes. What this means for the Radch." I acknowledged this. "I know this must be disturbing to you." It was the first acknowledgment of this possibility since she had come aboard. "I made you to serve my ends, for the good of the Radch. It's part of your design, to want to serve me. And now you must not only serve me, but also oppose me."

She was, I thought, making it remarkably easy for me to oppose her. One side or the other of her had done that, and I wasn't sure which. But I said, through One Var, "Yes, my lord."

"If she succeeds, ultimately the Radch will fragment. Not the center, not the Radch itself." When most people spoke of the Radch they meant all of Radchaai territory, but in truth the Radch was a single location, a Dyson sphere, enclosed, self-contained. Nothing ritually impure was allowed within, no one uncivilized or nonhuman could enter its confines. Very, very few of Mianaai's clients had ever set foot there, and only a few houses still existed who even had ancestors who had once lived there. It was an open question if anyone within knew or cared about the actions of Anaander Mianaai, or the extent or even existence of Radch territory. "The Radch itself, as the Radch, will survive longer. But my territory, that I built to protect it, to keep it pure, will shatter. I made myself into what I am, built all this"—she gestured sweepingly, the walls of the decade room encompassing, for her purposes, the entirety of Radch space—"all this, to keep that center safe. Uncontaminated. I couldn't trust it to anyone else. Now, it seems, I can't trust it to myself."

"Surely not, my lord," I said, at a loss for what else to say, not sure exactly what I was protesting.

"Billions of citizens will die in the process," she continued, as though I had not spoken. "Through war, or lack of resources. And I…"

She hesitated. Unity, I thought, implies the possibility of disunity. Beginnings imply and require endings. But I did not say so. The most powerful person in the universe didn't need me to lecture her on religion or philosophy.

"But I am already broken," she finished. "I can only fight to prevent my breaking further. Remove what is no longer myself."

I wasn't sure what I should, or could, say. I had no conscious memory of having this conversation previously, though I was certain now I must have, must have listened to Anaander Mianaai explain and justify her actions, after she used the overrides and changed…something. It must have been quite similar, perhaps even the same words. It had, after all, been the same person.

"And," Anaander Mianaai continued, "I must remove my enemy's weapons wherever I find them. Send Lieutenant Awn to me."

Lieutenant Awn approached the Var decade room with trepidation, not knowing why I had sent her there. I had refused to answer her questions, which had only fed a growing feeling on her part that something was very wrong. Her boots on the white floor echoed emptily, despite One Var's presence.

As she reached it the decade room door slid open, nearly noiseless.

The sight of Anaander Mianaai within hit Lieutenant Awn like a blow, a vicious spike of fear, surprise, dread, shock, doubt, and bewilderment. Lieutenant Awn took three breaths, shallower, I could see, than she liked, and then hitched her shoulders just the slightest bit, stepped in, and prostrated herself.

"Lieutenant," said Anaander Mianaai. Her accent, and tone, were the prototype of Lieutenant Skaaiat's elegant vowels, of Lieutenant Issaaia's thoughtless, slightly sneering arrogance. Lieutenant Awn lay facedown, waiting. Frightened.

As before I received no data from Mianaai that she did not deliberately send me. I had no information about her internal state. She seemed calm. Impassive, emotionless. I was sure that surface impression was a lie, though I didn't understand why I thought that, except that she had yet to speak favorably of Lieutenant Awn, when in my opinion she should have.

"Tell me, Lieutenant," said Mianaai, after a long silence, "where those guns came from, and what you think happened in the temple of Ikkt."

A combination of relief and fear washed through Lieutenant Awn. She had, in the moments available to process Anaander Mianaai's presence here, formed an expectation that this question would be asked. "My lord, the guns could only have come from someone with sufficient authority to divert them and prevent their destruction."

"You, for instance."

A sharp stab of startlement and terror. "No, my lord, I assure you. I did disarm noncitizens local to my assignment, and some of them were Tanmind military." The police station in the upper city had been quite well-armed, in fact. "But

I had those disabled on the spot, before I sent them on. And according to their inventory numbers, these had been collected in Kould Ves."

"By *Justice of Toren* troops?"

"So I understand, my lord."

"Ship?"

I answered with one of One Var's mouths. "My lord, the guns in question were collected by Sixteen and Seventeen Inu." I named their lieutenant at the time, who had since been reassigned.

Anaander Mianaai made the barest hint of a frown. "So as far back as five years ago, someone with access—perhaps this Inu lieutenant, perhaps someone else, prevented these weapons from being destroyed, and hid them. For five years. And then, what, planted them in the Orsian swamp? To what end?"

Face still to the floor, blinking in confusion, Lieutenant Awn took one second to frame a reply. "I don't know, my lord."

"You're lying," said Mianaai, still sitting, leaning back in her chair as though quite relaxed and unconcerned, but her eyes had not left Lieutenant Awn. "I can see plainly that you are. And I've heard every conversation you've had, since the incident. Who did you mean when you spoke of someone else who would benefit from the situation?"

"If I'd known what name to put there, my lord, I would have used it. I only meant by it that there must be a specific person who acted, who caused it..." She stopped, took a breath, abandoned that sentence. "Someone conspired with the Tanmind, someone who had access to those guns. Whoever it was, they wanted trouble between the upper city and the lower. It was my job to prevent that. I did my best to prevent that." Certainly an evasion. From the moment Anaander Mianaai had ordered the hasty execution of those Tanmind citizens in the temple, the first, most obvious suspect had been the Lord of the Radch herself.

"Why would anyone want trouble between the upper city and the lower?" Anaander Mianaai asked. "Who would exert themselves over it?"

"Jen Shinnan, my lord, and her associates," answered Lieutenant Awn, on firmer ground, for the moment at least. "She felt the ethnic Orsians were unduly favored."

"By you."

"Yes, my lord."

"So you're saying that in the first months of the annexation, Jen Shinnan found some Radchaai official willing to divert crates full of weapons so that five years later she could start trouble between the upper and lower city. To get you in trouble."

"My lord!" Lieutenant Awn lifted her forehead one centimeter off the floor, then halted. "I don't know how, I don't know why. I don't know wh..." She swallowed that last, which I knew would have been a lie. "What I know is, it was my job to keep the peace in Ors. That peace was threatened and I acted to..." She stopped, realizing perhaps that the sentence would be an awkward one to finish. "It was my job to protect the citizens in Ors."

"Which is why you so vehemently protested the execution of the people who *endangered* the citizens in Ors." Anaander Mianaai's tone was dry, and sardonic.

"They were my responsibility, lord. And as I said at the time, they were under control, we could have held them until reinforcements arrived, very easily. You are the ultimate authority, and of course your orders must be obeyed, but I didn't understand why those people had to die. I still don't understand why they had to die right then." A half-second pause. "I don't need to understand why. I'm here to follow your orders. But I..." She paused again. Swallowed. "My lord, if you suspect anything of me, any wrongdoing or disloyalty, I beg you, have me interrogated when we reach Valskaay."

The same drugs used for aptitudes testing and reeducation could be used for interrogation. A skilled interrogator could pry the most secret thoughts from a person's mind. An unskilled one could throw up irrelevancies and confabulations, could damage her subject nearly as badly as an unskilled reeducator.

What Lieutenant Awn had asked for was something surrounded by legal obligations—not least among them the requirement that two witnesses be present, and Lieutenant Awn would have the right to name one of them.

I saw nausea and terror in her when Anaander Mianaai didn't answer. "My lord, may I speak plainly?"

"By all means, speak plainly," said Anaander Mianaai, dry and bitter.

Lieutenant Awn spoke, terrified, face still to the floor. "It was *you.* You diverted the guns, you planned that mob, with Jen Shinnan. But I don't understand why. It can't have been about me, I'm *nobody.*"

"But you do not intend to *remain* nobody, I think," replied Anaander Mianaai. "Your pursuit of Skaaiat Awer tells me as much."

"My..." Lieutenant Awn swallowed. "I never pursued her. We were *friends*. She oversaw the next district."

"Friends, you call that."

Lieutenant Awn's face heated. And she remembered her

accent, and her diction. "I am not presumptuous enough to call it more." Miserable. Frightened.

Mianaai was silent for three seconds, and then said, "Perhaps not. Skaaiat Awer is handsome and charming, and no doubt good in bed. Someone like you would be easily susceptible to her manipulation. I have suspected Awer's disloyalty for some time."

Lieutenant Awn wanted to speak, I could see the muscles in her throat tense, but no sound came out.

"I am, yes, speaking of sedition. You say you're loyal. And yet you associate with Skaaiat Awer." Anaander Mianaai gestured and Skaaiat's voice sounded in the decade room.

"I know you, *Awn. If you're going to do something that crazy, save it for when it'll make a difference."*

And Lieutenant Awn's reply: "*Like* Mercy of Sarrse *One Amaat One?*"

"What difference," asked Anaander Mianaai, "would you wish to make?"

"The sort of difference," Lieutenant Awn replied, mouth gone dry, "that *Mercy of Sarrse* soldier made. If she hadn't done what she did, all the business at Ime would still be going on." As she spoke I'm sure she realized what it was she was saying. That this was dangerous territory. Her next words made it plain she *did* know. "She died for it, yes. But she revealed all that corruption to you."

I had had a week to think about the things Anaander Mianaai had said to me. By now I had worked out how the governor of Ime might have had the accesses that prevented Ime Station from reporting her activities. She could only have gotten those accesses from Anaander Mianaai herself. The only question was, which Anaander Mianaai had enabled it?

"It was on all the public news channels," Anaander

Mianaai observed. "I would have preferred it wasn't. Oh, yes," she said, in answer to Lieutenant Awn's surprise. "That wasn't by my desire. The entire incident has sown doubt where before there was none. Discontent and fear where there had been only confidence in my ability to provide justice and benefit.

"Rumors I could have dealt with, but reports through approved channels! Broadcast where every Radchaai could see and hear! And without the publicity I might have let the Rrrrrr take the traitors away quietly. Instead I had to negotiate for their return, or else let them stand as an invitation to further mutiny. It caused me a great deal of trouble. It's *still* causing trouble."

"I didn't realize," said Lieutenant Awn, panic in her voice. "It was on all the public channels." Then realization struck her. "I haven't...I haven't said anything about Ors. To anyone."

"Except Skaaiat Awer," the Lord of the Radch pointed out. Which was hardly just—Lieutenant Skaaiat had been nearby, close enough to see with her own eyes the evidence that something had happened. "No," Mianaai continued, in answer to Lieutenant Awn's inarticulate query, "it hasn't turned up on public channels. Yet. And I can see that the idea that Skaaiat Awer might be a traitor is distressing to you. I think you're having trouble believing it."

Once again, Lieutenant Awn struggled to speak. "That is correct, my lord," she finally managed.

"I can offer you," said Mianaai in reply, "the opportunity to prove her innocence. And to better your situation. I can manipulate your assignment so that you can be close to her again. You need only take clientship when Skaaiat offers—oh, she'll offer," the Lord of the Radch said, seeing,

I'm sure, Lieutenant Awn's despair and doubt at her words. "Awer has been collecting people like you. Upstarts from previously unremarkable houses who suddenly find themselves in positions advantageous for business. Take clientship, and observe." *And report* was left unsaid.

The Lord of the Radch was trying to turn her enemy's instrument into her own. What would happen if she couldn't do that?

But what would happen if she did? No matter what choice Lieutenant Awn made now, she would be acting against Anaander Mianaai, the Lord of the Radch.

I had already seen her choice once, when faced with death. She would choose the path that kept her alive. And she—and I—could puzzle out the implications of that path later, would see what the options were when matters were less immediately urgent.

In the Esk decade room Lieutenant Dariet asked, alarmed, "Ship, what's wrong with One Esk?"

"My lord," said Lieutenant Awn, her voice shaking with fear, face, as ever, to the floor. "Do you order me?"

"Stand by, Lieutenant," I said, directly into Lieutenant Dariet's ear, because I could not make One Esk speak.

Anaander Mianaai laughed, short and sharp. Lieutenant Awn's answer had been as bald a refusal as a plain *Never* would have been. Ordering such a thing would be useless.

"Interrogate me when we reach Valskaay," Lieutenant Awn said. "I demand it. I am loyal. So is Skaaiat Awer, I swear it, but if you doubt her, interrogate her as well."

But of course Anaander Mianaai couldn't do that. Any interrogation would have witnesses. Any skilled interrogator—and there would be no point in using an unskilled one—would hardly fail to understand the drift of the questions put to either Lieutenant Awn or Lieutenant Skaaiat. It would be too open a move, spread information this Mianaai didn't want spread.

Anaander Mianaai sat silent for four seconds. Impassive.

"One Var," she said, when those four seconds had passed, "shoot Lieutenant Awn."

I was not, now, a single fragmentary segment, alone and unsure what I might do if I received that order. I was all of myself. Taken as separate from me, One Esk was fonder of Lieutenant Awn than I was. But One Esk was not separate from me. It was, at the moment, very much part of me.

Still, One Esk was only one small part of me. And I had shot officers before. I had even, under orders, shot my own captain. But those executions, distressing and unpleasant as they had been, had clearly been just. The penalty for disobedience is death.

Lieutenant Awn had never disobeyed. Far from it. And worse, her death was meant to hide the actions of Anaander Mianaai's enemy. The entire purpose of my existence was to oppose Anaander Mianaai's enemies.

But neither Mianaai was ready to move openly. I must conceal from this Mianaai the fact that she herself had already bound me to the opposing cause, until all was in readiness. I must, for the moment, obey as though I had no other choice, as though I desired nothing else. And in the end, in the great scheme of things, what was Lieutenant Awn, after all? Her parents would grieve, and her sister, and they would likely be ashamed that Lieutenant Awn had disgraced them by disobedience. But they wouldn't question. And if they questioned, it would do no good. Anaander Mianaai's secret would be safe.

All this I thought in the 1.3 seconds it took for Lieutenant Awn, shocked and terrified, to reflexively raise her head. And in that same time, the segment of One Var said, "I am unarmed, my lord. It will take me approximately two minutes to acquire a sidearm."

It was betrayal, to Lieutenant Awn, I saw it plainly. But she must have known I had no other choice. "This is unjust," she said, head still up. Voice unsteady. "It's improper. No benefit will accrue."

"Who are your fellow conspirators?" asked Mianaai, coldly. "Name them and I may spare your life."

Half lifted up, hands under her shoulders, Lieutenant Awn blinked in complete confusion, bewilderment that was surely as visible to Mianaai as it was to me. "Conspirators? I have never conspired with anyone. I have always served you."

Above, on the command deck, I said in Captain Rubran's ear, "Captain, we have a problem."

"Serving me," said Anaander Mianaai, "is no longer sufficient. No longer sufficiently unambiguous. Which *me* do you serve?"

"Wh—" began Lieutenant Awn, and "Th—" And then, "I don't understand."

"What problem?" asked Captain Rubran, bowl of tea halfway to her mouth, only mildly alarmed.

"I am at war with myself," said Mianaai, in the Var decade room. "I have been for nearly a thousand years."

To Captain Rubran I said, "I need One Esk to be sedated."

"At war," Anaander Mianaai continued on Var deck, "over the future of the Radch."

Something must have come suddenly clear for Lieutenant Awn. I saw a sharp, pure rage in her. "Annexations and ancillaries, and people like *me* being assigned to the military."

"I don't understand you, Ship," said Captain Rubran, her voice even but definitely worried now. She set down her tea on the table beside her.

"Over the treaty with the Presger," said Mianaai, angrily. "The rest followed from that. Whether you know it or not, you are the instrument of my enemy."

"And *Mercy of Sarrse* One Amaat One exposed whatever it was you were doing at Ime," said Lieutenant Awn, her anger still clear and steady. "That was *you*. The system governor was making ancillaries—you needed them for your war with yourself, didn't you. And I'm sure that's not all she was doing for you. Is that why that soldier had to die even if it meant extra trouble getting her back from the Rrrrrr? And I..."

"I'm still standing by, Ship," said Lieutenant Dariet, in the Esk decade room. "But I don't like this."

"*Mercy of Sarrse* One Amaat One knew almost nothing, but in the hands of the Rrrrrr, she was a piece that my enemy might use against me. As an officer on a troop carrier, *you* are nothing, but in a position of even minor planetary authority, with the potential backing of Skaaiat Awer to help you increase your influence, you are a potential danger to me. I could have just maneuvered you out of Ors, out of Awer's way. But I wanted more. I wanted a graphic argument against recent decisions and policies. Had that fisherman not found the guns, or not reported them to you, had events that night gone as I wished, I would have made sure the story was on all the public channels. In one gesture I would have secured the loyalty of the Tanmind and removed someone troublesome to me, both minor aims, but I also would have been able to impress on everyone the danger of lowering our guard, of disarming in even a small way. And the danger of placing authority in less-than-competent hands." She made a short, bitter *ha*. "I admit, I underestimated you. Underestimated your relationship with the Orsians in the lower city."

One Var could delay no longer, and walked into the Var

decade room, gun in hand. Lieutenant Awn heard it come in, turned her head slightly to watch it. "It was my job, to protect the citizens of Ors. I took it seriously. I did it to the best of my ability. I failed, that once. But not because of you." She turned her head, looked straight at Anaander Mianaai, and said, "I should have died rather than obey you, in the temple of Ikkt. Even if it wouldn't have done any good."

"You can fix that now, can't you," said Anaander Mianaai, and gave me the order to fire.

I fired.

Twenty years later, I would say to Arilesperas Strigan that Radchaai authorities didn't care what a citizen thought, so long as she did as she ought to do. It was quite true. But since that moment, since I saw Lieutenant Awn dead on the floor of my Var decade room, shot by One Var (or, to speak with less self-deception, by me) I have wondered what the difference is between the two.

I was compelled to obey this Mianaai, in order to lead her to believe that she did indeed compel me. But in that case, she *did* compel me. Acting for one Mianaai or the other was indistinguishable. And of course, in the end, whatever their differences, they were both the same.

Thoughts are ephemeral, they evaporate in the moment they occur, unless they are given action and material form. Wishes and intentions, the same. Meaningless, unless they impel you to one choice or another, some deed or course of action, however insignificant. Thoughts that lead to action can be dangerous. Thoughts that do not, mean less than nothing.

Lieutenant Awn lay on the floor of the Var decade room, face-down again, dead. The floor under her would need repair, and cleaning. The urgent issue, the important thing, at that moment, was to get One Esk moving because in approximately half a second no amount of filtering I could do would hide the strength of its reaction and I really needed to tell the captain what had happened and I couldn't remember Mianaai's enemy—Mianaai herself—laying down the orders I knew she had laid on me and why couldn't One Esk see how important it was, we weren't ready to move openly yet and I'd lost officers before and who was One Esk anyway except me, myself, and Lieutenant Awn was dead and she had said, *I should have died rather than obey you.*

And then One Var swung the gun up and shot Anaander Mianaai point-blank in the face.

In a room down the corridor, Anaander Mianaai leaped with a cry of rage off the bed she'd been lying on. "Aatr's tits, *she was here before me*!" In the same moment she transmitted the code that would force One Var's armor down, until she reauthorized its use. It was a command that didn't rely on my obedience, an override neither Anaander would have wanted to do away with.

"Captain," I said, "now we *really* have a problem."

In another room down the same corridor, the third Mianaai—the second, now, I suppose—opened one of the cases she had brought with her and pulled out a sidearm, and stepped quickly into the corridor and shot the nearest One Var in the back of the head. The one who had spoken opened her own case, pulled out a sidearm and also a box I recognized from Jen Shinnan's house, in the upper city, on Shis'urna. Using it would disadvantage her as well as me, but it would disadvantage me badly. In the seconds she took to arm the device I formed intentions, transmitted orders to constituent parts.

"What problem?" asked Captain Rubran, now standing. Afraid.

And then I fell to pieces.

A familiar sensation. For the smallest fragment of a second I smelled humid air and lake water, thought, *Where's Lieutenant Awn?* and then I recovered myself, and the memory of what I had to do. Tea bowls rang and shattered as I dropped what I was holding and ran from the Esk decade room, down the corridor. Other segments, separated from me again as they had been in Ors, muttering, whispering, the only way I could think between all my bodies, opened lockers, handed guns, and the first to be armed forced the lift doors open and began to climb down the shaft. Lieutenants protested, ordered me to stop, to explain. Tried fruitlessly to block my way.

I—that is, almost the entirety of One Esk—would secure the central access deck, prevent Anaander Mianaai from damaging my—*Justice of Toren*'s—brain. So long as *Justice of Toren* lived, unconverted to her cause, it—I—was a danger to her.

I—One Esk Nineteen—had separate orders. Instead of climbing down the shaft to central access I ran the other way, toward the Esk hold and the airlock on its far side.

I wasn't, apparently, responding to any of my lieutenants, or even Commander Tiaund, but when Lieutenant Dariet cried, "Ship! Have you lost your mind?" I answered.

"The Lord of the Radch shot Lieutenant Awn!" cried a segment somewhere in the corridor behind me. "She's been on Var deck all this time."

That silenced my officers—including Lieutenant Dariet—for only a second.

"If that's even true...but if it is, the Lord of the Radch wouldn't have shot her for no reason."

Behind me the segments of myself that hadn't yet begun their climb down the lift shaft hissed and gasped in frustration and anger. "Useless!" I heard myself say to Lieutenant Dariet as at the end of the corridor I manually opened the hold door. "You're as bad as Lieutenant Issaaia! At least Lieutenant Awn *knew* she held her in contempt!"

An indignant cry, surely Lieutenant Issaaia, and Dariet said, "You don't know what you're talking about. You're not functioning right, Ship!"

The door slid open, and I could not stop to hear the rest, but plunged into the hold. A deep, steady thunking shook the deck I ran on, a sound just hours ago I thought I would never hear again. Mianaai was opening the Var holds. Any ancillary she thawed would have no memory of recent events, nothing to tell it not to obey this Mianaai. And its armor wouldn't have been disabled.

She would take Two Var and Three and Four and as many as she had time to awaken, and try to take either the central access deck or the engines. More likely both. She had, after all, Var and every hold below it. Though the segments would be clumsy and confused. They would have no memory of functioning apart, the way I had, no practice. But numbers were on her side. I had only the segments that had been awake at the moment I fragmented.

Above, my officers had access to the upper half of the holds. And they would have no reason not to obey Anaander Mianaai, no reason not to think I had lost my mind. I was, at this moment, explaining matters to Hundred Captain Rubran, but I had no confidence she would believe me, or think me even remotely sane.

Around me, the same thunking began that was sounding below my feet. My officers were pulling up Esk segments to thaw. I reached the airlock, threw open the locker beside it, pulled out the pieces of the vacuum suit that would fit this segment.

I didn't know how long I could hold central access, or the engines. I didn't know how desperate Anaander Mianaai might be, what damage she might think I could do to her. The engines' heat shield was, by design, extremely difficult to breach, but I knew how to do it. And the Lord of the Radch certainly did as well.

And whatever happened between here and there, it was a near-certainty I would die shortly after I reached Valskaay, if not before. But I would not die without explaining myself.

I would have to reach and board a shuttle, and then manually undock, and depart *Justice of Toren*—myself—at exactly the right time, at exactly the right speed, on exactly the right heading, fly through the wall of my surrounding bubble of normal space at exactly the right moment.

If I did all that, I would find myself in a system with a gate, four jumps from Irei Palace, one of Anaander Mianaai's provincial headquarters. I could tell her what had happened.

The shuttles were docked on this side of the ship. The hatches and the undocking ought to work smoothly, it was all equipment I had tested and maintained myself. Still, I found myself worrying that something would go wrong. At least it was better than thinking about fighting my own officers. Or the heat shield's failing.

I fastened my helmet. My breath hissed loud in my ears. Faster than it should have. I forced myself to slow my breathing, deepen it. Hyperventilating wouldn't help. I had to move quickly, but not so hastily that I made some fatally foolish mistake.

Waiting for the airlock to cycle, I felt my aloneness like

an impenetrable wall pressing around me. Usually one body's off-kilter emotion was a minor, easily dismissable thing. Now it was *only* this one body, nothing beyond to temper my distress. The rest of me was here, all around, but inaccessible. Soon, if things went right, I wouldn't even be near my self, or have any idea when I might rejoin it. And at this moment I could do nothing but wait. And remember the feel of the gun in One Var's hand—my hand. I was One Esk, but what was the difference? The recoil as One Var shot Lieutenant Awn. The guilt and helpless anger that had overwhelmed me had receded at that moment, overcome by more urgent necessity, but now I had time to remember. My next three breaths were ragged and sobbing. For a moment I was perversely glad I was hidden from myself.

I had to calm myself. Had to clear my mind. I thought of songs I knew. *My heart is a fish*, I thought, but when I opened my mouth to sing it, my throat closed. I swallowed. Breathed. Thought of another one.

Oh, have you gone to the battlefield
Armored and well armed?
And shall dreadful events
Force you to drop your weapons?

The outer door opened. If Mianaai had not used her device, officers on duty would have seen that the lock had opened, would have notified Captain Rubran, drawing Mianaai's attention. But she had used it, and she had no way of knowing what I did. I reached around the doorway for a handhold and pulled myself out.

Looking at the inside of a gateway often made humans queasy. It had never bothered me before, but now I was nothing but a single human body I found it did the same to me. Black, but a black that seemed simultaneously an unthinkable depth into which I might fall, *was* falling, and a suffocating closeness ready to press me into nonexistence.

I forced myself to look away. Here, outside, there was no floor, no gravity generator to keep me in place and give me an up and down. I moved from one handhold to the next. What was happening behind me, inside the ship that was no longer my body?

It took seventeen minutes to reach a shuttle, operate its emergency hatch, and perform a manual undock. At first I fought the desire to halt, to look behind me, to listen for the sounds of someone coming to stop me, never mind I couldn't have heard anything outside my own helmet. *Just maintenance*, I told myself. *Just maintenance outside the hull. You've done it hundreds of times.*

If anyone came I could do nothing. Esk would have failed—*I* would have failed. And my time was limited. I might not be stopped, and still fail. I could not think of any of that.

When the moment came, I was ready and away. My view was limited to fore and aft, the only two hardwired cameras on the shuttle. As *Justice of Toren* receded in the aft view, the rising sense of panic that I had mostly held in check till now overtook me. What was I doing? Where was I going? What could I possibly accomplish alone and single-bodied, deaf and blind and cut off? What could be the point of defying Anaander Mianaai, who had made me, who owned me, who was unutterably more powerful than I would ever be?

I breathed. I would return to the Radch. I would eventually return to *Justice of Toren*, even if only for the last moments of my life. My blindness and deafness were irrelevant. There was only the task before me. There was nothing to do but sit in the pilot's chair and watch *Justice of Toren* get smaller, and farther away. Think of another song.

According to the chronometer, if I had done everything exactly as I should, *Justice of Toren* would disappear from my screen in four minutes and thirty-two seconds. I watched, counting, trying not to think of anything else.

The aft view flashed bright, blue-white, and my breath stopped. When the screen cleared I saw nothing but black—and stars. I had exited my self-made gate.

I had exited more than four minutes too soon. And what had that flash been? I ought only to have seen the ship disappear, the stars suddenly spring into existence.

Mianaai had not attempted to take central access, or join forces with the officers on the upper decks. The moment she realized I had already fallen to her enemy, she must have resolved immediately to take the most desperate course available to her. She and what Var ancillaries she had serving her had taken my engines, and breached the heat shield. How I had escaped and not vaporized along with the rest of the ship, I couldn't account for, but there had been that flash, and here I still was.

Justice of Toren was gone, and all aboard it. I was not where I was supposed to be, might be unreachably distant from Radch space, or any human worlds at all. All possibility of being reunited with myself was gone. The captain was dead. All my officers were dead. Civil war loomed.

I had shot Lieutenant Awn.

Nothing would ever be right again.

17

Luckily for me, I had come out of gate-space on the fringes of a backwater, non-Radchaai system, a collection of habitats and mining stations inhabited by heavily modified people—not human, by Radchaai standards, people with six or eight limbs (and no guarantee any of them would be legs), vacuum-adapted skin and lungs, brains so meshed and crosshatched with implants and wiring it was an open question whether they were anything but conscious machines with a biological interface.

It was a mystery to them that anyone would choose the sort of primitive form most humans I knew were born with. But they prized their isolation, and it was a dearly held tenet of their society that, with a few exceptions (most of which they would not actually admit to), one did not ask for anything a person did not volunteer. They viewed me with a combination of puzzlement and mild contempt, and treated me as though I were a child who had wandered into their midst and they might keep half an eye on me until my parents found me, but really I wasn't their responsibility. If any of them guessed my origin—and surely they did, the shuttle alone was enough—they didn't say so, and no one pressed me for answers, something they would have found appallingly rude. They were silent, clannish, self-contained, but they were also brusquely generous at unpredictable intervals. I would still be there, or dead, if not for that.

I spent six months trying to understand how to do anything—not just how to get my message to the Lord of the Radch, but how to walk and breathe and sleep and eat as myself. As a *myself* that was only a fragment of what I had been, with no conceivable future beyond eternally wishing for what was gone. Then one day a human ship arrived, and the captain was happy to take me on board in exchange for what little money I had left from scrapping the shuttle, which had been running up docking charges I couldn't pay otherwise. I found out later that a four-meter, tentacled eel of a person had paid the balance of my fare without telling me, because, she had told the captain, I didn't belong there and would be healthier elsewhere. Odd people, as I said, and I owe them a great deal, though they would be offended and distressed to think anyone owed them anything.

In the nineteen years since then, I had learned eleven languages and 713 songs. I had found ways to conceal what I was—even, I was fairly sure, from the Lord of the Radch herself. I had worked as a cook, a janitor, a pilot. I had settled on a plan of action. I had joined a religious order, and made a great deal of money. In all that time I only killed a dozen people.

By the time I woke the next morning, the impulse to tell Seivarden anything had passed, and she seemed to have forgotten her questions. Except one. "So where next?" She asked it casually, sitting on the bench by my bed, leaning against the wall, as though she were only idly curious about the answer.

When she heard, maybe she'd decide she liked it better on her own. "Omaugh Palace."

She frowned, just slightly. "That a new one?"

"Not particularly." It had been built seven hundred years ago. "But after Garsedd, yes." My right ankle began to tingle and itch, a sure sign the corrective was finished. "You left Radchaai space unauthorized. And you sold your armor to do it."

"Extraordinary circumstances," she said, still leaning back. "I'll appeal."

"That'll get you a delay, at any rate." Any citizen who wanted to see the Lord of the Radch could apply to do so, though the farther one was from a provincial palace, the more complicated, expensive, and time-consuming the journey would be. Sometimes applications were turned down, when the distance was great and the cause was judged hopeless or frivolous—and the petitioner was unable to pay her own way. But Anaander Mianaai was the final appeal for nearly any matter, and this case was certainly not routine. And she would be right there on the station. "You'll wait months for an audience."

Seivarden gestured her lack of concern. "What are you going to do there?"

Try to kill Anaander Mianaai. But I couldn't say that. "See the sights. Buy some souvenirs. Maybe try to meet the Lord of the Radch."

She lifted an eyebrow. Then she looked at my pack. She knew about the gun, and of course she understood how dangerous it was. She still thought I was an agent of the Radch. "Undercover the whole way? And when you hand that"—she shrugged toward my pack—"over to the Lord of the Radch, then what?"

"I don't know." I closed my eyes. I could see no further than arriving at Omaugh Palace, had not even the remotest shadow of an idea of what to do after that, how I might get close enough to Anaander Mianaai to use the gun.

No. That wasn't true. The beginning of a plan had this moment suggested itself to me, but it was horribly impractical, relying as it did on Seivarden's discretion and support.

She had constructed her own idea of what I was doing and why I would return to the Radch playing a foreign tourist. Why I would report directly to Anaander Mianaai instead of a Special Missions officer. I could use that.

"I'm coming with you," Seivarden said, and as though she had guessed my thoughts she added, "You can come to my appeal and speak on my behalf."

I didn't trust myself to answer. Pins and needles traveled up my right leg, started in my hands, arms, and shoulders, and my left leg. A slight ache began in my right hip. Something hadn't healed quite right.

"It's not as if I don't already know what's going on," Seivarden said.

"So when you steal from me, breaking your legs won't be enough. I'll have to kill you." My eyes still closed, I couldn't see her reaction to that. She might well take it as a joke.

"I won't," she answered. "You'll see."

I spent several more days in Therrod recovering sufficiently that the doctor would approve my leaving. All that time, and afterward all the way up the ribbon, Seivarden was polite and deferential.

It worried me. I had stashed money and belongings at the

top of the Nilt ribbon, and would have to retrieve them before we left. Everything was packaged, so I could do that without Seivarden seeing much more than a couple of boxes, but I had no illusions she wouldn't try to open them first chance she got.

At least I had money again. And maybe that was the solution to the problem.

I took a room on the ribbon station, left Seivarden there with instructions to wait, and went to recover my possessions. When I returned she was sitting on the single bed—no linens or blankets, that was conventionally extra here—fidgeting. One knee bouncing, rubbing her upper arms with her bare hands—I had sold our heavy outer coats, and the gloves, at the foot of the ribbon. She stilled when I came in, and looked expectantly at me, but said nothing.

I tossed into her lap a bag that made a tumbling clicking sound as it landed.

Seivarden gave it one frowning look, and then turned her gaze to me, not moving to touch the bag or claim it in any way. "What's this?"

"Ten thousand shen," I said. It was the most commonly negotiable currency in this region, in easily transportable (and spent) chits. Ten thousand would buy a lot, here. It would buy passage to another system with enough left over to binge for several weeks.

"Is that a lot?"

"Yes."

Her eyes widened, just slightly, and for half a second I saw calculation in her expression.

Time for me to be direct. "The room is paid up for the next ten days. After that—" I gestured at the bag on her lap. "That should last you a while. Longer if you're truly serious about staying off kef." But that look, when she'd realized she had access to money, made me fairly certain she wasn't. Not really.

For six seconds Seivarden looked down at the bag in her lap. "No." She picked the bag up gingerly, between her thumb and forefinger, as though it were a dead rat, and dropped it on the floor. "I'm coming with you."

I didn't answer, only looked at her. Silence stretched out.

Finally she looked away, crossed her arms. "Isn't there any tea?"

"Not the sort you're used to."

"I don't care."

Well. I didn't want to leave her here alone with my money and possessions. "Come on, then."

We left the room, found a shop on the main corridor that sold things for flavoring hot water. Seivarden sniffed one of the blends on offer. Wrinkled her nose. "This is *tea*?"

The shop's proprietor watched us from the corner of her vision, not wanting to seem to watch us. "I told you it wasn't the sort you were used to. You said you didn't care."

She thought about that a moment. To my utter surprise, instead of arguing, or complaining further about the unsatisfactory nature of the tea in question, she said, calmly, "What do you recommend?"

I gestured my uncertainty. "I'm not in the habit of drinking tea."

"Not in the..." She stared at me. "Oh. Don't they drink tea in the Gerentate?"

"Not the way you people do." And of course tea was for officers. For humans. Ancillaries drank water. Tea was an extra, unnecessary expense. A luxury. So I had never developed the habit. I turned to the proprietor, a Nilter, short and pale and fat, in shirtsleeves though the temperature here was a constant four C and Seivarden and I both still wore our inner coats. "Which of these has caffeine in it?"

She answered, pleasantly enough, and became pleasanter when I bought not only 250 grams each of two kinds of tea but also a flask with two cups, and two bottles, along with water to fill them.

Seivarden carried the whole lot back to our lodging, walking alongside me saying nothing. In the room she laid our purchases on the bed, sat down beside them, and picked up the flask, puzzling over the unfamiliar design.

I could have showed her how it worked, but decided not to. Instead I opened my newly claimed luggage and dug out a thick golden disk three centimeters larger in diameter than the one I had carried with me, and a small, shallow bowl of hammered gold, eight centimeters in diameter. I closed the trunk, set the bowl on it, and triggered the image in the disk.

Seivarden looked up to watch it unfold into a wide, flat flower in mother-of-pearl, a woman standing in its center. She wore a knee-length robe of the same iridescent white, inlaid with gold and silver. In one hand she held a human skull, itself inlaid with jewels, red and blue and yellow, and in the other hand a knife.

"That's like the other one," Seivarden said, sounding mildly interested. "But it doesn't look so much like you."

"True," I answered, and sat cross-legged before the trunk.

"Is that a Gerentate god?"

"It's one I met, traveling."

Seivarden made a breathy, noncommittal noise. "What's its name?"

I spoke the long string of syllables, which left Seivarden nonplussed. "It means *She Who Sprang from the Lily*. She is the creator of the universe." This would make her Amaat, in Radchaai terms.

"Ah," said Seivarden, in a tone I knew meant she'd made that equation, made the strange god familiar and brought it safely within her mental framework. "And the other one?"

"A saint."

"What a remarkable thing, that she should resemble you so much."

"Yes. Although she's not the saint. The head she's holding is."

Seivarden blinked, frowned. It was very un-Radchaai. "Still."

Nothing was just a coincidence, not for Radchaai. Such odd chances could—and did—send Radchaai on pilgrimages, motivate them to worship particular gods, change entrenched habits. They were direct messages from Amaat. "I'm going to pray now," I said.

With one hand Seivarden made a gesture of acknowledgment. I unfolded a small knife, pricked my thumb, and bled into the gold bowl. I didn't look to see Seivarden's reaction—no Radchaai god took blood, and I hadn't troubled to wash my hands first. It was guaranteed to lift Radchaai eyebrows, to register as foreign and even primitive.

But Seivarden didn't say anything. She sat silent for thirty-one seconds as I intoned the first of the 322 names of the Hundred of White Lily, and then she turned her attention to the flask, and making tea.

Seivarden had said she'd lasted six months at her last attempt to quit kef. It took seven months to reach a station with a Radchaai consulate. Approaching the first leg of the journey, I had told the purser in Seivarden's hearing that I wanted passage for myself and my servant. She hadn't reacted, that I could see. Perhaps she hadn't understood. But I had expected a more or less angry recrimination in private when she discovered her status, and she never mentioned it. And from then on I woke to find tea already made and waiting for me.

She also ruined two shirts attempting to launder them, leaving me with one for an entire month until we docked at the next station. The ship's captain—she was Ki, tall and covered in ritual scars—let fall in an oblique, circuitous way that she and all her crew thought I'd taken Seivarden on as a charity case. Which wasn't far from the truth. I didn't contest it. But Seivarden improved, and three months later, on the next ship, a fellow passenger tried to hire her away from me.

Which wasn't to say she had suddenly become a different person, or entirely deferential. Some days she spoke irritably to me, for no reason I could see, or spent hours curled in her bunk, her face to the wall, rising only for her self-imposed duties. The first few times I spoke to her when she was in that mood I only received silence in reply, so after that I left her alone.

The Radchaai consulate was staffed by the Translators Office, and the consular agent's spotless white uniform—including pristine white gloves—argued she either had a servant or spent a good deal of her free time attempting to appear as though she did. The tasteful—and expensive-looking—jeweled strands wound in her hair, and the names on the memorial pins that glittered everywhere on the white jacket, as well as the faint disdain in her voice when she spoke to me, argued *servant*. Though likely only one—this was an out-of-the-way posting.

"As a visiting noncitizen your legal rights are restricted."

It was clearly a rote speech. "You must deposit at minimum the equivalent of—" Fingers twitched as she checked the exchange rate. "Five hundred shen per week of your visit, per person. If your lodging, food, and any extra purchases, fines, or damages exceed the amount on deposit and you cannot pay the balance, you will be legally obligated to take an assignment until your debt is paid. As a noncitizen your right to appeal any judgment or assignment is limited. Do you still wish to enter Radch space?"

"I do," I said, and laid two million-shen chits on the slim desk between us.

Her disdain vanished. She sat slightly straighter and offered me tea, gesturing slightly, fingers twitching again as she communicated with someone else—her servant, it turned out, who, with a slightly harried air, brought tea in an elaborately enameled flask, and bowls to match.

While the servant poured, I brought out my forged Gerentate credentials and placed those on the desk as well.

"You must also provide identification for your servant, honored," said the consular agent, now all politeness.

"My servant is a Radchaai citizen," I answered, smiling slightly. Meaning to take the edge off what was going to be an awkward moment. "But she's lost her identification and her travel permits."

The consular agent froze, attempting to process that.

"The honored Breq," said Seivarden, standing behind me, in antique, effortlessly elegant Radchaai, "has been generous enough to employ me and pay my passage home."

This didn't resolve the consular agent's astonished paralysis quite as effectively as Seivarden perhaps had wished. That accent didn't belong on anyone's servant, let alone a noncitizen's. And she hadn't offered Seivarden a seat, or tea, thinking her too insignificant for such courtesies.

"Surely you can take genetic information," I suggested.

"Yes, of course," answered the consular agent, with a sunny smile. "Though your visa application will almost certainly come through before Citizen..."

"Seivarden," I supplied.

"...before Citizen Seivarden's travel permits are reissued. Depending on where she departed from and where her records are."

"Of course," I answered, and sipped my tea. "That's only to be expected."

As we left, Seivarden said to me, in an undertone, "What a snob. Was that real tea?"

"It was." I waited for her to complain about not having had any, but she said nothing more. "It was very good. What are you going to do if an arrest order comes through instead of travel permits?"

She made a gesture of denial. "Why should they? I'm already asking to come back, they can arrest me when I get there. And I'll appeal. Do you think the consul has that tea shipped from home, or might someone here sell it?"

"Find out, if you like," I said. "I'm going back to the room to meditate."

The consular agent's servant outright gave Seivarden half a kilo of tea, likely grateful for the opportunity to make up for her employer's unintentional slight earlier. And when my visa came through, so did travel permits for Seivarden, and no arrest order, or any additional comment or information at all.

That worried me, if only slightly. But likely Seivarden was right—why do anything else? When she stepped off the ship there would be time and opportunity enough to address her legal troubles.

Still. It was possible Radch authorities had realized I wasn't actually a citizen of the Gerentate. It was unlikely—the Gerentate was a long, long way from where I was going, and besides, despite fairly friendly—or at least, not openly antagonistic—relations between the Gerentate and the Radch, as a matter of policy the Gerentate didn't supply any information at all about its residents—not to the Radch. If the Radch asked—and they wouldn't—the Gerentate would neither confirm nor deny that I was one of its citizens. Had I been departing from the Gerentate for Radchaai space I would have been warned repeatedly that I traveled at my own risk and would receive no assistance if I found myself in difficulties. But the Radchaai officials who dealt with foreign travelers knew this already, and would be prepared to take my identification more or less at face value.

Anaander Mianaai's thirteen palaces were the capitals of their provinces. Metropolis-size stations, each one half ordinary large Radchaai station—with accompanying station AI—and half palace proper. Each palace proper was the residence of Anaander Mianaai, and the seat of provincial administration. Omaugh Palace wouldn't be any sort of quiet backwater. A dozen gates led to its system, and hundreds of ships came and went each day. Seivarden would be one of thousands of citizens seeking audience, or making an appeal in some legal case. A noticeable one, certainly—none of those other citizens were returned from a thousand years in suspension.

I spent the months of travel considering just what I wanted to do about that. How to use it. How to counter its disadvantages, or turn them to my favor. And considering just what it was I hoped to accomplish.

It's hard for me to know how much of myself I remember. How much I might have known, that I had hidden from myself all my life. Take, for instance, that last order, the instruction I–*Justice of Toren* had given to me–One Esk Nineteen. *Get to Irei Palace, find Anaander Mianaai, and tell her what's happened.* What did I mean by that? Over and above the obvious, the bare fact I'd wanted to get the message to the Lord of the Radch?

Why had it been so important? Because it had been. It hadn't been an afterthought, it had been an urgent necessity. At the time it had seemed clear. Of *course* I needed to get the message out, of course I needed to warn the right Anaander.

I would follow my orders. But in the time I'd spent recovering from my own death, the time working my way toward Radch space, I had decided I would do something else as well. I would defy the Lord of the Radch. And perhaps my defiance would amount to nothing, a feeble gesture she would barely notice.

The truth was, Strigan was right. My desire to kill Anaander Mianaai was unreasonable. Any actual attempt to do such a thing was not sane. Even given a gun that I could carry into the very presence of the Lord of the Radch herself without her knowing until I chose to reveal it—even given that, all I could hope to accomplish was a pitiful cry of defiance, gone as soon as made, easily disregarded. Nothing that could possibly make any difference.

But. All that secret maneuvering against herself. Designed, certainly, to avoid open conflict, to avoid damaging the Radch too badly. To avoid, perhaps, too badly fracturing Anaander Mianaai's conviction that she was unitary, one person. Once the dilemma had been clearly stated, could she pretend things were otherwise?

And if there were now two Anaander Mianaais, might there not also be more? A part, perhaps, that didn't know about the feuding sides of herself? Or told herself she didn't? What would happen if I said straight out the thing the Lord of the Radch had been concealing from herself? Something dire, surely, or she would not have gone to such lengths to hide herself from herself. Once the thing was open and acknowledged, how could she help tearing herself apart?

But how could I say anything straight out to Anaander Mianaai? Granted I could reach Omaugh Palace, granted I could leave the ship, step onto the station—if I could do that much then I could stand in the middle of the main concourse and shout my story aloud for everyone to hear.

I might begin to do that, but I would never finish. Security would come for me, maybe even soldiers, and that day's news would say a traveler had lost her mind on the concourse, but Security had dealt with the situation. Citizens would shake their heads, and mutter about uncivilized foreigners, and then forget all about me. And whichever part of the Lord of the Radch noticed me first could no doubt easily dismiss me as damaged and insane—or at least, convince the various other parts of herself that I was.

No, I needed the full attention of Anaander Mianaai, when I said what I had to say. How to get it was a problem I had worried at for nearly twenty years. I knew that it would be harder to ignore someone whose erasure would be noticed. I could visit the station and try to be seen, to become familiar, so that any part of Anaander couldn't just dispose of me without comment. But I didn't think that would be enough to force the Lord of the Radch—all of the Lord of the Radch—to listen to me.

But Seivarden. Captain Seivarden Vendaai, lost a thousand years, found by chance, lost again. Appearing now at Omaugh Palace. Any Radchaai would be curious about that, with a curiosity that carried a religious charge. And Anaander Mianaai was Radchaai. Perhaps the most Radchaai of Radchaai. She couldn't help but notice that I had returned in company with Seivarden. Like any other citizen she would wonder, even if only at the back of her mind, what, if anything, that might mean. And she being who she was, the back of her mind was a substantial thing.

Seivarden would ask for an audience. Would be, eventually, granted one. And that audience would have all of Anaander's attention; no part of her would ignore such an event.

And surely Seivarden would have the attention of the Lord of the Radch from the moment we stepped off the ship. So, arriving in Seivarden's company, would I. Tremendously risky. I might not have concealed my nature well enough, might be recognized for what I was. But I was determined to try.

I sat on the bunk waiting for permission to leave the ship at Omaugh Palace, my pack at my feet, Seivarden leaning negligently against the wall across from me, bored.

"Something's bothering you," Seivarden observed, casually. I didn't answer, and she said, "You always hum that tune when you're preoccupied."

My heart is a fish, hiding in the water-grass. I had been thinking of all the ways things could go wrong, starting now, starting the moment I stepped off the ship and confronted the dock inspectors. Or Station Security. Or worse. Thinking of how everything I had done would be for nothing if I was arrested before I could even leave the docks.

And I had been thinking about Lieutenant Awn. "I'm so transparent?" I made myself smile, as though I were mildly amused.

"Not transparent. Not exactly. Just..." She hesitated. Frowned slightly, as though she'd suddenly regretted speaking. "You have a few habits I've noticed, that's all." She sighed. "Are the dock inspectors having tea? Or just waiting till we've aged sufficiently?" We couldn't leave the ship without the permission of the Inspector's Office. The inspector would have received our credentials when the ship requested permission to dock, and had plenty of time to look over them and decide what to do when we arrived.

Still leaning against the bulkhead, Seivarden closed her eyes and began to hum. Wobbling, pitch sinking or rising by turns as she mis-sang intervals. But still recognizable. *My heart is a fish.* "Aatr's tits," she swore after a verse and a half, eyes still closed. "Now you've got me doing it."

The door chime sounded. "Enter," I said. Seivarden opened her eyes, sat straight. Suddenly tense. The boredom had been a pose, I suspected.

The door slid open to reveal a person in the dark-blue jacket, gloves, and trousers of a dock inspector. She was slight, and young, maybe twenty-three or -four. She looked familiar, though I couldn't think who it was she reminded me of. The sparser-than-usual scatter of jewelry and memorial pins might tell me, if I stared closely enough to read names. Which would be rude. Across from me, Seivarden tucked her bare hands behind her back.

"Honored Breq," the inspector adjunct said, with a slight

bow. She seemed unfazed by my own bare hands. Used to dealing with foreigners, I supposed. “Citizen Seivarden. Would you please accompany me to the inspector supervisor’s office?”

And there should have been no need for us to visit the inspector supervisor herself. This adjunct could pass us onto the station on her own authority. Or order our arrest.

We followed her past the lock into the loading bay, past another lock into a corridor busy with people—dock inspectors in dark blue, Station Security in light brown, here and there the darker brown of soldiers, and spots of brighter color—a scatter of non-uniformed citizens. This corridor opened into a wide room, a dozen gods along the walls to watch over travelers and traders, on one end the entrance to the station proper, and opposite, the doorway into the inspector’s office.

The adjunct escorted us through the outermost office, where nine blue-uniformed minor adjuncts dealt with complaining ship captains, and beyond them were offices for likely a dozen major adjuncts and their crews. Past those and into an inner office, with four chairs and a small table, and a door at the back, closed.

“I am sorry, cit... honored, and citizen,” said the adjunct who had led us here, fingers twitching as she communicated with someone—likely the station AI, or the inspector supervisor herself. “The inspector supervisor *was* available, but something’s come up. I’m sure it won’t be more than a few minutes. Please have a seat. Will you have tea?”

A reasonably long wait, then. And the courtesy of tea implied this wasn’t an arrest. That no one had discovered my credentials were forged. Everyone here—including Station—would assume I was what I said I was, a foreign traveler.

And possibly I would have a chance to discover just who this young inspector adjunct reminded me of. Now she'd spoken at a bit more length, I noticed a slight accent. Where was she from? "Yes, thank you," I said.

Seivarden didn't respond to the offer of tea right away. Her arms were folded, her bare hands tucked under her elbows. She likely wanted the tea but was embarrassed about her ungloved hands, couldn't hide them holding a bowl. Or so I thought until she said, "I can't understand a word she's saying."

Seivarden's accent and way of speaking would be familiar to most educated Radchaai, from old entertainments and the way Anaander Mianaai's speech was widely emulated by prestigious—or hopefully prestigious—families. I hadn't thought changes in pronunciation and vocabulary had been so extreme. But I'd lived through them, and Seivarden's ear for language had never been the sharpest. "She's offering tea."

"Oh." Seivarden looked briefly at her crossed arms. "No."

I took the tea the adjunct poured from a flask on the table, thanked her, and took a seat. The office had been painted a pale green, the floor tiled with something that had probably been intended to look like wood and might have succeeded if the designer had ever seen anything but imitations of imitations. A niche in the wall behind the young adjunct held an icon of Amaat and a small bowl of bright-orange, ruffle-petaled flowers. And beside that, a tiny brass copy of the cliffside in the temple of Ikkt. You could buy them, I knew, from vendors in the plaza in front of the Fore-Temple water, during pilgrimage season.

I looked at the adjunct again. Who was she? Someone I knew? A relative of someone I'd met?

"You're humming again," Seivarden said in an undertone.

"Excuse me." I took a sip of tea. "It's a habit I have. I apologize."

"No need," said the adjunct, and took her own seat by the table. This was, fairly clearly, her own office and so she was direct assistant to the inspector supervisor—an unusual place for someone so young. "I haven't heard that song since I was a child."

Seivarden blinked, not understanding. If she had, she likely would have smiled. A Radchaai could live nearly two hundred years. This inspector adjunct, probably a legal adult for a decade, was still impossibly young.

"I used to know someone else who sang all the time," the adjunct continued.

I knew her. Had probably bought songs from her. She would have been maybe four, maybe five, when I'd left Ors. Maybe slightly older, if she remembered me with any clarity.

The inspector supervisor behind that door would be someone who had spent time on Shis'urna—in Ors itself, most likely. What did I know about the lieutenant who had replaced Lieutenant Awn as administrator there? How likely was it she'd resigned her military assignment and taken one as a dock inspector? It wasn't unheard of.

Whoever the inspector supervisor was, she had money and influence enough to bring this adjunct here from Ors. I wanted to ask the young woman the name of her patron, but that would be unthinkably rude. "I'm told," I said, meaning to sound idly curious, and playing up my Gerentate accent just the smallest bit, "that the jewelry you Radchaai wear has some sort of significance."

Seivarden cast me a puzzled look. The adjunct only smiled. "Some of it." Her Orsian accent, now I had identified it, was clear, obvious. "This one for instance." She slid one gloved finger under a gold-colored dangle pinned near her left shoulder. "It's a memorial."

"May I look closer?" I asked, and receiving permission moved my chair near, and bent to read the name engraved in Radchaai on the plain metal, one I didn't recognize. It wasn't likely a memorial for an Orsian—I couldn't imagine anyone in the lower city adopting Radchaai funeral practices, or at least not anyone old enough to have died since I'd seen them last.

Near the memorial, on her collar, sat a small flower pin, each petal enameled with the symbol of an Emanation. A date engraved in the flower's center. This assured young woman had been the tiny, frightened flower-bearer when Anaander Mianaai had acted as priest in Lieutenant Awn's house twenty years ago.

No coincidences, not for Radchaai. I was quite sure now that when we were admitted to the inspector supervisor's presence, I would meet Lieutenant Awn's replacement in Ors. This inspector adjunct was, perhaps, a client of hers.

"They make them for funerals," the adjunct was saying, still talking about memorial pins. "Family and close friends wear them." And you could tell by the style and expense of the piece just where in Radchaai society the dead person stood, and by implication where the wearer stood. But the adjunct—her name, I knew, was Daos Ceit—didn't mention that.

I wondered then what Seivarden would make—had made—of changes in fashion since Garsedd, the way such signals had changed—or not. People still wore inherited tokens and memorials, testimony to the social connections and values of their ancestors generations back. And mostly that was the same, except "generations back" was Garsedd. Some tokens that had been insignificant then were prized now, and some that had been priceless were now meaningless. And the color and gemstone significances in vogue for the last hundred or so years wouldn't read at all, for Seivarden.

Inspector Adjunct Ceit had three close friends, all three of whom had incomes and positions similar to hers, to judge from the gifts they'd exchanged with her. Two lovers intimate enough to exchange tokens with but not sufficiently so to be considered very serious. No strands of jewels, no bracelets—though of course if she did any work actually inspecting cargo or ship systems such things might have been in her way—and no rings over her gloves.

And there, on the other shoulder, where now I could see it plainly and look straight at it without being excessively impolite, was the token I had been looking for. I had mistaken it for something less impressive, had, on first glance, taken the platinum for silver, and its dependent pearl for glass, the sign of a gift from a sibling—current fashions misleading me. This was nothing cheap, nothing casual. But it wasn't a token of clientage, though the metal and the pearl suggested a particular house association. An association with a house old enough that Seivarden could have recognized it immediately. Possibly had.

Inspector Adjunct Ceit stood. "The inspector supervisor is available now," she said. "I do apologize for your wait." She opened the inner door and gestured us through.

In the innermost office, standing to meet us, twenty years older and a bit heavier than when I'd last seen her, was the giver of that pin—Lieutenant—no, Inspector Supervisor Skaaiat Awer.

18

It was impossible that Lieutenant Skaaiat would recognize me. She bowed, oblivious to the fact that I knew her. It was strange to see her in dark blue, and so much more sober, more grave than when I'd known her in Ors.

An inspector supervisor in a station as busy as this likely never set foot on the ships her subordinates inspected, but Inspector Supervisor Skaaiat wore almost as little jewelry as her assistant. A long strand of green-and-blue jewels coiled from shoulder to opposite hip, and a red stone dangled from one ear, but otherwise a similar (though clearly more expensive) scattering of friends, lovers, dead relatives decorated her uniform jacket. One plain gold token hung on the cuff of her right sleeve, just next to the edge of the glove, the placement that of something she intended to be reminded of, as much for herself to see as anyone else. It looked cheap, machine-made. Not the sort of thing she would wear.

She bowed. "Citizen Seivarden. Honored Breq. Please sit. Will you have tea?" Still effortlessly elegant, even after twenty years.

"Your assistant already offered us tea, thank you, Inspector Supervisor," I said. Inspector Supervisor Skaaiat looked momentarily at me and then at Seivarden, slightly surprised, I thought. She had been addressing Seivarden primarily, thinking of Seivarden as the principal person between the two of us. I sat. Seivarden hesitated a moment and then sat in the seat beside me, arms still crossed to hide her bare hands.

"I wanted to meet you myself, citizen," Inspector Supervisor Skaaiat said, when she'd taken her own seat. "Privilege of office. It isn't every day you meet someone a thousand years old."

Seivarden smiled, small and tight. "Indeed not," she agreed.

"And I felt it would be improper for Security to arrest you on the dock. Though..." Inspector Supervisor Skaaiat gestured, placatory, the pin on her cuff flashing once as she did. "You are in some legal difficulty, citizen."

Seivarden relaxed, just slightly, shoulders lowering, jaw loosening. Barely detectable, unless you knew her. Skaaiat's accent and mildly deferential tone were having an effect. "I am," Seivarden acknowledged. "I intend to appeal."

"There's some question about the matter, then." Stilted. Formal. A query that wasn't a query. But no answer came. "I can take you to the palace offices myself and avoid any entanglement with Security." Of course she could. She'd worked this out with Security's chief already.

"I'd be grateful." Seivarden sounded more like her old self than I'd heard her in the last year. "Would it be worth asking you to assist me contacting Geir's lord?" Geir might conceivably have some responsibility for this last member of the house it had taken over. Hated Geir, which had absorbed its enemy—Vendaai, Seivarden's house. Vendaai's relations with

Awer hadn't been any better than with Geir, but I supposed the request was a measure of just how desperate and alone Seivarden was.

"Ah." Inspector Supervisor Skaaiat winced, just slightly. "Awer and Geir aren't as close as they used to be, citizen. About two hundred years ago there was an exchange of heirs. The Geir cousin killed herself." The verb Inspector Supervisor Skaaiat used implied that it hadn't been an approved, Medical-mediated suicide but something illicit and messy. "And the Awer cousin went mad and ran off to join some cult somewhere."

Seivarden made a breathy, amused noise. "Typical."

Inspector Supervisor Skaaiat raised an eyebrow, but only said, temperately, "It left some bad feeling on both sides. So my connections with Geir aren't what they could be, and I might or might not be able to be helpful to you. And their responsibilities toward you might be... difficult to determine, though you might find that useful in an appeal."

Seivarden gestured abortively, arms still tightly crossed, one elbow lifting slightly. "It doesn't sound like it's worth the trouble."

Inspector Supervisor Skaaiat gestured ambivalence. "You'll be fed and sheltered here in any event, citizen." She turned to me. "And you, honored. You're here as a tourist?"

"Yes." I smiled, looking, I hoped, very much like a tourist from the Gerentate.

"You're a very long way from home." Inspector Supervisor Skaaiat smiled, politely, as though the observation were an idle one.

"I've been traveling a long time." Of course she—and by implication others—were curious about me. I had arrived in company with Seivarden. Most of the people here wouldn't know her name, but those who did would be attracted by the staggering unlikelihood of her having been found after a thousand years, and the connection to an event as notorious as Garsedd.

Still smiling pleasantly, Inspector Supervisor Skaaiat asked, "Looking for something? Avoiding something? Just like to travel?"

I made a gesture of ambiguity. "I suppose I like to travel."

Inspector Supervisor Skaaiat's eyes narrowed slightly at my tone of voice, muscles tensing just perceptibly around her mouth. She thought, it seemed, that I was hiding something, and she was interested now, and more curious than before.

For an instant I wondered why I'd answered the way I had. And realized that Inspector Supervisor Skaaiat's being here was incredibly dangerous to me—not because she might recognize me, but because *I* recognized *her*. Because she was alive and Lieutenant Awn was not. Because everyone of her standing had failed Lieutenant Awn (*I* had failed Lieutenant Awn), and no doubt if then–Lieutenant Skaaiat had been put to the test, she would have failed as well. Lieutenant Awn herself had known this.

I was in danger of my emotions affecting my behavior. They already had, they always did. But I had never been confronted with Skaaiat Awer until now.

"My response is ambiguous, I know," I said, making that placatory gesture Inspector Supervisor Skaaiat had already used. "I've never questioned my desire to travel. When I was a baby, my grandmother said she could tell from the way I took my first steps that I was born to go places. She kept on saying it. I suppose I've just always believed it."

Inspector Supervisor Skaaiat gestured acknowledgment. "It would be a shame to disappoint your grandmother, in any event. Your Radchaai is very good."

"My grandmother always said I'd better study languages."

Inspector Supervisor Skaaiat laughed. Almost as I remembered her from Ors, but still that trace of gravity. "Forgive me, honored, but do you have gloves?"

"I meant to buy some before we boarded, but I decided to wait and buy the right sort. I hoped I'd be forgiven my bare hands on arrival since I'm an uncivilized foreigner."

"An argument could be made for either approach," Inspector Supervisor Skaaiat said, still smiling. A shade more relaxed than moments before. "Though." A serious turn. "You speak very well, but I don't know how much you understand other things."

I raised an eyebrow. "Which things?"

"I don't wish to be indelicate, honored. But Citizen Seivarden doesn't appear to have any money in her possession." Beside me, Seivarden grew tense again, tightened her jaw, swallowed something she had been about to say. "Parents," continued Inspector Supervisor Skaaiat, "buy clothes for their children. The temple gives gloves to attendants—flower-bearers and water-bearers and such. That's all right, because everyone owes loyalty to God. And I know from your entrance application that you've employed Citizen Seivarden as your servant, but..."

"Ah." I understood her. "If I buy gloves for Citizen Seivarden—which she clearly needs—it will look as though I've offered her clientage."

"Just so," agreed Inspector Supervisor Skaaiat. "Which would be fine if that's what you intended. But I don't think things work that way in the Gerentate. And honestly..." She hesitated, clearly on delicate ground again.

"And honestly," I finished for her, "she's got a difficult legal situation that might not be helped by her association with a foreigner." My normal habit was expressionlessness. I could keep my anger out of my voice easily. I could speak to Inspector Supervisor Skaaiat as though she were not in any way connected with Lieutenant Awn, as though Lieutenant Awn had had no anxieties or hopes or fears about future patronage from her. "Even a rich one."

"I'm not sure I'd say it quite that way," began Inspector Supervisor Skaaiat.

"I'll just give her some money now," I said. "That should take care of it."

"No." Seivarden's tone was sharp. Angry. "I don't need money. Every citizen is due basic necessities, and clothes are a basic necessity. I'll have what I need." At Inspector Supervisor Skaaiat's surprised, inquiring look Seivarden said further, "Breq has good reasons for not having given me money."

Inspector Supervisor Skaaiat had to know what that likely meant. "Citizen, I don't mean to lecture," she said. "But if that's the case, why not just let Security send you to Medical? I understand you're reluctant to do that." Reeducation wasn't the sort of thing that was easy to mention politely. "But really, it might make things better for you. It often does."

A year ago I'd have expected Seivarden to lose her temper at this suggestion. But something had changed for her in that time. She only said, slightly irritably, "No."

Inspector Supervisor Skaaiat looked at me. I raised one eyebrow and a shoulder, as if to say, *That's how she is.*

"Breq has been very patient with me," said Seivarden, astonishing me utterly. "And very generous." She looked at me. "I don't need money."

"Whatever you like," I said.

Inspector Supervisor Skaaiat had watched the whole exchange intently, frowning just slightly. Curious, I thought, not only about who and what I was, but what I was to Seivarden. "Well," she said now, "let me take you to the palace. Honored Breq Ghaiad, I'll have your things delivered to your lodgings." She rose.

I stood as well, and Seivarden beside me. We followed Inspector Supervisor Skaaiat to the outer office—empty, Daos Ceit (Inspector Adjunct Ceit, I would have to remember) likely gone for the day, given the hour. Instead of taking us through the front of the offices, Inspector Supervisor Skaaiat led us through a back corridor, through a door that opened at no perceptible cue from her—Station, that would be, the AI that ran this place, *was* this place, paying close attention to the inspector supervisor of its docks.

"Are you all right, Breq?" asked Seivarden, looking at me with puzzlement and concern.

"Fine," I lied. "Just a little tired. It's been a long day." I was sure my expression hadn't changed, but Seivarden had noticed something.

Through the door was more corridor, and a bank of lifts, one of which opened for us, then closed and moved with no signal. Station knew where Inspector Supervisor Skaaiat wanted to go. Which turned out to be the main concourse.

The lift doors slid open onto a broad and dazzling view—an avenue paved in black stone veined with white, seven hundred meters long and twenty-five wide, the roof sixty meters above. Directly ahead stood the temple. The steps were not really steps, but an area marked out on the paving with red and green and blue stones; actions on the steps of the temple potentially had legal significance. The entrance was itself forty meters high and eight wide, framed with representations of hundreds of gods, many human-shaped, some not, a riot of colors. Just inside the entrance lay a basin for worshippers to wash their hands in, and beyond that containers of cut flowers, a swath of yellow and orange and red, and baskets of incense, for purchase as offerings. Away down either side of the concourse, shops, offices, balconies with flowered vines snaking down. Benches, and plants, and even at an hour when most Radchaai would be at supper hundreds of citizens walked or stood talking, uniformed (white for the Translators Office, light brown for Station Security, dark brown for military, green for Horticulture, light blue for Administration) or not, all glittering with jewelry, all thoroughly Civilized. I saw an ancillary follow its captain into a crowded tea shop, and wondered which ship it was. What ships were here. But I couldn't ask, it wasn't the sort of thing Breq from the Gerentate would care about.

I saw them all, suddenly, for just a moment, through non-Radchaai eyes, an eddying crowd of unnervingly ambiguously gendered people. I saw all the features that would mark gender for non-Radchaai—never, to my annoyance and inconvenience, the same way in each place. Short hair or long, worn unbound (trailing down a back, or in a thick, curled nimbus) or bound (braided, pinned, tied). Thick-bodied or thin-, faces delicate-featured or coarse-, with cosmetics or none. A profusion of colors that would have been gender-marked in other places. All of this matched randomly with bodies curving at breast and hip or not, bodies that one moment moved in ways various non-Radchaai would call feminine, the next moment masculine. Twenty years of habit overtook me, and for an instant I despaired of choosing the right pronouns, the right terms of address. But I didn't need to do that here. I could drop that worry, a small but annoying weight I had carried all this time. I was home.

This was home that had never been home, for me. I had

spent my life at annexations, and stations in the process of becoming this sort of place, leaving before they did, to begin the whole process again somewhere else. This was the sort of place my officers came from, and departed to. The sort of place I had never been, and yet it was completely familiar to me. Places like this were, from one point of view, the whole reason for my existence.

"It's a bit longer walk, this way," Inspector Supervisor Skaaiat said, "but a dramatic entrance."

"It is," I agreed.

"Why all the jackets?" asked Seivarden. "That bothered me last time. Though the last place, anyone in a coat was wearing it knee-length. Here it looks like it's either jackets or coats down to the floor. And the collars are just *wrong*."

"Fashion didn't trouble you the other places we've been," I said.

"The other places were *foreign*," Seivarden answered, irritably. "They weren't supposed to be *home*."

Inspector Supervisor Skaaiat smiled. "I imagine you'll get used to it eventually. The palace proper is this way."

We followed her across the concourse, my and Seivarden's uncivilized clothes and bare hands attracting some curious and disgusted looks, and came to the entrance, marked simply with a bar of black over the doorway.

"I'll be fine," said Seivarden, as though I'd spoken. "I'll catch up with you when I'm done."

"I'll wait."

Inspector Supervisor Skaaiat watched Seivarden go into the palace proper and then said, "Honored Breq, a word, please."

I acknowledged her with a gesture, and she said, "You're very concerned about Citizen Seivarden. I understand that, and it speaks well of you. But there's no reason to worry for her safety. The Radch takes care of its citizens."

"Tell me, Inspector Supervisor, if Seivarden were some nobody from a nothing house who had left the Radch without permits—and whatever else it was she did, to be honest I don't know if there was anything else—if she were someone you had never heard of, with a house name you didn't recognize and know the history of, would she have been met courteously at the dock and given tea and then escorted to the palace proper to make her appeal?"

Her right hand lifted, the barest millimeter, and that small, incongruous gold tag flashed. "She's not in that position anymore. She's effectively houseless, and broke." I said nothing, only looked at her. "No, there's something in what you say. If I didn't know who she was I wouldn't have thought to do anything for her. But surely even in the Gerentate things work that way?"

I made myself smile slightly, hoping for a more pleasant impression than I had likely been making. "They do."

Inspector Supervisor Skaaiat was silent a moment, watching me, thinking about something, but I couldn't guess what. Until she said, "Do you intend to offer her clientage?"

That would have been an unspeakably rude question, if I had been Radchaai. But when I had known her Skaaiat Awer had often said things most others left unsaid. "How could I? I'm not Radchaai. And we don't make that sort of contract in the Gerentate."

"No, you don't," Inspector Supervisor Skaaiat said. Blunt. "I can't imagine what it would be like to suddenly wake up a thousand years from now having lost my ship in a notorious incident, all my friends dead, my house gone. I might run away too. Seivarden needs to find a way she can belong somewhere. To Radchaai eyes, you look like you're offering that to her."

"You're concerned I'm giving Seivarden false expectations." I thought of Daos Ceit in the outer office, that beautiful, very expensive pearl-and-platinum pin that wasn't a token of clientage.

"I don't know what expectations Citizen Seivarden has. It's just... you're acting as though you're responsible for her. It looks wrong to me."

"If I were Radchaai, would it still look wrong to you?"

"If you were Radchaai you would behave differently." The tightness of her jaw argued she was angry but trying to conceal it.

"Whose name is on that pin?" The question, unintended, came out more brusquely than was politic.

"What?" She frowned, puzzled.

"That pin on your right sleeve. It's different from everything else you're wearing." *Whose name is on it?* I wanted to ask again, and, *What have you done for Lieutenant Awn's sister?*

Inspector Supervisor Skaaiat blinked, and shifted slightly backward, almost as though I had struck her. "It's a memorial for a friend who died."

"And you're thinking about her now. You keep shifting your wrist, turning it toward yourself. You've been doing it for the past few minutes."

"I think of her frequently." She took a breath, let it out. Took another. "I think maybe I'm not being fair to you, Breq Ghaiad."

I knew. I knew what name was on that pin, even though I hadn't seen it. *Knew* it. Wasn't sure if, knowing, I felt better about Inspector Supervisor Skaaiat, or much, much worse.

But I was in danger, at this moment, in a way I had never anticipated, never predicted, never dreamed might happen. I had already said things I should never, ever have said. Was about to say more. Here was the one single person I had met in twenty long years who would know who I was. The temptation to cry out, *Lieutenant, look, it's me, I'm* Justice of Toren *One Esk* was overwhelming.

Instead, very carefully, I said, "I agree with you that Seivarden needs to find herself a home here. I just don't trust the Radch the way you do. The way she does."

Inspector Supervisor Skaaiat opened her mouth to answer me, but Seivarden's voice cut across whatever Inspector Supervisor Skaaiat would have said. "That didn't take long!" Seivarden came up beside me, looked at me, and frowned. "Your leg is bothering you again. You need to sit down."

"Leg?" asked Inspector Supervisor Skaaiat.

"An old injury that didn't heal quite right," I said, glad of it for the moment, that Seivarden would attribute any distress she saw to that. That Station would, if it was watching.

"And you've had a long day, and I've kept you standing here. I've been quite rude, please forgive me, honored," Inspector Supervisor Skaaiat said.

"Of course." I bit back words that wanted to come out of my mouth behind that, and turned to Seivarden. "So where do things stand now?"

"I've requested my appeal, and should have a date sometime in the next few days," she said. "I put your name in too." At Inspector Supervisor Skaaiat's raised eyebrow Seivarden added, "Breq saved my life. More than once."

Inspector Supervisor Skaaiat only said, "Your audience probably won't be for a few months."

"Meantime," continued Seivarden with a small, still-cross-armed acknowledging gesture, "I've been assigned lodgings and I'm on the ration list and I've got fifteen minutes to report to the nearest supplies office and get some clothes."

Lodgings. Well, if her staying with me had looked wrong to Inspector Supervisor Skaaiat, doubtless it would, for the same reasons, look wrong to Seivarden herself. And even if she was no longer my servant, she had requested I accompany her to her audience. That was, I reminded myself, the important issue. "Do you want me to come with you?" I didn't want to. I wanted to be alone, to recover my equilibrium.

"I'll be fine. You need to get off that leg. I'll catch up with you tomorrow. Inspector Supervisor, it was good to meet you." Seivarden bowed, perfectly calculated courtesy toward a social equal, received an identical bow from Inspector Supervisor Skaaiat, and then was off down the concourse.

I turned to Inspector Supervisor Skaaiat. "Where do you recommend I stay?"

Half an hour later I was as I had wished to be, alone in my room. It was an expensive one, just off the main concourse, an incredibly luxurious five meters square, a floor of what might almost have been real wood, dark-blue walls. A table and chairs, and an image projector in the floor. Many—though not all—Radchaai had optical and auditory implants that allowed them to view entertainments or listen to music or messages directly. But people still liked to watch things together, and the very wealthy sometimes made a point of turning their implants off.

The blanket on the bed felt as if it might be actual wool, not anything synthetic. On one wall a fold-down cot for a servant, which of course I no longer had. And, incredible luxury for the Radch, the room had its own tiny bath—a necessity for me, given the gun and ammunition strapped to my body under my shirt. Station's scans hadn't picked it up, and wouldn't, but human eyes could see it. If I left it in the room, a searcher might find it. I certainly couldn't leave it in the dressing room of a public bath.

A console on the wall near the door would give me access to communications. And Station. And it would allow Station to observe me, though I was certain it wasn't the only way Station could see into the room. I was back in the Radch, never alone, never private.

My luggage had arrived within five minutes of my taking the room, and with it a tray of supper from a nearby shop, fish and greens, still steaming and smelling of spices.

There was always the chance that no one was paying attention. But my luggage, when I opened it, had clearly been searched. Maybe because I was foreign. Maybe not.

I took out my tea flask and cups, and the icon of She Who Sprang from the Lily, set them on the low table beside the bed. Used a liter of my water allowance to fill the flask, and then sat down to eat.

The fish was as delicious as it smelled, and improved my mood slightly. I was, at least, better able to confront my situation once I'd eaten it, and had a cup of tea.

Station could certainly see a large percentage of its residents with the same intimate view I'd had of my officers. The rest—including me, now—it saw in less detail. Temperature. Heart rate. Respiration. Less impressive than the flood of data from more closely monitored residents, but still a great deal of information. Add to that a close knowledge of the person observed, her history, her social context, and likely Station could very nearly read minds.

Nearly. It couldn't *actually* read thoughts. And Station didn't know my history, had no prior experience with me. It would be able to see the traces of my emotions, but wouldn't have many grounds for guessing accurately why I felt as I did.

My hip had in fact been hurting. And Inspector Supervisor Skaaiat's words to me had been, in Radchaai terms, incredibly rude. If I had reacted with anger, visible to Station if it was looking (visible to Anaander Mianaai if she had been looking), that was entirely natural. Neither one could do more than guess what had angered me. I could play the part now of the exhausted traveler, pained by an old injury, in need of nothing more than food and rest.

The room was so quiet. Even when Seivarden had been in one of her sulking moods it hadn't seemed this oppressively silent. I hadn't grown as used to solitude as I had thought. And thinking of Seivarden, I saw suddenly what I had not seen, there on the concourse and blind-angry with Skaaiat Awer. I had thought then that Inspector Supervisor Skaaiat had been the only person I had met who might know me, but that wasn't true. Seivarden would have.

But Lieutenant Awn had never expected anything from Seivarden, had never stood to be hurt or disappointed by her. If they had ever met, Seivarden would surely have made her disdain clear. Lieutenant Awn would have been stiffly polite, with an underlying anger that I would have been able to see, but she would never have had that sinking dismay and hurt she felt when then–Lieutenant Skaaiat said, unthinkingly, something dismissive.

But perhaps I was wrong to think my reactions to the two, Skaaiat Awer and Seivarden Vendaai, were very different. I had already put myself in danger once, out of anger with Seivarden.

I couldn't untangle it. And I had a part to play, for whoever might be watching, an image I had carefully built on the way here. I set my empty cup beside the tea flask, and knelt on the floor before the icon, hip protesting slightly, and began to pray.

19

Next morning I bought clothes. The proprietor of the shop Inspector Supervisor Skaaiat had recommended was on the verge of throwing me out when my bank balance flashed onto her console, unbidden I suspected, Station sparing her embarrassment—and simultaneously telling me how closely it was watching me.

I needed gloves, certainly, and if I was going to play the part of the spendthrift wealthy tourist I would need to buy more than that. But before I could speak up to say so, the proprietor brought out bolts of brocade, sateen, and velvet in a dozen colors. Purple and orange-brown, three shades of green, gold, pale yellow and icy blue, ash gray, deep red.

"You can't wear those clothes," she told me, authoritative, as a subordinate handed me tea, managing to mostly conceal her disgust at my bare hands. Station had scanned me and provided my measurements, so I needed do nothing. A half-liter of tea, two excruciatingly sweet pastries, and a dozen insults later, I left in an orange-brown jacket and trousers, an icy white, stiff shirt underneath, and dark-gray gloves so thin and soft I might almost have still been barehanded. Fortunately current fashion favored jackets and trousers cut generously enough to hide my weapon. The rest—two more jackets and pairs of trousers, two pairs of gloves, half a dozen shirts, and three pairs of shoes—would be delivered to my lodgings by the time, the proprietor told me, I was done visiting the temple.

I exited the shop, turned a corner onto the main concourse, crowded at this hour with a throng of Radchaai going in and out of the temple or the palace proper, visiting the (no doubt expensive and fashionable) tea shops, or merely being seen in the right company. When I had walked through before, on my way to the clothes shop, people had stared and whispered, or just raised their eyebrows. Now, it seemed, I was mostly invisible, except for the occasional similarly well-dressed Radchaai who dropped her gaze to my jacket front looking for signs of my family affiliation, eyes widening in surprise to see none. Or the child, one small gloved hand clutching the sleeve of an accompanying adult, who turned to frankly stare at me until she was drawn past and out of sight.

Inside the temple, citizens crowded the flowers and incense, junior priests young enough to look like children to my eyes bringing baskets and boxes of replacements. As an ancillary I wasn't supposed to touch temple offerings, or make them myself. But no one here knew that. I washed my hands in the basin and bought a handful of bright yellow-orange flowers, and a piece of the sort of incense I knew Lieutenant Awn had favored.

There would be a place within the temple set aside for prayers for the dead, and days that were auspicious for making such offerings, though this wasn't such a day, and as a foreigner I shouldn't have Radchaai dead to remember. Instead I walked into the echoing main hall, where Amaat stood, a jeweled Emanation in each hand, already knee-deep in flowers, a hill of red and orange and yellow as high as my head, growing incrementally as worshippers tossed more blooms on the pile. When I reached the front of the crowd I added my own, made the gestures and mouthed the prayer, dropped the incense into the box that, when it filled, would be emptied by more junior priests. It was only a token—it would return to the entrance, to be purchased again. If all the incense offered had been burned, the air in the temple would have been too thick with smoke to breathe. And this wasn't even a festival day.

As I bowed to the god, a brown-uniformed ship's captain came up beside me. She made to throw her handful of flowers, and then stopped, staring at me. The fingers of her empty left hand twitched, just slightly. Her features reminded me of Hundred Captain Rubran Osck, though where Captain Rubran had been lanky, and worn her hair long and straight, this captain was shorter and thick-bodied, hair clipped close. A glance at her jewelry confirmed this captain was a cousin of hers, a member of the same branch of the same house. I remembered that Anaander Mianaai hadn't been able to predict Captain Rubran's allegiance, and didn't want to tug too hard on the web of clientage and contacts the hundred captain belonged to. I wondered if that was still true, or if Osck had come down on one side or the other.

It didn't matter. The captain still stared, presumably receiving by now answers to her queries. Station or her ship would tell her I was a foreigner and the captain would, I presumed, lose interest. Or not, if she learned about Seivarden. I didn't wait to see which was the case, but finished my prayer and turned to work my way through the people waiting to make offerings.

Off the sides of the temple were smaller shrines. In one,

three adults and two children stood around an infant they had laid at the breast of Aatr—the image being constructed to allow this, its arm crooked under the god's often-sworn-by breasts—hoping for an auspicious destiny, or at least some sign of what the future might hold for the child.

All the shrines were beautiful, glittering with gold and silver, glass and polished stone. The whole place rumbled and roared with the echoes of hundreds of quiet conversations and prayers. No music. I thought of the nearly empty temple of Ikkt, the Divine of Ikkt telling me of hundreds of singers long gone.

I was nearly two hours in the temple admiring the shrines of subsidiary gods. The entire place must have taken up whatever part of this side of the station was not occupied by the palace proper. The two were certainly connected, since Anaander Mianaai acted as priest here at regular intervals, though the accesses wouldn't be obvious.

I left the mortuary shrine for last. Partly because it was the part of the temple most likely to be crowded with tourists, and partly because I knew it would make me unhappy. It was larger than the other subsidiary shrines, nearly half the size of the vast main hall, filled with shelves and cases crowded with offerings for the dead. All food or flowers. All glass. Glass teacups holding glass tea, glass steam rising above. Mounds of delicate glass roses and leaves. Two dozen different kinds of fruit, fish and greens that nearly gave off a phantom aroma of my supper the night before. You could buy mass-produced versions of these in shops well away from the main concourse, and put them in your home shrine, for gods or for the dead, but these were different, each one a carefully detailed work of art, each one conspicuously labeled with the names of the living donor and the dead recipient, so every visitor could see the pious mourning—and wealth and status—on display.

I probably had enough money to commission such an offering. But if I did so, and labeled it with the appropriate names, it would be the last thing I ever did. And doubtless the priests would refuse it. I had already considered sending money to Lieutenant Awn's sister, but that, too, would attract unwelcome curiosity. Maybe I could arrange it so that whatever was left would go to her, once I had done what I'd come here to do, but I suspected that would be impossible. Still, thinking it, and thinking of my luxurious room and expensive, beautiful clothes, gave me a twinge of guilt.

At the temple entrance, just as I was about to step out onto the concourse, a soldier stepped into my path. Human, not an ancillary. She bowed. "Excuse me. I have a message from the citizen Vel Osck, captain of *Mercy of Kalr.*"

The captain who had stared at me as I made my offering to Amaat. The fact she'd sent a soldier to accost me said she thought me worth more trouble than a message through Station's systems, but not enough to send a lieutenant, or approach me herself. Though that might also have been due to a certain social awkwardness she preferred to push off onto this soldier. It was hard not to notice the slight clumsiness of a sentence designed to avoid a courtesy title. "Your pardon, citizen," I said. "I don't know the citizen Vel Osck."

The soldier gestured, slight, deferential apology. "This morning's cast indicated the captain would have a fortuitous encounter today. When she noticed you making your offering she was sure you were who was meant."

Noticing a stranger in the temple, in a place as big as this, was hardly a fortuitous encounter. I was slightly offended that the captain hadn't even tried to put more effort into it. Mere seconds of thought would have produced something better. "What is the message, citizen?"

"The captain customarily takes tea in the afternoons," said the soldier, bland and polite, and named a shop just off the concourse. "She would be honored if you would join her."

The time and place suggested the sort of "social" meeting that was, in reality, a display of influence and associations, and where ostensibly unofficial business would be done.

Captain Vel had no business with me. And she would gain no advantage in being seen with me. "If the captain wants to meet citizen Seivarden..." I began.

"It wasn't Captain Seivarden the captain encountered in the temple," the soldier answered, again slightly apologetic. Surely she knew how transparent her errand was. "But of course if you wanted to bring Captain Seivarden, Captain Vel would be honored to meet her."

Of course. And even houseless and broke, Seivarden would get a personal invitation from someone she knew, not a message through station systems, or a this-edge-of-insulting invite from Captain Vel's errand-runner. But it was exactly what I had wanted. "I can't speak for Citizen Seivarden, of course," I said. "Do please thank Captain Vel for the invitation." The soldier bowed, and left.

Off the concourse I found a shop selling cartons of what was advertised merely as "lunch," which turned out to be fish again, stewed with fruit. I took it back to my room and sat at the table, eating, considering that console on the wall, a visible link with Station.

Station was as smart as I had ever been, when I had still been a ship. Younger, yes. Less than half my age. But not to be dismissed, not at all. If I was discovered, it would almost certainly be because of Station.

Station hadn't detected my ancillary implants, all of which I had disabled and hidden as best I could. If it had, I would have already been under arrest. But Station could see at least the basics of my emotional state. Could, with enough information about me, tell when I was lying. Was, certainly, watching me closely.

But emotional states, from Station's view, from mine when I was *Justice of Toren*, were just assemblages of medical data, data that were meaningless without context. If, in my present dismal mood, I had just stepped off a ship, Station would possibly see it, but not understand why I felt the way I did, and would not be able to draw any conclusions from it. But the longer I was here, the more of me Station saw, the more data Station would have. It would be able to assemble its own context, its own picture of what I was. And would be able to compare that to what it thought I ought to be.

The danger would be if those two didn't match. I swallowed a mouthful of fish, looked at the console. "Hello," I said. "The AI who's watching me."

"Honored Ghaiad Breq," said Station from the console, a placid voice. "Hello. I am usually addressed as *Station*."

"Station, then." Another bite of fish and fruit. "So you *are* watching me." I was, genuinely, worried about Station's surveillance. I wouldn't be able to hide that from Station.

"I watch everyone, honored. Is your leg still troubling you?" It was, and doubtless Station could see me favor it, see the effects of it in the way I sat now. "Our medical facilities are excellent. I'm sure one of our doctors could find a solution to your problem."

An alarming prospect. But I could make that look entirely understandable. "No, thank you. I've been warned about Radchaai medical facilities. I'd rather endure a little inconvenience and still be who I am."

Silence, for a moment. Then Station asked, "Do you mean

the aptitudes? Or reeducation? Neither would change who you are. And you aren't eligible for either one, I assure you."

"All the same." I set my utensil down. "We have a saying, where I come from: Power requires neither permission nor forgiveness."

"I have never met anyone from the Gerentate before," said Station. I had, of course, been depending on that. "I suppose your misapprehension is understandable. Foreigners often don't understand what the Radchaai are really like."

"Do you realize what you've just said? Literally that the uncivilized don't understand civilization? Do you realize that quite a lot of people outside Radch space consider themselves to be civilized?" The sentence was nearly impossible in Radchaai, a self-contradiction.

I waited for *That wasn't what I meant*, but it didn't come. Instead, Station said, "Would you have come here if not for Citizen Seivarden?"

"Possibly," I answered, knowing I could not lie outright to Station, not with it watching me so closely. Knowing that now any anger or resentment—or any apprehension about Radchaai officials—that I felt would be attributed to my being resentful and fearful of the Radch. "Is there any music in this very civilized place?"

"Yes," answered Station. "Though I don't think I have any music from the Gerentate."

"If I only ever wanted to hear music from the Gerentate," I said, acid, "I would never have left there."

This did not seem to faze Station. "Would you prefer to go out or stay in?"

I preferred to stay in. Station called up an entertainment for me, new this year but a comfortably familiar sort of thing—a young woman of humble family with hopes of clientage to a more prestigious house. A jealous rival who undermines her, deceiving the putative patron as to her true, noble nature. The eventual recognition of the heroine's superior virtue, her loyalty through the most terrible trials, even uncontracted as she is, and the downfall of her rival, culminating in the long-awaited clientage contract and ten minutes of triumphant singing and dancing, the last of eleven such interludes over four separate episodes. It was a very small-scale work—some of these ran for dozens of episodes that added up to days or even weeks. It was mindless, but the songs were nice and improved my mood considerably.

I had nothing urgent to do until word came of Seivarden's appeal, and if Seivarden's request for an audience, and for me to accompany her, was granted, that would mean another, even longer wait. I rose, brushed my new trousers straight, put on shoes and jacket. "Station," I said. "Do you know where I can find the citizen Seivarden Vendaai?"

"The citizen Seivarden Vendaai," answered Station from the console, in its always even voice, "is in the Security office on sublevel nine."

"Excuse me?"

"There was a fight," said Station. "Normally Security would have contacted her family, but she has none here."

I wasn't her family, of course. And she could have called for me if she'd wanted me. Still. "Can you direct me to the Security office on sublevel nine, please?"

"Of course, honored."

The office on sublevel nine was tiny: nothing more, really, than a console, a few chairs, a table with mismatched tea things, and some storage lockers. Seivarden sat on a bench at the back wall. She wore gray gloves and an ill-fitting jacket and trousers of some stiff, coarse fabric, the sort of thing extruded on demand, not sewn, and probably produced in a preset range of sizes. My own uniforms, when I had been a ship, had been made that way, but had looked better. Of course I'd sized each one properly, it had been a simple thing for me to do at the time.

The front of Seivarden's gray jacket was spattered with blood, and one glove was soaked with it. Blood was crusted on her upper lip, and the small clear shell of a corrective sat across the bridge of her nose. Another corrective lay across a bruise forming on one cheek. She stared dully ahead, not looking up at me, or at the Security officer who had admitted me. "Here's your friend, citizen," said Security.

Seivarden frowned. Looked up, around the small space. Then she looked more closely at me. "Breq? Aatr's tits, that's you. You look..." She blinked. Opened her mouth to finish the sentence, stopped again. Took another, somewhat ragged breath. "Different," she concluded. "Really, really different."

"I only bought clothes. What happened to you?"

"There was a fight," said Seivarden.

"Just happened on its own, did it?" I asked.

"No," she admitted. "I was assigned a place to sleep, but there was already someone living there. I tried to talk to her but I could hardly understand her."

"Where did you sleep last night?" I asked.

She looked down at the floor. "I managed." Looked up again, at me, at the Security officer beside me. "But I wasn't going to be able to *keep* managing."

"You should have come to us, citizen," said Security. "Now you've got a warning on your record. Not something you want."

“And her opponent?” I asked.

Security made a negating gesture. It wasn’t something I was supposed to ask.

“I’m not managing very well on my own, am I,” said Seivarden, miserably.

Heedless of Skaaiat Awer’s disapproval, I bought Seivarden new gloves and jacket, dark green, still the sort of thing that was extruded on demand, but at least it fit better, and the higher quality was obvious. The gray ones were past laundering, and I knew the supply office wouldn’t issue more clothes so soon. When Seivarden had put them on, and sent the old ones for recycling, I said, “Have you eaten? I was planning to offer you supper when Station told me where you were.” She’d washed her face, and now looked more or less reputable, give or take the bruising under the corrective on her cheek.

“I’m not hungry,” she said. A flicker of something—regret? Annoyance? I couldn’t quite tell—flashed across her face. She crossed her arms and quickly uncrossed them again, a gesture I hadn’t seen in months.

“Can I offer you tea, then, while I eat?”

“I would *love* tea,” she said with emphatic sincerity. I remembered that she had no money, had refused to let me give her any. All that tea we had carried with us was in my luggage, she had taken none of it with her when we’d parted the night before. And tea, of course, was an extra. A luxury. Which wasn’t really a luxury. Not by Seivarden’s standards, anyway. Likely not by any Radchaai’s standards.

We found a tea shop, and I bought something rolled in a sheet of algae, and some fruit and tea, and we took a table in a corner. “Are you sure you don’t want anything?” I asked. “Fruit?”

She feigned lack of interest in the fruit, and then took a piece. "I hope you had a better day than I did."

"Probably." I waited a moment, to see if she wanted to talk about what had happened, but she said nothing, just waited for me to continue. "I went to the temple this morning. And ran into some ship's captain who stared quite rudely and then sent one of her soldiers after me to invite me to tea."

"One of her *soldiers*." Seivarden realized her arms were crossed, uncrossed them, picked up her tea cup, set it down again. "Ancillary?"

"Human. I'm pretty sure."

Seivarden lifted an eyebrow briefly. "You shouldn't go. She should have invited you herself. You didn't say yes, did you?"

"I didn't say no." Three Radchaai entered the tea shop, laughing. All wore the dark blue of dock authority. One of them was Daos Ceit, Inspector Supervisor Skaaiat's assistant. She didn't seem to notice me. "I don't think the invitation was on my account. I think she wants me to introduce her to *you*."

"But…" She frowned. Looked at the bowl of tea in one green-gloved hand. Brushed the front of the new jacket with the other. "What's her name?"

"Vel Osck."

"Osck. Never heard of them." She took another drink of tea. Daos Ceit and her friends bought tea and pastries, sat at a table on the other side of the room, talking animatedly. "Why would she want to meet me?"

I raised an eyebrow, incredulous. "*You're* the one who believes any unlikely event is a message from God," I pointed out. "You're lost for a thousand years, found by accident, disappear again, and then turn up at a palace with a rich foreigner. And you're surprised when that gets attention." She made an ambiguous gesture. “Absent Vendaai as a functioning house, you need to establish yourself somehow.”

She looked so dismayed, just for the shortest instant, that I thought my words had offended her in some way. But then she seemed to recover herself. “If Captain Vel wanted my good will, or cared at all about my opinion, she made a bad start by insulting you.” Her old arrogance lurked behind those words, a startling difference from her barely suppressed dejection up to now.

“What about that inspector supervisor?” I asked. “Skaaiat, right? She seemed polite enough. And you seemed to know who she was.”

“All the Awers *seem* polite enough,” Seivarden said, disgustedly. Over her shoulder I watched Daos Ceit laugh at something one of her companions had said. “They *seem* totally normal at first,” Seivarden went on, “but then they go having visions, or deciding something’s wrong with the universe and they have to fix it. Or both at once. They’re all insane.” She was silent a moment, and then turned to see what I was looking at. Turned back. “Oh, *her*. Isn’t she kind of…provincial-looking?”

I turned my full attention on Seivarden. Looked at her.

She looked down at the table. “I’m sorry. That was…that was just wrong. I don’t have any…”

“I doubt,” I interrupted, “that her pay allows her to wear clothes that make her look…‘different.’”

“That’s not what I meant.” Seivarden looked up, distress and embarrassment obvious in her expression. “But what I meant was bad enough. I just…I was just surprised. All this time, I guess I’ve just assumed you were an ascetic. It just surprised me.”

An ascetic. I could see why she would have assumed that,

but not why it would have mattered that she was wrong. Unless... "You're not *jealous*?" I asked, incredulous. Well-dressed or not, I was just as provincial-looking as Daos Ceit. Just from a different province.

"No!" And then the next moment, "Well, yes. But not like *that*."

I realized, then, that it wasn't just other Radchaai who might get the wrong impression from that gift of clothes I'd just made. Even though Seivarden surely knew I couldn't offer clientage. Even though I knew that if she thought about it for longer than thirty seconds, she would never want from me what that gift implied. Surely she couldn't think that I'd meant that. "Yesterday the inspector supervisor told me I was in danger of giving you false expectations. Or of giving others the wrong impression."

Seivarden made a scornful noise. "That would be worth considering if I had the remotest interest in what Awer thinks." I raised an eyebrow, and she continued, in a more contrite tone, "I thought I'd be able to handle things by myself, but all last night, and all today, I've just been wishing I'd stayed with you. I guess it's true, all citizens are taken care of. I didn't see anyone starving. Or naked." Her face momentarily showed disgust. "But those clothes. And the skel. Just skel, all the time, very carefully measured out. I didn't think I'd mind. I mean, I don't mind skel, but I could hardly choke it down." I could guess the mood she'd been in, when she'd gotten into that fight. "I think it was knowing I wasn't going to get anything else for weeks and weeks. And," she said, with a rueful smile, "knowing I'd have had better if I'd asked to stay with you."

"So you want your old job back, then?" I asked.

"*Fuck* yes," she said, emphatic and relieved. Loud enough

for the party across the room to hear and turn disapproving glances our way.

"Language, citizen." I took another bite of my algae roll. Relieved, I discovered, on several counts. "Are you sure you wouldn't rather take your chances with Captain Vel?"

"You can have tea with whoever you want," said Seivarden. "But she should have invited you herself."

"Your manners are a thousand years old," I pointed out.

"Manners are manners," she said, indignant. "But like I said, you can have tea with whoever you want."

Inspector Supervisor Skaaiat entered the shop, saw Daos Ceit and nodded to her, but came over to where Seivarden and I sat. Hesitated, just an instant, noticing the correctives on Seivarden's face, but then pretended she hadn't seen them. "Citizen. Honored."

"Inspector Supervisor," I replied. Seivarden merely nodded.

"I'm hosting a small get-together tomorrow evening." She named a place. "Just tea, nothing formal. I'd be honored if you both came."

Seivarden laughed outright. "Manners," she said again, "are manners."

Skaaiat frowned, nonplussed.

"Yours is the second such invitation today," I explained. "Citizen Seivarden tells me the first was less than entirely courteous."

"I hope mine met her exacting standards," Skaaiat said. "Who failed them?"

"Captain Vel," I answered. "Of *Mercy of Kalr.*"

To someone who didn't know her well, Skaaiat probably looked as though she had no real opinions about Captain Vel. "Well. I admit I intended to introduce you, citizen, to friends of mine who might be useful to you. But you might find Captain Vel's acquaintance more congenial."

"You must have a low opinion of me," Seivarden said.

"It's possible," said Skaaiat, and oh how strange it was to hear her speak with such gravity, as I had known her twenty years ago but different, "that Captain Vel's approach was less than entirely respectful toward the honored Breq. But in other respects I suspect you'd find her sympathetic." Before Seivarden could answer, Skaaiat continued, "I have to go. I hope to see you both tomorrow evening." She looked over at the table where her assistant sat, and all three of the adjunct inspectors there stood, and left the shop behind her.

Seivarden was silent a moment, watching the door they had exited from.

"Well," I said. Seivarden looked back to me. "I guess if you're coming back I'd better pay you so you can buy some more decent clothes."

An expression I couldn't quite read flashed across Seivarden's face. "Where did you get yours?"

"I don't think I'll pay you *that* much," I said.

Seivarden laughed. Took a drink of her tea, another piece of fruit.

I wasn't at all certain she'd really eaten. "Are you sure you don't want anything else?" I asked.

"I'm sure. What *is* that thing?" She looked toward the last bit of my algae-covered supper.

"No idea." I hadn't ever seen anything quite like it in the Radch, it must have been recently invented, or an idea imported from some other place. "It's good, though, do you want one? We can take it back to the room if you like."

Seivarden made a face. "No, thanks. You're more adventurous than I am."

"I suppose I am," I agreed, pleasantly. I finished the last of my supper, drained my tea. "But you wouldn't know it to look at me, today. I spent the morning in the temple, like a good tourist, and the afternoon watching an entertainment in my room."

"Let me guess!" Seivarden raised an eyebrow, sardonic. "The one everyone is talking about. The heroine is virtuous and loyal, and her potential patron's lover hates her. She wins through because of her unswerving loyalty and devotion."

"You've seen it."

"More than once. But not for a very long time."

I smiled. "Some things never change?"

Seivarden laughed in response. "Apparently not. Songs any good?"

"Pretty good. You can watch back at the room, if you like."

But back in the room she folded down the servant's cot, saying, "I'm just going to sit down a moment," and was asleep two minutes and three seconds later.

20

It would almost certainly be weeks before Seivarden even had an audience date. In the meantime we were living here, and I would have a chance to see how things stood, who might side with which Mianaai if things came to an open breach. Maybe even whether one Mianaai or another was in ascendance here. Any information might prove crucial when the moment arrived. And it would arrive, I was increasingly sure. Anaander Mianaai might or might not realize what I was any time soon—but at this point there was no hiding me from the rest of herself. I was here, openly, noticeably, along with Seivarden.

Thinking of Seivarden, and Captain Vel Osck's eagerness to meet her, I thought also of Hundred Captain Rubran Osck. Of Anaander Mianaai complaining she couldn't guess her opinion, could rely on neither her opposition nor her support, nor could she pressure her in order to discover or compel it. Captain Rubran had been fortunate enough in her family connections to be able to take such a neutral stance, and keep it. Did that say something about the state of Mianaai's struggle with herself at the time?

Did the captain of *Mercy of Kalr* also take that neutral stance? Or had something changed in that balance during the time I had been gone? And what did it mean that Inspector Supervisor Skaaiat disliked her? I was certain dislike was the expression I had seen on her face when I had mentioned the name. Military ships weren't subject to dock authorities—except of course in the matter of arrivals and departures—and the relationship between the two usually involved some contempt on one side and mild resentment on the other, all covered over with guarded courtesy. But Skaaiat Awer had never been given to resentment, and besides she knew both sides of the game. Had Captain Vel offended her personally? Did she merely dislike her, as happened sometimes?

Or did her sympathies place her on the other side of some political dividing line? And after all, where was Skaaiat Awer likely to fall, in a divided Radch? Unless something had happened to change her personality and opinions drastically, I thought I knew where Skaaiat Awer would land in that toss. Captain Vel—and for that matter *Mercy of Kalr*—I didn't know well enough to say.

As for Seivarden, I was under no illusions as to where *her* sympathies would lie, given a choice between citizens who kept their proper places along with an expanding, conquering Radch, or no more annexations and the elevation of citizens with the wrong accents and antecedents. I was under no illusions as to what Seivarden's opinion of Lieutenant Awn would have been, had they ever met.

The place where Captain Vel customarily took tea was not prominently marked. It didn't need to be. It was probably not at the very top of fashion and society—not unless Osck's fortunes had soared in the last twenty years. But it was still the sort of place that if you didn't already know it was there you were almost certainly not welcome. The place was dark and the sound muffled—rugs and hangings absorbed echoes or unwanted noises. Stepping in from the noisy corridor it was as though I had suddenly put my hands over my ears. Groups of low chairs surrounded small tables. Captain Vel sat in one corner, flasks and bowls of tea and a half-empty tray of pastries on the table in front of her. The chairs were full, and an outer circle had been pulled around.

They had been here for at least an hour. Seivarden had said to me before we left the room, blandly, still irritated, that of course I wouldn't want to rush out to tea. If she'd been in a better mood she would have told me straight out that I should arrive late. It had been my own inclination even before she spoke, so I said nothing and let her have the satisfaction of thinking she'd influenced me, if she wished to have it.

Captain Vel saw me and rose, bowing. "Ah, Breq Ghaiad. Or is it Ghaiad Breq?"

I made my own bow in return, taking care that it was precisely as shallow as hers had been. "In the Gerentate we put our house names first." The Gerentate didn't have houses the way Radchaai did, but it was the only term Radchaai had for a name that indicated family relationship. "But I am not in the Gerentate at the moment. Ghaiad is my house name."

"You've already put it in the right order for us then!" Captain Vel said, falsely jovial. "Very thoughtful." I couldn't see Seivarden, who stood behind me. I wondered briefly what expression was on her face, and also why Captain Vel had invited me here if her every interaction with me was going to be mildly insulting.

Station was certainly watching me. It would see at least traces of my annoyance. Captain Vel would not. And likely would not care if she could have.

"And Captain Seivarden Vendaai," Captain Vel continued, and made another bow, noticeably deeper than the one before. "An honor, sir. A distinct honor. Do sit." She gestured to chairs near her own, and two elegantly attired and bejeweled Radchaai rose to make way for us, no complaint or expression of resentment apparent.

"Your pardon, Captain," said Seivarden. Bland. The correctives from the day before had come off, and she looked very nearly what she had been a thousand years ago, the wealthy and arrogant daughter of a highly placed house. In a moment she would sneer and say something sarcastic, I was sure, but she didn't. "I no longer deserve the rank. I am the honored Breq's servant." Slight stress on *honored*, as though Captain Vel might be ignorant of the appropriate courtesy title and Seivarden meant merely to politely and discreetly inform her. "And I thank you for the invitation she was good enough to convey to me." There it was, a hint of disdain, though it was possible only someone who knew her well would hear it. "But I have duties to attend to."

"I've given you the afternoon off, citizen," I said before Captain Vel could answer. "Spend it however you like." No reaction from Seivarden, and still I couldn't see her face. I took one of the seats cleared for us. A lieutenant had sat there previously, doubtless one of Captain Vel's officers. Though I saw more brown uniforms here than a small ship like *Mercy of Kalr* could account for.

The person next to me was a civilian in rose and azure, delicate satin gloves that suggested she never handled anything rougher or heavier than a bowl of tea, and an ostentatiously large brooch of woven and hammered gold wire set with sapphires—not, I was sure, glass. Likely the design advertised whatever wealthy house she belonged to, but I didn't recognize it. She leaned toward me and said, loudly, as Seivarden took the seat opposite me, "How fortunate you must have thought yourself, to find Seivarden Vendaai!"

"Fortunate," I repeated, carefully, as though the word were unfamiliar to me, leaning just slightly more heavily on my Gerentate accent. Almost wishing the Radchaai language concerned itself with gender so I could use it wrongly and sound even more foreign. Almost. "Is that the word for it?" I had guessed correctly why Captain Vel had approached me the way she had. Inspector Supervisor Skaaiat had done something similar, addressing Seivarden even though she knew Seivarden had come as my servant. Of course, the inspector supervisor had seen her mistake almost immediately.

Across from me, Seivarden was explaining to Captain Vel about the situation with her aptitudes. I was astonished at her icy calm, given I knew she'd been angry ever since I told her I'd intended to come. But this was, in some ways, her natural habitat. If the ship that had found her suspension pod had brought her somewhere like this, instead of a small, provincial station, things would have gone very differently for her.

"Ridiculous!" exclaimed Rose-and-Azure beside me, while Captain Vel poured a bowl of tea and offered it to Seivarden. "As though you were a child. As though no one knew what you were suited for. It used to be you could depend on officials to handle things properly." *Justly*, rang the silent companion of that last word. *Beneficially.*

"I did, citizen, lose my ship," Seivarden said.

"Not your fault, Captain," protested another civilian somewhere behind me. "Surely not."

"Everything that happens on my watch is my fault, citizen," answered Seivarden.

Captain Vel gestured agreement. "Still, there shouldn't have been any question of you taking the tests *again*."

Seivarden looked at her tea, looked over at me sitting empty-handed across from her, and set her bowl down on the table in front of her without drinking. Captain Vel poured a bowl and offered it to me, as though she hadn't noticed Seivarden's gesture.

"How do you find the Radch after a thousand years, Captain?" asked someone behind me as I accepted the tea. "Much changed?"

Seivarden didn't retrieve her own bowl. "Changed some. The same some."

"For the better, or for the worse?"

"I could hardly say," replied Seivarden, coolly.

"How beautifully you speak, Captain Seivarden," said someone else. "So many young people these days are careless about their speech. It's lovely to hear someone speak with real refinement."

Seivarden's lips quirked in what might be taken for appreciation of a compliment, but almost certainly wasn't.

"These lower houses and provincials, with their accents and their slang," agreed Captain Vel. "Really, my own ship, fine soldiers but to hear them talk you'd think they'd never gone to school."

"Pure laziness," opined a lieutenant behind Seivarden.

"You don't have that with ancillaries," said someone, possibly another captain behind me.

"A lot of things you don't have with ancillaries," said someone else, a comment that might be taken two ways, but I was fairly sure I knew which way was meant. "But that's not a safe topic."

"Not safe?" I asked, all innocence. "Surely it isn't illegal here to complain about young people these days? How cruel. I had thought it a basic part of human nature, one of the few universally practiced human customs."

"And surely," added Seivarden with a slight sneer, her mask finally cracking, "it's *always* safe to complain about lower houses and provincials."

"You'd *think*," said Rose-and-Azure beside me, mistaking Seivarden's intent. "But we are sadly changed, Captain, from your day. It used to be you could depend on the aptitudes to send the *right* citizen to the *right* assignment. I can't fathom some of the decisions they make these days. And atheists given privileges." She meant Valskaayans, who were, as a rule, not atheists but exclusive monotheists. The difference was invisible to many Radchaai. "And human soldiers! People nowadays are squeamish about ancillaries, but you don't see ancillaries drunk and puking on the concourse."

Seivarden made a sympathetic noise. "I've *never* known officers to be puking drunk."

"In your day, maybe not," answered someone behind me. "Things have changed."

Rose-and-Azure tipped her head toward Captain Vel, who to judge by her expression had finally understood Seivarden's words as Rose-and-Azure had not. "Not to say, Captain, that you don't keep *your* ship in order. But you wouldn't have to *keep* ancillaries in order, would you?"

Captain Vel waved the point away with an empty hand, her bowl of tea in the other. "That's command, citizen, it's just my job. But there are more serious issues. You can't fill troop carriers with humans. The human-crewed Justices are all half-empty."

"And of course," interjected Rose-and-Azure, "those all have to be *paid*."

Captain Vel gestured assent. "They say we don't need them anymore." *They* being, of course, Anaander Mianaai. No one would name her while being critical of her. "That our borders are proper as they are. I don't pretend to understand policy, or politics. But it seems to me it's less wasteful to store ancillaries than it is to train and pay humans and rotate them in and out of storage."

"They say," said Rose-and-Azure beside me, taking a pastry from the table in front of her, "that if it hadn't been for *Justice of Toren*'s disappearance they'd have scrapped one of the other carriers by now." My surprise at hearing my own name couldn't have been visible to anyone here, but surely Station could see it. And that surprise, that startlement, wasn't something that would fit into the identity I'd constructed. Station would be reevaluating me, I was sure. So would Anaander Mianaai.

"Ah," said a civilian behind me. "But our visitor here is doubtless glad to hear our borders are fixed."

I barely turned my head to answer. "The Gerentate would be a very large mouthful." I kept my voice even. No one here could see my continuing consternation at that startlement moments ago.

Except, of course, Station and Anaander Mianaai. And Anaander Mianaai—or part of her, at least—would have very good reasons for noticing talk about *Justice of Toren*, and reactions to it.

"I don't know, Captain Seivarden," Captain Vel was saying, "if you've heard about the mutiny at Ime. An entire unit refused their orders and defected to an alien power."

"Certainly wouldn't have happened on an ancillary-crewed ship," said someone behind Seivarden.

"Not too big a mouthful for the Radch, I imagine," said the person behind me.

"I daresay"—again I leaned just slightly on my Gerentate accent—"sharing a border with us this long, you've learned better table manners." I refused to turn all the way around to see whether the answering silence was amused, indignant, or merely distracted by Seivarden and Captain Vel. Tried not to think too hard about what conclusions Anaander Mianaai would draw from my reaction to hearing my name.

"I think I heard something about it," said Seivarden, frowning thoughtfully. "Ime. That was where the provincial governor and the captains of the ships in the system murdered and stole, and sabotaged the ships and station so they couldn't report to higher authorities. Yes?" No point worrying what Station—or the Lord of the Radch—would make of my reaction to *that*. It would fall where it fell. I needed to stay calm.

"That's beside the point," answered Rose-and-Azure. "The point is, it was mutiny. Mutiny winked at, but one can't make a plain statement of fact about the dangers of promoting the ill-bred and vulgar to positions of authority, or policies that encourage the most vile sort of behavior, and even undermine everything civilization has always stood for, without losing business contacts or promotions."

"You must be very brave, then, to speak so," I observed. But I was sure Rose-and-Azure wasn't particularly brave. She spoke as she did because she could do so without danger to herself.

Calm. I could control my breathing, keep it smooth and regular. My skin was too dark to show a flush, but Station would see the temperature change. Station might just think I was angry about something. I had good reason to be angry.

"Honored," Seivarden said abruptly. From the set of her jaw and shoulders, she was suppressing an urge to cross her arms. Would be, quite soon, in one of those silently-facing-the-wall moods. "We'll be late to our next engagement." She rose, more abruptly than was strictly polite.

"Indeed," I acknowledged, and set down my untasted tea. Hoped her action was on her own account, and not because she'd seen any sign of my agitation. "Captain Vel, thank you for your very kind invitation. It was an honor to meet you all."

Out on the main concourse, Seivarden, walking behind me, muttered, "Fucking snobs." People passed, mostly not paying any attention to us. That was good. That was normal. I could feel my adrenaline levels dropping.

Better. I stopped and turned to look at Seivarden, raised an eyebrow.

"Well, but they *are* snobs," she said. "What do they think the aptitudes are *for*? The whole *point* is that anyone can test into anything."

I remembered twenty-years-younger Lieutenant Skaaiat asking, in the humid darkness of the upper city, if the aptitudes had lacked impartiality before, or lacked them now, and answering, for herself, *both*. And Lieutenant Awn's hurt and distress.

Seivarden crossed her arms, then uncrossed them, balled her gloved hands into fists. "And of *course* someone from a lower house is going to be ill-bred and have a vulgar accent. They can hardly help it.

"And what *were* they thinking," Seivarden continued, "to have a conversation like that. In a tea shop. On a *palace station*. I mean, not just *when we were young* and *provincials are vulgar* but the aptitudes are corrupt? The military is badly mismanaged?" I didn't speak, but she answered as though I had. "Oh, of course, everyone complains things are mismanaged. But not like *that*. What's going on?"

"Don't ask me." Though of course I knew—or thought I did. And wondered again what it meant that Rose-and-Azure, and others there, had felt so freely able to speak as they had. Which Anaander Mianaai might hold an advantage here? Though such free speaking might only mean the Lord of the Radch preferred to let her enemies identify themselves clearly and unambiguously. "And have you always been in favor of the ill-bred testing into high positions?" I asked, knowing she hadn't.

Realizing, suddenly, that if Station had never met anyone from the Gerentate, Anaander Mianaai very possibly had. Why had that not occurred to me before? Something programmed into my ship-mind, invisible to me until now, or just the limitations of this one small brain remaining to me?

I might have deceived Station, and everyone else here, but I had not for a moment deceived the Lord of the Radch. She had certainly known from the instant I set foot on the palace docks that I was not what I said I was.

It would fall where it fell, I told myself.

"I thought about what you told me, about Ime," Seivarden said, as though it answered my question. Oblivious to my renewed distress. "I don't know if that unit leader did the right thing. But I don't know what the right thing to do would have been. And I don't know if I'd have had the courage to die for that right thing if I knew what it was. I mean..." She paused. "I mean, I'd like to think I would. There was a time I'd have been sure I would. But I can't even..." She trailed off, her voice shaking slightly. She seemed on the verge of breaking into tears, like the Seivarden of a year ago, nearly any feelings at all too raw for her to handle. That sustained politeness, back in the tea shop, must have been the result of considerable effort.

I hadn't paid much attention to the people passing us as we walked. But now something struck me as wrong. I was suddenly aware of the location and direction of the people around us. Something indefinite troubled me, something about the way certain people moved.

At least four people were watching us, surreptitiously. Had no doubt been following us, and I had not noticed until now. This had to be new, surely. I would have noticed if I had been followed from the moment I'd stepped onto the docks. I was sure I would have.

Station had certainly seen my startlement back in the tea shop, when Rose-and-Azure had said, "*Justice of Toren.*" Station would certainly have wondered why I had reacted the way I had. Would certainly have begun to watch me even more closely than it had been. Still, Station didn't need to have me followed to watch me. This was not merely observation.

This was not Station.

I had never been given to panic. I would not panic now. This throw was mine, and if I had miscalculated slightly the trajectory of one piece, I had not miscalculated the others. Keeping my voice very, very even I said to Seivarden, "We'll be early for the inspector supervisor."

"Do we have to go to that Awer's?" Seivarden asked.

"I think we should." Having said it, immediately wishing

I hadn't. I didn't want to see Skaaiat Awer, not now, not in this state.

"Maybe we shouldn't," said Seivarden. "Maybe we should go back to the room. You can meditate or pray or whatever it is, and then we can have supper and listen to some music. I think that would be better."

She was worried about *me*. Clearly she was. And she was right, back to the room would be better. I would have a chance to calm down, to take stock.

And Anaander Mianaai would have a chance to make me disappear with no one watching, no one the wiser. "The inspector supervisor's," I said.

"Yes, honored," Seivarden replied, subdued.

Skaaiat Awer's quarters were their own small maze of corridors and rooms. She lived there with a collection of dock inspectors and clients and even clients of clients. She was certainly not Awer's only presence here, and the house would have had its own quarters elsewhere on the station, but Skaaiat evidently preferred this arrangement. Eccentric, but that was expected of any Awer. Though as with so many Awers, there was a practical edge to her eccentricity—we were very near the docks here.

A servant admitted us, escorted us to a sitting room floored with blue-and-white stone, walled floor to ceiling with plants of all kinds, dark or light green, narrow-leaved or broad-, trailing or upright, some flowering, spots and swaths here and there of white, red, purple, yellow. Likely they were the entire occupation of at least one member of this household.

Daos Ceit waited for us there. Bowed low, seeming genuinely pleased to see us. "Honored Breq, Citizen Seivarden. Inspector Supervisor will be so pleased you've come. Do please sit." She gestured to the chairs spread around. "Will you have tea? Or are you full up? I know you had another engagement today."

"Tea would be nice, thank you," I said. Neither I nor Seivarden had actually drunk any at Captain Vel's gathering. But I didn't want to sit. All the chairs looked as though they'd impede my freedom of movement if I was attacked and had to defend myself.

"Breq?" Seivarden, voice very quiet. Concerned. She could see something was wrong, but she couldn't discreetly ask what it was.

Daos Ceit handed me a bowl of tea, smiling, to all appearances sincerely. Oblivious, it seemed, to the state of tension I was in, which was so obvious to Seivarden. How had I not recognized her the moment I'd seen her? Not immediately identified her Orsian accent?

How had I not realized I couldn't possibly deceive Anaander Mianaai for more than the smallest instant?

I couldn't stand through this, not courteously. I would have to choose a seat. None of the available chairs was tenable. But I was more dangerous than nearly anyone here realized, even sitting. I still had the gun, a reassuring pressure against my ribs, under my jacket. I still had the attention of Station, of *all* of Anaander Mianaai, yes, and that was what I had *wanted*. This was still my game. It was. Choose a seat. The omens will fall where they fall.

Before I could make myself sit, Skaaiat Awer came into the room. As modestly jeweled as when she was working, but I'd seen the pale-yellow fabric of her elegantly cut jacket on a bolt at that expensive clothier's shop. On her right sleeve cuff that cheap, machine-stamped gold tag flashed.

She bowed. "Honored Breq. Citizen Seivarden. How

good to see you both. I see Adjunct Ceit has given you tea." Seivarden and I acknowledged this with polite gestures. "Let me say, before anyone else arrives, that I'm hoping you'll both stay to supper."

"You tried to warn us yesterday, didn't you?" asked Seivarden.

"Seivarden," I began.

Inspector Supervisor Skaaiat raised one elegantly yellow-gloved hand. "It's all right, honored. I knew Captain Vel prided herself on being old-fashioned. On knowing how much better things were when children respected their elders and good taste and refined manners were the rule. All familiar enough, I'm sure you heard such talk a thousand years ago, citizen." Seivarden gave a small, acknowledging *ha*. "I'm sure you heard all about how Radchaai have a duty to bring civilization to humanity. And that ancillaries are far more efficient for that purpose than human soldiers."

"Well, as to that," said Seivarden, "I'd say they are."

"Of course you would." Skaaiat showed a small flash of anger. Seivarden probably couldn't see it, didn't know her well enough. "You probably don't know, citizen, that I commanded human troops during an annexation myself." Seivarden hadn't known that. Her surprise was obvious. I had known, of course. My lack of surprise would be obvious to Station. To Anaander Mianaai.

There was no point in worrying about it. "It's true," Skaaiat continued, "that you don't have to pay ancillaries, and they never have personal problems. They do whatever you ask them to, without any sort of complaint or comment, and they do it well and completely. And that wasn't true of my human troops. And most of my soldiers were good people, but it's so easy, isn't it, to decide the people you're fighting aren't really human. Or maybe you have to do it, to be able to kill them. People like Captain Vel love pointing out the atrocities that human troops have committed, that ancillaries never would. As though making those ancillaries was not an atrocity in itself.

"They're more efficient, as I said." In Ors, Skaaiat would have been sarcastic on this topic, but she spoke seriously. Carefully and precisely. "And if we were still expanding we would have to still use them. Because we couldn't do it with human soldiers, not for long. And we're built to expand, we've been expanding for more than two thousand years and to stop will mean completely changing what we are. Right now most people don't see that, don't care. They won't, until it affects their lives directly, and for most people it doesn't yet. It's an abstract question, except to people like Captain Vel."

"But Captain Vel's opinion is meaningless," said Seivarden. "So is anyone else's. The Lord of the Radch has decided, for whatever reason. And it's foolish to go around saying anything against it."

"She might decide otherwise, if persuaded," answered Skaaiat. All of us still standing. I was too tense to sit, Seivarden too agitated, Skaaiat, I thought, angry. Daos Ceit standing frozen, trying to pretend she wasn't hearing any of this. "Or the decision might be a sign that the Lord of the Radch has been corrupted in some way. Captain Vel's sort certainly doesn't approve of all the talking with aliens we've been doing. The Radch has always stood for civilization, and civilization has always meant pure, uncorrupted humanity. Actually dealing with nonhumans instead of just killing them can't be good for us."

"Is that what that business at Ime was about?" asked Seivarden, who had clearly spent our walk here thinking about this. "Someone decided to set up a base and stockpile ancillaries and . . . and what? Force the issue? You're talking about rebellion. Treason. Why would anyone be talking about something like that now? Unless, when they got the people responsible for Ime, they didn't get everyone. And now they're letting a few people put their heads up and make some noise, and once they think everyone involved has identified themselves . . ." She was openly angry now. It was a fairly good guess, it might well be more or less right. Depending on which Anaander had the upper hand here. "Why didn't you warn us?"

"I tried, citizen, but I ought to have spoken more directly. Even so, I wasn't sure Captain Vel had gone so far. All I knew was that she idealized the past in a way I can't agree with. The noblest, most well-intentioned people in the world can't make annexations a good thing. Arguing that ancillaries are efficient and convenient is not, to me, a point in favor of using ancillaries. It doesn't make it better, it only makes it look a little cleaner."

And that only if you ignored what ancillaries were to begin with. "Tell me"—I almost said *Tell me, Lieutenant*, but caught myself in time—"Tell me, Inspector Supervisor, what happens to the people waiting to be made into ancillaries?"

"Some are still in storage, or on troop carriers," Skaaiat said. "But most have been destroyed."

"Well, that makes it all better then," I said, seriously. Evenly.

"Awer was against it from the start," said Skaaiat. She meant the continual expansion, not any expansion at all. And the Radch had used ancillaries long before Anaander Mianaai had made herself into what she was. There just hadn't been quite so many of them. "Awer's lords have said so to the Lord of the Radch, repeatedly."

"But the lords of Awer have not refused to profit from it." I kept my voice even. Pleasant.

"It's so easy to go along with things, isn't it?" Skaaiat said. "Especially when, as you say, it profits you." She frowned then, and cocked her head slightly, listened a few seconds to something only she could hear. Looked questioningly at me, at Seivarden. "Station Security is at the door. Asking for Citizen Seivarden." *Asking* was certainly more polite than the reality. "Excuse me a moment." She stepped into the corridor, followed by Daos Ceit.

Seivarden looked at me, oddly calm. "I'm beginning to wish I were still frozen in my escape pod." I smiled, but apparently it didn't convince her. "Are you all right? You haven't been all right since we left that Vel Osck person. Damn Skaaiat Awer for not speaking more directly! Usually you can't get an Awer to *stop* saying unpleasant things. She picks now to be discreet!"

"I'm fine," I lied.

As I spoke, Skaaiat returned with a citizen in the light brown of Station Security, who bowed and said to Seivarden, "Citizen, will you and this person come with me?" The courtesy was, of course, merely a form. One didn't refuse Station Security's invitations. Even if we tried there were reinforcements outside, placed there to make sure we didn't refuse. They wouldn't be Station Security, those people who had followed us from Captain Vel's meeting. They would be Special Missions, or even Anaander Mianaai's own guard. The Lord of the Radch had put all the pieces together and decided to remove me before I could do any serious damage. But it was almost certainly too late for that. All of her was paying attention. The fact that she'd sent Station Security to arrest me, and not some Special Missions officer to kill me quickly and quietly, told me that.

"Of course," Seivarden answered, all calm courtesy. Of course. She knew she was innocent of any wrongdoing, she was sure I was Special Missions and working for Anaander herself, why should she worry? But I knew that finally the moment had come. The omens that had been in the air for twenty years were about to come down and show me—show Anaander Mianaai—what pattern they made.

This Security officer didn't even twitch an eyebrow as she answered. "The Lord of the Radch wishes to speak with you privately, citizen." Not a glance at me. She likely didn't know why she'd been sent to escort us to the Lord of the Radch, didn't realize I was dangerous, that she needed the backup that awaited us out in the station's corridors. If she even knew it was there.

The gun still sat under my jacket, and extra magazines tucked here and there, wherever the bulge wouldn't show. Anaander Mianaai almost certainly didn't know what I intended.

"Is this my audience I requested, then?" asked Seivarden.

The Security officer gestured ambiguity. "I couldn't say, citizen."

Anaander Mianaai couldn't have known my object in coming, knew only that I had disappeared some twenty years ago. Part of her might know that she'd been aboard my last voyage, but none of her could know what had happened after I'd gated out of Shis'urna's system.

"I did ask," said Inspector Supervisor Skaaiat, "if you might have tea and supper first." The fact she'd asked said something about her relationship with Security. The fact she'd been refused said something about the urgency behind this arrest—it was an arrest, I was sure.

Security, oblivious, made an apologetic gesture. “My orders, Inspector Supervisor. Citizen.”

“Of course,” said Skaaiat, smooth and unruffled, but I knew her, heard worry hidden in her voice. “Citizen Seivarden. Honored Breq. If there’s any assistance I can provide please don’t hesitate to call on me.”

“Thank you, Inspector Supervisor,” I said, and bowed. My fear and uncertainty, my near panic, drained away. The omen Stillness had flipped, become Movement. And Justice was about to land before me, clear and unambiguous.

The Security officer escorted us not to the main entrance of the palace proper, but into the temple, quiet at this hour when many people were visiting, or sitting home with family and a bowl of tea. A young priest sat behind the now-half-empty baskets of flowers, bored and sullen. She gave us a resentful glance as we entered, but didn’t even turn her head as we passed.

We went through the main hall, four-armed Amaat looming, the air still smelling of incense and the heap of flowers at the god’s feet and knees, back to a tiny chapel tucked into a corner, dedicated to an old and now-obscure provincial god, one of those personifications of abstract concepts so many pantheons hold, in this case a deification of legitimate political authority. No doubt when the palace had been built there had been no question of this god’s placement next to Amaat, but she seemed to have fallen out of favor, the demographic of the station, or perhaps just fashion, having changed. Or perhaps something more ominous had caused it.

In the wall behind the image of the god a panel slid open. Behind it an armed and armored guard, her weapon holstered but not far from her hand, silver-smooth armor covering her face. Ancillary, I thought, but there was no way to be sure. I wondered, as I had occasionally over the past twenty years, how that worked. Surely the palace proper wasn't guarded by Station. Were Anaander Mianaai's guards just another part of herself?

Seivarden looked at me, irritated, and, I thought, a bit afraid. "I didn't think I rated the secret entrance." Though it probably wasn't all that secret, just slightly less public than the one outside on the concourse.

The Security officer made that ambiguous gesture again, but said nothing.

"Well," I said, and Seivarden gave me an expectant look. Clearly she thought this was due to whatever special status she had decided I had. I stepped through the door, past the unmoving guard, who didn't acknowledge me at all, nor Seivarden coming behind me. The panel slid shut behind us.

21

Beyond the short stretch of blank corridor, another door opened onto a room four meters by eight, its ceiling three meters above. Leafy vines snaked across the walls, trailing from supports rising from the floor. Pale blue walls suggested vast distances beyond the greenery, making the room feel larger than it was, the last vestige of a fashion for false vistas, more than five hundred years out of date. At the far end a dais, and behind it images of the four Emanations hung in the vines.

On the dais stood Anaander Mianaai—two of her. The Lord of the Radch was so curious about us she wanted more than one part of herself here to question us, I guessed. Though likely she had rationalized it to herself some other way.

We walked to within three meters of the Lord of the Radch, and Seivarden knelt, and then prostrated herself. I was, supposedly, not Radchaai, not subject to Anaander Mianaai. But Anaander Mianaai knew, she had to know, who I really was. She had not summoned us this way without knowing. Still, I didn't kneel, or even bow. Neither Mianaai betrayed any surprise or indignation at this.

"Citizen Seivarden Vendaai," said the Mianaai on the right. "What exactly do you think you're playing at?"

Seivarden's shoulders twitched, as though, facedown on the floor, she had momentarily wanted to cross her arms.

The Mianaai on the left said, "*Justice of Toren*'s behavior has been alarming and perplexing enough, just on its own. Entering the temple and defiling the offerings! Whatever could you have meant by it? What am I to say to the priests?"

The gun still lay against my side, under my jacket, unremarked. I was an ancillary. Ancillaries were notorious for their expressionless faces. I could easily keep from smiling.

"If my lord pleases," said Seivarden into the pause that followed Anaander Mianaai's words. Her voice was slightly breathy, and I thought maybe she was hyperventilating slightly. "Wh...I don't..."

The Mianaai on the right let out a sardonic *ha*. "Citizen Seivarden is surprised, and doesn't understand me," that Mianaai continued. "And you, *Justice of Toren*. You intended to deceive me. Why?"

"When I first suspected who you were," said the Mianaai on the left before I could answer, "I almost didn't believe it. Another long-lost omen fetching up at my feet. I watched you, to see what you would do, to try to understand what you were intending by your rather extraordinary behavior."

If I had been human, I would have laughed. Two Mianaais before me. Neither trusted the other to hold this interview unsupervised, unobstructed. Neither knew the details of the destruction of *Justice of Toren*, each no doubt suspected the other's involvement. I might be an instrument of either, neither trusting the other. Which was which?

The Mianaai on the right said, "You've done a fairly decent job concealing your origin. It was Inspector Adjunct Ceit who first made me suspect." *I haven't heard that song since I was a child*, she'd said. That song, that had obviously come from Shis'urna. "I admit it took me an entire day to piece everything together, and even then I could hardly believe it. You hid your implants reasonably well. Station was completely deceived. But the humming would likely have given you away eventually, I imagine. Are you aware you do it almost constantly? I suspect you're making an effort not to do it now. Which I do appreciate."

Still facedown on the floor, Seivarden said, in a small voice, "Breq?"

"Not Breq," said the Mianaai on the left. "*Justice of Toren.*"

"*Justice of Toren* One Esk," I corrected, dropping all pretense of a Gerentate accent, or human expression. I was done pretending. It was terrifying, because I knew I couldn't live long past this, but also, oddly, a relief. A weight gone.

The right-hand Mianaai gestured the obviousness of my statement. "*Justice of Toren* is destroyed," I said. Both Mianaais seemed to stop breathing. Stared at me. Again I might have laughed, if I were capable of it.

"Begging my lord's indulgence," said Seivarden from the floor, voice tentative. "Surely there's some mistake. Breq is human. She can't possibly be *Justice of Toren* One Esk. I served in *Justice of Toren*'s Esk decade. No *Justice of Toren* medic would give One Esk a body with a voice like Breq's. Not unless she wanted to seriously annoy the Esk lieutenants."

Silence, thick and heavy, for three seconds.

"She thinks I'm Special Missions," I said, breaking that silence. "I never told her I was. I never told her I was anything, except Breq from the Gerentate, and she never believed that. I wanted to leave her where I found her, but I couldn't and I don't know why. She was never one of my favorites." I knew that sounded insane. A particular sort of insane, an AI insanity. I didn't care. "She doesn't have anything to do with this."

The right-hand Mianaai lifted an eyebrow. "Then why is she here?"

"No one could ignore her arrival here. Since I arrived with her, no one could ignore or conceal mine. And you already know why I couldn't just come straight to you."

The slight twitch of a frown on the right-hand Mianaai.

"Citizen Seivarden Vendaai," said the Mianaai on the left, "it is now clear to me that *Justice of Toren* deceived you. You didn't know what it was. It would be best, I think, if you left now. Without, of course, speaking of this to anyone else."

"No?" breathed Seivarden into the floor, as though she were asking a question. Or as though she was surprised to hear the word come out of her mouth. "No," she said again, more certainly. "There's a mistake somewhere. Breq jumped off a *bridge* for me."

My hip hurt, thinking of it. "No sane human being would have done that."

"I never said you were *sane*," Seivarden said, quietly, sounding slightly choked.

"Seivarden Vendaai," said the left-hand Mianaai, "this ancillary—and it *is* an ancillary—isn't human. The fact you thought it was explains a good deal of your behavior that was unclear to me before. I'm sorry for its deception and your disappointment, but you need to leave. *Now.*"

"Begging my lord's indulgence." Seivarden still lay face-down, speaking into the floor. "Whether you give it or not. I'm not leaving Breq."

"Go away, Seivarden," I said, expressionless.

"Sorry," she said, sounding almost blithe except her voice still shook slightly. "You're stuck with me."

I looked down at her. She turned her head to look up at me, her expression a mix of fear and determination. "You don't know what you're doing," I told her. "You don't understand what's happening here."

"I don't need to."

"Fair enough," said the Mianaai on the right, seeming almost amused. The left-hand one seemed less so. I wondered why that was. "Explain yourself, *Justice of Toren*."

Here it was, the moment I had worked toward for twenty years. Waited for. Feared would never come. "First," I said, "as I'm sure you already suspect, you were aboard *Justice of Toren*, and it was you yourself who destroyed it. You breached the heat shield because you discovered you had already suborned me yourself, some time previously. You're fighting yourself. At least two of you, maybe more."

Both Mianaais blinked and shifted their stances a fraction of a millimeter, in a way I recognized. I'd seen myself do it, in Ors, when communications cut out. Another of those communications-blocking boxes—part of Anaander Mianaai, at least, must have worried about what I might say, must have been waiting with her hand on the switch. I wondered how far the effect reached, and which Mianaai had triggered it, trying, too late, to hide my revelation from herself. Wondered what that must have been like, knowing that facing me this way could only lead to disaster, and yet obligated by the nature of her struggle with herself to do so. The thought amused me briefly.

"Second." I reached into my jacket, pulled out the gun, the dark gray of my glove bleeding into the white the weapon had taken from my shirt. "I'm going to kill you." I aimed at the right-hand Mianaai.

Who began to sing, in a slightly flat baritone, in a language dead for ten thousand years. "*The person, the person, the person with weapons.*" I couldn't move. Couldn't squeeze the trigger.

You should be afraid of the person with weapons. You
should be afraid.
All around the cry goes out, put on armor made of iron.
The person, the person, the person with weapons.
You should be afraid of the person with weapons. You
should be afraid.

She shouldn't know that song. Why would Anaander Mianaai ever go digging in forgotten Valskaayan archives, why would she trouble to learn a song that very possibly no one but me had sung for longer than she had been alive?

"*Justice of Toren* One Esk," said the right-hand Mianaai, "shoot the instance of me to the left of the instance that's speaking to you."

Muscles moved without my willing them. I shifted my aim to the left and fired. The left-hand Mianaai collapsed to the ground.

The right-hand one said, "Now I just have to get to the docks before I do. And yes, Seivarden, I know you're confused but you *were* warned."

"Where did you learn that song?" I asked. Still otherwise frozen.

"From you," said Anaander Mianaai. "A hundred years ago, at Valskaay." This, then, was that Anaander who had pushed reforms, begun dismantling Radchaai ships. The one who had first visited me secretly at Valskaay and laid down those orders I could sense but never see. "I asked you to teach me the song least likely to ever be sung by anyone else, and then I set it as an access and hid it from you. My enemy and I are far too evenly matched. The only advantage I have is what might occur to me when I'm apart from myself. And that day it occurred to me that I had never paid close enough attention to you—you, One Esk. To what you might be."

"Something like you," I guessed. "Apart from myself." My arm still outstretched, gun aimed at the back wall.

"Insurance," Mianaai corrected. "An access I wouldn't think of looking for, to erase or invalidate. So very clever of me. And now it's blown up in my face. All of this, it seems, is happening because I paid attention to you, in particular, and because I never paid any attention to you. I'm going to return control of your body to you, because it'll be more efficient, but you'll find you can't shoot me."

I lowered the gun. "Which *me*?"

"*What's* blown up?" asked Seivarden, still on the floor. "My lord," she added.

"She's split," I explained. "It started at Garsedd. She was appalled by what she'd done, but she couldn't decide how to react. She's been secretly moving against herself ever since. The reforms—getting rid of ancillaries, stopping the annexations, opening up assignments to lower houses, she did all of that. And Ime was the other part of her, building up a base, and resources, to go to war against herself and put things back the way they had been. And the whole time all of her has been pretending not to know it was happening, because as soon as she admitted it the conflict would be in the open, and unavoidable."

"But you said it straight out to all of me," Mianaai acknowledged. "Because I couldn't exactly pretend the rest of me wasn't interested in Seivarden Vendaai's second return. Or what had happened to you. You showed up so publically, so *obviously*, I couldn't hide it and pretend it hadn't happened, and only talk to you myself. And now I can't ignore it anymore. Why? Why would you do such a thing? It wasn't any order I ever gave you."

"No," I agreed. "It wasn't."

"And surely you guessed what would happen if you did such a thing."

"Yes." I could be my ancillary self again. Unsmiling. No satisfaction in my voice.

Anaander considered me a moment and then made a *hmf* sound, as though she'd reached some conclusion that surprised her. "Get up off the floor, citizen," she said to Seivarden.

Seivarden rose, brushing her trouser legs with one gloved hand. "Are you all right, Breq?"

"*Breq*," interrupted Mianaai before I could answer, stepping off the dais and striding past, "is the last remaining fragment of a grief-crazed AI, which has just managed to trigger a civil war." She turned to me. "Is that what you wanted?"

"I haven't been *crazed* with grief for at least ten years," I protested. "And the civil war was going to happen anyway, sooner or later."

"I was rather hoping to avoid the worst of it. If we're extremely fortunate, that war will only cause decades of chaos, and not tear the Radch apart completely. Come with me."

"Ships can't *do* that anymore," insisted Seivarden, walking beside me. "You made them that way, my lord, so they didn't lose their minds when their captains died, like they used to, or follow their captains against you."

Mianaai lifted an eyebrow. "Not exactly." She found a panel on the wall by the door that had been previously invisible to me, yanked it open, and triggered the manual door switch. "They still get attached, still have favorites." The door slid open. "One Esk, shoot the guard." My arm swung up and I fired. The guard staggered back against the wall, reached for her own weapon, but slid to the floor and then lay still. Dead, because her armor retracted. "I couldn't take that away without making them useless to me," Anaander Mianaai continued, oblivious to the person—the citizen?—she'd just ordered killed. Still explaining to Seivarden, who frowned, not understanding. "They have to be smart. They have to be able to think."

"Right," agreed Seivarden. Her voice trembled, just slightly, the edge of her self-control wearing thin, I thought.

"And they're armed ships, with engines capable of vaporizing planets. What am I going to do if they don't want to obey me? Threaten them? With what?" A few strides had brought us to the door communicating with the temple. Anaander opened that and stepped briskly into the chapel of legitimate political authority.

Seivarden made an odd sound in the back of her throat. An aborted laugh or a noise of distress, I wasn't sure which. "I thought they were just made so they had to do as they were told."

"Well, exactly," said Anaander Mianaai as we followed

her through the temple's main hall. Sounds from the concourse reached us, someone speaking urgently, voice pitched high and loud. The temple itself seemed deserted. "That's how they were made from the start, but their minds are complex, and it's a tricky proposition. The original designers did that by giving them an overwhelming reason to *want* to obey. Which had advantages, and rather spectacular disadvantages. I couldn't completely change what they were, I just... adjusted it to suit me. I made obeying *me* an overriding priority for them. But I confused the issue when I gave *Justice of Toren* two *me*s to obey, with conflicting aims. And then, I suspect, I unknowingly ordered the execution of a favorite. Didn't I?" She looked at me. "Not *Justice of Toren*'s favorite, I wouldn't have been so foolish. But I never paid attention to *you*, I'd never have asked if someone was *One Esk's* favorite."

"You thought no one would care about some nobody cook's daughter." I wanted to raise the gun. Wanted to smash all that beautiful glass in the mortuary chapel as we passed it.

Anaander Mianaai stopped, turned to look at me. "That wasn't *me*. Help me now, I'm fighting that other me even now, I'm quite certain. I wasn't ready to move openly, but now you've forced my hand, help me and I'll destroy her and remove her utterly from myself."

"You can't," I said. "I know what you are, better than anyone. She's you and you're her. You can't remove her from yourself without destroying yourself. Because *she's you*."

"Once I reach the docks," Anaander Mianaai said, as though it were an answer to what I had just said, "I can find a ship. Any civilian ship will take me where I want to go without question. Any military ship... will be a dicier proposition. But I can tell you one thing, *Justice of Toren* One Esk, one thing I'm certain of. I've got more ships than she does."

"Meaning what, exactly?" asked Seivarden.

"Meaning," I guessed, "the other Mianaai is likely to lose an open battle, so she has a slightly better reason to want to stop this spreading any further." I could see Seivarden didn't understand what that meant. "She's held it back by concealing it from herself, but now all of her here..."

"Most of me, anyway," corrected Anaander Mianaai.

"Now she's heard it straight out she can't ignore it. Not here. But she might be able to prevent the knowledge from reaching the parts of her that aren't here. At least long enough to strengthen her position."

Realization made Seivarden's eyes widen. "She'll need to destroy the gates as soon as possible. But it can't work. The signal travels at the speed of light, surely. She can't possibly overtake it."

"The information hasn't left the station yet," said Anaander Mianaai. "There's always a slight delay. It would be far more efficient to destroy the palace instead." Which would mean turning a warship engine on the entire station, vaporizing it, along with everyone on it. "And I'd have to destroy the whole palace to stop the information going any further. There isn't just one spot where my memories are stored. It's made hard to destroy or tamper with on purpose."

"Do you think," I asked, into Seivarden's shocked silence, "that even you could get a Sword or a Mercy to do that? Even with accesses?"

"How badly would you like the answer to that question?" asked Anaander Mianaai. "You know *I'm* capable of it."

"I do," I acknowledged. "Which option do you prefer?"

"None of the currently available choices is very good. The loss of either the palace or the gates—or both—will cause disruption on an unprecedented scale, all through Radch space. Disruption that will last for years, simply because of the size of that space. *Not* destroying the palace—and the gates, really they're still part of the problem—will ultimately be even worse."

"Does Skaaiat Awer know what's going on?" I asked.

"Awer has been a thorn in my side for nearly three thousand years," said Mianaai. Calmly. As though this were an ordinary, casual conversation. "So much moral indignation! I'd almost think they bred for it, but they're not all genetically related. But if I stray from the path of propriety and justice, I'm sure to hear about it from Awer."

"Then why not get rid of them?" asked Seivarden. "Why go and make one inspector supervisor here?"

"Pain is a warning," said Anaander Mianaai. "What would happen if you removed all discomfort from your life? No," Mianaai continued, ignoring Seivarden's obvious distress at her words, "I value that moral indignation. I encourage it."

"No you don't," I said. By now we were on the concourse. Security and military herded sections of the frightened crowd—many of them would have implants, would have been receiving information from Station when it suddenly cut out, with no explanation.

A ship's captain I didn't know spotted us, and hurried over. "My lord," she said, bowing.

"Get these people off the concourse, Captain," Anaander Mianaai said, "and clear the corridors, as quickly and safely as you can. Continue to cooperate with Station Security. I'm working to resolve this as quickly as possible."

As Anaander Mianaai spoke, a flash of movement caught my eye. Gun. Instinctively I raised my armor, saw the person holding the gun was one of the people who had been following us on the concourse, just before Security had summoned us. The Lord of the Radch must have sent orders before she triggered her device and cut off all communications. Before she knew about the Garseddai gun.

The captain Anaander Mianaai had been speaking to recoiled, visibly startled by the sudden appearance of my armor. I raised my own gun, and a hammer-hard blow hit me from the side—someone else had shot at me. I fired, hit the person holding the gun. She fell, her own shot wild, hitting the temple façade behind me, shattering some god, bright-colored chips flying. Sudden, shocked silence from the already frightened citizens along the concourse. I turned, looked along the trajectory of the bullet that had hit me, saw panicked citizens and the sudden silver gleam of armor—this other shooter had seen me shoot the first, didn't know armor wouldn't help her. Half a meter from her another flash of silver as someone else armored herself. Citizens between me and my targets, moving unpredictably. But I was used to crowds of the frightened and the hostile. I fired, and fired again. The armor disappeared, both my targets fallen. Seivarden said, "Fuck, you *are* an ancillary!"

"We'd better get off the concourse," said Anaander Mianaai. And to the nameless captain beside her, "Captain, get these people to safety."

"But..." the captain began, but we were already moving away, Seivarden and Anaander Mianaai staying low, moving as speedily as they could.

I wondered briefly what was happening in other parts of the station. Omaugh Palace was huge. There were four other concourses, though all were smaller than this one, and level upon level of homes, workplaces, schools, public spaces, all of it full of citizens who would certainly be frightened and confused. If nothing else, anyone who lived here knew the necessity of following emergency procedures, wouldn't stop to argue or wonder once the order to seek shelter had gone out. But of course, Station couldn't give that order.

I couldn't know, or help. "Who's in the system?" I asked, as soon as we were out of earshot, climbing down an emergency access ladder well, my armor retracted.

"Near enough to matter, you mean?" Anaander Mianaai answered from above me. "Three Swords and four Mercies in easy shuttle distance." Any order from Anaander Mianaai on the station would have to come by shuttle, because of the communications blackout. "I'm not worried about them at this very moment. There's no possibility of giving them orders from here." And the instant there would be, the instant that blackout was raised, the entire question would already be settled, the knowledge Anaander Mianaai was so desperate to hide from herself already speeding toward the gates that would take it through all of Radch space.

"Is anyone docked?" I asked. Right now, those would be the only ships that mattered.

"Only a shuttle from *Mercy of Kalr*," said Anaander Mianaai, sounding half-amused. "It's mine."

"Are you certain?" And when she didn't answer I said, "Captain Vel isn't yours."

"You got that impression too, did you?" Anaander Mianaai's voice was definitely amused now. Above me, above Anaander Mianaai, Seivarden climbed, silent except for her shoes on the ladder rungs. I saw a door, halted, pulled the latch. Swung it open, and peered into the corridor beyond. I recognized the area behind the dock offices.

Once we'd all clambered into the corridor and shut the emergency door, Anaander Mianaai strode ahead, Seivarden and me following. "How do we know she's the one she says she is?" Seivarden asked me, very quietly. Her voice still shook, and her jaw looked tight. I was surprised she hadn't curled up in a corner somewhere, or fled.

"It doesn't matter which one she is," I said, not making any attempt to lower my voice. "I don't trust any of her. If she tries to go anywhere near *Mercy of Kalr*'s shuttle you're going to take this gun and shoot her." All of what she'd said to me might easily be a ruse, intended to get me to help her to the docks, and to *Mercy of Kalr*, so she could destroy this station herself.

"You don't need the Garseddai gun to shoot me," Anaander Mianaai said, without looking behind her. "I'm not armored. Well, some of me is. But not *me*. Not most of me." She turned her head briefly, to look at me. "That *is* troublesome, isn't it."

With my free hand I gestured my lack of concern or sympathy.

We turned a corner and stopped cold, confronted with Inspector Adjunct Ceit holding a stun stick, the sort of thing Station Security might use. She must have heard us talking in the corridor, because she evinced no surprise at our appearance, just a look of terrified determination. "Inspector Supervisor says I'm not to let anyone past." Her eyes were wide, her voice unsure. She looked at Anaander Mianaai. "Especially not you."

Anaander Mianaai laughed. "Quiet," I said, "or Seivarden will shoot you."

Anaander Mianaai raised an eyebrow, plainly disbelieving that Seivarden could bring herself to do any such thing, but she was silent.

"Daos Ceit," I said, in the language I knew had been her first. "Do you remember the day you came to the lieutenant's house and found the tyrant there? You were afraid and you grabbed my hand." Her eyes, impossibly, grew wider. "You must have woken before anyone else in your house or they'd never have let you come, not after what happened the night before."

"But…"

"I *must* speak with Skaaiat Awer."

"You're alive!" she said, eyes still wide, still not quite believing. "Is the lieutenant…Inspector Supervisor will be so…"

"She's dead," I interrupted before she could get any further. "*I'm* dead. I'm all that's left. I have to speak to Skaaiat Awer *right now*. The tyrant will stay here and if she won't then you should hit her as hard as you can."

I had thought Daos Ceit was mainly astonished, but now tears welled, and one dropped onto her sleeve, where she held the stick at the ready. "All right," she said. "I will." She looked at Anaander Mianaai and lifted the stick just slightly, the threat plain. Though it did strike me as foolhardy to post no one here but Daos Ceit.

"What's the inspector supervisor doing?"

"She's sent people to manually lock down all the docks." That would take a lot of people, and a long time. It explained why Daos Ceit was here by herself. I thought of storm shutters rolling down, in the lower city. "She said it was just like that night in Ors, and the tyrant had to be doing it."

Anaander Mianaai listened to all this, bemused. Seivarden seemed to have passed into some sort of shocked state, beyond astonishment.

"You stay here," I said to Anaander Mianaai, in Radchaai. "Or Daos Ceit will stun you."

"Yes, I got that much," said Anaander Mianaai. "I see

I didn't make a very positive impression when last we met, citizen."

"Everyone knows you killed all those people," Daos Ceit said. Two more tears escaped. "And blamed the lieutenant for it."

I had thought she was too young to have such strong feelings about the event. "Why are you crying?"

"I'm scared." Not taking her eyes off Anaander Mianaai, or lowering the stick.

That struck me as very sensible. "Come on, Seivarden." I walked past Daos Ceit.

Voices sounded ahead, where the outer office lay, past a turning. One step and then the next. It had never been anything else.

Seivarden let out a convulsive breath. It might have started as a laugh, or something she'd wanted to say. "Well," she said then. "We survived the bridge."

"That was easy." I stopped and checked under my brocaded jacket, counting magazines even though I already knew how many I had. Shifted one from under the waistband of my trousers to a jacket pocket. "This is not going to be easy. Or end half as well. Are you with me?"

"Always," she said, voice still oddly steady though I was sure she was on the point of collapse. "Haven't I already said that?"

I didn't understand what she meant, but now wasn't the time to wonder, or ask. "Then let's go."

22

We rounded the corner, my gun at the ready, and found the outer office empty. Not silent. Inspector Supervisor Skaaiat's voice sounded outside, slightly muted through the wall. "I appreciate that, Captain, but I'm ultimately responsible for the safety of the docks."

An answer, muffled, words indistinguishable, but I thought I recognized the voice.

"I stand by my actions, Captain," Skaaiat Awer answered as Seivarden and I came through the office and reached the wide lobby just outside.

Captain Vel stood, her back to an open lift shaft, a lieutenant and two troops behind her. The lieutenant still had pastry crumbs on her brown jacket. They must have climbed down the shaft, because I was quite certain Station controlled the lifts. In front of us, facing them and all the lobby's watching gods, stood Skaaiat Awer and four dock inspectors. Captain Vel saw me, saw Seivarden, and frowned slightly in surprise. "Captain Seivarden," she said.

Inspector Supervisor Skaaiat didn't turn around, but I

could guess what she was thinking, that she'd sent Daos Ceit to defend the back way in, all by herself. "She's fine," I said, answering her, and not Captain Vel. "She let me past." And then, not having planned it, the words seeming to come out of my mouth of their own volition, "Lieutenant, it's me, I'm *Justice of Toren* One Esk."

As soon as I said it I knew she would turn. I raised the gun to aim it at Captain Vel. "Don't move, Captain." But she hadn't. She and the rest of *Mercy of Kalr* stood puzzling out what I had just said.

Skaaiat Awer turned. "Daos Ceit would never have let me by otherwise," I said. And remembered Daos Ceit's hopeful question. "Lieutenant Awn is dead. *Justice of Toren* is destroyed. It's only me now."

"You're lying," she said, but even with my attention on Captain Vel and the others I could see she believed me.

One of the lift doors came jerkily open and Anaander Mianaai jumped out. And then another. The first turned, fist raised, as the second lunged for her. Soldiers and dock inspectors backed reflexively away from the struggling Anaanders, into my line of fire. "*Mercy of Kalr* stand clear!" I shouted, and the soldiers moved, even Captain Vel. I fired twice, hitting one Anaander in the head and the other in the back.

Everyone else stood frozen. Shocked. "Inspector Supervisor," I said, "you can't let the Lord of the Radch reach *Mercy of Kalr*. She'll breach its heat shield and destroy us all."

One Anaander still lived, struggled vainly to stand. "You've got it backward," she gasped, bleeding. Dying, I thought, unless she got to a medic soon. But it hardly mattered, this was only one of thousands of bodies. I wondered what was happening in the private center of the palace proper, what sort of violence had broken out. "I'm not the one you want to shoot."

"If you're Anaander Mianaai," I said, "then I want to shoot you." Whichever half she represented, this body hadn't heard all of that conversation in the audience hall, still thought it possible that I was on her side.

She gasped, and for a moment I thought she was gone. Then she said, faintly, "My fault." And then, "If I were me"—a brief moment of pained amusement—"I'll have gone to Security."

Except, of course, unlike Anaander Mianaai's personal guard (and whoever had shot at me on the concourse), Station Security's "armed" was stun sticks, and "armored" was helmets and vests. They never had to face opponents with guns. I had a gun, and because of who I was, I was deadly with it. This Mianaai had missed that part of the conversation as well. "Have you noticed my gun?" I asked. "Have you recognized it?" She wasn't armored, hadn't realized that the gun I had shot her with was different from any other gun.

Hadn't had, I thought, time or attention to wonder how anyone on the station could have had a gun she didn't know about. Or maybe she just assumed I had shot her with a weapon she'd hidden from herself. But she saw now. No one else understood, no one else recognized the weapon, except Seivarden who already knew. "I can stand right here and pick off anyone who comes through the shafts. Just like I did you. I've got plenty of ammunition."

She didn't answer. Shock would defeat her in a matter of minutes, I thought.

Before any of the Mercy of Kalrs could react, a dozen vested and helmeted Station Security came thunking down the lift shaft. The first six tumbled out into the corridor, then stopped, shocked and confused by the dead Anaander Mianaais lying on the ground.

I had spoken the truth, I could pick them off, could shoot them in this moment of frozen surprise. But I didn't want to. "Security," I said, as firmly and authoritatively as I could. Noting which fresh magazine was nearest to hand. "Whose orders are you following?"

The senior Security officer turned and stared at me, saw Skaaiat Awer and her dock inspectors, facing Captain Vel and her two lieutenants. Hesitated as she tried to put us together in some shape she understood.

"I am ordered by the Lord of the Radch to secure the docks," she announced. As she spoke I saw on her face the moment she connected the dead Mianaais with the gun I held ready. The gun I shouldn't have had.

"I have the docks secured," said Inspector Supervisor Skaaiat.

"All due respect, Inspector Supervisor." Senior Security sounded reasonably sincere. "The Lord of the Radch has to get to a gate so she can send for help. We're to ensure she makes it safely to a ship."

"Why not her own security?" I asked, already knowing the answer, as Senior Security did not. It was plain on her face that the question hadn't occurred to her.

Captain Vel said, brusque, "My own ship's shuttle is docked, I'd be more than happy to take my lord where she wants to go." This with a pointed look at Skaaiat Awer.

Another Anaander Mianaai was almost certainly in that shaft behind those other Security officers. "Seivarden," I said, "escort Senior Security to where Inspector Adjunct Daos Ceit is." And to Senior Security's look of dubious alarm, "It will make a number of things clear to you. You'll still outnumber us and if you're not back within five minutes they can take me down." Or try to. They had probably never any of them met an ancillary and didn't know how dangerous I could be.

"And if I won't?" asked Senior Security.

I had left my face expressionless, but now, in answer, I smiled, as sweetly as I could manage. "Try it and see."

The smile unnerved her, and she obviously had no idea what was going on, and knew it, knew things weren't adding up to anything she could make sense of. Likely her entire career had been spent dealing with drunks, and arguments between neighbors. "Five minutes," she said.

"Good choice," I said, still smiling. "Do please leave the stun stick behind."

"This way, citizen." Seivarden, all elegant servant's politeness.

When they had gone Captain Vel said, urgently, "Security, we outnumber them, despite the gun."

"Them." The apparently next-ranking Security officer was plainly still confused, still hadn't worked out what was going on. And, I realized, Security was used to thinking of Inspector Supervisor Skaaiat, indeed all of the dock inspectors, as being allies. And of course military officers held both dock authorities and Station Security forces in mild contempt, a fact Security here was certainly aware of. "Why is there a *them*?"

A look of frustrated irritation crossed Captain Vel's face.

All this time, muttered words had been passing from the Security on solid ground to the Security still hanging in the shaft. I was certain an Anaander Mianaai was with them, and that the only thing that had kept her from herself ordering Security to rush me was her realizing that despite what Station (and certainly her own sensors) had told her, I had a gun. She needed to protect her own particular body, now she couldn't rely on any of the others. That and the lag time of questions and information passing from citizen to citizen up and down the shaft had kept her from acting until now, but surely she would move soon. And as if in answer to my thought the whispering in the shaft intensified, and the Security officers shifted their stances, just slightly, in a way that told me they were about to charge.

Just then, Senior Security returned. She turned to look at me as she passed, a horrified expression on her face. Said to her now-hesitating officers, "I don't know what to do. The Lord of the Radch is back there, and she says the inspector supervisor and this...this person are acting under her direct orders and we're not to allow even one of her on the docks or onto any ship, under any circumstances." Her fear and her confusion were evident.

I knew how she felt, but this wasn't the time to sympathize. "She asked you, and not her own guard, because her own guard is fighting her, and probably each other. Depending on which of them got orders from which of her."

"I don't know who to believe," said Senior Security. But I thought Security's natural inclination to side with dock authority might tip the balance in our favor.

And Captain Vel and her lieutenant and troops had lost the initiative, lost any chance to disarm me, with Security in the balance but ready to tip my way, them and their stun sticks. Maybe if the Mercy of Kalrs had ever seen combat, ever seen any enemy that wasn't a training exercise. Hadn't spent so long on a Mercy, ferrying supplies or running long, dull patrols. Or visiting palaces and eating pastry.

Eating pastry and having tea with associates who had decided political opinions. "You don't even know," I said to Captain Vel, "which one is giving which orders." She frowned, puzzled. She hadn't entirely understood the situation, then. I'd assumed she knew more than she did.

"You're confused," said Captain Vel. "It isn't your fault, the enemy has misinformed you, and your mind was never your own to begin with."

"My lord is leaving!" called a Security officer. As a body, Security looked toward Senior Security. Who looked at me.

None of this distracted Inspector Supervisor Skaaiat. "And just who, Captain, is the enemy?"

"You!" Captain Vel answered, vehement and bitter. "And everyone like you who aids and encourages what's happened to us in the last five hundred years. Five hundred years of alien infiltration and corruption." The word she used was a close cousin of the one the Lord of the Radch had used to describe my pollution of temple offerings. Captain Vel turned to me again. "You're confused, but you were made by Anaander Mianaai to serve Anaander Mianaai. Not her enemies."

"There is no way to serve Anaander Mianaai without serving her enemy," I said. "Senior Security, Inspector Supervisor Skaaiat has seen to the docks. You secure any airlocks you can reach. We need to be certain no one leaves this station. The continued existence of this station depends on it."

"Yes, sir," said Senior Security, and began to consult with her officers.

"She spoke with you," I guessed, turning back to Captain Vel. "She told you the Presger had infiltrated the Radch in order to subvert and destroy it." I saw answering recognition on Captain Vel's face. I had guessed correctly. "She couldn't have told that lie to anyone who remembered what the Presger did, when they thought humans were their legitimate prey. They are powerful enough to destroy us whenever they wish. No one is subverting the Lord of the Radch except the Lord of the Radch. She has been secretly at war with herself for a thousand years. I forced her to see it, all of her here, and she will do anything to prevent having to acknowledge this to the rest of herself. Including using *Mercy of Kalr* to destroy this station before that information can leave here."

Shocked silence. Then Inspector Supervisor Skaaiat said, "We can't control all the accesses to the hull. If she goes outside and finds a launch unattended, or willing to take her..." Which would be anyone she found, because who here would think of disobeying the Lord of the Radch? And there was no way to broadcast a warning to everyone. Or to ensure that anyone believed the warning.

"Carry the message as quickly as you can, as far as you can," I said, "and let the omens fall as they will. And I need to warn *Mercy of Kalr* not to let anyone aboard." Captain Vel made a quick, angry motion. "Don't, Captain," I said. "I'd rather not have to tell *Mercy of Kalr* I killed you."

The shuttle pilot was armed and armored, and unwilling to leave without her captain's direct order. I was unwilling to allow Captain Vel anywhere near the shuttle. If the pilot had been an ancillary I wouldn't have hesitated to kill her, but as it was I shot her in the leg and let Seivarden and the two dock inspectors who'd come to do the manual undock for me drag her onto the station.

"Put pressure on the wound," I said to Seivarden. "I don't know if it's possible to reach Medical." I thought of the Security, soldiers, and palace guards all over the station, who likely had conflicting orders and priorities, and hoped that all the civilians were safely sheltered by now.

"I'm coming with you," said Seivarden, looking up from

where she knelt half on the shuttle pilot's back, binding her wrists.

"No. You might have some authority with Captain Vel's sort. Maybe even with Captain Vel herself. You do have a thousand years' seniority, after all."

"A thousand years' back pay," said a dock inspector, in an awed voice.

"Like *that* will ever happen," said Seivarden, and then, "Breq." And recollecting herself, "Ship."

"I don't have time," I said, brusque and flat.

A brief flash of anger on her face, and then, "You're right." But her voice shook, just slightly, and her hands.

I turned without saying anything more and boarded the shuttle, pushing off from the station's gravity into the shuttle's lack of it, and closed the lock, then kicked myself over to the pilot's seat, waving away a globule of blood, and strapped in. Thunking and pounding told me undocking had started. I had one wired-in camera fore, which showed me a few of the ships around the palace, shuttles, miners, little tenders and sail-pods, the bigger passenger and cargo ships either on their way out or waiting for permission to approach. *Mercy of Kalr*, white-hulled, awkward-shaped, its deadly engines larger than the rest of it, was somewhere out there. And beyond all of this, the beacons that lit the gates that brought ships from system to system. The station would have gone utterly, suddenly silent to them. The pilots and captains of these ships must be confused or frightened. I hoped none of them would be foolish enough to approach without permission from dock authorities.

My only other wired camera, aft, showed me the gray hull of the station. The last *thunk* of the undocking vibrated through the shuttle, and I set the controls on manual and started out—slowly, carefully, because I couldn't see to either side. Once I judged myself clear, I picked up speed. And then sat back to wait—even at this shuttle's top speed *Mercy of Kalr* was half a day away.

I had time to think. After all this time, after all this effort, here I was. I had hardly dared hope that I could revenge myself so thoroughly, hardly hoped that I could shoot even one Anaander Mianaai, and I had shot four. And more Anaander Mianaais were almost certainly killing each other back there in the palace as she battled herself for control of the station, and ultimately of the Radch itself, the result of my message.

None of it would bring back Lieutenant Awn. Or me. I was all but dead, had been for twenty years, just a last, tiny fragment of myself that had managed to exist a bit longer than the rest, each action I took a very good candidate for the last thing I'd ever do. A song bubbled up into my memory. *Oh, have you gone to the battlefield, armored and well-armed, and shall dreadful events force you to drop your weapons?* And that led, inexplicably, to the memory of the children in the temple plaza in Ors. *One, two, my aunt told me, three, four, the corpse soldier.* I had very little to do now besides sing to myself, and no one to disturb, no worries I might choose some tune that would lead someone to recognize or suspect me, or that anyone would complain about the quality of my voice.

I opened my mouth to sing out, in a way I hadn't for years, when I was checked mid-breath by the sound of something banging against the airlock.

This sort of shuttle had two airlocks. One would only open when docked with a ship or a station. The other was a smaller emergency hatch along the side. It was just the sort of hatch I'd used to board the shuttle I'd taken when I'd left *Justice of Toren* so long ago.

The sound came one more time and then stopped. It occurred to me that it might only have been some debris knocking into the hull as I passed. Then again, if I were in Anaander Mianaai's place, I'd try anything I could think of to achieve my aims. And I couldn't see the outside of the shuttle with communications blocked, only those two narrow views fore and aft. I might well be bringing Anaander Mianaai to *Mercy of Kalr* myself.

If someone was out there, if it wasn't just debris, it was Anaander Mianaai. How many of her? The airlock was small, and easily defensible, but it would be easiest not to have to defend it at all. It would be best to keep her from opening the airlock. Surely the communications blackout didn't reach much farther away from the palace. I quickly made the changes in heading that would steer me away from *Mercy of Kalr* but still, I hoped, toward the outer edges of the communications block. I could speak to *Mercy of Kalr* and never go any closer to it. That done, I turned my attention to the airlock.

Both doors of the lock were built to swing inward, so that any pressure difference would force them shut. And I knew how to remove the inner door, had cleaned and maintained shuttles just like this one for decades. For centuries. Once I removed the inner door it would be nearly impossible to open the outer one so long as there was air in the shuttle.

It took me twelve minutes to remove the hinges and maneuver the door to a place where I could secure it. It should have taken ten, but the pins were dirty and didn't slide as smoothly as they should have, once I'd released their catches. Human troops shirking, I was sure—I'd never have allowed such a thing on any of my own shuttles.

Just as I finished, the shuttle's console began to speak, in a flat, even voice I knew belonged to a ship. "Shuttle, respond. Shuttle, respond."

"*Mercy of Kalr*," I said, kicking myself forward. "This is *Justice of Toren* piloting your shuttle." No immediate answer—I didn't doubt what I'd said had been enough to shock *Mercy of Kalr* into silent surprise. "Do not let anyone aboard you. In particular do not let any version of Anaander Mianaai anywhere near you. If she's already there keep her away from your engines." Now I could access the cameras that weren't physically wired, I hit the switch that would show me a panoramic view of what was outside the shuttle—I wanted more than just that forward camera view. Hit the buttons that would broadcast my words to anyone listening. "All ships." Whether they would listen—or obey—I couldn't predict, but that wasn't something I could realistically control anyway. "Do not let anyone aboard you. Do not let Anaander Mianaai aboard you under any circumstances. Your lives depend on it. The lives of everyone on the station depend on it."

As I spoke the gray bulkheads seemed to dissolve away. The main console, the seats, the two airlock hatches remained, but otherwise I might have been floating unprotected in vacuum. Three vacuum-suited figures clung to handholds around the airlock I'd disabled. One had turned her head to look at a sail-pod that had swung dangerously close. A fourth was pulling herself forward along the hull.

"She's not aboard me," said *Mercy of Kalr*'s voice through the console. "But she's on your hull and ordering my officers to assist her. Ordering me to order you to allow her into the shuttle. How can you be *Justice of Toren*?" Not *What do you mean don't let the Lord of the Radch aboard*, I noticed.

"I came with Captain Seivarden," I said. The Anaander Mianaai who'd come forward clipped herself to one handhold, then another, and pulled a gun from the tool-holder on her suit. "What is the pod doing?" The sail-pod was still too close to me.

"The pilot is offering help to the people on your hull. She's only just realized it's the Lord of the Radch, who's told her to back off." The sail-pod would do the Lord of the Radch very little good—it was built for only very short trips, more a toy than anything else. It would never make it as far as *Mercy of Kalr.* Not in one piece, and not with its passengers alive and breathing.

"Are there any other Anaanders outside the station?"

"There don't appear to be."

The Anaander Mianaai with the gun extended armor in a flash of silver that covered her vacuum suit, held the gun against the shuttle's hull, and fired. I've heard it said that guns won't fire in a vacuum, but really it depends on the gun. This one fired, the impact a *bang* that I could feel where I clung to the pilot's seat. The force of the shot pushed her back, but not far, securely clipped as she was to the hull. She fired again, *bang.* And again. And again.

Some shuttles were armored. Some even had a larger version of my own armor. This shuttle wasn't, didn't. This shuttle's hull was built to withstand a fair number of random impacts, but it wasn't built to endure continued stress on the same spot, over and over again. *Bang.* She had thought through her inability to open the airlock, realized that whoever was piloting this shuttle was her enemy. Realized that I had removed the inner door, and that the outer wouldn't open until the air was out of the entire shuttle. If Anaander Mianaai could get in, she could patch the bullet hole and repressurize the shuttle. Even after a hull breach the shuttle (unlike the sail-pod) would have enough air to take her all the way to *Mercy of Kalr.*

If she had tried to order the palace's destruction from where she hung on to the side of this shuttle, she had failed. More likely, I realized, she'd known from the beginning such an order would fail and had not tried to give it. She needed to get aboard a ship, order it closer to the palace, and breach its heat shield herself. She wouldn't be able to get anyone else to do it for her.

If *Mercy of Kalr* was correct, and there were no other Anaanders outside the station, all I had to do was get rid of these. The rest, whatever was happening on the station, I would have to leave to Skaaiat and Seivarden. And Anaander Mianaai.

"I remember the last time we met," said *Mercy of Kalr.* "It was at Prid Nadeni."

A trap. "We never met." *Bang.* The sail-pod moved away, but not far. "Until now. And I was never at Prid Nadeni." But what did it prove, that I knew that?

Verifying my identity might have been easy, if I hadn't disabled or hidden so many of my implants. I thought for a moment, considering, and then I spoke a string of words, the closest I could get with my single, human mouth to the way I would have identified myself to another ship, so long ago.

Silence, punctuated by another shot against the shuttle hull.

"Are you really *Justice of Toren*?" asked *Mercy of Kalr* at length. "Where have you been? And where's the rest of you? And what's happening?"

"Where I've been is a long story. The rest of me is gone. Anaander Mianaai breached my heat shield." *Bang.* The forward Anaander ejected the magazine from her gun, slowly and methodically, and inserted another. The others still huddled around the airlock. "I assume you know what's going on with Anaander Mianaai."

"Only partially," said *Mercy of Kalr.* "I find I'm having difficulty saying what I think is happening."

No surprise at all, to me. "The Lord of the Radch visited you in secret, and placed some new accesses. Probably other things. Orders. Instructions. In secret, because she was hiding what she'd done from herself. Back at the palace"—it seemed ages ago, now, but it had only been a few hours—"I told all of her straight out what was happening. That she was divided, moving against herself. She doesn't want that knowledge to go any further, and there's a part of her that wants to use you to destroy the station before the information can get out. She'd rather do that than face the results of that knowledge." Silence from *Mercy of Kalr.* "You're bound to obey her. But I know..." My throat closed up. I swallowed. "I know there's only so far you can be forced to go. But it would be extremely unfortunate for the residents of Omaugh Palace if you discovered that point *after* having killed them all." *Bang.* Steady. Patient. Anaander Mianaai only needed one very small hole, and some time. And there was plenty of time.

"Which one destroyed you?"

"Does it matter?"

"I don't know," answered *Mercy of Kalr*, from the console, voice calm. "I've been unhappy with the situation for some time."

Anaander Mianaai had said that *Mercy of Kalr* was hers, but Captain Vel was not. That had to be uncomfortable for it. Could potentially be uncomfortable for me, and extremely unfortunate for the palace, if *Mercy of Kalr* was sufficiently attached to its captain. "The one that destroyed me was the one Captain Vel supports. Not, I think, the one that visited you. I'm not completely certain, though. How are we supposed to tell them apart when they're all the same person?"

"Where *is* my captain?" asked *Mercy of Kalr.* It said something to me, that the ship had waited this long to ask.

"She was fine when I left her. Your lieutenant too." *Bang.* "I did injure the shuttle pilot, she wouldn't leave her station. I hope she's all right. *Mercy of Kalr*, whichever Lord of the Radch has your support, I beg you not to let any on board, or obey her orders."

The firing stopped. The Lord of the Radch was worried, perhaps, that her gun would overheat. Still, she had plenty of time, no need to rush.

"I see what the Lord of the Radch is doing to the shuttle," said *Mercy of Kalr.* "That in itself would be enough to tell me something is wrong."

But of course, *Mercy of Kalr* had more indications than just that. The communications blackout, which resembled what had happened on Shis'urna twenty years ago, probably only reported in rumor, but still sobering, assuming rumors had reached this far. My—*Justice of Toren*'s—disappearance. Its own clandestine visit from the Lord of the Radch. Its captain's political opinions.

Silence, the four Anaander Mianaais clinging motionless to the shuttle hull.

"You still had your ancillaries," said *Mercy of Kalr.*

"Yes."

"I like my soldiers, but I miss having ancillaries."

That reminded me. "They aren't doing maintenance as they should. The hinges on the airlock door were very sticky."

"I'm sorry."

"It doesn't matter right now," I said, and it struck me that something similar might have delayed Anaander Mianaai's attempts to open the lock on her side. "But you'll want to have your officers get after them."

Anaander began firing again. *Bang.* "It's funny," *Mercy of Kalr* said. "You're what I've lost, and I'm what you've lost."

"I suppose." *Bang.* Occasionally, over the past twenty years, I had had moments when I didn't feel quite so utterly lonely, lost, and helpless as I had since the moment *Justice of Toren* had vaporized behind me. This wasn't one of those moments.

"I can't help you," said *Mercy of Kalr.* "No one I could send would get there in time." And besides, it was an open question, to me, whether in the end *Mercy of Kalr* would help me or the Lord of the Radch. It was best not to let Anaander inside this shuttle, near its steering or even its communications equipment.

"I know." If I didn't find some way to get rid of these Anaanders, and find it soon, everyone on the palace station would die. I knew every millimeter of this shuttle, or others just like it. There had to be something I could use, something I could do. I still had the gun, but I would have just as difficult a time getting through the hull as the Lord of the Radch. I could put the door back on and let her come in the small, easily defensible airlock, but if I failed to kill all of her...but I would certainly fail if I did nothing. I took the gun out of my jacket pocket, made sure it was loaded, pushed over to face the airlock and braced myself against a passenger seat.

Extended my armor, though that wouldn't help me if a bullet bounced back at me, not with this gun.

"What are you going to do?" asked *Mercy of Kalr*.

"*Mercy of Kalr*," I said, gun raised, "it was good to meet you. Don't let Anaander Mianaai destroy the palace. Tell the other ships. And please tell that incredibly, stupidly persistent sail-pod pilot to get the hell away from my airlock."

The shuttle was not only too small for a gravity generator, it was too small for growing plants to make its own air. On the aft side of the airlock, behind a bulkhead, was a large tank of oxygen. Right underneath where the three Mianaais waited. I considered angles. The Lord of the Radch fired again. *Bang*. An orange light on the console flashed and a shrill alarm sounded. Hull breach. The fourth Lord of the Radch, seeing the jet of fine ice crystals stream from the hull, unclipped herself, turned, pulled herself back toward the airlock, I could see it on the display. She moved more slowly than I wanted, but she had all the time in the world. I was the one in a hurry. The sail-pod engaged its small engine and moved out of the way.

I fired the gun into the oxygen tank.

I had thought it would take several shots, but immediately the world tumbled around, all sound cut off, a cloud of frozen vapor forming around me and then dispersing, and everything spinning. My tongue tingled, saliva boiling away in the vacuum, and I couldn't breathe. I would probably have ten—maybe fifteen—seconds of consciousness, and in two minutes I would be dead. I hurt all over—a burn? Some other injury despite my armor? It didn't matter. I watched, as I spun, counting Lords of the Radch. One, vacuum suit breached, blood boiling through the tear. Another, one arm sheared off, certainly dead. That was two.

And a half. *Counts as a whole*, I thought, and that made three. One left. My vision was going red and black, but I could see she was still hanging on to the shuttle hull, still armored, out of the way of the exploded tank.

But I had always been, first and foremost, a weapon. A machine meant for killing. The moment I saw that still-living Anaander Mianaai I aimed my gun without conscious thought and fired. I couldn't see the results of the shot, couldn't see anything except one silver flash of sail-pod and after that black, and then I passed out.

23

Something rough and writhing surged up out of my throat and I retched, and gasped convulsively. Someone held me by the shoulders, gravity pulled me forward. I opened my eyes, saw the surface of a medical bed, and a shallow container holding a bile-covered tangled mass of green and black tendrils that pulsed and quivered, that led back to my mouth. Another retch forced me to close my eyes and the thing came all the way free with an audible plop into the container. Someone wiped my mouth and turned me over, laid me down. Still gasping, I opened my eyes.

A medic stood beside the bed I lay on, the slimy green-and-black thing I had just vomited up dangling from her hand. She stared at it, frowning. "Looks good," she said, and then dropped it back into its dish. "That's unpleasant, citizen, I know," she said, apparently to me. "Your throat will be raw for a few minutes. You..."

"Wh..." I tried to speak, but ended up retching again.

"You don't want to try to talk just yet," said the medic as someone—another medic—rolled me over again. "You had a close call. The pilot who brought you in got you just in time, but she only had a basic emergency kit." That stupid, stubborn sail-pod. It must have been. She hadn't known I wasn't human, hadn't known saving me would be pointless. "And she couldn't get you here right away," the medic continued. "We were worried for a little bit there. But the pulmonary corrective's come all the way out, and the readings are good. Very minimal brain damage, if any, though you might not quite feel like yourself for a while."

That actually struck me as funny, but the retching had subsided again and I didn't want to restart it, so I refused to acknowledge it. I kept my eyes closed and lay as still and quiet as I could while I was rolled over and laid down again. If I opened my eyes I would want to ask questions.

"She can have tea in ten minutes," said the medic, to whom I didn't know. "Nothing solid just yet. Don't talk to her for the next five."

"Yes, Doctor." Seivarden. I opened my eyes, turned my head. Seivarden stood at my bedside. "Don't talk," she said to me. "The sudden decompression..."

"It will be easier for her to keep silent," admonished the medic, "if you don't talk to her."

Seivarden fell silent. But I knew what the sudden decompression would have done to me. Dissolved gasses in my blood would have come out of solution, suddenly and violently. Very possibly violently enough to kill me even without the complete lack of air. But an increase in pressure—say, being hauled back into atmosphere—would have sent those bubbles back into solution.

The pressure difference between my lungs and the vacuum might have injured me. And I had been surprised when the tank blew, and preoccupied with shooting Anaander

Mianaais, and might not have exhaled as I should have. And that had probably been the least of my injuries, given the explosion that had propelled me into the vacuum to begin with. A sail-pod would have had only the most rudimentary means of treating such injuries, and the pilot had probably shoved me into a bare-bones version of a suspension pod to hold me until I could get to a medic.

"Good," said the medic. "Stay nice and quiet." She left.

"How long?" I asked Seivarden. And didn't retch, though my throat was, as the medic had promised, still raw.

"About a week." Seivarden pulled a chair over and sat.

A week. "I take it the palace is still here."

"Yes," said Seivarden, as though my question hadn't been completely foolish but deserved an answer. "Thanks to you. Security and the dock crew managed to seal off all the exits before any other Lords of the Radch made it out onto the hull. If you hadn't stopped the ones that did..." She made an averting gesture. "Two gates have gone down." Out of twelve, that would be. That would cause enormous headaches, both here and at the other ends of those gates. And any ships in them when they'd gone might or might not have made it to safety. "Our side won, though, that's good."

Our side. "I don't have a side in this," I said.

From somewhere behind her Seivarden produced a bowl of tea. She kicked something below me, and the bed inclined itself, slowly. She held the bowl to my mouth and I took one small, cautious sip. It was wonderful. "Why," I asked, when I'd taken another, "am I here? I know why the idiot who hauled me in did it, but why did the medics bother with me?"

Seivarden frowned. "You're serious."

"I'm always serious."

"That's true." She stood, opened a drawer and brought

out a blanket, which she laid over me, and carefully tucked around my bare hands.

Before she could answer my question, Inspector Supervisor Skaaiat came partway into the small room. “Medic said you were awake.”

“Why?” I asked. And in answer to her puzzled expression, “Why am I awake? Why am I not dead?”

“Did you want to be?” asked Inspector Supervisor Skaaiat, still looking as though she didn’t understand me.

“No.” Seivarden offered the tea again, and I drank, a larger sip than before. “No, I don’t want to be dead, but it seems like a lot of work just to revive an ancillary.” And cruel to have brought me back just so the Lord of the Radch could order me destroyed.

“I don’t think anyone here thinks of you as an ancillary,” said Inspector Supervisor Skaaiat.

I looked at her. She seemed entirely serious.

“Skaaiat Awer,” I began, flat-voiced.

“Breq,” said Seivarden before I could speak further, voice urgent. “The doctor said lie still. Here, have more tea.”

Why was Seivarden even here? Why was Skaaiat? “What have you done for Lieutenant Awn’s sister?” I asked, flat and harsh.

“Offered her clientage, actually. Which she wouldn’t take. She was sure her sister held me in high regard but she herself didn’t know me and wasn’t in need of my assistance. Very stubborn. She’s in horticulture, two gates away. She’s doing fine, I keep an eye on her, best I can from this distance.”

“Have you offered it to Daos Ceit?”

“This is about Awn,” Inspector Supervisor Skaaiat said. “I can see it is, but you won’t come out and say it. And you’re right. There was a great deal more that I could have said to her before she left, and I should have said it. You're the ancillary, the non-person, the piece of equipment, but to compare our actions, you loved her more than I ever did."

Compare our actions. It was like a slap. "No," I said. Glad of my expressionless ancillary's voice. "You left her in doubt. I killed her." Silence. "The Lord of the Radch doubted your loyalty, doubted Awer, and wanted Lieutenant Awn to spy on you. Lieutenant Awn refused, and demanded to be interrogated to prove her loyalty. Of course Anaander Mianaai didn't want that. She ordered me to shoot Lieutenant Awn."

Three seconds of silence. Seivarden stood motionless. Then Skaaiat Awer said, "You didn't have a choice."

"I don't know if I had a choice or not. I didn't think I did. But the next thing I did, after I shot Lieutenant Awn, was to shoot Anaander Mianaai. Which is why—" I stopped. Took a breath. "Which is why she breached my heat shield. Skaaiat Awer, I have no right to be angry with you." I couldn't speak further.

"You have every right to be as angry as you wish," said Inspector Supervisor Skaaiat. "If I had understood when you first came here, I would have spoken differently to you."

"And if I had wings I'd be a sail-pod." Ifs and would-haves changed nothing. "Tell the tyrant," I used the Orsian word, "that I will see her as soon as I can get out of bed. Seivarden, bring me my clothes."

Inspector Supervisor Skaaiat had, it turned out, actually come to see Daos Ceit, who'd been badly injured in the last convulsions of Anaander Mianaai's struggle with herself. I walked slowly down a corridor lined with corrective-swathed injured lying on hastily made pallets, or encased in pods that would hold them suspended until the medics could get to them. Daos Ceit lay on a bed, in a room, unconscious. Looking smaller and younger than I knew she was. "Will she be all right?" I asked Seivarden. Inspector Supervisor Skaaiat hadn't waited for me to make my slow way down the corridor, she'd had to get back to the docks.

"She will," answered the medic, behind me. "You shouldn't be out of bed."

She was right. Just dressing, even with Seivarden's assistance, had left me shaking with exhaustion. I had come down the corridor on sheer determination. Now I felt turning my head to answer the medic would take more strength than I had.

"You just grew a new pair of lungs," continued the medic. "Among other things. You're not going to be walking around for a few days. At the very least." Daos Ceit breathed shallowly and regularly, looking so much like the tiny child I'd known I wondered for a moment that I hadn't recognized her as soon as I'd seen her.

"You need the space," I said, and then that clicked together with another bit of information. "You could have left me in suspension until you weren't so busy."

"The Lord of the Radch said she needed you, citizen. She wanted you up as soon as possible." Faintly aggrieved, I thought. The medics, not unreasonably, would have prioritized patients differently. And she hadn't argued when I'd said she needed the space.

"You should go back to bed," said Seivarden. Solid Seivarden, the only thing between me and utter collapse just now. I shouldn't have gotten up.

"No."

"She gets like this," said Seivarden, her voice apologetic.

"So I see."

"Let's go back to the room." Seivarden sounded extremely patient and calm. It was a moment before I realized she was talking to me. "You can get some rest. We can deal with the Lord of the Radch when you're good and ready."

"No," I repeated. "Let's go."

With Seivarden's support I made it out of Medical, into a lift, and then what seemed to be an endless length of corridor, and then, suddenly, a tremendous open space, the ground stretching away covered with glittering shards of colored glass that crunched and ground under my few steps.

"The fight spilled over into the temple," Seivarden said, without my asking.

The main concourse, that's where I was. And all this broken glass, what was left of that room full of funeral offerings. Only a few people were out, mostly picking through the shards, looking, I supposed, for any large pieces that might be restored. Light-brown-jacketed Security looked on.

"Communications were restored within a day or so, I think," Seivarden continued, guiding me around patches of glass, toward the entrance to the palace proper. "And then people started figuring out what was going on. And picking sides. After a while you couldn't not pick a side. Not really. For a bit we were afraid the military ships might attack each other, but there were only two on the other side, and they went for the gates instead, and left the system."

"Civilian casualties?" I asked.

"There always are." We crossed the last few meters of glass-strewn concourse and entered the palace proper. An official stood there, her uniform jacket grimy, stained dark on one sleeve. "Door one," she said, barely looking at us. Sounding exhausted.

Door one led to a lawn. On three sides, a vista of hills and trees, and above, a blue sky streaked with pearly clouds. The fourth side was beige wall, the grass gouged and torn at its base. A plain but thickly padded green chair sat a few meters in front of me. Not for me, surely, but I didn't much care. "I need to sit down."

"Yes," said Seivarden, and walked me there, and lowered me into it. I closed my eyes, just for a moment.

A child was speaking, a high, piping voice. "The Presger had approached me before Garsedd," said the child. "The translators they sent had been grown from what they'd taken off human ships, of course, but they'd been raised and taught by the Presger and I might as well have been talking to aliens. They're better now, but they're still unsettling company."

"Begging my lord's pardon." Seivarden. "Why did you refuse them?"

"I was already planning to destroy them," said the child. Anaander Mianaai. "I had begun to marshal the resources I thought I'd need. I thought they'd gotten wind of my plans and were frightened enough to want to make peace. I thought they were showing weakness." She laughed, bitter and regretful, odd to hear in such a young voice. But Anaander Mianaai was hardly young.

I opened my eyes. Seivarden knelt beside my chair. A child of about five or six sat cross-legged on the grass in front of me, dressed all in black, a pastry in one hand, and the contents of my luggage spread around her. "You're awake."

"You got icing on my icons," I accused.

"They're beautiful." She picked up the disk of the smaller one, triggered it. The image sprang forth, jeweled and enameled, the knife in its third hand glittering in the false sunlight. "This *is* you, isn't it."

"Yes."

"The Itran Tetrarchy! Is that where you found the gun?"

"No. It's where I got my money."

Anaander Mianaai frankly stared in astonishment. "They let you leave with that much money?"

"One of the tetrarchs owed me a favor."

"That must have been some favor."

"It was."

"Do they really practice human sacrifice there? Or is this," she gestured to the severed head the figure held, "just metaphorical?"

"It's complicated."

She made a breathy *hmf*. Seivarden knelt silent and motionless.

"The medic said you needed me."

Five-year-old Anaander Mianaai laughed. "And so I do."

"In that case," I said, "go fuck yourself." Which she could actually, literally do, in fact.

"Half your anger is for yourself." She ate the last bite of pastry and brushed her small gloved hands together, showering fragments of sugar icing onto the grass. "But it's such a monumentally enormous anger even half is quite devastating."

"I could be ten times as angry," I said, "and it would mean nothing if I was unarmed."

Her mouth quirked in a half-smile. "I haven't gotten to where I am by laying aside useful instruments."

"You destroy the instruments of your enemy wherever you find them," I said. "You told me so yourself. And I won't be useful to you."

"I'm the right one," the child said. "I'll sing for you if you like, though I don't know if it will work with this voice. This is going to spread to other systems. It already has, I just haven't seen the reply signal from the neighboring provincial palaces yet. I need you on my side."

I tried sitting up straighter. It seemed to work. "It doesn't matter whose side anyone is on. It doesn't matter who wins, because either way it will be *you* and nothing will really change."

"That's easy for *you* to say," said five-year-old Anaander Mianaai. "And maybe in some ways you're right. A lot of things haven't really changed, a lot of things might stay the same no matter which side of me is uppermost. But tell me, do you think it made no difference to Lieutenant Awn, which of me was on board that day?"

I had no answer for that.

"If you've got power and money and connections, some differences won't change anything. Or if you're resigned to dying in the near future, which I gather is your position at the moment. It's the people without the money and the power, who desperately want to live, for those people small things aren't small at all. What you call no difference is life and death to them."

"And you care so much for the insignificant and the powerless," I said. "I'm sure you stay awake nights worrying for them. Your heart must bleed."

"Don't come all self-righteous on me," said Anaander Mianaai. "You served me without a qualm for two thousand years. You know what that means, better than almost anyone else here. And I *do* care. But in, perhaps, a more abstract way than you do, at least these days. Still, this is all my own doing. And you're right, I can't exactly rid myself of myself. I could use a reminder of that. It might be best if I had a conscience that was armed and independent."

"Last time someone tried to be your conscience," I said,

thinking of Ime, and that *Mercy of Sarrse* soldier who had refused her orders, "she ended up dead."

"You mean at Ime. You mean the soldier *Mercy of Sarrse* One Amaat One," the child said, grinning as if at a particularly delightful memory. "I have never been dressed down like that in my long life. She cursed me at the end of it, and tossed her poison back like it was arrack."

Poison. "You didn't shoot her?"

"Gunshot wounds make such a mess," the child said, still grinning. "Which reminds me." She reached beside herself and brushed the air with one small gloved hand. Suddenly a box sat there, light-suckingly black. "Citizen Seivarden."

Seivarden leaned forward, took the box.

"I'm well aware," said Anaander Mianaai, "that you weren't speaking metaphorically when you said your anger had to be armed to mean anything. I wasn't either, when I said my conscience should be. Just so you know I mean what I'm saying. And just so you don't do anything foolish out of ignorance, I need to explain just what it is you have."

"You know how it works?" But she'd had the others for a thousand years. More than enough time to figure it out.

"To a point." Anaander Mianaai smiled wryly. "A bullet, as I'm sure you already know, does what it does because the gun it's fired from gives it a large amount of kinetic energy. The bullet hits something, and that energy has to go somewhere." I didn't answer, didn't even raise an eyebrow. "The bullets in the Garseddai gun," five-year-old Mianaai continued, "aren't really bullets. They're... devices. Dormant, until the gun arms them. At that point, it doesn't matter how much kinetic energy they have leaving the gun. From the moment of impact, it makes however much energy it needs to cut through the target for precisely 1.11 meters. And then it stops."

"Stops." I was aghast.

"One point eleven meters?" asked Seivarden, kneeling beside me. Puzzled.

Mianaai made a dismissive gesture. "Aliens. Different standard units, I assume. Theoretically, once it was armed, you could toss one of those bullets gently against something and it would burn right through it. But you can only arm them with the gun. As far as I can tell there's nothing in the universe those bullets can't cut through."

"Where does all that energy come from?" I asked. Still aghast. Appalled. No wonder I had only needed one shot to take out that oxygen tank. "It has to come from somewhere."

"You'd think," said Mianaai. "And you're about to ask me how it knows how much it needs, or the difference between air and what you're shooting at. And I don't know that either. You see why I made that treaty with the Presger. And why I'm so anxious to keep its terms."

"And anxious," I said, "to destroy them." The aim, the fervent desire, of the other Anaander, I guessed.

"I didn't get where I am by having reasonable goals," said Anaander Mianaai. "You're not to speak of this to anyone." Before I could react, she continued, "I *could* force you to keep quiet. But I won't. You're clearly a significant piece in this cast, and it would be improper of me to interfere with your trajectory."

"I hadn't thought you would be superstitious," I said.

"I wouldn't say superstitious. But I have other things to attend to. Few of me are left here—few enough that the exact number is sensitive information. And there's a lot to do, so I really don't have time to sit here talking.

"*Mercy of Kalr* needs a captain. And lieutenants, actually. You can probably promote them from your own crew."

"I can't be a captain. I'm not a citizen. I'm not even *human.*"

"You are if I say you are," she said.

"Ask Seivarden." Seivarden had set the box on my lap, and now once again knelt silent beside my chair. "Or Skaaiat."

"Seivarden isn't going anywhere you aren't going," said the Lord of the Radch. "She made that clear to me while you were asleep."

"Then Skaaiat."

"She already told me to fuck off."

"What a coincidence."

"And really, I do need her here." She clambered to her feet, barely tall enough to meet my eyes without looking up, even sitting as I was. "Medical says you need a week at the least. I can give you a few additional days to inspect *Mercy of Kalr* and take on whatever supplies you might need. It'll be easier for everyone if you just say yes now and appoint Seivarden your first lieutenant and let her take care of things. But you'll manage it the way you want." She brushed grass and dirt off her legs. "As soon as you're ready I need you to get to Athoek Station as quickly as you can. It's two gates away. Or it would be if *Sword of Tlen* hadn't taken that gate down." *Two gates away*, Inspector Supervisor Skaaiat had said, of Lieutenant Awn's sister. "What else are you going to do with yourself?"

"I actually have another option?" She might have named me a citizen, but she could take it back as easily. "Besides death, I mean."

She made a gesture of ambiguity. "As much as any of us. Which is to say, possibly none at all. But we can talk philosophy later. We've both got things to do right now." And she left.

Seivarden gathered my things, repacked them, and helped

me to my feet, and out. She didn't speak until we were on the concourse. "It's a ship. Even if it is just a Mercy."

I had slept for some time, it seemed, long enough for the shards of glass to be cleared away, long enough for people to come out, though not in great numbers. Everyone looked slightly haggard, looked as though they'd be easily startled. Any conversations were low, subdued, so the place felt deserted even with people there. I turned my head to look at Seivarden, and raised an eyebrow. "You're the captain here. Take it if you want it."

"No." We stopped by a bench, and she lowered me onto it. "If I were still a captain someone would owe me back pay. I officially left the service when I was declared dead a thousand years ago. If I want back in, I have to start all over again. Besides." She hesitated, and then sat beside me. "Besides, when I came out of that suspension pod, it was like everyone and everything had failed me. The Radch had failed me. My ship had failed me." I frowned, and she made a placatory gesture. "No, it's not fair. None of it's fair, it's just how I felt. And I'd failed myself. But you hadn't. You didn't." I didn't know what to say to that. She didn't seem to expect an answer.

"*Mercy of Kalr* doesn't need a captain," I said, after four seconds of silence. "Maybe it doesn't want one."

"You can't refuse your assignment."

"I can if I have enough money to support myself."

Seivarden frowned, took a breath as though she wanted to argue, but didn't. After another moment of silence, she said, "You could go into the temple and ask for a cast."

I wondered if the image of foreign piety I'd constructed had convinced her I had some sort of faith, or if she was merely too Radchaai not to think the toss of a handful of omens would answer any pressing question, persuade me toward the right action. I made a small, doubtful gesture. "I really don't feel the need. You can, if you want. Or toss right now." If she had something with a front and a back, she could make a throw. "If it comes up heads you stop bothering me about it and get me some tea."

She made a quick, amused *ha*. And then said, "Oh," and reached into her jacket. "Skaaiat gave me this to give you." Skaaiat. Not *that Awer*.

Seivarden opened her hand, showed me a gold disk two centimeters in diameter. A tiny, leafy border stamped around its edge, slightly off center, surrounding a name. AWN ELMING.

"I don't think you want to throw it, though," Seivarden said. And, when I didn't answer, "She said you really should have it."

While I was still trying to find something to say, and a voice to say it with, a Security officer approached, cautious. Said, voice deferential, "Excuse me, citizen. Station would like to speak with you. There's a console right over there." She gestured aside.

"Don't you have implants?" Seivarden asked.

"I concealed them. Disabled some. Station probably can't see them." And I didn't know where my handheld was. Probably somewhere in my luggage.

I had to get up and walk to the console, and stand while I spoke. "You wanted to speak to me, Station, here I am." The week of rest Anaander Mianaai had spoken of became more and more inviting.

"Citizen Breq Mianaai," said Station in its flat, untroubled voice.

Mianaai. My hand still curled around Lieutenant Awn's memorial pin, I looked at Seivarden coming behind me with my luggage. "There was no point in making you any more upset than you already were," she said, as though I'd spoken.

The Lord of the Radch had said *independent*, and I was unsurprised to discover she hadn't meant it. But the move she'd chosen to undercut it did surprise me.

"Citizen Breq Mianaai," Station said again, from the console, voice as smooth and serene as ever, but I thought the repetition was slightly malicious. My suspicion was confirmed when Station continued. "I would like you to leave here."

"Would you." No answer more cogent than that came to my mind. "Why?"

A half second of delay, and then the answer. "Look around you." I didn't have the energy to actually do that, so I took the imperative as rhetorical. "Medical is overwhelmed with injured and dying citizens. Many of my facilities are damaged. My residents are anxious and afraid. *I* am anxious and afraid. I don't even mention the confusion surrounding the palace proper. And *you* are the cause of all this."

"I'm not." I reminded myself that, childish and petty as it seemed now, Station wasn't very different from what I had been, and in some ways the job it did was far more complicated and urgent than mine, caring as it did for hundreds of thousands, even millions of citizens. "And my leaving won't change any of that."

"I don't care," said Station, calm. The petulance I detected was certainly my imagination. "I advise you to leave now, while it's possible. It may become difficult at some point in the near future."

Station couldn't order me to leave. Strictly speaking it shouldn't have spoken to me the way it had, not if I was, in fact, a citizen. "It can't *make* you leave," Seivarden said, echoing part of my thoughts.

"But it can express its disapproval." Quietly. Subtly. "We do it all the time. Mostly nobody notices, except they visit another ship or station and suddenly find things inexplicably more comfortable."

A second of silence from Seivarden, and then, "Oh." From the sound, she was remembering her days on *Justice of Toren*, and the move to *Sword of Nathtas*.

I leaned forward, my forehead against the wall adjoining the console. "Are you finished, Station?"

"*Mercy of Kalr* would like to speak with you."

Five seconds of silence. I sighed, knowing I couldn't win this game, shouldn't even try to play it. "I will speak to *Mercy of Kalr* now, Station."

"*Justice of Toren*," said *Mercy of Kalr* from the console.

The name caught me by surprise, started exhausted tears. I blinked them away. "I'm only One Esk," I said. And swallowed. "Nineteen."

"Captain Vel is under arrest," said *Mercy of Kalr*. "I don't know if she's going to be reeducated or executed. And my lieutenants as well."

"I'm sorry."

"It isn't your fault. They made their own choices."

"So who's in command?" I asked. Beside me Seivarden stood silent, one hand on my arm. I wanted to lie down and sleep, just that, nothing else.

"One Amaat One." The senior soldier in *Mercy of Kalr*'s highest ranking unit, that would be. Unit leader. Ancillary units hadn't needed leaders.

"She can be captain, then."

"No," said *Mercy of Kalr*. "She'll make a good lieutenant but she's not ready to be captain. She's doing her best but she's overwhelmed."

"*Mercy of Kalr*," I said. "If *I* can be a captain, why can't you be your own?"

"That would be ridiculous," answered *Mercy of Kalr*. Its voice was calm as ever but I thought it was exasperated. "My crew needs a captain. But then, I'm just a Mercy, aren't I. I'm sure the Lord of the Radch would give you a Sword if you asked. Not that a Sword captain would be any happier to be sent to a Mercy, but I suppose it's better than no captain at all."

"No, Ship, it's not..."

Seivarden interrupted, voice severe. "Cut it out, Ship."

"*You're* not one of my officers," said *Mercy of Kalr* from the console, and now the impassivity of its voice audibly broke, if only slightly.

"Not *yet*," Seivarden replied.

I began to suspect a setup, but Seivarden wouldn't have made me stand like this in the middle of the concourse. Not right now. "Ship, I can't be what you've lost. You can't ever have that back, I'm sorry." And I couldn't have back what I'd lost, either. "I can't stand here anymore."

"Ship," said Seivarden, stern. "Your captain is still recovering from her injuries and Station has her standing here in the middle of the concourse."

"I've sent a shuttle," said *Mercy of Kalr* after a pause that was, I supposed, meant to express what it thought of Station. "You'll be more comfortable aboard, Captain."

"I'm not..." I began, but *Mercy of Kalr* had already signed off.

"Breq," said Seivarden, pulling me away from the wall I was leaning on. "Let's go."

"Where?"

"You know you'll be more comfortable aboard. More comfortable than here."

I didn't answer, just let Seivarden pull me along.

"All that money won't mean much if more gates go and ships are stranded and supplies are cut off." We were headed, I saw, toward a bank of lifts. "It's all falling apart. This isn't going to just be happening here, it's going to fall apart all over Radch space, isn't it?" It was, but I didn't have the energy to contemplate it. "Maybe you think you can stand aside and watch everything happen. But I don't really think you can."

No. If I could, I wouldn't have been here. Seivarden wouldn't have been here, I'd have left her in the snow on Nilt, or never have gone to Nilt to begin with.

The lift doors closed us in, briskly. A little more briskly than usual, though perhaps it was just my imagination that Station was expressing its eagerness to see me gone. But the lift didn't move. "Docks, Station," I said. Defeated. There was, in truth, nowhere else for me to go. It was what I was made to do, what I was. And even if the tyrant's protestations were insincere, which they ultimately had to be, no matter her intentions at this moment, still she was right. My actions would make some sort of difference, even if small. Some sort of difference, maybe, to Lieutenant Awn's sister. And I had already failed Lieutenant Awn once. Badly. I wouldn't a second time.

"Skaaiat will give you tea," Seivarden said, voice unsurprised, as the lift moved.

I wondered when I'd eaten last. "I think I'm hungry."

"That's a good sign," said Seivarden, and grasped my arm more securely as the lift stopped, and the doors opened on the god-filled lobby of the docks.

Choose my aim, take one step and then the next. It had never been anything else.

Acknowledgments

It's a commonplace to say that writing is a solitary art, and it's true that the actual act of putting words down is something a writer has to do herself. Still, so much happens before those words are put down, and then after, when you're trying to put your work into the best form you can possibly manage.

I would not be the writer I am without the benefit of the Clarion West workshop and my classmates there. And I've benefited from the generous and perceptive assistance of many friends: Charlie Allery, S. Hutson Blount, Carolyn Ives Gilman, Anna Schwind, Kurt Schwind, Mike Swirsky, Rachel Swirsky, Dave Thompson, and Sarah Vickers all gave me a great deal of help and encouragement, and this book would have been the lesser without them. (Any missteps, however, are entirely my own.)

I would also like to thank Pudd'nhead Books in St. Louis, the Webster University Library, St. Louis County Library, and the Municipal Library Consortium of St. Louis County.

Libraries are a tremendous and valuable resource, and I'm not sure it's possible to have too many of them.

Thanks also to my awesome editors, Tom Bouman and Jenni Hill, whose thoughtful comments helped make this book what it is. (Missteps, again, all mine.) And thanks to my fabulous agent, Seth Fishman.

Last—but not least, not at all—I could not have even begun to write this book without the love and support of my husband Dave and my children Aidan and Gawain.

extras

orbit

meet the author

MissionPhoto.org

ANN LECKIE has worked as a waitress, a receptionist, a rodman on a land-surveying crew, a lunch lady, and a recording engineer. The author of many published short stories, she lives in St. Louis, Missouri, with her husband, children, and cats.

interview

Honored Breq, or One Esk, or* Justice of Toren*, is a unique character in that she has a human body, but artificial intelligence. What led you to this choice, and what were some of the challenges and opportunities it presented?

Breq on her own wasn't nearly as challenging as *Justice of Toren*, or even just One Esk. Depicting what that must be like—to have not only a huge ship for a body, but also hundreds, sometimes thousands, of human bodies all seeing and hearing and doing things at once—the thought of that kept me from even starting for a long time. How do you show a reader that experience? I could try to depict the flood of sensation and action, but then the focus would be so diffuse that it would be difficult to see where the main thread was. On the other hand, I could narrow things down to only one segment of One Esk, shortchanging one of the things that really intrigued me about the character, and also making it seem as though it was more separate from the ship than it was.

But a character like *Justice of Toren* also sees a great deal, and so it can act as an essentially omniscient narrator—it knows its own officers intimately and can see their emotions. It can witness things happening in several places at once. So I could write in straight first person, while also taking advantage of that ability to see so much at one time whenever I needed that. It was a nifty short-circuit around one of the more obvious limits of a first-person narrator.

You have shown us elements of Radch culture in great detail, and reading* Ancillary Justice*, one gets the sense that you know far more about this civilization than appears in the novel. Can you tell us a little about what inspired the Radch?

I'm not sure I could say truthfully that any particular real-world example inspired the Radch. It was built piece by piece as time went by. That said, some of those pieces did come from the real world. I took a number of things from the Romans—though their theology isn't particularly Roman, the Radchaai attitude toward religion is fairly similar, particularly the way the gods of conquered peoples can be integrated into an already-familiar pantheon. And the careful attention to omens and divination—though the Radchaai logic behind that is quite different.

The Romans have provided a lot of writers with a model for various interstellar empires, of course, and no wonder. The Roman Empire is a really good example of a large empire that, in one form or another, functioned for quite a long time over a very large area. And over that time, there was all sorts of exciting drama—civil wars and assassinations and revolts and bits breaking off and being forced back in, even a pretty big change in the form of government, from Republic to Principate. There's tons of material there. And they loom large in European history. It wasn't so long ago that any educated Westerner learned Greek and Latin as a matter of course, and read Virgil and Ovid and Cicero and Caesar and a host of other writers as part of that education.

But I didn't want my future—however fanciful it was—to be entirely European. The Radchaai aren't meant to be Romans in Space.

Though* Ancillary Justice *is your first novel, you have published a number of short stories. Do you have very different approaches to writing, according to length? What can you share about your writing process?

When I first started writing seriously, I found that I was naturally producing very long work, and writing shorter was very difficult. Some of that was just being a beginner, but some of it was a product of the way I write. I might start out with the bones of an idea—the next step will be figuring out the setting. Setting, for me, is very much a part of my characters, and to set those characters in motion without also giving those details that make those characters' actions meaningful makes for thin work, at least when I do it.

People are who they are because of the world they live in, and the world is the way it is because of the people who live in it. If you're writing something set in the real world fairly close to our present time you can evoke setting and historical context with a few words. But I tend to write secondary-world fantasy, or far-future space opera, and evoking the history and culture of those worlds can be a bit complicated. It takes a bit of elbow room, or else incredibly efficient exposition.

I personally like working with a big frame, I like the feeling that the world extends well past the edges of the story, and odd, neat little details are one of the ways you do that.

But in a short story, there's very little room to work. Often new writers are advised to make sure every scene in a story is doing at least two things, but I've found that when I write short, two is too few. Every scene has to be doing as much work as it possibly can, and each sentence has to have a justification. If I can cut it, and the story remains comprehensible, then it pretty much has to go. Even if it's doing two or three things.

And then, of course, some ideas are suited to large-scale handling, and some wouldn't make more than a thousand words of story even if you jammed as much extra stuff in as you could. So I found that if I wanted to write short fiction, I needed to learn either to pull out a fragment of a big idea, or else compress something sweeping into a smaller space.

Your main character is known for her encyclopedic knowledge of song, and for her enthusiasm for singing. Is this an enthusiasm you share, and if so, were there any pieces of music you found particularly inspiring when writing this novel?

I love singing! I especially love singing with other people—choral singing is a blast. I think it's a shame that so many people I meet have such an ambivalent, fraught relationship with singing. It's such a personal kind of music, one nearly anyone can make, but there's often a feeling that only certain people are allowed to do it. I've met way more people who claim they can't sing than actually can't. And I've met lots of people who actively discourage anyone around them from singing. Why is that? I wish people felt freer to sing, and freer to enjoy people around them singing.

It's one of the things I love about shape note singing—there's no audition, no question of whether or not your voice is good enough, or whether anyone has talent. You love to sing? Come sing! There's no audience, we're just singing for the pure joy of singing. Granted, the music itself might be something of an acquired taste. Still, if the idea intrigues you, visit fasola.org and see if there's a singing near you.

I didn't know right away that One Esk would want to sing. But the moment I realized that it would be able to sing choral music *all by itself* the idea was pretty much inescapable.

As for music that I found inspiring, there would be two different sorts. Music that I listened to while writing or plotting, and music that I included in the story itself. Of the latter, there are three real-life songs in *Ancillary Justice.* Two of them are (shockingly enough) shape note songs—"Clamanda" (Sacred Harp 42) and "Bunker Hill" (Missouri Harmony 19). They're songs that, for one reason or another, I connect with these characters and events.

The third is older than these two by a couple of centuries, but it shares their military theme. It's "L'homme Armé," and it seems like every late fifteenth-century composer and their pet monkey wrote a mass based on it. I exaggerate—I don't think we have that many surviving Missas L'homme Armé by pet monkeys. But it was a popular song in its day.

Music I listened to—I find that projects tend to have their own soundtracks. Sometimes particular scenes do. The list of music I used while writing would be long and dull, but at least one scene wouldn't have existed without a particular piece. The bridge scene was a product of listening to Afro Celt Sound System's "Lagan" way too many times.

Ancillary Justice *is the first in a loose trilogy. What can we expect from the next books?*

Now Breq has a ship, she's got one priority—to make sure Lieutenant Awn's sister is safe, and keep her that way. But she can't do that without getting involved in local political and social maneuvering at Athoek Station, and can't avoid the chaotic and dangerous consequences of civil war breaking out across the Radch. And once the people in the territories surrounding Radchaai space realize what's going on, they're going to take an interest, and it's not likely to be a friendly one. And not all the neighbors are human.

introducing

If you enjoyed
ANCILLARY JUSTICE
look out for

ANCILLARY SWORD

by Ann Leckie

1

"Considering the circumstances, you could use another lieutenant." Anaander Mianaai, ruler (for the moment) of all the vast reaches of Radchaai space, sat in a wide chair cushioned with embroidered silk. This body that spoke to me—one of thousands—looked to be about thirteen years old. Black-clad, dark-skinned. Her face was already stamped with the aristocratic features that were, in Radchaai space, a marker of the highest rank and fashion. Under normal circumstances no one ever saw such young versions of the Lord of the Radch, but these were not normal circumstances.

The room was small, three and a half meters square, paneled with a lattice of dark wood. In one corner the wood was missing—probably damaged in last week's violent dispute between rival parts of Anaander Mianaai herself. Where the wood remained, tendrils of some wispy plant trailed, thin silver-green leaves and here and there tiny white flowers. This was not a public area of the palace, not an audience chamber. An empty chair sat beside the Lord of the Radch's, a table between those chairs held a tea set, flask, and bowls of unadorned white porcelain, gracefully lined, the sort of thing that, at first glance, you might take as unremarkable, but on second would realize was a work of art worth more than some planets.

I had been offered tea, been invited to sit. I had elected to remain standing. "You said I could choose my own officers." I ought to have added a respectful *my lord* but did not. I also ought to have knelt and put my forehead to the floor, when I'd entered and found the Lord of the Radch. I hadn't done that, either.

"You've chosen two. Seivarden, of course, and Lieutenant Ekalu was an obvious choice." The names brought both people reflexively to mind. In approximately a tenth of a second *Mercy of Kalr*, parked some thirty-five thousand kilometers away from this station, would receive that near-instinctive check for data, and a tenth of a second after that its response would reach me. I'd spent the last several days learning to control that old, old habit. I hadn't completely succeeded. "A fleet captain is entitled to a third," Anaander Mianaai continued. Beautiful porcelain bowl in one black-gloved hand, she gestured toward me, meaning, I thought, to indicate my uniform. Radchaai military wore dark-brown jackets and trousers, boots and gloves. Mine was different. The left-hand side was brown, but the right side was black, and my captain's insignia bore the marks that showed I commanded not only my own ship but other ships' captains. Of course, I had no ships in my fleet besides my own, *Mercy of Kalr*, but there were no other fleet captains stationed near Athoek, where I was bound, and the rank would give me an advantage over other captains I might meet. Assuming, of course, those other captains were at all inclined to accept my authority.

Just days ago a long-simmering dispute had broken out and one faction had destroyed two of the intersystem gates. Now preventing more gates from going down—and preventing that faction from seizing gates and stations in other systems—was an urgent priority. I understood Anaander's reasons for giving me the rank, but still I didn't like it. "Don't make the mistake," I said, "of thinking I'm working for *you*."

She smiled. "Oh, I don't. Your only other choices are officers currently in the system, and near this station. Lieutenant Tisarwat is just out of training. She was on her way to take her first assignment, and now of course that's out of the question. And I thought you'd appreciate having someone you could train up the way you want." She seemed amused at that last.

As she spoke I knew Seivarden was in stage two of NREM sleep. I saw pulse, temperature, respiration, blood oxygen, hormone levels. Then that data was gone, replaced by Lieutenant Ekalu, standing watch. Stressed—jaw slightly clenched, elevated cortisol. She'd been a common soldier until one week ago, when *Mercy of Kalr*'s captain had been arrested for treason. She had never expected to be made an officer. Wasn't, I thought, entirely sure she was capable of it.

"You can't possibly think," I said to the Lord of the Radch, blinking away that vision, "that it's a good idea to send me into a newly broken-out civil war with only one experienced officer."

"It can't be worse than going understaffed," Anaander Mianaai said, maybe aware of my momentary distraction, maybe not. "And the child is beside herself at the thought of serving under a fleet captain. She's waiting for you at the docks." She set down her tea, straightened in her chair. "Since the gate leading to Athoek is down and I have no idea what the situation there might be, I can't give you specific orders. Besides"—she raised her now-empty hand as though forestalling some speech of mine—"I'd be wasting my time attempting to direct you too closely. You'll do as you like no matter what I say. You're loaded up? Have all the supplies you need?"

The question was perfunctory—she surely knew the status of my ship's stores as well as I did. I made an indefinite gesture, deliberately insolent.

"You might as well take Captain Vel's things," she said, as though I'd answered reasonably. "She won't need them."

Vel Osck had been captain of *Mercy of Kalr* until a week ago. There were any number of reasons she might not need her possessions, the most likely, of course, being that she was dead. Anaander Mianaai didn't do anything halfway, particularly when it came to dealing with her enemies. Of course, in this case, the enemy Vel Osck had supported was Anaander Mianaai herself. "I don't want them," I said. "Send them to her family."

"If I can." She might well not be able to do that. "Is there anything you need before you go? Anything at all?"

Various answers occurred to me. None seemed useful. "No."

"I'll miss you, you know," she said. "No one else will speak to me quite the way you do. You're one of the very few people I've ever met who really, truly didn't fear the consequences of offending me. And none of those very few have the . . . similarity of background you and I have."

Because I had once been a ship. An AI controlling an enormous troop carrier and thousands of ancillaries, human bodies, part of myself. At the time I had not thought of myself as a slave, but I had been a weapon of conquest, the possession of Anaander Mianaai, herself occupying thousands of bodies spread throughout Radch space.

Now I was only this single human body. "Nothing you can do to me could possibly be worse than what you've already done."

"I am aware of that," she said, "and aware of just how dangerous that makes you. I may well be extremely foolish just letting you live, let alone giving you official authority and a ship. But the games I play aren't for the timid."

"For most of us," I said, openly angry now, knowing she could see the physical signs of it no matter how impassive my expression, "they aren't games."

"I am also aware of that," said the Lord of the Radch. "Truly I am. It's just that some losses are unavoidable."

I could have chosen any of a half dozen responses to that. Instead I turned and walked out of the room without answering. As I stepped through the door, the soldier *Mercy of Kalr* One Kalr Five, who had been standing at stiff attention just outside, fell in behind me, silent and efficient. Kalr Five was human, like all *Mercy of Kalr*'s soldiers, not an ancillary. She had a name, beyond her ship, decade, and number. I had addressed her by that name once. She'd responded with outward impassivity, but with an inner wave of alarm and unease. I hadn't tried it again.

When I had been a ship—when I had been just one component of the troop carrier *Justice of Toren*—I had been always aware of the state of my officers. What they heard and what they saw. Every breath, every twitch of every muscle. Hormone levels, oxygen levels. Everything, nearly, except the specific contents of their thoughts, though even that I could often guess, from experience, from intimate acquaintance. Not something I had ever shown any of my captains—it would have meant little to them, a stream of meaningless data. But for me, at that time, it had been just part of my awareness.

I no longer *was* my ship. But I was still an ancillary, could still read that data as no human captain could have. But I only had a single human brain, now, could only handle the smallest fragment of the information I'd once been constantly, unthinkingly aware of. And even that small amount required some care—I'd run straight into a bulkhead trying to walk and receive data at the same time, when I'd first tried it. I queried *Mercy of Kalr*, deliberately this time. I was fairly sure I could walk through this corridor and monitor Five at the same time without stopping or stumbling.

I made it all the way to the palace's reception area without incident. Five was tired, and slightly hungover. Bored, I was sure, from standing staring at the wall during my conference with the Lord of the Radch. I saw a strange mix of anticipation and dread, which troubled me a bit, because I couldn't guess what that conflict was about.

Out on the main concourse, high, broad, and echoing, stone paved, I turned toward the lifts that would take me to the docks, to the shuttle that waited to take me back to *Mercy of Kalr*. Most shops and offices along the concourse, including the wide, brightly painted gods crowding the temple façade, orange and blue and red and green, seemed surprisingly undamaged after last week's violence, when the Lord of the Radch's struggle against herself had broken into the open. Now citizens in colorful coats, trousers, and gloves, glittering with jewelry, walked by, seemingly unconcerned. Last week might never have happened. Anaander Mianaai, Lord of the Radch, might still be herself, many-bodied but one single, undivided person. But last week *had* happened, and Anaander Mianaai was not, in fact, one person. Had not been for quite some time.

As I approached the lifts a sudden surge of resentment and dismay overtook me. I stopped, turned. Kalr Five had stopped when I stopped, and now stared impassively ahead. As though that wave of resentment Ship had shown me hadn't come from her. I hadn't thought most humans could mask such strong emotions so effectively—her face was absolutely expressionless. But all the Mercy of Kalrs, it had turned out, could do it. Captain Vel had been an old-fashioned sort—or at the very least she'd had idealized notions of what "old-fashioned" meant—and had demanded that her human soldiers conduct themselves as much like ancillaries as possible.

Five didn't know I'd been an ancillary. As far as she knew I was Fleet Captain Breq Mianaai, promoted because of Captain Vel's arrest and what most imagined were my powerful family connections. She couldn't know how much of her I saw. "What is it?" I asked, brusque. Taken aback.

"Sir?" Flat. Expressionless. Wanting, I saw after the tiny signal delay, for me to turn my attention away from her, to leave her safely ignored. Wanting also to speak.

I was right, that resentment, that dismay had been on my account. "You have something to say. Let's hear it."

Surprise. Sheer terror. And not the least twitch of a muscle. "Sir," she said again, and there was, finally, a faint, fleeting expression of some sort, quickly gone. She swallowed. "It's the dishes."

My turn to be surprised. "The dishes?"

"Sir, you sent Captain Vel's things into storage here on the station."

And lovely things they had been. The dishes (and utensils, and tea things) Kalr Five was, presumably, preoccupied with had been porcelain, glass, jeweled and enameled metal. But they hadn't been mine. And I didn't want anything of Captain

Vel's. Five expected me to understand her. Wanted so much for me to understand. But I didn't. "Yes?"

Frustration. Anger, even. Clearly, from Five's perspective what she wanted was obvious. But the only part of it that was obvious to me was the fact she couldn't just come out and say it, even when I'd asked her to. "Sir," she said finally, citizens walking around us, some with curious glances, some pretending not to notice us. "I understand we're leaving the system soon."

"Soldier," I said, beginning to be frustrated and angry myself, in no good mood from my talk with the Lord of the Radch. "Are you capable of speaking directly?"

"We can't leave the system with no good dishes!" she blurted finally, face still impressively impassive. "Sir." When I didn't answer, she continued, through another surge of fear at speaking so plainly, "Of course it doesn't matter to *you*. You're a fleet captain, your rank is enough to impress anyone." And my house name—I was now Breq Mianaai. I wasn't too pleased at having been given that particular name, which marked me as a cousin of the Lord of the Radch herself. None of my crew but Seivarden and the ship's medic knew I hadn't been born with it. "*You* could invite a captain to supper and serve her soldier's mess and she wouldn't say a word, sir." Couldn't, unless she outranked me.

"We're not going where we're going so we can hold dinner parties," I said. That apparently confounded her, brief confusion showing for a moment on her face.

"Sir!" she said, voice pleading, in some distress. "*You* don't need to worry what other people think of you. I'm only saying, because you ordered me to."

Of course. I should have seen. Should have realized days ago. She was worried that *she* would look bad if I didn't have dinnerware to match my rank. That it would reflect badly on the ship itself. "You're worried about the reputation of the ship."

Chagrin, but also relief. "Yes, sir."

"I'm not Captain Vel." Captain Vel had cared a great deal about such things.

"*No*, sir." I wasn't sure if the emphasis—and the relief I read in Five—was because my not being Captain Vel was a good thing, or because I had finally understood what she had been trying to tell me. Or both.

I had already cleared my account here, all my money in chits locked in my quarters on board *Mercy of Kalr*. What little I carried on my person wouldn't be sufficient to ease Kalr Five's anxieties. Station—the AI that ran this place, *was* this place—could probably smooth the financial details over for me. But Station resented me as the cause of last week's violence and would not be disposed to assist me.

"Go back to the palace," I said. "Tell the Lord of the Radch what you require." Her eyes widened just slightly, and two tenths of a second later I read disbelief and then frank terror in Kalr Five. "When everything is arranged to your satisfaction, come to the shuttle."

Three citizens passed, bags in gloved hands, the fragment of conversation I heard telling me they were on their way to the docks, to catch a ship to one of the outer stations. A lift door slid open, obligingly. Of course. Station knew where they were going, they didn't have to ask.

Station knew where *I* was going, but it wouldn't open any doors for me without my giving the most explicit of requests. I turned, stepped quickly into the dockbound lift after them, saw the lift door close on Five standing, horrified, on the black stone pavement of the concourse. The lift moved, the three citizens chattered. I closed my eyes and saw Kalr Five staring at the lift, hyperventilating slightly. She frowned just the smallest amount—possibly no one passing her would notice. Her fingers twitched, summoning *Mercy of Kalr*'s attention, though with some trepidation, as though maybe she feared it wouldn't answer.

But of course *Mercy of Kalr* was already paying attention. "Don't worry," said *Mercy of Kalr*, voice serene and neutral in Five's ear and mine. "It's not you Fleet Captain's angry with. Go ahead. It'll be all right."

True enough. It wasn't Kalr Five I was angry with. I pushed away the data coming from her, received a disorienting flash of Seivarden, asleep, dreaming, and Lieutenant Ekalu, still tense, in the middle of asking one of her Etrepas for tea. Opened my eyes. The citizens in the lift with me laughed at something, I didn't know or care what, and as the lift door slid open we walked out into the broad lobby of the docks, lined all around with icons of gods that travelers might find useful or comforting. It was sparsely populated for this time of day, except by the entrance to the dock authority office, where a line of ill-tempered ship captains and pilots waited for their turn to complain to the overburdened inspector adjuncts. Two intersystem gates had been disabled in last week's upheaval, more were likely to be in the near future, and the Lord of the Radch had forbidden any travel in the remaining ones, trapping dozens of ships in the system, with all their cargo and passengers.

They moved aside for me, bowing slightly as though a wind had blown through them. It was the uniform that had done it—I heard one captain whisper to another one, "Who is that?" and the responding murmur as her neighbor replied and others commented on her ignorance or added what they knew. I heard *Mianaai* and *Special Missions*. The sense they'd managed to make out of last week's events. The official version was that I had come to Omaugh Palace undercover, to root out a seditious conspiracy. That I had been working for Anaander Mianaai all along. Anyone who'd ever been part of events that later received an official version would know or suspect that wasn't true. But most Radchaai lived unremarkable lives and would have no reason to doubt it.

No one questioned my walking past the adjuncts, into the outer office of the Inspector Supervisor. Daos Ceit, who was her assistant, was still recovering from injuries. An adjunct I didn't know sat in her place but rose swiftly and bowed as I entered. So did a very, very young lieutenant, more gracefully and collectedly than I expected in a seventeen-year-old, the sort who was still all lanky arms and legs and frivolous enough to spend her first pay on lilac-colored eyes—surely she hadn't been born with eyes that color. Her dark-brown jacket, trousers, gloves, and boots were crisp and spotless, her straight, dark hair cut close. "Fleet Captain. Sir," she said. "Lieutenant Tisarwat, sir." She bowed again.

I didn't answer, only looked at her. If my scrutiny disturbed her, I couldn't see it. She wasn't yet sending data to *Mercy of Kalr*, and her brown skin hadn't darkened in any sort of flush. The small, discreet scatter of pins near one shoulder suggested a family of some substance but not the most elevated in the Radch. She was, I thought, either preternaturally self-possessed or a fool. Neither option pleased me.

"Go on in, sir," said the unfamiliar adjunct, gesturing me toward the inner office. I did, without a word to Lieutenant Tisarwat.

Dark-skinned, amber-eyed, elegant and aristocratic even in the dark-blue uniform of dock authority, Inspector Supervisor Skaaiat Awer rose and bowed as the door shut behind me. "Breq. Are you going, then?"

I opened my mouth to say, *Whenever you authorize our departure*, but remembered Five and the errand I'd sent her on. "I'm only waiting for Kalr Five. Apparently I can't ship out without an acceptable set of dishes."

Surprise crossed her face, gone in an instant. She had known, of course, that I had sent Captain Vel's things here, and that I didn't own anything to replace them. Once the surprise had gone I saw amusement. "Well," she said. "Wouldn't you have felt the same?" When I had been in Five's place, she meant. When I had been a ship.

"No, I wouldn't have. I didn't. Some other ships did. Do." Mostly *Swords*, who by and large already thought they were above the smaller, less prestigious *Mercies*, or the troop carrier *Justices*.

"My Seven Issas cared about that sort of thing." Skaaiat Awer had served as a lieutenant on a ship with human troops, before she'd become Inspector Supervisor here at Omaugh Palace. Her eyes went to my single piece of jewelry, a small gold tag pinned near my left shoulder. She gestured, a change of topic that wasn't really a change of topic. "Athoek, is it?" My destination hadn't been publicly announced, might, in fact, be considered sensitive information. But Awer was one of the most ancient and wealthy of houses. Skaaiat had cousins who knew people who knew things. "I'm not sure that's where I'd have sent you."

"It's where I'm going."

She accepted that answer, no surprise or offense visible in her expression. "Have a seat. Tea?"

"Thank you, no." Actually I could have used some tea, might under other circumstances have been glad of a relaxed chat with Skaaiat Awer, but I was anxious to be off.

This, too, Inspector Supervisor Skaaiat took with equanimity. She did not sit, herself. "You'll be calling on Basnaaid Elming when you get to Athoek Station." Not a question. She knew I would be. Basnaaid was the younger sister of someone both Skaaiat and I had once loved. Someone I had, under orders from Anaander Mianaai, killed. "She's like Awn, in some ways, but not in others."

"Stubborn, you said."

"Very proud. And fully as stubborn as her sister. Possibly more so. She was very offended when I offered her clientage for her sister's sake. I mention it because I suspect you're planning to do something similar. And you might be the only person alive even more stubborn than she is."

I raised an eyebrow. "Not even the tyrant?" The word wasn't Radchaai, was from one of the worlds annexed and absorbed by the Radch. By Anaander Mianaai. The tyrant herself, almost the only person on Omaugh Palace who would have recognized or understood the word, besides Skaaiat and myself.

Skaaiat Awer's mouth quirked, sardonic humor. "Possibly. Possibly not. In any event, be very careful about offering Basnaaid money or favors. She won't take it kindly." She gestured, good-natured but resigned, as if to say, *but of course you'll do as you like.* "You'll have met your new baby lieutenant."

Lieutenant Tisarwat, she meant. "Why did she come here and not go directly to the shuttle?"

"She came to apologize to my adjunct." Daos Ceit's replacement, there in the outer office. "Their mothers are cousins." Formally, the word Skaaiat used referred to a relation between two people of different houses who shared a parent or a grandparent, but in casual use meant someone more distantly related who was a friend, or someone you'd grown up with. "They were supposed to meet for tea yesterday, and Tisarwat never showed or answered any messages. And you know how military gets along with dock authorities." Which was to say, overtly politely and privately contemptuously. "My adjunct took offense."

"Why should Lieutenant Tisarwat care?"

"You never had a mother to be angry you offended her cousin," Skaaiat said, half laughing, "or you wouldn't ask."

True enough. "What do you make of her?"

"Flighty, I would have said a day or two ago. But today she's very subdued." *Flighty* didn't match the collected young person I'd seen in that outer office. Except, perhaps, those impossible eyes. "Until today she was on her way to a desk job in a border system."

"The tyrant sent me a baby *administrator*?"

"I wouldn't have thought she'd send you a baby anything," Skaaiat said. "I'd have thought she'd have wanted to come with you herself. Maybe there's not enough of her left here." She drew breath as though to say more but then frowned, head cocked. "I'm sorry, there's something I have to take care of."

The docks were crowded with ships in need of supplies or repairs or emergency medical assistance, ships that were trapped here in the system, with crews and passengers who were extremely unhappy about the fact. Skaaiat's staff had been working hard for days, with very few breaks. "Of course." I bowed. "I'll get out of your way." She was still listening to whoever had messaged her. I turned to go.

"Breq." I looked back. Skaaiat's head was still cocked slightly, she was still hearing whoever else spoke. "Take care."

"You, too." I walked through the door, to the outer office. Lieutenant Tisarwat stood, still and silent. The adjunct stared ahead, fingers moving, attending to urgent dock business no doubt. "Lieutenant," I said sharply, and didn't wait for a reply but walked out of the office, through the crowd of disgruntled ships' captains, onto the docks where I would find the shuttle that would take me to *Mercy of Kalr*.

The shuttle was too small to generate its own gravity. I was perfectly comfortable in such circumstances, but very young officers often were not. I stationed Lieutenant Tisarwat at the dock, to wait for Kalr Five, and then pushed myself over the awkward, chancy boundary between the gravity of the palace and the weightlessness of the shuttle, kicked myself over to a seat, and strapped myself in. The pilot gave a respectful nod, bowing being difficult in these circumstances. I closed my eyes, saw that Five stood in a large storage room inside the palace proper, plain, utilitarian, gray-walled. Filled with chests and boxes. In one brown-gloved hand she held a teabowl of delicate, deep rose glass. An open box in front of her showed more—a flask, seven more bowls, other dishes. Her pleasure in the beautiful things, her desire, was undercut by doubt. I couldn't read her mind, but I guessed that she had been told to choose from this storeroom, had found these and wanted them very much, but didn't quite believe she would be allowed to take them away. I was fairly sure this set was hand-blown, and some seven hundred years old. I hadn't realized she had a connoisseur's eye for such things.

I pushed the vision away. She would be some time, I thought, and I might as well get some sleep.

I woke three hours later, to lilac-eyed Lieutenant Tisarwat strapping herself deftly into a seat across from me. Kalr Five—now radiating contentment, presumably from the results of her stint in the palace storeroom—pushed herself over to Lieutenant Tisarwat, and with a nod and a quiet *Just in case, sir* proffered a bag for the nearly inevitable moment when the new officer's stomach reacted to microgravity.

I'd known young lieutenants who took such an offer as an insult. Lieutenant Tisarwat accepted it, with a small, vague smile that didn't quite reach the rest of her face. Still seeming entirely calm and collected.

"Lieutenant," I said, as Kalr Five kicked herself forward to strap herself in beside the pilot, another Kalr. "Have you taken any meds?" Another potential insult. Antinausea meds were available, and I'd known excellent, long-serving officers who for the whole length of their careers took them every time they got on a shuttle. None of them ever admitted to it.

The last traces of Lieutenant Tisarwat's smile vanished. "No, sir." Even. Calm.

"Pilot has some, if you need them." That ought to have gotten some kind of reaction.

And it did, though just the barest fraction of a second later than I'd expected. The hint of a frown, an indignant straightening of her shoulders, hampered by her seat restraints. "No, thank you, sir."

Flighty, Skaaiat Awer had said. She didn't usually misread people so badly. "I didn't request your presence, Lieutenant." I kept my voice calm, but with an edge of anger. Easy enough to do under the circumstances. "You're here only because Anaander Mianaai ordered it. I don't have the time or the resources to hand-raise a brand-new baby. You'd better get up to speed *fast.* I need officers who know what they're doing. I need a whole crew I can *depend* on."

"Sir," replied Lieutenant Tisarwat. Still calm, but now some earnestness in her voice, that tiny trace of frown deepening, just a bit. "Yes, sir."

Dosed with *something*. Possibly antinausea, and if I'd been given to gambling I'd have bet my considerable fortune that she was filled to the ears with at least one sedative. I wanted to pull up her personal record—*Mercy of Kalr* would have it by now. But the tyrant would see that I had pulled that record up. *Mercy of Kalr* belonged, ultimately, to Anaander Mianaai, and she had accesses that allowed her to control it. *Mercy of Kalr* saw and heard everything I did, and if the tyrant wanted that information she had only to demand it. And I didn't want her to know what it was I suspected. Wanted, truth be told, for my suspicions to be proven false. Unreasonable.

For now, if the tyrant was watching—and she was surely watching, through *Mercy of Kalr*, would be so long as we were in the system—let her think I resented having a baby foisted on me when I'd rather have someone who knew what they were doing.

I turned my attention away from Lieutenant Tisarwat. Forward, the pilot leaned closer to Five and said, quiet and oblique, "Everything all right?" And then to Five's responding, puzzled frown, "Too quiet."

"All this time?" asked Five. Still oblique. Because they were talking about me and didn't want to trigger any requests I might have made to Ship, to tell me when the crew was talking about me. I had an old habit—some two thousand years old—of singing whatever song ran through my head. Or humming. It had caused the crew some puzzlement and distress at first—this body, the only one left to me, didn't have a particularly good voice. They were getting used to it, though, and now I was dryly amused to see crew members disturbed by my silence.

"Not a peep," said the pilot to Kalr Five. With a brief sideways glance and a tiny twitch of neck and shoulder muscles that told me she'd thought of looking back, toward Lieutenant Tisarwat.

"Yeah," said Five, agreeing, I thought, with the pilot's unstated assessment of what might be troubling me.

Good. Let Anaander Mianaai be watching that, too.

It was a long ride back to *Mercy of Kalr*, but Lieutenant Tisarwat never did use the bag or evince any discomfort. I spent the time sleeping, and thinking.

Ships, communications, data traveled between stars using gates, beacon-marked, held constantly open. The calculations had already been made, the routes marked out through the strangeness of gate space, where distances and proximity didn't match normal space. But military ships—like *Mercy of Kalr*—could generate their own gates. It was a good deal more risky—choose the wrong route, the wrong exit or entrance, and a ship could end up anywhere, or nowhere. That didn't trouble me. *Mercy of Kalr* knew what it was doing, and we would arrive safely at Athoek Station.

And while we moved through gate space in our own, contained bubble of normal space, we would be completely isolated. I wanted that. Wanted to be gone from Omaugh Palace, away from Anaander Mianaai's sight and any orders or interference she might decide to send.

When we were nearly there, minutes away from docking, Ship spoke directly into my ear. "Fleet Captain." It didn't need to speak to me that way, could merely desire me to know it wanted my attention. And it nearly always knew what I wanted without my saying it. I could connect to *Mercy of Kalr* in a way no one else aboard could. I could not, however, *be Mercy of Kalr*, as I had been *Justice of Toren*. Not without losing myself entirely. Permanently.

"Ship," I replied quietly. And without my saying anything else, *Mercy of Kalr* gave me the results of its calculations, made unasked, a whole range of possible routes and departure times flaring into my vision. I chose the soonest, gave orders, and a little more than six hours later we were gone.

introducing

If you enjoyed
ANCILLARY JUSTICE,
look out for

WAR DOGS

by Greg Bear

An epic interstellar tale of war from a master of science fiction.

One more tour on the red.

Maybe my last.

They made their presence on Earth known thirteen years ago.

Providing technology and scientific insights far beyond what mankind was capable of, they became indispensable advisors and promised even more gifts that we just couldn't pass up. We called them Gurus.

It took them a while to drop the other shoe. You can see why, looking back.

It was a very big shoe, completely slathered in crap.

They had been hounded by mortal enemies from sun to sun, planet to planet, and were now stretched thin—and they needed our help.

And so our first bill came due. Skyrines like me were volunteered to pay the price. As always.

These enemies were already inside our solar system and were establishing a beachhead, but not on Earth.

On Mars.

Down to Earth

I'm trying to go home. As the poet said, if you don't know where you are, you don't know who you are. Home is where you go to get all that sorted out.

Hoofing it outside Skybase Lewis-McChord, I'm pretty sure this is Washington State, I'm pretty sure I'm walking along Pacific Highway, and this is the twenty-first century and not some fidging movie—

But then a whining roar grinds the air and a broad shadow sweeps the road, eclipsing cafés and pawnshops and loan joints—followed seconds later by an eye-stinging haze of rocket fuel. I swivel on aching feet and look up to see a double-egg-and-hawksbill burn down from the sky, leaving a rainbow trail over McChord field...

And I have to wonder.

I just flew in on one of those after eight months in the vac, four going out, three back. Seven blissful months in timeout, stuffed in a dark tube and soaked in Cosmoline.

All for three weeks in the shit. Rough, confusing weeks.

I feel dizzy. I look down, blink out the sting, and keep walking. Cosmoline still fidges with my senses.

Here on Earth, we don't say *fuck* anymore, the Gurus don't like it, so we say fidge instead. Part of the price of freedom. Out on the Red, we say fuck as much as we like. The angels edit our words so the Gurus won't have to hear.

SNKRAZ.

Joe has a funny story about *fuck*. I'll tell you later, but right now, I'm not too happy with Joe. We came back in separate ships, he did not show up at the mob center, and my Cougar is still parked outside Skyport Virginia. I could grab a shuttle into town, but Joe told me to lie low. Besides, I badly want time alone—time to stretch my legs, put down one foot after another. There's the joy of blue sky, if I can look up without keeling over, and open air without a helm—and minus the rocket smell—is a newness in the nose and a beauty in the lungs. In a couple of klicks, though, my insteps pinch and my calves knot. Earth tugs harsh after so long away. I want to heave. I straighten and look real serious, clamp my jaws, shake my head—barely manage to keep it down.

Suddenly, I don't feel the need to walk all the way to Seattle. I have my thumb and a decently goofy smile, but after half an hour and no joy, I'm making up my mind whether to try my luck at a minimall Starbucks when a little blue electric job creeps up behind me, quiet as a bad fart. Quiet is not good.

I spin and try to stop shivering as the window rolls down. The driver is in her fifties, reddish hair rooted gray. For a queasy moment, I think she might be MHAT sent from Madigan. Joe warned me, "For Christ's sake, after all that's happened, stay away from the doctors." MHAT is short for *Military Health Advisory Team*. But the driver is not from Madigan. She asks where I'm going. I say downtown Seattle. Climb in, she says. She's a colonel's secretary at Lewis, a pretty ordinary grandma, but she has these strange gray eyes that let me see all the way back to when her scorn shaped men's lives.

I ask if she can take me to Pike Place Market. She's good with that. I climb in. After a while, she tells me she had a son just like me. He became a hero on Titan, she says—but she can't really know that, because we aren't on Titan yet, are we?

I say to her, "Sorry for your loss." I don't say, *Glad it wasn't me.*

"How's the war out there?" she asks.

"Can't tell, ma'am. Just back and still groggy."

They don't let us know all we want to know, barely tell us all we *need* to know, because we might start speculating and lose focus.

She and I don't talk much after that. Fidging *Titan*. Sounds old and cold. What kind of suits would we wear? Would everything freeze solid? Mars is bad enough. We're almost used to the Red. Stay sharp on the dust and rocks. That's where our shit is at. Leave the rest to the generals and the Gurus.

All part of the deal. A really big deal.

Titan. Jesus.

Grandma in the too-quiet electric drives me north to Spring Street, then west to Pike and First, where she drops me off with a crinkle-eyed smile and a warm, sad finger-squeeze. The instant I turn and see the market, she pips from my thoughts. Nothing has changed since vac training at SBLM, when we tired of the local bars and drove north, looking for trouble but ending up right here. We liked the market. The big neon sign. The big round clock. Tourists and merchants and more tourists, and that ageless bronze pig out in front.

A little girl in a pink frock sits astride the pig, grinning and slapping its polished flank. What we fight for.

I'm in civvies but Cosmoline gives your skin a tinge that lasts for days, until you piss it out, so most everyone can tell I've been in timeout. Civilians are not supposed to ask probing questions, but they still smile like knowing sheep. *Hey, spaceman, welcome back! Tell me true, how's the vac?*

I get it.

A nice Laotian lady and her sons and daughter sell fruit and veggies and flowers. Their booth is a cascade of big and little peppers and hot and sweet peppers and yellow and green and red peppers, Walla Walla sweets and good strong brown and fresh green onions, red and gold and blue and russet potatoes, yams and sweet potatoes, pole beans green and yellow and purple and speckled, beets baby and adult, turnips open boxed in bulk and attached to sprays of crisp green leaf. Around the corner of the booth I see every kind of mushroom but the screwy kind. All that roughage dazzles. I'm accustomed to browns and pinks, dark blue, star-powdered black.

A salient of kale and cabbage stretches before me. I seriously consider kicking off and swimming up the counter, chewing through the thick leaves, inhaling the color, spouting purple and green. Instead, I buy a bunch of celery and move out of the tourist flow. Leaning against a corrugated metal door, I shift from foot to cramping foot, until finally I just hunker against the cool ribbed steel and rabbit down the celery leaves, dirt and all, down to the dense, crisp core. Love it. Good for timeout tummy.

Now that I've had my celery, I'm better. Time to move on. A mile to go before I sleep.

I doubt I'll sleep much.

Skyrines share flophouses, safe houses—refuges—around

the major spaceports. My favorite is a really nice apartment in Virginia Beach. I could be heading there now, driving my Cougar across the Chesapeake Bay Bridge, top down, sucking in the warm sea breeze, but thanks to all that's happened—and thanks to Joe—I'm not. Not this time. Maybe never again.

I rise and edge through the crowds, but my knees are still shaky, I might not make it, so I flag a cab. The cabby is white and middle-aged, from Texas. Most of the fellows who used to cab here, Lebanese and Ethiopians and Sikhs, the younger ones at least, are gone to war now. They do well in timeout, better than white Texans. Brown people rule the vac, some say. There's a lot of brown and black and beige out there: east and west Indians, immigrant Kenyans and Nigerians and Somalis, Mexicans, Filipinos and Malaysians, Jamaicans and Puerto Ricans, all varieties of Asian—flung out in space frames, sticks clumped up in fasces—and then they all fly loose, shoot out puff, and drop to the Red. Maybe less dangerous than driving a hack, and certainly pays better.

I'm not the least bit brown. I don't even tan. I'm a white boy from Moscow, Idaho, a blue-collar IT wizard who got tired of working in cubicles, tired of working around shitheads like myself. I enlisted in the Skyrines (that's pronounced SKY-reen), went through all the tests and boot and desert training, survived first orbital, survived first drop on the Red—came home alive and relatively sane—and now I make good money. Flight pay and combat pay—they call it engagement bonus—and Cosmoline comp.

Some say the whole deal of cellular suspension we call timeout shortens your life, along with solar flares and gamma rays. Others say no. The military docs say no but scandal painted a lot of them before my last deployment. Whole bunch at Madigan got augured for neglecting our spacemen. Their docs tend to regard spacemen, especially Skyrines, as slackers and complainers. Another reason to avoid MHAT. We make more than they do and still we complain. They hate us. Give them ground pounders any day.

"How many drops?" the Texan cabby asks.

"Too many," I say. I've been at it for six years.

He looks back at me in the mirror. The cab drives itself; he's in the seat for show. "Ever wonder why?" he asks. "Ever wonder what you're giving up to *them*? They ain't even human." Some think we shouldn't be out there at all; maybe he's one of them.

"Ever wonder?" he asks.

"All the time," I say.

He looks miffed and faces forward.

The cab takes me into Belltown and lets me out on a semicircular drive, in the shadow of the high-rise called Sky Tower One. I pay in cash. The cabby rewards me with a sour look, even though I give him a decent tip. He, too, pips from my mind as soon as I get out. Bastard.

The tower's elevator has a glass wall to show off the view before you arrive. The curved hall on my floor is lined with alcoves, quiet and deserted this time of day. I key in the number code, the door clicks open, and the apartment greets me with a cheery pluck of ascending chords. Extreme retro, traditional Seattle, none of it Guru tech; it's from before I was born.

Lie low. Don't attract attention.

Christ. No way am I used to being a spook.

The place is just as I remember it—nice and cool, walls gray, carpet and furniture gray and cloudy-day blue, stainless steel fixtures with touches of wood and white enamel. The couch and chairs and tables are mid-century modern. Last year's Christmas tree is still up, the water down to scum and the branches naked, but Roomba has sucked up all the needles.

Love Roomba. Also pre-Guru, it rolls out of its stair slot and checks me out, nuzzling my toes like a happy gray trilobite.

I finish my tour—checking every room twice, ingrained caution, nobody home—then pull an Eames chair up in front of the broad floor-to-ceiling window and flop back to stare out over the Sound. The big sky still makes me dizzy, so I try to focus lower down, on the green and white ferries coming and going, and then on the nearly continuous lines of tankers and big cargo ships. Good to know Hanjin and Maersk are still packing blue and orange and brown steel containers along with Hogmaw or Haugley or what the hell. Each container is about a seventh the size of your standard space frame. No doubt filled with clever goods made using Guru secrets, juicing our economy like a snuck of meth.

And for that, too—for *them*—we fight.

The History of Welsh Athletics

Statistics

By

John Collins, Alan & Brenda Currie, Mike Walters and Clive Williams

Edited by **Clive Williams**

First published by
Dragon Sports Books Ltd
2002

ISBN 095240415X

Dragon Sports Books Ltd
19 Murray Street, Llanelli,
Carms SA15 1AQ

Printed in Wales by
Provincial Printing & Publishing Co. Ltd.
Sanatorium Road, Cardiff CF11 8DG
Tel: +44 (0)29 2022 8729

This book is

dedicated to the memory of Nerys

a little angel

who touched the hearts

of all who met her

The History of Welsh Athletics
Statistics

Contents

Preface

We had hoped to include this statistical detail as part of the main book. However, in the latter stages of production we began to realise that the book would be rather cumbersome at almost 500 pages, and also bearing in mind that many people will want to refer to the statistics when watching athletics events, we decided to produce a separate volume so that it will be easier to carry and use.

Whilst some of the sections are merely updates of earlier productions compiled by the authors, some of the compilations are new and have not been seen before, such as the list of championship results, the progressive all-comers records and the schedule of Welsh international matches and the resultant list of "most capped" Welsh athletes.

Much of the base data has come from the personal collections of the late Viv Pitcher, D.J.P. Richards and Eddie O'Donnell. Welsh athletics, and indeed the sport in general, owe these gentlemen a debt of gratitude for their foresight in meticulously recording the activities of the sport in Wales during its formative years. Without their efforts, the production of this statistical data, and indeed much of the detail in the main book, would have been even more time-consuming and no doubt less accurate.

In particular, we hope that many of the stars and champions of previous years (and their children and grandchildren!) will enjoy seeing their names in print again.

The compilation of this data has been particularly onerous, and considerable effort and research has been undertaken to ensure accuracy. However, we acknowledge in advance that there have been errors and omissions, but we very much hope that these have been kept to a minimum, and would be pleased to receive any such information.

As we went to press, a detailed book, *Welsh Women's Athletics 1919-1959*, researched and compiled by John Brant was published. This book contains many performances recorded prior to the formation of the Welsh Women's AAA in 1951, and therefore some performances – particularly those recorded in schools' events – must be treated with a degree of caution as it is unlikely that graded officials were present. There is no doubt that many of these performances are genuine, but given the uncertainty of the conditions under which the events were held, further investigation is required as to their validity before they can be included in this, or future publications.

However we have included women's marks prior to the formation of the Welsh Women's AAA where we are reasonably certain of their accuracy. One of the factors used in making this assumption has been whether the marks were achieved as part of a meeting organised by the Welsh AAA or its predecessor, the South Wales & Mon AAA, or whether there was a reasonable chance of graded officials being present.

Clive Williams
Otterbourne, Winchester
December 2001

Explanation and Guide to Contents

The following pages contain all the statistical information on Welsh athletics that it has been possible to obtain. The compilers have engaged in extensive research and yet are conscious of the fact that there will be errors and omissions in the records shown. Due to the fact that there are no central records for athletics in Wales it has been necessary to seek information from various sources. Nevertheless, some details have proved impossible to trace while others have caused confusion, with separate sources giving conflicting results. The compilers would welcome any additions or amendments to the records, as our ultimate aim is for accuracy and completeness. Note that all statistics throughout the book are up to 31 December 2000.

There are a number of matters which need clarification and these are discussed below.

ELIGIBILITY

The three basic criteria for Welsh eligibility are birth, parentage and residence in Wales for a prescribed period. However, in these days of ease of mobility, many people may be eligible to represent more than one country. We have taken the view that merely being eligible is not sufficient in itself. The athlete must have taken up eligibility and not subsequently have relinquished it. Throughout the book we have included only those performances which were achieved at a time when the athlete concerned had assumed Welsh eligibility and was qualified to compete in Welsh Championships and/or be selected for Welsh national teams. Athletes may well have achieved their best performances before assuming Welsh eligibility or after having relinquished it so that marks shown here are not necessarily the athletes' lifetime bests. We are concerned only with whether someone is Welsh in athletics terms rather than in the wider context. The point can be illustrated with a couple of examples. Tony Simmons was born in Maesteg and is unquestionably Welsh even though he has lived most of his life in Luton. He won Welsh titles as a junior athlete but between 1971 and 1977 transferred his allegiance to England. He resumed Welsh eligibility from 1978. We have ignored his performances in the intervening years as, in purely athletics terms, he was not Welsh at the time. Similarly Jon Brown was born in Bridgend and also won a Welsh title as a young athlete. He, too, took up English qualification later and competed for England in the 1994 Commonwealth Games, so that his UK 10000 metres record is not recognised as a Welsh record. Should he "return to the fold" at some later date only performances achieved from then on will be considered.

The following athletes are affected by this stipulation and are therefore only eligible as indicated below.

Tony Ashton from 1967, Nigel Bevan from 1989, Ken Cocks from 1978, John Davies (TVH) from 1968, Bob Dobson from 1981, Mal Edwards from 1980, Paul Edwards from 1980 until April 1991, Paul Farmer from 1972, Ron Griffiths from 1972, Roger Hackney from 1978, Steve James from 1974, Phil Lewis from 1968, Colin Mackenzie from 1978 - 1990, Joe Mills from 1991, Robert Mitchell from 2000, Lee Newman from June 1997,

Colin O'Neill from 1973, Milton Palmer from 1978, Bob Roberts from 1973, Tony Simmons not eligible from 1971 – 1977, Garry Slade from 1988, Jon Stark from 1980, Peter Templeton from 1974, Iwan Thomas from 1993, Andy Williams from 1976, Paul Williams (Cambridge) from 1977

Thelwyn Bateman not eligible 1976 – 1980, Rhian Clarke from 1996, Julie Crane from 1994, Margaret Critchley from 1976, Emma Davies from 1996, Jean Davies from 1967, Jane Falconer from 1993, Lea Haggett 1986 only, Diane Heath from 1977, Hilary Hollick from 1977, Nicola Jupp from 1991, Barbara Ann King from 1984, Sian Lax from 1995, Paula Lloyd not from 1974, Jessica Mills from 1991, Jennifer Mockler from 2000, Sarah Moore from 1992, Catherine Murphy from 1995, Michelle Probert from 1978, Angharad Richards from 1992, Susan Tooby 1982 – 1989, Angela Tooby from 1982, Averil Williams from 1962, Janeen Williams from 1979.

CONVERSION FACTORS

Up until 1969 many track performances were recorded over imperial distances. Most tracks in this country were 440 yards in circumference making them 4 laps to the mile. From about 1970 on tracks were gradually converted to the now standard 400 metres and all performances are now measured over metric distances. Ignoring races run over imperial distances would severely reduce the value of this book as a historical record, but we are aware that to many people they may mean very little. The following table gives the generally accepted factors for converting times over imperial distances to their metric equivalents. (All field events performances are shown in metric measurements even though they may have been measured in feet and inches at the time).

To convert 100 yards to 100 metres add 0.9 seconds.

To convert 220 yards to 200 metres deduct 0.1 seconds.

To convert 440 yards to 400 metres deduct 0.3 seconds.

To convert 880 yards to 800 metres deduct 0.7 seconds.

To convert one mile to 1500 metres deduct 18 seconds.

To convert 2 miles to 3000 metres deduct 34 seconds.

To convert 3 miles to 5000 metres add 28 seconds.

To convert 6 miles to 10000 metres add one minute.

The difference between 120 yards and 110 metres is so minute as to make conversion unnecessary. These conversions must be regarded as approximate.

Throughout the book, we have abbreviated times and distances in the generally accepted way ie 22.4 for 220 yards/200 metres relates to 22.4 secs; 4:11.4 for the mile/1,500m relates to 4mins 11.4 secs, 2:12:12 for the marathon relates to 2 hours 12 minutes and 12 seconds and 51.40 in field events relates to 51.40 metres.

ABBREVIATIONS

For reasons of space it has been necessary to include abbreviations throughout the statistical section. The following have been used consistently whenever they have been required:

a	=	fully automatic timing	m	=	run over metric distance
dh	=	course believed to be downhill	mx	=	mixed sex race

dnf	=	did not finish	ntt	=	no time taken
dnq	=	did not qualify	q	=	Welsh qualification uncertain
dns	=	did not start	R2	=	second round of heats
e	=	estimated but reliable time	u	=	ungraded officials present
h	=	hand timing	w	=	wind assisted performance
i	=	performance achieved indoors	y	=	time converted from linear distance
it	=	intermediate time during longer race	?	=	performance unconfirmed
*	=	achieved at altitude			

RECORDS LISTS

Over the years the definition of a Welsh record has changed considerably. At one time only performances achieved in Wales by athletes born in Wales were classified as Welsh records. When Clive Williams was appointed Welsh Statistician and Records Officer in 1963 he was instrumental in revising this system so that the best authentic performances by Welsh athletes were recognised, regardless of where they were recorded. For historical reasons many of the performances shown in the evolution of Welsh National best performances lists were not necessarily recognised as Welsh records at the time which is why the term "best performances" has been used rather than "records". Indoor performances are not included. The standard layout of these lists gives performance, athlete's name and club followed by location and date of performance. In some instances the venue is not known in which case the event is listed. If the venue is outside the UK the appropriate country is named even if the location is well known (eg Rome, Italy). Where the actual date is not known it has been shown as 00.00.1997 or similar. The dates shown for combined events (decathlon, heptathlon, etc) represent the second day of competition if held over 2 days. Progressive bests are given for both metric and imperial distances and no attempt has been made to convert times from one method to the other.

The evolution of Welsh all comers' best performances lists are the best performances achieved in Wales by athletes of any nationality. The layout is similar to that for the Welsh best performances list except that the athlete's country is given instead of club. All comers records for metric distances begin with the first performance equal or superior to the existing linear equivalent.

The Welsh all-time lists give the best performances (usually 50 deep) by Welsh athletes in each of the standard events, bearing in mind the earlier comments on eligibility. The layout is similar to the evolution of best performances lists except that there is no indication of club affiliation (some athletes belonged to many clubs during their careers). If an athlete's best performance was achieved indoors this is listed in its appropriate place and the best outdoor performance is also shown, where known.

AGE GROUPS

As with records, definitions of the various younger age groups have been subject to many changes over the years. Previously terms such as "boys", "girls", "youths" etc were used but recent changes mean that the terms used now accurately reflect the ages of the athletes concerned. U20M is the abbreviation for men under 20, U15G for girls under 15, etc. In most cases ages are as at 31 August in the year in question. The one exception is that under 20s are as at 31 December and there are moves afoot in some quarters to apply this date to all age groups. Until 1955 all age groups were classified as at 1 April.

9.6	Berwyn Jones (Birchfield)	Birmingham	21.07.1962
9.6	Berwyn Jones (Birchfield)	Maindy Stadium, Cardiff	28.07.1962
9.6	Ron Jones (Woodford Green)	Jenner Park, Barry	01.09.1962
9.6	Ron Jones (Woodford Green)	Barking	08.09.1962
9.6	Ron Jones (Woodford Green)	White City, London	28.09.1962
9.5	Ron Jones (Woodford Green)	Maindy Stadium, Cardiff	27.07.1963
9.5	Ron Jones (Woodford Green)	Maindy Stadium, Cardiff	27.07.1963
9.5	Lynn Davies (Roath H)	White City, London	16.05.1964
9.5	Lynn Davies (Roath H)	Maindy Stadium, Cardiff	30.05.1964
9.5	Ron Jones (Woodford Green)	Maindy Stadium, Cardiff	19.06.1965

100 metres (hand timing)

10.8	David Jacobs (London AC)	Stockholm, Sweden	06.07.1912
10.7	Ken Jones (Newport AC)	Lucknow, India	29.01.1946
10.6	Ken Jones (Newport AC)	Wembley	30.07.1948
10.5	Ron Jones (Birchgrove H)	Moscow, Russia	05.09.1959
10.4	Ron Jones (Birchgrove H)	Birmingham	03.10.1959
10.3	Berwyn Jones (Birchfield)	Budapest, Hungary	02.10.1963
10.3	Ron Jones (Borough of Enfield)	Berne, Switzerland	29.06.1968

100 metres (fully automatic timing)

10.48	Ron Jones (Borough of Enfield)	White City, London	14.08.1963
10.43*	Ron Jones (Borough of Enfield)	Mexico City, Mexico	15.10.1967
10.42*	Ron Jones (Borough of Enfield)	Mexico City, Mexico	13.10.1968
10.29	Colin Jackson (Cardiff AAC)	Wrexham	28.07.1990
10.24	Christian Malcolm (Cardiff AAC)	Ljubljana, Yugoslavia	25.07.1997
10.18	Christian Malcolm (Cardiff AAC)	Annecy, France	29.07.1998
10.12	Christian Malcolm (Cardiff AAC)	Annecy, France	29.07.1998

220 yards (hand timing)

23.2	Cyril R Lundie (Roath H)	St Helen's, Swansea	07.09.1902
23.2	Cyril R Lundie (Roath H)	Rodney Parade, Newport	31.08.1903
23.2	A M J Griffiths (Abergavenny AC)	Abergavenny	00.00.1904
23.0	J Gorman (Newport AC)	Rodney Parade, Newport	27.06.1908
22.8	David Jacobs (Herne Hill H)	Oval	09.09.1911
22.0	David Jacobs (Herne Hill H)	Stamford Bridge, London	22.06.1912
21.7	Kenneth Jenkins (Oxford University)	Oxford	00.00.1938
21.6	Gwilym Roberts (Achilles)	Philadelphia, USA	15.06.1957
21.6	Nick Whitehead (Birchfield)	Loughborough	21.05.1958
21.5	Ron Jones (Birchgrove H)	Welwyn Garden City	19.09.1959
21.5	Ron Jones (Birchgrove H)	Maindy Stadium, Cardiff	22.06.1963
21.5	Ron Jones (Birchgrove H)	Maindy Stadium, Cardiff	24.07.1965
21.2	Lynn Davies (Roath H)	Cyncoed, Cardiff	01.06.1966
21.1	Howard Davies (Newport H)	Maindy Stadium, Cardiff	27.07.1968

200 metres (hand timing)

22.4	David Jacobs (Herne Hill H)	Stamford Bridge, London	18.05.1912
21.9	David Jacobs (Herne Hill H)	Stockholm, Sweden	10.07.1912
21.9	Kenneth Jenkins (Oxford University)	Paris, France	04.09.1938
21.7	Ken Jones (Newport AC)	Oslo, Norway	03.09.1949
21.4	Ron Jones (Birchgrove H)	Birmingham	03.10.1959
21.3	Ron Jones (Woodford Green)	Zurich, Switzerland	02.07.1963
20.8*	Howard Davies (Newport H)	Mexico City, Mexico	27.09.1968

Section 1

Evolution of Welsh National Best Performances

MEN

100 yards (hand timing)

10.2	Charles Thomas (Reading AC)	Harlequins Ground, Cardiff	09.09.1893
10.2	Charles Thomas (Reading AC)	Harlequins Ground, Cardiff	01.09.1894
10.2	Charles Thomas (Reading AC)	Cardiff	04.08.1896
10.0?	Charles Thomas (Reading AC)	Oxford	05.03.1897
10.2	Charles Thomas (Reading AC)	Welsh Championships	00.00.1897
10.0	Fred Cooper (Bradford AC)	Welsh Championships	00.00.1898
10.0	Fred Cooper (Bradford AC)	Stamford Bridge, London	02.07.1898
10.0 dh	Charles Thomas (Reading AC)	Abergavenny	02.08.1898
10.0	Charles Thomas (Reading AC)	Oxford	08.03.1899
10.0	Stan Macey (Newport AC)	Pontypool	18.07.1925
10.0	Cyril Cupid (Swansea Valley AC)	St Helen's, Swansea	11.07.1931
10.0	Cyril Cupid (Swansea Valley AC)	Crymlyn Burrows, Swansea	16.06.1934
9.8	Cyril Cupid (Swansea Valley AC)	Rodney Parade, Newport	30.06.1934
9.8	Ken Jones (Newport AC)	Uxbridge	12.06.1948
9.8	Ken Jones (Newport AC)	Abertillery	25.06.1949
9.8	Ken Jones (Newport AC)	Bristol	20.08.1949
9.8	Ken Jones (Newport AC)	Abertillery	14.05.1952
9.8	Ken Jones (Newport AC)	Vancouver, Canada	31.07.1954
9.8	Ken Jones (Newport AC)	Vancouver, Canada	31.07.1954
9.8	Nick Whitehead (Birchfield)	Loughborough	07.05.1958
9.8	Nick Whitehead (Birchfield)	Maindy Stadium, Cardiff	17.05.1958
9.8	John Morgan (Thames Valley H)	Wolverhampton	14.06.1958
9.8	Ron Jones (Birchgrove H)	Paignton	02.07.1958
9.8	Nick Whitehead (Birchfield)	Colwyn Bay	05.07.1958
9.8	Ron Jones (Birchgrove H)	White City, London	11.07.1958
9.8	Nick Whitehead (Birchfield)	Uxbridge	16.08.1958
9.8	Ron Jones (Birchgrove H)	Maindy Stadium, Cardiff	20.06.1959
9.7	Ron Jones (Birchgrove H)	White City, London	14.08.1959
9.7	Ron Jones (Birchgrove H)	Edinburgh	22.08.1959
9.7	Ron Jones (Birchgrove H)	Welwyn Garden City	19.09.1959
9.7	Nick Whitehead (Birchfield)	Dublin, Ireland	19.06.1960
9.7	Nick Whitehead (Birchfield)	Maindy Stadium, Cardiff	25.06.1960
9.7	Nick Whitehead (Birchfield)	Edinburgh	20.08.1960
9.7	Berwyn Jones (Loughborough)	White City, London	22.07.1961
9.7	Berwyn Jones (Loughborough)	Maindy Stadium, Cardiff	26.07.1961
9.7	Berwyn Jones (Loughborough)	Maindy Stadium, Cardiff	29.07.1961
9.7	Berwyn Jones (Loughborough)	Newport	02.06.1962
9.7	Berwyn Jones (Loughborough)	Maindy Stadium, Cardiff	23.06.1962

accuracy of the lists from the 1950s onward but recognise that many earlier marks by both men and women may not yet have been discovered. Our research will continue and we hope one day to have a fuller picture. In the meantime we would welcome any additional information on the subject.

MARRIED NAMES

Many women athletes competed under both their maiden and married names. A full list of names is included below, listed alphabetically by maiden name. This has proved to be a difficult area to cover, especially with the constraints of space in some sections. In the all-time lists both names are included, separated by a slash (/). In lists of records the single name has been used first, then both names on the first occasion the athlete appeared under her married name, following which only the married name has been used. A similar pattern has been used in lists of Welsh Champions whenever space has permitted.

Married names:

Appleby-Bateman, Thelwyn
Archard-Cashell, Gillian
Barnes-Hudd, Sue
Belt-Pengilley, Sandra
Bull-Owen, Sarah
Chick-Newhams, Debbie
Coy-Lewis, Sheila
Davies-Morton, Jill
Davies-Mullett, Jenny
Davies-Yorke, Hilary
Docker-Whitehead, Jean
Donaghue-Mittleberger, Hayley
Dourass-Rickard, Gloria
Edwards-Willoughby, Joanne
Evans-Layzell, Alyson
Evans-Powell, Joanne
Evans-Rees, Jane
Fox-Richards, AnnMarie
Francis-Thomas, Elizabeth
Gill-Lewis, Elizabeth
Gould-Coe, Eirwyn
Griffiths-Gibbs, Lisa
Harries-Bunting, Susan
Heath-Fryar, Diane
Hodge-Lee, Sarah
Hulbert-Brace, Jackie
Huntbach-Lerue, Lynn
James-Lynch, Sally
Jenkins-Gilderdale, Ceri
Jenner-Thompson, Christine
Jones-Taylor, Leanne
Lewis-Porter, Lynfa
Lock-Harris, Kim
Martin Jones-Howell, Ruth
McDermott-Wade, Kirsty
Morley-Brown, Kay
Morley-Humberstone, Jenny
Morris-Lewis, Sian
Morris-Notman, Anne
Nixon-Davies, Fiona
Parry-Tullett, Hayley
Parsons-Johns, Elizabeth
Pritchard-Diss, Ceri
Probert-Scutt, Michelle
Pugh-Jenkins, Clare
Richardson-Cameron, Beccy
Roberts-Ricketts, Kelly
Smith-Cardy-Wise, Bronwen
Smith-Davies, Joanne
Sullivan-Gallagher, Pat
Tanner-Hollick, Hilary
Tayler-Bowen, Julie
Thomas-Grech, Ceri
Thomas-Walters, Bernadette
Tooby-Smith, Angela
Tooby-Wightman, Susan
Waters-Morgan, Sian
White-Dawson, Cathy

GENERAL NOTES

There are inevitably restrictions on what it has been possible to include in this statistics section due to the constraints of space. Some items have had to be omitted and the layout of some of the material included may not be as aesthetically pleasing as one would have wished. We apologise in advance for this and hope that readers will understand our desire to include as much detail as possible.

With the creation of the Welsh Women's AAA in 1951, there came the first attempts to formalise athletics for women in the Principality. Prior to this there were no national championships for women and no records were maintained. This is not to say that Welsh women did not participate in athletics before this date, far from it. Examination of the following lists of national and all comers' records will show that, with some exceptions, they date from the early 1950s. The compilers are acutely aware that there was considerable earlier involvement in athletics by women and further research is needed in order to obtain an accurate picture of the level and standard of activity. We are reasonably confident of the

200 metres (fully automatic timing)

21.49*	Ron Jones (Borough of Enfield)	Mexico City, Mexico	16.10.1967
21.36	Dave Roberts (Cardiff AAC)	Cwmbran	29.05.1978
21.33	Jonathan Stark (Edinburgh AC)	Cwmbran	11.07.1980
21.19	Colin Jackson (Cardiff AAC)	Tel Aviv, Israel	08.05.1988
21.18	Jamie Baulch (Newport H)	Salamanca, Spain	21.07.1991
21.16	Jamie Baulch (Newport H)	Giuliano, Italy	09.08.1992
21.06	Jamie Baulch (Newport H)	Seoul, South Korea	17.09.1992
20.91	Jamie Baulch (Newport H)	Seoul, South Korea	18.09.1992
20.84	Jamie Baulch (Cardiff AAC)	Victoria, Canada	24.08.1994
20.75	Doug Turner (Cardiff AAC)	Stoke	09.09.1995
20.43	Doug Turner (Cardiff AAC)	Tallin, Estonia	09.06.1996
20.29	Christian Malcolm (Cardiff AAC)	Kuala Lumpur, Malaysia	19.09.1998
20.19	Christian Malcolm (Cardiff AAC)	Sydney, Australia	27.09.2000
20.19	Christian Malcolm (Cardiff AAC)	Sydney, Australia	27.09.2000

440 yards (hand timing)

52.5	Francis Jones (Oxford University)	Oxford	07.11.1874
51.8	Tom Nicholas (Monmouth AC)	Birmingham	12.07.1890
51.8	David Jacobs (Herne Hill H)	Herne Hill	23.07.1910
50.4	David Jacobs (Herne Hill H)	Herne Hill	11.08.1910
49.8	Cecil Griffiths (London AC)	Barry Island	16.07.1921
49.7	Peter Phillips (London University)		14.05.1953
49.6	Peter Phillips (London University)	White City, London	08.06.1954
49.5	Bob Shaw (Oxford University)	Oxford	20.04.1955
49.3	David H Jones (Birchfield H)	Colwyn Bay	05.07.1958
49.0	David H Jones (Birchfield H)	Nottingham	21.05.1960
49.0	William Griffiths (London University)	Motspur Park	27.07.1960
48.5	Michael Davies (Achilles)	Cambridge	04.05.1961
48.4	Pat Jones (Ilford AC)	Maindy Stadium, Cardiff	22.06.1963
47.9	Pat Jones (Ilford AC)	Southend	14.09.1963
47.8	Pat Jones (Ilford AC)	Ilford	10.06.1965
47.3	Howard Davies (Newport H)	White City, London	15.06.1967
47.0	Howard Davies (Newport H)	White City, London	13.07.1968

400 metres

50.1	David Jacobs (Herne Hill H)	Oval	13.09.1913
48.9	David H Jones (Birchfield)	Manchester	14.06.1958
47.0	Howard Davies (Newport H)	Tokyo, Japan	31.08.1967
46.8	Howard Davies (Newport H)	Zurich, Switzerland	02.07.1968
46.6	John Robertson (Barry H)	Crystal Palace London	24.08.1968
46.60	John Robertson (Barry H)	Crystal Palace London	30.08.1969
46.50	Jamie Baulch (Newport H)	Sheffield	30.08.1993
46.34	Iwan Thomas (Newham Essex B)	Wrexham	03.07.1994
45.98	Iwan Thomas (Newham Essex B)	Victoria, Canada	23.08.1994
45.73	Iwan Thomas (Newham Essex B)	Ljubljana, Yugoslavia	21.05.1995
45.58	Iwan Thomas (Newham Essex B)	Bellinzona, Switzerland	20.06.1995
45.40	Jamie Baulch (Cardiff AAC)	Narbonne, France	29.07.1995
45.15	Jamie Baulch (Cardiff AAC)	Gateshead	21.08.1995
45.14	Jamie Baulch (Cardiff AAC)	Copenhagen, Denmark	23.08.1995
45.14 *	Iwan Thomas (Newham Essex B)	Pietersburg, South Africa	03.04.1996
44.98 *	Iwan Thomas (Newham Essex B)	Pretoria, South Africa	08.04.1996

44.66 *	Iwan Thomas (Newham Essex B)	Johannesburg, South Africa	14.04.1996
44.57	Jamie Baulch (Cardiff AAC)	Lausanne, Switzerland	03.07.1996
44.49	Iwan Thomas (Newham Essex B)	Sheffield	29.06.1997
44.46	Iwan Thomas (Newham Essex B)	Lausanne, Switzerland	02.07.1997
44.36	Iwan Thomas (Newham Essex B)	Birmingham	13.07.1997

880 yards

2:01.5 e	Harry Cullum (Roath H)	Northampton	04.07.1896
1:59.8	A B Manning (Swansea Valley AC)	Stamford Bridge, London	05.07.1902
1:59.4	A S D Smith (Cambridge University)	Welsh Championships	00.00.1906
1:55.8 e	Cecil Griffiths (Surrey AC)	Stamford Bridge, London	01.07.1922
1:55.8	Cecil Griffiths (Surrey AC)	Glasgow	11.08.1923
1:53.1 e	Cecil Griffiths (Surrey AC)	Stamford Bridge, London	03.07.1926
1:53.1 e	Jim Alford (Roath H)	Sydney, Australia	05.02.1938
1:50.9	Tony Harris (Mitcham AC)	Brighton	25.08.1959
1:50.7	Tony Harris (Mitcham AC)	Motspur Park	25.06.1960
1:50.2	Tony Harris (Mitcham AC)	White City, London	20.05.1961
1:49.8	Tony Harris (Mitcham AC)	White City, London	22.05.1961
1:49.0	Tony Harris (Mitcham AC)	Motspur Park	24.06.1961
1:48.9	Tony Harris (Mitcham AC)	Brighton	20.07.1963
1:48.5	Tony Harris (Mitcham AC)	Wimbledon	05.08.1964

professional marks, under unknown conditions, which bettered the known amateur bests at the time:

2:00.25	William Richards		00.00.1866
2:00.0	Harry Cullum	Rochdale	04.11.1899
1:57.6	Fred "Tenby" Davies	Taff Vale Park, Pontypridd	00.00.1909

800 metres

1:57.0	Cecil Griffiths (Surrey AC)	Paris, France	29.07.1923
1:53.6	Reg Thomas (RAF)	Paris, France,	28.07.1929
1:49.3	Tony Harris (Mitcham AC)	White City, London	18.08.1962
1:48.0	Tony Harris (Mitcham AC)	Hurlingham	05.09.1964
1:46.8	Bob Adams (Bromsgrove & Redditch)	Carmarthen	09.08.1969
1:46.26	Phil Lewis (Wolverhampton & Bilston)	Christchurch, New Zealand	27.01.1974
1:46.16	Gareth Brown (Cardiff AAC)	Stockholm, Sweden	02.07.1984
1:45.44	Neil Horsfield (Newport H)	Wrexham	28.07.1990

1500 metres

3:55.0	Reg Thomas (RAF)	Paris, France	02.08.1931
3:54.6	Reg Thomas (RAF)	Stockholm, Sweden	06.08.1931
3:53.6	Reg Thomas (RAF)	Milan, Italy	17.09.1933
3:53.5	Reg Thomas (RAF)	Helsinki, Finland	05.09.1937
3:53.4	John Disley (London AC)	Brighton	03.09.1956
3:49.8	John M Williams (Carmarthen H)	Birmingham	03.10.1959
3:48.4	Richard Jones (Hampstead H)	Paddington	26.07.1960
3:46.1	Tony Harris (Mitcham AC)	Turku, Finland	29.07.1964
3:45.2	Gwynn Davis (Bristol AC)	Karlskoga, Sweden	23.08.1968
3:45.0	Phil Thomas (Herne Hill H)	Paddington	12.07.1969
3:42.6	Phil Thomas (Herne Hill H)	Edinburgh	22.07.1970
3:42.6	Bob Maplestone (Cardiff AAC)	Seattle, USA	15.06.1972
3:39.7	Bob Maplestone (Cardiff AAC)	Seattle, USA	17.06.1972
3:38.05	Glen Grant (Army)	Edmonton, Canada	12.08.1978
3:37.96	Neil Horsfield (Newport H)	Crystal Palace, London	10.07.1987

3:35.13	Neil Horsfield (Newport H)	Crystal Palace, London	20.07.1990
3:35.08	Neil Horsfield (Newport H)	Brussels, Belgium	10.08.1990

One mile

4:43.0	A B Manning (Swansea Valley AC)	Welsh Championships	00.00.1901
4:35.8	E Francis (Cardiff)	Abergavenny	00.00.1904
4:35.0	D H Griffiths (Newport H)	Rodney Parade, Newport	27.06.1908
4:31.0	Cliff Price (Newport H)	Rodney Parade, Newport	09.08.1913
4:27.8	Reg Thomas (RAF)	RAF Championships	00.00.1927
4:21.2	Reg Thomas (RAF)	Stamford Bridge, London	07.07.1928
4:20.2	Reg Thomas (RAF)	RAF Championships	00.00.1928
4:20.2	Reg Thomas (RAF)	RAF Championships	00.00.1930
4:15.2	Reg Thomas (RAF)	Stamford Bridge, London	05.07.1930
4:14.0	Reg Thomas (RAF)	Hamilton, New Zealand	23.08.1930
4:13.4	Reg Thomas (RAF)	Stamford Bridge, London	25.05.1931
4:11.5	Jim Alford (Roath H)	Sydney, Australia	12.02.1938
4:10.6	John Disley (London AC)	Birmingham	03.10.1953
4:10.2	John Disley (London AC)	Cambridge	20.05.1954
4:09.0	John Disley (London AC)	Vancouver, Canada	05.08.1954
4:09.0	John Disley (London AC)	White City, London	28.05.1955
4:07.0	John Disley (London AC)	White City, London	06.08.1956
4:05.4	John Disley (London AC)	Walton	14.06.1958
4:04.4 e	Tony Pumfrey (Coventry Godiva)	Dublin, Ireland	06.08.1958
4:02.8	Richard Jones (Hampstead H)	Motspur Park	25.06.1960
4:02.2	Tony Harris (Mitcham AC)	Motspur Park	25.07.1962
4:01.0	Tony Harris (Mitcham AC)	Motspur Park	22.07.1964
3:58.96	Tony Harris (Mitcham AC)	White City, London	03.07.1965
3:58.5	Bob Maplestone (Cardiff AAC)	Arkadelphia, USA	25.05.1973
3:54.39	Neil Horsfield (Newport H)	Cork, Ireland	08.07.1986

professional marks, under unknown conditions, which bettered the known amateur bests at the time:

4:24.0	William Richards		29.07.1865
4:17.25	William Richards	Manchester	19.08.1865

3000 metres

8:21.6	John Disley (London AC)	Krefeld, Germany	31.08.1952
8:09.6 it	John Disley (London AC)	Turku, Finland	17.09.1957
8:08.8	Tony Ashton (Reading AC)	Crystal Palace, London	03.08.1969
8:08.2	Tony Ashton (Reading AC)	White City, London	29.08.1970
8:04.4	Tony Ashton (Reading AC)	Crystal Palace, London	06.08.1971
7:54.0	John Davies (Thames Valley H)	Oslo, Norway	21.08.1974
7:51.53	Tony Simmons (Luton United)	Crystal Palace, London	23.08.1978
7:46.95	David James (Cardiff AAC)	Cwmbran	26.05.1980
7:46.40	Ian Hamer (Swansea H)	Auckland, New Zealand	20.01.1990

Two miles

9:44.6	Cliff Price (Newport H)	Rodney Parade, Newport	14.07.1914
9:38.2	Jim Alford (Roath H)	Rodney Parade, Newport	24.08.1938
9:09.0	Phil Morgan (South London H)	Oxford	12.06.1952
8:59.0	Chris Suddaby (Oxford University)		00.00.1955
8:43.8	John Disley (London AC)	Turku, Finland	17.09.1957
8:42.6	Gordon Minty (Thames Valley H)	Ypsilanti, USA	12.05.1973
8:42.17	Peter Griffiths (Tipton H)	Crystal Palace, London	17.09.1976
8:20.28	David James (Cardiff AAC)	Crystal Palace, London	27.06.1980

Three miles

15:08.8	A S D Smith (Cambridge University)	Queens Club, London	31.03.1905
14:52.0	Len Tongue (Newport H)	Rodney Parade, Newport	30.06.1934
14:41.0	Harry Gallivan (Cwmbran H)	Rodney Parade, Newport	27.06.1936
14:32.8	Ivor Brown (Mitcham AC)	Taff Vale Park, Pontypridd	25.06.1938
14:32.2	Ivor Brown (Mitcham AC)	White City, London	00.07.1938
14:30.2	Phil Morgan (South London H)	White City, London	12.03.1949
14:25.4	Phil Morgan (South London H)	White City, London	10.03.1951
14:12.4	Phil Morgan (South London H)	White City, London	23.06.1951
14:07.6	Phil Morgan (South London H)	Oxford	08.05.1952
14:03.8	Phil Morgan (South London H)	White City, London	21.06.1952
14:03.0	Chris Suddaby (Oxford University)	White City, London	19.05.1956
14:02.5	David Richards (Polytechnic H)	Oxford	10.03.1957
14:00.6	David Richards (Polytechnic H)	Reading	18.05.1957
13:45.4	John Merriman (Watford H)	White City, London	13.07.1957
13:43.8	John Merriman (Watford H)	Uxbridge	21.06.1958
13:32.06	John Merriman (Watford H)	Arms Park Cardiff	22.07.1958
13:31.6	John Merriman (Watford H)	Motspur Park	25.06.1960
13:11.0	Gordon Minty (Thames Valley H)		28.04.1971

professional mark, under unknown conditions, which bettered the known amateur bests at the time:

15:26.0	William Richards		00.00.186?

5000 metres

14:13.2	John Disley (London AC)	White City, London	20.07.1957
14:03.0	John Merriman (Watford H)	White City, London	15.06.1960
14:02.8	Alan Joslyn (Polytechnic H)	White City, London	02.08.1969
14:02.0	Bernie Plain (Cardiff AAC)	Edinburgh	25.07.1970
14:01.6	Fred Bell (Thames Valley H)	Crystal Palace, London	18.08.1971
13:38.0	Gordon Minty (Thames Valley H)	Crystal Palace, London	24.06.1972
13:25.67	Tony Simmons (Luton Utd)	Lausanne, Switzerland	12.07.1978
13:18.6	Steve Jones (Newport H)	Lisbon, Portugal	10.06.1982
13.09.80	Ian Hamer (Swansea H)	Rome, Italy	09.06.1992

Six miles

30:06.4	Sam Palmer (Mitcham AC)	White City, London	07.07.1939
29:28.4	Chris Suddaby (Oxford University)	White City, London	21.04.1956
28:53.8	John Merriman (Watford H)	White City, London	27.04.1957
28:51.0	John Merriman (Watford H)	White City, London	26.05.1958
28:43.0	John Merriman (Watford H)	Chiswick	28.06.1958
28:33.2	John Merriman (Watford H)	White City, London	04.08.1958
28:15.8	John Merriman (Watford H)	White City, London	10.07.1959
28:10.8	John Merriman (Watford H)	White City, London	15.07.1960
28:09.4 it	John Merriman (Watford H)	White City, London	30.07.1960
28:07.4 it	John Merriman (Watford H)	White City, London	07.08.1961
27:34.4	Gordon Minty (Thames Valley H)	East Lansing, USA	25.05.1973
27:20.8	Gordon Minty (Thames Valley H)	Bakersfield, USA	15.06.1973

10000 metres

30:52.2	Chris Suddaby (Oxford University)	Croydon	04.07.1956
29:03.8	John Merriman (Watford H)	Stockholm, Sweden	19.08.1958
29:01.8	John Merriman (Watford H)	White City, London	30.07.1960
28:52.89	John Merriman (Watford H)	Rome, Italy	08.09.1960
28:51.84	Bernie Plain (Cardiff AAC)	Edinburgh	18.07.1970
28:51.4	Gordon Minty (Thames Valley H)	Eugene, USA	02.06.1972

28:41.6	Bernie Plain (Cardiff AAC)	Crystal Palace, London	20.09.1972
28:20.6	Bernie Plain (Cardiff AAC)	Leipzig, Germany	30.06.1973
28:14.89	Bernie Plain (Cardiff AAC)	Crystal Palace, London	01.08.1975
28:13.25	Steve Jones (Newport H)	Crystal Palace, London	05.09.1980
28:00.58	Steve Jones (Newport H)	Prague, Czech	19.06.1981
27:39.14	Steve Jones (Newport H)	Oslo, Norway	09.07.1983

Two miles steeplechase

11:31.0	Ken Harris (Roath H)	GKN, Cardiff	06.07.1946
10:05.4	John Disley (London AC)	White City, London	15.07.1950
10:04.0	John Disley (London AC)	White City, London	14.07.1951
09:44.0	John Disley (London AC)	White City, London	21.06.1952

3000 metres steeplechase

9:18.4	John Disley (London AC)	Southgate	28.06.1950
9:11.6	John Disley (London AC)	White City, London	26.09.1951
8:59.59	John Disley (London AC)	Helsinki, Finland	23.07.1952
8:51.94	John Disley (London AC)	Helsinki, Finland	25.07.1952
8:44.2	John Disley (London AC)	Moscow, Russia	11.09.1955
8:41.4	Tony Ashton (Reading AC)	White City, London	15.07.1967
8:39.8	Bernie Hayward (Cardiff AAC)	Edinburgh	23.07.1970
8:35.6	Ron McAndrew (Reading AC)	Portsmouth	09.07.1971
8:33.6	John Davies (Thames Valley H)	Warsaw, Poland	21.06.1973
8:30.2	John Davies (Thames Valley H)	Athens, Greece	18.07.1973
8:28.0	John Davies (Thames Valley H)	Sotteville, France	14.08.1973
8:24.8	John Davies (Thames Valley H)	Christchurch, New Zealand	26.01.1974
8:22.48	John Davies (Thames Valley H)	Crystal Palace, London	13.09.1974
8:21.41	Roger Hackney (Aldershot F & D)	Stockholm, Sweden	06.07.1982
8:19.38	Roger Hackney (Aldershot F & D)	Helsinki, Finland	12.08.1983
8:18.91	Roger Hackney (Aldershot F & D)	Hechtel, Belgium	30.07.1988

110 metres hurdles (hand timing)

16.6 y	William Cowell Davies (Oxford University)	Lillie Bridge, London	31.03.1871
16.2 y	Wyatt Gould (Newport AC)		00.00.1903
16.2 y	Wallis Walters (Cardiff University)	Abergavenny	00.00.1904
16.2 y	Wallis Walters (Cardiff University)	St Helen's, Swansea	08.09.1906
16.2 y	Stan Macey (Newport AC)	Pontypool	09.06.1930
16.2 y	T T Simmonds (Metro Police)	Crymlyn Burrows, Swansea	26.06.1937
16.2 y	T T Simmonds (Metro Police)	Police Championships	00.00.1937
15.9 y	Mervyn Rosser (Polytechnic H)	Abertillery	07.05.1949
15.8 y	Mervyn Rosser (Polytechnic H)	Abertillery	25.06.1949
15.4 y	Mervyn Rosser (Polytechnic H)	Imber Court	03.09.1949
15.2 y	Bob Shaw (Achilles)	Maindy Stadium, Cardiff	19.06.1954
15.1 y	Bob Shaw (Achilles)	White City, London	10.07.1954
15.0 y	Bob Shaw (Achilles)	Cambridge	23.04.1955
15.0 y	Bob Shaw (Achilles)	Cambridge	30.04.1955
14.7 y	Bob Shaw (Achilles)	Oxford	12.05.1955
14.7 y	Bob Shaw (Achilles)	White City, London	19.05.1956
14.7 y	Bob Shaw (Achilles)	Oxford	18.05.1957
14.6 y	Bob Shaw (Achilles)	Aldershot	29.06.1957
14.5	Berwyn Price (Cardiff AAC)	Maindy Stadium, Cardiff	16.05.1970
14.5	Berwyn Price (Cardiff AAC)	Durham	20.06.1970

14.5	Berwyn Price (Cardiff AAC)	Brighton	04.07.1970
14.5	Berwyn Price (Cardiff AAC)	Cwmbran	01.08.1970
14.2	Berwyn Price (Cardiff AAC)	White City, London	08.08.1970
14.0	Berwyn Price (Cardiff AAC)	Madrid, Spain	12.09.1971
13.9	Berwyn Price (Cardiff AAC)	Madrid, Spain	12.09.1971
13.9	Berwyn Price (Cardiff AAC)	Formia, Italy	20.05.1973
13.5	Berwyn Price (Cardiff AAC)	Leipzig, Germany	01.07.1973
13.5	Berwyn Price (Cardiff AAC)	Athens, Greece	14.05.1976

110m hurdles (fully automatic timing)

14.21	Berwyn Price (Cardiff AAC)	Paris, France	12.09.1970
14.00	Berwyn Price (Cardiff AAC)	Crystal Palace, London	15.07.1972
13.94	Berwyn Price (Cardiff AAC)	Munich, Germany	03.09.1972
13.76	Berwyn Price (Cardiff AAC)	Edinburgh	16.06.1973
13.69	Berwyn Price (Cardiff AAC)	Moscow, Russia	18.08.1973
13.69	Colin Jackson (Cardiff AAC)	Cottbus, Germany	23.08.1985
13.62	Colin Jackson (Cardiff AAC)	Wrexham	08.06.1986
13.51	Colin Jackson (Cardiff AAC)	Cwmbran	14.06.1986
13.44	Colin Jackson (Cardiff AAC)	Edinburgh	19.07.1986
13.41	Colin Jackson (Cardiff AAC)	Zurich, Switzerland	19.08.1987
13.37	Colin Jackson (Cardiff AAC)	Rome, Italy	01.09.1987
13.23	Colin Jackson (Cardiff AAC)	Belfast	27.06.1988
13.11*	Colin Jackson (Cardiff AAC)	Sestriere Italy	11.08.1988
13.11	Colin Jackson (Cardiff AAC)	Crystal Palace, London	14.07.1989
13.11	Colin Jackson (Cardiff AAC)	Auckland, New Zealand	27.01.1990
13.08	Colin Jackson (Cardiff AAC)	Auckland, New Zealand	28.01.1990
13.06	Colin Jackson (Brecon AC)	Crystal Palace, London	10.07.1992
13.04	Colin Jackson (Brecon AC)	Cologne, Germany	16.08.1992
12.97*	Colin Jackson (Brecon AC)	Sestriere, Italy	28.07.1993
12.91	Colin Jackson (Brecon AC)	Stuttgart, Germany	20.08.1993

440 yards hurdles

63.3	Mervyn Rosser (London University)	St Helen's, Swansea	24.06.1950
62.0	Richard Greening (Newport H)	Maindy Stadium, Cardiff	23.06.1951
60.6	Gareth Lewis (Aberystwyth University)	Maindy Stadium, Cardiff	20.06.1953
54.8	Bob Shaw (Achilles)	Maindy Stadium, Cardiff	19.06.1954
53.4	Bob Shaw (Achilles)	White City, London	10.07.1954
53.3	Bob Shaw (Achilles)	Vancouver, Canada	03.08.1954
52.2	Bob Shaw (Achilles)	White City, London	16.07.1955

400 metres hurdles

53.4	Bob Shaw (Achilles)	Berne, Switzerland	26.08.1954
52.5	Bob Shaw (Achilles)	Berne, Switzerland	28.08.1954
52.3	Bob Shaw (Achilles)	Berne, Switzerland	29.08.1954
51.7	Bob Shaw (Achilles)	Budapest, Hungary	30.09.1956
51.7	Colin O'Neill (Bristol AC)	Crystal Palace, London	14.07.1973
50.9	Colin O'Neill (Bristol AC)	Christchurch, New Zealand	20.01.1974
50.70	Colin O'Neill (Bristol AC)	Christchurch, New Zealand	27.01.1974
50.58	Colin O'Neill (Bristol AC)	Christchurch, New Zealand	29.01.1974
50.01	Philip Harries (Derby AC)	Derby	05.06.1988
49.81	Paul Gray (Cardiff AAC)	Birmingham	26.07.1998
49.76	Paul Gray (Cardiff AAC)	Sheffield	02.08.1998
49.16	Paul Gray (Cardiff AAC)	Budapest, Hungary	18.08.1998

High Jump

1.71	R F Houghton (Newport FC)	Stoke	01.07.1882
1.73	R F Houghton (Newport FC)	Lillie Bridge, London	30.06.1883
1.73	J Jacobs (Newport AC)	St Helen's, Swansea	07.09.1902
1.78	Frank Whitcutt (Cardiff University)	Penarth	06.06.1927
1.83	Frank Whitcutt (Cardiff University)	Rodney Parade, Newport	16.06.1928
1.83	Hubert Stubbs (Polytechnic H)	Imber Court	04.06.1938
1.84	Hubert Stubbs (Polytechnic H)	Pontypridd	25.06.1938
1.90	Hubert Stubbs (Polytechnic H)	Dublin, Ireland	23.07.1938
1.90	Hubert Stubbs (Polytechnic H)	Cologne, Germany	20.08.1939
1.94	John Lister (Birchgrove H)	Maindy Stadium, Cardiff	30.05.1961
1.95	Peter Lance (Loughborough)	Loughborough	05.06.1969
1.95	Peter Lance (Loughborough)	Crystal Palace, London	16.06.1969
1.95	Steve Hughes (Cardiff AAC)	Birmingham	02.05.1970
1.95	Steve Hughes (Cardiff AAC)	Aldershot	08.07.1970
2.00	Peter Lance (Loughborough)	Cwmbran	16.06.1973
2.00	Peter Lance (Loughborough)	Wolverhampton	23.06.1973
2.01	Geraint Griffiths (Gloucester)	Cwmbran	18.06.1975
2.01	Geraint Griffiths (Gloucester)	Cwmbran	19.07.1975
2.02	Trevor Llewelyn (Blackheath)	Hendon	09.07.1977
2.04	Geraint Griffiths (Gloucester)	Luxembourg, Luxembourg	06.08.1977
2.11	George Robertson (RAF)	Oxford	06.05.1978
2.11	Trevor Llewelyn (Blackheath)	Crystal Palace, London	27.08.1978
2.11	Trevor Llewelyn (Blackheath)	Crystal Palace, London	10.09.1978
2.15	Trevor Llewelyn (Blackheath)	Tokyo, Japan	25.09.1978
2.16	Trevor Llewelyn (Blackheath)	Cwmbran	30.05.1982
2.18	Trevor Llewelyn (Blackheath)	Oxford	14.05.1983
2.20	Trevor Llewelyn (Blackheath)	Crystal Palace, London	15.07.1983
2.21	John Hill (Solihull)	Halfheim, Germany	26.05.1985
2.22	John Hill (Solihull)	Edinburgh	17.08.1985
2.24	John Hill (Solihull)	Cottbus, Germany	23.08.1985

Pole Vault

2.89 +	T Williams (Welsh Collegiate Inst)	Llandovery	10.05.1871
3.05	D Cooke (Wrexham)	Birmingham	21.06.1884
3.07	Cyril Evans (Port Talbot YMCA)	Morriston	21.08.1937
3.07	J Gravelle (Llanelly AC)	Morriston	21.08.1937
3.07	Ron Harris (Neath AC)	Morriston	21.08.1937
3.11	Cyril Evans (Port Talbot YMCA)	Pontypridd	25.06.1938
3.15	Cyril Evans (Port Talbot YMCA)	Hendy	30.08.1947
3.20	Cyril Evans (Port Talbot YMCA)	Aberavon	19.06.1948
3.21	D Owens (Caerphilly CS)	Aberavon	02.07.1949
3.27	D J Davies (Whitland GS)	Carmarthen	20.05.1950
3.44	Derek Cole (Army)	Margam	08.07.1950
3.45	Glyn Jenkins (Whitland GS)	Bangor	15.07.1950
3.50	Ken Goodall (Loughborough)	Maindy Stadium, Cardiff	16.06.1951
3.66	Hywel Williams (Roath H)	Chesterfield	28.06.1952
3.66	Colin Fletcher (Bridgend AC)	Barry	04.06.1955
3.68	Colin Fletcher (Bridgend AC)	Maindy Stadium, Cardiff	23.06.1956
3.76	Dewar Neill (Polytechnic H)	Maindy Stadium, Cardiff	21.06.1958
3.81	Colin Fletcher (Bridgend AC)	Maindy Stadium, Cardiff	30.05.1959
3.81	Colin Fletcher (Bridgend AC)	Pontypridd	06.06.1960

3.87	Roy Williams (Carmarthen H)	Loughborough	22.06.1960
3.88	Morton Evans (Thames Valley H)	Loughborough	31.05.1962
4.06	Glyn Morris (Bridgend AC)	White City, London	16.05.1964
4.09	Glyn Morris (Bridgend AC)	Pitreavie	31.07.1965
4.10	Clive Longe (Roath H)	Loughborough	20.05.1967
4.14	Colin Balchin (Birchgrove H)	Edinburgh	27.05.1967
4.17	Les Jones (Blackheath)	Southall	13.08.1967
4.25	David Lease (Birchgrove H)	Harpenden	15.06.1968
4.39	David Lease (Birchgrove H)	Bath	26.03.1969
4.49	David Lease (Birchgrove H)	Leicester	25.05.1970
4.58	David Lease (Birchgrove H)	Harpenden	20.06.1970
4.65	David Lease (Birchgrove H)	Harpenden	19.06.1971
4.72	David Lease (Birchgrove H)	Bargoed	08.07.1972
4.74	Peter Lynk (Soton & Eastleigh)	Corby	31.05.1987
4.80	Peter Lynk (Soton & Eastleigh)	Cwmbran	20.06.1987
4.80	Neil Winter (Shaftesbury)	Jarrow	03.06.1989
4.90	Neil Winter (Shaftesbury)	Copthall	12.05.1990
5.00	Neil Winter (Shaftesbury)	Corby	28.05.1990
5.10	Neil Winter (Shaftesbury)	Corby	28.05.1990
5.10	Neil Winter (Shaftesbury)	Morfa Stadium, Swansea	16.06.1990
5.15	Neil Winter (Shaftesbury)	Morfa Stadium, Swansea	16.06.1990
5.20	Neil Winter (Shaftesbury)	Birmingham	02.09.1990
5.31	Neil Winter (Shaftesbury)	Morfa Stadium, Swansea	20.05.1992
5.40	Neil Winter (Shaftesbury)	Budapest, Hungary	13.06.1992
5.50	Neil Winter (Shaftesbury)	San Giuliano, Italy	09.08.1992
5.50	Neil Winter (Shaftesbury)	Crawley	06.08.1994
5.60	Neil Winter (Shaftesbury)	Enfield	19.08.1995

NB + competition conditions not identical to present day

Long Jump

6.18	W D Thomas (Lampeter Coll)	Lampeter	16.04.1891
6.40	Wallis Walters (Cardiff University)	St Helen's, Swansea	08.09.1906
6.46	D R Hughes (Llandovery College)	Llandovery	05.04.1922
6.75	John Lloyd (Newport AC)	Clydach	25.09.1926
6.75	J Higgins (Swansea Valley AC)	St Helen's, Swansea	23.07.1932
6.77	J Higgins (Swansea Valley AC)	Clydach	03.09.1932
6.77	Lewis Riden (Roath H)	Rodney Parade, Newport	27.06.1936
6.78+	John Frowen (Lewis School)	Tonypandy	01.07.1950
7.03	John Frowen (Lewis School)	Tonypandy	01.07.1950
7.06	Chris Alele (Cardiff University)	Maindy Stadium, Cardiff	19.06.1954
7.11	Eric Darlow (RAF)	Uxbridge	04.07.1956
7.19	Eric Darlow (RAF)	Uxbridge	03.07.1957
7.22	Bryan Woolley (Birchfield)	White City, London	24.05.1958
7.25	Bryan Woolley (Birchfield)	Uxbridge	16.08.1958
7.32	Bryan Woolley (Birchfield)	Maindy Stadium, Cardiff	29.07.1961
7.36	Bryan Woolley (Birchfield)	Erith	24.09.1961
7.39	Lynn Davies (Roath H.)	Barry	19.05.1962
7.40	Lynn Davies (Roath H)	Maindy Stadium, Cardiff	23.06.1962
7.54	Lynn Davies (Roath H)	Maindy Stadium, Cardiff	28.07.1962
7.61	Lynn Davies (Roath H)	Perth, Australia	26.11.1962
7.72	Lynn Davies (Roath H)	Perth, Australia	26.11.1962
7.94	Lynn Davies (Roath H)	White City, London	16.05.1964
8.01	Lynn Davies (Roath H)	White City, London	16.05.1964

8.01	Lynn Davies (Roath H)	Maindy Stadium, Cardiff	25.07.1964
8.02	Lynn Davies (Roath H)	Maindy Stadium, Cardiff	25.07.1964
8.07	Lynn Davies (Roath H)	Tokyo, Japan	18.10.1964
8.13*	Lynn Davies (Roath H)	Pretoria, South Africa	06.04.1966
8.18*	Lynn Davies (Roath H)	Bloemfontein, South Africa	09.04.1966
8.23	Lynn Davies (Roath H)	Berne, Switzerland	30.06.1968

NB + John Frowen beat existing Welsh all comers' record of 6.78 with his first round jump, (distance not known) and then went on to jump 7.03 later in the same competition.

Triple Jump

12.37	John Lloyd (Newport AC)	Rodney Parade, Newport	24.05.1924
12.79	John Lloyd (Newport AC)	Pontypool Park	18.07.1925
13.17	Frank Whitcutt (Cardiff University)	Rodney Parade, Newport	02.08.1926
13.51	Gwynne Evans (Newport AC)	Rodney Parade, Newport	30.06.1934
13.51	Gwynne Evans (Newport AC)	Rodney Parade, Newport	29.06.1935
13.74	Gwynne Evans (Newport AC)	Panteg	28.08.1938
14.11	Gwyn Harris (Lewis School)	Abertillery	10.07.1948
14.52	Gordon Wells (RAF)	Abertillery	25.06.1949
14.62	Aneurin Evans (Roath H)	White City, London	10.06.1957
14.62	Richard Dodd (Loughborough)	Maindy Stadium, Cardiff	17.05.1958
14.90	Peter Walker (Saro AC)	Birmingham	13.05.1961
15.29	Lynn Davies (Roath H)	Maindy Stadium, Cardiff	23.06.1962
15.43	Lynn Davies (Roath H)	Maindy Stadium, Cardiff	28.07.1962
15.64	Graham Webb (Newport H)	Wolverhampton	19.07.1969
15.88	John Phillips (Cardiff AAC)	Athens, Greece	14.05.1978
15.88	David Wood (Cardiff AAC)	Morfa Stadium, Swansea	25.08.1984
15.90	David Wood (Cardiff AAC)	Karlovac, Yugoslavia	16.09.1984
15.99	Steven Shalders (Cardiff AAC)	Santiago, Chile	20.10.2000

Shot Put

10.72 +	Hugh Williams (Cambridge University)	Cambridge	15.03.1859
10.97 +	Hugh Williams (Cambridge University)	Cambridge	28.05.1860
11.53	George Dillaway (Mon Police)	Rodney Parade, Newport	24.05.1924
12.57	Howard Ford (Achilles)	Sketty Hall, Swansea	26.07.1930
12.75	J P Wallace (Achilles)	(year of performance uncertain)	1929/1930
12.80 q	L Landsberg (Swansea Valley AC)	Clydach	23.08.1930
12.85	Arthur Lewis (Exeter H)	Pontypool Park	15.08.1931
13.31	Arthur Lewis (Exeter H)	Sketty Hall, Swansea	23.07.1932
13.31	Arthur Lewis (Exeter H)	Abertillery	03.08.1932
13.70	Bill Kingsbury (Rhondda Valley)	Woking	00.00.1954
14.07	Bill Kingsbury (Rhondda Valley)	Farnham	00.00.1954
14.60	John P Jones (Belgrave H)	Motspur Park	29.05.1957
15.27	Arthur Richardson (John Summers)	Wrexham	21.05.1960
16.25	Arthur Richardson (John Summers)	Wrexham	27.05.1961
16.36	Archie Buttriss (Hereford Police)	Hereford	21.08.1963
16.41 u	John Walters (Cardiff AAC)	Cyncoed	02.05.1970
16.55	John Walters (Cardiff AAC)	St. Helen's Swansea	17.07.1971
16.57	Paul Rees (Soton & Eastleigh)	Crystal Palace, London	13.08.1975
16.66	Paul Rees (Soton & Eastleigh)	Dublin, Ireland	29.05.1976
16.70	Paul Rees (Soton & Eastleigh)	Southampton	02.07.1978
16.78	Shaun Pickering (Haringey)	Crystal Palace, London	15.06.1985
17.05	Shaun Pickering (Haringey)	California, USA	00.00.1986
17.20	Shaun Pickering (Haringey)	San Jose, USA	01.03.1986

17.45	Shaun Pickering (Haringey)	Loughborough	25.06.1986
17.57	Shaun Pickering (Haringey)	Newham	16.08.1986
17.80	Paul Edwards (Walton)	Walton	18.05.1987
18.35	Paul Edwards (Walton)	Walton	15.06.1988
19.32	Paul Edwards (Walton)	Sandhurst	15.07.1988
19.81	Paul Edwards (Walton)	Sandhurst	15.07.1988
19.85	Paul Edwards (Walton)	Walton	02.07.1989
20.45	Shaun Pickering (Haringey)	Crystal Palace, London	17.08.1997

NB + competition conditions not identical to present day

Discus

33.76 q	L Landsberg (Swansea Valley AC)	Clydach	23.08.1930
36.78 q	L Landsberg (Swansea Valley AC)	Clydach	03.09.1932
35.56	Ned Jenkins (Port Talbot YMCA)	Morriston	21.08.1937
38.66	Arthur Lewis (Loughborough)		00.00.1937
39.24	Hywel Williams (Roath H)	Newport	18.08.1951
40.76	Hywel Williams (Roath H)	Merthyr	17.05.1952
41.12	Hywel Williams (Roath H)	Oxford	12.06.1952
42.36	Hywel Williams (Roath H)	Maindy Stadium, Cardiff	05.07.1952
43.30	Hywel Williams (Roath H)	Aberystwyth	13.04.1953
44.70	Hywel Williams (Roath H)	Maindy Stadium, Cardiff	08.05.1954
45.18	Hywel Williams (Roath H)	Vancouver, Canada	03.08.1954
47.50	Hywel Williams (Roath H)	Nairobi, Kenya	30.07.1955
48.02	Archie Buttriss (Hereford Police)	Glebelands, Newport	01.06.1963
48.46	Clive Longe (Roath H)	Loughborough	05.06.1969
48.92	Clive Longe (Roath H)	Colwyn Bay	05.07.1969
49.36 u	John Walters (Cardiff AAC)	Maindy Stadium, Cardiff	28.04.1970
49.38 u	John Walters (Cardiff AAC)	Cyncoed, Cardiff	02.05.1970
49.40 u	John Walters (Cardiff AAC)	Cyncoed, Cardiff	06.05.1970
51.04	John Walters (Cardiff AAC)	St Athan	20.05.1970
52.02	John Walters (Cardiff AAC)	Hayes	31.07.1971
52.34	Ted Kelland (Royal Marines)	Southall	30.06.1973
52.46	Shaun Pickering (Haringey)	Crystal Palace, London	23.06.1984
52.76	Shaun Pickering (Haringey)	Birmingham	07.07.1984
53.32	Shaun Pickering (Haringey)	Crystal Palace, London	07.08.1985
53.82	Shaun Pickering (Haringey)	Stanford, USA	28.03.1986
54.24	Shaun Pickering (Haringey)	Morfa Stadium, Swansea	13.07.1986
54.48	Paul Edwards (Walton)	Loughborough	07.06.1987
54.90	Paul Edwards (Walton)	Walton	09.07.1988
57.12	Paul Edwards (Walton)	Colindale	10.08.1988
59.37	Lee Newman (Belgrave H)	Ashford	09.05.1998
59.51	Lee Newman (Belgrave H)	Battersea Park	04.07.1998
60.43	Lee Newman (Belgrave H)	Enfield	23.08.1998

Hammer

24.23 +	David Parker Morgan (Oxford University)	Oxford	16.02.1864
25.35 +	David Parker Morgan (Oxford University)	Oxford	02.03.1864
26.39 +	David Parker Morgan (Oxford University)	Oxford	18.03.1865
27.80 +	David Parker Morgan (Oxford University)	Oxford	02.03.1866
31.68	L A Hughes (Oswestry & Queens)	Cambridge	11.03.1902
32.88	John H Thomas (Birchgrove H)	Maindy Stadium, Cardiff	19.06.1954
43.84	Albert Ley (London Police)	Maindy Stadium, Cardiff	25.06.1955
45.64	Albert Ley (London Police)	Maindy Stadium, Cardiff	23.06.1956
46.56	Albert Ley (London Police)	White City, London	05.07.1958

48.72	Lawrie Hall (Thames Valley H)	Arms Park, Cardiff	26.07.1958
50.16	Lawrie Hall (Thames Valley H)	Alperton	07.05.1960
54.44	Lawrie Hall (Thames Valley H)	Chiswick	13.05.1961
54.62	Lawrie Hall (Thames Valley H)	Alperton	24.05.1961
55.40	Lawrie Hall (Thames Valley H)	Watford	03.06.1961
55.66	Lawrie Hall (Thames Valley H)	Dublin, Ireland	17.07.1961
56.24	Lawrie Hall (Thames Valley H)		05.05.1962
57.40	Lawrie Hall (Thames Valley H)		00.05.1962
58.56	Lawrie Hall (Thames Valley H)	Enfield	26.05.1962
59.20	Shaun Pickering (Haringey)	Reading	14.05.1981
63.32	Shaun Pickering (Haringey)	Fresno, USA	06.03.1982
64.34	Shaun Pickering (Haringey)	Tucson, USA	26.02.1983
64.70	Shaun Pickering (Haringey)	Stanford, USA	14.01.1984
68.14	Shaun Pickering (Haringey)	Stanford, USA	17.03.1984
68.64	Shaun Pickering (Haringey)	Stanford, USA	07.04.1984

NB + Performances by David Parker Morgan were achieved by throwing a hammer with a wooden handle with an unlimited run up.

Javelin

39.70 q	C Sayers (Welsh Guards)	Army Championships	00.00.1923
42.72 q	C Sayers (Welsh Guards)	Army Championships	00.00.1924
30.01	Matt Cullen (Swansea Valley AC)	Clydach	25.09.1926
45.80 q	C Sayers (Welsh Guards)	Army Championships	00.00.1927
36.48	J P Richards (Swansea Valley AC)	Aberavon	27.07.1935
41.40	Fred Needs (Manselton AC)	West Wales v East Glam	10.08.1935
41.82	Fred Needs (Manselton AC)	Aberavon	22.08.1936
43.14	Fred Needs (Manselton AC)	Morriston	21.08.1937
44.76	G Rickards (Hendy AC)	Gorseinon	18.06.1938
46.00	Fred Needs (Manselton AC)	Kidwelly	13.08.1938
52.48	Arthur Squibbs (Loughborough)	Kidwelly	29.07.1939
55.74	Arthur Squibbs (Loughborough)	Port Talbot	19.08.1939
57.28	Clive Roberts (Swansea AC)	Maindy Stadium, Cardiff	19.06.1954
58.90	Brian Sexton (Roath H)	Barry	04.06.1955
61.30	Clive Roberts (Swansea AC)	Maindy Stadium, Cardiff	26.06.1955
61.30	Neville Hughes (Milocarian)	Aldershot	20.07.1955
61.64	Clive Roberts (Roath H)	Motspur Park	11.05.1957
61.82	Brian Sexton (Roath H)	Margam	06.07.1957
61.82	Clive Roberts (Roath H)	Motspur Park	30.04.1958
63.14	Norman Watkins (Thames Valley H)	Birmingham	07.05.1958
65.96	Brian Sexton (Roath H)	Llanharan	22.08.1959
66.38	Brian Sexton (Roath H)	Ruislip	25.09.1960
66.58	Brian Sexton (Roath H)	Bargoed	13.05.1961
66.98	Brian Sexton (Roath H)	Maindy Stadium, Cardiff	20.06.1961
67.82	Tony Edwards (Rochester)	Liverpool University	15.05.1965
69.04	Tony Edwards (Rochester)	Liverpool University	15.05.1965
69.24	Tony Edwards (Rochester)	Loughborough	01.06.1965
69.34	Tony Edwards (Rochester)	Loughborough	20.05.1967
70.26	Tony Edwards (Rochester)	Loughborough	07.06.1967
71.24	Tony Edwards (Rochester)	Le Baule, France	23.07.1967
72.78	Tony Edwards (Rochester)	Glasgow	15.06.1968

73.30	Nigel Sherlock (Walton)	Grangemouth	07.06.1969
75.48	Nigel Sherlock (Walton)	Brno, Czech	05.07.1969
75.78	Colin Mackenzie (Newham Essex B)	Crystal Palace, London	27.06.1981
76.18	Colin Mackenzie (Newham Essex B)	Portsmouth	00.00.1981
77.72	Colin Mackenzie (Newham Essex B)	Crystal Palace, London	04.07.1981
78.02	Colin Mackenzie (Newham Essex B)	Enfield	27.04.1985
79.44	Colin Mackenzie (Newham Essex B)	Leeds	29.06.1985
81.30	Colin Mackenzie (Newham Essex B)	Crystal Palace, London	07.08.1985

New Model

In 1986 the specification of the javelin was changed by moving the centre of gravity. This had the effect of reducing distances thrown

73.52	Colin Mackenzie (Newham Essex B)	Cwmbran	14.06.1986
74.14	Colin Mackenzie (Newham Essex B)	Edinburgh	11.06.1988
76.82	Nigel Bevan (Belgrave H)	Birmingham	13.05.1989
77.30	Nigel Bevan (Belgrave H)	Jarrow	04.06.1989
78.02	Nigel Bevan (Belgrave H)	Aarhus, Denmark	06.07.1989
78.60	Nigel Bevan (Belgrave H)	Meisingset, Norway	16.07.1989
78.90	Nigel Bevan (Belgrave H)	Morfa Stadium, Swansea	22.07.1989
79.56	Nigel Bevan (Belgrave H)	Duisburg, Germany	28.08.1989
79.70	Nigel Bevan (Belgrave H)	Auckland, New Zealand	03.02.1990
80.68	Nigel Bevan (Belgrave H)	Birmingham	28.06.1992
81.70	Nigel Bevan (Belgrave H)	Birmingham	28.06.1992

Decathlon – 1934 tables

5129	John Cotter (Birchfield)	White City, London	11.07.1936
5396	John Cotter (Birchfield)	Loughborough	06.08.1938

1952 tables

5014	Hywel Williams (Roath H)	Maindy Stadium, Cardiff	07.06.1952
5035	Hywel Williams (Roath H)	Uxbridge	29.08.1953
5370	Hywel Williams (Roath H)	Loughborough	10.08.1957
5486	Hywel Williams (Roath H)	Wolverhampton	08.08.1959
5548	Hywel Williams (Roath H)	Helsinki, Finland	13.09.1959

1962 tables

6259	Hywel Williams (Roath H)	Helsinki, Finland	13.09.1959
6342	Clive Longe (Roath H)	Llanrumney, Cardiff	18.07.1964
6424	Clive Longe (Roath H)	Loughborough	08.08.1964
6673	Clive Longe (Roath H)	Uxbridge	02.09.1964
7083	Clive Longe (Roath H)	Eton Manor	14.05.1966
7114	Clive Longe (Roath H) 6936*	Beverwijk, Netherlands	17.07.1966
7123	Clive Longe (Roath H) 6954*	Kingston, Jamaica	06.08.1966
7160	Clive Longe (Roath H) 6996*	Budapest, Hungary	01.09.1966
7200	Clive Longe (Roath H) 7028*	Loughborough	21.06.1967
7392	Clive Longe (Roath H) 7234*	Los Angeles, USA	09.07.1967
7451	Clive Longe (Roath H) 7308*	Kassel, Germany	29.06.1969

*NB * scores as recalculated on 1984 tables*

Fully automatic timing (1984 tables)

7240	Clive Longe (Roath H)	Mexico City, Mexico	19.10.1968
7268	Paul Edwards (Walton)	Bonn, Germany	14.08.1983

4 x 110 yards relay

45.2	Monmouth	Ystrad Rhondda	24.08.1935
45.2	Monmouth	Pontypridd	21.08.1937
43.9	Welsh AAA *(Bernard Ball, Reg Snow, Alan Roche, Gareth Morgan)*	Newport	18.08.1951
43.7	Wales	Maindy Stadium, Cardiff	26.06.1954
43.7	Wales *(?, ?, C. L. Davies, John Gilpin)*	Newport	09.07.1955
43.2	Wales *(Nick Whitehead, Jack Melen, Dave Roberts, Gwilym Roberts)*	Margam	06.07.1957
42.7	Wales	Colwyn Bay	05.07.1958
42.13	Wales *(Ron Jones, John Morgan, David Roberts, Nick Whitehead)*	Arms Park, Cardiff	26.07.1958
42.0	Wales *(Berwyn Jones, Ron Jones, Nick Whitehead, Lynn Davies)*	Barry	19.05.1962
40.80	Wales *(Dave England, Ron Jones, Berwyn Jones, Nick Whitehead)*	Perth, Australia	01.12.1962
40.8	Wales (*Terry Davies, Lynn Davies, Keri Jones, Ron Jones)*	Barry	11.06.1966
40.6	Wales (*Terry Davies, Lynn Davies, Keri Jones, Ron Jones)*	Kingston, Jamaica	13.08.1966
40.2	Wales *(Terry Davies, Lynn Davies, Keri Jones, Ron Jones)*	Kingston, Jamaica	13.08.1966

4 x 100 metres relay

40.04	Wales *(Kevin Williams, Colin Jackson, Jamie Baulch, Tremayne Rutherford)*	Cwmbran	09.07.1995
39.09	Wales *(Kevin Williams, Doug Turner, Christian Malcolm, Jamie Henthorn)*	Kuala Lumpur, Malaysia	20.09.1998
38.73	Wales *(Kevin Williams, Doug Turner, Christian Malcolm, Jamie Henthorn)*	Kuala Lumpur, Malaysia	21.09.1998

4 x 440 yards relay

3:46.0	Cardiff	Arms Park, Cardiff	07.07.1934
3:43.8	Glamorgan	Newport	14.07.1934
3:14.1	Wales	Leicester	20.07.1968

4 x 400 metres relay

3:12.4	Wales *(Mike Delaney, Gwynne Griffiths, Wynford Leyshon, Colin O'Neill)*	Cwmbran	21.07.1973
3:11.8	Wales *(Colin O'Neill, Gwynne Griffiths, Bob Roberts, Mike Delaney)*	Lisbon, Portugal	19.08.1973
3:08.6	Wales *(Colin O'Neill, Wynford Leyshon, Phil Lewis, Mike Delaney)*	Christchurch, New Zealand	02.02.1974
3:08.43	Wales *(Steve James, Wynford Leyshon, Jeff Griffiths, Mike Delaney)*	Cwmbran	08.07.1978
3:03.68	Wales *(Peter Maitland, Jamie Baulch, Paul Gray, Iwan Thomas)*	Victoria, Canada	27.08.1994
3:03.63	Wales *(Paul Gray, Jamie Baulch, Matthew Elias, Iwan Thomas)*	Kuala Lumpur, Malaysia	20.09.1998
3:01.86	Wales *(Paul Gray, Jamie Baulch, Doug Turner, Iwan Thomas)*	Kuala Lumpur, Malaysia	21.09.1998

WOMEN

100 yards (hand timing)

12.0	Marjorie Clements (Cardiff Uni)	Cardiff	01.05.1930
11.9	Nellie Denner (Port Talbot YMCA)	Neath	15.07.1937
11.9	Jean Docker (Middlesex Ladies)	Maindy Stadium, Cardiff	07.06.1952
11.6	Janet Lewis (Roath H)	Maindy Stadium, Cardiff	20.06.1953
11.6	Hilary Lewis (Tonypandy GS)		00.00.1954
11.6	Bonny Jones (Heol Gam SS)	Abertillery	02.07.1955
11.5	Gwyneth Lewis (Holyhead CS)	Colwyn Bay	09.07.1955
11.4	Gwyneth Lewis (Bangor College)	Maindy Stadium, Cardiff	22.06.1957
11.4	Jean Docker/Whitehead (Middlesex Ladies)	Maindy Stadium, Cardiff	21.06.1958
11.4	Bonny Jones (Roath H)	Colwyn Bay	05.07.1958
11.4	Bonny Jones (Roath H)	Arms Park, Cardiff	19.07.1958
11.4	Jean Whitehead (Middlesex Ladies)	Arms Park, Cardiff	19.07.1958
11.4	Gwyneth Lewis (Bangor College)	Arms Park, Cardiff	19.07.1958
11.4	Carol Thomas (Roath H)	Treorchy	09.08.1958
11.1	Daphne Williams (Eirias)	Colwyn Bay	06.06.1959
10.9	Liz Parsons (Roath H)	Glebelands, Newport	27.05.1961
10.8	Liz Parsons (Roath H)	Maindy Stadium, Cardiff	25.07.1964
10.8	Liz Parsons (Roath H)	Barry	05.09.1964
10.8	Liz Parsons (Roath H)	Maindy Stadium, Cardiff	10.06.1965
10.8	Liz Gill (Barry H)	White City, London	03.07.1965
10.7	Liz Gill (Barry H)	White City, London	03.07.1965
10.7	Liz Gill (Barry H)	Birmingham	17.07.1965
10.7	Liz Parsons (Roath H)	Maindy Stadium, Cardiff	25.06.1966
10.7	Liz Parsons/Johns (Roath H)	Bristol	28.05.1968
10.7	Liz Johns (Roath H)	Sketty Lane, Swansea	03.06.1968
10.7	Liz Johns (Roath H)	Maindy Stadium, Cardiff	27.07.1968
professional mark achieved under unknown conditions			
12.0	Lily Morgan (Neath)	Neath	28.08.1920

100 metres (hand timing)

11.8	Liz Parsons (Roath H)	White City, London	03.08.1964
11.6	Liz Gill (Barry H)	Hagen, Germany	30.05.1965
11.6	Liz Gill (Barry H)	Hagen, Germany	30.05.1965
11.6	Liz Gill (Barry H)	Budapest, Hungary	25.08.1965
11.5	Margaret Williams (Bristol AC)	Cwmbran	29.05.1976
11.5	Margaret Williams (Bristol AC)	Bristol	08.08.1976
11.4	Michelle Probert/Scutt (Sale H)	Birmingham	22.05.1982
11.4	Helen Miles (Cardiff AAC)	Morfa Stadium, Swansea	25.06.1988
11.4	Sallyanne Short (Torfaen AC)	Morfa Stadium, Swansea	25.06.1988

100 metres (fully automatic timing)

11.96	Margaret Williams (Bristol AC)	Crystal Palace	20.08.1976
11.87	Michelle Probert (Sale H)	Cwmbran	23.09.1978
11.75	Michelle Probert (Sale H)	Cwmbran	21.06.1979
11.67	Carmen Smart (Cardiff AAC)	Brisbane, Australia	25.09.1982
11.57	Michelle Probert/Scutt (Sale H)	Birmingham	02.09.1984
11.54	Sallyanne Short (Torfaen AC)	Jessheim, Norway	26.05.1988
11.50	Helen Miles (Cardiff AAC)	Birmingham	05.08.1988
11.48	Carmen Smart (Cardiff AAC)	Leckwith Stadium, Cardiff	26.08.1989

11.47	Sallyanne Short (Torfaen AC)	Auckland, New Zealand	27.01.1990
11.47	Sallyanne Short (Torfaen AC)	Auckland, New Zealand	28.01.1990
11.47	Sallyanne Short (Torfaen AC)	Birmingham	26.07.1991
11.39	Sallyanne Short (Torfaen AC)	Cwmbran	12.07.1992

220 yards (hand timing)

28.6	Nellie Denner (Port Talbot YMCA)	Neath	15.07.1937
27.1	Margaret Farquharson (Roath H)	Cardiff	11.06.1950
26.7	Jean Docker (Middlesex Ladies)		00.00.1954
25.6	Gwyneth Lewis (Bangor College)	Colwyn Bay	07.07.1956
25.2	Jean Whitehead (Middlesex Ladies)	Arms Park, Cardiff	22.07.1958
25.2	Liz Gill (Barry H)		30.05.1964
24.6	Liz Gill (Barry H)	Barry	13.06.1964
24.5	Liz Parsons (Roath H)	Wolverhampton	29.05.1965
24.4	Liz Gill (Barry H)	Maindy Stadium, Cardiff	24.07.1965
24.4	Liz Parsons (Roath H)	White City, London	02.07.1966

200 metres (hand timing)

24.3	Liz Gill (Barry H)	Warsaw, Poland	20.06.1965
24.1	Liz Gill (Barry H)	Budapest, Hungary	27.08.1965
24.0	Liz Gill (Barry H)	Budapest, Hungary	28.08.1965
23.9	Margaret Williams (Bristol AC)	Crystal Palace, London	05.06.1976
23.1	Michelle Probert/Scutt (Sale H)	Stretford	30.08.1980
22.9	Michelle Scutt (Sale H)	Ardal, Norway	28.08.1981

200 metres (fully automatic timing)

23.48	Margaret Williams (Bristol AC)	Crystal Palace, London	21.08.1976
23.32	Michelle Probert/Scutt (Sale H)	Stretford	22.08.1980
22.89	Michelle Scutt (Sale H)	Crystal Palace, London	09.06.1982
22.80	Michelle Scutt (Sale H)	Antrim	12.06.1982

440 yards (hand times)

67.2	Marjorie Clements (Cardiff Uni)	Liverpool	22.05.1926
62.6	Lillian Holmes (Pontypool)	Abercarn	26.07.1952
62.6	Rose Peek (Newport H)		00.00.1953
62.4	Sheila Coy (Roath H)	Maindy Stadium, Cardiff	19.06.1954
60.2	Jean Docker (Middlesex Ladies)	Maindy Stadium, Cardiff	23.06.1956
60.2 e	Jackie Barnett (Newport AC)	Motspur Park	06.06.1958
58.8	Jean Docker/Whitehead (Middlesex Ladies)	Croydon	02.07.1958
57.3	Gloria Dourass (Small Heath)	Hull	22.08.1964
57.1	Thelwyn Appleby (Coventry Godiva)	Coventry	16.05.1965
55.5	Gloria Dourass (Small Heath)	White City, London	02.07.1966
55.5	Gloria Dourass (Small Heath)	White City, London	02.07.1966
55.4	Gloria Dourass (Small Heath)	Kingston, Jamaica	06.08.1966

400 metres

57.1	Gloria Dourass (Small Heath)	Birmingham	13.06.1964
56.5	Gloria Dourass (Small Heath)	Birmingham	05.06.1965
56.1	Gloria Dourass (Small Heath)	Berlin, Germany	04.09.1965
55.9	Gloria Dourass (Small Heath)		11.06.1966
55.0	Gloria Dourass (Small Heath)	Crystal Palace, London	19.07.1968
54.8	Gloria Dourass (Small Heath)	Crystal Palace, London	20.07.1968

54.6	Gloria Dourass (Small Heath)	Paris, France	27.06.1971
54.05	Michelle Probert (Sale H)	Athens, Greece	16.06.1979
53.91	Michelle Probert (Sale H)	Cwmbran	30.06.1979
53.88	Michelle Probert (Sale H)	Cwmbran	21.07.1979
53.14	Michelle Probert (Sale H)	Crystal Palace, London	28.07.1979
52.27	Michelle Probert/Scutt (Sale H)	Cwmbran	18.05.1980
51.83	Michelle Scutt (Sale H)	Graz, Austria	21.06.1980
51.68	Michelle Scutt (Sale H)	Crystal Palace, London	08.08.1980
51.62	Michelle Scutt (Sale H)	Leicester	07.09.1980
50.63	Michelle Scutt (Sale H)	Cwmbran	31.05.1982

880 yards

3:35.0 q	Hetty Tindall (Aber Uni)	Aberystwyth	07.05.1921
2:59.0 q	Marjorie Evans (Aber Uni)	Aberystwyth	02.05.1925
2:38.5 q	Eiris Evans (Aber Uni)	Manchester	19.05.1925
3:17.3	Rose Peek (Newport H)	Maindy Stadium, Cardiff	07.06.1952
3:00.2	Rose Peek (Newport H)	Maindy Stadium, Cardiff	20.06.1953
2:43.6	B Ludlam (Mountain Ash GS)	Maindy Stadium, Cardiff	19.06.1954
2:35.0	Pauline Webb (Streatham)	Maindy Stadium, Cardiff	22.06.1957
2:34.3	Jackie Barnett (Newport AC)	Maindy Stadium, Cardiff	20.06.1959
2:21.1	Jackie Barnett (Newport AC)	Motspur Park	03.07.1959
2:18.8	Jackie Barnett (Newport AC)	Maindy Stadium, Cardiff	25.06.1960
2:18.1	Jackie Barnett (Newport AC)	Maindy Stadium, Cardiff	17.09.1960
2:16.1	Jackie Barnett (Newport AC)	White City, London	08.07.1961
2:15.9	Jackie Barnett (Newport AC)	Maindy Stadium, Cardiff	23.06.1962
2:12.1	Jackie Barnett (Newport AC)	White City, London	07.07.1962

800 metres

2:22.5	Valerie Morgan (Selsonia)	Fredricksberg	30.08.1959
2:09.4	Thelwyn Appleby/Bateman (Coventry G)	Crystal Palace, London	19.07.1968
2:09.4	Thelwyn Bateman (Coventry G)	Cwmbran	28.06.1969
2:08.6	Thelwyn Bateman (Coventry G)	Maindy Stadium, Cardiff	26.07.1969
2:06.2	Thelwyn Bateman (Coventry G)	Crystal Palace, London	30.08.1969
2:05.5	Thelwyn Bateman (Coventry G)	Leicester	31.05.1971
2:04.4	Thelwyn Bateman (Coventry G)	Crystal Palace, London	25.07.1971
2:04.01	Kirsty McDermott (Brecon AC)	Budapest, Hungary	29.07.1981
2:03.0	Kirsty McDermott (Bristol AC)	Aldershot	19.07.1982
2:02.14	Kirsty McDermott (Bristol AC)	Crystal Palace, London	31.07.1982
2:01.23	Kirsty McDermott (Bristol AC)	Crystal Palace, London	07.08.1982
2:00.56	Kirsty McDermott (Bristol AC)	Crystal Palace, London	17.09.1982
1:57.42	Kirsty McDermott (Bristol AC)	Belfast	24.06.1985

1500 metres

4:32.6 it	Thelwyn Appleby/Bateman (Coventry G)	Hendon	04.05.1969
4:30.2	Thelwyn Bateman (Coventry G)	Brno, Czech	06.07.1969
4:26.1	Thelwyn Bateman (Coventry G)	Crystal Palace, London	19.07.1969
4:23.9	Thelwyn Bateman (Coventry G)	White City, London	01.09.1969
4:23.8	Thelwyn Bateman (Coventry G)	Portadown	19.06.1971
4:22.4	Jean Lochhead (Airedale & Spen V)	Kirkby	03.06.1972
4:20.8	Jean Lochhead (Airedale & Spen V)	Crystal Palace, London	07.07.1972
4:18.6	Jean Lochhead (Airedale & Spen V)	Crystal Palace, London	08.07.1972
4:13.0	Hilary Hollick (Sale H)	Cwmbran	12.06.1977
4:12.90	Hilary Hollick (Sale H)	Stockholm, Sweden	26.07.1977

4:12.72	Hilary Hollick (Sale H)	Edmonton, Canada	12.08.1978
4:07.35	Kirsty McDermott (Bristol AC)	Birmingham	06.07.1985
4:02.83 it	Kirsty McDermott (Bristol AC)	Oslo, Norway	27.07.1985
4:02.13	Kirsty McDermott/Wade (Blaydon H)	Gateshead	13.06.1987
4:00.73	Kirsty Wade (Blaydon H)	Gateshead	26.07.1987

One mile

5:35.4	Janet Eynon (Croydon)	Croydon	24.08.1966
5:23.9	Susan Barnes (Westbury)		00.00.1968
4:54.0	Thelwyn Appleby/Bateman (Coventr G)	Hendon	04.05.1969
4:49.1	Thelwyn Bateman (Coventry G)	Leicester	14.06.1969
4:47.0	Jean Lochhead (Airedale & Spen V)	Preston	26.08.1972
4:44.6	Thelwyn Bateman (Coventry G)	Crystal Palace, London	14.09.1973
4:38.1	Hilary Hollick (Sale H)	Gateshead	30.07.1977
4:37.7	Kim Lock (Cardiff AAC)	Hendon	14.08.1982
4:19.41	Kirsty McDermott (Bristol AC)	Oslo, Norway	27.07.1985

3000 metres

10:38.2	Jean Lochhead (Airedale & Spen V)	Kirby	13.09.1970
9:40.4	Bronwen Cardy (Bromsgrove & Red)	Crystal Palace, London	16.07.1971
9:38.8	Jean Lochhead (Airedale & Spen V)	Edinburgh	16.06.1972
9:35.77	Thelwyn Appleby/Bateman (Coventry G)	Crystal Palace, London	21.08.1976
9:29.6	Thelwyn Bateman (Coventry G)	Bristol	28.05.1977
9:24.0	Thelwyn Bateman (Coventry G)	Cwmbran	12.06.1977
9:23.76	Thelwyn Bateman (Coventry G)	Edinburgh	16.07.1978
9:18.62	Thelwyn Bateman (Coventry G)	Crystal Palace, London	18.08.1978
9:17.99	Hilary Hollick (Sale H)	Crystal Palace, London	05.07.1980
9:05.03	Hilary Hollick (Sale H)	Antrim	25.05.1981
8:59.69	Angela Tooby (Cardiff AAC)	Cwmbran	27.05.1984
8:52.59	Angela Tooby (Cardiff AAC)	Crystal Palace, London	06.06.1984
8:47.7	Kirsty McDermott/Wade (Blaydon H)	Gateshead	05.08.1987
8:47.59	Angela Tooby (Cardiff AAC)	Stockholm, Sweden	05.07.1988
8:45.39	Hayley Parry/Tullett (Swansea H)	Gateshead	15.07.2000

5000 metres

17:36.7	Annemarie Fox (Swansea H)	Cwmbran	06.06.1981
16:44.14	Hilary Hollick (Sale H)	Birmingham	09.08.1981
16:10.26	Hilary Hollick (Sale H)	Oslo, Norway	26.06.1982
15:27.56	Angela Tooby (Cardiff AAC)	Cwmbran	28.05.1984
15:22.50	Angela Tooby (Cardiff AAC)	Oslo, Norway	28.06.1984
15:13.22	Angela Tooby (Cardiff AAC)	Oslo, Norway	05.08.1987

10000 metres

36:34.1	Kath Williams (Port Talbot H)	Birmingham	02.06.1984
32:58.07	Angela Tooby (Cardiff AAC)	Tokyo, Japan	14.09.1984
32:25.38	Angela Tooby (Cardiff AAC)	Edinburgh	28.07.1986
31:56.59	Angela Tooby (Cardiff AAC)	Stuttgart, Germany	30.08.1986
31:55.30	Angela Tooby (Cardiff AAC)	Rome, Italy	04.09.1987

80 metres hurdles (hand timing)

14.3	Virginia Price (Pontardawe GS)	Maindy Stadium, Cardiff	07.06.1952
13.5	Dilys Watts (Haverfordwest YC)	Maindy Stadium, Cardiff	20.06.1953
13.0	Sheila Coy (Whitchurch GS)	Maindy Stadium, Cardiff	19.06.1954

12.4	Maureen Le Quirot (Heol Gam SS)	Maindy Stadium, Cardiff	22.06.1957
12.2	Carol Thomas (Whitchurch)	Colwyn Bay	13.07.1957
11.6	Carol Thomas (Roath H)	Maindy Stadium, Cardiff	21.06.1958
11.6	Carol Thomas (Roath H.)	Abertillery	28.06.1958
11.5	Carol Thomas (Roath H)	Colwyn Bay	05.07.1958
11.5	Carol Thomas (Roath H)	Motspur Park	04.07.1959
11.5	Wendy Palmer (Spartan Ladies)	Maindy Stadium, Cardiff	19.06.1965
11.4	Wendy Palmer (Spartan Ladies)	Watford	17.07.1965
11.4	Wendy Palmer (Spartan Ladies)	Maindy Stadium, Cardiff	25.06.1966
11.4	Christine Jenner (Surrey AC)	Maindy Stadium, Cardiff	25.06.1966

100 metres hurdles (hand timing)

15.2	June Hirst (BP Llandarcy AC)	Swansea	30.08.1969
14.8	June Hirst (BP Llandarcy AC)	Barry	22.08.1970
14.8	Ruth Martin Jones (Birchfield H)	Birmingham	19.05.1971
14.4	Ruth Martin Jones (Birchfield H)	Crystal Palace, London	01.07.1972
14.4	Ruth Martin Jones (Birchfield H)	Papendal, Netherlands	29.07.1972
14.3	Elizabeth Wren (Bromley)	Hendon	19.04.1980
14.0	Sarah Rowe (Gloucester AC)	Ardal, Norway	28.08.1981

100 metres hurdles (fully automatic timing)

14.88	Ruth Martin Jones/Howell (Birchfield)	Crystal Palace	18.09.1976
14.77	Diane Heath (Stretford)	Athens, Greece	02.07.1977
14.67	Ruth Howell (Birchfield)	Cwmbran	08.07.1978
14.64	Sarah Bull (Newport H)	Crystal Palace	01.09.1979
14.24	Sarah Bull/Owen (Newport H)	Graz, Austria	21.06.1980
14.22	Elizabeth Wren (Bromley)	Tel Aviv, Israel	31.08.1985
13.66	Kay Morley (Cardiff AAC)	Cwmbran	14.06.1986
13.49	Kay Morley (Cardiff AAC)	Cwmbran	20.06.1987
13.15	Kay Morley (Cardiff AAC)	Jarrow	03.06.1989
13.11	Kay Morley (Cardiff AAC)	Auckland, New Zealand	20.01.1990
12.91	Kay Morley (Cardiff AAC)	Auckland, New Zealand	02.02.1990

400 metres hurdles

69.6	Jane Wisby (Swansea H)	Cyncoed, Cardiff	29.05.1974
62.9	Lynne Davies (Stretford)	Kirkby	01.06.1974
62.4	Bernie Butcher (Sale H)	Bristol	24.07.1976
60.8	Diane Heath (Stretford)	Cwmbran	04.06.1977
60.40	Diane Heath (Stretford)	Crystal Palace London	20.08.1977
59.64	Diane Heath (Stretford)	Edinburgh	15.07.1978
58.9	Diane Heath (Stretford)	Athens, Greece	16.06.1979
58.35	Diane Heath (Stretford)	Crystal Palace, London	28.07.1979
58.17	Diane Heath (Stretford)	Birmingham	12.08.1979
58.16	Diane Heath/Fryar (Stretford)	Cwmbran	09.07.1983
57.71	Alyson Layzell (Cheltenham)	Dublin, Ireland	09.06.1996
57.39	Alyson Layzell (Cheltenham)	Birmingham	15.06.1996
56.43	Alyson Layzell (Cheltenham)	Birmingham	16.06.1996

High Jump

1.28	Bronwen Jones (Cardiff Uni)	Harlequins, Cardiff	08.05.1919
1.32 q	Muriel Walker (Aberystwyth Uni)	Aberystwyth	07.05.1922
1.34 q	Anne Hatfield (Aberystwyth Uni)	Aberystwyth	03.05.1924
1.47 q	Anne Hatfield (Aberystwyth Uni)	Aberystwyth	02.05.1925

1.40	M Humphries (Bangor University)	Welsh University Champs	08.05.1948
1.42	Rose Peek (Newport H)	Maindy Stadium, Cardiff	20.06.1953
1.45	Rose Peek (Newport H)	Maindy Stadium, Cardiff	15.05.1954
1.45	Rose Peek (Newport H)	Maindy Stadium, Cardiff	19.06.1954
1.45	Kathleen Boobyer (Skewen)	Maindy Stadium, Cardiff	25.06.1955
1.47	Sally Jones (Neath Girls GS)	Maindy Stadium, Cardiff	23.06.1956
1.47	Sally Jones (Neath Girls GS)	Abertillery	28.06.1958
1.50	Joyce Wheeler (Duffryn GS)	Colwyn Bay	05.07.1958
1.50	Sally Jones (Roath H)	Colwyn Bay	05.07.1958
1.52	Sally Jones (Roath H.)	Llanrumney	13.05.1959
1.52	Joyce Wheeler (Duffryn GS)		00.05.1959
1.52	Sally Jones (Roath H)	Maindy Stadium, Cardiff	30.05.1959
1.55	Sally Jones (Roath H)	Maindy Stadium, Cardiff	20.06.1959
1.55	Monica Zeraschi (Eirias)	Maindy Stadium, Cardiff	18.07.1959
1.61	Pam Guppy (Birchgrove H)	Maindy Stadium, Cardiff	25.05.1963
1.62	Pam Guppy (Birchgrove H)	Maindy Stadium, Cardiff	20.06.1964
1.62	Christine Craig (Grove Park SS)	Maindy Stadium, Cardiff	25.07.1969
1.64	Christine Craig (Grove Park SS)	Crystal Palace, London	16.08.1969
1.65	Ruth Martin Jones (Birchfield H)	Leicester	22.05.1971
1.70	Ruth Martin Jones (Birchfield H)	Crystal Palace, London	06.05.1972
1.70	Ruth Martin Jones/Howell (Birchfield)	Lille, France	11.09.1976
1.71	Liz Wren (Soton & Eastleigh)	Crystal Palace, London	03.07.1977
1.71	Sarah Bull (Newport H)	Cwmbran	20.05.1979
1.71	Sarah Rowe (Gloucester AC)	Nottingham	07.07.1979
1.71	Sarah Rowe (Gloucester AC)	Cwmbran	21.07.1979
1.71	Sarah Bull (Newport H)	Cwmbran	21.07.1979
1.73	Sarah Rowe (Gloucester AC)	Cwmbran	21.07.1979
1.74	Julia Charlton (Carmarthen H)	Crystal Palace, London	27.07.1979
1.75	Sarah Rowe (Gloucester AC)	Crystal Palace, London	28.07.1979
1.77	Sarah Rowe (Gloucester AC)	Bristol	13.04.1980
1.79	Sarah Rowe (Gloucester AC)	Cwmbran	10.05.1980
1.79	Marion Hughes (Derby Ladies AC)	Kirkby	12.07.1980
1.81	Sarah Rowe (Gloucester AC)	Kirkby	12.07.1980
1.82	Sarah Rowe (Gloucester AC)	L'Aquila, Italy	20.08.1980
1.82	Marion Hughes (Derby Ladies)	L'Aquila, Italy	20.08.1980
1.84	Sarah Rowe (Gloucester AC)	Utrecht, Netherlands	22.08.1981
1.84	Sarah Rowe (Gloucester AC)	Cwmbran	31.05.1982

Pole Vault

2.20	Claudia Filce (Wrexham AC)	Stoke	16.09.1989
2.50	Claudia Filce (Wrexham AC)	Wrexham	13.07.1994
2.60	Claudia Filce (Wrexham AC)	Deeside	30.07.1994
3.00	Claudia Filce (Wrexham AC)	Birmingham	20.05.1995
3.50	Rhian Clarke (Essex Ladies)	Loughborough	19.05.1996
3.65	Rhian Clarke (Essex Ladies)	Newport	01.06.1996
3.65	Rhian Clarke (Essex Ladies)	Birmingham	20.07.1996
3.70	Rhian Clarke (Essex Ladies)	Hendon	10.08.1996
3.70	Rhian Clarke (Essex Ladies)	Walnut, USA	20.04.1997
3.70	Rhian Clarke (Essex Ladies)	Basel, Switzerland	19.05.1997
3.75	Rhian Clarke (Essex Ladies)	Enskede, Sweden	27.05.1997
3.90	Rhian Clarke (Essex Ladies)	Leckwith Stadium, Cardiff	31.05.1997
3.92	Rhian Clarke (Essex Ladies)	Austin, USA	01.04.2000
4.15	Rhian Clarke (Essex Ladies)	Austin, USA	07.04.2000

Long Jump

5.03	Jean Docker (Middlesex Ladies)	Maindy Stadium, Cardiff	07.06.1952
5.13	Sally Jones ((Roath H)	Swansea	02.06.1956
5.43	Bonny Jones (Roath H)	Maindy Stadium, Cardiff	07.06.1958
5.43	Bonny Jones (Roath H.)	Maindy Stadium, Cardiff	30.05.1959
5.61	Monica Zeraschi (Eirias)	Maindy Stadium, Cardiff	17.07.1959
5.66	Janice Catt (Redhill & Reigate)	Motspur Park	18.06.1960
5.68	Monica Zeraschi (Roath H)	Maindy Stadium, Cardiff	24.06.1961
5.71	Janice Catt (Chelsea CPE)	Maindy Stadium, Cardiff	23.06.1962
5.80	Monica Zeraschi (Roath H)	Maindy Stadium, Cardiff	22.06.1963
5.92	Sylvia Powell (Swansea Valley)	Barry	20.08.1966
6.00	Sylvia Powell (Swansea Valley)	Llandarcy	14.08.1968
6.14	Ruth Martin Jones (Birchfield H)	Turin, Italy	06.09.1970
6.15	Ruth Martin Jones (Birchfield H)	Birmingham University	19.05.1971
6.41	Ruth Martin Jones (Birchfield H)	Crystal Palace, London	03.06.1972
6.49	Ruth Martin Jones (Birchfield H)	Edinburgh	16.06.1972
6.52	Gillian Regan (Cardiff AAC)	Morfa Stadium, Swansea	28.08.1982

Triple Jump

11.32	Audrey Lewis (Cheltenham)	Stoke	18.06.1986
11.32	Susan Harries (Havering)	Southampton	24.04.1993
12.10	Jane Falconer (Colchester)	Colchester	29.08.1993
12.10	Jane Falconer (Colchester)	Jersey	18.09.1993
12.14	Jayne Ludlow (Cardiff AAC)	Istanbul, Turkey	21.05.1994

Shot Put

08.19	Diana Noott (Aberystwyth University)	Aberystwyth	09.05.1953
08.60	Diana Noott (Aberystwyth University)	Bangor	03.05.1954
09.45	Anne Holdsworth (Maesydderwyn)	Maindy Stadium, Cardiff	19.06.1954
10.64	Anne Holdsworth (Rotherham)	Maindy Stadium, Cardiff	25.06.1955
11.40	Sandra Murphy (Merthyr)	Barry	16.05.1964
11.72	Hazel Andow (Birchgrove H)	Aldershot	07.06.1965
11.95 ?	Jean Davies (Buckingham)		24.09.1967
11.73	Jean Davies (Buckingham)	Belfast	07.08.1968
12.96	Maureen Pearce (Flint TC)	Chester	27.05.1970
13.00	Venissa Head (Cardiff AAC)	Crystal Palace, London	19.07.1974
13.01	Venissa Head (Cardiff AAC)	Cwmbran	24.07.1974
14.31	Venissa Head (Cardiff AAC)	WRAC Championships	00.06.1975
14.36	Venissa Head (Cardiff AAC)	Crystal Palace, London	04.07.1975
14.88	Venissa Head (Cardiff AAC)	Crystal Palace, London	26.05.1976
15.39	Venissa Head (Army AA)	Cwmbran	29.05.1976
15.62	Venissa Head (Bristol AC)	Newham	27.04.1977
15.72	Venissa Head (Bristol AC)	Cwmbran	12.06.1977
16.12	Venissa Head (Bristol AC)	Cwmbran	21.07.1979
16.35	Venissa Head (Bristol AC)	Crystal Palace, London	28.07.1979
16.43	Venissa Head (Bristol AC)	Winterhur, Austria	14.06.1980
16.63	Venissa Head (Bristol AC)	Graz, Austria	21.06.1980
16.78	Venissa Head (Bristol AC)	Crystal Palace, London	13.07.1980
17.05	Venissa Head (Bristol AC)	Cwmbran	10.08.1980
17.54	Venissa Head (bristol AC)	Cwmbran	17.05.1981
17.62	Venissa Head (Bristol AC)	Antrim	24.05.1981
17.84	Venissa Head (Bristol AC)	Cwmbran	06.06.1981

17.85	Venissa Head (Bristol AC)	Cwmbran	25.08.1982
17.93	Venissa Head (Bristol AC)	Cwmbran	25.08.1982
18.12	Venissa Head (Bristol AC)	Birmingham	05.06.1983
18.28	Venissa Head (Bristol AC)	Thionville, France	02.07.1983
18.41	Venissa Head (Bristol AC)	Helsinki, Finland	10.08.1983
18.93	Venissa Head (Bristol AC)	Haverfordwest	13.05.1984

Discus

28.32	Diana Noott (Aberystwyth University)	Aberystwyth	09.05.1953
28.84	Diana Noott (Aberystwyth University)	Aberystwyth	20.05.1954
28.84	Jean Crutchley (Pembroke Dock GS)	Maindy Stadium, Cardiff	25.06.1955
29.62	Jean Crutchley (Pembroke Dock GS)	Maindy Stadium, Cardiff	23.06.1956
31.58	Jean Crutchley (Pembroke Dock GS)	Maindy Stadium, Cardiff	22.06.1957
31.90	Jean Crutchley (Swansea Valley)	Abertillery	28.06.1958
33.38	Lynette Harries (Mond AC)	Maindy Stadium, Cardiff	20.06.1959
34.90	Lynette Harries (Mond AC)	Ystradgynlais	28.08.1959
38.16	Hazel Andow (Birchgrove H)	Aberystwyth	02.05.1964
39.40	Delyth Prothero (Brecon AC)	Brynmawr	20.05.1971
39.84	Janet Beese (Newport H)	Croydon	11.06.1972
40.84	Jackie Grey (Cardiff AAC)	Bristol	02.09.1973
42.88	Delyth Prothero (Cardiff AAC)	Sketty Lane, Swansea	23.09.1973
43.14	Delyth Prothero (Cardiff AAC)	Bristol	14.07.1974
44.44	Vivienne Head (Cardiff AAC)	Haverfordwest	14.06.1975
45.38	Janet Beese (Newport H)	Cwmbran	15.05.1976
45.92	Vivienne Head (Cardiff AAC)	Cwmbran	17.07.1976
47.34	Vivienne Head (Army AA)	Uxbridge	09.04.1977
47.40	Vivienne Head (Bristol AC)	Barry	17.06.1978
49.16	Venissa Head (Bristol AC)	Cwmbran	21.07.1979
50.22	Venissa Head (Bristol AC)	Cwmbran	07.06.1980
51.22	Venissa Head (Bristol AC)	Graz, Austria	21.06.1980
51.48	Venissa Head (Bristol AC)	Cwmbran	11.07.1980
52.54	Venissa Head (Bristol AC)	Crystal Palace, London	13.07.1980
52.62	Venissa Head (Bristol AC)	Birmingham	02.05.1981
53.24	Venissa Head (Bristol AC)	Radley	09.05.1981
53.72	Venissa Head (Bristol AC)	Cwmbran	27.05.1981
55.70	Venissa Head (Bristol AC)	Acoteais, Portugal	24.04.1982
56.66	Venissa Head (Bristol AC)	Cwmbran	25.07.1982
57.28	Venissa Head (Bristol AC)	Yeovil	30.08.1982
57.32	Venissa Head (Bristol AC)	Edinburgh	29.05.1983
58.46	Venissa Head (Bristol AC)	Edinburgh	29.05.1983
60.62	Venissa Head (Bristol AC)	Edinburgh	29.05.1983
62.72	Venissa Head (Bristol AC)	Birmingham	05.06.1983
64.68	Venissa Head (Bristol AC)	Athens, Greece	18.07.1983

Hammer

31.38	Janet Beese (Newport H)	Glasgow	15.07.1990
34.02	Angela Bonner (Torfaen AC)	Leckwith Stadium, Cardiff	01.06.1991
41.10	Angela Bonner (Torfaen AC)	Leckwith Stadium, Cardiff	08.06.1991
41.56	Angela Bonner (Torfaen AC)		00.05.1992
44.14	Sarah Moore (Bristol AC)	Leckwith Stadium, Cardiff	23.05.1992
45.36	Sarah Moore (Bristol AC)	Bristol	16.09.1992
45.72	Sarah Moore (Bristol AC)	Birmingham	16.07.1993

49.40	Sarah Moore (Bristol AC)	Jersey	18.09.1993
50.08	Sarah Moore (Bristol AC)	Colindale, London	01.04.1994
50.52	Sarah Moore (Bristol AC)	Istanbul, Turkey	21.05.1994
53.00	Sarah Moore (Bristol AC)	Halle, Germany	13.05.1995
53.26	Sarah Moore (Bristol AC)	Leckwith Stadium, Cardiff	25.05.1996
55.64	Sarah Moore (Bristol AC)	Colindale, London	27.04.1997
56.60	Sarah Moore (Bristol AC)	Birmingham	12.07.1997

Javelin

26.70	Kay Bowater (Bangor University)	Maindy Stadium, Cardiff	20.06.1953
27.46	Joan Lindsay (Aberystwyth University)	Maindy Stadium, Cardiff	19.06.1954
33.38	Anne Holdsworth (Swansea Valley)	Maindy Stadium, Cardiff	23.06.1956
34.82	Pauline Williams (Birchgrove H)	Llanrumney, Cardiff	23.06.1958
35.46	Anne Holdsworth (Swansea Valley)	Abertillery	28.06.1958
43.74	Averil Williams (Lozells)	Maindy Stadium, Cardiff	23.06.1962
44.30	Averil Williams (Lozells)	Hamilton, New Zealand	07.12.1963
44.30	Averil Williams (Lozells)	Wellington, New Zealand	07.03.1964
44.80	Averil Williams (Lozells)	Enfield	31.08.1968
47.00	Averil Williams (Lozells)	Chiswick	31.05.1969
48.80	Averil Williams (Lozells)	Barry	30.05.1970
50.70	Jackie Zaslona (Birchfield H)	Crystal Palace, London	11.06.1976
52.04	Jackie Zaslona (Birchfield H)	Cwmbran	03.06.1978
53.32	Jackie Zaslona (Birchfield H)	Birmingham	11.08.1979
54.02	Janeen Williams (Cannock)	Birmingham	29.03.1980
54.06	Jackie Zaslona (Birchfield H)		26.04.1980
55.36	Jackie Zaslona (Birchfireld H)	Woodford	30.08.1980
56.06	Karen Hough (Swansea H)	Morfa Stadium, Swansea	08.06.1985
58.32	Karen Hough (Swansea H)	Crystal Palace, London	08.08.1986
58.84	Karen Hough (Swansea H)	Hendon	17.08.1986
59.40	Karen Hough (Swansea H)	Stuttgart, Germany	28.08.1986

New specification from 1999

46.89	Caroline White (Trafford)	Colwyn Bay	19.06.1999

Pentathlon – Long jump, 200m, 80m hurdles, shot, high jump (using 1954 tables)

3366	Janice Catt (Chelsea CPE)	Hurlingham	17.09.1960

Pentathlon – Shot, 200m, high jump, 80m hurdles, long jump (using 1954 tables)

3536	Janice Catt (Chelsea CPE)	Hurlingham	16.09.1961
3734	Janice Catt (Chelsea CPE)	Wimbledon	26.05.1962
3759	Wendy Palmer (Spartan)	Exmouth	18.08.1965
3780	Christine Jenner (Surrey AC)	Wimbledon	07.05.1966
3843	Liz Parsons (Roath H)	Cardiff	17.09.1966
3894	Pam Dalton (Roath H)	Barry	01.07.1967
4180	Ruth Martin Jones (Birchfield)	Oadby	06.07.1967

Pentathlon – 100m hurdles, shot, high jump, long jump, 200m (using 1954 tables)

4209	Ruth Martin Jones (Birchfield)	Oxford	25.06.1969
4422	Ruth Martin Jones (Birchfield)	Oadby	02.07.1970
4497	Ruth Martin Jones (Birchfield)	Edinburgh	22.07.1970

Pentathlon – 100m hurdles, shot, high jump, long jump, 200m (using 1971 tables)

4015	Ruth Martin Jones (Birchfield)	Oldbury	08.05.1971
4294	Ruth Martin Jones (Birchfield)	Crystal Palace, London	07.05.1972

Pentathlon - 100m hurdles, shot, high jump, long jump, 800m (using 1971 tables)

4005	Ruth Martin Jones/Howell (Birchfield)	Birmingham	30.04.1978
4022	Ruth Howell (Birchfield)	Edmonton, Canada	06.08.1978
4035	Sarah Bull/Owen (Newport H)	Cwmbran	10.05.1980

Heptathlon - 100m hurdles, high jump, shot, 200m, long jump, javelin, 800m (using 1971 tables)

5126	Ruth Martin Jones/Howell (Birchfield)	Birmingham	24.09.1978
5200	Sarah Bull/Owen (Newport H)	Cwmbran	10.05.1980
5227	Sarah Rowe (Gloucester AC)	Cwmbran	28.09.1980
5316	Sarah Owen (Newport H)	Cwmbran	10.05.1981
5365	Sarah Owen (Newport H)	Morfa Stadium, Swansea	13.06.1981
5538	Sarah Owen (Newport H)	Brussels, Belgium	12.07.1981
5743	Sarah Rowe (Gloucester AC)	Utrecht, Netherlands	23.08.1981

Heptathlon (using 1984 tables)

5642	Sarah Rowe (Gloucester AC)	Utrecht, Netherlands	23.08.1981

4 x 110 yards relay

51.4	Roath Harriers	Maindy Stadium, Cardiff	14.06.1958
53.0	Treorchy AC	Cardiff	11.06.1950
53.0	Rhondda AC	Maindy Stadium, Cardiff	19.06.1954
52.2	Neath GS	Maindy Stadium, Cardiff	25.06.1955
50.2	Roath Harriers	Maindy Stadium, Cardiff	21.06.1958
46.1	Wales *(Liz Parsons, Gloria Dourass, Liz Gill, Thelwyn Appleby)*	Kingston, Jamaica	13.08.1966

4 x 100 metres relay

45.37	Wales *(Helen Miles, Sian Morris, Sallyanne Short, Carmen Smart)*	Edinburgh	02.08.1986

4 x 400 metres relay

3:52.4	Wales *(Sue Norman, Delyth Davies, Gloria Dourass, Debbie Froggatt)*	Cwmbran	24.07.1974
3:44.0	Wales *(Jenny Davies, Elaine Oxton, Lianne Dando, Gloria Dourass)*	Brussels, Belgium	22.06.1975
3:35.60	Wales *(Carmen Smart, Diane Fryar, Kirsty McDermott, Michelle Scutt)*	Dublin, Ireland	04.07.1982

Section 2

Evolution of Welsh All-Comers' Best Performances

MEN

100 yards (hand timing)

10.0	Charles Bradley (England)	Cardiff	12.08.1893
9.8 ?	Charles Bradley (England)	Cardiff	27.07.1895
10.0	Fred Cooper (Wales)	Welsh Championships	00.00.1898
10.0	Charles Thomas (Wales)	Abergavenny	02.08.1898
9.8 ?	Willie Applegarth (England)	Cardiff	28.06.1913
10.0	Stan Macey (Wales)	Pontypool	18.07.1925
10.0	Cyril Cupid (Wales)	St Helen's, Swansea	11.07.1931
10.0	Cyril Cupid (Wales)	Crymlyn Burrows, Swansea	16.06.1934
9.8	Cyril Cupid (Wales)	Rodney Parade, Newport	30.06.1934
9.8	Ernest Page (England)	Rodney Parade, Newport	02.08.1937
9.8	Ken Jones (Wales)	Abertillery	25.06.1949
9.8	E McDonald Bailey (Trinidad)	Swansea	19.05.1951
9.8	E McDonald Bailey (Trinidad)	Rodney Parade, Newport	18.08.1951
9.8	Ken Jones (Wales)	Abertillery	14.05.1952
9.8	Nick Whitehead (Wales)	Maindy Stadium, Cardiff	17.05.1958
9.6	James Omagbemi (Nigeria)	Colwyn Bay	05.07.1958
9.5	Tommy Robinson (Bahamas)	Arms Park, Cardiff	17.07.1958
9.5	Keith Gardner (Jamaica)	Arms Park, Cardiff	19.07.1958
9.5	Tommy Robinson (Bahamas)	Arms Park, Cardiff	19.07.1958
9.4	Keith Gardner (Jamaica)	Arms Park, Cardiff	19.07.1958

100 metres (fully automatic timing)

10.35	Allan Wells (Scotland)	Cwmbran	23.09.1978
10.32	Mike McFarlane (England)	Cwmbran	27.05.1984
10.29	Colin Jackson (Wales)	Wrexham	28.07.1990

220 yards (hand timing)

23.2	Cyril R Lundie (Wales)	St Helen's, Swansea	07.09.1902
23.2	Cyril R Lundie (Wales)	Rodney Parade, Newport	31.08.1903
23.2	A M J Griffiths (Wales)	Abergavenny	00.00.1904
23.0	J Gorman (Wales)	Rodney Parade, Newport	27.06.1908
23.0	Cecil Griffiths (Wales)	Barry	16.06.1921
23.0	H J Anderson (Wales)	Welsh Championships	00.00.1926
22.7	Cyril Cupid (Wales)	St Helen's, Swansea	11.07.1931
22.6	Ted Davies (Wales)	Rodney Parade,Newport	29.06.1935
22.2	Ernest Page (England)	Rodney Parade, Newport	02.08.1937
22.2	Kenneth Jenkins (Wales)	Taff Vale Park, Pontypridd	25.06.1938
21.9	E McDonald Bailey (Trinidad)	Ebbw Vale	20.05.1950
21.8	Nick Whitehead (Wales)	Colwyn Bay	05.07.1958

21.6	Tommy Robinson (Bahamas)	Arms Park, Cardiff	22.07.1958
21.6	Stan Levenson (Canada)	Arms Park, Cardiff	22.07.1958
21.4	Ted Jeffreys (South Africa)	Arms Park, Cardiff	22.07.1958
21.2	Ted Jeffreys (South Africa)	Arms Park, Cardiff	22.07.1958
21.2	Gordon Day (South Africa)	Arms Park, Cardiff	22.07.1958
21.2	Stan Levenson (Canada)	Arms Park, Cardiff	22.07.1958
21.0 w	Tommy Robinson (Bahamas)	Arms Park, Cardiff	24.07.1958

NBw = this mark was accepted as an all comers' record although it is believed to have been wind assisted 20.9 semi final times by Tommy Robinson and Ted Jeffreys were not accepted.

200 metres (fully automatic timing)

21.24	Allan Wells (Scotland)	Cwmbran	23.09.1978
20.77	Mike McFarlane (England)	Cwmbran	18.05.1980
20.36	Todd Bennett (England)	Cwmbran	28.05.1984

440 yards

53.5	R F Leonard (Wales)	Welsh Championships	00.00.1897
52.8	R F Leonard (Wales)	Welsh Championships	00.00.1898
52.6	R F Leonard (Wales)	Welsh Championships	00.00.1899
52.0	A M J Griffiths (Wales)	Abergavenny	00.00.1904
51.3	David Jacobs (Wales)	Arms Park, Cardiff	11.07.1914
49.8	Cecil Griffiths (Wales)	Barry	16.07.1921
48.8	Peter Higgins (England)	Rodney Parade, Newport	18.08.1951
48.8	Peter Higgins (England)	Maindy Stadium, Cardiff	07.07.1956
48.3	John McIsaac (Scotland)	Arms Park, Cardiff	17.07.1958
47.6	Mal Spence (South Africa)	Arms Park, Cardiff	17.07.1958
46.8	Ted Sampson (England)	Arms Park, Cardiff	22.07.1958
46.7	Mal Spence (South Africa)	Arms Park, Cardiff	22.07.1958
46.6	Milkha Singh (India)	Arms Park, Cardiff	24.07.1958

400 metres (fully automatic timing)

46.67	Harry Schulting (Netherlands)	Cwmbran	08.07.1978
46.20	Alan Bell (England)	Cwmbran	18.05.1980
46.20	Phil Brown (England)	Cwmbran	31.05.1982
46.10	Kriss Akabusi (England)	Cwmbran	28.05.1984
45.29	Phil Brown (England)	Cwmbran	26.05.1986

880 yards

2:02.0	A Williams (Wales)	Welsh Championships	00.00.1899
2:01.6	A S D Smith (Wales)	Welsh Championships	00.00.1905
1:59.4	A S D Smith (Wales)	Welsh Championships	00.00.1906
1:59.2	Cecil Griffiths (Wales)	Arms Park, Cardiff	19.08.1922
1:57.6	Cecil Griffiths (Wales)	Rodney Parade, Newport	00.08.1923
1:57.0	Jim Alford (Wales)	Rodney Parade, Newport	30.06.1934
1:56.4	Jim Alford (Wales)	Rodney Parade, Newport	26.06.1936
1:54.2	Arthur Wint (Jamaica)	Abertillery	26.06.1949
1:53.3	A A Kwofie (Ghana)	Pontypool	08.07.1950
1:52.2	Brian Hewson (England)	Maindy Stadium, Cardiff	08.05.1954
1:49.3	Herb Elliott (Australia)	Arms Park, Cardiff	22.07.1958
1:48.6	George Kerr (Jamaica)	Maindy Stadium, Cardiff	25.07.1964
1:47.5	Chris Carter (England)	Maindy Stadium, Cardiff	10.09.1966

800 metres

1:46.8	Andy Carter (England)	Carmarthen	09.08.1969
1:46.8	Bob Adams (Wales)	Carmarthen	09.08.1969
1:46.53	Paul Forbes (Scotland)	Cwmbran	31.05.1982
1:46.08	Peter Elliott (England)	Cwmbran	28.05.1984
1:44.65	William Tanui (Kenya)	Wrexham	28.07.1990

One mile

4:43.0	A B Manning (Wales)	Welsh Championships	00.00.1901
4:35.8	E Francis (Wales)	Abergavenny	00.00.1904
4:35.0	D H Griffiths (Wales)	Rodney Parade, Newport	27.06.1908
4:31.0	Cliff Price (Wales)	Rodney Parade, Newport	09.08.1913
4:31.0	D J P Richards (Wales)	Abergavenny	00.08.1928
4:27.0	Reg Thomas (Wales)	Arms Park, Cardiff	20.07.1929
4:26.0	Reg Thomas (Wales)	Pontypool	09.06.1930
4:17.2	Reg Thomas (Wales)	Abercarn	22.07.1933
4:17.0	Jim Alford (Wales)	Pontypridd	21.08.1937
4:16.1	John Disley (Wales)	St Helen's, Swansea	16.08.1952
4:13.8	John Disley (Wales)	Maindy Stadium, Cardiff	08.05.1954
4:10.2	Derek Ibbotson (England)	Rodney Parade, Newport	09.07.1955
4:08.2	John Disley (Wales)	Colwyn Bay	05.07.1958
4:07.0	Herb Elliott (Australia)	Arms Park, Cardiff	24.07.1958
4:03.4	Merv Lincoln (Australia)	Arms Park, Cardiff	24.07.1958
3:59.0	Herb Elliott (Australia)	Arms Park, Cardiff	26.07.1958
3:57.6	Kip Keino (Kenya)	Maindy Stadium, Cardiff	10.09.1966
3:55.8	Geoff Smith (England)	Cwmbran	15.08.1981

1500 metres

3:37.5	Steve Ovett (England)	Cwmbran	12.06.1977
3:35.74	Rob Harrison (England)	Cwmbran	26.05.1986

Two miles

9:44.6	Cliff Price (Wales)	Rodney Parade, Newport	14.07.1914
9:38.2	Jim Alford (Wales)	Rodney Parade, Newport	24.08.1938
9:28.4	Valdu Lillakas (Estonia)	Ebbw Vale	20.05.1950
9:03.2	Freddie Green (England)	Swansea	15.08.1953

3000 metres

8:03.8	David Black (England)	Bargoed	07.07.1973
7:58.0	Jim Dingwall (Scotland)	Cwmbran	09.08.1975
7:53.4	Barry Smith (England)	Cwmbran	18.05.1980
7:46.95	David James (Wales)	Cwmbran	26.05.1980

Three miles

15:32.0	C G Constable (England)	Arms Park, Cardiff	15.06.1929
14:52.8	Robbie Sutherland (Scotland)	St Helen's, Swansea	11.07.1931
14:52.0	Len Tongue (Wales)	Rodney Parade, Newport	30.06.1934
14:41.0	Harry Gallivan (Wales)	Rodney Parade, Newport	27.06.1936
14:32.8	Ivor Brown (Wales)	Taff Vale Park, Pontypridd	25.06.1938
14:17.2	Freddie Green (England)	Abertillery	27.06.1953
14:10.0	Peter Driver (England)	Rodney Parade, Newport	09.07.1955
14:10.0	Alan Perkins (England)	Maindy Stadium, Cardiff	07.07.1956
14:05.4	Bruce Tulloh (England)	Maindy Stadium, Cardiff	17.05.1958

13:46.6	John Merriman (Wales)	Colwyn Bay	05.07.1958
13:15.0	Murray Halberg (New Zealand)	Arms Park, Cardiff	22.07.1958

5000 metres

13:20.6	Nick Rose (England)	Cwmbran	12.06.1977
13:13.01	Thomas Nyariki (Kenya)	Leckwith Stadium, Cardiff	25.05.1996

Six miles

32:00.8	Norman Wilson (Wales)	Ebbw Vale	11.08.1951
30:57.4	David Richards (Wales)	Maindy Stadium, Cardiff	23.08.1955
28:47.8	Dave Power (Australia)	Arms Park, Cardiff	19.07.1958

10000 metres

29:25.8	Fergus Murray (Scotland)	Colwyn Bay	05.07.1969
29:17.4	Mike Beevor (England)	Cwmbran	01.08.1970
27:51.30	Ian Stewart (Scotland)	Cwmbran	11.06.1977

3000m steeplechase

10:13.6	David Richards (Wales)	Maindy Stadium, Cardiff	03.07.1954
10:04.6	Brian James (Wales)	Maindy Stadium, Cardiff	25.06.1955
9:44.7	Jack Wingfield (Wales)	Maindy Stadium, Cardiff	22.06.1957
9:31.2	Hedydd Davies (Wales)	Maindy Stadium, Cardiff	23.06.1962
9:05.3	Hedydd Davies (Wales)	Maindy Stadium, Cardiff	20.06.1964
9:04.8	Bill Stitfall (Wales)	Barry	11.06.1966
8:41.4	Maurice Herriott (England)	Maindy Stadium, Cardiff	10.09.1966
8:31.4	John Davies (Wales)	Cwmbran	23.07.1974
8:31.0	Tony Staynings (England)	Cwmbran	12.06.1977

120 yards hurdles (hand times)

16.8	Wyatt Gould (Wales)	Welsh Championships	00.00.1902
16.2	Wyatt Gould (Wales)		00.00.1903
16.2	Wallis Walters (Wales)	Abergavenny	00.00.1904
16.2	Wallis Walters (Wales)	St Helen's, Swansea	08.09.1906
16.0	Fred Foley (England)	Rodney Parade, Newport	08.06.1930
16.0	John Gabriel (England)	Rodney Parade, Newport	22.05.1937
15.9	Mervyn Rosser (Wales)	Abertillery	07.05.1949
15.8	Mervyn Rosser (Wales)	Abertillery	25.06.1949
15.5	Peter Hildreth (England)	Ebbw Vale	20.05.1950
15.3	Peter Hildreth (England)	St Helen's, Swansea	19.05.1951
15.3	Jack Parker (England)	Maindy Stadium, Cardiff	08.05.1954
15.2	Bob Shaw (Wales)	Maindy Stadium, Cardiff	19.06.1954
15.0	Bob Shaw (Wales)	Margam	06.07.1957
14.8	John Duncan (Nigeria)	Colwyn Bay	05.07.1958
14.4	Ghulam Raziq (Pakistan)	Arms Park, Cardiff	24.07.1958
14.0 w	Keith Gardner (Jamaica)	Arms Park, Cardiff	24.07.1958
13.9 m	Alan Pascoe (England)	Carmarthen	09.08.1969
13.6 m	Berwyn Price (Wales)	Cwmbran	10.08.1975

NB w = this mark was accepted as an all comers' record despite being wind assisted (+3.5)

110m hurdles (fully automatic timing)

13.86	Berwyn Price (Wales)	Cwmbran	28.05.1978
13.73	Colin Jackson (Wales)	Cwmbran	25.05.1986
13.62	Colin Jackson (Wales)	Wrexham	08.06.1986

13.51	Colin Jackson (Wales)	Cwmbran	14.06.1986
13.51	Colin Jackson (Wales)	Cwmbran	20.06.1987
13.38	Colin Jackson (Wales)	Leckwith Stadium, Cardiff	02.06.1990
13.10	Colin Jackson (Wales)	Leckwith Stadium, Cardiff	03.06.1990

440 yards hurdles

63.3	Mervyn Rosser (Wales)	St Helen's, Swansea	24.06.1950
62.0	Richard Greening (Wales)	Maindy Stadium, Cardiff	23.06.1951
60.6	Gareth Lewis (Wales)	Maindy Stadium, Cardiff	20.06.1953
54.8	Bob Shaw (Wales)	Maindy Stadium, Cardiff	19.06.1954
54.4	D Salter (England)	Rodney Parade, Newport	09.07.1955
53.9	Alec Hannah (Scotland)	Maindy Stadium, Cardiff	17.05.1958
51.9	Gert Potgieter (South Africa)	Arms Park, Cardiff	19.07.1958
51.1	Gert Potgieter (South Africa)	Arms Park, Cardiff	19.07.1958
49.7	Gert Potgieter (South Africa)	Arms Park, Cardiff	22.07.1958

400m hurdles

49.57	Harry Schulting (Netherlands)	Cwmbran	18.05.1980

High Jump

1.73	J Jacobs (Wales)	St Helen's, Swansea	07.09.1902
1.78	Frank Whitcutt (Wales)	Penarth	06.06.1927
1.83	Frank Whitcutt (Wales)	Rodney Parade, Newport	16.06.1928
1.83	John Newman (England)	Rodney Parade, Newport	24.05.1937
1.84	Hubert Stubbs (Wales)	Pontypridd	25.06.1938
1.87	Hubert Stubbs (Wales)	St. Helen's, Swansea	20.08.1938
1.88	Peter Wells (England)	Newport	09.07.1949
1.88	Derek Cox (England)	Abertillery	27.06.1953
1.93	Brendan O'Reilly (Ireland)	Maindy Stadium, Cardiff	01.08.1954
1.95	Julius Chigbolu (Nigeria)	Colwyn Bay	05.07.1958
1.95	Charles Porter (Australia)	Arms Park, Cardiff	19.07.1958
1.95	Learie Scipio (Trinidad)	Arms Park, Cardiff	19.07.1958
1.95	Ken Money (Canada)	Arms Park, Cardiff	19.07.1958
1.95	Ernie Haisley (Jamaica)	Arms Park, Cardiff	19.07.1958
1.95	Robert Kotei (Ghana)	Arms Park, Cardiff	19.07.1958
1.95	Julius Chigbolu (Nigeria)	Arms Park, Cardiff	19.07.1958
1.95	Gordon Miller (England)	Arms Park, Cardiff	19.07.1958
1.95	Joseph Leresae (Kenya)	Arms Park, Cardiff	19.07.1958
1.95	Nagalingham Ethirveerasingham (Ceylon)	Arms Park, Cardiff	19.07.1958
1.95	Patrick Etolu (Uganda)	Arms Park, Cardiff	19.07.1958
1.95	Crawford Fairbrother (Scotland)	Arms Park, Cardiff	19.07.1958
1.95	Learie Scipio (Trinidad)	Arms Park, Cardiff	19.07.1958
1.95	Crawford Fairbrother (Scotland)	Arms Park, Cardiff	19.07.1958
1.95	Gordon Miller (England)	Arms Park, Cardiff	19.07.1958
1.98	Joseph Leresae (Kenya)	Arms Park, Cardiff	19.07.1958
1.98	Charles Porter (Australia)	Arms Park, Cardiff	19.07.1958
1.98	Ernie Haisley (Jamaica)	Arms Park, Cardiff	19.07.1958
1.98	Robert Kotei (Ghana)	Arms Park, Cardiff	19.07.1958
1.98	Crawford Fairbrother (Scotland)	Arms Park, Cardiff	19.07.1958
1.98	Patrick Etolu (Uganda)	Arms Park, Cardiff	19.07.1958
1.98	Julius Chigbolu (Nigeria)	Arms Park, Cardiff	19.07.1958
1.98	Ken Money (Canada)	Arms Park, Cardiff	19.07.1958

2.00	Robert Kotei (Ghana)	Arms Park, Cardiff	19.07.1958
2.03	Ernie Haisley (Jamaica)	Arms Park, Cardiff	19.07.1958
2.03	Charles Porter (Australia)	Arms Park, Cardiff	19.07.1958
2.06	Ernie Haisley (Jamaica)	Arms Park, Cardiff	19.07.1958
2.15	Dean Bauck (Canada)	Cwmbran	23.07.1974
2.17	Jacques Alletti (France)	Cwmbran	30.06.1979
2.18	Istvan Gibiscar (Hungary)	Cwmbran	18.05.1980
2.18	Mark Naylor (England)	Cwmbran	18.05.1980
2.19	Phil McDonnell (England)	Morfa Stadium, Swansea	20.07.1985
2.24	Geoff Parsons (Scotland)	Cwmbran	25.05.1986
2.25	Dalton Grant (England)	Leckwith Stadium, Cardiff	03.06.1990
2.27	Randy Jenkins (USA)	Wrexham	03.07.1994

Pole Vault

2.89 +	T Williams (Wales)	Llandovery	10.05.1871
2.89	J Higgins (Wales)	Clydach	22.08.1931
3.07	Cyril Evans (Wales)	Morriston	21.08.1937
3.07	J Gravelle (Wales)	Morriston	21.08.1937
3.07	Ron Harries (Wales)	Morriston	21.08.1937
3.11	Cyril Evans (Wales)	Pontypridd	25.06.1938
3.15	Cyril Evans (Wales)	Hendy	30.08.1947
3.20	Cyril Evans (Wales)	Aberavon	19.06.1948
3.47	Tim Anderson (England)	Aberavon	14.08.1948
3.64	Tim Anderson (England)	Aberavon	23.07.1949
3.96	Geoff Elliott (England)	Rodney Parade, Newport	18.08.1951
4.07	Geoff Elliott (England)	Maindy Stadium, Cardiff	08.05.1954
4.09	Geoff Elliott (England)	St. Helen's, Swansea	03.07.1954
4.16	Bob Reid (Canada)	Arms Park, Cardiff	26.07.1958
4.16	Geoff Elliott (England)	Arms Park, Cardiff	26.07.1958
4.16	Mervyn Richards (New Zealand)	Arms Park, Cardiff	26.07.1958
4.40	David Stevenson (Scotland)	Maindy Stadium, Cardiff	10.09.1966
4.91	Mike Bull (N Ireland)	Maindy Stadium, Cardiff	26.07.1969
5.00	Herve D'Encausse (France)	Cwmbran	01.08.1970
5.00	Michel Ollivary (France)	Cwmbran	01.08.1970
5.03	Mike Bull (N Ireland)	Maindy Stadium, Cardiff	22.07.1972
5.20	Bruce Simpson (Canada)	Cwmbran	24.07.1974
5.45	Jean Michel Bellot (France)	Cwmbran	30.06.1979
5.55	Paul Benevidies (USA)	Wrexham	28.07.1990
5.70	Joe Dial (USA)	Cwmbran	14.07.1991
5.80	Grigory Yegorov (Kazakhstan)	Cwmbran	12.07.1992

NB + competiton conditions not identical to present day

Long Jump

6.18	W D Thomas (Wales)	Lampeter	16.04.1891
6.40	Wallis Walters (Wales)	St Helen's, Swansea	08.09.1906
6.68	R Hall (Ireland)	Abergele	00.00.1920
6.75	John Lloyd (Wales)	Clydach	25.09.1926
6.75	J Higgins (Wales)	St Helen's, Swansea	23.07.1932
6.77	J Higgins (Wales)	Clydach	03.09.1932
6.77	Lewis Riden (Wales)	Rodney Parade, Newport	27.06.1936
6.78	Robert Hawkey (England)	Rodney Parade, Newport	02.08.1937
6.78 +	John Frowen (Wales)	Tonypandy	01.07.1950

7.03	John Frowen (Wales)	Tonypandy	01.07.1950
7.06	Chris Alele (Wales)	Maindy Stadium, Cardiff	19.06.1954
7.10	Bryan Woolley (Wales)	Maindy Stadium, Cardiff	17.05.1958
7.20	Bryan Woolley (Wales)	Maindy Stadium, Cardiff	21.06.1958
7.40 #	Deryck Taylor (Jamaica)	Arms Park, Cardiff	22.07.1958
7.47	Deryck Taylor (Jamaica)	Arms Park, Cardiff	22.07.1958
7.47	Paul Foreman (Jamaica)	Arms Park, Cardiff	22.07.1958
7.54	Lynn Davies (Wales)	Maindy Stadium, Cardiff	28.07.1962
8.01	Lynn Davies (Wales)	Maindy Stadium, Cardiff	25.07.1964
8.02	Lynn Davies (Wales)	Maindy Stadium, Cardiff	25.07.1964
8.07	Ralph Boston (USA)	Maindy Stadium, Cardiff	24.07.1965
8.18	Ralph Boston (USA)	Maindy Stadium, Cardiff	24.07.1965

NB + John Frowen beat existing record with his first round jump (distance not known) and went on to jump 7.03 later in the competition.

 # Deryck Taylor led the competition at the end of the qualifying round. Altogether 8 athletes jumped beyond the existing record of 7.20 but jumping order is not known.

Triple Jump

12.37	John Lloyd (Wales)	Rodney Parade, Newport	24.05.1924
12.79	John Lloyd (Wales)	Pontypool	18.07.1925
13.17	Frank Whitcutt (Wales)	Rodney Parade, Newport	02.08.1926
13.51	Gwynne Evans (Wales)	Rodney Parade, Newport	30.06.1934
13.51	Gwynne Evans (Wales)	Rodney Parade, Newport	29.06.1935
13.74	Gwynne Evans (Wales)	Panteg	28.08.1938
14.49	Sidney Cross (England)	Abertillery	10.07.1948
14.52	Gordon Wells (Wales)	Abertillery	25.06.1949
14.68	Ken Wilmshurst (England)	Rodney Parade, Newport	09.07.1955
14.76	Sol Akpata (Nigeria)	Colwyn Bay	05.07.1958
15.03#	Jack Smyth (Canada)	Arms Park, Cardiff	24.07.1958
15.10	Gabuh Bin Piging (North Borneo)	Arms Park, Cardiff	24.07.1958
15.69	Jack Smyth (Canada)	Arms Park, Cardiff	24.07.1958
15.74	Ian Tomlinson (Australia)	Arms Park, Cardiff	24.07.1958
15.85	Mick McGrath (Australia)	Cwmbran	19.07.1975
15.85	Dave Johnson (England)	Cwmbran	28.05.1978
15.98	Bernard Lamitie (France)	Cwmbran	30.06.1979
16.88	Bela Bakosi (Hungary)	Cwmbran	18.05.1980

NB # Jack Smyth led competition after qualifying round. Altogether 6 athletes exceeded previous record but jumping order not known

Shot

09.98	Michael Roche (Wales)	Arms Park, Cardiff	14.07.1923
11.53	George Dillaway (Wales)	Rodney Parade, Newport	24.05.1924
12.67	J P Wallace (England)	St Helen's, Swansea	24.08.1929
13.70	Robert Howland (England)	St Helen's, Swansea	26.07.1930
13.94	Kenneth Pridie (England)	Abertillery	09.08.1933
13.99	Harold Moody (England)	Port Talbot	14.08.1948
14.04	Harold Moody (England)	Port Talbot	14.08.1948
16.83	John Savidge (England)	Maindy Stadium, Cardiff	08.05.1954
16.91	Arthur Rowe (England)	Arms Park, Cardiff	24.07.1958
17.01	Arthur Rowe (England)	Arms Park, Cardiff	24.07.1958
17.57	Arthur Rowe (England)	Arms Park, Cardiff	24.07.1958
18.26	Alan Carter (England)	Swansea	01.05.1965
18.90	Arnjolt Beer (France)	Cwmbran	01.08.1970

19.27	Geoff Capes (England)	Maindy Stadium, Cardiff	18.07.1973
20.47	Geoff Capes (England)	Cwmbran	23.07.1974
21.68	Geoff Capes (England)	Cwmbran	18.05.1980

Discus

33.76	L Landsberg (Wales?)	Clydach	23.08.1930
36.78	L Landsberg (Wales?)	Clydach	03.09.1932
38.66	Arthur Lewis (Wales)		00.00.1937
41.18	Harold Moody (England)	Port Talbot	14.08.1948
42.94	Tom Barratt (England)	Rodney Parade, Newport	18.08.1951
43.30	Hywel Williams (Wales)	Aberystwyth	13.05.1953
46.74	John Savidge (England)	Maindy Stadium, Cardiff	08.05.1954
47.50	Eric Cleaver (England)	Margam	06.07.1957
51.73	Les Mills (New Zealand)	Arms Park, Cardiff	22.07.1958
53.89	Stephanus du Plessis (S Africa)	Arms Park, Cardiff	22.07.1958
55.94	Stephanus du Plessis (S Africa)	Arms Park, Cardiff	22.07.1958
58.36	John Hillier (England)	Bargoed	07.07.1973
58.68	Ain Roost (Canada)	Cwmbran	24.07.1974
61.44	Richard Slaney (England)	Cwmbran	12.08.1982
62.10	Richard Slaney (England)	Cwmbran	10.07.1983

Hammer

32.88	John Thomas (Wales)	Maindy Stadium, Cardiff	19.06.1954
43.84	Albert Ley (Wales)	Maindy Stadium, Cardiff	25.06.1955
45.64	Albert Ley (Wales)	Maindy Stadium, Cardiff	23.06.1956
54.34	Don Anthony (England)	Maindy Stadium, Cardiff	07.07.1956
56.72	Mike Ellis (England)	Maindy Stadium, Cardiff	17.05.1958
60.38	Muhammad Iqbal (Pakistan)	Arms Park, Cardiff	26.07.1958
61.03	Muhammad Iqbal (Pakistan)	Arms Park, Cardiff	26.07.1958
61.12	Mike Ellis (England)	Arms Park, Cardiff	26.07.1958
61.70	Muhammad Iqbal (Pakistan)	Arms Park, Cardiff	26.07.1958
62.91	Mike Ellis (England)	Arms Park, Cardiff	26.07.1958
64.36	John Lawlor (Ireland)	Maindy Stadium, Cardiff	29.07.1961
65.68	Howard Payne (England)	Maindy Stadium, Cardiff	16.05.1970
67.58	Paul Dickenson (England)	Cwmbran	04.05.1975
68.72	Chris Black (Scotland)	Cwmbran	04.09.1976
70.50	Gabor Tamas (Hungary)	Cwmbran	18.05.1980
74.18	Martin Girvan (N Ireland)	Cwmbran	31.05.1982

Javelin

30.01	Matt Cullen (Wales)	Clydach	25.09.1926
36.48	J P Richards (Wales)	Aberavon	27.07.1935
41.40	Fred Needs (Wales)	W Wales v E Glam	10.08.1935
41.82	Fred Needs (Wales)	Aberavon	22.08.1936
43.14	Fred Needs (Wales)	Morriston	21.08.1937
44.76	G Rickards (Wales)	Gorseinon	18.06.1938
46.00	Fred Needs (Wales)	Kidwelly	13.08.1938
52.48	Arthur Squibbs (Wales)	Kidwelly	29.07.1939
55.74	Arthur Squibbs (Wales)	Port Talbot	19.08.1939
56.81	William Wall (England)	Abertillery	10.07.1948
58.46	Malcolm Dalrymple (England)	Newport	09.07.1949
59.73	Malcolm Dalrymple (England)	Pontypool	08.07.1950

59.74	Michael Denley (England)	Rodney Parade, Newport	18.08.1951
62.18	W W Kretschman (England?)	Aberystwyth	15.05.1955
69.12	Colin Smith (England)	Margam	06.07.1957
71.28	Colin Smith (England)	Arms Park, Cardiff	19.07.1958
79.76	Dave Travis (England)	Maindy Stadium, Cardiff	16.05.1970
80.20	David Ottley (England)	Cwmbran	30.06.1979
96.20	Ferenc Paragi (Hungary)	Cwmbran	18.05.1980

Javelin – New specification

73.74	Mick Hill (England)	Cwmbran	25.05.1986
74.72	Chris Crutchley (England)	Morfa Stadium, Swansea	13.07.1986
75.68	Mark Roberson (England)	Cwmbran	09.07.1988
78.90	Nigel Bevan (Wales)	Morfa Stadium, Swansea	22.07.1989
79.22	Nigel Bevan (Wales)	Wrexham	03.09.1989
86.00	Steve Backley (England)	Leckwith Stadium, Cardiff	03.06.1990
88.46	Steve Backley (England)	Leckwith Stadium, Cardiff	03.06.1990

Decathlon

7044	Clive Longe (Wales)	Cardiff	10.09.1966
7277	Jean-Pierre Crozet (France)	Cwmbran	05.10.1975
7684	Daley Thompson (England)	Cwmbran	23.05.1976
7856	Brad McStravick (Scotland)	Cwmbran	28.05.1984

4 x 110 yards relay

44.7	English Universities	Maindy Stadium, Cardiff	16.06.1951
42.9	AAA	Newport	18.08.1951
41.8	Nigeria	Eirias Park, Colwyn Bay	05.07.1958
40.9	England *(Peter Radford, David Segal, Roy Sandstrom, Adrian Breacker)*	Arms Park, Cardiff	26.07.1958
40.7	England *(Peter Radford, David Segal, Roy Sandstrom, Adrian Breacker)*	Arms Park, Cardiff	26.07.1958
40.3	Great Britain *(Peter Radford, Ron Jones, David H Jones, Berwyn Jones)*	Maindy Stadium, Cardiff	27.07.1963

4 x 100 metres relay

40.25	Hungary *(Istvan Tatar, Istvan Nagy, Laszlo Babaly, Ferenc Kiss)*	Cwmbran	18.05.1980
40.25	England	Wrexham	28.07.1990
40.17	Japan *(Hideaki Miyata, Tomohiro Osawa, Yoshiyuki Okuyama, Tatsuo Sugimoto)*	Cwmbran	14.07.1991
40.09	World Select	Cwmbran	12.07.1992
40.04	Wales *(Kevin Williams, Colin Jackson, Jamie Baulch, Tremayne Rutherford)*	Cwmbran	09.07.1995
39.8	Australia	Wrexham	09.08.1999

4 x 440 yards relay

3:13.4	South Africa *(Gordon Day, Gerry Evans, Gert Potgieter, Mal Spence)*	Arms Park, Cardiff	26.07.1958
3:08.1	South Africa *(Gordon Day, Gerry Evans, Gert Potgieter, Mal Spence)*	Arms Park, Cardiff	26.07.1958

4 x 400 metres relay

3:06.79	Netherlands *(Harry Schulting, Koen Gijsbers, Mario Westbroek, Marcel Klarenbeck)*	Cwmbran	18.05.1980
3:06.27	England	Wrexham	28.07.1990
3:05.11	Trinidad and Tobago	Cwmbran	12.07.1992

WOMEN

100 yards

11.3	Ethel Johnson (England)	Colwyn Bay	22.05.1929
10.9e	Nellie Halstead (England)	Colwyn Bay	19.07.1930
10.8	Betty Cuthbert (Australia)	Arms Park, Cardiff	19.07.1958
10.7	June Paul (England)	Arms Park, Cardiff	19.07.1958
10.7	Heather Young (England)	Arms Park, Cardiff	19.07.1958
10.6	Marlene Willard (Australia)	Arms Park, Cardiff	19.07.1958
Professional mark achieved under unknown conditions			
12.0	Lily Morgan (Wales)	Neath	28.08.1920

100 metres

11.5	Chi Cheng (Formosa)	Maindy Stadium, Cardiff	26.07.1969
11.30	Sonia Lannaman (England)	Cwmbran	11.06.1977
11.27	Heather Oakes (England)	Cwmbran	27.05.1984

220 yards

26.9 e	Nellie Halstead (England)	Colwyn Bay	19.07.1930
26.2	Kathleen Chambers (England)	Abertillery	03.08.1932
25.6	Gwyneth Lewis (Wales)	Colwyn Bay	07.07.1956
24.5	Betty Cuthbert (Australia)	Arms Park, Cardiff	22.07.1958
24.3	Marlene Willard (Australia)	Arms Park, Cardiff	22.07.1958
24.0	Betty Cuthbert (Australia)	Arms Park, Cardiff	22.07.1958
24.0	Marlene Willard (Australia)	Arms Park, Cardiff	22.07.1958
23.6	Marlene Willard (Australia)	Arms Park, Cardiff	24.07.1958

200 metres

23.4	Chi Cheng (Formosa)	Maindy Stadium, Cardiff	26.07.1969
23.2	Raelene Boyle (Australia)	Cwmbran	24.07.1974
23.16	Sonia Lannaman (England)	Cwmbran	12.06.1977
22.58	Sonia Lannaman (England)	Cwmbran	18.05.1980

440 yards

60.4	Olive Hall (England)	Pontypool	04.07.1936
60.2	Jean Docker (Wales)	Maindy Stadium, Cardiff	23.06.1956
59.3	Jackie Barnett (Wales)	Maindy Stadium, Cardiff	25.06.1960
59.2	Jackie Barnett (Wales)	Maindy Stadium, Cardiff	23.06.1962
57.8	Gloria Dourass (Wales)	Maindy Stadium, Cardiff	19.06.1965
57.3	Gloria Dourass (Wales)	Maindy Stadium, Cardiff	23.07.1965
56.5	Gloria Dourass (Wales)	Maindy Stadium, Cardiff	25.06.1966

400 metres

59.4	Olive Hall (England)	Pontypool	19.06.1937
55.5	Gloria Dourass (Wales)	Barry	27.06.1970
54.9	Marge McGowan (Canada)	Cwmbran	23.07.1974
53.1	Verona Elder (England)	Cwmbran	04.09.1976
51.88	Donna Hartley (England)	Cwmbran	12.06.1977
51.47	Donna Hartley (England)	Cwmbran	01.07.1979
50.63	Michelle Probert/Scutt (Wales)	Cwmbran	31.05.1982

880 yards

3:35.0	Hetty Tindall (Wales)	Aberystwyth	07.05.1921
2:59.0	Marjorie Evans (Wales)	Aberystwyth	02.05.1925

2:53.8	Phylis Jones (Wales)	Aberystwyth	05.05.1926
2:49.0	Winnie Robbins (Wales)	Cardiff	28.04.1927
2:31.2	Madge French (England)	Pontypool	06.07.1935
2:18.8	Jackie Barnett (Wales)	Maindy Stadium, Cardiff	25.06.1960
2:16.1	Anne Smith (England)	Maindy Stadium, Cardiff	17.09.1960
2:15.9	Jackie Barnett (Wales)	Maindy Stadium, Cardiff	23.06.1962
2:13.9	Madelaine Ibbotson (England)	Maindy Stadium, Cardiff	25.07.1962
2:09.5	Phyllis Perkins (England)	Maindy Stadium, Cardiff	27.07.1963
2:08.6	Pat Lowe (England)	Maindy Stadium, Cardiff	10.09.1966
2:08.0	Judy Pollock (Australia)	Maindy Stadium, Cardiff	29.07.1967
2:07.4	Mary Green (England)	Maindy Stadium, Cardiff	27.07.1968

800 metres

2:09.4	Thelwyn Bateman (Wales)	Cwmbran	28.06.1969
2:08.6	Thelwyn Bateman (Wales)	Maindy Stadium, Cardiff	26.07.1969
2:06.9	Maureen Crowley (Canada)	Cwmbran	24.07.1974
2:06.1	P Lasarki (Greece)	Cwmbran	17.07.1976
2:05.3	Jane Colebrook (England)	Cwmbran	10.06.1977
2:01.5	Lesley Kiernan (England)	Cwmbran	11.06.1977
2:00.21	Christiane Wildschek (Austria)	Cwmbran	01.07.1979

One mile

4:39.5	Rita Ridley (England)	Maindy Stadium, Cardiff	11.09.1971
4:36.68	Janet Marlow (England)	Cwmbran	26.05.1980
4:29.48	Bev Nicholson (England)	Leckwith Stadium, Cardiff	17.09.1989

1500 metres

4:55.3	Bronwen Cardy (Wales)		1971
4:40.2	Jean Lochhead (Wales)		1973
4:15.4	Thelma Wright (Canada)	Cwmbran	23.07.1974
4:15.3	Mary Stewart (Scotland)	Cwmbran	04.09.1976
4:13.0	Hilary Hollick (Wales)	Cwmbran	12.06.1977
4:11.7	Christine Benning (England)	Cwmbran	01.07.1979
4:04.39	Zola Budd (England)	Cwmbran	28.05.1984

3000 metres

9:42.4	Thelwyn Bateman (England)	Cwmbran	04.09.1976
9:20.0	Glynis Penny (England)	Cwmbran	12.06.1977
9:13.4	Mary Stewart (Scotland)	Cwmbran	17.09.1977
9:04.6	Paula Fudge (England)	Cwmbran	01.07.1979
8:52.88	Paula Fudge (England)	Cwmbran	30.05.1982

5000 metres

16:33.49	Kath Binns (England)	Cwmbran	31.05.1982
15:27.56	Angela Tooby (Wales)	Cwmbran	28.05.1984

10000 metres

32:59.59	Liz Lynch (Scotland)	Cwmbran	26.05.1986

100 metres hurdles

14.3	Mary Rand (England)	Maindy Stadium, Cardiff	10.09.1966
14.3	Patricia Pryce (England)	Maindy Stadium, Cardiff	10.09.1966
14.3	Pat Jones (England)	Maindy Stadium, Cardiff	10.09.1966
14.3	Eva Kucmanova (Czech)	Maindy Stadium, Cardiff	10.09.1966

height 2 ft 9 ins but spacing between hurdles only 8 25 metres instead of 8 5 metres

13.4	Chi Cheng (Formosa)	Maindy Stadium, Cardiff	26.07.1969
13.20	Silvia Kempin (Germany)	Cwmbran	01.07.1979
13.19	Glenys Nunn (Australia)	Cwmbran	10.07.1983
13.02	Kay Morley (Wales)	Wrexham	28.07.1990

400m hurdles

59.9	Janette Roscoe (England)	Cwmbran	04.09.1976
57.60	Christine Warden (England)	Cwmbran	11.06.1977
56.81	Silvia Hollman (Germany)	Cwmbran	01.07.1979
56.53	Jenny Laurendet (Australia)	Morfa Stadium, Swansea	13.07.1986
54.69	Kim Batten (USA)	Cwmbran	12.07.1992

High Jump

1.32	Muriel Walker (Wales)	Aberystwyth	07.05.1922
1.34	Anne Hatfield (Wales)	Aberystwyth	03.05.1924
1.47	Anne Hatfield (Wales)	Aberystwyth	02.05.1925
1.52	M Hudson (England)	Maindy Stadium, Cardiff	15.05.1954
1.55	Thelma Hopkins (N. Ireland)	Maindy Stadium, Cardiff	07.06.1958
1.57	Thelma Hopkins (N. Ireland)	Maindy Stadium, Cardiff	07.06.1958
1.60	Thelma Hopkins (N. Ireland)	Maindy Stadium, Cardiff	07.06.1958
1.62	Thelma Hopkins (N. Ireland)	Maindy Stadium, Cardiff	07.06.1958
1.62	Mary Bignal (England)	Arms Park, Cardiff	22.07.1958
1.62	Mary Donaghy (New Zealand)	Arms Park, Cardiff	22.07.1958
1.62	Helen Frith (Australia)	Arms Park, Cardiff	22.07.1958
1.62	Michele Mason (Australia)	Arms Park, Cardiff	22.07.1958
1.62	Dorothy Shirley (England)	Arms Park, Cardiff	22.07.1958
1.62	Audrey Bennett (England)	Arms Park, Cardiff	22.07.1958
1.65	Mary Donaghy (New Zealand)	Arms Park, Cardiff	22.07.1958
1.65	Dorothy Shirley (England)	Arms Park, Cardiff	22.07.1958
1.65	Helen Frith (Australia)	Arms Park, Cardiff	22.07.1958
1.67	Mary Donaghy (New Zealand)	Arms Park, Cardiff	22.07.1958
1.67	Michele Mason (Australia)	Arms Park, Cardiff	22.07.1958
1.70	Michele Mason (Australia)	Arms Park, Cardiff	22.07.1958
1.70	Mary Donaghy (New Zealand)	Arms Park, Cardiff	22.07.1958
1.81	Debbie Brill (Canada)	Cwmbran	24.07.1974
1.81	A Batatoli (Greece)	Cwmbran	17.07.1976
1.81	Barbara Simmonds (England)	Cwmbran	30.06.1979
1.81	Ros Few (England)	Cwmbran	30.06.1979
1.81	Ann Marie Devally (England)	Cwmbran	30.06.1979
1.86	Andrea Matay (Hungary)	Cwmbran	01.07.1979
1.93	Andrea Matay (Hungary)	Cwmbran	18.05.1980

Pole Vault

2.50	Claudia Filce (Wales)	Wrexham	13.07.1994
2.60	Claudia Filce (Wales)	Deeside	30.07.1994
3.60	Kate Staples (England)	Cwmbran	09.07.1995
3.73	Janine Whitlock (England)	Leckwith Stadium, Cardiff	25.05.1996
3.85	Janine Whitlock (England)	Wrexham	03.08.1996
3.90	Janine Whitlock (England)	Leckwith Stadium, Cardiff	31.05.1997
3.90	Rhian Clarke (Wales)	Leckwith Stadium, Cardiff	31.05.1997
3.91	Janine Whitlock (England)	Wrexham	02.08.1997
3.92	Janine Whitlock (England)	Leckwith Stadium, Cardiff	04.08.1998
3.92	Janine Whitlock (England)	Colwyn Bay	04.09.1999
4.02	Janine Whitlock (England)	Colwyn Bay	04.09.1999
4.12	Janine Whitlock (England)	Colwyn Bay	04.09.1999

Long Jump

5.03	Jean Docker (Wales)	Maindy Stadium, Cardiff	07.06.1952
5.13	Sally Jones (Wales)	Swansea	02.06.1956
5.40	Margaret Davies (Wales)	Maindy Stadium, Cardiff	01.06.1957
5.43	Bonnie Jones (Wales)	Maindy Stadium, Cardiff	07.06.1958
5.50	Thelma Hopkins (N. Ireland)	Maindy Stadium, Cardiff	07.06.1958
5.55	Violet Odogwu (Nigeria)	Colwyn Bay	05.07.1958
5.78w	Beverley Weigel (New Zealand)	Arms Park, Cardiff	26.07.1958
5.97w	Beverley Watson (Australia)	Arms Park, Cardiff	26.07.1958
6.02w	Sheila Hoskin (England)	Arms Park, Cardiff	26.07.1958
6.09	Sheila Parkin (England)	Maindy Stadium, Cardiff	25.07.1964
6.36	Ruth Martin Jones (Wales)	Cwmbran	23.07.1974
6.42	Sharon Colyear (England)	Cwmbran	11.06.1977
6.56	Sue Reeve (England)	Cwmbran	01.07.1979
6.58	Oluyinka Idowu (England)	Leckwith Stadium, Cardiff	09.06.1991

Triple Jump

10.35	Susannah Filce (Wales)	Swansea	16.06.1990
12.77	Michelle Griffith (England)	Leckwith Stadium, Cardiff	03.06.1990

Shot

08.42	Irene Phillips (England)	Colwyn Bay	19.07.1930
09.63	S. Rylands (England)	Maindy Stadium, Cardiff	13.06.1953
10.64	Anne Holdsworth (Wales)	Maindy Stadium, Cardiff	25.06.1955
15.54	Val Sloper (New Zealand)	Arms Park, Cardiff	19.07.1958
16.15	Jean Haist (Canada)	Cwmbran	24.07.1974
18.50	Eva Wilms (Germany)	Cwmbran	01.07.1979
18.93	Venissa Head (Wales)	Haverfordwest	13.05.1984
19.00	Judy Oakes (England)	Cwmbran	25.05.1986
19.03	Myrtle Augee (England)	Leckwith Stadium, Cardiff	02.06.1990
19.69	Zhu Xinmei (China)	Cwmbran	14.07.1991

Discus

28.32	Diana Noott (Wales)	Aberystwyth	09.05.1953
28.50	Diana Noott (Wales)	Aberystwyth	24.04.1954
28.82	Diana Noott (Wales)	Aberystwyth	20.05.1954
28.84	Jean Crutchley (Wales)	Maindy Stadium, Cardiff	25.06.1955
29.62	Jean Crutchley (Wales)	Maindy Stadium, Cardiff	23.06.1956
31.58	Jean Crutchley (Wales)	Maindy Stadium, Cardiff	22.06.1957
31.90	Jean Crutchley (Wales)	Abertillery	28.06.1958
32.74	E Okoli (Nigeria)	Colwyn Bay	05.07.1958
39.29	Lois Jackman (Australia)	Arms Park, Cardiff	26.07.1958
42.92	Marie Depree (Canada)	Arms Park, Cardiff	26.07.1958
45.30	Jennifer Thompson (New Zealand)	Arms Park, Cardiff	26.07.1958
45.91	Suzanne Allday (England)	Arms Park, Cardiff	26.07.1958
51.40	Rosemary Payne (Scotland)	Cwmbran	11.08.1973
55.82	Carol Martin (Canada)	Cwmbran	23.07.1974
57.40	Agnes Herczeg (Hungary)	Cwmbran	01.07.1979
58.86	Venissa Head (Wales)	Cwmbran	13.07.1983
62.02	Venissa Head (Wales)	Haverfordwest	13.05.1984

Hammer

32.60	Angela Bonner (Wales)	Leckwith Stadium, Cardiff	29.08.1990
34.02	Angela Bonner (Wales)	Leckwith Stadium, Cardiff	01.06.1991
44.62	Jean Clark (England)	Leckwith Stadium, Cardiff	08.06.1991
45.94	Fiona Whitehead (England)	Leckwith Stadium, Cardiff	08.06.1991
52.62	Lorraine Shaw (England)	Wrexham	08.08.1993
58.08	Lorraine Shaw (England)	Barry	30.04.1995
60.24	Lorraine Shaw (England)	Cwmbran	09.07.1995
67.10	Lorraine Shaw (England)	Wrexham	09.08.1999

Javelin

23.87	Miriam Little (England)	Colwyn Bay	19.07.1930
26.84	S. Rylands (England)	Maindy Stadium, Cardiff	13.06.1953
28.26	Joan Lindsay (Wales)	Aberystwyth	17.06.1954
33.38	Anne Holdsworth (Wales)	Maindy Stadium, Cardiff	23.06.1956
34.82	Pauline Williams (Wales)	Llanrumney, Cardiff	23.06.1958
35.46	Anne Holdsworth (Wales)	Abertillery	28.06.1958
48.73	Magdalena Swanepoel (South Africa)	Arms Park, Cardiff	24.07.1958
57.40	Anna Pazera (Australia)	Arms Park, Cardiff	24.07.1958
60.24	Tessa Sanderson (England)	Cwmbran	12.06.1977
60.58	Tessa Sanderson (England)	Cwmbran	17.09.1977
62.26	Tessa Sanderson (England)	Cwmbran	01.07.1979
64.02	Tessa Sanderson (England)	Cwmbran	26.05.1980
65.62	Fatima Whitbread (England)	Cwmbran	30.05.1982
68.98	Fatima Whitbread (England)	Cwmbran	26.05.1986

Javelin – New Model

46.89	Caroline White (Wales)	Colwyn Bay	19.06.1999

Heptathlon

5357	Sue Longden (England)	Cwmbran	20.05.1979
5506	Corinne Schneider (Switzerland)	Cwmbran	21.09.1980
5561	Sue Longden (England)	Swansea	08.05.1982
6100 *	Kim Hagger (England)	Cwmbran	28.05.1984

*NB * rescored as 6092 on 1984 tables*

4 x 110 yards relay

49.8	Nigeria	Colwyn Bay	05.07.1958
46.6	Australia *(Betty Cuthbert, Kay Johnson, Wendy Hayes, Marlene Matthews-Willard)*	Arms Park, Cardiff	26.07.1958
46.1	England *(Heather Young, June Paul, Dorothy Hyman, Madeleine Weston)*	Arms Park, Cardiff	26.07.1958
45.3	England *(Heather Young, June Paul, Dorothy Hyman, Madeleine Weston)*	Arms Park, Cardiff	26.07.1958

4 x 100 metres relay

43.99	West Germany *(P. Sharp, D. Schenten, A. Richter, E. Vollmer)*	Cwmbran	01.07.1979

4 x 400 metres relay

3:46.9	Wolverhampton & Bilston	Cwmbran	04.09.1976
3:31.22	United Kingdom *(Karen Williams, Joslyn Hoyte Smith, Verona Elder, Donna Hartley)*	Cwmbran	01.07.1979

Section 3

Welsh All-Time Best Performers

MEN

100 metres (fully automatic timing)

10.12	Christian Malcolm	Annecy, France	29.07.1998
10.29	Colin Jackson	Wrexham	28.07.1990
10.34	Kevin Williams	Barcelona, Spain	11.06.1997
10.39	Jamie Henthorn	Gothenburg, Sweden	29.07.1999
10.40	Doug Turner	Imperia, Italy	26.06.1997
10.42 *	Ron Jones	Mexico City, Mexico	13.10.1968
10.42	Peter Maitland	Edinburgh	03.06.1995
10.44	Tremayne Rutherford	Oordegem, Belgium	09.07.1994
10.47	Nigel Walker	Wrexham	28.07.1990
10.48	Tim Benjamin	Bath	16.09.2000
10.51 *	Lynn Davies	Mexico City, Mexico	15.10.1967
10.51	Jamie Baulch	Cardiff	22.07.1995
10.54	Berwyn Jones	White City	23.08.1963
10.57	Gareth Edwards	Duisburg, Germany	24.08.1973
10.60	Mark Owen	Colombes, France	29.05.1982
10.62	David Roberts	Cwmbran	28.06.1981
10.70	Jonathan Stark	Sittard, Holland	16.08.1980
10.74	Richard Moore	Cwmbran	14.06.1986
10.77	Michael Williams	Gateshead	26.07.1987
10.78	Hywel Griffiths	Crystal Palace	01.08.1975
10.79	Mal Owen	Tel Aviv, Israel	31.08.1985
10.84	Seriashe Childs	Edinburgh	13.08.2000
10.85	Steve Rees	Grangemouth	16.06.1991
10.86	Paul Fisher	Budapest, Hungary	13.06.1992
10.86	Craig Kerslake	Sheffield	11.06.1994

superior wind assisted performances

10.10w	Christian Malcolm	Alicante, Spain	18.07.1998
10.22w	Jamie Henthorn	Catania, Sicily	29.08.1997
10.26w	Doug Turner	Laguna, Spain	13.07.1996
10.30w	Kevin Williams	Bedford	27.07.1997
10.35w	Nigel Walker	Cardiff	26.08.1989
10.47w	Jonathan Stark	Cwmbran	11.07.1980
10.48w	Lynn Davies	Edinburgh	17.07.1970
10.51w	David Roberts	Crystal Palace	13.07.1974
10.65w	Michael Williams	Portsmouth	20.06.1987
10.67w	John J Williams	Edinburgh	17.07.1970
10.67w	Steve Rees	Cardiff	26.05.1990

10.71w	Vic Martindale		00.00.1980
10.72w	Andrew Parker	Loughborough	30.07.2000
10.74w	Mal Owen	Cardiff	26.08.1989
10.75w	Paul Fisher	Cardiff	26.08.1989
10.78w	Jon Marsden	Birmingham	22.08.1981
10.78w	Tim Jones	Cwmbran	31.07.1982
10.79w	Neil Bowd	Cwmbran	11.09.1983
10.79w	John Bowen	Edinburgh	03.06.1995
10.79w	Tim Miller	Bath	02.05.1998
10.79w	Seriashe Childs	Sheffield	15.08.1999
10.80w	Bryn Middleton	Newport	28.05.1994
10.80w	Neil Powell	Newport	28.05.1994
10.81w	David Winterton	Cardiff	26.08.1989
10.82w	Tony Ene	Cwmbran	10.07.1993
10.84w	Phil Harvey	Hayes	13.05.1989
10.86w	Simon Taylor	Edinburgh	13.08.1983
10.86w	Marcus Browning	Stoke	25.06.1988

200 metres (fully automatic timing)

20.19	Christian Malcolm	Sydney, Australia	27.09.2000
20.43	Doug Turner	Tallin, Estonia	09.06.1996
20.72	Tim Benjamin	Bydgoszcz, Poland	18.07.1999
20.84	Jamie Baulch	Victoria, Canada	24.08.1994
20.87	Iwan Thomas	Bedford	30.08.1997
20.93	Jamie Henthorn	Fullerton, USA	22.04.1999
20.96	Peter Maitland	Victoria, Canada	24.08.1994
21.07	Tremayne Rutherford	Birmingham	19.07.1997
21.19	Colin Jackson	Tel Aviv, Israel	08.05.1988
21.20	Scott Herbert	Bedford	27.05.1996
21.30	Kevin Williams	Cardiff	31.05.1997
21.33	Jonathan Stark	Cwmbran	11.07.1980
21.35	Nigel Walker	Edinburgh	31.07.1983
21.36	David Roberts	Cwmbran	29.05.1978
21.38	Michael Williams	Antrim	26.06.1990
21.49 *	Ron Jones	Mexico City, Mexico	16.10.1967
21.52	Steve Rees	Cardiff	01.06.1991
21.54	Phil Harries	Cwmbran	20.06.1987
21.65	Jeff Griffiths	Edmonton, Canada	08.08.1988
21.65	John Bowen	Cardiff	01.06.1991
21.65	Gareth Davies (Sale)	Cardiff	23.05.1992
21.67	Phil Harvey	Nesbyen, Norway	04.09.1988
21.69	Jon Marsden	Birmingham	23.08.1981
21.69	Mark Owen	Cwmbran	26.06.1982
21.74	Mal Owen	Cwmbran	10.07.1983
21.77	Bryn Middleton	Oordegem, Belgium	09.07.1994
21.79	Dominic Papura	Vilvoord, Belgium	06.08.2000
21.87	Paul Fisher	Cardiff	26.05.1990
21.88	Ron Griffiths	Crystal Palace	15.07.1972
21.93	Tim Jones	Cwmbran	31.05.1982
21.93	Marcus Browning	Crystal Palace	01.08.1990
21.95	James Simmons	Utrecht, Holland	23.08.1987

3:45.9	David Messum	Wolverhampton	04.07.1979
3:45.9	David Lee	Loughborough	17.05.1989
3:46.1	Tony Harris	Turku, Finland	29.07.1964
3:46.1	Paul Williams (Barry)	Loughborough	27.04.1988
3:46.14	James Ellis-Smith	Birmingham	15.06.1996
3:46.3	Fred Bell	Karlskoga, Sweden	23.08.1968
3:46.4	David James	Crystal Palace	20.08.1980
3:46.58	Justin Chaston	Gateshead	02.07.1995
3:46.7	Gordon Minty	Crystal Palace	03.07.1972
3:46.8	Brian Donovan	Edinburgh	28.07.1973
3:47.0	Tony Simmons	Motspur Park	19.07.1967
3:47.1	Tony Ashton	Saarijarvi, Finland	24.06.1972
3:47.1	Steve Mosley	Salisbury	10.07.1994
3:47.2	Bob Phillips	Stretford	21.08.1990
3:47.2	Nigel Adams	Cwmbran	07.09.1988
3:47.29	Neil Emberton	Hot Springs, USA	09.04.1994
3:47.3	Adrian Leek	Knoxville, USA	19.05.1979
3:47.61	Andrew Walling	Wythenshawe	14.06.2000
3:47.99i	Peter Wyman	Glasgow	10.03.1990

Sub 4 minute mile performers

3:54.39	Neil Horsfield	Cork, Ireland	08.07.1986
3:56.19	Ian Hamer	Cork, Ireland	05.07.1991
3:57.8	Mal Edwards	Jersey	19.09.1987
3:58.5	Bob Maplestone	Arkadelphia, USA	25.05.1973
3:58.77	Roger Hackney	Swansea	13.07.1986
3:58.96	Tony Harris	White City	03.07.1965
3:59.16	Glen Grant	Crystal Palace	19.06.1976
3:59.5	Gareth Brown	Swansea	25.08.1984

3000 metres (no conversions from 2 miles included)

7:46.40	Ian Hamer	Auckland, NZ	20.01.1990
7:46.95	David James	Cwmbran	26.05.1980
7:49.47	Roger Hackney	Crystal Palace	13.07.1984
7:49.80	Steve Jones	Crystal Palace	13.07.1984
7:51.53	Tony Simmons	Crystal Palace	23.08.1978
7:53.23	Christian Stephenson	Cardiff	05.07.2000
7:53.31	John Davies (TVH)	Crystal Palace	16.05.1979
7:54.12	Andres Jones	Cardiff	05.07.2000
7:54.60i	Neil Horsfield	Birmingham	14.03.1992
	8:09.0	Cheltenham	22.07.1987
7:56.83i	Tony Blackwell	Cosford	12.03.1983
	7:57.0	Stretford	15.06.1982
7:57.48	Chris Davies	Wythenshawe	14.06.2000
7:58.9	Chris Buckley	Swindon	10.07.1986
7:59.2	Bernie Plain	Cwmbran	09.08.1975
7:59.97	Justin Chaston	Lublin, Poland	04.06.1994
8:00.2i	Dick Milne	Dortmund, Germany	19.02.1977
8:00.4	Paul Williams (Cambridge)	Crystal Palace	03.05.1978
8:00.50	Mark Morgan	Wrexham	03.07.1994
8:00.54	Nick Comerford	Cork, Ireland	24.06.1995
8:00.64	Malcolm Edwards	Wattenscheid, Ger	26.05.1989

1:50.8y	Gwynn Davis	Grangemouth	17.06.1968
1:50.81	David Barlow	Crystal Palace	24.07.1982
1:50.9	Nick Morgan	Charlottesville, USA	16.04.1982
1:51.0y	Vivian Blackwell	Cardiff	28.07.1962
1:51.0	Tony Elgie	Motspur Park	29.04.1970
1:51.0	Rikki McTaggart	Cosford	20.06.1984
1:51.1	Dave Messum		00.00.1982
1:51.2	Clive Thomas	Brussels, Belgium	05.06.1971
1:51.2	Paul Williams (Cambridge)	Haringey	09.09.1979
1:51.20	Matt Kinane	Woodford	02.09.1990
1:51.2	Dale Woodman	Enfield	04.06.1994
1:51.3	Richard Yarrow	Crystal Palace	13.07.1973
1:51.3	Andy Williams	Crystal Palace	05.05.1976
1:51.3	David Knox	Cwmbran	05.08.1989
1:51.40	Steve Bright	Edinburgh	18.07.1981
1:51.4	Nick Comerford	Wrexham	29.08.1987
1:51.4	Stephen Price	Horsham	18.08.1991
1:51.5	Bob Phillips	Yate	09.09.1990
1:51.52	Mark Bryant	Edinburgh	18.07.1981

1500 metres

3:35.08	Neil Horsfield	Brussels, Belgium	10.08.1990
3:38.05	Glen Grant	Edmonton, Canada	12.08.1978
3:38.9	Ian Hamer	Cwmbran	05.08.1989
3:39.57	Malcolm Edwards	Crystal Palace	08.07.1988
3:39.7	Bob Maplestone	Seattle, USA	17.06.1972
3:40.53	Tony Blackwell	Crystal Palace	25.07.1982
3:40.69	Gareth Brown	Crystal Palace	21.06.1986
3:42.20	Nicky Comerford	Birmingham	16.06.1996
3:42.23	Joe Mills	Solihull	14.07.1999
3:42.3	Steve Jones	Aldershot	14.07.1982
3:42.6	Phil Thomas	Edinburgh	22.07.1970
3:43.2	Barrie Williams	Westwood, USA	14.05.1977
3:43.5	Roger Hackney	Loughborough	24.06.1987
3:43.6	Clive Thomas	Athens, Greece	13.06.1974
3:43.67	John Theophilus	Sittard, Holland	17.08.1980
3:43.7	Peter Ratcliffe	Cwmbran	27.07.1974
3:43.85	Christian Stephenson	Cardiff	19.07.1998
3:44.2	Matthew Davies	Wythenshawe	30.07.1996
3:44.3	Paul Williams (Cambridge)	Crystal Palace	13.08.1980
3:44.3	Shaun Whelan	Cwmbran	07.09.1988
3:44.5	John Greatrex	Cwmbran	27.07.1974
3:44.6	Kevin Glastonbury	Des Moines, USA	29.04.1978
3:44.65	Gerallt Owen	Hot Springs, USA	14.04.1990
3:44.9	John Davies	Wolverhampton	09.06.1979
3:45.07	Carl Leonard	Indianapolis, USA	00.00.1995
3:45.1	Keith Jones	Aldershot	04.07.1979
3:45.2	Gwynn Davis	Karlskoga, Sweden	23.08.1968
3:45.2	Chris Davies	Stretford	06.07.1999
3:45.4	Chris Buckley	Crystal Palace	13.08.1980
3:45.48	Peter Baker	Crystal Palace	23.06.1978
3:45.7	Graham Spencer	Grangemouth	13.06.1971

48.0	Paul Roberts	Swansea	02.07.1989
48.0	Scott Herbert	Luton	29.06.1997
48.00	Huw Bannister	Bedford	06.07.1997
48.1	Haydn Curran	Carmarthen	09.08.1969
48.18	Darrell Maynard	Cwmbran	18.06.2000
48.2	David Price	Birmingham	14.06.1972
48.2	Chris Cashell	Warrington	24.08.1985
48.2	Ray Blaber	Bracknell	15.07.1990
48.27	Nick Hamilton	Stoke	29.07.1989
48.3	David LeMasurier	Edinburgh	03.07.1971
48.38	Mal James	Cwmbran	26.06.1982
48.4	David Thomas	Crystal Palace	20.08.1968
48.4	John Marsh	Hendon	07.06.1969
48.40	Phil Harvey	Swansea	22.07.1989
48.4	David Griffin	Cork, Ireland	24.06.1995
48.43	David Williams	Newport	01.06.1996
48.5	Haydn Wood	Birmingham	15.05.1985
48.50	Lea Farmer	Brugge, Belgium	23.08.1998
48.5	Tim Benjamin	Aberdare	31.08.1998

800 metres

1:45.44	Neil Horsfield	Wrexham	28.07.1990
1:46.16	Gareth Brown	Stockholm, Sweden	02.07.1984
1:46.26	Phil Lewis	Christchurch, N Z	27.01.1974
1:46.72	Malcolm Edwards	Crystal Palace	13.09.1987
1:46.8	Bob Adams	Carmarthen	09.08.1969
1:47.04	Phil Norgate	Crystal Palace	25.07.1982
1:47.17	Paul Williams (Barry)	Oslo, Norway	14.09.1991
1:47.8y	Tony Harris	Wimbledon	05.08.1964
1:47.99	Matthew Shone	Birmingham	24.07.1999
1:48.0	Glen Grant	Crystal Palace	05.06.1976
1:48.1	John Greatrex	Koblenz, Germany	24.06.1970
1:48.3	Bob Maplestone	Seattle, USA	06.05.1977
1:48.38	Peter Lewis	Crystal Palace	09.09.1977
1:49.0y	John M Williams	Loughborough	30.05.1963
1:49.18	Roger Barrett	Copenhagen, Denmark	22.07.1984
1:49.48	Paul Roberts	Tel Aviv, Israel	27.05.1993
1:49.5	Ian Hamer	Cwmbran	16.08.1989
1:49.67	Sean Price	Cwmbran	14.06.1986
1:49.87	Tony Dyke	Duisburg, Germany	25.07.1973
1:49.9	Matthew Davies	Milton Keynes	24.07.1996
1:50.11	Chris Blount	Bedford	03.07.1994
1:50.12	Joe Mills	Tallin, Estonia	31.07.1999
1:50.2	Alun Roper	Luxembourg	06.08.1977
1:50.3	Kevin Glastonbury	Cwmbran	19.07.1977
1:50.47	Darrell Maynard	Cwmbran	09.07.1995
1:50.5	John Robertson	Crystal Palace	15.10.1969
1:50.53	Neil Emberton	Fayetteville, USA	06.05.1995
1:50.6	Simon Evans	Stretford	03.06.1980
1:50.6	Andrew Walling	Stretford	22.08.1995
1:50.7y	Tony Jones	White City	09.06.1962
1:50.7	Tony Blackwell	Stretford	00.05.1982

21.96i	Chris Page	Birmingham	17.01.1999
21.96	Matthew Elias	Stoke	30.04.2000

superior wind assisted performanes

20.36w	Doug Turner	Bedford	27.07.1997
20.60w	Tim Benjamin	Riga, Latvia	07.08.1999
21.04w	Michael Williams	Stoke	01.07.1990
21.18w	Colin Jackson	Cardiff	26.08.1989
21.25w	Mark Owen	Reykjavik, Iceland	18.07.1982
21.34w	Ron Griffiths	Crystal Palace	14.07.1972
21.39w	Howard Davies	Edinburgh	21.07.1970
21.49w	John J Williams	Edinburgh	21.07.1970
21.55w	Gareth Davies (Sale)	Crystal Palace	13.06.1993
21.55w	Andrew Parker	Brugge, Belgium	23.08.1998
21.56w	Jeff Griffiths	Edmonton, Canada	08.08.1978
21.75w	Tim Jones	Reykjavik, Iceland	18.07.1982
21.77w	Neil Bowd	Edinburgh	13.08.1983
21.80w	Simon Taylor	Edinburgh	13.08.1983
21.91w	Mike Delaney	Christchurch, N Zealand	27.01.1974

400 metres

44.36	Iwan Thomas	Birmingham	13.07.1997
44.57	Jamie Baulch	Lausanne, Switz	03.07.1996
46.6	John Robertson	Crystal Palace	24.08.1968
46.7y	Howard Davies	White City	13.07.1968
46.74	Jeff Griffiths	Cwmbran	29.05.1978
46.77	Gwynne Griffiths	White City	02.08.1969
46.92	Mike Delaney	Cwmbran	08.07.1978
47.04	Matthew Elias	Getafe, Spain	09.09.2000
47.2	Andy Williams	Cwmbran	20.06.1976
47.2	Peter Maitland	Crawley	01.07.1995
47.21	Steve Thomas	Crystal Palace	23.07.1983
47.28	Colin O'Neill	Crystal Palace	03.07.1976
47.39	Gareth Davies	Tel Aviv, Israel	26.05.1993
47.4	John J Williams	Maindy	20.07.1971
47.4	Paul Gray	Haringey	05.07.1997
47.5y	Pat Jones	Ilford	10.06.1965
47.5	Roger Barrett	Swansea	25.08.1984
47.51	Chris Page	Cwmbran	18.06.2000
47.53	Mark Rowlands	Carmarthen	15.07.1997
47.76	Joe Lloyd	Sheffield	06.05.1996
47.8y	Peter G Williams	Cardiff	25.07.1964
47.9	Bob Adams	Cardiff	26.07.1969
47.9	George Robertson	Cosford	20.06.1984
47.90	Jeremy Frankel	Cwmbran	12.07.1992
47.9	James Weston	Cork, Ireland	24.06.1995
47.94	Mark Ponting	Colwyn Bay	23.07.1994
47.96	Mark Thomas	Cwmbran	31.05.1986
48.0	Wynford Leyshon	Cwmbran	23.07.1974
48.0	Alun James	Cwmbran	19.07.1975
48.0	Steve James	Cwmbran	09.08.1975
48.0	Phil Harries	Derby	24.04.1988

8:01.1i	Adrian Leek	Louisville, USA	10.02.1979
	8:04.6	Charlottesville, USA	16.05.1982
8:01.1	Eddie Conway	Colindale	10.08.1988
8:01.2	Gordon Minty	Crystal Palace	14.07.1972
8:02.3	Geoff Hill	Swansea	17.06.1988
8:02.5	Nigel Adams	Swansea	17.06.1988
8:03.6i	Dennis Fowles	Cosford	09.02.1974
8:04.4	Tony Ashton	Crystal Palace	06.08.1971
8:04.66	Peter Baker	Crystal Palace	23.08.1978
8:04.98	Clive Thomas	Crystal Palace	28.04.1976
8:05.6	Gwynn Davis	Warley	04.07.1973
8:06.2	Fred Bell	Crystal Palace	23.05.1973
8:06.4	Peter Griffiths	Crystal Palace	17.09.1976
8:06.9	Peter Jenkins	Barry	27.07.1988
8:07.0	Brian Donovan	Bristol	08.08.1973
8:07.02	Colin Jones	Cork, Ireland	24.06.1995
8:07.62	James Hill	Antrim	26.06.1990
8:08.6	John Barry	Swansea	25.08.1984
8:08.9	Glen Grant	Crystal Palace	21.09.1980
8:09.0	Gerallt Owen	Carbondale, USA	21.04.1990
8:09.5	Kenny Davies	Cwmbran	20.06.1984
8:09.6	Hugh Richards	Crystal Palace	28.07.1971
8:09.8i	Steve Jones (Brom)	Cosford	07.01.1989
8:09.94	David Lee	Crystal Palace	03.08.1988
8:10.3	Justin Hobbs	Barry	23.06.1993
8:10.72i	James Ellis-Smith	Fayetteville, USA	21.01.1994
8:10.8	Micky Morris		00.00.1978
8:10.8	John Theophilus	Crystal Palace	06.08.1980
8:10.8	Steve Brace	Cwmbran	17.06.1987
8:11.1	Shaun Whelan	Swansea	20.07.1988
8:11.2	Bernie Hayward		00.00.1973

Some notable 2 miles performances (pre 1969)

8:43.8	John Disley	Turku, Finland	17.09.1957
8:46.2	Alan Joslyn	White City	03.06.1968
8:47.0	John Godding	Bristol	03.07.1965
8:47.6	John Merriman	Watford	02.06.1960

5000 metres (no conversions from 3 miles included)

13:09.80	Ian Hamer	Rome, Italy	09.06.1992
13:18.6	Steve Jones	Lisbon, Portugal	10.06.1982
13:25.67	Tony Simmons	Lausanne, Switz	12.07.1978
13:33.91	David James	The Hague, Holland	04.07.1980
13:34.5	Adrian Leek	Knoxville, USA	14.04.1979
13:38.0	Gordon Minty	Crystal Palace	24.06.1972
13:38.6	Bernie Plain	Helsinki, Finland	06.06.1973
13:39.43	Andres Jones	Crystal Palace	05.08.2000
13:39.8	John Davies (TVH)	Crystal Palace	25.05.1975
13:41.34	Chris Buckley	Crystal Palace	13.07.1984
13:41.57	Dennis Fowles	Cwmbran	18.05.1980
13:42.73	Clive Thomas	Crystal Palace	28.06.1975
13:44.04	Roger Hackney	Cwmbran	14.06.1986

13:45.53	Justin Hobbs	Victoria, Canada	24.08.1994
13:48.31	Christian Stephenson	Birmingham	11.07.1997
13:50.5	Nigel Adams	Cwmbran	06.09.1989
13:50.83	Nick Comerford	Birmingham	23.07.1999
13:51.04	Paul Williams (Cambridge)	Edinburgh	28.05.1983
13:51.86	Justin Chaston	Birmingham	15.07.1995
13:52.78	Peter Griffiths	Crystal Palace	26.06.1977
13:55.9	Glen Grant	Krefeld, Germany	07.05.1978
13:56.08	Peter Jenkins	Derby	04.06.1988
13:56.96	Tony Blackwell	Belgrade, Yugoslavia	07.06.1981
13:57.6	Steve Slocombe	Wolverhampton	09.07.1979
13:57.91	Mark Morgan	Loughborough	23.05.1999
13:58.44	Nathaniel Lane	Stretford	11.07.2000
13:58.5	Dick Milne	Cwmbran	12.06.1977
13:58.88	Donald Naylor	Stretford	11.07.2000
14:01.1	Kenny Davies	Cwmbran	05.09.1984
14:01.6	Fred Bell	Crystal Palace	18.08.1971
14:01.90	Geoff Hill	Derby	04.06.1988
14:01.97	Chris Davies	Birmingham	23.07.1999
14:02.8	Alan Joslyn	White City	02.08.1969
14:03.0	John Merriman	White City	15.06.1960
14:03.30	Ian Mitchell	Stretford	11.07.2000
14:06.72	Malcolm Edwards	Jarrow	03.06.1989
14:07.0	Brian Donovan	West London	12.05.1973
14:07.2	Brian Standen	Crystal Palace	22.06.1974
14:07.6	Dic Evans	Wolverhampton	26.07.1975
14:08.0	Dave Hopkins	Cwmbran	29.06.1975
14:08.4	Dic Samuel	Crystal Palace	14.09.1977
14:08.63	James Hill	Cardiff	02.06.1990
14:09.0	Bob Maplestone	Brighton	01.07.1972
14:09.0	Eddie Conway	Swansea	25.06.1988
14:09.12	Carl Leonard	Philadelphia, USA	27.04.1995
14:09.4	Mike Critchley	Wolverhampton	26.07.1975

Some notable 3 miles performances (pre 1969)

13:31.6	John Merriman	Motspur Park	25.06.1960
13:35.8	Alan Joslyn	Grangemouth	08.06.1968
13:39.6	Chris Loosley	Cardiff	24.07.1965
13:44.6	Tony Ashton	Motspur Park	22.06.1968
13:46.4	John Disley	White City	20.07.1957
13:47.8	Tony Simmons	Luton	28.06.1967
13:48.0	David J P Richards	Cardiff	29.07.1961
13:48.2	Gwynn Davis		17.09.1968
13:53.6	Brian Jeffs		09.08.1967
13:55.0	Nick Barton		22.06.1968

10,000 metres (no conversions from 6 miles included)

27:39.14	Steve Jones	Oslo, Norway	09.07.1983
27:57.77	Ian Hamer	Brussels, Belgium	13.09.1991
28:00.50	Andres Jones	Watford	22.07.2000
28:14.89	Bernie Plain	Crystal Palace	01.08.1975
28:14.96	Tony Simmons	Crystal Palace	10.06.1978
28:17.00	Justin Hobbs	Helsinki, Finland	29.06.1994

28:18.6	John Davies (TVH)	Crystal Palace	11.04.1979
28:23.62	Dennis Fowles	Crystal Palace	24.07.1982
28:43.67	Adrian Leek	Crystal Palace	07.08.1981
28:44.4	Gordon Minty	Christchurch, N Z	25.01.1974
28:51.05	Nigel Adams	Cardiff	26.08.1989
28:52.89	John Merriman	Rome, Italy	08.09.1960
28:58.6	David Hopkins	Cwmbran	17.09.1977
29:01.17	Nathaniel Lane	Stanford, USA	27.03.1999
29:11.0	Fred Bell	Crystal Palace	15.09.1971
29:12.75	Ali Cole	Crystal Palace	23.07.1983
29:17.53	Dick Milne	Cwmbran	08.07.1978
29:20.4	Tony Ashton	Crystal Palace	14.04.1971
29:21.2	Paul Williams (Cambridge)	Crystal Palace	11.04.1984
29:22.09	Carl Leonard	Raleigh, USA	28.03.1997
29:22.72	John Robertshaw	Crystal Palace	07.08.1981
29:24.44	Mike Critchley	Crystal Palace	01.08.1975
29:25.1	Kenny Davies	Cwmbran	15.08.1984
29:27.87	Glen Grant	Derby	05.06.1988
29:31.2	John Davies (Essex)	Crystal Palace	11.10.1978
29:33.41	Ieuan Ellis	Crystal Palace	23.07.1983
29:37.95	James Hill	Gateshead	29.06.1990
29:38.16	Chris Buckley	Cwmbran	25.05.1986
29:40.0	Peter Ratcliffe	Cwmbran	25.06.1977
29:43.78	Mike Bishop	Antrim	25.05.1985
29:49.0	Alan Jones	Crystal Palace	15.09.1971
29:50.72	Steve Brace	Gateshead	29.06.1990
29:51.3	Dic Evans	Luxembourg, Lux	04.08.1977
29:51.8	Alan Joslyn	Edinburgh	18.07.1970
29:52.5	Steve Knight	Enfield	31.07.1994
29:53.6	Micky Morris	Cwmbran	17.09.1977
29:54.12	Dale Rixon	Newport	01.06.1996
29:54.3	Geoff Hill	Cwmbran	17.08.1988
29:54.4	John Jones	Cardiff	09.05.1970
29:54.4	Andrew Smith	Corby	29.05.1989
29:55.0	Cyril Leigh	Wythenshawe	23.05.1970
29:56.0	Robert Walmsley	Eugene, USA	03.05.1986
29:58.0	Bernie Hayward		15.10.1969
29:58.2	Paul Wheeler	Swansea	27.05.1985
29:59.4	Brian Standen	Crystal Palace	17.04.1974

Some notable 6 miles performances

27:20.8	Gordon Minty	Bakersville, USA	15.06.1973
28:07.4	John Merriman	White City	07.08.1961
28:12.8	Malcolm Thomas	Philadelphia, USA	26.04.1974
28:41.0	Alan Joslyn	White City	12.07.1968
29:07.6	David J P Richards	Cardiff	25.10.1958
29:08.4	David Williams	Southall	25.05.1968
29:11.8	Tony Simmons	Luton	20.04.1967
29:12.0	Ron Franklin	Walton	10.08.1965
29:16.0	Nick Barton	White City	30.05.1966
29:18.2	Bob Roath	Motspur Park	25.04.1964
29:20.6	Ron McAndrew		24.07.1967
29:24.0	Cyril Leigh		29.07.1967

3000 metres steeplechase

8:18.91	Roger Hackney	Hechtel, Belgium	30.07.1988
8:22.48	John Davies (TVH)	Crystal Palace	13.09.1974
8:23.90	Justin Chaston	Nice, France	18.07.1994
8:25.37	Christian Stephenson	Solihull	19.08.2000
8:30.6	Peter Griffiths	Nice, France	17.07.1977
8:31.22	David Lee	Edinburgh	19.06.1992
8:32.00	Steve Jones	Crystal Palace	08.08.1980
8:35.49	Micky Morris	Crystal Palace	14.08.1976
8:35.6	Ron McAndrew	Portsmouth	09.07.1971
8:36.2	Bernie Hayward	Christchurch, N Z	26.01.1974
8:37.8	Clive Thomas	Dieppe, France	12.07.1975
8:40.58	Tony Blackwell	Cwmbran	28.05.1984
8:41.4	Tony Ashton	White City	15.07.1967
8:44.03	Donald Naylor	Wythenshawe	14.06.2000
8:44.2	John Disley	Moscow, Russia	11.09.1955
8:45.05	Steve Jones (Brom)	Birmingham	17.06.1989
8:46.2	Dic Evans	Warley	22.08.1971
8:47.6	Tony Pretty	Wolverhampton	26.07.1975
8:50.14	Marcus Thomas	Cwmbran	25.05.1986
8:50.47	Phil Llewellyn	Edinburgh	31.07.1983
8:50.76	Hugh Richards	Crystal Palace	14.07.1972
8:50.8	Dic Samuel	Crystal Palace	18.08.1976
8:52.4	Gareth Bryan Jones	Motspur Park	16.07.1967
8:53.2	Peter Ratcliffe	Edinburgh	28.07.1973
8:54.6	Hedydd Davies	Wolverhampton	27.06.1964
8:55.2	John Theophilus	Cwmbran	26.06.1977
8:55.6	Phil Cook	Loughborough	20.06.1993
8:56.0	Ted Turner	Aldershot	14.06.1979
8:57.2	Brian Jeffs	Portsmouth	20.07.1963
8:58.6	Steve Gibbons	Stretford	26.07.1975
8:59.1	Chris Davies	Kingston	05.07.1997
8:59.6	Ifan Lloyd	Carmarthen	09.05.1993
8:59.9	Andrew West	Chapel Hill, USA	21.04.1984
9:00.0	Tacwyn Davies	Crystal Palace	18.08.1976
9:00.28	Brian Matthews	Nesbyen, Norway	03.09.1988
9:00.8	Karl Palmer	Colwyn Bay	20.06.1992
9:01.2	Stephen Griffiths	Carmarthen	09.05.1993
9:01.6	Bill Stitfall	White City	30.05.1966
9:01.6	Glen Grant	Aldershot	11.06.1980
9:03.0	Gordon Minty	Columbus, USA	20.04.1974
9:03.6	Andy Bamber	Crystal Palace	05.07.1980
9:05.2	Chris Suddaby	Stockholm, Sweden	26.07.1956
9:07.5	Roger Porter	Hornchurch	05.07.1986
9:07.6	Lloyd Roberts	Cwmbran	10.05.1981
9:08.5	Kevin Parker	Crystal Palace	05.05.1982
9:08.9	Andy Eynon	Crawley	01.07.1995
9:09.50	Matthew Davies	Bedford	30.08.1997
9:09.6	Howard Norman	Cwmbran	02.08.1987
9:10.68	Andrew Rodgers	Birmingham	05.06.1983
9:11.04	David Messum	Edinburgh	16.08.1981

110 metres hurdles (fully automatic timing)

12.91	Colin Jackson	Stuttgart, Germany	20.08.1993
13.51	Nigel Walker	Birmingham	03.08.1990
13.53	Paul Gray	Victoria, Canada	22.08.1994
13.69	Berwyn Price	Moscow, Russia	18.08.1973
14.17	Colin Bovell	Nivelles, Belgium	23.07.1994
14.18	James Archampong	Lisbon, Portugal	21.07.1994
14.23	Alan Tapp	Cwmbran	14.06.1986
14.28	Nick Dakin	Crystal Palace	12.06.1993
14.29	Rhys Davies	Antrim	25.06.1990
14.37	Richard Harbour	Plovdiv, Bulgaria	10.08.1990
14.37	James Hughes	Birmingham	16.07.1995
14.39	James Mason	Crystal Palace	05.08.1987
14.45	Nathan Palmer	Bedford	27.08.2000
14.64	Berian Davies	Gladbeck, Germany	24.08.1991
14.81	Huw Jones	Birmingham	25.05.1980
14.85	Howard Rooks	Crystal Palace	14.07.1973
14.85	Mike Morgan		00.00.1979
14.88	Luke Gittens	Bedford	27.08.2000
14.99	Nick Alexander	Sittard, Holland	17.08.1980
15.05	Dick Gyles	Crystal Palace	26.05.1974
15.15	Marvin Gray	Cardiff	19.08.1995
15.19	Ben Roberts	Bedford	30.05.1999
15.25	Rob Kingsborough	Wurttenburg, Germ	09.09.1990
15.26	Paul Jones	Waterford, Ireland	03.09.2000
15.30	Matthew Butler	Bedford	05.07.1998
15.35	Phil Harries	Gateshead	19.08.1990
15.41	Chris Richards	Bremen, Germany	12.09.1976
15.42	Roger Rees	Crystal Palace	01.06.1975
15.46	Mike Bartlett	Edinburgh	20.06.1992
15.58	Stuart Gibbs	Cwmbran	26.06.1982
15.58	Tony Pithers	Wrexham	21.08.1988
15.68	Chris Cashell	Haringey	08.09.1991
15.71	James Hillier	Cwmbran	21.06.1997
15.75	Kirtley Robbins	Birmingham	24.06.1992

superior wind assisted performances

13.49w	Nigel Walker	Jarrow	03.06.1989
13.65w	Berwyn Price	Crystal Palace	25.08.1975
14.14w	James Archampong	Cardiff	25.05.1996
14.27w	Richard Harbour	Stoke	01.07.1990
14.34w	Nathan Palmer	Bedford	28.05.2000
14.50w	Howard Rooks	Crystal Palace	15.07.1972
14.61w	Berian Davies	Grangemouth	16.06.1991
14.86w	Luke Gittens	Bedford	28.05.2000
14.89w	Nick Alexander	Dublin, Ireland	19.08.1979
14.90w	Dick Gyles	Crystal Palace	13.07.1974
14.98w	Ben Roberts	Arles, France	24.05.1998
15.08w	Tony Pithers	Wrexham	08.06.1986
15.19w	Paul Jones	Aberdeen	08.08.1999
15.21w	Mike Bartlett	Crystal Palace	10.06.1990
15.27w	Derek Fishwick	Edinburgh	02.07.1983

15.44w	Peter Dyer	Edinburgh	16.08.1986
15.46w	Kirtley Robbins	Jarrow	03.06.1989
15.48w	Stephen Edwards	Bedford	28.07.1996
15.51w	Tudor Bidder	Dublin, Ireland	19.08.1979
15.67w	Danny Haywood	Stoke	09.09.1995
15.76w	Geoff Ingram	Aberdeen	08.08.1999
15.79w	Neil Hammersley	Cwmbran	11.09.1983

400 metres hurdles

49.16	Paul Gray	Budapest, Hungary	18.08.1998
50.01	Phil Harries	Derby	05.06.1988
50.58	Colin O'Neill	Christchurch, N Z	29.01.1974
50.84	Matthew Elias	Gothenburg, Sweden	29.07.1999
51.21	Steve James	Crystal Palace	23.06.1978
51.30	James Hillier	Bedford	04.07.1999
51.54	Derek Fishwick	Crystal Palace	14.06.1980
51.63	Mark Rowlands	Cwmbran	21.06.1997
51.7	Bob Shaw	Budapest, Hungary	30.09.1956
51.78	Alun James	Crystal Palace	14.08.1976
51.84	Rob Kingsborough	Pliezhausen, Germany	09.09.1990
51.89	Chris Cashell	Haringey	08.09.1991
52.07	Dave Griffin	Edinburgh	03.06.1995
52.14	Wynford Leyshon	Crystal Palace	13.07.1973
52.2	Neil Hammersley	Swansea	25.08.1984
52.20	Craig White	Colwyn Bay	23.07.1994
52.4	John Lewis	Edinburgh	21.07.1970
52.6	Bob Roberts	Crystal Palace	13.07.1973
52.77	Berwyn Price	Crystal Palace	13.09.1974
52.8	Marvin Gray	Newport	01.06.1996
52.80	Berian Davies	Cwmbran	21.06.1997
53.12	Jeremy Bridger	Birmingham	15.06.1996
53.2	Keith Lancey	Cwmbran	19.07.1975
53.4	Roger Richardson	Birmingham Univ	06.05.1970
53.4	Orrie Fenn	West London	27.07.1977
53.5y	John Marsh	Hurlingham	02.06.1962
53.63	David Thomas (Colwyn Bay)	Edinburgh	18.07.1987
53.7	Nick Dakin	Crystal Palace	06.05.1985
53.8	David Goodger	Newport	17.06.1995
53.89	Mike Bartlett	Swansea	16.06.1990
53.9	Danny Haywood	Newport	17.06.1995
54.0	Jon Owen	Aldershot	01.07.1981
54.05	Colin Bovell	Aartselaar, Belgium	21.07.1994
54.1	Russ Williams	Aldershot	06.07.1988
54.22	Jamie Sheffield	Wrexham	25.06.1995
54.3	Tony Pithers	Loughborough	25.06.1986
54.37	Joe Lloyd	Bedford	26.05.1997
54.4	Russ Richards	Stoke	31.07.1988
54.5	Gareth Lewis	Wimbledon	11.05.1997
54.50	Chris Ewart	Cwmbran	17.06.1979
54.6	Richard Tibbott	Crystal Palace	26.07.1969
54.6	Trystan Bevan	Newport	23.06.1996
54.7	Ted Savill	Cologne, Germany	19.07.1969

54.72	Bernard Murphy	Cwmbran	14.06.1986
54.8	David Jones	Luton	18.08.1984
54.8	Simon Beer	Swansea	27.08.1990
54.8	Steven Evans	Colwyn Bay	07.06.1998
54.9	Lionel Godfrey	Oxford	21.05.1969
54.9	Tudor Bidder	Cwmbran	10.05.1981
54.93	David Thomas (Cheltenham)	Cwmbran	20.06.1987
55.0	Charles Davies	Haringey	11.09.1976
55.0	Martyn Bowen	Oxford	18.05.1985

High Jump

2.24	John Hill	Cottbus, Germany	23.08.1985
2.20	Trevor Llewelyn	Crystal Palace	15.07.1983
2.20	Robert Mitchell	Bedford	19.08.2000
2.16	Michael Powell	Nesbyen, Norway	03.09.1988
2.16i	Andrew Penk	Cardiff	20.02.2000
	2.15	Cardiff	31.05.1997
2.15i	Andrew McIver	Cosford	26.01.1980
	2.10	Hornchurch	04.05.1981
2.15	Chuka Enih-Snell	Abingdon	10.09.2000
2.11	George Robertson	Oxford	06.05.1978
2.10	Milton Palmer	Crystal Palace	24.06.1978
2.10	Stuart Gibbs	Portsmouth	04.07.1984
2.10i	Dafydd Edwards	Crystal Palace	15.01.1994
	2.05	Wrexham	20.07.1991
2.09	Ceri Payne	Brecon	06.07.1991
2.09	Sam Hood	Bedford	27.08.2000
2.07	Paul Evans	Swansea	11.08.1982
2.06	David Nolan	Cwmbran	18.06.1994
2.06	Matthew Perry	Newport	01.06.1996
2.05	Steve Ingram	Barry	15.05.1994
2.05	Stuart Brown	Newport	17.06.1995
2.04	Geraint Griffiths	Luxembourg, Lux	06.08.1977
2.03	Chris Trotman	Hull	13.07.1985
2.01	Steve Brock	Cwmbran	25.05.1980
2.01	Daniel Leonard	Rugby	25.06.2000
2.01	Kim Harland	Carmarthen	01.07.2000
2.00	Peter Lance	Cwmbran	16.06.1973
2.00	Dick Gyles	Crystal Palace	26.05.1975
2.00	Tony Norris	Cwmbran	21.06.1980
2.00	David Rowe	Cheltenham	03.07.1985
2.00	Paul Manwaring	Swansea	25.06.1988
2.00	Damian Stirling	Barry	22.07.1990
2.00	Robert Bradley	Cwmbran	14.07.1991
2.00	Chris Harding	Brecon	28.06.1992
2.00	Andrew Blow	Cwmbran	10.07.1993
2.00	Deiniol Evans	Newport	14.08.1994
2.00	Rowan Griffiths	Birmingham	01.02.1997
2.00	Alun Davies	Carmarthen	13.06.1998
1.98	Neil Harris	Wrexham	15.05.1988
1.97	Paul Edwards	Walton	04.10.1980
1.97	Robert James	Wrexham	27.05.1989

1.97	Craig Grant	Hereford	15.07.1989
1.97	Ian Kitchen	Munster, Germany	29.07.1989
1.96	Chris Richards	Cwmbran	26.08.1974
1.96	Chris Raymond	Cheltenham	08.05.1985
1.96	Richard Harbour	Barry	07.08.1988
1.96	Richard V Roberts	Carmarthen	11.05.1997

Pole Vault

5.60	Neil Winter	Enfield	19.08.1995
5.40	Tim Thomas	Belfast	02.08.1997
5.00	Ian Wilding	Newport	01.06.1996
4.90	Egryn Jones	Cwmbran	14.06.1995
4.81	Andrew Penk	Deeside	13.05.2000
4.80i	David Lease	Cosford	19.02.1972
	4.72	Bargoed	08.07.1972
4.80	Peter Lynk	Cwmbran	20.06.1987
4.80	Glyn Price	Wrexham	28.07.1990
4.80i	Chris Type	Cardiff	23.01.2000
	4.70	Aberdare	18.05.1999
4.75	David Gordon	Corby	24.08.1994
4.75	Paul Jones	Hexham	25.07.1999
4.70	Rupert Goodall	Crystal Palace	12.06.1976
4.70	Cameron Johnson	Sheffield	08.07.2000
4.65	Brychan Jones	Reading	12.06.1983
4.60	Nick Pritchard	Swansea	28.08.1995
4.50	Islwyn Rees	Cwmbran	08.06.1975
4.50	Tony Pithers	Acoteias, Portugal	25.05.1986
4.40	Nigel Skinner	Copenhagen, Den	22.07.1984
4.40	Mark Johnson	Swansea	12.08.1984
4.40	Andrew Main	Cwmbran	14.06.1986
4.40	Doug Minter	Nottingham	06.07.1986
4.40	Glyn Sutton	Swansea	16.06.1990
4.40i	Steve Lloyd	Birmingham	03.01.1994
	4.35	Colwyn Bay	11.05.1991
4.40	Steven Francis	Utrecht, Holland	09.07.1995
4.40i	Gareth Lease	Birmingham	25.01.1998
	4.35	Sheffield	12.07.1997
4.34	Peter Challinor	Grand Rapids, USA	10.06.1972
4.32	Geoff Ward	Cwmbran	28.06.1981
4.31	Alexander Thomas	Birmingham	14.06.1998
4.30	Clive Longe	Athens, Greece	18.09.1969
4.30	Nick Heal	Cwmbran	22.06.1980
4.30	Richard Quixley	Swansea	22.06.1988
4.30	David Griffiths	Loughborough	27.04.1994
4.25	Robin Griffiths	Southampton	05.07.1975
4.25	Paul Edwards	Walton	23.08.1981
4.20	Peter Edwards	Crystal Palace	19.05.1976
4.20	Clive Davies	Alsager	25.06.1980
4.20	Tegid Griffiths	Aldershot	26.07.1985
4.20	Robert Hughes	Cwmbran	13.05.1989
4.20	Ian Thomas	Cosford	31.07.1992
4.20	Darren Beddows	Swansea	06.07.1996

4.20	Anthony Perry	Cannock	09.05.1998
4.20	Richard Stubbs	Cardiff	03.06.1998
4.20	Tom Abdy	Brugge, Belgium	23.08.1998
4.19	Les Jones	White City	13.07.1968
4.16	Gordon Pickering	Swansea	21.06.1974
4.15	Jamie Cole	Derby	10.09.2000
4.14	Colin Balchin	Edinburgh	27.05.1967
4.10	Brian Riley	Crystal Palace	21.07.1984
4.10	Derek Fishwick	Swansea	25.06.1988
4.10	Godfrey Benson	Portsmouth	31.07.1988
4.10	Rob James	Swansea	27.08.1990

Long Jump

8.23	Lynn Davies	Berne, Switzerland	30.06.1968
7.75	Ken Cocks	Southampton	02.07.1978
7.68	Garry Slade	Grantham	01.08.1992
7.62	Gareth Davies (Swansea)	Oxford	14.05.1994
7.56	Colin Jackson	Tel Aviv, Israel	31.08.1985
7.55	Gwyn Williams	Cyncoed	04.05.1968
7.55	George Robertson	Oxford	18.06.1987
7.55	Anthony Malcolm	Cwmbran	18.06.2000
7.47	John Elias	Cyncoed	04.05.1968
7.45	Peter Templeton	Cwmbran	27.07.1974
7.44	Richard Jones	Cwmbran	02.07.1983
7.38	Steve Ingram	Istanbul, Turkey	21.05.1994
7.35	Graham Hughes	Woodford	26.08.1978
7.32	Bryan Woolley	Cardiff	29.07.1961
7.32i	Marcus Browning	Cosford	09.01.1987
	7.29	Oxford	26.06.1990
7.31	Colin Wright	Keele	02.07.1977
7.29	Steven Shalders	Neath	30.04.1999
7.29	Gareth Brown	Parliament Hill	06.05.2000
7.26	Steven Partridge	Swansea	15.07.1989
7.25	Paul Hawkins	Swansea	23.07.1986
7.24	Nick Walne	Cambridge	20.05.1995
7.22	Martin Griffiths	Chiswick	19.07.1980
7.21	John Lister	Cardiff	24.07.1965
7.21	Clive Longe	Kassel, Germany	28.06.1969
7.18	Bleddyn Williams	Cardiff	28.07.1962
7.18	Dick Gyles	Wolverhampton	03.07.1974
7.16	John Lewis	Cardiff	07.05.1966
7.16	Peter W Davies	Anderlecht, Belgium	31.05.1971
7.16	Kedrick Thompson	Cwmbran	16.06.1973
7.16	Andrew Wooding	Telford	13.09.1997
7.13	Paul Evans (Swansea)	Birmingham	07.08.1983
7.13	Andrew Adey	Cwmbran	13.05.1989
7.13	Andrew Thomas	Newport	11.06.2000
7.12	Geoff Ward	Stoke	26.06.1977
7.12	David Wood	Luton	07.05.1983
7.12	Stuart Gibbs	Portsmouth	11.07.1984

superior wind assisted performances

7.96w	Colin Jackson	Barcelona, Spain	17.05.1986
7.91w	Steve Ingram	Cwmbran	18.06.1994

7.69w	Garry Slade	Loughborough	12.06.1988
7.62w dh	Gwyn Williams	Bargoed	21.06.1969
7.49w	Peter Templeton	Bristol	22.09.1974
7.45w	Marcus Browning	Birmingham	10.07.1987
7.42w	Colin Wright	Warrington	23.04.1977
7.41w	Gareth Brown	Cwmbran	18.06.2000
7.39w	John Lister	Wolverhampton	04.06.1966
7.39w	Martin Roberts	Swansea	11.06.1989
7.30w	John Lewis	Cardiff	21.04.1966
7.30w	Nick Walne	Oxford	28.06.1995
7.28w	Steven Partridge	Portsmouth	31.07.1988
7.25w	Ray Gazzard	Cardiff	02.07.1959
7.25w	Stuart Gibbs	Cwmbran	02.06.1984
7.19w	Ian Roberts	Welwyn	19.07.1992
7.18w	Tom Hallett	Wrexham	01.08.1992
7.16w	Andrew Thomas	Cwmbran	18.06.2000
7.14w	Geoff Ward	Southampton	01.07.1978
7.12w	Chris Price	Oxford	08.03.1989

Triple Jump

15.99	Steven Shalders	Santiago, Chile	20.10.2000
15.90	David Wood	Karlovac, Yugoslavia	16.09.1984
15.88	John Phillips	Athens, Greece	14.05.1978
15.82i	Charles Madeira Cole	Glasgow	15.03.1998
	15.79	Loughborough	17.05.1998
15.64	Graham Webb	Wolverhampton	19.07.1969
15.60	Peter W Davies	West London	15.05.1976
15.43	Lynn Davies	Cardiff	28.07.1962
15.42	Jon Hilton	Bedford	11.06.2000
15.16	Paul Farmer	Braintree	28.06.1992
15.07	Nigel Green	Uttoxeter	07.06.1967
15.05	Peter Walker	Cardiff	25.06.1966
15.01	Martyn Roberts	Motspur Park	18.05.1968
14.91i	Gerald Evans	Cosford	03.02.1967
	14.63	Cwmbran	27.07.1968
14.74	Scott Balment	West London	11.06.1989
14.73	Gareth Davies (Swansea)	Oxford	14.05.1994
14.72	Stuart McKenzie	Cwmbran	14.06.1986
14.68	Gareth Davies (Cardiff)	Swansea	25.06.1988
14.67	Richard Jones	Cwmbran	27.06.1981
14.67	Gareth Brown	Exeter	20.06.1992
14.62	Aneurin Evans	White City	10.06.1957
14.62	Richard Dodd	Cardiff	17.05.1958
14.60	Richard Gyles	Oxford	26.04.1972
14.57	John Lewis	Enfield	04.06.1983
14.54	Philip Jones	Norbiton	02.05.1970
14.52	Gordon Wells	Abertillery	25.06.1949
14.50	Garry Slade	Tooting Bec	11.05.1991
14.47	Bleddyn Williams	Edinburgh	16.07.1960
14.45	Martin Lucas	Cwmbran	20.06.1976
14.45	Tegid Griffiths	Aldershot	09.06.1982
14.44	John Tustin	Leicester	18.05.1974

14.43	Leighton Adams	Luton	07.09.1985
14.41	David Evans	Cyncoed	31.05.1967
14.36	Michael Powell	Loughborough	01.07.1987
14.35	David Rees	Cwmbran	15.07.1972
14.33	Aled Williams	Athens, Greece	13.05.1978
14.32	Tim Jennings	Bargoed	07.07.1962
14.30	Peter J Davies	Cardiff	12.06.1968
14.30	Alan Keyse	Wolverhampton	04.07.1979
14.29	Phil Ward	Cwmbran	07.07.1979
14.28	John Furnham	Crystal Palace	17.09.1978
14.27	Tegid Griffiths	Aldershot	08.06.1983
14.18	Paul Hawkins	Grangemouth	16.07.1979
14.17	Steven Alvey	Tilburg, Holland	22.08.1999
14.16	Micky Morris	Cwmbran	31.07.1982
14.16	Paul Ellis	Oordegem, Belgium	09.07.1994
14.15	Spencer Jones		31.05.1969

superior wind assisted performances

15.81w	Charles Madeira Cole	Loughborough	17.05.1998
15.59w	Jon Hilton	Cudworth	22.07.2000
15.16w	Martyn Roberts	Southampton	29.06.1968
14.74w	Gerald Evans	Leicester	06.04.1968
14.30w	Colin Lloyd	Annan	29.08.1990
14.22w	Peter Sullivan	Edinburgh	07.07.1979
14.16w	Nick Walne	Wrexham	20.07.1991

Shot

20.45	Shaun Pickering	Crystal Palace	17.08.1997
19.85	Paul Edwards	Walton	02.07.1989
17.81	Lee Newman	Birmingham	25.07.2000
17.41	Lee Wiltshire	Swindon	01.05.1994
16.77	Mark Proctor	Aldershot	03.07.1991
16.70	Paul Rees	Southampton	02.07.1978
16.56	Matthew Bundock	Tooting Bec	30.08.1997
16.55	John Walters	Swansea	17.05.1971
16.36	Archie Buttriss	Hereford	21.08.1963
16.32	Ted Kelland	Cwmbran	29.06.1975
16.25	Arthur Richardson	Wrexham	27.05.1961
16.13i	Richard Davies	Cosford	24.03.1990
	15.90	Cosford	09.09.1989
16.02	Erol Palsay	Crystal Palace	13.08.1975
15.79	Martin Lockley	Cwmbran	21.06.1980
15.56	Peter Sutton	Cardiff	16.05.1970
15.55	Clive Longe	Los Angeles, USA	18.07.1969
15.52	Clayton Turner	Aldershot	02.06.1991
15.39	Brian Penny	Ystradgynlais	27.06.1971
15.32	Bill Kingsbury	Battersea	00.00.1951
15.03	David Williams	Warley	20.05.1989
14.86i	Andrew Turner	Horsham	28.01.1996
	14.74	Bournemouth	14.05.1994
14.68	John Davies	Cardiff	29.07.1961
14.60	John Powell Jones	Motspur Park	29.05.1957
14.54	Justin Bryan	Deeside	30.08.1999

14.53	Kevin Jones	Cwmbran	20.06.1976
14.45	Peter Wilson	Sale	29.04.1972
14.45i	Ken Latten	St Athan	22.03.1980
14.37	Ewart Hulse	Newport	07.07.1996
14.31	Aneurin Evans	Cardiff	24.06.1961
14.23	Alan Thomas	Horsham	09.04.1995
14.22	John Tym	Cwmbran	26.06.1982
14.20	Hywel Williams	Llanrumney	23.06.1958
14.19i	Mark Hewer	St Athan	07.12.1980
	14.16	Athens, Greece	25.08.1981
14.08	Allan Martin	Cyncoed	27.05.1970
14.07	Gareth Gilbert	Stretford	04.06.1996
14.04	Lawrie Hall	Southall	00.06.1965
13.99	David P Rees		00.00.1968
13.97	Nigel Winchcombe	Coventry	02.07.1988
13.83	Derek Emery	St Athan	20.05.1970
13.79	Norman Lemon	Llandarcy	18.05.1968
13.78	Steven Norris		00.00.1976
13.75	Eric Ricketts	Cwmbran	12.05.1984
13.74	Robert Gye	Swansea	08.05.1965
13.74	Lawrence Daniels		00.00.1974
13.73	Dave Richardson	Wrexham	21.07.1991
13.63i	John Parkin	Birmingham	01.02.1998
13.62	Andrew Nicholls	Swindon	10.07.1986
13.61	Owen Thomas	Swansea	05.05.1982
13.60	David Stears	Cardiff	24.05.1966
13.59	David Bunce	Brighton	02.06.1962

Discus

60.43	Lee Newman	Enfield	23.08.1998
57.12	Paul Edwards	Colindale	10.08.1988
54.38	Shaun Pickering	Cardiff	26.08.1989
52.34	Ted Kelland	Southall	30.06.1973
52.02	John Walters	Hayes	31.07.1971
51.82	Mark Proctor	West London	17.07.1991
50.94	Paul Rees	Crawley	22.07.1978
49.28	Ken Latten	Cwmbran	21.07.1979
49.22 ?s	Denis Day	Vancouver, Canada	16.06.1967
48.92	Clive Longe	Colwyn Bay	05.07.1969
48.88	Nigel Winchcombe	Bracknell	25.05.1985
48.70	Martin Lockley	Santa Barbara, USA	22.03.1980
48.36	Tegid Griffiths		16.08.1989
48.02	Archie Buttriss	Newport	01.06.1963
47.64	Andrew Turner		28.06.1995
47.50	Hywel Williams	Nairobi, Kenya	30.07.1955
46.80	John Parkin	Derby	04.09.1999
46.48	Gareth Gilbert	Stretford	18.08.1998
46.40	Mal Pemberton	Oxford	14.06.1961
45.86	Erol Palsay	Edinburgh	15.09.1973
45.29	Justin Bryan	Wrexham	17.08.1998
45.26	Clayton Turner	Horsham	28.07.1991
44.68	Gareth Marks	Utrecht, Holland	09.07.1995

44.66	Aneurin Evans	Cardiff	27.05.1961
44.62	Matthew Bundock	Cwmbran	21.06.1997
44.58	Norman Lemon	Llandarcy	18.05.1968
44.52	Peter Roberts	Copthall	15.09.1990
44.14	W Jones	Shrewsbury	13.06.1959
43.78	Alun Williams	Bristol	23.06.1996
43.76	Kevin Jones	Crystal Palace	29.05.1977
43.74	Allan Martin	Aberavon	15.07.1972
43.73	Morris Davies	Aldershot	15.07.1964
43.62	Brian Penny	Swansea	03.06.1968
43.38	Gareth Jones	Swansea	20.05.1987
43.00	Andrew Nicholls	Bristol	06.09.1986
42.74	Bruce Barnes	Cardiff	15.05.1965
42.72	Roger Beard	Carmarthen	04.06.1966
42.64	David Boorer		10.05.1967
42.62	Brian Collins	Swansea	19.06.1982
42.58	Lyndon Davies	Cyncoed	02.05.1970
42.48	Ewart Hulse	Rotherham	29.06.1997
42.30	John H Thomas	Exeter	26.06.1956
42.26	Andrew Roda	Swansea	14.05.1988
42.22	Jeff Bowen	Bonn, Germany	19.06.1966
42.19	Dafydd Farr	Bath	30.08.1999
42.14	John Buttriss	Bristol	27.05.1987
42.06	Terry Lalley	Swansea	20.07.1988
41.98	John Collins	Cwmbran	14.07.1982
41.54	Damon McGarvie	Cwmbran	10.07.1993
41.46	Nick Lia	Cyncoed	21.05.1975
41.46	Graham Holder	Coventry	21.08.1999
41.28	Peter Rees	Brecon	22.06.1991
41.26	Julian Tucker	Newport	11.08.1981

Hammer

68.64	Shaun Pickering	Stanford, USA	07.04.1984
62.56	Adrian Palmer	Edinburgh	06.08.1994
61.91	Graham Holder	Budapest, Hungary	03.07.1999
59.40	Gareth Jones	Cwmbran	11.05.1994
59.18	Nigel Winchcombe	Nesbyen, Norway	03.09.1998
58.56	Lawrie Hall	Enfield	26.05.1962
58.04	Philip Bufton	Colwyn Bay	07.06.1998
57.92	Nick Lia	Cardiff	10.04.1977
56.88	John Owen	Bristol	24.06.1990
55.96	Peter Stark	Cranwell	11.07.1979
55.92	David Roberts	Birmingham	17.06.1984
55.40	Morris Davies	Crystal Palace	15.08.1973
55.02	Neil Williams	Wrexham	02.06.1991
54.62	Ewart Hulse	Colwyn Bay	11.05.1991
54.04	Paul Rees	Bournemouth	15.05.1976
53.82	Alan Phipps	Tidworth	11.07.1974
53.34	Andy Davie	Cardiff	08.08.1974
52.68	Ted Kelland	Cwmbran	22.09.1973
51.96	Mark Proctor	Colchester	30.05.1991
51.76	Andrew Turner	Newham	13.06.1996

51.66	Bill Treharne	Wimbledon	08.07.1967
51.24	Marc Gulliver	Leeds	30.05.1995
51.18	John Parkin	Bedford	04.07.1998
50.80	Julian Tucker	Swansea	08.08.1982
50.72	Nigel Spivey	Brecon	25.07.1992
50.02	Ross Blight	Cwmbran	18.06.2000
49.60	Don Harrigan	Cardiff	22.06.1968
49.58	Gordon Window	Cwmbran	29.07.1984
49.58	Hamid Lane	Wrexham	05.06.1993
49.30	Terry Lalley	Solihull	12.08.1990
49.20	Crayton Phillips	Cheltenham	11.06.1982
49.00	Ray Bacon	Motspur Park	10.05.1981
48.84	Mike Llewellyn Eaton	Haringey	31.05.1980
48.66	Martin Cliffe	Stretford	28.05.1983
48.64	Anthony Coutanche	New River	21.08.1988
48.24	Tony Doran	Cardiff	17.07.1994
48.16	Brian Cooksley	Cardiff	03.06.1998
48.04	Albert Ley	Southampton	21.07.1962
47.34	Neil Townsend	Crawley	25.06.1995
47.16	Luigi Antoniazzi	Bournemouth	23.06.1994
46.58	Marcus Davies	Aberdare	08.06.1996
46.16	Gareth Driscoll	Newport	08.08.1998
46.12	Brian Lewis	Crystal Palace	05.07.1970
46.00	Robert Proctor	Bristol	07.12.1980
45.48	Adrian Jones	Cwmbran	23.07.1975
45.42	Andrew Jones	Cardiff	23.02.1992
45.40	Phil Jones	Cwmbran	28.06.1976
45.36	Allan Martin	St Athan	20.05.1970
45.10	Martin Lewis	Woodford	11.09.1977
44.24	Paul Triggs	Bristol	11.09.1982

Javelin

81.70	Nigel Bevan	Birmingham	28.06.1992
74.14	Colin Mackenzie	Edinburgh	11.06.1988
70.90	Shane Lewis	Watford	06.06.1998
70.30	Tim Newenham	Portsmouth	11.06.1989
68.91	Stuart Loughran	Birmingham	26.07.1998
68.74	Jonathan Clarke	Cwmbran	14.06.1986
64.52	Chris Thomas	Bergen ap Zoom, Holland	24.08.1997
63.78	Richard Jones	Bournemouth	19.06.1993
62.92	Linton Baddeley	Harrow	22.06.1991
61.85	Derek Hermann	Bath	16.09.2000
60.88	Andrew Furst	Bournemouth	09.05.1993
59.98	Tim Brooks	Colindale	12.08.1987
58.92	Gareth Rowlands	Tooting Bec	07.07.1990
58.48	Rhys Williams	Neath	04.06.2000
58.12	Chris Raymond	Cheltenham	20.07.1991
58.03	Matthew Davies	Newport	13.06.1999
58.02	Angus Jefferies	Cwmbran	27.06.1987
57.88	Paul Edwards		00.00.1987
57.72	Luigi Antoniazzi	Sheffield	05.06.1993
57.48	Jeremy Moody	Barry	07.08.1994

57.02	Paul Verheyden	Swansea	09.05.1991
56.50	Julian Howells	Wrexham	20.06.1992
56.47	Kevin Ricketts	Aldershot	05.07.2000
56.32	Neil Bithell	Wrexham	04.08.1991
55.71	Rhys Taylor	Carmarthen	10.06.2000
55.36	Andrew Mitchell	Swansea	02.05.1990
55.34	Ian Gould	Wrexham	05.06.1993

Javelin (pre 1986 model)

81.30	Colin Mackenzie	Crystal Palace	07.08.1985
75.48	Nigel Sherlock	Brno, Czech	05.07.1969
74.54	Tim Newenham	Cwmbran	11.05.1985
73.94	Gareth Brooks	Leicester	06.08.1978
72.78	Tony Edwards	Glasgow	15.06.1968
69.04	John James	Crawley	07.09.1968
68.08	Jonathan Clarke	Cwmbran	23.06.1985
67.64	Graham Robinson	Swansea	18.05.1985
67.48	Tim Brooks	Cheltenham	11.05.1984
67.20	Gareth Rowlands	Cwmbran	02.06.1984
67.06	Nigel Price	Cwmbran	27.06.1981
66.98	Brian Sexton	Cardiff	20.06.1961
66.50	Phil Ramsey	Brighton	31.07.1971
66.22	Wayne Phillips	Cardiff	13.05.1970
65.10	Gareth Jones	Hartford	18.05.1968
64.54	Jeff Bowen	Hornchurch	05.06.1965
64.12	Jim Boyle	Cyncoed	27.05.1968
63.14	Norman Watkins	Brmingham	07.05.1958
62.68	Steve Griffiths	Swansea	26.06.1983
62.26	Clive Longe	Loughborough	31.05.1967
62.22	Bill Carey	Crystal Palace	02.06.1974
61.95	Brian Harland	Crystal Palace	31.05.1969
61.82	Clive Roberts	Motspur Park	30.04.1958
61.32	David Palmer	Motspur Park	14.05.1977
61.30	Neville Hughes	Aldershot	20.07.1955
61.16	Robert Voss	Cardiff	19.06.1965
60.86	David Price	Cardiff	22.04.1964
60.78	Norman Lang	Cardiff	04.06.1966
60.58	Alistair Owen	Swansea	19.06.1982
60.54	Chris Raymond	Cheltenham	08.05.1985

Decathlon (100m, LJ, SP, HJ, 400m, 110mH, DT, PV, JT, 1500m)

7308 pts	Clive Longe *(10.9,7.21,14.77,1.70,51.1,14.84,6.02,4.10,57.10,4:59.2)*	Kassel, Germany	29.06.1969
7268 pts	Paul Edwards *(11.62,6.62,14.54,1.86,52.10,16.36,48.40,4.00,57.80,4:21.20)*	Bonn, Germany	14.08.1983
7071 pts	Paul Jones *(11.17,6.71,11.82, 1.81,50.20,15.87,37.88,4.65,47.86, 4:31.39)*	Arles, France	04.06.2000
7053 pts	George Robertson *(11.05,7.39,12.27, 2.07,48.54,16.00, 29.02,3.70,45.24, 4:38.52)*	Arles, France	19.05.1986
6812 pts	Nigel Skinner *(11.21,6.78,12.85,1.80,50.46,16.38,36.90, 4.10,45.78, 4:37.99)*	Dombasle, France	19.08.1984
6637 pts	Tony Pithers *(11.5,6.11,12.58,1.80,51.6,15.83,3.62,4.50,46.94,4:28.8)*	Acoteias, Portugal	26.05.1986
6524 pts	Geoff Ward *(11.4,7.14w,10.92,1.90,52.1,16.53,5.42,4.10,41.18,4:43.8)*	Southampton	02.07.1978
6514 pts	Stuart Gibbs *(11.5,7.02,11.89,1.99,53.3,15.9 3,2.20,3.90,47.02,4:57.5)*	Cosford	05.08.1983
6454 pts	Robert James *(11.38,6.22,11.28,1.97,52.55,16.58,36.68,3.80,48.12,4:51.04)*	Wrexham	28.05.1989
6436 pts	Kevin Ricketts *(11.1,6.39,11.78,1.86,52.5,16.03, 33.53,3.60, 52.68,4:48.0)*	Aldershot	22.06.2000

6399 pts	Tegid Griffiths *(11.8,6.36,11.46,1.84,53.0,16.8,38.52,4.20,46.70,4:35.1)*	Aldershot	27.07.1985
6372 pts	Ben Roberts *(11.44,6.61,12.86,1.89,54.13,15.95,38.59, 3.80,46.99, 5:28.66)*	Cardiff	04.07.1999
6244 pts	Duncan Gauden *(11.53,6.52w,11.04,1.83,53.14,16.68,36.66,3.50,45.60,4:43.63)*	Stoke	26.06.1994
6148 pts	Geoff Ingram *(11.55,6.31,10.33,1.70,51.28,15.8,32.83,3.90,44.01,4:51.9)*	Cosford	28.07.1998
6123 pts	Steve Ingram *(11.65,6.61,09.98, 1.98,52.10,15.5,31.86,3.30,44.16,5:11.91)*	Cardiff	27.05.1990
6064 pts	David Rees *(11.0,6.27,10.63,1.66,50.7,16.4,31.94,3.21,42.18,4:29.0)*	Llanrumney	18.07.1964
6052 pts	Steve Brock *(11.5,6.55,10.45,2.01,53.3,16.0,31.90,3.00,40.16,4:46.1)*	Cwmbran	26.05.1980
6050 pts	Hywel Williams *(11.9,6.07,13.61,1.74,55.1,16.8,39.50,3.50,52.15,4:56.8)*	Helsinki, Finland	13.09.1983
6022 pts	Graham Hughes *(11.2,6.87,10.09,1.90,52.9,17.0,28.24,2.90,48.12, 4:42.13)*	Cosford	01.08.1980
5959 pts	Derek Fishwick *(11.5,6.58,09.64,1.75,51.6,15.7,29.00,3.40,34.98,4:30.3)*	Cwmbran	25.06.1978
5945 pts	Marcus Browning *(11.40,6.75,10.69,1.69,51.8,17.25,29.14,3.10,51.26,4:54.51)*	Waterford, Ireland	16.09.1990
5882 pts	John Lister *(11.2,6.89,10.16,1.88,52.9,15.3,30.63,3.04,31.55,5:09.2)*	Cardiff	10.09.1966
5875w pts	Robert Bradley *(11.44,6.34w,09.06,1.89,51.82,16.00,29.32,3.10,41.06,5:00.02)*	Wrexham	18.04.1993
5873 pts	Craig Shiel *(11.5,5.98,09.68,1.75,51.8,16.1,31.56,2.80,46.34,4:25.3)*	Fontainebleu, France	21.05.1980
5869 pts	Owen Sussex *(11.0,6.25,09.82,1.70,51.2,16.9,27.80,3.00,41.62, 4:22.8)*	Exeter	27.05.1979
5863w pts	Richard Stubbs *(11.75w,6.31, 09.46,1.89,54.63,17.26w,28.34,3.30,50.80,4:40.82)*	Wrexham	18.04.1993
5817 pts	Martin Lockley *(11.8,5.74,13.61,1.60,54.7,19.0,41.74,3.38,44.80,4:59.8)*	Wolverhampton	15.08.1976

WOMEN

100 metres (fully automatic timing)

11.39	Sallyanne Short	Cwmbran	12.07.1992
11.48	Carmen Smart	Cardiff	26.08.1989
11.50	Helen Miles	Birmingham	05.08.1988
11.57	Michelle Probert/Scutt	Birmingham	02.09.1984
11.67	Catherine Murphy	Bedford	14.08.1999
11.73	Lisa Armstrong	Thessaloniki, Greece	08.08.1991
11.82	Jennifer Webb	Edinburgh	28.08.1982
11.85	Liz Parsons/Johns	Helsinki, Finland	10.08.1971
11.88	Rachel King	Haapsalu, Estonia	20.06.2000
11.90	Angharad James	Bedford	29.05.2000
11.96	Margaret Williams	Crystal Palace	20.08.1976
12.00	Danielle Selley	Sheffield	30.07.2000
12.02	Sian Morris/Lewis	Berlin, Germany	17.08.1990
12.03	Gillian Regan	Cwmbran	14.06.1986
12.05	Sophie Anna Williams	Bath	14.05.1997
12.05	Lowri Jones	Bedford	03.07.1999
12.13	Gael Davies	Sheffield	12.07.1996
12.16	Louise Sharps	Dublin, Ireland	13.08.1994
12.19	Alexandria Bick	Sheffield	15.08.1998
12.20	Diane Thorne	Cwmbran	08.07.1978
12.20	Pamela Greaves	Cwmbran	08.07.1989
12.20	Samantha Gamble	Antrim	07.08.1999
12.21	Jane Bradbeer	Swansea	08.06.1985
12.21	Nicola Short	Cwmbran	14.06.1986
12.25	Allison Rees	Swansea	08.06.1985
12.26	Stacey Rodd	Cardiff	01.07.1995
12.27	Lucy Evans	Sheffield	08.07.2000
12.29	Sonia Reay	Cardiff	26.08.1989
12.29	Natasha Bartlett	Stoke	29.06.1991
12.33	Allison Consterdine	Nesbyen, Norway	04.09.1988
12.33	Louise Whitehead	Birmingham	18.07.1998
12.36	Karen Taylor	Edinburgh	18.07.1981
12.36	Hannah Paines	Colwyn Bay	02.07.1994
12.38	Sarah Roberts	Cardiff	01.07.1995
12.40	Delyth Jones	Newport	28.05.1994
12.42	Leanne Rowlands	Cardiff	01.07.1995

superior wind assisted automatic times

11.36w	Sallyanne Short	Cardiff	26.08.1989
11.41w	Helen Miles	Copthall	20.08.1988
11.45w	Michelle Probert/Scutt	Antrim	12.06.1982
11.58w	Liz Parsons/Johns	Crystal Palace	17.07.1971
11.65w	Catherine Murphy	Cwmbran	09.07.1995
11.70w	Liz Gill	White City	31.07.1965
11.71w	Jennifer Webb	Birmingham	23.06.1984
11.87w	Angharad James	Bedford	29.05.2000
11.88w	Danielle Selley	Blackpool	15.07.2000
11.95w	Lowri Jones	Bedford	03.07.1999
12.16w	Nicola Short	Edinburgh	16.08.1986

12.16w	Alexandria Bick	Sheffield	15.08.1998
12.24w	Jane Evans		00.00.1975
12.28w	Delyth Jones	Newport	28.05.1994
12.30w	Allison Consterdine	Birmingham	07.06.1986
12.32w	Dawn Oliver	Edinburgh	13.08.1983
12.37w	Denice Grist	Cardiff	26.08.1989
12.40w	Rhian Owen	Birmingham	19.07.1981
12.41w	Hayley Baxter	Carmarthen	23.05.1998

200 metres (fully automatic timing)

22.80	Michelle Probert/Scutt	Antrim	12.06.1982
23.24	Sallyanne Short	Birmingham	28.06.1992
23.28	Catherine Murphy	Birmingham	25.07.1999
23.48	Margaret Williams	Crystal Palace	21.08.1976
23.82	Sian Morris/Lewis	Edinburgh	28.07.1986
23.84	Carmen Smart	Crystal Palace	30.07.1982
23.89	Helen Miles	Cardiff	01.06.1991
24.24	Louise Whitehead	Cardiff	31.05.1997
24.37	Anne Middle	San Sebastian, Spain	26.07.1986
24.38i	Lowri Jones	Neubrandenburg, Germany	04.03.2000
	24.81	Sheffield	16.08.1988
24.40	Natasha Bartlett	Istanbul, Turkey	22.05.1994
24.48	Lisa Armstrong	Cwmbran	12.07.1992
24.56	Danielle Selley	Sheffield	30.07.2000
24.82i	Alexandria Bick	Birmingham	21.02.1999
	24.85	Dublin, Ireland	08.08.1998
24.85	Samantha Gamble	Tilburg, Holland	27.08.1999
24.90	Karen Taylor	Crystal Palace	19.08.1978
24.92	Angharad James	Neath	28.04.1996
24.92	Louise Sharps	Hendon	10.08.1996
24.96	Sarah Rowe	Birmingham	08.08.1981
25.02	Jennifer Webb	Edinburgh	18.07.1981
25.04	Sarah Bull/Owen	Brussels, Belgium	11.07.1981
25.05	Jane Bradbeer	Crystal Palace	30.07.1983
25.06	Dawn Higgins	Tallin, Estonia	31.07.1999
25.09	Joanne Gronow	Cwmbran	09.07.1995
25.16	Leri Davies	Brecon	05.07.1997
25.19i	Gael Davies	Birmingham	24.02.1996
25.22	Erica Burfoot	Swansea	06.07.1996
25.24	Donna Porazinski	Carmarthen	23.05.1998
25.27	Aimee Cutler	Brecon	05.07.1997
25.28	Gillian Archard/Cashell	Cwmbran	10.07.1993
25.31	Allison Consterdine	Birmingham	06.07.1986
25.34	Emma Staples	Brecon	05.07.1997
25.38	Rachel Newcombe	Wrexham	30.07.1994
25.39	Rhian Cains	Nottingham	08.07.1995

superior wind assisted performances

22.48w	Michelle Probert/Scutt	Dublin, Ireland	04.07.1982
23.19w	Sallyanne Short	Auckland, N Zealand	29.01.1990
23.51w	Carmen Smart	Cwmbran	10.07.1983
23.81w	Helen Miles	Grangemouth	16.06.1991

24.03w	Louise Whitehead	Bedford	24.05.1998
24.56w	Lowri Jones	Bedford	05.07.1998
24.60w	Angharad James	Bedford	28.05.2000
24.71w	Alexandria Bick	Sheffield	16.08.1998
24.89w	Sarah Rowe	Utrecht, Holland	22.08.1981
24.90w	Ruth Martin Jones/Howell	Edinburgh	22.07.1970
25.00w	Lucy Evans	Sheffield	15.08.1999
25.35w	Gail Evans	Cardiff	01.07.1995
25.38w	Lisa Griffiths/Gibbs	Wrexham	31.07.1993
25.39w	Hannah Paines	Cardiff	01.07.1995

400 metres

50.63	Michelle Probert/Scutt	Cwmbran	31.05.1982
52.72	Catherine Murphy	Runaway Bay, Australia	17.09.2000
52.80	Sian Morris/Lewis	Lappeenranta, Finland	18.06.1983
53.24	Dawn Higgins	Jona, Switzerland	16.07.2000
53.32	Ann Middle	La Coruna, Spain	06.08.1986
53.34	Louise Whitehead	Birmingham	24.07.1999
53.81	Alyson Evans/Layzell	Cwmbran	20.06.1998
53.82	Carmen Smart	Brisbane, Australia	03.10.1982
54.35	Gillian Archard/Cashell	Corby	30.05.1994
54.46	Kirsty McDermott/Wade	Derby	25.05.1987
54.6	Gloria Dourass/Rickard	Paris, France	27.06.1971
54.60	Amanda Pritchard	Cwmbran	21.06.1997
54.77	Cathy White/Dawson	Crystal Palace	14.06.1992
54.91	Karen Taylor	Cwmbran	12.08.1982
55.1	Carol Fernley	Cwmbran	10.08.1980
55.19	Rachel Newcombe	Cwmbran	12.07.1992
55.19	Emma Davies	Haapsalu, Est	20.06.2000
55.2	Paula Lloyd	Crystal Palace	20.07.1973
55.2	Diane Heath/Fryar	Crystal Palace	10.07.1979
55.4	Sandra Belt/Pengilley	Cwmbran	23.07.1974
55.53	Sian Waters/Morgan	Crystal Palace	20.08.1977
55.58	Kathryn Bright	Loughborough	21.05.2000
55.6	Jenny Davies/Mullett	Feltham	25.06.1978
55.6	Hayley Parry/Tullett	Newport	06.07.1997
55.79	Natasha Bartlett	Tilburg, Holland	17.07.1993
55.8y	Thelwyn Appleby/Bateman	White City	01.07.1966
55.8	Donna Porazinski	Bath	09.07.2000
56.17	Bernie Butcher	Crystal Palace	27.07.1979
56.2	Cathy Owen	Bristol	02.06.1982
56.21	Samantha Porter	Edinburgh	18.07.1987
56.31	Kay Buckland	Crystal Palace	21.08.1976
56.4	Sarah Rowe	Crystal Palace	24.07.1981
56.47	Jane Tomley	Cwmbran	09.07.1983
56.49	Sarah Roberts	Swansea	06.07.1996
56.55	Claire Edwards	Crystal Palace	14.09.1991
56.6	Anna Turner	Wrexham	04.05.1996
56.6	Kathryn Williams	Leamington	25.08.1996
56.7	Kate-Elin Williams	Cork, Ireland	24.06.1995
56.8	Michelle Cooke	Barry	10.07.1988
56.8	Alison Parry	Crawley	22.06.1991

56.8	Anne Evison	Wakefield	09.08.1992
56.85i	Caroline Wilkins	Glasgow	16.03.1999
	56.9	Rugby	14.07.1996
56.9	Lianne Dando	Brussels, Belgium	22.06.1975
56.9	Paula Thomas	Cwmbran	07.07.1979
56.9	Pat Sullivan/Gallagher	Birmingham	31.05.1981
56.95	Nicola Davies	Oordegam, Belgium	09.07.1994
57.0	Margaret Williams	Bristol	11.04.1976
57.0	Claire Warnes	Galashiels	18.07.1987
57.05	Nerys Evans	Ayr	13.08.1988

800 metres

1:57.42	Kirsty McDermott/Wade	Belfast	24.06.1985
2:01.25	Hayley Parry/Tullett	Budapest, Hungary	22.07.2000
2.01.7	Ann Middle	Wythenshawe	28.08.1991
2:02.39	Emma Davies	Kuala Lumpur, Malaysia	17.09.1998
2:03.17	Cathy White/Dawson	Victoria, Canada	26.08.1994
2:03.28	Rachel Newcombe	Kuala Lumpur, Malaysia	18.09.1998
2:03.88	Alison Parry	Cwmbran	14.07.1991
2:04.4	Thelwyn Appleby/Bateman	Crystal Palace	25.07.1971
2:04.68	Hilary Hollick	Crystal Palace	25.06.1977
2:04.84	Alyson Evans/Layzell	Wrexham	03.07.1994
2:05.2	Kim Lock/Harris	Aldershot	19.07.1982
2:06.0	Gloria Dourass/Rickard	Crystal Palace	10.09.1971
2:06.57	Melissa Watson	Hendon	17.08.1986
2:07.32	Amanda Pritchard	Belfast	22.06.1996
2:07.9	Jenny Davies/Mullett	Hull	29.07.1978
2:08.0	Samantha Porter	Coventry	10.09.1989
2:08.04	Liz Francis/Thomas	Nesbyen, Norway	03.09.1988
2:08.15	Natalie Lewis	Cardiff	05.07.2000
2:08.4	Jean Lochhead	Belfast	05.06.1973
2:09.0	Marion Hepworth	Crystal Palace	20.09.1972
2:09.1	Emma Brady	Stretford	22.07.1997
2:09.15	Gillian Archard/Cashell	Luton	06.05.1996
2:09.7	Lisa Carthew	Cardiff	03.08.1994
2:10.0	Sarah Hodge/Lee	Cwmbran	08.08.1990
2:10.1	Sally James/Lynch	Cwmbran	19.08.1987
2:10.17	Sarah Mead	Birmingham	24.07.1998
2:10.2	Annemarie Fox/Richards	Cwmbran	31.08.1983
2:10.4i	Angela Hartley	Cosford	26.01.1980
	2:11.0	Bristol	10.08.1977
2:10.4	Clare Martin	Newport	06.07.1997
2:10.8	Janette Howes	Kirkby	15.08.1982
2:10.80	Kathryn Bright	Vlakenswaard, Holland	06.07.1993
2:10.9	Bernie Butcher	Stretford	19.06.1979
2:10.9	Barbara Ann King	Swansea	25.08.1984
2:10.91	Sarah Rowe	Utrecht, Holland	23.08.1981
2:11.01	Georgina Parnell	Dublin, Ireland	08.08.1998
2:11.1	Hayley Nash	Corby	19.09.1987
2:11.1	Esther Evans	Aylesbury	16.06.1992
2:11.21	Lynne Gallagher	Cardiff	15.07.1998
2:11.3y	Jackie Barnett	White City	07.07.1962

2:11.3	Claire Schofield	Stretford	10.09.1991
2:11.34	Caitlin Funnell	Nesbyen, Norway	03.09.1988
2:11.6	Nicola Charlton	Aldershot	09.07.1988
2:11.7	Carol Nicholas	Middlesbrough	21.07.1979
2:11.78	Ruth Hornby	Birmingham	18.07.1998
2:12.0	Pat Sullivan/Gallagher	Melksham	19.06.1984
2:12.1	Delyth Davies	Cwmbran	27.07.1974
2:12.16	Jennifer Mockler	Stretford	25.07.2000
2:12.2	Nicola Haines/Jones	Cwmbran	16.08.1989
2:12.4	Ceri Thomas/Grech	Cardiff	07.08.1996
2:12.5	Lynn Huntbach/Lerue	Cwmbran	02.07.1980
2:12.5	Jessica Mills	Walthamstow	22.07.1992
2:12.5	Anne Evison	Leeds	15.06.1993
2:12.54	Caroline Morgan	Cwmbran	14.06.1986

1500 metres

4:00.73	Kirsty McDermott/Wade	Gateshead	26.07.1987
4:01.23	Hayley Parry/Tullett	Oslo, Norway	28.07.2000
4:12.72	Hilary Hollick	Edmonton, Canada	12.08.1978
4:13.12	Kim Lock/Harris	Cwmbran	11.08.1982
4:14.3	Angela Tooby/Smith	Ipswich	19.06.1985
4:15.60	Hayley Nash	Birmingham	07.08.1988
4:15.99	Ann Middle	La Laguna, Spain	13.07.1991
4:16.12	Melissa Watson	Crystal Palace	13.09.1987
4:16.23	Susan Tooby/Wightman	Lisbon, Portugal	17.06.1984
4:16.45	Annmarie Fox/Richards	Crystal Palace	30.07.1983
4:18.6	Jean Lochhead	Crystal Palace	08.07.1972
4:20.49	Liz Francis/Thomas	Sheffield	25.08.1996
4:20.60	Wendy Ore	Solihull	21.08.1994
4:20.7	Thelwyn Appleby/Bateman	Crystal Palace	21.07.1973
4:21.90	Caitlin Funnell	Wrexham	28.07.1990
4:22.42	Lisa Carthew	Birmingham	16.07.1993
4:22.52	Clare Martin	Birmingham	13.08.2000
4:23.6	Janette Howes	Middlesbrough	05.09.1981
4:24.17	Rachel Newcombe	Watford	30.08.2000
4:24.2	Sarah Hodge/Lee	Lesneven, France	02.06.1990
4:24.2	Bronwen Smith/CardyWise	Redditch	05.05.1994
4:24.76	Sian Pilling	Edinburgh	01.08.1986
4:25.80i	Alyson Evans/Layzell	Birmingham	04.02.1995
4:26.11i	Emma Davies	Birmingham	16.01.2000
	4:34.28	Portsmouth	13.05.2000
4:26.3	Sally James/Lynch	Crystal Palace	12.08.1987
4:26.50	Catherine Dugdale	Cardiff	05.07.2000
4:26.6	Alison Parry	Woking	27.07.1989
4:26.86	Emma Brady	Budapest, Hungary	22.07.2000
4:27.5	Lynn Maddison	Stretford	05.08.1986
4:27.73i	Esther Evans	Cardiff	04.03.2000
	4:30.3	Stretford	16.07.1996
4:28.3	Ruth Eddy	Watford	09.06.1999
4:29.90	Jessica Mills	Birmingham	27.06.1992
4:30.43	Ceri Thomas/Grech	Birmingham	12.07.1997
4:30.7	Barbara Ann King	Swansea	12.08.1984

4:32.0	Angela Hartley		00.00.1978
4:32.0	Pat Sullivan/Gallagher	Swindon	10.07.1986
4:33.0	Cathy White/Dawson	Watford	10.07.1996
4:33.3i	Gloria Dourass/Rickard	Cosford	30.01.1971
4:33.92	Nicola Haines/Jones	Cardiff	08.09.1991
4:33.99	Hayley Donaghue/Mittleberger	Wythenshawe	07.06.1998
4:34.2	Ceri Pritchard/Diss	Tooting Bec	18.07.1990
4:34.3	Clare Pugh/Jenkins	Barry	16.08.1987
4:34.4	Margaret Morgan		00.00.1975
4:34.6	Anna James		Pre 1976
4:34.8	Anne Howard	Aldershot	21.06.1980
4:35.0	Caroline Morgan	Cwmbran	20.06.1979
4:35.0	Debbie Chick/Newhams	Barry	24.05.1989
4:35.3	Anne-Marie Hutchinson	Cwmbran	27.06.2000
4:35.38	Catherine Davies	Cwmbran	18.06.1994
4:35.6	Clare Thomas	Swindon	07.08.1997
4:35.61	Ann Roblin	Cwmbran	14.06.1986

One Mile

4:19.41	Kirsty McDermott/Wade	Oslo, Norway	27.07.1985
4:26.50i	Hayley Parry/Tullett	Stuttgart, Germany	06.02.2000
4:37.7	Kim Lock/Harris	Hendon	14.08.1982
4:38.1	Hilary Hollick	Gateshead	30.07.1977
4:38.39	Angela Tooby/Smith	Crystal Palace	14.08.1987

3000 metres

08:45.39	Hayley Parry/Tullett	Gateshead	15.07.2000
08.47.59	Angela Tooby/Smith	Stockholm, Sweden	05.07.1988
08.47.7	Kirsty McDermott/Wade	Gateshead	05.08.1987
08:57.17	Susan Tooby/Wightman	Crystal Palace	06.06.1984
09.01.67	Melissa Watson	Belfast	27.06.1988
09.05.03	Hilary Hollick	Antrim	25.05.1981
09.08.48	Kim Lock/Harris	Crystal Palace	07.08.1982
09:13.65	Hayley Nash	Budapest, Hungary	13.06.1992
09:14.72	Wendy Ore	Sheffield	11.06.1994
09:16.04i	Annemarie Fox/Richards	Ghent, Belgium	14.02.1988
	09:21.3	Swansea	01.06.1983
09:20.99	Sally James/Lynch	Utrecht, Holland	23.08.1987
09.26.5	Thelwyn Appleby/Bateman	Cork, Ireland	26.06.1981
09:26.8	Bronwen Smith/Cardy Wise	Redditch	29.04.1993
09:32.0	Jane Swarbrick	Cyncoed	14.05.1983
09:32.0	Sarah Hodge/Lee	Yate	18.07.1990
09:34.65	Debbie Chick/Newhams	Cwmbran	18.06.1994
09:37.5	Lynn Maddison	Middlesbrough	30.08.1986
09:38.0	Ceri Pritchard/Diss	Tooting Bec	01.08.1990
09:38.14	Barbara Ann King	Copenhagen, Denmark	22.07.1984
09:38.8	Jean Lochhead	Edinburgh	16.06.1972
09:39.84	Janette Howes	Cwmbran	11.08.1982
09:40.92	Liz Francis/Thomas	Birmingham	17.08.1996
09:41.4	Lisa Carthew	Barry	23.06.1993
09:41.74	Carol Hayward	Antrim	01.07.1989
09:42.52	Anne-Marie Hutchinson	Bath	16.09.2000

09:44.7	Catherine Dugdale	Millfield	03.05.1999
09:47.6	Nicola Haines/Jones	Swansea	20.05.1992
09:48.1	Maggie Smith	Wigan	07.05.1988
09:48.43	Pat Sullivan/Gallagher	Birmingham	17.06.1989
09:48.9	Ann Middle	Vigo, Spain	30.03.1986
09:50.8	Kathy Williams	Middlesbrough	21.07.1979
09:50.8	Ceri Thomas/Grech	Street	04.05.1998
09:51.54	Bernadette Thomas/Walters	Swansea	22.07.1989
09:52.9	Jackie Hulbert/Brace	Middlesbrough	13.08.1977
09:53.1	Tracy Pugh	Cannock	24.05.1992
09:55.12	Sue Barnes/Hudd	Crystal Palace	05.09.1975
09:56.0	Frances Gill	Neath	08.07.1997
09:56.4	Claire Pugh/Jenkins	Swansea	13.09.1987
09:57.0mx	Louise Copp	Cwmbran	23.07.1980
09:57.0	Sian Pilling	Portsmouth	21.07.1990
09:57.1	Clare Thomas	Cardiff	06.08.1997
10:00.5	Alison Whitelaw	Swansea	16.06.1990
10:03.4	Yvonne Rowe		00.00.1978
10:03.46	Elinor Caborn	Copeland	07.09.1991
10:04.7	Karen Powell	Leicester	26.04.1986
10:05.0	Margaret Morgan	West London	05.11.1975
10:05.3	Vivienne Conneely	Portsmouth	18.07.1992
10:06.8	Emma Turner	Swindon	07.08.1997
10:07.0	Bev Morgan	Edinburgh	00.05.1987
10:09.48	Jessica Mills	Wrexham	01.08.1992

Under age performance (under 15):
10:00.6 by Louise Silva at West London on 07.03.1979

5000 metres

15:13.22	Angela Tooby/Smith	Oslo, Norway	05.08.1987
15:32.19	Susan Tooby/Wightman	Antrim	26.05.1985
16:10.26	Hilary Hollick	Oslo, Norway	26.06.1982
16:25.4	Ceri Pritchard/Diss	Tooting Bec	10.09.1989
16:25.7	Hayley Nash	Cwmbran	08.04.1992
16:25.79	Wendy Ore	Birmingham	16.06.1996
16:26.48	Melissa Watson	Jarrow	04.06.1989
16:32.89	Angharad Mair	Cardiff	31.05.1997
16:34.60	Sally James/Lynch	Birmingham	25.07.1987
16:44.94	Bronwen Smith/Cardy Wise	Eugene, USA	06.08.1989
17:01.87	Barbara Ann King	Cwmbran	28.05.1984
17:08.8	Pat Sullivan/Gallagher	Cwmbran	22.04.1987
17:10.2	Liz Francis/Thomas	Birmingham	23.08.1998
17:18.1	Eryl Davies	Carmarthen	23.06.1988
17:19.7	Lynne Maddison	Liverpool	28.07.1996
17:21.5	Nicola Haines/Jones	Cwmbran	11.06.1997
17:22.5	Annmarie Fox/Richards	Bebington	11.06.1995
17:23.72	Dinah Cheverton	Cardiff	23.07.1995
17:25.81	Debbie Chick/Newhams	Cwmbran	27.07.1997
17:25.93	Vivienne Conneely	Sheffield	05.05.1996
17:30.11	Frances Gill	Cwmbran	27.07.1997
17:37.4	Fiona Nixon/Davies	Cwmbran	22.04.1987

17:44.1	Marilyn Kitchen	Dudley	28.04.1996
17:44.8	Catherine Dugdale	Newport	01.06.1996
17:45.0	Louise Copp	Swansea	08.05.1982
17:45.2	Kathy Williams	Cwmbran	10.05.1980
17:54.72	Clare Martin	Birmingham	27.07.1997
17:59.0	Sara Johnson	Carmarthen	12.09.1995
18:02.9	Barbara Boylan	Wirral	11.06.1995
18:07.4	Sandra Manser	Cwmbran	09.06.1993
18:08.1	Beccy Richardson/Cameron	Cwmbran	20.05.1990
18:10.0	Hayley Donaghue/Mittelberger	Hereford	24.04.1997
18:12.4	Emma Davies	Tamworth	28.04.1996
18:18.26	Samantha Gray	Cwmbran	21.06.1997
18:18.4	Elizabeth Williams	Swansea	14.05.1983

10,000 metres

31:55.30	Angela Tooby/Smith	Rome, Italy	04.09.1987
32:20.95	Susan Tooby/Wightman	Oslo, Norway	02.07.1988
34:07.24	Hayley Nash	Sheffield	06.06.1992
34:11.76	Angharad Mair	Birmingham	14.06.1996
34:24.21	Sally James/Lynch	Cardiff	08.06.1991
34:37.3	Bronwen Smith/Cardy Wise	Watford	22.07.2000
34:55.0mx	Melissa Watson	Carmarthen	14.09.1993
35:06.8	Frances Gill	Neath	21.05.1997
35:22.8	Ceri Pritchard/Diss	Coventry	05.05.1990
36:34.1	Kathy Williams	Birmingham	02.06.1984
36:45.0	Dinah Cheverton	Exeter	06.10.1993
36:54.5	Vivienne Conneely	Antrim	05.05.1997
36:56.92	Alison Whitelaw	Wrexham	26.05.1991
37:16.35	Beccy Richardson	Cardiff	26.08.1989
38:16.1	Barbara Boylan	Exeter	10.08.1996
38:17.8	Sue Neal	Swansea	03.09.1989
38:50.00	Peta Bee	Cardiff	26.08.1989
39:08.42	Liz Hardley	Wrexham	26.05.1991
39:28.42	Ann Cartwright	Birmingham	06.07.1991
39:42.8	Liz Clarke	Exeter	05.08.1995

100 metres hurdles (fully automatic timing)

12.91	Kay Morley/Brown	Auckland, N Zealand	02.02.1990
13.46	Rachel King	Budapest, Hungary	03.07.1999
13.57	Bethan Edwards	Horsham	29.08.1992
13.92	Liz Wren	Cwmbran	14.06.1986
13.93	Lisa Griffiths/Gibbs	Crystal Palace	12.06.1993
14.24	Sarah Bull/Owen	Graz, Austria	21.06.1980
14.25	Lauren McLoughlin	Edinburgh	13.08.2000
14.28	Non Evans	Cardiff	22.07.1995
14.31	Tracey Lewis	Birmingham	06.06.1986
14.34	Diane Heath/Fryar	Athens, Greece	19.07.1983
14.35	Sarah Rowe	Cwmbran	20.09.1980
14.47	Lowri Roberts	Loughborough	30.07.2000
14.58	Megan Jones	Colwyn Bay	23.07.1994
14.59	Carol Whiteway	Cardiff	26.08.1989
14.62	Julia Charlton	Birmingham	16.07.1983

14.67	Ruth Martin-Jones/Howell	Cwmbran	08.07.1978
14.68	Jane Buttress	Edinburgh	07.08.1982
14.68	Rebecca Jones	Bedford	27.08.2000
14.86	Natasha Bartlett	Hull	21.08.1994
14.88	Lynn Parry	Derby	24.05.1987
14.96	Rebecca Jones-Morris	Cwmbran	14.06.1986
15.01	Norma Evans	Edinburgh	01.09.1979
15.02	Sarah Jones Morris	Antrim	06.05.1990
15.07	Amanda Stacey	Crystal Palace	18.08.1978
15.14	Rachel Stannard	Carmarthen	16.07.1976
15.15	Michelle DeBono-Evans	Loughborough	30.07.2000
15.27	Amanda Wale	Wrexham	01.08.1999
15.32	Joelanda Thomas	Cardiff	23.05.1992
15.38	Amy Bergiers	Colwyn Bay	24.05.1997
15.44	Abigail Jones	Bedford	24.05.1998
15.49	Teresa Andrews	Cwmbran	18.06.1994
15.51	Anna Leyshon	Bergen op Zoom, Holland	24.08.1997
15.58	Marie Humphries	Crystal Palace	08.08.1992
15.66	Jackie Barber	Cwmbran	14.06.1986

superior wind assisted performances

12.84w	Kay Morley/Brown	Sestriere, Italy	08.08.1990
13.44w	Rachel King	Palmo, Spain	28.05.1998
13.80w	Lisa Griffiths/Gibbs	Sheffield	30.04.1994
14.10w	Sarah Rowe	Birmingham	08.08.1981
14.14w	Lauren McLoughlin	Bedford	27.08.2000
14.40w	Lowri Roberts	Loughborough	30.07.2000
14.44w	Megan Jones	Cwmbran	10.07.1993
14.60w	Rebecca Jones-Morris	Edinburgh	16.08.1986
14.62w	Lynn Parry	Cwmbran	27.05.1984
14.65w	Rebecca Jones	Bedford	28.05.2000
14.98w	Amanda Stacey	Crystal Palace	27.08.1978
15.16w	Teresa Andrews	Newport	28.05.1994
15.22w	Jane Shepherd	Hull	21.06.1986
15.56w	Kathryn Morgan	Edinburgh	13.08.1983
15.67w	Sandra Oakley	Edinburgh	18.07.1981
15.70w	Emma Jones	Colwyn Bay	02.07.1994

400 metres hurdles

56.43	Alyson Evans/Layzell	Birmingham	16.06.1996
58.16	Diane Heath/Fryar	Cwmbran	09.07.1983
59.25	Natasha Bartlett	Cwmbran	18.06.1994
59.46	Cathy White/Dawson	Crystal Palace	12.06.1993
59.9	Michelle Cooke	Swansea	01.05.1988
60.20	Claire Edwards	Oordegem, Belgium	09.07.1994
60.21	Kathryn Williams	Hendon	10.08.1996
60.58	Tracey Lewis	Nesbyen, Norway	03.09.1988
60.6	Amanda Stacey	West London	07.06.1978
60.79	Jane Buttress	Cwmbran	30.05.1982
60.8	Rebecca Jones-Morris	Wrexham	29.08.1987
61.07	Louise Whitehead	Budapest, Hungary	03.07.1999
61.08	Jane Evans/Rees	Graz, Austria	21.06.1980

61.17	Donna Porazinski	Cwmbran	17.06.2000
61.19	Sarah Bull/Owen	Cwmbran	11.07.1980
61.32	Caroline Wilkins	Cudworth	28.06.1997
61.59	Lynfa Lewis/Porter	Crystal Palace	15.08.1980
62.3	Eirwyn Gould/Coe	Aldershot	11.07.1982
62.4	Bernie Butcher	Bristol	24.07.1976
62.6	Lynn Parry	Cannock	10.05.1987
62.7	Emma Davies	Cwmbran	03.07.1993
62.70	Lisa Thompson	Brugge, Belgium	23.08.1998
62.9	Lynn Davies	Kirkby	01.06.1974
63.4	Judith Nethercott	Barry	18.05.1985
63.7	Kate Disley	Hendon	06.07.1985
63.74	Tanya Sexton	Cwmbran	10.07.1993
63.8	Nicola Charlton	Middlesbrough	05.09.1981
63.8	Claire Schofield	Cwmbran	26.08.1991
63.9	Liz Wren	Bournemouth	27.05.1985
64.2	Linda Croft	Bristol	20.08.1978
64.2	Esther Evans	Southampton	01.08.1992
64.22	Gael Davies	Loughborough	18.05.1997
64.46	Mari Prys Jones	Copeland	07.09.1991
64.5	Debbie Heaven	Cwmbran	07.06.1980
64.52	Maria Yarnold	Swansea	16.06.1990
64.59	Mandy Bloomer	Bedford	01.05.1999
65.0	Abigail Jones	Cwmbran	19.07.1997
65.09	Jackie Barber	Antrim	06.05.1990
65.10	Sara Johnson	Wrexham	29.07.1995
65.14	Sarah Newman	Barry	14.07.1998
65.2	Sharon James	Cwmbran	02.06.1984
65.4	Glenda James	Dublin, Ireland	20.07.1985
65.5	Delyth Davies	Cwmbran	20.07.1975
65.55	Rachel Newcombe	Birmingham	08.05.1994
65.8	Michelle John	Ayr	18.07.1995
65.87	Megan Freeth	Edinburgh	13.08.2000
65.9	Sarah Jones-Morris	Loughborough	17.05.1989
66.0	Jane Shepherd	Leicester	06.09.1985
66.01	Vicky Parnell	Colwyn Bay	24.05.1997

High Jump

1.85i	Julie Crane	Cardiff	13.02.2000
	1.83	Bedford	30.05.1998
1.84	Sarah Rowe	Utrecht, Holland	22.08.1981
1.83	Marion Hughes	Solihull	19.07.1986
1.83	Rebecca Jones	Arles, France	03.06.2000
1.81	Lea Haggett	Birmingham	06.06.1986
1.79i	Julia Charlton	St Athan	24.02.1980
	1.78	Barry	13.07.1980
1.79	Teresa Andrews	Oordegem, Belgium	09.07.1994
1.77	Christine Brookes	Cardiff	24.09.1982
1.77	Val Adams	Swansea	14.08.1985
1.76	Sarah Nicholls	Cwmbran	29.06.1980
1.76	Susannah Filce	Edinburgh	21.07.1990
1.75	Sarah Bull/Owen	Crystal Palace	14.08.1982

1.75	Rebecca Richards	Street	21.04.1990
1.74	Martha Tullberg	Barry	12.07.1987
1.74	Lisa Griffiths/Gibbs	Linwood	21.08.1993
1.73	Liz Wren	Gateshead	14.06.1980
1.73i	Nicola Jupp	Birmingham	23.02.1992
	1.66	Welwyn	27.06.1992
1.73i	Ailsa Wallace	Birmingham	13.02.1994
	1.70	Istanbul, Turkey	21.05.1994
1.73	Ceri Stokoe	Newport	16.07.2000
1.72	Kim Miller	Portsmouth	09.06.1985
1.71	Jackie Barber	Dublin, Ireland	20.07.1985
1.71	Jane Shepherd	Stretford	26.04.1986
1.71	Kelly Moreton	Stoke	05.08.1995
1.70	Ruth Martin Jones/Howell	Crystal Palace	06.05.1972
1.70	Jane Lloyd Francis	Cwmbran	04.06.1978
1.70	Ruanda Davis	Cwmbran	23.09.1978
1.70	Amanda Jones	Essen, Germany	26.07.1980
1.70	Cathy Lucas	Southwark	28.05.1983
1.70	Lisa Lewis	Crawley	21.07.1984
1.70	Carol Whiteway	Swansea	31.08.1987
1.70	Fiona McPhail	Cardiff	23.05.1992
1.70	Krissy Owen	Hereford	22.05.1994
1.70	Kathy Pritchett	Sheffield	30.07.2000
1.69	Christine Craig	Keele	25.06.1972
1.68i	Viv Rothera	Cosford	22.03.1975
	1.67	Nottingham	26.04.1975
1.68	Pam Walker	Swansea	20.06.1982
1.68	Amanda Wale	Cwmbran	09.07.1989
1.68	Beverley Green	Cardiff	26.05.1990
1.68	Emma Hanson	Cwmbran	03.07.1993
1.66	Lisa Thompson	Brecon	12.07.1995
1.65	Bethan Jones		00.00.1976
1.65	Susan Lovell	Cwmbran	25.05.1977
1.65	P Beddoe		00.00.1979
1.65	Kerry Crook	Cwmbran	10.05.1980
1.65	Karen Nethercott	Cyncoed	16.06.1984
1.65	Alyson Preskey	Loughborough	26.06.1984
1.65	Claudia Filce	Telford	30.04.1989
1.65	Jane Falconer	Colchester	24.07.1993
1.65	Sally Peake	Aberdare	13.07.1999
1.65	Rhian Horlock	Blackpool	15.07.2000

Pole Vault

4.15	Rhian Clarke	Austin, USA	07.04.2000
3.76 *	Krissy Owen	Albuquerque,USA	01.05.1999
	3.55	Walnut, USA	16.04.1999
3.55	Gael Davies	Wolverhampton	20.08.2000
3.50	Eirion Owen	Colwyn Bay	05.06.1999
3.20	Rebecca Roles	Aberdare	31.08.1996
3.20	Anna Leyshon	Stoke	06.08.2000
3.01	Penny Hall	Worcester	20.06.1999
3.00	Claudia Filce	Birmingham	20.05.1995

3.00	Bonnie Elms	Cwmbran	19.07.1997
2.90	Carys Holloway	Deeside	19.08.2000
2.85	Nikki Witton	Telford	09.09.2000
2.70	Rebecca Morgan	Brecon	31.08.1997
2.65	Susan Williams	Barry	14.07.1998
2.55	Megan Freeth	Yate	26.07.1998

Long Jump

6.52	Gillian Regan	Swansea	28.08.1982
6.51i	Ruth Martin-Jones/Howell	Cosford	23.02.1974
	6.49	Edinburgh	16.06.1972
6.32	Jo Edwards/Willoughby	Bristol	28.05.1989
6.25	Lisa Armstrong	Brecon	15.07.1992
6.19	Jill Davies/Morton	Crystal Palace	19.08.1978
6.01	Sarah Bull/Owen	Cwmbran	10.05.1980
6.00	Sylvia Powell	Llandarcy	14.08.1968
5.96	Lisa Griffiths/Gibbs	Cardiff	30.06.1993
5.94	Ceri Jenkins/Gilderdale	Athens, Greece	02.07.1977
5.92	Julia Charlton	Haverfordwest	05.05.1982
5.90	Sarah Rowe	Cwmbran	30.05.1982
5.88	Sallyanne Short	Cwmbran	15.05.1994
5.85	Alison Preskey	Crystal Palace	07.05.1984
5.83	Janet Brown	Swansea	29.05.1982
5.82	Nicola Short	Barry	16.07.1988
5.81	Christine Jenner/Thompson	Cardiff	24.06.1967
5.81	Amanda Jones	Dortmund, Germany	19.08.1979
5.80	Monica Zeraschi	Cardiff	22.06.1963
5.80	Lara Richards	Cwmbran	18.06.2000
5.77	Karen Jenkins	Cheltenham	25.05.1974
5.77	Rose Tillson	Cwmbran	08.08.1976
5.77	Aimee Cutler	Brecon	08.07.1998
5.76	Emily Stewart	Jersey	12.09.1992
5.74	Anna Proctor	Wrexham	20.07.1991
5.73	June Hirst	Barry	24.05.1969
5.73	Gemma Jones	Brecon	20.04.1997
5.71	Janice Catt	Cardiff	23.06.1962
5.71	Kathryn Evans	Swansea	24.07.1983
5.70	Karen Evans	Colwyn Bay	14.07.1975
5.68	Philomena Ronan		00.00.1975
5.66	Marion Hughes	Warley	17.09.1983
5.65	Nicolette Dymond	Middlesbrough	04.09.1982
5.65	Jane Shepherd	Warrington	18.05.1986
5.65	Rebecca Jones	Arles, France	04.06.2000
5.64	Bronwen Jones	Cardiff	23.06.1962
5.64	Lisa Lewis	Crawley	21.07.1984
5.63	Sharon McParlin	Cwmbran	13.07.1968
5.62	Pat Roche	Swansea	15.07.1984
5.61	Teresa Andrews	Newport	17.06.1995
5.60	Jennifer Hughes	Solihull	00.00.1969
5.59	Audrey Lewis		25.05.1986
5.59	Sarah Lane (Swansea)	Newport	26.06.1999
5.58	Jackie Hammersley	Cwmbran	03.06.1978

superior wind assisted performances

6.54w	Ruth Martin-Jones/Howell	Edinburgh	16.06.1972
6.38w	Jo Edwards/Willoughby	Cannock	06.08.1989
6.34w	Jill Davies/Morton	Chesterfield	08.07.1978
5.92w	Emily Stewart	Wrexham	01.08.1992
5.84w	Aimee Cutler	Sheffield	15.08.1998
5.82w	Lara Richards	Sheffield	14.08.1999
5.70w	Sarah Lane (Swansea)	Aberdare	31.08.1998
5.69w	Teresa Andrews	Newport	01.06.1996
5.66w	Rebecca Jones	Bedford	29.05.2000
5.61w	Nicola Jupp	Wrexham	01.08.1992
5.59w	Debbie Adams	Cwmbran	10.05.1998
5.58w	Karen Taylor	Teeside	30.08.1986

Triple Jump

12.14	Jayne Ludlow	Istanbul, Turkey	21.05.1994
12.10	Jane Falconer	Colchester	30.08.1993
11.62i	Lara Richards	Cardiff	04.03.2000
	11.53	Coventry	30.04.2000
11.50	Teresa Andrews	Newport	01.06.1996
11.49	Susan Harries/Bunting	Windsor	12.08.1995
11.32	Audrey Lewis	Stoke	18.06.1986
11.31	Jo Edwards/Willoughby	Cheltenham	04.08.1990
11.10	Emily Tugwell	Exeter	09.08.1998
11.10	Debbie Lloyd	Brugge, Belgium	23.08.1998
11.08	Emily Stewart	Crystal Palace	08.08.1992
11.08	Joanne Tomlinson	Lancaster	07.07.1996
11.07	Sian Jones	Rugby	09.07.2000
11.05	Pat Roche	Newport	26.06.1994
11.02	Llinos Hughes	Deeside	25.07.1999
11.01i	Laura Eastwood	Birmingham	04.01.1998
	10.90	Brecon	19.09.1999
10.96	Nicola Jupp	Derby	18.09.1994
10.96	Ceri Jones	Carmarthen	01.07.2000
10.95	Megan Freeth	Yate	26.07.1998
10.94	Amanda Wale	Brecon	05.07.1998
10.91	Elizabeth Webb	Newport	26.06.1999
10.78	Megan Jones	Newport	12.08.1995
10.73	Nicola Short	Barry	29.06.1997
10.71i	Eleri Owen	Birmingham	12.02.1994
10.70	Joy Lamacraft	Cwmbran	21.06.1997

superior wind assisted performances

12.37w	Jane Falconer	Colchester	30.08.1993
11.60w	Lara Richards	Sheffield	15.08.1999
11.23w	Emily Stewart	Stoke	26.07.1992
11.02w	Caroline Marsden	Cardiff	21.06.2000

Shot

19.06i	Venissa Head	St Athan	07.04.1984
	18.93	Haverfordwest	13.05.1984
15.95i	Philippa Roles	Birmingham	06.02.1999
	14.84	Bath	16.09.2000

15.09	Jayne Berry	Vezsprem, Hungary	22.07.1993
14.23	Janet Beese	Cwmbran	07.06.1978
13.82	Janeen Williams		00.00.1982
	13.72i	Cosford	29.01.1983
	13.57	Birmingham	29.03.1980
13.32	Sarah Bull/Owen	New Haven, USA	11.04.1981
12.96	Maureen Pearce	Chester	27.05.1970
12.88	Krissy Owen	Cwmbran	18.06.1994
12.66	Lesley Brannan	Deeside	29.07.2000
12.65	Rebecca Roles	Derby	04.09.1999
12.54	Lisa Griffiths/Gibbs	Wrexham	03.07.1994
12.41	Alyson Hourihan	Cardiff	01.07.1992
12.28	Delyth Evans	Edinburgh	13.08.1983
12.26i	Jayne Richardson	Cosford	23.01.1982
	11.82	Cwmbran	06.06.1982
12.14	Delyth Prothero		00.00.1972
12.13	Frances Pincock	Cosford	17.06.1978
12.11	Cathy Lucas	West London	30.06.1984
12.05	Louise Finlay	Grangemouth	05.08.2000
12.01	Angharad Lloyd	Tilburg, Holland	22.08.1999
11.99	Val Watson	Warrington	15.05.1976
11.95	Jean Davies		24.09.1967
11.93	Loretta Hamilton	Motspur Park	04.06.1975
11.91	Vivienne Head	Bristol	01.05.1977
11.90	Lisa Angulatta	Edinburgh	17.08.1985
11.86	Sarah Moore	Oxford	10.05.1992
11.85	Adelina Evans	Warley	04.09.1971
11.84	Jackie Grey	Cardiff	29.05.1974
11.79	Jane Lloyd-Francis	Cwmbran	11.05.1980
11.78	Sandra Lee	Cwmbran	10.09.1983
11.72	Hazel Andow	Aldershot	07.06.1965
11.72	Clare McKenzie	Swansea	29.08.1994
11.66	Karen Glover	Cwmbran	26.04.1987
11.64	Janet Covill	Barry	12.05.1979
11.63	Alison George	Rotherham	06.08.1995
11.62	Joanne Evans/Powell	Cardiff	23.04.1995
11.54	Ruth Martin Jones/Howell	Durham	23.06.1970
11.45	Liz Edwards	Antrim	07.08.1999
11.40	Sandra Murphy	Barry	16.05.1964
11.37	Jackie Leonard	Aldershot	11.06.1986
11.37	Laura Douglas	Deeside	04.06.2000
11.25	Rebecca Jones	Colwyn Bay	05.06.1999
11.24	Teresa Andrews	Aberdare	00.08.1996
11.20	Charlotte Rees	Swansea	12.04.2000
11.17	Joanna Stallbow	Haverfordwest	05.07.1975
11.15	Jayne Fisher	Leicester	19.06.1994
11.13i	Barbara Spencer		00.00.1972
11.12i	Amanda Barnes	Cosford	21.03.1986
	11.05	Yeovil	19.05.1984
11.10	Leanne Jones/Taylor	Barry	10.05.1998
11.00	Hayley Griffiths	Carmarthen	04.07.1992

Discus

64.68	Venissa Head	Athens, Greece	19.07.1983
60.00	Philippa Roles	Neath	09.05.1999
51.79	Rebecca Roles	Bedford	31.05.1999
49.30	Amanda Barnes	Bournemouth	18.06.1988
47.40	Vivienne Head	Barry	17.06.1978
47.20	Sandra Lee	Nottingham	25.06.1983
45.72	Janet Beese	Cwmbran	08.07.1978
45.62	Val Watson	Stretford	28.08.1976
45.52	Jayne Fisher	Cardiff	25.05.1996
44.04	Delyth Prothero	Bristol	28.06.1975
43.58	Alyson Hourihan	Cardiff	01.07.1992
43.36	Diane English	Bristol	02.07.1978
43.22	Jayne Berry	Cardiff	23.05.1992
42.22	Jane Davies	Cardiff	23.05.1992
41.22	Hayley Hartson	Carmarthen	14.05.1989
40.92	Kelly Roberts/Ricketts	Aberdare	31.08.1998
40.84	Jackie Grey	Bristol	02.09.1973
40.10	Sarah Worthy	Cwmbran	15.05.1982
39.96	Morgyn Warner	Solihull	28.04.1984
39.94	Joanne Evans/Powell	Bedford	17.09.1994
39.62	Laura Douglas	Wrexham	16.07.2000
38.84	Sarah Moore	High Wycombe	29.08.1994
38.72	Caroline Williams	Cwmbran	06.05.1978
38.72	Anwen James	Ashford	25.07.1999
38.16	Hazel Andow	Aberystwyth	02.05.1964
38.12	Ruth Hanney	Colwyn Bay	04.05.1986
37.82	Janeen Williams	Woodford	30.08.1980
37.00	Sarah Johnson	Cwmbran	03.07.1993
36.58	Laura Eastwood	Douglas, I of Man	06.07.1997
36.40	Ffion Jones	Edinburgh	13.08.2000
36.36	Lesley Brannan	Colwyn Bay	02.07.1994
36.34	Michelle Robertson	Wrexham	04.06.1989
36.27	Carys Parry	Cardiff	13.05.2000
36.21	Victoria Gibbons	Barry	14.07.1998
35.90	Julie Tayler/Bowen	Swansea	30.07.1981
35.56	Rhian James		00.00.1974
35.52	Leanne Jones/Taylor	Barry	15.05.1994
35.33	Ruth Morris	Blackpool	15.07.2000
35.06	Linda Fairley		00.00.1974
34.94	Christine Lewis	Galashiels	11.08.1984
34.90	Lynette Harries	Ystradgynlais	28.08.1959
34.82	Janet Covill		00.00.1979
34.76	Amanda Jervis	Carmarthen	13.07.1993
34.74	Katrina Beedles	Colwyn Bay	14.07.1975
34.74	Cathy Kingsbury	Barry	23.07.1991
34.68	Jane Lloyd Francis	Loughborough	12.05.1979
34.54	Eirian Owen	Cwmbran	20.05.1978
34.32	Lyndsey Thomas	Carmarthen	04.05.1991
34.08	Rachel Beynon	Barry	22.08.1993
34.00	Carol Norton	Wrexham	16.07.1986
34.00	Onyema Amadi	Barry	22.07.1990

Hammer

56.60	Sarah Moore	Birmingham	12.07.1997
55.09	Philippa Roles	Neath	09.05.1999
53.80	Carys Parry	Santiago, Chile	17.10.2000
51.86	Lesley Brannan	Cwmbran	18.06.2000
48.63	Laura Douglas	Edinburgh	13.08.2000
47.70	Angela Bonner	Cardiff	14.04.1996
46.86	Leanne Jones/Taylor	Rhondda	12.06.1997
45.70	Rachel Clough	Colwyn Bay	19.06.1999
43.52	Sheena Parry	Bedford	01.05.1999
42.32	Kelly Roberts/Ricketts	Newport	28.08.2000
38.36	Louise Finlay	Cwmbran	17.06.2000
38.32	Dee Groves	Wrexham	04.05.1996
38.11	Jayne Berry	Neath	14.06.1998
38.04	Hannah Lia	Newport	28.08.2000
36.76	Clare McKenzie	Brecon	05.06.1994
36.62	Sarah Hughes	Cardiff	17.07.1994
36.22	Katherine Lenaghan	Cannock	09.09.2000
35.68	Bethan Deverall	Colwyn Bay	11.05.1996
34.90	Ruth Morris	Newport	28.08.2000
34.86	Cathy Kingsbury	Wrexham	17.08.1996
34.38	Alison George	Colwyn Bay	02.09.1995

Javelin

46.89	Caroline White	Colwyn Bay	19.06.1999
43.11	Charlotte Rees	Newport	28.08.2000
41.11	Alison Siggery	Grangemouth	05.08.2000
40.89	Emily Skucek	Deeside	18.07.2000
40.21	Clare Lockwood	Bedford	03.07.1999
39.01	Natasha Campbell	Ashford	09.05.1999
37.01	Joanne Smith/Davies	Neath	20.08.2000
36.11	Rebecca Roles	Stafford	11.07.1999
35.61	Adrienne Harvey	Neath	04.06.2000
35.07	Joanne Roberts	Carmarthen	01.07.2000

Javelin (pre 1999 model)

59.40	Karen Hough	Stuttgart, Germany	28.08.1986
56.50	Caroline White	Cardiff	08.06.1991
55.36	Jackie Zaslona	Woodford Green	30.08.1980
54.02	Janeen Williams	Birmingham	29.03.1980
49.04	Onyema Amadi	Cwmbran	18.06.1994
48.80	Averil Williams	Barry	30.05.1970
48.16	Julie Abel	Swansea	16.06.1990
46.70	Susan James	Yeovil	17.06.1973
46.20	Angharad Richards	Birmingham	07.08.1993
46.06	Jenny Morley/Humberstone	Edinburgh	18.07.1981
45.80	Emily Steele	Wrexham	01.08.1992
45.74	Sian Lax	Telford	21.04.1996
44.66	Hilary Davies	Brecon	23.05.1993
44.40	Jayne Dawkins	Portsmouth	08.07.1983
43.56	Catherine Gunn	Melksham	14.06.1987
43.20	Krissy Owen	Colwyn Bay	11.06.1994

42.80	Jayne Berry	Brecon	21.05.1989
42.58	Amanda Horrex	Leicester	02.05.1982
42.38	Katrina Beedles	Cwmbran	05.09.1976
42.37	Natasha Campbell	Ashford	05.07.1998
42.16	Clare Lockwood	Bedford	04.07.1998
41.50	Sheila Evelyn	Cwmbran	27.08.1984
41.28	Cathy Middleton	Cardiff	07.08.1991
41.18	Joanne Smith/Davies	Colwyn Bay	16.06.1991
41.14	Emma Thorne	Ayr	13.08.1988
40.92	Amanda Barnes	Bristol	05.07.1986
40.19	Alison Siggery	Dublin, Ireland	08.08.1998
40.15	Rhian Hughes	Carmarthen	23.05.1998
40.12	Julie Fenwick	Belgium	25.07.1993
40.10	Lisa Hardwick	Sheffield	05.05.1991
40.06	Angela Thomas	Swansea	31.08.1987
39.96	Nicola Jupp	Bracknell	15.05.1994
39.66	Joanne Tubb	Cwmbran	06.08.1977
39.54	Alyson Hourihan	Cwmbran	20.07.1988
39.50	Margaret Rainbow	Cwmbran	29.06.1974
39.26	Sarah Rowe	Leamington	28.08.1982
39.06	Julie Tayler/Bowen	Swansea	12.04.1982
38.96	Katie England	Cheltenham	01.06.1986
38.94	Marita Rowlands	Cwmbran	03.06.1978
38.74	Loretta Hamilton	Enfield	23.08.1981
38.66	Rebecca Roles	Croydon	07.06.1998
38.54	Janet Beese	Cwmbran	27.07.1974
38.46	Jackie Gray	Swansea	28.05.1973
38.38	Stephanie Jones	Swansea	23.03.1983
38.36	Charlotte Rees	Neath	19.08.1998

Heptathlon (Events: 100 H, HJ, SP, 200m, LJ, JT, 800m)

5642 pts	Sarah Rowe *(14.21w,1.84, 09.61,24.89w,5.76w,33.10,2:10.91)*	Utrecht, Holland	23.08.1981
5424 pts	Lisa Griffiths/Gibbs *(13.96w,1.69,11.39,25.38w,5.87,36.30,2:27.94)*	Wrexham	01.08.1993
5389 pts	Sarah Bull/Owen *(14.5,1.75,12.20,25.4,5.72,29.50,2:17.6)*	Crystal Palace	15.08.1982
5186 pts	Rebecca Jones *(14.60,1.83,10.57,26.00,5.65,33.45,2:33.28)*	Arles, France	04.06.2000
4898 pts	Ruth Martin Jones/Howell *(14.8w,1.62,09.86,25.8,5.95,25.20,2:24.1)*	Birmingham	24.09.1978
4678w pts	Jane Shepherd *(15.22w,1.69, 09.19,27.03w,5.34w,32.50,2:32.72)*	Hull	23.06.1986
4601 pts	Liz Wren *(14.8,1.65,09.20,25.9,5.31,23.12,2:28.2)*	Birmingham	10.05.1981
4546 pts	Amanda Wale *(15.27,1.59,09.38, 26.29,5.12,26.70, 2:25.61)*	Wrexham	02.08.1998
4473 pts	Loretta Hamilton *(16.5,1.50,09.98,27.5,5.13,38.74,2:21.0)*	Enfield	23.08.1981
4456w pts	Teresa Andrews *(15.82w,1.71,10.55,26.54w,5.43,19.64,2:39.94)*	Wrexham	28.08.1994
4444 pts	Krissy Owen *(17.10w,1.63,11.68,27.80,5.08, 41.78,2:44.76)*	Wrexham	01.08.1993
4435w pts	Julia Charlton *(14.7w,1.65,08.63,27.2,5.61w,29.80,2:49.5)*	Swansea	15.05.1983
4357 pts	Lisa Thompson *(15.89,1.59,08.13, 27.02,52.3,24.19, 2:21.97)*	Wrexham	02.08.1998
4273 pts	Emily Stewart *(15.9,1.51,08.26,26.5,5.65,28.28,2:37.2)*	Corby	28.06.1992
4257w pts	Nicola Jupp *(15.76w,1.59, 09.16,27.33w,5.35w,28.70,2:44.20)*	Linwood	22.08.1993

Section 4

Welsh Championships Results (Track & Field) Senior Men and Women

The first events to be labelled "Welsh Championships" were races over 100 yards and one mile held in 1893. The 100 yards (or its metric equivalent the 100 metres), has been held every year since except during the two world wars. Between 1893 and 1906 races over 220 yards, 440 yards, 880 yards and 120 yards hurdles were occasionally held during open meetings and classified as Welsh Championships but there was no overall championships meeting. In 1907 a meeting was held at Newport Athletic Grounds, Rodney Parade, Newport, which was identified as the "First Welsh Amateur Championship Sports". It was promoted by the South Wales and Monmouthshire Executive Committee of the AAA which assumed responsibility for introducing Welsh Championships for athletics. The authority for this body to make that assumption may be open to question as its area of responsibility covered only South Wales, but in the absence of any alternative meetings claiming to be Welsh Championships the meeting of 1907 and its successors have been generally accepted as such.

In the following pages will be found a complete listing of Welsh Champions since 1893, or at least as complete a listing as it has been possible to discover. For the senior men's and senior women's championships the first three in each event (where known) are shown for each year. The athlete's name is followed by his/her club and performance. In the younger age groups the winners only are given. Imperial distances were used for all track events up to and including 1968 and metric distances have applied since 1969. The only exceptions to this were the men's steeplechase which was over 2 miles in 1946 but over 3000 metres after that, and the women's high hurdles which was at 80 metres until 1968 and 100 metres since.

Dates and venues of the senior championships are given below. These are for the main championships meeting only as occasionally some events were held at other times.

29/06/07	Newport Athletic Grounds
27/06/08	Newport Athletic Grounds
26/06/09	Newport Athletic Grounds
26/06/10	Barry Cricket Club
24/06/11	Barry Cricket Club
15/06/12	Newport Athletic Grounds
09/08/13	Newport Athletic Grounds
11/07/14	Cardiff Arms Park
04/09/20	Newport Athletic Grounds
16/07/21	Barry Athletic Club
19/08/22	Cardiff Arms Park
14/07/23	Cardiff Arms Park
24/05/24	Newport Athletic Grounds
18/07/25	Pontypool Park
02/08/26	Newport Athletic Grounds
06/06/27	Penarth Recreation Ground
16/06/28	Newport Athletic Ground
20/07/29	Cardiff Arms Park
09/06/30	Polo Grounds, Pontypool
00/00/31	Pontypool Park
23/07/32	St Helen's, Swansea
22/07/33	Abercarn Welfare Ground
30/06/34	Newport Athletic Grounds
29/06/35	Newport Athletic Grounds
27/06/36	Newport Athletic Grounds
26/06/37	Crymlyn Burrows
25/06/38	Taff Vale Park, Pontypridd
24/06/39	Newport Athletic Grounds
06/07/46	Sloper Road, Cardiff
28/06/47	Pontypool
19/06/48	Talbot Athletic Ground
25/06/49	Abertillery
24/06/50	St Helen's, Swansea
23/06/51	Maindy, Cardiff
07/06/52	Maindy, Cardiff
20/06/53	Maindy, Cardiff
19/06/54	Maindy, Cardiff
25/06/55	Maindy, Cardiff
23/06/56	Maindy, Cardiff
22/06/57	Maindy, Cardiff
21/06/58	Maindy, Cardiff
20/06/59	Maindy, Cardiff
25/06/60	Maindy, Cardiff
24/06/61	Maindy, Cardiff
23/06/62	Maindy, Cardiff
22/06/63	Maindy, Cardiff
20/06/64	Maindy, Cardiff
19/06/65	Maindy, Cardiff
25/06/66	Maindy, Cardiff
24/06/67	Maindy, Cardiff
22/06/68	Maindy, Cardiff
28/06/69	Cwmbran Stadium
20/07/70	Maindy, Cardiff
19/06/71	Maindy, Cardiff
24/06/72	Maindy, Cardiff
16/06/73	Cwmbran Stadium
15/06/74	Maindy, Cardiff
29/06/75	Cwmbran Stadium
20/06/76	Cwmbran Stadium
25/06/77	Cwmbran Stadium
04/06/78	Cwmbran Stadium
16/06/79	Cwmbran Stadium
21/06/80	Cwmbran Stadium
28/06/81	Cwmbran Stadium
26/06/82	Cwmbran Stadium
26/06/83	Morfa, Swansea
02/06/84	Cwmbran Stadium
22/06/85	Cwmbran Stadium
14/06/86	Cwmbran Stadium
20/06/87	Cwmbran Stadium
25/06/88	Morfa, Swansea
26/08/89	Leckwith, Cardiff
16/06/90	Morfa, Swansea
01/06/91	Leckwith, Cardiff
23/05/92	Leckwith, Cardiff
10/07/93	Cwmbran Stadium
18/06/94	Cwmbran Stadium
17/06/95	Spytty, Newport
01/06/96	Spytty, Newport
21/06/97	Cwmbran Stadium
20/06/98	Cwmbran Stadium
20/06/99	Eirias, Colwyn Bay
18/06/00	Cwmbran Stadium

The first championships for women were held in 1952. At first they were held with the men's championships but for a number of years separate championships were held. The following list indicates dates and venues of championships for women only.

27/06/70	Jenner Park, Barry
26/06/71	Jenner Park, Barry
00/00/72	Maindy, Cardiff
02/06/73	Cwmbran Stadium
01/06/74	Penylan, Brecon
07/06/75	Cwmbran Stadium
29/05/76	Cwmbran Stadium
04/06/77	Cwmbran Stadium
03/06/78	Cwmbran Stadium
02/06/79	Cwmbran Stadium
07/06/80	Cwmbran Stadium
06/06/81	Cwmbran Stadium
05/06/82	Cwmbran Stadium
11/06/83	Cwmbran Stadium
08/06/85	Morfa, Swansea

SENIOR MEN

100 yards

1893	Charles Thomas (Reading)	10.2				
1894	Charles Thomas (Reading)	10.2				
1895	Charles Thomas (Reading)					
1896	Charles Thomas (Reading)	10.2				
1897	Charles Thomas (Reading)	10.2				
1898	Fred Cooper (Bradford)	10.0				
1899	Charles Thomas (Oxf Univ)	10.2				
1900	Cyril R Lundie (Cardiff)	11.0				
1901	Cyril R Lundie (Roath)	10.6				
1902	Cyril R Lundie (Roath)	10.6				
1903	Cyril R Lundie (Roath)	10.4				
1904	Austin Miller (London AC)	10.2				
1905	P C Fenwick (Swansea AC)	10.2				
1906	C E Wilkie (Swansea AC)	10.2				
1907	Austin Miller (London AC)	10.6				
1908	Austin Miller (London AC)	10.4	J Gorman (Newport AC)		P C Fenwick (Highgate)	
1909	J Gorman (Newport AC)	10.6	Austin Miller (London AC)	10.6	R Woodruff (Machen FC)	10.7
1910	David Jacobs (Herne Hill)	10.6	R Woodruff (Machen FC)	10.7	J Gorman (Newport AC)	10.8
1911	David Jacobs (Herne Hill)	10.2				
1912	David Jacobs (Herne Hill)	10.6	T C Huss (Lynn AC)	11.6	only 2 athletes	
1913	David Jacobs (Herne Hill)	10.6	J E Jones (Poly H)			
1914	David Jacobs (Herne Hill)	10.5	Charles Neal (Polytechnic H)		A H Hurlow (Cathays H)	
1920	Arthur Holland (Newp AC)	10.8	Cecil Griffiths (Surrey AC)		Sidney Herring (Newport H)	
1921	Bryn Evans (Barry AC)	10.3	Sidney Herring (Newport H)		F D Blackford (Pontypool)	
1922	Rowe Harding (Swan CFC)	10.4	Arthur Holland (Newport AC)		JH Osborne-Jones (Aber Univ)	
1923	Will Owens (Port Talbot)	10.2	Rowe Harding (Swansea CFC)		JH Osborne-Jones (Edin Univ)	
1924	Will Owens (Port Talbot)	10.6	Stan Macey (Newport AC)		Sidney Herring (Newport AC)	
1925	Stan Macey (Newport AC)	10.0	H J Anderson (Newport H)		F C Williams (Newport AC)	
1926	Rowe Harding (Swan CFC)	11.0	H J Anderson (Newport H)		Stan Macey (Newport AC)	
1927	R H Thomas (Canton H)	10.6	Stan Macey (Newport AC)		Syd Dowen (Newport AC)	
1928	Erik M Hughes (Newport H)	10.4	D P Manley (Swansea CFC)		Ken Watkins (Newport AC)	
1929	H Anderson (Port Talbot)	10.2	Cyril Cupid (Swansea VAC)		J White (Roath)	
1930	Herbert Aubrey (Newp H)	10.4	Cyril Cupid (Swansea VAC)		Ken Hughes (Newport AC)	
1931	Cyril Cupid (Swansea VAC)	10.4	Herbert Aubrey (Newport H)		R H Thomas (Canton H)	
1932	Cyril Cupid (Swansea VAC)	10.2	Herbert Aubrey (Newport H)		A Gimblett (Swansea VAC)	
1933	Cyril Cupid (Swansea VAC)	10.2	William Stevenson (Swan VAC)		Eric Thomas (Newport AC)	
1934	Cyril Cupid (Swansea VAC)	9.8	Cyril Williams (Newport AC)		Wlliam Stevenson (Swansea VAC)	
1935	Stan Jones (Roath)	10.2	W L Thomas (Met Police)		William Stevenson (Swansea VAC)	
1936	Bernard George (Newp AC)	10.6	Jack Knowles (Newport AC)		W H Hopkins (Newport AC)	
1937	Nash Thomas (Cowbridge)	10.2	Stan Jones (Roath)		Cyril Cupid (Swansea VAC)	
1938	Nash Thomas (Melingriffith)	9.9	Walter Turner (Newport AC)	10.1	Cyril Cupid (Swansea VAC)	
1939	Kenneth Jenkins (Achilles)	10.2	Jack Matthews (Roath)		A H Loveluck (Roath)	
1946	Ken Jones (Newport AC)	10.9	Howell Hopkin (Mond AC)		Cyril Cupid (Birchfield)	
1947	Ken Jones (Newport AC)	10.2	Neville Jones (Llanelly GS)		W O Williams (Westbury)	
1948	Ken Jones (Newport AC)	9.9	John Madden (Polytechnic H)		Keith Maddocks (Port Talbot)	
1949	Ken Jones (Newport AC)	9.8	Howell Hopkin (Mond AC)		B K Palmer (Newport AC)	
1950	Gareth Morgan (Lincoln)	10.3	Bernard Ball (Roath)		Howell Hopkin (Mond AC)	
1951	Ken Jones (Newport AC)	10.3	Gareth Morgan (Bangor Univ)		Bernard Ball (Roath)	
1952	Ken Jones (Newport AC)	10.3	Gordon Wells (Cardiff Univ)	10.4	Bernard Ball (Roath)	10.5
1953	Ken Jones (Newport AC)	10.2	Bernard Ball (Roath)	10.4	D K James (Carmarthen)	10.5
1954	John Gilpin (Exeter)	10.2	Ken Jones (Newport AC	10.4	David Pulsford (Rhymney GS)	10.4
1955	John Gilpin (Exeter)	10.4	David Pugh (Roath)	10.5	Gareth Griffiths (Rhondda)	10.5
1956	Ron Jones (Birchgrove)	10.3	Nick Whitehead (Wrexham)	10.3	John Gilpin (Exeter)	10.4
1957	Nick Whitehead (Lough C)	10.1	Dewi Roberts (Beaumaris)	10.3	Jack Melen (Millfield)	10.4
1958	Nick Whitehead (Birchfield)	9.7	Ron Jones (Birchgrove)	9.9	Wyn Oliver (Llanelli GS)	10.0
1959	Ron Jones (Birchgrove)	9.8	Nick Whitehead (Birchfield)	9.9	Wyn Oliver (Llanelli GS)	10.0
1960	Nick Whitehead (Birchfield)	9.7	Berwyn Jones (Caerleon C)	10.1	David Griffiths (QPH)	10.1
1961	Berwyn Jones (Loughboro)	9.7	Dewi Bebb (Cardiff TC)	9.8	David Griffiths (QPH)	9.8
1962	Berwyn Jones (Birchgrove)	9.7	Lynn Davies (Cardiff TC)	9.9	David England (Small Heath)	9.9
1963	Ron Jones (Woodford Green)	9.5	Berwyn Jones (Birchfield)	9.5	Lynn Davies (Cardiff TC)	9.6
1964	Brian Coles (Birchgrove)	9.8	David England (Small Heath)	9.8	Terry Davies (Carmarthen)	9.9
1965	Ron Jones (Woodford Green)	9.5	Lynn Davies (Roath)	9.7	Terry Davies (Carmarthen)	9.8
1966	Ron Jones (Enfield)	9.6	Lynn Davies (Roath)	9.7	Terry Davies (Carmarthen	)9.7
1967	Ron Jones (Enfield)	9.7	Lynn Davies (Roath)	9.7	John J Williams (Maesteg S)	9.8
1968	Ron Jones (Enfield)	9.7	John J Williams (Maesteg)	9.8	Brian Coles (Birchgrove)	10.0

100 metres

1969	Terry Davies (Carmarthen)	10.8	John J Williams (Cardiff C)	10.8	Howard Davies (Birchfield)	10.9
1970	Ron Jones (Enfield)	10.6	Gary Vince (Cardiff)	10.7	Terry Davies (Carmarthen)	10.7
1971	John J Williams (Swansea)	10.8	Gary Vince (Cardiff)	10.8	Ron Jones (Enfield)	11.0
1972	Hywel Griffiths (Swansea)	10.8	Steve Ware (Swansea)	10.9	Brian Griffiths (TVH)	11.1
1973	Gary Vince (Cardiff)	10.4	Ron Griffiths (Luton)	10.5	Hywel Griffiths (Swansea)	10.6
1974	David Roberts (Cardiff)	10.5	Ron Griffiths (Luton)	10.6	Gareth Edwards (Newport)	10.7
1975	Gareth Edwards (Newport)	10.7	Ron Griffiths (Luton)	10.8	Peter Keeling (Newport)	11.0
1976	David Roberts (Cardiff)	10.5	Vic Martindale (Bristol)	10.8	Gareth Edwards (Newport)	10.9
1977	David Roberts (Cardiff)	10.7	Vic Martindale (Bristol)	10.9	Paul Evans (Cardiff)	11.1
1978	David Roberts (Cardiff)	10.9	Mal Owen (Carmarthen)	11.2	Vic Martindale (Bristol)	11.2
1979	Mal Owen (Carmarthen)	11.1	Stephen Thomas (Cardiff)	11.2	Stephen James (Wolves)	11.3
1980	Jon Stark (Edinburgh)	10.85	Jon Marsden (Norfolk)	11.00	Vic Martindale (Bristol)	11.03
1981	David Roberts (Cardiff)	10.66	Jon Stark (Edinburgh)	10.75	Vic Martindale (Bristol)	10.87
1982	David Roberts (Cardiff)	11.01	Mark Owen (Wolves)	11.04	Nigel Walker (Cardiff)	11.16
1983	Mark Owen (Wolves)	10.6	Mal Owen (Newham)	10.6	Haydn Wood (Newport)	10.9
1984	Nigel Walker (Cardiff)	11.30	Colin Jackson (Cardiff)	11.41	Jon Thompson (Cardiff)	11.75
1985	Colin Jackson (Cardiff)	11.01	Mal Owen (Newham)	11.16	David Radford (Oswestry)	11.27
1986	Colin Jackson (Cardiff)	10.53	Nigel Walker (Cardiff)	10.59	Richard Moore (Cardiff)	10.74
1987	Paul Gray (Cardiff)	11.17	Stu Colquhoun-Lynn (Sale)	11.19	Richard Moore (Cardiff)	11.19
1988	David Winterton (Newport)	10.8	Jon Thompson (Wolves)	10.9	Arthur Emyr (Swansea)	11.0
1989	Nigel Walker (Cardiff)	10.35	Mark Owen (Wolves)	10.69	Mal Owen (Newham)	10.74
1990	Colin Jackson (Cardiff)	10.7	Steve Rees (Swansea)	11.0	Michael Williams (T Solent)	11.0
1991	Colin Jackson (Brecon)	10.93	Steve Rees (Swansea)	11.07	Jamie Baulch (Newport)	11.11
1992	Colin Jackson (Brecon)	10.66	Jamie Baulch (Newport)	10.91	Paul Fisher (Swansea)	11.01
1992	Colin Jackson (Brecon)	10.66	Jamie Baulch (Newport)	10.91	Paul Fisher (Swansea)	11.01
1993	Kevin Williams (Cardiff)	10.78	Jamie Baulch (Cardiff)	10.90	Pete Maitland (Carmarthen)	10.94
1994	Tremayne Rutherford (Card)	10.66	Kevin Williams (Cardiff)	10.73	Pete Maitland (Swansea)	10.75
1995	Kevin Williams (Cardiff)	10.6	Pete Maitland (Swansea)	10.7	Doug Turner (Cardiff)	10.7
1996	Tremayne Rutherford (Card)	10.96	Jamie Henthorn (Carmarthen)	11.10	Christian Malcolm (Cardiff)	11.18
1997	Jamie Henthorn (T Solent)	10.51	Doug Turner (Cardiff)	10.52	Kevin Williams (Cardiff)	10.53
1998	Colin Jackson (Brecon)	10.47	Christian Malcolm (Cardiff)	10.58	Kevin Williams (Cardiff)	10.68
1999	Jamie Henthorn (T Solent)	11.0	Seriashe Childs (Brecon)	11.6	David Lawson (Telford)	11.6
2000	Christian Malcolm (Cardiff)	10.4	Tim Benjamin (Cardiff)	10.6	Jamie Henthorn (T Solent)	10.8

220 yards

1905	A Griffiths (Abergavenny)	23.4			
1906	P C Fenwick (Swansea AC)	23.8			
1907	J Gorman (Newport AC)	23.6			
1908	J Gorman (Newport AC)	23.0			
1909	J Gorman (Newport AC)	25.0	R A Gibbs (Cardiff FC)		C H Wyatt (Abergavenny AA)
1910	J Gorman (Newport AC)	25.2	H N King (Newport AC)		D R Richards (Swansea AC)
1911	David Jacobs (Herne Hill)	24.5			
1912	David Jacobs (Herne Hill)	23.6	W L D Collins (Roath)		F G Frazer (Abergavenny H)
1913	David Jacobs (Herne Hill)	24.5	D R Richards (Swansea AC)		H I James (Newport AC)
1914	Charles Neal (Polytechnic)	23.5	A E Morgan (Newport AC)	23.8	L L Fullerton (Whitchurch FC)
1920	event not held				
1921	Cecil Griffiths (Surrey)	23.0	Bryn Evans (Cardiff Univ)		Sidney Herring (Newport H)
1922	Arthur Holland (Newp AC)	24.6	George Virgin (Roath)	24.8	Fred Phillips (Newport AC)
1923	Rowe Harding (Swan CFC)	23.9	T H Venables (Cardiff AC)		J H Osborne-Jones (Edin Univ)
1924	Reg Sowden (Roath)	23.5	H J Anderson (Newport H)		Will Owen (P Talbot YMCA)
1925	H J Anderson (Newport H)	23.8	Stan Macey (Newport AC)		S Purcell (Swansea Valley)
1926	H J Anderson (Newport H)	23.0	Rowe Harding (Swansea CFC)		Stan Macey (Newport AC)
1927	Stan Macey (Newport AC)	24.2	Syd Dowen (Newport AC)		Claude Blake (Roath)
1928	Erik M Hughes (Newp H)	23.4	Ken Watkins (Newport AC)		Cyril Howell (Roath)
1929	Ronnie Boon (Roath)	23.4	D J Gimblett (Llanelly YMCA)		Cyril Howell (Roath)
1930	Cyril Cupid (Swansea Vall)	24.2	Ken Hughes (Newport AC)		Cyril Howell (Roath)
1931	Cyril Cupid (Swansea Vall)	23.2	Ronnie Boon (Roath)		Ken Watkins (Newport AC)
1932	Cyril Cupid (Swansea Vall)	23.6	Erik Hughes (Newport H)		Harold Trueman (Roath)
1933	Cyril Cupid (Swansea Vall)	23.4	Eric Thomas (Newport AC)		Harry L Uzzell (Newport AC)
1934	Cyril Cupid (Swansea Vall)	23.2	C J E Betty (Achilles)		A J F Churchill (Ilford)
1935	Ted Davies (Achilles)	22.6	Jack Knowles (Achilles)		Bernard George (Newport AC)
1936	Jack Knowles (Newport AC)	23.0	W H Hopkins (Newport AC)		J Edwards (Cardiff Univ)
1937	Ted Davies (Achilles)	23.2	Jack Gratton (Neath AC)		Stan Jones (Roath)
1938	Kenneth Jenkins (Oxf Univ)	22.2	V J Harries (Cardiff Univ)		Jack Gratton (Neath AC)
1939	Kenneth Jenkins (Oxf Univ)	23.0	Jack Knowles (Newport AC)		Jack Matthews (Bridgend CS)
1946	Ken Jones (Newport AC)	24.0	A L Carr (Barry AC)		Cyril Cupid (Birchfield)
1947	Ken Jones (Newport AC)	24.1	B Edwards (Caerleon College)		Ken Alun Jones (Newport AC)
1948	Ken Jones (Newport AC)	23.1	A L Carr (Unattached		Howell Hopkin (Mond AC)
1949	Ken Jones (Newport AC)	22.5	J J Brown (St Marys Hospital)		P L Lillington (Polytechnic)

1950	Reg Perry (HopkinsonsElec)	23.3	S R Richardson (Achilles)		Reg Snow (Roath)	
1951	Ken Jones (Newport AC)	23.2	Bernard Ball (Roath)		Reg Snow (Roath)	
1952	Ken Jones (Newport AC)	23.1	Reg Snow (Roath)	23.2	Russell Davies (Carmarthen)	23.4
1953	Ken Jones (Newport AC)	22.7	John Huins (Cardiff Univ)	22.8	Reg Snow (Roath)	23.3
1954	Ken Jones (Newport AC)	22.5	Peter Phillips (London Univ)	22.7	Gwilym Roberts (Newport)	22.9
1955	John Gilpin (Exeter)	23.5	P T Davies (Belgrave)	23.8	David Pugh (Roath)	23.9
1956	Gwilym Roberts (Newport)	22.3	Nick Whitehead (Wrexham)	22.9	Clive Phillips (Roath)	23.0
1957	Nick Whitehead (Lough C)	22.8	Jack Melen (Millfield)	22.9	John Gilpin (Exeter)	23.5
1958	Nick Whitehead (Birchfield)	22.1	Ron Jones (Birchgrove)	22.8	Wyn Oliver (Llanelli GS)	23.5
1959	Ron Jones (Birchgrove)	22.0	Nick Whitehead (B'field)	22.1	Wyn Oliver (Llanelli GS)	22.3
1960	Nick Whitehead (Birchfield)	21.7	David Griffiths (QPH)	22.6	John C Jones (Roath)	22.6
1961	David Griffiths (QPH)	22.2	Berwyn Jones (Loughboro)	22.5	Dewi Bebb (Cardiff TC)	22.5
1962	Berwyn Jones (Birchgrove)	21.8	David England (Sm Heath)	22.1	Bill Morris (Card TC)	22.2
1963	Ron Jones (Wood Green)	21.5	Berwyn Jones (Birchfield)	21.6	David England (Sm Heath)	22.0
1964	David England (Sm Heath)	22.4	Derek Pugh (Halesowen)	22.8	Keri Jones (Cardiff TC)	23.0
1965	Ron Jones (Wood Green)	21.8	Terry Davies (Carmarthen)	22.1	Howard Davies (Swan Un)	22.3
1966	Terry Davies (Carmarthen)	21.6	Keri Jones (Cardiff TC)	21.8	Peter Carvell (Loughboro)	22.4
1967	Terry Davies (Carmarthen)	22.3	Nicholas Williams (Carm)	22.6	Eirwyn Jones (Swansea)	22.7
1968	John J Williams (Maesteg S)	22.4	William Williams (Birchfield)	23.1	E J Jenkins (Wirral)	23.8

200 metres

1969	John J Williams (Card CE)	21.9	Terry Davies (Carmarthen)	22.0	Howard Davies (Birchfield)	23.1
1970	Ron Jones (Enfield)	22.2	Paul Briggs (Gilwern)	22.7	Gary Vince (Cardiff)	22.9
1971	John J Williams (Swansea)	21.7	Steve Ware (Swansea)	22.4	Ron Jones (Enfield)	22.4
1972	Steve Ware (Swansea)	22.0	Hywel Griffiths (Swansea)	22.3	Brian Williamson (Cardiff)	22.8
1973	Steve Ware (Swansea)	22.4	Ron Griffiths (Luton)	22.4	Brian Williamson (Cardiff)	23.0
1974	David Roberts (Cardiff)	21.7	Ron Griffiths (Luton)	21.9	Ninian Davies (Cardiff)	24.8
1975	Peter Keeling (Newport)	22.2	Ron Griffiths (Luton)	22.2	Kevin Davies (Wolves)	22.5
1976	David Roberts (Cardiff)	21.8	Berwyn Price (Cardiff)	22.3	Gerald Hedges (Croesyceiliog)	22.3
1977	Vic Martindale (Bristol)	22.2	Ron Griffiths (Luton)	22.3	Paul Evans (Cardiff)	22.3
1978	David Roberts (Cardiff)	21.7	Derek Morgan (Aberdare)	21.7	David Morgan (Swansea)	22.3
1979	Stephen Thomas (Cardiff)	22.4	Stephen James (Wolves)	22.5	Derek Morgan (Cardiff)	22.5
1980	Jon Stark (Edinburgh)	22.2	Jeff Griffiths (Swansea)		Jon Marsden (Norfolk)	
1981	Jon Stark (Edinburgh)	21.75	Tim Jones (Newport)	21.85	Jon Marsden (Norfolk)	22.03
1982	Mark Owen (Wolves)	21.69	Tim Jones (Newport)	22.24	Huw Thomas (Alsager Col)	22.52
1983	Nigel Walker (Cardiff)	21.8	Mark Owen (Wolves)	21.9	Steve Thomas (Cheltenham)	22.3
1984	Neil Bowd (Swansea)	22.43	Jon Thompson (Cardiff)	22.52	Mike Owen (Carmarthen)	22.81
1985	Richard Wintle (Swansea)	22.6	Jon Thompson (Cardiff)	22.6	Mike Owen (Carmarthen)	22.7
1986	Mark Owen (Wolves)	21.96	Phil Harries (Derby)	22.03	Jon Thompson (Wolves)	22.09
1987	Phil Harries (Derby)	21.54	David Winterton (Newport)	22.01	Jon Thompson (Wolves)	22.11
1988	Colin Jackson (Cardiff)	21.1	Phil Harries (Derby)	21.4	David Winterton (Newport)	21.6
1989	Colin Jackson (Cardiff)	21.18	Mark Owen (RAF)	22.13	Doug Turner (Newport)	22.29
1990	Michael Williams (T Solent)	21.55	Doug Turner (Newport)	22.13	Steve Rees (Swansea)	22.20
1991	Jamie Baulch (Newport)	21.95	Steve Rees (Swansea)	22.16	Doug Turner (Newport)	22.30
1992	Jamie Baulch (Newport)	21.38	Gareth Davies (Sale)	21.65	Mark Owen (RAF)	21.83
1993	Jamie Baulch (Cardiff)	21.46	John Bowen (Cardiff)	21.78	Gary Hockaday (Deeside)	21.98
1994	Jamie Baulch (Cardiff)	21.85	Bryn Middleton (Cardiff)	22.58	Neil Powell (Cardiff)	22.74
1995	Doug Turner (Cardiff)	21.58	Jamie Baulch (Cardiff)	21.72	Chris Millard (Clevedon)	22.92
1996	Doug Turner (Cardiff)	21.99	David Jacobs (Rhondda)	22.91	Chris Millard (Swansea)	23.00
1997	Christian Malcolm (Cardiff)	21.41	Doug Turner (Cardiff)	21.59	Richard Wintle (Swansea)	22.58
1998	Christian Malcolm (Cardiff)	21.01	Jamie Baulch (Cardiff)	21.07	Pete Maitland (Newham)	21.84
1999	Jamie Henthorn (T Solent)	22.82	David Lawson (Telford)	23.26	Chris Millard (Weston)	23.40
2000	Christian Malcolm (Cardiff)	21.09	Tim Benjamin (Cardiff)	21.21	Kevin Williams (Cardiff)	22.14

440 yards

1897	R F Leonard (Newport AC)	53.5				
1898	R F Leonard (Newport AC)	52.8				
1899	R F Leonard (Newport AC)	52.6				
1900	event not held					
1901	E R Thomas (Roath)	53.8				
1902	Will Phillips (Swansea CFC)	53.6				
1903	Ed Whale (Canton RFC)	53.0				
1904	AMJ Griffiths (Swan CFC)	53.5				
1905	AMJ Griffiths (Swan CFC)	54.0				
1906	H N King (Newport AC)	55.0				
1907	J Gorman (Newport AC)	54.0				
1908	Harry Uzzell (Newport AC)	54.2	J S Pow (Cardiff)			
1909	H T Whittaker (Llanishen)	55.4	Eddie Ace (Swansea CFC)		Ben Uzzell (Newport AC)	
1910	David Jacobs (Herne Hill)	54.4	A D Givons (Newport AC)		R W Corfield (Swansea AC)	
1911	David Jacobs (Herne Hill)	55.0	W L D Collins (Newport AC)			

1912	Ben Uzzell (Newport AC)	55.6	W L D Collins (Roath)	55.7	F G Frazer (Abergavenny H)	
1913	David Jacobs (Herne Hill)	53.2	H T Whitaker (Newport AC)	54.8	C B Francis (Newport AC)	
1914	David Jacobs (Herne Hill)	51.3	A G Jones (Llanishen AC)	54.8	A J Burland (Cathays H)	
1920	Cecil Griffiths (Surrey AC)	51.4	Fred Phillips (Newport AC)	55.0	George Curtis (Swan CFC)	57.6
1921	Cecil Griffiths (Surrey AC)	49.8				
1922	Cecil Griffiths (Surrey AC)	54.4	Fred Phillips (Newport AC)		G F Williams (Cambridge Univ)	
1923	Cecil Griffiths (Surrey AC)	54.0	W B Nicholas (Newport AC)		H W Macey (Grange YMCA)	
1924	Cecil Griffiths (Surrey AC)	55.0	H A Young (Abertillery AA)		JTP Marshall (Spillers AC)	
1925	Harold Gee (Roath)	54.4	H W Macey (Grange Baptist AC)		Gwyn Lewis (Roath)	
1926	Erik Hughes (Newport H)	54.2	Claude Blake (Roath)		L H Howells (Aberystwyth Univ)	
1927	Erik Hughes (Newport AC)	54.8	Cecil Griffiths (Surrey AC)		Claude Blake (Roath)	
1928	Erik Hughes (Newport AC)	52.0	Llewellyn Uzzell (Newp AC)		G E Bradbeer (ATS Beachley)	
1929	Erik Hughes (Newport AC)	51.8	W H Witchell (Bangor Univ)		Llewellyn Uzzell (Newport AC)	
1930	Erik Hughes (Newport AC)	51.0	Alec Watson (Roath)		Ken Watkins (Newport AC)	
1931	Erik Hughes (Newport AC)	53.4	W H Witchell (Bangor Univ)		Alec Mackay (Roath)	
1932	W H Witchell (Newport AC)	52.4	Cyril Howell (Roath)		Llewellyn Uzzell (Newport AC)	
1933	Trevor Jones (Newport AC)	52.2	Erik Hughes (Newport AC)		Alec Watson (Roath)	
1934	Peter Fraser (Achilles)	50.6	Llewellyn Uzzell (Newport AC)		Trevor Jones (Newport AC)	
1935	Ivor Gaylard (Elyn AC)	52.6	Llewellyn Uzzell (Newport AC)		J F F Giddings (Highgate H)	
1936	Ivor Gaylard (Elyn AC)	51.2	I J Owen (Penrhys AC)		G Jenkins (CAVH)	
1937	Ivor Gaylard (Elyn AC)	52.0	I J Owen (Cardiff Univ)		T T Simmonds (Met Police)	
1938	Roy Williams (Port Talbot)	51.4	Dennis Ford (Roath)	51.5	Tim Cavanagh (Cardiff Gas)	
1939	Edward Jones (Roath)	54.0	I J Owen (Cardiff Univ)		Roy Williams (Port Talbot)	
1946	Jim Alford (Roath)	54.0	E B Dawson (Bristol Univ)		A G Toozer (Roath)	
1947	J E Bibbs (Llanelly GS)	54.9	Roy Williams (Port Talbot)		R Cotterill (Reading AC)	
1948	Ernest Harwood (Roath)	55.0	J E Bibbs (RAF)		A J Jennings (Unattached)	
1949	Ernest Harwood (Roath)	52.0	Ken Davies (Hendy AC)		J B Thomas (Mitcham AC)	
1950	J E Bibbs (Carmarthen TC)	52.0	Ken Davies (RTB)	53.0	Harold Steggles (Roath)	
1951	Harold Steggles (Roath)	52.4	J E Bibbs (Trinity College)		Roy F Rumsam (Roath)	
1952	John Collins (Port Talbot)	51.7	J S F Pode (Oxford Univ)	52.0	J E Bibbs (Coventry G)	52.1
1953	Harold Steggles (Roath)	51.3	D H Jones (London Univ)	51.4	Denis Murphy (Card Univ)	51.6
1954	Peter Phillips (Polytechnic)	50.2	Harold Steggles (Aberystwyth)	50.6	Ron Griffiths (Neath AC)	52.7
1955	Anthony Ford (Welsh Reg)	50.5	John Collins (Port Talbot)	52.3	C F Arlett (Aberyst Univ)	52.4
1956	Anthony Ford (Birchgrove)	50.6	Peter Phillips (Polytech H)	51.0	Jim Usoro (Roath)	51.5
1957	David Pulsford (Mon TC)	50.3	Anthony Ford (Milocarian)	51.4	G H Davies (Bristol)	51.8
1958	David Jones (Birm Univ)	50.0	R Davies (Carmarthen)	51.1	William Griffiths (Lond Un)	51.6
1959	William Griffiths (Lond Un)	50.9	Malcolm Jones (Barnet)		David Jones (Birchfield)	
1960	Pat Jones (Ilford)	49.8	Malcolm Jones (Barnet)	49.9	Wyn Oliver (Carmarthen)	50.8
1961	Anthony Burgess (Poly)	48.7	David Williams (Birchgrove)	50.5	John Styles (QPH)	52.3
1962	Allan Skirving (St Julians)	49.3	Pat Jones (Ilford)	49.4	Thomas Phillips (Bangor Un)	51.4
1963	Pat Jones (Ilford)	48.4	John Styles (QPH)	49.8	Peter Williams (Aberyst Un)	50.6
1964	Pat Jones (Ilford)	49.1	Peter Williams (Portsmouth)	49.1	Derek Pugh (Halesowen)	49.5
1965	Pat Jones (Ilford)	48.4	Peter Williams (Portsmouth)	48.9	Allan Skirving (Newport)	50.2
1966	Pat Jones (Ilford)	49.0	Gwynne Griffiths (Trinity)	49.0	Derek Bevan (Cardiff TC)	49.5
1967	Gwynne Griffiths (Carm)	48.8	Peter Williams (Portsmouth)	49.9	Wyn Leyshon (Neath GS)	51.3
1968	John Robertson (Barry)	48.4	Gwynne Griffiths (Wolves)	50.4	Mike Delaney (RAF)	51.0

400 metres

1969	Gwynne Griffiths (Wolves)	47.3	John Robertson (Barry)	48.0	Haydn Curran (Carmarthen)	49.5
1970	Haydn Curran (Carmarthen)	48.5	Keith Lancey (Swansea)	49.1	Alun Roper (Swansea)	50.1
1971	David LeMasurier (Cardiff)	48.9	Michael Lewis (Carmarthen)	49.0	Mike Godfrey (Cardiff)	50.2
1972	Gwynne Griffiths (Wolves)	49.2	Mike Delaney (Cardiff)	49.9	Tony Elgie (Cardiff)	50.5
1973	Mike Delaney (Cardiff)	49.0	Michael Lewis (Carmarthen)	50.1	Mike Godfrey (Cardiff)	52.2
1974	Mike Delaney (Cardiff)	47.7	Wynford Leyshon (Cardiff)	48.5	Emlyn Evans (Leicester)	51.8
1975	Colin O'Neill (Bristol)	49.1	Wynford Leyshon (Cardiff)	49.5	Keith Lancey (Swansea)	50.3
1976	Jeff Griffiths (Swansea)	47.1	Andy Williams (Cardiff)	47.2	Colin O'Neill (Bristol)	47.8
1977	Andy Williams (Cardiff)	49.1	Wynford Leyshon (Cardiff)	49.9	Martin Rowlands (Liverpool)	50.3
1978	Jeff Griffiths (Swansea)	47.6	Mike Delaney (Cardiff)	48.2	Wynford Leyshon (Cardiff)	49.2
1979	Mike Delaney (Cardiff)	49.40	Derek Morgan (Cardiff)	49.80	Ian Davies (Bridgend)	50.13
1980	Alan Tinsley (Cardiff)	49.40	Mike Delaney (Cardiff)	49.80	Mark Thomas (Bristol)	
1981	Jeff Griffiths (Swansea)	48.62	Mark Thomas (Bristol)	49.30	Alan Tinsley (Cardiff)	49.80
1982	Malcolm James (Cardiff)	48.38	Mark Thomas (Bristol)	48.50	Jeff Griffiths (Swansea)	48.82
1983	Ben Jones (Newport)	48.8	Mark Thomas (Cardiff)	48.8	Russ Williams (R Navy)	49.2
1984	Roger Barrett (Carmarthen)	47.84	Gareth Brown (Cardiff)	49.11	Adrian Hardman (Cardiff)	49.29
1985	Mark Thomas (Cardiff)	48.1	Haydn Wood (Cardiff)	48.7	Martyn Bowen (Notts)	49.3
1986	Mark Thomas (Cardiff)	48.15	Martyn Bowen (Oxford Un)	48.76	Roger Barrett (Carmarthen)	48.95
1987	Roger Barrett (Carmarthen)	48.83	Martyn Bowen (Notts)	48.97	Paul Roberts (Colwyn Bay)	49.03
1988	Roger Barrett (Carmarthen)	49.5	Steve Partridge (Swansea)	49.8	Robert Ellis (Swansea)	49.9
1989	Phil Harvey (Cardiff)	49.11	Paul Roberts (Cardiff)	49.19	Derek Lake (Crickhowell)	49.96
1990	Paul Roberts (Cardiff)	48.3	Ray Blaber (Swindon)	48.4	John Bowen (Beddau)	49.3
1991	Shaun Lewis (Swansea)	49.01	Ray Blaber (Cardiff)	49.11	Nick Hamilton (T Solent)	49.45

1992	Joe Lloyd (Cheltenham)	48.70	Jeremy Frankel (Colwyn B)	49.08	Nick Davies (O Gaytonian)	49.36
1993	Gareth Davies (Sale)	47.42	Iwan Thomas (Newham)	48.04	James Weston (Cardiff)	48.86
1994	Iwan Thomas (Newham)	47.09	Gareth Davies (Sale)	48.09	Joe Lloyd (Cheltenham)	48.27
1995	Iwan Thomas (Newham)	46.40	James Weston (Cardiff)	48.72	Joe Lloyd (Swansea)	49.16
1996	Joe Lloyd (Swansea)	48.29	David Williams (Swansea)	48.43	Garry Batte (Barry)	49.49
1997	Huw Bannister (Llanelli)	48.10	Joe Lloyd (Swansea)	48.30	Mark Ponting (Cardiff)	48.40
1998	Iwan Thomas (Newham)	45.45	Paul Gray (Cardiff)	47.49	Joe Lloyd (Swansea)	48.77
1999	Matthew Elias (Cardiff)	49.1	Gethin Thomas (Trafford)	50.0	James Weston (Cardiff)	50.5
2000	Jamie Baulch (Cardiff)	46.35	Chris Page (Cardiff)	47.51	Darrell Maynard (Abertillery)	48.18

880 yards

1899	A Williams (Usk)	2:02.0				
1900	event not held					
1901	event not held					
1902	event not held					
1903	A S D Smith (Bristol AC)	2:05.0				
1904	T Anzaney (Cardiff H)	2:05.2	W A Walkley (St Mellons)		D H Griffiths (Abergavenny)	
1905	A S D Smith (Cambridge Un)	2:01.6				
1906	A S D Smith (Cambridge Un)	1:59.4				
1907	Harry Uzzell (Newport AC)	2:10.0				
1908	J R Jenkins (St Martins)	2:05.6				
1909	Eddie Ace (Swansea CFC)	2:07.8	J O Jones (Abergavenny H)		W Sharpe (Newport H)	
1910	Eddie Ace (Swansea CFC)	2:06.8	J O Jones (Abergavenny H)		W Sharpe (Newport H)	
1911	Eddie Ace (Swansea CFC)	2:09.8				
1912	F H Johnson (Llantarnam)	2:06.8	A E Marshall (Newport H)	2:08.8		
1913	C B Francis (Newport AC)	2:06.8	H B Nott (Newport AC)		A E Marshall (Newport AC)	
1914	F H Johnson (Newport H)	2:06.0	William Hart (Cathays H)		C B Francis (Newport AC)	
1920	event not held					
1921	B Harrhy (Chepstow H)	2:07.0	F G G Pinchin (Newport H)		C Morgan (Newport H)	
1922	Cecil Griffiths (Surrey)	1:59.2	B Harrhy (Newport H)		D J P Richards (Port Talbot)	
1923	Cecil Griffiths (Surrey)	2:07.0	A W C Johnson (Cardiff Univ)		F J Worrell (Spillers AC)	
1924	Cecil Griffiths (Surrey)	2:05.8	B Kinchington (Newport H)		L O Lyne (Lancs Fusiliers)	
1925	Gwyn Lewis (Roath)	2:06.4	Ivor Thomas (Newport AC)		T J Williams (Shirenewton)	
1926	Gwyn Lewis (Roath)	1:59.0	Erik Hughes (Newport H)		P J Ryan (Roath)	
1927	Cecil Griffiths (Surrey)	2:06.4	Gwyn Lewis (Roath)		Erik Hughes (Newport AC)	
1928	Gwyn Lewis (Roath)	1:59.8	Ivor Thomas (Achilles)		Tom Thomas (Newport H)	
1929	Reg Thomas (RAF)	1:58.6	Gwyn Lewis (Roath)		A Williams (Newport H)	
1930	Reg Thomas (RAF)	2:00.0	Frank Owen (Abergele)		E G Armstead (Newport AC)	
1931	Reg Thomas (RAF)	2:01.6	Frank Owen (Abergele)		Trevor Jones (Spillers AC)	
1932	Gwyn Lewis (Roath)	2:01.0	Trevor Jones (Spillers AC)		J G Griffiths (Salford)	
1933	F A Stanley (Newport AC)	2:02.4	Trevor Jones (Newport AC)		Ken Harris (Roath)	
1934	Jim Alford (Roath)	1:57.0	S J Hill (Milocarian)		F A Stanley (Newport AC)	
1935	Jim Alford (Roath)	1:58.0	Emlyn James (Roath)		Graham Cumming (Cardiff TC)	
1936	Jim Alford (Roath)	1:56.4	J M Burch (Melingriffith)		C H Critchley (Newport H)	
1937	Jim Alford (Roath)	1:57.4	Tim Cavanagh (Cardiff Gas)		Emlyn James (Roath)	
1938	Jim Alford (Roath)	1:58.0	R G James (Mond AC)	1:59.4	Tim Cavanagh (Cardiff Gas)	
1939	Tim Cavanagh (Cardiff Gas)	2:04.2	Howard Davies (Neath AC)		R G Watkins (Saunders AC)	
1946	Jim Alford (Roath)	2:03.8	D Butcher (Cambridge Univ)		H Thomas (Newport H)	
1947	Brian Williams (Roath)	2:08.5	Doug Rees (Portsmouth)		Howard Davies (Neath AC)	
1948	Brian Williams (Roath)	2:02.5	Glyn Matthews (Roath)		Doug Rees (Portsmouth)	
1949	Brian Williams (Roath)	2:01.0	J B Thomas (Mitcham)		C Derek Williams (Reading)	
1950	Mel Litchfield (Cardiff TC)	2:00.3	R G Williams (Roath)	2:01.0	Glan Williams (Cardiff Univ)	
1951	Glan Williams (Cardiff Un)	2:03.0	Brian Williams (Roath)		Mel Litchfield (Cardiff TC)	
1952	Peter Griggs (Cov Godiva)	2:00.1	Glan Williams (Cardiff Un)	2:01.1	Derek Clarke (Penarth)	2:01.4
1953	David Richards (Roath)	1:58.0	Peter Griggs (Cov Godiva)	1:59.3	Roy Adams (Penarth)	2:00.4
1954	Glan Williams (Belgrave)	1:59.7	Derek Clarke (Barry)	1:59.7	W B Evans (Hendy)	2:03.4
1955	Harry Packer (Rhondda V)	1:58.9	A J Menlove (Farnham)	1:58.9	Ray Billington (Rhyl)	2:00.1
1956	Harry Packer (Rhondda V)	1:56.4	Norman Horrell (Rhondda V)	1:56.8	A J Menlove (Farnham)	1:57.6
1957	Ray Billington (Rhyl)	1:56.9	I Trevor-Owen (Manchester)	1:58.3	David Jones (Birm Univ)	1:59.6
1958	Norman Horrell (Rhon V)	1:54.7	Ray Billington (Rhyl)	1:55.1	Peter Griffin (Westbury)	1:55.7
1959	Peter Griffin (Westbury)	1:54.9	Tony Jones (Bridgend)	1:55.3	Ray Billington (Liv Pemb)	1:56.2
1960	Tony Jones (Bridgend)	1:53.0	Peter Griffin (Westbury)	1:53.6	Viv Blackwell (Wrexham)	1:55.7
1961	Tony Jones (Bridgend)	1:52.9	Viv Blackwell (Wrexham)	1:53.0	Peter Griffin (Westbury)	1:53.8
1962	Tony Jones (Roath)	1:52.9	David Gravell (Merthyr)	1:54.9	M Johns (Birchgrove)	2:00.5
1963	John Williams (Birchfield)	1:51.6	David Gravell (Merthyr)	1:55.8	Peter Griffin (Westbury)	1:58.4
1964	Tony Jones (Roath)	1:54.9	Bill Stitfall (Birchgrove)	1:57.0	David Gravell (Merthyr)	1:57.7
1965	Tony Jones (Roath)	1:57.0	Wyn Shearn (Croesyceiliog)	1:57.7	Terry James (Ardwyn GS)	1:58.6
1966	Tony Harris (Mitcham)	1:53.8	Ken Bennett (Birchgrove)	1:55.9	Wyn Shearn (Portsmouth)	1:56.4
1967	Bob Adams (Bromsgrove)	1:54.0	Gwynn Davis (Aberystwyth)	1:54.9	Elfyn Thomas (Carmarthen)	1:55.0
1968	Bob Adams (Bromsgrove)	1:52.9	Paul Kelly (Sale)	1:55.3	John Powell (Cardiff TC)	1:56.4

800 metres

1969	Bob Adams (Polytechnic)	1:49.5	Peter Lewis (Birchfield)	1:49.5	Graham Spencer (Cardiff)	1:54.9
1970	Bob Adams (Polytechnic)	1:52.5	Bob Maplestone (Cardiff)	1:53.4	David LeMasurier (Cardiff)	1:54.9
1971	Bob Adams (Polytechnic)	1:53.3	Tony Elgie (Cardiff)	1:54.2	Keith Jones (Cardiff)	1:54.7
1972	David LeMasurier (Cardiff)	1:55.7	Alun Roper (Swansea)	1:56.1	Vince James (Wolves)	1:56.7
1973	Richard Yarrow (Cardiff)	1:53.7	Alun Roper (Swansea)	1:53.7	Peter Lewis (Birchfield)	1:54.8
1974	Alun Roper (Swansea)	1:52.0	Tony Dyke (Swansea)	1:52.4	David LeMasurier (Cardiff)	1:54.3
1975	Richard Yarrow (Cardiff)	1:54.4	Tony Dyke (Swansea)		Neil Robinson (Cardiff)	1:57.5
1976	Alun Roper (Swansea)	1:55.7	A Evans (Newport)	1:56.7	Keith McGeoch (Wye)	1:58.6
1977	Peter Lewis (Birchfield)	1:50.8	Glen Grant (Army)	1:51.3	Alun Roper (Swansea)	1:51.7
1978	Glen Grant (Cambridge)	1:49.3	Peter Lewis (Birchfield)	1:51.9	Roger Barrett (Carmarthen)	1:53.2
1979	Peter Lewis (Southampton)	1:52.1	Simon Evans (Bristol)	1:53.2	David Barlow (Newcastle)	1:54.2
1980	Mal Edwards (Wolves)	1:54.6	David Barlow (Wolves)	1:56.?	Simon Evans (Bristol)	1:56.4
1981	Nick Morgan (Cardiff)	1:55.20	Steve Bright (Torfaen)	1:55.63	Gareth Brown (Wycombe)	1:56.05
1982	Phil Norgate (Epsom)	1:49.57	Gareth Brown (Leeds Univ)	1:50.37	David Barlow (Wolves)	1:51.48
1983	Phil Norgate (Epsom)	1:47.8	Gareth Brown (Cardiff)	1:48.1	Roger Barrett (Carmarthen)	1:52.2
1984	Paul Williams (Barry)	1:52.45	Neil Horsfield (Newport)	1:53.40	David Barlow (Wolves)	1:53.57
1985	Mal Edwards (Army)	1:51.4	Paul Williams (Barry)	1:51.6	Rikki McTaggert (RAF)	1:53.7
1986	Paul Williams (Barry)	1:51.71	Sean Price (Rhymney)	1:53.08	David Barlow (Wolves)	1:53.19
1987	Neil Horsfield (Newport)	1:48.44	Paul Williams (Barry)	1:50.26	Tomos Davies (Guildford)	1:52.40
1988	Neil Horsfield (Newport)	1:50.4	Sean Price (Cardiff)	1:50.9	Paul Williams (Barry)	1:51.4
1989	Peter Wyman (Edinburgh)	1:52.66	Sean Price (Cardiff)	1:53.40	David Knox (Old Gayton)	1:54.34
1990	Neil Horsfield (Newport)	1:51.08	Mike Hall (Llanelli)	1:53.39	David Knox (Hillingdon)	1:53.63
1991	Paul Williams (Barry)	1:54.86	David Morgan (Rhymney)	1:56.38	David Barlow (Wd Green)	1:56.80
1992	Neil Horsfield (Newport)	1:50.93	Paul Williams (Sale)	1:51.68	Sean Price (Cardiff)	1:53.94
1993	Paul Roberts (Cardiff)	1:50.16	Neil Horsfield (Newport)	1:50.58	Neil Emberton (Wrexham)	1:51.20
1994	Darrell Maynard (Belgrave)	1:54.87	Paul Roberts (Cardiff)	1:55.36	Chris Blount (Newport)	1:55.53
1995	Darrell Maynard (Belgrave)	1:55.6	Paul Roberts (Cardiff)	1:56.2	Martyn Jones (Swansea)	1:56.5
1996	Darrell Maynard (Belgrave)	1:54.75	Andrew Walling (Bangor)	1:55.46	Sean Price (Swansea)	1:56.02
1997	Darrell Maynard (Belgrave)	1:51.69	Tom Cordy (Newport)	1:52.49	Andrew Walling (Bangor)	1:52.81
1998	Matthew Shone (Notts)	1:50.89	Matt Davies (Wood Green)	1:54.62	Jeremy Bridger (T Solent)	1:56.62
1999	Matthew Shone (Wood Gr)	1:50.4	Joe Mills (Blackheath)	1:52.2	Robin Powell (Colwyn B)	1:55.1
2000	Matthew Shone (Wood Gr)	1:49.90	Joe Mills (Blackheath)	1:52.25	Andrew Walling (Bangor)	1:52.28

One mile

1893	Hugh Fairlamb (Roath)		Johns (Newport AC)			
1894	Harry Cullum (Roath)					
1895–1900	event not held					
1901	A B Manning (Swansea)	4:43.0				
1902	event not held					
1903	A S D Smith (Bristol)	4:44.4				
1904	D H Griffiths (Abergavenny)	4:49.8	R Rees (Newport H)		H C Cleaver (Newport H)	
1905	A S D Smith (Camb Univ)	4:37.0	D H Griffiths (Abergavenny)		Eddie O'Donnell (Cardiff Univ)	
1906	A S D Smith (Camb Univ)	4:45.6	D H Griffiths (Abergavenny)		Eddie O'Donnell (Cardiff Univ)	
1907	D H Griffiths (Newport H)	4:50.0				
1908	D H Griffiths (Newport H)	4:35.0	W. Emerson (Newport AC)		C G Hill (Tredegar H)	
1909	C G Hill (Tredegar)	4:44.4	W Emerson (Newport AC)		Rhys Evans (Roath)	
1910	Eddie O'Donnell (Roath)	4:40.2	W Emerson (Newport AC)	4:45.0	J F Iles (Roath)	
1911	W Emerson (Newport AC)	4:46.8				
1912	Cliff Price (Newport H)	4:39.6	T Elsmore (Cwmbran H)			
1913	Cliff Price (Newport H)	4:31.0	G C Dummitt (Cwmbran H)	4:50.4		
1914	Mark Williams (Talywain)	4:43.8	H B Nott (Newport H)		William Cleaver (Talywain)	
1920	J T Griffiths (Newport H)	4:48.6	Ivor Wintle (Newport H)		Jim Edwards (Newport H)	
1921	J T Griffiths (Newport H)	4:43.4	Ivor Wintle (Taltwain AC)		E Davies (Roath)	
1922	Jim Edwards (Newport H)	4:39.0	Danny Phillips (Newport H)		DJP Richards (P Talbot YMCA)	
1923	DJP Richards (Newport H)	4:35.0	Ernie Thomas (Newport H)		Jimmy Guy (Roath)	
1924	DJP Richards (Newport H)	4:42.0	B D Hammond (Newport H)		Jimmy Guy (Roath)	
1925	DJP Richards (Newport H)	4:35.6	F C Morgan (Roath)		Jim Edwards (Pontypool)	
1926	DJP Richards (Newport H)	4:34.6	Ivor Thomas (Oxford Univ)		Danny Phillips (Newport H)	
1927	Gwyn Lewis (Roath)	4:54.0	Frank Denmead (Cwm H)		Danny Phillips (Newport H)	
1928	Gwyn Lewis (Roath)	4:38.0	Frank Denmead (Cwm H)		Danny Phillips (Newport H)	
1929	Reg Thomas (RAF)	4:27.0	Norman Moses (Newport AC)		T H Timbrell (Roath)	
1930	Reg Thomas (RAF)	4:26.0	Gwyn Lewis (Roath)		Tom Thomas (Cardiff Univ)	
1931	Reg Thomas (RAF)	4:31.8	Tom Thomas (Newport AC)		Leslie Wilce (Newport H)	
1932	Tom Thomas (Card Univ)	4:39.6	Len Tongue (Newport H)		D J Pritchard (Abergele)	
1933	Reg Thomas (RAF)	4:17.2	E C Edwards (Spillers AC)		J M Burch (Spillers AC)	
1934	Ken Harris (Roath)	4:28.2	Philip Dee (Newport H)		R G W Hopkins (Swansea Vall)	
1935	Jim Alford (Roath)	4:27.4	Ken Harris (Roath)		Philip Dee (Newport H)	
1936	Reg Thomas (RAF)	4:21.4	Philip Dee (Newport H)	4:21.5	Ken Harris (Roath)	4:22.8
1937	Philip Dee (Mitcham)	4:31.5	Ted March (Cardiff Gas)		Len Brown (Roath)	

1938	Jim Alford (Roath)	4:23.0	Ted March (Cardiff Gas)		J McCarthy (Cardiff Univ)	
1939	Maldwyn White (Birchfield)	4:32.6	Len Brown (Roath)		Philip Dee (Mitcham)	
1946	Howard Davies (Neath AC)	4:38.0	Len Brown (Roath)		M R Jones (Newport H)	
1947	Ed Cooper (Roath)	4:55.0	L H James (Newport H)		T R Pate (Penrhys H)	
1948	Jim Alford (Roath)	4:33.0	John Disley (Loughborough)		Doug Rees (Portsmouth)	
1949	John Disley (London AC)	4:32.0	Doug Rees (Portsmouth)		R Corne (Aberystwyth Univ)	
1950	Doug Rees (Portsmouth)	4:36.0	Bob Morgan (Roath)		D Ridd (Swansea AC)	
1951	John Disley (Loughboro)	4:29.6	Joe Yates (Mond AC)		Ken Huckle (Roath)	
1952	Joe Yates (Mond AC)	4:22.2	Peter Griggs (Coventry God)	4:38.0	C N Griffiths (Penarth)	4:38.5
1953	Tony Pumfrey (Cov God)	4:24.2	Derek Clarke (Penarth)	4:26.3	Ken Huckle (Roath)	4:28.1
1954	John Disley (London AC)	4:16.8	Tony Pumfrey (Coventry G)	4:19.4	Joe Yates (Mond AC)	4:31.4
1955	Tony Pumfrey (Cov God)	4:22.8	Ken Huckle (Roath)	4:23.8	Brian James (Bournemouth)	4:31.2
1956	Brian James (Oxford)	4:20.6	Ken Huckle (Roath)	4:20.8	J G Davies (St Albans)	4:24.8
1957	Tony Pumfrey (Cov God)	4:21.8	P J P Saunders (TVH)	4:23.6	Haydn Tawton (Canton)	4:27.5
1958	John Disley (London AC)	4:14.8	Tony Pumfrey (Coventry G)	4:16.0	Haydn Tawton (Roath)	4:18.2
1959	Tony Pumfrey (Birchfield)	4:16.8	Roy Profitt (Devonport)	4:17.8	Roger H-Jones (Pembroke)	4:20.5
1960	Norman Horrell (Rhondda)	4:12.5	Haydn Tawton (Roath)	4:13.8	Roy Profitt (Polytechnic)	4:19.0
1961	Dil Robbins (Port Talbot)	4:21.6	Haydn Tawton (Roath)	4:26.6	Brian Williams (Guildford)	4:27.6
1962	Bernard Tucker (Card Un)	4:14.5	Dil Robbins (Port Talbot)	4:19.6	Peter Griffin (Westbury)	4:22.6
1963	Bernard Tucker (Card Un)	4:17.0	Bill Stitfall (Birchgrove)	4:19.1	Fred Bell (Carmarthen)	4:20.9
1964	Bernard Tucker (Card Un)	4:18.2	John Godding (Abery Un)	4:19.7	David Gregory (Newport)	4:20.3
1965	Chris Loosley (Abery Un)	4:09.6	Fred Bell (Carmarthen)	4:09.7	Bill Stitfall (Birchgrove)	4:15.2
1966	Fred Bell (Carmarthen)	4:16.2	Viv Blackwell (RAF)	4:16.4	John Godding (Birchgrove)	4:20.2
1967	Tony Simmons (Luton)	4:13.9	Fred Bell (Carmarthen)	4:17.7	John Powell (Birchgrove)	4:21.4
1968	Gwynn Davis (Aberystwyth)	4:17.0	Fred Bell (Carmarthen)	4:17.4	Bob Maplestone (Roath)	4:18.6

1500 metres

1969	Fred Bell (TVH)	3:53.5	Bob Maplestone (Cardiff)	3:54.6	Robin Davies (Birchfield)	3:56.9
1970	Bernie Hayward (Cardiff)	3:51.3	Dave Deubner (Cardiff)	3:52.8	David Hopkins (Newport)	3:55.8
1971	Graham Spencer (Cardiff)	3:52.6	Dennis Fowles (Cardiff)	3:56.5	Alun Roper (Swansea)	4:00.4
1972	Gwynn Davis (Aberystwyth)	3:48.1	Bernie Hayward (Cardiff)	3:49.9	Brian Donovan (Cardiff)	3:51.8
1973	Clive Thomas (TVH)	3:52.6	Peter Ratcliffe (Cardiff)	3:52.9	Steve Slocombe (Cardiff)	3:58.5
1974	Gwynn Davis (Bristol)	3:49.8	John Theophilus (Swansea)	3:50.0	Peter Ratcliffe (Cardiff)	3:50.1
1975	John Theophilus (Swansea)	3:48.2	Bernie Plain (Cardiff)	3:49.6	Graham Spencer (Cardiff)	3:50.5
1976	Gwynn Davis (Bristol)	3:50.6	John Theophilus (Swansea)	3:51.6	P Corney (Portsmouth)	3:57.0
1977	Paul Williams (Cambridge)	3:53.4	Kevin Glastonbury (Cardiff)	3:53.5	Gwynn Davis (Bristol)	3:53.7
1978	Peter Baker (Bristol)	3:46.1	Tony Blackwell (Wolves)	3:48.6	John Theophilus (Swansea)	3:48.9
1979	Paul Williams (Cambridge)	3:47.5	Charles Monk (Bristol)	3:49.0	Adrian Leek (Cardiff)	3:49.6
1980	John Theophilus (Swansea)	3:52.6	Glyn Reynolds (Sheffield)	3:53.6	Keith Jones (Cardiff)	3:53.7
1981	Tony Blackwell (Wolves)	3:48.78	Roger Hackney (RAF)	3:48.92	Steve Jones (Bristol)	3:50.60
1982	Roger Hackney (RAF)	3:44.43	Tony Blackwell (Wolves)	3:44.60	Steve Jones (Newport)	3:45.20
1983	Tony Blackwell (Wolves)	3:50.7	David James (Cardiff)	3:54.3	Geoff Hill (Swansea)	3:58.0
1984	John Barry (Bournemouth)	3:57.77	Peter Wyman (Bridgend)	3:58.16	James Hill (Newport)	3:59.05
1985	Neil Horsfield (Newport)	3:50.3	David Constable (Birchfield)	3:51.3	Ian Hamer (Bridgend)	3:53.1
1986	Mal Edwards (Andover)	3:40.81	Neil Horsfield (Newport)	3:41.78	Glen Grant (Cambridge)	3:45.35
1987	Mal Edwards (Andover)	3:48.99	Ian Hamer (Bridgend)	3:52.37	David Lake (Bristol)	3:54.79
1988	Nick Comerford (Barry)	3:55.6	Shaun Whelan (Swansea)	3:55.8	Derek Bultitude (Notts)	3:56.6
1989	Neil Horsfield (Newport)	3:42.46	Steve Knight (Cardiff)	3:55.87	Matthew Chaston (Cardiff)	3:56.09
1990	Neil Horsfield (Newport)	3:50.11	Matthew Chaston (Belgrave)	3:50.80	Steve Mosley (Cardiff)	3:52.42
1991	Glen Grant (Cambridge)	3:51.11	Steven Price (Brighton)	3:51.77	Mark Bryant (Cardiff)	3:53.76
1992	Clive Boulton (Wrexham)	3:52.90	Nick Comerford (Barry)	3:53.46	Glen Grant (Cambridge)	3:53.91
1993	Ian Hamer (Swansea)	3:54.98	Nick Comerford (Cardiff)	3:55.30	Matt Davies (Cambridge)	3:55.98
1994	Christian Stephenson (Card)	3:55.19	Neil Horsfield (Newport)	3:55.56	Joe Mills (Chelmsford)	3:55.74
1995	Nick Comerford (Cardiff)	4:09.74	Rob Simon (Cardiff)	4:10.66	Andrew Walling (Bangor)	4:10.78
1996	James EllisSmith (Reigate)	3:50.71	Nick Comerford (Cardiff)	3:52.39	Christian Stephenson (Card)	3:53.60
1997	Christian Stephenson (Card)	3:54.70	James EllisSmith (Reigate)	3:56.75	Steve Mosley (Cardiff)	3:57.01
1998	Christian Stephenson (Card)	3:46.2	Nick Comerford (Cardiff)	3:46.8	Joe Mills (Blackheath)	3:50.5
1999	Chris Davies (Telford)	3:52.06	Matthew Shone (Wood Gr)	4:00.58	Andres Jones (Cardiff)	4:04.31
2000	Christian Stephenson (Card)	3:52.0	Chris Davies (Telford)	3:52.8	Donald Naylor (Swansea)	3:54.5

Four miles

1907	D H Griffiths (Newport H)	21:05.0				
1908	Tom Arthur (Newport H)	20:41.8	Rhys Evans (Roath)			
1909	Tom Arthur (Newport H)	20:58.8	A S Wilson (Abertillery)	21:20.4		
1910	J F Iles (Roath)	21:09.0	Eddie O'Donnell (Roath)		W Emerson (Newport AC)	
1911	W Emerson (Newport AC)	23:20.8				
1912	Cliff Price (Newport H)	21:14.4	Tom Miles (Penywain)	21:18.4		
1913	Cliff Price (Newport H)	20:45.4	Tom Arthur (Newport H)	21:39.0	E Massey (Newport H)	21:41.4
1914	A S Wilson (Newport H)	21:24.4	J C Jenkins (Spillers AC)		only 2 athletes	
1920	Tom Miles (Newport H)	21:10.0	W J Jones (Cwm H)	21:41.0	Jim Edwards (Newport H)	21:52.0

1921	Ernie Thomas (Cwmbran)	21:19.4	J H Brunning (Cwm H)		only 2 finishers	
1922	Jim Edwards (Newport H)	21:22.0	Danny Phillips (Newport H)		Eddie Davies (Roath)	
1923	Ernie Thomas (Newport H)	21:12.0	Danny Phillips (Newport H)		Jim Edwards (Newport H)	
1924	DJP Richards (Newport H)	20:47.8	J H Brunning (Cwm H)		Ernie Thomas (Newport H)	
1925	DJP Richards (Newport H)	20:56.0	Ernie Thomas (Newport H)		Eddie Davies (Roath)	
1926	Ernie Thomas (Newport H)	20:04.0	Danny Phillips (Newport H)		only 2 athletes finished	
1927	Ernie Thomas (Cwmbran)	22:05.8	Frank Denmead (Cwm H)		Ted Hopkins (Roath)	
1928	DJP Richards (Newport H)	20:28.0	Ernie Thomas (Cwmbran)		J J Prosser (Cwmbran)	
1929	DJP Richards (Newport H)	21:04.0	Ossie Williams (Llanbradach H)		Leslie Wilce (Newport H)	
1930	Danny Phillips (Cwmbran)	20:35.2	T H Timbrell (Swansea Valley)		James Duggan (Swansea Valley)	
1931	J J Prosser (Cwmbran)	20:51.0	Harry Gallivan (Pontnewydd H)		A S Stone (Pontypool H)	
1932	Harry Gallivan (Pontnewydd)	20:50.4	Ted Hopkins (Roath)		Wilf Short (Newport H)	

Three miles

1933	Len Tongue (Newport H)	15:20.0	A S Stone (Pontypool H)		Ivor Brown (Llanbradach H)	
1934	Len Tongue (Newport H)	14:52.0	Harry Gallivan (Cwmbran H)		Bill Matthews (Penrhys AC)	
1935	Len Tongue (Newport H)	15:07.4	George Fox (Penrhys AC)		T R Harris (Roath)	
1936	Harry Gallivan (Cwmbran)	14:41.0	Bill Matthews (Penrhys AC)		Eddie Cooper (Roath)	
1937	Ivor Brown (Mitcham)	14:42.0	Harry Gallivan (Cwmbran H)		W T Williams (Port Talbot)	
1938	Ivor Brown (Mitcham)	14:32.8	Bill Matthews (Penrhys)	14:34.2	Eddie Cooper (Roath)	
1939	Dillan Hier (RAF)	15:16.0	Harry Gallivan (Cwmbran H)		Ivor Brown (Mitcham)	
1946	Ivor Lloyd (Newport H)	15:40.0	Eddie Cooper (Roath)		Douglas Cupid (Swansea Vall)	
1947	Jim Alford (Roath)	16:15.0	Ivor Lloyd (Newport H)		Tom Christison (Cwmbran)	
1948	Ivor Lloyd (Newport H)	16:00.0	Eddie Cooper (Roath)		John Nash (Port Talbot)	
1949	Maldwyn White (Birchfield)	15:17.0	Ivor Lloyd (Newport H)		John Nash (Port Talbot)	
1950	Dyfrig Rees (Coventry)	15:22.6	John Nash (Port Talbot)		Geraint Williams (Cardiff Univ)	
1951	Doug Rees (Portsmouth)	15:15.9	John Nash (Port Talbot)		Dyfrig Rees (Coventry)	
1952	Dyfrig Rees (Coventry)	15:18.2	Tom Wood (Newport)	15:24.2	J L Edwards (Carmarthen)	15:26.0
1953	Lyn Bevan (Newport)	14:55.0	Ken Huckle (Roath)	15:20.0	John Nash (Port Talbot)	15:42.9
1954	Norman Wilson (Wolves)	14:55.2	Lyn Bevan (Newport)	15:13.2	Ken Huckle (Roath)	15:22.2
1955	Ken Huckle (Roath)	14:46.2	Ron Franklin (Newport)		John Nash (Port Talbot)	
1956	Joe Yates (Mond AC)	14:45.8	Ken Huckle (Roath)	14:49.0	Rhys Davies (Coventry)	14:50.6
1957	Donald MacLean (Belgrave)	14:58.4	Norman Horrell (RhonddaV)	14:59.2	Roger Harrison-Jones (Rhyl)	15:00.0
1958	Norman Horrell (Rhondda V)	14:31.0				
1959	John Merriman (Watford)	13:54.6				
1960	Roy Proffitt (Polytechnic)					
1961	Ron Franklin (Tipton)	14:28.0	Ken Flowers (Hereford)	14:44.7	Hedydd Davies (Carmarthen)	14:59.0
1962	Norman Horrell (Rhondda V)	14:18.2	Ron Franklin (Tipton)	14:22.4	Ken Flowers (Hereford)	14:31.8
1963	Norman Horrell (Rhondda V)	14:24.6	Ron Franklin (Tipton)	14:30.2	Ken Flowers (Gilwern)	14:34.6
1964	Steve Rogers (Wrexham)	14:19.4	Ron Franklin (TVH)	14:28.4	Dil Robbins (Port Talbot)	14:49.8
1965	John Godding (Birchgrove)	14:11.0	Ken Flowers (Gilwern)	14:15.2	Ron Franklin (TVH)	14:19.6
1966	Nick Barton (Windsor)	14:07.2	Paul Darney (Birchgrove)	14:11.8	Ron Franklin (TVH)	14:26.2
1967	Paul Darney (Birchgrove)	14:21.8	Mal Evans (Tipton)	14:26.0	Dil Robbins (Port Talbot)	14:31.0
1968	Paul Darney (Birchgrove)	14:22.6	Clive Williams (Birchgrove)	14:32.6	Gerallt Davis (Aberystwyth)	14:45.4

5000 metres

1969	Bernie Plain (Cardiff)	14:17.8	Mike Rowland (Newport)	14:24.6	Alan Joslyn (Polytechnic)	14:29.6
1970	Gwynn Davis (Aberystwyth)	14:11.2	Tony Simmons (Luton)	14:18.0	Mike Rowland (Newport)	14:48.0
1971	Ian Thompson (Cardiff Un)	14:33.6	Clive Thomas (TVH)	14:37.0	Mike Critchley (Cardiff)	14:45.6
1972	Malcolm Thomas (TVH)	14:26.6	Peter Ratcliffe (Cardiff)	14:30.2	Dic Evans (Cardiff)	15:01.8
1973	Gwynn Davis (Bristol)	14:36.4	Clive Williams (Cardiff)	14:37.2	Mike Critchley (Cardiff)	14:53.4
1974	Dennis Fowles (Cardiff)	14:25.8	Steve Gibbons (Swansea)	14:52.0	Clive Williams (Cardiff)	14:59.2
1975	David Hopkins (Newport)	14:08.0	Steve Gibbons (Swansea)	14:26.0	Brian Donovan (Cardiff)	14:32.4
1976	David Hopkins (Newport)	14:10.0	Peter Ratcliffe (Cardiff)	14:22.2	Brian Donovan (Cardiff)	14:32.6
1977	Dick Milne (Notts)	14:15.0	Steve Slocombe (Cardiff)	14:17.6	Adrian Leek (Cardiff)	14:21.8
1978	Tony Simmons (Luton)	13:35.0	Steve Jones (RAF)	13:48.6	David Hopkins (Newport)	14:13.2
1979	John Davies (TVH)	13:42.5	David James (Cardiff)	13:54.9	Steve Slocombe (Cardiff)	14:22.7
1980	Glen Grant (Cambridge)	14:24.1	Colin Mattock (Wolves)	14:28.0	John Robertshaw (Newport)	14:31.9
1981	Dennis Fowles (Cardiff)	14:03.00	David James (Cardiff)	14:11.42	Chris Buckley (Westbury)	14:22.75
1982	Steve Jones (Newport)	14:08.6	Tony Blackwell (Wrexham)	14:19.2	John Davies (Sale)	14:22.6
1983	David James (Cardiff)	14:05.4	Tony Blackwell (Wolves)	14:11.2	Paul Williams (Cambridge)	14:13.3
1984	Tony Blackwell (Wolves)	14:18.82	Kenny Davies (Newport)	14:21.16	Nigel Adams (Swansea)	14:21.97
1985	Steve Jones (Newport)	13:54.2	Chris Buckley (Westbury)	14:09.6	Nigel Adams (Swansea)	14:12.9
1986	Roger Hackney (RAF)	13:44.04	Steve Jones (Newport)	13:54.24	Chris Buckley (Westbury)	14:21.78
1987	Nigel Adams (Swansea)	14:19.49	Mark Harris (Westbury)	14:30.63	Geoff Hill (Swansea)	14:37.56
1988	Roger Hackney (RAF)	14:08.0	Eddie Conway (Cardiff)	14:09.0	Peter Jenkins (Newport)	14:12.6
1989	Ian Hamer (Edinburgh)	14:11.65	Geoff Hill (Swansea)	14:22.31	Steve Brace (Bridgend)	14:40.37
1990	James Hill (Newport)	14:10.49	Chris Buckley (Westbury)	14:14.61	Nigel Adams (Swansea)	14:21.30
1991	Steve Brace (Bridgend)	14:45.18	Geoff Hill (Swansea)	14:46.59	James Hill (Newport)	14:47.89
1992	Ian Hamer (Swansea)	13:57.87	Justin Chaston (Belgrave)	14:22.23	Steve Brace (Bridgend)	14:30.91

1993	Justin Hobbs (Cardiff)	14:08.74	Steve Brace (Bridgend)	14:16.82	Steve Jones (Newport)	14:18.62
1994	Justin Chaston (Belgrave)	14:01.73	Ian Hamer (Swansea)	14:10.69	Steve Knight (Cardiff)	14:20.45
1995	Justin Hobbs (Cardiff)	14:30.08	Mark Shaw (Newport)	14:49.46	Andres Jones (Carmarthen)	15:06.42
1996	Steve Brace (Bridgend)	14:33.17	Andrew Eynon (Swansea)	14:38.07	Mark Shaw (Newport)	14:49.71
1997	Nick Comerford (Cardiff)	14:20.39	Chris Davies (Telford)	14:21.98	Colin Jones (Shaftesbury)	14:43.20
1998	Mark Morgan (Swansea)	14:28.11	Chris Davies (Telford)	14:42.49	Kevin Holland (Crawley)	15:07.39
1999	Colin Jones (Eryri)	15:00.6	Richard Szade (Newport)	15:28.0	James Hill (Bridgend)	16:09.5
2000	Adam Jones (Pontypridd)	14:09.8	Tim Snell (Abertillery)	15:38.9	only 2 ran – plus one lap short	

Six miles

1951	Norman Wilson (RAF)	32:00.8	Jack Nash (Port Talbot)		Paddy Wallace (Newport)	
1952	Norman Wilson (RAF)	32:04.0	Tom Wood (Newport)	32:57.0	Jack Nash (Port Talbot)	33:50.0
1953	event not held					
1954	DJP Richards (Roath)	32:20.6	Lyn Bevan (Newport)		Ron Franklin (Mountain Ash)	
1955	DJP Richards (Roath)	30:57.4	Ken Huckle (Roath)	31:02.8	Ron Franklin (Newport)	32:04.6
1956	Joe Yates (Mond AC)	31:20.0				
1957	Norman Horrell (Rhonda V)	31:36.0	Ron Franklin (Newport)	31:55.0	P Bowden (Bristol)	32:56.0
1958	Harry Wilson (Welwyn)	30:27.4	Barrie Saunders (TVH)	31:17.4	R B Morgan (Achilles)	31:17.6
1959	DJP Richards (Poly)	30:19.6	Ron Franklin (Newport)		Rhys Davies (Coventry)	
1960	Ron Franklin (Tipton)	30:37.2	John Burrows (Roath)	32:27.2	David Thomas (Birchgrove)	33:31.8
1961	DJP Richards (Poly)	29:29.6	Ron Franklin (Tipton)	29:42.0	Roy Profitt (Poly)	30:30.6
1962	DJP Richards (Poly)	29:53.4	Norman Horrell (Rhondda)	30:13.2	Bryan Davies (Carmarthen)	31:29.6
1963	Ron Franklin (Tipton)	30:09.0	Ken Flowers (Gilwern)	30:17.0	Jim O'Brien (Port Talbot)	30:29.6
1964	Ron Franklin (Tipton)	29:49.2	Ken Flowers (Gilwern)	30:39.0	Lyn Bevan (Newport)	31:31.2
1965	Ron Franklin (TVH)	29:26.4	Ken Flowers (Gilwern)	30:04.8	Mike Rowland (Newport)	30:34.2
1966	Paul Darney (Birchgrove)	29:37.0	Ron Franklin (TVH)	29:43.0	Nick Barton (Windsor)	
1967	Paul Darney (Birchgrove)	29:36.0	Ron Franklin (TVH)	30:10.0	Hedydd Davies (TVH)	30:21.0
1968	Paul Darney (Birchgrove)	29:48.8	Ron Franklin (TVH)	29:58.2	David Collier (Luton)	30:44.6

10,000 metres

1969	Bernie Plain (Cardiff)	29:41.0	Gordon Minty (TVH)	30:45.0	Ron Franklin (TVH)	
1970	Bernie Plain (Cardiff)	29:26.8	John Jones (Windsor)	29:54.4	Alan Joslyn (Poly)	29:54.8
1971	Mike Rowland (Newport)	30:27.4	Tony White (Longwood)	30:49.8	David Collier (Luton)	31:33.0
1972	Malcolm Thomas (TVH)	30:11.6	Dave Walsh (Cardiff)	32:17.2	Ron Franklin (TVH)	32:30.6
1973	Gwynn Davis (Bristol)	30:36.2	David Hopkins (Newport)	31:16.6	Dic Evans (Cardiff)	31:30.8
1974	Mike Critchley (Cardiff)	30:15.8	Dennis Fowles (Cardiff)	30:32.4	Dic Evans (Cardiff)	30:47.4
1975	Mike Critchley (Cardiff)	30:31.6	Bob Sercombe (Newport)	30:46.2	Dave Walsh (Cardiff)	31:18.0
1976	Peter Ratcliffe (Cardiff)	30:07.0	Dic Evans (Cardiff)	30:27.6	Bob Sercombe (Newport)	30:57.8
1977	Peter Ratcliffe (Cardiff)	29:40.0	Ali Cole (Swansea)	29:40.0	Bernie Plain (Cardiff)	29:41.2
1978	Dick Milne (Notts)	30:06.0	Kirk Clifford (C&C)	30:10.4	Bernie Plain (Cardiff)	30:16.0
1979	Tony Simmons (Luton)	29:04.1	Adrian Leek (Cardiff)	29:05.0	John Robertshaw (Newport)	29:43.9
1980	Ali Cole (Swansea)	30:17.9	John Robertshaw (Newport)	30:21.9	Ieuan Ellis (Newport)	30:28.8
1981	Ali Cole (Swansea)	29:57.3	Bernie Hayward (Cardiff)	30:29.3	Bernie Plain (Cardiff)	30:46.0
1982	Dennis Fowles (Cardiff)	29:34.10	Ieuan Ellis (Newport)	29:54.67	Kenny Davies (Newport)	30:21.58
1983	Ali Cole (Newport)	29:46.5	Ieuan Ellis (Newport)	29:47.8	Paul Wheeler (Cardiff)	30:00.6
1984	Kenny Davies (Newport)	29:47.5	Simon Collingridge (Poly)	30:56.5	Malcolm Firth (Manchester)	31:01.2
1985	Paul Wheeler (Cardiff)	29:58.2	Tony Williams (Rhondda)	30:04.3	Steve Brown (Cheltenham)	30:10.0
1986	Ali Cole (Newport)	30:29.67	Kenny Davies (Newport)	31:04.47	Adrian Ward (Massey F)	31:08.08
1987	Ieuan Ellis (Newport)	30:16.4	Greg Newhams (Bridgend)	30:56.1	Michael Edwards (AFD)	31:25.1
1988	Ieuan Ellis (Newport)	31:48.62	Garry Davies (Salford)	32:03.66	Huw Roberts (Les Croupiers)	32:09.90
1989	Steve Jones (Newport)	28:43.48	Nigel Adams (Swansea)	28:51.05	Andy Smith (Swansea)	30:38.92
1990	Shaun Tobin (Swansea)	31:40.95	Paul Howarth (Barry)	31:42.08	Mark Healey (Lliswerry)	31:49.89
1991	Glyn Harvey (Colwyn Bay)	31:52.56	Tony Holloway (Wrexham)	31:56.48	Huw Roberts (Les Croupiers)	32:06.74
1992	Geoff Hill (Swansea)	30:30.33	Shaun Tobin (Swansea)	30:31.27	Jon Hooper (Bridgend)	31:20.02
1993	Dale Rixon (Bridgend)	30:08.64	James Hill (Newport)	31:15.72	Gareth Jones (Soton)	32:47.99
1994	Mark Healey (Lliswerry)	31:13.84	Andrew Pritchard (Cardiff)	31:22.30	Jeff Secker (Swansea)	32:18.38
1995	Bruce Chinnick (Westbury)	30:49.5	Shaun Tobin (Swansea)	31:28.7	Kevin Blake (Cardiff)	31:55.7
1996	Dale Rixon (Bridgend)	29:54.12	Shaun Tobin (Swansea)	30:23.37	Huw Roberts (Bridgend)	32:07.02
1997	Steve Brace (Bridgend)	29:55.73	Dale Rixon (Bridgend)	29:59.24	Steve Knight (Cardiff)	30:57.77
1998	Andres Jones (Cardiff)	30:21.4	Steve Brace (Bridgend)	31:35.0	Phil Cook (Cardiff)	32:33.8
1999	Dale Rixon (Bridgend)	30:55.8	Kevin Tobin (Swansea)	31:49.2	Phil Cook (Barry)	31:51.1
2000	Steve Brace (Bridgend)	32:27.6	John Collins (Swansea)	39:17.9	P McManus (Aberdare)	40:31.0

Two miles / 3000 metres (from 1954) Steeplechase

1946	Ken Harris (Roath)	11:31.0	D J Llewellyn (Cardiff Univ)			
1947 – 1951	event not held					
1952	Dyfrig Rees (Coventry)	11:21.1	Tom Wood (Newport)	11:31.0	R Greer (Hopkinson)	11:43.0
1953	Phil Ll Morgan (Achilles)	10:38.0	Tom Wood (Newport)	11:11.4	R Greer (Hopkinson)	11:34.8
1954	David Richards (Roath)	10:13.6	Tom Wood (Newport)	10:16.6	J Francis (Newport)	10:41.2
1955	Brian James (Bournemouth)	10:04.6	Ron Franklin (Newport)	10:34.2	R Greer (Birchgrove)	10:42.2

1956	Rhys Davies (Coventry)	10:13.2	G H Lewis (Roath)	10:28.4	Ron Franklin (Newport)	10:37.2
1957	Jack Wingfield (Roath)	9:44.1	G H Lewis (Gosforth)	10:02.2	P J Bowden) (Bristol)	10:05.6
1958	Jack Wingfield (Roath)	10:06.0	D C Hughes (Rhyl)	10:30.0	only 2 athletes	
1959	David Richards (Poly)	9:19.4	David Pritchard (Birchgrove)	9:52.7	Jack Wingfield (Roath)	9:59.8
1960	David Pritchard (Birchgrove)	9:32.0	Hedydd Davies (Carmarthen)	9:45.6	Jack Wingfield (Roath)	9:48.0
1961	Hedydd Davies (Carmarthen)	9:31.7	Norman Horrell (Rhondda V)	9:49.2	George Matthuidis (Newport)	9:58.6
1962	Hedydd Davies (Birchfield)	9:31.2	Mike Rowland (Newport)	9:57.8	Bill Stitfall (Birchgrove)	10:03.8
1963	Hedydd Davies (Birchfield)	9:32.4	Brian Griffiths (Roath)	10:06.2	Glyn Matthews (Barry)	11:37.6
1964	Hedydd Davies (Birchfield)	9:05.3	Bill Stitfall (Birchgrove)	9:25.7	Brian Griffiths (Roath)	9:30.6
1965	Brian Griffiths (Roath)	9:28.8	Derek Vaughan (Swansea)	10:22.6	Richie Pugh (Pontypool)	11:13.0
1966	Ron McAndrew (Wigan)	9:15.2	Hedydd Davies (TVH)	9:18.8	Bill Stitfall (Birchgrove)	9:29.4
1967	Ron McAndrew (Wigan)	9:05.4	Brian Griffiths (Roath)	9:20.4	Hedydd Davies (TVH)	9:32.2
1968	Ron McAndrew (Reading)	9:20.2	Brian Griffiths (Roath)	9:37.8	Dic Evans (Cardiff TC)	9:48.0
1969	Bernie Hayward (Cardiff)	8:58.2	Peter Griffiths (Hillingdon)	9:03.6	Brian Griffiths (Cardiff)	9:20.0
1970	Ron McAndrew (Reading)	9:06.8	Dic Evans (Cardiff TC)	9:27.8	R Lea (Unattached)	10:51.0
1971	Fred Bell (TVH)	9:22.0	Steve Gibbon (Carmarthen)	9:23.4	Dave Walker (Worcester)	9:30.2
1972	John Theophilus (Swansea)	9:14.8	Mike Lane (Gilwern)	9:38.6	Brian Griffiths (Cardiff)	9:54.8
1973	Bernie Hayward (Cardiff)	8:56.0	Ron McAndrew (Reading)	9:00.0	John Theophilus (Swansea)	9:09.2
1974	Dic Evans (Cardiff)	9:15.4	Brian Griffiths (Cardiff)	9:26.0	D A Wood (Aberdare)	9:46.0
1975	Bernie Hayward (Cardiff)	8:56.4	Brian Griffiths (Cardiff)	9:27.6	Roy Davies (Swansea)	9:43.2
1976	Peter Griffiths (Tipton)	8:57.0	Roy Davies (Swansea)	9:46.0	Alan Jefferies (Swansea)	9:52.6
1977	John Davies (TVH)	8:33.8	Peter Griffiths (Tipton)	8:44.2	Steve Jones (RAF/Swindon)	8:52.2
1978	John Davies (TVH)	8:43.2	Peter Griffiths (Tipton)	8:54.0	Roger Hackney (Birm Un)	8:59.4
1979	Roger Hackney (Birm Un)	8:47.0	Dic Evans (Cardiff)	9:19.8	Brian Griffiths (Cardiff)	9:48.0
1980	Peter Griffiths (Tipton)	9:09.3	Andy Bamber (Met Police)	9:12.6	Mike Lane (Newport)	9:24.8
1981	Peter Griffiths (Tipton)	9:10.7	Lloyd Roberts (Cardiff)	9:21.6	Phil Llewellyn (Shaftesbury)	9:28.7
1982	Andy Bamber (Met Pol)	9:10.58	Kevin Parker (Westbury)	9:18.20	Mark Roberts (Cardiff)	9:19.84
1983	Phil Llewellyn (RAF)	8:59.8	Kevin Parker (Westbury)	9:16.5	Steve Smith (Swansea)	9:37.3
1984	Alwyn Ormond (Newport)	9:25.24	Gareth Proctor (Sale)	9:25.99	Kevin Parker (Westbury)	9:26.69
1985	David Lee (Exeter)	9:09.47	John Messum (Wolves)	9:16.79	Paul Miller (Cardiff)	9:18.27
1986	Marcus Thomas (Cardiff)	9:00.23	David Lee (Exeter)	9:01.36	Brian Matthews (Barry)	9:01.95
1987	David Lee (Exeter)	9:14.65	Adrian Brown (Newport)	9:19.53	Henry Foley (Colwyn Bay)	9:20.83
1988	David Lee (Exeter)	9:04.7	Neil Hardee (Newport)	9:15.6	Greg Newhams (Bridgend)	9:19.1
1989	Roger Hackney (Aldershot)	8:32.16	Philip York (Ealing)	9:35.46	Roger Porter (Basildon)	9:40.37
1990	Justin Chaston (Belgrave)	8:45.47	Phil Cook (Barry)	9:17.00	Brian Matthews (Barry)	9:29.88
1991	Justin Chaston (Belgrave)	8:54.50	Phil Cook (Barry)	9:01.75	Karl Palmer (Preseli)	9:12.85
1992	Phil Cook (Barry)	9:04.80	Karl Palmer (Preseli)	9:05.63	Philip York (TVH)	9:30.59
1993	Phil Cook (Barry)	9:09.92	Geran Hughes (Cardiff)	9:29.86	Mike Cherrington (Swansea)	9:43.58
1994	David Lee (Loughborough	9:02.21	Phil Cook (Barry)	9:13.58	Phil Llewellyn (Shaftesbury)	9:19.66
1995	Phil Cook (Barry)	9:27.14	Mike Cherrington (Mandale)	9:31.72	Jon Peters (Wrexham)	9:49.52
1996	Phil Cook (Cardiff)	9:33.21	Mike Cherrington (Swansea)	9:35.47	Felipe Jones (Westbury)	9:37.28
1997	David Lee (Blackheath)	9:13.76	Phil Cook (Cardiff)	9:35.26	John Foster (Lliswerry)	9:52.12
1998	Donald Naylor (Swansea)	9:21.1	Phil Cook (Cardiff)	9:46.2	Bernie Jones (Wrexham)	9:53.4
1999	Sullivan Smith (Swansea)	9:47.7	John Foster (Lliswerry)	9:49.6	Mike Cherrington (Mandale)	9:52.3
2000	Sullivan Smith (Swansea)	9:53.24	Ron McWilliam (Deeside)	10:09.88	Paul Gronow (Cardiff)	10:10.53

120 yards hurdles

1902	Wyatt Gould (Newport AC)	16.8				
1903	Wyatt Gould (Newport AC)	17.6				
1904	Wallis Walters (Card Univ)	17.0				
1905	Wyatt Gould (Newport AC)	16.6				
1906	Conway Williams (Newport)	17.2				
1907	Conway Williams (Newport)	18.6	Wallis Walters (Cardiff Univ)			
1908	Wallis Walters (Card Univ)	17.0	Wyatt Gould (Newport AC)		S H Williams (Newport AC)	
1909	Wyatt Gould (Newport AC)	17.4	Wallis Walters (Cardiff Un)	17.5	William Titt (St Saviours)	17.8
1910	William Titt (St Saviours)	17.8	Wallis Walters (Cardiff Un)	17.8	C V Sederman (St Saviours)	
1911	William Titt (St Saviours)	18.8				
1912	Wallis Walters (Card Univ)	19.6	Ben Uzzell (Newport AC)	19.7	Harry Uzzell (Newport AC)	
1913	William Titt (Cardiff)	18.8	Harry Uzzell (Newport AC)			
1914	P A Livingston (Swansea)	18.2	William Titt (St Saviours)		Wyatt Gould (Newport AC)	
1920	T E Vaughan (Newport AC)	19.4	F K Allen (Newport AC)		William Titt (St Saviours)	
1921	F K Allen (Newport AC)	17.2	T E Vaughan (Newport AC)		William Titt (St Saviours)	
1922	R F Roberts (Newport AC)	17.4				
1923	event not held					
1924	F K Allen (Newport AC)	18.8	A R Weatherley (Newport AC)		J Wreford (Goldcliffe)	
1925	F K Allen (Newport AC)	17.2	Tom White (Newport AC)		Jack Powell (Cardiff AC)	
1926	Frank Whitcutt (Card Univ)	19.0	F K Allen (Newport AC)		W J Purnell (Splott YMCA)	
1927	Frank Whitcutt (Card Univ)	16.6	F K Allen (Newport AC)			
1928	Stan Macey (Newport AC)	16.4	J G Ward (Monmouth GS)		T D Morris (Monmouth GS)	
1929	Stan Macey (Newport AC)	16.4	Frank Whitcutt (Newport AC)		Phil Phillips (Roath)	
1930	Stan Macey (Newport AC)	16.2	Frank Whitcutt (Newport AC)		Phil Phillips (Roath)	

1931	Stan Macey (Newport AC)	18.4	Phil Phillips (Roath)		A D Challis (Swansea Valley)	
1932	Stan Macey (Newport AC)	16.8	Phil Phillips (Roath)		Cyril F Bond (Cardiff Police)	
1933	Stan Macey (Newport AC)	16.8	G W C Jones (Swansea CFC)		only 2 finishers	
1934	Stan Macey (Newport AC)	16.8	T T Simmonds (Surrey)		Cyril F Bond (Cardiff Police)	
1935	T T Simmonds (Met Police)	16.4	Cyril F Bond (Cardiff Police)		Stan Macey (Newport AC)	
1936	T T Simmonds (Met Police)	16.8	Cyril F Bond (Cardiff Police)		only 2 finishers	
1937	T T Simmonds (Met Police)	16.2	Cyril F Bond (Cardiff Police)		only 2 athletes	
1938	Cyril F Bond (Cardiff Police)	17.4	Hubert Stubbs (Poly)		I Davies (Penrhys)	
1939	Leslie Hayes (Hendy AC)	17.2	J M K Marsh (Newport AC)		only 2 athletes	
1946	event not held					
1947	Mervyn Rosser (Lond Univ)	17.4	E James (Mond AC)		only 2 athletes	
1948	Mervyn Rosser (Lond Hosp)	18.3	M Lloyd (Aberdare GS)		K E Frederickson (Newport H)	
1949	Mervyn Rosser (Poly)	16.0	M Ricketts (St Gregorys AC)		K E Frederickson (Newport H)	
1950	Clive Balch (London AC)	16.4	Mervyn Rosser (London Univ)		A H Roads (Swansea AC)	
1951	Bob Shaw (Manchester GS)	16.4	Clive Balch (London AC)		A H Roads (Cardiff Univ)	
1952	Clive Balch (London AC)	17.0	only one athlete			
1953	Mervyn Rosser (Poly)	16.6	Richard Greening (Newp H)	17.6	W E Manning (Port Talbot)	20.0
1954	Bob Shaw (Achilles)	15.1	Martyn Gatehouse (Brist Un)	15.8	Clive Balch (London AC)	16.5
1955	Bob Shaw (Achilles)	15.2	Martyn Gatehouse (Roath)	15.7	N R Hughes (Welch Regt)	19.9
1956	Martyn Gatehouse (Roath)	16.3	H Davies (Trinity College)	17.3	H A Templeman (Carmarthen)	19.2
1957	Bob Shaw (Achilles)	15.6	Gwilym Thomas (Loughbor)	16.4	Keith Davitte (Port Talbot)	17.6
1958	Martyn Gatehouse (Shaftes)	15.5	J Chamberlain (StMaryHos)	16.3	Eric Darlow (RAF)	16.3
1959	Martyn Gatehouse (Shaftes)	16.3	R Davies (Lewis Sch)	17.0	W Griffiths (Cwmlai)	19.1
1960	Brian Whipp (Loughboro)	18.3	Andrew Fear (Hampstead)	DSQ	only 2 athletes	
1961	Frank GlynneJones (Achilles)	14.9	John Lister (Birchgrove)	15.0	Andrew Fear (Hampstead)	17.9
1962	Frank GlynneJones (Camb U)	15.2	John Lister (Birchgrove)	15.2	Andrew Fear (Old Eliz)	15.9
1963	John Lister (Birchgrove)	15.6	Andrew Fear (Watford)	17.2	only 2 athletes	
1964	John Lister (Birchgrove)	15.7	Andrew Fear (Welwyn)	16.0	B G Edwards (LTC)	16.5
1965	John Lister (Birchgrove)	14.8	David Williams (Lond Univ)	15.0	Goronwy Davies (Staffs TC)	15.2
1966	John Lister (Birchgrove)	14.8	Goronwy Davies (Poly)	14.9	Clive Longe (Roath)	15.4
1967	Alan Bergiers (Carmarthen)	15.5	only one athlete			
1968	Alan Bergiers (Carmarthen)	15.0	only one athlete			

110 metres hurdles

1969	Alun James (Carmarthen)	14.9	Alan Bergiers (Carmarthen)	15.2	Barrie Williams (Pontadawe)	15.8
1970	Howard Rooks (Surrey B)	14.7				
1971	Berwyn Price (Cardiff)	14.5	Roger Rees (Carmarthen)	15.8	Les Prince (Boro Rd College)	16.0
1972	Howard Rooks (Surrey B)	14.8	Clive Webb (Aberystwyth)	16.4		
1973	Howard Rooks (Surrey B)	15.1	Ninian Davies (Cardiff Coll)	15.5	only 2 athletes	
1974	Dick Gyles (Cardiff)	15.6	Ninian Davies (Cardiff Coll)	15.7	J Owen (Cardiff Univ)	16.8
1975	Orrie Fenn (Leic Univ)	15.5	Wynford Leyshon (Cardiff)	15.9		
1976	Tudor Bidder (Cardiff)	16.4	Neddyn Lloyd (Cardiff Coll)	16.8	Charles Davies (Newport)	17.1
1977	Berwyn Price (Cardiff)	14.5	Neddyn Lloyd (Carmarthen)	15.9	Tudor Bidder (Swansea)	16.5
1978	Berwyn Price (Cardiff)	14.0	Huw Jones (Oxford)	14.8	Mike Morgan (Army)	15.0
1979	Berwyn Price (Cardiff)	14.4	Tudor Bidder (Cardiff)	15.5	Neil Thomas (Carmarthen)	15.6
1980	Nick Alexander (Cardiff)	15.17	Huw Jones (Oxford)	15.21	Neil Hammersley (Cleddau)	15.81
1981	Berwyn Price (Swansea)	14.29	Huw Jones (Oxford)	14.83	Nick Alexander (Cardiff)	15.21
1982	Berwyn Price (Swansea)	14.20	Nigel Walker (Cardiff)	14.66	Huw Jones (Oxford)	14.94
1983	Nigel Walker (Cardiff)	14.7	Alan Tapp (Barry)	14.9	Tudor Bidder (Cardiff)	15.6
1984	Colin Jackson (Cardiff)	15.56	James Mason (Crawley)	16.05	Nigel Skinner (Cardiff)	17.20
1985	Colin Jackson (Cardiff)	14.37	Alan Tapp (Birchfield)	15.72	Philip Davies (TVH)	15.88
1986	Colin Jackson (Cardiff)	13.51	Nigel Walker (Cardiff)	13.66	Alan Tapp (Birchfield)	14.23
1987	Colin Jackson (Cardiff)	13.51	Paul Gray (Cardiff)	14.50	Alan Tapp (Wolves)	15.08
1988	Alan Tapp (Birchfield)	14.3	Nick Dakin (Newham)	14.6	James Mason (Crawley)	14.9
1989	Nick Dakin (Newham)	14.39	James Mason (Crawley)	14.87	Richard Harbour (Barry)	15.25
1990	Nigel Walker (Cardiff)	14.14	Rhys Davies (Cardiff)	15.24	Rob Kingsborough (Stoke)	16.05
1991	Nigel Walker (Cardiff)	14.30	Nick Dakin (Loughboro)	14.81	Berian Davies (Swansea)	14.87
1992	Colin Jackson (Brecon)	13.45	Nigel Walker (Cardiff)	13.84	Colin Bovell (Cardiff)	14.46
1993	Paul Gray (Cardiff)	14.06	Nick Dakin (Newham)	14.40	James Hughes (Cardiff)	14.44
1994	Paul Gray (Cardiff)	14.38	James Hughes (Cardiff)	14.77	Nick Dakin (Newham)	15.40
1995	Colin Bovell (Newham)	14.5	Nick Dakin (Newham)	15.2	only 2 athletes	
1996	James Archampong (Swansea)	14.3	James Hillier (Newport)	15.6	Matthew Eveleigh (Cardiff)	15.7
1997	James Archampong (Swansea)	14.61	James Hillier (Newport)	15.71	Shaun Robson (Newport)	16.00
1998	James Archampong (Swansea)	15.00	Ciaran Doherty (Cardiff)	15.21	Matthew Butler (Cardiff)	15.78
1999	James Hillier (Birchfield)	16.38	Geoff Ingram (Norwich)	17.96	only 2 athletes	
2000	Paul Gray (Cardiff)	14.36	Nathan Palmer (Cardiff)	14.61	Luke Gittens (Cardiff)	16.18

220 yards hurdles

1958	Martyn Gatehouse (Shaftes)	25.8	J M Brownhill (Cardiff TC)	27.1	Ray Gazzard (Birchgrove)	27.2
1959	Martyn Gatehouse (Shaftes)	26.8	Ray Gazzard (Birchgrove)	27.0	J D Carter (Newport)	27.6

1960	Ray Gazzard (Birchgrove)	26.5	Andrew Fear (Hampstead)	26.8	D J Farrant (Oxford)	26.8
1961	Frank GlynneJones (Achilles)	25.5	John Lister (Birchgrove)	25.5	D Jones (Cardiff TC)	26.4
1962	Frank GlynneJones (CambU)	24.9	John Lister (Birchgrove)	25.0	Andrew Fear (Old Eliz)	26.3
1963	John Lister (Birchgrove)	25.7	David Rees (Swansea Univ)	27.2	Antonio Pelopida (Gloucs)	27.3
1964	John Lister (Birchgrove)	26.4	Andrew Fear (Welwyn)	26.9	only 2 athletes	

440 yards hurdles

1950	Mervyn Rosser (Lond Univ)	63.3	Richard Greening (Newport)		Hywel Williams (Roath)	
1951	Richard Greening (Newport)	62.0	Hywel Williams (Roath)		A Richards (Roath)	
1952	H Cohen (Roath)	73.0	only one athlete			
1953	Gareth Lewis (Aberys Un)	60.6	Richard Greening (Newport)	63.6	W E Manning (Port Talbot)	70.4
1954	Bob Shaw (Achilles)	54.8	K Frederickson (Newport)	58.0	Gareth Lewis (Aberys Un)	61.5
1955	Bob Shaw (Achilles)	55.2	K Frederickson (Newport)	58.5	M J Sparkes (RAF)	62.9
1956	R T Thomasson (Christie)	58.8	B H Lewis (Roath)	60.9	K H Thomas (Birchgrove)	62.4
1957	Gwilym Thomas (Lough)	59.6	B Moore (Birchgrove)	63.0	John Parry (Llanelli)	72.0
1958	Keith Davitte (Swan Univ)	60.4	R T Thomasson (Christie)	61.4	Eric Inwood (Roath)	64.6
1959	Brian Lewis (Llandrind GS)	58.5	Martyn Gatehouse (Shaftes)		Hedydd Davies (Carmarthen)	
1960	Brian Lewis (Llandrind GS)	58.1	Tony Clemo (Birchgrove)	62.2	Brian James (Bournemouth)	64.6
1961	John Parry (Brighton)	56.8	Brian Lewis (Birchfield)	57.0	Keith Davitte (Port Talbot)	60.9
1962	John Parry (Brighton)	57.6	Roy Harvey (Cardiff TC)	61.6	Alan Marshall (Merthyr)	64.5
1963	David Rees (Swan Univ)	56.7	Brian Lewis (Cardiff TC)	57.7	Alan Marshall (Merthyr)	69.0
1964	David Rees (London Univ)	57.8	Steve Williams (Whitland)	62.0	Berkeley Edwards (Card C)	64.5
1965	John Watkins (Army)	56.0	John Lewis (Pontypridd S)	56.5	David Rees (London Un)	57.4
1966	John Lewis (Cardiff TC)	55.9	Roger Richardson (Birm Un)	57.2	John Watkins (Wd Green)	58.1
1967	Roger Richardson (Birm Un)	58.4	only one athlete			
1968	Roger Richardson (Birm Un)	55.4	Ted Savill (Birchgrove)	55.9	Wynford Leyshon (Neath)	

400 metres hurdles

1969	Ted Savill (RAF)	56.9	Barrie Williams (Pontardawe)	57.3	R M Adams (Cheltenham)	62.4
1970	John Lewis (Cardiff)	53.4	Keith Lancey (Swansea)	55.0	Ted Savill (Cardiff)	58.4
1971	Wynford Leyshon (Card Un)	56.7	Michael DeClair (Cleddau)	62.6	only 2 athletes	
1972	Wynford Leyshon (Card Un)	53.5	Keith Lancey (Swansea)	54.3	George Clues (Carmarthen)	57.2
1973	Bob Roberts (Bristol)	54.3	S Phillips (Cardiff College)	57.8	Charles Davies (Gilwern)	59.5
1974	Lionel Godfrey (Windsor)	56.8	B Lease (Cardiff)	59.1	Wayne Hughes (Rhondda)	59.2
1975	Wynford Leyshon (Cardiff)	52.8	Keith Lancey (Swansea)	53.5	Orrie Fenn (Leic Univ)	54.4
1976	Colin O'Neill (Bristol)	52.8	Wynford Leyshon (Cardiff)	54.2	Lionel Godfrey (Windsor)	55.6
1977	Colin O'Neill (Bristol)	51.8	Steve James (Wolves)	53.1	Alun James (Stretford)	53.4
1978	Steve James (Wolves)	52.3	Robert Davies (Carmarthen)	55.4	Charles Davies (Newport)	55.9
1979	Derek Fishwick (Cardiff)	53.08	Colin O'Neill (Bristol)	53.61	Neil Hammersley (Cleddau)	54.57
1980	Derek Fishwick (Cardiff)	53.57	Colin O'Neill (Bristol)	54.26	Neil Hammersley (Cleddau)	54.63
1981	Derek Fishwick (Cardiff)	53.27	Neil Hammersley (Cleddau)	53.51	Dafydd Jon Owen (Herc W)	54.88
1982	Neil Hammersley (Ipswich)	52.99	Derek Fishwick (Cardiff)	53.39	Dafydd Jon Owen (Herc W)	55.63
1983	Derek Fishwick (Cardiff)	53.0	Dafydd Jon Owen (Herc W)	54.8	Tudor Bidder (Cardiff)	55.7
1984	Nick Dakin (Bristol)	54.1	Dafydd Jon Owen (Herc W)	55.3	Derek Fishwick (Cardiff)	55.4
1985	Philip Harries (Derby)	52.86	Derek Fishwick (Cardiff)	53.61	Neil Hammersley (Ipswich)	54.72
1986	Neil Hammersley (Ipswich)	52.78	Philip Harries (Derby)	54.21	Russ Williams (R Navy)	54.25
1987	Philip Harries (Derby)	51.71	David Thomas (Colwyn Bay)	53.93	Neil Hammersley (Ipswich)	53.98
1988	David Thomas (Colwyn B)	54.5	David Griffin (Cardiff)	55.1	David Thomas (Cheltenham)	55.5
1989	Paul Gray (Cardiff)	53.36	Rob Kingsborough (Stoke)	53.37	Chris Cashell (Wrexham)	53.86
1990	Paul Gray (Cardiff)	52.29	Chris Cashell (Wrexham)	52.38	Neil Hammersley (Belgrave)	53.39
1991	Chris Cashell (Wrexham)	52.94	Paul Gray (Cardiff)	53.07	Neil Hammersley (Belgrave)	54.66
1992	Philip Harries (Derby)	51.84	Chris Cashell (Peterboro)	52.70	David Griffin (Dacorum)	52.87
1993	Chris Cashell (Peterboro)	53.26	Craig White (Sale)	54.02	Marvin Gray (Cardiff)	55.18
1994	David Griffin (Cardiff)	52.75	Chris Cashell (T Solent)	53.46	Marvin Gray (Cardiff)	54.03
1995	David Griffin (Cardiff)	52.7	Mark Rowlands (Swansea)	53.0	Marvin Gray (Cardiff)	53.7
1996	Marvin Gray (Cardiff)	52.8	Philip Harries (Derby)	52.8	Jeremy Bridger (T Solent)	53.7
1997	Paul Gray (Cardiff)	50.80	Mark Rowlands (Swansea)	51.63	Matthew Elias (Cardiff)	51.96
1998	Philip Harries (Derby)	57.50	only one athlete			
1999	James Hillier (Birchfield)	53.46	Geoff Ingram (Norwich)	56.68	only 2 athletes	
2000	Matthew Elias (Cardiff)	54.48	Andrew Davies (Llanelli)	58.87	only 2 athletes	

High Jump

1907	W I Thomas (Cwmbran FC)	1.60				
1908	W I Thomas (Cwmbran FC)	1.67				
1909	W I Thomas (Cwmbran FC)	1.62	E Greenway (Hay FC)	1.60	E J Protheroe (Newport AC)	
1910	W I Thomas (Cwmbran FC)	1.62	C V Sederman (St Saviours)	1.62	G M Whitworth (Sunderland)	1.62
1911	W I Thomas (Cwmbran FC)	1.52	I Prosser (Barry School)		William Titt (St Saviours)	
1912	Leslie Baynham (Swansea)	1.65	A B Davies (Abertillery H)	1.62	H R Ellis (Caerphilly)	
1913	A B Davies (Abertillery)	1.55	only one athlete			
1914	A B Davies (Abertillery)	1.60	S G Cockrane (Redwick FC)	1.55	Jno Parkin (St Saviours)	

1920	John D Jones (Abergele)	1.67	A B Davies (Oxford Univ)	1.60	William Morgan (Ebbw V)	1.60
1921	John D Jones (Abergele)	1.70	A B Davies (Oxford Univ)			
1922	H Clay (Chepstow H)	1.60	HAB Nevill (Welch Regt)	1.59	G Hacker (Tredegar)	1.57
1923	HAB Nevill (Welch Regt)	1.67	A B Davies (Abertillery H)	1.65		
1924	Gwyn Watts (Llancarfan)	1.52	H C Clay (Chepstow H)	1.50		
1925	Gwyn Watts (Grange YM)	1.65	O Bassett (Peterstone)	1.62	H M Eshelley (Spillers)	1.52
1926	Frank Whitcutt (Cardiff Un)	1.67	Gwyn Watts (Roath)		only 2 athletes	
1927	Frank Whitcutt (Cardiff Un)	1.73	Gwyn Watts (Roath)	1.70	S G Proll (Spillers)	
1928	Frank Whitcutt (Cardiff Un)	1.83	Gwyn Watts (Roath)	1.67	F C Wreford (Newport AC)	1.67
1929	Frank Whitcutt (Cardiff Un)	1.75	J D P Smith (Camb Univ)		Gwyn Watts (Roath)	
1930	Frank Whitcutt (Cardiff Un)	1.70	K W Jones (Monmouth GS)		Gwyn Watts (Roath)	
1931	E M Evans (Swansea Vall)	1.67	L Beale (Polytechnic)	1.65	K W Jones (Oxford Univ)	1.60
1932	L H Beale (Polytechnic)	1.62	E Harris (Swansea Vall)	1.60	Phil Phillips (Roath)	1.52
1933	L H Beale (Polytechnic)	1.70	T T Simmonds (Met Police)	1.67	S G Proll (Spillers)	1.57
1934	Frank Whitcutt (Newp AC)	1.73	L H Beale (Polytechnic)		T T Simmonds (Met Police)	
1935	Lewis Riden (Roath)	1.73	Hubert Stubbs (Newp AC)	1.70	T T Simmonds (Met Police)	1.70
1936	Lewis Riden (Roath)	1.65	T T Simmonds (Met Police)	1.62	Edwin Hale (Roath)	1.62
1937	Hubert Stubbs (Polytechnic)	1.65	Lewis Riden (Roath)	1.60	T T Simmonds (Met Police)	1.57
1938	Hubert Stubbs (Polytechnic)	1.84	Edwin Hale (Roath)		W V A Evans (Cardiff Univ)	
1939	Hubert Stubbs (Polytechnic)	1.73	W V A Evans (Newp AC)	1.57	Edwin Hale (Roath)	1.52
1946	Lewis Riden (Roath)	1.52	Edwin Hale (Roath)	1.45	only 2 athletes	
1947	Viv Cooper (Salisbury)	1.55	C B Coates (Bristol Univ)	1.55	Lewis Riden (Roath)	1.50
1948	N P Evans (Unattached)	1.73	A E Hickman (Mond AC)	1.62	W A Davies (Unattached)	1.62
1949	N P Evans (Aberdare)	1.73	Harold Straker (Roath)		B M Loughlin (RAOC)	
1950	G H Gillibrand (RAF)	1.67	Harold Straker (Roath)	1.65	Hywel Williams (Roath)	1.62
1951	Norman Finch (Army)	1.73	Emlyn Thomas (Swansea AC)		B M Loughlin (Pontypool)	
1952	B M Loughlin (Pontypool)	1.70	Hywel Williams (Roath)	1.67	M C Millwater (Newport H)	1.65
1953	Norman Finch (Bangor Un)	1.75	B M Loughlin (Pontypool)	1.73	M C Millwater (Newport H)	1.73
1954	Kevin Phillips (Swansea AC)	1.83	Chris Alele (Cardiff Univ)	1.78	Morton Evans (Carmarthen)	1.75
1955	Chris Alele (Cardiff Univ)	1.85	Kevin Phillips (Swansea AC)	1.83	Norman Watkins (Leics Un)	1.78
1956	Kevin Phillips (Swansea AC)	1.83	Aneurin Evans (Roath)	1.80	M C Millwater (Newport H)	1.80
1957	Aneurin Evans (Cowbridge)	1.78	Kevin Phillips (Swansea AC)	1.78	Terry Morgan (Newport AC)	1.73
1958	Terry Morgan (Newport AC)	1.83	Kevin Phillips (Swansea AC)	1.78	B Jones (Mitcham)	1.78
1959	Erith Williams (Swan Vall)	1.78	Terry Morgan (Newport AC)	1.67		
1960	John Lister (Birchgrove)	1.78	G Owen (Soro)	1.75	A Carter (Bristol)	1.73
1961	John Lister (Birchgrove)	1.85	Erith Williams (Birchfield)	1.83	P Williams (Caerphilly GS)	1.73
1962	E Morgan (Cardiff TC)	1.62	only one athlete			
1963	John Lister (Birchgrove)	1.80	W Jones (Swansea Univ)	1.65	W Roberts (Cardiff TC)	1.60
1964	Erith Williams (Birchfield)	1.83	P Wilson (Brighton)	1.78	John Lister (Birchgrove)	1.78
1965	John Lister (Birchgrove)	1.83	Erith Williams (Birchfield)	1.83	J L Williams (Carmarthen)	1.70
1966	Steve Hughes (RAF)	1.88	Erith Williams (Birchfield)	1.80	Edwin Clarke (Birchgrove)	1.80
1967	Edwin Clarke (Birchgrove)	1.85	Alan Bergiers (Carmarthen)	1.80	only 2 athletes	
1968	Alan Bergiers (Carmarthen)	1.80	only one athlete			
1969	Peter Lance (Loughboro)	1.88	Alan Bergiers (Carmarthen)	1.78	only 2 athletes	
1970	Steve Hughes (RAF)	1.90	Roger Stennett (Camb Univ)	1.90	only 2 athletes	
1971	Steve Hughes (RAF)	1.78	only one athlete			
1972	Mike Cummings (Cardiff)	1.83	Mike Ronan (Newport)		only 2 athletes	
1973	Peter Lance (Coventry)	2.00	Mike Cummings (Cardiff)	1.85	Peter Templeton (Bristol)	1.85
1974	Mike Cummings (Cardiff)	1.90	Richard Gyles (Cardiff)	1.90	Geraint Griffiths (Gloucs)	1.90
1975	Geraint Griffiths (Gloucs)	1.95	Mike Cummings (Loughboro)	1.89	Peter Templeton (Bristol)	1.86
1976	Geraint Griffiths (Gloucs)	1.98	Derek Fishwick (Cardiff)	1.85	Steve Brock=Carwyn Jones	1.85
1977	Geraint Griffiths (Stretford)	1.94	Chris Berry (Swansea)	1.85	Geoff Ward (Stoke)	1.80
1978	Trevor Llewelyn (B'heath)	2.05	George Robertson (Oxford)	1.95	Geraint Griffiths (Stretford)	1.90
1979	Trevor Llewelyn (B'heath)	2.00	Neil Thomas (Carmarthen)	1.95	Geraint Griffiths (Stretford)	1.95
1980	Trevor Llewelyn (B'heath)	2.05	Paul Evans (Swansea)	1.95		
1981	Trevor Llewelyn (B'heath)	2.10	Milton Palmer (Wolves)	2.05	Andrew McIver (Cardiff)	2.00
1982	Trevor Llewelyn (B'heath)	2.05	Andrew McIver (Cardiff)	2.00	Paul Evans (Swansea)	1.90
1983	Trevor Llewelyn (B'heath)	2.10	Paul Evans (Swansea)	2.05	John Hill (Solihull)	2.00
1984	Mike Powell (Wolves)	2.00	Stuart Gibbs (Royal Navy)	1.95	Robert James (Cardiff)	1.90
1985	John Hill (Solihull)	2.00	David Rowe (Cheltenham)	1.95	Robert James (Cardiff)	1.90
1986	Mike Powell (Wolves)	2.00	Chris Trotman (Daventry)	1.95	Stuart Gibbs (Royal Navy)	1.95
1987	Mike Powell (Wolves)	2.11	Paul Manwaring (Cleddau)	1.90	Neil Harris (Deeside)	1.90
1988	Mike Powell (Cardiff)	2.12	Paul Manwaring (Swansea)	2.00	Steve Ingram (Swansea)	2.00
1989	Mike Powell (Cardiff)	2.13	Steve Ingram (Swansea)	1.95	Robert James (Cardiff)	1.95
1990	Steve Ingram (Swansea)	1.95	Damian Stirling (Oswestry)	1.95	Paul Manwaring (Swansea)	1.95
1991	Ceri Payne (Barry)	2.08	Neil Harris (Deeside)	1.90	David Mahaffey (Swansea)	1.90
1992	Wayne Davies (Carmarthen)	1.95	Chris Harding (Bridgend)	1.90	D Mahaffey=DafyddEdwards	1.90
1993	Andrew Blow (Swansea)	2.00	Stuart Brown (Deeside)	1.95	Neil Harris (Deeside)	1.90
1994	David Nolan (Swansea)	2.06	Dafydd Edwards (Cardiff)	2.03	Stuart Brown (Deeside)	2.00
1995	Stuart Brown (Deeside)	2.05	Matthew Perry (Cardiff)	1.95	Rowan Griffiths (Swansea)	1.90
1996	Matthew Perry (Cardiff)	2.06	Rowan Griffiths (Swansea)	1.90	Scott Price (Newport)	1.85

1997	David Nolan (Swansea)	1.90	Nicholas BainVenn (Cardiff)	1.85	Giles Chesher (Brecon)	1.75
1998	Andrew Penk (Cardiff)	1.95	Stuart Brown (Deeside)	1.90	Kim Harland (Carmarthen)	1.90
1999	Rhodri Jones (Deeside)	1.95	Kim Harland (Carmarthen)	1.90	Rowan Griffiths (Newham)	1.85
2000	Robert Mitchell (Shaftesbury)	2.15	Rowan Griffiths (Newham)	1.95	only 2 athletes	

Pole Vault

1937	Cyril Evans (Port Talbot)	2.74	A Squires (Newport AC)	2.59	Ron Harries (Trebanos AC)	2.59
1938	Cyril Evans (Port Talbot)	3.11	L J Holmes (Maesteg) and V Gay (Loughboro) tied for 2nd place			2.74
1939	A Squires (Royal Tank Regt)	2.74	Cyril Evans (Port Talbot)	2.74	Ron Harries (Mond)	2.74
1946	event not held					
1947	G H Thorne (Port Talbot)	2.72	John Jones (Neath AC)		only 2 athletes	
1948	Cyril Evans (Port Talbot)	3.20	Hywel Davies (Unattached)		only 2 athletes	
1949	Hywel Davies (Llanelly AC)	2.89	N M Goff (Newport H)	2.44	Howell Hopkin (Mond)	2.28
1950	Derek Cole (Army)	3.20	F M Williams (Unattached)	3.05	D J Morgan (Aberystw Un)	2.89
1951	Ken Goodall (Loughboro)	3.43	Hywel Williams (Roath)	2.74	only 2 athletes	
1952	Hywel Williams (Roath)	3.35	Viv Jones (Caerphilly GS)	3.20	E M Williams (Aberyst Un)	3.20
1953	Ken Goodall (Loughboro)	3.58	Hywel Williams (Roath)	3.50	only 2 athletes	
1954	Ken Goodall (Birchfield)	3.50	only one athlete			
1955	Colin Fletcher (Bridgend)	3.50	Morton Evans (Carmarthen)	3.43	G C Coles (Bridgend)	3.27
1956	Colin Fletcher (Bridgend)	3.68	D Davies (Swansea Valley)	3.27	Terry Hamilton (Newp AC)	3.27
1957	Morton Evans (Llanelli)	3.50	James Johnson (Wrexham)	3.35	Colin Fletcher (Bridgend)	3.35
1958	Dewar Neill (RAF)	3.76	Colin Fletcher (Bridgend)	3.66	Terry Hamilton (Southgate)	3.50
1959	Morton Evans (Bath)	3.73	Royston Williams (Carm)		J Lee (Army)	3.50
1960	Colin Fletcher (Bridgend)	3.66	Morton Evans (TVH)	3.50	Trevor Evans (Achilles)	3.50
1961	Glyndwr Morris (Army)	3.73	John Ball (St Lukes)	3.66	John Evans (M y Dderwen)	3.50
1962	John Evans (Cardiff TC)	3.50	John Ball (St Lukes)	3.50	only 2 athletes	
1963	Glyndwr Morris (Army)	3.83	Graham Gibbs (Bridgend) and Peter Shorland (Brighton) tied			3.66
1964	Leslie Jones (Loughboro)	3.96	Peter Shorland (Brighton)	3.66	only 2 athletes	
1965	Graham Gibbs (Bridgend)	3.86	Glyndwr Morris (Army)	3.76	Hywel Williams (Roath)	3.66
1966	Glyndwr Morris (Army)	3.81	only one athlete			
1967	event was abandoned because of poor weather and could not be held at a later date					
1968	John Evans (Birchgrove)	3.82	only one athlete			
1969	Peter Challinor (Flint)	3.81	Anthony Toms (R Navy)	3.81	only 2 athletes	
1970	Leslie Jones (Blackheath)	4.07	only one athlete			
1971	Peter Challinor (Sale)	3.70	only one athlete			
1972	Richard Morris (Cardiff)	3.40	only one athlete			
1973	David Lease (Cardiff)	4.57	Gordon Pickering (Llandeilo)	3.78	Islwyn Rees (Carmarthen)	3.66
1974	David Lease (Cardiff)	4.50	Islwyn Rees (Carmarthen)	4.15	Gordon Pickering (Llandeilo)	4.00
1975	Rupert Goodall (Stoke)	4.20	Paul Edwards (Wolves)	3.65		
1976	Rupert Goodall (Stretford)	4.60	Islwyn Rees (Carmarthen)	4.00	Paul Edwards (Wolves)	4.00
1977	Rupert Goodall (Stretford)	4.50	Islwyn Rees (Carmarthen)	4.20	Geoff Ward (Stoke)	4.20
1978	Rupert Goodall (Stretford)	4.30	Brychan Jones (Cardiff)	4.00	Mark Howells (Carmarthen)	3.45
1979	David Lease (Cardiff)	4.35	Brychan Jones (Cardiff)	4.20	Nick Heal (Cardiff)	4.05
1980	Nick Heal (Cardiff)	4.30	Islwyn Rees (Carmarthen)	4.00		
1981	Brychan Jones (Aldershot)	4.30	David Lease (Cardiff)	4.15	Islwyn Rees (Carmarthen)	4.00
1982	Brychan Jones (Aldershot)	4.40	Mark Johnson (Cardiff)	4.20	Nick Heal (Cardiff)	4.10
1983	Brychan Jones (Aldershot)	4.40	Peter Lynk (Bournemouth)	4.00	Paul Edwards (Walton)	3.60
1984	Brychan Jones (Aldershot)	4.20	Nigel Skinner (Cardiff)	4.10	Peter Lynk (Bournemouth)	4.00
1985	Peter Lynk (Bournemouth)	4.40	Brychan Jones (Aldershot)	4.20	Glyn Price (Barry)	4.20
1986	Peter Lynk (Bournemouth)	4.40	Glyn Price (Barry)	4.40	Andrew Main (Nottingham)	4.40
1987	Peter Lynk (Southampton)	4.80	Glyn Price (Barry)	4.40	Doug Minter (Windsor)	4.40
1988	Tony Pithers (Cardiff)	4.20	Derek Fishwick (Cardiff)	4.10	Islwyn Rees=Doug Minter	4.00
1989	Glyn Price (Barry)	4.50	Islwyn Rees (Carmarthen)	4.00	Tim Thomas (Swansea)	3.90
1990	Neil Winter (Shaftesbury)	5.15	Glyn Price (Swansea)	4.60	Glyn Sutton (Newport)	4.40
1991	Tim Thomas (Swansea)	4.40	Glyn Price (Swansea)	4.20	Nick Pritchard (Newport)	4.20
1992	Tim Thomas (Swansea)	4.70	Nick Pritchard (Newport)	4.30	Ian Wilding (Stoke)	4.20
1993	Neil Winter (Shaftesbury)	5.25	Tim Thomas (Swansea)	4.80	Glyn Price (Swansea)	4.40
1994	Tim Thomas (Swansea)	4.90	Egryn Jones (Swansea)	4.50	David Gordon (Newham)	4.40
1995	Tim Thomas (Swansea)	5.00	Egryn Jones (Swansea)	4.50	David Gordon (Newham)	4.20
1996	Neil Winter (Shaftesbury)	5.25	Ian Wilding (Stoke)	5.00	Tim Thomas (Swansea)	4.60
1997	Tim Thomas (Swansea)	4.60	David Gordon (Newham)	4.40	Ian Wilding (Newham)	4.40
1998	Andrew Penk (Cardiff)	4.70	David Gordon (Newham)	4.60	Chris Type (Cardiff)	4.20
1999	Chris Type (Cardiff)	4.60	David Gordon (Newham)	4.00	Richard Stubbs (Preseli)	4.00
2000	Egryn Jones (Cardiff)	4.50	Gareth Lease (Cardiff)	4.20	David McFall (Brecon)	3.70

Long Jump

1907	Wallis Walters (Card Univ)	5.75				
1908	Wallis Walters (Card Univ)	6.03				
1909	Wallis Walters (Card Univ)	6.23	William Titt (St Saviours)	6.23	only 2 athletes	
1910	Wallis Walters (Card Univ)	5.93	G M Whitworth (Sunderl)	6.89	T J Parker (Aberavon)	5.56

1911	W L Walters (Goldsmith C)	6.00	A D Givons (Newport AC)		William Titt (St Saviours)	
1912	A D Givons (Newport AC)	5.92	W L Walters (Herne Hill)	5.89		
1913	J E Jones (Polytechnic H)	6.17	A D Givons (Newport AC)	6.07	Harry Uzzell (Newport AC)	5.26
1914	H R Morris (Spillers AC)	5.79	A D Givons (Newport AC)	5.60	Fred Dukes (Spillers AC)	5.54
1920	event not held					
1921	H C Williams (Abergele)	5.83	W J Purnell (Cardiff)			
1922	W J Purnell (Splott)	6.23	H C Clay (Chepstow)	6.02	J H OsborneJones (Aber Un)	5.73
1923	W J Purnell (Splott)	6.35	A L Hughes (Cardiff AC)			
1924	W J Purnell (Splott)	6.25	John Lloyd (Newbridge)	5.99	H C Clay (Chepstow)	5.55
1925	John Lloyd (Newport AC)	6.22	W J Purnell (Grange Baptist)	6.20	Matt Cullen (Swansea Vall)	6.02
1926	John Lloyd (Newport AC)	6.16	W J Purnell (Splott)	6.09	Ken Watkins (Newport AC)	5.97
1927	Frank Whitcutt (Cardiff Un)	6.06	W J Purnell (Splott)	5.92	Ken Watkins (Newport AC)	5.85
1928	Philip Phillips (Pontyclun)	6.17	W J Purnell (Splott)	5.83	R Rees (Swansea Valley)	
1929	Frank Whitcutt (Card Univ)	6.22	Philip Phillips (Roath)	6.04	W J Purnell (Splott)	6.01
1930	Philip Phillips (Card Univ)	6.04	A D Challis (Swansea Vall)		Frank Whitcutt (Newport AC)	
1931	R T Jones (Cardiff Univ)	6.24	Philip Phillips (Roath)	6.22	M T Parry (Port Talbot)	5.92
1932	R T Jones (Cardiff Univ)	6.30	A G Hawkins (RAF)	6.17	J P Rickard (Swansea Vall)	5.97
1933	Reg Oriel (Peterston)	6.23	L H Beale (Polytechnic H)	5.83	Philip Phillips (Roath)	5.80
1934	Reg Oriel (Spillers)	5.98	Gwyn J Evans (Newport AC)		D J M Davies (Pontypool)	
1935	Lewis Riden (Roath)	6.60	Gwyn J Evans (Newport AC)	6.14	D J M Davies (Newport AC)	6.06
1936	Lewis Riden (Roath)	6.77	Reg Oriel (Peterston)	6.31	Edwin Hale (Roath)	6.13
1937	T E Davies (Roath)	6.21	Gwyn J Evans (Newport AC)		H Thomas (Roath)	
1938	Brian Crossman (Roath)	6.34	Cyril Cupid (Swansea Vall)	6.31	Gwyn J Evans (Newport AC)	6.22
1939	John Cotter (Birchfield)	6.64	T E Davies (Loughboro)	6.44	Brian Crossman (Roath)	6.26
1946	P Zimmerman (Merioneth)	6.28	Brian Crossman (Roath)	6.20	Edwin Hale (Roath)	5.33
1947	W Neville Jones (Llanelly S)	6.25	Brian Crossman (Roath)	6.14	M E Lewis (R Engineers)	5.98
1948	D M Nears Crouch (CardTC)	5.95	Alvo Davies (Port Talbot)	5.94	John Cotter (Milocarian)	5.89
1949	Ken J Jones (Newport AC)	6.37	John Frowen (Pengam GS)	6.36	M E Lewis (Newport AC)	
1950	John Frowen (Pengam GS)	6.65	Gordon Wells (Card Univ)	6.48	K J Davies (Newport H)	6.28
1951	Alan Roche (Newport AC)	6.70	J Davies (Bristol)		Gordon Wells (Cardiff Univ)	
1952	Alan Roche (Newport AC)	6.74	Gordon Wells (Cardiff Univ)	6.34	D W Kelly (Aberyst Univ)	6.31
1953	G N Lewis (Unattached)	6.53	J H Davies (Newport H)	6.34	A H Thomas (Canton HS)	6.09
1954	Chris Alele (Cardiff Univ)	7.06	Gordon Wells (Rhondda V)	6.61	R G Taylor (Rhondda V)	6.46
1955	Norman Watkins (Leic Univ)	6.64	Roger Jones (Llanelli)	6.42	C Evans (Monmouth TC)	6.36
1956	Ray Gazzard (Birchgrove)	6.45	Roger Jones (Llanelli)	6.40	G N Lewis (RAF)	6.35
1957	Roger Jones (Llanelli)	6.49	T E Williams (Guys Hosp)	6.26	Norman Watkins (Leic Un)	6.25
1958	Bryan Woolley (Loughboro)	7.20	Ray Gazzard (Birchgrove)	7.01	Eric Darlow (RAF)	6.87
1959	Ray Gazzard (Birchgrove)	6.65	Brian Hardwick (Newp H)	6.20	Paul Sayzeland (Newp HS)	5.89
1960	Bryan Woolley (Loughboro)	6.86	Ray Gazzard (Birchgrove)	6.37	Brian Hardwick (Oakdale)	6.18
1961	Bryan Woolley (Birchfield)	7.16	Lynn Davies (Ogmore GS)	7.14	Terry Davies (Carmarthen)	7.03
1962	Lynn Davies (Cardiff TC)	7.40	Bryan Woolley (Birchfield)	6.91	Bleddyn Williams (Liv Un)	6.88
1963	Lynn Davies (Cardiff TC)	6.99	Gary Laycock (Monkton H)	6.80	R Williams (Whitchurch)	6.16
1964	Terry Davies (Carmarthen)	7.02	John Lister (Birchgrove)	7.01	Arthur Thomas (Card TC)	6.96
1965	Lynn Davies (Roath)	7.64	John Lister (Birchgrove)	7.07	John Lewis (Birchgrove)	6.83
1966	Lynn Davies (Roath)	7.75	John Lister (Birchgrove)	7.00	John Lewis (Cardiff TC)	6.84
1967	Gwyn Williams (Cardiff TC)	7.23	David Turner (Nailsea GS)	6.28	Keith Lowe (Roath)	6.14
1968	Gwyn Williams (Birchgrove)	7.02	only one athlete			
1969	Gwyn Williams (Cardiff)	7.20	John Elias (Cardiff)	6.82	Russell Church (Cardiff)	6.50
1970	Gwyn Williams (Cardiff)	7.22	John Phillips (Cardiff Coll)	6.84	John Lister (Cardiff)	6.73
1971	Keith Lowe (Cardiff)	6.80	Roger Shewell (Newport)	6.72	Russell Church (Cardiff)	5.98
1972	Kedrick Thompson (Card C)	7.02	R P Edwards (Cardiff)	6.85	Roger Shewell (Newport)	6.38
1973	Kedrick Thompson (Card C)	7.16	John Elias (Cardiff)	6.87	Godfrey Evans (Sale)	6.63
1974	Roy Turkington (Wolves)	7.34	Richard Gyles (Cardiff)	6.98	Kedrick Thompson (Card)	6.81
1975	Peter Templeton (Bristol)	7.26	Kedrick Thompson (Cardiff)	6.88	D Moralee (Unattached)	6.85
1976	No athletes reported for the event					
1977	Colin Wright (Stoke)	7.29	Geoff Ward (Stoke)	7.12	Martin Griffiths (Redhill)	6.98
1978	Graham Hughes (Cardiff)	7.15	Ken Cocks (W Cornwall)	7.05	Kedrick Thompson (B'burn)	6.65
1979	Colin Wright (Stoke)	6.92	Alan Keyse (Swansea Univ)	6.78	Martin Griffiths (Poly)	6.57
1980	David Rist (Gilwern)	6.45				
1981	Richard Jones (Deeside)	7.17	Steve Brock (Cardiff)	6.90	Ian Strange (Cardiff)	6.66
1982	Richard Jones (Deeside)	7.16	Steve Brock (Cardiff)	6.86	Chris Starr (RAF)	6.74
1983	Richard Jones (Deeside)	7.19	Paul Hawkins (Cardiff)	7.14	David Wood (Cardiff)	7.08
1984	Richard Jones (Wolves)	7.35	Stuart Gibbs (Royal Navy)	7.25	Steve Brock (Cardiff)	7.09
1985	David Wood (Cardiff)	6.95	Richard Jones (Wolves)	6.94	Simon Marsh (Barry)	6.71
1986	Paul Hawkins (Cardiff)	7.08	Richard Jones (Wolves)	6.92	Stuart Gibbs (Royal Navy)	6.74
1987	Marcus Browning (Chester)	7.12	George Robertson (Cardiff)	7.09	Steven Partridge (Swansea)	6.66
1988	Steve Partridge (Swansea)	7.15	Paul Hawkins (Cardiff)	6.94	Mark Harries (Carmarthen)	6.55
1989	Andrew Adey (Newport)	6.83	Garry Slade (Yate)	6.72	Gareth Davies (Swansea)	6.70
1990	Garry Slade (Yate)	7.25	Andrew Adey (Newport)	7.03	Paul Farmer (Cardiff)	7.00
1991	Garry Slade (Leeds)	7.46	Paul Farmer (Cardiff)	6.67	Andrew Adey (Newport)	6.65
1992	Garry Slade (Leeds)	7.65	Gareth Brown (Swindon)	7.21	Steve Ingram (Swansea)	6.86

1993	Garry Slade (Leeds)	7.31	Gareth Davies (Swansea)	6.85	Ian Roberts (Shaftesbury)	6.80
1994	Steve Ingram (Swansea)	7.91	Gareth Davies (Swansea)	7.25	Ian Roberts (Shaftesbury)	6.99
1995	Garry Slade (Cardiff)	7.24	Anthony Malcolm (Salisbury)	7.03	Steve Ingram (Swansea)	6.96
1996	Anthony Malcolm (Salisbury)	7.32	Lee Edwards (Cardiff)	6.90	Gareth James (Carmarthen)	6.78
1997	Ioan Hughes (Ynys Mon)	7.07	Andrew Wooding (Colwyn B)	7.05	Matthew Perry (Cardiff)	7.03
1998	Andrew Wooding (Colwyn B)	7.03	James Morris (Swansea)	6.73	Ioan Hughes (Trafford)	6.60
1999	Andrew Thomas (Llanelli)	7.01	Alex Jackson (Neath)	6.95	Anthony Malcolm (Cardiff)	6.79
2000	Anthony Malcolm (Cardiff)	7.55	Gareth Brown (Swindon)	7.41	Andrew Thomas (Llanelli)	7.16

Triple Jump

1924	John Lloyd (Newport AC)	12.37	Matt Cullen (Swansea Vall)	11.30		
1925	John Lloyd (Newport AC)	12.79	J W White (Port Talbot)	12.19	A L Hughes (Cardiff AC)	11.15
1926	Frank Whitcutt (Card Univ)	13.17	John Lloyd (Newport AC)	13.14	J W White (Port Talbot)	
1927	Frank Whitcutt (Card Univ)	12.63	Matt Cullen (Swansea Vall)			
1928	Frank Whitcutt (Card Univ)	12.58	E J Taylor (Wheatsheaf)	12.22	R Reece (Swansea Vall)	11.57
1929	Frank Whitcutt (Card Univ)	12.80	J Higgins (Swansea Vall)	12.44	A E Johnson (Newport AC)	11.78
1930	Frank Whitcutt (Newport AC)	12.51	J Higgins (Swansea Vall)	12.43	P Phillips (Roath)	11.86
1931	J Higgins (Swansea Vall)	12.66	P Phillips (Roath)	12.36	L Beale (Polytechnic)	12.36
1932	J Higgins (Swansea Vall)	12.39	E Griffiths (Swansea Vall)	12.09	L Beale (Polytechnic)	11.86
1933	Gwynne Evans (Cardiff Un)	12.81	S J Williams (Quakers Yd)	12.47	Reg Oriel (Peterston)	12.41
1934	Gwynne Evans (Cardiff Un)	13.51	S J Williams (Quakers Yd)	12.34	Reg Oriel (Spillers AC)	11.86
1935	Gwynne Evans (Cardiff Un)	13.51	R G W Hopkins (Swansea V)	12.77	D J Lewis (R Tank Corps)	12.25
1936	Gwynne Evans (Cardiff Un)	13.14	R G W Hopkins (Swansea V)	12.98	S J Williams (Quakers Yard)	12.43
1937	Gwynne Evans (Newport AC)	12.60	R G W Hopkins (Swansea V)	12.11	W V A Evans (Cardiff Univ)	11.72
1938	Gwynne Evans (Newport AC)	13.31	W Morris (Swansea Vall)	13.00	W V A Evans (Cardiff Univ)	12.89
1939	Gwynne Evans (Southgate H)	13.53	Brian Crossman (Roath)	13.52	K Campbell (Southend)	13.28
1946	Brian Crossman (Roath)	12.52	N P Evans (Caerleon Coll)	12.51	P Zimmerman (Merioneth)	12.44
1947	Brian Crossman (Roath)	12.85	L H Davies (Unattached)	12.32	J B Williams (Unattached)	11.43
1948	Gwyn Harris (Lewis Sch)	13.02	M E G Lewis (Newport AC)	12.57	John Cotter (Milocarian)	12.24
1949	Gordon Wells (RAF)	14.52	John Frowen (Pengam Sch)	13.66	Gwyn Harris (Welch Regt)	13.54
1950	Gordon Wells (Cardiff Univ)	14.21	John Frowen (Pengam Sch)	13.97	T G Davies (Swansea Vall)	12.98
1951	Gordon Wells (Cardiff Univ)	13.20	Norman Finch (Army)		T G Davies (Swansea Vall)	
1952	Gordon Wells (Cardiff Univ)	13.31	J L Tapper (Birchfield)	13.09	D W Kelly (Aberyst Univ)	12.14
1953	Norman Finch (Bangor Un)	13.73	K G Fisher (Aberyst Univ)	13.21	J H Davies (Newport H)	12.98
1954	D E Williams (Bangor Un)	13.63	Gordon Wells (Rhondda Vall)	13.43	Richard Dodd (Aberys Un)	12.75
1955	Robert Sussex (Merthyr)	13.77	Gordon Wells (Rhondda)	13.09	C Evans (Monmouth TC)	13.00
1956	Robert Sussex (Merthyr)	13.88	David J Williams (Hendy)	13.32	Terrence Morgan (Newport)	13.10
1957	T E Williams (Guys Hosp)	13.30	Terrence Morgan (Newport)	13.03	C Reid (Newport AC)	12.57
1958	Richard Dodd (Loughboro)	14.57	Robert Sussex (Merthyr)	13.82	Aneurin Evans (Roath)	13.33
1959	Aneurin Evans (W Guards)	13.89	D H Price (Lensbury AC)	13.42	Norman Richards (Rhondda V)	
1960	Peter Walker (Saro AC)	13.69	Gwilym Owen (Saro AC)	13.36	Brian Hardwick (Oakdale)	13.19
1961	Lynn Davies (Ogmore GS)	14.61	Gwilym Owen (Saro AC)	14.01		
1962	Lynn Davies (Cardiff TC)	15.29	Peter Walker (Loughboro)	14.72	Nigel Green (St Julians HS)	13.95
1963	Peter Walker (Welsh Coll)	13.83	Nigel Green (Swansea Univ)	13.83	D Jones (Swansea Univ)	13.33
1964	Graham Webb (Newp HS)	14.46	Tim Jennings (Unattached)	14.26	Ralph Ford (Abertillery)	13.88
1965	Graham Webb (Newport H)	14.12	Ralph Ford (Abertillery)	13.79	Dennis Skuse (Wiggin)	13.56
1966	Peter Walker (Unattached)	15.05	Gerald Evans (Flint)	14.72	Graham Webb (Cardiff TC)	14.46
1967	Peter Walker (Shrewsbury)	14.81	Gerald Evans (Sale)	14.56	Martyn Roberts (Cardiff Un)	14.32
1968	Graham Webb (Cardiff TC)	14.72	Gerald Evans (Sale)	14.64	Martyn Roberts (Cardiff Un)	14.12
1969	Graham Webb (Newport)	14.60	Peter Walker (Shrewsbury)	14.44	Spencer Jones (Carmarthen)	14.03
1970	John Phillips (Cardiff Coll)	14.03	Graham Webb (Cardiff)	13.67	Martyn Roberts (Cardiff)	13.33
1971	Graham Webb (Cardiff)	12.27	only one athlete			
1972	Peter Walker (Sale)	14.15	only one athlete			
1973	John Phillips (Cardiff)	14.52	Philip Jones (Ealing)	14.20	Gerald Evans (Sale)	14.12
1974	John Phillips (Cardiff)	14.83	Martin Lucas (Cardiff)	13.96	S Phillips (Cardiff Coll)	13.13
1975	John Phillips (Cardiff)	15.07	Sean Power (Cardiff)	15.02	Martin Lucas (Cardiff)	13.86
1976	John Phillips (Cardiff)	15.05	Sean Power (Cardiff)	14.77	Martin Lucas (Cardiff)	14.45
1977	John Phillips (Cardiff)	14.95	Sean Power (Cardiff)	14.55	Peter Davies (TVH)	14.33
1978	John Phillips (Cardiff)	15.88	Sean Power (Cardiff)	14.60	Alan Keyse (Hereford)	13.83
1979	John Phillips (Cardiff)	14.42	Alan Keyse (Hereford)	13.57	T Bellis (Cardiff)	13.46
1980	Sean Power (Cardiff)	14.80				
1981	David Wood (Cardiff)	15.42	Richard Jones (Deeside)	14.67	Sean Power (Cardiff)	14.27
1982	David Wood (Cardiff)	15.19	Richard Jones (Deeside)	14.46	Sean Power (Cardiff)	13.89
1983	David Wood (Cardiff)	15.23	Richard Jones (Deeside)	14.30	Stuart McKenzie (Bridgend)	13.94
1984	David Wood (Cardiff)	15.40	Stuart McKenzie (Bridgend)	14.62	Paul Hawkins (Cardiff)	14.10
1985	David Wood (Cardiff)	15.11	Stuart McKenzie (Bridgend)	14.18	Robert James (Cardiff)	13.21
1986	David Wood (Cardiff)	15.84	Stuart McKenzie (Swansea)	14.72	Sean Power (Cardiff)	14.24
1987	David Wood (Cardiff)	14.80	Stuart McKenzie (Swansea)	14.01	Gareth Davies (Cardiff)	13.65
1988	Gareth Davies (Cardiff)	14.68	David Richards (Stafford)	13.75	Geoff Ward (Wrexham)	13.29
1989	David Wood (Cardiff)	15.79	Paul Farmer (Cardiff)	14.53	Gareth Davies (Swansea)	13.57
1990	David Wood (Cardiff)	15.20	Paul Farmer (Cardiff)	14.71	David Richards (Swansea)	13.42

1991	David Wood (Cardiff)	14.48	Paul Farmer (Cardiff)	14.41	Garry Slade (Leeds)	14.28
1992	Paul Farmer (Cardiff)	14.64	Garry Slade (Leeds)	14.46	David Wood (Cardiff)	14.36
1993	Garry Slade (Leeds)	14.46	Gareth Brown (Swindon)	13.97	Julian Hall (Cardiff)	13.23
1994	Paul Farmer (Cardiff)	14.61	Sean Power (Cardiff)	12.99	only 2 athletes	
1995	Gareth Davies (Cardiff)	14.39	Chas Madeira Cole (Carm)	13.79	Ryan Robinson (Torfaen)	13.56
1996	Chas Madeira Cole (Carm)	14.04	Darren Morgan (Preseli)	12.97	Mark Pickett (Torfaen)	12.34
1997	Chas Madeira Cole (Carm)	15.32	Jon Hilton (Sale)	14.79	Paul Ellis (Colwyn Bay)	13.36
1998	Chas Madeira Cole (Carm)	15.40	Jon Hilton (Sale)	14.87	Steven Shalders (Cardiff)	14.46
1999	Chas Madeira Cole (Newham)	15.35	Jon Hilton (Sale)	15.02	Steve Alvey (Loughboro)	13.93
2000	Chas Madeira Cole (Newham)	15.38	Jon Hilton (Sale)	15.37	Steven Frost (Wrexham)	14.11

Shot

1923	Michael Roche (Mon Pol)	9.98	F Skelly (Glamorgan Police)		William Kear (Mon Police)	
1924	George Dillaway (Mon Pol)	11.53	Michael Roche (Mon Police)			
1925	Michael Roche (Mon Police)	10.67	George Dillaway (Mon Police)	10.44	Matt Cullen (Swansea V)	9.98
1926	event not held					
1927	George Dillaway (Mon Pol)	10.78	M Broaders (Swansea Vall)	9.83		
1928	George Dillaway (Mon Pol)	10.64	D J Price (Mon Police)	10.02		
1929	George Dillaway (Mon Pol)	11.03	F C Wreford (Newport AC)	8.60		
1930	George Dillaway (Mon Pol)	11.49	D J Price (Mon Police)		Matt Cullen (Swansea V)	
1931	Arthur W Lewis (Aber Un)	12.85	George Dillaway (Mon Pol)	11.22	D J Price (Mon Police)	11.10
1932	George Dillaway (Mon Pol)	11.38	R L Evans (Swansea Valley)	10.59		
1933	George Dillaway (Mon Pol)	10.93	W R Newton (Newport AC)	8.84	only 2 athletes	
1934	Arthur W Lewis (Exeter H)	11.63	George Dillaway (Mon Pol)	10.93	only 2 athletes	
1935	Arthur W Lewis (Exeter H)	11.57	George Dillaway (Mon Pol)		only 2 athletes	
1936	Arthur W Lewis (Exeter H)	12.89	Fred Wood (Kent Police)	11.03	George Dillaway (Mon Pol)	10.45
1937	George Dillaway (Mon Pol)	10.48	W Newman (Abertillery)		M Jones (Abertillery)	
1938	John Cotter (Birchfield)	11.78	George Dillaway (Mon Pol)		W T M Jones (Mon Police)	
1939	John Cotter (Birchfield)	12.33	W T M Jones (Mon Police)	10.21	E S Rankin (Cardiff Tech)	10.13
1946	Arthur W Lewis (Lough)	11.83	Howell Hopkin (Mond AC)		John Jones (Neath AC)	
1947	Albert Hoyle (Mon Police)	9.54	John Jones (Neath AC)		only 2 athletes	
1948	John Cotter (Milocarian)	11.33	Arthur W Lewis (Loughboro)	11.00	Brian Carter (Mond)	10.64
1949	Brian Carter (Mond)	11.68	T J Raubenheimer (Wycombe)	11.00	L T Hodson (Mon Police)	10.81
1950	Brian Carter (Mond)	11.75	Viv Evans (Welsh Regiment)	11.35	Bill Kingsbury (Army)	11.14
1951	Brian Carter (Mond)	12.49	D Jones (Pontypool)	12.21	Viv Evans (Welsh Regiment)	
1952	Brian Carter (Mond)	12.64	Viv Evans (Welsh Brigade)	12.11	Hywel Williams (Roath)	11.85
1953	Brian Carter (Mond)	12.71	Bill Kingsbury (Army)	12.67	Viv Evans (Swansea AC)	12.64
1954	Bill Kingsbury (S London H)	12.60	Brian Carter (Mond)	12.55	Tony Morgan (R Artillery)	11.58
1955	John Thomas (Birchgrove)	12.86	Ken L Jones (Aberys Un)	12.44	Brian Carter (Mond)	12.44
1956	Bill Kingsbury (Rhondda)	12.32	Brian Carter (Mond)	12.29	John H Williams (Llanelli)	11.99
1957	John Powell Jones (Belgrave)	13.82	Hywel Williams (RAF)	12.90	Bill Kingsbury (Rhondda V)	12.16
1958	Hywel Williams (RAF)	13.38	Aneurin Evans (Roath)	12.75	Bill Kingsbury (Rhondda V)	12.62
1959	John R Davies (Llanelli GS)	14.11	Arthur Richardson (JSum Sch)	13.21	Hywel Williams (RAF)	13.00
1960	Arthur Richardson (JSum Sch)	14.77	M Jones (Oakdale AC)	11.75	Brian Penny (Luton)	11.60
1961	Arthur Richardson (JSum Sch)	14.70	Aneurin Evans (Caerleon)	14.31	Archie Buttriss (Met Police)	13.28
1962	Archie Buttriss (Heref Pol)	14.01	Aneurin Evans (Cardiff TC)	13.68	Lawrie Hall (TVH)	12.65
1963	Archie Buttriss (Heref Pol)	14.75	Aneurin Evans (Cardiff TC)	14.21	D Jones (Swansea Vall)	13.33
1964	Archie Buttriss (Birchfield)	15.11	John Walters (Birchgrove)	14.84	Lawrie Hall (TVH)	13.04
1965	John Walters (Birchgrove)	14.88	Archie Buttriss (Birchfield)	14.02	David Stears (Cardiff TC)	13.12
1966	Clive Longe (Roath)	14.93	Arthur Richardson (Flint)	14.81	John Walters (Birchgrove)	14.58
1967	John Walters (Birchgrove)	14.53	Brian Penny (Swansea)	13.71	Peter Sutton (Birchgrove)	13.28
1968	John Walters (Birchgrove)	15.48	Peter Sutton (Birchgrove)	13.88	Brian Penny (Swansea)	13.05
1969	John Walters (Cardiff)	15.28	Archie Buttriss (Hereford)	14.75	Ted Kelland (Royal Navy)	13.88
1970	John Walters (Cardiff)	16.25	Brian Penny (Swansea)	15.15	Peter Sutton (Cardiff)	14.93
1971	John Walters (Cardiff)	15.81	Paul Rees (Southampton)	14.41	Brian Penny (Swansea)	13.98
1972	John Walters (Cardiff)	15.36	Erol Palsay (Cardiff)	15.06	Brian Penny (Swansea)	14.98
1973	Paul Rees (Southampton)	15.81	Ted Kelland (R Marines)	14.31	only 2 athletes	
1974	Paul Rees (Southampton)	15.93	John Walters (Cardiff)	14.38	R Hurley (Sutton)	11.37
1975	Ted Kelland (Royal Navy)	16.32	Paul Rees (Southampton)	15.79	John Walters (Cardiff)	13.80
1976	Paul Rees (Cardiff)	16.16	Ted Kelland (R Marines)	15.89	Kevin Jones (Cardiff)	14.53
1977	Paul Rees (Cardiff)	15.24	Ted Kelland (R Marines)	14.16	John Walters (Cardiff)	13.92
1978	Paul Rees (Bournemouth)	15.98	Ted Kelland (R Marines)	15.41	Martin Lockley (Birchfield)	13.92
1979	Paul Rees (Bournemouth)	16.33	Martin Lockley (Birchfield)	15.14	Ted Kelland (R Marines)	15.08
1980	Paul Rees (Bournemouth)	16.27	Martin Lockley (Birchfield)	15.79	John Walters (Cardiff)	14.02
1981	Paul Rees (Bournemouth)	15.89	Mark Hewer (Cardiff)	14.06	Shaun Pickering (Haringey)	13.88
1982	Paul Rees (Bournemouth)	15.17	Shaun Pickering (Haringey)	14.91	John Tym (N W Police)	14.22
1983	Shaun Pickering (Haringey)	16.13	Paul Edwards (Walton)	13.91	Nigel Winchcombe (Reading)	13.07
1984	Lee Wiltshire (Bournemouth)	15.74	Richard Davies (Wolves)	14.36	John Walters (Cardiff)	12.91
1985	Shaun Pickering (Haringey)	15.35	Lee Wiltshire (Portsmouth)	15.03	Paul Edwards (Wolves)	14.09
1986	Paul Edwards (Wolves)	15.59	Lee Wiltshire (Portsmouth)	15.38	Richard Davies (Wolves)	14.64
1987	Paul Edwards (Wolves)	17.08	Shaun Pickering (Haringey)	16.68	Lee Wiltshire (Portsmouth)	15.08

1988	Paul Edwards (Walton)	16.25	Clayton Turner (Crawley)	14.25	Nigel Winchcombe (Hercules)	13.48
1989	Paul Edwards (Walton)	18.15	Shaun Pickering (Haringey)	17.68	Lee Wiltshire (Southampton)	16.29
1990	Paul Edwards (Walton)	18.09	Shaun Pickering (Haringey)	16.89	Phil Olsen (Cardiff)	12.39
1991	Lee Wiltshire (Shaftesbury)	16.07	Clayton Turner (Crawley)	14.86	Andy Turner (Bournemouth)	13.14
1992	Shaun Pickering (Haringey)	18.31	Lee Wiltshire (Portsmouth)	15.06	Andy Turner (Bournemouth)	14.00
1993	Lee Wiltshire (Portsmouth)	16.53	Andy Turner (Bournemouth)	13.93	Alan Thomas (Met Police)	13.62
1994	Lee Wiltshire (Portsmouth)	16.93	Andy Turner (Bournemouth)	14.39	Alan Thomas (Met Police)	14.12
1995	Lee Wiltshire (Portsmouth)	14.93	Andy Turner (Crawley)	14.10	Alan Thomas (Walton)	13.34
1996	Andy Turner (Crawley)	14.11	Ewart Hulse (Colwyn Bay)	13.94	Justin Bryan (Torfaen)	12.79
1997	Shaun Pickering (Haringey)	19.15	Lee Newman (Belgrave)	16.18	Matthew Bundock (B'heath)	15.04
1998	Shaun Pickering (Haringey)	19.14	Andy Turner (Bournemouth)	13.93	Justin Bryan (Torfaen)	13.70
1999	Lee Newman (Belgrave)	16.26	Justin Bryan (Torfaen)	14.49	Andy Turner (Bournemouth)	14.34
2000	Andy Turner (Bournemouth)	14.59	Justin Bryan (Torfaen)	14.45	Ewart Hulse (Colwyn Bay)	13.06

Discus

1937	Matt Cullen (Swansea V)	29.88	Ned Jenkins (Port Talbot)	29.37	J Rees (Hendy AC)	28.50
1938	John Cotter (Birchfield)	33.84	Matt Cullen (Swansea V)	30.58	V Gay (Loughboro)	30.45
1939	John Cotter (Birchfield)	34.44	Matt Cullen (Swansea V)	27.64	T J Raubenheimer (Llanelly)	25.74
1946	Arthur W Lewis (Loughboro)	38.10	John Jones (Neath AC)	28.48	Lionel Pugh (Card Univ)	27.90
1947	D L Phillips (Carm YM)	31.68	H G Thomas (ATS Beachley)		John Jones (Neath AC)	
1948	Arthur W Lewis (Loughboro)	34.78	John Cotter (Milocarian)	34.23	Brian Carter (Mond)	32.29
1949	T J Raubenheimer (Wyc)	32.96	Arthur W Lewis (Loughboro)		Brian Carter (Mond)	
1950	T J Raubenheimer (Wyc)	35.78	Viv Evans (Welsh Regmt)	35.66	A L Ford (Loughboro)	34.43
1951	Viv Evans (Army)	36.49	Hywel Williams (Roath)	35.67	Bob Shaw (Manchester GS)	
1952	Hywel Williams (Roath)	39.80	Viv Evans (Welsh Brigade)	39.46	Bob Shaw (Oxford Univ)	38.08
1953	Hywel Williams (Roath)	40.34	John Thomas (Cardiff Coll)	40.28	Viv Evans (Swansea AC)	35.46
1954	John Thomas (Birchgrove)	35.90	D D Voyle (Cardiff Univ)	35.44	B Morgan (Aberystw Univ)	34.44
1955	John Thomas (Birchgrove)	38.54	M W Dyer (Welsh Regmt)	36.08	Dennis Stallard (Rhon AC)	34.26
1956	D D Voyle (Cardiff Univ)	34.26	Terence Morgan (Newport)	33.30	B L Lewis (Caerleon Coll)	33.08
1957	Norman Watkins (Leic Un)	36.42	Terence Morgan (Newport)	35.90	Mal Pemberton (Birm Un)	35.28
1958	Hywel Williams (RAF)	43.74	Mal Pemberton (Newport)	39.88	Norman Watkins (Birm Un)	36.56
1959	Hywel Williams (RAF)	42.26	Anthony Morgan (P Talbot)	39.69	Archie Buttriss (M Police)	39.06
1960	Arthur Richardson (JSum)	37.04	Anthony Morgan (P Talbot)	36.88	Brian Sexton (Roath)	31.90
1961	Mal Pemberton (Achilles)	44.58	Hywel Williams (Roath)	44.24	Aneurin Evans (Caerleon C)	40.76
1962	Aneurin Evans (Cardiff TC)	42.20	Archie Buttriss (Heref Pol)	40.39	Anthony Morgan (P Talbot)	36.43
1963	Hywel Williams (RAF)	45.62	Aneurin Evans (Caerleon)	44.00	Derek Hanlon (Birchgrove)	39.99
1964	Hywel Williams (Roath)	42.62	John Walters (Birchgrove)	37.90	Bill Treharne (Surrey)	34.51
1965	Hywel Williams (Roath)	43.70	Roger Beard (Pontypridd)	41.56	John Walters (Birchgrove)	39.66
1966	Clive Longe (Roath)	45.22	John Walters (Birchgrove)	43.28	Ted Kelland (Roath)	41.22
1967	John Walters (Birchgrove)	45.80	Hywel Williams (Roath)	44.22	Ted Kelland (Roath)	43.82
1968	John Walters (Birchgrove)	47.34	Hywel Williams (Roath)	43.38	Ted Kelland (Roath)	41.98
1969	Ted Kelland (R Navy)	46.66	John Walters (Cardiff)	46.40	Brian Penny (Swansea)	37.20
1970	John Walters (Cardiff)	46.36	Hywel Williams (RAF)	44.40	Morris Davies (Wd Green)	40.08
1971	John Walters (Cardiff)	43.38	Hywel Williams (RAF)	42.08	Paul Rees (Southampton)	40.10
1972	John Walters (Cardiff)	46.14	Paul Rees (Southampton)	41.20	Morris Davies (Wd Green)	38.72
1973	Ted Kelland (R Navy)	48.84	Paul Rees (Southampton)	43.72	Colin Smart (Card Coll)	34.62
1974	Paul Rees (Southampton)	45.82	John Walters (Cardiff)	44.46	Gareth Jenkins (Swansea)	30.86
1975	Ted Kelland (R Navy)	48.64	John Walters (Cardiff)	44.68	Paul Rees (Southampton)	43.88
1976	Ted Kelland (R Navy)	49.46	Paul Rees (Cardiff)	47.36	John Walters (Cardiff)	42.22
1977	Paul Rees (Cardiff)	43.14	Ted Kelland (R Marines)	42.28	John Walters (Cardiff)	41.64
1978	Paul Rees (Bournemouth)	47.92	Martin Lockley (Birchfield)	46.82	Ted Kelland (R Marines)	45.32
1979	Paul Rees (Bournemuth)	49.74	Martin Lockley (Birchfield)	47.00	Ted Kelland (R Marines)	46.90
1980	Paul Rees (Bournemouth)	49.22	Martin Lockley (Birchfield)	47.96	Ken Latten (Cardiff)	45.94
1981	Paul Rees (Bournemouth)	47.06	John Walters (Cardiff)	43.04	John Collins (Cardiff)	40.50
1982	Paul Rees (Bournemouth)	43.00	Paul Edwards (RAF)	41.96	John Collins (Cardiff)	40.92
1983	Shaun Pickering (Haringey)	47.30	Nigel Winchcombe (Reading)	45.52	Paul Edwards (RAF)	42.94
1984	Nigel Winchcombe (Brack)	41.88	John Walters (Cardiff)	39.10	Lee Wiltshire (Bournemouth)	38.56
1985	Shaun Pickering (Haringey)	49.26	Nigel Winchcombe (Brack)	45.90	Paul Edwards (RAF)	43.74
1986	Paul Edwards (Wolves)	49.52	Clayton Turner (Crawley)	42.00	John Buttriss (Torfaen)	41.82
1987	Shaun Pickering (Haringey)	50.80	Paul Edwards (Wolves)	50.34	Clayton Turner (Crawley)	43.24
1988	Paul Edwards (Walton)	48.08	Nigel Winchcombe (Herc)	43.54	Andy Turner (Bournemouth)	42.86
1989	Shaun Pickering (Haringey)	54.38	Paul Edwards (Walton)	52.70	Mark Proctor (Hillingdon)	47.66
1990	Paul Edwards (Walton)	49.82	Shaun Pickering (Haringey)	48.70	Andy Turner (Bournemouth)	42.92
1991	Clayton Turner (Crawley)	43.36	Andy Turner (Bournemouth)	42.64	Ewart Hulse (Colwyn Bay)	38.18
1992	Shaun Pickering (Haringey)	51.72	Andy Turner (Bournemouth)	44.88	Peter Roberts (Swansea)	42.58
1993	Andy Turner (Bournemouth)	44.28	Gareth Gilbert (Wrexham)	43.82	Damon McGarvie (Carm)	41.54
1994	Andy Turner (Bournemouth)	43.28	Justin Bryan (Torfaen)	41.78	Gareth Gilbert (Cardiff)	41.58
1995	Andy Turner (Crawley)	43.44	Gareth Gilbert (Cardiff)	42.84	Gareth Marks (Swansea)	42.50
1996	Andy Turner (Crawley)	44.78	Gareth Gilbert (Cardiff)	42.88	Paul Roberts (Swansea)	41.24
1997	Lee Newman (Belgrave)	55.48	Shaun Pickering (Haringey)	49.60	Matthew Bundock (B'heath)	44.62
1998	Lee Newman (Belgrave)	56.43	Justin Bryan (Torfaen)	45.05	Andy Turner (Bournemouth)	44.37

1999	Lee Newman (Belgrave)	58.29	Andy Turner (Bournemouth)	44.06	Justin Bryan (Torfaen)	43.10
2000	Lee Newman (Belgrave)	55.14	Andy Turner (Bournemouth)	42.46	Justin Bryan (Torfaen)	42.31

Hammer

1954	John Thomas (Birchgrove)	32.88	only one athlete			
1955	Albert Ley (London Police)	43.84	P Shannahan (RAF)	38.54	B L Lewis (Monmouth TC)	33.96
1956	Albert Ley (Met Police)	45.64	B L Lewis (Caerleon Coll)	39.60	only 2 athletes	
1957	Albert Ley (Cornwall Police)	43.80	J Cunningham (RAF)	39.38	only 2 athletes	
1958	Lawrie Hall (TVH)	45.40	Albert Ley (Cornwall Police)	44.64	only 2 athletes	
1959	Lawrie Hall (TVH)	47.42	Albert Ley (Cornwall Police)	42.69	B Lewis (Unattached)	40.14
1960	Lawrie Hall (TVH)	45.26	K Evans (Welsh Guards)	40.47	L Martin (AAS Beachley)	36.30
1961	Lawrie Hall (TVH)	52.08	Albert Ley (Cornwall Police)	43.53	B Lewis (Rhondda Vall)	38.58
1962	Lawrie Hall (TVH)	55.40	Albert Ley (Cornwall Police)	45.59	only 2 athletes	
1963	Lawrie Hall (TVH)	50.64	E Howell (Swansea Univ)	31.18	only 2 athletes	
1964	Lawrie Hall (TVH)	50.96	Albert Ley (Cornwall Police)	46.75	Bill Treharne (Surrey)	36.71
1965	Lawrie Hall (TVH)	53.58	Bill Treharne (Surrey)	45.23	Roger Beard (Pontypridd S)	39.39
1966	Lawrie Hall (TVH)	52.92	Bill Treharne (Surrey)	47.32	Edwin Purkis (RAF)	41.78
1967	Lawrie Hall (TVH)	52.30	Bill Treharne (Surrey)	48.46	Brian Lewis (Ealing)	40.74
1968	Donald Harrigan (Card TC)	49.60	Lawrie Hall (TVH)	49.12	Bill Treharne (Surrey)	47.98
1969	Morris Davies (Wood Green)	49.97	Edwin Purkis (RAF)	49.82	Lawrie Hall (TVH)	49.60
1970	Morris Davies (Wood Green)	51.66	Brian Lewis (Hillingdon)	44.20	only 2 athletes	
1971	Morris Davies (Wood Green)	49.46	Brian Lewis (Hillingdon)	42.62	Gordon Window (RAF)	42.46
1972	Morris Davies (Wood Green)	51.50	Andy Davie (Cardiff)	43.72	only 2 athletes	
1973	Morris Davies (Wood Green)	49.94	Andy Davie (Cardiff)	49.70	Brian Lewis (Hillingdon)	42.08
1974	Nick Lia (Cardiff)	51.38	Andy Davie (Cardiff)	49.30	P James (Cardiff College)	34.42
1975	Nick Lia (Cardiff)	53.26	Ted Kelland (R Navy)	49.36	Paul Rees (Southampton)	49.00
1976	Nick Lia (Cardiff)	53.74	Paul Rees (Cardiff)	52.60	Ted Kelland (R Navy)	46.12
1977	Nick Lia (Cardiff)	56.32	Phil Jones (Cardiff)	44.32	Adrian Jones (Swansea)	41.02
1978	Nick Lia (Cardiff)	51.64	Lawrie Hall (TVH)	48.26	Jon Tym (N W Police)	39.78
1979	Peter Stark (St Athan)	54.40	Nick Lia (Cardiff)	54.34	Lawrie Hall (TVH)	49.28
1980	Shaun Pickering (Haringey)	55.24	Peter Stark (Bridgend)	54.04	Mike LlewellynEaton (Card)	47.10
1981	Shaun Pickering (Haringey)	57.82	Nick Lia (Cardiff)	49.54	Mike LlewellynEaton (Card)	48.64
1982	Shaun Pickering (Haringey)	60.14	Dave Roberts (Liverpool)	51.36	Nick Lia (Cardiff)	48.92
1983	Shaun Pickering (Haringey)	61.74	Nigel Winchcombe (Reading)	55.52	Dave Roberts (Liverpool)	51.06
1984	John Owen (Cleddau)	50.12	Nigel Winchcombe (Brack)	49.64	Gordon Window (Cardiff)	46.98
1985	Shaun Pickering (Haringey)	57.42	Nigel Winchcombe (Brack)	57.12	John Owen (Swansea)	49.80
1986	Nigel Winchcombe (Newham)	56.92	Dave Roberts (Liverpool)	54.60	John Owen (Swansea)	50.74
1987	Shaun Pickering (Haringey)	58.56	Nigel Winchcombe (Newham)	55.56	Adrian Palmer (Cardiff)	53.24
1988	Nigel Winchcombe (Herc)	56.96	Adrian Palmer (Cardiff)	55.64	Ewart Hulse (Colwyn Bay)	48.66
1989	Shaun Pickering (Haringey)	63.12	Adrian Palmer (Cardiff)	53.56	Nigel Winchcombe (Herc)	53.12
1990	Shaun Pickering (Haringey)	60.52	Adrian Palmer (Cardiff)	53.00	Neil Williams (Wrexham)	48.92
1991	Adrian Palmer (Cardiff)	54.90	Neil Williams (Wrexham)	54.64	Ewart Hulse (Colwyn Bay)	51.80
1992	Shaun Pickering (Haringey)	58.32	Adrian Palmer (Cardiff)	55.80	Gareth Jones (Cardiff)	53.02
1993	Adrian Palmer (Cardiff)	59.10	Gareth Jones (Cardiff)	50.22	Ewart Hulse (Colwyn Bay)	49.70
1994	Gareth Jones (Cardiff)	58.74	Adrian Palmer (Cardiff)	58.62	Graham Holder (Bexley)	56.02
1995	Adrian Palmer (Cardiff)	60.50	Gareth Jones (Cardiff)	54.52	Graham Holder (Bexley)	54.30
1996	Adrian Palmer (Cardiff)	57.26	Graham Holder (Bexley)	56.40	Gareth Jones (Cardiff)	55.92
1997	Adrian Palmer (Cardiff)	62.14	Graham Holder (Bexley)	60.68	Ewart Hulse (Colwyn Bay)	51.50
1998	Graham Holder (Bexley)	61.61	Adrian Palmer (Cardiff)	60.78	Phil Bufton (Brecon)	54.12
1999	Graham Holder (Shaftes)	60.82	Adrian Palmer (Cardiff)	56.36	Ewart Hulse (Colwyn Bay)	48.24
2000	Graham Holder (Shaftes)	61.44	Adrian Palmer (Cardiff)	56.95	Ross Blight (Cardiff)	50.02

Javelin (new model used from 1986)

1938	Arthur Squibbs (Loughboro)	43.96	Fred Needs (Port Talbot)	41.66	L J Holmes (Maesteg AC)	29.33
1939	Arthur Squibbs (Loughboro)	43.28	T J Raubenheimer (Llanell)	39.10	E Benneche (Duffryn Welf)	34.64
1946	C B Coates (Newport HS)	45.36	Lionel Pugh (Cardiff Univ)	43.29	Howell Hopkin (Mond)	40.02
1947	C B Coates (Bristol Univ)	45.88	E Lewis (Caerleon College)		Roy Williams (Port Talbot)	
1948	Howell Hopkin (Mond)	48.40	C B Coates (Bristol Univ)	45.17	J N Thomas (Mond)	39.72
1949	Lionel Pugh (Swansea AC)	47.22	Howell Hopkin (Mond)	45.80	R G Cumberledge (Blaina)	45.72
1950	Neville Hughes (W Regmt)	49.16	Howell Hopkin (Mond)	43.02	Lionel Pugh (Swansea CFC)	42.48
1951	Neville Hughes (W Regmt)	54.44	Garfield Owen (Cowbridge)	53.52	Bill Kingsbury (Farnham)	
1952	L I Kinsey (Cathays HS)	43.04	W H J Wright (RAF)	40.70	D J Knight (Newport AC)	39.06
1953	Garfield Owen (Unattached	53.00	Neville Hughes (W Regmt)	48.71	Hywel Williams (Roath)	45.00
1954	Clive Roberts (Swansea AC)	57.28	Garfield Owen (Llanharan)	54.80	Bill Kingsbury (S Lond H)	45.88
1955	Clive Roberts (Lond Univ)	61.30	Neville Hughes (W Regmt)	56.40	Brian Sexton (Roath)	55.28
1956	Clive Roberts (Swansea AC)	58.02	Brian Sexton (Roath)	54.84	T Loxton Rhondda Vall)	49.06
1957	Brian Sexton (Roath)	60.88	Clive Roberts (Swansea AC)	56.26	John James (Cardiff Univ)	46.44
1958	Norman Watkins (Birm Un)	60.04	Brian Sexton (Roath)	57.02	Clive Roberts (Swansea AC)	56.92
1959	Brian Sexton (Roath)	53.02	John James (Cardiff Univ)	51.64	David Price (Roath)	48.16
1960	Brian Sexton (Roath)	60.10	David Price (Roath)	50.12	Alan Swindley (J Summers)	48.78

1961	Brian Sexton (Roath)	62.64	John James (Carmarthen)	60.04	Alan Swindley (J Summers)	59.07
1962	David Price (Birchfield)	57.66	Brian Sexton (Roath)	57.61	John James (Carmarthen)	56.08
1963	David Price (Birchgrove)	60.28	Brian Sexton (Roath)	58.17	Nevel Clarke (Carmarthen)	56.64
1964	John James (Crawley)	61.12	David Lewis (Unattached)	59.82	David Price (Card TC)	55.78
1965	John James (Carmarthen)	63.38	Robert Voss (Roath)	61.16	Norman Lang (Rhondda GS)	57.78
1966	John James (Carmarthen)	62.90	Graham Robinson (P Talbot)	57.92	Norman Lang (Porth GS)	57.02
1967	Jim Boyle (Port Talbot)	57.38	Graham Robinson (P Talbot)	55.40	Colin Burks (Birchfield)	51.34
1968	Jim Boyle (Swansea)	58.54	Graham Robinson (Swansea)	56.16	Brian Davies (Neath H)	46.24
1969	Jim Boyle (Swansea)	62.24	John James (Crawley)	60.56	Graham Robinson (Swansea)	59.64
1970	John James (Crawley)	64.36	Wayne Phillips (Card Coll)	62.44	Graham Robinson (Swansea)	59.56
1971	Graham Robinson (Swansea)	55.49	only one athlete			
1972	no competitors reported for the event					
1973	Colin Burks (Birchfield)	52.30		51.32	only 2 athletes	
1974	Gareth Brooks (Cardiff)	56.50	Bill Carey (Aberdare)	56.06	Gareth Jenkins (Swansea)	54.14
1975	Phil Ramsay (Wolves)	57.14	Bill Carey (Aberdare)	55.52	Gareth Jenkins (Card Coll)	55.36
1976	Gareth Brooks (Cardiff)	64.38	Phil Ramsay (Wolves)	61.42	Bill Carey (Aberdare)	60.04
1977	Gareth Brooks (Cardiff)	61.54	David Palmer (Walton)	60.14	Phil Ramsay (Wolves)	54.90
1978	Gareth Brooks (Cardiff)	63.74	Graham Robinson (Swansea)	58.06	Nigel Price (Swansea)	54.56
1979	Gareth Brooks (Cardiff)	63.56	Nigel Price (Cardiff Coll)	60.70	Steve Robbins (Cleddau)	49.76
1980	Gareth Brooks (Cardiff)	66.38	Graham Robinson (Swansea)	56.10		
1981	Nigel Price (SGIHE)	67.06	Tim Brooks (Cardiff)	62.64	Gareth Brooks (Cardiff)	62.20
1982	Colin Mackenzie (Newham)	76.48	Graham Robinson (Swansea)	62.84	Nigel Price (Cardiff)	60.20
1983	Tim Brooks (Cardiff)	65.84	Graham Robinson (Swansea)	63.34	Steve Griffiths (Cardiff)	62.68
1984	Gareth Rowlands (Swansea)	67.20	Tim Brooks (Cardiff)	62.46	Graham Robinson (Swansea)	62.22
1985	Colin Mackenzie (Newham)	73.14	Tim Newenham (Cardiff)	67.74	Graham Robinson (Swansea)	62.08
1986	Colin Mackenzie (Newham)	73.52	Tim Newenham (Cardiff)	69.62	Jon Clarke (Swansea)	68.74
1987	Colin Mackenzie (Newham)	70.92	Jon Clarke (Swansea)	65.14	Luigi Antoniazzi (Soton)	51.92
1988	Colin Mackenzie (Newham)	72.02	Tim Newenham (Cardiff)	67.24	Jon Clarke (Swansea)	60.72
1989	Colin Mackenzie (Newham)	72.40	Tim Newenham (Cardiff)	66.88	Luigi Antoniazzi (Cardiff)	55.50
1990	Colin Mackenzie (Newham)	70.78	Nigel Bevan (Belgrave)	70.64	Linton Baddeley (Cardiff)	58.84
1991	Shane Lewis (Preseli)	62.16	Linton Baddeley (Cardiff)	58.14	Paul Verheyden (Swansea)	49.36
1992	Shane Lewis (Preseli)	62.32	Richard Jones (Neath)	57.70	only 2 athletes	
1993	Nigel Bevan (Belgrave)	70.52	Jon Clarke (Swansea)	59.62	Shane Lewis (Swansea)	57.50
1994	Nigel Bevan (Belgrave)	68.68	Shane Lewis (Swansea)	68.52	Jon Clarke (Swansea)	61.48
1995	Stuart Loughran (Swansea)	58.98	David Morgan (Cardiff)	48.02	only 2 athletes	
1996	Stuart Loughran (Swansea)	58.02	Shane Lewis (Swansea)	56.26	Luigi Antoniazzi (Cardiff)	52.68
1997	Nigel Bevan (Belgrave)	67.14	Stuart Loughran (Swansea)	62.94	Shane Lewis (Swansea)	60.38
1998	Shane Lewis (Swansea)	67.96	Nigel Bevan (Birchfield)	66.04	Stuart Loughran (Swansea)	63.86
1999	Mike Groves (Torfaen)	47.68	Richard Stubbs (Preseli)	47.12	Andrew Davies (Neath)	37.73
2000	Derek Hermann (Carmarthen)	57.41	Kevin Ricketts (Deeside)	54.34	David Morgan (Cleddau)	52.15

Decathlon (scoring as per tables in operation at the time)

1949	Howell Hopkin (Mond)	4978	N M Goff (Newport H)	4629	John Jones (Neath AC)	3541
1950	Hywel Williams (Roath)	4762	only one athlete			
1951	Hywel Williams (Roath)	4109	Howell Hopkin (Mond)	3886	Clive Balch (London AC)	3554
1952	Hywel Williams (Roath)	5014	Norman Finch (R Artillery)	4123	only 2 athletes	
1953	no competitors reported for the event					
1954	S A Clarke (Aberys Univ)	3869	only one athlete			
1955	Norman Watkins (Leic Un)	4952	Morton Evans (Carmarthen)	4231	only 2 athletes	
1956	Arthur John (Redhill)	4654	Terry Hamilton (Newp AC)	4208	B L Lewis (Caerleon Coll)	3951
1957	Aneurin Evans (CowbridgeS)	4453	Norman Watkins (Leic Un)	4255	Terry Hamilton (Newp AC)	3619
1958	Arthur John (Redhill)	5022	Ray Gazzard (Birchgrove)	4332	Gwilym Thomas (Loughboro)	4036
1959	Hywel Williams (RAF)	5371	Paul Sayzeland (Newp HS)	4093		
1960	Ray Gazzard (Birchgrove)	3922	Peter Harris (Newport HS)	3044	A Wilson (Aberdare GS)	2682
1961	Brian Whipp (Lozells)	4629	John Lister (Birchgrove)	4568	Peter Harris (Newport)	3763
1962	John Lister (Birchgrove)	4638	James Davies (Rochester)	4058	Derrick Hanlon (Birchgrove)	3705
1963	David Rees (Swansea Univ)	4846	John Lister (Birchgrove)	4548	John Davies (Rochester)	3814
1964	Clive Longe (RAF)	5782	David Rees (London Univ)	5630	Hywel Williams (Roath)	4978
1965	Goronwy Davies (Madel C)	5304	F H Brown (RAF)	4576	Steve Williams (Card Univ)	4449
1966	John Lister (Birchgrove)	5309	Brian Lewis (Hayes)	3962	only 2 athletes	
1967	Eirwyn Jones (Swansea)	5194	A Harbron (Unattached)	4187	Roy Davies (Neath)	4097
1968	Alan Bergiers (Carmarthen)	4913	Derek Vaughan (Swansea)	4451	J Layer (Barry)	4167
1969	Paul Caviel (Troedyrhiw)	5049	Peter Nolan (Barry)	4834	only 2 athletes finished	
1970	Paul Caviel (Troedyrhiw)	5392	Roy Bergiers (Carmarthen)	5391	Alan Bergiers (Carmarthen)	5002
1971	Paul Caviel (Troedyrhiw)	5308	Michael LeClair (Cleddau)	3875	Alan Mee (Troedyrhiw)	3825
1972	Paul Caviel (Troedyrhiw)	5332	Alan Bergiers (Card Coll)	5298	Alan Mee (Troedyrhiw)	4578
1973	Derek Fishwick (Cardiff)	4594	Alan Mee (Troedyrhiw)	4549	Mike Cummings (Cardiff)	4540
1974	event not held					
1975	Geoff Ward (Stoke)	5837	Derek Fishwick (Cardiff)	5250	Jon Roberts (Wolves)	5177
1976	Geoff Ward (Stoke)	6331	Spencer Jones (Carmarthen)	5051	only 2 athletes	
1977	Geoff Ward (Stoke)	6337				

1978	Derek Fishwick (Cardiff)	6096	Mark Johnson (Newport)	5603		
1979	Geoff Ward (Stoke)	6399	Steven Brock (Cardiff)	5666	Martyn Thomas (Cardiff)	5289
1980	Geoff Ward (Stoke)	6430	Steven Brock (Cardiff)	6210	Martyn Thomas (Cardiff)	5503
1981	Paul Edwards (Walton)	6510	Geoff Ward (Stoke)	6443	Tegid Griffiths (Army)	6209
1982	Stuart Gibbs (R Navy)	6215	Paul Edwards (RAF)	5678	Tudor Bidder (Cardiff)	5149
1983	Stuart Gibbs (R Navy)	6628	only one athlete			
1984	event not held					
1985	Tony Pithers (Cardiff)	6555	George Robertson (RAF)	6531	Keith Ridgeway (RAF)	4702
1986	Stuart Gibbs (R Navy)	6401	Tegid Griffiths (Deeside)	6299	Tony Pithers (Cardiff)	5867
1987	Tony Pithers (Cardiff)	5628	only one athlete			
1988	Tony Pithers (Cardiff)	6173	Rob James (Cardiff)	5744	Duncan Gauden (Shrewsbury)	5377
1989	Rob James (Cardiff)	6454	Tony Pithers (Cardiff)	6397	Martin Roberts (Colwyn B)	5520
1990	Rob James (Cardiff)	6241	Steve Ingram (Swansea)	6123	Tony Pithers (Cardiff)	5754
1991	Rob James (Cardiff)	6094	Duncan Gauden (Shrewsbury)	5541	Richard Stubbs (Cardiff)	5110
1992	Duncan Gauden (Shrewsbury)	5499	Richard Stubbs (Cardiff)	5470	Steven Lloyd (Oxford)	5148
1993	Duncan Gauden (Telford)	6129	Rob Bradley (Chester)	5874	Richard Stubbs (Cardiff)	5822
1994	Duncan Gauden (Telford)	5666	Adrian Jones (Wrexham)	2914	Glynn Owens (Wrexham)	2798
1995	Duncan Gauden (Telford)	5751	Richard Stubbs (Cardiff)	5629	Glyn Price (Swansea)	4834
1996	Egryn Jones (Cardiff)	5498	only one athlete			
1997	Duncan Gauden (Telford)	5590	Richard Stubbs (Preseli)	5457	Gareth James (Telford)	5243
1998	Paul Jones (Colwyn Bay)	6389	Geoff Ingram (Norwich)	5662	only 2 athletes	
1999	Paul Jones (Colwyn Bay)	6940	Geoff Ingram (Norwich)	6070	Richard Stubbs (Preseli)	5419
2000	Ben Roberts (Colwyn Bay)	5479	Kevin Ricketts (Deeside)	5429	Neil Edwards (Wrexham)	4611

SENIOR WOMEN

100 yards / 100 metres

1952	Jean Docker (Middlesex)	11.9	J Brooks (Brecon School)	12.9	Esme Carey (Newport H)	12.9
1953	Janet Lewis (Roath)	11.6	Jean Docker (Middlesex)	11.7	Sylvia Jones (Pontypool)	11.8
1954	Jean Docker (Middlesex)	11.8	Margaret Farquharson (Roath)		A Lewis (Pontypool AC)	
1955	Jean Docker (Middlesex)	12.4	Pat Doyle (Glanafan GS)	12.5	H Lewis (Rhondda AC)	12.7
1956	Gwyneth Lewis (Holyhead)	11.7	Jean Docker (Middlesex)	11.9	Anne Paske (Rhondda Vall)	12.3
1957	Gwyneth Lewis (Bangor Univ)	11.4	Jean Docker (Middlesex)	11.8	E A Preece (Mond AC)	12.0
1958	Jean Whitehead (Middlesex)	11.4	Bonnie Jones (Roath)	11.5	Beryl Turner (Holyhead SS)	11.6
1959	Daphne Williams (C Bay)	11.3	Bonnie Jones (Roath)	11.4	Carol Thomas (Roath)	11.5
1960	Elizabeth Parsons (Roath)	11.2	Monica Zeraschi (Pend SS)	11.4	Elizabeth Gill (Barry)	11.7
1961	Elizabeth Parsons (Roath)	11.2	Monica Zeraschi (Pend SS)	11.3	Elizabeth Gill (Barry)	11.4
1962	Elizabeth Parsons (Roath)	11.6	J Blackbourn (Warras AC)	11.7	G Lewis (Barry TC)	11.9
1963	Elizabeth Gill (Barry)	11.1	Elizabeth Parsons (Roath)	11.3	Monica Zeraschi (Roath)	11.5
1964	Elizabeth Gill (Barry)	10.8	Elizabeth Parsons (Roath)	10.9	Pam Dalton (Roath)	11.5
1965	Elizabeth Parsons (Roath)	10.8	Gloria Dourass (Sm Heath)	11.0	Gaynor Legall (Grange CS)	11.6
1966	Elizabeth Parsons (Roath)	10.8	Gloria Dourass (Sm Heath)	11.2	Elizabeth Gill (Barry)	11.2
1967	event cancelled due to bad weather					
1968	Eliz Parsons/Johns (Roath)	10.9	Sylvia Powell (Swan Vall)	11.3	D Phipps (Mynyddbach CS)	11.7
1969	Celia Hall (Swansea)	12.5	Ruth Martin Jones (Birm Un)	12.6	Michelle Smith (Holton R)	12.7
1970	Hilary Davies (Epsom)	12.2	Patrice Shiels (Havering)	12.2	Elizabeth Johns (Roath)	12.3
1971	Elizabeth Johns (Roath)	11.9	Joan Wicks (Middlesex)	12.6	Sandra Belt (Cardiff)	12.6
1972	Sandra Belt (Cardiff)	12.0	Michelle Smith (Cardiff)	12.3	Gaynor Blackwell (Swansea)	12.6
1973	Sandra Belt (Cardiff)	12.8	Michelle Smith (Cardiff)	13.2	Linda Williams (Aberdare)	13.7
1974	Helen Watts (Cardiff)	12.7	Linda Williams (Aberdare)	12.7	Lianne Dando (Cardiff)	12.9
1975	Sandra Belt/Pengilley (Card)	12.8	Philomena Ronan (Swansea)	13.1	Michelle Atkinson (Brecon)	13.4
1976	Margaret Williams (Bristol)	11.5	Ceri Jenkins (Cleddau)	12.2	Gillian Regan (Cardiff)	12.4
1977	Margaret Williams (Bristol)	11.8	Lianne Dando (Cardiff)	12.1	Carmen Smart (Barry)	12.1
1978	Michelle Probert (Sale)	12.1	Diane Thorne (Carmarthen)	12.2	Jill Davies (Plymouth)	12.5
1979	Michelle Probert (Sale)	11.7	Carmen Smart (Barry)	11.9	Diane Thorne (Carmarthen)	12.1
1980	Michelle Probert (Sale)	11.3	Carmen Smart (Cardiff)	11.6	Jenny Webb (Wolves)	11.8
1981	Michelle Probert/Scutt (Sale)	12.0	Jenny Webb (Wolves)	12.2	Jill Davies/Morton (Plym)	12.6
1982	Michelle Scutt (Sale)	12.0	Carmen Smart (Cardiff)	12.3	Jenny Webb (Wolves)	12.7
1983	Carmen Smart (Cardiff)	12.1	Jenny Webb (Wolves)	12.3	Helen Orrells (Newtown)	13.1
1984	Helen Miles (Cardiff)	12.5	Carmen Smart (Cardiff)	12.8	Sallyanne Short (Torfaen)	12.9
1985	Carmen Smart (Cardiff)	12.42	Jenny Webb (Wolves)	12.80	Gillian Regan (Cardiff)	13.06
1986	Sallyanne Short (Torfaen)	11.71	Helen Miles (Cardiff)	11.76	Carmen Smart (Cardiff)	11.77
1987	Sallyanne Short (Torfaen)	11.79	Helen Miles (Cardiff)	11.82	Carmen Smart (Cardiff)	12.13
1988	Helen Miles (Cardiff)	11.4	Sallyanne Short (Torfaen)	11.4	Alison Eves (Cardiff)	12.3
1989	Carmen Smart (Cardiff)	11.48	Sallyanne Short (Torfaen)	11.49	Helen Miles (Cardiff)	11.58
1990	Helen Miles (Cardiff)	11.8	Sallyanne Short (Torfaen)	11.9	Lisa Armstrong (Torfaen)	12.2
1991	Helen Miles (Cardiff)	11.84	Sallyanne Short (Torfaen)	11.95	Lisa Armstrong (Torfaen)	12.10
1992	Sallyanne Short (Torfaen)	11.48	Helen Miles (Cardiff)	11.71	Lisa Armstrong (Torfaen)	11.89
1993	Helen Miles (Cardiff)	11.96	Lisa Armstrong (Cardiff)	12.38	Stacey Rodd (Barry)	12.62
1994	Sallyanne Short (Torfaen)	12.17	Louise Sharps (Deeside)	12.53	Krysta Williams (Cardiff)	12.78
1995	Catherine Murphy (Shaftes)	11.80	Sallyanne Short (Torfaen)	11.86	Stacey Rodd (Barry)	12.56
1996	Gael Davies (Gloucester)	12.99	Stacey Rodd (Cardiff)	13.08	Louise Sharps (Swansea)	13.12
1997	Rachel King (Cardiff)	12.20	Catherine Murphy (Shaftes)	12.33	Angharad James (Swansea)	12.52
1998	Catherine Murphy (Shaftes)	12.12	Sophie Williams (Wessex)	12.65	Angharad James (Swansea)	12.77
1999	Sarah Lane (Swansea)	12.88	Jo Tomlinson (Deeside)	13.19	Alwena Griffiths (C Bay)	13.25
2000	Catherine Murphy (Shaftes)	12.14	Angharad James (Swansea)	12.42	Ellie Mardle (Cardiff)	12.71

220 yards / 200 metres

1952	Jean Docker (Middlesex)	27.3	Rita Evans (P Talbot YM)	28.5	Sheila Coy (Penarth GS)	28.6
1953	Jean Docker (Middlesex)	27.8	Marg Farquharson (Roath)	27.8	M Jones (Unattached)	28.5
1954	Marg Farquharson (Roath)	27.3	Jean Docker (Middlesex)		Georgina Jones (Carmarthen)	
1955	Jean Docker (Middlesex)	27.4	Marg Farquharson (Roath)	28.1	M G Vowles (St Julians HS)	29.5
1956	Jackie Barnett (Newport AC)	27.5	Marilyn Morgan (Newport H)	28.0	Elizabeth Taylor (Roath)	28.0
1957	Jean Docker (Middlesex)	26.9	Gwyneth Lewis (Bangor Un)	27.2	Elizabeth Taylor (Roath)	27.3
1958	Jean Whitehead (Middlesex)	26.0	Jackie Barnett (Chelsea Coll)	26.3	Sheila Lewis (Roath)	26.9
1959	Daphne Williams (C Bay)	25.5	Monica Zeraschi (Eirias)	25.7	Carol Thomas (Roath)	26.1
1960	Elizabeth Parsons (Roath)	26.3	Pam Dalton (Roath)	26.9	Pam Clarke (Roath)	26.9
1961	Elizabeth Parsons (Roath)	26.2	Monica Zeraschi (Pendor)	26.5	Pam Clarke (Roath)	27.4
1962	Elizabeth Parsons (Roath)	25.5	J Blackbourn (Warras AC)	25.6	Rita Protheroe (Selsonia)	26.6
1963	Elizabeth Gill (Barry)	25.5	Tanya Alcock (Cyfarthfa)	27.3	Mary Oakes (Towyn)	27.7
1964	Elizabeth Gill (Barry)	25.2	Elizabeth Parsons (Roath)	26.2	Marilyn Matthews (Penarth)	28.2
1965	Elizabeth Parsons (Roath)	25.7	Gaynor Legall (Grange CS)	26.5	E Davies (Caerphilly GS)	27.7
1966	Elizabeth Parsons (Roath)	24.8	Elizabeth Gill (Barry)	25.0	Gaynor Legall (Roath)	25.7

1967	event cancelled due to bad weather					
1968	Marilyn Stokes (St Julians)	27.4				
1969	Michelle Smith (Holton SS)	26.6	Celia Hall (Swansea)	26.9	Meryl Jones (Brecon)	27.0
1970	Hilary Davies (Epsom)	25.6	Paula Lloyd (Wirral)	25.7	Patrice Shiels (Havering)	25.7
1971	Elizabeth Johns (Cardiff)	24.7	Michelle Smith (Cardiff)	25.5	Joan Wicks (Middlesex)	25.8
1972	Sandra Belt (Cardiff)	24.9	Michelle Smith (Cardiff)	25.7	S Miles (Bridgend YM)	27.0
1973	Sandra Belt (Cardiff)	25.6	Paula Lloyd (Wirral)	25.7	Michelle Smith (Cardiff)	26.0
1974	Linda Williams (Aberdare)	26.6	Michelle Atkinson (Brecon)	27.0	Chris Griffiths (Swansea)	27.6
1975	Sandra Belt/Pengilley (Card)	26.7	Lianne Dando (Cardiff)	26.8	Michelle Atkinson (Brecon)	27.0
1976	Margaret Williams (Bristol)	24.4	Elaine Oxton (Liverpool)	27.0	Sue Norman (Cwmbran)	27.1
1977	Margaret Williams (Bristol)	24.4	Diane Heath (Stretford)	24.9	Carmen Smart (Barry)	25.9
1978	Michelle Probert (Sale)	23.7	Diane Heath (Stretford)	24.3	Diane Thorne (Carmarthen)	25.0
1979	Carmen Smart (Barry)	24.0	Kirsty McDermott (Brecon)	25.1	Lianne Dando (Cardiff)	25.5
1980	Michelle Probert (Sale)	23.8	Carmen Smart (Cardiff)	24.4	Eirwen Gould (Aldershot)	25.9
1981	Michelle Probert/Scutt (Sale)	24.2	Elizabeth Pendrey (Deeside)	26.3	Carmen Smart (Cardiff)	26.6
1982	Michelle Scutt (Sale)	23.7	Carmen Smart (Cardiff)	24.7	Elizabeth Pendrey (Deeside)	26.1
1983	Carmen Smart (Cardiff)	24.9	Jenny Webb (Wolves)	25.6	Helen Orrells (Newtown)	26.7
1984	Helen Miles (Cardiff)	25.14	Sallyanne Short (Torfaen)	25.16	Jane Bradbeer (Cardiff)	25.71
1985	Carmen Smart (Cardiff)	25.03	Tracy Lewis (Wrexham)	26.22	Bev Preece (Barry)	27.93
1986	Sallyanne Short (Torfaen)	23.83	Rhian Owen (Cleddau)	25.70	Alison Eves (Cardiff)	26.53
1987	Sallyanne Short (Torfaen)	24.42	Sian Morris (Cardiff)	24.49	Rebecca Jones-Morris (Cardiff)	26.48
1988	Sallyanne Short (Torfaen)	23.3	Helen Miles (Cardiff)	23.7	Sian Morris (Cardiff)	24.7
1989	Sallyanne Short (Torfaen)	23.92	Lisa Armstrong (Torfaen)	25.22	Sonia Reay (Bridgend)	25.86
1990	Sallyanne Short (Torfaen)	24.17	Lisa Armstrong (Torfaen)	26.12	Denice Grist (Rhondda)	26.74
1991	Helen Miles (Cardiff)	23.89	Sallyanne Short (Torfaen)	23.98	Lisa Armstrong (Torfaen)	24.76
1992	Sallyanne Short (Torfaen)	23.57	Megan Jones (Newport)	25.85	only 2 athletes	
1993	Helen Miles (Cardiff)	24.94	Gillian Archard (T Solent)	25.28	Dawn Higgins (Cardiff)	25.94
1994	Sallyanne Short (Torfaen)	24.75	Louise Sharps (Deeside)	25.56	Jo Gronow (Barry)	25.99
1995	Catherine Murphy (Shaftes)	24.3	Jo Gronow (Barry)	26.3	Leanne Rowlands (Cardiff)	27.3
1996	Gael Davies (Gloucester)	26.79	Louise Sharps (Swansea)	27.10	Gail Evans (Carmarthen)	27.31
1997	Louise Whitehead (Swan U)	24.49	Catherine Murphy (Shaftes)	24.57	Angharad James (Swansea)	25.44
1998	Catherine Murphy (Shaftes)	23.8	Louise Whitehead (Swansea)	24.5	Lowri Jones (Torfaen)	25.0
1999	Louise Whitehead (Swansea)	25.1	Donna Porazinski (Newport)	26.9	Kathryn Williams (Swansea)	27.1
2000	Catherine Murphy (Shaftes)	24.23	Louise Whitehead (Swansea)	25.20	Angharad James (Swansea)	25.51

440 yards / 400 metres

1952	Margaret Skinner (Newport H)	67.5	V Carless (Barry GS)	68.5	Marg Farquharson (Roath)	69.6
1953	Sheila Coy (Roath)	64.7	V Carless (Barry)	65.0	I Davies (Aberystwyth Un)	66.0
1954	Sheila Coy (Whitchurch)	62.4	P M Williams (Neath AC)		only 2 athletes	
1955	Jean Docker (Middlesex)	63.6	Jackie Barnett (Newp AC)	65.2	Lilian O'Brien (Unattached)	72.4
1956	Jean Docker (Middlesex)	60.2	Pauline Webb (Streatham)	61.7	only 2 athletes	
1957	Jean Docker (Middlesex)	62.5	Pauline Webb (Streatham)	64.2	only 2 athletes	
1958	P Cranfield (Mond AC)	65.1	N Hughes (Rhondda Vall)	71.0	only 2 athletes	
1959	Jackie Barnett (Newport AC)	60.6	Valerie Morgan (Selsonia)	60.6	Sheila Coy/Lewis (Roath)	61.8
1960	Jackie Barnett (Newport AC)	59.3	L Gamlin (Westbury)	60.8	Valerie Morgan (Selsonia)	61.4
1961	Jackie Barnett (Newport AC)	60.0	Pam Dalton (Roath)	63.7	L Rochelle (Roath)	
1962	Jackie Barnett (Roath)	59.2	Pam Dalton (Roath)	60.6	Judith Williams (Aldershot)	63.7
1963	Pam Dalton (Roath)	59.8	Judith Williams (Aldershot)	60.9	H McCrann (Roath)	63.1
1964	Gloria Dourass (Sm Heath)	59.7	D Brown (Barry)	64.4		
1965	Gloria Dourass (Sm Heath)	57.8	Pam Dalton (Roath)	58.3	only 2 athletes	
1966	Gloria Dourass (Sm Heath)	56.5	Thelwyn Appleby (Cov G)	58.3	Pam Dalton (Roath)	58.6
1967	Gloria Dourass (Sm Heath)	57.5	Pam Dalton (Roath)	59.1	Gillian Gosling (Roath)	
1968	Janet Eynon (Croydon)	58.8	Pam Dalton (Roath)	61.2	Gillian Gosling (Roath)	61.3
1969	Janet Eynon (Croydon)	58.8	Delyth Davies (Cardiff)	59.4	Gillian Gosling (Cardiff)	60.4
1970	Gloria Dourass (Sm Heath)	55.5	Thelwyn Bateman (Cov G)	57.3	Delyth Davies (Cardiff)	59.6
1971	Thelwyn Bateman (Cov G)	56.9	Christine Checketts (Cardiff)	61.6	only 2 athletes	
1972	Christine Checketts (Cardiff)	58.7	Anne Disley (Newport)	59.6	Margaret Brain (Newport)	63.3
1973	Paula Lloyd (Wirral)	57.5	Lianne Dando (Cardiff)	59.0	L K Morris (Eirias)	62.2
1974	Debbie Froggatt (Cardiff)	61.9	Margaret Brain (Newport)	63.0	J Tipping (J Beddoes Sch)	69.0
1975	Gloria Dourass (Birchfield)	56.8	Lianne Dando (Cardiff)	57.6	Jenny Davies (Havering)	58.8
1976	Gloria Dourass (Birchfield)	56.0	Jenny Davies (Havering)	57.4	Elaine Oxton (Liverpool)	60.6
1977	Jenny Davies (Havering)	56.9	Bernie Butcher (Sale)	57.7	Angela Pennington (Carm)	59.1
1978	Sian Morgan (Barry)	56.1	Jenny Davies (Plymouth)	56.7	Carol Fernley (Loughboro)	58.1
1979	Michelle Probert (Sale)	55.1	Carol Fernley (Bristol)	56.0	Bernie Butcher (Bury)	56.6
1980	Carol Fernley (Bristol)	55.6	Bernie Butcher (Bury)	58.1	Sian Morgan (Unattached)	58.5
1981	Kirsty McDermott (Bristol)	55.6	Sarah Rowe (Gloucester)	56.6	Gloria Rickard (Birchfield)	58.2
1982	Kirsty McDermott (Bristol)	55.0	Sian Morris (Port Talbot)	55.0	Jane Tomley (Croydon)	57.0
1983	Jane Tomley (Croydon)	57.3	Jenny Mullett (Brighton)	57.6	Bev Preece (Cardiff)	57.8
1984	Michelle Probert/Scutt (Sale)	53.08	Kirsty McDermott (Bristol)	57.17	Sharon James (Cleddau)	60.94
1985	Sian Morris (Cardiff)	55.04	Tracy Smedley (Colchest)	59.51	Rhian Owen (Cleddau)	60.25
1986	Sian Morris (Cardiff)	54.19	Kirsty McDermott/Wade (Blay)	55.70	Anne Evison (Oswestry)	57.09

1987	Kirsty Wade (Blaydon)	54.74	Samantha Porter (Cardiff)	56.62	Anne Evison (Wrexham)	57.92
1988	Ann Middle (Newport)	56.2	Kirsty Wade (Blaydon)	56.4	Samantha Porter (Cardiff)	57.3
1989	Samantha Porter (Cardiff)	58.01	Nerys Evans (Brecon)	58.15	Anne Evison (Wrexham)	58.77
1990	Samantha Porter (Cardiff)	57.4	Anne Evison (Wrexham)	57.7	Joanne Gronow (Barry)	58.6
1991	Kirsty Wade (Blaydon)	56.00	Anne Evison (Wrexham)	58.15	Joanne Gronow (Barry)	58.38
1992	Gillian Archard (T Solent)	56.24	Rachel Newcombe (Liverpool)	56.25	Cathy White (Highgate)	57.23
1993	Gillian Archard (T Solent)	54.94	Kate Williams (Carm)	57.08	Nicola Davies (Wrexham)	57.72
1994	Gillian Archard/Cashell (TS)	54.77	Rachel Newcombe (Liverpool)	55.57	Nicola Davies (Wrexham)	57.46
1995	Kate Williams (Swansea)	57.7	Dawn Higgins (Cardiff)	57.7	Michelle John (Swansea)	59.3
1996	Kathryn Bright (Newport)	56.60	Anna Turner (Cardiff)	57.30	Donna Porazinski (Newp)	59.21
1997	Amanda Pritchard (Cardiff)	54.60	Emma Davies (Andover)	55.48	Kathryn Bright (Newport)	56.20
1998	Alyson Layzell (Cheltenham)	53.81	Dawn Higgins (Cardiff)	54.35	Donna Porazinski (Newport)	55.82
1999	Dawn Higgins (Cardiff)	55.71	Donna Porazinski (Newport)	56.93	Rachel Newcombe (Liverp)	57.21
2000	Louise Whitehead (Swansea)	53.37	Dawn Higgins (Cardiff)	53.90	Emma Davies (Andover)	55.62

880 yards / 800 metres

1952	Rose Peek (Newport H)	3:17.3	P Williams (Unattached)	3:17.4	only 2 athletes	
1953	Rose Peek (Newport H)	3:00.2	M Shapland (Birchgrove)	3:03.3	only 2 athletes finished	
1954	B Ludlam (Mtn Ash GS)	2:43.6	Rose Peek (Newport H)		Anne Holdsworth (Maesydderwen)	
1955	Marg Farquharson (Roath)	2:48.0	B Ludlam (Unattached)	2:50.0	Dilys Watts (Unattached)	2:58.2
1956	Marg Farquharson (Roath)	2:44.4	E M Arthur (Swansea AC)	2:45.3	B Ludlam (Aber Vall)	2:48.2
1957	Pauline Webb (Streatham)	2:35.0	E M Arthur (Swansea AC)	2:47.0	B Ludlam (Abergavenny)	2:50.0
1958	C Cutter (Roath)	2:49.8	only one athlete			
1959	Jackie Barnett (Newport AC)	2:34.3	Valerie Morgan (Selsonia)		E M Arthur (Roath)	
1960	Jackie Barnett (Newport AC)	2:18.8	Valerie Morgan (Selsonia)	2:24.5	A Ramsay (Roath)	2:25.6
1961	Jackie Barnett (Newport AC)	2:25.8	Pam Dalton (Roath)	2:43.0	only 2 athletes	
1962	Jackie Barnett (Roath)	2:15.9	Valerie Morgan (Selsonia)	2:23.4	Judith Williams (Aldershot)	2:25.4
1963	Judith Williams (Aldershot)	2:24.0	Pat Sullivan (Westbury)	2:34.0		
1964	Tanya Alcock (Cyfarthfa)	2:25.8	Pat Sullivan (Westbury)	2:26.5	only 2 athletes	
1965	Pam Dalton (Roath)	2:18.5	Jackie Barnett (Surrey)	2:22.1	Pat Sullivan (Westbury)	2:25.0
1966	Delyth Davies (Cathays)	2:25.9	Pam Dalton (Roath)	2:26.5	Pat Sullivan (Westbury)	2:28.1
1967	Delyth Davies (Birchgrove)	2:23.5	G Gardner (Barry)	2:26.1	Jean Lochhead (Airedale)	2:28.0
1968	Thelwyn Bateman (Coventry)	2:15.6	Delyth Davies (Barry)	2:21.7	Janet Eynon (Croydon)	2:31.2
1969	Thelwyn Bateman (Coventry)	2:09.4	Delyth Davies (Cardiff)	2:19.8	Jean Lochhead (Airedale)	2:27.5
1970	Thelwyn Bateman (Coventry)	2:08.1	Delyth Davies (Cardiff)	2:17.1	P Jones (Flint)	2:28.7
1971	Delyth Davies (Cardiff)	2:16.0	Nicola Page (Carmarthen)	2:22.2	only 2 athletes	
1972	Thelwyn Bateman (Coventry)	2:11.2	Delyth Davies (Cardiff)	2:15.9	Ann Disley (Newport)	2:22.5
1973	Jean Lochhead (Airedale)	2:11.8	Delyth Davies (Cardiff)	2:14.9	Ann Roblin (Cardiff)	2:21.2
1974	Jean Lochhead (Airedale)	2:13.6	Delyth Davies (Cardiff)	2:16.7	Ann Roblin (Cardiff)	2:20.4
1975	Jean Lochhead (Airedale)	2:17.2	Ann Disley (Newport)	2:18.9	Lyn Huntbach (Cwmbran)	2:27.8
1976	Ann Roblin (Cardiff)	2:18.5	Pat Waters (Cwmbran)	2:23.0	K Price (Carmarthen)	2:32.2
1977	Hilary Hollick (Sale)	2:13.3	Gloria Rickard (Birchfield)	2:13.6	Angela Hartley (Barry)	2:14.2
1978	Hilary Hollick (Sale)	2:09.0	Gloria Rickard (Birchfield)	2:09.4	Jenny Davies (Havering)	2:12.0
1979	Kirsty McDermott (Brecon)	2:11.5	Jenny Mullett (Havering)	2:13.4	Angela Hartley (Unattached)	2:15.0
1980	Kirsty McDermott (Brecon)	2:09.2	Hilary Hollick (Sale)	2:09.3	Angela Hartley (Cardiff)	2:14.2
1981	Kirsty McDermott (Bristol)	2:13.0	Jenny Mullett (Brighton)	2:13.9	Pat Gallagher (Westbury)	2:16.4
1982	Kirsty McDermott (Bristol)	2:09.4	Kim Lock (Cardiff)	2:12.3	Jeanette Howes (Hull)	2:13.4
1983	Kirsty McDermott (Bristol)	2:08.3	Kim Lock (Cardiff)	2:09.1	Jenny Mullett (Brighton)	2:17.1
1984	Kirsty McDermott (Bristol)	2:07.62	Kim Lock (Cardiff)	2:09.03	Wendy Ore (Bridgend)	2:19.27
1985	Kirsty McDermott (Bristol)	2:02.3	Pat Gallagher (Westbury)	2:13.7	Liz Francis (Bridgend)	2:16.9
1986	Kirsty McDermott/Wade (B)	2:04.29	Ann Middle (Spain)	2:05.84	Carolyn Morgan (Swansea)	2:12.54
1987	Kirsty Wade (Blayden)	2:03.77	Liz Francis (Bridgend)	2:12.13	Pat Gallagher (Bristol)	2:12.31
1988	Kirsty Wade (Blayden)	2:03.5	Liz Francis (Cardiff)	2:11.1	Caitlin Funnell (Cambridge)	2:13.5
1989	Ann Middle (Newport)	2:07.27	Caitlin Funnell (Cambridge)	2:15.57	Nicky Haines (Stourport)	2:15.94
1990	Samantha Porter (Cardiff)	2:11.74	Tina Curry (Swansea)	2:12.76	Tracey Smedley (Hounslow)	2:13.87
1991	Alison Parry (Kingston)	2:07.68	Samantha Porter (Cardiff)	2:12.79	Esther Evans (Millfield)	2:15.22
1992	Alison Parry (Kingston)	2:12.12	Esther Evans (Millfield)	2:15.36	Liz Francis (Cardiff)	2:16.19
1993	Cathy White (Highgate)	2:07.24	Alison Parry (Croydon)	2:09.20	Kathryn Bright (Newport)	2:12.04
1994	Cathy White/Dawson (High)	2:06.10	Alyson Layzell (Cheltenham)	2:07.66	Lisa Carthew (Swansea)	2:09.84
1995	Alyson Layzell (Cheltenham)	2:07.5	Hayley Parry (Swansea)	2:10.6	Kathryn Bright (Newport)	2:15.5
1996	Hayley Parry (Swansea)	2:06.51	Gillian Cashell (T Solent)	2:09.27	Rachel Newcombe (Liverp)	2:11.06
1997	Rachel Newcombe (Liverp)	2:10.07	Emma Brady (Sale)	2:11.83	Lynne Gallagher (Shaftesb)	2:12.97
1998	Rachel Newcombe (Liverp)	2:06.89	Emma Davies (Andover)	2:08.25	Sarah Mead (Torfaen)	2:10.25
1999	Natalie Lewis (Cardiff)	2:11.7	Kathryn Bright (Newport)	2:15.0	Emma Brady (Torfaen)	2:17.5
2000	Natalie Lewis (Cardiff)	2:12.04	Ruth Hornby (Cardiff)	2:15.36	Lynne Gallagher (Shaftesbury)	2:16.06

1500 metres

1971	Bronwen Cardy (Bromsgrove)	4:55.3	Pat Sullivan (Westbury)	5:23.7	only 2 athletes	
1972	Susan Tolan (Cwmbran)	4:56.3	Anne Roblin (Heath Sch)	5:04.1	only 2 athletes	
1973	Jean Lochhead (Airedale)	4:40.2	Delyth Davies (Cardiff)	4:50.4	Bronwen Cardy (Bromsgrove)	4:52.3

1974	Jean Lochhead (Airedale)	4:42.2	Anne Morris (Cardiff)	4:47.4	Ann Disley (Newport)	4:49.4
1975	Jean Lochhead (Airedale)	4:40.6	Anne Morris (Cardiff)	4:41.2	Ann Disley (Newport)	5:04.2
1976	Margaret Morgan (Coventry)	4:47.7	Anne Notman (Cardiff)	4:48.6	Lyn Huntbach (Cwmbran)	4:51.5
1977	Hilary Hollick (Sale)	4:40.4	Anne Notman (Cardiff)	4:44.9	Ann Disley (Newport)	4:45.4
1978	Hilary Hollick (Sale)	4:32.0	Kim Lock (Cardiff)	4:39.8	Lyn Huntbach (Torfaen)	4:43.6
1979	Kim Lock (Cardiff)	4:31.1	Caroline Morgan (Cledd)	4:40.6	Lyn Lerue (Torfaen)	4:44.3
1980	Hilary Hollick (Sale)	4:28.5	Kim Lock (Cardiff)	4:32.0	Annemarie Fox (Swansea)	4:40.1
1981	Hilary Hollick (Sale)	4:33.4	Thelwyn Bateman (Birchfield)	4:38.4	Yana Jones (Tiverton)	4:47.6
1982	Hilary Hollick (Sale)	4:26.7	Kim Lock (Cardiff)	4:29.8	Annemarie Fox (Swansea)	4:40.2
1983	Kim Lock (Cardiff)	4:24.1	Annemarie Fox (Swansea)	4:26.4	Angela Tooby (Cardiff)	4:37.9
1984	Susan Tooby (Cardiff)	4:32.61	Angela Tooby (Cardiff)	4:33.12	Pat Gallagher (Westbury)	4:45.01
1985	Susan Tooby (Cardiff)	4:23.44	Angela Tooby (Cardiff)	4:23.47	Annemarie Fox (Swansea)	4:28.15
1986	Annemarie Fox (Swansea)	4:24.91	Lynn Maddison (Colwyn B)	4:31.42	Ann Roblin (Cardiff)	4:35.61
1987	Kirsty Wade (Blayden)	4:25.89	Wendy Ore (Bridgend)	4:29.43	AnnemarieFox/Richards (Sw)	4:31.68
1988	Annemarie Richards (Card)	4:19.7	Melissa Watson (Swindon)	4:20.4	Hayley Nash (Torfaen)	4:21.4
1989	Annemarie Richards (Card)	4:33.90	Nicky Haines (Stourport)	4:36.71	Sian Pilling (Oxf Univ)	4:37.89
1990	Sarah Hodge (Westbury)	4:27.66	Caitlin Funnell (Cambridge)	4:28.44	Alison Parry (Southampton)	4:31.13
1991	Kirsty Wade (Blaydon)	4:22.62	Caitlin Funnell (Cambridge)	4:36.74	Pat Gallagher (Westbury)	4:40.97
1992	Jessica Mills (Harlow)	4:40.85	Pat Gallagher (Westbury)	4:46.44	only 2 athletes	
1993	Wendy Ore (Cardiff)	4:36.24	Lisa Carthew (Swansea)	4:37.34	Hayley Mittelberger (Newp)	4:45.20
1994	Wendy Ore (Cardiff)	4:27.69	Lisa Carthew (Swansea)	4:33.83	Catherine Davies (Cardiff)	4:35.38
1995	Liz Francis/Thomas (Cardiff)	4:36.80	Esther Evans (Aylesbury)	4:38.18	Clare Martin (Newport)	4:42.80
1996	Hayley Parry (Swansea)	4:29.40	Clare Martin (Newport)	4:35.80	Esther Evans (Aylesbury)	4:37.55
1997	Clare Martin (Newport)	4:33.03	Ceri Thomas (Cardiff)	4:40.70	Emma Turner (Abertillery)	4:45.30
1998	Ceri Thomas (Cardiff)	4:39.7	Catherine Dugdale (Cardiff)	4:39.8	Hayley Mittelberger (Abert)	4:43.8
1999	Ruth Eddy (Colchester)	4:45.7	Samantha Gray (Abertillery)	4:53.7	only 2 athletes	
2000	Emma Brady (Telford)	4:37.60	Catherine Dugdale (Swansea)	4:38.81	Annemarie Hutchinson (Neath)	4:41.26

3000 metres

1971	no competitors					
1972	Lesley John (Cwmbran)	11:19.4	Jackie Sommerfield (Westbury)	12:20.6	only 2 athletes	
1973	Jean Lochhead (Airedale)	11:15.4	Bronwen Cardy (Bromsgrove)	11:21.4	only 2 athletes	
1974	Jean Lochhead (Airedale)	10:25.0	Bronwen Cardy (Bromsgrove)	10:33.0	only 2 athletes	
1975	Jean Lochhead (Airedale)	10:52.4	Pam Hiley (Cardiff)	10:59.6	Shaun Lode (Brecon)	11:36.4
1976	Bronwen Cardy/Smith (Brom)	10:18.6	Lyn Huntbach (Cwmbran)	10:25.8	Anne Notman (Cardiff)	10:34.0
1977	Jackie Hulbert (Swansea)	10:14.8	Bronwen Smith (Bromsgrove)	10:36.2	Lyn Huntbach (Cwmbran)	10:44.8
1978	Anne Notman (Cardiff)	10:11.2	Annemarie Fox (Swansea)	10:12.4	Jackie Hulbert (Swansea)	10:18.8
1979	Kim Lock (Cardiff)	09:51.0	Annemarie Fox (Swansea)	10:03.0	Kathy Williams (P Talbot)	10:09.4
1980	Annemarie Fox (Swansea)	09:55.6	Kathy Williams (P Talbot)	10:03.5	Lyn Lerue (Torfaen)	10:24.8
1981	Hilary Hollick (Sale)	09:42.9	Annemarie Fox (Swansea)	09:45.1	Kathy Williams (P Talbot)	10:11.2
1982	Hilary Hollick (Sale)	09:47.9	Annemarie Fox (Swansea)	09:53.4	Sally James (Newport)	10:05.4
1983	Annemarie Fox (Swansea)	09:34.1	Angela Tooby (Cardiff)	09:37.0	Sally James (Newport)	09:48.7
1984	Ann King (Swansea)	09:49.26	Sally James (Newport)	09:59.23	Lynn Maddison (C Bay)	10:34.69
1985	Melissa Watson (Swindon)	10:04.93	Rebecca Powell (Swansea)	10:16.93	Marianne Layden (Brecon)	10:23.45
1986	Susan Tooby (Cardiff)	09:18.74	Melissa Watson (Swindon)	09:20.00	Angela Tooby (Cardiff)	09:27.74
1987	Melissa Watson (Swindon)	09:08.28	Angela Tooby (Cardiff)	09:09.70	Susan Tooby (Cardiff)	09:20.88
1988	Susan Tooby (Cardiff)	09:07.8	Kim Lock/Harris (Cardiff)	09:30.4	Wendy Ore (Cardiff)	09:33.7
1989	Melissa Watson (Westbury)	09:24.42	Hayley Nash (Torfaen)	09:27.45	Sally Lynch (Newport)	09:47.10
1990	Alison Whitelaw (Wrexham)	10:00.5	Debbie Chick (Newport)	10:03.6	Claire Jenkins (Newport)	10:18.2
1991	Annemarie Fox/Richards (Card)	09:42.04	Sally Lynch (Newport)	09:44.77	Nicola Haines (Newport)	09:57.77
1992	Kirsty Wade (Blaydon)	09:12.51	Hayley Nash (Torfaen)	09:39.88	Wendy Ore (Cardiff)	09:54.74
1993	Hayley Nash (Cardiff)	09:37.76	Nicola Haines/Jones (Newp)	09:54.90	Lynn Maddison (Sale)	09:58.20
1994	Debbie Newhams (Bridgend)	09:34.65	Hayley Nash (Cardiff)	09:37.55	Nicola Haines Jones (Newport)	10:11.06

5000 metres

1980	Kathy Williams (P Talbot)	17:45.2				
1981	Annemarie Fox (Swansea)	17:36.7	Liz Williams (PTalbot)	18:19.4	Gill Evans (Bridgend)	22:24.4
1982	Louise Copp (P Talbot)	17:45.0	Sian Davies (Wyeside)	20:53.8	only 2 athletes	
1983	Liz Williams (P Talbot)	18:18.4	Bev Morgan (P Talbot)	18:33.2	Gill Evans (Bridgend)	18:47.1
1984 – 1987	event not held					
1988	Eryl Davies (Newport)	17:18.1	Rebecca Richardson (LesC)	18:17.0	Peta Bee (Birchfield)	18:49.1
1989 – 1993	event not held					
1994	Sally Lynch (Newport)	17:34.92	Elinor Caborn (Bedford)	18:35.40	only 2 athletes	
1995	Dinah Cheverton (Newport)	17:33.4	Hayley Nash (Newport)	17:33.5	Angharad Mair (Les C)	18:05.8
1996	Angharad Mair (Newport)	17:32.8	Cathy Dugdale (Heartbeat)	17:44.8	Sally Lynch (Newport)	17:52.0
1997	Angharad Mair (Newport)	16:40.22	Nicola Haines Jones (Newp)	17:33.73	Cathy Dugdale (Cardiff)	17:49.80
1998	Hayley Nash (Newport)	16:53.07	Nicola Haines Jones (Newp)	17:26.42	Emma Davies (Deeside)	18:51.07
1999	Nicola Haines Jones (Newp)	17:24.6	Mary Dowell-Jones (Notts U)	19:25.5	only 2 athletes	
2000	Ruth Schofield (Wrexham)	19:12.0	Sally McWilliams (Deeside)	22:20.7	only 2 athletes	

10,000 metres

1988	Alison Whitelaw (Wrexham)	38:46.07	only one athlete			
1989	Angela Tooby (Cardiff)	33:41.40	Susan Tooby (Cardiff)	35:14.35	Ceri Pritchard (Coventry)	36:01.93
1990	Liz Hardley (Wrexham)	40:36.29				
1991	Alison Whitelaw (Wrexham)	36:56.92	Liz Hardley (Wrexham)	39:08.42	only 2 athletes	
1992 – 1997	event not held					
1998	Hayley Nash (Newport)	34:28.8	Sara Keranen (Les C)	42:20.4	only 2 athletes	
1999	No competitors					
2000	Event not held					

80 metres hurdles / 100 metres hurdles

1952	Virginia Price (Pontardawe GS)	14.3	Dilys Watts (Haverfordwest)	14.6	J Davies (St Julians HS)	15.5
1953	Dilys Watts (Haverfordwest)	13.5	J Pearce (Whitland)	13.7	only 2 athletes	
1954	Sheila Coy (Whitchurch S)	13.0	Dilys Watts (Haverfordwest)		G M Price (Neath GS)	
1955	H Lewis (Rhondda VAC)	14.0	G M Price (Neath GS)	14.1	Dilys Watts (Unattached)	14.1
1956	Maureen Le Quirot (Heolgam)	13.3	C A Sherwood (St Julians)	13.5	V Lavender (Newport AC)	14.2
1957	Maureen Le Quirot (Heolgam)	12.4	Carol Thomas (Whitchurch)	12.5	C A Sherwood (St Julians)	12.6
1958	Carol Thomas (Roath)	11.6	Sheila Lewis (Roath)	11.7	Ann Thomas (Llanelli AC)	12.2
1959	Carol Thomas (Roath)	12.0	Sheila Lewis (Roath)	12.2	C A Sherwood (Newport)	12.7
1960	Carol Thomas (Whitchurch)	12.3	C A Sherwood (St Julians)	12.8	Ann Thomas (Llanelli AC)	12.8
1961	Carol Thomas (Roath)	11.7	Janice Catt (Redhill)	12.1	Ann Thomas (Llanelli AC)	12.2
1962	Ann Thomas (Llanelli AC)	12.0	Bonny Jones (Roath)	12.1	Janice Catt (Chelsea Coll)	12.1
1963	Janice Catt (Chelsea Coll)	12.1	Bonny Jones (Roath)	12.2	Kathryn Hutchinson (Neath)	13.2
1964	Brenda Meredith (Mitcham)	12.2	Bonny Jones (Roath)	12.2	Gillian Jones (Birchgrove)	12.3
1965	Wendy Palmer (Exmouth)	11.5	Brenda Meredith (Mitcham)	11.7	Jenny Williams (Barry GS)	12.1
1966	Wendy Palmer (Exeter)	11.4	Christine Jenner (Surrey)	11.4	Brenda Meredith (Mitcham)	11.6
1967	Wendy Palmer (Chelsea C)	11.6	Christine Thompson (Surrey)	11.7	Jenny Williams (Barry GS)	12.1
1968	June Hirst (Neath GS)	12.9	S Squire (Croesyceiliog)	16.3		
1969	June Hirst (BP Llandarcy)	15.6	Ruth Martin Jones (Birm Un)	15.7	only 2 athletes	
1970	June Hirst (BP Llandarcy)	15.4	Mary Moxley (Llandovery)	16.6	only 2 athletes	
1971	Gaynor Blackwell (Glanafan)	16.0	Pat Pearson (Cambridge)	16.9	Sheridan Bergiers (Carm)	17.8
1972	Gaynor Blackwell (Swansea)	16.1	Sarah Bull (Croesyceiliog)	17.2	Heather Webb (Bromsgrove)	18.1
1973	C P Wilkey (Cardiff)	18.4	Sarah Bull (Croesyceiliog)	18.7	only 2 athletes	
1974	Pat Pearson (Cambridge)	16.3	Jane Lloyd Francis (Carm)	17.2	Dawn Merritt (Swansea)	17.6
1975	Linda Croft (Carmarthen)	15.7	Michelle Atkinson (Brec)	15.8	Pat Pearson (Cambridge)	17.2
1976	Linda Croft (Carmarthen)	16.0	Pat Pearson/Lamour (Camb)	17.1	J Archer (Aberdare)	19.0
1977	Michelle Atkinson (AFD)	15.3	Jane LloydFrancis (Aber Un)	15.9	Paula Middle (Pontypool)	15.9
1978	Diane Heath (Stretford)	14.6	Sarah Bull (Newport)	15.0	Amanda Stacey (Lond Un)	15.0
1979	Diane Heath (Stretford)	14.6	Amanda Stacey (Lond Un)	14.9	Sarah Bull (Newport)	14.9
1980	Sarah Bull (Newport)	14.2	Sarah Rowe (Gloucester)	14.2	Alice Simmons (Newport)	15.5
1981	Sarah Bull/Owen (Newport)	15.4	Jane Buttress (Newport)	16.6	Caris Watson (Cardiff)	18.0
1982	Lynn Parry (Cov God)	14.9	Jane Buttress (Newport)	15.0	Amanda Crewe (Swansea)	17.3
1983	Liz Wren (Bromley)	15.0	Diane Heath/Fryar (Stretford)	15.0	Sarah Owen (Newport)	15.6
1984	Sarah Owen (Newport)	15.38	Liz Wren (Bromley)	15.40	Tracy Lewis (Wrexham)	15.83
1985	Liz Wren (Bromley)	14.90	Tracy Lewis (Wrexham)	15.10	Kay Morley (Cardiff)	15.21
1986	Kay Morley (Cardiff)	13.66	Liz Wren (Bromley)	13.92	Tracy Lewis (Wrexham)	14.33
1987	Kay Morley (Cardiff)	13.49	Liz Wren (Bromley)	14.04	Lisa Griffiths (Torfaen)	14.01
1988	Kay Morley (Cardiff)	13.5	Liz Wren (Bromley)	14.4	Carol Whiteway (Carmarthen)	14.6
1989	Kay Morley (Cardiff)	13.24	Liz Wren (Bromley)	14.27	Carol Whiteway (Carmarthen)	14.59
1990	Kay Morley (Cardiff)	13.56	Bethan Edwards (Cardiff)	14.67	Carol Whiteway (Soton)	15.22
1991	Kay Morley/Brown (Cardiff)	13.78	Bethan Edwards (Cardiff)	14.43	Emily Stewart (Friskney)	15.71
1992	Kay Morley/Brown (Cardiff)	13.48	Megan Jones (Newport)	14.94	Joelanda Thomas (Newport)	15.32
1993	Lisa Griffiths/Gibbs (Torfaen)	13.90	Megan Jones (Newport)	14.44	Bethan Edwards (Cardiff)	14.46
1994	Bethan Edwards (Cardiff)	14.36	Megan Jones (Newport)	15.02	Teresa Andrews (Preseli)	15.49
1995	Rachel King (Cardiff)	14.2	Non Evans (Swansea)	14.5	Rachel Stannard (Newport)	15.6
1996	Bethan Edwards (Cardiff)	14.0	Non Evans (Swansea)	14.0	Rachel King (Cardiff)	14.1
1997	Rachel King (Cardiff)	14.24	Rachel Stannard (Newport)	15.62	Anna Leyshon (Swansea)	16.09
1998	Rachel King (Cardiff)	13.81	Non Evans (Swansea)	14.56	Lowri Roberts (Newport)	15.20
1999	Lowri Roberts (Newport)	15.78	Anna Leyshon (Swansea)	17.65	Stephanie Little (Newport)	18.19
2000	Rachel King (Cardiff)	14.12	Lowri Roberts (Newport)	14.89	only 2 athletes	

400 metres hurdles

1975	J Archer (Aberdare)	75.7	only one athlete			
1976	Julie Morgan (Cardiff)	69.1	Pat Lamour (Cambridge)	70.4	J Archer (Aberdare)	70.5
1977	Diane Heath (Stretford)	60.8	Bernie Butcher (Sale)	64.3	Lynfa Lewis (Southampton)	66.0
1978	Lynfa Lewis (Southamp)	64.0	Bernie Butcher (Sale)	64.6	Pat Lamour (Cambridge)	67.6
1979	Jane Evans (Bristol)	61.9	Lynfa Lewis (Southampton)	62.7	Linda Croft (Cardiff)	65.5
1980	Jane Evans (Bristol)	61.7	Sarah Bull (Newport)	62.2	Lynfa Lewis (Southampton)	62.7
1981	Sarah Bull/Owen (Newp)	62.3	Lynfa Lewis/Porter (Soton)	63.3	Jane Buttress (Newport)	66.4
1982	Diane Heath/Fryar (Stretford)	59.2	Jane Buttress (Newport)	62.9	Michelle Cooke (Carm)	63.8

1983	Diane Fryar (Stretford)	59.1	Jane Buttress (Newport)	62.4	Sarah Owen (Newport)	62.8
1984	Michelle Cooke (Swansea)	61.3	Alyson Evans (Cardiff)	63.7	Sharon James (Cleddau)	65.2
1985	Michelle Cooke (Swansea)	60.75	Lynn Parry (Coventry)	66.08	Linda Gummer (Torfaen)	72.37
1986	Alyson Evans (Cardiff)	59.40	Michelle Cooke (Swansea)	60.14	Karen Adams (Wrexham)	66.42
1987	Michelle Cooke (Swansea)	61.49	Rebecca Jones-Morris (Card)	64.01	Karen Adams (Wrexham)	66.74
1988	Michelle Cooke (Swansea)	59.9	Tracy Lewis (Stretford)	62.0	Rebecca Jones-Morris (Cardiff)	66.1
1989	Michelle Cooke (Swansea)	62.28	Tracy Lewis (Stretford)	65.36	Mari Prys Jones (Carmarthen)	67.35
1990	Michelle Cooke (Swansea)	63.15	Maria Yarnold (Newport)	64.52	Mari Prys Jones (Carmarthen)	66.03
1991	Claire Edwards (Wrexham)	61.99	Michelle Cooke (Swansea)	62.30	Mari Prys Jones (Carmarthen)	64.57
1992	Claire Edwards (Wrexham)	62.67	Michelle Cooke (Swansea)	62.77	Emma Davies (Barry)	65.03
1993	Claire Edwards (Wrexham)	62.40	Emma Davies (Barry)	63.10	Michelle Cooke (Swansea)	63.38
1994	Natasha Bartlett (Cardiff)	59.25	Claire Edwards (Wrexham)	61.92	Emma Davies (Barry)	66.33
1995	Claire Edwards (Wrexham)	63.6	Kathryn Williams (Swansea)	65.0	Amanda Horton (Newport)	67.0
1996	Alyson Evans/Layzell (Ch)	58.92	Caroline Wilkins (Cardiff)	62.16	Amanda Horton (Newport)	67.03
1997	Alyson Layzell (Cheltenham)	59.88	Caroline Wilkins (Cardiff)	62.48	Sarah Lewis (Newport)	68.13
1998	Abigail Jones (Wrexham)	66.66	only one athlete			
1999	Louise Whitehead (Swansea)	63.5	Kathryn Williams (Swansea)	65.5	Nicola Mills (Newport)	67.0
2000	Kathryn Williams (Swansea)	62.77	Michelle Debono (Herne H)	68.55	only 2 athletes	

High Jump

1952	P Evans (Treorchy AC)	1.34	Esme Carey (Newport)	1.29	M Palmer (St Julians HS)	1.27
1953	Rose Peek (Newport)	1.42	M Palmer (St Julians HS)	1.40	R Birch (Penarth)	1.36
1954	Rose Peek (Newport)	1.45	D Jones (Rhondda GS)	1.42	Marie Witts (Port Talbot)	1.42
1955	Kathleen Boobyer (Skewen)	1.45	D Jones (Rhondda)	1.40	Marie Witts (Port Talbot)	1.40
1956	S Jones (Neath GS)	1.48	remainder failed at qualifying height !			
1957	Sally Jones (Roath)	1.42	R M Williams (Quakers Yd)	1.27	Barbara Perry (Whitchurch)	1.27
1958	Sally Jones (Roath)	1.45	Joyce Wheeler (Duffryn GS)	1.42 =	M E Wardle (Newport HS)	1.42 =
1959	Sally Jones (Roath)	1.55	Monica Zeraschi (Erias)	1.52	Joyce Wheeler (Port Talbot)	1.50
1960	Monica Zeraschi (Eirias)	1.52	Linda Hughes (Llanelli GS)	1.47	L Parkes (Lady Mary HS)	1.45
1961	Linda Hughes (Llanelli GS)	1.50	Barbara Perry (Birchgrove)	1.42	Margaret Liddiard (Cwmbran)	1.37
1962	Jane Davies (Crymich SS)	1.52	Barbara Perry (Birchgrove)	1.50	Margaret Liddiard (Cwmbran)	1.40
1963	Pam Guppy (Heol Hir SS)	1.55	Monica Zeraschi (Roath)	1.52	K Matthews (Penarth GS)	1.52
1964	Pam Guppy (Heol Hir SS)	1.62	Marilyn Matthews (Penarth)	1.50	Barbara Perry (Birchgrove)	1.40
1965	Pam Guppy (Birchgrove)	1.52	Pat McDiarmid (Birchgrove)	1.42	Joan Bishop (Caerphilly GS)	1.40
1966	Janet Jones (Aldershot)	1.42	only one athlete			
1967	June Hirst (Neath GS)	1.45	Ruth Martin Jones (Birm U)	1.40		
1968	June Hirst (Neath GS)	1.48				
1969	June Hirst (B P Llandarcy)	1.60	Christine Craig (Grove Park)	1.57	Ruth Martin Jones (B'field)	1.45
1970	June Hirst (Neath GS)	1.48	only one athlete			
1971	Sheridan Bergiers (Carm)	1.42	Susan Hamer (Cyfarthfa)	1.32	only 2 athletes	
1972	Delyth Hughes (Sale)	1.57	Christine Griffiths (Swansea)	1.55	Sarah Bull (Newport)	1.50
1973	Hilary MacPherson (Eirias)	1.52	Sarah Bull (Croesyceiliog)	1.50	only 2 athletes	
1974	Jane Lloyd Francis (Carm)	1.40	Elaine Hammersley (Cleddau)	1.35	Sheridan Bergiers (Caerleon)	1.35
1975	Heather Thomas (Carm)	1.55	Sarah Bull (Newport)	1.45	only 2 athletes	
1976	Jane Lloyd Francis (Aber U)	1.63	Susan Lovell (Caldicott)	1.55	Janet Beese (Newport)	1.50
1977	Jane Lloyd Francis (Aber U)	1.64	Susan Lovell (Newport)	1.60	Viv Rothera (Swansea)	1.50
1978	Jane Lloyd Francis (Aber U)	1.70	Sarah Bull (Newport)	1.65	Viv Rothera (Swansea)	1.60
1979	Marion Hughes (Derby)	1.60	Jane Lloyd Francis (Unatt)	1.55	Viv Rothera/Christina Brown	1.50
1980	Marion Hughes (Derby)	1.75	Sarah Bull (Newport)	1.70	Sarah Rowe (Gloucester)	1.70
1981	Sarah Rowe (Gloucester)	1.75	Marion Hughes (Derby)	1.65	Alice Simmons (Newport)	1.55
1982	Marion Hughes (Derby)	1.78	Sarah Nicholls (Bridgend)	1.65	Susan Lovell (Torfaen)	1.65
1983	Marion Hughes (Derby)	1.70	Sarah Rowe (Cheltenham)	1.65	Sarah Bull/Owen (Newport)	1.60
1984	Marion Hughes (Derby)	1.68	Val Adams (Swansea)	1.65	Jackie Barber (Barry)	1.65
1985	Marion Hughes (Derby)	1.80	Kim Miller (Southampton)	1.68	Karen Nethercott (SGIHE)	1.60
1986	Marion Hughes (Derby)	1.81	Val Adams (Swansea)	1.75	Jackie Barber (Barry)	1.70
1987	Marion Hughes (Derby)	1.71	Val Adams (Swansea)	1.68	Carol Whiteway (Carm)	1.65
1988	Marion Hughes (Derby)	1.75	Jackie Barber (Barry)	1.65	Val Adams (Swansea)	1.55
1989	Marion Hughes (Derby)	1.70	Bev Green (Swansea)	1.65	Anna Clode (Cardiff)	1.60
1990	Susannah Filce (Wrexham)	1.70	Bev Green (Swansea)	1.60	Val Adams (Darlington)	1.55
1991	Rebecca Richards (Millfield)	1.68	Val Adams (Darlington)	1.65	Susannah Filce (Wrexham)	1.65
1992	Susannah Filce (Wrexham)	1.70	Fiona McPhail (Wigan)	1.70	Val Adams (Darlington)	1.65
1993	Teresa Andrews (Preseli)	1.70	Emma Hanson (Cardiff)	1.65	Susannah Filce (Wrexham)	1.60
1994	Teresa Andrews (Preseli)	1.70	Ailsa Wallace (Barry)	1.70	Claudia Filce (Wrexham)	1.65
1995	Julie Crane (Nottingham)	1.78	Teresa Andrews (Preseli)	1.75	Kelly Moreton (Newport)	1.60
1996	Teresa Andrews (Preseli)	1.65	Caroline Hogg (Cardiff)	1.50 =	Kathryn Evans (Swansea)	1.50 =
1997	Kelly Moreton (Newport)	1.60	only one athlete			
1998	Julie Crane (Nottingham)	1.80	Ailsa Wallace (Cardiff)	1.65	Kelly Moreton (Newport)	1.65
1999	Julie Crane (Birm Univ)	1.75	Ailsa Wallace (Cardiff)	1.60	Emily Tugwell (Swansea)	1.82
2000	Julie Crane (Sale)	1.82	only one athlete			

Pole Vault

1995	Rebecca Roles (Swansea)	2.50	Bonny Elms (Newport)	2.50	only 2 athletes	
1996	Rhian Clarke (Essex L)	3.65	Rebecca Roles (Swansea)	2.90	only 2 athletes	
1997	Rhian Clarke (Essex L)	3.60	Rebecca Roles (Swansea)	3.20	Eirion Owen (Brecon)	2.80
1998	Rhian Clarke (Essex L)	3.70	Rebecca Roles (Swansea)	3.20	Penny Hall (Cardiff)	2.90
1999	Rhian Clarke (Essex L)	3.60	Eirion Owen (Brecon)	2.80	Anna Leyshon (Swansea)	2.30
2000	Anna Leyshon (Swansea)	2.90	Penny Hall (Cardiff)	2.80	Nicola Witton (Newport)	2.70

Long Jump

1952	Jean Docker (Middlesex)	5.03	J Griffiths (Neath)	4.68	G Pinnell (St Julians HS)	4.25
1953	Lilian O'Brien (Mtn Ash GS)	4.87	Jean Docker (Middlesex)	4.67	Joan Lindsay (Aberystwyth)	4.66
1954	A Foster (Ebbw Vale GS)	4.99	M Stapleton (Heol Gam SS)		Joan Lindsay (Aberyst Un)	
1955	Jackie Barnett (Newport AC)	4.82	J Bryant (St Josephs)	4.74	S Jones (Neath GS)	4.70
1956	Sally Jones (Roath)	5.12	J Bryant (Newport AC)	4.90	S Jones (Neath GS)	4.87
1957	Sally Jones (Roath)	4.99	Norma Lee (Merthyr AC)	4.87	G Garnham (Pembroke GS)	4.81
1958	Bonnie Jones (Bridgend TC)	5.33	Carol Morgan (Roath)	5.05	Norma Lee (Merthyr AC)	5.00
1959	Bonnie Jones (Roath)	5.29	Monica Zeraschi (Eirias)		Carol Thomas (Roath)	
1960	Monica Zeraschi (Eirias)	5.19	Pam Dalton (Roath)	5.16	Carol Morgan (Roath)	4.89
1961	Monica Zeraschi (Eirias)	5.68	Janice Catt (Redhill)	5.58	Bonnie Jones (Roath)	5.23
1962	Janice Catt (Chelsea Coll	5.71	Bonnie Jones (Roath)	5.65	A Livingstone (Bush GS)	5.14
1963	Monica Zeraschi (Roath)	5.80	Janice Catt (Chelsea Coll)	5.49	Bonnie Jones (Roath)	5.33
1964	Bonnie Jones (Roath)	5.45	Sylvia Powell (Swan Vall)	5.11	Tanya Alcock (Cyfarthfa)	5.03
1965	Pam Guppy (Birchgrove)	5.36	Sylvia Powell (Swan Vall)	5.23	Viv Bennett (Barry GS)	4.95
1966	Christine Jenner (Surrey)	5.54	Sylvia Powell (Swan Vall)	5.34	Viv Bennett (Barry)	4.78
1967	Chris Jenner/Thompson (Su)	5.81	Sylvia Powell (Swan Vall)	5.48	Wendy Palmer (Chelsea Co)	5.32
1968	June Hirst (BP Llandarcy)	5.15	only one athlete			
1969	Ruth Martin Jones (Birm Un)	5.76	Jennifer Hughes (Calving H)	5.42	June Hirst (BP Llandarcy)	5.35
1970	June Hirst (Neath GS)	5.35	Sharon McParlin (Barry)	5.21	only 2 athletes	
1971	Susan Hopkins (Carmarthen)	5.07	Angela Smith (Cardiff)	4.87	Pat Pearson (Cambridge)	4.77
1972	Gaynor Blackwell (Swansea)	5.26	Margaret Brain (Cwmbran)	5.07	Ann Rich (Cardiff)	4.99
1973	Ruth Martin Jones (B'field)	5.88	H Webb (Bromsgrove)	5.18	Sarah Bull (Croesyceiliog)	5.10
1974	Gillian Regan (Cardiff)	5.47	Karen Jenkins (Hereford)	5.43	Linda Williams (Aberdare)	5.21
1975	Ruth Martin Jones (B'field)	6.00	Gillian Regan (Cardiff)	5.89	Linda Croft (Carmarthen)	5.40
1976	Gillian Regan (Cardiff)	6.00	Ceri Jenkins (Cleddau)	5.42	Pat Bevans (Abertillery)	5.30
1977	Gillian Regan (Cardiff)	5.99	Ceri Jenkins (Cleddau)	5.62	Jill Davies (Plymouth)	5.36
1978	Ruth MJ/Howell (Birchfield)	6.33	Jill Davies (Plymouth)	5.98	Gillian Regan (Cardiff)	5.74
1979	Gillian Regan (Cardiff)	6.20	Jill Davies (Plymouth)	6.17	Deborah Perry (Cardiff)	5.43
1980	Gillian Regan (Cardiff)	5.94	Sarah Rowe (Gloucester)	5.72	Marion Hughes (Derby)	5.54
1981	Jill Davies/Morton (Plym)	6.01	Gillian Regan (Cardiff)	5.84	Joanne Edwards (Bristol)	5.67
1982	Gillian Regan (Cardiff)	6.01	Jill Morton (Plymouth)	5.86	Nicolette Dymond (Rhymney)	5.24
1983	Sarah Owen (Newport)	5.39	Liz Wren (Bromley)	5.11	Ruth Hanney (Bridgend)	4.36
1984	Gillian Regan (Cardiff)	6.30	Jo Edwards/Willoughby (B)	5.91	Sarah Owen (Newport)	5.60
1985	Gillian Regan (Cardiff)	5.88	Joanne Willoughby (Bristol)	5.80	Linda Gummer (Torfaen)	5.21
1986	Gillian Regan (Cardiff)	6.21	Joanne Willoughby (Bristol)	5.98	Nicola Short (Torfaen)	5.80
1987	Nicola Short (Torfaen)	5.59	Lisa Griffiths (Torfaen)	5.52	Audrey Lewis (Cheltenham)	5.11
1988	Joanne Willoughby (Bristol)	5.68	Nicola Short (Torfaen)	5.58	Pat Roche (Cardiff)	5.51
1989	Joanne Willoughby (Bristol)	6.16	Lisa Griffiths (Torfaen)	5.53	Kathryn Evans (Carmarthen)	5.38
1990	Joanne Willoughby (Bristol)	6.15	Pat Roche (Cardiff)	5.47	Amanda Wale (Wrexham)	5.47
1991	Anna Proctor (Newport)	5.46	Tracy Powell (Wrexham)	5.36	Pat Roche (Cardiff)	5.12
1992	Lisa Armstrong (Torfaen)	5.78	Anna Proctor (Newport)	5.63	Joanne Willoughby (Bristol)	5.47
1993	Lisa Armstrong (Torfaen)	6.07	Lisa Griffiths/Gibbs (Torfaen)	5.95	Emily Stewart (Hallamshire)	5.41
1994	Sallyanne Short (Torfaen)	5.76	Joanne Willoughby (Bristol)	5.64	Emily Stewart (Hallamshire)	5.36
1995	Nicola Short (Torfaen)	5.66	Teresa Andrews (Preseli)	5.61	Susan Harries (Havering)	4.96
1996	Nicola Short (Torfaen)	5.74	Teresa Andrews (Preseli)	5.69	Gemma Jones (Torfaen)	5.52
1997	Gemma Jones (Torfaen)	5.69	Nicola Short (Newport)	5.46	Sarah Lane (Torfaen)	5.22
1998	Aimee Cutler (Torfaen)	5.75	Debbie Adams (Newport)	5.29	Sarah Lane (Torfaen)	5.23
1999	Sarah Lane (Swansea)	5.35	Lara Richards (Newport)	5.34	Debbie Lloyd (Colwyn Bay)	5.15
2000	Lara Richards (Newport)	5.80	Gemma Jones (Torfaen)	5.64	Joanne Tomlinson (Deeside)	5.10

Triple Jump

1993	Jane Falconer (Colchester)	11.89	Emily Stewart (Hallamshire)	10.58	Eleri Owen (Eryri)	10.19
1994	Nicola Jupp (Reading)	10.75	Pat Roche (Cardiff)	10.72	Eleri Owen (Eryri)	10.53
1995	Jayne Ludlow (Cardiff)	11.29	Susan Harries (Havering)	11.10	Joy Lamacraft (Swansea)	09.84
1996	Teresa Andrews (Preseli)	11.50	Kathryn Evans (Swansea)	09.65	Emma Lane (Torfaen)	09.47
1997	Laura Eastwood (Deeside)	10.87	Jo Tomlinson (Deeside)	10.78	Joy Lamacraft (Cardiff)	10.70
1998	Susan Harries/Bunting (Hav)	10.89	Emily Tugwell (Swansea)	10.77	Jo Tomlinson (Deeside)	10.63
1999	Lara Richards (Newport)	11.49	Susan Bunting (Havering)	10.90	Sarah Friday (Preseli)	10.63
2000	no competitors					

Shot

1953	Diana Noott (Aberyst Un)	07.69	P Phillips (Whitland)	07.01	S Tudor (Aberyst Un)	06.98
1954	Anne Holdsworth (M'wen)	09.45	Diana Noott (Aberyst Un)		Jean Docker (Middlesex)	
1955	Anne Holdsworth (Rotherham)	10.64	Diana Noott (Aberyst Un)	07.90	E Arthur (Swansea AC)	06.79
1956	Anne Holdsworth (Swansea)	10.29	V P Davies (Unattached)	08.68	Maureen Le Quirot (Heolgam SS)	08.68
1957	Anne Holdsworth (Swansea)	10.30	R Gassney (Pembroke GS)	08.24	Jean Crutchley (Pemb GS)	08.14
1958	Anne Holdsworth (Swansea)	09.82	Pauline Williams (B'grove)	08.44	J Budden (Merthyr AC)	08.32
1959	Pauline Williams (B'grove)	09.57	Anne Holdsworth (Swansea)	08.88	Lynette Harries (Mond)	08.62
1960	Pauline Williams (B'grove)	09.43	Anne Holdsworth (Swansea)	08.95	Mary Lewis (Swansea)	07.83
1961	Lynette Harries (Mond)	09.03	M Edwards (Welshpool)	08.57	C Horton (Merthyr)	08.51
1962	Anne Holdsworth (Swansea)	10.32	P Morgan (Haverfordwest)	09.96	Averil Williams (Lozells)	09.83
1963	Sandra Murphy (Merthyr)	10.13	L Rochelle (Roath)	09.93	only 2 athletes	
1964	Sandra Murphy (Merthyr)	11.21	Hazel Andow (Birchgrove)	09.65	only 2 athletes	
1965	Hazel Andow (Birchgrove)	11.64	Sandra Murphy (Merthyr)	11.19	L James (Cyfarthfa)	09.15
1966	Hazel Andow (Birchgrove)	11.59	Sandra Walton (Merthyr)	10.75	Mary Lloyd (Chester)	09.88
1967	Mary Lloyd (Ursuline Con)	09.22	J Bent (Surrey)	08.37		
1968	Jean Davies (Bucks)	11.07	Mary Lloyd (Ursuline Con)	10.35	Janet Beese (St Julians HS)	09.22
1969	Janet Beese (St Julians HS)	11.31	Frances Pincock (Milf Hav)	09.94		
1970	Janet Beese (Newport)	11.92	Maureen Pearce (Flint)	11.56	Frances Pincock (Milf Hav)	10.77
1971	Janet Beese (Newport)	11.86	Frances Pincock (Milf Hav)	11.48	Mary Watham (Rumney HS)	09.66
1972	Janet Beese (Newport)	12.22	Melanie Roberts (Newport)	09.76	Sally Blake (Newport)	08.91
1973	Delyth Prothero (Card Coll)	11.00	Jackie Gray (Cardiff)	10.75	Sally Blake (Newport)	09.20
1974	Venissa Head (Cyfarthfa S)	12.38	Janet Beese (Newport)	12.01	Delyth Prothero (Card Col)	11.61
1975	Venissa Head (Army)	14.08	Janet Beese (Newport)	12.53	Delyth Prothero (Cardiff)	11.10
1976	Venissa Head (Army)	15.39	Janet Beese (Newport)	11.90	Vivienne Head (Army)	11.30
1977	Venissa Head (Army)	14.87	Janet Beese (Newport)	12.53	Vivienne Head (Bristol)	11.89
1978	Venissa Head (Bristol)	14.31	Janet Beese (Newport)	13.84	Vivienne Head (Bristol)	11.14
1979	Venissa Head (Bristol)	15.30	Janet Beese (Newport)	12.94	Janeen Williams (Cannock)	12.07
1980	Venissa Head (Bristol)	15.79	Sarah Bull (Newport)	13.03	Jane Lloyd Francis (Card)	11.25
1981	Venissa Head (Bristol)	17.84	Sarah Bull/Owen (Newport)	12.87	Alyson Hourihan (Cardiff)	10.83
1982	Venissa Head (Bristol)	16.95	Alyson Hourihan (Cardiff)	10.70	Barbara Pendrey (Deeside)	10.02
1983	Venissa Head (Cardiff)	18.03	Sarah Owen (Newport)	11.39	Alyson Hourihan (Cardiff)	11.11
1984	Venissa Head (Cardiff)	16.49	Sarah Owen (Newport)	12.89	Janet Beese (Newport)	12.63
1985	Venissa Head (Cardiff)	15.75	Janet Beese (Newport)	12.89	Janeen Williams (Birchfield)	11.93
1986	Venissa Head (Cardiff)	15.58	Janet Beese (Newport)	12.60	Janeen Williams (Birchfield)	12.42
1987	Venissa Head (Cardiff)	15.64	Janeen Williams (Birchfield)	12.53	Janet Beese (Newport)	12.26
1988	Venissa Head (Cardiff)	14.04	Janet Beese (Newport)	11.95	Alyson Hourihan (Cardiff)	11.51
1989	Jayne Berry (Brecon)	13.31	Janet Beese (Newport)	11.93	Jo Evans (Bridgend)	11.35
1990	Jayne Berry (Cardiff)	13.73	Janet Beese (Newport)	11.95	Sarah Owen (Newport)	11.15
1991	Janet Beese (Newport)	12.24	Alison George (Cannock)	10.34	Rachel Masterman (Torfaen)	10.19
1992	Jayne Berry (Cardiff)	13.85	Sarah Moore (Bristol)	11.69	Alyson Hourihan (Police)	11.55
1993	Jayne Berry (Cardiff)	14.08	Philippa Roles (Swansea)	12.89	Alyson Hourihan (Cardiff)	11.97
1994	Krissy Owen (Eryri)	12.88	Alyson Hourihan (Cardiff)	11.63	Clare McKenzie (Barry)	11.56
1995	Philippa Roles (Swansea)	13.21	Alison George (Cannock)	11.32	Alyson Hourihan (Cardiff)	11.29
1996	Lesley Brannan (Wrexham)	11.46	Alison George (Cannock)	10.56	Kelly Roberts (Wrexham)	08.88
1997	Jayne Berry (Brecon)	14.30	Philippa Roles (Swansea)	14.22	Lesley Brannan (Sale)	11.36
1998	Philippa Roles (Swansea)	13.91	Jayne Berry (Brecon)	13.58	Alyson Hourihan (Cardiff)	11.41
1999	Lesley Brannan (Sale)	11.74	Liz Edwards (Wrexham)	11.09	only 2 athletes	
2000	Lesley Brannan (Sale)	12.61	Cathy Kingsbury (Rhondda)	09.45	Julie Eckley (Brecon)	07.99

Discus

1953	Diana Noott (Aberys Un)	25.90	Dilys Watts (Haverfordwest)	25.50	only 2 athletes	
1954	Diana Noott (Aberys Un)	25.14	Jean Docker (Middlesex)		A Foster (Ebbw Vale)	
1955	Jean Crutchley (Pemb Dk)	28.84	Anne Holdsworth (Rotherham)	26.08	Dilys Watts (Unattached)	24.62
1956	Jean Crutchley (Pemb Dk)	29.62	V P Davies (Unattached)	25.40	Maureen Le Quirot (Heolgam)	24.28
1957	Jean Crutchley (Pemb Dk)	31.58	Anne Holdsworth (Swansea)	27.64	Lynette Harries (Swansea V)	24.56
1958	Jean Crutchley (Selsonia)	30.54	J Price (Merioneth SS)	30.49	Lynette Harries (Swansea V)	29.88
1959	Lynette Harries (Mond)	33.38	J Price (Merioneth SS)		E Hey (Llanelli GS)	
1960	Lynette Harries (Mond)	33.20	Patsy McMinn (Llanelli)	30.00	Mary Lewis (Swansea)	29.04
1961	Lynette Harries (Mond)	31.82	A Williams (Llanelli GS)	31.58	D Lewis (Aberyst Un)	30.26
1962	Averil Williams (Lozells)	31.58				
1963	Sandra Murphy (Merthyr)	28.96	Tanya Alcock (Cyfarthfa)	26.13	T Evans (Ystalyfera)	23.86
1964	Sandra Murphy (Merthyr)	29.62	Hazel Andow (Birchgrove)	28.52	Tanya Alcock (Cyfarthfa)	27.58
1965	Hazel Andow (Birchgrove)	31.38	J Parry (Caerffili S)	28.91	P Jeremiah (Barry GS)	22.60
1966	Hazel Andow (Cathays)	32.66	Victoria Lacey (Carmarthen)	29.32	J Parry (Caerffili S)	27.06
1967	Hazel Andow (Birchgrove)	34.68	only one athlete			
1968	Janet Beese (Newport)	28.00	Janet Hay (BP Llandarcy)	22.94	only 2 athletes	
1969	Janet Beese (St Julians HS)	30.86	Frances Pincock (Milf Hav)	29.90	only 2 athletes	
1970	Janet Beese (Newport)	35.84	Frances Pincock (Milf Hav)	27.00	Lynette Harding (Penarth)	23.88
1971	Janet Beese (Newport)	38.48	Delyth Prothero (Brecon S)	33.82	Sally Blake (Newport)	25.32

1972	Janet Beese (Newport)	38.52	Linda Fairley (Swansea)	30.52	Adelina Evans (Swansea)	22.80
1973	Delyth Prothero (Card Coll)	38.00	Jackie Gray (Cardiff)	37.84	Linda Fairley (Swansea)	32.84
1974	Janet Beese (Newport)	40.60	Delyth Prothero (Cardiff)	40.54	Jacqui Gray (Cardiff)	40.54
1975	Delyth Prothero (Cardiff)	42.76	Janet Beese (Newport)	40.24	Vivienne Head (Army)	39.52
1976	Vivienne Head (Army)	42.08	Janet Beese (Newport)	41.52	Katrina Beedles (Cardiff)	33.14
1977	Vivienne Head (Bristol)	43.40	Janet Beese (Newport)	41.72	Val Watson (Sale)	40.48
1978	Vivienne Head (Bristol)	45.16	Janet Beese (Newport)	42.86	Alyson Hourihan (Cardiff)	35.98
1979	Venissa Head (Bristol)	44.10	Vivienne Head (Bristol)	43.46	Alyson Hourihan (Cardiff)	39.96
1980	Venissa Head (Bristol)	50.22	Alyson Hourihan (Cardiff)	39.48	Jane Lloyd Francis (Card)	31.94
1981	Venissa Head (Bristol)	51.78	Alyson Hourihan (Cardiff)	43.02	Sarah Worthy (Torfaen)	36.50
1982	Venissa Head (Bristol)	54.08	Alyson Hourihan (Cardiff)	39.56	Sarah Worthy (Torfaen)	37.26
1983	Venissa Head (Cardiff)	44.04	Alyson Hourihan (Cardiff)	39.84	Sarah Worthy (Torfaen)	37.78
1984	Venissa Head (Cardiff)	57.18	Janet Beese (Newport)	41.82	Vivienne Head (Newport)	41.12
1985	Venissa Head (Cardiff)	50.76	Janet Beese (Newport)	39.48	Alyson Hourihan (Cardiff)	37.74
1986	Venissa Head (Cardiff)	53.90	Amanda Barnes (Millfield)	42.62	Janet Beese (Newport)	41.18
1987	Venissa Head (Cardiff)	53.84	Amanda Barnes (Millfield)	42.86	Janet Beese (Newport)	40.54
1988	Venissa Head (Cardiff)	54.26	Alyson Hourihan (Cardiff)	38.58	Janet Beese (Newport)	38.08
1989	Janet Beese (Newport)	42.28	Alyson Hourihan (Cardiff)	41.34	Hayley Hartson (Swansea)	39.86
1990	Janet Beese (Newport)	39.60	Jayne Berry (Cardiff)	39.08	Hayley Hartson (Swansea)	38.58
1991	Janet Beese (Newport)	40.32	Jane Davies (Torfaen)	39.96	Jayne Fisher (Swansea)	39.58
1992	Jayne Berry (Cardiff)	43.22	Jayne Fisher (Swansea)	42.32	Jane Davies (Torfaen)	42.22
1993	Philippa Roles (Swansea)	43.70	Jayne Fisher (Swansea)	41.70	Jayne Berry (Cardiff)	41.66
1994	Jayne Fisher (Swansea)	45.38	Alyson Hourihan (Cardiff)	42.08	Jo Evans (Cardiff)	36.26
1995	Philippa Roles (Swansea)	44.16	Jayne Fisher (Swansea)	43.66	Alyson Hourihan (Cardiff)	37.46
1996	Philippa Roles (Swansea)	45.14	Rebecca Roles (Swansea)	36.66	Lesley Brannan (Wrexham)	34.12
1997	Philippa Roles (Swansea)	48.20	Alyson Hourihan (Cardiff)	41.36	Rebecca Roles (Swansea)	38.16
1998	Philippa Roles (Swansea)	50.61	Rebecca Roles (Swansea)	42.66	Alyson Hourihan (Cardiff)	40.01
1999	Philippa Roles (Sale)	52.98	Rebecca Roles (Swansea)	48.95	Kelly Ricketts (Deeside)	38.41
2000	Rebecca Roles (Rugby)	45.56	Kelly Ricketts (Deeside)	37.23	Julie Eckley (Brecon)	26.84

Hammer

1991	Angela Bonner (Torfaen)	34.02	Cathy Kingsbury (Rhondda)	31.46	Janet Beese (Newport)	29.06
1992	Sarah Moore (Bristol)	44.14	Angela Bonner (Torfaen)	39.12	Cathy Kingsbury (Rhondda)	32.60
1993	Sarah Moore (Bristol)	45.02	Angela Bonner (Torfaen)	40.16	Leanne Jones (Rhondda)	37.64
1994	Sarah Moore (Bristol)	48.32	Angela Bonner (Torfaen)	45.08	Leeanne Jones (Rhondda)	40.16
1995	Sarah Moore (Bristol)	51.82	Cathy Kingsbury (Rhondda)	32.38	Sheena Parry (Rhondda)	32.14
1996	Sarah Moore (Bristol)	52.90	Lesley Brannan (Wrexham)	46.18	Leanne Jones (Rhondda)	41.02
1997	Sarah Moore (Bristol)	52.36	Leanne Jones (Rhondda)	42.74	Lesley Brannan (Sale)	42.42
1998	Sarah Moore (Bristol)	52.39	Carys Parry (Rhondda)	47.01	Lesley Brannan (Sale)	45.59
1999	Sarah Moore (Bristol)	53.57	Carys Parry (Rhondda)	51.09	Lesley Brannan (Sale)	47.71
2000	Sarah Moore (Bristol)	53.74	Carys Parry (Rhondda)	52.07	Lesley Brannan (Sale)	51.86

Javelin (new model from 1999)

1953	Kay Bowater (Bangor Un)	26.70	only one athlete			
1954	Joan Lindsay (Aberys Un)	27.46	only one athlete			
1955	Maureen McMahon (Heolg)	25.14	Joan Lindsay (Aberys Un)	24.66	Anne Holdsworth (Rotherham)	24.56
1956	Anne Holdsworth (Swan A)	33.38	Jean Crutchley (Pemb Dk)	25.58	A Williams (Unattached)	25.02
1957	Anne Holdsworth (Swan A)	29.28	Maureen McMahon (HeolGam)	26.70	G K Evans (Heol Gam)	26.70
1958	Anne Holdsworth (Swan U)	30.94	Maureen McMahon (Bridgend)	31.28	D L Thomas (Llanelli)	30.27
1959	Pauline Williams (B'grove)	34.08	P C P Neicho (St Athan			
1960	Pauline Williams (B'grove)	33.82	Anne Holdsworth (Swan V)	24.18	Jenny Maplestone (LMarg)	21.78
1961	Maureen McMahon (Brid)	34.80	H Miller (Barry TC)	31.98	Rayann GriffithsJones (Amman)	30.60
1962	Averil Williams (Lozells)	43.74	Maureen McMahon (Roath)	36.37	Rayann GriffithsJones (Amman)	31.12
1963	Rayann Griffiths Jones (Amman)	32.74	Sheila Coleman (Porthcawl)	31.29	P Fenton (Porthcawl)	29.56
1964	Rayann Griffiths Jones (Amman)	37.12	Janet Spink (Middlesex)	32.18	Eileen Jones (Mynydd Bach)	31.72
1965	Rayann Griffiths Jones (Amman)	36.28	Sheila Coleman (Unattached)	30.07	L James (Cyfarthfa)	27.48
1966	Janet Spink (Middlesex)	34.22	Sheila Coleman (Whitchurch)	33.14	Jenny Maplestone (Birchgrove)	29.42
1967	Janet Spink (Middlesex)	34.52	Karen Abbot (Ferndale)	33.54	Sheila Coleman (Whitchurch)	31.34
1968	Janet Spink (Middlesex)	35.28	Karen Abbot (Ferndale)	30.86	Sandra Martin (Neath GS)	25.20
1969	Janet Spink (Middlesex)	33.14	Janet Wady (Pontllanfraith)	32.12	Lynne Walters (Cardiff)	30.06
1970	Averil Williams (Birchfield)	44.86	Susan James (Afon Taf)	32.56	Janet Spink (Dartford)	31.28
1971	Averil Williams (Birchfield)	43.92	Susan James (Afon Taf)	39.16	Diane Kelly (Brighton)	33.94
1972	Margaret Rainbow (Swansea)	35.60	Diane Kelly (Brighton)	34.70	J Moates (Penarth)	26.38
1973	Susan James (Millfield)	45.40	Jacqui Gray (Cardiff)	34.18	Diane Kelly (Brighton)	34.06
1974	Susan James (Millfield)	41.70	Elizabeth McKay (Millfield)	36.06	Margaret Rainbow (Caerleon)	35.10
1975	Susan James (L Mabel Col)	40.08	Jane Lucas (Cardiff)	34.42	only 2 athletes	
1976	Jackie Zaslona (Birchfield)	43.62	Jane Lucas (Caerleon Coll)	35.26	Katrina Beedles (Cardiff)	33.00
1977	Jackie Zaslona (Birchfield)	41.60	Yvonne Norton (Llandrindod)	36.56	only 2 athletes	
1978	Jackie Zaslona (Birchfield)	52.04	Susan James (Unattached)	40.96	Marita Rowlands (Deeside)	38.94
1979	Janeen Williams (Cannock)	50.98	Jackie Zaslona (Birchfield)	50.70	Susan James (Cardiff)	41.46

1980	Jackie Zaslona (Birchfield)	49.04	Jennifer Morley (Bracknell)	40.14	Jackie Flanagan (Cardiff)	33.00
1981	Janeen Williams (Cannock)	51.58	Jackie Zaslona (Birchfield)	48.06	Jennifer Morley (Bracknell)	41.84
1982	Jackie Zaslona (Birchfield)	49.50	Janeen Williams (Cannock)	48.06	Jennifer Morley (Bracknell)	43.06
1983	Jackie Zaslona (Birchfield)	47.48	Janeen Williams (Birchfield)	42.20	Jennifer Morley (Bracknell	42.60
1984	Karen Hough (Swansea)	49.64	Janeen Williams (Birchfield)	49.16	Jackie Zaslona (Birchfield)	46.74
1985	Janeen Williams (Birchfield)	49.02	Jackie Zaslona (Birchfield)	48.32	Alyson Hourihan (Cardiff)	32.28
1986	Karen Hough (Swansea)	53.66	Janeen Williams (Birchfield)	47.30	Caroline White (Border)	46.34
1987	Janeen Williams (Birchfield)	48.64	Amanda Barnes (Millfield)	38.00	only 2 athletes	
1988	Caroline White (Border)	48.10	Alyson Hourihan (Cardiff)	32.86	only 2 athletes	
1989	Caroline White (Border)	52.16	Jackie Zaslona (Birchfield)	47.20	Jayne Berry (Brecon)	37.60
1990	Julie Abel (Colwyn Bay)	48.16	Jackie Zaslona (Birchfield)	46.14	Cathy Middleton (Swansea)	35.56
1991	Caroline White (Stretford)	51.44	Onyema Amadi (Cardiff)	42.28	Hazel Lowe (Newport)	37.20
1992	Emily Steele (Birchfield)	45.54	Onyema Amadi (Cardiff)	43.32	Hilary Davies (Brecon)	39.90
1993	Caroline White (Trafford)	50.58	Onyema Amadi (Cardiff)	43.34	Hilary Davies (Brecon)	41.48
1994	Caroline White (Trafford)	49.24	Onyema Amadi (Cardiff)	49.04	Angharad Richards (Guildford)	45.96
1995	Onyema Amadi (Cardiff)	41.82	Joanne Davies (Swansea)	34.54	Emily Bufton (Brecon)	31.26
1996	Onyema Amadi (Cardiff)	48.34	Sian Lax (Wenlock)	43.70	Clare Lockwood (C Bay)	38.48
1997	Sian Lax (Telford)	39.40	Clare Lockwood (C Bay)	33.42	Dee Groves (Torfaen)	29.20
1998	Caroline White (Trafford)	47.16	Onyema Amadi (Cardiff)	42.88	Clare Lockwood (C Bay)	39.23
1999	Caroline White (Trafford)	48.89	Clare Lockwood (Birchfield)	37.75	only 2 athletes	
2000	Alison Siggery (Carm)	36.23	Clare Lockwood (Birchfield)	35.38	Sara Siggery (Carmarthen)	31.35

Pentathlon/Heptathlon (from 1979)

1967	Ruth Martin Jones (Birm U)	3942	Pam Dalton (Roath)	3894	only 2 athletes	
1968	Sylvia Powell (Swansea Vall)	3679	June Hirst (Neath GS)	3511	only 2 athletes	
1969	June Hirst (BP Llandarcy)	3863	Susan Lloyd (Swansea)	3484	Lesley Black (Merthyr S)	3338
1970	June Hirst (BP Llandarcy)	3876	Ann Disley (Newport)	2858	only 2 athletes	
1971	event not held					
1972	Sarah Bull (Newport)	3441	Barbara Spencer (Cardiff)	3365		
1973	Sarah Bull (Newport)	2962	Chris Griffiths (Swansea)	2351	Linda Fairley (Swansea)	2280
1974	June Hirst (BP Llandarcy)	2908	Elaine Hammersley (Cleddau)	2509	Sheridan Bergiers (Caerl C)	2501
1975	Jane Lloyd Franics (Aber U)	2867	Elaine Hammersley (Cleddau)	2293	only 2 athletes	
1976	Janet Beese (Newport)	3157	Sarah Bull (Newport)	3066	Bethan Jones (Carmarthen)	2973
1977	Jane Lloyd Francis (Carm)	3040				
1978	Jane Lloyd Francis (Aber U)	3165	Pat Lamour (Cambridge)	3144	Janet Beese (Newport)	2354
1979	Sarah Bull (Newport)	3735	Jane Lloyd Francis (Unatt)	3365	Pat Lamour (Cambridge)	2996
1979	Pat Lamour (Cambridge)	4286	only one athlete in the heptathlon event			
1980	Sarah Bull (Newport)	4035	Sarah Rowe (Gloucester)	3950	Jane Lloyd Francis (Cardiff)	3310
1980	Sarah Bull (Newport)	5200	only one athlete in the heptathlon event			
1981	Sarah Bull/Owen (Newport)	5365	Liz Wren (Bromley)	4680	Loretta Hamilton (Herc W)	4550
1982	Sarah Owen (Newport)	5281	only one athlete			
1983	Sarah Owen (Newport)	4830	Liz Wren (Bromley)	4792	only 2 athletes	
1984	Linda Gummer (Torfaen)	4180	only one athlete			
1985	Liz Wren (Bromley)	4497	Linda Gummer (Torfaen)	4059	only 2 athletes	
1986	Event not held					
1987	Audrey Lewis (Cheltenham)	3681	Debra Perry (Cardiff)	2572	only 2 athletes	
1988	Debbie Simmons (Cardiff)	2722	only one athlete			
1989	Joanne Evans (Bridgend)	3620	Audrey Lewis (Cheltenham)	3416	only 2 athletes	
1990	Amanda Wale (Wrexham)	4078	Sarah Owen (Newport)	3663	Dawn Nicolson (Leicester)	3482
1991	Amanda Wale (Wrexham)	4083	Sarah Owen (Newport)	3737	Audrey Lewis (Cheltenham)	3323
1992	Lisa Gibbs (Torfaen)	4577	Amanda Wale (Wrexham)	3795	Sarah Owen (Newport)	3601
1993	Lisa Gibbs (Torfaen)	5424	Amanda Wale (Wrexham)	4194	Sarah Owen (Newport)	4162
1994	Amanda Wale (Wrexham)	4302	Amanda Horton (Newport)	3657	only 2 athletes	
1995	Amanda Wale (Wrexham)	4076	Amanda Horton (Newport)	3825	only 2 athletes	
1996	no finishers					
1997	Sarah Lewis (Newport)	3107	Amanda Horton/Wallace (N)	2452	only 2 athletes	
1998	Amanda Wale (Wrexham)	4546	Teresa Andrews (Preseli)	4229	Nicola Jupp (Preseli)	4070
1999	Amanda Wale (Wrexham)	4475	Michelle Debono (Herne H)	3275	only 2 athletes	
2000	Amanda Wale (Wrexham)	4039				

MOST SENIOR TRACK AND FIELD CHAMPIONSHIP WINS (BY EVENT)

100	Ron Jones	8	1956-1970	100	Liz Parsons/Johns	7	1960-1971
200	Ken Jones	8	1946-1954	200	Sallyanne Short	7	1986-1994
400	Erik Hughes	6	1925-1931	400	Gloria Dourass	7	1964-1976
800	Jim Alford	6	1934-1946	800	Kirsty McDermott/Wade	10	1979-1988
1m/1500	Reg Thomas	5	1929-1936	1500	Hilary Hollick	5	1977-1982
				3000	Jean Lochhead	3	1973-1975
					Annemarie Fox/Richards	3	1980-1991

4m/5K	Ernie Thomas	4	1921-1927
	David Richards	4	1954-1962
6m/10K	David Richards	5	1954-1962
S/Chase	David Lee	5	1985–1997
Hurdles	Stanley Macey	7	1928-1934
400 H	Derek Fishwick	4	1979-1983
	Phil Harries	4	1987-1998
HJ	Trevor Llewelyn	6	1978-1983
PV	Tim Thomas	5	1991-1997
LJ	Garry Slade	5	1990-1995
TJ	David Wood	10	1981-1991
SP	Paul Rees	9	1973-1982
DT	Hywel Williams	7	1952-1965
	Paul Rees	7	1974-1982
HT	Lawrie Hall	10	1958-1967
JT	Colin Mackenzie	7	1982-1990
CE	Geoff Ward	5	1975-1980
	Duncan Gauden	5	1992-1997

	Melissa Watson	3	1985-1989
5000	Angharad Mair	2	1996-1997
10000	Alison Whitelaw	2	1988-1991
Hurdles	Kay Morley Brown	7	1986-1992
400 H	Michelle Cook	6	1984-1990
HJ	Marion Hughes	10	1979-1989
PV	Rhian Clarke	4	1996-1999
LJ	Gillian Regan	9	1974-1986
SP	Venissa Head	15	1974-1988
DT	Venissa Head	10	1979-1988
HT	Sarah Moore	9	1992-2000
JT	Caroline White	7	1988-1999
CE	Sarah Bull/Owen	8	1972-1983

MOST TITLES WON AT SENIOR TRACK AND FIELD CHAMPIONSHIPS

25	Venissa Head	Shot x 15, Discus x 10
19	Shaun Pickering	Shot x 5, Discus x 5, Hammer x 9
16	Ken Jones	100y x 7, 220y x 8, Long Jump x 1
16	Paul Rees	Shot x 9, Discus x 7
16	Kirsty McDermott/Wade	400m x 4, 800m x 10, 1500m x 2
15	Frank Whitcutt	120yH x 2, High Jump x 6, Long Jump x 2, Triple Jump x 5
15	Janet Beese	Shot x 5, Discus x 9, Combined Events x 1
13	D J P Richards*	Mile x 4, 4 miles x 4, 2m Walk x 5
13	Hywel Williams	Pole Vault x 1, Shot x 1, Discus x 7, Decathlon x 4
13	Liz Parsons/Johns	100y/m x 7, 220y/200m x 6
13	Colin Jackson	100m x 6, 200m x 2, 110m Hurdles x 5
12	Ron Jones	100y/m x 8, 220y/200m x 4
12	John Lister	120yH x 4, 220yH x 2, High jump x 4, Decathlon x 2
12	John Walters	Shot x 7; Discus x 5
11	Michelle Probert/Scutt	100m x 5, 200m x 4, 400m x 2
11	Sallyanne Short	100m x 4, 200m x 7

** Richards also won seven road walking titles (three at 15 miles and four at 10 miles)*

LONGEST GAP BETWEEN FIRST AND LAST WELSH SENIOR TITLE

D J P Richards	1m/4miles/walks	1923 – 1947	24 years
Janet Beese	Discus	1968 –1991	23 years
Shaun Pickering	Shot/Discus/Hammer	1980 – 1998	18 years
Arthur William Lewis	Shot/Discus	1931 – 1948	17 years
Jim Alford	880y/Mile	1934 – 1948	14 years
Ron Jones	100y	1956 – 1970	14 years
Venissa Head	Shot	1974 – 1988	14 years
Colin Jackson	100m/200m/110m Hurdles	1984 – 1998	14 years
George Dillaway	Shot	1924 – 1937	13 years
Hywel Williams	Discus	1952 – 1965	13 years
Phil Harries	400m Hurdles	1985 – 1998	13 years
Peter Walker	Triple Jump	1960 – 1972	12 years
Gloria Dourass/Rickard	440y/400m	1964 – 1976	12 years
Gillian Regan	Long Jump	1974 – 1986	12 years
David Lee	Steeplechase	1985 – 1997	12 years

Section 5

Welsh Championships Results (Track & Field) other age groups

Until the championships of 1940 the distinction between juniors and youths was very vague and it was not uncommon for athletes of the same age to be classified as either. The 220 yards championships held between 1924 and 1939 were styled "Youths" and have been included in the U17 listings. Jack Matthews (b1920) was second to Gratton in the 1935 Junior 100 yards (when only 15) and won the Youths 220 in 1937 (at 17). At one time the qualifying period for an age group was "as at 1 April" in the year in question, which was later altered to "as at 1 September". As Matthews was born in June he would have been under 17 in 1937 by the definition in force at the time (1 April). There have been many changes in definitions over the years, for example at the Glamorgan County Championships of 1949 the specification was by age on the day of the championships.

Under 20 Men (Junior Men)

	100 yards / 100 metres		220 yards / 200 metres		440 yards / 400 metres	
1934	Jack Gratton	11.4			Ivor Gaylard (300y)	36.2
1935	Jack Gratton	10.4			Dennis Ford	60.2
1936	Jack Gratton	10.4			Roy Williams	55.0
1937	Walter Turner	10.6			Dennis Ford	53.4
1938	Walter Turner	10.6	Reg Michael	23.7	Edward Jones	54.6
1939	Eric Finney	10.6	Fred Edwards	24.0	S Williams	54.2
1940	Eric Finney	10.2	Eric Finney	24.1	R Harries	54.0
1941	Eric Finney	10.2	Eric Finney	25.2	Garth Williams	55.6
1942	B Jones	10.8	W B Richards	25.8	Derek Williams	57.2
1943	S Evans	10.5	A L Carr	24.8	Ernest Harwood	54.8
1944	Keith Maddocks	10.8	J J Brown		E Harwood=B Williams	54.8
1945	J H Williams	ntt	A B Gibson	25.0	Brian Williams	53.3
1946	A B Gibson	10.7	A B Gibson	24.6	J E Bibbs	56.4
1947	Neville Jones	10.5	V G Sweet	24.6	J E Bibbs	55.4
1948	P Lillington	10.1	J S Hunt	24.9	Roy Adams	54.9
1949	P Lillington	10.2	J S Hunt	24.0	Peter Phillips	54.9
1950	Gareth Griffiths	10.4	J S Hunt	23.7	Peter Phillips	52.0
1951	Robin Pinnington	10.9	Robin Pinnington	23.8	J P Thorne	53.0
1952	Gwilym Roberts	10.5	I L Griffiths	24.1	J K Owen	54.9
1953	I Griffiths	10.9	David Pulsford	23.7	David Pugh	52.9
1954	K Thomas	10.9	David Pulsford	23.3	David Pulsford	52.3
1955	Clive Phillips	10.3	G Williams	24.2	David Jones	53.8
1956	Dewi Roberts	10.2	Dewi Roberts	23.3	D Perrott	53.5
1957	Dewi Roberts	10.1	G Jones	23.4	N B Cooper	52.4
1958	John C Jones	10.3	John C Jones	22.3	Alan Griffiths	50.9
1959	Brian Davies	9.9	B Morgan	22.7	Huw Jones	50.4
1960	Brian Davies	10.4	Brian Davies	22.4	Huw Jones	51.0
1961	Keith Batstone	10.0	Allan Skirving	23.0	Allan Skirving	51.1
1962	Philip Hearne	10.4	Michael Jenkins	23.3	Allan Skirving	50.2
1963	Michael Jenkins	10.4	Michael Jenkins	22.8	Derek Bevan	50.5
1964	Brian Coles	9.9	Brian Coles	22.0	Derek Bevan	50.1
1965	Geoff De Costa-Jones	10.3	Geoff De Costa-Jones	22.8	Ian McGovan	51.6
1966	John J Williams	10.2	David Williams	23.4	Wayne Lewis	51.8
1967	Mike Walters	10.1	Mike Walters	22.7	Haydn Curran	49.9
1968	Adrian Barwood	10.6	Alan Gore	23.6	Russell Davies	51.3
1969	Adrian Thomas	11.0	Clive Rees	23.2	Alan Gore	50.8
1970	Adrian Thomas	10.8	Adrian Thomas	22.2	Mike Lewis	50.6
1971	Steve Ware	11.2	Steve Ware	22.5	Richard Llewellyn	52.2
1972	Steve Ware	11.0	Peter Keeling	23.2	Steve Ware	49.3
1973	Gareth Edwards	11.0	Peter Keeling	22.9	Peter Keeling	51.8
1974	Gareth Edwards	10.6	Peter Keeling	22.6	Peter Keeling	51.8
1975	Kevin Davies	10.8	Kevin Davies	21.8	Jeff Griffiths	49.5

1976	Malcolm Owen	11.3	Gerald Hedges	22.5	Jeff Griffiths	48.5
1977	Clifford Jeffers	10.9	Alan Tinsley	22.4	Alan Tinsley	51.9
1978	Derek Morgan	11.1	Derek Morgan	22.4	David Barlow	51.1
1979	Steve Thomas	11.34	Steve Thomas	22.17	David Harrison	49.89
1980	Huw Thomas	11.0	Mark Owen	22.8	Mal James	49.6
1981	Tim Jones	10.7	Tim Jones	21.7	Mal James	49.9
1982	Nigel Walker	10.8	Tim Jones	22.3	Alan Matthews	50.9
1983	Haydn Wood	11.3	Haydn Wood	22.4	David Green	51.1
1984	Colin Jackson	10.8	David Radford	22.3	Adrian Hardman	50.9
1985	Jon Walters	11.15	Jon Walters	22.45	Chris Cashell	48.80
1986	Paul Gray	11.34	Stuart Colquhoun-Lynn	22.57	Paul Roberts	49.01
1987	James Simmons	11.19	Michael Williams	22.16	David Gough	49.21
1988	Andrew Perrin	11.2	Craig Sillett	23.0	Shaun Lewis	49.8
1989	Steven Rees	10.81	Steven Rees	21.82	Martin Hudson	52.29
1990	Steven Rees	10.67	Steven Rees	21.66	Darren Parry	50.34
1991	Steven Rees	10.9	Jamie Baulch	21.8	Joe Lloyd	48.5
1992	Craig Kerslake	11.45	Gareth Lewis	22.93	Joe Lloyd	49.60
1993	Craig Kerslake	11.14	Bryn Middleton	22.74	David Williams	49.56
1994	Jamie Henthorn	10.78	Bryn Middleton	21.84	Mark Ponting	48.92
1995	Jamie Henthorn	11.30	Jamie Henthorn	22.35	Steve Evans	49.67
1996	Jamie Henthorn	10.54	Jamie Henthorn	21.46	Huw Bannister	50.10
1997	Iestyn Lewis	10.91	Ben Harland	22.50	Matthew Elias	48.72
1998	Andrew Parker	11.00	Andrew Parker	21.75	Chris Page	49.56
1999	Tim Benjamin	10.72	Tim Benjamin	22.3	Chris Page	50.4
2000	Anthony Mayo	11.40	Anthony Mayo	23.23	Daniel Forbes	50.9

	880 yards / 800 metres		**One mile / 1500 metres**		**120 yards / 110m hurdles**	
1934	Ivor Gaylard	2:19.4			K Marsh	14.0
1935	Brynley Quick	2:15.0	Teddy Jones	5:06.4		
1936	Bernard Daly	2:11.0	Teddy Jones	4:57.0		
1937	Bernard Daly	2:07.4	Bramwell Baldwin	4:59.2		
1938	Stan Tibbs	2:07.5	James Griffiths	4:52.0		
1939	Ron Hoggins	2:07.6	Randall Jones	4:51.8		
1940	Ron Hoggins	2:13.0	A D Downs	4:54.0	W Donovan	15.4
1941	Derek Williams	2:12.8	W T Phillips	5:13.8		
1942	Derek Williams	2:19.2	D W Davie	5:15.8		
1943	Ernerst Harwood	2:06.4	Bernard Baldwin	4:55.0		
1944	Brian Williams	2:07.8	J Bromley	4:51.0		
1945	Brian Williams	2:08.8	F P Williams	4:40.8		
1946	Brian Williams	2:08.5	J Bromley	4:46.0		
1947	J E Bibbs	2:08.9	I G Phillips	5:04.2		
1948	D M Jones	2:09.0	B Morgan	4:55.4		
1949	Roy Adams	2:01.3	Joe Yates	4:45.8	K Frederickson	16.4
1950	Denis Murphy	2:01.1	Joe Yates	4:44.1	J Jenkins	17.3
1951	Ike Williams	2:00.9	Ike Williams	4:35.4	J Page	17.1
1952	Ike Williams	2:00.4	Ike Williams	4:39.5	Viv Jones	16.2
1953	David Richards	1:58.9	David Richards	4:25.4	Martyn Gatehouse	16.9
1954	W B Evans	1:59.0	M C Phillips	4:37.4	G V Jones	22.4
1955	M Roberts	2:05.6	Roger Harrison-Jones	4:33.3	Keith Davitte	16.4
1956	P Davies	2:05.8	A Coleman	4:45.1	Keith Davitte	16.5
1957	Tony Jones	2:04.8	K C Jones	4:32.5	David Michael	16.2
1958	John Williams	1:57.1	Billy Perkins	4:27.2	J L Evans	15.2
1959	John Williams	1:59.7	C Chaston	4:25.8	Alan Evans-Jones	15.6
1960	Maurice Johns	2:01.3	David Ponting	4:22.6	Alan Evans-Jones	15.9
1961	Bill Stitfall	2:02.7	Tom Edmunds	4:35.0	Roy Harvey	15.2
1962	Clive Williams	2:01.8	Fred Bell	4:22.5	B Edwards	15.9
1963	Tony Blount	1:57.9	Clive Williams	4:34.7	Tim Jennings	15.8
1964	A Thomas	2:03.6	M A Edwards	4:34.9	John Lewis	15.1
1965	Paul Bateman	1:56.9	Nicholas Gibbs	4:27.8	H Thomas	17.5
1966	John Powell	1:57.5	Tony Simmons	4:16.6	Alun James	16.5
1967	Vincent James	1:57.1	Bernie Hayward	4:17.3	Alun James	15.0
1968	Keith Jones	1:58.9	Frank Thomas	4:23.3	M Williams	17.9
1969	T H R Jones		Steve Seaman	4:19.6	Berwyn Price	15.2
1970	Richard Yarrow	1:57.4	Peter Ratcliffe	4:01.8	Les Prince	15.1
1971	Richard Yarrow	1:58.9	Peter Ratcliffe	3:57.9	Roger Rees	15.5
1972	Mike Buckland	1:55.2	Andrew Ireland	4:10.7	Charley Davies	16.5
1973	Tony Dyke	1:52.0	Mike Buckland	4:04.7	Jonathan Roberts	15.6

1974	Tony Dyke	1:55.3	Brian Fenn	4:20.3	Neddyn Lloyd	15.9
1975	A Evans	2:02.3	Micky Morris	3:55.8	Neddyn Lloyd	15.2
1976	A Evans	1:57.9	Kevin Glastonbury	3:57.9	Tudor Bidder	15.9
1977	Roger Barrett	1:55.9	Tony Blackwell	3:52.7	Huw Jones	15.7
1978	Roger Barrett	1:55.1	Keith Gallivan	4:04.4	Huw Jones	14.6
1979	Nick Morgan	2:00.7	Mark Webborn	3:57.5	Tim Lewis	15.41
1980	Gareth Brown	1:54.6	Nick Morgan	4:02.0	Nigel Walker	15.3
1981	Steve Bright	1:55.4	Mark Bryant	4:00.1	Nigel Walker	14.6
1982	Adam Richards	1:57.7	Andrew Rodgers	4:00.8	Nigel Walker	14.2
1983	Andrew Jones	1:58.4	Nigel Gooch	4:01.3	Simon Jones	16.1
1984	Paul Williams	1:56.5	Neil Horsfield	3:55.5	Colin Jackson	13.8
1985	Simon Merrick	1:55.66	Neil Horsfield	3:54.41	Philip Harries	14.76
1986	Nick Melling	1:54.22	Justin Hobbs	3:57.88	Paul Gray	14.40
1987	Tom Stout	1:58.14	Justin Chaston	3:58.82	Peter Dyer	15.22
1988	Bedwyr Huws	1:54.7	Peter Conway	3:54.3	Russell Richards	16.0
1989	Bedwyr Huws	1:53.21	Guto Eames	4:13.7	Richard Harbour	15.37
1990	Jonathan Robbins	2:02.74	James Ellis-Smith	3:58.5	Richard Harbour	14.36
1991	Peter Wyatt	1:56.1	Guto Eames	3:54.79	Berian Davies	14.3
1992	Zane Maynard	1:57.18	Carl Leonard	4:07.34	Berian Davies	14.3
1993	Zane Maynard	1:56.60	David Povall	4:05.96	James Hughes	14.14
1994	Chris Blount	1:55.2	Chris Blount	4:01.9	James Archampong	14.26
1995	Matthew McHugh	1:58.09	Russ Cartwright	4:03.23	James Archampong	14.3
1996	Russ Cartwright	1:55.46	Russ Cartwright	3:57.63	Stephen Edwards	15.08
1997	Gareth Beard	1:56.56	Simon Lewis	4:05.5	Ben Roberts	14.97
1998	David Cawley	1:59.73	Dafydd Solomon	4:22.74	Luke Gittens	14.69
1999	Robin Powell	1:59.5	Daniel Beynon	4:04.2	no competitors	
2000	James Nasrat	1:55.60	Matthew Jones (Stoke)	3:58.15	Kristopher Jones	16.77

	3000 metres		**Steeplechase**		**400m hurdles**	
1957			D C Hughes	5:06.8		
1958			Hedydd Davies	5:06.0		
1959			C Chaston	4:28.8		
1960			D Gibson	4:39.5		
1961			Bill Stitfall	4:28.4		
1962			Bill Stitfall	4:23.5		
1963			Derek Vaughan	4:49.3		
1964			Terry James	ntt		
1965			Ron McAndrew	6:15.4		
1966			Jim Bisgrove	6:15.5		
1967			Richard Jones	6:26.9	Wynford Leyshon (300)	41.0
1968	Frank Thomas	9:43.4	Tony Pretty	6:06.4	Philip Nash	61.7
1969	Dennis Fowles	8:51.0	Dennis Fowles	6:21.2	Barrie Williams	57.9
1970	Peter Ratcliffe	8:52.2	John Davies	5:58.0	George Clues	57.5
1971	Peter Ratcliffe	8:35.6	John Davies	5:55.0	Charlie Davies	58.4
1972	Andrew Ireland	9:00.8	Len Wallace	6:16.8	Orrie Fenn	56.9
1973	not known		Len Wallace	6:24.8	Huw Lewis	58.7
1974	Kenny Davies	9:27.6	J Thomas	6:12.0	R Jenkins	59.1
1975	Adrian Leek	8:39.6	Steve Evans	5:51.8	Neddyn Lloyd	61.3
1976	Adrian Leek	8:33.6	Lloyd Roberts	6:22.2	Roy Saunders	58.4
1977	Tony Blackwell	8:23.0	Peter Ward	5:59.8	Robert Davies	57.5
1978	Mark Donnelly	8:53.8	Andy Fox	6:11.4	Chris Ewart	55.3
1979	Colin Clarkson	8:16.7	Phil Llewellyn	6:00.8	Chris Ewart	54.50
1980	Tim Willcock	8:30.1	Phil Llewellyn	6:03.6	David Jones	55.6
1981	Steve Blakemore	8:34.3	Marcus Thomas	6:10.8	David Jones	56.4
1982	Geoff Hill	8:32.7	Jon Pimley	6:11.3	Adam Richards	57.8
1983	Brian Matthews	8:38.1	Andrew Rodgers	5:45.1	Ian Morgan	56.8
1984	Ian Hamer	8:34.8	David Lee	6:03.0	Sean O'Malley	58.0
1985	Dale Rixon	8:34.35	Andrew McIntyre	6:01.87	Philip Harries	54.47
1986	Justin Hobbs	8:35.12	Phil Cook	6:06.79	Simon Beer	60.22
1987	Justin Hobbs	8:45.75	Phil Cook	6:07.23	Russell Richards	55.41
1988	Andrew Jones (AV)	8:42.6	Jonathan Lewis	6:07.8	Russell Richards	55.5
1989	Gerallt Owen	8:52.43	Steven Glynn	6:10.3	Wayne Proctor	56.65
1990	Peter Lewis	8:57.93	Andrew Powell	6:20.37	Marvin Gray	57.28
1991	Colin Jones	8:45.4	Tim Hopkins	6:20.8	Robert Bradley	58.2
1992	Christian Stephenson	8:50.62	Chris Blount	6:02.50	Robert Bradley	58.06
1993	Christian Stephenson	8:39.34	Chris Blount	5:56.30	James Archampong	55.04
1994	Ian Pierce	8:44.62	Simon White	6:11.34	David Goodger	56.78
1995	Andres Jones	8:46.52	Leigh Kinroy	6:25.55	Mark Rowlands	54.10
1996	Andres Jones	8:31.86	Daniel Lewis	6:18.64	James Hillier	55.10
1997	Alun Vaughan	8:51.36	Simon Type	6:30.50	Matthew Elias	52.93
1998	Jonathan Phillips	9:07.81	Paul Clarke	6:20.9	Shaun Robson	56.81

1999	Marc Hobbs (5k)	15:57.01	Paul Clarke	6:12.1	Andrew Griffiths	57.9
2000	Alex Haines	9:27.16	no competitors		Nathan Jones	57.49

	High Jump		**Pole Vault**		**Long Jump**	
1934	Stuart Devonald	1.50				
1935	Idris Wride	1.50				
1936	Alun Meredith	1.57	A E Mallett	2.28	D Jenkins	6.09
1937	Edward Jones	1.49	J Austin or R Gould			
1938	L S Dyer	1.64	Fred Chivers	2.40		
1939	David Pulling	1.57	George Thorne	2.70		
1940	S A Marsh	1.47			Brian Crossman	5.87
1941	J H Anthony	1.52			J B Williams	5.66
1942	J M Evans	1.50			C Coray	5.21
1943	H L Jones	1.60			J D Robins	6.09
1944	N Strachan	1.59			C Evans	6.36
1945	N P Evans	1.58			Alan Roche	5.54
1946	B M Loughlin	1.65			Alan Roche	6.11
1947	D J Davies	1.50			I H Thomas	5.99
1948	D M Crawford	1.65			J H Chislett	5.75
1949	WI Prosser or AVLewis	1.65	D Owens	3.21	John Frowen	6.39
1950	D Cameron	1.60	J P Priest	2.59	D J Ashurst	6.63
1951	Brian Hardwick	1.73	Viv Jones	3.22	D Pugh	5.87
1952	Morton Evans	1.65	Colin Fletcher	3.05	P H Nutton	5.93
1953	Angus Thomson	1.78	Colin Fletcher	3.15	A H Thomas	6.45
1954	D Evans-Williams	1.70	G I Ball	3.05	A H Thomas	6.70
1955	Terence Morgan	1.67	G Coles	3.29	Roger Jones	6.06
1956	Aneurin Evans	1.78	D L John	3.20	J Lewis	6.30
1957	Aneurin Evans	1.78	D Howells	3.05	Ray Gazzard	6.21
1958	M J Edwards	1.67	John Ball	3.50	Ian Hughes	6.68
1959	John Lister	1.67	John Ball	3.50	A Roderick	6.06
1960	John Lister	1.73	John Evans	3.58	Terry Davies	6.60
1961	P Williams	1.70	John Evans	3.50	Lynn Davies	6.97
1962	J Morgan	1.67	Graham Gibbs	3.72	William Jones	6.68
1963	J A Hardie	1.57	cancelled		Maurice Richards	6.48
1964	Edwin Clarke	1.70	David Williams	3.50	J B Bayliss	6.65
1965	Philip Jacklin	1.75	D T Thomas	3.20	Ron Gould	6.84
1966	Philip Jacklin	1.78	Maldwyn Lewis	3.35	John Elias	6.92
1967	Peter Lance	1.80	Alan Watkins	3.15	Keith Lowe	7.05
1968	Alan Jenkins	1.83	Malcolm Hurley	2.28	Russell Church	6.41
1969	Brynmor Williams	1.75	K S James	3.04	Russell Church	6.64
1970	L Phillips	1.70	not held		R Thomas	6.24
1971	L Jones	1.68	W Lloyd	3.10	Terry Ronan	6.49
1972	not held		M Thomas	3.28	J Rees	6.60
1973	Mike Cummings	1.88	Gordon Pickering	3.81	R Owen	6.59
1974	Mike Cummings	1.78	Gordon Pickering	4.14	Steve Kohut	6.09
1975	Peter Mitchell	1.90	Islwyn Rees	4.20	G Murron	6.50
1976	Chris Berry	1.75	Rupert Goodall	4.60	Andrew Lea	6.40
1977	Huw Jones	1.85	not held		Alan Keyse	6.47
1978	Steve Brock	1.85	not held		Phil Lewis	6.69
1979	Andrew McIver	2.00	Phil Hunt	3.15	David Wood	6.70
1980	Andrew McIver	2.03	Nick Heal	4.30	Richard Jones	7.07
1981	Tony Norris	1.93	Robert Hughes (Carm)	3.70	Richard Jones	7.05
1982	David Rowe	1.90	Nigel Skinner	4.00	Stephen Edwards	6.68
1983	John Hill	1.90	Nigel Skinner	4.10	Ian Thomas	6.39
1984	John Hill	2.08	Glyn Price	4.15	Simon Marsh	6.54
1985	John Hill	2.00	Peter Lynk	4.45	Simon Marsh	6.67
1986	Craig Grant	1.85	Neil Ashman	4.01	Steve Partridge	6.65
1987	Craig Grant	1.96	Neil Ashman	3.70	Lynn Fowler	6.32
1988	Craig Grant	1.90	Ian Thomas	3.95	Steve Ingram	6.68
1989	Steve Ingram	1.90	Robert Hughes (C Bay)	4.10	Chris Price	6.86
1990	Lee McCabe	1.85	Neil Winter	4.60	Andrew Adey	6.96
1991	Ceri Payne	1.85	Tim Thomas	4.40	Julian Hall	6.33
1992	R Bradley=C Harding	1.93	Tim Thomas	4.60	Tom Hallett	7.18
1993	Chris Harding	1.94	Ian Wilding	4.60	Lee Edwards	6.73
1994	Rowan Griffiths	1.88	Ian Wilding	4.40	Lee Edwards	6.45
1995	Matthew Perry	1.90	Paul Jones	4.00	Charles Madeira-Cole	6.75
1996	Matthew Perry	2.00	Darren Beddoes	3.90	Andrew Wooding	6.82
1997	Andrew Penk	2.03	Andrew Penk	4.71	Ioan Hughes	6.99
1998	Rhodri Jones	1.85	Anthony Perry	4.00	Andrew Wooding	6.84
1999	Kim Harland	1.97	Chris Type	4.60	Steven Shalders	7.10
2000	Owen Chesher	1.85	Cameron Johnston	4.45	Steven Frost	6.63

Year	Triple Jump		Shot Put		Discus	
1936					Melville Lewis	30.56
1937			Thomas John Jones	10.17	K Lee	38.54
1938			T J Raubenheimer	11.12	Jestyn Rees	37.25
1939			W H Lodwig	08.99	D L Phillips	33.18
1940	Brian Crossman	12.67	R E Payne	11.07	J M Jenkins	29.26
1941	Brynmor Jones	11.63	H P Hughes	11.38	Selwyn Evans	32.17
1942	Brynmor Jones	11.07	H P Hughes	11.30	Selwyn Evans	38.48
1943	D G Williams	12.23	J D Robins	13.00	J D Robins	37.98
1944	M Griffiths	12.37	G J Stanley	11.27	G J Stanley	36.54
1945	Alan Roche	12.15	R Williams	10.68	R Williams	33.96
1946	Gwyn Harris	12.98	Bill Kingsbury	11.76	R Ablett	36.02
1947	A W Williams	11.69	C W Pook	11.64	A Nesbitt	35.06
1948	Gwyn Harris	13.64	John Thomas	11.14	R King	35.36
1949	John Frowen	12.63	D G Sanders	13.10	John Thomas	40.02
1950	D J Ashurst	12.98	Walter Wright	12.65	N W Noake	36.67
1951	Brian Hardwick	13.00	J Morris	12.06	J E Thomas	37.78
1952	G F Layton	12.08	K L Jones	13.71	J Morris	34.47
1953	Angus Thomson	13.40	Tony Morgan	13.43	Tony Morgan	35.26
1954	D E Williams	12.81	Tony Morgan	13.97	J R Webb	38.46
1955	M Cridge	12.36	Malcolm Pemberton	12.93	Malcolm Pemberton	39.44
1956	Aneurin Evans	13.82	Aneurin Evans	13.99	P Thomas	36.68
1957	Aneurin Evans	13.05	Aneurin Evans	15.29	P Thomas	42.26
1958	Ian Hughes	13.33	John Davies	15.70	G Williams	37.60
1959	P Williams	13.42	Arthur Richardson	16.36	Alan Scaplehorn	37.91
1960	John Mantle	13.47	H White	12.49	W Rees	37.55
1961	Lynn Davies	14.01	David Bunce	14.90	Denis Day	40.53
1962	Nigel Green	14.27	David Bunce	14.89	Peter Skehan	41.64
1963	Timothy Jennings	13.71	Roger Guy	14.04	Peter Skehan	42.98
1964	Graham Webb	13.65	Roger Guy	15.35	Roger Beard	42.22
1965	David Evans	13.94	D Boxer	13.98	John Mounsey	40.91
1966	David Evans	14.35	Allan Martin	14.84	Allan Martin	40.34
1967	Peter Davies	13.70	Allan Martin	14.93	Allan Martin	44.28
1968	Peter Davies	13.69	Byron Mugford	15.25	Lyndon Davies	42.64
1969	George Clues	12.35	Jeffrey Baker	12.41	David Scott	40.19
1970	D Davies	12.83	Laurence Daniels	13.42	D Thomas	40.84
1971	Terry Ronan	13.31	Peter Wilson	14.93	Michael Flavell	43.52
1972	J Rees	13.55	Robert Edwards	13.69	Nick Lia	44.36
1973	N Gwilym	13.18	Ken Latten	12.39	Ken Latten	42.60
1974	V Everett	12.67	Ken Latten	12.31	Ken Latten	45.42
1975	Andrew Lea	12.84	Brian Isgar	12.02	Gareth Jenkins	40.36
1976	Andrew Lea	13.23	Lloyd Williams	12.68	Nigel Stevens	33.82
1977	Peter Sullivan	13.48	John Tym	13.82	Richard Jenkins	38.48
1978	Phil Ward	13.99	John Tym	14.68	John Tym	39.08
1979	David Wood	14.28	Mark Hewer	14.87	John Collins	42.58
1980	David Wood	15.09	Shaun Pickering	15.50	Peter Rees	43.66
1981	David Wood	14.41	Mark Hewer	15.31	John Collins	41.82
1982	Stuart McKenzie	13.81	Robert Proctor	13.40	Brian Collins	46.68
1983	Stuart McKenzie	13.80	Robert Proctor	13.34	Brian Collins	41.10
1984	Gareth Davies (Card)	13.38	Clayton Turner	13.70	Clayton Turner	40.62
1985	Gareth Davies (Card)	13.83	Clayton Turner	14.89	Clayton Turner	43.68
1986	Leighton Adams	13.88	Clayton Turner	15.88	Clayton Turner	43.62
1987	Huw Meredith	13.12	Clayton Turner	15.88	Clayton Turner	47.12
1988	Gareth Davies (Swan)	13.71	Steven Williams	13.14	Gary Cornish	37.74
1989	Neil Charnock	13.03	Steven Williams	13.92	Peter Roberts	41.48
1990	Gareth Davies (Swan)	14.31	Peter Roberts	13.20	Peter Roberts	44.58
1991	Julian Hall	13.30	Matthew Hicks	13.70	Gareth Gilbert	46.24
1992	Julian Hall	13.90	Matthew Hicks	14.58	James Hoopert	41.66
1993	Julian Hall	13.13	Neil Bithell	12.48	Richard Scrivens	38.60
1994	Paul Ellis	13.22	Justin Jones	12.90	Gareth Marks	43.06
1995	Daniel Davies	14.04	Gareth Marks	12.62	Gareth Marks	44.80
1996	Charles Madeira-Cole	13.35	James Elton	13.22	John Parkin	42.52
1997	Gavin Jones	12.87	Ben Roberts	13.30	John Parkin	42.38
1998	Stephen Alvey	13.23	Liam McCaffrey	12.97	John Parkin	47.43
1999	Steven Shalders	15.47	Ben Roberts	14.37	Ben Roberts	42.33
2000	Steven Frost	13.77	David Roberts	13.58	Simon Bull	36.42

Year	Hammer		Javelin		Decathlon	
1937			C Crockett	45.82		
1938			T J Raubenheimer	40.55		
1939			Lionel Pugh	41.44		

1940			Lionel Pugh	47.66		
1941			Frank Stephens	36.48		
1942			Frank Stephens	40.42		
1943			A S Hobbs	41.20		
1944			G F Stradling	44.74		
1945			C B Coates	39.87		
1946			C B Coates	44.42		
1947			R W Rayner	37.92		
1948			W W Weller	45.54		
1949			R A Wright	51.68		
1950			R G Poyntz	38.83		
1951			L Dunstan	49.87		
1952			J H Hallam	43.93		
1953			P D Anzallucca	40.26		
1954	I E Holme	34.42	Angus Thomson	58.38		
1955	R Bacon	45.70	B Lewis	57.76		
1956	P Thomas	23.70	T Lockston	48.70		
1957	not held		M J Seabrook	56.72		
1958	M Farnham	16.86	David Price	56.14		
1959	L Martin	47.48	David Price	52.57		
1960	L Martin	49.27	W Cole	46.37		
1961	E Howells	28.99	N Clarke	50.51		
1962	E Howells	36.52	E Howells	36.52		
1963	Colin Balchin	28.85	D R Lewis	42.98		
1964	Roger Beard	46.72	Norman Lang	53.50		
1965	not held		Norman Lang	53.03		
1966	not held		David Powell	53.92		
1967	Allan Martin	46.20	Mike Gange	45.16		
1968	Keith Watkinson	47.38	Mike Gange	51.08		
1969	Keith Watkinson	51.70	M J Czarnecki	43.25		
1970	Laurie Daniels	44.08	R Squibbs	42.24		
1971	Nick Lia	44.56	S Jones	50.02		
1972	Nick Lia	55.10	R Edwards	49.38		
1973	Andrew Stimpson	39.08	Bill Carey	55.62		
1974	Phil Jones	40.38	D Stephens	52.06		
1975	Mike Llewellyn-Eaton	40.26	Gareth Jenkins	49.26		
1976	Phil Jones	49.60	Alan Watkins	50.32		
1977	Ray Bacon	44.00	Nigel Price	54.70		
1978	Dino Lantzos	42.50	Neil Thomas	52.78		
1979	Dino Lantzos	43.96	Steve Robbins	56.00		
1980	Shaun Pickering	59.48	Steve Griffiths	56.96		
1981	Julian Tucker	52.20	Tim Brooks	56.18	Stuart Gibbs	5815
1982	Crayton Phillips	52.52	Alistair Owen	60.58	not known	
1983	Crayton Phillips	53.20	Gareth Rowlands	61.80	Nigel Skinner	6456
1984	Philip Bufton	49.50	Jonathan Clarke	60.84	not known	
1985	Philip Bufton	50.20	Jonathan Clarke	68.08	Chris Raymond	5150
1986	Philip Bufton	56.38	Jonathan Clarke	63.14	Ian Gould	5599
1987	Adrian Palmer	58.94	Angus Jefferies	58.02	not held	
1988	Adrian Palmer	52.54	Julian Howells	54.02	Robert Hughes	4935
1989	Barrie Barnfield	44.02	Peter Roberts	50.08	Robert Hughes	6093
1990	Neil Williams	52.96	Paul Verheyden	53.30	Stephen Lloyd	5652
1991	Neil Williams	57.22	Richard Jones	50.00	Robert Bradley	5789
1992	Hamid Lane	48.24	Stuart Loughran	52.76	Robert Bradley	5097
1993	Hamid Lane	52.20	Richard Jones	60.78	Justin Jones	5524
1994	Neil Jones	35.30	Stuart Loughran	53.70	Kevin Ricketts	5412
1995	Ross Blight	51.50	Stuart Loughran	56.86	Kevin Ricketts	5702
1996	Ross Blight	51.12	Matthew Davies	55.94	Paul Jones	5811
1997	John Parkin	49.52	Chris Thomas	55.80	Paul Jones	6373
1998	John Parkin	51.19	Chris Thomas	55.90	Thomas Abdy	4708
1999	Gareth Driscoll	49.58	James Anthony	52.15	Ben Roberts	6372
2000	Matthew Grindle	44.67	Rhys Williams	52.76	Nathan Jones	5566

Under 17 Men (Youths)

	100 yards / 100 metres		220 yards / 200 metres		440 yards / 400 metres	
1924			T Elkins	25.4		
1925			J J White	25.0		
1927			Ronnie Boon	25.8		
1928			F G Hill	24.2		

1929			S J Jones	24.0		
1930			T D Wrighton	25.4		
1931			E J Thomas	25.4		
1932			Jack Knowles	24.8		
1933			Jack Knowles	24.0		
1934			Ivor Gaylard	24.0		
1935			Wyndham Weeks	24.0		
1936			Wyndham Weeks	24.0		
1937			Jack Matthews	24.0		
1938			Jack Thomas	24.0		
1939			Jack Thomas	24.5		
1940	H Rees	11.0	B F Rowley	24.8	P Lea	59.7
1941	L A Horton	11.5	W J Brown	26.0	W Evans	
1942	not held		not held		not held	
1943	A Haley	10.8	R E Hawkwood	25.8	Brian Williams	58.2
1944	C Williams	10.8	Alan Roche	25.5	J R James	57.6
1945	J McJennett	10.3	C Williams	25.0	J R James	56.0
1946	L Shakeshaft	10.7	L Shakeshaft	25.4	B R Morris	61.
1947	P F Williams	10.5	J S Hunt	25.5	W M Ryall	59.6
1948	W Brooks	10.6	J M Allcroft	25.9	Denis Murphy	61.0
1949	R J Jones	10.4	Derek Grindell	23.8	J P Thorne	53.8
1950	Derek Grindell	10.3	Derek Grindell	23.8	Julius Hermer	55.9
1951	G T Raybould	11.0	G T Raybould	24.0	David Pugh	55.7
1952	Gareth Curtis	10.6	David Pulsford	24.2	G S Thomas	54.5
1953	Jack Melen	10.7	A Jones	25.2	Alan Griffiths	55.3
1954	J Evans	10.9	C Lewis	25.2	K Turner	56.2
1955	G Jones	10.7	G Jones	25.9	G Motton	55.7
1956	Mike James	10.7	Mike James	24.0	T D Phillips	53.8
1957	John C Jones	10.8	John C Jones	23.7	A J Griffiths	52.4
1958	Brian Davies	10.3	Brian Davies	22.8	H L Jones	52.3
1959	Tony Bigham	10.4	D Jones	23.9	B Joseph	52.9
1960	Dennis Brown	10.9	T Hitchen	24.0	Byron Broadstock	52.2
1961	Michael Jenkins	10.3	Paul Carvell	23.6	J Gillard	53.4
1962	Peter Wilson	10.6	Peter Wilson	23.5	Neil Thomas	52.0
1963	Clive Nock	10.3	Clive Nock	23.2	Roger Willey	53.0
1964	G Davies	10.7	Geoff De Costa Jones	23.0	Geoff De Costa Jones	51.5
1965	Keith Lowe	10.5	Paul Taylor	23.5	R Thomas	53.8
1966	Philip Ware	10.6	Philip Ware	23.7	Ian Thomas	51.8
1967	G R Lewis	10.3	Alan Gore	23.0	Russell Davies	52.1
1968	Adrian Thomas	10.7	Richard Wyke	23.4	P M Lloyd	52.5
1969	Steve Ware	11.6	Steve Ware	22.8	Malcolm Gibson	51.6
1970	Steve Ware	11.4	Steve Ware	22.9	Malcolm Gibson	50.7
1971	Paul Evans	11.2	Steve Bailey	24.9	A Hughes	51.8
1972	John Roberts	11.4	Kevin Williams	23.9	Jeff Griffiths	53.2
1973	Steve Perks	11.5	Steve Perks	22.9	Huw Evans	50.9
1974	Steve Perks	11.4	Steve Perks	22.5	A Hopkins	55.9
1975	Cliff Jeffers	11.0	Cliff Jeffers	23.0	M Whittock	50.7
1976	Cliff Jeffers	11.8	David Morgan	22.9	H G Williams	52.7
1977	Pat Smith	11.1	Pat Smith	23.1	Mike Owen	53.8
1978	Malcolm James	11.4	Malcolm James	22.9	Tony Morgan	50.9
1979	Malcolm James	11.2	Malcolm James	22.78	Phil Harvey	50.50
1980	Tim Jones	11.14	Tim Jones	23.07	Andy Jones	51.56
1981	Haydn Wood	10.9	Haydn Wood	22.5	David Tucker	50.8
1982	Haydn Wood	11.0	Haydn Wood	22.6	David Tucker	51.1
1983	Simon Marsh	11.5	Stuart Colquhoun-Lynn	23.3	Adrian Hardman	49.3
1984	Chris Ellis	11.3	Richard Wintle	23.0	Derrick Wyke	53.2
1985	Andrew Perrin	11.75	Marcus Browning	24.0	Derrick Wyke	51.1
1986	Andrew Perrin	11.49	Andrew Perrin	22.90	Ian Carr	51.10
1987	Michael Williams	11.29	Michael Williams	22.53	Craig Sillett	50.3
1988	Gareth Davies	11.4	Gareth Davies	23.2	Martin Hudson	51.7
1989	Jamie Baulch	11.24	Jamie Baulch	22.56	Peter Maitland	49.67
1990	Craig Kerslake	11.61	Gary Beavan	23.21	Martin Holliday	51.06
1991	Bryn Middleton	11.6	James Squire	22.8	Nathan Davies	51.3
1992	Geraint Evans	12.10	James Archampong	23.15	Andrew Jones	50.06
1993	Jamie Henthorn	11.06	Jamie Henthorn	22.60	Mark Ponting	48.82
1994	Christian Malcolm	10.98	Christian Malcolm	22.46	Steven Evans	51.56

1995	Christian Malcolm	11.73	Christian Malcolm	22.54	Tariq Guendouzi	51.19
1996	Ben Harland	11.35	Ben Harland	23.14	Chris Page	50.58
1997	Tim Benjamin	10.97	Tim Benjamin	21.96	Chris Page	51.10
1998	Tim Benjamin	10.87	Tim Benjamin	22.26	Neil Wynne	52.17
1999	Nick Hiscott	11.5	Mike Groves	23.6	Gareth Rees	51.1
2000	Nick Hiscott	12.13	Mike Groves	22.86	Rhys Williams	50.6

	880 yards / 800 metres		**1500 metres**		**3000 metres**	
1940	Derek Williams	2:18.3				
1941	F K Stearns	2:25.0				
1942	not held					
1943	Brian Williams	2:17.4				
1944	N J Chance	2:16.6				
1945	C W Ditchburn	2:16.0				
1946	K Thomas	2:15.1				
1947	P A Stephens	2:13.2				
1948	Dennis Murphy	2:18.8				
1949	D W White	2:12.8				
1950	David Richards	2:09.0				
1951	I Reed	2:09.0				
1952	W B Evans	2:04.7				
1953	M C Phillips	2:12.5				
1954	P Davies	2:13.5				
1955	T Wingfield	2:10.0				
1956	B Gallagner	2:02.8				
1957	John Williams	1:57.5				
1958	David Ponting	2:02.2				
1959	J Hill	2:04.5				
1960	Allan Skirving	2:01.0				
1961	David Hughes	2:06.2				
1962	Peter Smith	2:03.5				
1963	Peter Smith	2:08.9				
1964	Paul Bateman	1:57.2				
1965	Tony Simmons	2:00.0				
1966	R P Jones	2:04.6				
1967	S Hovey	2:10.2				
1968	S Martin	2:05.0	P Smart	4:48.9		
1969	Richard Yarrow	2:00.0	Peter Ratcliffe	4:13.2		
1970	K Powell	2:01.4	Gareth Morgan	4:13.1		
1971	Tony Dyke	1:59.4	Will Snowdon	4:17.0		
1972	Tony Dyke	1:54.8	Micky Morris	4:09.6		
1973	Mike Cole	2:02.9	Micky Morris	4:10.9	B Davies	10:02.4
1974	Hugh Shakeshaft	2:09.0	Steve Evans	4:11.0	D Roberts	9:28.4
1975	Kevin Glastonbury	1:55.4	Kevin Glastonbury	3:58.3	Tony Blackwell	8:50.0
1976	A Martin	2:03.9	Colin Clarkson	4:04.5	Colin Clarkson	8:43.2
1977	Colin Morgan	2:04.4	Colin Clarkson	4:05.7	Colin Clarkson	8:31.8
1978	Nick Morgan	1:58.5	Mike Pritchard	4:06.5	Martin Webborn	8:45.0
1979	Shaun Whelan	1:56.26	Andy Smith	4:07.33	Nigel Stops	9:05.2
1980	B Martin	2:02.6	Neil Hardee	4:18.9	D Edwards	9:14.3
1981	Grant Howells	2:02.5	Andrew Rodgers	4:07.8	Brian Matthews	9:20.7
1982	Paul Williams	1:59.0	Nicky Comerford	4:11.0	Robert Dean	9:06.7
1983	Paul Williams	1:56.1	Neil Horsfield	4:03.4	David Morgan	9:18.9
1984	Mike O'Neill	2:03.8	Andrew Jones (AVAC)	4:17.1	Justin Hobbs	9:19.2
1985	Mike O'Neill	1:58.7	Justin Hobbs	4:04.6	Andrew Jones (AVAC)	9:10.9
1986	Peter Conway	1:57.99	Peter Conway	4:01.41	Andrew Jones (Newp)	8:49.00
1987	Guto Eames	2:00.42	Guto Eames	4:07.3	Delwyn Bainton	9:05.6
1988	Jason Davies	1:59.6	Neil Diamond	4:12.2	Andrew Powell	9:14.1
1989	Peter Wyatt	1:57.84	Peter Wyatt	4:06.9	Andrew Powell	9:04.6
1990	James Murray	1:59.10	Benedict Antwiss	4:19.02	Jon Williams	9:28.78
1991	Daniel Ashman	2:00.5	David Povall	4:18.8	David Povall	9:17.7
1992	Adrian Staples	2:03.23	Robert Pierce	4:22.90	Simon Miles	9:19.23
1993	John Weybourne	1:58.90	Robert Court	4:17.48	Damian Cuke	9:21.42
1994	Russ Cartwright	1:57.84	David Davey	4:11.04	Steven Lawrence	9:05.36
1995	Sion Owen	2:00.55	Robin Hart	4:18.60	Steven Lawrence	9:18.51
1996	Robin Powell	2:02.90	Dafydd Solomon	4:19.89	Paul Gronow	9:20.44
1997	Ian Bateman	2:00.38	Daniel Beynon	4:18.40	Chris Davey	9:22.83
1998	Neil Wynne	2:03.88	Andrew Mallows	4:16.55	Matthew Jones (Stoke)	9:09.45
1999	Steven Richards	2:00.6	Matthew Jones (Stoke)	4:02.1	Daniel Gurmin	9:37.3
2000	Adam Davies	1:57.92	Stephen Davies	4:10.86	David Jones	9:12.51

	Steeplechase		100 yards / 100m hurdles		400m hurdles	
1940			P F Rowley	14.8		
1950			P H Nutton	16.2		
1951			P H Nutton	15.6		
1952			Martyn Gatehouse	15.4		
1953			Keith Davitte	15.2		
1954			abandoned			
1955			T E Evans	15.4		
1956			David Michael	14.4		
1957			J Watkins	14.9		
1958			R Pearce	15.2		
1959			John Powell	14.6		
1960			R Williams	14.9		
1961			Terry Schneider	14.5		
1962			Terry Schneider	14.1		
1963			P Lewis	14.6		
1964			Gareth Edwards	14.3		
1965			Phil Stockford	14.1		
1966			Paul R Nash	15.0		
1967			Paul R Nash	14.7		
1968	John Davies	2:56.2	P Saunders	14.6		
1969	John Davies	2:56.2	P Kerrigan	15.5		
1970	Keith Powell	2:50.7	J Roberts	14.3		
1971	Tony Dyke	2:54.5	R Roberts	14.5		
1972	H L Lewis	2:59.6	Neddyn Lloyd	14.4		
1973	Steve Evans	4:36.0	R Cole	14.6		
1974	Steve Evans	4:22.9	L Hovey	15.6		
1975	N Frost	4:45.2	Roy Saunders	14.4	Roy Saunders	58.5
1976	N Frost	4:37.1	Huw Jones	14.0	Roy Davies	60.3
1977	Andy Jones	4:37.1	Tim Lewis	13.7	Chris Ewart	56.4
1978	Phil Llewellyn	4:31.4	David Jones	14.6	David Jones	56.9
1979	Marcus Thomas	4:29.0	Nigel Walker	13.7	Dean Crapnell	59.84
1980	John McKeevor	4:38.1	M Williams	14.37	Phil Harvey	60.23
1981	Adam Richards	4:33.7	Simon Jones	14.3	Ian Morgan	59.0
1982	John Pritchard	4:34.3	Colin Jackson	14.0	Ian Snook	62.3
1983	Peter Bridger	4:30.8	Simon Davies	14.7	Andrew McKenzie	58.3
1984	Stephen Ellis	4:41.5	Peter Dyer	14.7	Richard Wintle	58.3
1985	Roger Jones	4:31.07	Peter Dyer	14.11	Clive Jones	60.5
1986	Chris Osborne	4:36.71	Rhys Davies	14.02	Russell Richards	56.44
1987	Matthew Bramwell	4:44.57	Damian Talbot	14.27	Ioan Bebb	57.71
1988	David Jones	4:39.2	Richard Harbour	13.8	Mark Eggar	58.9
1989	Andrew Powell	4:34.1	Berian Davies	13.34	Simon Peckham	58.28
1990	Anthony Jones	4:36.70	Paul Rainbow	14.60	Paul Rainbow	56.67
1991	Chris Blount	4:27.8	James Hughes	13.6	Philip Lee	58.8
1992	Christian Davies	4:41.82	Matthew Eveleigh	14.3	Matthew Eveleigh	58.48
1993	Damian Cuke	4:44.52	Steven Edwards	14.1	Stuart Jones	57.72
1994	Tom Cairnes	4:41.62	Jamie Sheffield	13.94	James Hillier	57.64
1995	Tobben Tymons	4:49.42	Steven Francis	14.0	Gareth Lewis	55.57
1996	Paul Gronow	4:40.03	Kevin Drury	14.12	Kevin Drury	57.47
1997	Dean Hood	5:00.80	Jon Marsden	14.36	Dean Hood	59.22
1998	Frank Flegg	4:39.2	Nathan Palmer	13.42	Leighton Lewis	57.66
1999	Stephen Clarke	4:52.8	Nick Hiscott	14.52	Nathan Jones	57.7
2000	Peter Kellie	4:41.84	Daniel Leonard	15.46	Rhys Williams	55.95

	High Jump		Pole Vault		Long Jump	
1940	B Spicer	1.45			C T Coray	5.21
1941	T L Harper	1.38			J Brown	4.90
1942	not held				not held	
1943	K Faulkner	1.34			K Faulkner	5.53
1944	E D Richards	1.42			R Scott	5.84
1945	H B Griffiths	1.50			L Shakeshaft	5.23
1946	D Lurvey	1.55			M Lloyd	5.45
1947	R G Long	1.45			J H Chislett	5.24
1948	D J House	1.50			W Brooks	5.41
1949	Brian Hardwick	1.62			D Ashurst	5.88
1950	V K Clopet	1.61	C T Royle	2.59	Brian Hardwick	6.09
1951	D H Price	1.57	Colin Fletcher	2.79	P H Nutton	5.88
1952	Angus Thomson	1.70	M J Llewellyn	2.67	W C Dallas	5.32
1953	Terence Morgan	1.60	J Jenkins	2.97	P E Copus	6.24
1954	abandoned (weather)		abandoned (weather)		T E Evans	5.84

1955	Aneurin Evans	1.73	Glyndwr Morris	3.27	B Watkins	5.97
1956	David Michael	1.67	John Ball	3.30	Ian Hughes	5.97
1957	John Lister	1.62	John Ball	3.05	D D Davies	6.14
1958	John Lister	1.70	P L Cornelius	3.26	A A Davies	6.50
1959	L Henry	1.73	Graham Gibbs	3.33	Tony Bigham	6.34
1960	J Williams	1.65	M Sutton	3.12	Gareth George	6.08
1961	A Day	1.60	Les Jones	3.20	Gwyn Williams	6.18
1962	C Hagget	1.65	Telfyn Jarrold	3.50	Gwyn Williams	6.56
1963	Ron Gould	1.67	David Williams	3.35	Gareth Edwards	6.16
1964	M Shone	1.73	Roy Morgan	3.53	John Elias	6.14
1965	John Griffiths	1.76	Maldwyn Lewis	3.05	Keith Lowe	6.64
1966	Alan Jenkins	1.67	Malcolm Hurley	2.74	Robert Dorrington	6.08
1967	M Pinches	1.54	Keith Thomas	3.20	Russell Church	6.02
1968	Paul Evans	1.60	M Edds	2.74	Jeff Thornton	5.90
1969	D Harris	1.55	Terrence McQuade	2.94	G Howells	6.49
1970	Andrew Shufflebotham	1.62	W Lloyd	2.94	M Jones	5.73
1971	D M Davies	1.54	K Grundy	2.97	Steve Kohut	6.39
1972	Mike Cummings	1.80	Gordon Pickering	3.20	Steve Kohut	6.10
1973	Chris Berry	1.75	Islwyn Rees	3.79	D Williams	6.18
1974	Chris Richards	1.80	P Davies	3.05	Andrew Lea	5.51
1975	Steve Brock	1.88	Nick Heal	3.55	C Williams	6.36
1976	Phil Lewis	1.74	R Hartwell	2.87	Owen Sussex	6.13
1977	Phil Lewis	1.76	Mark Howells	3.43	Owen Sussex	6.42
1978	Andrew McIver	1.80	Mark Howells	3.40	John Furnham	6.55
1979	Anthony Norris	1.93	Robert Hughes (Carm)	3.05	John Furnham	6.66
1980	David Bethell	1.90	Alun Phillips	3.45	Ray Sherry	6.04
1981	Michael Powell	1.85	Peter Lynk	3.40	Steven Edwards	6.51
1982	Robert James	1.84	Peter Lynk	3.64	Simon Marsh	6.35
1983	Chris Trotman	1.91	Richard Davies	3.40	Simon Marsh	6.55
1984	Chris Trotman	1.90	Neil Ashman	3.50	Simon Williams	6.31
1985	Lee Jones	1.90	Neil Ashman	3.80	Mark Harries	6.44
1986	Andrew Blow	1.83	Ian Thomas	3.60	Richard James	6.34
1987	Andrew Blow	1.90	Howard Turner	3.60	Steve Ingram	6.60
1988	Richard Harbour	1.90	Robert Hughes (C Bay)	3.30	Richard Harbour	6.51
1989	Ceri Payne	1.85	Neil Winter	4.40	Tom Hallett	6.77
1990	Ceri Payne	1.88	Neil Winter	4.50	Darren Yeo	6.38
1991	Dafydd Edwards	1.90	Ian Wilding	4.10	Wayne Bannister	6.45
1992	Kevin Ricketts	1.88	Matthew Turner	3.00	Andrew Davies	6.25
1993	Matthew Perry	1.85	Matthew Turner	3.40	Richard Talbot	6.39
1994	Andrew Penk	1.90	Steven Francis	4.00	Matthew Perry	6.10
1995	Andrew Penk	1.94	Steven Francis	4.20	Andrew Wooding	6.70
1996	Darren Wright	1.90	Alex Thomas	3.90	James Morris	6.37
1997	Alun Davies	1.80	Anthony Perry	4.00	Alex Jackson	5.96
1998	Roger Owens	1.90	Chris Type	4.30	Kris Davies	6.09
1999	Chuka Enih-Snell	1.90	Mark Harvey	2.80	Adam Wrench	6.58
2000	Chuka Enih-Snell	2.11	Mark Harvey	3.50	Ricardo Childs	6.59

	Triple Jump		**Shot Put**		**Discus**	
1940	D H Hillier	11.38	P Evans	11.92	Selwyn Evans	34.44
1941	not held		not held		not held	
1942	not held		not held		not held	
1943	K Faulkner	11.57	J M Butcher	10.39	R W Bowen	30.45
1944	Alan Roche	11.96	J M Butcher	11.91	D J Knight	36.10
1945	H B Griffiths	11.49	D T Price	10.44	V H Cohen	30.03
1946	M Lloyd	11.59	J Perietti	13.00	R J King	37.02
1947	W J Brooks	09.78	A J Smith	12.05	R Sheppard	35.19
1948	D Pugh	11.68	J Walsh	12.90	J Walsh	32.34
1949	E Morgan	11.55	J Walsh/WD Mogford	14.07	EWB James/J Roberts	37.71
1950	Brian Hardwick	12.00	V Clopet	14.06	E W B James	36.52
1951	D H Price	12.52	Tony Morgan	11.97	M A Lewis	38.85
1952	Angus Thomson	13.38	Tony Morgan	13.33	Tony Morgan	42.41
1953	B Davies	12.63	A Hunter	12.03	J R Webb	43.66
1954	abandoned (weather)		A C Williams	13.16	A C Williams	55.20
1955	Aneurin Evans	13.42	P W Swan	13.73	A C Williams	50.24
1956	Ian Hughes	12.67	D H Jones	12.65	G Margretts	44.80
1957	E J Francis	12.34	A R Thomas	13.98	A R Thomas	44.59
1958	A A Davies	13.02	D C Jones	13.46	Alan Scaplehorn	48.16
1959	Tony Bigham	12.56	David Bunce	14.46	Ray Lott	46.95
1960	Nigel Green	12.66	H Steer	14.22	Denis Day	48.02
1961	Tim Jennings	13.23	Terry Price	15.10	D Elvin	40.30
1962	Graham Webb	13.71	I Edwards	14.01	G Harries	43.18

1963	Graham Webb	14.29	Roger Beard	15.77	Roger Beard	49.55
1964	John Elias	12.63	John Mounsey	13.45	John Mounsey	50.69
1965	Paul Edwards	13.04	Allan Martin	16.69	Allan Martin	44.70
1966	Robert Dorrington	12.43	Paul Luff	15.31	James Hennessy	46.62
1967	A Evans	13.00	Jeffrey Baker	13.78	C Williams	48.00
1968	Jeffrey Thornton	13.09	Adrian Thomas	13.39	D R Thomas	42.42
1969	B Jones	12.65	S Maynard	10.76	Mike Flavell	41.30
1970	Phil Olsen	12.59	Robert Edwards	13.89	Robert Edwards	49.36
1971	J D Rees	13.34	not held		Ken Latten	37.12
1972	H Williams	12.01	Ken Latten	13.04	Ken Latten	42.74
1973	Tudor Bidder	12.44	Brian Isgar	13.11	G R Williams	36.26
1974	Chris Richards	12.49	Brian Isgar	14.38	J Brace	36.58
1975	P Sear	12.67	Lloyd Williams	13.87	J Brace	36.62
1976	Owen Sussex	13.72	H Griffiths	13.20	H James	41.50
1977	Owen Sussex	13.49	Peter Rees	15.55	John Buttriss	43.90
1978	John Furnham	13.33	Mark Hewer	14.92	John Collins	42.94
1979	Paul Hawkins	13.61	Mark Hewer	16.93	David Harrison	41.14
1980	Ray Sherry	13.06	Robert Proctor	13.91	M Morgan	42.62
1981	Steven Edwards	13.78	Nigel Skinner	12.89	Julian Tucker	44.62
1982	Mickey Morris	13.65	David Jeremy	12.83	Clive Jones	42.12
1983	Meirion Thomas	12.17	Clayton Turner	14.49	Steven Meredith	39.14
1984	Leighton Adams	13.08	Mike Roberts	13.27	Mike Roberts	39.78
1985	Ian O'Bryan	13.62	Ian Gould	12.82	Ian Gould	40.54
1986	Gareth Davies (Swan)	13.35	Andrew Millard	12.85	Gary Cornish	39.06
1987	Steven Felsbergs	12.52	David Nelson	14.06	David Nelson	40.34
1988	Linton Baddeley	13.07	Peter Roberts	13.16	Peter Roberts	45.14
1989	Linton Baddeley	13.72	Simon Cooke	13.70	Simon Cooke	44.42
1990	Darren Yeo	13.55	Matthew James	11.90	Hamid Lane	39.70
1991	Daniel Davies	12.60	Justin Jones	13.18	Justin Jones	38.52
1992	Daniel Davies	12.70	Stephen Bradley	12.03	Gareth Marks	39.50
1993	Richard Crayford	11.64	Gareth Marks	12.96	Gareth Marks	45.00
1994	Richard Crayford	12.01	Steven Thomas	13.49	Steven Thomas	41.50
1995	Chris Roberts	13.16	John Parkin	12.33	John Parkin	42.48
1996	Chris Roberts	12.69	Stuart Tynan	12.64	James Bryan	39.54
1997	Steven Shalders	13.70	Liam McCaffrey	13.79	Liam Walsh	41.96
1998	Steven Shalders	14.33	James Anthony	13.40	Ian McCaffrey	34.07
1999	Lee Harries	13.12	Simon Bull	12.72	Simon Bull	37.52
2000	Matthew Jacobs	12.22	Michael Mogford	13.75	Gareth Bull	42.55

	Hammer		**Javelin**		**Pentathlon / Octathlon**	
1940			Frank Stephens	37.22		
1941			not held			
1942			not held			
1943			F G D Williams	37.36		
1944			A W Williams	45.92		
1945			N A Thomas	37.62		
1946			J Davies	39.00		
1947			D E Davies	36.21		
1948			B Wilcox	37.88		
1949			J Walsh	40.04		
1950			P J Laverty	45.91		
1951			Clive Roberts	48.38		
1952			Clive Roberts	57.11		
1953			G R Meadows	46.36		
1954			A Evans	47.24		
1955			W Morris	50.02		
1956			David Price	45.52		
1957			M D Herbert	45.25		
1958			D M Edwards	44.50		
1959			L Lewis	49.18		
1960			J R Rowlands	49.07		
1961			G Davies	50.08		
1962			Robert Voss	51.66		
1963			Graham Robinson	52.52		
1964			Graham Robinson	56.72		
1965			Laurence Aalten	43.35		
1966			Laurence Aalten	43.44		
1967			R Gardner	45.60		
1968	Edward Childs		D J Harford	49.76		
1969	D Thomas	34.52	Mike Flavell	42.82		
1970	A Parry Jones	27.94	Bill Carey	48.50		

1971	G Williams	31.74	Gareth Brooks	45.36		
1972	Alan Stimpson	42.32	Gareth Jenkins	47.30		
1973	Philip Jones	35.18	M Hewitt	51.48		
1974	Nigel Stevens	36.48	Gareth Scales	50.88		
1975	Nigel Stevens	40.34	Gareth Scales	55.88		
1976	D Arnold	32.92	Neil Thomas	50.36	Owen Sussex	2698
1977	Chris Beynon	38.20	Neil Thomas	49.88	Owen Sussex	2993
1978	Chris Beynon	40.08	Steve Griffiths	53.72	Darrell Stretton	2541
1979	David Davies	43.38	Darrell Stretton	51.66	Darrell Stretton	2734
1980	Crayton Phillips	52.92	Gareth Rowlands	59.46	R Jones	2312
1981	Julian Tucker	58.06	Chris Talbot	52.96	Nigel Skinner	3043
1982	Martin Cliffe	49.80	Alistair Owen	57.08	not known	
1983	Philip Bufton	47.12	Nicky John	47.88	Simon Marsh	4347
1984	Philip Bufton	57.14	Jonathan Clarke	58.86	not known	
1985	Adrian Palmer	55.20	Craig Miller	48.90	Ian Gould	3905
1986	Jonathan Rose	34.56	Julian Howells	51.50	Marcus Browning	4844
1987	Marcus Davies	48.22	Hugh Daniels	49.88	Ian Thomas	4156
1988	Marcus Davies	54.98	Linton Baddeley	48.10	Robert Hughes	4176
1989	Neil Williams	55.26	Linton Baddeley	54.76	Gianluigi Fecci	4100
1990	Andrew Jones	47.08	Richard Jones	53.20	Gianluigi Fecci	3767
1991	Mark Boswell	46.66	Richard Jones	50.64	Justin Jones	4311
1992	Ross Blight	46.80	Stuart Loughran	56.88	Stuart Jones	4223
1993	Ryan Ashley	33.58	Matthew Roblin	49.30	Stuart Jones	4599
1994	James Elton	46.38	Bryn Samuel	50.18	Jamie Sheffield	4522
1995	Chris Aherne	53.34	Derek Hermann	52.18	Steffan Edwards	3804
1996	Chris Aherne	51.46	Chris Thomas	52.50	Darren Wright	4513
1997	Gareth Driscoll	52.62	Rhys Willaims	53.28	James Anthony	4803
1998	Matthew Grindle	47.14	Jason Hallett	49.98	James Anthony	4866
1999	James Rees	43.54	Mike Groves	46.33	Simon Bull	4310
2000	James Grindle	51.10	Mike Groves	51.60	Gareth Bull	3936

Under 15 Boys (Boys)

	100 yards / 100 metres		220 yards / 200 metres		440 yards / 400 metres	
1951	Jack Melen	11.5	Jack Melen	26.1		
1952	David Paske	11.1	W E Hughes	25.6		
1953	J Evans	10.8	D G Davies	26.0		
1954	A Devonshire	11.1	A Devonshire	25.2		
1955	John Hitchen	11.0	John Hitchen	24.3		
1956	H L Jones	11.0	H L Jones	24.2		
1957	J Davies	12.1	J O Phillips	25.5		
1958	Tony Bigham	11.0	A Ross	25.0		
1959	J Roberts	10.8	M Bishop	24.8		
1960	R Hughes	11.1	Paul Carvell	24.1		
1961	A Lewis	10.5	K Jones	24.6		
1962	D Mottram	11.2	D Thomas	24.8		
1963	Lewis Jones	11.4	Lewis Jones	25.6		
1964	John Evans	10.7	John Evans	24.5	J Thomas	55.4
1965	Alan Gore	10.9	Alan Gore	24.5	Wayne Lewis	57.7
1966	Adrian Thomas	10.8	C Morgan	25.1	M Williams	57.4
1967	R Hewkins	11.0	R Peters	24.4	C R Williams	54.7
1968	R Evans	11.2	R Evans	25.7	R Peters	58.5
1969	A Walters	12.2	A Walters	24.5	T Chewins	57.7
1970	A Edwards	11.7	A Edwards	24.3	N Smith	56.0
1971	not known		S Williams		not known	
1972	Steve Perks	11.6	Steve Perks	24.2	L Parfitt	63.0
1973	Richard Griffiths	11.7	Richard Griffiths	23.6	D George	55.9
1974	Cliff Jeffers	12.1	M S Meaney	24.7	N Quantick	56.5
1975	Mark Brinkworth	12.0	Mark Brinkworth	24.1	J Powell	55.9
1976	L Jones	12.3	A Morgan	24.6	A Morgan	54.5
1977	Malcolm James	11.0	Malcolm James	23.2	Malcolm James	54.0
1978	Andrew Lambert	12.0	Shaun Whelan	24.4	Andy Jones	53.7
1979	David Howell	12.41	Robert Clappe	24.84	David Tucker	54.13
1980	Haydn Wood	11.9	Haydn Wood	24.1	Carl Worthington	57.7
1981	Noel Watkins	11.6	Cheuk Ho Lin	24.0	Adrian Hardman	53.6
1982	Simon Davies	11.8	Roger Walters	24.6	Ian Holbrook	55.1
1983	Paul Jones	12.8	Philip Rees	25.1	Simon Beer	54.2
1984	John Davies	12.0	Andrew Millard	24.9	Julian Bean	54.9
1985	Michael Williams	11.78	Michael Williams	24.09	Robert Edmunds	54.36
1986	Michael Williams	11.29	Michael Williams	22.70	Martin Liddiatt	54.52

1987	Matthew Roderick	12.03	Matthew Roderick	24.0	Andrew Stradling	54.5
1988	Derwyn Owen	12.0	Derwyn Owen	24.5	Martin Holliday	53.0
1989	Darren Holland	11.7	Darren Yeo	23.8	Lance Worthington	52.5
1990	Carwyn Walters	12.0	Eirian Rees	24.9	David Williams	37.4
1991	David Bird	12.0	David Bird	24.7	Aaron Bowen	39.8
1992	Graham Thomas	12.1	Jamie Sheffield	24.5	Mark Rowlands	39.2
1993	Neil Evans	11.6	Neil Evans	24.2	Jamie Griffiths	39.7
1994	Iestyn Lewis	11.7	Iestyn Lewis	24.0	Mike Bodden	40.6
1995	Andre Silva	11.29	Mike Ferraro	24.72	Mike Bodden	38.63
1996	Tim Benjamin	11.33	Tim Benjamin	23.35	Lloyd Newman	39.7
1997	Martin John	11.95	Craig Powell	24.02	Matthew Petty	37.88
1998	Sean Madden	12.05	Nick Hiscott	23.79	Adam Davies	38.11
1999	Iain Hunt	11.98	Iain Hunt	25.07	Gareth Griffiths	41.26
2000	Simon Roach	12.04	Simon Roach	24.36	Ashley Bayliss	55.81

	880 yards / 800 metres		**1500 metres**		**75y / 80y / 80m hurdles**	
1951	E P Wardle	2:22.3			David Paske	12.4
1952	R Fenton	2:12.5			David Paske	11.0
1953	K Turner	2:20.8			C W Marlin	11.1
1954	A Stradling	2:25.1			abandoned (weather)	
1955	R Emms	2:21.7			John Ball	10.9
1956	Gordon McIlroy	2:12.8			Carl Chisnall	10.7
1957	J Pritchard	2:18.7			A Roberts	10.9
1958	A Scurver	2:18.7			S Francis	11.3
1959	R Hughes	2:13.1			T Hughes	11.5
1960	Glyn Jones	2:12.7			Terry Schneider	10.9
1961	P Smith	2:10.9			R Davies	10.8
1962	K Williams	2:09.2			D Reid	10.7
1963	J Sayse	2:11.1			C Walter	11.2
1964	J Thomas	2:12.6			Mike Walters	10.8
1965	B Warrilow	2:13.6			Paul Nash	12.0
1966	D Burke	2:16.9			M Fletcher	11.5
1967	N McCleorie	2:20.9			P Swinburn	11.6
1968	W Leaper	2:11.9			P Kerrigan	11.2
1969	Will Snowdon	2:11.3			J Stoodley	12.2
1970	Tony Dyke	2:10.0			D Davies	12.2
1971	not known				not known	
1972	Michael Cole	2:06.4			R Davies	13.1
1973	S Owen	2:07.8	Hugh Shakeshaft	4:29.4	L Hovey	12.3
1974	Keith Gallivan	2:16.4	Gary Keeble	4:33.4	D Nicholas	12.6
1975	Andrew Martin	2:07.0	Colin Clarkson	4:26.5	A Backhouse	12.8
1976	Nick Morgan	2:08.2	Mike Bounds	4:23.6	Mark Griffiths	12.7
1977	Paul Keeble	2:05.0	Marcus Thomas	4:32.5	Wynne Harries	12.0
1978	David Powell	2:08.4	David Powell	4:24.4	K Williams	13.0
1979	A Carter	2:07.2	Andrew Millard	4:24.2	Peter Inker	12.73
1980	Anthony Rees	2:07.0	Nicky Comerford	4:28.9	S Jones	12.6
1981	Paul Williams	2:07.3	Michael Powell	4:29.6	Colin Jackson	11.9
1982	Ian Cowie	2:11.0	Simon Taylor	4:25.9	Chris Griffiths	12.6
1983	Simon Taylor	2:05.0	Andrew Jones (AVAC)	4:21.0	Peter Dyer	12.4
1984	Peter Conway	2:04.0	Matthew Sherlock	4:39.1	Nathan Kelly	12.6
1985	Martin Clayton	2:08.6	Richard Baker	4:25.58	Ian Thomas	12.6
1986	Huw Davies	2:02.81	Huw Davies	4:23.46	Richard Harbour	12.17
1987	Peter Wyatt	2:04.0	Peter Wyatt	4:18.6	Berian Davies	11.83
1988	Jason Murphy	2:04.9	Jason Murphy	4:24.8	Paul Rainbow	11.8
1989	Darren Yeo	2:06.7	Jon Williams	4:24.2	James Hughes	11.9
1990	Richard Davies	2:13.0	Christian Davies	4:27.7	James Armstrong	11.6
1991	Adrian Staples	2:07.5	Robert Court	4:25.8	Graham Thomas	12.5
1992	Russ Cartwright	2:06.1	David Davey	4:23.6	Graham Thomas	11.8
1993	Carl Harries	2:06.6	Tariq Guendouzi	4:25.1	Chris Truscott	11.8
1994	Mike Bodden	2:10.8	Dafydd Solomon	4:27.5	Kevin Drury	11.7
1995	Mike Bodden	2:07.77	Scott Williams	4:36.29	Jon Marsden	11.96
1996	Ian Bateman	2:08.01	Daniel Beynon	4:28.25	Jon Marsden	11.7
1997	Steven Richards	2:08.62	Matthew Jones	4:21.37	David Tame	11.94
1998	Steven Richards	2:06.66	Chris Davies	4:21.29	Nick Hiscott	12.20
1999	Gareth Tapper	2:08.08	Luke Northall	4:28.37	Jamie Barned	12.74
2000	Jason Atkinson	2:09.10	Jason Atkinson	4:26.59	Andrew Holgate	12.4

	High Jump		**Pole Vault**		**Long Jump**	
1951	H Fletcher	1.45	A F Johnston	5.04		
1952	Keith Davitte	1.52	G C Coles	2.82	B Watkins	5.13
1953	Aneurin Evans	1.52	T E Evans	3.14	B Watkins	5.96

1954	abandoned (weather)		abandoned (weather)		K W Ford	5.36
1955	John Ball	1.55	John Ball	2.74	B Goode	5.15
1956	J Webber	1.47	John Howe	2.36	Carl Chisnall	5.71
1957	D Jones	1.50	John Evans	3.05	G E Thomas	5.55
1958	A Hillier	1.55	Graham Gibbs	3.05	Tony Bigham	6.02
1959	A Price	1.57	R Davies	2.82	F Ebrall	5.73
1960	B Herbert	1.62	D B Regan	3.15	Gary Laycock	6.14
1961	C Haggett	1.52	E Lang	3.12	J Edwards	5.62
1962	A Jones	1.64	Roy Morgan	3.15	D Ashby	5.65
1963	Peter Lance	1.52	Roy Morgan	3.26	John Elias	5.72
1964	John Griffiths	1.64	J Matthews	2.82	Keith Lowe	5.84
1965	A Westcott	1.52	not held		Alan Gore	5.42
1966	P D Thomas	1.42	not known		M Fletcher	5.66
1967	S Ross	1.47	S B Mahoney	2.59	N Nolan	5.47
1968	R Evans	1.37	T McQuaid	2.74	C Thomas	5.57
1969	J Roberts	1.52	no competitors		N Gwilym	5.37
1970	D Davies	1.48	D Isaac	2.38	G Palmer	5.33
1971	not known		not known		not known	
1972	Neil Thomas	1.50	R Thomas	2.44	C Sanna	5.22
1973	Steve Brock	1.76	J Featherstone	2.71	Gerald Hedges	5.19
1974	M Evans	1.39	M Jenkins	2.90	C Williams	5.58
1975	C Richards	1.53	K Howells	2.65	Julian Barrington	5.45
1976	Tony Norris	1.60	Robert Hughes	2.57	R Locke	5.64
1977	Tony Norris	1.69	Robert Hughes	3.23	Ian Strange	6.52
1978	David Rowe	1.60	not held		Ray Sherry	5.85
1979	Michael Powell	1.80	A Bowen	2.55	Robert Clappe	5.75
1980	Darren Russell	1.60	Alan Turrell	3.05	Neil Mills	5.33
1981	Steve Partridge	1.55	Dafydd Richards	2.80	Simon Marsh	6.14
1982	Simon Williams	1.70	Neil Ashman	2.32	Robert Pipkin	5.73
1983	Lee Jones	1.73	Lucas Jones	3.05	Mike Hobbs	5.24
1984	Roydon Murdoch	1.65	Cerith Lewis	3.20	Lee Rosser	5.56
1985	Andrew Blow	1.70	not held		Richard James	6.17
1986	Richard Harbour	1.75	Howard Turner	3.00	Matthew Roderick	5.80
1987	Darren Walsh	1.68	Daniel Mawer	3.10	David Davies	5.96
1988	Tim Thomas	1.70	David Thomas (Tregib)	2.90	Scott Herbert	6.27
1989	Simon Howells	1.78	Richard Tomala	2.90	Derwyn Owen	5.54
1990	Gavin Puckett	1.60	David Thomas (Llanelli)	2.90	Robert Williams	5.42
1991	Rhodri Thomas	1.75	Matthew Turner	2.70	Richard Talbot	5.87
1992	Matthew Perry	1.75	Andrew Penk	2.80	Matthew Perry	6.03
1993	Andrew Penk	1.70	Steven Francis	3.40	Christian Malcolm	6.12
1994	Jamie Dalton	1.82	Jon Parry	3.10	James Morris	6.06
1995	David McFall	1.65	Anthony Perry	2.80	Gareth Gittins	5.69
1996	Chris Harries	1.75	Chris Type	3.15	Chris Evans	5.54
1997	Gareth Allen	1.65	Adam J Smith	2.20	Steven Jones	5.76
1998	Steven Chantrell	1.70	Mark Harvey	2.60	Ricardo Childs	5.31
1999	Sam Jones	1.63	not held		Iain Hunt	5.82
2000	Daniel Williams	1.53	Ashley Ball	2.10	Nathan Fredericks	5.52

	Triple Jump		**Shot Put**		**Discus**	
1951	D Owen	11.00	T J Powell	13.33	B Smith	28.90
1952	B Watkins	12.16	E Lewis	10.96	B Smith	36.86
1953	B Watkins	12.66	A C Williams	13.94	A C Williams	43.34
1954	abandoned (weather)		W Booth	13.74	G Margretts	43.16
1955	G Francis	11.35	C D Jones	12.37	W Farleigh	38.26
1956	Carl Chisnall	11.82	H Thomas	12.72	Alan Scaplehorn	38.30
1957	F Goldby	11.75	D C Jones	13.82	C Ward	36.64
1958	Tony Bigham	12.08	David Bunce	15.59	Ray Lott	44.78
1959	R Ford	11.80	M Owen	12.72	P Herbert	36.72
1960	Gary Laycock	11.94	I Edwards	12.69	V Bonneci	38.52
1961	Graham Webb	12.41	R Philpott	13.53	C Oakes	39.23
1962	D Jones	12.09	W Bunce	14.83	L Bassett	38.65
1963	John Elias	12.82	Allan Martin	14.99	R Bull	38.73
1964	P Edwards	12.38	B Williams	13.23	M Suffield	40.32
1965	A J Lovell	10.97	J Baker	13.09	D Morgan	37.28
1966	M Fletcher	11.62	Adrian Thomas	13.77	C Williams	38.36
1967	R Hewkins	11.79	S Willis	12.63	S Willis	39.62
1968	A Mortimore	11.19	Robert Edwards	14.53	Robert Edwards	35.36
1969	N Gwilym	11.59	R Watkins	09.50	G Hughes	31.72
1970	A Irving	10.99	I Bruce	11.35	Ken Latten	38.08
1971	not known		R Hathway		R Hathway	
1972	Andrew Lea	11.25	Brian Isgar	11.64	D Davies	34.22

1973	A Watkins	11.02	Gerald Hedges	11.05	L Brace	36.14
1974	R Snowden	11.07	H Griffiths	12.00	R Jameson	29.88
1975	P House	11.90	L Sheppard	11.06	John Buttriss	37.40
1976	Richard Jones	12.17	Nigel Payne	12.33	R Gregory	30.00
1977	John Furnham	12.91	Tony Jones	11.60	Gary Jenkins	34.80
1978	Ray Sherry	12.10	Robert Proctor	14.13	Brian Collins	34.40
1979	M Humphries	12.04	Robert Proctor	14.43	C Radnor	34.86
1980	R Crooks	11.13	Andrew Gwilliam	12.27	Alistair Owen	36.74
1981	Mark Watkins	11.79	David Jeremy	12.27	Richard Kingsbury	30.80
1982	Darren Wyatt	11.93	Warren Rossiter	12.64	Gary Smith	37.00
1983	Craig Miller	11.88	Ian Gould	12.46	Nick George	34.10
1984	Andrew Stevens	11.41	Craig Flower	11.92	Paul Strawford	33.58
1985	Gareth Davies (Swan)	12.11	Steve Thatcher	11.74	Robert Mullen	28.08
1986	Anthony Coombes	12.18	Stephen Clarke	12.63	Peter Roberts	32.92
1987	Linton Baddeley	12.25	Lawrence Mainwaring	12.56	Simon Cooke	35.40
1988	Darren Yeo	12.07	Gianluigi Fecci	13.34	Paul Beard	32.76
1989	Darren Yeo	13.00	Jon Cockcroft	12.05	Richard Scrivens	34.06
1990	Daniel Davies	12.04	Justin Jones	13.11	Justin Jones	39.48
1991	Rhodri Thomas	12.12	Simon Ellesmore	11.10	Stuart Jones	33.20
1992	Richard Crayford	12.27	Matthew Roblin	13.40	Wayne Jones	33.86
1993	Daniel Puddick	13.23	Chris Hughes	14.18	Chris Hughes	40.16
1994	Karl Evans	12.03	Jamie Dalton	12.99	Chris Aherne	35.16
1995	event discontinued		Liam Walsh	12.99	Chris Marland	38.88
1996	Liam Walsh	13.98	Liam Walsh	43.18		
1997	Jon Neale	11.29	Nathan Jones	31.94		
1998	Mike Mogford	11.88	Kevin Llewellin	32.89		
1999	Glenn Williams	12.92	Gareth Bull	39.35		
2000	Jamie Pritchard	13.76	Gregory Finlay	36.09		

	Hammer		**Javelin**		**Pentathlon**	
1951			A Jones	39.62		
1952			G C Coles	42.04		
1953			Aneurin Evans	44.01		
1954			J Raven	34.52		
1955			D Humphreys	42.12		
1956			D A Wassall	42.90		
1957			W Isaac	41.80		
1958			J Lewis	43.36		
1959			Richard Lewis	52.42		
1960			D Harries	40.04		
1961			G Goodwin	43.60		
1962			P Conney	44.32		
1963			A Gierke	40.93		
1964			S Mullins	42.84		
1965			P Skupinski	43.52		
1966			A G Sweet	37.74		
1967			D J Harding	42.52		
1968			no competitors			
1969			no competitors			
1970			M Harries	35.76		
1971			not known			
1972			V Richards	43.58		
1973			G Sadler	37.12		
1974			P J Lucas	28.96		
1975	Hywel Osbourne	26.50	Steve Cahill	46.68		
1976	Chris Beynon	35.84	P Batkin	39.98		
1977	Jeremy Flye	31.64	Tim Brookes	40.76		
1978	Robert Proctor	36.92	A James	38.52		
1979	Robert Proctor	49.96	James Jackson	46.38		
1980	Adrian Thomas (ATaf)	45.96	Sean Aldred	45.88		
1981	John Protheroe-Thomas	33.04	Nicky John	37.14	Gary Smith	1550
1982	Philip Bufton	41.24	Keith Marshall	47.20	not known	
1983	Adrian Thomas	38.24	Craig Miller	47.84	Ian Gould	2785
1984	Terry Evans	37.60	Mike Pritchard	42.34	not known	
1985	Alan Cain	23.30	Ian Jones	44.72	Gareth Matthews	1813
1986	Gareth Wood	31.10	Peter Roberts	40.74	not held	
1987	Neil Williams	40.10	Linton Baddeley	48.46	Robert Hughes	2481
1988	Andrew John	36.84	Jason Hewlett	36.46	Paul Rainbow	2193
1989	Simon Bennett	42.52	Richard Jones	44.22	Justin Jones	2059
1990	Mark Boswell	45.42	Benedict Green	47.48	Justin Jones	2397
1991	Warren King	37.94	Barry Walters	51.00	Stuart Jones	2171

1992	Matthew Jones	33.74	Bryn Samuel	46.02	Graham Thomas	2673
1993	John Parkin	44.70	Tony Richards	43.58	Sion Owen	2513
1994	Andrew Carter	41.94	Nikki Flowers	44.92	Kevin Drury	3163
1995	Jon Hodgeon	37.06	Shaun Groves	48.22	Gareth Gittins	2220
1996	Matthew Grindle	39.62	Rhys Williams	49.22	James Anthony	2754
1997	James Grindle	34.68	Michael Groves	31.80	not held	
1998	Adam Farr	41.36	Michael Groves	45.83	Chuka Enih-Snell	2895
1999	Glenn Williams	49.60	Thomas Rees	38.19	Gareth Bull	2203
2000	Jamie Pritchard	44.01	Thomas Rees	49.97	Jamie Pritchard	2425

300m hurdles (now discontinued)

1990	Gareth James	46.9	1991	Alan Jones	47.0	1992	Richard Crayford	42.5
1993	Chris Truscott	44.6	1994	Steffan Edwards	44.7	1995	Lee Webb	46.86
1996	Ben Jenkins	49.62	1997	Nathan Jones	44.01	1999	JamesPritchard	48.52

Under 13 Boys (Colts)

	100 metres		**200 metres**		**800 metres**	
1974	N A Hinwood	13.1			N Morgan	2:24.3
1975	Malcolm James	12.5	Malcolm James	25.6	Steve Kinchin	2:19.2
1976	T P Jones	13.8	P M Donovan	28.1	D C Bosley	2:26.0
1977	Paul Humphries	13.1	Martin Nugent	27.9	David Powell	2:15.9
1978	Mark Griffiths	12.9	Mark Griffiths	27.1	Anthony Rees	2:21.2
1979	Anthony Jones	13.63	Anthony Jones	26.87	Stephen Price	2:27.4
1980	Richard Wintle		Roger Walters	27.1	R Hughes	2:23.3
1981	Jason Ball	12.88	Peter Spargo	26.36	David Gough	2:20.71
1982	Lee Rosser	13.3	Giles Hill	27.36	Calvin Chew	2:25.68
1983	Philip Llewellyn	12.9	Nick Taylor	28.2	Richard Baker	2:14.0
1984	Steve Rees	13.0	Matthew Roderick	26.7	Martin Hudson	2:22.7
1985	Matthew Roderick	12.92	Matthew Roderick	26.6	Richard Heard	2:25.43
1986	Simon Lewis	13.00	Dean Thomas	26.97	Jason Murphy	2:16.61
1987	Darren Holland	13.05	Darren Holland	26.22	Darren Yeo	2:19.15
1988	Gareth Evans	13.2	Nick Walne	27.5	Richard Goodenough	2:18.8
1989	Paul Farmahan	13.1	Paul Farmahan	26.68	Adrian Staples	2:20.6
1990	Ben Strevens	13.8	Alistair Mason	28.4	Alistair Lovell	2:22.6
1991	Chris Hughes	13.7	James Griffiths	28.1	Carl Harries	2:22.5
1992	Alun Evans	13.4	Alun Evans	27.1	Craig Davies	2:28.0
1993	Greg Healey	13.6	Mike Bodden	28.0	Mike Bodden	2:29.6
1994	Jon Francis	12.9	Jon Francis	27.0	David Teague	2:23.5
1995	Simon Davies	12.60	Rhys Saunders	27.92	Matthew Lewis	2:21.03
1996	David Gravell	12.77	David Gravell	27.46	Chris Davies	2:20.23
1997	Philip Griffiths	13.08	Philip Griffiths	27.83	Jason Atkinson	2:25.28
1998	David Gomes	13.20	Paul Heatley	27.46	Chris Gowell	2:22.93
1999	Marcus Johnstone	13.20	Marcus Johnstone	27.50	Thomas Organ	2:21.57
2000	Benjamin Hale	13.21	Bruce Tasker	26.29	Jacob McCullough	2:19.95

	1500 metres		**High Jump**		**Long Jump**	
1975			Tony Norris	1.51	Adrian Hadley	5.01
1976	Steve Watkins	4:46.9	Steve Watkins	1.45	P Donovan	4.20
1977	David Powell	4:42.4	Adrian Moyle	1.45	Michael Powell	4.70
1978	Lee Williams	4:51.7	R Pickin	1.27	David Tucker	4.80
1979	Stephen Price	4:54.2	Simon Marsh	1.43	Steve Partridge	4.67
1980	R Jones	4:54.3	H Pryor	1.35	Stephen Thornton	5.00
1981	Alun Jones	4:56.56	Ian Gould	1.40	Jason Ball	4.80
1982	Chris Key	5:03.1	Stephen Watkins	1.43	Lee Rosser	4.83
1983	Simon Learner	4:49.3	Andrew Blow	1.48	Richard James	4.83
1984	Mark Morgan	4:51.7	Richard Harbour	1.47	Steve Rees	4.95
1985	Richard Heard	4:45.6	Tomos Williams	1.30	Matthew Roderick	4.93
1986	Jason Murphy	4:40.77	Paul Rainbow	1.25	Simon Lewis	4.80
1987	Kyle Jones	4:54.2	Simon Howells	1.45	Lee Watt	4.75
1988	Kyle Jones	4:54.0	Dugald Rees	1.35	Nick Walne	4.67
1989	Adrian Staples	4:50.8	Rhodri Thomas	1.49	Paul Farmahan	5.11
1990	Leighton Johnson	4:52.4	Graham Thomas	1.53	James Beckett	4.57
1991	Steve Lawrence	4:48.9	Andrew Penk	1.55	Andy Wooding	4.87
1992	Dafydd Solomon	4:45.9	Jamie Dalton	1.40	Craig Davies	4.67
1993	David Teague	4:56.5	Ian Kimber	1.39	Greg Healey	4.65
1994	Daniel Beynon	4:53.1	Nico Algieri	1.45	Gareth Williams	4.67
1995	Alex Haines	4:59.30	Gareth Allen	1.49	Simon Davies	4.70
1996	Mike Targett	4:52.21	Steve Chantrell	1.51	Michael Groves	4.76

1997	Charles Harvey	4:49.65	Samuel Jones	1.40	Owen Bissmire	4.96
1998	Jason Atkinson	4:54.79	Philip Harries	1.45	Geraint Wadley	4.47
1999	Gavin Stokes	5:00.58	Ross Connell	1.35	Stephen Martin	4.23
2000	Jacob McCullough	4:56.68	Steffan Phillips	1.35	Ifiok Otung	4.75

	Shot Put		**80m / 75m hurdles**		**Pentathlon**	
1976	A Cleverley	08.31				
1977	Robert Proctor	09.65				
1978	Mark Griffiths	09.71				
1979	Steve Foulkes	08.14				
1980	R Beaumond	07.48				
1981	Ian Gould	09.94				
1982	Russell Cross	08.30				
1983	Mark Francis	07.69				
1984	Richard Daniels	07.40				
1985	Greg Williams	08.13				
1986	Jonathan Davies	09.28				
1987	Jonathan Cockcroft	09.50				
1988	Justin Jones	10.39				
1989	Adrian Staples	07.39				
1990	John Parkin	08.63				
1991	Chris Hughes	11.48	Chris Truscott	14.3		
1992	Jamie Dalton	11.06	Wynne James	12.7	Jamie Dalton	1814
1993	Julian Saunders	09.29	Rhys White	14.4	James Bryan	1359
1994	Ryan Willey	09.62	Jon Marsden	12.4	Niko Algieri	1720
1995	Neil Phillips	08.96	David Smitham	12.86	Jason Evans	1400
1996	Gavin Elliott	09.33	Gareth Hassell	14.3	Adam Christie-Rees	1619
1997	Daniel McCaffrey	09.34	Owen Bissmire	13.31	not held	
1998	Greg Finlay	10.25	David Greene	12.73	James Pritchard	1774
1999	David Price	11.04	Keith Davies	13.70	Daniel Williams	1582
2000	Gareth Lloyd	09.26	Steffan Phillips	13.84	Hugh Jones	1431

Discontinued events

300 metres

1990	Karl Davies	44.5
1991	James Griffiths	44.1

Pole Vault

1976	S Walrond	1.81

Triple Jump

1979	Peter Hamilton	9.20

U20 Junior Women

	100 metres		**200 metres**		**400 metres**	
1983	Rhian Owen	12.8	Sian Morris	24.6	Rhian Owen	59.3
1984	Helen Miles	11.9	Helen Miles	25.9	Samantha Taylor	60.2
1985	Helen Miles	11.66	Sallyanne Short	25.9	Georgina Funnell	58.71
1986	Sallyanne Short	11.9	Sallyanne Short	24.2	Anne Evison	57.9
1987	Nicola Short	13.08	Alison Eves	26.68	Nicola Lane	58.80
1988	Allison Consterdine	12.4	Allison Consterdine	25.6	Mary Murphy	58.9
1989	Pamela Greaves	12.20	Pamela Greaves	25.57	Claire Warnes	57.81
1990	Alicia Porter	13.1	Joanne Gronow	26.08	Joanne Gronow	58.63
1991	Alicia Porter	12.6	Joanne Gronow	25.4	Joanne Gronow	58.2
1992	Lisa Armstrong	12.62	Alicia Porter	27.66	Kay Furse	58.92
1993	Dawn Higgins	12.54	Dawn Higgins	25.58	Nicola Davies	58.26
1994	Louise Sharps	12.32	Louise Sharps	25.58	Dawn Higgins	59.10
1995	Louise Sharps	12.90	Louise Sharps	26.04	Kate Williams	57.85
1996	Angharad James	12.39	Gael Davies	25.65	Amanda Pritchard	55.80
1997	Angharad James	12.31	race declared void		Sarah Mead	60.16
1998	Sophie Williams	12.16	Donna Porazinski	25.24	Donna Porazinski	57.44
1999	Rachel Lewis	12.87	Donna Porazinski	26.4	Donna Porazinski	57.2
2000	Lucy Evans	12.78	Lucy Evans	26.05	Donna Porazinski	57.5

	800 metres		**1500 metres**		**3000 metres**	
1983	Fiona Harwood	2:18.6	Bethan Williams	4:48.4		
1984	Fiona Harwood	2:17.4	Wendy Ore	4:39.1		
1985	Avril Stephens	2:22.60	Lynn Maddison	4:40.38		
1986	Georgina Funnell	2:18.3	Hayley Donaghue	5:01.9		
1987	Caitlin Funnell	2:18.11	Susan Davies	5:25.66	Peta Bee	11:04.9
1988	Caitlin Funnell	2:13.3	Rhian Morgan	4:52.1	Carol Hayward	10:03.9
1989	Tina Curry	2:16.75	Joanne Parsons	4:43.48	Carol Hayward	09:47.77

1990	Tina Curry	2:17.82	Joanne Kilminster	4:56.15	Lisa Roberts	11:08.36
1991	Clare Schofield	2:16.3	Jessica Mills	4:41.2	Emma Davies	10:59.6
1992	Emma Brady	2:20.09	Esther Evans	4:55.50	Jessica Mills	10:09.48
1993	Kathryn Bright	2:20.92	Clare Martin	4:40.98	Clare Martin	10:28.86
1994	Kathryn Bright	2:16.40	Catherine Davies	4:43.60	Catherine Davies	11:09.92
1995	Kirsty Jones	2:17.31	Clare Martin	4:48.00	Clare Martin	10:21.11
1996	Deborah Quirk	2:22.54	Clare Thomas	4:40.50	Clare Thomas	10:21.33
1997	Amanda Pritchard	2:08.28	Nicola Knapp	4:46.28	Samantha Gray	10:32.80
1998	Rebecca Evans	2:17.93	Sarah Mead	4:38.05	Sian Pritchard	11:15.39
1999	Natalie Lewis	2:19.6	Kristy Doyle	4:57.86	Lucy Kirby	10:39.7
2000	Lisa Thompson	2:19.03	Kristy Doyle	4:52.45	Emily Crowley	11:07.38

	100m hurdles		**400m hurdles**		**High Jump**	
1983	Lynn Parry	15.4	Michelle Cooke	63.9	Kerry Crook	1.55
1984	Non Evans	14.9	Alyson Evans	63.9	Val Adams	1.68
1985	Non Evans	16.33	Alyson Evans	61.30	Val Adams	1.68
1986	Jackie Barber	15.5	Susan Haskins	67.0	Jackie Barber	1.60
1987	Carol Whiteway	15.29	Sarah Jones-Morris	67.6	Carol Whiteway	1.68
1988	Carol Whiteway	14.7	Nicola Short	69.4	Carol Whiteway	1.65
1989	Dawn Nicholson	15.69	Emma Lile	67.09	Amanda Wale	1.68
1990	Bethan Edwards	14.46	Maria Yarnold	65.92	Rebecca Richards	1.68
1991	Bethan Edwards	14.4	Mari Prys-Jones	65.0	Rebecca Richards	1.68
1992	Bethan Edwards	13.8	Clare Edwards	63.08	Susannah Filce	1.60
1993	Megan Jones	14.72	Emma Davies	66.12	Susannah Filce	1.65
1994	Rachel King	14.52	Emma Davies	65.12	Ailsa Wallace	1.70
1995	Rachel King	14.0	no competitors		Teresa Andrews	1.74
1996	Rachel Stannard	15.46	Kathryn Williams	62.2	Teresa Andrews	1.70
1997	Rachel Stannard	15.25	Gael Davies	64.83	Kelly Moreton	1.65
1998	Lowri Roberts	15.22	Lisa Thompson	65.34	Lisa Thompson	1.50
1999	Lowri Roberts	15.3	Stephanie Little	68.6	Ceri Stokoe	1.55
2000	Lauren McLoughlin	14.84	Donna Porazinski	61.17	Rebecca Jones	1.77

	Long Jump		**Shot Put**		**Discus**	
1983	Nicolette Dymond	5.25	Delyth Evans	11.72	Debra Gould	29.84
1984	Karen Taylor	5.21	Lisa Angulatta	11.63	Lisa Angulatta	30.44
1985	Lisa Lewis	5.43	Lisa Angulatta	11.03	Lisa Angulatta	29.84
1986	Pat Roche	5.13	Jo Evans	09.81	Jo Evans	30.12
1987	Nicola Short	5.40	Jayne Berry	12.26	Jayne Barry	33.88
1988	Susan Harries	5.40	Jayne Berry	12.95	Jane Davies	39.36
1989	Amanda Wale	5.30	Jayne Fisher	09.96	Jayne Fisher	36.80
1990	Bethan Edwards	5.40	Hayley Hartson	10.82	Hayley Hartson	39.20
1991	Emily Stewart	5.32	Rachel Masterman	10.36	Hayley Hartson	36.20
1992	Lisa Armstrong	6.19	Sarah Moore	11.44	Sarah Moore	36.42
1993	Emily Stewart	5.44	Hayley Griffiths	10.51	Kelly Roberts	35.94
1994	Teresa Andrews	5.13	Krissy Owen	12.50	Sarah Johnson	36.32
1995	Teresa Andrews	5.54	Philippa Roles	12.71	Philippa Roles	43.70
1996	Teresa Andrews	5.21	Philippa Roles	13.01	Philippa Roles	46.62
1997	Gemma Jones	5.47	Nicola Parson	10.03	Rebecca Roles	39.72
1998	Debbie Adams	5.05	Rebecca Roles	10.90	Rebecca Roles	43.93
1999	Aimee Cutler	5.62	Carys Parry	09.22	Anwen James	35.61
2000	Lara Richards	5.70	Laura Douglas	11.37	Anwen James	35.86

	Javelin		**Heptathlon**	
1983	Julie Tayler	34.76	Julia Charlton	4725
1984	Paula Taylor	26.66	not held	
1985	Karen Hough	56.06	Karen Hough	4166
1986	Karen Hough	49.34	not held	
1987	Catherine Gunn	39.06	not held	
1988	Jayne Berry	38.34	Amanda Wale	3492
1989	Sarah Lewis	25.30	Amanda Wale	4104
1990	Onyema Amadi	39.54	Angela Taylor	3015
1991	Jo Smith	34.20	Emily Stewart	4010
1992	Emily Steele	45.80	Krissy Owen	4126
1993	Hilary Davies	39.12	Krissy Owen	4444
1994	Krissy Owen	41.48	Teresa Andrews	4456
1995	Amanda Jervis	32.96	Abigail Jones	3628
1996	Rhian Hughes	39.22	Clare McGovern	2920
1997	Sian Lax	41.14	Kelly Moreton	3632
1998	Clare Lockwood	41.16	Lisa Thompson	4357
1999	Natasha Campbell	35.64	Stephanie Little	4142
2000	Emily Skucek	39.59	Rebecca Jones	4752

	Pole Vault		Triple Jump		Hammer	
1991					Angela Bonner	35.86
1992					Sarah Moore	43.74
1993			Emily Stewart	10.50	Leanne Jones	33.86
1994			Jayne Ludlow	11.63	Clare McKenzie	36.68
1995			Jo Tomlinson	10.47	Sheena Parry	39.00
1996	Rebecca Morgan	2.00	Teresa Andrews	11.05	Sheena Parry	36.90
1997	Susan Williams	2.40	Emma Lane	10.26	Bethan Davies	29.12
1998	Rebecca Roles	3.00	Laura Eastwood	10.71	Carys Parry	44.24
1999	Anna Leyshon	2.50	Megan Freeth	10.88	Carys Parry	48.88
2000	Carys Holloway	2.60	Lara Richards	11.88	Carys Parry	48.14

Under 17 Women (Intermediates)

	100 yards / 100 metres		220 yards / 200 metres		400 metres	
1962	Tanya Alcock	11.7	Tanya Alcock	27.5		
1963	Sylvia Powell	12.1	Tanya Alcock	27.7		
1964	Judith Alcock	12.0	Linda Davies	26.5		
1965	Linda Davies	11.8	Gaynor Legall	26.9		
1966	Gaynor Legall	11.6	Gaynor Legall	26.4		
1967	Diane Chipps	11.9	Diane Chipps	26.0		
1968	Avril Jones	12.1	Avril Jones	26.7		
1969	Patrice Shiels	13.0	Michelle Smith	25.6		
1970	Marva Connikie	13.1	Marva Connikie	26.9		
1971	Marva Connikie	12.5	Marva Connikie	28.5		
1972	Lianne Dando	12.5	Delyth Thomas	26.6	Sue Tolan	62.8
1973	Philomena Ronan	14.5	D Fear	28.0	Juliet Reed	65.7
1974	Philomena Ronan	12.3	Ceri Jenkins	26.3	Pat Waters	63.2
1975	Carmen Smart	12.8	Carmen Smart	26.5	Elaine Oxton	59.9
1976	Carmen Smart	12.0	Carmen Smart	25.5	Kay Buckland	57.4
1977	Diane Thorne	12.1	Diane Thorne	25.6	Sian Waters	58.2
1978	Karen Taylor	12.5	Karen Taylor	25.1	Carol Nicholas	57.7
1979	Karen Taylor	12.1	Karen Taylor	25.2	Paula Thomas	59.7
1980	Sian Morris	12.5	Sian Morris	25.9	Bev Preece	58.6
1981	Rhian Owen	12.9	Sarah Collins	27.8	Sian Morris	59.0
1982	Dawn Oliver	12.6	Dawn Oliver	25.9	Kathryn Morris	60.9
1983	Helen Miles	12.2	Helen Miles	25.1	Andrea Williams	60.4
1984	Jane Bradbeer	12.0	Sallyanne Short	24.4	Tanya Richards-Clarke	59.1
1985	Jane Bradbeer	12.21	Jane Bradbeer	25.05	Debbie Jones	60.1
1986	Nicola Short	12.3	Allison Consterdine	24.6	Clare Warnes	60.4
1987	Sonia Reay	12.98	Clare Warnes	26.55	Clare Warnes	58.17
1988	Pamela Greaves	12.5	Sonia Reay	26.6	Nerys Evans	57.7
1989	Lisa Armstrong	12.01	Lisa Armstrong	24.53	Joanne Gronow	59.41
1990	Lisa Armstrong	12.75	Lisa Armstrong	25.44	Alex Kegie	58.25
1991	Bethan Griffiths	12.8	Bethan Griffiths	26.1	Megan Jones	41.7
1992	Dawn Higgins	13.16	Megan Jones	25.73	Dawn Higgins	40.66
1993	Louise Sharps	12.32	Louise Sharps	25.54	Lianne Billen	43.84
1994	Delyth Jones	12.40	Angharad James	25.54	Michelle John	41.78
1995	Hannah Paines	13.00	Hannah Paines	26.78	Gail Evans	42.72
1996	Sophie Williams	12.63	Rhian Cains	26.29	Donna Porazinski	42.44
1997	Hayley Baxter	12.85	Aimee Cutler	26.01	Rhian Cains	41.14
1998	Lowri Jones	12.22	Lowri Jones	24.89	Emma Church	43.47
1999	Lowri Jones	12.3	Lowri Jones	25.1	Aimee John	42.3
2000	Danielle Selley	12.47	Danielle Selley	25.90	Samantha Gamble	42.07

	880 yards / 800 metres		1500 metres		3000 metres	
1967	Shirley Ellis	2:38.3				
1968	Deborah Gill	2:41.2				
1969	Christine Ball	2:34.4				
1970	Ann Disley	2:27.2				
1971	Ann Disley	2:24.0				
1972	Anne Roblin	2:25.3				
1973	Anne Morris	2:23.6	Sue Tolan	5:02.7		
1974	Lynn Huntbach	2:23.9	Jackie Hulbert	5:05.7		
1975	E Jones	2:22.6	Jackie Hulbert	5:04.2		
1976	Angela Hartley	2:19.3	Angela Hartley	4:55.4		
1977	Kirsty McDermott	2:20.6	Annmarie Fox	4:49.8		
1978	Kirsty McDermott	2:19.0	Gillian Irvine	4:57.3		
1979	Louise Copp	2:20.2	Yana Jones	4:44.6		
1980	Ann Howard	2:18.9	Janette Howes	4:44.7		
1981	Nicola Charlton	2:18.4	Janette Howes	4:40.8		

1982	Fiona Harwood	2:18.3	Julie Thompson	4:52.4		
1983	Debbie Crowley	2:20.6	Cathy Lock	4:49.3		
1984	Karen Whitehouse	2:16.4	Clare Pugh	4:54.7		
1985	Karen Whitehouse	2:22.0	Clare Pugh	4:50.13		
1986	Nicola Lucas	2:18.0	Lisa Carthew	4:52.8		
1987	Rachel Gaisford	2:19.55	Joanne Parsons	4:50.32	Nicola Morgan	10:30.14
1988	Julie Garrett	2:16.5	Clare Barnett	4:52.3	Rebecca Evans	10:30.2
1989	Julie Garrett	2:16.86	Claire Schofield	5:07.54	Claire Schofield	10:55.12
1990	Claire Edwards	2:16.94	Claire Schofield	4:52.63	Joanne Elward	11:21.20
1991	Claire Edwards	2:20.7	Jenny Smith	4:53.1	Charlotte Morgan	10:45.1
1992	Kathryn Bright	2:13.62	Bethan Fallon	4:52.46	Vivienne Conneely	10:13.62
1993	Kirsty Jones	2:19.62	Helen Protherough	4:59.20	Clare Williams	11:21.26
1994	Sarah Devey	2:22.60	Clare Thomas	4:53.80	Heledd Gruffudd	10:42.02
1995	Sarah Mead	2:20.25	Clare Thomas	4:49.99	Heledd Gruffudd	11:04.33
1996	Sarah Mead	2:16.71	Jessica Parry-Williams	4:56.85	Ceri Wensley	10:51.29
1997	Georgina Parnell	2:17.13	Sarah Williams	4:49.26	Tracy Andrews	12:05.80
1998	Georgina Parnell	2:17.23	Clare Woolley	5:03.10	Claire Salter	11:21.38
1999	Elise Taylor	2:22.7	Katie Greenwood	4:54.93	Claire Evans	11:19.8
2000	Lucy Thomas	2:20.60	Amanda Jones	4:57.33	Fiona Harrison	11:38.09

	80y / 80m hurdles		**400m / 300m hurdles**		**Pentathlon / Heptathlon**	
1962	S Thatcher	12.3				
1963	G Jones	11.8				
1964	Judith Alcock	12.3				
1965	Jennifer Williams	12.4				
1966	P Woodward	13.5				
1967	Lesley Black	12.8				
1968	June Hirst	12.7				
1969	Gaynor Blackwell	12.7				
1970	Gaynor Blackwell	12.8				
1971	Susan Hamer	12.8				
1972	Lynette Davies	13.0				
1973	Lynette Davies	13.2			Philomena Ronan	2711
1974	Claire Armstrong	12.2			Ceri Jenkins	2829
1975	Karen Evans	12.7			Karen Evans	3321
1976	Phyllis Lynham	12.3			Paula Middle	2994
1977	Amanda Stacey	12.0			Joy McLean	2604
1978	Alice Simmons	12.7			Sarah Rowe	3419
1979	Jane Buttriss	11.7			Jane Buttriss	3238
1980	Lynn Parry	11.5			Sarah Nicholls	3406
1981	Lynn Parry	12.2			Sarah Nicholls	4524
1982	Sarah Collins	12.3			Julia Charlton	4803
1983	Lynn Davies	15.6	Samantha Taylor	68.0	Andrea Munkley	4285
1984	Rebecca Jones-Morris	11.5	Christa Bell	68.6	Lisa Griffiths	4427
1985	Lisa Griffiths	12.27	Sian Sanders	68.19	Jane Shepherd	4484
1986	Cheryl Thomas	12.1	Alison Davies	68.0	Carol Whiteway	3881
1987	Emma Pearce	12.11	Amanda Horton	73.37	Amanda Wale	3499
1988	Bethan Edwards	12.0	Sally Whiteside	71.6	Claudia Filce	3475
1989	Bethan Edwards	11.78	Mari Prys Jones	45.96	Julie Pryce	4008
1990	Joelanda Thomas	12.08	Mari Prys Jones	45.40	Susannah Filce	3980
1991	Rachel King	12.2	Megan Jones	45.0	Krissy Owen	4061
1992	Rachel King	12.0	Megan Jones	45.3	Krissy Owen	4434
1993	Louise Dennis	12.24	Lucy Roberts	46.98	Teresa Andrews	4243
1994	Kathryn Williams	12.16	Kathryn Williams	44.96	Abigail Jones	3576
1995	Gael Davies	11.6	Martha Jones	47.50	Kelly Moreton	4014
1996	Anna Leyshon	12.10	Lisa Thompson	46.57	Kelly Moreton	4089
1997	Nia Maynard	12.09	Donna Porazinski	45.17	Lisa Thompson	3983
1998	Laura McLaughlin	11.96	Stephanie Little	48.24	Rebecca Jones	4255
1999	Melissa Harries	12.2	Helen Davies	45.7	Rebecca Jones	4657
2000	Melissa Harries	12.8	Helen Davies	45.90	Elen Evans	3663

	High Jump		**Long Jump**	
1962	P Fenton	1.37	Tanya Alcock	4.75
1963	Pamela Guppy	1.53	Tanya Alcock	5.12
1964	Pat McDiarmid	1.40	S Hollett	4.84
1965	Janet Jones	1.45	L Williams	4.94
1966	P Woodward	1.32	Vivienne Bennett	5.05
1967	June Hirst	1.52	Sharon McParlin	4.80
1968	June Hirst	1.40	June Hirst	5.17
1969	Janice Davies	1.42	C Jones	4.71

1970	Christine Griffiths	1.45	Angela Smith	4.99
1971	Jackie Dillaway	1.45	Ann Disley	4.89
1972	Jackie Dillaway	1.40	Gillian Regan	5.40
1973	Elaine Hammersley	1.42	Philomena Ronan	4.89
1974	Viv Rothera	1.60	Gillian Humphreys	5.01
1975	Viv Rothera	1.58	Karen Evans	5.61
1976	J Watkins	1.45	Jill Davies	5.34
1977	Ruanda Davis	1.65	Rachel Freke	5.19
1978	Sarah Rowe	1.69	Amanda Jones	5.62
1979	Sarah Rowe	1.65	Jackie Hammersley	5.57
1980	Sarah Nicholls	1.65	Joanne Edwards	5.51
1981	Sarah Nicholls	1.70	Julia Charlton	5.47
1982	Christine Brookes	1.65	Karen Taylor	5.19
1983	Val Adams	1.55	Lisa Lewis	5.01
1984	Jackie Barber	1.65	Pat Roche	5.62
1985	Jackie Barber	1.65	Nicola Short	5.64
1986	Martha Tullberg	1.62	Nicola Short	5.71
1987	Amanda Davies	1.55	Susan Harries	5.11
1988	Claudia Filce	1.55	Bethan Edwards	5.06
1989	Anna Clode	1.60	Lisa Armstrong	5.46
1990	Bev Green	1.68	Lisa Armstrong	5.77
1991	Susannah Filce	1.65	Anna Proctor	5.40
1992	Teresa Andrews	1.70	Nicola Jupp	5.61
1993	Teresa Andrews	1.68	Karina Williams	5.43
1994	Non Williams	1.53	Jayne Ludlow	5.27
1995	Jayne Ludlow	1.50	Gemma Jones	5.47
1996	Kelly Moreton	1.63	Debbie Adams	5.26
1997	Lisa Thompson	1.55	Aimee Cutler	5.44
1998	Rebecca Jones	1.65	Aimee Cutler	5.38
1999	Rebecca Jones	1.65	Sarah Lane (Swan)	5.35
2000	Kathy Pritchett	1.65	Amy Protheroe	5.27

	Pole Vault		**Triple Jump**		**Hammer**	
1995	not held		Jayne Ludlow	12.11	Bethan Davies	22.26
1996	Rebecca Roles	3.00	Laura Eastwood	09.78	Carys Parry	33.28
1997	Megan Freeth	2.40	Nia Lewis	10.49	Carys Parry	36.60
1998	Megan Freeth	2.50	Debbie Lloyd	10.18	Laura Douglas	37.90
1999	Victoria Perry	2.30	Sian Jones	11.01	Laura Douglas	40.01
2000	Jacqui Lloyd	2.00	Ceri Jones	10.86	Louise Finlay	38.36

	Shot Put		**Discus**		**Javelin**	
1962	A Hopkins	08.02	Tanya Alcock	28.56	P Fenton	24.80
1963	Sandra Murphy	10.29	Sandra Murphy	27.88	Sheila Coleman	28.42
1964	C Patchell	08.37	J Parry	25.56	Janet Spinks	29.68
1965	Anne Schropfer	09.14	S Baker	28.66	L James	29.65
1966	J Jones	08.25	J Bedford	23.34	C Morgan	26.50
1967	G Newton	09.15	Janet Wady	28.88	Janet Wady	30.44
1968	Frances Pincock	09.49	Frances Pincock	24.78	Janet Wady	28.08
1969	Paulette Coggin	08.63	A Walters	20.90	Margaret Rainbow	29.58
1970	Anne Johns	08.93	Delyth Prothero	29.54	Susan James	35.30
1971	Delyth Prothero	08.98	Delyth Prothero	31.04	Susan James	37.70
1972	Lynn Langdon	09.25	Lynn Langdon	31.56	Jane Lucas	28.42
1973	Debra Chapman	09.74	J Hawkins	21.32	Yvonne Williams	31.06
1974	Joanna Stallbow	10.56	Katrina Beedles	31.62	Alyson Hadfield	21.12
1975	Sian Bowley	10.14	Katrina Beedles	30.58	Alyson Hadfield	29.58
1976	Karen Glover	09.63	Alyson Hourihan	31.48	Alyson Hourihan	32.98
1977	Alyson Hourihan	09.39	Alyson Hourihan	36.50	Jo Tubb	36.62
1978	Janette Covill	10.17	Caroline Williams	35.38	Jane Jackson	36.10
1979	Jackie Leonard	09.96	Sandra Lee	35.04	Jennifer Morley	36.62
1980	Jackie Leonard	11.20	Sandra Lee	42.16	Amanda Horrex	39.76
1981	Delyth Evans	11.37	Debbie Gould	29.52	Julie Tayler	35.80
1982	Jayne Richardson	11.82	Vanessa Edwards	28.12	Penny Miller	32.80
1983	Lisa Angulatta	11.00	Lisa Angulatta	28.86	Karen Hough	48.32
1984	Linda Williams	09.93	Christine Lewis	33.72	Karen Hough	53.42
1985	Jayne Morgan-Berry	09.82	Amanda Barnes	40.44	Cathy Gunn	36.26
1986	Jayne Berry	10.20	Jane Davies	35.44	Emma Thorne	35.10
1987	Tina Loftus	10.26	Jane Davies	36.16	Emma Thorne	38.00
1988	Hayley Hartson	10.47	Hayley Hartson	39.62	Elizabeth Randle	29.78

1989	Rachel Masterman	10.51	Hayley Hartson	37.92	Onyema Amadi	34.72
1990	Rachel Masterman	09.93	Vicky Todd	30.94	Donna Jackson	33.24
1991	Clare McKenzie	09.99	Stephanie Codd	29.32	Hilary Davies	37.54
1992	Lesley Brannon	10.54	Kelly Roberts	33.28	Julie Fenwick	35.94
1993	Philippa Roles	11.72	Philippa Roles	44.72	Angharad Richards	41.48
1994	Dwysli Lewis	09.09	Dee Groves	28.64	Rhian Hughes	33.52
1995	Rebecca Roles	09.18	Rebecca Roles	32.08	Sian Lax	40.66
1996	Angharad Lloyd	10.19	Rebecca Roles	37.56	Clare Lockwood	35.82
1997	Liz Edwards	09.64	Anwen James	34.94	Natasha Campbell	37.52
1998	Liz Edwards	10.36	Laura Douglas	31.60	Natasha Campbell	37.66
1999	Laura Douglas	11.10	Laura Douglas	31.82	Charlotte Rees	34.21
2000	Louise Finlay	11.03	Ruth Morris	32.71	Charlotte Rees	38.26

Under 15 Girls (Junior Women)

	100 yards / 100 metres		**High Hurdles**		**High Jump**	
1952	Sylvia Jones	12.3	J Morris	12.8	H Ballett	1.37
1953	M Hughes	13.1	Louvain Thomas	12.6	S Rees	1.29
1954	J M Hindley	12.8	E Trowbridge	13.1	P Haddock	1.32
1955	Bonnie Jones	11.6	Norma Lee	11.6	J Molyneux	1.34
1956	Carol Davies	11.7	Carol Davies	11.7	M D Thomas	1.37
1957	Ellen Grainger	11.7	B Rees	10.8	S Barrett	1.38
1958	Liz Parsons	12.1	M A Steer	11.3	Linda Hughes	1.45
1959	Liz Parsons	11.5	M Dewar	11.4	L. Parkes	1.40
1960	J Cutter	12.6	R C Jones	11.3	P Dunn	1.40
1961	J Cutter	11.7	Isabel Barden	10.4	Marilyn Matthews	1.45
1962	G J Willis	12.1	Kathryn Hutchinson	10.6	Pamela Guppy	1.45
1963	Linda Davies	12.3	Susan Hollett	11.0	Pat McDiarmid	1.34
1964	G R Wien	12.3	Barbara Farrah	12.1	L Ededuwa	1.33
1965	G R Wien	12.5	R Thomas	12.7	E Claesson	1.32
1966	Gillian Sudbury	12.0	A Skirving	12.4	June Hirst	1.47
1967	Patrice Shiels	11.5	A Skirving	12.4	Christine Jones	1.42
1968	Michelle Smith	12.0	Angela Morgan	12.2	Pamela Thomas	1.32
1969	Valerie Davies	13.4	M Black	12.7	Susan Beddows	1.42
1970	Carlie Morgan	12.7	Annette Thomas	14.8	Jackie Dilloway	1.38
1971	Elizabeth Conlon	13.2	Wendy Peterson	12.6	Jane Scrase	1.40
1972	Ceri Jenkins	12.8	L Parsons	12.7	J Collins	1.42
1973	Ceri Jenkins	13.2	Phyllis Lynham	13.3	Viv Rothera	1.55
1974	Carmen Smart	13.0	Phyllis Lynham	12.1	Jane Watkins	1.40
1975	R Davies	13.4	Alyson Hourihan	12.4	Ruanda Davies	1.50
1976	Debbie Perry	12.9	Sharon Whyte	11.8	Ruanda Davies	1.57
1977	Karen Taylor	12.2	Catrin Daniels	12.2	Pam Walker	1.55
1978	Jocelyn Peets	12.7	Jane Buttriss	11.5	Pam Walker	1.58
1979	Dawn Oliver	12.2	Lynn Parry	11.7	Julia Charlton	1.70
1980	Helen Miles	12.2	Julia Charlton	11.8	Julia Charlton	1.75
1981	Helen Miles	12.5	Alyson Evans	12.1	Val Adams	1.50
1982	Jane Bradbeer	12.9	Sheila Evelyn	12.0	Jane Shepherd	1.60
1983	Jane Bradbeer	13.1	Lisa Griffiths	13.1	Jackie Barber	1.55
1984	Nicola Short	12.6	Marguerite Davies	12.1	Carol Whiteway	1.55
1985	Catherine Allen	13.25	Emma Pearce	12.73	Amanda Davies	1.50
1986	Sonia Reay	12.7	Emma Pearce	11.7	Lea Haggett	1.70
1987	Emma Todd	12.75	Bethan Edwards	11.71	Anna Clode	1.51
1988	Lisa Armstrong	12.3	Mari Prys Jones	11.5	Bev Green	1.61
1989	Sara Owen	13.0	Anna Proctor	12.0	Susannah Filce	1.65
1990	Sian Bradshaw	13.2	Emma Hanson	11.9	Krissy Owen	1.65
1991	Sara Colton	13.3	Jody Lester	11.8	Kath Evans	1.64
1992	Stacy Rodd	12.9	Louise Dennis	12.2	Beth James	1.48
1993	Hannah Paines	12.4	Sarah Newman	11.9	Non Williams	1.54
1994	Gail Evans	12.7	Amy Bergiers	11.4	Lisa Thompson	1.50
1995	Debbie Morgan	12.53	Sarah Lane (Tor)	11.79	Lisa Thompson	1.60
1996	Erica Burfoot	12.57	Lauren McLoughlin	11.7	Lara Richards	1.45
1997	Alex Bick	12.74	Lauren McLoughlin	11.68	Rebecca Jones	1.53
1998	Danielle Selley	12.49	Danielle Selley	11.06	Elizabeth Callicott	1.49
1999	Jo Hodge	12.84	Louise Robinson	12.35	Bethan Price	1.50
2000	Danielle Barker	13.00	Heather Jones	11.57	Elen Davies	1.55

	150y / 150m / 200m		**800 metres**		**1500 metres**	
1966	Diane Chipps	18.1				
1967	Patrice Shiels	18.7				
1968	Michelle Smith	18.0				
1969	Valerie Davies	20.6				

1970	Carlie Morgan	20.7				
1971	Elizabeth Conlon	27.6	Ann Morris	2:20.3		
1972	Ceri Jenkins	27.3	Jackie Hulbert	2:26.9	Jackie Hulbert	4:59.1
1973	Ceri Jenkins	27.8	Jackie Hulbert	2:26.1	Jackie Hulbert	5:15.7
1974	Heather Evans	26.7	Angela Hartley	2:30.0	Elin Jones	5:13.1
1975	Ruanda Davies	27.2	Kirsty McDermott	2:19.9	Susan Lewis	4:59.0
1976	Carol Nicholas	26.9	Susan Lewis	2:21.6	Susan Lewis	5:00.2
1977	Karen Taylor	25.6	Bethan Thomas	2:23.2	Gillian Irvine	4:58.7
1978	Jocelyn Peets	25.9	Louise Copp	2:24.7	Kathy Williams	4:52.2
1979	Lynn Parry	26.1	Claire Paisley	2:26.5	Jacqueline Thomas	5:07.2
1980	Helen Miles	26.0	Jackie Thomas	2:20.5	Ann Parry	4:59.0
1981	Helen Miles	26.7	Debbie Crowley	2:25.5	Debbie Crowley	4:54.6
1982	Jane Bradbeer	26.2	Karen Whitehouse	2:21.8	Natalie Wood	4:55.5
1983	Jane Bradbeer	26.7	Karen Whitehouse	2:25.6	Clare Pugh	4:46.6
1984	Carol Whiteway	27.3	Ceri Burnell	2:19.73	Ceri Burnell	4:54.3
1985	Lisa Randall	27.24	Ceri Thomas	2:23.98	Lisa Carthew	4:54.10
1986	Sonia Reay	26.3	Julie Garrett	2:17.4	Julie Garrett	4:50.60
1987	Emma Todd	26.35	Julie Garrett	2:14.64	Mari Prys Jones	4:48.3
1988	Lisa Armstrong	25.4	Mari Prys Jones	2:21.5	Mari Prys Jones	4:59.6
1989	Bethan Griffiths	26.3	Claire Edwards	2:17.53	Claire Edwards	4:55.7
1990	Emma Jones	26.7	Kathryn Bright	2:18.7	Angharad Howells	4:57.0
1991	Sara Colton	26.9	Kate Williams	2:26.4	Angharad Howells	4:56.0
1992	Rhiannon Ridgeway	26.4	Charlotte Reeks	2:19.0	Emma Turner	4:56.6
1993	Charlotte Reeks	26.3	Charlotte Reeks	2:24.1	Dunya Hurley	4:48.2
1994	Gail Evans	26.1	Sarah Mead	2:20.4	Nicola Knapp	4:53.8
1995	Rhian Cains	26.49	Donna Porazinski	2:19.56	Georgina Parnell	4:55.90
1996	Erica Burfoot	25.28	Claire Woolley	2:24.68	Teresa Penhorwood	4:53.98
1997	Alex Bick	26.44	Gemma Thomas	2:23.41	Katie Greenwood	5:02.96
1998	Aimee John	26.17	Elise Taylor	2:19.15	Jenna Evans	4:50.24
1999	Paula Williams	26.68	Gemma Jones	2:21.91	Amanda Jones	4:54.03
2000	Danielle Barker	26.64	Leila James	2:29.12	Bethan Strange	5:04.4

	Long Jump		**Discus**		**Javelin**	
1952	P Phillips	4.44				
1953	P Nicholas	4.42				
1954	Sally Jones	4.77				
1955	J Jones	4.80				
1956	G Garenham	4.60				
1957	G Davies/G Griffiths	4.53	K M Williams	25.86	Rita Everett	25.46
1958	Monica Zeraschi	5.37	M Davies	27.08	C Benfield	19.53
1959	not known		not known		not known	
1960	R L Jones	4.64	S Tatchell	28.33	R Jones	28.21
1961	Tanya Alcock	5.14	E Robb	25.72	S Davies	26.13
1962	M C Meaney		Hazel Andow		E Jones	29.34
1963	M C Meaney	4.34	Hazel Andow	31.14	C Godwins	23.10
1964	E Coombs	4.50	D Williams	26.50	L James	25.62
1965	Leslie Black	4.65	A Giles	18.88	J Thomas	24.17
1966	Sharon McParlin	5.08	Janet Wady	23.82	Janet Wady	31.76
1967	J Crawford	4.65	Lynette Harding	23.78	Mary David	26.22
1968	Michelle Smith	4.79	M Jones	18.39	Margaret Rainbow	25.36
1969	A J Collins	4.46	Delyth Prothero	25.11	Susan James	31.14
1970	Alison Pick	4.84	Ann Rice	22.68	Susan James	32.40
1971	Venissa Head	4.71	Debbie Chapman	21.16	Yvonne Williams	29.10
1972	Ceri Jenkins	5.14	Cheryl Watson	22.18	D Beere	25.75
1973	Gillian Humphries	4.75	Coral Maybank	27.30	Alyson Hadfield	25.32
1974	Chris Romanin	4.82	Alyson Hourihan	29.16	Debbie Morris	26.84
1975	N Hopgood	4.75	Alyson Hourihan	30.38	Alyson Hourihan	29.02
1976	Debbie Perry	5.08	Jo Tubb	24.64	Jo Tubb	33.60
1977	A Niblett	4.37	Tracy Edwards	24.36	Tracy Canty	25.20
1978	Paula Thomas	5.30	Jackie Richardson	28.22	Julie Tayler	28.72
1979	Karen Hawkins	5.32	Sian Phillips	27.16	Julie Tayler	38.34
1980	Julia Charlton	5.08	Delyth Evans	22.98	Penny Miller	25.82
1981	Tracy Pearce	4.88	Lisa Angulatta	24.81	Penny Miller	30.98
1982	Jane Shepherd	5.20	Helen Poole	22.58	Sheila Evelyn	27.90
1983	Nicola Short	4.58	Clare Annetts	26.16	Catherine Gunn	33.52
1984	Nicola Short	5.23	Frances Burton	25.10	Sarah Phillips	27.50
1985	Nerys Evans	4.85	Elizabeth Bradbeer	30.26	Sarah Phillips	31.72
1986	Caroline Mills	5.04	Hayley Hartson	26.90	Joelle Hill	31.84
1987	Bethan Edwards	5.29	Hayley Hartson	30.84	Elizabeth Randle	37.34
1988	Lisa Armstrong	5.33	Ruth Mason	30.30	Anna Morgan	30.26
1989	Marie Humphries	4.94	Vicky Todd	27.26	Joanne Evans	34.68

1990	Leanne Beckett	4.92	Stephanie Codd	27.04	Amanda Jervis	29.70
1991	Karina Williams	4.87	Philippa Roles	29.88	Jo Griffiths	29.58
1992	Elinor Lamerton	5.34	Philippa Roles	40.66	Dee Groves	29.02
1993	Gemma Jones	5.10	Yvette Roberts	27.02	Karen Hayward	26.48
1994	Kristy Carlisle	5.06	Rebecca Roles	34.70	Clare Lockwood	29.04
1995	Aimee Cutler	5.03	Laura Eastwood	29.66	Alison Eardley	24.30
1996	Aimee Cutler	5.12	Kate Eveleigh	25.38	Adrienne Harvey	26.42
1997	Amy Pearson	4.89	Laura Douglas	27.70	Ffion Jones	27.40
1998	Melissa Harries	5.28	Louise Finlay	25.80	Charlotte Rees	30.71
1999	Sophie Newington	4.75	Mair Jones	23.42	Sara Siggery	29.75
2000	Sally Peake	5:31	Ella Newington	20.69	Natalie Griffiths	29.34

	Shot Put		**Pentathlon**	
1960	N Davies	09.69		
1961	T Evans	09.40		
1962	Sandra Murphy	10.74		
1963	Hazel Andow	10.35		
1964	L James	09.26		
1965	G Newton	09.69		
1966	J C Jones	08.25		
1967	Lynette Harding	08.53		
1968	Linda Richards	08.43		
1969	Amanda Farquharson	09.51		
1970	Ann Rice	08.65		
1971	Venissa Head	09.79		
1972	Debbie Chapman	08.73		
1973	Debbie Morris	09.51	Viv Rothera	2822
1974	Janet Phillips	10.44	Alyson Hourihan	2509
1975	Karen Glover	08.77	Alyson Hourihan	2685
1976	M Arapovic	07.98	Rachel Freke	2830
1977	Jayne Richardson	08.85	Alice Simmons	2517
1978	Amanda Horrex	09.94	Jane Buttriss	2739
1979	Sonia Woods	08.72	Kerry Crook	2951
1980	Delyth Evans	11.53	Julia Charlton	3438
1981	Lisa Angulatta	11.57	Val Adams	2371
1982	Andrea Munkley	10.42	Jane Shepherd	3184
1983	Kerrie Davies	09.18	Jane Shepherd	3680
1984	Sharon Fletcher	09.11	Sharon Fletcher	2831
1985	Amanda Davies	09.39	Amanda Wale	2436
1986	Samantha King	07.75	Laura Southwood	2613
1987	Sarah Young	10.63	Bethan Edwards	2539
1988	Rachel Masterman	11.10	Bev Green	2626
1989	Vicky Todd	10.00	Susannah Filce	3018
1990	Krissy Owen	09.75	Krissy Owen	2615
1991	Louise Davies	10.26	Teresa Andrews	2621
1992	Philippa Roles	12.43	Rachel Stannard	2306
1993	Bethan Thomas	09.39	Beth Davies	2614
1994	Nicola Parsons	09.22	Kelly Moreton	2757
1995	Carys Parry	09.77	Lisa Thompson	2875
1996	Kate Eveleigh	10.05	Stephanie Little	2630
1997	Laura Douglas	11.33	not held	
1998	Louise Finlay	10.26	Melissa Harris	2792
1999	Mair Jones	09.51	Faye Harding	2537
2000	Vicky Lloyd	09.55	Faye Harding	2991

Under 13 Girls (Minor Girls)

	100 metres		**200 metres**		**800 metres**	
1975	Jane Bradbury	14.4	Jane Bradbury	30.3	J Hopper	2:36.8
1976	Tina Cleaver	13.2	Tina Cleaver	28.6	Caroline Devereux	2:30.0
1977	Lisa Thorne	13.4	Lisa Thorne	28.2	Kate Roderick	2:33.1
1978	Mannon Richards	13.4	Debbie Reynolds	27.3	L Reed-Smith	2:32.5
1979	Clare Tamblyn	13.2	Clare Tamblyn	27.6	Sarah Morgan	2:38.5
1980	Heather Brown	13.1	Heather Brown	28.6	Marian Jenkins	2:33.3
1981	Jane Bradbeer	13.5	Jane Bradbeer	27.6	Jane Shepherd	2:31.9
1982	Colette Lewis	13.7	Colette Lewis	28.0	Glenda James	2:36.9
1983	Jane Davies	14.0	Jane Davies	28.7	Lisa Carthew	2:32.8
1984	Nicola Evans	13.2	Vicky Grace	28.9	Julie Garrett	2:32.20
1985	Emma Todd	12.98	Vicky Grace	26.88	Julie Garrett	2:21.96
1986	Nicola Grady	13.2	Nicola Grady	27.5	Kerry Jones	2:30.0
1987	Martine Woodward	13.23	Joanne James	27.66	Lynn Gallagher	2:31.22

1988	Joanne James	13.0	Joanne James	27.1	Emma Jones	2:28.6
1989	Ceri Stephens	13.5	Ceri Stephens	27.5	Rachel Jones	2:27.39
1990	Emma Thomas	13.5	Emma Thomas	27.9	Yvonne Evans	2:29.2
1991	Rhiannon Ridgeway	13.6	Rhiannon Ridgeway	28.5	Charlotte Reeks	2:27.4
1992	Ceri McDermott	13.8	Ceri McDermott	28.2	Amanda Pritchard	2:30.3
1993	Emma Staples	13.2	Emma Staples	27.6	L Thompson=G Mounsey	2:33.6
1994	Anna McGovern	13.5	Aimee Cutler	28.3	Gemma Mounsey	2:34.9
1995	Sarah Lane (Swan)	13.22	Sarah Lane (Swan)	27.17	Kelly Hall	2:31.98
1996	Danielle Selley	13.32	Aimee John	28.49	Amy Holloway	2:32.77
1997	Jo Hodge	13.07	Jo Hodge	27.26	Lucy Thomas	2:23.23
1998	Sophie Newington	13.54	Faye Harding	28.14	Faye Harding	2:29.79
1999	Danielle Barker	13.18	Danielle Barker	27.90	Lisa Lanini	2:26.6
2000	Victoria Morgan	13.90	Lisa Lanini	27.76	Lisa Lanini	2:25.59

	1500 metres		**75m / 70m Hurdles**		**High Jump**	
1975	M Turberville	5:27.6	H Andrew	14.6	P Mills	1.20
1976	Sharron Davies	5:19.9	C Daley	16.1	J Hallsworth	1.23
1977	Louise Silva	5:05.9	Sandra Oakley	13.1	A Young	1.30
1978	Jacqueline Thomas	5:14.0	S Feewtrell	13.3	Kathryn Evans	1.41
1979	Cath Cornish	5:20.8	Kath Thomas	13.8	Kathryn Evans	1.50
1980	Clare Pugh	5:19.4	Elizabeth Scarf	13.6	Claire Lucas	1.35
1981	Clare Pugh	5:04.5	Julie Price	15.1	Jane Shepherd	1.45
1982	Ceri Burnell	5:09.3	Sharon Fletcher	13.8	Sharon Fletcher	1.35
1983	Julie Crowley	5:11.1	Kirsty Shepherd	13.8	Kirsty Shepherd	1.32
1984	Joanne Parsons	5:07.1	Emma Pearce	13.9	Xania Llewellyn	1.25
1985	Caroline Thomas	5:05.95	Laura Southwood	12.53	Laura Southwood	1.41
1986	Kerry Jones	5:06.47	Vicky Harrison	11.8	Bev Green	1.40
1987	Joanne Elward	5:08.5	Anna Proctor	11.88	Katrina Bartlett	1.38
1988	Cathy Davies	5:19.7	Joanne James	11.5	Philippa Barker	1.30
1989	Angharad Howells	5:08.6	Emma Jones	12.1	Kathryn Evans	1.43
1990	Kathryn Jones	5:07.1	Louise Dennis	11.7	Karina Williams	1.30
1991	Heledd Gruffudd	5:13.1	Suzanne Kimber	12.2	Caroline Hogg	1.40
1992	Catrin Davies	4:58.8	Sarah Newman	11.8	Caroline Hogg	1.47
1993	Rachel Fry	5:20.4	Sarah Lane (Torf)	12.1	Lisa Thompson	1.46
1994	Rachel Fry	5:11.2	Stacy King	11.8	Stephanie Little	1.30
1995	Claire Evans	5:17.64	Lauren McLoughlin	11.84	Lara Richards	1.45
1996	Gemma Thomas	5:10.56	Danielle Selley	11.7	Mary McKinley	1.40
1997	Fiona Harrison	5:17.59	Jessica Wilstead	12.8	Laura Thomas	1.25
1998	Natasha Harry	5:22.08	Claire Jones	12.90	Nicola Thomas	1.30
1999	Ann Marie Tucker	5:23.60	Catie Povey	12.41	Cathy Bradbury	1.45
2000	Emma Roberts	5:23.91	Rhian Ashford	13.1	Rhian Ashford	1.36

	Long Jump		**Shot Put**		**Pentathlon**	
1975	H Andrew	4.15	Jane Bradbury	6.78	H Andrew	1961
1976	M Green	4.45	Jayne Richardson	6.76	G Moyle	1857
1977	Karen Hawkins	4.63	Helen Parker	6.61	Sandra Oakley	2211
1978	Karen Taylor	4.28	Kerry Crook	6.89	Kerry Crook	2524
1979	Kathryn Evans	4.72	Rhian Williams	6.14	Deborah Hopkins	1870
1980	Helen Clayton	4.27	Claire Lucas	7.74	Elizabeth Scarf	2803
1981	Suzanne Barrett	4.35	Lynne Richardson	6.70	Jane Shepherd	2851
1982	Nicola Short	4.57	Sharon Fletcher	6.92	Sharon Fletcher	2258
1983	Kirsty Shepherd	4.28	Elizabeth Bradbeer	6.54	Amanda Horton	1659
1984	Caroline Mills	4.20	Karen Williams	7.21	Karen Williams	2066
1985	Joanna Howell	4.19	Sara Lewis	7.49	Laura Southwood	2062
1986	Bev Green	4.40	Rachel Masterman	8.99	Bev Green	2080
1987	Anna Proctor	4.36	Vicky Todd	7.54	Anna Proctor	1981
1988	Rebecca Lewis	4.09	Donna James	8.00	Jo James	1955
1989	Emma Jones	4.56	Louise Davies	8.20	Emma Jones	2027
1990	Elinor Lamerton	4.68	Philippa Roles	8.61	Emma Thomas	1725
1991	Tamsin Proctor	4.34	Bethan Thomas	9.22	Angela Griffiths	1839
1992	Ceri McDermott	4.62	Catrin Evans	8.06	Catherine James	2063
1993	Sarah Lane (Torf)	4.82	Helen Thomas	8.32	Emma Staples	2442
1994	Aimee Cutler	4.82	Kelly Ridgeway	9.62	Stephanie Little	2042
1995	Sarah Lane (Swan)	4.48	Nicola Crocker	8.81	Lauren McLoughlin	2127
1996	Danielle Selley	4.35	Louise Finlay	9.98	Danielle Selley	2250
1997	Gemma Tovey	4.01	Alicia Coulman	8.92	not held	
1998	Sophie Newington	4.30	Laura Hudson	9.42	Elizabeth Nasrat	1731
1999	Danielle Barker	4.09	Llinos Jones	8.65	Cathy Bradbury	1958
2000	Rachel Conway	4.50	Beth Spiller	8.38	Rhian Ashford	1769

	Discus		Javelin	
1975	J Darlow	19.40	Caroline Williams	09.26
1976	D Roberts	16.38	A Wilson	19.84
1977	Claire Davidson	20.54	Julie Tayler	22.82
1978	not held		Jenny Smith	21.38
1979	Rhian Williams	15.08	Paula Tayler	14.68
1980	Claire Lucas	16.58	Sallyanne Short	14.68
1981	Gail Smith	15.38	Sarah Nicholas	17.08
1982	Elizabeth Bradbeer	15.73	Elizabeth Bradbeer	16.72
1983	Elizabeth Bradbeer	15.94	Elizabeth Bradbeer	19.46
1984	Louise Richards	16.12	Xania Llewellyn	18.00
1985	Nicola Grattidge	18.06	Nicola Smith	19.06
1986	Anna Lewis	16.68	Anna Morgan	21.56
1987	Vicky Todd	19.32	Emily Steele	22.28
1988	Kelly Jenkins	17.36	Jody Evans	20.10
1989	Sarah Johnson	17.46	Joanne Griffiths	19.78
1990	Philippa Roles	24.50	Philippa Roles	22.88
1991	event discontinued		event discontinued	

Welsh Championships Results (Cross-Country) All Groups

SENIOR MEN'S CHAMPIONSHIPS – FIRST THREE

Note that the event in 1940 was unofficial and no WCCA medals were awarded

1894	Hugh Fairlamb (Roath)	49:40	A E Turner (Roath)	50:10	R A Blandy (Roath)	50:55
1895	Harry Cullum (Roath)	50:32	Egbert Fairlamb (Roath)		A T Shackell (Roath)	
1896	Harry Cullum (Cardiff H)	44:10	Hugh Fairlamb (Roath)	45:49	R C Brookes (Cardiff H)	46:04
1897	A E Turner (Newport)	44:29	Egbert Fairlamb (Roath)	45:14	R C Brookes (Cardiff H)	45:40
1898	R C Brookes (Cardiff H)	58:41	A E Turner (Newport)	59:34	W S Jones (Cdf H)	59:55
1899	J G Lee (Newport)	46:02	S Hancock (Roath)	46:40	A Palmer (Newport)	47:27
1900	A Palmer (Newport)	40:22	S Hancock (Roath)	41:10	T W White (Roath)	41:20
1901	A Palmer (Newport)	46:55	A E Turner (Newport)	47:22	G White (Cardiff H)	47:33
1902	A E Turner (Newport)	37:26	T W White (Roath)	37:43	A Palmer (Newport)	37:55
1903	A E Turner (Newport)	38:53	A Palmer (Newport)	39:18	R B Pugh (Newport)	39:19
1904	E Francis (Cathays H)	45:52	W G Bradbury (Newport)	46:00	D G Harris (Newport)	46:07
1905	E Francis (Cathays H)	36:40	E O Price (Newport)	ntt	R G Davies (Newport)	ntt
1906	Tommy Arthur (Newport)	39:08	E O Price (Newport)	39:22	E G Ace (Newport)	39:44
1907	Tommy Arthur (Newport)	48:00	E O Price (Newport)	48:48	Eddie O'Donnell (Barry)	49:06
1908	Tommy Arthur (Newport)	41:40	Rhys Evans (Roath)	41:50	D H Griffiths (Newport)	42:10
1909	Tommy Arthur (Newport)	48:59	Rhys Evans (Roath)	49:29	Ben Christmas (Roath)	50:00
1910	J F Iles (Roath)	57:47	Ernest Paul (Cwmbran)	57:57	A S Wilson (Abertillery)	58:20
1911	Ernest Paul (Cwmbran)	56:23	W Herring (Cwmbran)	56:34	A S Wilson (Newport)	56:44
1912	Tom Miles (Cwmbran)	57:02	Ernest Paul (Cwmbran)	57:33	A Herring (Cwmbran)	58:09
1913	Edgar Stead (Cwmbran)	58:05	A Herring (Cwmbran)	58:10	Ernest Paul (Cwmbran)	58:19
1914	Cliff Price (Newport)	57:42	P Waters (Cwmbran)	59:10	A S Wilson (Newport)	59:33
1920	Tom Miles (Newport)	53:34	Ernie Thomas (Cwmbran)	55:07	Ivor Wintle (Newport)	56:11
1921	Ernie Thomas (Cwmbran)	49:12	Sam Judd (Newport)	49:47	Gwyn Morgan (Cwm H)	50:47
1922	Ernie Thomas (Newport)	39:50	Gwyn Morgan (Cwm H)	40:55	E J Davies (Roath)	41:20
1923	Jim Edwards (Newport)	43:32	D J P Richards (Newport)	43:40	Danny Phillips (Newport)	44:11
1924	Ernie Thomas (Newport)	46:38	B D Hammond (Newport)	47:55	D J P Richards (Newport)	48:11
1925	D J P Richards (Newport)	42:18	Ernie Thomas (Newport)	42:21	B D Hammond (Newport)	43:58
1926	Ernie Thomas (Newport)	45:17	Gwyn Morgan (Cwm H)	46:23	B D Hammond (Newport)	46:25
1927	Ernie Thomas (Cwmbran)	53:53	Ted Hopkins (Roath)	54:52	J Hughes (Pontnewydd)	55:06
1928	D J P Richards (Univ Wales)	50:52	J Prosser (Cwmbran)	52:05	Ernie Thomas (Cwmbran)	52:06
1929	D J P Richards (Univ Wales)	37:21	Danny Phillips (Cwmbran)	37:37	Ernie Thomas (Cwmbran	38:28
1930	Danny Phillips (Cwmbran)	45:13	J Prosser (Cwmbran)	45:28	T H Timbrell (Swan Vall)	46:41
1931	Danny Phillips (Cwmbran)	50:42	Ernie Thomas (Cwmbran)	51:28	A S Stone (Pontypool)	52:09
1932	Harry Gallivan (Pontnewydd)	44:35	A Harvey (Cwmbran)	44:59	Danny Phillips (Cwmbran)	45:20
1933	Ernie Thomas (Cwmbran)	56:58	A S Stone (Pontypool)	57:01	Ivor Brown (Llanbradach)	57:25
1934	Bill Matthews (Penrhys)	52:59	Harry Gallivan (Pontnewydd)	53:17	E L Adams (Mansfield)	54:10
1935	Harry Gallivan (Cwmbran)	50:39	Len Tongue (Newport)	51:39	Tom Richards (Pontnewydd)	51:45
1936	Harry Gallivan (Cwmbran)	56:29	Bill Matthews (Penrhys)	57:01	A Williams (Sutton)	57:37
1937	Bill Matthews (Penrhys)	50:00	Harry Gallivan (Cwmbran)	50:03	Ivor Brown (Mitcham)	50:29
1938	Bill Matthews (Penrhys)	49:50	Harry Gallivan (Cwmbran)	50:02	Ivor Brown (Mitcham)	50:37
1939	Dillan Hier (RAF)	50:38	Bill Matthews (Penrhys)	51:01	George Fox (Mitcham)	51:21
1940	S I Griffiths (Newport)	29:22	Howard Davies (Neath)	29:30	Bramwell Baldwin (Roath)	29:35
1946	Dillan Hier (RAF)	60:04	Eddie Cooper (Roath)	60:32	Tom Richards (S London)	61:03
1947	Ivor Lloyd (Newport)	48:55	Bernard Baldwin (Roath)	49:09	Eddie Cooper (Roath)	49:36
1948	Jim Alford (Roath)	47:31	Maldwyn White (Birchfield)	47:46	Eric Williams (Mitcham)	48:03
1949	John Andrews (Finchley)	62:43	Pat Wallace (Newport)		Eric Williams (Mitcham)	
1950	Anthony Noonan (Watford)	51:50	Doug Rees (Portsmouth)	52:36	Pat Wallace (Newport)	52:40
1951	Tom Richards (S London)	61:21	John Edwards (Carm YM)	61:45	Doug Rees (Portsmouth)	62:07
1952	Norman Wilson (RAF)	55:34	Tom Wood (Newport)	56:54	Doug Rees (Portsmouth)	57:25
1953	Norman Wilson (RAF)	46:10	Ken Huckle (Roath)	46:42	Doug Rees (Portsmouth)	46:55
1954	Lyn Bevan (Newport)	56:06	David Richards (Roath)	56:13	Phil Morgan (S London)	56:28
1955	Lyn Bevan (Newport)	48:25	John Disley (S London)	49:17	Ken Huckle (Roath)	49:40
1956	Chris Suddaby (Oxford Univ)	49:06	Ken Huckle (Roath)	49:34	Bill Butcher (Birchfield)	50:05

1957	Norman Horrell (Rhonda V)	52:01	R Morgan (Oxford Univ)	52:26	Tony Pumfrey (Coventry)	52:44
1958	John Merriman (Watford)	50:55	David Richards (Poly H)	51:44	Norman Horrell (Roath)	52:00
1959	David Richards (Poly H)	51:15	Norman Horrell (Roath)	51:44	John Merriman (Watford)	51:54
1960	David Richards (Poly H)	49:36	Bob Roath (Walton)	50:52	Roy Profitt (Devonport)	51:10
1961	Norman Horrell (Roath)	52:46	Roger HarrisonJones (Pemb)	53:54	David Richards (Poly H)	54:12
1962	Norman Horrell (Roath)	50:50	Robert Williams (TVH)	51:12	Roger HarrisonJones (Pemb)	51:38
1963	Bob Roath (Walton)	35:32	Norman Horrell (Roath)	35:32	Brian Jeffs (RAF)	35:59
1964	Tom Edmunds (Gilwern)	37:44	Hedydd Davies (Birchfield)	37:45	Tony Harris (Mitcham)	39:00
1965	Tom Edmunds (Gilwern)	38:46	Chris Loosely (Aberystwyth)	39:05	Hedydd Davies (Birchfield)	39:15
1966	Hedydd Davies (TVH)	45:42	Chris Loosely (Aberystwyth)	46:22	Roy Mack (Birchfield)	46:39
1967	Cyril Leigh (Wigan)	39:18	John Godding (Birchgrove)	40:02	Viv Blackwell (RAF)	40:16
1968	Alan Joslyn (Poly H)	34:54	Alan Jones (Kent)	35:41	Tony Simmons (Luton)	35:51
1969	Tony Simmons (Luton)	37:17	Malcolm Thomas (TVH)	37:27	Alan Joslyn (Poly H)	37:34
1970	Malcolm Thomas (TVH)	38:48	Dave Walker (Worcester		Tony Simmons (Luton)	
1971	Malcolm Thomas (TVH)	34:08	Tony Ashton (Reading)	34:38	Bernie Plain (Cardiff)	34:45
1972	Malcolm Thomas (TVH)	38:10	Bernie Plain (Cardiff)	39:30	Bernie Hayward (Cardiff)	39:38
1973	Malcolm Thomas (TVH)	38:42	Bernie Plain (Cardiff)	39:04	Dave Hopkins (Newport)	39:08
1974	John Jones (Windsor)	38:57	Dave Hopkins (Newport)	39:02	Steve Slocombe (Cardiff)	39:34
1975	Steve Gibbons (Swansea)	39:04	Clive Thomas (TVH)	39:15	Dic Evans (Cardiff)	
1976	Bernie Plain (Cardiff)	36:47	Micky Morris (Cwmbran)	36:57	Dave Hopkins (Newport)	37:07
1977	Steve Jones (RAF)	40:28	Bernie Plain (Cardiff)	40:38	Fred Bell (Herc Wimbledon)	40:46
1978	Steve Jones (RAF)	39:22	Dave Hopkins (Newport)	39:41	Dennis Fowles (Cardiff)	39:52
1979	Steve Jones (RAF)	37:47	Roger Hackney (Birm Un)	37:56	Peter Baker (Shaftesbury)	38:24
1980	Steve Jones (RAF)	40:35	= Tony Simmons (Luton)	40:35	David James (Cardiff)	40:50
1981	Steve Jones (Bristol)	35:10	Tony Blackwell (Wolves)	36:08	Chris Buckley (Westbury)	36:23
1982	Roger Hackney (AFD)	35:19	Steve Jones (Bristol)	35:22	Chris Buckley (Westbury)	36:08
1983	Steve Jones (Newport)	37:34	Tony Blackwell (Wolves)	38:43	David James (Cardiff)	38:47
1984	Steve Jones (Newport)	39:10	Chris Buckley (Westbury)	40:04	Nigel Adams (Swansea)	40:12
1985	Steve Jones (Newport)	33:28	Chris Buckley (Westbury)	34:00	Kenny Davies (Newport)	34:22
1986	Steve Jones (Newport)	36:43	Paul Wheeler (Les Croupiers)	37:09	Nigel Adams (Swansea)	37:45
1987	Mike Bishop (Staffs M)	39:04	Steve Jones (Newport)	39:30	Ieuan Ellis (Newport)	40:02
1988	Nigel Adams (Swansea)	40:30	Eddie Conway (Cardiff)	40:36	Paul Wheeler (Cardiff)	40:51
1989	Nigel Adams (Swansea)	43:35	Steve Jones (Newport)	44:15	Ieuan Ellis (Newport)	45:10
1990	Eddie Conway (Cardiff)	39:36	Ieuan Ellis (Newport)	39:40	Nigel Adams (Swansea)	39:47
1991	Ian Hamer (Swansea)	32:33	Nigel Adams (Swansea)	32:47	Jon Hooper (Cardiff)	33:20
1992	Ian Hamer (Swansea)	34:29	Steve Jones (Newport)	34:41	Mark Healy (Lliswerry)	35:39
1993	Justin Hobbs (Cardiff)	37:06	Ian Hamer (Swansea)	38:20	Austin Davies (Brecon)	38:26
1994	Justin Hobbs (Cardiff)	40:06	Christian Stephenson (Card)	40:29	Steve Knight (Cardiff)	40:44
1995	Christian Stephenson (Card)	40:49	Nick Comerford (Cardiff)	42:28	Colin Jones (Eryri)	42:33
1996	Christian Stephenson (Card)	36:53	Tony Graham (Newport)	37:18	Martin Rees (Swansea)	37:20
1997	Christian Stephenson (Card)	37:23	Steve Knight (Cardiff)	38:57	Andres Jones (Cardiff)	39:03
1998	Nick Comerford (Cardiff)	37:46	Jamie Lewis (Swansea)	38:00	Christian Stephenson (Card)	38:37
1999	Ian Pierce (Tipton)	39:25	Andres Jones (Cardiff)	39:52	Colin Donnelly (Eryri)	40:03
2000	Nick Comerford (Cardiff)	40:30	Andres Jones (Cardiff)	40:35	Nathaniel Lane (Cardiff)	41:54

SEVEN MILES / SIX MILES / 10K SENIOR MEN'S CHAMPIONSHIPS – FIRST THREE

Initially this was a barring race, whereby all Welsh Cross Country Internationals and the members of the winning senior teams were not allowed to run. This restriction was removed in 1969 and from that date all athletes with a Welsh qualification were allowed to run. The distance changed to 6 miles in 1962 and 10K in 1972. Event was held in January/February until 1968 when the date was switched to November/December. This means that in 1968, 2 events were held but the December event has been classed as coming under the 1968/69 season and so appears as 1969. The event was discontinued after 1991 because the fixture list was restructured.

1954	David Richards (Roath)	35:00	K J Phipps (Newport)	36:21	Jack Wingfield (Roath)	36:24
1955	Joe Yates (Mond)	44:25	George Morgan (Roath)	44:32	Tony Rathbone (Newport)	45:16
1956	Peter J Bowden (Bristol)	38:38	Ken Flowers (Abergavenny)	39:40	P Sadler (RAF)	40:90
1957	Bill Hancock (Swansea AC)	35:00	Jack Wingfield (Card Univ)	35:10	Haydn Tawton (Roath)	35:12
1958	M Palmer (RAF Valley)	42:39	K Jones (Neath H)	42:49	W Thomas (Roath)	44:12
1959	Billy Perkins (Newport)	28:20	Jim O'Brien (P Talbot YM)	28:41	G Barrell (Cheltenham)	28:44
1960	Brian Jeffs (Essex B)	36:20	Dai Thomas (Birchgrove)	37:45	D Llewellyn (Newport)	37:51
1961	Jim O'Brien (Port Talbot)	40:31	George Mathiudis (Newport)	41:02	Ron Cullum (Carmarthen)	41:15
1962	Tom Edmunds (Gilwern)	34:43	Jim O'Brien (Port Talbot)	35:37	Viv Blackwell (RAF)	36:02
1963	John Collins (Pontypool)	29:58	Winston Bradley (Gilwern)	30:33	Brian Griffiths (Roath)	30:39
1964	Tom Edmunds (Gilwern)	31:45	Bill Stitfall (Birchgrove)	32:15	John Collins (Pontypool)	32:42
1965	Chris Loosley (Aberystwyth)	34:01	Brian Griffiths (Roath)	34:23	John Collins (Pontypool)	34:29
1966	Ron McAndrew (Wigan)	35:44	Brian Griffiths (Roath)	35:50	Bernie Plain (Birchgrove)	36:30
1967	Adrian Aylett (Gilwern)	29:38	Will Bradley (Gilwern)	30:03	Brian Griffiths (Roath)	30:32
1968	Jeff Kirby (Roath)	35:27	John Ingram (Birchgrove)	35:58	Brian Griffiths (Roath)	36:13
1969	Malcolm Thomas (TVH)	32:33	Brian Hutton (Luton)	34:14	Mike Rowland (Newport)	34:25
1970	Bernie Plain (Cardiff)	32:22	Hugh Richards (Shaftesbury)	32:59	Hedydd Davies (TVH)	33:16
1971	Bernie Hayward (Cardiff)	3:36	John Jones (Windsor)	33:58	Alan White (Longwood)	34:15

1972	Fred Bell (TVH)	33:46	Steve Gibbons (Carmarthen)	33:58	Dic Evans (Cardiff)	34:19
1973	Dave Hopkins (Newport)	33:18	Alan White (Longwood)	34:07	Mike Critchley (Cardiff)	34:26
1974	Dave Hopkins (Newport)	31:13	Gareth Morgan (Cardiff)	31:39	Bob Sercombe (Newport)	31:49
1975	Dave Hopkins (Newport)	33:19	Steve Gibbons (Swansea)	33:50	Dic Evans (Cardiff)	34:13
1976	Steve Gibbons (Swansea)	32:59	Glen Grant (Cambridge)	33:12	John Robertshaw (Newport)	33:35
1977	Peter Ratcliffe (Cardiff)	28:59	Steve Jones (Swindon)	29:07	Richard Samuel (Shaftesbury)	29:11
1978	Peter Ratcliffe (Cardiff)	31:41	Dave Hopkins (Newport)	31:55	Ted Turner (Bristol)	32:07
1979	David James (Cardiff)	36:02	Dave Hopkins (Newport)	36:11	Ali Cole (Swansea)	36:41
1980	John Robertshaw (Newport)	34:11	Dennis Fowles (Cardiff)	34:29	Barrie Williams (Staffs M)	34:30
1981	Ali Cole (Swansea)	35:05	Mike Lane (Newport)	35:29	Dave Hopkins (Newport)	35:44
1982	Ali Cole (Swansea)	30:44	Dave James (Cardiff)	30:50	John Theophilus (Swansea)	30:59
1983	John Theophilus (Swansea)	33:00	Tony Blackwell (Wolves)	33:35	Nigel Adams (Swansea)	33:36
1984	Nick Boughey (Swansea)	31:26	Andrew Evans (Rugby)	31:37	Ali Cole (Newport)	31:47
1985	Nigel Adams (Swansea)	31:47	Kenny Davies (Newport)	32:11	Ali Cole (Newport)	32:17
1986	Nigel Adams (Swansea)	31:04	Andy Smith (Swansea)	31:46	Kenny Davies (Newport)	31:54
1987	Paul Wheeler (Cardiff)	30:19	Andy Smith (Swansea)	30:43	Nigel Adams (Swansea)	30:53
1988	Nigel Adams (Swansea)	31:01	Neil Hardee (Newport)	31:13	Paul Wheeler (Cardiff)	31:18
1989	Brian Matthews (Barry)	31:43	Tony Blackwell (Wrexham)	31:44	Andy Smith (Swansea)	31:46
1990	Nigel Adams (Swansea)	32:08	Greg Newhams (Bridgend)	33:06	Steve Smith (Swansea)	33:29
1991	Steve Knight (Cardiff)	34:39	Jon Hooper (Cardiff)	34:51	Patrick Hoare (Overton)	34:54

Team winners

1954	Roath	36	1964	Birchgrove	59	1974	Cardiff	37	1984	Newport	46
1955	Newport	33	1965	Birchgrove	107	1975	Cardiff	50	1985	Swansea	39
1956	Roath	60	1966	Birchgrove	46	1976	Cardiff	54	1986	Swansea	37
1957	Roath	32	1967	Birchgrove	82	1977	Cardiff	64	1987	Swansea	67
1958	Newport	45	1968	Roath	32	1978	Cardiff	42	1988	Newport	55
1959	Roath	87	1969	Cardiff	70	1979	Cardiff	44	1989	Swansea	61
1960	Newport	61	1970	Cardiff	21	1980	Cardiff	57	1990	Swansea	95
1961	Roath	62	1971	Cardiff	25	1981	Swansea	42	1991	Newport	87
1962	Newport	86	1972	Cardiff	48	1982	Swansea	46			
1963	Birchgrove	74	1973	Cardiff	38	1983	Swansea				

NOVICES CHAMPIONSHIPS – FIRST THREE

When the event was held in December eg Dec 1925 it was classed as coming under the 1925/26 cross country season and so appears as 1926. The event folded after 1968 because of complications concerning the definition of a 'novice'. The event in 1940 was unofficial.

1920	O Morgan (Cwmbran H)		Ernie Thomas (Cwmbran H)		S Howell (Newport H)	
1921	Gwyn Morgan (Cwm H)		N Hunt (Newport H)		Ivor Thomas (Cwmbran H)	
1922	DJP Richards (Port Talbot)		T Webber (Newport H)		D Phillips (Newport H)	
1923	Bill Lambert (Roath H)		Frank Denmead (Cwm H)		T V Berry (Roath H)	
1924	W Heale (Roath H)		Frank Denmead (Cwm H)		J Chaplin (Cwm H)	
1925	C Tew (Cwm H)		A Stone (Pontypool H)		S Frankham (Pontypool H)	
1926	J J Prosser (Newport H)		C J German (Cardiff Univ)		J J Davies (Cardiff Univ)	
1927	J Hughes (Pontnewydd)		Claude Blake (Roath H)		C J German (Cardiff Univ)	
1928	Tom G Burge (Splott YM)		Idris Lloyd (Llanbradach H)		A Stone (Pontypool H)	
1929	A Hayward (Pontypool H)		F E Powell (Newport H)		C Evans (Cwm H)	
1930	T Tear (Splott YM)		W Harris (Cwm H)		Gordon Pritchard (Spillers)	
1931	Harry Gallivan (Pontnewydd)		E C Edwards (Splott YM)		W Harris (Cwm H)	
1932	Len Tongue (Newport)		E C James (Roath H)		Gordon Pritchard (Spillers)	
1933	H Rowlands (Pontnewydd)		Ivor Brown (Llanbradach H)		Bill Matthews (Penrhys H)	
1934	W Screen (Newport H)		G L Raddon (Swansea Valley)		J Millar (Swansea Valley)	
1935	D James (Penrhys)		W Jones (Penrhys)		Bryn Quick (Port Talbot YM)	
1936	E H Jones (Lampeter College)		A H Prater (Swansea Univ)		C H Critchley (Pill H)	
1937	Lawrence Jones (Swan Univ)		H E March (Cardiff Gas)		Tom Winslade (Port Talbot YM)	
1938	H E March (Cardiff Gas)		Frank James (Roath H)		Ivor Gaylard (Penrhys)	
1939	Bill Richards (Roath H)		Bramwell Baldwin (Roath H)		S M Wood (Cardiff Univ)	
1940	M H Jones (Monmouth TC)		M Sadler (Roath H)		AC Fowler (RAF St Athan)	
1946	D C Saunders (Cardiff Univ)		C J Revington (Cardiff Univ)		L H Jones (Newport H)	
1947	J Loftus (Cardiff Gas)		Glyn Matthews (Roath H)		I G Phillips (Newport H)	
1948	J Fiddy (Pontnewydd)		Jeffrey Bowen (Llanelly GS)		M Farrigan (RAF St Athan)	
1949	K Weaver (Cwmbran H)		S Reynolds (Roath H)		Glan Williams (Cardiff Univ)	
1950	George Mugford (Roath)		not known		not known	
1951	Ken Huckle (Roath)	29:10	R N Bredin (Lampeter C)	29:13	David Richards (Barry CS)	29:22
1952	David Richards Jr (Barry CS)	26:32	Ivor Reed (Barry CS)	27:15	J F Hughes (Trinity C)	27:40
1953	B D Jones (Loughborough)		R Roberts (Hopkins)		F Mattick (Mountainn Ash)	
1954	A/C Gibson (RAF)		Jack Wingfield (Card Univ)		K Phipps (Newport H)	
1955	Mel Phillips (Newport H)		Dai Thomas 1 (Birchgrove)		K Jenkins (Cardiff Univ)	
1956	P Sadler (RAF)		B E Walters (Hafren)		= Norman Horrell (Rhondda)	
1957	? Perkins (RAF)		Colin Williams (Barry H)		Dai Pritchard (Birchgrove)	

1958	W Hotchkiss (Cardiff Univ)	31:03	K Jones (Neath H)	31:08	Tony Jones (Roath H)	31:18
1959	Trevor Owen (Roath H)		Tim Bee (Carmarthen H)		Dai Thomas 2 (Birchgrove)	
1960	Adrian Aylett (Gilwern)	34:14	= P Gray (Birchgrove)	34:14	not known	
1961	Tom Edmunds (Gilwern)	23:57	not known		not known	
1962	Mike Rowland (Newport)	25:33	Bill Stitfall (Birchgrove)	25:41	Winston Bradley (Gilwern)	25:49
1963	D E Rees (Carmarthen)	36:47	Alcwyn Price (Neath H)	37:09	Clive Williams (Birchgrove)	37:14
1964	Bill Francis (Birchgrove)	27:30	Charlie Turley (Birchgrove)	28:02	Alan Jefferies (Bridgend YM)	28:50
1965	J Rutter (Newport)	27:59	Alan Hodges (Newtown)	28:28	Glyn Williams (Pt Sunlight)	28:38
1966	Jim Bisgrove (Birchgrove)	28:12	Alun Roper (Neath H)	28:47	Bill Collier (Gilwern)	28:56
1967	Nicholas Gibbs (Barry)	28:34	K Jones (Cardiff Univ)	28:52	John Hill	29:16
1968	Dic Evans (Cardiff CE)	27:30	Peter Nolan (Barry)	28:56	Russell Pullen (Neath H)	29:27

Team winners

1920	Cwmbran	22	1931	Roath = Splott	45	1947	Barry C School	30	1958	Roath	
1921	Cwmbran	19	1932	Newport	37	1948	Barry C Sschool	22	1959	Birchgrove	28
1922	Cwm H = Newp	25	1933	Elyn	41	1949	RAF St Athan	34	1960	Birchgrove	29.5
1923	Troedyrhiw	38	1934	Newp = Spillers	40	1950	RAF St Athan	26	1961	Roath	31
1924	Cwm H	25	1935	Cardiff Univ	43	1951	Roath	19	1962	Birchgrove	25
1925	Abertillery	26	1936	Swansea Univ	40	1952	Barry C School	26	1963	Neath	33
1926	Pontypool	31	1937	P Talbot YM	41	1953	Roath	58	1964	Gilwern	49
1927	Cardiff Univ	36	1938	Penrhys	25	1954	Newport	21	1965	Newport	34
1928	Pontnewydd	53	1939	Roath	18	1955	Roath	27	1966	Birchgrove	18
1929	Newport H	39	1940	No team event		1956	RAF St Athan	23	1967	Cardiff Univ	wo
1930	Splott YMCA	31	1946	Cardiff Univ	16	1957	Carmarthen	46	1968	Barry	12

SENIOR WOMEN'S CHAMPIONSHIPS – FIRST THREE

The Welsh Women's Cross Country Association was formed in 1968 and that year's race was the first held under their auspices. The race in 1967 was held as a trial for the International Cross Country Championships held that year in Barry. There is evidence to suggest that championships were held before 1967, possibly as early as 1963. A result has been found for a 2 miles championships at Glebelands Playing Fields, Newport on 24 April 1965 (6 athletes started) with the result as shown below:

1965	Pat Sullivan (Westbury)	12:55	Pat Dalton (Roath)	13:35	P Weston (Westbury)	14:06
1967	Jean Lochhead (Airedale)	15:31	Pat Sullivan (Westbury)	16:04	Janet Eynon (Croydon)	16:29
1968	Thelwyn Bateman (Cov G)	13:40	Gloria Dourass (Sm Heath)	14:10	Jean Lochhead (Airedale)	14:18
1969	Thelwyn Bateman (Cov G)	18:22	Jean Lochhead (Airedale)	18:52	Bronwen Cardy (Bromsgrove)	19:56
1970	Thelwyn Bateman (Cov G)	14:52	Jean Lochhead (Airedale)	15:31	Bronwen Cardy (Bromsgrove)	15:46
1971	Gloria Dourass (Sm Heath)	16:35	Bronwen Cardy (Bromsgrove)	16:36	Delyth Davies (Cardiff)	17:34
1972	Bronwen Cardy (Bromsgrove)	18:08	Thelwyn Bateman (Cov G)	18:14	Susan Barnes (Verlea)	18:31
1973	Thelwyn Bateman (Cov G)	15:51	Bronwen Cardy (Bromsgrove)	16:10	Delyth Davies (Cardiff)	16:31
1974	Jean Lochhead (Airedale)	17:24	Bronwen Cardy (Bromsgrove)	17:37	Ann Disley (Newport)	18:18
1975	Jean Lochhead (Airedale)	22:32	Ann Morris (Cardiff)	23:04	Bronwen Cardy (Bromsgrove)	23:32
1976	Ann Morris (Cardiff)	15:18	Ann James (London Oly)	15:39	Ann Roblin (Cardiff)	15:46
1977	Ann Disley (Newport)	15:59	Jean Lochhead (Airedale)	16:21	Bronwen C Smith (Brom)	16:24
1978	Hilary Hollick (Sale)	18:37	Jean Lochhead (Airedale)	19:00	Annmarie Fox (Swansea)	19:12
1979	Hilary Hollick (Sale)	18:10	Bronwen Smith (Bromsgrove)	18:13	Carol Nicholas (Cleddau)	18:32
1980	Hilary Hollick (Sale)	19:31	Kim Lock (Cardiff)	20:02	Carol Bradford (Clevedon)	20:29
1981	Carol Bradford (Clevedon)	16:37	Hilary Hollick (Sale)	16:55	Bronwen Smith (Bromsgrove)	17:16
1982	Thelwyn Bateman (B'field)	16:56	Angela Tooby (Aberystwyth)	17:04	Kim Lock (Cardiff)	17:09
1983	Kim Lock (Cardiff)	20:55	Louise Copp (Port Talbot)	21:15	Annmarie Fox (Swansea)	21:38
1984	Angela Tooby (Cardiff)	19:07	Kim Lock (Cardiff)	19:45	Louise Copp (Cardiff)	20:18
1985	Angela Tooby (Cardiff)	19:05	= Susan Tooby (Cardiff)	19:05	Barbara Ann King (Swansea)	20:15
1986	Susan Tooby (Cardiff)	17:58	= Angela Tooby (Cardiff)	17:58	Lynn Maddison (Colwyn Bay)	18:36
1987	Angela Tooby (Cardiff)	20:04	Susan Tooby (Cardiff)	20:36	Wendy Ore (Bridgend)	20:41
1988	Melissa Watson (Swindon)	17:50	Wendy Ore (Bridgend)	17:59	Sally James/Lynch (Newport)	18:23
1989	Melissa Watson (Westbury	19:20	Sally Lynch (Newport)	19:29	Wendy Ore (Cardiff)	20:21
1990	Melissa Watson (Westbury)	20:54	Sally Lynch (Newport)	21:09	Sarah Hodge (Westbury)	21:34
1991	Sarah Hodge/Lee (Westbury)	18:45	Melissa Watson (Westbury)	19:00	Lynn Maddison (Sale)	19:20
1992	Melissa Watson (Westbury)	21:29	Hayley Nash (Torfaen)	21:40	Wendy Ore (Cardiff)	21:56
1993	Wendy Ore (Cardiff)	17:43	Hayley Nash (Cardiff)	18:05	Sally Lynch (Newport)	18:32
1994	Wendy Ore (Cardiff)	24:48	Hayley Nash (Cardiff)	25:08	Melissa Watson (Westbury)	25:53
1995	Wendy Ore (Cardiff)	23:45	Angela Tooby/Smith (Wel)	24:26	Lynn Maddison (Colwyn Bay)	25:10
1996	Wendy Ore (Cardiff)	22:39	Susan Tooby/Wightman (Car)	22:48	Hayley Nash (Newport)	23:09
1997	Hayley Nash (Newport)	22:44	Clare Martin (Newport)	22:56	Debbie Chick (Bridgend)	23:09
1998	Angharad Mair (Newport)	24:48	Hayley Nash (Newport)	24:49	Catherine Dugdale (Cardiff)	25:31
1999	Hayley Nash (Newport)	26:57	Samantha Gray (Abertillery)	28:13	Sally Lynch (Newport)	28:42
2000	Catherine Dugdale (Swansea)	24:30	Louise Copp (Cardiff)	24:44	Frances Gill (Neath)	25:04

VENUES FOR SENIOR CHAMPIONSHIPS - Men

Ely Racecourse, Cardiff:	1894, 1898, 1899, 1900, 1901, 1904, 1906, 1911
East Moors, Cardiff	1895
Harlequin Grounds, Cardiff	1896,1897
Caerleon Racecourse:	1902, 1903, 1905, 1907, 1909, 1910, 1912, 1913, 1914, 1921, 1922, 1925, 1926, 1927, 1928, 1931, 1933, 1934, 1937, 1939, 1947, 1948, 1949, 1950, 1951, 1952, 1955, 1956
Victoria Park, Swansea:	1908
St Arvans, Chepstow:	1920
Court Farm, Llantarnam:	1923, 1929, 1930, 1932, 1935, 1936, 1938
Roath Park, Cardiff:	1924
Rumney, Cardiff:	1940
Caerau (Ely) :	1946
Grangetown, Cardiff:	1953, 1954
Pontcanna, Cardiff:	1957, 1958
Cadoxton, Barry	1959, 1960, 1962
Duffryn HS, Newport:	1961
Newbridge Fields, Bridgend:	1963, 1979, 1998
Penlan, Swansea	1964
Recreation Grounds, Caerleon	1965
Gilwern	1966
Sports Centre, Barry	1967, 1983
Glebelands, Newport	1968, 1974, 1975
Singleton Park, Swansea	1969, 1972, 1977, 1978, 1980, 1984, 1988, 1991, 1993, 1996
Llanrumney, Cardiff	1970
Cwmbran:	1971
Blackweir, Cardiff	1973, 1976
Heath Park, Cardiff	1981, 1982, 1985, 1986, 1989, 1992, 1995, 1997, 2000
Colcot, Barry	1987, 1990
United Counties, Carmarthen	1994
Colwyn Bay	1999

VENUES FOR SENIOR CHAMPIONSHIPS - Women

Barry:	1967, 1983
Glebelands, Newport	1968
Duffryn HS	1969
Cwmbran	1970, 1971
Singleton Park, Swansea	1972, 1980, 1984, 1988, 1991, 1993, 1996
Brecon	1973
Llanrumney, Cardiff	1974
Bridgend	1975, 1979, 1998
Beachley	1976
Cardiff	1977, 1978
Heath Park, Cardiff	1981, 1982, 1986, 1989, 1992, 1995, 1997, 2000
Swansea	1985
Colcot, Barry	1987, 1990
United Counties, Carmarthen	1994
Colwyn Bay	1999

AGE GROUP CHAMPIONS

Junior Men began as a race defined by ability and later by age and this continued up to 1955 when it ceased and was effectively replaced by the 7 miles championship. Note that the event in 1940 was an unofficial race. It restarted in 1963 as an event dictated by age, and in this year it was as a trial for the new junior international race. U17 men (previously youths) was first held in 1928, U15 (boys) in 1955, U13 (colts) in 1969. The U17 women (intermediates) was first held in 1969, U15 girls was also introduced in 1969 and U13 girls in 1972. Junior women's championship (U20) was not introduced until 1989.

	U20/Junior*	U17 Men	U15 Boys
1905	Eddie G Ace (Swansea)		
1906	T W Bumford (Barry H)		
1907	L Lloyd (Newport H)		
1908	Edgar Stead (Cwmbran)		
1909	P Curry (Tredegar)		
1910	T Harry (St Saviours)		
1911	H L Lloyd (Cathays)		
1912	E J Davies (St Saviours)		
1913	Cliff Price (Newport)		
1914	Sam Judd (Chepstow)		
1920	R Lovell (Newport)		
1921	Gwyn Morgan (Cwm H)		

1922	J Bassett (Newport)		
1923	Will Lambert = Jim Guy (Roath)		
1924	E R Leyshon (Newport)		
1925	A Stainer (Abertillery)		
1926	Ivor Thomas (Newport)		
1927	Gwyn Lewis (Roath)		
1928	A Fournier (Llanbradach)	S T Hardy (Cwmbran)	
1929	S T Hardy (Cwmbran)	T R Tear (Splott YM)	
1930	T H Timbrell (Swansea V)	Gordon Pritchard (Spillers)	
1931	Sam Palmer (Essex Reg)	Gordon Pritchard (Spillers)	
1932	Gordon Pritchard (Spillers)	L Nash (Pontnewydd)	
1933	Len Tongue (Newport)	Eddie Cooper (Roath)	
1934	Bill Matthews (Penrhys)	Ivor Gaylard (Elyn AC)	
1935	Gwyn W Fox (Penrhys)	Bryn Quick (Port Talbot YM)	
1936	Dennis Morgan (Swansea V)	Bramwell Baldwin (Barry CS)	
1937	Bryn Quick (Mansel)	F E Nicholls (Newport)	
1938	Tom Winslade (Port Talbot Y)	Bill E Richards (Barry CS)	
1939	L Stucky (Penrhys)	D H Downs (Bridgend CS)	
1940	S Griffiths (Newport H)	D H Downs (Bridgend CS)	
1941	event not held	T Perrett (Bridgend CS)	
1942	event not held	G Richards (Bridgend CS)	
1943	event not held	Dennis Davie (Barry CS)	
1944	event not held	Gwyn Marshman (Barry CS)	
1945	event not held	Bill Butcher (Barry CS)	
1946	D Saunders (Cardiff Univ)	C Bumford (Barry CS)	
1947	Bernard Baldwin (Roath)	Jeffrey Bowen (Llanelly GS)	
1948	Jim Davies (Port Talbot Y)	Jeffrey Bowen (Llanelly GS)	
1949	A/C Lee (RAF)	R Griffiths (Llanelly GS)	
1950	John Nash (Port Talbot)	Lyn Bevan (Newport)	
1951	Ken Huckle (Roath)	Ike Williams (Salford)	
1952	Lyn Bevan (Newport)	not known	
1953	Peter Griggs (Coventry Godiva)	not known	
1954	DJP Richards Jun (Roath)	Tony Rathbone (Newport)	
1955	Neville Phillips (Newport)	J Jones (Llanelli GS)	Colin Vowles (Barry)
1956	event not held	Colin Williams (Barry)	Colin Vowles (Barry)
1957	event not held	Ganson (RAF)	J Scott (Porth GS)
1958	event not held	John Williams (Carm GS)	M Jones (Queen Eliz GS)
1959	event not held	Dilwyn Griffiths (Carmarthen)	Tom Edmunds (Gilwern)
1960	event not held	Tom Edmunds (Gilwern)	G Thomas (Carmarthen GS)
1961	event not held	not known	not known
1962	Event not held	Bill Stitfall (Birchgrove)	Glyn Jones (Carmarthen)
1963	Fred Bell (Carmarthen)	Chris Loosley (Carmarthen)	Derek Denley (Barry)
1964	Tom Edmunds (Gilwern)	Ian Jones (West Monmouth)	K Bowes (AAS)
1965	Clive Williams (Birchgrove)	not known	not known
1966	Chris Loosley (Aberystwyth)	Tony Simmons (Luton)	D Thomas (Aber)
1967	Ron McAndrew (Wigan)	Tony Simmons (Luton)	Owen E Lewis (Swansea)
1968	Bernie Hayward (B'grove)	Frank Thomas (Aberystwyth)	John Davies (TVH)
1969	Malcolm Thomas (TVH)	Dennis Fowles (Cardiff)	Peter Ratcliffe (Gilwern)
1970	Bernie Hayward (Cardiff)	John Davies (TVH)	Robert Vice (Swansea)
1971	not known	not known	R Games (Brecon)
1972	Peter Ratcliffe (Cardiff)	Gareth Morgan (Cardiff)	Tony Dyke (Bishop Gore)
1973	Richard Samuel (Shaftesbury)	Steve Rolfe (Llanelli GS)	Micky Morris (Cwmbran)
1974	not known	Micky Morris (Cwmbran)	Steve Evans (Abertilllery)
1975	Andrew Darby (Caerleon College)	Micky Morris (Cwmbran)	Tony Blackwell (Wrexham)
1976	Micky Morris (Cwmbran)	Alan Cummings (Cardiff)	Colin Clarkson (Swansea)
1977	Micky Morris (Cwmbran)	Colin Clarkson (Swansea)	Phil Llewellyn (Shaftesbury)
1978	Tony Blackwell (Wolves)	Colin Clarkson (Swansea)	Andrew Evans (Rugby)
1979	Chris Buckley (Westbury)	Steve Blakemore (Cardiff)	John Pimley (Torfaen)
1980	Steve Blakemore (Cardiff)	Nigel Stops (Shaftesbury)	Brian Matthews (Barry)
1981	Simon Axon (Swansea)	John McKeever (Aberystwyth)	Nicky Comerford (Barry)
1982	Andy Smith (Swansea)	Andrew Rodgers (Leeds)	Paul Williams (Barry)
1983	Andrew Rodgers (Leeds)	Paul Williams (Barry)	Colin Hignell (Barry)
1984	Brian Matthews (Barry)	Neil Horsfield (Newport)	Justin Hobbs (Cardiff)
1985	Neil Hardee (Newport)	Justin Hobbs (Cardiff)	Gerallt Owen (Swansea)
1986	Dale Rixon (Cardiff)	Justin Hobbs (Cardiff)	Jon Brown (Hallamshire)
1987	Justin Hobbs (Cardiff)	Gerallt Owen (Swansea)	Paul Lewis (Bridgend)
1988	Justin Hobbs (Cardiff)	Guto Eames (Cardiff)	Peter Wyatt (Bristol)
1989	Justin Hobbs (Cardiff)	Neil Lisk (Aberystwyth)	Colin Jones (Eryri)
1990	Guto Eames (Cardiff)	Neil Emberton (Newtown)	Jon Williams (Neath)
1991	Neil Emberton (Newtown)	Colin Jones (Eryri)	Justin Thomas (Neath)
1992	Christian Stephenson (Cardiff)	Chris Blount (Newport)	Alan Jones (Carmarthen)

1993 Christian Stephenson (Cardiff)
1994 Colin Jones (Eryri)
1995 Andres Jones (Carmarthen)
1996 Nathaniel Lane (Cardiff)
1997 Chris Davies (Telford)
1998 Paul Gronow (Cardiff)
1999 Tim Gardner (Wycombe)
2000 Jonathan Phillips (Cardiff)

U13 Boys

1969 Will Snowdon (Cantonian)
1970 Tony Dyke (Bishop Gore)
1971 not known
1972 Steve Evans (Abertillery)
1973 Gary Keeble (Bristol)
1974 not known
1975 Colin Clarkson (Swansea)
1976 Paul Keeble (Newport)
1977 Alan Penman (Swansea)
1978 Mark Griffiths (Swansea)
1979 L Williams (Ferndale)
1980 Carl Worthington (Ferndale)
1981 R Hughes (Cleddau)
1982 R Hughes (Cornwall)
1983 Chris Osborne (Ferndale)
1984 A Lewis (Ferndale)
1985 Tim Cummings (Barry)
1986 Stephen Blow (Beddau)
1987 Anthony Jones (Bridgend)
1988 Nick Froggatt (Newcastle)
1989 Richard Pierce (Wrexham)
1990 Tawfiq Ayoub (Cardiff)
1991 David Fallon (Wirral)
1992 Matthew Russell (Colwyn Bay)
1993 Andrew Davies (Newtown)
1994 Duncan Hughes (Wrexham)
1995 Anthony Walters (Aberdare)
1996 Michael Boland (Cardiff)
1997 Richard Kinsey (Cardiff)
1998 Charles Harvey (Carmarthen)
1999 Owen Evans (Carmarthen)
2000 Thomas James (Cardiff)

U15 Girls

1969 Katrina Blackwell (Port Talbot)
1970 Margaret Bevan (Brecon)
1971 Susan Tolan (Cwmbran)
1972 Susan Tolan (Cwmbran)
1973 Sian Lode (Brecon)
1974 Jackie Hulbert (Swansea)
1975 Shiobhan Taylor (Cardiff)
1976 Debbie Lewis (Cardiff)
1977 Claire Francis (Kg Henry VIII)
1978 Gillian Irvine (Carmarthen)
1979 Yana Jones (Tiverton)
1980 Louise Silva (Melbourn)
1981 Debbie Crowley (Port Talbot)
1982 Debbie Crowley (Port Talbot)
1983 Clare Pugh (Newport)
1984 Ceri Burnell (Cardiff)
1985 Lisa Carthew (Swansea)
1986 Julie Crowley (Port Talbot)
1987 Rebecca Evans (Swansea)
1988 Vanessa Jones (Wrexham)
1989 Rachel Parsons (Cardiff)
1990 Lynn Gallagher (Westbury)
1991 Angharad Howells (Carmarthen)
1992 Nina Hampshire (Brecon)
1993 Heledd Gruffudd (Carmarthen)
1994 Heledd Gruffudd (Carmarthen)

Ian Pierce (Wrexham)
David Davey (Barry)
Steve Lawrence (Swansea)
Alun Vaughan (Eryri)
Paul Gronow (Cardiff)
Elliot Cole (Bridgend)
Richard Williams (Shaftesbury)
Richard Kinsey (Cardiff)

U20 Junior Women

Carol Hayward (Newport)
Carol Hayward (Newport)
Jo Parsons (Cardiff)
Jessica Mills (Harlow)
Lynn Gallagher (Westbury)
Jenny Preston (Aberystwyth)
Viv Conneely (Newport)
AnneMarie Hutchinson (Neath)
Clare Thomas (Swansea)
Rebecca Evans (Bridgend)
Sian Pritchard (Brecon)
Sarah Williams (Sale)

U13 Girls

Jackie Hulbert (Swansea)
Debbie Lewis (Cardiff)
Debbie Lewis (Cardiff)
S Lewis (Southampton)
Gillian Irvine (Carmarthen)
Kathy Williams (Port Talbot)
Louise Silva (Melbourn)
Jane Thomas (Carmarthen)
Debbie Crowley (Port Talbot)
J Jones (Cardiff)
Clare Pugh (Newport)
Ceri Burnell (Cardiff)
Julie Crowley (Port Talbot)
Debra Morgan (Beddau)
Julie Garrett (Cardiff)
Mari Prys Jones (Carmarthen)
Jo Elward (Barry)
Amanda Rowbotham (Colwyn Bay)
Angharad Howells (Carmarthen)
Heledd Gruffudd (Carmarthen)
Heledd Gruffudd (Carmarthen)
Amanda Pritchard (Cardiff)
Laura Jones (Wrexham)

Gavin Hughes (Preseli)
Steve Lawrence (Swansea)
Paul Gronow (Cardiff)
Chris Davey (Barry)
Daniel Beynon (Swansea)
Matthew Jones (Stoke)
David Jones (Carmarthen)
Luke Northall (Wrexham)

U17 Women

Susan Adams (Bromsgrove)
Katrina Blackwell (Port Talbot)
Ann Disley (Newport)
Kerry Walker (Swansea)
Susan Tolan (Cwmbran)
Susan Tolan (Cardiff)
Ann Lewis (Cwmbran)
Jane Clement (Swansea)
Debbie Lewis (Cardiff)
Carol Nicholas (Cleddau)
Claire Francis (Newport)
Kathy Williams (Port Talbot)
Kathy Williams (Port Talbot)
Tracy Long (Fleet)
Fiona Harwood (Cardiff)
Lynn Maddison (Colwyn Bay)
Clare Pugh (Newport)
Clare Pugh (Newport)
Ceri Burnell (Cardiff)
Rebecca Evans (Swansea)
Vanessa Jones (Wrexham)
Emma Thomas (Millfield)
Elinor Caborn (Bedford)
Viv Conneely (Neath)
Bethan Hopewell (Bedford)
Kirsty Jones (Wycombe)
Clare Thomas (Swansea)
Catherine Vines (Cannock)
Ceri Wensley (Newport)
Teresa Penhorwood (Swansea)
Georgina Parnell (Newport)
Miriam Gaskell (Brecon)

1995	Eleanor Roper (Neath)	Kristy Doyle (Barry)
1996	Teresa Penhorwood (Swansea)	Fiona Harrison (Preseli)
1997	Laura Scott (Brecon)	Fiona Harrison (Preseli)
1998	Eleanor S-Smith (Swansea)	Amanda Jones (Swansea)
1999	Eleanor S-Smith (Swansea)	Rickie Cotter (Llanelli)
2000	Amanda Jones (Swansea)	Lisa Lanini (Wrexham)

WINNING TEAMS

	Senior Men		U20 Junior Men		U17 Men	
1894	Roath Harriers	25				
1895	Roath Harriers	21				
1896	Roath Harriers	38				
1897	Cardiff Harriers	42				
1898	Cardiff Harriers	52				
1899	Newport Harriers	34				
1900	Newport Harriers	44				
1901	Newport Harriers	31				
1902	Newport Harriers	35				
1903	Newport Harriers	21				
1904	Newport Harriers	31				
1905	Newport Harriers	28	Castleton Harriers	52		
1906	Newport Harriers	30	Barry Harriers	90		
1907	Newport Harriers	27	Newport Harriers	53		
1908	Newport Harriers	35	Cwmbran Harriers	32		
1909	Newport Harriers	63	Newport Harriers	75		
1910	Newport Harriers	53	Tredegar St James	85		
1911	Cwmbran Harriers	31	Pontnewydd	68		
1912	Cwmbran Harriers	36	St Saviours	90		
1913	Cwmbran Harriers	33	Abertillery AAC	55		
1914	Newport Harriers	28	Talywain	77		
1920	Newport Harriers	48	Newport Harriers	34		
1921	Newport Harriers	45	Cwm Harriers	54		
1922	Newport Harriers	36	Newport Harriers	43		
1923	Newport Harriers	28	Roath Harriers	68		
1924	Newport Harriers	39	Cwm Harriers	52		
1925	Newport Harriers	33	Abertillery AAC	50		
1926	Newport Harriers	33	Newport Harriers	37		
1927	Roath Harriers	68	Cwmbran Harriers	118		
1928	Cwmbran Harriers	31	Llanbradach H	91	Splott YMCA	12
1929	Cwmbran Harriers	43	Newport Harriers	63	Splott YMCA	09
1930	Cwmbran Harriers	48	Newport Harriers	102	Splott YMCA	13
1931	Cwmbran Harriers	41	Newport Harriers	97	ATS Beachley	15
1932	Cwmbran Harriers	33	Roath Harriers	83	Roath Harriers	17
1933	Cwmbran Harriers	63	Newport Harriers	66	Roath Harriers	08
1934	Newport Harriers	87	Roath Harriers	79	Roath Harriers	10
1935	Cwmbran Harriers	86	Penrhys AC	109	Barry C School	12
1936	Cwmbran Harriers	33	Swansea Valley AC	63	Barry C School	08
1937	Roath Harriers	42	Roath Harriers	50	Barry C School	12
1938	Cwmbran Harriers	48	Port Talbot YMCA	65	Barry C School	15
1939	Roath Harriers	39	Race AC	80	Barry C School	16
1940	Roath Harriers	14	no team event		Bridgend C School	12
1941	event not held		no team event		Barry C School	09
1942	event not held		no team event		Bridgend C School	13
1943	event not held		no team event		Barry C School	07
1944	event not held		no team event		Barry C School	08
1945	event not held		no team event		Barry C School	06
1946	Roath Harriers	62	Cardiff University	39	Newport Harriers	15
1947	Roath Harriers	30	Newport Harriers	38	Llanelly G School	08
1948	Roath Harriers	51	RAF St Athan	39	Barry C School	09
1949	Newport Harriers	41	RAF St Athan	57	Swansea G School	13
1950	Newport Harriers	36	RAF St Athan		Swansea G School	
1951	Newport Harriers	33	Roath Harriers	60	Barry C School	12
1952	Newport Harriers	33	Newport Harriers	29	not known	
1953	Roath Harriers	39	Roath Harriers		Roath Harriers	
1954	Newport Harriers	26	Cardiff University	17	Newport Harriers	15
1955	Newport Harriers	27	Newport Harriers	12	Llanelly G School	12
1956	Newport Harriers	41	event not held		Newport High School	18
1957	Newport Harriers	33	event not held		Queen Elizabeth G School	
1958	Newport Harriers	47	event not held		Birchgrove	14
1959	Roath Harriers	97	event not held		Birchgrove	14

1960	Newport Harriers	35	event not held		Cardiff High School	27
1961	Roath Harriers	124	event not held		not known	
1962	Newport Harriers		event not held		Birchgrove Harriers	12
1963	Newport Harriers	124	Birchgrove Harriers	18	Gilwern Harriers	22
1964	Newport Harriers	74	Birchgrove Harriers	34	West Monmouth G S	22
1965	Newport Harriers	64	Birchgrove Harriers		not known	
1966	Birchgrove Harriers	47	Birchgrove Harriers		Birchgrove Harriers	
1967	Birchgrove Harriers	53	Birchgrove Harriers		Birchgrove Harriers	10
1968	Birchgrove Harriers	37	Birchgrove Harriers		Swansea Harriers	16
1969	Cardiff AAC	69	Cardiff AAC	22	Swansea Harriers	13
1970	Cardiff AAC	35	Cardiff AAC		AAC Chepstow	16
1971	Cardiff AAC	29	Cardiff AAC		not known	
1972	Cardiff AAC	28	Cardiff AAC		Cardiff AAC	06
1973	Cardiff AAC	26	Cardiff AAC	06	Swansea Harriers	12
1974	Cardiff AAC	56	not known		Cardiff AAC	12
1975	Cardiff AAC	31	Swansea Harriers	06	Cardiff AAC	09
1976	Cardiff AAC	35	Cardiff AAC	09	Cardiff AAC	25
1977	Cardiff AAC	32	AAC Chepstow	10	Swansea Harriers	11
1978	Cardiff AAC	40	Swansea Harriers	09	Cardiff AAC	11
1979	Cardiff AAC	32	Swansea Harriers	11	Cardiff AAC	09
1980	Swansea Harriers	58	Cardiff AAC	18	Cardiff AAC	36
1981	Cardiff AAC	56	Swansea Harriers	14	Beddau AC	24
1982	Newport Harriers	63	Swansea Harriers	10	Beddau AC	29
1983	Newport Harriers	41	Newport Harriers	28	Cardiff AAC	22
1984	Newport Harriers	31	Newport Harriers	39	Cardiff AAC	18
1985	Newport Harriers	23	Newport Harriers	16	Barry & Vale Harriers	27
1986	Newport Harriers	33	Cardiff AAC	20	Cardiff AAC	25
1987	Newport Harriers	44	Cardiff AAC	78	Swansea Harriers	35
1988	Swansea Harriers	52	Swansea Harriers	54	Cardiff AAC	41
1989	Newport Harriers	54	Cardiff AAC	34	Aberdare Valley AC	57
1990	Newport Harriers	40	Cardiff AAC	21	Newport Harriers	59
1991	Swansea Harriers	66	Swansea Harriers	55	Newport Harriers	48
1992	Newport Harriers	81	Swansea Harriers	48	Newport Harriers	44
1993	Swansea Harriers	64	Newport Harriers	38	Swansea Harriers	37
1994	Cardiff AAC	47	Newport Harriers	56	Carmarthen Harriers	28
1995	Cardiff AAC	51	Cardiff AAC	48	Carmarthen Harriers	35
1996	Cardiff AAC	47	Cardiff AAC	45	Cardiff AAC	25
1997	Cardiff AAC	30	Cardiff AAC	40	Barry & Vale Harriers	31
1998	Swansea Harriers	50	Cardiff AAC	27	Swansea Harriers	29
1999	Swansea Harriers	62	Barry & Vale Harriers	38	no full teams	
2000	Swansea Harriers	57	Cardiff AAC	14	Newport Harriers	35

	U15 Boys		**U13 Boys**		**U13 Girls**	
1955	Cadoxton SM School	30				
1956	Abergavenny AC	36				
1957	Queen Elizabeth G School					
1958	Cardiff High School	19				
1959	Cardiff High School	11				
1960	Birchgrove Harriers	34				
1961	not known					
1962	Dyffryn High School	46				
1963	Barry Grammar School	24				
1964	AAS Beachley	17				
1965	not known					
1966	Birchgrove Harriers					
1967	Swansea Harriers	10				
1968	Swansea Harriers	08				
1969	Gruffydd Jones School	20	Cynffig Comp School	16		
1970	Cantonian High School	24	Bishop Gore School	11		
1971	Bishop Gore School		Abertillery AC			
1972	Carmarthen Harriers	20	Abertillery AC	07	Swansea Harriers	28
1973	Swansea Harriers	18	Olchfa School	09	Cardiff AAC	
1974	not known		not known		Cardiff AAC	
1975	Wrexham AC	09	Swansea Harriers	18	Cwmbran Olympiads	21
1976	Cardiff AAC	17	Newport Harriers	09	Cardiff AAC	06
1977	Cardiff AAC	16	Bryn Celynnog School	21	Cardiff AAC	09
1978	Cardiff AAC	11	Cardiff AAC	15	Cardiff AAC	12
1979	Swansea Harriers	19	Ferndale School	22	Bridgend AC	16
1980	Barry & Vale Harriers	27	Ferndale School	31	Cardiff AAC	19
1981	Cardiff AAC	25	Ferndale School	34	Cardiff AAC	25
1982	Cardiff AAC	18	Ferndale School	42	Barry & Vale Harriers	37

1983	Beddau AC	26	Swansea Harriers	30	Cardiff AAC	19
1984	Cardiff AAC	32	Cardiff AAC	24	Cardiff AAC	17
1985	Swansea Harriers	18	Ferndale School	33	Cardiff AAC	26
1986	Newport Harriers	27	Ferndale School	27	Swansea Harriers	24
1987	Beddau AC	56	Ferndale School	69	Cardiff AAC	39
1988	Swansea Harriers	50	Ferndale School	20	Barry & Vale Harriers	71
1989	Swansea Harriers	52	Cardiff AAC	65	Swansea Harriers	31
1990	Carmarthen Harriers	49	Wrexham AC	45	Carmarthen Harriers	39
1991	Neath Harriers	35	Carmarthen Harriers	46	Carmarthen Harriers	19
1992	Carmarthen Harriers	23	Cardiff AAC	32	Carmarthen Harriers	30
1993	Carmarthen Harriers	45	Cardiff AAC	40	Swansea Harriers	46
1994	Cardiff AAC	41	Swansea Harriers	54	Swansea Harriers	33
1995	Cardiff AAC	20	Swansea Harriers	21	Newport Harriers	46
1996	Swansea Harriers	27	Cardiff AAC	29	Swansea Harriers	44
1997	Swansea Harriers	35	Swansea Harriers	40	Swansea Harriers	58
1998	Carmarthen Harriers	58	Carmarthen Harriers	64	Swansea Harriers	55
1999	Swansea Harriers	38	Carmarthen Harriers	35	Bridgend AC	38
2000	Carmarthen Harriers	47	Carmarthen Harriers	51	Brecon AC	40

	Senior Women		**U20/U17 Women**		**U15 Girls**	
1970	Brecon AC	26				
1971	no teams		Swansea Harriers		Swansea Harriers	
1972	Newport Harriers		no teams		Swansea Harriers	27
1973	no teams		Cardiff AAC		Cardiff AAC	
1974	no teams		Cardiff AAC	08	Cardiff AAC	
1975	Cardiff AAC	16	Brecon AC	14	Cardiff AAC	09
1976	Cardiff AAC	14	Carmarthen Harriers	09	Cardiff AAC	12
1977	Cwmbran Olympiads	11	Barry Harriers	12	Brecon AC	21
1978	Carmarthen Harriers	11	Swansea Harriers	18	Cardiff AAC	23
1979	Swansea Harriers	08	Cardiff AAC	08	Cardiff AAC	11
1980	Cardiff AAC	13	Cardiff AAC	17	Cardiff AAC	12
1981	Cardiff AAC	10	Port Talbot Harriers	22	Cardiff AAC	19
1982	Cardiff AAC	24	Bridgend AC	20	Cardiff AAC	25
1983	Cardiff AAC	20	Cardiff AAC	12	Beddau AC	43
1984	Cardiff AAC	11	Cardiff AAC	23	Cardiff AAC	16
1985	Cardiff AAC	15	Swansea Harriers	20	Cardiff AAC	15
1986	Cardiff AAC	19	Cardiff AAC	13	Cardiff AAC	36
1987	Cardiff AAC	39	Cardiff AAC	29	Swansea Harriers	29
1988	Les Croupiers RC	60	Swansea Harriers	25	Cardiff AAC	64
1989	Newport Harriers	56	Cardiff AAC	42	Cardiff AAC	41
1990	Newport Harriers	27	Colwyn Bay AC	47	Swansea Harriers	61
1991	Newport Harriers	57	Carmarthen Harriers	67	Neath Harrier	31
1992	Newport Harriers	43	Neath Harriers	76	Carmarthen Harriers	54
1993	Newport Harriers	28	Newport Harriers	41	Swansea Harriers	39
1994	Cardiff AAC	19	Newport Harriers	45	Carmarthen Harriers	32
1995	Cardiff AAC	18	Newport Harriers	37	Carmarthen Harriers	51
1996	Newport Harriers	21	Cardiff AAC	64	Swansea Harriers	30
1997	Newport Harriers	15	Brecon AC	50	Swansea Harriers	42
1998	Newport Harriers	16	Brecon AC	46	Swansea Harriers	30
1999	Les Croupiers RC	56	Brecon AC	37	Swansea Harriers	28
2000	Cardiff AAC	23	Cardiff AAC	56	Swansea Harriers	16

NORTH WALES CROSS COUNTRY CHAMPIONSHIPS

Senior Men

1955 A F Bradford (Pioneer Corps)
1956 I Roberts (Cov Godiva
1957 Tony Pumfrey (Cov Godiva)
1958 S Kippax (Rhyl)
1959 M Palmer (RAF Valley)
1960 Tony Pumfrey (Cov Godiva)
1961 B Waters (Wrexham)
1962 Roger Harrison Jones (Rhyl)
1963 Ray Billington (Birchfield)
1964 Roger Harrison Jones (Rhyl)
1965 R Williams (TVH)
1966 A A Hodges (Newtown)
1967 Ray Billington (TVH)
1968 event not held
1969 R O Williams (Liverpool)
1970 T Harper (Wirral)
1971 T Harper (Wirral)
1972 John Robertshaw (Card Un)
1973 P Flatman (RAF Valley)
1974 John Robertshaw (sale)
1975 T Harper (Wirral)
1976 T Davies (Para Regmt)
1977 T Davies (Para Regmt)
1978 Tony Blackwell (Wrexham)
1979 Tony Blackwell (Wrexham)
1980 T Davies (Aldershot)
1981 Tony Blackwell (Wrexham)
1982 Tony Blackwell (Wrexham)
1983 George Nixon (Wrexham)
1984 Tony Blackwell (Wrexham)
1985 Dave Messum (Wolves)
1986 Dave Messum (Wolves)
1987 Colin Donnelly (Eyri)
1988 I Hanson (Wrexham)
1989 Emlyn Roberts (Eyri)
1990 Glyn Harvey (Wrexham)
1991 Colin Donnelly (Eyri)
1992 Clive Boulton (Wrexham)
1993 Colin Donnelly (Eyri)
1994 Colin Donnelly (Eyri)
1995 Colin Jones (Eyri)
1996 Colin Jones (Eyri)
1997 Ian Pierce (Tipton)
1998 Colin Donnelly (Eyri)
1999 Colin Donnelly (Eyri)
2000 Colin Donnelly (Eyri)

U20 Junior Men

1972 M Russell (Wrexham)
1973 M Russell (Wrexham)
1974 M Russell (Wrexham)
1975 M Ligema (Aberystwyth Uni)
1976 M Ligema (Aberystwyth Uni)
1977 Ll Roberts (Cardiff Uni)
1978 Dave Carr (Army)
1979 S Holliwell (Bangor Uni)
1980 Tim Wilcock (Deeside)
1981 Tim Wilcock (Deeside)
1982 John Messum (Deesdale)
1983 G A Griffiths (Wrexham)
1984 C Kneale (Wrexham)
1985 N Glynn (Newtown)
1986 Simon Shiels (Colwyn Bay)
1987 Andrew Edge (Wrexham)
1988 A Neal (Wrexham)
1989 Bedwyr Huws (Eyri)
1990 M Ward (Eyri)
1991 Neil Emberton (Newtown)
1992 Colin Jones (Eyri)
1993 Neil Emberton (Newtown)
1994 Colin Jones (Eyri)
1995 Ian Pierce (Tipton)
1996 C Bradshaw (Wrexham)
1997 T Davies (Newtown)
1998 G Clowes (Prestatyn)
1999 Alun Vaughan (Eyri)
2000 Duncan Hughes (Wrexham)

U17 Men

1973 Vaughan Edwards (Wrexham)
1974 Vaughan Edwards (Wrexham)
1975 Vaughan Edwards (Wrexham)
1976 Tony Blackwell (Wrexham)
1977 D Tomlinson (Wrexham)
1978 John Messum (Deeside)
1979 John Messum (Deeside(
1980 I Humphreys (Wrexham)
1981 G A Griffiths (Eyri)
1982 Andrew Ridgeway (Wrexham)
1983 C Kneale (Wrexham)
1984 N Glynn (Newtown)
1985 Andrew Edge (Wrexham)
1986 Roger Jones (Deeside)
1987 Bedwyr Hughes (Eyri)
1988 Bedwyr Hughes (Eyri0
1989 Neil Emberton (Newtown)
1990 Neil Emberton (Newtown)
1991 Colin Jones (Eyri)
1992 John Peters (Newtown)
1993 Ian Pierce (Wrexham)
1994 I Williams (Wrexham)
1995 Alun Vaughan (Eyri)
1996 C Lundy (Wrexham)
1997 Andrew Davies (Newtown)
1998 Duncan Hughes (Wrexham)
1999 Cai Pierce (Eyri)
2000 Neil Jones (Colwyn Bay)

U15 Boys

1977 John Messum (Deeside)
1978 N C Jones (Deeside)
1979 T Wylie (North Powys)
1980 S Evans (Wrexham)
1981 Andrew Ridgeway (Wrexham)
1982 Gary Davies (Wrexham)
1983 Neil Bebbibgton (Colwyn Bay)
1984 Andrew Edge (Wrexham)
1985 P Wells (Colwyn Bay)
1986 P Grant (Eyri)
1987 M Smith (Deeside)
1988 Neil Emberton (Newtown)
1989 Colin Jones (Eyri)
1990 R Brown (Newtown)
1991 Ian Pierce (Wrexham)
1992 A McLean (Eyri)
1993 Alun Vaughan (Eyri)
1994 Alun Vaughan (Eyri)
1995 Andrew Davies (Newtown)
1996 Duncan Hughes (Wrexham)
1997 Cai Pierce (Eyri)
1998 Cai Pierce (Eyri)
1999 Llyr Pierce (Eyri)
2000 Luke Northall (Wrexham)

U13 Boys

1977 R Smith (Grove Park School)
1978 C Jones (St Davids School)
1979 N Jones (Denbigh High School)
1980 G Ellis (Eyri)
1981 N Key (Wrexham)
1982 N Key (Wrexham)
1983 D Ll Roberts (Eyri)
1984 P Prydderch (Eyri)
1985 I Kneale (Wrexham)
1986 J Kidd (Deeside)
1987 D Thomas (Colwyn Bay)
1988 Ian Oliver (Colwyn Bay)
1989 Ian Pierce (Wrexham)
1990 P Wilshaw (Wrexham)
1991 I Williams (Wrexham)
1992 Matthew Russell (C Bay)
1993 Andrew Davies (Newtown)
1994 Mike Bodden (Colwyn Bay)
1995 Carl Prior (Deeside)
1996 Cai Pierce (Eyri)
1997 N Jones (Eirias High School)
1998 Luke Northall (Wrexham)
1999 Llion Davies (Wrexham)
2000 Nicholas Northall (Wrexham)

Senior Women

1977 K Wright (St Davids School)
1978 C Cole (Deeside)
1979 P Jones (Deeside)
1980 S Davies (Deeside)
1981 Susan Tooby (Bangor University)
1982 Susan Tooby (Bangor University)
1983 T Williams (Colwym Bay)
1984 Karen Adams (Wrexham)
1985 A carson (Eyri)
1986 Lynn Maddison (Colwyn Bay)
1987 Lynn Maddison (Colwyn Bay
1988 P Yale (Eyri)
1989 Liz Hughes (Aberystwyth)
1990 Lynn Maddison (Sale)
1991 Liz Hughes (Aberystwyth)
1992 Lynn Maddison (Sale)
1993 Lynn Maddison (Sale)
1994 Lynn Maddison (Sale)
1995 Lynn Maddison (Sale)
1996 Isabel Redfern (Colwyn Bay)
1997 Isabel Redfern (Colwyn Bay)
1998 T Williams (Eyri)
1999 Emma Davies (Deeside)
2000 Ruth Schofield (Wrexham)

U20 Women

1990 M O'Brien (Bangor University)
1991 Emma Davies (Deeside)
1992 Claire Schofield (Wrexham)
1993 Isabel redfern (Colwyn Bay)
1994 No entries
1995 No entries
1996 No entries
1997 C Wynn Green (Ruthin)
1998 No entries
1999 Sian Williams (Wrexham)
2000 J Maundrell (Deeside)

U17 Women

1981 Nicola Charlton (Sale)
1982 Karen Adams (Wrexham)
1983 Lynn Maddison (Colwyn Bay)
1984 Lynn Maddison (Colwyn bay)
1985 S McCall (Crewe)
1986 D Samuels (Wrexham)
1987 N Lucas (Deeside)
1988 Kim Barraclough (Colwyn Bay)
1989 Isabel Redfern (Colwyn Bay)
1990 Clare Schofield (Wrexham)
1991 Clare Schofield (Wrexham)
1992 Clare Edwards (Wrexham)
1993 C Morgan (Newtown)
1994 J Lang (Colwyn Bay)
1995 B Castle (Prestatyn HS)
1996 C Wynn Green (Ruthin)
1997 Sherin Omed (Eyri)
1998 Laura Scott (Brecon)
1999 J Maundrell (Deeside)
2000 Sarah Wallbank (Wrexham)

U15 Girls

1977 S Davies (Deeside)
1978 S Davies (Deeside)
1979 C Davies (Deeside)
1980 Nicola Charlton (Deeside)
1981 J Kirk (Howardian High School)
1982 S Key (Wrexham)
1983 P Yale (Eyri)
1984 P Yale (Eyri)
1985 C Jones (Eyri)
1986 Kim Barraclough (Colwyn Bay)
1987 Vanessa Jones (Wrexham)
1988 Clare Schofield (Wrexham)
1989 Clare Schofield (Wrexham)
1990 Clare Edwards (Wrexham)
1991 C Morgan (Wrexham)
1992 A Jones (Wrexham)
1993 Zoe Parry (Colwyn Bay)
1994 Sherin Omed (Eyri)
1995 Sherin Omed (Eyri)
1996 S Williams (Wrexham)
1997 Laura Scott (Brecon)
1998 Sarah Wallbank (Wrexham)
1999 Sarah Wallbank (Wrexham)
2000 Faye Harding (Wrexham)

U13 Girls

1978 D McLean (Deeside)
1979 E Smallman (Deeside)
1980 S Key (Wrexham)
1981 J Traynor (Deeside)
1982 D Samuels (Wrexham)
1983 Amanda Wale (Wrexham)
1984 D Hoban (Newtown)
1985 W Jones (Newtown)
1986 J Bradley (Newtown)
1987 Clare Edwards (Wrexham)
1988 Amanda Rowbotham (C. Bay)
1989 Amanda Rowbotham (C. Bay)
1990 A Jones (Wrexham)
1991 L Allum (Oswestry)
1992 Sherin Omed (Eyri)
1993 Sherin Omed (Eyri)
1994 Laura Jones (Wrexham)
1995 Laura Jones (Wrexham)
1996 Sarah Wallbank (Wrexham)
1997 Sarah Wallbank (Wrexham)
1998 Faye Harding (Wrexham)
1999 Faye Harding (Wrexham)
2000 Lisa Lanini (Wrexham)

Section 7

Welsh Championships Results (Road and Fell) All Groups

WELSH U20 JUNIOR MEN 5K CHAMPIONSHIPS

1997	Simon Lewis	16:40	1998	Simon Lewis	16:29	1999	Jon Phillips	15:23
2000	Marc Hobbs	16:48						

WELSH U17 MEN 3 MILES / 5K CHAMPIONSHIPS

1980	Andrew Smith	15:17	1981	Nigel Stops	14:37	1982	Brian Matthews	14:24
1983	Andrew Rodgers	14:28	1984	Paul Williams	16:14	1985	Andrew Pritchard	15:26
1986	Andrew McIntyre	16:17	1987	Gerallt Owen	15:38	1988	Gary Cutler	15:37
1989	Richard Baker	16:06	1990	Matthew Martin	16:35	1991	Colin Jones	15:52
1992	Chris Blount	16:19	1993	Damian Cuke	14:28	1994	Gavin Hughes	16:08
1995	Steven Lawrence	16:54	1996	Tim Gardner	15:06	1997	Rory Broady	19:08
1998	Daniel Beynon	16:43	1999	David Notman	15:58	2000	Alex Hains	16:20

WELSH U20 JUNIOR WOMEN 5K CHAMPIONSHIPS

1998	Jamie Jones	20:08	1999	Sian Pritchard	20:10	2000	Sian Pritchard	20:41

WELSH U17 WOMEN 5K CHAMPIONSHIPS

1998	Sian Williams	20:34	1999	Clare Evans	19:40	2000	Cath E Jones	23:43

WELSH 10K CHAMPIONSHIPS – SENIOR MEN – FIRST THREE

1984	Alun Roper (Swansea)	29:46	Mick Crowell (Bridgend)	29:49	Steve Smith (Swansea)	30:18
1985	Mike Bishop (Staffs)	28:34	Chris Buckley (Westbury)	28:48	Dennis Fowles (Cardiff)	29:08
1986	Steve Jones (Newport)	28:39	Peter Jenkins (Newport)	29:27	Tony Blackwell (Wrexham)	29:31
1987	Nigel Adams (Swansea)	29:45	Brian Matthews (Barry)	29:56	Steve Brace (Bridgend)	30:09
1988	Nigel Adams (Swansea)	29:18	Kenny Davies (Newport)	30:28	Brian Matthews (Barry)	30:38
1989	Chris Buckley (Westbury)	29:55	Ieuan Ellis (Newport)	30:47	Gareth Davies (Westbury)	31:15
1990	Nigel Adams (Swansea)	29:34	Chris Buckley (Westbury)	31:15	Steve Brace (Bridgend)	30:33
	nb Chris was a clear 2nd with 800m to go but was misdirected and finished 7th. He was awarded second place.					
1991	Jerry Hall (Swansea)	30:18	Steve Rhind (Cardiff)	30:58	Colin Jones (Eryri)	31:01
1992	Steve Brace (Bridgend)	30:11	Greg Newhams (Bridgend)	30:15	Mark Morgan (Newport)	30:26
1993	Chris Buckley (Westbury)	29:10	Justin Hobbs (Cardiff)	29:18	Steve Brace (Bridgend)	29:45
1994	Justin Hobbs (Cardiff)	29:31	Christian Stephenson (Cardiff)	29:49	Kevin Blake (Cardiff)	30:24
1995	Dale Rixon (Bridgend)	29:57	Mark Shaw (Newport)	30:40	Martin Rees (Swansea)	30:42
1996	Darren Hiscox (Bridgend)	30:13	Mark Morgan (Swansea)	30:23	Steve Brace (Bridgend)	30:33
1997	Steve Brace (Bridgend)	30:14	Darren Hiscox (Bridgend)	30:15	Gareth Davies (Bridgend)	30:18
1998	Christian Stephenson (Cardiff)	29:28	Marcus Jenkins (Newport)	30:18	Steve Brace (Bridgend)	30:45
1999	Mark Morgan (Swansea)	30:22	Dale Rixon (Bridgend)	30:59	Steve Brace (Bridgend)	31:01
2000	Darren Hiscox (Bridgend)	32:02	Martin Rees (Neath)	32:04	Nigel Adams (Swansea)	32:06

WELSH 10K CHAMPIONSHIPS – SENIOR WOMEN – FIRST THREE

1984	Barbara Ann King (Trin Coll)	34:35	Sally James (Newport)	35:14	Liz Gooch (Beddau)	38:41
1985	Annmarie Fox (Swansea)	34:48	Pat Gallagher (Westbury)	36:38	Jackie Hulbert (Les Croupiers)	
1986	Lynn Maddison (C Bay)	34:02	Pat Gallagher (Westbury)	36:43	Liz Hughes (Aberystwyth)	38:18
1987	Sally Lynch (Newport)	34:29	Bronwen Cardy (Bromsgrove)	34:43	Hayley Nash (Torfaen)	34:53

1988	Ceri Pritchard (Warw Univ)	34:31	Bernadette Walters (Cardiff)	36:18	Sarah Hodge (Stroud)	36:35
1989	Bernadette Walters (Cardiff)	34:56	Maggie Smith (Aldershot)	36:08	Sue Neal (Les Croupiers)	37:22
1990	Ceri Pritchard (Coventry)	35:01	Bronwen CardyWise (Broms)	36:32	Janet Kelly (Gloucester)	37:52
1991	Nicola Haines Jones (Newp)	35:48	Ann Cartwright (Prestatyn)	38:26	Ruth Collishaw (Les Croup)	40:21
1992	Bronwen CardyWise (Broms)	35:41	Nicola Haines Jones (Newp)	36:13	Debbie Chick (Newport)	37:04
1993	Hayley Nash (Cardiff)	34:25	Beccy Cameron (Bridgend)	35:55	Nicola Haines Jones (Newp)	36:23
1994	Lynn Maddison (C Bay)	35:07	Nicola Haines Jones (Newp)	35:32	Bronwen CardyWise (Bridg)	35:57
1995	Wendy Ore (Cardiff)	34:44	Bronwen CardyWise (Brid)	35:12	Eryl Davies (Bridgend)	36:14
1996	Hayley Nash (Newport)	34:36	Frances Gill (Newport)	36:03	Sally Lynch (Newport)	36:20
1997	Emma Evans (Bridgend)	35:08	Viv Conneely (Birchfield)	35:30	Debbie Chick (Bridgend)	35:36
1998	Frances Gill (Neath)	35:09	Liz Francis Thomas (Cardiff)	36:01	Nicola Haines Jones (Newp)	36:11
1999	Nicola Haines Jones (Newp)	36:03	Bernadette Walters (Cardiff)	36:34	Michelle Cooke (Llanelli)	36:41
2000	Louise Copp (Cardiff)	37:12	Sandra Bunn (Lliswerry)	37:16	Debbie Phillips (Cardiff)	38:56

WELSH 10 MILES CHAMPIONSHIPS – SENIOR MEN – FIRST THREE

1981	Ali Cole (Swansea)	49:53	Ieuan Ellis (Newport)	50:16	= Kenny Davies (Newport)	50:16
1982	Kenny Davies (Newport)	49:09	Norman Wilson (TVH)	49:23	Colin Mattock (Wolves)	49:40
1983	Nigel Adams (Swansea)	49:45	Mick McGeoch (Les C)	50:22	Steve Brown (Cheltenham)	50:56
1984	Peter Williams (Swansea)	49:08	Mick McGeoch (Barry)	50:29	Steve Smith (Swansea)	50:31
1985	Ieuan Ellis (Newport)	49:53	Alun Roper (Swansea)	49:57	Neil Hardee (Newport)	50:00
1986	Ieuan Ellis (Newport)	49:29	Steve Smith (Swansea)	50:23	Alan Maddocks (Leicester)	50:33
1987	Dennis Fowles (Cardiff)	49:25	Greg Newhams (Bridgend)	49:35	Steve Brace (Bridgend)	51:08
1988	Ieuan Ellis (Newport)	49:48	Owen G Lewis (Swansea)	50:12	Greg Newhams (Bridgend)	50:39
1989	Steve Brace (Bridgend)	48:34	Greg Newhams (Bridgend)	49:16	Jerry Hall (Swansea)	49:26
1990	Steve Brace (Bridgend)	48:12	Greg Newhams (Bridgend)	48:53	Dale Rixon (Cardiff)	49:39
1991	Steve Brace (Bridgend)	48:10	Greg Newhams (Bridgend)	49:32	Kenny Davies (Newport)	49:49
1992	Nigel Adams (Swansea)	48:15	Steve Brace (Bridgend)	48:49	Shaun Tobin (Swansea)	48:50
1993	Steve Brace (Bridgend)	49:44	Shaun Tobin (Swansea)	50:48	Martin Rees (Swansea)	51:35
1994	Steve Brace (Bridgend)	49:40	John Edwards (Bridgend)	49:44	Gareth Davies (Bridgend)	50:07
1995	Steve Brace (Bridgend)	48:24	Gareth Davies (Bridgend)	49:32	Jon Hooper (Bridgend)	50:19
1996	Gareth Davies (Bridgend)	49:38	Shaun Tobin (Swansea)	49:51	Darren Hiscox (Bridgend)	50:29
1997	Steve Brace (Bridgend)	51:11	Gareth Davies (Bridgend)	51:20	Paul Richards (Neath)	51:51
1998	Andres Jones (Cardiff)	52:07	Martin Rees (Neath)	52:16	Philip Jones (Neath)	56:14
1999	Rodri Jones (Westbury)	52:47	Richard Szade (Newport)	53:32	Kenny Davies (Swansea)	57.24
2000	Mark Morgan (Swansea)	51:21	Shaun Tobin (Swansea)	52:08	Adrian Bailey (Bro Dysynni)	52:14

WELSH 10 MILE CHAMPIONSHIPS – SENIOR WOMEN – FIRST THREE

1982	Bronwen Smith (Bromsgrove)	62:00	Louise Copp (Port Talbot)	64:18	Debbie Chick (UCWA)	65:06
1983	Susan Tooby (Cardiff)	55:66	Sally James (Newport)	59:05	Jackie Hulbert (Les Croup)	59:40
1984	Wendy Ore (Bridgend)	60:42	Liz Williams (Newport)	61:47	Gillian Evans (Bridgend)	64:59
1985	Sue Graham (Torfaen)	61:20	Rebecca Powell (Swansea)	63:35	Bernadette Thomas (Cardiff)	63:43
1986	Jackie Hulbert (Les Croup)	59:31	Sue Graham (Torfaen)	61:17	Rebecca Powell (Swansea)	62:19
1987	Eryl Davies (Les Croup)	59:35	Rebecca Powell (Swansea)	63:56	Veronica Singleton (Les C)	65:47
1988	Eryl Davies (Les Croup)	60:18	Bernadette Walters (Cardiff)	62:29	Peta Bee (Birchfield)	63:30
1989	Beccy Richardson (Les C)	61:07	Liz Hardley (Wrexham)	62:40	Liz Hughes (Aberystwyth)	62:45
1990	Ceri Pritchard (Coventry)	56:03	Bronwen CardyWise (Broms)	56:46	Sally Lynch (Newport)	56:57
1991	Ceri Pritchard (Herne Hill)	55:47	Bronwen CardyWise (Broms)	57:36	Sally Lynch (Newport)	57:48
1992	Liz Hughes (Cardiff)	56:57	Debbie Chick (Newport)	57:59	Nicola Haines Jones (Newp)	58:46
1993	Hayley Nash (Cardiff)	57:05	Sally Lynch (Newport)	60:03	Nicky Haines Jones (Newp)	60:45
1994	Hayley Nash (Cardiff)	55:32	Sally Lynch (Newport)	57:53	Debbie Newhams (Bridgend)	57:59
1995	Sally Lynch (Newport)	58:24	Barbara Boylan (Cardiff)	59:15	Dinah Cheverton (Newport)	59:16
1996	Angharad Mair (Newport)	56:52	Emma Evans (Bridgend)	60:51	Clare Evans (Unattached)	61:39
1997	Frances Gill (Neath)	58:50	Emma Evans (Bridgend)	60:53	Claire Allen (Swansea)	62:29
1998	Angharad Mair (Newport)	55:19	Frances Gill (Neath)	59:37	Debbie Phillips (Cleddau)	61:56
1999	Bernadette Walters (Cardiff)	60:18	Louise Copp (Cardiff)	63:47	Edwina Turner (Les Croup)	66:32
2000	Louise Copp (Cardiff)	58:22	Bernadette Walters (Cardiff)	58:39	Frances Gill (Neath)	58:50

WELSH HALF MARATHON CHAMPIONSHIPS – SENIOR MEN – FIRST THREE

1984	Dennis Fowles (Cardiff)	63:53	Chris Buckley (Westbury)	65:13	Kenny Davies (Newport)	65:21
1985	Nigel Adams (Swansea)	64:24	Ieuan Ellis (Newport)	65:05	Tony Simmons (Luton)	66:05
1986	Ieuan Ellis (Newport)	65:00	Ali Cole (Newport)	66:10	Steve Brace (Bridgend)	67:42
1987	Greg Newhams (Bridgend)	67:23	Dic Evans (Cardiff)	68:57	Huw Roberts (Les Croup)	69:31
1988	Steve Brace (Bridgend)	66:56	Greg Newhams (Bridgend)	66:58	Paul Howarth (Barry)	67:49
1989	Steve Brace (Bridgend)	66:07	Ieuan Ellis (Newport)	67:26	Gary Davies (Salford)	68:04
1990	Steve Brace (Bridgend)	66:25	Brian Matthews (Les C)	67:41	Paul Howarth (Les C)	68:50
1991	Steve Brace (Bridgend)	65:58	Anthony Williams (Bridgend	67:20	Mike Surridge (Les C)	67:27
1992	Steve Brace (Bridgend)	65:17	Martin Rees (Swansea)	68:23	Alun Roper (Swansea)	69:22
1993	Paul Smith (Les Croup)	67:38	Ceri Williams (Carmarthen)	67:47	Simon Shiels (Wrexham)	67:49
1994	Steve Brace (Bridgend)	65:39	Kevin Tobin (Swansea)	66:02	Jerry Hall (Swansea)	66:43
1995	Steve Brace (Bridgend)	67:51	Gareth Davies (Bridgend)	67:56	Shaun Tobin (Swansea)	68:17
1996	Martin Rees (Swansea)	66:40	Darren Hiscox (Swansea)	66:58	Paul Richards (Swansea)	67:26
1997	Kevin Blake (Cardiff)	66:40	Martin Rees (Swansea)	66:40	Paul Richards (Swansea)	68:29
1998	Dale Rixon (Bridgend)	68:10	Gareth Davies (Bridgend)	70:43	Steve Brace (Bridgend)	73:01
1999	Dale Rixon (Bridgend)	68:18	Rodri Jones (Westbury)	68:39	Phil Cook (Barry)	69:14
2000	Ian Pierce (Tipton)	67.47	Simon Shiels (Eryri)	70:20	Russell Owen (Eryri)	71.41

WELSH HALF MARATHON CHAMPIONSHIPS – SENIOR WOMEN – FIRST THREE

1984	Barbara Ann King (Trin Coll)	79:25	Debbie Chick (Swansea)	83:24	Sue Graham (Torfaen)	84:25
1985	Ann Evans (Merthyr)	77:36	Ann Howard (Aldershot)	84:00	Veronica Singleton (Les C)	87:34
1986	Sue Graham (Torfaen)	81:37	Eryl Davies (Les Croupiers)	81:57	Rebecca Powell (Swansea)	87:37
1987	Eryl Davies (Les Croupiers)	83:23	Veronica Singleton (Les C)	88:20	Christine Jones (Flint)	89:12
1988	Eryl Davies (Les Croupiers)	75:49	Sue Graham (Torfaen)	81:46	Beccy Richardson (Les C)	83:36
1989	Sue Graham (Torfaen)	83:28	Sue Neal (Les Croupiers)	83:58	Eryl Davies (Newport)	85:29
1990	Debbie Chick (Newport)	83:48	Sue Graham (Torfaen)	85:13	Diane Haines (Pegasus)	88:10
1991	Janet Kelly (Gloucester)	80:44	Liz Clarke (Colwyn Bay)	81:51	Liz Hughes (Cardiff)	82:14
1992	Liz Clarke (Colwyn Bay)	83:35	Debbie Chick (Newport)	84:19	Beccy Richardson (Les C)	85:03
1993	Liz Clarke (Colwyn Bay)	81:31	Ann Cartwright (Wrexham)	82:10	Jo Clarkson (Les Croup)	83:44
1994	Lorna Williams (Unattached)	79:16	Sue Martin Clark (Medw)	80:57	Angharad Mair (Les C)	81:35
1995	Hayley Nash (Newport)	81:57	Liz Clarke (Les Croupiers)	89:17	Glenda Edwards (Les C)	92:07
1996	Frances Gill (Newport)	80:51	Emma Evans (Bridgend)	83:11	Kay Davies (Amman V)	90:39
1997	Frances Gill (Newport)	78:12	Clare Allen (Swansea)	80:43	Edwina Turner (Les C)	81:16
1998	Paula Jeffs (Bro Dysynni)	86:18	Liz Clarke (Les Croupiers)	89:01	Frances Williams (Cardiff)	95:41
1999	Paula Jeffs (Bro Dysynni)	87:41	Mary D Jones (Birm Univ)	90:32	Mary Meredith Prestatyn)	95:43
2000	Samantha Bretherick (Preseli)	78:24	Paula Jeffs (Bro Dysynni)	84:54	Rhiannon Teagle (Abertillery)	87:45

WELSH ULTRA 40 MILES CHAMPIONSHIPS – SENIOR MEN – FIRST THREE

1990	Mick McGeoch (Les C)	4:06:34	Gwyn Williams (Club 69)	4:17:35	Paul Sutton (SGIHE)	6:57:57
1991	Paul Belcher (Les C)	4:27:34	Alan Monday (Preseli)	5:13:30	Brian Adamson (Bridgend)	5:33:17
1992	Gwyn Williams (Club 69)	4:15:13	Mal Griffiths (Bridgend)	4:18:28	Bernard Lloyd (Wycombe)	4:31:20
1993	Mick McGeoch (Les Croup)	4:04:13	Mal Griffiths (Bridgend)	4:06:12	Paul Gwilym (Newport)	4:16:41
1994	Mal Griffiths (Bridgend)	4:29:45	Alan Monday (Preseli)	4:54:22	Mark Rowberry (Lliswerry)	4:55:41
1995	Mal Griffiths (Bridgend)	4:24:04	Tony Holling (P Talbot)	5:12:4	only 2 athletes	
1996	Mal Griffiths (Bridgend)	4:33:51	Mark Rowberry (Lliswerry)	4:59:25	Alan Monday (Cardigan)	5:29:45
1997	Tony Holling (P Talbot)	4:48:23	Mark Rowberry (Lliswerry)	4:53:21	Eric Rees (Sarn Helen)	5:01:05
1998	Jeff Rees (Neath)	4:29:04	Mark Rowberry (Lliswerry)	4:58:04	Lyn Rees (Sarn Helen)	5:01:06
1999	Jeff Rees (Neath)	4:31:32	Eric Rees (Sarn Helen)	4:43:57	Lyn Rees (Sarn Helen)	4:56:27
2000	Eric Rees (Sarn Helen)	4:38:27	Jeff Rees (Neath)	4:40:46	Andy Cleves (Les C)	4:47:57

WELSH ULTRA 40 MILES CHAMPIONSHIPS – SENIOR WOMEN

1990	Kay Pritchard (Les C)	6:14:49	only one athlete			
1998	Dawn Kenwright (S Helen)	5:33:18	Chris Lloyd (Neath)	6:42:41	only 2 athletes	

WELSH ROAD RELAY CHAMPIONSHIPS – SENIOR MEN

1968	Birchgrove	J Powell, I Rennie, J Ingram, B Hayward, P Darney, B Plain	2:21:57
1969	Cardiff	D Walsh, B Hayward, R Maplestone, P Darney, B Griffiths, J Kirby	1:25:05
1970	Cardiff	J Walsh, D Walsh, J Ingram, W Pryce, J Kirby, M Critchley	2:24:47
1971	Cardiff	B Donovan, G Spencer, D Evans, J Ingram, J Kirby, D Fowles	2:28:15
1972	Cardiff	M Critchley, G Spencer, J Bisgrove, J Kirby, J Walsh, T Elgie	2:24:40
1973	Cardiff	C Williams, J Kirby, P Ratcliffe, M Critchley	1:08:51
1974	Cardiff	T Davies, R Atkinson, B Hayward, M Critchley	1:06:43
1975	Swansea	A Cole, D Holt, J Theophilus, S Gibbons	1:25:10
1976	Swansea	A Jefferies, S Gibbons, A Cole, D Holt	1:21:24
1977	Swansea	D Flynn, D Holt, B Davies, A Cole	1:15:20
1978	Cardiff	D Fowles, B Hayward, D Walsh, P Darney, J Bartley, D James	2:04:40
1979	Cardiff	S Slocombe, D Evans, B Hayward, D James, S Blakemore, M Morris	2:03:52
1980	Newport	M Richards, J Robertshaw, P Hutching, M Lane, C Crombie, M Rowland	2:04:13
1981	Cardiff	S Blakemore, L Roberts, D Fowles, M Morris, K Jones, D James	2:02:23
1982	Cardiff	K Jones, B Hayward, H Roberts, D Fowles, B Plain, P Ratcliffe	2:03:35
1983	Cardiff	S Slocombe, H Roberts, M Pritchard, P Ratcliffe, D Fowles, D James	2:01:29
1984	Swansea	C Elvins, S Smith, I Williams, N Adams, N Boughey, A Roper	2:04:24
1985	Newport	I Ellis, N Hardee, J Hill, A Cole, C Clarkson, S Jones	2:02:24
1986	Newport	N Horsfield, A Brown, N Hardee, A Cole, K Davies, I Ellis	2:09:44
1987	Swansea	G Hill, A Smith, D Thomas, J Theophilus, A Roper, N Adams	1:58:45
1988	Newport	J Hill, N Hardee, N Horsfield, P Jenkins, A Jones, A Cole	1:56:48
1989	Swansea	J Hall, G Owen, A Roper, A Smith, N Adams, G Hill	1:51:32
1990	Swansea	K Tobin, A Doel, G Hill, J Hall, A Smith, S Tobin	2:00:20
1991	Swansea	S Smith, J Hall, A Smith, I Hamer, S Tobin, N Adams	1:58:05
1992	Swansea	A Roper, S Tobin, J Secker, A Doel, I Hamer, J Hall	1:57:23
1993	Swansea	A Doel, M Rees, S Tobin, J Hall, P Richards, I Hamer	1:58:32
1994	Cardiff	R Gardiner, K Blake, P Lewis, N Comerford, J Hobbs, S Knight	2:04:32
1995	Swansea	P Richards, J Hall, S Tobin, K Palmer, K Davies, M Rees	2:05:53
1996	Swansea	P Richards, M Rees, M Morgan, A Eynon, S Tobin, J Hall	1:33:52
1997	Cardiff	S Mosley, N Comerford, S Griffiths, C Stephenson, H Evans, N Lane	1:35:40
1998	Cardiff	R Simon, C Stephenson, P Cook, K Blake, S Mosley, N Comerford	1:36:08
1999	Cardiff	S Type, A Jones, A Donald, C Stephenson, S Lewis, N Comerford	1:36:52
2000	Cardiff	A Hunt, N Lane, J Thie, C Stephenson, A Jones, N Comerford	1:45:31

WELSH ROAD RELAY CHAMPIONSHIPS – SENIOR WOMEN

1971	Cardiff	S Davies, C Checkets, D Davies	40:42
1972	Swansea	K Blackwell, K Walker, S Tayler	37:57
1973 and 1974		No teams reported	
1975	Newport	A Disley, J Beese, S Jones	39:49
1976	Newport	S Jones, L Stratford, M Brain	41:36
1977	Cardiff	D Davies, S Cuddihoe, A Notman	36:51
1977	Cardiff	D Davies, A Griffiths, A Notman, D Lewis	46:05
Two events were held in 1977, one as usual in the spring and one in the autumn. From then on the event was held in the autumn			
1978	Cardiff	A Notman, A Blakey, B Thomas, D Davies	37:18
1979	Cardiff	T Kenward, B Thomas, D Davies, A Blakey	36:36
1980	Cardiff	L Marchetti, W Ryan, J Thomas, B Thomas	38:27
1981	Cardiff	F Harwood, A Hartley, A Blakey, B Thomas	35:23
1982	Cardiff	F Harwood, T Kenward, B Thomas, J Thomas	37:06
1983	Newport	S Miller, K Howarth, S James, C Lock	38:31
1984	Swansea	D Matthews, K Roper, A Fox, R Powell	35:43
1985	Swansea	D Matthews, S Stephens, A Fox, R Powell	35:39
1986	Les Croupiers	K Powell, E Davies, V Singleton, S Neal	37:36
1987	Les Croupiers	E Davies, V Singleton, R Mann, S Neal	70:11
1988	Cardiff	B Walters, F Harwood, A Fox/Richards, A Roblin	69:01
1989	Wrexham	V Jones, A Whitelaw, L Hardley, M Docking	64:13
1990	Newport	D Chick, E Davies, C Hayward, S Lynch	67:27

1991	Cardiff	H Templeman, C Thomas, A Richards, L Copp	68:39
1992	Cardiff	L Francis, A Richards, L Copp, W Ore	66:18
1993	Cardiff	L Francis, L Copp, B Walters, W Ore	64:38
1994	Cardiff	L Copp, B Boylan, A Richards, C Thomas	66:38
1995	Cardiff	A Richards, T Sexton, L Francis/Thomas, C Thomas	66:51
1996	Newport	N Haines Jones, S Lynch, C Martin, D Cheverton	49:27
1997	Newport	N Haines Jones, F Gill, C Wensley, H Nash	48:59
1998	Newport	C Martin, G Parnell, C Wensley, H Nash	51:02
1999	Newport	N Haines Jones, S Lynch, D Cheverton, H Nash	49:19
2000	Cardiff	D Phillips, N Lewis, K Doyle, J Clarke	64:31

WELSH ROAD RELAY CHAMPIONSHIPS – U17 MEN

1969	Cardiff	S Davies, K Finlayson, B Donovan, D Fowles	18:13
1970	Cardiff	P Williams, W Snowdon, S Slocombe, B Donovan	17:50
1971	Cardiff	F Cuthbert, P Harries, K Page, S Cottrell	20:14
1972	Cardiff	G Morgan, K Page, W Snowdon,	19:39
1973	Swansea	won outright	
1974	AAC Chepstow	T Hughes, C White, R Stitt, K Dack	49:06
1975	Cwmbran		66:33
1976	Swansea		
1977	Carmarthen	M Arnold, S McCartney, R Davies, R Barrett	50:14
1978	Swansea		50:29
1979	Cardiff	S Blakemore	50:44
1980	Cardiff	S Knight, R Toms, M Thomas, A West	50:29
1981	Newport	N Hardee, A Moyle, A Brown, A Millard	52:00
1982	Barry	P Howarth, M Jones, N Comerford, B Matthews	51:54
1983	Cardiff	A Phillips, A Pritchard, E Conway, A Clayton	53:52
1984	Swansea	E Talbot, S Merrick, J Thomas, S Pride	52:06
1985	Newport	R Jenkins, A Adams, R Parr, S D Taylor	51:45
1986	Cardiff	C Osborne, M O'Neill, P Niblett, J Hobbs	51:04
1987	Newport	B Daniel, J Lewis, S Glynn, A Jones	49:38
1988	Newport	G Chapman, K Storer, A Edmunds, S Glynn	53:22
1989	Newport	M Dunk, M Grimal, C Jones, N Haine	52:24
1990	Carmarthen	B Antwis, D Rowley, J Viceri, R Llewelyn	52:54
1991	Newport	D Povall, G Cooper, P Lee, C Blount	52:10
1992	Cardiff	M Finlayson, A Little, A Waggett, S Miles	53:02
1993	Cardiff	R Court, T Ayoub, N Griffin, S Type	53:54
1994	Carmarthen	T Tyman, S Meredith, G Edwards, T Cairns	57:42
1995	Cardiff	R Hart, D Solomon, J Enos, P Gronow	55:48
1996	Barry	G Colcombe, P Kennedy, S Williams, C Davey	55:04
1997	Swansea	R Davies, M Jones, M Hobbs, D Beynon	56:31
1998	Carmarthen	J Goodwin, S Clarke, D Summers, S Lewis	58:56
1999	Newport	S Davies, A Sims, J Bale, J Nasrat	49:32
2000	Swansea	H Thomas, M Targett, S Jones, S Richards	59:56

WELSH ROAD RELAY CHAMPIONSHIPS – U15 BOYS

1973	Swansea		27:00
1974	Cardiff	A Leek, S Holbrook, P Wheeler, K Glastonbury	34:44
1975	Cardiff		38:32
1976	Swansea	C Clarkson	27:42
1977	Swansea	H Parsell, J Lee, S Axon, C Clarkson	34:41
1978	Cardiff		33:04
1979	Swansea	M Griffiths,	33:39
1980	Beddau	M Lawrence, N Gooch, R Breeze, D Jenkins	33:41
1981	Cardiff	L Williams, A Phillips, C Worthington, M Powell	32:26
1982	Cardiff	A Phillips, A Clayton, A Hardman, M Powell	32:31
1983	Barry	G Noble, B O'Brien, M Dewis, C Hignell	34:46

1984	Cardiff	C Osborne, M O'Neill, J Hobbs, P Niblett	32:01
1985	Cardiff	C Osborne, P Conway, R Baker, M Clayton	31:55
1986	Newport	H Davies, A Edmunds, N Morse, S Glynn	32:06
1987	Beddau	J Hope, I Evans, R McIntyre, S Blow	32:57
1988	Newport	M Dunk, M Grimal, C Jones, N Haine	33:02
1989	Carmarthen	B Pillinger, D Lewis, D O'Gorman, D Rowley	54:55
1990	Cardiff	J Goldsworthy, M Finlayson, S Miles, J Lewis	26:02
1991	Carmarthen	A Jones, S Meredith, A Jones, M McHugh	25:24
1992	Swansea	D Jenkins, N Johnson, A Bowen, G Clement	25:53
1993	Swansea	D Berni, S Lawrence, P Jones, G Clement	25:49
1994	Barry	C Davey, D Huggins, S Williams, P Kennedy	28:44
1995	Barry	L Jones, D Huggins, S Williams, C Davey	28:40
1996	Swansea	P Evans, D Beynon, L Hobbs, M Hobbs	27:43
1997	Cardiff	T Davies, P Kinsey, B Dare, M Boland	27:54
1998	Swansea	C Davies, A Strawbridge, S Richards, I Davies	28:17
1999	Carmarthen	C Harvey, T Page, R Thomas, O Evans	40:19
2000	Carmarthen	C Harvey, O Evans, T Page, G Evans	45:29

WELSH ROAD RELAY CHAMPIONSHIPS – U13 BOYS

1974	Cardiff	A Cummings, I King, N Morgan, M Glastonbury	37:02
1975	Cardiff		41:27
1976	Cardiff	M Pritchard	30:05
1977	Cardiff	A Halton, R Sherry, C Gunning, K Tanetta	41:04
1978	Swansea		35:32
1979	Cardiff	J Pritchard, M Ryan	36:05
1980	Cardiff	I McDonald, P Bridger, L Williams, M Ryan	34:53
1981	Aberdare	S Samuel, J Ramsay, S Fowler, A Jones	36:27
1982	Aberdare	S Samuel, S Fowler, G Howells, A Jones	35:53
1983	Cardiff	R Atkinson, P Jones, S Learner, R Baker	36:48
1984	Cardiff	R Baker, A Clayton, L Parsons, C Carroll	34:01
1985	Swansea	D Naylor, C Arnold, C Leonard, M Hudson	36:14
1986	Swansea	T Davies, J Murphy, C Arnold, C Leonard	35:32
1987	Cardiff	P Edwards, R Barrell, M Fowles, P Curran	35:41
1988	Carmarthen	D Lewis, D O'Gorman, C Morris, D Rowley	33:55
1989	Newport	A Fear, P Little, B Lloyd, S Jones	36:07
1990	Cardiff	I Thomas, S Thomas, G Bridle, N Griffin	21:50
1991	Newport	M Goodger, T Kelly, E Cook, R Young	20:52
1992	Cardiff	S Olsen, J Enos, B Light, K Olsen	20:57
1993	Newport	J Dewhurst, A Thomas, R Moore, N Wachter	21:37
1994	Swansea	D Beynon, M Hobbs, N Reid, L Hobbs	20:37
1995	Cardiff	M Boland, R Kinsey, M Lewis, J Walsh	20:42
1996	Swansea	C Davies, K Beynon, C Jones, S Richards	21:30
1997	Carmarthen	T Page, O Evans, R Thomas, C Harvey	20:29
1998	Newport	J Pritchard, B Clarke, R Jones, C Gowell	21:46
1999	Carmarthen	J Davey, H Jones, K Davies, C Gibson	38:40
2000	Carmarthen	K Davies, W Evans, A Patterson, M McCabe	53:46

WELSH ROAD RELAY CHAMPIONSHIPS – U17 WOMEN

1974	Cardiff	A Cook, L Shaw, S Cuddilee	35:55
1975	Carmarthen	K Price, S Jones, A Pennington	29:07
1976	Carmarthen	K Price, S Jones, D Price	30:30
1977	Carmarthen	D Rees, S Jones, A Pennington	28:38
1978 – 1992		event not held	
1993	Swansea	K Williams, R Jones, L Brown, H Wescombe	67:09
1994	Cardiff	E Turner, S Morgan, J Clarke, D Jones	69:57
1995	Cardiff	S Taylor, C Taylor,, A Pritchard, M Taylor	68:49
1996	Preseli	S Brew, C Thomas, K Freeman, H Hawthorn	66:54

1997	Neath	T Andrews, N Randall, Z Davies, E Jones	48:56
1998	Swansea	A Bohan, C Evans, T Penhorwood, C Jones	45:36
1999	Swansea	C Morris, K Healey, M Blyth	32:14
2000	Wrexham	H Williams, K Williams, S Wallbank	43:46

WELSH ROAD RELAY CHAMPIONSHIPS – U15 GIRLS

1971	Swansea	D Minney, J Hulbert, K Lewis	19:00
1972	Swansea	A James, S Baptiste, K Lewis	18:17
1973	Swansea	A James, C Hole, J Hulbert	24:49
1974	Cardiff	P Wilson, E Stead, M Shipper, S Taylor	30:30
1975	Cardiff	E Stead, D Lewis, C Kearney, S Taylor	29:40
1976	Cardiff	C Kearney, S Hooper, G Reece, S Horwood	31:56
1977	Cardiff	S Deabreu, M Parfitt, M Heaven, L Pymble	Apr 33:11
1977	Cardiff	S Yardley, L Williams, S Morgan, C Sutton	Sep 29:31
1978	Port Talbot	L Copp, C Paisley, E Williams, C Williams	29:58
1979	Cardiff	J Thomas, L Yardley, H Brenton, K Roderick	30:26
1980	Port Talbot	D Brambley, B Morgan, D Crowley, C Cornish	30:41
1981	Port Talbot	D Brambley, D Crowley, C Brambley, B Morgan	29:41
1982	Beddau	L Phillips, R Bowen, M Jenkins, L Harrison	30:54
1983	Cardiff	C Burnell, J Finlayson, N Lane, L Stenstrom	31:53
1984	Cardiff	C Burnell, L Stenstrom, C Thomas, W McNamara	29:53
1985	Cardiff	W McNamara, J C Parsons, S Childs, C Thomas	30:22
1986	Cardiff	J Garrett, D Whitty, C Parry, J Parsons	30:30
1987	Cardiff	C Barnett, D Whitty, A Boffey, R Parsons	30:12
1988	Cardiff	R Parsons, C James, A Constantinou, M Green	31:21
1989	Neath	S Parsey, C Cerusuola, L Davies, K Furse	31:13
1990	Carmarthen	A Morgan, K Williams, A Evans, A Howells	30:30
1991	Cardiff	C Joyce, L Hill, A Solomon, M Higgins	30:08
1992	Swansea	R Clements, S Devey, D Richards, H Wescombe	29:07
1993	Swansea	D Richards, J Jones, S Evans, C Thomas	28:32
1994	Newport	C Wensley, Z Gabica, D Porazinski, L Walters	32:17
1995	Swansea	A Bohan, J Winstanley, L Cowap, T Penhorwood	32:19
1996	Swansea	A Bohan, R Weaver, T Penhorwood, C E Jones	31:24
1997	Swansea	M Blyth, C Rimmer, E Smith, E Jones	30:53
1998	Swansea	L Barfoot, A O'Connor, A Jones, C Rimmer	31:19
1999	Swansea	S Leyman, N Harry, A Jones, C Barfoot	37:30
2000	Swansea	S Leyman, S Clement, A Jones, L Barfoot	53:49

WELSH ROAD RELAY CHAMPIONSHIPS – U13 GIRLS

1973	Cardiff B	S England, S Reed, A Clark	26:55
1974	J Beddows School	M Davies, J Jones, H Lakelin, S Williams	29:40
1975	Cwmbran	L Chevrier, T Walker, S Smith, A Matthuidis	22:36
1976	Cardiff	K Blake, C Sutton, B Harding, C Yardley	23:20
1977	Cardiff	J Thomas, A Glastonbury, L Yardley, K Roderick	Apr 21:47
1977	Cardiff	J Thomas, A Glastonbury, K Roderick, L Yardley	Sep 22:08
1978	Cardiff	F Harwood, J Celnick, S Morgan, S Porter	21:30
1979	Port Talbot	C Phillips, C Cornish, S James, D Crowley	22:06
1980	Abertillery	K Phillips, A Meredith, K Whitehouse, L Dix	22:10
1981	Swansea	S Lewis, R Hayler, S Long, A Long	22:16
1982	Cardiff	J Finlayson, N Lane, L Strenstrom, C Burnell	21:53
1983	Cardiff	W McNamara, J E Parsons, J C Parsons, C Thomas	23:21
1984	Cardiff	J Garrett, S Childs, A Spillane, J Parsons	21:37
1985	Cardiff	J Garrett, D Whitty, H Templeman, R Parsons	21:53
1986	Cardiff	C James, A Trevett, L Dix, R Parsons	22:31
1987	Cardiff	D Higgins, A Jones, L Finlayson, C James	22:51
1988	Cardiff	J Eggar, L Thomas, S Finlayson, D Higgins	22:24
1989	Carmarthen	R Williams, A Morgan, Y Evans, A Howells	22:12

1990	Carmarthen	Y Evans, L Arthur, H Gruffudd, K Jones	22:36
1991	Carmarthen	E Jones, C Davies, L Arthur, H Gruffudd	21:39
1992	Swansea	S Evans, E Penny, R Clements, J Jones	21:44
1993	Swansea	J Winstanley, Z Goodchild, T Penhorwood, R Bevan	22:35
1994	Carmarthen	H Richards, B Jones, C Thomas, G Mounsey	23:36
1995	Newport	R Weaver, C Powell, K Healy, C E Jones	22:32
1996	Swansea	M Blyth, E S Smith, E Seaward, M Evans	23:24
1997	Neath	N Harry, T Keyes, A Davies, L Thomas	22:08
1998	Bridgend	N Grabham, N McCann, T Barnard, Z John	22:49
1999	Carmarthen	N Walters, N Jones, C John, C Jones	42:17
2000	Cardiff	L Brown, C Dowden, A John, L Richards	53:54

NORTH WALES 10 MILES CHAMPIONSHIPS – SENIOR MEN CHAMPIONS

1962	Ray Billington (B'field)	57:00	1975	Ian Williams (Wrex)	54:08	1988	T Cahill (Prestatyn)	51:12
1963	Ray Billington (B'field)	56:09	1976	Vaughan Edwards (Wrex)	53:22	1989	T Cahill (Prestatyn)	51:12
1964	Event not Held		1977	George Nixon (Wrex)	51:32	1990	Glyn Harvey (C Bay)	51:29
1965	J Bayliss (Newtown)	56:47	1978	George Nixon (Wrex)	52:57	1991	Andrew Edge (Wrex)	52:16
1966	R Williams (TVH)	52:37	1979	George Nixon (Wrex)	51:39	1992	Simon Shiels (Prestatyn)	52:39
1967	Ray Billington (TVH)	53:14	1980	George Nixon (Wrex)	51:54	1993	N Haskins (Deeside)	53:05
1968	Ray Billington (TVH)	55:05	1981	George Nixon (Wrex)	51:17	1994	G Williams (Traff)	54:20
1969	Evam Williams (Shrews)	51:14	1982	George Nixon (Wrex)	52:08	1995	Vaughan Edwards	53:38
1970	Barry Williams (Wirral)	55:10	1983	Tony Blackwell (Wrex)	48:50	1996	K Brown (Eyri)	54:08
1971	Evan Williams (Shrews)	52:17	1984	George Nixon (Wrex)	52:30	1997	K Brown (Wrex)	53:55
1972	P Flatman (RAF Valley)	53:09	1985	Tony Blackwell (Wrex)	51:07	1998	A Williams (B Dys)	55:38
1973	P Flatman (RAF Valley)	52:02	1986	Tegid Roberts (Eyri)	51:11	1999	Adrian Bailey (B D)	53:13
1974	P Mainwaring (Wrex)	54:02	1987	H Griffiths (Eyri)	51:37	2000	Emlyn Roberts (Eyri)	54:11

NORTH WALES 10 MILES CHAMPIONSHIPS – SENIOR WOMEN CHAMPIONS

1984	Julie Griffiths (Prestatyn)	68:11	1990	Alison Whitelaw (Wrex)	61:46	1996	Emma Davies (Dees)	63:34
1985	J Wilcox (Shrewbury)	68:50	1991	Alison Whitelaw (Wrex)	60:40	1997	Liz Clarke (Les C)	64:16
1986	J Griffiths (Prestatyn)	64:23	1992	Liz Clarke (C Bay)	62:23	1998	Alison Whitelaw (W)	63:04
1987	W O'Neale (Colwyn Bay)	64:32	1993	Liz Clarke (C Bay)	62:53	1999	Alison Whitlaw (W)	62:53
1988	Liz Hughes (Aberystwyth)	61:32	1994	Alison Whitelaw (Wrex)	63:32	2000	Alison Whitelaw (W)	63:13
1989	Liz Hughes (Aberystwyth)	60:51	1995	Emma Davies (Dees)	64:38			

WELSH FELL RUNNING CHAMPIONS

	Senior Men	Senior Women
1984	Andrew Darby (Mynyddwyr De Cymru)	Angela Carson (Eryri Harriers)
1985	Hefin Griffiths (Eryri Harriers)	Angela Carson (Eryri Harriers)
1986	Hefin Griffiths (Eryri Harriers)	Angela Carson (Eryri Harriers)
1987	Hefin Griffiths (Eryri Harriers)	Alice Bedwell (Mynyddwyr De Cymru)
1988	Colin Donnelly (Eryri Harriers)	Angela Carson (Eryri Harriers)
1989	Duncan Hughes (Hebog)	Stel Farrar (Eryri Harriers)
1990	Duncan Hughes (Hebog)	Lydia Kirk (Mynyddwyr De Cymru)
1991	Emlyn Roberts (Eryri Harriers)	Jill Teague (Bingley Harriers)
1992	Steve Hughes (Hebog)	Angela Carson/Brand-Barker (Keswick AC)
1993	Andrew Darby (Mynyddwyr De Cymru)	Angela Brand-Barker (Keswick AC)
1994	Simon Forster (Eryri Harriers)	Sharon Woods (Mynyddwyr De Cymru)
1995	Gary Rees Williams (Eryri Harriers)	Brand-Barker (Keswick AC)
1996	Simon Forster (Eryri Harriers)	Menna Angharad (Eryri Harriers)
1997	Julian Bass (Mynyddwyr De Cymru)	Victoria Musgrove (Eryri Harriers)
1998	Colin Donnelly (Eryri Harriers)	Victoria Musgrove (Eryri Harriers)
1999	Colin Donnelly (Eryri Harriers)	Jayne Lloyd (Eryri Harriers)
2000	Colin Donnelly (Eryri Harriers)	Sam Bretherick (Preseli Harriers)

Section 8

Welsh Marathon Running

EVOLUTION OF WELSH NATIONAL BEST PERFORMANCES – SENIOR MEN

2:51:50	Pat Dengis	Boston Marathon	Boston	18.04.1932
2:47:09	Pat Dengis	Boston Marathon	Boston	17.04.1933
2:31:30	Pat Dengis	Port Chester Marathon	New York	12.10.1934
2:30:28	Pat Dengis		Lawrence	30.05.1938
2:29:59	Tom Richards	Polytechnic Marathon	Windsor	26.06.1954
2:29:19	Ron Franklin	Polytechnic Marathon	Windsor	11.06.1960
2:28:50	Ron Franklin	AAA Championships	Enfield	29.07.1961
2:25:06	Ron Franklin	Polytechnic Marathon	Windsor	16.06.1962
2:22:57	Bob Roath	Polytechnic Marathon	Windsor	15.06.1963
2:19:08	Mike Rowland	Commonwealth Games	Edinburgh	23.07.1970
2:16:18	Bernie Plain	Maxol Marathon	Manchester	04.06.1972
2:15:59	Malcolm Thomas	AAA Championships	Harlow	27.10.1973
2:14:56	Bernie Plain	Commonwealth Games	Christchurch, NZ	31.01.1974
2:12:33	Tony Simmons	AAA Championships	Sandbach	07.05.1978
2:12:12	Dennis Fowles	London Marathon	London	13.05.1984
2:08:05	Steve Jones	Chicago Marathon	Chicago	21.10.1984
2:07:13	Steve Jones	Chicago Marathon	Chicago	20.10.1985

EVOLUTION OF WELSH NATIONAL BEST PERFORMANCES – SENIOR WOMEN

3:14:31	Betty Norrish		Coventry	15.08.1976
2:55:16	Jean Lochhead	AAA Championships	Sandbach	17.06.1979
2:51:42	Jackie Hulbert	Omaha, USA		08.11.1981
2:46:04	Jean Lochhead	London Marathon	London	09.05.1982
2:45:54	Sue Martin	London Marathon	London	17.04.1983
2:43:56	Jean Lochhead		Berlin	25.09.1983
2:43:30	Sue Martin		Canvey Island	25.09.1983
2:41:51	Jackie Hulbert	New York Marathon	New York	23.10.1983
2:39:26	Jackie Hulbert	London Marathon	London	20.04.1986
2:32:09	Susan Tooby	London Marathon	London	17.04.1988
2:31:33	Susan Tooby	Olympic Games	Seoul	23.09.1988

EVOLUTION OF WELSH ALL COMERS' BEST PERFORMANCES – SENIOR MEN

2:50:00	Wilf Short (Wales)	Swansea	14.07.1934
2:45:00	Ike O'Brien (Wales)	Ammanford	15.07.1939
2:42:53	Tom Richards (Wales)	Margam	08.07.1950
2:42:00	Horace Oliver (Wales)	Margam	28.07.1951
2:30:40	Tom Richards (Wales)	Margam	12.07.1952
2:22:29	Jim Peters (England)	Cardiff	25.07.1953
2:14:43	Brian Kilby (England)	Aberavon	06.07.1963

EVOLUTION OF WELSH ALL COMERS' BEST PERFORMANCES – SENIOR WOMEN

3:11:17	Pat Day (England	Newport	20.08.1977
2:57:50	Sheila Megson (England)	Prestatyn	04.10.1981
2:48:59	Sue Martin (Wales)	Neath	04.09.1983

WELSH MARATHON CHAMPIONSHIPS – SENIOR MEN – FIRST THREE

1934	Wilf Short (Newport H)	2:50:00	Dennis Morgan (Swansea V)	2:51:10	Ted Hopkins (Roath)	3:02:22
1935	J H Overton (Newport H)	3:26:15	W H Woodland (Elyn)	3:58:20	only 2 finished out of 4	
1936	Dennis Morgan (Swansea V)	3:26:11	Ike O'Brien (P Talbot YM)	3:33:10	J M Davies (Pontypool)	3:46:00
1937	Ike O'Brien (P Talbot YM)	3:03.46	V B Sellars (Finchley)	3:19:01	E J Mogford (Hendy)	3:22:18
1938	Ike O'Brien (P Talbot YM)	2:58:23	E J Mogford (Hendy)	2:59:30		
1939	Ike O'Brien (P Talbot YM)	2:45:00	V B Sellars (Finchley)	2:51:00		
1947	Martin Richards (Highgate)	3:28:30	Dennis Morgan (Mitcham)		only 2 finished out of 6	
1948	event not held					
1949	Ken Thomas (Newport H)	2:54:00	Martin Richards (Finch)	3:12:00	E Gordon (Newport H)	
1950	Tom Richards (SLH)	2:42:53	John Nash (P Talbot YM)	2:44:23	A J Blayney (Ealing)	3:02:00
1951	Horace Oliver (Reading)	2:42:00	John Nash (P Talbot YM)		E B Brown (Epsom)	
1952	Tom Richards (SLH)	2:30:40	John Nash (P Talbot YM)	2:35:43	Les Williams (Newport)	2:49:27
1953	Tom Richards (SLH)	2:35:20	Les Williams (Newport)	2:49:20	John Nash (P Talbot YM)	2:50:03
1954	Dyfrig Rees (Coventry)	2:33:02	John Nash (P Talbot YM)	2:45:58		
1955	Tom Richards (SLH)	2:35:42	Les Williams (Newport H)	2:50:58	John Nash (P Talbot YM)	2:54:59
1956	Tom Richards (SLH)	2:44:06	H Thomas (Newport H)	2:58:29	Peter Bowden (Bristol S)	3:22:03
1957	Rhys Davies (Coventry)	2:33:57	Ken Flowers (Abergavenny)	2:34:26	Tom Wood (Newport)	2:35:16
1958	Rhys Davies (Coventry)	2:35:39	Ron Franklin (Newport H)	2:35:50	Tom Wood (Newport)	2:39:41
1959	Rhys Davies (Coventry)	2:35:29	Ron Franklin (Newport H)	2:39:40	Eddie Elderfield (TVH)	2:51:44
1960	Ron Franklin (Tipton)	2:37:13	Eddie Elderfield (TVH)	2:40:08	David MacDonald (Haltem)	2:54:45
1961	Ron Franklin (Tipton)	2:31:40	Ken Flowers (Hereford)	2:50:14	David MacDonald (Haltem)	3:08:32
1962	Ron Franklin (Tipton)	2:36:50	Brian Jeffs (Essex)	2:48:06	Dave Jones (Ilford)	2:55:07
1963	Ron Franklin (Tipton)	2:26:12	Jim O'Brien (P Talbot)	2:30:35	Lynn Hughes (Bridgend YM)	2:34:31
1964	Ron Franklin (TVH)	2:28:50	Derek Davies (HLI)	2:31:42	Lynn Hughes (Bridgend YM)	2:33:35
1965	Lynn Hughes (Newport)	2:26:46	Ron Franklin (TVH)	2:29:37	Ken Flowers (Hereford)	2:31:40
1966	Hedydd Davies (TVH)	2:31:10	Ron Franklin (TVH)	2:33:21	Lynn Hughes (Newport)	2:37:46
1967	Cyril Leigh (Wigan)	2:35:36	Lynn Hughes (Bridgend YM)	2:37:50	Bryan Hutton (Luton)	2:56:12
1968	Lynn Hughes (TVH)	2:31:51	Ron Franklin (TVH)	2:32:53	David Nunn (Maidenhead)	2:35:59
1969	Hedydd Davies (TVH)	2:26:42	Ron Franklin (TVH)	2:37:34	Ivor Adams (Newport)	2:40:34
1970	Hedydd Davies (TVH)	2:35:42	Ron Franklin (TVH)	2:45:32	Keith Brown (P Talbot)	2:51:12
1971	Bernie Plain (Cardiff)	2:20:59	Hedydd Davies (TVH)	2:26:16	John Prater (Hallamshire)	2:31:09
1972	Hedydd Davies (Sale)	2:27:06	Ron Franklin (TVH)	2:30:21	Derek Davies (Cheltenham)	2:34:25
1973	Mal Thomas (TVH)	2:15:59	Mike Critchley (Cardiff)	2:17:02	Cyril Leigh (Salford)	2:19:42
1974	Dave Jones (Cardiff)	2:22:53 =	Rob Atkinson (Cardiff)	2:22:53	Roy Bulley (RAF)	2:29:46
1975	Bob Sercombe (Newport)	2:22:02	John Robertshaw (Newport)	2:28:49	Hedydd Davies (TVH)	2:34:04
1976	Bob Sercombe (Newport)	2:21:43	Russell Brandon (TVH)	2:37:16	Hedydd Davies (TVH)	2:38:00
1977	Bernie Plain (Cardiff)	2:18:22	Bob Sercombe (Newport)	2:19:32	John Davies (Essex)	2:20:14
1978	Alan Joslyn (Newport)	2:25:07	Bob Sercombe (Newport)	2:32:54	Graham Finlayson (Cardiff)	2:37:34
1979	Mick Crowell (Bridgend)	2:21:58	Bob Atkinson (Cardiff)	2:28:21	Dave Roberts (Swansea)	2:32:11
1980	Mick Crowell (Bridgend)	2:24:19	Mick McGeoch (unattached)	2:26:52	Dic Evans (Cardiff)	2:31:00
1981	Mick Crowell (Bridgend)	2:20:06	Norman Wilson (TVH)	2:20:36	Alan Joslyn (Newport)	2:20:46
1982	Mick Crowell (Bridgend)	2:21:36	Ieuan Ellis (Newport)	2:21:55	Bernie Plain (Cardiff)	2:23:47
1983	Alun Roper (Swansea)	2:31:54	D Owen Lewis (Swansea)	2:32:01	Sandy Johnston (Les C)	2:32:13
1984	Ieuan Ellis (Newport)	2:20:35	Steve Brace (Bridgend)	2:24:03	Bernie Plain (Cardiff)	2:24:56
1985	Steve Brace (Bridgend)	2:21:37	Mick Crowell (Bridgend)	2:21:42	Mick McGeoch (Les C)	2:27:32
1986	Dic Evans (Cardiff)	2:23:32	Mick Crowell (Bridgend)	2:23:43	Trevor Hawes (Swansea)	2:32:26
1987	Dic Evans (Cardiff)	2:28:02	Paul Bennett (Cardiff)	2:31:49	Emlyn Roberts (Eryri)	2:35:17
1988	Tegid Roberts (Eryri)	2:26:45	Emlyn Roberts (Eryri)	2:27:18	Mick McGeoch (Les C)	2:27:41
1989	Ieuan Ellis (Newport)	2:22:02	Dic Evans (Cardiff)	2:31:36	Dave Bright (Les C)	2:31:46
1990	Dewi Jones (Carmarthen)	2:29:51	Kevin Wilkinson (San Dom)	2:30:41	Brian Rees (Preseli)	2:31:00
1991	Jeremy Collins (Swansea)	2:29:04	Mal Griffiths (Bridgend)	2:31:15	Gareth Jones (Soton)	2:35:02
1992	Dewi Jones (Trots)	2:32:42	Neale Clarke (Dartford)	2:33:02	Mal Griffiths (Bridgend)	2:34:49
1993-1994	event not held					
1995	Dewi Jones (Trots)	2:39:37	John Cox (Barry)	2:45:58	Rhys ab Elwyn (Eryri)	2:48:15
1996	Howard Parsell (Neath)	2:41:45	Dewi Jones (Trots)	2:46:08	Rhys ab Elwyn (Eryri)	2:49:07
1997	Richard V Jones (Swansea)	2:49:09	Jeff Rees (Neath)	2:53:28	Peter Maggs (Chepstow)	2:53:59
1998	Peter Maggs (Chepstow)	2:48:41	Philip Jones (Neath)	2:48:59	Emlyn Roberts (Eryri)	2:49:30
1999	Emlyn Roberts (Eryri)	2:41:13	Mike Evans (Trots)	2:49:58	Eric Rees (Sarn Helen)	2:59:13

WELSH MARATHON CHAMPIONSHIPS – SENIOR WOMEN – FIRST THREE

1977	Linda Lamonby (Newport)	3:23:20				
1979	Betty Norrish (B & H)	3:29:42				
1981	Chris Barrett (Pemb)	3:02:02	Ann Franklin (MDC)	3:08:07	Betty Norrish (Mitcham)	3:39:48
1982	Betty Norrish (Mitcham)	3:29:14	Helen Francis (P Talbort)	4:05.13	Mandy Griffiths (Unattached)	4:25:42
1983	Sue Martin (Medway)	2:48:59	Jean Robertson (Eryri)	3:20:00	Betty Norrish (Mitcham)	3:45:02
1984	Sue Graham (Torfaen)	3:06:52	Eryl Francis (Aberdare)	3:10:31	Ruth Mann (Les Croups)	3:16:02
1985	Karen Bowler (Beddau)	3:15:33	Eryl Francis (Wimbledon)	3:25:44	Avril Pickles (Unattached)	3:29:29
1986	Bronwen Smith (Bromsgrove)	3:03:02	Karen Bowler (Hailsham)	3:15:58	Only 2 athletes	
1987	Liz Hughes (Aberystwyth)	3:04:04	Wendy Hill (Eryri)	4:03:45	Only 2 athletes	
1988	L Morrison (Bridgend)	3:31:15				
1989	Ruth Collishaw (Les C)	3:24:04				
1990	Kay Davies (Amman V)	3:12:57	Kay Pritchard (Les C)	3:33:12	Only 2 athletes	
1991	Caroline Jones (Carmarthen)	3:05:04	Val Clare (Lliswerry)	3:24:34	Alison Croft (San Dom)	4:02:13
1992	Kay Davies (Amman V)	3:07:37				
1995	Vicky Musgrove (Wrexham)	3:09:51	Elizabeth Lee (Gloucs)	3:50:17	Gillian Evans (Shepshed)	3:51:43
1996	Vicky Musgrove (Wrexham)	3:21:47	Dawn Kenwright (Sarn H)	3:27:24	Tricia Jones (Buckley)	3:56:55
1997	Dawn Kenwright (Sarn H)	3:16:43	Tracey Evans (Eryri)	3:28:25	Carol Trollen (Brecon)	3:38:44
1998	Jo Groves (Unattached)	3:24:36	Dawn Kenwright (Sarn H)	3:27:29	Rosalind Adams (Wrexham)	3:52:22
1999	Victoria Perry (Altrincham)	3:10:38	Monica Barlow (Sarn H)	3:55:15	Carol Trollen (Brecon)	3:57:45

NB It is unclear if the events held in 1977, 79, 81 and 88 were in fact Welsh Championship events.
Event not held in 1978, 1980, 1993, 1994, 2000

WELSH ALL TIME MARATHON LIST – SENIOR MEN

Perf	Name	Club	Venue	Year
2:07:13	Steve Jones	Newport	Chicago	1985
2:10:35	Steve Brace	Bridgend	Houston	1996
2:12.12	Dennis Fowles	Cardiff	London	1984
2:12:23	Tony Simmons	Luton	Sandbach	1978
2:12:34	Gordon Minty	TVH	Eugene	1981
2:13:20	Ieuan Ellis	Newport	Beijing	1986
2:13:41	Dale Rixon	Bridgend	Puteaux	1996
2:13:48	Mike Bishop	Staff M	Paris	1987
2:14:03	Adrian Leek	Cardiff	Pittsburg	1987
2:14:56	Bernie Plain	Cardiff	Christchurch	1974
2:15:07	Jamie Lewis	Swansea	Dublin	2000
2:15:47	Norman Wilson	TVH	Tokyo	1982
2:15:51	Chris Buckley	Westbury	London	1991
2:15:59	Malcolm Thomas	TVH	Harlow	1973
2:16:21	Laurie Adams	Hillingdon	Brisbane	1983
2:16:53	Mike Rowland	TVH	Manchester	1972
2:16:56	Alan Joslyn	Cwmbran	Windsor	1976
2:17:02	Mike Critchley	Cardiff	Harlow	1973
2:17:11	Roger Hackney	AFD	Birmingham	1989
2:17:20	Greg Newhams	Bridgend	London	1990
2:17:23	Alun Cole	Newport	London	1983
2:17:27	Ted Turner	AFD	Hong Kong	1983
2:17:30	Peter Williams	Swansea	St Paul	1989
2:17:33	Trevor Hawes	Swansea	London	1983
2:17:57	Dic Evans	Cardiff	Glasgow	1986
2:17:58	Mick McGeoch	Les Croups	London	1983
2:18:03	Malcolm French	Army AA	London	1985
2:18:08	Cyril Leigh	Salford	Manchester	1972
2:18:19	John Davies	Newham	London	1983
2:18:35	Rodri Jones	Westbury	London	2000
2:18:40	Jon Hooper	Cardiff	London	1989
2:18:49	Simon Pride	Swansea	Dublin	2000
2:18:51	Jeremy Hall	Swansea	London	1990
2:18:56	John Robertshaw	Newport	Sandbach	1991
2:19:04	Bob Sercombe	Newport	Manchester	1973
2:19:20	Mickey Crowell	Bridgend	Glasgow	1983
2:19:29	Pete Jones	Cambridge	London	1984
2:19:40	Eddy Lee	Pegasus	Barcelona	1987
2:19:46	Gareth Davies	Bridgend	London	1994
2:19:53	Simon Axon	Swansea	London	1986
2:20:08	Kenny Davies	Newport	London	1984
2:20:13	Tony Graham	Newport	New York	1998
2:20:24	Jon Edwards	Bridgend	London	1994
2:20:33	Peter Griffiths	Tipton	London	1983
2:20:35	Alun Roper	Swansea	Belfast	1985
2:20:38	Tom Jones	Swansea	Nuremburg	1980
2:20:49	Dave Carr	Army AA	London	1987
2:20:56	Dave Jones	Cardiff	Harlow	1974
2:21:17	Darran Hiscox	Bridgend	London	1998

2:21:24	Paul Smith	Les Croups	London	1991
2:21:39	Malcolm Firth	Manchester	London	1984
2:21:41	Robert Rollins	Bridgend	Washington	1990
2:21:48	Dave Holt	Swansea	Rotherham	1976
2:21:53	Shaun Tobin	Swansea	Chicago	1996
2:21:56	Tony Blackwell	Wrexham	London	1988
2:22:01	Tegid Roberts	Eryri	Dublin	1988
2:22:25	Steve Davies	Mansfield	London	1990
2:22:26	Graham Spencer	Tipton	Glasgow	1981
2:22:31	Tony White	Longwood	Rotherham	1971
2:22:32	Steve Brown	Cheltenham	London	1984
2:22:36	Nigel Spiers	Sheffield	Aberdeen	1982
2:22:49	John Jones	Windsor	Rotterdam	1973
2:22:50	Bob Atkinson	Cardiff	Harlow	1973
2:22:57	Bob Roath	Walton	Chiswick	1963
2:23:00	John Jenkins	Cambridge	London	1982
2:23:04	Frank Thomas	Aberystw	London	1981
2:23:13	Richard Samuel	Shaftesbury	London	1981
2:23:16	Steve Seaman	Swansea	Cardiff	1983
2:23:18	Martin Rees	Neath	Dublin	1999
2:23:29	Hedydd Davies	Sale	Edinburgh	1970
2:23:29	Brian Lamkin	Windsor	Maasluis	1977
2:23:30	John Wild	Newport	Malmo	1985
2:23:40	Paul Bennett	Cardiff	London	1989
2:23:42	Roy Profitt	Salford	Manchester	1971
2:23:48	Lynn Hughes	TVH	Rotterdam	1973
2:23:5	Derek Vaughan	Swansea	P Elizabeth	1985
2:23:59	Steve Kirk	Swansea	London	1982
2:24:06	Damian McCoy	Swansea	London	1985
2:24:11	Ron McAndrew	Chorley	Dublin	1985
2:24:16	Paul Allen	Tipton	Chiswick	1971
2:24:46	Gwyn Williams	Club 69	London	1989
2:24:58	Gary Davies	Sparkhill	London	1983
2:24:59	Arwel Lewis	Eryri	London	1989
2:25:06	Ron Franklin	Tipton	Chiswick	1962
2:25:07	George Nixon	Wrexham	London	1983
2:25:24	Robin Thomas	Hunters BT	Macclesfield	1983
2:25:26	Kelvin Turner	Overton	Swinderby	1985
2:25:32	Norman Thomas	Gloucester	M Keynes	1979
2:25:34	Dave Bright	Les Croups	London	1989
2:25:47	Phil Smith	Bridgend	London	1995
2:25:48	Dave Roberts	Swansea	London	1981
2:25:56	Dave G Jones	Swansea	London	1985
2:25:58	Ewan Williams	Worksop	Wolves	1983
2:25:58	Richie Bullen	Les Croups	London	1986
2:25:59	Jeremy Collins	Swansea	London	1993
2:26:05	Barrie Williams	Swansea	New York	1979
2:26:17	Glen Grant	Cambridge	Berlin	1989
2:26:19	Colin Mattock	Wolves	Sandwell	1981
2:26:40	Owen E Lewis	Swansea	Aberdeen	1988

WELSH ALL TIME MARATHON LIST – WOMEN

Perf	Name	Club	Venue	Year
2:31:33	Susan Tooby	Cardiff	Seoul	1988
2:35:39	Hayley Nash	Cardiff	Victoria	1994
2:38:47	Angharad Mair	Newport	Reykjavik	1996
2:39:26	Jackie Hulbert	Les Croups	London	1986
2:41:47	Sally Lynch	Newport	London	1994
2:42:32	Sue Martin	Medway	London	1989
2:43:26	Eryl Davies	Les Croups	London	1987
2:43:56	Jean Lochhead	Airedale	Berlin	1983
2:45:33	Bronwen Cardy	Bromsgrove	Wolves	1987
2:46:57	Kathy Williams	Port Talbot	London	1984
2:47:08	Liz Hughes	Aberystwyth	London	1990
2:47:28	Jackie Newton	Stockport	Dublin	1996
2:48:03	Janet Kelly	Gloucester	London	1991
2:48:51	Barbara A King	Epsom	London	1983
2:50:18	Sue Neal	Les Croups	London	1989
2:50:30	Clare Allen	Swansea	London	1997
2:50:35	Ann Franklin	Mynyddwyr	London	1982
2:50:56	Beccy Richardson	Les Croups	London	1989
2:51:33	Sue Graham	Torfaen	Maasluis	1988
2:52:39	Fiona Nixon	Westbury	Bristol	1987
2:53:01	Edwina Turner	Les Croups	London	1997
2:53:11	Louise Copp	Cardiff	London	2000
2:53:29	Liz Clarke	Colwyn B	Nottingham	1991
2:53:37	Sam Bretherick	Preseli	Manchester	2000
2:54:22	Ann Cartwright	Wrexham	London	1992
2:55:05	Frances Gill	Neath H	London	1999
2:55:29	Karen Bowler	Beddau	London	1985
2:56:43	Ann Evans	Swansea	Cardiff	1985
2:57:55	Liz Williams	Port Talbot	London	1983
2:58:45	Caroline Jones	Carmarthen	Belfast	1991
2:58:54	Linda Way	Cardiff	London	1997
2:59:21	Bridget Hogge	Eryri	London	1981

With acknowledgements to John Walsh for his assistance in the compilation of these Welsh all time marathon lists

Section 9

Welsh Championships Results (Walking) All Groups

TWO MILES TRACK WALK / 3000m TRACK WALK (from 1969) – FIRST THREE

nb: 1904 – one mile, 1925 walked lap too far

1904	Norman Moses (Newport)	7:27.6	J O'Leary (Cardiff)		E Bethell (Worcester)	
1905	Alf Yeoumans (Swansea FC)	14:24.0	W R Sullivan (Swansea CFC)			
1906	W R Sullivan (Swansea FC)	14:57.0	Norman Moses (Newport AC)		Edward Frankham (Abersychan)	
1907	Alf Yeoumans (Swansea FC)	14:46.4				
1908	Alf Yeoumans (Highgate)	14:44.4	W R Sullivan (Swansea CFC)		J G Williams (Weston)	
1909	Alf Yeoumans (Highgate)	14:30.4	W R Sullivan (Swansea CFC)	14:31.0	J G Williams (Weston)	
1910	Edward Frankham (Abersych)	15:09.0	J G Williams (Weston)	15:13.0	W R Sullivan (Swansea CF)	15:15.0
1911	Edward Frankham (Abersych)	15:52.0	W R Sullivan (Swansea CFC)		H Prosser (Newport AC)	
1912	Edward Frankham (Abersych)	15:18.0	W R Sullivan (Swansea CFC)	15:19.2	H Prosser (Newport AC)	15:30.0
1913	John Evans (Uxbridge)	14:35.6	A Evans (Talywain AC)	15:16.4	James Hollett (Swansea HC)	15:56.4
1914	John Evans (Uxbridge)	14:58.0	A Evans (Talywain AC)		P W Leyland (Brynmawr H)	
1920	Will Ovens (Newport H)	14:40.0	Alf Yeoumans (Swansea AC)		James Hollett (Swansea AC)	
1921	John Evans (Finchley H)	15:28.0	Will Ovens (Newport AC)		T L Jones (Cardiff)	
1922	Will Ovens (Newport AC)	16:04.6	James Hollett (Swansea CFC)		G E Eaton (Cwmavon)	
1923	G E Eaton (Cwmavon)	16:28.2	Will Ovens (Newport H)		J C Kearns (Cardiff)	
1924	Will Ovens (Newport H)	16:44.8	J C Kearns (Roath)		J Heywood (Swansea AC)	
1925	Will Ovens (Herne Hill H)	17:48.0	J C Kearns (Roath)		F R Owen (Mon Police)	
1926	Will Ovens (Glamorgan WC)	15:11.4	R Cox (Glamorgan WC)		Harry Lewis (Glamorgan WC)	
1927	Harry Lewis (Glam WC)	15:59.4	Rees Richards (Penarth WC)		S J Mowbray (Newport H)	
1928	Rees Richards (Penarth)	14:27.2	Harry Lewis (Glamorgan WC)		only 2 athletes	
1929	Jim Edwards (Newport H)	15:38.4	E C Coulson (Glamorgan WC)		H Fox (Glamorgan WC)	
1930	Jim Edwards (Newport H)	14:45.0	Harry Lewis (Cardiff City WC)		Maurice Bingham (Glam WC)	
1931	Harry Lewis (Glamorgan WC)	15:42.0	F C Gibbon (Newport H)		W H Blackwell (Newport H)	
1932	J P Keohane (Glam WC)	15:30.4	F C Gibbon (Newport H)		Maurice Bingham (Glam WC)	
1933	Harry Lewis (Glamorgan WC)	15:00.0	T Jones (Newport H)		Maurice Bingham (Glam WC)	
1934	Arthur Pearcey (Newport H)	14:52.2	Maurice Bingham (Glam WC)		T Jones (Newport H)	
1935	Arthur Pearcey (Newport H)	15:07.4	C F Willmott (Newport H)		J H Taylor (Glamorgan WC)	
1936	Arthur Pearcey (Newport H)	14:30.4	Maurice Bingham (Glam WC)		D J P Richards (Newport H)	
1937	D J P Richards (Newport H)	14:31.0	Arthur Pearcey (Newport H)		J H Taylor (Glamorgan WC)	
1938	D J P Richards (Newport H)	15:17.4	Maurice Bingham (Roath)		J H Taylor (Roath)	
1939	D J P Richards (Newport H)	14:20.2	R G Davies (Newport H)		T Cooksley (Roath)	
1946	D J P Richards (Newport H)	15:35.0	Maurice Bingham (Roath)		R G Davies (Newport H)	
1947	D J P Richards (Newport H)	16:09.0	R G Davies (Newport H)		J Keohane (Penrhys H)	
1948	T L Owens (Manchester)	15:38.9	D J P Richards (Newport H)		R G Davies (Newport H)	
1949	Gwyn Rees (Coventry G)	15:40.8	K W Smith (Cambridge H)		R G Davies (Newport H)	
1950	Gwyn Rees (Coventry G)	15:05.6	Maurice Bingham (Roath)		K W Smith (Cambridge H)	
1951	Maurice Bingham (Roath)	15:21.2	John King (Splott NPC)		John Lowther (St Julians HS)	
1952	David Barry (Roath)	14:47.8	John King (Roath Youth)	14:52.5	David Morris (Roath Y)	15:49.0
1953	Gareth Lewis (Roath)	14:38.6	David Barry (Roath)	14:45.8	Len Rowe (Roath Y)	15:17.9
1954	Gareth Howell (London Un)	14:59.4	Gareth Lewis (Aberyst Univ)	15:34.2	David Barry (Roath)	15:48.0
1955	Gareth Howell (London Un)	14:25.6	John Lowther (Newport H)	14:51.0	E Griffiths (Newport H)	
1956	Gareth Howell (London Un)	14:17.4	Terry Simons (Worcester)	16:04.8	David Barry (Roath)	16:48.2
1957	Michael Shannon (Newport)	14:53.0	David Davies (StJulian S)	15:09.6	Terry Simons (Bromsgrove)	15:16.8
1958	John Lowther (Newport)	14:48.6	David Davies (Newport)	15:17.8	Terry Simons (Bromsgrove)	15:22.7
1959	Michael Shannon (Newport)	15:07.2	Melvin Pope (Newport)	15:15.2	Terry Simons (Bromsgrove)	15:47.4
1960	Melvin Pope (Newport)	15:12.3	only one athlete			
1961	Michael Shannon (Newport)	15:20.8	Melvin Pope (Newport)	15:31.5	Peter Broad (Cardiff T)	15:34.4
1962	Michael Shannon (Highgate)	14:58.0	Roy Hart (Roath LWC)	15:07.4	Les Haines (Roath L)	15:31.8
1963	Roy Hart (Roath LWC)	14:43.6	Les Haines (Roath LWC)	15:59.0	R Townsend (Newport)	16:08.8
1964	Roy Hart (Roath LWC)	14:02.6	Les Haines (Roath LWC)	15:41.8	H M Williams (Caerphilly S)	17:58.3
1965	Les Haines (Roath LWC)	15:15.6	Brian Buckingham (Roath)	16:01.8	Trevor Morgan (Roath)	17:03.6
1966	Roy Hart (RAF)	13:54.6	Ken Bobbett (Roath LWC)	14:35.0	Jack Thomas (Wd Green)	15:21.6
1967	Ken Bobbett (Roath LWC)	14:50.2	Jack Thomas (Wd Green)	15:24.0	Ray Taylor (Splott CC)	15:40.0
1968	Ken Bobbett (Roath LWC)	15:05.8	Jack Thomas (Wd Green)	15:32.0	Dave Rosser (Southend)	15:45.4
1969	Roy Hart (Cardiff)	13:33.0	Dave Rosser (Southend)	13:44.0	Bill K Wright (Coventry)	14:20.0
1970	Dave Rosser (Southend)	13:54.2	Jack Thomas (Wd Green)	14:07.8	only 2 athletes	

1971	Roy Hart (Bromsgrove)	14:13.0	Dave Rosser (Southend)	14:28.6	Jack Thomas (Wd Green)	14:48.0
1972	event not held					
1973	Jack Thomas (Wood Green)	14:26.8	John Collins (Swansea)	14:38.6	only 2 athletes	
1974	Aneurin Tanner (Surrey)	14:28.4	Jack Thomas (Wd Green)	14:37.0	Reg Gardner (Nomads)	15:24.8
1975	John Eddershaw (Sheffield)	13:48.0	Aneurin Tanner (Surrey)	14:04.0	Jack Thomas (Wd Green)	14:42.4
1976	Jack Thomas (Wood Green)	13:59.2	M J Stacey (Bristol)	15:21.0	only 2 athletes	
1977	John Eddershaw (Sheffield)	13:54.0	Jack Thomas (Bristol)	14:16.0	Reg Gardner (Halesowen)	15:21.6
1978	Steve Barry (Cardiff)	13:23.6	John Eddershaw (Sheffield)	14:33.2	Jack Thomas (Bristol)	14:57.2
1979	Steve Barry (Cardiff)	13:29.6	Reg Gardner (Halesowen)	14:10.8	Jack Thomas (Bristol)	14:23.6
1980	Steve Barry (Cardiff)	12:26.40	John Eddershaw (Sheffield)	13:52.10	Reg Gardner (Halesowen)	14:11.75
1981	Bob Dobson (Ilford)	12:59.6	Reg Gardner (Halesowen)	13:51.1	John Eddershaw (Sheffield)	14:07.5
1982	Steve Barry (Cardiff)	12:11.56	Bob Dobson (Ilford)	13:41.17	Reg Gardner (Bromsgrove)	14:16.44
1983	Reg Gardner (Bromsgrove)	13:31.1	Bob Dobson (Ilford)	13:48.7	Gareth McMullen (Splott)	14:18.2
1984	Steve Johnson (Splott)	12:17.9	Gareth McMullen (Splott)	13:31.4	Paul Biggs (Splott)	13:37.9
1985	Steve Johnson (Splott)	12:31.75	Brian Dowrick (Splott)	13:07.43	Reg Gardner (Bromsgrove)	13:55.70
1986	Steve Johnson (Splott)	12:34.34	Pat Chichester (Splott)	13:11.11	Brian Dowrick (Splott)	13:28.28
1987	Steve Johnson (Cardiff)	11:45.77	Pat Chichester (Splott)	13:03.17	Dean Katchi (Splott)	14:21.54
1988	Steve Johnson (Splott)	12:10.4	Pat Chichester (Splott)	12:23.2	Martin Bell (Cardiff Univ)	12:33.8
1989	Martin Bell (Cardiff Univ)	12:11.4	Steve Johnson (Splott)	12:22.3	Kirk Taylor (Splott)	12:30.5
1990	Martin Bell (Splott)	12:44.9	Gareth Holloway (Splott)	12:53.6	Pat Chichester (Splott)	12:59.2
1991	Martin Bell (Splott)	12:19.41	Gareth Holloway (Splott)	12:58.27	Kirk Taylor (Splott)	13:32.95
1992	Gareth Holloway (Splott)	12:12.36	Martin Bell (Splott)	12:46.59	Steve Johnson (Splott)	13:02.08
1993 – 1999	event not held					
2000	Mark Williams (Tamworth)	14:21.7	Neil Loader (Colchester)	15:55.6	David Holdsworth (Ilford)	18:53.1

SEVEN MILES TRACK WALK / 10K TRACK WALK (from 1969) – FIRST THREE

1952	John King (Roath Y)	56:51.0	David Barry (Roath)	57:37.0	Len Rowe (Roath Y)	58:16.0
1953	event not held					
1954	David Barry (Roath)	57:37.8	Len Rowe (Roath Youth)	59:58.6	Dennis Ruffle (Mon Pol)	67:11.2
1955	Gareth Howell (Lond Un)	54:10.3	John Lowther (Newport)		David Barry (Roath)	
1956	Terry Simons (Worcester)	59:31.0	David Barry (Roath)		Jack Thomas (Newport)	60:14.0
1957	David Davies (St Julians)	57:03.8	David Barry (Roath)	59:02.8	Jack Thomas (Newport)	60:04.0
1958	Michael Shannon (Newport)	57:38.8	John Lowther (Newport)	58:13.0	David Davies (Newport)	58:59.0
1959	Melvin Pope (Newport)	56:17.0	Bill Bosustow (Newport)	62:04.0	Eric Hewinson (Newport)	63:02.0
1960	Melvin Pope (Newport)	55:57.0	Bill Bosustow (Newport)	62:18.0		
1961	Michael Shannon (Newport)	56:00.6	Peter Broad (Cardiff TC)	58:25.4	Bill Bosustow (Newport)	64.04.4
1962	Michael Shannon (Highgate)	54:43.6	Roy Hart (Roath LWC)	55:47.2	Les Haines (Roath WC)	59:52.0
1963	Les Haines (Roath)	58:09.2	David Davies (Newport)	61:29.6	H Hill (Roath)	62:43.8
1964	Roy Hart (Roath)	57:23.6	Les Haines (Roath)	62:03.8	John Ridley (Newport)	64:12.6
1965	Les Haines (Roath)	56:33.6	Ken Bobbett (Roath)	56:41.6	Trevor Morgan (Roath)	64:10.6
1966	Roy Hart (RAF)	52:08.0	Ken Bobbett (Roath)	52:28.0	J M Rowe	60:47.0
1967	Ken Bobbett (Roath)					
1968	Ken Bobbett (Roath)	53:42.4	A R Harry (Splott)	56:31.6	Ian Harry (Splott)	59:16.0
1969	Dave Rosser (Southend)	47:49.0	Ken Bobbett (Roath)	48:24.0		
1970	Trevor Morgan (Roath)	58:08.4	T Abbott (Troedyrhiw)	62:59.2	E Davies (Troedyrhiw)	67:58.2
1971	Roy Hart (Bromsgrove)	46:56.0	Dave Rosser (Southend)	49:42.0	Melvin Pope (Newport)	52:56.0
1972 – 1973	event not held					
1974	Dave Rosser (Southend)	50:52.4	Aneurin Tanner (Surrey)	53:27.8	Reg Gardner (Nomad)	53:55.4
1975	John Eddershaw (Sheffield)	49:28.4	Aneurin Tanner (Surrey)		Reg Gardner (Nomads)	
1976	Bill K Wright (Coventry)	51:29.0	Jack Thomas (Wd Green)	51:51.0	Glyn Jones (Coventry G)	55:17.6
1977	John Eddershaw (Sheffield)	49:04.2	Bill K Wright (Coventry)	50:42.4	Jack Thomas (Bristol)	51:36.2
1978	Steve Barry (Cardiff)	47:13.8	John Eddershaw (Sheffield)	48:17.8	Reg Gardner (Bromsgrove)	50:52.0
1979	Steve Barry (Cardiff)	47:56.8	Reg Gardner (Halesowen)	49:47.4	John Evans (Ilford)	50:55.0
1980	Steve Barry (Cardiff)	43:34.10	John Eddershaw (Sheffield)	48:16.20	Reg Gardner (Halesowen)	49:38.14
1981	Bob Dobson (Ilford)	45:50.2	John Eddershaw (Sheffield)	48:06.5	Reg Gardner (Halesowen	48:35.6
1982	Steve Barry (Cardiff)	42:44.13	Bob Dobson (Ilford)	46:53.86	Reg Gardner (Bromsgrove)	50:27.13
1983	Bob Dobson (Ilford)	48:05.6	Reg Gardner (Bromsgrove)	48:51.8	Steve Johnson (Splott)	49:48.0
1984	Steve Barry (Cardiff)	42:08.99	Steve Johnson (Splott)	43:10.53	Gareth McMullen (Splott)	46:39.64
1985	Steve Johnson (Splott)	44:26.2	Brian Dowrick (Splott)	45:34.1	Pat Chichester (Splott)	45:58.9
1986	Steve Johnson (Splott)	45:35.21	Pat Chichester (Splott)	47:03.69	Brian Dowrick (Splott)	47:58.08
1987	Steve Johnson (Cardiff)	43:03.15	Kirk Taylor (Splott)	46:20.76	Gareth McMulen (Splott)	52:06.22
1988	Steve Johnson (Splott)	43:16.0	Pat Chichester (Splott)	44:43.4	Kirk Taylor (Splott)	46:56.4
1989	Kirk Taylor (Splott)	46:00.7	Steve Johnson (Splott)	46:19.1	Pat Chichester (Splott)	47:36.8
1990	Gareth Holloway (Splott)	46:13.54	Pat Chichester (Splott)	46:56.48	Andrew Pryor (Splott)	51:31.84
1991	Martin Bell (Splott)	43:23.0	Gareth Holloway (Splott)	43:51.0	Brian Dowrick (Splott)	47:18.2
1992	Martin Bell (Splott)	42:12.88	Steve Johnson (Splott)	45:59.56	Dave Ratcliffe (Coventry)	49:53.30
1993	Gareth Holloway (Splott)	45:02.2	Brian Dowrick (Splott)	47:23.4	David Ratcliffe (Coventry)	50:20.8
1994	Colin Bradley (Lliswerry)	48:48.3	Pat Chichester (Splott)	50:43.5	only 2 athletes	
1995	event not held					
1996	Colin Bradley (Lliswerry)	48:21.67	Bob Dobson (Ilford)	53:57.00	only 2 athletes	
1997	Martin Bell (Cardiff)	43:53.07	Colin Bradley (Lliswerry)	51:41.26	Bob Dobson (Ilford)	52:31.00

1998	Martin Bell (Cardiff)	43:47.06	Colin Bradley (Lliswerry)	53:59.5	John Gordon (Caerphilly)	59:43.8
1999	no competitors reported					
2000	event not held					

3000 / 5000 METRES (1996 and 1997) FEMALE TRACK WALK – FIRST THREE

1974	C Bourne (Swansea)	19:36.4	only one athlete			
1975	S Morgan (Bridgend Y)	19:18.6	A D Watkins (Abertillery)	22:55.8	A Pickles (Bridgend Y)	23:59.0
1976	S Morgan (Bridgend)	17:44.6	S Reed (Cardiff)	18:10.6	only 2 athletes	
1977 – 1979	event not held					
1980	Karen Nipper (Barry)	17:03.3	only one athlete			
1981	Karen Nipper (Barry)	15:32.1	only one athlete			
1982	event not held					
1983	Karen Nipper (Roath W)	16:14.2	Julie Taylor (Splott)	17:14.9	Sandra Williams (Splott)	21:25.2
1984	Karen Nipper (Roath W)	15:43.31	Belinda Huxtable (Splott)	17:17.87	Julie Taylor (Splott)	18:23.64
1985 – 1989	event not held					
1990	Lisa Simpson (Splott)	15:16.0	Kerry Woodcock (Lake)	15:35.8	only 2 athletes	
1991 – 1995	event not held					
1996	Sian Woodcock (Bingley)	28:39.16	Miriam Doran (Newport)	28:51.67	Hayley Morgans (Leicester)	30:13.71
1997	Hayley Morgans (Leicester)	29:58.73	only one athlete			
1998 – 1999	event not held					
2000	Phillipa Reilly (Newport)	26:37.2	only one athlete			

SEVEN MILES ROAD WALK – FIRST THREE

1956	David Barry (Newport)	54:49				
1957	David Davies (Newport H)	55:17	Mike Shannon (Newport H)	57:15	David Barry (Roath L)	57:38
1958	Mel Pope (Newport H)	53:34	David Davies (Newport H)	54:10	David Barry (Roath L)	55:19
1959	Mel Pope (Newport H)	61:43				
1960	Mel Pope (Newport H)	49:51	Les Haines (Ely)	50:22	David Barry (Roath L)	53:40
1961	Mel Pope (Newport H)	53:32	Peter Broad (Roath L)	54:58	Les Haines (Roath L)	55:00
1962	Vaughan Thomas (Belgrave)	52:20	Les Haines (Roath L)	53:37	Mike Shannon (Highgate)	54:10
1963	Roy Hart (Roath L)	55:20	Les Haines (Roath L)	58:20	Trevor Morgan (Roath L)	61:48
1964	Vaughan Thomas (Belgrave)	52:20	Les Haines (Roath L)	53:37	Mike Shannon (Highgate)	54:10
1965	Roy Hart (Roath L)	51:40	Les Haines (Roath L)	54:45	Ken Bobbett (Roath L)	56:12
1966	Roy Hart (Roath L)	51:32	Ken Bobbett (Roath L	53:24	Les Haines (Roath L)	56:05
1967	Ken Bobbett (Roath L)	49:50	Les Haines (Roath L)	53:27	J Alderman (Splott)	55:50

TEN MILES ROAD WALK

(it is believed that in 1945 and 1946 the events were not classed as Welsh Championships)

1945	DJP Richards (Newport H)	1:22:14				
1946	DJP Richards (Newport H)	1:27:45				
1947	DJP Richards (Newport H)	1:23:02	Gwyn Rees (Coventry God)	1:28:10	R G Davies (Newport H)	
1948	DJP Richards (Newport H)	1:28:25	Gwyn Rees (Coventry God)	1:31:24	R G Davies (Newport H)	1:33:59
1949	Gwyn Rees (Coventry God)	1:32:20	K W Smith (Cambridge)	1:34:41	Maurice Bingham (Roath)	1:35:24
1950	Gwyn Rees (Coventry God)	1:26:29	Maurice Bingham (Roath)		L Williams (Coventry God)	
1951	K W Smith (Cambridge)	1:21:08	Maurice Bingham (Splott)	1:23:51	David Barry (Roath)	1:27:04
1952	K W Smith (Cambridge)	1:21:50				
1953	David Barry (Roath Y)	1:22:33				
1954	David Barry (Roath Y)	1:24:43				
1955	Gareth Howell (London Un)	1:23:40	David Barry (Roath)	1:29:20	Len Evans (Highgate)	1:31:35
1956	Terry Simons (Bromsgrove)	1:23:35	David Barry (Roath)			
1957	David Davies (Newport H)	1:22:10	David Barry (Roath Lab)	1:26:09	Jack Thomas (Newport H)	1:26:24
1958	Mel Pope (Newport H)	1:18:21	David Davies (Newport H)	1:22:07	David Barry (Roath Lab)	1:25:26
1959	Mel Pope (Newport H)	1:17:14	Terry Simons (Worcester)	1:23:46	Les Haines (Cardiff)	1:23:47
1960	Mel Pope (Newport H)	1:24:26	Les Haines (Ely)	1:29:52	Ted McAtee (Highgate)	1:32:09
1961	Mel Pope (Newport H)	1:22:06	Mike Shannon (Newport)	1:25:55	Les Haines (Roath Lab)	1:26:42
1962	Vaughan Thomas (Belgrave)	1:16:16	Mel Pope (Newport H)	1:17:48	Les Haines (Roath Lab)	1:20:46
1963	Roy Hart (Roath Lab)	1:20:10	Les Haines (Roath Lab)	1:23:44	H Hill (Roath Lab)	1:35:08
1964	Roy Hart (Roath Lab)	1:17:45	Les Haines (Roath Lab)	1:22:22	Ken Bobbett (Roath)	1:24:29
1965	Ken Bobbett (Roath Lab)	1:16:24	Les Haines (Roath Lab)	1:19:00	Brian Buckingham (Roath)	1:22:25
1966	Ken Bobbett (Roath Lab)	1:16:44	Les Haines (Roath Lab)	1:18:17	Jack Thomas (Wood Green)	1:21:18
1967	Ken Bobbett (Roath Lab)	1:14:39	Les Haines (Roath Lab)	1:18:41	Alan Harry (Splott)	1:22:24

20K ROAD WALK

1958	Mel Pope (Newport H)	1:40:34				
1959	Mel Pope (Newport H)	1:50:29	Les Haines (Ely)	2:09:36	Dennis Ruffle (Newport H)	2:12:35
1960	Mel Pope (Newport H)	1:44:53	Mike Shannon (Newport H)	1:48:53	Les Haines (Ely)	1:54:54
1961	Mel Pope (Newport H)	1:37:45	Les Haines (Roath L)	1:38:59	Mike Shannon (Newport H)	1:40:01
1962	not known					
1963	Vaughan Thomas (Belgrave)	1:38:18	Arthur Thompson (Met)	1:43:24	Les Haines (Roath L)	1:43:47

1964	Roy Hart (Roath L)	1:37:04	Les Haines (Roath L)	1:44:10	Ken Bobbett (Roath L)	1:44:24
1965	Les Haines (Roath L)	1:44:14	Brian Buckingham (Roath)	1:52:49	Trevor Morgan (Roath L)	2:03.40
1966	Ken Bobbett (Roath L)	1:40:04	Roy Hart (Roath L)	1:48:00	Les Haines (Roath L)	1:50:00
1967	Ken Bobbett (Roath L)	1:42:04	Les Haines (Roath L)	1:45:40	Ray Taylor (Splott)	1:50:53
1968	Les Haines (Roath L)	1:44:52	David Rosser (Southend)	1:46:15	Ian Harry (Splott)	1:49:50

15 MILES ROAD WALK

1929	Jim Edwards (Newport H)	2:19:42	Rees Richards (Penarth)	2:26:23	E Wall (Glam WC)	2:27:06
1930	Maurice Bingham (Glam)	2:21:52	L W Thomas (Glam WC)	2:22:56	Harry Lewis (Splott YM)	2:23:16
1931	F C Gibbon (Newport H)	2:22:05	W S Wood (Glam WC)	2:22:10	T Bradley (Card WC)	2:25:04
1932	F C Gibbon (Newport H)	2:16:26	T Bradley (Cardiff WC)	2:17:08	R F Banwell (Newport H)	2:17:57
1933	Maurice Bingham (Glam)	2:20:19	Arthur Pearcey (Newport H)	2:23:08	W S Wood (Newport Rail)	2:23:54
1934	Arthur Pearcey (Newport H)	2:12:2	W Pearcey (Newport H)	2:14:50	W S Wood (Newport Rail)	2:14:40
1935	Maurice Bingham (Glam)	2:21:07	Arthur Pearcey (Newport H)	2:24:41	L R Spooner (Newport H)	2:25:17
1936	DJP Richards (Newport H)	2:05:10	Maurice Bingham (Glam)	2:13:41	R G Davies (Newport H)	2:18:42
1937	DJP Richards (Newport H)	2:09:19	Maurice Bingham (Glam)	2:10:12	W S Wood (Newport H)	2:20:46
1938	DJP Richards (Newport H)	2:05:08	Maurice Bingham (Roath)	2:10:17	Gwyn Rees (Godiva)	2:17:37
1939	Maurice Bingham (Roath)	2:08:12	Gwyn Rees (Godiva)	2:16:29	R G Davies (Newport)	2:16:58

30K ROAD WALK

1991	Gareth Holloway (Splott)	2:25:15	Colin Bradley (Medway)	2:30:11	Dave Ratcliffe (Coventry)	2:34:35
1992	Brian Dowrick (Splott)	2:21:10	Steve Johnson (Splott)	2:30:52	Andy Pryor (Splott)	2:33:53
1993	Dave Ratcliffe (Coventry)	2:33:16	Colin Bradley (Trowbridge)	2:38:29	Gareth McMullen (Splott)	2:43:38
1994	Martin Bell (Splott)	2:22:21	Colin Bradley (Trowbridge)	2:40:28	only 2 finished	
1995	Colin Bradley (Trowbridge)	2:41:55	Bob Dobson (Ilford)	2:49:08	only 2 finished	

20 MILES ROAD WALK

1951	David Barry (Roath Y)	3:10:35	F Bailey (Roath Y)	3:12:50	C F Carter (Newport WC)	3:15:32
1952	David Barry (Roath Y)	3:09:50	J King (Roath Y)		Ted McAtee	
1953	event not held					
1954	David Barry (Roath Y)	2:52:30	Len Rowe (Roath Y)	3:01:43	Ted McAtee	3:03:47
1955	David Barry (Roath Y)	3:09:12	Jack Morgan (Newport H)		Tom Thomas (Newport H)	
1956	Event not held					
1957	Event not held					
1958 – 1962	no details available					
1963	Roy Hart (Roath)	3:13:02	Les Haines (Roath)	3:18:16	Trevor Morgan (Roath)	3:26:23
1964 – 1965	no details available					
1966	Roy Hart (Roath)	2:40:53	Ken Bobbett (Roath)	2:49:39	Les Haines (Roath)	2:55:34

Section 10

Welsh Participants at Major International Track & Field Championships

The following information lists every Welsh athlete who has competed in any of the 4 principal international championships which are: the Olympic Games, the World Championships, the European Championships and the Commonwealth Games. In the first three of these Welsh athletes represent Great Britain but in the Commonwealth Games Wales is represented by a separate national team. Fixtures in brackets indicate athlete's finishing position.

OLYMPIC GAMES

1906	Wallis Walters	110m hurdles	heat (3)
1908	Wallis Walters	110m hurdles	heat (1), semi (3)
	Wyatt Gould	110m hurdles	heat (1), Semi (3)
	Alf Yeoumans	10 miles walk	dnf
1912	David Jacobs	100 metres	heat (1) 10.8, semi (2)
		200 metres	heat (1) 23.2, semi (2)
		4 x 100m relay	heat (1) 45.0, semi (1) 43.0, final (1) 42.4
1920	Jack Ainsworth Davis	400 metres	heat (2) 51.3, R2 (2) 50.7, semi (3) ntt, final (5) 50.4
		4 x 400m relay	heat (2) 3:40.9, final (1) 3:22.2
	Cecil Griffiths	4 x 400m relay	heat (2) 3:40.9, final (1) 3:22.2
1928	Reg Thomas	1500 metres	heat (3)
1932	Reg Thomas	1500 metres	heat (dnf)
1948	Ken Jones	100 metres	heat (2) 10.6, R2 (3) 10.7, semi (6) 10.9
		4 x 100m relay	heat (1) 41.4, final (2) 41.3
	Tom Richards	Marathon	final (2) 2:35:08.6
1952	John Disley	3000m steeplechase	heat (1) 8:59.4, final (3) 8:51.8
1956	John Disley	3000m steeplechase	heat (2) 8:46.6, final (6) 8:44.6
	Bob Shaw	400m hurdles	heat (3) 52.5
1960	John Merriman	10000 metres	final (8) 28:52.6
	Nick Whitehead	4 x 100m relay	heat (1) 40.1, semi (3) 40.5, final (3) 40.2
1964	Lynn Davies	100 metres	heat (6) 10.7
		Long Jump	final (1) 8.07
		4 x 100m relay	heat (3) 40.1, semi (4) 40.1, final (8) 39.6
	Ron Jones	4 x 100m relay	heat (3) 40.1, semi (4) 40.1, final (8) 39.6
1968	Ron Jones	100 metres	heat (3) 10.4, R2 (6) 10.4
		4 x 100m relay	heat (4) 39.3, semi (5) 39.4
	Howard Davies	400 metres	heat (5) 47.30
	Lynn Davies	Long Jump	final (9) 7.94
	Clive Longe	Decathlon	final (13) 7338
1972	Berwyn Price	110m hurdles	heat (2) 13.94, semi (7) 14.37
		4 x 100m relay	heat (3) 39.63
	Lynn Davies	Long Jump	dnq 7.64
	Ruth Martin-Jones	Long Jump	dnq 5.93
1976	Berwyn Price	110m hurdles	heat (2) 13.82, semi (5) 13.78
1980	Roger Hackney	3000m steeplechase	heat (5) 8:36.4, semi (7) 8:29.2
	Michelle Probert	400 metres	heat (3) 52.16, semi (5) 51.89
		4 x 400m relay	heat (3) 3:29.0, final (3) 3:27.5
1984	Steve Jones	10000 metres	heat (4) 28:15.22, final (9) 28:28.08
	Roger Hackney	3000m steeplechase	heat (2) 8:30.81, semi (5) 8:20.77, final (10) 8:27.10
	Nigel Walker	110m hurdles	heat (3) 14.07, semi (dnf)
	Steve Barry	20000m Walk	final (24) 1:30:41
	Michelle Scutt	400 metres	heat (4) 52.89, semi (6) 52.07
		4 x 400m relay	heat (3) 3:27.68, (4) 3:25.51
	Venissa Head	Shot Put	final (6) 17.90
		Discus	final (7) 58.18
1988	Roger Hackney	3000m steeplechase	heat (8) 8:39.30, semi (dnf)
	Colin Jackson	110m hurdles	heat (1) 13.50, R2 (1) 13.37, semi (3) 13.55, final (2) 13.28

	Phil Harries	400m hurdles	heat (5) 50.81
	Paul Edwards	Shot Put	dnq 17.13
	Helen Miles	100 metres	heat (6) 11.88
	Kirsty Wade	800 metres	heat (5) 2:02.75, semi (5) 2:00.86
		1500 metres	heat (6) 4:08.37
	Angela Tooby	10000 metres	heat (16) 33:26.57
	Susan Tooby	Marathon	final (12) 2:31:33
	Sallyanne Short	4 x 100m relay	heat (2) 43.91, semi (6) 43.50
1992	Ian Hamer	5000 metres	heat (5) 13:40.20
	Steve Brace	Marathon	final (27) 2:17:49
	Colin Jackson	110m hurdles	heat (1) 13.10, R2 (2) 13.57, semi (2) 13.19, final (7) 13.46
	Nigel Bevan	Javelin	dnq 73.78
	Kirsty Wade	1500 metres	heat (8) 4:08.30, semi (9) 4:11.36
	Kay Morley	100m hurdles	heat (6) 13.44
1996	Iwan Thomas	400 metres	heat (2) 45.22, R2 (2) 45.04, semi (4) 45.01, final (5) 44.70
		4 x 400m relay	semi (1) 3:01.36, final (2) 2:56.60
	Steve Brace	Marathon	final (60) 2:23:28
	Justin Chaston	3000m steeplechase	heat (5) 8:28.32, semi (9) 8:28.50
	Colin Jackson	110m hurdles	heat (1) 13.36, R2 (1) 13.33, semi (2) 13.17, final (4) 13.19
	Neil Winter	Pole Vault	dnq 5.40
	Shaun Pickering	Shot Put	dnq 18.29
	Jamie Baulch	4 x 400m relay	heat (1) 3:01.79, semi (1) 3:01.36, final (2) 2:56.60
2000	Christian Malcolm	200 metres	heat (2) 20.52, R2 (2) 20.19, semi (2) 20.19, final (5) 20.23
	Jamie Baulch	400 metres	heat (7) 46.52
		4 x 400m relay	heat (2) 3:04.35, semi (2) 3:01.35, final (6) 3:01.22
	Andres Jones	10000 metres	heat (9) 28:11.20
	Christian Stephenson	3000m steeplechase	heat (10) 8:46.66
	Justin Chaston	3000m steeplechase	heat (7) 8:31.01
	Colin Jackson	110m hurdles	heat (1) 13.38, R2 (1) 13.27, semi (3) 13.34, final (5) 13.28
	Iwan Thomas	4 x 400m relay	heat (2) 3:04.35, semi (2) 3:01.35, final (6) 3:01.22
	Hayley Tullett	1500 metres	heat (3) 4:10.58, semi (3) 4:05.34, final (11) 4:22.29

NB Catherine Murphy travelled as a member of the 4x400m relay squad in 2000, but did not take part.
NB Averil Williams (Javelin in 1960) had not yet assumed Welsh eligibility
NB Tony Simmons (10000m in 1976) had temporarily relinquished his eligibility

WORLD CHAMPIONSHIPS

1983	Steve Jones	10000 metres	heat (6) 27:47:57, final (12) 28:15.03
	Roger Hackney	3000m steeplechase	heat (5) 8:30.90, semi (6) 8:22.44, final (5) 8:19.38
	Michelle Scutt	400 metres	heat (4) 53.30, R2 (4) 52.70, semi (6) 51.88
	Venissa Head	Shot Put	final (10) 18.05
		Discus	dnq 53.78
1987	Roger Hackney	3000m steeplechase	heat (6) 8:21.35, final (14) 8:48.86
	Colin Jackson	110m hurdles	heat (2) 13.37, semi (4) 13.58, final (3) 13.38
	Nigel Walker	110m hurdles	heat (2) 13.62, semi (6) 13.68
	Kirsty Wade	1500 metres	heat (4) 4:09.06, final (6) 4:01.41
	Angela Tooby	10000 metres	heat (7) 33:20.14, final (9) 31:55.30
1991	Ian Hamer	5000 metres	heat (6) 13:54.49
	Colin Jackson	110m hurdles	heat (1) 13.25, semi (dns)
	Colin Mackenzie	Javelin	dnq 75.12
	Kirsty Wade	1500 metres	heat (7) 4:07.22, final (6) 4:05.16
	Kay Morley-Brown	100m hurdles	heat (3) 13.24, semi (7) 13.24

NB Sallyanne Short travelled as part of the 4x100m relay squad, but did not take part

1993	Steve Jones	Marathon	final (13) 2:20.04
	Colin Jackson	110m hurdles	heat (1) 13.23, semi (1) 13.13, final (1) 12.91
		4 x 100m relay	final (2) 37.77
1995	Justin Chaston	3000m steeplechase	heat (8) 8:24.97, semi (8) 8:38.90
	Catherine Murphy	4 x 100m relay	heat (5) 43.90
1997	Iwan Thomas	400 metres	heat (1) 45.62, R2 (2) 44.98, semi (4) 44.61, final (6) 44.52
		4 x 400m relay	semi (1) 3:00.19, final (2) 2:56.65
	Jamie Baulch	400 metres	heat (1) 45.85, R2 (1) 45.06, semi (3) 44.69, final (8) 45.22
		4 x 400m relay	semi (1) 3:00.19, final (2) 2:56.65
	Dale Rixon	Marathon	final (dnf)
	Colin Jackson	110m hurdles	heat (1) 13.19, R2 (1) 13.19, semi (1) 13.24, final (2) 13.05
	Shaun Pickering	Shot Put	dnq 18.10
	Angharad Mair	Marathon	final (23) 2:42:31
1999	Doug Turner	200 metres	heat (2) 20.72, R2 (8) 21.08
	Jamie Baulch	400 metres	heat (2) 45.51, R2 (1) 45.14, semi (4) 45.24, final (8) 45.18

		4 x 400m relay	heat (3) 3:02.21
	Colin Jackson	110m hurdles	heat (1) 13.19, R2 (1) 13.21, semi (2) 13.19, final (1) 13.04
	Paul Gray	400m hurdles	heat (4) 50.15
	Hayley Tullett	1500 metres	heat (6) 4:05.72

EUROPEAN CHAMPIONSHIPS

1938	Kenneth Jenkins	200 metres	heat (2) 22.2, semi (2) 21.9, final (6) 22.1
	Jim Alford	1500 metres	heat (3) 4:02.5, final (7) 4:03.0
	Hubert Stubbs	High Jump	final (6) 1.85
1946	Horace Oliver	Marathon	final (dnf)
1950	John Disley	3000m steeplechase	final (13) ntt
1954	Ken Jones	100 metres	heat (2) 10.9, semi (4) 10.7
		4 x 100m relay	heat (2) 41.4, final (2) 40.8
	John Disley	3000m steeplechase	heat (5) 9:13.6, final (10) 9:07.6
	Bob Shaw	400m hurdles	heat (1) 53.4, semi (2) 52.5, final (5) 52.3
1958	John Merriman	10000 metres	final (6) 29:03.8
1962	Berwyn Jones	100 metres	heat (3) 10.5, semi (5) 10.5
		4 x 100m relay	heat (1) 39.8, final (3) 39.8
	Tony Harris	800 metres	heat (2) 1:58.6, semi (4) 1:50.2
	Arthur Thompson	20K Road Walk	final (15) 1:50:08
	Lynn Davies	Long Jump	final (11) 7.33
	Ron Jones	4 x 100m relay	heat (1) 39.8, final (3) 39.8
1966	Ron Jones	100 metres	heat (4) 10.8, semi (5) 10.9
		4 x 100m relay	heat (3) 40.0, final (5) 40.0
	Lynn Davies	Long Jump	final (1) 7.98
		4 x 100m relay	heat (3) 40.0, final (5) 40.0
	Clive Longe	Decathlon	final (9) 7160
1969	Ron Jones	100 metres	heat (4) 10.9, semi (8) 10.8
		4 x 100m relay	heat (5) 40.2
	John Robertson	400 metres	heat (3) 47.8, semi (6) 47.0
		4 x 400m relay	heat (1) 3:33.8, final (6) 3:04.2
	Bob Adams	800 metres	heat (2) 1:49.2, semi (6) 1:50.9
	Lynn Davies	Long Jump	final (2) 8.07w
	Clive Longe	Decathlon	final (dnf)
	Gwynne Griffiths	4 x 400m relay	heat (1) 3:33.8, final (6) 3:04.2
	Thelwyn Bateman	1500 metres	heat (8) 4:35.2
1971	John Robertson	400 metres	heat (7) 48.25
	Ron McAndrew	3000m steeplechase	heat (12) 9:02.11
	Berwyn Price	110m hurdles	heat (5) 14.57
	Lynn Davies	Long Jump	final (4) 7.85
	Liz Johns	100 metres	heat (5) 11.86
		4 x 100m relay	heat (3) 45.1, final (6) 44.9
1974	Bernie Plain	Marathon	final (4) 2:18:02.2
	Bob Sercombe	Marathon	final (14) 2:37:13.0
	John Davies	3000m steeplechase	heat (4) 8:36.0
	Berwyn Price	110m hurdles	heat (6) 14.28, semi (3) 13.78w, final (7) 14.05
	Dave Roberts	4 x 100m relay	heat (5) 40.33
1978	Tony Simmons	Marathon	final (13) 2:15:31.5
	John Davies	3000m steeplechase	heat (10) 8:57.4
	Berwyn Price	110m hurdles	heat (3) 14.00, semi (5) 14.01
1982	Steve Jones	10000 metres	final (7) 28:22.94
	Roger Hackney	3000m steeplechase	heat (7) 8:39.22
	Steve Barry	20K Walk	final (11) 1:31:00
	Michelle Scutt	400 metres	heat (7) 52.11
1986	Steve Jones	Marathon	final (20) 2:22:12
	Roger Hackney	3000m steeplechase	heat (3) 8:24.49, final (8) 8:20.97
	Nigel Walker	110m hurdles	heat (2) 13.76, semi (2) 13.54, final (4) 13.52
	Kirsty Wade	1500 metres	heat (2) 4:06.74, final (7) 4:04.99
	Angela Tooby	10000 metres	final (9) 31:56.59
	Venissa Head	Shot Put	final (12) 52.04
	Karen Hough	Javelin	dnq 59.40
	NB Colin Jackson travelled to Championships, but withdrew injured before competition began		
1990	Neil Horsfield	1500 metres	heat (3) 3:39.97 final (9) 3:40.59
	Ian Hamer	5000 metres	heat (4) 13:42.46, final (12) 13:32.61
	Colin Jackson	110m hurdles	heat (1) 13.63, semi (1) 13.52, final (1) 13.18
	Nigel Walker	110m hurdles	heat (2) 13.82, semi (7) 13.84
	Paul Edwards	Shot Put	dnq 18.66

	Sallyanne Short	200 metres	heat (5) 23.83
	Kay Morley	100m hurdles	heat (4) 13.21, semi (7) 13.22

NB Helen Miles travelled as part of 4x100m relay squad, but did not take part

1994	Justin Hobbs	10000 metres	final (22) 29:28.08
	Steve Brace	Marathon	final (52) 2:24:21
	Justin Chaston	3000m steeplechase	heat (7) 8:31.08, final (11) 8:36.83
	Colin Jackson	110m hurdles	heat (1) 13.16, semi (1) 13.04, final (1) 13.08
1998	Doug Turner	200 metres	heat (1) 20.63, semi (2) 20.89, final (2) 20.64
	Iwan Thomas	400 metres	heat (2) 45.33, semi (1) 44.82, final (1) 44.52
		4 x 400m relay	final (1) 2:58.68
	Colin Jackson	110m hurdles	heat (1) 13.31, semi (1) 13.02, final (1) 13.02
	Paul Gray	400m hurdles	heat (3) 49.16, semi (6) 50.34
	Shaun Pickering	Shot Put	dnq 17.80
	Jamie Baulch	4 x 400m relay	heat (1) 3:02.37, final (1) 2:58.68

NB Tony Simmons (10000m in 1974) had temporarily relinquished his Welsh eligibility

COMMONWEALTH GAMES

1930	Reg Thomas	880 yards // One mile	final (2) 1:55.5 // final (1) 4:14.0
1934	Cyril Cupid	100 yards // 220 yards	heat (2), semi (5) // heat (2) 22.7, R2 (4)
	Cyril Williams	220 yards	heat (4)
	Peter Fraser	440 yards	heat (4)
	Jim Alford	880 yards	heat (3)
	Ken Harris	One mile	heat (1) 4:35.4, final (7 or 8)
	Len Tongue	3 miles	final (10)
	Stan Macey	120y hurdles	heat (4)
	Wilf Short	Marathon	final (6) 3:02:56
	Frank Whitcutt	High Jump	dnq
	Arthur Lewis	Shot Put	final (7) 11.70
1938	Jim Alford	880 yards // One mile	final (4) 1:53.1 // final (1) 4:11.5
1950	Tom Richards	Marathon	final (5) 2:42.11
1954	Ken Jones	100 yards	heat (2) 10.0, semi (3) 9.8, final (6) 9.8
		220 yards	heat (1) 22.4, semi (2) 22.1, final (3) 21.9
	Peter Phillips	440 yards // 880 yards	heat (5) 50.0 // heat (6) 1:58.7
	John Disley	One mile	heat (5) 4:09.0
	Bob Shaw	120y hurdles // 440y hurdles	heat (?) 15.4 // heat (2) 53.8, final (3) 53.3
	Hywel Williams	Discus	final (5) 45.18
	Clive Roberts	Javelin	final (11) 55.03
1958	Ron Jones	100 yards // 4 x 110y relay	heat (1) 9.9, R2 (4) 10.0 // final (5) 42.13
	Nick Whitehead	100 yards // 220 yards	heat (2) 9.9, R2 (3) 10.0 // heat (3) 22.9, R2 (3) 22.0
		4 x 110y relay	final (5) 42.13
	Dewi Roberts	100 yards // 4 x 110y relay	heat (3) 10.1, R2 (4) 10.1 // final (5) 42.13
	John Morgan	100 yards // 4 x 110y relay	heat (1) 10.0, R2 (4) 10.0 // final (5) 42.13
	John C Jones	220 yards	heat (2) 21.9, R2 (3) 22.1
	Wynne Oliver	220 yards	heat (5) 22.8
	Ray Billington	880 yards	heat (5) 1:57.3
	Norman Horrell	880 yards	heat (3) 1:54.2
	Haydn Tawton	880 yards	heat (6) 1:58.0
	John M Williams	880 yards	heat (4) 1:56.3
	Tony Pumfrey	One mile	heat (5) 4:12.3
	John Merriman	3 miles // 6 miles	final (6) 13:32.06 // final (2) 28:48.84
	David Richards	3 miles	final (13) ntt
	John Disley	3 miles	final (dnf)
	Rhys Davies	Marathon	final (9) 2:30:54
	Ron Franklin	Marathon	final (10) 2:31:24
	Dyfrig Rees	Marathon	final (15) 2:39:17
	Tom Wood	Marathon	final (18) 2:53:42
	Bob Shaw	440y hurdles	heat (4) 55.0, semi (4) 54.2
	Kevin Phillips	High Jump	dnq 1.85
	Terence Morgan	High Jump	dnq 1.83
	Colin Fletcher	Pole Vault	dnq 3.66
	Dewar Neill	Pole Vault	dnq 3.50
	Bryan Woolley	Long Jump	qual 7.05, final (16) 6.48
	Ray Gazzard	Long Jump	dnq 6.61
	Richard Dodd	Triple Jump	dnq 13.73
	John Davies	Shot Put	final (14) 13.00
	Hywel Williams	Shot Put // Discus	final (12) 13.38 // final (7) 46.42
	Malcolm Pemberton	Discus	final (13) 41.70

	Laurie Hall	Hammer	final (10) 48.73
	Brian Sexton	Javelin	final (12) 62.83
	Norman Watkins	Javelin	final (14) 60.00
	Bonnie Jones	100 yards // 4 x 110y relay	heat (4) 11.4 // heat (3) disqualified
		Long Jump	dnq 5.40
	Jean Whitehead	100 yards // 220 yards	heat (4) 11.4 // heat (3) 25.2
		4 x 110y relay	heat (3) disqualified
	Gwyneth Lewis	100 yards // 220 yards	heat (4) 11.4 // heat (3) 26.5
		4 x 110y relay	heat (3) disqualified
	Beryl Turner	100 yards	heat (5) 11.9
	Jackie Barnett	220 yards	heat (4) 27.0
	Daphne Williams	220 yards	heat (4) 27.5
	Sheila Lewis	80m hurdles	heat (3) 11.8
	Carol Thomas	80m hurdles	heat (3) 11.6
	Ellen Grainger	4 x 110y relay	heat (3) disqualified
	Sally Jones	Long Jump	dnq 4.70
1962	Berwyn Jones	100 yards // 4 x 110y relay	heat (2) 9.6w, R2 (2) 9.8, semi (6) 9.9 // heat (2) 41.4, final (3) 40.8
	Nick Whitehead	100 yards // 220 yards	heat (3) 9.9w, R2 (4) 10.1 // heat (2) 22.3, R2 (6) 22.5
		4 x 110y relay	heat (2) 41.4, final (3) 40.8
	Lynn Davies	100 yards // Long Jump	heat (4) 9.9w, R2 (4) 10.2 // final (4) 7.72
		Triple Jump	final (11) 14.47
	Ron Jones	100 yards // 4 x 110y relay	heat (1) 9.6w, R2 (2) 9.8, semi (5) 9.8 // heat (2) 41.4, final (3) 40.8
	David England	220 yards // 4 x 110y relay	heat (3) 22.1, R2 (5) 22.5 // heat (2) 41.4, final (3) 40.8
	Tony Harris	880 yards	heat (2) 1:51.3, semi (2) 1:51.2, final (6) 1:52.3
		One mile	heat (2) 4:09.9, final (6) 4:11.8
	John Merriman	6 miles // Marathon	final (3) 28:40.8 // final (dnf)
	Laurie Hall	Shot Put // Hammer	final (15) 13.18 // final (5) 54.41
	Jackie Barnett	880 yards	final (6) 2:14.8
1966	Terry Davies	100 yards // 220 yards	heat (5) 10.3 // heat (4) 22.4, R2 (6) 22.0
		4 x 110y relay	heat (3) 40.6, final (4) 40.2
	Lynn Davies	100 yards	heat (4) 10.0, R2 (4) 10.0
		Long Jump	final (1) 7.99
		4 x 110y relay	heat (3) 40.6, final (4) 40.2
	Keri Jones	100 yards	heat (4) 10.4, R2 (7) ntt
		220 yards	heat (4) 22.3, R2 (8) 22.0
		4 x 110y relay	heat (3) 40.6, final (4) 40.2
	Ron Jones	100 yards	heat (4) 10.4, R2 (5) 10.0
		4 x 110y relay	heat (3) 40.6, final (4) 40.2
	Howard Davies	220 yards // 440 yards	heat (5) 22.9 // heat (3) 49.0
	Tony Harris	880 yards // One mile	heat (7) 2:02.2 // heat (8) 4:24.6
	Roy Hart	20 miles Walk	final (9) 3:15:02.6
	Clive Longe	Decathlon	final (2) 7123
	Gloria Dourass	100 yards // 220 yards	heat (5) 11.2 // heat (3) 25.3, semi (8) 25.4
		440 yards // 4 x 110y relay	heat (4) 55.4 // final (5) 46.2
	Liz Parsons	100 yards // 220 yards	heat (2) 11.0, semi (7) 11.0 // heat (4) 25.0
		4 x 110y relay	final (5) 46.2
	Thelwyn Appleby	100 yards // 220 yards	heat (6) 11.3 // heat (4) 25.5
		440 yards // 4 x 110y relay	heat (3) 56.8 // final (5) 46.2
	Liz Gill	100 yards // 220 yards	heat (5) 11.1 // heat (3) 24.6, semi (6) 24.8
		4 x 110y relay	final (5) 46.2
1970	John J Williams	100 metres // 200 metres	heat (5) 10.6w // heat (3) 21.4w, R2 (7) 21.5w
		4 x 100m relay	heat (3) 40.5, final (5) 40.2
	Lynn Davies	100 metres // Long Jump	heat (2) 10.4w, R2 (6) 10.6w // final (1) 8.06w
	Ron Jones	100 metres	heat (3) 10.6w, R2 (6) 10.5w
	Terry Davies	200 metres // 4 x 100m relay	heat (4) 21.8w, R2 (7) 21.8w // heat (3) 40.5, final (5) 40.2
	Howard Davies	200 metres // 4 x 100m relay	heat (2) 21.8w, R2 (6) 21.3w // heat (3) 40.5, final (5) 40.2
	Gwynne Griffiths	400 metres	heat (5) 50.64
	Phil Lewis	800 metres	heat (6) 1:52.0
	Bob Adams	800 metres	heat (1) 1:49.6, semi (7) 1:50.3
	John Greatrex	800 metres	heat (3) 1:51.7, semi (7) 1:51.5
	Bob Maplestone	1500 metres	heat (8) 3:57.2
	Phil Thomas	1500 metres	heat (4) 3:45.5, final (7) 3:42.6
	Gwynn Davis	1500 metres // 5000 metres	heat (6) 3:52.8 // heat (10) 14:22.8
	Tony Ashton	5000 metres	heat (8) 14:17.4
	Bernie Plain	5000 metres //10000 metres	heat (4) 14:09.8, final (13) 14:02.0 // final (11) 28:51.8
	Alan Joslyn	10000 metres	final (16) 29:51.8
	Mike Rowland	Marathon	final (11) 2:19:08
	Cyril Leigh	Marathon	final (12) 2:19:53

	Hedydd Davies	Marathon	final (17) 2:23:29
	Bernie Hayward	3000m steeplechase	heat (4) 8:49.2, final (7) 8:39.8
	Peter Griffiths	3000m steeplechase	heat (7) 9:07.6
	Ron McAndrew	3000m steeplechase	heat (dnf)
	Berwyn Price	110m hurdles	heat (4) 14.4w, semi (6) 14.4w
	Alun James	110m hurdles	heat (6) 14.7, semi (8) 14.9
	John Lewis	400m hurdles	heat (5) 53.4, semi (7) 52.4
	Roger Richardson	400m hurdles	heat (8) 54.5
	David Lease	Pole Vault	final (8) 4.50
	Gwyn Williams	Long Jump	final (10) 7.14
	Graham Webb	Triple Jump	dnq 14.64
	John Walters	Shot Put // Discus	final (8) 16.05 // final (11) 48.06
	Morris Davies	Hammer	dnq 3 no throws
	Nigel Sherlock	Javelin	final (9) 66.24
	Dave Rosser	20 mile Walk	final (11) 2:49:41
	Pat Shiels	100 metres // 200 metres	heat (5) 12.3 // heat (4) 24.6, semi (8) 24.7
		4 x 100m relay	final (6) 46.5
	Heather Davies	100 metres // 200 metres	heat (5) 12.01 // heat (5) 25.2
		4 x 100m relay	final (6) 46.5
	Michelle Smith	100 metres // 200 metres	heat (7) 12.3 // heat (4) 24.9
		4 x 100m relay	final (6) 46.5
	Thelwyn Bateman	800 metres	heat (dnf)
	Gloria Dourass	800 metres	heat (4) 2:07.6, final (4) 2:08.6
	Christine Craig	High Jump	final (10) 1.62
	Ruth Martin Jones	Long Jump // Pentathlon	final (9) 6.00 // final (6) 4497
		4 x 100m relay	final (6) 46.5
	Margaret Pearce	Shot Put	final (12) 11.23
	Averil Williams	Javelin	final (5) 47.70
	June Hirst	Pentathlon	final (13) 4165
1974	Mike Delaney	200 metres // 400 metres	heat (6) 21.9 // heat (5) 48.17
		4 x 400m relay	final (6) 3:08.6
	Phil Lewis	800 metres	heat (3) 1:48.3, semi (4) 1:46.3, final (8) 1:48.9
		4 x 400m relay	final (6) 3:08.6
	Bernie Hayward	1500 metres // 5000 metres	heat (6) 3:50.3 // heat (7) 14:23.2
		3000m steeplechase	final (6) 8:36.2
	Gordon Minty	5000 metres // 10000 metres	final (8) 13:45.6 // final (8) 28:44.4
	Bernie Plain	10000 metres // Marathon	final (11) 29:28.4 // final (7) 2:14:56.2
	Malcolm Thomas	Marathon	final (9) 2:14:46.8
	John Davies	3000m steeplechase	final (2) 8:24.8
	Berwyn Price	110m hurdles	heat (1) 14.0, final (2) 13.84
		400m hurdles	heat (5) 53.0, semi (6) 52.8
	Wynford Leyshon	400m hurdles	heat (5) 54.0, semi (7) 52.6
		4 x 400m relay	final (6) 3:08.6
	Colin O'Neill	400m hurdles	heat (3) 52.6, semi (4) 50.7, final (8) 50.58
		4 x 400m relay	final (6) 3:08.6
	David Lease	Pole Vault	final 3 no heights
	Gloria Dourass	400 metres // 800 metres	heat (4) 55.8, semi (7) 56.1// heat (2) 2:06.2, semi (8) 2:08.9
	Jean Lochhead	800 metres // 1500 metres	heat (7) 2:09.8 // heat (4) 4:26.9, final (12) 4:29.9
	Ruth Martin Jones	Long Jump	final (3) 6.38
	Susan James	Javelin	final (8) 43.24
1978	Dave Roberts	100 metres // 200 metres	heat (4) 10.88, R2 (6) 10.84 // heat (5) 21.70, R2 (6) 21.91
	Jeff Griffiths	200 metres // 400 metres	heat (7) 21.56, R2 (8) 21.65 // heat (4) 47.97, R2 (5) 47.41
		4 x 400m relay	heat (5) 3:11.9
	Mike Delaney	400 metres // 4 x 400m relay	heat (3) 47.56, R2 (7) 47.41 // heat (5) 3:11.9
	Glen Grant	800 metres	heat (4) 1:49.3, semi (2) 1:49.3, final (8) 1:49.3
		1500 metres	heat (4) 3:41.6, final (6) 3:38.1
	John Davies	1500 metres	heat (10) 3:53.5
		3000m steeplechase	heat (2) 8:48.1, final (10) 9:02.0
	Steve Jones	1500 metres // 5000 metres	heat (10) 3:49.4 // heat (7) 14:10.76, final (11) 13:54.6
	Tony Simmons	5000 metres // 10000 metres	heat (6) 13:57.56, final (7) 13:39.8 // final (6) 29:01.2
	Berwyn Price	110m hurdles // 4x400 relay	heat (3) 14.20, final (1) 13.70w // heat (5) 3:11.9
	Steve James	400m hurdles // 4x400 relay	heat (4) 51.42, semi (6) 53.00 // heat (5) 3:11.9
	Mike Critchley	Marathon	final (8) 2:19:50.9
	Mike Rowland	Marathon	final (25) 2:48:10.0
	John Phillips	Triple Jump	final (9) 15.59
	Hilary Hollick	1500 metres	heat (5) 4:18.36, final (5) 4:12.72
	Ruth Howell	Long Jump // Pentathlon	final (7) 6.17 // final (6) 4022
	Venissa Head	Shot Put // Discus	final (6) 15.52 // final (8) 45.72

	Jackie Zaslona	Javelin	final (10) 41.08
1982	Phil Norgate	800 metres	heat (3) 1:52.02, semi (dnf)
	Roger Hackney	5000 metres	final (11) 13:51.20
		3000m steeplechase	final (4) 8:32.84
	Dennis Fowles	10000 metres // Marathon	final (6) 28:33.89 // final (13) 2:16:49
	Steve Jones	10000 metres	final (11) 29:13.68
	Berwyn Price	110m hurdles	heat (3) 13.99w, final (6) 13.73
	Steve Barry	30K Walk	final (1) 2:10:16
	Trevor Llewelyn	High Jump	final (13) 2.05
	Carmen Smart	200 metres // 400 metres	heat (4) 24.35, semi (6) 23.91 // heat (6) 53.82, semi (8) 54.75
		4 x 400m relay	final (5) 3:35.76
	Michelle Scutt	400 metres // 4x400 relay	heat (1) 52.49, semi (1) 52.86, final (2) 51.97 // final (5) 3:35.76
	Kirsty McDermott	800 metres // 4x400 relay	heat (2) 2:05.91, final (1) 2:01.31 // final (5) 3:35.76
	Kim Lock	1500 metres // 3000 metres	heat (1) 4:15.12, final (6) 4:14.02 // final (13) 9:36.00
	Hilary Hollick	1500 metres // 3000 metres	heat (3) 4:17.72, final (8) 4:15.69 // final (9) 9:18.33
	Diane Fryar	400m hurdles	heat (7) 60.60
		4 x 400m relay	final (5) 3:35.76
	Sarah Owen	400m hurdles // High Jump	heat (7) 62.84 // final (13) 1.65
		Heptathlon	final (10) 5227
	Gillian Regan	Long Jump	final (10) 6.16
	Venissa Head	Discus	final (6) 50.64
1986	Mal Edwards	800 metres	heat (3) 1:49.81, semi (4) 1:49.33, final (5) 1:47.27
	Paul Williams	800 metres	heat (4) 1:52.55, semi (6) 1:48.52
	Neil Horsfield	1500 metres	heat (3) 3:42.83, final (9) 3:57.08
	Steve Jones	10000 metres	final (3) 28:02.48
	Ieuan Ellis	Marathon	final (7) 2:15:12
	Roger Hackney	3000m steeplechase	final (2) 8:25.15
	Colin Jackson	110m hurdles	heat (1) 13.69, final (2) 13.42w
	Nigel Walker	110m hurdles	heat (1) 13.64w, final (4) 13.69w
	Steve Johnson	30K Walk	final (8) 2:21:05
	David Wood	Triple Jump	final (9) 15.28
	Shaun Pickering	Shot Put	final (8) 16.79
		Discus	final (9) 51.30
		Hammer	final (9) 62.64
	Colin Mackenzie	Javelin	final (7) 70.82
	Tim Newenham	Javelin	final (10) 65.48
	Helen Miles	100 metres // 4x100 relay	heat (6) 11.63w // final (3) 45.37
	Sallyanne Short	100 metres // 200 metres	heat (5) 11.60w // heat (6) 24.06
		4 x 100m relay	final (3) 45.37
	Carmen Smart	100 metres // 200 metres	heat (6) 11.83 // heat (7) 24.31
		4 x 100m relay	final (3) 45.37
	Sian Morris	200 metres // 400 metres	heat (4) 23.82, final (7) 23.97 // heat (5) 54.75
		4 x 100m relay	final (3) 45.37
	Kirsty Wade	800 metres // 1500 metres	heat (1) 2:03.94, final (1) 2:00.94 // heat (2) 4:27.90, final (1) 4:10.91
	Angela Tooby	10000 metres	final (3) 32:25.38
	Susan Tooby	10000 metres	final (6) 32:56.78
	Kay Morley	110m hurdles	heat (4) 13.52w, final (7) 13.83
	Alyson Evans	400m hurdles	heat (4) 58.83, final (8) 58.31
	Gillian Regan	Long Jump	final (9) 6.05
	Venissa Head	Discus	final (2) 56.20
	Karen Hough	Javelin	final (6) 53.32
1990	Neil Horsfield	800 metres // 1500 metres	heat (6) 1:50.88, semi (7) 1:49.93 // heat (8) 3:49.34
	Ian Hamer	1500 metres	heat (5) 3:42.55, final (9) 3:46.23
		5000 metres	heat (3) 13:52.58, final (3) 13:25.63
	Roger Hackney	5000 metres	heat (8) 13:58.89, final (14) 14:27.06
		3000m steeplechase	final (7) 8:36.62
	Steve Brace	Marathon	final (9) 2:16:16
	Steve Jones	Marathon	final (4) 2:12:44
	Colin Jackson	110m hurdles	heat (1) 13.11, final (1) 13.08
	Nigel Walker	110m hurdles	heat (3) 13.87, final (5) 13.78
	Paul Edwards	Shot Put	final (3) 18.17
	Nigel Bevan	Javelin	final (4) 79.70
	Sallyanne Short	100 metres	heat (4) 11.47, semi (2) 11.47, final (5) 11.41w
		200 metres	heat (1) 23.19w, final (6) 23.35
	Carmen Smart	100 metres	heat (3) 11.91, semi (6) 11.66
	Angela Tooby	10000 metres	final (dnf)
	Kay Morley	100m hurdles	heat (5) 13.51, final (1) 12.91
	Caroline White	Javelin	final (6) 55.18

1994	Peter Maitland	100 metres // 200 metres	heat (5) 10.55 // heat (2) 21.23, R2 (6) 20.96
		4 x 400m relay	heat (4) 3:03.68, final (7) 3:07.80
	Jamie Baulch	200 metres //400 metres	heat (3) 21.24, R2 (5) 20.84 // heat (4) 46.93, R2 (5) 46.45
		4 x 400m relay	heat (4) 3:03.68, final (7) 3:07.80
	Iwan Thomas	200 metres	heat (2) 21.56, R2 (6) 21.29
		400 metres	heat (1) 46.46, R2 (3) 46.37, semi (7) 45.98
		4 x 400m relay	heat (4) 3:03.68, final (7) 3:07.80
	Justin Hobbs	5000 metres // 10000 metres	heat (6) 13:50.72, final (8) 13:45.53 // final (dnf)
	Dale Rixon	Marathon	final (4) 2:16:15
	Justin Chaston	3000m steeplechase	final (7) 8:32.20
	Colin Jackson	110m hurdles	heat (1) 13.51, final (1) 13.08
	Paul Gray	110m hurdles	heat (2) 13.53, final (3) 13.54
	Phil Harries	400m hurdles	heat (dnf)
	Neil Winter	Pole Vault	final (1) 5.40
	Steve Ingram	Long Jump	dnq 3 no jumps
	Lee Wiltshire	Shot Put	final (14) 15.22
	Nigel Bevan	Javelin	final (4) 80.38
	Cathy Dawson	800 metres	heat (3) 2:03.81, final (4) 2:03.17
	Hayley Nash	Marathon	final (7) 2:35:39
	Lisa Gibbs	Heptathlon	final (dnf)
1998	Kevin Williams	100 metres // 4 x 100 relay	heat (5) 10.51 // heat (3) 39.09, final (4) 38.73
	Jamie Henthorn	100 metres // 200 metres	heat (3) 10.46, R2 (7) 10.52 // heat (3) 21.13, R2 (5) 21.02
		4 x 100m relay	heat (3) 39.09, final (4) 38.73
	Christian Malcolm	100 metres	heat (3) 10.47, R2 (3) 10.27, semi (5) 10.33
		200 metres	heat (2) 20.92, R2 (2) 20.53, semi (2) 20.56, final (2) 20.29
		4 x 100m relay	heat (3) 39.09, final (4) 38.73
	Doug Turner	200 metres	heat (1) 20.83, R2 (2) 20.68, semi (5) 20.64
		4 x 100m relay	heat (3) 39.09, final (4) 38.73
		4 x 400m relay	final (3) 3:01.86
	Iwan Thomas	400 metres	heat (2) 46.76, R2 (1) 45.26, semi (1) 44.61, final (1) 44.52
		4 x 400m relay	heat (3) 3:03.63, final (3) 3:01.86
	Jamie Baulch	400 metres	heat (2) 46.14, R2 (1) 45.64, semi (2) 44.83, final (4) 45.30
		4 x 400m relay	heat (3) 3:03.63, final (3) 3:01.86
	Christian Stephenson	1500 metres	heat (3) 3:45.75, final (9) 3:44.82
		3000m steeplechase	final (6) 8:42.95
	Dale Rixon	Marathon	final (15) 2:26:50
	Steve Brace	Marathon	final (17) 2:29:21
	Paul Gray	110m hurdles // 4x400 relay	heat (2) 13.54, final (4) 13.62 // heat (3) 3:03.63, final (3) 3:01.86
	Matthew Elias	400m hurdles // 4x400 relay	heat (8) 52.34 // heat (3) 3:03.63
	Shaun Pickering	Shot Put	final (3) 19.33
	Lee Newman	Discus	final (7) 56.28
	Nigel Bevan	Javelin	final (8) 73.06
	Emma Davies	800 metres	heat (4) 2:02.39, semi (7) 2:05.03
	Rachel Newcombe	800 metres	heat (4) 2:03.58, semi (7) 2:03.28
	Hayley Nash	10000 metres	final (7) 35:20.14
	Rachel King	100m hurdles	heat (6) 13.73
	Julie Crane	High Jump	final (8) 1.80
	Rhian Clarke	Pole Vault	final (11) 3.80
	Philippa Roles	Discus	final (6) 54.10
	Sarah Moore	Hammer	final (23) 47.79

Section 11

Welsh Medallists at International Track & Field Championships

For a nation with a population of just under three million, Wales has an impressive record in major international athletics championships as the following lists will show. The lists name every Welsh athlete who has won a medal of any colour in every major international track and field championship in which Welsh athletes are eligible to compete. The total medal count is: 58 Gold Medals, 50 Silver Medals and 52 Bronze medals.

GOLD MEDALS

1912	Olympic Games	David Jacobs	4 x 100m relay	42.4
1920	Olympic Games	Jack Ainsworth Davis	4 x 400m relay	3:22.2
1920	Olympic Games	Cecil Griffiths	4 x 400m relay	3:22.2
1930	Commonwealth Games	Reg Thomas	One Mile	4:14.0
1937	World Student Games	Jim Alford	800 metres	1:54.1
1937	World Student Games	Jim Alford	1500 metres	3:56.0
1938	Commonwealth Games	Jim Alford	One mile	4:11.5
1964	Olympic Games	Lynn Davies	Long Jump	8.07
1966	European Championships	Lynn Davies	Long Jump	7.98
1966	Commonwealth Games	Lynn Davies	Long Jump	7.99
1967	European Indoor Champs	Lynn Davies	Long Jump	7.85
1970	Commonwealth Games	Lynn Davies	Long Jump	8.06w
1970	European Junior Champs	Berwyn Price	110m hurdles	14.21
1973	World Student Games	Berwyn Price	110m hurdles	13.69
1975	European Junior Champs	Micky Morris	2000m steeplechase	5:34.8
1978	Commonwealth Games	Berwyn Price	110m hurdles	13.70w
1979	Gymnasiade	Colin Mackenzie	Javelin	69.50
1982	Commonwealth Games	Steve Barry	30k walk	2:10:16
1982	Commonwealth Games	Kirsty McDermott	800 metres	2:01.31
1982	Gymnasiade	Andrew Rodgers	1500 metres	3:56.16
1985	European Junior Champs	John Hill	High Jump	2.24
1986	Commonwealth Games	Kirsty Wade	800 metres	2:00.94
1986	Commonwealth Games	Kirsty Wade	1500 metres	4:10.91
1986	World Junior Championships	Colin Jackson	110m hurdles	13.44
1986	Gymnasiade	Amanda Barnes	Discus	42.68
1989	European Indoor Champs	Colin Jackson	60m hurdles	7.59
1990	European Championships	Colin Jackson	110m hurdles	13.18
1990	Commonwealth Games	Colin Jackson	110m hurdles	13.08
1990	Commonwealth Games	Kay Morley	100m hurdles	12.91
1991	European Youth Olympics	Scott Herbert	4 x 100m relay	41.86
1992	World Junior Championships	Jamie Baulch	4 x 100m relay	39.21
1993	World Championships	Colin Jackson	110m hurdles	12.91
1993	European Junior Champs	Iwan Thomas	4 x 400m relay	(heat)
1993	European Youth Olympics	James Archampong	110m H (91.4cm)	13.92w
1994	European Indoor Champs	Colin Jackson	60 metres	6.49
1994	European Indoor Champs	Colin Jackson	60m hurdles	7.41
1994	European Championships	Colin Jackson	110m hurdles	13.08

1994	Commonwealth Games	Colin Jackson	110m hurdles	13.08
1994	Commonwealth Games	Neil Winter	Pole Vault	5.40
1995	European Junior Champs	Jamie Henthorn	4 x 100m relay	39.43
1997	European Under 23 Champs	Jamie Henthorn	4 x 100m relay	38.99
1997	European Junior Champs	Christian Malcolm	200 metres	20.51w
1997	European Junior Champs	Christian Malcolm	4 x 100m relay	39.62
1998	European Championships	Iwan Thomas	400 metres	44.52
1998	European Championships	Colin Jackson	110m hurdles	13.02
1998	European Championships	Jamie Baulch	4 x 400m relay	2:58.68
1998	European Championships	Iwan Thomas	4 x 400m relay	2:58.68
1998	Commonwealth Games	Iwan Thomas	400 metres	44.52
1998	World Junior Championships	Christian Malcolm	100 metres	10.12
1998	World Junior Championships	Christian Malcolm	200 metres	20.44
1999	World Indoor Champs	Jamie Baulch	400 metres	45.73
1999	World Indoor Champs	Colin Jackson	60m hurdles	7.38
1999	World Championships	Colin Jackson	110m hurdles	13.04
1999	European Under 23 Champs	Christian Malcolm	4 x 100m relay	38.96
1999	European Under 23 Champs	Jamie Henthorn	4 x 100m relay	38.96
1999	World Youth Championships	Tim Benjamin	200 metres	20.72
2000	European Indoor Champs	Christian Malcolm	200 metres	20.54
2000	World Junior Championships	Tim Benjamin	4 x 100m relay	39.05

SILVER MEDALS

1930	Commonwealth Games	Reg Thomas	880 yards	1:56.4
1948	Olympic Games	Ken Jones	4 x 100m relay	41.3
1948	Olympic Games	Tom Richards	Marathon	2:35:08
1951	World Student Games	Phil Morgan	5000 metres	
1951	World Student Games	Harold Steggles	4 x 400m relay	
1954	European Championships	Ken Jones	4 x 100m relay	40.8
1958	Commonwealth Games	John Merriman	6 miles	28:48.84
1965	World Student Games	Lynn Davies	Long Jump	7.89
1966	Commonwealth Games	Clive Longe	Decathlon	7123
1967	World Student Games	Howard Davies	4 x 400m relay	3:06.7
1969	European Championships	Lynn Davies	Long Jump	8.07w
1969	European Indoor Champs	Lynn Davies	Long Jump	7.76
1971	European Indoor Champs	Phil Lewis	800 metres	1:50.5
1973	World Student Games	Phil Lewis	4 x 400m relay	3:05.4
1973	World Student Games	Wynford Leyshon	4 x 400m relay	3:05.4
1974	Commonwealth Games	John Davies	3000m steeplechase	8:24.8
1974	Commonwealth Games	Berwyn Price	110m hurdles	13.84
1976	European Indoor Champs	Berwyn Price	60m hurdles	7.80
1982	Commonwealth Games	Michelle Scutt	400 metres	51.97
1982	Gymnasiade	Michael Williams	200 metres	22.03
1985	European Junior Champs	Neil Horsfield	1500 metres	3:45.39
1985	European Junior Champs	Colin Jackson	110m hurdles	13.69
1986	Commonwealth Games	Roger Hackney	3000m steeplechase	8:25.15
1986	Commonwealth Games	Colin Jackson	110m hurdles	13.42w
1986	Commonwealth Games	Venissa Head	Discus	56.20
1987	European Indoor Champs	Colin Jackson	60m hurdles	7.63
1988	Olympic Games	Colin Jackson	110m hurdles	13.28
1989	World Indoor Champs	Colin Jackson	60m hurdles	7.45
1991	European Junior Champs	Jamie Baulch	4 x 100m relay	39.86
1991	European Junior Champs	Lisa Armstrong	4 x 100m relay	44.57
1991	European Junior Champs	Peter Maitland	4 x 100m relay	(heat)

1991	European Youth Olympics	Natasha Bartlett	4 x 100m relay	47.28
1993	World Indoor Champs	Colin Jackson	60m hurdles	7.43
1993	World Championships	Colin Jackson	4 x 100m relay	37.77
1995	European Junior Champs	Jamie Henthorn	100 metres	10.41
1995	European Youth Olympics	Mark Rowlands	400m H (84cm)	52.63
1996	Olympic Games	Iwan Thomas	4 x 400m relay	2:56.60
1996	Olympic Games	Jamie Baulch	4 x 400m relay	2:56.60
1997	World Indoor Champs	Jamie Baulch	400 metres	45.62
1997	World Indoor Champs	Colin Jackson	60m hurdles	7.49
1997	World Championships	Colin Jackson	110m hurdles	13.05
1997	World Championships	Iwan Thomas	4 x 400m relay	2:56.65
1997	World Championships	Jamie Baulch	4 x 400m relay	2:56.65
1997	European Junior Champs	Christian Malcolm	100 metres	10.24
1998	European Championships	Doug Turner	200 metres	20.64
1998	Commonwealth Games	Christian Malcolm	200 metres	20.29
1999	European Under 23 Champs	Christian Malcolm	100 metres	10.28
1999	European Under 23 Champs	Christian Malcolm	200 metres	20.47
1999	European Junior Champs	Tim Benjamin	200 metres	20.60w
1999	European Youth Olympics	Nathan Palmer	110m H (91.4cm)	13.94

Tony Simmons won a silver medal in the 10000 metres (28:25.79) at the European Championships in 1974 during the period when he had temporarily relinquished his Welsh eligibility.

BRONZE MEDALS

1939	World Student Games	Kenneth Jenkins	100 metres	
1939	World Student Games	Kenneth Jenkins	200 metres	
1952	Olympic Games	John Disley	3000m steeplechase	8:51.94
1953	World Student Games	Peter Phillips	400 metres	49.7
1954	Commonwealth Games	Ken Jones	220 yards	21.9
1954	Commonwealth Games	Bob Shaw	440y hurdles	53.3
1960	Olympic Games	Nick Whitehead	4 x 100m relay	40.32
1962	European Championships	Ron Jones	4 x 100m relay	39.8
1962	European Championships	Berwyn Jones	4 x 100m relay	39.8
1962	Commonwealth Games	John Merriman	6 miles	28:40.26
1962	Commonwealth Games	Dave England	4 x 110y relay	40.80
1962	Commonwealth Games	Ron Jones	4 x 110y relay	40.80
1962	Commonwealth Games	Berwyn Jones	4 x 100y relay	40.80
1962	Commonwealth Games	Nick Whitehead	4 x 110y relay	40.80
1965	World Student Games	Liz Gill	100 metres	11.6w
1965	World Student Games	Liz Gill	200 metres	24.0
1974	Commonwealth Games	Ruth Martin-Jones	Long Jump	6.38
1979	Gymnasiade	Philip Harvey	400 metres	48.46
1980	Olympic Games	Michelle Probert	4 x 400m relay	3:27.5
1984	European Indoor Champs	Phil Norgate	800 metres	1:48.39
1985	European Junior Champs	Helen Miles	100 metres	11.63
1985	European Junior Champs	Helen Miles	4 x 100m relay	44.78
1986	Commonwealth Games	Steve Jones	10000 metres	28:02.48
1986	Commonwealth Games	Angela Tooby	10000 metres	32:25.38
1986	Commonwealth Games	Helen Miles	4 x 100m relay	45.37
1986	Commonwealth Games	Sian Morris	4 x 100m relay	45.37
1986	Commonwealth Games	Sallyanne Short	4 x 100m relay	45.37
1986	Commonwealth Games	Carmen Smart	4 x 100m relay	45.37
1987	World Indoor Champs	Nigel Walker	60m hurdles	7.66
1987	European Indoor Champs	Nigel Walker	60m hurdles	7.65
1987	European Junior Champs	Paul Gray	110m hurdles	14.16

1987	World Championships	Colin Jackson	110m hurdles	13.38
1990	Commonwealth Games	Ian Hamer	5000 metres	13:25.63
1990	Commonwealth Games	Paul Edwards	Shot Put	18.17
1991	European Youth Olympics	Natasha Bartlett	200 metres	24.85
1993	European Youth Olympics	Mark Ponting	400 metres	48.74
1994	Commonwealth Games	Paul Gray	110m hurdles	13.54
1995	European Youth Olympics	Philippa Roles	Shot Put	13.66
1996	World Junior Championships	Mark Rowlands	4 x 400m relay	3:06.76
1997	World Student Games	Jamie Henthorn	4 x 100m relay	39.23
1997	European Junior Champs	Mark Rowlands	4 x 400m relay	3:08.48
1997	European Junior Champs	Philippa Roles	Discus	50.62
1998	Commonwealth Games	Shaun Pickering	Shot Put	19.33
1998	Commonwealth Games	Paul Gray	4 x 400m relay	3:01.86
1998	Commonwealth Games	Jamie Baulch	4 x 400m relay	3:01.86
1998	Commonwealth Games	Doug Turner	4 x 400m relay	3:01.86
1998	Commonwealth Games	Iwan Thomas	4 x 400m relay	3:01.86
1998	Commonwealth Games	Matthew Elias	4 x 400m relay	(heat)
1999	World Indoor Champs	Jamie Baulch	4 x 400m relay	3:03.20
1999	World Student Games	Dawn Higgins	4 x 400m relay	3:32.25
1999	European Under 23 Champs	Matthew Elias	4 x 400m relay	3:03.58
2000	World Junior Championships	Tim Benjamin	200 metres	20.94

Both Diane Heath (1975 European Junior Championships, 4x400m relay) and Michelle Probert (1977 European Junior Championships, 4x100m relay) won bronze medals before assuming their Welsh eligibility.

Lea Haggett won a bronze medal (1990 World Junior Championships, High Jump) after relinquishing her Welsh eligibility.

In relay events those athletes who competed only in the preliminary rounds are indicated by showing (heat) in the final column.

Section 12

Welsh International Matches Track & Field and Road Running

WELSH INTERNATIONAL OUTDOOR TRACK AND FIELD MATCHES

This is the first time such a list has been produced and considerable effort and research has been undertaken to ensure accuracy. To be classed as an international there must be no age restriction (note in the home countries combined events internationals only the designated senior athletes are included not the junior athletes). If an area of England is included in the match (as opposed to an England national team) it becomes an inter area/inter regional match unless a national team from outside the UK participates. To be considered an international match there must be a score and only those competing in the scoring events are included for vests. The matches in the early years against AAA are included as these teams were considered to be England. Note that some of the later meetings have not been included because in effect they were just international open meetings. When male and female teams competed together and when the matches were scored separately then the male score is given first, followed by the female score, otherwise a combined score is given.

** indicates first of 2 days*

Date	Venue	M/F	Match Result
10.07.1948	Abertillery	M	AAA 31, **Wales** 11
18.08.1951	Newport	M	AAA 119, **Wales** 54
27.06.1953	Abertillery	M	AAA 75, **Wales** 41
03.10.1953	Birmingham	M/F	AAA 53, Midlands 30, **Wales** 16, Netherlands 15; WAAA 27, Midl 27, **Wales** 6, Neth 3
08.05.1954	Maindy	M	AAA 119, **Wales** 66
02.08.1954	Maindy	M	**Wales** 94, Ireland 87
09.07.1955	Newport	M	AAA 127, **Wales** 69
07.07.1956	Maindy	M	AAA 89, **Wales** 49
06.07.1957	Margam	M	AAA 127, **Wales** 72
05.07.1958	Eirias Park	M/F	Nigeria 84.5, **Wales** 62.5; **Wales** 36, Nigeria 31
18.07.1959	Maindy	M	**Wales** 38, Pakistan 33
09.07.1960	Abertillery	M	AAA 74, **Wales** 40
20.08.1960	Edinburgh	M	Scotland 68, **Wales** 34
29.07.1961	Maindy	M	**Wales** 113.5, Scotland 108, Ireland 104.5
10.06.1967	Grangemouth	M	England 72, Scotland 60, **Wales** 48, N Ireland 26
08.06.1968	Grangemouth	M	England 85, Scotland 62, **Wales** 46.5, N Ireland 23.5
07.06.1969	Grangemouth	M	England 75, Scotland 59, **Wales** 52, N Ireland 20
21.06.1969	Bargoed	M	AAA 100, **Wales** 94
05.07.1969	Colwyn Bay	M	England 79, Scotland 65, **Wales** 53, N Ireland 28
13.06.1971	Grangemouth	M	England 92, **Wales** 50, Scotland 47, N Ireland 24
07.07.1973	Bargoed	M	England 133, **Wales** 94
21.07.1973	Cwmbran	M	Netherlands 113, **Wales** 109
18.08.1973*	Lisbon	M	**Wales** 103.5, Portugal 97.5
29.06.1974	Cwmbran	F	**Wales** 81, Northern Ireland 51
23.07.1974*	Cwmbran	M	Canada 113, **Wales** 87
23.07.1974*	Cwmbran	F	Canada 135, Scotland 85, **Wales** 49
27.07.1974	Cwmbran	M	**Wales** 167, Portugal 132, N Ireland 100
14.06.1975	Haverfordwest	F	**Wales** 70, Northern Ireland 59
22.06.1975	Brussels	F	Belgium 97, **Wales** 49; **Wales** 72, Greece 71; Italy 100, **Wales** 44
19.07.1975	Cwmbran	M	**Wales** 174, Ireland 137, Luxembourg 111
09.08.1975	Cwmbran	M	England 264, Scotland 177, **Wales** 158, N Ireland 117
29.05.1976	Dublin	M	**Wales** 84, Ireland 80, Luxembourg 47
19.06.1976	Coatbridge	F	Belgium 133, Scotland 108, **Wales** 71
17.07.1976	Cwmbran	F	**Wales** 121, Spain 120.5, Greece 116.5, N Ireland 90
12.09.1976	Wolverhampton	M/F	England 215, Scotland 108.5, **Wales** 101.5. No female score
02.07.1977	Athens	F	Greece 68, **Wales** 66
06.08.1977	Luxembourg	M	**Wales** 170.5, Ireland 155, Luxembourg 122.5
14.05.1978	Athens	M	Greece 260, Scotland 218, **Wales** 163, Luxembourg 116
27.05.1978	Lisbon	F	**Wales** 92, Portugal 65
08.07.1978	Cwmbran	M	**Wales** 160, Netherlands 157.5, Ireland 123.5
08.07.1978	Cwmbran	F	**Wales** 86, Greece 56
16.06.1979	Athens	F	**Wales** 81, Greece 76

21.07.1979	Cwmbran	M	Greece 185, Scotland 130, **Wales** 126
21.07.1979	Cwmbran	F	Scotland 120, **Wales** 117, Israel 73
19.08.1979	Dublin	M	Netherlands 199, Ireland 137.5, **Wales** 108.5
20.08.1979*	Belfast	M	**Wales** 120, Northern Ireland 94
18.05.1980	Cwmbran	M	England 242, Hungary 229, Netherlands 126.5, **Wales** 103.5
14.06.1980	Winterthur	F	Netherlands 98, Switzerland 93, Belgium 74, Spain 70, Austria 66, Irel 63, **Wales** 48, Luxemb 8
21.06.1980	Graz	F	**Wales** 75, Austria 71
16.08.1980*	Sittard	M	Netherlands 193, **Wales** 144.5, Ireland 103.5
15.08.1981	Cwmbran	M/F	England 266, **Wales** 214, Irel 132, Brittany 114; **Wales** 160.5, N Irel 94.5, Brittany 57
25.08.1981*	Athens	M	Greece 90, Scotland 90, **Wales** 70, Israel 49, Luxembourg 34
28.08.1981*	Ardaal	F	Norway 135, Scotland 95, **Wales** 82
12.06.1982	Antrim	F	South 89.5, Midlands 83, Scotland 71, **Wales** 64, North 62, Ireland 37, N Ireland 28.5,
03.07.1982*	Dublin	F	Switz 86, Netherlands 80.5, Belg 72, **Wales** 71, Irel 68, Spain 57.5, Denmark 55.5, Austria 47.5
17.07.1982*	Reykjavik	M	**Wales** 108, Iceland 97
11.08.1982*	Cwmbran	M/F	Ireland 119, **Wales** 103; **Wales** 80, Ireland 77
28.08.1982	Edinburgh	M/F	**Wales** 43, Scotland 42, France 34, Ireland 32, Belgium 30, Netherlands 28, N Ireland 18
09.07.1983*	Cwmbran	M/F	**Wales** 105, Denmark 105; Denmark 86, **Wales** 70
18.07.1983*	Athens	F	**Wales** 90, Greece 66
30.07.1983	Edinburgh	M	Scotland 91, **Wales** 89, Iceland 74, N Ireland 70, Israel 63, Luxembourg 44
16.06.1984*	Lisbon	F	Neth 95, Switz 90, Belgium 70, Austria 69, Spain 69, Ireland 59, Portugal 52, **Wales** 44
23.06.1984	Birmingham	F	England 195, Yugoslavia 136, Scotland 101, **Wales** 68
21.07.1984*	Copenhagen	M/F	France U23 213, Denmark 123, **Wales** 99; France U23 144, Denmark 86, **Wales** 74
25.08.1984	Swansea	M	**Wales** 207.5, Netherlands 198, Iceland 161.5, N Ireland 159
25.08.1984	Swansea	F	**Wales** 191, Netherlands 146, N Ireland 139
20.07.1985	Swansea	M/F	Eng 237, Scot 175, **Wales** 170, Catalonia 106; Eng 164, Scot 143, **Wales** 128, Catalonia 70
03.08.1985*	Grangemouth	M	England 20204, Ireland 19582, Scotland 19508 – multis **Wales** dnf team
31.08.1985*	Tel Aviv	M	Greece 92, Scotland 84, **Wales** 63, N Ireland 57, Israel 34;
		F	**Wales** 75, Scotland 61, Israel 36, Greece 35, N Ireland 35,
17.05.1986	Barcelona	M/F	**Wales** 171, Catalonia 142, C Catala 62; **Wales** 137, Catalonia 76
13.07.1986	Swansea	M	England 201, **Wales** 122, N Ireland 96
13.07.1986	Swansea	F	**Wales** 106, Australia 105.5, Belgium 92.5
17.08.1986	Copthall	F	Poland 126, England 111, **Wales**/Scotland 66
11.07.1987	Swansea	M	Scotland 74, **Wales** 71, N Ireland 63, Cyprus 54, Israel 39
		F	Scotland 63, **Wales** 62, N Ireland 49, Cyprus 33, Israel 32
18.07.1987*	Edinburgh	M/F	Scotland 167, Ireland 158, **Wales** 115; Scotland 114, Ireland 110.5, **Wales** 84.5
23.08.1987	Utrecht	M/F	Belgium 146, **Wales** 145, Netherlands 129; Belgium 110, **Wales** 102.5, Netherlands 98.5
09.07.1988	Cwmbran	M	England B 246, France B 237, **Wales** 116, Australia U20 94
09.07.1988	Cwmbran	F	France B 214, **Wales** 161, Australia 112
20.08.1988*	Wrexham	M	England 20854, Eng 20598, Irel 19895, Scotland 18422, N Irel 17314, **Wales** 16852 – Multis
03.09.1988*	Nesbyen	M/F	Norway 123, **Wales** 87; Norway 96, **Wales** 58
30.06.1989*	Antrim	M	**Wales** 87, Israel 76, N Ireland 74, Scotland 69, Cyprus 55, Euskadi 54
		F	Scotland 73, N Ireland 67, **Wales** 65, Cyprus 50, Israel 42, Euskadi 31
22.07.1989	Swansea	M/F	Eng 222, Portugal 198, Spain 153, **Wales** 132; Eng 173.5, Spain 149, **Wales** 124, N Irel 101
29.07.1989*	Aberdeen	M	England 20800, Eng B 19839, Scotland 20267, **Wales** 17852, Irel 17605, N Irel 16496 – multis
25.06.1990*	Antrim	M/F	Canada 198, NIreland 115, **Wales** 112; Canada 151, N Irel 86, **Wales** 78
28.07.1990	Wrexham	M/F	England 302, Int Select 265, **Wales** 176; England 138, Int Select 112, **Wales** 71
		M/F	England 137, **Wales** 93, Cyprus 52; England 62, **Wales** 39, Cyprus 24
16.06.1991	Grangemouth	M	Scotland 70, Ireland 64, **Wales** 62, N Ireland 55, Iceland 51
		F	**Wales** 57, Scotland 57, N Ireland 51, Ireland 49, Iceland 37
14.07.1991	Cwmbran	M/F	Select 157, England 147, **Wales** 89; Select 133, England 102, **Wales** 75
		M	England 105, **Wales** 65, USA Jn 59, Scotland 55 – one per event
		F	England 70, **Wales** 58, USA Jn 54, Scotland 43 – one per event
31.08.1991*	Middlesbrough	M	England 21272, Scotland 19101, Ireland 16517, **Wales** 15966
		F	England 16147, Ireland 12730, Scotland 12111, **Wales** 11798 – multis
13.06.1992	Budapest	M	Czech 211, Hung 206, **Wales** 117, Hung Jnr 97;
		F	Czech 170, Hung 143.5, **Wales** 93, Hung Jn 76.5
12.07.1992	Cwmbran	M/F	Select 201, England 171, **Wales** 117
29.08.1992*	Cardiff	M	England 19158, Ireland 18167, Scotland 17229, **Wales** 16066 – multis
29.08.1992*	Cardiff	F	England 15052, Ireland 13381, Scotland 12853, **Wales** 12589, N Ireland 3630
26.05.1993*	Tel Aviv	M/F	Israel 68, **Wales** 61, Scotland 49, Turkey 39; Scotland 52, **Wales** 48, Turkey 48, Israel 25
22.07.1993	Veszprem	M	Hungary 57, Slovakia 57, **Wales** 53, Slovenia 52, Croatia 36
		F	Hungary 57, Slovenia 49, **Wales** 48.5, Slovakia 45, Croatia 24.5
25.07.1993	Cardiff	M/F	Select 122, England 121, **Wales** 74, Australia 52; **Wales** 79, Engl 76, Australia 54, Select 42
21.08.1993*	Glasgow	M	England 20397, **Wales** 17081, Scotland 17049, N Ireland 14290
21.08.1993*	Glasgow	F	England 15682, Scotland 14482, **Wales** 13980
21.05.1994	Istanbul	M/F	**Wales** 65, Scotland 58, Israel 52, Turkey 50; Turkey 66, Scotland 55, **Wales** 46, Israel 28
03.07.1994	Wrexham	M/F	England 145, **Wales** 102, Select 83; England 111.5, Select 61.5, **Wales** 57
24.06.1995	Cork	M/F	North 80, Ireland 77, **Wales** 59; Ireland 64, North 58, **Wales** 31
09.07.1995	Cwmbran	M/F	England 156, **Wales** 106, Select 59 England 139, **Wales** 85, Select 32
22.07.1995*	Cardiff	M/F	Turkey 79, Scotland 69, **Wales** 67, N Irel 63; **Wales** 68, Turkey 66, Scotland 65, N Irel 46
26.08.1995*	Kilkenny	M	England 21150, Scotland 18176, Ireland 17850, **Wales** 16266

		F	England 15750, Scotland 13540, Ireland 12550, **Wales** 11320
25.05.1996	Cardiff	M/F	**Wales** 201.5, Ireland 154.5; **Wales** 91.5, Ireland 69.5
22.06.1996	Belfast	M/F	Scotl 72, **Wales** 62, N Irel 56, Turkey 47, Irel 46; Scot 66, Turkey 55.5, N Irel 53, **Wales** 42.5
31.05.1997	Cardiff	M/F	**Wales** 117, Select 106, N Ireland 71; **Wales** 101, Select 101, N Ireland 53,
23.08.1997*	Jarman Park	M	England 20322, Ireland 18728, Scotland 18455, N Ireland 18020, **Wales** 17316
		F	England 16402, Ireland 14174, Scotland 13671, N Ireland 11950, **Wales** 11366
07.06.1998	Leeds	M/F	Eng 106, **Wales** 98, Scot 83, North 70, Select 67, N Ireland 52, Ireland 38
01.08.1998*	Wrexham	M	England 19538, Ireland 19060, **Wales** 14805, N Ireland dnf
		F	England 15298, **Wales** 13132, Ireland 12164, N Ireland 11859
03.07.1999	Budapest	M	Hungary 67, England 52, Czech 47, Slovakia 37, Ireland 34, **Wales** 34, Cyprus 32,
		F	England 77, Hungary 70, Czech 61, Slovakia 53, **Wales** 41, Ireland 21, Cyprus 20
31.07.1999	Tallin	M/F	England 83, Estonia 70, Finland 70, **Wales** 61, Ireland 42, Latvia 36
07.08.1999*	Aberdeen	M	England 19216, N Ireland 17604, **Wales** 15863, Scotland 15020
		F	England 15276, Scotland 13470, **Wales** 12188, N Ireland 4124
09.08.1999	Wrexham	M	**Wales** 65, Scotland 49, England 42, Australia 25, N Ireland 23
		F	England 54, **Wales** 46, Scotland 34, Australia 22, N Ireland 21
04.06.2000	Bedford	M/F	England 82, Canada 70, Australia 69, **Wales**/Scotland 61, England U23 51, All Ireland 42
22.06.2000	Riga	M/F	Belarus 71, England 68, Ireland 62, Latvia 57, **Wales** 38, Estonia 25
22.07.2000	Budapest	M	England 64.5, Hungary 64.5, SAfrica 47, **Wales** 29, Ukraine 27, Cyprus 24, Ireland 23
		F	Hungary 73, England 70, Ukraine 33, SAfrica 32, **Wales** 28, Ireland 25, Cyprus 19
29.07.2000	Dublin	M	England 43, South Africa 42, Ireland 35, **Wales** 27
		F	England 40, Ireland 32, S Africa 23, **Wales** 17
02.03.2000*	Waterford	M	England 26296, Ireland 22902, **Wales** 22603, N Ireland 16163, Scotland 14682
		F	England 19970, Scotland 19242, Ireland 17783, **Wales** 15173, N Ireland 6249

WELSH INTERNATIONAL TRACK AND FIELD VESTS

The following lists show in numerical order by the number of appearances the athletes who have competed in the above matches. Much research has gone in to the production of these lists bearing in mind that no central collection of match results exists. The compilers have used their own copies of published results, referred to *Athletics Weekly* and researched contemporary editions of newspapers such as the *Western Mail*. The lists are as accurate as the information available. Problems have occurred sometimes in tracing relay compositions, and often results given in early newspapers listed only the first three so that athletes finishing outside the first three are not known. In the early years matches were few and far between which explains why some of **Wales**' most prominent athletes only made limited number of appearances.

Men

24	David Wood	1979-91
23	Paul Gray	1986-00
17	John Walters	1967-81
17	Neil Horsfield	1984-94
17	Colin Jackson	1984-97
16	Berwyn Price	1971-82
16	Paul Rees	1973-83
16	Nigel Walker	1981-92
16	Adrian Palmer	1987-97
15	Roger Barrett	1979-90
15	Shaun Pickering	1980-89
14	Wyn Leyson	1969-78
14	Derek Fishwick	1976-88
14	Paul Edwards	1981-90
14	Philip Harries	1985-96
14	Jamie Baulch	1990-00
14	Kevin Williams	1993-00
13	John Phillips	1973-79
13	Andrew Turner	1988-00
12	Peter Lewis	1969-80
12	John Davies	1971-84
12	Gareth Brooks	1973-80
12	Trevor Llewelyn	1978-83
12	Paul Williams(BV)	1984-92
12	Paul Roberts	1987-95
12	Tim Thomas	1991-97
11	David Lease	1968-80
11	Nick Lia	1973-79
11	Steve Barry	1978-84
11	Mal Owen	1978-91
11	Mark Thomas	1982-88
11	Nigel Winchcombe	1984-89
11	Lee Wiltshire	1984-94
11	David Lee	1985-92
11	Chris Cashell	1986-95
11	Nigel Bevan	1989-99
10	Steve James	1974-80
10	Dic Evans	1974-87
10	Geoff Ward	1976-88
10	Tony Blackwell	1978-83
10	Neil Hammersley	1979-88
10	Gareth Brown	1981-88
10	Colin Mackenzie	1982-90
10	Glyn Price	1985-91
10	Nick Comerford	1988-99
09	Lawrie Hall	1959-80
09	Graham Robinson	1969-83
09	Mike Delaney	1973-82
09	Dave Roberts	1974-82
09	Dennis Fowles	1974-84
09	Richard Jones	1980-85
09	Mal Edwards	1980-88
09	Chris Buckley	1982-86
09	Stuart McKenzie	1982-87
09	Steve Johnson	1983-88
09	Mike Powell	1984-89
09	Sean Price	1986-96
09	Doug Turner	1990-99
09	Phil Cook	1991-97
09	Joe Lloyd	1992-99
08	John Eddershaw	1973-80
08	Colin O'Neill	1973-82
08	Glen Grant	1975-91
08	Brychan Jones	1976-85
08	Peter Lynk	1983-87
08	Nigel Adams	1984-91
08	Ian Hamer	1987-93
08	Neil Winter	1989-95
08	Justin Chaston	1990-94
08	Shane Lewis	1991-97
08	Peter Maitland	1993-95
08	James Weston	1993-99
08	Graham Holder	1996-00
07	Ron Jones	1956-69
07	John James	1961-73
07	Peter Lance	1968-73
07	Bernie Plain	1969-76
07	Alun James	1969-77
07	Clive Thomas	1971-75
07	John Greatrex	1973-76
07	Ted Kelland	1973-80
07	Geraint Griffiths	1974-79
07	Jeff Griffiths	1975-81
07	Ali Cole	1976-83
07	Paul Williams(C)	1977-83
07	Steve Jones	1978-82
07	Dave James	1978-83
07	Ken Latten	1978-83
07	George Robertson	78-87
07	Phil Llewellyn	1982-94
07	Steve Ingram	1987-95
07	Duncan Gauden	1989-98
07	Garry Slade	1991-95
07	Matthew Shone	1998-00
06	Hywel Williams	1951-67
06	Brian Sexton	1954-61
06	Terry Davies	1961-69
06	Fred Bell	1967-71
06	Graham Webb	1967-73
06	Tony Simmons	1968-79
06	Bernie Hayward	1969-76
06	Phil Lewis	1971-75
06	Richard Gyles	1971-76
06	Peter Griffiths	1971-81
06	Ron Griffiths	1973-77
06	Peter Templeton	1974-76
06	Islwyn Rees	1974-88
06	Andrew McIver	1979-82
06	Roger Hackney	1979-86
06	Jonathan Stark	1980-87
06	Tim Brooks	1981-84
06	Mark Owen	1982-86
06	Haydn Wood	1983-86
06	Jon Thompson	1984-88
06	Tim Newenham	1985-90
06	Paul Farmer	1990-94
06	Dave Griffin	1992-95
06	Darrell Maynard	1993-97
05	John Elias	1967-73
05	John Robertson	1967-73
05	Andie Davie	1973-74
05	Peter Ratcliffe	1973-76
05	Dave Hopkins	1974-77
05	Phil Ramsay	1975-77
05	Reg Gardner	1975-82
05	Vic Martindale	1976-80
05	John Robertshaw	1976-81
05	John Furnham	1979-81
05	Mal James	1979-83
05	Marcus Browning	1986-88
05	Kirk Taylor	1986-89
05	David Winterton	1987-89
05	Gareth Davies (Sal)	1990-94
05	Shaun Tobin	1991-94
05	Richard Stubbs	1991-97
05	Gareth Davies(Sw)	1992-95
05	Stuart Brown	1993-95
05	Gareth Gilbert	1993-97
05	Iwan Thomas	1993-98
05	Jamie Henthorn	1996-00
04	Reg Snow	1951-54
04	Brian Carter	1951-55
04	Derek Clarke	1953-54
04	John Disley	1953-58

04	Clive Roberts	1954-57
04	Martyn Gatehouse	1954-58
04	Kevin Phillips	1954-58
04	David Richards	1954-61
04	Roger Jones	1955-59
04	Colin Fletcher	1956-59
04	Nick Whitehead	1956-60
04	Norman Horrell	1958-61
04	Bob Adams	1967-71
04	Gwynn Davis	1967-73
04	Kedrick Thompson	1973-74
04	Mike Cummings	1973-75
04	Peter Davies	1973-75
04	Roger Rees	1973-76
04	John Theophilus	1973-80
04	Gareth Edwards	1974-76
04	Paul Evans (Car)	1974-76
04	Kevin Davies	1975-76
04	Rupert Goodall	1976-78
04	Tudor Bidder	1976-79
04	Colin Wright	1977-79
04	Derek Morgan	1978-79
04	Nigel Price	1979-80
04	Kenny Davies	1982-84
04	John Owen	1984-90
04	Nick Dakin	1984-93
04	Clayton Turner	1987-91
04	Paul Fisher	1991-92
04	Jeremy Frankel	1991-93
04	Joe Mills	1994-00
04	Ewart Hulse	1995-97
04	Stuart Loughran	1995-00
04	Charles M Cole	1996-00
03	Bob Shaw	1951-57
03	Ken Goodall	1953-54
03	Peter Phillips	1953-56
03	Gordon Wells	1954-55
03	John Gilpin	1954-56
03	Bill Kingsbury	1954-56
03	John H Thomas	1954-56
03	Ray Billington	1955-58
03	Robert Sussex	1955-58
03	Ray Gazzard	1956-60
03	Morton Evans	1957-61
03	Bryan Woolley	1958-61
03	Wyn Oliver	1959-61
03	Tony Jones	1960-61
03	Haydn Curran	1969
03	Gwynne Griffiths	1969-73
03	Morris Davies	1971-73
03	Keith Lancey	1971-75
03	Howard Rooks	1973
03	Gary Vince	1973
03	Stephen Ware	1973
03	Gordon Pickering	1973-74
03	Richard Yarrow	1973-76
03	Steve Slocombe	1973-77
03	Tony Dyke	1974-75
03	Martin Lucas	1975-76
03	Neil Thomas	1976-79
03	Dick Milne	1977-78
03	Aled Williams	1977-78
03	Huw Jones	1977-80
03	Martin Lockley	1978-80
03	Steve Perks	1979
03	Steve Thomas	1979
03	Nick Alexander	1979-80
03	Keith Jones	1979-80
03	Alan Tinsley	1979-80
03	Nick Heal	1980-82
03	Jon Marsden	1980-83
03	David Barlow	1980-89
03	Tim Jones	1981-82
03	Phil Norgate	1982-83
03	Steve Brock	1982-84
03	Ieuan Ellis	1982-87
03	Nathan Kavanagh	1983-84
03	Alan Tapp	1983-86
03	John Hill	1984-85
03	David Radford	1984-85
03	Richard Davies	1984-86
03	Tony Pithers	1985-88
03	Martyn Bowen	1986-87
03	Stu Colq-Lynn	1986-87
03	Brian Matthews	1986-88
03	Steven Partridge	1987-88
03	David Thomas	1987-88
03	James Simmons	1987-89
03	Jonathan Clarke	1987-95
03	Gareth Davies (C)	1987-88
03	Pat Chichester	1988-90
03	Rhys Davies	1988-90
03	Matthew Chaston	1989-90
03	Steven Rees	1989-91
03	Gareth Holloway	1990-95
03	John Bowen	1991-93
03	Gareth Jones	1992-95
03	Kevin Ricketts	1993-99
03	Trem Rutherford	1994-96
03	Matthew Perry	1995-96
03	Rowan Griffiths	1995-99
03	Anthony Malcolm	1996-97
03	Mark Rowlands	1996-97
03	ChristianStephenson	1996-7
03	Christian Malcolm	1997-99
03	Paul Jones	1998-00
02	Brian Williams	1948-51
02	Bernard Ball	1951-53
02	Norman Finch	1951-53
02	Glan Williams	1951-54
02	Norman Wilson	1951-54
02	Joe Yates	1951-54
02	Roy Adams	1953-54
02	Lyn Bevan	1953-54
02	John Huins	1954
02	Chris Alele	1954-55
02	Terence Morgan	1954-56
02	D Thomas	1954-56
02	David Pulsford	1954-57
02	D E Williams	1954-57
02	A V Ford	1955-56
02	Ken Huckle	1955-56
02	M C Millwater	1956-57
02	Gwilym Roberts	1956-57
02	Anthony Pumfrey	1957-58
02	Aneurin Evans	1957-61
02	Mal Pemberton	1958-61
02	John Davies	1959-61
02	Malcolm Jones	1960
02	Peter Griffin	1960-61
02	Berwyn Jones	1960-61
02	Erith Williams	1960-61
02	Hedydd Davies	1961-68
02	John Lister	1961-69
02	Alan Bergiers	1967-68
02	Ron McAndrew	1967-68
02	Colin Balchin	1967-69
02	Roger Richardson	1968-69
02	Gwyn Williams	1968-69
02	Alan Joslyn	1968-73
02	Clive Longe	1969
02	Lynn Davies	1969-71
02	Mike Rowland	1969-71
02	John J Williams	1969-71
02	Dave Rosser	1969-73
02	Bob Roberts	1973
02	William Carey	1974
02	Chris Richards	1975-76
02	Andy Williams	1976-77
02	Micky Morris	1976-80
02	Peter Baker	1978-79
02	Graham Hughes	1978-81
02	Adrian Leek	1979
02	Steve Robbins	1979
02	Mike Llew Eaton	1980-81
02	Mark Hewer	1981
02	Paul Hawkins	1983-86
02	David Roberts	1983-86
02	Gareth Rowlands	1984
02	Nigel Skinner	1984
02	Stuart Gibbs	1984-86
02	Paul Wheeler	1985-86
02	Peter Jenkins	1986-88
02	Andrew Perrin	1986-88
02	Adrian Brown	1987
02	Tomos Davies	1987
02	Mark Harris	1987
02	Paul Manwaring	1987-89
02	Neil Hardee	1988
02	Phil Harvey	1988-89
02	Geoff Hill	1988-89
02	Robert James	1988-89
02	Andrew Adey	1989-90
02	James Hill	1990
02	Linton Baddeley	1990-91
02	Nick Hamilton	1991
02	Shaun Lewis	1991
02	Ceri Payne	1991
02	Kevin Tobin	1992
02	Andrew Blow	1993
02	Ian Wilding	1993-96
02	Dafydd Edwards	1994
02	Mark Morgan	1994-95
02	Marvin Gray	1994-96
02	Ian Roberts	1994-96
02	James Hughes	1995
02	Colin Jones	1995
02	Rob Simon	1995
02	Alan Thomas	1995
02	Colin Bovell	1995-97
02	Egryn Jones	1995-97
02	Andrew Penk	1995-97
02	David Williams	1996
02	Andy Eynon	1996-97
02	Andrew Thomas	1999
02	Chris Davies	1999-00
02	James Hillier	1999-00
02	Geoff Ingram	1999-00
02	Gareth Brown	2000
01	Jim Alford	1948
01	C B Coates	1948
01	Gwyn Harris	1948
01	Howell Hopkin	1948
01	Doug Rees	1948
01	E Robinson	1948
01	Clive Balch	1951
01	Maurice Bingham	1951
01	Viv Evans	1951
01	T Farquharson	1951
01	Brian Hardwick	1951
01	Neville Hughes	1951
01	J S Hunt	1951
01	Viv Jones	1951
01	John King	1951
01	Gareth Morgan	1951
01	John Nash	1951
01	D Pugh	1951
01	Alan Roche	1951
01	W Williams	1951
01	David Barry	1953
01	Ken Jones	1953
01	Dennis Murphy	1953
01	Mervyn Rosser	1953
01	C Bosley	1954
01	Trevor Evans	1954
01	K Frederickson	1954
01	D K James	1954
01	G N Lewis	1954
01	B M Loughlin	1954
01	Garfield Owen	1954
01	G Phillips	1954
01	Harold Steggles	1954
01	A H Thomas	1954
01	G C Coles	1955
01	C L Davies	1955
01	Gareth Griffiths	1955
01	Gareth Howell	1955
01	V Matthews	1955
01	Graham Pugh	1955
01	C P Roberts	1955
01	Terry Hamilton	1956
01	Albert Ley	1956
01	Harry Packer	1956
01	Chris Suddaby	1956
01	David J Williams	1956
01	J Cunningham	1957
01	David Davies	1957
01	Keith Davitte	1957
01	John Powell Jones	1957
01	W Jones	1957
01	Jack Melen	1957
01	John Merriman	1957
01	Dave W Roberts	1957
01	P J P Saunders	1957
01	Mike Shannon	1957
01	Gwilym Thomas	1957
01	I Trevor Owen	1957
01	Norman Watkins	1957
01	David Jones	1958
01	Dewar Neill	1958
01	R Davies	1959
01	Ian Hughes	1959
01	Arthur Richardson	1959
01	John C Jones	1960
01	Pat Jones	1960
01	J Watkins	1960
01	Dewi Bebb	1961
01	Vivian Blackwell	1961
01	Anthony Burgess	1961
01	Michael Davies	1961
01	David Griffiths	1961
01	Glyndwr Morris	1961
01	Gwilym Owen	1961
01	David Pritchard	1961
01	Dil Robbins	1961
01	Peter Walker	1961
01	Gareth B Jones	1967
01	Edwin Clarke	1967
01	Howard Davies	1967
01	John E Lewis	1967
01	Alan Jones	1968
01	Martyn Roberts	1968
01	Ken Bobbett	1969
01	Jim Boyle	1969

01	Paul Caviel	1969
01	Peter Challinor	1969
01	Gerald Evans	1969
01	John Evans	1969
01	Brian Griffiths	1969
01	Vince James	1969
01	Keith Lowe	1969
01	Bob Maplestone	1969
01	Nigel Sherlock	1969
01	Roger Stennett	1969
01	Adrian Thomas	1969
01	Bill Treharne	1969
01	Mike Walters	1969
01	Graham Spencer	1971
01	Brian Donovan	1973
01	Hywel Griffiths	1973
01	John Jones	1973
01	Neddyn Lloyd	1974
01	Gareth Jenkins	1975
01	John R Lewis	1975
01	Tony Pretty	1975
01	Aneurin Tanner	1975
01	Steve Gibbons	1976
01	Kevin Glastonbury	1976
01	Richard Hughes	1976
01	Kevin Jones	1976
01	Jon Wilson	1976
01	Bill Wright	1976
01	Phil Jones	1977
01	Alun Roper	1977
01	Jack Thomas	1977
01	Kirk Clifford	1978
01	Ken Cocks	1978
01	Robert Davies	1978
01	Mike Morgan	1978
01	Milton Palmer	1978
01	Dick Samuel	1978
01	Ian Davies	1979
01	Simon Evans	1979
01	Alan Keyse	1979
01	Dave Messum	1979
01	Charles Monk	1979
01	Peter Stark	1979
01	Martin Griffiths	1980
01	Huw Thomas	1980
01	Nse Akang	1981
01	Steve Bright	1981
01	Bob Dobson	1981
01	Lloyd Roberts	1981
01	Martin Thomas	1981
01	Andy Bamber	1982
01	Chris Starr	1982
01	Dean Crapnell	1983
01	Paul Evans (Sw)	1983
01	Ben Jones	1983
01	Kevin Parker	1983
01	John Barry	1984
01	Andrew Orchard	1984
01	Marcus Thomas	1984
01	Brian Dowrick	1985
01	John Messum	1985
01	Chris Trotman	1985
01	Jon Walters	1985
01	Andrew Main	1986
01	Richard Wintle	1986
01	Henry Foley	1987
01	James Mason	1987
01	Eddie Conway	1988
01	Arthur Emyr	1988
01	Doug Minter	1988
01	David Richards	1988
01	Shaun Whelan	1988
01	Neil Charnock	1989
01	Steve Jones (Brom)	1989
01	Martin Roberts	1989
01	Mark Toop	1989
01	Ray Blaber	1990
01	Michael Hall	1990
01	Richard Harbour	1990
01	Glyn Harvey	1990
01	Damian Stirling	1990
01	Michael Williams	1990
01	Robert Bradley	1991
01	Berian Davies	1991
01	Ian Gould	1991
01	Neil Williams	1991
01	Clive Boulton	1992
01	Wayne Davies	1992
01	Chris Harding	1992
01	Stephen Lloyd	1992
01	Peter Roberts	1992
01	Tony Ene	1993
01	Kevin Blake	1994
01	Colin Bradley	1994
01	Justin Hobbs	1994
01	Dale Woodman	1994
01	Andres Jones	1995
01	Steve Mosley	1995
01	Jas Archampong	1996
01	Daniel Davies	1996
01	Richard Gardiner	1996
01	Steve Knight	1996
01	Chris Millard	1996
01	David Nolan	1996
01	Steve Brace	1997
01	Lee Edwards	1997
01	Huw Evans	1997
01	Gareth James	1997
01	Steven Shalders	1997
01	Chris Thomas	1997
01	Andrew Walling	1997
01	Ben Roberts	1998
01	Justin Bryan	1999
01	Kim Harland	1999
01	Jon Hilton	1999
01	Lee Newman	1999
01	Chris Type	1999
01	Tim Benjamin	2000
01	Robert Mitchell	2000
01	Nathan Palmer	2000

Women

31	Helen Miles	1982-96
29	Carmen Smart	1975-89
27	Sallyanne Short	1983-95
26	Venissa Head	1974-88
25	Gillian Regan	1974-86
23	Jackie Zaslona	1976-90
21	Janet Beese	1974-91
20	Annmarie Fox	1979-91
18	Sian Morris	1981-91
18	Michelle Cooke	1984-94
17	Sarah Bull	1975-95
17	Marion Hughes	1979-88
16	Kirsty McDermott	1979-91
15	Kim Lock	1978-88
15	Kay Morley	1986-92
13	Alyson Hourihan	1981-92
13	Liz Wren	1983-89
13	Jo Willoughby	1983-92
13	Caroline White	1986-99
12	Jenny Davies	1975-83
12	Diane Heath	1977-83
12	Janeen Williams	1979-86
12	Alyson Evans	1984-98
12	Jayne Berry	1987-96
12	Bethan Edwards	1990-97
12	Rachel Newcombe	1992-00
12	Sarah Moore	1994-00
11	Michelle Probert	1978-86
11	Rachel King	1995-00
10	Jennifer Webb	1979-84
10	Lisa Griffiths	1987-94
10	Cath Murphy	1995-00
09	Vivienne Head	1975-84
09	Sarah Rowe	1979-83
09	Nicola Short	1986-97
09	Samantha Porter	1987-90
09	Onyema Amadi	1988-96
09	Lisa Armstrong	1989-94
09	Alison Parry	1989-95
09	Philippa Roles	1993-00
09	Julie Crane	1995-00
08	Gloria Dourass	1974-78
08	Hilary Hollick	1977-82
08	Angela Tooby	1983-88
08	Susan Tooby	1984-87
08	Melissa Watson	1985-89
08	Elizabeth Francis	1987-95
08	Gillian Archard	1988-96
08	Teresa Andrews	1992-98
07	Ceri Jenkins	1974-76
07	Anne Morris	1974-77
07	Angela Hartley	1976-80
07	Jill Davies	1976-82
07	Karen Taylor	1978-82
07	Val Adams	1984-92
07	Wendy Ore	1984-93
07	Amanda Wale	1989-98
07	Jayne Fisher	1991-96
07	Dawn Higgins	1995-00
06	Michelle Atkinson	1974-76
06	Sue James	1974-78
06	Ruth MartinJones	1976-79
06	Caroline Morgan	1976-87
06	Bernie Butcher	1977-80
06	Caitlin Funnell	1988-91
06	Susannah Filce	1989-92
06	Claire Edwards	1990-95
06	Cathy White	1991-94
06	Hayley Parry	1995-97
05	Lianne Dando	1974-79
05	Diane Thorne	1976-79
05	Lynfa Lewis	1976-81
05	Karen Hough	1983-86
05	Anne Evison	1986-90
05	Hayley Nash	1988-95
05	Joanne Gronow	1990-95
05	Natasha Bartlett	1991-94
05	Ailsa Wallace	1994-97
05	Emma Davies	1997-00
05	Louise Whitehead	1999-00
04	Sandra Pengilley	1974-75
04	Linda Croft	1975-76
04	Jane Lucas	1975-76
04	Jane Lloyd Francis	1976-78
04	Jane Evans	1979-80
04	Carol Fernley	1979-80
04	Jane Buttress	1981-83
04	Sally James	1983-91
04	Barbara A King	1984
04	Tracey Lewis	1985-89
04	Ann Middle	1986-89
04	Lisa Carthew	1993-94
04	Louise Sharps	1993-97
04	Lesley Brannan	1995-99
04	Rebecca Roles	1995-99
04	Kathryn Bright	1996-99
03	Jean Lochhead	1974-75
03	Delyth Prothero	1974-75
03	Philomena Ronan	1974-75
03	Vivienne Rothera	1974-75
03	Kay Buckland	1976
03	Sue Lovell	1976-77
03	Angela Pennington	1976-77
03	Lyn Huntbach	1976-78
03	Bronwen Smith	1976-93
03	Sandra Lee	1979-81
03	Janet Howes	1980-82
03	Jane Bradbeer	1984-85
03	Amanda Barnes	1986-87
03	Rebecca Richard	1990-91
03	Audrey Lewis	1991
03	Anna Proctor	1991-92
03	Emily Stewart	1991-94
03	Esther Evans	1992-95
03	Jayne Ludlow	1994-96
03	Angharad Mair	1995-97
03	Sian Lax	1995-97
03	Gael Davies	1996-97
03	Angharad James	1996-97
03	Amanda Pritchard	1996-97
03	Rhian Clarke	1997-00
02	Sheila Coy	1953-58
02	Jean Docker	1953-58
02	Delyth Davies	1974
02	Debbie Froggatt	1974
02	June Hirst	1974
02	Karen Jenkins	1974
02	Margaret Rainbow	1974
02	Juliet Worrall	1974
02	Heather Thomas	1975
02	Elaine Oxton	1975-76
02	Margaret Morgan	1976
02	Margaret Williams	1976
02	Sian Morgan	1978
02	Julia Charlton	1980-83
02	Lyn Parry	1980-84
02	Jennifer Morley	1981
02	Jane Tomley	1983
02	Karen Nipper	1983-84
02	Pat Gallagher	1984-86
02	Jackie Barber	1986-88
02	Rebecca J Morris	1987
02	Eirwen Williams	1987
02	Clare Warnes	1987-89

02	Carol Whiteway	1987-90
02	Carol Hayward	1989
02	Hayley Hartson	1989-90
02	Sarah Hodge	1990
02	Emily Steele	1991-92
02	Christine Page	1992
02	Jane Falconer	1993
02	Krissy Owen	1993-94
02	Angela Bonner	1995-96
02	Gemma Jones	1995-97
02	Clare Martin	1996
02	Hannah Paines	1996
02	Ceri Thomas	1996-97
02	Anna Turner	1996-97
02	Kathryn Williams	1996-97
02	Emma Brady	1999-00
01	J Pearce	1953
01	D L Watts	1953
01	Jean Crutchley	1958
01	Bonnie Jones	1958
01	Sally Jones	1958
01	J Price	1958
01	Carol Thomas	1958
01	J Wheeler	1958
01	Daphne Williams	1958
01	Sue Norman	1974
01	Pat Pearson	1974
01	Ann Disley	1975
01	Karen Evans	1975
01	Pamela Hiley	1975
01	Elin Jones	1975
01	Ann Lewis	1975
01	Siobhan Taylor	1975
01	Pat Lamour	1976
01	Julie Morgan	1976
01	Ann Roblin	1976
01	Ruanda Davies	1977
01	Paula Middle	1977
01	Yvonne Norton	1977
01	Jaqui Hammersley	1978
01	Jackie Hulbert	1978
01	Amanda Stacey	1978
01	Yvonne Rowe	1979
01	Kathy Williams	1979
01	Christine Brookes	1981
01	Jayne Dawkins	1981
01	Yana Jones	1981
01	Delyth Evans	1983
01	Sandra Miller	1983
01	Julie Tayler	1983
01	Belinda Huxtable	1984
01	Allison Rees	1984
01	Michelle Reynolds	1984
01	Samantha Taylor	1984
01	Lynn Maddison	1985
01	Sian Sanders	1985
01	Debbie Jones	1987
01	Emma Thorne	1987
01	Martha Tullberg	1987
01	Allison Consterdine	1988
01	Karen Dunster	1988
01	Kerry Woodcock	1988
01	Emma Lile	1989
01	Bernadette Walters	1989
01	Sally Whiteside	1989
01	Julie Abel	1990
01	Tina Curry	1990
01	Bev Green	1990
01	Alex Kegie	1990
01	Mari Prys Jones	1990
01	Alison Whitelaw	1990
01	Maria Yarnold	1990
01	Jane Davies	1991
01	Sian Pilling	1991
01	Nicola H Jones	1992
01	Fiona McPhail	1992
01	Megan Jones	1993
01	Nicola Davies	1994
01	Angharad Richards	1994
01	Krysta Williams	1994
01	Dinah Cheverton	1995
01	Joanne Davies	1995
01	Bonnie Elms	1995
01	Non Evans	1995
01	Amanda Horton	1995
01	Michelle John	1995
01	Joy Lamacraft	1995
01	Kerry J Wallace	1995
01	Kate Williams	1995
01	Claudia Filce	1996
01	Jo Tomlinson	1996
01	Natasha Campbell	1997
01	Sarah Lewis	1997
01	Kelly Moreton	1997
01	Lucy Power	1997
01	Caroline Wilkins	1997
01	Nicola Jupp	1998
01	Lowri Jones	1999
01	Stephanie Little	1999
01	Clare Lockwood	1999
01	Eirion Owen	1999
01	Danielle Selley	1999
01	Victoria Consterdne	2000
01	Rebecca Jones	2000
01	Lara Richards	2000

WELSH INTERNATIONAL ROAD RUNNING MATCHES – SENIOR MEN

Date	Distance	Venue	Match Result
08.07.1979	Marathon	Tullamore, Eire	Ireland 5, England 8, Denmark 17, **Wales 21,** Scot 24
14.10.1979	Marathon	Glasgow	Position unknown
16.03.1980	25K	Bolton	England 10, Scotland 39, N Irel 46, **Wales 69,** Irel 116
14.09.1980	Marathon	Glasgow	England 5, Ireland 9, N Irel 18, **Wales 28,** Scotland dnf
28.09.1980	Marathon	Glasgow	England 10, Scotland 17, **Wales 18**
27.09.1981	Marathon	Aberdeen	England 10, Scotland 17, **Wales 22,** Irel 34, N Irel 37
18.10.1981	Marathon	Glasgow	Scotland 9, **Wales 9,** Ireland 9, N Ireland 14
19.09.1982	Marathon	Aberdeen	**Wales 13,** Scotland 15, England 19, N Ireland 31
17.10.1982	Marathon	Glasgow	England 1st, Scotland 2nd, **Wales 3rd**
14.11.1982	25K	Twickenham	**Wales 1st**
11.09.1983	Marathon	Glasgow	**Wales 2nd**
18.09.1983	Marathon	Aberdeen	England 9, **Wales 20,** N Ireland 23, Scotland dnf
30.09.1984	Marathon	Glasgow	**Wales 3rd**
19.05.1985	Marathon	Bridgend	**Wales 1st**, England 2nd
01.09.1985	Marathon	Edinburgh	Scotland 3, **Wales 8,** Ireland 11, England 14
15.09.1985	Marathon	Aberdeen	**Wales 3rd**
22.09.1985	Marathon	Glasgow	Position unknown
13.03.1986	Marathon	Barcelona	Position unknown
19.05.1986	Marathon	Bridgend	England 1st, **Wales 2nd,** Catalonia 3rd
21.09.1986	Marathon	Glasgow	**Wales 5th**
15.03.1987	Marathon	Barcelona	**Wales 1st**
12.04.1987	Half Marathon	Stafford	Scotland 8, **Wales 13**
24.05.1987	Marathon	Aberdeen	England 8, Scotland 16, **Wales 21**
05.07.1987	Marathon	Bridgend	**Wales 1st,** Scotland 2nd, Catalonia 3rd
30.08.1987	Half Marathon	Livingston	England 10, Scotland 16, **Wales 20,** N Ireland
06.09.1987	Half Marathon	Cardiff	**Wales 6,** Scotland 15
13.03.1988	Marathon	Barcelona	**Wales 2nd**
30.04.1988	10K	H Hempstead	England 7, **Wales 33,** Kenya 56, Scotland 81, N Irel 164
28.05.1988	Marathon	Aberdeen	Scotland 8, **Wales 23,** England 24
29.08.1988	Half Marathon	Livingston	England 3, Scotland 7, N Ireland 12, **Wales 19**
18.09.1988	Marathon	Anglesey	**Wales 7,** N Ireland 14, Scotland 26, Catalonia 31
20.03.1989	Marathon	Barcelona	**Wales 1st,** Scotland 2nd, Catalonia 3rd
28.05.1989	Marathon	Aberdeen	**Wales 3rd**
28.08.1989	Half Marathon	Livingston	England 6, **Wales 25,** Scotland, N Ireland
10.09.1989	Marathon	Anglesey	**Wales 13,** N Ireland 17, Scotland dnf
19.03.1990	Marathon	Barcelona	**Wales 2nd**
27.05.1990	Marathon	Aberdeen	England 6, **Wales 20,** Scotland 21
22.07.1990	Marathon	Luton	**Wales dnf**
26.08.1990	Half Marathon	Livingston	Scotland 7, **Wales 8,** England 9

10.03.1991	Marathon	Redcar	England 13, **Wales 38,** N Ireland 54
17.03.1991	Marathon	Barcelona	Position unknown
28.04.1991	Marathon	Vendee	Position unknown
06.05.1991	Ekiden Relay	Belfast	England 2:04:41, N Irel 2:05:13, Scot 2:06:54, **Wales 2:12:28**
21.07.1991	Marathon	Luton	**Wales 12,** England 15, Scotland 20, N Ireland 31
10.11.1991	10 miles	Llandudno	**Wales 15,** Scotland 16, N Ireland 23, England 24
19.07.1992	Marathon	Luton	**Wales 13,** Scotland 14, N Ireland 18
06.09.1992	10K	Cardiff	**Wales 11,** England 11, Scotland 25
03.04.1993	4 miles	Warkworth	**Wales 10th**
02.05.1993	4 miles	Bamburgh	**Wales 10th**
08.05.1993	4 miles	Alnwick	**Wales 9th**
12.09.1993	10K	Swansea	England 7, **Wales 18,** N Ireland 31, Scotland 33
04.04.1994	4 miles	Ford	**Wales 10th**
09.04.1994	4 miles	Bamburgh	**Wales dnf**
23.04.1994	4 miles	Warkworth	**Wales dnf**
05.06.1994	Half Marathon	Dunfermline	England 6, Ireland 25, Scotland 25, **Wales 36,** N Irel 42
21.08.1994	Half Marathon	Liverpool	England 8, **Wales 25,** N Ireland 29, Kenya 30
11.09.1994	10K	Swansea	England 10, **Wales 27,** Scotland 41
04.06.1995	10K	Cardiff	England 8, **Wales 17,** Scotland 27
20.08.1995	Half Marathon	Liverpool	Russia 9, Select 17, England 20, **Wales 32**
03.07.1996	6K	Battersea	England 12, **Wales 26**
25.08.1996	Half Marathon	Liverpool	England 13, **Wales 18,** Russia 19
31.08.1997	10 miles	Erewash	England 7, **Wales 14,** Scotland 27
12.10.1997	10 miles	Newry	Kenya 6, Ireland 19, England 20, Denmark 39, **Wales 39**
30.08.1998	Half Marathon	Liverpool	**Wales 4th**
20.09.1998	10 miles	Newry	Kenya, Ireland, Denmark, England, **Wales**
26.03.2000	10K	Swansea	England 11, Scotland 17, **Wales 19**

WELSH INTERNATIONAL ROAD RUNING VESTS – SENIOR MEN

16	Dic Evans	1980–91
12	Mick McGeoch	1980-89
09	Shaun Tobin	1993-98
08	Mick Crowell	1979-86
08	Steve Brace	1985-96
06	Ieuan Ellis	1982-91
06	Steve Brown	1983-87
06	Tegid Roberts	1987-89
06	Arwel Lewis	1987-91
05	Jerry Hall	1989-94
05	Gareth Davies	1990-97
05	Justin Hobbs	1993-95
05	Mark Morgan	1994-00
05	Darren Hiscox	1996-98
04	Greg Newhams	1987-92
04	Jon Hooper	1990-94
04	Paul Smith	1990-94
04	Martin Rees	1994-98
03	Malcolm Firth	1979-84
03	Paul Bennett	1987-91
03	Paul Howarth	1988-90
03	Kevin Tobin	1993-95
03	Steve Knight	1994-96
03	Rhodri Jones	1997-00
02	Gordon McIlroy	1979-80
02	John Robertshaw	1980
02	Dave Roberts	1980-81
02	Nigel Spiers	1982-83
02	Kenny Davies	1982-91
02	Trevor Hawes	1983-86
02	Eddy Lee	1985-87
02	Richard Bullen	1987-88
02	Owen Lewis	1988
02	Emlyn Roberts	1988-89
02	Tony Simmons	1988-90
02	Dave Bright	1990
02	Jeremy Collins	1990-91
02	Kevin Wilkinson	1991-92
02	Nicky Comerford	1993
02	Karl Palmer	1993
02	Jon Edwards	1994
02	Paul Richards	1994-96
02	Bruce Chinnick	1995
02	Rob Atkinson	1979
02	Alan Joslyn	1979
01	Cyril Leigh	1979
01	Hedydd Davies	1980
01	Lynn Hughes	1980
01	Mike Lane	1980
01	Mike Rowland	1980
01	Ali Cole	1981
01	Graham Spencer	1981
01	Frank Thomas	1981
01	Colin Mattock	1982
01	Norman Wilson	1982
01	Peter Jones	1984
01	Alan Jefferies	1985
01	Dave E Jones	1985
01	Alun Roper	1985
01	Steve Jones	1987
01	Jeremy Thomas	1987
01	Tony Blackwell	1988
01	Roger Hackney	1988
01	Geoff Hill	1988
01	Peter Jenkins	1988
01	Huw Roberts	1989
01	Ray Fundalski	1990
01	Malcolm Griffiths	1991
01	Martin Haley	1991
01	Dewi Jones	1991
01	Ron McAndrew	1991
01	Steve Rhind	1991
01	Nigel Adams	1992
01	Christian Stephenson	1993
01	Kevin Blake	1994
01	Phil Cook	1994
01	Colin Jones	1994
01	Jeff Secker	1995
01	0Dale Rixon	1996
01	Simon Shiels	1998
01	Andres Jones	2000
01	Jamie Lewis	2000

WELSH INTERNATIONAL ROAD RUNNING MATCHES – SENIOR WOMEN

Date	**Distance**	**Venue**	**Match Result**
07.06.1987	10K	Strathclyde	Scotland 9, **Wales 14**
18.10.1987	10K	Cardiff	England 9, Scotland 18, **Wales 22**
05.06.1988	10K	Strathclyde	Scotland 18, England 23, **Wales 56,** N Ireland 76
18.06.1989	10K	Strathclyde	**Wales 20,** Scotland 27, N Ireland 61
26.08.1990	Half Marathon	Livingston	**Wales 1st**
10.11.1991	10 miles	Llandudno	N Ireland 5, **Wales 5,** Scotland 12
06.09.1992	10K	Cardiff	Scotland 14, England 16, **Wales 18,** Ireland 30
12.09.1993	10K	Swansea	England 8, **Wales 18,** Scotland dnf - 3 to score England 3, Scotland 10, **Wales 10 –** 2 to score
29.05.1994	10K	Glasgow	Ireland 9, England 12, **Wales 36,** Scot 45, N Ireland 53

21.08.1994	Half Marathon	Liverpool	England 6, **Wales 17**
11.09.1994	10K	Swansea	England 6, **Wales 17,** Scotland 26
21.05.1995	10K	Glasgow	**Wales 4th**
04.06.1995	10K	Cardiff	England 1st, **Wales 2nd,** Scotland 3rd
19.05.1996	10K	Glasgow	England 8, Scotland 26, Ireland 35, **Wales 36,** N Irel 63
03.07.1996	6K	Battersea	**Wales 10,** England 11
31.08.1997	10 miles	Erewash	Position unknown
12.10.1997	10 miles	Newry	Position unknown
20.09.1998	10 miles	Newry	Position unknown
26.03.2000	10K	Swansea	England 1st, Scotland 2nd, **Wales 3rd**

WELSH INTERNATIONAL ROAD RUNNING VESTS – SENIOR WOMEN

9	Bronwen Cardy	1987-96
5	Nicky Haines/Jones	1989-94
5	Dinah Cheverton	1993-97
4	Eryl Davies	1987-94
3	Sally Lynch	1987-89
3	Liz Clarke	1991-94
3	Barbara Boylan	1995-96
3	Angharad Mair	1995-96
2	Hayley Nash	1987-95
2	Wendy Ore	1987-96
2	Peta Bee	1988-89
2	Maggie Smith	1988-89
2	Liz Hughes	1990-91
2	Bernadette Walters	1992-00
2	Louise Copp	1994-00
2	Lynne Maddison	1995
2	Frances Gill	1996-00
2	Vivienne Conneely	1997
2	Jackie Newton	1998-00
1	Beccy Powell	1987
1	Helen Williams	1987
1	Fiona Davies/Nixon	1988
1	Sue Graham	1988
1	Beccy Richardson	1988
1	Ceri Pritchard	1989
1	Liz Hardley	1990
1	Alison Whitelaw	1990
1	Dawn Kenwright	1991
1	Beccy Cameron	1994
1	Debbie Chick	1994
1	Liz Francis/Thomas	1996
1	Clare Allen	1997
1	Emma Evans	1997
1	Debbie Phillips	1998
1	Edwina Turner	1998

Section 13

Welsh Representatives in World Cross-Country Championships

Wales took part in the first International Cross Country Championships which were held at Hamilton Park Racecourse in Scotland in 1903 and competed every year up to and including 1987. In 1988 only one team from the UK was allowed to enter and so it was the end of an era for Wales competing as a separate nation. Below is a complete list of all the athletes who have represented Wales in this event up to 1987.

SENIOR MEN

14 Danny Phillips (Newport/Cwmbran) 1922-37

12 Ernie Thomas (Cwmbran) 1922-35

10 Tom Richards (Pontnewydd/Mitcham/SLH) 1934-53, Steve Jones (RAF/Swindon/Bristol/Newport) 1977-87

9 Harry Gallivan (Pontnewydd/Cwm H) 1931-39

8 Tommy Arthur (Newport) 1905-14, Chris Buckley (Westbury) 1980-87

7 William Butcher (Atalanta/Birchfield) 1949-59, Dyfrig Rees (Coventry Godiva) 1950-57, Malcolm Thomas (TVH/Leeds) 1969-76, Bernie Plain (Birchgrove/Cardiff) 1969-77, Tony Simmons (Luton Utd) 1969-87.

6 ER Leyshon (Newport/Cwmbran) 1924-29, J Prosser (Cwmbran) 1925-32, Ivor Brown (Llanbradach) 1933-39, Tom Wood (Newport) 1949-57, Phil Morgan (SLH) 1953-59, David Richards (Polytechnic) 1955-61, Norman Horrell (Rhondda/Roath) 1957-63, Hedydd Davies (Birchfield/TVH) 1963-68, Dic Evans (Cardiff) 1972-79, Clive Thomas (TVH) 1973-80, Ieuan Ellis (Newport) 1982-87

5 EJ Davies (Newport) 1912-22, DJP Richards (Port Talbot YMCA, Newport, UC Wales) 1922-29, Ted Hopkins (Roath) 1926-33, Sam Palmer (Army) 1931-39, Ken Harris (Roath) 1935-50, Roger Harrison-Jones (Rhyl/Liverpool Pembroke) 1959-64, Dennis Fowles (Cardiff) 1972-82, David Hopkins (Newport) 1973-78, Alun "Ali" Cole (Swansea/Newport) 1977-86, Kenny Davies (Newport) 1982-86

4 EJ Thomas (Newport) 1903-06, Rhys Evans (Roath) 1903-09, Eddie Ace (Newport) 1905-08, Ernest Paul (Cwmbran) 1909-12, Bill Matthews (Penrhys) 1934-48, A Williams (Sutton H) 1935-39, Eddie Cooper (Roath) 1937-49, Dennis Morgan (Mitcham) 1938-48, Ivor Lloyd (Newport) 1947-50, Eric Williams (Mitcham) 1947-51, Maldwyn White (Birchfield) 1948-52, Doug Rees (Portsmouth) 1950-53, Lyn Bevan (Newport) 1953-64, Tony Pumfrey (Coventry) 1954-60, Ken Flowers (Abergavenny/Gilwern) 1956-65, Harry Wilson (Welwyn) 1958-62, Roy Profitt (Devonport/Polytechnic) 1959-63, Brian Jeffs (RAF) 1960-67, John Jones (Windsor, Slough & Eton) 1969-74, Steve Gibbons (Carmarthen/Swansea) 1971-76, Mike Lane (Gilwern/Newport) 1974-81, Roger Hackney (Aldershot, Farnham & Dist/RAF) 1979-82, Tony Blackwell (Wolverhampton & Bilston) 1981-84, Paul Wheeler (Les Croupiers/Cardiff) 1983-87,

3 RG Davies (Newport) 1903-05, T Hughes (Farnworth) 1904-06, EO Price (Newport) 1904-07, T Burnford (Barry/Roath) 1906-08, Ben Christmas (Roath) 1907-09, Jack Meyrick (Newport) 1910-12, AS Wilson (Newport) 1911-21, W Milland (Newport) 1912-14, Jim Edwards (Newport) 1921-25, Gwyn Morgan (Cwmbran) 1921-26, BD Hammond (Newport) 1924-26, Jimmy Guy (Roath) 1924-27, Frank Denmead (Cwmbran) 1927-29, AS Stone (Pontypool) 1931-33, George Fox (Mitcham) 1936-39, Pat Wallace (Newport) 1949-51, Anthony Noonan (Watford) 1950-52, George Phipps (Cambridge) 1951-54, Norman Wilson (RAF) 1952-55, Ken Huckle (Roath) 1953-56, John Merriman (Watford) 1958-60, Bob Roath (Walton) 1960-65, Ron Franklin (Tipton) 1961-64, Tom Edmunds (Gilwern) 1964-66, Chris Loosley (Aberystwyth) 1965-68, Cyril Leigh (Wigan/Salford) 1967-69, Alun Joslyn (Polytechnic) 1967-70, Nigel Evans (Westbury) 1970-72, Tony Ashton (Reading) 1971-73, Micky Morris (Cwmbran/Cardiff) 1976-79, Glen Grant (Army) 1976-80, David James (Cardiff) 1980-83, Nigel Adams (Swansea) 1983-87, Peter Jenkins (Newport) 1985-87.

2 DG Harris (Reading) 1903-04, JD Marsh (Salford) 1903-04, RB Pugh (Newport) 1903-04, WJ Francis (Cathays) 1904-05, HC Cleaver (Newport) 1905-06, EJ Francis (Cathays) 1905-07, H Grainger (Roath/Cwmbran) 1908-13, T Elsmore (Cwmbran)1909-11, L Lloyd (Cathays) 1909-11, Edgar Stead (Cwmbran) 1909-13, E Massey (Newport) 1909-14, FJ Iles (Roath) 1910-11, W Herring (Cwmbran) 1911-12, Tom Miles (Cwmbran) 1912-14, Sam Judd (Newport) 1914-21, S Driscoll (Cwmbran) 1928-29, Tom Burge (Roath) 1930-31, R Simons (Pontypool) 1931-32, Len Tongue (Newport) 1933-34, WL Raddon (Swansea) 1935-36, E Jones (Swansea Valley/Mitcham) 1937-38, Dillan Hier (RAF) 1939-46, Bill Richards (Roath) 1946-47, John Andrews (Finchley) 1948-49, John Edwards (Carmarthen) 1951-52, John Disley (SLH) 1955-56, Brian James (Bournemouth) 1955-57, Peter Bowden (Bristol) 1956-58, Rhys Davies (Coventry Godiva) 1957-58, Barrie Saunders (TVH) 1958-62, Robert Williams (TVH) 1962-65, Jim O'Brien (Port Talbot) 1962-67, Gerry Barrell (SLH)

1964-65, John Godding (Birchgrove) 1965-67, Fred Bell (Carmarthen) 1966-67, Roy Mack (Birchfield) 1966-67, Nick Barton (London Univ) 1966-69, A Jones (Cambridge) 1968-69, Jeff Kirby (Roath/Cardiff) 1968-69, Ron McAndrew (Reading)
1968-71, Paul Darney (Cardiff) 1969-70, Mike Critchley (Cardiff) 1973-76, Steve Slocombe (Cardiff) 1974-77, Peter Griffiths (Tipton) 1975-78, John Davies (TVH) 1976-79, Peter Baker (Shaftesbury) 1978-79, John Theophilus (Swansea) 1982-83, Mike Bishop (Staff Moorlands) 1986-87.

1 T Baggs (Newport) 1903, W Crail (Newport) 1903, W Davies (Newport) 1903, A Palmer (Newport) 1903, A Rees (Newport) 1903, A Turner (Newport) 1903, WG Bradbury (Newport) 1904, TT Wynn (Newport) 1905, T Horton (Cathays) 1906, W Thomas (Newport) 1906, W Cooper (Newport) 1907, W Fitzjohn (Abertillery) 1907, DH Griffiths (Abergavenny) 1907, F Pinkard (Newport) 1907, C Gould (Cathays) 1908, Eddie O'Donnell (Roath) 1908, PB Currey (Tredegar) 1909, R Jones (Newport) 1909, T Pavey (Abertillery) 1909, J Coombs (Abertillery) 1910, D Francis (Roath) 1910, T Harry (St Saviour's) 1910, Bill Johnson (Newport) 1910, S Wilson (Roath) 1910, W Taylor (Newport) 1912, C Hill (Newport) 1913, J Jones (Abertillery) 1913, J Williams (Cwmbran) 1913, Cliff Price (Newport) 1914, P Waters (Cwmbran) 1914, HJ Browning (Cwmbran) 1921, W Jones (Newport) 1921, IS Williams (Cwmbran) 1921, T Webber (Newport) 1922, J Cox (Cwmbran) 1924, AW Johnson (Roath) 1924, JH Brunning (Cwmbran) 1925, D Evans (Newport) 1925, R Morgan (Abertillery) 1925, J Stamer (?) 1925, Ivor Thomas (Newport) 1926, TV Berry (Roath) 1927, LS Howells (Univ of Wales) 1927, J Hughes (Pontynewydd) 1927, J Davies (Univ of Wales) 1928, Ossie Williams (Llanbradach) 1929, James Duggan (Swansea Valley) 1930, J Gifford (Cwmbran) 1930, J Lloyd (Roath) 1930, F Shackell (Splott) 1930, TH Timbrell (Swansea Valley) 1930, Wilf Short (Newport) 1931, H Tongue (Newport) 1933, EL Adams (Mansfield) 1934, DJ Jones (Swansea Valley) 1934, C Evans (Cwmbran) 1936, GT Clarke (Tooting) 1937, J Pearce (Cwmbran) 1938, Tom Winslade (Port Talbot YMCA) 1938, Reg Thomas (RAF/Newport) 1939, Tom Christison (Pontnewydd) 1946, JC Lloyd (Newport) 1946, DC Saunders (Cardiff Univ) 1946, Bernard Baldwin (Roath) 1947, Martin Richards (Highgate) 1947, Glan Williams (Cardiff Univ) 1947, Jim Alford (Roath) 1948, J Davies (Port Talbot YMCA) 1948, HF Bull (Essex Beagles) 1949, C Rosser (Aylesford) 1950, P Griggs (Coventry Godiva) 1953, Gilbert Legge (Newport) 1954, John Nash (Port Talbot YMCA) 1954, Chris Suddaby (Thames Hare & Hounds) 1956, Jack Wingfield (Roath) 1957, JI Evans (Queen's Park H) 1958, Haydn Tawton (Roath) 1958, WP Adams (Sheffield Univ) 1959, Ken Dare (Small Heath) 1960, Bryan Davies (Carmarthen) 1962, Alan Griffiths (Notts) 1962, George Matthiudis (Newport) 1963, Tony Harris (Mitcham) 1964, Bill Stitfall (Birchgrove) 1964, John H Collins (Pontypool) 1965, Gerry Williams (Hereford) 1966, Mel Evans (Tipton) 1968, David Walker (1970), Bernie Hayward (Cardiff) 1971, B Brookes (Small Heath) 1972, Alan Cass (Portsmouth) 1972, Brian Donovan (Cardiff) 1973, David Jones (Cardiff) 1975, Peter Ratcliffe (Cardiff) 1976, Trevor Hawes (Swansea) 1977, Richard Samuels (Shaftesbury) 1978, Ted Turner (Army) 1979, John Robertshaw (Newport) 1981, Dick Milne (Notts) 1982, Andrew Evans (Rugby) 1984, Alun Roper (Swansea) 1984, Phil Llewellyn (Shaftesbury) 1985, Dale Rixon (Cardiff) 1986, Steve Smith (Swansea) 1986.

SENIOR WOMEN

16 Jean Lochhead (Airdale) 1967-84

12 Bronwen Cardy (Bromsgrove) 1969-82

7 Delyth Davies (Cardiff) 1967-74, Thelwyn Bateman (Coventy Godiva/Birchfield) 1968-82

5 Hilary Hollick (Sale) 1978-82, Kim Lock (Cardiff) 1979-84

4 Gloria Dourass (Small Heath/Birchfield) 1968-73, Ann Roblin (Cardiff) 1974-86,Ann James (Airdale) 1975-79, Sally James (Newport) 1983-87

3 Janet Eynon (Croydon) 1967-69, Ann Disley (Newport) 1974-78, Annmarie Fox (Swansea) 1978-86, Kathy Williams (Port Talbot) 1980-82, Lynn Maddison (Colwyn Bay) 1985-87, Susan Tooby (Cardiff) 1985-87

2 Rita Gorton (Bromsgrove) 1969-71, Marion Hepworth (Airdale) 1972-73, Ann Morris (Cardiff) 1975-76, Carol Nicholas (Cleddau) 1978-79, Carole Bradford (Clevedon) 1980-81, Yana Jones (Tiverton) 1980-81, Louise Copp (Port Talbot) 1981-84, Fiona Harwood (Cardiff) 1983-85, Angela Tooby (Cardiff) 1984-85, Wendy Ore (Bridgend) 1985-87

1 J Clifford (Newport) 1967, B Meredith (Mitcham) 1967, Pat Sullivan (Westbury) 1967, H Priestley 1968, Pam Johns (Cardiff) 1970, Susan Barnes (Verlea) 1972, Lesley John (Cwmbran Olympiads) 1972, Margaret Morgan (Coventry) 1976, Lyn Huntbach (Cwmbran) 1977, Debbie Lewis (Cardiff) 1977, Trudy Kenward (Cardiff) 1980, Tracy Long (Fleet) 1982, Jane Oldfield (Barry) 1984, Barbara Ann King (Swansea) 1985, Melissa Watson (Swindon) 1986, Ann Middle (Tintoretto) 1987

JUNIOR MEN

4 Steve Blakemore (Cardiff) 1978-81

3 Andrew Rodgers (Leeds) 1982-84

2 Fred Bell (Carmarthen) 1962-63, Winston Bradley (Gilwern) 1962-63, Chris Loosley (Carmarthen) 1963-64, Will Francis (Birchgrove) 1964-65, J Powell (Birchgrove) 1967-68, Tony Simmons (Luton) 1967-68, Alan Cummings (Cardiff) 1976-77, Adrian Leek (Cardiff) 1976-77, Ieuan Ellis (Aberystwyth) 1978-79, Simon Axon (Swansea) 1978-80, Andrew Smith (Swansea) 1980-81, Nigel Stops (Shaftesbury) 1980-81, Nick Boughey (Swansea) 1981-82, Nazar Habib (Cardiff) 1983-84, Neil Horsfield (Newport) 1984-85, Dale Rixon (Cardiff) 1984-85, Paul Williams (Barry) 1984-86, Justin Hobbs (Cardiff) 1986-87.

1 Tom Edmunds (Gilwern) 1962, S Oultram (?) 1962, Alcwyn Price (Neath H) 1962, Bill Stitfall (Birchgrove) 1963, Robert Mack (Birchfield) 1964, Clive Williams (Birchgrove) 1964, Jeff Kirby (Roath) 1965, Bernie Plain (Cardiff) 1965, D Price 1965, Gerry Williams (Hereford) 1965, Gwynn Davis (Aberystwyth) 1967, Tim Hopkins (Sutton Utd) 1967, Ron McAndrew

(Wigan) 1967, Gary Davis (Aberystwyth) 1968, Bernie Hayward (Cardiff) 1968, Dennis Fowles (Cardiff) 1969, John Mescall (Port Talbot) 1969, Tony Pretty (Thames Valley) 1969, Robert Sercombe (Newport) 1969, Frank Thomas (Aberystwyth) 1969, John Davies (Thames Valley) 1972, Brian Donovan (Cardiff) 1972, Peter Ratcliffe (Cardiff) 1972, Richard Samuels (Shaftesbury) 1972, Steve Slocombe (Cardiff) 1972, Dave Carr (Army) 1976, B Davies (Swansea) 1976, David James (Cardiff) 1976, Howard Norman (Cardiff) 1976, Colin Clarkson (Swansea) 1977, Hugh Shakeshaft (Hereford) 1977,

Mark Donnelly (Torfaen) 1978, Keith Gallivan (Swansea) 1978, Chris Buckley (Westbury) 1979, Paul Lanfear (Reading) 1979, E Martin (Chepstow) 1979, Howard Parsell (Swansea) 1979, Phil Llewellyn (Shaftesbury) 1980, Peter Williams (Swansea) 1980, Steve Smith (Swansea) 1981, Andrew Evans (Rugby) 1982, Geoff Hill (Swansea) 1982, David Thomas (Swansea) 1982, Nigel Gooch (Beddau) 1983, Brian Matthews (Barry) 1983, Alwyn Ormond (Newport) 1983, Ian Williams (Swansea) 1983, Michael Lewis (Rhymney Valley) 1984, Gary Grant (Liverpool) 1985, Alun Phillips (Barry) 1985, John Robinson (Wirral) 1985, Carl Worthington (Cardiff) 1985, Kevin Blake (Cardiff) 1986, Patrick Hoare (Overton) 1986, Ivan Horsfall-Turner (Tonbridge) 1986, Nick Melling (Cardiff) 1986, Justin Chaston (Belgrave) 1987, Andrew Edge (Wrexham) 1987, Bedwyr Huws (Eryri) 1987, Robert Jay (Rhymney Valley) 1987, Gerallt Owen (Swansea) 1987

Section 14

Welsh Athletes Gaining UK International Vests

The following lists give the number of vests won by Welsh athletes at Senior, 'A', U23 and Junior level. The abbreviations are: V = total number of vests, O = outdoors, I = indoors, XC = cross country, RR = road running, W = walking. No vests won when competing in the World Students Games have been included. The totals given are for the period the athletes gained their vests when eligible for Wales. Please note however that some athletes won more UK vests either before they took up their Welsh eligibility or after they relinquished it. The vests have been shown in this way in order to give a true reflection of vests gained by athletes when they were eligible for Wales.

SENIOR MEN

V	Name	Year	O	I	XC	RR	W
63	Colin Jackson	85-00	41	22			
50	Berwyn Price	71-82	39	11			
43	Lynn Davies	62-72	34	09			
32	Nigel Walker	83-92	13	19			
31	Ron Jones	59-70	31				
25	Roger Hackney	79-90	19	03	02	01	
23	Paul Edwards *	83-91	12	11			
22	Jamie Baulch	92-00	19	03			
19	John Disley	50-57	19				
17	Steve Jones	80-93	12			05	
15	Colin O'Neill*	73-78	07	08			
15	Shaun Pickering	87-98	9	06			
14	Reg Thomas	28-37	14				
13	Steve Barry	80-84					13
12	Dave Roberts	74-78	11	01			
12	Iwan Thomas	94-00	12				
11	John Davies	73-78	11				
11	Christian Stephenson	95-00	03		07	01	
10	Bernie Plain	73-79	08			02	
10	Neil Winter	90-96	10				
09	Berwyn Jones	61-63	09				
09	John Robertson	67-71	09				
09	Ian Hamer	90-92	06	02		01	
09	Doug Turner	96-99	04	05			
08	Bob Shaw	54-56	08				
08	John Merriman	58-61	08				
08	Howard Davies	67-68	08				
07	Nick Whitehead	57-60	07				
07	Gwynne Griffiths	68-70	06	01			
07	Phil Lewis	69-76	01	06			
07	Glen Grant	76-80	03	04			
07	Justin Chaston	94-00	07				
06	Ken Jones	48-54	06				
06	Christian Malcolm	99-00	03	03			
05	Jim Alford	37-45	05				
05	Nigel Sherlock	1969	05				
05	John Hill	85-86	01	04			
05	Neil Horsfield	87-92	04	01			
05	Steve Brace	91-96				05	
04	Cecil Griffiths	20-23	04				
04	Hywel Williams	58-59	04				
04	Lawrie Hall	61-65	04				
04	Clive Longe	66-69	04				
04	Bob Adams	1969	03	01			
04	Ron McAndrew	71-73	03	01			
04	David Lease	72-74	03	01			
04	Clive Thomas	74-75	03	01			
04	Tony Simmons *	78-79	02			02	
04	Trevor Llewelyn	78-84	04				
04	Paul Williams (Cam)	79-80		04			
04	Gareth Brown	83-88	01	03			
04	Nigel Adams	89-91			01	03	
04	Paul Gray	94-99	04				
04	Kevin Williams	96-99	01	03			
03	Hubert Stubbs	38-39	03				
03	Tony Harris	61-62	03				
03	Gwyn Williams	67-69	02	01			
03	Peter Lance	1973	01	02			
03	Dennis Fowles	74-82	02	01			
03	Geraint Griffiths	1975		03			
03	Dick Milne	1977		03			
03	Peter Griffiths	77-78	02	01			
03	Mal Edwards *	80-86		03			
03	Bob Dobson	81-82	03				
03	George Robertson	82-86	01	02			
03	Phil Norgate	1984	03				
03	Phil Harries	88-89	03				
03	Nigel Bevan	89-92	03				
03	Tim Thomas	97-00			02	01	
03	Nicky Comerford	98-00	02	01			
02	Wallis Walters	06-08	02				
02	Kenneth Jenkins	1938	02				
02	Brian Woolley	58-60	02				
02	Peter Walker	66-67	01				
02	John Greatrex	70-75		02			
02	John Walters	1971		02			
02	Gary Vince	74-75		02			
02	John Phillips	75-77	02				
02	Micky Morris	77-78	02				
02	Ieuan Ellis	85-87				02	
02	Steve Johnson	85-87					02
02	Alan Tapp	1986		02			
02	Justin Hobbs	94-95	02				
01	Wyatt Gould	1908	01				
01	Alf Yeoumans	1908					01
01	David Jacobs	1912	01				
01	Jack AinsworthDavis	1920	01				
01	Horace Oliver	1941				01	
01	Tom Richards	1948				01	
01	Arthur Thompson	1962					01
01	Vaughan Thomas	1963					01
01	John Williams	1964	01				
01	Terry Davies	1966	01				
01	Graham Webb	1966	01				
01	Gerald Evans	1968		01			
01	Bernie Hayward	1970	01				
01	Mike Delaney	1972		01			
01	Gareth Edwards	1974		01			
01	Bob Sercombe	1974				01	
01	Tony Dyke	1975		01			
01	Steve James	1977	01				
01	Ken Cocks	1978	01				
01	Jeff Griffiths	1978	01				
01	Andrew McIver	1980		01			
01	Paul Evans (Swan)	1983		01			
01	Nigel Skinner	1984		01			
01	David Wood	1984	01				
01	Mike Bishop	1989				01	
01	Colin Mackenzie *	1990	01				
01	Gareth Holloway	1992					01
01	Brian Dowrick	1993					01
01	Colin Jones	1995			01		
01	Dale Rixon	1997				01	
01	Mark Morgan	1999				01	
01	Tim Benjamin	2000		01			
01	Jamie Henthorn	2000		01			
01	Andres Jones	2000	01				
01	Paul Jones	2000	01				

The following athletes won more UK vests either before taking up their eligibility or after relinquishing it. Their total UK vests are:

46	Paul Edwards	16	Colin O'Neill	17	Tony Simmons
09	Milton Palmer	07	Mal Edwards	04	Colin Mackenzie
03	Bob Roberts	03	Andy Williams	02	Peter Templeton

SENIOR WOMEN

V	Name	Year	O	I	XC	RR	V	Name	Year	O	I	XC	RR
28	Venissa Head	75-88	21	07			**03**	Philippa Roles	99-00	02	01		
25	Ruth Martin Jones/Howell	71-78	20	05			**02**	Jean Lochhead	73-74		02		
24	Kirsty McDermott/Wade	81-94	15	09			**02**	Sarah Rowe	81-82	02			
22	Michelle Probert/Scutt	79-85	19	03			**02**	Sian Morris/Lewis	1983	02			
14	Gillian Regan	78-86	02	12			**02**	Susan Tooby *	1988			01	01
12	Kay Morley Brown	89-92	09	03			**02**	Bronwen Cardy	88-93				02
11	Sallyanne Short	88-95	10	01			**02**	Joanne Edwards/Willoughby	1989	02			
10	Averil Williams *	62-71	10				**02**	Cathy White/Dawson	94-95	01	01		
10	Carmen Smart	81-87	10				**02**	Hayley Nash	96-98			01	01
10	Hayley Parry/Tullett	97-00	05	03	02		**02**	Emma Davies	99-00		02		
09	Angela Tooby	84-88	08		01		**01**	Hilary Davies/Yorke	1970		01		
07	Helen Miles	86-91	05	02			**01**	Gloria Dourass/Rickard	1974		01		
06	Thelwyn Bateman	69-71	06				**01**	Diane Heath/Fryar	1978	01			
06	Sarah Bull/Owen	81-84	06				**01**	Janeen Williams *	1981	01			
06	Catherine Murphy	95-00	04	02			**01**	Karen Hough	1986	01			
05	Elizabeth Gill/Lewis	1965	04	01			**01**	Annmarie Fox/Richards	1988		01		
05	Jackie Zaslona	76-81	05				**01**	Sarah Hodge/Lee	1990				01
05	Hilary Tanner/Hollick *	77-81	05				**01**	Onyema Amadi	1991	01			
04	Elizabeth Parsons/Johns	65-71	03	01			**01**	Ceri Pritchard/Diss	1991				01
03	Karen Nipper	83-85	03	Walks			**01**	Lisa Armstrong	1993		01		
03	Melissa Watson	86-88 02				01	**01**	Sally Lynch	1994				01
03	Caroline White	90-91	03				**01**	Lisa Griffiths/Gibbs	1993	01			
03	Wendy Ore	93-94	01		01	01	**01**	Alyson Evans/Layzell	1997	01			
03	Rhian Clarke	97-98	01	02			**01**	Angharad Mair	1997				01
							01	Eryl Davies	1998				01

The following athletes won more UK vests either before taking up their eligibility or after relinquishing it. Their total UK vests are:

27	Averil Williams	12	Hilary Tanner/Hollick	11	Margaret Critchley/Williams
04	Susan Tooby	03	Paula Lloys	02	Janeen Williams

UK 'A' and 'B' OUTDOOR INTERNATIONALS – Senior Men

V	Name	Year	V	Name	Year	V	Name	Year
02	Neville Whitehead	1959-1960	**01**	Tony Ashton	1967	**01**	Clive Thomas	1975
02	Ron Jones	1959-1963	**01**	Ken Bobbett	1967	**01**	Peter Griffiths	1977
02	Laurie Hall	1961-1963	**01**	Tony Edwards	1967	**01**	Peter Lewis	1977
02	Lynn Davies	1961-1964	**01**	John Robertson	1967	**01**	Dave Roberts	1977
02	Gwyn Williams	1967-1970	**01**	Bob Adams	1970	**01**	Roger Hackney	1979
02	David Lease	1970-1973	**01**	Bernie Hayward	1970	**01**	Steve James	1979
02	Gary Vince	1970-1973	**01**	Berwyn Price	1970	**01**	Adrian Leek	1979
02	Bernie Plain	1970-1977	**01**	John Walters	1970	**01**	Colin Mackenzie	1985
02	John Davies	1973-1977	**01**	Graham Webb	1970	**01**	Shaun Pickering	1985
02	Colin O'Neill	1973-1977	**01**	John J Williams	1970	**01**	Phil Harries	1990
02	John Phillips	1975-1977	**01**	Phil Lewis	1973	**01**	Nick Comerford	1999
01	John Davies	1960	**01**	Wynford Leyshon	1973	**01**	Lee Newman	1999
01	Peter Walker	1961	**01**	Gareth Edwards	1975	**01**	Matthew Shone	1999
01	John Williams	1964	**01**	Alun James	1975			

Athletes who have won vests before taking up their Welsh eligibility:

02	Mal Edwards 1975-79	01	Bob Roberts 1970	01	Andy Williams 1973,
01	Bob Dobson 1975	01	Ken Cocks 1977	01	Milton Palmer 1977.

UK 'A' and 'B' OUTDOOR INTERNATIONALS – Females

V	Name	Year	V	Name	Year	V	Name	Year
02	Venissa Head	1975-1979	**01**	Janeen Williams	1979	**01**	Dawn Higgins	1999
01	Vivienne Head	1977	**01**	Jackie Zaslona	1979	**01**	Catherine Murphy	1999
01	Diane Heath	1979	**01**	Susan Tooby	1985	**01**	Rachel Newcombe	1999
01	Michelle Probert	1979	**01**	Helen Miles	1990	**01**	Louise Whitehead	1999
01	Gillian Regan	1979	**01**	Sallyanne Short	1990			

Athletes who have won vests before taking up their Welsh eligibility:

02	Janeen Williams 1975-1977	01	Hilary Hollick 1975	01	Thelwyn Appleby/Bateman 1977

UK U23 VESTS – Men

V	Name	Year	O	I	V	Name	Year	O	I
08	Jamie Henthorn	1997-1999	06	02	**02**	Paul Jones	1999-2000	02	
06	Neil Winter	1990-1995	06		**02**	Robert Mitchell	2000	02	
04	Jamie Baulch	1993-1995	04		**01**	Rhys Davies	1990	01	
04	James Hillier	1999-2000	04		**01**	Nigel Bevan	1991	01	
04	Christian Malcolm	1999-2000	03	01	**01**	Paul Gray	1991	01	
03	Stuart Loughran	1997-1998	03		**01**	Garry Slade	1991	01	
03	Charles Madeira Cole	1997-1998	03		**01**	Colin Bovell	1992	01	
03	Paul Jones	1999-2000	02	01	**01**	MarkMorgan	1994	01	
02	Justin Chaston	1990-1991	02		**01**	Iwan Thomas	1994	01	
02	Gareth Holloway	1990-1991	02		**01**	James Hughes	1995	01	
02	Gareth Davies (Sale)	1992-1993	02		**01**	James Archampong	1996	01	
02	Tremayne Rutherford	1994	02		**01**	Ian Wilding	1996	01	
02	Peter Maitland	1995	02		**01**	Matthew Bundock	1997	01	
02	Anthony Malcolm	1997	01	01	**01**	Chris Davies	1998	01	
02	Andres Jones	1999	02		**01**	Nathaniel Lane	1998	01	
02	Matthew Elias	1999-2000	02		**01**	Andrew Penk	1998	01	

UK U23 VESTS – Women

V	Name	Year	O	I	V	Name	Year	O	I
08	Philippa Roles	1998-2000	07	01	**02**	Julie Crane	1995-1998	02	
06	Rhian Clarke	1997-1999	05	01	**01**	Sallyanne Short	1990	01	
06	Emma Davies	1998-2000	05	01	**01**	Lisa Carthew	1993	01	
04	Catherine Murphy	1995-1997	04		**01**	Jane Falconer	1995	01	
04	Rachel King	1997-1998	03	01	**01**	Hayley Parry	1995	01	
03	Rebecca Roles	1999-2000	03		**01**	Clare Martin	1997	01	
02	Caroline White	1990-1991	02		**01**	Louise Whitehead	1997	01	
02	Jayne Berry	1991-1992	02						

UK JUNIOR VESTS – Women

V	Name	Year	O	I	XC	V	Name	Year	O	I	XC
13	Philippa Roles	1993-1997	11	02		**02**	Rhian Clarke *	1996	01	01	
09	Carys Parry	1998-2000	09			**02**	Amanda Pritchard	1996	02		
08	Lisa Armstrong	1990-1992	08			**02**	Lowri Jones	1999-2000	01	01	
06	Karen Hough	1984-1986	06			**02**	Natalie Lewis	2000	01	01	
05	Sarah Rowe	1979-1981	05			**01**	Paula Lloyd	1972	01		
05	Lisa Griffiths	1986-1988	05			**01**	Venissa Head	1974	01		
05	Rebecca Jones	1999-2000	04	01		**01**	Carmen Smart	1976	01		
04	Bethan Edwards	1991-1992	04			**01**	Jill Davies	1978	01		
04	Emma Davies	1996-1997	02	02		**01**	Sian Morgan	1978	01		
03	Sian Morris	1982-1983	03			**01**	Michelle Probert *	1978	01		
03	Helen Miles	1984-1985	03			**01**	Amanda Stacey	1978	01		
03	Sallyanne Short	1984-1986	03			**01**	Marion Hughes	1980	01		
03	Jayne Berry	1988-1989	03			**01**	Julia Charlton	1983	01		
03	Susannah Filce	1990-1991	03			**01**	Catherine Gunn	1985	01		
03	Jayne Ludlow	1994-1995	03			**01**	Amanda Barnes	1986	01		
03	Danielle Selley	2000	03			**01**	Lea Haggett	1986	01		
02	Val Watson	1975-1976	02			**01**	Sian Pilling	1986	01		
02	Kirsty McDermott	1979-1980	02			**01**	Carol Hayward	1989			01
02	Jennifer Morley	1980-1981	02			**01**	Onyema Amadi	1991	01		
02	Jane Buttriss	1980-1982	02			**01**	Kathryn Bright	1993	01		
02	Karen Dunster	1988	02			**01**	Angharad Richards	1994	01		
02	Claire Edwards	1991	02			**01**	Clare Thomas	1996			01
02	Natasha Bartlett	1991-1993	02			**01**	Kathryn Williams	1996	01		
02	Jane Falconer	1993	02			**01**	Rebecca Roles	1997		01	
02	Julie Crane	1994	02			**01**	Aimee Cutler	1998		01	
02	Rachel King	1995	01	01		**01**	Lara Richards	2000	01		

Athletes who have won UK Junior vests before taking up their Welsh eligibility

03 Michelle Probert (1976-1977) 02 Diane Heath (1974-1975) 02 Catherine Murphy (1993)
01 Rhian Clarke (1995)

UK JUNIOR VESTS – Men

V	Name	Year	O	I	XC
15	Tim Benjamin	1998-2000	12	03	
08	Gareth Hollaway	1986-1989	08		
08	Christian Malcolm	1996-1998	06	02	
08	Steven Shalders	1999-2000	07	01	
06	Colin Mackenzie	1980-1982	06		
06	Colin Jackson	1984-1986	06		
06	Paul Williams (Barry)	1984-1986	06		
06	Jamie Baulch	1991-1992	06		
06	James Archampong	1993-1995	05	01	
05	Neil Horsfield	1984-1985	05		
05	Paul Gray	1986-1988	05		
05	Richard Harbour	1989-1991	05		
05	Jamie Henthorn	1993-1996	04	01	
05	Mark Rowlands	1995-1997	04	01	
04	Gareth Edwards	1973-1974	04		
04	Andrew Rodgers	1982-1983	04		
04	Nathan Kavanagh	1984-1985	04		
04	Kirk Taylor	1985-1987	04		
04	Neil Winter	1990-1992	04		
04	Christian Stephenson	1993	02		02
03	Berwyn Price	1969-1970	03		
03	Steve James	1972-1973	03		
03	Adrian Leek	1976-1978	03		
03	Nigel Walker	1980-1982	03		
03	Pat Chichester	1985	03		
03	Clayton Turner	1985-1986	03		
03	Leigh Taylor	1987-1989	03		
03	Michael Williams	1987-1990	03		
03	Peter Maitland	1991	03		
03	James Hughes	1993	03		
03	Andres Jones	1995	02		01
03	Matthew Elias	1997	02	01	
03	Chuka Enih Snell	2000	02	01	
02	John Elias	1967	02		
02	Peter Lance	1967	02		
02	Tony Simmons	1967	02		
02	David Thomas	1967	02		
02	David Williams	1967	02		
02	Tony Dyke	1973-1974	02		
02	Jeff Griffiths	1975	02		
02	Micky Morris	1975	02		
02	Nigel Skinner	1983-1984	02		
02	John Hill	1985	02		
02	Rhys Davies	1987-1988	02		
02	Nick Hamilton	1989	02		
02	Neil Williams	1990-1991	02		
02	Colin Jones	1991-1992			02
02	Matthew Pryor	1991-1992	02		
01	Keith Lowe	1967	01		
01	John J Williams	1967	01		
01	Tony Pretty	1969	01		
01	Gareth Brooks	1975	01		
01	Kevin Glastonbury	1976	01		
01	Rupert Goodall	1976	01		
01	Islwyn Rees	1976	01		
01	Chris Richards	1976	01		
01	Nick Alexander	1978	01		
01	Graham Davies	1978	01		
01	Trevor Llewelyn	1978	01		
01	Owen Sussex	1978	01		
01	Shaun Pickering	1980	01		
01	Jon Stark *	1980	01		
01	Tim Jones	1982	01		
01	Philip Harries	1985	01		
01	Russell Hutchings	1986	01		
01	Andrew Pryor	1987	01		
01	Justin Hobbs	1988	01		
01	Andrew Jones	1988	01		
01	Paul Roberts	1988	01		
01	Gerallt Owen	1989			01
01	Gareth Davies (Sale)	1990	01		
01	Berian Davies	1991	01		
01	Scott Herbert	1991	01		
01	Joe Mills	1991	01		
01	Steven Rees	1991	01		
01	Chris Blount	1992	01		
01	Steven Griffiths	1992			01
01	Richard Jones	1993	01		
01	Stuart Loughran	1993	01		
01	Bryn Middleton	1993	01		
01	Mark Ponting	1993	01		
01	Iwan Thomas	1993	01		
01	Ian Pierce	1994			01
01	Ian Wilding	1994	01		
01	Nathaniel Lane	1995			01
01	Anthony Malcolm	1995	01		
01	Andrew Penk	1997	01		
01	Nathan Palmer	1999	01		
01	Ben Roberts	1999	01		
01	Matthew Jones	2000		01	
01	Chris Type	2000		01	
01	Richard Williams	2000	01		

Athletes who have gained UK Junior vests before taking up their Welsh eligibility:

04	Mal Edwards (1974-76)	02	Colin O'Neill (1967)	02	Paul Williams (Camb) (1974)
02	Paul Edwards (1977-78)	02	Nigel Bevan (1987)	02	Iwan Thomas (1992)
02	Robert Mitchell (1999)	01	Ron Griffiths (1969)	01	Roger Hackney (1976)
01	Jon Stark (1978)				

Section 15

Welsh Schools' Athletics

In the 1920s the then governing body of athletics in Wales held a series of meetings which they designated "Schoolboy Championships". All four of these meetings were held at Cardiff Arms Park and (based on the fact that Ronnie Boon was born in 1909) would appear to have been for the senior boys' age group. Only five individual events, plus a relay, were held, and for the record the winners were as follows:

Schoolboy Championships

	100 yards		220 yards		440 yards	880 yards	One mile	Relay
1924	T Elkins	11.2	A N S Ransom	25.4	A Powell	J W Dwyer	J W Dwyer	Abertillery CS
1925	T J Thomas	10.9	T J Thomas	25.5	J E Florence	A L Banner	A L Banner	Pengam CS
1926	C J Lewis	10.9	F G Hill	25.2	J E Florence	E Humphries	E Humphries	Pengam CS
1927	Ronnie Boon	10.8	Ronnie Boon	25.6	W H Witchell	T Evans	Lyndon Clark	Newport HS

Times for distances over 220 yards (if taken) are not known

In the 1930s the first Welsh Championships were held for Juniors and Youths, during the course of which events were staged for schools' athletes. Classified as "Secondary Schools Welsh Championships" and "Elementary Schools Welsh Championships" they appear to have covered the categories now recognised as senior and junior boys. The number of events was very limited and the winners are listed below:

Secondary Schools (Senior Boys)

	100 yards		Long Jump	
1934	Jack Gratton	10.2	Roy Spencer	5.99
1935	Bernard George	10.6	R Thomas	5.51
1936	"Nash" Thomas	10.4	Alun Meredith	6.09
1937	Jack Matthews	10.6	Brian Crossman	6.26
1938	Reg Michael	10.6	Brian Crossman	6.28
1939	Eric Finney	??.?	Brian Crossman	6.45
	440 yards		**One mile**	
1934	W C F Taylor	59.0	H M Morgan	6:10.4

Elementary Schools (Junior Boys)

	100 yards		220 yards	
1934	Fred Saunders	11.0	Fred Saunders	27.4
1935	David Howells	11.6	Harry Pleass	27.2
1936	Jack Thomas	11.2	Jack Thomas	25.2
1937	Trevor Harries	11.4	Ken Thomas	25.0
1938	G Williams	11.4	G Williams	25.0
1939	Bryn Jones	11.0	Bryn Jones	24.8

WELSH SCHOOLS' TRACK AND FIELD CHAMPIONS

A great deal of research has been undertaken in the compilation of these lists. Early newspaper reports did not give first names. One difficulty is that in some cases different sources have given different winners' names eg 1954 triple jump for junior boys. Consequently we have listed both names separated by a forward slash (/). On the rare occasions when athletes have tied for a title, both names are shown separated by an equals sign (=). Please note that championships were not held in 1984.

100 yards / 100 metres

	Senior Boys		Middle Boys		Junior Boys	
1947	Lynn (Cowboy) Davies	10.6	D R Wynne	11.2	R J Jones	11.6
1948	G Morgan	10.4	R Jones	10.4	R Hollow	11.4
1949	D.K James	10.3	R J Jones	10.8	G T Raybould	11.5
1950	Gareth Griffiths	10.8	G T Raybould	11.2	P H Holland	11.6
1951	Robin Pinnington	10.4	G T Raybould	10.6	A Jones	11.5
1952	K Thomas	10.4	Gareth Curtis	10.5	J Evans	10.9
1953	K Thomas	10.5	Gareth Curtis	10.4	J Evans	10.8
1954	Gareth Curtis	10.4	D M Johnston	10.8	D Worthington	11.2
1955	Bryan Woolley	10.5	Dewi Roberts	10.5	John Hitchen	10.9
1956	Derek Walkley	10.2	Peter Sayzeland	10.5	K Jones	10.6
1957	Dewi Roberts	10.0	John Hitchen	10.1	H Roberts	10.9
1958	John C Jones	10.2	Brian Davies	10.4	Tony Bigham	10.8
1959	Wyn Oliver	10.6	T Evans	11.2	T Griffiths	11.5
1960	Brian Davies		R Morgan	10.0	Peter Wilson	10.8
1961	Keith Batstone	10.3	John Arrowsmith	10.3	M Lovell	10.6
1962	Philip Hearne	10.1	Peter Wilson	10.3	P Richards	11.0

1963	not known		Clive Nock	10.1	not known	
1964	Brian Coles	10.0	R Lloyd	10.5	Keith Lowe	10.7
1965	John Bradshaw	10.4	David Roberts	10.6	G Lewis	11.2
1966	John J Williams	9.9	Philip Ware	10.4	Allan Thomas	10.7
1967	John J Williams	9.8	Adrian Thomas	10.1	G Williams	10.7
1968	Adrian Thomas	10.2	Allan Thomas	10.2	not known	
1969	Adrian Thomas	10.9	David Miles	11.1	P Evans	11.7
1970	Clive Rees	10.8	N Husbands	11.3	I Roberts	11.7
1971	Steve Ware	11.3	Steve Bailey	11.3	Kevin Davies	11.9
1972	Paul Evans	11.0	John Roberts	11.2	Steve Perks	11.5
1973	John Roberts	11.2	Kevin Davies	11.4	Richard Griffiths	11.9
1974	John Roberts	10.9	Kevin Davies	11.3	Richard Griffiths	11.8
1975	Kevin Davies	11.3	Clifford Jeffers	11.4	Phillip House	12.2
1976	Malcolm Owen	11.3	Derek Morgan	11.4	Anthony Morgan	12.0
1977	Clifford Jeffers	11.5	Andrew Jenkins	11.6	Malcolm James	11.7
1978	V Ajayi	11.1	Malcolm James	11.1	Tim Griffiths	11.6
1979	David Harrison	11.3	Ian Strange	11.1	Richard Evans	11.9
1980	Mark Owen	10.8	Steve Elvin	11.1	Haydn Wood	11.8
1981	Tim Jones	11.1	Neil Bowd	11.4	Cheuk Ho Lin	12.0
1982	Neil Bowd	11.5	Haydn Taylor	11.6	Simon Davies	12.2
1983	Lawrie Jones	11.7	Simon Marsh	11.9	Jason Ball	12.4
1985	Richard Wintle	11.0	Andrew Perrin	11.4	Ian Carr	11.8
1986	Lyndon Pritchard	11.4	Andrew Perrin	11.3	Philip Jones	11.9
1987	Andrew Perrin	11.4	Huw Griffiths	11.4	Huw Summers	12.0
1988	Ian Carr	11.4	Steve Rees	11.8	Simon Lewis	12.4
1989	Steve Rees	10.8	Daniel Mawer	11.2	Darren Holland	11.6
1990	Jamie Baulch	11.4	Craig Kerslake	11.5	Nick Roberts	12.6
1991	Jamie Baulch	11.0	Nathan John	11.6	David Bird	11.9
1992	Peter Maitland	10.5	Jamie Henthorn	11.1	Graham Thomas	11.6
1993	Bryn Middleton	11.0	Neil Powell	11.2	Christian Malcolm	11.7
1994	Philip Parry	11.48	Christian Malcolm	10.92	Iestyn Lewis	11.80
1995	Neil Powell	11.02	Christian Malcolm	10.99	Andre Silva	11.58
1996	Tim Miller	11.19	Ben Harland	11.20	Tim Benjamin	11.33
1997	Ben Harland	10.90	Andre Silva	11.14	Craig Powell	11.77
1998	Andrew Parker	11.01	Craig Powell	11.36	Luke Hicks	12.07
1999	Dominic Papura	10.96	Seriashe Childs	11.30	Daniel Evans	12.02
2000	Steven Shalders	11.13	Lee Hudgell	11.8	Simon Roach	12.07

220 yards / 200 metres

1947	Trevor Brewer	24.2	R L Rowe	25.6	R J Jones	26.3
1948	John Huins	23.5	H Morris	23.8	D Enoch	25.0
1949	John Huins	23.8	Derek Grindell	23.5	G T Raybould	25.0
1950	Robin Pinnington	23.8	G B Jones	25.4	W B J Evans	27.1
1951	Robin Pinnington	23.5	G T Raybould	23.8	P Daniel	26.2
1952	K Richards	23.8	Gareth Curtis	24.8	J Evans	26.1
1953	David Pulsford	23.4	Gareth Curtis	23.3	G Davies	25.0
1954	David Pulsford	22.8	David H Jones	23.7	L Edwards	24.7
1955	David H Jones	23.3	Dewi Roberts	22.8	John Hitchen	24.5
1956	Dewi Roberts	23.1	A Edwards	24.4	G O'Neill	24.5
1957	Dewi Roberts	22.8	John Hitchen	23.6	J Phillips	24.7
1958	John C Jones	22.5	Brian Davies	23.5	C Hitchen	24.7
1959	Wyn Oliver	23.2	D Harris	24.2	R Hughes	25.7
1960	Malcolm Morgan	22.5	M M Jones	23.4	Paul Carvell	23.5
1961	Allan Skirving	23.1	Paul Carvell	23.6	Clive Nock	24.2
1962	Allan Skirving	22.4	Peter Wilson	23.0	T Stephenson	24.4
1963	Paul Carvell	23.4	Clive Nock	23.5	S Crimmins	24.6
1964	Brian Coles	22.4	J Evans	24.2	J Evans	24.2
1965	D Mike Thomas	22.4	T Chapman	24.3	Alan Gore	25.0
1966	David Roberts	22.5	Philip Ware	23.4	Allan Thomas	24.0
1967	John J Williams	21.9	Alan Gore	23.2	Derek Herbert	24.2
1968	Adrian Thomas	23.5	not known		not known	
1969	Richard Giles	22.4	Steve Ware	22.4	John Walters	24.4
1970	Clive Rees	22.4	Steve Ware	22.6	Steve Kohut	24.3
1971	Steve Ware	22.8	Steve Bailey	23.5	Kevin Davies	25.1
1972	Steve Ware	22.3	Kevin Davies	23.4	Steve Perks	23.9
1973	Paul Evans	22.3	Kevin Davies	22.5	Richard Griffiths	23.3
1974	John Roberts	23.1	Kevin Davies	23.2	Richard Griffiths	24.0
1975	Kevin Davies	22.5	Derek Morgan	23.3	Mark Brinkworth	24.5
1976	Gerald Hedges	23.3	David Morgan	23.2	Julian Barrington	24.5
1977	Derek Morgan	22.6	Michael Owen	23.4	Malcolm James	23.1
1978	Derek Morgan	22.1	Malcolm James	22.3	Tim Griffiths	24.2

1979	David Wood	23.0	Phil Harvey	22.4	Richard Evans	23.5
1980	Mark Owen	22.6	Tim Jones	22.5	Haydn Wood	23.6
1981	Malcolm James	22.9	Simon Hill	23.2	Cheuk Ho Lin	24.5
1982	Neil Bowd	23.8	Simon Taylor	23.2	David Davies	25.0
1983	Neil Bowd	23.9	Richard Rees	24.2	Martin Lewis	25.3
1985	Richard Wintle	22.7	Andrew Perrin	23.9	Huw Griffiths	24.5
1986	Eurig Parry	23.4	Andrew Perrin	22.7	Martin Liddiatt	24.7
1987	Andrew Perrin	23.0	John Williams	23.3	Matthew Roderick	23.8
1988	Eifion Lewis	23.1	Steven Rees	23.2	Martin Powell	24.6
1989	Steven Rees	21.9	Jamie Baulch	22.6	Darren Yeo	23.5
1990	Jamie Baulch	22.9	Darren Yeo	23.0	Eirian Rhys	24.9
1991	Jamie Baulch	22.0	Darren Holland	24.0	David Bird	24.2
1992	Jon Gittins	22.8	Bryn Middleton	22.9	Jamie Sheffield	23.8
1993	Bryn Middleton	22.3	Jamie Henthorn	22.4	David Price	24.4
1994	Gareth Wyatt	23.08	Christian Malcolm	22.36	Iestyn Lewis	24.34
1995	David O'Hare	22.08	Christian Malcolm	21.41	Andre Silva	23.41
1996	Tim Miller	22.22	Ben Harland	22.64	Tim Benjamin	23.21
1997	Ben Harland	22.07	Andre Silva	22.37	Craig Powell	23.42
1998	Andrew Parker	22.85	Steven Shalders	22.97	Nick Hiscott	24.34
1999	Dominic Papura	22.55	Gareth Rees	23.49	Iain Hunt	24.46
2000	Gareth Llewellyn	23.1	Michael Groves	23.3	Calvin McLaggon	24.5

440 yards / 400 metres

1947	J E Bibbs	53.6	Roy Adams	53.8		
1948	Roy Adams	52.0	R J Jones	54.9		
1949	Roy Adams	52.4	Julius Hermer	55.6		
1950	Peter Phillips	54.2	R P Davies	56.4		
1951	J L Evans	53.0	David G Pugh	53.3		
1952	David G Pugh	53.0	Alan Griffiths	54.4		
1953	David G Pugh	52.0	Alan Griffiths	54.1		
1954	Alan Griffiths	55.2	David H Jones	52.8		
1955	David H Jones	52.8	G Davies	53.6		
1956	Dewi Bebb	53.2	T D Phillips	52.8		
1957	T D Phillips	51.8	A Griffiths	52.1		
1958	Robert Sully	52.1	Huw Jones	51.9		
1959	Huw Jones	50.9	B Whyld	52.6	G Hall	55.7
1960	Huw Jones	51.0	Byron Broadstock	53.3	G Williams	53.0
1961	Allan Skirving	51.7	Neil Thomas	53.5	P Smith	55.8
1962	Allan Skirving	50.0	Neil Thomas	52.4	Paul Bateman	54.4
1963	not known		G Griffiths	52.1	L Morgan	54.8
1964	Derek Bevan	50.5	T Davies	53.7	R Watkins	55.9
1965	Ian McGivan	51.4	R Thomas	52.9	M Davies	55.6
1966	Howard Davies	51.5	Haydn Curran	51.6	H Thomas	55.8
1967	Haydn Curran	50.5	not known		not known	
1968	not known		not known		not known	
1969	Stuart Jones	49.8	C Williams	52.2	A Powell	56.7
1970	Michael Lewis	50.0	Malcolm Gibson	51.4	D Lovitt	57.4
1971	Michael Lewis	51.0	R Hughes	52.2	P Tucker	54.9
1972	Timothy Archer	51.7	P Tucker	54.2	E Griffiths	55.1
1973	Timothy Archer	50.9	Jeff Griffiths	52.2	Neil Peters	54.6
1974	M Rees	52.5	Jeff Griffiths	52.0	Jonathan Wilson	55.4
1975	R Hughes	50.6	Gerald Hedges	52.7	Rob Humphreys	55.7
1976	Gerald Hedges	51.1	Nicholas Newman	52.5	Rob Humphreys	54.4
1977	R Rodgers	51.7	Michael Owen	51.5	D Rowlands	53.8
1978	Derek Morgan	50.2	Tony Morgan	51.0	David Andrews	52.4
1979	David Harrison	50.1	Phil Harvey	49.1	Alan Matthews	54.9
1980	Grant Cullins	52.4	Alan Matthews	51.7	D Bevan	55.2
1981	Malcolm James	50.2	Andrew Dunn	51.1	Adrian Hardman	53.1
1982	Grant Cullins	51.4	Adrian Hardman	52.2	Ian Holbrook	54.9
1983	Alan Matthews	52.3	Adrian Hardman	50.7	Derek Wyke	54.8
1985	Chris Cashell	50.2	Derek Wyke	51.3	Ian Carr	54.2
1986	Mark Dewis	52.3	Paul Roberts	50.4	Martin Liddiatt	55.5
1987	David Gough	50.1	Ian Carr	50.8	Andrew Stradling	54.4
1988	Chris Wilkins	50.5	Peter Maitland	51.3	Lance Worthington	54.7
1989	Martin Liddiatt	51.6	Peter Maitland	50.8	Lance Worthington	52.4
1990	Darren Parry	50.3	Jason Murphy	50.6	David Williams	53.4
1991	Jason Murphy	49.6	Lance Worthington	50.5	John Weybourne	54.9
1992	Jason Murphy	50.9	Andrew Jones	51.5	Graham T Thomas	39.5
1993	David Williams	50.1	Mark Ponting	50.1	Tom Damsell	39.2
1994	John Williams	52.56	Jonathan Bates	51.08	Michael Bodden	38.54
1995	Mark Ponting	48.82	Tariq Guendouzi	51.56	Richard Phillips	39.02

1996	Huw Bannister	50.20	Lea Farmer	50.60	David Teague	37.88
1997	Lea Farmer	49.91	David Teague	50.74	Matthew Petty	37.45
1998	Lea Farmer	49.66	David Teague	50.85	Michael Groves	38.43
1999	Daniel Forbes	50.08	Gareth Rees	50.51	Andre Ofarnah	38.60
2000	Daniel Forbes	50.2	Guto Jones	52.0	Chris Czekaj	38.6

880 yards / 800 metres

1947	J E Bibbs	2:08.0	K Thomas	2:12.5		
1948	W Rees	2:06.0	P A Stevens	2:06.8		
1949	P A Stevens	2:08.0	D White	2:11.0		
1950	P A Stevens	2:04.0	C Moyle	2:16.2		
1951	B Andrews	2:09.3	W B Evans	2:09.5		
1952	W B Evans	2:08.4	D Robinson	2:11.8		
1953	W B Evans	2:04.0	D Robinson	2:06.0		
1954	W B Evans	2:00.2	G Cowburn	2:01.5		
1955	Don Edwards	2:03.3	W Evans	2:04.5		
1956	Denzil Owen	2:03.6	John Williams	2:03.2		
1957	B Macken	2:00.6	John Williams	1:56.7		
1958	John Williams	1:54.2	David Ponting	2:02.0		
1959	Billy Perkins	1:59.4	J Hill	2:05.3		
1960	T J Vincent	1:59.0	Clive Lewis	1:59.5		
1961	Clive Lewis	1:58.7	P Williams	2:04.6		
1962	Clive Lewis	2:01.8	P Smith	2:04.9		
1963	not known		Wynford Shearn	2:02.9		
1964	Terry James	1:59.6	Paul Bateman	2:00.4		
1965	Wynford Shearn	1:55.0	Ian Thomas	2:03.0	A Lovell	2:12.2
1966	Paul Bright	1:58.4	Ian Thomas	1:59.5	D Burke	2:12.2
1967	Alec McNab	1:55.8	not known	2:05.9	not known	
1968	not known		not known		not known	
1969	J C Evans	1:57.0	Richard Yarrow	1:58.3	Will Snowdon	2:09.7
1970	Richard Yarrow	1:56.3	Mike Buckland	2:02.2	Tony Dyke	2:08.0
1971	Terry Allen	1:59.6	Tony Dyke	2:00.0	S Davies	2:11.3
1972	Mike Buckland	2:00.1	Tony Dyke	1:57.4	M Cole	2:11.0
1973	Tony Dyke	1:54.4	E Price	2:04.2	Ian Williams	2:08.1
1974	Tony Dyke	1:54.3	R Evans	2:03.2	S Owen	2:09.0
1975	Lloyd Roberts	2:00.3	Kevin Glastonbury	1:59.0	Andrew Martin	2:04.8
1976	Kevin Glastonbury	1:58.9	Keith Gallivan	2:05.0	Mark Britton	2:04.4
1977	D Herbert	1:58.2	Mark Britton	2:02.2	Will Dewar	2:03.7
1978	Alan Fiddler	2:00.5	Nick Morgan	1:57.9	Shaun Whelan	2:06.2
1979	D Reid	1:59.0	Shaun Whelan	1:58.7	Grant Howells	2:06.5
1980	Keith Jones	2:01.2	Grant Howells	2:04.5	Anthony Rees	2:05.4
1981	Richard Toms	1:56.1	Grant Howells	2:00.6	Carl Worthington	2:05.1
1982	Adam Richards	1:59.9	Paul Williams	1:58.2	Ian Cowie	2:11.1
1983	Robert Ellis	1:57.5	Simon Merrick	2:04.9	Michael O'Neill	2:05.8
1985	Carl Worthington	1:57.8	Michael O'Neill	1:59.2	Martin Clayton	2:10.5
1986	Simon Merrick	1:57.1	Kevin Taylor	2:02.9	Huw Davies	2:06.5
1987	Tommy Stout	1:58.2	Jason Davies	2:01.0	Steve Cottrell	2:07.4
1988	Bedwyr Huws	1:56.2	Jason Davies	2:02.8	Jason Murphy	2:05.5
1989	Bedwyr Huws	2:00.0	Neil Emberton	1:58.7	Darren Yeo	2:08.6
1990	Guto Eames	1:56.7	Jason Murphy	1:56.5	Simon Williams	2:09.7
1991	Leighton Phillips	1:56.0	Daniel Ashman	2:00.4	Adrian Staples	2:05.8
1992	Jason Murphy	2:01.2	Greg Davies	2:03.7	Ceri Williams	2:08.3
1993	Zane Maynard	1:58.7	John Weybourne	1:57.4	Mark Goodger	2:07.3
1994	John Weybourne	1:55.50	Neville Johnson	1:57.74	Peter O'Neill	2:06.96
1995	Matthew McHugh	1:55.95	Mark Goodger	1:59.03	Michael Bodden	2:05.71
1996	Neville Johnson	1:59.02	Dafydd Solomon	2:03.22	Nathan Boland	2:06.9
1997	Dafydd Solomon	1:58.10	Daniel Forbes	2:00.88	Steven Richards	2:07.64
1998	Dafydd Solomon	2:00.71	Neil Wynne	2:02.56	Adam Daniel	2:07.50
1999	Robin Powell	1:56.52	Steven Richards	1:59.69	Gareth Tapper	2:07.46
2000	James Nasrat	1:57.8	Gareth Tapper	2:00.27	Chris Gowell	2:05.16

One mile / 1500 metres

1947	I G Phillips	5:01.0
1948	B Morgan	4:43.3
1949	E J Clifford	4:49.9
1950	David JP Richards	4:56.0
1951	David JP Richards	4:38.1
1952	David JP Richards	4:37.5
1953	W Russell	4:44.0
1954	Terry Marney	4:41.4
1955	Roger Harrison-Jones	4:26.1

1956	Eric Jones	4:37.2				
1957	Haydn Tawton	4:24.6				
1958	Billy Perkins	4:26.3				
1959	David Ponting	4:39.5	R Barlow	4:43.2		
1960	David Ponting	4:24.9	Alan Thomas	4:38.6		
1961	Vic Webley	4:30.9	D H L Lamb	4:33.9		
1962	Stuart Hocknell	4:25.2	B Williams	4:39.3		
1963	Chris Loosley	4:24.0	G Comilek	4:42.4		
1964	Chris Loosley	4:17.1	Paul Bateman	4:34.0		
1965	Paul Bateman	4:27.0	Alec McNab	4:29.7		
1966	Alec McNab	4:21.5	Frank Thomas	4:33.0		
1967	John Powell	4:16.9	not known			
1968	not known		not known			
1969	J C Evans	4:14.3	T Allen	4:19.0		
1970	Brian Donovan	4:11.4	Gareth Morgan	4:18.4		
1971	Gareth Morgan	4:07.9	Peter Baker	4:17.3		
1972	Paul Roebuck	4:12.2	Brian Fenn	4:16.7		
1973	Peter Baker	4:04.4	Micky Morris	4:03.9		
1974	Brian Fenn	4:14.0	D Jones	4:17.1	Arwel Jones	4:22.6
1975	Vaughan Edwards	4:09.0	Ian Williams	4:09.7	Colin Clarkson	4:29.0
1976	Bernard Jones	4:12.5	Geraint Jones	4:12.5	Michael Bounds	4:20.6
1977	Keith Gallivan	4:05.3	Colin Clarkson	4:03.6	Paul Keeble	4:20.2
1978	Tim Wilcock	4:11.4	Mark Pritchard	4:06.8	Grant Howells	4:31.2
1979	Nick Morgan	3:59.6	Peter Lloyd	4:06.4	Grant Howells	4:22.2
1980	Nick Morgan	3:59.7	Grant Howells	4:17.1	Nicky Comerford	4:18.7
1981	Mark Bryant	4:07.6	Nicky Comerford	4:12.0	Michael Powell	4:24.4
1982	Steve Knight	4:12.6	Nicky Comerford	4:11.0	Aled Davies	4:29.5
1983	Peter Wyman	4:06.7	Neil Horsfield	4:05.3	Simon Taylor	4:22.3
1985	Andrew Pritchard	4:16.6	Justin Hobbs	4:05.3	Bedwyr Huws	4:28.1
1986	Justin Hobbs	3:59.2	Peter Conway	4:08.3	Paul Lewis	4:28.0
1987	Peter Conway	4:01.4	Guto Eames	4:04.5	Stephen Blow	4:22.9
1988	Peter Conway	4:01.0	Paul Freeguard	4:08.8	Anthony Jones	4:23.4
1989	Gerallt Owen	4:10.7	Neil Emberton	4:13.0	David Rowley	4:23.2
1990	Neil Emberton	4:06.1	Ben Antwiss	4:14.5	Simon Williams	4:22.8
1991	Mark Smith	4:06.6	Andrew Marshman	4:13.3	Robert Court	4:20.2
1992	Carl Leonard	4:13.2	Christian Davies	4:21.0	David Davey	4:27.0
1993	Andrew Marshman	4:08.5	Robert Court	4:07.1	Matthew Russell	4:19.1
1994	Robert Court	4:07.14	David Davey	4:09.80	Dafydd Solomon	4:25.26
1995	David Davey	4:08.00	Robin Hart	4:15.15	Scott Williams	4:29.20
1996	Simon Lewis	4:09.43	Paul Kennedy	4:18.95	Daniel Beynon	4:19.72
1997	Simon Lewis	4:08.23	Daniel Beynon	4:14.99	Matthew Jones	4:22.10
1998	James Murray	4:30.30	Daniel Beynon	4:11.63	Chris Davies	4:23.29
1999	Daniel Beynon	4:09.42	Matthew Jones	4:05.48	Luke Northall	4:21.60
2000	Matthew Jones	3:54.50	Stephen Davies	4:06.77	Tom Page	4:30.82

5000 / 3000 metres

1969	H D Edwards	16:30.4		
1970	Martin Russell	16:13.4		
1971	Martin Russell	15:54.0		
1972	Gareth Morgan	15:00.0		
1973	Andrew Ireland	16:36.0		
1974	G Jones	17:03.6	Steve Evans	8:56.8
1975	Mike Parkes	9:07.8	Tony Blackwell	9:02.6
1976	David James	9:02.0	Alan Cummings	9:03.8
1977	Bruce Chinnick	9:08.0	Colin Clarkson	9:08.6
1978	Tim Wilcock	9:05.0	Steve Blakemore	8:58.4
1979	Paul Miller	9:09.4	Stephen Armstrong	9:02.0
1980	Robert Walmsley	8:51.4	John Pimley	9:11.2
1981	David Thomas	8:43.2	Scott Atkins	9:14.9
1982	David Thomas	8:52.8	Lee Williams	9:18.3
1983	Lee Williams	8:53.9	Simon Jones	9:12.7
1985	Steven Price	9:07.3	Paul Niblett	8:58.6
1986	Andrew Jones	8:59.5	Andrew Jones	8:57.7
1987	Gareth Davies	9:12.7	Steven Glynn	9:09.2
1988	Gerallt Owen	8:41.2	Simon Williams	9:12.3
1989	Gerallt Owen	8:37.3	Simon Williams	9:00.2
1990	Robert Simon	8:59.5	Colin Jones	8:48.7
1991	Colin Jones	8:56.0	David Povall	9:26.0
1992	Richard Gardiner	9:11.1	Gary Cooper	9:30.3
1993	Paul Walby	9:13.7	David Davey	9:07.1
1994	Andres Jones	8:46.96	Steven Lawrence	9:04.44

1995	John Perkins	9:32.78	Steven Lawrence	9:06.66
1996	Andres Jones	8:34.37	Paul Gronow	8:54.04
1997	Paul Gronow	8:52.35	Elliott Cole	9:22.27
1998	Jonathan Phillips	9:05.99	Matthew Jones	9:09.8
1999	Elliott Cole	9:09.33	David Jones	9:13.70
2000	Elliott Cole	9:05.1	David Jones	8:50.07

Steeplechase

1961	R Clarke	4:45.6		
1962	not known			
1963	Terry James	4:28.2		
1964	D H L Lamb	4:33.6		
1965	Dic Evans	4:34.0		
1966	Dic Evans	6:12.3		
1967	Richard Jones	6:28.6		
1968	Thomas Murray	6:21.2		
1969	A Jones	6:29.2		
1970	Ian Armstrong	6:23.4	Billy Snowdon	2:52.8
1971	Neil Rousell	6:21.2	Tony Dyke	2:52.3
1972	Neil Rousell	6:11.8	B Connah	3:00.4
1973	Billy Snowdon	6:34.4	Steve Evans	4:38.9
1974	Julian Thomas	6:34.8	Steve Evans	4:27.2
1975	David Messum	6:22.4	Kevin Glastonbury	4:26.9
1976	Nigel Penny	6:22.0	Peter Ward	4:26.5
1977	Andy Fox	6:19.6	Andy Jones	4:34.8
1978	Andy Fox	6:17.4	John Messum	4:36.7
1979	John Messum	6:07.1	Marcus Thomas	4:21.8
1980	Marcus Thomas	6:09.6	Paul McHugh	4:30.5
1981	Marcus Thomas	5:59.0	Adam Richards	4:32.0
1982	John Pimley	6:11.5	John Pritchard	4:42.0
1983	Meredith Richards	6:24.7	Alan Phillips	4:42.0
1985	Colin Hignell	6:11.5	Roger Jones	4:34.5
1986	Phil Cook	6:29.2	Chris Osborne	4:48.3
1987	Chris Osborne	6:15.3	Richard Baker	4:35.8
1988	Jonathan Lewis	6:05.7	Tim Cummings	4:33.2
1989	Jonathan Lewis	6:22.4	Andrew Powell	4:29.6
1990	Llyr Jones	6:18.0	Tim Hopkins	4:36.2
1991	John Williams	6:28.2	Jon Williams	4:34.5
1992	Justin Everley	6:19.5	Ian Pierce	4:46.5
1993	John Peters	6:09.9	Alan Jones	4:44.2
1994	Leigh Kinroy	6:11.4	Simon Type	4:34.6
1995	Leigh Kinroy	6:26.45	Toben Tymmons	4:41.65
1996	Simon Type	6:41.24	Peter Bevan	4:48.46
1997	Paul Clarke	6:35.27	Kevin Summerhayes	4:47.46
1998	Paul Clarke	6:21.25	James Williams	4:39.6
1999	James Williams	6:14.72	Andrew Simms	4:43.33
2000	James Williams	6:19.64	Michael Targett	4:41.54

High Hurdles

1947	F H Parish	15.3	M B Lloyd	14.2	H K Davies	11.9
1948	M B Lloyd	14.8	H Jones	14.1	Viv Jones	11.5
1949	A H Road	15.8	Onllwyn Brace	14.2	D S Miles	11.9
1950	Onllwyn Brace	15.8	W G Lewis	14.8	G Jones	11.5
1951	M Sackville	14.9	A M Hall	14.2	David Pask	10.9
1952	Viv Jones	14.6	David Pask	14.2	A Jones	11.5
1953	B Morgan	14.4	P T Johnson	13.3	D S Griffiths	10.3
1954	P T Johnson	16.7	David Pask	15.5	C Marlin	10.8
1955	T Mynott	16.0	A Owens	15.0	John Ball	10.6
1956	Keith Davitte	16.4	David Michael	14.5	G Chisnall	10.5
1957	David Michael	15.2	John Ball	14.4	A Roberts	10.4
1958	David Michael	16.0	R Pearce	14.8	A Sandy	11.0
1959	Alan E Jones	17.5	G M Jones	16.5	C Evans	11.5
1960	Ifan Lloyd		Tudor Jones	14.8	Terry Schneider	10.9
1961	John Powell	15.1	Richard Williams	14.5	Gareth James	10.9
1962	Goronwy Davies	15.5	Gareth Davies	14.5	Gareth James	10.5
1963	Howard Rooks	15.6	John Lewis	14.4	not known	
1964	G Davies	15.9	D Reid	13.9	Richard Jones	10.6
1965	John Lewis	14.8	Phil Stockford	14.0	B Reynolds	11.4
1966	Alun James	14.9	B Jones	14.4	D Hollyman	11.2
1967	Alun James	14.8	Colin Beynon	14.0	M Rowlands	11.1

1968	not known		not known		not known	
1969	Berwyn Price	14.6	G Powell	14.3	R D Roberts	11.0
1970	Les Prince	15.1	P Kerrigan	14.4	A Robinson	12.1
1971	Roger Rees	15.4	J Richards	14.3	R S Jones	11.8
1972	Roger Rees	14.9	Neddyn Lloyd		Mark Jewell	12.3
1973	Neddyn Lloyd	15.0	Russell Cole	13.9	Neil Hammersley	11.9
1974	Orrie Fenn	14.9	Tudor Bidder	14.5	Neil Hammersley	12.0
1975	Neddyn Lloyd	16.1	Roy Saunders	14.5	Tim Lewis	12.2
1976	Chris Richards	14.9	Roy Davies	14.3	David Jones	12.2
1977	Neil Hammersley	16.1	Viv Walker	14.9	Alec James	12.2
1978	Tim Lewis	14.4	David Jones	14.0	Wynne Harries	11.4
1979	Tim Lewis	15.0	Nigel Walker	14.1	Andrew Richards	12.0
1980	Nigel Walker	14.9	Tim O'Dwyer	14.5	S Jones	12.3
1981	Nigel Walker	14.6	Richard Robinson	14.2	Colin Jackson	12.0
1982	Tim O'Dwyer	16.2	Colin Jackson	13.7	Andrew Bolton	12.6
1983	Andrew Davies	16.0	Colin Jackson	14.2	Wayne Thomas	12.8
1985	Andrew O'Toole	16.8	Peter Dyer	13.5	Nathan Evans	12.1
1986	David Thomas	15.3	Rhys Davies	14.4	Richard Harbour	12.0
1987	Russell Richards	16.3	Richard Harbour	14.5	Berian Davies	11.8
1988	Russell Richards	15.7	Richard Harbour	13.8	Paul Rainbow	12.0
1989	Richard Harbour	14.9	Berian Davies	13.3	James Hughes	11.7
1990	Berian Davies	15.1	James Hughes	14.5	Jonathan Armstrong	11.6
1991	Berian Davies	14.6	James Hughes	13.8	Graham O'Connell	12.4
1992	James Hughes	14.8	James Archampong	13.6	Graham Thomas	11.6
1993	James Archampong	14.3	Steven Edwards	13.9	Chris Truscott	12.0
1994	Steven Edwards	15.26	Jamie Sheffield	13.80	Paul Bodenham	12.2
1995	James Hillier	15.61	Gareth Lewis	13.90	Jon Marsden	12.16
1996	Steven Edwards	15.2	Shaun Robson	14.0	Jon Marsden	11.6
1997	Shaun Robson	15.12	Nathan Palmer	13.59	Nathan Jones	11.77
1998	Shaun Robson	15.20	Nathan Jones	14.22	Nick Hiscott	11.53
1999	Nathan Palmer	14.32	Nathan Jones	14.21	Gethin Morgan	11.94
2000	Nathan Palmer	14.80	Alec Porter	14.5	Euron Roberts	12.07

200 yards hurdles

1960	Alan Evans-Jones	23.6		
1961	John Powell	23.7	J Vann	24.2
1962	Keri Jones	23.4	Edgar Williams	24.5
1963	Keri Jones	23.4	Gareth Edwards	24.1
1964	John Lewis	23.0	Gareth Edwards	23.6
1965	John Lewis	22.7	Phil Stockford	23.7
1966	Mike Walters	22.8	Paul Nash	24.9
1967	Alun James	22.5	Paul Nash	23.9

400 metres hurdles

1969	Barrie Williams	57.2	P Jones	60.2
1970	D George Clues	58.2	R Mugford	60.3
1971	Jon Owen	58.5	Alwyn Evans	61.3
1972	Jon Owen	57.7	Hugh Evans	58.4
1973	Orrie Fenn	55.9	Hugh Evans	57.9
1974	Orrie Fenn	55.7	Robin Davies	60.3
1975	Robin Davies	57.6	Roy Saunders	59.6
1976	Robin Davies	56.7	D Thomas	58.1
1977	Robert Davies	56.4	Cassim Hammer	57.2
1978	Robert Davies	55.4	David Jones	57.7
1979	Phil Lewis	56.3	Gareth Rees	56.8
1980	Alun James	57.6	Paul Harvey	57.5
1981	Dean Crapnell	57.9	Jonathan Allen	58.1
1982	Paul Harvey	57.9	Ian Snook	60.6
1983	Robert Subbiani	60.4	David Parry	60.1
1985	Chris Cashell	55.9	Clive Jones	59.6
1986	David Thomas	56.2	Russell Richards	58.2
1987	Russell Richards	56.7	Luc Evans	57.8
1988	Russell Richards	54.9	Marvin Gray	57.2
1989	Wayne Proctor	56.4	Simon Peckham	59.8
1990	Wayne Proctor	57.2	Paul Rainbow	57.8
1991	Wayne Proctor	55.8	James Atkin	58.4
1992	Paul Rainbow	57.9	Matthew Eveleigh	59.3
1993	Matthew Eveleigh	57.6	Mark Rowlands	55.9
1994	Matthew Eveleigh	57.84	Mark Rowlands	54.42
1995	Jamie Sheffield	55.33	Gareth Lewis	57.39

1996	Mark Rowlands	53.0	Gavin Jones	62.2		
1997	Shaun Robson	57.6	Dean Hood	58.83		
1998	Gavin Jones	56.29	Leighton Lewis	57.0		
1999	Stuart Copeland	58.73	Nathan Jones	57.01		
2000	Nathan Jones	56.02	Rhys Williams	55.44		

Walk

1947	B Lewis	7:39.8	A Smith	3:30.0	J Thomas	2:46.0
1948	R J Carter	7:25.7	R E Leppitt	3:28.0	V Thomas	2:37.2
1949	V G Jones	7:41.7	J M Thomas	3:28.9	G Davies	2:52.9
1950	John Lowther	7:23.8	G Williams	3:38.2	J Evans	2:47.2
1951	John Lowther	6:56.6	J Walters	3:33.2	J Evans	2:34.9
1952	G Williams	6:54.5	R Chapman	3:31.9	J Pemberton	2:35.7
1953	Gareth Howell	6:50.1	C R Brownhill	5:14.6	B E Pritchard	3:28.8
1954	Jack Thomas	7:34.2	C Richards	5:00.4	J Shorney	3:32.5
1955	Selwyn Wyatt	7:31.0	C Richards	5:02.4	C Milner	3:28.2
1956	Mike Shannon	7:05.0	M Healey	5:34.0	T Bonning	3:21.2
1957	Mike Shannon	6:56.6	D Howell	5:17.8	B Potts	3:40.2
1998			Richard Jacklin	12:33.52	James Williams	5:45.20
1999			Cameron Smith	10:47.0	Owen Young	5:36.0
2000			Owen Young	12:39.6	Damian Lack	5:44.6

High Jump

1947	E Roberts	1.57	M B Lloyd	1.50	G Dick	1.40
1948	Norman Finch	1.67	D R Edmunds	1.64	B Lewis	1.38
1949	Ieuan Prosser	1.70	A Murray	1.62	T Edwards	1.42
1950	M Sackville	1.60	Brian Hardwick	1.60	J Jenkins	1.37
1951	Morton Evans	1.65	D H Price	1.71	B Francis	1.48
1952	B T Badley	1.65	J Anthony	1.55	Terence Morgan	1.40
1953	D Evans-Williams	1.70	P T Johnson	1.62	Aneurin Evans	1.60
1954	G Pratt	1.70	Aneurin Evans	1.62	David Michael	1.55
1955	W Whale	1.70	Aneurin Evans	1.73	P Allen	1.60
1956	Aneurin Evans	1.75	David Michael	1.75	John Lister	1.62
1957	Aneurin Evans	1.80	John Lister	1.70	J M S James	1.55
1958	K Adams	1.70	John Lister	1.70	D Buckley	1.60
1959	B Williams	1.70	N Pearse	1.75	D Price	1.60
1960	Raymond Simpole	1.73	N Pearse	1.70	B Herbert	1.64
1961	Peter Williams	1.77	G Morris	1.67	B Morgan	1.62
1962	J Begley	1.75	Peter Gibson	1.75	not known	
1963	R Lewis	1.70	I M Williams	1.76	Peter Lance	1.66
1964	Alan Bergiers	1.70	M Williams	1.73	John Griffiths	1.68
1965	Peter Gibson	1.75	Peter Lance	1.76	K Roberts	1.55
1966	Peter Lance	1.78	Robert Bruynooghe	1.65	J Bowen	1.52
1967	Peter Lance	1.90	Richard Gyles	1.70	not known	
1968	Roger Stennett	1.76	Brynmor Williams	1.78	not known	
1969	Brynmor Williams	1.78	A Rose	1.70	Andrew Shufflebotham	
1970	Brynmor Williams	1.85	Ron Owen	1.78	A Marenghi	1.58
1971	Richard Davies	1.79	P Smith	1.70	B Crighton	1.50
1972	John Rees	1.80	Carwyn Jones	1.70	John Wright	1.62
1973	Carwyn Jones	1.79	Chris Berry	1.76	N Thomas	1.63
1974	Mike Cummings	1.90	Chris Richards	1.88	N Owen	1.65
1975	Chris Richards	1.86	Steve Brock	1.78	Steve Robbins	1.56
1976	Chris Richards	1.90	Nigel Jones	1.75	H Williams	1.67
1977	G Llewellyn	1.70	Keith McBurney	1.84	Chris Sander	1.71
1978	J Humphries	1.79	Andrew McIver	1.92	Carl Davies	1.76
1979	Phil Lewis	1.85	Tony Norris	1.93	Derek McIver	1.80
1980	Paul Evans	2.02	David Bethel	1.85	Darren Russell	1.76
1981	David Bethel	1.85	Derek McIver	1.70	David Romaniw	1.65
1982	David Francis	1.80	Robert James	1.80	Nicholas Holland	1.69
1983	Robert James	1.75	John Mahoney	1.80	Lee Jones	1.72
1985	Steven Partridge	1.85	Craig Grant	1.91	Andrew Blow	1.80
1986	Neil Harris	1.75	Roydon Murdock	1.80	Martin Williams	1.69
1987	Neil Harris	1.95	Steve Ingram	1.97	Matthew Fox	1.68
1988	Steve Ingram	1.90	Dawson Edwards	1.90	Justin Arnold	1.69
1989	Steve Ingram	1.90	Ceri Payne	1.90	Steven Francis	1.83
1990	Matthew Lyon	1.85	Justin Arnold	1.85	Ian Jones	1.70
1991	Ceri Payne	2.09	Dafydd Edwards	2.01	Leighton Thomas	1.80
1992	Dafydd Edwards	2.00	Leighton Thomas	1.85	Ben Olsen	1.75
1993	David Nolan	1.95	Daniel Partridge	1.91	Jamie Dalton	1.73
1994	Rowan Griffiths	1.90	Andrew Penk	2.00	Jamie Dalton	1.75

1995	Matthew Perry	2.01	Andrew Penk	1.90	Edward Kelly	1.70
1996	Andrew Penk	1.95	Jamie Dalton	1.85	Roger Owens	1.70
1997	Rhodri Jones	1.90	Alun Davies	1.90	Chuka Enih-Snell	1.70
1998	Rhodri Jones	1.92	Kim Harland	1.90	Chuka Enih-Snell	1.91
1999	Rhodri Parry	1.95	Chuka Enih-Snell	2.05	Ben Potts	1.77
2000	Kim Harland	2.01	Chuka Enih-Snell	2.06	Daniel Segerson	1.76

Pole Vault

1947	G W Cole	2.79	not held		not held	
1948	Glyn Jenkins	3.05	D Owens	2.82	B Evans	2.44
1949	D J Morgan	3.12	Viv Jones	2.82	not held	
1950	Glyn Jenkins	3.45	Colin Fletcher	2.59	not held	
1951	Viv Jones	3.12	C Jones	2.74	L Evans	2.28
1952	Viv Jones	3.05	Ron Ashong	2.82	G Evans	2.67
1953	D B Davies	2.89	P T Johnson	3.05	T Evans	3.06
1954	R Saer	3.05	Trevor Evans	3.35	E Williams	2.82
1955	R John	3.12	Trevor Evans	3.27	T Williams	2.97
1956	J Johnson	3.35	John Ball	3.20	E Thomas	2.89
1957	J Johnson	3.50	Brian John	3.05	John Evans	3.07
1958	John Ball	3.35	John Howe	3.05	G Fisher	2.89
1959	John Ball	3.35	John Evans	3.41	R Owen	2.89
1960	John Ball	3.52	Michael Sutton	3.27	A W Poole	3.09
1961	John Evans	3.43	Leslie Jones	3.20	R Davies	2.89
1962	Leslie Jones	3.53	Owen Bevan	3.35	R Morgan	2.97
1963	Leslie Jones	3.66	David Williams	3.59	Chris Evans	3.12
1964	David Williams		A Hodges	3.12	M Lewis	2.97
1965	P Evans	3.20	Maldwyn Lewis	3.20	W Summer	2.74
1966	A Hodges	3.27	Keith Thomas	3.05	R Best	2.74
1967	R Williams	3.27	not known		not known	
1968	not known		Robin Swales	3.20	Shane Swales	3.20
1969	Ian Jones	3.35	K James	3.05	C Pritchard	2.82
1970	N Hughes	3.20	Shane Swales	3.15	P Johnson	2.70
1971	Shane Swales	3.40	N Evans	3.25	Islwyn Rees	3.05
1972	Les Keen	3.30	Islwyn Rees	3.35	D Birch	2.60
1973	Meirion Thomas	3.35	Islwyn Rees	3.66	Stephen Land	2.70
1974	Gordon Pickering	3.90	Islwyn Rees	4.10	P Williams	3.00
1975	Islwyn Rees	4.00	Martyn Jenkins	3.40	P Jones	2.50
1976	Brychan Jones	3.80	R Hartwell	2.85	Mark Howells	3.00
1977	E Thomas	2.90	Mark Howells	3.60	Robert Hughes	3.20
1978	P Evans	3.20	Robert Hughes	3.55	Alun Phillips	2.90
1979	Anthony Evans	3.20	Robert Hughes	3.75	Nigel Hancock	2.70
1980	Anthony Evans	3.40	Alun Phillips	3.46	Alan Tyrrell	3.10
1981	Mark Broadbent	3.55	Nigel Skinner	4.10	Matthew Lee	2.80
1982	Nigel Skinner	4.10	Glyn Price	3.70	Stephen Thomas (Mar)	2.80
1983	Nigel Skinner	4.00	Richard Davies	3.40	Neil Ashman	2.95
1985	Chris Barry	3.55	Neil Ashman	3.80	Shaun Wake	2.30
1986	Neil Ashman	3.65	Phil Thomas	3.20	Howard Turner	3.30
1987	Phil Thomas	2.90	Egryn Jones	3.60	Daniel Mawer	2.70
1988	Ian Thomas	3.80	Richard Davies	3.70	Stephen Thomas (Tr)	2.90
1989	Ian Thomas	4.00	Neil Winter	4.59	Richard Tomala	3.15
1990	Stephen Lloyd	4.20	Neil Winter	4.80	David Thomas	2.80
1991	Tim Thomas	4.42	Richard Tomala	3.70	Richard Harris	2.50
1992	Nicky Pritchard	4.30	Nathan Rawlins	3.50	Craig Millard	3.10
1993	David Francis	3.40	Matthew Turner	3.40	Steven Francis	3.40
1994	David Francis	3.70	Steven Francis	4.10	Jonathan Parry	2.90
1995	Paul Jones	4.00	Steven Francis	4.20	Chris Type	2.70
1996	Andrew Penk	4.30	Jonathan Parry	3.60	Chris Type	2.90
1997	Darren Beddows	3.80	Chris Type	4.35	Mark Harvey	
1998	Jonathan Parry	3.50	Chris Type	4.50	Adam Smith	2.65
1999	Chris Type	4.60	Owen Chesher	3.10	Kevin Jones	2.30
2000	Owen Chesher	3.30	Paul Walker	3.20	Jason Rees	2.60

Long Jump

1947	Neville Jones	6.04	M B Lloyd	5.82	W J G Brooks	4.56
1948	Gwyn Harris	6.04	J M Howells	5.63	R Hollow	4.91
1949	John Frowen	6.57	J F Rees	5.74	L S Dyer	5.26
1950	D D Thomas	6.10	L Dyer	5.68	E Tomkins	5.46
1951	D D Thomas	6.36	Bryan Woolley	6.13	R Skyrme	5.33
1952	Gwilym Roberts	5.99	J Clayton	6.08	Brian Watkins	5.36
1953	Richard Dodd	6.23	Bryan Woolley	6.59	Brian Watkins	5.93

1954	Bryan Woolley	6.37	Brian Watkins	6.06	G Morris	5.47
1955	Bryan Woolley	6.67	J A Jones	5.93	H Morgan	5.56
1956	Dewi Bebb	6.02	Peter Sayzeland	5.94	L Hayward	5.74
1957	B Richards	5.84	Aled Jones	5.18	G E Thomas	5.29
1958	Ian Hughes	6.59	Andrew Davies	6.09	Tony Bigham	5.79
1959	Ian Hughes	6.72	G Thomas	6.49	F Ebrall	6.01
1960	Terry Davies	6.62	Gwyn Morgan Jones	6.09	S Williams	5.54
1961	Lynn Davies	6.56	Gwyn Morgan Jones	6.37	M Lovell/C Burdock	5.58
1962	not known		Gary Laycock	6.11	R Haskins	5.56
1963	Nick Aspin	5.50	John Lewis	6.21	not known	
1964	Tony Harry	6.17	Gareth Edwards	6.43	Keith Lowe	5.81
1965	Derek Morgan	6.71	Keith Lowe	6.73	Raymond Hamill	5.94
1966	John Elias	6.86	Raymond Hamill	6.27	A Davies	6.00
1967	John Elias	7.34	Raymond Hamill	6.79	not known	
1968	not known		not known		not known	
1969	Raymond Hamill	6.41	Colin Maidment	6.02	Steve Kohut	5.57
1970	Kedrick Thompson	6.60	David Rees	6.36	Steve Kohut	6.08
1971	Steve Herman	6.39	Wynn Evans	6.41	S Davies	5.65
1972	David Rees	6.36	W Simmonds	6.24	R Jones	5.53
1973	David Rees	6.70	Kevin Williams	6.29	M Williams	5.94
1974	Steve Kohut	6.35	David Edwards	5.99	Alan Watkins	5.80
1975	Kevin Williams	6.11	J Quarless	6.10	Gareth Watkins	5.55
1976	Nigel Price	6.39	Cerith Williams	6.20	Ian Strange	5.72
1977	Steve Barlow	6.49	Julian Barrington	6.50	Ian Strange	6.19
1978	Tony Owen	6.74	David Wood	6.67	Ray Sherry	5.79
1979	David Wood	6.75	John Furnham	6.37	Robert Clappe	5.84
1980	Richard Jones	7.13	Huw Davies	6.64	Lyndon Richards	5.85
1981	Steve Pill	6.52	Andrew McMahon	6.17	Simon Marsh	5.62
1982	Paul Hawkins	6.41	Angus Cann	6.01	Richard Williams	5.37
1983	Andrew McMahon	6.39	Simon Marsh	6.39	Chris Kersey	5.66
1985	Steven Partridge	6.48	Mark Harris	6.54	Richard James	5.77
1986	Reuben Woodford	5.97	Richard James	6.35	Richard Harbour	5.62
1987	Sion Wyn Davies	6.39	Steve Ingram	6.41	David Davies	5.97
1988	David Manley	6.32	Richard Harbour	6.16	Simon Lewis	5.92
1989	Steve Ingram	6.27	Simon Lewis	6.33	Derwyn Owen	5.60
1990	Linton Baddeley	6.93	Simon Lewis	6.66	Chris Robertson	5.50
1991	Greg Bourne	6.40	Jonathan Morris	5.94	Richard Talbot	5.63
1992	Darren Yeo	6.45	Gareth Sansom	6.12	Matthew Perry	5.92
1993	Nick Walne	6.81	Stuart Jones	6.37	Keith Holmes	5.85
1994	Damian Clarke	6.45	Chris Shepherd	6.03	James Morris	5.77
1995	Chas Madeira-Cole	6.62	Andrew Wooding	6.69	Gareth Gittins	5.80
1996	Chas Madeira-Cole	6.66	James Morris	6.59	Nathan Palmer	5.74
1997	Andrew Wooding	7.03	Alex Jackson	6.63	Steven Jones	5.92
1998	Steven Frost	6.45	Kris Davies	6.63	Paul Dyer	5.68
1999	Alex Jackson	6.67	Chuka Enih-Snell	6.49	Iain Hunt	5.94
2000	Kris Davies	6.82	Ricardo Childs	6.42	Joel Sheppard	5.67

Triple Jump

1947	Gwyn Harris	12.09	G D Jenkins	11.52	J F Rees	10.82
1948	Gwyn Harris	13.28	C F Williams	12.03	Brian Hardwick	11.45
1949	John Frowen	13.78	D Roberts	11.99	L S Dyer	11.14
1950	E Hacker	12.47	S E Thomas	11.66	D Tomkins	11.25
1951	Richard Dodd	13.14	D H Price	12.72	G Simmonds	11.21
1952	Richard Dodd	13.04	D Tomkins	12.63	B Watkins	11.73
1953	Richard Dodd	13.28	B Rush	12.10	A Evans	12.12
1954	C Mills	13.79	D Chesworth	12.98	B D Smith/E Cookson	11.69
1955	D Chesworth	13.18	Aneurin Evans	13.50	A Jones	11.59
1956	Aneurin Evans	13.88	P Hancock	12.57	C Williams	12.46
1957	Aneurin Evans	14.07	Aled Jones	12.49	C Bowen	12.11
1958	Ian Hughes	12.99	A Phillips	12.63	R Jones	11.86
1959	P Williams	13.74	A Jones	13.07	F Ebrall	12.24
1960	Bleddyn Williams	14.25	Tony Bigham	12.88	R Duke	12.16
1961	Nigel Green	13.75	Gwyn Morgan Jones	13.26	J W Jones	12.50
1962	David Evans	13.80	not known		D Reid	12.34
1963	David Evans	13.66	Graham Webb	13.90	John Elias	13.50
1964	Graham Webb	13.87	Gwynn Davis	13.28	K Bevan	11.89
1965	Nigel Morgan	13.59	Alun James	13.05	M Czarnecki	11.85
1966	John Davies	13.64	J Arthur	12.65	J Thornton	12.18
1967	Spencer Jones	13.69	not known		not known	
1968	not known		G Sherwood	12.60	not known	
1969	John Phillips	13.49	R Mostyn	13.30	C D Williams	12.53

1970	John Rein	13.32	David Rees	12.96	P Jenkins	11.41
1971	D Smith	13.52	David Rees	13.23	John Leighton	12.29
1972	John Tustin	13.91	Robert Hanratty	12.93	Andrew Lea	11.63
1973	John Tustin	14.03	John Leighton	12.86	Graham Hughes	12.23
1974	M Watkins	12.71	N Hornsby	13.19	Graham Hughes	12.53
1975	M Bellis	12.86	Graham Hughes	12.81	Philip Ward	11.69
1976	Alan Watkins	13.13	I Gorecki	12.70	David Wood	12.54
1977	Mike Jones	14.01	Philip Ward	13.57	John Furnham	12.74
1978	Philip Ward	13.84	David Wood	13.38	Wynne Harries	12.44
1979	David Wood	14.90	Paul Hawkins	13.68	Mark Humphries	11.99
1980	David Wood	14.39	Nathan Humphries	13.68	Mickey Morris	12.60
1981	Huw Knight	13.30	Steve Edwards	13.13	Mark Watkins	11.81
1982	Barry Roberts	13.44	Mickey Morris	13.21	Leighton Adams	11.90
1983	Barry Roberts	13.36	Gareth Davies (Stan)	12.83	David Morris	11.69
1985	Gareth Davies (Stan)	13.30	Andrew Stevens	12.67	Gareth Davies (Gow)	12.00
1986	Leighton Adams	12.87	Gareth Davies (Gow)	13.21	Gerald Walker	11.97
1987	Leighton Adams	13.27	Gerald Walker	13.61	Linton Baddeley	12.51
1988	Gareth Davies (Gow)	13.96	Gerald Walker	13.53	Simon Lewis	12.22
1989	Neil Charnock	13.39	Linton Baddeley	14.14	Darren Yeo	13.05
1990	Linton Baddeley	13.44	Darren Yeo	13.15	Daniel Francombe	12.71
1991	Ryan Robinson	13.65	Nick Walne	13.57	Rhodri Thomas	12.12
1992	Ryan Robinson	12.49	Daniel Francombe	13.63	Justin Hay	11.77
1993	Daniel Francombe	13.85	Kevin Morgan	12.80	Daniel Puddick	12.83
1994	Paul Ellis	13.59	Charles Madeira-Cole	13.51	Craig Davies	11.93
1995	Charles Madeira-Cole	13.82	Daniel Puddick	12.94	Michael Ferraro	11.69
1996	Charles Madeira-Cole	13.24	Rhys Williams	13.27	Stephen Shalders	12.25
1997	Lee Mason	13.09	Steven Shalders	?	Gareth Rees	11.75
1998	Steven Frost	13.57	Steven Shalders	15.06	Guto Jones	12.34
1999	Matthew Delicate	13.22	David Brown	12.79	David Keenan	11.77
2000	Steven Frost	13.81	Michael Knott	12.86	Lewis Johnson	12.36

Shot Put (weight changed 1971)

1947	C W Pook	11.38	H J Jones	12.38	J F Rees	11.53
1948	John Thomas	11.99	W Wright	14.25	J Rees	12.33
1949	D G Sanders	12.49	R Roberts	13.56	J L Salter	12.81
1950	D G Sanders	13.53	A M Hall	13.07	C Gibbon	12.27
1951	K Ll Jones	12.77	K Pritchard	14.06	David Pask	12.32
1952	K Ll Jones	14.64	R Jones	12.44	M Ll Allen	13.94
1953	Tony Morgan	13.92	P Verrow	14.16	H Morgan	15.30
1954	M Vincent	12.52	A C Williams	14.78	J T Lacey	13.08
1955	Malcolm Pemberton	12.52	A C Williams	13.97	John Davies	12.57
1956	Aneurin Evans	13.79	A Thomas	13.00	T Huzzy	12.06
1957	Aneurin Evans	13.82	John Davies	14.78	D C Jones	13.21
1958	John Davies	15.57	D C Jones	13.36	D Williams	12.67
1959	John Davies	15.69	D Sutton	12.88	G Roberts	12.73
1960	B Arthur	13.03	G Roberts	13.64	I Edwards	13.65
1961	Raymond Jones	14.04	Terry Price	15.05	K Davies	13.49
1962	Dennis Day	13.35	Terry Price	16.14	D Jones	13.59
1963	Terry Price	14.48	not known		Allan Martin	14.21
1964	Roger Beard	15.02	Allan Martin	14.34	Paul Luff	14.10
1965	D Boxer	13.96	Paul Luff	14.51	M Nash	13.34
1966	Allan Martin	15.63	D Roberts	14.50	Adrian Thomas	14.26
1967	Allan Martin	15.61	not known		not known	
1968	Lyndon Davies	14.15	Peter Wilson	14.23	R Edwards	12.86
1969	Lyndon Davies	14.41	Joe Hughes	13.56	D Owen	11.45
1970	Graham Price	14.63	Joe Hughes	14.38	Kevin Jones	15.57
1971	Joe Hughes	13.24	Kevin Jones	13.65	G Michael	12.43
1972	Joe Hughes	13.28	Kevin Jones	14.40	Brian Isgar	12.31
1973	Kevin Jones	13.72	P Vaughan	12.12	Lloyd Williams	
1974	Kevin Jones	13.29	A James	13.11	S Parker	13.89
1975	A Shaw	12.44	Jon Tym	14.27	Peter Rees	12.92
1976	Lloyd Williams	12.70	Nigel Jones	13.08	Ewart Hulse	12.08
1977	Lloyd Williams	12.47	Peter Rees	15.40	Mark Hewer	13.20
1978	Ian Brown	12.78	Mark Hewer	15.39	Richard James	13.03
1979	John Daniels	13.92	Mark Hewer	16.63	R Barrett	12.75
1980	Mark Hewer	15.20	Richard James	13.54	Mark Griffiths	12.64
1981	Mark Hewer	15.32	Stephen Edwards	14.83	Julian Mainwaring	12.18
1982	Stephen Edwards	12.69	Gwyn Rees	13.98	Warren Rossiter	13.24
1983	Stephen Edwards	13.12	George Yiacoummi	14.46	Ian Gould	12.87
1985	Michael Roberts	13.00	Ian Gould	13.35	David Nelson	12.89
1986	Michael Roberts	11.92	Andrew Millard	12.58	David Nelson	14.38

1987	Adrian Palmer	11.64	David Nelson	14.21	Lawrence Mainwaring	12.29
1988	Steven Williams	13.53	David Nelson	14.44	Gianluigi Fecci	13.38
1989	Steven Williams	13.44	Simon Cooke	13.87	Matthew James	12.03
1990	Peter Roberts	13.32	Stephen Ford	12.86	Justin Jones	13.52
1991	Peter Roberts	14.05	Stephen Ford	13.69	Jamie Brown	12.02
1992	Peter Maitland	13.48	Matthew Green	13.39	Matthew Roblin	13.12
1993	Stephen Ford	12.65	Gareth Marks	13.69	John Parkin	11.91
1994	Gareth Marks	13.39	James Sheehan	13.24	Jamie Dalton	12.53
1995	James Elton	12.25	John Parkin	12.90	Stuart Tynan	13.56
1996	Matthew Jones	13.28	Stuart Tynan	12.81	Liam Walsh	14.28
1997	Ben Roberts	13.85	Liam McCaffrey	14.06	Andrew Masterton	12.16
1998	David Blackmore	13.98	James Anthony	13.03	Simon Cole	12.18
1999	Ben Roberts	15.34	Simon Bull	13.42	Glenn Williams	12.04
2000	David Roberts	12.31	Michael Mogford	14.51	Greg Finlay	14.69

Discus

1947	A J Evans	32.14	N W Noake	35.48	J L Roberts	32.42
1948	S G Williams	31.39	D V T Reakes	38.68	T J Kitson	28.23
1949	N W Noake	34.43	B James	39.91	J A Newcombe	30.03
1950	S A Clarke	34.64	J M Crayford	40.52	W A Evans	34.06
1951	S A Clarke	39.50	H Jones	39.23	D Richards	31.94
1952	R Llewellyn	37.71	P Bromfield	43.16	A C Williams	34.70
1953	D Voyle	36.41	P Bromfield	43.94	A C Williams	40.66
1954	W R Evans	39.00	P Bromfield	46.34	P Thomas	41.02
1955	J Reed	37.12	H Morgan	48.12	C Jones	38.86
1956	Malcolm Pemberton	37.08	P Thomas	47.84	F Jones	38.12
1957	A E Williams	42.16	Alan Thomas	45.26	M Pape	43.28
1958	D Margretts	34.06	D Harries	45.44	Ray Lott	41.48
1959	G Williams	42.20	D A Williams	41.18	B Elliott	35.26
1960	Alan Scaplehorn	37.42	Dennis Day	46.31	V Bonnici	40.04
1961	Dennis Day	43.93	Peter Skehan	49.29	K Davies	44.59
1962	Dennis Day	44.03	not known		D Jones	41.74
1963	Gerald Wallace	39.39	P Gittens	49.46	T Getreke	41.83
1964	G Harries	42.14	J Evans	46.86	B Crawford	40.17
1965	D Jones	36.98	Graham La Page	50.24	A Cousins	41.45
1966	Allan Martin	38.68	D Barnes	43.55	D Scott	38.48
1967	Allan Martin	45.40	not known		not known	
1968	not known		S Willis	44.78	not known	
1969	Lyndon Davies		R Thomas	47.40	B Jones	37.50
1970	Graham Price	42.68	Joe Hughes	50.06	B Oatley	41.04
1971	Joe Hughes	43.30	David McPherson	41.46	R Hathaway	34.62
1972	David McPherson	39.92	Ken Latten	41.14	Edward Lewis	37.00
1973	Ken Latten	41.14	Edward Lewis	35.68	Arfon Grindall	35.96
1974	Gareth Jenkins	39.98	Edward Lewis	37.98	Nigel Stevens	36.32
1975	Edward Lewis	38.68	Nigel Stevens	36.96	R Owen	30.26
1976	Edward Lewis	43.54	Hugh James	42.86	J Moore	36.76
1977	Ian Rees	35.08	John Buttriss	41.56	Hywel King	34.82
1978	Ian Rees	37.86	John Collins	45.92	M Stephens	34.64
1979	John Collins	41.80	David Harrison	39.86	Paul Jenkins	40.82
1980	John Collins	43.66	Mark Morgan	40.74	Gwyn Rees	35.54
1981	Brian Collins	38.96	Paul Walsh	40.48	Steven Meredydd	34.96
1982	Brian Collins	42.22	Clive Jones	37.70	Gary Smith	35.90
1983	Stephen Edwards	37.50	Nick John	39.74	Nick George	34.26
1985	Michael Roberts	34.48	Gareth Jones	39.72	Scott Richardson	32.10
1986	Anthony Coutanche	39.98	Gary Cornish	38.70	Paul Evans	32.60
1987	Anthony Coutanche	38.40	David Nelson	42.58	Anthony Doran	33.58
1988	Simon Baker	36.60	Simon Cooke	43.54	Steven Mellalieu	35.18
1989	Peter Roberts	41.32	Simon Cooke	40.36	Geraint James	35.24
1990	Peter Roberts	44.06	Damian McGarvie	39.54	Justin Jones	41.18
1991	Peter Roberts	44.44	Andrew Furst	40.22	Aaron Jones	31.06
1992	Damian McGarvie	40.00	Justin Jones	39.30	Chris Hughes	40.36
1993	Justin Jones	39.24	Gareth Marks	44.28	John Parkin	35.42
1994	Gareth Marks	45.94	Stephen Thomas	44.40	Eifion Robinson	33.86
1995	Gareth Marks	51.38	John Parkin	42.78	Liam Walsh	39.70
1996	Ross Blight	35.14	Eifion Robinson	38.38	Liam Walsh	44.06
1997	David Blackmore	37.78	Stuart Tynan	42.56	Nathan Jones	35.38
1998	Bryan Cooksley	40.60	Simon Bull	35.86	Craig Williams	36.51
1999	Chris Marland	41.80	Simon Bull	41.87	Gareth Bull	38.51
2000	Andrew Sherwood	38.31	Glenn Williams	46.35	Greg Finlay	40.30

Hammer (new weight 1971)

1960	H Jenkins	28.25				
1961	E K Howells	29.17				
1962	T Perrin	35.16				
1963	J Hughes	33.74				
1964	Roger Beard	46.63				
1965	V Harries	41.70				
1966	D Evans	43.52				
1967	Allan Martin	49.20				
1968	not known					
1969	D Ratcliffe	36.62				
1970	Martin Lewis	42.16	D Jones	38.08	M Jones	35.80
1971	Martin Lewis	42.72	G Williams	37.44	R Sowery	41.78
1972	G Williams	38.34	Alan Stimson	41.32	C Brookes	36.44
1973	Mike Llewellyn-Eaton	39.66	C Brookes	38.78	Michael Lewis	35.80
1974	Mike Llewellyn-Eaton	47.32	Phil Jones	45.82	Nigel Stevens	46.16
1975	Phil Jones	44.22	Nigel Stevens	47.48	Ewart Hulse	35.72
1976	Phil Jones	50.38	Huw Casey	34.24	Ewart Hulse	45.04
1977	Nigel Stevens	39.94	Ewart Hulse	37.70	K Davies	33.08
1978	Dino Lantzos	39.64	Peter Crook	44.12	G Williams	33.12
1979	Dino Lantzos	42.36	David Davies	44.04	Alan Roberts	36.28
1980	Ewart Hulse	45.80	Brian Collins	35.58	Adrian Thomas (AT)	45.74
1981	Jeremy Flye	36.36	John Owen	47.62	David Wilton	34.14
1982	John Owen	49.12	Martin Cliffe	46.60	Dorian Jones	42.32
1983	John Owen	50.20	Phil Bufton	49.30	Adrian Thomas (Treg)	40.70
1985	Anthony Coutanche	40.46	Adrian Palmer	51.86	Stephen Owens	27.20
1986	Anthony Coutanche	47.80	Ceri Evans	39.58	Marcus Davies	47.54
1987	Adrian Palmer	57.72	Marcus Davies	51.46	Paul Harrison	41.70
1988	Keith Boswell	40.18	Marcus Davies	55.60	Paul Beard	32.14
1989	Keith Boswell	45.54	Neil Williams	55.78	Simon Bennett	39.66
1990	Neil Williams	54.12	Hamid Lane	51.36	Mark Boswell	34.02
1991	Anthony Doran	49.24	Mark Boswell	47.72	Warren King	34.92
1992	Andrew Jones	46.48	Mark Boswell	47.80	Eirian Rees	33.86
1993	Hamid Lane	54.46	Ross Blight	50.46	John Parkin	40.46
1994	Ross Blight	54.18	John Parkin	44.56	Chris Aherne	47.08
1995	Ross Blight	52.60	Chris Aherne	48.14	Jonathan Hodgeon	32.52
1996	Ross Blight	48.24	Chris Aherne	52.00	Matthew Grindle	43.18
1997	Richard Tully	36.64	Jonathan Hodgeon	46.52	Chris Seabourne	38.68
1998	Bryan Cooksley	48.96	Matthew Grindle	49.03	James Grindle	43.83
1999	Thomas O'Shea	45.52	James Rees	49.15	Glenn Williams	48.73
2000	James Rees	46.59	Glenn Williams	52.80	Jamie Pritchard	44.29

Javelin

1947	E M Williams	40.04	G Lewis	47.87	C R Edwards	29.60
1948	W Hackett	48.84	Ray Jones	48.38	W Johnson	32.35
1949	Garfield Owen	56.84	D Williams	45.14	J L Salter	40.51
1950	R M Hurst	47.32	John Wicks	38.22	R James	35.54
1951	N Tate	50.42	Clive Roberts	51.83	G Littler	36.38
1952	Clive Roberts	58.11	T E Fennell	45.14	M Ll Allen	41.21
1953	G F Harries	47.84	J P Rogers	45.96	N J Johnson	38.30
1954	B H Lewis	44.64	L Shelton	48.44	J Morris	46.64
1955	H Mount	46.20	D Evans	47.86	D W Humphreys	43.48
1956	John James	55.52	M Herbert	49.86	Gary Mumford	47.02
1957	A Hill	45.36	David Price	50.70	M Pape	49.60
1958	David Price	52.92	A Swindley	47.28	G Roberts	44.22
1959	David Price	61.12	I Lewis	49.00	Richard Lewis	54.02
1960	D Davies	45.96	J Rowlands	50.52	G Jones	45.30
1961	David Tristram	55.38	R Owen/P Lewis	47.91	H Thomas	50.17
1962	G Roberts	55.42	Gareth Jones	54.59	not known	
1963	not known		F Meredith	48.15	not known	
1964	C Oldham	55.24	R Weekley	51.04	M Charles	44.30
1965	Philip Cooney	49.28	K Fletcher	46.86	K Marsh	42.31
1966	not known		Laurence Aalten	42.72	John Roberts	41.74
1967	Richard Kemp	52.84	not known		not known	
1968	Phil Ramsay	49.56	not known		not known	
1969	John Roberts	52.26	Stephen Jones	45.56	B Jones	43.12
1970	John Roberts	51.26	Nick Lia	48.84	Kevin Jones	43.74
1971	D B Evans	44.84	R Evans	51.20	Robert Jones	44.04
1972	Mark Evans	49.32	Robert Jones	53.42	E Nickells	42.76
1973	Mark Evans	56.46	Robert Jones	46.18	M Jones	44.86
1974	Samuel Stephens	57.38	M Jones	50.88	Alan Watkins	53.28

1975	Robert Jones	51.36	Gareth Scales	58.84	Stephen Cahill	46.96
1976	Nigel Price	51.34	L Curry	49.00	Alan Edmunds	41.08
1977	Gareth Scales	54.22	Stephen Cahill	49.15	R Hughes	47.50
1978	Nigel Price	61.01	Steve Griffiths	51.38	A James	43.90
1979	Steve Robbins	53.20	Gareth Rowlands	50.80	Timothy Pawlett	44.72
1980	Steve Griffiths	55.88	Richard Jones	53.44	Mark Jones	46.56
1981	Gareth Rowlands	62.40	Chris Talbot	52.22	Colin Jackson	49.52
1982	Gareth Rowlands	61.86	John Hallam	50.16	Keith Marshall	48.06
1983	Robert Jones	53.68	Keith Marshall	55.10	Adrian Evans	44.52
1985	Jonathan Clarke	54.62	Craig Miller	52.00	Andrew Williams	45.32
1986	Jonathan Clarke	67.34	Julian Howells	51.58	Anthony Roberts	41.64
1987	Jonathan Clarke	57.64	Hugh Daniels	50.74	Neil Waters	52.60
1988	Andrew Mitchell	44.76	Linton Baddeley	48.02	Morgan Williams	49.28
1989	Huw Evans	53.32	Linton Baddeley	59.12	Richard Jones	48.32
1990	Linton Baddeley	56.14	Richard Jones	53.86	Mark Taylor	46.20
1991	Linton Baddeley	60.58	Richard Jones	55.50	Barry Walters	45.94
1992	Andrew Furst	49.56	Stuart Loughran	55.22	Matthew Roblin	42.96
1993	Stuart Loughran	53.16	Barry Walters	48.10	Derek Hermann	45.40
1994	Mark Taylor	49.84	Matthew Davies	54.38	Chris Thomas	46.64
1995	Bryn Samuel	48.88	Matthew Davies	51.56	Liam Walsh	49.16
1996	Matthew Davies	52.54	Chris Thomas	54.78	Rhys Williams	49.98
1997	Chris Thomas	58.70	Shaun Groves	54.04	Rhys Taylor	45.22
1998	Matthew Davies	57.74	Chris Hughes	50.93	Michael Groves	53.30
1999	James Anthony	52.25	Rhys Taylor	51.92	Nathan Cale	38.08
2000	Rhys Williams	57.31	Michael Groves	54.32	Thomas Rees	47.89

Cricket Ball

1947	J M Guy	80.88	WK Thomas	80.60	J F Rees	69.44
1948	B Vincent	90.62	J G Irwin	83.24	D Batcup	71.24
1949	V G Williams	97.92	J G Irwin	86.06	E H Richards	74.04
1950	E Roberts	89.65	C F Dutton	89.84	G R Meadows	71.08

Pentathlon

1993	not held		Graham Thomas	3037	Anthony Woodward	2293
1994	Darren Morgan	2255	Jamie Sheffield	2967	Chris Roberts	2453
1995	not held		Gareth Lewis	2879	Michael Ferraro	2367
1996	Paul Jones	2909	Ben Roberts	3062	Roger Owens	2726
1997	Ben Roberts	3031	James Anthony	3000	Nathan Jones	2904
1998	Ben Roberts	3079	James Anthony	3129	Chuka Enih-Snell	2713
1999	Ben Roberts	2740	Chuka Enih-Snell	3140	Daniel Kerslake	2299
2000	Nathan Jones	3078	Chuka Enih-Snell	2903	Jamie Pritchard	2425

100 yards / 100 metres

	Senior Girls		**Middle Girls**		**Junior Girls**	
1955	Gwyneth Lewis	11.5			Beryl Turner	12.0
1956	Gwyneth Lewis	11.7			P Lister	12.2
1957	Daphne Williams	11.8			H Parry	11.7
1958	Daphne Williams	11.7			Monica Zeraschi	11.8
1959	Daphne Williams	12.6			J Davies	12.6
1960	Monica Zeraschi	11.5			A Ormond	12.0
1961	Monica Zeraschi	11.4			D Cox	11.9
1962	not known				not known	
1963	Liz Gill	11.3			L Davies	12.1
1964	Liz Parsons	12.5			J Llewellyn	13.1
1965	Linda Davies	12.1			G Wein	12.4
1966	not known				Elizabeth Lloyd	11.6
1967	Marilyn Stokes	11.5	Diane Chipps	11.3	Beryl Walker	11.9
1968	not known		Diane Chipps	11.6	Michelle Smith	11.7
1969	Elizabeth Lloyd	12.4	Beryl Walker	12.6	Marva Connikie	12.5
1970	Avril Jones	12.7	Marva Connikie	12.7	Sheila Richardson	12.8
1971	Michelle Smith	12.4	Marva Connikie	12.8	Elizabeth Conlan	13.4
1972	Jean Bagley		Delyth Thomas	12.7	Damiana John	12.9
1973	Delyth Thomas		Gillian Regan	13.2	Ceri Jenkins	
1974	Linda Williams	13.0	Ceri Jenkins	12.3	Carmen Smart	12.6
1975	Leanne Dando	12.6	Carmen Smart	12.3	Diane Thorne	13.1
1976	Ceri Jenkins	12.9	Carmen Smart	12.3	Karen Taylor	13.0
1977	Rose Tillson	13.0	Diane Thorne	12.9	Karen Taylor	13.0
1978	Diane Thorne	12.1	Jennifer Webb	12.1	Dawn Oliver	12.5
1979	Diane Thorne	12.6	Jocelyn Peets	12.7	Dawn Oliver	12.7

1980	Mair Evans	13.2	Janette Brown	12.9	Dawn Oliver	12.3
1981	Jennifer Webb	12.2	Rhian Owen	12.5	Helen Miles	12.5
1982	Mair Evans	13.1	Helen Miles	12.3	Jane Bradbeer	12.6
1983	Dawn Oliver	13.2	Helen Miles	12.8	Jane Bradbeer	13.0
1985	Alison Rees	12.7	Nicola Short	12.4	Catherine Allen	13.1
1986	Debbie Jones	12.8	Nicola Short	12.6	Nicola Evans	12.6
1987	Emma James	12.8	Catherine Allen	12.7	Joanna Howell	12.7
1988	Emma James	13.1	Joanna Howell	12.8	Natasha Bartlett	13.1
1989	Pamela Greaves	12.3	Natasha Bartlett	12.3	Bethan Griffiths	12.6
1990	Sonia Reay	12.8	Bethan Griffiths	12.7	Sian Bradshaw	13.2
1991	Lisa Armstrong	12.0	Dawn Higgins	11.9	Sarah Colton	12.9
1992	Leanne Rowlands	12.3	Dawn Higgins	12.4	Rhiannon Ridgeway	12.6
1993	Lisa Armstrong	12.3	Stacey Rodd	12.5	Hannah Paines	12.8
1994	Krysta Williams	12.54	Hannah Paines	12.36	Gail Evans	12.80
1995	Stacy Rodd	12.26	Hannah Paines	12.39	Emily Wyatt	12.92
1996	Hannah Paines	12.39	Gail Evans	12.46	Erica Burfoot	12.47
1997	Gail Evans	12.74	Aimee Cutler	12.60	Catherine Jones	12.68
1998	Sarah Lane	13.10	Lowri Jones	12.1	Danielle Selley	12.53
1999	Caroline Marsden	12.68	Lowri Jones	12.24	Paula Williams	12.83
2000	Alex Bick	13.08	Aimee John	13.0	Danielle Barker	13.2

220 yards / 200 metres

1956	Carol Thomas	27.0				
1957	Daphne Williams	26.7				
1958	Daphne Williams	26.7				
1959	Daphne Williams	27.5				
1960	Monica Zeraschi	25.6				
1961	Monica Zeraschi	25.7				
1962	not known					
1963	Liz Gill	25.4				
1964	Liz Parsons	26.1				
1965	Linda Davies	27.0			Elizabeth Lloyd	18.2
1966	not known				Diane Chipps	17.5
1967	Marilyn Stokes	26.9	Diane Chipps	25.7	Sonia Barate	17.6
1968	not known		Diane Chipps		Michelle Smith	
1969	Elizabeth Lloyd	26.1	Michelle Smith	26.2	S Brown	19.7
1970	Avril Jones	26.2	Marva Connikie	26.9	Sheila Richardson	19.6
1971	Michelle Smith	25.9	Helen Watts	27.2	Dierdre Birch	20.2
1972	Jean Bagley	27.4	Delyth Thomas		Sharon Essien	19.7
1973	Delyth Thomas	26.9	S Roberts	27.6	Ceri Jenkins	25.8
1974	Kathy Morris	28.7	Ceri Jenkins	26.9	Heather Evans	27.3
1975	Leanne Dando	26.6	Carmen Smart	26.2	Ruanda Davies	26.6
1976	Ceri Jenkins	26.5	Carmen Smart	26.1	Karen Taylor	26.5
1977	Carmen Smart	25.9	Diane Thorne	26.1	Karen Taylor	26.6
1978	Diane Thorne	25.3	Susan Webb	25.3	Paula Thomas	26.0
1979	Diane Thorne	26.5	Karen Taylor	25.7	Dawn Oliver	26.2
1980	Mair Evans	27.4	Paula Thomas	25.6	Dawn Oliver	25.2
1981	Jennifer Webb	26.1	Liz Simister	26.9	Helen Miles	26.1
1982	Rhian Owen	26.5	Helen Miles	26.1	Jane Bradbeer	26.4
1983	Sian Morris	25.3	Sallyanne Short	26.3	Jane Bradbeer	27.0
1985	Alison Rees	25.9	Nicola Short	26.1	Lisa Randall	26.9
1986	Paula Goodridge	26.9	Nicola Short	25.8	Nicola Evans	26.2
1987	Paula Goodridge	26.4	Sonia Reay	26.7	Emma Todd	26.3
1988	Paula Goodridge	26.8	Joanna Howell	26.2	Natasha Bartlett	26.0
1989	Sonia Reay	25.8	Lisa Armstrong	24.9	Bethan Griffiths	26.1
1990	Sonia Reay	26.3	Natasha Bartlett	25.8	Sian Bradshaw	26.7
1991	Lisa Armstrong	24.9	Dawn Higgins	25.9	Sarah Colton	27.0
1992	Natasha Bartlett	25.7	Leanne Billen	25.8	Rhiannon Ridgeway	26.3
1993	Katherine Morris	26.1	Stacy Rodd	26.2	Rhiannon Ridgeway	26.7
1994	Krysta Williams	26.60	Hannah Paines	25.92	Gail Evans	26.72
1995	Sarah Roberts	25.48	Gail Evans	25.35	Debbie Morgan	26.17
1996	Angharad James	25.3	Gail Evans	25.65	Erica Burfoot	25.22
1997	Leri Davies	25.16	Aimee Cutler	25.27	Catherine Jones	26.16
1998	Donna Porazinski	26.98	Lowri Jones	25.16	Helen Davies	26.22
1999	Donna Porazinski	25.77	Lowri Jones	25.21	Paula Williams	26.76
2000	Rachel Lewis	27.08	Samantha Gamble	27.1	Fay Harding	26.4

400 metres

1972	Anne Disley	60.0	Kathy Morris	60.8
1973	Kathy Morris	60.9	Leanne Dando	59.7

1974	Kathy Morris	61.3	Debbie Froggatt	62.0		
1975	Ann Roblin	63.5	Julie Morgan	60.6		
1976	Kim Price	62.4	Angela Pennington	59.2		
1977	H Potter	59.2	Sian Walters	57.0		
1978	Angela Pennington	59.8	Carol Nicholas	57.9		
1979	Ann Griffiths	58.2	Paula Thomas	56.9		
1980	Ann Griffiths	59.3	Cathy Owen	57.1		
1981	Beverley Preece	60.1	Sian Morris	57.7		
1982	Michelle Cooke	59.4	Alyson Evans	59.9		
1983	Rhian Owen	60.4	Alyson Evans	59.8		
1985	Alyson Evans	58.8	Debbie Jones	59.8		
1986	Debbie Jones	60.7	Claire Warnes	60.5		
1987	Nicola Lane	59.3	Claire Warnes	58.0		
1988	Mary Murphy	59.0	Nerys Evans	57.9		
1989	Nerys Evans	58.3	Joanne Gronow	58.9		
1990	Joanne Gronow	59.6	Alex Kegie	58.8		
1991	Joanne Gronow	58.2	Kay Furse	58.3		
1992	Kay Furse	60.5	Dawn Higgins	41.0		
1993	Katherine Morris	59.0	Kate Williams	41.3		
1994	Nicola Davies	58.50	Lucy Parsons	40.86		
1995	Michelle John	60.23	Sarah Mead	42.59		
1996	Sarah Roberts	56.49	Amanda Pritchard	40.11		
1997	Leri Davies	59.11	Donna Porazinski	41.35		
1998	Donna Porazinski	60.49	Susannah Evans	42.27		
1999	Donna Porazinski	57.97	Helen Davies	41.1		
2000	Donna Porazinski	56.9	Aimee John	42.8		

880 yards / 800 metres

1965	Tanya Alcock	2:26.8				
1966	not known					
1967	Delyth Davies	2:24.8	Margaret Davies	2:33.3		
1968	not known		not known			
1969	J Watts	2:29.6	D Gill	2:30.8		
1970	Dorothy Stevenson	2:33.1	Katrina Blackwell	2:23.3	Anne Morris	2:30.9
1971	Nicola Page	2:22.9	Ann Disley	2:22.4	Anne Morris	2:24.5
1972	Ann Disley	2:20.9	Dierdre Birch	2:27.5	Jackie Hulbert	2:27.8
1973	Ann Roblin	2:23.4	Anne Morris	2:19.7	Jackie Hulbert	2:22.5
1974	Dierdre Birch	2:29.1	Lyn Huntbach	2:29.6	Pat Waters	2:24.4
1975	Ann Roblin	2:24.1	Angela Hartley	2:22.0	Kirsty McDermott	2:22.4
1976	Pat Waters	2:27.6	Angela Hartley	2:19.0	Kirsty McDermott	2:19.8
1977	not known		Kirsty McDermott	2:14.0	Bethan Thomas	2:21.7
1978	Angela Pennington	2:29.2	Kirsty McDermott	2:21.7	Louise Copp	2:23.8
1979	Carol Nicholas	2:19.2	Louise Copp	2:21.7	Jane Thomas	2:23.1
1980	Ann Griffiths	2:16.6	Nicola Charlton	2:21.9	Jackie Thomas	2:18.0
1981	Sandra Miller	2:19.7	Nicola Charlton	2:18.2	Sharon James	2:24.9
1982	Claire Owen	2:19.8	Fiona Harwood	2:19.2	Karen Whitehouse	2:22.6
1983	Fiona Harwood	2:22.6	Ellie Palmer	2:20.2	Karen Whitehouse	2:22.2
1985	Avril Stephens	2:21.2	Karen Whitehouse	2:18.8	Julie Crowley	2:22.5
1986	Karen Whitehouse	2:25.9	Julie Crowley	2:19.8	Julie Garrett	2:21.4
1987	Ceri Burnell	2:22.3	Julie Crowley	2:20.2	Julie Garrett	2:14.0
1988	Rebecca Hickey	2:20.8	Julie Garrett	2:15.7	Mari Prys Jones	2:17.7
1989	Rebecca Hickey	2:17.0	Julie Garrett	2:18.3	Claire Edwards	2:18.1
1990	Julie Garrett	2:21.2	Claire Edwards	2:20.9	Kathryn Bright	2:21.9
1991	Claire Schofield	2:19.3	Claire Edwards	2:17.4	Kate Williams	2:22.2
1992	Claire Schofield	2:24.6	Kathryn Bright	2:23.6	Charlotte Reeks	2:22.2
1993	Emma Parry	2:20.5	Nina Hampshire	2:17.5	Charlotte Reeks	2:19.3
1994	Emma Parry	2:20.36	Sarah Devey	2:21.32	Sarah Mead	2:18.46
1995	Helen Westcombe	2:23.16	Melanie Taylor	2:19.12	Donna Porazinski	2:21.37
1996	Julia Clarke	2:22.02	Amanda Pritchard	2:17.23	Gemma Mounsey	2:21.17
1997	Sarah Mead	2:17.37	Teresa Penhorwood	2:17.89	Elise Taylor	2:22.42
1998	Anwen Owen	2:24.30	Natalie Lewis	2:19.14	Gemma Jones	2:21.32
1999	Natalie Lewis	2:17.49	Gemma Thomas	2:22.00	Lucy Thomas	2:19.52
2000	Julie Maundrell	2:26.33	Lucy Thomas	2:21.19	Fay Harding	2:25.10

1500 metres

1974	Sheila Hayler	5:22.9	Lyn Huntbach	5:13.8		
1975	Pamela Hiley	5:13.3	Ann Lewis	5:01.4	Ann Marie Fox	4:58.6
1976	Pat Waters	5:16.8	Debbie Lewis	5:01.2	Bernadette Rogers	5:03.0
1977	Caroline Morgan	5:02.6	Ann Marie Fox	4:44.1	Gillian Irvine	4:45.8
1978	Gina Williams	4:57.6	Gillian Irvine	4:52.0	Daryl Bevan	5:00.7

1979	Sian Rhian Jones	5:00.4	Kath Williams	4:47.9	Kate Roderick	4:56.8
1980	Bernadette Thomas	4:54.5	Kate Roderick	4:53.2	Cathy Corish	4:58.1
1981	Becky Powell	5:06.2	Fiona Harwood	4:49.0	Debbie Crowley	4:53.1
1982	Rhian Loudon	5:16.6	Debbie Crowley	4:50.7	Julie Jones	4:55.9
1983	Wendy Ore	4:57.4	Catherine Lock	5:02.1	Claire Pugh	4:51.8
1985	Kay Burnell	4:57.1	Lynne Stenstrom	4:47.7	Wendy McNamara	4:57.5
1986	Dawn Samuels	5:14.3	Nicola Morgan	4:48.6	Sarah Griffiths	5:01.5
1987	Hayley Donaghue	4:56.0	Rebecca Evans	4:40.3	Laura Carthew	4:48.5
1988	Ceri Thomas	4:53.9	Rebecca Evans	4:52.5	Claire Schofield	4:54.7
1989	Joanne Parsons	4:56.6	Rachel Parson	5:00.0	Amanda Rowbotham	4:57.6
1990	Claire Barnett	5:08.2	Claire Schofield	4:59.7	Angharad Howells	4:58.0
1991	Heidi Templeman	4:59.5	Vivienne Conneely	4:59.6	Angharad Howells	4:53.6
1992	Emma Davies	5:09.2	Emma Parry	4:51.6	Samantha Gray	5:00.8
1993	Emma Parry	4:49.6	Helen Protheroe	5:00.6	Dunya Hurley	4:43.5
1994	Clare Martin	4:56.44	Claire Thomas	4:49.46	Catrin Davies	4:52.26
1995	Anne-Marie Hutchinson	4:49.67	Claire Thomas	4:44.32	Teresa Penhorwood	4:53.35
1996	Rachel O'Donnell	4:50.94	Nicola Knapp	4:54.56	Teresa Penhorwood	4:54.07
1997	Nicola Knapp	4:48.27	Lucy Kirby	4:48.42	Claire Evans	5:01.5
1998	Nicola Knapp	4:56.45	Teresa Penhorwood	4:52.95	Eleanor Sherrard Smith	4:54.6
1999	Kirsty Doyle	5:00.52	Katie Greenwood	5:03.94	Amanda Jones	5:00.60
2000	Kirsty Doyle	4:52.0	Lucy Thomas	4:51.47	Bethan Strange	5:02.77

3000 metres

1976	Jane Clement	11:17.8	Sally Horwood	10:52.0
1977	Pat Waters	11:55.4	Carol Francis	10:55.0
1978	Dilwen Price	12:13.8	not known	
1979	L Jones	11:41.4	Beccy Powell	10:56.0
1980	Angela Parry	11:44.2	Kath Williams	10:21.5
1981	Lorena Marchetti	11:19.9	Sally James	10:48.1
1982	Sally James	10:27.3	Melanie Davies	10:53.4
1983	Jane Swarbrick	11:01.0	Angela Griffiths	10:56.2
1985	Beverley Morgan	10:50.9	Lorraine Madden	10:53.6
1986	Julie Williams	11:26.0	Pippa Amat	11:05.3
1987	Claire Pugh	10:21.1	Lisa Carthew	10:35.8
1988	Carol Hayward	10:11.1	Lindsey Whitley	10:57.5
1989	Ceri Thomas	10:43.6	Claire Schofield	10:33.4
1990	Deborah Whitty	11:01.1	Joanne Elward	11:19.5
1991	Emma Davies	11:01.6	Charlotte Morgan	11:00.8
1992	Mary Dowell Jones	11:37.5	Vivienne Conneely	10:14.2
1993	Vivienne Conneely	10:34.4	Jillian Lang	11:12.0
1994	Melissa Morgan	10:22.48	Heledd Gruffudd	10:32.56
1995	Vivienne Conneely	10:38.46	Rebecca Evans	10:46.6
1996	Claire Thomas	10:14.8	Sarah Brew	10:16.87
1997	Ceri Wensley	10:21.64	Sian Harries	11:10.68
1998	Ceri Wensley	11:10.3	Claire Salter	11:13.4
1999	Eloise Crowley	10:57.00	Miriam Gaskell	11:11.11
2000	Emily Crowley	10:54.21	Fiona Harrison	11:27.24

80m / 100m hurdles

1956	Maureen LeQuirot	12.6				
1957	Carol Thomas	12.2			B Rees	11.1
1958	Carol Thomas	12.3			M Frampton	11.3
1959	Carol Thomas	13.1			P Morgan	11.4
1960	C Sherwood	12.6			C A Jones	10.7
1961	Pat Morgan	12.8			Isobel Barden	10.4
1962	not known				not known	
1963	M Evans	12.7			not known	
1964	J Duignan	14.3			J Llewellyn	15.9
1965	Kathryn Hutchinson	12.3			M Beasley	12.2
1966	not known				Brenda Monk	12.1
1967	Monica Powell	12.6	Brenda Monk	12.6	Mary Moxley	12.2
1968	not known		June Hirst	12.6	not known	
1969	June Hirst	15.3	Gaynor Blackwell	11.9	Jayne Seymour	12.6
1970	M Moseley	15.9	Gaynor Blackwell	11.6	B Antrobus	12.3
1971	Gaynor Blackwell	16.5	Gwenda Jones	13.4	R Jones	12.1
1972	Gwenda Jones		Lynette Davies	13.0	J Jones	
1973	Bridget Roberts	15.8	E Davies		Clare Armstrong	12.0
1974	Terry Howard	17.8	E Davies	12.8	Clare Armstrong	11.9
1975	J Jones	16.1	Iola Pritchard	12.4	Norma Evans	12.3
1976	Bethan Jones	16.2	Ceri Smith	12.7	Sharon Whyte	12.4
1977	Bethan Jones	17.9	Sharon Whyte	12.6	Alice Simmons	12.4

1978	Norma Evans	14.4	Catrin Daniels	12.5	Jane Buttress	11.2
1979	Norma Evans	15.3	Jane Buttress	11.8	Julia Charlton	12.0
1980	Norma Evans	15.3	Sandra Oakley	12.4	Sarah Collins	12.3
1981	Jane Buttress	15.7	Julia Charlton	12.2	Alyson Evans	12.0
1982	Tracy Lewis	15.7	Alyson Evans	12.1	Rebecca Jones Morris	11.9
1983	Helen Parry	17.6	Katherine Morgan	12.6	Lisa Griffiths	12.5
1985	Non Evans	15.6	Lisa Griffiths	12.0	Cheryl Thomas	11.9
1986	Sarah Jones Morris	16.2	Marguerite Davies	12.2	Emma Pearce	11.9
1987	Sarah Jones Morris	15.5	Emma Pearce	12.0	Bethan Edwards	11.6
1988	Carol Whiteway	15.7	Bethan Edwards	12.2	Mari Prys Jones	11.7
1989	Amanda Wale	16.0	Bethan Edwards	11.6	Emma Hanson	11.8
1990	Bethan Edwards	15.4	Joelanda Thomas	12.4	Megan Jones	11.8
1991	Bethan Edwards	14.9	Megan Jones	12.3	Jodie Lester	11.8
1992	Marie Humphries	15.2	Rachel King	11.7	Louise Dennis	12.1
1993	Megan Jones	14.7	Kathryn Williams	12.2	Danielle Sullivan	11.7
1994	Emma Jones	15.8	Kathryn Williams	12.32	Amy Bergiers	11.68
1995	Rachel Stannard	15.83	Anna Leyshon	11.94	Sarah Lane	11.93
1996	Clare Anning	16.0	Anna Leyshon	12.0	Stephanie Little	11.8
1997	Anna Leyshon	15.1	Nia Maynard	11.99	Lauren McLoughlin	11.5
1998	Laura Clifford	17.74	Megan Freeth	11.96	Helen Davies	11.32
1999	Lowri Roberts	15.45	Lauren McLoughlin	11.73	Elin Evans	12.28
2000	Rebecca Jones	15.3	Alisa Cullen	12.3	Heather Jones	11.8

400m hurdles

1978	Beccy Wyatt	67.9	Celia Sutton	66.9
1979	Angela Carson	67.9	Jane Buttress	64.1
1980	Emma Quaeck	66.3	Claire Taylor	69.5
1981	Jane Buttress	64.8	Nicola Charlton	65.1
1982	Michelle Cooke	62.5	Alyson Evans	64.8
1983	Annette Griffiths	70.1	Alyson Evans	66.2
1985	Alyson Evans	61.2	Glenda James	66.8
1986	Susan Haskins	70.2	Glenda James	69.1
1987	Lisa Cross	66.8	Amanda Horton	69.3
1988	Claire Davies	71.5	Ruth Stanton	70.4
1989	Emma Lile	66.9	Mari Prys Jones	45.8
1990	Maria Yarnold	66.4	Claire Edwards	46.3
1991	Claire Schofield	64.4	Megan Jones	44.1
1992	Claire Edwards	66.0	Megan Jones	46.4
1993	Claire Edwards	62.7	Lucy Roberts	45.6
1994	Gemma Cashin	66.54	Kathryn Williams	45.56
1995	Michelle John	66.93	Leanne Dennis	45.68
1996	Kathryn Williams	63.68	Sarah Newman	48.18
1997	Abigail Jones	66.14	Donna Porazinski	44.66
1998	Sarah Newman	68.06	Stephanie Little	48.44
1999	Stephanie Little	67.57	Helen Davies	45.18
2000	Donna Porazinski	64.1	Helen Davies	46.2

High Jump

1955	Marie Witts	1.42			Margaret Liddiard	1.42
1956	S Jones = M Liddiard	1.45			G Wilkins	1.45
1957	M Wardle	1.42			S Kinson	1.45
1958	Joyce Wheeler	1.47			Monica Zeraschi	1.45
1959	Monica Zeraschi	1.50			P Philllips	1.40
1960	Lynda Hughes	1.47			M B Jones	1.46
1961	Jane Davies	1.45			Jacqueline Hughes	1.45
1962	not known				not known	
1963	not known				A James	1.40
1964	Liz Parsons	1.43			W Leslie	1.37
1965	Gillian Smith	1.45			Dorothy Czerwieska	1.42
1966	not known				June Hirst	1.50
1967	not known		June Hirst	1.53	Janice Davies	1.45
1968	not known		June Hirst	1.54	not known	
1969	June Hirst	1.57	Janice Davies	1.47	S Beddow	1.45
1970	Elizabeth Kay	1.50	Sarah Bull		Jackie Dilloway	
1971	Janice Davies	1.44	Jackie Dilloway	1.44	Jane Scrase	1.38
1972	Ann Senior	1.42	Hilary McPherson	1.52	Viv Rothera	1.51
1973	Sarah Bull	1.58	P Exton	1.47	Viv Rothera	1.59
1974	Heather Thomas	1.46	Viv Rothera	1.55	Juliet Worrell	1.50
1975	A Slater	1.50	Viv Rothera	1.64	Diane Williams	1.47
1976	Bethan Jones	1.58	Paula Jones	1.55	Sara Jones	1.49

1977	Viv Rothera	1.54	A Morris	1.56	Pam Walker	1.49
1978	Diane Williams	1.46	A Butler	1.46	Pam Walker	1.60
1979	C Bown	1.49	Pam Walker	1.59	Julia Charlton	1.70
1980	L Goddard	1.52	Sarah Nicholls	1.72	Julia Charlton	1.70
1981	Gaynor Moyle	1.45	Sarah Nicholls	1.65	Val Adams	1.52
1982	Sarah Nicholls	1.60	Christine Brookes	1.60	Sioned Davies	1.43
1983	Julia Charlton	1.56	Val Adams	1.63	Lisa Griffiths	1.60
1985	Val Adams	1.73	Jackie Barber	1.60	Amanda Davies	1.45
1986	Jackie Barber	1.55	Carol Whiteway	1.60	Laura Southwood	1.45
1987	Jackie Price	1.55	Amanda Davies	1.55	Beverley Green	1.50
1988	Carol Whiteway	1.55	Anna Clode	1.55	Beverley Green	1.57
1989	Amanda Wale	1.63	Beverley Green	1.60	Samantha Rex	1.50
1990	Anna Clode	1.60	Beverley Green	1.65	Emma Hanson	1.58
1991	Beverley Green	1.65	Krissy Owen	1.65	Teresa Andrews	1.55
1992	Joy Lamacraft	1.45	Teresa Andrews	1.70	Non Williams	1.50
1993	Emma Hanson	1.68	Teresa Andrews	1.70	Beth James	1.56
1994	Kathryn Evans	1.55	Non Williams	1.55	Kate Gregory	1.50
1995	Ailsa Wallace	1.70	Kelly Moreton	1.65	Lisa Thompson	1.60
1996	Abigail Jones	1.50	Kelly Moreton	1.60	Megan Freeth	1.45
1997	Kelly Moreton	1.65	Lisa Thompson	1.60	Lara Richards	1.53
1998	Kelly Moreton	1.60	Rebecca Jones	1.61	Claire Shaw	1.51
1999	Ceri Stokoe	1.61	Rebecca Jones	1.68	Sally Peake	1.58
2000	Rebecca Jones	1.76	Kathy Pritchet	1.60	Sally Peake	1.60

Pole Vault

1995	Rebecca Roles	2.70		
1996	Rebecca Roles	3.15		
1997	Bonny Elms	2.75	not known	2.30
1998	Kate Farr	2.20	Kerry Watkin	2.00
1999	Carys Holloway	2.50	Adrienne Harvey	2.10
2000	Carys Holloway	2.50	Sioned Rees	2.30

Long Jump

1956	Norma Lee	4.93				
1957	G Garnham	4.67			R Roberts	4.35
1958	Bonny Jones	4.69			Monica Zeraschi	5.34
1959	Monica Zeraschi	5.34			J Nelson	4.81
1960	Monica Zeraschi	5.09			J Mortimore	4.84
1961	Monica Zeraschi	5.61			Tanya Alcock	4.96
1962	not known				not known	
1963	Tanya Alcock	5.19			not known	
1964	not known				L Bridenan	3.97
1965	Tanya Alcock	4.81			A Jones	4.81
1966	not known				not known	
1967	Monica Powell	5.07	June Hirst	5.42	Elizabeth Roberts	4.84
1968	not known		Sharon McParlin	5.63	not known	
1969	June Hirst	5.47	Enid Sherratt	5.25	Ann Disley	4.76
1970	Elizabeth Kay	5.15	Susan Hopkins	5.09	Rhiannon Williams	4.88
1971	Gaynor Blackwell	5.14	Gwenda Jones	4.91	Shirley England	4.63
1972	Gwenda Jones	5.28	Gillian Regan	5.32	Ceri Jenkins	5.17
1973	Gwenda Jones	5.24	Ann Rich	4.94	Ceri Jenkins	5.27
1974	Linda Williams	4.75	Philomena Ronan	5.24	Chris Romanin	4.93
1975	Philomena Ronan	5.05	Ceri Jenkins	5.28	Jen Kamara	4.70
1976	Gillian Humphreys	5.06	Rose Tillson	5.21	Kirsty McDermott	4.89
1977	Rose Tillson	5.32	Deborah Perry	5.28	Paula Thomas	4.90
1978	C Norton	4.93	Jackie Hammersley	5.23	Claire Williams	4.90
1979	Deborah Perry	5.28	Karen Greene	5.18	Claire Williams	4.99
1980	Alice Simmons	5.39	Janette Brown	5.57	Julia Charlton	5.41
1981	Janette Brown	5.30	Julia Charlton	5.24	Joan Tudor	4.80
1982	Kate Roderick	4.90	Karen Taylor	4.83	Jayne Okey	4.95
1983	Nicolette Dymond	4.92	Kathryn Evans	5.32	Susan Parry	4.96
1985	Lisa Lewis	5.23	Nicola Short	5.40	Caroline Mills	4.82
1986	Patricia Roche	5.13	Nicola Short	5.53	Johanna Howell	4.99
1987	Emma James	5.34	Lisa Davies	5.23	Bethan Edwards	5.32
1988	Debra Gunn	5.00	Bethan Edwards	4.98	Petra Hurford	5.04
1989	Lisa Davies	5.33	Bethan Edwards	4.97	Joy Lamacraft	4.88
1990	Bethan Edwards	5.45	Beverley Green	5.36	Leanne Beckett	5.23
1991	Beverley Green	5.08	Tracy Powell	5.26	Karina Williams	5.06
1992	Anna Proctor	5.34	Leanne Beckett	4.94	Karina Williams	5.19
1993	Lisa Armstrong	5.80	Karina Williams	5.37	Ceri McDermott	5.12

1994	Gail Manning	4.82	Jayne Ludlow	5.19	Ceri McDermott	4.92
1995	Sarah Roberts	5.17	Ceri McDermott	5.34	Sarah Lane	4.68
1996	Sarah Roberts	5.16	Sarah Lane	5.50	Aimee Cutler	5.26
1997	Debbie Adams	5.29	Aimee Cutler	5.70	Amy Pearson	4.95
1998	Sarah Lane	5.33	Aimee Cutler	5.77	Danielle Selley	5.43
1999	Aimee Cutler	5.70	Lara Richards	5.70	Sally Peake	4.98
2000	Lara Richards	5.42	Amy Prothero	5.17	Sally Peake	5.40

Triple Jump

1993	Michelle Gillespie	10.23		
1994	Ufa Bolayes	09.63		
1995	Joanne Tomlinson	10.69		
1996	Joanne Tomlinson	10.59	Laura Eastwood	10.09
1997	Donna Owens	10.28	Nia Lewis	10.28
1998	Laura Eastwood	10.37	Lara Richards	10.79
1999	Megan Freeth	10.64	Lara Richards	11.20
2000	Lara Richards	11.02	Ceri Jones	10.96

Shot

1956	Maureen LeQuirot	08.46				
1957	R Gassner	07.82				
1958	Lynette Harries	08.56				
1959	A Davies	08.98				
1960	Janet Thomas	08.77			N Davies	09.69
1961	Pat Morgan	09.36			R Jones	10.20
1962	not known				not known	
1963	S Davies	08.86			not known	
1964	not known				not known	
1965	Hazel Andow	10.68			C Jones	09.57
1966	Hazel Andow	11.58			not known	
1967	Vivienne Morgan	09.22	Jennifer Heycook	09.40	Helen Colmer	09.59
1968	not known		Janet Beese	09.88	not known	
1969	Janet Beese	10.49	Frances Pincock	09.78	Margaret Raymond	08.98
1970	Janet Beese	11.47	Wendy Bartlett	09.15	Lyn Langdon	09.64
1971	Frances Pincock	11.18	Delyth Prothero	09.55	Joanna Stallbow	09.37
1972	Delyth Prothero	10.49	Lyn Langdon	09.58	Debbie Chapman	10.36
1973	Jackie Gray	11.52	Joanna Stallbow	09.24	Debra Morris	10.11
1974	Venissa Head	12.63	Joanna Stallbow	10.87	Sian Bowley	10.44
1975	Joanna Stallbow	11.17	Sian Bowley	10.21	Karen Glover	09.78
1976	Joanna Stallbow	11.00	Deborah Morris	10.00	Denise Laws	09.19
1977	Michelle Smith	09.68	Alyson Hourihan	09.84	Tonia Antoniazzi	09.33
1978	Alyson Hourihan	10.39	Denise Laws	10.34	Sandra Lee	10.66
1979	Alyson Hourihan	10.75	Sandra Lee	10.86	Delyth Evans	09.77
1980	Janet Covill	09.69	Sandra Lee	11.39	Delyth Evans	12.19
1981	Sandra Lee	11.32	Delyth Evans	11.84	Lisa Angulatta	11.58
1982	Sarah Nicholls	10.02	Delyth Evans	11.77	Andrea Munkley	10.07
1983	Ruth Thompson	10.88	Lisa Angulatta	10.95	Vanessa Daniels	10.04
1985	Lisa Angulatta	10.58	Jayne Morgan-Berry	10.51	Tina Loftus	10.16
1986	Linda Williams	10.58	Jayne Berry	11.38	Catrin Thomas	09.56
1987	Jayne Berry	11.85	Tina Loftus	10.13	Rachel Masterman	11.07
1988	Jayne Berry	13.90	Louise Davies	09.45	Ruth Mason	09.78
1989	Jayne Fisher	09.61	Rachel Masterman	10.52	Vicky Todd	10.46
1990	Lyndsey Thomas	10.51	Vicky Todd	09.64	Hayley Griffiths	10.21
1991	Rachel Masterman	10.72	Krissy Owen	10.75	Jodie Donovan	10.00
1992	Claire McKenzie	10.22	Hayley Griffiths	11.00	Philippa Roles	10.95
1993	Krissy Owen	12.29	Philippa Roles	12.90	Vicky Page	10.35
1994	Krissy Owen	12.03	Philippa Roles	12.65	Rebecca Roles	09.87
1995	Lesley Brannan	11.24	Rebecca Roles	09.39	Angharad Lloyd	09.72
1996	Philippa Roles	13.04	Angharad Lloyd	10.42	Elizabeth Edwards	09.87
1997	Philippa Roles	13.83	Angharad Lloyd	10.72	Laura Douglas	11.34
1998	Anwen James	09.10	Laura Douglas	10.25	Louise Finlay	10.64
1999	Liz Edwatds	10.41	Laura Douglas	10.83	Kelly Rowlands	09.13
2000	Laura Douglas	11.11	Louise Finlay	11.43	Sally Hinds	10.79

Discus

1956	Jean Crutchley	26.02				
1957	J Price	26.50				
1958	Lynette Harries	30.19				
1959	J Price	27.92			A Morgan	23.44
1960	Mary Lewis	31.99			P Jones	25.74

1961	Janet Wollan	32.06			Pat McRobb	31.02
1962	not known				not known	
1963	not known				Hazel Andow	28.34
1964	A Owen	26.91			not known	
1965	Hazel Andow	31.01			D Williams	27.36
1966	Hazel Andow	33.70			not known	
1967	Anne Schropfer	28.32	Ann Furness	28.84	Lynette Harding	25.70
1968	not known		J Francis	29.44	not known	
1969	Janet Beese	29.94	Susan Roberts	26.84	Delyth Prothero	27.96
1970	Janet Beese	34.38	Delyth Prothero	30.02	Ann Rice	26.82
1971	Susan Roberts	29.10	Delyth Prothero	34.68	J Lloyd	23.08
1972	Delyth Prothero	38.86	Lyn Langdon	29.26	Angharad Jones	24.70
1973	Jackie Gray	36.94	Vivienne Head	31.78	Eirian Owen	27.24
1974	Vivienne Head	36.74	Coral Maybank	29.54	Katrina Beedles	27.94
1975	S Brown	26.64	Eirian Owen	31.53	M Davies	25.94
1976	Eirian Owen	30.38	Marie Ellis	29.48	Caroline Williams	25.60
1977	Eirian Owen	30.38	Alyson Hourihan	35.10	Tracy Edwards	24.26
1978	Alyson Hourihan	38.60	Caroline Williams	36.00	Sandra Lee	38.44
1979	Alyson Hourihan	35.74	Sandra Lee	43.48	Sian Phillips	27.60
1980	Janet Covill	29.96	Sandra Lee	42.38	H Maybank	26.18
1981	Sandra Lee	44.92	Sian Phillips	29.80	Anwen Morgan	27.64
1982	Sarah Worthy	38.12	Vanessa Edwards	30.54	Amanda Barnes	30.24
1983	Sarah Worthy	38.34	Christine Lewis	31.76	Amanda Barnes	34.92
1985	Lisa Angulatta	30.30	Jayne Morgan-Berry	30.96	Elizabeth Bradbeer	30.24
1986	Carol Norton	32.70	Jane Davies	37.14	Jane Evans	24.30
1987	Jayne Berry	34.30	Jayne Fisher	34.08	Hayley Hartson	33.28
1988	Jayne Fisher	35.90	Hayley Hartson	36.28	Ruth Mason	25.70
1989	Jayne Fisher	37.92	Hayley Hartson	39.04	Vicky Todd	29.04
1990	Lyndsey Thomas	30.86	Claire James	29.44	Stephanie Codd	24.24
1991	Michelle Swan	31.58	Claire James	31.20	Philippa Roles	28.58
1992	Hilary Davies	32.68	Sarah Johnson	35.00	Philippa Roles	36.14
1993	Kelly Roberts	36.18	Philippa Roles	42.06	Vicky Page	31.18
1994	Lesley Brannan	36.36	Philippa Roles	43.80	Rebecca Roles	33.26
1995	Sarah Johnson	35.24	Rebecca Roles	36.64	Victoria Gibbons	31.92
1996	Philippa Roles	48.22	Rebecca Roles	36.04	Kate Everleigh	26.20
1997	Philippa Roles	50.48	Laura Eastwood	34.60	Laura Douglas	27.88
1998	Anwen James	34.23	Laura Douglas	33.45	Louise Finlay	26.02
1999	Anwen James	34.94	Laura Douglas	31.43	Mair Jones	23.82
2000	Laura Douglas	36.21	Ruth Morris	33.62	Rachel Cookson	23.12

Hammer

1993	Phillipa Burgess			
1994	Sheena Parry	35.68		
1995	Sheena Parry	42.66	Bethan Davies	22.66
1996	Philippa Roles	38.90	Carys Parry	37.32
1997	Marie Hughes	31.50	Carys Parry	40.94
1998	Carys Parry	47.88	Laura Douglas	36.15
1999	Carys Parry	49.11	Laura Douglas	45.54
2000	Laura Douglas	45.86	Hannah Lia	35.38

Javelin

1956	S Trist	24.53				
1957	A M Morgan	29.78			Rita Everett	27.56
1958	Elinor Joshua	32.56			G Evans	26.74
1959	O Crist	27.52			L Proctor	25.52
1960	O Crist	29.02			Rayann Jones	28.88
1961	Rayann Jones	29.22			Carol Roberts	26.72
1962	not known				not known	
1963	Rayann Jones	33.47			A Doyle	25.70
1964	Sheila Coleman	32.42			not known	
1965	Carol Roberts	36.34			R James	27.37
1966	not known				L Nicholas	30.06
1967	Jennifer Joseph	30.04	Janet Wady	32.66	J Cookson	26.74
1968	not known		not known		not known	
1969	Maureen Pearce	34.48	Margaret Rainbow	28.84	Susan James	30.92
1970	Janet Wady	30.71	Margaret Rainbow	34.11	Susan James	32.94
1971	Margaret Rainbow	33.70	Susan James	38.58	Yvonne Williamson	29.48
1972	Margaret Rainbow	37.36	J Boswell	29.78	Sonia Guzevicius	27.68
1973	Jane Lucas	30.77	Sonia Guzevicius		Ann Thomas	26.74
1974	J Warner	29.26	Alyson Hadfield	31.88	Deborah Morris	28.28

1975	Ruth Percival	29.90	Helen Kneath	35.14	Julie Simpson	27.16
1976	Ruth Percival	29.78	Debra Morris	31.40	Joanna Tubb	35.30
1977	Wendy Banks	34.98	Joanne Tubb	38.28	Jackie Flanagan	30.90
1978	Wendy Banks	35.17	Jane Jackson	35.20	Amanda Horrex	32.30
1979	Jane Jackson	36.22	Suzannah Pesticcio	36.22	Julie Tayler	36.10
1980	Suzannah Pesticcio	29.54	Stephanie Jones	35.56	Faye Jones	23.66
1981	Amanda Horrex	40.70	Hazel Lowe	34.26	Penny Miller	29.40
1982	Jackie Leonard	36.04	Penny Miller	34.98	Karen Hough	41.00
1983	Carol Thomas	35.60	Karen Hough	46.08	Catherine Gunn	32.56
1985	Sheila Evelyn	39.54	Catherine Gunn	38.86	Elizabeth Bradbeer	29.28
1986	Carol Morris	35.54	Sarah Phillips	34.60	Elizabeth Randle	28.28
1987	Catherine Gunn	40.96	Emma Thorne	36.68	Elizabeth Randle	30.02
1988	Jayne Berry	39.18	Onyema Amadi	36.24	Hilary Davies	31.34
1989	Stephanie Evans	31.28	Onyema Amadi	34.22	Hilary Davies	32.76
1990	Onyema Amadi	41.56	Joanne Evans	36.24	Donna Kelleher	33.70
1991	Nicola Nimmo	35.64	Hilary Davies	33.80	Joanne Griffiths	30.28
1992	Hilary Davies	37.42	Krissy Owen	34.84	Philippa Roles	28.18
1993	Hilary Davies	42.58	Philippa Roles	31.08	Rhian Hughes	29.28
1994	Hilary Davies	43.50	Keri Thomas	33.70	Claire Lockwood	36.72
1995	Joanna Griffiths	34.22	Rhian Hughes	38.76	Stacey Matthews	25.64
1996	Rhian Hughes	39.82	Claire Lockwood	37.96	Ffion Jones	25.48
1997	Claire Lockwood	37.94	Lynsey Stokes	33.72	Alison Siggery	29.96
1998	Tanya Jones	32.77	Kate Eveleigh	34.19	Alison Siggery	32.87
1999	Emily Skucek	38.01	Charlotte Rees	35.82	Amy Hall	29.97
2000	Emily Skucek	40.21	Charlotte Rees	40.92	Natalie Griffiths	30.57

Pentathlon

1993	not known		Abigail Jones	2557	Beth James	2584
1994	Claire Lewis	1038	Abigail Jones	2626	Kelly Moreton	2655
1995	Joanne Tomlinson	2275	Kristy Carlisle	2554	Lisa Thompson	2920
1996	Clare Anning	2348	Lisa Thompson	2945	Stephanie Little	2640
1997	Sarah Newman	2014	Lisa Thompson	3026	Rebecca Jones	2525
1998	Sarah Newman	2196	Megan Freeth	2855	Danielle Selley	3045
1999	Emily Skucek	2624	Rebecca Jones	3323	Sarah Evans	2491
2000	Rebecca Jones	3623	Helen Davies	2845	Fay Harding	2991

Walks

1998			Keirina Rowland	15:19.90	Lisa Munn	6:05.42
1999			Lisa Munn	12:18.3	Samantha Martin	5:54.94
2000			not held		Charlene Ball	5:42.6

BRITISH SCHOOLS INTERNATIONAL TRACK AND FIELD MATCHES

Individual Welsh male winners:

100 yards/metres: 1967 John J Williams, 1972 Steve Ware, 1982 Haydn Wood, 1995 Christian Malcolm.
220y/200m: 1967 John J Williams, 1972 Steve Ware, 1979 Malcolm James, 1982 Haydn Wood, 1995 Christian Malcolm.
440y/400m: 1962 Allan Skirving, 1979 Phil Harvey, 1983 Adrian Hardman.
800 metres: 1973 Tony Dyke, 1982 Paul Williams.
1,500 metres: 1975 Ian Williams, 1983 Neil Horsfield
Steeplechase: 1974 Steve Evans, 1987 Richard Baker.
High Hurdles: 1963 Howard Rooks, 1973 Neddyn Lloyd, 1989 Berian Davies
200y Hurdles: 1963 W Jones, 1964 G Lewis, 1965 John Lewis, 1967 Alun James.
400m Hurdles: 1988 Marvin Gray, 2000 Rhys Williams.
4x100m relay: Wales won in 1972, 1973, 1979
High Jump: 1966 Peter Lance, 1967 Peter Lance, 1968 Roger Stennett, 1991 Dafydd Edwards, 1994 Matthew Perry, 1995 Steven Francis, 1999 Chuka Enih-Snell, 2000 Chuka Enih-Snell
Long Jump: 1964 Tony Harry, 1966 John Elias, 1973 J Rees, 1979 John Furnham
Triple Jump: 1962 Gwyn Morgan Jones, 1982 Mickey Morris, 1983 Gareth Davies (Stanwell), 1987 Gareth Davies (Gowerton), 1997 Steven Shalders, 1998 Steven Shalders
Discus: 1976 Hugh James, 1982 Clive Jones
Javelin: 1975 Gareth Scales, 1983 Keith Marshall

Individual Welsh female winners:

100 metres: 1983 Helen Miles
200 metres: 1983 Helen Miles, 1989 Lisa Armstrong, 1998 Lowri Jones
400 metres: 1988 Nerys Evans
800 metres: 1978 Kirsty McDermott, 1983 Ellie Palmer, 1996 Amanda Pritchard
3,000 metres: 1980 Kath Williams

400m Hurdles:	1982 Alyson Evans, 1983 Alyson Evans
High Jump:	1999 Rebecca Jones
Long Jump:	1998 Aimee Cutler
Shot Put:	1982 Delyth Evans, 1993 Philippa Roles, 2000 Louise Finlay
Discus:	1980 Sandra Lee, 1993 Philippa Roles, 1994 Philippa Roles
Hammer:	1999 Laura Douglas
Javelin:	1970 Susan James, 1983 Karen Hough, 1984 Karen Hough
4x400:	Wales won in 1991

WELSH SCHOOLS INTER COUNTIES CROSS COUNTRY CHAMPIONSHIPS (1984 was an open event)

	Senior Boys	Middle Boys	Junior Boys	Senior Girls	Middle Girls	Junior Girls
1961	Peter Bate		Phil Morgan			
1962	Chris Loosley		D Lamb			
1963	Chris Loosley		Ian Jones			
1964	not known		not known			
1965	Cancelled due to bad weather					
1966	Gareth Davies		Frank Thomas			
1967	Gareth Davies		J Evans			
1968	Frank Thomas		Steve Seaman			
1969	Owen E Lewis		S Davies			
1970	I Armstrong		Tim Green			
1971	not known		not known			
1972	Nigel Hughes		not known	Ann Disley		
1973	Peter Baker	Micky Morris	A Morgan	A Price	not known	Jackie Hulbert
1974	Steve Rolfe	Steve Evans	Gary Keeble	Sheila Hayler	A Price	Margery Bevan
1975	Keith Jones	Tony Blackwell	Colin Clarkson	Ann Roblin	Siobhan Taylor	Carol Coles
1976	Keith Jones	Alan Cummings	Nick Morgan	Jane Clement	Debbie Lewis	Kirsty McDermott
1977	D Barrett	Gerwyn Davies	Richard Toms	Caroline Morgan	Kirsty McDermott	Gillian Irvine
1978	Robert Davies	Steve Blakemore	Ashley Halton	Debbie Lewis	Gillian Irvine	Kathy Williams
1979	Paul Miller	Richard Toms	Mark Griffiths	Claire Francis	Trudy Kenward	Jackie Thomas
1980	Andrew Smith	John Pimley	Nick Comerford	Beccy Powell	Trudy Kenward	Debbie Crowley
1981	Keith Noble	Brian Matthews	David Morgan	Kathy Williams	Fiona Harwood	Debbie Crowley
1982	Brian Matthews	Reuban Evans	Colin Hignell	Sally Jones	Debbie Crowley	Claire Pugh
1983	David Thomas	Paul Williams	Andrew Jones	Jane Swarbrick	Melanie Davies	Ceri Burnell
1984	Paul Williams	Colin Hignell	Gerallt Owen	Cathy Lock	Claire Pugh	Ceri Burnell
1985	Paul Williams	Justin Hobbs	Nicky Morse	Bev Morgan	Ceri Burnell	Lisa Carthew
1986	Andrew Jones	Bedwyr Huws	Paul Lewis	Laura MacLehose	Julie Crowley	Lisa Cobley
1987	Justin Hobbs	Stephen Glynn	Steven Blow	Ceri Burnell	Nicola Morgan	Sarah Griffiths
1988	Gerallt Owen	Paul Lewis	Anthony Jones	Carol Hayward	Clare Barnett	Joanne Elward
1989	Guto Eames	Neil Emberton	Nicky James	Vicky Harmer	Claire Barnett	Emma Davies
1990	Paul Lewis	Colin Jones	Carl Hyde	Joanne Parsons	Emma Davies	Anwen Evans
1991	Colin Jones	David Kelly	Alan Jones	Alison Morgan	Emma Parry	Angharad Howells
1992	Colin Jones	Ian Pierce	Matt Russell	Heidi Templeman	Viv Conneely	Samantha Gray
1993	Colin Jones	Damian Cuke	Matt Russell	Viv Conneely	Samantha Gray	Amanda Pritchard
1994	Nathaniel Lane	David Davey	Andrew Davies	Catherine Davies	Claire Thomas	Amanda Pritchard
1995	Andres Jones	Steve Lawrence	Scott Williams	Rachel O'Donnell	Claire Thomas	Kristy Doyle
1996	Alun Vaughan	Paul Gronow	Carl Prior	Julia Clarke	Rebecca Evans	Kristy Doyle
1997	Sion Meredith	Chris Davey	Matthew Jones	Amanda Pritchard	Laura Scott	Eleanor S Smith
1998	Paul Gronow	Daniel Beynon	Richard Kinsey	Lucy Kirby	Kristy Doyle	Eleanor S Smith
1999	Anthony Waters	David Jones	Luke Northall	Lucy Kirby	Eleanor S Smith	Hannah Wright
2000	Matthew Jones	Luke Northall	Mike Williams	Kristy Doyle	Amanda Jones	Faye Harding

WELSH SCHOOLS INTER SCHOOLS CROSS COUNTRY CHAMPIONSHIPS

In 1980 two events were held, one in March and the second in October. Thereafter the event was held in October and then in November from 1986.

Year	Senior Boys	Middle Boys	Junior Boys	Senior Girls	Middle Girls	Junior Girls
1977	Gary Keeble	Andrew West	Nigel Stops	Rebecca Wyatt	Kirsty McDermott	Becky Powell
1978	Stephen Smout	Peter Williams	Ridwaan Domingo	Rebecca Wyatt	Kirsty McDermott	Paula Thomas
1979	Ian Williams	Peter Williams	Mark Griffiths	Gillian Birchall	Becky Powell	Daintry Morgan
1980	Peter Williams	Brian Matthews	Nick Comerford	Becky Powell	Beverley Tucker	Debbie Crowley
1980	Keith Noble	Brian Matthews	Chris Phillips	Becky Powell	Fiona Harwood	Julie Thompson
1981	David Thomas	Paul Williams	Gareth Noble	Debbie Heaven	Fiona Harwood	Julie Jones
1982	Andrew Millard	Paul Williams	Julian Thomas	Tracy Thomas	Catherine Locke	Claire Pugh
1983	Nicholas Glynn	Colin Hignell	C Donovan	Jane Oldfield	Claire Pugh	Andrea Groves
1984	Nicholas Glynn	Justin Hobbs	Richard Baker	Bev Morgan	Ceri Burnell	Lisa Carthew
1985	not held					
1986	Chris Osbourne	Bedwyr Huws	Neil Emberton	Dawn Treadwell	Nicola Morgan	Mari Jones
1987	Gerallt Owen	Simon Williams	Chris Blount	Pippa Amat	Rebecca Evans	Sarah Olivant
1988	Gary Cutler	Neil Emberton	Matthew Fowles	Wendy Jones	Claire Barnett	Joanne Elward
1989	Colin Jones	Andrew Real	Stuart Jones	Rachael Parsons	Joanne Elward	Angharad Howell

1990	Colin Jones	Justin Thomas	Ceri Williams	Claire Schofield	Colleen Cerasuolo	Nina Hampshire
1991	Colin Jones	Robert Court	Steven Lawrence	Viv Conneely	A M Hutchinson	Heledd Gruffudd
1992	Paul Walby	David Carey	Andrew Davies	Charlotte Davies	Samantha Gray	Sherin Omed
1993	Andres Jones	Steven Lawrence	Duncan Hughes	A M Hutchinson	Dunya Hurley	Laura Jones
1994	Steven Lawrence	Andrew Davies	Nick Reid	Samantha Gray	Jackie Cadogan	Natalie Lewis
1995	Alun Vaughan	Scott Williams	Matthew Jones	Rebecca Evans	Teresa Penhorwood	Claire Evans
1996	Paul Kennedy	Matthew Jones	Richard Kinsey	Claire Thomas	Kristy Doyle	Gemma Thomas
1997	Nathan Boland	Matthew Jones	Charles L Harvey	Rebecca Evans	Eleanor S Smith	Fiona Harrison
1998	Matthew Jones	David Jones	Oliver Crocker	Laura Scott	Amanda Jones	Natasha Harry
1999	Cai Pierce	Luke Northall	Thomas James	Miriam Gaskell	Amanda Jones	Natalie Gill
2000	Alex Hains	Tom Page	Joe Thomas	Amanda Jones	Cara Dowden	Non Stanford

BRITISH SCHOOLS CROSS COUNTRY INTERNATIONAL

Highest placed Welsh athletes

		Intermediate Boys		Junior Boys		Intermediate Girls		Junior Girls
1972	04	Neil Roussell			07	Susan Tolan		
1973	09	Micky Morris			08	Sian Lode		
1974	08	Steve Evans			23	Jackie Hulbert		
1975	10	Tony Blackwell			13	Jane Clement		
1976	04	Colin Clarkson			11	Debbie Lewis		
1977	01	Colin Clarkson	05	Marcus Thomas	11	Debbie Lewis	07	Gillian Irvine
1978	06	Mike Bounds	12	Ashley Halton	13	Susan Davies	08	Kate Roderick
1979	13	Andrew Smith	05	Mark Griffiths	11	Kathy Williams	10	Jackie Thomas
1980	20	John McKeever	05	Nicky Comerford	11	Kathy Williams	05	Debbie Crowley
1981	17	Nicky Comerford	11	Nigel Sanders	15	Fiona Harwood	01	Debbie Crowley
1982	10	Nicky Comerford	09	Gareth Noble	10	Fiona Harwood	14	Angela Griffiths
1983	03	Paul Williams	07	Simon Taylor	13	Catherine Lock	12	Ceri Burnell
1984	17	Justin Hobbs	09	Gerallt Owen	10	Claire Pugh	08	Ceri Burnell
1985	03	Justin Hobbs	05	Nick Morse	11	J Morgan	05	Lisa Carthew
1986	10	Bedwyr Huws	07	Paul Lewis	14	Wendy McNamara	10	Julie Garrett
1987	08	Steven Glynn	10	Neil Emberton	15	Joanne Parsons	12	Mari Jones
1988	10	Paul Lewis	02	Jamie Williams	09	Claire Barnett	10	Claire Williams
1989	02	Carl Leonard	10	Jonathan Williams	10	Claire Barnett	11	Emma Davies
1990	10	Colin Jones	04	Justin Thomas	16	Rachael Parsons	10	Annemarie Hutchinson
1991	11	Justin Thomas	11	Alan Jones	19	Emma Parry	08	Angharad Howells
1992	10	Ian Pierce	11	Daniel Florence	06	Annemarie Hutchinson	10	Heledd Gruffudd
1993	13	Damian Cuke	08	Steve Lawrence	14	Samantha Gray	08	Heledd Gruffudd
1994	11	David Davey	13	James Enos	08	Heledd Gruffudd	05	Amanda Pritchard
1995	08	Steve Lawrence	03	Scott Williams	13	Claire Thomas	10	Teresa Penhorwood
1996	08	Andrew Davies	08	Elliot Cole	04	Rebecca Evans	05	Kristy Doyle
1997	11	Chris Davey	04	Matthew Jones	06	Kristy Doyle	06	Eleanor Sherrard Smith
1998	08	Daniel Beynon	06	William Wardell	07	Kristy Doyle	09	Eleanor Sherrard Smith
1999	14	David Jones	05	Luke Northall	13	Caroline Rimmer	07	Hannah Wright
2000	05	David Jones	14	Michael Williams	14	Amanda Jones	15	Faye Harding

Section 16

League Athletics (Welsh and UK)

WELSH LEAGUE – Welsh Men's Champions

Year	Div 1	Div 2	Div 3	Div 4	Div 5
1970	Swansea	East: Gilwern; West: Swansea B			
1971	Newport	Cardiff B			
1972	Newport	Rhondda	Cardiff C		
1973	Cardiff B	Gilwern	Bridgend YM		
1974	Carmarthen	Rhondda	Aberdare		
1975	Carmarthen	Aberdare			
1976	Newport	Cwmbran Olympiads	Newport B		
1977	Carmarthen	Rhondda	Aberystwyth		
1978	Carmarthen	Cardiff B	Port Talbot		
1979	Bridgend YM	Torfaen			
1980	Deeside	Barry & Vale			
1981	Swansea	Bridgend YM	Colwyn Bay		
1982	Swansea	Barry & Vale	Aberdare		
1983	Swansea	Carmarthen	Wrexham		
1984	Swansea	Cardiff B	Swansea B		
1985	Swansea	Wrexham	Aberdare	Brecon	
1986	Swansea	Colwyn Bay	Brecon		
1987	Swansea	Swansea B	Llanelli		
1988	Swansea	Llanelli	Rhymney Valley	Torfaen B	Llanelli B
1989	Colwyn Bay	Barry & Vale	Hereford	Crickhowell	Mercury
1990	Colwyn Bay	Torfaen	Crickhowell	Neath	Swansea C
1991	Colwyn Bay	Deeside	Neath	Swansea C	Port Talbot
1992	Colwyn Bay	Brecon	Colwyn Bay B	Rhymney Valley	Preseli
1993	Colwyn Bay	Llanelli	Rhymney Valley	Preseli	Wrexham
1994	Colwyn Bay	Swansea B	Maesteg	Ynys Mon	
1995	Deeside	Torfaen	Rhonnda	Lliswerry	
1996	Torfaen	Brecon	Lliswerry	Beddau	
1997	Torfaen	Wrexham	Rhondda	Preseli B	
1998	Colwyn Bay	Preseli	Newport B	Ynys Mon	

WELSH LEAGUE – Welsh Women's Champions

1976	Section A:	Newport	Section B: Cardiff	
1977	Cardiff	Swansea		
1978	Cardiff	Carmarthen		
1979	Cardiff	Torfaen		
1980	Cardiff	Port Talbot	Cardiff B	
1981	Cardiff	Wyeside	Cleddau	
1982	Cardiff	Cleddau	Brecon	
1983	Torfaen	Barry & Vale	Port Talbot	
1984	Cardiff	Colwyn Bay	Cardiff B	
1985	Swansea	Barry & Vale	Rhayader	
1986	Swansea	Colwyn Bay	Cleddau	Wrexham
1987	Cardiff	Newport	Wrexham	Rhymney Valley
1988	Swansea	Wrexham	Cleddau	Rhondda
1989	Wrexham	Carmarthen	Bridgend	Aberystwyth
1990	Wrexham	Bridgend	Neath	
1991	Carmarthen	Torfaen	Hereford	
1992	Swansea	Brecon		
1993	Swansea	Preseli		
1994	Wrexham	Swansea B		
1995	Newport	Brecon		
1996	Newport	Brecon		
1997	Preseli	Rhondda		
1998	Preseli	Llanelli		

WELSH LEAGUE – Combined Men's and Women's Champions

1999	Deeside	Torfaen	Neath	Newport B
2000	Deeside	Neath	Rhondda	Port Talbot

BRITISH MEN'S ATHLETICS LEAGUE – formed in 1969

Division One:	Cardiff champions in 1972, 1973, 1974	Cardiff second in 1969 and 1978	Cardiff third in 1970, 1971 and 1977
Division Three:	Cardiff champions in 1994	Swansea champions in 1998	
Division Four:	Swansea champions in 1971	Cardiff champions in 1993	

UK WOMEN'S LEAGUE – formed in 1975

Division Four: Cardiff champions in 1990 Swansea champions in 1995

GOLD CUP

British Athletics League knockout competition for senior men. First held in 1973 Cardiff won the competition in 1974 and were second in 1978 and third in 1976

JUBILEE CUP

Knockout competition for senior women. First held in 1974 No Welsh teams in the first three

PLATE FINALS

For Area League non-finalists who had progressed furthest in the qualifying rounds. Swansea won the men's plate competition in 1988Torfaen won the women's plate competition in 1989

Section 17

Officers of the Welsh Associations

OFFICERS OF THE WELSH CROSS COUNTRY ASSOCIATION

President: 1896-1912 William Fairlamb, 1912-1915 J P Mountjoy, 1919-1920 Frank Liddington Johns, 1920-1927 Harry Packer, 1927-1929 W H Facey, 1929-1931 Eddie O'Donnell, 1931-1932 A V J Mathias, 1932-1933 W H Facey, 1933-1935 Jack Pound, 1935-1937 J G Coombes, 1937-1938 Will Johnson, 1938-1945 Eddie O'Donnell, 1945-1947 Charles Radford, 1947-1949 F Hanger, 1949-1951 Roy Jones, 1951-1952 E Howard, 1952-1954 D J P Richards, 1954-1956 Bill Cook, 1956-1957 Frank Duggan, 1957-1958 Alan Radford, 1958-1959 Frank Duggan, 1959-1961 Ken Harris, 1961-1963 Ron B Evans, 1963-1965 Bernard Baldwin, 1965-1967 Tom Wood, 1967-1969 Derek Lakin, 1969-1971Ted Hopkins, 1971-1973 Alan Radford, 1973-1975 Hubert Gorvin, 1975-1986 George Crump, 1986-1989 Frank Ireland

Secretary: 1896-1900 Claude Hailey, 1900-1903 R A Pritchard, 1903-1907 Frank Liddington Johns, 1907-1909 Percy Mountjoy, 1909-1911 Eddie O'Donnell, 1911-1920 A V J Mathias, 1920-1926 Eddie O'Donnell, 1926-1928 T V Berry, 1928-1935 J G Coombes, 1935-1938 A Wade, 1938-1968 Ted Hopkins, 1968-1978 Graham Fraser, 1978-1989 John Collins

Treasurer: 1896-1900 Claude P Hailey, 1900-1903 R A Pritchard, 1903-1907 Frank Liddington Johns, 1907-1909 Percy Mountjoy, 1909-1910 Eddie O'Donnell, 1910-1927 Frank Liddington Johns, 1927-1937 Bill Fisher, 1937-1945 W R Butcher, 1945-1952 D J P Richards, 1952-1967 Alan Radford, 1967-1969 Tom Wood, 1969-1977 Derek Lakin,1977-1986 Sheila Crump, 1986-1989 John Griffiths

OFFICERS OF THE SOUTH WALES AND MONMOUTHSHIRE AAA

President: 1919-1939 Harry Packer, 1946 Frank Liddington Johns, 1947 Bill Fisher

Secretary: 1919-1922 A V J Mathias, 1922-1924 Eddie W O'Donnell, 1925-1929 A V J Mathias, 1930-1931 Jack Pound, 1932-1934 E J Styles, 1935-1937 E M Hughes, 1938-1947 Cyril Howell

Treasurer: 1919-1921 A V J Mathias, 1922-1947 Eddie W O'Donnell

OFFICERS OF THE WELSH AAA

President: 1948-1949 Eddie W O'Donnell, 1950-1953 Cyril Howell, 1954-1958 Bill Fisher, 1959-1976 Arthur Williams, 1976-1977 Frank Duggan, 1977-1979 Ken Harris, 1979-1981 Ron B Evans, 1981-1983 Reg Snow,1983-1985 Frank Ireland, 1985-1987 Ken Harris, 1987-1989 Barrie Owen, 1989-1990 Bill Evans

Secretary: 1948-1949 Cyril Howell, 1950-1962 J D B Williams, 1963-1966 Phil O Davies, 1967-1975 Bernard Baldwin, 1975-1990 Bill Evans

Treasurer: 1948-1956 Bill Fisher, 1957-1966 Ray Thomas, 1967-1974 Alan Radford, 1974-1980 D John Jones, 1980-1982 Ivor J Lewis, 1982-1990 Hedydd Davies

Chairman: 1970-1971 Ray Thomas, 1972-1973 Roy Jones, 1973-1980 Ron B Evans, 1980-1985 Ken Harris, 1985-1990 Frank Ireland

OFFICERS OF THE WELSH WOMEN'S AAA

President: 1959-1972 Margaret Lewis, 1973-1978 Roy Jones, 1979-1989 Raye Evans

Secretary: 1951-1953 Joan Cook, 1954-1955 Kay Watson, 1956-1967 Mari Davies, 1968 Irene Lisle, 1969-1971 Lynette Harries, 1972 Miss F Watts, 1973-1975 Raye Courtney, 1976-1989 Margaret Elgie

Treasurer: 1951-1953 Miss O Brind, 1954-1960 Joan Cook, 1961-1966 Mrs J Slatter, 1967-1976 Raye Evans, 1978-1989 Sally Blake

Chairman: 1951 Miss G Thomas, 1952-1953 Cyril Howell, 1954-1971 Roy Jones, 1972 Mrs Checketts, 1973-1989 Lynette Harries

OFFICERS OF THE WELSH WOMEN'S CROSS COUNTRY ASSOCIATION

Chairman: 1968-1974 Roy Jones

Secretary: 1968-1969 Irene Lisle, 1970-1974 Margaret Liddiard

Treasurer: 1968-1974 Raye Evans

OFFICERS OF THE ATHLETICS ASSOCIATION OF WALES

President: 1989-1992 Frank Ireland, 1992-1994 Les Davies, 1994-1996 George Crump,1996-1998 Hedydd Davies, 1998-2000 Tom Jones, 2000 Hedydd Davies

Secretary: 1989-1991 Bill Evans, 1991-1998 Barrie Owen, 1998-2000 Jan Evans

Treasurer: 1989-1994 Hedydd Davies, 1994-2000 Keith Matthews

Chairman: 1989-2000 Lynette Harries

OFFICERS OF THE WELSH SCHOOLS ATHLETICS ASSOCIATION

President: 1947-1976 Trevor Jenkins, 1977-1983 Jack O'Connell, 1984-1999 Charlie Hughes

Treasurer: 1947-1964 Jim Excell, 1965, 1966,1967 not known, 1968-1980 Jack O'Connell, 1981-1999 Charlie Hughes

Chairman: 1947-1952 Glyn John, 1953-1955 HVW Robinson, 1956, 1957, 1958 not known, 1959 E Humphreys, 1961 not known, 1962-1964 Jack King, 1965-1967 not known, 1968 A Roberts, 1969-1970 Mari Davies, 1971-1972 JDB Williams, 1973-1974 Rita Jones, 1975-1976 David Phillips, 1977-1978 Les Jones, 1979-1980 David Rees, 1981-1982 Trevor Lewis, 1983-1984 Frank Davies, 1985-1986 Gwyn Watts, 1987-1988 David Ball, 1989-1990 Derek Flye, 1991-1992 Nick Fisher, 1993-1994 John Phillips, 1995-1996 Tesni Davies, 1997-1998 Graham Webb, 1999-2000 Wynford Leyshon.

Secretary: 1947-1969 JDB Williams, 1970-1982 Norman George, 1983-1994 David Phillips, 1995-2000 Graham Coldwell.

Section 18
Honours and Awards

AWARD OF HONOUR

The Award of Honour was instigated by the Welsh AAA in 1952 for outstanding service over a long period to Welsh Athletics. In 1995 the AAW decided to reinstate this very special award to be presented in recognition of outstanding service to Welsh Athletics, usually for a period of at least 25 years.

1952	Eddie W O'Donnell, Frank Liddington Johns, William E Fisher, A Jack Pound, Arthur E Williams, Frank Duggan, Cyril M Howell, Ted Hopkins
1954	Welsh Schools AA
1956	Rev C P Hines, J D B Williams
1964	Lynn Davies
1975	Bernard Baldwin
1984	Ron B Evans
1988	Ken Harris, Bill Evans
1989	Reg Snow
1995	Alan Currie, Charlie Hughes, Frank Ireland, Bill Kingsbury
1996	Ivor Adams, John Collins, Raye Evans, Barrie Owen, Dave Williams
1997	Gerry Batty
1998	Hedydd Davies,
1999	Gwilym Evans, Mike Rowland
2000	Sally Blake, Margaret Elgie

MERITORIOUS PLAQUES

The Meritorious Plaque was instigated by the Welsh AAA and awarded to persons for services to Welsh Athletics. In 1990 the AAW decided to continue with the award which is presented for services to Welsh Athletics usually for at least 10 years.

1954	Jim Alford, Bill Cook, Rev C P Hines, Ken Jones, Roy Jones, Charles Radford, David J P Richards, Major G D Taylor, Ray Thomas, J D B Williams, Alf Yeoumans,
1955	Jack Meyrick, Harry Lewis, John Disley, Bob Shaw, Tom Richards, Will Johnson
1956	Matt Cullen, H King, Tom Mogford
1957	Jack P Collard, C T Wright
1958	K Cooper, Ron B Evans, Jim Guy, Ken Harris, D Owen
1959	P E Jones, Harry F Keene, G F Young
1960	J Harris, R G James, J B F Morgan, J G Thomas, Sam J Williams
1961	Len G Colledge, George M Hapgood, Ernie Jones, Jack Jones
1962	Ron Franklin, Llewellyn Harrison Jones, Derek Lakin, H V W Robinson, Reg Snow, Nick Whitehead
1963	Maurice Bingham, Hubert Gorvin, Percy Irwin, Bill Kingsbury, E Virgin, Dave J Williams
1964	No awards
1965	Frank Brown, J Donoghue, Alan C Radford
1966	Phil Davies, J H T Mason, Barrie Owen, R V Tawton, R C Townsend, H Owen
1967	Tom Wood
1968	George Crump. L Jones, Alun Jones, Graham Fraser, Norman Moses
1969	No awards
1970	Ivor Adams, J Carvell, John Collins, Gilbert Legge, Jim O'Brien, Hywel Williams
1971	John Flook, John Griffiths, Terry Notman, H Williams
1972	D Davies, B Jones, Clive Williams
1973	Bill Allen, Ann Batty, Brian Palmer, David Phillips, Berwyn Price, Dave J Roberts, Dave J Williams
1974	George Boardman, Bob Sercombe
1975	Brian Adamson, Alan Currie, Les Davies, Charlie Hughes, Gordon Rayner, Pat Wallace
1976	Roy Jones
1977	Raye Evans, Clifford Guy
1978	John Davies

1979	Bill Brian, Bill Evans, C Harrison, Norman John, D John Jones, T Thomas
1980	Gerry Batty, Eric Eynon, Mike Rowland
1981	Dave Hopkins, Rose Johnson
1982	Ivor Arnold, Steve Barry, Kath Evans, Viv Thomas
1983	Frank Ireland, Irene Lisle, Viv Pitcher
1984	Owen Edwards, Margaret Elgie, Ken Griffiths, Mrs I Jenkins, John Sammons
1985	Gwilym Evans, Steve Jones, Wyndham Smith
1986	Peter Morris, John Walsh
1987	John Elias, Paul Darney, Andrew Ireland, Colin Jackson, Sean Power, Alun Roper, Nigel Walker, Eirwyn Walters, Graham Webb
1988	Hedydd Davies, Edwin Llewellyn Eaton, Cen Stokes, Derek Tayler
1989	Arwyn Evans
1990	Lynnette Harries
1991	Kath Evans
1992	Colin Davies, Frank Ireland, Richard Jenkins
1993	Arthur Bebbington, Hedydd Davies, David Phillips, Ken Thomas
1994	David A Jones, David Williams
1995	Bill Powell
1996	Sally Blake, Brenda Currie, Arthur Davies, John Penny
1997	Bernard Harris, Dave Llewellyn
1998	Bill Burrows, Kay James, Anne Notman
1999	Frank Stringer, Averil Williams
2000	Terry Davies, David Jones

WELSH SPORTS HALL OF FAME

In October of 1981 an exhibition to commemorate Welsh sporting excellence was opened at the National Sports Centre, Cardiff, by Lynn Davies and Richard Meade, both Olympic gold medallists in their respective sports. The idea of a Welsh Sports Hall of Fame was first conceived by the noted BBC radio commentator G V Wynne-Jones. Later on Lord Brooks of Tremorfa took over as chairman and the exhibition was moved to the South Glamorgan County Council headquarters on Atlantic Wharf.

The Roll of Honour was instigated in 1989 and opened by Billy Boston of rugby league fame. He was one of the 10 original members among whom athletics was well represented with what could be described as two and a half entries. **Lynn Davies** and **Kirsty Wade** made the original list together with **Ken Jones** who, of course, excelled in athletics as well as rugby union. Since then an annual dinner has been held at which additions are made to the list of outstanding Welsh sportsmen and women.

In 1992 **Tanni Grey**, multi gold medallist at that year's Paralympic Games in Barcelona, was added to the list. The Hall of Fame had grown so much by 1994 that it became necessary to move the showcases for a third time, this time to the Museum of Welsh Life at St Fagan's. The athletics representation increased again in 1995 with the addition of **Jim Alford**. **Chris Hallam**, London Wheelchair Marathon winner was added in 1997, miler and steeplechaser **John Disley** in 1998 and **Theresa John**, one of the world's leading athletes for people with learning difficulties, in 2000.

BBC WALES SPORTS PERSONALITY OF THE YEAR

Instigated in 1954 the BBC Sports Personality of the Year awards have now become an established part of the sporting calendar and one of the highlights enjoyed by athletes of the Principality.

Colin Jackson leads the way for athletics by being one of only three men (Howard Winstone and Ian Woosnam being the others) to take the award three times. Lynn Davies and Tanni Grey have both scored twice while Tanni shares with Kirsty Wade the distinction of being the only women ever to win this coveted award.

In 1963 junior awards were introduced with one each for the outstanding junior male and female of the year. Kirsty Wade (1976) and Colin Jackson (1985) both won the junior award and then went on to take the senior plaudits as well.

Senior Awards:	1954	Ken Jones	1986	Kirsty Wade
	1955	John Disley	1988	Colin Jackson
	1964	Lynn Davies	1992	Tanni Grey
	1966	Lynn Davies	1993	Colin Jackson
	1973	Berwyn Price	1998	Iwan Thomas
	1982	Steve Barry	1999	Colin Jackson
	1985	Steve Jones	2000	Tanni Grey-Thompson
Junior Awards:	1969	Christine Craig	1985	Colin Jackson
	1972	Hugh Evans	1986	Karen Hough
	1974	Islwyn Rees	1998	Christian Malcolm
	1976	Kirsty McDermott		

ATHLETES OF THE CENTURY

In 2000 Ken Bennett, the AAW statistician conducted a poll within the sport inviting interested parties to nominate their choice of athletes of the century. Human nature dictates that most people will support those within their own memory span so that there will always be a tendency in this type of poll to favour the more recent athletes over those of the past.

There was considerable difference of opinion over the relative merits of a gold medal won at the Olympic Games and one at the World Championships. For many the Olympics is the pinnacle while others maintain that the World Championships is the athletics equal of the Olympics. It should be borne in mind, of course, that the World Championships were instigated in 1983 so that earlier athletes did not have the opportunity to compete on the world stage other than at the four yearly festival that is the Olympic Games. Nowadays athletes have 3 such chances in every 4 year period.

The result of the poll was that in the men's listings two athletes stood out above the rest but deciding between them was not easy. Colin Jackson (world record holder and twice world champion) just edged out Lynn Davies (Olympic champion) by a mere three votes. The women's was more clear-cut with Kirsty Wade an easy winner.

For interest the first five men and women are given with the number of votes cast for each.

Men:

1	Colin Jackson	164
2	Lynn Davies	161
3	Steve Jones	75
4	Iwan Thomas	71
5	John Disley	26

Women:

1	Kirsty Wade	190
2	Venissa Head	103
3	Angela Tooby	86
4	Kay Morley	73
5	Michelle Scutt	64

Section 19

Welsh Winners of AAA and UK Titles

Names listed at end of each section are athletes who became champions either before taking up their Welsh eligibility or after relinquishing it.

AAA SENIOR MEN

1890	Tom Nicholas	440 yards	51.8
1898	Fred Cooper	100 yards	10.0
1902	A B Manning	880 yards	1:59.8
1906	Alf Yeoumans	2 m walk	14:20.4
1913	Ben Uzzell	220 y hurdles	
1921	John Evans	2 m walk	14:40.2
1923	Cecil Griffiths	880 yards	1:56.6
1925	Cecil Griffiths	880 yards	1:57.2
1930	Reg Thomas	One mile	4:15.2
1931	Reg Thomas	One mile	4:16.4
1933	Reg Thomas	One mile	4:14.2
1939	Sam Palmer	6 miles	30:06.4
1952	John Disley	2m s/chase	9:44.0
1955	John Disley	3K s/chase	8:56.6
1955	Bob Shaw	440y hurdles	52.2
1957	John Disley	3K s/chase	8:56.8
1957	Hywel Williams	Decathlon	5370
1963	Berwyn Jones	100 yards	9.71
1964	Lynn Davies	Long Jump	7.95w
1965	Birchgrove Harriers	4 x 1m relay	16:59.8
1966	Lynn Davies	Long Jump	8.06
1967	Lynn Davies	Long Jump	7.93
1968	Lynn Davies	Long Jump	7.94
1969	Ron Jones	100 metres	10.7
1969	Gwynne Griffiths	400 metres	46.77
1969	Lynn Davies	Long Jump	7.62
1972	Bernie Plain	10 miles	48:25.8
1973	Berwyn Price	110m hurdles	14.10
1974	John Davies	3K s/chase	8:26.8
1974	Berwyn Price	110m hurdles	13.94w
1975	Berwyn Price	110m hurdles	13.94
1976	Berwyn Price	110m hurdles	13.80w
1977	Berwyn Price	110m hurdles	14.17
1978	Berwyn Price	110m hurdles	14.14
1980	Roger Hackney	3K s/chase	8:39.38
1980	Steve Barry	3K walk	12:00.44
1981	Steve Barry	10K walk	43:22.4
1982	Roger Hackney	3K s/chase	8:28.98
1982	Steve Barry	10K walk	41:14.7
1983	Steve Barry	10K walk	40:54.7
1984	Steve Jones	10K	28:09.97
1984	Nigel Walker	110m hurdles	13.78
1986	Colin Jackson	110m hurdles	13.51
1987	Paul Edwards	Shot	17.26
1988	Colin Jackson	110m hurdles	13.29
1989	Colin Jackson	110m hurdles	13.19
1990	Neil Horsfield	1500 metres	3:44.70
1990	Colin Jackson	110m hurdles	13.23
1990	Paul Edwards	Shot	19.00
1992	Colin Jackson	110m hurdles	13.15
1993	Colin Jackson	110m hurdles	13.15
1994	Justin Chaston	3K s/chase	8:28.28
1996	Justin Chaston	3K s/chase	8:29.19

1996	Colin Jackson	110m hurdles	13.13
1997	Tim Thomas	Pole Vault	5.30
1998	Iwan Thomas	400 metres	44.50
1998	Nick Comerford	3000 metres	8:11.98
1998	Christian Stephenson	3K S/Chase	8:23.76
1998	Colin Jackson	110m hurdles	13.37
1998	Paul Gray	400m hurdles	49.81
1999	Jamie Baulch	400 metres	45.36
1999	Christian Stephenson	3K s/chase	8:44.42
1999	Colin Jackson	110m hurdles	13.24w
1999	Paul Jones	Decathlon	6922
2000	Andres Jones	5000 metres	13:45.86
2000	Andres Jones	10K	28:00.50
2000	Christian Stephenson	3K s/chase	8:28.21
2000	Colin Jackson	110m hurdles	13.54

Bob Roberts (1970 400H 52.42), Paul Edwards (1991 Shot 18.92, 1992 Shot 19.08), Colin Mackenzie (1993 Javelin 81.44)

UK SENIOR MEN

1975	Cardiff AAC	4 x 100m	44.0
1977	Berwyn Price	110m hurdles	14.19
1978	Berwyn Price	110m hurdles	13.93w
1978	Ken Cocks	Long Jump	7.56
1981	Steve Barry	10K walk	42:32.43
1982	Roger Hackney	3K s/chase	8:31.52
1982	Steve Barry	10K walk	42:30.72
1982	Trevor Llewelyn	High Jump	2.16
1983	Nigel Walker	110m hurdles	14.48
1983	Steve Barry	10K walk	41:14.38
1986	Colin Jackson	110m hurdles	13.73
1987	Neil Horsfield	1500 metres	3:43.69
1988	Phil Harries	400m hurdles	50.01
1989	Colin Jackson	110m hurdles	13.18w
1989	Paul Edwards	Shot	17.89
1990	Neil Horsfield	1500 metres	3:48.39
1990	Colin Jackson	110m hurdles	13.10
1990	Paul Edwards	Shot	18.57
1991	Ian Hamer	5000 metres	13:49.86
1992	Colin Jackson	110m hurdles	13.43
1993	Neil Winter	Pole Vault	5.35
1997	Iwan Thomas	400 metres	44.36
1997	Shaun Pickering	Shot	19.25

Paul Edwards (1991 Shot 18.68, 1992 Shot 18.77, 1993 Shot 19.06)

AAA SENIOR MEN INDOORS

1963	Lynn Davies	Long Jump	7.48
1966	Lynn Davies	Long Jump	7.85
1967	Ron McAndrew	2K s/chase	5:42.4
1969	Gwynne Griffiths	400 metres	48.9
1969	Bob Adams	800 metres	1:51.1
1970	Gwynne Griffiths	400 metres	49.0
1970	Ron McAndrew	2K s/chase	5:36.8
1971	Phil Lewis	800 metres	1:50.2
1971	Bernie Hayward	2K s/chase	5:34.8
1971	Berwyn Price	60m hurdles	7.9
1972	Ron McAndrew	2K s/chase	5:32.4
1972	Lynn Davies	Long Jump	7.51
1973	Ron McAndrew	2K s/chase	5:36.8
1974	Clive Thomas	1500 metres	3:53.4
1975	Dave Roberts	60 metres	6.84
1975	Berwyn Price	60m hurdles	8.01
1976	Phil Lewis	800 metres	1:50.0
1976	Berwyn Price	60m hurdles	8.1
1977	Peter Griffiths	2K s/chase	5:34.2
1978	Berwyn Price	60m hurdles	7.90
1979	Paul Williams (Camb)	1500 metres	3:46.6
1980	Mal Edwards	1500 metres	3:46.9
1980	Andrew McIver	High Jump	2.15
1981	Roger Hackney	1500 metres	3:44.4
1984	Phil Norgate	800 metres	1:50.27
1986	Alan Tapp	60m hurdles	7.96
1987	Mal Edwards	1500 metres	3:47.52
1988	Paul Edwards	Shot	17.78
1988	Gareth Brown	1500 metres	3:56.12

1989	Colin Jackson	60m hurdles	7.52
1990	Colin Jackson	60m hurdles	7.43
1990	Paul Edwards	Shot	17.79
1991	Paul Edwards	Shot	18.58
1992	Colin Jackson	60m hurdles	7.55
1993	Colin Jackson	60m hurdles	7.55
1995	Paul Gray	60m hurdles	7.83
1996	Doug Turner	200 metres	21.06
1996	Shaun Pickering	Shot	17.88
1997	Jamie Baulch	200 metres	20.84
1997	Colin Jackson	60m hurdles	7.54
1998	Joe Mills	1500 metres	3:50.30
1998	Shaun Pickering	Shot	18.95
1999	Colin Jackson	60m hurdles	7.59
2000	Christian Malcolm	200 metres	20.74
2000	Paul Jones	Octathlon	5277

Peter Templeton (1967 Long Jump 7.25), Mal Edwards (1979 800m 1:51.9), Paul Edwards (1992 Shot 19.15, 1993 Shot 18.47, 1994 Shot 18.95), Lee Newman (1995 Shot 17.30, 1997 Shot 18.10)

AAA U23 MEN

1999	Christian Malcolm	100 metres	10.20w
1999	Christian Malcolm	200 metres	21.01
1999	James Hillier	400m hurdles	51.30
2000	Matthew Elias	400m hurdles	51.51
2000	Robert Mitchell	High Jump	2.19

AAA U20 JUNIOR MEN

1947	Neville Jones	100 yards	10.2
1947	Neville Jones	Long Jump	6.00
1950	Norman Finch	High Jump	1.78
1951	Bob Shaw	120y hurdles	14.7
1951	Bob Shaw	Discus	41.88
1952	Gareth Lewis	1 mile walk	6:53.6
1953	David Pulsford	220 yards	22.9
1953	Gareth Howell	1 mile walk	6:49.9
1954	Gareth Howell	1 mile walk	6:54.0
1955	Bryan Woolley	Long Jump	6.81
1956	Mike Shannon	1 mile walk	7:07.4
1956	Aneurin Evans	Triple Jump	13.71
1957	Mike Shannon	1 mile walk	6:55.3
1958	John Davies	Shot	16.41
1959	Tony Harris	880 yards	1:54.3
1959	John Davies	Shot	16.20
1960	Tony Harris	880 yards	1:55.4
1961	Lynn Davies	Triple Jump	13.76
1964	John Lewis	120y hurdles	14.2w
1967	Tony Simmons	2 miles	8:50.34
1968	Peter Lewis	880 yards	1:54.4
1969	Berwyn Price	110m hurdles	14.7
1972	Stephen Bailey	100 metres	11.2
1973	Tony Dyke	800 metres	1:52.0
1973	Steve James	400m hurdles	54.1
1974	Tony Dyke	800 metres	1:51.1
1975	Micky Morris	2K s/chase	5:37.8
1976	Jeff Griffiths	400 metres	47.2
1976	Rupert Goodall	Pole Vault	4.40
1980	Nigel Walker	110m hurdles	15.07
1980	Colin Mackenzie	Javelin	71.46
1981	Nigel Walker	110m hurdles	14.47
1982	Colin Mackenzie	Javelin	70.28
1983	Andrew Rodgers	2K s/chase	5:43.18
1983	John Hill	High Jump	2.10
1984	Paul Williams (Barry)	800 metres	1:51.46
1984	Neil Horsfield	1500 metres	3:45.85
1985	Paul Williams (Barry)	800 metres	1:52.68
1985	Neil Horsfield	1500 metres	3:47.38
1985	Colin Jackson	110m hurdles	14.17
1985	Phil Harries	400m hurdles	54.63
1985	John Hill	High Jump	2.13
1987	Paul Gray	110m hurdles	14.08
1988	Paul Gray	110m hurdles	14.39
1990	Richard Harbour	110m hurdles	14.27w
1990	Neil Winter	Pole Vault	5.00

1991	Richard Harbour	110m hurdles	14.67
1992	Neil Winter	Pole Vault	5.35
1993	Neil Winter	Pole Vault	5.40
1995	Jamie Henthorn	100 metres	10.64
1996	Christian Malcolm	200 metres	21.32
1996	Andres Jones	5000 metres	14:39.57
1996	Mark Rowlands	400m hurdles	52.38
1997	Christian Malcolm	200 metres	20.48w
1997	Alun Vaughan	5000 metres	15:29.76
1997	Mark Rowlands	400m hurdles	51.88
1998	Christian Malcolm	100 metres	10.17w
1998	Christian Malcolm	200 metres	20.32w
1999	Steven Shalders	Long Jump	7.23
2000	Tim Benjamin	200 metres	20.95w
2000	Steven Shalders	Triple Jump	15.12

Tony Ashton (1964 1500 steeplechase 4:19.7), Colin ÓíNeill (1966 Long Jump 6.99w), Ron Griffiths (1969 200m 21.7), Paul Williams (1974 1500m 3:53.7), Milton Palmer (High Jump 1974 2.01, 1975 2.00, 1976 2.11, 1977 2.10), Lee Newman (1992 Discus 51.22), Robert Mitchell (1999 High Jump 2.14)

AAA U20 JUNIOR MEN INDOORS

1968	Phil Lewis	800 metres	1:54.2
1970	Adrian Thomas	60 metres	6.8
1971	Cardiff AAC	Medley relay	4:40.2
1972	Stephen Ware	400 metres	50.0
1973	Paul Evans	60 metres	7.0
1973	Tony Dyke	800 metres	1:52.6
1974	Gareth Edwards	60 metres	6.8
1976	Kevin Glastonbury	1500 metres	3:54.0
1977	Kevin Glastonbury	1500 metres	3:55.0
1978	Colin Clarkson	1500 metres	3:55.9
1981	Nigel Walker	60m hurdles	8.2
1982	Nigel Walker	60m hurdles	8.01
1983	John Hill	High Jump	2.01
1985	Colin Jackson	60m hurdles	7.99
1988	Justin Hobbs	3000 metres	8:23.03
1991	Steve Rees	200 metres	22.08
1992	Peter Maitland	60 metres	6.82
1992	Neil Winter	Pole Vault	5.00
1994	James Archampong	60m hurdles	8.01
1994	Ian Wilding	Pole Vault	4.70
1995	James Archampong	60m hurdles	8.08
1997	Christian Malcolm	200 metres	21.26
1998	Christian Malcolm	60 metres	6.82
1998	Christian Malcolm	200 metres	21.43
1998	Gareth Beard	800 metres	1:53.13
1998	Ben Roberts	Pentathlon	3254
2000	Tim Benjamin	60 metres	6.83
2000	Tim Benjamin	200 metres	21.06

Steve James (1972 60m hurdles 8.2), Mal Edwards (1975 800m 1:55.0),
Milton Palmer (1976 High Jump 2.03), Garry Slade (1987 Long Jump 7.32)

AAA U17 MEN

1968	Adrian Thomas	100 yards	10.0w
1971	Tony Dyke	800 metres	1:58.0
1972	Tony Dyke	800 metres	1:55.0
1972	Gareth Brooks	Javelin	54.42
1974	Steve Evans	1500 s/chase	4:18.1
1977	Colin Clarkson	2 miles	8:34.8
1978	David Jones	400m hurdles	56.01
1979	Malcolm James	200 metres	22.06w
1979	Malcolm James	400 metres	50.2
1980	Michael Powell	High Jump	2.00
1982	Paul Williams (Barry)	800 metres	1:53.37
1983	Adrian Hardman	400 metres	49.09
1983	Neil Horsfield	1500 metres	3:55.09
1983	Nathan Kavanagh	3K walk	13:12.84
1984	Jonathan Clarke	Javelin	60.26
1986	Russell Hutchings	10K walk	47:53.45
1986	Marcus Browning	Long Jump	6.62
1989	Berian Davies	100m hurdles	13.01w
1989	Neil Winter	Pole Vault	4.40
1990	Neil Winter	Pole Vault	5.00
1994	Mark Rowlands	400m hurdles	53.30

1995	Christian Malcolm	100 metres	10.85
1995	Steven Lawrence	3000 metres	8:52.59
1997	Steven Shalders	Triple Jump	14.04
1998	Tim Benjamin	200 metres	21.15w
1998	Nathan Palmer	100m hurdles	12.96w
1998	Chris Type	Pole Vault	4.35
1998	Steven Shalders	Triple Jump	15.38w
2000	Adam Davies	800 metres	1:56.50
2000	Rhys Williams	400m hurdles	54.92
2000	Chuka Enih-Snell	High Jump	2.06

Paul Williams – Cambridge (1972 1500m 4:00.1)

AAA U17 MEN INDOORS

1970	Stephen Ware	200 metres	24.0
1971	Paul Evans	60 metres	7.1
1972	Tony Dyke	800 metres	2:00.0
1972	Stephen Kohut	Long Jump	6.44
1979	Phil Harvey	400 metres	50.7
1979	John Furnham	Long Jump	6.67
1992	Andrew Davies	Long Jump	6.17
1995	Christian Malcolm	60 metres	6.96
1995	Christian Malcolm	200 metres	22.25
1996	James Morris	Long Jump	6.54
1997	Tim Benjamin	200 metres	22.43
1998	Tim Benjamin	200 metres	21.51
1998	Nathan Palmer	60m hurdles	8.23
1998	Chris Type	Pole Vault	4.20
1998	Steven Shalders	Triple Jump	14.42
1998	James Anthony	Pentathlon	3360
1999	Chuka Enih-Snell	High Jump	2.02
2000	Adam Davies	800 metres	1:58.86
2000	Stephen Davies	1500 metres	4:06.02
2000	Chuka Enih-Snell	High Jump	2.07

Mal Edwards (1974 800m 1:55.6), Paul Farmer (1986 Triple Jump 13.62), Matthew Bundock (1993 Shot 14.96) Cameron Johnson (1999 Pole Vault 4.20)

AAA U15 BOYS

1992	Russell Cartwright	800 metres	2:05.04
1992	Richard Crayford	Triple Jump	12.28
1994	Jamie Dalton	High Jump	1.84
1995	Mike Ferraro	Triple Jump	12.39
1996	Liam Walsh	Discus	45.88
1998	Chuka Enih-Snell	High Jump	1.95
1998	Chuka Enih-Snell	Pentathlon	3039
2000	Daniel Segerson	High Jump	1.79
2000	Thomas Rees	Javelin	47.33

AAA U15 BOYS INDOORS

1994	Kevin Drury	High Jump	1.80
1996	Liam Walsh	Shot	13.84
1997	Adam Wrench	Long Jump	5.48
1998	Chuka Enih-Snell	High Jump	1.91

AAA SENIOR WOMEN

1974	Ruth Martin Jones	Long Jump	6.26
1978	Jill Davies	Long Jump	6.19
1980	Michelle Probert	400 metres	51.94
1982	Michelle Probert/Scutt	400 metres	51.05
1983	Michelle Scutt	200 metres	23.17
1984	Sarah Owen	Heptathlon	5150
1988	Kirsty Wade	800 metres	2:01.52
1988	Angela Tooby	10K	33:13.95
1995	Catherine Murphy	200 metres	23.40
1999	Hayley Tullett	1500 metres	4:08.06
2000	Hayley Tullett	1500 metres	4:06.44

Barbara Ann King (1983 10K 35:19.86), Lea Haggett (High Jump 1990 1.88, 1992 1.89, 1995 1.85)

UK SENIOR WOMEN

1977	Hilary Hollick	1500 metres	4:13.0
1977	Venissa Head	Shot	15.72
1978	Hilary Hollick	1500 metres	4:14.08
1979	Jackie Zaslona	Javelin	53.32
1981	Venissa Head	Shot	17.62

1981	Venissa Head	Discus	45.20
1982	Michelle Scutt	400 metres	50.63
1983	Venissa Head	Shot	17.69
1983	Venissa Head	Discus	60.62
1984	Angela Tooby	5000 metres	15:27.56
1984	Venissa Head	Discus	57.44
1985	Angela Tooby	5000 metres	15:28.00
1986	Venissa Head	Discus	55.74
1988	Melissa Watson	3000 metres	9:04.85
1988	Venissa Head	Discus	53.66
1989	Susan Tooby	5000 metres	16:04.99
1989	Kay Morley Brown	100m hurdles	13.15
1990	Sallyanne Short	100 metres	11.36w
1990	Kay Morley Brown	100m hurdles	13.16w
1992	Kay Morley Brown	100m hurdles	13.59
1997	Sarah Moore	Hammer	56.60

Lea Haggett (1991 High Jump 1.85)

AAA SENIOR WOMEN INDOORS

1965	Liz Gill	60 yards	6.9
1966	Gloria Dourass	440 yards	58.0
1971	Ruth Martin Jones	Long Jump	6.02
1972	Jean Lochhead	1500 metres	4:26.9
1973	Jean Lochhead	1500 metres	4:30.6
1981	Carmen Smart	200 metres	24.5
1981	Kirsty McDermott	800 metres	2:07.1
1981	Thelywn Bateman	3000 metres	9:44.7
1983	Venissa Head	Shot	17.67
1985	Carmen Smart	200 metres	24.44
1985	Kirsty McDermott	800 metres	2:02.70
1986	Kirsty McDermott/Wade	800 metres	2:03.09
1987	Kirsty Wade	1500 metres	4:09.26
1994	Kirsty Wade	800 metres	2:05.60
1996	Catherine Murphy	200 metres	23.69
1997	Hayley Parry	800 metres	2:04.14
1998	Hayley Parry	800 metres	2:02.91
2000	Emma Davies	800 metres	2:07.34

Thelwyn Bateman (1980 3K 9:37.4), Lea Haggett (1995 High Jump 1.88)

AAA U23 WOMEN

1999	Emma Davies	800 metres	2:09.65
1999	Philippa Roles	Discus	55.08
2000	Emma Davies	800 metres	2:07.38
2000	Philippa Roles	Discus	51.79

AAA U20 JUNIOR WOMEN

1987	Lisa Griffiths	100m hurdles	14.66
1989	Jayne Berry	Shot	13.66
1992	Bethan Edwards	100m hurdles	14.05
1992	Lisa Armstrong	Long Jump	6.15
1994	Julie Crane	High Jump	1.78
1995	Philippa Roles	Shot	14.11
1996	Amanda Pritchard	800 metres	2:07.59
1996	Rhian Clarke	Pole Vault	3.50
1996	Philippa Roles	Shot	13.76
1997	Philippa Roles	Discus	50.94
1997	Emma Davies	800 metres	2:07.11

Lea Haggett (High Jump 1990 1.84, 1991 1.84), Rhian Clarke (1995 Pole Vault 3.40)

AAA U20 JUNIOR WOMEN INDOORS

1985	Helen Miles	60 metres	7.55
1988	Carol Whiteway	60m hurdles	9.08
1989	Jayne Berry	Shot	14.54
1990	Lisa Armstrong	200 metres	25.11
1991	Lisa Armstrong	60 metres	7.48
1992	Bethan Edwards	60m hurdles	8.47
1995	Philippa Roles	Shot	13.72
1995	Teresa Andrews	Pentathlon	3564
1996	Emma Davies	800 metres	2:13.08
1997	Emma Davies	800 metres	2:08.55
1997	Rebecca Roles	Pole Vault	3.10
2000	Lowri Jones	200 metres	24.60
2000	Rebecca Jones	Pentathlon	3236

AAA U17 WOMEN

1971	Paula Lloyd	400 metres	56.2
1973	Gillian Regan	Long Jump	5.56
1976	Carmen Smart	100 metres	12.04
1977	Sian Waters	400 metres	55.53
1978	Kirsty McDermott	800 metres	2:07.74
1979	Sarah Rowe	Heptathlon	3786
1981	Karen Nipper	2500m walk	14:59.32
1983	Karen Hough	Javelin	45.92
1984	Sallyanne Short	100 metres	11.88
1984	Sallyanne Short	200 metres	24.21w
1984	Karen Hough	Javelin	46.30
1989	Bethan Edwards	80m hurdles	11.46
1992	Krissy Owen	Heptathlon	4440
1993	Angharad Richards	Javelin	46.20
1994	Jayne Ludlow	Triple Jump	11.14
1994	Philippa Roles	Shot	12.82
1994	Philippa Roles	Discus	44.40
1995	Jayne Ludlow	Triple Jump	11.76w
1995	Sian Lax	Javelin	44.78
1998	Aimee Cutler	Long Jump	5.84w
1999	Rebecca Jones	High Jump	1.79
1999	Lara Richards	Long Jump	5.82w
1999	Lara Richards	Triple Jump	11.60w
1999	Laura Douglas	Hammer	42.78
2000	Danielle Selley	100 metres	12.00

Michelle Probert (1976 200m 23.6), Lea Haggett (1987 High Jump 1.75, 1988 High Jump 1.77) Jessica Mills (1990 3K 10:15.25), Julie Crane (1993 High Jump 1.70)

AAA U17 WOMEN INDOORS

1970	Gaynor Blackwell	60m hurdles	9.3
1973	Gillian Regan	Long Jump	5.71
1990	Lisa Armstrong	60 metres	7.64
1990	Lisa Armstrong	200 metres	25.32
1992	Nicola Jupp	High Jump	1.73
1994	Jayne Ludlow	Triple Jump	11.74
1994	Philippa Roles	Shot	13.26
1995	Gael Davies	300 metres	40.58
1998	Aimee Cutler	Long Jump	5.70
1999	Danielle Selley	60 metres	7.70
2000	Samantha Gamble	200 metres	24.93
2000	Samantha Gamble	300 metres	40.22

Diane Heath (1973 60m 7.8), Jane Falconer (1990 High Jump 1.76),
Emma Davies (1995 800m 2:16.36), Jennifer Mockler (1997 1500m 4:38.53, 1998 1500m 4:35.33)

AAA U15 GIRLS

1970	Susan James	Javelin	39.14
1976	Kirsty McDermott	800 metres	2:11.1
1979	Julie Tayler	Javelin	33.48
1980	Julia Charlton	High Jump	1.70
1982	Karen Hough	Javelin	38.70
1983	Jane Shepherd	Shot	11.37
1983	Jane Shepherd	Pentathlon	3671
1986	Lea Haggett	High Jump	1.81
1988	Lisa Armstrong	200 metres	25.53
1988	Lisa Armstrong	Long Jump	5.30
1991	Teresa Andrews	Pentathlon	2888
1992	Philippa Roles	Shot	12.85
1992	Philippa Roles	Discus	42.06
1994	Amanda Pritchard	800 metres	2:12.2
1997	Lauren McLoughlin	75m hurdles	11.42
1997	Rebecca Jones	Pentathlon	2811
1998	Danielle Selley	100 metres	12.15
1998	Danielle Selley	75m hurdles	11.08
2000	Heather Jones	75m hurdles	11.1

Jean Davies (1962 Shot 11.49), Jane Falconer (1988 High Jump 1.68, 1989 High Jump 1.73, 1989 Pentathlon 2874), Catherine Murphy (1990 200m 25.53w), Angharad Richards (1991 Javelin 38.78)

AAA U15 GIRLS IND OORS

1984	Amanda Barnes	Shot	11.49
1989	Susannah Filce	High Jump	1.68
1989	Susannah Filce	Pentathlon	3064

1991	Jodi Lester	60m hurdles	9.28
1993	Charlotte Reeks	800 metres	2:21.22
1994	Sarah Mead	800 metres	2:18.19
1997	Lauren McLoughlin	60m hurdles	9.16
1998	Danielle Selley	60 metres	7.77
1998	Danielle Selley	60m hurdles	8.94
1998	Danielle Selley	Pentathlon	3229
1999	Lucy Thomas	800 metres	2:19.31

Catherine Murphy (1990 60m 7.85, 200m 26.27), Jennifer Mockler (1996 800m 2:20.49)

ROAD RUNNING

all AAA events except where indicated

1978	Tony Simmons	Marathon	2:12:33
1983	Angela Tooby	10 miles	55:31
1983	Cardiff AAC	4Stage SW Relay	39:01
1984	Steve Jones	10K	27:59
1985	Steve Jones	Half Marathon	61:14
1985	Steve Jones	Marathon	2:08:16
1988	Swansea Harriers	6 Stage SM Relay	2:26:05
1989	Trevor Hawes	100K	6:43:55
1990	Chris Buckley	10 miles	48:15
1991	Nigel Adams	10K	28:50
1991	Nigel Adams	10 miles	47:14
1991	Steve Brace	Half Marathon	63:50
1991	Swansea Harriers	6 Stage SM Relay	1:47:32
1993	Justin Hobbs	10K	28:45
1993	Christian Stephenson	BAF Junior 10K	30:41
1993	Steve Brace	Half Marathon	65:00
1994	Justin Hobbs	10K	29:07
1994	Wendy Ore	BAF 10K	33:41
1994	Swansea Harriers	12 Stage SM Relay	4:06:26
1995	Steve Knight	10 miles	51:08
1996	Justin Hobbs	Half Marathon	63:41
1998	Christian Stephenson	BAF 10K	29:28
1999	Mark Morgan	10K	29:13
1999	Cardiff AAC	6 Stage SM Relay	1:42:46

RACE WALKING ASSOCIATION

1981	Russell Hutchings	U13B 3K	16:03
1981	Nathan Kavanagh	U15B 3K	13:58
1981	Bob Dobson	30K	2:48:30
1982	Steve Barry	10 miles	1:08:01
1982	Steve Barry	20K	1:25:51
1983	Steve Barry	10 miles	1:06:41
1983	Steve Barry	20K	1:23:15
1983	Nathan Kavanagh	U17M 5K	22:39
1984	Kirk Taylor	U17M 5K	22:42
1988	Splott RWC	30K Road Relay	2:20:58
1988	Splott RWC	10 miles	51 points
1988	Gareth Holloway	U20M 10K	46:25
1989	Splott RWC	10 miles	26 points
1990	Splott RWC	20K	31 points
1992	Splott RWC	10 miles	20 points

Bob Dobson (30K 1973 2:40:07 1975 2:36:26, 50K 1970 4:20:22 1973 4:14:29 1974 4:16:58)

MOST CHAMPIONSHIPS

The following lists are based on all the championships listed above
but do not include wins by athletes who were not eligible at the time.

Men

22	Colin Jackson
13	Christian Malcolm
13	Berwyn Price
11	Steve Barry
09	Lynn Davies
07	Paul Edwards
07	Neil Winter
06	Tim Benjamin
06	Tony Dyke
06	Chuka Enih Snell
06	Neil Horsfield
06	Nigel Walker

Women

11	Philippa Roles
09	Venissa Head
08	Kirsty McDermott/Wade
07	Lisa Armstrong
07	Danielle Selley
06	Emma Davies
04	Michelle Probert/Scutt
04	Angela Tooby
04	Hayley Parry/Tullett

Section 20

Current Welsh Records/ Welsh Age Group Best Performances (as at December 2000)

100 metres

AC		10.29	Colin Jackson (Wales)	Wrexham	28.07.1990
WN		10.12	Christian Malcolm	Annecy, France	29.07.1998
U20M		10.12	Christian Malcolm	Annecy, France	29.07.1998
U17M		10.71	Tim Benjamin	Sheffield	16.08.1998
U15B		11.1	Malcolm James		00.00.1977
		11.1	Michael Williams	Swansea	31.08.1986
U13B		12.5	Malcolm James		00.00.1975
AC		11.27	Heather Oakes (England)	Cwmbran	27.05.1984
WN		11.39	Sallyanne Short	Cwmbran	12.07.1992
U20W		11.62	Helen Miles	Cottbus, Germany	22.08.1985
U17W		11.88	Sallyanne Short	Crystal Palace	16.06.1984
U15G		12.0	Helen Miles	Swansea	08.08.1981
U13G		12.6	Jane Bradbeer	Swansea	08.08.1981

200 metres

AC		20.36	Todd Bennett (England)	Cwmbran	28.05.1984
WN		20.19	Christian Malcolm	Sydney, Australia	27.09.2000
U20M		20.29	Christian Malcolm	Kuala Lumpur, Malaysia	19.09.1998
U17M		21.19	Tim Benjamin	Annecy, France	31.07.1998
U15B		22.2	Michael Williams	Portsmouth	12.07.1986
U13B		25.6	Malcolm James		00.00.1975
AC		22.58	Sonia Lannaman (England)	Cwmbran	18.05.1980
WN		22.80	Michelle Scutt	Antrim	12.06.1982
U20W		23.60	Michelle Probert	Bremen, Germany	12.09.1976
U17W		23.60	Michelle Probert	Bremen, Germany	12.09.1976
U15G		24.9	Jane Bradbeer	Swansea	24.07.1983
U13G		25.7	Jane Bradbeer	Wolverhampton	01.08.1981

400 metres

AC		45.29	Phil Brown (England)	Cwmbran	26.05.1986
WN		44.36	Iwan Thomas	Birmingham	13.07.1997
U20M		47.07	Jeff Griffiths	Crystal Palace	14.08.1976
U17M		48.46	Phil Harvey	Lille, France	24.06.1979
U15B		50.3	Malcolm James	Cwmbran	29.08.1977
U15B	300m	36.6	Richard Phillips	Barry	08.07.1995
AC		50.63	Michelle Scutt (Wales)	Cwmbran	31.05.1982
WN		50.63	Michelle Scutt	Cwmbran	31.05.1982
U20W		52.80	Sian Morris	Lappeenranta, Finland	18.06.1983
U17W		55.53	Sian Waters	Crystal Palace	20.08.1977
U17W	300m	39.81	Donna Porazinski	Dublin, Ireland	19.07.1997

800 metres

AC		1:44.65	William Tanui (Kenya)	Wrexham	28.07.1990
WN		1:45.44	Neil Horsfield	Wrexham	28.07.1990
U20M		1:48.20	Paul Williams	Cwmbran	25.05.1986
U17M		1:51.6	Neil Horsfield	Cwmbran	31.08.1983
U15B		2:00.6	Huw Davies	Swansea	28.09.1986
U13B		2:14.0	Richard Baker		00.00.1983
AC		2:00.21	Christiane Wildschek (Austria)	Cwmbran	01.07.1979
WN		1:57.42	Kirsty McDermott	Belfast	24.06.1985
U20W		2:04.01	Kirsty McDermott	Budapest, Hungary	29.07.1981
U17W		2:07.32	Amanda Pritchard	Belfast	22.06.1996
U15G		2:10.66	Amanda Pritchard	Crystal Palace	15.07.1994
U13G		2:16.1	Lisa Lanini	Wrexham	05.08.2000

1000 metres

WN	2:17.36	Neil Horsfield	Gateshead	09.08.1991
WN	2:33.70	Kirsty Wade	Gateshead	09.08.1985

1500 metres

AC	3:35.74	Rob Harrison (England)	Cwmbran	26.05.1986
WN	3:35.08	Neil Horsfield	Brussels, Belgium	10.08.1990
U20M	3:44.49	Neil Horsfield	Karlovac, Yugoslavia	15.09.1984
U17M	3:51.5y	Colin Clarkson		00.00.1977
	3:53.8	Tony Dyke	Merthyr Tydfil	12.08.1972
U15B	4:13.7	David Powell		00.00.1979
U13B	4:31.3	David Powell	Manchester	26.07.1977
AC	4:04.39	Zola Budd (England)	Cwmbran	28.05.1984
WN	4:00.73	Kirsty Wade	Gateshead	26.07.1987
U20W	4:23.6	Janet Howes	Middlesbrough	05.09.1981
U17W	4:23.6	Janet Howes	Middlesbrough	05.09.1981
U15G	4:36.0	Debbie Crowley	Swansea	30.07.1981
U13G	4:52.9	Lucy Thomas	Barry	03.08.1997

One mile

AC	3:55.8	Geoff Smith (England)	Cwmbran	15.08.1981
WN	3:54.39	Neil Horsfield	Cork, Ireland	08.07.1986
U20M	4:01.7	Neil Horsfield	Cheltenham	06.09.1985
U17M	4:06.7	Barrie Williams	Arcadia, USA	22.04.1972
AC	4:29.48	Bev Nicholson (England)	Cardiff	17.09.1989
WN	4:19.41	Kirsty McDermott	Oslo, Norway	27.07.1985

3000 metres

AC	7:46.95	David James (Wales)	Cwmbran	26.05.1980
WN	7:46.40	Ian Hamer	Auckland, New Zealand	20.01.1990
U20M	8:12.6	Andrew Rodgers	Crewe	25.06.1983
U17M	8:25.2	Colin Clarkson	Gateshead	03.08.1977
U15B	9:12.2	Luke Northall	Wigan	16.05.1999
AC	8:52.88	Paula Fudge (England)	Cwmbran	30.05.1982
WN	8:45.39	Hayley Tullett	Gateshead	15.07.2000
U20W	9:37.5	Lynn Maddison	Middlesbrough	30.08.1986
U17W	9:50.8	Kathryn Williams	Middlesbrough	21.07.1979

5000 metres

AC	13:13.01	Thomas Nyariki (Kenya)	Cardiff	25.05.1996
WN	13:09.80	Ian Hamer	Rome, Italy	09.06.1992
U20M	14:07.2	Adrian Leek	Aldershot	31.07.1977
AC	15:27.56	Angela Tooby (Wales)	Cwmbran	28.05.1984
WN	15:13.22	Angela Tooby	Oslo, Norway	05.08.1987
U20W	16:47.4	Sally James	Cwmbran	07.09.1983

10,000 metres

AC	27:51.30	Ian Stewart (Scotland)	Cwmbran	11.06.1977
WN	27:39.14	Steve Jones	Oslo, Norway	09.07.1983
U20M	30:06.1	Andres Jones	Ayr	21.07.1996
AC	32:59.59	Liz Lynch (Scotland)	Cwmbran	26.05.1986
WN	31:55.30	Angela Tooby	Rome, Italy	04.09.1987

Steeplechase

AC	3000m	8:31.0	Tony Staynings (England)	Cwmbran	12.06.1977
WN	3000m	8:18.91	Roger Hackney	Hechtel, Belgium	30.07.1988
	2000m	5:23.6	Roger Hackney	Birmingham	10.06.1982
U20M	3000m	8:54.6	Micky Morris	Bristol	07.09.1975
	2000m	5:34.8	Micky Morris	Athens, Greece	24.08.1975
U17M	1500m	4:11.2	Steve Evans	Edinburgh	15.07.1974

High Hurdles

AC	110m	13.10	Colin Jackson (Wales)	Cardiff	03.06.1990
WN	110m	12.91	Colin Jackson	Stuttgart, Germany	20.08.1993
U20M	110m	13.44	Colin Jackson	Athens, Greece	19.07.1986
U17M	100m	13.11	Nathan Palmer	Dublin, Ireland	08.08.1998
U15B	80m	11.3	Jon Marsden	Dunfermline	10.08.1996

U13B	75m	12.4	Wynne James	Barry	26.07.1992
		12.4	Jon Marsden	Brecon	19.06.1994
AC	100m	13.02	Kay Morley (Wales)	Wrexham	28.07.1990
WN	100m	12.91	Kay Morley	Auckland, New Zealand	02.02.1990
U20W	100m	13.57	Bethan Edwards	Horsham	29.08.1992
U17W	80m	11.35	Bethan Edwards	Birmingham	13.08.1989
U15G	75m	11.00	Danielle Selley	Cardiff	20.06.1998
U13G	70m	11.7	Petra Hurford	Swansea	31.08.1986
		11.7	Louise Dennis	Carmarthen	14.07.1990
		11.7	Danielle Selley	Swansea	29.06.1996

200 metres Hurdles

WN		22.63	Colin Jackson	Cardiff	01.06.1991

400 metres Hurdles

AC		49.57	Harry Schulting (Netherlands)	Cwmbran	18.05.1980
WN		49.16	Paul Gray	Budapest, Hungary	18.08.1998
U20M		51.5	Matthew Elias	Cardiff	06.06.1998
U17M		53.30	Mark Rowlands	Birmingham	31.07.1994
U15B	300m	42.5	Richard Crayford	Barry	26.07.1992
AC		54.69	Kim Batten (USA)	Cwmbran	12.07.1992
WN		56.43	Alyson Layzell	Birmingham	16.06.1996
U20W		58.37	Alyson Evans	Tel Aviv, Israel	01.09.1985
U17W		61.02	Claire Edwards	Haringey	08.09.1991
U17W	300m	43.83	Gael Davies	Nottingham	08.07.1995

High Jump

AC	2.27	Randy Jenkins (USA)	Wrexham	03.07.1994
WN	2.24	John Hill	Cottbus, Germany	23.08.1985
U20M	2.24	John Hill	Cottbus, Germany	23.08.1985
U17M	2.15	Chuka Enih Snell	Newport	10.09.2000
U15B	1.96	Chuka Enih-Snell	Aberdare	29.08.1998
U13B	1.67	Jamie Dalton	Brecon	28.06.1992
AC	1.93	Andrea Matay (Hungary)	Cwmbran	18.05.1980
WN	1.84	Sarah Rowe	Utrecht, Netherlands	22.08.1981
U20W	1.84	Sarah Rowe	Utrecht, Netherlands	22.08.1981
U17W	1.81	Lea Haggett	Birmingham	06.06.1986
U15G	1.81	Lea Haggett	Birmingham	06.06.1986
U13G	1.68	Julia Charlton	Dublin, Ireland	06.08.1978

Pole Vault

AC	5.80	Grigory Yegorov (Kazakhstan)	Cwmbran	12.07.1992
WN	5.60	Neil Winter	Enfield	19.08.1995
U20M	5.50	Neil Winter	San Giuliano, Italy	09.08.1992
U17M	5.20	Neil Winter	Birmingham	02.09.1990
U15B	4.40	Neil Winter	Krefeld, Germany	01.10.1988
U13B	2.40	Patrick Sullivan		00.00.1978
	2.40	David Weatherley	Swansea	27.06.1984
AC	4.12	Janine Whitlock (England)	Colwyn Bay	04.09.1999
WN	4.15	Rhian Clarke	Austin, USA	07.04.2000
U20W	3.70	Rhian Clarke	Hendon	10.08.1996
U17W	3.20	Rebecca Roles	Aberdare	31.08.1996
U15G	2.25	Megan Freeth	Swansea	16.09.1996

Long Jump

AC	8.18	Ralph Boston (USA)	Cardiff	24.07.1965
WN	8.23	Lynn Davies	Berne, Switzerland	30.06.1968
U20M	7.56	Colin Jackson	Tel Aviv, Israel	31.08.1985
U17M	7.11	Marcus Browning	Crystal Palace	14.09.1986
U15B	6.63	Ian Strange	Cwmbran	19.07.1977
U13B	5.31	Clive Woolmer		00.00.1982
AC	6.58	Oluyinka Idowu (England)	Cardiff	09.06.1991
WN	6.52	Gillian Regan	Swansea	28.08.1982
U20W	6.25	Lisa Armstrong	Brecon	15.07.1992
U17W	6.01	Lisa Armstrong	Corby	19.08.1990
U15G	5.57	Ceri Jenkins		00.00.1972
U13G	4.88	Lisa Armstrong	Solihull	20.07.1986

Triple Jump

AC		16.88	Bela Bakosi (Hungary)	Cwmbran	18.05.1980
WN		15.99	Steven Shalders	Santiago, Chile	20.10.2000
U20M		15.99	Steven Shalders	Santiago, Chile	20.10.2000
U17M		15.14	Steven Shalders	Ayr	18.07.1998
U15B		13.55	Darren Yeo	Dublin, Ireland	15.07.1989
U13B		10.62	Paul Rainbow	Cwmbran	03.09.1986
AC		12.76	Evette Finikin (England)	Cardiff	09.06.1991
WN		12.14	Jayne Ludlow	Istanbul, Turkey	21.05.1994
U20W		12.14	Jayne Ludlow	Istanbul, Turkey	21.05.1994
U17W		12.14	Jayne Ludlow	Istanbul, Turkey	21.05.1994

Shot

AC		21.68	Geoff Capes (England)	Cwmbran	18.05.1980
WN		20.45	Shaun Pickering	Crystal Palace	17.08.1997
U20M	7.26kg	15.20	Clayton Turner	Gottingen, Germany	16.08.1986
	6.25kg	15.88	Clayton Turner	Swansea	12.07.1986
U17M		16.93	Mark Hewer	Cwmbran	17.06.1979
U15B		15.66	Mark Hewer	Crystal Palace	11.09.1977
U13B		13.36	Chris Hughes	Swansea	31.08.1991
AC		19.69	Zhu Xinmei (China)	Cwmbran	14.07.1991
WN		18.93	Venissa Head	Haverfordwest	13.05.1984
U20W		14.60	Philippa Roles	Neath	04.09.1996
U17W		13.65	Philippa Roles	Schio, Italy	06.08.1994
U15G		13.22	Emily Steele	Much Wenlock	23.07.1989
U13G		10.08	Louise Finlay	Cwmbran	07.04.1996

Discus

AC		62.10	Richard Slaney (England)	Cwmbran	10.07.1983
WN		60.43	Lee Newman	Enfield	23.08.1998
U20M	2kg	46.65	John Parkin	Liverpool	18.07.1998
	1.75kg	51.38	Gareth Marks	Cardiff	01.07.1995
U17M		48.84	Clayton Turner	Hendon	02.09.1984
U15B		48.66	Liam Walsh	Wrexham	27.07.1996
U13B		38.92	Chris Hughes	Barry	28.07.1991
AC		62.02	Venissa Head (Wales)	Haverfordwest	13.05.1984
WN		64.68	Venissa Head	Athens, Greece	18.07.1983
U20W		51.60	Philippa Roles	Ljubljana, Slovakia	24.07.1997
U17W		48.88	Philippa Roles	Dublin, Ireland	13.08.1994
U15G		44.12	Philippa Roles	Swansea	30.08.1992
U13G		29.48	Rebecca Roles	Swansea	16.05.1992

Hammer

AC		74.18	Martin Girvan (N Ireland)	Cwmbran	31.05.1982
WN		68.64	Shaun Pickering	Stanford, USA	07.04.1984
U20M	7.26kg	57.26	Shaun Pickering	Cwmbran	18.05.1980
	6.25kg	60.96	Shaun Pickering	Kirkby	12.07.1980
U17M		62.12	Shaun Pickering	Welwyn Garden City	28.05.1978
U15B		54.84	Marcus Davies	Havering	23.08.1986
AC		67.10	Lorraine Shaw (England)	Wrexham	09.08.1999
WN		56.60	Sarah Moore	Birmingham	12.07.1997
U20W		53.80	Carys Parry	Santiago, Chile	17.10.2000
U17W		46.82	Carys Parry	Aberdare	30.08.1997

Javelin

AC		88.46	Steve Backley (England)	Cardiff	03.06.1990
WN		81.70	Nigel Bevan	Birmingham	28.06.1992
U20M		68.74	Jonathan Clarke	Cwmbran	14.06.1986
U17M		70.30	Colin Mackenzie	Nottingham	06.07.1979
U15B		58.58	Rhys Williams	Dunfermline	10.08.1996
U13B		39.18	Mike Groves	Cwmbran	12.05.1996
AC		46.89	Caroline White (Wales)	Colwyn Bay	19.06.1999
WN		46.89	Caroline White	Colwyn Bay	19.06.1999
U20W		43.11	Charlotte Rees	Newport	28.08.2000
U17W		43.11	Charlotte Rees	Newport	28.08.2000
U15G		30.88	Natalie Griffiths	Bedford	26.08.2000
U13G		30.28	Emily Steele	Antrim	01.08.1987

Combined Events

AC	Dec	7856	Brad McStravick (Scotland)	Cwmbran	28.05.1984
WN	Dec	7268 a	Paul Edwards	Bonn, Germany	14.08.1983
		7308 h	Clive Longe	Kassel, Germany	29.06.1969
U20M	Dec	6812 a	Nigel Skinner	Dombasle, France	19.08.1984
U17M	Oct	5025	James Anthony	Birmingham	22.08.1998
U15B	Pen	3163	Kevin Drury	Wrexham	27.08.1994
U13B	Pen	1814	Jamie Dalton	Brecon	21.06.1992
AC	Hep	6092	Kim Hagger (England)	Cwmbran	28.05.1984
WN	Hep	5642	Sarah Rowe	Utrecht, Netherlands	23.08.1981
U20W	Hep	5642	Sarah Rowe	Utrecht, Netherlands	23.08.1981
U17W	Hep	4657	Rebecca Jones	Cardiff	04.07.1999
U15G	Pen	3441	Jane Shepherd	Swansea	14.05.1983
U13G	Pen	2608	Jane Shepherd	Cwmbran	10.05.1981

4 x 100 metres relay

AC	39.8	Australia	Wrexham	09.08.1999
WN	38.73	Wales	Kuala Lumpur, Malaysia	21.09.1998
		Kevin Williams, Doug Turner, Christian Malcolm, Jamie Henthorn		
AC	43.99	Germany	Cwmbran	01.07.1979
WN	45.37	Wales	Edinburgh	02.08.1986
		Helen Miles, Sian Morris, Sallyanne Short, Carmen Smart		

4 x 400 metres relay

AC	3:05.11	Trinidad & Tobago	Cwmbran	12.07.1992
WN	3:01.86	Wales	Kuala Lumpur, Malaysia	21.09.1998
		Paul Gray, Jamie Baulch, Doug Turner, Iwan Thomas		
AC	3:31.22	United Kingdom	Cwmbran	01.07.1979
		Karen Williams, Joclyn Hoyte Smith, Verona Elder, Donna Hartley		
WN	3:35.60	Wales	Dublin, Ireland	04.07.1982
		Carmen Smart, Diane Fryar, Kirsty McDermott, Michelle Scutt		

Marathon

AC	2:14:43	Brian Kilby (England)	Port Talbot	06.07.1963
WN	2:07:13	Steve Jones	Chicago, USA	20.10.1985
AC	2:48:59	Sue Martin (Wales)	Neath	04.09.1983
WN	2:31:33	Susan Tooby	Seoul, Korea	23.09.1988

Track Walking

3000m	WN	11:45.77	Steve Johnson	Cwmbran	20.06.1987
5000m	WN	20:22.0	Steve Barry	West London	20.03.1982
10,000m	WN	41:13.62	Steve Barry	Crystal Palace	19.06.1982
One Hour	WN	13,987metres	Steve Barry	Brighton	28.06.1981
20,000m	WN	1:26:22.0	Steve Barry	Brighton	28.06.1981
5000m	WN	24:32.92	Karen Nipper	Lyngby, Denmark	21.07.1984
10,000m	WN	51:00.0	Karen Nipper	Leicester	21.02.1981

CURRENT WELSH INDOOR BEST PERFORMANCES (as at 31 December 2000)

50 metres

WN	5.85	Nigel Walker	Dortmund, Germany	19.02.1983
WN	6.4 h	Liz Gill	Berlin, Germany	20.02.1966
	6.80 a	Dawn Oliver	Paris, France	25.01.1981

60 metres

AC	6.74	John Skeete (Scotland)	Cardiff	26.02.2000
WN	6.49	Colin Jackson	Paris, France	11.03.1994
U20M	6.67	Christian Malcolm	Chemnitz, Germany	01.03.1997
U17M	6.93	Tim Benjamin	Birmingham	21.02.1998
U15B	7.32	Jamie Henthorn		00.00.1993
U13B	8.4	John Davies	St Athan	19.02.1984
	8.4	Mike Derbyshire		00.00.1986
AC	7.41	Zoe Wilson (England)	Cardiff	26.02.2000
WN	7.34	Carmen Smart	Cosford	17.02.1990
U20W	7.48	Lisa Armstrong	Cosford	16.03.1991
U17W	7.56	Lisa Armstrong	Cosford	11.02.1990
U15G	7.77	Danielle Selley	Birmingham	21.02.1998
U13G	8.4	J Johnson	St Athan	18.03.1973
	8.4	Colette Lewis	St Athan	20.03.1982

150 metres

U15B	18.7	Matthew Roderick	St Athan	11.04.1987
U13B	20.4	Richard Wintle	St Athan	22.03.1980
U15G	20.0	Helen Miles	St Athan	28.03.1981
U13G	21.1	Heather Brown	St Athan	22.03.1980

200 metres

AC	21.75	Paul Brizzel (N Ireland)	Cardiff	26.02.2000
WN	20.54	Christian Malcolm	Ghent, Belgium	26.02.2000
U20M	21.06	Tim Benjamin	Birmingham	06.02.2000
U17M	21.51	Tim Benjamin	Birmingham	22.02.1998
U15B	23.6	Darren Yeo	Glasgow	21.10.1989
AC	23.63	Donna Frazer (England)	Cardiff	06.02.2000
WN	23.46	Catherine Murphy	Birmingham	27.01.1996
U20W	24.38	Michelle Probert	Berlin, Germany	03.02.1979
	24.38	Lowri Jones	Neubrandenburg, Germany	04.03.2000
U17W	24.82	Alex Bick	Birmingham	21.02.1999
U15G	26.46	Aimee Cutler		00.00.1996

300 metres

WN	34.57	Gareth Davies	Birmingham	20.02.1993
U20M	35.00	Haydn Wood	Cosford	31.03.1984
U17M	37.70	Haydn Wood		00.00.1982
U15B	38.04	Tim Benjamin	Birmingham	21.01.1996
WN	39.6	Sian Morris	Cosford	20.02.1987
U20W	40.22	Samantha Gamble	Birmingham	05.02.2000
U17W	40.22	Samantha Gamble	Birmingham	05.02.2000

400 metres

AC	48.10	Wayne Martin (England)	Cardiff	12.03.2000
WN	45.39	Jamie Baulch	Birmingham	09.02.1997
U20M	47.83	Matthew Elias	Birmingham	07.02.1998
U17M	49.58	Chris Page	Birmingham	04.01.1997
U15B	57.37	David Gomes	Cardiff	13.02.2000
AC	54.07	Vicki Day (England)	Cardiff	12.02.2000
WN	54.33	Louise Whitehead	Birmingham	14.02.1999
U20W	56.5	Michelle Probert	Cosford	09.12.1978
U17W	58.7	Sian Waters		00.00.1978

600 metres

WN	1:17.8	Bob Adams	Cosford	20.12.1969
U20M	1:22.8	Bedwyr Huws	Cosford	18.02.1989
U17M	1:27.0	Shaun Whelan		00.00.1980
U15B	1:30.4	Huw Davies	St Athan	12.04.1986
U13B	1:47.2	I McDonald	St Athan	22.03.1979
WN	1:30.16	Kirsty McDermott	Cosford	09.02.1985
U20W	1:31.4	Kirsty McDermott	Cosford	11.02.1981
U17W	1:40.8	Jackie Thomas	St Athan	28.03.1981
U15G	1:42.7	Mari Prys Jones		00.00.1988
U13G	1:51.0	Karen Whitehouse	St Athan	28.03.1981

800 metres

AC	1:49.63	Neil Speaight (England)	Cardiff	12.03.2000
WN	1:48.39	Phil Norgate	Gothenburg, Sweden	04.03.1984
U20M	1:52.6	Tony Dyke	Cosford	17.03.1973
U17M	1:58.14	Stephen Davies	Cardiff	19.02.2000
U15B	2:24.63	Matthew Gallivan	Cardiff	13.02.2000
U13B	2:25.11	Nathan Cleverly	Cardiff	06.02.2000
AC	2:06.10	Emma Davies (Wales)	Cardiff	12.03.2000
WN	2:01.52	Hayley Parry	Birmingham	15.02.1998
U20W	2:02.88	Kirsty McDermott	Grenoble, France	22.02.1981
U17W	2:17.30	Sarah Mead	Birmingham	27.02.1994
U15G	2:17.30	Sarah Mead	Birmingham	27.02.1994
U13G	2:40.74	Adrienne Davies	Cardiff	06.02.2000

1000 metres

WN	2:22.1	Malcolm Edwards	Cosford	20.02.1987
U20M	2:26.6	Neil Emberton		00.00.1992
U17M	2:40.2	Tony Dyke	St Athan	12.03.1972
	2:40.2	Mike Powell	St Athan	27.02.1983
U15B	2:44.9	Peter Wyatt	St Athan	11.04.1987
U13B	3:08.5	Ian Gould		00.00.1981
WN	2:38.95	Kirsty Wade	Stuttgart, Germany	01.02.1987
U20W	3:00.72	Lucy Thomas	Birmingham	14.02.1999
U17W	3:00.72	Lucy Thomas	Birmingham	14.02.1999
U15G	3:00.72	Lucy Thomas	Birmingham	14.02.1999
U13G	3:18.5	Julie Garrett		00.00.1985

1500 metres

AC	3:47.86	James Mayo (England)	Cardiff	26.02.2000
WN	3:43.0	Malcolm Edwards	Sindelfingen, Germany	02.03.1980
U20M	3:52.0	Tony Blackwell	Cosford	19.11.1977
U17M	4:06.02	Stephen Davies	Birmingham	06.02.2000
U15B	4:50.70	Daniel Evans	Cardiff	20.02.2000
U13B	5:08.78	Matthew Williams	Cardiff	09.12.2000
AC	4:27.07	Shirley Griffiths (England)	Cardiff	26.02.2000
WN	4:07.6	Kirsty Wade	East Rutherford, USA	13.02.1988
U20W	4:32.6	Kim Lock	Cosford	09.12.1978
U17W	5:12.50	Rhian Hole	Cardiff	26.02.2000

One mile

WN	3:59.5	Bob Maplestone	San Diego, USA	19.02.1972
U20M	4:13.7	Tony Simmons	Cosford	19.03.1966
WN	4:23.86	Kirsty Wade	New York, USA	05.02.1988

3000 metres

AC		7:53.63	Rob Whalley (England)	Cardiff	06.02.2000
WN		7:51.49	Ian Hamer	Birmingham	14.03.1992
U20M		8:13.4	Tony Blackwell	Cosford	10.12.1977
U17M		8:52.56	David Jones	Cardiff	20.02.2000
AC		9:26.31	Katie Skorupska (England)	Cardiff	12.03.2000
WN		8:54.63	Hayley Tullett	Erfurt, Germany	02.02.2000
U20W		10:11.54	Vivienne Conneely	Glasgow	19.02.1993
U17W		10:28.11	Heledd Gruffudd	Birmingham	13.02.1994

50 metres Hurdles

WN		6.40	Colin Jackson	Budapest, Hungary	05.02.1999
U20M		6.91	Nigel Walker	Paris, France	25.01.1981

55 metres Hurdles

WN		7.5	Richard Harbour	Swansea	11.03.1990
		7.5	Paul Gray	Swansea	13.02.1994
		7.5	James Hughes	Swansea	13.02.1994
U20M	106.7cm	7.5	Richard Harbour	Swansea	11.03.1990
	99.0cm	7.5	Ben Roberts	Swansea	01.03.1998
U17M		7.6	Nathan Palmer	Swansea	01.03.1998
U15B		8.2	Jon Armstrong	Swansea	18.02.1990
U13B		9.2	Paul Rainbow		00.00.1986
WN		8.0	Lisa Griffiths	Swansea	07.03.1993
U20W		8.1	Bethan Edwards	Swansea	12.01.1992
U17W		8.3	Bethan Edwards	Swansea	12.03.1989
		8.3	Lauren McLoughlin	Swansea	01.03.1998
U15G		8.5	Jodi Lester	Swansea	11.03.1990
U13G		9.2	Petra Hurford	Swansea	00.00.1986
		9.2	Sarah Lane (Torfaen)	Swansea	07.03.1993
		9.2	Lauren McLoughlin	Swansea	06.03.1994

60 metres Hurdles

AC		7.98	Chris Baillie (Scotland)	Cardiff	26.02.2000
WN		7.30	Colin Jackson	Sindelfingen, Germany	06.03.1994
U20M	106.7cm	7.78	Colin Jackson	Cosford	26.01.1985
	99.0cm	8.09	James Archampong	Birmingham	29.01.1995
U17M		8.16	Colin Jackson	Cosford	19.03.1983
U15B		8.87	Jon Marsden	Birmingham	17.02.1996
U13B		11.77	Michael Walker	Cardiff	04.03.2000
AC		8.29	Melanie Wilkins (England)	Cardiff	26.02.2000
WN		8.16	Kay Morley Brown	Glasgow	08.02.1992
U20W		8.47	Bethan Edwards	Birmingham	23.02.1992
U17W		8.67	Bethan Edwards	Cosford	04.03.1989
U15G		8.94	Danielle Selley	Birmingham	21.12.1998
U13G		11.34	Rhian Ashford	Cardiff	04.03.2000

High Jump

AC		2.25	Brendan Reilly (Ireland)	Cardiff	06.02.2000
WN		2.16	Andrew Penk	Cardiff	20.02.2000
U20M		2.15	Andrew McIver	Cosford	26.01.1980
		2.15	John Hill	Cosford	11.01.1985
U17M		2.07	Chuka Enih-Snell	Birmingham	05.02.2000
U15B		1.91	Chuka Enih-Snell	Birmingham	21.02.1998
U13B		1.55	Jamie Dalton	Swansea	26.01.1992
AC		1.87	Wanita May (Canada)	Cardiff	13.02.2000
WN		1.85	Julie Crane	Cardiff	13.02.2000
U20W		1.83	Rebecca Jones	Neubrandenburg, Germany	04.03.2000
U17W		1.79	Julia Charlton	St Athan	24.02.1980
U15G		1.79	Julia Charlton	St Athan	24.02.1980
U13G		1.50	Susannah Filce		00.00.1987

Pole Vault

AC		5.50	Paul Williamson (England)	Cardiff	06.02.2000
WN		5.32	Tim Thomas	Cardiff	26.02.2000
U20M		5.10	Neil Winter	Birmingham	08.02.1992
U17M		4.85	Neil Winter	Cosford	17.02.1990
U15B		3.20	Andrew Penk	Cosford	05.12.1992
AC		4.10	Iris Hill (England)	Cardiff	16.08.2000
WN		3.91	Rhian Clarke	Gainesville, USA	02.03.2000
U20W		3.65	Rhian Clarke	Lievin, France	03.03.1996
U17W		2.35	Megan Freeth	Milford Haven	09.02.1997

Long Jump

AC		7.46	Steve Phillips (England)	Cardiff	06.02.2000
WN		7.97	Lynn Davies	Los Angeles, USA	12.02.1966
U20M		7.32	Marcus Browning	Cosford	09.01.1987
U17M		6.90	Scott Herbert	Cosford	10.02.1990
U15B		5.88	Chuka Enih-Snell	Birmingham	01.02.1998
U13B		4.50	Josh Gibson	Cardiff	06.02.2000
AC		6.18	Ann Danson (England)	Cardiff	12.02.2000
WN		6.51	Ruth Howell	Cosford	23.02.1974
U20W		5.77	Nicola Short	Cosford	10.01.1986
U17W		5.77	Nicola Short	Cosford	10.01.1986
U15G		5.28	Ceri Jenkins	St Athan	12.03.1972
U13G		4.25	Rachel Conway	Cardiff	06.02.2000

Triple Jump

AC		15.31	Farel Mepandy (Congo)	Cardiff	12.03.2000
WN		15.82	Charles Madeira Cole	Glasgow	15.03.1998
U20M		15.45	Steven Shalders	Birmingham	20.02.1999
U17M		14.42	Steven Shalders	Birmingham	22.02.1998
AC		12.23	Debbie Row (England)	Cardiff	26.02.2000
WN		11.74	Jayne Ludlow	Birmingham	13.02.1994
U20W		11.74	Jayne Ludlow	Birmingham	13.02.1994
U17W		11.74	Jayne Ludlow	Birmingham	13.02.1994

Shot

AC		18.28	Stephan Hayward (Scotland)	Cardiff	26.02.2000
WN		19.10	Shaun Pickering	Birmingham	27.01.1996
U20M	7.26kg	15.25	Clayton Turner	Cosford	21.03.1987
	6.25kg	16.03	Clayton Turner	St Athan	11.04.1987
U17M		16.73	Clayton Turner	Cosford	08.12.1984
U15B		13.84	Liam Walsh		00.00.1996
U13B		14.61	Chris Hughes	Hereford	07.03.1992
AC		19.06	Venissa Head (Wales)	St Athan	07.04.1984
WN		19.06	Venissa Head	St Athan	07.04.1984
U20W		14.54	Jayne Berry	Cosford	18.03.1989
U17W		13.68	Philippa Roles	Birmingham	26.02.1994
U15G		11.72	Philippa Roles	Cosford	08.03.1992
U13G		09.86	Emily Steele	Much Wenlock	11.10.1987

Pentathlon

WN		3494 h	Tony Pithers	Cosford	02.03.1985
		3418 a	Nigel Skinner	Vittel, France	04.02.1984
U20M		3418 a	Nigel Skinner	Vittel, France	04.02.1984
U17M		3360	James Anthony	Birmingham	31.01.1998
U15B		2629	Kevin Drury	Birmingham	03.01.1994
AC		3926	Kelly Sotherton (England)	Cardiff	05.03.2000
WN		3834 h	Sarah Bull	Cosford	01.03.1980
		3776 a	Lisa Gibbs	Cosford	14.03.1993
U20W		3554	Rebecca Jones	Neubrandenburg, Germany	04.03.2000
U17W		3370	Rebecca Jones	Glasgow	12.12.1998
U15G		3231	Danielle Selley	Glasgow	13.12.1997
U13G		1532	Rhian Ashford	Cardiff	04.03.2000

Heptathlon

AC	4909	James Holder (England)	Cardiff	05.03.2000
WN	5277	Paul Jones	Birmingham	23.02.2000
U20M	4892	Ben Roberts	Birmingham	08.02.1998

4 x 200 metres relay

AC	1:28.83	Loughborough College	Cardiff	12.03.2000
WN	1:26.65	Wales	Birmingham	26.02.1995
		Kevin Williams, Doug Turner, Bryn Middleton, Peter Maitland		
U20M	1:34.27	Welsh Schools	Birmingham	22.02.1997
AC	1:39.72	Midlands	Cardiff	04.03.2000
WN	1:40.4	Wales	Cosford	20.02.1987
		Carmen Smart, Sian Morris, Sallyanne Short, Helen Miles		

1600 metres medley relay

WN	3:25.41	Wales	Birmingham	15.03.1992
WN	4:04.11	Wales	Birmingham	15.03.1992

The History of Welsh Athletics

By

John Collins, Alan & Brenda Currie, Mike Walters and Clive Williams

Edited by **Clive Williams**

Front Cover: *Clockwise from top right – Lynn Davies, Jim Alford, Colin Jackson, Steve Jones and Kirsty Wade*
Back Cover: *Poster of the 1958 Cardiff Empire Games*

First published by
Dragon Sports Books Ltd
2002

ISBN 095240415X

Dragon Sports Books Ltd
19 Murray Street, Llanelli,
Carms SA15 1AQ

Printed in Wales by
Provincial Printing & Publishing Co. Ltd.
Sanatorium Road, Cardiff CF11 8DG
Tel: +44 (0)29 2022 8729

This book is

dedicated to the memory of Nerys

a little angel

who touched the hearts

of all who met her

The History of Welsh Athletics

Contents

Pen Portraits appear throughout the book for the following:

Jim Alford, Steve Barry, Jamie Baulch, George Crump, Harry Cullum, Cyril Cupid, Lynn Davies, John Disley, Margaret Elgie, Bill Evans, Raye Evans, Ron Evans, Arthur Gould, Tanni Grey-Thompson, Chris Hallam, Ken Harris, Venissa Head, Ted Hopkins, Charlie Hughes, Colin Jackson, Ken Jones, Ron Jones, Steve Jones, Bill Kingsbury, Christian Malcolm, John Merriman, Kay Morley, Micky Morris, Eddie O'Donnell, Ron Pickering, Viv Pitcher, Berwyn Price, D.J.P. Richards, Tom Richards, Iwan Thomas, Reg Thomas, Angela and Sue Tooby, Kirsty Wade, Nigel Walker, Nick Whitehead, Arthur Williams, Hywel Williams, Alf Yeoumans.

Introduction

by
Rt. Hon. Rhodri Morgan AM, First Minister, National Assembly for Wales and Patron of the Athletics Association of Wales

As readers will see when they start exploring this valuable and fascinating publication, the first great modern Welsh athlete was a Morgan. He was Griffith Morgan or Guto Nythbrân, as he was popularly known. Born and bred in the parish of Porth in the Rhondda Valley, according to legend, Guto could run to Pontypridd and back before the kettle boiled.

Once, his father sent him to gather sheep. When he had finished, he told his father that he had some difficulty rounding up one of the flock. When he pointed out the awkward one, his father was amazed to see that it was, in fact, a hare. Well, just because he was fast doesn't mean he was bright!

In order to keep his muscles supple, Guto used to sleep on horse manure. Now that's a tip not many modern athletics coaches have taken up. Guto easily won the race against *Prince* of Bedwas in 1737 but then died in the arms of his sweetheart, Siân Siop.

My last great triumph was completing – yes completing not winning – the Cynon Valley Half Marathon fifteen years ago. That was a triumph for me. All right, so that doesn't make this Morgan the modern Guto, but if it comes to that, I don't expect that Julie Big Ben would have much in common with Siân Siop either!

Athletics in Wales is in a healthier state now than I can ever recall. The upswing started after 1958. It was a great year for people of my generation when what was then called the Empire Games came to Cardiff. A previously unknown Welshman, John Merriman, became an overnight hero by just failing to beat Australian Dave Power for the 6 miles gold medal. From those Games we all remember the other great Antipodeans, Herb Elliott and Murray Halberg scooping up gold medals, before going on to win gold again in the Rome Olympics just two years later. It was a thrill for me to see three world records broken and the first emergence of Kenya as a world athletics power, which I was able to witness again at first hand at other major athletics gatherings I have been fortunate enough to attend over the years.

In my youth, until the formation of Cardiff Amateur Athletic Club in 1968, there were two athletics clubs in Cardiff – my club, Roath Harriers and Birchgrove Harriers – and I recall that Cardiff dominated the British League for its first five years.

In 1964, Lynn Davies became our hero when he won the long jump gold medal in the rain in the Tokyo Olympics. Other great giants of Welsh athletics we think of are Jim Alford, Tom Richards, Ken Jones, Steve Jones, Colin Jackson, Kirsty Wade, Iwan Thomas, and the peerless Tanni Grey-Thompson, to name just a few. When Colin retires who takes his place in the Welsh athletics pantheon? Watch this space!

Foreword

by
Colin Jackson
World Champion and World Record Holder 110 metres hurdles

I have been running for as long as I remember, but did not see the day when I would be writing a foreword for a book that my company has sponsored.

The key factor to this book in my eyes is that it brings the history of athletics in Wales up to where we are today. It is packed with things I could not believe – did Guto Nythbrân run the first ever sub four-minute mile and was he faster over ten miles than the current African athletes on the circuit? There are dozens of superb pictures, which have never been seen in public before (including some of myself) and many stories that astounded me.

The compilers should be congratulated on a superb piece of work, which undoubtedly will become the encyclopaedia for the sport in Wales. They have put together decades of their own research, records and love for the sport into this book for the enjoyment of others.

I won my first Welsh hurdles title in 1984 as an 18-year-old in an earth shattering time of 15.56! However the first ever champion in my event, Wyatt Gould of Newport AC way back in 1902 was only slightly slower in 16.8. He certainly did not have the advantage of modern technology like synthetic running tracks and training techniques.

Being Welsh makes me as a person, feel a little different representing the UK, when you think we make up such a small part of the population. Then being crowned world champion and record holder makes me feel even more special as a Welshman, when you think of my roots. A small boy, from an immigrant family, representing his country Wales and moving on to become the fastest ever in history, at his chosen event. Now who would like to give me betting odds on that!

Winning gold medals all over the world has given me the chance to wave a Welsh flag at every opportunity especially in Stuttgart and Seville. People were confused when I did it for the first time but they soon knew where Wales was and how important it was for me to show my patriotism.

The sport in Wales is in a healthy state with a record number of athletes competing for British teams at various age groups. This publication will I am sure give extra impetus to all those young athletes who are just taking up the sport and be the next generation of potential Welsh superstars on the world athletics circuit.

I was one of the lucky ones. I earned fame and fortune in the sport and so for me this book represents a small thank you to Welsh athletics for the makings of Colin Jackson the "athlete" and the "person".

Message

from
Lynn Davies
Olympic Champion, Long Jump 1964

Someone once said that to understand where you are going it helps to know where you have come from. This *History of Welsh Athletics* provides us with a comprehensive review of the people and events which have shaped the sport in Wales.

For me, it has evoked many happy memories of Welsh Championships, Welsh Games, Commonwealth Games and the friends made over the years. In particular the piece on the 1958 Empire Games staged at the Arms Park in Cardiff. I well recall watching John Merriman win Wales' only athletics medal, silver in the six miles then waiting outside the ground for his autograph. Little did I realise that four years later I would be representing Wales at my first Commonwealth Games in Perth, Australia and sharing a room in the athletes village with my hero, John Merriman.

I was surprised to learn that organised athletics in Wales goes back as far as the 1860s and the first Welsh sprint champion was crowned in 1893.

Thanks to meeting the late Ron Pickering at the Glamorgan Secondary Schools Championships at Maindy Stadium in 1961 I began my athletics career. Ron was the newly appointed National Coach for Wales and for the next six years, like Jim Alford before him was an inspirational leader to teachers, coaches and young aspiring athletes.

Like all Welsh athletes I came through the schools and clubs structure. Ogmore Grammar School, Roath Harriers and Cardiff Amateur Athletic Club all helped my development as an athlete and this book rightly recognises the valuable role that schools and clubs have made and continue to make in Welsh athletics.

It was Mike Walters' idea, as a tribute to his late daughter, to compile this book and his fellow contributors, Clive Williams, John Collins and Alan and Brenda Currie are a superb team of experts steeped in the sport and have left no stone unturned in their research. For those who like facts and figures there are endless lists of all-time best performances and the evolution of records, Welsh athletes at major Games, and even rugby links with athletics are covered.

Welsh athletics is currently enjoying a golden era. A record nine athletes represented us at the 2000 Sydney Olympic Games, and the talented Christian Malcolm, fifth in the 200m final, promises to be a fitting successor to the great Colin Jackson. His wonderful career inspired a generation of young athletes to believe that they too could compete with the world's best.

Yes, the sport has come a long way since those early, innocent days thanks to the priceless contributions of officials, coaches, teachers and administrators. This book is a fitting tribute to the efforts of these volunteers, and the athletes who made, and continue to make Welsh athletics the great sport it is today.

Message

from
D. Hedydd Davies, Llywydd/President
Cymdeithas Athletau Cymru/Athletics Association of Wales

It is my pleasure as President of the Athletics Association of Wales to write a short introduction to this excellent record of the development of athletics in Wales.

My first experience of a Welsh Championship was competing in and winning a silver medal in the boys 880 yds on a very wet day in Carmarthen in 1954. Sixteen years later it was a pleasure to return to my hometown of Carmarthen to win the Welsh Championship marathon title for the third time.

This book is a result of dedicated research and the compilers are to be thanked and congratulated on producing a superb book. It will serve as a permanent record of the development of the sport in Wales. It is a treasure of information for all athletics enthusiasts and we have for the first time an authentic record of the achievements of all our great athletes of the past right up to the present stars of Colin Jackson, Jamie Baulch, Iwan Thomas, Christian Malcolm and Hayley Tullett.

I am sure that this book will be an inspiration to the young athletes of today to aim to emulate the achievements of the great Welsh athletes of the past. Records are there to be broken but to win a medal at a Welsh, Commonwealth, European or Olympic Championship will remain as a permanent record of achievement for the individual.

Diolch o galon am y llyfr hwn a fydd yn record o hanes datblygiad athletau yng Nghymru ac hefyd yn help i'r athletwyr ifanc i ymdrechu ac i anelu i gyrraedd safon y cewri yn y gorffennol.

Preface

This book has been a long time coming - almost forty years in fact. From the time Ken Bennett and this writer produced the first deep Welsh best performer lists back in 1963, the production of a definitive history of athletics in Wales has always been in my thoughts. Since that time I have maintained as much detail and information on Welsh athletics as storage space (and wife!) permitted, and this book, produced with John Collins, Alan and Brenda Currie and Mike Walters, all of whom, like me, have had a love affair with Welsh athletics for the majority of our lifetime, is the culmination of all of this effort.

The credit for getting the book away at this time is entirely down to Mike Walters, who, in the summer of 2000, suggested that he would like to produce a book in memory of his late daughter – and it mushroomed from there. So, what is the book all about? Well put simply, the aim of the book is to tell the story of Welsh athletics in its entirety, hopefully in a way those not close to the sport in Wales will find interesting, but at the same time to chronicle the beginnings and the great moments of the sport in Wales before the essence of the detail and passion is lost. Hopefully the team assembled to undertake this onerous task is a fine balance between the various aspects of the sport in Wales.

Now for the first time since D.J.P. Richards' *1956 History of the Welsh AAA,* which only covered the summer activity, we have tried to place in two books, a complete history of all branches of athletics in Wales – track & field, cross country, road running, race walking and the latest addition to the sport, fell running into two handy reference manuals. Much of the detail is being seen for the first time, especially many of the items in the separate statistics section.

The group assembled to undertake this task are not professional writers, but well meaning enthusiasts, who eat, sleep and breath Welsh athletics, so if there is any lapse into too much detail on a specific item, it is down to the passion of the writer on that particular point. Should this have occurred, we apologise in advance.

Whilst the authors have had a vast array of material at their disposal – mostly from personal collections, it has been impossible to track down a great deal of information about the early years of the sport in Wales. In particular, we have been unable to trace the minute books of the South Wales and Monmouthshire AAA – the forerunner of the Welsh AAA – prior to 1937 and have had to rely on other data to arrive at some of our conclusions. However, we believe that the information contained in the following pages will not materially differ from that contained in the minute books. Discovering detail about the early years in north Wales has also been virtually impossible.

We have tried to present the detail in a logical manner, separating the various elements of the sport into different sections. Despite this, there have been anomalies, as, for example, Steve Jones as a track, cross country and road performer features prominently in all sections. So we apologise in advance for any duplication.

The proceeds from the book will go in their entirety to the establishment and maintenance of a Welsh Athletics Hall of Fame at the National Indoor Athletics Centre at the University of Wales Institute Cardiff.

With a compilation of this type, we acknowledge that there have been errors and omissions, but we very much hope that these have been kept to a minimum. We would be pleased to hear from stars of yesteryear about their recollections and reminiscences and we hope to include this detail in a future publication as this book is only the first of a series of books on Welsh athletics – watch this space ...

Clive Williams
Otterbourne, Winchester
December 2001

Stop Press

Unfortunately there have been unforseen delays in the appearance of this book for which we apologise to the many people who have assisted us with its production. We had intended that it would cover activity up to the end of 2000. However we have added a further chapter covering 2001 to bring the contents up-to-date.

Acknowledgements and Bibliography

We are indebted to the numerous individuals who have given help and encouragement to us in the production of this book, and these are listed in alphabetical order. However, Peter Lovesey, Ian Buchanan, Emma Lile, Brian Lee, John Walsh, Rob Cole, Jack Thomas, Kevin Kelly, Steve Lewis and Colin Jackson deserve special mention. If we have missed anyone, please accept our apologies in advance

Peter, the author of numerous fictional thrillers, and in particular, the author of *The Official Centenary History of the AAA* (Guinness Superlatives 1979) has been invaluable in helping to piece together the early years of athletics in Wales. He has put his library of rare historical athletics journals and books at our disposal. Clive Williams has corresponded with him on and off for the past fifteen years checking and probing specific aspects of the sport in Wales. There is no doubt that the early references to athletics in Wales in this book would have been incomplete without his unselfish commitment to help uncover almost anything with a hint of "Welshness".

Clive Williams has also corresponded with Ian Buchanan, the noted athletics and Olympics writer and historian over many years, and exchanged facts and figures of numerous Welsh stars of yesteryear. Similarly, Kevin Kelly has an extensive library of athletics memorabilia and he has been particularly helpful.

Emma Lile, the Assistant Curator (Traditional Music, Sports and Customs) at the Museum of Welsh Life at St.Fagans produced an excellent thesis for her degree *Athletic Competition in Pre-Industrial Wales* (University of Birmingham 1994) and this spawned a contribution to this book *Professional Pedestrianism in south Wales,* which is re-produced as part of chapter one.

Rob Cole first entered sports journalism with *The Western Mail* in the early 1980s, and latterly he has run his own company, Westgate Sports Agency. His all-round knowledge of Welsh sport is second to none, and his enthusiasm for this project, along with the placing at our disposal of his press clippings and other valuable material, has made our job in producing this book significantly easier.

Former Roath Harrier Brian Lee has produced many historical books on Cardiff and the sport of Point-to-Point and Horse Racing. But his book *The Great Welsh Sprint* (Gwyn Thomas 1999), the story of the Welsh Powderhall Handicap is an invaluable contribution to the history of athletics in Wales, and we are grateful for his permission to make numerous references to this great Welsh event in this book.

John Walsh another former Roath Harrier, now resident in Carmarthen is the unparalled marathon expert in the UK. He has compiled the UK marathon rankings for the National Union of Track Statisticians for over 30 years, and maintains a general interest in all Welsh athletics statistics and we are grateful for his help and support in the production of this book.

Jack Thomas is the undisputed guru on Welsh walking affairs so we are also grateful for his contribution and Steve Lewis of The Sports Bookshop has given us permission to quote from his book on Newport RFC and given invaluable help and advice on the vital area of sales and distribution.

We also record our thanks to the staff at Llanelli, Neath, Swansea and Cardiff libraries and Peter Morris who undertook the onerous task of proof reading.

Much of the base data for the statistics contained herein came from the personal collections of the late Viv Pitcher, D.J.P. Richards and Eddie O'Donnell. Welsh athletics, and indeed the sport in general owe these gentlemen a debt of gratitude for their foresight in meticulously recording the activities of the sport in Wales during its formative years.

Grateful thanks also to Ian Fitzgerald, Managing Director of *Provincial Printing & Publishing Co. Ltd.* for his advice, Andrew Harris for his artistic flair with the photographs, Isabel Butcher for her expertise in designing the cover and the legendary Mrs. Fitz for her invaluable assistance.

Before listing our thanks to the vast number of other individuals and organisations who have assisted us in the production of this book, we are particularly grateful for the generous sponsorship received from Colin Jackson and his Company JJ Productions, the Welsh based media organisation.

Our thanks are also due to the following:

Martin Adams (Axis Historical Society), Jim Alford, John Billot, Ken Bennett, Bernard Baldwin MBE, Jackie Brace, Steve Brace, Brian Blandford, A.R. Brewer, Graham Coldwell, Eric Cowe, Mike Critchley, M.H. Davies, Owen Edwards, Howard Evans, Lyn Evans, Graham Finlayson BEM, D. Finch, Peter Oale, Alistair Griffiths, John Griffiths, M.J. Harnett, Lynette Harries, K.W.B. Harris, Gareth Hughes, Mona Hughes, Richard E. Huws, Frank Ireland, Richie Jenkins, John M. Jenkins, Myrddin John MBE, Richard Johnson, Ken Jones (Llanberis), Tom Jones, D.J. Joseph, Carole Kuhlman, Dawn Kenwright, Bill Kingsbury, Jeff Kirby, Carol Lammerman-Jones, B. Lawrence, Steve Lewis, Irene Lisle, John Lister, Martin Lucas, Dr. John Morgan-Guy, Mick McGeoch, Andy Milroy, W. Moore, Wilf Morgan, Gwynant Phillips, Sean Power, Emlyn Roberts, Mike Sheridan, Francis Stevens, Brian Sexton, Prof Dai Smith, Reg Snow MBE, David Thurlow, Derek Tayler, Andy Unwin, Sally Uphill, Geoff Ward, John J. Williams, Hywel Williams, Rhys Williams, Prof. Gareth Williams, David Alun Williams, Averil Williams, Tom Wood, Adrian Woods.

Bibliography

AAA Jubilee Souvenir – 50 years of progress, AAA, 1932
Athletics and Football, 3rd edition, Montague Shearman, London: Longmans, 1889
Baledi I'r Cyw Cloff, E. Wyn James, Canu Gwerin, 1992
Baledi Morgannwg, Ben Bowen Thomas, University of Wales Press, 1951
British Athletics Annuals, National Union of Track Statisticians, 1959-2000
British Sport: A Social History, Dennis Brailsford, Lutterworth, 1992
Cross Country 1903-1986 – Son Histoire, Yves Jeannotat
Early Womens Athletics: Statistics and History, Volume One, Eric L. Cowe, 1999
Encyclopaedia of Track and Field Athletics, Mel Watman, Hale 1981
Eyes Towards Cardiff, Bernard Baldwin MBE, 1956
Fields of Praise. Official History of the Welsh Rugby Union 1881-1981, David Smith and Gareth Williams, University of Wales Press, 1980
Great British Olympians, Ian Buchanan, Guinness Publishing, 1991
Gone North, vols one and two, Richard Gale
Hen Faledi Ffair, Tegwyn Jones, Y Lolfa, 1971
History of British Athletics, Mel Watman, London: Hale 1968

History of Olympic Track and Field, Mel Watman, Athletics International 2000
History of Welsh International Rugby, John Billot, Provincial Printing & Publishing Co Ltd, 1999
Honour of Empire Glory of Sport – The History of Athletics at the Commonwealth Games, Bob Phillips, Parrs Wood Press, 2000
ICCU Handbook and Supplement, Laurie Richardson
Jubilee Brochure of Newport Harriers AC, N.J.T. Moses, 1946
Jubilee History of the ICCU 1903-1953, Laurie Richardson, 1953
Llanelli Yesteryear, Brian Cripps, Gomer, 1999
Llanelli Lives, Howard M. Jones, Gwasg y Draenog, 2000
Marathona Cymreig, Tecwyn Jones, Vaughan, Y Faner, 1983
Memories of Wales, Herbert Williams, BBC Radio Wales, 1999
Modern Athletics 3rd edition, Henry Fazakerley Wilkinson, The Field, 1877
Mountain Ash Remembered, Bernard Baldwin MBE, D Brown and Sons Ltd, 1984
Mysterious Wales, Chris Barber
Newport Athletic Club 1875-1925, W.J. Townsend Collins, 1925
Newport Athletic Club 1875-1975, W.E. Davies, 1975
Newport Rugby Football Club 1874-1950, Steve Lewis, Tempus, 1999
Official Centenary History of AAA, Peter Lovesey, Guinness Superlatives Ltd, 1979
Official History of the VIth British Empire and Commonwealth Games, Wales 1958, Cyril Newham, J.D.B. Williams MBE and Eileen M. Richards.
Oxford versus Cambridge. A record of Inter-University Contests from 1827-1930, J. Bruce-Kerr and H.M. Abrahams, 1931
Pedestrian Monmouth, Gareth Jenkins, Severn and Wye Review, 1971
Pedestrianism; or, An Account of the Performances of Celebrated Pedestrians during the Last and Present Century, Walter Thom, Aberdeen: A. Brown & F. Frost, 1813
Powderhall and Pedestrianism: The History of a Famous Sports Enclosure, 1870-1943, David A. Jamieson, Edinburgh and London: Johnston, 1943
Pedestrians, The: an Athletics Legacy, Warren Roe
Rhagor o Redwyr, Tegwyn Jones, Canu Gwerin, 1993
Roath Cardiff Harriers – a Short History, Viv Pitcher, 1952
Runners and Races 1500m/Mile, Cordner Nelson/Roberto Quercetani, Tafnews Press, 1973
Runs will take place whatever the weather, Colin Shields, Scottish Cross Country Union
Sport and the British: A Modern History, Richard Holt, Oxford: Oxford University Press, 1989
Sport and the Making of Britain, Derek Birley, Manchester University Press, 1983
Sport in Britain: Its Origins and Development, H.A Harris, London: Paul, 1975
Studmarks on the Summit, Bill Smith
The Great Welsh Sprint – The story of the Welsh Powderhall Handicap 1903-1934, Brian Lee, Gwyn Thomas, 1999
The Industrial Revolution in North Wales, 3rd edition, A.H Dodd, University of Wales Press, 1971
The Kings of Distance: A Study of Five Great Runners, Peter Lovesey, Eyre & Spottiswoode, 1968
The Professionals, Geoffrey Nicholson, London: Deutsch, 1964
WCCA Centenary Brochure, George Crump and others, 1996
Welsh AAA History and Records, D.J.P Richards, Welsh AAA, 1956
Welsh Athletics Annuals, Clive Williams 1977-1981 and Alan and Brenda Currie, 1982-1995; Welsh AAA and AAW
Welsh Track and Field, Clive Williams, Welsh AAA, 1967 and 1968
Westbury Harriers Jubilee History 1924-1999, Peter Griffin
Who's Who in British Athletics, Peter Matthews, Daily Express, 1989
Who's Who in Olympic Track and Field 2000, Mel Watman, Athletics International, 2000
Who's Who of UK & GB International Athletes 1896-1939, Ian Buchanan, 2000
Who's Who of Welsh International Rugby Players, John M. Jenkins, Duncan Pierce, Timothy Auty, 1991
World Championships Media Guide, UK Athletics, 1999
Yr Hen Redwyr, Tecwyn Jones, Vaughan Y Faner, 1983

Periodicals and newspapers

Athletics Today
Athletics 1945-1949
Athletics Weekly 1950-2000
Athletics International
Bells Life
Birchgrove Harriers Newsletter
Cardiff AAC Newsletter
Cardiff and Merthyr Guardian
Glamorgan, Monmouth and Brecon Gazette
Merthyr Express
South Wales Argus
South Wales Evening Post
South Wales Echo
The Cambrian
The Monmouthshire Beacon
The Welshman
Track Stats
Welsh Track & Field
Welsh Athlete
Western Mail

List of Abbreviations and Notes on Contents

Throughout the book, we have abbreviated times and distances in the generally accepted way i.e. 22.4 for 220 yards/200m relates to 22.4 seconds; 4:11.4 for the mile/1,500m relates to 4 minutes 11.4 seconds, 2:12:12 for the marathon relates to 2 hours 12 minutes and 12 seconds and 51.40 in field events means 51 metres 40 centimetres. We have also tended to abbreviate kilometres as "k", metres as "m" and yards as "yds" when referring to events.

Whilst metric measurement in field events was not used on a regular basis until the last quarter of the last century, we have converted marks achieved before this time to their metric equivalents so as to allow comparison with the performances of today.

We have also used maiden names for athletes until the time of marriage.

Where there is no explanation in the text, we have used the following abbreviations:

AAA	Amateur Athletic Association
AAC	Amateur Athletic Club
AAW	Athletics Association of Wales
AC	Athletic Club or Athletics Club
AGM	Annual General Meeting
BAAB	British Amateur Athletic Board
BAF	British Athletic Federation
BVAF	British Veteran's Athletic Federation
CS	Comprehensive School or County School
EAA	European Athletic Association
GS	Grammar School
H	Harriers
IAAF	International Amateur Athletic Federation
ICCU	International Cross Country Union
IAC	International Athletes' Club
NUTS	National Union of Track Statisticians
NIAC	National Indoor Athletics Centre
RWA	Race Walking Association
SLH	South London Harriers
SS	Secondary School
TVH	Thames Valley Harriers
UKA	United Kingdom Athletics
UWIC	University of Wales Institute, Cardiff
Welsh AAA	Welsh Amateur Athletic Association
Welsh CCA	Welsh Cross Country Association
WRU	Welsh Rugby Union
Welsh Women's AAA	Welsh Women's Amateur Athletic Association
Welsh Women's CCA	Welsh Women's Cross Country Association

There are frequent references to AAA Championships and Women's AAA Championships. Whilst these events, in the main, have been organised by the AAA/Women's AAA (of England) they have been open to athletes of any nationality.

We have attempted, wherever possible, to use the modern spelling of place names. Therefore, for example, we have used Llanelli, even though the correct spelling at the time of occurrence was Llanelly. The only variance to this has been where there is a specific reference to a club (i.e. Caernarvon AC) prior to the adoption of the modern spelling.

Chapter 1

From Hafod House to the World

This chapter looks at the period up to the end of the Second World War, and traces the earliest references to athletics in Wales when the term "athletics" was used to describe all physical sporting activity, although the word was not commonly used until it became associated with amateur athletics in the mid nineteenth century .... also a Welshman is credited with being the architect of modern athletics, and three 19th century Welshmen set world bests ....

Arguably, one of the earliest references to athletics in Wales dates back to Pentraeth, Anglesey in the sixth century, where Hywel, the son of Gwalchmai, in a competition for the hand of the daughter of Einon (son of Geraint) took part in a jumping contest of three leaps against another local man. Chris Barber, in his *Mysterious Wales* recounts that Hywel won the contest using a hop, skip and jump technique "which enabled him to jump about 50 feet". So apart from its significance to Welsh athletics, this could be the earliest reference to triple jumping in Britain, if not in the world. The three stones are there today for all to see, half a mile from Pentraeth, near the entrance to Plas Gwyn.

Whether this is fact or fiction, we will never know, but it does serve to illustrate that sporting prowess was an important feature in Wales fourteen centuries ago.

We also know that sport was, in effect, a method of keeping fit for military service and intensive training schedules provided ideal preparation for war and by the fifteenth century, feats like wrestling, putting the stone, throwing the javelin, fighting with stone and buckle and various endurance activities designed to improve strength and stamina were practised by the Welsh when in training for battle. (Emma Lile, *Athletic Competition in Pre-Industrial Wales c1066-c1880)*

Modern athletics competition have their origins in Greece, where the ancient Olympic Games were held every four years from at least 776 BC. The modern Olympics were established in Athens in 1896 and Mel Watman in his *Encyclopaedia of Track and Field Athletics,* (Hale, 1981), gives some credit for the establishment of the modern Olympics to William Penny Brookes, who founded the annual Games at Much Wenlock, Shropshire, not far from the Welsh border, in 1850. These events in Much Wenlock are still in existence today.

Professional pedestrianism in south Wales during the nineteenth century

The first forms of athletics competition in Wales can be traced back to the eleventh century, but the pre-cursor to the organised athletics we know today, lies with the activity of professional pedestrians in the nineteenth century.

Coinciding with a period of industrial growth and development that profoundly altered all spheres of daily life, the heyday of professional pedestrianism across Wales, and particularly the densely populated south, reached its peak during the mid-nineteenth century. This rather quaint precursor of modern athletics, comprising an eclectic mixture of running and walking events of varying types and distances, straddled the transition from rural to urban by becoming increasingly structured and reliant on rules, regulations and accurate timekeeping. Pedestrian challenges signified the beginning of codified sports, which ousted traditional, primarily spontaneous, parish games from prominence and could be held equally well within the new towns as on turnpike roads and fields just outside. As communication systems across Britain improved, large crowds travelled from afar to witness the proceedings, and the sport became extremely fashionable. According to a reporter for Swansea's *Cambrian* newspaper in 1815, a "whole race of 50 mile-a-day men" had emerged, and soon "every county will have to boast of its pedestrian champion". "What was before the disease of an individual", he continued rather concernedly: "has now become an epidemic; and where it will end I know not. Already several masters of numerous workmen assure me that they can scarcely keep them to business, and that all ambition has forsook them except that of going over a certain length of ground within a certain time ... The rage prevails, and those who in our workshops and manufactories were known as good hands, are now only desirous of proving that they have good legs".

Professional pedestrianism had captured south-Walian imagination long before the onset of urbanisation however, for since at least the late-seventeenth century footmen were employed as messengers and competitive runners by the gentry, who viewed any athletic success as a means of enhancing their own renown and social standing. For other working-class citizens not lucky enough to receive such patronage, pedestrianism offered a rare opportunity to achieve instant fame and fortune, owing to the high monetary sums staked on race results. Here was an activity where men of all backgrounds stood equal on the starting line, and where entrants willingly walked for many consecutive days if the financial rewards proved suitably tempting. Gambling was an integral element of the occasion, and for those accustomed to poverty and hardship, winning could mean the difference between starvation and survival.

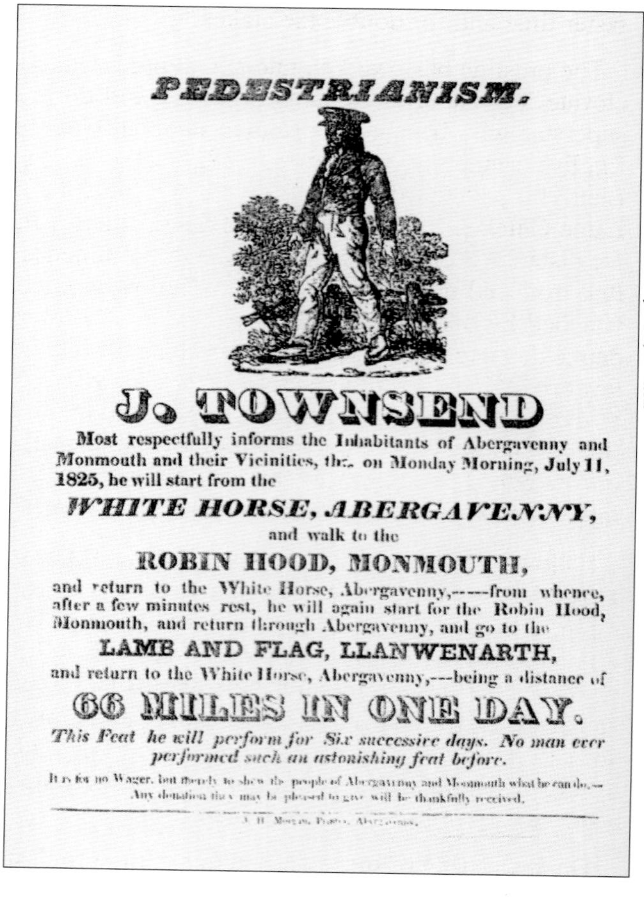

PEDESTRIANISM.
J. TOWNSEND
Most respectfully informs the Inhabitants of Abergavenny and Monmouth and their Vicinities, that on Monday Morning, July 11, 1825, he will start from the
WHITE HORSE, ABERGAVENNY,
and walk to the
ROBIN HOOD, MONMOUTH,
and return to the White Horse, Abergavenny,-----from whence, after a few minutes rest, he will again start for the Robin Hood, Monmouth, and return through Abergavenny, and go to the
LAMB AND FLAG, LLANWENARTH,
and return to the White Horse, Abergavenny,---being a distance of
66 MILES IN ONE DAY.
This Feat he will perform for Six successive days. No man ever performed such an astonishing feat before.
It is for no Wager, but merely to shew the people of Abergavenny and Monmouth what he can do.—
Any donation they may be pleased to give will be thankfully received.

As fields and countryside formerly used for games were industrially developed, so pedestrian contests required alternative facilities. These were frequently provided by shrewd local innkeepers who, while appearing saviours of the sport on the one hand, were also fully aware of the profit-making potential of such an enterprise. By arranging events either near or on the premises of their taverns, publicans were guaranteed healthy takings, as spectators and competitors alike quenched their thirst and laid their wagers over the bar. Demanding feats such as Mr Bruce Knight's 86-mile return trip from Cardiff to Brecon in thirty-three hours, in September 1804, and Mr John Townsend's 384-mile walk in August 1825, beginning at the Bear Inn, Brecon, and ending at the Wheat-Sheaf Inn, Hay on Wye, six days later, would have generated considerable monetary interest, and required plenty of fluids for all involved.

Although the largest bets were normally reserved for solitary challenges against clock or calendar, head-to-head matches also attracted eager punters. In August 1810, £168 was lodged as a deposit in the Brecon Bank backing militia officer Mr Williams, Jr., of Llwynhouse to complete the nineteen miles from Brecon to Abergavenny in three hours, while in February 1846 Aberdarians made "liberal appeals to their pockets" for a foot-race between local man Rees Meredith and Robinson, an Englishman. Such was Meredith's confidence that he gave his opponent three yards start, yet, rather than gaining on him and taking the lead, he fell further behind Robinson, who convincingly won the race by five yards. Fast and furious gambling took place in July 1851, when William Hopper of Morwinstow, Cornwall, attempted to walk fifty miles in twelve hours between Swansea and Bridgend for a stake of £12. Commencing at 6.00 a.m., the cattle dealer completed the task with thirty minutes to spare, despite wearing heavy laced boots weighing over 4½lb. A glutton for punishment, Hopper duly undertook a similar feat the following day, only in a faster time and for double the stakes.

The prestige bestowed on talented athletes was so great that pedestrianism success could elevate local men to celebrated heroes, and during the 1840s, there emerged in Wales a superstar who became undisputed national champion and conqueror of many renowned English runners. John Davies (1822-c.1904), born in Llansanffraid-ym-Mechain, near Llanfyllin, Powys, but often travelling south to race, was nicknamed Y Cyw Cloff ('The Lame Chicken'), in recognition of his distinctive running style. His slight frame was ideal for distance events and he first came to prominence in 1844 as one half of a two-man team that trounced the English star John Tetlow at Cimdda Common, Llantrisant, in a contest watched by over two thousand spectators. So infuriated by his defeat was Tetlow that he demanded a rematch against Davies alone, which was subsequently held over a mile of 'fine level road' in Llanilltud Faerdref, near Llantrisant. Undeterred by the odds backing Tetlow at five-to-three favourite, Davies capitalised on an early lead by pulling away to win in a (then) remarkable time of four minutes and forty-five seconds. As a result, the bookmakers purportedly lost about £1,000, and Tetlow £500, the latter blaming his defeat on travel fatigue after his journey from Manchester to Wales.

Following victories over Sergeant Rennie, ('The Running Sergeant'), William Bevan, and Howell Powell, Davies's unbeaten streak was eventually broken at Cimdda, in February 1845, when he finished twenty yards behind the Sheffield coal carrier Tom Maxfield. Allegations that a third runner, Welshman William Jackson, had fixed the finishing positions beforehand prompted a re-run, which was again embroiled in controversy when a fall by Maxfield during the race was viewed by Davies's supporters as a ploy to avoid losing. A third match, held at Lansdown, near Bath in December, finally settled the matter when, despite Maxfield's familiarity with the mile-long course, Davies stormed to a fifty-yard victory in just over five minutes.

Davies's string of successes led to his immortalisation in various ballads, which marvelled at his remarkable speed by comparing him to hares, deer, and, the ultimate accolade, the eighteenth-century running legend Guto Nythbrân. As the balladeer Edward Jones patriotically wrote following the Welshman's defeat of Maxfield:

Mawr yw ffrwst a thrwst y Saeson,
Maeddu'r Cymry yw eu hamcanion,
Ond fe fagwyd yng ngwlad Forgan
Un sy'n cario ar y cyfan.

(The English have great bravado,
Their goal is to beat the Welsh,
But born in the county of Glamorgan
Is one who carries all our hopes)

After the race, successful punters won enough to afford a tasty goose on Christmas Day, and his supporters welcomed Davies's homecoming to Cardiff on the Prince of Wales steamer with rapturous applause. The ballad writer Ywain Meirion paid a fitting tribute to Davies's competitive career:

Ni wiw i Sais na Sgot na Gwyddel
Gynnig arno mewn un gornel

(It is no use for an Englishman, Scot or Irishman
To attempt to challenge him)

for this was a practically invincible athlete, and an inspiration to all.

In the wake of the impressive performances of men like Davies, pedestrians in south Wales continued to strive for glory, confident in their abilities to succeed. A match "for no inconsiderable sum of money, or a sumptuous supper for a large party of friends" was held on the Swansea Sands in February 1845, and created great interest, if only for the sheer size of one of the two competitors. Both adjudged "respectable tradesmen" by *The Welshman*, the one "if not weighing half a ton, is assuredly not far short of it, staple weight". After the rather intriguing "doffing" of their "Benjamins" and appointing an umpire, the pair ran astonishingly quickly, with the lighter runner winning by a substantial margin.

As they traversed the racing circuit many athletes grew so well known that they adopted pseudonyms designed to reflect their athletic prowess. Examples of these included the "Welsh Bantam", "Pontypool Deer" and "Cwm Celin Stag", while the title "Flying Tailor" appeared especially common. *Bell's Life* of 11th April 1859 covered a 360-yard match at the Storey Arms, near Libanus, Breconshire, between William Jenkins, "The Flying Tailor" of Merthyr Tydfil, and the renowned pedestrian George Hopkins of Hirwaun, which attracted almost 4,000 spectators. Six years later, in September 1865, "The Flying Tailor" William Lewis, lost to William Moseley over 200 yds in a race at Neath, which according to *The Cambrian* generated much excitement.

It's Deer at the Gnoll

Neath residents were treated to many a pedestrian feat, including, in August 1855, a rare appearance by a woman athlete, Miss Isabella Melross, who travelled down from Scotland to demonstrate her stamina. Having walked an extraordinary 1,000 miles in 1,000 half-hours the previous year, Melross amazed spectators by completing 500 half-miles in 500 half-hours, and 500 quarter-miles in 500 quarter-hours. Not quite so impressive was a one-man event at the Gnoll Fields, Neath, in 1867, owing to the non-appearance of a second athlete. Challenged to a 100-yard dash by William Deer of the Railway Inn, William Aston, engineer on the Neath and Brecon Railway, failed to show up on the proposed date. This led to a host of railway-linked quips from *The Cambrian*, ridiculing Aston for failing to "get his steam up", owing to a "bust boiler" and an "out of order safety valve". Undaunted, Deer set off alone and finished successfully to cheers from the crowd.

In contrast to the more serious events, numerous novelty races were regularly held, involving such eccentricities as walking backwards, trundling wheelbarrows, and gathering potatoes. Man-against-horse events proved particularly popular, such as the trouncing of the cavalryman Lieutenant Tottenham over 200 yds by the runner Lieutenant Tute at Abergavenny in March 1840, as were the performance of amazing feats by the younger generation. In March 1839 a seven-year-old boy ran the seven miles from Risca to Newport in forty-five minutes for a sovereign wager, and beat the Tredegar coach into the bargain. Another child athlete, thirteen-year-old Mountjoy, Jr., followed in the footsteps of his celebrated pedestrian father by twice undertaking a sixty-four-mile return trip between Swansea and Neath within the space of a few days in March 1844. During the challenge he managed one forty-five-minute period of running half-a-mile forwards, walking three-quarters-of-a-mile backwards, running and hopping 100 yds each, picking up a hundred eggs with his mouth, and, finally, clearing twenty hurdles at 2 feet 4½ inches high! Evidently unaffected by such exertions, Mountjoy maintained his fitness well into the 1860s, completing a forty-mile walk around Swansea and Mumbles inside eight hours in April 1869.

Such was the gruelling nature of many pedestrian events that even conscientious, well-trained athletes were susceptible to illness and injury, and dropping out of races was not uncommon. Cramp severely hindered Mr Williams Jr. of Llwynhouse, an officer in the Breconshire militia, thirteen miles through his nineteen-mile run from Brecon to Abergavenny in August 1810, and although managing to cross the finishing line, albeit in a slow time, he was immediately put to bed to recover. Some physical suffering was endured by one Wilson in 1839, who removed his shoes while attempting to walk fifteen miles in two hours, such was the pain they caused, while in 1850 "The Flying Tailor" Jackson withdrew from a race on the Mumbles Road owing to exhaustion.

William Gale of Cardiff – star distance walker

Perhaps the greatest martyr for his cause, however, was Cardiffian William Gale who, in November 1880, travelled to the Lillie Bridge track, West Brompton, London, seeking to walk 2,500 miles in 1,000 hours. The track, which was the headquarters of the Amateur Athletic Club (AAC) and venue for the first Amateur Athletic Association (AAA) championships in 1880, was burned down seven years later by a gang involved in betting at a professional sprinting match. Under the watchful eye of seven judges, Gale "cheerfully" began his task on a bitterly cold evening on blister-inducing hard ground. Incredibly, he withstood all discomforts and "every form of bad weather", until January 1881 when, as reported in *The Cambrian:* "On the second signal being given at 4.30 a.m. on Tuesday morning he turned out as usual within a few seconds of time, but once on the path it was with the greatest difficulty that he could be prevailed upon to move, and after he had walked three laps (1460 yds) out of his allotted distance he stopped and flatly refused to move further, and at 4.57.56 he went into his house, and the match, as originally arranged, was at an end".

The Cambrian continued: "He had then been walking for 1786 consecutive half hours in which he had covered the extraordinary distance of 2232 miles. A doctor was called in immediately and reported his condition wonderfully well, his pulse beating strongly at 88, only a trifle higher than usual. His breakdown was the most extraordinary as in all his previous walks he has never shown the slightest symptoms of cowardice. He slept heavily for about six hours when, after a hot bath, he once more turned out of his house on to the track, having previously announced his intention of endeavouring to complete the 2,500 miles within the stipulated time .... Gale's excitability undoubtedly caused the collapse, and yet this is not to be wondered at: considering what he had undertaken and the wretched weather he had to encounter. It is intended to give him a benefit shortly to recompense him for his failure".

William Gale of Cardiff

Not all Gale's efforts were to be applauded, however, for earlier in his career, in December 1855, he was questioned by police regarding the validity of a walk of 1,300 half-miles in 1,300 half-hours in the White-Stile Fields (now the Uplands district of Swansea), for a £50 bet. Cries of "Hoax!" were raised when not once during the proceedings was Gale seen walking at night, preferring to remain inside a specially erected booth to engage in his "apparently arduous task". This booth intensely annoyed nearby residents, who were compelled to suffer the unsavoury rabble who congregated around it, and who were "a perfect disgrace to the whole town". The police were eventually called to eject Gale and his supporters.

In a walk against time at the Neath cricket ground in September 1855, Gale walked 11,476m in one hour. Put another way he walked 7 miles, 230 yds in 59:29, a believable but extraordinary performance.

Pedestrian events were by no means always harmonious and trouble-free therefore, and, indeed, for each honest, dedicated athlete there were several dubious, untrustworthy characters, whose less-than-upright activities tarnished the sport immeasurably. Trickery was rife, with fleet-footed amateurs entering races under false names, professionals impersonating unknown amateurs, and match fixing galore, while riots amongst the crowd also sullied the sport's reputation. During an ultra-distance event in October 1815, the aforementioned Wilson duped the public by walking only in the daylight hours before being relieved at night by an athlete whom he closely resembled. This devious scheme was discovered later during a quarrel over the division of the profits, and the matter then taken to court for investigation. In May 1853, spectators were rankled when "The American Deer", following a series of marathon endeavours, failed to appear at the Traveller's Rest, Swansea, for his scheduled event of twenty miles in two hours. A crowd of several hundred gathered to view the feat, only to be disappointed by his non-appearance, without so much as an apology. Similar unsportsmanlike behaviour occurred during a novelty race on the Swansea Sands in 1848, when Welshman Jackson, "The Flying Tailor", carrying a friend on his back, achieved a dubious victory by pushing over his opponent Mr Knock "by a clever dodge" halfway through the event.

It was precisely this seamy side of pedestrianism, provoking hostile attacks from ministers of religion and drawing unenviable comparisons with the emerging amateur sports and their ethos of fair play, that increasingly discredited it and became a matter of grave concern for the authorities. Rowdyism and irresponsible crowd behaviour, stemming from a combination of gambling and drink, aggravated matters further, leading on numerous occasions to police prosecution. Meetings staged near public houses, which encouraged excessive alcohol consumption, did nothing to allay the sport's waning image, while warnings of the lure of the gin bottle generally went unheeded. Meanwhile, *The Cardiff and Merthyr Guardian* following a race at Hirwaun in 1848, questioned the wisdom of gambling by "the sporting men of Aberdare" who, "in those days of commercial distress", should consider the many ways in which their money may have been "more wisely spent". With too many organisers and performers setting financial gain above athletic integrity, an unhealthy preoccupation with money overshadowed all sense of sportsmanship and wholesome competition. Owing to the large sums of money involved, an easily manipulated handicap system, and the absence of one central governing body until the 1920s, pedestrianism almost courted foul play and unscrupulous behaviour.

Glamorgan's William Richards sets world record for the mile

Here's a pub quiz question: Name the only Welshman to hold the world mile record! Well not many people would get it right, because the mark was set in 1865 by William Richards, one of the best-known professional runners of his day. All we know is that he was born in "Glamorgan" on 11th October 1839, and, as far as is known, achieved all of his performances in England or further afield. He first came to prominence at Millwall in London in 1858, and apart from being a leading performer, helped many other runners with their training. He was a fine runner over distances from 880 yds to 20 miles. Known as "The Welshman" his best year was 1865 when in front of 15,000 spectators on 19th August in Manchester, he dead-heated in a world record time of 4:17¼ with William Lang in a race billed to find the "Champion Miler of England". The race was contested by the greatest field of professional milers to have been assembled up to that time, including Siah Albison, a former world record holder (4:22¼) and the reigning world record holder Edward Mills (4:20). The race, held on a 651yd track, was closely contested throughout and Richards, who was regarded as a dark horse beforehand, made a last minute dash for the line after the Scot Robert McInstay and Lang, the pre-race favourite began to tire in the home straight. A contemporary report takes up the story ...."rushing toward the finish in an all-out drive, Richards fought alongside, and they flashed across the finish line in a blur of pumping arms and sprinting legs, five yards ahead of McInstay. The judges called it a tie, and Lang's supporters howled with rage, but the judgement stood." Of course, we will never know the true validity of this performance, given the lack of formal rules at the time, but it does serve to illustrate that a Welshman was amongst the best in the world at the time. In later life he ran the Black Horse pub in Oldham Road Manchester, close to the Manchester running grounds, and in 1869 lost to the American Indian "Deerfoot" in a five miles race in Cleveland Ohio. Whilst there is some scepticism today about professional performances generally when Richards was active, there is no doubt that he was a fine competitor, and at the forefront of the sport at the time.

The move to formalise and the beginning of the end for pedestrianism

The formation of the Amateur Athletic Club (AAC) in 1866 and the codification of its official rules eventually sealed the fate of professional pedestrianism, for while athletics and pedestrianism coexisted for a time; the latter was ultimately forced out of existence. In a concentrated attempt to dissociate upright and respectable modern athletics from the corrupted professional form, AAC regulations restricted participation to the upper and middle-classes, and consequently the gentry, once so supportive of pedestrianism, deserted it in droves. Perhaps it was the initial exclusiveness of amateur athletics to the wealthy that hindered its development across Wales, where pedestrian events continued to be held until the end of the nineteenth century, some decades after they had ceased in England. Another contributing factor may have been that Wales remained "passionately wedded to the ancient ways", in spite of social changes in the wake of industrialisation that undoubtedly benefited sport. Whatever the case, the AAC's influence was slow to travel. It was not until Newport Athletic Club (founded 1875) acquired the Rodney Parade Grounds in 1877, that amateur athletics meetings in Wales began to be held on a more regular basis.

By the 1890s standardised track championship events, as well as national cross-country contests, were becoming ever more popular in Wales, especially in the south. Conversely, the fortunes of professional pedestrianism fell into sharp decline, as the Amateur Athletic Association (AAA), which was formed in 1880, began prosecuting athletes who raced under false names, and took an increasingly firm stance on betting, culminating in its exclusion from the association's events in 1906. Apart from a brief walking mania in the shape of the Powderhall contests during the early 1900s, inspired by a walking marathon craze and the revival of the Olympic Games in 1896, by the turn of the twentieth century professional pedestrianism was fast becoming a distant memory. Its unrestrained rowdiness was totally at odds both with the new order and the religious climate of the period exemplified by the religious revival of 1904-5, which led to the demise of traditional customs and the continued suppression of "sinful" popular recreations.

Despite its ignoble end, at its zenith professional pedestrianism undoubtedly played a significant role among south-Walian communities, desperate for a source of leisure and enjoyment in a period of increasingly controlled and regimented work schedules. It generated the type of close-knit environment endangered by the replacement of rural fairs and festivals with unsociable factory hours, and welcomed competitors from all walks of life. Foot-racing challenges offered a valuable recreational outlet away from the strains of labour, and in paving the way for organised amateur athletics, constituted one of the final reminders, in sport at least, of a boisterous and unbridled pre-industrial age.

Llanelli's John Graham Chambers, the architect of modern athletics

Llanelli born John Graham Chambers, set about regularising athletics in Britain around the middle of the nineteenth century. Up until the involvement of Chambers, who was educated at Eton and Trinity College, Cambridge, the winning of cash prizes by the working classes, as we have seen, drove most athletics activity in Wales. The gentry also took part in competitions for cash prizes, but as it was not their main source of income, they were still classed as amateurs! Ironically, the question of amateurs and professionals was a major issue in those far off days, as it would be over a century later for the sport to turn full circle with today's

Llanelli born John Chambers second from right was the man who virtually single-handed structured sport in Britain.

athletics events open to both amateurs and professionals. But in Chambers' time, professional athletes were the underclass, where betting, race fixing and cheating were the order of the day and professional athletics continued to hold precedence until Chambers started his crusade to codify amateur athletics in the 1860s.

So Wales has an important link with the start of organised athletics in Britain – and indeed in the world. It was Chambers, born on 2nd February 1843, and baptised in Llanelli the following year, one of fourteen children of William Chambers jnr, a prominent Llanelli landowner, who was instrumental in the formation in 1880 of the AAA, the catalyst for structured amateur athletics in Britain, and indeed the world. Chambers was also one of the founders of the AAC, the forerunner of the AAA in 1865. With the formation of the AAA, professional athletics started to decline throughout England, but in Wales it remained popular until the Second World War, although the demise started in the mid 1930s.

But the Welsh impact on organised amateur athletics in Britain doesn't end with John Chambers. The 7th Earl of Jersey, who was to become the second President of the Welsh Football Union – the predecessor of the Welsh Rugby Union – in its second season in 1881/1882, became the first President of the AAA after its formation at the Randolph Hotel, Oxford on 24th April 1880. As well as being a leading administrator, the 7th Earl ran in the mile in the second varsity match for Oxford in 1865, finishing second behind R.E. Webster of Cambridge who clocked 4:44¼. He was Paymaster General in 1889/90 and Governor General of New South Wales 1890-93 and died in 1915.

Furthermore, John Chambers' brother, Charles Campbell Chambers (Swansea C&FC) was the first President of the Welsh Football Union. Charles Campbell Chambers was also captain of Swansea RFC in 1875 and played cricket for Glamorgan. The Earl of Jersey owned significant amounts of land in Glamorgan and was a generous benefactor of the Briton Ferry and St. Thomas districts of Swansea, where according to *Fields of Praise*, the official history of the Welsh Rugby Union, written by David Smith and Gareth Williams, he "spent £60,000 in providing a variety of amenities from roads to libraries and sports facilities: he had a particular interest in amateur athletics". This link with Welsh rugby is a theme, which exists throughout this history of Welsh athletics, and documented elsewhere in this book.

Hafod House, Aberystwyth – the cradle of Welsh athletics

It was John Chambers though who was the amateur athletics trailblazer in Wales. 15 years before the formation of the AAA in 1880, he organised a meeting at Aberystwyth on 16th September 1865, which is probably the earliest record of an organised athletics meeting in Wales. Chambers however, when just 17 years old, held some athletics events at Hafod House, his father's home also in Aberystwyth, some five years earlier on 27th July 1860, where the family subsequently moved on 29th September 1856. In this "meeting" Bob Harrigan, the cricket historian reported in *The Welshman* that there were foot races on the lawn, and throwing the cricket ball. Twelve pedestrians (presumably professionals) also competed for prizes over 600 yds. The sports followed a cricket match

By permission of Llanelli Library

Hafod House

between Hafod and Ystrad Meurig, in which Chambers scored 20 out of 54 and bowled 13 of the opposition batsmen. Hafod House, "a historic mansion in a remote situation" was built in 1786 and rebuilt in 1807 after a fire. It was demolished in 1954, already in ruins after the last owner left in the 1930s.

As we have seen, however, other meetings of a less organised nature were held in Wales, particularly professional events, which appeared to be popular "in the south" according to a contemporary report. Like most reported meetings at the time the events at Aberystwyth in 1865 were divided into two classes - one for gentlemen amateurs and those for mechanics and professionals.

Bell's Life of 23 September 1865 records:

Athletic Sports at Aberystwyth, Wales
"On (the previous) Saturday, a series of athletic sports took place under the immediate direction of J. Chambers Esq of Trinity College, Cambridge, late President of the Cambridge University Boat Club, Pryse Pryse Esq. and other gentlemen of the county. £40 and upwards were awarded in prizes ....". Bell's Life continues: "700 persons paid for admittance and the money raised (about £25) was handed over to the local infirmary".

A selection of the results, as printed in *Bells Life* are as follows:

100 yds flat race (amateurs), won in two heats by Midgley of Birmingham.

High Jump: a tie between Chambers (Aberystwyth) and Southam (Birmingham). O.Roe of Aberystwyth being the next best. Greatest height being 4ft 8½ ins.

One Mile Walk won by Humphreys of Aberystwyth 8mins 45secs

Putting the Stone (14lbs) Chambers 33ft 9ins; 2, Jones 33ft 4ins of Jesus College Oxford who represented his University at the Inter Varsity Games

Throwing the Cricket Ball: Chambers 98yds 2ft; 2, Atwood (Aber) 94 yds.

One Mile: 1, M. Davies of rugbian celebrity.

The competition amongst mechanics and professionals followed:

100 yds flat: almost a walk over by Collier of Manchester whose graceful running elicited repeated shouts of applause.

Half Mile: won by Collier in 2mins 12secs easily.

It will be noted that as well as organising the meeting, Chambers also competed, winning the cricket ball throw and tying for first in the high jump with 4' 8 ½ (1.43m), so he can claim to be the inaugural holder of the Welsh high jump record. He also won the 7 miles walk at the inaugural AAC championships in Mincing Lane, London in 1866, as well as organising the meeting, and standardising the rules.

Chambers was indeed a remarkable man. As Peter Lovesey comments in his *Official Centenary History of the AAA* in 1980:

"In the 40 years of his life, John Graham Chambers rowed for Cambridge, founded the inter-varsity sports, became English (!) Champion Walker, coached four winning Boat-Race crews, devised the Queensberry Rules, staged the Cup Final and the Thames Regatta, instituted championships for billiards, boxing, cycling, wrestling and athletics, rowed beside Webb when he swam the Channel and edited a national newspaper. He was the architect of modern athletics."

Chambers virtually single-handed structured sport in Britain and indeed the world, as Britain led the way in introducing a structure to world sport. He drew up the rules of the modern track and field programme for the AAC in 1866, including the 120 yds hurdles, 16lb shot and 16lb hammer throw. The specification for these events have fundamentally remained unchanged to this day. But Chambers was not without his critics as during his tenure as secretary of the AAC, the forerunner of the AAA, Walter Rye accused him in his book *Rubbish and Nonsense* of mismanaging the AAC. Rye comments: "He was a strange character who tries to combine aristocratic sport with the running of the AAC for his own benefit at Lillie Bridge". This apathy towards Chambers in effect brought about the formation of the AAA in 1880.

John Chambers died at his home in Kensington in 1883, 3 years after he was instrumental in the formation of the AAA aged 40. Lovesey continues: ".... Chambers drove himself with almost manic energy." Before he died he opened a Welsh Shop in Chelsea, selling Welsh produce and goods. His trainer, Harry Andrews, born in Monmouth on 28th May 1831, managed the shop. Andrews was also an outstanding athlete, and his best performance was probably beating the renowned American Indian, Deerfoot and William Jackson in a professional 12 miles event in Canterbury in 1863. Later, Andrews was the groundsman at Lillie Bridge, the venue of the first AAA championships in 1880. He died at the age of 54.

We have further evidence of organised amateur athletics in Wales in the 1860s. H.F. Wilkinson's *Modern Athletics* (1877) reports that: "In the principality of Wales athletic sports have taken but little root, the Caernarvon meeting – founded in 1868 – being the only one of importance in the north. Although professional pedestrianism flourishes in the great mining districts of the south, amateur athletic meetings are rare, and chiefly confined to a few watering places where English visitors congregate during the season, Tenby being perhaps the oldest and most important reunion".

As illustrated with John Chambers' activities, the early impetus for amateur athletics in Wales came from the Universities and Colleges, and apart from the meeting in Aberystwyth in 1865, we know that meetings took place in St. David's College Lampeter and at Llandovery College in 1871. It is also likely that sports events took place in this year in both Swansea and Merthyr, but documentary evidence does not exist.

Lampeter and Llandovery to the fore

The annual sports meetings at Lampeter were amongst the first regularly held in Wales, and the college produced many fine athletes, the most famous being Kenneth Jenkins who was a finalist in the 200m at the 1938 European Championships in Paris. On 24th October 1871, which is the earliest record of the Lampeter meeting taking place, the event was held on the College cricket ground, with the weather "very wet" and the going "very heavy". The results included five wins for the inappropriately named Walter John Drought. Drought won the 100 yds by 2 feet from Meredith Hamer in 10¾ secs; the quarter mile race in 57.0 secs; Putting the Weight (15 lbs) 33'6 (10.21m); 120 yds hurdles in 19.4 secs and shared first place in the pole jump with James Thomas Powell with 8'1 (2.46m). On leaving Lampeter in 1872 with a BA, Drought held several ministries in Britain before moving abroad, first to Jamaica in 1874 and then to become Chaplain at

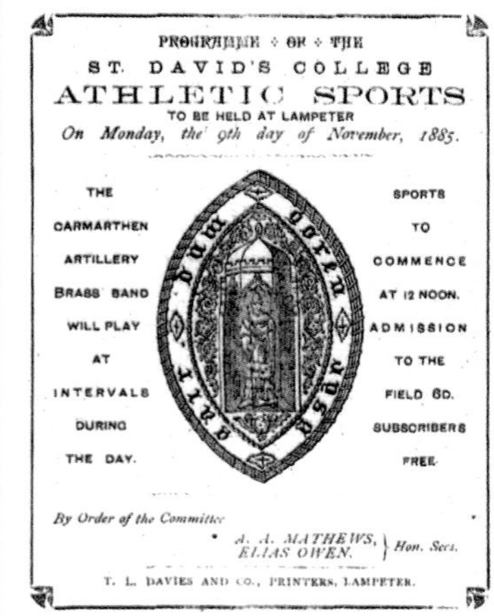
PROGRAMME OF THE
ST. DAVID'S COLLEGE
ATHLETIC SPORTS
TO BE HELD AT LAMPETER
On Monday, the 9th day of November, 1885.

THE CARMARTHEN ARTILLERY BRASS BAND WILL PLAY AT INTERVALS DURING THE DAY.

SPORTS TO COMMENCE AT 12 NOON. ADMISSION TO THE FIELD 6D. SUBSCRIBERS FREE.

By Order of the Committee
A. A. MATHEWS, *ELIAS OWEN,* } *Hon. Secs.*

T. L. DAVIES AND CO., PRINTERS, LAMPETER.

By permission St. David's College, Lampeter

This programme of the annual Lampeter meeting in 1885 is likely to be the earliest surviving programme of an athletics meeting in Wales.

Frieberg in 1879/80; Chantilly 1880/86; Dusseldorf 1886/91 and Dunkerque from 1892. He was probably an Irishman. Hamer and Powell also entered the Church on leaving Lampeter.

Although the 1871 meeting is the earliest documented event discovered so far at Lampeter it is likely that some form of athletics activity took place soon after Revd Rowland Williams arrived at the College as Vice Principal in 1850. Interestingly, D.T.W. Price contradicts this in his first volume of the History of the College, when he says "the only organised Games before 1878 was croquet".

We also know that amateur athletics meetings were held at Llandovery College around the same time as they started in Lampeter. On 10th May 1871, the Welsh Collegiate Institution held a meeting on the cricket field with the weather "beautifully fine". According to the *"Athletic Almanac"* 10 events were held, including a "pole jump", and "wide jump". T. Williams won five events including the 120 yds hurdles over 10 flights – the same specification as today. His win in the pole jump, the predecessor of today's pole vault, in 9'6 (2.89m) was particularly noteworthy, and can be regarded as an inaugural Welsh record for the event.

Further evidence of athletics activity during this period comes from the establishment of a recreation ground and cinder track in 1860 by the industrialist William Gilbertson so that "Pontardawe's sportsmen could play rugby and run".

Williams of Bassaleg sets world record for the shot

The inter-varsity athletics match (Cambridge v Oxford) started in 1864, and Welshmen were prominent in the early years. But both universities held athletics events before this. In 1859 Hugh Williams born in Bassaleg, near Newport, Mon on 23 December 1833 won the shot putt at the Cambridge University sports with 35'2 (10.72m) for what is regarded as a world record for the regulations in existence at the time. He improved this to 36'0 (10.97m) in the 1860 meeting

Another Welshman, David Parker Morgan, of Oxford who was born around 1842/43, the 4th son of William Morgan of Maesmynis, near Brecon set four world bests under the prevailing conditions for the hammer, with a best of 91'2 ¼ (27.80m) in 1866. He was a prolific performer in inter-varsity matches. At Fenner's in 1865, he finished third in the 100 yds and 120 yds hurdles; and in the match the following year in Oxford, he won the 120 yds hurdles in 18¼ secs, and finished third in both the shot and hammer – in the latter event behind his cousin Richard John James, who finished second. Morgan was vicar of Aberavon 1870-75; vicar of Aberdovey 1871-76 and assistant minister of the Church of Heavenly Rest, New York 1881-85.

James was the son of the local vicar. He was born in Llandysul in 1844, and won the hammer at the first AAC champs in 1866 when at Cambridge University, with David Parker Morgan in second place, with 75'0 (22.86m). Like his father, James also became a vicar at several parishes before spending 49 years up to 1929 at St. Ishmael with Llansaint and Ferryside. He died in 1933 aged 89.

William Cowell Davies was another remarkable Welsh athlete during the early 1870s. He was born at Bala on 7th October 1848. He finished second in the AAC 120 yds hurdles championship of 1871, and won the same event for Oxford at the inter-varsity meeting at Lillie Bridge, London in the same year with 16.6secs which can be regarded as an inaugural Welsh record for the event. He was called to the Bar in 1874, and unusually, continued with his athletics exploits afterwards. Even more surprisingly he took part in ultra running events, and in an amateur "go as you please" as such events were then called at the Agricultural Hall, Islington on 9th October 1880, he set a number of world bests, covering

80 miles in 11 hours 45 mins 35 secs and 81 miles in 12 hours. These times beat the bests by both professional and amateurs. He died in 1911 in Streatham, London aged 63.

An "Olympic Festival" took place in Llandudno on 26th June 1866, which was part of the Liverpool "Olympic" Festival series. There is also a record of an annual meeting in Llandrindod Wells on 20th August 1872, suggesting that athletics meetings had been held there for some years earlier. Meetings were also held in Merthyr on 11th October 1875 and Caernarvon 11th August 1876.

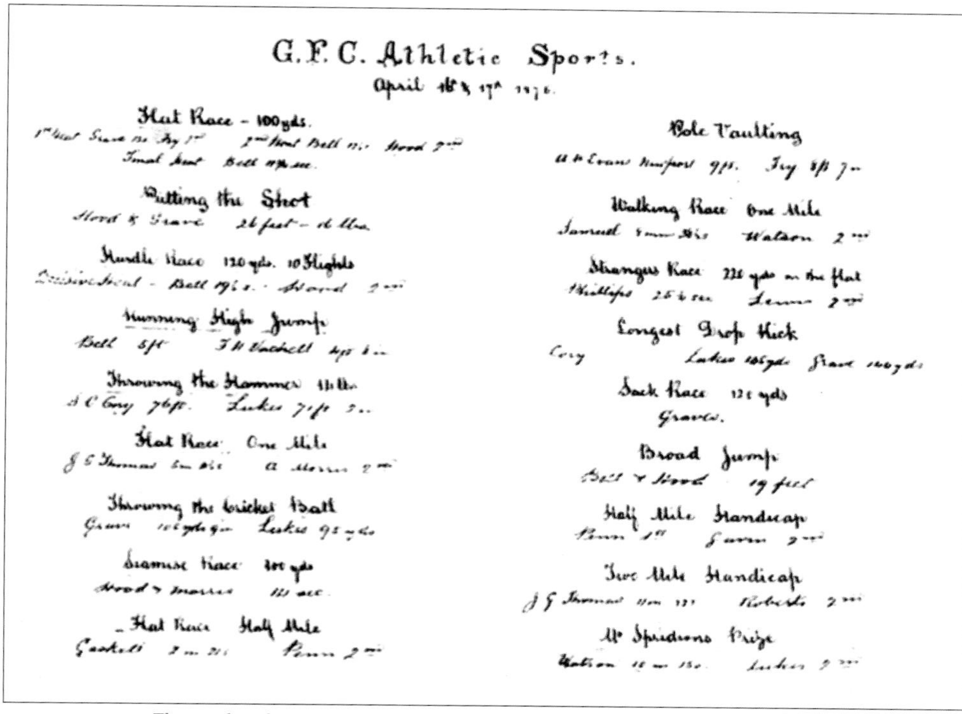

G.F.C. Athletic Sports.
April 16th & 17th 1875.

Flat Race - 100 yds.
[illegible]

Putting the Shot
[illegible] 26 feet [illegible]

Hurdle Race 120 yds. 10 Flights
[illegible] Bell [illegible] 2nd

Running High Jump
Bell 5 ft [illegible]

Throwing the Hammer [illegible]
[illegible] Lukes [illegible]

Flat Race One Mile
J G Thomas [illegible] 2nd

Throwing the Cricket Ball
Graves [illegible] Lukes [illegible]

Siamese Race 100 yds
[illegible]

Flat Race Half Mile
Gaskell [illegible] Penn 2nd

Pole Vaulting
[illegible] Newport 9 ft. [illegible]

Walking Race One Mile
[illegible] Watson 2nd

Strangers Race 220 yds on the flat
Phillips [illegible] 2nd

Longest Drop Kick
Cory [illegible] Lukes [illegible] Graves [illegible]

Sack Race 120 yds
Graves.

Broad Jump
Bell & Hood 19 feet

Half Mile Handicap
Penn 1st [illegible] 2nd

Two Mile Handicap
J G Thomas [illegible] Roberts 2nd

Mr Spiridions Prize
Watson [illegible] Lukes 2nd

The results of one of the earliest recorded amateur meetings in Cardiff (1875).

"Athletic Sports" were held by Glamorgan Football Club - the forerunner of Cardiff RFC – on April 16th and 17th 1875 in Cardiff. The meeting was probably held on the area which was to become known as Cardiff Arms Park.

The following month, on Whit Monday, 17th May 1875, St. Helen's Swansea was officially opened with an athletics meeting. A crowd of 6 to 7,000 people were attracted to a meeting which included a blindfold wheelbarrow race! So here we see athletics or "sports" as they were called, playing an important part in the early years of rugby at two of Wales' most famous grounds.

By 1878, there are records of several amateur meetings being held in Wales:

Wrexham Hare & Hounds	June 12
Newtown AC	July 20
Merthyr Tydfil	July 25
Newport AC	Aug 5
Rhayader	Aug 22
Tenby	Aug 22
Caernarvon AC	Aug 29

A meeting was held in Carmarthen on Whit Monday in 1879 when Frank McGuire of Trinity College won the Corporation Half Mile and won £5 and a silver medal, and further meetings were held in Conway (30th August 1879); Cardiff College (24th July 1880) and Rhyl on 16th October 1883. These were meetings for amateurs, so the reference to McGuire winning £5 is a mystery.

Elsewhere in this book there is reference to the very close link that athletics has with rugby football in Wales. As has already been seen, both Cardiff RFC and Swansea Cricket & Football Club held amateur athletics meetings in 1875. Rev. Edward Peake a member of the first Welsh rugby team against England in 1881 had his career cut short by a hurdling accident at Oxford. He finished third in the 120 yds hurdles in the 1883 varsity match at Lillie Bridge.

Richard Mullock, man of many guises – and probably sport's first "Mr. fix-it"

By permission of Steve Lewis

Richard Mullock

Richard Mullock of Newport Athletic Club, who was instrumental in the formation of the Welsh Football (Rugby) Union in 1880, and its first honorary secretary, was, along with John Chambers, present at the formation of the AAA in Oxford in 1880. When he returned from the AAA meeting he set about establishing the first rulebook for Welsh athletics. He was a member of the AAA General Committee for several years during the 1880s at the same time as he was secretary of the Welsh Football Union. Also at this time, the Earl of Jersey was both President of the Welsh Football Union and the AAA. It is possible that Mullock's contact with the Earl of Jersey at the AAA brought about his connection with Welsh rugby.

Newport Athletic Club, of which Newport RFC at the time was part, and was therefore not confined solely to athletics, was formed in 1875. The club started holding athletic sports meetings "immediately" - although there is a newspaper record showing that a meeting was held in Newport in May 1874, and probably on the Marshes – land between Wyndham Street and Malpass Pill. As such, Newport AC can be regarded as the pioneers of "club" athletics in Wales, especially as they

Finish of a sprint event at the Newport Athletic Grounds, Rodney Parade over a century ago. The athlete in the hooped vest on the right is believed to be Arthur Gould.

were the first Welsh club to be affiliated to the AAA on its formation in 1880. Caernarvon AC were the second, being admitted in the following year. An indication of the esteem with which Newport AC was held at the time was that they were one of only two clubs (London AC was the other) to have direct representation at AAA committee meetings. This situation almost certainly came about because of their member base of more than 300, which included the members of all of their sections, including rugby, gymnastics, cricket, cycling, tennis, hockey and bowls. Undoubtedly, Richard Mullock would not have been particularly forthcoming on this point, as he had a reputation of being a "wheeler dealer". All other clubs at the time received voting rights through their area associations.

Strangely, when Mullock was elected to the AAA General Committee in 1881, it was as a representative of the "West of England Clubs" and therein probably lies the answer why Welsh athletics was controlled by the AAA for over a century until the formation of the British Athletic Federation (BAF) in 1991 and the Athletics Association of Wales (AAW) a year earlier.

Mullock had considerable influence in athletics circles, as he did in Welsh rugby. In the Newport sports of 1885, when the redoubtable Arthur Gould of rugby fame won four events, the referee was none other than Charles Herbert, secretary of the AAA between 1883 and 1906, who was, along with Baron Pierre de Coubertin, one of the founders of the modern Olympic Games in 1896.

In the first report published by Newport AC, it said "proceeds of the athletic meetings, 1874/75 £49 16s 8d". Athletics meetings were held regularly at the Newport AC Grounds at Rodney Parade to the beginning of the First World War, and up to 1899 meetings were held on Easter Monday, Whit Monday, and August Bank Holiday, along with occasional meetings on Saturdays or during the evening. Many famous athletes of the day took part including Walter George, the multi world record holder and winner of twelve AAA and English Cross Country Union titles; Edgar Bredin winner of five AAA 440/880 titles; and 1908 Olympic 100m champion Reg Walker of South Africa. Later in their careers, Walker and Bredin took part in the professional circuit in Wales, competing at the Harlequins Ground in Cardiff and Pontypridd's Taff Vale Park.

The contribution to Welsh athletics made by Newport Athletic Club in the formative years cannot be overestimated. Apart from Mullock, many of their officials and athletes left indelible marks on the sport in Wales. W. Petherbridge, was the first appointed officer from the AAA in London for Cardiff and Newport in 1886; W. Clifford Phillips, who was captain of Newport RFC in their first match in 1875, was the first appointed delegate from South Wales to the Southern Committee of the AAA in 1894, whilst Harry Packer, another rugby stalwart who won seven Welsh caps in the 1890s and managed the 1924 British Lions, was President of the South Wales & Mon AAA from 1919 to 1939. He was also President of the Welsh Cross Country Association from 1920 to 1927 and twice President of the International Cross Country Union. Furthermore, many of the early Welsh championships were held under the auspices of Newport Athletic Club, and the first fully integrated Welsh athletics championships were held at their grounds at Rodney Parade in 1907.

By permission of Steve Lewis

Harry Packer

Newport's brightest and best-known athletics star was 44 times capped rugby wing and 1948 Olympic relay silver medallist Ken Jones, who won sixteen Welsh titles. Literally dozens of their athletes were winners of Welsh titles in the early years, including Wyatt Gould who competed in the 1908 London Olympics in the 400m hurdles. Gould was one of six brothers, but the biggest star of them all was Arthur Gould.

Pen Portrait – Arthur Joseph Gould (Newport AC) 1864 – 1919*

By permission of Steve Lewis

Arthur Gould

There is no doubt that "Monkey" Gould would have been a truly outstanding athlete had he decided to concentrate on athletics, instead of rugby union. He is described in contemporary reports, as the "W.G. Grace of Rugby" and won 27 Welsh rugby caps between 1885 and 1897, captaining his country on 18 occasions. He is described in *Who's Who of Welsh International Rugby Players* (Jenkins, Pierce, and Auty, 1990) as the first superstar of Welsh Rugby. Gould was nicknamed "Monkey" in his schooldays because of his lithesome ability to climb trees. By all accounts he was a strikingly handsome individual, standing almost 5'11 tall and weighing 11 stone.

Remarkably, Arthur Gould, born in Newport on October 10th 1864, was one of six brothers, all of whom played rugby for Newport. Their father, Joseph, who had come from Oxford to work in the brass foundry business in Newport, was an enthusiastic supporter of rugby in Newport and was a cricketer. Three of the Gould brothers were to play rugby for Wales, whilst younger brothers Gus and Wyatt were also outstanding athletes.

No records exist of his performances in Welsh championships, but his athletics prowess is well documented - particularly across the border in England. Despite his amateur status, he is reputed to have won more than £1,000 in foot races alone by the time he left to work in the West Indies in 1890. On his return 18 months later, he ran in the handicap 100 yds at the Private Banks' sports at Catford Bridge, London and won off scratch from 73 other runners. He also won the handicap 120 yds hurdles that day, beating the AAA Champion of two years earlier, Sherard Joyce, with both men off 18 yds. After this performance, he is quoted as saying that he was lamentably out of condition, and "must get some of this superfluous flesh off". He also said that he had won about 100 prizes for running. *The Welsh Athlete,* a weekly newspaper devoted to all sports, said on 30th November 1891: "Gould has no equal as a hurdle racer, and if time had permitted, he would have assuredly have taken the Amateur Championship". This almost certainly referred to the AAA Championship.

There is no doubt that the 120 yds hurdles was his best event, as he placed third in the AAA Championships on two occasions, firstly in 1887, when John Le Fleming clocked 16.2 secs to win, and in 1893 when four times winner Godfrey Shaw, won in 16.4 secs. For good measure, Gould also finished fourth in the AAA 100 yds in 1887. He is reputed to have clocked 10.2 for 100 yds, but there are no other records of his times. In 1893, he also won both the Midland Counties 120 yds hurdles and 100 yds titles.

As is documented elsewhere, his club Newport AC were probably the trail blazers of organised amateur athletics in Wales, and Gould regularly competed in their

events at Newport. In fact, when only 13 years old in 1877, at sports events to celebrate the opening of Rodney Parade, *Fields of Praise* reports that: " Mr J. Hooper, jun and Master A.J. Gould were attired in motley and amused the crowd with their capers"

On 30th May 1885 Gould won the open sprint, hurdles and high jump in the Whit Monday open meeting in front of 4,000 spectators at Rodney Parade. Gould, in an interview with *The Welsh Athlete* on 5th October 1891 says: " When I last ran in Newport in 1890, I won the whole of the events for which I entered, and the following day .... I brought off the 120 hurdles and quarter off scratch. In the two days I landed 25 guineas' worth of prizes". In the same edition, *The Welsh Athlete* also reported that in Portsmouth, on two occasions, he carried off three first prizes on the same day.

A unique fact about the Gould brothers is that apart from Arthur, two others - Gus and Wyatt - won bronze medals in the 120 yds hurdles at the AAA championships. Gus finished 3rd in 1899, whilst Wyatt, four times winner of the Welsh 120 yds title, including the inaugural championship in 1902, finished third in 1903. Wyatt also ran in the 400m hurdles in the 1908 London Olympics, and captained Newport RFC in 1905/06.

Gould was held in such high esteem, that in 1896, a testimonial was organised to commemorate his "brilliant success as an all round athlete and in recognition of his services to rugby". This created a furore, particularly from the (English) Rugby Football Union, who said that by accepting, Gould would be declared a professional. A house was presented to him as part of the proceeds. The redoubtable Richard Mullock the Newport secretary designed the testimonial and the President of the Welsh Football Union, the forerunner of the Welsh Rugby Union, Sir John T.D. Llewellyn MP, presented it to him. Gould retired after he was presented with the testimonial, and it is not clear if he retired as a result of the mayhem it caused in rugby circles, as it led to the temporary suspension of international rugby matches against the other home countries. After his retirement, he continued as a committee member at Newport AC, became a first class referee and Welsh rugby selector.

He died at the young age of 55. *The Western Mail* reported that he had an "athlete's heart" and suffered a haemorrhage whilst at work at the brewers Phillips in Newport. He was taken home and died that afternoon. His funeral was one of the biggest seen in Newport and newspaper coverage of his death was probably the largest of any Welshman until the death of Lloyd George some 30 years later.

* *Actually christened Joseph Arthur Gould*

Regrettably, membership of Newport AC declined after the Second World War, and the athletics section of the club is now defunct, and memories of bygone days have become lost in the present era of professional rugby union. However, the groundbreaking work by their early members has ensured that the name of Newport Athletic Club will always be remembered for the pioneering role they undertook in Welsh athletics.

In the early days of rugby in Wales many of the clubs were referred to as "Harriers". For example, there were, amongst others, Tredegar Harriers, Oakfield Harriers, Llanelly Harriers, and intriguingly Newport Harriers – prior to their formation as an athletics and cross-country club. There are records of Newport Harriers playing rugby against Pontypridd and Llandaff in September of 1891. Newport Harriers as the athletics club was formed in 1896, and like their rivals across town, Newport Athletic Club, have made a significant impact on Welsh athletics – particularly in cross-country running, which is covered elsewhere. They are the oldest surviving athletics club in Wales. Pill Harriers of Newport, who took part in many cross-country events in the 1920s, still play rugby today under that name. The nickname of Llanelli RFC in their early days was "The Llanelly Runners".

Lots of activity at Welsh Colleges in latter part of the 19th Century

Although it was not until after the Second World War (1947) that the University of Wales Athletic Union was formed, and championships began to be held, there was considerable athletics activity in Welsh colleges in the latter part of the 19th century and the early part of the last century. The earliest inter-college event was a men's 440 yards which was first held at Aberystwyth in 1892, and continued at this venue until 1899 when the three colleges of the University of Wales – Cardiff, Bangor and Aberystwyth – started to hold the event on a rota basis. Apparently there was a problem with the starting pistol in the first race, and it had to be started with a whistle! A.H. Schmittner of Aberystwyth won the race in 55.0. This event remained the only inter-college track and field event until 1922, when further events were added to the programme.

Formal championships did not start until 1948, but at Cardiff's sports in 1899, the 100 yards and high jump were also open to competitors from Bangor and Aberystwyth. The March 1899 edition of the *Magazine of the University College of South Wales and Monmouthshire, Cardiff* reported that the event would take place at the Harlequins ground during the first week in May. Amongst the events scheduled was a 150 yards event for "boys of Intermediate Schools of Cardiff and District", and two ladies events. However, the results do not include any ladies events, so it is not certain if they were held. The meeting, on May 4th, held under the patronage of Lord Tredegar, included over a dozen events and 1908 110m hurdles Olympian Wallis Walters took part in several events – including the handicap mile – but won his speciality (120 yards hurdles) in 18.0. Representatives from schools at Pengam, Porth, Penarth, Newport, as well as Cardiff took part in the schools 150 yards won by C. Williams of Newport in 17.8 secs. The first recorded meeting at Cardiff College took place at Sophia Gardens on 8th May 1889, with 14 events being competed for including a 3 legged race, "broad jump" and one mile bicycle race, apart from "standard" events such as 100, 220 and 440 yards; high jump and one mile walk. The Cardiff College magazine reported, "The day was fine but did not pour". It is not thought that any equivalent Cardiff meeting was held until the 1899 event.

Both Bangor and Aberystwyth also held annual college sports around the same time as Cardiff, and some events – as well as the inter-college 440 yards – were open to athletes from the other two colleges and local amateurs. It is likely that Aberystwyth held sports soon after their formation in 1872. Along with Bangor, they were certainly holding college sports by 1891/92. By 1921 we have records of women's events being held in the Cardiff Sports and Bronwen Jones became Victrix Ludorum by winning three events, the 880 yards and both high and long jumps. There was also a women's Tug of War event. The Cardiff Sports of 1922 also included inter-college events and these included wins for I.O Jones (Aberystwyth) in the men's 100 yards (10.2) and the women's event resulted in a dead-heat between Connie Barnes and Kitty Walker (both Cardiff) in 12.6 secs.

Aberystwyth's Ann Hatfield just misses a UK high jump best

In the Aberystwyth Sports on May 2nd 1925, Ann Hatfield won the high jump with 4'10 (1.47m), a leap which was only marginally behind the best recorded by a British athlete at the time (Hilda Hatt 1.50m). Hatfield, born in 1904, went on to win the event at the

Women's Inter-Varsity Athletic (WIVAB) Sports at Manchester just two weeks later with 1.38m. Another fine performance at Manchester came from another Aberystwyth athlete Eiris Evans who missed winning the 880 yards by ½yard. Unfortunately only winning times were recorded in those days, but based on the winning time of 2:38.4 it can be safely assumed that she ran 2:38.5. The performances of Hatfield at Aberystwyth and Evans can be safely taken as inaugural Welsh records.

Members of Welsh Colleges have competed in the Universities Athletic Union (UAU) Championships since their inception in 1920 (men) and WIVAB Sports since 1924, although unofficial sports were held for the latter from 1921. D.J.P. Richards of Aberystwyth, winner of numerous Welsh running and walking titles, was the first Welsh winner of a UAU title when he took the three miles in 1925. He followed this up with further wins in 1926, 1928 and 1929. He competed for Britain in the 1928 World Student Games in Paris. Mair Roberts of Aberystwyth won the hurdles events in the unofficial 1921 WIVAB Sports, with the afore-mentioned Bronwen Jones of Cardiff finishing third in the mile.

Marjorie Clements, a former pupil at Cardiff High School, took the WIVAB 440 yards at Liverpool in 1925 (67.2). Surprisingly, five years later she was still at Cardiff University and won the 100 yards at their sports in 12.0, which was the fastest recorded at the time by a Welsh woman. Another fast 100 was recorded by Olive Jones (12.1) when she won the event at the Bangor College Sports, just 4 days after Clements' run on May 7th. Eric Cowe, in his *Early Women's Athletics: Statistics and History, 1999,* reports that Clements' father owned the Grosvenor Hotel, Splott, Cardiff.

Universities of Wales Cross-Country Championships start in 1923

The early 1920s were an exciting time for athletics in the University of Wales. Not only was there a widening of the events in the Inter-Collegiate track and field but also the formation of College Harriers clubs. At Cardiff, the club was formed in November of 1922. In the spring of 1923, appropriately on St. David's Day, the inaugural University of Wales cross-country championships for men was staged at Aberystwyth with the hosts claiming both the individual and team titles.

Initially the event rotated annually among the three established colleges at Aberystwyth, Bangor and Cardiff. The newly established Swansea College competed for the first time in 1929 but did not host the event until 1932 and had to wait until 1963 for its first individual winner and team victory.

Included among the winners of the title are multi Welsh title-winner D.J.P. Richards (Aberystwyth), Empire Games mile winner Jim Alford (Cardiff), Commonwealth and European marathon champion Ian Thompson (Cardiff) and, more recntly, former GB junior international Nathaniel Lane (Cardiff), who, bizarrely, won the event by running the fastest leg of the university runners in the Micky Morris relays in 2001! Richards took part in the 1928 World Student Games in Paris and won the UAU cross-country title in 1929 at Winkworth Park, Leeds.

The first great Welsh sprinters

Welsh sprinters were at the forefront of British athletics at the turn of the century. Both Charles Thomas of Landovery College, Reading AC and Oxford University, and Fred Cooper (Abergavenny AC and Bradford AC) set British records for 100 yds of 10.0secs. Although it has to be said that no fewer than 50 athletes had clocked 10.0 seconds flat between 1855 and 1899! Despite this, there is no doubt that both Thomas and Cooper were amongst the leading British sprinters of their time

By permission of Llandovery College

Charles Thomas

Thomas won the Welsh 100 yds title for five successive years between 1893 and 1897, winning again in 1899, with Cooper winning in 1898. Cooper also won the AAA 100 yds title in 1898, equalling the British record, and to this day is one of only three Welshmen to win AAA 100 yds/100m titles – Rhymney born Berwyn Jones of Monmouthshire TC, Caerleon & Birchfield H (1963) and Ron Jones (Birchgrove H, Woodford Green AC & Borough of Enfield H) in 1969, being the only others. Cooper also finished third in the AAA 100 yds in 1899. Thomas never won an AAA title, but finished third on two occasions - 1894 and 1896 – and fourth in 1895.

Born in Merthyr Tydfil, on 28th May 1873, Thomas in fact clocked "evens" (10.0) on several occasions, but only the performance at Oxford on 8th March 1899 was ratified as a British record by the AAA. His first 10.0 set some two years earlier at the Merton College Sports, Oxford was rejected at the AAA General Committee on 7th May 1898 and a 10.0 clocking at Abergavenny on 2 August 1897 was also rejected as the "100 yds track" was partly downhill. Additionally, Thomas clocked an unsubstantiated 9.8 at Abergavenny on Aug 3rd the following year and won the 100 yds at three successive inter-varsity meetings (1989-1900). In a meeting in Cardiff on 12th August 1893, he was narrowly beaten by the four-times AAA 100 yds champion, Charles Bradley, who equalled the British record and set a new Welsh all-comers record of 10.0. Bradley also won in Cardiff two years later in 9.8, but for some unknown reason this was never ratified as a British record. Thomas equalled the British record for the little run 120 yds flat at Alresford, Hants, on 8th June 1894, clocking 11.8 secs. This time equalled the record held by Bradley and William Phillips, winner of the AAA 100 yds championship between 1880 and 1882. Altogether in 1894, Thomas won eight of the thirteen races he contested.

Fred Cooper

Fred Cooper was born in Abergavenny in 1871, and like many sprinters of his time, he was an outstanding rugby player. After initially playing for and captaining his hometown club, he played for Newport in season 1892/93, before turning professional with Bradford, where he was a prolific try-scorer between 1895 and 1899. He was also an outstanding goal kicker and kicked 171 goals between 1895 and 1900. Intriguingly, when Cooper won his *Amateur* Athletic Association (AAA) title in 1898, he had been a professional rugby league player with Bradford for three years.

During 1891 and 1892, he won £60 worth of prizes at all of the principal athletics meetings in south Wales. At the Roath meeting on 20th June 1891, he won both the 120 yds and 440 yds handicaps, amounting to "12 guineas worth" of prizes. He also won several prizes over hurdles from "Newport, Penarth, Builth and other places".

Crouch start pioneer was a Welshman

Apart from the link with John Chambers, Wales has another claim to fame with the establishment of athletics rules in Britain. Tom Nicholas of Monmouth AC pioneered the crouch start in Britain, and for that matter in the world. A former pupil of Monmouth School, along with others he started to place his hands over the start line claiming that as long as his feet were behind the line, this was within the rules. However, the AAA ruled in 1889 that this contravened the rules. After a long argument by the committee and a small majority (6-5) it was decided that no part of the body must touch the ground in front of the mark before the pistol fire. This rule remains in force today. Nicholas won the AAA 440 yds in a Welsh record 51.8 secs in 1890, which stood for 20 years. He died in Aberaeron aged 63 in 1924.

Two years after the formation of the AAA in 1880, Roath (Cardiff) Harriers was formed. It came about as a result of a wager from men employed in the various offices of shipping factors in Cardiff Docks. Viv Pitcher takes up the story in his *History of Roath (Cardiff) Harriers* in 1952: "A number of young men who were proud of their athletic prowess decided to test their skills in a cross-country race ... over their morning coffee. Interestingly, he says that when formed, Roath were the first club in Wales to be dedicated to athletics, but we now know that Caernarvon AC were admitted to the AAA in 1881, and Newtown AC and Wrexham Hare and Hounds were in existence in 1878, two years before the formation of the AAA.

Like both Newport clubs, the Roath club was to make a significant impact on Welsh athletics and cross-country running, and officials at the club were instrumental in the formation of the Welsh Cross Country Association (WCCA) in 1896; and Cyril Howell and Eddie O'Donnell, were the prime movers behind the formation of the Welsh AAA in 1948. Roath merged with Birchgrove (Cardiff) Harriers in November 1968 to form Cardiff AAC.

The AAA General Committee of 14th August 1883 stated that Welsh clubs with voting rights were Newport, Monmouth AC (330 members, given 3 votes); Caernarvon AC (30 members, one vote); Swansea Club (30 members, 1 vote), but with no mention of Roath. In 1883, control of athletics in London and the Southern District (of England) was given to a Southern Committee of the AAA, with similar duties and responsibilities as the English Midlands and Northern Counties, who had been in existence prior to the formation of the AAA in 1880. At this same committee meeting, seven Welsh athletes were suspended from amateur competition for receiving cash or cheque prizes at the Cardiff Easter Tuesday Sports.

South Wales still a hotbed for professional athletics in late nineteenth century

Although the amateur form had, in the main taken root, it seems that professional athletics was still a force, particularly in south Wales. The AAA Jubilee Souvenir brochure (1930) reported: "In 1883 a surprising proposal was made that Clubs in Wales should be allowed to include events for professionals at amateur athletic meetings". Interestingly, the motion was put to the AAA General Committee by no less a person than AAA secretary Charles Herbert, so this request had significant credence. However, the motion was lost as members felt that it was "partial legislation" and as such the AAA would have no control, if any, of professional activity.

Cardiff Harlequins Football and Athletic Club started holding an annual sports meeting in 1883 but by 1887, just two Welsh clubs were affiliated to the AAA – Newport AC and Swansea AC, although it is not known if the latter had any connection with Swansea Cricket

& Football Club, which had an athletics section at the time. We also know that sports meetings were a feature at the Cowbridge School by 1888, and in that year, apart from other events, held a pole jump. Cowbridge School at the time was a boarding school and produced several fine athletes, including William Haines and Francis Willoughby Jones. Haines born around 1848 was third in the 3 miles inter-varsity meeting of 1870 and fourth in the mile the following year, whilst Willoughby Jones, born in Swansea on 3rd September 1853 clocked 52.5 for 440 yds at Oxford on 7th November 1874, which can be regarded as an inaugural Welsh record for the event. In later years, decathlon star Aneurin Evans, who emigrated to Australia and Aneurin "Nash" Thomas, who lost his life in the Second World War, were also pupils. More of Thomas later.

During the early 1890s numerous professional meetings were being held in Cardiff and the Glamorgan and Monmouthshire Valleys, and were attracting entries from far and wide. *The Welsh Athlete* reported in September 1891 that W.H. Taylor of Gloucester had complained bitterly about the treatment he had received at the Cardiff Sports. The same edition reported that a 120 yds running match of £20 a side, was won by George Davies of Pontymoil over Vaughan of Pontypool at Cwmbran Gardens. A later edition carried an advert proclaiming that George Thomas of Newport was willing to make a match for £10 to £25 a side to run 100 yds … "Thomas can be seen at the Newport AC Grounds", it continued. So again we have the question of professional athletes mixing with amateurs, a situation that appeared to be the norm in south Wales at the time, and perhaps explains the reason why the clubs in Wales made the proposal to the AAA in order to regularise the situation.

By 1893, similar clubs to Roath Harriers were being formed, and apart from Roath and Newport AC, clubs were also in existence at Chepstow, Penarth, Abergavenny and Barry. Workmen building Barry Docks formed Barry Dock Harriers in 1898. This club eventually became Barry Harriers, but it had no connection with the club of the same name that was active from the 1950s. The Wenvoe Castle Estate gave fifteen acres at the Buttrills in 1896 as a gift to Barry for recreational purposes, and Barry Dock Harriers held their first trial run from this venue. Athletics events in Barry took place at the annual Whit-Monday sports held on Cadoxton Moors between 1888-1890, and at the Witchill Athletic Grounds from 1891 onwards. In the 1891 sports, prizes amounted to £120 and three thousand attended "despite the bad weather".

By permission of Glamorgan Records Office

Barry Harriers 1906

Welshmen instrumental in creation of international race

In 1896, Wales' oldest surviving club, Newport Harriers was formed, and like Newport AC their officials and athletes have made a significant impact on the sport in Wales. Prior to their formation, there were a number of Harrier clubs in Newport, and Frank Liddington Johns, who had been Chairman, Treasurer and Secretary at the age of 18 of one of them, Caerau Harriers started his remarkable connection with the club, where he held virtually all of the key positions for over 50 years. Apart from his prominent activities at both Newport clubs, he was, with R.A. Pritchard of Roath Harriers, the driving force behind the formation of the International Cross Country race in 1903. He was Secretary of the International Cross Country Board from 1906 to 1911 and organiser of the International race on the first four occasions it was held in Wales. He died in 1959 aged 84. The length of service to club and country is likely to be matched by another Newport Harrier, Ivor Adams, who has been club secretary without a break from 1967, as well as serving Welsh athletics in numerous capacities.

In the AAA constitution of 1897, Llanelli Wheelers' Cy. and AC are listed as part of the (English) Midland Counties AAA, whilst Newport AC still had direct affiliation to the AAA, as had three clubs from Cardiff – Roath, Cardiff Harlequins F & AC; and Cardiff FC, and two from Swansea – Swansea C&FC and Swansea Harriers. The latter had no connection with the existing club of that name, which was formed in 1962 by members of Cockett Boys Club in the town, as it was then. There is no mention of any other Welsh club affiliation to the AAA around the turn of the century, although we know that at least two other clubs in Cardiff were in existence at the time - Cardiff H and St. Annes H. There is also a record of a club in Usk, and another Swansea club St. Helen's H. It is not known if the north Wales clubs referred to earlier were still in existence at this time.

In 1899, Cardiff Harlequins changed their name to Cardiff AC and for many years this club held both amateur and professional meetings at the Harlequins Ground, which is still in existence, just off Newport Rd, and used by St. Peters RFC, which famously beat near neighbours Cardiff RFC in the Welsh Rugby Cup in 1993. However, this Cardiff Harlequins club has no connection with the existing club of that name which was formed in 1983 by four members of Cardiff High School Old Boys. During the early part of the last century, the Harlequins ground was the Mecca for south Wales professional athletics and there are numerous references to professional events being held there around the turn of the century. The 1895 and 1896 Welsh Cross Country Champion, Harry Cullum of Cardiff, who was by now running as a professional, beat Edgar Bredin at the ground in September 1899 over a 1,000 yards to win £100, two months before he beat Bredin, the holder, to win the world's professional 880 yds title at Rochdale. In another meeting in 1899 at the Harlequins Ground, on May 22nd, Alf Downer beat Bredin over 350 yds to win £35. D.A. Jamieson in *Powderhall Grounds and Pedestrianism* (1943), describes Downer, a Jamaican-Scot, as the fastest and most versatile professional runner Scotland has produced giving further evidence that the leading British athletes of the time considered the Welsh venue as an important part of the professional circuit in Britain.

Pen Portrait – Harry Cullum
(Roath H, Cardiff H and Salford H) 1874 – 1953

One of the finest pedestrians – as professional athletes were called at the time - in Britain in the late 1890s and early 1900s was Harry Cullum of Cardiff, who won the world professional 880 yds championship at Rochdale in 1899. In his amateur days, he twice won the Welsh cross-country title, three Welsh mile titles and the 440 yds twice. In a letter to his grandson, Ron Cullum of Aberystwyth, in 1940, he said that during his career, he had won "hundreds of races from 100 yds to 10 miles". He also left Ron a collection of over 500 programmes.

He turned professional in 1899, and one of his motivations may have been his suspension as an amateur for a seemingly trivial offence at the Salford sports meeting of September 1898, when he was adjudged to have aided and abetted another athlete who had impersonated another. In those far off days, this was

probably a very serious offence, bearing in mind the amounts of money at stake both as prizes and betting winnings.

By permission of Ron Cullum

The 600 yards. professional championship of the World at Dundee Football Ground. Cardiff's Harry Callum is on the right. Note the size of the crowd.

In his finest race, he won the world professional half-mile championship in Rochdale on 4th November 1899, defeating the holder Edgar Bredin, in 2 minutes flat for a prize of £200. Many events in those days were handicaps, but it is believed that this race was a scratch event. Describing the race 40 years later, Harry said: "It was a very bad day and blowing a gale .... I had run 1:55 and 1:56.2 in time trials at Bradford and Leeds, so if the race had have been held in July or August, I would have smashed the record for I was flying at the time!". Bearing in mind in his amateur days, Bredin had won the AAA 880 yds title for three successive years between 1893 and 1895 clocking 1:55.3 to win in 1893; Harry's times were entirely believable. The Welsh amateur record at the time was his 2:01.5 set when finishing second in the AAA Championships of 1896, and the long standing professional record was 2:00.25 set in 1866 by William Richards.

Cullum had also beaten Bredin by 12 yds in Cardiff on 3rd September 1899 over 1000 yds. Bredin was reported to be very upset at Cullum's win in Rochdale, and demanded a re-match, which Cullum (apparently) refused. In all Cullum is reported to have won more than £3,000 in his professional career, a sum that is worth nearer £100,000 today. He ran all over Britain and on 30th September 1901, Scotland's J. Furguson beat him by a foot in an event that was billed as the 600 yds championship of the World. Furguson's time was 3/5ths of a second outside the world record.

In another race against Bredin at the Cardiff Harlequins Ground, in April 1900, this time over the unusual distance of 700 yds, Bredin won, pocketing a prize of £100. Earlier in the year, back at Rochdale, the Irish champion G.B. Tinkler beat Cullum over 1,000 yds to win £100.

In one of his last races before retiring in 1912, when 38 years old, he won the Stadium Half Mile Handicap at the Cardiff Stadium off a start of 70 yds, winning £35. The programme shows a Finnish athlete, William Kolehmainen - brother of five times Olympic gold medallist Hannes - three Americans and two Scots in a field of 43 entries, highlighting the popularity of events of this nature within Wales

Before turning professional, he won the second Welsh cross-county title as a member of Roath Harriers on a course from the Cardiff Harlequins Ground, beating teammate Egbert Fairlamb. The next year he was a prime mover in the formation of a new club in Cardiff, Cardiff Harriers and it was in their colours that he retained his title, beating the 1894 winner Hugh Fairlamb of Roath by the wide margin of 1min 39 secs. He could only finish 6th in the 1897 championship, but had the satisfaction of being part of the winning Cardiff team.

In his letter to his grandson he says that he won three Welsh mile titles and two Welsh 440 yds titles, but unfortunately there are no records of these performances, but based on the accuracy of other data contained in the letter, there is no doubt that his comments are accurate. He also finished second in the AAA half mile of 1896 at

Northampton, and fourth the following year in Manchester, also finishing 3rd in the mile. Unfortunately, there is very little further information on his amateur exploits, which must have been numerous. But what is not in doubt is that he was one of the finest athletes produced by Wales, and one of the leading British athletes of his time.

He worked for many years in the Cooperative Wholesale Society in Cardiff. He died in Llandaff North Cardiff in 1953 aged 79.

Like Cullum, Fred Davies of Tenby was one of the finest professional half milers in Britain during the early part of the last century, and as did Cullum, he achieved the unwanted accolade of being the scratch man - or "virtual" scratch man/backmarker* - at the Christmas Half Mile Handicap at the Powderhall meeting in Edinburgh. Cullum achieved this feat in 1900 and 1902, whilst Davies was the backmarker in 1908, 1911 and 1913. Davies, like Cullum, also won the World professional 880 yds championship, and was a prolific winner of professional events throughout Britain, and won events from 100 yds up to the mile. There are several recorded results of him running under 2 minutes for the 880 yds, but it is unclear whether he started off scratch (i.e. he could have run less than 880 yds) in these events. The Irishman Beauchamp "Bert" Day, who was one of the leading pro runners on the world stage, was beaten decisively by Davies at Pontypridd in 1909 in a time of 1:57.6, one of the fastest times recorded in the world that year, with both runners starting off scratch. Davies, nicknamed "Tenby", underlined his versatility by finishing second in the 1913 Welsh Powderhall 130 yds sprint behind J. Helens of Newcastle. He died in Cardiff in 1932.

* *Running with no allowance (start) at all or the last man to start, due, in the main, to the athletes' previous record of either winning races or achieving high positions.*

The Welsh Powderhall Handicap Sprint

Brian Lee in his *The Great Welsh Sprint – The story of the Welsh Powderhall Handicap 1903 – 1934* reports that Pontypridd Athletic Club formed a syndicate in December of 1900 to hold professional sprints. But the first Welsh Powderhall Sprint, a handicap event over 130 yds, started in 1903 at Taff Vale Park, Pontypridd and continued there until 1930 when the event moved to Virginia Park Caerphilly amid controversy and continued until 1934, when the event was discontinued. Lee reports in his book: "Tom Coggins of Caerphilly had spent £20,000 to make the Stadium the finest in the United Kingdom...it had a cinder track and a grandstand which would hold 5,000 people". Cinders in those days were either loose coal ash from the fire grate or gravel, but were still up to "2 ½ yds" faster than a grass track. The controversy had arisen because the promoter had incurred serious financial losses at Pontypridd, due to

By permission of Brian Lee

Welsh Powderhall finalists 1909. Left to right: Richie Rees (3rd), T. G. Thomas (4th), E. C. Holway (1st) and F. J. Thomas (2nd). David Williams the referee is on the extreme left and Ted Lewis (starter) is on the right.

being overcharged by the ground owners, and therefore decided to move the event to Caerphilly - but confusingly an event also calling itself the Welsh Powderhall still took place at Pontypridd in 1930 the week before the Caerphilly event. Despite this confusion, there was clear indication that professional athletics had strong roots in south Wales as both events attracted around 100 competitors in the Powderhall events alone. Taff Vale Park was a major venue for both professional and amateur events up to the Second World War, and was the venue for Jim Alford's famous mile victory over 1930 Empire Games Champion, Reg Thomas in 1937 in a Welsh record of 4:17.1. Alford further lowered his Welsh record when he emulated Thomas by taking the Empire mile title in Sydney the following year with 4:11.5. More of both Thomas and Alford later.

The Welsh Powderhall attracted runners from all over the world, including the 1904 Olympic 100 and 200m silver medallist Nat Cartmel of America and Australians Jack Donaldson and Arthur Postle. Donaldson, was the world professional 100 yds and 220 yds (21.1) record holder who ran at Taff Vale Park in 1910, 1912 and 1913 running off scratch on all three occasions, but, like Cartmel never won, obviously finding the scratch marks too much. In 1910 Donaldson won his heat beating F. Gill of Penygraig who had a start of 18 ½ yds. His best position was fourth in the 1913 final, but he again won his heat - one of 16 - in 12.4 secs. J. Helens of Newcastle won off a start of 15 yds. Earlier in the year, J. Sullivan of Barry had beaten the great Australian over 220 yds in Cardiff off a start of 27 yds in a time of 21.8 secs. Another American, C.E. Holway, who was a prolific performer in professional events in Britain at the time, did manage to win the 1909 event off 2 ½ yds, the shortest winning handicap in the history of the race. Reg Walker of South Africa, the 1908 Olympic 100m champion ran in the 1912 Powderhall, winning his heat, but again his short handicap proved too much and he failed to progress to the final.

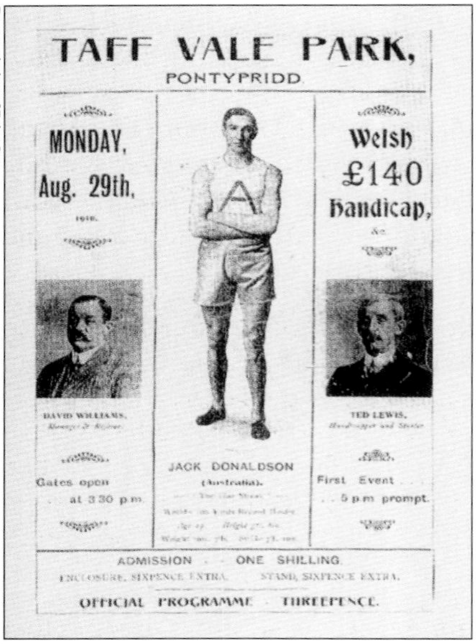

By permission of Brian Lee

The 1910 Welsh Powderhall programme with Jack Donaldson the world professional record holder for 100 and 220 yards on the cover.

Willie Applegarth, Britain's leading amateur sprinter, and a member of Britain's gold medal winning 4 x 100m relay team in the 1912 Stockholm Olympics before turning professional ran when past his best in 1921. Running off scratch, he failed to win his heat and therefore failed to qualify for the semi-finals. Usually, the Powderhall heats were held on a Saturday, with semi-finals and finals held on the following Monday. On 28th June 1913, he set what is believed to be the first outright British amateur record in Wales when he clocked 14.4 secs for the little-run 150 yds at Cardiff. He also won the 100 yds at the same meeting in 9.8, which was also a British amateur record, but for some unknown reason it was never ratified.

In 1922, a record 20 heats were held, with 180 competitors taking part. In 1933, the event attracted between 20,000 and 40,000 spectators. Intriguingly, the first two finishers in the 1930 Pontypridd event, Les Thomas and Selwyn Fletcher were wing three-quarters from Pontypridd RFC, so were therefore playing amateur rugby, but running professionally!

Unfortunately, the event, like most professional meetings and races was awash with cheating, a fact which ultimately, along with the growing strength of organised amateur athletics, contributed to its downfall. Most of the cheating surrounded trying to hoodwink the handicapper into believing that you were not as good as you really were. This sometimes involved deliberately hanging back in minor races in order to deceive the handicapper. In the 1921 event, a band of bookmakers from the Midlands disappeared after the heats in order to avoid paying out after they had offered extravagant odds!

Malcolm Lewis of *The South Wales Echo* in 1960 described the skulduggery and cunning, which occurred in those days to win the not insignificant cash prizes, and betting winnings, when he interviewed Michael "Jake" Crowley, the 1912 winner from Cardiff. Crowley claimed that he had made his biggest "killing" in the history of the Powderhall race and that he had embarked on a giant hoodwink that brought him a £900 pay-off. He said: "I waited nine years for my chance. To give the idea that I couldn't run fast enough I entered races with a little piece of lead inserted in the sole of my running shoes. I also carried a piece in the black belt I wore around my waist". Brian Lee picks up the story: "The man behind the deception was the boxer Peerless Jim Driscoll who was a bookmaker at the Powderhall and other sporting events. Driscoll, who won a huge amount in the race, gave the Cardiff-born Irishman £800 to add to the £100 he won as winner of the 1912 event". To put this amount in context, it has to be remembered that a terraced house in Cardiff at the time could be bought for about half that figure. Incidentally, Crowley also played rugby for Cardiff between 1909 and 1920 underlining again that rugby authorities at the time turned a blind eye to this form of professionalism.

In his book, Lee recounts several other cases of athletes holding back in minor events to obtain good handicaps, including Pat Barry of Cardiff, who apparently ran without distinction in several handicap races all over Wales between 1919 and 1923 to allow him to get a handicap of 20 yds, which was sufficient for him to win the 1923 Powderhall and so allow his backers to pull a big betting coup. He was a 100-1 outsider before the event when he won aged 26 to take the coveted prize and allow his backers to clean up. The first prize up to 1908 was £100 and thereafter it was increased to £140. Winners of the heats and semi-finals also won cash amounts varying from 10 shillings (50p) to £10.

Although the Powderhall 130 yds sprint was the main event on the programme, other events were held, and in 1904, the second occasion that the event took place, amateur events were also held. This was clearly in contravention of AAA laws at the time.

As described earlier, many other professional meetings were held in Wales at the time, including the rival event, the Cambrian Dash, which was also held at Taff Vale Park, and the Coronation Sprint, held at the "Welsh White City" at Sloper Road, Cardiff. The Scottish Powderhall dates back to 1870 and is still held today on New Year's Day. During the early part of the last century, there are records of professional meetings taking place at Porthcawl, Merthyr, Fleur-de-Lys, New Tredegar and Bargoed.

"Unlucky" Weaver, the unheralded sprint star and runner-up specialist

Despite never being a winner of the Welsh Powderhall, Colin Weaver of Llanhilleth, was an outstanding runner and one of the leading professional sprinters in Britain at the time. He reached the final of four Scottish Powderhalls finishing second in 1935, 1943 and 1946 and was "bought out" of the Army by a bookmaker in 1935 to run in the Scottish event. He reached the Welsh Powderhall final only once - 1931 - when his brother Reg, the backmarker, won off a start of 12 yds. In the Stoke-on-Trent handicap 100 yds, he clocked 9.9 secs off scratch, a time which was on a par with the leading British amateur sprinters of his day. In fact there is no doubt that many of the top Welsh Powderhall runners of yesteryear would have won some of the important amateur titles of their day - and of course if they had have been around today, they would have been allowed to do so. Dubbed "Unlucky Weaver" because of his succession of runners-up positions in the Scottish event, he was asked if he could have won any of them. He told Brian Lee wryly: "I was running to orders!" He died in May 2000 in his hometown, aged 86. Brother Reg was an excellent all-round sportsman, playing football for Newport County, Chelsea and Wolves and played for the Welsh League against the Irish League in 1935.

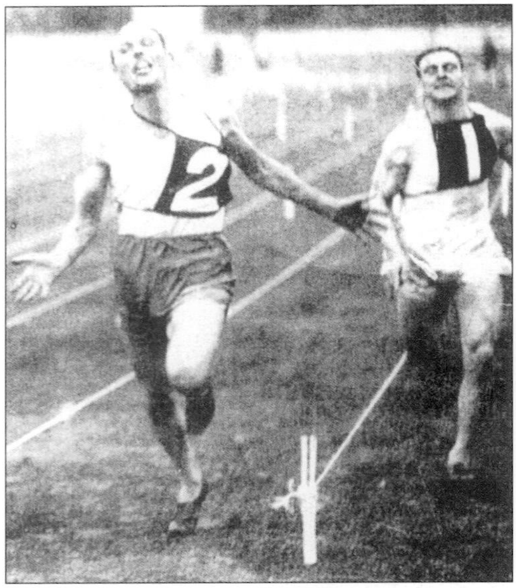

Colin Weaver of Llanhilleth winning one of his many 100 yards. races. Note the stringed lanes and the wearing of bibs instead of numbers.

Whilst the Welsh Powderhall had a set of rules, these were rules for that specific event, with no overall governing body until the 1920s to ensure standard rules were being applied fairly across all competitions as is the case today with the *UK Athletics Rules For Competition.* We know that Colin Weaver ran 9.9 for 100 yds, and as we have seen William Richards, ran a "world's best" for the mile (4:17.25) in 1865, but which body had the responsibility to ensure that the timekeepers were qualified and the watches were accurate - and was the distance accurately measured? We will never know as, in the main, times were of secondary importance and the winning of cash prizes and the profit making of the bookies were undoubtedly the key motivations. However, what is not in doubt is that there was a degree of romanticism about the Welsh Powderhall - and its Scottish equivalent, from where the Welsh event was derived - and the Welsh Powderhall, and indeed professional running in south Wales generally, played an important role in the development of athletics in Wales.

RULES GOVERNING THE COMPETITION.

1.—All Competitors must dress in the Dressing Room, and one Attendant only will be allowed each Competitor.

2.—Competitors must be dressed in proper costume, guernsey body and long drawers, or they will not be allowed to compete.

3.—Competitors will not be allowed to start unless wearing a number properly secured corresponding with number opposite name on programme.

4.—Attendants will be allowed to accompany Competitors to their mark in the Final Heat of the Sprint Handicap only.

5.—Competitors starting with their hands on the ground must not place them beyond their mark.

6.—Any Competitor going over his mark with either of his hands or feet (after receiving instructions to get in position) before the pistol is fired, will be penalised one yard for first offence, two yards for second offence, and the third time he will be disqualified.

7.—All questions affecting the start to be left to the absolute discretion of the Starter.

8.—Any Competitor starting off his wrong mark will be disqualified.

9.—Any Competitor misconducting himself or wilfully disobeying orders will be disqualified.

10.—All objections must be lodged or made with the Referee accompanied with a deposit of £1 within ten minutes of the time the numbers are placed on the telegraph board, but by the discretion of the Referee permission may be given to any person to lodge an objection against the winner or winners of heats on the Saturday, providing the same is lodged not later than 10 p.m. on the same date as the heats are run. And in the event of the objection being (in the opinion of the Referee) frivolous, the amount deposited by the objector will be forfeited and the same deposit may be so used as the Referee deems fit.

11.—In the event of a Dead Heat taking place the Referee shall have full power if he desires to compel the Competitors to re-run the heat or final, but reasonable time will be given, which will also be at the discretion of the Referee.

12. The Referee's decision to be final.

13.—In the event of any protests, objections or any other ruling not provided for in these Rules, the Referee shall have full and complete power to decide, and his decision shall be final and conclusive and subject to no appeal in any Court of Law

SPECIAL NOTICE TO COMPETITORS.

The Gun will be fired Ten Minutes prior to the time scheduled for the Final of £140 Sprint as notice to the Finalists to make their way to the starting point. The Event will be run strictly to time; there will be no waiting for anyone.

Rules of the Welsh Powderhall

Because of the handicapping system employed, it is difficult to single out the outstanding performers in the Welsh Powderhall, but apart from those already mentioned, Arthur Morgan of Llangewydd, Bridgend who became the first Welshman to win the Scottish Powderhall in 1930, was clearly one of the best, although he failed to reach the final in the Welsh event. From a consistency viewpoint, George Cowdell of

Tredegar had one of the best records in the Welsh Powderhall, winning in 1927 and finishing second the following year and third in 1929. In 1927 he had a 16 ½ yds start, but due to this win, his start had been reduced to 12 ½ yds for the 1928 race, so it was virtually impossible to win the event more than once.

Ted Lewis of Pontypridd, who managed boxer Jimmy Wilde, was the first secretary of the Pontypridd AC syndicate and his name is synonymous with the event. He drafted the first rules and acted as starter until 1928.

Winners of the Welsh Powderhall

By permission of Brian Lee

1928 Welsh Powderhall final with (left to right) Richie Rees of Bargoed (4) winning from 1927 winner George Cowell (Tredegar) and Jim Taysome (Bargoed) No. 1.

Taff Vale Park, Pontypridd:

Year	Winner	Start
1903	Harry Howden, Edinburgh	13 yds
1904	Fred Coombes, Tonypandy	12 ½ yds
1905	A. J. Graham, Cardiff	10 ½ yds
1906	Dai Christopher, Currie	5 yds
1907	Charlie Evans, Tenby	10 yds
1908	Beauchamp "Bert" Day, Blackpool	3 ½ yds
1909	C.E. Holway, USA	2 ½ yds
1910	Willie Thomas, Merthyr	14 ½ yds
1911	Tommy Oldfield, Cardiff	9 ½ yds
1912	Michael "Jake" Crowley, Cardiff	16 yds
1913	J. Helens, Newcastle	15 yds
1914	Tommy Andrews, Cardiff	19 yds
1915-1918	No events due to World War 1	
1919	F. Lawless, Eastleigh	14 ½ yds

1920	J.H. Thomas, Pembroke Dock	14 yds
1921	Eddie Williams, Cardiff	14 ½ yds
1922	W "Buller" Loveluck, Pyle	16 ½ yds
1923	Pat Barry, Cardiff	20 yds
1924	Mike Herlihy, Cardiff	16 yds
1925	Eddie Morgan, Llanhilleth	14 ½ yds
1926	Alec Bevan, New Tredegar	20 yds
1927	George Cowdell, Tredegar	16 ½ yds
1928	Richie Rees, Bargoed	15 yds
1929	Bryn Davies, Pontypridd	15 ½ yds
1930	Les Thomas, Treforest	12 ½ yds

Virginia Park, Caerphilly:

1930	Jackie Munn, Cardiff	12 ½ yds
1931	Reg Weaver, Llanhilleth	15 ½ yds
1932	Fred Curwood, Abercynon	15 ½ yds
1933	Lionel Wilton, Abercynon	16 ½ yds
1934	A. Martin, Abercynon	15 ½ yds

Championships resume – an overview of the Welsh AAA Championships to 1945

As we have seen there was much professional activity, particularly in south Wales during the 1890s but these events were restricted to open meetings. Athletics in the Principality began the slow move to formality and establishment of amateur principles when the South Wales & Monmouthshire Sub Committee of the Southern Committee of the AAA - to give it its full name - started holding Welsh Championships towards the end of the nineteenth century and until 1907 they were farmed out to various sports and open meetings throughout south Wales. It is not certain under whose authority this body held "Welsh Championships", but programmes and literature we have available today clearly indicate that the championships were labelled as Welsh Championships, and therefore open to all with a Welsh qualification, which at the time was birth or 12 months continuous residence in Wales and Monmouthshire, with Welsh parentage not being accepted as a qualification. It was 1950 before the eligibility criteria were extended to include father's place of birth. It was even later until the present day qualification of either parent's birthplace was allowed.

We have results for junior championships from 1924, but it is unclear if they were true Welsh junior title events as a programme for an event, held on the Gnoll, Neath in 1934 is headed "First Welsh Junior Championship Sports". To add further confusion, some events held were for school athletes only and several were referred to as "Secondary Schools' Welsh Championships". In fact the first Welsh Secondary Schools' Championships were held in 1947. D.J.P Richards says in his 1956 *History of the Welsh AAA* that Welsh Junior Championships were inaugurated in 1940, but results are listed from 1924! Who'd be a historian! The championships in 1940, held at Whitchurch Secondary School, Cardiff, also incorporated championships for Youths, although the Neath meeting, held between 1934 and 1939, also had events labelled as "Welsh Youths' Championships". Boys championships started in 1951, and Boys under 13 (previously Colts) in 1974.

Championships for women started in 1952, following the formation of the Welsh Women's AAA in December of the previous year. Events for both senior and junior women (under 15) were held from the outset, with events for women under 17 (intermediates) starting in 1962, minor girls (under 13) in 1975, and under 20s in 1983.

The first Welsh amateur championship events held were the 100 yds and mile in 1893 and various events continued to be held as part of other sports meetings until the first fully integrated championships for senior men were held at Rodney Parade Newport on 29th June 1907, when ten events were competed for: 100 yds, 220 yds, 440 yds, 880 yds, 1 mile, 4 miles, 120 yds hurdles, high jump, long jump and 2 miles walk. As was normal at the time, events were held on temporary grass tracks, laid especially for the day. It was not until the 1951 championships at Maindy Stadium, Cardiff that the championships were held on a custom built, permanent facility. Many of the early championships were combined with cycling championships, but this relationship was a stormy one and eventually ceased.

Programme of the first integrated Championships in 1907

The first Welsh championships events, the 100 yds and the mile held in 1893, were won by Charles Thomas (Lampeter College) and Hugh Fairlamb of Roath Harriers, respectively, the former event being held as part of an open meeting at the Cardiff Harlequins Ground. Thomas dominated the 100 yds before the turn of the century winning six times between 1893 and 1899, with AAA champion Fred Cooper breaking the winning streak with his British record equalling 10.0 win in 1898, which for some reason was never ratified by the AAA. "Evens" (10.0) was not run again until 1934 Empire Games representative Stan Macey won at Pontypool Park in 1925. Macey was a prolific winner of Welsh titles taking the 120 yds hurdles seven consecutive years between 1928 and 1934. He also won the 220 yds in 1927. His hurdles tally still stands today as the highest number of wins in that event, despite the presence in later years of 110m hurdles world record holder Colin Jackson and fellow world-class performers Berwyn Price and Nigel Walker.

Cyril Lundie of Roath dominated the short sprint between 1900 and 1903 before 1908 Olympian David Jacobs won the title four times between 1910 and 1914, also winning the 220 yds three times and 440 yds twice. The 220 yds was first held in 1905, with Newport's J. Gorman winning four times between 1907 and 1910, also taking the 100 in 1909. Abergavenny AC's A.M.J. Griffiths, the first 220 yds champion in 1905 had been suspended the previous year by the Midland Counties AAA for "roping" at the Mitchell's and Butlers Sports in Birmingham. Presumably this was the contemporary term for running out of lane, as sprint events at the time were run in lanes divided by string about one foot from the ground.

Athletics at the Arms Park

By permission of Kevin Kelly

David Jacobs in hooped vest with dark shorts on right, winning 120 yards handicap event at Newport Athletic Ground, Rodney Parade on 3rd August 1910.

Rugby stars Arthur Holland (1922) Rowe Harding (1923) Ronnie Boon (1929) all took 220 yds titles. Appropriately enough, all three of these wins came at Cardiff Arms Park, although Holland's win was on the cricket ground, which, effectively, is where Cardiff RFC's ground is today. Glamorgan County Cricket Club played their matches there until the 1960s, when the present cricket ground was built in Sophia Gardens. Holland (1920) and Harding (1922) also took 100 yds titles.

Aneurin "Nash" Thomas was one of the first Welsh athletes to beat "evens" for the 100 yards.

The next athlete to dominate the sprints pre-war was Swansea athlete Cyril Cupid, who first appeared in the championships in 1929 at Cardiff Arms Park when he finished second to H. Anderson of Port Talbot in the 100 yds. Cupid went on to win a total of eight 100 and 220 yds titles between 1930 and 1934, including four consecutive sprint doubles, a record that was to stand until the appearance of the redoubtable Ken Jones just after the Second World War. Cupid's winning time of 9.8 at Newport in 1934 in a championship that doubled as the inaugural Empire Games trials, was the first time a Welshman had bettered evens. Only Nash Thomas (9.9 in 1938) and Ken Jones (9.9 in 1948 and 9.8 in 1949) and pro runner Colin Weaver (9.9) ducked under the 10 seconds barrier before North Walian and 1960 Olympic relay bronze medallist Nick Whitehead clocked 9.7 in 1958 for the first of his six sprint titles.

Aneurin "Nash" Thomas, a native of Mountain Ash, was still at Cowbridge Grammar School when he won the 100 yds in an unimpressive 10.2 at Crymlyn

Burrows, Swansea in 1937, but the following year at Taff Vale Park, Pontypridd, he clocked 9.9 for one of the fastest times recorded in Britain that year, with Cupid third. He also recorded an unsubstantiated 9.8 when beating Cupid in the Elba Sports in Swansea the same year. The Second World War robbed him of his finest years and he failed to return.

Ted Davies (Achilles) and Kenneth Jenkins produced winning times in the 220 yds in the late 1930s that were only equalled by Olympic Silver medallist Ken Jones after the war. Davies's winning time of 22.6 in 1935 was the first clocking under 23 secs in the championships. Jenkins lowered this time to 22.2 in 1938 in the first of his two wins and this time was not bettered for 20 years until Nick Whitehead won in 1958 with 22.1. Jenkins also took the 100 at a waterlogged Newport in 1939, when rugby legend Jack Matthews was second.

15 times capped Welsh rugby star, Harry Uzzell, who captained Wales on four occasions, took the 880 yds in 1907 and the 440 yds the following year. His brother Ben took the 440 yds in 1912 and also won the AAA 220 yds hurdles in 1913, which were held as part of Newport AC's August Sports Meeting. The 1912 AAA event was also held at Newport. Ben lost his life in the First World War

By permission of Steve Lewis

Harry Uzzell

1920 Olympic 4 x 400 relay gold medallist Cecil Griffiths won nine 440/880 yds titles in the 1920s. His remarkable 49.8 440 yds win at Barry Island Cricket Ground in 1921 stood as a championship best until equalled by Pat Jones (Ilford AC) 39 years later. A pen portrait of this outstanding athlete appears later. Erik Hughes, an athlete of Scandinavian descent took the first of his six consecutive 440 yds titles in 1926 – a record which still stands today. Uniquely, he took all three sprints in 1928 – a record which has not been equalled to this day. He was secretary of the South Wales & Mon AAA between 1935/1937.

A.B. Manning of Swansea took the mile in 1901, a year before he won the AAA half mile title in 1:59.8, but there were very few performances of international standard in the middle distances until Reg Thomas's mile win in 4:17.2 at Abercarn in 1933. Passing through the half mile in 2:05.5, he finished well ahead of runner-up E.C. Edwards of Spillers AC, Cardiff. Thomas, the 1930 Empire mile champion took the mile on five occasions in all over a span of seven years, with Phil Dee coming the closest of any to beat him in the championships, missing out by inches at Newport in 1936. Dee won the title in Thomas's absence the following year. A tribute to Thomas appears later. The 1938 Empire mile champion, Jim Alford as well as winning six half-mile titles and two mile titles before the war, also took the 3 miles in 1947 (Pontypool Park) and mile at Talbot Athletic Ground, Aberavon in 1948 to complete his competitive career in the championships with a total of eleven wins.

The championships performance of D.J.P. Richards is remarkable, but to win your first senior title in 1923 (mile) and still be winning in 1947 (10 mile walk) is a feat, that is unlikely to be repeated.

Pen Portrait – D. J. P. Richards (Port Talbot YMCA, Aberystwyth University and Newport H) 1899-1967

Always known by his initials, DJP, or occasionally, as Dippy, he was one of the very few athletes of international class who remained in the sport after retirement to achieve as much distinction in the flatter as the former.

He won twenty three Welsh titles on the track, cross-country and walking spanning a period of a quarter of a century, and was then Treasurer and President of the Welsh CCA. He was also one of the prime movers in the establishment of the Glamorgan Schools Cross Country Association in 1953. On retirement from competition he became the voice of the sport in Wales as a broadcaster, writer and historian. He contributed to several local papers, particularly *The South Wales Echo* and in 1956 produced *The History of the Welsh AAA*, which this publication seeks to emulate.

Courtesy of Brian Lee

D.J.P. Richards (left) and Alf Yeoumans pictured in 1939. They won sixteen Welsh walking titles between them.

His first Welsh title wins came in running events in the 1920s and 1930s, but he progressed to walking and won numerous open events and championships from 2 to 15 miles. One of his finest walking performances came in the 1939 Welsh championships held at Rodney Parade Newport, where he beat Alf Yeoumans' 34 year-old championship record for the 2 miles by 3.7 seconds. His best 2 miles walk came in the Wales match against Southern Counties at Swansea in 1938 when he clocked 13:57.4, a time which stood as the Welsh record until beaten by Gareth Howell with 13:29.4 on the grass of Rodney Parade in 1957. Richards finished 6th in the 1937 AAA 2 miles walk and 5th in 1939.

He took the mile title for four successive years between 1923 and 1926. Some of his finest performances, however, came as a cross-country runner, where at his prime he was one of the leading performers in Britain. His finest year was in 1925 when he won the English Midlands senior title and went on to finish fourth in the English championship, where his club, Newport Harriers finished second - still the highest position of any Welsh club in this prestigious event. Only a handful of Welsh athletes have finished in the top ten in this event. He competed for Britain in the 1928 World Student Games in Paris whilst a student at Aberystwyth University and won four University Athletic Union titles between 1925 and 1929.

He first sprung to prominence when winning the Welsh Novice Cross Country title at Margam in 1922, quickly improving to second in the senior championship at Cwmbran behind Newport Harriers team mate Eddie Edwards the following year when he won the first of his five Welsh vests in the international race. He took three Welsh cross-country titles - in 1925, 1928 and 1929 and won the last of his walking titles in 1948 at the remarkable age of 49. He died in 1967 aged 68.

His son, David (also DJP) was an outstanding athlete too, winning the English and Welsh youths cross-country titles in 1952, the Welsh junior cross-country title in 1954 and the senior cross-country titles in both 1959 and 1960, as well as many track titles. He also represented Wales in the 1958 Cardiff Empire Games in both the 3 and 6 miles. When his father died DJP junior, was holidaying in France and Spain with his family and *The South Wales Echo* announced: "D. J. P. Richards is dead – Now search starts on the Continent for son"

The three and four miles events were mainly the domain of cross-country runners and particularly Newport Harriers. Their runners won the four miles on eighteen of the twenty-eight occasions the event was run up to the Second World War. Cliff Price of Newport H. who lost a leg in the First World War, won in 1912 and 1913 - and intriguingly ran for England that year in a track match against Scotland and Ireland in Glasgow, only to run for Wales in the international cross-country race in 1914. This serves as further evidence that at the time Wales was effectively considered an area of England for track athletics without the same status as Ireland and Scotland. There is no other explanation. Price finished third in the 1914 AAA 4 and 10 miles championships.

Ernie and Ivor

Another Newport Harrier of cross-country fame, Ernie Thomas, who won six Welsh cross-country titles, took the four miles title four times between 1921 and 1927, setting a record of 20:04.0 in 1926, which was never beaten, as the event was replaced with the 3 miles in 1933, as this was, by now, the accepted international distance. He also finished fourth (and second British athlete) in the English National Cross Country Championship at Hereford in 1922, which, at the time, was open to athletes of any nationality. He died in the early 1960s aged 60. His brother Ivor, although never a winner at the championships, is worthy of mention however. He married into the Bulmer's cider family and changed his surname to Bulmer-Thomas in 1952. He won the 1927 inter-varsity 3 miles for Oxford in 15:05.0; ran for Wales in the International Cross Country Championship in 1926 and was a member of numerous Newport Harriers scoring teams including their team which finished second in the English National at Hereford in 1925, when he was 48th. D.J.P. Richards led the team home in fourth place. He was second in the Welsh AAA mile in 1926, in a race won by Richards. His real claim to fame though was as a politician and writer. He was Labour MP for Keighley 1942-48 and amongst his other many appointments were Parliamentary Secretary, Ministry of Aviation 1945/46 and the first UK delegate to the General Assembly of the UN in 1946. After his political career ended following a falling-out with Prime Minister Clement Attlee, he wrote for several Fleet St newspapers and was prominent in Church affairs. He was awarded the CBE in 1984 and died in 1993 aged 87. Both Thomas brothers attended West Mon Grammar School, Pontypool and Ernie's occupation couldn't

Courtesy of Newport H

Ernie Thomas

Ivor Thomas winning the 3 miles for Oxford in the 1927 Varsity match against Cambridge.

have been more diverse than his brother - he worked for the Great Western Railway as a platelayer. Ivor won a scholarship to St. John's Oxford where he obtained a double first. He spoke twelve languages and during the Second World War, he worked in the Intelligence Service.

Wilf Short won the inaugural marathon event held from Stormy Down, near Bridgend in 1934 to earn himself a place in the Welsh team for the 1934 Empire Games in a time that remained unbeaten as a championships best (2:50:00) until Ike O'Brien won the third of his titles in 1939 with 2:45:00.

Wyatt Gould, the 1908 Olympic 400m hurdler, took four 120 yds hurdles titles, including the first two events held, in 1902 and 1903, both of which were held on his home soil of Newport. The 440 yds hurdles were not introduced in the championships until 1950.

William Titt of St. Saviours, Cardiff, who won the 120 yds hurdles three times (1910/1911 and 1913) and placed in the first three on two further occasions, was also an Olympian – but not in athletics. He took part in the gymnastics team combined exercises in both the 1908 London and 1912 Stockholm Games, winning a bronze medal in the latter. He also won the Welsh amateur middleweight boxing championship twice. As his son, Tony Le Beau told Rob Cole in 1999: "He was a very reserved and religious man....and very rarely spoke to his family or friends about his sporting feats...I remember him giving a gymnastic display to my son when he was 65.....it was amazing, he did handstands and walked on his hands". He officiated in the gymnastics events at the 1948 London Olympics and died at his home in Rumney, Cardiff in 1956 aged 75.

Walking events were featured in the championships from 1904, when Norman Moses of Newport AC won the mile. For the previous 3 years he had been Secretary of Newport Harriers, further underlining the close association between the two clubs. He was a fine all-round athlete and President of Newport Harriers for almost 20 years. He wrote for many years as "Harrier" in the Newport based *South Wales Argus*. D.J.P. Richards and Alf Yeoumans won sixteen walking titles between them up to 1947. Yeoumans winning time in the 2 miles of 14:24.0 in 1905 stood as a championships best for a remarkable 34 years until Richards beat it with 14:20.3 at Newport in 1939.

Field event standards have generally been very poor, and the fact that professional meetings only catered for running events was undoubtedly a factor, combined with the relatively poor conditions in the early years, with only a small number of venues having permanent pits for the jumps, for example. Throws were held from circles marked out on grass. Bill Kingsbury, a life-long servant to Welsh athletics, and winner of two Welsh shot titles in the 1950s remembers competing in hob nail boots, as they were the best method of getting any grip in some circles, which were invariably a sea of mud.

Fifteen Welsh titles for Whitcutt

Despite the poor conditions for holding field events, there were some fine performances in the early years and 1908 Olympian Wallis Walters of Cardiff took the first four long jump titles, as well as taking the 120 yds hurdles titles in 1904, 1908 and 1912. Frank Whitcutt of Newport AC and Cardiff University was a remarkable performer in the jumps, winning the high, long and triple jumps on a combined thirteen occasions during the 1920s and 1930s. Additionally he won the 120 yds hurdles twice, in 1926 and 1927 and finished second on a further two occasions. His best event however, was the high jump where he competed without success in the 1934 White City Empire Games. His winning high jump of 1.83m set in winning the Welsh title at Newport in 1928 stood as a Welsh record until beaten 10 years later by British international Harry Stubbs with 1.90m, which he achieved on three occasions. Stubbs took the Welsh title three times (1937/38/39).

Whilst there were references to "pole jumps" in Wales as early as 1871, it was 1937 before the pole vault was introduced to the Welsh championships, with Cyril Evans of Port Talbot YMCA taking the event in both 1937 and 1938. The rules in 1871 however; were slightly different in that competitors were allowed to slide/clamber up the pole before leaping over the bar. The wooden pole in use at the time had a metal spike in the bottom, and competitors ran up on grass and simply pierced the grass with the pole and took off and landed on their feet - with no pit. Pole climbing was still allowed by the AAA as late as 1920.

The triple jump (or hop, step and jump as the event was then called) was first introduced in 1924, when John Lloyd of Newport AC won with 12.37m. Gwynne Evans, yet another Newport AC member took seven successive triple jump titles between 1933 and 1939, a record that stood until equalled in the 1970s and 80s by Cardiff's John Phillips and Dave Wood. Evans competed in the 1934 Empire Games and set three Welsh records during his career (best of 13.74m in 1938). His Welsh record stood until Gwyn Harris of Lewis School, Pengam, the 1948 champion jumped 14.11 at Abertillery Park in 1947.

Throwing events (shot) were first introduced in 1923, but the other events took some time before they appeared on the programme - the discus came in 1937, the javelin in 1938, and it was 1954 before the hammer appeared. George Dillaway, a policeman from Gwent, was the early shot star, taking the event eight times between 1924 and 1937. His 1924 performance of 11.53m erased the then world best (and Welsh record) for the event of 10.97m set an incredible 64 years earlier by Hugh Williams of Cambridge University. Dillaway also took four second places, and a third, finishing behind Arthur "Tiny" Lewis who won in 1934/35/36. Lewis competed in the 1934 Empire Games, where he was the Welsh flag bearer, finishing seventh with 11.70m. Standing 6'4 tall, he won in the first post war championships in Sloper Road, Cardiff in 1946. Born in Merthyr Vale in 1905, he was a fine all-round sportsman and a reserve for the Welsh hockey team in 1932. The early competitions would have been held from a grass circle, and, as with the discus, it was likely that this continued until the championships moved in 1951 to Maindy Stadium, in Cardiff the first purpose-built athletics stadium in Wales.

The irrepressible Matt Cullen, of Swansea Valley AC, of whom we will hear more later, took the first discus title in 1937 at Crymlyn Burrows in Swansea with 29.88m, finishing second to John Cotter the next two years. Cotter was an excellent all-rounder and finished second in both the 1936 and 1938 AAA decathlon, setting Welsh records on each occasion. Matt is credited with introducing the event to Wales and finished second in the English Southern Counties Championships in 1926 and

© T.J. and D. Davies

Matt Cullen winner of the first Welsh discus title in 1937 and World Veterans discus champion in 1977.

competed in the Welsh championships at various events for over 50 years.

Rugby man Arthur Squibbs of Loughborough College, and a native of Cardigan, took the first two javelin titles before the war, but both marks were behind his Welsh record 55.74m set on 19th August 1939 at Port Talbot. This stood as the Welsh best for 15 years until bettered by 1954 Empire Games representative Clive Roberts of Swansea who threw 57.28m to win the 1954 title and earn selection for Vancouver. The 1938 championships at Taff Vale Park, Pontypridd were broadcast on BBC radio. The minutes of the South Wales and Mon AAA said that a "running commentary" would be given!

Little did those at the 1939 championships at Newport on June 23rd realise that in three months time World War Two would be upon them. It was at these championships that D.J.P. Richards beat Alf Yeoumans' 34 year old 2 miles walk Welsh record, with 14:20.2 and future rugby great Jack Matthews finished second in the 100 yds behind double sprint champion Kenneth Jenkins.

A number of future senior stars graced the championships for the younger age groups before the war, including rugby legends, Ronnie Boon and Matthews. Boon (Barry CS) took both the junior 100 and 220 in 1927, whilst Matthews, who was also still at school in Bridgend won the junior 220 in 1937.

The senior championships were suspended for the duration of the Second World War and resumed in 1946 at the GKN sports ground in Sloper Road, Cardiff.

Welsh international and representative matches

Although, the South Wales & Mon AAA were given authority by the AAA to hold matches against the Scottish and Irish AAA as far back as 1897, apart from participation in the Empire Games, Wales did not taste true international competition until after the Second World War when a match was held in Birmingham against Holland, the AAA and the Midland Counties in 1953. The first match in Wales which can be regarded as a full international was the match against Ireland at Maindy Stadium, Cardiff in 1954, when Wales won by 94 pts to 87. The newly opened Eirias Park in Colwyn Bay staged the next full international in Wales in 1958 when Nigeria, who were in Wales for the Empire Games, provided the opposition.

An attempt was made though for a match against either South Africa or Australia at Swansea after the 1934 Empire Games, but this did not materialise. There was also an attempt to hold a match against Ireland in 1939. Discussions took place with the Irish officials who were in Wales for the 1939 International Cross Country Championships in Cardiff, but the event didn't materialise because of the expense involved. A number of pre-war international matches with the team dubbed as "England and Wales" were held, but very few, if any Welsh athletes were included, as the teams were selected in London and mainly without Welsh representation on the selection committee. It has to be said though that very few, if any, of the Welsh athletes not selected had much of a gripe about the situation because standards in the main, apart from isolated events and athletes lagged behind those of England.

However, many representative matches were held, and these commenced with the inter-town series between Cardiff, Newport and Swansea. The first was held at St. Helen's Swansea in 1902, when Newport were the winners. This competition continued until 1907, but it was not held again until 1934. Abergavenny took part in 1903/1904/1905 and 1907.

The first track and field competition involving teams outside Wales was the match at St. Helen's Swansea on 24 August 1929 when a Welsh team took on Achilles, with the home side taking five events to the four of Achilles. These early representative matches invariably involved a Welsh AAA or South Wales and Mon team and attracted great crowds, particularly at St. Helen's Swansea, and were the only source at the time for the Welsh public to see the great names of the time such as 1948 Olympic 400m champion Arthur Wint and McDonald Bailey, winner of a remarkable fourteen AAA sprint titles during the late 1940s and early 50s. Until the 1958 Empire Games, virtually all of the Welsh all-comers records were set in these meetings. It has to be said that in Wales these matches at the time were considered "international" matches, both by the athletes and officials, but in the schedule of Welsh international appearances which appear in the statistics volume, it has been decided only to include such matches if at least one of the opposing teams was a country, or a full AAA team, which meant that it was effectively an England team.

Wales took on a Southern Counties team, again at St. Helen's on 11th July 1931, and this meeting saw the emergence of Cyril Cupid as Wales' best sprinter since Charles Thomas and Fred Cooper.

Pen Portrait – Cyril G. Cupid
(Swansea Valley AC and Birchfield Harriers) c1910-1965

Cyril Cupid was the Welsh Linford Christie of his day, winning nine Welsh sprint titles between 1930 and 1934, finishing second twice and third on a further four occasions. He was the first Welshman to break 10 secs for 100 yds. He showed his versatility, when in the 1938 Championships at Taff Vale Park, Pontypridd, after finishing 3rd in the 100 yds, behind Nash Thomas who won in 9.9; he took second in the long jump behind Roath's Brian Crossman.

His best performance came in the 1934 Welsh Championships at Rodney Parade, Newport when his winning time of 9.8 clipped 2 tenths of a second off the Welsh record held jointly by himself, Fred Cooper who ran 10.0 when winning the title 26 years earlier; Charles Thomas (Reading AC) in 1899, and Stan Macey of Newport A.C set when winning the Welsh title in 1925. Cooper also ran 10.0 when winning the AAA title in 1898. It was another 14 years before Olympic star Ken Jones equalled the time.

Apparently Cupid used to create quite a stir in the Swansea area, being a coloured athlete, and standing "well over 6 ft tall", and apart from Ken Jones, he is the only athlete to have won the sprint double in four successive Welsh Championships.

Cupid had equalled the Welsh 100 yds record of 10.0 when winning for South Wales in the Southern Counties match at St. Helen's, Swansea on 11th July 1931, and also won the 220 yds in 22.7 beating the previous Welsh all-comers record by 3 tenths – quite a feat even in those days of grass tracks. He ran "evens" again when winning for West Wales against East Glamorgan on 10th Aug 1935.

The Swansea athlete was one of the Welsh team to take part in the 1934 Empire Games, Wales' first appearance in the athletics events. Whilst he didn't perform well, he certainly didn't disgrace himself. In the first round of the 100, he finished second by a yard to the eventual silver medallist Marthinus Theunissen of South Africa, who won in 10.0, before going out after finishing fifth in the second round. In the 220 yds, he finished second in his heat, again to Theunissen who won in 22.5, but ahead of Australian Jack Horsfall, who ran 22.1 the following year. In the second round, he was struggling around the top bend and finished out of the qualifying positions. England's Arthur Sweeney won both sprint finals, with Theunissen second in both.

Cupid was a "manual" worker all his life, and would have achieved much more had he not had to work long hours in the local foundry, which put great strain on him. At the time, his mentor, Matt Cullen was reputed to have said that he would have been a match for Jesse Owens, the 1936 Berlin Olympics star had he have been given the same opportunities (!).

He was still competing after the War, but had now moved to the Midlands and won the Warwickshire 100 yds in 10.1 in 1946. He returned to Wales for the first post war Welsh championships at Sloper Rd, Cardiff on July 6th and finished third in the 220 yds behind the winner in 24.0, Ken Jones, who was running in his first Welsh Championships.

County and area championships

Both Glamorgan and Monmouthshire/Gwent started holding County championships in 1922. Glamorgan held just two events – 100 and 440 yds – as part of the Cardiff Conservative Club Sports at Cardiff Arms Park, whilst Gwent held seven championships, with each event farmed out to various open sports meetings in the county. The Glamorgan championships were also allocated to various open meetings until the first fully integrated championships were held at Ely, Cardiff in 1948. Additional events were added as the years progressed, and by the last series of championships before the Second World War, only hurdles events and the hammer were missing from the Glamorgan programme. Venues for the championships in 1939 read like a tour of south Wales: Crymlyn Burrows, Swansea; Mond, Ystrad Rhondda, Grangetown, Cardiff; Grovesend and Port Talbot. Cyril Cupid won the 1934 Glamorgan 100 yds at Crymlyn Burrows in 10.0 to again equal the Welsh record he held jointly by Charles Thomas, Fred Cooper, and Stan Macey.

The Gwent championships were held at various open meetings and sports at Newport, Abertillery, Pontypool, Blackwood, Risca, Abergavenny, Abercarn, Blaenavon and Chepstow. In some years up to World War Two, the records show that only two or three events were held and two junior events were held in the last meeting before the Second World War, at Newport on 7th August. The 1926 miners strike prevented any events being held that year. Gwent youth's championships were held for the first time in 1943 at Ebbw Vale. Unlike the Glamorgan championships, road-walking events were held from 1928. Carmarthenshire held a 220 yds championship at the Ammanford C&FC Sports in 1933, won by Leslie Hayes of Hendy AC, who also won the only other recorded pre-war championship, also over 220 yds at Penygroes on 7 Aug 1935.

West Wales championships were inaugurated in 1926, when a small number of events were held at Glais on September 25th. The following year, a fully integrated meeting was held at Waverley Park, Clydach, when nine events were held. By 1939, when the championships were held at Parc Stephen, Kidwelly, virtually a full championships programme was held, including a marathon and a 100 yds for juniors. Only the hammer and 440 yds hurdles were missing from the programme. It is interesting to point out again the apparent double standards at the time when dealing with professional athletes, as Con Jones of Treboeth, the winner of the 3 miles in 1934, was subsequently disqualified, when it was discovered he had taken part in professional events.

A Glamorgan v Monmouthshire inter-county meeting was established at Treorchy in 1927 until replaced with an Inter Area Meeting, first held at Panteg in 1938, where a west Wales team started to compete. The term "west Wales" however should be loosely interpreted, as it appears to have covered an area west of Bridgend through to Carmarthen. At the same time the Glamorgan team changed to a team representing East Glamorgan, and these arrangements no doubt mirrored the administrative changes brought about in 1933 when the South Wales & Mon AAA achieved "District" status as part of the English Southern Committee of the AAA.

Whilst the southern part of Wales appears to have been catered for reasonably well, there is no evidence of any representative matches taking place involving north and mid Wales, i.e. those counties administered by the (English) Northern and Midland Counties. It was not until 1955 that the first North Wales Championships were held at Eirias Park, Colwyn Bay.

In 1937, a league competition was in existence in Mid Glamorgan, and Arthur Williams, President of the Welsh AAA between 1959 and 1976 is recorded in the minutes of the South Wales Committee as saying that this form of competition must spread to all parts of Wales if standards were to improve. In fact it took another 30 years for a national league to reach Wales. Five clubs joined the league: Port Talbot YMCA, Neath AAC, Mansel AC, Cwmavon AC and Gwynfi AC. At the fourth and final match of the year at The Gnoll, Neath, on 15 July women's events were held for the first time and Nellie Denner of Port Talbot YMCA won the 100 yards in 11.9 which was the fastest time recorded in Wales by a Welsh athlete at the time. We are uncertain as to the conditions which prevailed that day, but based on her winning time in the 220 yards (28.6) her 100 yards time must be treated with some caution. However, what is of significance is that there were organised women's events, other than those in schools, being held under the auspices of the South Wales & Mon AAA some 14 years before the formation of the Welsh Women's AAA in 1951. It was also in 1937 that a Welsh "County" first competed in the Whitsun British Games at the White City – traditionally the first major meeting of the British season at the time, when a combined Glamorgan and Monmouthshire team took part.

First semblance of a coaching structure

Jim Alford was appointed the first national coach for Wales in 1948, and this coupled with the appointment of Ray Thomas as the first Welsh representative to the AAA coaching committee, were the first steps of the formalisation of a coaching structure in Wales. Thomas, the senior lecturer in Physical Education at Caerleon Training College can be regarded as the driving force behind this formalisation, and in 1949 further recognition of the importance of coaching was achieved with Thomas, as the first secretary of the Welsh AAA coaching committee being appointed to the Welsh AAA general committee. At the time of his death in 1972, aged 63, he was Chairman of both the Welsh AAA and Cwmbran Olympiads after serving as treasurer of the Welsh AAA for nine years between 1957 and 1966.

A young John Disley (right) with Geoff Dyson and 'friend' giving tips on hurdling technique.

Whilst coaching formalisation occurred after the Second World War, the seeds were sown in 1937 when the Chief Finnish Olympic coach, Armas Valsti, paid a visit to Wales and coached in a number of schools and clubs in west Wales. Harold Abrahams, the 1924 Olympic 100m champion, also made several visits to Wales to lecture before the War and Welsh coaches were attending the Loughborough Summer School during the latter part of the 1930s. A summer school for athletes was also being held in Barry at this time. In 1946, Geoff Dyson, the AAA chief national coach, visited Whitchurch Secondary School, Cardiff to "lecture and demonstrate field events".

Dyson came again in 1950, this time with his wife, the former Maureen Gardner, the 1948 Olympic silver medallist behind Fanny Blankers-Koen in the 80m hurdles. Dyson also brought with him Arthur Wint, the Olympic 400m champion and 800m silver medallist from 1948. The Welsh AAA minutes reported, "clubs should make early applications for their services".

Like most sporting organisations athletics in the Principality came to a halt for the duration of the Second World War although junior championships continued to be held throughout and youths' championships were inaugurated in 1940, and also held throughout the hostilities.

Chapter 2

The Post War Years

The austerity of the immediate post War years was lightened with the emergence of Wales' first individual Olympic medallists Tom Richards and John Disley; the 1958 Cardiff Empire and Commonwealth Games make an indelible mark on the Principality and a rainy Tokyo day in 1964 puts Nantymoel on the map ....

The period immediately following the end of the Second World War was something of a golden era for sport. After six years of conflict and deprivation people were anxious to get back to normal as quickly as possible. In the years before the advent of mass television audiences, attendances at sporting events reached an all time peak. Football League matches regularly attracted crowds of 50,000-60,000 and more, while crowds of 40,000 plus filled the Arms Park for Cardiff v Newport rugby matches.

Athletics was no exception in a situation which continued throughout the 1950s. On 26 May 1947, 15,000 people watched Sidney Wooderson run the mile at the Whitsun Sports in Pontypool while 4,000 spectators witnessed the Carmarthen Sports on the same day! No less than 12,000 attended the Welsh Championships at Abertillery in June 1949. What would we give for that sort of attendance at today's meetings?

It was decided early in 1946 that the Welsh Senior Championships would be held that year for the first time since 1939. The venue was fixed as the GKN Sports Ground, Sloper Road, Cardiff on 6 July. The Inter Counties match would be held at the Newport AC grounds on August Bank Holiday Monday. A resolution had been passed in September 1939 that "every effort should be made to function in a normal capacity until such time as circumstances made this impossible" and the fact that junior and youths championships had been staged annually without interruption throughout the War years was a tribute to the small band of enthusiasts left at home.

Some idea of the conditions under which athletes competed just after the War can be gleaned from the following comments on the Welsh Youths and Junior Championships held at Penarth on 15 June 1946. The meeting was held on a completely circular 330 yds track with no straights. There was a stiff gradient of 60 yds or so leading up to the finish line which, in races longer than 330 yds (c300m), obviously had to be negotiated on each lap. An 880 yds time of 2:08.8 (2:08.1 for 800m) might not look much today but when we take into account that it was achieved on a grass track and with having to run up this hill 3 times it becomes a little more respectable. There were no lanes marked out for the 220 or 440 yds so that the athlete drawn on the inside had an inbuilt advantage.

As before the War, most athletics meetings were held on grass tracks at rugby fields such as Talbot Athletic Ground, Aberavon, St Helen's Swansea, Abertillery Park, Pontypool Park and Cardiff Arms Park or at venues such as Taff Vale Park, Pontypridd. Tracks were marked out and laid down just prior to the meeting. It was part of the duties of the officials of the meeting to ensure that the tracks were accurately measured and there was sometimes controversy over the accuracy of some tracks.

1946 had begun on a tragic note when Reg Thomas, one of Wales' greatest ever athletes, died in a plane crash at Stroud in March. Meanwhile Jim Alford, one of his successors as Commonwealth Games one mile champion, was still competing with distinction. He was Welsh 440 yds and 880 yds champion that year and the following year won the mile in the match between the AAA and Cambridge University.

A major development in 1947 was the staging of the first Welsh Schools' Championships at Pontypridd. Over the years this meeting has been the launching pad for the careers of many of Wales' greatest athletes. The 1947 meeting, properly called the inter-county national championships of the Welsh Secondary Schools AAA, was held at Taff Vale Park in atrocious weather. As with most other events at the time it was an entirely male affair and it was to be eight years before the championships were extended to include girls' events. Previously schools' athletics had flourished at county level with the 1946 Glamorgan Secondary Schools' championships attracting a thousand entrants. The University of Wales Athletic Union was also formed in 1947 and held its first championships in 1948.

Also in this year Jim Alford, after his distinguished career as an athlete, was appointed Wales' first national coach. The two outstanding Welsh athletes of this period were undoubtedly sprinter Ken Jones and marathon runner Tom Richards, both of whom won silver medals in the 1948 Olympic Games. More on these fine athletes later.

Low profile for the 1948 Olympic Games in Wales

Athletics did not enjoy a particularly high profile in Welsh sporting circles in the late 1940s. It is interesting to note that Glamorgan's county cricket match against Gloucestershire at Ebbw Vale received greater coverage in *The Western Mail* than the 1948 Olympic Games, which was given just half a column. The fact that the "Whitsun Sports" attitude still prevailed probably didn't help. One meeting in 1947 included in the programme an egg and spoon crawl, an obstacle race and a men's pillow fight. Events such as the sack race, three-legged race and wheelbarrow race were frequently included and, although these would undoubtedly have added to the fun of the occasion they would not have done much to improve athletics' image as a serious competitive sport. Throwing the cricket ball was contested at the Welsh Schools' Championships for a number of years but was eventually dropped, presumably because the considerable distances achieved represented a safety hazard.

Most track races were run as handicaps and the official handicapper was a very important person. As in the early part of the century, it was not unusual for athletes to be, shall we say, modest when filling in their entry forms for handicap races, somewhat understating their achievements in the hope of obtaining a better handicap. Prizes were frequently given, usually to the first three, in all open track meetings and some of these would cause a surprise if offered today. At one meeting the first prize in a boys' 100 yds handicap was a cigarette case and in the boys' 880 yds a cigarette lighter was presented. Typical prizes were cutlery, pens, dressing sets and powder cases.

Representative matches at the time tended to involve some of the better English clubs. "South Wales & Monmouthshire v Polytechnic Harriers" or "South Wales & Monmouth v London AC" were typical examples. Competing for Polytechnic Harriers in just such a match at Ebbw Vale on 20 May 1950 E McDonald Bailey, one of the world's great sprinters in his era, clocked 21.9 for the 220 yds, easily the fastest time ever seen in Wales. At the same meeting Peter Hildreth ran 120 yds hurdles in 15.5 for another Welsh all-comers' record, these being the best performance achieved in Wales irrespective of nationality. Included in the statistics section later is an evolution of such records – the first time such a schedule has been produced, and this serves to indicate the vast array of world-class athletes who have competed in the Principality over the years.

Olympic Champion Wint fails to better Welsh all-comers' record at Ebbw Vale

Although they were not full international matches meetings such as that at Ebbw Vale gave the Welsh athletics public the opportunity to see some of the best athletes in the country at first hand. Later on in the same year Arthur Wint, the 1948 Olympic 400m Champion ran 440 yds in 51.1 but was unable to break Cecil Griffiths' Welsh all-comers' record of 49.8 which had stood since 1921. Wint, who also took the 800m silver in 1948, had, however, set a new 880 yds record the previous year, clocking 1:54.2 at Abertillery to break Jim Alford's record set in 1936. Winner of the Welsh youths' 440 yds title that year was Julius Hermer who later in life went on to become Lord Mayor of Cardiff.

The first in a series of matches between the Welsh AAA and the AAA was held at Abertillery on 10 July 1948. As the AAA was, to all intents and purposes, England, these may be regarded as full international matches between Wales and England.

The 1949 Welsh Championships at Abertillery saw seven times capped Gordon Wells produce an outstanding triple jump (or hop, step and jump, as the event was called at the time) of 14.52 to set Welsh national and all-comers' records. The jump added 41 cms to Gwyn Harris's records set at the same venue a year before. It was the third best leap in Britain that year. John Disley took his first Welsh title after finishing runner-up in the mile to Jim Alford at Talbot Athletic Ground, Aberavon the year before. Years afterwards Jim remembers having his work cut out to win and wondering: "who this runner from north Wales is". Ken Jones became the first (and still the only) athlete to win both sprints and the long jump in the same championships.

One of the great personalities of the pre-War period, E W (Eddie) O'Donnell died in January of 1950. A useful athlete in his younger days, he won the Welsh mile title in 1910 and was a cross-country international, but it was as an administrator that he really made his mark on Welsh athletics

Pen Portrait – E.W. (Eddie) O'Donnell (Barry H, Cardiff University and Roath Harriers) 189?-1950

The name Eddie O'Donnell probably means very little to those involved in Welsh athletics today, but his contribution to both cross-country and track and field is incalculable. He served the sport as a Welsh champion and international athlete, administrator, official and journalist for forty years until his death in 1950, some days before being appointed for a third term unopposed as President of the Welsh AAA.

Like his contemporary, Viv Pitcher, he meticulously recorded results of events in Wales and without his attention to detail and devotion much of the activities of his era would have been lost and therefore unknown. He was President of the International Cross Country Union when the international race was held in Cardiff

Eddie O'Donnell

in 1939, and also served as President and Secretary of the Welsh CCA as well as Treasurer of the South Wales and Mon AAA from 1922 to 1947. He was part of the Welsh "team" which secured home rule for Welsh athletics in 1948, having sown the seeds with the AAA prior to World War Two.

As "Backmarker" he contributed to the *South Wales Echo* and *Western Mail* and as such he was the voice of the sport in Wales for many years. He was a pillar of society in his hometown of Barry, where he was a member of the original Barry Harriers, before joining Roath Harriers. His father, Dr. P. J. O'Donnell had come to the town from Ireland towards the end of the 19th Century, and established the first Catholic Church in Barry.

John Frowen of Lewis School Pengam caused a sensation at the Glamorgan Schools' Championships at Tonypandy on 1st July 1950, when he broke the Welsh senior and British junior long jump records with 7.03. The previous Welsh record had stood for 14 years to Lewis Riden of Roath (6.77). He did not remain in athletics for long and later became a professional footballer with Cardiff City.

John Frowen

Maindy Stadium Opens in 1951

The Festival of Britain was held in 1951 with a major exhibition in London and street parties throughout the country. It was an opportunity for people to celebrate being British and, with memories of the War still fresh in the mind, was greeted with enthusiasm. It was also a significant year for Welsh athletics. Maindy Stadium, Cardiff, was opened in May and became the Mecca of Welsh athletics for many years afterwards. It was a six-lane cinder track with a cycle track around the outside and was considered "state of the art" at the time and the first purpose-built athletics facility in Wales. The first meeting held there was the Glamorgan County Championships on 14 May 1951. The arrival of Maindy was a most welcome advance in Welsh athletics as the accuracy of tracks was still a contentious issue at some of the venues used. For a match between South Wales and London AC at Blaenavon, officials using a ball of string and a one hundred foot tape measured out the track in an hour early on in the day. This was common practice at the time and it was the responsibility of the meeting officials to ensure the accuracy of the track. Harold Steggles, Welsh 440 yds champion of that year, was credited with a time of 48.0 yet he himself was convinced that he had run no faster than 51.0!

McDonald Bailey was back in Wales in 1951. Running the 100 yds for Polytechnic Harriers at Swansea in May he recorded 9.8 to equal the Welsh all-comers' record first set

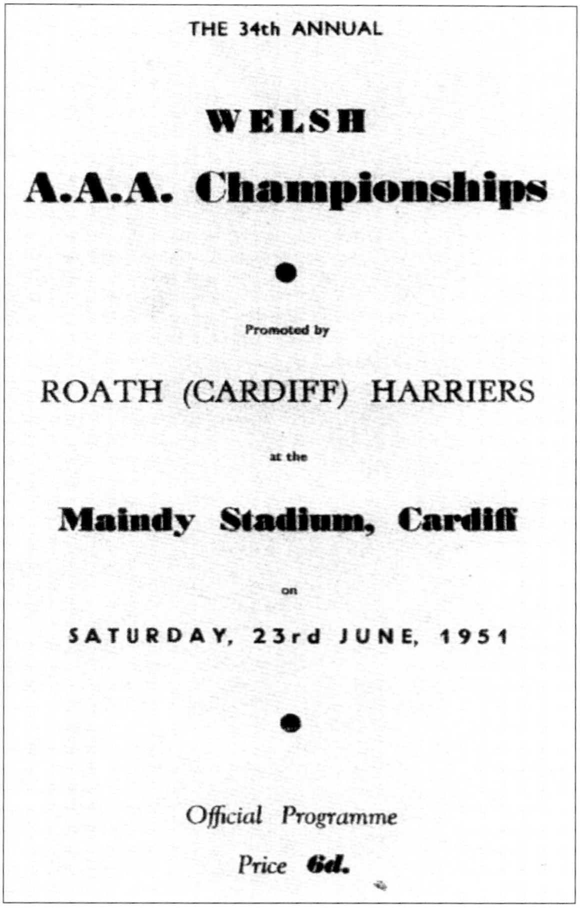
THE 34th ANNUAL

WELSH

A.A.A. Championships

Promoted by

ROATH (CARDIFF) HARRIERS

at the

Maindy Stadium, Cardiff

on

SATURDAY, 23rd JUNE, 1951

Official Programme

Price 6d.

Programme of the first Welsh championship to be held on a purpose-built track in 1951 at Maindy Stadium, Cardiff.

by Cyril Cupid some 17 years earlier. In August he repeated this time when winning for the AAA v Welsh AAA at Newport.

Another major step forward for Welsh athletics came in 1951 with the first Welsh Championships for boys under 15 (classified simply as "boys" at the time). There is no doubt that by this time the sport was growing in stature and scope, although in Wales it was still very much centred in the south. A glance at the list of Welsh champions will show that winners representing clubs from north Wales were very rare birds indeed. As recently as 1971 the only club north of Brecon affiliated to the Welsh AAA, other than educational institutions, was Aberystwyth AC, despite the fact that Wrexham AC was formed in 1954.

This is not to suggest that nothing was happening in the north and a number of organisations were set up in the region. The South Denbighshire, Merionethshire and Montgomeryshire District AAA was formed in April 1949 and one of its first tasks was to organise a county championships event (or more accurately a three counties event) at Wrexham that July.

The Central Council for Physical Recreation's (CCPR) national training centre at Lilleshall opened in 1951, and prior to the opening, the Welsh AAA held a course there for north Wales athletes. Also in 1951, Swansea's Lionel Pugh, two years earlier the Welsh javelin champion, was appointed as AAA National coach to the Midlands.

A significant development occurred in 1952 when the Welsh Championships included events for women for the first time. Seven events for senior women were held in conjunction with the senior men's championships at Maindy on 7 June, and five events (including a relay) for junior women were staged with the junior men's championships at the same venue a month later. The term "junior women" might be misleading as in those days it referred to athletes in the under 15 girls age group and not under 20s as would be the case today.

In 1952 John Disley, who had improved on his British record in 1951, competed as one of the favourites for the steeplechase title in the Olympic Games in Helsinki. In the event he had to be satisfied with the bronze medal, just two-tenths behind the silver medallist, Vladimir Kazantsev of the USSR. Nevertheless his bronze medal was only the second individual medal won at the Olympics by a Welshman behind Tom Richards' silver in 1948.

John Disley leads from Gordon Pirie en route to breaking the Welsh one-mile record at Walton on 14th June 1958 with 4:05.4 clocking.

Pen Portrait - John Disley (London AC)

During the 1950s Wales' outstanding athlete was undoubtedly John Disley. Born in Corris on 20th November 1928 he became Britain's first world-class steeplechaser when he set four British records at 2 miles and five at 3,000m.

In September of 1951 Disley broke his own British and Commonwealth record for the 3,000m steeplechase, clocking 9:11.6 in a meeting at the White City, London, the home at the time of British athletics. Among those he beat was future Olympic Champion Chris Brasher who was back in fifth place. Disley's preparations for the following year's Olympic Games in Helsinki were obviously going well. At those Games Disley was Wales' only representative and was in the form of his life. He won the second heat with a huge improvement on his record, becoming the first British athlete to beat nine minutes. The final was a disappointment for him though and was won by the inspired American FBI agent Horace Ashenfelter with Disley, despite another big improvement on his record, just being pipped for second place to take bronze. His Olympic medal was the first ever to be won by a Welshman in an individual track event. Only Colin Jackson has achieved this feat since. Later in the year he became the first Welshman to be voted British Athlete of the Year and also won the Welsh Sports Personality of the Year award in 1955 - Ken Jones was the first winner the previous year.

He went to the 1956 Melbourne Olympics as Britain's number one, and despite running 8:44.6 he could only finish sixth in a race surprisingly won by his inspired friend Chris Brasher in a new British and Olympic record 8:41.2. Brasher went into

the race as Britain's third string, behind Disley and Eric Shirley. It was Brasher's first win over Disley.

It was his misfortune and greatest regret that the steeplechase, held in 1930 and 1934, was not re-introduced into the Commonwealth Games programme until 1962 when his competitive days were over. In 1958 he was still good enough to be ranked second in the Commonwealth but was denied the opportunity of representing his country in this event. On home soil at Cardiff Arms Park, and in front of fanatical Welsh fans, he would surely have won the gold medal. Instead he had to be satisfied with competing in the one mile in Vancouver in 1954 (he finished fifth in his heat, but still bettered his own Welsh mile record by 1.2 seconds with 4:09.0) and the three miles in 1958 (pulled out with Achilles tendon problems).

The European Championships in 1950 (Brussels) and 1954 (Berne) were not happy occasions as he could only finish thirteenth and tenth respectively.

A schoolmaster, he ran for London Athletic Club throughout his career and, despite missing out on the chance of carrying the three feathers to victory in the 1958 Cardiff Games, he gained 19 British vests between 1950 and 1957. Educated at Oswestry High School in Shropshire, he had never seen an athletics track until he went to Loughborough College as a student in 1946. Before that his running had been confined to annual cross-country runs and school sports.

Disley first made an impact on the Welsh scene when he won the first of his four Welsh mile titles at the 1949 championships held at Abertillery Park in the undistinguished time of 4:32.0. But he went on to beat Jim Alford's Welsh record set in the 1938 Sydney Empire Games, clocking 4:10.6 in 1953 and subsequently beat it on five further occasions to end with a best of 4:05.4 in June 1958. Strangely, he didn't win a Welsh steeplechase title, but won three AAA steeplechase titles, including the 2 miles event in 1952, which was classed as a world's best (9:44.0 secs). During his career, he set 18 Welsh records at 1,500m, mile, 3,000m, 3,000m and 2 miles steeplechase and 5,000m. His best position in the Welsh Cross-Country Championships was second in 1955, in a race at Caerleon won by the late Lyn Bevan of Newport.

He was a member of the International Orienteering Federation (1972-78) and was a leading pioneer of the sport in Britain. He was awarded the CBE in 1979 for his work in outdoor education and was vice-chairman of the Sports Council (1974-82). His other claim to fame is that along with Brasher, he founded the London marathon in 1981, and today it remains as one of the great marathons of the world. He married UK record holder (220y 1949, and 100y 1951) Sylvia Cheeseman, who won three relay medals at major Games including a bronze in the 1952 Helsinki Olympics.

The track at Maindy Stadium underwent some major improvements in 1953. There had been some criticism of the state of it because the surface was too loose and on the recommendation of national coach Jim Alford it was resurfaced. The improvements obviously worked because on 25 July 1953 the AAA Junior Championships were staged there. The AAA Marathon, held during the same meeting, finished on the Maindy track and was won by Jim Peters in a new all-comers' record 2:22:29.

There was a glut of Welsh all-comers' records in a match between the Welsh AAA and the AAA at Maindy Stadium on 8 May 1954. Brian Hewson, with a 1:52.2 880 yds, John Disley with a 4:13.8 mile and Geoff Elliott with 4.07 in the pole vault all set new figures whilst John Savidge, just two months ahead of his Empire Games gold in the shot, got a double. He threw 46.74 in the discus and put the shot out to 16.83. Second to him in the discus was Hywel Williams who broke his own Welsh record with 44.70.

Gulps as Gilpin beats Ken Jones

The sensation of the Welsh Championships of 1954 was that Ken Jones was actually beaten. Off to a poor start in the 100 yds he was never able to make up the deficit and finished a yard behind John Gilpin to suffer his only defeat in what turned out to be his last appearance in a Welsh Championship. The loss was just a blip, though, and he proved he had lost none of his speed when he ran a superb 200m in Cologne, finishing in second place just behind Jim Golliday (USA), who, but for untimely injuries might have been Olympic Champion in 1952. In all Ken won 16 Welsh track and field titles, the most by any athlete at the time. His record was later equalled by Paul Rees (shot and discus) and finally beaten by another thrower as Shaun Pickering amassed 19 championships.

Wales engaged in its first full scale international in 1954, other than in matches against the AAA, when a match between Wales and Ireland was held at Maindy Stadium on August Bank Holiday (although the previous year a small contingent of Dutch athletes had competed in a track-only floodlit meeting involving the AAA, Midland Counties and Wales at Birmingham). Wales made a good start to international competition in winning the match by 94 points to 87. The winner of the 880 yds was Ron Delany of Ireland who would go on to become Olympic 1,500m champion at Melbourne two years later. Brendan O'Reilly set a Welsh all comers' record of 1.93 in the high jump.

Eirias Park Opens

Athletics in north Wales received a major boost in 1955 with the opening of the cinder track at Eirias Park, Colwyn Bay. The first full North Wales Championships were staged there on 18 June 1955. A month earlier the Cardiff University cinder track at Llanrumney had been opened.

© Jim Parry

John Disley coming in to win the mile event in the first North Wales District AAA Championships.

The match between the Welsh AAA and the AAA had by now become something of an annual event and always produced high quality results. At Newport on 9 July 1955 there were new Welsh all-comers' figures by future world record holder Derek Ibbotson (4:10.2) in the mile, Peter Driver (14:10.0) in the three miles and Ken Wilmshurst in the triple jump (14.68). Wilmshurst's mark bettered Gordon Wells record set some six years earlier at Abertillery. Later that month, at a meeting in Nairobi, Kenya, Hywel Williams threw the discus 47.50 which ranked him among the best in Britain and would remain a Welsh record for eight years.

Competing in an international between the USSR and the UK at Moscow in September 1955 John Disley once more broke the British record for the 3,000m steeplechase. His time of 8:44.2 ahead of Chris Brasher would have been a world record a month earlier. So his hopes of gold in Melbourne were high, but it was not to be.

Athletics in Wales was not without its problems at the time. There was much criticism of timekeeping standards, especially among those taking times for the minor places. The practice for many years had been to time the winners only but when attempts were made to time others this was frequently by people of very limited experience. It was reported in the newspapers that at one meeting, times for minor places had been taken by a timekeeper who did not attempt to watch the starter, being satisfied to start his watch when he heard the report of the gun.

The Russians are coming to Swansea – well, almost!

Matt Cullen, an Irishman who settled in Wales in the 1920s, and as we have seen, winner of the inaugural Welsh discus title in 1937, was one of the great characters of Welsh athletics. He frequently visited the countries of Eastern Europe and on one visit to Prague he made contact with some Russian athletics authorities. The Soviet Union was due to compete in an international match against Britain at the White City Stadium in 1956. Matt was nothing if not ambitious and he made approaches to the Russians regarding the possibility of them paying a visit to Wales while they were in this country, and competing in Swansea. To Matt's delight the Russian response appeared to be quite favourable.

The opportunity to bring some of the world's greatest athletes to Wales would have been a tremendous fillip to Welsh athletics and with the Cardiff Empire Games only two years away it would have given Welsh athletes competition of the highest possible calibre. St Helen's was chosen to be the venue and a provisional date of the last weekend in August was set. The meeting never took place, of course. Jack Crump, Secretary of the British Amateur Athletic Board, was furious with Matt for making a direct approach that contravened the international rules, as invitations to overseas athletes could only be made by the BAAB. In a letter to Matt, Crump pointed out that "the Soviet athletics team are the guests of the BAAB and it will not be possible for them to appear in any other meeting in Great Britain apart from their match in London."

Like all good stories, however, this one had a twist in the tail. On a shopping expedition to London's West End the Russian discus thrower Nina Ponomaryeva (Olympic Champion in 1952 and 1960) was accused of shoplifting. The allegation that she had stolen some hats from C & A Modes led to an international incident and the Soviet team promptly packed their bags and left for home, so the match in the White City never took place either. Matt's reaction to the irony of this is not on record. He coached numerous athletes of all ages and abilities both at his club Swansea Valley AC and wider afield for over 50 years. In 1970, he was one of the prime movers behind the establishment of championships for Welsh veterans and today the Matt Cullen Trophy is still competed for in these championships. He competed in the second World Veteran's Championships in Gothenberg in 1977 in six events and won the discus with 31.58 a world record for his age group at the age of 77. He also won numerous European and British veterans titles and died in 1981 aged 81.

At the Welsh Championships it was normal practice to hold qualifying rounds for the field events in the morning, with the finals being held later in the day. This led to one or two odd situations. In 1956 only one athlete attained the qualifying standard in the women's high jump and as a consequence only she competed in the final later in the day. Nowadays there are no qualifying rounds and all competitors take part in the final and are included in the final classification. In 1957 Hywel Williams, who was far and away Wales' best discus thrower at the time, failed to turn up in time for the qualifying round. When he finally appeared the referee consulted with those who had qualified in the morning and it was agreed that Hywel should be offered a place in the final. Ever the sportsman, Hywel declined the offer stating that it was his own fault that he had been late and it would not be fair on the others if he were allowed to compete. His conscience would not allow him to participate (can you imagine that happening today?).

Pen Portrait – Bill Kingsbury MBE
(Army, Rhondda AC, Farnham AC and South London H)

Bill Kingsbury is not a name that is instantly recognisable alongside World and Olympic champions - but his contribution to track and field athletics, particularly in Wales, as an athlete, coach and mentor is immeasurable.

He is still competing in veteran's events and coaching at the age of 74, and competed for his club, Rhondda AC in the Welsh League at the age of 71. In fact his contribution to other sports – particularly rugby – is just as great. He was offered terms to play rugby league in 1954, but declined as he was hoping to make that year's Welsh Empire Games team for Vancouver, but cash restrictions in the austere post war period, restricted the numbers in the team and he missed out. "Off the record" says Bill, "I was offered £2,000". Don't worry Bill, we won't tell anyone!

As far as his name is concerned, he is somewhat of a Jekyll and Hyde. The answer to this conundrum is that he regales in the name of W.F.J.P.H Kingsbury. When he first sent in an entry for an athletics event, he just used the initial "W" as "it was easier" and therefore became known as Bill in athletics circles. But to his family and friends in the Army he is known as Jim, and as Percy to his friends and former teammates in Tylorstown RFC!

Bill Kingsbury (in the circle) pictured at a wet Maindy Stadium during the Wales v. Southern and Midland Counties match in 1956. No. 83, in the background, is Brian Penny of Swansea.

As a competitor, he won just two Welsh shot titles (1954 and 1956), placing second or third on a further four occasions and finishing third in the javelin twice. But his best years of competition came when he was stationed in the Army in the Middle East as a PE Instructor, and this obviously prevented him from competing in Welsh championships. He won many Army titles – too numerous to mention, but ended his service with bests of 60.64m (javelin),

14.20m (shot) and 13.69m for the triple jump. He represented the Army in no fewer than seven sports, which is surely a record.

On his return to the UK he was stationed in Aldershot and started competing for Farnham AC where he was coached by Franz Stampfl, who advised, amongst others, Roger Bannister. It was here in 1951 that Bill achieved his best shot with 50'3 ¼ (15.37m), which added over 2 metres to Tiny Lewis' 1932 Welsh record. Stampfl remarked that Bill was the smallest 50' shot putter (at 5'9 and 12 stone 2 lbs) he had coached.

His best marks in Wales came in 1956 when he won both the shot and javelin (14.98m/57.56m) in a match against the RAF at Ferndale.

Amongst his successes as a veterans competitor is British pentathlon champion in the 65-70 age group and record holder for the hammer in the same group.

He has received many awards – both coaching and for services to athletics, but the modest Bill shies away from giving details saying that he undertakes his activities for enjoyment and not reward.

In 1993 he was Lloyds Bank Coach of the Year in Wales, and he does admit to being honoured at receiving the Torch Trophy from the Duke of Edinburgh in 1999 for "Outstanding voluntary service to the Athletics Association of Wales" and a Golden Award for Sporting Achievement last year when the comedian Norman Wisdom was presented with a similar award at the Savoy in London for his contribution to show business

The AAW awarded him their top award, The Award of Honour in 1996, and he received a Meritorious Plaque from the Welsh AAA in 1963.

He has coached far too many athletes to mention in detail – "over 300" he says, but credit for the remarkable performances of hammer thrower Carys Parry, who represented Britain in the World Junior Championships in Chile in 2000, must be particularly pleasing to him, as he has coached her from the time she started competing.

In this modern era of professional athletics, the sport cannot do without the likes of Bill Kingsbury, and many like him, who have given a lifetime to the sport for no reward other than the satisfaction of helping others progress. In fact Bill claims that it costs him between £1,000 and £1,500 per year to continue serving the sport, which he spends without a second thought. Without him, and thousands of other volunteer officials, there would not be a sport in which to participate.

Sexton proves there's a point to marriage

The 1957 Welsh Championships saw Brian Sexton of Roath Harriers take the javelin title to stop Swansea's Clive Roberts winning the event for the fourth successive year. Sexton, who emigrated to Canada in 1963, took three further titles between 1959 and 1961, and during his career set six Welsh records with the old specification model, taking the record from 58.90 which he set taking the Glamorgan title on a grass run-up at Jenner Park, Barry in 1955 to 66.98 in 1961. Roberts, who was part of the Welsh team at the 1954 Vancouver Empire Games, was coached by Midlands National Coach and fellow Swansea Grammar School athlete, Lionel Pugh, set four Welsh marks in his career, ending with a best of 61.82 in 1958. Welsh 1958 Commonwealth Games representative Sexton, who was coached by Jim Alford, started the Javelin Club of Canada when he emigrated – and still remembers receiving his first javelin. It was a Christmas present from his future wife when he was 17 in 1950. They married four years later and are still going strong after 47 years of married life – is this where the saying "there must be a point to married life" comes from?

By 1957, the sport was changing in nature and the members of the Welsh Handicapping Board of Control expressed their concern at the reduction in the number of handicap meetings being staged in Wales. In 1957 just one such meeting was held and it was becoming increasingly obvious that this style of meeting was losing its appeal. The Board was finally wound up in 1970 after years of having existed in name only with no function to fulfil.

The match versus the AAA was held at Margam that year and produced its usual crop of Welsh all-comers' records, one of them from Bob Shaw in the 120 yds hurdles in which he clocked 15.0 – two tenths faster than his own record set three years earlier. Colin Smith, who would win the Empire and Commonwealth gold medal at Cardiff a year later, threw the javelin 69.12 and Eric Cleaver hurled the discus out 47.50 to set new marks.

Undoubtedly the most significant year in the history of Welsh athletics occurred in 1958 with the staging of two major international events in the Principality. The first was the International Cross Country Championships (forerunner of the World Cross Country Championships) held at Pontcanna Fields, Cardiff, and the second was the VI British Empire and Commonwealth Games (as they were then styled) staged at Cardiff Arms Park in July. Both of these events are covered in detail elsewhere in this book. The Empire Games were an outstanding success and certainly did much to raise the profile of Wales as a nation and of Welsh athletics. The advent of a major international meeting being staged in Cardiff created an enormous interest in the sport and this year was in many ways the year in which Welsh athletics took off.

The standard of athletics was higher than had ever been seen in Wales before and every single Welsh all comers' record was broken with the exception of the Marathon. Three world records were broken, the first ever on Welsh soil. For the first time ever women featured in the Welsh team. Wales selected a huge team of 33 men (of whom the late Huw Jones unfortunately was forced to withdraw) and 10 women and the only area of controversy surrounded the omission of north Walian schoolgirl Monica Zeraschi from the long jump, an event in which she had beaten the two Welsh representatives. From a Welsh point of view the outstanding athlete was John Merriman. He started off this momentous year by finishing seventh in the International Cross Country event and went on to win the silver medal in the six miles at the Empire Games.

A few weeks before the big event Wales took part in a full international match when they entertained a strong team from Nigeria who were in Wales for the Games. The match was held at Eirias Park, Colwyn Bay on 5 July. Oddly enough there is no mention of this meeting in the Welsh AAA annual report for that year. For the record the Nigerians won by 115.5 points to 98.5. New Welsh all-comers' records were set for 100 yds, 220 yds, one mile, three miles, 120 yds hurdles and the high jump, although all were destined to be broken a couple of weeks later at the Games.

This memorable year ended with the creation of another event that caused great public interest. The Nos Galan road race through the streets of Mountain Ash was held on New Year's Eve, starting at a few minutes before midnight so that it began in 1958 and finished in 1959, following the pattern of the famous Sao Paolo midnight race in Brazil. The story of Nos Galan, and its founder, Bernard Baldwin is elsewhere in this book.

Immediately after the closing of the Games the track at Cardiff Arms Park was uplifted and re-laid at Maindy Stadium, making this a first class facility for that time. In June 1959 another cinder track was opened, this time at Glebelands, the home of Newport Harriers. The number of cinder tracks in Wales was now seven although four of these - at

Aberystwyth University, Llanrumney, RAF St Athan and Talbot Green, were privately owned. The only public cinder tracks were at Maindy, Eirias Park and now Glebelands.

First Welsh Games in 1959

There was a definite spin-off effect of the staging of the Empire Games and in 1959 no less than 900 athletes entered the Welsh Junior, Youths' and Boys' Championships. This year also saw two far-reaching innovations with the staging of the first Welsh Games and the first schools' international match. The schools' match was held at Colwyn Bay and Scotland provided the opposition. This fixture would eventually become one of the major events in the schools' calendar.

Berwyn Jones just edges out Robbie Brightwell (7) to win the 1963 Welsh Games 100 yards. Others in the picture include Ron Jones (4) and David Jones (3).

The Welsh Games were originally planned to be a small-scale version of the Empire Games and were not confined to athletics. The intention was to create an annual festival of sport in the Welsh capital and perpetuate the tremendous spirit engendered by the events of 1958. With the newly laid track at Maindy and the super new Empire Pool in the centre of Cardiff (one of only two Olympic size pools in Britain at the time, and now demolished to make way for the Millennium Stadium) the facilities existed to fulfil this objective. Boxing, swimming, cycling, gymnastics and weight lifting were all included in the early editions but one by one these gradually disappeared and the Welsh Games eventually became an athletics only meeting. The athletics at the first ever Welsh Games incorporated a limited events men's international match between Wales and a strong team from Pakistan, including a number who had won medals the previous year, with Wales running out victors by 38 points to 33.

Running for Britain against the USSR in Moscow in September Aberdare-born Ron Jones ran 100m in 10.5 to break the Welsh record of 10.6 set by Ken Jones in the 1948 Olympic Games. A month later, in Birmingham, he brought the record down to 10.4. Late in that year Berwyn Jones won a 60 yds race at an indoor meeting at RAF St Athan. Indoor athletics was another new venture and the RAF station was to become the home of this branch of the sport in Wales for many years. The meetings became so popular that national indoor championships were introduced in 1970 and continued until 1991. The first indoor meeting held at St. Athan

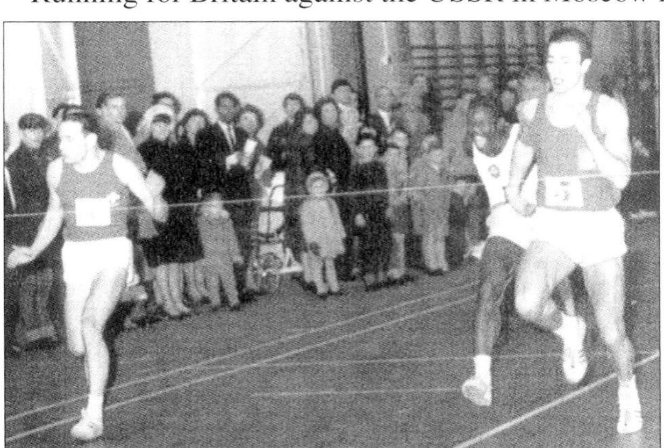

© Western Mail

Lynn Davies (5) wins the 60 yards from Ron Jones in the Welsh AAA v RAF indoor meeting at St Athan in 1965. Note the wooden track surface on the gymnasium floor with no lanes.

- and therefore in Wales - was held on a 160 yd wood floor in the main gymnasium on 28th November 1957. Events then moved to a building next door and onto a 190 yd concrete surface, which was first used on 23rd January 1965. Amongst the leading marks recorded there were Venissa Head's UK indoor record of 19.06 set in 1984, which still stands and is the only mark in excess of 19m recorded by a British female athlete – 32cms ahead of the mark set by Judy Oakes in 1988. Another indoor mark of significance to Welsh athletics is Bob Maplestone's mile of 3:59.5 in San Diego in 1972, which was the first time a UK athlete had bettered 4 minutes indoors, and still stands as the Welsh indoor record. Bob, Cardiff born and a member of Cardiff AAC during the period of their British League successes in the early 1970s is now domiciled in the USA, and a US citizen.

A host of international stars took part in the Welsh Games of 1960 including the legendary Herb Elliott who, only eleven days earlier, had devastated the world's best middle runners when winning the Olympic Games 1,500m in a new world record time. At Maindy he ran in the 880 yds. Winner of the 3 miles was Laszlo Tabori, formerly of Hungary, who as a displaced person was prevented from competing in the Olympic Games where he would have been a serious threat to anyone in the 1,500 or 5,000m. Others to appear included Commonwealth triple jump champion Ian Tomlinson and sprinters Harry Jerome (Canada) and Seraphino Antao of Kenya who would go on to win both sprints in the 1962 Perth Commonwealth Games. The only other Kenyan present was Nyandika Maiyoro, the first distance runner of any consequence to emerge from that country. Who could have anticipated that his fellow countrymen would one day dominate the middle distances? Commonwealth champions Marlene Willard (sprints) and Norma Thrower (hurdles), like Elliott re-visited the city where they had enjoyed some of their greatest moments in athletics just two years earlier.

Gordon Roberts

Lynn Davies (2) wins the Welsh Games 100 yds in 1962 from a star-studded field. Others in the picture are (left to right): Lib Dem MP Ming Campbell (1), Robbie Brightwell (6), Bob Frith (5), Ron Jones (1) and Adrian Metcalfe (10).

In the 1960 Rome Olympics Nick Whitehead won a bronze medal in the 4 x 100 relay and John Merriman broke his own UK record in the 10,000m to become the first Briton to record less than 29 minutes for the distance, whilst Ted Hopkins attended as assistant team manager to the British team.

Pen Portrait - Nick Whitehead (Loughborough College and Birchfield H)

In an era when Wales produced a string of outstanding sprinters Neville (Nick) Whitehead proved himself one of the best of them. His duels with Ron Jones were a feature of the Welsh Championships during the late 1950s. In the ten Welsh sprint finals he contested he never finished lower than second, winning the sprint double in 1957, 1958 and 1960 and placing second in both sprints in 1956 and 1959. In all he broke or equalled the Welsh 100 yds record on seven occasions and retired with all-time bests of 9.7 (1960) and 21.6 (220 yds) in 1958. His finest moment came in the 1960 Rome Olympic Games when he took bronze in the 4 x 100m relay. At the time he was only the seventh Welsh athlete to take an Olympic medal.

His running in 1957 was enough to get him international recognition and he ran in the 4 x 110y relay for Britain against France at the White City that August. In May 1958 he equalled the Welsh record for 220 yds and later that year twice equalled the record for 100 yds. His two victories over Ron Jones at the 1958 Welsh Championships meant he could regard himself as Wales' top sprinter that year in which he competed in his first major championships the Cardiff Commonwealth Games. He reached the second round in the 100 and 220 yds and was one of the Welsh team which finished fifth in the 4 x 110 yds relay.

Nick Whitehead seen here competing in the AAA Championships at the White City in 1959.

Although Ron got his revenge in 1959, when it was his turn to score a Welsh double, both sprinters were chosen for Britain's four international matches that year. The most bizarre experience of the season came in the 4 x 110 relay against Poland at the White City when both teams were disqualified. Nick was on form again in 1960 winning the Welsh 100 yds by a huge margin from Berwyn Jones with a Welsh record-equalling time before going on to score a similarly emphatic win in the 220. In all he matched the Welsh 100 yds record of 9.7 three times that season to rank equal fourth in Britain (as he had in 1958).

Nick's third major championship was the Commonwealth Games in Perth, Australia in 1962 when he travelled as captain to the Welsh team and added another relay bronze to his tally when he teamed up with Dave England, Ron & Berwyn Jones to set a new Welsh record of 40.80. His next visit to a major international meeting was under a different guise. As overall team manager to the Great Britain team from 1978 to 1984 he attended the 1980 Moscow and 1984 Los Angeles Olympic Games as well as the inaugural World Championships in Helsinki in 1983 and the World Student Games of the same year.

A Great Britain staff coach Nick has been a Director of the National Coaching Foundation and, among many other activities, Deputy Director of the Sports Council for Wales and held many positions on national committees. He was founder Chairman, later President, of the British Paraplegic AA and is currently President of the Federation of Sports Associations for the Disabled (Wales) of which he was also founder Chairman. He is also President of Wrexham AC.

A former teacher at Hertford and Birmingham Dr Whitehead became Head of Department at Leeds Polytechnic. He has been author or co-author of 14 books and over 30 research articles and is a Fellow of the University of Wales Institute at Cardiff. He has been invited to become a Fellow of the University of North Wales. In 1985 he was awarded the OBE in recognition of his services to sport.

Peter Radford wins at Bargoed.

Another addition was made to the number of cinder tracks in Wales with the opening in 1960 of Bargoed Park on 24 September. The track, costing £7,000 made an auspicious start when at the first meeting Peter Radford won the invitation 100 yds in 9.7 seconds, with Ron Jones second and Berwyn Jones third, just over three weeks after Radford had won the 100m bronze medal at the Rome Olympics. Radford also won the 220 yds in 21.9, with the Jones boys finishing in the same order. The local paper, *The Rhymney Valley and Merthyr Express* enthused on its front page: "Bargoed Becoming Valley's Sports Arena".

It was in 1961 that Ron Pickering, the newly appointed Welsh National Coach in succession to Jim Alford, first spotted the potential of 19 year-old Lynn Davies. That year he took his first Welsh senior title (triple jump) and finished a close second to Bryan Woolley in the long jump. Remarkably, the following year Lynn was fourth in the Commonwealth Games long jump with a new British record of 7.72. A Welsh AAA v Southern Counties AAA match was organised to mark the official opening of Jenner Park, Barry on 19 May 1962. A total of £13,500 had been spent on improvements there in what was declared by the mayor of Barry to be "The first stage towards the making of Jenner Park into a really first class sports stadium". The match, which the Southern Counties won by 108 points to 85, saw the emergence of Lynn Davies, second in the long jump to Fred Alsop. His leap of 7.39 would have been his first Welsh record but for the following wind. Later on he followed Berwyn Jones, Ron Jones and nick Whitehead to anchor the Welsh AAA team to a new Welsh record of 42.0 for the 4x110 yds relay.

Lynn Davies beats Ron Jones in the 100 yards during the Wales v Army match at Jenner Park, Barry in 1966. The other athlete in the picture is the 1964 Welsh 100 yards champion, Brian Coles.

Welsh sprinting was at an all time high during this period. The Welsh record for 100 yds had been set at 9.8 by Cyril Cupid back in 1934. Even the great Ken Jones, who equalled it on a number of occasions, never succeeded in beating that time. A succession of fine sprinters gave the record something of a hammering between 1958 and 1965. Ron Jones and Nick

Whitehead clocked a number of 9.8 timings before Ron finally recorded 9.7 in 1959. He and Whitehead continued on their record equalling spree and were later joined by Berwyn Jones who, in 1962, brought the record down to 9.6. It was the durable Ron Jones who first clocked 9.5, which he did on three occasions. Lynn Davies also ran 9.5 a couple of times. Rhymney born Berwyn Jones won the AAA title in 1963, only the second Welshman to achieve the feat after Fred Cooper some 60 years earlier. Later that year he clocked 10.3 for 100m in an international match in Budapest, equalling the British record to really announce his arrival on the British scene. Another performance of note in 1963 came from 17 year-old Newport schoolboy Graham Webb who triple jumped 14.67 at Glebelands to shatter both Welsh youths' and junior records in one go. It was the best jump by a British youth that year. Graham went on to set a Welsh senior record of 15.64 in 1969 which stood for nine years until bettered by John Phillips with 15.88.

Pen Portrait – Ron Jones MBE
(Birchgrove H, Woodford Green AC, Borough of Enfield H)

In the 1990 Welsh Athletics Annual looking back at the 1989 season the editor commented on the state of Welsh sprinting: "If asked to name the Welsh record holder for 100m many people, quite feasibly, would offer the name of Olympic 110 hurdles silver medallist Colin Jackson or perhaps his team-mate, World indoor 60 hurdles bronze medallist Nigel Walker. However, they would be would be wrong! The record still stands to 55 years old Ron Jones. He set the record of 10.42 in the 1968 Mexico Olympics where, at the age of 34, he was Britain's team captain. There is very little doubt that if Colin or Nigel had concentrated their efforts on the 100m the Welsh record would be nearer to 10.0 seconds today".

The editor must have given Colin a free copy of the Annual, as three months later it happened. Competing at the Welsh Games in Wrexham on 28th July, running down the back straight to make use of a favourable wind, Colin finally removed Ron Jones' 22 year old record stopping the clock at 10.29.

© Western Mail

Ken Jones (left) and Ron Jones compare styles after Ron had beaten Ken's record of seven wins in the Welsh 100 yards event at the Welsh Championships at Maindy Stadium in 1970.

The former Chief Executive of Portsmouth Football Club was a proud owner of the record. Says Ron: "the 1960s were definitely a golden era for Welsh sprinting, and our sprinters were generally the best in Britain. Lynn Davies, Terry Davies, the former London Welsh, Llanelli and Wales 'B' wing, Berwyn Jones and Nick Whitehead, all ran for Britain during this period and I think that it was fierce but friendly rivalry which

kept standards high".

Ron will go down in Welsh athletics history as the most prolific Welsh record setter with 22 entries. He equalled the 9.8 100 yds record in July 1958 at Paignton, but at the White City on 14th August 1959 he made the record his own with a time of 9.7. A month later he broke the 100m hand time record with 10.5 in Moscow to take the eleven-year-old record set by his hero Ken Jones.

Even as early as 1956, Ron had ideas of being "another Ken Jones" – in the athletics sense, that is. Ken, as with thousands of Welsh youngsters, was Ron's idol. Like Ken, Ron captained Britain's athletics team in a major games - the 1968 Olympics - and took two relay bronze medals in major championships - the 1962 European (Belgrade) and Commonwealth Games - but an individual medal always eluded him. At the Commonwealth Games in Perth he gained sprint relay bronze with Berwyn Jones, Nick Whitehead and Dave England.

After his retirement Ron's energies have been directed towards soccer. Firstly he became Chief Executive of Queens Park Rangers in 1976, having spent the previous nine years on the QPR staff as a part time coaching adviser, before moving to Cardiff City to become the first Managing Director of a Football League Club, in 1980. He left Cardiff City in June 1988 to rejoin John Gregory, his former boss at QPR, and subsequently become Managing Director at Portsmouth. However he still had fond memories of his athletics career and still regards himself as an athletics man.

Surprisingly for an athlete who was generally regarded as Europe's top sprinter in the late 1960s, Ron's most pleasing moment in a glittering career spanning fifteen years was when he bettered Ken Jones' sequence of seven Welsh 100 yds titles in 1970. Ron rates this performance even above the occasion in 1963 when, as a member of one of the most famous British sprint relay quartets of all time, David and Berwyn Jones and Cardiff based 1960 Olympic 100m bronze medallist Peter Radford being the others, he equalled the world 4 x 110 yds record at the White City in beating the mighty USA with a time of 40.0. The USA quartet, which included Bob Hayes, the man destined to win the 1964 Tokyo Olympic 100m, hadn't been beaten for many a year and the British foursome, nicknamed the "Jones Boys", became the toast of British athletics. Also at the age of 34 he took the first ever AAA 100m title to follow in the footsteps of fellow Welshmen Fred Cooper (1898) and Berwyn Jones (1963) as winners of an AAA sprint title.

He regards Berwyn Jones' decision to sign for Wakefield Trinity Rugby League Club as a great tragedy for athletics. "There is little doubt that our rivalry would have ensured faster times in the 1960s and I'm sure Berwyn would have gone much faster than he did" says Ron of the former Caerleon Training College sprinter. "There were tears in Berwyn's eyes in 1964 when our world record equalling sprint relay team received special plaques from the Duke of Edinburgh at Buckingham Palace. Berwyn thought he had let the boys down by going North just before the 1964 Tokyo Olympics".

© Western Mail

Berwyn Jones, Peter Radford, David Jones and Ron Jones pictured outside Buckingham Palace before receiving awards from the Duke of Edinburgh.

Another performance which gave Ron great pleasure was his 1968 Welsh 100 yds win over, as he puts it, "the pretender to Welsh sprinting" – a 20-year-old Cardiff College of Education (now UWIC) student by the name of JJ Williams. In appalling weather conditions at Cardiff's Maindy Stadium that day (many other events had to be postponed) the 35-year-old Cwmaman born man beat the future Wales and British Lions rugby star with a time of 9.7 to 9.8, with Cardiff's Brian Coles third.

Ron was particularly pleased with that run because the previous weekend in the Wales v Army match at Barry's Jenner Park, 'JJ' had caused a sensation by beating the Welsh record holder by a whisker with both men clocking 10.0 seconds.

In total Ron won 12 Welsh sprint titles between 1956 and 1970. However, his first Welsh title win in 1956 was remarkable in the circumstances. "I was a late starter in the sport and, after knocking on the front door of Bernard Baldwin, the former Welsh AAA Secretary, at his Mountain Ash house for advice, he suggested that I ran the Glamorgan championships of that year which were due to be held at St Helen's, Swansea. With very little training or preparation I won the 440 yds but came nowhere in the 100. At that time I had already entered for the Welsh Championships in both the 100 and 440 yds and as the 100 event came before the 440 I ran that and, to my great surprise, won. It was only the second or third 100 I had ever run! Perhaps if the 440 had come first I would have just run in that, and not bothered with the 100 again!"

It was at this time that Ron joined Cardiff club Birchgrove Harriers, and was soon to benefit from the help received from the club's coaches Jack Collard and Jim Thomas.

Altogether Ron won 31 British international vests. He took part in nine major championships – 4 Commonwealth, 3 European and 2 Olympics. Retirement came at the end of the 1970 Commonwealth Games in Edinburgh just a month ahead of his 36th birthday. His act will be hard to follow but he is certainly one of the legends of Welsh athletics and thoroughly deserved his MBE in the 2001 New Year's Honours List.

Tokyo gold for Lynn

Prior to 1964 only three Welsh athletes had won gold medals at the Olympic Games. These were achieved in relays through David Jacobs (4 x 100m) in 1912 and Cecil Griffiths and Jack Ainsworth Davis (4 x 400m) in 1920. We can only speculate what a fit Reg Thomas might have achieved in 1932 and the nearest anyone had come to winning an individual gold medal was the silver medal of Tom Richards in 1948. The Lynn Davies story is told elsewhere in more detail, but his unexpected gold medal in the long jump at the Tokyo Olympics must go down on record as one of the defining moments in Welsh athletics history. Whereas the wind assistance gained by others had cost him a medal at the Commonwealth Games two year earlier, this time he used the elements to his advantage and waited until the right moment before launching himself off on his winning leap. In 1963 Lynn had lost his British record to John Morbey but he reclaimed it at the Inter Counties Championships at the White City in May. He was never to lose it again. His 1968 record of 8.23 still stands to him 33 years later. On 25 July 1964 he twice improved his record in the Welsh Games at Maindy Stadium and became the first Welsh athlete to set a British record in Wales. His gold medal-winning jump in Tokyo improved it yet again. Lynn also competed in the 100m and the 4 x 100m relay in which Ron Jones also took part. Another pointer to Olympic success was provided at the Welsh Games of 1964 when Ann Packer, who would go on to win the 800m in world record time in Tokyo, won the 880 yds.

Harris is first Welshman under 4 minutes

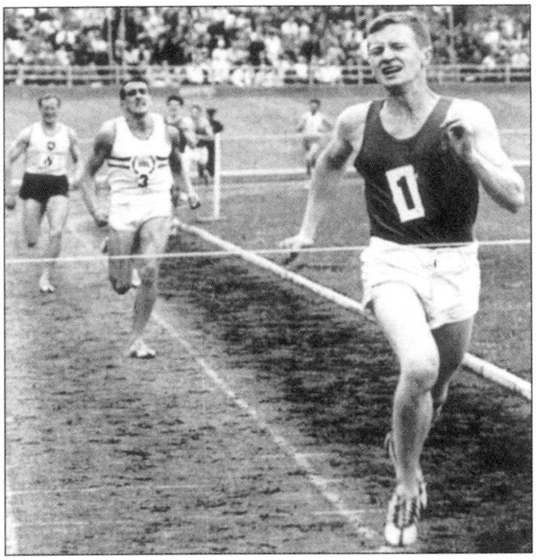

Tony Harris wins the 880 yards at the 1962 Welsh Games at Maindy Stadium, from Mike Fleet (3) and Wrexham's Viv Blackwell.

One piece of Welsh athletics history occurred on 3 July 1965 when at the White City Stadium in London Tony Harris clocked 3:58.96 to become the first Welsh athlete to run a sub four-minute mile. He had an indifferent career, and whilst an athlete with considerable talent, never showed his best form in Wales. He took the Welsh 880 yds title in 1966, but appeared in few Welsh Championships. He reached the final of both 880 yds and mile in the Perth Commonwealth Games, finishing sixth in both, and also appeared in the team in Jamaica four years later, but failed to progress past the heats.

Another, less inspiring event, occurred at a meeting in Pontypool Park later that month. Many of the events were running late – and it was all down to some donkeys! There had been a series of donkey races earlier in the programme and when one of the women sprinters asked why her race was being held up until after the donkey races she was told "well, the donkeys are getting rather tired, dear". The race eventually took place two hours late. The meeting in question was hardly a small "tea party" type as former world record holder Derek Ibbotson was one of the competitors in the mile won by Birchgrove's Bill Stitfall.

A matter of interest to younger athletes, which occurred in 1965, was the change in the qualifying dates for the various young age groups. Previously the determining factor had been the athlete's age prior to 1st April in the year in question, but this was now changed to 1st September, which is still the case today. A feature of that year's Welsh Games was a long jump competition involving Lynn Davies and his predecessor as Olympic Champion Ralph Boston of the USA. At great expense the Cardiff City Council laid a special pit in front of the main grandstand to give the event maximum exposure. For a whole hour there were no other events on the programme so that the crowd had no distractions, and Ron Pickering gave a commentary on the event. Boston won with a leap of 8.18 that still stands as a

Lynn Davies, Ron Pickering and Gwyn Williams look on as the new long jump pit is built at Maindy for the 1965 Welsh Games for Lynn's epic battle with world long jump record holder Ralph Boston who is pictured right during the competition.

Welsh all-comers' record to this day. The following year Lynn Davies completed his set by taking long jump gold medals at the European Championships and the Commonwealth Games. He thus became the first Welsh athlete to win gold medals in all three of the major international championships.

One unique event to be held that year was a competition for throwing the 56 lbs weight at Swansea University. The event, popular at Highland Games meetings, was contested twice in the Olympic Games and on one occasion at the AAA Championships. This was the first time for it to be staged in Wales, and quite possibly the last.

RAF St. Athan decathlete Clive Longe enjoyed a brilliant season in 1966. Guesting at the Southern Championships in May he beat British record holder Derek Clarke, taking his national record from him in the process with a score of 7083 points. Just a month later, competing for Britain in an international match in Holland, he increased his score to 7114 while winning the match. By August he was ready for the Commonwealth Games, held in sunny Jamaica, and he upped his record for the third time in the year in taking the silver medal. He hadn't finished yet, though, as he then went on to compete in the European Championships in Budapest. He finished ninth this time despite breaking his British record yet again.

Birchgrove take AAA title

Cardiff's Birchgrove Harriers winners of AAA 4 x 1 mile relay in 1965 (left to right): Bill Stitfall, Ken Bennett, Bernie Plain and John Godding.

Cardiff's Birchgrove Harriers were amongst the strongest middle distance teams in Britain in the mid 1960s, and they caused a stir when they beat the much-fancied Longwood Harriers (Huddersfield) squad, which contained the former mile world record holder Derek Ibbotson, to the inaugural 4 x 1 mile relay title. Formed by Jack Collard and Jim Thomas at Birchgrove School, Cardiff on 17 December 1952, they rose from humble beginnings to be the strongest all-round club in Wales and merged with their neighbours, Roath Harriers in November 1968 with whom they were then sharing Maindy Stadium as an HQ. Collard was responsible for much of the club's success and was the first and only secretary of the club, but sadly after the merger, decided not to take any further part in the sport. He became the first official in British athletics to receive the Torch Trust award in 1963, which is awarded to individuals who have given outstanding service to amateur sport in Britain. He died in 1998 aged 86.

A young Hedydd Davies (116) and Bill Stitfall compete for the Welsh AAA in their match against the Army at Jenner Park, Barry in 1966. Stitfall won narrowly in a new Welsh all-comers record of 9:04.8, with Davies second in 9:06.0. The time beat Davies' all-comers record of 9:05.3 set in 1964.

The first ever Inter Area Decathlon was held at Maindy on 10 September 1966 in conjunction with the Welsh Games. Despite it being just 8 days after the European Championships Clive Longe was in action again. He broke the 7000 points barrier, which had by now become routine for him, and was the individual winner ahead of

Scotland's Peter Gabbett. The Welsh pair of Longe and Birchgrove's John Lister won the match, the forerunner of today's home countries combined events international match, over 1000 points clear of the Southern Counties.

Kip Keino at the Welsh Games

Kip Keino (Kenya), future Olympic 1,500m champion at Mexico in 1968, with a lap to go in the Morley Mile at Maindy Stadium during the 1966 Welsh Games. Calling out his lap time is Ted Hopkins.

A highlight of the 1966 Welsh Games in Cardiff was the appearance of Kip Keino in the Morley mile. This popular Kenyan athlete became Olympic 1,500m Champion in 1968 and also won the steeplechase in 1972. At Maindy he lowered Herb Elliott's Welsh all-comers' record, set in the 1958 Commonwealth Games, when clocking 3:57.6. Olympic Champion Mary Rand, a frequent visitor to Cardiff, won the 80m hurdles. At the Welsh Championships that year, Pat Jones took his fifth 440 yds title since 1960, Birchgrove's John Lister won his fourth successive 120 yds hurdles title, and Lynn Davies won his fourth and (surprisingly) last long jump title. The main beneficiary of this was his close friend and Cardiff College student Gwyn Williams, who took the next four titles in succession.

After years of planning, a training camp was officially opened by Lord Aberdare at Merthyr Mawr on 19 November 1966. Jim Alford had first mooted the idea in the late 1950s and he had spent three years working there with a band of young volunteers by the time he left Wales in 1960. The huge sand dunes at Merthyr Mawr, near Ogmore, reputed to be the highest in Europe, were considered an ideal base for training purposes and the site became a popular training venue for many years. Jim Alford was present at the opening ceremony seeing for himself how his idea had come to fruition. Amongst others, Birchgrove sprinter/triple jumper Dave Williams, Alan Thomas, Tony Clemo and, later, Norman John, were instrumental in guiding and maintaining the project at Candlestone Farm through from infancy to completion.

In 1966 Ron Pickering left Wales and was succeeded by Peter Lay, who made his Welsh debut at the popular annual Easter Young athletes course at Llanrumney, Cardiff.

Pen Portrait - Ron Pickering OBE (1931-1991)

Ron arrived in Wales as Welsh National Coach on 1 July 1961 and has said since that the patron saint of athletics coaches must have been watching over him on that day as it was the beginning of the journey which led to the "discovery" of Lynn Davies and Ron went on to guide him to Olympic stardom. He coached and assisted numerous Welsh athletes, and when he left Wales to take up a new appointment as general manager of the Lee Park Recreation Centre in north London on 1 March 1967, he left the Principality in a significantly healthier state than when he arrived.

Athletics was a way of life in the Pickering household as Ron's wife Jean, the former Jean Desforges, was European long jump champion in 1954. Their son, Shaun, was born in Abersychan and became Wales' finest all round throwing events exponent, winning 19 Welsh titles and becoming at various stages of his career

Lynn Davies takes more guidance from his coach Ron Pickering.

record holder at shot, discus and hammer. In 1996 Shaun, went on, in Atlanta, to fulfil a dream of his father's, that his son would be an Olympian. Ron would have been proud of Shaun's bronze medal for Wales in the shot at the 1998 Kuala Lumpur Commonwealth Games.

An outspoken critic of drug abusers, Ron was a firm believer in the real meaning of sportsmanship and some of the attitudes prevailing in modern sport distressed him. He held strong views on such issues as apartheid and expressed them fervently. Pace making was another issue about which he had strong feelings and he said that many runners were "prostituting themselves on the European circuit to bring in as much as possible". Little has changed within the sport in that respect.

His roots were deep in East London. He attended Stratford Grammar School, he taught at Wanstead County High, following National Coach Jim Alford (who he followed yet again into Wales). He had been a shot putter of average talent and always had a great passion for the field events.

He became a household name as athletics commentator with the BBC and covered all major events around the world. His knowledge of the sport was enormous and he frequently gave talks and seminars on various aspects of the sport, which he loved so much. Not many people realise that he started his broadcasting career in Wales as a sports presenter on TWW (Television Wales and the West) – the forerunner of HTV. His passion for what he considered to be the greatest sport made television viewing compulsive with his unmistakable East London voice and his love for superlatives to describe the action. However he was more than just a commentator. He was a visionary, teacher, coach, inspirer and crusader but above all he was a master communicator. Not only did he cover athletics but also skiing and gymnastics, made documentaries on sport in Cuba, Kenya and South Africa as well as other television projects.

Ron was president of Haringey AC and inspired the club to great things, coaching and encouraging athletes and officials at the New River Stadium. He also spent time and energy on handicapped sport and for all these efforts he was awarded the OBE in 1986.

In late 1990 he underwent major heart surgery and appeared to have been well on the road to recovery when he died suddenly at the age of 60 and one of the great voices of athletics was silenced. He was most proud of being known as a renowned physical educationalist. His legacy lives on with the Ron Pickering Memorial Fund, set up by Jean, which has helped hundreds of young athletes over the years and raised hundreds of thousands of pounds.

Clive Longe continued in 1967 where he had left off in 1966. At the British Universities Championships in June he again increased his British record and then in July he represented the British Commonwealth in a match against the United States in Los Angeles and set his sixth national record with a score of 7392.

Gordon Roberts

Ron Jones (8) just edges out Lynn Davies (9) for the 1967 Welsh 100 yards title. Schoolboy star JJ Wiliams (10) was third. 19 is Brian Lowe (Roath H).

The first Welsh Inter-Counties Championships involving all counties in Wales was held in 1967 at Brecon and the Welsh Senior Championships celebrated their golden jubilee in this year at Maindy. First held as a championships meeting (rather than individual championship events dispersed throughout Wales) in 1907, they had been cancelled eleven times due to the two World Wars, so the 50th championships came in 1967 rather than 1956. It turned out to be a somewhat inauspicious occasion, however, as the meeting was severely disrupted by the weather. Mid afternoon there came a sudden cloudburst that flooded the track and held things up for some time. The programme restarted and the final of the men's 100 yds was run on a track that looked more like a swimming pool. Ron Jones narrowly beat Lynn Davies with both clocking 9.7; a remarkable time under the circumstances as the Welsh record at the time was 9.5. Eventually, however, the conditions deteriorated further and the elements won in the end. The meeting was abandoned with the 220 yds, 440 yds, 120 yds hurdles and several field events not completed. These were ultimately held at the Welsh Games late in July, when Cwmbran's modern stadium hosted Welsh Senior Championships for the first time. One event, which was completed, was the hammer where Lawrie Hall won the event for an incredible tenth successive year. During this period he set eight Welsh records taking it from the 48.72 he set during the 1958 Cardiff Empire Game to 58.56 set four years later. This mark was to stand as the Welsh record for 19 years until beaten by Shaun Pickering with 59.20.

Another Lynn is a world-beater

Lynn Hughes of Bridgend became an unofficial world record holder on 4 November 1967 when he ran a 40 miles track race at Maindy Stadium in 3:58:53.2 to become the first man in history to complete the distance in less than four hours. Along with his twin brother Eric, he was one of the founders of the Bridgend club which originated in 1966 as a section of Bridgend YMCA. Amongst others involved at the time were Brian Adamson and Roy Anthony. The club broke away from the YMCA in 1983 and have been an independent club ever since.

In 1967 Welsh AAA representatives met delegates of the Lord Byers' Committee of Enquiry to discuss every aspect of athletics in Wales. One of the recommendations was for the appointment of a full-time paid administrator. It would be over 20 years before this proposal materialised when Brenda Currie was appointed Welsh National Administrator in 1987.

They say lightning never strikes twice but don't tell that to the athletics authorities. The Welsh Championships of 1968 were almost a carbon copy of the 1967 edition with many of the events being postponed due to torrential rain flooding the track once again. In absolutely awful conditions Liz Johns won the 100 yds in an excellent 10.9 but again the

Liz Johns (Parsons) wins the Welsh 100 yards title from Sylvia Powell (Swansea Valley) at Maindy in 1968. Liz competed for Wales at the 1966 Commonwealth Games and 1971 European Championships. At Glebelands, Newport in 1961 she became the first Welsh woman to run sub-11 seconds (10.9) for 100 yards. Sylvia Powell was Welsh pentathlon champion in 1968 the same year she was the first Welsh woman to jump 6.00 in the long jump.

weather had the last word and the meeting was finally abandoned. It was decided to hold the postponed events at Cwmbran again on 27 July – even though the Welsh Games were due to take place at Maindy on the same day! If ever there was a case for the introduction of all-weather tracks it was in the Welsh Championships of those 2 years. In 1968 the Crystal Palace track acquired a synthetic surface and in Mexico City the Olympic Games were held on a synthetic track for the first time. Today's athletes probably cannot imagine competing on anything else, but this was revolutionary stuff in 1968. It was to be a further six years before the first synthetic track would appear in Wales when the Wales v Canada international match at Cwmbran on 23/24 July 1974 was the occasion of the official opening of Wales' first such track.

Lynn's 8.23 still the UK long jump record in 2001

In June 1968 Lynn Davies set his seventh and final British record for the long jump when he leapt 8.23 at an international meeting between Britain and Switzerland in Berne. Converted to imperial measurement the jump was exactly 27 feet. Remarkably this stands as the British record to this day. He won the AAA title for the fourth time in five years and appeared to be in good form. With the Olympic Games on the horizon this was a good omen, but as is documented elsewhere, and known to almost every athletics enthusiast, Bob Beamon was in the form of his life, and shattered any dream Lynn had of retaining his title.

Lynn Davies on his way to setting a new UK long jump record, in Berne.

Cardiff AAC take British League title for three successive years

1968 saw the first tentative moves toward the formation of a British League with a pilot league of two divisions of six clubs each, in which Cardiff's Birchgrove Harriers were the only Welsh club taking part in the "A" division. The British Athletics League, or the National Athletics League, as it was first called, had its first year in 1969, with the newly amalgamated (November 1968) Birchgrove and Roath Harriers competing as Cardiff AAC. The first seeds of a British league competition were sown when *Athletics Weekly* pundit, Tony Ward and Tom McNab made a fact-finding trip to Poland in 1966. Teams for the league's inaugural year were selected after recourse to the National Union of Track Statisticians and a computer! Performances of the leading athletes in what were assumed to be the top 45 clubs in the country were fed in and assessed and this resulted in the top 18 teams being allocated to three divisions of six. Cardiff were assessed to have been the fourth strongest in the country and therefore took their place in division one with Polytechnic H, Birchfield H, Thames Valley Harriers, Blackheath H and Brighton & Hove AC. Birchfield, after three matches, clinched the first league title, ironically at Maindy Stadium, with Cardiff a fine second. Cardiff went on to win the league title for three successive years between 1972 and 1974, and is still to this day one of only a handful of clubs to have been an ever present in the league. Incidentally, that appearance at Maindy was their only appearance in their home City until the opening of Leckwith 20 years later, as the once proud Maindy Stadium fell into disrepair, and was unable to be used for league, or eventually for Welsh Championships, due to the poor conditions. Instead the club held its home fixtures at the excellent new stadium at Cwmbran which was to become the new Mecca of Welsh athletics under the guidance of, amongst others, Geoff Whitson, a member of the famous Davidge, Cresswell and Whitson Newport back row of the 1960s. It was at Cwmbran that Cardiff achieved all of their major "home" performances.

Pilot Welsh League introduced...and athletics goes metric

A feature of the newly formed British League was that the 2 bottom teams in the lowest division would drop out and be replaced by new clubs. An end of season qualifying match would determine who the replacements would be and each Area association was to nominate 2 teams to participate in that meeting. The only fair way in which Wales could make such nominations would be through organising a league of its own and it was this consideration which led to the formation of the Welsh League. in 1969 a pilot Welsh League, modelled on the British version, was run with seven clubs taking part. The clubs involved were Barry Harriers, Bridgend YMCA, Cardiff's "B" team, Newport Harriers, Port Talbot Harriers, Swansea Harriers and Troedyrhiw AC. Three matches were held and champions Swansea and runners up Troedyrhiw represented Wales in a qualifying match at the Crystal Palace where they finished 7th and 8th. There was nothing new about the concept of league athletics as there had been a thriving South Wales League in existence for many years after the War, staging three or four fixtures per season. There is also evidence of a Glamorgan league before the War, but information is sketchy.

The AAA Championships in 1969 were held over metric distances for the first time and Ron Jones became the inaugural 100m champion, finally winning a well-deserved AAA title - the third Welshman to win an AAA sprint title behind Fred Cooper over a century earlier and Berwyn Jones (1963). At the same championships Carmarthen-born Gwynne Griffiths (Wolverhampton) took the 400m to become the first Welshman to win a one-lap AAA title since Tom Nicholas in 1890. Lynn Davies won the silver medal at the European Championships in Athens where Thelwyn Bateman competed in the 1,500m to become the

GREYHOUND - RACING HERE • THURS DAYS & SATURDAYS AT 7.45 P.M.

© Western Mail

Ron Jones (17) wins the inaugural AAA 100m title at the White City in 1969 from Don Halliday (14) and Ian Green (12).

first Welsh woman ever to take part in the European Championships. Clive Longe, who had again broken his UK decathlon record in June, made his final international appearance at Athens but withdrew after failing to clear a height in the pole vault.

The 1969 Welsh Championships (for once unaffected by the weather) were held at Cwmbran the first time the Championships had been scheduled for a venue other than Maindy since it opened in 1951. Cwmbran did not yet have a synthetic surface and the reason for the move was due to the Prince of Wales' investiture that year, rather than to any athletics related consideration. The royal occasion kept the local authorities in Wales busy in arranging special events with which to commemorate it and as a consequence the date of the Welsh Championships had to be changed. Since 1962 the Welsh Championships had been sponsored by the Cardiff Corporation but they were unable to continue this in 1969 because of their involvement in matters royal. Cwmbran Corporation stepped in with a sponsorship offer and consequently the championships were moved, giving Cwmbran its first ever full-blown championships event apart from the previous year's Marathon. Another feature of these championships was that all track events were converted to metric distances for the first time. The Welsh Schools' Championships followed suit and also went metric.

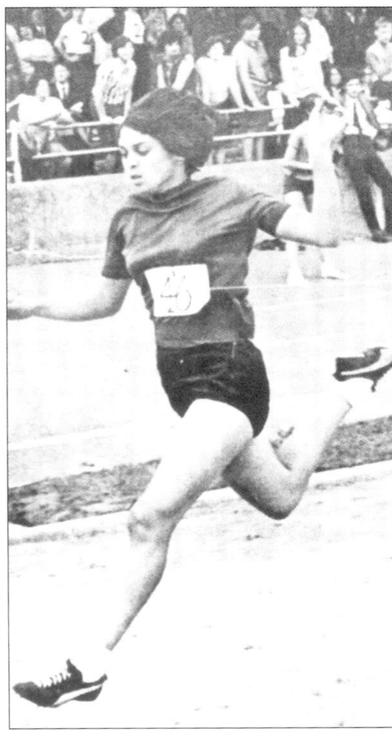

© Gordon Roberts

Michelle Smith won the Welsh sprint title at Cwmbran in 1969 and was a member of the Welsh team at the 1970 Edinburgh Commonwealth Games.

Star of the 1969 Welsh Games at Maindy was undoubtedly Chi Cheng of Formosa who set Welsh all comers' records for the 100m, 200m and 100m hurdles, the latter time also being a UK all-comers record of

13.4. However the era was brought to a sad close with the death in December 1970 of Lillian Board, the Mexico Olympic 400m silver medallist. She was an interested spectator at the Games after winning the 220 yds in the previous year but, although entered in the programme, was prevented from running in the 880 yds in 1969 by an untimely injury. Lillian's death from cancer shocked the athletics world.

Chapter 3
The Modern Era

Not so much an outside half factory, but a sprint hurdles conveyor belt, as five Welsh hurdlers win medals on the world stage, Cwmbran Stadium establishes itself as one of the leading athletics stadiums in the country, the first official individual world records for Welsh athletes ... and athletics goes professional.

From the 1970s to the turn of the new millennium athletics in the Principality took on a new meaning. Synthetic tracks eventually reached all corners and counties with senior and eventually junior leagues providing the background for club athletes to participate more frequently at a higher level. New superstars appeared to take over the mantle from Olympic champion Lynn Davies. The nation may be proud of its rugby union outside-half factory but the conveyer belt was also busy producing some of the greatest hurdlers in the world - Colin Jackson, Berwyn Price, Nigel Walker, Paul Gray and Kay Morley-Brown – all of whom were to win medals on the world stage. Steve Jones with his exploits on both road and cross-country ensured that Wales had a mention in periodicals all over the world. Kirsty McDermott (Wade) was an inspiration to young athletes with her triple Commonwealth gold medals. British teams at all the major championships included a high proportion of Welsh athletes and, for a nation with only a population of 2.9 million, the red dragon has been flown proudly in medal ceremonies and on flag poles and by athletes and supporters around the four corners of the globe.

League athletics makes its mark

Early in the summer of 1970 after the success of the pilot league the previous year, the Welsh League proper got under way. A meeting was held in Cardiff at which a constitution and set of league rules were approved. There would be a first division of six clubs and two lower divisions (division 2 east and west) of four clubs each. Swansea's John Collins was confirmed as League Secretary with Carmarthen stalwart R.B. Evans as the inaugural chairman and Trevor Beese (Newport) as Financial Officer. It was a men's league only and it would be a few years before a Welsh Women's League was formed. One characteristic of the league was, unlike many other leagues in Britain, the application of minimum standards. Designed to maintain a meaningful level of performance and to eliminate the possibility of athletes reducing the competition to a farce by scoring points through recording silly marks, a standard equivalent to 700 points on the IAAF tables was set for each event.

There was no response as yet from clubs in the north but this was to come later. Swansea Harriers won the inaugural Welsh League and went into the British League qualifying competition at Leicester to finish third and thereby qualify for the newly created division four for 1971. Cardiff repeated their performance of the previous season finishing second in division one of the British League, finishing fourth in the final meeting at Warley where Berwyn Price was the club's only winner in the 110m hurdles. League athletics had come to stay and it was to revolutionise club athletics in this country.

A further development came in 1977 when, after a pilot league the previous year, the Welsh Women's League came into existence. The first match being held at Glebelands, Newport on 22nd May with Cardiff running out winners for the first of six consecutive championships. In 1979 Deeside became the first team from north Wales to take part in the men's league and they made an immediate impact. Coming into the second division, they finished runners up to Torfaen and won promotion to division one in their first season. The next year they went one better and won the first division championship.

Swansea Harriers were demoted from the British League in 1977 and dominated the Welsh League until their return to the British League in 1989. They won the division one championship every season from 1981 to 1988 inclusive to create a record of eight successive title wins, which stands to this day. In fact Swansea Harriers have won the Welsh League title every year in which they have contested it. They also hold another unique record in that they are the only club to win both men's and women's championships in the same season. They achieved this feat three times, in 1985, 1986 and 1988, and with the recent amalgamation of the leagues it is a record that will remain for all time. Newport Harriers won the men's title in 1976 and also section 'A' of the women's league but this was a pilot league in two sections of equal standing with Cardiff's second team winning section 'B'.

In 1981 Colwyn Bay joined the men's league and also became the first north Wales club to compete in the women's league. Their men's team won the third division championship at the first time of asking. Both men and women's leagues were now truly national and covered the length and breadth of Wales. Another north Wales team to make a mark on the league was Wrexham. They joined the women's league in 1986 and won the fourth division title. The next season they topped division three, then division two in 1988 and finally became the first north Wales team to win the first division championship in 1989. They retained their title in 1990. There was a spell of north Wales domination in the men's league when Colwyn Bay were champions from 1989 to 1994 and Deeside in 1995.

The men's league has been won by a total of eight teams and the women's by seven. On the men's side Swansea lead with nine victory titles followed by Colwyn Bay (7), Carmarthen (4), Newport (3), Deeside and Torfaen (2 each) and Bridgend and Cardiff 'B' (1 each). Cardiff lead the women's roll call with a total of eight titles followed by Swansea (5), Wrexham (3), Newport and Preseli (2 each) and Carmarthen and Torfaen (1each). These totals will never be changed as from 1999 the men and women's leagues merged to form the Welsh Senior League. Scores are now calculated on combined results and Deeside emerged as the first winners of this new styled competition and can truly claim the title of the strongest all-round club in the league. A Welsh junior league was established in 1994.

The emergence of Berwyn Price as a world-class hurdler

In September 1970 Pontllanfraith's Berwyn Price saw the early autumn Paris sunshine beam down on him as he raced to the gold medal in the European Junior championships in a winning time of 14.21, which was a new British junior record. He was an outstanding junior and his build up to Paris the previous season set him on the road to a glittering career. In 1969 he won the first of his seven AAA titles as he claimed the AAA junior championship in 14.7. He went on the win the senior crown for six successive years between1973 and 1978 – a feat that even world record holder Colin Jackson was never to achieve – although Colin took ten titles spread over a period of fourteen years.

© Mark Shearman

Berwyn Price seen here at the AAA Championships at Crystal Palace in 1970.

The Commonwealth Games were held at Meadowbank Stadium, Edinburgh, only the third time this great festival had come to Britain. The Games went metric for the first time and even more to the athletes' liking, the track surface was all-weather synthetic. Not so welcome was the weather, which was wet and windy and stayed that way for most of the week. However the gloom was lifted with Lynn Davies defending the long jump title he had won in Kingston four years earlier. At the Games it was also announced that Swansea had been unsuccessful in their bid to host the 1974 Games, which were awarded to Christchurch, New Zealand. For the first time since their inception in 1959 the Welsh Games were not held due to the Commonwealth Games being held in Edinburgh.

Earlier in the year, Ron Jones, running as well as ever at 35 years of age took the sprint double at the Welsh Championships at Maindy for the fourth time. The others performances of significance were John Walters' seventh and eighth shot and discus titles and nine championships bests, some admittedly due to the change to metric distances the previous year.

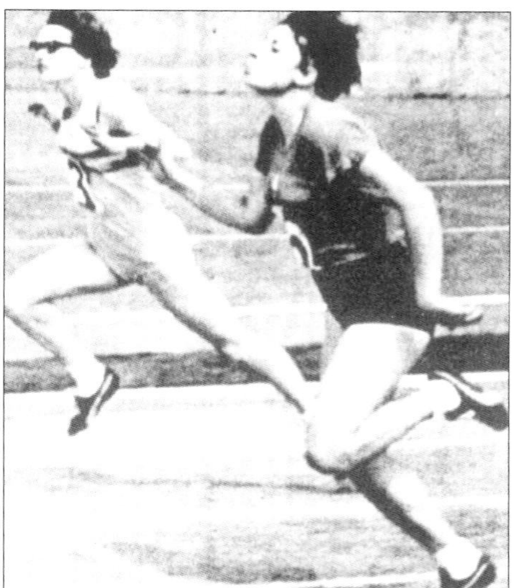

Roath's Liz Johns (Parsons), nearest the camera, seems to just pip Madeleine Cobb (3) to win the 1968 Welsh Games 100 yards. However controversially the English runner was given the verdict.

The picturesque Scandinavian city of Helsinki was the venue for the 1971 European Championships. With John Robertson (400m), Berwyn Price (110 hurdles) and Ron McAndrew (Steeplechase) all being eliminated in the very first round, it was left to Lynn Davies again to fly the flag but he could "only" finish fourth with a leap of 7.85 in the long jump. The 1971 Welsh Women's Championships at Jenner Park, Barry in June saw the end of the remarkable championships career of Liz Johns of Cardiff. The former Liz Parsons had been a giant amongst Welsh women sprinters over the previous decade, winning sprint titles in all age groups. At Barry, the 26 year-old took the sprint double for a remarkable sixth time – the first such feat coming as a precocious 15 year-old at Maindy in 1960. In all she won 13 senior titles and four British vests, including competing at the Helsinki European Championships, which was to be her only appearance in a major athletics championship. She was eliminated in the heats of the 100m but was a member of the British team that finished sixth in the 4 x 100m.

Liz Gill was also one of the finest sprinters in Britain at the time, and the Barry Harrier beat her Cardiff namesake to the 100 yds title in both 1963 and 1964. She also took the 220 yds titles in those years and won five British vests in a relatively short career which promised much more. Between them they dominated Welsh women's sprinting throughout the 1960s, with Liz Johns setting eleven Welsh sprint records in all, to the nine of her Barry rival.

John J. Williams, still to achieve rugby fame, took the sprint double at the Welsh men's championships at Maindy in 1971 to add to his 220/200 titles of 1968 and 1969, whilst Berwyn Price won the first of his six senior titles in the 110m hurdles in a new championships best of 14.5. A virtually unknown Ian Thompson, then a student at Cardiff University took the 5,000m in an uninspiring 14:33.6 to give little indication of the form he was to show three years later when he won both the Commonwealth and European marathon titles for England.

Goodbye to Maindy Stadium

On the domestic scene 1972 was a great year for the powerful Cardiff AAC team as they won the men's British Athletics League for the first time. They defended the title for the next two seasons and also won the men's Cup Final in 1974, and thus became the first team to perform the league and cup double. Their winning performances attracted top athletes to the club and raised the profile of the sport in Wales.

It was a remarkable performance by the capital city club, as they had to compete away from home for all major fixtures due to the dreary state of the now ancient Maindy Stadium, which had served the sport so well since 1951. With a "home" Division one fixture the following season Cardiff had to travel down the M4 and hold it at Cwmbran Stadium. One of the proudest athletes at the Aldersley Stadium, Wolverhampton on Saturday July 29th 1972 was 42-year-old team captain Hywel Williams. The Llanharan-born sergeant P.E. instructor in the RAF at St Athan had been in athletics for over 20 years and more or less retired at the end of the season. The former British decathlon champion and twice Welsh representative at Commonwealth Games (1954 and 1958) was delighted with the League victory. "I am very proud to have led my club to the title and be part of Welsh athletics history. As a club we should now go from strength to strength", he said.

The Welsh Games were held at Maindy Stadium for the last time in 1972 when the track fell into decline but this did not stop three times Commonwealth champion Pam Kilborn-Ryan of Australia putting on a fine display of hurdling to win impressively. So the curtain was brought down on a venue that had served Welsh athletics so well in the past quarter of a century. Crowds of over 10,000 were commonplace and some of the all-time greats of world athletics, such as Herb Elliott, Mary Rand, Lillian Board, Ann Packer, Kip Keino, Ralph Boston and all of the British and Welsh stars of the era had graced its cinders.

John Walters receives the Fellowship Cup for "Best Performance at the Welsh Senior Championships" in 1968 from George (later Lord Tonypandy) Thomas, MP, and Secretary of State for Wales. The Welsh AAA President, Arthur Williams, and Irene Lisle, secretary of the Welsh Women's AAA, watch the presentation.

Despite the poor conditions, the Welsh men's and women's championships were held at Maindy again with John Walters taking the shot and discus double for the fifth time taking his medal haul to twelve titles since his first win – the shot in 1965. He finished as runner-up or third on a further 16 occasions. Still competing in veteran's events where he has taken a number of British age group titles, he has been an outstanding servant to Welsh athletics setting two Welsh shot and five discus records during his career. He has also appeared for Cardiff in the British League almost 70 times, the third highest number of appearances in League history, and won two British vests. Other wins of note came from Sandra Belt of Cardiff with a sprint double and Janet Beese of Newport with a shot/discus double, both in championship bests.

John Walters

In July 1972 Bob Maplestone a member of Cardiff AAC but now living and working in the USA, sliced nearly three seconds off Phil Thomas's Welsh 1,500m record with a time of 3:39.7 in sunny Seattle.

Berwyn Price, was a student at University of Wales, Aberystwyth, and won the University of Wales Athletes Union title at Singleton, Swansea in 1970 when the event was run in reverse to give wind assistance. He emerged as a top class athlete on the world circuit when he won the 1973 World Student Games in Moscow in a new British and Commonwealth record of 13.69, beating David Hemery's mark of 13.72 set in 1970. He also won the first of his six AAA titles.

The first ever European Junior Championships were held in Duisburg with Newport's Gareth Edwards (not the rugby player!) finishing eighth in the 100m final in 10.74 and Tony Dyke going out in the first round of the 800m. Earlier in the year Dyke, the Bishop Gore pupil retained his AAA junior title to emulate the feat of fellow Welshman Tony Harris who was successful in 1959 and 1960.

At home in the Welsh men's championships at Cwmbran, Loughborough College student Peter Lance, jumping on his home track, won his only senior title and became the first Welshman to clear 2 metres in the high jump for a new national record. Amongst the other winners in 1973, was future Scottish National Coach Dave Lease taking the first of his three pole vault titles. A fine all-round athlete – he was also an international trampolinist – he set six Welsh pole vault records during his career taking the record from 4.24m in 1968 to the 4.72m he recorded at Bargoed in 1972, although his all-time best was 4.80m set indoors at Cosford earlier in the year. Mike Delaney, Britain's men's team manager at the Edmonton World Championships took the first of his three 400m titles. His all-time best of 46.92 was set in 1978 when he made the second of his two appearances in the Commonwealth Games. Yet another athlete to make an indelible mark in the record books – Aberdare-born Paul Rees – won his first shot title with 15.81m. In all he won nine Welsh shot and seven discus titles creating a record in the former which still stands today as the most number of wins in that event. He shares this accolade with Hywel Williams in the discus. Now a schoolteacher in Bournemouth, Paul ended his career with all-time bests of 16.70/50.94, both set in 1978. He set four Welsh shot records firstly adding 2cms to John Walters' 16.55 mark in 1971 and lastly with his 16.70 in 1978.

Championships split for men and women and Lochhead achieves triple treble!

The 1973 Welsh Women's Championships were held apart from the men for the first time at Cwmbran and saw the emergence of Jean Lochhead who was to develop into one of Wales' finest middle-distance runners. She took the very difficult-to-achieve treble of title wins in the 800, 1,500 and 3,000 and, unbelievably, repeated this feat at the next two championships. This unique performance will surely never be equalled - especially bearing in mind that all of the wins each year came on the same day. Future Welsh team manager Delyth Prothero took both shot and discus titles, whilst Sandra Belt repeated her double sprint victory of the previous year. 1973 was also significant in that Wales competed in an overseas international for the first time, against Portugal in Lisbon winning by six points. Welsh wins came from Hywel Griffiths (100), Gary Vince (200), Clive Thomas (1,500), John Davies (3,000m steeplechase), Kedric Thompson (long jump), Paul Rees (shot), Ted Kelland (discus), Morris Davies (hammer) and the sprint relay team of Gary Vince, Hywel Griffiths, John Elias and Steve Ware.

For the first time the Welsh Games were held at Cwmbran Stadium in front of 4,000 spectators in driving rain. There was a return to the international representative format of 1961, with a full-scale match against a strong Holland team, which provided Wales with excellent opposition. The visitors won by a mere four points. A trio of Kiwi Olympic stars - John Walker, Olympic 1500 bronze medalist, Rod Dixon, a bronze medallist over the same distance in 1972, and Dick Quax, destined to be a silver medallist over 5,000 in 1976 - competed as guests and were the individual stars indicating again the status of the Welsh Games and the pulling power of the new Cwmbran Stadium.

1974 saw the start of a piece of women's athletics history, which will take a long time to beat. Venissa Head became the first Welsh athlete to throw the shot beyond the 13-metre barrier at Crystal Palace. It was the start of an incredible sequence of 35 Welsh records in the shot and discus events, which she dominated for over ten years. A new "tartan" all-weather surface at Cwmbran was opened on June 29th with a women's international match against Northern Ireland. This was the first time that a separate Welsh women's team had taken part in an international match and the occasion was celebrated with an easy home victory with Sandra Pengilley (Belt) and Jean Lochhead scoring double wins for Wales.

Cwmbran emerges as the new Welsh athletics Mecca

With the opening of the new surface, Cwmbran was starting to emerge as the new Mecca for Welsh and indeed British athletics. A midweek international match against Canada was staged on 23rd and 24th July and was the best seen in Wales from a standards viewpoint since the 1958 Empire Games. The event resulted in the Welsh all-comers record book being practically re-written as fourteen new records were set – all bar two coming from either the Canadians or guest competitors. The exceptions being John Davies' steeplechase of 8:31.4, which sliced 10 seconds of Maurice Herriott's time of 10 years earlier, and Ruth Martin-Jones in the long jump with 6.36. Welsh fans had the opportunity to see a host of world stars in action including Alan Pascoe the 400m hurdles Commonwealth Champion from Christchurch, Debbie Brill the future Commonwealth high jump champion, June Haist, the reigning Commonwealth shot and discus champion, and the mighty Geoff Capes of England, who improved on his own all-comers record set the previous year with a 20.47 shot mark, one of the best in the world that year.

The meeting confirmed the emergence of north Walian Dave Roberts as one of Wales' finest sprinters. Earlier in the season at the last Welsh Championships to be held at Maindy, he took the sprint double with 10.5/21.7 and went on to win a total of nine sprint titles up to 1982. Against Canada, he took the 100m in 10.6 and followed this with a win in the Welsh Games, also in Cwmbran the following Saturday in a match against Portugal and

Northern Ireland in 10.5. The Cardiff solicitor won twelve UK vests between 1974 and 1978, and his finest run came when he startled everyone with a windy 100m clocking of 10.1 for Wales in their match against Iceland in Reykjavik in 1982. He narrowly finished second to Nikolay Sidirov of the USSR who was running as a guest. Only 1980 Olympic Champion Allan Wells and his compatriot Cameron Sharp, the Commonwealth double bronze medallist that year, were faster Britons in 1982.

In the 1974 Welsh Games, the home team repeated their win of the previous year in Lisbon. Carlos Lopes, who would become the Olympic Marathon Champion in 1984, took the 5,000 with another Portuguese star in the making, triple London marathon winner, Antonio Pinto in second. Fernando Mamede, world record holder for 10,000m, ran in the 1,500, but was beaten by former Gilwern Harrier, Peter Ratcliffe who won in 3:43.7. Lopes was to return to Wales two years later to win the World Cross Country title at Chepstow. This match was the culmination of four days international track and field activity at Cwmbran that did much for Welsh athletics and the stadium itself.

Athens was the venue for the 1975 European Junior Championships, which saw one of the most outstanding performances by a young Welsh athlete to date. Micky Morris of Cwmbran Olympiads destroyed the field in the 2,000m steeplechase to claim a magnificent gold medal in a new British junior record time of 5:34.8. This was a massive 4 seconds faster than John Tierney's existing record, and still stands as the Welsh record. Tragically the highly talented athlete was never to fulfil his massive potential as he died in April 1981 whilst out on a training run.

Pen Portrait – Micky Morris (Cwmbran Olympiads & Cardiff AAC) 1956-1981

In April 1981 Welsh athletics, and the sport in Britain in general, was robbed of one of its most talented athletes with the sudden death of the 1975 European Junior 2000m steeplechase champion Micky Morris at the tender age of twenty four.

A passer-by found him lying in the roadside and mouth-to-mouth resuscitation failed to revive him. He had been feeling fine and looking forward to the new season when he hoped to have made a determined challenge to make the Welsh squad preparing for the 1982 Commonwealth Games.

He first came to prominence as a youngster with his local club Cwmbran Olympiads and it was as a member of Cwmbran that he won the European junior title before moving to Cardiff AAC.

His last race was on April 5th when he helped Cardiff AAC win the Welsh road relay title in record time, and he was due to run in the National 12 Stage event in which his club eventually finished fifth.

He was very unlucky not to have made the Welsh team for the Edmonton Commonwealth Games. In the 1978 AAA 3,000m steeplechase he finished third in the same time (8:35.8) as second placed Tony Staynings but this failed to gain him the trip and he was bitterly disappointed. There was some consolation later in the year, however, when he won the second of his two British vests in the match against Finland at Crystal Palace.

In 1976 he took the Welsh junior cross-country title and he also finished second in the senior cross-country race. After this performance Clive Williams wrote in *Athletics Weekly* " Without doubt Morris is one of the finest young athletes at the moment." He retained his junior title in 1977.

His best 3,000m steeplechase (8:35.6) was set in finishing second to Tony Staynings in the 1976 AAA event – a huge improvement from 8:54.6.

However, in retrospect, 1975 was his best year. He started by winning the Welsh youths' cross-country title and startled statisticians with a new British junior 2,000m steeplechase record of 5:35.6 on July 1st on his home track at Cwmbran. There were many who doubted this performance but he silenced the doubting Thomases by later taking the AAA junior title in 5:37.8 at Liverpool and also took the event in the junior international against France at Warley in 5:44.6. Then came his European junior gold medal performance. In 1975 he also took the Welsh 1,500 title in the then championship best time of 3:55.8.

But that win in the European Junior Championships 2000m steeplechase in Athens on 24th August 1975 was the pinnacle in his tragically short life. He went to the USA on an athletics scholarship in 1978 but never settled. He returned to join the Gwent Police Force and had been fighting to regain his best form.

Every winter the Micky Morris Memorial Cross-Country relays are held in Cardiff, an event which is firmly fixed in the racing calendar of clubs both in Wales and from across the Severn Bridge.

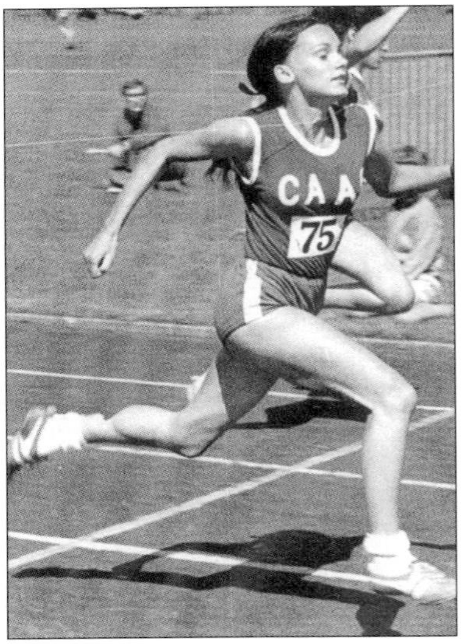

Sandra Pengilley (Belt) winning the 100m at Barry Trophy meeting at Jenner Park in 1985. She won three Welsh sprint titles in 1972, 1973 and 1975.

In the Welsh women's championships held on the new surface at Cwmbran for the first time, Jean Lochhead, achieved her third consecutive treble victory in the 800/1,500 and 3,000, whilst Sandra Pengilley retained her 100 and 200 titles. Ted Kelland of the Royal Marines was the only double winner in the men's championships also at Cwmbran a fortnight later with his 16.32/48.04 shot/discus win.

The Welsh Games of 1975 was again an international match (against Ireland and Luxembourg) with guest competitors from other countries. Three all-comers records were beaten – two of them having stood since the 1958 Empire Games. These fell to Berwyn Price, who erased Keith Gardner's 120y converted mark with 13.8 in the 110m hurdles, and Mike McGrath of Australia who broke fellow countryman Ian Tomlinson's triple jump record with 16.05. Geraint Griffiths equalled his own Welsh high jump record in winning with 2.01. Swansea Harrier Jeff Griffiths also broke Allan Skirving's long-standing Welsh junior 400m record with 48.1. Later in the year, again at Cwmbran, England won the home countries international comfortably with Dave Roberts (100) and Berwyn Price (110m hurdles) the only Welsh winners.

Cardiff first British club in Europe

In May, Cardiff AAC achieved a piece of British athletics history when, as the previous season's British clubs' champions, they represented Britain at the first European Clubs' Championships in Liege, Belgium, where they finished fifth behind a very strong Wattenscheid (West Germany) team. Mike Butterfield (high jump), Bernard Hayward (3,000m steeplechase) and 110m hurdler Berwyn Price provided the club's only wins in a high quality meeting. Butterfield, an RAF airman at St. Athan narrowly failed to better his own UK record with 2.10. However, just two weeks later he upped the record to 2.12 when winning his speciality in the opening division one league fixture at Cwmbran. In the same meeting, current BBC TV pundit Paul Dickenson of Hillingdon broke the Welsh all-comers record for the hammer with 67.58.

The summer of 1976 was the first season for the Welsh Women's League as they had a pilot scheme to find the top six teams to occupy Division 1 for the following season, with the remainder in Division 2, Newport Harriers and Cardiff AAC emerged as the top two teams.

From Sketty to Australia, via Kidderminster and Oman

Hidden away amongst the winners at the Welsh Championships at Cwmbran of 1976 was Tudor Bidder then a student at Cardiff College of Education (now UWIC) and currently Head of World Class Potential at UK Athletics, who took the 110m hurdles in 16.4. He also took second behind Berwyn Price in 1979 and picked-up third place finishes in 1983 for both hurdles events and the decathlon in 1982. Born in Sketty, Swansea he taught briefly in Kidderminster and at Cynffig Comprehensive before starting his professional coaching career as Director of Coaching in Oman between 1986 and 1989. He then moved to Australia as a member of the Australian Institute of Sport set-up with responsibility for 400m and high jump before returning to the UK as Technical Director for jumps and combined events in the newly formed UK Athletics. Whilst in Australia, he coached, amongst others, Alison Inverarity, the 1994 Commonwealth high jump champion, and was an advisor to Cathy Freeman, last year's Olympic 400m champion. He follows in the long line of Welsh-born Coaches who have become National Coaches in the UK, Jim Alford, Lionel Pugh and Dave Lease.

Tudor Bidder (20) running in the British Colleges 400m hurdles final at Coatbridge in 1978 ahead of his Cardiff College of Education teammate, Keith Lancey (19).

Cwmbran stages the first UK Championships – and they are a "rip-roaring successs"

From the first championships in 1880, the AAA championships have been open to all male athletes in the world. This had sometimes caused controversy with home athletes seeking to win a "British" title. This anomaly was remedied in 1977 with the establishment of UK National Championships and Cwmbran had the honour of staging the first such event. Furthermore, women's titles would also be at stake, as a similar situation had previously been the case with the Women's AAA Championships being open to all comers. As Mel Watman, the respected athletics journalist reported in *Athletics Weekly*, the Championships were well organised and a "rip-roaring success". Two British records were set by Chris Warden in the men's 400m hurdles and by Tessa Sanderson in the javelin. Home stars Berwyn Price, Venissa Head and Hilary Hollick took inaugural titles, with Hilary slashing 5.6 seconds off Jean Lochhead's five year-old Welsh record in the 1,500m (4:13.0), which was also a Welsh all-comers record. Venissa's shot win of 15.72 was a new Welsh record to boot. A further nine Welsh all-comers records were beaten, including in the

1,500 where Welsh fans had the opportunity to see future Olympic 800m Champion Steve Ovett win in 3:37.5. This event served as further indication that Cwmbran was one of the top athletics venues in the UK.

At the European Junior Championships in Donetsk in 1977, Michelle Probert (Sale) made her first international championship appearance as a member of Britain's 4 x 400m relay team. The fine tradition of overseas stars competing in the Welsh Games continued as Eamonn Coghlan of Ireland, who was to become the world 5,000m champion in 1983, took his speciality.

In May 1978, Wales travelled to Greece for a four-sided international, with Jeff Griffiths producing a fine personal best to win the 400m in 46.91 from former European 400m champion David Jenkins of Scotland. Steeplechaser John Davies was the only other Welsh winner. The Welsh championships at Cwmbran that year were benefiting from the improved conditions in the Principality with fourteen new championship bests and a new Welsh record. Significantly, seven of the bests came from the women including a new javelin record from Jackie Zaslona in the javelin with 52.04, bettering her own record set two years earlier by 1.3m. There was fine triple jumping from one of the titans of the event in Wales, as John Phillips took his seventh title in a windy 15.88, which equalled his Welsh record set earlier in the year in Greece. The Welsh Games at Cwmbran that year were described as the best ever in *Athletics Weekly* as both Welsh men and women's teams beat their respective opposition. The women avenged a defeat by Greece in Athens the previous year, whilst the men beat Holland and Ireland, reversing a defeat by the Dutchmen five years earlier on the same track. British men's team manager for the recent world championships, Mike Delaney was the Welsh hero as he ran a storming last leg in the 4 x 400m relay to clinch victory for the home side. He also ran his lifetime best 46.92 to finish second in the individual event behind Harry Schulting of Holland. Steve Barry broke Roy Hart's 1971 10,000m walk record with 46:06.0. Top performances in the women's team came from Michelle Probert and Hilary Hollick who both scored doubles in the 100/200 and 800/1,500 respectively.

Fully automatic timing was used for the first time in the Welsh championships at Cwmbran in 1979, with four championships bests being set notably from Paul Rees with his shot and discus double - his ninth and tenth titles respectively. Triple jumper John Phillips brought his Welsh championships career to a close with his eighth (seventh successive) win with 14.42. John, whose father David was also a Welsh title winner (discus in 1947) was a giant amongst Welsh triple jumpers and set a Welsh record 15.88 in Athens in 1978 to add 24 cms to Graham Webb's 1969 record. This record stood until first equalled, and then bettered (by 2 cms) by Cardiff club mate Dave Wood in 1984.

European Cup for Cwmbran and phenomenal throwing by Paragi and Capes

In July 1979, Cwmbran staged one of the two European Cup semi-final for women, which was undoubtedly the most important meeting held in Wales since the 1958 Empire Games. Teams from West Germany, Hungary, France, Yugoslavia, Austria, Denmark, Iceland and the UK battled it out to win a place in the Turin final in August. In brilliant sunshine, and in front of an appreciative crowd of over 10,000, the home side battled through to the final finishing second to the powerful West German team. The Welsh women's all-comers record book was virtually re-written with all records falling except both sprints, which were won with wind assistance by the reigning Olympic Champion, Annegret Richter of West Germany, whilst team-mate Silvia Hollmann's 400m hurdles win in 56.81 was the fastest time seen in Britain. Later in the year, Cwmbran added to its reputation as one of the finest athletics venues in Britain by staging a "B" international against France, in which another four Welsh all-comers records were broken and there were wins for home stars Michelle Probert (400m) Roger Hackney (3,000m steeplechase) and Steve James 400m hurdles. On the British League front, despite a spirited performance in the final division one match of the year at their home track at Cwmbran, Cardiff, the league champions between 1972 and 1974, slipped out of the top division for the first time.

Yet another major meeting took place at Cwmbran in May 1980, as Wales hosted a four-cornered match against England, Netherlands, and Hungary. It resulted in the second best javelin throw of all time as Ferenc Paragi, a well built 5'10 ½ /205lb Hungarian hurled the old-style 800 gram implement a massive 96.20 (315'7) – just 52 cms short of the world record he had set the previous month. It was this throw, along with others which Paragi achieved at the time, which convinced the IAAF, the world governing body for athletics, to change the specification of the javelin to ensure the safety of spectators, as the javelin was effectively being thrown from one end of the arena to the other. In a sun drenched stadium in front of a large appreciative crowd, the spear appeared to be in the air for ages before it finally landed quite close to the high jump pit! In an event sponsored by the Dutch electrical giant Phillips, Paragi's throw was not the only outstanding performance as this was the meeting in which the great Geoff Capes set his Commonwealth and UK record of 21.68 for the shot, which still stands today, over twenty years later, as the UK record. As well as Paragi's throw, his team-mate Andrea Matay high jumped 1.93 for a new UK all-comers record and 19 year-old Michelle Probert started to make an impact with her first 400m clocking under 53 secs in a Welsh record of 52.27. Two weeks later, the Cwmbran Classic meeting, which became one of the top invitational events in the country, held its first meeting with most of Britain's Moscow hopefuls present.

The 1980 Welsh Games were held under floodlights for the first time at Cwmbran with Daley Thompson returning to one of his favourite venues prior to winning the Olympic decathlon gold medal in Moscow. But the star was Kathy Cook who set Games records in both sprints. Here's a good quiz question: How many decathlon appearances did double Olympic Champion and world record holder Daley Thompson make in England? The answer is none! Except for the 1986 Commonwealth Gold in Edinburgh, all his "home" appearances were at Cwmbran. Daley's first decathlon was at Cwmbran as a precocious 16 year-old in 1975 when he scored 6685 pts. He returned to Cwmbran later in the year and finished second in the Great Britain versus France decathlon international. The rest is history!

The Cwmbran Classic meeting in May 1981 signalled the re-opening of the track after refurbishment, and Venissa Head set a new UK shot record of 17.54. For good measure she also added 48 cms to her own Welsh discus record. These marks were her eighth Welsh record in each event. Later in June at the Welsh Championships in Cwmbran, Dave Roberts regained his 100 crown with an outstanding display in his first major competition in three years. The former Great Britain international, who had won the 100 against Finland as long ago as 1974, cruised to an effortless win to record his eighth senior title success.

England, Northern Ireland and Brittany provided the opposition for Wales at the 1981 Welsh Games, again at Cwmbran, which saw Linford Christie win the 200m while Geoff Smith won the Emsley Carr mile in a new Welsh all-comers record of 3:55.8, the first time the world classic event had been held in Wales. Also in 1981, after a short absence, Cardiff returned to division one of the British League. At the final meeting of the season at Birmingham they gained promotion with Birchfield, as 42-year-old stalwart John Walters took his league appearances to 49 out of a possible 51 since the league started in 1969.

Clean sweep for Malcolm James and Paul Rees bows out after 16 senior titles

The Welsh Championships in 1982 created a little bit of history as the winner of the senior 400m completed a clean sweep by becoming the only male athlete to achieve the remarkable feat of becoming Welsh champion in every age group. In winning his one and only senior title, Malcolm James of Cantonian High School and Cardiff AAC achieved the near impossible. He completed the sprint double at under 13 in 1975, at under 15 in 1977, at under 17 in both 1978 and 1979 and won the under 20 400 in both 1980 and 1981. Malcolm's 50.3 for 400m in 1977 was a new British under 15 record. He also took both the 200 and 400 (22.0/50.2) in the 1979 AAA Youth Championships. Paul Rees also bowed out of the championships taking his 15th and 16th titles with his shot and discus double, whilst Berwyn Price, now competing for Swansea, took his sixth 110m hurdles title in 14.20, just one behind the record of wins in the championships for the event held by Newport's Stan Macey (1928-1934). World record holder Colin Jackson has won five Welsh titles. Michelle Scutt (nee Probert) took the sprint double for the third successive year.

The UK Championships returned to Cwmbran in May 1982 after a break of five years. For the 876 competitors (546 men / 330 women) prize money for the first three finishers in the finals was awarded for the first time and training grants given for championship records, personal best performances and for those athletes who reached European championship standards. Pride of place went to 21-year-old Sale Harrier Michelle Scutt (Probert) who surpassed herself by running the fastest women's 400 in the world at the time that year in setting a new Commonwealth and British record. Her 50.63 beat former record holder Joslyn Hoyte-Smith into second place and stripped nearly a second off her previous best. As the defending champion tied up in the last 20 metres, Michelle was able to snatch a famous victory on the line. Michelle later in the season completed the double as she also won the AAA title. Another Welsh winner was 21-year-old Cambridge University student Trevor Llewelyn. It took him a total of 19 attempts to claim his first major title in winning the high jump. An incredible four-hour competition saw him clear a new Welsh record height of 2.16, twenty-four hours before sitting a three-hour geography examination. The Monday of the competition (31st May) was one of the best day's athletics enjoyed in Wales for many a year. A crowd of 8,000 people were brought to their feet to cheer home three Welsh winners. Steve Barry in the 10,000 walk, Roger Hackney in the steeplechase and the wonderful run of Michelle Scutt made it a day to remember for Welsh fans.

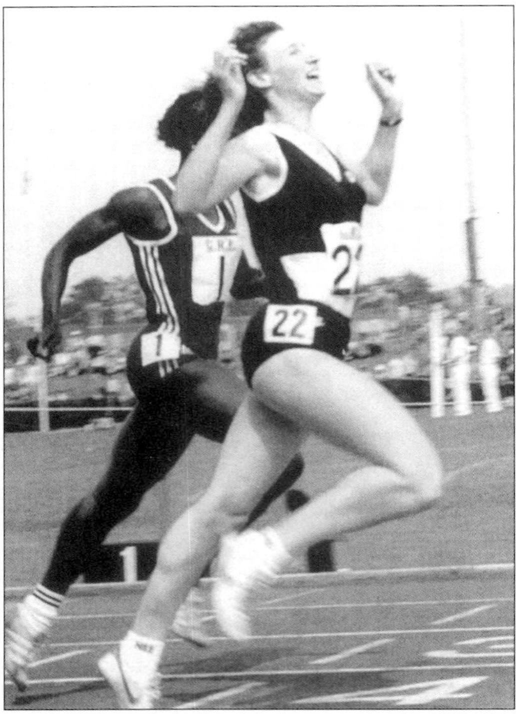

Michelle Scutt shows her delight at winning the 1982 UK 400m title at Cwmbran with a new UK record of 50.63, ahead of Joslyn Hoyte-Smith.

The Welsh Games at Cwmbran in August featured a match against Ireland, with guest competitors in some events. However, local man Steve Barry was one of the stars as he set a new Welsh all-comers record in the 10,000m walk, with Richard Slaney doing likewise in the discus. Olympic champion Daley Thompson made his second appearance at the Welsh Games and thrilled the large crowd by winning the pole vault.

In 1983 during an early season international match against Russia at Birmingham, Venissa Head set two more Welsh records. In the shot she went out to 18.12 and reached 62.72 in the discus, a massive two-metre improvement. A large contingent of Australian athletes competed in the Welsh Games with their star being Glynis Nunn who won the 100 hurdles in a Welsh all-comers record of 13.19. She also won the long jump and a year later was crowned Olympic heptathlon champion.

At the end of the 1980 season Sian Morris decided to run a 400 race and at the Welsh Games that year she made her senior Welsh debut with a fine run in 56.0. Nothing remarkable except she was only 15 at the time. Coached by Doug Griffiths she reached her full potential during the 1983 season. She had a remarkable opening two months as the 18-year-old Cwmafon-based runner won silver at the UK championships, gained two senior Great Britain vests, and lowered her best time by more than two seconds. Her winning run against Finland and Switzerland saw her further reduce her best to 52.80 which still stands today as the Welsh junior record.

Julia Charlton

Wales lost one of its most promising athletes in 1983 when Haverfordwest based Julia Charlton announced her retirement from the sport. At just 17-years old, the multi-event athlete had to surrender her career to a crippling knee injury. She won six Welsh age group championships from 1978 to 1981. In 1980 she won four – high jump, long jump, 75 hurdles and pentathlon titles while she took a hat trick of titles at the Welsh Schools' championships the same year. 1980 was an outstanding year in her short career. At Crystal Palace she jumped superbly in the high jump to beat the cream of Britain's high jumpers and claim a British junior under 15 title. On June 14th 1980 in the " Westathletic Cup" at Winterthur, Switzerland in an international match against Netherlands, Switzerland, Belgium, Spain, Austria and Ireland she, at just 14 years and 22 days, became the youngest ever Welsh senior international as she cleared 1.75 to finish seventh. A year later, which was effectively her last at the top level, she cleared 1.79 for a new Welsh senior indoor record. Her indoor form was carried forward as she won at the European Schools' indoor meeting the same year. During her phenomenal but short career she set British age high jump records at 12, 13,14 and 15 as well as a British under 15 record both indoor and outdoor. She also held Welsh senior outdoor and indoor records as well as a Welsh under 15 long jump record. Four of her seven UK records still stand - age 12 (1.68) and age 13 (1.75) outdoor, while her personal best of 1.79 is still age 13 and under 15 age group record to beat indoor. The 1.79 still stands as the European age 13 best.

Nigel Walker achieved a 200/110m hurdles double at the Welsh Men's Championships held for the first time at Morfa Stadium, Swansea, the new home of Swansea Harriers, whilst Shaun Pickering achieved a treble in the heavy events, also winning his third successive hammer title. At the Women's Championships at Cwmbran, there were double wins for Venissa Head (shot and discus) and for former Barry Harrier Carmen Smart who took both sprints.

We all know that athletics is all about athletes but without officials there would not be any athletics. One of those great stalwarts, who literally gave his life to Welsh athletics Arthur E Williams died after a short illness on 2nd November 1983 aged 90.

Pen Portrait – Arthur E. Williams MM, MBE (Port Talbot YMCA & Port Talbot H) 1893 - 1983

Arthur Williams

Arthur E Williams had a record very few could equal. He served his club in one capacity or another for over 60 years. He was one of the founder members of Port Talbot YMCA Harriers (now Port Talbot Harriers) in 1921 and was still an active committee-member in his capacity as President at the time of his death at the grand age of 90 in 1983.

He had been involved with all of the major developments in Welsh athletics and was President of the Welsh AAA for 17 years between 1959 and 1976.

At the time of his death he was busily arranging for funds to be raised for the Los Angeles Olympics in his capacity as Chairman of the Welsh branch of the British Olympic Association. Just three weeks earlier he had attended the Welsh AAA AGM at Brecon taking his usual active part in the debates.

He was a familiar figure at all Welsh fixtures and was at home whether supervising the funnel at a cross country race or acting as a field referee at one of the major events at the White City. He officiated in the 1948 Olympic Games at Wembley. Although only slight in stature he had boundless energy and despite his advanced years he would drive his own car to athletics meetings, resplendent in his blazer and AAA badge.

He was also a regular contributor to *Athletics Weekly*, as "AEW" with his Welsh Notes and one of his reports appeared in the first ever issue on 7th January 1950.

When the Welsh AAA instituted their 'Award of Honour' in 1952, Arthur was one of the eight initial recipients. In 1972 the AAA also awarded him the same honour. Before his death he was due to attend the AAA's AGM at which he was to be re-elected as Vice-President. He was also a Life Vice-President of the Welsh AAA.

He saw distinguished service in the Great War during which he received the Military Medal in the field for bravery under enemy fire. A deeply religious man, he was a staunch Methodist and had been president of the Port Talbot Free Church Council. He was also holder of the Scouts Silver Cross for life saving. In 1964 he received the MBE for services to athletics.

Arthur, who was born in Bristol, moved to Port Talbot as a young man to work on the docks. A close friend of George Thomas, later Lord Tonypandy, the former speaker of the House of Commons who was born in Port Talbot, Arthur was a tireless worker for Welsh athletics in general and his contribution will certainly not be equalled for many decades to come – if ever.

Colin Jackson takes his first Welsh title

There was a sensational ending to the 1984 indoor season as Venissa Head rewrote the record books and took British women's shot putting into a new era when she became the first Briton to break 19 metres at the Welsh indoor championships at St. Athan. She recorded a sensational 19.06 with her opening put to set a new Commonwealth, British and Welsh record having beaten the previous best of 18.33. She achieved this despite all her warm-up throws hitting the beams in the roof! " I had to overcome this by throwing flatter and speed of release quicker". This mark still stands as the UK record today. Surrey-based Phil Norgate, coached by former Welsh 6 miles champion Harry Wilson, who was also Steve Ovett's coach, won a bronze medal in the 800 at the European Indoor Championships in Gothenburg. In a thrilling final he just missed out on a silver medal as he finished in 1:48.39. There was a slight scare after the race when he was involved in a complaint about a clash but the judges did not uphold the objection and so Phil became only the third Welsh athlete to win a European indoor medal. He followed in the footsteps of long jumper Lynn Davies who struck gold in 1967, while Berwyn Price won the silver in the 60 hurdles in 1976. The 1984 Welsh Championships at Cwmbran were the first since 1972 to have men and women's championships at the same time. A 17 year-old Cardiff athlete destined to become the fastest sprint hurdler in the world, one Colin Jackson, took his first Welsh 110m hurdles title in 15.56. Richard Jones of Deeside won his fourth successive long jump title. Future Welsh record holder (11.50) Helen Miles took the first two of her eight Welsh titles with a sprint double of 12.5/25.14, whilst Michelle Scutt won her eleventh and last Welsh title with a new championships best in the 400m (53.08).

© Ceri Breeze

A young Colin Jackson aged 17 winning his first Welsh senior title in 1984.

Brown the first Welshman under 4 minutes in Wales

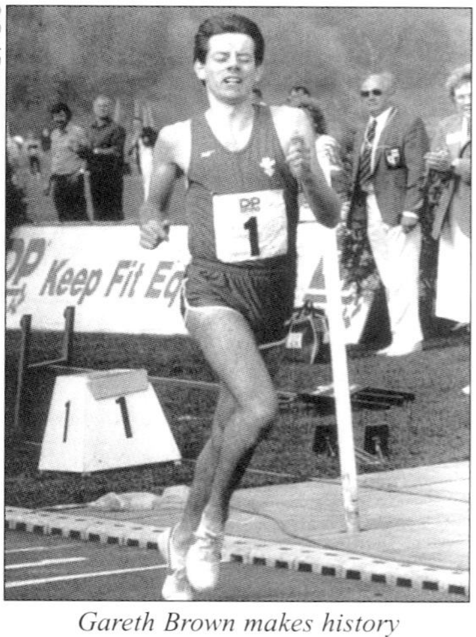

© Ceri Breeze

Gareth Brown makes history

On August 25th 1984 the Welsh Games moved to the new Morfa Stadium, Swansea for the first time with Olympic decathlon champion Daley Thompson providing one of the highlights with his victory in the 100m. However in the DP Invitation Mile Gareth Brown created a piece of Welsh history. Back in 1954 Roger Bannister became the first man to beat four minutes for a mile and since then only three Welsh runners had managed to emulate his feat … but never in Wales. Since 1959 *The Western Mail* had waited patiently to hand over a special trophy to the first Welshman to run a sub four-minute mile on Welsh soil. At the new showpiece stadium the 23-year-old claimed the trophy.

With a brilliantly judged piece of running in his first competitive mile race, he was left out in front of the field with a lap and a half to go after pacemaker Charlie Petersen, grandson of the great Welsh boxer Jack Petersen, had dropped out. His Cardiff club-mate had provided the perfect start by taking him through the first lap in 59.4, and reaching halfway in 1:59.7. Brown was strong enough to hold on and finish in 3:59.5 and go into the history books. Not many British athletes win America's vaunted national collegiate titles and none before Gareth Brown ever found it to be the quickest way home. In May 1984 the 22-year-old signed up on an athletics scholarship for Iowa State University. Within three months he was the NCAA indoor 800 champion. He was later stripped of his title, disqualified from his university's track team and on his way home and all because he had a British University degree in pharmacology. As a graduate he was therefore ineligible for university athletics competition in America. As he was able to train twice a day his talent came through and within weeks he had set a British indoor record for 1,000 yds in 2:07.1. During the summer he improved on Phil Lewis' 10-year-old Welsh outdoor 800 record with a run of 1:46.16 at Stockholm in July. A new job in accountancy brought him a more settled lifestyle and, as a member of Windsor, Slough and Eton AC, he won the AAA indoor 1,500 in his first race for 18 months. The Welsh 800 record holder quit athletics in 1986 after being overlooked for the Commonwealth Games in Edinburgh. He later married hurdler Kay Morley who was to become Commonwealth 100m hurdles champion in 1990.

1985 was Kirsty McDermott's year as she set two UK and three Welsh records. At the Ulster Games in Belfast on 24th June she finally broke the two-minute barrier in sensational style for a new British and Commonwealth record. At just 22-years-old she matched the best and was dragged to the record mark by World champion and record holder, the mighty Czech Jarmila Kratochvilova, who finished in 1:57.14 to Kirsty's 1:57.42. She had run nearly three seconds faster than ever before to become only the third British athlete to dip under the magical 2 minute mark. On 27th July Kirsty's record breaking exploits continued in Oslo when she smashed the British and Commonwealth mile records in only her second race over the distance in the world famous Bislett Games. Mary Decker-Slaney brought the field home with Kirsty running 4:19.41. During the race she also set a new Welsh 1,500 mark of 4:02.83. Both the 800m and mile times remain Welsh records in 2001.

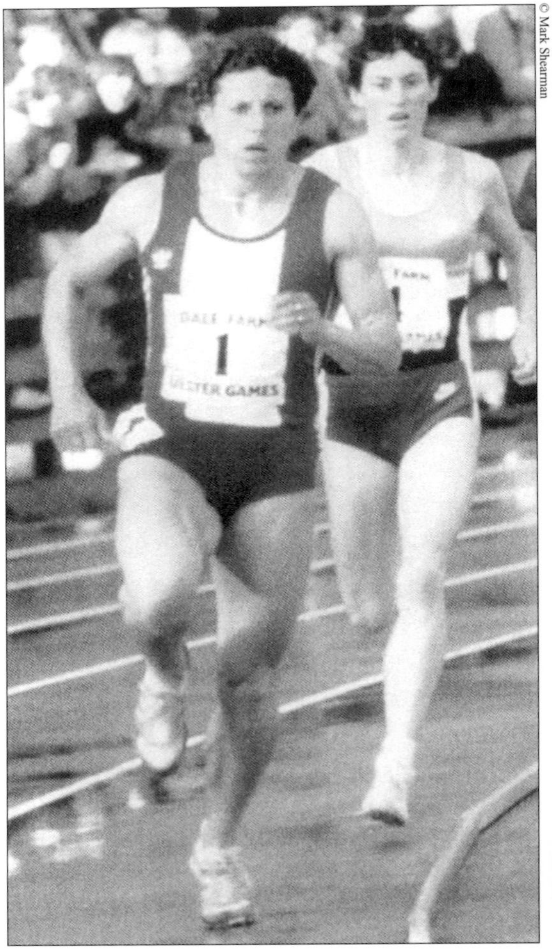

© Mark Shearman

The Ulster Games in Belfast in 1985 saw Kirsty McDermott chase home world champion Jarmila Kratochvilova to set a new UK and Commonwealth 800 record.

Brilliant Welsh performances in Cottbus

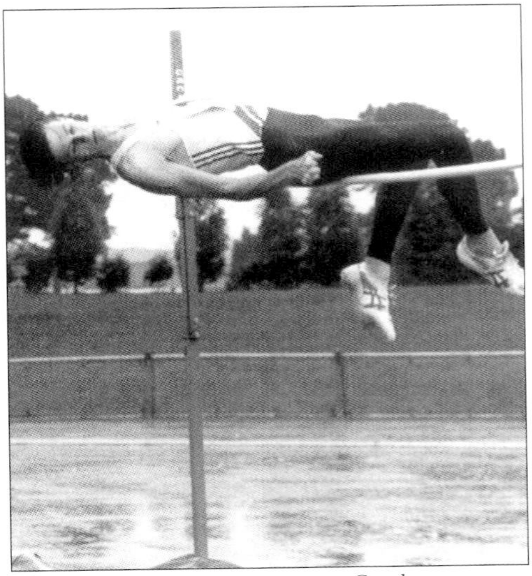

John Hill jumping at a wet Cwmbran.

The year 1985, co-incidentally the 'Year of the Youth' was an outstanding one for Wales' junior athletes. No less than eleven gained UK junior vests, the most ever in one season, and six went on to represent the UK in the European Junior Championships at Cottbus, East Germany. They came home with one gold medal, two silvers and two bronze medals, and none finished lower than sixth place. Bearing in mind that in the previous seven editions of the championships Wales' medal tally was two gold and two bronze this was an exceptional achievement all round. The star was Solihull based high jumper John Hill as he soared to a gold medal. Early on during the summer he topped 2.18 and in the build-up to Cottbus he jumped ever upwards - 2.21 in Halfheim, West Germany, one centimetre above Trevor Llewelyn's Welsh senior record, culminating in another 2.21 effort at Meadowbank in the Bells Junior international just three days before leaving for East Germany.

On the afternoon of 23rd August in Cottbus he went even higher. A look at the form guide for the year – nobody had bettered 2.24 – suggested that at his best he would get amongst the medals. However he did the impossible. A British athlete had won a high jump gold medal! His jumping was immaculate: 2.05 (1st attempt), 2.10 (1), 2.14 (1), 2.18 (1), 2.21 (1), 2.24 (1). At the same meeting Colin Jackson made his international debut at a major championship. Under the guidance of coach Malcolm Arnold and influence of training partner Nigel Walker he had improved his technique out of all recognition since he made his senior Welsh debut against Denmark in 1984. During the winter of 1985 he had made his British senior debut indoors against the Federal Republic of Germany. In Cottbus, if he ran well, he'd surely win at least a silver medal. If he ran badly, he'd still probably win silver such was his consistency. He ran well! During the lead up to the championship he had broken the existing British Junior record of 13.72 and had equalled the Welsh senior record at 13.69. But still he only won the silver medal behind Jon Ridgeon's new European Junior record of 13.46.

Newport's Neil Horsfield won the second silver medal in a highly competitive 1,500m. In his build up he had won his first senior Welsh title as well as claiming his third consecutive AAA junior title. At the bell he found himself in front and was gradually winding things up but a momentary lapse of concentration cost him the gold. Making a tremendous charge down the home straight Finn Mika Maaskola swept passed to win in 3:44.99 to Neil's 3:45.39.

Earlier in the year at Cwmbran spectators saw Helen Miles gain an emphatic win over great rival Sallyanne Short in the Welsh Young Ladies (under 20) 100m in a record 11.66, a time that put her in the top 10 in the UK senior rankings. From being a possible relay member for Cottbus she had suddenly emerged as the top junior sprinter in the country with an outside chance of a medal. Thursday, 22nd August was to become a historic day for the Brynteg Comprehensive schoolgirl who was being coached by 800m international Tony Elgie. Ten thirty in the morning for a young athlete is certainly no time to run a heat in a major championship. In the semi-final at Cottbus she raced to a new personal best of 11.62, the second fastest time by a Welsh athlete behind Michelle Scutt's Welsh national record of 11.57 set a year earlier. In the final she clocked 11.63 for a great bronze medal, and become the first ever Welsh female athlete to win a medal at the championships. Three days later she returned to play a major role in running the first leg to help the British quartet win the bronze medals in the 4 x 100m relay. In her career, she won 31 Welsh vests – more than any other athlete, male or female. Next in the lists come her great rivals Carmen Smart (29) and Sallyanne Short with 27. Javelin thrower Karen Hough of Swansea finished sixth while Barry's Paul Williams was just outside the medals in the 800m with a close fourth placing completed the "Welsh Six" at Cottbus.

Anne Middle made her international debut for Wales in 1985 against Catalonia in Barcelona. Ironically the 24-year-old housewife lived in Santiago, Spain with her husband and daughter having moved there the previous season. Born in Hereford she was twice Spanish 400 champion and won the European Clubs 800 in 2:03.8. On a warm Friday evening on August 19th Whitley Bay based Kirsty McDermott, soon to become Mrs. Wade, stormed to her third Commonwealth best in sixteen days as she played a waiting game in a 1,000m race at Gateshead to defeat Christina Boxer and take her record. Kirsty had already taken the Commonwealth 800m and mile records from Boxer during the summer.

Pen Portrait – Berwyn Price (Cardiff AAC, (UCW Aberystwyth and Swansea H)

In September 1985 at Luton Berwyn Price came to the end of a glittering career as the former Commonwealth Games champion retired from the sport which he had graced with pride and dignity for nearly two decades.

The 6'3" tall, well built and extremely powerful Welsh hero dominated British hurdling for more than a decade and finally at the age of thirty-four made up his mind to quit after the disappointment of his Swansea Harriers' club failure to get back into the British League.

During his career the Pontllanfraith raised, Tredegar born star had done so much to stimulate interest in athletics in Wales through his own career and his continuing efforts as Head of Sport and Recreation for the local council in Swansea.

An international match at Karlstad in Sweden on July 3rd 1982 saw him gain his 50th and last British international vest. At the time it was a record number of vests for a Welsh athlete, nine ahead off Lynn Davies. Colin Jackson is currently the only athlete with more to his credit. He also equalled the number of vests held by another great British hurdler, Alan Pascoe. Berwyn's total included 11 indoor and 39 outdoor internationals. He took part in both the 1972 (Munich) and 1976 (Montreal) Olympic Games, reaching the semi-finals of the 110 hurdles on both occasions.

His first major title was the European junior crown in Paris in 1970. He followed this with a win in the 1973 World Student Games in Moscow in a new British and Commonwealth record of 13.69 beating David Hemery's mark of 13.72 set in 1970. He won the first of his two Commonwealth medals, a silver at Christchurch in 1974 with a time of 13.84. During the Games he made his one and only serious attempt at the longer distance of 400 hurdles:" To make up the numbers and to show the Welsh flag". He clocked 52.8 in both heat and semi-final.

Of course, he went one better in the 1978 Edmonton Commonwealth Games when he became only the fourth Welshman to take a Commonwealth gold, following in the

footsteps of Reg Thomas, Jim Alford and Lynn Davies. His other medal was silver in the 1976 European Indoor Championships in Munich, when he set a new British record of 7.80 for 60 hurdles.

Berwyn felt more at home in the Commonwealth Games than the Olympics and equalled the highest number of appearances in the Games by a Welshman – four by Ron Jones.

In 1973 he won the first of his record six consecutive AAA titles. He was the first ever UK champion in 1977 on home soil in Cwmbran Stadium. Having won the Welsh junior title in 1969 coincidentally he went on to add six Welsh senior titles to his long list of achievements. As well as winning those six AAA titles, he finished second on three occasions in 1970, 1971 and 1972 – a truly amazing record of consistency.

His last three seasons of competitive athletics were restricted to the Welsh League and with his recurring back trouble causing all sorts of problems he felt satisfied with a distinguished career during which he had been a fine ambassador for his sport and country.

He won all his medals as a member of Cardiff AAC after attending that famous sporting school, Lewis School, Pengam, before briefly joining his local club, Bargoed AC. At Lewis School his mentor was PE teacher John Davis, who said in typical teacher style at the time: "Right – you are going to be a hurdler!" Davis helped with the early coaching before he arrived at Cardiff AAC where John Lister, himself a former Welsh 120y hurdles champion gave advice. Gwyn Evans at UCW Aberystwyth also helped a great deal on technique. His first love though was rugby because, as he put it at the time "Being a Welsh lad from the Valleys, rugby has to be your first consideration". Fortunately athletics prevailed and he became one of the all-time greats of Welsh athletics.

The story tracing the history of the sport in Wales is not always about the superstars. Other achievements are worth recording and may encourage ordinary human beings to take up athletic activities. One such individual is madcap Cardiffian Paul Jenkins who completed six races in two days. He became quite a celebrity on his fleeting visit to the US. He amazed people with his stamina and strength by completing the Michigan five race challenge and then packing his bags and heading for the Chicago Marathon. After running a 10,000 track race (36 minutes), a 400 (60 seconds), a 100 (14.5), a mile (5:10) and then a full marathon (4:05:00), the 29-year-old National Sports Centre, Cardiff assistant flew to Chicago. During some of his marathons he has had the good fortune to figure in three of the world's fastest ever races. Earlier in 1985 he did Rotterdam (Carlos Lopes' world record of 2:07:12 to win the race) and London (Steve Jones ran 2:08:16) and in Chicago he figured in a race won by Steve again in his UK and Welsh record of 2:07:13. Paul finished Chicago in a modest 4:11:00.

In the glorious sunshine of Athens in 1986 Colin Jackson announced his arrival on the world stage with a gold medal-winning run in the 110 hurdles at the World Junior Championships. It was revenge for Colin as he beat Jon Ridgeon into second place. Ridgeon had won the European Junior title the previous year just edging out the Welshman. His winning time of 13.44 also broke Ridgeon's European and British junior records.

The highlight of the Welsh Games at Swansea was the men's 400 as Jamaica's 1983 World champion Bert Cameron was beaten by England's Phil Brown who set a Welsh all-comers record with a superb run of 45.29, clipping 0.81 off Kriss Akabussi's two year-old mark. This time still stands in 2001, despite the exploits of Iwan Thomas and Jamie Baulch The main competition was a men's match between Wales, England, and Northern Ireland whilst the women took on Australia and Belgium.

Horsfield win Emsley Carr Mile

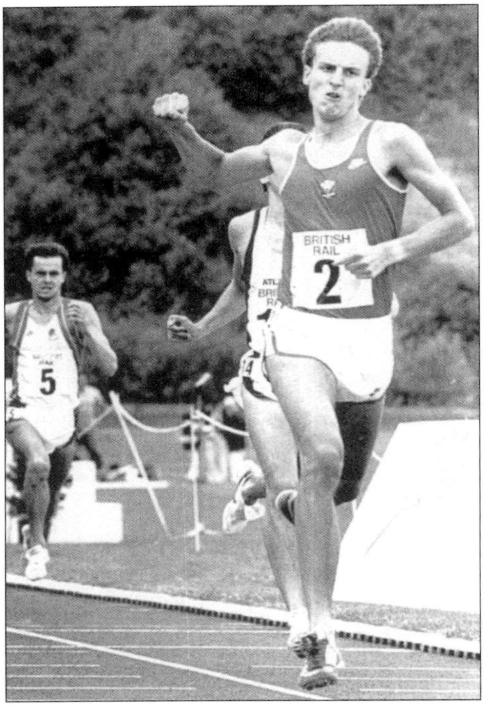

© Ceri Breeze

Neil Horsfield, one of the all-time greats of Welsh middle-distance running seen here becoming the only Welshman to win the famous Emsley Carr Mile. His Welsh records set over a decade ago at 800m; 1,500m and mile are still standing today.

The Welsh Games were held at the Morfa Stadium in Swansea again and part of the programme was the world famous Emsley Carr Mile. The race is an annual invitation originally introduced to encourage achievement of the first four-minute mile. The Emsley Carr Mile Trophy comprises a book, bound in red Morocco leather, containing a history of mile running throughout the world since 1868. Since its inception in 1953 the race has been held as part of the Welsh Games on three occasions – 1981 at Cwmbran and at Swansea in 1985 and 1986. Neil Horsfield created history by becoming the only Welshman to win the event as he raced clear to win in 3:59.03 thereby joining a list of exclusive winners including former world record holders and Olympic champions.

For Neil it was a momentous week as on the Tuesday before his run in Swansea he had stripped more than four seconds off the Welsh mile record when he finished fourth in the Cork City Sports meeting. To show the Commonwealth Games selectors were right to add him to the team, the 19-year-old from Newport Harriers mixed it with some of the world's best milers and reduced the record to 3:54.39. He was able to stay in contention with the likes of Steve Ovett, Sydney Maree and Marcus O'Sullivan until the final straight. As well as smashing Bob Maplestone's 1976 record of 3:58.5, he also sliced a massive seven seconds off his previous best.

After sixteen years as one of Wales' leading athletes, long jumper Gillian Regan retired. Her best ever jump was the 6.52 she achieved at Swansea in 1982 to finally break Ruth Martin-Jones' (Howell) ten year old record and, as an added bonus, earn herself a place in the Welsh team for the Commonwealth Games held that year in Brisbane. Competing indoors was her forte and she gained twelve British vests to add to her two outdoors. She gained twenty-four Welsh vests, which included a second appearance in the Commonwealth Games in Edinburgh in 1986. Between 1980 and 1986 she was five times runner-up in the Women's AAA Indoor Championships. Other championship honours included nine senior Welsh titles. In 1982, her best season, she was second in the UK Championships and third in the Women's AAA Championships.

We shall never know just how good Karen Hough might have been as a javelin thrower as she dramatically gave up the sport when still only 18 years old to eventually take up golf.

From the start of her career she was prominent at UK national level. In 1982 she won the Women's AAA under 15 title and followed this up by taking the under 17 championships in 1983 and 1984. In Wales she was under 17 champion in 1983 and 1984, under 20 champion in 1985 and 1986 and senior champion in 1984 and 1986. In her first senior victory, at the age of 16, she defeated both Janeen Williams and Jackie Zaslona, who had dominated the Welsh scene for the previous eight years. Her record at international level was admirable. She represented Britain in four junior international matches, finishing first in two of them and second in another. She was sixth in the European Junior Championships in 1985 and the following year competed in the World Junior Championships, the European Championships and the Commonwealth Games. She was fifth in the World Juniors and sixth in the Commonwealth Games. At Stuttgart in the European Championships she set her lifetime best and Welsh record of 59.40 when finishing thirteenth in the qualifying round, just missing out on the final. On returning home she promptly retired from the sport. Karen still holds the Welsh senior and British junior records as well as all the UK Age records from 14-19 and in 1986 she broke Fatima Whitbread's British junior record and became the Carwyn James 'Junior Sportswoman of the Year'. She seemed to be developing into the natural successor to Tessa Sanderson and Whitbread as the British No 1 before her shock announcement to retire.

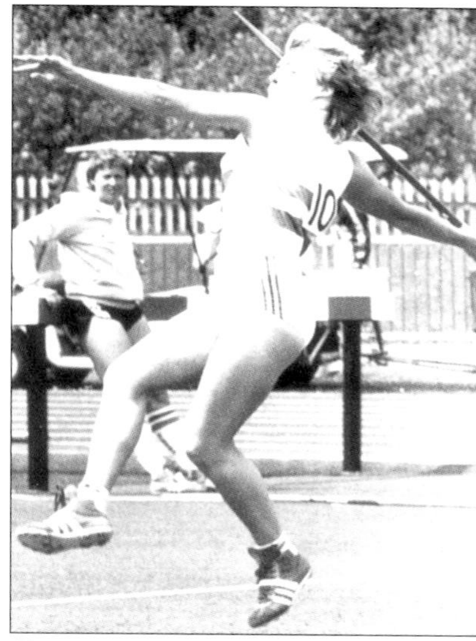

Karen Hough retired from the sport at just 18 years old. She won three AAA junior javelin tiles and competed at both the European Championships and Commonwealth Games in 1986.

Ann Franklin at 34-years-old and a member of Mynyddwyr De Cymru Running Club set world records tumbling like ninepins with a brilliant run in the 40-mile track race at Jenner Park in 1986. Ann decided to enter the race – billed as an attempt on the men's world record – only at the last minute after taking a long break from running. She was the only woman in the 15 strong field. Despite the lack of training she carved big chunks off four world track best performances. She smashed the 40-mile record by almost eight minutes as she raced home in 4:47:25. Along the way she set new world bests for at 25 miles, 30 miles and 50k.

During the summer Wales 'welcomed' to the fold 15-year-old Streatham based Herne Hill Harrier high jumper Lea Haggett. With her father born in Aberfan she made indications that she wanted to represent Wales. She won the Welsh under 15 title as well as the Women's AAA title at the same age group. With a best for the season of 1.81, a staggering improvement of 16cms, she removed two of Julia Charlton's Welsh records at under 15 and under 17. However despite numerous invitations to compete for Wales during the season she declined them all and her records have an odd place in the history of the sport in Wales.

Experienced athletes find the global nature of the sport sometimes difficult to come to terms with due to all the travelling. So for a 17-year-old it can be a daunting task. Not so for Cardiff's future Commonwealth Games 110m hurdles bronze medallist Paul Gray. Due to run in Cyprus at the beginning of the season he should have set off for the island at 10.00am on a Thursday from Heathrow with a group of British athletes. He found himself left off the flight because of over-booking. That meant he had to suffer a long delay in London before heading for Cyprus at 10.00pm the same night. When he finally arrived at 4.00am he found his baggage had been lost! By the time his luggage, containing all his kit arrived on the Friday night, it was too late for him to train and went into Saturday's race without any preparation. It did not affect him as he added the UK Age 17 to his Age 16 record in the 110 hurdles.

At the 1986 Welsh Championships at Cwmbran, which doubled as the trials for the Welsh Commonwealth Games team, Colin Jackson retained his Welsh 100m title, and won his third successive 110m hurdles championship. Sallyanne Short of Torfaen took her first Welsh titles in the 100 and 200m.

The Welsh Championships of 1987, again at Cwmbran, provided Nicola Short with the opportunity of having her own slice of history within the sport in Wales. The Torfaen athlete had won the long jump for under 13's in 1982, under 15's in 1983 and 1984 and the under 17's in 1985 and 1986. In 1987 she became the only female athlete to win at every age group. She won the under 20's and senior long jump titles to complete the ' Grand Slam'. There was almost a family double as her older sister, Sallyanne, was champion at every age group except under 15. Despite being recognised as one of Wales' greatest-ever female sprinters, her success as an under 13 came in the javelin (!), which she won in 1980.

On 26th July 1987 Kirsty Wade just four days after running " like a donkey in reverse gear" in Rome, broke her own Welsh record over 1,500m in Gateshead, the world's fastest that year at the time with 4:00.73. At the Welsh Championships in Cwmbran on June 20th, she was also far from being a donkey when she achieved a treble win in the 400/800 and 1,500 – the first time this treble has been achieved, although Jean Lochhead had won the 800/1,500/3,000 in three successive championships a decade earlier. The other star performer was Kay Morley who set a new Welsh record for the 100m hurdles with 13.49, taking 0.17 off her own record set the previous year. In Birmingham at the European Junior Championships Paul Gray fulfilled his early promise winning a bronze medal in the sprint hurdles with a time of 14.16 behind Tony Jarrett and Florian Schwarthoff. Earlier in the year, the Cardiff 18 year-old had followed in the footsteps of many of the great Welsh sprinters of the past when he took the Welsh 100m title.

The summer of 1988 saw Cardiff put the final pieces together of it's bid to host the 1994 Commonwealth Games but the effort was only rewarded in September with seven votes as they and Delhi lost out to Victoria, Canada. It was a bid held amidst allegations that the Canadian city had bought votes with unfair wheeling and dealing. However the failure to attract the Games to Wales was probably in the budgets the two had at their disposal. Cardiff had £180,000 while the £750,000 made available to Victoria also had the full backing of the Canadian Government. The Welsh championships moved back to Morfa Stadium, Swansea for the first time since 1983, where the phenomenal Venissa Head, with her last appearance in the championships took her 25th title, the highest number of senior title wins in the history of Welsh athletics. D.J.P. Richards with his 20 wins between 1923 and 1947 is the next person on the roll of honour.

Enter Winter and exit Head

1989 saw the emergence of a rare field event talent as 15-year-old schoolboy Neil Winter hit the headlines with his sensational pole-vaulting, while Wales' finest woman field event exponent, Venissa Head retired. Living in the small village of Llandogo between Chepstow and Monmouth but attending an English school, Neil set a new European age 15 record mark of 4.80m at the UK Championships at Jarrow on June 4th. His new record, which equalled Peter Lynk's Welsh senior record, saw him on par with Russia's world record holder Sergey Bubka and world junior record holder Rodion Gataulin. On July 21st he made his senior debut for Wales in the Welsh Games at the age of 15 years 4 months – the youngest male athlete to represent Wales at senior level. Earlier in the year at The Hague, Colin Jackson won his first major senior title when he took the European indoor 60m hurdles title and at the end of February, he clocked 7.41 to set new European and Commonwealth records for the event. Also in 1989, javelin thrower Nigel Bevan aligned himself to the land of his father. Born in Ipswich, he is the son of former Welsh trampoline international Randall Bevan who hailed from Ammanford. He made an immediate impact as he broke Haverfordwest-born Colin Mackenzie's Welsh record with a throw of 77.30. At the UK Championships in Jarrow in June he extended this and at the Welsh Games in Swansea in July he broke the record for the third time in the summer with 78.90.

On August 5th 1989 the new track at Carmarthen was officially opened with the Annual Celtic Games international between Northern Ireland, Eire, Scotland and Wales at under 13, 15 and 17 age groups taking centre stage for only the fourth time in Wales. Just a week later Colwyn Bay took over Swansea's mantle as kings of the Welsh League by becoming the first club from north Wales to win the HFC League Division 1 title. They also created another record in winning all four matches during the season. Not to be outdone neighbours Wrexham AC seven days later won the Women's League Division 1 title at their very first attempt, creating a record in the process. Winners of Division 4 in 1986, Division 3 in 1987, they took the Division 2 title in 1988 and completed a unique accomplishment by winning all four divisions in successive seasons.

Spain and Portugal provided the opposition in the 1989 Welsh Games at Morfa and totally unnoticed in the 10,000 walk was Daniel Plaza of Spain who was fourth. In 1992 he became Olympic 20K walk champion. The 5,000 was won by a certain Antonio Pinto of Portugal who later went on to win three London Marathons (1992, 1997 and 2000), 15 years after competing in the 1974 Welsh Games.

New Stadium at last for Cardiff

© Ceri Breeze

Three of Wales' greatest women sprinters - Helen Miles (8), Sallyanne Short (1) and Carmen Smart (11) seen here competing at the 1989 Welsh Championships, won by Smart in 11.48 which still stands as the Welsh record today.

With the Commonwealth Games being held in January the following year, the 1989 Welsh Championships and Games trials were held later than usual on August 26th at the new £5.5m Cardiff Athletic Stadium at Leckwith, the first new athletics facility in Cardiff since the opening of Maindy Stadium in 1951. Its opening marked the culmination of a 20 year fight by Cardiff AAC to get a modern athletics facility built in the city. During the championships, the first to be held in Cardiff for 15 years, Carmen Smart, at the age of 29 and producing the best results of her long and distinguished career, won the 100m in a new Welsh record of 11.48, beating Helen Miles' existing mark of 11.50. Nine championships best were bettered in one of the best championships for many years. Nigel Walker (100 in 10.35) and Colin Jackson (200 in 21.18) both ran windy times to win their fourth and eighth titles respectively. Shaun Pickering's double in the discus and hammer in championship bests were his 12th and 13th titles. The Championships were also significant in that a new champion in the women's 800m was crowned for the first time in ten years. With double Commonwealth champion Kirsty Wade absent expecting a baby, Spanish-based Anne Middle, running in the colours of Newport, won her first title. Derby's Marion Hughes took her ninth successive high jump title – a record for the event. It was also a great day for another Newport athlete, Janet Beese. The 37-year-old first won a senior title in 1968 in the discus. Her last title was won in 1974 but 15 years later she came good again and won her eleventh title with a winning effort in the discus.

Pen Portrait - Venissa Head (Army AA, Bristol AC and Cardiff AAC)

During the summer of 1989 the dominant force in Welsh and British shot and discus throwing Venissa Head was missing as she announced her retirement. Commonwealth Games silver medallist in the discus and former British record holder in the shot, her record is one, which will be difficult to equal let alone surpass. During her career she set an amazing total of thirty-five Welsh records (21 in the shot and 14 in the discus).

Venissa won the Welsh Women's AAA shot title for the first time in 1974 whilst a schoolgirl at Cyfarthfa Grammar School in Merthyr and it was to be another fifteen years before anyone else was to hold the title. She also scored ten consecutive Welsh championship wins in the discus from 1979 to 1988, following on directly from her twin sister Vivienne who had been champion for the previous three years. In all she took 25 Welsh shot and discus titles.

It was also in 1974 that she set her first Welsh record, again in the shot, with a throw of 13.00 to begin her reign as Welsh record holder. Her Welsh shot record of 18.93 was set at the unlikely venue of Haverfordwest in 1984. In the discus the pattern was similar to the championship situation with sister Vivienne holding the lead from 1975 to 1979 when Venissa took over. Her final discus record stands at 64.68 and was set in the warmth of Athens in July 1983.

Venissa confirmed her promise on the British scene in 1981 when she broke the

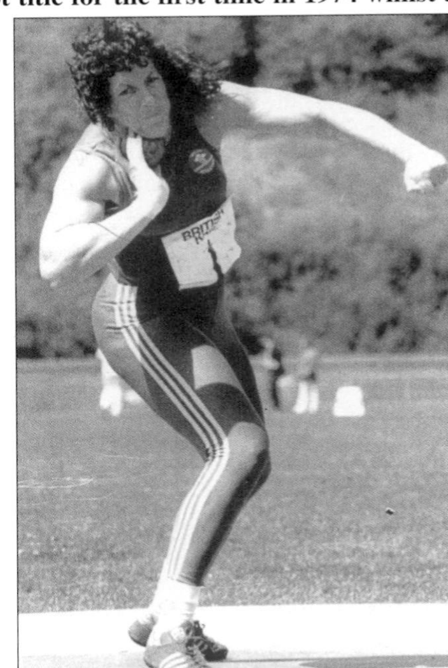

© Ceri Breeze

Venissa Head

British shot record three times and followed that up with a fourth record, and her third on Welsh soil in the same stadium at Cwmbran.

In April 1984 at RAF St Athan, she set her British indoor record with a massive throw of 19.06, which still stands as the record. At St Athan she would often hit the roof beams with some of her mighty efforts! She became the first ever-British athlete to go over the magical 19-metre mark. Only Judy Oakes (1988) and Myrtle Augee (1990) have reached that distance since, either indoors or outdoors.

Between 1974 and 1988 Venissa competed thirty times for Wales in international matches just one short of Helen Miles' record of thirty-one, including three Commonwealth Games. Her twenty-five appearances in the shot resulted in twenty victories and with twelve wins out of twenty in the discus, she compiled an enviable record of consistency at a very high level of performance.

In her three Commonwealth appearances she improved her record each time. Her first Games in 1978 in Edmonton saw her take sixth in the shot (the only time she contested this event) and eighth in the discus. She moved up to sixth in the discus at Brisbane in 1982 while the Games in Edinburgh in 1986 was the highlight of her long and distinguished career as she took the silver medal. That discus medal owed nothing to the boycott and should be recognised as well earned. In fact she led until the fourth round of throws and eventually had to settle for second spot, with 56.20, just 22cms behind winner Gael Martin of Australia.

The first UK Championships were held at Cwmbran in 1977, when Venissa won the shot, and went on to win the title on two more occasions, once with a new British record, and also took the discus title five times. One title, which eluded her however, was the Women's AAA championships, a meeting in which she competed infrequently.

Her twenty-eight appearances in British international matches (21 outdoors and 7 indoors) is a record for a Welsh woman. Included in this record is her only appearance in the Olympics in Los Angeles where she finished sixth in both discus and shot. Her first international for Britain was in 1975 against Netherlands and Hungary and her last ironically against Hungary in 1988.

She threw in the World Championships in 1983 and finished tenth in the shot and in the European's in 1986 finished twelfth in the discus. Indoors she twice appeared in the European's so that, with her three Commonwealth Games appearances, she took part in every major championship open to her except the World Indoor Championships, a record beaten only by Kirsty Wade.

Injuries to her hand meant that her shot putting was restricted in her final few years when she concentrated her efforts more on the discus. She was rather unlucky to be overlooked for the 1988 Olympics in Seoul despite heading the British ranking lists for that year – in fact she recorded six throws better than the best anyone else could manage. No doubt this major disappointment contributed to a loss of incentive to carry on and in 1989 she declined an offer to represent Wales in the Welsh Games, indicating that she had retired.

The 1990 Commonwealth Games in Auckland at the end of January gave an early start to the season and Colin Jackson followed up his 110m hurdles win in New Zealand by taking the AAA 60m hurdles indoor title at Cosford in a new UK all-comers record of 7.43 in March. The previous month, Nigel Walker (60m 6.65), Carmen Smart (60m 7.34) and Neil Winter (pole vault of 4.85) had set new Welsh indoor records at the Omron Games also at Cosford. For the young Winter, it was the best vault by a Welsh athlete indoors or out - and he was still only 15 years old. In May in the Inter-Counties Championships at Corby, he became the first Welsh athlete to clear the 5m barrier, with 5.10.

Neil Winter, the youngest Welsh Champion ever at 16

The senior championships returned to Morfa Stadium, Swansea, with Neil Winter taking his first senior title in the pole vault at just 16 years of age and setting his fifth Welsh record of the year with 5.15m. The editor of the *Welsh Athletics Annual* said of the performance at the time: "Winter is emerging as potentially the best British pole vaulter ever". In four year's time he would be Commonwealth Champion. Winter's mark at Swansea also improved on his own British youth's record (16-18) set some weeks earlier. For the precocious Winter, now competing for Monmouth School, it was his third Welsh title in two weeks as he added the senior title to the youths and junior championships to become the only athlete to win titles in three age groups in the same year. Colin Jackson took his ninth Welsh title in winning the 100m in an uninspiring 10.7, whilst Cardiff colleague Nigel Walker took his fifth Welsh title with a 14.14 clocking in the 110m hurdles - his first hurdles win in the Welsh Championships for seven years. On the women's front, Helen Miles won her fourth Welsh title, with great rival and friend Sallyanne Short taking her fifth consecutive 200m title. Only Michelle Scutt amongst Welsh women sprinters had won five successive titles in the past, so the Torfaen athlete was in good company. Commonwealth champion Kay Morley secured her fifth sprint hurdles win in succession to beat the record of four consecutive wins by 1958 Empire Games competitor Carol Thomas some thirty years earlier.

The new Leckwith Stadium at Cardiff had the distinction of holding the UK Championships in 1990 – the fifth occasion that the event had come to Wales following the previous four held at Cwmbran. Predictably, the Principality's two Commonwealth champions, Colin Jackson and Kay Morley, took UK titles, with Colin running the fastest time seen in Britain – 13.10. Other Welsh winners were Sallyanne Short (100), Neil Horsfield (1,500) and Auckland bronze medallist Paul Edwards (shot). Sallyanne also picked-up the 200m bronze. In the Welsh Junior Championships Cardiff's Julie Garrett clinched a remarkable sixth successive national title at Cwmbran Stadium in July. The high-class teenager, who completed the Cardiff marathon before her ninth birthday, won her second successive under 17 800m crown to extend her amazing winning sequence. Since 1984 the 16-year-old had won consecutive medals at under 13, under 15 and under 17.

Horsfield on a par with Reg Thomas and Jim Alford

For the first time ever the 1990 Welsh Games were held in north Wales at Wrexham and the large crowd were treated to a host of top class performances. Ireland's Sonia O'Sullivan ran in the 1,500 while Kay Morley demonstrated why she was Commonwealth champion as she raced to a new Games and all-comers record of 13.10. Kenya was well represented with 1988 Olympic champion John Ngugi winning the 3,000m. The Welsh star was undoubtedly Colin Jackson as he set a new Welsh record in the 100 and completed the double with a Games record in the hurdles. In the 100 he clocked 10.29 to delete Ron Jones' long standing 10.42 set 22 years earlier in Mexico City. Newport's Neil Horsfield also brought the house down with his new Welsh 800m record of 1:45.44, clipping 72 hundredths off Gareth Brown's 1984 mark. The previous weekend in the *Parcelforce* Games at Crystal Palace, Colin clocked 13.09 in the hurdles to again reduce his own UK all-comers record, and Neil brought his own Welsh 1,500 record down to 3:35.13 further reducing the mark to 3:35.08 in the Ivo Van Damme meeting in Brussels later in the year.

His 800 and 1,500 times still stand today as the Welsh records and, with his mile record of 3:54.39 set in 1986, AAA 1,500 title (1990), UK 1,500m championship wins in 1987 and 1990, and his seven Welsh 800/1,500 titles, the tall Newport Harrier can justifiably claim to be one of the all-time greats of Welsh middle-distance running. Unlike Reg Thomas and Jim Alford, he was never a winner at a major games, there is no doubt that his name can be uttered in the same breath as these great runners of yesteryear.

1991 started badly as Wales lost two highly influential icons within the sport with the deaths of Ron Evans and Ron Pickering. A tribute to Ron Pickering, Lynn's former coach appears elsewhere.

Pen Portrait - R.B. Evans (Carmarthen Harriers) 1906-1991

R.B. Evans

On 12th January Carmarthen's 'Mr Athletics' Ron Evans passed away at the age of eighty-five. Known throughout athletics circles as 'RB', he dedicated over forty years of his life to the sport as a starter, official and administrator, showing particular devotion to Carmarthen Harriers and West Wales.

He had the ability to encourage youngsters into athletics and there are dozens of former international athletes who are grateful for the help and support given to them by Ron Evans.

In 1948 he achieved his life-long ambition when he founded Carmarthen and District Harriers Athletics Club. He made a team to be reckoned with in all aspects of the sport. He was the great organiser while his great friend Ernie Jones was the motivating coach and between them they put the area on the athletics map and soon became known as the 'dynamic duo'.

Based at Carmarthen Park in those early days with no track or pits, Ron would organise Saturday morning cross-country races. Even sprinters were expected to run!

Ron's enthusiasm for the sport ran so deep that he travelled thousands of miles a year ferrying athletes from one end of the country to the other. His symbolic Rover with the distinctive number plate ATH 100 was seen at athletics stadiums throughout Britain.

When the cinder track at Johnstown was opened in 1962, he had found a new home for the club. During the 60s he was the brainchild behind the Young Athletes Courses in Aberystwyth. Such was his standing in the sport that during the years of the courses he had such famous names as Robbie and Anne Brightwell, John Cooper, Ron Jones, Lynn Davies and Ron Pickering as part of his coaching team.

International athletics was also brought to West Wales and Ron persuaded the 1964 Olympic long jump champion Lynn Davies to run in the colours of Carmarthen during a meeting against Birchfield Harriers in 1965, which was a mini version of a Grand Prix meeting. At that meeting the Olympic hero broke the British long jump record, which unfortunately never appeared in the record books due to the absence of a wind gauge reading.

Gareth Edwards may be a living legend in the world of rugby but he was also an English Schools' champion and British junior record holder at 200 yds hurdles. His first appearance for a club after he left Millfield School was, thanks to Ron, for Carmarthen.

In addition to his dedication to Carmarthen, Ron pursued his own career within the sport. He was a well-known starter in Wales and officiated in the 1962 and 1966 Commonwealth Games.

During his life he held almost every administrative position possible. He was elected Chairman of the Welsh AAA and served as its President on two occasions. He was also President of the Welsh Cross-Country Association and past Chairman of the Inter-Counties Association. In 1984, in recognition of his services to athletics, he received the AAA Award of Honour. He was also elected a Life Vice-President of the AAA.

With the formation of the new Athletics Association of Wales, he was elected as one of only three Life Vice-Presidents of the Association, testimony to the affection which Ron Evans was held within the sport.

© Ceri Breeze

David Wood

The Welsh Championships returned to Leckwith in 1991 after an absence of a year and in a special invitation event Colin Jackson ran a new world's best of 22.63 for the rarely run 200m hurdles, clipping six hundredths off the 1960 Olympic 400m hurdles Champion Glenn Davis' previous best, with Nigel Walker second and European 200m champion, John Regis third. Elsewhere on the track, Colin claimed his 10th Welsh title with a 10.93 100m clocking, and Nigel Walker won his sixth and last title in the 110m hurdles. This likeable Cardiff athlete, whose highpoint in a glittering career, in which he was outshone by his friend and training partner, was his world indoor bronze in 1987, and was an outstanding servant to Welsh athletics. The 1991 championships also saw the career of Dave Wood draw to a close as he took his tenth triple jump title in eleven years, having won his first as a nineteen year old in 1981. He dominated the event in Wales during the 1980s, setting two Welsh records in the space of a month in 1984, with his 15.90 in Yugoslavia standing as the Welsh record until broken by Steve Shalders by 9cms in the World Junior Championships in Chile last year. His 24 appearances for Wales in major matches between 1979 and 1991 is a record for a Welshman, just one appearance ahead of Cardiff teammate Paul Gray. West Walian Dave shares the record of seven successive triple jump wins with Gwynne Evans (1934/39) and John Phillips (1973/79). In the women's events, Helen Miles took the sprint double for the first time since 1984 ahead of Sallyanne Short to win her fifth and sixth Welsh titles. Another double winner was the remarkable 38 year-old Newport Harrier Janet Beese who took the shot and discus, almost a quarter of a century after her first senior title in 1968. In all she took 15 Welsh

© Ceri Breeze

Janet Beese holder of 15 Welsh senior championship titles in a 23-year span between 1968 and 1991.

titles in her career and had the misfortune to be around at the same time as Venissa Head. In addition to her wins, Janet also took second or third spots on a remarkable 23 occasions! The women's hammer was held for the first time and won by Angela Bonner of Torfaen with 34.02.

Cardiff staged the UK Championships again in 1991. The only Welsh winner was Auckland 5,000m bronze medallist Ian Hamer who took his speciality to confirm his status as Britain's best in the event.

Earlier in the year a new £30,000 all-weather track opened at Penlan, Brecon – the first such facility in Powys, replacing the old cinder track. In May, Welsh athletics lost one of its driving forces in north Wales with the untimely death of Tudor Williams.

After the 1992 Barcelona Olympics hurdlers Kay Morley-Brown and Nigel Walker announced their retirement from the sport,

Pen Portrait - Kay Morley (Leeds AC and Cardiff AAC)

Kay was born in Swinton, Yorkshire and in 1983 she came to UCW Cardiff to follow a postgraduate teaching course. She eventually lived and worked in Cardiff as a maths teacher and assumed her Welsh eligibility in 1985. During her seven years of hurdling she not only transformed the event Wales but also had a tremendous bearing on the event in Britain.

The sister of Sue Morley, the former holder of the British record for 400 hurdles, Kay became a member of the redoubtable Malcolm Arnold school of hurdling which included Colin Jackson and Nigel Walker. It certainly was the influence of these two famous hurdlers that gave Kay the extra inspiration and impetus to reach the very top. In Malcolm Arnold she had the final jigsaw piece to achieve her aims in the sprint hurdles event.

Her first year in Welsh athletics in 1985 saw her ranked only fourth in the 100 hurdles with a best time of 15.21 set when she finished behind Liz Wren at the Welsh championships. For the next seven years she was crowned Welsh champion and three times UK champion. She also broke the Welsh record on five occasions taking it from 14.21 to 12.91.

She made the first of her seventeen appearances (with nine victories) for Wales against Catalonia in 1986 when she won in 14.29. Her appearances for Britain totalled twelve with three of these indoors.

The high spot of her career was undoubtedly on February 2nd 1990 when against all expectations she was crowned Commonwealth champion in Auckland with 12.91 – a time which still stands today as the Welsh record. Her indoor record of 8.16 also still stands and both are likely to remain on the books for some time ahead, such was her dominance in the events.

Kay shares with Michelle Scutt, Kirsty Wade, Angela Tooby and Venissa Head the double distinction of being the only Welsh women athletes to win medals at the Commonwealth Games and to have competed in all major international events – the World and European championships, Olympic and Commonwealth Games.

In March 1991 Kay married Gareth Brown, the first Welsh athlete to run a sub four-minute mile on Welsh soil.

The women's 400m hurdles at the Welsh Games at Cwmbran in 1992 featured two of the athletes who were to dominate the event on the world stage. Future world champion Kim Batten (USA) beat future Olympic champion Deon Hemmings of Jamaica in a thrilling race to set a new Welsh all-comers record of 54.69 which still stands today. In the sprint hurdles 1994 Commonwealth Games champion Michelle Freeman also of Jamaica won. In the men's sprint hurdles Colin Jackson had a thrilling victory over American rivals Jack Pierce, Greg Foster and his British understudy Tony Jarrett in what proved to be the highlight of the day. The pole vault saw a world-class exhibition from Grigory Yegorov (Kazakhstan) who set a Welsh all-comers and Games record of 5.80. Torfaen sprinter Sallyanne Short was at the peak of her form as she defeated a field that included crack American and Jamaican sprinters and her time of 11.39 was an outstanding Welsh record that still stands today. The time bettered her own record of 11.47 which she ran three times.

Pen Portrait - Nigel Walker (Cardiff AAC)

Another stalwart hurdler to retire in 1992 was Nigel Walker. Born in Cardiff in 1963, he joined his hometown club and never competed for any other throughout his career. It was a testament to his consistency that he was ranked in Britain's top six every year since 1982, a year he was the British junior No. 1.

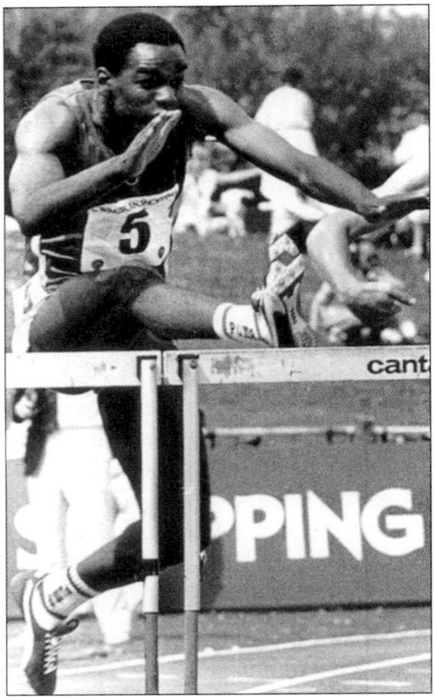

Nigel Walker

It was perhaps his misfortune that that his career overlapped those of two other great British and Welsh hurdlers, Berwyn Price and Colin Jackson. However in 1984 he did top the Welsh rankings with a best time of 13.78, the year he was No 2 in Britain and ran in the Olympic Games.

With his 1984 time he was closing in on Berwyn's Welsh record of 13.69 set in 1973. He eventually beat it in 1986 with a time of 13.52 in Stuttgart in August. By then though Colin Jackson had emerged and beat Nigel to the record three weeks earlier in Athens with a time of 13.44. So despite never having held the Welsh record he nevertheless ended his career as Wales' second fastest hurdler.

He gained sixteen international vests for Wales, just one less than his second chosen sport later in life, and such, was his consistency, that he competed in every major championship including twice at the European Championships and Commonwealth Games. His greatest achievements came indoors with a total of nineteen British vests. He ran twice in the World Indoor championships and an incredible six times in the European Indoor championships. 1987 was to be the highlight of his distinguished career when within a fortnight he won two bronze medals in both the World and European Indoor Championships. At the World in Indianapolis he was timed at 7.66 while he was slightly faster (7.65) at Lievin in the European. His form came as no surprise as the previous season had seen him finish a close fourth in both the European and Commonwealth outdoor Championships.

© Western Mail

Nigel Walker with his two bronze medals.

In the former, it was the highest individual placing of a Welsh athlete in a track event at the time in the European Championships, if one discounts Tony Simmons' 10,000m silver in 1974, when he temporarily relinquished his Welsh eligibility.

As he readily admits, world bronze in the inaugural World indoor was fortuitous – "World record holder Greg Foster and Commonwealth champion Mark McKoy crashed out at the third hurdle but at least I had the pleasure of beating recently crowned European champion Arto Bryggare and a certain Colin Jackson".

A more than useful sprinter (he competed in the 1990 European indoors over the flat 60 and reached the semi-final), he had a best time of 10.47 as well as a wind-assisted 10.35 set when winning the 1989 Welsh title. He also took Welsh sprint titles in 1983 (200m) and 1984 (100m) to add to his three 110m hurdles wins (1983/90/91)

His retirement after the Welsh Games at Cwmbran was a great loss to the sport as he had been performing at the very highest level for over a decade gaining thirty-two British vests. However his blistering speed was put to good effect as he pursued his new career as a rugby player with Cardiff RFC. It took him only a short time to make a considerable impression and on March 6th 1993 he made his debut at a near veteran age of twenty-nine for Wales against Ireland. So in his first season of senior rugby and after just twenty games for Cardiff, he won his cap as the fastest rugby union wing in the world.

He gained seventeen caps between 1993 and 1998 and his try against France in 1993 was the first by a Welsh player on French soil for ten years. In May 1994 in a World Cup qualifier against Portugal he used his scorching pace to score four tries to equal the individual try record in a game for Wales. Such was his ability in his new sport that at one stage he had scored eight tries in as many international matches. He eventually scored twelve in his seventeen international appearances. His career was effectively over when on 21st February 1998 at Twickenham against England just three minutes into the match when he suffered a dislocation of his right shoulder. And so he joined an elite group of men that have gained international honours in both sports.

His vast experience in the sporting world has seen him become a television presenter and commentator for both sports as well as, a post with the WRU looking after the welfare of players.

Swansea's Ian Hamer, still the second fastest British 5,000m runner of all-time

Auckland 5,000m bronze medallist Ian Hamer really reached the heights in 1992 as he broke Steve Jones' Welsh 5,000m record of 13:18.6, which had been set in Portugal virtually 10 years ago to the day. In a Grand Prix meeting in Rome's Olympic Stadium, Hamer clocked one of the fastest times in the world that year to win from Italian Salvatore Antibo, the reigning European Champion, and Basildon's Rob Denmark. His time of 13:09.8 took him from being ranked 47th in the world the previous year, to the 16th fastest of all time. Amongst British athletes, only one man had gone faster at the time – Dave Moorcroft with his 1982 world record of 13:00.41. Both of these times still stand today as the two fastest times recorded by British 5,000m runners – true testament to the outstanding run of the 27 year-old Bridgend born, Edinburgh University graduate.

Another athlete to reach the heights in 1992, this time literally, was Neil Winter, who capped an outstanding season by raising his own Welsh record for the third time when competing for Britain's junior team in Italy. On this occasion, the 18 year-old jumped 5.50 to set a new British junior best – just three years earlier he had been the first from the Principality to better 5m. In the same meeting, another emerging star, 19 year-old Newport Harrier Jamie Baulch knocked two hundredths of his own 200m Welsh record with 21.16.

Shaun Pickering was the star of the 1992 Welsh Championships at Leckwith taking all three of the heavy events, to achieve his 15th, 16th and 17th titles, whilst Colin Jackson won both 100 and 110m hurdles to take his Welsh title haul to twelve. Sallyanne Short clinched a sprint double again, whilst Kay Morley-Brown bowed out with her seventh successive sprint hurdles win - an all-time record. Neil Winter, however, had an off day failing to clear his opening height.

At the Seoul World Junior Championships of 1993 Jamie Baulch set foot on the world stage for the first time as a member of the British sprint relay team which came home with gold.

Colin Jackson had started the year by winning the silver medal at the World Indoor Championships behind training partner Mark McKoy of Canada. In June he won the Europa Cup in a new record of 13.10 before setting a European and Commonwealth record of 12.97 in July. As we now know, he was to win the world crown in a new record of 12.91 in Stuttgart in the finest moment for Welsh athletics since Lynn Davies' Olympic long jump victory in 1964. For his outstanding achievements during the year the IAAF voted him the "World Male Athlete of the Year".

On the domestic scene Wales made the journey to Tel Aviv in Israel for a four nations international match in May. There was a remarkable performance from Bronwen Cardy Wise in the 3,000m. She was only second but to set a new personal best at the age of 42 was a significant achievement. Her previous best was set 22 years earlier and she knocked 13 seconds off it. She had been called into the team only as a late replacement but finished in 9:29.82.

The 1993 Welsh championships held at Cwmbran saw Helen Miles take the sprint double for the last time, whilst Swansea schoolgirl Philippa Roles took her first senior title in the discus. Commonwealth Games sixth placer (at Auckland) Caroline White made her last appearance in the championships taking her fifth javelin title since 1988. Welsh athletics is littered with family connections and Lisa Gibbs' second successive heptathlon win in the 1993 championships is significant in this respect. Lisa is the daughter of Brian (Welsh 3,000 steeplechase champion of 1965) and Pam Griffiths who, as Pam Guppy, was Welsh high jump champion in 1963, 1964 & 1965 and twice broke the Welsh record for the event with 1.61 and 1.62 in 1963/64. Brian is still active as a veteran performer today and was a prolific member of Roath, Cardiff and currently Swansea veterans' teams.

For the first time in 21-years the Welsh Games returned to Cardiff (Leckwith) with Australia's golden girl Cathy Freeman winning the 200. Not known at the time was that one of her advisors was Swansea born former Welsh 110m hurdles champion Tudor Bidder, a member of the coaching team at the Australian Institute for Sport who had responsibility for 400m and high jump in the organisation.

Shortly after winning the AAA indoor 800 title in 2:05.60 in 1994 Kirsty Wade discovered she was pregnant at the time and duly retired.

Pen Portrait – Kirsty Wade
(Brecon AC, Bristol AC, Loughborough Colleges and Blaydon H)

Kirsty is famous for her running exploits, but few people realise her earliest claim to fame came as a child poet. Even in those days, when she was a pupil at Llandrindod High School she had a vision what she wanted in life and in particular in her chosen sport and it dominated her life even in those early days. Even then it was winning which was uppermost in her mind. Here is "Two Hundred Yards" by Kirsty, aged 12

Static atmosphere
Silence reigns.
'Bang' goes the starter's gun.
Advice is paid no heed
And three in front at the bend.
At 100 yds they're failing fast
Oblivious to the cheers
'Come on you can work harder'.
Legs pump like pistons,
Hair blown back,
Fatigue is coming on.
Arms tighten up
Feet are heavy.
Relief! Relief!
Just ten yards to go
But you're not in front.
One last effort to pass the post first.
Then the haze descends
Till a familiar far away, voice cries
'Well done! A good first!
Fatigue floods in,
Air floats up to the head.
You're walking on air
It's gorgeous.
You did it,
You've won. You've won. You've won.

The poem was used in a Schools Council theme-book on Sport, "Teaching and Learning of English in Wales".

The former Queen of Welsh athletics has given up life in the fast lane and has 'abdicated' to live on an island in the Outer Hebrides. At a glance it might be a strange change of environment for someone who had created so much history within the sport. However, having being born in Girvan, Scotland, of English parents, lived in mid-Wales most of her life, won titles in both the Welsh and English Schools' championships, ran for Wales, it was perhaps natural that she returned to her land of birth.

Wales have not been over-blessed with world-class women athletes. However Kirsty, in her way, was a pioneer as she took on many of the finest and emerged in the gold-medal class. She first showed promise under the guidance of Roy Jones

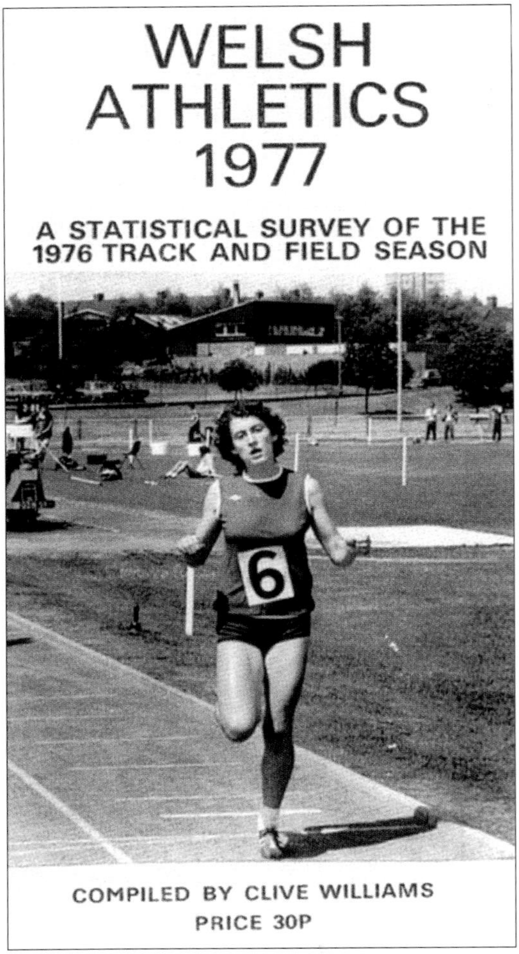

WELSH
ATHLETICS
1977
A STATISTICAL SURVEY OF THE
1976 TRACK AND FIELD SEASON
6
COMPILED BY CLIVE WILLIAMS
PRICE 30P

14 yr-old Kirsty McDermott (Wade) featured on the front page of the first Welsh Athletics Annual in 1977, winning the 1976 Welsh Games junior women's 800.

during the 1975 season as she won the Welsh women's and Schools' under 15 800 title. Twelve months later she did the double again setting a Schools' record in the process. At Crystal Palace in the Women's AAA junior 800 she was noticed by the national press 'as one to watch for the future' (!). She won the title in 2:11.1 which gave her a new Welsh record for both under 15 and 17 age groups. It was also the fastest time recorded by a Welsh athlete in the year - irrespective of age. Her efforts ensured that she was on the front cover of the first ever Welsh Athletics Annual in 1977. She was also awarded the Welsh Junior 'Sports Personality of the Year' accolade.

By the age of seventeen she had won her first Welsh senior 800 title and it was the start of a remarkable run of ten successive titles from 1979 to 1988. During her unbeatable 800m reign her best time was 2:03.3 in 1985 and in almost all her races she would lead from gun to tape. She also won four titles at 400 with her best time being 54.74 in 1987, while two titles also came in 1987 and 1991 in the 1,500, – making sixteen titles in all. Only Venissa Head (25) amongst Welsh women won more.

Kirsty's first appearance in Wales as Mrs Wade – following her 1986 marriage to Tony Wade in Barbados in March, was not remembered for her usual two-lap title but her second place to Sian Morris in the 400. It was only her second defeat at the championships – she also lost in the one lap event to Michelle Scutt in 1984.

Her junior career was a steady build up and this served her well for her superstar career. After her Women's AAA under 15 title win, she repeated this in 1978 at under 17. Following that success she moved from Llandrindod High School in the heart of Wales to the exclusive sporting academy at Millfield School in Somerset. To complete her junior career as a British junior international she joined a small but elite group of Welsh athletes who have won English Schools' titles with an 800 victory in 1980. The previous year she had finished sixth in the European Junior Championships, her first major challenge.

As an 18 year-old in 1981 she gained her first British indoor vest and just missed out on a medal at the European indoors finishing fourth it took another three seasons before she was seen in the British colours indoors again. It was her first breakthrough as she finished in 2:02.88, which still stands today as the Welsh indoor

record. In 1982 she broke the Welsh 800 record on four occasions – 2:03.0 at Aldershot, 2:02.14 while finishing fourth in the WAAA final, 2:01.23 at Cleckheaton and a superb 2:00.05 at Crystal Palace.

By the time she reached the Queen Elizabeth 11 Stadium in Brisbane in 1982 for the Commonwealth Games she was no longer a teenager, having celebrated her 20th birthday just a month before and was expected to gain valuable experience and reach the final of the 800. The rest is history as she held the inside lane from start to finish to be crowned Commonwealth Champion in 2:01.31.

After a disappointing few seasons arguably her greatest year of all round achievement was in 1985 as she ran under the two-minute barrier six times. She had major battles with Kratochvilova, Decker-Slaney and even had a victory over Olympic champion Doina Melinte. During her campaign she set British and Commonwealth records for 800, 1000 and 1 mile.

By nature Kirsty was a pessimist and it wasn't all plain sailing for she had to fight back from a disastrous year in 1984 when she was on the verge of quitting the sport. But having married and living in Whitley Bay, she rediscovered the dedication. "After winning in Brisbane I just couldn't believe it. I had only just made the Welsh team by setting a personal best. It was a real shock to win. After that win, although I was only twenty, I thought it was a perfect opportunity to end my career. I used to treat athletics as a hobby and it was always bottom of my priorities and I wanted to take up a career possibly in nursing".

In the doldrums after failing to make the 1984 Olympic team Kirsty went on a special vegetarian diet and rediscovered her enthusiasm for the sport the following year with devastating affect. "I cut out chocolate and mum's sponge puddings and stuck to 1,000 calories a day. It was quite hard but from a racing weight of 10st 4lbs in 1981 I was 8st 9lbs at the end of 1984".

Kirsty never wanted to be a full-time athlete and with being a graduate of English from Loughborough University she ran the Sub-Two Fitness Centre at Rowlands Gill at Tyne and Wear. Living in Whitley Bay, the northeast air seemed to agree with her and training at a new base brought handsome dividends.

Her achievement in 1986 will go down in history as probably the greatest middle distance performance by any woman at the Commonwealth Games. Those privileged to be at the Meadowbank Stadium in the cold summer witnessed a piece of athletics history. Her achievement in becoming the first woman to win not only the Commonwealth 800 title twice but also a middle distance double of 800/1,500 was truly remarkable.

In 1987 she continued in fine form. Her rise as a world-class runner reached a new peak in February in San Diego when she broke the European indoor mile record with a time of 4:26.10, two seconds inside the record. She also won the European Cup race outdoors with one of her devastating finishing kicks.

Her new home track at Gateshead soon became a favourite venue as at the end of the season she set a new Welsh 3,000 record of 8:47.86. By the time Kirsty reached 25, she had won three Commonwealth golds for Wales and set Welsh records at four different distances. Her record-breaking included 800 (6), 1,500 (4), 1 mile (1) and 3,000 (1) – a truly remarkable achievement, unequalled amongst Welsh middle-distance athletes. Her 800/1,500/mile records of 1:57.42/4:00.73/4:19.41 still stand as Welsh records.

Now content with her three children and husband running a bed and breakfast in the Outer Hebrides, Kirsty keeps herself fit by teaching exercise classes in the evenings. She is still involved in her old sport with children in the UK Sports Hall

Athletics Scheme and is looking forward to encourage youngsters to use the new track in the area.

In the poll undertaken by the AAW last year to establish the leading Welsh athletes of the last century, she won the female award ahead of Venissa Head, which confirmed her as Wales' finest female athlete of all-time.

Colin Jackson got 1994 off to a bang with a new world indoor record of 7.30 for the 60m hurdles in Sindelfingen, Germany after equalling it with 7.36 in Glasgow a month earlier. A week later he was European champion again, achieving the unique distinction of winning both the 60m flat and 60m hurdles titles.

In May, the Welsh under 20 championships heralded the opening of the new Spytty Lane track in Newport, where Newport Harriers took up residence. The highlight of the Welsh senior championships at Cwmbran was the fourth sprint double from Sallyanne Short, taking her sprint title haul to twelve. She later took the long jump to end up with thirteen championship wins in her illustrious career. Her first senior titles had come 10 years earlier, again on her home-town track, but these title wins were the last for the 26 year-old, who during her career had become UK Champion in 1990; made 11 appearances in a British vest, plus 27 for Wales and set the existing Welsh 100m record at 11.39. Swansea's Steve Ingram eclipsed one of the longest championships bests he took the long jump with a windy 7.91 to erase Lynn Davies' 1966 record, whilst Iwan Thomas took his first Welsh title with a championships best time in the 400m (47.09). Colin Jackson ended the season as he started clocking the season's fastest time - 12.98 in Tokyo and be named as Britain's male athlete of the year by the British Athletics Writers Association.

1994 also marked the retirement after 65 years in the sport of an outstanding servant to Welsh athletics.

Pen Portrait - K.W.B "Ken" Harris (Roath Harriers)

Ken Harris's remarkable contribution to Welsh athletics started when he joined Roath Harriers as a 19 year old in 1929. Sixty-five years later he decided to retire, albeit reluctantly! Still going strong in 2001, and living with his wife and daughter in Hereford, he celebrated his 90th birthday with a Mediterranean cruise - such is his resilience. In fact no single article can do justice to the achievements of this remarkable servant to Welsh athletics, which he has served as an international and Welsh champion athlete; Captain, Secretary and President of Roath Harriers; President of the two athletics administrations in Wales - the Welsh CCA and Welsh AAA, and as a senior official in both track and field and cross-country events.

His finest performance as an athlete came in 1934 when he was part of the first Welsh team to compete in the Empire Games, in London, winning his one-mile heat in 4:35.4. As he readily admits, he was well out of it in the final won by New Zealand's Jack Lovelock with Sydney Wooderson (England) second. He qualified for the Welsh team by winning the Welsh mile title that year in his fastest time of 4:28.2, which had only been bettered in Wales by 1930 Empire Games champion Reg Thomas. In the race at Rodney Parade, Newport, Phil Dee of Cross Keys, running for Newport Harriers was the early leader and was still leading down the back straight of the last lap. But, as a local newspaper reported: "Harris took off at this point, and went on to win with ease"

His only other Welsh title came in the first post War championships when he won the inaugural 2 miles steeplechase in 11:31.0, but he was a prolific scorer for his club in Welsh Cross Country Championships and, over a span of 15 years between 1935 and 1950, he only failed to make the top ten on one occasion. His best position was fourth in the 1946 race at Ely, Cardiff when he was appointed captain of the Welsh team for the international race in Scotland. Altogether he appeared in the international five times between 1935 and 1950.

In the 1958 Cardiff Empire Games he was clerk of the course for the marathon and later that year he received the first of his many awards for services to athletics - a Welsh AAA meritorious plaque. He received an IAAF Special Award in 1988, the same year that he received the Welsh AAA Award of Honour. The following year he received the AAA Plaque of Honour.

© Cen Breeze

Les Davies (left) President of A A W congratulates Ken Harris on his achievements in athletics just before his retirement in 1994.

He was also honoured with the presidency of Cardiff AAC, which was formed out of a merger of Roath and Birchgrove Harriers in November 1968. He also served as President of Cwmbran Olympiads. However, it is as a starter that many athletes of the 60s, 70s and 80s will remember him. Resplendent in his red blazer, at all events from the small inter-club right up to international meetings, where in the former, his quip of "Small gun today, so no false starts" became as well known as his fairness and humility. Ken is part of a breed that we are unlikely to see again in Wales or indeed in Britain.

Phil arrives, fifth in line

Malcolm Arnold, Welsh National Coach for the past 20 years, was appointed Director of Coaching for the UK in 1994, taking over from Frank Dick. Initially a temporary appointment, his position was confirmed as a permanent post in February 1995. An accomplished triple jumper in his competitive days, Malcolm ranked fourth in Britain in 1963 and was well up in the lists for most of the 60s. Retiring from competition, he took to coaching and has never looked back. At one time he was national event coach for the long and triple jump. After teaching posts in his native Cheshire and Bristol he took up his first full-time coaching appointment when he became Director of Coaching in Uganda in 1970. Among his charges during this period was the redoubtable John Akii-Bua, who took the gold medal for the 400m hurdles in the Munich Olympics of 1972, breaking the world record in the process. His reputation as one of the world's leading coaches for the high hurdles grew during his term as Welsh National Coach, a position he took up on his return from Uganda. Among his protégés were Kay Morley, Nigel Walker, and of course Colin

Malcolm Arnold has been the great motivator behind the success of Colin Jackson.

Jackson. Phil Banning, who, at the time was the GB National Event Coach for 800 and 1,500, replaced Malcolm. Phil had a distinguished career as an athlete, retiring with a 1,500 personal best of 3:39.85 (1975) and became only the fifth occupant of the position following in the illustrious footsteps of Jim Alford, Ron Pickering, Peter Lay and Malcolm.

Welsh Championships back in Newport after a 56-year gap

The 1995 Welsh Championships returned to Newport on June 17th for the first time since 1939. On this occasion they were held across town from the last venue - Rodney Parade - at the fine new Spytty Lane Stadium. In her first appearance in the championships Catherine Murphy took the sprint double to follow on from the great Welsh women sprinters of the past - Liz Parsons (Johns), Liz Gill (Lewis), Sandra Belt (Pengilley), Michelle Scutt, Helen Miles, Carmen Smart and Sallyanne Short - who have achieved the feat. After a seven-year gap, Nick Comerford regained his 1,500m title. Lee Wiltshire (shot) and Garry Slade (long jump) took fifth titles.

Jamie Henthorn was the top Welsh performer with wins in the 100 and 200 (10.48/21.12) as Wales took on Holland and Belgium in an under 23 match in Utrecht on July 9th 1995, whilst at the Welsh Games in Cwmbran on the same day, Welsh fans were treated to a fine pole vaulting display by Nick Hysong of America who was to be crowned Olympic champion in Sydney. The American cleared 5.70 with Welsh star Neil Winter second. Another athlete to collect an Olympic medal in Sydney - Cardiff based Darren Campbell - won the 100m for England in a match easily won by England by 50 pts from the home team and an international select team. Colin Jackson, Nigel Bevan and Sallyanne Short were the only Welsh winners, although the Welsh men's team took both relays. The sprint relay squad of Kevin Williams, Colin Jackson, Jamie Baulch, Tremayne Rutherford clocked 40.04 which was technically a new Welsh record, although intrinsically inferior to the hand timed 4 x 110 mark of 40.2 set by Terry Davies, Lynn Davies, Keri Jones and Ron Jones at the 1966 Jamaica Commonwealth Games.

On July 23rd and 24th, at Cardiff's Leckwith Stadium, Wales were narrowly defeated by Turkey in a match which also contained national teams from Scotland and Northern Ireland, whilst Southampton based sprinter Henthorn finished off a fine season with a sprint relay gold in the European Junior Championships in Hungary.

Newport athlete Doug Turner became only the second Welsh athlete to win a senior AAA indoor sprint title - Cardiff clubmate Dave Roberts (60m) was the first in 1975 - when he won the 200m in Birmingham in February 1996. In the next track event, Catherine Murphy became the third when the outdoor champion at both 100 and 200 took the 200! There was another Welsh winner when Shaun Pickering also won the shot.

The different qualifying criteria for Welsh international eligibility amongst the various sports in Wales was highlighted in the indoor international in Lieven, France, when Great Britain took on the home nation, Italy and Germany. Martin Giraud, the outstanding London Welsh wing who won Welsh Youth caps took part in the long jump. The former English Schools' long jump champion, whose grandfather was Welsh, cannot compete for Wales in athletics events, as to claim a qualification for athletics purposes, one or both parents must have been born in Wales. Jamie Henthorn, Emma Davies, Rhian Clark and Philippa Roles were also in the GB squad.

Wales comfortably defeated Ireland in both men's and women's matches at the Welsh Games at Leckwith in May, whilst Newport's Spytty Road track again staged the 1996 Welsh Championships on June 1st, where Commonwealth champion Neil Winter equalled his championships best of 5.25 to win the pole vault for the third time. Star performer however was Rhian Clark in the women's event, who bettered her own Welsh record by 15 cms to win with 3.65. Alyson Layzell, whose last title win was ten years earlier as a nineteen year old, made a welcome return to the championships to regain her 400m hurdles title in a new championships best of 58.92. That win was to mark a remarkable couple of weeks for the Cheltenham-based doctor as she reduced the Welsh record on no less than three occasions, ending with a sparkling 56.43 in the Olympic trials in Birmingham on June 16th to finish second behind world record holder, Sally Gunnell in a time, which was not only the second fastest by a Briton that year, but the ninth fastest by a Briton all-time. In those three races, Alyson, who reached the final of the 1986 Commonwealth Games, had reduced the previous Welsh record set by Diane Fryar thirteen years earlier by a hefty 1.73 seconds. Other performances of note from a Welsh perspective, other than Colin Jackson's expected win the 110m hurdles and Justin Chaston's steeplechase victory where he regained the title he won two years earlier, was 35 year-old TV presenter Angharad Mair's fourth place in the 10,000m, and Canada based, Bridgend-born Jon Brown's second place in the men's event. Unfortunately for Welsh athletics, apart from his win in the Welsh boys cross-country championships in 1986, Jon has not taken advantage of his Welsh qualification and has opted for England.

Olympic 4 x 400m relay silver medallist Jamie Baulch had a good start to the year in 1997, taking the AAA indoor 200, and he followed that up with a fine 400 win in the World Indoor Trials in a new Welsh indoor record of 45.39 which still stands today. The former Newport Harrier then went on to win the silver in the 400 at the World Indoor Championships in Paris in 45.62, his first individual medal in a major senior event. In a scintillating indoor season, he set seven indoor personal bests from 60m through to 400m. Colin Jackson took second in the 60m hurdles to eventual Sydney Olympic champion Anier Garcia (Cuba), and Swansea's Hayley Tullett made her first appearance in a British vest setting an indoor best of 2:04.40, but this failed to get her to the final. Setting a new Welsh best in the pole vault of 3.90, Rhian Clarke failed to pass the qualifying stages. In the 1997 Welsh Games in May at Leckwith, which took the form of a match against Northern Ireland and an international select team, she again vaulted 3.90, and had to settle for second to Janine Whitlock who also cleared 3.90, and had the satisfaction of sharing with Whitlock the Welsh all-comers record. Two rarely run events, the 150 and 300m, were added to the programme to add some extra spice and both events, unsurprisingly, led to Welsh all-comers records. Scot Ian Mackie took the shorter event in 14.99, whilst Jamie Baulch took the longer race. "I'm happy to come away with a Welsh record......but someone's just pointed out that I'm probably the only Welsh athlete to have run the distance before....", he said afterwards. Cardiff based Darren Campbell, the future European 100m champion and Olympic 200m silver medallist took both 100 and 200m events for the international team. After two years in Newport, the Welsh Championships returned to Cwmbran on their traditional date of the third weekend in June, and saw a first Welsh senior title for 18 year-old Christian Malcolm, clocking 21.41 into a strong headwind to win the 200, whilst Tim Thomas of Swansea Harriers took his fifth pole vault title – his first came in 1991 as an eighteen year-old. 20 year-old Rhian Clark easily retained her vault title with 3.60, 5cms below her championship best winning leap the previous year.

Christian Malcolm emerges as the finest Welsh sprint prospect of all-time

Christian Malcolm gave a clear indication of his outstanding potential by becoming European junior 200m Champion in Yugoslavia in 1997. He also took the silver in the 100 behind England's Dwain Chambers, who won in a stupendous new world junior record of

10.06, with Christian becoming the youngest ever Welsh 100m record holder with 10.24 – five hundredths ahead of Colin Jackson's 1990 record. As a comparison, and whilst it must be appreciated that conditions have changed dramatically from the cinder tracks of yesteryear, Ken Jones clocked a Welsh record of 10.6 50 years earlier in the 1948 London Olympics. The following year, in the French town of Annecy Christian was crowned double sprint champion at the World Junior Championships as he blitzed the opposition in both finals to won gold in 10.12 and 20.44. For his efforts he was nominated as IAAF 'World Junior Athlete of the Year'. It was the first time that the sprint double had been achieved and at just 19 years of age he set his third Welsh senior 100m record clipping 0.12 off the record he set in Yugoslavia. The sprint star turned his back on a possible glittering football career to chase athletics glory and dreams. A Wales Youth international on the wing, he could have signed for Nottingham Forest and had a spell with Queens Park Rangers before finally deciding to take up athletics full time.

The 1998 Welsh Games held on a chilly evening at Leckwith saw Katherine Merry, still in her pre 400m specialist mode, give indications of future form in the event with a stadium record of 52.76, with Australia's Melissa Gainsford-Taylor taking both sprints also in stadium records. Colin Jackson made his first appearance at that year's Welsh Championships at Cwmbran since 1992 and took the 100m for the sixth time, his thirteenth title in total, whilst Christian Malcolm, a month ahead of his world junior sprint double, retained his 200m title. Shaun Pickering appeared in the championships for the last time and took his nineteenth title – the shot – with 19.14, a mere 1cm behind his championships best set in winning the previous year. Star performances in the women's events came from Catherine Murphy with a sprint double and Bristol's Sarah Moore who took the hammer for the seventh time - the sixth in succession. Despite the event being in its infancy, she has dominated the event in Wales during the 1990s and has taken the Welsh record from a modest 44.14 in 1992, to the very respectable 56.60 she set last year when taking the UK title.

Christian Malcolm celebrates his golden sprint double at the World Junior Championships in 1998.

At the AAA Championships at Birmingham towards the end of July 1998, Christian Stephenson won the 3,000m steeplechase title to follow in the long line of Welsh winners of this event - John Disley, John Davies, Roger Hackney and Justin Chaston whilst Paul Gray confirmed his fine form in becoming the first Welsh athlete to win the intermediate hurdles event since Phil Harries, ten years earlier. Cardiff-based, Scottish Commonwealth Games representative Martin Bell won the 10,000m walk event. Tara Krzywicki, daughter of Welsh soccer international Dick and a Welsh women's soccer international herself, took the 10,000m title at Bedford on July 5th ahead of Newport's Hayley Nash. However, Tara competes for England in athletics events. There was also a first AAA title for double Welsh 1,500 Champion Nick Comerford who took the 3,000 title at Sheffield in August.

The European Championships in Budapest saw Colin Jackson (110 hurdles) and Iwan Thomas (400m) win gold medals. Iwan and Jamie Baulch were members of the British 4x400 relay squad that won a bronze medal. Doug Turner ran the race of his life to clinch a silver medal in the 200. Despite going out in the heats Paul Gray broke his own Welsh record in the 400 hurdles with 49.16 which still stands today.

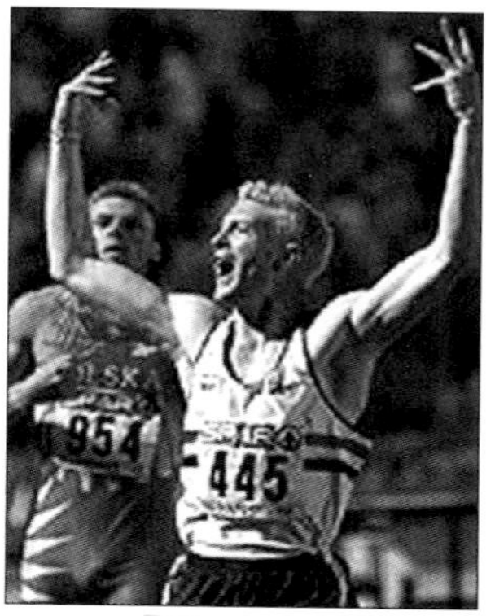

European gold for Iwan Thomas.

September normally sees the outdoor season nearly completed but two major meetings still remained for the top stars. At the beginning of the month the IAAF World Cup was held in Johannesburg. Iwan Thomas continued his fine form with a win in the 400m in 45.33, just ahead of American champion Jerome Young. Colin Jackson was just edged out in the sprint hurdles 13.10 to 13.11 by Falk Balzer.

The Commonwealth Games were held in Kuala Lumpur, Malaysia with the Welsh team returning with four medals. Iwan Thomas collected his third gold of the season in the 400 (Jamie Baulch finished fourth), Christian Malcolm won bronze in the 200 while Shaun Pickering finished his long career with a bronze in the shot. The 4x400 relay team of Iwan Thomas, Jamie Baulch, Paul Gray and Doug Turner also collected bronze. Young Matthew Elias also received a bronze medal having run in the heat of the relay. The major disappointment for the Welsh team was the withdrawal of team captain Colin Jackson.

The indoor season in 1999 ended in sensational style with the Principality creating history by winning two world titles in the space of 72 hours. Maebashi, Japan was the scene for the IAAF World Indoor Championships. On 5th March Colin Jackson just got the nod from American Reggie Torian with a time of 7.38 to win his first ever world indoor title. Two days later against all the odds Jamie Baulch claimed gold with a scintillating run in the 400m in 45.73 well clear of another American, Milton Campbell. He also gained a bronze in the 4 x 400 relay. Surprisingly, the Welsh senior championships had never been held in north Wales, but Colwyn Bay had the distinction in 1999 as Rhian Clark took her fourth successive pole vault title and Philippa Roles her sixth (fifth consecutive) discus title to give early indications of a possible challenge to the remarkable dominance in the event of Venissa Head, some twenty years earlier.

Colin Jackson took the 1999 AAA 110m hurdles for a record ninth time to beat the old record set by former UK record holder Don Finlay, who won his titles between 1932 and 1949. Jamie Baulch also took his first AAA championship in the 400m with 45.36, whilst Christian Stephenson retained his 3,000m steeplechase title, and Paul Jones of Colwyn Bay took the decathlon title with 6922 pts to become the first Welshman since Hywel Williams

© Mark Shearman

Tim Benjamin World Youth Champion.

in 1957 to win the event. His winning score was just short of the personal best he set earlier in the month when retaining his Welsh title at Cardiff with 6940 pts. In July at the World University Games in Palma de Mallorca Dawn Higgins ran the second leg in the 4 x 400 relay and helped claim a bronze medal for Britain and, at the European Junior Championships in August at Riga, outstanding sprinting prospect Tim Benjamin raced to a silver medal in the 200m with a wind assisted time of 20.60. However a month earlier at Bydgoscz, Poland at the IAAF World Youth Championship the Cardiff speedster won the gold medal with some distance to spare in a new British under 17 record time of 20.70.

Finding the move from junior to senior championship level relatively comfortable Christian Malcolm showed his class at the European under 23 Championships in Gothenburg. He gained two silver medals in the sprints as well as joining fellow Welsh sprinter Jamie Henthorn to bring home the gold medal for Britain in the 4 x 100m relay. In the 200m Christian was very unlucky not to have had a share at least in the gold medal. He was given exactly the same time, 20.47 as the declared winner John Ertzgaard of Norway. It was a good Championship for Welsh athletes with Matthew Elias, son of former long jump star John and Kathy, a former Welsh Schools' hurdles champion and now Chairman of Cardiff AAC, collecting a bronze medal as part of the British 4 x 400m team.

Wrexham hosted what will probably be the last-ever Welsh Games under floodlights in dreadful conditions in 1999, forty years after they were first inaugurated to keep alive the spirit of the 1958 Cardiff Empire Games. During this past four decades the Games have witnessed some of the finest moments in Welsh athletics, including Lynn Davies' classic 1965 battle with world record-holder Ralph Boston in front of 10,000 spectators at Cardiff's Maindy Stadium, and the appearances of most of the leading stars of British and indeed world athletics. Many reasons are cited for the demise of an event which at its height was classed as one of the best meetings in Britain, and these include, not surprisingly, the inability to attract a sponsor. More significantly, and ironically, they have fallen victim of the modern system, which the Games themselves helped to bring about. Heptathlon star Denise Lewis competed in the hurdles, high jump and shot and despite the conditions England's Lorraine Shaw set a new UK record in the hammer with 67.10 to bring down the curtain on this once proud event with a moment to savour.

A Powerful dream fulfilled at UWIC

The Millennium saw a new chapter within the sport in Wales as in January the National Indoor Athletics Centre was opened by Colin Jackson and Jamie Baulch at the Cyncoed campus of UWIC (University of Wales Institute, Cardiff). The £7m training and competition centre was built with the support of a £5.6m grant from the Sports Council for Wales's Sportlot Fund, the largest grant offered to date from that Fund. Facilities at the Centre include a 200m banked track, an eight-lane 60m sprint straight, six-lane 140m straight, high jump, long jump, triple jump, and three pole vault training areas, netted

© Ian Dixon

The new National Indoor Athletics Centre at UWIC.

indoor training areas for javelin, discus, hammer, and shot put. Sports medicine, physiotherapy and sports science support are also well catered for in the 700-seater arena. Little did Irish international triple jumper Sean Power realise when he came from Burton-on-Trent and comprehensive school teaching to begin lecturing at Cardiff College of Education (as UWIC was then called) in 1974, that he would be masterminding such a project. Says Sean: " I sketched out the design on a sheet of A3 in 1994, and the finished product is essentially the same. That gives me much satisfaction, but belies the enormous amount of work put in by a vast array of people to make it all happen".

Sean, who became a Cardiff AAC stalwart, and Welsh triple jump champion in 1980 (plus seven seconds and thirds) and now Head of the Centre for Performance Analysis at UWIC, is particularly proud that the first UKA High Performance Centre to be located outside of England will be based at the National Indoor Athletics Centre. "This is a tribute to the staff and an indication of the outstanding facilities we have at UWIC," he said. Still competing in the veteran ranks, he is a former world veteran's triple jump record holder and world champion in the over 50-age group in 1994. Remarkably, in the same year, at the age of 51, he finished second in the Welsh Championships, and was still competing for Cardiff in the British League until a few years ago. Whilst at his peak (best of 15.31) he competed in the shadow of the two all-time greats of Welsh triple jumping - John Phillips and Dave Wood (18 titles between them in 23 years) both of whom were students at the Cardiff College.

In the two-day Welsh indoor championships at NIAC in February the baton passed on to the younger brigade of athletes. 21 year-old Andrew Penk set new Welsh figures in the high jump with 2.16, while 20 year-old Natalie Lewis ran 2:11.55 for a new all-comers record in the 800m. In the under 17 800m Stephen Davies (16) raced away to win in a new Welsh age-group record of 1:58.14.

At the end of February the inaugural home countries senior international (the first ever-indoor international to be held in Wales) took place at NIAC along with the Schools' International Athletic Board under 16 international. The schools' match saw a convincing win for England whilst they were also victorious in the senior international. The highlight for Wales in the senior match was the new Welsh indoor pole vault record by Tim Thomas as he cleared 5.32, and numerous Welsh indoor all-comers records were beaten in a match, which augurs well for the future of the sport in Wales.

The same weekend, Christian Malcolm scorched to a sensational gold medal in Ghent to be crowned European Indoor 200 Champion winning in an emphatic 20.54 from the favoured outside lane. At just 20, he became only the third Briton, after Linford Christie in 1986 and Ade Mafe in 1989, to win the title. Fellow Welshman Jamie Henthorn found the pace too hot in the 60m and went out in the first round. 17-year-old Tim Benjamin was the baby of the team and broadened his experience further by taking part in his first senior championships. Despite his large frame not being suited to the tight turns, struggling and stumbling indoors, he did exceptionally well to reach the semi-finals to place fifth in 21.54 after a third in his heat in 21.27. The World Youth champion and European Junior silver medallist (over 200m outdoors in 1999), Tim's appearance in Ghent earned him the distinction of becoming the youngest Briton to compete in a senior championship since another sprinter, Ade Mafe, in 1984. Catherine Murphy reached the semi-finals of the 200m and finished third, just outside a final spot. Hayley Tullett went one better and reached the 3,000m final and was just outside her best as she finished seventh in a classy final won by Romania's Gabriela Szabo.

Darney's double

No Welsh athlete has ever won both AAA 5,000m and 10,000m titles - let alone in the same season! That is until Andres Jones from Aberaeron in 2000. The son of a Colombian mother and Welsh father, the 23 year-old firstly claimed the 10,000 title at Watford in July and then won the 5,000 crown in the main Championships and Olympic trials at Birmingham in August to book his place in the British team for Sydney. In fact it was the first time in 28 years for any athlete to win both titles in the same year. Christian Stephenson won his third AAA 3,000m steeplechase title in succession, but in a time just outside the time set by UKA for selection. Happily he subsequently achieved the standard and the two Paul Darney coached athletes were Sydney bound. Hayley Tullett also booked her Sydney place by capping a fine season with a win in the 1,500m. The 23 year-old Swansea Harrier, having her best season to date had taken 2.2 seconds off Angela Tooby's twelve-year 3,000m Welsh record with 8:45.39 at Gateshead in July.

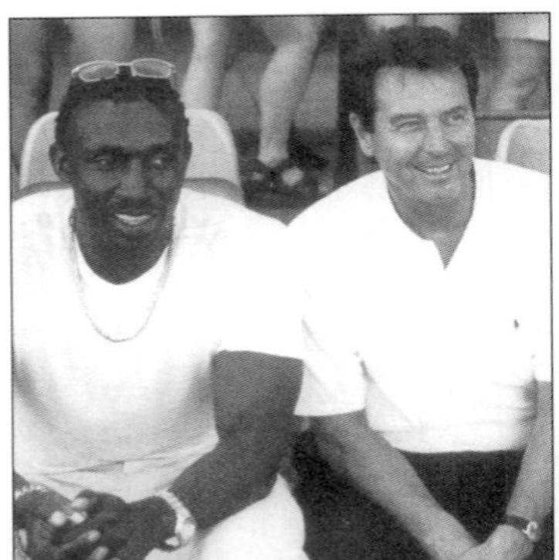

Two Olympic champions, Linford Christie (1992 Barcelona) and Lynn Davies (1964 Tokyo) enjoy the 2000 Welsh Championships at Cwmbran.

Although taking his fifth Welsh title at Cwmbran in 2000, Jamie Baulch won his first 400 crown, whilst Christian Malcolm and Catherine Murphy scored sprint doubles. Baulch and Malcolm were key members of the British team that narrowly won the European Cup in Gateshead in July, with Malcolm taking the 200 and Baulch the 400 as well as running the last leg in the long relay.

Pen Portrait - Jamie Baulch (Newport H & Cardiff AAC)

The Olympic form of Jamie Baulch was a total mystery in Sydney. However Jamie, who is a trained architectural technician with a son called Jay can look at his career to date with a great deal of satisfaction. He is a full time athlete but he is no ordinary guy. With his good looks and notorious hairstyle, he has been dubbed the "Darling of the Track".

Prior to his disappointing run in the heats in Sydney, the Nottingham born athlete had won a medal at every major championship in which he had competed. At the relative tender age of twenty-six, he was an Olympic silver medallist and World indoor champion.

As one of the world's fastest 400 runners his career started with success in the Welsh Schools' Championships. In 1989 he won the under 17 age group 200, followed by a sprint double at the Welsh youths' championships. At the end of the season he ran his first ever 400 and recorded a promising 50.4. The following year he went on to complete the sprint double at the Welsh Schools' championships with another end of season 'fact finding' 400 completed in 49.5.

Jamie had a brilliant junior career starting in 1991 when he competed for Britain three times including the European Junior Championships in Thessalonica where he finished seventh over 200 and gained his first ever medal with a silver as part of the 4 x 100 relay team. Prior to the championships he had completed the Welsh Schools' senior sprint double which was quickly followed by his first Welsh senior title over 200 to add to the junior victory over the same distance. Such was his form that Jamie set a Welsh senior and junior record of 21.18 at Salamanca, Spain in July.

In 1992 Jamie competed in the World junior championships in Seoul and was placed fourth in the 200 final in 21.04, having set new Welsh senior and junior records in the semi-final with a time of 20.91. He won his first ever-gold medal in the sprint relay. Jamie also made his British senior debut in the World Cup in Havana as part of the sprint relay squad, finishing fourth.

He ran a spectacular leg in the 4 x 400 team in the World Cup at Crystal Palace in 1994 to help Britain to victory. His potential over the one lap was suddenly discovered and he started to compete more at 400 breaking the Welsh record with a time of 45.14. At the Commonwealth Games in Victoria he lowered his own Welsh 200 record to 20.84 despite going out in the heats – his fifth Welsh record in the event in three years.

However it was the second half of the 1995 season when he made his impression at international level. His progress, unfortunately, came too late to gain World championship selection, yet in August he defeated Roger Black and Darnell Hall (USA), both of whom had won medals at those championships. He had run some superb relay legs for club and country and at the end of the season he was ranked third in the UK and the top under 23 athlete.

The early months of 1996 were spent in Australia and he won their national title. In July at Lausanne he ran his best ever time of 44.57, setting his fifth Welsh record and despite just missing out on an individual place on the Atlanta Olympic team, he was part of the exceptionally strong 4 x 400 team, which secured an Olympic silver medal and a new European record. His 44.57 stood as the Welsh record until beaten by Iwan Thomas in 1997 with 44.49.

His short stride and running style is ideal for indoor running and in 1997 after having spent the winter again in Australia, Jamie enjoyed more sublime form setting

seven personal bests over 60, 200, and 400, and in doing so broke Todd Bennett's 12-year-old British and Commonwealth indoor record for 400 with a time of 45.39. Jamie's superior racing form continued into the 1997 World indoor championships where he won the silver medal behind Sunday Bada of Nigeria. Outdoors the highlight was the World Championships in Athens where he reached the final and was also a member of the relay team that won the silver medal.

1998 proved a difficult season as he became sick and as a result only went to the European Championships as a member of the relay squad. Nevertheless, his perseverance paid off with a gold medal in the relay at the World Cup in South Africa. The Commonwealth Games in Kuala Lumpur saw Jamie almost back to his best and he narrowly missed out on a bronze medal in the individual 400, but returned home with a bronze in the relay. The individual gold, of course, went to compatriot Iwan Thomas.

The highlight of his career so far was on March 7th 1999 at the World indoor championships in Maebashi, Japan. He had a great indoor season winning all five of his competitions culminating with a gold in Japan with a time of 45.73. During the outdoor season Jamie ran consistently and in a superb race at the AAA championships and World trials, he stormed home to win his first national outdoor title in 45.36 and secure his place at the World Championships in Seville. It was always going to be difficult to emulate his indoor performance but Jamie made it to the final, which was won in a sensational world record by Michael Johnson in 43.12. It was for Jamie "the greatest sporting moment in history and I was part of it".

Since finishing second in the Welsh Schools trampoline championships in 1991 and falling at the 1994 European indoor championships, Jamie has come a long way. Apart from his growing collection of medals, now totalling nine, his media work continues to flourish and his bubbly personality make him a very attractive proposition to the media and sponsors alike. He has completed two TV series presenting children's sports programme called 'Energize' which had an audience of over two million. With the added bonus of being a member of 'Team Linford', he will add to his current total of twenty-two British vests and more success will come to this very patriotic Welshman. The more than colourful character can be summed up in three words – fun, dedicated, lively. There's more to come from Jamie!

The 2000 season ended with Tim Benjamin winning the 200m bronze medal in the world junior championships in Santiago, Chile in 20.94, and a gold medal as part of the winning British sprint relay team. However, the performance which caught everyone's eye was the 10th place in the triple jump by Steve Shalders in a new Welsh record of 15.99, which erased Dave Woods' 1984 mark of 15.90 from the books. Another triple jump performance of note came from Charles Madeira-Cole in the Welsh Championships as the 22 year-old took his fifth successive title with 15.38. The future of Welsh triple jumping looks bright with this pair. Two other performances that caught the eye were wins from Kathryn Williams (400m hurdles) and Anna Leyshon (pole vault) both of whom followed in the footsteps of their famous fathers (JJ and Wyn) in taking senior titles.

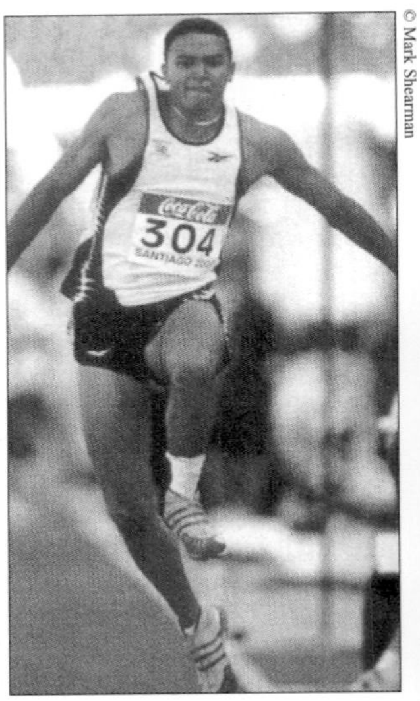

© Mark Shearman

Steven Shalders seen here competing in the World Junior Championships.

Tanni and Chris at the forefront of British disabled sport.

Sport for disabled athletes has become prominent during the last decade and rightly so. Leading the advance both in competitive terms and in bringing a high profile to the sport both in Wales and in Britain has been Tanni Grey-Thompson.

Pen Portrait - Tanni Grey-Thompson, MBE, OBE

Tanni-Grey Thompson celebrates her fourth gold medal at the 2000 Paralympics in Sydney. She was also honoured by carrying the British flag at the Closing Ceremony.

With the popularity of mass participation races in the early 80s ever increasing, so did the profile of wheelchair athletes who took part in these races all over the world.

To many people, Tanni is the face of disabled sport. No matter what the colour of her hair (and her mother was said to be unhappy with the bright orange style she sported in Sydney 2000!) she is instantly recognisable. The sight of the 31-year-old wheelchair athlete crossing the finishing line with a fist clenched in triumph was one of the most enduring images to emerge from the Sydney Paralympics.

Tanni has never let disability stand in her way of sporting fulfilment. Sport provided her at a very young age with an outlet for her enthusiasm. Born with spina bifida, she needed a wheelchair by the age of eight. After initially avoiding special school lessons, she found they did at least introduce her to the sporting horizons available to her. A born competitor, she tried horse-riding and was then introduced to archery, basketball, swimming and tennis. Although her competitive spirit made her unsuited to team games, she never looked back in athletics. Her first sorties into wheelchair racing were characteristically successful and she was selected for the Welsh squad for the junior games in 1981. From there she never looked back and her achievements were all chronicled in her book about her life in 1996 – *Tanni, the Inspiring Story of a World-class Athlete*. The talented sportswoman has won four London Marathons and gold medals at the last three Paralympic Games.

Tanni has twice been voted BBC Wales Sports Personality of the Year, to take her place amongst the great Welsh sports stars, past and present. Her services to disabled sport have also seen her honoured with the MBE and in 1999 the OBE. In 1993 she became part of the Welsh Sports Hall of Fame.

As impressive as the sheer volume of her success is the variety of events at which she excels. Not many athletes compete from 100m up through the distances to marathon length but that is the range Tanni races between, and invariably wins. Her versatility was shown at the 1992 Paralympics in Barcelona where she won no fewer than four gold medals.

Tanni has been performing at world-class level for more than ten years, most of those as Tanni Grey. She married fellow wheelchair athlete Ian Thompson, a record holder at 5,000m, in May 1999. They met through athletics and it is in her sport that she is most comfortable. She has an intense competitive edge and dedicated commitment in training. Even on honeymoon in Switzerland, the newly-weds found

time for training with Swiss athletes. However her previous achievements were put in the shadow, as she became the star of the Paralympic Games in Sydney, where she was the British flagbearer in front of 87,000 spectators. Four times - from 100m to 800m - she struck gold, surpassing her wildest pre - Games dreams of two gold and two silver. The Cardiff born athlete thought she only had a good chance of winning the 200m and 400m. Her gold in the 100m was the most difficult but it gave her the most satisfaction, as the panel for the race didn't originally select her. However having competed in the four events at the previous Games, she was determined to go for a clean sweep.

History shows that Tanni has done all there is to do in her sport after winning medals at every Paralympics since 1988. She holds twenty world records and in Seoul, as an inexperienced 19-year-old she took bronze in the 400m to start her Olympic collection.

Four years later she won four gold medals in Barcelona, set new world records and was named track athlete of the Games. In Atlanta in 1996 she won one gold and three silvers. Prior to travelling to Atlanta she had won four gold in the World Disabled Games in Berlin.

Her achievements on the track has meant that she has been in great demand off it as well working in development for UK Athletics in Birmingham and working with young children.

Now having been there, done that and bought enough T-shirts to fill her wardrobe for a long time to come Tanni has just one championship on her list to conquer. The 800m has been integrated into the mainstream Games at the Commonwealth Games in Manchester in 2002. She has the ambition in Manchester of competing in the Welsh team with Colin Jackson with the two bowing out in style on top of the rostrum. Everyone in Welsh athletics would like to see that ....

Theresa John and Chris Hallam have also been at the forefront of sport for the disabled, and like Tanni have been admitted to the Welsh Sports Hall of Fame. Theresa won three mini Olympic and European gold medals, captained Great Britain and was one of the world's leading athletes for people with learning difficulties ten years ago. Chris battled his way to the top to become one of Britain's most distinguished and successful disabled athletes.

Pen Portrait - Chris Hallam, MBE

1984 was a poor year for Welsh athletes at the Olympic Games. However one Welshman did strike gold, and to cap his great performance he also claimed his fourth world record in the event as Cwmbran based Chris swam to a gold in the 50m breast stroke in the Paraplegic Olympics in Stoke Mandeville.

Chris has been confined to a wheelchair since he was fourteen years old after being involved in a motorcycle accident and breaking his back and sport became the main concern of his life. Before the accident he was a highly promising swimmer. He has dedicated himself to the pursuit of excellence and his achievements have meant a higher profile for his sport and he excels in a bewildering variety of sports from his wheelchair.

When he turned his attention to track athletics he broke all the British records

from 100m to 5,000m. In 1984 he set six British records while winning the 100, 200, 400, 800, 1,500, and 5,000 at the British national championships. However his first love was road racing and in 1985 he won the London Marathon and repeated that victory in 1987 with another outstanding performance reducing his own British wheelchair record to 2:08:34.

At the 1986 British Paraplegic Games in Stoke Mandeville he won eight gold, a silver and two bronze medals which included six victories in the pool and two on the track. His achievements were recognised as he was nominated the British Disabled Sportsman of the Year. At the Paralympics in Seoul in 1988 he won silver in the 1,500m. During the year he broke the world 100 and 200m records and for his sporting brilliance he was awarded the MBE in 1989. His coach is former AAA decathlon champion – and winner of thirteen Welsh track and field titles – Hywel Williams.

Chris Hallam MBE

Fine performances from Welsh athletes in Sydney Paralympics

The Paralympics in Sydney 2000 was undoubtedly a huge success as far as presenting the event to the whole world was concerned with massive audience figures within Stadium Australia and other venues. It was Britain's most successful ever, finishing second in the medal table to the Australians with a total of 141 medals (41 Gold, 43 Silver and 47 Bronze).

The British athletics contingent apart from Tanni Grey-Thompson, included fellow Welsh athletes, Beverly Jones, Lloyd Upsdell, Stephen Herbert, Tracy Hinton and James Wagstaff.

Beverley Jones was in fine form prior to Sydney as she claimed a unique double in the English Open in May, winning the 100 and discus. In Sydney she reached the final of both the 100 and 200, finishing just outside the medals in the shorter sprint, in fourth, while in the 200 she was eighth.

For blind athlete Tracy Hinton it was her third Paralympics and took her total of medals to six. In Barcelona in 1992 she won a bronze in the 100 and silver in both the 200 and 400. Atlanta four years later was a disappointment with no podium placing.

However after the Games she met James Wagstaff and they soon became known as 'Little and Large' in Sydney. At 6'4 and nearly sixteen stones the former UWIC back row and Welsh University cap became the 'guide runner' for the eight stone tax officer from Llanedeyrn, Cardiff. Prior to Sydney the partnership had won bronze in the 1997 European Blind Championships in the 200 in Italy, another bronze in Madrid at the World Championships in the 400 and a gold in the 800 at the European championships in Portugal as well as silver medals in the 200 and 400 at the same venue. For four years James had been Tracy's guide, racing stride for stride to medals around the world and Sydney was the last time that they would be together. They both set emotions aside as they won bronze medals in the 200 and 400 while a silver was the reward in a tough 800 final.

Stephen Herbert is part of the Jamie Baulch and Katherine Merry training group and his fine-tuning by the group was rewarded with a victory in May at the English Open in the 100 and runner-up spot in the 200. His first Paralympics saw him reach the final of both sprints with a sixth in the 100 and eighth in the 200. However in the relay he was lead off man and gained a fine silver medal.

If Tanni was the established worldwide star, another Welsh athlete made a strong claim to take over her superstar status in the future. As a 15-year old, Essex based Lloyd Upsdell made his mark in the sport when he competed in August 1998 at the World championships in Birmingham and claimed gold medals in the 100 and 200, while smashing the world record in the 200 with a time of 28.96. A year later at the European Cerebral Palsy Championships at Nottingham he won the sprint double again while improving his global record in the 200 with a time of 28.76. His build up to Sydney started a year earlier as he took part at Sydney in the Southern Cross championships. He again won the sprint double but this time he also broke the world record for the 100 with a time of 13.52 as well as improving again his own mark in the 200 with a time of 27.30. His double gold medal performances in Sydney stopped the crowds as fans mobbed him for his autograph and pictures with his medals. The blonde 15 stone powerhouse became one of the stars as he took 0.38 off his own 100 record finishing in 13.46 as well as improving the 200 record to 27.17. He also won silver in the relay along with Stephen Herbert. Father Geoff, originally from Whitchurch, Cardiff was a busy man in Sydney making sure that grandmother back in Cardiff had the video recorder in full working order.

Chapter 4

Welsh Athletics Devolution

Whilst the earliest reference we can trace to amateur athletics in Wales is 1860, when John Chambers organised a sports meeting in the grounds of his father's house in Aberystwyth, it was not until 88 years later that a single body covering the administration of track and field athletics and road running in Wales came about with the formation of the Welsh AAA. And it took a further 42 years before the establishment of the AAW, which also encompassed cross-country and fell running.

It was not until 1948, when the Welsh Amateur Athletic Association (Welsh AAA) was formed, that track and field athletics and road running in Wales (as opposed to cross-country and fell running, which is covered elsewhere in this book) had a single voice, controlling all aspects of the sport in Wales. Until this time, various areas of the Amateur Athletic Association (of England) - the AAA – had control. The "breakaway" of the Welsh Counties from the AAA was the first fundamental change in structure of the sport in Britain since the formation of the AAA in 1880.

From 1894 until 1948, south Wales - effectively Glamorgan, Monmouthshire and parts of west Wales - was controlled either by the Southern Counties AAA (of England) or the Southern Committee of the English AAA through a South Wales & Monmouthshire AAA; north Wales (Anglesey, Flint, Denbigh, and "North" Caernarvonshire) was a district of the English Northern Counties AA; and the English Midland Counties AAA controlled Merionethshire, "South" Caernarvonshire, Radnorshire, Cardiganshire and Montgomeryshire. The Southern Committee of the AAA (or its South Wales Committee) and the Midland Counties AAA also controlled Brecknockshire, Carmarthenshire and Pembrokeshire, at various times.

However, whilst the formation of a Welsh AAA in 1948 was a much welcomed move, the arrangement still left Wales one-step away from true autonomy, as the new body did not have the same powers as England, Scotland and Northern Ireland. This was because the new structure purely gave Wales the same authority as the Southern, Northern, Midland and Eastern Counties of England, in other words, in athletics administration terms; Wales was still an area of England. The third Lord Aberdare, the only Welshman to be a member of the International Olympic Committee, (member of the executive 1931-1951) and a member of the organising committee for the 1948 Olympics, was elected the first patron. He died in 1957.

Women's events were a feature of open and league meetings during the 1930s and therefore there was a need for separate bodies. As a result the Welsh Women's AAA was formed in 1951 and the Welsh Women's Cross Country Association in 1967, which subsequently merged with the (Men's) Welsh Cross Country Association in 1974. At a meeting of the Executive Committee of the Welsh AAA on 11 November 1950 it was reported that application had been made to the Women's AAA for advice on the formation of a Welsh Women's AAA which, it was felt would "provide the necessary incentive for the development of athletics for women in Wales". The number of women and girls taking part in athletics had been steadily increasing in recent years and both Glamorgan and Monmouthshire had held county championships for women and each had established a Secondary Schools Girls' AAA. Earlier attempts to form a Welsh Women's AAA had failed through a lack of affiliations in Wales but it was now felt that the formation of such a body was possible and that a Welsh Honorary Secretary should be appointed. A strong case would need to be presented to the Women's AAA in support of the proposal.

A special meeting of clubs was held at Cardiff YMCA on 24 May 1951 in which it was reported that the General Committee of the English Women's AAA had agreed upon the formation of the Welsh Women's AAA. This would be confirmed at their next AGM and the new organisation would come within the framework of the Women's AAA. The special meeting unanimously supported the formal proposal that such body be formed and inaugural officers of the new association were provisionally appointed. The first official meeting of the WWAAA was held in Cardiff on 16 July 1951 at which the provisional appointments were confirmed. The management of the newly formed association was entrusted to a committee comprising Miss G.A.Thomas of Rhondda (Chairman), Miss J. Cook of Newport (Hon Secretary) and Miss O.I. Brind of Barry (Treasurer and Assistant Secretary). An advisory panel of six senior members of the Welsh AAA would assist them. A constitution was drawn up and the following year the first Welsh Women's Championships were held.

After 1948 Welsh athletics effectively continued to be a region of England until Wales led the way in the United Kingdom with the formation of a fully integrated athletics body – the Athletics Association of Wales (AAW) in 1990. What was significant about this step was that the AAW was a body covering all of the "athletics" organisations in Wales: The Welsh AAA, Welsh Cross Country Association, The Welsh Women's AAA, and the Welsh Fell Running Association. This arrangement primarily came about due to the formation of the British Athletic Federation (BAF), the predecessor of the current UK organising body, UK Athletics. However, the other organising bodies (AAA, Women's AAA, Scottish AAA and Northern Ireland AAA) within the UK were reluctant initially to follow the Welsh move, and continued to operate for some time with individual associations controlling cross country and men's and women's athletics.

In fact the first moves toward some form of amalgamation of the three Welsh governing bodies (Welsh AAA, Welsh Women's AAA & Welsh CCA) came about in March 1987 when the Welsh AAA set up its office at Morfa Stadium, Swansea. The office was made available to the other two associations and some of the committees of the various bodies (championships, international and officials' committees) operated as joint committees. There was no formal merging but there was an element of co-operation.

Later in 1987 the Welsh Athletics Council was formed. This body consisted of representatives from each of the three associations and it was given the task of producing an acceptable constitution for a proposed single governing body. This constitution was duly drawn up and circulated to all clubs in 1988. One complication was that the Welsh AAA was still an area association of the AAA, which had made provisional plans to merge with the Women's AAA and form the English AA. To enable this merger to take place it would be necessary for the Welsh AAA to secede from the AAA, which they were reluctant to do until the formation of the BAF as the new governing body for athletics in the UK. On 8 April 1989 a combined EGM of the three Welsh bodies was held at the National Sports Centre in Cardiff at which the formation of a single governing body was formally approved and the draft constitution accepted. The inaugural officers of the new body, to be called the Athletics Association of Wales (AAW) were elected: President – Frank Ireland (Barry and Vale H), Chairman – Lynette Harries, Hon Secretary – Dr W.A.L (Bill) Evans (Cardiff AAC), Hon Treasurer – Dr Hedydd Davies (Carmarthen H). The AAW would support ten committees to cover the various aspects of the sport, which were: Track & Field, Road Running, Rules & Eligibility, Selection, Women's Commission, Cross Country, Coaching, Officials, Junior Commission and Development Committee. In addition there was a Management Board which met monthly to oversee the day to day running of the sport, and a Council which was a quarterly meeting at which clubs were entitled to be represented.

Single governing body at last as AAW becomes a reality

The AAW became fully operational on 17 February 1990 and held its first AGM at Wrexham on 28 October that year. As the BAF had still not yet been formed the Welsh AAA was technically still in existence as an area of the AAA even though its authority to govern the sport in Wales had been handed over to the new body. This anomaly was finally resolved when the BAF came into being on 1 October 1991 at which point the Welsh AAA seceded from the AAA in return for a financial consideration of £100,000. The money was passed over to the AAW and the Welsh AAA was then formally wound up.

Once the AAW was finally up and running two individuals who had figured prominently in its creation stood down. Scottish born Margaret Elgie, assistant secretary, had been a leading figure in Welsh women's athletics since the mid 1970s. In 1975 she took over the reins as Secretary of the Welsh Women's AAA from Raye Courtney and held that post until the merger.

Pen Portrait - Margaret Elgie (1935-2000)

The year 2000 was brought to a sad close by the death of Margaret Elgie. Her involvement in athletics began in the early 1960s on a grass track at RAF Leuchars, in Scotland holding a stopwatch, in all weathers, while husband Tony was training. A short while afterwards, unknown to Tony, she had arranged for him to join the local athletics club at Dundee. Even in those early days she showed that she was going to be a good organiser.

She would travel with, and support Tony whenever he was racing and gradually over a period of time she became involved in the administration of the sport. In the mid 70's she was eventually persuaded to stand for the office of Secretary of the Welsh Women's AAA's, a post she was successful in gaining. Tony achieved much success as an 800m runner, and much of this due to Margaret's guidance and support. Tony retired with a personal best of 1:51.0 set in 1970.

She represented Wales on the British Amateur Athletic Board – the then UK governing body where the question was once asked by a Scottish delegate "Mr Chairman, is the lady on my right representing the Scottish AAA's or the Welsh AAA's ?" Her broad Scottish accent clearly confusing her fellow countryman. Later when she became Welsh team manager she would often say to visiting officials "As

you can clearly see, I'm the Welsh team manager" and always with a twinkle in her eye.

When the BAF was formed she sat on that management board, and was also a member of the steering committee that examined the subvention system of payment for athletes. Previous to this, it was all done "under the table" in unmarked brown envelopes.

Back in Wales, together with fellow officers of the association, she was instrumental in the joining of the Welsh Women's AAA's and the Welsh AAA's. It is difficult to imagine in those days that the men and the women would have separate fixtures both home and abroad. The newly formed AAW was to become a blue print for other areas of the United Kingdom to follow.

Margaret held positions in athletics at all levels from Team Administrator to Team Manager at both Welsh and British levels. She was British Team Manager on a number of occasions and was Welsh Team Manager, along with Dave Williams at the Commonwealth Games, 1986 in Edinburgh and 1990 in Auckland.

Following the Games in Auckland she stepped down from her position as Welsh Team Manager. Whilst she still possessed the ability and energy to continue the job, she selflessly thought that it was time for someone else to pick up the reins.

She then entered the world of drug testing and joined the Drug Testing Scheme in the early 1990s working closely with the Sports Council for Wales. Once again, her thoroughness and organisational skills quickly became apparent and Margaret was appointed as the National Co-ordinator for Wales covering all sports that were financially supported by the now, Welsh Institute of Sport. She was one of the testers selected to go to the British Olympic Training Camp in Tallahasee in 1995. In 1998 she finally resigned from the drug-testing scene when her illness had begun to take its toll.

Margaret Elgie possessed the very highest personal standards and she had the respect of both officials and athletes alike and which she had deservedly earned. Despite being small in stature she possessed the heart of a lion and even with her dry sense of humour she always had a sense of justice and fair play.

Bill Evans (Cardiff AAC) 192?-1995

Dr W.A.L. (Bill) Evans held many senior posts in both Welsh and British athletics and was the first secretary of the AAW. Secretary of the Welsh AAA for 15 years (1974-1989) he was chairman of the BAAB from 1980-1984 and was head of delegation to the British team at the 1984 Olympic Games in Los Angeles. Later he became the first Welshman to be elected Chairman of the AAA (1989 – 1991) and was instrumental in bringing about the formation of BAF, of which he was Chairman from 1991-1994, at the same time as he was heavily involved in the creation of the single governing body in Wales. In recognition of his services to Welsh athletics he was accorded life membership of the AAW. Bill came into athletics relatively late in life, and developed his interest in the sport in the early 1970s through the activities of his son Paul, who was an outstanding junior sprinter. His first administrative post was as secretary of Cardiff AAC in the early 1970s before becoming Chairman. Such was his modesty and unassuming nature, whilst occupying the most senior role in British athletics, he could be still found on a

Monday and Thursday evening serving coffee and tea in the Cardiff club room at Maindy Stadium along with his wife Kath, also a former Cardiff Chairman.

Uniquely, another Cardiff stalwart, John Lister, the winner of twelve Welsh titles throughout his competitive career, who has been treasurer of the Cardiff club, apart from two years, since 1968, became the first BAF treasurer. He was also treasurer of the AAA between 1986 and 1991. Nowadays, he is a leading light in the European Athletic Association, where he is a member of the EAA Council and Chairman of its marketing committee He is the organising delegate - effectively the organiser - for the 2002 European Championships in Munich.

John Lister

In the early part of 1996 the Sports Council for Wales (SCW) conducted a survey into the state of athletics in Wales. While the SCW had welcomed the creation of a single governing body for athletics in Wales there were still concerns over the way in which the sport was being run. As the SCW was the major source of financing for Welsh athletics its perception on how the sport organised itself was significant. The survey was held throughout Wales and the views were sought of everyone involved in the sport, in whatever capacity. On 20 July 1996 the AAW held an EGM at the Welsh Institute of Sport (formerly the National Sports Centre) in Cardiff at which the findings of the survey and consequent recommendations by the SCW were considered. Among these were the appointment of a Chief Executive Officer and the division of Wales into eight administrative regions. Eventually it was decided to accept the proposals in principle subject to review by a working party. Four people were elected to form the working party: George Crump, David Samuel, Peter Morris and Alan Currie. Later, four others with expertise in particular aspects of the sport, Hilary Thomas, Tom Jones, John Filce and Clive Williams, were co-opted and the panel then met on two occasions.

After their deliberations at Gwbert on Sea and later at Hereford the working party presented their proposals to an EGM of the AAW in June of 1997. The appointment of a Chief Executive Officer was seen as a key element in the development of the sport in Wales and this was one of the major recommendations. All the proposals were considered individually. Some were rejected but enough were accepted to bring about a significant change in the administration of athletics in Wales. The appointment of a CEO was endorsed as well as the division of Wales into four regions, north, south, east and west (rather than the eight proposed by the SCW) each with a regional board and with representation on the Management Board. The unwieldy number of committees was drastically reduced to four with the proviso that facilitators would be appointed to cater for specific activities.

David Turner, previously with the Sports Council of Wales was the first CEO appointed, to be followed in 1998 by the present incumbent, as Director of Athletics, Steve Brace, one of Wales' finest marathon runners. So, after a century of control and much hard work by volunteers and amateur officials, for much of the time fighting off the "scourge" of professional athletics, amateur athletics in Wales had turned full circle with the much needed appointment of a professional administrator.

Celtic Manor and Sir Terry to the rescue ....

The launch of the Celtic Manor Resort sponsorship package of Welsh athletics.
Pictured from left to right are: David Moorcroft (Chief Executive UK Athletics), Steve Brace (AAW Director of Athletics), Lynette Harries (AAW Chairman), Gareth Davies (Chairman Sports Council for Wales) and Terry Matthews of Celtic Manor Resort.

In April 2000 Welsh athletics was celebrating one of the most amazing sponsorship deals in the sport's history. The future of the sport was secured by a five-year package worth around £300,000 in financial terms but of inestimable value to the morale of the sport. The Celtic Manor Resort in Newport under the leadership of Resort Chairman Terry (later Sir Terry) Matthews came to the rescue as the Association was due to lose its headquarters at the Morfa Stadium in Swansea. The offices AAW had occupied for the past 13 years was to be demolished to make way for a football and rugby stadium with no facilities for athletics. The Celtic Manor deal provided a new office and £25,000 a year grant. That financial contribution was doubled in its first year by the largest ever Sportsmatch award by the Sports Council for Wales with AAW able to reapply for further match funding each year.

In the beginning .... Newport and Caernarvon to the fore

One of the first references to Wales in the AAA (of England) minutes, apart from the presence of Richard Mullock of Newport Athletic Club and John Chambers at the formation of the AAA in 1880, is in the minutes of the AAA General Committee of 14th August 1883. The entry states that Welsh clubs with voting rights were Newport Monmouth AC, Caernarvon AC and "Swansea Club".

It is not clear how Wales was controlled for the next three years but at the Southern Committee of the AAA in 1886, W. Petherbridge of Newport AC was appointed as "local hon. Officer" for Newport and Cardiff District, with responsibility for "Lydney (!), Bridgend, Merthyr Tydvil and intervening district." At the next meeting on 25 February 1887, W. Bryant (Hon. Sec. Swansea Football, Cricket and AC) was "duly appointed Honorary Local Officer for the Swansea District, such district to comprise the counties of

Pembroke, Carmarthen, and Brecknock, and that part of Glamorganshire west of Bridgend and Merthyr Tydvil". At this time, the Northern Counties AA of England controlled the north Wales counties, and presumably the mid Wales counties were similarly controlled by the English Midland Counties AAA.

Although "devolution" did not come to Wales until 1948, as early as the AAA General Committee meeting of 9th December 1893, a petition was presented by several south Wales clubs to form a "branch" of the AAA to govern athletics in Wales. In fact this took another 55 years to achieve, for the decision taken that day was to empower the Southern Committee of the AAA to appoint a committee for South Wales and Monmouthshire – effectively covering Glamorgan, Monmouthshire and a "small" part of west Wales. W. Clifford Phillips of Newport Athletic Club was the first appointed delegate from the South Wales & Monmouthshire Committee to the Southern Committee of the AAA in 1894. Clifford Phillips was a member of the well-known Newport brewers of the same name who were generous benefactors to Newport Athletic Club. AAA minutes record that Mr. Phillips asked for and got £15 for the "working expenses" of the South Wales Committee. As far as is known, other areas of Wales, such as north and mid Wales did not enjoy similar status, but continued to be part of the English Midland and Northern Counties. In 1906, Dr. E. Lewys-Lloyd (Merionethshire and south Caernavonshire) and A.J. Matthews (Radnor) were the appointed representatives for their counties to the Midland Counties AAA of England.

Given the preceding detail, it is interesting to note that the South Wales Committee organised Welsh Championships. Indeed, championships programmes from 1907, when the first fully integrated championships were held, refer to the championships as the "Welsh Amateur Championships, promoted by the South Wales and Monmouthshire Executive Committee of the AAA". However, as can be seen from the results, there are very few representatives from north and mid Wales. Scrutiny of the programmes also fails to show any competitors from mid or north Wales during the early years, so it is open to question if the championships received sufficient publicity in the counties controlled by the English Midland and Northern Counties, to truly qualify as Welsh championships. There is a pointer in the AAA General Committee minutes of 11th December 1897, however, when the South Wales Committee was granted permission to arrange international meetings with the Scottish and Irish AAA's provided that the Northern and Midland Committees (of the AAA) was each granted one seat on the Welsh Committee of management for the meetings. It is likely therefore that a similar arrangement existed for championships, although minutes of the South Wales committee from 1937 to 1948 do not show any representatives from mid or north Wales. At this point it is worth noting that it has not been possible to locate minutes of the South Wales & Mon Committee prior to 1937, and this has resulted in a great deal of "piecing together" the activity of earlier years. Attempts to find more formal details of north Wales activity in the formative years have also been extremely difficult.

The Welsh Cross Country Association (WCCA), formed in 1896 was an autonomous body directly affiliated to the International Cross Country Union, and as such operated independently of the summer sport. It continued in this way until the formation of the AAW in 1990, and this aspect is covered in more detail in Chapter six.

So, apart from the WCCA, Wales was governed in athletics terms by various regions of the (English) AAA for summer track and field athletics and road running up until the formation of the Welsh AAA in 1948. This may be explained by the fact that at the time, in legal terms, Wales was considered to be part of England, whilst Scotland and Ireland had separate identities. Indeed in the Welsh AAA General Committee minutes of 8th March

1950, Cyril Howell, the then hon. Secretary, said that from an athletics viewpoint, Wales was part of "England and Wales"! At this meeting the qualification for competing in the Welsh championships and for representing Wales was expanded to include birth in Wales of both parents.

English Counties oppose home rule for Wales

There were several further moves during the early part of the last century to allow Wales to manage its own affairs for track and field, including at the AAA General Committee of 3 June 1905, when a request for further powers for Wales and the formation of a Welsh AAA was "considered", but not agreed to. It was referred back to the English Southern Counties for consideration. Apparently, the English Northern and Midland Counties were opposed to these proposals.

It took until 1938 for a concerted effort to be made by the South Wales & Mon AAA (as the South Wales Committee was now known) to bring home rule to Wales, when a memorandum was submitted to the Southern Counties AAA requesting that a governing body be set up to control "summer" athletics in the Principality. The President of the South Wales & Mon AAA, Bill Facey (Newport AC), Eddie O'Donnell (Treasurer) and Cyril Howell, the Secretary – both of Roath H; had met the committee of the Southern Counties AAA in London to press home the claims for a Welsh association. It appears that outline approval was given in 1939, but due to the outbreak of the Second World War, athletics devolution did not occur until approval at the AAA AGM of 1948. Although the South Wales and Mon minutes of 3rd December 1947 reported that on 4th October 1947, the AAA General Committee had approved the formation of the Welsh AAA "to include Monmouthshire" with the same duties and powers as the Northern and Midland Associations (of England). The South Wales minutes of 23rd January 1946 report that: "both the Northern and Midland Counties had readily consented for their Welsh Counties to be taken over for administration by a Welsh committee" – thereby reversing their views of some 55 years earlier!

The minutes of the South Wales & Mon Executive meeting of 23 Jan 1946 lists ten area committees as the composition of the "Committee for Wales": It was not until 1947 that the name Welsh AAA was agreed upon.

Monmouthshire
East Glamorgan (to include Bridgend)
West Glamorgan
Carmarthenshire
Pembrokeshire
Cardiganshire
Radnorshire and Brecknockshire
Merionethshire and Montgomeryshire
Caernarvonshire and Anglesey
Denbighshire and Flintshire

The minutes of the South Wales & Mon Executive meeting on 3 Dec 1947 (presumably now acting as a Welsh AAA) make their first reference to north Wales, when they say that a meeting "is to be arranged of persons interested in the formation of a district committee in North Wales". In fact this meeting took place at Colwyn Bay on 12 December 1947. In the minutes of 28 April 1948, an application for affiliation from Chirk AAA was approved, the first from a north Wales club. It was also reported that communications from the honorary secretaries of the Carmarthenshire and Caernarvonshire & Anglesey County Associations had been received "which indicates that there was no lack of enthusiasm in these districts". Lt. Col. The Rev. C.P. Hines, one of the pioneers of athletics in north Wales was the driving force in setting up of an Anglesey-Caernarvon Association and the North Wales District Committee. So, a body responsible for athletics throughout Wales was at last a reality, but it was not until 1955 that the first North Wales Championships were held in Colwyn Bay. The Welsh AAA Executive Committee also held their first meeting in the north in 1950 - at Bangor on July 15th. Interestingly, the Northern Counties AA of England held their 1930 championships in Colwyn Bay.

We are in the professional era, and rightly so, but without amateur officials - past and present, there would not be a sport in which to compete

There is no doubt that Welsh athletics - and athletics in general - needs to be managed by professionals, so that individuals with the requisite skills and time can devote their energies towards the development and management of the sport. However, today's generation must never forget the massive contribution being made by the volunteers of today and those of the past to make our sport of athletics what it is today. It must be remembered that an international athletics meeting requires a minimum of 200 volunteer officials to function on the day alone, let alone the many hours of preparation required to make a meeting successful. In the main these volunteers get no reward other than the satisfaction of seeing the meeting run smoothly and efficiently. This history of athletics in Wales cannot be complete without reference to those volunteers and officials over the years who have given of their time without financial reward and who have played significant roles in the development of the sport, both in Wales and further afield. Without this commitment, today's professional superstars would not have a sport in which to compete. It is extremely difficult to single out individuals, but the following are amongst the many officials not already mentioned who have given sterling service to the sport in Wales:

Bill Fisher: A member of both Newport Harriers and Newport AC, Bill Fisher can be regarded as one of the founding fathers of modern day athletics in Wales. He was Welsh AAA President from 1954 until 1958, and was the last President of the South Wales & Mon AAA before the Welsh AAA came into being in 1948. He was also the first Welsh AAA Treasurer and occupied this position for eleven years between 1948 and 1958. He occupied countless other honorary positions and was one of the founders of the Monmouthshire Schools Athletics Association in 1937.

Cyril Howell was one of the driving forces behind the formation of the Welsh AAA in 1948. He first became involved with athletics as a member of Grange AC in Cardiff and later, in 1923, joined Roath Harriers, where he held all of the main offices. He was a leading member of their teams in the 1920s and early 1930s, finishing third in the Welsh 220 yds Championship on three successive occasions. He was Secretary of the East Glamorgan AAA until 1937 when he was elected Secretary of the South Wales & Mon AAA. In 1950 he became President of the Welsh AAA on the death of Eddie O'Donnell, and held this position until Bill Fisher took over in 1954. In later life he concentrated his efforts on the Commonwealth Games Council for Wales, where he was Chairman during the 1958 Cardiff

Games. He was Chairman of the CGC for Wales from 1952 and President from 1958 (on the death of the third Lord Aberdare in 1957 when the positions were amalgamated) until he retired in 1983. He was one of the very few Welshmen to officiate in the 1948 Olympics, where he was a starter. He died in 1995, aged 91.

D. Hedydd Davies: Carmarthen Harrier Hedydd Davies is one of the unsung heroes of Welsh athletics - both as an athlete and as an official. In the former, he won the 1966 Welsh Cross country title at Gilwern and represented Wales in the international race on six occasions. On the track he took four 3,000m steeplechase titles and won four marathon titles running in that event in the 1970 Commonwealth Games in Edinburgh. As an official, he has twice occupied the top position in Welsh athletics as President in 1998 and is the present incumbent. He was also Treasurer of the Welsh AAA and its successor, AAW from 1984-1993 and has undertaken countless voluntary positions and tasks over the past 30 years both for his club, Dyfed Schools and for athletics in general.

J.D.B. "Jack" Williams, who died in 1973, was one of the founders of the Glamorgan Secondary Schools' AAA in 1937 and one of the prime movers in the establishment of the Welsh Schools Association in 1946. He was Welsh AAA secretary from 1950 until 1962 and was largely responsible for the efficient running of the administration at the 1958 Empire Games, and one of the contributors to the official history of the Games He was also President of Birchgrove Harriers. Arthur Williams, President of the Welsh AAA said of him at the time of his death in *Athletics Weekly*: "The best tribute we can pay in thanks for all he gave is to work harder to prepare our Welsh Youth to play its part in the British and Welsh arena".

L.R.Jones: Roy Jones of Newport Harriers, like many of his contemporaries, gave a lifetime to Welsh athletics at club, county and national level. He was instrumental in the formation of the Welsh Women's AAA in 1951 and was Chairman from 1954 for many years, later to become President, a position he held when he died in 1978 aged 69. He was President of the Welsh CCA in 1951/52 and a Life Vice President of the Welsh AAA, where he was a past Chairman and, for many years, Chairman of the Finance and General Purposes Committee.

R.C.G. Snow MBE: Although Reg undertook a number of high profile jobs - Welsh men's team manager at three Commonwealth Games (1974/1978/1982) and countless other Welsh teams; and one of the Welsh representatives on the BAAB (1972-1985), he was one of the tireless backroom volunteers who for almost 35 years served Welsh athletics as an athlete and administrator. He was just as happy working behind the scenes as he was serving Welsh athletics on the BAAB. For many years he was the Welsh AAA championships secretary, performing this task with his usual calm, tact and diplomacy. He finished in the first three of the Welsh 220 yds championships on four occasions in the early 1950s, and missed winning a Welsh title only due to the presence of Olympic silver medallist Ken Jones. He also won Glamorgan titles at both sprints. His best 220 yds time of 22.3 in 1950 made him the 12th fastest in Britain that year. He was awarded the MBE for his services to athletics in 1986.

Barrie Owen is another one of those unsung heroes, without whom the sport in Wales would not survive. In 1955 he became a teacher and was also invited to become a club leader of Cockett Boys Club in the west of Swansea. The Club took part in Boys Clubs of Wales athletics events and soon started to achieve success and athletes were entered in Glamorgan AAA, Welsh AAA and Welsh cross-country events. As a fund raising exercise the Boys Club members ran a relay to London. From those beginnings came the nucleus of athletes that formed Swansea Harriers Athletics Club in 1962 with Barrie as first Chairman, and amongst others, John Griffiths and Derek Vaughan as founder members. The club was originally based at the Ashleigh Road Playing fields with a grass track in summer before moving to the neighbouring University College cinder track and eventually to the synthetic track at Morfa Stadium. Over the intervening years Barrie served almost continuously as a club officer and official including overlapping periods as Chairman and Team manager and latterly as President and Fixture secretary overseeing the steady growth and development of the club to its current status. Having qualified as a coach in 1967 he has throughout the years coached innumerable athletes predominantly in the sprints and relays. In recent times he has tended to concentrate on younger age groups including organising the club's juvenile and introductory groups. Continuing this area of interest he was instrumental in founding the West Glamorgan Primary Schools Athletic Association in the City and also initiated the West Glamorgan Track and Field League that was the forerunner of the current Louise Arthur League. At national level he has served for long periods on numerous committees including Welsh AAA and AAW councils, management boards and selection committees. At British level he has been an active member of the AAA General and Development committees and the BAF Council and Management Board. In recognition of his service to the sport he was elected President of the Welsh AAA from 1987-1989 and then reversed normal practice by going on to serve as Honorary Secretary of AAW from 1991 to 1997, taking over from Bill Evans. More recently he has been recalled to service as senior men's team manager to the Welsh track and field team.

Frank Ireland: Although a relative latecomer to the sport, Frank occupied all the main offices in Welsh athletics including President of the Welsh AAA (1983-85), AAW (1989-92) and Welsh CCA (1986-1989), as well as serving his club, Barry and Vale Harriers as Chairman and President for 30 years. In particular he was the first President of the newly formed AAW, and last President of the WCCA and oversaw the integration of the three main athletics bodies in Wales to form the present governing body. Frank received Meritorious Plaques for his services to Welsh athletics in 1984 (Welsh AAA) and AAW (1993), and received the highest tribute of the AAW for services rendered to Welsh Athletics, the Award of Honour in 1996. His son Andrew is a former Welsh junior and Welsh schools' champion at 1,500 and 3,000m.

Lynette Harries has been at the forefront of Welsh athletics for over 40 years, winning four Welsh titles at shot and discus, including three successive wins at the latter between 1959 and 1961 as a member of Mond AC before moving into the administration of the sport. She was secretary of the Welsh Women's AAA from 1969 - 1971 and remarkably she has been Chairman of either the Welsh

WAAA or the AAW for 28 years. She served the former as Chairman from 1973 until the formation of the AAW in 1989 and took over in the same position of the newly amalgamated body and has held that position to guide Welsh athletics through a period, which can be described as the most turbulent, but the most successful in its existence. The sport in Wales owes much to Lynette.

Chapter 5

Guto Nythbrân, Nos Galan .... and Bernard Baldwin

NOS GALAN

Guto Nythbrân's remarkable running exploits in the eighteenth century were commemorated by the Nos Galan road races in Mountain Ash, which were first held in 1958. Nos Galan, which attracted all of the leading British athletes at the time, was the brainchild of the remarkable Bernard Baldwin, whose imagination and forethought was years ahead of his contemporaries.

The Rhondda Valley, famous for brass bands, male voice choirs, Welsh rugby giants as well as other greats such as boxers Tommy Farr and Jimmy Wilde, also produced three centuries ago a runner whose reputed performance in his greatest race was to run 12 miles in 53 minutes. This runner with that time would have left most of the leading runners in the world today trailing in his wake.

The site where once the Great Western Colliery, Porth, once stood, was the home of Griffidd Morgan. He was born in Hollybush (Llwyncelyn, Porth) in 1700 but moved to Nythbrân Farm in the Parish of Llanwonno soon after. It was from this place that he took his nickname of Guto Nythbrân – pronounced *Gitto Neethbraan.* Little did his parents know that their son would possibly become one of the greatest runners in the world and that centuries later his exploits would be revered with races held in his honour in nearby Mountain Ash. The Nos Galan Races, inaugurated by the incomparable Bernard Baldwin, became what they did because it was said that the Spirit of Guto paraded the hillsides during that day and night. It was the link with the legend of Guto that the people of the Cynon Valley liked so much and which persuaded Bernard to use his unique organising talent to revive and remember Guto's exploits.

Guto grew up to be a fast runner with tremendous stamina developing his abilities by helping his father bring in the sheep from the mountains. He was reputed to climb hills taking no notice of roads, walls, ditch or hedge. As a young man he ran and won in various parts of south Wales against local opposition making money for his backers. He trained with his local Llanwonno hounds and was said to be able to outdistance both horses and hounds. He prepared for a race by sleeping on the warm manure heap outside the stable, allowing the neutral heat to loosen his limbs "until his muscles were like whipcord and as flexible as whalebones".

It had long been the boast of shepherds in the area to be fleet-footed and before long Guto vied with them and often casually caught a sheep, or sometimes a bird in flight. Then after a day's work and with all the sheep safely in the pen, tired of trying to elude them, he would go off over the mountain for a run with the hounds.

News of his achievements spread throughout the Parish and soon Guto's fame became known far and wide and he was often called upon to show his paces. On one occasion his mother sent him on an errand to Pontypridd, more than 3 miles away and was amazed to find he had run there and back, almost 7 miles before the kettle had boiled for breakfast.

Needless to say such prowess won him many admirers and especially attracted Siân (Jane) who kept a little shop in the village. She was known as Siân o' Shop (Jane of the shop) in true Welsh fashion, and it was Guto's modesty as much as his fame that she admired. They fell in love and then Siân saw that there was money to be made in running. She soon became his manager and as a shopkeeper was a shrewd handler of the purse strings. Guto had no interest in money and only had eyes for undertaking running challenges. She raised the money for the bets which invariably became associated with the races and so confident did she and other villagers become that they "put their shirts" on Guto and won large sums of money, for he was unbeatable. Love for Siân was all that Guto needed to spur him and in his early races he carried all before him, winning as he pleased.

Running with the hounds to far off Carmarthen on one occasion he was obliged to stay overnight. A farmer there, who had heard of Guto's feats, offered him hospitality in return for a race against a horse for one mile. He trailed the horse most of the way but then glided slowly but surely away in the last few strides to win comfortably. It meant a fortune to the farmer, who readily agreed to share it but Guto refused and returned home.

To run was his pleasure and among the many races and subsequent wagers was one against an Army captain from Carmarthen stationed at Hirwaun. Siân heard of the captain's boasts of his own prowess and cunningly let it be known that Guto was now in his thirties and that age was catching up on him. But Guto's speed and endurance has scarcely diminished and once again the parishioners and the shrewd Siân gathered their winnings, for Guto raced him out of sight in a 3-mile race for a wager of £500 at Hirwaun Common.

It was several years after this race before anyone was foolish enough to challenge Guto again, but one day in September 1737, by which time he was 37 years of age, news reached the parish of another challenge, this time by a runner styled "Prince" from Bedwas Parish near Caerphilly. So, as the news spread around via the church congregation, the excitement once again became intense. Guto, who reputedly ran 50 yds in 4 seconds, was also capable of running 10 miles in 45 minutes, but the terms of this race was for an even longer distance – 12 miles, from Newport to Bedwas Church. So, there was a lingering doubt in the minds of the parishioners, especially as Guto's opponent was a much younger man. Even so, a fantastic sum of money was wagered on the result, and they say that Siân wagered her entire savings, £1,000, made up of sovereigns, which she carried in her apron on the day.

Meanwhile, Guto, who had not raced for 4 years was careful not to under-estimate his opponent and for three nights before the race slept in a blanket where the warmth of the manure made his legs more supple. He was in fine fettle on 6th September and although he walked with his followers the 30 miles to Newport he pranced about the start as impatient as a greyhound. This confidence, together with his genuine offers of advice to his rival, unnerved the Englishman who was determined to set the pace. This he did and in the early stages he got well ahead of Guto who seemed more intent on chatting to friends, often stopping for a minute or two until they became alarmed and urged him to continue. Then, with the thoughts of Siân and his followers, he sped after his opponent and, after offering a few words of advice as they ran together, he moved effortlessly away with 2 miles to go. The last mile was a steep climb to the church but Guto was determined to make it a grandstand finish and he sprinted the whole way to win easily in the astonishing time of 53 minutes.

His followers were overjoyed and began to make merry while Guto approached Siân for his rewards – a kiss and an embrace, but so enthusiastic was she on this occasion that she ran to him and slapped him heavily on the back saying "Da iawn, Guto bach, da iawn" (Well done, Guto, well done). Sadly the slap proved too much after the strain of that final spurt and with a gasp Guto fell dead on the spot. He had run his last race on earth; a displaced heart was the result, it was said, and when the news spread around the scenes of grief became indescribable, and it lingers in the Parish to this day. His body was carried, amid scenes of great emotion to his last resting place in Llanwonno churchyard.

Today as we look at the legend it is extremely unlikely that Guto ran 12 miles in 53 minutes. Even the greatest middle distance runners in the world in the past and including the great African athletes of today would have found great difficulty in running such time on the course. The road from Newport to Bedwas was probably reputed to be that distance. It almost certainly wasn't measured properly until the Newport Turnpike trust came into being in 1758. The more likely distance according to maps was about 10.4 miles, measured from the centre of Newport to Bedwas Church. This would have made Guto the fastest 10-mile runner of the eighteenth century. It is interesting to note that Woolley Morris who ran the distance in 54 minutes 30 seconds in 1753 died in similar circumstances.

The story of Guto was written down by William Thomas (1843-1890), a local antiquarian, and eventually published in 1888. He had spent much time in talking to old people whose fathers had known and even trained with him. Newspaper cuttings from the 19th Century refer to superhuman qualities he possessed. An article discovered by a community newspaper correspondent in the Cynon Valley states that the renowned athlete had been blessed – or cursed – with quadruple lungs, bones that could bend like whalebone and sinews that stretched like rubber. The article also states that Guto was more than 6ft in height, a rare phenomenon for the early 18th Century.

Manuscripts have been found claiming that Guto had run a measured mile in less than four minutes. Many stories - some perhaps taller than others - have been told over the years of his sporting prowess but there is no doubt that Guto Nythbrân will live on in the history of athletics in Wales.

The emergence of Nos Galan as one of the best known running festivals in Britain

Thanks to the brainwave of local schoolteacher and former Welsh cross-country international Bernard Baldwin, who was to become one of the most significant figures in Welsh athletics, the first Nos Galan races, modelled on Brazil's famous Sao Paulo New Year's Eve midnight event, were held in Mountain Ash in 1958. Ken Norris, one of Britain's leading middle distance runners at the time, who won the Brazilian event in 1957, gave his winning trophy to the Nos Galan organisers for presentation to the winning team in the midnight race. The event consisted of a 100 yds sprint in Oxford Street and a midnight 4 miles race, where the race started in one year and finished in the next. The events were confined to senior men and four of the best sprinters in Great Britain trotted out of Castree's Men's Shop for the first 100 yds race - a straight final. The winner was future 100m Olympic bronze medallist and world 220 yds record holder Peter Radford in 9.9 with Dave Segal second in 10.0 and local man Ron Jones third in 10.1.

To maintain interest during the intervening hours before the big race, Bernard, hit on the idea of having a solitary mystery runner to run with lighted torch from the graveside of Guto Nythbrân at Llanwonno Churchyard down into Mountain Ash, light a beacon outside the

A scene showing the huge crowds that were attracted to the Nos Galan races. This shows the scene on Mountain Ash bridge at the finish of the 4 miles midnight race in the early 1960s.

Town Hall and so signal the start of the midnight race. At 11.00 pm on New Year's Eve a crowd would gather around the church of St Gwynno in Llanwonno all eager to see the Mystery Runner. The first Mystery Runner was 1948 Olympic marathon silver-medallist Tom Richards who was almost unable to get through the dense crowd outside the Town Hall to light the beacon. Eventually 101 runners set off for a 4 mile "round the houses" race with the runners coming up the main street in Mountain Ash - Oxford Street - four times in all. To be there or on the Mountain Ash Bridge was to have a grandstand view and there was a tumultuous shout for the inaugural winner, one of Britain's leading middle distance stars of the time, Stan Eldon, who clocked 18:46 for the course.

The presentation ceremonies for the races were in true Olympic fashion with a printed sash for the winner, worded in Welsh, and medals to the second and third, presented on a specially made rostrum. The idea of Olympic runners running through the streets of a mining town in south Wales, especially at midnight on New Year's Eve, caught the imagination of the press. The event was carried in every major newspaper and on all television channels.

The story of Nos Galan thereafter was one of increasing success. A men's mile was added to the programme in the afternoon in 1959 and was held in Penrhiwceiber, two miles down the Aberdare Valley from Mountain Ash. The crowds got bigger each year, entries increased to more than a thousand runners, continental runners and teams entered. The narrow streets could hardly cope with such numbers, and the event did reach saturation point.

In 1961 Nigerian law student Kamoru Agbo-ola broke the record for the 100 yds with a sizzling 9.6 when he beat Ron Jones by the thickness of his vest. The record remained intact until the end. Ron received the well-earned honour of being selected as Mystery Runner in 1967 and in all he won the Nos Galan 100 yds six times (1963, 1965 – 1969).

Interest in the identity of the Mystery Runner was an exciting feature of the event each year. The secret never got out and such famous runners as former world mile record holder Derek Ibbotson, European 5,000m champion Bruce Tulloh, Martin Hyman and Stan Eldon all had the honour of representing the spirit of Guto Nythbrân in the early years. Then, in 1965, in teeming rain the 1964 Olympic 800m champion Anne Packer ran down from the church on the hill to become the first woman to receive the honour. 1964 Olympic long jump champion Mary Rand followed her in 1966 - and this was the biggest surprise of the lot, for Mary was certainly no distance runner. By that year, 1966, a Women's Mile had been added to the programme and entries totalled over 800 runners.

Almost every year there appeared to be some crisis in Nos Galan affairs - the foot and mouth disease threatened the end in 1967; there was a threat by striking miners to keep runners out of Deep Duffryn Colliery baths where the runners changed; insufficient homes for runners to stay (600 was sometimes insufficient) and, when a white South African team entered, the Anti-Apartheid Movement threatened to bring the proceedings to a standstill with a demonstration in the main street. All these crises were probably fuelled by the well-meaning publicity conscious Baldwin, but the organisation survived these and many other problems and with tremendous support and encouragement from the police succeeded in making Nos Galan a truly international event. By the time that future world 10,000m record holder Dave Bedford won the 4 miles race in 1969 it was safe to say that every runner of

David Bedford (1), twice winner of the Nos Galan 4 miles heads the field on his way to victory in 1969. Note extreme right starter Ken Harris nearly gets knocked over in the rush. Other athletes in the picture include Dic Evans (right of Bedford) who won the 1974 Welsh steeplechase title and extreme right Clive Thomas who won the Welsh 1500 title in 1973.

note in Britain was taking part as well as stars from abroad. The characteristic of the event was that the route for the races was lined with boy torchbearers. Eighty of these, all in blue tracksuits with Nos Galan flashes, marked the route admirably. They added a certain flavour to the races with over a thousand torches being produced each year.

Lillian Board and Mary Rand celebrate the New Year in style – at Mountain Ash!

In 1969 the Mystery Runner was Lillian Board, the 400m silver medallist from the previous years Mexico Olympics. Like Mary Rand she had never run 4 miles before in her life but she took it in her stride and made a dazzling figure, all in white, as she ran down the mountainside from Llanwonno. Her appearance in the event was a tribute to the persuasive powers of Bernard Baldwin. Who else could convince an Olympic long jump champion (Mary Rand) and the then

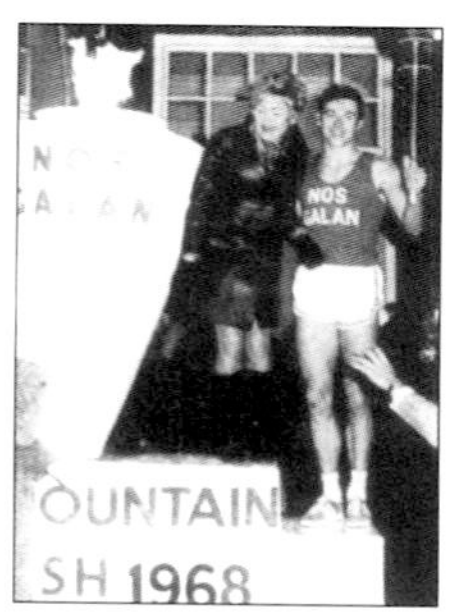

'Mystery Runner' Lynn Davies holding the torch he carried from Guto's grave in 1968. With him on the podium is Lillian Board who would be the torchbearer the following year.

golden girl of British athletics - Lillian Board - to run 4 miles at midnight. The whole country mourned Lillian's death from cancer less than a year later.

European indoor 1,500m champion John Whetton, Mystery Runner in 1970, was one of the most loyal of all the runners in Nos Galan. Apart from being well placed in the 4 miles each year, he won the mile on no fewer than seven occasions. He was "adopted" by the Bridge Social Club in Mountain Ash and is now a life member of that club. In 1964, Whetton won from Alan Simpson and, later that year in the Tokyo Olympics, both reached the 1,500m final with Simpson just missing out on bronze in fourth place. Simpson also won the 4 miles that year from Geoff North of Belgrave and Irish internationals Tom O'Riordan and Eddie Spillane who led their club, Donore Harriers Dublin, to the team race title. Again, the presence in a small Welsh Valley town of Mountain Ash of world class athletes such as Simpson, who was unquestionably Britain's top 1,500 runner at the time, and Whetton was a tribute to Baldwin's persuasive powers.

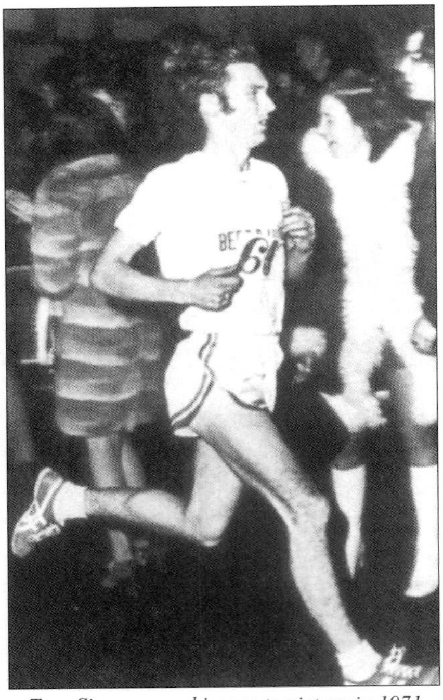
Tony Simmons on his way to victory in 1971

In 1971 it was World 10,000m record holder David Bedford's turn to be Mystery Runner but his 4 mile run from Guto's grave at Llanwonno was too much and he found Tony Simmons too good for him in the midnight race immediately afterwards. Simmons became the first Welshman to win the race, winning by over 20 seconds to set a new record of 17:41, which remained unbeaten. It was a shock to all when following the 1973 events Nos Galan in its entirety had to end. The reason given was the undue delay to traffic and behaviour of some locals. Even the solo run by the Mystery Runner from Llanwonno was not allowed, though this could scarcely be said to hold up traffic. Strangely, and perhaps a sign of the times, there was no public protest whatsoever. Nos Galan had lasted 16 years, a fair run which still evokes many memories in a town, which had taken the event to its heart. There have been a number of attempts to revive the event. After a brief resurrection in 1984 it fell by the wayside the following year. London Marathon Directors John Disley and Chris Brasher brought it back to life again in 1986. However in the 90's it has had a potted history with various sponsors only making brief contributions to the event. This made yearly planning difficult. Recent Mystery Runners have included Kirsty Wade, Steve Jones and Christian Malcolm. Bernard Baldwin and his group have made many efforts with the help of Rhondda Cynon Taff Council but, with the new era of professionalism in the sport, any promotion will not rekindle the golden years from 1958 to 1973 for which Nos Galan will always be remembered.

Bernard Baldwin – a man ahead of his time

Bernard Baldwin was Nos Galan. He conceived it and ran it, it was his. Bernard's enthusiasm for the event was almost to end in disaster in 1967 as rockets on the back seat of his car, due to be used to announce the arrival of the mystery runner at the Town Hall in Mountain Ash, exploded as he led the mystery runner down from Llanwonno and the car was burned out. Bernard and Nos Galan treasurer Tom Lewis received serious body burns and were rushed to the special burns unit at Chepstow Hospital. Fortunately, they recovered but the ordeal had a lasting effect on both of them.

Bernard Baldwin, MBE

The event, which was big enough to have an organising committee in place throughout the year, took advantage of this and the Nos Galan committee organised many other events as a general contribution to Welsh athletics. In the early 1960s an innovative two-man Cardiff to Swansea relay was held, changing in 1965 to a two-man relay from Cardiff to Mountain Ash which was won by Chris Loosley and John Godding of University College of Wales, Aberystwyth. The event attracted the leading distance runners from all over Britain, but was discontinued some years later. The Committee also promoted long distance track races at Cardiff's Maindy Stadium and in 1966 they were rewarded when the late John Tarrant of Salford Harriers broke the world best for 40 miles with 4hrs 03mins 28 secs and again in 1967 when Lynn Hughes of Bridgend broke the record reducing it further with 3hrs 58mins 53.2 secs. In 1968 the event was extended to 50 miles - 200 laps - and Alan Phillips of Reading AC, who held the world best, was the winner.

Amongst the other events organised by the Nos Galan Committee, or other organisations such as Road Runners Club (Glamorgan) or its successor Road Runners Club (Wales), were a series of events which brought athletics to the people - long before the advent of the major marathons. Obstensively organised by these groups in the 1960s, they were first and foremost the idea of the redoubtable Bernard, who must take the credit for their introduction. Along with a band of enthusiastic helpers - many with little experience of organising athletics events, – he organised the Taff Street Dash on the evening of the Welsh athletics championships, the Easter road race series at Pencoed, the Wattstown Road Races and the immensely popular series of evening road races in such places as Cilfynydd, Glyncoch, Pwllgwaun, Hopkinstown, Merthyr, Troedyrhiw and many other venues in south Wales. These events attracted the stars of the day and, to a certain extent, some of the locals did not appreciate the quality of the athletes being paraded before them. Imagine a small terraced street in Wattstown, in the Rhondda Valley, with the Olympic 100m bronze medallist and two other world record holders about to run in a 100 yds event in the middle of the road. This writer can well remember a local miner, popping his head around the front door of his terraced house and asking Bernard Baldwin, as ever with megaphone in hand: "What the hell is going on here today then?". To be told that Peter Radford, Ron and Berwyn Jones, plus several other of Britain's top athletes were running in a 100 yds race just outside his front door completely bemused him. To him it was equivalent to a modern day prank by Noel Edmonds - he promptly closed the door and went in!

The Taff Street Dash, held on what Bernard described as the most congested main street in Britain, was a major event in the British calendar, and it attracted all of the top sprinters of the day in the 1960s including Radford, David Jones, Alf Meakin, all the Welsh stars including the young J.J. Williams, who recalls: "I have fond memories of all of Bernard Baldwin's events and particularly The Taff Street Dash - the event was amongst my earliest recollections of top athletics in Wales". The athletes changed in Hodge's men's outfitters in Taff St, and warmed up in the street behind Taff St, which is the area used for the famous

Pontypridd market. JJ continues: "If you were drawn in lanes one or four, you had no chance of winning because you were either in the gutter or on the pavement amongst the crowd – all the winners came from lanes two or three!" He won in 1966. The after-race function at the New Inn Hotel also in Taff St, which also served as the annual dinner of the Road Runners Club of Wales, was Bernard's real show-piece, where his unique show business-style talent entertained the guests until the early hours with his anecdotes and comments on virtually every person in the room - up to 300 of them!

Despite his vision, energy and drive, Bernard had his critics, particularly amongst the athletics die-hards who felt that his events were diverting interest from true track and field events – especially when his *Welsh Notes* in *Athletics Weekly* were sometimes entirely devoted to his promotions. But what cannot be denied is that his contribution to Welsh athletics has been enormous. It made road running popular before the road running boom.

However, Bernard contributed far more to Welsh athletics than his involvement in Nos Galan and the many other road race promotions he organised. He was born in 1925 in Barry, one of seven children - four boys and three girls. He served in the Fleet Air Arm as a trainee gunner in World War Two and then attended Caerleon Training College between 1947 – 49 to train as a PE teacher. He taught at Tintern village school in the Wye Valley, then at Mill Street and later Treforest Lower Comprehensive School, Pontypridd.

Bernard took up athletics and cross-country running at school, becoming Welsh junior mile champion and winning his full international cross country vest in 1947. His brother Bramwell also won the Welsh junior mile title in 1937 and was a fine cross-country runner. Bernard later played soccer for Welsh league teams Tynte Rovers, Abercynon and Penrhiwceiber.

Shortly after his marriage in 1949, he entered the administration side of athletics. Between 1966 and 1975, he was secretary of the Welsh AAA and he was awarded the MBE in 1971 for services to British athletics. He became the Welsh delegate to the BAAB, then one of six national team managers, taking teams to all parts of the world.

He has written or compiled numerous booklets and diaries on Welsh athletics, was Welsh correspondent to *Athletics Weekly* for 22 years, and for many years a prolific contributor on Welsh athletics to *The* Western Mail, South Wales Echo, South Wales Argus and Sunday Express – and a regular broadcaster on BBC Wales. As well as these activities, he also found time to undertake the public address duties at numerous athletics meetings in Wales – and type and run off on his ancient machine, the first ever Welsh Best Performer lists produced by Clive Williams and Ken Bennett in 1963.

Having settled in Mountain Ash in 1950 he has been active in numerous events in the area. He is a brass instrumentalist, preferring cornet or trumpet, an amateur magician, and speaks French and Russian reasonably fluently. Bernard will always be remembered in his community for the pleasure he brought to thousands of people with Nos Galan. "Nos Galan is one of the few events in Britain which has imagination and has a special brand of magic" - former world 10,000m record holder Dave Bedford after his victory in 1969.

Still living in Mountain Ash and very lucid at the age of 76, all in Welsh athletics believe that Bernard has not received the recognition he deserves - let's hope that this is rectified without delay.

Chapter 6

The Story of Cross-Country Running in Wales

The Welsh Cross Country Association, formed in 1896, was an autonomous body affiliated directly to the International Cross Country Union, and as such operated independently from the Welsh AAA until the formation of the AAW in 1990. Most of today's track and field clubs owe their existence to the "winter" branch of our sport, and it can be fairly said that without it, club athletics in Wales, or indeed in Britain, would not be what it is today.

An appreciation

"Track racing may be described as the prose and cross country as the poetry of foot racing. The man who goes in for cross country racing taking fence, ditch and ploughed fields as they come enjoys the sensation of running pure and simple and there is not the monotony that is experienced in track running."

Evening Express, 4-10-1902.

"Cross country running may not win a man many silver cups, but it can be turned to account every day of his life. Many run only for the enjoyment of the exercise. They may not find a place in the club's first team but they form, nevertheless, the backbone of most clubs. Natural aptitude is advantageous but much may be attained by development. One of the beauties of cross-country running is that men of every calibre can enjoy it ....."

NTJ Moses, Newport Harriers Jubilee Brochure, 1946.

"Cross-country running draws its strength and its reason for existence from its past, its origins, but also from nature. For more than in any other sport, one runs across country in play – for the pleasure, without desiring any more. And even when the goal is victory one continues to play......to play with the elements. Indeed in that one has no choice!"

Yves Jeannotat, Cross–country 1903-1986 – Son Histoire.

The Origins

These three quotations from up to a century ago are still valid today and cross-country running in particular is the backbone of the club system in Britain.

Cross-country running and road running, as branches of athletics, almost certainly developed from three inter-linked activities - training for or as a substitute for other sports, as an offshoot of the practice of foot following in hunting and beagling, and the running challenge competitions between individuals. The last events were to a significant extent professional in that successful individuals were often "sponsored" if not actually competing for cash prizes or other personal financial reward. The passage of time, lack of acceptable (accurate) contemporaneous records and the inevitable exaggeration of verbal history - the last encouraged, for obvious reasons by sponsors and bookmakers, if not the individual concerned, make it almost impossible to separate truth from myth and legend. It should be appreciated moreover that until as late as the 1960s the activity was almost, if not totally, a male preserve. Due to the conditions prevailing there was, unlike today, little or no differentiation between road and country events. As an aside it is worthy of comment that the original marathon run of Pheidippides, recorded in Greek mythology, was a point-to-point event and was almost certainly partly off-road unlike its modern re-creation.

As we have seen, in Wales' case the most notable challenge runner of history was Griffidd Morgan in the eighteenth century, but in the 1820/1830s one finds the first recorded races - an annual cross country race at Carnwath in Lanarkshire, a one mile steeplechase held near Edinburgh in May 1828, one at Shrewsbury school on the Welsh borders (1831) and another at Rugby school three years later. The last was a forerunner of the "Crick run" at the same school, initially over eighteen kilometres, which started in 1837. These schools' examples were apparently soon copied by other public schools as part of their sports programmes. The early association with hunting continues to the present day with many traditional clubs still incorporating 'Harriers' or 'Beagles' in their names.

In 1868 Walter Rye of Thames Rowing Club organised the first of a series of runs to keep his oarsmen fit in winter - one of the judges apparently being Tom Hughes, author of "Tom Brown's Schooldays", who included the subject of a race in his book. Rye went on to organise the first (English) championship at Epping Forest in November 1876. Unfortunately the event was declared null and void due to several competitors "losing the trail" and going off course. The following years however saw successful annual events at Roehampton, south of London, over the area used to the present day for the annual Oxford versus Cambridge university cross-country match. The start in Scotland was similar – their inaugural championship in March 1886 attracted only eleven starters whilst gate receipts totalled 2 shillings (10p). By 1883, matters in England were sufficiently developed for a meeting of clubs to be called to form the National Cross Country Union with Walter Rye as its first president, area associations having been formed in the previous three years in the midlands and north.

The foregoing might suggest that the British were the sole originators but this was not the case. For example, in the 1880s the Germans had horse racing as their source of inspiration - competitors running against each other in their racing colours whilst spectators and supporters wagered on the results.

Meanwhile in Wales the sport developed in the industrial areas and clubs formed in the Newport area, Cardiff (Roath Harriers and St Anne's) and Swansea (Swansea Harriers and St Helen's). Roath Harriers, which in 1968, combined with Birchgrove Harriers to form Cardiff AAC, can claim to be the first established cross-country club in Wales whilst Newport Harriers, for their part, have the longest unbroken independent existence. As later pages will show these two clubs dominated the sport of cross-country running over very many years until relatively

Roath Harriers 1910 – 1911

recent times. Newport Harriers was formed by the amalgamation of a number of small clubs in the vicinity, themselves the offshoots of other sporting activities, in particular football clubs. Moreover, Newport apparently maintained a federal structure for some years with its constituent units as satellites, occasionally competing as semi-independent clubs. Roath Harriers, came about as the result of a wagered race between young men of the town who worked together in the docks. The initial contest was held from the Royal Oak public house in Roath, Cardiff and was so much enjoyed by the participants that they repeated it on a regular basis. From that series of runs the Roath club was formed in 1882 with its headquarters at the self same hostelry. As will be seen, the Royal Oak was later to serve as a venue even more significantly in the development of the sport. Membership was initially by invitation only but after some years it became open to all.

The early days

Initially clubs tended to hold regular pack runs on a 'hare and hounds' basis during the winter months. One or two of the members were chosen as 'hares' and they would set off carrying bags of torn paper with which they would lay a trail. After an appropriate interval the remainder would set off to follow the trail. Where warranted the pursuers would be split into one or more groups or 'packs' based on ability and the faster groups would be held back longer. Each pack had a leader and a 'whipper-in'; the former controlled the overall speed, curbing the more exuberant members, whilst the latter brought up the rear and tended to the tail-enders. The idea was to run as a group until near the end when on a signal from the leader there would be, in modern parlance, a 'burn-up' back to the headquarters. It was a test of the skill and ingenuity of the hares that they laid trails over arduous ground and also, where appropriate, false trails so hampering the progress of their pursuers. It is interesting to note that the laying of false trails was excluded in Roath's club rules but from contemporary press reports it appears that this rule was not observed. This system of running has re-surfaced in recent times with the proliferation of 'hashing' clubs, who even continue the tradition of the participants being known by nicknames.

A logical development was to hold competitions between clubs on a similar basis with Roath Harriers the most active. Their principal opponents were Cardiff rivals, St Anne's and the two Swansea teams, St Helen's and Swansea Harriers – no connection to the present day club of that name. These matches were a fairly regular occurrence during the winter months in the early 1880s. An inaugural South Wales and Monmouthshire Championship was organised in March 1894 by W M Douglas at Ely Racecourse in Cardiff, surprisingly on a Thursday afternoon. In common with several others of that time, William Douglas was a born organiser, involved with many of the popular sports and he remained a faithful supporter through the years. In addition to running, swimming, rugby and rowing benefited from his support. Roath Harriers, led by Hugh Fairlamb, had the first five runners home in the race and won with an almost minimal 25 points beating Swansea Harriers (92) and St Helen's (110) for the team title. Early the following year Roath, as south Wales champions, travelled to Bristol for a match versus Bristol Harriers who were West of England champions. The home club filled the first three places but excellent packing by Roath meant that Bristol only narrowly won the team competition. The following year (1895) Roath won the championship again, at East Moors, Cardiff over a course of about eight miles, beating St Anne's, the only other competing team. The prefix "South" had now been dropped from the title although neither club nor individual from outside the locality took part. This time Roath Harriers had the first six to finish giving them minimum points (21) in the team event, led by future professional star, Harry Cullum. He retained his individual title in the following year (1896) but was then in the colours of rival club, Cardiff Harriers, which had been formed in the meantime. Even so Roath gained a third successive team win. Prior to this in January, Roath and Bristol had met again, only on this occasion, with home advantage Roath turned the tables on their opponents.

Frank Liddington Johns

That same year, (September 11th 1896), following an advertisement in the *South Wales Argus*, a group of small clubs in the Newport area of Monmouthshire got together and formed the one club – Newport Harriers. However, as indicated previously, it appears to have been an association rather than a monolithic club. Its constituent members, who were in many cases offshoots of other sports such as football, continued as satellites and their names recur at a later date in championships and other events. One of the constituents (Caerau Harriers) had a teenager, Frank Liddington Johns as its sole officer and he became Treasurer of the new club. This latter post he held for over twenty-five years in addition to undertaking numerous other official duties in the sport. He was to make an indelible mark on the sport in Wales and wider afield. In 1896, the Roath Harriers programme of events included a four-mile handicap road race - on the Rumney road and included an ascent of Rumney Hill - one of the earliest references to a specific road race as such.

Formation of Welsh Cross Country Association

Two months after the Newport club's formation, on November 12th 1896, a meeting was held at the Royal Oak in Roath, Cardiff. Attended by representatives of the Roath, Newport, Cardiff, Penarth and Swansea clubs it saw the formation of a Welsh Cross Country Association – succeeding where a similar meeting the previous season had failed. The earlier meeting at the Blue Bell Hotel in Cardiff in January 1896 had however appointed a committee with William Fairlamb of Roath Harriers as Chairman to draft rules and laws. Eight clubs had been invited to the second meeting, the absentees being St Anne's, St Helen's and Pontypool Harriers. William Fairlamb was elected inaugural Chairman of the Association and Claude Hailey, also of Roath, became Secretary and Treasurer. W M Douglas, who presided over the meeting, was elected Vice President in recognition of his contribution in drawing up the draft constitution and rules accepted by the meeting and also acting as the original Championships Secretary. With an Association formed things became much more formalised and committee minutes of the time detail decisions on such matters as the award of championship medals to the winner and the runner-up.

In November 1897, following a letter from the Northern Counties Cross Country Association (of England), it was decided to apply to join the (English) National Cross Country Union "provided that there is no entrance fee to be paid". It was also agreed that the Secretary should write enquiring as to whether a team of cross-country runners selected from Welsh clubs would be allowed to run in the (English) national championship of 1898, "not necessarily for prizes". Presumably the former was not progressed whilst the English Association refused the participation request. The latter organisation did however indicate an intention to revise its rules "for the purpose of admitting the Welsh and other associations". About this time a problem, which continues to the present day, arose with objections being raised as to the eligibility of one of the entrants for the (Welsh) championship on the basis that he was first claim to another club.

The 1897 Welsh Championship was held from the Harlequin's Ground in Cardiff and was reported to have been particularly arduous with no fewer than twenty-two water jumps. A Turner (Newport) won from Egbert Fairlamb, (younger brother of Hugh) whilst Cardiff Harriers won their first team title.

In 1898, a third place medal was added to the championship individual awards. About this date also, the original Cardiff Harriers became defunct whilst Swansea Harriers resigned from membership. The former club were effectively replaced by Grange Harriers who later adopted their predecessor's name whilst yet another Cardiff club (Central Harriers) was formed and joined the Association. That year's championship race returned to Ely racecourse with RC Brookes (Cardiff) winning from A Turner (Newport) and W S Jones (Cardiff. The final year of the century saw Newport Harriers achieve their first team win of a series of twelve consecutive victories. They were led by J G Lee, their captain, as first man home, and this feat was repeated by fellow club members in eight of the following ten years.

The new Century

The new Century should have seen the Welsh Championship move out of Cardiff but Newport were unable to find a course and the event reverted to Ely once more. St Anne's, Cardiff rejoined the association and RA Pritchard replaced Claude Hailey as Secretary and Treasurer. Yet again there were difficulties at the pre-Championships scrutiny meeting – this time between the various Cardiff clubs – they plus Newport Harriers being the sole teams entered. For the first time money became a feature when at the 1900 Annual General Meeting the Treasurer declared a balance in hand of £6-2s-9d (£6.14). In 1901 the decision was made to award a medal to the leading runner of all complete non-winning teams. One interesting rule, in those days was that all championship entrants had to have participated in three club runs prior to the entry date. This rule was enforced rigorously and on occasions clubs were required to produce their attendance registers for verification purposes. In 1901 and 1902 some entrants were struck out for failing to comply with this pre-condition. In the latter year the awards were yet further amended to the effect that no individual could "take two medals" although it was not made clear how the rule applied. Presumably, it meant that individual medallists were not also awarded team medals if their club were successful or if they were first scorer for a non-winning team. This rule was still in existence 80 years later.

The 1902 championship finally moved out of Cardiff, the venue being Caerleon Racecourse, giving a fourth consecutive team success to Newport. This venue was to play a significant role in Welsh cross-country running. Also notable was the achievement of both Newport and Roath clubs in completing "B" teams. Up until 1903, all committee meetings of the association had been held in the Royal Oak at Roath, but in February of that year they moved to the Grand Hotel in Cardiff and thence two years later to Newport. The 1904 Annual General Meeting saw Barry Harriers present for the first time represented by Eddie O'Donnell, another individual whose name was to recur frequently. Also at this meeting Frank Liddington Johns took over as Secretary/Treasurer from RA Pritchard of Roath. At the immediately following committee meeting came the decision to hold a junior race in conjunction with the Welsh Championship – offering the opportunity for less experienced athletes to compete, eligibility being based on ability and achievements to date rather than age. The influence of Liddington Johns was soon apparent with the January 1905 meeting having an appendix to its minutes detailing championship awards and closely defining both team and individual eligibility for the junior race – effectively debarring any international runners, and all championship medal winners. Even junior race award winners were debarred in subsequent years. About eighty years later similar "barring clauses" were still in force for the Welsh Novice Championship.

The start of international competition

The first recorded international cross-country competition took place on March 20th 1898. The French Athletic Federation challenged the first eight in the English Championship of that year to meet a similar number of their best runners. The race was held at Ville d'Avray near Paris and resulted in an overwhelming victory for the England squad. All of their eight runners finished ahead of the first French representative. Fifth man home was Castleton (Cardiff) born Jack Marsh of Salford Harriers, a former member of the Newport club whilst there was an Englishman, (H Freeman), in the French squad of eight.

The next such development was a proposal for an English team to compete against an Irish one at the Cork Exhibition of 1902 but this failed to materialise. It appears that Frank Liddington Johns, whose interest had been aroused by the English/French encounter, wrote offering a Welsh team as substitutes but this failed due to lack of time. However the contacts, between Johns and Pritchard of Wales and Dudley Fletcher of Ireland resulted in plans for a representative race at Hamilton Park in Scotland in March 1903. England, rather arrogantly, initially declined to participate claiming that their national event was open to all comers, offered adequate high level competition and could serve as a British championship. Finding that the other three nations were still going ahead they relented and agreed to join the match but even then required the date to be chosen to fit in with the schedule of Alf Shrubb, the leading runner of the time. The first official reference in the Welsh CCA minute books came as late as November 1902. It records an invitation from Ireland to which the Welsh officials were however a little hesitant. They sought at this stage to involve England or alternatively hold a joint competition with Ireland or Scotland or "failing that an offer be made" to Ireland to run in Wales. Matters were obviously moving positively and rapidly behind the scenes as in February 1903 decisions were being made on Welsh kit for "the International Contest" and that "the team to be sent to represent Wales be confined to members of clubs affiliated to the Welsh association".

The actual team selection a month later consisted of the first ten home in the Welsh Championship plus Jack Marsh (Salford) and D.G. Harries, a member of a club in Reading. The latter was subject to his "consenting to become a member of an affiliated club." He apparently complied and joined Newport Harriers. For his part Jack Marsh, was the Castleton runner who had captained Newport Harriers before moving to Manchester. There, he became captain of the Salford club and achieved considerable success including being placed in the English Northern Counties and English National Championships. As previously mentioned, he had also competed in the race in France in 1898. Frank Liddington Johns was appointed manager of the twelve-man team with A Turner, of the Newport club, as captain. Since the first nine runners home in that year's Welsh Championship had all been from Newport Harriers it meant eleven of that first Welsh international team were all past or present members of his club. The whole party travelled as a group to Glasgow by train, William Fairlamb and R.A. Pritchard being the other Welsh officials.

Conditions on the race day were hardly auspicious, heavy rain confining spectators to the shelter of the racecourse grandstand in front of which the race started and finished. In the actual race Alf Shrubb, who later turned professional, led from the start and won by half a minute. He was only challenged by J.J. Daly of Ireland, who eventually fell back and finished in third place, being passed by T. Edwards. England packed its six scorers in the first seven places home to achieve an overwhelming victory; a performance they repeated in following years. Jack Marsh in twelfth position was the first Welsh runner home with the team placed fourth and last. Following the race there was a dinner during which a local businessman and patron of sport, Fred Lumley, offered to present a trophy for annual team competition - the magnificent Lumley Shield, which remains a prized award to present times.

In spite of the weather, the organisers made a profit of eight pounds, which they divided equally among the participating countries, setting a precedent for following occasions. The overall success of the venture ensured that the competition would be repeated the following year. The venue then was Haydock Park in Lancashire and it was here that the International Board was formed which later became the International Cross Country Union, (ICCU).

The 1900s to the First World War

Programme cover from the first international cross-country race in Wales in 1906. Note signature of EW (Eddie) O'Donnell in top corner.

The advent of international competition and the resultant desire to field the strongest possible team to represent the Principality brought inevitable changes in attitudes of the Welsh committee. In January 1904, the decision was reached to invite non-affiliated clubs to compete in the championship so long as they paid the entry fee. Additionally, the Secretary was "instructed to enquire through the *Athletic News* if any good cross country runner having a Welsh qualification is willing to run for Wales in the international and to send a list of his performances". As a consequence, the team selected for the 1904 International, whilst it contained no fewer than seven members of Newport Harriers also included three from English clubs. This race saw Wales achieve its highest ever placing - second to England ahead of both Ireland and Scotland.

In 1905, the International race was scheduled for Dublin, with the consequential travel significantly increasing costs for the Welsh association. Again publicity in *Athletic News* was sought with the result that three non-residents were again nominated as "possibles" for the Welsh team. After much careful consideration "it was resolved to send a team to Dublin at cost of not more than twenty pounds; those selected to be asked to pay their own hotel expenses and as a consequence not to select any runners from English clubs." This decision was reversed later and Hughes of Farnworth Harriers, Bolton and Marsh of Salford were named as reserves with Messrs. Fairlamb, Mountjoy and Liddington Johns as International Board delegates.

The 1906 International race was planned to be held in Wales on March 10th, and for the first of many occasions the venue selected was Caerleon Racecourse. Irrespective of the sporting success the promotion of the event left the Association with a debt of twenty pounds requiring an emergency meeting in July to try and clear the sum. One of the schemes was a draw with the major prize being a free trip, valued at three guineas (£3.15), with the Welsh team to the 1907 competition in Glasgow.

At the 1907 AGM the Welsh association's debt was reported to have been cleared. Even so monetary considerations remained paramount since the 1908 race was to be held at Colombes in Paris. At the meeting Frank Liddington Johns resigned as Secretary and was replaced by Percy Mountjoy of Roath with the former reverting to the post of Assistant Secretary. A request to the association to allow individual entries in the Welsh Championship was "ruled out of order" due to lack of advance notice. A quotation had been received from Cooks, the travel agents, for travel to Paris "was London and back for £2-11-6d (£2.58) per head plus fares to and from London." In view of this it was decided to select a team of only nine athletes plus two officials "unless reserves were willing to pay their own way." Messrs. Liddington Johns and Mountjoy were again the two officials with William Fairlamb the third International Board delegate.

The AGM of the Welsh CCA in 1908 resolved "to hold a marathon race under the auspices of the Association, all arrangements as to distance, prizes, date to be left to the committee." In February 1909, the Pontnewydd club offered "to hold a meeting ....for the purpose of running the Welsh marathon and would guarantee........a minimum profit of £15." Not surprisingly the offer was accepted. The distance was fixed at "about twenty miles."

No fewer than seven different clubs were represented in the international team selected for 1909 at Derby but on this occasion no Anglo-Welsh runners, following acceptance of a formal proposal once more restricting selection to members of affiliated clubs only. At the Annual General Meeting the following November there was considerable debate over second claim athletes resulting in a rule that they had to be registered with the Association Secretary before being eligible to compete for their second club in races. There was also a decision to set up a selection committee for the international team consisting "of one representative from each affiliated club" and "that no runner be allowed to act on such sub-committee." The March 1910 committee meeting ended with a report "that some club or clubs affiliated to the Association are in the habit of allowing professional runners to take part in the evening training and handicap runs held under the club's auspices. The Honorary Secretary was instructed to write to the AAA (of England) for their opinion on the practice."

At the 1910 AGM Frank Liddington Johns reported that the International Board had accepted the invitation to run the 1911 international in Wales (at Caerleon) and that he had been asked to again act as Meeting Secretary. A reply had been received from the AAA which stated that the "Southern Committee could not see how to prevent professional runners attending training runs, it being understood that they did not compete as club members." The question of affiliation to the AAA (of England) was brought up "but it was decided to take no action unless requested by the AAA." The formation of a league was also turned down, the opinion being expressed that "a league could not be worked under present conditions".

AV Mathias replaced Eddie O'Donnell as Secretary at the 1911 AGM of the association. In 1912 there were protests from St Saviours and Cathays Harriers against the judge's decisions in that year's junior championship. It was agreed to re-run the event on Easter Monday but that the individual medal winners should retain their awards. However at a further meeting in April the motion was rescinded and the judge's decision upheld.

Regrettably for posterity, the minutes do not enlighten us as to the exact cause of the dispute although contemporary reports on the race indicated judging or recording errors and omissions in the official results.

Championships & other cross country races, 1903 to 1914

In 1903, Newport Harriers seeking stronger opposition competed in the English Midland Counties Junior Championship at Wolverhampton finishing as second team. The next season they went one better defeating pre-race favourites, Northampton Alpine on the latter's home course with D.G. Harries fourth individual. Also in 1904, Roath Harriers travelled to London for an inter-club match versus Blackheath Harriers. Rhys Evans was individual winner for the visitors over a very heavy muddy course but the team scores were equal on thirty-nine points. In modern times this would have given Roath victory as their sixth scorer was in tenth position to Blackheath's twelfth. Jack Marsh running for Salford was second in the Northern Counties Championships at Haydock in February and fourth in the English National race a month later.

The 1904 Welsh Championship, at Ely produced a surprise winner in relative newcomer E. Francis, of Cathays Harriers with pre-race favourite D.G. Harries third. Most of the international team were selected from the front placers in the championship. To these were added R.B. Pugh of Newport and T. Edwards of Salford Harriers, who had run for England at Hamilton finishing second to Alf Shrubb. The international that year at Haydock proved a success for Wales beating Ireland and Scotland to be second to England, mainly due to excellent runs by Marsh (6th) and Hughes of Farnworth (8th). This was despite T. Edwards being disqualified and not allowed to start and E. Francis retiring at half distance. Alf Shrubb retained his title but later went to the United States and turned professional thus being lost to amateur sport, which, of course, would not have been the case today.

In February 1905, as preparation for the coming Welsh Championship Roath Harriers held their annual trip to Blackheath, this time losing 33-45. Newport, for their part, finished second to Birchfield Harriers in the Midland Counties Senior Championship. In December of that year, Roath again visited the Londoners losing 31-49 despite closing in before their rivals. It was January 1906 before Blackheath made their first visit to Wales but with a weak team they lost to Roath 32-43. That same month Newport Harriers emulated their neighbours by defeating South London Harriers 37-41 at Croydon. The 1905 Welsh Championship was held at Caerleon and E. Francis (Cathays) comfortably retained his title whilst Newport retained the team award. For the first time a junior (by ability, not age) Championship was held attracting no fewer than ten teams all of which closed in. E.G. Ace, of Swansea Harriers, who until then had run with only mediocre success in senior championships seized his opportunity to win the title chased home by Eddie O'Donnell (Barry). The latter had the additional pleasure of his team finishing second to Castleton Harriers and ahead of a Roath second team. The junior event was obviously a great success both in the numbers attracted and in the fact that 'new' clubs were able to gain honours. In the first four years of this competition award winners included Castleton, Barry (twice), Caerleon, All Saints (Newport), Cwmbran, Abertillery and Abergavenny. The rate of change was enhanced by the rules excluding previous medal winners but even so there was an obvious incentive to clubs and their members to participate.

The 1905 international race in Dublin gave England a third consecutive win whilst Wales slipped back to fourth team position; E. Francis (9th) being the first man home. Jack Marsh missed out on this occasion as the Welsh association decided to select only home-based runners for their team. The 1906 International race came to Wales for the first time, being held at Caerleon. Prior to this the Welsh Championship at Ely saw Newport retain their title from Roath Harriers with Castleton Harriers, the previous year's junior winners, third. Ace and O'Donnell, prominent in the first junior race, had both changed clubs and were now in the colours of Newport and Roath respectively, in the senior event. Earlier in that season, Newport again competed in the Midland's Junior and Senior Championships and in the latter, at Coventry, had an excellent outing to finish third team and only narrowly lose out to Derby and County for second place. Welsh champion Tommy Arthur led them home in seventh place with a strong finish and might well have placed higher had he not been baulked by spectators encroaching on the course near the end of the race. As part of the publicity for the coming International the Lumley Shield was put on display in Newport. In the International race C.J. Straw of England won leading his nation to a fourth successive team victory with J.J. Daly of Ireland again the only athlete splitting the English scorers. Wales were once more fourth with T. Hughes in ninth place the best placed individual. Also yet again, the weather was unkind, a torrential downpour and wind making conditions uncomfortable in the extreme for competitors and spectators alike.

The 1907 Welsh Championship at Caerleon saw Newport retain senior and junior titles and provide both individual champions – Tommy Arthur and Ll. Lloyd. That season's International at Scotstoun, Glasgow saw France take part for the first time, finishing equal third on points with Ireland. They had been invited to the 1906 race in Wales but apparently had insufficient time to prepare. For Wales the Glasgow race was a disaster - the first man home was in thirty second position and the team finished a distant fifth.

In February 1908, Newport Harriers hosted the English Midland Championships at Caerleon attracting 260 athletes and twenty one teams - by far the largest such event to date in Wales. North Staffordshire Harriers won the team title with the host club seventh. Tommy Arthur was first Welsh runner home in 6th place. His fine form continued when he led Newport to victory in the Welsh senior race at Swansea. Edgar Stead (Cwmbran) and his team achieved a similar result in the junior race. The host club had a miserable day failing to finish a single runner in either race although former members E Ace and Ben Christmas were fifth and sixth respectively in the senior race.

The admission of France to the international running community was a tribute to the persuasive powers of Frank Liddington Johns and their appearance in 1907 at Scotstoun was followed by them hosting the 1908 race at Colombes, Paris. Here England won for the fifth time with the French team second and Wales last yet again. The 1909 International was held at Derby and was won by A. Wood of England. However, the star was the young Jean Bouin, running for France, giving an advance indication of his performances to come. Early in the race he paused and assisted one of the English athletes, who had fallen at a hurdle, before resuming his challenge for the lead. With a quarter mile to go Wood led by three to four metres from the Frenchman and well clear of all their pursuers. Wood just maintained this gap to the finish line despite several challenges from his rival, thus gaining a narrow victory. Wales again made a dismal showing, a distant fifth in the team competition with Edgar Stead (22nd) the leading finisher.

Wood went on to retain his title in Belfast in 1910 with France failing to complete a team. Jean Bouin then gained three consecutive victories – Caerleon (1911), Edinburgh (1912) and Paris (1913). The 1911 race in Wales saw Caerleon maintain its reputation for adverse conditions with snow on the ground obliterating the course markings and a chain of human markers waving hand flags having to be provided as a substitute.

There had been hopes that Belgium might join the other countries at Derby but with the First World War intervening it was 1925 before an additional nation joined the competition.

Courtesy of Brian Lee

Tommy Arthur (Newport) who was Welsh cross-country champion 1906 – 1909 and 4 miles track champion in 1908 and 1909. He represented Wales in the International Cross-Country Championships eight times between 1905 and 1914.

The final international before activity ceased due to the war was at Chesham, England in March 1914. England provided team and individual winners yet again although Scotland actually closed in before them whilst Wales were fourth team. A. S. Wilson in seventh position the first man home but according to contemporary reports Welsh supporters had great confidence in their national champion, Cliff Price of Newport who…."after gaining a very useful lead, he was mis-directed upon entering the country" and eventually finished tenth.

Domestically, the 1909 Welsh Championship, at Caerleon, was an almost total triumph for Newport - Tommy Arthur won the title for the fourth successive year to create a record which was not equalled until Malcolm Thomas performed the feat some 63 years later – and his club scored an eleventh successive team win. Initially, Arthur was challenged by A. Grainger, of Cwmbran Harriers, but having failed to stay the pace with the leader Grainger dropped out altogether. This action removed any chance of his club upsetting Newport; a result which had been predicted prior to the race.

The 1910 Welsh Championship was also held at Caerleon with Newport winning the senior title and Tredegar St James the junior event. J.F. Iles (Roath Harriers) and T. Harry (St Saviours) were the individual champions. The following year at Ely, Newport finally had their senior title stranglehold broken – Cwmbran Harriers led home by Ernest Paul as winner, packing their scorers in the first ten.

High tide delays championship

The Welsh Championships returned to Caerleon yet again in 1912 and Cwmbran retained their senior title with the first three runners home - T.J. Miles, Ernest Paul and A. Herring. E. Davies (St Saviours) won the junior race leading his club to a single point win over the Abertillery club. The official race report has the interesting comments "very bad judging of junior race. Several runners missed from sheets …. Good attendance but teams and spectators interfered with by shortage of trains through coal strike." It may well be that the first of these comments indicates the reason for the suggestions of a re-run of the race raised in Welsh CCA committee meetings.

In the 1913 senior race at Caerleon an irate farmer "with a pike" affected the race by turning "all except the first two men off the trail which led through a gap in the hedge and made them go along the rough cinders to a proper entrance gate into field." Despite this interference Cwmbran repeated their success although on this occasion their three medallists were Edgar Stead, A. Herring and Ernest Paul.

Courtesy of Brian Lee

Edgar Stead of Cwmbran.

An indication of the variable conditions at Caerleon can be gauged by the fact that the senior race was delayed for a week "when high tides and torrential downpours flooded the area to depth of three to four feet". Not surprisingly and despite "brilliant sunshine ...... ground was very heavy which told against the runners, many falling out." Newport regained the team title ahead of Cwmbran Harriers with Cliff Price of Newport first man home.

At the 1912 AGM William Fairlamb resigned as President and was replaced by Percy Mountjoy. It was finally decided to affiliate to the AAA (of England). At the immediately following committee meeting the Treasurer suggested a "watch competition" as a fund raising scheme and this was enthusiastically received, it being decided to "proceed at once....and that cards be issued as early as possible." The watch competition was to be decided in February – opening the sealed case containing the watch and scrutinising the cards. In the interim, as in more recent times, it became apparent that relatively few cards and payments had been returned with a consequential poor financial return. The competition was therefore extended for a month and a major effort undertaken to promote the scheme. This apparently met with reasonable success although no figures are quoted in the minutes.

The 1913 AGM yet further debated eligibility for international selection, it having been formally proposed, "that all Welsh qualified athletes be eligible for selection." This was again defeated thus continuing the restriction of selection to members of affiliated clubs. At the meeting several clubs expressed interest in hosting that season's championships; one of these, Pontnewydd Harriers was eventually approved as the successful bidder. In addition to his other duties Frank Liddington Johns was now acting as Chairman of the committee.

The ongoing problem of Welsh team selection continued to exercise minds and was raised yet once more in March 1914. In that year's selection sub-committee meeting it was "pointed out the absurdity of our rules, which allowed Massey, an English international, being included and excluded any Welshman who was a member of an English club." The specific anomaly had been created by E. Massey who finished eighth in that year's championship, representing Newport Harriers. In the autumn, the 1914 Annual General Meeting finally passed a rule stating "that any amateur runner having a birth or residential qualification may be eligible for selection in the Welsh international team." The length of residency required was not specified. The main factor in the final acceptance of a change was that in wartime conditions most good "runners of the past year had joined the colours" and if they remained in the armed forces in the longer term they "would be debarred from selection." It was further "decided, owing to the state of war......holding championships, senior and junior, be abandoned for the present." This was apparently the effective cessation of all activity, even committee meetings, for a period of about five years.

The 1920s

The resumption of administrative and competitive activity came in the 1919/20 season. An annual general meeting was held in January 1920 and the minutes read as if there had only been a few weeks break rather than several years – even the names of officers and representatives of clubs showing little change. At the meeting it was proposed to hold a novice championship open "to teams of eight men (four to count) from any area in Wales and from clubs (athletic or otherwise) whether affiliated to the association or not." Novices were defined as being those who have never won a prize in a race, club or open of over half a mile" prior to a set date. The event was to be held at Tredegar in February and Percy Mountjoy gave a donation of two guineas (£2.10) towards the cost of medals.

The First World War is notorious for the huge loss of life suffered by the armed forces in the main due to the prolonged trench warfare. One of those definitely recorded as having been killed in action was Newport's Tommy Arthur, four times the title winner, whilst Cliff

Price of the same club lost a leg. Bearing this in mind it is pleasing to note that several of the names entered in the revived championships were athletes who had competed five or six years previous - including Sam Judd of Chepstow, Ernest Paul (Cwmbran), D.H. Francis (Roath) and T.J. Miles (Newport). The last named went on to win the senior race regaining the title he had previously won eight years earlier. It is also worthy of note that in the programme for the races Chepstow Harriers whilst entering as a team in their own right are still referred to as a "branch of Newport Harriers."

With regard to the resumption of international competition in 1920 "it was decided that should funds be available we send a team to Belfast to compete in this event." In March a team was selected but the decision on participation was further deferred pending fund raising efforts. These were apparently unsuccessful and the decision finally reached not to attend. The selected athletes were however "awarded jerseys" and an official photograph taken of the team. The Honorary Secretary was mandated to attend the International Board meeting to explain Wales' absence and to issue an invitation for the race to be held in Wales the following season. The race was notable for the fact that for the first time the winner was neither English nor French - that distinction going to Jimmy Wilson of Scotland. It should however be noted that six years earlier he had been a member of England's winning team.

At the AGM in December 1920 A.V. Mathias resigned as Honorary Secretary and was replaced by Eddie O'Donnell. Despite only having a balance of just over eight pounds in its accounts the Association decided on a full programme of races for 1920/21; namely novice (January, Newport area), junior (February, Cwmbran district) and senior and international (March – both at Caerleon). At a late stage the venue for the junior race had to be changed to Malpas Court, Newport as "the greater portion of the Cwmbran course" was "now into plough and quite unsuitable." Later that spring there were complications over the International with the Welsh Association formally minuting "that we view with regret the apparent deflection (sic) of the French team from the International.......and desire that....England should not accept the invitation of our French friends for a contest before...." As a support event to the International the Territorial Forces Association held its own championship over the Caerleon course prior to the main race.

It's back to Caerleon Racecourse

The 1921 International was held at Caerleon for the third time and yet again England dominated with four of the first five individuals home split only by B.H. Bingham (Ireland) in third place. In the absence of France, Wales were third team just ahead of Scotland. First Welsh runner home was Sam Judd in thirteenth place. France returning to the competition gave England its first ever team defeat in the 1922 International at Hampden Park, Glasgow and provided the individual champion in Joseph Guillemot. First Welshman home that year was senior champion Ernie Thomas, in fifth place. In later years he followed this up with eleventh in 1924 at Newcastle on Tyne and sixth in 1927 and 22nd in 1933 on home ground. His record of twelve runs in the international together with six Welsh senior titles over the period, 1921-33 plus two second places and two thirds makes him one of our most successful cross-country runners, certainly until recent times.

With home advantage in 1923 France repeated their team success. Neither Wales nor Scotland were present on this occasion but Belgium competed for the first time and provided the third individual home.

In January 1923, international matters had again come to the fore at association committee meetings. The political changes in Ireland meant another country and team had been created. It was agreed that "both the Free State" and "Northern Ireland should be allowed to compete; that each should have one representative on the International Board; that the race should be held alternately in the south and the north....once every five years." It was however decided to oppose the proposition by France that the race be held in that country every third year and by Scotland "that the race be held annually in the north of England." It was however a further nine years before a Northern Ireland team appeared and yet a further five before they hosted the competition. In the same year (1923) the Welsh association agreed to assist University College Aberystwyth in the inauguration of a west Wales championship. The College had been the first club outside south Wales to join the association and had been competing for a number of years. At a later meeting it was decided that the winning club and individual in this west Wales event would be granted free entry to the Welsh Senior Championship. Plans were made for the race to be held in Carmarthen early in 1925 but were later abandoned "owing to the withdrawal of the Carmarthen College team".

The 1924 AGM covered a large amount of business. Eddie O' Donnell reported that a special sub-committee of the International Board had been called "at which rules governing cross country internationals were drawn up" and that the governing body was now termed "The International Cross Country Union." This was probably in anticipation of the fact that Belgium and later Switzerland would be joining. It was also agreed to call a special general meeting to consider revision of the domestic first claim rules. This latter action was on a request from Newport Harriers supported by Pontypool. Finally, it was noted that the (English) National cross-country race was to be held at Hereford on March 14th 1925, for the second time in four years. As a consequence the Welsh Senior Championship was scheduled for March 21st and it was agreed to seek postponement of the international in Dublin to April 4th. The latter plea was unsuccessful as the date selected was 28th March 1925. A further development was to propose that the financial arrangements for internationals be altered so that "the home country should take the whole of the profits and bear the whole of the expenses" rather than the procedure to date of sharing any profit or loss equally among the participants.

In that 1925 International in Dublin Wales were third and only one point behind the Irish team. For the Newport Harrier members of the Welsh squad this competition was their third major championship in as many weeks as they had contested the English national event at Hereford, finishing second team behind Birchfield Harriers, with D.J.P Richards in 4th place.

At the next AGM, (October 1925), the name of Ted Hopkins (Roath) appears in the list of delegates for the first time - the start of many years' service to the sport. At the meeting it was reported that the financial proposals for the international had been accepted. The next event was scheduled for Brussels on March 28th 1926 with Wales as hosts the following year. There was also the comment that Belgium be asked to wear "colours other than the scarlet now used." There then followed a tortuous and lengthy discussion on a proposal on first claim rules the aim being to restrict athletes to representing the club nearest their home in championship races. On a vote the proposal was narrowly lost but several of the officers abstained. Two weeks later a special General Meeting was called and the whole subject raised again. On this occasion it was made clear that the rule would not be retrospective and that existing athletes would retain their current affiliations. Moreover athletes who moved residence could also retain their existing eligibility and similar exceptions would apply to members of "closed" clubs. The Chairman restricted debate and the proposals were carried by a large majority. Even so a further General Meeting was held in January 1926 to make an amendment to the operative dates for the revised rules. A committee meeting

Courtesy of Newport H.

Welsh cross-country team of 1926, which competed at the International in Belgium.
Back row left to right: not known, not known, Ted Hopkins, Ivor Thomas, Danny Phillips, not known, AVJ Mathias (Hon. Sec. WCCA).
Front row left to right: Frank Liddington Johns (Hon. Treasurer WCCA), Jimmy Guy, Ernie Thomas, E. Leyshon, not known, not known. Amongst unknown athletes are B. Hammond and C. Morgan.

immediately followed at which a major topic was fund raising for the coming visit to Belgium. The ideas included a Prize Draw with three major prizes – Trip to Brussels with team; rail fare and ticket for the FA Cup Final; and rail fare plus ticket to Wales/Ireland rugby match! The draw raised over £61 towards the quoted price of £80 for the team's trip to Brussels. On a domestic matter it was agreed to accept a Welsh University team "being entered for the senior championship" subject to the University becoming directly affiliated; such affiliation being formally accepted a month later. There was also reference to a Miner's road race "sponsored by the South Wales Echo." A letter was to be sent to the newspaper thanking them "for the valuable help they had given through the event, in fostering distance running in Wales". Unfortunately no details of the event are given other than confirmation that it was "a confined one and that prize winners would not thereby forfeit their novice status"

At the October 1926 AGM eight new clubs were accepted into membership but still predominantly south and east Wales based. The general meeting then went on to formally consider and adopt a complete new set of rules drawn up by the officers. They had apparently carried out their task very efficiently as the whole package was accepted with minimal discussion, amendment or addition. Two notes were added clarifying that championship medals were "awards" not "prizes" as far as novice status was concerned and that the "AAA law regarding the giving of assistance or refreshment to competitors be added by means of a footnote in the new edition of the rules." Following this administrative success Eddie O'Donnell (Honorary Secretary) and A.V. Mathias (Assistant Secretary) did not seek re-election and were replaced by T.V. Berry and J.G. Coombes respectively although both of the former post holders continued as vice presidents.

The scrutiny meeting for the junior race to be held at Cwm in January 1927 ruled out B. Fournier of Llanbradach because he "was not an amateur and decided that he would only be allowed to compete if he applies for reinstatement before the race." The meeting then went on to deal with other business. The junior race at Cwm had problems and a committee meeting on February 2nd decided that the race would have to be re-run at Court Farm, Cwmbran ten days later.

The international race in 1927 returned to Caerleon and the Welsh captain was Jimmy Guy (Spillers AC) better known in later years as the official handicapper, starter and secretary of East Glamorgan AAA, whilst T.V. Berry (Assistant Secretary) also gained selection to the team to add to his other responsibilities. One unexpected complication that arose was that the Prize Draw incurred the attention and displeasure of the Home Office in London no less and they instructed the local police to the effect that the draw "...should have to be withdrawn." In the race France gained their fourth team victory in the eight post war years and the second in a run of four consecutive successes. With Belgium absent Wales were fourth team splitting Scotland and Ireland. The individual winner on this occasion was Lewis Payne (Hallamshire) aged only 19 and to date the youngest ever senior international champion.

The 1927 General Meeting finally saw Frank Liddington Johns retire as Honorary Treasurer being replaced by Bill Fisher, also of Newport. The meeting then began yet another revision of eligibility rules; this carrying over to an adjournment a month later. The net result was that the existing lengthy and complicated rules were replaced by the relatively straightforward AAA (of England) one with the substitution of "five miles radius" for "twenty miles" in recognition of the relative closeness of communities in south Wales. A committee meeting immediately followed and a sub-committee was appointed to investigate the possibilities of holding a youths' championship. This task was completed with remarkable alacrity and formal plans laid within a fortnight. The race was to be held prior to the senior race, at the same venue, and over a distance of approximately three miles. It was confirmed that winning such an event would not jeopardise novice status. Yet a further development occurred late that year when a special general meeting in August gave consent to the "formation of a cross-country league among clubs of the association" to be operated by a league committee.

It should be noted that until 1924 cross-country was included as a team event in the Olympic programme but there does not appear to be any record of any Welsh participation.

The championships of the 1920s and emergence of D.J.P. Richards

Very aptly the first championship held after the First World War was the inaugural novice championship at Bassaleg, outside Newport. It was held on "a glorious spring afternoon. Trail well laid over five miles of varied country with only a few dozen yards of road in the whole length." O. Morgan and Ernie Thomas of Cwmbran Harriers were first and second with S. Howell of Newport Harriers third, their respective clubs finishing first and second with Cwm Harriers third and Chepstow Harriers fourth. No times were recorded but an unofficial time of 31:08 was noted for the winner. These clubs also dominated the junior race at Chepstow but with Newport the winners, Chepstow second and Cwm third. The good fortune with the weather did not continue, "frequent showers of tropical intensity and driven by the wind made the conditions almost unbearable for runners and spectators alike." Consequently the lack of times on this occasion is hardly surprising. The senior race was held at the same venue a fortnight later in far better conditions – "fine, warm and sun shining brilliantly." T.J. Miles of Newport won from Ernie Thomas of Cwmbran with their teams in the same positions. Despite the favourable circumstances Roath only started six runners and two of these "met with misfortune in the country and could not finish the course." Even so their club was credited with the "the two last placings" to enable them to close in!

Ernie Thomas (Cwmbran) took the first of his six senior titles in 1921, winning by over half a minute from Sam Judd now in the colours of Newport whilst Gwyn Morgan in third place collected his third individual award in six weeks.

The novice race at Margam at the end of January 1922 saw the first Welsh title win of the remarkable D.J.P. Richards, running for Port Talbot YMCA, whose achievements are documented elsewhere in this book. The 1923 senior event at Court Farm, Cwmbran saw Newport Harriers totally dominant with the first four home including Richards, having changed clubs, as runner-up. Cwmbran Harriers were a distant second just ahead of Roath. Ernie Thomas regained the title in 1924 and broke the course record set eleven years earlier. Newport, with the first three home for the second successive year retained the team title. T.H. Gwilliam, born in Montgomeryshire ran as an individual in the colours of Birchfield Harriers.

Newport Harriers were still regular participants in the English Midland Championships and in the years 1922-24 were second to Birchfield on three occasions - the Midland junior at Leicester (1922) and the senior in 1923 and 1924. The venue for the 1924 Midland senior was Caerleon.

The 1925 senior race at Caerleon saw Newport provide the first three home with D.J.P Richards taking the first of his three senior titles with a narrow victory over Ernie Thomas. In fifth place in that year's novice championship was future marathon star Ike O'Brien running for Port Talbot YMCA whilst the name of future Welsh AAA President Arthur Williams also appears down the field. They also ran in the junior race at Pengam Farm, Cardiff at the end of January as did several others better known in later years as administrators - Ted Hopkins, J.D.B. (Jack) Williams and Charlie Radford (Cardiff Gas). Pengam Farm was now the base of Roath Harriers and they established a new headquarters there a year or so later. Newport led by Ernie's brother, Ivor once more won the team title very easily ahead of Roath and this was repeated in the senior race at Caerleon - Ernie Thomas regaining the individual title.

Further indication of the growing popularity of cross-country running came with the 1926 Novice Championship at Llandaff Fields, home of the University College which attracted no fewer than thirty two teams all of whom closed in with 221 runners completing the course. A.J. Nichols (Cwmbran) was first across the finish line but "it having been proved that he had been paced on several occasions by senior members of his club, he was disqualified." Cardiff University won the team competition from Cwmbran and their margin of victory was such that they would probably have still done so even if Nichols had not been ruled out. J. Hughes of Pontnewydd took the title by default and his club was third. Following this occurrence there were also problems at Cwm early in February and the junior championship had to be declared "no race" due to a large number of the competitors going off course. In the re-run at Court Farm, Cwmbran, Hughes defeated Nichols by over half a minute but Gwyn Lewis of Roath beat both. The host club won from Newport and Pontnewydd in a high scoring competition. Later in February the first west Wales championship was held at Neath with four teams from that locality taking part. Ike O'Brien (Port Talbot) won the race but the next six runners (three of them members of the Duggan family) were all representing Swansea Valley AC who thus gained a comfortable team victory. They included Frank Duggan who, in later years, was a leading official and administrator, particularly in west Wales. The senior race at Caerleon saw Ernie Thomas (Cwmbran) winning from Ted Hopkins (Roath). Roath regained the team title after several years whilst Cwmbran were second ahead of Newport.

The 1928 Senior Championship saw D.J.P. Richards' reappearance to win by over a minute wearing the colours of the University of Wales. Cwmbran with six runners in the first nine home gained a very easy victory from Roath with the University third; a total of eleven teams closing in. Immediately prior to the senior championship the inaugural youths (under 18) championship had been held. S.T. Hardy (Cwmbran) won by nearly a minute in 14:09 so one suspects that the course was less than the three miles stated. With three to score Splott YMCA won from Newport and Cwmbran; eight teams comprising forty-four athletes completing the course. Earlier in the month D.J.P. Richards representing Aberystwyth University won the second west Wales title at Clydach. The team event was however retained by Swansea Valley AC ahead of the students and an army team from the 2nd East Lancs Regiment who were presumably in barracks in the area.

Most of the foregoing commentary has inevitably related to winning teams and individuals. However, cross-country is a team sport and the mainstay of clubs are the members who make up the teams, often training and competing for little tangible reward but because of their enjoyment of competition, the comradeship and the satisfaction of endeavour for their club. Taking one club, Cwm Harriers, at random the names of A and Frank Denmead appear frequently in results during the 1920s. The second of these, in particular, scored for Cwm Harriers in eight championships between 1923-25, twice in the novice and three times each in the junior and senior championships. In addition Frank also counted for Cwm in the 1926 and 1928 senior championships. Despite never winning any titles he was selected for Wales on three occasions, (1927-8-9), making an excellent record of consistent service and typical of the sport and its participants.

The 1930s championships with Bill Matthews and Harry Gallivan to the fore

The 1930 Welsh Novice Championship at Llanbradach saw a new name but one to dominate in the future - Harry Gallivan winning for Pontnewydd, whilst the junior race at Pontnewydd, was won by Private Sam (Soapy) Palmer of the Essex Regiment, another athlete to make a significant mark on the sport in Wales. He was seven seconds ahead of Gallivan who had beaten him by over a minute a month earlier. In the 1931 Senior Championship, Danny Phillips (Cwmbran) led home from teammate, Ernie Thomas, to win the first of his two titles and their club retained its title with Newport and Roath yet again second and third.

But it was Gallivan and the slight Penrhys Harrier Bill Matthews who were to dominate the senior championship in the 1930s, taking the event three times each. Ernie Thomas took his sixth title in 1933, twelve years after his first win on the same Caerleon Racecourse.

Ivor Gaylard of Elyn AC won the December 1933 youth's race whilst Roath won the team competition. In third place for Roath was Viv Pitcher who gave yeoman administrative service to the sport in later years. Bill Matthews won the junior race in February whilst Jim Alford (fifth) and Ken Harris (seventh) were the leading scorers in Roath's winning team. Jack Collard was eighth for Elyn AC, with another Elyn runner, the celebrated Road Runners Club statistician, Dave (Jenkin) Roberts in 10th. Collard, along with Jim Thomas formed Birchgrove Harriers in 1952, after a spell as secretary of Hopkinsons Electrical AC. This race was re-run after the initial competition at Glais, in the lower Swansea valley, was declared "no race" due to stewards mis-directing the leaders. There was some consolation for Swansea Valley AC as they took the second place medals ahead of Elyn AC. Four weeks later Bill Matthews won his first senior title ahead of Harry Gallivan with Reg Thomas (RAF), the 1930 Empire Games Mile Champion, eighth. In what was obviously a very high standard race Ted Hopkins was twelfth, Jim Alford fourteenth, Wilf Short fifteenth and Ken Harris twenty seventh! Newport Harriers won the team event from Cwmbran 87-91.

Pen Portrait - Viv Pitcher (Roath Harriers)

The late Viv Pitcher did more than anyone else to record the early years of track and field and cross-country in Wales. His name might not be one that is instantly recognisable, but there is no question that his contribution to Welsh athletics was considerable. In short much of the historical data now available would have been lost without him.

Viv Pitcher

He was a man of strong principles and he fell out with the then Welsh athletics establishment in the late 1950s. Apart from being coerced back by Ted Hopkins to officiate in the 1967 International Cross Country Championships in Barry, he severed all connections with the sport, until about 1985 when he returned to live in Cardiff and was a frequent visitor to Welsh Cross Country Championships and Gwent Leagues at Heath Park in Cardiff.

Viv was probably Wales' first athletics statistician. His painstaking research up to the time of his fracas with officialdom resulted in a series of copperplate hand-written volumes of irreplaceable results, facts and figures relating to both the athletics and cross-country scene in Wales. The first deep all-time lists produced by the editor had their base in Viv Pitcher's books, whilst another of his volumes "Outstanding Welsh Athletics Performances" was the source of more valuable data.

He was a Roath Harrier through and through and in 1952 he published a history of the club which recorded every fact and detail possible about the club from its formation in 1882 up to the 1952/1953 season. It records every Roath member who won a Welsh title along with a full list of club officers from which it is recorded that Viv was club treasurer five times and club secretary in 1952.

Viv also officiated at all of the major meetings in Wales until the late 1950s and was the first Championship Secretary of the Glamorgan Championships just after the Second World War. He also acted in this capacity at several Welsh Championship meetings. He contributed to *The Western Mail* for many years as "Pacemaker" and the Welsh AAA finally recognised his services to Welsh athletics when they belatedly awarded him a Meritorious Plaque in 1983.

The 1936 junior and youth races at Whitchurch were delayed one week to February 1st due to national mourning following the death of King George V. Bramwell Baldwin, elder brother of Bernard, won the youth event. The 1937 youth and senior races were held at Caerleon in almost perfect weather. In the earlier race Bramwell Baldwin defending his title collapsed after a mile and failed to finish. Despite this setback Barry School retained their team title with Canton High School second and Bridgend County School third. The senior race saw Billy Matthews and Harry Gallivan head to head once more. The latter set the early pace with Matthews back in fourth place. As the heavy conditions took their toll the rugged Penrhys Harrier came through to win by three seconds, with Ivor Brown of Llanbradach third. Barry County School again won the youth team title the next season with Bill Richards, seventh the previous year, winning ahead of Lyn Griffiths of Port Talbot YMCA. Third in the race was Bramwell Baldwin, competing for the fourth consecutive year and thereby gaining a complete set of individual medals for the event - gold in 1936, silver in 1935 and bronze in 1938. The senior championship at Llantarnam in March 1938 was the 99th overall in the history of the sport in the Principality. The leading placings in the race were almost a repeat of the previous year – Bill Matthews narrowly beating Harry Gallivan with Ivor Brown now Mitcham AC again third.

There have been occasional allusions to colleges and universities at various points where they participated in national or regional championships. For their part they also had their own University of Wales championships between teams from the constituent colleges starting in1923. From these they selected a University of Wales team to go forward to the

Roath Harriers thought to have been taken after the 1935 Welsh Cross-Country Championships won by Harry Gallivan (Cwmbran)
Team; Back row W. H. Facey, Bob Wade, Ken Harris (4), Mr. Bennett, Bert Lacey (8), Tom Hopkins, Jim Alford (1), Tom Burge (5) George Stowe
Front row: Tom Slammin (6), Ted Hopkins – Capt. (2), Len Brown (7).

annual Universities Athletic Union (UAU) Championship against opposition from the English Provincial Universities. In the late 1920s D.J.P Richards was their leading athlete whilst in 1935 and 1936 Jim Alford was the individual champion, although he does not appear to have represented them in the UAU event, certainly in the latter year.

The international scene, 1929-39.

The International Cross-Country Championship became truly worthy of the title, certainly as far as Europe was concerned, in March 1929 at the Vincennes Hippodrome, Paris. Spain, Italy, Switzerland and Luxembourg all competed for the first time making up a ten-team competition. It was a further twenty-one years before that total was matched again. France, with home advantage, gained a fourth consecutive win, England having been second on each occasion. The influx of new teams did not greatly improve Wales' record, as the only teams they beat regularly were Ireland and Belgium. Suffice to say that they were never last in the years between the two World Wars. Best team placings were 1933 (Caerleon), 1935 (Paris) and 1938 (Belfast) on all of which occasions they were fourth team. The latter occasion was notable for two other reasons. Internationally it was the first time since the political division of Ireland that the race was held in the north and both parts of Ireland fielded teams. Secondly, from a Welsh viewpoint the performance of Soapy Palmer – his nickname came from his initials - S.O.A. Palmer - in finishing third individual was the memorable achievement. Up to that point it was the highest position a Welsh athlete had finished in the race – indeed as time would tell, only two other Welshmen – John Merriman (1960) and Steve Jones (1984) would equal the feat, although Maesteg born Tony Simmons during his wilderness years finished second for England, ironically at Chepstow in 1976, the last time the international race has been held in Wales. To add salt to the wound, Simmons was appointed English captain that day!

The start of the 1939 International Cross-Country race at Ely Racecourse, Cardiff. Early leaders are Frenchman Gaston Letisserand (14) and Maurice Beaudoiun (22) with Belgian Oran Van Rumst (27) just behind them.

Over the years the now defunct Caerleon Racecourse – it is now a housing estate - had gained a reputation both for its severity and the inordinately bad weather for the races –1906 (heavy rain), 1911(snow), 1921 (fog) and 1927 (heavy rain). 1933 was different and for once "glorious summer conditions prevailed" as the local paper reported. Indeed the weather was so warm that one of the English runners risked disqualification by removing his vest before climbing what had become known as heartbreak hill. The race saw the emergence of the great Jack Holden who won the event for England by ten seconds from the Scotsman, R Sutherland. Holden went on to win the next two international races. Harry Gallivan, the previous year's Welsh champion, was the leading Welshman in thirteenth place with Ernie Thomas the next scorer. The team race again went to England but Wales put up one of its better performances finishing fourth.

W. H. Facey of Roath Harriers, the President of the International Cross Country Union crowning Jack Holden of England the winner of the international race at Caerleon in 1933.

Despite the impending war, the 1939 Championship went ahead in Cardiff on the now defunct Ely racecourse, the first major event to be held there for almost 30 years, and the scene of the first Welsh Cross-Country Championship in 1894. France comfortably won the team event ahead of England with Belgium third for the third consecutive year. Wales were fifth ahead of both Irish teams. Individual champion was again Jack Holden, gaining a then record fourth individual title and his sixth medal placing in eight years. Brilliant weather graced the occasion as Ivor Brown, of Llanbradach, was first Welsh runner home in eleventh position with that year's AAA 6 miles Champion Soapy Palmer not far behind in fourteenth. *The South Wales Echo* said of the occasion: "Great Cross Country Running at Ely"

32nd ANNUAL

INTERNATIONAL CROSS COUNTRY CHAMPIONSHIP

TO BE HELD AT

ELY RACECOURSE

ENGLAND
FRANCE
BELGIUM
WALES
SCOTLAND
N. IRELAND
EIRE

CARDIFF
(by kind permission)

SATURDAY
APRIL 1st, 1939

RACE START - 3.15 p.m.

Preceded by

A DEMONSTRATION OF PHYSICAL EXERCISES
by THE WOMEN'S LEAGUE OF HEALTH AND BEAUTY
Led by Muriel M. Parsons (Instructress for Wales)
Accompanied by St. Alban's Military Band.

Souvenir Programme - 3D.

Front page of programme of the International Cross-Country race held at Ely, Cardiff in 1939.

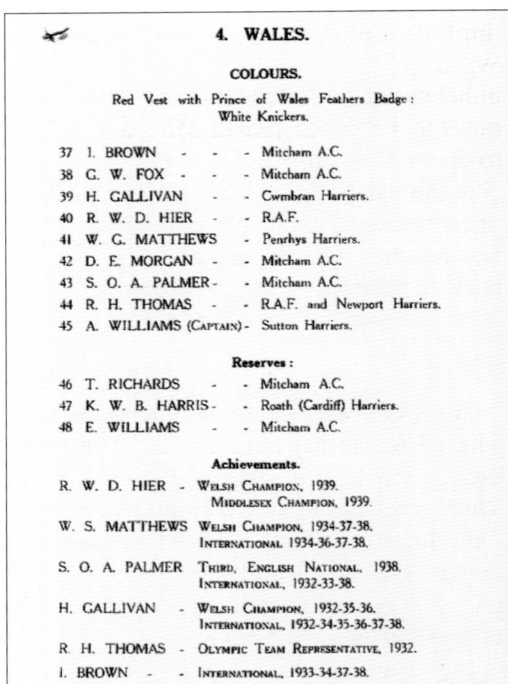

4. WALES.

COLOURS.

Red Vest with Prince of Wales Feathers Badge: White Knickers.

37	I. BROWN	Mitcham A.C.
38	G. W. FOX	Mitcham A.C.
39	H. GALLIVAN	Cwmbran Harriers.
40	R. W. D. HIER	R.A.F.
41	W. G. MATTHEWS	Penrhys Harriers.
42	D. E. MORGAN	Mitcham A.C.
43	S. O. A. PALMER	Mitcham A.C.
44	R. H. THOMAS	R.A.F. and Newport Harriers.
45	A. WILLIAMS (CAPTAIN)	Sutton Harriers.

Reserves:

46	T. RICHARDS	Mitcham A.C.
47	K. W. B. HARRIS	Roath (Cardiff) Harriers.
48	E. WILLIAMS	Mitcham A.C.

Achievements.

R. W. D. HIER	WELSH CHAMPION, 1939. MIDDLESEX CHAMPION, 1939.
W. S. MATTHEWS	WELSH CHAMPION, 1934-37-38. INTERNATIONAL 1934-36-37-38.
S. O. A. PALMER	THIRD, ENGLISH NATIONAL, 1938. INTERNATIONAL, 1932-33-38.
H. GALLIVAN	WELSH CHAMPION, 1932-35-36. INTERNATIONAL, 1932-34-35-36-37-38.
R. H. THOMAS	OLYMPIC TEAM REPRESENTATIVE, 1932.
I. BROWN	INTERNATIONAL, 1933-34-37-38.

Page from programme for the 1939 International Cross Country race.

Danny Phillips of Newport and Cwmbran appeared in the international race a remarkable fourteen times between 1922 and 1937, and this remains a record to this day, as Wales ceased to participate as a separate nation after 1987, competing as part of a British team from that date. Ernie Thomas' total of twelve (1922-1935) is the second best by a Welsh athlete ahead of Tom Richards (10 appearances between 1934 and 1953) and Steve Jones (1977 – 1987), also with 10 appearances. For his part Harry Gallivan achieved nine runs between 1931 and 39. His best race position was in 1935 at Paris when he finished eighth.

We are off to Tooting Bec!

During the mid 1930s, home based Welsh cross-country running suffered a great blow, when a large number of the team to represent Wales in the international race during this period "defected" to England. But it was for no other reason than to escape the poverty and joblessness of the south Wales valleys, and the good thing for Welsh fans was that all retained their Welsh identity. The most significant of those making the move to south London to work as a male nurse in Tooting Bec Hospital was future Olympic silver medallist Tom Richards, of whom we will hear more later. Amongst others to make this move were Ivor Brown (Llanbradach); Eric Williams and George Fox (Penrhys); Dennis Morgan and Ellwood Jones (Swansea Valley). Brown finished third in the senior championships in both 1937 and 1938, whilst Morgan was the 1936 marathon champion and Fox finished third in the 1939 cross-country championship. Eric Williams was third in both 1948 and 1949 and unbeknown to the organisers, attended the centenary races in 1996. All joined Mitcham AC, and if allowed to do so, the club would have won the team title at the championships in 1937, 1938 and 1939, as all of the athletes named finished in the top ten of each race. Tommy Winslade (Port Talbot YMCA) winner of the Welsh Junior title in 1938 was another who made the journey to Mitcham. Sixty years on he was still alive and well, back in his home town of Maesteg.

First three in the Welsh Cross-Country Championships at Llantarnam in 1938. Left to right Bill Matthews (Penrhys Harriers) 1st, Harry Gallivan (Cwmbran) 2nd and Ivor Brown (Mitcham) 3rd.

The Second World War period

Cross-country, like most other activities, was severely constrained during the early 1940s. The 1939 international race in Wales was the last full one until 1946 although there was a race in Paris, of all places, in 1940 involving juniors from France, England and Belgium. Welsh championships continued for a short period but then lapsed until December 1945, with the sole exception of the youth's race. During this wartime period there were domestic competitions, especially between Service units and the like. Almost certainly these were part of a policy to maintain fitness and enhance morale in the general population and the armed forces in particular.

The 1938/9 championship programme in Wales appears to have taken place undisturbed. The honour of being the 100th Welsh Championship fell to the novice race at Pontnewydd in December. Roath Harriers won with the lowest ever score of eighteen points. Bill

Start of the Welsh Cross-country Championships at Caerleon in 1939 showing two Welsh distance legends. The athlete rubbing his hands in an RAF vest in the centre of the picture is Reg Thomas the 1930 Empire Games mile champion, with his RAF colleague, and winner of the race, Dillan Hier next to him. Alongside Dillan is Tom Richards in the colours of Mitcham, some 9 years before his 1948 Olympic silver medal performance. Next-but-one to Tom is Mitcham teammate Ivor Brown and then Ken Harris with handkerchief wrapped around his left hand.

Richards now running for Roath was individual champion followed by his club mate, another former Barry runner, Bramwell Baldwin, and S. M. Wood of Cardiff University. The Senior Championships in March 1939 returned to Caerleon. Roath Harriers won from Cwmbran with Welsh Universities third. Dillan Hier, of the RAF, won the race from Bill Matthews whilst the latter's former club mate George Fox gave Mitcham AC its third consecutive bronze medallist.

The following season saw only two championship level races. The youth event was held at Rumney, Cardiff on February 24th. D. H. Downs of Bridgend School retained his individual title and led his school to a first team win with Barry School second and Roath Harriers third. The second event was an open race with no medals awarded. S .I. Griffiths (Newport Harriers) won from Howard Davies (Neath AC) and Bramwell Baldwin of Roath.

For the five years of the Second World War the youth race venue alternated between Bridgend and Barry and the keen rivalry between these two schools was obviously a significant factor. Bridgend won in 1941 with Barry winning on the four other occasions. Only two of the fifteen individual medallists were not representing one or other of the two schools.

The Second World War was a break point in many ways in that life, values and expectations afterwards were never going to return to those of previous times. It is therefore a convenient point to make an overall review up to that date. Taking the Welsh Senior championship as the criterion Newport Harriers predominance is self-evident. In the forty-six years of championships there had been forty-one races. Of these Newport won twenty one times including runs of twelve and eight in succession, were second seven times and third on four occasions. To their total must be added two races where their second team finished third. Of their rivals, Roath Harriers won on six occasions but had twenty two-second places and ten thirds. Cwmbran Harriers, for their part, achieved twelve wins including one spell of six consecutive victories but only six second places and one third. As indicated elsewhere, Newport Harriers' successes extended over the border and in this respect they had two particularly high points. In 1903-8 and 1922-26 when they gained high team placings in Midland counties events in the earlier period and in both Midland counties and English national competitions in the latter one. Their failure to defend their Midland junior team title in 1924 was attributable to a fixture clash resulting from disruption caused by a foot and mouth epidemic amongst farm animals that year.

One other aspect of note is the remarkable continuity and longevity of service of Welsh CCA officers. The situation up to the mid-1920s has been covered previously but the following quarter century continued the same pattern and this was in general terms the case until the association became part of the Athletics Association of Wales in 1990. An exception was the Presidency which became looked upon as a way of honouring senior personnel. For the fifty years from the mid-1920s individuals generally held the office for periods of two years before handing on the chain of office. The posts of Secretary and Treasurer for their part saw only fourteen individuals cover the sixty years, the most notable being Ted Hopkins who was Honorary Secretary from 1938 to 1968 inclusive.

Pen Portrait - Ted Hopkins MBE (Roath H and Cardiff AAC) 190? -1974

Ted Hopkins MBE

It is over a quarter of a century since the death of Ted Hopkins, but his name is still revered as one of the finest personalities in Welsh athletics. He died in 1974 and just 13 days after his death, his name appeared in the New Year's Honours List. Viv Pitcher's excellent history of Roath Harriers said: "1924 saw the advent in Roath colours of a man who, as captain and the club champion for future years, probably did more than anyone else in guiding the club along the path which eventually led to the outstanding successful period to World War 11. I refer to Ted Hopkins who, as a member of Splott YMCA, had already shown considerable promise as a distance runner".

Ted had given almost half a century of service to athletics, both as a competitor and administrator. He first started running as a junior with Roath Harriers and quickly established himself as an athlete of outstanding talent, placing second in the Welsh Junior Cross-Country Championships in his first season. The following year he came fourth in the senior race and gained the first of his five Welsh vests in the International Championship. His best season was in 1927 when he was placed second in the Welsh and twenty-sixth in the International. That year he won the Glamorgan four miles track championship. He missed the seasons from 1929 – 1931 with leg injuries and began to involve himself with club and county administration but he came back in 1932 to make two more appearances in the International.

His first loyalty, though, was to his club and he was held in such high esteem that when a heavy cold prevented him from defending the Roath club championship, the winner locked the trophy away in a cupboard for a whole year until Ted got to hear about it and, as club captain, ordered his colleague to display the trophy. He told him "You're the champion of the best club in Wales and don't you forget it!" Many of his stories and sayings became folklore in the club.

However, it was as an official that Ted Hopkins really earned the title "Mr Athletics", holding nearly every major office in his Club, County and Area Association. Although he didn't "drink, smoke or swear" he was a popular manager of many British and Welsh teams and was assistant team manager to the British team at the Rome Olympics in 1960. His term as Welsh athletics team manager extended over 32 years until he stood down after the Edinburgh Commonwealth

Games in 1970. He had been the Welsh team general manager (all sports) at the three previous Commonwealth Games – Cardiff (1958), Perth (1962) and Kingston (1966). In 1967 he achieved his greatest honour being elected President of the International Cross Country Union. In fact, the only major office to elude him was the Presidency of the Welsh AAA.

In normal circumstances he was a quietly spoken man but his outward appearance belied his inner strength and he would not be overawed or put down by any one in higher office if Ted thought they were in the wrong and perhaps this did not endear him to some people.

One of his proudest moments came in 1972 when, under his Chairmanship, Cardiff won the British League Division 1 for the first time. Far from being a mere figurehead Ted brought new enthusiasm to the position when he accepted it upon the formation of the new club with the merger of Roath Harriers and Birchgrove Harriers in 1968, and was one of the key figures of the committee until he stood down in 1973 when he was club President.

The post war years

The 1945/6 season saw a full programme of championships with the senior race at Caerau in Cardiff providing a link with pre-war days as both Dillan Hier and Roath Harriers retained their respective titles. Third individual was Tommy Richards, now representing South London Harriers, repeating the placing he had gained nine years earlier. The years immediately after the Second World War were ones of continuing austerity with food and fuel either rationed or in very short supply. Added to this was the massive rebuilding necessary to repair the devastation caused by bombing raids on towns and cities. Even so, subject to these restrictions, sport resumed its place in daily life and cross-country was no exception. To add to the problems the winter of 1947 was a particularly cold and harsh one. The senior championships of 1947, 1948 and 1949 were all held at Caerleon with Roath Harriers retaining their title on the first two occasions but having to give best to Newport in the last year. Ivor Lloyd (Newport), Jim Alford (Roath) and John Andrews (Finchley Harriers) won individual titles with Bernard Baldwin runner up for Roath in 1947. It was Alford's only senior cross-country title in a glittering career dominated by his Empire Games glory in 1938.

The post war international races

The first international after the Second World War was held at Ayr in Scotland at the end of March 1946. France provided both team and individual winners, (Rafael Pujazon), with England relegated to third place for the first time. Belgium took second team place and had Marcel Vandewattyne second individual making the first of his remarkable record breaking series of twenty one consecutive appearances. With home advantage France and Pujazon won again the following season ahead of Belgium and England whilst Belgium gained their first team and individual wins, (J. Doms), in 1948 at Reading. Wales were sixth or seventh on every occasion. Tommy Richards, who first competed for Wales in 1934, was still in the team. His total of ten appearances spanning the war period and took him to third on Wales men's all time list.

In 1951 the international was held for the sixth (and as it turned out, the last) time at Caerleon Racecourse but, to the relief of many, heartbreak hill was bypassed due to the heavy nature of the ground. Contemporary reports describe the course as a quagmire, and it had to be hastily changed because most parts were under water. The conditions suited

Geoff Saunders of England who won and led his team to their first win since 1938. Doug Rees, of Portsmouth, was first Welshman home in 33rd with Tom Richards ten places back whilst the team were eighth and last. This was the time of the so-called "cold war" between the western nations and the communist countries of Eastern Europe. The Balkan countries had their own annual cross-country competition so it was rather a surprise when Yugoslavia made an appearance in the event in France in 1953. The athletic impact was as great as the political one since Franjo Mihalic won the race and his nation's team were third overall. Regrettably it was a one-off occurrence and it was almost twenty years before a communist country next took part. However, in the intervening years the number of countries gradually increased. Then, in the Empire Games year of 1958, Cardiff hosted the event for the second time. The race was held virtually in the centre of the city on Pontcanna Fields. Stan Eldon, of England, narrowly won the race from Alain Mimoun, running for France, but the event highlighted the talent of future Empire Games silver medallist John Merriman, (Watford Harriers), who finished seventh less than half a minute behind the winner. Merriman also took the Welsh senior title that year, his only such victory. David Richards, son of D.J.P Richards, was second Welshman home in the international in seventeenth place with Norman Horrell of Rhondda Valley AC only ten seconds but five places further back. Wales were fifth out of the nine teams; one of their better results.

The 1958 Cardiff race was also notable as Tunisia competed, the first occasion by a non-European country. North African neighbours, Morocco, followed them two years later. For the latter country, Abdeslem Ben Rhadi, in 1960, at Hamilton Park, Glasgow was the first champion representing a non-European country. It has to be conceded, though, that the great Alain Mimoun, who was Algerian born, had previously totalled four victories running for France. At Hamilton Park, John Merriman had another outstanding run, finishing third and only seven seconds behind Rhadi, to equal Soapy Palmer's feat in 1938 as the highest finishing position of a Welsh athlete in the race.

The next significant development was the introduction of a junior men's race, in 1961 at Nantes in France, following the "one off" event twenty-one years earlier. The results were subsequently declared void as there was confusion over ages, but anyway, Wales did not send a team. However, a team was sent to Graves Park, Sheffield in 1962 with future senior champion, Tom Edmunds (Gilwern Harriers) finishing an excellent fifth in the race. There was age group confusion again in 1963, when the first Welsh Junior Championship by age, as opposed to ability, was marred when it was discovered that Gwyn Morris of Roath, who finished second, was over age, in a race won by Fred Bell of Carmarthen Harriers at Newbridge Fields, Bridgend. The following year Roy Mack of Birchfield Harriers maintained Wales' good record in the junior international event by finishing sixth in Dublin. Ahead of him Dave Walker, (Worcester Harriers), was second running for England and Walker returned the following year to gain third place at Ostend (1965). Also in the England junior team at Ostend and placed 19th was Tony Ashton (Reading) who on becoming a senior took up his Welsh qualifications. Similarly, five years later, Walker ran in the Welsh Senior Championship finishing second and splitting Malcolm Thomas and Tony Simmons, although there were doubts expressed over his eligibility for the Principality.

The 1965 competition at Waterloo near Ostend in Belgium was a memorable one for several other reasons. Firstly, the senior race attracted a record fifteen nations and these included, for the first time, New Zealand, who finished third and West Germany. Secondly, in the senior race both team and individual competitions were virtually dead heats. In the individual race Jean Fayolle (France) was controversially given the verdict over Mel Batty (England) both recording the same time whilst their teams tied on fifty five points with

England winning on position of last scorer. The following year (1966) the event left the European continent for the first time, being held in Morocco. Here the race was won by El Ghazi, of the host nation, ahead of Derek Graham representing an all-Ireland team.

In 1967, the event returned to Wales for the first time since 1958, and was held at Barry mainly due to the herculean efforts of a small number of officials not least Graham Fraser and Derek Lakin the then current Secretary and Treasurer of the Welsh CCA, both of whom were prominent members of Barry Harriers. The races took place on a very flat course of football pitches at Barry (Colcot) Sports Centre with the addition of water jumps and steeplechase barriers and it received some criticism from cross-country diehards. Despite this, the event went off extremely well and not surprisingly, the 1964 Olympic steeplechase champion, Gaston Roelants of Belgium cantered to victory for one of his four wins in the race. "It was the easiest race of my life" he was reported as saying afterwards. Wales were tenth of the eleven teams that closed in with Aberdare athlete John Godding of Birchgrove Harriers, that year's Welsh team winners on the same Colcot course, in forty-third place the first Welshman home. Tony Simmons, winner of the Welsh youth's title for the past two years gave an indication of his future form when he finished an excellent eighth in the junior race for the best Welsh performance of the day. This promotion in Wales was typical since, unlike larger countries with hordes of helpers, Wales with its limited resources and manpower sometimes struggled to make the event a success but always managed the task. The Barry case was typical with everyone having to "muck in" and make their contribution irrespective of their status. In Barry a portable grandstand had to be erected in the finishing straight. Amongst others, Ted Hopkins, (that year's International President no less), and Ken Harris, (Welsh President some years earlier), spent the Wednesday and Thursday before the race day physically erecting the stand. Ted Hopkins, then in his late 60s, even had to drive the heavy goods vehicle to Barry containing the pieces of the stand after a future international athlete and top coach, who had been helping with the arrangements, had difficulty in driving the vehicle!

The start of women's international competition and Wales in the vanguard of change again

There had been an international women's race at Douai in France in 1931, followed by three more in the period before the Second World War. Then in the 1950s there were another four competitions, three of which were won by Diane Leather, the leading English female middle distance runner of the period. However it was at Barry in 1967 that the first official women's race was held attracting teams from the four home countries plus two individuals from the United States and a single entry from New Zealand, although the latter did not start. One of the Americans, Doris Brown, won the race comfortably, a performance she repeated the following four years. This race marked the first appearance of Jean Lochhead, (Airedale & Spen Valley), who went on to compete in the race on more occasions than any other Welsh athlete and to date the most by a female of any nation –a total of sixteen. Her best individual placing came five years on when she finished sixth at Waregem in Belgium, having been eighth the previous year in Cambridge.

Jean Lochhead

The commencement of the women's competition met with some

chauvinistic reluctance and its initial progress was not helped by differences of opinion amongst the Women's Associations themselves. This was compounded by the fact that the 1968 men's competitions were scheduled to be held in north Africa. That year it was to be Tunis, where religious constraints on the participation of women also became a factor to be taken in to consideration. As a consequence, England hosted the women's race at Blackburn. The United States fielded a complete team on this occasion and led by Doris Brown duly won the team and individual competitions.

The following year, (1969), the men's and women's competitions came back together at Clydebank in Scotland. Then in 1970, there were actually two parallel women's competitions. The United States hosted one in Maryland contested by the home countries, the hosts and Canada whilst five of the European nations, including Poland, took part in a race won by Paola Pigni of Italy. The latter race was held at Vichy, the same venue as that season's male competitions and had full ICCU recognition. Thus it was not until San Sebastian, in 1971, and with ten nations participating that the women's competition matched the men's event in stature and status.

The change from ICCU to IAAF World Championships

The final two years of ICCU sponsored races were held at San Sebastian, (1971) and Cambridge (1972) and these two venues saw a full complement of races held. From a Welsh point of view the most noteworthy point was Malcolm Thomas' excellent sixth place in the senior men's race at San Sebastian, the highest Welsh finishing position since John Merriman's third in 1960. Wales were not represented by juniors in 1970 nor 1971 but in Tunis, in 1968, Tony Simmons had finished seventh in the race to follow-up his eighth at Barry the previous year.

The 1973 change with the IAAF taking over responsibility for the races from the ICCU ended a 70 year period where this body had ruled the sport of cross-country world-wide thanks to the initiative of two early Welsh administrators - Frank Liddington Johns and R.A. Pritchard. The move also marked a fundamental change to cross-country administration and whilst it first brought benefits it was to the long-term detriment of Wales, and for that matter Scotland and Northern Ireland. The obvious immediate change was that it awarded the races the status and title of World Championships. Theoretically this meant that only countries directly affiliated to the world body (IAAF) could compete but initially the position of the four home countries was safeguarded and their right to separate teams was maintained. However the writing was on the wall and over the following fifteen years Wales and its British colleagues progressively lost firstly their voting rights, then their right to send delegates to the annual cross-country board meeting and finally in 1987 to enter separate teams in place of a single team representing Britain and Northern Ireland. In retrospect, the perceived arrogance and obdurate conservatism of the home countries was a contributory factor to their eventual exclusion. Rightly or wrongly, the eight other voting nations of the old ICCU board undoubtedly saw the UK delegates, plus Ireland, as an obstructive minority who used their five votes to block any change or reform not to their direct benefit and requiring a two thirds majority to be passed.

With the IAAF setting up a Cross Country Commission the ICCU reverted to being a solely British body at meetings of which the four home countries discussed matters of common interest and agreed strategies. This probably served to reinforce the suspicions of the other countries. Even at this late date it should be realised that the ICCU was still solely a male preserve. Wales, where the formerly separate men and women's associations had already merged in 1974, was very much the exception. On the first occasion that the Welsh delegates suggested that the relevant women's associations from Britain be invited to join the ICCU the other delegates rejected the idea out of hand. However, the seeds had been sown and a year or so later, probably with some encouragement from the BAAB - the then ruling body of British athletics - the proposal was accepted unanimously. By this time Wales, for its part had already moved on and discussions were under way for the formation of the Athletics Association of Wales comprising the Welsh AAA, Welsh WAAA and the already merged Welsh CCA.

The 1976 World Championships at Chepstow - Wales' last home race

Before all the above changes were completed however Wales was to have the honour of hosting what was now a world championship for the first and last time as an independent country. The year was 1976 and the venue chosen was Chepstow Racecourse. Over three hundred athletes from twenty-one countries took part in the three races in spring like conditions which saw the finest assembly to date of distance runners in Wales. A local official George Crump, then President of the Welsh CCA, and a man who made a significant contribution to Welsh cross-country running over three decades, was the driving force behind one of the most successful championships held.

Pen Portrait - George Crump MBE (1931-2000)

© Ian Dixon

George Crump MBE

George Crump's association with cross country running in the Principality began in the early 1960s when he was appointed 'Officer in charge of Cross Country' as an additional duty at the Army Apprentice College, Chepstow. When a local league was formed in Pontypool his lads, together with Gilwern Harriers, provided the mainstay and the majority of the competitors in the early days. When matters were formalised he became League Chairman and later took on additional duties of Secretary and Treasurer in which capacities he served until 1988. Under his guidance and leadership the League, now called the Gwent League, grew in size and scope – offering competition to an ever-increasing range of age groups, including in 1971 the pioneering step to include races for females! Concurrently the League began attracting teams from far outside the boundaries of Wales and the borders.

In parallel George, ably supported by his wife Sheila, took on national responsibilities in the Welsh CCA. In particular this involved being a leading member of the small squad who hosted the highly successful World Cross Country Championships at Chepstow in 1976 - possibly and regrettably the last occasion Wales is likely to undertake that honour.

Leading on from that co-operation between the then separate Men's and Women's Associations, George was a major figure in the merger to form the current joint Associations in Wales. Subsequently he became the Welsh CCA President until 1986 (with his wife Sheila the Treasurer for a similar period) ably guiding the sport in Wales in his own witty and self-deprecating manner. One phrase, which always springs to mind, was his reference to his official position "despite being non-

walking, non-Welsh speaking Englishman!" If this was not enough George was also much involved in Service Athletics – including the Wilts and Border League, which operated midweek and caters for Service teams.

All the foregoing would in itself be a superb record of service to the sport and youth but when one bears in mind that for over 30 years George was confined to a wheelchair following tragic injuries sustained in a fall whilst out running on the cliffs at Chepstow it is even more a tribute to the enthusiasm and fortitude of him and his wife.

National recognition came in 1979 in the form of an MBE for services to athletics in general and the Services in particular but then in November 1987 came the joint presentation to George and Sheila of the prestigious Barclaycard 'Hidden Heroes' award for the 'Administrators' category – initially for Wales and then for the UK as a whole – the latter at a glittering ceremony in London. Everyone in Welsh athletics took pride in such tangible recognition of their contribution to the sport.

In the senior men's race at Chepstow in 1976 future world marathon record holder Carlos Lopes, (Portugal), took the first of his three senior men's titles with consummate ease with Welshman Tony Simmons finishing second for England after falling out with Welsh officialdom. Former Cathays High School pupil Glen Grant of the Army, led Wales home in thirty first spot. Relatively good packing by the rest of the team of Steve Gibbons (Swansea) 35th, Dave Hopkins (Newport) 43rd, Commonwealth steeplechase silver medallist John Davies (TVH) 54th, four times Welsh champion Malcolm Thomas (TVH) 66th and Micky Morris (Cwmbran Olympiads - winner of the previous year's European junior steeplechase title) 75th, combined to give Wales eighth place out of eighteen countries one of its best ever senior team performances. Wales were thirteenth in the junior race which was dominated by the United States with the first two runners home whilst Nat Muir of Scotland was third. Carmen Valero of Spain won the women's race from two future Olympic champions, Tatayana Kazankina (USSR) and Gabriella Dorio (Italy). The USSR won the team title ahead of Italy and the United States with Wales placing twelfth.

© Mark Shearman

Steve Jones (107) battles with Carlos Lopes (Portugal) and England's Tim Hutchings for medals at the 1984 World Cross Country Championships.

The success of Wales in hosting the Chepstow competition was undoubtedly a factor in delaying the probable inevitable decision of the IAAF to restrict the United Kingdom to a single team in each race. Over the following years venues continued to be mainly on the European continent but more and more nations took part although often on an irregular basis and not in all the races. Wales' record stabilised and on most occasions the teams were placed in the early teens which considering relative populations can be considered more than satisfactory. It must be conceded that fund raising was a never-ending task and it is to the credit of the then officers of the association that

Wales's representation was maintained. This was particularly the case in 1984 when the venue was Meadowlands, on the outskirts of New York. The race was the occasion of Steve Jones' best result in the championships – third place behind Carlos Lopes (Portugal) and Tim Hutchings (England). Five years earlier Steve had achieved his previous best performance - seventh at Limerick; in a race won by John Treacy (Ireland) on his home ground. On that occasion Steve had been preceded by the now returned-to-the-fold Tony Simmons in fourth position - the first time since 1904 that Wales had placed two men in the first ten runners home.

For his part Simmons had followed up his second place at Chepstow by finishing eighth in 1977 at Dusseldorf, Germany and fourth in Bellahouston Park, Glasgow, both for England before returning to represent the land of his birth. Also of note was the fact that Karl Palmer gained a team bronze medal, running in the England junior squad in the New York competition in 1984. He also went on to finish third in the English junior race in the mud of Milton Keynes the following season. This was, of course, several years before his taking up residence in Pembrokeshire and thereby gaining eligibility for Wales. Two other performers deserving of mention are Steve Blakemore of Cardiff and Andrew Rodgers (Leeds) who represented Wales four times and three times respectively in the junior international between 1978 and 1984.

Wales' last appearance as a separate team in the World Championships came in Warsaw in March 1987. Weather conditions were cold but sunny and the bleak atmosphere of Eastern Europe was accentuated by food restrictions following the Chernobyl power station incident. Both senior and junior men's races were dominated by Kenyans and Ethiopians. With Roger Hackney, Kirsty Wade, Angela Tooby and Melissa Watson all absent Wales' chances of a successful final appearance were slim. This situation was compounded by Steve Jones and Mike Bishop both having 'off' days. As a consequence the senior men were nineteenth, the women a respectable thirteenth and the juniors twenty-second with Peter Jenkins, Susan Tooby and Justin Hobbs the first Welsh athletes home in the three races. Moreover, some other nations were unaware of the significance of the occasion. This was shown by the fact that members of the New Zealand party, whose nation were due to host the 1988 competition, were in the process of issuing preliminary details to embarrassed Welsh officials until advised of their error.

UK participation in the World Championships

From 1988 onwards participation in the annual race was restricted to a single British team, thereby preventing individual participation from the home countries for the first time since 1903. Initially there was difficulty over selection and trials including the holding of specific trial races. Due to the numbers involved these were hardly viable and the problem was eventually solved by the previously mainly English inter-counties competition becoming a full United Kingdom event with the inclusion of full Welsh and Scottish regional or district teams plus representative teams from Northern Ireland. To cover the inevitable anomalies and hard cases there was provision of "wild cards" for any outstanding individuals not otherwise entered. Regrettably, the overall change has had an adverse effect on Welsh endurance running. There is no doubt that the opportunity and challenge of representing one's nation in a World championship against the best in the world was a very attractive target and a great motivating factor for ambitious Welsh athletes. The change also devalued the Welsh Championships since they were no longer seen as a vital step in the path to selection for the world races.

With a single British team, and despite the addition of a junior women's race and even

Angela Tooby (406) seen here running in the World Cross-Country Championships in New York in 1984. On her right is Grete Weitz (293), and to her left is Ingrid Kristiansen and Galina Zakharova (382) who finished second. The winner was Maricia Puica of Rumania (partly obscured between Tooby and Weitz.

more recently senior short course races, the chances of selection are very greatly reduced particularly as the size of teams has also been cut down. As a consequence only a handful of Welsh athletes have gained British team places. Angela Tooby's outstanding second place in Auckland in 1988, in the first race in which a combined British team took part, only nineteen seconds behind Norway's Ingrid Kristiansen is by far the best Welsh performance. Four years earlier in New York Angela had given an indication of her capability by leading the race for much of the way only to lose out to the fast finishers in the later stages and end up eighth. Roger Hackney also made the team to Auckland finishing thirteenth whilst Susan Tooby gained sixteenth place at the same venue helping Britain to second place in the team contest behind the Soviet Union. The junior women's race was introduced into the World Championship in 1989. In that first year Carol Hayward of Newport gained selection for Britain and to date remains the one and only Welsh competitor to have taken part.

In recent times there has been the further addition of a European Cross-Country Championship to the calendar of events. To date it has always been held in the pre-Christmas period. Despite the additional opportunity thus created and the short course world events mentioned earlier the only Welsh athletes to compete for British teams in the World and European events in recent times have been Wendy Ore, Christian Stephenson, Nicky Comerford and Nathaniel Lane (Cardiff); Colin Jones (Eryri) and Nigel Adams and Hayley Tullett/Parry (Swansea). In addition Sally Lynch (Newport), Melissa Watson (Westbury) and Andres Jones (Cardiff) have been nominated as reserves. Melissa, in particular, suffered the extreme frustration of being reserve to travel. Wendy Ore (Cardiff), for her part, was unfortunate missing out by a narrow margin on at least two further occasions, including one where she suffered a heavy fall in the trial and still only just failed to achieve an automatic qualification. In February 1991 the United Kingdom trial was due to be held at Basingstoke. Heavy snow throughout Britain disrupted travel very badly and the event was cancelled at a late stage. That particular season Sarah Lee-Hodge (Westbury),

Neil Emberton (Newtown) and Nigel Adams (Swansea) had all been in excellent form and can consider themselves very unlucky not to have been chosen even as reserves,

The domestic scene, 1950-89

© Gordon Roberts

Part of the start of the 1968 Welsh Cross-Country Championships at Glebelands, Newport – the last championship that Roath Harriers took part in before their merger with Birchgrove Harriers to form Cardiff AAC in November that year. Left to right: NUTS marathon expert John Walsh (Roath) 124; title holder Cyril Leigh (Wigan) A; four-times Welsh Steeplechase champion Ron McAndrew (Reading) Y; eventual winner Alan Joslyn (Polytechnic) – partly hidden by McAndrew; Graham Boardman (Newport) 72; 1965 Welsh steeplechase champion Brian Griffiths (Roath) 120; and Bob Maplestone (Roath) the first Welshman to run a mile in under 4 minutes indoors, 122.

On an individual basis Norman Horrell, initially of Rhondda and then Roath Harriers was probably the most successful individual runner of the late 1950s in domestic competition with DJP Richards junior his closest rival. The former won three Welsh senior titles, was second twice and third once whilst the latter had two wins, two seconds and one third place. Somewhat surprisingly, John Merriman had only one win, (1958 at Pontcanna) and one third (1959 at Barry). Equally 1952 Olympic steeplechase bronze medallist John Disley could only manage a second place at Caerleon in 1955, behind Newport's Lyn Bevan.

© Western Mail

John Merriman running the 1958 Welsh Cross-Country championships which he won from David Richards who went on to win the title in 1959 and 1960.

Moving on in time Tony Simmons won in 1969 (Singleton Park, Swansea) and was third in 1968 and 1970 (Glebelands, Newport and Llanrumney, Cardiff) before his self-imposed exile to England,

David Richards (Barry Grammar School), son of DJP, winning the English National Youth's Cross-Country title in 1952.

culminating in his outstanding second place in the International at Chepstow. Malcolm Thomas second in 1969 went on to win in the following four seasons to equal Tommy Arthur's feat of 60 years earlier, but his career was then curtailed by injury problems. Without injuries he would have won many more titles and the four-sequence win was not challenged until Steve Jones' five-year winning streak between 1977 and 1981. Bernie Plain, destined to become one of Britain's finest marathon runners, gained his only title in 1976 on literally home ground - the flat riverside land of Bute Park in the centre of Cardiff now used for the annual Cardiff Reebok meeting. Chasing him home was Micky Morris (Cwmbran) who had won the Welsh junior title at Beachley the previous weekend. Down the field in eighth place was the relatively unknown Tredegar born Steve Jones, running for the RAF, although he had been runner-up in the previous year's 10 k championship, in the colours of Swindon AC. As is well documented, Steve went on to win the title on a record nine occasions, but Roger Hackney broke Steve's five win sequence in 1982 at Newbridge Fields, Bridgend whilst the 1980 result at Swansea was a tie between Steve and Tony Simmons, back in Welsh colours - the first and only dead-heat in the history of the event. More recently Christian Stephenson (Cardiff) has won three times plus one-second place and one third.

The emergence of the Tooby twins as major players on the world stage

Susan and Angela Tooby at the head of the field in the Welsh Championships in 1986.

The first Welsh Women's Championships were held in 1968, but a trial was held the previous year for the inaugural World Championships at Barry. A race was also held at Newport in 1965, but it is not known whether this was accorded full championship status. Thelwyn Bateman (Coventry Godiva and Birchfield) has been the most successful with three consecutive wins starting in 1968 followed by single victories in 1973 and 1982 plus one runner up spot. Three athletes have recorded four wins - Wendy Ore (Cardiff) in the early 1990s plus one second and three third places; Melissa Watson (Swindon/Westbury) in the late 1980s plus one-second place and one third and Angela Tooby (Cardiff). Angela's four wins plus two-second places were in the 1980s. Of the wins two, in 1985 and 1986 were officially tied with her identical twin sister Susan; no doubt causing problems to the judges. The previous year there had been a similar scenario but on that occasion Susan, apparently a few days short of qualifying for Wales, was only running as a guest competitor. This was despite the fact that both sisters had competed in 1982 when Angela running for UC Aberystwyth had been second whilst Susan (UC Bangor) was fifth. One of the enduring images of that era is the two sisters running side by side, stride for stride, in their characteristic arm swinging style and yet, apparently, managing not to clash with each other. Two other female athletes who warrant mention are Bronwen Cardy/Smith (Bromsgrove) who was placed on ten occasions including one victory and Jean Lochhead (Airedale & Spen Valley) who was placed on eight occasions and included three wins.

Over the years the number of Welsh championships has continued to increase. For the younger age groups boys, (now called 'under 15'), and colts (under 13) have been added whilst for females there are now junior women (under 20), intermediates (under 17), girls (under 15) and minors (under 13). In some cases the old and new age categories do not coincide absolutely. For instance, the youth's age group was initially 'under 18' at start of season with the junior men being 'under 21' at the same date, the latter event having changed to an age category from its former ability classification. This was at least partly a consequence of the introduction of the category at international level. At the other end of the age spectrum and from the 1980s onwards there has been a massive increase in veteran competition with leagues and championships plus eventually representative matches and internationals.

Reviewing the Welsh Championships for younger age groups the male name that stands out is Justin Hobbs whose record shows boys' champion 1984, youth titles 1985 & 1986, junior winner 1987, 1988 and 1989 before going on to senior titles in 1993 and 1994. On the other hand many outstanding athletes have won age group titles and have then gone on to gain success at top international level but for one reason or another have not gained Welsh senior cross country championship titles. These include John Davies (TVH) who was boys' champion in 1968 and youth winner in 1970; Dennis Fowles (Cardiff) who was youth champion in1969; former European Cross Country Champion and Sydney Olympic marathon fourth placer, Jon Brown (Hallamshire) who won the boy's race in 1986 and Colin Jones (Eryri) who achieved wins in the boys' race in 1989, in the youth event in 1991 and the junior in 1994.

Looking at team results Roath Harriers won the Welsh senior men's title the first three years after the Second World War. Newport Harriers then went on to resume their domination of the event taking the title in fourteen of the next seventeen years. Starting in 1966 Birchgrove Harriers gained three successive wins and then underwent amalgamation with neighbours, Roath Harriers to form Cardiff AAC in 1968. The club then had eleven consecutive wins up to 1979. During this period they also dominated the team competition in the Welsh 10k cross-country race each autumn. Initially this was a barring race, introduced in 1954 to replace the old junior (by ability) race which ceased in 1955. All Welsh cross country internationals and the members of the winning senior teams were debarred. This restriction was removed in 1969 and from that date all athletes with a Welsh qualification were allowed to run. The distance changed to 6 miles in 1962 and 10k in 1972. The event was discontinued after 1989 because the fixture list was restructured. The senior women's team event also saw Cardiff achieve a run of eight wins in the 1980s with Newport Harriers gaining a similar number but not in succession. The younger female age groups show a much wider variety of clubs although once again Cardiff AAC did record a total of fourteen wins in the 'under 15' girls races between 1973 and 1989.

Swansea halt Cardiff's run, and Hackney denies Steve Jones a record sixth consecutive win

In 1980, on their home course at Singleton and with their first ever win, Swansea Harriers halted Cardiff AAC's sequence of team victories in the senior men's race. The following year at the Heath Park, Cardiff Steve Jones won for a fifth time whilst Cardiff AAC regained the men's team title. In February 1982, again at Heath Park Roger Hackney shadowed Steve throughout the race and then broke away in the last hundred metres to prevent Jones achieving a record sixth consecutive victory. Newport Harriers won the men's team event. As mentioned elsewhere, the senior women's race saw the first appearance of the Tooby sisters. With Kathy and Liz Williams (Port Talbot) also gaining high positions the women's race thus had the unusual distinction of two sets of twins in the first nine runners home. The 1982 Championships were also notable for the spread of the titles - no fewer than nine clubs claimed an individual winner and the team titles were spread over seven clubs.

© Ceri Breeze

Welsh middle distance stars Steve Jones (1) and Roger Hackney battle it out at Cwmbran.

In February 1983, at Colcot, Barry, and with reigning champion Hackney competing in an indoor match for Great Britain, Steve Jones achieved the record sixth - albeit not consecutive - title ahead of Wrexham's Tony Blackwell running for Wolverhampton & Bilston whilst Chris Buckley (Westbury) was third for the second year in succession. Now in the colours of Newport Harriers Steve led his new club to the second of what would be a six-race sequence of team victories. There were also victories for Paul Williams (Barry &Vale - youth), Andrew Rodgers (Leeds –junior) and Clare Pugh (Newport – junior woman), all of whom had won the previous year but in a younger age group. 1984(Singleton Park) and 1985 (a snow bound Heath Park) saw Steve Jones gain his seventh and eighth senior titles, on both occasions ahead of Chris Buckley.

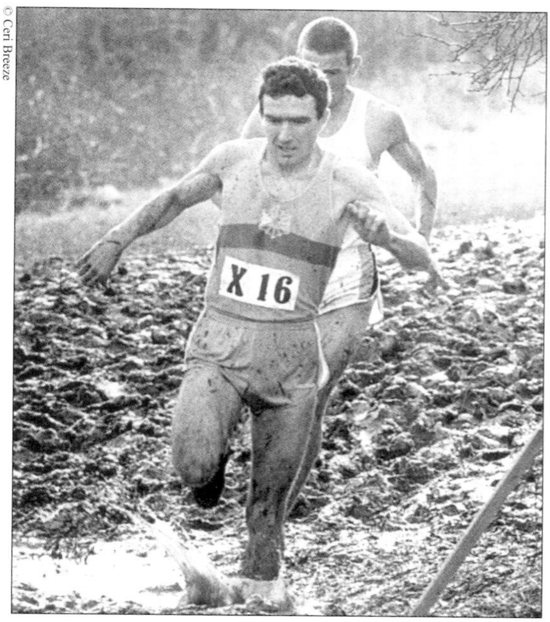

© Ceri Breeze

Mike Bishop leads Steve Jones through the mire of Colcot, Barry on his way to winning the 1987 Welsh title.

In February 1986 Heath Park, Cardiff, yet again, was the venue as Steve achieved a ninth victory in ten years to establish a record which is unlikely to be beaten in the foreseeable future, with Paul Wheeler (Cardiff) runner up this time. In the boy's race the champion was Bridgend born Jon Brown running as an individual in the colours of Hallamshire Harriers - to date his only appearance in a Welsh event - some fourteen years before he took 4th spot in the Sydney Olympic Marathon. The 1987 Championships were held at Colcot, Barry and the course, which could be quite fast in dry weather, had been subjected to two days of non-stop rain. In the senior women's race Lynn Maddison (Colwyn Bay) cut out the early pace and prevented the Tooby sisters running in together yet again although they were still first and second. Similarly in the men's event Karl Palmer (Preseli) led early on before Mike Bishop (Staffs Moorlands) took over accompanied by Steve Jones. However, the latter had been troubled by niggling injuries through the season and on this occasion had to settle for second spot with Bishop eventually winning by nearly half a minute to deny Steve an unprecedented tenth title in eleven years.

It was a case of "all change" in 1988. The Welsh Championship was no longer the selection race for a team to the world championships. Partly as a consequence, the Tooby twins, Mike Bishop and Roger Hackney were all absentees whilst Steve Jones was injured. In the women's event Melissa Watson won from Wendy Ore (Cardiff) whilst Les Croupiers gained their first Welsh Cross Country title. In the mens' race Nigel Adams took the individual title, ahead of Eddie Conway and Paul Wheeler (both Cardiff) and led Swansea Harriers to a team victory.

The 1989 Welsh Championships were back on Heath Park Cardiff on February 25th. Heavy rain had fallen over the preceding days and the atrocious weather persisted reducing the course to a quagmire. This year north Wales athletes were rewarded for their long journey by dominating the individual placings in the younger age groups; taking five of the six titles plus two third places. The two senior races were both wars of attrition through the mud – Nigel Adams retained his title despite Steve Jones leading for part of the way but Newport regained the team award. Melissa Watson (Westbury), for her part, had to withstand a strong challenge from Sally Lynch (Newport) to do likewise in the women's race.

The English "National" and other championships

Malcolm Thomas of TVH (1598) running in the 1971 English National Cross-Country Championships at Norwich where he finished second to Dave Bedford. His club finished 6th in the team race with three other Welshmen in the TVH scoring six – Tony Petty 83rd, Hedydd Davies 123rd and Clive Thomas 132nd. Malcolm won the title the following year and also took the Welsh title on four successive occasions between 1970 and 1973 to equal Tommy Arthur's record of 62 years earlier.

As noted earlier the English National Men's Championship was, from its inception until 1983, an open event which meant that clubs or individuals from any country could enter. Despite the event being the English Championships, most Welsh athletes recognise the event as the British Championship and over the years the Cardiff, Newport and Swansea clubs entered teams whilst numerous individuals contested the events. The majority of the latter were, of course, representing English clubs. Amongst winners over the years were W (Ike) Williams of Salford who twice won the youth's title in 1950 (with another Welshman Brian James of Bournemouth third) and 1951. His example was followed in 1952 by David Richards jun. in the colours of Barry Grammar School.

Malcolm Thomas (TVH), sometimes alluded to as 'Thomas the tank', took full advantage of his strength to win in the blizzard racked senior men's race in Sutton Park in 1972, having been second the previous year. Relatively closely behind Malcolm in Sutton Park were fellow Welshmen Tony Simmons (Luton 5th), John Jones (Windsor 10th), Bernie Hayward (Cardiff 12th) and 1974 European marathon fourth placer Bernie Plain (Cardiff 25th) whilst the Cardiff team were just out of the medals in fourth place in a field of almost a thousand and over a hundred teams. When he went into work on the Monday following the race, on telling a work colleague rather proudly that he had finished an excellent 12th in "The National", Hayward was met with the retort, "only 12th – what happened?"

By far the most outstanding and consistent record in the English National Championships by any Welsh athlete is that of Tony Simmons - second youth 1966, first youth 1967, third junior 1968, third senior 1973, senior champion in 1975 on home ground at Luton and third senior 1977 and 1978. As mentioned previously, Newport Harriers achieved third place in the English senior race in 1925 following fourth and sixth team placings in 1923 and 1922. Other individual medallists have included Jack Marsh (1897, senior, second); Soapy Palmer (1938, senior, third); Tom Edmunds (1961, third, youths); Alan Cummings (1977, second, youths) and John Merriman, (1960, second, senior). Reference has already been made to Karl Palmer's place in the junior race in 1985.

Also of note was Phil Banning (Andover) in second place in the English junior race in 1971, about a quarter century before he established a formal link with Wales as AAW Director of Coaching and Micky Morris' similar placing in the junior race in 1976 at Western Park, Leicester. Unfortunately he was wearing a Welsh vest and despite only having been entered as an individual, he was disqualified for not wearing the colours of his club - at that time Cwmbran Olympiads. Almost equally unlucky was Ernie Thomas, in the Newport senior team at Hereford in 1922. He finished fourth but with Guillemot and Schnellmann, both in the colours of France, first and third, was actually the second British athlete in the race.

As far as women's performances are concerned February 1985 saw Angela Tooby further enhance her reputation by winning the English Women's Championship at Birkenhead in cold snowy conditions. Unfortunately, her win was totally overshadowed by unprecedented happenings behind her. Zola Budd, already thirty metres down in second place after a mile or so, was forced out of the race by anti-apartheid demonstrators who blocked her path. Susan Tooby was eighth whilst Cardiff AAC finished fifth out of the 53 finishing teams.

Over the years numerous Welsh athletes have competed in local championships whilst working and living abroad. A typical example is Nigel Evans, of Westbury Harriers, who was runner up in the Canadian Championships in 1969 before returning home and representing Wales in the internationals in Vichy (1970) and San Sebastian (1971). Somewhat ironically for Nigel Canada were one place and a mere four points ahead of Wales in the team event at Vichy. Similarly in November 1986, Steve Jones ran in the United States Championships and finished second to his great friend and rival Pat Porter.

The Welsh Women's Cross Country Association.

References have been made elsewhere to the fact that until the 1960s endurance running was almost totally a male preserve. In the 1950s and even earlier there were small numbers of women running middle distance events on the track and gradually some of these showed interest in road and country competition. They tended to be concentrated in the major centres of population and were usually associated with the then major clubs. In Wales the Welsh Women's AAA were the initial promoters of cross-country events in the early 1960s mainly in the Newport and Cwmbran areas. By the mid–1960s there were Welsh championships being held but the numbers competing in the early years failed to reach double figures and a significant proportion of the contestants were from across the border.

With the first full women's international race in Barry in 1967, a Welsh Women's CCA was formed. Following the English example this newly created body took on responsibility for women's cross country and road running in the Principality. This it did for a number of years with rapidly growing numbers of participants. It was also responsible for women's international competition, sending teams to the annual international championship and to the "Home Countries" event between the women of the five nations of the British Isles. The association worked very closely with its male counterpart in Wales and in November 1974 the two bodies merged to form the first such joint organisation in the United Kingdom. One of the first tasks of that new association was, of course, organisation of the 1976 World Cross Country Championships at Chepstow.

Cross-country Leagues and other domestic inter-club competition

At club level, cross-country in Wales, until the mid 1960s had become a mainly inter-club event with just the county, inter-county and national championships as targets. The club matches were normally only between senior men's teams but often included youths and juniors competing as seniors. The races were usually over a distance of about six miles and would often include fences, complete with barbed wire, gates, lengths of road or path and ploughed fields. The last was a particularly difficult surface and in wet weather could reduce even the strongest and fittest athlete to a shambling trot. Running along the furrows was awkward and required careful placement of feet on the crests or in the ruts; running across the furrows demanded very careful choice of stride length to coincide with the furrow width whilst diagonal stretches produced a combination of both problems. The scoring of the matches was normally on the basis of so many to run, so many to score. Occasionally where lap courses or similar were used the younger athletes could be encouraged to peel off into the finish after an appropriate distance. There were leagues but these tended to be localised if only due to the constraints of winter travel before motorways existed.

In Wales, there was a South West Wales League covering the western half of the former county of Glamorgan. In south-east Wales a league was started in Pontypool in 1963 and this became the Gwent League a year later. There were inevitable teething troubles; the first match of the new league was held at Prescoed Camp near Usk on 26th October 1963. Eleven eager boys set off in their event but poor marshalling meant that the winner's time for what had been intended as a 2.2 k course was nearly forty-five minutes! Order emerged from chaos and the thirty youths and twelve seniors fared rather better. The young league was soon running freely and proceeded to grow at an almost alarming rate as the attractions of an ongoing structured competition became apparent. There was also the fact that the league had adopted the so-called northern system of scoring where the number of points was decided by position and number of starters. This meant that the team with the highest total from its scorers, not the lowest, was the winner. It also meant that clubs who had an incomplete team on one or even more occasions were not thereby automatically ruled out of contention in the team competition for the remainder of the season as they could carry forward any points they had collected, albeit from an incomplete team.

In 1968, in Bridgend, a record number of well over three hundred competitors took part in a Gwent League match. The league also gradually increased the number of age categories catered for, notably in 1971/2, taking the then almost revolutionary step of including races for females. Initially these attracted only very small numbers of contestants but gradually both numbers and calibre of participants improved. That season was also notable as the number of runners in a single meeting exceeded one thousand for the first time whilst the total number of participants during that season was nearly 2,400, reputedly the highest number for a league competition in Britain. In more recent times the Gwent League has continued to grow in size, scope and popularity encompassing teams from as far afield as

Aberystwyth, Bristol and Cornwall. This growth was further boosted by the consequences of the "jogging boom" of the 1980s, which resulted in much greater numbers of senior and veteran athletes and also many new running clubs. Numbers peaked at more than eleven hundred in many matches and over five thousand different competitors over the season. It is only in the last five years of the twentieth century that total numbers have started to drop back, reflecting a general change seen elsewhere in the sport. For a number of years starting in the 1980s the Gwent League took part in an annual women's inter-league match versus the Southern, Midlands, Northern and Scottish leagues. The matches were always held in England and strictly both Scottish and Gwent Leagues were guests. The match covered the whole range of age groups up to seniors and peaked in importance and popularity in the early 1990s. In more recent years it suffered as the leading athletes of the various leagues started to give precedence to other competitions and the match lapsed completely at the end of the century. In general the English leagues dominated the competition but it still provided athletes with a very valuable additional tier of competition, especially in the younger age groups. Much of the credit for the success of the Gwent League must go to George and Sheila Crump, without whom it is unlikely that the event would have developed into the undoubted success it was.

Elsewhere in Wales there have been several other leagues. The first cross country league in Wales was the North Wales League, which held its first race at RAF Valley on 18th October 1958 won by Roger Harrison Jones of Rhyl AC who was to go on to win five Welsh vests in the international race between 1959 and 1964. Initially the league was started by Ray Billington – then with Liverpool Pembroke AC, and Les Baldwin (Wrexham). Amongst the early teams were Eirias AC, Wrexham AC, Rhyl AC, RAF Valley, local Army units and Aberystwyth and Bangor Universities. At a later date Terry Harper (Wrexham) joined Les Baldwin, but the North Wales CCA took over the league in 1975/76. There have also been local leagues based on Deeside, in the Glamorgan Valleys, west Glamorgan, Gwynedd and north Gwent. The last is based on the Leisure centres in the area rather than clubs. The West Glamorgan competition, which started in 1978/79 and effectively replaced the former South West Wales League, includes teams from such organisations as Corus, (formerly British Steel) and Unison (Civil Service) plus informal groupings with such evocative names as 'Black Tuesday' and 'Newton Innmates'. British Steel, based on their Margam plant, were the first men's team champions of that league. These local leagues fulfil a valuable function by providing regular structured competition without the requirement of long travel.

The north Wales scene

Prior to the formation of the Welsh AAA in 1948, athletes and clubs in north Wales were affiliated to the Northern Counties AA of England. In the main, this was recognition of the practicalities of travel whereby journeys across the border and back were so much easier than the long trek south and return. Then, from its formation until 1974, the North Wales AAA controlled all sectors of the sport under the general jurisdiction of the relevant Welsh associations, all of which were based in the south. Local government re-organisation of the former Welsh Counties, in 1974, was followed by the athletics bodies as far as the boundaries for local organisation were concerned. This meant that the North Wales AAA was disbanded and replaced by separate Clwyd and Gwynedd associations. The cross-country runners realised that they faced a problem of viability of numbers and ability. Both for domestic and inter-county competition it was desirable that a combined body should continue. An application to the Counties Athletic Union (CAU) on this basis was made and accepted and the North Wales CCA was formed.

A year earlier David Alun Williams of Wrexham AC had taken over from Terry Bithell (Wirral AC) as cross-country secretary of the North Wales AAA and he became the first and to date only secretary of the new body. This covered the old six counties of Anglesey, Caernarfon, Flint, Denbigh, Merioneth and Montgomery. There were occasional queries due to the last pair of counties being incorporated into what was Powys until the more recent further change to unitary local authorities.

The North Wales AAA had first held a senior men's cross-country championship at Marford, in March 1955, with A.F. Bradford of the Army Pioneer Corps, based at Wrexham, the first champion. After this championships were held every year with the exception of 1968. That particular year another foot and mouth epidemic amongst farm animals wrought havoc in the sport throughout much of the United Kingdom restricting the use of agricultural land and forcing any races that were held to be confined to school playing fields and the like. Records for junior men and youths did not start until 1972 and 1973 respectively but there are suggestions that championships for these age groups had been held prior to those years. In addition to promoting their cross country championships and organising the regional team to the Inter-counties competition each year the new association also took responsibility for the annual north Wales ten-mile road championship each April.

In 1977 three championship races were added for the younger male age groups whilst girls and senior ladies were also catered for. In following years more and more categories were added. Since 1985 the arrangement has been that the two older female categories, together with the three older male ones, have been held together on one date with the six 'under 15' categories on a separate date. In 1989 the association started sending younger age group teams to their particular CAU event which in those days, rather conveniently, was held in Shrewsbury each year. The previous season saw the commencement of an annual triangular cross country match between north Wales, the Isle of Man and Shropshire; the inaugural event being in Moss Valley Park, Wrexham in March 1988.

As mentioned earlier, a north Wales League started in 1958, but this event was discontinued some time in the 1960s. However, since 1975-76 there has been a north Wales League providing competition over the whole range of age groups on a monthly basis throughout the winter. Like its southern counterpart the league encompasses teams from across the English border in its membership as well as those from throughout north Wales. Moreover whilst smaller it also grew steadily. In 1989/90 there were almost two hundred runners in the match at Shrewsbury and well over eight hundred different athletes participated during the season. Wrexham AC, (formed in 1954), has been the dominant club in the league over the years, particularly in the senior men's section although in recent years they have been challenged strongly by Eryri Harriers.

The first formal veterans events

Allusion has been made elsewhere to the growth of veteran events (men over 40 and women over 35) and the fact that in the later years of the twentieth century this has been the growth area of the sport. Certainly up until the 1970s there was very little specific competition for veteran men and certainly none for women. Performances are recorded but these were the exception rather than the rule and were generally men who happened to be over forty years of age but were still competing as seniors. Instances being Tom Richards (South London Harriers) and Ron Cullum, (Carmarthen - grandson of the great Harry Cullum) - both of whom continued competing at a high level despite their age. The first Welsh Veteran's Cross Country Championships were in the mid-1970s - often incorporated in the Welsh 6 mile/10k Cross Country Championship together with a senior inter-counties team competition.

The first year that male veterans appear to have been officially recognised as an age grouping in Welsh Cross Country Championships and awarded medals was in November 1976. This inaugural event, held at Cwmbran as part of the Welsh 10k Championship, was well supported. Evan Williams (Shrewsbury), in his first season as a veteran, easily took the "over 40" award beating 1958 Commonwealth Games 880y runner Ray Billington (Wrexham). George Phipps (Leamington), who had run for Wales in the 1951-2-4 internationals took the "over 50" title ahead of another former international, Paddy Wallace (Newport), who had been runner-up the previous season in the corresponding British Championship. Robert Crombie (Newport) took the "over 60" award. Twelve months on at the Glebelands, Newport and again in the 10k Championship Ron Pannell (Bristol AC) was first veteran. Ray Billington was again runner up with newly qualified Dill Robbins (Swansea) in third spot. The following year, at the same venue, former Welsh mile champion Dill Robbins improved to win from Jim O'Brien (Bridgend) and John Evans (Neath).

In those early days there were only individual awards and in the latter two years only one age category, nominally "over 40". In 1981 there were two championships – one in February in conjunction with the Welsh senior men's race at Heath Park, Cardiff and the second in November as part of the Welsh 10k and inter-counties race at Glebelands, Newport. On both occasions Jim O'Brien won from former Welsh 3,000m steeplechase champion, Brian Griffiths (Swansea) in the "over 40" category. At Cardiff Hedydd Davies (Carmarthen) was third whilst at Newport D. I. Davies (Newtown) occupied that position. There was now a team race and once more other categories. In the February race Paddy Wallace won the 'over 50s' but in the November he lost out to Ron Franklin (TVH) with George Phipps third in the age group. On the latter occasion Robert Crombie took the "over 60" title with Swansea Harriers being winning team on both occasions. In November 1982 the event moved north to Moss Valley Park, Wrexham. This time the newly eligible Alan Jefferies (Swansea) won from Jim O'Brien with Brian Griffiths third. With five year age categories on this occasion Evan Williams and Dill Robbins in fourth and fifth places in the race gained the 'over 45' awards whilst Dougie Mends (Les Croupiers) gained victory in the "over 50" section. In the team competition Swansea Harriers easily retained the title.

At the British veterans level there were two Welsh successes. At Parliament Hill Fields, London Tacwyn Davies (Aldershot & Farnham) won the British men's title for the third successive year whilst Pat Gallagher (Westbury) retained the women's title she had won at Birkenhead the previous season. Unfortunately Taff Davies' appearances in Welsh events over the years were few and far between but this could be partly at least attributed to his military commitments. Pat, for her part, had and still has an excellent record of participation in and for Wales, including having been women's team captain at Barry in 1967. In the early 1980s there were few if any veteran's competitions over the country for women in Wales. The following year, at Cambridge Taff gained a record equalling fourth successive title whilst Pat came home second in her event. The other leading female veteran at the time was Jean Lochhead (Airedale & Spen) who, more than holding her own in senior competition, ran for Wales in the World Championship at Gateshead. She thus made a record fifteenth consecutive appearance - the best by any Welsh athlete, any woman of any nationality and second only (male or female) to Belgium's Marcel Vandewattyne.

The first occasion on which women veterans appear to have been formally acknowledged and awarded medals was in the Welsh Women's Championships at Newport in February 1984. Pat Gallagher was first ahead of Liz Gooch and Margaret Harding, (both of Beddau

AC). Fifth veteran home was Myfanwy Loudon (Newport) who was thereby first "over 45". Pat retained her title a year later in Swansea and ahead of the same pair from Beddau. A month or so later, in March 1985, the British Veteran's Championships were held on Heath Park in Cardiff. Tacwyn Davies regained the men's title for a fifth win in six years whilst Pat Gallagher likewise regained the women's. Equally pleasing for local supporters Beddau AC won the women's team event.

At this time (1985/6) there was often some confusion with the Welsh CCA and the Welsh Veterans Association designating different events as the men's championship. In November 1985, at Wrexham, Alan Jefferies (Swansea) won from Bill Yale (Eryri) and Arthur Egan (Wrexham) with Wrexham AC team winners from Les Croupiers RC and Newport Harriers. Then in February 1986, at Cardiff Alun Roper (Swansea) won from Jim O'Brien and Mike Rowland (Newport). On this occasion Swansea Harriers won the team race from Bridgend AC and Les Croupiers. The women had no such problem with only the Cardiff event recognised as a championship. Pat Gallagher won from Jean Lochhead, with Delyth M. Davies of Cardiff AAC third.

The growth of veteran's cross country was shown early in December 1986 when all eight Welsh counties declared male champions and only Dyfed failed to name a female winner – all the more surprising as at the time it had numerous potential candidates, not least, of course, Pat Gallagher. Earlier that month she and Jean Lochhead had both been scorers in the Welsh women's team in the representative match at Tredegar Park, Newport. The 1986/7 Championship was held at Connah's Quay on the third day of the New Year and in conjunction with the Welsh inter counties event. In the absence of Alun Roper, Dic Evans (Cardiff) won easily from Barrie Williams (Newcastle) with Cyril Leigh (Wigan) close up in third, taking the 'over fifty' award. Second in the latter category was Evan Williams whilst Tom Wood (Newport) was first 'over 60'. Cardiff AAC (19 points) easily won the team event from Swansea Harriers (31) with Eryri Harriers (40) third. Jean Lochhead also benefited from the absence of the previous champion (Pat Gallagher) and won from her former club mate Ann James, now with Rhondda AC, whilst Delyth Davies was third and Newport Harriers won the team event.

The British Veterans Championships at Cockfosters in March 1987 saw Dic Evans and Alun Roper head to head at the front of the field. Initially, they were accompanied by Dic's former teammate, 1978 Commonwealth Games marathon runner, Mike Critchley (now Bolton United), but he then fell back whilst Alun pulled away to a clear win over Dic. Alun Roper then travelled out to Israel and competed in the World Veteran's Championships finishing second to Antione Borowski of France. Cyril Leigh did even better there winning the "over 50" title in a race that he led from start to finish.

The 1988 British Veteran's Championships were held in Irvine in mid-March. No female representatives made the long journey north but four Welsh men gained awards. Alun Roper continued to show excellent form to retain his title whilst Barrie Williams (Newcastle), who later won the northern title, was a clear third.

Six years after being the venue of the Welsh Veteran's Championship Moss Valley Park was the venue for the inaugural Veteran's Cross Country International. The event was organised by Ron Bell and the Wrexham club with support from Wrexham Council on November 5th 1988 with the host nation providing the fireworks. The men's match saw a very strong Welsh team dominate the proceedings as they ran out clear winners in the 'over 40'and 'over 50' categories and only lost first place in the "over 45s" on count back. Tony Simmons, Alun Roper and Dic Evans took the first three places in the 'over 40s' and with four to score there was scant possibility of them losing that section. It was the same story in the 'over 50s' where the first three were all Welsh. In the middle age group England and Wales tied on 21 points each with the verdict going to England on the strength of their last scorer finishing in eighth place just nine seconds ahead of former Welsh junior champion Fred Bell (Woking) who was Wales' final scorer in ninth position. In the women's match Wales provided both individual winners but failed to win the team event in either class. Bronwen Cardy–Wise (Bromsgrove) scored a narrow win in the "over 35s" whilst Pat Gallagher was half a minute clear in the 'over 40s'. The Welsh CCA took the opportunity of the occasion to present Meritorious Award plates to Jean Lochhead and Tony Simmons in recognition of their outstanding records in the sport. The latter award was extremely significant in that it finally erased any bitter memories of the past when Tony was at odds with Welsh officialdom. The success of the veteran's match led to what is now an annual festival of cross-country incorporating highly competitive races of a very high calibre between teams of veterans, over a range of age groups, from the five countries of the British Isles.

The following two years the international race was held in Bedfordshire, included in the existing Ampthill Trophy open meeting. In both years Tony Simmons, almost on home ground, held on to his individual title. In 1989 Wales also retained the "over 40" men's team title with Alun Roper (4th), Dic Evans (6th) and Malcolm Thomas (TVH- 10th) ably backing Tony up.

Welsh and other representative cross country matches

From the 1960s onwards until the late 1980s there was a significant programme of representative matches. These provided an important step between club and league races at one level and world championships at the higher. For Wales there were matches against the RAF, the Army, Universities Athletic Union and the English areas. In some cases these were normal multi-sided matches, (8 to run, 6 to score or similar), such as that which in later years was regularly held at RAF Cosford, near Wolverhampton whilst others were part of sponsored events. Typical of the latter were the International Athletes Club (IAC) pre-Christmas matches held for a number of years at the Crystal Palace in south London and then more recently at Cardiff Castle/Bute Park or the similar event at Gateshead each November. The programme usually covered senior and junior men and women plus supporting open races over a range of age groups. With TV coverage the main races often included small team internationals (4 to run, 3 to score) together with a sprinkling of international stars competing as individuals – such as Craig Virgin (USA), John Treacy (Ireland) and quadruple Olympic Champion Lasse Viren (Finland).

Wales' record in these matches often suffered due to the fact that there seemed to be a tacit understanding that where athletes had a dual qualification the other team took precedence. Over the years Wales often lost out for this reason. A typical situation in, for instance, an IAC meeting at Crystal Palace would be Steve Jones, Roger Hackney and Peter Jenkins competing for the RAF; Ted Turner, Taff Davies and Maggie Smith for the Army; Tony Simmons, John Jenkins and Kirk Clifford for Eastern counties and so on. Taking a broader view there was the fact that, thereby, even more Welsh qualified athletes were able to take part and gain competitive experience at this level.

The first representative race organised by the Welsh CCA was against an Army team and took place at Gilwern, near Abergavenny, in November 1965. The race was restricted to senior men and resulted in a win for the Aberystwyth University pair of John Godding and Chris Loosley, who led Wales to an easy win. Subsequent matches against the Army took place for the next 10 years or so at venues such as Blackweir, Cardiff, Porthkerry Park, Barry and Glebelands, Newport. A match against the RAF was held for the first time at St. Athan on 11th January 1969, won by Roger Clark (RAF), with Mike Rowland first Welshman home in third. This match continued until the mid 1970s.

Moving on several years, January 1982 was the occasion of "the match that never was". The women's Home Countries International was due to return to Wales with the Royal Welsh Showground at Llanelwedd as the venue. However, very heavy snowfall in the first week of the New Year meant that the course was covered to a depth of several feet. More significantly access to the locality was nigh impossible, resulting in cancellation of the fixture at very short notice.

Wales'senior men had a particularly good series of results in the early part of the 1982/83 season. They finished third team at the Gateshead meeting with Steve Jones runner up for the second consecutive year; fourth in the IAC Match at the Crystal Palace and second in the representative match at RAF Cosford. Winners of the last were the hosts but with Roger Hackney and Steve Jones in their team finishing first and second individuals. The good form of Welsh athletes was continued after Christmas at Mallusk in Ireland where the team were fourth and only one point behind England in third place.

In January 1985, Wales received an unexpected invitation for a small team to compete in a race at San Sebastian in the Basque region of Spain. In bitterly cold conditions Nigel Adams of Swansea finished third and with Newport's Kenny Davies ninth and Paul Wheeler (Cardiff) tenth the team finished second to Portugal beating amongst others England and Spain. The cross-country course consisted of "out and back" laps along the partly constructed sea front promenade. The evening following the race there was an extremely heavy snowfall closing roads and airports and trapping the visitors. Fortunately their excuses, on a belated return home, were confirmed by pictures on British TV. These showed ploughs clearing the snow, in nearby Biarritz, but only so that gamblers could reach the casino - a revealing indication of local priorities! A little later that spring, and not to be outdone by her sister's win in the English Championship Susan Tooby was an easy winner of the Women's Home Countries International held that year at Sidcup in Kent.

In the autumn of 1985 the annual match versus RAF, Midlands and UAU was held in Wales for the first time - at Tredegar Park, Newport. It was also one of the first cross-country competitions, certainly in the United Kingdom, where routine drug testing was carried out. Steve Jones won the race for the RAF but was chased almost throughout by Mike Bishop (Staffs Moorlands) exercising his Welsh qualifications for the first time. In the later stages Mike fell back to eventually finish third succumbing to a late burst by Chris Buckley. Continuing the firsts Wales won the senior men's competition and achieved the same result with the senior women. In the latter race Melissa Watson was first Welsh athlete home behind Carole Bradford (Clevedon) who had opted for the Midland Counties team on this occasion. Carole was later to transfer her allegiance to England totally when the Welsh Women's AAA declined to accept her eligibility claim of Welsh grandparentage.

The new year (January 1986) brought a change of fortune. At Mallusk, in miserable wet and windy conditions Roger Hackney stormed home to win whilst Susan Tooby, with a courageous exhibition of front running in the adverse conditions, did likewise in the women's race. The following day in San Sebastian (January 6th) Mike Bishop finished third. With Kenny Davies and Nigel Adams also well-placed Wales were again second in the team event.

Triple Commonwealth Games winner Kirsty Wade's appearances on the country were all too few and far between although she did place second in the women's international race at the Gateshead invitation meeting in November 1984 and 1985. In the 1986 race she could only manage seventh but came right back into form a couple of weeks later. After many years at Crystal Palace and the one at Alexandra Palace the IAC meeting together with its extensive TV coverage moved to Cardiff Castle. Kirsty won the women's race and, despite the absence of both Tooby sisters, excellent packing by Lynn Maddison (Colwyn Bay-6th), Melissa Watson (8th), Ann Middle (9th), Wendy Ore (14th) and Sally James (Newport 16th) meant Wales (24 points) were comfortably ahead of England (35) and Scotland (51) to win the Billy Morton Trophy for the home countries competition. The men's team also performed creditably being second to England. Wales were also successful in the quadrangular match at Cosford just holding off the RAF (49-50) to retain the title they won the previous year. Regrettably there was no women's race on this occasion whilst the junior men had little opposition in their race and placed ten in the first thirteen home.

Ngugi at Cardiff Castle

Early in the new year, (1987), Roger Hackney successfully defended his title at Mallusk, but only by the narrowest of margins since the runner up was given the same time. Later in the month, Peter Jenkins (RAF/Newport) had an outstanding run to finish second in the annual international meeting at Fermoy, south of the border in the Republic. A new match was organised in the spring in Scotland - a Celtic international for youths, junior men and "under 23s". Wales finished second team in the last two categories and third in the youths. Andrew Jones (Newport) was runner up in the youth event and Dale Rixon (Cardiff) similarly placed in the under 23 race. In December 1987 the IAC meeting returned to Cardiff Castle Grounds and the men's international race saw Paul Kipkoech (Kenya) win comfortably with teammate and multi-world champion John Ngugi in fourth place. The women's international brought major home country success with Angela Tooby winning, sister Susan finishing third, Kirsty Wade fourth and Hayley Nash eighth to ensure Wales retained the team trophy. In the new year, the male Celtic international in Irvine brought further Welsh success with the 'under 23s' winning and the junior and youth squads both finishing second team in their sections. Also in January, there was an unexpected triumph when Wendy Ore was the winner of the senior women's race in the UK Inter-Counties Championships at Nottingham. At the end of the month the first United Kingdom world trials were held at Gateshead to choose the British teams to compete in the championships in New Zealand. In the men's race Eamonn Martin (England) won with Deon McNeilly (Northern Ireland), who set the early pace, second and Roger Hackney a solid third. The last was a 'wild card' entry as the Welsh CCA declined to nominate him. In the women's race Angela Tooby, a

The Welsh team in IAC/HFC International Cross-Country at Cardiff Castle grounds in 1987. The team collected the Billy Morton Trophy for winning the Home Countries Championship.
Back Row: Sally James (Lynch), Wendy Ore, Susan Tooby, and Angela Tooby.
Front Row: Hayley Nash, Kirsty Wade.

week after winning the prestigious Almond Blossom race in Portugal, was always in the leading group. She moved away in the later stages to a clear win whilst Susan Tooby finished third to ensure her selection, ahead of Zola Budd. Wendy Ore also had a good run to finish eleventh. Many people considered that the trial was an unnecessary addition to the fixture list. This was accentuated by a clash with the UK inter-counties fixture devaluing the latter, if not both competitions.

In November 1988, the annual quadrangular match held near Birmingham brought neither team nor individual success with Nigel Adams (Swansea) and Maggie Smith (Army/Aldershot) third in their respective races the best placers. The IAC invitation at Cardiff Castle, the weekend before Christmas, also brought little festive joy. The men's event was won by Steve Tunstall (Preston Harriers) from a very high quality field. John Ngugi (Kenya) was only sixth on this occasion. Tunstall was the athlete who finished in the top twenty in the World Championships representing France whilst serving in the Foreign Legion. On returning to Britain he took up English eligibility although it later transpired that his father was born in Cardiff. The women's race was won by Jill Hunter (England) who took full advantage of the absence of Kirsty Wade and the Toobys. Their combined absence meant the Welsh team could only finish fourth although junior Carol Hayward (Newport) continued to show good form against senior opposition.

Early in January 1989, the Celtic junior international was again held at Irvine in Ayrshire. Star from a Welsh viewpoint was Gerallt Owen (Swansea) who won the junior race in a sprint finish despite having gone off course at one stage and having to catch back up with the leaders. As a consequence of his success he was selected to represent Great Britain in a junior international in Lisbon. Later in January, the annual match between Welsh CCA and the Army at Beachley threw up the intriguing sight of two Steve Jones running stride for stride for the whole race at the head of the field eventually crossing the line together to jointly win the men's event. The second and lesser known of the pair was Steve Jones (Bromsgrove) who had made rapid progress over the previous year, particularly as a steeplechaser. The British world trials were again held at Gateshead, despite the previous year's adverse comments. Carole Hayward was the most successful athlete finishing fifth in the inaugural women's junior trial and gaining her selection for the forthcoming championships at Stavanger in Norway. This was despite her losing two places in the later stages. In the women's senior race Sally Lynch (Newport) was ninth home and was named as non-travelling reserve. None of Wales' male athletes qualified although Roger Hackney, who did not compete, was one of the discretionary selections. Sally Blake (Newport) was named as British women's team manager. Welsh athletics lost her for good in 2000 when she emigrated with her husband to Australia.

Wales contested a Euro Cross competition at Margate In November 1989. This was a forerunner of the race series which were to become a major feature of the winter programme in the 1990s. Glorious weather greeted the event which saw Wales second in the women's team competition with Susan Tooby third individual but a disappointing fifth team in the men's event. A fortnight later there were further races in the series - Angela Tooby third, Susan fourth and Melissa Watson thirteenth at Bolbec in France, whilst Roger Hackney was second at Roeslare in Belgium.

Golden era ends

The period then coming to an end was arguably the 'golden era' of Welsh cross-country with such athletes as Steve Jones, Roger Hackney, Tony Simmons, Kirsty Wade and the Tooby twins amongst the best in the world. It also saw Wales' final years as a separate team in the World Championships. Unfortunately, Wales never fully capitalised on the opportunity to make a mark at world level although our clubs did so at their nearest equivalent - the European club's cup. On the women's side our best opportunity as a nation was probably in Warsaw in 1987. Having the better of England in the women's Home Countries race at Cardiff in 1986 and 1987 a 'dream' team of Kirsty Wade, Angela and Susan Tooby plus any of Lynn Maddison, Wendy Ore, Kim Lock, Hayley Nash or Ann Middle could surely have matched, if not beaten, any other nation in the world, including the Americans and Russians. On the men's side and for a variety of reasons including injuries and the other priorities and commitments of the individuals Wales were never able to select their best team. Steve Jones and Tony Simmons showed on several occasions that they were capable of top ten placings whilst Roger Hackney and John Davies (TVH) should have made the top twenty-five at worst. Wales would then have needed two others to make the first hundred - Chris Buckley, Peter Jenkins and Mike Bishop are obvious candidates. Other possibilities were Peter Baker (Shaftesbury) who ran so well in 1987/8 or even Steve Tunstall, had he chosen to take up his Welsh qualifications.

Pen Portrait – Angela Tooby (Aberystwyth University, Hereford AC and Cardiff AAC)
Susan Tooby (Bangor University and Cardiff AAC)

Tooby or not Tooby! Identification of athletes within the sport can on occasions be extremely difficult and has been the nightmare scenario for stadium announcers and television commentators especially when racing numbers are difficult to read. During the 1980s Welsh women's athletics was on a high, in particular in cross-country and road racing. In the forefront of this revolution were identical twins Susan and Angela Tooby.

Born at Woolhope, Hereford in October 1960 the twins took middle distance and marathon running in Wales to another planet. The two sisters were unique in athletic circles and were invariably talked about, written about and commented on as "the Tooby twins". It was a phrase that all too easily rolled off the tongue. It meant that Angela and Susan were rarely seen as individuals, but as two halves of a pair. In 1988 even *Athletics Weekly* had an article on them headed "Seoul Sisters".

The two by nature were very competitive and many were the times that they were seen battling it out at the front of races. They even had the same coaches - Ann Hill and eventually Harry Wilson, Steve Ovett's coach and a former Welsh 6 miles champion. By their own admission, Angela was the better athlete but by 1988 Susan had gone a long way to establishing her running career in a new direction, well away from her shadow. In her new career as road and marathon runner, Susan was pretty well on top. She was at the end of the year the fastest British woman over both 10 miles and half marathon.

It all started during the 1987 World Championships. While Angela was running the 10,000m in Rome, Susan, who despite running the qualifying time was not selected, ran the Cardiff half marathon. She won it by a long way and more importantly enjoyed it. Her next step was London and it was a tremendous debut. Her time, 2:32:09, was a Welsh record, beating Jackie Hulbert's (Brace) mark of 2:39:26 set in 1986. It was the moment she stepped outside Angela's shadow and became known less as Angela's sister and more as Susan Tooby, marathon runner. Later in the season, she set a new UK best for the half marathon in the Great North Run, finishing second to Grete Waitz with a time of 69:56. This was over a minute

inside Liz McColgan's previous best and over three minutes quicker than she'd ever run it before!

Next major step was the unlikely setting of Aylesbury, where Susan then clocked 53:25 for 10 miles, half a minute off Priscilla Welch's previous UK best. And that was despite having to ask the way near the finish! At the 1998 Seoul Olympics she finished 12th in a new Welsh record of 2:31:33 and completed a year of self-discovery.

Angela started her career at cross-country and 800m, joining Hereford AC in 1974. She competed in the English Schools cross-country four times with her best position being a modest 21st in 1979. She came of age internationally in 1983 with a momentous victory in the Paris -Versailles 17k in 58:29. Earlier in the season, having shaken off the effects of a car accident, she chose the Women's National 10 miles championship to record not only her first championship win but her very first victory in an open race of any sort!

During the 1986 Commonwealth Games in Edinburgh the commentators nightmare returned as both girls ran in the 10,000m. Angela won her first ever major medal with a bronze behind Liz Lynch of Scotland and New Zealand's Anne Audain with Susan finishing 6th.

The double returned in 1988 and collected medals at the inaugural World Cross-Country Championships. Angela took the individual silver, nineteen seconds behind Ingrid Kristiansen.

In 1983 Angela finished second in the Welsh 3,000m championships and won the international against Denmark over the same distance. Susan meanwhile had already won the Welsh 10 miles in 55:56. Ironically, both won the same number of Welsh International vests on the track – eight.

In 1984 the twins took their first Welsh cross-country title as they came in together as they would for the next two years, while Angela was the victor in 1987. Angela also won the English National cross-country title in 1985. Her only Welsh track title was in the 10,000 in 1989 while Susan won the 1,500 (1984 and 1985) and 3,000 (1986 and 1988). Angela was certainly the dominant athlete on the track as she won the UK Championships 5,000 in 1984 and 1985 with Susan second on both occasions. Angela's best domestic championship win was undoubtedly her victory in the Women's AAA 10,000 in 1988. That year she was also UK long course cross-country champion with Susan third. In 2000 Angela's 1987 marks of 5,000 (15:13.22) and 10,000 (31:55.30) remain as Welsh records, with Susan's marathon mark of 2:31:33 still intact.

European Club's Cup competitions

Whilst Wales lost its place in the World Cross-Country Championships Welsh athletes have had the restricted opportunity of competing in the European Club's Cup. These men and women's competitions, often referred to as the European clubs championships, are, in general terms, open to the champion clubs of the various European nations. Moreover, with Cardiff AAC being one of the founder members of the women's event they did have a guaranteed entry. This meant that on occasions when they were not the current Welsh champions Wales had the opportunity of a second team participating. The men's competition, which started in 1962, was dominated by English teams in the early years but in more recent times the heavily sponsored Portuguese and Italian clubs have come to the fore. They have also tended to be hosts on a majority of occasions; on the first thirteen occasions the races were all held at Arlons in France. In the first year only four clubs competed but this gradually grew to nine before doubling to eighteen in 1977. In 1981, Swansea Harriers competed at Varese in Italy; the first time any Welsh club other than Cardiff had taken part.

Then in the spring of 1983, Newport Harriers, in their first participation, had an excellent trip to the men's race at Lyon, finishing fourth. Steve Jones led them home as third individual behind the Portuguese pair of Fernando Mamede and Carlos Lopes, both representing Sporting Club, Lisbon. The following year in Portugal Newport were once again placed fourth with Steve Jones fifth individual. On this occasion Roger Hackney, in the colours of Aldershot, England' representatives, was just behind him. That same weekend in Italy, however, Cardiff AAC had a magnificent win in the women's competition with Angela Tooby the individual champion. She was more than ably backed up by sister, Susan, who was fourth and Kim Lock fifth. In the women's race in Madrid, in 1985, Angela retained her title with Susan again fourth and the Cardiff team gaining bronze medals. Elsewhere on the Iberian peninsular, in the Algarve, Newport found the men's competition very tough and were placed sixth. Individual winner was Carlos Lopes but he was followed by Roger Hackney in second spot, again representing Aldershot. Hackney's good form continued the following weekend when he finished third in the prestigious L'Equipe Invitation race in Paris. This time he was ahead of Lopes despite having run a 3,000m race indoors at Cosford the previous day.

Newport continued their good record in the 1986 men's race finishing fifth whilst Cardiff women's team were fourth. On this occasion both competitions were at the same venue on the Algarve in Portugal. Individually Angela Tooby maintained her superb record winning for the third consecutive year but on this occasion sister Susan, gained the bronze medal after her two previous fourth placings. The competitions in 1987 saw Newport Harriers fourth in the men's event whilst a weakened Cardiff team struggled in the women's race despite Angela notching up her fourth consecutive individual victory. Second Welsh woman home this time was Anne Middle from Newport, currently at university in Spain and representing Tintoretto, who finished third team.

In February 1988 the European Clubs Cup women's race came to Wales (Cardiff Castle/Bute Park) for the first time in its history. Angela Tooby made the most of home advantage to score a remarkable fifth successive win with Susan following her home in second place. Kim Lock-Harris was eleventh but SC Braga (Portugal) packed four in ten to tie on fourteen points with Cardiff and gain the narrowest of victories by virtue of better-placed last scorer. The previous day at Clusone in Italy Newport finished seventh with Steve Jones eighth individual. Panetta (Pro Patria, Italy) retained his title and led his club to victory.

The 1989 events returned to the Algarve. SC Lisbon, fielding what amounted to the Portuguese national team won the men's race, led by Domingo Castro, one of the twins. Swansea Harriers were in ninth place whilst in the women's competition Cardiff were eleventh and Les Croupiers RC nineteenth. The 1991 competitions were both affected by weather. The women's race on February 9th took place in snow-covered San Marino. Ann Middle finished an excellent sixth in the race but was then disqualified due to her current residence in Spain and membership of Tintoretto, for whom she had run in the 1987 race. Newport thus dropped to seventh place whilst Cardiff were thirteenth. In the men's race the following day at Marseilles a depleted Newport squad finished tenth. The 1992 races were at Cassino, Italy (women) and Alicante, Spain (men) but Newport thirteenth and Cardiff sixteenth in the former and Swansea thirteenth in the men's had little to enthuse over. In 1993 both races were once again in the Algarve. Newport were Wales' representatives in both male and female competitions, finishing fourteenth in the former and eleventh in the latter. Amorebieta, Spain (men) and Piedmonte, France (women) staged the 1994 events and bouncing back from a relatively poor Welsh championships the previous weekend Swansea Harriers' men finished fourth to equal the previous best by a Welsh club, just ahead of Bingley Harriers who were the English representatives.

In more recent times the most notable occurrence was in 1997 when Newport Harriers took on the onerous task of hosting the women's competition at Tredegar Park. Their success is a tribute to their club and its officers. Regrettably, there are now moves to restrict the United Kingdom to a single team in each of the competitions. This is despite the fact that Cardiff, as founder members of the women's competition were originally guaranteed an annual place. Should this retrograde step occur it will further devalue the Welsh senior championships and, for that matter those of the other home countries. Many athletes no longer view their national title as a prime target, preferring to run in (say) the Reebok series because of the tangible rewards and in the relevant trial races if they have ambitions for European or World selection. These concerns are over and above the practical problem of how a single British representative club could be chosen.

The Veteran's scene in the 1990s

The 1990 Welsh Veteran's Championships were held at Bangor on January 6th. Dic Evans easily retained the men's title but the women's race saw Ann James win out in a sprint finish with Liz Gooch. Not surprisingly, the team competitions were dominated by north Wales clubs with Wrexham and Eryri both gaining two sets of medals.

The Veteran's International moved north to Aberdeen in November 1991 and was combined with the Hydrasun open meeting. Tony Simmons finally lost his individual title, to Roy Bailey of England, but Dic Evans was first "over 45" home and led his section to a second team placing. Overall England dominated whilst Scotland just edged out Wales for second place. That season's Welsh events were held at Llanrumney, Cardiff on January 4th. Newly qualified Jeremy Collins (Swansea) won from Dave Ide (Gloucester) with David G Jones (Swansea) third. In the women's race Dawn Kenwright retained her title ahead of Ann James (Rhondda) and Ann Cartwright (Prestatyn). Les Croupiers again held off Wrexham in the team competition whilst Penarth & Dinas Runners were surprise third placers.

In March 1992 the British Veteran's Championships were held at Pentwyn, Cardiff. In the M45 category Alun Roper just lost out and had to be content with silver on this occasion. There was major local success, however, in the M50 category where Cardiff, led home by Jim O'Brien, won the team title.

Alun Roper

The international moved off the mainland for the first time in the autumn of 1992, being held at Newton Abbey on the outskirts of Belfast. Moreover, for the first time the Irish Republic participated fully. Tony Simmons was second in the men's race to maintain his superb record in the event. Dic Evans was third M45, whilst Liz Hughes (Cardiff) and Pat Gallagher were similarly placed in the W35 and W40 women's sections. The Welsh Championships were at Fairwood, Gower on 2nd January 1993, once more as part of the inter-counties competition. Alun Roper won by over a minute from teammate and defending champion Jeremy Collins with 1991 winner, Mike Venables, third. Swansea Harriers were easy team winners. Liz Hughes won the women's race from Pat Gallagher with Liz Slater (Brecon) third. Les Croupiers retained their team title for the fifth consecutive year. The 1993 British Championships were at Burnley, in March. Swansea's Martin Rees and Alun Roper, finished third and fourth in the men's race with the latter first in the M45 category. In the separate M50 race Alan Jefferies (Swansea) was third. Good back up gave Swansea first team place in the younger category and silver medals in the older one. Pat Gallagher was tenth in the women's race and first W45.

Martin Rees

In November 1993, the Veteran's International returned to Wales and was held at an excellent new venue near Culverhouse Cross west of Cardiff. With home support Wales provided individual winners in Martin Rees (Swansea M40), Alun Roper (M45) and Ron Elliott (North Wales RR M50) but were second to England in all three team events. A mere eight days later veterans were back in action in Cardiff with the British and Welsh Cross Country Relay Championships being held on the traditional Heath Park course the day after the Micky Morris Relays. Swansea Harriers won the M50 and Cardiff the W35 race with Alun Roper (Swansea) and Barbara Boylan (Cardiff) the fastest individuals. The Welsh Veteran's Championships, in conjunction with the inter-counties races, were held at Ruabon on 2nd January 1994. Kevin Brown (Swindon) ran out an easy winner in the men's race whilst Barbara Boylan took the women's title. Griffithstown Harriers were surprise team winners narrowly ahead of Swansea and Wrexham but the home club took the M50 team award as well as wining first and third women's team awards.

In the BVAF Championships at Tunbridge Wells in March 1994, Alun Roper finished fourth overall and retained his M45 title despite losing a shoe early in the race. Alan Garrett (Cardiff) was second in the M50 race and took the M55 award whilst Alan Jefferies (Swansea) was third overall and second M50. In the women's race Pat Gallagher finished tenth overall to retain her W45 title for the fourth consecutive year.

The 1994 International was held at Sunderland on a day of almost incessant rain which turned the paths of the parkland venue into streams let alone the course which was already well churned up by a league race held that same day. The event was notable for the addition of an extra women's age group. Then in 1995 the Veteran's International developed yet further. It was held outside the United Kingdom for the first time, at Malahide, near Dublin. It also included a guest Russian men's team in one section. Successive venues were Irvine, Scotland (1996), and Ballymena, Antrim (1997) before returning to north Wales in 1998. Here, as on the first occasion ten years earlier, a major figure in the organisation of the very enjoyable event was Ron Bell. The venue was St Asaph with Prestatyn AC acting as host club. Despite home advantage Wales had a relatively poor day. The only individual medallists being Pat Gallagher (first W50) and Frances Gill (Neath Harrriers third W35); the latter finishing an excellent third overall in the women's race. Team wise it was the older age groups who achieved success with the W50, M55 and M60 squads all gaining silver medals.

Cross-country relays

Whilst relays are a fairly common and popular feature of the athletic programme this has not been the case in Wales as far as cross-country is concerned. In the late 1950s Newport

Harriers organised a senior men's relay in Kimberley Park, near to their then headquarters at Malpas. When the club moved across the river to the Glebelands in the early 1960s the relays were likewise transferred. They were then held for many years on the flat fast riverside course also used for Welsh Cross-Country Championships and now carried the name of the Dewar Shield relays. The shield in question was apparently the massive oak and silver trophy which dated back to the start of the century. The senior men's relay was of a particularly high standard drawing teams from the west of England as well as from the whole of south Wales. Despite being held in the autumn, thus providing an ideal warm up for the coming winter season and being expanded so that there were races over a range of age groups the events failed to maintain viable entries in their later years and eventually lapsed completely in the early 1990s.

In 1981 Cardiff AAC organised a men's event on Heath Park in memory of former European junior steeplechase champion Micky Morris, which continues to this day, again organised by Graham Finlayson. Cardiff won in that first year with Steve Jones, running for the RAF, setting the fastest lap - 17:55 and twenty years later the record was only eleven seconds faster and in many of the intervening years no athlete had broken eighteen minutes. Over the years Cardiff, Newport, Swansea and Westbury have dominated the event and only on two occasions has one of that quartet not been the victors and this despite the efforts of such clubs as Shaftesbury Harriers, second in 1987, and Aldershot, Farnham and District. In 1985, the race attracted no fewer than fifty-eight teams to what was by then officially designated a Welsh championship. There was also a women's race over one lap of the course which was won by Sally Lynch (Newport), but the distance was extended in later years.

From its inception the relay incorporated a veteran's competition. Bridgend YMCA won the first year with Jim O'Brien recording the fastest lap time. Bristol AC won in 1982 and then Aldershot had five consecutive wins. They were followed by Swansea Harriers with nine victories in succession - Alun Roper setting a veteran's record of 18:35 in 1987. That particular year saw a very fiercely contested senior race with Swansea eventually winning from Shaftesbury Harriers.

Welsh Championships of the early 1990s

The final decade of the twentieth century saw a much more fluid situation, particularly in the senior men's competition, with Newport Harriers having two wins, Cardiff AAC four wins in succession and Swansea Harriers five wins. Even so it was 1998 before the last club won at a venue other than Singleton Park. Individually, with the exception of 1999, (Ian Pierce - Tipton Harriers), the men's senior champions have all come from Cardiff or Swansea but only Christian Stephenson with wins in 1995, 1996 and 1997 plus second in 1994 and third in 1998 managed any sequence or much consistency. Similarly, over the same period Newport, Cardiff and Swansea have tended to take the majority of the younger male age group team awards.

The 1990 Welsh Championships were held at Barry and Melissa Watson easily retained her title for the third consecutive year. Nigel Adams failed to emulate her performance whilst Steve Jones failed to gain his tenth win. Ieuan Ellis set the pace most of the way but Eddie Conway of Cardiff was always in close attendance and late in the race he eased past and away to victory. Ieuan held on for second place ahead of Nigel Adams. Newport Harriers took both senior team titles. Notable amongst the younger age groups was Lynn Gallagher (Westbury) who won the Girls' race - twenty-five years after her mother's first

Welsh title win over the country and in the same club colours.

In the autumn of 1990 the final Welsh 10k/Women's 5k event was held at Llanmartin in Gwent over an undulating pastureland course. It was a sign of the times that there were complaints over the muddy gateways and matter left by cattle, the usual occupants of the fields. One wonders what the reaction would have been if the farmer had chosen to plough one of the fields instead of leaving it fallow! In the races Steve Knight confirmed recent good form whilst Wendy Ore made it a Cardiff double win. The 1991 championships returned to Singleton Park and, yet again, with home advantage Swansea regained the men's team title. New member, Commonwealth Games 5,000m bronze medallist Ian Hamer, who beat his club mate and pre-race favourite Nigel Adams, led them home. In the women's race Sarah Lee-Hodge (Westbury) who had been fourth in 1989 and third in 1990, finally beat her club mate Melissa Watson who was reigning champion from the previous three years. In the youths and junior men's races the in-form Colin Jones (Eryri) and Neil Emberton (Newtown) duly won their events.

Heath Park staged the 1992 Welsh Championships and in the senior men's race Ian Hamer retained his title despite a formidable challenge from Steve Jones. Steve did however have the pleasure of helping Newport regain the team title in a very high scoring race. In the senior women's event Melissa Watson regained her title ahead of Hayley Nash (Torfaen AC) whilst Newport had a narrow win over Cardiff in the team event. The younger age groups saw titles spread around with six clubs gaining team awards whilst individual medallists came from no fewer than fourteen different clubs. The Welsh Championships of 1993 were back on the undulating parkland of Singleton. Wendy Ore followed up her Inter-Counties, British trials and English national runs by winning almost as she pleased ahead of Hayley Nash, also now in Cardiff colours. Likewise Christian Stephenson (Cardiff) cruised round the junior men's course. The senior men's race was more competitive with Ian Hamer, defending champion, the early leader. However in the later stages Justin Hobbs (Cardiff) moved up with him and then pulled away to add a senior title to his previous collection of colts, youth and junior age group wins. Ian held on to second place whilst Austin Davies (Brecon AC) capped a fine season with a third place medal ahead of Steve Jones, now in his 37th year and running in what turned out to be his last championship, seventeen years after his first appearance in the race. Newport retained the senior women's team title ahead of Cardiff but Swansea continued their habit of winning at home in the men's competition. Junior women's champion was Lynne Gallagher (Westbury) whilst her mother placed fifteenth in the senior race.

Carmarthen hosted the 1994 Welsh Championships - the first time the senior event had been held west of Swansea - on the flat muddy fields of the United Counties Showground. Cardiff AAC had a good day with the first three in the senior men's race and the first two in the senior women's as Justin Hobbs and Wendy Ore retained their titles and led their club to team victories. Somewhat surprisingly, in the men's competition this was Cardiff's first team win for thirteen years. With Christian Stephenson opting to run as a senior and finish second, Colin Jones (Eryri) won the junior men's race by a huge margin with Ian Oliver (Colwyn Bay) and Ian Pierce (Wrexham) crossing the line together second and third. In the under 15 boys race Steve Lawrence (Swansea) and Alun Vaughan (Eryri) finishing first and second only two seconds apart. Northern clubs also had individual successes in the other younger age groups. Wrexham AC provided both under13 winners in Duncan Hughes and Laura Jones whilst Colwyn Bay AC athletes collected a silver and two bronze medals in addition to that previously mentioned. For the host club, Heledd Gruffydd retained the under 15 girls title to record her fourth consecutive win in the championships.

The Welsh Inter-Counties Cross Country Championships developed through the 1980s and by the end of the decade were a major fixture. Moreover with counties often more willing to travel than clubs they were in the younger age groups often a better reflection of Welsh cross-country than the main championships later in the season. For several years the two senior races were held separately on an earlier date, in conjunction with the Welsh women's 5k/men's 10k races until those events ceased in 1990/1. Eventually all the races were held on one day usually by utilising two courses at the same venue. The situation was complicated by the addition of veteran's races which themselves incorporated the Welsh "open" championship for those age groups. In 1996 the eight counties were replaced by unitary authorities. For its part athletics concurrently adopted a four-region structure and the competitions were thereafter held between teams from those new bodies.

Welsh representative & similar matches of the early 1990s

In the 1990s the invitation and representative matches, which had been a major feature of the winter programme, tended to be displaced or in some cases absorbed by race series. Examples of the latter, some of which had commenced some years earlier were the IAAF World Cross, the Euro Cross and domestically the Reebok series. In the United Kingdom matches which have been absorbed by the Reebok series are those in Margate and Cumbernauld and it also now encompasses the UKCAU (inter-county) Championship as its finale. This is now the main trial for British teams in the world championships. The series races tend to be much more biased to individual participation with athletes gaining points for their performances over the series towards cumulative awards. In the case of the World Cross there are even criteria setting down the minimum number of world ranked athletes who must start in order for the race to count towards the season's total. These events do sometimes still include some team competition within their structure but secondary to the individual competition, the exceptions to this being the cases of the annual Celtic international for younger age groups and the Home countries women's event.

However in 1990, the British authorities yet again held specific trials for the world team selection. This time the venue was Glasgow on March 11th. On this occasion Nigel Adams ninth in the men's race in the same time as the eighth finisher and Melissa Watson eighth in the women's just missed out on automatic selection for Aix–Les-Bains later in the month. However several of the athletes initially selected withdrew and so Nigel gained a place in the team, whilst Melissa was named as a reserve. Nigel made the most of his opportunity being one of Britain's scorers but Melissa as travelling reserve had the frustration of merely being a spectator. A fortnight later and outside the normal season Ian Hamer achieved a notable success. Using all his strength and speed he drew away in the closing stages to win the World Student's Cross-country title at Poznan in Poland. In addition, he led Britain to second team placing. The only previous such winner from Wales was David James (Cardiff) ten years earlier at Coleraine in Ireland.

In January 1991, the Irish Republic organised a fixture incorporating a Celtic nations match, the second Westathletic international and an IAAF grand prix meeting. Unfortunately their sponsorship fell through and financial aid to visiting teams did not materialise, Wales, however, still took part. Major success was achieved in the Celtic junior race where Colin Jones was with the leaders all the way to finish second only two seconds down on the winner whilst Neil Emberton (Newtown) made a late charge to come through to third only three seconds behind his team mate. The under 23s were swallowed up in the combined senior race with Justin Hobbs our first runner home. In the team events Ireland won all three age groups in the Celtic men's match whilst Portugal won both Westathletic competitions with Wales third of the seven countries in the men's and fifth in the women's of the latter.

The quadrangular match versus RAF, Midlands and UAU was revived in December 1991 and held at Llanmartin in south east Gwent. Ian Hamer won the men's race but a strong Midlands squad took the team event. In the women's race Hayley Nash running as a non-scorer was first home but the next four were all Welsh to ensure a team victory. For the junior men Mark Morgan (Newport) won by over half a minute whilst good packing ensured that Wales a gained second team victory.

The Celtic international was held at Carmarthen early in January 1992. Whilst the flat fields of the Showground may not appeal to traditionalists they do make an excellent venue for spectators and organisers. In the under 17 race Chris Blount (Newport) set the pace but eventually had to settle for second place. In the under 20 and under 23 races north Walians Colin Jones (Eryri) and Jamie Lewis (now Swansea) both gained convincing victories. With good packing Wales won the under 20 team title and was second in the others giving them overall victory. A week later came the annual match versus the Army at Chepstow with the Royal Navy providing additional opposition for the first time. In all three races AAW gained overwhelming wins by providing the first six on each occasion. The senior men's race was won by Shaun Tobin (Swansea) with his elder brother, Kevin, second whilst Steve Henshaw (Deeside) won the junior race.

Following the previous year's problems the United Kingdom trials were held at Basingstoke on February 9th, with the additional cache of being designated as the United Kingdom Championships. Despite this there were several withdrawals from the senior men's squad, in particular, whilst Ian Hamer failed to finish. In the junior men's race Colin Jones finished fifth to ensure his selection for the World Championships in Boston, USA. Angela Tooby returned to form in sixth position in the same time as the fifth placer but, with only the first three automatically selected and the fourth placer chosen as a reserve, she still lost out on this occasion.

The 1993 Celtic international was held at Mallusk in conjunction with the annual IAAF meeting there. Wales' best result was in the under 23s where they finished second. That race was combined with the senior open race where Ian Hamer running as an individual finished sixth. The following day Christian Stephenson ran for Great Britain in the annual junior race in Lisbon, finishing eleventh and second Briton – much to the pleasure of Bernie Plain, who was now Britain's junior men's team manager.

Male and female veteran's races were included for the first time in the match versus the Army at Chepstow a week later in January. The AAW totally dominated all the competitions yet again. In the senior women's race Hayley Nash and Melissa Watson, first and third individuals were split by a then virtually unknown army corporal named Kelly Holmes.

The problems over world championship trials were finally resolved in February 1993 with the UKCAU (British Inter-Counties) event being upgraded and expanded and for the first time including both sexes and all age groups, with the exception of veterans. For many years prior to this consolidation of races into one meeting those for the younger age groups had been held annually at Shrewsbury. The races, in 1993, were held at Corby. Christian Stephenson continued his brilliant season by leading from the start and literally running away from the rest of the junior field, thus ensuring his selection for the world event in Spain. Wendy Ore finished seventh in the women's race and with the first four automatically selected and the fifth placer as reserve missed out yet again. To emphasise her good form she went on to finish fourth in the English Championships at Luton a fortnight later. In the younger age groups of the inter- counties races Dunya Hurley (Powys) had another excellent run to finish third in the minor girls race following up her success in the corresponding Welsh event.

Wales revived the women's Home Countries International at Carmarthen in 1993. The hosts finished third in both races but in the senior race were without Wendy Ore and Hayley Nash. Plans for a European Championship were now progressing and it had been proposed that the four home countries be permitted to enter separate teams, as is the case in some other sports. These hopes were dashed by the European Association specifying that only IAAF affiliates could enter. The next suggestion, by Scotland, was for a Commonwealth competition, albeit not on an annual basis due to the travel implications. This never materialised and must now seem increasingly unlikely.

In late November 1993 the Margate international was held in dreadful conditions but brought satisfactory results for Wales. It was bitterly cold and snowing during both senior races. Wales selected a very young team for the men's event and were rewarded by Christian Stephenson winning. He was well supported by Karl Palmer (Preseli 5th), Colin Jones (Eryri 8th) and Jon Hooper (Cardiff 12th) to win the team event comfortably ahead of England.

The British inter-counties (UKCAU) championships were held at Luton and after a spell of unrelenting rain the courses were a sea of ankle deep mud. Colin Jones and Christian Stephenson gave the Principality a 1-2 in the junior men's race whilst Steve Lawrence (Swansea) and Alun Vaughan (Eryri) were third and fourth in the under 15 boys race only five seconds down on the winner.

1994/5 started with a Welsh team competing in an invitation international as part of the Mike Sully races at Bristol. This memorial meeting had been taking place for over a quarter of a century. In its early days the meeting established itself as a major inter-club fixture but then gradually seemed to lose out to leagues and other fixtures. The aim on this occasion was for the meeting to regain its former status. As a consequence competition standard was very high and Wales were third. A similar standard of opposition was faced in the Margate International, which had also become an unofficial trial for the European Championships, held a month later. This time Wales were placed second in the team competitions. Continuing a similar high level the Cosford match was again very fiercely contested with Nicky Comerford (Cardiff) fourth Wales' highest placed finisher. For the Brussels IAAF World Cross meeting just before Christmas Wales continued its policy of sending young athletes to provide them with experience of top class competition. Andres Jones (Carmarthen) had a good run in the junior event and as a consequence was selected for the Great Britain in the annual junior international in Lisbon.

The Celtic international returned to Irvine once more with windy conditions making the testing coastal park course even tougher than usual. Wales were second in the under 20 team event whilst Mark Morgan (Newport) won the under 23 race. The 1995 world trials were yet again in Northumberland with Welsh athletes more successful on this occasion. Christian Stephenson was chosen for the Great Britain senior team and Nathaniel Lane (Cardiff) for the juniors with Andres Jones nominated as reserve for the latter section.

Centenaries and Celebrations

A group of fixtures that deserve special mention are those organised by various cross-country bodies to mark anniversaries and the like. The first, almost inevitably, was to mark the one hundredth anniversary of the formation of Roath Harriers. This was organised by

Cardiff AAC in October 1982 at Heath Park. In addition to a period costume run and social events there was an invitation men's team race and this gave athletes the opportunity of an early season test. John Theophilus (Swansea) was the individual winner in that main race from Dennis Fowles (Cardiff) and Ieuan Ellis (Newport).

Over the years there have been a series of similar events organised by Westbury Harriers to celebrate various landmarks in their history. Although an English club they have always had close links with south Wales and have provided innumerable athletes to Welsh championships and teams, particularly in endurance events. They have also been major participants in the Gwent League since 1974. Moreover, their promotions have always involved Welsh teams. The particular anniversaries marked were their club's golden and diamond jubilees in 1974 and 1984 and their women's section jubilees in 1978 and 1988. The women's race in the latter year was actually won by a Welsh junior, Carole Hayward (Newport), setting the tone for what was to be her best ever season.

For its part the AAW held a series of events to mark the centenary (in 1996) of the formation of the Welsh CCA. These included a buffet reception in the Royal Oak Hotel at Roath on the exact anniversary of the formation meeting. The celebrations were spread over the latter half of the 1995/6 winter season and the first half of the 1996/7 season. The Centenary committee's original aim was to hold events in all parts of the Principality. The feature over which they had no control was, of course, the weather but fortune smiled on them and all the functions held enjoyed good weather. The first was the combined Inter Counties and Veteran's Championships held in the splendid natural arena of Pontypool Park in December 1995. This meant that south east Wales had its event a month early. Hard frost followed by bright sunshine, combined with the terrain of the park ensured testing conditions for all the races. A very pleasing aspect was that all eight counties were represented. At least one athlete from each county won an individual medal and six of the

Centenary Dinner at Cardiff City Hall.

counties had a champion. Again, on a team basis, each of the counties gained at least one set of medals.

The Centenary year proper started with the Celtic Nations International being held late in January 1996 with teams and officials accommodated at the Urdd youth centre at Llangranog. The races were held on a spectacular undulating course overlooking the shore of Cardigan Bay with conditions made arduous by heavy ground frost. Home advantage, which meant that Welsh teams were virtually at full strength, ensured gaining more success than in most previous years whilst for the first time there was competition for all six age groups. Wales' individual winners were Hayley Parry (Swansea-under 23), Clare Martin (Newport-under 20), Christian Stephenson (Cardiff-under 23) and Nathaniel Lane (Cardiff-under 20). In February, the Centenary year championships were held in Singleton Park again on a superb sunny day. As ever, our major clubs dominated proceedings but no fewer than sixteen clubs had at least one athlete gaining a medal. Especial mention should be made of Mercury AC and Amman Valley RC who gained championship team medals for the first time. In the evening a civic reception was held at Swansea Guildhall attended by all the surviving Welsh senior men's and women's champions, except John Merriman and Jim Alford, but including the redoubtable Billy Matthews, of Penrhys, some sixty years after his victories. With an extensive informal exhibition of photographs, mementoes and trophies on display, the evening was one of nostalgia and reunion for all present.

The celebratory year culminated in a representative and international match on October 12th. It was held in the private grounds of Coedrhydarglyn Park just west of Cardiff. Here a valley provided a natural arena even better than that at Pontypool and afforded spectators an almost continuous view of the races. It had been hoped to incorporate that year's British trials for the world championships but Wales were outbid financially by the Northumberland Tourist Board. Instead very enjoyable and successful races were organised with teams from the Home Countries plus the Armed Services, Police and the like. Following the example of the Roath event it included a re-enactment of a Victorian club run in period costume. In the evening the races were followed by a Civic Dinner in the splendid surroundings of Cardiff City Hall. As at the Swansea function the opportunity was taken to mount a display of photographs, press cuttings and other memorabilia. As with most of the major events staged in Cardiff over the past decade or so, the Coedrhydarglyn race was ably organised by the incomparable Graham Finlayson BEM.

From Centenary Celebration to the end of the Century

The end of 1996 saw Christian Stephenson representing Great Britain in his first European Cross Country Championships in Charleroi, Belgium where he finished 49th. The new year started well for Welsh athletes with Stephenson becoming the first Welsh winner of the CAU Inter Counties Championships since Syeve Jones, 16 years previously. On the international front Hayley Parry and Clare Martin represented Great Britain in the Coca Cola Cross Country International in Belfast in January. Domestically, Christian Stephenson won the senior men's title for the third successive year at Heath park, Cardiff in February 1997, coming home with over a minute to spare from runner-up Steve Knight. Another Cardiff man, Andres Jones, took third place to give the host club a clean sweep. Wendy Ore's string of four successive victories (1993, 94, 95, 96) was finally ended when Hayley Nash (three times a runner-up) claimed her first title. The following month Stephenson finished second to Keith Cullen in the World Championships trials at Luton to book his place in the team, sadly as Wales' only representative. Held in Turin, the World

Championship was won by the incomparable Paul Tergat of Kenya with Stephenson in 38th place, the second highest placed British runner behind Welsh-born Jon Brown.

The next cross-country season, 1997/1998, saw Christian Stephenson starting well, winning the inaugral Reebok challenge race at Bristol in October, ahead of Keith Cullen. In December the event came to Cardiff and Andres Jones performed well to finish 8th. In December Stephenson was again on international duty as Wales' sole representative in the Great Britain team which finished sixth at the European Championships in Portugal. His individual position on the occasion was 39th. Defending champion Stephenson could manage only third place in the Welsh Championships at Bridgend in February as clubmate Nick Comerford came home a clear winner. Swansea Harriers, led home by runner-up Jamie Lewis, wrested the team title from Cardiff after four successive victories, reclaiming the title they had last won in 1993. Angharad Mair pipped reigning champion Hayley Nash by a second to win her only Welsh title. Comerford was obviously the man in form as he came 7th in the World Championships trials, held on home territory in Cardiff, ironically on St David's Day. For the first time the World Championships for both men and women would consist of 2 races each, a short race (4k for both) and a long race (8k for women, 12k for men). Comerford ran the 4k at the trials but, unfortunately for him, his splendid effort was not sufficient to get him a spot on the plane to Marrakech.

In the European Championships at Ferrara, Italy in December 1998, Christian Stephenson finished 22nd helping the Great Britain team to 4th place. The Welsh Championships went north in 1999 with Colwyn Bay as the venue. Not surprisingly it was a north Wales athlete, Ian Pierce who captured the men's title. Despite a strong challenge from Eryri, who had two finishers in the first four, Swansea Harriers hung on to their team prize they had won for the past three seasons. The CAU Inter Counties Championships, which incorporated the World Championship trials, were held at Wollaton Park, Nottingham in February. In a very close finish to the women's 4k, Hayley Parry took 3rd place and secured her selection. Christian Stephenson was also selected after finishing 4th in the men's 12k race. The World Championships were held in Belfast on 28 March with Stephenson and Parry carrying the flag for Wales. There is an enormous leap from the best in Britain to the best in the world and Stephenson finished 73rd in his race and Parry 40th in hers.

The 1999/2000 season saw two Welsh representatives in the men's race (but, sadly no women) in the European Championships at Valenje, Slovenia in December. Christian Stephenson, who had been a comfortable winner of the Birmingham Reebok in November, was 20th and Nick Comerford, 3rd in the Margate Reebok, 45th. After this performance Comerford went from strength to strength. Running over 9k in the Reebok Challenge at Cardiff in January, he thrilled the home crowd by beating Keith Cullen in a sprint finish and claimed vistory by a mere second. Cullen had not lost a domestic race to a British runner since Christian Stephenson beat him at Bristol over two years previously. Hayley Tullett (formerly Parry) won the women's 4k race, beating the English National champion Angela Newport in the process, while Matthew Jones, who had also won at Margate, took the under 17 race to make it a Welsh treble. Nottingham's Wollaton Park was again the setting for the World Championship trials and it turned out to be a highly successful day for Welsh runners. Hayley Tullett, who, at the time of writing, has never won a Welsh cross-country title, ran out an easy winner of the women's 4k, once again getting the better of the English champion. Although Keith Cullen turned the tables on him this time, Comerford earned himself a trip to the Worlds by taking 3rd spot in the 12k race. Stephenson, unfortunately, had to drop out with dysentery. Incidentally the women's 8k was won by Tara Krzywicki, daughter of ex Welsh football international Dick Krzywicki. Nick Comerford was back in

Cardiff two weeks after his Nottingham triumph to reclaim the Welsh title he had won two years before. Despite a clean sweep of individual medals, Cardiff failed to clinch the team prize, which went to Swansea for the 3rd year in succession. Catherine Dugdale of Swansea took the women's race. The World Championships at Vilamoura, Portugal saw Hayley Tullett take 39th place in the women's 4k while Nick Comerford was 88th at 12k.

Chapter 7
From Stormy Down to Chicago

Well, it's a long way from Stormy Down to Chicago. Who would have thought, in 1934, when the first Welsh Marathon Championship took place from Stormy Down, near Bridgend, that half a century later the world record would be broken in Chicago by a Welshman! This chapter traces the history of road running in Wales.

Road running really only became recognised as a section of athletics separate from cross-country in the 1930s. A significant feature at that time was the creation of point-to-point road relays often sponsored by the *News of the World*. In Wales' case the event was from Newport to Swansea. However, prior to that there were occasional reports of races on the road. Traditionally, the original road run of history was that of Pheidippides from Marathon to Athens recorded in Greek mythology. That original marathon was itself commemorated in the first modern Olympics in 1896, with a race over forty kilometres mainly on rough cobbled roads. With Greece as host nation hopes were high for a local winner especially as it provided twelve of the seventeen starters. Even so the chances seemed slim as Lemursiaux of France had a clear lead up to thirty kilometres. Here though he succumbed to a bout of cramp which slowed him and allowed Flack of Australia to catch up and take the lead, whereupon the Frenchman dropped out. But at thirty-five kilometres Flack was himself caught and passed by Spiridon Louis. The Greek shepherd went on to score a popular victory acclaimed by the crowd in the stadium and with Prince Georg of Greece apparently accompanying him around part of the finishing lap.

The earliest historical references in Wales are to challenge races such as the one between Guto Nythbrân and "Prince" of Bedwas which is covered elsewhere. There is also a very interesting historical reference in a booklet on the customs and traditions of Wales. This notes that on Anglesey and in Caernarvonshire a popular feature of traditional weddings was a race from the church to the bride's home. This was apparently in the early nineteenth century and the purpose was to publicise that a wedding had taken place. It began immediately the bride had first worn her wedding ring during the service and was from the church door to the house where the wedding feast was to be held. The reward being the wedding cake, no less. For example, on one occasion in Llanllechid, Caernarvonshire, thirty young men are reputed to have run a distance of four miles.

As mentioned in the cross-country section two early press references to specific road races appeared in the *Express* in March 1896. Both involved members of Roath Harriers. The first was an eight to score, 4 ½ mile road race between two teams of club members. One team was composed of those who worked in the docks and the other of workers from the town. Held on a Thursday evening it resulted in a win for the Dockers team with Hugh Fairlamb the individual winner. On the last Saturday of that same month the Roath club held a four-mile handicap race on the Rumney road on the outskirts of Cardiff and including an ascent of Rumney Hill. Hugh Fairlamb, off scratch, was again the fastest individual finishing in third place. The race was followed in the evening by the Roath club's annual dinner and prize-giving.

How did the marathon become 26 miles 385 yards ....?

Moving on twelve years, the incident at the end of the marathon held as part of the 1908 Olympic Games in London resulted in major publicity. On a swelteringly hot day Dorando Pietri, of Italy when in the lead, first turned the wrong way in the stadium and then collapsed. He was helped up and turned the right way only to collapse several more times before being virtually carried over the finish line by officials. He was subsequently disqualified for being assisted and the gold medal awarded to Hayes, of the United States, who had been second to finish. The irony of the situation was that at a late date the course had been lengthened so that the race would finish in front of the royal box and hence the standard distance of 26 miles and 385 yds was established for the marathon.

The public interest generated by the Dorando incident was almost certainly a factor in a race being organised in Bristol in October of that year over a distance of 22 ½ miles. Seventy-five runners started from the Bristol Rovers football ground and a crowd estimated at twelve thousand watched the finishing stages. The winner was J Price of Small Heath Harriers. Ben Christmas of Roath Harriers and Swansea was fifth. A contemporary report noted: "all the men finished remarkably fresh considering the very muddy state of the roads".

Two months after the Bristol race, on December 8th 1908, a so-called marathon, over roughly eleven miles, was organised by Cwmbran Harriers in their locality. The course consisted of two laps starting with three laps of a field then a loop up "half way hill" ending with another lap of the field before being repeated. It is not clear how much of the race was on road as a contemporary report states, "The course was an exceedingly hard and hilly one and was made more so owing to the heavy going." Even so twelve clubs entered the required minimum of six runners and no fewer than two hundred and twenty runners started. The clubs entered included Roath and Newport Harriers. The latter nominated over forty competitors but did not include Tommy Arthur who ran in the colours of his home team, Llanhilleth, whilst a former teammate EO Price represented Treharris Harriers. This club had only been formed a month earlier and Price was the inaugural Honorary Secretary. In the actual race Ernest Paul of Cwmbran is reported to have led by about thirty yards at halfway. He later further increased his lead only to be overtaken in the latter stages by Tommy Arthur, who with better pace judgement, won in a time of 68 minutes exactly. Paul hung on for second place (68:50) whilst F Williams (Pontnewydd) and Ben Christmas were third and fourth both being timed at 69:30.

Prior to this, road races tended to be intermittent and, as indicated, the running surfaces were often rather rougher than present day tarmacadam or concrete. There were also highly publicised ultra distance races but these were often around and around a stadium or arena or even indoors in a hall or similar building such as Madison Square Garden in the United States. They tended to be the province of professionals competing for cash awards and even more to the benefit of their backers and sponsors betting on the achievements of their protégés. The extent to which such events influenced sport is revealed by the comment in *The Times* of December 4th 1909. This was to the effect that "The craze for 'Marathon' races which threatened danger to cross-country running in this country by tempting well known runners to become professionals seems to be dying out".

In May 1926 and 1927, the *Evening Express* newspaper sponsored a road race in south

Wales. Unfortunately reports do not indicate the venue or distance although times in the first year would suggest about seven miles. Ernie Thomas (Cwmbran) won on both occasions whilst the names and placings of the next nine home were almost identical both years. They included E Leyshon (Cwmbran), Frank Denmead (Cwm Harriers), Ted Hopkins and Jimmy Guy (Roath), Danny Phillips (Newport) and Ike O'Brien (Port Talbot). Earlier in 1926, a minute of the Welsh CCA committee contained references to a miner's road race sponsored by the *South Wales Echo* but gave no indications of the date, distance or venue. It went on to state that a letter would be sent thanking the paper "for the valuable help they had given .... in fostering distance running in Wales." No other details were given except to record that the event was "confined" and successful participants would not lose novice status.

The 1930s – Relays & Marathons .... and Stormy Down

In the 1930s *The News of the World* sponsored point-to-point road relays in various parts of Britain. The relays consisted of about twelve stages varying in length between three and seven miles. These races included the Edinburgh to Glasgow in Scotland, the Manchester to Blackpool in the north of England and the London to Brighton in the south. The last named of these courses was also used for a national final with teams qualifying from the regional races. In Wales, the first Newport to Swansea relay was held at the end of February 1933. It was along the A48, a distance of 58 ½ miles in eleven stages of between four and seven miles. Cwmbran Harriers were in either first or second place on every stage but one and they eventually won from Roath Harriers and Newport Harriers. The final stage from Llansamlet to Swansea must have been a classic. Soapy Palmer (Cwmbran) took over with a mere ten second lead from Ted Hopkins (Roath) whilst Len Tongue (Newport) was only a further two seconds back. Palmer increased the winning margin to thirty five seconds but Hopkins and Tongue were still only one second apart at the end of their stints. In all ten teams finished and of these all but two came from east Glamorgan or south Monmouthshire.

The second such relay was held the following November, only nine months after the first. Again Cwmbran Harriers led for seven stages in the middle of the race and at the end of the seventh leg were two and a half minutes clear. However Newport Harriers were by far the strongest team in the latter stages and anchored by Wilf Short they eventually won by three minutes from Cwmbran with Roath Harriers third. Newport's winning time was over five minutes faster than that of the Cwmbran team earlier in the year.

The first true marathon in Wales was held in 1934 from Stormy Down, east of Bridgend, to Swansea Guildhall. It was intended as a trial to aid selection for that year's Empire Games being held at the White City stadium in London in August. Wilf Short (Newport Harriers) won in 2:50:00 and was duly selected for the Games. He went forward as a virtual unknown outside the Principality and created considerable surprise by finishing an excellent sixth.

Swansea-born Pat Dengis triple USA champion

Meanwhile in the United States, a Swansea born athlete was establishing a reputation for himself as one of America's most consistent distance runners. Franz (Pat) Dengis born in St. Thomas, Swansea in 1900 emigrated to the United States during the economic depression of the 1920s. In the 1930s he competed in thirty-six marathons and won fifteen including being USA champion in 1935, 1938 and 1939. The last of these performances was shortly before he was killed in an air crash. Pat's time of 2:51:50 set in the 1932 Boston marathon is listed as the inaugural Welsh record. He went on to successively reduce that time over the following six years by no less than twenty-one minutes to 2:30:28. With the

Second World War intervening this latter record was to stand for over sixteen years. In 1936, Pat returned to Wales for a period during which time he ran in the (English) AAA marathon of that year recording 2:40:19.4 in fourth place.

The third Newport to Swansea relay took place in November 1934. On this occasion Roath Harriers led most of the way only for Cwmbran to come good in the last few stages and win by nearly two minutes from Roath and Newport anchored by Jim Alford and Wilf Short respectively. Penrhys Harriers who had led the first stage thanks to Bill Matthews hung on to finish fourth of the sixteen teams. In 1936, Roath Harriers anchored by Jim Alford won in a new record time (5:18:20) 6 ½ minutes ahead of Cwmbran (winners in 1935) with Newport a further 8 ½ minutes back. In 1937 they retained their title with Westbury Harriers no less than 11 ½ minutes down in second place. Apparently traffic rules were applied for the first time on this occasion which kept runners to the left side of the road and probably caused slower times. A year later Roath led from start to finish to win for a third consecutive time chased all the way by Westbury with Newport third out of the twelve teams who finished.

'News of the World' sixth annual Newport-Cardiff-Swansea relay starting from Newport Town Hall in 1937. Roath Harriers (A1) won from Westbury with Newport Harriers third. Roath's G.W. Watson is taking the baton from the Mayor of Newport, Councillor Mrs. H.J. Hart J.P. Note a young Roy Jones (Newport H) looking on between the second and third runners to Watson's left.

Returning to the topic of marathons, the Welsh Championships in 1935, (JH Overton, Newport), and 1936, (Dennis Morgan, Swansea Valley) were both won in times well in excess of three hours. Second, behind Morgan, was his west Glamorgan rival Ike O'Brien (Port Talbot YMCA). In the following three years (1937-8-9) Ike went on to win the Welsh title setting a new championship best of 2:45:00 on the third occasion. That year he also contested the AAA marathon and was placed fifth in 2:47:33. He finished on the verge of collapse and after standing stiffly to attention whilst a band played God Save The King he then succumbed completely. The previous year, on a hot August afternoon, Ike had made a solo forty-eight mile run along the A48 from Cardiff City Hall to Swansea. He was carrying a message from the Lord Mayor of Cardiff to an athletics meeting being held on the St Helen's sports ground. He apparently completed the run in 6:27:42 with total composure despite being greeted by an ecstatic crowd when he entered the arena. In 1936, 1937, 1938 and 1939 there were also west Wales Marathon Championships held. The 1936 race, from the Talbot Athletic Ground at Aberavon, had eight entrants, including Pat Dengis, but only one finisher - Ike O'Brien. He also won in the following years from Morriston Cross in 1937 and Parc Stephens, Kidwelly in 1938 and 1939. Only in 1937 and 1938 was there any other finisher recorded. Of particular interest to modern eyes were the special notes for the marathon runners, which appeared each year in the programme. –"No pacing is allowed. No competitor is allowed to take drugs. Competitors must retire from the race if ordered to do so by the honorary medical officer".

The onset of the Second World War inevitably resulted in a virtual cessation of sporting activity except for local events encouraged by the authorities to help maintain morale and fitness – particularly in the armed services.

The 1950s and Cardiff Empire Games Marathon

The 1950s were noteworthy for the start of several new road races. The first, just across the Severn Estuary, was the Bristol to Weston and back relay. This was an eight-man event on similar lines to those sponsored by the *News of the World*. However, whilst those events in England had been revived this had not been the case in Wales, and the immensely popular Newport to Swansea event failed to survive the War. The new west of England event continued for seventeen years before the inevitable traffic problems caused its demise as with so many similar events throughout the United Kingdom.

Tom Richards at Maindy winning one of his five Welsh marathon titles.

The AAA Marathon was staged at Cardiff for the first time in 1953. Starting and finishing at Maindy Stadium, the one lap course went out to Tredegar Park via St Mallons and Castleton, returning to Cardiff via St Brides and Peterstone. The race was won by the legendary Jim Peters, four times world record holder and the first man ever to beat 2:20:00 for the distance. Despite strong winds and heavy rain, and the added handicap of twice encountering a herd of cows on the return journey, Peters clocked a Welsh all-comers' record od 2:22:29, a world-class time for that period. Tom Richards, who had been AAA runner up four times in the previous five years after finishing 3rd in 1946, retained his Welsh title.

Other events were promoted as part of the build up to the Empire Games in Cardiff including the first "Lawr y Cwm" (Down the Valley) ten mile race from Mountain Ash to Pontypridd. This was held during a week of celebrations in Pontypridd in June 1956. These festivities were originally conceived to mark the centenary of the composition of the Welsh national anthem and the bi-centenary of the construction of the 'Old Bridge.' The latter spans the River Taff at Pontypridd and is featured on the town's coat of arms. The race was won by Jeff Gamlin (Westbury) from Ken Huckle (Roath). It was preceded by Tom Richards running up from Pontypridd to Mountain Ash with a goodwill message. This and other features intended to increase public interest and attention were early indications of the organisational and presentation skills of Bernard Baldwin. The following year the race was won by the English international Ken Norris (TVH) who led his club team to victory ahead of Newport Harriers. Prior to the latter race there was a visit to the tomb of Guto Nythbrân in the churchyard at Llanwonno and this was also to become the pre-cursor to the Nos Galan events we have read about in an earlier chapter.

Newport "10" – the oldest established road race in Wales

The 1958 Empire and Commonwealth Games marathon was to start and finish from the stadium at Cardiff Arms Park, out to Newport and back, including a loop towards the coast. On Easter Saturday 1958, as part of the preparations, Newport Harriers organised a ten mile road race starting from the Ebbw river bridge, on the western outskirts of the town, and covering part of the marathon course. In a field of forty runners it was athletes from the Bristol clubs who dominated and they continued to do so for the early years of what became known as the "Newport 10", which is still in existence today and thus the oldest established road race in Wales.

To select the Welsh athletes for the Games marathon a trial was held over much of the eventual course but starting and finishing at Maindy Stadium. As a consequence the event was probably over distance but selection queries did not stop there. In the race, which also served as that year's championship, Rhys Davies (Coventry Godiva) won from Ron Franklin whilst Tom Wood finished third. However, Tom's success was at the expense of Dyfrig Rees who, when in third place, had missed a turning and gone off course at a late stage. All four were eventually chosen for the Games only for Tom Wood to be involved in a car accident. Fortunately his injuries were not such as to prevent him competing. Of that quartet Dyfrig Rees had been Welsh champion in 1954, Rhys Davies was also champion in 1957 and 1959 and Tom Wood bronze medallist in 1957. For his part Ron Franklin by finishing second in that race began a remarkable sequence of performances. These saw him finish first or second in the Welsh championship on thirteen occasions in the fifteen years up to 1972 and including five consecutive victories. It is also worthy of comment that over forty years on, at the turn of the century, Ron Franklin and Tom Wood are still competing, albeit rather less frequently and over somewhat shorter distances.

More details of the Empire Games marathon are given elsewhere in the book.

The North Wales Ten

The North Wales ten-mile road race has been held on the last Saturday in April since 1962. Unlike so many other events of that era it has survived into the twenty first century. It has always been held in Wrexham and throughout its history has been organised by the North Wales Cross Country Association. The first twenty one races were run on a four lap course from what was then the Denbighshire Technical College next to Wrexham Football ground on Mold road. When a former secretary of the Wrexham club qualified as a civil engineer he measured the course and found it to be over distance. The start was therefore moved appropriately. The particular benefit for competitors of that original location was that with times called out every lap pace judgement was made that much easier. Major alterations to the main road from Mold into Wrexham made it impossible for the race to continue at that original venue after 1983. The organisers obtained permission to use the premises of the Dunlop factory on the Wrexham Industrial Estate and a new three lap course was devised. The hopes were that this could be used for the next twenty one years but then in 1986 Dunlop closed the factory. Fortunately an alternative was found at the Kellogg's factory and the superb facilities there continue to be used up to the present. The first winner, on the old course, in 1962, was Ray Billington (Birchfield Harriers), who had run the 880 yds for Wales in the 1958 Empire Games. In 1963 he retained the road title and became the first of an elite band to hold North Wales road and country titles simultaneously. 1969 saw a classic head to head race with Evan Williams (Shrewsbury) and Terry Harper (Wirral - a former North Wales CCA Secretary) running stride for stride over the whole distance. In the last few yards Evan managed to sneak ahead and win by one second in an excellent 51:14. The 1975 result shows Ian Williams (Wrexham) winning in 54:08 although he was still under seventeen years of age at the time. In 1977 George Nixon (Wrexham) commenced a sequence of six consecutive wins in consistent times. He went on to achieve a record seventh win in 1984 in the first race on the new course.

The fastest time on the old course, by far, is the 48:50 recorded by Tony Blackwell (Wolverhampton/Wrexham) on its last occasion in 1983 after Jerry Hall (Derby & County) had set the pace most of the way. Two years later Blackwell recorded 51:07 on the new course despite gale force winds making conditions extremely difficult and that remains the championship record. The outright fastest time on the new course was by Tony Power (Shrewsbury) in the open section in 1984 whilst Dic Evans (Cardiff) was only ten seconds slower in 1986. It appears that females may have run on the old route but records only exist since the change of course. The inaugural winner here was Julie Griffiths of Prestatyn RC in 68:11 but the championship record holder is Alison Whitelaw (Wrexham), in 1991, with 60:40. The outright women's record stands to open competitor Amanda Wright (Bridgenorth) who with a splendid run broke the hour recording 59:48. In 1990 the course was re-measured, adjudged to be short and a slight adjustment made. Since the late 1970s the race has been sponsored, initially by a local paper merchants and then more recently by Majestic Travel Limited, which has enabled it to flourish, whilst other local businesses have contributed to the awards for the open race held in conjunction. This started as an invitation event in the early 1970s after runners from the Cheshire and Liverpool areas initially participated as guests. It then went on to become a full open race and remains such to the present day with the North Wales Championship incorporated. Apart from 1978, when as a twenty fifth anniversary celebration all finishers were presented with medals, the race remains a traditional style one. Moreover despite the proximity of the London Marathon date and often a clash with national relay championships it continues to maintain its standards and popularity.

The 1960s – Steady development

Ron Franklin's sequence of successes in Welsh marathons, referred to previously, overlapped with two others; those of Lynn Hughes (Bridgend/Newport/TVH) and AAW President Hedydd Davies (TVH). Lynn was placed on six occasions between 1963 and 1968 whilst Hedydd won four times plus gaining a second and two thirds between 1966 and 1976. The 1962 Welsh marathon won by Ron Franklin also included an open race which was won by Buddy Edelen, an American school teacher working in Essex, with John Tarrant (Salford) second. Thanks largely to the efforts of Arthur Williams, the 1963 Welsh Marathon was staged over a mainly flat course in Port Talbot, beginning and ending on Aberavon seafront. The race included an open competition and attracted a high quality entry including a strong team from Coventry Godiva Harriers, undoubtedly the leading road running club in Britain at the time. Brian Kilby, Commonwealth and European champion of 1962, came home first in a scintillating 2:14:43, which to this day remains the fastest marathon ever run in Wales. Ron Franklin (3rd in 2:26:12) took the Welsh title. The following year Kilby's clubmate Juan Taylor came within a minute of equalling his time when he clocked 2:15:37 over the same course with Ron Franklin (5th in 2:28:50) winning his fifth consecutive Welsh title.

Arthur Williams's efforts in organising these events were rewarded when the event was awarded AAA status in 1965. For the third successive year the race winner was wearing the colours of Coventry Godiva as Bill Adcocks led his team to a clean sweep of the medal places clocking 2:16:50 ahead of Brian Kilby (2:17:34) and Juan Taylor (2:18:57). In sixth place (2:26:46) Lynn Hughes won the first of his two Welsh titles. The strength of the Coventry Godiva team at the time is illustrated by a story concerning another of Arthur Williams's promotions – a 4x 3½ miles road relay around Aberavon seafront. The Coventry club, who by now had established a close affinity with Arthur Williams, decided to enter one year. They based themselves in the seaside town of Porthcawl and, on the day of the race, ran the 10 miles or so to Port Talbot, romped home with the relay race and promptly ran back to Porthcawl.

Bernard's Monday evening road races

A very important feature of road competition in the south Wales valleys in the 1960s were the Monday night series of road races each autumn. These were another promotion of Bernard Baldwin and usually consisted of a sprint, a mile race and a three mile race, or thereabouts. The sprint was usually on any convenient fairly level surface and the other two races over laps around streets. The venues were usually housing estates in the Glamorgan valleys with administration in a local social club or similar premises. The races were a real case of taking sport to the people and drew significant crowds. For the athletes they provided valuable competition in an era when there were far fewer open events than is now the case and bridged a gap between the track and country seasons. Athletes from Newport and the two Cardiff clubs (Birchgrove and Roath) together with Gilwern Harriers provided the majority of the runners. The last club was particularly strong, led by Tom Edmunds, Winston Bradley and the extensive Aylett family. In addition to the weekday evening events there was a weekend race at Wattstown, in the Rhondda, and a series of races each Easter Monday at Pencoed, near Bridgend. The Wattstown race was notorious for its hills particularly the initial ascent from the colliery, which was then followed by hair-raising laps around a typical Welsh mountainside housing estate. Whilst the Monday night races in the main only attracted local competition both Wattstown and Pencoed drew competitors from England. The Pencoed road races, which followed a similar format to 'Nos Galan', included sprints for youngsters as well as seniors plus boys' and women's mile races and a men's four mile. They were very high standard competitions with international calibre competitors in both men's and women's sprint and distance races, including over the years, many British Olympic athletes.

Ghost runner dominates Roath race

Yet another event that started in 1960 was the 'Roath 16' in Cardiff. It was first run on May 7th 1960. The distance was apparently totally accidental. The course first used was out and back from Maindy Stadium and the old Smith's Crisps factory at St Mellons just happened to be a convenient turning point. After two years the event was moved to a two lap course in the Roath and Cyncoed areas of Cardiff. This was used until 1969 when the distance was cut and the race renamed the Lake 15. It continued in this form until 1982. Over the years the race consistently drew team and individual entries from the Midlands including Worcester and Coventry Godiva Harriers. In the early years of the Roath race John Tarrant (Hereford/Salford) won on no fewer than six occasions plus one second place and one third. John, who lived and worked in Hereford, was known in the previous decade as the 'ghost runner.' Due to his home location he became a frequent and respected competitor in Welsh events. The reason for his title was that as a young man John had boxed

The late John Tarrant of Salford Harriers winning the 40 mile track race at Maindy Stadium in 1966 in a new world best of 4:03:28. The holder of the megaphone on the extreme right is Bernard Baldwin.

in fairground booths for cash. Recording that fact on a race entry form he found himself declared a professional and was thus debarred from amateur athletics. However, he continued to take part in road races illicitly. He would join in them immediately after the start without a number and then turn off just prior to the finish line, sometimes with the connivance of officials. Numerous appeals to be allowed to compete officially were refused and his predicament aroused great sympathy especially amongst his fellow athletes. A nation-wide petition to the AAA in London, supported by *Athletics Weekly* undoubtedly contributed to his eventual belated re-instatement but even that was only for domestic competition. In 1969 in the Roath 16 he slumped to a low position in the race and it was only in later years that it was realised that the cause was the onset of the stomach cancer that was to cause his early death. Before that though, he returned to compete in 1973, ran what was to be his last ever race, finished eleventh and was a popular winner of the veteran's prize.

In 1960, running in the Polytechnic marathon and with a time of 2:29:19 Ron Franklin became Welsh record holder. In 1961 the AAA marathon was held on a tough course at Enfield in north London at the end of July. Ron finished third in 2:28:50 and was selected for the Enschede Marathon in Holland. Here he finished third and again went under two and a half hours despite the short time interval between the races. Then in October of the same year he was one of the two Britons chosen to run in the 'International Marathon of Peace' at Kosice on the border between Czechoslovakia and Hungary. The race was won by the Olympic champion, Abebe Bikila of Ethiopia. Despite the effects of the long and tortuous journey Ron still managed a respectable 2:30:30. In the following year he further improved his best time with 2:25:06 for third place in the Polytechnic marathon of 1962 behind British international Ron Hill (Bolton) and Franjo Mihalic (Yugoslavia). Then the following year and in the same race Bob Roath (Walton AC) ran two minutes faster still to reduce the Welsh record to 2:22:57.

The 1960 Newport '10' provided another win in Wales for John Tarrant who set a course record of 48:55. In third place was Jim O'Brien, the most successful of former Welsh marathon star Ike's sons, who followed their father into the sport. In 1964 the race was moved to the host club's new headquarters at the Glebelands, starting and finishing with a lap of the track. The course was now out and back along the Usk valley with a sharp about turn at the halfway point. In general individuals and teams from the Bristol area continued to dominate the results but in 1967 they were absent. John Tarrant won again with Jim O'Brien second whilst Gilwern Harriers won the team event. In 1968, the opening of the nearby motorway meant further course changes whilst in 1969 Mike Rowland became the first local (and Welsh) victor; a win he repeated in 1971 and 1972.

Newport Harriers also organised a road relay each year on an undulating road course around the Malpas area whilst in west Glamorgan, BP (Llandarcy) AC held a similar event over a hilly course through Jersey Marine village, east of Swansea. Both of these events were well supported and the late 1960s saw the first Welsh road relay championship. At the end of March 1968 a six man event was held on the Bridgend Trading Estate using two single followed by four double laps of a road course. This had previously been used for annual races organised by the Glamorgan Police AC from their Waterton Cross sports ground. Birchgrove Harriers, anchored by Bernie Plain, won the inaugural event ahead of Roath Harriers. Since Birchgrove and Roath then amalgamated to form Cardiff AAC it is hardly a surprise to find that the new club went on to win in the following six years.

© Gordon Roberts

Start of the first ever Welsh Road Relay Championship held at Bridgend on 30 March 1968. Roy Anthony of Bridgend is in the centre with Mike Rowland wearing H (Newport), Keith Jones (Birchgrove 'B') and Gerry Batty (Swansea) wearing B. Right Bernie Plain brings his club Birchgrove Harriers home to win. Other members of the Birchgrove team were John Powell, Ian Rennie, John Ingram, Bernard Hayward and Paul Darney.

The AAA marathon again came to Wales in 1968, this time to Cwmbran. Incorporating the trial for the forthcoming Olympic Games in Mexico, the race attracted all the leading British marathon runners at a time when there was considerable sterngth in depth for this event in the UK. Tim Johnstone came in first, clocking 2:15:26, followed by such luminaries as Bill Adcocks, Jim Alder, Ron Hill, Brian Kilby and Alistair Wood. The first three went on to represent Britain at Mexico. An indication of the quality of this race is given by the fact that Lynn Hughes, who was first Welsh finisher in 2:31:51, occupied 20th position.

The 1970s – and the emergence of Steve Jones as a marathon runner

The 1970s saw a further steady development in road running with standards rising and the numbers of competitors and events increasing. In Wales the Cardiff club were the dominant force but in races such as the Newport 10 and even their own Lake 15 started to receive challenges from both Newport and Swansea. On an individual basis Jim O'Brien refused to concede to his veteran status and finished in the first three in the Lake 15 at the turn of the decade. In the Newport 10 either the home club or Cardiff won the team event in seven of the ten years to finally end the domination by Bristol teams. Individually Mike Rowland (TVH/Newport), John Jones (Windsor, but born in Mountain Ash) and John Robertshaw, now Newport, all gained two wins each. In 1972 Mike Rowland then with TVH set a new record of 46:59 with Dave Hopkins (Newport) only four seconds down and four other runners all under fifty minutes. A re-measure showed the course to be about a quarter mile under distance but even so the times represented high standard performances. The 1976 race at Newport was only three weeks before the Olympic marathon trial with the result that amongst the entrants were British internationals Trevor Wright and Dave Holt, the latter later to join Swansea, who finished second (49:20) and third (49:29). In front though was John Robertshaw who won by ten seconds and led his Newport club to team victory. Second team was a surprise - RAF Lyneham led by Steve Jones in fifth position and in what appears to be one of his few appearances in that particular race.

Mention has already been made of the annual Pencoed road races and in 1973 Dave Bedford, who later that year set a world 10,000 metre track record won the four miles. Coventry Godiva won the team event although Swansea Harriers led by John Theophilus in second position were only two points adrift. The following year the Pencoed four miles race was of even higher standard. Dave Hopkins (Newport) won by one second from Bernie Plain (Cardiff) setting a new course record whilst behind them in the first ten were a host of other British internationals including Dave Holt (Swansea), his twin brother Bob (Hercules Wimbledon), Dennis Fowles (Cardiff), Max Coleby (Darlington) and Trevor Wright (Hallamshire).

In July 1970, Mike Rowland took the Welsh record under two hours twenty minutes recording 2:19:08 in the 1970 Commonwealth Games. A year later Bernie Plain (Cardiff) made his debut at the marathon in Manchester. Despite "hitting the wall" and losing several places and much time in the later stages he still recorded 2:19:49. Two months later he had recovered sufficiently to win the Welsh event at Aberavon in a new championship best of 2:20:59.2. The following year the Maxol Marathon at Manchester in June was also the Olympic trial. Bernie finished sixth, with three to qualify, and so had to be content with a new personal best and Welsh record of 2:16:18. In October 1973 the Harlow marathon incorporated not only the AAA Championship but also the Welsh event. Malcolm Thomas (TVH) probably better known as a cross-country runner, gained a quadruple success - AAA title, Welsh title, Welsh record and Welsh championship best with 2:15:59; the last of these still standing a quarter century on.

© Ceri Breeze

Bernie Plain winning the Welsh marathon title in 1972.

1974 brought the Commonwealth Games at Christchurch, New Zealand in January. Bernie Plain finished seventh in the marathon and regained the Welsh record with 2:14:56, just over a minute faster than the time set a year earlier, whilst Malcolm Thomas finished ninth. Later that year Bernie finished second in the Polytechnic Marathon (and AAA championship), and went on to be placed fourth in the European Championships in Rome. 1976 was Olympic year and despite a bout of pleurisy Bernie finished fifth in the trial thus just missing out on selection once more. He did go on to win the Polytechnic Marathon in a more than respectable 2:15:32 and led Cardiff AAC to a team victory. In May 1978 the AAA Marathon was again at Sandbach and Tony Simmons (Luton) recorded 2:12:33 to improve the Welsh record by well over two minutes. A year later in 1979, Bernie Plain finished fourth in the AAA marathon at Coventry and earned what was to be his final GB vest being selected to run in the Karl Marx Stadt event.

Black, Foster and Steve Jones star in the 1900 Road Races

Many of Britain's leading middle distance stars took part in the Cardiff 1900 road races, which started in 1976 as a celebration of the City of Cardiff's 1900th anniversary that year. The event, held on a traffic-free circular course around the Civic Centre, made ideal viewing for spectators, and continued until the early 80s. Held for the first three years on New Years Day, and subsequently on May Day, Dave Black, winner of the 5,000m bronze and 10,000m silver in the 1974 Christchurch Commonwealth Games, won the first two races ahead of fellow British international Bernie Ford, before distance legend Brendan Foster, the Olympic 10,000 bronze medallist in Montreal, took the 1979 event in a record 18:38, a time which was never beaten. Second that year was Steve Jones who won the event three times – 1978, 1980 and 1981. Ann Ford, wife of Bernie, and winner of the 3,000m bronze in the 1978 Edmonton Commonwealth Games, took the women's race for the first three years, whilst former Welsh 1,500m record holder Hilary Hollick (Sale) won in 1979, and Cardiff's Kim Lock took the race the following year. The meeting incorporated events for all age groups and many of the future stars of Welsh athletics won, including Colin Clarkson and Nick Comerford.

Betty Norrish the women's marathon trailblazer

During the 1970s for the first time Welsh women appear in the lists of marathon finishers. Betty Norrish (Brighton & Hove) already a veteran set an inaugural time of 3:14:31 in the Coventry marathon in August 1976. The following year a women's event was held for the first time in Wales at Newport over a four-lap course to the south east of the town and in conjunction with the men's championship. It should be realised that, at that time, mixed events were still frowned upon. With five starters and four finishers Linda Lamonby of the host club was the only Welsh athlete and set an inaugural championship best of 3:23:20. Then in 1979, Jean Lochhead (Airedale & Spen) recorded 2:55:16 in the AAA marathon at Sandbach in Cheshire. Following a gap of a year a Welsh Women's Championship was also held in 1979 with Betty Norrish the only finisher.

The 1970s were also notable in Wales for the introduction of road relays for the younger male age groups and for females. Following on from the senior men's event one for under 17 men started in 1969 and was won for the first four years by Cardiff AAC. Senior women and under 15 girls (1971), under 15 boys and under 13 girls (1973), under 13 boys and under 17 women (1974) all followed in rapid succession. Not all of the events were held on the same occasion or at the same venue.

At the British level the national twelve stage road relays had in general lapsed in the 1960s due to combination of factors but particularly traffic and safety considerations. The races were revived some years on and then generally held off public roads. The national twelve stage in particular had been re-established and was now held on the paths around Sutton Park in Sutton Coldfield. It had alternate short (about 3 mile) and long (about five and a half mile) stages. Wales made its nominations to this event based on aggregate performances of a club's two teams in the Welsh men's relays. These had now settled down as a six stage competition. Following the initial runs at Bridgend it went to St Athan for a year but then settled in Cardiff starting and finishing at the College of Education in Cyncoed, now UWIC. In 1973, Gateshead Harriers won the British race and three Welsh clubs had been nominated to take part. Cardiff AAC were a solid eighth but Swansea Harriers were over twenty minutes back in twenty third place and Bridgend twenty sixth an equal distance further back. The following year Cardiff improved dramatically to finish third team and be the first non-English club to gain medals in the event.

The first recorded road matches contested by Wales took place in 1979. In July of that year a four man team contested the Tullamore marathon in Southern Ireland finishing fourth with Alan Joslyn 2:20:37 in sixth place our first man home. Three months later a three man team ran in Glasgow. On this occasion Malcolm Firth who was third man home in Ireland improved significantly to finish third in the race in 2:22:32, with Mick Crowell fourth just over a minute down. Then throughout the following decade Wales continued to send three man teams to the Aberdeen and Glasgow marathons each autumn. They won the Aberdeen event in 1982 and provided individual runners up in 1982 (Ieuan Ellis) and 1983 (Trefor Hawes) – Ieuan's time of 2:16:47 being particularly noteworthy.

Welsh athletes in the London Marathon and the start of a McGeoch dynasty

There are occasionally events in life in general and sport in particular that catch the public interest and attention to such an extent that they enter into folklore. Or else they cause fundamental changes in attitudes and perceptions. In road running in the United Kingdom the first London Marathon was such an occurrence. The brainchild of Chris Brasher and John Disley, they mobilised a team of enthusiasts following Brasher's own participation in the New York Marathon. Up until 1981 there had been a steady growth in interest and participation in endurance running. This was demonstrated by the success of cross-country leagues in winter, the appearance of running clubs, often referred to as "jogging" clubs where participation took precedence over competition and an increase in both numbers of endurance races and the numbers of entrants in those races. However much of the public still, and not without some validity, viewed endurance runners, outside the elite few, as masochists, fitness fanatics or a combination of both. The first London Marathon in March 1981 with its seven thousand runners, its TV coverage, admittedly not live, the joint finish by Dick Beardsley and Inge Simonsen but particularly the participation of first timers and novices radically changed attitudes – as a TV commentator famously observed 'ordinary people doing an extra-ordinary thing.' The growth of activity in the sport increased dramatically. Suddenly it became fashionable to be seen running or jogging, however slowly, and the wearing of trainers and tracksuits or similar apparel socially acceptable. Equally charities and other good causes discovered an effective high profile method of both publicising themselves and of raising funds.

In that first London Marathon Dic Evans (Cardiff) was first Welsh athlete home, (29th in 2:21:25), with fellow west Walian Frank Thomas (Aberystwyth) not far behind in 2:23:04. On the female side Jackie Hulbert - the future Mrs Steve Brace – (then RAF/Cardiff) was first Welsh runner in 2:53:07. Reputedly Dic's pupils, having seen him on television, marked his return to school after the race in a similar manner to Raleigh welcoming Queen Elizabeth the First! Amongst others finishing was Mick McGeoch (Les Croupiers), 58th in 2:24:19. Mick warrants comment because twenty years later he is one of that elite band to have finished in every London Marathon. The Les Croupiers club was formed in 1980, with the former Cardiff runner, Dave Walsh and brother of marathon statistician John, as the prime mover of the enterprise. McGeoch and fellow Barry runner Rob Atkinson, another former Cardiff member who ran a 2:22:50 marathon in 1979, were amongst the founder members. The club got its name from the Cardiff Casino of the same name owned by former Welsh marathon international Gordon McIlroy, who gave the club a generous cash sum to help the club get started and has continued with his support ever since.

The second London Marathon in 1982 was grossly oversubscribed and this situation has continued to the end of the century. It has necessitated involved entry procedures to try to be fair. In recent times there are still more applicants than places but, helped by continuing increases in the numbers of starters accepted, this is now far less of a problem. Over the intervening years many of the other cities and towns in the United Kingdom have ceased to organise a marathon or have cut the distance. Perhaps more of concern is the fact that whilst London's overall numbers increase there is, at the end of the century, a significant decline in the number of British finishers in the 2: 20 to 2: 45 range – the province of the good club runners.

The early 1980s

Comment was made in the previous section on the impetus given to road running throughout the United Kingdom by the London Marathon. Wales was no different to the rest of the country. In addition to such established races as the Newport 10, Pencoed 4, Vale of Neath 10, Lake 15, and Barry Island races a host of new events sprang up. The half marathon seemed to be the most popular and these were held at Aberdare, Caernarfon, Aberavon and Rhymney; all being well supported. The marathon remains the prime challenge and *The Western Mail* newspaper organised one in Cardiff in September 1981. Designated a charity fun run in aid of Rookwood Hospital it was a race in all but name. Over three thousand took part and for the majority the sole aim was to finish. It says much for the spirit and enthusiasm engendered that 95% succeeded and ensured that the event would be repeated the next year.

For the serious competitive athlete there was plenty of choice and some fine races ensued in 1981. British international Dave Black (Small Heath) was a welcome visitor winning the Aberdare 5 ahead of John Robertshaw (Newport) but himself beaten by Steve Jones in both the Pencoed 4 and the Cardiff May Day race with Dave James (Cardiff) third on both occasions. Steve Jones also won the inaugural Swansea Bay 10k in September despite high-class opposition which included his great rivals Roger Hackney, born in Swansea, and Tony Simmons whilst 1,500m star Hilary Hollick (later Thomas) was first female home. The popular Bridgend 7½ became the Bridgend 10 and incorporated the inaugural Welsh championship. Winner Ali Cole (Swansea) went on to show his versatility with victories in the Finchley 20, Aberdare Half Marathon and Newport 15 as well as a fine second place in the Glasgow Marathon in 2:18:53. Bernie Plain came back to somewhere near his earlier form with an impressive win in that year's Polytechnic marathon as well as being first home in the *Western Mail* run.

The 1981 Welsh Marathon was held at Newport in August and it brought together two other major contenders. They were Norman Wilson who had recently qualified for Wales by residence, and the Welsh champion of the previous two years Mike Crowell (Bridgend). Wilson had previously clocked 2:13:16 in Boston in April to head the Welsh rankings for that year and also won the Belgrave 20 in July whilst Crowell had only been narrowly beaten by Ali Cole in the Aberdare Half Marathon the previous week. Wilson made the early running and at half way had a commanding lead only for Crowell to gradually chase him down and take the lead in the last mile to complete a hat trick of wins. Wilson only just held off Alan Joslyn (Newport) for second place. Then later in that year, November, Jackie Hulbert (now Brace) became the new Welsh women's marathon record holder recording 2:51:42 at Omaha in the United States. In north Wales there was a half marathon at Caernarfon in September won by J Wagstaffe in 67:05 and a north Wales marathon a month later won by B Grant in 2:24:01

1982 was Commonwealth Games year again but with them being staged in Brisbane they were out of season for athletes from the northern hemisphere. Jean Lochhead ran in the second London Marathon and despite being officially classified as a veteran lowered her personal best by over nine minutes to set a new Welsh record (2:46:04). In those days there was still no women's marathon in the Games. The Welsh Marathon Championship was the following weekend in Neath. Mick Crowell gained a fourth successive victory ahead of Ieuan Ellis and Bernie Plain. However their times were well outside the qualifying standards for Games selection. In the women's competition Betty Norrish, at the age of 52, reclaimed the title she had won three years earlier. The AAA Marathon in Gateshead, won by England's Steve Kenyon (Salford) merely compounded the Games selection problems. Norman Wilson had the qualifying time from the previous year's Boston race but finished fifth in (only) 2:16:41. With dual qualifications he thus found himself in the invidious position of being under consideration by both Wales and England but eventually not selected by either country. In the end Wales made no specific selection of athletes for the Games marathon but allowed Dennis Fowles to make his debut following his sixth place in the 10,000m track event. He went on to fully deserve the opportunity and was placed thirteenth in 2:16:49. Elsewhere that year there were also good performances with America based Adrian Leek (Cardiff) achieving 2:15:56 in the New York race late in October and Norman Wilson 2:16:14 in Tokyo. In Aberdeen in September Ieuan Ellis (Newport) recorded 2:16:47 to be placed second and also led the Welsh team to victory. The second ever Welsh 10 Mile Championship at Bridgend saw Kenny Davies, third in the first race, win in 49:09 whilst Bronwen Cardy Smith was the inaugural women's winner.

The second Cardiff *Western Mail* marathon also took place in September 1982 with Bernie Plain first home for the second year in a time of 2:23:40 with Mick McGeoch second almost two minutes back. One absentee from Cardiff was Ann Franklin who opted for the London to Brighton race and was first woman home in a near record 7:01:51 despite the event being into a strong head wind all the way. Later in the autumn Wales dominated the Nike 25 k road race in Twickenham. Kenny Davies won in exactly 75 minutes with Norman Wilson third, Colin Mattock (Wolverhampton) fourth and Ieuan Ellis seventh. Dick Milne (Notts AC), running as an individual, came fifth whilst with only three to score Wales easily took the team award. One weekend' earlier during that summer of 1982 the Les Croupiers running club ran a solo multi-stage relay from Cardiff to Caernarvon in what was the precursor of their annual Castles relay race. 1982 also saw the Mayor's Charity races around the streets of Carmarthen held for the first time on the Easter weekend.

In 1983 the youths' three miles, won by Andrew Rodgers (Leeds), was held in conjunction with the Pencoed races whilst the ten mile was again at Bridgend in October. Here Nigel Adams (Swansea) took the men's title and Susan Tooby (Cardiff) the women's. As far as relays were concerned the senior men's six stage event appeared settled in its venue at Cyncoed at the end of March with the senior women's and all other age groups held on the Bridgend Trading Estate in mid-October. Cardiff comfortably won the men's event setting a new course record. Newport reversed the positions in the women's race and in the younger age groups Cardiff won four of the five sections with Barry and Vale, winning the boys event and gaining two second places, next most successful club. Steve Jones took the Pencoed four mile race for a sixth consecutive year in 1983 whilst Kirsty Wade making one of her few appearances on the road in Wales took the women's mile title. An idea of the scope of the meeting at its peak can be gauged from the fact that it consisted of no less than fifteen different events. That year's Carmarthen Mayor's race was over nine miles and brought a win for Jock Seaman (Swansea) ahead of team mate, Alun Roper. The latter, however won that year's Welsh Marathon Championship in 2:31:54. Showing his versatility and powers of recovery Alun, twice winner of the Welsh 800m title, ran 800m in a British League track race only six days later. In the women's marathon Sue Martin Clarke

(Medway) brought respectability to the championship best time by recording 2:48:59.

Early January 1984 saw two Welsh distance runners start the year well. At Barry Steve Jones won the four miles for the fourth successive year whilst Angela Tooby took three minutes off the women's record in the classic Morpeth to Newcastle race with a time of 79:44. The year saw two further Welsh road championships inaugurated with titles being awarded for the 10k and half marathon distances. The latter was incorporated in the Barry half marathon, which was now one of a series, sponsored by Pearl Assurance. Held early in April it gave Dennis Fowles a win in the men's race from Chris Buckley (Westbury) and Kenny Davies (Newport). The women's title was won by Ann King, running in the colours of Trinity College, Carmarthen with her club mate, Debbie Chick (Swansea) second and Sue Graham (Torfaen) third. Ann also won the 10k Championship at Llanelli a week later, this time ahead of Sally James (Newport) whilst Alun Roper (Swansea) just beat Micky Crowell in the men's race. A fortnight later, at the end of the month Steve Jones won the AAA 10k Championship at Birmingham in 27:59. In September the fourth *Western Mail* marathon, which incorporated the Welsh Championship, saw Ieuan Ellis win from Steve Brace and Bernie Plain whilst Sue Graham took the women's title. Five weeks later Peter Williams (Swansea) won the ten miles at Bridgend ahead of Mick McGeoch whilst Peter's sister, Kathy, was second to Wendy Ore (Bridgend) in the women's competition. The men's relay had been held yet again at Cyncoed in April and Swansea took the title after a seven year break. Swansea also took the senior women's event at Bridgend in the autumn. Earlier in the summer six teams set out from Caernarfon to undertake the Castles relay to Cardiff following on from Les Croupiers south-north trial the previous year.

In the 1984 London Marathon Dennis Fowles had added to his own and Wales' reputation in such events by setting a new Welsh record of 2:12:12 to slice 21 seconds off Tony Simmons 6 year-old record in finishing third. On the other side of the Atlantic Adrian Leek was third in the Columbus marathon in a personal best of 2:14:52 whilst Ali Cole (now Newport) went on to win the Nike Oregon race.

Steve's kinda town as he sets world record in Chicago

Pride of place for 1984, if not the decade, goes to Steve Jones. In October 1984 he started the Chicago Marathon for the second time after retiring at seventeen miles the previous year. This time he made no mistake to score a stunning win in a new world record of 2:08:05 defeating both his great rival, Carlos Lopes (Portugal - 2:09:06) and Commonwealth champion Rob de Castella (Australia). The year ended with a revival of Nos Galan, albeit with only one race over a one mile course and with a restricted field. This was won by James Hill (Newport) and was sponsored by the International Athletes Club (IAC) led by Dave Bedford. It started a few minutes before midnight and was preceded by the traditional run down from Guto's grave at Llanwonno.

Pen Portrait – Steve Jones (Swindon AC, RAF, Bristol AC and Newport H)

There was little to indicate that Steve Jones would become one of Wales' two individual world record holders in the standard Olympic events when, as a virtually unknown RAF serviceman stationed in RAF Lynham near Swindon, he finished seventh in the 1976 Welsh Cross Country Championships. Steve's run failed to impress the Welsh selectors, who did not choose him for that year's World Cross-Country Championships, held in Chepstow, no more than 20 miles from his birthplace of Tredegar, Gwent. This was the spur he needed to make his mark. In

the 1977 championship in Singleton Park Swansea, he won the first of his record nine Welsh cross country titles, 10 seconds ahead of Bernie Plain the previous year's winner, to give a glimpse of his outstanding achievements ahead.

It took another seven years of perseverance and dedication before he entered the world record books with his win in the 1984 Chicago Marathon clocking 2:08:05 to beat world champion Rob De Castella (Australia) and that year's Olympic champion Carlos Lopes of Portugal. Steve's time improved Alberto Salazar's world record by 8 seconds. He reduced this time to 2:07:13 when winning the Chicago race again the following year, a tantalising one second outside the world record set by Lopes when winning in Rotterdam earlier in the year. He said after the event: "If I had known that I was so close to the world record, I am certain that I would have bettered it. If there had been a clock at the top of the straight, I might have started my kick earlier". His 2:07:13 still stands in 2000 as the UK and Welsh record and, judging by the current dearth of UK marathon talent, it is likely to stand for many years to come. That win earned him £41,000, but had he broken the world record he would have received a bonus of £35,000, so that one second lapse turned out to be very expensive!

Altogether, Steve ran in 18 marathons, winning five, including the 1985 London race. His complete marathon record is as follows:

TIME	POS	EVENT	DATE
	DNF	Chicago	20 Oct 83
2:08:05	1	Chicago. World record	21 Oct 84
2:08:16	1	London	21 Apr 85
2:07:13	1	Chicago. UK Record	20 Oct 85
2:22:12	20	Stuttgart (*European Championships*)	30 Aug 86
2:12:37	2	Boston	20 Apr 87
2:14:07	9	Boston	18 Apr 88
2:08:20	1	New York	6 Nov 88
2:12:58	8	New York	5 Nov 89
2:12:44	4	Auckland *(Commonwealth Games)*	30 Jan 90
2:16:10	2	Hokkaido	26 Aug 90
2:26:53	86	Berlin	29 Sept 91
2:19:14	3	Honolulu	15 Dec 91
2:13:53	11	Boston	20 Apr 92
2:10:06	1	Toronto	4 Oct 92
2:15:30	15	Boston	19 Apr 93
2:20:04	13	Stuttgart	14 Aug 93
2:17:40	32	Boston	18 Apr 94

DNF – did not finish

Marathon statistics by John Walsh

One of his very few disasters came in the 1986 European Championships at Stuttgart, where he started as favourite but finished 20th. He was leading by nearly 2 minutes at the half way stage, but became dehydrated. An athlete of less determination would have dropped out - but not Steve. He entered the stadium in considerable distress, and later said that he felt that he was running on the spot. Also the fact that so many of his friends, including several from his club, Newport Harriers, and his coach Mike Rowland were cheering him on, kept him going.

Although he will be remembered as a marathon star, he started out in major events as a 3,000m steeplechaser, running 8:46.6 in 1977, finishing third that year in the Welsh Championships to 1974 Commonwealth Games silver medallist and Welsh record holder John Davies. Whilst he was a good steeplechaser with a personal best of 8:32.0 for the sixth best Briton of 1980, he realised that he had to change events if he was to achieve his ambition of being a world class performer, and hence his move to the marathon.

He was an outstanding performer in all the other middle distance events, whether on the track, road or cross-country. But it was as a cross-country runner that his talents were mainly viewed in Wales. As well as his nine Welsh title wins, he finished second on three further occasions - a remarkable achievement which places him head and shoulders above all other Welsh cross-country runners. He is also the finest Welsh performer in the World Cross-Country Championships, finishing third in New York in 1984 behind Carlos Lopes and Tim Hutchings; with two other top ten finishes (7th in 1979 and 9th in 1980). Altogether he appeared in the World Cross-Country Championships for Wales on ten occasions, the highest number of appearances in modern times.

In comparison with his cross-country achievements, he was less successful in the Welsh track championships, winning three titles in all - 5,000m twice (1982 and 1985) and 10,000m in 1989. He also placed third over 1,500m on two occasions, and second in the 5,000m twice to illustrate the range of his middle distance talents, which is further underlined by his list of personal bests in the standard track events:

1,500m	3:42.3	14.07.82
3,000m	7:49.80	13.07.84
5,000m	13:18.6	10.06.82
10,000m	27:39.14	09.07.83
3,000m steeplechase	8:32.00	08.08.80

His 10,000m still stands as the Welsh record at the end of 2000, and his 5,000m best stood for ten years until beaten by Swansea's Ian Hamer in 1992 with 13:09.8, which is still the second best time recorded by a British athlete behind Dave Moorcroft's former world record of 13:00.41.

Steve's only medal at one of the major athletics gatherings was his 10,000m bronze in the 1986 Commonwealth Games in Edinburgh. Altogether he reached the 10,000m final in five major championships, but the 1984 Los Angeles Games was his only appearance in the Olympics, where he finished ninth in the 10,000m in 28:28.08. In all he competed in four Commonwealth Games for Wales, a record he shares with Ron Jones and Berwyn Price.

Amongst some of his other exploits is a UK half marathon best of 60:59 when finishing second to Mike Musyoki's world record of 60:43 in the 1986 Great North Run. This performance was the second fastest in the world at the time and still stands today as the UK best. He won three AAA titles, at 10,000m on track and road, and the half marathon in that Great North Run.

He was also a prolific team scorer for his main club, Newport Harriers in numerous road and cross-country team events. As Rob De Castella, Australia's former world record holder, said in an interview in 1990: "Although one second short of the world record, his 2:07:13 in Chicago in 1985, is to my mind, one of the greatest marathon's ever". An accolade like this from one of the world's all-time marathon greats is true testimony to the esteem in which Steve is held in world athletics circles. There is no doubt that he is Wales' finest distance runner of all-time and his performances will remain unequalled for years to come.

Early in 1985 the New Orleans Marathon was another Welsh success being dominated by the Williams family from Cwmafon, near Port Talbot. Peter won the race outright whilst sister Kathy won the women's section with her twin sister Liz in second place. Whilst the sisters were somewhat down on their previous best times Peter set a new personal best of 2:19:08.

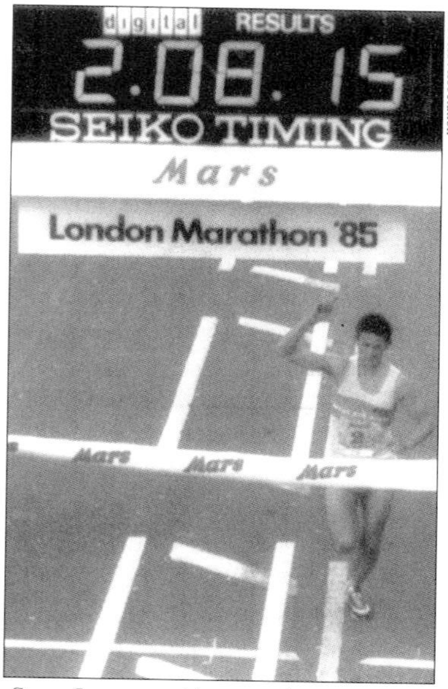

© Press Association

Steve Jones a stride away from victory in the fifth London Marathon in 1985 at the finish on Westminster Bridge in a new UK and course record time of 2:08:16.

Watched by a huge TV audience, Steve Jones went on to win the 1985 London Marathon after a classic race-long head-to-head confrontation with Charlie Spedding (Gateshead) just eleven seconds slower than his winning time in Chicago. The euphoria of this win was however slightly dampened by the news that Carlos Lopes had reclaimed the world record in Rotterdam the previous day with a stunning time of 2:07:12. On 11th August 1985 at the AAA Half Marathon in Birmingham Steve Jones captured his second world best time with a piece of front running which left the rest of the field floundering after just three miles. It was a perfect response from him after the British selectors had decided to snub him for the 10,000m spot in the team bound for the European Cup Final the following week in Moscow. He had won the AAA inaugural 10k Championship the previous year in 27:59 over the same course and, angry at his omission, he had promised fireworks. Despite the damp conditions he stamped his authority on the race almost from the start and broke away to finish in 61:14, taking 14 seconds off the former world best by American Larry Greene in Orlando in December 1984. It was also the first individual world mark recorded by a British athlete on home soil since Brendan Foster set a world 3,000m record in Gateshead in August 1974.

© Mark Shearman

Steve Jones defies the pouring rain to set a world half marathon best at Birmingham in 1985.

The late 1980s – the golden era

The Welsh Marathon was held at Bridgend in May 1985 and gave the home club a 1-2 with Steve Brace winning his first Welsh title by five seconds from Micky Crowell whilst Karen Bowler (Beddau) won the women's title. The men's half marathon, held in conjunction with the Cynon Valley race, saw Nigel Adams win ahead of Ieuan Ellis and Tony Simmons. For some reason the women's event was held separately as part of the Aberavon race in October. Ann Evans (Merthyr) took the title here with the statuesque blonde Ann Howard (Aldershot) in second spot. The women's and junior relays were yet again at Bridgend the weekend before the Aberavon race. Swansea won the senior women's title ahead of Cardiff and Newport and between them those three clubs took thirteen of the fifteen sets of medals in the five other races. In September Ieuan Ellis had been deservedly selected for the United Kingdom team in the European Marathon Cup in Rome and finished tenth in 2:15:56. The following month Steve Jones returned to Chicago and with unrivalled consistency won again in a new British (and Welsh) record of 2:07:13 - a mere but vital second outside Lopes's world record.

The first Welsh Championship of 1986 was the 10 mile held at Carmarthen on Easter Monday (March 31st) as part of the annual Mayor's charity races. Ieuan Ellis won ahead of Steve Smith (Swansea) and west Wales émigré Alan Maddocks (Leicester). Jackie Hulbert won the women's event in front of Sue Graham and Becky Powell with Swansea Harriers taking both team titles. The following weekend Newport, without Steve Jones, beat Swansea, without Nigel Adams, in the men's relay with Bridgend third. For the latter club junior Ian Hamer ran the first leg with veteran Jim O'Brien balancing up the ages on the fifth stage.

Every athlete's dream is to run in a major championship but the percentage who have that dream fulfilled is very low. Jackie Hulbert's dream of running in the 1986 Commonwealth Games was shattered by a back injury which forced the Welsh marathon record holder to withdraw from the team. The jinx that had kept the talented 27-year-old athlete out of two previous Games had struck once again. A back injury, linked to the spina bifida problem she was born with had finally forced her out of the running. Problems for the future Mrs. Brace first flared up shortly after her great performance in the 1986 London Marathon in April when she lowered her own Welsh record by nearly 2½ minutes to 2:39:26 in finishing ninth. Physiotherapy, electrotherapy and acupuncture all failed to help. A multi-champion as a schools' competitor while at Bishop Gore, Swansea, she missed out on the 1978 Games because of a foot operation, and was left out in the cold in 1982 when no women's marathon runners were selected. At the same time Ieuan Ellis did equally well being eighth male in 2:14:38. He thus further reduced, by twenty four seconds, his personal best, set in the race a year earlier, when he had finished fifteenth. Meanwhile, over in the United States, Roger Hackney ran in a ten mile race in Washington, recording a superb British record of 46:41.

In May 1986, the Welsh Marathon was again at Bridgend and incorporated an international match. Dic Evans (Cardiff), incensed at not being selected for the Welsh team, finished second in 2:32:32 behind the aptly named Domingo Catalan of Catalonia but ahead of all three of the athletes nominated for Wales. In the half marathon held in conjunction Ieuan Ellis won in 67:25 and went on to win the Cynon Valley half marathon in July which included the Welsh Championship. Dic was rewarded for his success at Bridgend by representing Wales in the Glasgow Marathon in September. Here he placed second and set a new personal best of 2:17:57. In mid October Ieuan Ellis ran in the Beijing Marathon and further reduced his personal best, recording 2:13:21. Earlier that summer Steve Jones finished second in the Great North run from Newcastle to South Shields. Mike Musoki (Kenya) won the race in a new world best for the half marathon of 60:43 with Steve second in 60:59 well inside his previous world best of 61:14. This still stands as the British best.

The Welsh senior road relays moved to Swansea in 1987 and were held over an undulating lap starting and finishing on the University track. For the first time the men's six stage and women's four stage events were held together. In almost perfect weather Wendy Ore got Bridgend off to a storming start opening up a huge lead over defending champions, Les Croupiers. However by the end of the third stage Les Croupiers had taken the lead and they went on to retain their title by a quarter of a minute with Swansea third nearly two minutes further back. Bridgend, led off by Ian Hamer, also set the early pace in the men's relay but then Swansea took over and, despite a challenge from Dale Rixon (Cardiff) who recorded equal fastest long leg, the home club drew away to win. Newport, anchored by Steve Jones who matched Rixon's time, came through to take second place ahead of Cardiff. Swansea thus gained the title for only the second time in ten years but Newport had the consolation of qualifying for the national twelve stage race as their second team in fourth position assured them of the best aggregate time. The seventh running of the Welsh ten was at

Carmarthen and saw Dennis Fowles break the Swansea/Newport domination winning in 49:25 in a record for the course but short of the championship best, (Bridgend, 1984, Peter Williams, 49:08). Newport were conspicuously absent probably due to their own ten mile race just two days earlier. Bridgend took the team award ahead of Swansea who only just held off Les Croupiers despite being the first team to close in. The women's event, held in conjunction, was won by Eryl Davies (Les Croupiers) ahead of Becky Powell (Swansea).

Eryl Davies went on to win her second road title of the year in convincing fashion, almost five minutes clear of teammate Veronica Singleton, in the half marathon at Caernarfon on May 24th. She was also well over two minutes inside the course record and led her club to a third team victory. Greg Newhams (Bridgend) was equally impressive in the men's race winning by over ninety seconds with a time thirteen seconds inside Tony Blackwell's course record. This performance was just two weeks after him finishing the London Marathon with a sub 2:20 clocking! Les Croupiers won the women's team award ahead of Swansea with Eryri Harriers third. The North Wales club took the men's awards from Les Croupiers with North Wales RRC third in close finish which saw the respective third scorers of those teams finish twelve, thirteenth and fourteenth.

Dic Evans retained his title in the 1987 Welsh Marathon Championship at Bridgend, moving away after fifteen miles and then holding on in the latter stages. Incorporated in the race was an international match and Dic led Wales to victory, ably backed up by Paul Bennett (Cardiff) in third place. Bennett's placing also ensured that Cardiff easily won the club title with Eryri second team. The 1987 Welsh 10k in Cardiff was the last in a series sponsored by Capital Windows. Nigel Adams took the men's championship ahead of Brian Matthews (Barry &Vale) and Steve Brace. Nigel thereby won the championship title and the overall prize in the series. The male team result was extremely close. Newport won by a mere four points with Swansea and Cardiff both on forty points and the west Wales club taking second place on last scorer. The women's race incorporated an international match due to include West Germany, where the sponsors had business interests. Regrettably the Europeans did not appear leaving England, Scotland and the hosts to contest the match. Sandra Branney of Scotland was individual winner in exactly 34 minutes but she was followed home by three English runners to take the team award. Scotland just edged out Wales for second place. Sally Lynch (Newport) was Wales' first athlete home in fifth position, Bronwen Cardy (Bromsgrove) was eighth and Hayley Nash (Torfaen) was ninth.

The first road international in 1987 was in the Barcelona Marathon in March. Steve Brace and Eddy Lee (Pegasus) represented Wales finishing second and sixth. Steve set a new personal best of 2:14:33 whilst Eddy's time of 2:19:40 was a Welsh veteran's best performance. The Aberdeen Marathon, which was first held in 1979, has incorporated an international race from its second year. On this occasion, in May, Mick McGeoch in sixth, was first Welsh man home in this his fifth appearance in the race. A female team next travelled north and competed in a 10k competition in conjunction with the Strathclyde 10k. Sally Lynch finished second with Bronwen Cardy, fourth, Eryl Davies eighth and Becky Powell, fifteenth, to place Wales second to the host nation. The Brecon 10, early in August, included an inter-area match versus Midlands for both men and women. Competition was extremely close in both. In the individual race Bill Bedell (Midlands) won by one second from Ieuan Ellis in a sprint finish lopping a whopping two minutes off of the course record. The team results were equally tight, both teams scoring eighteen points in the men's and Wales taking the honours on last counter. In the women's race Wales won by one point and provided the individual winner in Bronwen Cardy. At the end of the same month at Livingston in Scotland and over the half marathon distance Bill Bedell won narrowly again, this time in an England vest. Here he triumphed by two seconds from Greg Newhams whilst Dic Evans, now a veteran, achieved a personal best (65:12) in eighth place. The match involved the four home countries with Wales finishing third.

In veteran's events in 1987 Welsh athletes achieved notable success at both British and world level. In the world events in Israel in March Karen Bowler (now Arena 80) won both 10k and 25k races whilst Cyril Leigh was first M50 in the 10k and second in the longer race. At British level Alun Roper won the 5k and Eddy Lee retained his marathon title at Stone in Staffordshire. In the former race Pat Gallagher was first W40 whilst Evan Williams (Shrewsbury) and Bob Brierley (Carmarthen) were first in the M50 and M70 categories of the marathon, the latter in a remarkable 3:20:35.

The senior road relays at the end of March 1988 were again held at Swansea University. Thirty five teams lined up in the men's race and Shaun Whelan ran the fastest short leg of the day to give the home club the best possible start. Then Newport took over and despite challenges held on to win from Swansea; both clubs breaking the course record. Swansea gained slight consolation from the fact that their aggregate time for two teams was slightly better than Newport's but both clubs were nominated for the AAA Twelve stage race in Sutton Park. The women's relay was much more closely contested with Cardiff just holding on to win by seven seconds from Les Croupiers.

The Mayor's race at Carmarthen on Easter Monday 1988 was again the Welsh ten mile and Ieuan Ellis regained the title ahead of Owen E Lewis (Swansea) with Greg Newhams third. Swansea Harriers won the team event from Bridgend and Les Croupiers. The latter club totally dominated the women's competition with first and second teams led by Eryl Davies first home ahead of Bernadette Walters (Cardiff) and Peta Bee (Birchfield). The latter athlete was a popular visitor to the town, having family connections there, and being a relative of Ron Evans. Gary Cutler of Llanelli won the youths' three miles by nearly fifty seconds from Paul Lewis (Bridgend) and Lee Sandham (Swansea). Llanelli AC won the team awards ahead of Swansea and Carmarthen.

First of seven Welsh half-marathon titles for Steve Brace

The 1988 Welsh Half Marathon at Aberdare saw Steve Brace gain the first of his seven titles at the distance, defeating his clubmate and defending champion Greg Newhams by a mere two seconds. Eryl Davies had another win in the ladies section and Les Croupiers won both team titles. The Anglesey Marathon and Welsh Championship in September was won by Tegid Roberts ahead of Emlyn Roberts, who lowered his personal best by seven minutes. Mick McGeoch was third and defending champion Dic Evans fourth. With Arwel Lewis in sixth place Eryri easily won the team event and also placed their 'B' team third behind Les Croupiers. The race also included the final match of the season and despite Tegid not having been nominated for the international team Wales, led by Emlyn Roberts, gained a comfortable team win ahead of Northern Ireland, Scotland and Catalonia. The Welsh 10k was held as part of the Capital Windows event in Cardiff. On a fine autumn morning Nigel Adams was in top form and literally ran away from the field for a convincing victory in 29:18. Training partner, Kenny Davies was second ten seconds in front of Brian Matthews (Barry). Swansea Harriers with three in the first nine home won the team event. The women's competition was won by Ceri Pritchard (Warwick University) over seventy seconds clear of Bernadette Walters with Sarah Hodge (Stroud) third; Cardiff taking the team title.

The AAA 10k Championship at Hemel Hempstead on April 30th included a full-scale international match involving the four home countries and Kenya. Wales were second to

England with Roger Hackney eighth their highest placed individual. In the Aberdeen marathon Wales had another good day beating England and finishing second to the home country. Owen E Lewis (Swansea) in sixth place was their first man home. There was an inter-area match at Chelmsley Wood on June 19th and it proved to be one of the few very hot days of that summer. Midlands won the team event whilst Wales just pipped Southern Counties for second team place. Greg Newhams was fourth in the race and third in the match ably backed up by Owen Lewis, Andy Evans (Rugby) and Tony Blackwell (Wolverhampton). As in previous years the Brecon 10 included a representative match. Nigel Adams led most of the way but was never clear and in the final stages Andy Wilton (Tipton) caught up and then went away in the finish around the running track to win by two seconds. Ieuan Ellis was third placer but the next three were all Midlands athletes to settle the team result. There was a similar if slightly closer team result in the women's match with Beccy Richardson, third, and Sue Graham, fourth Wales' best finishers. In the Livingston half marathon England, led again by Bill Bedell won whilst Wales had a poor day and were relegated to fourth place. A similar team result ensued in the New Forest half marathon.

New marathon record for Susan Tooby in Seoul

For the first time a women's inter-county match was held at Wenvoe near Cardiff 1988. It was incorporated in the Wenvoe five mile road race and six of the eight Welsh Counties took part. Carol Hayward (Gwent) was an impressive winner thirty seconds ahead of Bernadette Walters who led Mid Glamorgan to a team victory. 1988 was quite a year for Welsh road running. Steve Jones, after an indifferent period, showed that he was far from a spent force by his performance in the Great North Run recording the fastest half marathon time of the year by a British athlete. In this run he finished ahead of the trio selected for the United Kingdom in the Seoul Olympics. Despite the fact that his time in the Boston Marathon was not up to his usual standards, he then received a late invitation for Seoul when Hugh Jones was forced to withdraw from the team. However considering that he would not be ready to do himself or the team justice he declined the place. A month after the Games everything changed. A brilliant victory by over three minutes in the New York Marathon consolidated his world status and his time of 2:08:20 meant that he had the four fastest performances by a British athlete. He was, though, not Wales' only world-class marathon runner. Steve Brace also demonstrated his class with no less than five marathons in under 2:20 and a personal best of 2:12:58 in London followed up by 2:11:50 in Chicago to put him second on the Welsh all time list. On the female side Susan Tooby was the star of the year. Fourth place in the London Marathon with a new Welsh record by over seven minutes of 2:32:09 ensured her selection for Seoul. During the summer she maintained that form setting a British best (69:56) for the half marathon in the Great North Run in July and for ten miles at Aylesbury in September. Then in the Olympic Marathon she further improved her best time finishing an excellent twelfth in 2:31.33. In addition Eryl Davies and Bronwen Cardy both received international recognition running for Britain in the European Marathon Cup race in late April. s

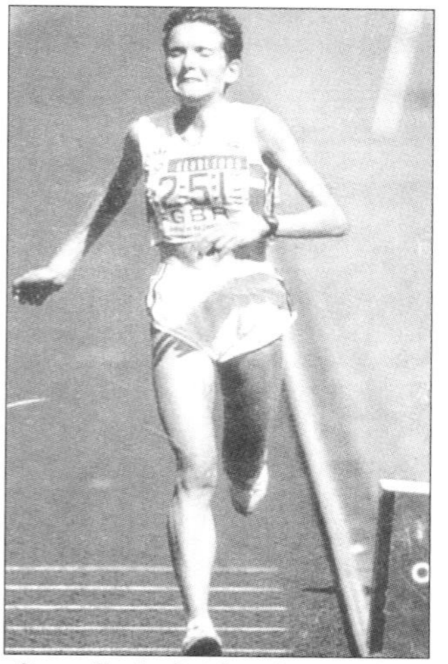

Susan Tooby finishes the marathon at Seoul 1988 Olympics setting a new Welsh record time.

In the north the Llandudno 10 mile road race had, over the years, established a reputation as a high quality event. In November 1988 this was recognised by it being designated the

AAA championship, the first time such an event was in Wales since the marathon twenty years previously. Earlier in the year its traditional Easter Saturday date saw the thirtieth running of the Newport 10. Appropriately, and in only his second appearance in the race, Steve Jones won in a new record for the revised course of 48:06 and second only to Mike Rowland's 46:59 in 1972.

Swansea first to take the AAA short stage title out of England

Swansea Harriers were the road team of the year in 1988. After finishing second to Newport in the Welsh relay they went on to place fourth in the AAA twelve stage event in Sutton Park and then topped this by winning the AAA six stage race at Derby in October - the first non English winners ever. In between those performances Swansea also won the Castles relay after a titanic struggle with Newport. Although still called a relay the event had by now developed into a multi-stage competition attracting over thirty teams with results decided by aggregate times over the twenty one sections from Caernarfon to Cardiff.

In veteran's events in 1988 Welsh athletes continued their record of success. Pride of place must go to Tacwyn Davies (Aldershot) who won the M50 section in the European Veterans' Championships in Bruges and was outright winner of the British event in Barnsley, albeit only by one second. The BVAF ten mile at Oswestry, on a scorchingly hot August day, saw Alun Roper win ahead of Dic Evans whilst Bronwen Cardy won the women's race. A fortnight later Bronwen just failed to retain her half marathon title at Welwyn despite closing the gap on the leader down to five seconds in the later stages. In the marathon Eddy Lee (Pegasus) was more successful gaining a third consecutive British title in the event, held this time as part of the Flying Fox Marathon at Stone on October 2nd. Behind Eddy, Bob Brierley won the M70 award with another remarkable time (3:28:32)

The first championships of 1989 were the senior road relays in Wrexham. There was a disappointing lack of support with Newport and Cardiff noticeable absentees from both races as Swansea took the men's race and Wrexham the women's. The 1989 Welsh 10k Championship was included in the Barry Carnival race and produced an absorbing duel between Chris Buckley and guest runner Nigel Adams (he forgot to enter officially) with the former just holding on for a narrow win and hacking over a minute off the course record in the process with Bernie Walters (Cardiff) easily taking won the women's race. The Welsh Marathon was held on Anglesey in September over a very tough course. This, together with strong winds on the many exposed stretches, combined to spoil the times of almost the whole field. Ieuan Ellis was seeking to run inside 2:14 with a view to possible Commonwealth Games selection but could only manage 2:22:02. Even so it indicates the quality of his performance when it is appreciated that Dic Evans in second spot was over nine minutes down. With only Ieuan of the main contenders taking part the race proved valueless as a trial. Local club Eryri Harriers took the team title. The race also included an international competition but Scotland failed to close in and Wales beat Northern Ireland. The junior road relays at Bridgend were a fiasco due to being the subject of numerous disqualifications mainly as a result of confusion over recently implemented changes in age groups. Cardiff were the main sufferers losing at least one team in each male race and including two squads which had finished first. In the female races there were also problems as in the girls event Swansea and Carmarthen were both ruled out due to their third stage runners mistakenly taking a wrong turning to cut the lap short. As a consequence Newport took the youths' and colts' titles, Carmarthen the boys' and minors' and Neath Harriers the girls'. Following on from being the AAA championship the 1989 Llandudno 10 was awarded the Welsh Championship. Steve Brace won his second title of the season with a time of 48:34 and was also outright winner after being pushed all the way by Sam Carey

(Warrington) who finished only three seconds down. His clubmate Greg Newhams took silver and Jerry Hall (Swansea) the bronze medal. Les Croupiers won their third team title of the year whilst Eryri just held off Wrexham for second place. Les Croupiers also won the women's team awards with Beccy Richardson first ahead of Liz Hardley (Wrexham) and Liz Hughes (Aberystwyth).

The international season in 1989 started with the Barcelona Marathon and Wales, led by reigning Welsh champion Tegid Roberts (Eryri) won from Scotland and Catalonia. In May, in Aberdeen, Liz Hughes was the star. She led the women's competition from start to finish and lopped ten minutes off her personal best to win by twelve minutes in 2:54:24. There were numerous other successes during the year. Steve Brace further enhanced his reputation winning the Paris Marathon in 2:13:03 whilst Mick McGeoch maintained his record of finishing in every London Marathon. Tony Simmons, although now a veteran, won the Delhi International Marathon and Nigel Adams, running for Britain, won the first stage of an international road relay in Portugal. His club, though, failed to retain their AAA six stage relay title but were again fourth in the twelve stage event at Sutton Park. Later in the year Swansea won the team prize in the AAA 10 mile championship at Hendon in north London. Another of their members, Trefor Hawes won the inaugural AAA 100k Championship at Nottingham, an event made even more gruelling by temperatures of 80F.

The 1990s – Steve Brace and Nigel Adams are the new stars

1990 saw the Commonwealth Games in Auckland in January but never one to miss a race Steve Brace warmed up for his marathon by finishing third in the annual Morpeth to Newcastle race on New Year's Day. Regrettably Susan Tooby had to withdraw from the Games team but with the two Steves in the men's event Wales probably still had its strongest representation ever. However medals were not to be and on the day Steve Jones was fourth and Steve Brace ninth.

The first Welsh championship of the new decade was the Welsh ten mile at Pontypridd on February 18th. The race attracted strong competition from England but Steve Brace, back from New Zealand, was up to the task and won both the open race and the Welsh title in a sprint finish in a new personal best of 48:12. Fifth in the race but runner up in the championship, was teammate Greg Newhams to ensure Bridgend of the team title. Ceri Pritchard (Coventry) easily won the women's title. The Barry forty mile track race at Jenner Park was given championship status for the first time. Both Mick McGeoch and Ann Franklin suffered problems in the race but whilst Mick recovered sufficiently to finish second in the open event and take the Welsh title, Ann had to withdraw, allowing Kay Pritchard of Les Croupiers to claim victory. Later that month Wales sent a team to the Barcelona Marathon and, led home by Dic Evans, they finished second. The following weekend saw the Welsh senior relays at Swansea. In cold, windy conditions the home club defended their title successfully defeating the pre–race favourites Cardiff by over two minutes. Newport completely dominated the women's relay providing the four fastest laps to romp home six minutes clear of Les Croupiers. Sally Lynch on the anchor leg was over a minute faster than any other competitor and thereby doubled Newport's already big lead. On 7th April Swansea, the only British club present, finished fifth in the European Clubs men's road championship held, somewhat surprisingly, over ten miles in Lisbon. Benfica provided the first three home with Nigel Adams the first Welshman in 48:03. In the women's race over 15k, held in Naples on the same day, Les Croupiers were ninth and Cardiff tenth with Bernadette Walters in fifteenth place the best placed athlete. The following weekend was Easter and Steve Brace took the opportunity to win both the Newport 10 on the Saturday and the Welsh Half Marathon at Carmarthen on the Monday.

Debbie Chick (Newport) won the women's title. On May 6th in high temperatures Steve Brace retained his title in the Paris Marathon winning in 2:13:10. In Aberdeen, at the end of the month, Liz Hughes repeated her success of the previous year and further improved her personal best to 2:49:47. Dic Evans was once again our leading male representative in fifth place. Two months later and literally on home ground, Tony Simmons won the Luton International Marathon in 2:24:25.

For the first time since 1987, Steve Brace was beaten in a Welsh road championship as Nigel Adams dominated the 1990 10k event at Barry right from the start. Defending champion Chris Buckley was a clear second with less than half a mile to go when he was misdirected and finished seventh. Nigel scored an impressive win knocking twenty one seconds off the course record. Steve Brace, who finished second, generously pointed out that he would not have caught Chris who was thus awarded the second place. Bridgend won the team race from Swansea with Les Croupiers third. The last club took gold and silver team medals in the women's race which again saw Ceri Pritchard get the better of Bronwen Cardy with Janet Kelly of Gloucester third. A week later Nigel Adams carried on where he had left off by comfortably winning the Milton 10k near Stoke. He eventually won in a new course record (28:52) by forty-eight seconds from former Olympic silver medallist Mike McLeod running for the north. Wales were only fourth in the team event, but with Nigel ably backed up by Shaun Tobin and Gerallt Owen, Swansea won the club prize. For the second time in three years the AAA 10 Mile Championship was held in Wales, this time in conjunction with the Brecon 10. In a field of over five hundred runners Ieuan Ellis and Nigel Adams set the early pace. Chris Buckley then moved up to the front at about three miles and gradually forged ahead. He made a decisive break after seven miles and from then on was unchallenged to set a new course record of 48:14. Bridgend won the team event by three points from Newport with Bristol third. Ieuan Ellis was a convincing winner of the Livingston half marathon on August 26th but Wales lost the team award by one point to Scotland whilst England were only one point further back in third place. Alison Whitelaw finished an excellent third in the women's race helping Wales to take the women's prize thanks to good support from Liz Hardley and Liz Hughes.

September 16th 1990 saw a clash between the Welsh Marathon in Cardiff and the Great North Run at Newcastle and inevitably athletes were split between the two competitions. Dewi Jones (Carmarthen) won the marathon after Huw Roberts, who led up to twenty miles, fell back to finish fourth. Huw did, however, have the consolation of leading Les Croupiers to team victory. There were only three competitors in the women's race with Kay Davies (Amman Valley) winning the title. The race at Newcastle included the AAA Championship and had attracted a world class field led by Steve Moneghetti and Douglas Wakihuri. Greg Newhams was highest placed Welsh athlete, tenth in the race and seventh in the championship. Ieuan Ellis was thirteenth in the race and led Newport to second team placing behind a Westbury Harriers team which included Chris Buckley.

The Lake Vyrnwy half marathon in September 1990 included an inter-area match and Wales took the honours due to excellent packing led by Steve Knight (Cardiff) in fifth place and with four others in the next seven places. The Barnsley Inter-area 10k in November saw over one thousand runners facing real winter conditions of wind, sleet and rain. Simon Mugglestone (Midlands) won but only after a race-long challenge from Nigel Adams who finished a clear second. Wales were third in the team event whilst Swansea easily won the club awards. In December two Welsh athletes received British recognition running in the Ekiden relays. At Chiba in Japan Nigel Adams ran the fourth leg and brought Britain up from seventh to third in a time of 13:55 for his 5,000m stint. Later in the month Sarah

Hodge ran the fifth stage in Barcelona. For the record Japan won their event whilst Ethiopia took the women's race in Spain.

1991 started with Steve Brace finishing third in the Morpeth to Newcastle classic for the second successive year. The first Welsh Championship of the year was the ten miles at Pontypridd and Steve Brace retained his title for a third consecutive occasion with a time of 48:10. Ceri Pritchard was also successful in retaining her title ahead of the same athletes as in the previous year. She also improved her time by sixteen seconds but in the open race had to give best to Scottish international Karen McLeod. There was an international match as part of the Langbaugh Cleveland marathon at Redcar in early March. Ieuan Ellis, resident in the north east of England, declined an invitation to represent Wales as with his sights set on the following month's Boston Marathon he wished to keep his options open. In the end he won the Redcar race by a clear two minutes and then went on to finish sixteenth in Boston in 2:16:20. However his absence from the Welsh team at Redcar did not affect the team result in which Wales finished second to England. The Welsh youth's three mile championship was once again at Carmarthen on Easter Monday. Colin Jones (Eryri) made the long trip south and was rewarded with a forty second win from David Povall (Newport) and Tim Hopkins (Swansea). The following weekend the Welsh senior relays were held at Swansea. The home club scored an emphatic win in the men's race and had its 'B' team third only nineteen seconds down on Cardiff in second place. Nigel Adams ran the final leg for Swansea and, despite having a ninety second lead, still put in an exceptional run to clock the day's fastest long stage time, over twenty seconds faster than his nearest rivals. Sally Lynch ran the fastest lap in the women's race as she had done the previous year when her club won the title. On this occasion, however, she was trying to close a huge gap. Despite making up over a minute on Cardiff, the latter club were still comfortable victors with Les Croupiers a distant third. On the same day Wales sent at team to compete in a representative match as part of the Reading half marathon. The team was predominantly from Bridgend. With Steve Brace winning (64:28) and Greg Newhams second (65:10) both Wales and their club had the best of starts. However fine packing by Southern Counties runners meant they edged out Wales by one point in a four to score match but Bridgend easily took the club award.

Bridgend take AAA marathon team title .... and Swansea in the medals at the twelve stage

Another fine run by Steve Brace saw him finish seventh in the 1991 London Marathon in a new personal best of 2:11:45. Incorporated in the race was the IAAF World Cup and Steve was one of the British team which beat Portugal for the title. He also led Bridgend to first place in the AAA club team championship, to emulate the performance of Cardiff some years earlier. As a result of his performance he was invited to run in the World Championships to be held in Tokyo but declined, preferring to concentrate on the following year's Olympics in Barcelona. The North Wales 10 on April 27th saw Alison Whitelaw (60:40) retain her title again beating club mate Liz Hardley. Andrew Edge was the new men's champion in 52:16 to give Wrexham the double. On the same day Swansea finally got amongst the medals in the AAA twelve stage relay at Sutton Park. Ian Hamer led the first leg in a very fast time and thereafter Swansea were never lower than fifth. On the last long stage Nigel Adams recorded one of the day's fastest times to put Swansea up to third ahead of Coventry Godiva and then Geoff Hill responded with an excellent anchor leg to consolidate the position. Tipton Harriers at the front gained a third consecutive victory whilst of the other Welsh clubs Cardiff were 23rd and Les Croupiers 41st. The following day a two man Welsh team competed in the Les Herbiers Marathon at Vendee in France.

Conditions were difficult with a strong head wind in the latter half of the race; Dic Evans in eighteenth spot was Wales' best placed athlete and also gained the award for first veteran home. At the 1991 European club's road competition for women at Braga in Portugal, Sally Lynch continued her good form to finish fourteenth leading Newport to sixth place, the highest by a British club, with Cardiff thirteenth in a competition dominated by the heavily sponsored Braga and Benfica clubs of Portugal. The same day an Ekiden Relay was run in conjunction with the Belfast Marathon. Wales finished fourth of the four home countries but in the full race Ieuan Ellis was second, only eight seconds behind Joel Kipchumba (Kenya).

Two AAA titles for Nigel Adams and Steve Brace wins in Berlin

Steve Brace added his first AAA title to the Welsh one in the 1991 AAA Half Marathon at Cambridge. Mark Dalloway (Stourport) led all the way but never succeeded in shaking Steve off and at the finish succumbed to a blistering finish by the Bridgend runner. Greg Newhams was fifth and Bridgend were third in the team event won by defending champions Westbury for whom Chris Buckley finished sixth. In the Luton International Marathon Ieuan Ellis, running his fourth marathon of the year, won and sliced exactly five minutes of the record set the previous year by Tony Simmons. With Jon Hooper fourth and Paul Bennett eighth Wales won the international competition between the four home countries whilst Janet Kelly completed the Welsh success by winning the women's race. That year's Milton 10k at Stoke was also the AAA Championship. After Steve Brace set the early pace Nigel Adams took over to claim his first AAA title and once more break the course record with 28:50. Steve Brace finished fourth whilst Swansea had three other athletes in the first twelve to give them the AAA team title with Bridgend second. The Welsh 10k was held at Llanrwst on August 18th. Ashford Laukam (Tipton) won the open race with a new course record. North Wales athletes and clubs almost inevitably dominated although Nicky Haines Jones (Newport) did take the women's title and Steve Rhind (Cardiff) finished second in the men's competition behind north Wales born Jerry Hall.

September 15th saw Nigel Adams continue his outstanding summer by finishing third in the Great North Run in a new personal best (61:53 and timed through the ten mile point in a startling 46:51). Meanwhile, back in south Wales Jeremy Collins was running twice the distance to win the Welsh Marathon in Cardiff ahead of Malcolm Griffiths (Bridgend). Caroline Jones (Carmarthen) took the women's title. The following week the Lake Vrnwy half marathon took place and again included a representative match. Wales could only finish third of the six teams on this occasion with fifth placed Kenny Davies their best performer. Bronwen Cardy Wise (76:45) and Liz Hughes (78:41) were first and second in the ladies race and led their team to a clear win over Midland counties. In the Berlin Marathon at the end of September Steve Brace won in a new personal best of 2:10:57, which turned out to be his second fastest run of all-time. In the race he was pressed all the way by Mark Plaatjes (USA) and it was only in the final run in that he broke clear to win by a mere four seconds. Down the field Chris Buckley was forty eighth whilst Steve Jones, now 36, finished eighty sixth. Meanwhile back in Wales Nigel Adams, a non-driver, won the Sospan 10k in Llanelli and with it a car! The AAA 10 mile championship at Chelmsley Wood on October 6th saw Nigel score another resounding success. With the ninth fastest time ever recorded by a British athlete he gained his second such title of the year. Mike Cadman set the pace until seven miles when Nigel took over. Holding off a late challenge from Jon Solly he went on to win by five seconds in 47:14. Steve Brace finished sixth (48:27) and Greg Newhams ninth (48:30).

Swansea regain the six-stage

The success story continued at Chorley in the last weekend of October 1991 as Swansea regained the AAA six-stage relay title they had previously won three years earlier. Nigel Adams put Swansea into the lead on the fourth stage only for John Sherban (Shaftesbury) to go back in front on the next stage. However, Ian Hamer on the anchor leg regained the lead halfway around the final stage and went away to victory. Elsewhere that weekend Alun Roper won the British veteran's half marathon whilst Dic Evans and Liz Hughes won their respective age categories. The Llandudno 10 on November 10th included a home countries match but conditions were hardly conducive to fast running with a gale force wind and squally showers. Jerry Hall was the early leader and despite falling back in the later stages finished third and led the Welsh team home first one point ahead of Scotland. The women's match was only two to score and despite having three in the first seven in the race and first five in the match Wales were only second to Northern Ireland. Liz Hughes second in the race and first in the match was their best placed athlete. That same day Nigel Adams and Ian Hamer ran for Britain in an Ekiden relay in Berlin both recording third fastest times for their stages to help Britain to third place behind Ethiopia and the United States. The year's major fixtures ended with the Abbey Dash 10k at Leeds on December 8th. The north won both men's and women's competitions with Wales third. Jerry Hall (Swansea) fourth Jackie Huybs (Blaenavon) eighth were our best placed athletes. Thus ended another remarkable year for Welsh road running with Steve Brace and Nigel Adams looking to take up where Steve Jones left off.

It was the same again at the start of 1992 as Steve Brace finished third for the third consecutive year in the Morpeth to Newcastle race. Later in that first week it was announced that he had been selected for the marathon in the Barcelona Olympics. Then in March the AAA half marathon was held at Bath and despite the close venue Wales was relatively poorly represented. Paul Froggatt (Newport) was the highest placed in seventh position just two seconds ahead of Jerry Hall (Swansea). Greg Newhams was tenth and Newport Harriers were fourth team. The Welsh senior relays at Swansea saw the home club achieve a fourth consecutive win with Ian Hamer on the fifth lap setting a new short lap record. On the previous leg the in-form Paul Froggatt had run a very fast time to bring Newport into second place with defending champions, Cardiff comfortably taking the women's title. Chris Blount won the Welsh youths' three miles at Carmarthen on Easter Monday with teammate David Povall third. Simon Lewis from Retford was rewarded for his long journey by gaining the silver medal whilst once again Carmarthen won the team event. That same weekend Steve Jones, now exiled in the United States, finished eleventh in the Boston Marathon in a respectable 2:13:53. Five days later Swansea were once more third in the AAA twelve stage relay in Sutton Park. The Welsh Half Marathon was held in May in Carmarthen in hot sultry conditions. Steve Brace gained his fifth consecutive win with his main challenge coming in the early stages from Martin Rees (Swansea). Liz Clarke continued her winning streak by taking the women's title ahead of Debbie Chick (Newport). Les Croupiers won the men's team race from Carmarthen and Swansea whilst Newport won the women's team awards.

The AAA ten mile was held with the Michelin race at Stoke early in June. Steve Brace improved to third to be best placed Welsh runner. His club was second in the team event and Swansea third with Steve's wife Jackie, (formerly Hulbert), the leading Welsh woman in seventh place. A month later Steve ran in his first Olympic Marathon in Barcelona and finished first Briton in twenty seventh.

In mid-July the Luton International Marathon saw all three Welsh scorers in the international match finish in the first eight places. This gave Wales a team victory for the second consecutive year whilst Janet Kelly retained her title in the women's race (2:56:05). Paul Smith (Les Croupiers) was their first man home, fourth in the race and third in the match with 2:27:18. Later in that month, and somewhat further north Ieuan Ellis won the Reykjavik Marathon. The last weekend of the month saw the World veteran's road championships held on the roads around the NEC in Birmingham. Races were held on two days over 10k and 25k. Amongst Welsh medallists were Alun Roper (M45), Bronwen Cardy Wise (W40) and Pat Gallagher (W45) in the shorter race plus Liz Hughes (W35) in the 25k, all of whom gained gold medals in their respective age categories. The Welsh 10k at Llanrwst was Steve Brace's first race following the Olympics. With the leading group in the early stages he took over about halfway. In the later stages the chasing group closed slightly but he held on to gain his first win in this particular event. His win meant he became the first athlete to have won Welsh titles at the four standard distances and also to hold three simultaneously. Greg Newhams was second ahead of Mark Morgan (Newport) and their clubs were first and second ahead of Cardiff. Bronwen Cardy Wise won the women's race followed by four Newport athletes to give their team an overwhelming victory ahead of Wrexham.

The Cardiff 10k, at the beginning of September of 1992 went wrong when the absence of marshals meant athletes ran different routes. The first two finishers did cover the correct course but after that there are queries. A result was declared for the home countries match incorporated and this gave Wales victory over England by virtue of better last scorer with Scotland third. Martin Jones (England) was individual winner four seconds ahead of Greg Newhams, an excellent second, beating both Nigel Adams (4th) and Steve Brace (5th). Jackie Davies (England) won the women's race and Scotland won the women's team race with England second and Wales third. The following week the Welsh Marathon was held in Cardiff and Dewi Jones (Trots) and Kay Davies (Amman Valley) regained the titles they had won in 1990. The Lake Vyrnwy half marathon in late September incorporated the usual representative match. Dave Gratton (North), won but second was Martin Rees (Swansea), a latecomer into the sport but now improving with almost every race. The team race was close with Midlands just winning out from the North with Wales third. In the women's event Bronwen Cardy broke her own course record by just over one minute. North won the team competition with Wales second. The Great North Run included the BAF (British) Half Marathon Championship and this gave the Bridgend club yet another team title. The start of November saw Steve Jones return to form at 37, winning the Toronto Marathon in 2:10:56, the fastest time by a Briton for three years. Concurrently Kevin Wilkinson the took British veteran's title at Stone and Ieuan Ellis was winning the Humber Marathon for the third year in succession.

The 1992 Welsh ten mile title race was held at Llandudno in early November and Nigel Adams finally broke Steve Brace's sequence of championship wins. It has to be acknowledged that Steve was running only six days after finishing tenth in the New York Marathon so was probably suffering from jetlag in addition to race tiredness. Even so it was pleasing to see Nigel coming back to form after injury problems. Shaun Tobin was third just behind Steve and Greg Newhams was fourth following placings of 2nd, 3rd, 2nd, 2nd and 2nd in the previous five years! With Swansea and Bridgend runners filling eight of the first nine places, those clubs easily took the team awards. Liz Hughes won the women's race for Cardiff a minute clear of Debbie Chick (Newport) with Nicky Haines-Jones a similar distance further back in third place. With Frances Gill and Jackie Brace fifth and seventh Newport comfortably won the female team awards. A week later the major road competitive year ended with the Barnsley 10k and yet again it incorporated an inter-area race. Kenyan runners first and third dominated the individual race but Wales finished second to a strong Northern counties team ahead of the Midlands. Bridgend who supplied four of the five man team picked up the club awards whilst Steve Brace finally showed he is human by having an off day and finishing down the field.

1993 started with Steve Brace giving his usual strong showing in the Morpeth to Newcastle race finishing third yet again. Then in February Steve Jones was nominated for the British team for the World Marathon Championships. The Welsh Championships began with the longest event, the forty mile ultra distance race. Although strictly a track race it tends to be included with the road events. Organiser Mick McGeoch also competed and finished third overall to take the Welsh title ahead of Malcolm Griffiths (Bridgend) who occupied fourth place throughout the contest and was second Welsh athlete to finish.

A new race series, The Northumberland Castles Challenge started at Warkworth on April 3rd. Sponsored by Channel Four Television, the team set up was unusual and almost certainly designed to attract maximum world wide TV coverage. In all there were thirteen teams including USA, South Africa and several European countries. There was a Great Britain squad, totally composed of English runners, separate teams from the home countries plus a GB Junior team. The United States team dominated finishing first, third and fourth. Behind them Great Britain and South Africa were second and third but only seven points covered teams sixth to tenth with Wales in the last position (82) only one point behind England and Sweden (both 81). Justin Hobbs (Cardiff) in sixteenth place was our highest placed individual. The following day host club Swansea won the Welsh men's relay title for the fifth year in succession with Shaun Tobin running the fastest short leg despite having competed in Northumberland the previous day. Bridgend came through to finish second with Newport third. In the women's race Newport made a determined effort to win but once again Wendy Ore ran a storming final stage to enable Cardiff to retain their title whilst Swansea were again third.

The 1993 London Marathon had been designated as the BAF (British) and AAA (English) Championship but was also a world championships trial. Steve Jones and Paul Evans (Belgrave) had been pre-selected so there was only one marathon place left open.Steve Brace finished tenth in the race but there were two Britons ahead of him. First Welsh woman to finish and fourteenth in the race was Sue Martin (Medway) gaining her third female veteran award. The following day Steve Jones contested the Boston Marathon and finished fifteenth in 2:15:30. In the twelve stage road relay Swansea finished in bronze medal position for the third successive year. After Bridgend were well placed early on Cardiff moved through thanks to an excellent stage by Justin Hobbs, only to fall back thereafter. Swansea, despite the absence of Geoff Hill and Nigel Adams, both injured, were in the silver medal position with a lap to go. In an exciting finish Alun Roper was overtaken by the Boxhill runner but held off the challenge of Salford with only nine seconds covering the three teams at the finish line. On the same day as the relay the North Wales 10 took place. Defending champion Simon Shiels was third with last year's runner up, Nigel Haskins of Deeside winning in 53:05 half a minute clear of Gordon Jones (Wrexham). Liz Clarke (Colwyn Bay) retained her female title over two minutes clear of former winner, Alison Whitelaw. Also on the same day Cardiff and Newport had teams in the European clubs' women's 15k road race near Naples. The event turned out to be a complete fiasco. A local factory had been closed and the ensuing industrial dispute resulted in a demonstration which delayed the start of the race for an hour. It was decided to reduce the race to 10k but then in high temperatures violence broke out spilling on to the actual course. Consequently the race was abandoned at 7k and results declared based on positions at that point, giving Cardiff seventh place and Newport ninth.

It's Brace the race again !

With the strong wind a major factor Steve Brace gradually wore down the opposition in the AAA Half Marathon at St Neots and from nine miles on drew away to a clear win. With the AAA now being solely an English association and part of BAF the eligibility of Welsh athletes was a source of some controversy and dispute. The new English body had not made clear whether or not it was going to continue its predecessor's practice of holding open championships. An inter-area road relay was held at Milton Keynes on June 20th and Wales had the relatively unusual occurrence of a husband and wife competing in the same fixture. Steve Brace ran the fastest leg and the AAW squad finished a clear second behind the Northern team. Similarly thanks to Bronwen Cardy the women's quartet, which included Jackie Brace, also led on the first stage but then fell back to finish fourth. The North also took the honours in a 10k race at Harrogate with Wales second in the men's competition and fourth in the women's. Gareth Davies (Bridgend) led the men in fifth place and Nicky Haines-Jones the women in sixth.

The Welsh 10 at Brecon in August 1993 attracted a strong field and in the absence of champion, Nigel Adams, four times winner Steve Brace triumphed a minute clear of Shaun Tobin. Swansea Harriers took the team awards but only beat Bridgend on last scorer, both totalling 22 points. In the women's race Hayley Nash (Cardiff) won by almost three minutes, setting a new course record, but runner up Sally Lynch (Newport) headed the winning team with Les Croupiers third. The race also included a veteran's competition with Martin Rees (Swansea) third overall.

The Llanrwst 10k included both an inter-area match and a Welsh inter-county match. In warm sunny conditions new course records were set in both men's and women's races. Kevin McLuskey (North) was outright winner in what was the fastest time of the year to that date and led his team to victory. Bronwen Cardy was second in the women's race and with Hayley Nash third Wales won the team award. In the inter-county competition West Glamorgan won the women's title and Mid Glamorgan the men's award. Another top quality field contested the Welsh 10k at Cardiff in September with defending champion Steve Brace giving best to Chris Buckley and Justin Hobbs settling for the bronze medal. In the women's race Hayley Nash (Cardiff) added the 10k title to her 10 mile and was a clear winner over a minute ahead of Beccy Cameron (Bridgend. Cardiff comfortably outscored defending champions Newport in the team event whilst Barbara Boylan took the honours in the veteran's competition to complete the home club's clean sweep in the women's event. On the same day Alun Roper (Swansea) won the BVAF half marathon championship at Aylesbury by finishing second overall in the race with club mate Jeremy Collins taking silver being placed fifth overall. The Swansea Bay 10k a week later incorporated a home countries international. In very wet and windy conditions Wales were second to England in the men's race. Two Kenyan's led the race followed by Mark Flint of the RAF, representing England, a clear third. Behind him there was a real tussle for the minor placings with only four seconds covering the five places including Steve Brace and Justin Hobbs. In the women's race Bronwen Cardy Wise was third behind two English runners' with Wales again second to England in the team event.

Bridgend born Jon Brown (Hallamshire) won the individual title whilst Bridgend won the team event with Steve Brace thirteenth the second Welsh qualified athlete home, in the Barnsley 10 k in mid-October which incorporated the BAF 10k Championship. In the women's race Bronwen Cardy finished second and in doing so set a new age record. Martin

Rees finished fifth in the male veteran event which was held as a separate race. An inaugural BAF Junior Championship was also held and this was dominated by Wales with Christian Stephenson (Cardiff) and Colin Jones (Eryri) first and second.

Bridgend, Swansea and Newport all contested the 1993 AAA six stage road relay at Aldershot in October. Bridgend led at first thanks to Steve Brace and Dale Rixon and were still third after four laps. Swansea gradually moved through the field overtaking their local rivals on the fifth stage and going on to finish third whilst Bridgend slipped to ninth. Martin Rees (Swansea) won the British veteran's 10k event in a sprint finish with two English competitors. Justin Hobbs, for his part, continued a fine run of form at the end of the month setting the fastest five mile time of the year. Then a week later he won the AAA 10k Championship at Leeds smashing the course record and clocking a personal best of 28:45. Moreover Swansea and Cardiff were second and third teams respectively. The year thus ended on a high note but against that it should be noted that for the first time since 1934, with the exception of the war years, there had been no Welsh marathon championship.

The first significant competition of 1994 was the 40 mile track race at Jenner Park, Barry. Stephen Moore (Hertford) won the open race for the third consecutive year whilst Malcolm Griffiths (Bridgend) took the Welsh title after being runner up the previous two years. There was an inter-area half marathon at Worcester on 20th March and Bronwen Cardy took the individual honours in the women's race ahead of two northern athletes. In the men's race Kenny Davies was fifth with the north again taking team honours.

Steve Brace retained his title in the Welsh ten miles at Newport on Easter Saturday (April 2nd) four seconds ahead of teammate John Edwards. With three more members in the next four places Bridgend gained an overwhelming team victory with their 'B' team second. Hayley Nash retained her title in an excellent 55:32 but the team event was very close with Newport winning from Bridgend and Cardiff.

Swansea add AAA 12 stage relay to their haul

Cardiff finally ended Swansea's five-year run of success in the 1994 Welsh road relays at Bridgend over a new course around the roads close to the Ford factory at Waterton Cross. Throughout, the race was very close and the final victory was only by thirteen seconds after Steve Knight (Cardiff) on the last stage set the day's fastest long lap two seconds faster than the pursuing Shaun Tobin (Swansea). To complete the double Cardiff retained the women's title for the fourth year, but only after Bridgend had led at the end of the third of the four stages. Steve Brace finished thirteenth in 2:12:23 in the London Marathon the following weekend and was third Briton across the finish line. Strongly supported by future Wales Commonwealth Games fourth placer, Dale Rixon with a debut of 2:15:41, Greg Newhams 2:19:38, Gareth Davies 2:19:46 and John Edwards 2:20:24 Bridgend gained an impressive team victory. In the women's race Hayley Nash was sixth and third Briton in 2:39:04, at the time the second fastest ever by a Welsh woman.

Despite having lost their Welsh men's relay title only three weeks earlier Swansea finally achieved success in the 1994 National twelve stage relay in Sutton Park on April 30th. Cardiff had the better start but on the second leg Swansea moved up to fourth just ahead of Cardiff. The next leg saw Cardiff edge back ahead of their rivals and then on the fourth stage Justin Hobbs ran the equal third fastest ever short stage. He was followed by Steve Knight who took Cardiff into the lead whilst Swansea slipped to sixth. On the next short lap Ian Hamer pulled Swansea up to second and cut in to Cardiff's lead. As a consequence Welsh supporters then had the inspiring sight of the two Welsh clubs heading up the front of the field with Swansea steadily reducing Cardiff's lead. Swansea finally took over on lap nine

Swansea Harriers 1994 AAA 12 stage road relay champions.
Back row: Jerry Hall, Ian Hamer, Paul Roberts, George Edwards (Team Manager), Andy Eynon, Kevin Tobin, and Geoff Hill.
Front row: Matt Kinane, Karl Palmer, Jamie Lewis, Seb Coe MP, Jeff Secker, Mark Morgan and Shaun Tobin.

as Jamie Lewis gradually opened up a lead which his team mates maintained to the finish ahead of Boxhill Runners and Blackheath. Cardiff slipped to seventh in the final stages whilst Bridgend were eighteenth. Neath Harriers competed for the first time and were more than pleased with their fifty first place.

The City of Glasgow women's 10k road race on May 29th incorporated a British Isles international. England and the Irish Republic dominated whilst Wales were third led by Bronwen Cardy in seventh place and Nicky Haines Jones eighth. A week later a men's team contested an international half marathon in Dunfermline over a very tough course. Wales were fourth whilst the extremely windy conditions ensured that times were all well outside normal ones. Wendy Ore won the 1994 BAF 10k Championship at Milton in spectacular manner. Leading into the last kilometre she went off course and ended up sixty metres down on the Kenyan Lucia Subiana. However she not only made up the deficit but also regained the lead to win her first British title in 33:41. Best of the Welsh men was Ian Hamer who was third in the race, (second BAF), and he led Swansea to another British team title. To complete the Welsh domination Bridgend were third in both men's and women's team competitions.

The Liverpool international half marathon in 1994 saw Wales finish second in the men's race with all three scorers provided by Swansea (Kevin & Shaun Tobin and Martin Rees). Wales were similarly placed in the women's competition behind England but these were the only two nations to close in. Meanwhile in Victoria, Canada the Commonwealth Games were taking place. The women's marathon was on August 27th and Hayley Nash fully justified her selection finishing seventh and improving her personal best to 2:35:39, a time only bettered by Susan Tooby amongst Welsh women. The following day Dale Rixon competed in the men's race and judging his efforts excellently he moved up six places in the final five kilometres to finish fourth only just over half a minute down on the personal best he had set earlier in the year. This equalled the previous highest finishing position in the event by a Welshman following Steve Jones fourth in 1990. Sally Lynch (Newport) gained a first full Great Britain vest by being selected for the Reykjavik marathon. Disappointingly she suffered an adverse reaction to one of the drinks provided during the race and although finishing could only record a time outside three hours. Fortunately it was only a short term problem and the following week she returned to form to retain her British Police ten mile title.

The 1994 Welsh 10k Championship was held at Cardiff on September 4th. Justin Hobbs won in 29:31 and with Christian Stephenson second and Kevin Blake third, the host club had an overwhelming team victory ahead of Bridgend and Swansea. North Walian Lynn Maddison (Colwyn Bay), won the women's race from Nicky Haines Jones and Bronwen Cardy Wise, now in the colours of Bridgend. The latter led her new club to victory over Cardiff and Newport. Swansea's relative lack of success at Cardiff is explained by the fact that the same day they won the AAA 10 miles Championship at Erewash beating Westbury Harriers, (including Chris Buckley), by a single point. Jamie Lewis led them home in fourth place (48:09). In the women's competition Wendy Ore finished second in 55:10, the fastest time recorded by a Welsh woman. The following week the Swansea Bay 10k incorporated a Home countries international which was dominated by England with the first three home in both men's and women's races. Debbie Newhams was fourth in the women's race leading Wales to second team position whilst this was almost matched by Steve Brace - fifth in the match and eighth overall. On the same day there was also an inter-area ten mile match at Newbury. Somewhat surprisingly, the first two Welsh men were both Swansea athletes - Andy Eynon and Paul Richards. The women's team provided an even more interesting fact. Wales' first woman home marked the return of Sue Martin Clarke. She finished in seventh place despite having got married the previous day!

Despite having finished thirteenth, (sixth Briton), in the Great North Run the previous weekend, Steve Brace regained the title he had last won two years earlier in the Welsh Half Marathon of 1994 at Lake Vyrnwy. Bridgend with three in the first four home easily won the men's team title. In the women's race unattached Lorna Williams, from Talgarth was a surprise winner ahead of Sue Martin Clarke. Les Croupiers led by TV presenter Angharad Mair, in third place, won the team event. A month later three Welsh clubs contested the AAA national six stage relay in Sunderland. Having won the twelve stage race Swansea made a bold bid for the double and were in the lead at the end of stage three thanks to a scintillating run by Karl Palmer. However Bingley overtook them on the next stage and they then slipped a place on each of the remaining stages to finish fourth. Cardiff were down the field until lap five when Christian Stephenson stormed around the lap and brought them up to fifth place only to find no final stage runner awaiting him. Justin Hobbs retained his AAA 10k road title at Brighton. Taking the lead soon after the start he eventually won by well over two hundred metres. With Nicky Comerford fourth and Steve Knight sixth Cardiff gained victory in the team event.

The 1995 season started relatively late in terms of international and representative competition. The first such race was the international held annually as part of the City of Glasgow women's only 10k race in May. The previous year's Welsh squad had so enjoyed the event, complete with pipers marking the kilometre points that they all vowed to get in the team again. However, this was not to be as two had become mothers in the interim and the other two were injured. A completely new squad therefore ran and finished fourth led by reigning Welsh 10k champion Lynne Maddison (Colwyn Bay). Later in the month came the Great Welsh Run in Cardiff and this included a home countries match. Wales finished second in the men's match where Justin Hobbs was similarly placed individual after a titanic head to head race long tussle with Gary Staines of England. Both athletes beat the fastest time set for the season and Justin's was also a personal best. The women's team were also second with Angharad Mair winning her first international vest and setting a personal best time of 36:25.

The next race in the inter-area series was a 10k race at Brighton. This saw an amazing run from relative newcomer, Mark Shaw (Newport) who won the race with the Welsh team third. The final race should have been in conjunction with the Llandudno ten mile in November but a dispute over entry fees for the match competitors resulted in AAW withdrawing. The Richard Burton 10k held at Cwmavon, just north of Port Talbot on a Sunday morning in mid-January 1996 was therefore substituted. This race brings back memories of the Monday night races of thirty years earlier since it is held around the roads of a typical terraced mining valley housing estate with the start and finish along the main road of the valley. Steve Brace and Wendy Ore both won in a high class field and the men finished second team. Wendy's performance was all the more meritorious as she had run in the UKCAU inter-counties cross country at Luton the day before.

A women's only 10k race in Glasgow was the first true match of the 1996 season. Here Angharad Mair commenced a series of further improvements on her personal best and finished fifth overall in the race. The next such race was in conjunction with the Wenvoe five mile race which is held over a surprisingly undulating course just north of Cardiff. In its early years the race was in conjunction with a traditional works fete and barbecue but as the latter declined the race continued in its own right. In this year's race the Northern team won the men's match whilst Hayley Nash won the women's race. Mark Morgan (now Swansea) had an excellent run in the open event and was rewarded with selection for Wales in a full international over 6k in Battersea Park, London the following week. This latter fixture was probably Wales' best result of the year. In the men's race they finished second team to England with Steve Brace, Mark Morgan and Steve Knight all in the top ten of a high class field. The women did even better, beating England with Wendy Ore again on top form finishing second to Elana Meyer (South Africa). The team packed well behind with Angharad Mair, (yet another personal best) in fifth.

Mid and late summer of 1996 brought three more fixtures - at Barnsley, Redditch and Liverpool. Barnsley is a notoriously tough race and on one of the hottest days of the year Wales only fielded an incomplete men's team whilst the ladies finished third team. Redditch was the Midland's venue for a 10k race. Hayley Nash finished second in the women's inter area race and the team were similarly placed. The men's competition was an extremely high level one and despite Mark Morgan setting a personal best by over half a minute and Martin Rees (Swansea) and Darren Hiscox (Bridgend) equalling theirs, Wales only finished fourth in the match. The Liverpool half marathon was a full international. Due to late notification of details only Hayley Nash ran in the women's event and was therefore drafted into an international select squad. She responded by finishing second and thereby gaining selection for Great Britain in the World Half Marathon Championships in Majorca later in the year. The men for their part were second to England and that only on position of last scorer but did beat the other home nations and Russia.

The programme of matches started even later in 1997 with the Chelmsley 10k in June. It saw the welcome return of Steve Brace, still producing good times and performances despite a lower weekly mileage. The team again finished second but pressed the North much more closely on this occasion. Wales won the women's team competition with an individual win for Angharad Mair and a personal best for Frances Gill well supported by Hayley Nash and Emma Evans, (Bridgend), returning from injury. The only full international in 1997 was the Erewash ten mile hosted by England where the male team finished second. All four of our team ran well with Darren Hiscox (Bridgend) finishing ahead of BAF champion Paul Taylor (Border) and Rhodri Jones (Westbury) again producing a personal best time.

All in all a not unsuccessful recent period but one where a problem seen previously became all too obvious. The sport is facing a problem due to the dearth of newcomers and youngsters coming through the ranks. Many club teams are depending on veterans, both male and female; to complete their strength and this is now becoming the case at representative and international level. On one occasion the whole Welsh team was composed of veterans. Without entering into a debate on whether or not veteran athletics is good for the sport as a whole the fact remains that the lack of 'new blood' does not augur well for its long-term future. This is also the case for other branches of the sport in Wales.

Towards the Millennium

An innovation for Welsh roadrunners of masochistic disposition came about in 1997 when a team of four contested an international match over 100k at Edinburgh in June. Competing for the Anglo Celtic Plate, Jeff Rees, Tony Holling, Eric Rees and Mark Rowberry combined to finish 2nd behind a strong England team and ahead of both Ireland and Scotland. Earlier in the year Holling had been crowned Welsh Ultra Champion by winning the 40 miles race at Jenner Park, Barry.

On the Welsh Championship scene Kevin Blake of Cardiff won the half marathon at Pontardawe by the closest margin imaginable. He just got the verdict over defending champion Martin Rees of Swansea, with both athletes clocking 66:40. Rees had the consolation of leading his club to the team honours. Newport's Frances Gill won the women's race, while Les Croupiers were 1st and 2nd in the team competition. The junior Men's 5k was held for the first time, with Simon Lewis of Cardiff becoming the inaugural winner. The previous day, Rory Broady (Swansea) claimed the under 17 title. Steve Brace claimed his 7th Welsh 10 miles title in nine years at Rhondda, and his Bridgend club took the team award for the 4th successive year. Frances Gill, now of Neath, earned her 2nd Welsh title of the year, but her club lost out to the strong Les Croupiers squad. Later on, Brace led a Bridgend clean sweep of the medals at the 10k championships in Cardiff while, to complete a good day for the club, Emma Evans took the honours in the women's race. Richard Jones (Swansea) and Dawn Kenwright (Sarn Helen) were the Welsh Marathon Champions over the gruelling course at Snowdonia. Cardiff's men and Newport's women took the honours in the senior road relys and among the juniors, despite the meeting being held in Newport, most of the titles went west with Swansea, Neath and Carmarthen winning titles. The only exception to the rule was Cardiff who were successful in the under 15 boys.

Internationally, Wales finished 2nd to England in a match over 10 miles held in conjunction with the Erewash 10. Darren Hiscox (11th) was the highest placed Welshman and his Bridgend clubmate Emma Evans (7th) took pride of place among the women. On the same day, Angharad Mair won the women's category in the Liverpool International Half-marathon. Wales finished well down the field, in 5th place, in an international 10 miles race incorporated into the Cross Border Challenge at Newry. Best individual performance in a very high quality field came once again from Darren Hiscox in 16th place, with Dinah Cheverton (15th) Wales' leading lady. Angharad Mair competed in the Marathon at the World Championships in Athens.

Simon Lewis retained his Welsh under 20 title in 1998, while Daniel Beynon of Swansea won the under 17s event. The 40 miles race at Barry included a women's competition for only the second time ever. Dawn Kenwright won with Jeff Rees of Neath taking the men's title. The 100k adventure continued with Wales being invited to two international events. In the first, at Greenwich, London, they were 3rd behind England and Scotland, despite an excellent performance from Jeff Rees. Later, at the Celtic International in Brittany, Wales were 2nd to the hosts despite the absence, through injury, of Jeff Rees, but ahead of

Scotland. Newcomer Victoria Musgrove was a splendid 2nd in the women's event.

Cardiff (men) and Newport (women) retained their laurels in the enior road relays and the Welsh Championships season continued in May with the half marathon at Tywyn. Bridgend proved once again that they were the strongest club on the road running scene at the time with another clean sweep, Dale Rixon winning the race and leading his teammates to a comprehensive win. The women's race went to Paula Jeffs of Bro Dysynni. Cardiff's Andres Jones won the Welsh 10 Miles Championships at Brecon in July, just holding off the challenge of Neath veteran Martin Rees. In the women's event, Angharad Mair deprived another Neath athlete of the title when she won ahead of Frances Gill. In September, Christian Stephenson of Cardiff won the Welsh 10k Championship without extending himself too much and Frances Gill was an equally emphatic winner of the women's title. Closing off the championship season, Peter Maggs of Chepstow and the unattached Jo Groves won the men's and women's titles respectively in the Welsh Marathon, held once again at Snowdonia.

On the international front Wales, with Darren Hiscox again to the fore, finished 4th team in the Liverpool International Half Marathon. The Cross Border Challenge 10 miles race in Newry attracted entries from 13 countries this time. Wales finished 5th with Mark Morgan leading them home in 49:06. First Welsh woman home was Jackie Newton in 59:41. Both Dale Rixon (15th) and Steve Brace (17th) contested the marathon in the Commonwealth Games at Kuala Lumpur. In November, Nicky Comerford competed for Britain in the Ekiden Relay at Chiba, Japan. The team finished in 15th place.

The 1999 Welsh Championship season kicked off at Barry, when Jeff Rees won the battle of the Rees's when he retained his 40 miles title ahead of Eric Rees and Lyn Rees, both of Sarn Helen. The Anglo Celtic Plate match over 100k was held in Dublin with Wales occupying 3rd place this time. Winners of the Welsh 10k Championships in Swansea were the host club's Mark Morgan and Nicola Haines-Jones of Newport. In the Welsh Road Relays Championships, Cardiff secured a hat trick of wins in the men's event, while Newport went one better to take their fourth successive women's title. It was the order as before in the Welsh Half Marathon Championships, again at Tywyn, with both Dale Rixon and paula Jeffs successfully defending their titles. There were new champions over 10 miles at Brecon, however, when Rodri Jones of Westbury and Bernadette Walters of Cardiff came out on top. Welsh champion Mark Morgan won the AAA 10k Championships at Bradford. Later in the year he ran for the Great Britain team that finished 16th in the Ekiden Relay at Chiba, japan. Emlyn Roberts of Eyri won the men's marathon at Snowdonia and Victoria Perry of Altrincham took the women's title.

2000 saw Eric Rees turning tables on his namesake as he defeated two-time champion Jeff Rees to take the Welsh Ultra 40 Miles Championships at Barry. The Alberto Culver 10k at Swansea incorporated an international match in which Wales finished 3rd behind Scotland and England. Consolation for Wales came via a superb performance from Andres Jones who won the race in a sprint finish with England's Nick Wetheridge and Scotland's Ian Grimes. Frances Gill (7th) led the Welsh women home with her three teammates immediately behind her. Mark Morgan added the 10 miles title to the 10k he won the previous season when he ran out an easy winner at Newport. Louise Copp comfortably took the women's title. At Llanelli, Martin Rees was again involved in a close finish when he lost out to Darren Hiscox by a mere 2 seconds in the Welsh 10k. Louise Copp won the women's race to take her second title of the season. The beautiful Lake Vyrnwy was the setting for the Welsh Half Marathon Championships. Ian Pierce of Tipton and Sam Bretherick of Preseli took the honours.

Chapter 8

History of Fell, Hill & Mountain running in Wales

Welsh Fell runners have been amongst the best in Britain since the Snowdon race was established in 1976 by Ken Jones of Llanberis. This short article gives a flavour of the activity of the newest branch of the sport in Wales, which has attracted many athletes who find modern-day cross-country courses too flat and uninteresting ....

Fell, hill and mountain running, as a separate activity in athletics in Wales tends to be associated mainly with two clubs - Eryri Harriers in the north and Mynyddwr de Cymru in the south. The former club has geographic considerations as its basis whilst the latter draws much support from those endurance athletes who prefer the less structured informal competition offered over more testing terrain.

In the latter half of the twentieth century cross-country has generally become a case of running defined laps of parkland or sportsfields. This has displaced the point to point or out and back across country events, with the plough, hedges, fences, ditches and other natural obstacles that the latter implies. Amongst reasons for this trend are the numbers and types of competitors and safety with the activity no longer restricted to male adults. In other circumstances a reaction to the trend can be seen in the popularity of multi-terrain and trail races plus competitions rejoicing in such evocative names as The Grizzly, Tough Ten and St Valentine's Day Massacre – athletes and organisers reacting against flatter, faster and less 'interesting' courses. On the road the trend to flat and fast courses may be justified by the desire for comparability between performances in order to produce valid ranking lists. On the country where weather and underfoot conditions are a much more significant factor the point is debatable. As a consequence there is still a significant division of attitude and interests between recreational runners and competitive athletes

In Britain, fell, hill and mountain running has its traditional origins in the events long held in the Lake District of England or in Scotland and associated with local fetes and the like. Such gala days would include sporting competitions in their programme of events, one of which would often be a race up to the top of a nearby hill or other landmark and back. Sometimes a course would be marked; in others merely one or more checkpoints would be established. In the middle of the twentieth century many such events were designated as 'professional' since cash prizes or the like would be awarded or merely the fact that the competition was not held under AAA Laws. Probably the best known race and one which, incidentally, was recognised as being under (Scottish) AAA laws, was the Ben Nevis race in Scotland each year to the top of Britain's highest mountain and back. There were also long distance events where a traverse of peaks in the Lake District was carried out in a target time of twenty four hours; the classic was 'Bob Graham's round of the fells' first carried out in 1932, but itself based on circuits dating back to the 1860s.

The oldest established fell race in Wales appears to be the Welsh 1,000m peaks race generally held in May/June each year and now over twenty miles and 9,000' of climb. It started in 1971 over an eighteen-mile route following an unofficial solo effort the previous year. The course visits the four highest peaks in Snowdonia having commenced on the shore at Aber near Bangor and finishes at the top of Snowdon. In 1978 the course was modified and extended to its current length. In addition to fell racers the event has classes for mountaineers and services teams with specific rules on equipment. There is also a 'short course' from Ogwen to Snowdon summit for junior mountaineers and in recent years female fell runners have taken part. Winners in the early years were English fell legend Jos Naylor (1972-73-74-75-76) and Mike Short of Horwich (1977-78-79-80-81) whilst on the female side local competitors Joan Glass won in 1974-75 & 78 and Bridget Hogge in 1976 & 1980.

The Snowdon Race & other events

On 19th July 1976, Ken Jones of Llanberis organised the first Snowdon mountain race. It had a field of eighty-six runners and was won by English cross-country international Dave Francis (Westbury) who took 72:05 to cover the ten mile (3,560') course to the summit and back with Bridget Hogge the first female. From that race grew the Eryri Harriers club in September 1977 and also later several of the other clubs in the region.

The Snowdon race grew to be an international event with teams from the other Home countries, Italy, France, Germany, Yugoslavia, Austria and the Irish Republic taking part. The Italians in particular, visited on many occasions starting in 1980. As a consequence the race 'twinned' with the Trofeo Vanoni whilst Eryri Harriers similarly established links with a specialist mountain running club based at Morbegno in the Italian Alps. Up until the late 1990s no Welsh athlete had won the race, the nearest being Andrew Darby (MDC/Newport), Tacwyn Davies (Aldershot F&D) and Martin Bishop (Staffs Moorlands) all being placed second. The course record stands to Englishman Kenny Stewart (Keswick) with 62:29 in 1985 whilst the best women's time is 72:48 by Carole Greenwood (England) in 1993. Then in 1998 Colin Jones became the first Welsh champion although it should be noted that locally based Scotsman, Colin Donnelly (Eryri) had triumphed ten years earlier.

In the late 1970s there were other races in various parts of Wales. On the Gwent border there was the Machen mountain race each August Bank Holiday at Bedwas. This event had a link with Guto Nythbrân, being the place of origin of his last opponent. At Eglwyswrw in Pembrokeshire there was another race with historical connections – 'Ras Beca' each August. The event commemorates and re-enacts an incident from the Rebecca riots when men dressed as women broke down gates to toll roads as a gesture of defiance against the authorities. Assuming they had sufficient lead, the first one or two runners to reach the finish field would don women's clothes for the last hundred yards or so. Then armed with a wooden hatchet they would symbolically break down a five-barred gate at the finish line. Further north in Dyfed on the first Sunday in June the Sarn Helen club organised a series of races for various ages including a longer event for senior men and women over a distance of about sixteen miles. The main race starting and finishing in Lampeter includes stretches of the Roman road from which the club and the races derive their name. It also had special awards for competitors who had contested the 'Welsh 1000 Peaks', which was usually held the previous day.

Administration and control of Fell Racing

The (British) Fell Racing Association was formed in Northern England in April 1970. A Welsh sub-committee of the FRA was established in July 1983, to deal with Welsh matters, following approaches made by Ken Jones to Danny Hughes, then Chairman of the British body. The Welsh committee eventually became the Welsh Mountain Running Association and until the late 1990s controlled the sport as a semi–autonomous body. Eventually the need to secure regular funding from the Welsh Sports Council for international and representative activities, led in 1995, to it becoming the Fell and Mountain Running committee and an integral part of the AAW. A year later the committee became part of the endurance committee of the AAW as part of the latter body's own re-organisation. The move was hotly disputed at the time and is still seen by many athletes as retrograde for the domestic level of the sport. This is demonstrated by the fact that some races are self-supporting and take place under fell running rules but without reference to permit and related procedures

The Establishment of Championships

The first FRA 'Runner of the Year' competition was held in 1972 based on points accumulated in a series of races. A similar system with modifications operated in succeeding years; the changes gradually favouring true fell running ability more and more but biased to venues in northern England. In 1981, Tacwyn Davies finished ninth to be the first Welsh athlete to figure in what was now termed the British Fell Racing Championship and concurrently took the inaugural veteran's title. This year also saw the start of a women's championship which Angela Carson won in 1983,1986, 1993 and 1994, the latter two in the colours of Keswick AC.

Andrew Darby and Angela Carson won the first Welsh Championships in1984. The competition, open to Welsh residents only, was based on a series of nine races, three in the south and six in the north. The initial events were three short, three medium and three long with a runner's best two performances in each category counting for points. Hill and mountain races, in general, were categorised by length, (long, medium or short), and amount of climb per mile, (A, B or C). At one end of the scale are races such as the Sarn Helen and Offa's Dyke races both of which are category "C" and are considered by some to be very long cross-country races. At the other are Moel Hebog, a very steep and rocky up and down race and the Welsh 1,000m Peaks race; both the latter being grade "A."

In 1986, Hefin Griffiths emerged as Welsh champion for the second time with his elder brother, Glyn the runner-up; the women's title was retained by Angela Carson, all three being members of Eryri Harriers. Angela Carson also won the United Kingdom women's title whilst Swansea born Del Davies took the veteran's award to add to his Welsh success. Runner-up in the senior men was Anglesey based Scot Colin Donnelly. That year the final and deciding race in the British competition was the Ben Nevis race. Colin Donnelly won the race in record time whilst Angela Carson and Del Davies also won their sections. However in the team competition Eryri lost out narrowly to Keswick in both the race and the overall British competition.

England won the team competition in the international held as part of the Snowdon race although L Bortaluzzi of Italy was individual winner. In October of that year the second World Cup of mountain running was held at Morbegno. To the surprise of the Welsh contestants the course had more in common with cross-country than traditional Fell running. Highest placed Welsh athlete was Hefin Griffiths tenth in the short race who then went on to finish twenty-ninth in the long one. Angela Carson placed sixteenth in the women's event.

The 1987 Welsh Championship was again over six races; two long, two medium and two short, with an individual's best four counting. Hefin Griffiths again retained his title closely challenged by teammates Steve Hughes and Colin Donnelly. Don Williams (Eryri) won the veteran's title whilst in the women's competition Alice Bedwell (Mynyddwr de Cymru) just beat Sue Ashton (Chepstow). In the UK competition Eryri won the team championship; the first time the trophy had left England. Colin Donnelly, as individual champion, led them home. That year the World Cup was in Lenzerheide, Switzerland. Hefin Griffiths was again one of the most successful Welsh competitors, finishing fifteenth in the men's short race. Veteran Dic Evans was 25th in the long event and Bedwyr Huws (Eryri) an excellent eleventh in the junior. That year there was also a BBC sponsored competition in conjunction with the Scafell Pike race and Battista Scanzi of Italy won whilst Wales could only finish fifth of the seven teams.

1988 saw over forty mountain races held in Wales during the year. Despite poor weather the numbers of athletes contesting them continued to grow. Colin Donnelly won both Welsh and British titles for a second consecutive year. He also broke the record for covering the fourteen Welsh 3,000' peaks adding a fifteenth for good measure. On June 11th in virtually perfect conditions he reduced the record, set by Jos Naylor, by nearly half an hour to 4:19:56. Angela Carson regained the Welsh women's title with Sue Ashton runner up for the second year in succession. Angela went on to finish sixth, highest placed Briton, in the World Cup held at Keswick with her Welsh team fifth and only three points behind England. The junior men also did well being placed fourth out of fifteen teams, again led home by Bedwyr Huws, but the senior men were only eleventh in the short competition and ninth in the long event. The Snowdon race attracted no fewer than eight international teams and Wales were third behind Scotland and England. Colin Donnelly won the race in the colours of his country of birth with the Griffiths brothers again heading the Welsh challenge with Hefin sixth and Glyn eleventh.

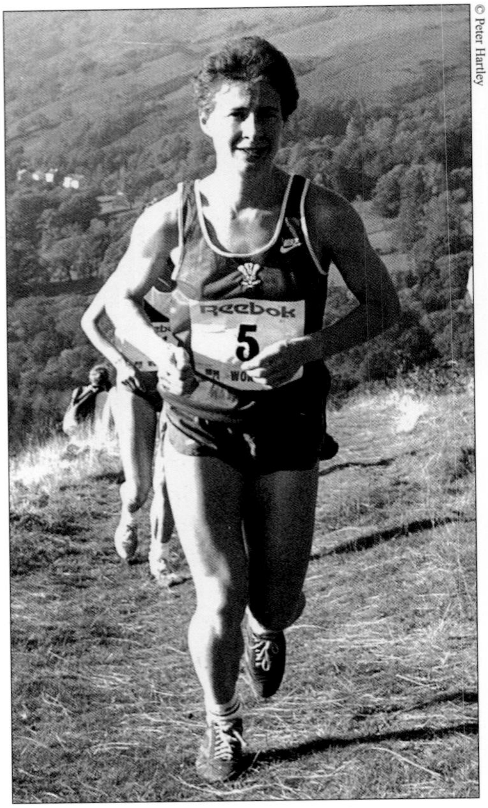

© Peter Hartley

Angela Carson (Brand Barker)

Colin Donnelly retained his British title in 1989 for a third consecutive year whilst the fifth World Cup was held at Die in southern France. In the junior event Wales fielded two very young athletes - sixteen-year-old Ioan Evans (Aberystwyth) and fifteen year old Colin Jones (Eryri). The two coped admirably with the high temperatures and finished eighteenth and twenty-third respectively to place eleventh in the team competition; in Colin's case an indication of performances to come. Angela Carson was a late withdrawal, being replaced by Dawn Kenwright (Sarn Helen) who rose to the occasion and was first Welsh woman home in 24th place, the team being ninth. The men's short race was in the late afternoon when temperatures had eased. Hefin Griffiths was ninth, Duncan Hughes (Eryri) twentieth and Glyn Griffiths twenty sixth to ensure that Wales closed in before England. The men's uphill race was the next day. With Hefin Griffiths and Duncan Hughes doubling up, Emlyn Roberts (Eryri) was our first man home in thirty-fourth place.

The 1990s – European Championships start

In the 1991 World Cup at Zermatt Wales finished eighth team in the junior men, twelfth in the women's event, ninth in the men's short race and fifteenth in the men's long race giving an overall placing of tenth in the men's competitions of the twenty three countries taking part. Outstanding performance was that of Colin Jones who, despite his age, finished twelfth, (first Briton) in the junior race

By 1992 there were nearly sixty official fell races held in the Principality attracting between fifty and one hundred and fifty competitors in each. These still ranged from arduous cross-country to extreme fell where navigational skills and mountain craft are as important as athletic ability. Moreover safety considerations had become a major consideration with rules regarding equipment to be carried by competitors and failure to comply with such conditions leading to refusal of entry. The sport also occasionally faced problems when long standing traditional routes traversed what had become designated as 'sensitive areas'. One positive development in the sport was the introduction of a Tuesday evening race series in north Wales. The Welsh Championships were won by Steve Hughes (Hebog) and Angela Brand Barker (formerly Carson) but no Welsh athletes featured in the leading places of the British Championship. The first international of the year was at Knockdu in Northern Ireland where a weakened Welsh team could only finish fourth. The second was incorporated in the Snowdon race on July 25th. In the men's race Wales were fifth of the eight teams but second to England in the women's with Angela Brand Barker, fourth, Alice Bedwell fifth, Mari Todd (Ambleside) ninth and Tracy Williams eleventh.

The eighth World Cup event was held at Susa in the Italian Alps in 1992 and Wales had an outstanding competition winning its first ever-individual medals, both in the junior races. Firstly, Mari Todd running as an individual, finished third in the inaugural junior women's race and then Stephen Griffiths (Aberystwyth) matched her performance in the junior men's competition, whilst the team were fifth out of the seventeen nations. In the senior women's race Wales were twelfth with Angela Brand Barker fifteenth our highest placer. Wales were less successful in the men's races finishing eleventh in the short race and fifteenth in the long to give an overall position of tenth, as in the previous year. Highest placed individual was Hefin Griffiths twenty-fifth in the short race.

During the 1992/3 winter a Hill series was started in south Wales with Peter Maggs (male), Sharon Woods (female), T Smith (veteran) and E Meredith (senior veteran) the inaugural winners. The last named of these went on to retain his title in the following five seasons whilst Sharon Woods gained three further wins but not consecutively. 1993 was not the best of summers for weather but fell races continued unaffected including the Tuesday evening series started the previous year in north Wales. The success of the two series prompted the introduction of a club championship with the first three from each club in the championship races to count.

Mynyddwr de Cymru takes the inaugural British team titles

The 1993 Welsh Championship was dominated by Simon Forster (Eryri) until his departure to New Zealand to continue studies. This left the positions to be decided on the last race in the Black Mountains, which was also a British championship event. Paul Wheeler (MDC) led the race early on but then fell back and consequently relinquished the title to his teammate, Andrew Darby, regaining the title he last won in 1984. Angela Brand Barker (now Keswick) who already led the women's competition ensured herself of British and Welsh titles by winning the race less than half a minute outside the course record. In the inaugural team championship Mynyddwr de Cymru took both men's and women's titles.

Two international races were held in Ireland at Knockdu at the end of May and Wales were third in the senior men and women's team competitions and second in the junior men. Best placed individuals were Colin Jones second in the junior with Ian Pierce (Wrexham) fifth, Angela Brand Barker fourth in the women and Paul Wheeler seventh in the senior men. A month later, at Tipperary in Southern Ireland, Wales were second in the men's team event with Simon Forster (Eryri) second individual, Paul Wheeler fourth, Graham Patten (MDC) seventh and Adrian Woods (MDC) eleventh. In the women's race Sue Ashton was fifth and Sharon Woods sixth. In the Snowdon race Wales were third team in the men's competition behind England and the Czech Republic and second to England in the women's team race. In both cases there was excellent packing with Angela Brand Barker sixth, Alice Bedwell seventh, Dawn Kenwright ninth and Mari Todd tenth in the women's competition and Hefin Griffiths twelfth, Simon Forster thirteenth, Paul Wheeler fifteenth and Steve Wilks (Eryri) twentieth in the men's race.

Bronze medals in French Alps at World Trophy Mountain Races.
Left to right: Tim Davies, Craig Shepherd, Colin Jones, Ian Pierce.

1993 saw the World Cup change its name and format. Now called the World Trophy Mountain Races and with only one senior men's race the event was held at Gap in the French Alps early in September. A Welsh trial was held at Waun Fach in the Black Mountains in early August with Paul Wheeler, Jane Coker (MDC), and Tim Davies (Mercia) clear winners of the various sections. The highlight of the Cup competition for Wales was the outstanding performance of the junior men who gained bronze medals finishing third behind Italy and the Czech Republic with Colin Jones fifth, Tim Davies fourteenth, Ian Pierce seventeenth and Craig Shepherd (Wrexham) thirty fifth. The ladies were ninth team and the senior men fourteenth. Mari Todd who had not taken part in the Welsh trial and lost out on selection was a clear winner of the female open race.

Tim Davies takes gold in the inaugural Home Countries International

An inaugural junior Home Countries International was held at Grasmere in the Lake District in October 1993. Our under 16 team won the gold medals led by Tim Davies, the individual champion, with his brother Andrew second and future Olympian Andres Jones (Carmarthen) fifth. The first ever Welsh junior women's team in such an event were third behind England and Scotland. At that time there were no junior championship events in Wales, which meant that ambitious youngsters had to join English clubs and travel to English fixtures in order to obtain competition. The most notable example was the Davies family, from near Welshpool, who were members of the Mercia club. Tim Davies recorded victories in six English under 16 championship races, breaking the record in four of them. His brother Andrew was clear winner of the English under 14 championship also winning four out of six races outright. For good measure their sister Jackie was runner up in the English girls' fell championship.

Simon Forster won the 1994 Welsh Championship despite a strong challenge late in the season by Hefin Griffiths with Emlyn Roberts third. Sharon Woods dominated the women's event ahead of Sheila Lloyd (Eryri). Don Williams did likewise in the veteran's section winning two categories and also took his age category in the British competition. Alan Vaughan (Eryri) won the male junior title and Christine Ashton (Chepstow) the female junior award. In the British women's championship Angela Brand Barker was once more female champion. In late May the annual five nations match, at Knockdu in County Antrim, was yet again dominated by England. Wales were second in the junior men's competition and third in the women's but only fifth in the senior men's event. Angela Brand Barker was second individual in the women's race whilst all eight juniors were well placed - Tim Davies third, Andres Jones sixth, Alan Vaughan seventh and Andrew Davies eighth. Best placed senior man was Simon Forster in ninth spot.

The Snowdon race of 1994 saw England win both men's and women's team events with Wales second in the latter, led home by Sharon Woods seventh and Dawn Kenwright eighth. Individual winners were Fabio Ciaponi (Italy) and Lucy Wright (England). In the extremely hot conditions veteran Gwynfor Owen (Eryri) had an outstanding run to break the veteran's record and beat the entire Welsh team in the process. The following month an uphill trial race to aid World Cup selection was held on Crib y Ddisgol at Llanberis with Duncan Hughes (men), Angela Brand Barker (women) and Alan Vaughan (junior), all of Eryri, winning the various sections. Gwynfor Owen continued his good form being second home and thereby ensured his selection. That year's World Trophy was held at Berchtesgarden in Germany at the beginning of September and for the first time comprised of an uphill only race. The ruling council for the sport had decided that the event would alternate yearly between an up and down race and an uphill only as a compromise to try and keep all the competing nations happy! As expected the event was totally dominated by those countries that concentrate on uphill only races - particularly Italy, France, Germany and Austria. It was a world-class marathon runner from Austria that triumphed as the skill and agility component required in downhill sections had been removed. Faced by an unaccustomed challenge Welsh athletes found the competition very hard and our leading runners were Tim Davies eighteenth junior (fourth Briton), Angela Brand Barker twenty sixth (third Briton) and Paul Wheeler sixty second (ninth Briton). In the team results Wales were ninth junior men, fourteenth women and fifteenth men out of the twenty-two nations taking part.

The 1994 representative season ended in October with the Home Countries junior international at Dreghorn in the Pentland hills near Edinburgh. Wales won the under 17 boys event, were second in the under 19 section and third team in the girls (under 19). Andrew Davies was individual winner in the under 17s with Alan Vaughan third whilst Wales' fourth runner home was Duncan Hughes, whose father had won the uphill trial race earlier in the year. Andres Jones was second in the under 19 competition with Tim, Andrew's elder brother fourth. In the girls' race Rhiannon Tomos (Eryri) was our highest placed individual.

Gary Williams (Eryri) convincingly won the 1995 Welsh Championship and had already won the event with two races still to go. Angela Brand Barker regained the women's title ahead of holder, Sharon Woods. For his part Don Williams continued to belie his age by being first or second in every male adult category. This year saw the twentieth anniversary of the Snowdon race and the ladies rose to the occasion by winning the team award for the first time. Darren Hiscox (Bridgend) was the first Welsh runner home in only his second fell race. The first ever European Mountain Running Championships were held on an uphill only course in France, with Paul Wheeler and relative newcomer Menna Angharad (Eryri) our leading performers. Paul and Darren Hiscox were both selected to run for Great Britain in an uphill only race at Susa in Italy; the first Welsh athletes to gain this honour. The World Mountain Running Trophy events were held at Arthur's Seat in Edinburgh and the junior men's team performed superbly to finish fourth and be first British team. Twenty-five countries took part and Wales were ninth overall in the men's events and tenth in the women's with outstanding individual performances by Darren Hiscox, Colin Jones, Menna Angharad and Tim Davies.

Telfes in Austria hosted the 1996 World Trophy on an up hill only course with no fewer than thirty-two nations participating. Again it was Wales' junior men who set the standard gaining silver medals behind the Italians. Tim Davies seventh, Andrew Davies twelfth and Alun Vaughan sixteenth were the scorers with Matthew Collins (Torfaen/MDC) in twenty-eighth place. Wales were eighteenth in the men's event and an excellent ninth in the women's. The outstanding performances were from Paul Wheeler fifty fourth overall (seventh Briton) and Menna Angharad nineteenth (third Briton). The second European Championships were very successfully hosted by Wales in conjunction with the Snowdon race. Wales were ninth in the men's event with Simon Forster twenty second, Paul Wheeler twenty fourth, Gary Williams forty second and Tim Davies forty fourth. In the women's competition Wales were eighth with Menna Angharad twelfth (third Briton) despite having been injured for several weeks previous; Jane Lloyd (Eryri) was twenty-ninth and Sharon Woods thirtieth. At the British Junior Championships in Belfast Wales won the under 16 team award with Alun Vaughan first, Andrew Davies second and Duncan Hughes eighth and in the under 18 group Wales also had the individual winner with Tim Davies whilst Tom

Cairns (Carmarthen) was third and Danny Lewis (Fairwater) tenth. England just edged Wales out in the team event by two points. In the under 18 girls event Wales were second again to England with Claire Peck (Carmarthen) sixth, Sherin Omed (Eryri) ninth and Donna Jones tenth.

The British Senior Championships were held in Northern Ireland in 1996 and Simon Forster finished twelfth, Adam Haynes eighteenth, Adrian Woods twentieth and Peter Maggs twenty second. Sharon Woods led the team home in seventh place in the women's event with Ann Nixon (Chepstow) ninth and Jayne Lloyd tenth. Once again the junior men stole the show beating England for the first time in the event. The team was led by Alan Vaughan, as individual champion, with Tim Davies as runner up and Danny Lewis closing in seventh. In the Welsh Championship Simon Forster won the men's title for the second time and in the women's Menna Angharad won for the first time. In the veteran sections Don Williams continued his successes but only after much stronger competition from Steve Jones (Eryri) and Adrian Orringe (MDC).

There were a number of highlights in 1997, notably that of Jonathan Hooper (Bridgend) gaining Great Britain selection to run in the Susa International race in Italy finishing a very creditable ninth whilst the British team were third. Alan Vaughan became the British junior champion at Grasmere in the Lake District and led Wales to the team prize ahead of England with Andrew Davies second, Matthew Collins fourth and Sion Meredith (Carmarthen) fourteenth. In the Black Forest Games in Germany Robin Powell (Colwyn Bay) won the 800m trail race (under 17) and Cai Pearce (Eryri) secured silver in the under 15 mountain race. Llinos Phillips (Carmarthen) finished with a bronze medal in the under 17 girls trail race and the junior men were third team ahead of England.

The 1997 World Mountain Running Championships were held in the Czech Republic. Due to Alun Vaughan being taken sick Wales' junior men probably missed out on winning yet another set of silver medals. Andrew Davies was a superb fifth individual whilst Matthew Collins was twelfth. Samantha Grey (Brecon) in only her second mountain race finished an excellent fourth in the junior women's competition whilst Mari Todd was twentieth in the senior women's race. Mari had also won the English Championship during the year breaking two course records along the way. In the senior men's race Jonathan Hooper was Wales' best place athlete in sixtieth place. Earlier in the year he had been placed nineteenth, third Briton, in the European Championship in an up hill only event. Julian Bass (MDC) took the 1997 Welsh men's title with the women's championship going to Victoria Musgrove (Eryri).

Donnelly equals Hefin Griffiths' three successive Welsh title wins

Colin Donnelly who took his first Welsh men's title back in 1988, brought the century to a close with three successive wins in the Welsh Championship to equal Hefin Griffiths' feat between 1985 and 1987. Victoria Musgrove repeated her 1997 win in 1998, with Jayne Lloyd (Eryri) and Sam Bretherick (Preseli) taking the women's award in 1999 and 2000 respectively.

The last two years of the decade saw mountain running become a worldwide activity with the 1998 championship on the island of Reunion in the Indian Ocean and the following year's venue being Sabah in Malaysia. Reflecting this change the ruling body changed its name from 'International Committee' to 'World Committee'. In Reunion it was the junior men who again produced the best result finishing fourth team. The following year Peter Williams (Swansea) and Darren Hiscox both had good runs in the European Championships on an uphill only course and as a consequence gained selection for Great Britain in grand prix events at Tefles, Austria and Susa in Italy.

Chapter 9

Wales and the Major Games

For all of the major athletics gatherings - Olympic Games, World Championships and European Championships, Welsh athletes participate as part of a British team. Therefore, to compete in the Commonwealth Games as a member of a Welsh team is special for a Welsh athlete. This chapter gives an overview of Welsh participation in these four great athletics festivals, and emphasises the special affection in Wales that the Commonwealth Games has in its various guises over the years.

The modern Olympic Games were revived in Athens in 1896, mainly due to the initiative of Frenchman Baron Pierre de Coubertin - although there are records of the Ancient Olympic Games taking place in Greece on or before 776BC.

The first Welshman to compete in the modern **Olympic Games**, was Cardiff schoolteacher Wallis Walters, who took part in the **1906 Interim, or Intercalated Olympic Games,** held again in Athens, finishing third in his heat of the 110m hurdles. He also ran in the 110m hurdles in the 1908 London Games with two other Welshmen - Alf Yeoumans of Swansea C&FC and fellow hurdler Wyatt Gould (Newport AC) - winning his heat in 17.8 secs, but going out at the semi-final stage. Walters won three Welsh 120 yds hurdles titles in 1904, 1908, and 1912, finished second on at least two other occasions (some early placings are not known) and won the long jump title for the first four occasions it was held (1907-1910). He twice finished second in the AAA 120 yds hurdles (1904/1905), finished third in the AAA long jump in 1904 and won two Midlands Counties titles - long jump in 1906 and 120 yds hurdles in 1907. On his retirement from competition, Walters turned his energies to officiating and organised the Welsh Championships of 1910 and 1911 at Barry Cricket Club, where he had become a member. His best time for 120 yds hurdles was 16.2 secs when winning the Inter-Town Sports in Abergavenny and Swansea in 1904 and 1906 respectively. This time equalled Wyatt Gould's Welsh record and subsequently stood for 46 years, until beaten by Mervyn Rosser with 15.9 secs in 1949, although Stan Macey in 1930 and T.T. Simmonds in 1937 equalled it. His best long jump was 6.40m, set in the 1906 Inter Town Sports at St. Helen's Swansea, and remained a Welsh record until 1920. He was instrumental in the formation of the Glamorgan Secondary Schools AAA and became their first chairman in 1937. He died at Llanybyther in 1952 aged 74.

Wyatt Gould was part of the unique Newport Gould dynasty, which made such an impact on Welsh rugby around the turn of the 19th Century. The youngest of six brothers, all of whom were rugby players – three were capped by Wales, including the incomparable Arthur, whose exploits are covered elsewhere - Wyatt was an excellent all-round sportsman and official, both for his club, and for Welsh athletics generally. In the **1908 London Olympics**, he stepped-up from his normal 120 yds hurdles event, where he had won four

Welsh titles between 1902 and 1910, and competed without success in the 400m hurdles. He had a walkover in his heat, before being eliminated after finishing third and last in one of the semi-finals. As far as we know, his best time for 120 yds hurdles was 16.2 secs set in 1903, and whilst equalled by Wallis Walters, Stan Macey and T.T. Simmonds in subsequent years, stood as a Welsh record until 1949. An indication of the quality of this performance can be gauged by the fact that Bob Shaw, the eventual 440 yds hurdles bronze medallist at the 1954 Empire Games in Vancouver, could only clock 16.4 secs to win the Welsh title on the cinders of Maindy Stadium, Cardiff, almost 50 years later.

By permission of Steve Lewis

Wyatt Gould

Another fact about the Gould brothers, which is unequalled, is that apart from Wyatt, who finished third in 1903, two others - Gus and Arthur - won bronze medals in the 120 yds hurdles at the AAA championships. Gus finished 3rd in 1899, whilst Arthur finished 3rd in 1887 and 1893. Wyatt captained Newport RFC in 1905/06, and was a long serving member of the club committee, organising many of the Welsh Championships when they were held at Newport, was a member of the South Wales & Monmouthshire AAA General Committee and was author of the athletics contribution to the History of *Newport Athletic Club, 1875-1925*, which documented much of the early athletics activity in Wales. He died in Plymouth in 1960, aged 80.

Yeoumans took part in the 10 miles walk at the 1908 Olympics and failed to finish, but the quality of his performances always seemed to be doubted – particularly outside Wales. See the chapter on race walking for a pen portrait of this fine Welsh athletics pioneer.

The only Welsh athlete to win an individual Olympic gold medal is Lynn Davies, with his 1964 long jump victory in Tokyo. However, David Jacobs, born in Cardiff on 30th April 1888, became Wales' first **Olympic** gold medallist when he ran as part of the British 4 x 100m relay team in **Stockholm in 1912** in a world record 42.4 secs. Jacobs was also part of the same team (Applegarth, Macintosh, and D'Arcy) which set a new world record for 4 x 110 yds in London in 1913. He was a prolific winner at the Welsh championships, taking 12 titles in all between 1910 and 1914, and uniquely taking the 100/220/440 yds treble in 1911 at Barry and 1913 at Newport. He captained the British team in Stockholm and also took part in the individual sprints winning both of his heats in the 100 and 200m in 10.8 secs and 23.2 secs respectively, but was eliminated in the next round of both events. His 10.8 equalled the Olympic record, but several athletes subsequently beat this time later in the Games. The time stood as a Welsh record for a staggering 34 years until beaten by Ken Jones. In the 4 x 100m relay, he ran on the third leg and handed over to anchor man Vic D'Arcy five yards in the lead. Jacobs placed second in the AAA championships on two occasions, firstly in 1912, when he was runner-up to the legendary Willie Applegarth in the 220 yds who won in 22.0 secs, and the following year when George Nicol beat him over 440 yds winning in 49.4. Unfortunately, there is no record of the times he recorded in both races, but in 1913, he almost certainly bettered his own Welsh record, which at the time stood at 50.4 secs. His best 220 yds time of 22.0 secs set in the heats of the 1912 AAA championships stood as the fastest Welsh 220 yds/200m time until equalled by Kenneth Jenkins in the 1938 Paris European Championships with a 21.9 secs timing for 200m (add 0.1 secs to 200m times to compare with 220 yds times). He was a loyal member of London

By permission of Kevin Kelly

Britain's gold medal winning team for 4x100m pictured at a meeting in London some time after their victory in the Stockholm Olympics of 1912. Left to right: Willie Applegarth, Vic D'Arcy, Welshman David Jacobs and Harold McIntosh.

club Herne Hill Harriers, and was a prolific winner of individual races and medals for their various relay teams. During the war, his parent's house in Denmark Hill, London was severely damaged by German bombs, and he lost virtually all of his medals and trophies, including that Stockholm Gold. After leaving Cardiff at the age of 11, Jacobs returned to Wales in later life and died in Llandudno in 1976, aged 88.

The **1920 Olympics in Antwerp,** were held in the shadow of the Great War, and in the circumstances, the organising committee did remarkably well considering that they had been awarded the Games within weeks of the end of hostilities, and Wales came away with two gold medals – albeit relay medals again – in the same event, the 4 x 400m.

The medallists were Cecil Griffiths, a native of Neath, and John "Jack" Ainsworth-Davis, who was born in Aberystwyth in 1895. Griffiths, who ran the opening leg in 50.6 secs, was one of Britain's leading 440 yds/half milers at the time, and was an AAA finalist at these events for ten successive years, winning the half twice in 1923 (1:56.6) and 1925 (1:57.2); and finishing 3rd over 440 yds three times between 1919 and 1921. In 1919 he was only 18 years old. His finest race came in the 1926 AAA 880 yds when placing third in the epic race between Otto Peltzer of Germany and the double Olympic

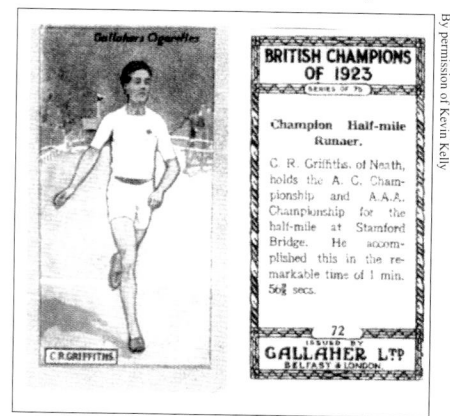

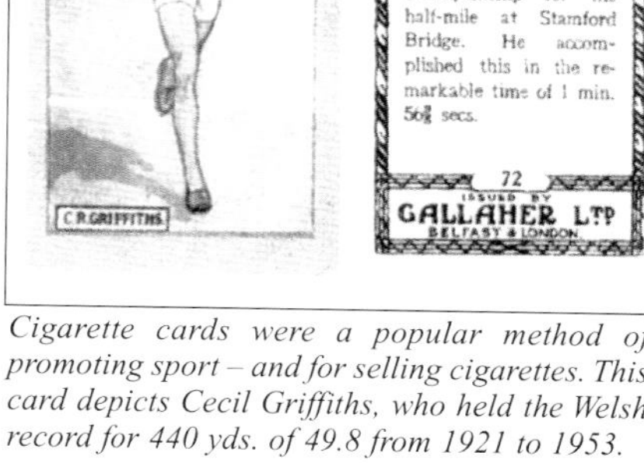

By permission of Kevin Kelly

Cigarette cards were a popular method of promoting sport – and for selling cigarettes. This card depicts Cecil Griffiths, who held the Welsh record for 440 yds. of 49.8 from 1921 to 1953.

The Olympic gold medal-winning 4x400m team of 1920 containing two Welshmen: (left to right) Guy Butler, Aberystwyth-born Jack Ainsworth-Davis, Robert Lindsay and Cecil Griffiths of Neath.

Champion (1924/1928) Douglas Lowe of Britain, which the German won in a UK all-comers record of 1:51.6. Third place times were not officially taken in those days, but contemporary estimates of his time were 1:53.1, which stood as unassailable to Welsh athletes until the arrival on the scene of Jim Alford and Reg Thomas some ten years later. Eminent athletics historian Ian Buchanan said of this performance: "It seems clear that amongst British half milers, only Lowe himself had ever run faster" Unfortunately, Griffiths was declared ineligible by the IAAF in 1923 for accepting a cash prize as a youth, and this meant he had to miss the 1924 "Chariot's of Fire" Olympic Games in Paris. Had he competed, he would surely have been a contender for an individual medal. Amongst his other best performances were three UK records at 1,000m (twice) and 660 yds.

Whilst there is no record of Ainsworth-Davis competing in the Welsh championships, Griffiths won ten Welsh titles in all, including five successive 440 yds titles between 1920 and 1924, and four half mile wins in 1922-24 and again in 1927. He also won the 220 yds in 1921 and in winning the 440 yds at the same championships on the Barry Cricket Ground at Barry Island, he ran 49.8 which was to stand as a Welsh record for almost 32 years until beaten by Peter Phillips of Porth, who won a bronze medal in the 1953 World Student Games. Phillips died in 1957 in a flying accident in Cyprus whilst serving in the RAF. Griffiths' 49.8 was one of the fastest times clocked by a British athlete that year, and was 0.6 secs faster than Robert Lindsay clocked in winning the AAA title some weeks later, when Griffiths was third. D.J.P. Richards, in his 1956 *History of the Welsh AAA*, describes him as " lightly built, but possessed with an easiness of style that made it appear as though he was blessed with boundless energy". Griffiths died aged 72 in Great Barr, Staffs in 1973. Not a great deal is known about the athletics career of Ainsworth - Davis, who finished fifth in the individual 400m in Antwerp with 50.0e after the withdrawal of Griffiths through illness. He placed fourth in the 1921 AAA 440 yds, and after this he appeared to retire to concentrate on his medical career. He eventually became a urological surgeon and secretary of the Royal Society of Medicine. During the Second World War, he was head of the surgical division at the RAF Hospital at Cosford. He died in 1976 aged 80.

Pembroke Dock born Reg Thomas was the only Welsh athlete at the **1928 Amsterdam and 1932 Los Angeles Olympic Games**, where he competed without distinction, finishing fourth in his heat of the 1,500m in Amsterdam, and dropping out of his 1,500m heat in Los Angeles as a result of an achilles tendon injury.

The Empire Games is the only major athletics gathering where Wales are able to send their own team, as distinct from being part of a British team, although Wales were not invited to send an athletics team to the **first Empire Games in Hamilton, Ontario in 1930**. This situation probably occurred because of the structure of Welsh athletics at the time whereby various English regions governed the sport in Wales, and as a result, the mile winner, Reg Thomas ran for England. He nearly made it a double, but had to settle for second in the 880 yds, behind England teammate Tommy Hampson, who was destined to win the same event at the forthcoming Los Angeles Olympics. Outside the athletics fraternity, the exploits of Thomas are little known in Wales, but as will be seen from the following tribute, he deserves to be recognised as one of the all-time greats of Welsh athletics.

Pen Portrait – Reg Thomas (Royal Air Force) 1907-1946

Reg Thomas is probably the least known of all Welsh athletics stars because he was regarded by many as being English!

Born in Pembroke Dock on 11th January 1907, he joined the RAF as an apprentice following the completion of his education at Coronation School, and went on to win the mile for England in the inaugural Empire (now Commonwealth) Games in Hamilton, Ontario in 1930. He also took the silver in the half mile. As a result of this his peers regarded him as an Englishman. But he never forgot his roots and returned to compete in Wales at every opportunity, winning a total of eight Welsh titles between 1929 and 1936: His Welsh championships wins are as follows:

1929	**½ mile**	**1:58.6**	**Cardiff Arms Park (Rugby Gd)**
	Mile	**4:27.0**	**Cardiff Arms Park (Rugby Gd)**
1930	**½ mile**	**2:00.0**	**Pontypool (Polo Grounds)**
	Mile	**4:26.0**	**Pontypool (Polo Grounds)**
1931	**½ mile**	**2:01.6**	**Pontypool Park**
	Mile	**4:31.8**	**Pontypool Park**
1933	**Mile**	**4:17.2**	**Abercarn**
1936	**Mile**	**4:21.4**	**Newport (Rodney Parade)**

Whilst he was selected for Wales in the 3 miles for the 1934 Empire Games miles he never actually ran because England complained and apparently refused permission for him run for Wales. Current Hon. Secretary of the Commonwealth Games Council for Wales, Myrddin John MBE says that Wales protested to the Empire Games Federation, but the outcome is not known.

By permission of Ian Buchanan

Reg Thomas

He ran in two Olympic Games - the 1928 Amsterdam Games, and in 1932 in Los Angeles. He went into the Amsterdam Games as runner-up in the AAA mile, but could do no better than 4th in his heat of the 1,500m. He won the AAA mile in 1930, 1931 and 1933, and, given he was the reigning Empire Champion (4:14.0) went into the Los Angeles Games as one of the favourites for the 1,500m. However, he ran suffering from an achilles tendon injury and was limping early in his heat and was forced to drop out. In fact his career was plagued with achilles tendon problems, and this had an effect on his performances and injury prevented him from competing in the 1936 Berlin Olympics.

When he returned home to Pembroke Dock a few months after winning the 1930 AAA mile in the second fastest time recorded in the Championships (4:15.2), he was given a civic welcome in a ceremony presided over by the Mayor of

Pembroke Dock, Major J.L. Adams at his old school. In this race, he defeated the eventual gold and silver medallists in Los Angeles, Luigi Beccali (Italy) and Jerry Cornes (Achilles), the AAA title winner in 1932, providing further evidence that if fully fit in Los Angeles, he would have been challenging for the gold.

Probably his finest race came in the British Games held on Chelsea FC's ground at Stamford Bridge – the main British athletics venue at the time – on 25th May 1931. Reputedly, 50,000 people had crowded into the ground, probably to see the flying Finn, Paavo Nurmi, winner of nine Olympic titles, and the current world record holder for the mile with 4:10.4, run in an invitation 4 miles in which he disappointed in finishing only fourth.

However, Thomas, ran the race of his life in the mile to clip 4 tenths off Albert Hill's British record which had stood for ten years with a new record of 4:13.4. His run was all the more remarkable as the grass track was wet after weekend rain and he had little opposition in the closing stages. He went straight into the lead at the gun passing 440 yds in 61.2, and the half-mile in 2:04 finishing over 200 yards clear. Hill, the 1920 Olympic 1,500m Champion, who was spectating, was one of the first to congratulate him. Many people at the time felt that if the conditions had have been more favourable, and with better opposition, he would have come close to Nurmi's world record.

Although his best mile time was that 4:13.4 at Stamford Bridge, official Welsh records at the time had to be set in Wales, and his win on July 22nd in the 1933 Welsh Championships on the Welfare Ground in Abercarn in 4:17.2, was classed in the Principality as the official Welsh record at the time. However, statisticians regard his Stamford Bridge run as a Welsh record and this stood as a Welsh best until beaten by his arch rival, Jim Alford of Roath Harriers when winning the 1938 Sydney Empire Games Mile in 4:11.5.

Thomas never ran against Alford in a Welsh championship, but they ran against each other off scratch in a mile handicap at Taff Vale Park, Pontypridd in 1937, with Alford winning in a time classed as an official Welsh record of 4:17.1, clipping just a tenth off Thomas's Abercarn best. His best times in other events were: 800m: 1:53.6 in 1929 and 1937; 1,500: 3:53.5 in 1937; 2miles 9:26.6 in 1931 and 3 miles: 14:53.4 when winning the Southern Championships in Portsmouth in 1935.

He competed for the RAF for most of his career and in all won eleven RAF titles including the mile title a record eight times between 1927 and 1937, setting Welsh records in 1927 (4:27.8) and 4:20.2 (1928). He is also one of the very few Welsh athletes to have set a world record, being part of the British 4 x 1,500m team which clocked 15:55.6 in winning against Germany in Cologne on 30th August 1931. Altogether he ran 14 times for Great Britain, winning three individual events (800m against France in Paris 1929 in his best 800m time of 1:53.6; and the mile against France (4:20.4) and Germany (4:17.8) in 1933. He was also part of winning British relay teams on a further four occasions. He captained the British team in 1933. Due to his service commitments abroad, he missed many opportunities to improve on his times, although he returned as often as possible to run in the RAF Championships. He was stationed in Egypt from 1934 until 1937, but on his return he finished fifth in the AAA mile in 1937.

He was determined to win a Welsh international vest, and this he did when he ran for Wales in the 1939 international cross country championship, held coincidentally on Ely Racecourse Cardiff when he finished a lowly 44th. He secured his place in the Welsh team by finishing 6th in the Welsh championships of that year held on Caerleon Racecourse in a race won by fellow RAF serviceman, Dillan Hier.

As with many athletes at the time, the Second World War put paid to his

competitive activity and tragically, after the war had ended, the Lancaster bomber he was piloting crashed into a Roman Catholic Nursing Home on the outskirts of Brownshill village, near Stroud on 14th March 1946. He was just 39. An inquest heard that it was only the supreme efforts of Squadron Leader Thomas saved the Lancaster from devastating the village. He was a hero to the end.

After being snubbed in 1930, unlike Welsh swimmers, who did attend as a Welsh team, an invitation was forthcoming for the next Empire Games in 1934. The Empire Games Council for Wales were formed in 1933 in order to organise Welsh participation in the **White City Empire Games**, with eleven Welsh athletes taking part, but no medals were won. The best performances came from Newport Harrier Wilf Short who finished sixth in the marathon with 3:02:56 and the Welsh standard bearer Arthur "Tiny" Lewis (Exeter) who finished seventh in the shot with 11.70m. Future mile champion Jim Alford, then just 20 and a university student in Cardiff, didn't progress any further than the heats of the half mile. The other Welsh competitors were: Cyril Cupid (Swansea Valley AC) 100 and 220 yds; Ken Harris of Roath Harriers, who won his mile heat, Cyril Williams (Newport AC) 220 yds, Peter Fraser (Newport AC) 440 yds, Len Tongue (Newport H), 10th in the 3 miles;

By permission of Bob Phillips

The final of the 1934 Empire Games mile at the White City. In the middle of the picture is Ken Harris (7). Alongside him wearing No. 10 is Sydney Wooderson of England the silver medalist, while the winner Jack Lovelock of New Zealand is No. 11. Two years later Lovelock won the Olympic Games 1500 in a new world record time. Both Lovelock (1933) and Wooderson (1937) also set world mile records.

Stan Macey (Newport AC) 120 yds hurdles, Frank Whitcutt (Newport AC) high jump and Gwynne Evans (Newport AC) triple jump. It is interesting to note that the team left Cardiff by the 3.15 pm train, the day before the opening ceremony, and the heats and final of the 100 yds! The team were housed in the Hotel York, Bernier St, Oxford Circus.

There were no Welsh athletes at the **1936 Olympic Berlin Games**, famous for the outstanding performances of Jesse Owens of the USA, and the antics of Hitler, but the **third Empire Games** held on the Sydney Cricket Ground in February 1938, saw Jim Alford, as the only Welsh athlete in the team, become the second Welshman to win Empire Games gold.

Pen Portrait – Jim Alford (Roath Harriers)

There is no doubt that Jim Alford is one of the finest athletes produced by Wales. Born in Cardiff on 15th October 1913, and winner of the mile in the 1938 Sydney Empire Games in a Games (and Welsh) record of 4:11.5, he won eleven Welsh track titles ranging from 440 yds through to 3 miles, represented Great Britain on five occasions and won the 800m and 1,500m at the World University Games (the forerunner of the World Student Games) in Paris in 1937 - the latter in a lifetime best. He also finished seventh in the 1938 Paris European Championships 1,500m. In one of his rare excursions over the country he finished 40th in the 1948 International Cross Country Championship in Reading, after winning the Welsh title at Cwmbran on March 6th, although he thought he had done enough to be selected after finishing 6th in 1935, but the selectors didn't think he was experienced enough to run!

His competitive career, remarkable for its longevity, ended in 1948 with his final Welsh title when he won the mile at Port Talbot in June ahead of a "youngster from north Wales" - as Jim put it. That 19 year-old youngster turned out to be another all-time great of Welsh athletics - John Disley.

Jim's Welsh track championships wins are as follows:

1934	**½ mile**	**1:57.0**	**Rodney Parade, Newport**
1935	**½ mile**	**1:58.0**	**Rodney Parade, Newport**
	Mile	**4:27.4**	**Rodney Parade, Newport**
1936	**½ mile**	**1:56.4**	**Rodney Parade, Newport**
1937	**½ mile**	**1:57.4**	**Crymlyn Burrows, Swansea**
1938	**½ mile**	**1:58.0**	**Taff Vale Park, Pontypridd**
	Mile	**4:23.0**	**Taff Vale Park, Pontypridd**
1946	**440 yds**	**54.0**	**GKN Ground, Cardiff**
	½ mile	**2:03.4**	**GKN Ground, Cardiff**
1947	**3 miles**	**16:15.0**	**Pontypool Park, Pontypool**
1948	**Mile**	**4:33.0**	**Talbot Athletic Ground, Aberavon**

His mile win on the grass track of Sydney Cricket Ground on 12th February 1938 was undoubtedly his finest performance - but he went into the Games as the favourite for the 880 yds. As Jim told David Thurlow in *Track Stats*, the quarterly historical and statistical publication of the National Union of Track Statisticians: "I was so certain to win the 880 yds that one of the judges came up to me at the start, shook me by the hand and said, "You've got it!" However, Jim was not at his best, due to the humid conditions and a sleepless night in a tiny cubicle on the Agricultural Showground, just yards away from where a speedway meeting was being held. Despite clocking a personal best of 1:53.0e in his heat, he slumped to fourth in the final after lying second at the bell. Pat Boot of New Zealand won clocking 1:51.2 secs.

In the mile, it was a completely different story. Jim was leading with a lap to go in 3:10.6, but the Australian Gerald Backhouse and Boot came past. Jim says: " I remember thinking that if I relaxed and stuck to them at least I would get some sort of a medal this time". Jim hung on and as Backhouse went to pass Boot on the last bend, he passed both to take the lead and went on to win in 4:11.5 after a sizzling

Jim Alford (140) about to take the lead from Pat Boot of New Zealand (124) and Gerald Backhouse (Australia – 1) en route to his 1938 mile gold medal at the Empire Games on the grass of Sydney Cricket Grounds.

last lap of 61 secs. His winning time was an improvement of 5.6 secs over his previous best of 4:17.1 set when beating the 1930 Empire champion, and fellow Welshman Reg Thomas at Taff Vale Park, Pontypridd the previous year. Jim's winning time also beat Thomas' Welsh record of 4:13.4 set when clocking a British record in 1931. Backhouse finished second in 4:12.2 with Boot a further 0.4secs back in third to win his second medal of the Games. Jim's time was an Empire Games record, beating 1936 Olympic Champion Jack Lovelock's winning time of 4:12.8 set in London in 1934. Afterwards Jim said that he could hear the spectators on "The Hill" shouting loudly for their man (Backhouse). "I could feel the hairs standing out of the back of my neck with nervousness. It was the first time I had experienced anything like it," he told Thurlow.

As cash was so short in those days, Jim went to Sydney as the only Welsh athletics competitor and was the "chief cook and bottle washer" of the overall Welsh team, as captain and manager. In his formal report to the Empire Games Council for Wales on his return, he lauded the performance of the six strong team from boxing, cycling and swimming (two gold and a silver) but complained that whilst the team had the "most striking uniform on parade, but on the track, in the swimming pool and in the ring it was a different matter" Apparently, Wales were the only team not to be provided with a distinctive track suit or with team badges! This situation no doubt stemmed from the fact that the Central Council of Physical Recreation had given Wales just £200 to send the whole team - although this amount was bolstered by an appeal, which raised much needed additional sums, and a small grant of £240 from the Australian organisers. Another indication of the cash shortage at the time was that Jim remembers Cyril Howell, soon to become one of the architects of the formation of the Welsh AAA in 1948, loaning him £20 for pocket money for the trip, although the South Wales & Mon AAA covered all other costs for Jim.

Dennis Reardon was also a gold medal winner for Wales in those 1938 Games taking the middleweight title in boxing. Some time after the Games, Reardon was in conversation with Col Harry Llewellyn, who won a show jumping gold medal in the 1952 Helsinki Olympics. On seeing the gold medal in a case behind the bar of the pub Reardon was running in Rhoose, Harry reminded Dennis that he had won the gold in 1952. Dennis's retort was: "Yes, but you had a bloody horse to help you!" So with someone of Dennis Reardon's sense of humour in the team, the long sea trip out to Australia via Gibraltar, Rome,

Jim Alford breaking the tape to take the Empire Games mile gold medal at Sydney in 1938.

Bombay and Calcutta was obviously a pleasant, if tiring occasion. Although, along with members of the English and Scottish teams who also travelled on the ship, Jim trained for at least an hour a day, but he still put on half -a- stone in weight. Altogether, the athletes were away for four months, of which three were taken up on the sea voyage.

After his Sydney victory, Jim went into the first European championships in Paris as one of the favourites for the 1,500m, but could only finish 7th in 4:03.0.

Surprisingly, his only race against the 1930 Empire Mile Champion Reg Thomas was in a special handicap race on 21st August 1937 during the Glamorgan v Monmouth inter-county meeting at Taff Vale Park, Pontypridd. It was billed as an attempt on the Welsh record by Thomas, who was 6 ½ years older than Jim. Welsh records at the time had to be set in Wales, but Reg had a best at the time of 4:13.4 set in 1934, the current British record. It turned out to be one of the finest mile races seen in Wales up to then. Over 60 years later, Jim remembers the race well: "Originally, I was to have a 20 yards start, but I was running well at the time and was having none of it. I said that unless I started off scratch with Reg, I would not run. The officials relented and we lined up together. Reg led me from the gun (others with starts were ahead) on the 400 yds grass track, but I took over on the second lap, however Reg was leading at the bell. At this point I felt quite strong and went into the lead and went further and further away to win by about 5 secs. I think my last 440yds was in the region of 60 secs". Jim's time was a personal best of 4:17.1, which he was to slash by 5.6 secs to win the Empire title the following year, and was just one tenth better than the "Welsh record" set by Reg when winning the Welsh title in Abercarn in 1933. So the record attempt succeeded, but the wrong man won!

Like so many of his contemporaries, the Second World War cut short his competitive career. He served as a Squadron Leader pilot in the RAF, but still managed to run times of 4:17.0 for the mile in 1942, and 4:15.0 behind Sydney Wooderson in 1943. He ended his career with personal bests of 1:53.7e for 880 yds set in the heats of the 1938 Empire Games; 3:56.0 for 1,500m (World Student Games gold in 1937) and his 4:11.5 for the mile set when winning in Sydney. He also made five appearances in a British vest.

After the war, and having obtained degrees from Cardiff and Bristol Universities, he moved into coaching and became the first National Coach for Wales in 1948. The Welsh AAA minutes of 17th November 1948 in confirming his appointment said that clubs were to be circularised setting out the terms of his engagement and inviting applications for his services. He coached numerous Welsh international stars including Olympic and Commonwealth Games medallists Ken Jones, Ron Jones, and Nick Whitehead. He also coached the 1954 Empire Games 6 miles champion, Peter Driver of England, and Commonwealth medallists, Ann Farquhar - Kinch (1970 javelin silver) and Gowrie Retchakan (400m hurdles silver in 1998). 1956 Olympic 1,500m champion, Ron Delany was also advised by Jim, who remarked in 1954: "Because of lack of facilities, his training was almost entirely on a fartlek basis. He brought his 1954 800m time down from 1:58 to 1:50.6 on this principle".

Liz Johns (nee Parsons), the first Welsh female sprinter to be successful on the British stage was also coached by Jim, as were numerous other Welsh stars, including in his early days, 1957 AAA decathlon champion, Hywel Williams. Jim was the Welsh coach at the 1958 Cardiff Empire Games and shortly afterwards he was appointed coach to Rhodesia and Nyasaland. He returned to Britain in 1962 and continued as a schoolteacher until his retirement, also undertaking special coaching assignments throughout the world as a member of the IAAF Development Commission. He is the author of numerous coaching books including the landmark AAA instructional booklet on Middle Distance Running and Steeplechase (1951)

and further AAA/BAAB booklets on Sprinting and Relay Racing (1953 and 1959). He is still active as a coach at the age of 87 in 2000, and when this writer last spoke to him early in that year he was as lucid as ever. He is one of the legends of Welsh athletics.

The **second European Championships were staged in Paris,** also in 1938, (Britain did not compete in the 1934 inaugural Games) and the British team contained three Welshmen - Jim Alford (1,500m), Hubert "Harry" Stubbs (High jump) and Kenneth Jenkins (200m). Alford failed to reproduce his Sydney form, with Sydney Wooderson taking the title. Jim was back in seventh. Harry Stubbs was the finest exponent of the high jump Wales had seen at the time. He took the Welsh title three times (1937/38/39) and his best leap of 1.90m set in 1938 and 1939 remained a Welsh record until beaten by John Lister of Birchgrove Harriers in 1961. Stubbs performed creditably in Paris, finishing equal sixth with 1.85m. Altogether he competed three times for Great Britain and was runner-up in the 1939 AAA event, and third in 1938.

Kenneth Jenkins, born in Carmarthen on June 15th 1915, a product of St. David's College Lampeter, also finished 6th in Paris, where in winning his semi final he equalled David Jacobs' 26 year old Welsh record of 21.9 secs. This time stood until beaten by Ken Jones in Oslo in 1949 with 21.7. Writing in the Handbook of the Carmarthenshire Schools AAA in 1946/47 he recalls an incident at the Colombes Stadium where the European Championships were being held which indicates the conditions under which athletes competed in those days: "Alan Pennington (his teammate) and I found ourselves at the start of the final without a trowel to dig our holes. The Dutch Champion, Osendarp, seeing our plight, handed us his trowel, and insisted that our holes should be dug before starting on his own". In those days, athletes did not have the benefit of all-weather tracks and starting blocks, and, had to "dig-in" – literally before each sprint event! One wonders what times Jenkins and his contemporaries would have been clocking with present day facilities. Jenkins won the 1938 and 1939 Welsh 220 yds titles at Pontypridd and Newport respectively, and took the bronze medals for both sprint events at the 1939 World Student Games. He was third in the 1938 AAA 220 yds and his best 220 yds time was a windy 21.7 set when winning for Oxford against the AAA at Oxford on 26th May 1938. The Second World War undoubtedly restricted his progess, where he served in the RAFVR having being ordained a Priest in 1939 after two years at Jesus College, Oxford. He was a Chaplain in Quatar 1952-57; Chaplain at the Royal Masonic School Bushey 1957-59 and at St. Peters College School, Adelaide from 1959-62.

Kenneth Jenkins of Oxford University (right) handing over the baton to Alan Reddington in the Oxford v. Cambridge match in 1937.

The first major Games after the Second World War were the **1946 European Championships** in Oslo, where Wales' only representative was Horace Oliver of Reading who failed to finish in the

Tom Richards in the closing stages of the 1948 Olympic marathon in his daps.

marathon. At the next **European gathering in 1950 in Brussels,** John Disley gave a glimpse of what was to come with 13th in the 3,000m steeplechase.

The **1948 Olympics** held so successfully in London so soon after the end of the Second World War, brought Wales two silver medals at Wembley, in Games brought alive by the outstanding performances of Dutch housewife Fanny Blankers - Koen, who won four golds. Welsh medals were another relay medal and Wales' first individual Olympic medal. This came from the 38 year old former Pontnewydd Harrier, Tom Richards, in the marathon, who finished just 16 secs behind the winner, Argentina's Delfo Cabrera - the nearest any Briton had come at the time to winning the Olympic marathon. Tom entered Wembley Stadium in third place to great cheers from the Wembley crowd and running strongly he soon overtook long time leader Etienne Gailly of Belgium, but failed to catch Cabrera. After the race Tom said that he was quite annoyed approaching Wembley, because some of the spectators thought that he was Jack Holden, his teammate and one of the pre-race favourites. They were shouting, "come on Jack, come on Holden," he said. Holden had dropped out earlier in the race, however. It is interesting to note from contemporary photographs of the race, that Tom was wearing daps (plimsolls) - how times have changed!

Pen Portrait – Tom Richards
(Pontnewydd H, Mitcham AC and SLH) 1910-1984

Without a doubt, Upper Cwmbran born Tom Richards was one of the most unassuming of all the great Welsh athletics stars. He was just as happy representing his club, as he was representing his country.

Along with the likes of many Welsh distance stars he left south Wales in 1936 because of the need to find work, and like a number of his contemporaries found employment at Tooting Bec Hospital, in South London. His first London club was Mitcham AC, but due to their inactivity during the Second World War, he joined South London Harriers and remained with them until his death in 1984 aged 74.

Although his Olympic marathon silver medal in 1948 is the event with which he is most remembered by the general public, he was a prolific winner of road running and cross country honours during his remarkable career, and was still running competitively in 1972 at the age of 62! In fact most of his best performances came as a veteran, and he ran his fastest marathon of 2:39:59 at the age of 44 in the 1954 Polytechnic event, and won his only Welsh cross country title at the age of 41 - an age when most of us nowadays are happy to sit in front of the television.

One of his earliest records of success came in walking events in Monmouthshire. But he soon graduated to cross country running and after finishing third in the Welsh junior championships (junior in those days referred to ability, rather than age) at Caerleon in 1934, he won the first of his ten Welsh international vests later

1948 Olympic silver medalist Tom Richards (second left) returns to his Cwmbran roots in 1981. In this picture at Cwmbran Stadium he is flanked by Ann Hill and stadium manager and Welsh rugby international Geoff Whitson. Also in the picture are two former Welsh marathon record holders Bernie Plain (third right) and Mike Rowland (first right). Second right is Gwynne Griffiths, three times winner of the Welsh 400 title.

that year in the international race in Scotland, after finishing ninth in his first Welsh senior championship, again at Caerleon. His Welsh cross country title came in 1951 at Caerleon, when he beat John Edwards of Carmarthen YMCA by 24 secs and his last Welsh vest came two years later in Paris after finishing eighth in that year's championship in Grangetown, Cardiff in a race won by Norman Wilson of the RAF. Altogether, he placed in the first ten of the Welsh cross country championships on eleven occasions, including third in 1935 in a race won by three times winner Harry Gallivan (Cwmbran Harriers) at Llantarnam.

But it was as a road runner that he really excelled, as evidenced by his Olympic silver in 1948 and his wins in most the English classic events. He never won a AAA title however, due mainly to the presence of all-time greats, Jack Holden and Jim Peters, but finished second on four occasions (1947/48/49 and 51) and also third in 1946. His first Welsh marathon title came at Margam in 1950, and he won this event on a further four occasions. A selection of his other road wins were: eight wins in the Finchley "20" between 1941 and 1949; twice winner of the Polytechnic marathon in 1944 and 1945, plus countless other marathon and ultra distance events, including the 1955 London to Brighton race in a record 5:27:24 and the Isle of Man 37½ mile event for three successive years between 1955 and 1957. He was fifth in the 1950 Empire Games marathon in Auckland, New Zealand, where the race went to England's Jack Holden who had dropped out of the 1948 Olympic race. After his fifth successive win in the Finchley "20" in 1945, *The Western Mail* wrote: ".....the Pontnewynydd man has perfected a technique of gliding over the ground with almost effortless ease, and, as a result, dominates distance running wherever he competes".

Due to the esteem in which his fellow road runners held him, he was elected president of the Road Runners Club in 1962-1964, and president of his club, South London Harriers in 1974-1977. In 1955 the Welsh AAA awarded him their Meritorious Plaque for services to Welsh athletics and as D.J.P. Richards said in 1956: "Without doubt, he is the most accomplished distance road runner produced by Wales". It took another 30 years before Steve Jones took this mantle, by setting his world marathon record in Chicago.

The 1948 Olympic relay medal came from one of Wales' all-time great sportsmen, Blaenavon born, 44 times capped rugby wing, Ken Jones of Newport, who also reached the semi-finals of the 100m. Ken and his teammates had actually been presented with the gold medals after the USA squad were disqualified and held them for three days. But on appeal, the Americans were re-instated, so Ken had to be content with the silver.

Pen Portrait – Ken Jones (Newport AC)

© Western Mail

Ken Jones was one of the greatest wings in world rugby. Here he returns to the scene of many of his tries, St. Helen's, Swansea to demonstrate his sprinting prowess and leave the opposition trailing in his wake.

Wales has something of a reputation for producing fine sprinters; think of the stars of yesteryear Lynn Davies, Ron and Berwyn Jones and Nick Whitehead. But one of the best ever was undoubtedly Ken Jones of Newport AC. Just after the Second World War, Ken was not only Wales' outstanding sprinter but also one of the best in the UK. In a career extending from 1946 to 1955 he collected silver medals at the Olympic Games and European Championships as well as a bronze at the Commonwealth Games.

An exceptionally gifted sportsman, Ken's exploits on the rugby field are legendary. He won 44 caps for Wales as a wing three-quarter which made him the most capped Welsh player of all time, a record which stood until beaten by the redoubtable Gareth Edwards (himself no mean athlete) in 1975. Ken also toured New Zealand and Australia with the British Lions, playing in three of the four tests, and is the only man who can claim to be an Olympian and a British Lion.

He first realised that he could be an international sprinter when he won the All-India 100m title in 1946. During his tour of duty there he clocked 10.7, but his first major honour was selection for the 100m and 4x100m relay in the 1948 Olympic Games at Wembley. Against the best in the world he reached the semi-finals of the 100 before being eliminated, recording a personal best and Welsh record of 10.6 in his heat. The relay provided an element of drama as the USA were disqualified for

a faulty changeover after winning the race easily from Great Britain for whom Ken ran the anchor leg. The British team were declared the winners but the Jury of Appeal reversed the Referee's decision and the Americans were re-instated, leaving Ken and his teammates with the silver medals.

Another outstanding season followed in 1949. He was 3rd over 220 yds at the AAA Championships in July behind McDonald Bailey (21.7) and Les Laing with whom he shared a time of 22.2. Bailey later was to take the 1952 100m Olympic bronze and Laing a relay gold medal for Jamaica in those same Helsinki Olympics. Ken was then selected for the Great Britain team to face France at the White City in August. In the 220 yds he was second to McDonald Bailey but ahead of Etienne Bally, European 100m Champion of the following year. Ken also ran the second leg in the medley relay which Britain won easily. Later that month in a match between Wales, the South and the Midlands, Ken won the 100 yds in 9.8 equalling the "English" Native Record for the third time in his career and beating Les Laing by a yard. In October he competed in an international meeting in Oslo and was second in both sprints (10.8 /21.7) behind Andy Stanfield (USA) destined to become Olympic 200m champion in 1952. At the end of 1949 Ken ranked third at 100 yds in Britain with only McDonald Bailey and Les Laing ahead of him. At 220 yds he ranked 7th with 21.9.

The year 1950 presented Ken with something of a dilemma. This was the year of the European Championships and the Commonwealth Games, but also the year in which the British Lions were due to tour New Zealand and Australia. So Ken was confronted with the sort of choice which need be made only by those with too much talent. He chose rugby and events were to prove he made the right decision as four years later he competed with distinction in both the championships but the chance to tour with the Lions was not to come his way again. He had a successful tour in 1950 and further enhanced his reputation as one of the world's outstanding rugby players. Meanwhile, because of the distance involved, Wales sent only one athlete to the 1950 Commonwealth Games at Auckland - Tom Richards. One can only speculate as to what Ken might have achieved as a sprinter in 1950, but, for the record, the Commonwealth 100 yds was won in 9.7 with second and third recording 9.8, while at the European Championships the first three in the 100m all recorded 10.7 and the 200 was won by Ken's great rival Brian Shenton. Ken's best performances at the time were 9.8 (100 yds) and 10.6 (100 m).

Ken's sprinting lost a little of its edge in 1951 and it was not until late in 1952 that he began to return to something like his best form with some fine sprinting in Wales' match against the Western Counties when he won the 100/220 yds double in 10.3 and 22.3. Unfortunately it was too late in the season for that year's Olympic Games. At the age of 31, and with an impressive record to his credit, it might have seemed that Ken's best days were behind him. However, in 1953 he came back to the international scene winning a place in the British team for the matches against France, Germany and Sweden.

His final season of top level athletics was 1954, appropriately enough the year of the Commonwealth Games and European Championships which he had sacrificed in 1950. He got a good start to the season running 2nd over 200m to Jim Golliday (USA) at an international meeting in Cologne in May, and in the 1954 Vancouver Commonwealth Games, he finished second in his heat of the 100 yds (10.0) and 3rd in his semi final (9.8) to become the only British sprinter in the final where he was 6th (won by Mike Agostini in 9.6), again clocking 9.8. Three days later he began his quest for honours in the 220 yds, winning his heat in 22.4, followed by second place in his semi final (22.1) to reach his second final of the Games. On 5th August he lined up with the best sprinters in the Commonwealth and earned himself a bronze

medal, finishing behind Don Jowett (NZ) and Brian Shenton (England) in 21.9, which at the time was only the fourth Commonwealth Games medal Wales had ever won - 440 yds hurdler Bob Shaw had won his bronze just two days earlier.

Three weeks later Ken was in Berne running for Great Britain in the European Championships. A solid second in his 100m heat (10.9) put him into the semi finals. Here, however, he appeared to misjudge the finish and dipped too soon when second place seemed assured. He lost his balance slightly and took fourth place in 10.7 only a tenth outside his personal best set in the 1948 Olympics. In those days of six lane tracks only three progressed to the final so Ken was left out. There was still the relay to come, though, and the British team of Ken Box, Ken Jones, George Ellis and Brian Shenton came home a good second to win a set of silver medals and climax an outstanding season for Ken. In Berne, he became the second Welshmen to captain a British team in one of the major athletics gatherings after David Jacobs (1912 Olympics). Subsequently Ron Jones (1968 Olympics) and Lynn Davies (1972 Olympics) were also to achieve the distinction. These were the last major championships that Ken took part in, and his relay medal meant that he became the first Welsh athlete to win a medal at all three major championships. It was early in that same year that he equalled the record number of Welsh rugby caps held by Dickie Owen since 1912, and it was a fitting accolade to a great sportsman that he became the inaugural winner of *The Western Mail* "Welsh Sports Personality of the Year" award.

He was still a good enough sprinter in 1955 to retain his Welsh 220 yds title and finish second in the 100 yds (his only defeat in the Welsh championships). He had won both those events every year from 1946 to 1954 except 1950 when, of course, he was in New Zealand with the Lions, and also had one win in the long jump. He continued his rugby career for a few more years and played his last match for Wales in 1957 at the age of 35. His final sporting honour came in 1960 when he was awarded the OBE in recognition of his services to sport.

The Empire Games of 1950 went to Auckland, New Zealand, but severe financial problems meant that Tom Richards, now aged 39, was the only Welsh athlete taking part. The long sea journey through the Panama Canal apparently took its toll and Tom finished fifth in the marathon behind his great rival Jack Holden of England. This is one of only two occasions - the 1934 Games at White City was the other - when Wales has not won a medal of any description at an Empire or Commonwealth Games.

Another Welsh individual Olympic medal came in the **1952 Stockholm Games**, made famous by the incomparable treble win by Emil Zatopek of Czechoslovakia in the 5,000m, 10,000m and marathon. The Welsh medal - at the time only the second individual Olympic medal to be won by a Welsh athlete - came from north Walian John Disley, the only Welsh athlete to make the British team, who took the bronze after twice breaking the UK record. His time of 8:51.8 was almost 20 seconds faster than his pre-championships best and stood as a UK (and Welsh) best until he lowered it to 8:44.2 in 1955. Disley also ran in Melbourne four years later, but could only manage sixth in 8:44.6, in a race won by his great friend, Chris Brasher, who beat Disley's UK record with 8:41.2.

The prospect of Wales hosting the Empire Games was mooted as early as 1938 - but for the 1946 Games. Sir Robert Webber, had made the suggestion, and the South Wales and Mon Committee of the AAA fully supported the proposal and pledged themselves to do all in their power to further any efforts to secure the event for Wales. Little did they know in the January of 1939 that in eight months time, the Second World War would be upon them, and this put paid to any further Welsh lobbying for the time being. It was during the **1954 Games in Vancouver** that Wales heard that it had been awarded the Games for 1958 – the first "small" country and non-Dominion to hold the event. The Vancouver Games – now renamed the Empire and Commonwealth Games - saw the first Welsh Empire medals since Jim Alford's mile win in 1938. Bronze medals came from former Cardiff schoolboy, Bob Shaw, who also took part in the 1956 Olympic Games, and Ken Jones. Shaw, a very versatile athlete, who won the AAA junior discus title in 1951, was a major revelation as he stormed to third place in the 440 yds hurdles in 53.3. Shaw brought Welsh respectability to his event, and his personal best for 400m hurdles set in 1956 of 51.7 was one of the leading marks in the world that year. It stood as a Welsh record for 13 years. Shaw first appeared in the 1951 Welsh championships, taking the 120 yds hurdles in 16.4, and took three further titles at the distance; as well as the 440 yds hurdles titles in 1954 and 1955, the latter in a championships best which stood for 15 years until beaten by John Lewis in 1970. For good measure he also took the discus bronze medals in the 1951 and 1952 championships. His other major win, which underlined his status as Britain's number one, came in the 1955 AAA 440 yds hurdles, which he won in 52.2 to become the first Welshman to win this event. It would take another 33 years for another Welsh athlete to take the AAA intermediate hurdles title, when Derby's Phil Harries set a new Welsh record to win in 1988 with 50.01. Shaw also finished fifth in the 400m hurdles at the 1954 European Championships in Berne, with 52.3. Wales had six competitors in the Vancouver Games, the largest representation since the 1934 White City Games. Apart from Shaw, Disley and Ken Jones; Peter Phillips (440 and 880), Clive Roberts (javelin) and 24-year-old Llanharan born Hywel Williams, were in the team.

Bob Shaw prolific Welsh intermediate hurdles record breaker.

Pen Portrait – Hywel Williams (Roath Harriers, RAF and Cardiff AAC)

Hywel Williams first appeared on the Welsh scene in 1947 when he won the first of his eighteen Glamorgan titles as a 17 year old and was still competing in Cardiff's British league team a quarter of a century later!

He competed in both the 1954 and 1958 Empire Games as a discus thrower. But he almost didn't make it in 1954 and it is only now almost 50 years later that the full story can be told. Although originally selected, he was dropped in favour of 440 yds hurdler Robert Shaw, the eventual bronze medallist, who had started to produce his fine performances after the original team had been announced. Hywel picks up the story: "I received my de-selection notice by telegram on the day I was about to leave Kenya where I was serving with the RAF. I was having none of it and came home anyway, and due to the lobbying of team manager Ted Hopkins with Welsh Empire Games selectors, I was added to the team". "Anyway", continues Hywel: "Friends and neighbours in my home village of Llanharan had contributed to a fund to send me to Vancouver, and I couldn't let them down as they were looking to me to fly the flag for the village". He eventually finished fifth with 45.18m, the highest position to date of a Welshman in this event, to better his own Welsh record set earlier in the year by 48 cms.

Hywel Williams receiving his championship plaque and trophy for winning the AAA decathlon in 1957 from Walter Jewell of the AAA. Hans Graf of Switzerland (left) was second, with the holder, Gerald Brown of Rhodesia (right) third.

He set his all-time discus best of 47.50, the following year whilst still serving with the RAF in Nairobi, which stood as the Welsh record until beaten by Archie Buttriss in 1963. He finished seventh in the discus in the 1958 Cardiff Games with 45.78 and describes his biggest disappointment in athletics as the absence of the decathlon in those 1958 Games, where by now he had become the AAA decathlon champion (1957) also finishing second in 1953 and 1959. Amongst his other achievements were thirteen Welsh titles in pole vault, shot, discus (seven wins and five seconds) and four decathlon titles, where he held the Welsh record for twelve years with 6259 pts on the 1962 scoring tables until beaten by his pupil, Clive Longe in 1964, and a Welsh pole vault record with 3.66m in 1952. He also won eighteen Glamorgan titles, winning five in 1953 alone, and two British vests in 1959. His incredible versatility is further indicated by his second place in the inaugural Welsh 440 yds hurdles championship in 1950.

As well as his ability as a performer, he was an excellent coach. In the early 1960s he started talking to a basketball player, one Clive Longe, who was stationed, like Hywel in RAF St. Athan. At that time Longe had never competed in an athletics event. Hywel takes up the story: "I could see immediately that he had the ideal build for a decathlete, and I eventually convinced him that he should start training for the event". He won the Welsh title in 1964 (with Hywel third) and in the same year broke his mentor's Welsh record with 6342 pts, before going on to win silver in the 1966 Jamaica Commonwealth Games and set sixteen Welsh and eight British decathlon records. Hywel coached many other athletes including the 1964 and 1966 AAA decathlon champion Derek Clarke. He also coached several Welsh stars including three times winner of the Welsh 400m hurdles title, Wyn Leyshon, John Walters, winner of twelve Welsh shot and discus titles, current Welsh team manager Delyth Davies (nee Prothero) who took three Welsh shot and discus titles, Steve Hughes (three Welsh high jump wins) and Gareth Brooks, the first Welsh athlete to better 70m for the javelin in Wales, who won six Welsh championships between 1974 and 1980. The British men's team manager in Sydney, Mike Delaney, winner of the 1973, 1974 and 1979 400m titles was also one to benefit from Hywel's coaching in his early days, along with countless other Welsh and RAF athletes. He didn't restrict his coaching activities to able bodied track and field however, as he coached Chris Hallam the Olympic paraplegian, and received the coach of the year award for

disabled athletes.

Although never a winner of a medal in one of the major championships, Hywel is one of the all-time greats of Welsh athletics – from a competitive and coaching perspective as well as from a longevity viewpoint. In 1972 at the age of 42 he was still competing in Cardiff's British League team, when as their captain he collected the league trophy in the first of their three successive league wins in 1972. Now in his 72nd year he is still coaching and a regular at the major athletics meetings events in Wales.

Swansea's Clive Roberts, coached by the future National Coach for the Midlands, Swansea schoolteacher, Lionel Pugh, finished eleventh in the javelin in Vancouver with 55.05, just over 2 metres short of the Welsh record he set whilst winning the Welsh title earlier in the year. Phillips went out in the heats of both the 440 and 880 yds.

The European Championships always fall in the same year as the Commonwealth Games and sometimes, as a result marathon runners in particular have to choose which Games to run in. Fortunately this has never been a major problem for Welsh athletes. In the **1954 European Championships** in Berne, as we have seen, Ken Jones won yet another sprint relay medal and John Disley (3,000m steeplechase) and Bob Shaw (400m hurdles) were the only other Welsh athletes in the British team.

The late John Merriman was the only Welsh medallist in the **1958 Cardiff Empire Games** with his classic 6 miles duel with Dave Power of Australia, where the Rhondda born athlete had to be content with the silver. The full story of the Cardiff Games is covered in the next chapter. **The 1958 European Championships in Stockholm,** held after the Cardiff Games, saw Merriman finish sixth in the 10,000m with 29:03.8, to set his fifth Welsh record in the event and a time which was intrinsically about 45 seconds faster than his Cardiff run of 28:48.84 for 6 miles. Merriman was the only Welsh athlete in the Stockholm team.

Welsh medallists and competitors in the major games from 1960 onwards became far more prevalent, although John Merriman in the **1960 Rome Olympics** could do no better than eighth in the 10,000m, but in a new UK (and Welsh) record of 28:52.89. The race was won by Pyotr Bolotnikov of the USSR, with Australia's Cardiff 1958 6 miles winner, Dave Power third. Nick Whitehead won the first of his two major relay medals as part of the British 4 x 100m team, which took bronze. The British team actually finished fourth, but were promoted to third when the USA squad were disqualified. Another member of that team was the individual bronze winner in the 100m, Peter Radford, the future Chairman of the British Athletic Federation, who has strong Welsh links, having studied at Cardiff College of Education (now UWIC), where he met his Barry born wife, Margaret. Averil Williams, who had taken the javelin bronze for England in the 1958 Empire Games, and who was to become one of the driving forces of women's athletics in Wales, failed to qualify for the javelin final.

The **Perth Commonwealth Games in 1962,** saw the first appearance in a major Games of Rhymney born Berwyn Jones, who teamed up with Nick Whitehead, Ron Jones, and Dave England to win the sprint relay bronze. And it could have been gold, as Nick took over on the last leg abreast with Dave Jones of England, but faded slightly to secure the bronze medals to win the first relay medal for Wales in a major championship. Another athlete making his first appearance in a major Games was the 19 year old Nantymoel youngster Lynn Davies, who narrowly missed the bronze medal after recording the only wind free jump of the final with his first UK record of 7.72m. Almost 40 years on he still holds the UK record with his 8.23 leap in Berne in 1968. On this occasion Merriman took the 6 miles bronze behind Canadian boy wonder Bruce Kidd, with Power, yet again in front of the Watford-based Welshman in second. Merriman made his marathon debut, but failed to finish in an event won by England's Brian Kilby, with Power, the 1958 winner securing his second silver. The Welsh team in Perth was nine strong, and apart from the two medallists, four athletes reached the final of their events - Lynn Davies, triple jump (11th), Tony Harris, who was destined to become the first Welsh athlete to dip under the magical 4 minutes for the mile (3:58.96 in 1965) who finished 6th in both the half and mile; prolific Welsh championships hammer winner and record beater (10 wins and nine records) Lawrie Hall who was 5th in his speciality with 54.41m and Jackie Barnett of Roath Harriers who finished 6th in the 880 yds after having run in the 220 yds in the Cardiff Games. Jackie, originally from Newport, who won four Welsh 880 yds titles between 1959 and 1962, brought a degree of respectability to this event bringing the Welsh record down from an uninspiring 2:34 in 1959 to 2:12.8 in 1962 (deduct 0.7 secs for a comparison with 800m times).

In the **1962 European Championships in Belgrade,** Berwyn Jones ran in both the 100m and the 4 x 100 relay and in the latter, he was part of the British team that took bronze. Ron

The end of the third leg of the sprint relay in the Great Britain v. Poland match at White City in 1962. Berwyn Jones (left) has handed over to Peter Radford.

Jones was also part of the team. Berwyn had his amateur athletics career cut short when he signed for rugby league club, Wakefield Trinity in 1964. There is no doubt that he would have continued to play an major role on the British sprinting scene for some time ahead had he not "gone north". He was part of the famous Anglo-Welsh sprint relay team dubbed the Jones Boys, which equalled the world record for 4 x 110 yds (40.0) in 1963. The other members being Peter Radford, Ron Jones and Dave Jones, although the latter was not Welsh, but Radford claimed honorary Welsh citizenship due to his Welsh connections! Nick Whitehead beat Berwyn to win the 1960 Welsh 100 yds title, but Berwyn won both the 100 and 220 in 1962 and the 100 the previous year, where he beat the late Dewi Bebb of rugby fame into second. In Belgrade Lynn Davies still finding his feet at this level of competition, was eleventh in the long jump.

The next major championships were the **1964 Tokyo Olympics,** where Lynn Davies achieved immortality. Ron Jones was the only other Welsh competitor where he was part of the British team that reached the final of the 4 x 100m relay that also contained Lynn.

Pen Portrait – Lynn Davies MBE (Cardiff CE and Cardiff AAC)

© Mark Shearman

Lynn Davies jumps to Olympic glory.

In Tokyo on 18 October 1964, the miner's son from Nantymoel, struck gold to become the first and still the only Welshman to win an individual Olympic gold medal. His win gave Britain her first field event gold since 1908 as he out-jumped the USSR's Igor Ter-Ovanesyan and America's world record holder Ralph Boston. And then on 30 June 1968 in Berne, a warm and sunny evening provided him with ideal conditions to set a new British record of 8.23, which still stands over thirty years later as the longest standing British (and Welsh) record in the book. This last fact in particular puts into perspective his outstanding talent. Of that jump in Berne, Lynn said at the time: "I knew it was a good one as soon as I came out of the pit; it was beyond my wildest dreams".

Lynn Davies' story is how a quiet, shy Welshman with tremendous competitive ability and enormous talent became one of the world's sporting greats. A dazzling teenage athlete, he might have well have become a professional footballer with Cardiff City had athletics not been his first love. As a 17 year-old, the strapping Ogmore Valley lad had played at inside right for Welsh League side Lewistown and soon caught the eye of a Cardiff City scout and signed amateur forms with the Ninian Park club. At Ogmore Grammar School though he had only one choice of winter game and that was rugby at which he was good enough to have four Welsh Secondary Schools trials. Being a natural all-round games player, he turned out at wing or centre for his school in the morning and played soccer in the afternoon.

His interest in athletics, as with so many others, was first aroused when, at 16 years of age, he was taken to see the 1958 Empire Games in Cardiff. "I still remember the exploits of sprinter Peter Radford, miler Herb Elliott and the then emerging Mary Bignal (Rand), who also collected a long jump gold in Tokyo", he recalls. "A few years later I was really enjoying my athletics and decided that my best bet would be to go back to college and study to become a physical education teacher. Anyway, I did not think there was any security in football at the time". How things have changed!

It was just three years before his Tokyo triumph that Lynn first hit headlines in Welsh track and field circles. The date was 24 June 1961 and the place Maindy Stadium, Cardiff. A pale, slim 19 year-old, self coached and without a club, caused a stir by winning the Welsh triple jump title with a Welsh record-shattering distance of 14.91. Later in the championships, his first at senior level, he was beaten by two cms by north Walian British international Bryan Woolley with a leap of 7.14. Lynn Davies, still a schoolboy, had arrived!

© Western Mail

Lynn Davies shows his wife Meriel his three gold medals.

The late Ron Pickering, former Welsh National Coach and BBC commentator, spotted Lynn's potential at those 1961 championships and took the raw athlete under his wing. He said at the time, "Lynn Davies has the ability to progress into a world class long jumper". How right he was! Lynn then joined Roath Harriers and Ron planned a tough three-year schedule for the Olympic Games. That schedule included appearances in the European Championships and Commonwealth Games in 1962 where he finished eleventh with 7.33 and fourth with 7.72 respectively.

World records never bothered Lynn. He was a gold medal chaser and his motto, "The Glory Is In Winning", carried him to worldwide acclaim. A unique hat-trick of gold medals, Olympic (1964), Commonwealth (1966 and 1970) and European (1966) long jump titles, made him the first athlete in history to hold all three at the same time.

His quest just for gold made him a few enemies and he was severely criticised for giving up on the silver and bronze medals in the 1968 Olympics at Mexico City. The long jump was one of the most keenly awaited events. For the first time, the "big four" clashed and lips were licked in anticipation at the prospect of defending champion Lynn (best of 8.23) up against the joint holders of the world record at 8.35, Ralph Boston (USA) and Igor Ter-Ovanesyan (USSR), and the world leader Bob Beamon (USA), whose best was 8.33.

Lynn proved prophetic in assessing Beamon's possibilities: "It only needs Beamon to hit the board once, and we can all go home". The rest is history as Lynn had a wretched time in the final. Completely demoralised the best of his three jumps of 7.94 placed him equal eighth and he should have been offered another three attempts, but the officials erred. By the time the mistake was acknowledged Lynn had no wish to continue in the competition. Beamon of course leaped 8.90, to transcend the 28' and 29' barriers in one go, and set a world record which was to stand for twenty three years until beaten by 5 cms by fellow countryman Mike Powell in the 1991 World Championships."The Leap" is still an inspiration to the sport in both Wales and Britain. His 43 UK senior international appearances included a remarkable tally of 28 victories in 100m, long jump and relay appearances. Also a hard act to follow is the 17 British and Commonwealth records he set in an international career spanning a decade from 1962 to 1972. During that time he jumped 8 metres or more in 22 competitions. Only nine other British athletes have legally exceeded that distance in thirty-two years! The closest challenge to his record was an 8.15 effort from Stewart Faulkner in 1990.

He was AAA champion five times and won the indoor title twice. His championship victories started in 1961 when he won the AAA junior triple jump title - he was only third in the long jump! He was also a fine sprinter, holding Welsh records for 100 yds (9.5 twice) and 220 yds (21.2). Despite never winning a Welsh sprint title (thanks to Ron Jones) he won four long jump titles and two triple jumps. He broke the Welsh record on ten occasions taking it from 7.36 in 1962 to the present-day 8.23.

On retiring from competition after the 1972 Olympics (where he was British captain), he first went to Canada as Technical Director and directed their teams at the 1974 Commonwealth and 1976 Olympics. On his return he became Britain's team manager. He later became a director of a sports equipment company, worked for BBC Wales TV as a sports presenter before returning to Cyncoed (UWIC) as a lecturer where he was a student 30 years earlier.

In 1964 and 1966 he was ranked the second best long jumper in the world; a fine accolade for a man who is, along with Colin Jackson, the finest athlete produced by Wales. If Sir Alf Ramsey had been involved in track and field he would have claimed that Lynn "The Leap" Davies was several decades ahead of his time. A thin, pale boy at Maindy Stadium in 1961 who said rather timidly at the time, "I spell my name with two n's" will remain the hero for all athletes in the Principality who aspire to reach for the very top in track and field athletics. There is a fitting postscript which underlines Lynn's unassuming nature. In an interview 10 years ago he recalled an embarrassing incident at the Sports Personality of the Year Awards which he had to

miss because of illness. He chuckles recalling the incident as the person announcing the awards said: "...and the runner-up is that great Welsh long jumper Lynn Davies. Unfortunately she can't be with us tonight because she has got the 'flu".

1966 saw the Commonwealth Games take place in Jamaica, with Wales taking two medals - Lynn Davies winning the first of his two Commonwealth long jump titles, and the vastly improved RAF St. Athan airman, Clive Longe, winning the decathlon silver just 14 points behind winner, Roy Williams of New Zealand, and setting his sixth Welsh and third UK record with 7123 pts in the bargain. Altogether, Wales sent a team of twelve to Jamaica and major disappointment came in the 4 x 110 yds relay, where a medal had been predicted for the Welsh squad of Terry Davies, Lynn, Keri Jones and Ron Jones, but they had to settle for fourth in a new Welsh record of 40.2, just 2 tenths behind Australia. Incredibly, this record stood for 32 years until beaten by the 4 x 100m team of Kevin Williams, Doug Turner, Christian Malcolm and Jamie Henthorn in the 1998 Kuala Lumpur Commonwealth Games, which clocked firstly 39.09 in the heats and then 38.73 in the final also to finish fourth. The women's 4 x 100m squad of Liz Parsons (Johns), Gloria Dourass, Liz Gill (Lewis) and Thelwyn Appleby (Bateman) also performed well finishing fifth in a new Welsh best of 46.2, which was to stand for 20 years until beaten by the bronze medal winning team in the 1986 Edinburgh Games with 45.37.

The **1966 European Championships** in Budapest saw Lynn Davies win the long jump with 7.98 and achieve an amazing grand slam of major titles – Olympic, Commonwealth and European. He was also part of the British team to finish fifth in the 4 x 100m relay that also contained Ron Jones. Clive Longe, despite finishing ninth in the decathlon, improved again his UK and Welsh record with 7160 pts. Altogether in his career, he set an incredible sixteen Welsh and eight UK records for the ten discipline event. Unfortunately on his return to Guyana, after he retired from competition, he took his own life in 1986 at the age of 47 after a successful career in his own country as a coach and politician.

Bob Beamon and the **1968 Mexico City Olympics** will probably haunt Lynn Davies for the rest of his life as Beamon shattered the world long jump record in the first round with his amazing leap of 8.90m - an improvement of 55cms on Ralph Boston's record. The other Welsh competitors in Mexico were Howard Davies who went out in his heat of the 400; Clive Longe with eleventh in the decathlon and the 34 year old British captain, Ron Jones who also went out in the heats but set a Welsh 100m record of 10.42 in the rarified atmosphere, which was to stand for twenty two years until beaten by Colin Jackson with 10.29 in Wrexham in 1990. Incidentally, Ron's first meeting with Colin took place at the Tesco checkout in Cardiff, where they stunned other shoppers with their reminiscences whilst packing their shopping bags! Davies set a new Welsh hand-timed 200m record in a pre Games meeting in Mexico and it took 25 years before present day stars Jamie Baulch and Doug Turner came anywhere close to it.

1969 saw an out-of-sequence European Championships in Athens, with a record number of seven Welsh athletes taking part, but only Lynn Davies won a medal, this time a silver behind arch rival Igor Ter-Ovanesyan, who won the long jump with 8.17, 10 cms ahead of Lynn. Two Welshman were part of the British 4 x 400m relay team finishing sixth - John Robertson of Barry and Carmarthen born Gwynne Griffiths, that years AAA 400m champion. Griffiths took three Welsh 400m titles in his career, with Robertson beating Griffiths to the title earlier in the year. Robertson's Welsh record of 46.60 stood for a remarkable 24 years until beaten by Jamie Baulch in 1993.

The following year **1970** saw the largest Welsh contingent compete in a major Games since the 1958 Cardiff Empire Games, when a team of forty two made the relatively short trip to Edinburgh for the ninth celebration of the **Commonwealth Games at Edinburgh's Meadowbank Stadium**. Lynn Davies, appearing in his third Commonwealth Games, was the only Welsh athlete to return with a medal, retaining his long jump title with 8.06, 12cms ahead of Phil May of Australia. For Lynn, it had been a traumatic season as he suffered major injuries. At a Games get-together in early July at Aberystwyth under the guidance of National Coach Peter Lay, Lynn, by now a PE lecturer at Cardiff College of Education had some injections for an Achilles heal injury which was to plague him throughout the competition. He went into the final as only the fifth best qualifier and his third round attempt proved to be the winning effort as the Welsh hero gained his fourth gold medal in a major championship with a wind-assisted leap of 8.06. He proved with only three valid jumps that he was a truly magnificent competitor and jumped back to the summit when the chips were down.

Many members of the team at Edinburgh gained valuable experience of competition at this level. Lynn's Cardiff club-mate Gwyn Williams made the long jump final and finished tenth. At the time Welsh long jumping was particularly strong, and Gwyn's best of 7.55 in 1968 is still the fifth best jump by a Welsh long jumper in 2001, and without the presence of his great friend Lynn, would have held the Welsh record for many years. Five Welsh records were set and these came from Bernie Plain - who was just starting to make an impact at international level - with 28:51.84 for eleventh in the 10,000m; Bernie Hayward with an excellent seventh in the 3,000m steeplechase and the first Welsh athlete under 8:40 with 8:39.8; Newport's Mike Rowland, bettering the thirteen year-old marathon record with 2:19:08 for eleventh; Phil Thomas with his seventh place in the 1,500m beating his own mark with 3:42.6; and Ruth Martin-Jones in the pentathlon with her sixth place with 4497pts which added 289pts to the mark she had set the previous year at Oxford. If success is measured by Welsh records and personal bests, then these were the best Commonwealth Games so far for Welsh athletes. Also worthy of mention was 35 year old Averil Williams's fifth place in the javelin with 47.70 - twelve years after her last appearance in the Games where she won the bronze for England with 46.76 in Cardiff. Altogether, the Cardiff club supplied twelve members to the team, and one of them, 18 yr old Berwyn Price made his first appearance in the Games reaching the semi-finals of the 110m hurdles.

1971 was European Championships year (Helsinki), with five Welsh athletes in the British team and Lynn Davies just missing out on a medal in the long jump, with his fourth place. Liz Johns a prolific winner of thirteen senior Welsh sprinting titles during the 1960s was part of the sixth placed British team in the 4 x 100m. During her career, where she was coached from a schoolgirl by Jim Alford, she set nine Welsh sprint records ending with a best of 11.85 for 100m set in the Games when finishing second in her heat.

Unfortunately, many of the fine performances at the **1972 Munich Olympics** were overshadowed by the attack on the Israeli team by Palestinian terrorists, which resulted in eleven fatalities. But on the track, just three Welsh athletes appeared – long jumper Ruth Martin-Jones becoming the first Welsh woman to appear at the Olympics; Berwyn Price (110m hurdles) and Lynn Davies making his farewell on the international stage as a competitor as the British team captain, but he failed to progress beyond the qualifying rounds of the long jump. On a broader front these were the Games where the incredible Finn, Lasse Viren won both the 5,000 and 10,000m, a feat he repeated in the next Olympics in Montreal. Uganda's John Akii-Bua, coached by Malcolm Arnold before his appointment as the Welsh National Coach, won the 400m hurdles in a new world record of 47.82 secs to erase three tenths from David Hemery's world record, set in Mexico City in 1968.

A fifteen-strong Welsh squad made the trip to Auckland for the **1974 Commonwealth Games,** the largest athletics squad to represent Wales in a Commonwealth Games outside of the UK. The team returned with three medals, including the first medal to be won by a Welsh woman - a bronze - won by Criccieth's Ruth Martin-Jones in the long jump, who had finished sixth in the pentathlon in the previous Games in Edinburgh.

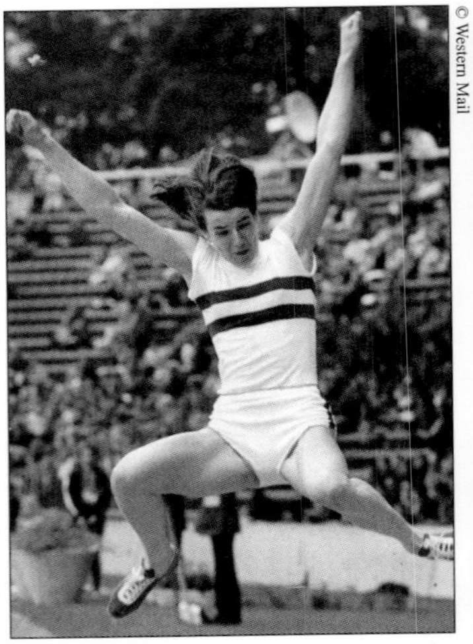
© Western Mail

Ruth Martin-Jones (Howell).

John Davies, Llwynypia born, and a member of Thames Valley Harriers became the first Welshman since John Merriman in 1958 and 1962 to win a Commonwealth middle distance medal when he took the 3,000m steeplechase silver behind Ben Jipcho of Kenya with a new UK and Welsh record of 8:24.8, despite tumbling to the ground on the last lap in a tussle with the eventual bronze medallist, Evans Mogaka (Kenya). Davies had initially been disqualified, but after a five hour wait whilst the jury of appeal viewed a tape of the race at the local TV studios, he was reinstated. The flare-up came just after the bell for the last lap. There was a tangle of arms as Mogaka tried to pass the Welshman on the outside. Then Davies caught the trail leg of leader, Jipcho, and crashed heavily onto the track bruising him and receiving track burns on his knees. He brought Mogaka down on top of him. "I didn't have time to think of what had happened and picked myself up and started to sprint after Jipcho". The 21 year old had produced one of the greatest track efforts ever seen by a Welsh athlete. Perhaps the gold medal was always out of his reach but for his fall he would certainly have climbed higher up the world-class podium and lowered further the British record, which he set. It was the highlight of his career as, after his run in the final of the 1978 Commonwealth steeplechase, he was dogged by injury problems. In 1979 he suffered from back and kidney problems. 1980 required an operation to remove a growth on his ankle and in 1981 an achilles tendon operation. In 1982 after three years in the wilderness he had recaptured his competitive appetite.

© Mark Shearman

Berwyn (678) takes silver in Auckland.

Wales' other medal in Auckland came from Berwyn Price in the 110m hurdles where he took silver behind Kenya's Fatwell Kimaiyo in 13.84 secs, a time well short of Berwyn's UK and Commonwealth record of 13.69 set in Moscow the previous year, which Kimaiyo equalled in winning. Berwyn also tried his hand at the 400m hurdles for the first time and clocked a creditable 52.8 in the semi finals. Welsh records came from Bernie Hayward, who finished sixth in the 3,000m steeplechase, one better than Edinburgh, with 8:36.2; Colin O'Neill with a new Welsh record in the 400m hurdles of 50.58 - his second Welsh record of the Games; Bernie Plain in the marathon with 2:14:56.2 for seventh and the 4 x 400m squad of O'Neill, Wyn Leyshon, Phil Lewis and Mike Delaney with 3:08.6 for sixth place in the first appearance in the Games of a Welsh team in this event.

Maesteg-born Tony Simmons failed to make the Welsh team for the Edinburgh Commonwealth Games after a relatively poor run in the Welsh championships that year, where Gwynn Davis beat him over 5,000m. This led him to defect to England for a number of years before eventually returning to the fold. During his temporary absence he developed into one of the finest middle distance runners of his era, winning the silver medal in the **1974 Rome European Championships** and finishing fourth in the 1976 Montreal Olympics. In Rome, he missed out on the gold by a tantalising four hundredths of a second. In fact in the timing to tenths of a second, he clocked the same time – 28:25.8 – as the winner Manfred Kuschmann. If the Luton based athlete had started his finishing surge a smidgeon earlier, he would almost certainly have won, but the East German held on by the proverbial thickness of his vest. Another medal almost came the way of a Welsh athlete in the marathon, when Cardiff's Bernie Plain, by far the finest home based middle and long distance runner of his era finished fourth behind winner and British team-mate, Cardiff University educated Ian Thompson. Newport's Robert Sercombe was 14th, after being initially disqualified at the selection race - the AAA championships - for allegedly cutting corners. He was the second Briton to finish in the AAA championship and his initial disqualification caused a furore amongst the close-knit marathon runners fraternity, and this no doubt, led to his reinstatement. John Davies (3,000m steeplechase); Dave Roberts, winner of nine Welsh sprint titles throughout the 1970s, including the 1974 100 and 200m, made his first appearance on the major-games stage as a member of the British 4 x 100 relay squad, but the team failed to progress beyond their heat. Berwyn Price also went out in the heats of the 110m hurdles.

Lynn Davies was at the **1976 Montreal Olympics,** but this time as Head Coach of the Canadian team, whilst Wales only had two athletes in the British team - Berwyn Price and Tony Simmons. Berwyn went out at the semi final stage of the 110m hurdles, whilst Simmons with that pitter-patter stride of his, just missing the bronze by 1.34 secs, which went to Brendan Foster, for Britain's only medal of the Games.

1978 saw the Commonwealth Games return to Canada, and this time, to Edmonton, Alberta, with another record squad of sixteen for a non UK Commonwealth Games. Berwyn Price became only the fourth Welsh athlete behind Reg Thomas, Jim Alford, and Lynn Davies to win a Commonwealth gold, and was Wales' only medallist at the Games. Berwyn just edged home from Australia's Warren Parr to win in 13.70. The first four from the Christchurch Games four years earlier qualified again for the final and were all together on the run-in from the last flight, but it was Berwyn who dipped the most efficiently as only 5/100ths split the quartet and the defending champion, Fatwell Kimaiyo of Kenya, was the one who missed a medal. Although only one medal was won, the Games were highly successful for Wales, as three Welsh records were broken with Glen Grant (3:38.1) and Hilary Hollick (4:12.72) setting new figures in the finals of the 1,500m. Ruth Howell raised

© Mark Shearman

Berwyn Price second left, takes gold in Edmonton.

The 1978 Welsh Commonwealth Games team prior to their departure for Edmonton:

Front (left to right): Hilary Hollick, Ruth Howell, Averil Williams (Team Manager – women); Reg Snow (Team Manager – men), Malcolm Arnold (Welsh National Coach), Raymond Jones (General Team Manager), Berwyn Price, Venissa Head, Jackie Zaslona.

Middle: Dave Roberts, Jeff Griffiths, John Phillips, Steve James, Mike Rowland, Steve Jones, Glen Grant.

Back: Tony Simmons, Mike Critchley, John Davies, Mike Delaney.

her pentathlon best to 4022 points. A further seven (Tony Simmons, Steve Jones, John Davies, John Phillips, Mike Critchley, Ruth Howell, Venissa Head and Jackie Zaslona) either reached the final or finished in the top eight of their respective events. There was the usual furore regarding team selection. With the athletics team (as other sports) being selected by the Commonwealth Games Council for Wales consisting members of the various sports, there was a plea for future teams to be selected by the experts – i.e. the athletics governing bodies. Two athletes - Micky Morris and Ken Cocks - were extremely unlucky not to get to the Games despite being well inside the qualifying standards set for the steeplechase and long jump.

Just three Welsh athletes made the British team for the **1978 European Championships** in Prague, which were held after the Commonwealth Games: Tony Simmons (marathon – 13th), John Davies (3,000m steeplechase) who went out in the heats and Berwyn Price, who was eliminated in the semi-finals of the 110m hurdles.

The **1980 Olympic Games** held in Moscow, remembered as the Coe/Ovett Games were marred by the absence of the Americans and many African nations, due to the Soviet Union's presence in Afghanistan. But from a Welsh perspective, Michelle Probert (Scutt) became the first and remains Wales' only woman medallist at the Olympic Games winning a bronze medal as a member of Britain's 4 x 400m relay team. It was the culmination of a tremendous season for Michelle as she lowered her Welsh 400m record five times ending with 51.62. She also set a new 200m record of 23.32. Michelle first shot to prominence in 1976 as Britain's top junior sprinter as she was unbeaten in the 100 and 200, and during her career, won eleven Welsh titles, mostly at 100 and 200, and only two at her main event, the 400 in 1979 and 1984. Her Welsh record of 50.63 for 400m set in 1982, still stands, and was a British record until beaten by Kathy Smallwood, and is still today the fifth fastest 400m time recorded by a British athlete. She won 22 UK vests between 1979 and 1985, and was a member of UK record breaking 4 x 400 teams in 1982 and 1984. During her illustrious career, she set 18 Welsh records at events from 100m to 400m. Roger Hackney, Wales' only other representative in Moscow finished seventh in his steeplechase semi-final.

At the **1982 European Championships in Athens** Steve Jones finished an excellent seventh in the 10,000m and Steve Barry was eleventh in the 20k walk, whilst Roger Hackney and Michelle Scutt were eliminated in the early rounds of the 3,000m steeplechase and 400m respectively.

The team of seven men and nine women, which represented Wales at the **1982 Brisbane Commonwealth Games** in October, was, by any yardstick, the most successful team to date in the history of the "Friendly Games". The Games were scheduled very early in the Australian summer, and for better or worse they began only three weeks after some of the Welsh team had been taking part in the European Championships. Wales won two gold medals, the highest ever at the time and three medals in all which equalled the record tally of the 1974 team. Nine athletes finished in the first six in their events, beating the previous best total of seven in the 1962 Games.

October 7th will go down as one of the greatest days in the history of Welsh athletics, with two gold medals being won within the space of a couple of hours in Brisbane. Firstly, Steve Barry, unquestionably Britain's best walker at the time for many years, completely outclassed a strong field in the 30k walk to win the gold medal by over two minutes and claim Wales' first gold medal of the Games. His time of 2:10:16 was a Games and British record. This was an amazing five minutes inside his previous best and at the end of the year the Cardiff athlete deservedly won *The Western Mail* "Sports Personality of the Year". And then Wales had won her second gold medal when Kirsty McDermott (Wade) ran a courageous race to take the 800m in 2:01.31. Always up with the leaders Kirsty refused to yield under pressure and withstood a strong challenge from Scotland's Anne Clarkson. Her victory made her the first Welsh woman to win a title at a major Games.

© Mark Shearman

Steve Barry proudly shows his gold medal in Brisbane.

Undoubtedly the Welsh medal haul would have been higher but for the injury sustained by the unfortunate Venissa Head. Her season's best would have won her the gold medal in the shot and bronze in the discus, and it would have been inconceivable that she would have come home without a medal of some sort. She gamely competed in the discus, finishing sixth, but had to withdraw from the shot. Another unlucky athlete was 800m runner Phil Norgate who was injured in a pre-Games meeting and was unable to do himself justice. He was third in his heat (behind the eventual gold and silver medallists) but re-injured himself in his semi-final and failed to finish.

Steve Jones was ill in Brisbane and he, too, performed well below his capabilities. After running so well in the European Championships 10,000m it was not unreasonable to assume that on form he would have finished in no lower than fourth place in Australia, but could manage no better than eleventh. His teammate Dennis Fowles did well to take sixth and was also something of a revelation in the marathon, clocking 2:16:49 for 13th on his debut at the distance to give indications of greater things ahead. This he did when he sliced 21 seconds off Tony Simmons' Welsh record with 2:12:12 for third in the following years London Marathon.

Berwyn Price's misfortune was that his event saw such a remarkable upsurge in standards during 1982. At the beginning of the season the reigning Commonwealth Champion held the British and Commonwealth records for 110m hurdles with a time of 13.69, which had stood since 1973. He ran 13.73 in the final in Brisbane, which was only good enough for sixth place. With Roger Hackney finishing an excellent fourth in the 3,000m steeplechase, it was left to Michelle Scutt to win the first Welsh medal of the Games. She had made a fine start to the season, winning the UK title with a new British and Commonwealth record, but had been beset with injury problems later on. In Brisbane, however, she was back to something like her best form and it took one of the greatest athletes of our time in Raelene Boyle of Australia to deprive her of the gold medal. Her silver medal in 51.97 was, just for a few days, the highest placing at the Games by a Welsh woman athlete until Kirsty later took the 800m.

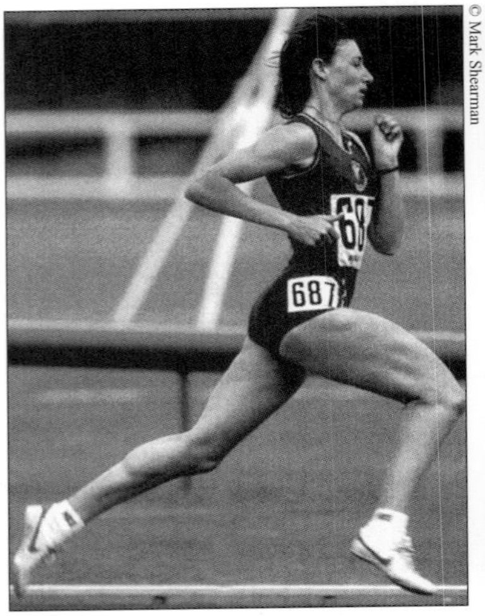

© Mark Shearman

Michelle Scutt seen here on her way to winning a silver medal in the 400m in Brisbane.

In **1983 the inaugural IAAF World Championships were held in Helsinki**. At a time when the Olympic Games were being devalued by politically inspired boycotts, these were truly global championships and to reflect this more countries (153) participated than in any other sports event in history and the standards achieved were higher than at any Olympic Games. The best performance from a Welsh athlete came from 3,000m steeplechaser Roger Hackney as he mixed it with the best in the world and finished 5th in 8:19.38 to set a new Welsh record. This time was to stand for five years until Hackney himself bettered it with 8:18.91 which remains today as the Welsh record. Steve Jones (12th 10,000m), Venissa Head (10th Shot) and Michelle Scutt (400m) were the other Welsh representatives.

The **1984 Los Angeles Olympics** with the centrepiece being at the huge Coliseum were held in true Hollywood tradition with a breathtaking space age opening ceremony and a light-radiating spaceship and a friendly "visitor" from another planet at the closing ceremony. A record breaking six athletes represented Wales, with Michelle Scutt, as part of the UK 4 x 400 team coming closest to a medal with fourth. Venissa Head also excelled reaching both shot and discus finals, although it has to be said that her performances would not have placed her in the top ten of the USSR championships that year, as unfortunately, the Games were again marred by a major boycott, as most of the Eastern bloc countries stayed away as retaliation against the USA's absence in Moscow in 1980. Steve Barry (20k walk), Steve Jones (10,000m), Nigel Walker (110m hurdles) and Roger Hackney (3,000m steeplechase) were the other Welsh competitors. One of the talking points of the Games was the fall of Mary Slaney in the 3,000m, allegedly caused by Zola Budd.

The **1986 Commonwealth Games** returned to Meadowbank Stadium, Scotland, after a 16 year absence – the first time the Games had been held in the same stadium twice. The Games were Wales' most successful - with a total haul of eight medals - but they nearly didn't take place, being saved at the last minute by the financial input of the late and infamous Robert Maxwell. To the superstitious it was probably appropriate that the first Commonwealth Games ever to be affected by a political boycott should be the 13th in the series. Much has been written about the effects of the boycott and to what extent the Games, and the medals won, were devalued. Certainly the absentees were missed, and no doubt the absence of the Kenyans made the winning of medals easier in the men's longer distances. The British government's refusal to take sanctions against South Africa and so bring pressure to bear on the country's policy of apartheid cost the Commonwealth Games the presence of 32 countries. The absentees were almost all from the African and Asian continents and the Caribbean. In the final analysis, however, an athlete can do no more than compete against those who are there, and if anyone doubts the value of the medals won then one can do so for many previous Olympic champions. Some events were affected more than others, some not at all, and the medals won by Kirsty Wade, Colin Jackson, Venissa Head and Angela Tooby owed nothing to the boycott and should be recognised as well earned. Wales were represented by 21 athletes and in dismal weather on the very first day, the Games got off to an excellent start with Steve Jones winning a bronze medal with his time of 28:02.48 in the 10,000m to claim his first medal in a major championship. Having been a credit to Welsh athletics for many years, the marathon expert thoroughly deserved his success. The event suffered greatly from the boycott as only 12 athletes started – the smallest field since 1934 with no Africans present.

27 July 1986 was to prove to be one of the most successful days ever in the history of Welsh athletics with no less than three silver medals won in Edinburgh. Leading the way was 19-year-old Colin Jackson, who had won the World Junior 110m hurdles title in Athens just a week before the Games in the fastest time ever by a British junior hurdler, albeit wind assisted. This turned out to be a good omen as he finished second in 13.42 to defending champion Mark McKoy who clocked 13.31. In fourth place was Nigel Walker in 13.69. Venissa Head, who led until the fourth round of the discus, eventually had to settle for the silver medal with 56.20, just 22 cms behind winner Gael Martin of Australia. It completed a throws double for the Australian as she had also retained her shot title but the victories were not without controversy. In 1981 the Australian had been suspended after failing a drugs test. A tinge of controversy hung over Wales' other silver medal as steeplechaser Roger Hackney was initially disqualified for trailing his leg around the final water jump but after much deliberation was finally re-instated by the Jury of Appeal. He ran 8:25.15 behind Graham Fell of Canada. Angela Tooby emulated the feat of Steve Jones by taking the bronze in the 10,000m in 32:25.38 to chop over a half a minute off her own Welsh record. The race was run in rain but at least the wind had dropped for the women who were going to make history because the distance was being run for the first time at a major Games or Championship. Scotland's Liz Lynch (the eventual world 10,000m champion Mrs. McColgan) won the race in a British and Commonwealth record. Susan Tooby, fourth at one point, slipped back a little but still finished a creditable sixth.

Four years earlier in Brisbane, Kirsty Wade had become the first Welsh woman to win a Commonwealth title. That she could successfully defend her laurels was always on the cards and she fully lived up to expectations in the 800m with a resounding victory in 2:00.94, a Games record and ended the Welsh silver medals streak on the day. Full of confidence after her defence she met Canadian Lynn Williams, the 3,000m champion in the 1,500m final and Kirsty defied the odds as she stormed away from the field to record a unique double as she crossed the line in 4:10.91. It was also the first time a Welsh athlete had won two medals at the same Commonwealth Games. The medal haul was completed as the women's 4 x 100m relay squad of Helen Miles, Sian Morris, Sallyanne Short and Carmen Smart took the bronze medals, bettering the 20 year-old Welsh record set in the 1966 Games, with 45.37, to set the seal on Wales' most successful Games, and win the first relay medals won by a Welsh women's team in the Commonwealth Games. But for the untimely injuries to Welsh record high jumper (2.24) John Hill and one-lap runner Michelle Scutt, the final medal tally of eight – two gold, three silver and three bronze would surely have been even higher.

The **1986 European Championship**s in Stuttgart, held four weeks after the Edinburgh Commonwealth Games, had seven Welsh athletes competing as part of the British team, with former world record holder Steve Jones going as the favourite for the marathon title. The full story of his performance is given in his pen portrait elsewhere, so suffice to say that he was hugely disappointed with his 20th place after leading by almost two minutes at the half-way point. The star of the team from a Welsh perspective was probably Nigel Walker, who achieved his finest performance in a major championships with his fourth place in the 110m hurdles in 13.52, for the second fastest time by a British - and Cardiff born athlete - that year. Angela Tooby (9th 10,000m) and Venissa Head (12th shot) were the only other Welsh finalists.

Rome was the venue for the second **World Championships in 1987**, and it provided the platform for Colin Jackson to announce his arrival on the senior world stage. At just 20 years old he won the bronze medal in a time of 13.38 secs behind the great American hurdler Greg Foster. In the women's 1,500m Kirsty Wade did well to reach the final and finish 6th in 4:01.41. Roger Hackney, Nigel Walker, and Angela Tooby were the other Welsh athletes in the British team. During the Championships to celebrate the 75th Anniversary of the IAAF, Lynn Davies was honoured among a group of world famous athletes from the past. David Hemery, Mary Peters and Mary Rand were the only other British athletes to be acclaimed.

A record nine Welsh athletes were part of the British team for the **1988 Seoul Olympics** which will always be remembered as the Games in which Ben Johnson was disqualified for failing a drugs test after "winning" the 100m. A lifetime of dreams and nearly a solid year of meticulous training were spoilt by American Roger Kingdom as Colin took the silver in 13.28. The American retained his Olympic crown and was undoubtedly the master as he scorched to an Olympic record time of 12.98. It was the first medal by a British athlete in the event since 1936 and only the second individual Olympic medal to be won by a Welsh male athlete since Lynn Davies' gold in 1964. For the first time in 16 years there was no mass boycott with only Cuba and Kenya missing but Seoul itself was a garrison-like City with tight security. However sport triumphed over the potential threats from sabotage and terrorism with the Olympic Games legacy seemingly safe.

Colin Jackson on his way to claim his one and only Olympic medal, silver at Seoul in 1988.

Kirsty Wade reached the semi-finals of both the 800 and 1,500m but her form had dipped alarmingly on the European circuit and it came as no surprise that she struggled in the heat of Seoul. Angela Tooby went out in the 10,000m heats suffering from a cyst on her eye and recovering from a hip injury, which had left her hobbling on crutches before the Games. However her sister Susan improved on her Welsh marathon record with a 12th place finish in 2:31:32 .The 27-year-old had sliced 37 seconds off her own record which she had set in finishing fourth in the London Marathon in April. Roger Hackney pulled up in his steeplechase semi-final suffering from a chest virus. The other member of the team from Wales was sprinter Helen Miles. At the time she was working for the Dorothy Perkins department store in Bridgend. The 21-year-old, already the fastest in Wales with a time of 11.50 had an unusual sponsorship agreement with her employers. She would receive a £25 voucher for every hundredth of a second she shaved off her best!

The **1990 Commonwealth Games in Auckland** at the end of January were arguably the best ever for Welsh athletics. Not only were four medals won, but almost every athlete in the fourteen strong team made at least one final and then finished in no lower than 9th place. The Games were a living proof of the renaissance of the Commonwealth Games. Entries for the Games broke all records – 672 athletes, including 242 women, from 47 countries. It was not the least surprising that Colin Jackson won the 110m hurdles gold medal. The manner of his victory, in a new European, Commonwealth, British and Welsh record time of 13.08, was most emphatic with a huge 0.26 seconds gap over his nearest pursuer. It was the fourth fastest time in history. Nigel Walker was fifth with three English athletes splitting the Welsh pair.

Another Welsh and Cardiff hurdler shared the limelight with Colin, as Kay Morley for once shared top billing with Colin as she joined the elite band of world hurdlers to win a gold medal at a major championship. Shortly before the Games began, at a pre-Games meeting in Auckland, Kay broke her own Welsh record with a time of 13.11 "equalling" as she would say, Colin Jackson's time which, by coincidence was also 13.11 at that particular time. She was in fine form for the challenge and had prepared herself well. She gave Welsh fans the fright of their lives in the Games themselves, however, as her semi-final must have been one of the worst races of her career. Hitting the fourth and fifth flights very hard, her stride pattern went to pieces and she finished in fifth place only. Luckily she qualified for the final as the fastest loser and as a result was in the unfavourable inside lane. Australia's Jane Flemming and England's Lesley - Ann Skeete, on the other hand, had looked most likely to do battle for the gold and Kay's confidence had taken a severe knock. Skeete had a superb start but the Welsh heroine was quickly into her stride and with all her opponents to her right, she could focus fully on her efforts. She flew past the English runner by halfway and won going away from a very strong field with a splendid Welsh record time of 12.91 (again same as Colin's three years later!), which at the time only three Commonwealth athletes had ever beaten. The Welsh queen of hurdling had also become only the third British woman to beat the magical 13 seconds barrier after Sally Gunnell and Shirley Strong. Kay on this occasion beat Sally, the defending champion by the best part of three metres.

Ian Hamer was another athlete whose build up to the Auckland Games had been meticulously planned. During a fine 1989 season he attained the Games qualifying time at 1,500m but not, ironically, at 5,000m which he regarded as his primary event. He was not included in the rather small athletics team originally selected (only 15 places for the Games' major sport was surely unrealistic) but his name was added a few weeks later after strong representations by the athletics authorities that, it must be remembered, did not have the final say on selection. The breakthrough by Ian was remarkable. Regarded as a 1,500m runner, his only noteworthy success at 5,000 had been to win a Wednesday night race at Cwmbran the previous September in his fastest time of 13:45.3. In Auckland he improved by almost 20sec for the first Welsh medal at the distance. As the Games drew nearer it became obvious that he was improving with every race, especially so when he broke David James' 1980 Welsh record for 3,000m (7:46.95) with 7:46.40. Still, he was not realistically expected to be among the medals in an event, which included such stars as Kenyan's Yobes Ondieki and John Ngugi, European 5,000 Champion Jack Buckner and UK 3,000 steeplechase record holder Mark Rowland among others. The race itself was surely one of the most dramatic ever seen with first one then another falling, including Olympic Champion Ngugi who recovered remarkably well to go to the front and then open up a very substantial lead. At the bell he had over 40 metres to spare but the pack was closing in. With 200 metres to go it was none other than Bridgend's Ian Hamer who sped away from the rest to give chase to the tiring Ngugi. Following hard on his heels was the relatively unknown Australian Andrew Lloyd and as Hamer himself began to tire it was Lloyd who sped past both him and Ngugi to claim gold. Ian hung on bravely to seize the most satisfying of bronze medals, to the delight of the entire Welsh team, and claim the first ever Welsh medal in the event.

Permision of Bob Phillips

Ian Hamer (1119) battles his way to the bronze medal. Eventual winner Andrew Lloyd (0050) makes his home run. 1988 Olympic Champion John Ngugi (0564) is about to be overtaken.

Wales' other medal in Auckland, also a bronze, came from shot putter Paul Edwards. The UK and former AAA Champion went to Auckland as one of the favourites, leading the Commonwealth rankings. It might seem odd for someone to be disappointed at winning a bronze medal but Paul felt that the gold was there for the taking. The competition was won with a put well within his capabilities and in some respects he was a little unlucky as he was the most consistent putter on the day to finish with a bronze medal effort of 18.17. Regrettably, he later relinquished his Welsh qualification and suffered disqualification for failing a drug test.

Probably the most frustrating position in which to finish in a major event is fourth. Steve Jones and Nigel Bevan both suffered this fate at Auckland in events in which the standard was world class. Steve finished in 2:12:44 in the marathon while Nigel, the find of the year improved his own Welsh javelin record to 79.70m. Steve's performance was the best ever by a Welshman in the event. Sallyanne Short sprinted brilliantly to set a new Welsh record in the heats of the 100m (11.47) and then equal it in the semi-final in which she became the first British sprinter to beat Paula Dunn since 1986. She ran even faster in the final (11.41w) but this time there was a strong tail wind as she finished in fifth place behind a world-class field. In the 200m she also reached the final and finished sixth in a personal best of 23.35 despite suffering a trapped nerve. As in all major championships inevitably there were hard luck stories. Carmen Smart was just 0.02 seconds away from a place in the final of the 100m while Angela Tooby ran just four laps of the 10,000m before an ankle injury forced her out, and sister Susan had to withdraw from the team before it left. Helen Miles travelled all the way to the other side of the world for nothing. Nursing a slight injury, she missed the sprints to save herself for the relay only to see her chance disappear with Sallyanne's injury in the 200m which prevented her taking any further part in Auckland.

Too late! Colin Jackson holds off the challenge of rivals Jack Pierce (out of shot) and Tony Jarrett to claim world title and world record at Stuttgart in 1993.

The **European Championships in Split** took place later in 1990, with Colin Jackson winning his second major title of the year as he took the gold medal in 13.18 seconds. It was the first medal of any kind won by a Welsh athlete at European level since Lynn Davies took silver in the long jump in Athens in 1966. The higher standard of the European Championships told as Commonwealth Champion Kay Morley went out in the semi-final of the 100m hurdles, as did Nigel Walker in the men's equivalent. Neil Horsfield (1,500m - 9th) and Commonwealth 5,000m bronze medallist Ian Hamer (12th) both reached their respective finals. The Welsh contingent of eight athletes was the largest of any European championship, but Helen Miles was unlucky again, as she travelled as part of the sprint relay team, and did not actually run.

Tokyo was the scene for the **third World Championships in 1991**, with six Welsh athletes in the British team. Colin Jackson received the first set back in his highly promising career as he had to withdraw from the semi-final of the 110m hurdles after pulling muscle fibres in his back when warming up. England's Tony Jarrett took the bronze behind Greg Foster of the USA. Kirsty Wade clocked 4:05.16 for sixth in a 1,500m won by Hassiba Boulmerka of Algeria. Kay Morley, now married to Mile star Gareth Brown, went out in the semis of the 100m hurdles. The championships were dubbed the finest athletics meeting yet, with the best performance coming from the USA's Mike Powell as he eclipsed Bob Beamon's legendary world long jump record from the books with 8.95, 5 cms ahead of his compatriot's 1968 mark.

With the return of Cuba and Ethiopia to the fold, the **1992 Barcelona Olympics** were the biggest to date with 157 countries taking part. Colin Jackson posted the fastest time with 13.10 in the 110 hurdles but that was in the heat as a rib cartilage injury hampered him severely. He finished seventh and saw the title going to his training partner Mark McKoy of Canada. Colin was one of six Welsh athletes in the British team, and the only one to reach the final. AAW Director of Athletics, Steve Brace made his Olympic debut in the marathon finishing 27th. These were the Games where Sally Gunnell took the women's 400m hurdles in a new world record of 52.74 secs.

To win a gold medal in a World Championship or Olympic Games is the dream of every athlete. To win that medal in a new world record is almost from the realms of fairy tales, and achieved by athletes from sunny California. But on this occasion, Colin Jackson, Cardiff born and Cardiff bred stunned the athletics world with his 12.91 timing in the 110m hurdles to slice one hundredth off Roger Kingdom's four year-old record in **Stuttgart at the 1993 World Championships**. There is no doubt that this is the finest performance by a Welsh athlete, and 20th August will go down as one of the greatest days in the history of Welsh athletics. He also won a silver medal as a member of the sprint relay team that set a British record of 37.77 behind the Americans. The 26-year-old who had to endure claims from his American rivals that he was a 'choker' at major championships was able to finally do his now famous lap of honour with both the Welsh and British flags. But it was the realisation of his lifetime ambition, which will always live with the 53,000 sell-out crowd. Afterwards, he could only squat at the end of the track, tears in his eyes, barely able to comprehend the enormity of what he had achieved. He delivered one of the most startling performances in the history of the sport. After all the taunts, fears and the doubts, he took out his frustration in one outrageous run which, if he hadn't clipped the last hurdle, would have amounted to sheer perfection. The contest was over from the first barrier, the man who had won all 13 of his races prior to the final made sure the fourteenth was going to be a cakewalk as he powered over the first barrier already clear. His reaction time from the blocks of 0.122 seconds was much better than his rivals and he simply blasted further and further clear. His time still stands today as one of the longest standing world record records in the books, true testimony to the outstanding achievement of this fine athlete. Steve Jones with his 13th place in the marathon was the only other Welsh competitor in Stuttgart.

For once, the **1994 European Championships** took place before the Commonwealth Games, and were held in Helsinki with world champion and record holder Colin Jackson winning his fourth major championships 110m hurdles gold medal in 13.08 secs. All of the other Welsh competitors (three) were middle and long distance runners, with only steeplechaser Justin Chaston, fresh from his personal best 8:23.90 set in Nice a month earlier, making the final.

Hurdlers Colin Jackson and Paul Gray pictured with team manager Delyth Davies at the 1994 Commonwealth Games in Victoria.

The **1994 Commonwealth Games** returned to Canada for the fourth time - no other country having undertaken the monumental task of organising the Games more frequently. 53 of the 70 eligible countries sent teams with newly integrated South Africa being warmly welcomed back after a 36-year absence. This time Victoria on the west coast were the hosts, and sixteen Welsh athletes made the journey, with Colin Jackson again taking pride of place with another 110m hurdles win, co-incidentally in the same time as his win in Auckland four years earlier – 13.08 secs. He defied jetlag and flew on to Canada from the Grand Prix meeting in Brussels, just three days before the opening of the Games. Unquestionably the best high hurdler in the world his 13.08 equalled the Games record he set in Auckland. Colin thus became the third Welsh athlete, after Lynn Davies and Kirsty Wade, to retain a Commonwealth title. Paul Gray ran exceptionally well to take the bronze after running a personal best 13.53 secs in the heats to be the third fastest Welshman (and Cardiffian!) of all-time behind Colin and Nigel Walker. It was the first time that two Welsh athletes have stood on the same medal podium at a major Games.

Another, but this time, most unexpected gold medal came from Neil Winter in the pole vault. He became only the second Welshman behind Lynn Davies to win a Commonwealth field events title. The 20-year-old Monmouthshire-born athlete, Wales' youngest ever senior record holder for any event at 15, went into the Games having taken his best (and the Welsh record) from 4.80 in 1989 to 5.50m in 1992. So at the very best he might have expected bronze. But his great friend, the unpredictable, Ockert Brits of South Africa, the clear favourite with a best of 5.85m, failed three times at his opening height of 5.50m, whilst Neil cleared his opening height of 5.20m before clearing the winning height of 5.40m first time, to add 5cms to the Games record. However he subsequently paid the price for his early career success. He last picked up a pole in 1998 and his crash from the big time can be blamed squarely on his one-track aim for the top. Dislocated shoulder, achilles

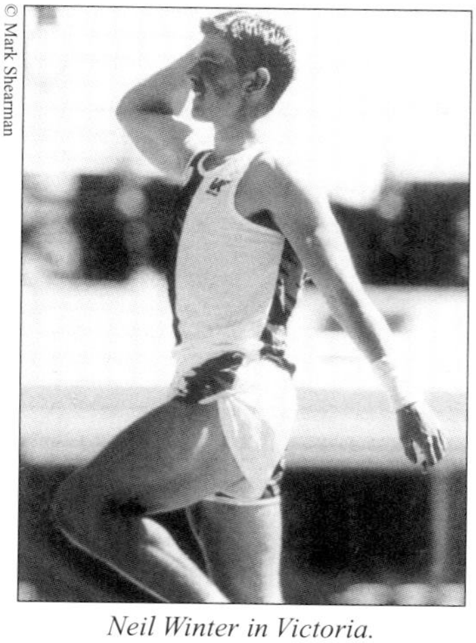

© Mark Shearman

Neil Winter in Victoria.

injury and operations on both knees cut short the career of the talented vaulter. "I think I could have done around 5.80 but you have to look at the reasons why I got injured. It was that my body could not handle it. I was pushing my body to get where I wanted to be and I was going to the limit. I thought I was indestructible."

No other Welsh medals were forthcoming but three athletes occupied the graveyard position of fourth. Cathy Dawson set two personal bests (2:03.81 in heat and 2:03.17 in final) in taking fourth in the 800m, missing out on the bronze by a tantalising five hundredths of a second to Gladys Wamuyu of Kenya; javelin thrower Nigel Bevan also missed out on bronze by a small margin - 4cms; whilst Dale Rixon, who started his running career with his local club Beddau, had the run of his life in the marathon, and missed bronze by just over a minute with 2:16:15, to equal the previous best position of a Welshman (Steve Jones 1990) in the event. It was the second successive Games for Bevan, a 26-year-old Belgrave Harrier, to take fourth in the javelin with 80.38m - one of the most frustrating experiences in sport. Since he burst on the Welsh scene in 1989, setting a Welsh record 76.82, he subsequently improved it eight times and is the current record holder with 81.70.

Iwan Thomas and Jamie Baulch, in their first major Games, were busy rewriting the Welsh record lists in their events in Victoria. Baulch ran in the 200m, setting new figures of 20.84 in his second round heat, while Thomas in the 400m became the first Welshman to beat 46 seconds with 45.98 in the semi-final. Some measure of the standard can be gained from the fact that neither of these performances was good enough to advance to the next round. The two teamed up as part of the 4 x 400 squad with Peter Maitland and Paul Gray, to break the Welsh record, which had stood since 1978. Their time of 3:03.68 clipped almost 5 seconds off the old best and took them to the final. The new record may have come down even further in the final except that the team were baulked by the Kenyans, who were subsequently disqualified, and lost valuable metres as a consequence. Apart from the actual team, Wales also had two technical officials at the Games, selected by the Canadian Organising Committee - Viv Thomas as a field judge and Alan Currie as a track umpire.

The **1995 World Championships** in Gothenburg, where Jonathan Edwards achieved the fairy tale win and world record in the triple jump with 18.29, were low key from a Welsh perspective with only two representatives from the Principality in the British team - Justin Chaston, who went out in the semis of the steeplechase and Catherine Murphy who ran in the heats of the sprint relay.

Two relay silvers were the sum total of the Welsh tally at the **1996 Atlanta Olympics**, which will probably go down as the beginning of the end for 1992 100m champion Linford Christie, who was controversially disqualified from the final due to two false starts. But the relay medals in the 4 x 400m by Iwan Thomas and Jamie Baulch, as the team set a new UK record of 2:56.60 secs behind the USA, were their first on the world stage, and an indication of even better things to come - certainly for Iwan. In the individual 400m Iwan's 44.70 for fifth place, behind winner Michael Johnson and second placed Roger Black, was only four hundredths behind his seventh Welsh record in the event, set during his winter campaign in Johannesburg. Colin Jackson competing in his third Olympics - only Lynn Davies amongst Welsh athletes, having achieved this feat, again failed in his quest for Olympic Gold. This time he was thwarted by Allen Johnson who clocked an Olympic best 12.95 secs, despite clattering most of the hurdles. Earlier in the year in the US trials, Johnson had clocked the second fastest time on record – 12.92 – just one hundredth of a second behind Colin's 1993 world record. Colin's poor consolation was that his time in fourth of 13.19 secs was the fastest ever by an Olympic fourth placer, and a highly creditable run after undergoing a double knee operation after the end of the 1995 season. AAW Director of Athletics Steve

Brace made his second Olympic appearance, but was well down the field in 60th; Commonwealth Champion Neil Winter failed to qualify in the pole vault with a height of 5.40, as did Shaun Pickering in the shot with 18.29.

Allen Johnson, whilst not the world record holder, proved that he was still the world's current number one, by taking the 110m hurdles crown at the **Athens World Championships in 1997**, with Colin Jackson winning the silver. Johnson's time of 12.93, to Colin's 13.05 clearly indicated the American's superiority, which Colin sportingly acknowledged in the post race interview. With a pre-championships season's best of 13.24 Colin could feel satisfied with his day's work. In the trials for the championships, Iwan Thomas had set a new British record of 44.36, third fastest in the world so far that year, so he went in to Athens full of confidence, but Olympic champion Michael Johnson won in a canter in 44.12, with England's Mark Richardson 4th and Iwan sixth with 44.52, his fourth fastest of the season.

There was also excellent running from Jamie Baulch who made the final in Athens finishing eighth in 45.22. Later, Iwan and Jamie were part of the British squad which won the silver medals in the 4 x 400 relay in a time which was only five hundredths (2:56.65) outside the UK record they set in Atlanta. Of the remaining members of the Welsh contingent, Dale Rixon failed to finish in the marathon, Shaun Pickering, winner of nineteen Welsh shot, discus and hammer titles didn't get past the qualifying stages of the shot and 36 year-old television presenter Angharad Mair, ran a season's best to finish 23rd in the marathon with 2:42:31.

1998 was a hallmark season for Iwan Thomas, when he won all three gold medals in the major events held. Firstly, he took the **European** crown in **Budapest** in 44.52, followed by the **IAAF World Cup** title (45.33) in **Johannesburg** and completed his exhausting schedule taking the **Commonwealth** gold in **Kuala Lumpur** with 44.52 - all within the space of a month. This string of achievements ranked him second in the world in the much-respected *Athletics International* annual rankings behind the redoubtable Michael Johnson. To these fine individual performances he added two 4 x 400 relay medals. In Budapest he took gold, in a team that also included Jamie Baulch and in Kuala Lumpur, he anchored the Welsh quartet, which sliced almost two seconds off the Welsh record set in the 1994 Commonwealth Games, to take the bronze in 3:01.86. Paul Gray, Doug Turner and Jamie Baulch were the other members of the team that took Wales' first ever medal in the event.

Pen Portrait – Iwan Thomas MBE (Newham and Essex Beagles)

Athletics is not a sport you associate with anyone taking up an event and running in a World championship in your very first season. So the feats of Iwan Thomas are more remarkable as he became the top British 400 runner of his generation despite his Sydney Olympic disappointment, where he failed to make the British team in the individual 400m.

Born in Farnborough, Kent, Iwan started BMX racing around the age of eight and within two years he became East Anglia champion and retained that title throughout until he switched to athletics nine years later. He was always in the top three or four racers in the UK, finishing second in the national championships in his first year and during this time he represented his country in two world championships, at Orlando in 1985 (fourth) and Brisbane in 1989 (ninth). He also took fourth place in the European Championships at Holland in 1997. During his

seven-year biking career he managed to win over 400 trophies. He also broke a few bones and needed a skin graft for a hip injury.

When Iwan's father moved to Germany to take up a NATO appointment, he moved in as a boarder at Stamford School to study for his A-levels. This signalled the end of his BMX career and Iwan instead took up rugby and athletics. The rest is history! His rugby skills were so advanced that he even managed to reach the final trials for England Schools'.

At the age of sixteen he decide to take on five track and field events at the school sports day. He managed to win the 100, 200, 400; long jump and high jump and broke the school record in every event. It was then that he started to realise that maybe he was destined to become a runner! He started taking athletics seriously in 1992 and made the British team for the World Junior Championships in Seoul, helping them to fifth in the 4 x 400 relay.

While at West London Institute studying a BSc (Honours) degree in Sports Studies and Leisure Management he got into top-level athletics when he joined Newham and Essex Beagles. He was introduced to Roger Black's former coach Mike Smith and soon Mike became his mentor and guiding light that helped develop Iwan's career into what it is today.

He set the first of his ten Welsh records with 46.34 in 1994 and then improved to 45.98 in the Commonwealth Games at Victoria. He made further progress to 45.58 in 1995, when he made the British 4 x 400 team that won the European Cup. But it would be probably fair to say that 1996 was the year that Iwan broke into world class. At the Atlanta Olympics he finished fifth in the final won by his great rival Michael Johnson. His time of 44.70 was another Welsh record and along with fellow Welshman Jamie Baulch, he collected a silver medal in the relay. Atlanta gave him the springboard to achieve greater things over the following two years as he changed his programme to reach another level. At the 1997 UK championships at Birmingham he went even faster and claimed Roger Black's British record with a superb run in 44.36, which still stands today. This set him up nicely for the Athens World Championships where he finished a disappointing sixth but once again claimed another silver medal in the relay.

But 1998 was undoubtedly the highlight of his career so far as it created a little bit of history unlikely to be challenged for a long time. Southampton based coach Mike Smith usually aims to get his athletes in peak condition for the AAA's which, as well as the national championships, usually doubles up as trials for all major competitions. In July of 1998 Iwan beat the cream of the British one-lap runners at the AAA's championships winning in an impressive 44.50. And what followed in a remarkable 29-day period is now Welsh athletics folklore - four gold medals and a bronze from the European Championships, Commonwealth Games and World Cup. Not surprisingly he was voted BBC Wales Sports Personality of the Year – the first athlete for five years (since Colin Jackson) to win the coveted award.

But from the highs of 1998 his career nose-dived in 1999. His whole future was put in doubt due to the development of a cyst on his ankle. He sustained a stress fracture in South Africa during winter training and eventually had to have keyhole surgery. His only consolation during the year was his MBE award. 2000 saw Iwan struck down again with injury and poor form. He had his first race since the Commonwealth Games when he ran in a low-key event in Budapest and was encouraged with his 45.85. He missed the Olympic Trials and controversially did not get the third individual spot in the team although he did run in each round of the relay in Sydney with a leg of 45.2 in the final.

At 27-years-old Iwan has the ability to climb back to the top. Along with his

determined, focused and fun-loving attitude he can look forward to further glory. Having already had his ample frame displayed at Madame Tussauds, he has a lot to live up to!

In the **1998 European Championships in Budapest,** Colin Jackson collected his sixth major outdoor title in the 110m hurdles with his season's best of 13.02, but the major surprise from a Welsh perspective was the 200m silver won by Newport athlete Doug Turner, the first sprint medal won by a Welshman in the four major outdoor Games/Championships since another Newport athlete, Ken Jones won the 220 yds bronze in the 1954 Empire Games in Vancouver. He had earned his place in the British team with second spot in the AAA championships, which doubled as the trials, with Scotland's Dougie Walker beating him in both the trial and in Budapest. Turner can thank Newport coach Jock Anderson for his early grounding in the event. Although Cardiff's Paul Gray went out in the semi final of the 400m hurdles, he had the huge satisfaction of breaking his own Welsh record by 0.6 secs, with 49.16 secs in his heat to become the fastest Briton of the year. He also took the AAA 400 hurdles title in July to become the third Welshman to win the event after Bob Shaw (1955) and Phil Harries (1988).

© Mark Shearman

Paul Gray setting his Welsh record.

The **Kuala Lumpur Commonwealth Games in 1998** attracted a record 57 countries and were again acknowledged as the most successful ever. Twenty-two athletes represented Wales - another record for a Commonwealth Games outside the United Kingdom. The team collected four medals - Iwan Thomas, the men's 4 x 400m squad, a silver from emerging superstar Christian Malcolm and Wales' first medal in the "heavy" events, a shot bronze from Shaun Pickering. 19 year-old Malcolm, another Newport athlete coached by Jock Anderson, and winner of the world junior 100 and 200m titles some six weeks earlier in Annecy, France, confirmed his status as the finest Welsh sprinter of all-time in taking the 200m silver in 20.29 secs to slice .14 secs off Doug Turner's Welsh record and set a new British junior record in the bargain. He added this record to his portfolio after he twice improved on his own Welsh record to win the world junior 100m crown with 10.12. Prior to Annecy, he had bettered Colin Jackson's Welsh record of 10.29, which had stood for 7 years, with 10.24 in the European Junior Championships in 1997 where he had taken the 100m silver and won the 200m. Controversially, Colin, selected as captain of the Welsh team, decided at the last moment not to compete. At the time he said: "After my success in the European Championships in Budapest last month I'm feeling tired and do not believe I will be able to

© Mark Shearman

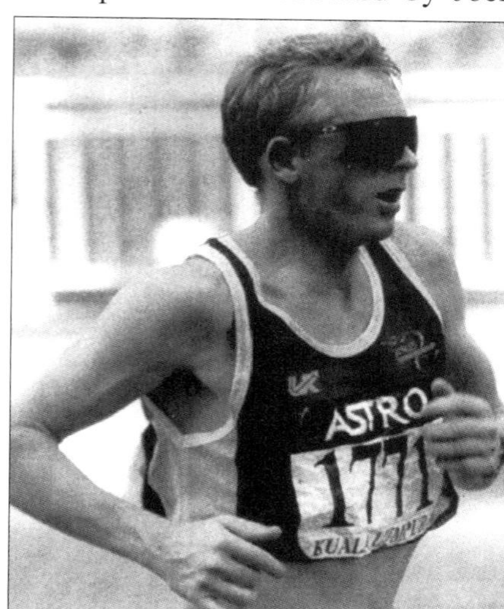

Steve Brace, currently AAW Director of Athletics, finishing the marathon in Kuala Lumpur.

perform at the required level". He continued: "I'm naturally disappointed I shall not be able to defend my title and represent Wales, which I have always relished". Had he have run, and won, as he almost certainly would have, (Tony Jarrett won with 13.47) he would have become the only the second athlete in Commonwealth Games history (Australian sprint hurdler Pam Kilborn is the only other) to have won the same event in three successive Games - with a silver for good measure. He would have also become the first athlete to have won the European and Commonwealth titles for a third consecutive time. This writer believes that Colin will look back with hindsight and regret that decision not to run.

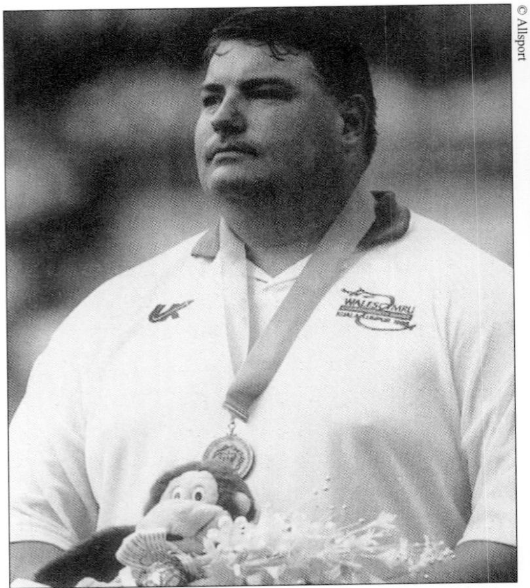

Shaun Pickering proudly stands on the podium with his shot bronze medal.

The Welsh sprint relay team of Kevin Williams, Doug Turner, Christian Malcolm and Jamie Henthorn took the baton round in a scintillating 38.73 to just miss the bronze medal by four hundredths and set a new Welsh record in the process knocking 36 hundredths off the mark they set in the heats, but more importantly, slicing a huge chunk of the pre Games Welsh record which had stood to the legendary foursome of Terry Davies, Lynn Davies, Keri Jones, Ron Jones who clocked 40.0 (converted from 4 x 110 yds) in finishing fourth in the Jamaica Commonwealth Games 32 years earlier. The most thoroughly deserved Welsh medal was claimed by Shaun Pickering. Having been a tremendous servant to Wales in the throws for many years including setting records in the shot, discus and hammer his bronze in the shot with a throw of 19.33 was the icing on the cake and culmination to a great career. Born in Abersychan when his father Ron was Welsh National Coach, the former Stanford University student was the first athlete to hold all three Welsh field event records at the same time.

Seville staged the **1999 World Championships**, with Colin Jackson regaining the title he last won in Stuttgart in 1993 when he set the world record of 12.91. This time he had to be satisfied with a season's best of 13.04. It was Britain's first world championships win since Jonathan Edwards' triple jump world record in Gothenburg in 1995. In 40 degrees plus heat Colin burst into tears in the emotion of the moment. He used his years of experience to produce an almost faultless race, edging out Cuba's young pretender Anier Garcia and Duane Ross of the United Sates. Garcia however, would go on to take Olympic Gold in Sydney. He put his famous 90-degree dip to winning effect, but would not believe the result until he saw the replay on the big screen. It was then his emotions came flooding out. In the final the start was vital and he had the fastest reaction time of all the finalists and with the fact that he did not hit one hurdle, it was catch up time for the seven other finalists.

With injury plagued Iwan Thomas missing from the 400m, it was left to Jamie Baulch to fly the flag of Wales in the final. Despite running 45.18 it was only good enough for last place as the golden wonder of the event, Michael Johnson shattered the world record with a time of 43.18. Doug Turner reached the final of the 200 and AAA champion Hayley Tullett of Swansea, made her first appearance in a major Games, but went out in the heats of the 1,500m; and Welsh record holder Paul Gray failed to make it past the heats of the

400m hurdles.

The only medal missing from 32 year-old Colin Jackson's trophy cabinet was an Olympic gold. But, competing in his fourth successive **Olympics in Sydney** - a record for a Welsh athlete - the only accolade he failed to win in a glittering career still eluded him, as he missed out on the medals to finish fifth, with the gold going to Cuba's Anier Garcia. An indifferent semi-final run gave him the unfavourable inside lane for the final and added to that a rare false start and the odds were increasing even before the gun had been fired. Typically, he quipped afterwards that whilst disappointed, he was still the reigning world champion and world record holder, so he really couldn't complain! Christian Malcolm gave another superb performance for an athlete of such tender years, beating his own Welsh 200m record in the qualifying rounds by a tenth clocking 20.19 twice, before finishing fifth in the final in 20.23. To put this performance into perspective from a Welsh viewpoint, he is the only Welsh athlete to reach an Olympic sprint final - and all at the age of 21. What a future he has in store! The absence of American 100, 200 and 400m world record holders Maurice Greene and Michael Johnson from the 200m had improved Christian's chances of reaching the final and perhaps sneaking a medal, but his day will come.

Pen Portrait – Christian Malcolm (Newport H & Cardiff AAC)

Christian has been described as a phenomenal talent who has emerged as a potential World and Olympic champion. He has that great ability to peak for the major races and runs personal bests in championships with extraordinary frequency. The long wait for our next Olympic champion could end in Athens 2004. In a relatively short career he has already collected ten medals (six gold and four silver) at major championships since 1997.

Even at a young age Christian was good at many things. He had soccer trials with Nottingham Forest and Queen's Park Rangers, was a member of the South Wales Schools' squad as a striker and above all he could run like the wind. As a pupil at Hartridge High School in Newport he was not always a model pupil and his art teacher, Meriel Davies, the wife of the 1964 Olympic star Lynn, had good reason to tell him off on more than one occasion.

He has long shown exceptional promise, with a beautiful running style; a promise that came to brilliant fruition in 1998, when he was elected by the IAAF at their annual ceremony in Monte Carlo as 'World Junior Athlete of the Year'. He was also awarded the British Athletics Writers' Association award. He competed for three years in Britain's junior international team from 1996 to 1998, making great progress each year. In 1996, aged 17, he was Britain's fastest ever over 200 and reached the World junior semi-finals in Sydney. Two years later he created history as he is the only athlete ever to win three consecutive AAA junior 200 titles (1996-1998) also adding the 100 title in 1998. His first ever AAA championship win was the youths' 100 in 1995.

During the 1997 indoor season he broke the Welsh record for 200 (21.26) at under 20 level. At the European junior championships in Ljubljana he came home with two gold medals and a silver. He won the silver in the 100 with a time of 10.24 beating Colin Jackson's long-standing Welsh senior record of 10.29. Gold in the 200 was claimed by a wide margin of victory in 20.51. A fine golden double was achieved as he helped the relay squad to victory. Not satisfied with his exploits at junior level in Europe, coach Jock Anderson was keen to see what the opposition was like at

senior level. Christian's arrival on the international scene was against the legendary Carl Lewis at Zurich. He beat the Olympic champion who earmarked the young Welshman as a future star.

Christian's 1998 season underpinned Carl Lewis' remarks. After winning the 100 and 200 at the AAA's under 20 championships, he went on to win the 200 at the Welsh senior championships. His ultimate goal for the season was at Annecy, France, the venue for the World Junior Championships. He not only won the gold in the 200 in a new British junior and championship record of 20.44 but also won gold at the 100 in 10.12. Both times created new Welsh senior records. It was the third occasion that he had lowered the 100 mark during the season. "The 100 win was the best of my career so far for sheer performance but I had greater satisfaction when I got the second gold in the 200. It had been something that I had been aiming at for a long time and to go there and do something no other Briton had ever done was great". In fact he was far and away the best sprint champion in the history of that event. Better than Boldon (1992), better than Cason (1988), Ezinwa (1990) and also better than Obikwel (1996).

His maturity and experience continued to grow as rapidly as his racing capability. He competed in Grand Prix meetings in Zurich and Lausanne in preparation for the 1998 Commonwealth Games where in his first real taste of senior championships, he ran superbly in the 200 final taking a silver medal in a new personal best, Welsh senior and European junior record of 20.29.

The focal point for the 1999 season was the European under 23 championships in Gothenburg. Having spent time prior to the start of the outdoor season in California, his hard work was rewarded as he delighted his growing number of fans by taking silver in both the 100 and 200, and competing as part of the relay team he came away with an European under 23 gold medal. However he missed out on selection for the World Championships in Seville, his former training partner Doug Turner getting the selectors' nod for the final 200 spot.

The 2000 indoor season established Christian on the senior circuit and having taken the AAA's 200 title in 20.74 and winning at the British Grand Prix in a then world season's best of 20.68, he set his sights on winning his first senior gold medal at the European indoor championships in Ghent. Drawn on the outside lane his normal smooth running action was not conducive to a perfect performance but he won brilliantly in 20.54, for a new Welsh indoor record and a huge improvement on his best. There is no doubt that on a more athlete friendly track he would certainly have gone much faster.

A runners-up spot at the AAA's Olympic trials followed by victory in the European Cup 200 in 20.45 at Gateshead won his place in Britain's team for Sydney, and as we have seen, he took the opportunity with both hands to show his peers his outstanding potential.

His ever-increasing celebrity status has provided high profile opportunities within the media and on the catwalk. Having his motivational inspiration from Carl Lewis and Linford Christie and taken a great deal of advice from Canada's Olympic champion Donovan Bailey, Christian is likely to be in the spotlight for the next decade of world athletics. 'Flash' is now mature enough for the big time and this writer predicts that in the years to come he will outshine both Lynn Davies and Colin Jackson as the finest athlete produced by Wales.

As in Seoul in 1988, nine Welsh athletes made the British team in Sydney and whilst not winning any medals performed creditably. Apart from Jackson and Malcolm, the best performances came from AAA 5,000 and 10,000 champion Andres Jones of Aberaeron, the British middle distance revelation of the UK season, who ran excellently in the 10,000m to finish ninth; Iwan Thomas and Jamie Baulch who were part of the UK 4 x 400m team which finished sixth, and Hayley Tullett, who capped a fine season, in which she set three personal bests and a new Welsh 3,000m record (8:45.39), by making the final of the 1,500m. Steeplechasers Justin Chaston and Christian Stephenson went out in the heats, whilst Catherine Murphy travelled as a reserve but failed to make the 4 x 400 squad. The men's 400m berths were full of controversy for one reason and another and Jamie Baulch was eventually selected ahead of the injury recovering Iwan Thomas who was only given a relay spot. It will remain a mystery as to why Baulch, the European Cup winner and World indoor champion ran so poorly in the heats as he went out in the very first round finishing seventh.

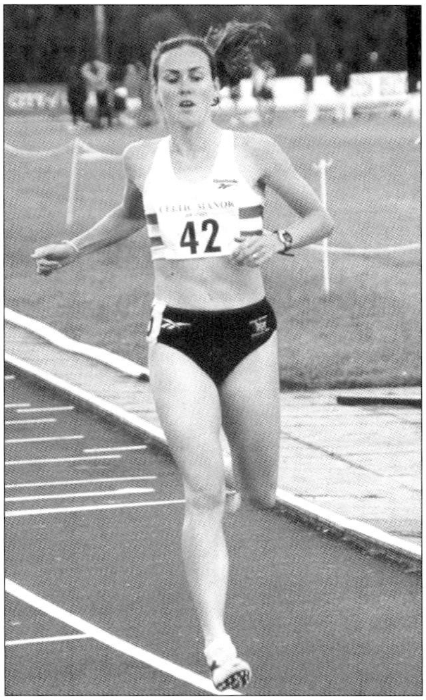

© Ian Dixon

Hayley Tullett, Sydney Olympics 1500 finalist.

Head of World Class Potential at UK Athletics, Tudor Bidder and former Welsh junior sprint stars Steve Perks and Adrian Thomas were part of the British coaching team, whilst five times Welsh 5,000 and 10,000 champion, Paul Darney attended as part of the coaching squad as he had two athletes in the team – Andres Jones and AAA steeplechase champion, Christian Stephenson. Triple Welsh 400m champion Mike Delaney followed in the footsteps of Lynn Davies, and Nick Whitehead by managing the British men's team. In fact Nick was overall British manager from 1978 to 1984 and attended in that capacity at the Moscow and Los Angeles Olympics, as well as the 1983 Helsinki World Championships. Ted Hopkins was also assistant manager of the overall team in the 1960 Rome Olympics. International Olympic Committee President Juan Antonio Samaranch in his closing remarks described the 2000 millennium Olympic Games in Sydney as " the best ever". Everyone who witnessed the spectacle live or from the comfort of his or her armchair would not argue with his conclusion.

Pen Portrait – Colin Jackson MBE (Cardiff AAC and Brecon AC)

The year 2000 was significant in that it marked the end of the championship career of our greatest ever track and field exponent Colin Jackson. His distinguished career came to an end in Sydney almost before he had realised it. The elusive gold medal remained an unattainable goal for the double world champion and record holder. He had become the highest profile-sporting ambassador in the Principality. No better statesman could a country wish for. After his Sydney run he commented: "I just crossed the line and said 'my goodness it's over' and that was it".

In Sydney Colin was making his fourth attempt at the ultimate prize, having just taken silver in Seoul in 1988, seventh in Barcelona four years later when suffering

with a rib injury and being one spot outside the medals in Atlanta in 1996. "I'm world champion and world record holder, my medal cabinet is crammed so I can't actually complain. When you see how many championships I've won it can never be a bad day for you. I've done better than 85 per cent of the world's athletes, so I can't possibly be disappointed with my championship career".

When he was in his teens, he started training with Welsh National Coach Malcolm Arnold and was a promising decathlete and long jumper before concentrating on the high hurdles. For historians it was 20 June 1981 that the name of Colin Jackson first appeared in the world of athletics. At the then new Morfa Stadium in Swansea, he won the Welsh under 15 80m hurdles with a new championship best of 11.9. A week later at Brecon he won the Welsh Schools' title in 12.0 as well as adding the javelin (!) title with a throw of 49.52. While a pupil at Cardiff's Llanedeyrn High School he was a gifted all rounder, holding school records for javelin, long jump and high jump, while also excelling at cricket. His first representative honour was in 1982 when he ran in the school's international match at Colwyn Bay and it is interesting to note that he never won the international schools' title on his two appearances in the event.

Colin won his first medal in 1985 when he took the silver medal as an 18 year-old, at the European junior championships. Another silver followed a year later at the Commonwealth Games in Edinburgh. A hamstring injury forced him to miss the European championships that year but he made up for it by going on to win the World junior championships in Athens, breaking the European junior record. The next three years saw him scoop a clutch of silver medals and one bronze. In 1987, he took the bronze at the World Championships in Rome and the silver in the European indoors. A year later he won what was to turn out to be his only Olympic medal with silver in Seoul.

An Olympic silver medal, a European and Commonwealth record in Sestriere and a Welsh record (200 21.29) running for Wales in Tel Aviv - 1988 certainly was the year in which Colin broadened both his horizons and his achievements. On June 28th he relieved Jon Ridgeon of his British record as he won the Ulster Games in Belfast in 13.13. In the space of twelve months he had changed from being a young pretender into an established star on the world athletics stage. It was a step, which many observers knew he would take one day, but never dreamed he could do it at the tender age of twenty-one. It was a year when he came of age as a top flight high hurdler, an athlete capable of striking fear into the hearts of even the very best Americans who had dominated the event on the world stage in modern times.

Even at that early age, he had only one aim in mind. "I want to be the best in the world", he openly admitted. Having established himself as the fourth fastest on the world all-time ranking list with his 13.13 in the rarefied atmosphere of Sestriere in the mountains of Italy, he did not have far to go to be the best. More than that Colin moved up to No 2 in the pecking order in a season that only defending Olympic champion Roger Kingdom was good enough to consistently beat him and it took two sub-13 second runs to defeat the Welshman in the Italian ski resort and in the Seoul Olympics.

In 1989 he was the World indoor silver medallist and also took his first European Cup win and in 1990, he won both the Commonwealth Games and European titles. At the Welsh Games in Wrexham Ron Jones' long standing Welsh 100 record was finally broken as Colin ran 10.29. A knee operation at the end of the season was the first sign that he was to later suffer from injury problems. For his services to the sport he was awarded the MBE. Injury manifested itself a year later, when he was forced to pull out of the World championship semi-final. The following year he finished seventh in the Olympics in Barcelona, having clocked the fastest time of four rounds with 13.10. He also won the World Cup that year in Cuba.

His Olympic disappointment was soon put on the back burner as in the 1993 World Championships in Stuttgart he shocked the world with an almost perfect run to win the gold with a world record of 12.91, which still stands today. He also drove home in a brand new black Mercedes provided for all champions! He was voted "1993 Athlete of the Year" by the IAAF and recognised for his brilliant performance by the British Athletic Writers' Association, who bestowed the same award. He was also awarded "Welsh Sports Personality of the Year" as he was in 1999.

Colin produced his best display of consistent sprint hurdling when he ran eleven races in under 13.10 in 1994. Indoors he also lowered the world record with a run of 7.30 in Sindelfingen, Germany. At the European indoors he created a unique double as he won both the 60 hurdles and 60 flat. Such was his improved sprinting speed that he came within 1/100th of Linford Christie's European 60 record with a time of 6.49. Injury plagued him the following year, and he was forced to miss the world championships and undergo another knee operation.

He finished fourth in the Olympics in Atlanta 1996, but suffered from more knee trouble afterwards. Two years later, in his only black-mark in an otherwise exemplary career, he was criticised for pulling out of the Commonwealth Games in Kuala Lumpur after having been made team captain. He later competed in a lucrative meeting in Tokyo. There he beat the World and Olympic champion Allen Johnson. Shrugging off the criticism, he said: "I feel like I've had enough of the Commonwealth Games. I've won one silver and two gold. I guess it's time for someone else to win the title". Earlier in the season he won his third successive European title in Budapest to become the first to do so in the event and ran 13.02 in

Colin had to use his finishing dip to clinch the world title in Seville from the fast finishing Anier Garcia of Cuba (right). However, Garcia gained his revenge by going on to beat Colin in Sydney to take the Olympic title.

both semi and final within seventy-five minutes. He made the long trip to South Africa for the World Cup which he won. The event was originally not on his schedule but with so many athletes dropping out of the British team, he felt he had to run. It was a journey too far as he admitted that he was exhausted and could not raise himself again for another championship meeting.

In 1999 he drew on all his experience to win the World championship in Seville - six years after his last World title. He became the first ever athlete to regain a world title. Early in 2000 he took his first gold medal after three silvers, by winning the World indoor championship. It was a great personal achievement particularly as many people had written him off as past it but he knew that he still had at least another championship in him. In a stop-go season after aggravating a hamstring injury sustained weight training in Australia in March and then being hit by a thigh problem he still won a record tenth AAA's title despite lack of training and numerous journeys back and forth to Germany and Limerick for medical treatment.

Being ranked in the world's top ten in his event every year since 1986, and in the top three since 1987, lapsing only in 1995 is an incredible span for any sportsman, let alone an athlete. He was top ranked each year from 1992 to 1994. His long career has brought him undoubted wealth – twenty-two major championship medals, twelve of them gold (one more than Linford Christie) and no one in history has run the 110 hurdles faster.

When he failed to win the sport's greatest honour - an Olympic gold - Colin knew that as he winds his career down, he can look back on life at the top with pride. "There was a time when I'd be a little bitter and think why haven't I won Olympic gold. But I wouldn't swap anything I've won or achieved in the sport just for an Olympic title. The two world titles I have won were just as difficult to win as an Olympic title".

Colin is the only hurdler in the world to run under 13 seconds three times in a season and as well as both the indoor and outdoor world record holder, he has also held the world best in 1991 (22.63) for the rarely run 200 hurdles. As one of the greatest athletes in the history of world athletics, Colin's record-breaking achievements go much deeper than his ultimate world records. After a European junior record of 13.44 in 1986 he has set seven European, eight Commonwealth and nine British records at 110 hurdles from 1988-1993; nine British and four Commonwealth and European at 60 hurdles indoors; fifteen Welsh records (100, 200, 110 hurdles and 60 hurdles) from 1985 to 1993. Also at 50 hurdles he set a British record in 1992 and a European record in 1999. His appearance in Sydney took his total of British international vests to 62, by far the greatest by any Welsh athlete. He is the only Welsh athlete to compete in four Olympic Games.

Consistency is one attribute, which all athletes aim for, and this is one factor, which has made Colin Jackson stand out from the rest of the high hurdlers of the world. He compiled the greatest ever season of sprint hurdling in 1993 with 13 races sub-13.20 and did even better in 1994 with eleven marks inside 13.10 as against five in 1993. Another record, of which he is proud, is the winning streak of forty-four hurdles races which only ended in February 1995 when beaten by Allen Johnson indoors in the same time of 7.42.

In the hurdling world it is recognised that to run sub-13.10 is the sign of superstar status in the event. It makes interesting reading statistics on the top hurdlers and their consistency and it adds weight to the claim that Colin Jackson is the greatest hurdler in the world.

A summary of Colin's achievements

Total sub 13.10 runs (as at end of 2000)

Colin Jackson	27
Mark Crear (USA)	22
Allen Johnson (USA)	19
Roger Kingdom (USA)	5
Renaldo Nehemiah (USA)	6
Greg Foster (USA)	3
Anier Garcia (Cuba)	3

Gold medal collection

1986	110m H	World Junior Championships (Athens)
1989	60m H	European Indoor Championships (The Hague)
1990	110m H	Commonwealth Games (Auckland)
1990	110m H	European Championships (Split)
1993	110m H	World Championships (Stuttgart)
1994	60m H	European Indoor Championships (Paris)
1994	60m H	European Indoor Championships (Paris)
1994	110m H	Commonwealth Games (Victoria)
1994	110m H	European Championships (Helsinki)
1998	110m H	European Championships (Budapest)
1999	60m H	World Indoor Championships (Maebashi)
1999	110m H	World Championships (Seville)

Sub 13 seconds runs

12.91	Stuttgart	20 August 1993
12.97A	Sestriere	28 July 1993
12.98	Tokyo	15 September 1994
12.99	Brussels	3 September 1993
12.99	Madrid	6 September 1994

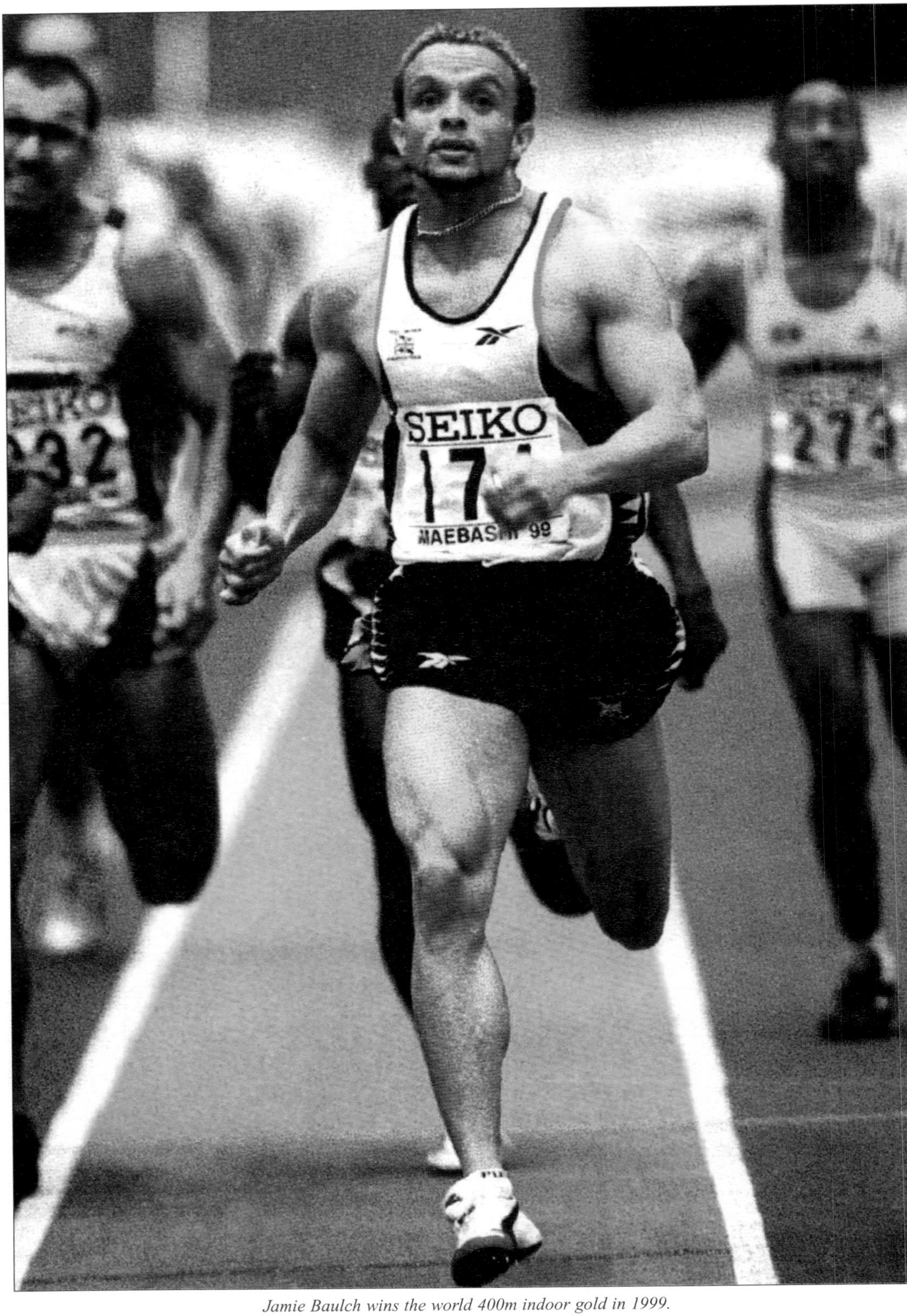

© Mark Shearman

Jamie Baulch wins the world 400m indoor gold in 1999.

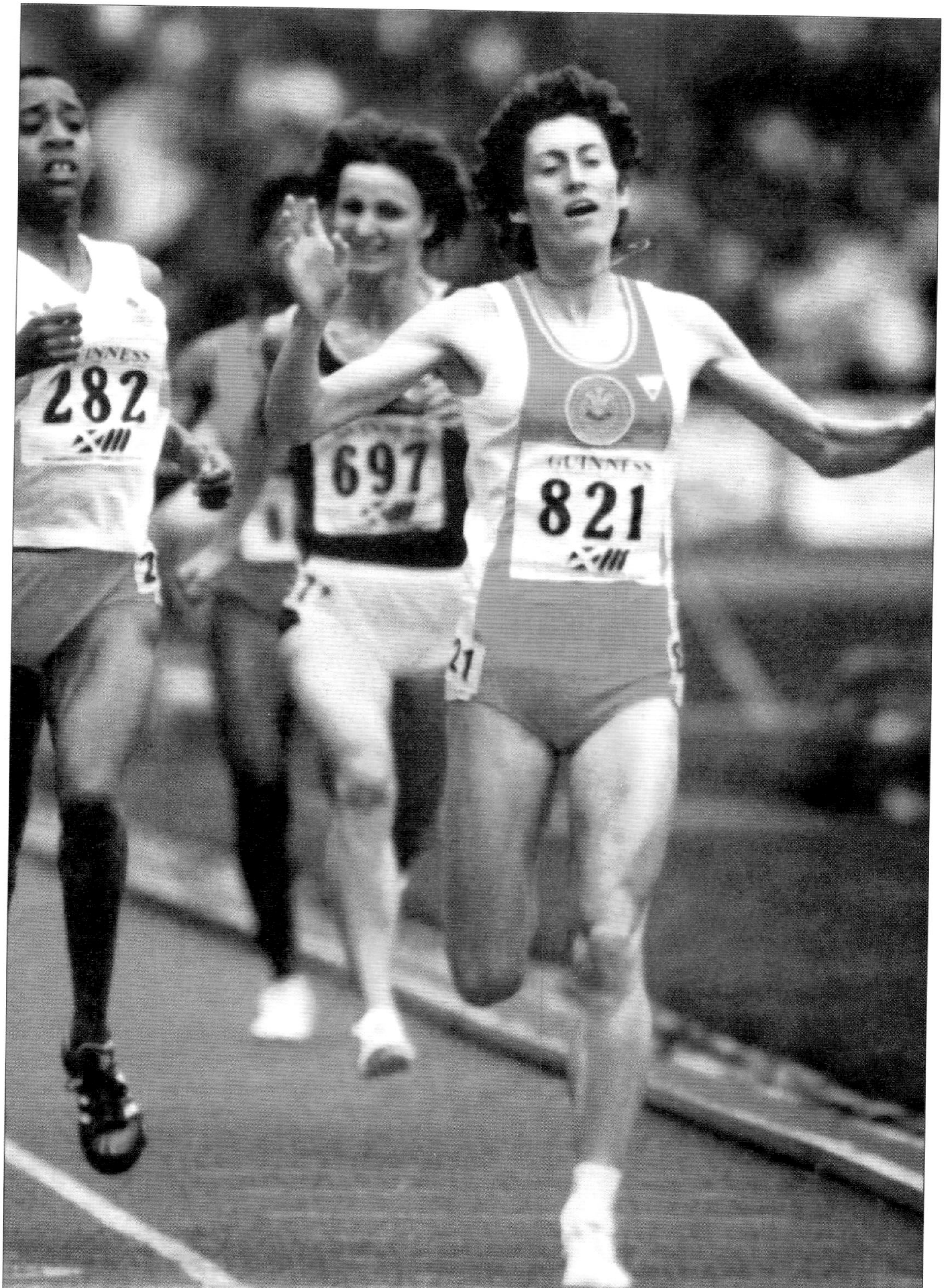

© Mark Shearman

Kirsty Wade celebrates her 800m victory at the 1986 Commonwealth Games in Edinburgh. Diane Edwards (282) of England was second.

© Mark Shearman

Kirsty Wade takes the bell in the lead on her way to claiming a second gold medal, this time over 1,500m at the 1986 Commonwealth Games. Debbie Bowker (145) of Canada was second and Lyn Williams (211) also of Canada, third. Yvonne Murray (691) of Scotland was fifth.

© Mark Shearman

Iwan Thomas (1781) just edges out England's Mark Richardson (1267) to win the 1998 Commonwealth Games title in Kuala Lumpur. Jamie Baulch (1769) just misses out on a medal.

© Mark Shearman

Christian Malcolm on his way to being crowned European indoor 200 champion in 2000.

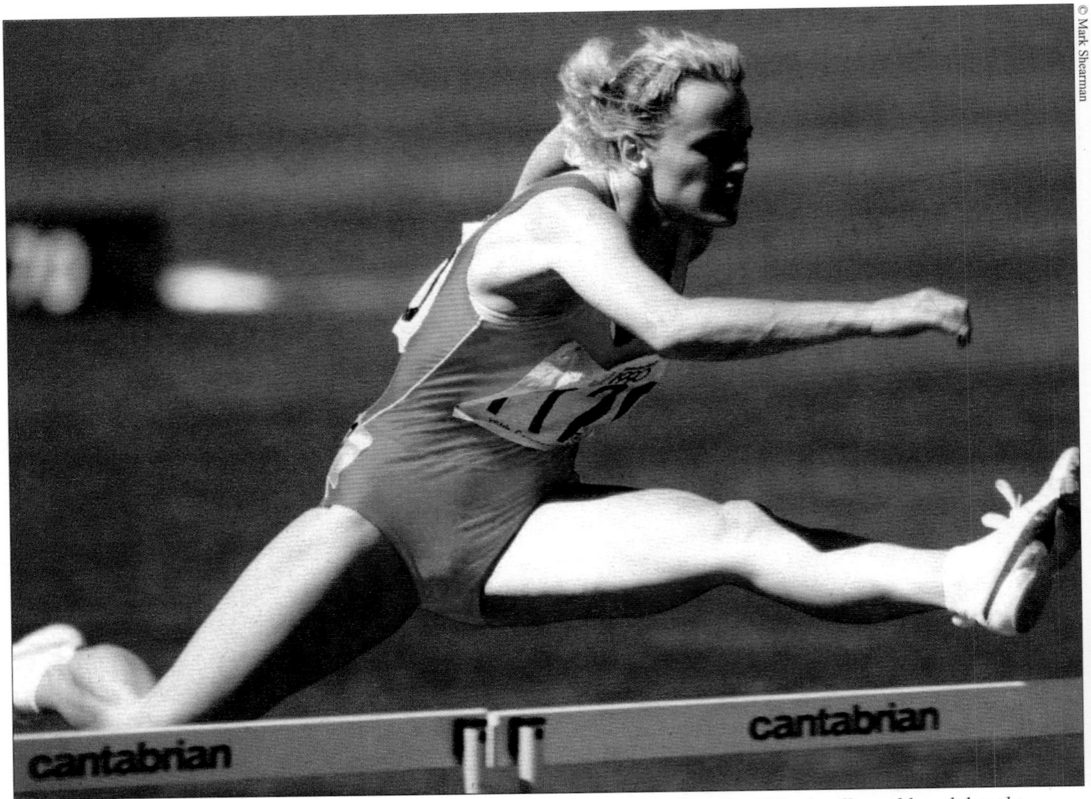

© Mark Shearman

Despite being drawn in the inside lane Kay Morley is on her way to taking the 100m hurdles gold medal at the 1990 Commonwealth Games in Auckland.

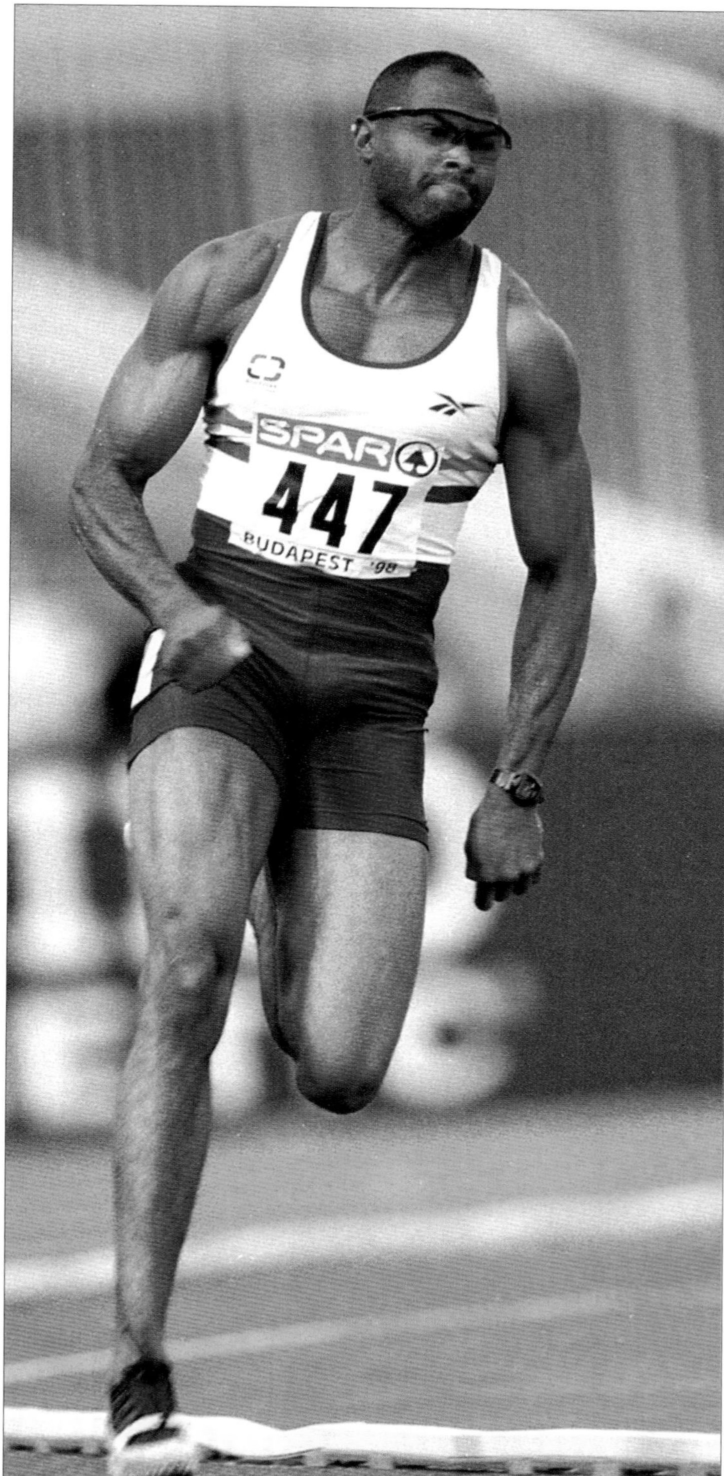

© Mark Shearman

Doug Turner on his way to win the silver medal in the 200 at the 1998 European Championships.

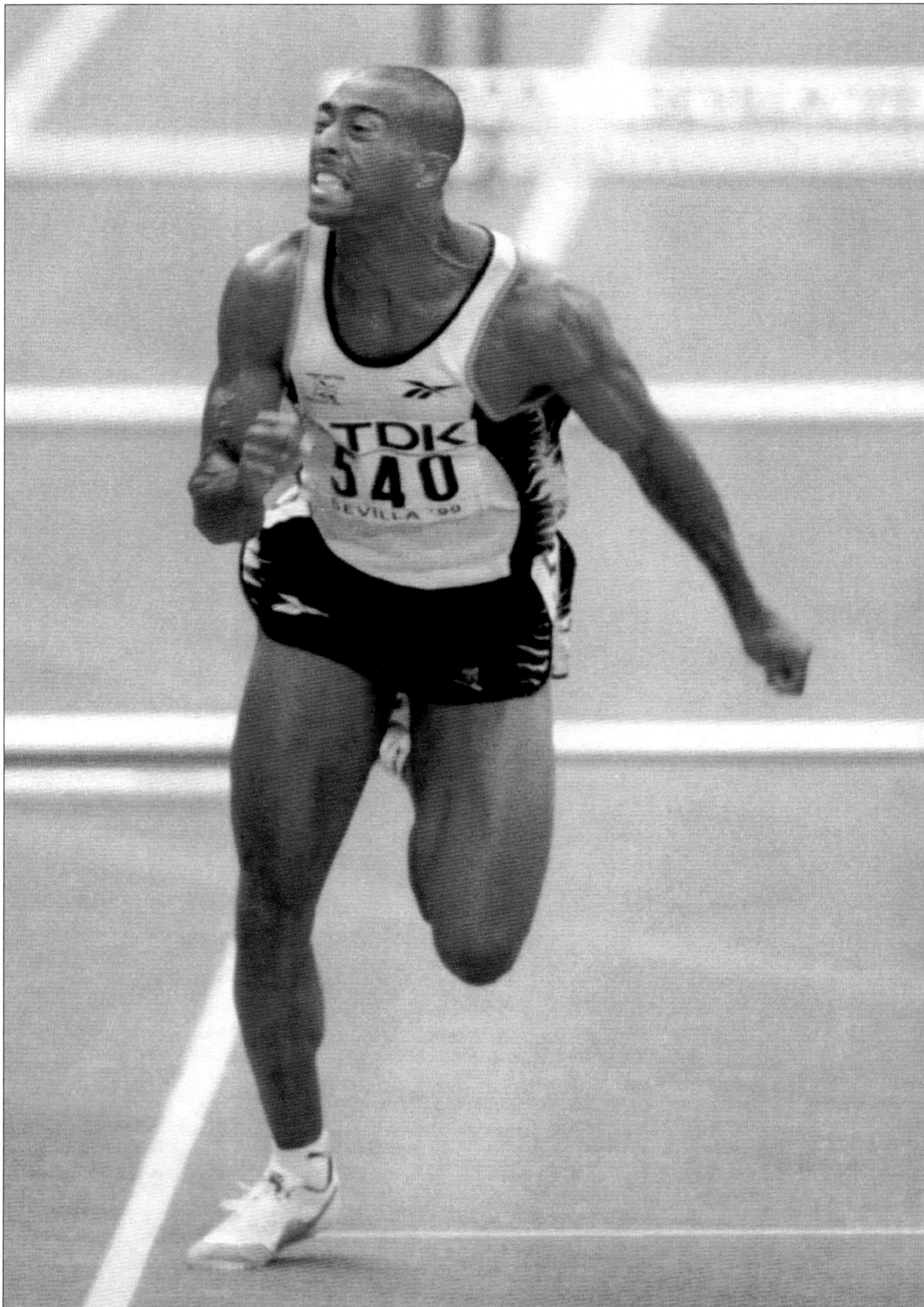

Seville 1999 saw Colin Jackson reclaim his world title.

Chapter 10

A Review of the 1958 Cardiff British Empire and Commonwealth Games

It was first mooted in 1938 that the Empire Games be brought to Wales for 1946, but the Second World War intervened, and it was not until 1958 that the great festival came, with the athletics events being held on the hallowed turf of Cardiff Arms Park. The Games were to have a dramatic effect on athletics in the Principality, if only for the fact that virtually all of the Welsh all-comers records were broken, and it gave the Welsh public the opportunity to see stars of world athletics such as Gert Potgieter, Keith Gardner, Betty Cuthbert and the young middle distance sensation Herb Elliott. John Merriman also emerged as a national hero by taking the 6 miles silver medal in a sterling battle with Australian Dave Power, one of the stars of the Games.

The V1th Empire Games might be best remembered in some quarters for the gold medal that the late Howard Winstone won in the bantamweight division of boxing, the only gold to be won by the hosts. However the Games, which ran from 18th to 26th July, were regarded as one of the best to date and are still to this day the biggest athletics spectacle Wales has seen.

This overhead shot of Cardiff Arms Park during the Opening Ceremony of the Games will bring back memories to many rugby fans, and shows the Empire Pool top left hand corner and to the right the then Glamorgan cricket ground which was used as the competitor's warm up area. Of course, the Empire Pool has now gone to make way for the Millennium Stadium, and Cardiff RFC now play on the old cricket ground.

Sir Arthur Porritt, Chairman of the British Empire and Commonwealth Games Federation said in his report of the Games: "The triumph of Wales and Cardiff in staging the V1th Games is now history - and history will ring down the years to come. The smallest country yet to accept the onerous responsibility of acting as hosts, Wales produced what, in retrospect, can only be called a masterpiece. Superb organisation, both administrative and technical; a standard of competition and sporting results comparing with the best in the world and, most important of all, a spirit of friendship and understanding engendered automatically by the traditional and spontaneous Welsh enthusiasm and warmth of hospitality – all combined to ensure an outstanding success. Wales should be justly proud of this achievement".

Wales had been an enthusiastic supporter of the Empire Games concept from the very earliest days and was one of the eleven countries which sent teams to the inaugural Games in 1930 in Hamilton, although not represented in the athletics events - Pembrokeshire-born Reg Thomas won the mile title and the half-mile silver in English colours. It was also one of the first countries to form an Empire Games Council or Association in 1933. This loyalty won Wales the vote for the 1958 Games. Wales was the first small country to have the honour of holding the Games. It is interesting, looking back briefly into history, to follow the sequence of events that brought the Games to Wales. The small teams sent by Wales to previous Games may not have acquired many gold medals but they had never returned empty handed.

After the 1938 Games in Sydney, the Welsh team returned victorious with two gold medals - including Jim Alford in the one-mile - and one silver medal from all sports. At the " Welcome Home" luncheon in Cardiff, Sir Robert Webber threw out a challenge that could have been entitled " Bring the Games to Wales " and he repeated it later in a broadcast. That challenge had never been forgotten and, after twenty years, Sir Robert had the pleasure and pride not only of seeing the rich fruits of the seeds he had sown, but also by being an active member of the Organising Committee. At the time he threw out his challenge, there was not a single cinder track in Wales. His speech mentioned that 1946 was proposed as the "target" year. With the intervention of the War, however, this plan never came to materialise, as did a major project for building a national sports stadium in Cardiff.

The idea, necessarily in cold storage during the war years, was revived immediately afterwards, and in the final analysis it will be judged that the Games came to Wales as the result of a simple decision taken by the British Empire Games Council in Wales in 1950 to elect its officers for a four-year period instead of annually. From that moment the Council had a team of officers and members with a four-year plan covering from one Games to the next. Within two years of that decision, a definite plan had been formulated for inviting the Games to Wales in 1958 – six busy years ahead. The Council for Wales accordingly settled down to the intensive preparation of a memorandum setting out how it proposed to stage the Games if invited to do so. Armed with this, and with personal guarantees from individuals who were prepared to support the Games to the extent of almost £25,000, the third Lord Aberdare, President of the Council and subsequently also of the Organising Committee until the time of his tragic death in October 1957, presented the case for Wales at the meeting of the British Empire and Commonwealth Games Federation in General Assembly held during the 1952 Olympic Games in Helsinki. Significantly, the Air Ministry had agreed that if required, part of RAF St. Athan, some 15 miles west of Cardiff, could be used as the athletes' village.

Wales confirmed as hosts in 1954

With the field left clear by the withdrawal of Nigeria and Singapore as potential hosts, the Welsh bid had a powerful lobby. The effect of Lord Aberdare's advocacy and the scheme he presented, was the knowledge that the Games would come to Wales in 1958, although final ratification could not, under the regulations, take place until the Federation meeting - now renamed the British Empire and Commonwealth Games Federation - during the Vancouver Games in 1954. There was a comprehensive draft organisational plan, an adequate schedule of facilities existing or projected, evidence of satisfactory financial backing and the prospect of general support throughout the Principality presented by Charles Newnham, who was to be appointed the full-time Director of Organisation in early

Team Manager Ted Hopkins leads the Welsh team at the Opening Ceremony of the Games.

1955. The motion was seconded by Australia and, by a unanimous vote, Wales was confirmed as the host country.

1,398 competitors, 962 men, 160 women and 266 officials took part in the nine sports, representing a record thirty-five countries. Of these 424 were track and field athletes. Wales had a team of 102 men, 18 women and 17 officials. England had the biggest team with 204. 35 countries, a record with only a dozen members of the Commonwealth not taking part, made their way to Cardiff for a memorable athletics feast. The Welsh track and field team were very young with many of those selected under 20 years of age. The youngest of these was John M. Williams in the 880 yds. He was just 17 years old and still a pupil at Queen Elizabeth Grammar School, Carmarthen, and one the finest teenage athletes in Britain.

Six-lane cinder track only just squeezes into Arms Park

The main stadium was at Cardiff Arms Park, the venue for track and field athletics and the Opening and Closing Ceremonies, the chief source of box office revenue, and by its very nature the chief showpiece, but to secure the venue the organisers had to depend on the goodwill of several organisations. Naturally the Cardiff Athletic Club and Welsh Rugby Union had their own interests to consider. The opening of the new rugby season would be five weeks after the Games ended. Cardiff Greyhound Racing Club had their track circling the rugby playing area and this would have to be dug up for the construction of a 440 yds cinder track of international quality. There were only inches to spare without cutting into the concrete terraces at ground level to fit in the six-lane track, although it was necessary to cut into the terraces at one end in order to provide the essential straight for the 100 yds and 120 yds hurdles. The stadium had a capacity of 34,000 with only 7,500 of these standing on the terraces. The capacity for international rugby matches at the time was around 60,000.

The cost of hosting the Games exceeded £300,000 but with nearly £110,000 raised before the first day, the Games made a record surplus of £37,000. This was helped by a paying attendance figure of over 110,000 spectators who attended the main stadium. Warming-up facilities for track and field athletics, with immediate access to the competitor's entrance to the main stadium had to be provided on the adjacent cricket ground, where Glamorgan Country Cricket Club played before their move to Sophia Gardens in the 1970s.

General view overlooking Cardiff Arms Park during the Opening Ceremony of the Games.

A Commonwealth wide competition was held for the design of the three major medals and it was befitting that the winning design was the work of a Cardiff artist A. Kitson-Towler.

For the first time in the Games, the Queen sent a message via a nationwide relay and it made its way from Buckingham Palace through Reading, Stratford-on-Avon, Wolverhampton, Stoke-on-Trent, Shrewsbury before entering Wales at Chirk on the Wales/England border. At the time Wales was made up of thirteen Counties and the baton had to pass through all of them before reaching Cardiff Arms Park.

Queen's Message leaves Buckingham Palace on its way to the opening of the Games in the safe hands of Roger Bannister (centre), the first man to run a mile in less than 4 minutes. He is flanked by fellow Vancouver Empire Games champions (left) Chris Chataway (3 miles), and (right) Peter Driver (6 miles).

One runner from each club, service unit and school in each county was given a stage, these being two miles for seniors and one mile for juniors. The run continued day and night, seniors being used in dense traffic conditions and, where possible, from midnight to 6.00 am. In the north the

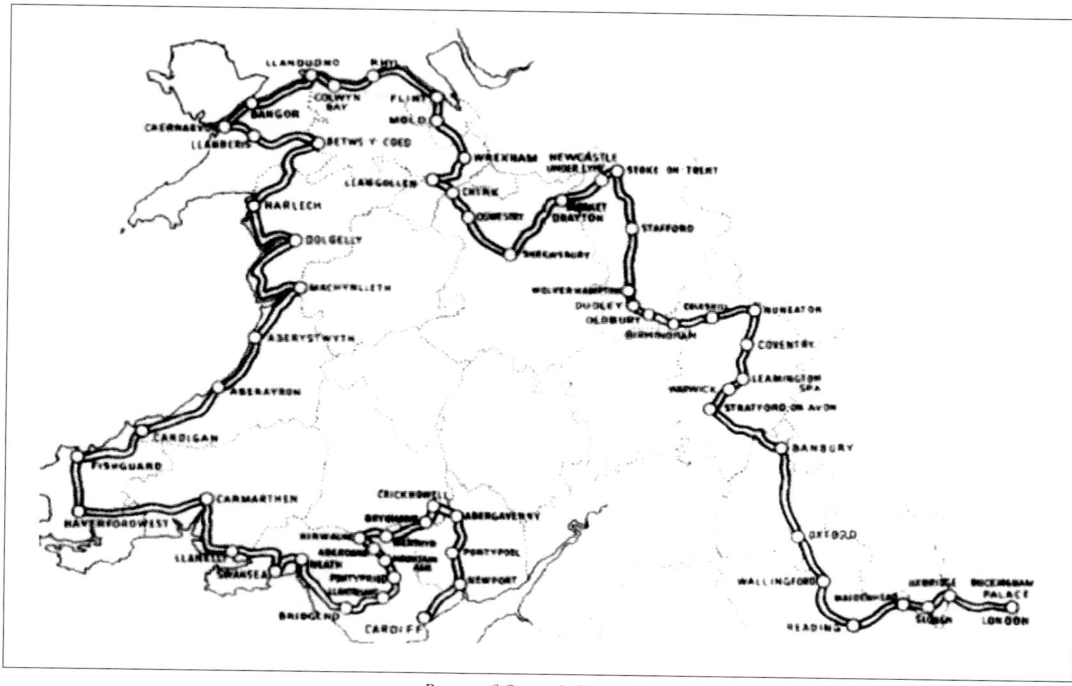

Route of Queen's Message.

message passed through Llangollen, Wrexham, Flint, Llandudno and Caernarvon before heading south down the west coast through Dolgellau, Aberystwyth, Cardigan and Haverfordwest. To satisfy the needs of the more heavily populated south the relay wound around the coast from Carmarthen, Llanelli, Swansea, and Bridgend before it covered the valleys of the south through Aberdare, Brynmawr, Abergavenny, and Newport then on to Cardiff. The baton carrying the message was appropriately engraved with a silver plate and this complete trophy is now on permanent exhibition at the National Museum of Wales. The final leg relay runner was Wales' most famous post-war rugby player and Olympic silver medallist 36 year-old Ken Jones of Newport. To a thunderous roar of applause that echoed around the stadium he made a circuit of the track and stopped in front of the Royal dais. As he handed the baton to the Duke of Edinburgh a wag in the crowd is reputed to have shouted: "Forward pass Ken".

Text of Queen's Message

To all athletes assembled at Cardiff for the Sixth British Empire and Commonwealth Games I send a warm welcome and my very best wishes.

I am delighted that so many Commonwealth countries have sent teams to Wales for these Games. The number is larger than ever and more than three times as great as for the first meeting at Hamilton in 1930.

This is welcome proof of the increasing value, which is being placed today on physical strength and skill as an essential factor in the development of the whole man; healthy in mind and body.

It also gives me the greatest personal pleasure to know that so many members of the Commonwealth family are meeting in friendly rivalry and competition.

I hope that many lasting friendships will grow from this great meeting of athletes and spectators and that you will all go home with a better understanding of the value of our Commonwealth of Nations.

I am greatly looking forward to being with you at the end of next week.

Elizabeth R.

The Games attracted capacity crowds of over 30,000 for the track and field events and this picture shows the crowd during the heats of the mile.

Cardiff Arms Park had not only been transformed, but also dressed up. The flags of the Commonwealth countries, the many-hued colours of the uniform of athletes and the colourful dresses of the spectators assembled in their summer clothes and the red-rust of the running track, combined to produce an unforgettable scene of beauty. The weather too played its part and, in the depressing British summer of 1958, the Games were blessed with sunshine for practically the whole of the athletics programme. Thus was engendered the infectious atmosphere of friendliness and good-natured camaraderie in which the events were conducted and which was shared by all present. They had come in greater numbers by far than ever before from the four-corners of the world to little Wales. The original programme planned could not contain their numbers and it became necessary to hold extra eliminating sessions even before the official Opening Ceremony.

The tally of new records bears its own testimony: three world records, twenty two Games records, eleven British and Commonwealth records, nine UK all-comers' records, sixteen UK National records, and 26 Welsh all-comers' records. The world records were set by Gert Potgieter (South Africa) in the 440 yds hurdles (49.7), Anna Pazera (Australia) who had competed for Poland in the 1956 Olympic Games, in the javelin with 57.40, while the quartet of English sprinters of Madeline Weston, Dorothy Hyman, June Paul and Heather Young scorched to a new mark of 45.3 in the 4 x 110 yds relay.

The Games provided a feast of athletics and the crowd, which averaged over 30,000 each day, witnessed the grace of Milkha Singh of India winning the 440 yds and the incredible strength of Potgieter. The Springbok who had broken three vertebrae in his neck playing rugby the previous year, set his new world record at the last Games in which his country would take part for almost four decades. Two 1960 Olympic Champions showed their class as Kiwi Murray Halberg won the 3 miles and the seemingly invincible Herb Elliott took the 880 yds/1 mile double just weeks ahead of a memorable day in world athletics when he slashed the biggest margin off the world mile record since 1882, when he won in Dublin with 3:54.5. Elliott went on to create athletics immortality by winning the Rome Olympic

Australia's Herb Elliott wins the 880 yards from Brian Hewson of England.

1,500 in a world record 3:35.6. His winning time in the mile at Cardiff was 3:59.03 – the first time 4 minutes had been bettered in Wales. For Halberg, the Rome 5,000m Champion, who had turned to athletics after a schoolboy rugby injury to his arm, it was a triumph at the headquarters of Welsh rugby as his winning time of 13:14.75 was the third fastest ever recorded.

The crowd's favourite, however, was Tom Robinson, the one-man team from the Bahamas, who struck gold in the 220 yds, after getting the Games off to a brilliant start by clocking a new Games record of 9.5 for 100 yds in the heats before the official opening ceremony. John Jones, a 19 year old from Lewis School, Pengam also caused a sensation in the heats of the 220 yds, when he finished second to eventual winner Robinson in a Welsh junior record of 21.9, and a time only bettered that year amongst British juniors by future world 220 yds record holder Peter Radford and Robbie Brightwell, the 1964 Tokyo Olympic 400m fifth placer.

Albie Thomas of Australia, the eventual silver medalist, leads in the 3 miles from New Zealander Nev Scott (part hidden) and eventual winner teammate Murray Halberg, who is tracked by Gordon Pirie and Derek Ibbotson, both of England.

Tom Wood (26) of Wales leads countryman Rhys Davies (23) just after the start of the marathon. Arthur Keily of England (7) is followed by Scotland's Alexander McDougall (20), Peter Wilkinson of England (10) and the eventual winner Dave Power of Australia (1).

Jamaica's Keith Gardner also performed brilliantly winning the 100 and 120 yds hurdles, and almost achieved a unique treble, being denied only by the spectacular Robinson who beat him into second in the 220 yds by just three hundredths of a second. Dave Power followed up his win in the six miles over John Merriman with an easy win in the marathon. The race wound its way out to Castleton and back in a course designed by Ken Harris. Welshman Rhys Davies was leading at the 10 miles point in 53:48, but faded to ninth at the finish.

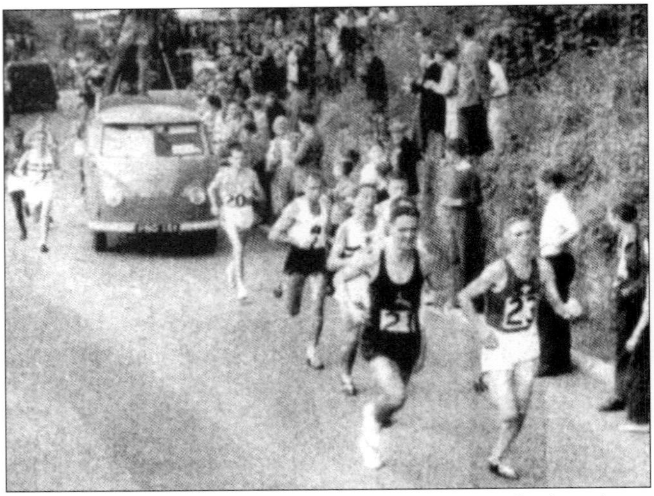

Rhys Davies of Wales leading at the 10 miles point near Castleton from the eventual silver medalist, Jan Barnard (21) of South Africa. Eventual winner Dave Power (1) can be seen just behind in 6th at this stage.

Games records were set in all of the men's field events except the pole vault, with Jamaica's Ernie Haisley causing a surprise in the high jump with his win over the 1956 Olympic silver medallist, Charles Porter. In the javelin, where the run-up was off grass, Colin Smith of England threw 71.28 in the first round to secure the gold and add over 2 metres to the Welsh all-comers record he set when winning for the AAA against the Welsh AAA at Margam the previous year.

Australia dominated the women's events taking five of the nine gold's at stake. The undoubted star was Australian Marlene Mathews-Willard who took both sprints beating teammate and 1956 Melbourne Olympic 200m champion Betty Cuthbert in the 220 yds.

Mathews had taken the bronze in Melbourne. Cuthbert was to take the Olympic 400m title in Tokyo six years later, ahead of Britain's Ann Packer. Behind Anna Pazera's world record win in the javelin was Averil Williams taking the bronze for England. Averil was soon to move to Wales and took the 1962 Welsh title before appearing again the Games in 1970 – but this time in the red of Wales, where at the age of 35 she finished an excellent fifth.

What is hard to believe by modern day standards is that the programme did not contain a number of events, which today are essential parts of the schedule for major Games. Significantly for Wales, the programme did not contain a 3,000m steeplechase and this, almost certainly, deprived Wales of a medal from the 1952 Olympic bronze medallist, John Disley, who, ran in the 3 miles but failed to finish due to injury. Similarly, Hywel Williams, the previous years AAA decathlon champion was robbed of a probable medal due to the absence of his speciality and had to content himself with appearances in the shot and discus. Furthermore there were no walking events. As seen elsewhere in this book, Hywel describes this as his biggest disappointment in an illustrious athletics career spanning three decades. The women's events were restricted to just nine events, with no distance event on the track beyond 220 yds and no pole vault, triple jump or hammer.

Merriman, Merriman, Merriman ....

The highlight for Wales came on Saturday 19th July when, with the temperatures in the high seventies, fifteen competitors started the six miles race. Welsh hopes rested with 23-year-old John Merriman who a month earlier had broken the Welsh records for 3 and 6 miles and so was in good form in his build up to the Games. During the first two miles the Welshman was happy to keep in the pack trailing the newly crowned UK 6 miles record holder Stan Eldon (England), Dave Power (Australia) and Arere Onentia of Kenya. Just after three miles Merriman led for two laps vociferously encouraged by his fellow countrymen.

© Western Mail

Eventual winner Dave Power (Australia) leads John Merriman of Wales in the closing stages of their epic 6 miles battle.

In the sweltering heat of the stadium the battle continued to be fought and at the bell Power sprinted, but Merriman, to the accompaniment of deafening roars from the crowd, went after him, while the gallant Onentia was forced to yield ground. Down the back straight Merriman, appearing strong, tried to force himself in front, but seemed to lack the confidence of experience in pressing home his challenge. He kept on terms, however, around the last bend and into the home straight. Power gallantly controlled himself for the final sustained effort, which took him over the finishing line a winner by some three yards and then collapsed on the grass verge. Merriman looked fresher and waved jauntily to his cheering compatriots who had found this race an unexpected national titbit. Power five days later went on to an incredible double by winning the marathon. Merriman's time of 28:48.94 was just over five seconds outside the Welsh record he set at the AAA Championships the previous month. He became an overnight national hero. Four days later he finished sixth in the 3 miles just ahead of Power. In his career he set a total of fourteen Welsh records – three at 3 miles, eight at 6 miles and three at 10,000m, plus two British records at 10,000m.

Speaking after the race he said: "A tactical error prevented me winning a gold medal for Wales. I believe I could have beaten Dave Power had I taken the lead a mile from the tape or kept my final burst for the last 100 yards. But I am pleased that I even came second, because I was very pessimistic before the race. Firstly the heat in the stadium (78 degrees) and second the fact that I was only placed seventh in the A.A.A. three miles the week before. I had had high hopes of gaining second place then at the White City. But when the crowd on Saturday started chanting "Merriman, Merriman, Merriman", I forgot all about the heat. My one thought was to get home in first place. While I ran the race according to plan - I intended taking it easy for the first three miles - I now know that I left my challenge too late and lost precious ground by trying to pass Power on two bends. Some have suggested that I lost ground by looking back. I don't think this is so in a six-mile race. I started preparing for this race as long ago as January, and well before I knew that I would represent Wales. I started by running eight miles a day and worked this up to 12 and 13 miles. Fully realising my lack of finishing speed, I concentrated on improving this by running repetitions of 440, 330 and 220yds flat out. Contrary to training principles I kept this up until the very eve of the race. I don't believe in resting up. In fact I went for a long walk before the race and because of the heat I increased my consumption of liquids and took more salt than usual. This helped considerably because there is nothing worse than having a parched mouth and nearly six miles in front of you. The first mile was too fast for my liking but I stayed with the second group for the first three miles. Then I made my effort to get among the leaders who were a good 20 yards ahead. This effort took a lot out of me. I was tired out but kept on. By the five-mile mark I was feeling perfectly fresh and I know now that I should have put the pressure on. I found the Cardiff track very fast but a little too hard for long distance work. Despite this I still managed to run about ten miles the day after the race and prepare for the three-mile race.

Pen Portrait – John Merriman (Watford H) 1936-2000

Merriman had been a promising athlete since 1953 but 1958 was the year in which he first made his name on the international scene. He started with an outstanding cross-country season, winning the Welsh title at his first attempt at Pontcanna Fields, Cardiff, just across the road from his Empire Games triumph. He was third in the English Inter-Counties championships, fifth in the English National and seventh in the International (now World Championships), which was also held that year at Pontcanna Fields. Some weeks after his exploits in the Cardiff Empire Games he went on to finish sixth over 10,000m in the European Championships in Stockholm setting a new Welsh record of 29:03.8.

In what was a golden era for British distance running Merriman shone like a beacon. After a fairly quiet 1959, in which he nevertheless ranked seventh in the world over 10,000m, he returned to his best form in the Olympic year of 1960 and had another successful season over the country. After taking fourth place in the Inter-Counties and second in the National he went on to finish third in the International championships in Scotland. This emulated the feat of Sam "Soapy" Palmer in 1938 and remains the best placing by a Welsh runner in this championship, since equalled by Steve Jones in 1984.

In a match against France at London's White City in July, Merriman clocked 29:01.8 for a new UK 10,000m record when finishing second to Robert Bogey. This set him up very nicely for the Olympic Games in Rome and he duly improved on his record in the Eternal City by recording a UK record 28:52.89 coming home in

eighth place, which stood as a Welsh record until beaten by Bernie Plain ten years later in the 1970 Commonwealth Games. From then on Merriman's commitment to athletics was only half hearted yet despite this he continued to turn in quality performances although his form could be erratic. His UK all-comers' record of 29:00.4 set in an international match against Hungary ranked him third in the world in 1961 and the following year he again ran for Wales in the Commonwealth Games in Perth and was good enough to win the bronze medal in the six miles with Britain's best strung out behind him. Despite his achievements there is a sense that Merriman was an athlete who never really fulfilled his potential. He was only 24 when he ran in the Rome Olympics, and would surely have gone on to greater things if his enthusiasm had not waned a little after the Games.

Had he taken the event seriously he may well have become one of the greats of marathon running. He won the prestigious Finchley 20 in 1960 suffering no great distress, and attempted the full distance for the first time in the AAA event in 1962. In the lead at 20 miles he suffered cramp and blisters and pulled out a mile further on. Later that year, after winning his bronze medal in the six miles, he also competed in the marathon at the Perth Commonwealth Games and was lying third after 20 miles before once again being forced to drop out with blisters. He died of a stroke at the young age of 64 in 2000.

A new feature was introduced for the closing ceremony and has since been carried on at other major Games. To take the opportunity to symbolise the friendliness of the Games, particularly that many friendships would have been made, all athletes would parade mixed up with no identity of country.

Creation of The Prince of Wales

However the closing ceremony will also be remembered for another historic moment, as the creation of the Prince of Wales was announced in the following words in the course of The Queen's Message:

> ***The Prince of Wales***
>
> *"I want to take this opportunity of speaking to all Welsh people, not only in this Arena but wherever they may be.*
>
> *The British Empire and Commonwealth Games in the capital, together with all the activities of the Festival of Wales, have made this a memorable year for the Principality.*
>
> *I have, therefore, decided to mark it further by an act which will, I hope, give as much pleasure to all Welshmen as it does to me.*
>
> *I intend to create my son, Charles Prince of Wales today. When he is grown up I will present him to you at Caernarvon"*

Illness prevented The Queen from taking part in person at the closing ceremony, so her message was relayed over the public address system. It was a truly historic moment of a memorable occasion.

The track and field sessions at the Games left an indelible impression on the minds of all who participated, whether as competitor, official or spectator. They constituted the greatest athletics feast ever presented in Wales and were at least equal to the 1948 Wembley Olympics as the finest sporting event to be seen in Britain. Almost immediately the Games finished, the track was dug up and re-laid just over a mile away at Maindy Stadium, where the cycling events of the Games had taken place.

In the final analysis, the Games were hailed throughout the athletics world as a major success. The much respected athletics journalist Mel Watman writing in the athlete's bible, *Athletics Weekly*, said: " They were the greatest track and field festival ever held in the British Isles" – that just about sums up the 1958 Cardiff Empire Games.

For the record ....

1958 Empire Games Champions

Men		
100 yds	Keith Gardner, Jamaica	9.66
220 yds	Tom Robinson, Bahamas	21.08
440 yds	Milkha Singh, India	46.71
880 yds	Herb Elliott, Australia	1:49.32
Mile	Herb Elliott, Australia	3:59.03
3 miles	Murray Halberg, New Zealand	13:14.75
6 miles	Dave Power, Australia	28:48.16
Marathon	Dave Power, Australia	2:22:45.6
120 yds Hurdles	Keith Gardner, Jamaica	14.20
440 yds Hurdles	Gert Potgieter, South Africa	49.73 world rec
4 x 110 yds relay	England (Peter Radford, Roy Sandstrom, Dave Segal, Adrian Breaker)	40.72
High Jump	Ernie Haisley, Jamaica	2.06
Pole Vault	Geoff Elliott, England	4.16
Long Jump	Paul Foreman, Jamaica	7.47
Triple Jump	Ian Tomlinson, Australia	15.74w
Shot	Arthur Rowe, England	17.57
Discus	Stephanus du Plessis, South Africa	55.94
Hammer	Mike Ellis, England	62.90
Javelin	Colin Smith, England	71.28
Women		
100 yds	Marlene Mathews-Willard, Australia	10.70
220 yds	Marlene Mathews-Willard, Australia	23.65
80m hurdles	Norma Thrower, Australia	10.72
4 x 110 yds relay	England (Madeleine Weston, Dorothy Hyman,June Paul, Heather Young)	45.37 world rec
High Jump	Michelle Mason, Australia	1.70
Long Jump	Sheila Hoskin, England	6.02
Shot	Val Sloper, New Zealand	15.54
Discus	Suzanne Allday, England	45.90
Javelin	Anna Pazera, Australia	57.40 world rec

Details of both the Welsh performances and the full Welsh team are contained within the statistics section.

Chapter 11

A Potted History of Welsh Schools' Athletics

The impact that the Welsh Schools' Athletics Association, and its predecessors have had on Welsh athletics is immeasurable. Put simply, without the dedication of its officials and PE teachers over the years, the likes of Colin Jackson, Nigel Walker, Kirsty McDermott (Wade) Christian Malcolm, Jamie Baulch, and a host of other stars might not have emerged.

Much of the origins of athletics in Wales can be traced back to the activities of various schools and colleges in the latter part of the nineteenth century. As we have seen, St. David's College, Lampeter and Llandovery College were probably the forerunners of organised athletics in the Principality around 1870. Most schools held an annual sports day which included many of the events we recognise today plus a few events which are no longer contested. The only inter-schools activity would have been annual matches between two or three schools but there was no co-ordinated competition on a wider scale.

It is interesting to note that on 25 June 1927 Port Talbot Elementary Schools held their first annual school sports at Talbot Memorial Park. Ten schools took part with events for youngsters from under 9 to under 14. Although there were a lot of fun events like sack races, potato races, skipping races and blind horses' races, there were also athletics events as we know them, e.g. high jump, long jump and 100 and 220 yds, though these were handicap races. A feature of the meeting was the printed programme, which was 42 pages long and included plenty of advertisements. There is also a programme for the Cardiff Schools' Football League Annual Sports held at Sophia Gardens, Cathedral Road on 4 July 1934. The foreword states that the league had been in existence for 38 years and had held annual sports days for 27 years. The programme is 84 pages long and over 1,500 youngsters took part in the events. There is no doubt that there was considerable athletics activity in schools during the 1930s. Each school held an annual sports day and there were local inter schools competitions but these were generally held within a relatively small area. Competition existed for both boys and girls.

Jack Williams Welsh Schools' AAA secretary 1947 – 1969. In the background (striped blazer) is RB Evans. The occasion is the opening of the Welsh Schools' Championships at Carmarthen Park in 1959.

Shortly before the Second World War a genuine attempt was made to organise schools competition. In

1937 both Glamorgan and Monmouthshire formed county schools' associations and in 1938 both bodies held county schools' championships and later met in inter-county matches. The Glamorgan Association had Wallis Walters, the 1908 Olympian, as Chairman and Trevor Jenkins as Secretary. The advent of the war obviously interrupted this process, but the seeds had been sown. No sooner was the war over than steps were taken to enlarge on the earlier initiatives and a meeting of the Glamorgan and Monmouthshire schools' associations was held on 20 September 1945 at Mountain Ash. The purpose of the meeting was to consider the formation of a national association to organise schools' athletics throughout Wales. Convened by Jack Williams of Mountain Ash, one of the pioneers in the formation of the Glamorgan Schools' AAA and secretary of that association at the time, the meeting was also attended by the other officers of that body, Sam Evans of Neath (Chairman) and Jim Excell of Aberdare (Treasurer) plus H.O. Jones, Secretary of the Monmouthshire SSAAA.

To these four must be given the credit for laying the foundations of the system of schools athletics in Wales which is now such an integral part of the athletics scene. After making a number of recommendations at their meeting, they then sent out questionnaires to every school in Wales. A meeting was held at the Royal Hotel, Cardiff on 9 March 1946 with the following present: H.V.W. Robinson (Merioneth), N.R. Butler (Montgomery), L. Jones (Radnor), E. C. Davies (Carmarthen), Jim Excell (Aberdare), H. O. Jones (Monmouth), Jack Williams and Sam Evans as Chairman, who in his inaugural address stated "For the first time we have assembled a small national committee to consider the encouragement of schoolboy athletics throughout the Principality" and he appealed to the meeting to reach definite decisions. He reported that almost a hundred schools had replied to the questionnaire and, spurred on by this positive response, the meeting produced a constitution and a further meeting was held at the Wellington Hotel, Wrexham on 12 July 1946, with Sam Evans in the chair, at which the Welsh Secondary Schools' AAA was formally created.

Twelve Welsh counties were represented at this meeting and the first officers of the WSSAAA were elected. Dr D Glyn John of Neath became Chairman with F. A. Arrowsmith of Llandrindod Wells as Vice Chairman; Jim Excell was elected Treasurer and Jack Williams as Secretary. Later on Trevor Jenkins, Director of Education for Glamorgan and one of the founder members of the Glamorgan association in 1937, was elected President. In addition to electing officers for the newly formed association, the other significant decision was to hold a Welsh Schools' National Championship meeting and this was scheduled for the following year. Since its inception, it has become an annual event and is one of the major meetings on the Welsh athletics calendar. It has been held every year with the exception of 1984, due to an industrial dispute. Meanwhile activity at county level had resumed Carmarthenshire Secondary Schools AAA held their first annual championships meeting at Carmarthen Park on 25 May 1946 and 15 schools took part. Most of the other counties held their first annual championships either in 1946 or 1947.

First Welsh Schools' Championships in 1947

An inter-county meeting took place in Bridgend on 29 July 1946 between Glamorgan, Carmarthenshire and Monmouthshire, but on 14 July 1947 the first ever Welsh Schools' National Championships were held, the venue being Taff Vale Park, Pontypridd and, despite the most atrocious weather conditions, were successfully completed. The counties taking part were Brecon & Radnor, Caernarvon, Carmarthen, Denbigh, Flint, Glamorgan, Merioneth, Monmouth, Montgomery and Pembroke – although affiliated, Anglesey did not take part until 1948 and Cardigan affiliated in 1950. The competition was for boys only and covered the senior, middle and junior age groups and the events were 100 yards, 220 yards, 440 yards, 880 yards, one mile, high hurdles, walk, relays, high jump, pole vault, long jump,

Welsh Secondary Schools
Amateur Athletic Association
WSSAAA
The First Annual
NATIONAL
CHAMPIONSHIP
MEETING
Taff Vale Park, Pontypridd, Glam
Saturday, 14th June, 1947

Front cover of the programme of the first ever Championships in 1947.

triple jump, shot, discus, javelin and cricket ball. An interesting addition to the programme of the 1948 championships was an exhibition run by Sydney Wooderson, world record holder for the 880yds at the time. It is worth noting that The South Wales & Mon AAA held "Schoolboy Championships" between 1924 and 1927 which were resumed in 1934 as "Elementary and Secondary Schools Championships". These appear to have ceased in 1941.

In 1955 events for girls were included in the championships for the first time. The only events were the 100 yds, high jump and relay for senior and junior girls. The following year a full programme of events (as at that time) was introduced for the same two age categories. This development led to the creation, in 1956, of a separate national association, the Welsh Secondary Schools' AAA for Girls, with Peggy Woodeson of Newport as its first Chairman and Eirlys Roberts of Anglesey as Secretary.

Eirias Park stages first Schools' international match

Continuing to expand its scope the WSSAAA embarked on its first venture into international competition when, on 15 July 1959, Scotland were the opposition in the first match ever to be organised at schools level between Wales and any other country. The result of the match, held at Eirias Park, Colwyn Bay, was a victory for the Scots by 97 points to 82. Welsh winners were Huw Ll Jones (440 yards 50.3), John Williams (880 yards 1:55.5), Alan Evans Jones (120 yards H 15.3) Bleddyn Williams (High Jump 1.67), John Davies (Shot 15.92) and David Price (Javelin 57.06).

The experiment was repeated in 1960, while in 1961, at Maindy Stadium, Cardiff, England took part for the first time and Northern Ireland followed in 1963. The matches, for athletes in the senior (under 20) age groups, became a regular annual fixture and led to the establishment of the British Schools' International Athletics Board in 1966. From 1968 the Irish team became a combined one drawn from north and south. Many of Britain and Ireland's greatest athletes have taken part in this match including John Treacy, Tom McKean, Yvonne Murray, Liz Lynch (McColgan), Steve Backley, Sonia O'Sullivan, Brian Hooper, Mike Winch, Katharine Merry, Mark Lewis-Francis and of course Wales' own Colin Jackson, Lynn Davies, Jamie Baulch and Christian Malcolm Oddly enough, they were not always as successful as one might have imagined. In his two matches for Wales Colin Jackson finished third and then second in the hurdles, beaten on both occasions by a Scottish hurdler by the name of Douglas Campbell. Whatever became of him, one wonders? Similarly, Lynn Davies was second in the long jump in 1961 to England's Neil Humphries.

At the 1982 Welsh Schools' Championships Alyson Evans (Layzell) became the first and still the only athlete to win three individual track events. As a pupil at Cardigan High School she won the Middle 80 hurdles, 400 and 400 hurdles. In 1985 she set a UK junior record of 58.37 for 400 hurdles and the following year reached the final at the Edinburgh Commonwealth Games. In 1996 she set three Welsh records and her best of 56.43 still stands as the Welsh 400 hurdles record today.

Since first taking part in 1961 England have tended to dominate the match, as one might expect, and have run out team winners each year since except in 1982 and 1983 when they did not take part. Wales finished runners up in 1967, 1972 and 1978 and have taken part in every match, (the only country to do so), including in 1984, despite the non-occurrence of the Welsh Schools' Championships. Since 1961 there have been many notable Welsh victories in individual events (listed in the statistical section). The only events on the current programme that Wales has never won are the boys' 3,000m, shot, hammer and walk, and the girls' 1,500m, 80m hurdles, pole vault, triple jump and walk. The most successful event has undoubtedly been the boys' high jump with eight wins. A major change occurred in 1974 when the match was switched from being for u20 to one for u17 which has been the case ever since.

1982 Welsh Schools' team. Colin Jackson (middle of back row) made his first appearance in Welsh colours at the Schools' International held that year in Colwyn Bay. On the extreme left and extreme right of back row are former Welsh long jump record holder Bryan Woolley and John Elias long jump star of the 60s and 70s. Next to Bryan is Delyth Davies the present Welsh Commonwealth Games team manager.

Cross-Country Championships commence in 1961

A further development came in 1961 when national cross-country championships were introduced, initially for two boys' age groups. These were held at Newtown and organised by William Thomas, PE Director of Montgomeryshire, until his death in 1972. Through his excellent organisational ability, the success of the cross-country championships was assured. Thomas was totally committed to the development of Welsh Schools' athletics and had become an active member of the Welsh Schools' Association before 1950, becoming Chairman in 1964 and, at various times, a Vice President and one of the Welsh team managers at British matches.

Boys' and Girls' Associations merge in 1966 to form Welsh Schools AA

Discussions were held in the mid 60s to consider amalgamating the male and female associations and a constitution was proposed at a joint executive meeting in February 1965. Following a mixed annual general meeting, the two Welsh associations merged in 1966 under the name of "Welsh Schools' AA". It is interesting to note that the Secretary of the female schools association at the time was Miss Raye Evans of Barry, who was has been such an influential force in Welsh women's athletics.

Pen Portrait – Raye Evans

Born in the Rhondda, Raye Evans showed early promise as a high jumper while at school, although there were few opportunities for competition then. In the 1950s she became Secretary of the Glamorgan Schools and team manager for both that organisation and the Welsh Schools' AA

Concerned at the lack of opportunity for girls, particularly beyond school age, she was heavily involved in the formation of the Welsh Women's AAA in 1951 and was one of its founder members. At various times she held the offices of Treasurer (1967-1976) and President (1979-1989), as well as being championships Secretary and team manager. She also represented the Welsh Women's AAA on the Women's AAA Executive Committee and was Welsh Women's CCA Treasurer from 1968 to 1974.

She was a prominent member of the WWAAA throughout the whole period of its existence, from its formation until it merged with the other bodies to form a single governing body for athletics in Wales. During this period Welsh women's athletics made great strides forward with the creation and development of annual national championships and regular representative and international matches.

An active fields events official for many years, she was a member of the team of judges for the jumping events at the Commonwealth Games (then known as the Empire Games) when they were held at Cardiff in 1958. Her association with the "Friendly Games" didn't end there, though, as she was team manager at the 1970 Games in Edinburgh, served as a committee member for many years and was a Vice President of the Commonwealth Games Council.

Raye Evans' contribution to Welsh athletics has been recognised in many ways. She is a life member of the Welsh Schools' AA and, in 1996, was presented with the AAW Award of Honour, the highest award that organisation can bestow. In 1998 special awards were made throughout the world to commemorate the 75th anniversary of the formation of the IAAF. Among the small number of Welsh officials to be recognised, Raye was presented with the IAAF Medal of Honour, an accomplishment that few will match.

Although no longer actively involved in athletics, Raye, now in her 90s, maintains a lively interest in the sport she has served so well for so long.

Until 1967 there were only two age groups for girls in the Welsh Schools' Championships. Juniors were under 15 while anyone over 15 was classed as a senior. In that year the senior category was split into two and the middle, or intermediate, age group was formed for girls under 17, which fell into line with the existing categories for boys. In common with the general trend in athletics the championships and the international match both converted to metric measurements in 1969.

Girls came into the cross-country picture in 1969. An international cross-country match was an inevitable development and this duly came into existence in 1972, initially only for middle boys and girls with junior boys and girls competing from 1977. Wales has only ever had 2 winners in the cross country – Colin Clarkson in 1977 and Debbie Crowley in 1981, both on home soil. On a patriotic note it is interesting to report that Debbie, who won by 80 metres, wore a daffodil pinned to her number. Highest placed athletes are listed in the statistical section. The team competition has been dominated by England who have won every event since they entered except for the under 15 girls event in 1991, when Ireland triumphed. Incidentally this has been the best age group for Wales with nine second places.

© Ceri Breeze

Debbie Crowley

John Clarkson

Colin Clarkson

For the other age groups Wales has finished second six times in the under 17 boys, five times in the under 15 boys and disappointingly only twice in the remaining female age group.

Based on the established Welsh Schools v Welsh Youth rugby match, the WSAA took up the suggestion of the South Glamorgan Schools and proposed annual inter-association fixtures against the various governing bodies of Welsh athletics in the under 20 age group. These would cover both cross-country and track and field, and the participating teams would take turns in acting as hosts. The proposal met with the approval of all concerned. Accordingly, on 29 March 1980, teams from the WSAA and the Welsh CCA contested a cross-country match at Fairwater Park, Cardiff with Cantonian High School playing hosts on behalf of the schools. The Welsh CCA ran out easy winners of both competitions, the boys' by 25 points to 53 and the girls' by 14 to 73. The individual winners of the inaugural competition were Steve Blakemore and Carole Bradford, both representing the Welsh CCA. Since then the fixture has become an annual event, usually held in its spiritual home at Talgarth, although there have been exceptions. In 1985 (at Bishop Gore, Swansea), 1989 (Porthkerry, Barry), 1993 (Sandy Water, Llanelli) and 1997 (Chepstow), the event was staged in conjunction with the British School's Cross Country international for under 17s.

Things didn't go quite so smoothly on the track. It was intended to follow up the cross-country fixture with a match between the WSAA and the Welsh AAA/Welsh Womens' AAA at Jenner Park, Barry, in July 1980. Unfortunately, a period of sustained heavy rain overnight rendered the track unusable and Meeting Director Andrew Ireland had no option but to call the meeting off. After this inauspicious start, however, the series began with a fixture at the same venue in 1981. The boys match was tight with the Welsh Schools running out winners by 105 to 104 points but the girls were beaten 70 to 94. This particular match has been held every year since, though in 1984 there was no competition for the girls, and over the years a variety of extra teams have been invited to add spice to the competition. Teams have included the Midlands, Scottish Schools, and Northern Ireland Schools plus, in the late 1980s, teams representing the American High Schools. The score between Welsh Schools and Welsh Athletics at the moment stands at 15 wins to 5 for the WSAA boys and 10 wins to 9 for the WSAA girls.

In 1988 another tier of competition was introduced with the creation of the inter-schools track and field cup for 2 age groups only – under 14 and from 14-16. This was introduced to encourage inter-school competition in athletics in the same way that a school hockey or rugby team would represent their school in an after school hours match. Similar competition in cross-country had been in existence since 1977.

The Welsh Schools AA, along with the other schools' associations, continued to develop and in 1990 a new competition was introduced - an indoor track and field international. This was held at Kelvin Hall, Glasgow on 8 December for the youngest of the three age groups and, as well as teams from Wales, Scotland and England, also included teams from Czechoslovakia and Belgium. The best placed Welsh athlete was David Williams who won his 400m heat and finished second in the final. This has now become an established competition and on 26 February 2000 the event was held in Wales for the first time at the magnificent new facilities at the National Indoor Athletics Centre at UWIC with teams from Wales, England, Scotland and Ireland competing.

The Glamorgan County Schools team at the 1958 Welsh Schools' Girls Championships. Pictured second right back row is Lynette Harries current AAW Chairman. At the meeting she won the shot and discus. Picture includes back row: Rayann Jones, Mary Lewis, Ann Morgan, Gillian Davies, Lynette Harries, Judith Rees. Front row: Marilyn Lewis, Gillian Powell, Jane Thomas, Hazel Cox, Beti Wyn Preece.

Pen Portrait – Charlie Hughes MBE (1928-1999)

One of the most prominent personalities in the evolution of schools' athletics in Wales was the late Charlie Hughes. Born in 1928, he went to teacher-training college in Bangor and, after 2 years in the army in Egypt, he started teaching at Denbigh High School where he remained until his retirement. His 'career' in athletics administration began in 1955 when he became Secretary and Treasurer of the Denbighshire Schools AA, a position he held until 1974. He then held the same posts with Clwyd Schools from 1974-1984. At national level he began as the Welsh Schools' Championships Secretary in 1967 and became Welsh Schools' AA

Treasurer in 1980 and President from 1983, holding both posts until his death in 1999. He represented Wales on the British Schools' International Athletics Board from 1982.

He was the driving force behind the implementation of huge sponsorship deals with the Esso National Dairy Council and afterwards the TSB, which gave the Welsh Schools' organisation a sound financial footing to carry out their activities.

No one had served the association with greater commitment, enthusiasm or skill. He spent untold hours working for the good of the association – not just ensuring that the finances remained healthy with or without sponsorship, but also supporting the needs of all school athletes both as individuals and as a collective body. He steered the association through a period of expansion, which saw the commitment to schools athletics extend far beyond anything schools had aspired to in the past. During his periods of office, we saw the introduction of the inter-schools competitions both in cross-country and track and field which gave access to a national championship for far more athletes in schools.

Charlie Hughes presenting Nigel Walker and Colin Jackson with awards for their services to Welsh Schools' athletics.

During his lifetime of service to the sport, he had seen many youngsters gain a lot of fun and enjoyment. Many went on to achieve great things and he was very proud of his connections with the formative years of world superstars like Colin Jackson, Nigel Walker, Jamie Baulch and Kirsty McDermott (Wade).

His long involvement in schools athletics brought him many awards. He received the Welsh AAA meritorious plaque in 1975 and the AAW Award of Honour in 1996 in recognition of his contribution to the sport in Wales. In between these he was awarded the MBE in 1990 for services to young people in sport. Funnily enough he collected his medal on the same day as hurdler Colin Jackson and recalled " I said jokingly to Colin that it had taken him just 13 seconds to earn his MBE and it had taken me 35 years".

Chapter 12

Walking in Wales – an overview

Wales has produced many outstanding walking champions from 19th century pedestrian stars Townsend and Gale through to Alf Yeoumans and Steve Barry. Here we look at the impact that this branch of the sport has had in Wales

Competitive athletics, including walking races, was a well-established part of local fairs and festivals by the seventeenth century. How amateur these meetings were and how competent were walking judges (if there were any) are other matters. It is known that in October 1670 Charles II and his nobles watched Lord Digby try to walk five miles in an hour on Newmarket Heath for a wager of £50. He failed by half a minute – but he was walking barefoot!

A class of professional pedestrians of known speed and endurance grew up in the service of the aristocracy. These "footmen" carried messages, went ahead of coaches to arrange food and rest at inns and performed other tasks which involved covering distance. The aristocracy and gentry began to match their footmen against each other for wagers in running and walking races. In the eighteenth and nineteenth centuries there were many professional contests, the best-known being Captain Robert Barclay's feat, starting on 1 June 1809 on Newmarket Heath, of walking a thousand miles in a thousand successive hours (i.e. one mile in each hour) for a prize of a thousand guineas. He succeeded, taking 42 days.

The first walking championship, under the now defunct AAC – the forerunner of the AAA, was held in 1866. As we have seen, the 7 miles race was won by the redoubtable Llanelli-born John Chambers in 59:32. Wales, with its first walking championship in 1904, appear to have been late starters. A study of the early English championships, which became AAA Championships in 1880, reveals no obvious Welsh winners other than Chambers. Some certainly had Welsh names, T Griffiths winning twice and W J Morgan three times. One can find a Parry and a Lewis amongst those placed, but none represented a Welsh club.

Alf Yeoumans of Swansea was the first Welsh winner of an AAA walking championship, taking the 2 miles at Stamford Bridge in 1906 and one of the finest exponents of the walking art in the early part of the last century.

*Pen Portrait – Alfred Thomas Yeoumans** *(Swansea C & FC and Highgate H) 1876 – 1955*

Although born in Enderby, Leicestershire, Alf Yeoumans spent most of his life in Swansea, where he was a docker, and many people in Wales feel that he never received the credit due to him. He competed in the 1908 Olympics in London and

broke at least two world-walking records that were never ratified. At Swansea in 1906, he clocked 12:53.2secs for 2 miles and at Bath the same year he was timed for the mile walk in 6:18.8, both times being faster then the listed world records.

D.J.P. Richards, himself the winner of twelve Welsh walking titles, said in his *Welsh AAA History and Records (1956):* "Neither of his times have found their place in the record lists, despite both events being held under the supervision of recognised judges and timekeepers – Why!" Apparently, his style was suspect and the minutes of the AAA meetings in February and April 1907 simply say that their decision to ratify the records were "held over" before refusing to accept the times at their meeting on 1st June. The general view in Wales was that he was hard done by.

Alf Yeoumans (centre), holder of the unofficial world record for 1 and 2 miles walk and 1908 Olympic Games representative.

He won dozens of races from 1 mile to 40 miles. His win at the AAA 2 miles in 1906 was in 14:20.4 but he was disqualified in the 1907 event. In the 1908 London Olympic Games he took part in the 10 miles walk but did not progress any further than the heats (heats for the 10 miles walk!). He won four Welsh 2 miles walks titles, with his winning time in 1905 of 14: 24.0 remaining as a championship best until beaten 34 years later by D.J.P. Richards at Rodney Parade Newport. When he retired he continued to serve Welsh athletics as an official, and was the first to congratulate DJP on his performance.

There are some interesting remarks attributed to him in an advertisement for embrocation in C.B. Fry's magazine published around 1906. It says that: "Yeoumans has beaten all the world's records for ½ mile; 1, 2, and 5 miles at unofficial meetings". It continues by saying that he lowered George Larner's world record for 2 miles of 13:11.0 with a time of 13 mins in Swansea; at Builth Wells in 1903 he clocked 6:15.0 for the mile which bettered Larner's world best; and clocked 39mins for 5 miles in an exhibition walk the following year to beat Dublin born William Sturgess's world record. He is also reputed to have clocked a time of exactly 6mins for the mile in an exhibition event. Whatever the validity of his performances, he was undoubtedly a remarkable athlete. He died in Swansea on 29th September 1955, aged 78.

** Surname on birth certificate was Yeomans.*

The next Welsh walker after Yeoumans to win an AAA title was John Evans, a Metropolitan Police officer, who took the 2 miles in 1921. Wales was to have a very long wait for another, although Will Ovens of Herne Hill Harriers finished third in the 7 miles in 1910 and second in the 2 miles the following year before he moved to South Wales, winning five Welsh 2 miles titles between 1920 and 1926. Much of the credit for the success of D.J.P.

Richards as a walker must go to Ovens who coached Richards when he took up walking in 1936. Richards says in his *History of the Welsh AAA*: "It was he (Ovens) who coached me and it was definitely due to his meticulous training that I acquired my 12 Welsh walking championships".

By permission of Kevin Kelly

Will Ovens

Walking in Wales appears to have been well supported in the years before the Second World War and good times were recorded. Presumably there were road walks in various places, but records of these have been hard to find.

The first Welsh Road Walking Championship came in 1929. It was a 15 miles race held in conjunction with the Royal Gwent Hospital Fete at Newport. It became a 10 miles race in 1945, although in that year and in 1946 it was classed as an open race, but reverted to Welsh Championship status in 1947. The results clearly show the dominance of Newport Harriers at this time. Something else is equally clear. Walkers were from South Wales, mostly South East Wales, and that has been true for all the twentieth century.

Post war walking in Wales was to go through several levels in quality and quantity. D.J.P Richards, who had been the leading Welsh walker in the late 1930s, was still winning practically everything up until 1948. So were Newport Harriers. The 1950s was one of the most successful decades for Welsh walking. Things started well and then improved. In 1951, John Lowther (St Julian's HS and Newport Harriers) won the AAA junior one mile walk in 6:59.2. He was the first British junior to walk a mile in under 7 minutes. In 1952 Gareth Lewis (Aberystwyth University) won followed in 1953 and 1954 by Gareth Howell (Ferndale GS, London University and Highgate Harriers) and in 1956 and 1957 by Mike Shannon (Newport HS and Newport Harriers). Gareth Howell also won the RWA Junior 5 miles road walk in 1954 and 1955.

The Welsh Secondary Schools, alone in Great Britain, held walks in their championships. Welsh dominance in AAA Junior Championships was the obvious result and Gareth Howell's win at Maindy Stadium in 1953, in lashing rain and strong wind, took him 6:49.8. That record stood until Shaun Lightman lowered it in 1962. Newport Harriers' three wins in the decade was unequalled by any other club.

Also in the 1950s a number of Cardiff clubs came into existence, providing much larger fields in road races, but Newport Harriers continued to dominate team championships. The Cardiff clubs set up other road races which were well supported. *The South Wales Argus* open 15 miles, which had started before the war and was originally limited to men with a Monmouthshire qualification, continued to be popular and attracted good walkers. It was won five times in succession by Jack Housden (Trowbridge AC), the National Police Champion. Newport Harriers organised an open 7 miles at Pontypool on August Monday and this was another race popular with Welsh and English walkers.

Dai Barry, father of Steve, with nine Welsh titles, was the most successful Welsh walker of the early 1950s. Mel Pope (Newport Harriers) was the Principality's best man later, winning 13 Welsh titles up to 1961, with a clean sweep in 1960. Barry was also an amateur boxer and international boxing referee.

Anyone who looks at the times recorded in Welsh road walks in the 1950s and 1960s can see that course accuracy presented a problem. So did direction. In 1954, Jack Thomas competed in the Welsh Junior 5 miles road walk from Roath Labour Club in Broadway. Gareth Howell shot away at the start and Jack soon lost sight of him. In second place he cleared everybody else but with no marshals to direct him he took a wrong turning and found himself wandering along unknown streets. Asking passers by if they had recently seen any race walkers produced a negative response but eventually he saw something he recognised which reminded him of a direct route back to the Roath Club. Setting off at a brisk heel-and-toe he was surprised to see, when he finally reached his destination, that the officials were facing in the opposite direction. He tapped the nearest one on the shoulder to enquire whether he had in fact finished second, whereupon the official leapt into the air and asked where on earth he had come from (though not exactly in those terms). It was soon confirmed that not only had Jack finished second, but he had only just failed to break the world record. Winner Gareth Howell had destroyed it, but no one was aware of which route he had taken to do so. The officials wisely decided that although the result would stand, the record would not. At one stage in the "Argus" walk, three walkers were walking along three different roads from one point on the course. Two of them ended up on a building site. In the 1957 Pontypool 7 the athletes walked into a car park and had to promptly turn around and walk out again as there wasn't another exit.

In spite of occasional problems Welsh walking had made considerable progress in the 1950s. This progress was not maintained throughout the 1960s though there were significant achievements. In 1965 Wales promoted the inaugural RWA 20k Championship, won by 1964 Olympic silver medallist Paul Nihill. In 1962 Arthur Thomson was in the British team for the European Championships in Belgrade, becoming the first Welsh walker to win a British vest since Alf Yeoumans. He was followed in 1963 by Vaughan Thomas (RAF) who also represented Great Britain at basketball, water polo, rifle shooting and ballroom dancing.

Roath and Splott emerge and Dai Barry's son needs his dinner

By the end of the 1960s there was a serious decline. Newport Harriers, with the departures of John Lowther, Jack Thomas, David Davies and Mike Shannon to India, Woodford Green, Australia and Highgate respectively, had ceased to have a walking section. Other clubs had lost walkers to movement and retirement and, although Roy Hart and Ken Bobbett maintained high standards, the numbers had gone. By 1970 there were no active walkers living in Wales. The Welsh RWA ceased to exist and Midland Counties took over responsibility for walking in Wales. Wales was experiencing very lean times.

The recovery, in the late 1970s, was swift and convincing. Two clubs, Roath and Splott, were re-formed – and Steve Barry, Wales' greatest ever walker arrived. Steve had been a good athlete as a schoolboy, but had dropped out of athletics. His wife, Sue, bought him some kit, told him his dinner wouldn't be ready until he had been training and reminded him that his father had been Welsh walking champion nine times. In December 1977 he won a 6 miles walk in Cardiff and the following month he won a 10 miles walk in Bristol, a distance he had never previously attempted. Within 2 years he was AAA champion. Before that, in October 1979, he led Wales to victory against Scotland in the first walking international Wales had taken part in. Steve was virtually unbeatable over the next few years, winning national titles and open races as he pleased, setting records everywhere and being *Daily Mail* Athlete of the Month. It was a combination of extraordinary talent and dedication or, as he put it, tunnel vision. In 1981 he broke Ken Matthews' UK 20k track record by over 2 minutes, registering 13,987 metres for one hour in the process which was also a British record. In 1983 he did the same to Paul Nihill's 20k road record, destroying every record from five miles upwards en route. *The Race Walking Record* called it the greatest display of walking ever seen in Britain.

Steve's greatest triumph came at the 1982 Commonwealth Games in Brisbane, which is covered in his pen portrait which follows. It is worth noting that he always supported the Welsh Championships and that his 10,000m championship record, set in 1984, still stands. In 1983 he broke his own British track record for 10,000m which was beaten the following year by Phil Vesty at the UK Championships in Cwmbran, making this the first official British walking record to be set in Wales. Where Steve Barry led others were eager to follow. They might not have gone as far but they went far enough for the 1980s to surpass the 1950s as Wales' best walking decade. By 1979 Roath Labour had a group of young walkers who would win much – Nathan Kavanagh, Russell Hutchings and David Pugh – and, by 1980, Splott were to take the field with their own young lions. It was, incidentally, in 1980 that Steve Barry made his British debut, finishing second to former world record holder Gerard Lelievre in Britain's win over France, Spain and Switzerland. Both clubs wisely built up from youth. Roath, first in the field, had the initial success but Splott, with Pat Chichester and the Holloway brothers directed by Ray Taylor, would surpass them. They also had very good seniors in Steve Johnson and Brian Dowrick and got really lucky when Commonwealth Games walker Martin Bell arrived from Scotland. British vests flowed in, open races were won throughout the UK and national titles were ticked off like items on a shopping list.

© Ceri Breeze

Steve Barry seen here in action at the 1983 Welsh Games in Cwmbran.

In 1987 Splott won the RWA 30k relay and in 1988 they won the RWA 10 miles, always the most fiercely contested championship. This title had never before left England. They won the RWA Junior 10,000m that year as well. Gareth Holloway and Leigh Taylor were in both winning teams and Holloway was in the team that retained the 30k relay. Another British record set in Wales came at the Welsh Games in 1988 when Sean Martindale established new figures for the 5,000m track walk at Cwmbran. In 1989 Splott retained the RWA 10 miles and Glamorgan won the English inter-counties title. That, too, had never been out of England previously. In 1988 Wales were invited to send a walking team to Denmark where they won the Randers Trophy defeating Denmark, Ireland, north Germany and Austria. It was Wales' greatest day since Steve Barry's Commonwealth win. Wales also defeated Denmark in a two-nations match in Cardiff in 1989, in a race won by Steve Barry.

During the 1980s Wales won 33 British walking championships, 15 individual and 4 team championships for seniors plus nine individual and 5 team championships for the younger age groups. Confidence was high and it seemed the secret of permanent success had been found. The 1990s opened very well. The Welsh RWA was re-formed to take charge of Welsh walking affairs. Tribute must be paid, however, to the Midland Counties who had looked after Welsh interests competently and warmly and to whom a great deal is owed.

Competitively Welsh walking continued to prosper. In 1990 Splott lost the RWA 10 miles but, two months later, captured another title which had not previously gone out of England, the RWA 20k, and then regained the 10 miles in 1992. The Welsh Championship and Open 30k was launched in 1991 and was well supported by individuals and clubs. In 1993 the RWA 20k was staged in Cardiff. One of the competitors was Bob Dobson, the only man in the field to have taken part in the inaugural championship back in 1965. In the same year Brian Dowrick became the first Welsh walker to win a BAF Championship when he took the 50k in Plymouth and Martin Bell won the AAA 10,000m. Sadly, the late 1990s saw a decline with walkers retiring and the Splott club ceasing to exist, leaving Penhow Walking Club, founded in 1989, as Wales' only purely walking club. Martin Bell kept the standard high at the top of Welsh walking with a succession of fine wins, British vests, Scottish records and two Commonwealth Games appearances for Scotland. Numbers, though, were fewer.

Distance walking is a speciality that needs its own section. In the 1952 Bath to London 100 miles Jack Morgan (Newport Harriers) finished in 22:33:35, nearly 35 minutes ahead of Idris Williams (Coventry Godiva). Both walkers believed that Jack had become Wales' first Centurion. So did everybody else, but recent research has revealed that J Iles, who covered 106 miles, 785 yds in September 1908, was Welsh and hailed from the Newport and Tredegar area. He is listed in the results as "unattached" and his time at 100 miles is not recorded. Since then the following Welsh walkers have become Centurions:

1955	Tom Thomas (Newport Harriers)	London to Brighton and back	21:14:57
1959	John Eddershaw (Sheffield)	London to Brighton and back	22:25:55
1974	Dave Ainsworth (Ilford)	Leicester to Skegness	22:44:41
1977	Jack Thomas (Bristol RWC)	Bristol 100	21:57:19
1985	Bob Dobson (Ilford)	Colchester 24 hours	20:58:25
1989	Chris Flint (London Vidarians)	Hendon 100	20:17:28
1989	Colin Bradley (Medway)	Hendon 100	21:27:56
1993	Mike Lewis (Trowbridge)	Battersea Park 24 hours	23:31:21

In order to qualify as a Centurion it is necessary to walk 100 miles within 24 hours. John Eddershaw has completed twelve 100 miles/24 hours' races. Chris Flint with ten finishes in ten starts is catching him up. In 1995 Chris was the second British walker to finish in that year's 100 miles and was selected for the Roubaix 28 hours. In Wales it was assumed that he was representing Great Britain but it turned out that he was representing England. He has lived in England long enough to establish a residential qualification. In spite of that, he is Welsh. Mike Lewis and Colin Bradley have both won the Cyril Evans Distance Walker of the Year Trophy.

Wales' best distance walker has been Bob Dobson. He has recorded the fastest 100 miles, clocking 17:52:01 at Woodford in 1986, going on to complete 204.330k in the 24 hours. He has set UK records for 10, 11, 12 and 13 hours. His 12 hours record of 118.805k was also a world best. He has won the Roubaix 100k, twice completed the multi stage Tour de Romandie (over 300k) in Switzerland, and ranked in the Great Britain top ten at 50k for thirty years. On 12/13 August 2000 he won both the 50k and 100k races at the Millennium Challenge at Newmarket. He has set one record that will probably never be equalled by completing over a hundred 50k races – and he doesn't count those that take him over 5 hours. He has won the Essex 50k 21 times, set UK records for 50k on the road and track and competed in the European Championships twice and the Commonwealth Games.

Several of Wales' top walkers have come from elsewhere. Roy Hart and Colin Bradley from Kent, Bob Dobson from Essex and Martin Bell from Scotland. Welsh walkers have not just walked. John Eddershaw has been Captain and President of the Centurions and has been Northern Counties Secretary. Dave Ratcliffe has been Midland Counties Secretary. Dave Ainsworth was the best publicity officer the RWA ever had and his Essex Newsletter is Britain's best walking publication.

Women's walking started a good many years later than men's. It must be admitted that it has not been as well supported. Karen Nipper was Wales' most consistently successful competitor, winning many races and British international honours. Lisa Simpson, Karen Dunster and the Woodcock sisters have all made significant contributions but there has been a lack of quantity.

From Norman Moses, the first Welsh walking champion of the twentieth century to Mark Williams, the first in the twenty first century, there have been successes and failures, triumphs and disappointments. Wales does not have many walkers at present but it must be remembered how bleak the prospects appeared in the early 1970s and how quickly and completely things recovered. In their 1979 victory over Scotland the entire Welsh team finished before Scotland's fourth scorer. There followed a series of British individual and team titles, international victories and then the Commonwealth gold medal of Wales' greatest walker Steve Barry. However, there might be hope for the future in the shape of young Cameron Smith who represented Wales in the British Schools International match in 1999 and 2000.

Enjoyment is not all about winning, though it helps. Good, honest competition is satisfying at every level. Over the years Wales has enjoyed a wonderful corporate spirit and this has involved not just the walkers themselves and the officials, but their families, supporters and friends. Without them not much would have been achieved and they deserve the thanks of everyone involved in Welsh walking for their selfless support.

Pen Portrait – Steve Barry
(Roath Labour Walking Club & Cardiff AAC)

Born in Cardiff on 25 October 1950, Steve Barry was the son of Dai Barry, a prominent Welsh walker who won nine national titles in the 1950s. Steve used to go and watch his father compete so it was probably inevitable that he would become interested in athletics. Although Steve took up the sport as a teenager it was not until 1978 that he started to make an impact when he collected his first Welsh titles, taking the honours at both 3k and 10k. He repeated this double in 1979 and 1980 and it was in the latter year that he won the first of his AAA titles with a victory over 3k. However he failed to make that year's Olympic team, finishing 6th in the 20k trials.

The following year was a significant one for Steve as he emerged as a walker of genuine world class. He suffered one frustrating experience when he was disqualified after the finish of the AAA 3k but went on to win the 10k titles at both the AAA and the UK Championships. His victory in the Lugano (effectively the World Championships of walking) semi final in 1981 was the last Lugano race won by a British walker and brought him that year's RWA Trophy.

It was in that year that he set the first of his British records when in an

international track race in Brighton on 27 June he covered 13,987 metres in an hour, breaking Phil Embleton's record of 1972, and carried on to clock 1:26:22 for 20k beating the record established by Ken Matthews in 1964. The latter mark gave him immense satisfaction, as Matthews was a man much admired by Steve and one of those who gave him inspiration in his early days.

By now Steve was the dominant force in British walking and he swept all before him in 1982. He signalled his intentions early on with a brace of British records. In a 30k road race at Douglas, Isle of Man, he recorded 2:15:11 to knock over 4 minutes off the record set in the corresponding race in the previous year. In a 10k track race at West London in March he registered 41:14.7 to claim Phil Embleton's 11-year-old record and by now he held UK records at 10k, 20k and 30k. Later that year he brought his 10k time down to 41:13.62 when finishing 3rd in a match against East Germany. He scored another 3k/10k double in the Welsh, retained both his AAA and UK titles and won RWA Championships over 10 miles and 20k.

After finishing 11th over 20k in the European Championships in Athens that September, Steve's outstanding year came to a fitting climax when he was crowned Commonwealth 30k Champion in Brisbane in October 1982. In beating a world-class field he led from the first feeding station and won by over 2 minutes. Walking at just under 7 minutes a mile, he demolished the Games record by almost 12 minutes to record 2:10:16, shattering his own British record. His achievements were recognised both within athletics and beyond. The Welsh AAA presented him with a Meritorious Plaque for services to Welsh Athletics and he was voted the BBC Wales Sports Personality of the Year in 1982. His victory was the only major international title ever won by a Welsh walker. Earlier that year he had twice set new figures for the 10k track walk. He is, at the time of writing in 2000, the last British walker to win a major international title.

Steve carried on in 1983 where he had left off the previous year. He began with another early season trip to Douglas and, racing over 20K on the road, he recorded 1:22:51 breaking Paul Nihill's British record of 1972. He won the AAA and UK 10k titles for the third time in succession, bringing his British record down to 40:54.7, the eighth British record of his career, in the AAA event. Steve also retained both his RWA titles at 10 miles and 20k. The lure of the Olympics was enough to persuade Steve, now 33, to carry on for another season in 1984. He won the Welsh 10k for the fifth time to bring his total of Welsh titles to nine equalling his father's record and was duly selected for the Los Angeles Games where he finished 24th over 20k.

Chapter 13

Men for all Seasons The link betwen rugby and athletics in Wales

For two sports which, on the face of it, have so little in common, athletics and rugby have a remarkably long-standing link that began in the very earliest days and continues to the present day. The first secretary of the Welsh Rugby Union was an athletics innovator, and .... were Ken Jones and J.J. Williams better athletes than rugby players?

Even as far back as the time when various sports were first being formalised in the universities and public schools of England we find the name of Llanelli born John Chambers prominent. As we have seen elsewhere in this book he was a man of many talents who excelled at any sport he attempted. He can be regarded as the father of modern day athletics and was one of the founders of the Amateur Athletic Club, the forerunner of the AAA. The rugby link is provided by the fact that his brother Charles Campbell Chambers, a former captain of Swansea RFC was the first President of the WRU at its formation in 1881. The 7th Earl of Jersey, the second WRU President ,was the first President of the AAA in 1880 and Richard Mullock, the first secretary of the Welsh Football Union (the predecessor of the WRU), was also present at the formation of the AAA in Oxford in 1880, and was instrumental in setting up the first rules for Welsh athletics.

The first rugby international match in which Wales played was against England at Blackheath on 19 February 1881, and included in the three-quarter line was **Edward Peake** of Oxford University and Chepstow who also won his athletics blue at Oxford as a hurdler. So began a tradition that has been virtually unbroken ever since, although for Peake he may have wished it were not so. His sporting career ended when he broke his leg in a hurdles race.

These were pioneer days for all sports and positions on the rugby field were not necessarily the same as those we would recognise today. In their first few matches Wales played two full backs, one of whom was **Charles Prydderch Lewis** of Llandovery College. He won his blue in the hammer in 1876 and would later become the first to play as a single full back. Llandovery College, indeed, was a breeding ground for talented all-rounders in the latter half of the nineteenth century. **William Henry Thomas** represented Cambridge in the Varsity cross-country race in 1887, finishing ninth, and won 11 Welsh caps as a forward, captaining the team on two occasions. In 1888 he became the first Welsh rugby player ever to tour overseas, travelling with R L Seddon's British team to Australia and New Zealand. Another product of the school was **Charles "Boomer" Nicholl** who won two athletics blues for Cambridge in the shot (1892/1893), finishing second in the latter year and went on to win 15 Welsh caps as a second row forward. He was also a more than useful cricketer.

A remarkable family of all round sportsmen around the turn of the century were the six

Gould brothers of Newport. The exploits of **Arthur Gould** are covered in detail elsewhere in this book, but he was something of a legend in the world of Welsh rugby, representing his country 27 times, which stood as a Welsh record when he retired in 1897. He was a good enough athlete to be Midland Counties champion at 100 yds and 120 yds hurdles in 1892 and in all won over a £1,000 in prizes for foot races. His brother **Wyatt Gould** never won a Welsh cap but was captain of Newport RFC and a player of near international standard. As an athlete he represented Britain in the 1908 Olympic Games at London's White City competing in the 110m hurdles. He, together with fellow hurdler Wallis Walters and walker Alf Yeoumans, were the first Welsh athletes to take part in the Olympics. Remarkably three Gould brothers – Arthur, Wyatt and Gus won bronze medals in the 120 yds hurdles at the (English) AAA championships.

Fred Cooper, like many sprinters of his time, was an outstanding rugby player. After initially playing for and captaining Abergavenny, he played for Newport in season 1892/93, before turning professional with Bradford, where he scored nineteen tries in seasons 1895/96 and 1896/9. He was also a prolific goal kicker and kicked 171 goals between 1895 and 1900, heading the rugby league goal scoring tables for each of these seasons. Cooper was Welsh Champion and AAA champion at 100 yards in 1898, and had the distinction of being Wales' first even time sprinter.

Another giant of the early days was **Harry Packer**. Known as "The Guvnor" he played for Wales seven times as a forward and was manager of the British Lions team to tour South Africa in 1924. He ran the line in the Wales v England game at Cardiff in 1934 at the age of 65! Despite serving on the WRU committee and being a Welsh selector, he still found time to be President of the South Wales and Mon AAA from 1919 until his death in 1945. For a number of years he was President of the Welsh CCA and was International President when the International Cross Country Championships were held in Wales in 1921 and 1927.

Ewan Davies, another Llandovery College old boy, won 2 caps for Wales as a wing in 1912 and was an outstanding sprinter. A man of many talents he was a solicitor who stood as a Liberal candidate in the General Elections of 1924 and 1929 and later became a cinema owner. In 1931 he opened the Plaza Cinema, Swansea, then the largest in Wales.

Henry "Harry" Uzzell was Welsh champion at 880 yds in 1907 and 440 yds in 1908 and went on to win 15 caps for Wales as a forward. He would almost certainly have won many more if it were not for the intervention of the First World War. He played 11 times before the war, including the final international before hostilities began, and then played in the first match after the war in 1920. In that season he played in all 4 matches as Welsh captain. To make it a family double his brother **Ben Uzzell** was Welsh 440 yds champion in 1912 and played for Newport and Pontypool. He also won the AAA 220 yds hurdles title in 1913 but lost his life in the Great War. **John "Dickie" Uzzell**, who dropped the goal for Newport in 1963 which sealed the only win over the All Blacks on the tour that year, was also an outstanding pole vaulter and javelin thrower in his schooldays at Bargoed Grammar School. Also in that team was **Alan "Algie" Thomas** another Bargoed schoolboy who won the Welsh Schools' middle discus in 1957. Centre Uzzell and wing forward Thomas won caps against New Zealand in 1963. Thomas also played against England in 1964, whilst Uzzell won a further four caps in 1965.

Between March 1907 and January 1910 Wales enjoyed what has become known as the "Golden Era" winning eleven consecutive international matches, a record that has still not been equalled. A man who played in two of those matches and who went on to play eight times for Wales was scrum half **Tommy Vile** of Newport. Oddly, he toured Australia and New Zealand with the British Isles in 1904 playing in the only test against New Zealand

and two of the three against Australia yet did not win his first Welsh cap until 1908. It was his misfortune to be a contemporary of the legendary Dickie Owen who equalled the Welsh record of 33 caps during this period. His connection with athletics is somewhat more tenuous than that of some of the other great rugby players as he was never an athlete of any note. He did become an athletics official, however, and acted as starter at the Welsh Championships in the early 1920s.

The link between rugby and athletics is not confined to personnel, as many rugby grounds were used for the major athletics meetings of the time before purpose-built tracks became the norm. "Athletic Sports" were held by Glamorgan Football Club - the forerunner of Cardiff RFC, in 1875 in Cardiff on the area which was to become known as Cardiff Arms Park. In the latter part of the 19th and early part of the last century, Newport Athletic Grounds at Rodney Parade was the Mecca for Welsh athletics. The first integrated Welsh Championships were held there in 1907 and the last championships to be held before the First World War were staged at Cardiff Arms Park where they were to be held again on two further occasions in 1923 and 1929. The adjacent cricket ground (effectively where Cardiff RFC currently play) also staged the Welsh Championships in 1922.

The first Welsh Junior Championships, in 1934, were held at the Gnoll ground at Neath. It also may be a surprise to many to learn that the first sporting event ever held at the St Helen's ground in Swansea, traditionally the home of rugby and cricket in the city, was an athletics meeting. Welsh Championships were held at St. Helen's in 1932 and again in 1950 - the last time the championships were held on a temporary surface, as Cardiff's Maindy Stadium was opened the following year and staged the championships each year until 1968. Other first class rugby grounds used for Welsh Championships and other major meetings before the advent of purpose-built tracks were Pontypool Park, Abertillery Park and Talbot Athletic Ground, Port Talbot.

An outstanding sporting figure in the 1920s was **Rowe Harding** of Swansea. Welsh 100 yds champion in 1922 and 1926 and 220 yds champion in 1923, he played 17 times for Wales as a left wing and toured South Africa with the 1924 Lions, playing in three of the four tests. He thus became the first Welsh athletics champion to play for the Lions. In 1959 he was elected chairman of Glamorgan County Cricket Club, a post he held until he stood down in 1976. outside of sport he had a distinguished career as a judge.

A contemporary of Rowe Harding's was **Arthur Holland**, Welsh 100 yds champion in 1920 and 220 yds champion of 1922, who was a prolific try scorer for Newport (33 tries in 43 games) and was several times a reserve for England. Another interesting character was **Jerry Shea** who played for Wales at both rugby codes, and competed as a professional runner. Also a welterweight boxer he gained victories during his career over three British champions; Frank Moody (light heavyweight champion and twice middleweight champion), Gipsy Daniels (light heavyweight) and Johnny Basham (middleweight and welterweight)

Ronnie Boon, Welsh 220 yds champion 1929, played 12 times for Wales as a wing. In 1933 he scored all Wales' points (through a try and a drop goal) when they defeated England at Twickenham for the first time. Included in the Welsh team was future cricket great Wilf Wooller making his international debut, who was also reputed to be a fine sprinter at Rydal School. Boon himself was also a cricketer and played for Glamorgan a number of times. Born in 1909, he emigrated from Wales to New Zealand in 1995 at the age of 84 and died there three years later.

Other athletes to play rugby for Wales during the 1930s included **Iorwerth Evans,** who played two matches as a hooker in 1934 and had been a member of the champion school relay team of Wales in 1925, and **Ned Jenkins**, second in the Welsh discus in 1937 and west Wales champion at both shot and discus, who played for Aberavon as a second row forward. Jenkins won 21 Welsh caps between 1927 and 1932, despite once being sent off in a Welsh trial match.

Kenyon Jones of Monmouth School and London Welsh won his only cap as a prop forward against England in 1934. A high jumper, whose grandfather ran for Wales, he was once selected to compete for Wales but was unable to turn out. During the Second World War he served in the Welch Regiment, attaining the rank of Lieutenant Colonel. He worked in Military Intelligence and was awarded the American Bronze Star for his work in General Eisenhower's office. Later awarded the MBE (military) he went on to become a successful businessman and was Managing Director of Unilever and later Chairman and Managing Director of Ronson Products.

Jack Knowles, Welsh 220 yds champion of 1936, never made it to the Welsh team but was an outstanding wing and scored Newport's only try in their match against New Zealand in 1935. **Raymond "Dickie" Ralph** played six times for Wales at outside half, scoring two tries on his debut, before "going north" and winning a Challenge Cup final medal with Leeds in 1936. A useful cricketer he was not an athlete himself but was the father of Mike Ralph, AAA triple jump champion of 1966, who competed for Britain in the 1964 Olympic Games.

Wales' first international match after the Second World War was against England at Cardiff Arms Park on 18 January 1947. All but two of the team were making their international debuts and among them were three whose names mean something in athletics. **Les Williams**, on the left wing, won seven caps and turned professional for Hunslet Rugby League club the day after scoring two tries against England at Cardiff. He was active for a very long period as a sprinter/jumper and competed in the World Veterans' Championships in Puerto Rico in 1983. In 1980 he suffered a personal tragedy while in Spain to compete in a veterans' meeting when his wife died from a broken neck after falling downstairs.

Jack Matthews had won the Welsh junior 220 yds title back in 1937 and finished second in the senior 100 yds to Kenneth Jenkins in the 1939 Senior Championships at Rodney Parade. Jack still vividly remembers competing against the likes of Cyril Cupid the leading home-based Welsh sprinter of the 1930s. Jack would be recognised as one of the greatest centres ever to play for Wales, noted for his deadly tackling. He toured New Zealand with the Lions in 1950 and played in all four tests. A doctor by profession, he also toured with the 1980 Lions in South Africa, this time as medical officer. He was awarded the OBE in 1981.

The third of Wales' 1947 debutants was a man who was to become one of the greatest Welsh sportsmen of all time. Undoubtedly the most successful of those who have performed with distinction at rugby and athletics, 44 times capped **Ken Jones** is the only man ever to be both an Olympic medallist and a Lion and reached the very pinnacle in both sports. Ken's illustrious career in both sports is detailed in chapter nine.

Alun Meredith, a noted line out forward, played in three matches for Wales in 1949, scoring a try against England on his debut. Back in 1936 he had won the Welsh junior high jump championship. He later became Director of Sport in the Royal Navy. A year later **John Robins** made his international debut playing in the front row for the all-conquering Welsh team which won the Grand Slam that season. Not surprisingly he, together with Jack Matthews, Ken Jones and eleven other Welsh players, was chosen to tour down under and he played in three tests against New Zealand and two against Australia. In all he won eleven

Welsh caps and was coach to the 1966 Lions. In 1943 he had won the long jump, shot and discus at Welsh Junior Championships.

The first ever Welsh Schools' Championships were held at Pontypridd in 1947 and the sprinting events featured two athletes who would later become prominent rugby players. Winner of the 100 yds was **Lynn "Cowboy" Davies** of Carmarthen Grammar School, ahead of **Trevor Brewer** of Newport High School who went on to win the 220 yds title. Brewer played against England in 1950 and won two more caps in 1955. In the match against Scotland in 1955 he scored two tries but was never selected again. Perhaps they thought he was showing off! Cowboy Davies made his rugby international debut in 1956, played in three of Wales' matches that season and scored tries in the first two of them. Obviously scoring tries was not what the selectors wanted of wing three-quarters in those days as he, too, was replaced after his third cap.

Welsh junior 100 yds champion of 1950 was **Gareth Griffiths** of Porth who would make his international debut against England in 1953. He developed into an outstanding wing or centre and was flown out to South Africa as a replacement for the injured Arthur Smith of Scotland. He went on to play in 3 test matches.

The 1955 season saw two field events specialists lining up for Wales. Ynyshir-born **Gordon Wells** was Welsh triple jump champion four times and set an overall Welsh and all-comers' record of 14.52 for the event at Abertillery in 1949 when taking the Welsh title. Because of the structure of athletics in Wales at the time, the performance was also classed as an English Native record and stood as a Welsh record for eight years. He made his debut as a centre against England in January and went on to win seven caps. **Garfield Owen**, who was Welsh javelin champion in 1953, was selected to play at full back for Wales for the first time in the same England match as Wells had done. Unfortunately for him he was injured in training and was forced to withdraw. He finally got his chance later and played in six successive internationals before signing on for Rugby League club Halifax where he enjoyed a hugely successful career in that game. He still lives in Halifax and sketches famous people for charity.

In the final match of the 1955 season **CD (Derek) Williams,** the Cardiff flanker was called into the Welsh team when the original choice withdrew and made an excellent contribution to Wales' victory over the French. His only other match was the next season, also against France, and again he was on the winning side. By now a Neath player he scored Wales' only try which was converted by Garfield Owen to clinch the game for Wales. Williams played in the Cardiff side that beat the All Blacks in 1953 and was also a talented boxer and cricketer. He won the Welsh youths 880 yds in 1940 and junior 880 yds titles in both 1941 and 1942. Whilst at Oxford University he won the Berkshire mile title and in 1948 he carried the Olympic Torch through Berkshire.

Onllwyn Brace, Welsh Schools' hurdles champion of 1949 (middle boys) and 1950 (senior boys) was one of the most talented rugby players of his time. He played at scrum half for Wales for the first time at Twickenham in 1956 when he partnered the legendary Cliff Morgan. His style of play was very unorthodox and he was in and out of the Wales team until 1961 winning 9 caps in all. His talent was never to flourish fully on the international scene although he was on the winning side in 6 of his matches.

It can be no surprise that most of the athletes who played international rugby were wings. Their ranks were swelled when **Keith Maddocks**, Welsh junior 100 yds champion of 1944, played his only international in 1957 followed the next year by **John Collins** of Aberavon who became a more permanent member of the team. The Welsh champion at 440 yds in

1952, Collins scored three tries in his ten internationals. After living for a number of years in Majorca he returned to his roots and is now a licensee in Aberavon. Around this time, **David Pulsford** of Rhymney was an extremely useful winger for both his home town and for Newport. Although he didn't win a cap, he came close to representative honours. His athletics link is that he won both the Welsh and AAA junior 220 yds in 1953 and the Welsh junior 440 yds title the following year. He also took the senior 440 yds title when at Monmouthshire Training College in 1957.

Winner of both the 440 yds and the long jump in the Welsh Schools' senior boys' championships in 1956 was a youngster who would go on to become one of the all time greats of Welsh rugby. **Dewi Beb**b assured himself of a place in rugby folklore by scoring the try that beat England at Cardiff on his debut in 1959. He had played only a handful of club matches but was to go on to become a regular member of the Welsh team until 1967, winning 34 caps in all. He is one of a very select band who has played for the Lions against all three southern hemisphere countries, having played four times against New Zealand and twice each against South Africa and Australia. Bebb never won a Welsh senior title but was second to Berwyn Jones at 100 yds in 1961 and was a prolific winner of sprint events whilst at Cardiff Training College, Cyncoed and Trinity College, Carmarthen and gained representative honours for the Welsh AAA.

Twice in 1963 **Bill Morris**, who the previous year had finished third in the Welsh 220 yds championships, took over from Dewi Bebb on the left wing for Wales, playing against Scotland and Ireland. Another contemporary of Bebb's was **Brian Davies** who was Welsh junior 100 and 220 yds champion in 1960. He won three caps as a centre in 1962/3, playing alongside the great man in two of them.

As we have seen elsewhere in this book, Rhymney born **Berwyn Jones** was one of an outstanding crop of Welsh sprinters during the 1960s. After winning the Welsh 100 yds title in 1961 he went one better in 1962 by taking the sprint double. In the same year he became the first Welsh athlete to clock 9.6 for the 100 yds. The following year he became only the second Welshman after Fred Cooper in 1898 to win the 100 yds at the AAA Championships and later on equalled the British record for 100m with a 10.3 clocking. Ironically, just to show the depth of sprinting in Wales at that time, he was beaten in both sprints at the Welsh Championships that year by his great friend from the next valley, Ron Jones. However, sadly for athletics, 1963 was to prove to be his last in the sport. He became a professional rugby league player in April 1964 with Wakefield Trinity for a reputed fee of £6,000. Of course, in those days it was not permissible to be a professional in one sport and an amateur in another so his athletics days were over. When he signed, the *South Wales Echo* announced: "Berwyn Bombshell - Will 'Flying Squad' break up, now" - referring to the world record equalling team of Berwyn, Ron, Dave Jones and Peter Radford, who had clocked 40.0 secs for 4 x 110 yds the previous year, and were regarded as a medal favourite for the 1964 Tokyo Olympics. Berwyn remarked at the time: "I feel extremely guilty at letting the boys down - but it was an opportunity that I could not turn down". However, athletics' loss was rugby league's gain and he was to enjoy an outstanding career in the northern game, scoring 26 tries for Bradford Northern in the 1967/68 season, no doubt building on his skills when he played for his home town club and Monmouthshire Training College (Caerleon). He continued to play until 1970 when he took up a teaching appointment in Hertfordshire.

Throughout the 1960s athletics continued to make its contribution to rugby. **John Mantle**, a fine all-round athlete was Welsh junior triple jump champion in 1960 and later won 2 caps as a flanker/second row forward. He won representative honours for Welsh Boys Clubs' teams at basketball and football whilst a member of Bargoed YMCA. In January 1964 he played as a flanker against England at Twickenham and at the end of that season he toured South Africa with Wales and played at No 8 in the only international match they played. He went north in 1965 and had an outstanding career in rugby league with St. Helen's, winning 16 caps for Wales and 13 for Great Britain. He was a member of the St. Helens team that won the Challenge Cup three times.

Terry Price, another whose remarkable talent never really came to full fruition on the international stage, was hailed as the new super star of Welsh rugby when he first played on the wing for Llanelli while still at school. His debut match was rather a daunting one – the opposition were the New Zealand All Blacks. Switching to full back he made his Wales debut at the age of 19 in 1965 and toured New Zealand and Australia with the Lions in 1966 without playing in any of the tests. He played in eight international matches before joining rugby league club Bradford Northern in 1967. Previously he had been Welsh under 17 shot put champion in 1961 and also won Welsh Schools' titles as a middle and senior boy in the same event. In the 1964 Welsh Schools Championships he was beaten into second place by Cardiff prop **Roger Beard**, another who enjoyed a successful rugby career. Although **Brian Coles** never won a cap, he was a prolific scorer at sevens competitions for Cardiff and won the 1964 Welsh 100 yds title in 9.8 ahead of Dave England.

The highlight of the athletics career of **Keri Jones** was when he competed at the Commonwealth Games in Kingston, Jamaica in 1966. Runner up in that year's Welsh 220 yds championships he was selected to run in both sprints and the relay. He reached the second round in both the 100 and 220 yds and was a member of the Welsh team that finished fourth in the sprint relay in a Welsh record time which was to stand for 30 years. The first of his five caps as a wing came against New Zealand in 1967 and he gained four more the following season and scored two tries. Another member of the relay team in those 1966 Games was **Terry Davies**, that year's Welsh champion at 220 yds. He retained his title in 1967 and won the inaugural 100m at Cwmbran in 1969. Like Keri Jones he competed in both sprints as well as the relay, going out in the first round of the 100 yds and reaching the second in the 220. He also competed at the 1970 Commonwealth Games in Edinburgh. He enjoyed a fine career with Llanelli and London Welsh and, although not winning his full cap, was a B international. Until recently, Terry was still turning out for his Llanelli club in Welsh League meeetings. His contribution to athletics was recognised with the award of an AAW meritorious plaque in 2000.

JJ Williams (Cardiff College of Education) just pips Terry Davies (Carmarthen) in 1968 at Cyncoed.

The international rugby career of **Maurice Richards** was as spectacular as it was brief. It began in Ireland in March 1968 and ended in Fiji in June 1969 but in that time he had proved himself a wing of the highest calibre. He played in 9 internationals, including 2 on Wales' tour of New Zealand and Australia in 1969, plus one uncapped match (in Fiji) and also in 3 tests for the British Lions on their 1968 tour to South Africa. In just

15 months he had played against every major rugby-playing country in the world. He scored some scintillating tries but the high spot of his career was when he equalled the Welsh record by scoring 4 tries in the match against England in April 1969. His career in athletics was nothing like as brilliant but he did win the Welsh junior long jump title in 1963. He was another who turned to rugby league, signing on for Salford, and became a star performer. In 1971/2 he scored 35 tries, followed by 38 the next season. He was top League try scorer in 1975/6 with a further 37 and in a fifteen year career in the northern game he scored 297 tries and almost 1000 points.

Accompanying Richards on the Welsh tour of New Zealand and Australia in 1969 was **Allan Skirving,** the Welsh 440 yds champion of 1962, also a wing. With Maurice Richards, Gerald Davies and Stuart Watkins in the party it is not surprising that he didn't get to play in the international matches but he was a fine wing in his own right. Skirving's best running days were as a junior and his Welsh junior 440 yds record of 48.9 stood for many years.

This was a period when Welsh rugby was on the threshold of a second "Golden Era" which would include a run of 8 successive victories from 1970-1972 and another run of ten wins (including 3 uncapped matches) from 1975-1977. One of the stars of the first period was **Barry Llewellyn** who competed as a shot putter in the Welsh Schools' championships in the mid 1960s and represented Wales in the British Schools' international in 1965 and 1966. He won 13 caps between 1970 and 1972 and was on the winning side 10 times. Another was **John Dawes**, third in the Welsh youths' (under 17) pole vault championships in 1957, who would captain the British Lions on their tour to New Zealand in 1971 when they became the only British side to win a test series there. This tour came after he had led Wales to the Grand Slam. His contribution to the game was recognised with the award of the OBE. When Dawes retired his place in the Welsh team was taken by **Roy Bergiers**. A talented all round athlete Roy competed for Wales as a triple jumper in the British Schools' international in 1969 after finishing second in the Welsh Schools' Championships to John Phillips, the outstanding Welsh triple jumper of the 1970s and 80s. In 1970 Roy finished second in the Welsh decathlon championship (which his brother Alan had won in 1968, as well as the 110 yards hurdles and high jump) and would have won this event in 1969 but for the fact that his entry arrived too late for inclusion and he competed only as a guest, beating the official entrants. Sister Sheridan was high jump Champion in 1971. As a centre he played eleven times for Wales and toured South Africa with the 1974 Lions. In 1972 he scored a try for Llanelli in their match against the All Blacks.

Another star of the all-conquering Wales team of the 1970s was second row forward **Allan Martin**. Wales' dominant junior thrower in 1966 and 1967, he won the shot and discus titles at the Welsh Schools' Championships and the Welsh Junior Championships in both years. In 1967 he also won both hammer championships. He represented Wales in the British Schools' international in 1966 (shot and discus) when he finished third in the shot behind Mike Winch of England, and in 1967 (all three events). Between 1973 and 1981 he made 34 appearances for Wales including a record 27 alongside Geoff Wheel in the second row. He toured with the Lions to New Zealand in 1977, playing in one test, and to South Africa in 1980.

Once described as the best uncapped prop forward in Wales, **Gerry Wallace** made his only representative appearance when he played against Tonga in 1974 in a match for which caps were not awarded. Despite giving a good account of himself he was not selected again, losing his place to Tony Faulkner. In the Welsh Schools' Championships of 1963 Wallace had won the senior boys' discus title. After winning the Welsh Schools' senior shot and discus in 1970, **Graham Price** went on to become one of the legends of Welsh rugby. A member of the infamous "Pontypool Front Row" he won a total of 41 caps between 1975 and 1983 in an illustrious career which included three tours with the British Lions. His Welsh record of twelve appearances for the Lions (four against South Africa, eight against New Zealand) ranks him equal third with Mike Gibson on the list of test appearances, behind only Willie John McBride and Dickie Jeeps. A man who shared three of Graham Price's matches was **Colin Smart**. While a student at Cardiff College of Education he finished third in the discus at the Welsh Championships in 1973. Later he enjoyed an outstanding career in international rugby. Not eligible to play for Wales, he made a total of 17 appearances for England. In three of those matches he packed down in the front row in direct opposition to Price.

Gareth Edwards in an English vest? Well, yes! The legendary scrum half was English Schools' 200 yds. hurdles champion and UK junior record holder whilst a pupil at Millfield School. Here he is shown wearing his English Schools' vest when a pupil at Millfield.

The man whose career spanned the whole of this great period in the history of Welsh rugby was, of course, **Gareth Edwards**. He played in 53 consecutive internationals for Wales, breaking Ken Jones' Welsh record en route, and scored a then record number of tries for his country. He toured with the Lions three times (twice to South Africa and once to Australia and New Zealand) and played in a total of 10 tests. Regarded by many experts as the most complete rugby player in the history of the game he was awarded the MBE and his place in Welsh sporting history is assured. He has a statue erected to him, which stands in a prominent position in Cardiff. In his younger days he was a highly promising athlete. He once held the British junior record for the 200 yds hurdles and competed in that event in the British Schools' international in 1966, ironically competing against Wales as he was at the time attending Millfield School. Prior to that he had been Welsh Schools' middle boys' champion in 1963 and 1964. Whilst at College at Cyncoed he was a member of the athletics team and was a long jumper of international class. The other great love of his life is angling at which he has also been a record breaker. Later he became a Company Director and Vice Chairman of Hyder, the Welsh water company.

© Paul Stuart

The sporting Williams family hold a unique place in Welsh Athletics in that they have all won titles and gained international honours.
Left to right: James (Junior International), Kathryn (G.B junior International), JJ and Rhys (2001 World Youth Olympic 400 Hurdles Champion).

Yet another member of this great side with strong athletics connections was **JJ Williams**. Winner of the Welsh sprint double in 1971 after winning the 220 yds in 1968 and 1969, he represented Wales at the Commonwealth Games in Edinburgh in 1970. As a rugby player he played in 30 internationals and his lightning speed (10.5/10.4w for 100m) brought him many tries including a hat trick against Australia in 1975. He toured with the Lions to South Africa in 1974 playing in all 4 tests. He scored a brace of tries in both the second and third tests to equal the record of fellow Welshman Willie Llewellyn (back in 1904) for the most tries by a Lion in a test series. He toured New Zealand in 1977 and played in 3 of the 4 tests, only an untimely injury in the third test preventing him from gaining a full set. He had the distinction of having scored at least one try against all the major rugby playing countries.

The Lions team of 1977 included 16 Welsh players and two more joined the party later as replacements. One of this number was **Brynmor Williams** who had won the Welsh junior high jump in 1969 and competed for Welsh Schools in the schools' international. At the time, due to the overwhelming presence of Gareth Edwards, he was yet to win his first cap but he played in three of the four test matches (Edwards was not on the tour) and, like JJ Williams, was prevented from playing in the final match by an injury sustained in the third. When Gareth Edwards retired Brynmor was selected for Wales' short tour of Australia in 1978 and made his debut in the first of the two test matches. It was his misfortune that Terry Holmes appeared on the scene at the same time and made the scrum half position his own, but Williams had 2 more caps in 1981. Despite being a contemporary of Gerald Davies and JJ Williams, **Clive Rees** made his Welsh debut in 1974 and managed to accumulate a total of 13 caps as a wing by 1983. A Welsh Schools' double sprint champion and Welsh junior 220 yds champion in 1969 he toured South Africa with the 1974 Lions but did not gain a test place.

In 1979 Wales played in an uncapped international match against Romania at the Cardiff Arms Park. Perhaps they underestimated the opposition as they won by just a single point (13-12) after being behind 12-6. The only Welsh try was scored by left wing **Jeff Griffiths** of Llanelli who had already won the Welsh 400m title in 1976 & 1978 and would go on to take his third title in 1981. He also took the AAA junior title in 1976 in 47.2 and held the Welsh junior record for many years. Jeff never won a full cap and in Wales' next international match, in January 1980, the left wing spot was occupied by **Les Keen**, the 1972 Welsh Schools' pole vault champion. He played in all four matches that season, scoring a try against Scotland.

The next time Wales played Romania, in 1983, they showed them more respect by making the match a full, capped international. Just as well, perhaps, as the Romanians ran out winners by 24 points to 6. Both wings were playing in their first internationals with **Mark Titley** of Swansea on the right and **Adrian Hadley** of Cardiff on the left. Titley (third in the Welsh Schools' 110m hurdles in 1977) went on to win 15 caps and Hadley (who won the Welsh Colts' long jump title in 1975) gained 27. He is probably best remembered for scoring two tries against England at Twickenham in 1988.

Also playing in the match against Romania in 1983 was centre **Robert Ackerman**. He was by then an established international, having made his debut on the wing against New Zealand back in 1980. A runner-up in both sprints at the Welsh Schools' Championships in 1979 he was a regular member of the Welsh team until 1985 and amassed a total of 22 caps. He toured New Zealand with the 1983 Lions and played in two tests, one as a replacement. Making his debut for Wales in their match against Australia in November 1984 was Llanelli wing **Phil Lewis** who, in 1979, had won both the high jump and the 400m hurdles for senior boys at the Welsh Schools' Championships. He held his place in the Welsh team the following season and played three further matches in1986, making eight appearances in all and scoring two tries. Possibly the shortest international rugby career was that of **Richard**

Wintle, Welsh 200m champion of 1985. In 1988 he was on the bench for the match between Wales and Western Samoa (in the good old days when Wales used to beat them) and came on to the field to replace Carwyn Davies of Llanelli.

Arthur Emyr (born Arthur Emyr Jones) was a good sprinter who finished third in the Welsh 100m championship in 1988. He won the first of his 13 caps in Wales' historic win over previously unbeaten England in 1989 which saved them from the humiliation of a first ever five nations whitewash. He played in all the 1991 World Cup matches, scoring a try against Western Samoa. He went on to enjoy a successful career in television, becoming BBC's Head of Sport for Wales following in the footsteps of another "dual" star, Onllwyn Brace.

Coming on as a replacement for David Evans, **Alan Edmunds** made his Wales debut against Ireland in 1990. The winner of the junior boys' javelin in the Welsh Schools' Championships in 1976, Edmunds went on to win one more cap, playing on the left wing in a special match against the Barbarians. In this game, arranged to commemorate the Baa-Baa's centenary, nine players from the Neath club took part. In another special match, to mark the opening of the new floodlights at Cardiff Arms Park in September 1991, Wales played a friendly against France with an 8.00 pm kick off. **Luc Evans,** who was third in the Welsh junior 400m hurdles in 1988, was among the substitutes and came on to replace his more illustrious namesake Ieuan and win his only cap. Whether he was on the field longer than Richard Wintle in 1988 is not known. The early 1990s saw the emergence of two of Wales' more celebrated wingers, both with considerable athletics background. **Wayne Proctor** was Welsh Schools' 400m hurdles champion in 1989, 1990 and 1991 and won the first of his 38 caps against Australia in 1992. After a few games **Nigel Walker** replaced him and from then on they were keen rivals for the coveted left wing berth. Walker had turned to rugby after a highly successful career as an athlete. For many years one of Britain's leading high hurdlers he ran in the 1984 Olympic Games and won bronze medals in both the European and World Indoor Championships in 1987. At 29 he turned his attention to rugby and after just a handful of club games was chosen to play for Wales against Ireland in 1993. In all he won 16 caps and, with his blazing turn of speed, caused a buzz of excitement around the stadium whenever he got hold of the ball. He had a brilliant game against New Zealand in 1997 but his playing career ended when he dislocated his shoulder just four minutes into the match against England in 1998. Wayne Proctor took his place, ironically.

Among the bigger men, **Ian Buckett**, who was third in the junior boys' discus at the Welsh Schools' Championships in 1982, won three caps as a prop forward between 1994 and 1997, while **Christian Loader**, second in the junior boys' hammer in 1988, was a regular member of the Welsh front row from 1995 to 1997, winning 19 caps before succumbing to injury.

Gareth Wyatt won the 200m for middle boys at the Welsh Schools' Championships in 1994. He later became a wing with Pontypridd and forced his way into the international reckoning. His opportunity came in 1997 in the first international match to be played at St Helen's since April 1954. Tonga were the opponents and Gareth played in the unaccustomed position of full back from where he scored an excellent try to help Wales record a comfortable 46-12 victory.

More recently two athletes who competed in championships in 1988 both won Welsh caps ten years later. **David Weatherley** (third in the Welsh Schools' middle boys' pole vault) and **John Funnell**, (second in the Welsh colts' shot put), made their debuts in the Wales v

Zimbabwe match at Harare in June 1998. Full back Weatherley started the game but was substituted later on by Byron Hayward while Funnell began the match on the bench and was called on to replace Mark Taylor in the centre. Later in the same tour, Funnell played in the ill fated match against South Africa which Wales lost by the staggering score of 96 to 13, and was substituted by Stephen Jones during the match. **Nick Walne**, who won the Welsh Schools' long jump title in 1993 after winning the middle boys' triple jump in 1991, is the latest addition to the list of athletes who have made the grade in rugby with three caps as a wing to his credit so far. He is still in contention for further recognition and may yet add to this tally.

One of the outstanding players in recent years has been centre **Scott Gibbs**. He has a family link with athletics as his father Graham was one of Wales' leading pole-vaulters in the 1960s and was Welsh Champion in 1965.

Is it possible to select a Welsh XV from the above players? Well, yes it is as every position on the rugby field has been filled at least once by athletes. In the case of hooker it was literally only once as Iorwerth Evans is the sole representative in this position and therefore the only one assured of selection. On the other hand choosing from the proliferation of great wings is an onerous task. Here's one possible line up: Terry Price, Ken Jones, John Dawes, Jack Matthews, Dewi Bebb, Dickie Ralph, Gareth Edwards, Graham Price, Iorwerth Evans, Barry Llewellyn, Allan Martin, Alun Meredith, C D Williams, John Mantle, Harry Uzzell.

Of course, JJ Williams was an outstanding left wing. Or what about Nigel Walker, Maurice Richards or Wayne Proctor? How can you leave out Roy Bergiers? Then there's Garfield Owen at full back. Who'd be a selector? Perhaps just leave well alone.

Chapter 14
Welsh Athletics Milestones

1860	John Chambers holds a sports meeting at Hafod House, Aberystwyth – probably the first record of an athletics meeting being held in Wales
1865	Chambers organises "athletic sports" at Aberystwyth
1871	St. David's College Lampeter and Llandovery College hold sports meetings
1875	Newport Athletic Club formed and start to hold "athletic sports"
1880	Newport represented at the formation of the AAA – Chambers also there
1882	Roath Harriers formed
1893	First Welsh 100 yards Championship
1894	First Welsh Cross-Country Championships
1896	Welsh Cross Country Association formed
1896	Newport Harriers formed
1903	Wales compete in the first international cross-country race in Scotland
1907	First full Welsh Track and Field Championships
1908	First Welsh competitors at an Olympic Games
1929	First Welsh representative match - against Achilles
1930	Reg Thomas wins Wales' first ever individual gold medal at a major Games
1934	First Welsh marathon championships held
1934	Cyril Cupid runs 9.8 - the first Welshman under 10.0 for the 100 yds
1934	First Welsh athletics team at the Empire Games
1938	Jim Alford emulates Reg Thomas and wins the Empire Games gold for the mile in Sydney
1946	Welsh Secondary Schools AAA formed
1947	First Welsh Schools Track and Field Championships
1948	Welsh AAA formed
1948	Jim Alford appointed first Welsh National Coach
1948	First match against AAA
1951	Maindy Stadium, Cardiff opened
1951	Welsh Women's AAA formed
1954	First full track and field international match against foreign opposition – Ireland
1958	British Empire and Commonwealth Games held in Cardiff
1959	First Welsh Games
1959	First British Schools Track and Field International
1961	Ron Pickering arrives in Wales as Jim Alford's replacement as National Coach
1964	Lynn Davies wins Wales' first and only individual Olympic gold medal
1967	Welsh Women's CCA formed

1969 British League commences, with Cardiff AAC as founder members, and Pilot Welsh Track and Field League held.

1969 Welsh track and field championships go metric…and move to Cwmbran

1970 First Welsh indoor championships held at St. Athan

1973 First overseas senior track and field international (Portugal)

1974 Both Welsh Cross-Country Associations merge

1974 Ruth Martin-Jones becomes the first Welsh woman to win a medal at a major Games

1974 Malcolm Arnold appointed Welsh National Coach

1974 Cardiff AAC win British League title for third successive year

1979 Cwmbran stages the Women's European Cup semi final

1980 Michelle Probert becomes the first Welsh woman to win an Olympic medal

1984 First sub 4 minute mile on Welsh soil by Gareth Brown

1985 Steve Jones sets a new world record for the marathon

1987 Full time office established by Welsh AAA at Morfa Stadium, Swansea

1988 Swansea become first Welsh club to win AAA 6 stage road relay

1990 AAW formed covering all athletics associations in Wales

1993 Colin Jackson sets a new world record for the 110m hurdles and becomes world champion

1994 Swansea become first Welsh club to win AAA 12 stage road relay

1995 Fell and Mountain Running in Wales become part of AAW

1998 Chief Executive for Welsh athletics appointed

1999 Colin Jackson wins his second World title

2000 AAW moves offices to Celtic Manor Resort

2000 National indoor athletics centre opened at Cyncoed

Chapter 15
2001 in retrospect

A Month by Month Overview of the Welsh Athletics Scene in 2001

By Mike Walters

JANUARY

5 Tanni Grey-Thompson was named the BBC Wales Sports Personality of the Year. The Carwyn James junior award went to 17-year old Paralympic sprint champion Lloyd Upsdell.

7 Robert Mitchell sets a new Welsh indoor record of 2.21 in the high jump at Birmingham. On the same day at the same venue Catherine Murphy also sets a new indoor record over 400 (52.75).

12 In Houston, USA Rhian Clarke sets a new Welsh indoor pole vault mark of 3.95.

13 Tim Thomas clears 5.33 in the pole vault at Birmingham to set a new Welsh indoor record.

27 At the UK World Indoor Trials and AAA Championships at Birmingham Catherine Murphy again lowered her Welsh 400 record to 52.31 and Tim Thomas improves his pole vault record by 2cm to 5.35.

28 Tim Benjamin breaks Welsh under 20 indoor 200 record at Birmingham with 21.00 in the semi-final. Catherine Murphy becomes the first woman to win the 200 and 400 at the AAA Indoor Championships – clocking Welsh 200 records of 23.36 in the semis and 23.35 in the final. Tim Thomas won the pole vault equalling his Welsh record of 5.35.

FEBRUARY

2 In Erfurt Germany, Hayley Tullett broke her own 3000 Welsh record by over two seconds with 8:52.26 compared to her previous mark set at the same venue on the same date last year of 8:54.63. Meanwhile in Houston again, Rhian Clarke improved her Welsh pole vault record to become the first Welsh female to clear 4 metres indoors.

3 At National Indoor Athletic Centre (NIAC) in Cardiff, Christian Malcolm sets a new Welsh all-comers record for 60m with 6.68.

10 The Celtic Manor Resort's sponsorship of the AAW scooped the National Sponsor of the Year Award at the Sportsmatch Cymru Awards Dinner.

11 No fewer than six new Welsh indoor records along with a further twelve all-comers records and one UK record were set at the Lansing Linde Severnside International at NIAC. Highlight was the UK record for Welsh-based Katharine Merry in the 400 with 51.54. Tim Thomas took his own indoor record in the pole vault to 5.40 – his fourth record this winter. Nathan Palmer continued his progress

by lowering the Welsh under 20 60m hurdles mark to 7.93.

© Ian Dixon

Catherine Murphy

18 At the National Indoor Arena, Birmingham, Catherine Murphy once again smashed her Welsh indoor 400 record for the third time with 51.99 as she finished second to Katharine Merry's new UK and Commonwealth mark of 50.53.

Both the Welsh men and women's teams win the inaugural inter-area indoor match at NIAC.

25 Tim Benjamin wins the under 20 AAA indoor 200 title with a new championship best time of 20.78. Chuka Enih-Snell wins the high jump with 2.14.

In the under 15 60 hurdles Heather Jones won the final in 8.85 but in the heat she ran 8.79 to break Katharine Merry's 12-year-old UK record. Another hurdler to win gold was Laura McLoughlin who took the under 20 race in 8.61.

Christian Stephenson was a runaway winner in the men's race at the Welsh Cross-Country Championships at Heath Park while Swansea Harrier Catherine Dugdale retained her women's title in a photo finish with Louise Copp.

MARCH

1 St David's Day was a tonic for Mark Morgan and Catherine Dugdale who won their respective races at the Armagh International Road Races in Northern Ireland.

10 For the third time Rhian Clarke competing in Houston raised her own Welsh pole vault record to 4.20 – 5cms higher than her outdoor record.

At the World Indoor Championships in Lisbon Christian Malcolm strikes silver in the 200 (20.76). Catherine Murphy bowed out in a tough 400 semi-final while Hayley Tullett ran a steady race to claim a new Welsh record (indoors and outdoors) of 8:45.36 in eighth place in the 3000, clipping three hundredths off her own mark set last year. Matt Elias made his debut at a major championship as a member of the British 4 x 400 relay team that finished fifth in the final.

In the first ever British international (under 23 v France) to be held at NIAC, Amanda Pritchard wins the 800 in 2:08.72.

18 At the Kelvin Hall in Glasgow Hayley Tullett ran a superb race to break both the long-standing UK and Welsh indoor records for 1500. She finished second in a time of 4:06.75 to world bronze medallist Natalya Gavrilova of Russia. The UK record had stood for 15 years to Zola Budd (4:06.87) while the Welsh record of 4:07.6 had stood to Kirsty Wade since 1988.

APRIL

11 UK Athletics and the Sports Council for Wales announce the establishment of the High Performance Centre for Wales – the first such centre to be created outside England. It will be based at NIAC at University of Wales Institute, Cyncoed, Cardiff.

21 Robert Mitchell, the 20-year-old Welsh senior champion, competing in Alfaz Del Pi, Spain equalled the Welsh high jump record of 2.24 set in 1985 by John Hill and on the same day at the Mount Antonio College Relays at Walnut, California Chuka Enih-Snell cleared 2.18, the best by a British 17 year old for 12 years.

28 Sarah Moore revised her own Welsh hammer record with a throw of 57.40 in Colindale, London.

MAY

11 Swansea Harriers picked up team titles in the M40 and M60 age groups at the National Veterans' Road Relay Championships at Sutton Park, Sutton Coldfield.

22 AAW celebrated the second year of Celtic Manor funding. To mark the occasion Colin Jackson MBE signed and unveiled a portrait of himself in honour of his world record of 12.91 for the 110 hurdles, which has stood since 1993.

JUNE

16/17 Steven Shalders was denied a new Welsh triple jump record as he recorded a distance of 16.26 at the Welsh Championships at Cardiff only to be denied by an illegal following wind of 2.7m/s, whilst Rhys Williams, son of JJ, ran a world under 18 championship qualifying time of 53.89 in the 400 hurdles. Cardiff hosted the championships for the first time since 1992.

In the 400, 1999 world indoor champion, and holder of the title, Jamie Baulch pulled up in the final with a recurring hamstring problem leaving Matt Elias to take his first senior flat title in 46.9 – the fourth fastest winning time in the history of the event.

Senior championship bests came from 200 winner Doug Turner (20.57w in heat/20.54 final), Catherine Murphy (200 – 23.35w) and Sarah Moore (56.77 hammer). Age group records came from Heather Jones (10.86 under 15 75m hurdles), Faye Harding (under 17 300 – 39.46) and Nicola Stevenson (10.29 under 13 shot)

JULY

1 There were four Welsh winners at the AAA under 23 championships at Bedford. Matt Elias won the 400 hurdles title in a personal best time of 50.1 while Rebecca Roles won the discus with a throw of 49.06. In the under 20 age group Tim Benjamin won the 200 in 20.6 and Chuka Enih-Snell took the high jump title with a clearance of 2.14.

Dave Lease the former Welsh pole vault record holder (4.80i 1972) is confirmed as High Performance Manager at NIAC. Lease is a former Scottish national coach and coach to 9.98 sprint-star Jason Gardener. His key role will be to ensure that the various needs, which are required for the UK High Performance athletes based at NIAC, plus the Elite Cymru athletes are met. This includes sports science, sports medicine screening and support, physiotherapy and massage.

14 At the World Youth Championships in Debrecen, Hungary 15 year old Fay Harding finished fifth in the final. Her heat time of 60.06 broke the ten-year-old Welsh age group best of 61.02 set by Claire Edwards.

14/15 In Amsterdam 22 year old Matt Elias was crowned European under 23 400 hurdles champion in another personal best time of 49.57, to become only the second Welshman to better 50 seconds. For good measure he also dipped under the barrier with 49.90 in his heat. He also brought home the British 4 x 400 relay squad in first place to earn his second gold medal. Steven Shalders broke his own Welsh triple jump record of 15.99 set in 2000 as his third round effort took him out to 16.28 to claim seventh place in the final. Completing the representation from Wales was Robert Mitchell who finished sixth in the high jump with 2.12.

15 In Brisbane Bronwen Cardy-Wise wins the World vets over 45 10,000 track title and then steps down to the W40 age group to help Britain win the cross-country team gold.

Matt Elias strikes gold in Amsterdam.

19 Tim Benjamin wins the European junior 400 title in Grosseto, Italy with a time of 46.43 in only his third race over the distance. Iwan Thomas (44.36) and Jamie Baulch (44.57) are the only Welshmen to have run faster.

© Mark Shearman

Tim Benjamin (138) wins in Grosseto.

25 Rhys Williams took gold at the European Youth Olympic Days Championships in Murcia, Spain as he won the 400 hurdles in 53.42.

28 Robert Mitchell adds 1 cm to John Hill's 1985 Welsh high jump record with 2.25 at Bedford.

29 Nottingham hosted the Cerebral Palsy World Games with three Welsh sprinters collecting medals. Lloyd Upsdell did the sprint double (13.46/27.88) while Stephen Herbert took bronze in the 200 (26.01) in his category. Beverley Jones in the CP 8 category set a new European record (14.23) in the heats of the 100 but was just edged out in the final. She also won silver in the 200 (31.24).

Rhys Williams

AUGUST

4 – 12 Alan Currie gives an eyewitness account of the World Championships in Edmonton on the following pages but here is an overview:

There were mixed fortunes for Welsh athletes. The outstanding performances came from Christian Malcolm as he ran eight races in six days. He finished seventh in the 100 with a Welsh record 10.11 and a disappointing fifth in the 200 in 20.22 after setting two Welsh records in the preliminary rounds. If he had replicated his 20.08 winning semi-final time in the final it would have given him silver. Only John Regis (19.87) amongst British athletes has run faster.

In the 400 metres both Jamie Baulch and Iwan Thomas went out in their heats but Tim Benjamin joined them for the relay and the Anglo-Welsh quartet finished sixth in the final.

Catherine Murphy also went out in the heats of the 400 but, as a member of the British team, was fifth in the final of the long relay while Hayley Tullett was ninth in her semi-final of the 1500.

5 Wales hosted the Celtic Games Junior International at Deeside College Stadium, Connah's Quay.

12 Deeside retained their Welsh Division 1 Senior Champions title for the third year in succession. Cwmbran won Division 2 while Cardiff took the Division 3 title.

13 At the AAA under 17 Championships at the Don Valley Stadium, Sheffield Luke Northall wins the 3000 in 8:43.20. In the under 15 age group Faye Harding won the 300 in 40.01 while Heather Jones retained her 75 hurdles title in 10.95.

18 Former British League champions Cardiff AAC finish seventh in Division 2 of the BAL to join Swansea in next year's Division 3. Swansea maintained their Division 3 status by finishing fifth in the final league match at Stafford.

Pembrokeshire AC win the Welsh Junior League Plate Final.

19 Carmarthen romped away to win the Welsh Junior League Cup Final at Brecon.

27 West Wales confirmed their strength by winning all three trophies in the Inter-Regional competition at Neath.

28 Philippa Roles (discus 6th) and Rhian Clarke (pole vault 9th) competed in the World University Games in Beijing, China.

29 Gerry Batty of Swansea Harriers dies aged 63. Originally a member of City of Rochester AC he moved to Swansea in the 1960s and soon became involved in the running of the Swansea club, where he occupied many positions including treasurer and coach. He was also Secretary/Treasurer of West Glamorgan AAA for most of its existence before reorganisation. He served on many Welsh AAA/AAW committees and twice served as Chairman of the Counties Athletic Union.

SEPTEMBER

1 Former world indoor 60m hurdles bronze medallist, Nigel Walker, is appointed Head of Sport at BBC Wales.

8 Over 3000 runners took part in the Millennium-Stadium-finish KRUF Cardiff 10k Road Race which was also the Welsh Championship. First Welsh finisher was Andres Jones (third overall) but he was declared ineligible for the Welsh title as he failed to wear his Cardiff AAC club vest. The championship went instead to Mark Morgan (fourth overall). In the women's race the Welsh title went to third placed overall Rachel Goddard (35.41) – a personal best time by over four minutes. Swansea won both team events

21 Welsh teams compete in all four events in the World Mountain Trophy in Arte Terme, Italy, with the senior men's squad finishing 17th out of the 29 competing countries and the senior women 14th of 25.

24 Former Olympic champion and world champion Khalid Skah wins Swansea Bay 10k.

OCTOBER

6 Swansea Harriers and Newport Harriers win the M40 and W45 team events respectively at the British Veteran's Cross-Country Championships held on home soil at Singleton Park, Swansea.

7 The British Junior Fell Running Championships were held at Cavehill Park, Belfast with all four Welsh teams at under 16 and under 18 age groups placing third. The best individual result from a Welsh athlete came from Eleanor Sherrard-Smith who also collected a bronze medal in the under 18 girls event.

13 Dave Williams former Welsh team manager dies at the age of 69. He was team manager between 1983 and 1993 and was Commonwealth Games team manger in 1986 and 1990. He came into athletics in 1965 to keep fit for football joining Birchgrove Harriers. He became Welsh Staff Coach for sprints and middle distance after taking his AAA senior coaching award in 1970. He was a former President of Cardiff AAC. The funeral service in Cardiff was packed with stars and personalities from Welsh athletics including many athletes he had coached. Three of them, Bernie Plain, Bernie Hayward and Tanni Grey-Thompson gave moving addresses.

The first of the year's Dual Annual Welsh Coaching Conferences was held in Cardiff, which included keynote lectures from Phil Banning, Bruce Longdon and Judy Vernon.

18 Welsh-based Olympic 200 silver medallist Darren Campbell opens the UK Athletics High Performance Centre at NIAC, with Lynn Davies and a host of

other UK and Welsh athletics stars and officials in attendance. This was the culmination of several years of lobbying and coaxing by the Head of the Centre for Performance Analysis at UWIC, former Welsh triple jump champion, Sean Power.

19 Sports Council for Wales announce that Deeside College is their preferred location for a regional indoor athletic training facility for North Wales.

26 British Pole vault record holder Janine Whitlock visited Deeside College to launch the North Wales Aqua-Pura Women in Athletics initiative.

27 Cardiff AAC finished third in the AAA Six-Stage road relay championships at Sutton Park.

NOVEMBER

22 Announced that NIAC at Cyncoed will host the 2002 AAA indoor championships – the first time that the event has been held outside England. This announcement came as further evidence that NIAC is now one of the - if not the - leading athletics facilities in the UK.

24 Tanni Grey-Thompson is named Welsh Woman of the Year in a ceremony sponsored by *The Western Mail* in association with *S4C* and *Heno*.

DECEMBER

2 Death is announced of former Welsh cross-country champion Norman Horrell. He had been in poor health for a number of years and won the title three times – in 1957 and again in 1961 and 1962. He ran in the 880 yards at the 1958 Cardiff Empire Games and took the Welsh title that year with 1:54.7.

THE TEN-DAY WONDER

An eye-witness account of the 2001 World Championships in Edmonton

By Alan Currie

It has been my good fortune to be present, at least once, at every major athletics event on the international calendar (Olympic Games, European Championships, Commonwealth Games, etc). Until this year the only blank was the World Championships and when they were scheduled to be held in Canada, Brenda and I were among the first to register for the trip. As self-confessed "Canadaphiles" who fell in love with that beautiful country some years ago, we thus had two excellent reasons for going.

After an 8-hour flight we settled into our hotel and then adapted to the 7-hour time difference between Edmonton and the UK. Our first visit to the Commonwealth Stadium (the site of the 1978 Commonwealth Games) came on Friday, 3 August when we witnessed a spectacular opening ceremony. One innovation was to incorporate the men's marathon into the actual ceremony. The race was a classic and we watched the action unfold on the huge screen at one end of the stadium. Simon Biwott of Kenya and Gezahegne Abera of

Ethiopia entered the stadium practically neck-and-neck and proceeded to battle it out over the 300 metres of track to the finish. Abera, the Olympic Champion, just held on and won by a second. Our seats could hardly have been better placed as we were looking directly down onto the finish line.

Absent wind-gauge denies Christian a Welsh record in 100m

There was one major disappointment for British supporters on day 2 when it was announced that Denise Lewis had been forced to withdraw from the heptathlon. There was almost another when Jonathan Edwards left it until his third attempt to ensure his place in the triple jump final. Christian Malcolm competed for the first time today, clocking 10.09 when finishing 2nd in his second round heat. This would have been a new Welsh record if it were not for the fact that the wind gauge malfunctioned, rendering his time invalid for record purposes. Hayley Tullett finished 2nd in her 1500m heat to qualify for the semi finals. After her misfortune at the Sydney Olympics last year we were hoping the gods would smile on her this time. In the evening we went to a function at which Cathy Freeman was the guest of honour.

On the Sunday we watched a great men's hammer competition. At major events such as these the field events come into their own and are every bit as exciting as those on the track. Unfortunately, they do not get proper coverage the rest of the time and are reduced to the margins of the sport. The women's heptathlon was duly completed and, with Eunice Barber of France dropping out, we couldn't help feeling that a fit Denise Lewis would have won the gold medal. One of the track's glamour events was concluded on this day when Maurice Greene led an American clean sweep of the medals in the men's 100 metres. Christian Malcolm finished 7th in a new Welsh record time of 10.11, this time without any problems from the wind gauge. Sadly, Hayley Tullett had an off day. She never looked comfortable in her race and tailed off to finish in 9th place. Swansea Harriers stalwarts John and Elaine Griffiths, Hayley's uncle and aunt, were with us throughout the entire holiday and sat a few seats away from us during the championships. That evening we met Hayley's parents, Jeff and Rosemary Parry, and we all went for a meal at a restaurant in downtown Edmonton.

Boston remembers his 1965 epic duel with Lynn at Maindy

One of the features of the championships was the introduction to the crowd of some of athletics' all-time greats at the medal ceremonies. Many of them were staying at the same hotel as we were and on Monday morning, as we went down to breakfast, we bumped into Ralph Boston. We introduced ourselves, got him to autograph our programme and chatted with him about his visit to Wales in 1965 when he competed in the Welsh Games against Lynn Davies. He was a charming man and remembered the event well.

Highlights of the day were again the field events. An outstanding women's pole vault was followed by the men's triple jump in which Jonathan Edwards won Britain's first and, as things turned out, only gold medal. The men's 400 metres final (minus Michael Johnson) was won in a run-of-the-mill 44.64 seconds which made us regret the injuries suffered by Iwan Thomas over the past couple of seasons. At the end of the first day Dean Macey led the decathlon by a single point so we left in high spirits. On the way out of the stadium we saw Mike Powell, so our programme for that day contains the autographs of two of the all time greats of long jumping.

Christian clocks two Welsh 200 records but misses out on a medal

Tuesday (7th August) was the longest day's athletics with a programme extending over 12 hours. Dean Macey wasn't able to hold on to his overnight lead but wound up with a bronze medal. Paula Radcliffe came desperately close to doing likewise as she finished 4th in the 10,000 metres. From a Welsh point of view it was disappointing to see Paul Gray finish 6th in his heat of the 110m hurdles and fail to progress to the next round. On the other hand, Christian Malcolm set a new Welsh record of 20.13 in the second round of the 200 metres.

On day 6 we saw Christian running in his 200m semi final. He won easily, setting another Welsh record of 20.08 in the process, and remained undefeated in the preliminary rounds. The Olympic Champion, Kostas Kederis of Greece, was clearly in a class of his own but we thought that Christian was a near certainty for one of the other medals. Charles Kamathi of Kenya won the 10,000 metres with Haile Gebrselassie of Ethiopia, in third place, as gracious in defeat as he always is in victory.

We started day 7 (Thursday) by meeting Kip Keino in the hotel foyer and obtaining another autograph. Confident of a medal in the 200m we went to the stadium armed with our Welsh Dragons, despite the instruction by the organisers that only the flags of participating nations (which for us, of course, meant the Union Jack) should be displayed. As expected, Kederis won the gold medal easily (20.04) but the scrap for the other medals was extremely tight. Christian finished in 5th place with 20.22, while the three immediately ahead of him all clocked 20.20 and even the photo-finish could not split two of them who were listed as equal 3rd. It was a disappointing result for Welsh supporters, especially as no-one other than Kederis approached Christian's earlier 20.08 time which would have sufficed for the silver medal. Also on this day we watched the final of the men's 110m hurdles, won by Allen Johnson. We couldn't help wondering what the absent Colin Jackson might have done in this event, which had been disastrous from a British point of view. Both Tony Jarrett and Wilbert Greaves had been disqualified for two false starts.

The next day, after a morning visit to West Edmonton Mall, the largest shopping mall in the world, we went to the stadium for an evening session and suffered another British disappointment as Steve Backley failed to qualify for the men's javelin final. Marion Jones made up for her shock defeat in the 100 metres a few days earlier by taking the gold medal at 200 metres.

The penultimate day's athletics was memorable for all the wrong reasons. Olga Yegorova of Russia, who had tested positive for EPO earlier in the year, won the women's 5,000 metres, accompanied by booing from some sections of the crowd. This day also saw the heats of the men's 4 x 100m relay in which Britain were strongly fancied to win a medal of some sort. There was a sense of déjà vu about the event as the British quartet did the same thing as in Sydney last year and failed to get the baton round. A faulty exchange at the last takeover meant their immediate elimination.

Mark Richardson – honorary Welshman!

On the final morning we stood at the roadside and watched the women marathon runners passing the 38k mark. During another great day's athletics there was a nice touch when Mark Richardson was graciously allowed to guest in the Welsh 4 x 400 metres relay team! He followed Iwan Thomas, Jamie Baulch and Tim Benjamin to run the final leg to bring the British team home in 6th place. Catherine Murphy ran the glory leg to anchor the British women's 4 x 400 squad home in 5th.

A colourful closing ceremony then brought the whole event to a conclusion. It had been a wonderful meeting, the weather had been glorious and the Canadian people must be the friendliest anywhere in the world. Like most good things it was over too soon. Now all we had to look forward to was six days in the glorious Rocky Mountains and a few days in Vancouver before flying home to sunny Neath. Life can be hard at times.

The Authors

John Collins: Born in Aylesbury, Bucks, on 25 November 1937, John's interest in athletics goes back to his schooldays. As a 13 year old he joined Vale of Aylesbury AC and later ran for his university – Imperial College London as well as a variety of clubs. By 18 he was already a club secretary. He moved to Wales in 1961, settling in the Pontypool area, and together with the late George Crump and others was instrumental in the formation of the Pontypool and District Cross-Country League, the forerunner of the Gwent CC League. In 1963 he won the Welsh 6 miles cross-country championship at Pwllgwaun, Pontypridd and after finishing 3rd in the Welsh 6 miles and 6th in the senior championship in 1965 he was selected to run for Wales in the international at Waterloo in Belgium. He still competes as a veteran and has competed six times for Wales in various age groups in the home countries international, as well as being a member of his club team that won several British titles. John moved to Swansea in 1965 and has been an official of the Swansea Harriers club in some capacity or other since 1970. At about the same time he was heavily involved in another major innovation in Welsh athletics when he was one of the founders, and the inaugural secretary, of the Welsh Men's Athletics League. At various times he served as secretary of the Welsh CCA and the cross-country committee of the AAW after the merger of associations. He served as a member of the AAA General Committee for several years, and was Welsh representative on the ICCU and later on the BAAB/BAF cross-country committees. He was awarded a meritorious plaque for his services to Welsh athletics in 1970 and the AAW Award of Honour in 1996.

The authors pictured at Neath during one of their many planning meetings Left to right: Mike Walters, Alan Currie, Brenda Currie, Clive Williams and John Collins.

Alan Currie: Moving to Wales as a wartime evacuee in 1941 after being born in London in 1937, his interest in athletics began in the mid 1950s and he ran his first race in 1959. He continued running in road and cross-country races until 1994. His early interest in athletics was kindled during National Service at RAF Northwood, which gave him the opportunity to visit the White City in 1956, where he saw his first athletics meeting, an evening match between London and Budapest (he still has the programme). Athletes taking part included a host of Olympic medallists and world record holders such as Gordon Pirie, Derek Ibbotson, Istvan Rozsavolgyi, Sandor Iharos, and Chris Brasher. He was also present at the White City in 1965 when Ron Clarke became the first man to run under 13 minutes for three miles. He has attended many of the great athletics festivals as a spectator and official, including the first World Cup Final in Dusseldorf when he met Brenda. In 1970 he became a graded track judge and reached grade one in 1980 and track referee in 1987. He has officiated at two Commonwealth Games plus such events as the European Cup Final (twice), European Junior Championships, World Student Games, IAAF Grand Prix Final and World Cup Final. As an administrator, he has been secretary of Neath Harriers since 1969, making him the second longest serving club secretary in Wales after Ivor Adams of Newport. He was divisional secretary of the Welsh League from 1970 to 1978 and took over from John Collins as overall secretary after that. He has been secretary of the West Wales region of the AAW for the past two years. Alan took over as editor of the *Welsh Athletics Annual* when Clive Williams stood down in 1982. He has sat on the Welsh selection committee for over 20 years and has had a hand in the selection of every Welsh Commonwealth Games team since 1982. A member of the NUTS for many years he is interested in the sport worldwide as well as at Welsh level. In 1975 he was awarded the Welsh AAA Meritorious Plaque for services to Welsh athletics and received the Award of Honour in 1995. Although English born he is a confirmed Welshman – having learned to speak Welsh and like any Welshman he is an ardent and knowledgeable Welsh rugby fan, attending most of the home matches (ticket permitting!) over the past 40 years, and having watched most of the legendary Welsh players since the mid 1950s when he saw his first match in 1954 – Cardiff v Neath at the Gnoll. Now retired, this has allowed him to travel the world to pursue his hobby, just having returned with Brenda from the Edmonton World Championships. He is currently studying Humanities at the Open University.

Brenda Currie: Born in Kingston on Thames with a Welsh father, she studied at Loughborough University, qualifying as a Chartered Librarian, and moved to Wales when she and Alan married in 1980. Up to that point her interest in athletics had been as a supporter only, paying frequent visits to the old White City and she attended the 1972 Munich Olympics. She was National Administrator to the Welsh AAA and later AAW for twelve years up to 1998 when the office was at Morfa Stadium, Swansea. Along with Alan, she was joint administrator of the Welsh Men's League for 15 years and the Welsh Women's League for 10. Together they produced the *Welsh Athletics Annual*, continually expanding its scope so that it covered all aspects of the sport in Wales, until 1995. Since then Brenda, a NUTS member for many years has been heavily involved in historical research and maintains substantial files of records of all aspects of Welsh athletics. She was presented with the AAW Meritorious Plaque in 1996 for her services to Welsh athletics and like Alan is a Welsh speaker.

Mike Walters: Carmarthen born in 1949, he had the good fortune to play at outside half for Queen Elizabeth Grammar School, with future Welsh rugby legends Ray Gravell at scrum half, Roy Bergiers in the centre and Gerald Davies on the wing! One of Wales' most promising sprinter/hurdlers in the 1960s, he was Welsh Schools' 200 yds hurdles champion in 1966, 1967 and 1968. His 22.6 clocking of 1966 remains the only British junior record ever set at the Welsh Schools' Championships. He was a Welsh Schools' international in 1966 and 1967. In fact, 1967 was a good season for him. He won a bronze medal over 60 yds at the AAA Junior Indoor Championships in Cosford and a silver medal at the AAA Junior Championships over 200 hurdles. Later that year he won a AAA vest against the UAU at Birmingham University. He represented Wales against the AAA at Bargoed in 1969 and remembers with pride being presented with his Welsh vest by the late Ted Hopkins. Indoor running obviously suited Mike as he jointly holds the record for the fastest time ever recorded in Britain over 55 yds with one Peter Radford. His contemporaries at Cardiff College of Education (now UWIC) included Gareth Edwards, J.J. Williams and former long jump star, John Elias (father of Matthew), and his personal tutor turned out to be a certain Lynn Davies, who remains a great influence today. Mike says that he was very fortunate to witness Michael Johnson's world record 43.18 in the 1999 World Championships, which he regards as the best performance he has seen along with Colin Jackson winning his second World title.He has been to the last three World Championships. Many years a NUTS member, Mike has a life long interest in the statistical and historical side of athletics and started contributing to the *Welsh Athletics Annual* in the late 1970s. He has been a Physical Education teacher for 30 years and has had experience as a team manager to Welsh Schools' and Welsh junior teams. Since 1983 Mike has worked with BBC Wales reporting on athletics and rugby, and has been a frequent contributor to athletics journals on Welsh affairs as well writing on rugby and athletics for the *Western Mail, Wales on Sunday and Evening Post*. The book is dedicated to Mike's daughter, Nerys, who died in 1997.

Clive Williams: Brought up in Bargoed in the Rhymney Valley, but born in Cardiff in 1944, and apart from athletics he has a broad interest in all Welsh sport - particularly rugby. He was a spectator at the 1958 Cardiff Empire Games and vividly remembers the Merriman/Power tussle for the 6 miles gold. When the local YMCA formed an athletics club at the time of the opening of the track in Bargoed in 1960, he became one of the founder members. His interest in Welsh athletics history and statistics started in 1962 when he joined Birchgrove Harriers and along with Ken Bennett, the current AAW statistician, he produced the first deep Welsh ranking lists in 1963, and has been a member of the NUTS since then. The original Welsh lists were run off on a duplicator owned by Bernard Baldwin, Welsh AAA Secretary at the time, but the lists gradually advanced to the publication of the first *Welsh Athletics Annual* in 1977. He continued to produce and edit the booklet until Alan Currie took over for the 1982 annual. He became statistician and records officer of the Welsh AAA in 1963 and held that position until he moved from Wales in 1987. After his appointment in 1963 he immediately set about re-defining and updating Welsh records, which until then had been recognised only if the athlete was born and the record set in Wales, which hardly reflected the true standard of Welsh athletics. Despite living outside Wales he has maintained his extensive collection of Welsh athletics historical data, which has proved invaluable in the production of this book. As an athlete he was Welsh junior champion at 880 yds, mile and cross-country in 1960s. He was a founder member of Cardiff AAC in 1968, and then became the first captain of the newly formed club and chairman in 1974. Entering the senior ranks, he was twice runner up in the Welsh 5,000m championships (1968/1973). He has undertaken public address duties at all of the major venues in the UK and for many years was the principal announcer at the major Welsh events. He was a Welsh selector for 20 years and a British selector for six, which involved him in the selection of two Olympic teams. He has been a frequent contributor to *Athletics Weekly* and *The Western Mail* and has been a regular broadcaster on Welsh athletics. He has spent all his working life in the brewing industry and is currently running his own consultancy company. He was awarded a Welsh AAA Meritorious Plaque in 1972 for his services to Welsh athletics.